"THE BEST THI‖ COME OUT OF SINCE THE SUPREMES. LEONARD MALTIN, WATCH YOUR BEHIND."

— NEW YORK POST

"Its breadth is unsurpassed. ★★★★"—USA TODAY

VideoHound's
GOLDEN
MOVIE
RETRIEVER
1997

THE COMPLETE GUIDE TO MOVIES ON
VIDEOCASSETTE, LASERDISC AND CD

New Web Site Guide
in every book!

Fortified with Cinematographer
and Alternate Format Indexes!

Bold new design
matches any decor!

"One of the most trusted home
video reference guides."
— *Video Store*

"Highly recommended."
— *Video Business*

"By far the best."
— *Houston Chronicle*

"One of the most comprehensive
guides in print."
— *Chicago Tribune*

"If one can't find a video film in
this book, it probably isn't worth
finding."
— *The Ottawa Citizen*

"Worth its weight in rental fees."
— *Stanten Island Advance*

"A consumer stand-by."
— *New York Times*

"You get the most for your
money... plus plenty of chutzpa."
— *USA TODAY*

VISIBLE
INK
PRESS

VideoHound's
FAMILY
VIDEO
GUIDE

SECOND EDITION

VideoHound's
FAMILY
VIDEO GUIDE

Edited by Martin F. Kohn

Foreword by Brian Henson

DETROIT   NEW YORK   TORONTO   LONDON

VideoHound's®
FAMILY
VIDEO
GUIDE

Copyright © 1995 by Visible Ink Press

Published by Visible Ink Press®, a division of
Gale Research Inc., 835 Penobscot Building,
Detroit, MI 48226-4094

Visible Ink Press and *VideoHound* are registered
trademarks of Gale Research Inc.

Most Visible Ink Press books are available at special quantity discounts when purchased in bulk by corporations, organizations, or groups. Customized printings, special imprints, messages, and excerpts can be produced to meet your needs. For more information, contact Special Markets Manager, Gale Research Inc., 835 Penobscot Bldg., Detroit, MI 48226.

Cover photographs courtesy of The Kobal Collection.

ISBN 0-7876-0984-6

CREDITS

LEADER DOGS
Martin F. Kohn
Martin Connors
Devra M. Sladics

CONTRIBUTING CANINES
Michelle Banks
Beth A. Fhaner
Julia Furtaw
Terri Schell
Carol Schwartz
Christine Tomassini

TECHNOHOUNDS
Don Dillaman
Theresa Rocklin

INK SPOTTERS
Judy Hartman,
General Graphic Services

DESIGN BIG DAWG
Cynthia Baldwin

DESIGNER RARE BREED
(COVER AND PAGE DESIGN)
Mary Krzewinski

PHOTOHOUNDS
Barbara Yarrow
Randy Bassett
Pam Hayes

CAT'S PAJAMAS (PRODUCTION)
Dorothy Maki
Evi Seoud
Shanna Heilveil

MARKETING AND PUBLICITY
HOUNDS
Cyndi Naughton
Betsy Revegno
Susan Stephani
Jenny Sweetland
Lauri Taylor

HELPING HOUND
Mary Alice Rattenbury

Photos courtesy of The Kobal Collection

A Cunning Canine™ Production

Contents

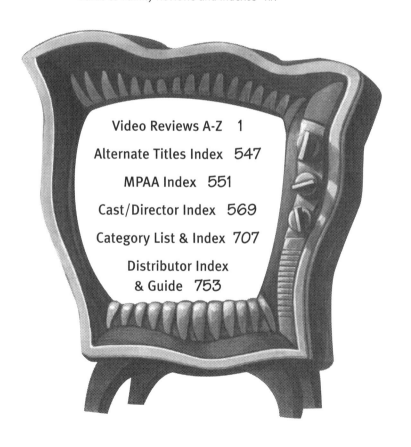

Foreword

By Brian Henson

©Jim Henson Productions, Inc.

My first professional collaboration with my father, Jim Henson, occurred when I was five years old and he cast me in "The Counting Film - Number Three" for *Sesame Street*. I sat at a table and distinctively said "three peas," as the numbers 1, 2 and 3 appeared next to the peas on my plate. It was a virtuoso performance and one that undoubtedly stands out as a high point in the annals of vegetable counting. For me, it served as a wonderful introduction to the simple edict that my father applied to all his work—that good family entertainment should be both fun and enlightening for children and adults. As he once wrote, "I believe that we can use television and film to be an influence for good; that we can help shape the thoughts of children and adults in a positive way." Over the years, I have tried to never lose sight of that fundamental rule.

Today, the influence that television programs and home videos have over children is greater than ever as kids are spending more and more time in front of the TV set. Too often, children and parents are in separate rooms watching different programs. Besides the fact that children might be viewing programs inappropriate, families lose quality time spent together. I believe that this vast amount of time watching movies and television can be especially enjoyable and educational when parents view with their children. As such, it is vital that parents make informed choices about what their children are watching, as well as choose videos that they will enjoy themselves. The good news is that there is an increasing amount of family entertainment—movies and television that please all ages. Conversely, the bad news is that identifying "good" family entertainment can be a challenge.

Given that, it is my pleasure to write this foreword for *VideoHound's Family Video Guide*. This guide provides a comprehensive listing of over 4,000 movies and special features, reviewing each title in terms of content, age-group recommendations and even adult interest. This information allows parents to judge each entry as to whether or not it is appropriate for their youngsters, and whether or not they themselves will find it engaging.

In addition to providing a means of vetting their children's entertainment, *VideoHound's Family Video Guide* can also assist parents in identifying videos that cover specific top-

©Jim Henson Productions, Inc.

ics of interest. If a child is particularly excited by dinosaurs, then the guide can help determine which movies might spark his or her imagination. If a kid is a Teenage Mutant Ninja Turtle fanatic, the guide provides a listing of the different film versions that deal with the Turtles' exploits. And perhaps, by flipping through *VideoHound's Family Video Guide,* parents will remember some favorite movie from their own childhood that they want to share with their children.

But the real fun is picking videos together as a family and watching them together as a family. Seeing *The Wizard of Oz* or *The Thief of Bagh-dad* again through the eyes of a child is a wonderful experience, and one that can help pave the way to healthy family dialogue on a full range of topics. Movies open youngsters up to new worlds and new ideas, and can help familiarize them with a wide variety of life's experiences. All in all, they provide a great adventure for parents to share with their children.

Introduction

BY MARTIN F. KOHN

Nine thousand.

That's the number of different titles in a typical video superstore. How long would it take to watch all of them? Let's crunch some numbers. Put away the calculator; it's our treat.

6,570.

That's the number of days in 18 years. A person who's one day old won't get much from a video, but let's assume that little baby watches 1.4 videos every day until, on her 18th birthday, she has seen every tape in the store, from *Aaron Loves Angela* through *Zuma Beach*.

Congratulations, kid. Here's your high school diploma. It seems to have been signed by H. Wayne Huizenga, the founder of Blockbuster. Party on, Wayne.

But hold the cell-phone.

While you were putting Wayne's kids through graduate school, another thousand tapes were being released each year. That's 18,000 more. You've got a lot of catching up to do. Let's see.

If 9,000 videos took 18 years to watch, then 18,000 videos ought to take . . .

Okay, you get the idea. Speaking realistically, "You couldn't view them in one lifetime," says Robert Finlayson. Not that he would mind if you tried. Finlayson is the vice president of the Video Software Dealers Association, the trade organization for people who rent and sell videotapes.

Here's another number.

5,280.

That's the number of feet in the extra mile we've gone to bring you this book. Why? Because kids today have never known life without video, and whether that's a good thing or a bad thing is pretty much up to you. If you've read this far you probably aren't that parental rarity who has banished television from the household; you realize that while video is sometimes the babysitter, it is more often the family activity, the conversation stimulator, the shared experience that can bring pleasure, knowledge and understanding. Or the joy of family-wide derision.

And even if it is just the babysitter, don't you want to know who's watching the kids?

Children today learn things backwards. They will watch *The Muppet Christmas Carol* or *Mr. Magoo's Christmas Carol* before they ever attend a theatrical production of "A Christmas Carol" or open the Dickens original. They will see *West Side Story* before they get to "Romeo and Juliet" or read Shakespeare. And no way are they ever going to read "The Hunchback of Notre Dame."

Children learn from everything, and like it or not, video is the teacher who comes home with them, hangs out at their friends' houses and, sometimes, even shows up in school. Nature, and the Video Software Dealers Association, abhor a vacuum. "That's the beauty of the industry," says Robert Finlayson. "There's something for everybody."

Indeed. But which of those somethings is right for you and your family? No, not everybody likes The Three Stooges. So, think of this volume as the guidebook you take to a strange city. It will direct you to the White House or the Louvre or Walt Disney's domain and tell you why a particular sight may appeal to a two-year-old and what makes another a must-see for older teens. It will also suggest which neighborhoods should be approached with caution.

Most of the videos scrutinized herein are intentionally aimed at children or are rated G, PG, or PG-13, but some R rated movies are included. How come? Because peer pressure, normal curiosity and sleepovers at Michael's or Alison's mean your child may be exposed prematurely to the collected works of Arnold Schwarzenegger or the best of Demi Moore. Armed with foreknowledge, you could explain why a certain film is inappropriate, or suggest to your child that you watch it together. (That alone may dissuade them.)

Additionally, some R rated films are appropriate for mature young people, and deserve to be included in a book about family videos. The blood and gore that earns an R for a film like *Glory* is the historical violence of the Civil War. It wouldn't be as affecting a movie if the slaughter had taken place off-screen. The sexuality in *The Birdcage* is essential to the story of two gay men who, at heart, represent the best kind of family values.

By letting you know about a video before you rent or buy it for your family, *VideoHound's Family Video Guide's* aims are the same as the film industry's—to entertain and to help you relax.

So . . . Be selective. Set an example. Pass the popcorn.

ACKNOWLEDGMENTS

VideoHound and friends would like to thank Brian Henson, Stephanie Greenhut and others at Jim Henson Productions for the contribution of the guest forword. We appreciate the patience and skills of Don Dillaman, Theresa Rocklin, Evi Seoud, Dorothy Maki and Judy Hartman. The Kobal Collection is much appreciated for their fast turnaround and notable photo selection. Mary Krzewinski shared her creative skills and her usual flair for the page and cover designs.

Thank you also to Christine Tomassini and Michelle Banks for help in gathering research, Beth Fhaner for help in writing the photo captions and Carol Schwartz, Terri Schell and Julia Furtaw for guidance and direction. And a thank you to Martin Kohn and Devra Sladics for their work on the contents.

Martin Kohn would also like to thank his wife Laura and daughters Maggie and Anna for their insight and expertise.

ABOUT THE EDITOR

Martin F. Kohn is an award-winning writer and editor for the *Detroit Free Press* (since 1977) and a contributor and reviewer for several different publications, including *Parents Magazine, Entertainment Weekly, Parenting* and *Family Life*. He has written two books based on his Detroit Free Press column: *Family Fare* (1988) and *Family Fare 2* (1993), both guides to family traveling fun in and around Michigan.

In 1990 and 1992, Kohn won the Society of American Travel Writers award and in 1995, he won the ASCAP-Deems Taylor Award for music journalism.

Originally from Brooklyn, NY, he resides with his wife Laura and daughters Maggie and Anna (all native Detroiters) in Huntington Woods, MI.

Guide to Family Reviews and Indexes

(1) **(2)**

Aladdin ♫♫♫◞

(3) (4) **(G/Family)** Disney naturally took the crown for the most financially successful cartoon of its time. Boy meets princess, loses her, finds her, wins her from evil **(5)** vizier and nasty parrot. Superb animation triumphs over mostly average songs and storyline by capitalizing on Williams' talent for ad-libbing with lightning speed as Aladdin's irrepressible big blue genie, though one wonders if his celebrity spoofs (Arsenio Hall, for example) will endure for as long as the imagery in "Pinocchio" or "Beauty and the Beast." For all ages: adults will enjoy the 1,001 Williams impersonations while kids will get a kick out of the genie, the romantic storyline, and the songs.

(6) ♫ A Whole New World; Prince Ali; Friend Like Me; One Jump Ahead; Arabian Nights.

BEWARE: Genie roughhousing. Be forewarned: very **(7)** small children may be frightened by some of **(8)** **(9) (10)** the later sequences. **(11)** **(12)**

1992 90m C D: Ron Clements, John Musker; W: **(14)** Clements, John Musker, Ted Elliot, Terry Rossio; **(13)** M: Alan Menken, Howard Ashman, Tim Rice; V: Robin Williams, Scott **(15)** Weinger, Linda Larkin, Jonathan Freeman, Frank Welker, Gilbert Gottfried, Douglas Seale, Brad Kane, Lea Salonga **Award Nominations:** Academy Awards 92: Best Song ("Friend like Me"), Best Sound, Best **(16)** Sound Effects Editing; **Awards:** Academy Awards 92: Best Original Score, Best Song ("A Whole New World"); Golden Globe Awards '93: Best Song ("A Whole New World"), Best Score; MTV Movie Awards 93: Best Comedic Performance (Williams). **VHS, Beta, LV, CDV** *DIS, BTTV, WTA* **(17)** **(18)**

(1) **Title**—The book is arranged alphabetically by title on a word by word basis, including articles, prepositions, and conjunctions (the ampersand (&) is alphabetized as "and"). Leading articles (*A, An, The*) are ignored in English-language titles. The equivalent foreign articles are not ignored, however: *The Addams Family* appears under "A" while *Les Miserables* appears under "L." **Other points to keep in mind:**

- Acronyms appear alphabetically as if regular words. For example, *D.A.R.Y.L.* is alphabetized as *Daryl*.
- Common abbreviations in titles file as if they are spelled out. For instance, *Mrs. Doubtfire* follows *Miss Firecracker*.
- Proper names in titles are alphabetized beginning with the individual's first name; for example, *Ollie Hopnoodle's Haven of Bliss* is under "O."
- Titles with numbers (*13 Ghosts*) are alphabetized as if the number was spelled out under the appropriate letter, in this case, "Thirteen." When numeric titles gather in close proximity to each other (*2000 Year Old Man, 2001: A Space Odyssey, 2010: The Year We Make Contact*), the titles will be arranged in a low (*2000*) to high (*2010*) sequence.
- In the event that more than one version of a title exists (for instance, *20,000 Leagues Under the Sea* has four versions listed while *A Christmas Carol* has three), the order will be chronological ranging from the earliest version to the most recent version.

(2) **Critical Rating**—VideoHound rates movies on a sliding scale from one to four bones, with the truly bad earning a Woof! Movies are rated within their genres (and occasionally large sub-genres), with comedies being rated against comedies, action-adventure against action-adventure, disaster flicks against other disasters, and so on. Kidvid, short subjects, recycled cartoons, or TV episodes generally are not rated. The scale:

WOOF! Stinky, often in a memorable way. Director often uses pseudonym. Actors wear disguises. Credits list "Bubba" as caterer/security/costume designer. Filmed in a vacant warehouse.

🦴 One bone—Quality control efforts lacking. Crew checks may have bounced. Director recently escaped from prison and had to work fast. Actors mystified by lack of script. Lighting guy had a few loose bulbs.

🦴ᵇ One and a half bones—Perhaps worth a look-see if enormous amounts of time on hands is a problem.

🦴🦴 Two bones—Toying with respectability, though it has a myriad of weak spots that may create the need for a mid-film snooze.

🦴🦴ᵇ Two and a half bones—Average film with average entertainment value for the average viewer. By law of averages, someone should like these. Beauty may be in eye of the average beholder.

🦴🦴🦴 Three bones—Better quality goods with fewer lows and more frequent highs. Storyline is good, cast knows how to act, and lighting technicians enjoy their work.

🦴🦴🦴ᵇ Three and a half bones—A delicacy, to be tasted like the finest morsel of day-old food left in the bowl. Among the best the movie-world has to offer.

🦴🦴🦴🦴 Four bones—Must be a masterpiece or a classic or a work of art or at the very least, a really good movie. Writer, director, actors, photographer, and yes, the lighting technicians all conspire to create a cinematic gem.

3 **MPAA Rating**—G, PG, PG-13, and R (no NC-17 movies are listed). The MPAA rating will not be present within the kidvid reviews.

4 **Age Range**—Approximate age ranges that video may be appropriate for, as follows:
  Preschool (ages 2-4)
  Primary (ages 5-10)
  Jr. High (ages 11-13)
  Sr. High (ages 14-17)
  Adult (ages 18 and over)
  Family (suitable for all ages)

5 **Description/review**—all the facts and some of the trivia that are fit to print. Contains information on colorized versions, sequels, remakes, and sources of adaptations.

6 **Songs**—a list of episodic singing and dancing occurring during musicals.

7 **Beware/Hound Advisory**—an indication of content areas to which the viewer may be sensitive. Generally, if a film has content that may be inappropriate for some ages, *VideoHound* will indicate what kind of offensive material may be present, usually taking into consideration the following topics: salty language or profanity, alcohol talk or drunkenness, drug use, sex talk, explicit or discreet sex shown on-screen, brief nudity or extensive nudity, roughhousing, mild violence or brutal violence and mature themes such as death, relationships and morals and ethics.

8 **Year released**—year of original release, either theatrically, on television, or direct to video.

9 **Length**—running time.

10 **Black and white** (B) or **color** (C)

11 **Director** (W/D: indicates writer/director)

12 **Writers**—Guys and gals who wrote or helped write the script.

13 **Composers/Lyricists**—They wrote or arranged or, occasionally, selected the music.

14 Cast—"C" or "V"; V indicates voiceovers. Also notes cameos.

15 Award Nominations—nominations from major award-giving bodies that did not result in actual awards.

16 Awards—including Academy Awards, Golden Globe, Cannes Film Festival, Canadian Genie, British Academy of Film and Television Arts, Australia Film Institute, French Cesar, Independent Spirit, and the MTV awards.

17 Format—Beta, VHS, CDV (CD-I and other compact disc formats) and/or LV (laserdisc)

18 Distributor code(s)—up to three distributor codes are listed. Check the Distributor Guide in the back of VideoHound for full contact information.

INDEXES

ALTERNATE TITLE INDEX A number of videos, particularly older or B-type releases, may have variant titles. This index lists these variant names and refers you to the primary titles as listed in the review section.

MPAA INDEX The MPAA index lists the titles of videos with their respective MPAA Rating of G, PG, PG-13, or R. A list of Unrated features is also included.

CAST/DIRECTOR INDEX The Cast/Director index provides videographies for actors and directors listed in the credits of the family reviews. Although listed in a first name, last name sequence, the names are alphabetized by last name. Film titles, complete with initial year of release, are arranged in alphabetic order. **Tipped triangle indicates a director.**

CATEGORY INDEX A wide range of terms ranging from the serious to silly permit you to video sleuth your favorite categories. The mix, arranged alphabetically by category, includes traditional film genres and sub-genres as well as a feast of *VideoHound* exclusives. Integrated into the index are cross-references, while preceding the index is a list of category definitions. **Bullet indicates a movie rated three bones or above.**

DISTRIBUTOR GUIDE Codes appear at the end of reviews signifying distributors. The full address and phone, toll-free and fax numbers of the distributors can be found in the Distributor Guide. A caution: a small number of distributors lead a nomadic lifestyle that includes frequent address changes. A tiny minority on the list in any given year will also go out of business. Studio distributors do not sell to the general public, they generally act as wholesalers, selling only to retail outlets.

Videohound's Family Video Guide

Abbott and Costello Cartoon Festival

Family Compilation of episodes from a syndicated Hanna-Barbera TV cartoon, putting animated editions of the comedy team in assorted wide-ranging adventures. Abbott provided his own voice, while a stand-in imitated Costello, who had passed away years earlier. Best to stick with real live versions, whose movies and live-action comedy show of the '50s are available on videocassette (and uncannily manage to make it to the front of every reference book).

1966 60m/C V: Bud Abbott, Mel Blanc, Don Messick. **VHS, Beta** *VCI*

Abbott and Costello Meet Captain Kidd 🦴🦴

Family With pirates led by Captain Kidd on their trail, Abbott and Costello follow a treasure map. Bland A&C swashbuckler spoof might hold children's attention, but the usually reliable Laughton seems distinctly disinterested as Kidd. One of the comedy duo's few color films.

1952 70m/C Bud Abbott, Lou Costello, Charles Laughton, Hillary Brooke, Fran Warren, Bill Shirley, Leif Erickson; **D:** Charles Lamont. **VHS, Beta, LV** *NOS, VCI*

Abbott and Costello Meet Dr. Jekyll and Mr. Hyde 🦴🦴

Family Abbott and Costello take on evil Dr. Jekyll, who has transformed himself into the wolfmanish Mr. Hyde and is terrorizing London. An attempt at recapturing the success of "Abbott and Costello Meet Frankenstein" that falls short.

1952 77m/B Bud Abbott, Lou Costello, Boris Karloff, Craig Stevens, Helen Westcott, Reginald Denny; **D:** Charles Lamont. **VHS, Beta** *MCA*

Abbott and Costello Meet Frankenstein 🦴🦴🦴

Family Big-budget A&C classic is one of their best efforts and was, until "Ghostbusters," the nimblest big screen mix of horror and comedy (well, that's if you don't count "Young Frankenstein"). Two unsuspecting baggage clerks deliver a crate containing the not quite dead remains of Dracula and Dr. Frankenstein's monster to a wax museum. The fiends are revived, wreaking havoc with the clerks. Chaney—the wolfman—makes a special appearance to warn the boys that trouble looms, and Price has a unique 'cameo' at the end. Last and most kid-friendly film to use the Universal creatures pioneered in the 1930s.

 *Monster roughhousing.*

1948 83m/B Bud Abbott, Lou Costello, Lon Chaney Jr., Bela Lugosi, Glenn Strange, Lenore Aubert, Jane Randolph; **D:** Charles T. Barton; **V:** Vincent Price. **VHS, Beta, LV** *MCA*

Abel's Island

Family Chasing his wife's scarf on a blustery day, a mouse is whooshed off to an uninhabited isle, where he 'eeks' out a simple, castaway existence and learns to appreciate the basic things in life. Fine version of William Steig's book, animated by Michael Sporn. Ages 4 to 10.

1988 28m/C D: Michael Sporn; **V:** Tim Curry, Lionel Jeffries. **VHS, Beta** *KUI, RAN, LME*

Above the Rim 🦴🦴 ⌐

R/Sr. High-Adult Vulgar, violent hoopster drama about a fiercely competitive inner-city playground game. Kyle-Lee Watson (Martin), a self-involved high school star raised by a saintly single mom (Pinkins), is torn between the lure of the streets and his college recruiting chances.

If you like *Ace Ventura: Pet Detective* (1993), you'll love:

Ace Ventura: When Nature Calls (1995)

Beverly Hills Cop (1984)

Beverly Hills Cop 2 (1987)

Beverly Hills Cop 3 (1994)

Clean Slate (1994)

Curse of the Pink Panther (1983)

Dragnet (1987)

Fletch (1985)

K-9 (1989)

Kuffs (1992)

The Naked Gun: From the Files of Police Squad (1988)

The Pink Panther (1964)

The Pink Panther Strikes Again (1976)

The Return of the Pink Panther (1974)

Revenge of the Pink Panther (1978)

Stop or My Mom Will Shoot! (1992)

Turner & Hooch (1989)

Who Framed Roger Rabbit? (1988)

His odds aren't made any easier by homeboy hustler Birdie (Shakur), who wants to improve his chances of making money on the local games by making sure Watson plays for his team. Energetic b-ball sequences, strong performances lose impact amid formulaic melodrama and the usual courtside obscenities. Debut for director Pollack.

BEWARE *Violence and courtside obscenities may be too strong for even some teens.*

1994 97m/C Duane Martin, Tupac Shakur, Leon, Marlon Wayans, Tonya Pinkins, Bernie Mac; **D:** Jeff Pollack; **W:** Jeff Pollack, Barry Michael Cooper; **M:** Marcus Miller. **VHS, LV** *COL*

The Absent-Minded Professor
🦴🦴🦴 ᵇ

Family Classic Disney fantasy of the era. Professor Brainard forgets his wedding day to invent an anti-gravity substance called flubber (flying rubber, get it?), causing inanimate objects and people to become airborne. Will his fiancee understand? Will the villain Wynn succeed in stealing the stuff? Great sequence of the losing school basketball team taking advantage of flubber during a game. Newly colorized version also available on cassette. The movie which helped popularize flubber-like products such as Silly Putty and Whammo Superballs (the early sixties were a very flubberized era). Followed by "Son of Flubber."

1961 97m/C Fred MacMurray, Nancy Olson, Keenan Wynn, Tommy Kirk, Leon Ames, Ed Wynn; **D:** Robert Stevenson. **VHS, Beta, LV** *DIS, BTV*

Ace Ventura: Pet Detective
🦴🦴 ᵇ

PG-13/Jr. High-Adult Shamelessly silly detective satire casts human cartoon Carrey, he of the rubber limbs and spasmodic facial muscles, as Ace, the guy who'll find missing pets, big or small. When the Miami Dolphins' mascot Snowflake is kidnapped, he abandons his search for an albino pigeon to save the lost dolphin just in time for the Super Bowl. Brain candy running full throttle with juvenile humor, some charm, and the hyper-energetic Carrey, not to mention Young as the police chief with a secret. With the look of a small budget and trashed by the critics, box office smash laughed all the way to the bank, along with Carrey, who catapulted into nearly instant superstardom after seven seasons as the geeky white guy on "In Living Color." Alrighty indeed.

BEWARE *Gross scatological humor, profanity. Ideal for 7th grade boys of all ages and genders who may never grow up.*

1993 87m/C Jim Carrey, Dan Marino, Courteney Cox, Sean Young, Tone Loc; **D:** Tom Shadyac; **W:** Jim Carrey, Tom Shadyac, Jack Bernstein; **M:** Ira Newborn. **VHS, LV, 8mm** *WAR*

Ace Ventura: When Nature Calls 🦴 ᵇ

PG-13/Jr. High-Adult The Aceman cometh again as America's pet pet detective (Carrey) leaves a Himalayan retreat and heads for Africa, there to recover a tribe's sacred animal, a repulsive white bat. Despite hostile indigenous people, an inept translator, sneaky colonialists and numerous poison darts in his posterior, Ace Carreys on. Physical comedy drives the movie but only a few gags are outstanding, particularly one with Ace inside a mechanical rhino, another with a Slinky and a long stairway. Mindless fun, emphasis on "mindless."

BEWARE *Masturbation jokes, sexual references, fake mucous.*

1995 94m/C Jim Carrey, Ian McNeice, Simon Callow, Maynard Eziashi, Bob Gunton, Sophie Okonedo, Tommy Davidson; **D:** Steve Oedekerk; **W:** Steve Oedekerk; **C:** Donald E. Thorin; **M:** Robert Folk. **VHS, LV** *WAR*

Across the Great Divide ♪♪ ♭

G/Family Two orphans must cross the rugged snow-covered Rocky Mountains in 1876 to claim their inheritance—Salem's lot. Well, a 400-acre plot of land in Salem, Oregon. Pleasant and scenic nature adventure, with lots of bears and deer. Ages 4 to 10.

1976 102m/C Robert F. Logan, George Flower, Heather Rattray, Mark Hall; **D:** Stewart Raffill; **W:** Stewart Raffill; **M:** Angelo Badalamenti. **VHS, Beta** *MED, VTR*

Across the Tracks ♪♪

PG-13/Sr. High-Adult Two brothers, one a rebel, the other a straight-A jock, are at odds when the black sheep is pressured into selling drugs. In an attempt to save his brother from a life of crime, the saintly one convinces him to join the school track team, and the two face off in a big meet. Fairly realistic teen drama about a 'good' kid who's not so perfect and a 'bad' kid who's really not such a bad guy. Strong story elements make this tape available in both R and PG-13 versions.

> **BEWARE** *Drunkenness and drug use, violence, profanity, and inferences of irresponsible sex.*

1989 101m/C Rick Schroder, Brad Pitt, Carrie Snodgress; **D:** Sandy Tung; **W:** Sandy Tung; **M:** Joel Goldsmith. **VHS** *ACA*

Adam's Rib ♪♪♪♪

Family Classic war between the sexes cast Tracy and Hepburn as married attorneys on opposite sides of the courtroom in the trial of blonde bombshell Holliday, charged with attempted murder of the lover of her philandering husband. The battle in the courtroom soon takes its toll at home as the couple is increasingly unable to leave their work at the office. Sharp, snappy dialogue by Gordon and Kanin with superb direction by Cukor. Perhaps the best of the nine movies pairing Tracy and Hepburn. Also available colorized.

1950 101m/B Spencer Tracy, Katharine Hepburn, Judy Holliday, Tom Ewell, David Wayne, Jean Hagen, Hope Emerson, Polly Moran, Marvin Kaplan, Paula Raymond, Tommy Noonan; **D:** George Cukor; **W:** Garson Kanin, Ruth Gordon; **M:** Miklos Rozsa. **VHS, Beta, LV** *MGM, HMV*

The Addams Family ♪♪ ♭

PG-13/Jr. High-Adult The TV ghouls gets a high-octane Hollywood treatment (much closer to the original Charles Addams comics than the popular sitcom actually was) that's funny in fits and starts, but no big deal except the budget. Weirdo claiming to be long-lost Uncle Fester shows up at the Addams' home to swindle the family out of their immense fortune. Never mind the thin plot, it's all a series of twists to highlight the morbid clan's eccentricities. Ultimately disappointing but the ensemble cast, sets, and special effects are terrific, and some critics noted ironically that the Addamses were the least dysfunctional

family on the big screen in quite some time. Box office hit that inspired a satisfactory sequel.

> **BEWARE** *Supernatural roughhousing, salty language. Grim jokes about electric chairs, torture and so forth are completely offset by the Addams' unflagging cheeriness.*

1991 102m/C Anjelica Huston, Raul Julia, Christopher Lloyd, Dan Hedaya, Elizabeth Wilson, Judith Malina, Carel Struycken, Dana Ivey, Paul Benedict, Christina Ricci, Jimmy Workman, Christopher Hart, John Franklin; **Cameos:** Marc Shaiman; **D:** Barry Sonnenfeld; **W:** Larry Thompson, Caroline Thompson; **M:** Marc Shaiman. **VHS, Beta, LV** *PAR*

Addams Family Values ♪♪♪

PG-13/Jr. High-Adult The creepy Addams' are back, but this time they leave the dark confines of the mansion to meet the "real" world. New baby Pubert inspires homicidal jealousy in sibs Wednesday and Pugsley, causing Gomez and Morticia to hire a gold-digging, serial-killing nanny with designs on Fester. A step above its predecessor, chock full of black humor, subplots, and one-liners. Cusack fits right in with a salaciously over the top performance and Ricci nearly steals the show again as the deadpan Wednesday.

> **BEWARE** *Profanity, sex talk, but the family is fundamentally decent and won't corrupt anyone's kids and they're not as gruesome as they'd like to be.*

1993 93m/C Anjelica Huston, Raul Julia, Christopher Lloyd, Joan Cusack, Carol Kane, Christina Ricci, Jimmy Workman, Kaitlyn Hooper, Kristen Hooper, Carel Struycken, David Krumholtz, Christopher Hart, Dana Ivey, Peter MacNicol, Christine Baranski, Mercedes McNab; **D:** Barry Sonnenfeld; **W:** Paul Rudnick; **M:** Marc Shaiman. **VHS, Beta** *PAR*

Adios Amigo ♪♪

PG/Jr. High-Adult Offbeat, nearly all-black western comedy has ad-libbing Pryor hustling as a perennially inept con man. Excessive violence and vulgarity are avoided in an attempt to provide good clean family fare; too bad the results aren't more rewarding.

1975 87m/C Fred Williamson, Richard Pryor, Thalmus Rasulala, James Brown, Robert Philip, Mike Henry; **D:** Fred Williamson; **W:** Fred Williamson. **VHS, LV** *SIM, VMK*

Adventures in Babysitting ♪♪

PG-13/Jr. High-Adult During a babysitting job, suburban teen Chris gets a distress call to pick up her runaway friend and has to drag three little kids with her downtown. Flat tire on the freeway starts a chain of perilous encounters with gangsters, prostitutes, African Americans (horrors!), and the unsuspecting parents of the supposedly at-home kids. One of those new, 'sophisticated' Disney comedies (made under their Touchstone banner) featuring a slight, borderline distasteful plot hinging mainly on Shue's enormous charm. Naturally, she delivers the anti-drug message at the start of the tape.

> **BEWARE** *Roughhousing, alcohol use, profanity beyond the call of duty. Sex talk (no action) includes running gags about a Playboy-type magazine whose centerfold model happens to resemble Chris.*

1987 102m/C Elisabeth Shue, Keith Coogan, Maia Brewton, Anthony Rapp, Calvin Levels, Vincent D'Onofrio, Penelope Ann Miller, George Newbern, John Ford Noonan, Lolita David, Albert Collins; **D:** Chris Columbus; **W:** David Simkins; **M:** Michael Kamen. **VHS, Beta, LV, 8mm** *TOU*

Adventures in Dinosaur City &

PG/Primary-Adult Low-budget kiddie movie made it to videocassette before "Jurassic Park" arrived in theaters but loses in nearly every other respect. Invention transports adolescents to a fantasy realm paralleling their favorite TV cartoon—about crime-fighting dinosaurs in the prehistoric era—and the kids assist a heroic T.Rex and his partners against their paper-mache foes. Certainly designed to be less scary than the Spielberg spectacle, but entertainment value verges on extinction.

1992 88m/C Omri Katz, Shawn Hoffman, Tiffanie Poston, Pete Koch, Megan Hughes, Tony Doyle, Mimi Maynard; **D:** Brett Thompson; **W:** Willie Baronet, Lisa Morton; **M:** Fredric Teetsel. **VHS, LV** *REP*

Adventures in Dinosaurland

Family Animated story of a little dinosaur who takes kids back to the stone age.

1983 44m/C VHS *FHE*

Adventures in Odyssey: The Knight Travellers

Family Nicely-animated cartoon in which young Dylan comes to the aid of a kindly inventor whose time-travelling "imagination station," designed for moral instruction, has been stolen and misused by the evil Fred Faustus.

1991 30m/C VHS

Adventures in Spying & &

PG-13/Jr. High-Adult Brian McNichols is on his summer vacation when he discovers a notorious drug lord lives in his neighborhood. There's a $50,000 reward for the villain's apprehension, so Brian and friends try to get the man's picture for the police. Action-packed and geared towards the junior high set, but relies too heavily on coincidence and other plot connivances to compete with espionage flicks aimed at an older market.

1992 92m/C Jill Schoelen, Bernie Coulson, Seymour Cassel, G. Gordon Liddy, Michael Emil; **D:** Hil Covington; **W:** Hil Covington; **M:** James Stemple. **VHS** *NLC*

Adventures in Wonderland: Hare-Raising Magic

Primary Live action modern-day version of Alice's adventures, from Disney, with good special effects and music. Emmy winner. Other volumes in series are Helping Hands (Vol. 2) and The Missing Ring (Vol 3). Ages 3 to 7.

1993 45m/C VHS *TOU*

The Adventures of a Gnome Named Gnorm &

PG/Primary-Adult Subterranean hobbit-like dwarf digs his way to "Upworld" (the original title), modern Los Angeles. Immediately Gnorm the gnome witnesses a murder and a young LAPD detective pals around with him to find out who did it. You'll barely care; clumsy hybrid of cop and fantasy cliches doesn't satisfy either way. Gaps on the audio are remains of profanity removed in an evident attempt to peddle this as a "family" film. Snout-faced Gnorm (only semi-convincingly designed by director and f/x ace Winston) may hold kids' interest for a short while.

⚠ BEWARE ⚠ *Violence, sex talk (even smarmier coming from a gnome).*

1993 86m/C VHS *PGV*

The Adventures of a Two-Minute Werewolf

Family When a teenage boy watches a scary horror movie, he turns into a werewolf, for a while. A comic alternative to "Teen Wolf," based on the book by Gene DeWeese; originally aired as an ABC Weekend Special.

1991 60m/C Lainie Kazan, Melba Moore, Barrie Youngfellow. **VHS** *VTR, AIM*

The Adventures of an American Rabbit & ▷

Family Feature cartoon adventure of unassuming young Rob Rabbit who finds himself receiving the Legacy from a bunny wizard. Before he knows it, Rob has become the superpowered, patriotic protector of animals the world over. All you need to know is that American Rabbit was fully animated—in Japan.

1986 85m/C VHS *BAR*

The Adventures of Babar

Family The charming elephant leaves the jungle to see the outside world in this adaptation of Jean and Laurent de Brunhoff storybooks. Not a cartoon like one would expect; this French adaptation features live actors in elaborate pachyderm costumes.

1985 60m/C VHS, Beta *VCD*

The Adventures of Baron Munchausen & & & ▷

PG/Jr. High-Adult The director of "Time Bandits" reached a high point with this imaginative, chaotic, and under-appreciated marvel based on the tall tales of the Baron, an adventurous aristocrat of European folklore. Interrupting a stage play based on his exploits, the elderly Munchausen recounts mighty battles, perilous bets, meetings with the King of the Moon (Williams), the god Vulcan and his wife Venus, and other odd, fascinating, and funny characters. Wonderful special f/x and visually stunning sets occasionally dwarf the actors but add up to a sumptuous, epic treat in the "Wizard of Oz" tradition.

🚸 *BEWARE* *Surrealistic roughhousing. Some nightmare imagery (including a bony, flying Angel of Death) may be too much for tiny tots. Storyline demands a fair amount of concentration to follow.*

1989 126m/C John Neville, Eric Idle, Sarah Polley, Valentina Cortese, Oliver Reed, Uma Thurman, Sting, Jonathan Pryce, Bill Paterson, Peter Jeffrey, Alison Steadman, Charles McKeown, Dennis Winston, Jack Purvis; *Cameos:* Robin Williams; *D:* Terry Gilliam; *W:* Terry Gilliam; *M:* Michael Kamen. **VHS, Beta, LV, 8mm** COL, CRC

The Adventures of Batman & Robin: Robin

Family From the recent TV cartoon series. "Robin's Reckoning, Parts I & II" finds the boy wonder discovering the man who killed his parents and deciding to take revenge—against Batman's wishes. Ages 7 to 11.
1995 46m/C VHS *WAR*

The Adventures of Batman & Robin: The Joker

Family From the recent TV cartoon series. The Joker breaks out of the asylum in "Christmas with The Joker," bent on destroying Batman's holiday cheer. A lethal chemical compound will be turned loose on Gotham City unless The Joker gets his way in "The Laughing Fish." Ages 7 to 11.
1995 46m/C VHS *WAR*

The Adventures of Batman & Robin: The Riddler

Family More from the recent TV cartoon series. "If You're So Smart, Why Aren't You Rich" finds The Riddler out for revenge and it's up to Batman and Robin to stop him. "Riddler's Reform" (yeah, right) finds the Dynamic Duo's nemesis up to his old tricks. Ages 7 to 11.
1995 45m/C VHS *WAR*

The Adventures of Batman & Robin: Two-Face

Family More from the recent TV cartoon series. "Shadow of the Bat, Parts I & II" finds Batman and Robin trying to clear Police Commissioner Gordon, who's been arrested for corruption. Batman goes undercover to find criminal mastermind Two-Face, and Gordon's daughter turns up as Batgirl to help out. Ages 7 to 11.
1995 46m/C VHS *WAR*

Adventures of Black Beauty

Primary-Jr. High Some of the chapters in Anna Sewell's famous "autobiography of a horse" are presented in a new, animated edition.
1988 58m/C VHS *RHU*

The Adventures of Blinky Bill

Preschool Animated Australian TV series about a mischievous little koala in red overalls who may hide his teacher's spectacles but who always comes through in a crisis, whether it's organizing a fund-raising footrace for a hospital, or fighting a bush fire with is equally cute mates, a kangaroo, a platypus, a wombat and other fauna from down under. Two episodes per tape. Ages 4 to 8.
1994 50m/C VHS *VMK*

The Adventures of Buckaroo Banzai Across the Eighth Dimension 🎞️🎞️🎞️

PG/Family A man of many talents, Buckaroo Banzai (Weller) travels through the eighth dimension in a jet-propelled Ford Fiesta to battle Planet 10 aliens led by the evil Lithgow. Buckaroo incorporates his vast knowledge of medicine, science, music, racing, and foreign relations to his advantage. Offbeat and often humorous cult sci-fi trip.
1984 100m/C Peter Weller, Ellen Barkin, Jeff Goldblum, Christopher Lloyd, John Lithgow, Lewis Smith, Rosalind Cash, Robert Ito, Pepe Serna, Vincent Schiavelli, Dan Hedaya, Yakov Smirnoff, Jamie Lee Curtis; *D:* W.D. Richter; *M:* Michael Boddicker. **VHS, Beta, LV** VES, LIV

The Adventures of Bullwhip Griffin 🎞️🎞️ 🎞️

Family Rowdy, family comedy-adventure set during the California Gold Rush. Proper English butler accompanies his mistress from Boston to San Francisco to find her gold-panning brother. Series of unlikely events soon make the servant into Bullwhip Griffin, the most feared hero in the west. Amusing Disney effort, based on Sid Fleischman's book "By the Great Horn Spoon."

 *Roughhousing.*

1966 110m/C Roddy McDowall, Suzanne Pleshette, Karl Malden, Harry Guardino; *D:* James Neilson. **VHS, Beta** DIS

Adventures of Buster the Bear

Preschool-Primary Joe the Otter doesn't want to share the fish in the stream with Buster, until Grandfather Bullfrog shows him that sharing makes life fun. From the Thornton W. Burgess characters in his "Fables of the Green Forest."
1978 52m/C VHS, Beta *FHE*

The Adventures of Captain Marvel 🎞️🎞️ 🎞️

Family Well-remembered cliff-hanging serial featuring a comic-strip titan who, for a while, was more popular than Superman. Exploring ancient ruins, mild-mannered archaeologist Billy Batson meets a mystic who gives him the awesome powers to say "Shazam!" and transform into

the caped, flying Captain Marvel. The superhero battles against a masked villain out to steal a deadly weapon of antiquity. On tape in two cassettes. Live-action Saturday-morning TV show of the '70s, "Shazam!" is also available.

1941 240m/B Tom Tyler, Frank "Junior" Coghlan, Louise Currie; **D:** William Witney. **VHS, LV** *VCN, REP, MLB*

The Adventures of Curious George

Preschool-Primary Includes two animated episodes based on the series by Margaret and H.A. Rey. In "Curious George," the Man in the Yellow Hat captures George in Africa and brings him home where the monkey tries to learn a new lifestyle. "Curious George Goes to the Hospital" has George eating a puzzle piece, getting a tummyache, and seeking help at the hospital.

1993 30m/C VHS

Adventures of Droopy

Family Cartoondom B-list dog has his day in seven vintage 'toons assembled here, including "Dumb-Hounded," "Wags to Riches," and "Deputy Droopy." Ages 4 to 8.

1955 53m/C D: Tex Avery. **VHS, Beta** *MGM*

The Adventures of Dudley the Dragon: Dudley and the Genie

Preschool The big green costumed character's heart is in the right place—with the environment—but in his attempts to do right, Dudley the Dragon comes off as something of a dud, and his goofy voice makes Barney sound suave by comparison. In this episode of the Canadian TV series the curious dragon meets up with a genie who tries to trick him into using more power than he needs in this gentle introduction to energy conservation. Ages 2 to 7.

1994 30m/C VHS *GKK*

The Adventures of Dudley the Dragon: Dudley Finds His Home

Preschool More adventures of a dragon who awakens after a 100-year nap and becomes fast friends with two 10-year-olds. In this episode Dudley and his friends learn about his new forest home. Ages 2 to 7.

1994 30m/C VHS *GKK*

The Adventures of Dudley the Dragon: Dudley's Tea Party

Preschool A gentle lesson in water conservation with the lazy dragon using so much water for his bath that he doesn't have enough left to make tea for his friends and has to search for more. Ages 2 to 7.

1994 30m/C VHS *GKK*

The Adventures of Dudley the Dragon: Mr. Crabby Tree

Preschool Dudley discovers why old Mr. Crabby Tree (Graham Greene, from "Dances With Wolves") is such a grouch. It seems folks have been taking trees for granted ever since he was a twig. The message is laudable but the singing can get hard to take. Ages 2 to 7.

1994 30m/C Graham Greene. **VHS** *GKK*

The Adventures of Frank and Jesse James

Family Republic Pictures, home of some of the slickest Saturday-matinee serials, made this cowboy saga portraying the outlaw James brothers of the west as good guys, trying to compensate for crimes committed in their names by hitting paydirt in a silver mine. Followup to "Jesse James Rides Again." A double cassette, with 13 action-packed chapters.

1948 180m/B Steve Darrell, Clayton Moore, Noel Neill, Stanley Andrews; **D:** Yakima Canutt. **VHS** *REP, MOV*

The Adventures of Frontier Fremont 🦴🦴

Family A rough and tumble story of a man who leaves the city, grows a beard, and makes the wilderness his home (and the animals his friends). Mountain life, that's the life for me. Almost indistinguishable from Haggerty's "Grizzly Adams," with the usual redeeming panoramic shots of majestic mountains.

1975 95m/C Dan Haggerty, Denver Pyle; **D:** Richard Friedenberg. **VHS, Beta** *VCI*

The Adventures of Huck Finn 🦴🦴🦴

PG/Jr. High-Adult Decent Disney attempt at Mark Twain's complex classic. Mischievous Huck and runaway slave Jim travel down the muddy Mississippi, getting into all sorts of close scrapes and adventures in the pre-Civil War era. The Disney touch dominates: racial slurs are eliminated, Twain's rich dialogue paraphrased (a mistake) and Tom Sawyer written out. Gorgeous photography.

⚠️ BEWARE *Violence, alcohol use. Huck attacked by his brute of a father, Jim faces a lynch mob.*

1993 108m/C Elijah Wood, Courtney B. Vance, Robbie Coltrane, Jason Robards Jr., Ron Perlman, Dana Ivey, Anne Heche, James Gammon, Paxton Whitehead, Tom Aldredge, Curtis Armstrong, Mary Louise Wilson, Frances Conroy; **D:** Stephen Sommers; **W:** Stephen Sommers; **M:** Bill Conti. **VHS, Beta, LV** *DIS, BTV*

The Adventures of Huckleberry Finn 🦴🦴

Family Twain's classic about the original American punk rebel Huck Finn, running away down the Mississippi in a raft and saving a fugitive slave, gets the same bland treatment MGM gave their later "Our Gang" shorts. Rooney is ideally cast, if overaged, as the incorrigible but good-hearted hero, and the script is sometimes funny, but far from Twain—Tom Sawyer doesn't even appear.

1939 89m/B Mickey Rooney, Lynne Carver, Rex Ingram, William Frawley, Walter Connolly; **D:** Richard Thorpe. **VHS, Beta** *MGM, HMV*

The Adventures of Huckleberry Finn 🦴🦴 ᵛ

Family Lively adaptation of the Twain saga in which Huck and runaway slave Jim raft down the Mississippi in search of freedom and adventure. Miscasting of Hodges as Huck hampers the proceedings, but Randall shines as the treacherous King. Strong supporting cast includes silent-era star Buster Keaton as a lion-tamer and real-life boxing champ Moore as Jim.

1960 107m/C Tony Randall, Eddie Hodges, Archie Moore, Patty McCormack, Neville Brand, Mickey Shaughnessy, Judy Canova, Andy Devine, Sherry Jackson, Buster Keaton, Finlay Currie, Josephine Hutchinson, Parley Baer, John Carradine, Royal Dano, Sterling Holloway, Harry Dean Stanton; **D:** Michael Curtiz. **VHS, Beta** *MGM, FCT*

The Adventures of Huckleberry Finn 🦴🦴

Family Classic adventure by Mark Twain of an orphan boy and a runaway slave done again as a TV movie and starring alumni of the sitcom "F-Troop." Lacks the production values of earlier versions.

1978 100m/C Forrest Tucker, Larry Storch, Kurt Ida, Mike Mazurki, Brock Peters; **D:** Jack B. Hively. **VHS, Beta** *NO*

The Adventures of Huckleberry Finn 🦴🦴🦴 ᵛ

Family Made for PBS-TV and closer than any other version in capturing the mighty Mark Twain novel—and it's still just two-thirds of the original story, following Huck's escape from abusive Pap and his journey down the Mississippi with the runaway slave Jim, whom Huck rescues (sort of) with the dubious help of visiting Tom Sawyer. Also here: Huck's view of a bloody feud between two 'grand' plantation families, a grim episode left out of many adaptations. This one doesn't avoid the racism, injustice and rampant religious hypocrisy that Samuel Clemens attacked. As Huck, Day just doesn't look scruffy and ill-bred enough for the role. Strangely, Oakes, who's Tom Sawyer, does! On tape in a two-volume set; a 121-minute condensed version is also available on one cassette.

🛑 BEWARE *Violence, alcohol use, and depiction of slavery and racism.*

1985 240m/C Sada Thompson, Lillian Gish, Richard Kiley, Jim Dale, Barnard Hughes, Patrick Day, Frederic Forrest, Geraldine Page, Butterfly McQueen, Samm-Art Williams; **D:** Peter Hunt. **VHS, Beta** *MCA*

The Adventures of Mark Twain 🦴🦴🦴 ᵛ

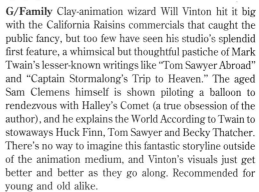

G/Family Clay-animation wizard Will Vinton hit it big with the California Raisins commercials that caught the public fancy, but too few have seen his studio's splendid first feature, a whimsical but thoughtful pastiche of Mark Twain's lesser-known writings like "Tom Sawyer Abroad" and "Captain Stormalong's Trip to Heaven." The aged Sam Clemens himself is shown piloting a balloon to rendezvous with Halley's Comet (a true obsession of the author), and he explains the World According to Twain to stowaways Huck Finn, Tom Sawyer and Becky Thatcher. There's no way to imagine this fantastic storyline outside of the animation medium, and Vinton's visuals just get better and better as they go along. Recommended for young and old alike.

🛑 BEWARE *Mature themes lurk around the edges, just as in Twain's own work. Note the chilling portrayal of Satan as an angel devoid of conscience in "The Mysterious Stranger" adaptation.*

1985 86m/C D: Will Vinton; **W:** Susan Shadburne; **V:** James Whitmore, Chris Ritchie, Gary Krug, Michele Mariana. **VHS, Beta, LV** *BAR*

The Adventures of Mary-Kate & Ashley: The Case of the Fun House Mystery

Primary Olsen twins must solve a at an amusement park involving an unusual funhouse. Ages 4 to 9.

1996 ?m/C VHS *KID, AVE*

The Adventures of Mary-Kate & Ashley: The Case of the Logical Ranch

Primary Olsen twins Mary-Kate and Ashley investigate strange goings-on at a ranch. Ages 4 to 9.

1996 ?m/C VHS *KID, AVE*

The Adventures of Mary-Kate & Ashley: The Case of the Mystery Cruise

Primary A cruise ship is the setting for this musical, mystery adventure for Olsen twins, Mary-Kate and Ashley. Ages 4 to 9.

1996 ?m/C VHS *KID, AVE*

TV's Favorite Twins Hit the Big Screen

The extremely popular twins from TV's "Full House" fame are capitalizing on their eight-year stint on the popular sitcom. Mary-Kate and Ashley Olsen have released their own albums, appeared on TV specials, and even released their own mystery video series, "The Adventures of Mary-Kate and Ashley Olsen." And most recently they've hit the big time, making the move to the silver screen in their first feature film, *It Takes Two.*

It's a rich girl/poor girl tale co-starring Kirstie Alley and Steve Guttenberg. The two girls from opposite sides of the track play Cupid to the two adults with interesting effects. This is the icing on the cake for the twosome, who have deals with Warner Bros. for more feature films, a new ABC series, and more detective videos. Watch out for these two—they'll probably be in your house soon.

The Adventures of Mary-Kate & Ashley: The Case of the Sea World Adventure

Primary Olsen twins, Mary-Kate and Ashley, head to Sea World for fun but end up solving a mystery, and providing lots of publicity for Shamu and company. Ages 4 to 9.
1996 ?m/C VHS *KID, AVE*

The Adventures of Mary-Kate & Ashley: The Case of the Shark Encounter

Primary Mary-Kate and Ashley are on the case involving a great white shark. Filmed at Sea World. Ages 4 to 9.
1996 ?m/C VHS *KID, AVE*

The Adventures of Mary-Kate & Ashley: The Case of the U.S. Space Camp Mission

Primary Mary-Kate and Ashley must solve a space mystery before it destroys the next rocket launch. Our money's on them. Filmed at Space Camp. Ages 4 to 9.
1996 ?m/C VHS *KID, AVE*

The Adventures of Mary-Kate & Ashley: The Case of Thorn Mansion

Primary Olsen twins, Mary-Kate and Ashley take their by now finely-honed investigative skills to a local mansion. Ages 4 to 9.
1996 m/C VHS *KID, AVE*

The Adventures of Mary-Kate & Ashley: The Christmas Caper

Primary The exceedingly cute Olsen twins must solve a mystery that threatens to destroy their Christmas. Ages 4 to 9.
1996 ?m/C VHS *KID, AVE*

Adventures of Mighty Mouse, Vol. 1

Family Animated cartoons featuring the super mouse, vintage animator Paul Terry's most popular Terrytoon star, a takeoff on the newly minted Superman character. Mighty Mouse made his debut in 1942, and these shorts hail from that era. Additional volumes available.
194? 30m/C VHS, Beta *FOX*

The Adventures of Milo & Otis
🦴🦴🦴

G/Family Milo is a trouble-prone tabby kitten, and Otis is his best pal, a pug-nosed pup. They romp on a farm until Milo is accidentally swept off in a box on a river. Otis follows, and after many adventures both come home with families of their own. Delightful live-action children's adventure in which no humans appear isn't strong on plot but compensates with comedian Dudley Moore's priceless narration (he also does all the character voices). Edited from a 1986 Japanese production, "Koneko Monogatari," that was record-breaking success in its homeland, but universal in appeal. Also known as "Milo & Otis."
1989 89m/C D: Masanori Hata; **W:** Mark Saltzman; **M:** Michael Boddicker. **VHS, Beta, LV** *COL, RDG, HMV*

The Adventures of Oliver Twist

Primary Animated version of Dickens' masterpiece about the wildly changing fortunes of an impoverished orphan cast out on the streets of London.
1993 91m/C VHS *VTR*

The Adventures of Peter Cottontail

Primary Animated series featuring the mischievous rabbit created by Thornton W. Burgess, and his continuing exploits throughout 26 two-episode tapes.

1986 30m/C VHS, Beta *AIM*

The Adventures of Peter Cottontail and His Friends of the Green Forest

Preschool-Primary Series of 26 videotapes with two stories on each chronicling the adventures of Peter Cottontail and other Thornton W. Burgess characters.

1988 60m/C VHS, Beta *AIM*

Adventures of Pinocchio

Primary-Jr. High Group of tales about the puppet who wants to become a real boy.

1988 63m/C VHS *NO*

The Adventures of Pinocchio

G/Family Live-action version of Carlo Collodi's story about woodcarver Gepetto (Landau) who carves himself a puppet son (Thomas) who longs to be a real boy. Check out Schneider as the fox and Neuwirth as the cat. Jim Henson's Creature Shop provided the animatronic magic to bring Pinocchio to life and he really looks life-like, too! So life-like was the puppet that crew members and Landau himself treated him as part of the gang.

1996 96m/C Martin Landau, Jonathan Taylor Thomas, Rob Schneider, Bebe Neuwirth, Udo Kier; **D:** Steven Barron; **W:** Steven Barron, Tom Benedek, Sherry Mills. **VHS** *NLC*

The Adventures of Raggedy Ann & Andy: Pirate Adventure

Preschool Raggedy Ann and Andy recover leprechaun's stolen pot of gold in this excerpt from the TV cartoon. Additional volumes available.

1994 30m/C VHS *FOX*

Adventures of Red Ryder ♫♫

Family The thrills of the rugged west are presented in this 12-episode serial. Based on the then-famous comic strip character.

1940 240m/B Donald (Don "Red") Barry, Noah Beery Sr.; **D:** William Witney. **VHS, Beta** *VCN, MLB*

Adventures of Reddy the Fox

Preschool-Primary While Granny Fox is away, Reddy the Fox gets into all kinds of trouble, until, much to his relief, Granny returns to set everything right. Based on Thornton W. Burgess' "Fables of the Green Forest."

1978 52m/C VHS, Beta *FHE*

The Adventures of Robin Hood
♫♫♫♫

Family Rollicking Technicolor tale of the legendary outlaw, regarded as the Mother of All Swashbucklers. The justice-minded rebel of Sherwood Forest battles the Normans, outwits evil Prince John, duels Sir Guy of Gisbourne, and gallantly romances the initially scornful Maid Marian. Grand castle sets and lush forest photography display ample evidence of the huge (in 1938) budget of $2 million plus. Flynn's youthful enthusiasm as the Saxon hero is contagious, and he performed most of his own stunts. Also available in letter-box format.

⚠ BEWARE *Violence.*

1938 102m/C Errol Flynn, Olivia de Havilland, Basil Rathbone, Alan Hale, Una O'Connor, Claude Rains, Patric Knowles, Eugene Pallette, Herbert Mundin, Melville Cooper, Ian Hunter, Montagu Love; **D:** Michael Curtiz; **W:** Norman Reilly, Seton I. Miller; **M:** Erich Wolfgang Korngold. **Award Nominations:** Academy Awards '38: Best Picture; **Awards:** Academy Awards '38: Best Film Editing, Best Interior Decoration, Best Original Score. **VHS, Beta, LV** *MGM, FOX, CRC*

The Adventures of Rocky & Bullwinkle: Birth of Bullwinkle

Family Jay Ward's classic TV 1959 cartoon "Rocky and His Friends" proved that a 'kiddie' show could have a fun dose of sophisticated satire for grownups too. The antics of Bullwinkle Moose and Rocky the Flying Squirrel (plus supporting performers like Dudley Do-Right, Aesop and Son, Mr. Peabody and Sherman) are on tape courtesy of Disney. Note that "Birth of Bullwinkle" in no way means this is an original episode; it's a reference to the classical painting parody on the box, a gag continued in ensuing volumes: "Blue Moose," "Canadian Gothic," "La Grande Moose," "Mona Moose," "Norman Moosewell," "Vincent Van Moose," and "Whistler's Moose."

1991 38m/C V: June Foray, William Conrad, Bill Scott. **VHS, Beta, LV** *TOU, FCT*

The Adventures of Sherlock Holmes' Smarter Brother ♫♫♫

PG/Jr. High-Adult The unknown brother of the famous Sherlock Holmes takes on some of his brother's more disposable excess cases and makes some hilarious moves. Moments of engaging farce borrowed from the Mel Brooks school of parody (and parts of the Brooks ensemble as well).

⚠ BEWARE *Sexual innuendo.*

1978 91m/C Gene Wilder, Madeline Kahn, Marty Feldman, Dom DeLuise, Leo McKern, Roy Kinnear, John Le Mesurier, Douglas Wilmer, Thorley Walters; **D:** Gene Wilder; **W:** Gene Wilder. **VHS, Beta** *FOX*

The Adventures of Sinbad the Sailor 🦴🦴

Preschool-Primary Sinbad receives a map to a treasure island where fabulous stores of jewels are hidden, and, in his search, falls in love with the King's daughter in this animated adventure.
1973 88m/C VHS, Beta *LIV, FHE*

Adventures of Smilin' Jack

Family WWII flying ace Smilin' Jack Martin comes to life in this action-packed serial. Character from the Zack Moseley comic strip about air force fighting over China.
1943 90m/B Tom Brown, Sidney Toler; *D:* Ray Taylor. **VHS, Beta** *SNC, NOS, VAN*

The Adventures of SuperTed

Family Four animated adventures from Britain featuring the teddy bear transformed by a friendly alien into a flying, intergalactic super bear.
1990 ?m/C VHS, Beta *TTC*

The Adventures of Teddy Ruxpin

Preschool Teddy Ruxpin and his friend Grubby the Octopede set out on a search for a fabulous treasure, but are captured by the grime-encrusted Mudblups. Commercialism-encrusted cartoon intended to promote the talking Teddy Ruxpin toys.
1986 44m/C VHS, Beta *LIV*

The Adventures of the Little Koala and Friends

Family Excerpt from the cable-TV cartoon stars Roobear, a koala cub, caught up in a mystery Down Under with messages about conservation and animal protection implicit.
1987 47m/C VHS *FHE*

The Adventures of the Wilderness Family 🦴🦴

G/Family Modern-day family, the Robinsons (as in Swiss Family, hint, hint) are fed up with the city and retreat to the mountains of Colorado, build a log cabin and adopt a pioneer lifestyle. First and best-known of several back-to-nature pics that migrated through regional theaters in the mid-70s.
1976 100m/C Robert F. Logan, Susan Damante Shaw; *D:* Stewart Raffill; *W:* Stewart Raffill. **VHS, Beta, LV** *MED, VTR*

The Adventures of Timmy the Tooth: Big Mouth Gulch

Preschool Timmy and his friends travel back to the wild west town of Big Mouth Gulch where the folks gather at the Dry Mouth Saloon. But mean Goony the Kid is stir-ring up trouble and it's up to Sheriff Timmy to save the day (thanks to a spelling bee). Yippee. Ages 2 to 6.
1994 30m/C VHS *MCA*

The Adventures of Timmy the Tooth: Lost My Brush

Preschool Brushbrush, a doglike toothbrush (talk about your canines), wanders off to chase butterflies and gets lost, leading Cavity Goon and Ms. Sweety to hatch a plot to capture Timmy when he goes searching for his pal. But Timmy's Flossmore Valley friends come to the rescue. Ages 2 to 6.
1994 34m/C VHS *MCA*

The Adventures of Timmy the Tooth: Molar Island

Preschool Timmy and Brushbrush take a vacation to an island paradise, which turns out to be sinking—or maybe stinking, thanks to the Gingivitis Tribe. Ages 2 to 6.
1994 30m/C VHS *MCA*

The Adventures of Timmy the Tooth: Operation: Secret Birthday Surprise!

Preschool Timmy's worried that everyone's forgotten his birthday but Mr. Wisdom's magical dream tells Tim what Flossmore Valley would be like without him. Then Timmy realizes just how much he means to all his friends. Sort of "It's a Wonderful Life" for rinse-and-spit fans. Ages 2 to 6.
1994 30m/C VHS *MCA*

The Adventures of Timmy the Tooth: Timmy in Space

Preschool "Commander" Timmy and his best friend Brushbrush boldly go where no tooth has gone before—into a far-off galaxy to fight the evil Cavity Goon and Ms. Sweety. Seems they've stolen a space station and it's up to Timmy to return the ship to its rightful owners. Ages 2 to 6.
1994 29m/C VHS *MCA*

The Adventures of Tom Sawyer 🦴🦴

Family Tom Sawyer, mischievous Missouri boy, gets into all kinds of trouble in this white-washed, made-for-TV adaptation of the Mark Twain classic. Everyone (except for Tyler as the homeless Huck Finn) seems remarkably well-groomed; even Injun Joe wears his Sunday best.

[BEWARE] *Violence and alcohol use.*

1973 76m/C Jane Wyatt, Buddy Ebsen, Vic Morrow, John McGiver, Josh Albee, Jeff Tyler. **VHS, Beta** *MCA*

The Adventures of Ultraman

Family Revised version of the Japanese series "Ultraman," a futuristic hero from a distant planet who is able to get quite large when necessary and battle Godzilla lookalikes.

1981 90m/C VHS, Beta *FHE*

The Adventures of Walt Disney's Alice

Family Three early Disney shorts featuring Lewis Carroll's cast of characters: "Alice's Egg Plant," "Alice's Orphan," and "Alice the Toreador." Silent.

1925 35m/B VHS, Beta *JEF*

Aesop's Fables

Preschool-Primary Cool Cos presents this cartoon special with morals, ideal for teaching kids what's right and wrong. From the same producers as Cosby's "Fat Albert" series.

1988 30m/C Bill Cosby. **VHS** *SVE, WAR*

Aesop's Fables, Vol. 1: The Hen with the Golden Egg

Family Nine cartoon fables are retold in this collection, including "The Lion in Love," "The Dog and His Image," and "The Crow and the Fox." Plus 6 more. Additional volumes available.

1987 50m/C VHS, Beta *VES, LIV*

Africa Screams 🦴🦴 ▷

Family Abbott and Costello go on an African safari in possession of a secret map. Unheralded independent A&C film is actually quite good in the stupid vein, with lots of jungle slapstick, generally good production values and a supporting cast of familiar comedy faces.

1949 79m/B Lou Costello, Bud Abbott, Shemp Howard, Hillary Brooke, Joe Besser, Clyde Beatty; **D:** Charles T. Barton. **VHS, Beta, LV** *KAR, MRV, CNG*

Africa Texas Style 🦴🦴

Family East African rancher hires an American rodeo star and his faithful Navajo sidekick to help run his wild game ranch. Decent family adventure from "Flipper" creator Ivan Tors, which served as the pilot for the TV series "Cowboy in Africa." Features lots of wildlife footage (actually shot at Africa U.S.A. outside Los Angeles).

1967 109m/C Hugh O'Brian, John Mills, Nigel Green, Tom Nardini; *Cameos:* Hayley Mills; **D:** Andrew Marton; **M:** Malcolm Arnold. **VHS** *REP*

African Journey

Family A moving, cross-cultural drama of friendship. A young black American goes to Africa for the summer to be with his divorced father who is working in the dia-

TV Shows and Classics Hit the Video Market

Kids these days spend hours upon hours in front of the TV and savvy video companies are giving them more of what they want. A trend of more direct-to-video release of popular TV series and classic titles has hit the shelves. And kids can watch their favorite shows over and over again. (Like they didn't already.)

One of the most obvious and successful stories in the crossover to video world is MCA/Universal's "Timmy the Tooth." But successes have also been made in the land of Saban's "Mighty Morphin Power Rangers" and the Lyons Group's "Barney." Other groups, including Sony Wonder, Nickelodeon, PolyGram, and the Cartoon Network are also catching the video craze bus.

Popularity of the shows as a TV series can make or break its video release. Kidvision recognized the popularity of TV's "Full House" stars Mary-Kate and Ashley Olsen and released a video series following the girls on mysterious adventures. Companies are also releasing and re-releasing classics like ABC's "Schoolhouse Rock" and CBS/Fox's "Dr. Seuss." And keep in mind, once these videos are out there, kids will be encouraged to tune in on TV, too. So, it's a win-win situation for TV and video producers. So, look for more of your favorites on video.

mond mines. There he meets a young black African like himself; they overcome cultural clashes and learn respect for one another. Beautiful scenery, filmed in Africa. Part of the "Wonderworks" series.

1989 174m/C Jason Blicker, Pedzisai Sithole. **VHS** *PME, HMV, BTV*

The African Queen ♪♪♪♪

Family After bible-thumping spinster Hepburn's missionary brother is killed in WWI Africa, hard-drinking, dissolute steamer captain Bogart offers her safe passage. Not satisfied with sanctuary, she persuades him to destroy a German gunboat blocking the British advance. The two spend most of their time battling aquatic obstacles and each other, rather than the Germans. Time alone on a African river turns mistrust and aversion to love, a transition effectively counterpointed by the continuing suspense of their daring mission. Classic war of the sexes script adapted from C.S. Forester's novel makes wonderful use of natural dialogue and humor. Shot on location in Africa.

BEWARE *Alcohol use, a massacre, and (Yeccch!) leeches.*

1951 105m/C Humphrey Bogart, Katharine Hepburn, Robert Morley, Theodore Bikel, Peter Bull, Walter Gotell; **D:** John Huston; **W:** John Huston, James Agee. **Award Nominations:** Academy Awards '51: Best Actress (Hepburn), Best Director (Huston), Best Screenplay; **Awards:** Academy Awards '51: Best Actor (Bogart). **VHS, Beta, LV** *FOX, FCT, TLF*

African Story Magic

Primary Kwaku, a boy from the inner city travels magically to Africa and hears intriguing folk tales which underlying message is that all hearts are the same color. Ages 3 to 10.

1992 27m/C VHS *LIV, FAF*

Against A Crooked Sky ♪♪

G/Family During the frontier days a 15-year-old boy sets out with an elderly trapper to rescue his sister, captured by Apaches. Family oriented western with an element of danger but otherwise standard ingredients.

BEWARE *Violence, including the killing of a heroic dog.*

1975 89m/C Richard Boone, Stewart Peterson, Clint Ritchie, Geoffrey Land, Jewel Blanch; **D:** Earl Bellamy. **VHS, Beta** *LIV, VES*

The Age of Innocence ♪♪♪

PG/Jr. High-Adult Magnificently lavish adaptation of Edith Wharton's novel of the pasion thwarted by convention is visually stunning, but don't expect action since these people kill with a word or gesture. Lead performances are strong though perhaps miscast, with Ryder an exception. Outwardly docile and conventional, she nevertheless holds on to her husband with steely manipulation. Woodward's narration of Wharton's observations helps sort out what goes on behind proper facades. Although slow, see this one for the beautiful authenticity, thanks to Scorsese, who obviously labored over the small details. He shows up as a photographer; his parents appear in a scene on a train.

1993 138m/C Daniel Day-Lewis, Michelle Pfeiffer, Winona Ryder, Richard E. Grant, Alec McCowen, Miriam Margolyes, Sian Phillips, Geraldine Chaplin, Stuart Wilson, Mary Beth Hurt, Michael Gough, Alexis Smith, Jonathan Pryce, Robert Sean Leonard; **Cameos:** Martin Scorsese; **D:** Martin Scorsese; **W:** Jay Cocks, Martin Scorsese; **M:** Elmer Bernstein. **Award Nominations:** Academy Awards '93: Best Adapted Screenplay, Best Art Direction/Set Decoration, Best Supporting Actress (Ryder); Directors Guild of America Awards '93: Best Director (Scorsese); Golden Globe Awards '94: Best Actress—Drama (Pfeiffer), Best Director (Scorsese), Best Film—Drama; **Awards:** Academy Awards '93: Best Costume Design; British Academy Awards '94: Best Supporting Actress (Margolyes); Golden Globe Awards '94: Best Supporting Actress (Ryder); National Board of Review Awards '93: Best Director (Scorsese), Best Supporting Actress (Ryder). **VHS, LV, 8mm** *COL*

Ah, Wilderness! ♪♪♪ ♪

Jr. High-Adult Well-done comedy based on the Eugene O'Neill play about a teenage boy (Linden) in small-town America, learning to be a man in the course of one summer. His father is of little help on the topic, so a rascally uncle pushes the youth to experiment with booze and girls. A minor classic, with Rooney in a supporting role as an underaged brat; in the mediocre 1948 musical remake "Summer Holiday" (also on video) he played the lead.

BEWARE *Alcohol use.*

1935 101m/B Wallace Beery, Lionel Barrymore, Aline MacMahon, Eric Linden, Cecilia Parker, Spring Byington, Mickey Rooney, Charley Grapewin, Frank Albertson; **D:** Clarence Brown. **VHS** *MGM, BTV*

The Air Up There ♪♪ ♪

PG/Jr. High-Adult Jimmy Dolan (Bacon) is an assistant college basketball coach who's a little down-on-his-luck. Figuring he needs a career boost, he heads to the African village of Winabi to recruit talented (and tall) Saleh (Maina) to play b-ball at his college. But Saleh is next in line to be the tribe's king and doesn't want to leave. Stupid American in foreign country learning from the natives story is lighthearted, but relies heavily on formula—and borders on the stereotypical, though climatic game is a lot of fun.

BEWARE *On-the-court profanity and fighting.*

1994 108m/C Kevin Bacon, Charles Gitona Maina, Sean McCann, Dennis Patrick; **D:** Paul Michael Glaser; **W:** Max Apple; **M:** David Newman. **VHS, LV** *HPH*

Airborne ♪ ♪

PG/Jr. High-Adult It's dueling in-lines as cool California dude Mitchell gets transplanted to Cincinnati for a school year, and has to prove himself when those midwestern school bullies come after him. Skating race allows Mitchell to show the Ohioans a thing or two about rollerblades. Wee wheel epic appealing largely to ball-bearing brained.

1993 91m/C Shane McDermott, Seth Green, Brittney Powell, Edie McClurg, Pat O'Brien; **D:** Rob Bowman; **W:** Bill Apablasa; **M:** Stewart Copeland. **VHS, Beta, LV** *WAR*

Airheads ♪♪ ♪

PG-13/Jr. High-Adult "Wayne's World" meets "Dog Day Afternoon." Silly farce has three metal heads (Buscemi, Fraser, Sandler) holding a radio station hostage in order to get their demo tape played. Events snowball and they receive instant fame. Cast and crew rich with subversive comedic talents, including Sandler and Farley from "Saturday Night Live." Metal-heavy soundtrack authenticity supplied by White Zombie and The Galactic Cowboys.

> **BEWARE** *Profanity, adolescent sexual droolings. If Beavis and Butthead were real people they'd be these guys.*

1994 91m/C Brendan Fraser, Steve Buscemi, Adam Sandler, Chris Farley, Michael McKean, Judd Nelson, Joe Mantegna, Michael Richards, Ernie Hudson, Amy Locane, Nina Siemaszko, John Melendez; **D:** Michael Lehmann; **W:** Rich Wilkes; **M:** Carter Burwell. **VHS** *NYR*

Airplane! 🦴🦴🦴 ▽

PG/Family Classic lampoon of disaster flicks is stupid but funny and launched a bevy of wanna-be spoofs. But it's still the best. Former pilot who's lost both his girl (she's the attendant) and his nerve takes over the controls of a jet when the crew is hit with food poisoning. The passengers become increasingly crazed and ground support more surreal as our hero struggles to land the plane. Clever, fast-paced, and very funny parody mangles every Hollywood cliche within reach. The gags are so furiously paced that when one bombs it's hardly noticeable. Launched Nielsen's second career as a comic actor. And it ain't over till it's over: don't miss the amusing final credits. Followed by lower flying "Airplane 2: The Sequel."

> **BEWARE** *Some profanity, innuendo. Best for kids who have seen "real" midair melodramas because so much here depends on parody.*

1980 88m/C Robert Hays, Julie Hagerty, Lloyd Bridges, Peter Graves, Robert Stack, Leslie Nielsen, Stephen Stucker, Ethel Merman; **Cameos:** Kareem Abdul-Jabbar, Barbara Billingsley; **D:** Jerry Zucker, Jim Abrahams, David Zucker; **W:** Jerry Zucker, Jim Abrahams, David Zucker; **M:** Elmer Bernstein. **VHS, Beta, LV, 8mm** *PAR*

Airplane 2: The Sequel 🦴🦴

PG/Jr. High-Adult Not a Zucker, Abrahams and Zucker effort, and sorely missing their slapstick and script finesse. The first passenger space shuttle has taken off for the moon and there's a mad bomber on board. Given the number of stars mugging, it's more of a loveboat in space than a fitting sequel to "Airplane." Nonetheless, some funny laughs and gags.

> **BEWARE** *Profanity, innuendo. See comments about "Airplane!"*

1982 84m/C Robert Hays, Julie Hagerty, Lloyd Bridges, Raymond Burr, Peter Graves, William Shatner, Sonny Bono, Chuck Connors, Chad Everett, Stephen Stucker, Rip Torn, Ken Finkleman, Sandahl Bergman; **D:** Ken Finkleman; **M:** Elmer Bernstein. **VHS, Beta, LV** *PAR*

Airport 🦴🦴🦴

G/Family Old-fashioned disaster thriller built around an all-star cast, fairly moronic script, and an unavoidable accident during the flight of a passenger airliner. A box-office hit that paved the way for many lesser disaster flicks (including its many sequels) detailing the reactions of the passengers and crew as they cope with impending doom. Considered to be the best of the "Airport" series; adapted from the Arthur Hailey novel.

> **BEWARE** *Someone is carrying someone else's child. This is the movie to see BEFORE the kids see "Airplane!"*

1970 137m/C Dean Martin, Burt Lancaster, Jean Seberg, Jacqueline Bisset, George Kennedy, Helen Hayes, Van Heflin, Maureen Stapleton, Barry Nelson, Lloyd Nolan; **D:** George Seaton; **W:** George Seaton. **Award Nominations:** Academy Awards '70: Best Adapted Screenplay, Best Art Direction/Set Decoration, Best Cinematography, Best Costume Design, Best Film Editing, Best Picture, Best Sound, Best Supporting Actress (Stapleton), Best Original Score; **Awards:** Academy Awards '70: Best Supporting Actress (Hayes); Golden Globe Awards '71: Best Supporting Actress (Stapleton). **VHS, Beta, LV** *MCA, BTV*

Airport '75 🦴🦴

PG/Jr. High-Adult After a mid-air collision, a jumbo 747 is left pilotless. Airline attendant Black must fly da plane. She does her cross-eyed best in this absurd sequel to "Airport" built around a lesser "all-star cast." Safe on the ground, Heston tries to talk the airline hostess/pilot into landing, while the impatient Kennedy continues to grouse as leader of the foam-ready ground crew. A slick, insincere attempt to find box office magic again (which unfortunately worked, leading to two more sequels).

1975 107m/C Charlton Heston, Karen Black, George Kennedy, Gloria Swanson, Helen Reddy, Sid Caesar, Efrem Zimbalist Jr., Susan Clark, Dana Andrews, Linda Blair, Myrna Loy; **D:** Jack Smight. **VHS, Beta** *GKK*

Airport '77 🦴🦴

PG/Jr. High-Adult Billionaire Stewart fills his converted passenger jet with priceless art and sets off to Palm Beach for a museum opening, joined by an uninvited gang of hijackers. Twist to this in-flight disaster is that the bad time in the air occurs underwater, a novel (and some might say, desperate) twist to the old panic in the plane we're all gonna die formula. With a cast of familiar faces, some of them stars and some of them just familiar faces, this is yet another sequel to "Airport" and another box-office success, leading to the last of the tired series in 1979.

> **BEWARE** *Violence in the air, which will not sit well with those afraid to fly.*

1977 114m/C Jack Lemmon, James Stewart, Lee Grant, Brenda Vaccaro, Joseph Cotten, Olivia de Havilland, Darren McGavin, Christopher Lee, George Kennedy, Kathleen Quinlan; **D:** Jack Smight. **VHS, Beta, LV** *MCA*

Aladdin 🦴

PG/Jr. High-Adult Spencer, a massive guy who usually plays roughneck cowpokes in spaghetti westerns, does the genie bit for a little boy in this silly Italian comedy that modernizes the Aladdin fable—but not the primitive f/x.

1986 97m/C Bud Spencer, Luca Venantini, Janet Agren, Julian Voloshin, Umberto Raho; **D:** Bruno Corbucci. **VHS, Beta** *MED*

Aladdin 🦴🦴🦴 ▽

G/Family Disney naturally took the crown for the most financially successful cartoon of all time. Boy meets prin-

cess, loses her, finds her, wins her from evil vizier and nasty parrot. Superb animation triumphs over mostly average songs and storyline by capitalizing on Robin Williams' talent for ad-libbing with lightning speed as Aladdin's irrepressible big blue genie, though one wonders if his celebrity spoofs (Arsenio Hall, for example), will endure for as long as the imagery in "Pinocchio" or "Beauty and the Beast." Adults will enjoy the 1,001 impersonations while kids will get a kick out of the adventure. ♫ A Whole New World; Prince Ali; Friend Like Me; One Jump Ahead; Arabian Nights.

1992 90m/C D: Ron Clements, John Musker; **W:** Ron Clements, John Musker, Ted Elliot, Terry Rossio; **M:** Alan Menken, Howard Ashman, Tim Rice; **V:** Robin Williams, Scott Weinger, Linda Larkin, Jonathan Freeman, Frank Welker, Gilbert Gottfried, Douglas Seale, Brad Kane, Lea Salonga. **Award Nominations:** Academy Awards '92: Best Song ("Friend Like Me"), Best Sound, Best Sound Effects Editing; **Awards:** Academy Awards '92: Best Song ("A Whole New World"), Best Original Score; Golden Globe Awards '93: Best Song ("A Whole New World"), Best Score; MTV Movie Awards '93: Best Comedic Performance (Williams). **VHS, Beta** *DIS, BTV*

Aladdin and His Magic Lamp

Family Another version of the classic tale brought to life via animation, before the conclusive Disney edition.
1969 72m/C D: Jean Image. **VHS** *RHI*

Aladdin and His Wonderful Lamp 🦴🦴 ▷

Family In this excellent "Faerie Tale Theatre" version, Aladdin is Robert Carradine, the Princess is Valerie Bertinelli and, best of all, the Genie is James Earl Jones. Most entertaining. Directed by Tim Burton, before he became famous for "Beetlejuice," "Batman" and "Edward Scissorhands." Ages 5 and up.
1984 60m/C Valerie Bertinelli, Robert Carradine, Leonard Nimoy, James Earl Jones; **D:** Tim Burton. **VHS, Beta** *KUI, FOX, FCT*

Aladdin and the King of Thieves

Family Second direct-to-video saga based on Disney's "Aladdin," once again features Robin Williams as the voice of the genie (after he settled his dispute with Disney). Aladdin's married Jasmine but gets involved with a search for his family. Other volumes available.
1996 m/C V: Robin Williams. **VHS** *DIS*

Aladdin and the Wonderful Lamp

Family Japanese-animated version of the classic tale wherein Aladdin must summon his magical genie to defeat the wicked wizard and own the most valuable treasures in the land.
1982 65m/C VHS, Beta *MED*

Alakazam the Great! 🦴 ▷

Preschool American version of the Japanese cartoon feature "Saiyu-ki" wasn't all that great once it had been

dubbed in English. Plot deals with a boastful monkey sent on a dangerous quest which teaches him humility.
1961 84m/C D: Lee Kresel; **V:** Frankie Avalon, Dodie Stevens, Jonathan Winters, Arnold Stang, Sterling Holloway. **VHS** *CNG*

Alan & Naomi 🦴🦴🦴

PG/Jr. High-Adult In 1944, 14-year-old Brooklyn kid Alan Silverman is asked to befriend a child refugee of the war raging across Europe. Naomi witnessed the Nazis killing her father and has retreated into a world of her own. Reluctantly, the boy builds a nurturing friendship with the fragile girl that becomes a growing experience for him as well. Fine performances elevate an earnest but somewhat cliched coming-of-age tale. Based on the novel by Myron Levoy.

> **BEWARE!** *Brutal Holocaust memories. Shouldn't be a problem for teens and mature pre-teens.*

1992 95m/C Lukas Haas, Vanessa Zaoui, Michael Gross, Amy Aquino, Kevin Connolly, Zohra Lampert; **D:** Sterling Van Wagenen; **W:** Jordan Horowitz; **M:** Dick Hyman. **VHS, LV** *COL*

Alaska 🦴🦴 ▷

PG/Family Brother and sister tackle the treacherous Alaskan wilderness after their bush-pilot father's plane crashes in the icy mountain regions. When searchers give up, the two teens take matters into their own hands and set out on a search party of their own. Along the way, they battle the weather and the outdoors, an evil poacher, and they rescue an orphaned polar bear, who returns the favor. Kids may be interested to learn that the two teen actors were trained in rock climbing, sea kayaking, and whitewater canoeing in preparation for the film and performed a lot of the stunts themselves.

> **BEWARE!** *Some mild language and adventure/peril.*

1996 ?m/C Thora Birch, Vincent Kartheiser, Dirk Benedict, Charlton Heston; **D:** Fraser Heston; **W:** Andy Burg. **VHS** *NYR*

Alex 🦴🦴 ▷

Jr. High-Adult Just in time to ride the coattails of the Olympics, this inspirational story follows a 15-year-old New Zealand swimmer, circa 1959, whose path to the Olympics is threatened by puberty, injury, and tragedy. Based on the novel by Tessa Duder.
1992 92m/C Chris Haywood, Josh Picker, Catherine Godbold, Elizabeth Hawthorne, Lauren Jackson; **D:** Megan Simpson. **VHS** *ORI*

Alex Mack: In the Nick of Time

Family Alex is your average 13-year-old girl, with two working parents, a brainy older sister, a loyal best friend (who happens to be a boy) and, thanks to a mysterious chemical spill, some paranormal abilities. She can give off electricity and turn herself into water (not, fortunately, at the same time). In these two episodes of the Nickelodeon TV show, Alex (engagingly played by Larisa Oleynik) tries to evade the chemical company meanies responsible

for her unusual state, and, normal kid that she is, strives for her dad's affection. Ages 8 to 13.
199? ?m/C VHS

Ali Baba and the Forty Thieves

Jr. High-Adult Ali Baba, small son of the Caliph of Baghdad, escapes the massacre of his family by Mongol invaders and finds refuge with Merry-Men bandits. Once grown to manhood, Ali leads the Forty Thieves to try and recapture his kingdom. Colorful, swashbuckling hit that helped save Universal Pictures from bankruptcy, though for modern audiences it's a bit short on magic (the 'open Sesame' cave is all that passes for f/x), long on palace romance. Universal spinoffs and imitations followed, also available on video, including 1952's "Son of Ali Baba" and others which reused extensive footage from this flick.

BEWARE *Ages 8 and up.*

1943 87m/C Jon Hall, Turhan Bey, Maria Montez, Andy Devine, Kurt Katch, Frank Puglia, Fortunio Bonanova, Moroni Olsen, Scotty Beckett; *D:* Arthur Lubin; *W:* Edmund Hartmann. **VHS** *MCA, FCT*

Ali Baba and the Forty Thieves

Family The thieves and Ali Baba are set loose in this animation based on Arabian folklore.
1991 25m/C VHS *VTR, WKV, MCA*

Ali Baba's Revenge

Preschool-Jr. High Efforts of Al Huck, his rodent sidekick, and a goofy genie combine to overthrow the tyrannical king of Alibaba. The Alibaban peasants (all cats) revolt behind Huck's leadership in response to unfair taxes.
1984 53m/C *D:* H. Shidar; *V:* Jim Backus. **VHS, Beta** *MPI*

Alice in Wonderland

Family French-produced version of the Lewis Carroll classic which combines the usage of Lou Bunin's puppets and live action to tell the story, with actors portraying both Carroll and Queen Victoria. Released independently to cash in on the success of the Disney version, this takes a more adult approach to the story and is worth viewing on its own merits. Uncle Walt was not enchanted, though, and sought legal action. History does not record whether he uttered "Off with their heads!"
1950 83m/C Carol Marsh, Stephen Murray, Pamela Brown, Felix Aylmer, Ernest Milton; *D:* Dallas Bower. **VHS, Beta** *MON*

Alice in Wonderland

G/Family Classic Disney dream version of Lewis Carroll's famous children's story about a girl who falls down a rabbit hole into a magical world populated by strange creatures. Beautifully animated with some startling images, but served with a strange dispassion, warmed by a fine batch of songs, including "I'm Late," "A Very Merry Un-Birthday," and the title song. Wynn's vocals perfectly

If you like *Alaska* (1996), you'll love:

The Amazing Panda Adventure (1995)

The Bear (1989)

Call of the Wild (1972)

Charlie, the Lonesome Cougar (1967)

Gentle Ben (1969)

Gentle Giant (1967)

Grizzly Adams: The Legend Continues (1990)

Mountain Family Robinson (1979)

Nikki, the Wild Dog of the North (1961)

White Fang (1991)

White Fang 2: The Myth of the White Wolf (1994)

suit the Mad Hatter. ♫ Alice in Wonderland; I'm Late; A Very Merry Un-Birthday.
1951 75m/C *D:* Clyde Geronimi; *V:* Kathryn Beaumont, Ed Wynn, Sterling Holloway, Jerry Colonna, Hamilton Luske, Wilfred Jackson. **VHS, Beta, LV** *DIS, FCT, KUI*

Alice in Wonderland

Family All-star updated adaptation of the Lewis Carroll classic, made for network TV. This time instead of Alice tumbling down a rabbit hole she falls through her television set (natch). But her adventures still include the White Rabbit, Mad Hatter, March Hare, Cheshire Cat, and the King and Queen of Hearts, many of whom insist on singing some unenthralling songs. Followed by "Alice Through the Looking Glass."
1985 90m/C Red Buttons, Anthony Newley, Ringo Starr, Telly Savalas, Robert Morley, Sammy Davis Jr., Steve Allen, Steve Lawrence, Eydie Gorme; *D:* Harry Harris. **VHS** *FCT*

Alice's Adventures in Wonderland

Family British adaptation of Lewis Carroll's timeless fantasy of the little girl who falls into a rabbit hole and, in this case, meets an all-star ensemble decked out in gaudy makeup and costumes, singing forgettable songs. The curious may check it out just for that amazing cast.

1972 96m/C Fiona Fullerton, Michael Crawford, Ralph Richardson, Flora Robson, Peter Sellers, Robert Helpmann, Dudley Moore, Michael Jayston, Spike Milligan, Michael Hordern; **D:** William Sterling; **W:** William Sterling; **M:** John Barry. **VHS, Beta** *VES*

Alive 🐾🐾 🎵

R/Sr. High-Adult Recounts the true-life survival story of a group of Uruguayan rugby players in 1972. After their plane crashes in the remote, snowy Andes (in a spectacular sequence) they're forced to turn to cannibalism during a 10-week struggle to stay alive. Marshall doesn't focus on the gruesome idea, choosing instead to focus on all aspects of their desperate quest for survival. The special effects are stunning, but other parts of the film are never fully realized, including the final scene. Based on the nonfiction book by Piers Paul Read.

> ⚠ **BEWARE** *Profanity, a vivid plane crash, starvation, death, friends eat friends; pretty much in that order.*

1993 127m/C Ethan Hawke, Vincent Spano, Josh Hamilton, Bruce Ramsay, John Haymes Newton, David Kriegel, Kevin Breznahan, Sam Behrens, Illeana Douglas, Jack Noseworthy, Christian Meoli, Jake Carpenter; **Cameos:** John Malkovich; **D:** Frank Marshall; **W:** John Patrick Shanley; **M:** James Newton Howard. **VHS, Beta, LV** *TOU*

All Dogs Go to Heaven 🐾

G/Family Beautifully animated musical mess from Bluth shows the perils of having 10—count 'em—credited writers. Dog crook Charlie is killed by his canine boss and goes to Heaven, but he's bored and heads back to Earth, where he becomes top dog in the rackets via an orphan girl who can predict horse races. But he turns into a good guy at the end in a plot that's all over the place; there's an alligator who befriends Charlie for no more reason than to be a convenient rescuer later on, and if the story takes place in 1939 Louisiana, why do the bad guys have a ray gun? Ad-heavy cassette also sags with a public service announcement for the Boys & Girls Clubs of America and a fabric softener commercial.

> ⚠ **BEWARE** *Depiction of doggy Hades may frighten small children; overall, film may make parents think they're already there.*

1989 85m/C D: Don Bluth; **W:** Don Bluth, David A. Weiss; **M:** Ralph Burns; **V:** Burt Reynolds, Judith Barsi, Dom DeLuise, Vic Tayback, Charles Nelson Reilly, Melba Moore, Candy Devine, Loni Anderson. **VHS, Beta, LV, 8mm** *MGM, RDG*

All Dogs Go to Heaven 2 🐾🐾

G/Family There's life after death, but not much, in this wan sequel, which finds dead dogs Charlie (Charlie Sheen's voice, replacing Burt Reynolds') and Itchy (DeLuise) sent to San Francisco to retrieve Gabriel's horn, which has fallen and can't get up. Along the way Charlie falls for Sasha (Sheena Easton), a singing setter, and makes a deal with the devil, who turns out to be a cat. Good songs by Barry Mann and Cynthia Weil enliven the otherwise routine proceedings.

> ⚠ **BEWARE** *Parents, get ready to explain doggy heaven to those young ones.*

1995 82m/C D: Paul Sabella, Larry Leker; **W:** Arne Olsen, Kelly Ward, Mark Young; **M:** Mark Watters, Barry Mann, Cynthia Weil; **V:** Charlie Sheen, Sheena Easton, Ernest Borgnine, Dom DeLuise, George Hearn, Bebe Neuwirth, Hamilton Camp, Wallace Shawn, Bobby DiCicco, Adam Wylie. **VHS, LV** *MGM*

All I Want for Christmas 🐾🐾

G/Family Paramount bet there was a market for low-budget G-rated fare with this holiday quickie, only to get eggnog on their faces from the low audience turnout. Blame the squishy, low intensity script about a little girl wanting to reunite her estranged parents, so she and her brother play various tricks to bring the ex-spouses together. Heavy xmas-in-New York ambiance, and charming performers, but be aware that comic actor Nielsen, star of the ad campaign, barely has two minutes onscreen as a department story Santa.

1991 92m/C Thora Birch, Leslie Nielsen, Lauren Bacall, Jamey Sheridan, Harley Jane Kozak, Ethan Randall, Kevin Nealon, Andrea Martin; **D:** Robert Lieberman; **W:** Richard Kramer, Thom Eberhardt, Gail Parent; **M:** Neal Israel, Bruce Broughton. **VHS, LV** *PAR*

All New Adventures of Tom Sawyer: Mischief on the Mississippi

Family The continuing adventures of Mark Twain's Tom Sawyer, Huck Finn, and Becky Thatcher in cartoon form. Additional volumes available.

1980 95m/C VHS *JFK*

All the President's Men 🐾🐾🐾 🎵

PG/Jr. High-Adult True story of the Watergate break-in that led to the political scandal of the decade, based on the best-selling book by Washington Post reporters Bob Woodward and Carl Bernstein. Intriguing, terse thriller is a nail-biter even though the ending is no secret. Expertly paced by Pakula with standout performances by Hoffman and Redford as the reporters who slowly uncover and connect the seemingly isolated facts that ultimately lead to criminal indictments of the Nixon Administration. Deep Throat Holbrook and Robards as executive editor Ben Bradlee lend authenticity to the endeavor, a realistic portrayal of the stop and go of journalistic investigations.

> ⚠ **BEWARE** *Profanity, disillusioning (though accurate) portrayal of government misconduct at high levels.*

1976 135m/C Robert Redford, Dustin Hoffman, Jason Robards Jr., Martin Balsam, Jane Alexander, Hal Holbrook, F. Murray Abraham, Stephen Collins, Lindsay Crouse; **D:** Alan J. Pakula; **W:** William Goldman; **M:** David Shire. **Award Nominations:** Academy Awards '76: Best Director (Pakula), Best Film Editing, Best Picture, Best Supporting Actress (Alexander); **Awards:** Academy Awards '76: Best Adapted Screenplay, Best Art Direction/Set Decoration, Best Sound, Best Supporting Actor (Robards); New York Film Critics Awards '76: Best Director (Pakula), Best Film, Best Supporting Actor (Robards). **VHS, Beta, LV** *WAR, BTV*

All the Right Moves 🐾🐾 🎵

R/Sr. High-Adult Stefan is a high school football hero hoping for a college athletic scholarship so he can vacate the Pennsylvania mill town where he grew up. But his rebellious attitude and feuds with the ambitious coach (who wants a change of scenery himself) jeopardize Stef's career plans. Familiar material, yet strong performances and a sympathetic teen hero—who knows that football isn't the only thing in life—push this serious-minded restless youth drama into field goal range.

BEWARE *That R rating is deserved, for profanity and for one scene in which Stef and his girlfriend, who'd been trying to save herself for marriage, finally have sex. Nudity, profanity, alcohol use.*

1983 90m/C Tom Cruise, Lea Thompson, Craig T. Nelson, Christopher Penn; **D:** Michael Chapman; **W:** Michael Kane. **VHS, Beta, LV** *FOX, FXV*

All This and Tex Avery Too!

Primary-Jr. High Animation great Tex Avery and his wild sense of humor changed the style and boundaries of cartoons forever. This two-hour compilation contains 14 'toons done by Avery, featuring some of the best-known creations from the Bugs Bunny/Warner Brothers stable; a must for aficionados.

1992 120m/C D: Tex Avery. **LV** *MGM*

Allan Quartermain and the Lost City of Gold

PG/Jr. High-Adult While trying to find his brother, Quartermain (Richard Chamberlain) discovers a lost African civilization, in this weak adaptation of an H. Rider Haggard adventure. An ostensible sequel to the marginally better "King Solomon's Mines."

1986 100m/C Richard Chamberlain, Sharon Stone, James Earl Jones; **D:** Gary Nelson; **W:** Gene Quintano, Lee Reynolds. **VHS, Beta** *FHE, MED, VTR*

Allegro Non Troppo

PG/Family Energetic and bold collection of animated skits mixed with live-action and set to classical music. No, not Disney's "Fantasia," but a worthy Italian imitator. Watch for the evolution of life set to Ravel's "Bolero," or the memories of an abandoned housecat set to "Valse Triste" of Sibelius. Some animation fans believe this even surpasses Walt's efforts, though the appeal is to a slightly older crowd, and non-cartoon segments lack sparkle. Animator Bruno Bozetto's individual segments are also available separately on short cassettes.

1976 75m/C Maurizio Nichetti; **D:** Bruno Bozzetto. **VHS, LV** *BMG, IME, INJ*

Alligator

R/Jr. High-Adult Dumped down a toilet 12 long years ago, lonely alligator Ramon resides in the city sewers, quietly eating and sleeping. In addition to feasting on the occasional stray human, Ramon devours the animal remains of a chemical plant's experiment involving growth hormones and eventually begins to swell at an enormous rate. Nothing seems to satisfy Ramon's ever-widening appetite: not all the people or all the buildings in the whole town, but he keeps trying, much to the regret of the guilt-ridden cop and lovely scientist who get to know each other while trying to nab the gator. Mediocre special effects are only a distraction in this witty eco-monster take.

BEWARE *People devoured by voracious gator, violence.*

1980 94m/C Robert Forster, Lewis Teague, Jack Carter, Henry Silva, Robin Riker, Dean Jagger; **D:** Lewis Teague; **W:** John Sayles, Frank Ray Perilli. **VHS, Beta** *LIV*

Alligator Pie

Preschool-Primary Flight of fancy from the imagination of a six-year old boy involved with one adventure after another along with a bevy of make-believe friends. Originally a CBC Children's Television teleplay; based on the book by Dennis Lee.

1992 48m/C VHS *BFI*

Almos' a Man

Sr. High-College Black teenager feels he needs a gun to assert himself, but the first shot he fires causes a tragedy that changes his life. Another "Boyz N the Hood" L.A. rap opera? No, a wrenching adaptation of a Richard Wright short story set on a farm in the 1930s. Ambiguous ending provokes much thought even as it exasperates. From the PBS-TV "American Short Story" series, intro'd by Henry Fonda.

BEWARE *Violence.*

1978 51m/C Madge Sinclair, Robert Dogui, LeVar Burton. **VHS, Beta** *MON, MTI, KAR*

Almost an Angel

PG/Jr. High-Adult Another in a recent spat of angels and ghosts assigned back to earth by the head office. Lifelong criminal (Hogan) commits heroic act before final exit and finds himself a probationary angel returned to earth to gain permanent angel status. He befriends a wheelchair-bound man, falls in love with the guy's sister, and helps her out at a center for potential juvenile delinquents. Melodramatic and hokey in many places, driven by Hogan's crocodilian charisma.

BEWARE *Salty language.*

1990 98m/C Paul Hogan, Linda Kozlowski, Elias Koteas, Doreen Lang, Charlton Heston; **D:** John Cornell; **W:** Paul Hogan. **VHS, LV** *PAR*

Almost Angels

Family Two boys romp in Austria as members of the Vienna Boys Choir. Lesser sentimental Disney effort that stars the actual members of the Choir; not much of a draw for today's Nintendo-jaded young viewers, and not to be confused with the better known convent-school comedy "The Trouble With Angels" and its sequel.

1962 85m/C Vincent Winter, Peter Weck, Hans Holt; **D:** Steve Previn. **VHS, Beta** *DIS*

Charlie and friends help a little boy in "All Dogs Go to Heaven 2."

Almost Partners

Family Comedy whodunit matches an amateur detective (Mary Wickes) with the real thing, a no-nonsense New York police detective (Paul Sorvino, who later played a similar role on TV's "Law & Order"). The case: Her late grandpa's ashes and burial urn have been stolen. From the PBS "Wonderworks" television series. Ages 9 and up.

1987 58m/C Paul Sorvino, Royana Black, Mary Wickes; **D:** Alan Kingsberg. **VHS** *PME, HMV, FCT*

Aloha, Bobby and Rose ♫♫ ♡

PG/Sr. High-Adult A mechanic and his girlfriend in L.A. become accidentally involved in an attempted robbery and murder and go on the run for Mexico, of course. Semi-satisfying drama in the surf, with fine location photography.

1974 90m/C Paul LeMat, Dianne Hull, Robert Carradine, Tim McIntire, Edward James Olmos, Leigh French; **D:** Floyd Mutrux. **VHS, Beta** *MED*

Aloha Summer ♫♫

PG/Jr. High-Adult Six surfing teenagers of various ethnic backgrounds learn of love and life in 1959 Hawaii while riding the big wave of impending adulthood, with a splash of kung fu thrown in for good measure. Sensitive but somewhat bland.

BEWARE *Fighting, nudity, sex.*

1988 97m/C Chris Makepeace, Lorie Griffin, Don Michael Paul, Sho Kosugi, Yuji Okumoto, Tia Carrere; **D:** Tommy Lee Wallace. **VHS, Beta, LV** *WAR, ORI*

Alvin & the Chipmunks: A Chipmunk Christmas

Family The classic Chipmunk Christmas tale has Alvin giving away his beloved harmonica to a little boy. Unfortunately, Dave has booked the trio for a Christmas concert at Carnegie Hall and expects Alvin to perform a harmonica solo. The Chipmunks perform "Christmas Don't Be Late" and more traditional Christmas carols.

1981 25m/C VHS, Beta *TOU*

Alvin & the Chipmunks: A Christmas Celebration

Family Alvin, Simon, and Theodore are supposed to perform at a community play. But when things go wrong, the three try to figure out a way to get out of the show. Too bad they couldn't. Ages 3 to 7.

1995 25m/C VHS *TOU*

Alvin & the Chipmunks: Alvin's Christmas Carol

Family Dicken's "A Christmas Carol" is given the Chipmunk spin when Alvin is a Scroogelike little chipmunk visited by three ghosts, Dave, Simon, and Theodore.

19?? 30m/C VHS *TOU*

Alvin & the Chipmunks: Batmunk

Family The famous television cartoon Chipmunks spoof "Batman" features Simon as Batmunk, the Caped Crimefighter, and Alvin as the villainous Jokester, whose criminal cohorts have been stealing all the toys in the city. Additional volumes available.

199? 25m/C VHS, Beta *TOU*

Always 🎵🎵 ♡

PG/Jr. High-Adult Hotshot fire-fighting pilot Dreyfuss flies low over one too many burning bushes and meets a fiery end. In the afterlife, he discovers from ethereal presence Hepburn that his spirit is destined to become a guardian angel to greenhorn fire-fighting flyboy Johnson who steals his girl's heart. Warm remake of "A Guy Named Joe," one of Spielberg's favorite movies, displays a certain self-conscious awareness of its source that occasionally becomes tiresome in spite of all those forest fires. Though both seem fresh from an over-acting seminar, Dreyfuss and Hunter eventually ignite some sparks, but Goodman steals the flaming scenery as the good bud. Old-fashioned tree-burning romance includes actual footage of the 1988 Yellowstone fire.

BEWARE *Tame sexual situations; brief profanity.*

1989 123m/C Holly Hunter, Richard Dreyfuss, John Goodman, Audrey Hepburn, Brad Johnson, Marg Helgenberger, Keith David, Roberts Blossom; **D:** Steven Spielberg; **W:** Jerry Belson; **M:** John Williams. **VHS, Beta, LV** *MCA, FCT*

Amadeus 🎵🎵🎵 ♡

PG/Jr. High-Adult Entertaining adaptation by Shaffer of his play about the intense rivalry between 18th century composers Antonio Salieri and Wolfgang Amadeus Mozart. Abraham's Salieri is a man who desires greatness but is tortured by envy and sorrow. His worst attacks of angst occur when he comes into contact with Hulce's Mozart, an immature, boorish genius who, de-spite his gifts, remains unaffected and delighted by the beauty he creates while irking the hell out of everyone around him. Terrific period piece filmed on location in Prague; excellent musical score, beautiful sets, nifty billowy costumes, and realistic American accents for the 18th century Europeans. 🎵 Concert No. 27 for Pianoforte and Orchestra in B Flat Major; Ave Verum Corpus; A Quintet For Strings in E Flat; A Concerto for Clarinet and Orchestra in A Major; Number 39 in E Flat Major; Number 40 in G Minor; Number 41 in C Major.

BEWARE *When he's not composing, Mozart is a babbling, bubbling font of risque remarks; illness and poverty shown realistically.*

1984 158m/C F. Murray Abraham, Tom Hulce, Elizabeth Berridge, Simon Callow, Roy Dotrice, Christine Ebersole, Jeffrey Jones, Kenny L. Baker, Cynthia Nixon, Vincent Schiavelli; **D:** Milos Forman; **W:** Peter Shaffer. **Award Nominations:** Academy Awards '84: Best Actor (Hulce), Best Cinematography, Best Film Editing; **Awards:** Academy Awards '84: Best Actor (Abraham), Best Adapted Screenplay, Best Art Direction/Set Decoration, Best Costume Design, Best Director (Forman), Best Makeup, Best Picture, Best Sound; Cesar Awards '85: Best Foreign Film; Directors Guild of America Awards '84: Best Director (Forman); Golden Globe Awards '85: Best Actor—Drama (Abraham), Best Director (Forman), Best Film—Drama, Best Screenplay. **VHS, Beta, LV** *REP, GLV, BTV*

Amahl and the Night Visitors

Jr. High-Adult Dramatization of Gian Carlo Menotti's English-language Christmas opera that was written specifically for TV in 1951. Amahl is a poor, crippled boy in ancient Jerusalem whose widowed mother has unexpected guests—the Three Kings on their way to visit to the newborn Christ. Beautifully filmed on location in Israel, and a rare example of opera that's accessible to younger viewers. For some others, see "The Maestro's Company" and "The Tales of Hoffmann."

1978 120m/C Teresa Stratas, Giorgio Tozzi, Willard White, Robert Sapolsky. **VHS, Beta** *HMV, MVD, KAR*

Amazing Adventures of Joe 90

Preschool-Primary Another of Britain's 'Super Marionation' spectaculars from Gerry and Sylvia Anderson, who perfected a painstaking but undeniably popular method of doing live-action sci-fi epics using miniature sets, expert special f/x, and casts made up entirely of puppets. In this sample, Joe is a 9-year-old secret agent who is the equal of any adult when it comes to an appetite for adventure. These tapes include three outings; for other puppet productions by Andersons, see "Thunderbirds" and "Stingray."

1968 90m/C VHS, Beta *FHE*

Amazing Bone and Other Stories

Preschool-Primary John Lithgow narrates four delightful animated stories by different authors. William Steig's "The Amazing Bone," Jenny Wagner's "John Brown, Rose and the Midnight Cat," Crockett Johnson's "A Pic-

ture for Harold's Room," and Ezra Jack Keats' "The Trip." Ages 3 to 10.

1988 32m/C VHS, Beta *FCT, CCC, BTV*

The Amazing Dobermans

G/Family Family-oriented pooch performance piece featuring longtime song-and-dance favorite Astaire in one of his odder roles as a reformed con man whose five trained dobermans help an undercover agent in foiling a gambling and extortion racket. The last in a series that includes "The Daring Dobermans" and "The Doberman Gang."

1976 96m/C Fred Astaire, Barbara Eden, James Franciscus, Jack Carter, Billy Barty; **D:** Byron Ross Chudnow; **M:** Alan Silvestri. **VHS, Beta** *MED*

Amazing Grace & Chuck

PG/Family Upon visiting a missile site in Montana, 12-year-old Little Leaguer Chuck begins a passive protest against nuclear weapons by refusing to play until nations forge a peace agreement. Hearing the news, pro-basketball star Amazing Grace Smith (Denver Nugget English) also quits his team. Soon athletes everywhere join the movement, US and Soviet leaders take notice. Hey, it could happen . . . right? Gentle, somewhat outdated political fantasy with good intentions but lacking coherence and plausibility.

⚠ BEWARE *Salty language.*

1987 115m/C Jamie Lee Curtis, Gregory Peck, William L. Petersen, Joshua Zuehlke, Alex English; **D:** Mike Newell; **M:** Elmer Bernstein. **VHS, Beta, LV** *HBO*

Amazing Mr. Blunden

G/Family "Back to the Future" British-style, as two children in 1918 are beseeched by phantom kids from a century earlier to journey back via time-travel potion to stop a murder plot by wicked 1818 in-laws. Fine Dickensian atmosphere at times (actors personally wish the viewer a hearty "Goodbye!" at the end), but slow-moving. Lousy f/x make one appreciate the first-rate production values in even the dreariest Disney fantasies. Adapted from Antonia Barber's novel, "The Ghosts."

⚠ BEWARE *Alcohol use and fighting.*

1972 100m/C Laurence Naismith, Lynne Frederick, Garry Miller, Marc Granger, Rosalyn London, Diana Dors; **D:** Lionel Jeffries; **M:** Elmer Bernstein. **VHS, Beta** *MED*

The Amazing Panda Adventure

PG/Family Ryan (Slater) is off to China during his spring break to visit dad Michael (Lang), who's working on a project to rescue the dwindling panda population. But there's poacher trouble and Ryan and young translator Ling (Ding) decide to rescue the preserve's panda cub, which has been animal-napped. If there's one thing

we don't want, it's poached panda (and where's Ace Ventura when you need him). Family fare, with a mixture of totally adorable real and animatronic pandas; filmed in the Sichuan province of China, home to the Wolong Nature Reserve which is famous for its successful breeding of the endangered giant pandas. Slater, in his first starring role, is the younger brother of Christian.

⚠ BEWARE *Adventure action and brief mild language.*

1995 84m/C Ryan Slater, Stephen Lang, Yi Ding, Wang Fei; **D:** Christopher Cain; **W:** Laurice Elehwany, Jeff Rothberg; **C:** Jack N. Green; **M:** William Ross. **VHS, LV** *WAR*

The Amazing Spider-Man

Family Collection of Spider-Man's most exciting adventures from Saturday-morning cartoons.

1982 100m/C VHS, Beta *MCA*

American Anthem

PG-13/Jr. High-Adult Young gymnast must choose between family responsibilities or the parallel bars. Olympic gymnast Gaylord makes his movie debut but doesn't get the gold. Good fare for young tumblers, but that's about it. Followed by two of the films' music videos and tape-ads featuring Max Headroom.

⚠ BEWARE *Athletes trying to act. Sort of like Orson Welles attempting a routine on the pommel horse, or vice versa.*

1986 100m/C Mitch Gaylord, Janet Jones, Michelle Phillips, Michael Pataki; **D:** Albert Magnoli; **M:** Alan Silvestri. **VHS, Beta, LV** *ORI, WAR*

American Boyfriends

PG-13/Jr. High-Adult Lackluster sequel to "My American Cousin," nevertheless of interest to viewers following the emotional travails of restless rural Canadian girl Sandy, now a teenager. Voyaging south to Oregon for the wedding of her bad-boy cousin Butch (on whom she had a crush in the original), Sandy and a friend spar with first romance.

⚠ BEWARE *Profanity, sex talk.*

1989 90m/C Margaret Langrick, John Wildman, Jason Blicker, Lisa Repo Martell; **D:** Sandy Wilson; **W:** Sandy Wilson. **VHS, Beta, LV** *LIV*

An American Christmas Carol

Family Charles Dickens' classic story retold with limited charm and tacked-on history lessons in a made-for-television effort starring the Fonz. This time a miserly Depression-era industrialist (young Winkler, in heavy age makeup) learns the true meaning of Christmas through the usual trio of ghosts.

1979 98m/C Henry Winkler, David Wayne, Dorian Harewood; **D:** Eric Till; **M:** Hagood Hardy. **VHS, Beta** *VES, LIV*

American Dreamer 🐾🐾 ▷

PG/Sr. High-Adult Housewife wins a trip to Paris as a prize from a mystery writing contest. Silly from a blow on the head, she begins living the fictional life of her favorite literary adventure. Sporadic comedy with a good cast wandering about courtesy of a clumsy screenplay.

BEWARE *Mild violence, sexual situations (nothing explicit).*

1984 105m/C JoBeth Williams, Tom Conti, Giancarlo Giannini, Coral Browne, James Staley; **D:** Rick Rosenthal; **M:** Lewis Furey. **VHS, Beta** *FOX*

American Flyers 🐾🐾 ▷

PG-13/Jr. High-Adult Two competitive brothers train for a grueling three-day bicycle race in Colorado while tangling with personal drama, including fears that one of them may have inherited dad's health problems and is sure to drop dead during the home stretch. Written by bike movie specialist Steve Tesich (who scripted the far superior "Breaking Away") with a lot of the usual cliches—the last bike ride, battling siblings, eventual understanding—gracefully overridden by fine photography. Interesting performances, especially Chong as a patient girlfriend.

BEWARE *A dying character and fear of death. Profanity. For ages 12 and up.*

1985 113m/C Kevin Costner, David Marshall Grant, Rae Dawn Chong, Alexandra Paul, John Amos, Janice Rule, Robert Townsend, Jennifer Grey, Luca Bercovici; **D:** John Badham; **W:** Steve Tesich; **M:** Lee Ritenour, Greg Mathieson. **VHS, Beta, LV** *WAR*

American Graffiti 🐾🐾🐾 ▷

PG/Family Teens of every era can relate to George Lucas' take on the more innocent early '60s. It's all one hectic but typical summer night; California high school friends have just graduated, unsure what the next big step is. They spend the hours cruising, dating, listening to rock'n'roll radio (legendary D.J. Wolfman Jack's appearance is magic) and meeting at the drive-in. Honest, humane, and consistently brilliant, with a cast of mostly unknowns who went on to stardom. Partial inspiration for TV's "Happy Days" was followed by less successful, "More American Graffiti."

BEWARE *Alcohol use and smoking, kids staying out late and breaking some rules.*

1973 112m/C Richard Dreyfuss, Ron Howard, Cindy Williams, MacKenzie Phillips, Paul LeMat, Charles Martin Smith, Suzanne Somers, Candy Clark, Harrison Ford, Bo Hopkins, Joe Spano, Kathleen Quinlan, Wolfman Jack; **D:** George Lucas; **W:** George Lucas, Gloria Katz, Willard Huyck. **Award Nominations:** Academy Awards '73: Best Director (Lucas), Best Film Editing, Best Picture, Best Story & Screenplay, Best Supporting Actress (Clark); **Awards:** Golden Globe Awards '74: Best Film—Musical/Comedy. **VHS, Beta, LV** *MCA, FCT*

American Heart 🐾🐾🐾

R/Sr. High-Adult Jack (Bridges) is a suspicious ex-con, newly released from prison, with few prospects and little hope. He also has a teenaged son, Nick (Furlong), he barely remembers but who desperately wants to have his father back in his life. Jack is reluctantly persuaded to let Nick stay with him in his cheap hotel where Nick befriends fellow resident, Molly, a teenage hooker, and other castoff street kids. Superb performances by both male leads Furlong, both yearning and frustrated as he pursues his dream of having a family, and Bridges as the tough parolee, unwilling to open his heart. Hardboiled, poignant, and powerful.

BEWARE *Profanity; brutality; brief nudity; alcohol use; drug use, prostitution..*

1992 114m/C Jeff Bridges, Edward Furlong, Lucinda Jenney, Tracey Kapisky, Don Harvey, Margaret Welsh; **D:** Martin Bell; **W:** Peter Silverman; **M:** James Newton Howard. **Award Nominations:** Independent Spirit Awards '94: Best Cinematography, Best First Feature, Best Supporting Actor (Furlong), Best Supporting Actress (Jenney); **Awards:** Independent Spirit Awards '94: Best Actor (Bridges). **VHS, LV** *LIV, BTV*

An American in Paris 🐾🐾🐾🐾

Family Lavish, imaginative musical features a sweeping score, and knockout choreography by Kelly. Ex-G.I. Kelly stays on in Paris after the war to study painting, supported in his efforts by rich American Foch, who hopes to acquire a little extra attention. But Kelly loves the lovely Caron, unfortunately engaged to an older gent. Highlight is an astonishing 17-minute ballet which holds the record for longest movie dance number—and one of the more expensive, pegged at over half a million for a month of filming. For his efforts, the dance king won a special Oscar citation. While it sure looks like Paris, most of it was filmed in MGM studios. 🎵 S'Wonderful; I Got Rhythm; Embraceable You; Love Is Here To Stay; Tra-La-La; I'll Build a Stairway to Paradise; Nice Work If You Can Get It; By Strauss; Concerto in F (3rd Movement).

1951 113m/C Gene Kelly, Leslie Caron, Oscar Levant, Nina Foch, Georges Guetary; **D:** Vincente Minnelli; **W:** Alan Jay Lerner; **M:** George Gershwin, Ira Gershwin. **Award Nominations:** Academy Awards '51: Best Director (Minnelli), Best Film Editing; **Awards:** Academy Awards '51: Best Art Direction/Set Decoration (Color), Best Color Cinematography, Best Costume Design (Color), Best Picture, Best Story & Screenplay, Best Score; Golden Globe Awards '52: Best Film—Musical/Comedy; National Board of Review Awards '51: 10 Best Films of the Year. **VHS, Beta, LV, 8mm** *MGM, TLF, BTV*

The American President 🐾🐾🐾

PG-13/Sr. High-Adult Widower president (Douglas) with 13-year-old daughter decides it's time to get back into the dating game. But just what woman wants to find her romance in the public eye? Environmental lobbyist Sydney Wade (Bening), that's who. Movie takes the refreshingly un-cynical position that there are idealistic people in government (and elsewhere) who really do want to serve the public.

BEWARE *Contains sexual situations and some strong language, and Bening wearing a Presidential shirt and not much more.*

1995 113m/C Michael Douglas, Annette Bening, Martin Sheen, Michael J. Fox, David Paymer, Samantha Mathis, John Mahoney, Anna Deavere Smith, Nina Siemaszko, Wendie Malick, Shawna

Ryan Tyler (Ryan Slater) rescues a baby panda from poachers in "The Amazing Panda Adventure."

Waldron, Richard Dreyfuss; **D:** Rob Reiner; **W:** Aaron Sorkin; **C:** John Seale; **M:** Marc Shaiman. **VHS** *NYR*

An American Summer 🦴🦴

Family Chicago kid Tom is stuck with his spacey aunt in California during the summer of '78. At first this convivial coming-of-age tale looks like a exercise in nostalgia, then you note a familiar fence-painting gag, a rascal named Fin, an abandoned mine . . . It's really an unpretentious adaptation of Mark Twain's "Adventures of Tom Sawyer," twisted to fit modern times. Clever gimmick, but no improvement over the original.

⚠ BEWARE *While Tom and Huck smoked forbidden tobacco, their counterparts here do marijuana with glass-eyed satisfaction. The Injun Joe character, meanwhile, is a killer pusher. Profanity.*

1990 100m/C Brian Austin Green, Joanna Kerns, Michael Landes. **VHS** *NO*

An American Tail 🦴🦴🦴

G/Family While emigrating to America in the 1880s, young Russian mouse Fievel gets separated from his family and learns to live by his wits in old New York's nooks and crannies. The bad guys are of course cats, who exploit the newcomer mice as cheap labor. Obviously producer Steven Spielberg had a high-minded history lesson planned with the sentimental, metaphorical plot, but the kids will keep watching for the excellent animation (by the Don Bluth Studios, a collection of expatriate Disney artists) and lively character voices. Aggressive marketing tried to create Fievel Fever, but the kid's no Mickey (though he did earn a sequel). Soundtrack includes the platinum selling song "Somewhere Out There."

1986 81m/C D: Don Bluth; **M:** James Horner; **V:** Dom DeLuise, Madeline Kahn, Phillip Glasser, Christopher Plummer, Nehemiah Persoff, Will Ryan, John Finnegan, Cathianne Blore. **VHS, Beta, LV** *MCA, APD, JCF*

An American Tail: Fievel Goes West 🦴🦴🦴

G/Family Fievel and the Mousekewitz family head west to seek their fortune, and the boy hero learns his hero Marshall Wylie Burp, a once-mighty lawdog, has almost given up fighting bad guys. The second Fievel epic got treated like vermin by critics, but it's actually a bit better than the first "American Tail," with superior animation and clever genre spoofs that older viewers will enjoy (like a great cover version of "Rawhide.") The first cartoon feature made entirely by Steven Spielberg's Amblimation studio. Laser edition is letterboxed and features chapter stops.

1991 75m/C D: Phil Nibbelink, Simon Wells; **W:** Flint Dille; **M:** James Horner; **V:** John Cleese, Dom DeLuise, Phillip Glasser, Amy Irving, Jon Lovitz, Cathy Cavadini, Nehemiah Persoff, Erica Yohn, James Stewart. **VHS, Beta, LV** *MCA*

Amos and Andrew 🦴🦴 🦴

PG-13/Jr. High-Adult Occasionally embarrassing attempt at comedy stops short of endorsing the stereotypes it tries to parody. Prizewinning African-American author Andrew Sterling (Jackson) is seen moving into a house on an island previously reserved for uptight white folks, and the neighbors call the cops, assuming he's a thief. Chief of police Coleman eagerly gets into the act, then exploits drifter Amos (Cage) in a cover-up attempt when he realizes his mistake. Amos and Andrew are soon housemates under siege by the police, resulting in chaos, comedy, and a mighty poor lesson in race relations.

> 🚫 BEWARE *Violence, profanity, racial stereotyping, really dumb cops (even by Hollywood standards).*

1993 96m/C Nicolas Cage, Samuel L. Jackson, Michael Lerner, Margaret Colin, Giancarlo Esposito, Dabney Coleman, Bob Balaban, Aimee Graham, Brad Dourif, Chelcie Ross, Jodi Long; **D:** E. Max Frye; **W:** E. Max Frye; **M:** Richard Gibbs. **VHS, LV** *COL, IME, NLC*

Amy 🦴🦴🦴

G/Family Superior Disney drama that was originally intended for television but was judged special enough for theaters. In the early 1900s, young housewife Amy, following the death of her deaf son, finds a sense of purpose in life that makes her leave behind a domineering husband to teach at a school for the deaf and blind. Eventually she organizes a football game between the handicapped kids and the other children in the neighborhood. Not as sentimental as one might dread.

1981 100m/C Jenny Agutter, Barry Newman, Kathleen Nolan, Margaret O'Brien, Nanette Fabray, Chris Robinson, Lou Fant; **D:** Vincent McEveety. **VHS, Beta** *DIS*

Anansi

Family Anansi is a spider who manages to outwit a prideful snake but then gets caught up in his own lies. Adaptation of a Jamaican folktale which features the reggae music of UB40. One of a terrific video storybook series "Rabbit Ears: We All Have Tales," with celebrities reciting folk legends and fairytales from different nations and cultures to wonderful (non-animated) illustrations. Other productions include "The Boy Who Drew Cats," "Br'er Rabbit and the Wonderful Tar Baby," "The Fool and the Flying Ship," "The Emperor's New Clothes," "Finn McCoul," "King Midas and the Golden Touch," "Koi and the Kola Nuts," "The Legend of Sleepy Hollow," "Paul Bunyan," "Pecos Bill," "Puss in Boots," "Stormalong," "Thumbelina," "The Ugly Duckling," and many others; see individual listings for descriptions.

1991 30m/C VHS *RAB, FCT, MLT*

Anchors Aweigh 🦴🦴🦴

Family Snappy big-budget (for then) musical about two horny sailors, one a girl-happy dancer and the other a shy singer. While on leave in Hollywood they return a lost urchin to his sister. The four of them try to infiltrate a movie studio to win an audition for the girl from maestro Iturbi. Kelly's famous dance with Jerry the cartoon Mouse (of "Tom and Jerry" fame) is the second instance of combining live action and animation. The young and handsome Sinatra's easy crooning and Grayson's near operatic soprano are blessed with music and lyrics by Styne and Cahn. Lots of fun, with conductor-pianist Iturbi contributing. 🎵 We Hate to Leave; I Fall in Love Too Easily; The Charm of You; The Worry Song; Jalousie; All of a Sudden My Heart Sings; I Begged Her; What Makes the Sun Set?; Waltz Serenade.

1945 139m/C Frank Sinatra, Gene Kelly, Kathryn Grayson, Jose Iturbi, Sharon McManus, Dean Stockwell, Carlos Ramirez, Pamela Britton; **D:** George Sidney; **M:** Jule Styne, Sammy Cahn. **Award Nominations:** Academy Awards '45: Best Actor (Kelly), Best Color Cinematography, Best Picture, Best Song ("I Fall in Love Too Easily"); **Awards:** Academy Awards '45: Best Score. **VHS, Beta, LV** *MGM*

And Baby Makes Six 🦴🦴 🦴

Jr. High-Adult Not exactly the newest idea in the world (see the 1965 release "Never Too Late"). TV drama about an unexpected pregnancy that creates new challenges for a middle-aged couple (Warren Oates and Colleen Dewhurst) with three grown children. Dewhurst is excellent as usual. Followed by "Baby Comes Home." Insider's note: Timothy Hutton plays one of the grown children; his father, Jim Hutton, played a similar role in "Never Too Late." Ages 9 and up.

1979 100m/C Colleen Dewhurst, Warren Oates, Maggie Cooper, Mildred Dunnock, Timothy Hutton, Allyn Ann McLerie; **D:** Waris Hussein; **W:** Shelley List. **VHS, 8mm** *NO*

And Now for Something Completely Different 🦴🦴🦴

PG/Sr. High-Adult A compilation of skits from BBC-television's "Monty Python's Flying Circus" featuring Monty Python's own, weird, hilarious brand of humor. Sketches include "The Upper Class Twit of the Year Race," "Hell's Grannies" and "The Townswomen's Guild Reconstruction of Pearl Harbour." A great introduction to Python for the uninitiated, or a chance for the converted to see their favorite sketches again.

> 🚫 BEWARE *Profanity, especially in reference to a certain deceased parrot.*

1972 89m/C John Cleese, Michael Palin, Eric Idle, Graham Chapman, Terry Gilliam, Terry Jones; **D:** Ian McNaughton; **W:** John Cleese, Michael Palin, Graham Chapman, Terry Gilliam, Terry Jones. **VHS, Beta, LV** *COL, TVC*

And Now Miguel 🦴🦴

Family Plodding tale of a young boy who wants to take over as head shepherd of his family's flock and must prove himself on the grazing trail. Filmed in New Mexico, it's scenic but a bit of a drag in spite of child actor Cardi's competent performance. Based on the novel by Joseph Krumgold.

1966 95m/C Pat Cardi, Michael Ansara, Guy Stockwell, Clu Gulager, Joe De Santis, Pilar Del Rey, Buck Taylor; **D:** James B. Clark. **VHS** *NOS*

And the Children Shall Lead

Family News of Martin Luther King's civil rights movement comes to a small town in Mississippi in 1964, dividing two once-peaceful families. One is affluent and white, the other are the kinfolk of their longtime black cook. The point is made that hope for racial equality lies with the attitudes of their children—well, some of their children, anyway. This drama done for the "WonderWorks" TV series is special in that it never simplifies the issues of racism, nor disrespects its characters, even the most bigoted ones.

1985 60m/C Danny Glover, LeVar Burton, Pam Potillo, Denise Nicholas, Andrew Prine; **D:** Michael Pressman. **VHS** *PME, PTB, HMV*

And You Thought Your Parents Were Weird! 🦴🦴

PG/Jr. High-Adult Whiz kids invent an R2D2-style robot that gets possessed by the spirit of their deceased dad. The cutie gadget provides fatherly guidance and companionship for mom. When it turns out his demise wasn't an accident, machine and sons set out to foil the evildoers. Silly family fantasy, in slightly questionable taste but harmless.

1991 92m/C Marcia Strassman, Joshua Miller, Edan Gross, John Quade, Sam Behrens, Susan Gibney, Gustav Vintas, Eric Walker; **D:** Tony Cookson; **W:** Tony Cookson; **M:** Randall Miller; **V:** Alan Thicke, Richard Libertini. **VHS** *VMK*

Andre 🦴🦴 🦴

G/Family Feel-good human-animal interaction from the man from snowy river. True story of a seal with an inclination to swim hundreds of miles every summer to visit the family in Maine that saved his life. Sort of a "Free Willy" in reverse with an appealing smaller sea mammal who does clever tricks while consorting with likewise appealing small human Majorino, portraying a shy little girl who blossoms with the arrival of Andre. Created a brief moment of controversy when it was revealed that Andre was actually a sea lion, not a seal as depicted in the original story.

> **BEWARE** *Mild profanity; sea lion gives folks the razzberry, young viewers may follow suit.*

1994 94m/C Keith Carradine, Tina Majorino, Chelsea Field, Keith Szarabajka, Shane Meier; **D:** George Miller; **W:** Dana Baratta. **VHS** *NYR*

Androcles and the Lion 🦴🦴 🦴

Jr. High-Adult Stagebound Hollywood production of the George Bernard Shaw play that uses the famous Aesop's fable as a jumping-off point for a satire of imperial Rome,

where a tailor saves Christians from a hungry lion he had previously befriended. Sharp dialogue, geared more for adult sensibilities than kids, but still a semi-satisfying experience.

1952 105m/B Jean Simmons, Alan Young, Victor Mature, Robert Newton, Maurice Evans; **D:** Chester Erskine. **VHS, Beta** *COL*

The Andromeda Strain 🦴🦴 🦴

G/Family A satellite falls back to earth carrying a deadly bacteria that must be identified in time to save the population from extermination. The tension inherent in the bestselling Michael Crichton novel is talked down by a boring cast. Also available in letter-box format.

> **BEWARE** *Potential global epidemic that could destroy every human.*

1971 131m/C Arthur Hill, David Wayne, James Olson, Kate Reid, Paula Kelly; **D:** Robert Wise. **VHS, Beta, LV** *MCA*

Andy and the Airwave Rangers 🦴🦴

Family Sci-fi thriller scaled down for kid viewers. Anna discovers she has telepathic powers. Her mother reveals the schoolgirl's actually a clone, psychically in tune with her widely scattered identical 'sisters.' Based on the young-adult novel by Mildred Ames.

> **BEWARE** *Violence.*

1989 75m/C Dianne Kay, Vince Edwards, Bo Svenson, Richard Thomas, Erik Estrada; **D:** Deborah Brock. **VHS, LV** *COL*

Andy Hardy Gets Spring Fever 🦴🦴

Family Andy falls for a beautiful acting teacher, and then goes into a funk when he finds she's engaged. Judge Hardy and the gang help heal the big wound in his heart. A lesser entry (and the seventh) from the popular series.

1939 88m/B Mickey Rooney, Lewis Stone, Ann Rutherford, Fay Holden, Cecilia Parker, Sara Haden, Helen Gilbert; **D:** Woodbridge S. Van Dyke. **VHS, Beta** *MGM*

Andy Hardy Meets Debutante 🦴🦴 🦴

Family Garland's second entry in series, wherein Andy meets and falls foolishly for glamorous debutante Lewis with Betsy's help while family is on visit to New York. Judy/Betsy sings "I'm Nobody's Baby" and "Singing in Rain." Also available with "Love Finds Andy Hardy" on laser disc.

1940 86m/B Mickey Rooney, Judy Garland, Lewis Stone, Ann Rutherford, Fay Holden, Sara Haden, Cecilia Parker, Diana Lewis, Tom Neal; **D:** George B. Seitz. **VHS, Beta, LV** *MGM*

Andy Hardy's Double Life 🦴🦴 🦴

Family In this entertaining installment from the Andy Hardy series, Andy proposes marriage to two girls at the same time and gets in quite a pickle when they both accept. Williams makes an early screen splash.

1942 91m/B Mickey Rooney, Lewis Stone, Ann Rutherford, Fay Holden, Sara Haden, Cecilia Parker, Esther Williams, William Lundigan, Susan Peters, Robert (Bobby) Blake; **D:** George B. Seitz. **VHS, Beta** *MGM, MLB*

Andy Hardy's Private Secretary 🦴🦴

Family After Andy fails his high school finals, he gets help from a sympathetic faculty member. As the secretary, Grayson makes a good first impression in one of her early screen appearances. The Hardy series was often used as a training ground for new MGM talent.

1941 101m/B Mickey Rooney, Kathryn Grayson, Lewis Stone, Fay Holden, Ian Hunter, Gene Reynolds, Sara Haden; **D:** George B. Seitz. **VHS, Beta** *MGM*

The Angel and the Soldier Boy

Family A wonderful wordless story for the whole family, featuring the animation of Alison De Vere and based on Peter Collington's wordless book about a little girl, pirates from a book, a toy soldier, and a toy angel. Soundtrack performed by Irish band Clannad. Ages 3 to 8.

1990 25m/C **VHS** *BMG, IGP*

Angel Square 🦴🦴

Jr. High-Adult Set in Canada in 1945. Sammy's father, a railroad watchman, is beaten and taken to the hospital in a coma. Sammy and his pal Tommy try to find the culprit, with the help of a policeman and others in the neighborhood. Ages 11 and up.

BEWARE *Subject matter includes anti-Semitism, Down syndrome and sexual curiosity (but no sex).*

1992 106m/C Ned Beatty; **D:** Anne Wheeler; **W:** James DeFelice. **VHS** *NO*

Angela's Airplane

Preschool-Primary Two five year-old girls find themselves in the middle of exciting, animated adventures. Angela sneaks into a plane and flies it with the help of Ralph, her stuffed rabbit. In "The Fire Station" Sheila talks Michael into hiding in a fire engine that gets sent out to a fire. Stories by Bob Munsch. Ages 3 to 7.

1993 25m/C **VHS**

Angelo My Love 🦴🦴🦴

R/Sr. High-Adult Compassionate docudrama about New York's modern gypsy community. Follows the adventures of 12-year-old Angelo Evans, the streetwise son of a fortune teller, who, with a fresh view, explores the ups and downs of his family's life. Duvall financed the effort and cast non-professional actors in this charming tale of reality and fairy-tale.

BEWARE *Profanity.*

1983 91m/C Angelo Evans, Michael Evans, Steve "Patalay" Tsiginoff, Cathy Kitchen, Millie Tsiginoff; **D:** Robert Duvall; **M:** Michael Kamen. **VHS, Beta, LV** *COL*

Angels in the Outfield 🦴🦴 🦴

PG/Family Remake of the 1951 fantasy about a lowly baseball team who, along with some heavenly help animated by Disney, find themselves on a winning streak. The new lineup includes Glover as manager of the hapless California Angels, Danza as a washed-up pitcher, and Lloyd as captain of the celestial spirits. Gordon-Levitt plays the foster child who believes he'll get his family back together if the Angels win the pennant. Familiar ground still yields good, heartfelt family fare. Oakland A's third baseman Carney Lansford served as technical advisor, molding actors into fair semblance of baseball team. Excellent special effects from Magic Lantern.

BEWARE *Profanity. A child without parents; Gordon-Levitt's father is uncaring.*

1994 102m/C Danny Glover, Tony Danza, Christopher Lloyd, Brenda Fricker, Ben Johnson, Joseph Gordon-Levitt, Jay O. Sanders; **D:** William Dear; **W:** Holly Goldberg Sloan. **VHS**

Angus 🦴🦴 🦴

PG-13/Jr. High-Adult Teen comedy about self-esteem revolves around the overweight Angus (Talbert), a friendly kid tormented by the usual school bullies. His best bud is twerp Troy (Owen), who tries to help Angus out with his crush on cute blonde Melissa (Ariana). There's even a schmaltzy prom scene. The profanity, though mild, and the boys' sexual interests make this questionable for the pre-teen audience that could actually enjoy it.

BEWARE *Some coarse adolescent language, fat jokes, and lots of grossness from sidekick Troy. A main character dies.*

1995 87m/C Charlie Talbert, Kathy Bates, George C. Scott, Chris Owen, Ariana Richards, Lawrence Pressman, Rita Moreno, James Van Der Beek, Anna Thompson; **D:** Patrick Read Johnson; **W:** Jill Gordon; **C:** Alexander Grusynski; **M:** David E. Russo. **VHS** *TTC*

Animal Alphabet

Preschool Film (by National Geographic) of animals in the wild plus animated sequences help youngsters learn the alphabet. There's an animal for each letter, and a song for each animal by Broadway composer Elizabeth Swados. Ages 1 to 4.

1985 30m/C **VHS, Beta** *ORI, WAR*

Animal Babies in the Wild

Preschool-Primary Splendid National Geographic footage of baby animals in their natural habitats as songs, stories, and dialogue familiarize children with less often seen wildlife. Ages 1 to 5.

1987 30m/C **VHS** *MLT*

Animal Behavior 🦴 🦴

PG/Jr. High-Adult Speech researcher and a music professor have a rocky campus romance, brought together in part by a lab chimp with a sign-language vocabulary, kept apart by dumb mixups. The monkey (and a subplot

Everyone is astounded when Angus (Charlie Talbert) is chosen as the king of the dance in "Angus."

about an autistic child) may get kids slightly interested, but adults will find this flaccid farce an unrewarding experiment.

🚫 BEWARE *Profanity, sex talk.*

1989 79m/C Karen Allen, Armand Assante, Holly Hunter, Josh Mostel, Richard Libertini; *D:* Jenny Bowen; *W:* Susan Rice; *M:* Cliff Eidelman. **VHS, Beta, LV** *HBO*

Animal Crackers 🦴🦴🦴

G/Family Kid viewers haven't embraced the Marx Brothers comedy team as enthusiastically as they have the Stooges. But give movie Marxism a chance, especially with this freeform hilarity loosely plotted around the theft of a painting at a wealthy estate where Capt. Rufus T. Spaulding (Groucho) is a houseguest and Zeppo, Chico and Harpo are party crashers. Only a boring romantic/musical subplot without the Brothers (a common Hollywood time-filler in those days) prevents this from being nonstop laughs. The one that gave the world the line "One morning I shot an elephant in my pajamas ... "

1930 98m/B Groucho Marx, Chico Marx, Harpo Marx, Zeppo Marx, Lillian Roth, Margaret Dumont, Louis Sorin, Hal Thompson, Richard

Greig; *D:* Victor Heerman; *W:* Morrie Ryskind. **VHS, Beta, LV** *MCA, FCT*

Animal Farm 🦴🦴🦴

Family British feature cartoon (a rarity all in itself) based on the George Orwell allegorical satire of Communism. Barnyard animals successfully overthrow their masters. Now what to do? Napoleon the power-crazed pig knows, and using propaganda and mob psychology, he takes control and turns the farm into a totalitarian dictatorship even worse than before. A bit talky for kiddie viewers, but it puts across Orwell's important ideas with some success.

1955 73m/C *D:* John Halas, Joy Batchelor; *V:* Maurice Denham, Gordon Heath. **VHS, Beta, LV, 8mm** *VYY, KUI, VTR*

Animal Stories

Preschool An animated collection of animal stories for the young: "Andy and the Lion," "Why Mosquitos Buzz in People's Ears" and "Petunia." Ages 3 to 8.

1984 30m/C VHS, Beta *FCT*

Animals Are Beautiful People

Family After Jamie Uys became known worldwide for "The Gods Must Be Crazy," home video revived this earlier theatrical documentary feature, a hit in his native South Africa. Uys brings his trademark wit and thoughtful sentiment to footage of baboons, elephants, cheetahs and other wildlife of the veldt.

1984 92m/C D: Jamie Uys. **VHS, Beta** *WAR*

Animalympics: Winter Games

Primary-Jr. High Made-for-TV cartoon companion to the feature "Animalympics" with the characters of the ZOO Network covering the first Animal Winter Games.

1982 30m/C V: Gilda Radner, Billy Crystal, Harry Shearer, Michael Fremer. **VHS** *LIV, FHE*

Anne Frank Remembered ♫♫♫♫

PG/Jr. High-Adult Oscar-winning documentary, narrated by Kenneth Branagh, tells the story of the Frank family before—and after—the two years of hiding Anne described in her famous diary. Includes the only known footage of Anne, age 12, filmed inadvertently as she gazed out her apartment window at a wedding party; conversations with eyewitnesses and an interview with Anne's father, Otto Frank, who survived Auschwitz and died in 1980. Written and directed by Jon Blair. Glenn Close reads excerpts from the diary.

BEWARE *Vivid and realistic depictions of the Holocaust.*

1995 122m/C VHS *NYR*

Anne of Avonlea ♫♫♫ ♪

Family Equally excellent mini-series sequel to "Anne of Green Gables" in which the heroine grows up and discovers romance. The same cast returns and Sullivan continues his tradition of lavish filming on Prince Edward Island and beautiful costumes. Based on the characters from L.M. Montgomery's classic novels "Anne of Avonlea," "Anne of the Island," and "Anne of Windy Poplars." The Canadian Broadcasting Corporation, PBS, and Disney worked together on this WonderWorks production. On two tapes.

1987 224m/C Megan Follows, Colleen Dewhurst, Wendy Hiller, Frank Converse, Patricia Hamilton, Schuyler Grant, Jonathan Crombie, Rosemary Dunsmore; **D:** Kevin Sullivan; **W:** Kevin Sullivan; **M:** Hagood Hardy. **VHS, Beta, LV** *KUI, TOU, DIS*

Anne of Green Gables ♫♫♫

Family Lonely Canadian couple adopt orphan girl Anne, who keeps them on their toes with her lively imagination and wins a permanent place in their hearts. Warm but loose adaptation of Lucy Maud Montgomery's popular novel is entertaining, though no match for the 1985 remake. Lead actress was previously known as Dawn

O'Day but identified with the fictional heroine so closely she assumed Anne's name in real life.

1934 79m/B Anne Shirley, Tom Brown, O.P. Heggie; **D:** George Nicholls Jr.; **M:** Max Steiner. **VHS, Beta** *TTC*

Anne of Green Gables ♫♫♫ ♪

Family Splendid production of the famous Lucy Maud Montgomery classic about a young orphan girl growing to young adulthood with the help of a crusty old brother and sister. With beautiful Prince Edward Island as a backdrop and splendid period costumes, the characters come to life under Sullivan's direction. One of the few instances where an adaptation lives up to (if not exceeds) the quality of the original novel. A WonderWorks presentation that was made with the cooperation of the Disney channel, the Canadian Broadcasting Corporation, and PBS. Followed by "Anne of Avonlea." On two tapes.

1985 197m/C Megan Follows, Colleen Dewhurst, Richard Farnsworth, Patricia Hamilton, Schuyler Grant, Jonathan Crombie, Marilyn Lightstone, Charmion King, Rosemary Radcliffe, Jackie Burroughs; **D:** Kevin Sullivan; **W:** Kevin Sullivan, Joe Weisenfeld; **M:** Hagood Hardy. **VHS, Beta, LV** *KUI, TOU, IGP*

Annie ♫♫ ♪

PG/Family Stagy big-budget adaptation of the comic-strip-derived Broadway musical has an ideal cast, ideal music, less-than-ideal script that tends to sag under the weight of colossal production values (did they really need the roller-skating elephants?). Entertaining nonetheless, with Burnett a standout as orphanage superintendant Miss Hannigan, scheming to part Little Orphan Annie from her adoptive millionaire Daddy Warbucks. ♫ Tomorrow; It's the Hard Knock Life; Maybe; I Think I'm Gonna Like It Here; Little Girls; We Got Annie; Let's Go to the Movies; You're Never Fully Dressed Without a Smile; Easy Street.

BEWARE *Alcohol use.*

1982 128m/C Aileen Quinn, Carol Burnett, Albert Finney, Bernadette Peters, Ann Reinking, Tim Curry; **D:** John Huston; **M:** Ralph Burns. **VHS, Beta, LV, 8mm** *COL, FCT, MLT*

Annie Hall ♫♫♫

PG/Sr. High-Adult Acclaimed coming-of-cinematic-age film for Allen is based in part on his own life. His love affair with Hall/Keaton is chronicled as an episodic, wistful comedy commenting on family, love, loneliness, communicating, maturity, driving, city life, careers, and various other topics. Abounds with classic scenes, including future star Goldblum and his mantra at a cocktail party; Allen and the lobster pot; and Allen, Keaton, a bathroom, a tennis racket, and a spider. The film operates on many levels, as does Keaton's wardrobe, which started a major fashion trend. Don't blink or you'll miss several future stars in bit parts. Expertly shot by Gordon Willis.

BEWARE *Alcohol use, conversation about sex, existential dialogue, a lobster loose in the kitchen.*

Anne Shirley and Gilbert Blythe smile for the camera in "Anne of Avonlea."

1977 94m/C Woody Allen, Diane Keaton, Tony Roberts, Paul Simon, Shelley Duvall, Carol Kane, Colleen Dewhurst, Christopher Walken, Janet Margolin, John Glover, Jeff Goldblum, Sigourney Weaver, Marshall McLuhan, Beverly D'Angelo, Shelley Hack; **D:** Woody Allen; **W:** Woody Allen, Marshall Brickman. **Award Nominations:** Academy Awards '77: Best Actor (Allen); **Awards:** Academy Awards '77: Best Actress (Keaton), Best Director (Allen), Best Original Screenplay, Best Picture; British Academy Awards '77: Best Actress (Keaton), Best Director (Allen), Best Film; Directors Guild of America Awards '77: Best Director (Allen); Golden Globe Awards '78: Best Actress—Musical/Comedy (Keaton); National Board of Review Awards '77: 10 Best Films of the Year, Best Actress (Keaton); National Society of Film Critics Awards '77: Best Actress (Keaton), Best Film. **VHS, Beta, LV** MGM, FOX, CRC

Annie O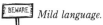

PG/Primary-Adult 15-year-old girl runs into problems when she joins the boys' basketball team. Her teammates are jealous and so are her brother and boyfriend.

 *Mild language.*

1995 93m/C Coco Yares, Chad Willet, Robert Stewart; **D:** Michael McClary. **VHS** HMK

Annie Oakley

Family This biography of the acclaimed shooting star covers her career from age 15 to retirement, including

some actual silent footage of Miss Oakley filmed by Thomas Edison in 1923. Made for television. From the "Tall Tales & Legends" series by Shelly Duvall.

1985 52m/C Jamie Lee Curtis, Cliff DeYoung, Brian Dennehy; **D:** Michael Lindsay-Hogg. **VHS, Beta** FOX

Another Stakeout

PG-13/Sr. High-Adult Sequel six years after the original finds Dreyfuss and Estevez partnered again for another stakeout, this time to keep an eye on Moriarty, a reluctant witness against the Mob. The two spying and squabbling detectives find themselves in an upscale neighborhood where blending in proves difficult. O'Donnell is a breath of fresh air as a wisecracking assistant district attorney tagging along on the stakeout, much to the boys' distress. Stowe briefly reprises her role as Dreyfuss' girlfriend. Writer Kouf reportedly had difficulty penning the script, obviously settling for the tried and true.

Profanity and cop and mob violence.

1993 109m/C Richard Dreyfuss, Emilio Estevez, Rosie O'Donnell, Cathy Moriarty, Madeleine Stowe, John Rubinstein, Marcia Strassman, Dennis Farina, Miguel Ferrer; **D:** John Badham; **W:** Jim Kouf. **VHS, LV** TOU

The Ant and the Aardvark

Preschool-Jr. High Collection of theatrical short cartoons by the animators of the "Pink Panther" series, featuring a endless struggle for supremacy between the title ant-agonists.

1969 32m/C VHS, Beta MGM

Antarctica

Family Unique adventure, based on a true incident of a Japanese 1957 Polar expedition forced by storms to evacuate and abandon their loyal team of sled dogs to certain death. Much later humans returned to find some huskies still surviving. Movie speculates what happened in between, as the canines battle against starvation, icequakes, killer whales, the unknown—and not always winning. Whenever a dog dies its freeze-frame 'obit' is posted for maximum impact, and young pooch-lovers may be upset. A Far East box-office sensation, worth discovering on cassette, although the US video version (dubbed in English) is technically uneven. Fine musical score by Vangelis.

Animal violence.

1984 112m/C Ken Takakura, Masako Natsume, Keiko Oginome; **D:** Koreyoshi Kurahara; **M:** Vangelis. **VHS, Beta** FOX

Any Which Way You Can

PG/Jr. High-Adult Those with an interest in rowdy orangutan adventures will appreciate sequel to "Every Which Way But Loose." Bad brawler Philo Beddoe and his buddy Clyde, the orangutan, return for another of life's little lessons. This time Philo is tempted to take part in a big bout for a large cash prize. Clyde steals scenes, brightening up the no-brainer story.

 *Cartoony and monkey violence.*

1980 116m/C Clint Eastwood, Sondra Locke, Ruth Gordon, Harry Guardino; *D:* Buddy Van Horn. **VHS, Beta, LV** *WAR*

Apollo 13 🦴🦴🦴

PG/Jr. High-Adult Adults should know how the 1970 Apollo lunar mission ended, but many youngsters will find this excellent film reenactment not just fascinating but suspenseful. Some 205,000 miles away from Earth, an explosion leaves the three astronauts (led by Hanks) tumbling in a damaged spacecraft. Director Howard concentrates on the personalities involved in the seven-day adventure up there and at Mission Control as all scramble to devise Plan One from Outer Space. Weightless shots are the real thing: Cast and crew made 600 dives in a NASA jet, each plunge creating 25 seconds of weightlessness. Based on the book "Lost Moon," by Apollo 13's Jim Lovell, seen as the Navy captain greeting the astronauts aboard the recovery ship.

 *Mild language and edge-of-the-sofa emotional intensity. Very young kids may not be able to sit through it.*

1995 140m/C Tom Hanks, Kevin Bacon, Bill Paxton, Gary Sinise, Ed Harris, Kathleen Quinlan, Brett Cullen, Emily Ann Lloyd, Miko Hughes, Max Elliott Slade, Jean Speegle Howard, Tracy Reiner, Michelle Little, David Andrews, Mary Kate Schellhardt; *D:* Ron Howard; *W:* William Broyles Jr., Al Reinert; *M:* James Horner, Dean Cundey. **Award Nominations:** Academy Awards '95: Best Adapted Screenplay, Best Art Direction/Set Decoration, Best Film Editing, Best Picture, Best Sound, Best Supporting Actor (Harris), Best Supporting Actress (Quinlan), Best Score; British Academy Awards '95: Best Cinematography; Directors Guild of America Awards '96: Best Director (Howard); Golden Globe Awards '96: Best Director (Howard), Best Film—Drama, Best Supporting Actor (Harris), Best Supporting Actress (Quinlan); **Awards:** Screen Actors Guild Award '95: Best Supporting Actor (Harris), Cast. **VHS, LV** *MCA*

The Apple Dumpling Gang 🦴🦴

G/Family Three frisky, too-cute children in the Wild West find a giant gold nugget and stage a bank robbery to protect their interests, but things don't go quite as planned. Unmistakably mid-70s Disney (not much of a compliment), marking the first of several collaborations between Knotts and Conway as a kiddie-comedy team.

 *Roughhousing.*

1975 100m/C Bill Bixby, Susan Clark, Don Knotts, Tim Conway, David Wayne, Slim Pickens, Harry (Henry) Morgan; *D:* Norman Tokar; *M:* Buddy Baker. **VHS, Beta** *DIS*

The Apple Dumpling Gang Rides Again 🦴🦴

G/Family Would-be outlaws Amos and Theodore continue terrorizing the West in their bungling attempt to go straight. Fans of Conway or Knotts may appreciate this

Kevin Sullivan Delights Audiences With a Family Classic

Reading the "Anne" books by Canadian author Lucy Maud Montgomery, which follow orphan Anne Shirley from childhood through adulthood on her beloved Prince Edward Island, is a fond memory for many little girls, their mothers, and their grandmothers. Today, Anne has an even larger following worldwide, ever since fellow Canadian Kevin Sullivan brought her vividly to life in the 1985 miniseries *Anne of Green Gables*. As producer, director, and co-writer of the screenplay, Kevin gained almost as many fans as Anne because his dedication to quality entertainment for viewers of all ages is so evident. *Anne* enjoyed enormous success in Canada and the U.S. as well as worldwide; the sequel, *Anne of Avonlea,* was equally successful and both enjoy status as family classics, an achievement earned in little more than a decade.

Kevin's attention to detail shows up in everything from the costumes, to the sets, to the casting of each character. Though neither production follows the books they are based on verbatim, each one stays true to the spirit of the original. A weekly television series based on more of Montgomery's characters from the town of Avonlea, "Road to Avonlea" (also called "Avonlea") recently wrapped its seventh and final season on CBC and is still running on the Disney Channel.

For more information on Kevin Sullivan and Sullivan Entertainment (formerly Sullivan Films), the company he founded in 1979, visit the Sullivan site on the World Wide Web at *http://www.sullivan-ent.com/*.

The crew of the trouble-bound lunar mission in "Apollo 13."

sequel to Disney's "The Apple Dumpling Gang"; others will decide this VCR's not big enough for the two of them.

1979 88m/C Tim Conway, Don Knotts, Tim Matheson, Kenneth Mars, Harry (Henry) Morgan, Jack Elam; **D:** Vincent McEveety; **M:** Buddy Baker. **VHS, Beta** *DIS*

The Apprenticeship of Duddy Kravitz 🦴🦴🦴 ⬠

PG/Jr. High-Adult Jewish teenager in Montreal circa 1948 is driven by an insatiable need to be the "somebody" everyone has always told him he will be. Series of get-rich-quick schemes backfire in different ways, and he becomes most successful at driving people off, even as he attains his superficial goals. Young Dreyfuss, then on the verge of stardom, is at his best. Made in Canada with thoughtful detail, and great performances. Script by Mordecai Richler, from his novel.

⚠ BEWARE! *Sex, alcohol use, circumcision, and meaningless ambition.*

1974 121m/C Richard Dreyfuss, Randy Quaid, Denholm Elliott, Jack Warden, Micheline Lanctot, Joe Silver; **D:** Ted Kotcheff; **W:** Mordecai Richler, Lionel Chetwynd. **Award Nominations:** Academy Awards '74: Best Adapted Screenplay; **Awards:** Berlin International Film Festival '74: Golden Berlin Bear. **VHS, Beta** *PAR*

Aquaman

Family A collection of eight animated adventures featuring that superhero human submarine, Aquaman. Ages 5 to 8.

1967 60m/C VHS, Beta *WAR*

Arabian Knight 🦴🦴

G/Family Animated story of a Princess Yum Yum (Beals) and a cobbler (Broderick) whose lives are forever changed by a thief (Winters). Other than the animation, which was a three-decade labor of Richard Williams from "Who Framed Roger Rabbit?" fame, the plot is a stinker and the songs even worse. Vincent Price supplies the voice of the villain, which he has done better many other times.

1995 ?m/C D: Richard Williams; **W:** Richard Williams; **V:** Matthew Broderick, Jennifer Beals, Vincent Price, Jonathan Winters, Clive Revill. **VHS** *NYR*

Arachnophobia 🦴🦴🦴

PG-13/Jr. High-Adult First theatrical release from Disney's Hollywood Pictures division is a seriocomic version of a nature-on-the-rampage horror story. Lethal South American spiders wind up breeding in a California com-

VIDEOHOUND'S FAMILY VIDEO GUIDE

munity somewhere off the beaten track. There they wreak havoc on two-legged antagonists, including utterly arachnophobic town doctor Daniels and gung-ho insect exterminator Goodman. Script's a bit yawn-inspiring but effective shocks and gore-venom effects make this a cautious choice for youngsters.

BEWARE *Terrifying spider attacks (in other words, if you're afraid of spiders, don't see this one), profanity (often cause-and-effect).*

1990 109m/C Jeff Daniels, John Goodman, Harley Jane Kozak, Julian Sands, Roy Brocksmith, Stuart Pankin, Brian McNamara, Mark L. Taylor, Henry Jones, Peter Jason, James Handy; **D:** Frank Marshall; **W:** Wesley Strick, Don Jakoby; **M:** Trevor Jones. **VHS, Beta, LV** *HPH*

Arena 🎵🎵

PG-13/Sr. High-Adult Remember old boxing melodramas about good-natured palookas, slimy opponents, gangsters and dames? This puts those cliches in a garish sci-fi setting, with handsome Steve Armstrong battling ETs and the astro-mob to be the first human pugilistic champ in decades. A really cute idea (from the screenwriters of "The Rocketeer"), but it conks out at the halfway point. Worth a look for buffs.

1988 97m/C Paul Satterfield, Claudia Christian, Hamilton Camp, Marc Alaimo, Armin Shimerman, Shari Shattuck, Jack Carter; **D:** Peter Manoogian; **W:** Danny Bilson, Paul DeMeo; **M:** Richard Band. **VHS, LV** *COL*

Ariel's Undersea Adventure, Vol. 1: Whale of a Tale

Family Maintaining the high standards of "The Little Mermaid," this video series reaffirms that nobody is in Disney's league under the sea. Both principal voices from the movie, Jodi Benson (Ariel) and and Sam Wright (Sebastian the crab), are along for the voyage. In "A Whale of a Tale," Ariel adopts a lost baby whale, and with the help of Sebastian and Flounder, tries to reunite him with his family. In "Urchin," Ariel makes friends with a mer-boy who has been swimming with gangsters and their friendship is put to the test. Ages 4 to 9.

1992 44m/C VHS, LV *DIS*

Ariel's Undersea Adventure, Vol. 2: Stormy the Wild Seahorse

Preschool-Primary In "Stormy the Wild Seahorse," Ariel tries to tame a wild seahorse against her father's and Sebastian's advice. "The Great Sebastian" follows Sebastian as he travels through shark-infested waters with Ariel and Flounder in tow. Ages 4 to 9.

1993 44m/C VHS, LV *TOU*

Ariel's Undersea Adventure, Vol. 3: Double Bubble

Preschool-Primary "Double Bubble" finds Ariel with her fins full babysitting mer-twins, while trying to foil the kidnapping schemes of Lobster Mobster and Da Shrimp (don't be short with him). In "Message in a Bottle," Ariel meets Simon the Sea Monster who may not be as scary as he seems. Ages 4 to 9.

1993 44m/C VHS, LV *TOU*

Ariel's Undersea Adventure, Vol. 4: In Harmony

Preschool-Primary "In Harmony" finds Ariel mistakenly freeing the evil Manta from a dormant undersea volcano and the creature tries to destroy Atlantica. Next, Ariel is warned by her father Triton never to play with things from the human world in "Charmed." But when she finds a beautiful charm bracelet she can't resist putting it on and it leads her into trouble. Ages 4 to 9.

1993 44m/C VHS, LV *DIS*

Ariel's Undersea Adventure, Vol. 5: Ariel's Gift

Preschool-Primary Sort of "Big" in reverse. A magic Stone of Youth turns King Triton into a young boy who calls himself "Red" and Ariel tries to keep him out of mischief until she can find a way to remove the magic spell. In "Trident True" Ariel wants to give Triton a special gift for Father's Day but she winds up in trouble as usual. Ages 4 to 9.

1993 44m/C VHS, LV *DIS*

The Aristocats 🎵🎵🎵

Family An eccentric woman bequeaths her fortune to her cat, Duchess (Eva Gabor) and her kittens in this animated Disney charmer, but there's a catch. Should the cats die, the money goes to the faithful butler. So, he takes them for a little ride in the country and dumps them there. At least he doesn't kill them; that would litter-ally be the end of the movie. With the help of a tough but friendly alley cat (Harris), the odds shift in favor of the good guys. It's pretty much the feline version of "101 Dalmatians." Maurice Chevalier sings the theme so memorably that many people think he's a character in the movie. Harris sings the almost-as-memorable "Everybody Wants To Be a Cat." Because a cat's the only one who knows where it's at, that's why.

1970 78m/C D: Wolfgang Reitherman; **M:** George Bruns; **V:** Eva Gabor, Phil Harris, Sterling Holloway, Roddy Maude-Roxby, Bill Thompson, Hermione Baddeley, Carol Shelley, Pat Buttram, Nancy Kulp, Paul Winchell. **VHS** *DIS*

Army of Darkness 🎵🎵🎵

R/Sr. High-Adult Campbell returns for a third "Evil Dead" round as the square-jawed, none too bright hero,

Duchess, her beau, and kittens look down from a window in "The Aristocats."

Ash, in this comic book extravaganza. He finds himself hurled back to the 14th-century through the powers of an evil book. There he romances a babe, fights an army of skeletons, and generally causes all those Dark Age knights a lot of grief, as he tries to get back to his own time. Raimi's technical exuberance is apparent and, as usual, the horror is graphic but still tongue-in-cheek.

⚠ BEWARE 『 *Graphic gore and violence all delivered with a smile.*

1992 77m/C Bruce Campbell, Embeth Davidtz, Marcus Gilbert, Ian Abercrombie, Richard Grove, Michael Earl Reid, Tim Quill, Patricia Tallman, Theodore (Ted) Raimi, Ivan Raimi; *Cameos:* Bridget Fonda; *D:* Sam Raimi; *W:* Ivan Raimi, Sam Raimi; *M:* Danny Elfman, Joseph Lo Duca. **VHS, Beta, LV** *MCA, FCT*

Arnold of the Ducks

Family Animated adventure, sort of a Tarzan-of-the-Apes spoof, about a lost baby rescued by ducks and raised as one of their own. Part of the CBS Storybreak series done for network TV and hosted by Captain Kangaroo himself, Bob Keeshan.

1985 25m/C VHS *KUI, FOX*

Around the World in 80 Days
🐾 🐾 🐾

G/Family Niven is Jules Verne's unflappable Victorian Phileas Fogg, who wagers that he can circumnavigate the Earth in four-score days. With his faithful manservant Passepartout they set off on a spectacular race against the clock. Perpetual favorite provides ample entertainment, although the small screen definitely diminishes its impact. More than 40 cameo appearances by many of Hollywood's biggest names occasionally slow the action.

1956 178m/C David Niven, Shirley MacLaine, Cantinflas, Robert Newton, Charles Boyer, Joe E. Brown, Martine Carol, John Carradine, Charles Coburn, Ronald Colman; *Cameos:* Melville Cooper, Noel Coward, Andy Devine, Reginald Denny, Fernandel, Marlene Dietrich, Hermione Gingold, Cedric Hardwicke, Trevor Howard, Glynis Johns, Buster Keaton, Evelyn Keyes, Peter Lorre, Mike Mazurki, Victor McLaglen, John Mills, Robert Morley, Jack Oakie, George Raft, Cesar Romero, Gilbert Roland, Red Skelton, Frank Sinatra, Ava Gardner; *D:* Michael Anderson Sr.; *W:* James Poe, John Farrow, S.J. Perelman; *M:* Victor Young. **Award Nominations:** Academy Awards '56: Best Art Direction/Set Decoration (Color), Best Costume Design (Color), Best Director (Anderson); **Awards:** Academy Awards '56: Best Adapted Screenplay, Best Color Cinematography, Best Film Editing, Best Picture, Best Original Score; Golden Globe Awards '57: Best Actor—Musical/Comedy (Cantinflas), Best Film—Drama; National Board of Review Awards '56: 10 Best Films of the Year; New York Film Critics Awards '56: Best Film. **VHS, Beta, LV** *WAR, BTV, HMV*

Around the World in 80 Days

Family The Jules Verne classic is brought to life via animation.
1991 47m/C VHS *VTR*

Arthur

PG/Jr. High-Adult Spoiled, alcoholic billionaire Moore stands to lose everything he owns when he falls in love with a waitress. He must choose between wealth and a planned marriage, or poverty and love. Surprisingly funny, with an Oscar for Gielgud as Moore's valet, and great performance from Minnelli. Arguably the best role Moore's ever had, and he makes the most of it, taking the one-joke premise to a nomination for Oscar actor.

BEWARE *Extreme alcohol use. Vulgar humor.*

1981 97m/C Dudley Moore, Liza Minnelli, John Gielgud, Geraldine Fitzgerald, Stephen Elliott, Jill Eikenberry, Lou Jacobi; **D:** Steve Gordon; **M:** Burt Bacharach. **Award Nominations:** Academy Awards '81: Best Actor (Moore), Best Original Screenplay; **Awards:** Academy Awards '81: Best Song ("Arthur's Theme"), Best Supporting Actor (Gielgud). **VHS, Beta, LV, 8mm** *WAR, FCT, BTV*

Arthur 2: On the Rocks

PG/Adult When Arthur finally marries his sweetheart, it may not be "happily ever after" because the father of the girl he didn't marry is out for revenge. When Arthur discovers that he is suddenly penniless, a bit of laughter is the cure for the blues and also serves well when the liquor runs out. A disappointing sequel with few laughs.

BEWARE *Mild profanity.*

1988 113m/C Dudley Moore, Liza Minnelli, John Gielgud, Geraldine Fitzgerald, Stephen Elliott, Ted Ross, Barney Martin, Jack Gilford; **D:** Bud Yorkin; **M:** Burt Bacharach. **VHS, Beta, LV, 8mm** *WAR, FCT*

Aspen Extreme

PG-13/Jr. High-Adult Former Aspen ski instructor writes and directs a movie on (what else?) ski instructors in (where?) Aspen. Long on ski shots and short on plot, this movie never leaves the bunny hill. Two Detroiters leave Motown for Snowtown to pursue a life on the slopes. T.J (Gross) soon has his hands full with two beautiful women (Polo and Hughes) who encourage his dream of becoming a writer. His friend Dexter (Berg), however, acquires a few bad habits, and the whole movie just goes downhill from there.

BEWARE *Profanity; suggested sex; alcohol use (which is a no-no on the slopes).*

1993 128m/C Paul Gross, Peter Berg, Finola Hughes, Teri Polo, Martin Kemp, Nicolette Scorsese, William Russ; **D:** Patrick Hasburgh; **W:** Patrick Hasburgh; **M:** Michael Convertino. **VHS, Beta, LV** *HPH, TOU*

Astronomy 101: A Beginner's Guide to the Night Sky

Primary An 11-year-old girl and her mother explore the night sky and learn about the hobby of star-gazing. They're pretty serious about it; they use a telescope to view heavenly bodies and set their alarm clock for the middle of the night to catch the planets at their best and brightest. Children with a genuine interest in astronomy will enjoy this video the most, and children who think they might be interested in astronomy may be inspired to learn more. Ages 10 and up.
1994 25m/C VHS *MAZ*

At the Circus

Family The Marx Brothers invade the circus to save it from bankruptcy and cause their usual comic insanity, though they've done it better before. Beginning of the end for the boys, a step down in quality from their classic work, though frequently darn funny. ♫ Lydia the Tattooed Lady; Step Up and Take a Bow; Two Blind Loves; Blue Moon.

1939 87m/B Groucho Marx, Chico Marx, Harpo Marx, Margaret Dumont, Kenny L. Baker, Florence Rice, Eve Arden, Nat Pendleton, Fritz Feld; **D:** Edward Buzzell. **VHS, Beta, LV** *MGM*

At the Earth's Core

PG/Jr. High-Adult A Victorian scientist invents a giant burrowing machine, which he and his crew use to dig deeply into the Earth. To their surprise, they discover a lost world of subhuman creatures and prehistoric monsters. Based on Edgar Rice Burrough's novels.

BEWARE *Violence.*

1976 90m/C Doug McClure, Peter Cushing, Caroline Munro; **D:** Kevin Connor. **VHS, Beta** *WAR, OM*

Atom Man vs. Superman

Family Serial followup to "The Adventures of Superman" (on video as "Superman: The Serial"), shows Clark Kent changing into the Man of Steel to take on arch-villain Lex Luthor, in a storyline more faithful than most to the vintage comic books. In 15 chapters.

BEWARE *Roughhousing.*

1950 251m/B Kirk Alyn, Lyle Talbot, Noel Neill, Tommy "Butch" Bond, Pierre Watkin; **D:** Spencer Gordon Bennet. **VHS, Beta** *WAR, MLB*

Attack of the Killer Tomatoes **WOOF!**

PG/Jr. High-Adult Candidate for worst film ever made, deliberate category. Horror spoof that defined "low budget" stars several thousand ordinary tomatoes that suddenly turn savage and begin attacking people. No sci-fi cliche remains untouched in this dumb parody. A few

musical numbers are performed in lieu of an actual plot. Followed by "Return of the Killer Tomatoes."

🔲 BEWARE *Incredibly stupid.*

1977 87m/C D: John DeBello. **VHS, Beta** *MED*

Attic In the Blue

Family Animated story about an ancient whaler who goes on a dangerous mission to find his lost love, accompanied only by his octopus-like companion.
1992 27m/C VHS *FCT, PIC*

Au Revoir Les Enfants 🎵🎵🎵🎵

PG/Jr. High-Adult During the Nazi occupation of France, the headmaster of a Catholic boarding school hides three Jewish boys among the students by altering their names and identities. One gentile boy, Julien, forms a friendship with one of the fugitives that ends tragically in a Gestapo raid. Compelling and emotional coming-of-age tale, based on an incident from director Malle's own history. Both French-language subtitled and English-dubbed versions are available.

🔲 BEWARE *Depictions of Nazis during World War II, profanity, sex talk, and alcohol use. Mature theme makes it more suitable for older kids.*

1987 104m/C Gaspard Manesse, Raphael Fejto, Francine Racette, Stanislas Carre de Malberg, Philippe Morier-Genoud, Francois Berleand, Peter Fitz, Francois Negret, Irene Jacob; **D:** Louis Malle; **W:** Louis Malle; **M:** Franz Schubert, Camille Saint-Saens. **Award Nominations:** Academy Awards '87: Best Foreign Language Film, Best Original Screenplay; **Awards:** British Academy Awards '88: Best Director (Malle); Cesar Awards '88: Best Director (Malle), Best Film; Los Angeles Film Critics Association Awards '87: Best Foreign Film; Venice Film Festival '87: Best Film. **VHS, Beta, LV** *INJ, ORI, FCT*

Audrey Rose 🎵🎵

PG/Sr. High-Adult Ivy's parents are terrified when their daughter has dreadful dreams. A mystery man steps in and declares that his deceased little Audrey Rose has been reincarnated in their child. Result is a New-Age courtroom custody drama, not the horror flick the advertising claims; interesting in that aspect, as adults argue over what's best for the girl(s). Adapted by Frank DeFelitta from his novel.

🔲 BEWARE *Reincarnation as a theme.*

1977 113m/C Marsha Mason, Anthony Hopkins, John Beck, John Hillerman; **D:** Robert Wise; **W:** Frank De Felitta. **VHS, Beta** *MGM*

The Aurora Encounter 🎵🎵

PG/Jr. High-Adult Small spaceman lands his flying jalopy in Texas around 1900, befriending Earth kids but panicking authorities (one villain played by the original George "Spanky" McFarland!). Warmhearted but ragged cheapie claims a basis in fact, but inspiration was "E.T." all the way. Potentially disturbing note: alien is portrayed by a little boy with a very real genetic disorder that gave him a gnomelike appearance.

🔲 BEWARE *Violence—though resurrection follows, natch.*

1985 90m/C Jack Elam, Peter Brown, Carol Bagdasarian, Dottie West, George "Spanky" McFarland; **D:** Jim McCullough. **VHS, Beta** *NWV, VTR, HHE*

Author! Author! 🎵🎵 ♭

PG/Jr. High-Adult Sweet, likable comedy about a playwright who is about to taste success with his first big hit. Suddenly his wife walks out, leaving him to care for her four children and his own son. He soon learns to juggle being father and writer without compromising either one.
1982 100m/C Al Pacino, Tuesday Weld, Dyan Cannon, Alan King, Andre Gregory; **D:** Arthur Hiller; **W:** Israel Horovitz; **M:** Dave Grusin. **VHS, Beta** *FOX*

Avalanche 🎵 ♭

PG/Jr. High-Adult Disasterama as vacationers at a new winter ski resort find themselves at the mercy of a monster avalanche leaving a so-called path of terror and destruction in its wake. Talented cast is buried by weak material, producing a snow-bound adventure yawn.
1978 91m/C Rock Hudson, Mia Farrow, Robert Forster, Rick Moses; **D:** Corey Allen. **VHS, Beta**

Avalon 🎵🎵🎵 ♭

PG/Sr. High-Adult Powerful but quiet portrait of the break-up of the family unit as seen from the perspective of an immigrant clan settled in Baltimore at the close of WWII. Initially, the family is unified in their goals, thoughts, and social lives. Gradually, all of this disintegrates; members move to the suburbs and television replaces conversation at holiday gatherings. Based on Levinson's experiences within his own family of Russian Jewish origins.

🔲 BEWARE *Profanity. Kids play with matches with a disastrous result. Adults in the family squabble like children.*

1990 126m/C Armin Mueller-Stahl, Aidan Quinn, Elizabeth Perkins, Joan Plowright, Lou Jacobi, Leo Fuchs, Eve Gordon, Kevin Pollak, Israel Rubinek, Elijah Wood, Grant Gelt, Bernard Hiller; **D:** Barry Levinson; **W:** Barry Levinson; **M:** Randy Newman. **VHS, Beta, LV, 8mm** *COL, FCT*

Ava's Magical Adventure 🎵🎵 ♭

PG/Family Ten-year-old Eddie decides to take Ava on a little adventure. Too bad she's a 2-ton elephant he's stolen from the circus. Based on the Mark Twain story "The Stolen White Elephant."
1994 97m/C Timothy Bottoms, Georg Stanford Brown, Patrick Dempsey, Priscilla Barnes, David Lander, Kaye Ballard, Remi Ryan; **D:** Patrick Dempsey, Rocky Parker; **W:** Susan D. Nimm; **M:** Mark Holden. **VHS, LV** *PSM*

Awakenings 🎵🎵🎵 ♭

PG-13/Jr. High-Adult Touching and fascinating tale, based on fact, of how Dr. Oliver Sacks' (Williams) drug therapy restored consciousness to semi-comatose patients, some of whom had been "asleep" for decades. De Niro is fabulous as a patient taking his first steps into a

 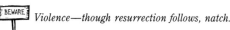

reality he had left as a boy. An achingly sad film—there's no guarantee the transformations will be permanent—but an uplifting one about the humanity that exists even in those who seem less than alive. Williams is touching as the shy doctor who in his own way awakens.

BEWARE *Catatonic patients (actors) could upset children.*

1990 120m/C Robin Williams, Robert De Niro, John Heard, Julie Kavner, Penelope Ann Miller, Max von Sydow, Anne Meara; *D:* Penny Marshall; *W:* Steven Zaillian; *M:* Randy Newman. **Award Nominations:** Academy Awards '90: Best Actor (De Niro), Best Adapted Screenplay, Best Picture; **Awards:** National Board of Review Awards '90: Best Actor (De Niro), Best Actor (Williams). **VHS, Beta, LV, 8mm** *COL, FCT*

Away We Go!

Preschool-Primary A boy, a girl and a salamander puppet named Newt the Newt scoot through New York to catch a flight home in this lively, live action video—a mini-musical, really, since boy, girl and Newt are constantly on the move and there's a song about each mode of transportation they use: an elevator, a taxi, a bus, the Staten Island Ferry and so on. Filmed on location. The songs are by Bob Golden and the late Jonathan Larson ("Rent"). Larson also directed "Away We Go" and he's the big guy dancing in the elevator. Ages 5 to 10.
1996 30m/C VHS *NYR*

Babar and Father Christmas

Family Canadian cartoon depiction of Babar-ism, this time in a holiday mode as Father Christmas (a sort of Euro-Santa) pays a visit to Babar's African kingdom.
1986 30m/B VHS, Beta *MED, VTR, APD*

Babar Comes to America

Family Babar, Celeste, and Artur head to Hollywood to make a movie but get sidetracked several times along the way.
1984 23m/C VHS *FCT*

Babar: Monkey Business

Family Babar the little elephant finds himself up to his trunk in fun thanks to a mischievous simian.
1991 30m/C VHS, Beta *FHE*

Babar Returns

Family Excerpts from the Babar TV cartoon series from Canada's Nelvana Productions. Here the pachyderm potentate tells his daughter Flora the story of how he was crowned king of the elephant herd.
1989 49m/C VHS, Beta *FHE, FCT*

Babar the Elephant Comes to America

Family Further cartoon adventures of de Brunhoffs' famous character depicts Babar setting out for Hollywood by balloon and seeing much of the USA in the process.

Done by the Bill Melendez team responsible for prime time "Peanuts" cartoon specials.
1985 25m/C VHS, Beta *LIV, INJ*

Babar the Little Elephant

Family Actor Ustinov narrates Jean de Brunhoff's story of the wise elephant's younger days, in one of the Babar tales animated by the "Peanuts" team.
1987 25m/C VHS, Beta *VES, LIV*

Babar: The Movie ♫ ♪

G/Family Babar, crowned king of the elephants while merely a boy (kid? cub? calf? that's it, calf) must devise a plan to outwit an angry hoard of rhinos attacking the village of his lady love Celeste. Canada's Nelvana animation studios did this adaption of the classic characters of Jean and Laurent de Brunhoff, but storybook-style visuals feel largely TV grade.
1988 75m/C D: Alan Bunce; **W:** Alan Bunce; **V:** Gavin Magrath, Gordon Pinsent, Sarah Polley, Chris Wiggins, Elizabeth Hanna. **VHS, Beta, LV, 8mm** *FHE, IME*

Babar's First Step

Family In this recent Babar tale, the elephant king tells his grandchildren the painful story of his mother's death and his own acceptance of loss. Could be upsetting to youngsters, but is also possibly an excellent vehicle for inviting children to talk about the death of a loved one.
1990 49m/C VHS *FHE*

Babar's Triumph

Family Babar gathers together all his animal friends to discuss ways in which they can save their jungle.
1989 51m/C VHS *FHE*

The Babe ♫♫ ♪

PG/Jr. High-Adult Follows the life of legendary baseball player Babe Ruth, portrayed as a sloppy drunkard whose appetites for food, drink, and sex were as large as he was. Alvarado and McGillis do well as the Babe's first and second wives, but this is Goodman's show from start to finish. Though a lackluster script laced with soap opera fails to complete the game, Goodman's amazing turn as the party-animal Bambino is reason enough to watch. That last at-bat is inspiring.

BEWARE *Abundant alcohol use by the title character. Sexual situations, bullying, and profanity. Ruth cheats on his wife.*

1992 115m/C John Goodman, Kelly McGillis, Trini Alvarado, Bruce Boxleitner, Peter Donat, J.C. Quinn, Richard Tyson, James Cromwell, Joe Ragno, Bernard Kates, Michael McGrady, Stephen Caffrey; **D:** Arthur Hiller; **W:** John Fusco; **M:** Elmer Bernstein. **VHS, LV** *MCA*

Babe ♫♫♫ ♪

G/Family This little piggy went whee-whee-whee! all the way to popular and critical success and a trough-full of Academy Award nominations. Using real and robotic animals, charming fable has intelligent piglet Babe (wonderfully voiced by Cavanaugh) raised on a farm by matriarch sheepdog Fly, and learning the art of sheep herding. Babe faces sheep rustlers and wild dogs and learns to communicate with his woolly charges. Taciturn farmer Hoggett (the splendid Cromwell) recognizes Babe's talents and comes up with a surprising way to show them off. Filmed in Australia and based on Dick King-Smith's book known variously as "The Sheep Pig" and "Babe, the Gallant Pig."

⚠️ BEWARE *A story to delight the entire family (adults, too!) with a message about overcoming incredible odds and ignoring stereotypes. A likeable animal dies.*

1995 91m/C James Cromwell, Magna Szubanski; **D:** Chris Noonan; **W:** Chris Noonan, George Miller; **C:** Andrew Lesnie; **M:** Nigel Westlake; **V:** Christine Cavanaugh, Miriam Margolyes, Danny Mann, Hugo Weaving. **Award Nominations:** Academy Awards '95: Best Adapted Screenplay, Best Art Direction/Set Decoration, Best Director (Noonan), Best Film Editing, Best Picture, Best Supporting Actor (Cromwell); Writers Guild of America '95: Best Adapted Screenplay; **Awards:** Golden Globe Awards '96: Best Film—Musical/Comedy; National Society of Film Critics Awards '95: Best Film. **VHS, LV** *MCA*

Babes in Arms 🦴🦴

Family Hey, let's put on a show! The children of several vaudeville performers team up to put on a show to raise money for their financially impoverished parents. Judy and Mickey work, worry, and kick up their heels. Loosely adapted from the Rodgers and Hart Broadway musical of the same name though featuring few of the songs. 🎵 Babes in Arms; I Cried for You; Good Morning; You Are My Lucky Star; Broadway Rhythm; Where or When; Daddy Was a Minstrel Man; I'm Just Wild About Harry; God's Country.

1939 91m/B Judy Garland, Mickey Rooney, Charles Winninger, Guy Kibbee, June Preisser; **D:** Busby Berkeley; **M:** Richard Rodgers, Lorenz Hart. **VHS, Beta, LV** *MGM*

Babes in Toyland 🦴🦴🦴

Family Lavish Disney production of Victor Herbert's timeless operetta, with Toyland being menaced by the evil Barnaby and his Bogeymen. Yes, Annette had a life after Mickey Mouse and before the peanut butter commercials. Somewhat charming, although the roles of the lovers seem a stretch for both Funicello and Kirk. But the flick does sport an amusing turn by Wynn.

1961 105m/C Annette Funicello, Ray Bolger, Tommy Sands, Ed Wynn, Tommy Kirk; **D:** Jack Donohue. **VHS, Beta** *DIS*

Babes in Toyland 🦴🦴

Family Young girl must save Toyland from the clutches of the evil Barnaby and his monster minions. Bland TV remake (with new songs by Bricusse) of the classic doesn't approach the original, even with the way-out cast. The good news; video release was trimmed down from the original broadcast version, a 150 minute ordeal.

1986 96m/C Drew Barrymore, Noriyuki "Pat" Morita, Richard Mulligan, Eileen Brennan, Keanu Reeves, Jill Schoelen, Googy Gress; **D:** Clive Donner; **M:** Leslie Bricusse. **VHS, LV** *ORI*

Babes on Broadway 🦴🦴🦴

Family Hey, let's put on another show! Mickey and Judy put on a show to raise money for a settlement house. Nearly the best of the Garland-Rooney series, with imaginative numbers staged by Berkeley. 🎵 Babes on Broadway; Anything Can Happen in New York; How About You?; Hoe Down; Chin Up! Cheerio! Carry On!; Mama Yo Quiero; F.D.R. Jones; Waiting for the Robert E. Lee.

1941 118m/B Mickey Rooney, Judy Garland, Fay Bainter, Richard Quine, Virginia Weidler, Ray Macdonald, Busby Berkeley; **D:** Busby Berkeley. **VHS, Beta, LV** *MGM*

Babies at Play

Preschool Regular toddlers do ordinary things: pet puppies, stir cookie dough, run around the park. These are the sort of videos you wish you could always take— well composed, nicely lighted, no camera jiggle and nobody's head gets chopped off. At best, preschoolers may be prompted to try new activities. At worst, they'll have something pleasing to watch when they can't be active. Ages 1 to 3.

1995 39m/C VHS *WAR*

Baby Animals

Preschool Few things are cuter than baby animals, and here we have cuteness overflowing as we visit baby animals on the farm—chicks, lambs, piglets, calves, colts, even emus and llamas. Ages 1 to 5.

1994 30m/C VHS

Baby Animals Just Want to Have Fun

Preschool-Primary Songs and stories about you know what. Film footage of animals is edited to fit the stories. Creatures featured include puppies, skunks, deer, rabbits and ponies. Ages 1 to 5.

1987 30m/C VHS *MLT*

Baby Boom 🦴🦴🦴

PG/Sr. High-Adult When a hard-charging female executive becomes the reluctant guardian of a baby girl—a gift from a long-lost relative—she adjusts with difficulty to motherhood and life outside the rat race. Fairly harmless collection of cliches helped by Keaton's witty, nervous performance as the New York business lady vastly transformed by tot. To best appreciate flick, see it with a bevy of five- and six-year-olds (a good age for applauding the havoc that a baby creates).

⚠️ BEWARE *Sex talk in the doctor's office and profanity (but not much).*

1987 103m/C Diane Keaton, Sam Shepard, Harold Ramis, Sam Wanamaker, James Spader, Pat Hingle, Mary Gross, Victoria Jackson, Paxton Whitehead, Annie Golden, Dori Brenner, Robin Bartlett, Christopher Noth, Britt Leach; **D:** Charles Shyer; **W:** Charles Shyer, Nancy Meyers; **M:** Bill Conti. **VHS, Beta, LV** *MGM, FCT, FOX*

Farmer Hoggett meets the little piglet that could in "Babe."

Baby, It's You: Dirty Diaper Dancing

Preschool The "Baby, It's You" series is for babies who love to watch other babies, and hopefully join in the fun themselves. In "Dirty Diaper Dancing," toddlers hit the dance floor to strut their stuff and get moving with fancy footwork to "Footloose," "Rock Around the Clock," and "Locomotion."
1996 30m/C VHS

Baby, It's You: Giggles and Gurgles

Preschool Babies dance and have fun to favorite tunes such as "Diamonds Are a Girl's Best Friend," "Please, Mr. Postman," and "Itsy Bitsy Teeny Weeny Yellow Polka Dot Bikini."
1996 30m/C VHS

Baby, It's You: Multiple Madness

Preschool Twins and triplets move to the groove of such hits as "Just the Two of Us," "1-2-3," and "Knock Three Times." Features babies dancing to upbeat music in fun, brightly colored settings.
1996 30m/C VHS

Baby on Board 🎵🎵

PG/Jr. High-Adult Kane plays the wife of a Mafia bookkeeper who is accidentally killed in a gangland murder. Out for revenge, she tracks her husband's killer to JFK airport with her four-year old daughter in tow. Just as she pulls the loaded gun from her purse and takes aim, a pickpocket snatches her purse, accidentally firing the gun. Now she's on the run and she jumps into the first cab she can find, driven by Reinhold. New York City is turned upside down as mother, daughter, and cabbie try to elude the mob in this predictable comedy.

🛑 BEWARE *Violence.*

1992 90m/C Carol Kane, Judge Reinhold, Geza Kovacs, Errol Slue, Alex Stapley, Holly Stapley; **D:** Francis Schaeffer. **VHS, Beta, LV** *PSM*

Baby ... Secret of the Lost Legend 🎵🎵

PG/Family Writer and his paleontologist wife, following reports of dinosaurs still lurking in the African jungle, risk their lives to reunite a hatchling brontosaurus with its giant mother. The Volkswagen-sized baby is (obviously a puppet) cute but hardly convincing by "Jurassic Park" standards; neither is the script of this Disney adventure.

🛑 BEWARE *Dinosaur violence (Baby's dad gets the Bambi's-mother treatment so beloved at Disney), topless native women, sex between the married protagonists.*

1985 95m/C William Katt, Sean Young, Patrick McGoohan, Julian Fellowes; **D:** Bill W.L. Norton. **VHS, Beta, LV** *TOU*

The Baby-Sitter's Club

Primary-Sr. High The phenomenally popular series of juvenile paperbacks by Ann M. Martin have been brought faithfully and frothfully to video in a series of half-hour cassettes, in which the organized group of neighborhood baby-sitters (six adolescent girls and one guest boy) learn various life lessons on and off the job. Tapes include: "The Baby-Sitters and the Boy Sitters," "Claudia and the Mystery of the Secret Passage," "Dawn and the Dream Boy," "Dawn and the Haunted House," "Dawn Saves the Trees," "Jessi and the Mystery of the Stolen Secrets," "Mary Anne and the Brunettes," "The Baby-Sitters Club Special Christmas," "Stacey Takes a Stand," "Stacey's Big Break," and "The Baby-Sitters Remember."
1990 30m/C VHS *GKK*

The Baby-Sitters Club 🎵🎵 ♭

PG/Primary-Adult Girls 8-13 are likely to enjoy this movie about early teen friendship based on the best-selling book series by Ann Martin. The pals spend the summer running a day camp for young kids in town. They also come to terms with issues in their lives. One girl's natural father shows up after a long absence. Another girl has to work on her academic skills in order to pass science. A third has diabetes and worries that it stands in the way of her attracting a boyfriend. Nothing very profound, but main characters are likeable and even get along with parents. Note: Schuyler Fisk, who plays one of the girls, is the daughter of Sissy Spacek. Another young actress, Larisa Oleynik, stars in the kids' TV series "Alex Mack."

🛑 BEWARE *Brief mild language.*

1995 92m/C Schuyler Fisk, Bre Blair, Rachel Leigh Cook, Larisa Oleynik, Tricia Joe, Stacey Linn Ransower, Zelda Harris, Brooke Adams, Peter Horton, Bruce Davison, Ellen Burstyn, Austin O'Brien, Aaron Michael Metchik; **D:** Melanie Mayron; **W:** Dalene Young; **C:** Willy Kurant; **M:** David Michael Frank. **VHS, LV** *COL*

Baby Songs

Preschool Hap Palmer writes songs that toddlers love and parents may find themselves humming at odd moments, which can be embarrassing if the song is "Today I Took My Diapers Off." When turned into music videos the tunes become even better. On this tape they include "My Mommy Comes Back," "Shout & Whisper" and "Sittin' in a High Chair" which features funny footage of a chimpanzee in a high chair acting silly. Ages 1 to 4.
1987 30m/C M: Hap Palmer. **VHS, Beta** *MLT*

Baby Songs Christmas

Family A charming array of holiday songs for infants. Ages 1 to 4.
1991 23m/C VHS, Beta

Baby Songs: Follow Along Songs

Preschool-Primary Children are introduced to colors, the alphabet and musical instruments all through the use of music. Be prepared to march along. Ages 1 to 4.
19?? ?m/C VHS

Baby Songs Presents: Baby Rock

Family A Rock-fest for kids, this edition of Baby Songs features rock classics performed by the original artists including "Blue Suede Shoes," "The Loco-Motion," "Twist & Shout," "I'm Walkin'" and "Wooly Bully." All ages.
1990 30m/C VHS *MED*

Baby Songs Presents: John Lithgow's Kid-Size Concert

Family Actor Lithgow turns out to be a songwriter, too, and a singer-guitarist. Songs and subjects include "I Can Put My Clothes on By Myself," "Getting Up Time," and "What a Miracle I Am." Easy to follow songbook included. Fine fun. Ages 2 to 5.
1990 32m/C John Lithgow. **VHS** *MED, VTR*

Baby Songs: Sing Together

Preschool-Primary Nine sing-along songs for the wee set. Ages 1 to 4.
1992 25m/C VHS

Baby Songs: Turn on the Music

Family In addition to the usual song-fest, this edition of Baby Songs features a clay animation segment. Ages 1 to 4.
1989 30m/C VHS *MED, VTR*

Baby, Take a Bow 🎵🎵

Family Temple's first starring role. As a cheerful Pollyanna-type she helps her father, falsely accused of theft, by finding the true thief. She's cute as a dimple, she is.
1934 76m/B Shirley Temple, James Dunn, Claire Trevor, Alan Dinehart; **D:** Harry Lachman. **VHS, Beta** *FOX*

BabyMugs

Preschool Some very clever Moms came up with this one. How can you occupy your toddler for minutes on end without worrying about them viewing something on the TV that will scar them for life?? Have them watch screen after screen of baby faces. Yes, it's that simple. Babies are fascinated by other babies, hence, the creation of BabyMugs, a video containing babies smiling gurgling, and laughing at the camera. Your little one will be so amazed that s/he may even wonder how those kids got into the TV set.
1994 30m/C VHS *TPV*

Baby's Day Out 🎵🎵

PG/Family Poor man's "Home Alone" refits tired Hughes formula using little tiny baby for original spin. Adorable Baby Bink crawls his way onto the city streets, much to his frantic mother's dismay, and unwittingly outsmarts his would-be kidnappers. As in HA I and II, the bad guys fall victim to all sorts of cataclysmic Looney Tunes violence. Small kids will get a kick out of this one. Particular problem for the moviemakers was that the nine-month old Worton twins were past the year mark by the end of the shoot, a world of difference in infantdom. Blue screens and out-of-sequence shooting were used to overcome the developmental gap.

> **BEWARE** *Cartoony violence involving a baby in peril and bumbling kidnappers. Profanity.*

1994 98m/C Adam Worton, Jacob Worton, Joe Mantegna, Lara Flynn Boyle, Joe Pantoliano, Fred Dalton Thompson, John Neville, Brian Haley, Matthew Glave; **D:** Patrick Read Johnson; **W:** John Hughes; **M:** Bruce Broughton. **VHS** *NYR*

Baby's First Workout: The Gerard Method

Family Patti Gerard Hanna offers a systematic program for motor skills development in a child's first year. Furthermore, the video shows parents the way to monitor their children's physical development through creative play. Parents and babies.
1989 42m/C VHS *KAR*

Bach & Broccoli 🎵🎵🎵🎵

Preschool-Primary Rather than go to a foster home, Fanny tries to charm her bachelor uncle, a self-centered musician, into adopting her and her skunk Broccoli. But the man turns out to have a deep personal reason for his discomfort around her that has nothing to do with the odiferous pet. Sentimental comedy-drama with expert poignancy and the rare virtue of equal respect for both its young and grownup characters. Third in Canadian producer Rock Demers' "Tales for All" series of quality family films.
1987 96m/C Mahee Paiement; **D:** Andre Melancon. **VHS, Beta** *FHE, LIV, FCT*

The Bachelor and the Bobby-Soxer 🎵🎵🎵

Family Playboy Grant is brought before Judge Loy for disturbing the peace and sentenced to court her teen-age sister Temple. Cruel and unusual punishment? Maybe, but the wise Judge hopes that the dates will help Temple

The members of "The Baby-Sitters' Club" celebrate their friendship.

over her crush on handsome Grant. Instead, Loy and Grant fall for each other.

1947 95m/B Cary Grant, Myrna Loy, Shirley Temple, Rudy Vallee, Harry Davenport, Ray Collins, Veda Ann Borg; **D:** Irving Reis; **W:** Sidney Sheldon. **VHS, Beta, LV** *CCB, MED, MLB*

Bach's Flight to Freedom

Family Forget the dour man peering out beneath a powdered wig. Bach must have been young once. In this splendid drama he's vigorous, 30-ish and our Johann Sebastian's in a batch of trouble. He wants to compose music his own way but his patron, a stuffy duke, prefers old-fashioned tunes. Bach (played well by Ted Dykstra) discovers a kindred spirit in a servant boy, Frederick, and together they prove the value of making one's own choices. The music, by you know who, is terrific. Ages 8 and up.

1996 ?m/C VHS *NYR*

Back Home ♪♪ ♭

Family Disney TV period drama about an English girl sent to America for her own safety during the darkest days of WWII. After the Allied victory she returns to Great Britain and boarding school, and must adjust to a family and society now foreign to her.

1990 103m/C Hayley Carr, Hayley Mills, Jean Anderson, Rupert Frazer, Brenda Bruce, Adam Stevenson, George Clark; **D:** Piers Haggard. **VHS** *DIS*

Back to Hannibal: The Further Adventures of Tom Sawyer and Huckleberry Finn ♪♪ ♭

Family Disney TV-movie reunites Twain's characters as adults (15 years after events in "The Adventures of Huckleberry Finn"). Huck is a tabloid reporter, while Tom is a Chicago lawyer; both are brought together to save their freed-slave friend Jim, falsely accused of murder in the killing of Becky Thatcher's husband. Indisputably intriguing premise, but merely mediocre treatment. Contrived script even brings back those con-artists, the King and the Duke, for an unnecessary encore.

⚑ BEWARE *Fighting and alcohol talk.*

1990 92m/C Raphael Sbarge, Mitchell Anderson, Megan Follows, William Windom, Ned Beatty, Paul Winfield; **D:** Paul Krasny; **M:** Lee Holdridge. **VHS** *DIS*

Back to School ♪♪ ♭

PG-13/Sr. High-Adult Under-educated, obnoxious millionaire Dangerfield enrolls in college to help his wimpy son, Gordon, achieve campus stardom. His motto seems to be "if you can't buy it, it can't be had." At first, his antics embarrass his shy son, but soon everyone is clamoring to be seen with the pair as Gordon develops his own self-confidence. Typical rude and silly Dangerfield enterprise proves a consistent chucklefest.

 Vulgar humor.

1986 96m/C Rodney Dangerfield, Keith Gordon, Robert Downey Jr., Sally Kellerman, Burt Young, Paxton Whitehead, Adrienne Barbeau, M. Emmet Walsh, Severn Darden, Ned Beatty, Sam Kinison, Kurt Vonnegut Jr., Robert Picardo, Terry Farrell, Edie McClurg, Jason Hervey; **D:** Alan Metter; **W:** Will Aldis, Steven Kampmann, Harold Ramis, Peter Torokvei, Steven Kampmann; **M:** Danny Elfman. **VHS, Beta, LV** *HBO*

Back to the Beach

PG/Jr. High-Adult Frankie and Annette return to the beach as self-parodying, middle-aged parents with rebellious kids, and the usual run of sun-bleached, lover's tiff comedy ensues. Plenty of songs and guest appearances from television past. Tries to bring back that surf, sun, and sand feel of the original "Beach Party" movies, but instead seems nostalgia wound around a mid-life crisis. Absolute Perfection; California Sun; Catch a Ride; Jamaica Sky; Papa-Oom-Mow-Mow; Sign of Love; Sun, Sun, Sun, Sun, Sun; Surfin' Bird; Wooly Bully.

 Salty language.

1987 92m/C Frankie Avalon, Annette Funicello, Connie Stevens, Jerry Mathers, Bob Denver, Barbara Billingsley, Tony Dow, Paul (Pee Wee Herman) Reubens, Edd Byrnes, Dick Dale, Don Adams, Lori Loughlin; **D:** Lyndall Hobbs; **M:** Stephen Dorff. **VHS, Beta, LV** *PAR*

Back to the Future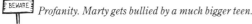

PG/Family When the neighborhood mad scientist constructs a time machine from a sportscar, his youthful companion Marty McFly accidentally transports himself to 1955—and immediately fouls up history by preventing his own future parents from meeting. Marty must do all he can to bring the mismatched mates together again, elude the local bully, and get back ... to the future. Crammed with rich details and a comic pace almost too frenzied, this Spielberg production was a megahit that made a superstar out of Fox, perfectly cast as the resourceful '80s boy who introduces rock 'n roll to the uncomprehending '50s high schoolers. Followed by two sequels and a cartoon TV series, all available on video.

 Profanity. Marty gets bullied by a much bigger teen.

1985 116m/C Michael J. Fox, Christopher Lloyd, Lea Thompson, Crispin Glover, Wendie Jo Sperber, Marc McClure, Thomas F. Wilson, James Tolkan, Casey Siemaszko, Billy Zane, George DiCenzo, Courtney Gains, Claudia Wells, Jason Hervey, Harry Waters Jr., Maia Brewton, J.J. Cohen; **Cameos:** Huey Lewis; **D:** Robert Zemeckis; **W:** Robert Zemeckis, Bob Gale; **M:** Alan Silvestri. **Award Nominations:** Academy Awards '85: Best Original Screenplay, Best Song ("The Power of Love"), Best Sound; **Awards:** People's Choice Awards '86: Best Film. **VHS, Beta, LV** *MCA, FCT, TLF*

Back to the Future, Part 2

PG/Jr. High-Adult The Doc and Marty McFly are time-hopping again after they find the present radically changed because of their earlier trips to future and past. Three generations of McFlys are visited by the pair while they try to set things straight. Fast, furious, and funny, but not quite as memorable as the first BTTF (which you need to watch immediately before this in order to comprehend storyline). Leads to a cliffhanger ending, setting the stage for Part III.

 Profanity and mild sex talk.

1989 107m/C Michael J. Fox, Christopher Lloyd, Lea Thompson, Thomas F. Wilson, Harry Waters Jr., Charles Fleischer, Joe Flaherty, Elisabeth Shue, James Tolkan, Casey Siemaszko, Jeffrey Weissman, Flea, Billy Zane, J.J. Cohen, Darlene Vogel, Jason Scott Lee, Crispin Glover, Ricky Dean Logan; **D:** Robert Zemeckis; **W:** Robert Zemeckis, Bob Gale; **M:** Alan Silvestri. **VHS, Beta, LV** *MCA*

Back to the Future, Part 3

PG/Jr. High-Adult Marty learns Doc Brown met an early death in a gunfight after being flung to 1885 in Part II. The boy time-warps back to the Wild West era of his hometown to save his friend, meets his own ancestors, the future villain's ancestors, and so on. Filmed simultaneously with Part II, but you wouldn't know it; pace is slower, more romantic and wheezier than the lickety-spit action of earlier two chapters. It's like slowing from 85 mph to 20 in a school zone. Gets an extra half-bone for completing all the storylines tidily. Complete trilogy is available as a boxed set.

 Old West alcohol use and profanity.

1990 118m/C Michael J. Fox, Christopher Lloyd, Mary Steenburgen, Thomas F. Wilson, Lea Thompson, Elisabeth Shue, Matt Clark, Richard Dysart, Pat Buttram, Harry Carey Jr., Dub Taylor, James Tolkan, Marc McClure, Wendie Jo Sperber, J.J. Cohen, Ricky Dean Logan, Jeffrey Weissman; **D:** Robert Zemeckis; **W:** Bob Gale, Robert Zemeckis; **M:** Alan Silvestri. **VHS, Beta, LV** *MCA*

Backbeat

R/Sr. High-Adult Explores the Beatles' early days between '60 and '62, when they were playing Hamburg's underground music scene. Storyline driven by the triangle of John Lennon, his best friend and original bass player, Stu Sutcliff, more painter than musician, and the woman Stu left the band for, Astrid Kirchherr, the photographer who came up with the band's signature look. Hart's dead-on as Lennon, playing him a second time (check out "The Hours and Times"). Energetic, enjoyable debut for director Softley is best when the music takes center stage. Produced by Don Was, the soundtrack captures the Fab Four's early bar band sound with a "supergroup" comprised of alternative rockers from current hot bands.

 Profanity, nudity, sex, and drug use in the tradition of the early days of rock'n'roll.

1994 100m/C Stephen Dorff, Sheryl Lee, Ian Hart, Gary Bakewell, Chris O'Neill, Scot Williams, Kai Wiesinger, Jennifer Ehle; **D:** Iain Softley; **W:** Michael Thomas, Stephen Ward, Iain Softley; **M:** Don Was. **VHS, LV** *PGV*

Bad Boys 🎷🎷 ◌

R/Sr. High-Adult And you thought the old buddy-cop formula was played out. Smith and Lawrence are Miami cops who must track down $100 million dollars worth of heroin stolen from their evidence room before internal affairs shuts down the precinct. Hey, this is no "Fresh Prince of Bel Air." High energy and dazzling action sequences will appeal to your "Lethal Weapon"-loving teen. Loud adventure is made louder still by cranking soundtrack.

BEWARE *Intense violent action; pervasive strong language. Those who don't like killings and the phrase "Oh, s—-!" should steer clear.*

1995 118m/C Martin Lawrence, Will Smith, Tcheky Karyo, Tea Leoni, Theresa Randle, Marg Helgenberger, Joe Pantoliano; **D:** Michael Bay; **W:** Michael Barrie, Jim Mulholland; **C:** Howard Atherton. **VHS, LV** *COL*

Bad Company 🎷🎷🎷 ◌

PG/Jr. High-Adult Thoughtful study of two very different teens in the old west, both Civil War draft dodgers, who roam the vast, often bleak frontier and turn to a fruitless life of crime. Cast and script are perfect in a realistic, unglamorized portrait of young men of the 'wild west.' A movie that really hasn't gotten the attention it deserves. Try it rather than the later R-rated "Young Guns" series.

BEWARE *Wild West violence, danger and gunplay.*

1972 94m/C Jeff Bridges, Barry Brown, Jim Davis, John Savage; **D:** Robert Benton; **W:** David Newman. **VHS, Beta, LV** *PAR*

Bad Medicine WOOF!

PG-13/Jr. High-Adult A youth who doesn't want to be a doctor is accepted by a highly questionable Latin American school of medicine. The kind of movie for which Steve Guttenberg is famous—sort of Police Academy Goes To Med School. Remember that it was for medical students like these that the U.S. liberated Grenada.

BEWARE *Profanity, sex and ethnic jokes.*

1985 97m/C Steve Guttenberg, Alan Arkin, Julie Hagerty, Bill Macy, Curtis Armstrong, Julie Kavner, Joe Grifasi, Robert Romanus, Taylor Negron, Gilbert Gottfried; **D:** Harvey Miller. **VHS, Beta** *FOX*

The Bad News Bears 🎷🎷🎷 ◌

PG/Family Misfit Little League team gets whipped into shape by a cranky, sloppy, beer-drinking coach who scandalizes winning-is-everything parents by recruiting a tomboy girl pitcher. O'Neal and Matthau score home runs with their cantankerous, sometimes touching relationship, and the supporting juvenile cast displays great teamwork as they pull together for the big game. Megahit spawned two sequels, a TV series and many imitators.

This was the first mainstream movie to showcase kids with realistic sandlot mouths, so be forewarned—the kids display a certain anti-authority attitude and let choice remarks fly, pioneering the era of rebellious toilet-talking tykes on the silver screen. By later standards these samples of 1976 profanity ("hell" and "damn") are mild indeed. On the positive values side, there's the usual, though skillfully subtle, lesson on sportsmanship and co-operation. At any rate, it's darn funny and kinda touching.

BEWARE *Continuous beer drinking; ballpark language, morally complex kids and adults.*

1976 102m/C Walter Matthau, Tatum O'Neal, Vic Morrow, Joyce Van Patten, Jackie Earle Haley; **D:** Michael Ritchie. **VHS, Beta, LV, 8mm** *PAR*

The Bad News Bears Go to Japan 🎷

PG/Family Second sequel to the classic in which the famed Little Leaguers volunteer to represent the USA on the field against an undefeated team of Japanese tykes. But the Bears need money for the Tokyo trip, and in steps publicity hungry talent agent Curtis. Dull comedy/travelogue, without much time devoted to baseball, or even to the kids themselves. See the original.

BEWARE *Alcohol use. The foul language of earlier Bears adventures is nearly absent.*

1978 102m/C Tony Curtis, Jackie Earle Haley, Tomisaburo Wakayama, George Wyner; **D:** John Berry. **VHS, Beta, LV** *PAR*

The Bad News Bears in Breaking Training 🎷 ◌

PG/Family Minor-league sequel with the Bears, lacking the social commentary of the first film, coming across as just another ragtag kiddie sports franchise—the Mighty Ducks without ice. With a chance to take on a Houston team, the kids devise a way to get to Texas and play at the famed Astrodome. Followed halfheartedly by "The Bad News Bears Go to Japan" (1978).

BEWARE *Baseballish Bear language.*

1977 105m/C William Devane, Clifton James, Jackie Earle Haley, Jimmy Baio; **D:** Michael Pressman; **W:** Paul Brickman. **VHS, Beta, LV** *PAR*

The Bad Seed 🎷🎷 ◌

Jr. High-Adult Mother makes tortuous discovery all parents hope to avoid: her cherubic eight-year-old daughter harbors an innate desire to kill. Based on Maxwell Anderson's powerful Broadway stage play (with many in the cast reprising their roles), it's stiff but anxiety inspiring. Remade for television in 1985.

BEWARE *A murderous child and many scary scenes.*

1956 129m/B Patty McCormack, Nancy Kelly, Eileen Heckart, Henry Jones, Evelyn Varden, Paul Fix; **D:** Mervyn LeRoy; **M:** Alex North. **Award Nominations:** Academy Awards '56: Best Actress (Kelly), Best Black and White Cinematography, Best Supporting Actress (Heckart, McCormack); **Awards:** Golden Globe Awards '57: Best Supporting Actress (Heckart). **VHS, Beta** *WAR*

Bagdad Cafe 🦴🦴🦴

PG/Jr. High-Adult A large German woman, played by Sagebrecht, finds herself stranded in the Mojave desert after her husband dumps her on the side of the highway. She encounters a rundown cafe where she becomes involved with the off-beat residents. A hilarious story in which the strange people and the absurdity of their situations are treated kindly and not made to seem ridiculous. Spawned a short-lived TV series with Whoopi Goldberg.

BEWARE *Eccentrics best appreciated by adults.*

1988 91m/C Marianne Sagebrecht, CCH Pounder, Jack Palance, Christine Kaufmann, Monica Calhoun, Darron Flagg; **D:** Percy Adlon; **W:** Percy Adlon; **M:** Bob Telson. **Award Nominations:** Academy Awards '88: Best Song ("Calling You"); **Awards:** Cesar Awards '89: Best Foreign Film. **VHS, Beta** *FCT, VTR*

The Ballad of Paul Bunyan

Family TV special uses animation to retell the legend of the legendary lumberjack, from his discovery as a baby in an extra-large floating crib to the day he dug Niagara Falls as part of a logging competition. Also on tape in a double-feature cassette with another Rankin/Bass rendering of an American legend, "Johnny Appleseed."

1972 30m/C D: Arthur Rankin Jr., Jules Bass. **VHS** *VTR, PSM*

Ballet Shoes 🦴🦴 ⌐

Family Cheerful all-ages entertainment set in Victorian London, where three adopted sisters in a struggling, eccentric family look to a career on the stage, and their guardian Sylvia goes to extremes to ensure that girls can afford to remain in the dance academy. BBC-TV production based on the book by Noel Streatfeild.

19?? 120m/C VHS *VCO, HMV*

Balto 🦴🦴 ⌐

G/Family Alaska, 1925. A diphtheria epidemic imperils the children of Nome but there is no serum left in the whole town. Enter sled dog Balto (voiced by Bacon), half-wolf, half-husky and all heart, leading his team on a 600-mile trek to deliver medicine to the stricken city. Animated adventure packs plenty of excitement and personality, with polar bears Muk and Luk voiced by Phil Collins and Boris the goose brought to life by animation veteran Bob Hoskins providing comic relief. Based on a true story; there's a statue of the real Balto in New York's Central Park, and the Iditarod dogsled race commemorates the harrowing journey.

BEWARE *Depiction of sick children, animals fighting, Balto kisses his girlfriend, Jenna (mush!).*

1995 78m/C D: Simon Wells; **W:** Cliff Ruby, Elana Lesser, David Steven Cohen, Roger S.H. Schulman; **M:** James Horner; **V:** Kevin Bacon, Bob Hoskins, Bridget Fonda, Jim Cummings, Phil Collins, Juliette Brewer, Danny Mann, Miriam Margolyes. **VHS, LV** *MCA*

Bambi 🦴🦴🦴🦴

G/Family True Disney classic, detailing the often harsh education of a newborn deer and his friends in the forest. Proves that Disney animation was—and still is—the best to be found. Thumper still steals the show and the music is delightful, including "Let's Sing a Gay Little Spring Song," "Love is a Song," "Little April Shower," "The Thumper Song," and "Twitterpated." Stands as a genuine perennial from generation to generation. Based very loosely on the book by Felix Salten.

BEWARE *Bambi's mama dies, a tragedy that still evokes discussion today when compared to death scenes in such movies as "The Lion King."*

1942 69m/C D: David Hand; **W:** Larry Morey; **M:** Frank Churchill, Edward Plumb; **V:** Bobby Stewart, Peter Behn, Stan Alexander, Cammie King, Donnie Dunagan, Hardie Albright, John Sutherland, Tim Davis, Sam Edwards, Sterling Holloway, Ann Gillis, Perce Pearce. **VHS, Beta, LV** *DIS, APD, RDG*

Bananas 🦴🦴🦴

PG/Jr. High-Adult Intermittently hilarious pre-"Annie Hall" Allen fare is full of the director's signature angst-ridden philosophical comedy. A frustrated product tester from New York runs off to South America, where he volunteers his support to the revolutionary force of a shaky Latin-American dictatorship and winds up the leader. Don't miss cameos by Stallone and Garfield. Witty score contributes much.

BEWARE *Howard Cosell calls the play-by-play of a couple in bed.*

1971 82m/C Woody Allen, Louise Lasser, Carlos Montalban, Howard Cosell, Charlotte Rae, Conrad Bain; **Cameos:** Sylvester Stallone, Allen (Goorwitz) Garfield; **D:** Woody Allen; **W:** Woody Allen; **M:** Marvin Hamlisch. **VHS, Beta, LV** *MGM, FCT, FOX*

The Band Wagon 🦴🦴🦴 ⌐

Family Theater set is cleverly satirized as Hollywood song-and-dance man with sagging career finds trouble when he is persuaded to star in a Broadway musical. Faust-obsessed director (Buchanan) falls prey to arthouse demons and the female lead (Charisse) doesn't seem to think much of the dancing partnership. Engaging, witty look behind the scenes has great numbers written by Howard Dietz and Arthur Schwartz and wonderful dancing. 🎵 That's Entertainment; Dancing in the Dark; By Myself; A Shine On Your Shoes; Something to Remember You By; High and Low; I Love Louisa; New Sun in the Sky; I Guess I'll Have to Change My Plan.

1953 112m/C Fred Astaire, Cyd Charisse, Oscar Levant, Nanette Fabray, Jack Buchanan, Bobby Watson; **D:** Vincente Minnelli; **M:** Arthur Schwartz, Jason James Richter. **VHS, Beta, LV** *MGM, FCT*

Bandolero! 🦴🦴 ⌐

PG/Family In Texas, Stewart and Martin are two fugitive brothers who escape the gallows, take Welch as a hostage, and run into trouble with their Mexican counterparts. Straight-ahead western is an enjoyable romp with fine performances.

"Balto" courageously leads his team through the icy mountains.

1968 106m/C James Stewart, Raquel Welch, Dean Martin, George Kennedy, Will Geer, Harry Carey Jr., Andrew Prine; **D:** Andrew V. McLaglen; **M:** Jerry Goldsmith. **VHS, Beta** *FOX*

Bang the Drum Slowly 🦴🦴🦴🦴

PG/Jr. High-Adult Touching story of a journeyman major league catcher who discovers that he is dying of Hodgkins disease and wants to play just one more season. Weakening ball player De Niro is supported by star pitcher Moriarty through thick and thin. Well-made locker room tearjerker (hey, there's no crying in baseball!) is based on a novel by Mark Harris and had been adapted earlier for television with Paul Newman and Albert Salmi.

 *A terminal illness.*

1973 97m/C Robert De Niro, Michael Moriarty, Vincent Gardenia, Phil Foster, Ann Wedgeworth, Heather MacRae, Selma Diamond, Danny Aiello; **D:** John Hancock. **Award Nominations:** Academy Awards '73: Best Supporting Actor (Gardenia); **Awards:** National Board of Review Awards '73: 10 Best Films of the Year; New York Film Critics Awards '73: Best Supporting Actor (De Niro). **VHS, Beta, LV** *PAR, FCT*

Barbarosa 🦴🦴🦴

PG/Family Offbeat western about an aging, legendary outlaw constantly on the lam who reluctantly befriends a naive farmboy and teaches him survival skills. Nelson and Busey are a great team, solidly directed. Lovely Rio Grande scenery.

 *Outlaw violence and gunplay.*

1982 90m/C Willie Nelson, Gilbert Roland, Gary Busey, Isela Vega; **D:** Fred Schepisi; **M:** Bruce Smeaton. **VHS, Beta, LV** *FOX*

The Barefoot Executive 🦴🦴

G/Family Mailroom boy who works for a national television network discovers that his girlfriend's pet chimpanzee has a knack for picking hit TV shows. He uses the critter to rise through the corporate ranks, a story based on the real-life climb of many present day execs. Bland Disney family comedy could have used the primate's help in its joke selection.

1971 92m/C Kurt Russell, John Ritter, Harry (Henry) Morgan, Wally Cox, Heather North; **D:** Robert Butler. **VHS, Beta** *DIS, OM*

Barnaby and Me 🦴🦴

Family Let's see, you and da kids are looking for something different in the engaging animal category. You've seen dogs, cats, seals, dolphins, chimpanzees, maybe a kangaroo or two, but never an adorable koala bear? Have we got a movie for you. The Six Flags amusement park empire tried to enter the family film biz by producing this seldom-seen made for TV marsupial adventure from Down Under. An international con man being pursued by the mob complicates his life by falling for a lovely young woman whose daughter has a pet koala named Barnaby. **1977 90m/C** Sid Caesar, Juliet Mills, Sally Boyden; **D:** Norman Panama. **VHS, Beta** *ACA*

Barney & Friends: Barney Rhymes with Mother Goose

Preschool Big purple dinosaur is back with a dozen classic songs and rhymes, including "Polly Put the Kettle On" and "Little Jack Horner."
1993 30m/C VHS *LGV*

Barney & Friends: Barney's Best Manners

Preschool Big purple dinosaur and his pals have a picnic with games and songs to teach manners, including "Please and Thank-You," "Snackin' on Healthy Food," "Does Your Chewing Gum Lose Its Flavor," and for fun "Three Little Fishies."
1993 30m/C VHS *LGV*

Barney & Friends: Families are Special

Preschool Adored by preschoolers, ridiculed by their older siblings, and either loved or loathed by parents, the genial purple dinosaur with the perpetually frozen smile has become a cultural icon. He may not be hip, but he's the closest thing to a hug you can find on video. In this installment of the Barney oeuvre, Barney and his friends explore family values. Meanwhile, Tosha is excited by the new birth in her family. Ages 1 to 5.
1995 30m/C VHS *LGV*

Barney Live in New York City

Preschool The Purple One hits Radio City Music Hall for an evening (okay, late afternoon) of songs and general niceness. Parents may want to take something for their queasiness before viewing. Ages 1 to 5.
1994 60m/C VHS *LGV*

Barney's Alphabet Zoo

Preschool Purple dinosaur and friends take trip to imaginary zoo. Ages 1 to 5.
1994 30m/C VHS *LGV*

Barney's Christmas Surprise

Preschool This Barney is not the purple dinosaur but a lovable English sheepdog with a mouse friend named Roger. Six animated short stories are told of Barney's adventures with Christmas, skiing, and dieting.
1992 30m/C VHS *GKK*

Barney's Imagination Island

Preschool Tosha and Min sail with Barney and friends to Imagination Island where they meet toy inventor Professor Tinkerputt who doesn't want anyone to play with his toys. Betcha Barney straightens him out. Ages 1 to 5.
1994 48m/C VHS *LGV*

Baron Munchausen 🦴🦴🦴

Sr. High-Adult Not to be confused with the Terry Gilliam's "Munchausen," this costly epic about the adventurous aristocrat of Teutonic lore was done for the 25th anniversary of Germany's UFA film studios. Contemplative, sometimes ponderous plot finds a modern descendent of Baron Munchausen retelling tall tales of his immortal ancestor in uncanny detail. Can he possibly be . . . ? Paced and nuanced for adults rather than kids, and showcasing the biggest stars of the era—which happened to be that of the Third Reich, the reason this seldom screened outside of wartime Germany. Now available for reappraisal thanks to video, in subtitled or English-dubbed editions.

🚸 BEWARE 🚸 *Brief nudity in a sultan's harem. Fantasy violence, and a tearjerking death scene.*
1943 120m/C Hans Albers, Kaethe Kaack, Hermann Speelmanns, Leo Slezak; **D:** Josef von Baky. **VHS, Beta** *INJ, VCD, GLV*

Basil Hears a Noise

Preschool-Primary Basil's metabolism rises as the fuzzy Muppet bear treks through an enchanted forest to find out who'd been playing tricks on everybody. Along the way, timid Basil also discovers the courage within himself. A charmer with nifty Muppet songs. Ages 3 to 6.
1993 28m/C VHS *REP, CTW, BTV*

The Basketball Diaries 🦴🦴

R/Sr. High-Adult Adaptation of underground writer/musician Jim Carroll's 1978 cult memoirs, with DiCaprio starring as the teen athlete whose life spirals into drug addiction and hustling on the New York streets. Carroll and friends Mickey (Wahlberg), Neutron (McGaw), and Pedro (Madio), form the heart of St. Vitus' hot hoopster team. But the defiant quartet really get their kicks from drugs, dares, and petty crime—leading to an ever-downward turn. The book takes place in the '60s but the film can't make up its mind what the decade is, although DiCaprio (and Wahlberg) are particularly effective in a self-conscious first effort from Kalvert.

🚸 BEWARE 🚸 *Stars have kid appeal, but this is not a movie for anyone under 16. Graphic depiction of drug addiction with related strong violence, sexuality and profanity.*
1994 102m/C Leonardo DiCaprio, Mark Wahlberg, Patrick McGaw, James Madio, Bruno Kirby, Ernie Hudson, Lorraine Bracco, Juliette Lewis, Josh Mostel, Michael Rapaport, Michael Imperioli; **Cameos:** Jim Carroll; **D:** Scott Kalvert; **W:** Bryan Goluboff; **C:** David Phillips; **M:** Graeme Revell. **VHS** *PGV*

Batman

Family The caped crusader and his faithful sidekick Robin battle crime in Gotham City in this collection of eight animated adventures from the old days. Ages 5 to 10.
1967 60m/C VHS, Beta *WAR*

Batman 🦴🦴🦴

PG-13/Jr. High-Adult Blockbuster fantasy epic that brought a dark, adult perspective to the comic book. Keaton plays the mild-mannered Bruce Wayne with enough nervous tics (he sleeps hanging upside down) to suggest a damaged personality when he steps into his Caped Crusader costume to fight the crime that long ago took his parents' lives. Nicholson steals the show as the disfigured, genuinely sadistic Joker whose connection to Batman turns out to be very personal. Some said this was too violent for kids, but marketing made it a moot point, with Batman toys and souvenirs gleefully peddled to youngsters, and the same problem arose with the sequel "Batman Returns." Best for older kids only, though nearly all age ranges have thus far taken a peek.

BEWARE *Frequent violence isn't realistic but often crosses the line into gruesome, especially the Joker's fondness for deadly chemicals. Profanity, sex.*

1989 126m/C Michael Keaton, Jack Nicholson, Kim Basinger, Robert Wuhl, Tracey Walter, Billy Dee Williams, Pat Hingle, Michael Gough, Jack Palance, Jerry Hall; **D:** Tim Burton; **W:** Sam Hamm, Warren Skaaren; **M:** Danny Elfman, Prince. **VHS, Beta, LV, 8mm** *FOX, WAR*

Batman Forever 🦴🦴

PG-13/Jr. High-Adult Not quite the equal of the sequel, at least the Batman threequel, with Kilmer in the title role, isn't as grim as its predecessors. And it makes an appeal to a younger audience by introducing Robin (O'Donnell) as the Caped Crusader's sidekick. Kidman is fun as sultry shrink Chase Meridian, whose name sounds like a worldwide banking conglomerate. Carrey's maniacal Riddler gets tedious in a hurry, but Jones's Two-Face—he blames Batman for his disfigurement and wants revenge—is fun to watch. Their weapon: A new form of TV that sucks out the brainpower of all who watch it. Whaddya mean, that's not new? Besides, it's a Batman movie. Who needs a plot?

BEWARE *Strong stylized violence in the comic book tradition. Some sexual innuendos between Batman and the shrink. Death may need to be explained to younger viewers. (Robin becomes an orphan.) Gauge this one on the first two, except not quite as dark.*

1995 121m/C Val Kilmer, Tommy Lee Jones, Jim Carrey, Chris O'Donnell, Nicole Kidman, Drew Barrymore, Debi Mazar, Michael Gough, Pat Hingle; **D:** Joel Schumacher; **W:** Janet Scott Batchler, Akiva Goldsman, Lee Batchler; **C:** Stephen Goldblatt; **M:** Elliot Goldenthal. **VHS, LV** *WAR*

Batman: Mask of the Phantasm

PG/Jr. High-Adult Feature-length theatrical release based on the '90s TV cartoon series that rendered Batman in 'toon form with some of the flair (and none of the mean spirit) of the Tim Burton movies. Major complaint was the bigscreen animation was identical to the small screen's, but on home video that matters not. Story illuminates Bruce Wayne's past more than the live-action epics, as Batman gets blamed for the murders of Gotham City gangsters, and there's a predictable connection to his long-lost first love. Interesting stuff for Batfans, but tale concludes like a comic book—full of infuriating, 'stay-tuned' loose ends. Yes, that is "Star Wars" Jedi Hamill doing the voice of the evil Joker.

⚑ BEWARE *Violence.*

1993 77m/C D: Eric Radomski, Bruce W. Timm; **W:** Michael Reeves, Alan Burnett, Paul Dini, Martin Pako; **M:** Shirley Walker; **V:** Kevin Conroy, Dana Delany, Mark Hamill, Stacy Keach, Hart Bochner, Abe Vigoda, Efrem Zimbalist Jr., Dick Miller. **VHS** *WAR*

Batman Returns ♪♪ ▷

PG-13/Jr. High-Adult More of the same from director Burton, with Batman/Bruce Wayne in a supporting role overshadowed by provocative villains. There's the cruelly misshapen Penguin, whose own father (former Pee Wee Herman Rubens, of all people) tried to kill him at birth; now he has a nightmare plot against Gotham City's children. And there's the exotic, dangerous Catwoman—a wickedly sexy character with more than a passing interest in Batman. Plotting takes a distant second to special effects, grotesque sets, thunderous music. Despite a big budget, grandiose sequel is of the love it or leave it variety, and insanely dark elements really make one wonder what age group it was intended for. A certain fast food chain caught flak for pushing "Batman Returns" merchandise onto kids.

⚑ BEWARE *Violence, profanity, sex talk, and grotesque characters. Very dark setting.*

1992 126m/C Michael Keaton, Danny DeVito, Michelle Pfeiffer, Christopher Walken, Michael Gough, Michael Murphy, Cristi Conaway, Pat Hingle, Vincent Schiavelli, Jan Hooks, Paul (Pee Wee Herman) Reubens, Andrew Bryniarski; **D:** Tim Burton; **W:** Daniel Waters; **M:** Danny Elfman. **VHS** *WAR*

*batteries not included ♪♪ ▷

PG/Family As a real estate developer schemes to demolish a city tenement, the few remaining residents are aided by flying china. Turns out the levitating dishes are aliens with a talent for home improvement. Steven Spielberg produced this sci-fi reworking of the old elves-and-the-shoemaker fairy tale, with the usual superb special f/x, awed stares, and utter schmaltz. Of the human actors, only crusty Cronyn doesn't get carried away by the cutes.

Meet the Star of Batman Forever, Chris O'Donnell

When Chris O'Donnell played a straight-laced prep school student corrupted by Al Pacino in *Scent of a Woman,* it wasn't much of a stretch: O'Donnell was a straight-laced preppie. In fact, his mother had to bribe him with the promise of a new car to get him to forsake his suburban Chicago prep-school rowing crew and fly to Los Angeles to audition for his first film, *Men Don't Leave.*

Growing up in a conservative Catholic family, O'Donnell had a mother who was a real estate broker and a father who owned a radio station. The charismatic one among seven children, at 13 he started making commercials. While filming *Fried Green Tomatoes, School Ties, Scent of a Woman* and *The Three Musketeers,* O'Donnell was completing his marketing degree at Boston College. Well-groomed and well-grounded, he still lives in Illinois and loves golf. His favorite actor is down-to-earth Jimmy Stewart.

Making *Mad Love* with Drew Barrymore, O'Donnell started to grow out of his clean-cut image. Playing a leather-suited, teasingly sexual Robin in *Batman Forever,* O'Donnell began sporting a buzz cut and a more dangerous image. Alternating between a romantic lead in "small" films such as *Circle of Friends* and roles in commercial blockbusters, O'Donnell by 1996 was making $2-3 million a film while still in his mid-20s and his future seems bright.

BEWARE *Violence, sex talk—there's a pretty embarrassing scene in which the two main space creatures get intimate, extraterrestrial-style.*

1987 107m/C Hume Cronyn, Jessica Tandy, Frank McRae, Michael Carmine, Elizabeth Pena, Dennis Boutsikaris; **D:** Matthew Robbins; **W:** Matthew Robbins, Brad Bird, Brent Maddock, S.S. Wilson; **M:** James Horner. **VHS, Beta, LV** *MCA*

Battle Beyond the Stars

PG/Primary-Adult The planet Akir must be defended against alien raiders, so Thomas recruits a team of spacegoing mercenaries. Sci-fi takeoff on the Japanese adventure "The Seven Samurai" is one of the better "Star Wars" ripoffs, thanks to the pen of John Sayles. Producer Roger Corman later used excerpts of it in more kid-oriented features "Space Raiders" and "Andy and the Airwave Rangers."

BEWARE *Space violence.*

1980 105m/C Richard Thomas, Robert Vaughn, George Peppard, Sybil Danning, Sam Jaffe, John Saxon, Darlanne Fluegel; **D:** Jimmy T. Murakami; **W:** John Sayles; **M:** James Horner. **VHS, Beta, LV** *VES, LIV*

Battle for Moon Station Dallos

Family Confusing but well-drawn Japanese cartoon feature about a guerilla war for independence waged by slave-like 'colonists' on the moon. Dallos is a mysterious lunar city the freedom fighters actually worship as a god. Inconclusive ending leaves room for lots of sequels. Notable as an example of 'adult' japanimation (deadly serious, with no silly robot or talking animal sidekicks) that's safe for kids; it avoids the sex, graphic carnage, profanity and nudity that have made the genre notorious. Also reportedly the first Japanese animated feature made for their domestic direct-to-video market, rather than the theater or TV.

BEWARE *Violence.*

1986 84m/C D: Mamoru Oshii. **VHS, Beta** *JFK*

Battle for the Planet of the Apes

G/Family Final chapter is the least interesting in the five-movie simian saga. Tribe of human atomic bomb mutations are out to make life miserable for the peaceful ape tribe. The story is told primarily in flashback with the opening and closing sequences taking place in the year 2670 A.D.

BEWARE *Violence.*

1973 96m/C Roddy McDowall, Lew Ayres, John Huston, Paul Williams, Claude Akins, Severn Darden, Natalie Trundy; **D:** J. Lee Thompson. **VHS, Beta** *FOX*

Battle of Britain

G/Family A powerful retelling of the most dramatic aerial combat battle of WWII, showing how the understaffed Royal Air Force held off the might of the German Luftwaffe.

1969 132m/C Michael Caine, Laurence Olivier, Trevor Howard, Kenneth More, Christopher Plummer, Robert Shaw, Susannah York, Ralph Richardson, Curt Jurgens, Michael Redgrave, Nigel Patrick, Edward Fox; **D:** Guy Hamilton. **VHS, Beta, LV** *MGM, FOX*

Battle of the Bullies WOOF!

Family Canadian TV special about an unsalvageable nerd who plots a high-tech revenge upon a slew of high school bullies.

1985 45m/C Manny Jacobs, Christopher Barnes, Sarah Inglis. **VHS, Beta** *NWV*

Battlestar Galactica

PG/Family Pilot episode (later released to theaters) of the glitzy family-hour sci-fi TV series. Crew of the last great starship must survive the human-exterminating, robot Cylons while questing for the legendary lost home, Earth. Grand f/x by the original "Star Wars" team, but George Lucas was not amused by the obvious imitation. TV episodes and feature-length cassette compilations are also available, but the costly saga was cancelled before telling the ultimate fate of mankind. Sorry.

BEWARE *Space violence.*

1978 125m/C Lorne Greene, Dirk Benedict, Karen Jensen, Jane Seymour, Patrick Macnee, Terry Carter, John Colicos, Richard A. Colla, Laurette Spang, Richard Hatch; **D:** Richard A. Colla. **VHS, Beta, LV** *MCA, MOV*

The Bay Boy

R/Sr. High-Adult Set in the 1930s in Nova Scotia, this period piece captures the coming-of-age of a rural teenage boy. Young Sutherland's adolescent angst becomes a more difficult struggle when he witnesses a murder, and is tormented by the secret.

1985 107m/C Liv Ullmann, Kiefer Sutherland, Peter Donat, Matthieu Carriere, Joe MacPherson, Isabelle Mejias, Alan Scarfe, Chris Wiggins, Leah K. Pinsent; **D:** Daniel Petrie; **M:** Claude Bolling. **VHS, Beta, LV** *ORI*

B.C.: A Special Christmas

Family TV cartoon short based on the sarcastic newspaper comic strip by Johnny Hart, about a gang of sophisticated cave-dwellers and their assorted follies. In this holiday-themed special, two of the tribe members (voices provided by the comedy team of Bob & Ray) scheme to get rich through inventing Santa Claus, only to be thwarted when the real thing shows up.

1971 25m/C V: Bob Elliott, Ray Goulding. **VHS, Beta, LV** *COL, NLC*

B.C.: The First Thanksgiving

Family Another cartoon version of the fave Johnny Hart comic strip (though with a different animation team than the earlier "A Special Christmas"). The caveman B.C. and his friends discover fire, meaning hot soup for Thanksgiving. The tribe goes in search of a turkey for flavoring, but the bird has other ideas.

1972 25m/C V: Don Messick, Daws Butler, Bob Holt. **VHS, Beta, LV** *NLC*

Be My Valentine, Charlie Brown/Is This Goodbye, Charlie Brown?

Family Two Peanuts specials: In "Be My Valentine, Charlie Brown," Charlie waits by his mailbox hoping for a valentine. Linus and Lucy are moving because of their father's job transfer to another city in "Is This Goodbye, Charlie Brown?"

1983 50m/C VHS, Beta *SHV*

Beach Blanket Bingo 🦴🦴🦴

Family Fifth entry in the "Beach Party" series (after "Pajama Party") is by far the best and has achieved near-cult status. Both Funicello and Avalon are back, but this time a very young Evans catches Avalon's eye. Throw in a mermaid, some moon-doggies, skydiving, sizzling beach parties, and plenty of nostalgic golly-gee-whiz fun and you have the classic '60s beach movie. Totally implausible, but that's half the fun when the sun-worshipping teens become involved in a kidnapping and occasionally break into song. Followed by "How to Stuff a Wild Bikini." 🎵 Beach Blanket Bingo; The Cycle Set; Fly Boy; The Good Times; I Am My Ideal; I Think You Think; It Only Hurts When I Cry; New Love; You'll Never Change Him.

1965 96m/C Frankie Avalon, Annette Funicello, Linda Evans, Don Rickles, Buster Keaton, Paul Lynde, Harvey Lembeck, Deborah Walley, Jody McCrea, Marta Kristen, Timothy Carey, Earl Wilson, Bobbi Shaw; **D:** William Asher; **W:** Sher Townsend, Leo Townsend; **M:** Les Baxter. **VHS, Beta, LV** *NO*

Beach Party 🦴🦴

Family Started the "Beach Party" series with the classic Funicello/Avalon combo. Scientist Cummings studying the mating habits of teenagers intrudes on a group of surfers, beach bums, and bikers, to his lasting regret. Typical beach party bingo, with sand, swimsuits, singing, dancing, and bare minimum in way of a plot. Followed by "Muscle Beach Party." 🎵 Beach Party; Don't Stop Now; Promise Me Anything; Secret Surfin' Spot; Surfin' and a-Swingin'; Treat Him Nicely.

1963 101m/C Frankie Avalon, Annette Funicello, Harvey Lembeck, Robert Cummings, Dorothy Malone, Morey Amsterdam, Jody McCrea, John Ashley, Candy Johnson, Dolores Wells, Yvette Vickers, Eva Six; **D:** William Asher; **W:** Lou Rusoff; **M:** Les Baxter. **VHS, Beta** *NO*

Beanstalk 🦴🦴🦴

PG/Family Modern-day version of the fairy tale finds young Jack Taylor (Daniels) scheming to make it big to help his hardworking single mom.He meets up with a wacky scientist (Kidder), who gives Jack some recently discovered seeds that naturally grow into an enormous beanstalk. And what does Jack find when he climbs the beanstalk—why an entire family of silly giants.

BEWARE *Rated PG for mild, comic violence and some language.*

1994 80m/C J.D. Daniels, Margot Kidder, Richard Moll, Amy Stock-Poynton, Patrick Renna, Richard Paul, David Naughton, Stuart Pankin, Cathy McAuley; **D:** Michael Paul Davis; **W:** Michael Paul Davis; **M:** Kevin Bassinson. **VHS, Beta** *PAR*

The Bear 🦴🦴🦴

PG/Jr. High-Adult Breathtaking moments in this innovative, somewhat slow nature drama about an orphan bear cub tagging after a grown male grizzly and dealing with hunters. The humans have almost no personality; a near-wordless narrative unfolds essentially from the cub's-eye-view, right down to some curious dream sequences. Jim Henson designed remote-controlled bears for more difficult scenes, and the differences are undetectable from animal thespians Bart and Douce (a cub as lovable as any "E.T." special effect). French-made, in English, and a huge money maker in Europe. Based on an even better novel by James Oliver Curwood.

BEWARE *Sex between consenting bears. Bambious death of parental bear; also violence and, believe it or not, accidental drug use, as the cub eats an amanita mushroom and trips out. At least he doesn't make a habit of it.*

1989 92m/C Jack Wallace, Tcheky Karyo, Andre Lacombe; **D:** Jean-Jacques Annaud; **W:** Gerard Brach, Michael Kane; **M:** Bill Conti. **VHS, Beta, LV** *COL, RDG, HMV*

The Bears & I 🦴🦴

G/Family Young Vietnam vet helps Indians regain their land rights while raising three orphan bear cubs. Beautiful photography in this Disney sanitization of the nonfiction book by Robert Franklin Leslie.

1974 89m/C Patrick Wayne, Chief Dan George, Andrew Duggan, Michael Ansara; **D:** Bernard McEveety; **M:** Buddy Baker. **VHS** *DIS*

Bear's Barnyard: It's a Dog's Life

Preschool-Primary First of all, Bear is a dog, and though he's billed as the star he's more of an excuse for building a story around some excellent nature photography. Bear, who looks like a shepherd-collie mix, wants to make some friends in "Barnyard," and in footage seen from his viewpoint he (and we) meet deer, ducks, sheep, lizards, horses, pigs, birds, bugs and we watch a baby chick hatching. The voice actors are amateurish but the visuals are super. Ages 1 to 5.

1994 30m/C VHS *NYR*

Bear's Big Lake

Preschool-Primary In "Lake," Bear gets lost on a camping trip but finds his way back with the help of a turtles, raccoons, frogs, a woodpecker, a caterpillar and a sort of guardian catfish. Ages 1 to 5.

1995 30m/C VHS

Beastmaster

PG/Jr. High-Adult Dumb but watchable barbarian adventure, with cutesy-critter appeal and lacking the explicit brutality of "Conan" and others of its ilk. Beastmaster Singer is a young warrior with the power to communicate with animals. Accompanied by a small posse of furry and feathered friends and slave girl Roberts, he battles evil cult tyrant Torn. An unrecognizable adaption (by director Coscarelli and co-producer Paul Pepperman) of Andre Norton's sci-fi novel of the same title.

BEWARE *Barbarian violence, nudity, sex.*

1982 119m/C Marc Singer, Tanya Roberts, Rip Torn, John Amos, Josh Milrad, Billy Jacoby; **D:** Don A. Coscarelli. **VHS, Beta, LV** *MGM*

Beastmaster 2: Through the Portal of Time

PG-13/Jr. High-Adult This time the laughs are intentional as the Beastmaster follows an evil monarch through a dimensional gate to modern-day L.A., where the shopping is better for both trendy clothes and weapons. Fun for genre fans, with a behind-the-scenes featurette on the tape.

BEWARE *Violence.*

1991 107m/C Marc Singer, Kari Wuhrer, Sarah Douglas, Wings Hauser, James Avery, Robert Fieldsteel, Arthur Malet, Robert Z'Dar, Michael Berryman; **D:** Sylvio Tabet; **M:** Robert Folk. **VHS, LV** *REP*

Beat Street

PG/Family Intended as a quick cash-in on the break dancing trend, this essentially plotless musical features kids trying to break into local show biz with their rapping and dancing skills. Features the music of Afrika Bambaata and the Soul Sonic Force, Grand Master Melle Mel and the Furious Five, and others. ♫ Beat Street Breakdown; Baptize the Beat; Stranger in a Strange Land; Beat Street Strut; Us Girls; This Could Be the Night; Breakers Revenge; Tu Carino (Carmen's Theme); Frantic Situation.

BEWARE *Street profanity and violence.*

1984 106m/C Rae Dawn Chong, Leon Grant, Saundra Santiago, Guy Davis, Jon Chardiet, Duane Jones, Kadeem Hardison; **D:** Stan Lathan. **VHS, Beta, LV** *VES, LIV*

Beautiful Girls

R/Sr. High-Adult A 10-year reunion brings together five high school buddies, each with his own problems with women and with growing up. They ice-fish, drink, sing Neil Diamond songs (yes, it's true!), and talk about the gentler gender (about which they haven't a clue). Shedding some light are the visiting and visually tantalizing cousin of a friend and a 13-year-old wise beyond her years. A great cast, including several heartthrobs (though Hutton could use a bath and a comb) will appeal to young women. Boys will think it stinks.

BEWARE *Strong language, especially during O'Donnell's very funny tirade on femininity. One character has an unusual collection of nude pin-ups and the relationship between Hutton and his 13-year-old neighbor (Portman) will either strike you as cute or leave a bad taste in your mouth.*

1996 110m/C Matt Dillon, Timothy Hutton, Michael Rapaport, Max Perlich, Noah Emmerich, Lauren Holly, Uma Thurman, Natalie Portman, Mira Sorvino, Martha Plimpton, Rosie O'Donnell, Annabeth Gish, Pruitt Taylor Vince, Sam Robards, David Arquette, Anne Bobby, Richard Bright; **D:** Ted Demme; **W:** Scott Rosenberg; **C:** Adam Kimmel; **M:** David A. Stewart. **VHS** *NYR*

Beauty and the Beast

Family Classic live-action French version of the famous story. Belle, completely devoted to her father, yields to fate when the old man picks a rose from an accursed Beast's garden and must surrender a daughter or die. But as she dwells in the Beast's bizarre castle Belle feels the monster's pain and loneliness. Meanwhile, her old suitor (Marais, also playing the Beast) schemes to steal the Beast's treasures. Not always comprehensible, especially at the end, and this compliant Belle seems weak-willed compared with Disney's spunky heroine. But for dreamlike, visual poetry you won't find a better talespinner than Cocteau. The Beast's estate, full of helpful, disembodied arms (a la Thing in "The Addams Family") and baleful, staring statues won't soon be forgotten, especially by nightmare-prone toddlers. In French with English subtitles.

1946 90m/B Jean Marais, Josette Day, Marcel Andre, Mila Parely, Nane Germon, Michel Auclair, Georges Auric; **D:** Jean Cocteau. **VHS, Beta, LV** *INJ, MLB, CRC*

Beauty and the Beast

Family The "Faerie Tale Theatre" version, with Susan Sarandon and Klaus Kinski as the title characters. Ages 6 to 10.

1983 60m/C Susan Sarandon, Anjelica Huston, Klaus Kinski, Stephen Elliott; **D:** Roger Vadim. **VHS, Beta, LV** *FOX, FCT*

Beauty and the Beast

Family Non-Disney animated version of the Brothers Grimm fairy tale classic which first aired on the Nickelodeon cable-TV channel.

1988 47m/C VHS *FHE*

Beauty and the Beast

G/Family Wonderful Disney musical combines superb animation, splendid characters, and lively songs in the legendary story about beautiful, willful Belle who becomes the unwilling guest of the fearsome and disagreeable Beast. Supporting cast includes the castle servants, a delightful bunch of singing household objects. Notable as the first animated feature to be nominated for the Best Picture Oscar. Awarding-winning title song as well as other Menken/Ashman tunes were good enough that this was soon transmuted into a smash Broadway stage musical. The deluxe video version features a work-in-progress rough film cut, a compact disc of the soundtrack, a lithograph depicting a scene from the film, and an illustrated book. ♫ Beauty and the Beast; Belle; Something There; Be Our Guest.

1991 84m/C D: Kirk Wise, Gary Trousdale; **M:** Alan Menken, Howard Ashman; **V:** Paige O'Hara, Robby Benson, Rex Everhart, Richard White, Jesse Corti, Angela Lansbury, Jerry Orbach, David Ogden Stiers, Bradley Michael Pierce, Jo Anne Worley, Kimmy Robertson. **Award Nominations:** Academy Awards '91: Best Picture, Best Song ("Belle", "Be Our Guest"), Best Sound; **Awards:** Academy Awards '91: Best Song ("Beauty and the Beast"), Best Score; Golden Globe Awards '92: Best Film—Musical/Comedy. **VHS, LV** *DIS, OM*

Bebe's Kids 🎬🎬 ☞

PG-13/Family The first black-oriented cartoon feature is based on characters created in routines by the late comedian Robin Harris. He's personified as an ineffectual ladies' man who takes a lovely woman out on their first date, but there's a surprise—five kids, her own and four little terrors she's baby-sitting. Their trip to a restrictive amusement park takes some funny shots at both black and white culture and Disneyland. Not entirely successful, but a notable 'toon change of pace with rapper Tone Loc's vocals (for a tough-talking diapered infant) stealing the show, just as he did in "Ferngully." The video includes the seven-minute animated short "Itsy Bitsy Spider," that accompanied the feature in most theaters.

> ⚠ BEWARE *Alcohol use, but the PG-13 rating seems highly unfair.*

1992 74m/C D: Bruce Smith; **W:** Reginald Hudlin; **M:** John Barnes; **V:** Faizon Love, Vanessa Bell Calloway, Wayne Collins, Jonell Green, Marques Houston, Tone Loc, Nell Carter, Myra J. **VHS, Beta, LV** *PAR*

Bed of Roses 🎬🎬

PG/Jr. High-Adult A widowed Wall Street whiz (Slater) ditches high finance and becomes a florist. One evening he spies Lisa (Masterson), a lonely workaholic financier, and bingo, it's love at first sight. He delivers flowers to her, pretending they're from a secret admirer. One thing leads to another, although the path of love is, of course, thorny. Highly romantic or excessively sappy, depending on your point of view. Young Slater fans will be mesmerized.

> ⚠ BEWARE *Mild profanity, hugging and kissing, conversation about childhood abuse.*

1995 88m/C Christian Slater, Mary Stuart Masterson, Pamela Segall, Josh Brolin, Ally Walker, Debra Monk; **D:** Michael Goldenberg; **W:** Michael Goldenberg; **C:** Adam Kimmel; **M:** Michael Convertino. **VHS, LV** *NLC*

Bedknobs and Broomsticks 🎬🎬 ☞

G/Family During WWII, three London kids are evacuated to the country home of prim Miss Eglantine Price, who turns out to be studying witchcraft by mail order. Her shaky command of magic takes them on a variety of adventures, some animated, and obviously intended to recall "Mary Poppins," though this overlong Disney romp isn't quite in that classic league until a wild ending pitting Nazi invaders against marching suits of clothes. Based on stories by Mary Norton.

1971 117m/C Angela Lansbury, Roddy McDowall, David Tomlinson, Bruce Forsyth, Sam Jaffe; **D:** Robert Stevenson. **Award Nominations:** Academy Awards '71: Best Art Direction/Set Decoration, Best Costume Design, Best Song ("The Age of Not Believing"), Best Original Score; **Awards:** Academy Awards '71: Best Visual Effects. **VHS, Beta, LV** *DIS*

Bedrock Wedlock

Family Compilation of Hanna-Barbera cartoon episodes, led by a notable "Flintstones" flashback episode in which a young Fred's wedding plans to Wilma nearly go awry. Also included are segments with characters like Wally Gator, Yogi Bear, Loopy D'Loop and more.

1989 80m/C V: Mel Blanc, Jean VanDerPyl, Alan Reed. **VHS, Beta** *TTC*

Bedrockin' and Rappin'

Family Join your favorite Hanna-Barbera cartoon characters, including the Flintstones, Scooby-Doo and Top Cat, for an exciting, unique rap session.

1991 30m/C VHS, Beta *TTC*

Bedtime for Bonzo 🎬🎬 ☞

Family College professor (Reagan) raises a chimp at home to bolster his theories about environment being more important than heredity. Cute comedy became a surrealistic footnote to history when the actor who co-starred with a chimp became President of the United States. The kids may not believe you when you tell them. It makes the movie that much more fun.

1951 83m/B Ronald Reagan, Diana Lynn, Walter Slezak, Jesse White, Bonzo the Chimp; **D:** Fred de Cordova. **VHS, Beta** *MCA, FCT*

Beethoven 🎬🎬

PG/Family Anxious St. Bernard pup escapes dognappers and wanders to the home of the Newtons, who adopt him over dad's objections. Beethoven grows into a huge, slobbering dog, a favorite—even a substitute parent—to the kids, but a headache for persnickety Mr. Newton, until a rematch with those dognappers (longtime Disney good guy Jones is ironically cast as the murderous ringleader). A hit, though it's most a case of teaching a new dog some very old tricks. Every dumb gag and pathos detail can be sniffed out long in advance, and the ending fails to make a case for film realism. Written by "Home Alone" creator John Hughes, under a pseudonym.

> ⚠ BEWARE *Dogs pee and characters are named after food (Ryce, Brie). An evil veterinarian (is nothing sacred?!) keeps dogs in cages for experimental purposes and hits them.*

1992 89m/C Charles Grodin, Bonnie Hunt, Dean Jones, Oliver Platt, Stanley Tucci, Nicholle Tom, Christopher Castile, Sarah Rose Karr, David Duchovny, Patricia Heaton, Laurel Cronin; **D:** Brian Levant; **W:** John Hughes, Amy Holden Jones. **VHS, LV** *MCA, FCT*

Belle gazes into the eyes of the enchanted Beast in "Beauty and the Beast."

Beethoven Lives Upstairs 𝄢𝄢𝄢 ▷

Family Moving, charming, fictional story of friendship between the great composer and his landlady's 10-year-old son, Christoph, in 19th century Vienna. At first Christoph resents the lodger, who is loud and eccentric and removes the legs of his piano so he can play it on the floor (to better feel its vibrations because he can't hear). But Christoph learns that it takes an extraordinary person to create extraordinary music. Includes more than two dozen excerpts of Beethoven's music. Most delicious moment has Beethoven at the piano, picking out with one hand the melody to "Ode To Joy," revising as he goes. Neil Munro is outstanding as the master composer. The part of Vienna is played by Prague. Ages 8 and up.

1992 52m/C Neil Munro, Illya Woloshyn, Fiona Reid, Paul Soles, Sheila McCarthy, Albert Schultz; *D:* David Devine; *W:* Heather Conkie. **VHS** *BMG, MVD*

Beethoven's 2nd 𝄢𝄢 ▷

PG/Family Sequel has awwww factor going for it as new daddy Beethoven slobbers over four adorable and appeal-

ing St. Bernard pups and his new love Missy. Same basic evil subplot as the first, with wicked kidnappers replacing evil vet. During the upheaval, the Newtons take care of the little yapping troublemakers, providing the backdrop for endless puppy mischief and exasperation on Grodin's part. Silly subplots and too many human moments tend to drag, but the kids will find the laughs (albeit stupid ones).

🦴 BEWARE 🦴 *Just like the first, dogs are in danger; alcohol use.*

1993 87m/C Charles Grodin, Bonnie Hunt, Nicholle Tom, Christopher Castile, Sarah Rose Karr, Debi Mazar, Christopher Penn, Ashley Hamilton; *D:* Rod Daniel; *W:* Len Blum; *M:* Randy Edelman. **VHS, LV** *MCA*

Beetle Bailey: Military Madness

Family The long-running Mort Walker comic strip about the antics of sad-sack slacker Bailey and his bunkmates at Camp Swampy were animated for an early '60s TV cartoon show. Four additional half-hour collections are available: "Pranks in the Ranks," "Pride of Camp Swampy," "Sarge's Last Stand," and "You're in the Army Now."

1963 30m/C *V:* Howard Morris. **VHS** *BFV*

Beetlejuice 𝄢𝄢𝄢

PG/Adult Recently deceased young couple become novice ghosts faced with scaring an obnoxious new family out of their old home. They hire a weirdo pro poltergeist for the job, but the afterlife becomes more complicated when the maniacal Beetlejuice becomes distracted by Router, the gloomy teen daughter befriended by the ghostly marrieds. Gaudy, funny, surreal and somewhat incoherent comedy of spooks, with inventive makeup f/x, music, and set designs. Followed by a cartoon TV series for kids.

🦴 BEWARE 🦴 *Salty language, supernatural violence—rapid aging, shrinking heads, that sort of stuff, not exactly realism.*

1988 92m/C Michael Keaton, Geena Davis, Alec Baldwin, Sylvia Sidney, Catherine O'Hara, Winona Ryder, Jeffrey Jones, Dick Cavett; *D:* Tim Burton; *W:* Michael McDowell, Warren Skaaren; *M:* Danny Elfman. **VHS, Beta, LV, 8mm** *WAR, FCT, TLF*

Beetlejuice, Vol. 1

Family Be careful—you know what happens when you say his name three times!! All kinds of fun and imagination surrounds this animated series spun off of the popular feature movie about "the ghost with the most." These six entertaining compilations will delight children, and some children at heart, too. Check out any of the six volumes from the Emmy-nominated series, including "Critter Sitters, The Big Faceoff and Skeletons in the Closet" or "Worm Welcome, Out of My Mind and A Dandy Handy Man."

1989 45m/C VHS, Beta *WAR*

Before and After 🦴🦴ᵒ

PG-13/Jr. High-Adult Parents Streep and Neeson, a doctor and a sculptor, are thrown into chaos when their teenaged son (Furlong) is accused of fatally bludgeoning a girlfriend they never knew about. Protective Neeson further complicates matters by destroying evidence that appears to incriminate his son. Well-acted but slow moving story of a family trying to hang together in the face of tragedy. Based on the novel by Rosellen Brown.

BEWARE *Some disturbing images of violence, strong language and some sensuality in the front seat of a parked car.*

1995 107m/C Meryl Streep, Liam Neeson, Edward Furlong, Alfred Molina, John Heard, Julia Weldon, Daniel von Bargen, John Heard, Ann Magnuson, Alison Folland, Kaiulani Lee; **D:** Barbet Schroeder; **W:** Ted Tally; **C:** Luciano Tovoli; **M:** Howard Shore. **VHS**

Before Sunrise 🦴🦴ᵒ

R/Sr. High-Adult Light, "getting-to-know-you," romance unfolds as two twenty-somethings share an unlikely 24-hour date. American Gen X-er Jesse (Hawke) and French beauty (Delpy) meet on a train and he convinces her to join him in exploring Vienna (and their mutual attraction) before he heads back to the States in the morning. The two exchange life experiences and philosophies. Cinematographer Daniel captures the Old World with finesse, especially in the inevitable "first kiss" atop the Ferris wheel made famous in Orson Welles' "The Third Man".

BEWARE *Realistic profanity. The couple shares a bottle of wine attained in an unorthodox method and talk about sex.*

1994 101m/C Ethan Hawke, Julie Delpy; **D:** Richard Linklater; **W:** Richard Linklater, Kim Krizan; **C:** Lee Daniel. **Award Nominations:** MTV Movie Awards '95: Best Kiss (Ethan Hawke/Julie Delpy); **Awards:** Berlin International Film Festival '94: Best Director (Linklater). **VHS, LV** *COL*

Being Human 🦴🦴ᵒ

PG-13/Jr. High-Adult Ambitious comedy drama. Hector (Williams) is a regular guy continuously reincarnated throughout the millennia. He's a caveman, a Roman slave, a Middle Ages nomad, a crew member on a 17th century new world voyage, and a modern New Yorker in separate vignettes that echo and extend the main themes of family, identity, and random fate. One of Williams' periodic chancy ventures away from his comedic roots occasionally strikes gold, but this one seems overly restrained.

BEWARE *Language, elements of violence, and elements of sensuality.*

1994 122m/C Robin Williams, John Turturro, Anna Galiena, Vincent D'Onofrio, Hector Elizondo, Lorraine Bracco, Lindsay Crouse, Kelly Hunter, William H. Macy, Grace Mahlaba, Theresa Russell, Charles Miller, Helen Miller; **D:** Bill Forsyth; **W:** Bill Forsyth; **M:** Michael Gibbs. **VHS, LV** *WAR*

Being There 🦴🦴🦴ᵒ

PG/Jr. High-Adult A feeble-minded gardener, whose entire knowledge of life comes from watching television, is sent out into the real world when his employer dies. Equipped with his prize possession, his remote control unit, the gardener unwittingly enters the world of politics and is welcomed as a mysterious sage. Sellers is wonderful in this satiric treat adapted by Jerzy Kosinski from his novel.

BEWARE *When Sellers says he likes to watch (meaning TV), Shirley MacLaine masturbates.*

1979 130m/C Peter Sellers, Shirley MacLaine, Melvyn Douglas, Jack Warden, Richard Dysart, Richard Basehart; **D:** Hal Ashby. **Award Nominations:** Academy Awards '79: Best Actor (Sellers); Cannes Film Festival '80: Best Film; **Awards:** Academy Awards '79: Best Supporting Actor (Douglas); Golden Globe Awards '80: Best Actor—Musical/Comedy (Sellers), Best Supporting Actor (Douglas); National Board of Review Awards '79: 10 Best Films of the Year, Best Actor (Sellers). **VHS, Beta, LV** *FOX, FCT, WAR*

The Bellboy 🦴🦴ᵒ

Family MDA Telethons aren't the only connection between Lewis and children; the comedian's frenetic screen persona resembles a nine-year-old kid running wild, and there's quite a similarity between early Jerry and the later Pee Wee Herman. Young viewers should especially enjoy Jerry's slapstick antics here. Plotless but clever outing is set at Miami's grand Fountainbleau Hotel, with the star/writer/director in a nearly wordless role as a goofball bellhop whose every errand turns into disaster.

1960 72m/B Jerry Lewis, Alex Gerry, Bob Clayton, Sonny Sands; **Cameos:** Milton Berle, Walter Winchell; **D:** Jerry Lewis; **W:** Jerry Lewis. **VHS, Beta, LV** *LIV*

The Belle of New York 🦴🦴

Family A turn-of-the-century bachelor falls in love with a Salvation Army missionary in this standard musical. 🎵 Naughty But Nice; Baby Doll; Oops; I Wanna Be a Dancin' Man; Seeing's Believing; Bachelor's Dinner Song; When I'm Out With the Belle of New York; Let a Little Love Come In.

1952 82m/C Fred Astaire, Vera-Ellen, Marjorie Main, Keenan Wynn, Alice Pearce, Gale Robbins, Clinton Sundberg; **D:** Charles Walters. **VHS, Beta** *MGM, FHE*

The Belles of St. Trinian's 🦴🦴🦴

Family Classic British comedy based on a popular comic strip by Ronald Searle about a girls' school and its rampaging inmates. The little hellions are mainly the background here; star is master character actor Sim in a gender-bending dual role as both the head mistress and her petty-crook twin brother, who scheme to save the school from financial ruin. The dreadful St. Trinian's tykes had more prominent parts in later sequels: "Blue Murder at St. Trinian's," "The Pure Hell of St. Trinian's," and "The Great St. Trinian's Train Robbery."

BEWARE *Alcohol talk.*

1953 86m/B Alastair Sim, Joyce Grenfell, Hermione Baddeley, George Cole, Eric Pohlmann, Renee Houston, Beryl Reid; **D:** Frank Launder; **M:** Malcolm Arnold. **VHS, Beta** *HMV*

The Bells of St. Mary's 🦴🦴🦴 🦴

Family Easy-going priest finds himself in a subtle battle of wits with the Mother Superior over how the children of St. Mary's school should be raised. It's the sequel to "Going My Way." Songs include the title tune and "Aren't You Glad You're You?" Also available in a colorized version.

1945 126m/B Bing Crosby, Ingrid Bergman, Henry Travers; **D:** Leo McCarey. **Award Nominations:** Academy Awards '44: Best Actress (Bergman); Academy Awards '45: Best Actor (Crosby), Best Director (McCarey), Best Film Editing, Best Picture, Best Song ("Aren't You Glad You're You"), Best Original Score; **Awards:** Academy Awards '45: Best Sound; Golden Globe Awards '46: Best Actress—Drama (Bergman); New York Film Critics Awards '45: Best Actress (Bergman). **VHS, Beta, LV** *REP, IGP*

The Belstone Fox 🦴🦴

Family Plodding British animal drama from the same producer as "Born Free." Not a complete success but an interesting comparison with Disney's superficially similar (and sunnier) "The Fox and the Hound." A fox cub is raised by a hunter for the sole purpose of being someday chased down and killed for sport in one of England's traditional country pastimes. Will a hunting dog who has befriended the fox carry out the foul deed? Might be a bit disturbing for young children. Based on the novel "Ballad of the Belstone Fox" by David Rook.

1973 103m/C Eric Porter, Rachel Roberts, Jeremy Kemp; **D:** James Hill. **VHS, Beta**

Ben and Me

Primary-Jr. High Classic Disney cartoon short in which Amos the mouse befriends Benjamin Franklin and takes his own look at events leading up to the American Revolution. Also available with "Bongo" on laserdisc.

1954 25m/C D: Hamilton Luske; **V:** Sterling Holloway. **VHS, Beta** *MTI, DSN*

Beneath the Planet of the Apes 🦴🦴 🦴

G/Family In the first sequel to the sci-fi classic, another Earth astronaut passes through the warp. He follows the same paths as Taylor, through Ape City and to the ruins of bomb-blasted New York's subway system, where warhead-worshipping human mutants are found living. Strain of sequelling shows instantly, though the next in the series, "Escape from the Planet of the Apes." improves matters.

 Violence.

1970 108m/C Charlton Heston, James Franciscus, Kim Hunter, Maurice Evans, James Gregory, Natalie Trundy, Jeff Corey, Linda Harrison, Victor Buono; **D:** Ted Post. **VHS, Beta, LV** *FOX, FUS*

The Beniker Gang 🦴🦴 🦴

G/Family Five orphans are sprung from the big house and become an extended family. They're supported by the eldest who writes a syndicated advice column. Sincere drama will likely interest the kids.

1983 87m/C Andrew McCarthy, Jennie Dundas, Danny Pintauro, Charlie Fields; **D:** Ken Kwapis. **VHS, Beta** *WAR*

Benji 🦴🦴🦴

G/Family Surprise hit that came out of nowhere (no Hollywood company wanted to release it) and became a minor classic. Successfully tells its simple tale from a dog's point-of-view, as a resourceful neighborhood stray mutt saves two children from kidnappers and finds romance with a pampered pooch named Tiffany. Benji is still one of the most sympathetic and winning animal actors ever. And yes, that is Aunt Bea from TV's "Andy Griffith Show" as the lady whose cat Benji routinely chases. Followup: "For the Love of Benji."

1974 87m/C Benji, Peter Breck, Christopher Connelly, Patsy Garrett, Deborah Walley, Cynthia Smith; **D:** Joe Camp. **Award Nominations:** Academy Awards '74: Best Song ("Benji's Theme (I Feel Love)"); **Awards:** Golden Globe Awards '75: Best Song ("I Feel Love"). **VHS, Beta** *VES, FCT, APD*

Benji at Work

Preschool-Primary Behind-the-scenes documentary look at how the lovable dog learns how to act, done in connection with the feature "Oh Heavenly Dog."

1993 30m/C Chevy Chase, Jane Seymour. **VHS** *NO*

Benji the Hunted 🦴🦴 🦴

G/Family Humans are virtually absent in this Benji adventure, released through Disney, but the critters make up for it as the heroic canine discovers some adorable orphaned cougar cubs, and battles terrain and predators to bring the kitties to safety. Not as fast-paced as others in the series, but solidly entertaining. Unusual touch: Benji isn't just a stray mutt here, he's playing himself, the superstar dog lost in the Oregon woods during a location shoot. Frank Inn, Benji's Santa-lookalike owner, also appears.

1987 89m/C Benji, Red Steagall, Frank Inn; **D:** Joe Camp. **VHS, Beta, LV** *DIS*

Benji's Very Own Christmas Story 🦴🦴

Family Canine thespian Benji and his friends go on a magic trip and meet Kris Kringle and learn how Christmas is celebrated around the world. Also included: "The Phenomenon of Benji," a documentary about Benji's odyssey from the animal shelter to international stardom. **1983 60m/C VHS, Beta** *BFV*

Benny & Joon 🦴🦴🦴

PG/Jr. High-Adult Depending on your tolerance for cute eccentrics and whimsy, this will either charm you with sweetness or send you into sugar shock. Masterson is Joon, a mentally disturbed young woman who paints and has a habit of setting fires. She lives with overprotective brother Benny (Quinn). Sam (Depp) is the outsider who charms Joon, a dyslexic loner who impersonates his heroes Charlie Chaplin and Buster Keaton with eerie accuracy. Depp is particularly fine with the physical demands of his role, but the film's easy dismissal of Joon's mental illness is a serious flaw. The laserdisc version is letterboxed.

BEWARE *Sex talk and portrayal of mentally ill young adults.*

1993 98m/C Johnny Depp, Mary Stuart Masterson, Aidan Quinn, Julianne Moore, Oliver Platt, CCH Pounder, Dan Hedaya, Joe Grifasi, William H. Macy, Eileen Ryan; **D:** Jeremiah S. Chechik; **W:** Barry Berman; **M:** Rachel Portman. **VHS, Beta, LV** *MGM*

The Berenstain Bears' Christmas

Family The distinctive cartoon bear clan from the creative team of Stan and Jan Berenstain act out little morality plays within their rollicking animated adventures. In this holiday offering, Papa Bear decides that this year he will find his perfect Christmas tree, but during his bumbling trek through the wintery woods he realizes how important a simple spruce is to the critters who dwell in it. The cassette also includes "Inside Outside Upside Down" and "The Bike Lesson."

1990 30m/C VHS, Beta *RAN, VEC*

Berenstain Bears' Comic Valentine

Family Brother Bear receives a mysterious Valentine from Miss Honey Bear, a secret admirer; but can he keep his mind on the upcoming holiday hockey match against the Beartown Bullies?

1982 25m/C VHS, Beta

Berenstain Bears' Easter Surprise

Family Boss Bunny, who usually controls the seasons, has quit; Poppa Bear's vainglorious effort to construct an Easter egg machine is a failure; and Brother Bear anxiously awaits his "Extra Special" Easter Surprise.

1981 25m/C VHS, Beta

Berenstain Bears Meet Big Paw

Family Brother and Sister Bear meet up with the legendary monster Big Paw and find out he is not such a bad beast after all. Additional volumes available.

1980 25m/C VHS, Beta, LV

The Berenstains Celebrate a 50-Year Partnership

Stan and Jan Berenstain have not only illustrated more than 150 books with an estimated 220 million copies in print, but they have recently celebrated 50 years of marriage. They met on the first day of art school in 1941 and it has been a wonderful partnership ever since. Their sons, Leo and Michael have even joined the team. The Berenstain Bears (the name suggested by none other than Dr. Seuss himself) have delighted and entertained children for years.

The adventures of Mama Bear, Papa Bear and the two cubs are loved and cherished by children of all ages. Over the years they have experienced everyday adventures such as messy rooms, new babies, and celebrating popular holidays. And thanks to their widespread popularity, they are also available on video to enjoy at home. Stan and Jan, both 72, believe teamwork has fueled their success. And what a team — 50 years is something to be proud of.

Bernard and the Genie 🦴🦴 ᵛ

G/Family Fired from his job, jilted by his girlfriend at Christmas, Bernard's troubles seemed to be solved—or are they just beginning?—when he rubs a magic lamp and becomes the surprised master of a funky genie. Holiday TV comedy from Britain is aimed at young and old alike, meaning a curious mix of childish elements (including a genuine Teenage Mutant Ninja Turtle cameo) and bawdy stuff. Great cast; Henry, the lamp occupant, is a comic superstar in England, as is Atkinson.

BEWARE *Sex talk, roughhousing.*

1991 70m/C Alan Cumming, Lenny Henry, Rowan Atkinson; **D:** Paul Weiland. **VHS** *FOX, BTV*

The Best Christmas Pageant Ever

Primary-Adult Troublemaking kids participate in the school Christmas pageant, guaranteeing a manger scene that nobody will soon forget. Lukewarm holiday heartwarmer, made for TV, based on the book by Barbara Robinson.
1986 60m/C Dennis Weaver, Karen Grassle. **VHS** *RHV*

The Best of Betty Boop, Vol. 1

Family Sweet Betty Boop sashays through 11 of her classic cartoon adventures in this collection of original shorts. Mastered from the original negatives.
1939 90m/C V: Mae Questel. **VHS** *REP*

The Best of Betty Boop, Vol. 2

Family Another collection of original cartoons starring the "Boop-Oop-a-Doop" girl, assisted by Bimbo and Koko the Clown. These black-and-white cartoons have be recolored for this release.
1939 85m/C V: Mae Questel. **VHS, Beta** *REP*

Best of Bugs Bunny & Friends

Family Collection of classics from great cartoon stars Bugs Bunny, Daffy Duck, Tweetie Pie, and Porky Pig. Includes "Duck Soup to Nuts," "A Feud There Was," and "Tweetie Pie."
1940 53m/C D: Isadore "Friz" Freleng, Chuck Jones, Robert McKimson. **VHS, Beta** *MGM*

The Best of Gumby

Family Special 30th Anniversary celebration of Art Clokey's 1957 television solo show for the Gumbster, following his debut the previous year on "Howdy Doody." Contains seven all-time favorite episodes of Gumby at his best. See also "Gumby" and "The World According to Gumby."
1987 45m/C VHS, Beta *FHE*

The Best of Roger Rabbit

Family Compilation of the original theatrical cartoons featuring Baby Herman and bedeviled babysitter Roger Rabbit. Includes "Tummy Trouble," "Roller Coaster Rabbit," and "Trail Mix-Up." Old-fashioned cartoon mayhem.
1995 ?m/C VHS *DIS*

The Best of Times 🎜🎜

PG/Jr. High-Adult Two grown men (Williams and Russell) attempt to redress the failures of the past by reenacting a football game they lost in high school 20 years ago due to Williams' dropped pass. With this cast, it should have been better, but film fumbles, too. Ages 12 and up.

BEWARE *Profanity and suggested sex.*

1986 105m/C Robin Williams, Kurt Russell, M. Emmet Walsh, Pamela Reed, Holly Palance, Donald Moffat, Margaret Whitton, Kirk Cameron; **D:** Roger Spottiswoode; **W:** Ron Shelton. **VHS, Beta, LV, 8mm** *NLC*

Bethie's Really Silly Clubhouse

Preschool-Primary Bethie's Clubhouse isn't in Mr. Rogers' neighborhood but somewhere between Eureeka's Castle and Pee-wee's Playhouse. Singer-songwriter Bethie (Beth Marlin Lichter) has talking appliances, furniture that clashes and some kids who come to visit. And although she speaks the one line all kids hate— "Put on your thinking caps"—she sings some pretty neat songs about vain iguanas, rock 'n roll mice and other intriguing animals. Ages 3 to 6.
1994 30m/C VHS *BMG*

Better Off Dead 🎜🎜 ▷

PG/Jr. High-Adult Compulsive teenager's girlfriend leaves him and he decides to end it all. After several abortive suicide attempts, he decides instead to out-ski her obnoxious new boyfriend. Uneven but funny, thanks largely to Cusack's charm and Armstrong's support. Not as tasteless as it might sound at first, with some genuine heart.

BEWARE *Profanity and suicide attempts. Touchy subject is made fun of.*

1985 97m/C John Cusack, Curtis Armstrong, Diane Franklin, Kim Darby, David Ogden Stiers, Dan Schneider, Amanda Wyss, Taylor Negron, Vincent Schiavelli, Demian Slade, Scooter Stevens; **D:** Steve Holland; **W:** Steve Holland; **M:** Rupert Hine. **VHS, Beta, LV** *FOX*

Betty Boop

Family The Fleischer Brothers' classic cartoon flapper character is probably best known to modern audiences for her cameo (as a has-been!) in "Who Framed Roger Rabbit?" Betty in her prime can be found on tape in several collections, including three volumes of "Betty Boop Festival" (sadly, no longer distributed).
193? 30m/C V: Mae Questel, Mel Blanc. **VHS, LV** *CNG*

Betty Boop Special Collector's Edition: Volume 1

Family Betty Boop returns in this collection of vintage cartoons, presented in glorious, original B&W, with appearances by jazz greats Cab Calloway and Don Redman. Vol. 2 features an additional 90 minutes of Boop-oop-a-doop, plus more with Calloway and his orchestra.
1935 90m/B D: Dave Fleischer, Max Fleischer; **V:** Louis Armstrong, Mae Questel. **VHS, LV** *REP*

The Beverly Hillbillies 🎜🎜 ▷

PG/Jr. High-Adult Big-screen transfer of the long-running TV show may appeal to fans. Ozark mountaineer Jed Clampett discovers oil, becomes an instant billionaire, and packs his backwoods clan off to the good life in California. Minimal plot finds dim-bulb nephew Jethro and daughter Elly May looking for a bride for Jed. Not that any of it matters. Everyone does fine by their imper-sonations, particularly Varney as the good-hearted Jed and Leachman as stubborn Granny. Ebsen, the original Jed, reprises another of his TV roles, detective Barnaby Jones. And yes, the familiar strains of the "Ballad of Jed Clampett" by Jerry Scoggins starts this one off, too.

 Salty language.

1993 93m/C Jim Varney, Erika Eleniak, Diedrich Bader, Cloris Leachman, Dabney Coleman, Lily Tomlin, Lea Thompson, Rob Schneider, Linda Carlson, Penny Fuller, Kevin Connolly; *Cameos:* Buddy Ebsen, Zsa Zsa Gabor, Dolly Parton; *D:* Penelope Spheeris; *W:* Larry Konner, Mark Rosenthal, Jim Fisher, Jim Staahl; *M:* Lalo Schifrin. **VHS** *FXV*

Beverly Hills Brats

PG-13/Jr. High-Adult Lonely Hollywood kid hires a bumbling burglar to kidnap him, in order to gain his parents' attention. Then both of them are snatched by real crooks. How did a great cast like this get involved in such a dimwitted farce?

 The neglectful father is a cosmetic surgeon, prompting gags and photos of female body parts. Profanity, sex talk.

1989 90m/C Martin Sheen, Burt Young, Peter Billingsley, Terry Moore; *D:* Dimitri Sotirakis; *M:* Barry Goldberg. **VHS, Beta, LV** *LIV, IME, VTR*

Beverly Hills Cop

R/Sr. High-Adult When a close friend of smooth-talking Detroit cop Axel Foley is brutally murdered in L.A., he traces the murderer to the posh streets of Beverly Hills. There he must stay on his toes to keep one step ahead of the killer and two steps ahead of the law. Better than average Murphy vehicle is followed by two lesser sequels.

 Abundant profanity and violence.

1984 105m/C Eddie Murphy, Judge Reinhold, John Ashton, Lisa Eilbacher, Ronny Cox, Steven Berkoff, James Russo, Jonathan Banks, Stephen Elliott, Bronson Pinchot, Paul Reiser, Damon Wayans, Rick Overton; *D:* Martin Brest; *W:* Danilo Bach, Dan Petrie Jr.; *M:* Harold Faltermeyer. **Award Nominations:** Academy Awards '84: Best Original Screenplay; **Awards:** People's Choice Awards '85: Best Film. **VHS, Beta, LV, 8mm** *PAR*

Beverly Hills Cop 2

R/Sr. High-Adult The highly successful sequel to the highly successful original repeats formula with essentially the same plot, dealing this time with Foley infiltrating a band of international munitions smugglers. Spawned a hit soundtrack and yet another sequel in a successful attempt to run a good thing straight into the ground.

 Abundant violence and profanity; brief nudity.

1987 103m/C Eddie Murphy, Judge Reinhold, Juergen Prochnow, Ronny Cox, John Ashton, Brigitte Nielsen, Allen (Goorwitz) Garfield, Paul Reiser, Dean Stockwell; *D:* Tony Scott; *W:* Larry Ferguson, Warren Skaaren; *M:* Harold Faltermeyer. **VHS, Beta, LV, 8mm** *PAR*

Beverly Hills Cop 3

R/Sr. High-Adult Yes, Detroit cop Axel Foley (Murphy) just happens to find another case that takes him back to his friends on the Beverly Hills PD. This time he uncovers a criminal network fronting WonderWorld, an amusement park with a squeaky-clean image. Fast-paced action, lots of gunplay, and Eddie wisecracks his way through the slow spots. Reinhold returns as the still impossibly naive Rosewood, with Bronson briefly reprising his role as Serge of the undeterminable accent. Critically panned box office disappointment relies too heavily on formula and is another disappointing followup.

 Abundant violence and profanity.

1994 109m/C Eddie Murphy, Judge Reinhold, Hector Elizondo, Timothy Carhart, Stephen McHattie, Theresa Randle, John Saxon, Alan Young, Bronson Pinchot; *Cameos:* Al Green, Gil Hill; *D:* John Landis; *W:* Steven E. de Souza; *M:* Nile Rodgers. **VHS** *PAR*

Beverly Hills Teens

Primary Compilation of episodes from a syndicated TV cartoon series about obscenely wealthy California kids and their zany adventures. Additional volumes available.

1989 120m/C VHS, Beta *JFK*

Beyond the Stars

Jr. High-Adult Adventurous young whiz kid Erik Nichols meets ex-astronaut Col. Paul Andrews and begins to investigate the NASA cover-up of a deadly accident that occurred during the Apollo 11 lunar landing. The movie reflects a lot on Erik's relationship with his father. (His parents are divorced.) Directed by the author of "Cocoon".

 There is some harsh language and arguing between Erik's father and the Colonel. Erik's divorced parents are amiable to each other.

1989 94m/C Martin Sheen, Christian Slater, Olivia D'Abo, F. Murray Abraham, Robert Foxworth, Sharon Stone; *D:* David Saperstein. **VHS, Beta, LV** *LIV*

The B.F.G. (Big Friendly Giant)

Preschool-Primary Another adaptation of a Roald Dahl work in the form of an animated tale finds young orphan Sophie making friends with the 25-foot-tall B.F.G., a fairy prince whose job is to catch dreams and blow the good ones into the minds of sleeping children. But lately, ugly, bad, bigger giants (who like to eat children) are stopping him.

1990 95m/C *D:* Brian Cosgrove; *W:* John Hambley; *M:* Keith Hopwood, Malcolm Rowe; *V:* David Jason, Amanda Root, Angela Thorne, Don Henderson, Frank Thornton. **VHS** *CEL*

Big

PG/Family Charming modern fable of an impatient 12-year-old boy who makes a wish to be 'big.' When he awakens the next morning he's got the body of a 30-year-old man. Thrown out by his terrified mom, the hero must learn to live as a grownup. His talent for evaluating toys gets him a job in a big corporation, a luxury apartment—even an office romance. Hanks is totally believable as a guileless man-child, while Perkins scores in the perilous role of the yuppie cynic attracted to him. Marshall directs with humanity, and the whole thing clicks from the beginning. Toy store scene with the giant piano keyboard is a classic.

BEWARE *Yes, the hero has a love affair with the high-powered businesslady, an episode handled with taste and conscience. Alcohol use, salty language.*

1988 98m/C Tom Hanks, Elizabeth Perkins, John Heard, Robert Loggia, Jared Rushton, David Moscow, Jon Lovitz, Mercedes Ruehl; **D:** Penny Marshall; **W:** Gary Ross; **M:** Howard Shore. **Award Nominations:** Academy Awards '88: Best Actor (Hanks), Best Original Screenplay; **Awards:** Golden Globe Awards '89: Best Actor—Musical/Comedy (Hanks); People's Choice Awards '89: Best Film—Musical/Comedy. **VHS, Beta, LV** *FOX, HMV*

Big Bird in China

Family "Sesame Street" mainstay Big Bird is guided through China by a six-year-old in search of the legendary phoenix. Along the way, they visit Chinese schools, children, watch a T'ai Ch'i demonstration, and learn Chinese words, traditions, and culture.

1987 75m/C VHS *KUI, RAN*

Big Bird in Japan

Family Big Bird and his pal Barkley the Dog lose their way while visiting Tokyo. As they wander about, they meet all sorts of interesting people, including a young girl who could be the legendary Bamboo Princess. Includes four new songs.

1991 60m/C VHS, Beta *RAN*

Big Bully 🐾

PG/Primary-Adult Arnold and Moranis—guess which one's the bully—find themselves teaching at the same school. Moranis soon realizes that Arnold was the aggressive kid (you guessed!) who made his childhood a living heck. The two adults quickly revert to the ways of their youth, with Arnold administering noogies and other assorted torments. Some fun, eh?

BEWARE *Mean-spirited pranks, some crude humor and language.*

1995 93m/C Tom Arnold, Rick Moranis, Julianne Phillips, Don Knotts, Carol Kane, Jeffrey Tambor, Curtis Armstrong, Faith Prince, Tony Pierce, Blake Bashoff; **D:** Steve Miner; **W:** Mark Steven Johnson; **C:** Daryn Okada; **M:** David Newman. **VHS** *WAR*

The Big Bus 🐾🐾

PG/Jr. High-Adult The wild adventures of the world's first nuclear-powered bus as it makes its maiden voyage from New York to Denver. Clumsy disaster-movie parody.

1976 88m/C Joseph Bologna, Stockard Channing, Ned Beatty, Ruth Gordon, Larry Hagman, John Beck, Jose Ferrer, Lynn Redgrave, Sally Kellerman, Stuart Margolin, Richard Mulligan, Howard Hesseman, Richard B. Shull; **D:** James Frawley; **M:** David Shire. **VHS, Beta** *PAR*

Big Business 🐾🐾🐾

PG/Jr. High-Adult Strained high-concept comedy about two sets of identical twins, each played by Tomlin and Midler, mismatched at birth by a near-sighted country nurse. One set is raised in the city amid wealth and splendor while the other grows up in a less auspicious rural setting. Fate conspires to bring the twins together, as the city duo tries to buy out the factory where the country twins work. From there on, it's a one-joke series of zany consequences and episodes of mistaken identity. Nice cast, some fairly funny moments, great technical effects, semi-lame script suffers from case of the repeats.

BEWARE *Profanity; condescending portrayals of rural folk.*

1988 98m/C Bette Midler, Lily Tomlin, Fred Ward, Edward Herrmann, Michele Placido, Barry Primus, Michael Gross, Mary Gross, Daniel Gerroll, Roy Brocksmith; **D:** Jim Abrahams. **VHS, Beta, LV, 8mm** *TOU*

Big Cable Bridges

Preschool-Jr. High Follows Lee and Nikki on an adventure that teaches how big cable-stayed bridges are built. Featured in the National Building Museum in Washington, D.C. Informative, but you really have to be interested in this stuff to appreciate it. Ages 6 to 11.

1994 30m/C VHS

Big Girls Don't Cry . . . They Get Even 🐾

PG/Jr. High-Adult Teenage Laura flees her oft-broken home because of her odious stepfamily. She joins her one nice relation at his wilderness retreat, but the whole much-remarried clan arrives to look for her. At last the bimbo mistress, lusty ex-husbands, spoiled ex-wives, and bratty half-siblings learn to get along. Icky, ineffective "family comedy" gives the bad-sitcom treatment to divorce and adultery, yet pretends to have insights.

BEWARE *Sex talk, profanity, and an unpleasant family.*

1992 98m/C Hillary Wolf, Griffin Dunne, Margaret Whitton, David Strathairn, Ben Savage, Adrienne Shelly, Patricia Kalember; **D:** Joan Micklin Silver. **VHS, LV** *COL, NLC*

The Big Green 🐾🐾

PG/Family Sorry to be bad news bearers, but the world didn't need another ragtag-kids-find-self-respect-through-sports movie, not even one about soccer. It begins promisingly, with a quartet of youngsters lying in a field and pouring Cheetos over themselves to attract birds. That's what passes for thrills in sleepy Elma, Texas, until a new teacher (D'Abo) comes to town from England and teaches the kids to play soccer. The tale is tattered but at least girls and boys play as equals and nobody blocks a shot with his crotch.

BEWARE *Some mild language.*

1995 100m/C Olivia D'Abo, Steve Guttenberg, Jay O. Sanders, John Terry, Chauncey Leopardi, Patrick Renna, Billy L. Sullivan, Yareli Arizmendi, Bug Hall; **D:** Holly Goldberg Sloan; **W:** Holly Goldberg Sloan; **C:** Ralf Bode; **M:** Randy Edelman. **VHS, LV** *TOU*

Big Jake

PG/Family Aging Texas cattle man who has outlived his time swings into action when outlaws kidnap his grandson and wound his son. He returns to his estranged family to help them in the search for Little Jake. O'Hara is once again paired up with Wayne and the chemistry is still there.

> **BEWARE** *Violence.*

1971 90m/C John Wayne, Richard Boone, Maureen O'Hara, Patrick Wayne, Chris Mitchum, Bobby Vinton; **D:** George Sherman; **M:** Elmer Bernstein. **VHS, Beta, LV** *FOX*

Big Mo

G/Family True story of the friendship that developed between Cincinnati Royals basketball stars Maurice Stokes and Jack Twyman after a strange paralysis hit Stokes.

1973 110m/C Bernie Casey, Bo Svenson, Stephanie Edwards, Janet MacLachlan; **D:** Daniel Mann. **VHS, Beta** *VES*

The Big Plane Trip

Preschool-Jr. High Live-action, featuring different aspects of the airline industry. Covers pilot training, the control tower, the cockpit, and flying. Also provides mini-tour of Switzerland, including toy museum, chocolate factory, medieval castle and Alpine train. Ages 5 to 10.

1994 45m/C **VHS** *TPV*

Big Red

Family Solid Disney adaptation of the favorite Jim Kjelgaard novel, filmed on location against the spectacular beauty of French Canada's Quebec Province. Orphan boy is hired by a grumpy adult to care for a champion Irish setter. The kid saves the dog, who later repays the favor during an attack by a mountain lion.

1962 89m/C Walter Pidgeon, Gilles Payant; **D:** Norman Tokar. **VHS, Beta** *DIS*

Big Shots

PG-13/Jr. High-Adult Two 12-year-old kids, one naive and white, the other black and streetwise, search the seamy side of town for a stolen watch. Intermittently fun, but with detours into violence and crime that take a great deal of delight out of what should have been a childish romp.

> **BEWARE** *Violence, profanity.*

1987 91m/C Ricky Busker, Darius McCrary, Robert Joy, Paul Winfield, Robert Prosky, Jerzy Skolimowski; **D:** Robert Mandel; **W:** Joe Eszterhas; **M:** Bruce Broughton. **VHS, Beta, LV** *ORI, WAR*

The Big Store

Family Marx Brothers vehicle has some big laughs, but lacks the rapid-fire hilarity that made them famous, as Groucho, Chico and Harpo work as department-store detectives and foil a kidnapping and takeover attempt. Unfortunately, they don't foil the some pointless musical numbers dropped in to kill time, though one of them gives Harpo an especially charming pantomime at the harp, accompanying two non-identical mirror images of himself. Tape includes the short subject "A Night at the Movies," with humorist Robert Benchley showing what could go wrong for a filmgoer in days before VCRs.

> **BEWARE** *Roughhousing.*

1941 96m/B Groucho Marx, Harpo Marx, Chico Marx, Tony Martin, Margaret Dumont, Virginia Grey, Virginia O'Brien; **D:** Charles Riesner. **VHS, Beta** *MGM, CCB*

Big Top Pee Wee

PG/Jr. High-Adult Herman's second feature following the success of "Pee Wee's Big Adventure" hasn't got the manic hilarity of its predecessor. Slightly out-of-character Herman owns a farm, has a girlfriend (!) and is the only resident of his community with the properly childlike nature to welcome a traveling circus into town. Eventually Pee Wee joins the show for a dreamlike finale that adds a quality of magic mostly lacking in the rest of the picture.

> **BEWARE** *Yes it's true, Pee Wee has sex, but it's handled in a discreet, offscreen manner.*

1988 86m/C Paul (Pee Wee Herman) Reubens, Kris Kristofferson, Susan Tyrrell, Penelope Ann Miller; **D:** Randal Kleiser; **W:** Paul (Pee Wee Herman) Reubens; **M:** Danny Elfman. **VHS, Beta, LV, 8mm** *PAR*

Big Trouble in Little China

PG-13/Jr. High-Adult Trucker plunges beneath the streets of San Francisco's Chinatown to battle an army of spirits. Comic-book-film parody with plenty of action and sophomoric sarcasm. Ages 14 and up.

> **BEWARE** *Supernatural violence.*

1986 99m/C Kurt Russell, Suzee Pai, Dennis Dun, Kim Cattrall, James Hong, Victor Wong, Kate Burton; **D:** John Carpenter; **W:** Gary Goldman, W.D. Richter; **M:** John Carpenter, Alan Howarth. **VHS, Beta, LV** *FXV, FOX*

Bigfoot and Wildboy

Family Two volumes of live-action adventures from a Sid & Marty Krofft Saturday-morning show of the '70s, in which Sasquatch teams up with a Tarzan-type kid to fight assorted fiends.

1977 72m/C Ray Young, Joseph Butcher, Yvonne Regalado, Monica Ramirez. **VHS, Beta** *NLC*

The misfit soccer team and coach look onto the field in "The Big Green."

Bigfoot: The Unforgettable Encounter 🎵🎵 ♭

PG/Primary-Adult Young boy heads off into the woods, comes face to face with Bigfoot, and sets off a media frenzy and a band of ruthless bounty hunters determined to capture his hairy friend.

> 🛑 *BEWARE Mild adventure action; some language. Bigfoot may scare some very young viewer, but he's harmless.*

1994 89m/C Zachery Ty Bryan, Matt McCoy, Barbara Willis Sweete, Clint Howard, Rance Howard, David Rasche; **D:** Corey Michael Eubanks; **W:** Corey Michael Eubanks; **M:** Shimon Arama. **VHS** *REP*

Bikini Beach 🎵🎵 ♭

Family Surfing teenagers of the "Beach Party" series follow up "Muscle Beach Party" with a third fling at the beach and welcome a visitor, British recording star "Potato Bug" (Avalon in a campy dual role). But, golly gee, wealthy Wynn wants to turn their sandy, surfin' shores into a retirement community. What to do? Sing a few songs, dance in your bathing suits, and have fun. Classic early '60s nostalgia is better than the first two efforts; followed by "Pajama Party." 🎵 Because You're You; Love's a Secret Weapon; Bikini Drag.

1964 100m/C Annette Funicello, Frankie Avalon, Martha Hyer, Harvey Lembeck, Don Rickles, Stevie Wonder, John Ashley, Keenan Wynn, Jody McCrea, Candy Johnson, Danielle Aubry, Meredith MacRae, Dolores Wells, Donna Loren, Timothy Carey; **D:** William Asher; **W:** William Asher, Leo Townsend, Robert Dillon; **M:** Les Baxter. **VHS, Beta**

Bill 🎵🎵🎵

Jr. High-Adult Made-for-TV movie based on a true story about a mentally retarded man who sets out to live independently after 44 years in an institution. Rooney gives an affecting performance as Bill and Quaid is strong as the filmmaker who befriends him. Awarded Emmys for Rooney's performance and the well written script. Followed by "Bill: On His Own."

1981 97m/C Mickey Rooney, Dennis Quaid, Largo Woodruff, Harry Goz; **D:** Anthony Page. **VHS, Beta** *LIV*

Bill and Coo 🎵🎵

Family Award-winning novelty short feature was celebrated in its day, but once you get the gimmick that's it; a melodramatic love story with a villain and hero—using an all bird cast.

1947 61m/C D: Dean Riesner. **VHS, Beta, 8mm** *VYY, MRV, NOS*

Bill & Ted's Bogus Journey 🦴🦴

PG/Jr. High-Adult Big-budget sequel to B & T's first movie has better f/x but a lesser quota of laughs for all that effort. Slain—bloodlessly—by lookalike robot duplicates from the future, the airhead heroes pass through Heaven (a Mt. Olympus-style kingdom) and Hell (a military academy). Finally, they trick the Grim Reaper into bringing them back for a second duel with their heinous terminators. Episodes of a Bill & Ted cartoon series are also available on tape.

1991 98m/C Keanu Reeves, Alex Winter, William Sadler, Joss Ackland, Pam Grier, George Carlin, Amy Stock-Poynton, Hal Landon Jr., Annette Azcuy, Sarah Trigger, Chelcie Ross, Taj Mahal, Roy Brocksmith, William Shatner; *D:* Pete Hewitt; *W:* Chris Matheson, Edward Solomon; *M:* David Newman. **VHS** *ORI*

Bill & Ted's Excellent Adventure 🦴🦴🦴

PG/Jr. High-Adult Utopian future of the Earth rests on whether two '80s boys pass their high-school history final. Time-traveling troubleshooter Rufus comes to the rescue in his cosmic phone booth, and Bill and Ted share a field trip through time as they goof up the lives of important world figures. Fun, brainless comedy earns its bones because the slang-speaking heroes are the most innocuous teen twits in recent movies. They may look like Beavis & Butthead and adore heavy-metal music, but there's no malice in these dudes and considerable humor as they set Lincoln, Napoleon, and Joan of Arc loose in a Southern California shopping mall.

> **BEWARE** *Profanity; don't look to these guys as role models.*

1989 105m/C Keanu Reeves, Alex Winter, George Carlin, Bernie Casey, Dan Shor, Robert Barron, Amy Stock-Poynton, Ted Steedman, Ted Steedman, Rod Loomis, Al Leong, Tony Camilieri; *D:* Stephen Herek; *W:* Chris Matheson, Edward Solomon; *M:* David Newman. **VHS, Beta, LV, 8mm** *COL, NLC*

Bill Cosby, Himself 🦴🦴🦴

PG/Family An alternative to the popular (but foul-mouthed) comedy concerts starring Richard Pryor or Eddie Murphy or Robert Townsend, cool Cos offers this record of his congenial standup act. Cosby shares his funny observations on marriage, drugs, alcohol, dentists, child-bearing and child-rearing. Performance was recorded at Toronto's Hamilton Place Performing Arts Center; the video includes some of Cosby's own home movies. Also available: "Bill Cosby: 49."

> **BEWARE** *Subjects include sex and drugs (addressed in fairly good taste). Some profanity.*

1981 104m/C Bill Cosby; *D:* Bill Cosby. **VHS, Beta, LV** *FOX*

Bill: On His Own 🦴🦴🦴

Jr. High-Adult Rooney is again exceptional in this sequel to the Emmy-winning TV movie "Bill." After 44 years in an institution, a mentally retarded man copes more and more successfully with the outside world. Fine supporting cast and direction control the melodramatic potential.

1983 100m/C Mickey Rooney, Helen Hunt, Teresa Wright, Dennis Quaid, Largo Woodruff, Paul Leiber, Harry Goz; *D:* Anthony Page. **VHS** *LIV*

Billie 🦴🦴

Family Duke stars as a tomboy athlete who puts the boys' track team to shame. Some amusing but very predictable situations, plus a few songs from Miss Duke. Based on Ronald Alexander's play "Time Out for Ginger."

1965 86m/C Patty Duke, Jim Backus, Jane Greer, Warren Berlinger, Billy DeWolfe, Charles Lane, Dick Sargent, Susan Seaforth Hayes, Ted Bessell, Richard Deacon; *D:* Don Weis; *W:* Ronald Alexander. **VHS, Beta, LV** *MGM*

The Billion Dollar Hobo 🦴🦴

G/Family Vernon, unsuspecting heir of a multimillion dollar fortune must duplicate his benefactor's experience as a hobo during the Depression in order to collect his inheritance. Slow-moving stuff, scripted in part by Conway, targeted at the young.

1978 96m/C Tim Conway, Will Geer, Eric Weston, Sydney Lassick; *D:* Stuart E. McGowan. **VHS, Beta** *FOX*

A Billion for Boris 🦴🦴🦴

Jr. High-Adult TV fixed by Boris' kid brother carries news broadcasts from the future, so the boy hero plans to make money for his widowed mom by betting on the next day's horse races. The mother-son relationship is fresh and interesting, more so than the familiar stuff about precognition, gambling and kidnappers. Based on a book by "Freaky Friday" author Mary Rodgers.

> **BEWARE** *Salty language.*

1990 89m/C Lee Grant, Tim Kazurinsky; *W:* Mary Rogers. **VHS, Beta** *IMP*

Billy Bunny's Animal Song

Family Muppet characters Billy Bunny, Cecil, Percival, Edgar Bear, the Termite, and the Porcupine share eight songs with onscreen lyrics to which children can sing and dance. Hosted by Kermit the Frog.

1993 30m/C **VHS, Beta** *JHV, TOU, BTV*

Billy Galvin 🦴🦴🦴

PG/Jr. High-Adult Independently made drama with heart, if not many surprises. Billy wants to be just like his father, a blue-collar ironworker. But bullheaded dad wants his kids to do better in life, not just the same grind, and the stubborn pair square off over the boy's future.

> **BEWARE** *Profanity.*

1986 95m/C Karl Malden, Lenny Von Dohlen, Joyce Van Patten, Toni Kalem, Keith Szarabajka, Alan North, Paul Guilfoyle, Barton Heyman; *D:* John Gray; *W:* John Gray; *M:* Joel Rosenbaum. **VHS, Beta** *LIV, VES*

Billy Jack 🦴🦴

PG/Sr. High-Adult On an Arizona Indian reservation, a half-breed ex-Green Beret with pugnacious martial arts skills (Laughlin) stands between a rural town and a school for runaways. Laughlin stars with his real-life wife Taylor. Features the then-hit song "One Tin Soldier," sung by Coven. The movie and its marketing by Laughlin inspired a "Billy Jack" cult phenomenon. A Spanish-dubbed version of this film is also available. Followed by a sequel in 1974, "Trail of Billy Jack," which bombed.
1971 112m/C Tom Laughlin, Delores Taylor, Clark Howat; *D:* Tom Laughlin; *W:* Tom Laughlin. **VHS, Beta, LV** *WAR*

Billy Madison 🦴 🦴

PG-13/Jr. High-Adult Billy (Sandler), cretinous, ne'er-do-well son of a hotelier (McGavin), must prove himself worthy of running the family business by repeating grades 1-12 in sixth months. Seems he only graduated high school the first time because his dad bribed the teachers. Back in school, Billy's a lot better at dodge ball than the rest of the first graders, has the hots for his teacher and generally acts dumb until crunch time. A lot of scenes that only make sense to the writers and cast (or the very dim-witted) are included.

> ⚠ **BEWARE** *Much joking about sex, crude humor, profanity. Lots of alcohol and heavy hang-overs.*

1994 90m/C Adam Sandler, Darren McGavin, Brigitte Wilson, Bradley Whitford, Josh Mostel, Norm MacDonald, Mark Beltzman, Larry Hankin, Theresa Merritt; *Cameos:* Chris Farley, Steve Buscemi; *D:* Tamra Davis; *W:* Adam Sandler; *M:* Randy Edelman. **VHS, LV** *MCA*

Billy Possum

Preschool Three animated episodes from the creator of Peter Cottontail, Thornton W. Burgess, here with other characters from his "Fables of the Green Forest." Segments include "Uncle Billy Regrets," "Whose Footprint Is That?" and "Lost in the Green Forest."
1979 60m/C VHS, Beta *FHE*

Bingo 🦴🦴 🦴

PG/Jr. High-Adult Much-needed spoof of hero-dog movies. The resourceful Bingo is left behind when his adopted family moves from Denver to Green Bay. During his incredible journey to rejoin them, the superintelligent mutt skateboards, solves math problems, performs CPR, and even has the villains cheering for him in the absurd finale. Some very funny moments as time goes by.
1991 90m/C Cindy Williams, David Rasche, Robert J. Steinmiller Jr., David French, Kurt Fuller, Joe Guzaldo, Glenn Shadix; *D:* Matthew Robbins; *W:* Jim Strain; *M:* Richard Gibbs. **VHS, LV** *COL*

Bingo Long Traveling All-Stars & Motor Kings 🦴🦴🦴

PG/Family Set in 1939, this follows the comedic adventures of a lively group of black ball players who have defected from the old Negro National League. The All-Stars travel the country challenging local white teams and disarming racial tension with humor. Warm and winning, with an undercurrent of seriousness.

> ⚠ **BEWARE** *Salty barnstorming ballpark language, violence, sex talk.*

1976 111m/C Billy Dee Williams, James Earl Jones, Richard Pryor, Stan Shaw; *D:* John Badham; *W:* Matthew Robbins; *M:* William Goldstein. **VHS, Beta** *MCA, FCT*

Bio-Dome 🦴

PG-13/Jr. High-Adult How many people does it take to write a truly stupid movie? Five: Three to come up with the story, and two to do the screenplay. You were expecting a joke? That's the trouble with "Bio-Dome": no jokes. Desperately seeking a men's room, junior college students Bud (Shore) and Doyle (Baldwin) stumble into the 'Dome, and are locked in with the scientists for a year. Dome and Domer—uh, Bud and Doyle—proceed to trash the place in a most unamusing fashion, spitting out their food, trying to plant marijuana, scratching their crotches, and bungee-jumping all the ding-dong day.

> ⚠ **BEWARE** *Crude language, a bare backside, blatant sex talk, four people riding in the front seat of a car. Your typical lude, crude Pauly Shore junk.*

1996 94m/C Pauly Shore, Stephen Baldwin, William Atherton, Henry Gibson, Joey Adams, Teresa Hill, Kylie Minogue, Kevin West, Denise Dowse, Dara Tomanovich; *D:* Jason Bloom; *W:* Kip Koenig, Scott Marcano; *C:* Phedon Papamichael; *M:* Andrew Gross. **VHS, LV** *MGM*

The Birch Interval 🦴🦴🦴

PG/Jr. High-Adult It's 1947, and 11-year-old Jesse is sent to live with Amish kinfolk in their isolated Pennsylvania community. Even in the bucolic setting the girl senses adult passions and prejudices in her secretly troubled family. Heartfelt little movie from the creators of "Sounder," with a respectful but never patronizing or simplistic portrayal of the Amish way of life. Based on the novel by Joanna Crawford.

> ⚠ **BEWARE** *Mature themes.*

1978 104m/C Eddie Albert, Rip Torn, Ann Wedgeworth; *D:* Delbert Mann; *W:* Joanna Crawford. **VHS, Beta** *MED*

The Birdcage 🦴🦴🦴

R/Sr. High-Adult Nightclub owner Armand (Williams) and female impersonator Albert (Lane) are a devoted gay couple in Miami's South Beach. Their lives are comically disrupted when Armand's son comes home from college and announces that (A) he's engaged and (B) his fiancee and her politically conservative parents are coming and couldn't flamboyant Albert try to act less swishy or just go away for a few days. Williams and Lane are funny and dear as the homosexual pair who truly exemplify family values. Based on the French movie "La Cage aux Folles."

> ⚠ **BEWARE** *Men (and a few women) in G-strings, brief shot of a topless woman on a beach. Alcohol flows like water. Be prepared to explain what's so funny about dinner plates that appear to depict men playing leapfrog.*

1995 118m/C Robin Williams, Nathan Lane, Gene Hackman, Dianne Wiest, Hank Azaria, Dan Futterman, Christine Baranski, Calista Flockhart, Tom McGowan; **D:** Mike Nichols; **W:** Elaine May; **C:** Emmanuel Lubezki. **VHS** *NYR*

The Birds 🐦🐦🐦

Jr. High-Adult Hitchcock attempted to top the success of "Psycho" with this terrifying tale of Man versus Nature, in which Nature alights, one by one, on the trees of Bodega Bay to stage a bloody act of revenge upon the civilized world. Only Hitchcock can twist the harmless into the horrific while avoiding the ridiculous; this is perhaps his most brutal film, and one of the cinema's purest, horrifying portraits of apocalypse. Based on a short story by Daphne Du Maurier; screenplay by novelist Evan Hunter (aka Ed McBain).

🚸 *Ordinary birds attack humans. You'll never think of Polly or Tweety the same way again.*

1963 120m/C Rod Taylor, Tippi Hedren, Jessica Tandy, Veronica Cartwright, Suzanne Pleshette; **D:** Alfred Hitchcock. **VHS, Beta, LV** *MCA*

Bizet's Dreams

Primary A Parisian schoolgirl takes piano lessons from composer Bizet as he works on staging the first production of "Carmen." Story of the opera parallels the affair the girl's mother is having, which may not be something small children need to face. Ages 9 and up.

1995 ?m/C **VHS**

The Black Arrow 🐦🐦

Family Exiled bowman returns to England to avenge the injustices of a villainous nobleman. Disney's made-for-cable version of the Robert Louis Stevenson medieval romp lacks the panache of their (shorter) 1948 adaptation.

1984 93m/C Oliver Reed, Benedict Taylor, Georgia Slowe, Stephan Chase, Donald Pleasence; **D:** John Hough. **VHS, Beta** *DIS*

Black Beauty 🐦🐦

Family Very loose adaptation of Anna Sewell's horse's point-of-view novel. Young girl develops a kindred relationship with an extraordinary colt, then has to go in search of the animal when they're separated.

1946 74m/B Mona Freeman, Richard Denning, Evelyn Ankers; **D:** Max Nosseck. **VHS, Beta** *CCB, MED, VTR*

Black Beauty 🐦🐦 🔖

G/Family Anna Sewell's oft-filmed 'Autobiography of a Horse' gets a respectable treatment, following the title mare from one owner until she's finally reunited with her favorite master. Perhaps the biggest surprise is off-screen; movie came from a British outfit otherwise specializing in low-grade horror and exploitation pictures.

1971 105m/C Mark Lester, Walter Slezak; **D:** James Hill. **VHS, Beta, LV** *PAR, FCT*

Black Beauty

Family Animated version of the classic children's tale that follows a magnificent horse from one owner to another.

1978 49m/C **VHS**

Black Beauty 🐦🐦🐦

G/Family Remake of the classic Anna Sewell children's novel about an oft-sold horse whose life has its shares of ups and downs. Timeless tale still brings children and adults to tears. Six-year-old quarterhorse named Justin gives a nuanced portrayal as the Black Beauty, recalling Olivier in "Hamlet." Directorial debut of "Secret Garden" screenwriter Thompson.

🚸 *Mistreatment of horses.*

1994 85m/C Andrew Knott, Sean Bean, David Thewlis, Jim Carter, Alun Armstrong, Eleanor Bron, Peter Cook, Peter Davison, John McEnery, Nicholas Jones; **D:** Caroline Thompson; **W:** Caroline Thompson. **VHS, LV** *WAR*

The Black Hole 🐦🐦

G/Family Disney's answer to "Star Wars" was this high-tech space adventure about a mad genius planning to pilot his starship right into a black hole. Except for the top quality special effects, it's creaky vehicle much in love with its own gadgetry, like two cutesy robots (one with a western drawl) who are plenty annoying but still the best-drawn characters. Dig that wild religious ending.

🚸 *Ray gun battles had some parents questioning the violence and overall darkness, but it's strictly video game stuff.*

1979 97m/C Maximilian Schell, Anthony Perkins, Ernest Borgnine, Yvette Mimieux, Joseph Bottoms, Robert Forster; **D:** Gary Nelson; **M:** John Barry. **VHS, Beta, LV** *DIS, OM*

Black Magic 🐦🐦

PG-13/Jr. High-Adult Insomniac Alex, haunted by the nightly appearances of his dead cousin Ross, goes to Ross' hometown to see if he can find a way to make the apparition disappear. On the way, he runs into his cousin's ex-girlfriend Lilian and falls in love. Problem is, Lilian's a witch, maybe. Lightweight made for cable TV fare.

1992 94m/C Rachel Ward, Judge Reinhold, Brion James, Anthony LaPaglia; **D:** Daniel Taplitz; **W:** Daniel Taplitz. **VHS, LV** *MCA*

The Black Planet 🐦🐦

Family Offbeat Australian cartoon feature, an environmentalist satire of the Cold War. Scientists discover a mystery 'Black Planet' orbiting nearby, and a Kennedy-like president finances a space program to explore it. But a senator and a general wanted that money for war; they conspire to sabotage the rocket, while an ecologist and a feminist repeatedly bumble into the way. Not as strident or overbearing as it sounds, though simplistic animation and jokes limit this to smaller viewers.

Alcohol use.

1982 78m/C D: Paul Williams. **VHS, Beta**

Black Sheep 🎵

PG-13/Jr. High-Adult Bah! Bah! "Black Sheep" is long on doo-doo jokes and short on wit and imagination. Chris Farley, who should have stuck with "Saturday Night Live" plays a politician's idiot brother—sort of Billy Carter without the refinement—who gets hidden away while the politico runs for governor. David Spade (also from "SNL") is the candidate's unctuous aide who becomes his brother's keeper. A sample of the repartee . . . Spade: "That was a chunk in the road." Farley: "I just chunked in my pants."

 Crude language, bathroom humor, marijuana and alcohol use, sexual innuendo, fingers smashed by a car trunk lid. And there's lots more idiocy where that came from.

1996 87m/C Chris Farley, David Spade, Tim Matheson, Christine Ebersole, Gary Busey, Grant Heslov, Timothy Carhart, Bruce McGill; **D:** Penelope Spheeris; **W:** Fred Wolf; **C:** Daryn Okada; **M:** William Ross. **VHS, Beta** *PAR*

The Black Stallion 🎵🎵🎵 ♭

PG/Family Young Alec Ramsey and a majestic Arabian stallion are the only survivors of a shipwreck, and the two develop a deep affection for each other while stranded on a desert island in an exceptionally beautiful (almost wordless) first half. Rescued, they return to Alec's suburban home in the U.S., and the Black (as he's called) seems to be an unmanageable misfit until he fulfills his destiny at the racetrack. Superb, visionary entertainment for adults and kids, based on the book by Walter Farley. The PG rating is ridiculous.

1979 120m/C Kelly Reno, Mickey Rooney, Teri Garr, Clarence Muse; **D:** Carroll Ballard; **W:** William D. Wittliff, Melissa Mathison, Jeanne Rosenberg; **M:** Carmine Coppola. **Award Nominations:** Academy Awards '79: Best Film Editing, Best Supporting Actor (Rooney); **Awards:** Academy Awards '79: Best Sound Effects Editing. **VHS, Beta, LV** *MGM, FOX, TLF*

The Black Stallion Returns 🎵🎵 ♭

PG/Family Sequel to "The Black Stallion" follows the adventures of young Alec as he travels to the Sahara to search for his beautiful horse, which was stolen by an Arab chieftain who claims rightful ownership. Expect a typical boy's adventure, nothing near the mystical quality of the first "Black Stallion" and the kids won't be disappointed—though some of the dialogue really hurts.

 Mild profanity and fighting. Arabs in general are portrayed as fearsome but sympathetic

1983 103m/C Kelly Reno, Teri Garr, Vincent Spano; **D:** Robert Dalva; **M:** Georges Delerue. **VHS, Beta, LV** *FOX*

The Black Tulip

Preschool-Primary Alexandre Dumas' classic tale is told here as a man grows the world's first black tulip, only to have it stolen.

1991 50m/C VHS *VTR*

The Black Widow

Family Fortune-teller plots to steal scientific secrets and take over the world, in this Republic serial in thirteen episodes. Forman plays the villainess, known as Sombra the Spider Woman (pic's alternate title), sort of a takeoff on her role as the Spider Lady in the original "Superman" chapter play.

1947 164m/B Bruce Edwards, Carol Forman, Anthony Warde; **D:** Spencer Gordon Bennet. **VHS** *VCN, REP, MLB*

Blackbeard's Ghost 🎵🎵 ♭

Family Middling Disney comedy in which Dean Jones conjures up the famed 18th-century pirate's spirit (Peter Ustinov) to prevent an old family home from being turned into a casino. Sort of foreshadows what happened 25 years later when Disney tried to take historic Virginia countryside and turn it into a theme park. Ages 4 to 10.

1967 107m/C Peter Ustinov, Dean Jones, Suzanne Pleshette, Elsa Lanchester, Richard Deacon; **D:** Robert Stevenson. **VHS, Beta, LV** *DIS*

Blackberry Subway Jam

Primary Based on the Robert Munsch story, "Jonathan Cleaned Up-Then He Heard A Sound," this nicely animated film focuses on a boy's whose mom tells him to clean up the place. Somehow a subway station pops up in Jonathan's living room; hundreds of passengers walk through and make a mess. Jonathan goes to City Hall to seek redress and discovers the secret of the municipal computer. Ages 4 to 7.

1987 9m/C VHS, Beta *NFB*

Blackstar

Preschool-Jr. High Saturday-morning-cartoon recycling of the adventures of John Blackstar, an astronaut who passes through a black hole and finds Sagar, a perilous new world of friends and foes awaiting. This empty-headed stuff came from the producers of the similar "He-Man and the Masters of the Universe" show, but fortunately proved not at all as popular. Additional volumes available.

1981 60m/C VHS, Beta *FHE*

Blacula 🎵🎵

PG/Sr. High-Adult The African Prince Mamuwalde stalks the streets of Los Angeles trying to satisfy his insatiable desire for blood. Mildly successful melding of blaxploitation and horror that spawned a sequel, "Scream, Blacula, Scream."

 Violence. Racial stereotyping.

1972 92m/C William Marshall, Thalmus Rasulala, Denise Nicholas, Vonetta McGee; *D:* William Crain. **VHS, Beta, LV** *ORI*

Blake of Scotland Yard

Family Byrd, also the screen's early Dick Tracy, plays a former Scotland Yard inspector who battles against The Scorpion, a mystery villain with a death ray. A serial in 15 episodes, also available under the same title in a condensed 70-minute edition.

1936 70m/B Ralph Byrd, Herbert Rawlinson, Joan Barclay, Lloyd Hughes; *D:* Robert F. "Bob" Hill. **VHS, Beta** *VYY, DVT, VCN*

Blame It on the Night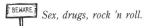

PG-13/Jr. High-Adult Rock star inherits his illegitimate military-cadet son after the boy's mother dies. Taking the kid on the road during a concert tour, with all the pressures and temptations of the rock 'n' roll lifestyle, turns into a growing experience for them both, but not enough of one. Mick Jagger helped write the story for this maudlin, tune-filled drama.

BEWARE *Sex, drugs, rock 'n roll.*

1984 85m/C Nick Mancuso, Byron Thames, Leslie Ackerman, Billy Preston, Merry Clayton; *D:* Gene Taft. **VHS, Beta** *FOX*

Blank Check 🦴🦴

PG/Jr. High-Adult 11-year-old Preston, bullied at school and scorned by his big brothers, figures out that money means power and respect. When he gets a blank check from a mobster who ran over his bike, the savvy lad cashes it for a million bucks, and goes on a spending orgy under an assumed name. Nice setup, but when the mobster and his goons come snooping around Preston's new toy-crammed castle, this Disney romp devolves into a blatant "Home Alone" ripoff. Preston should have set aside a couple grand to buy more inspiration.

BEWARE *Bullying by bigger kids. Hey, where is this kid's parents?*

1993 93m/C Brian Bonsall, Miguel Ferrer, Michael Lerner, Tone Loc, Rick Ducommun, Karen Duffy; *D:* Rupert Wainwright; *W:* Colby Carr, Blake Snyder; *M:* Nicholas Pike. **VHS, LV** *DIS*

Blankman 🦴🦴

PG-13/Jr. High-Adult Self-appointed superhero Wayans makes up in creativity what he lacks in superpowers, fighting crime in his underwear and a cape made from his grandmother's bathrobe. Life is simple, until an ambitious TV reporter (Givens) finds out about him. Silly one-joke premise is carried as far as it will go. Fans of Wayans will appreciate, as will those in the mood for some stupid fun.

BEWARE *Superhero violence and profanity.*

1994 92m/C Damon Wayans, Robin Givens, David Alan Grier, Jason Alexander, Jon Polito; *D:* Mike Binder; *W:* Damon Wayans, J.F. Lawton. **VHS** *NYR*

Blast-Off

Family Introduces kids to the history of space exploration and the space program with historical photos and film footage. Ages 8 to 12.

1995 30m/C **VHS** *HMK*

Bless the Beasts and Children 🦴🦴 🦴

PG/Jr. High-Adult Six misfit adolescent boys dumped by their parents at an Arizona dude ranch for the summer do some growing up when they determine to save a majestic herd of buffalo from authorized slaughter. Message-laden drama still manages to work. Based on the novel by Glendon Swarthout.

BEWARE *Violence, salty language, mature themes.*

1971 109m/C Billy Mumy, Barry Robins, Miles Chapin, Darel Glaser, Bob Kramer, Ken Swofford, Jesse White; *D:* Stanley Kramer. **VHS, Beta** *COL*

Blood Brothers

Family Single episode from the network mountain man drama "The Life and Times of Grizzly Adams," in which the hero recounts his first encounter with his Indian blood brother Nakuma. Beautiful scenery.

1977 50m/C Dan Haggerty, Denver Pyle, Don Shanks. **VHS, Beta** *MCG*

The Blue Bird 🦴🦴🦴

Family When Miss Shirley missed a chance to star in "The Wizard of Oz," the 20th Century Fox studios holding her contract came up with this misfire fantasy, based on Maurice Maeterlinck's story, as an "Oz" competitor. The child star plays a peasant girl who vainly seeks the fabled Blue Bird of Happiness in various fantasy lands inhabited by numerous Hollywood guest stars. Strangely (perhaps appropriately) joyless and stiff, it became Temple's first major box-office disappointment. Long ignored and worth a look on tape as a real curio.

1940 98m/C Shirley Temple, Gale Sondergaard, John Russell, Eddie Collins, Nigel Bruce, Jessie Ralph, Spring Byington, Sybil Jason; *D:* Walter Lang. **VHS, Beta** *FOX, MLB*

Blue Chips 🦴🦴 🦴

PG-13/Jr. High-Adult Nolte does Indiana coach Bobby Knight in this saga of Western U basketball coach Pete Bell, suffering through his first losing season. What follows is a tug of war between rich alumni who want to win at any cost and his ethics as he recruits for a new season. Larger than life hoopster O'Neal's film debut. McDonnell and Woodard are merely afterthoughts, but look for cameos from many real life gamesters, including Knight, Dick Vitale, and Larry Bird. Average script is bolstered by exciting game footage, shot during real games for authenticity.

BEWARE *Courtside and coach-like profanity.*

1994 108m/C Nick Nolte, Shaquille O'Neal, Mary McDonnell, Ed O'Neill, J.T. Walsh, Alfre Woodard; *Cameos:* Larry Bird, Bobby Knight, Rick Pitino; *D:* William Friedkin; *W:* Ron Shelton; *M:* Nile Rodgers, Jeff Beck, Jed Leiber. **VHS, Beta** *PAR*

Blue Fin

PG/Family Young boy and his semi-estranged fisherman father learn lessons of love and courage when their tuna boat is disabled and both have to work together to save the ship. Set in the waters off Australia.
1978 93m/C Hardy Kruger, Greg Rowe; *D:* Carl Schultz. **VHS, Beta**

Blue Fire Lady ♫♫

Family Girl's love of horses meets opposition from her father, so she sets out on her own, getting a job at a seedy racetrack and turning an unmanageable mare into a champion through her tender care. Okay equine fare from Australia, hindered by a muddy, low-budget look.

⚠ BEWARE ⚠ *Alcohol use.*

1978 96m/C Cathryn Harrison, Mark Holden, Peter Cummins. **VHS, Beta** *MED*

Blue Murder at St. Trinian's
♫♫♫

Jr. High-Adult Second in a series of madcap British comedies (after "Belles of St. Trinian's") about a ferocious pack of English schoolgirls, first rendered in the cartoon drawings of Ronald Searle. This time they take a field trip to Europe and make life miserable for a jewel thief. Fantasy scene in ancient Rome shows the girls thrown to the lions—and terrifying the lions.
1956 86m/B Joyce Grenfell, Terry-Thomas, George Cole, Alastair Sim, Lionel Jeffries, Thorley Walters; *D:* Frank Launder; *M:* Malcolm Arnold. **VHS** *VYY, VDM, FUS*

Blue Skies Again ♫♫

PG/Jr. High-Adult Spunky young woman determined to play major league baseball locks horns with the chauvinistic owner and the gruff manager of her favorite team. Ages 8 to 12.

⚠ BEWARE ⚠ *Sex talk.*

1983 91m/C Robyn Barto, Harry Hamlin, Mimi Rogers, Kenneth McMillan, Dana Elcar, Andy Garcia; *D:* Richard Michaels. **VHS, Beta** *WAR*

The Blue Yonder

Family Disney TV feature about an 11-year-old boy who travels back in time to meet his grandfather, an early pilot who disappeared flying solo across the Atlantic, just before Charles Lindberg. Should little Jonathan try to warn his ancestor or let history go unaltered? The answer isn't too satisfying, and the low-intensity yarn will interest mainly aviation buffs.
1986 89m/C Art Carney, Peter Coyote, Huckleberry Fox; *D:* Mark Rosman. **VHS, Beta** *DIS*

Blues Busters ♫ ♭

Family Late entry in the "Bowery Boys/East Side Kids" series of short-feature comedies that began in the 1930s with a crew of young urban wise guys and their antics, a fave with kids of the era. In this one, eternal doofus Sach (Hall) emerges from a tonsillectomy with a velvety singing voice. Slip (Gorcey), the boys' leader and eternal purveyor of get-rich-quick schemes, tries to use Sach's new crooning abilities to turn their neighborhood soda shop into a nightclub.
1950 68m/B Leo Gorcey, Huntz Hall, Adele Jergens, Gabriel Dell, Craig Stevens, Phyllis Coates, Bernard Gorcey, David Gorcey; *D:* William Beaudine. **VHS** *WAR*

Bluetoes the Christmas Elf

Family Yuletide cartoon about Bluetoes, an elf who's just too clumsy to help Santa on Christmas eve. Yet fate gives the little fella the break he deserves.
1988 27m/C **VHS** *FHE, FCT*

BMX Bandits ♫♫

Family Three adventurous Aussie teens put their BMX skills to the test when they witness a crime and are pursued by the criminals.
1983 92m/C Nicole Kidman, David Argue, John Ley, Angelo D'Angelo; *D:* Brian Trenchard-Smith; *W:* Patrick Edgeworth. **VHS** *IMP*

The Boatniks ♫♫ ♭

G/Family Accident-prone Coast Guard ensign finds himself in charge of the "Times Square" of waterways, Newport Harbor. Adding to his already "titanic" problems is a gang of ocean-going jewel thieves who lose their loot overboard and try to get it back. Shipshape Disney comedy.
1970 99m/C Robert Morse, Stefanie Powers, Phil Silvers, Norman Fell, Wally Cox, Don Ameche; *D:* Norman Tokar. **VHS, Beta** *DIS*

Bob the Quail

Preschool-Primary Taken from the "Fables of the Green Forest," this tale follows Bob's hunt for a good tree that will safely house his family.
1978 60m/C **VHS, Beta** *FHE*

Bobby Goldsboro's Easter Egg Mornin'

Family The entertainer hosts a special holiday program of fun and music.
1992 27m/C **VHS** *FHE*

Bobby Raccoon

Family Bobby learns to trust and respect his friendly neighborhood forest critters in this cartoon program.
1985 60m/C **VHS, Beta** *FHE*

Bobby's World: Fish Tales and Generics Under Construction

Family Two episodes from the Fox Kids Network Bobby's World animated series. In "Fish Tales," Bobby (voiced by Howie Mandel) shows everyone how they can use their imagination to overcome boredom on a camping trip in Canada. In the second, "Generics Under Construction," Bobby saves the day when a photographer shows up to take a family portrait but a construction crew has made a mess of the house. Ages 5 to 10.
1995 50m/C VHS *TCF*

The Bollo Caper

Family Cartoon story of Bollo and his mate Nefertiti who are the last golden leopards; all the others have been killed for their pelts. He saves himself and his species from extinction with the help of the President of the United States and the King of his own country. An ABC Weekend Special and adaptation of the book by the acclaimed humorist and columnist Art Buchwald.
1992 23m/C VHS *AIM*

Bon Voyage, Charlie Brown
🦴🦴🦴

G/Family Selected members of the "Peanuts" comic strip kids become exchange students in France, but Charlie Brown and Linus can't figure out why they have to sleep in the stables outside their unseen host's mysterious chateau. Untypical travelogue for the series, perhaps explained by the fact that cartoonist Charles M. Schultz himself relocated to France. Plot reveals some of Charlie Brown's family background, but Snoopy and Woodstock easily steal the show.
1980 76m/C *D:* Bill Melendez; *W:* Charles M. Schulz. VHS, Beta, LV *PAR*

Bonanza: The Return 🦴🦴

PG/Family Made for TV update to the classic television series has the son of original cast member Michael Landon portraying the son of the original cast member, a novel premise. In 1905, the children of various members of the Cartwright clan fight among themselves before uniting to keep the Ponderosa from falling into the hands of an unscrupulous businessman. Rather bland, though cast and nostalgia (and the occasional film clip from the series) keep it somewhat interesting.

🚫 BEWARE 🚫 *Violence.*

1993 96m/C Michael Landon Jr., Dirk Blocker, Emily Warfield, Alistair MacDougall, Brian Leckner, Dean Stockwell, Ben Johnson, Richard Roundtree, Linda Gray, Jack Elam. **VHS, LV** *VMK*

Bongo 🦴🦴

Family Originally a part of the Disney cartoon anthology "Fun and Fancy Free." Follows the adventures of a circus bear who flees the big time for the wonders of the forests.

Narrated by Dinah Shore. Also available with "Ben and Me" on laserdisc.
1947 36m/C Bill Roberts, Hamilton Luske; *D:* Jack Kinney. **VHS, Beta** *DIS, TOU*

Boo-Busters

Family Selection of recent Disney cartoon shorts with spooky themes: The Goof Troup discover a haunted house that's home to a Dixieland band of ghosts in "Hallow-Weenies." Chip 'n' Dale head off to jolly old England in "Ghost of a Chance" and find a prankish spook. See also "Monster Bash" and "Witcheroo," released simultaneously.
1993 44m/C VHS *DIS*

Book of Love 🦴🦴

PG-13/Jr. High-Adult "Zany" hijinks as a teenager struggles with friendship, girls, and those all-important hormones when he moves to a new neighborhood in the mid-50's. Average rehash of every 50's movie cliche in existence. Surprise! There's a classic rock 'n' roll soundtrack. Adapted by Kotzwinkle from his novel "Jack in the Box."

 🚫 BEWARE 🚫 *Sex talk.*

1991 88m/C Chris Young, Keith Coogan, Aeryk Egan, Josie Bissett, Tricia Leigh Fisher, Danny Nucci, Michael McKean, John Cameron Mitchell, Lewis Arquette; *D:* Robert Shaye; *W:* William Kotzwinkle; *M:* Stanley Clarke. **VHS, LV, 8mm** *COL*

Bopha! 🦴🦴🦴

PG-13/Jr. High-Sr. High Father-son strife set against the anti-apartheid movement as the Senior township police officer Mikah takes pride in his peaceful community, particularly in light of the growing unrest in the other townships. Son Zweli has become an activist and wife Rosie must be the family peacemaker. Then a prominent freedom movement member is arrested and two officers of the secret police make their sinister appearance. Directorial debut of Freeman is well acted. Adapted from the play by Percy Mtwa, although the hopeful ending has been changed in the movie. The title, a Zulu word, stands for arrest or detention. Filmed on location in Zimbabwe.

🚫 BEWARE 🚫 *Violence, cruelties of apartheid.*

1993 121m/C Danny Glover, Maynard Eziashi, Alfre Woodard, Malcolm McDowell, Marius Weyers, Malick Bowens, Robin Smith, Michael Chinyamurindi, Christopher John Hall, Grace Mahlaba; *D:* Morgan Freeman; *W:* Brian Bird, John Wierick; *M:* James Horner. **VHS, Beta, LV** *PAR*

Boris and Natasha: The Movie 🦴🦴

PG/Jr. High-Adult Long unreleased oddity that premiered on cable. The inept spies from the classic "Rocky and Bullwinkle" TV 'toon star in a mediocre live-action plot about the nogoodniks sent by "Fearless Leader" to America to capture a time weapon. Main actors are per-

fect in their incarnations of Boris Badenov and Natasha Fatale (Kellerman even sings the closing theme), but slow-starting script never really takes off, even with a cameo, sort of, by Agents Moose and Squirrel. The original animated versions are also widely available on cassette.

BEWARE *Salty language, alcohol use, cartoonish violence. Believe it or not, Boris and Natasha end the platonic phase of their relationship, but discreetly offscreen.*
1992 88m/C Sally Kellerman, Dave Thomas, Paxton Whitehead, Andrea Martin, Alex Rocco, Larry Cedar, Arye Gross, Christopher Neame, Anthony Newley; **Cameos:** John Candy, John Travolta, Charles Martin Smith; **D:** Charles Martin Smith. **VHS** *ACA, NLC*

Born Free 🎞🎞🎞

Family The touching story of a game warden and his wife in Kenya raising Elsa the orphaned lion cub. When the cub reaches maturity, they work to return her to life in the wild. Great family entertainment based on Joy Adamson's book. Theme song became a hit.
1966 95m/C Virginia McKenna, Bill Travers; **D:** James Hill; **M:** John Barry. **VHS, Beta, LV** *COL, HMV*

Born to Be Wild 🎞 ♭

PG/Jr. High-Adult A simian "Free Willy." Rebellious teenager Rick (Hornoff) befriends Katie, the 3-year-old gorilla his behavioral scientist mom (Shaver) is studying. When Katie's owner (Boyle) decides she would make a better sideshow attraction than science project, Rick busts her out and they head for the Canadian border. Animal slapstick and bodily function jokes ensue. Strictly for elementary school-age kids.

BEWARE *Mild language, gorilla flatulence.*

1995 98m/C Wil Horneff, Helen Shaver, Peter Boyle, Jean Marie Barnwell, John C. McGinley, Marvin J. McIntyre; **D:** John Gray; **W:** John Bunzel, Paul Young; **C:** Donald M. Morgan. **VHS, LV** *WAR*

Born to Run 🎞🎞

Family Young Australian boy dreams of restoring his grandfather's run-down horse farm to its former glory. Made-for-TV Disney feature, filmed on location.
1977 87m/C VHS, Beta *DVT*

Born Wild 🎞🎞 ♭

PG/Family Documentary filmmaker Christine Shaye (Shields) is assigned to capture the beauty of Africa. Christine arrives at the South African game preserve of Londolozi where she meets passionate conservationist John Varty (who plays himself). Varty has filmed one leopard family for 12 years but when the mother leopard is killed, he violates his own ethical code and rescues her two orphaned cubs.

BEWARE *Mild language, jungle violence. Be ready to explain the "Bambi syndrome" when the mother leopard is killed.*

1995 98m/C Brooke Shields, Martin Sheen, John Varty, David Keith; **D:** Duncan McLachlan; **W:** Duncan McLachlan, Andrea Buck. **VHS, LV** *COL*

Born Yesterday 🎞🎞

PG/Jr. High-Adult Remake of the 1950 classic suffers in comparison, particularly Griffith, who has the thankless task of surpassing (or even meeting) Judy Holliday's Oscar-winning mark as not-so-dumb blonde Billie Dawn. Her intellectual inadequacies are glaring when she hits the political world of D.C. with obnoxious tycoon boyfriend Goodman. To save face, he hooks her up with a journalist (Johnson) willing to coach her in Savvy 101, a la Eliza Doolittle. What worked well in post-WWII America seems sadly outdated today; stick with the original.

BEWARE *Profanity and sex talk.*

1993 102m/C Melanie Griffith, John Goodman, Don Johnson, Edward Herrmann, Max Perlich, Fred Dalton Thompson, Nora Dunn, Benjamin C. Bradlee, Sally Quinn, Michael Ensign, William Frankfather, Celeste Yarnall, Meg Wittner; **D:** Luis Mandoki; **W:** Douglas McGrath; **M:** George Fenton. **VHS, Beta, LV** *TOU, HPH*

Bound for Glory 🎞🎞🎞 ♭

PG/Jr. High-Adult The award-winning biography of American folk singer Woody Guthrie set against the backdrop of the Depression. Superb portrayal of the spirit and feelings of the period featuring many of his songs encased in the incidents that inspired them. Haskell Wexler's award-winning camera work is superbly expressive.
1976 149m/C David Carradine, Ronny Cox, Melinda Dillon, Randy Quaid; **D:** Hal Ashby; **W:** Robert Getchell. **Award Nominations:** Academy Awards '76: Best Adapted Screenplay, Best Costume Design, Best Film Editing, Best Picture; Cannes Film Festival '77: Best Film; **Awards:** Academy Awards '76: Best Adapted Score, Best Cinematography; National Board of Review Awards '76: Best Actor (Carradine). **VHS, Beta, LV** *MGM*

The Bounty 🎞🎞🎞

PG/Jr. High-Adult Cinematically impressive new version of "Mutiny on the Bounty" takes on water at times, but still sails with integrity. Emphasis is on a more realistic relationship between Fletcher Christian and Captain Bligh—and a more sympathetic portrayal of the captain, too. As the conflict-ridden captain, Hopkins delivers a first-rate performance eclipsing that of his shipmate Gibson as Christian. The sensuality of Christian's relationship with a Tahitian beauty also receives greater importance.

BEWARE *Violence on the high seas, brief nudity and authority is questioned.*

1984 130m/C Mel Gibson, Anthony Hopkins, Laurence Olivier, Edward Fox, Daniel Day-Lewis, Bernard Hill, Philip Davis, Liam Neeson; **D:** Roger Donaldson; **W:** Robert Bolt. **VHS, Beta, LV** *VES, LIV*

Bowery Blitzkrieg 🎞

Family This lesser "East Side Kids" entry has Gorcey opting to enter the boxing ring rather than turn to crime.
1941 62m/B Leo Gorcey, Huntz Hall, Bobby Jordan, Warren Hull, Charlotte Henry, Keye Luke; **D:** Wallace Fox. **VHS** *NOS, VEC, HEG*

Bowery Buckaroos 🦴🦴

Family The Bowery Boys take their act west in search of gold, meeting up with the usual amounts of goofy characters and hilarious misunderstandings.

1947 66m/B Leo Gorcey, Huntz Hall, Bobby Jordan, Gabriel Dell, Billy Benedict, David Gorcey, Julie Briggs, Bernard Gorcey, Chief Yowlachie, Iron Eyes Cody; **D:** William Beaudine. **VHS** *WAR*

Box of Delights 🦴🦴 ⌐

Family English TV treat (based on the novel by John Masefield) about a schoolboy on Christmas Eve assigned to protect a small box, "the greatest magical device of all time," from a cabal of crooks led by an evil wizard. The Box of Delights lets the boy shrink to minuscule size, talk to animals, fly and travel to the past in a long, twisting plot that's not exactly easy to follow and filled with Briticisms (give yourself a Christmas cracker if you know who Herne the Hunter is). Abundant special effects mix animation with live-action and computer-generated visuals; this might have done better as a feature cartoon—where are Hanna-Barbera Studios when you need them?

1983 120m/C Jon Pertwee. **VHS** *PAR*

The Boy Friend 🦴🦴🦴

G/Family Russell pays tribute to the Busby Berkeley Hollywood musical. Lots of charming dance numbers and clever parody of plot lines in this adaptation of Sandy Wilson's stage play. Fun! 🎵 The Boy Friend; I Could Be Happy; Won't You Charleston With Me?; Fancy Forgetting; Sur La Plage; A Room in Bloomsbury; Safety in Numbers; It's Never Too Late to Fall in Love; Poor Little Pierette.

1971 135m/C Twiggy, Christopher Gable, Moyra Fraser, Max Adrian, Vladek Sheybal, Georgina Hale, Tommy Tune; **D:** Ken Russell; **W:** Ken Russell. **VHS** *MGM*

The Boy God WOOF!

Jr. High-Adult Philippines-made loser about a pudgy kid descended from magical beings, in battle against monsters and fiends. Shabby takeoff on Greek mythology, good only for laughs. That ultra-sexy girl on the cassette box never appears in the film.

 *Fantasy violence.*

1986 100m/C Nino Muhlach; **D:** Erastheo J. Navda. **VHS, Beta** *VCD*

Boy of Two Worlds 🦴🦴

G/Family The petty prejudice of people in a small town compels a fatherless boy to embark on the adventurous life of a junior Robinson Crusoe.

1970 103m/C Jimmy Sternman, Edvin Adolphson; **D:** Astrid Henning Jensen. **VHS, Beta** *GEM*

Boy Takes Girl 🦴🦴

Family Adolescent girl finds hardship and romance when she's left to work on an Australian farming cooperative over the summer recess.

1983 93m/C Gabi Eldor, Hillel Neeman, Dina Limon; **D:** Michal Bat-Adam. **VHS, Beta** *MGM*

The Boy Who Could Fly 🦴🦴 ⌐

PG/Jr. High-Adult After a plane crash kills his parents, Eric withdraws into a trance state, pretending to fly. The girl next door befriends him, tries to prevent his incarceration in a loony bin—then events hint that Eric can really fly after all. Sentimental drama, rather like the troubled "Radio Flyer"; you either accept intrusion of fantasy in a somewhat grim reality, or you don't. There's no in-between, though fine cast works hard to limit the sap.

BEWARE *Mild profanity, alcohol use, autism, scenes from a mental institution.*

1986 120m/C Lucy Deakins, Jay Underwood, Bonnie Bedelia, Colleen Dewhurst, Fred Savage, Fred Gwynne, Louise Fletcher, Jason Priestley; **D:** Nick Castle; **W:** Nick Castle; **M:** Bruce Broughton. **VHS, Beta, LV** *WAR, ORI*

The Boy Who Drew Cats

Family Narrated Japanese folktale about a young artist whose skills come in handy when black magic threatens. Not animated, but told against vivid (and in this case, a little scary) storybook illustrations; from the award-winning series "Rabbit Ears: We All Have Tales," first aired on Showtime cable TV.

1991 35m/C M: Mark Isham. **VHS** *RAB, MVD*

The Boy Who Left Home to Find Out About the Shivers

Family From "Faerie Tale Theatre" comes a lesser known Brothers Grimm tale about Martin, a young resident of Transylvania who never learned fear. Tossed out by his superstitious father, Martin accepts an offer to spend three nights at a haunted castle. Cast of horror movie vets make this a cute retelling that actually improves on the original's ending. Some zombie ghosts turn out to be playful, Addams-Family level ghouls.

1981 60m/C Peter MacNicol, Christopher Lee, Vincent Price; **D:** Graeme Clifford. **VHS, Beta, LV** *KUI, FOX*

The Boy Who Loved Trolls

Family Paul's fantastic dreams come true when he meets Ofoeti, a real, live troll. The only problem is Ofoeti only has a day to live, and Paul must find a way to save him. Aired on PBS as part of the "Wonderworks" series.

1984 58m/C Sam Waterston, Susan Anton, Matt Dill; **D:** Harvey Laidman. **VHS** *PME, HMV, FCT*

The Boy with the Green Hair

🦴🦴 🐾

Family When young Peter learns his relief-worker parents were killed in an air raid, his hair turns green overnight. He declares he's become a living reminder of war's terrible cost, but town adults don't want his message and other kids chase and harass him. Considered a thought-provoking statement in its day; now seems outmoded and simplistic (with an utterly pointless musical number early on). Still worth seeing for child-actor Stockwell's haunted determination.

1948 82m/C Pat O'Brien, Robert Ryan, Barbara Hale, Dean Stockwell; **D:** Joseph Losey. **VHS, Beta, LV** *IME*

Boyd's Shadow 🦴🦴

Preschool-Primary Boy learns about preconceptions and acceptance through the town recluse, who was thought to "boil children and feed them to his snakes." In actuality, the recluse is an accomplished folk musician and friend of the boy's dead father. Filmed adaptation of a play by William Stevens who, along with his family, stars in the production (directed by his brother John).

1992 45m/C Bill Stevens, Becca Stevens, Katie Stevens, Carolyn Stevens, William Stevens; **D:** John Stevens; **W:** John Stevens; **M:** William Stevens. **VHS** *BTV*

Boys 🦴

PG-13/Jr. High-Adult Only for teens and adults, this "mature" story about a couple who haphazardly meet and fall in love will likely only appeal to young women. You see, young John (Haas) saves older woman Patty (Ryder) when she falls from her horse while riding by his New England prep school. John hides her in his dorm room and swears to protect her. Romance blooms, but Patty is hiding a secret (and it's not just her age). Based on the short story "Twenty Minutes" by James Salter.

> 🪧 **BEWARE!** *There is a sex scene between Patty and John, which isn't explicit, but it's obvious what's going on. Also, the students at the school smoke, swear, and make sexual jokes and there is a drunk driving scene.*

1996 89m/C Winona Ryder, Lukas Haas, John C. Reilly, William Sage, Skeet Ulrich; **D:** Stacy Cochran; **W:** Stacy Cochran; **C:** Robert Elswit. **VHS** *NYR*

Boys of the City 🦴🦴

Family The East Side Kids run amuck in an eerie mansion while trying to solve the murder of a judge.

1940 63m/B Leo Gorcey, Bobby Jordan; **D:** Joseph H. Lewis. **VHS, Beta** *NOS, SNC, DVT*

Boys on the Side 🦴🦴 🐾

R/Sr. High-Adult Star power and a cool rock soundtrack may entice teen viewers, so consider this: one of the three lead characters (Barrymore) brains her abusive boyfriend with a baseball bat. Also, she's pregnant. The other two? Well, one's a lesbian (Goldberg), the other (Parker) has AIDS, neither of which would be objectionable except that it makes for a sex-obsessed movie. Sort of a three-woman Thelma and Louise, the trio head for California in a car. A huge tear-jerker with plenty of female bonding.

> 🪧 **BEWARE!** *Physical abuse and retaliation, a great deal of profanity. A vivid drunken close-to-sex scene and lots of sex talk. The three women deal with very real issues involving relationships, AIDS, lies, and murder.*

1994 117m/C James Remar, Anita Gillette, Matthew McConaughey, Whoopi Goldberg, Mary-Louise Parker, Drew Barrymore; **D:** Herbert Ross; **W:** Don Roos; **C:** Donald E. Thorin. **VHS, LV** *WAR*

Boys Town 🦴🦴🦴 🐾

Family Hollywood's famous, righteous portrayal of the soft-spoken but two-fisted Father Flanagan, who founded Boys Town as a progressive, self-governing community for disadvantaged boys and juvenile delinquents, just outside Omaha. Plot covers the struggling, early years of the facility, underfunded and facing public skepticism. Somewhat slow until the incandescent Rooney shows up as Whitey Marsh, nervy punk who poses a challenge to Father Flanagan's assertion that "There's no such thing as a bad boy." You'll be cheering by the finish. Sequelized in "Men of Boys Town" and "Miracle of the Heart: A Boys Town Story."

> 🪧 **BEWARE!** *Alcohol use, fighting, orphans, corn; inspired Newt Gingrich to advocate putting troubled children in institutions.*

1938 93m/B Spencer Tracy, Mickey Rooney, Henry Hull, Gene Reynolds, Sidney Miller, Frankie Thomas Jr.; **D:** Norman Taurog. **Award Nominations:** Academy Awards '38: Best Director (Taurog), Best Picture, Best Screenplay; **Awards:** Academy Awards '38: Best Actor (Tracy), Best Original Screenplay. **VHS, Beta, LV** *MGM, BTV, IGP*

Boyz N the Hood 🦴🦴🦴 🐾

R/College-Adult Extraordinary drama (Singleton's debut as a writer and director) explains with chilling clarity what a lot of America still can't grasp; how ghetto kids end up becoming their own criminal predators. In South Central L.A., four young black high school students with different backgrounds, aims, and abilities grow up in a neighborhood terrorized by crime, gangs and racist cops. Of the quartet, Tre has the best chance of reaching adulthood, because he's the only one with a strong and deeply concerned father. Raw language and brutality, but all in the service of a nonviolent, pro-family message. Singleton was the youngest director ever nominated for an Oscar. The laserdisc version includes two extra scenes and an interview with him.

> 🪧 **BEWARE!** *Brutality, raw language, sex talk, drug talk, and dysfunctional families. All about the dangers of life in the street of the ghettos.*

1991 112m/C Laurence "Larry" Fishburne, Ice Cube, Cuba Gooding Jr., Nia Long, Morris Chestnut, Tyra Ferrell, Angela Bassett; **D:** John Singleton; **W:** John Singleton; **M:** Stanley Clarke. **Award Nominations:** Academy Awards '91: Best Director (Singleton), Best Original Screenplay; **Awards:** Chicago Film Critics Awards '91: Most Promising Actor (Ice Cube); MTV Movie Awards '92: Best New Filmmaker

Award (Singleton); National Board of Review Awards '91: 10 Best Films of the Year. **VHS, Beta, LV, 8mm** *COL, CRC, FCT*

Bozo the Clown: Ding Dong Dandy Adventures

Family Animated adventures of the world's most famous clown, compiled from TV. Additional volumes available.
1959 90m/C Larry Harmon. **VHS, LV** *JFK, IME*

The Brady Bunch Movie 🦴🦴🦴

PG-13/Jr. High-Adult Grunge and CDS may be the norm in the '90s, but the Bradys still live in the eight-track world of the '70s, where Davy Jones rocks and every day is a sunshine day. Then greedy developer McKean schemes to cash in on Mike and Carol's financial woes. (Hawaii! The Grand Canyon! What were they thinking?) Great ensemble cast capably fills the white platform shoes of the originals—Cole sounds just like Mr. Brady, Cox hilariously channels Jan's tormented middle child angst, and Taylor's self-absorbed Marcia, Marcia, Marcia is dead-on, right down to the frosty pursed lips. Look for neat-o cameos from some original Bradys and most of the Monkees.

🔲 BEWARE! *Sly references to sex that most kids probably won't understand; Marcia's girlfriend has a crush on her, Alice wears a leather teddy during the final credits. Florence Henderson says "crap." Horrors!*

1995 88m/C Shelley Long, Gary Cole, Michael McKean, Jean Smart, Henriette Mantel, Christopher Daniel Barnes, Christine Taylor, Paul Sutera, Jennifer Elise Cox, Jesse Lee, Olivia Hack, David Graf, Jack Noseworthy, Shane Conrad, RuPaul; **Cameos:** Ann B. Davis, Florence Henderson, Davy Jones, Barry Williams, Christopher Knight, Michael Lookinland, Mickey Dolenz, Peter Tork; **D:** Betty Thomas; **W:** Bonnie Turner, Terry Turner, Laurice Elehwany, Rick Copp; **M:** Guy Moon. **VHS, Beta** *PAR*

Brain Donors 🦴🦴 ▷

PG/Jr. High-Adult Goofy and uneven effort reminiscent of the Marx Brothers stars Turturro as a sleazy lawyer trying to take over the Oglethorpe Ballet Company by sweet talking its aged patroness. He is helped by two eccentric friends, and together they have plentiful opportunities to crack bad but witty jokes. The action culminates with an hilarious ballet scene featuring someone giving CPR to the ballerina playing the dying swan, an actor in a duck suit, duck hunters, and a pack of hounds. Occasionally inspired silliness.

🔲 BEWARE! *Sex talk and brief nudity. And very, very silly.*

1992 79m/C John Turturro, Bob Nelson, Mel Smith, Nancy Marchand, John Savident, George de la Pena, Juli Donald, Spike Alexander, Teri Copley; **D:** Dennis Dugan; **W:** Pat Proft; **M:** Ira Newborn. **VHS, Beta, LV** *PAR*

Brain 17 🦴🦴

Preschool-Primary 10-year-old lad named Stevie helps a giant robot, "Brain 17," battle an evil scientist who is bent on world domination.
1982 72m/C VHS, Beta *FHE*

The Brave Little Frog 🦴🦴 ▷

G/Family Tree frog Jonathan, the new amphibian at Rainbow Pond, is having trouble making friends until his pipe music and a friendly female frog help him out.
1994 90m/C VHS *HMD*

The Brave Little Toaster 🦴🦴 ▷

Family When a young boy leaves his cottage, the electrical appliances grow concerned and journey to the big city in search of him. Disney released (but didn't animate) this clever cartoon takeoff on "Incredible Journey" type stories, with a lamp, radio, electric blanket, vacuum and, of course, toaster, in lieu of the usual loyal housepet. Brilliant character voices, even if the gimmick wears pretty thin at feature length. Based on a novella by Thomas M. Disch.
1988 90m/C D: Jerry Rees; **V:** Jon Lovitz, Phil Hartman. **VHS, Beta, LV** *DIS, TOU, FCT*

Braveheart 🦴🦴🦴 ▷

R/Sr. High-Adult Three-hour epic set in 13th century Scotland won the 1996 Oscar as Best Picture and another for Gibson as Best Director. Gibson stars as folk hero William Wallace, leading his outnumbered clansmen in revolt against British oppression. Marceau and McCormack are elegant as Wallace's women, and McGoohan is loathsomeness personified as English King Edward I. Extremely violent but not inappropriately so; freedom comes at a high price. There is romance and some comic relief—watch as the king's army gets mooned en masse. Script is based on 300 pages of rhyming verse attributed to a blind poet. Film has done wonders for Scottish tourism.

🔲 BEWARE! *Brutality toward people and horses. Not for the squeamish as throats are cut and soldiers are impaled. Fairly discreet sex. Some will not be able to sit through the three-hour saga.*

1995 178m/C Mel Gibson, Sophie Marceau, Patrick McGoohan, Catherine McCormack, Brendan Gleeson, James Cosmo, David O'Hara, Angus McFadyen, Peter Hanly; **D:** Mel Gibson; **W:** Randall Wallace; **C:** John Toll; **M:** James Horner. **Award Nominations:** Academy Awards '95: Best Cinematography, Best Costume Design, Best Director (Gibson), Best Film Editing, Best Makeup, Best Picture, Best Screenplay, Best Sound, Best Score; British Academy Awards '95: Best Cinematography, Best Director (Gibson), Best Score; Directors Guild of America Awards '95: Best Director (Gibson); Golden Globe Awards '96: Best Film—Drama, Best Screenplay, Best Score; Writers Guild of America '95: Best Original Screenplay; **Awards:** Golden Globe Awards '96: Best Director (Gibson). **VHS, Beta** *PAR*

Bravestarr: The Legend Returns

Family Animated series finds a western marshal upholding the law on a barren, outlaw planet. In this eposde Bravestarr and his pals take on Tex Hex and his evil gang in a battle for New Texas. Additional volumes available.
1987 120m/C VHS *JFK*

The Breakfast Club 🦴🦴🦴 ▷

R/Sr. High-Family Five students from different cliques at a Chicago suburban high school spend a Saturday together in detention, learn more about each other than they ever did in regular class. Rather well done teenage culture study; these characters delve a little deeper than the standard adult view of adolescent stereotypes. One of Hughes' best movies. Soundtrack features Simple Minds and Wang Chung.

⚠️ **BEWARE** *High school profanity, sex talk, and the group gets high on marijuana while in detention.*

1985 97m/C Ally Sheedy, Molly Ringwald, Judd Nelson, Emilio Estevez, Anthony Michael Hall, Paul Gleason, John Kapelos; **D:** John Hughes; **W:** John Hughes; **M:** Gary Chang, Keith Forsey. **VHS, Beta, LV** *MCA, FCT*

Breakin' Through 🦴

Family Disney TV-movie based around the less-than-evergreen breakdancing craze, in which the choreographer of a troubled Broadway musical decides to energize his shows with a troupe of street dancers.

1984 73m/C Ben Vereen, Donna McKechnie, Reid Shelton; **D:** Peter Medak. **VHS, Beta** *DIS*

Breaking Away 🦴🦴🦴 ▷

PG/Family Fine coming-of-age drama about a working-class high school graduate, crazy over bicycle racing, whose dreams are tested against the realities of a crucial tournament. An honest, open look at present Americana with tremendous insight into the minds of average youth; shot on location at Indiana University. Great performances, touching family relationships. Writer Steve Tesich revisited the bike-racing motif in "American Flyers."

⚠️ **BEWARE** *Roughhousing.*

1979 100m/C Dennis Christopher, Dennis Quaid, Daniel Stern, Jackie Earle Haley, Barbara Barrie, Paul Dooley, Amy Wright; **D:** Peter Yates; **W:** Steve Tesich. **Award Nominations:** Academy Awards '79: Best Director (Yates), Best Picture, Best Supporting Actress (Barrie), Best Original Score; **Awards:** Academy Awards '79: Best Original Screenplay; Golden Globe Awards '80: Best Film—Musical/Comedy; National Board of Review Awards '79: 10 Best Films of the Year, Best Supporting Actor (Dooley). **VHS, Beta, LV** *FOX, HMV*

Breaking Free 🦴🦴

PG/Primary-Adult Teenaged loser forms an unlikely friendship with a bitter gymnast who's been blinded and forced to give up her dreams.

⚠️ **BEWARE** *Brief scene of mild violence.*

1995 106m/C Jeremy London, Gina Philips, Christine Taylor, Megan Gallagher. **VHS** *AVE*

Breaking the Ice 🦴🦴

Family Outdated combination of music and ice-skating spectacle stars child crooner Breen as a boy whose vocal talents are going to waste in his strict, rural religious community. He runs away from the farm and winds up a singing star at a Philadelphia ice show.

1938 79m/B Bobby Breen, Charlie Ruggles, Dolores Costello, Billy Gilbert, Margaret Hamilton. **VHS, Beta** *NOS, VYY, DVT*

Breaking the Rules 🦴🦴

PG-13/Jr. High-Adult Predictable buddy-road movie with a tearjerking premise and comedic overtones. Rob, Gene, and Phil were best buds growing up in Cleveland but young adulthood has separated them. They're reunited by Phil, who is dying of leukemia, and whose last wish is a cross-country road trip to California so he can appear as a contestant on "Jeopardy" (the game show last figured prominently in a movie in "White Men Can't Jump"). Along the way they meet brassy waitress Mary, who impulsively decides to join them and winds up bringing the trio's shaky friendship back together. Potts sparkles as the big-haired, big-hearted Mary, the rest of the crew is tuned and ready, but script goes down the road well traveled.

⚠️ **BEWARE** *Profanity and suggested sex. One of the characters is dying.*

1992 100m/C Jason Bateman, C. Thomas Howell, Jonathan Silverman, Annie Potts, Kent Bateman, Shawn Phelan; **D:** Neal Israel; **W:** Paul Shapiro; **M:** David Kitay. **VHS, LV** *HBO*

Brenda Starr 🦴🦴

PG/Jr. High-Adult While the long unreleased adaptation of the comic strip by Dale Messick is hardly as bad as the critics said, it's still a notch below average. Shields is well cast as fictional glamour girl reporter Brenda Starr, who declares she's quitting the funnies. A cartoonist (not Dale Messick, one of the first female comics creators—that would have been interesting) jumps into the page, a la "Last Action Hero," and trails Brenda on a typically campy adventure in the South American jungle searching for a scientist with a secret rocket fuel. Accurately conveys the silly, two-dimensional feel of the original strip, for what good that does.

⚠️ **BEWARE** *Fighting; portrays journalism as a viable career choice.*

1986 94m/C Brooke Shields, Timothy Dalton, Tony Peck, Diana Scarwid, Nestor Serrano, Jeffrey Tambor, June Gable, Charles Durning, Eddie Albert, Henry Gibson, Ed Nelson; **D:** Robert Ellis Miller; **W:** James David Buchanan. **VHS** *COL*

Brer Rabbit and Boss Lion

Preschool-Primary An adaptation of the American folk tale about how brains always overcome brawn, told through delightful illustrations and narration with a lilting musical score by Dr. John. Part of the "Rabbit Ears: American Heroes and Legends" series.

1992 34m/C VHS *UND, RAB, MVD*

The Brady clan and Alice show off their groovy duds in "The Brady Bunch Movie."

Mel Gibson as William Wallace leads the Scots to battle in "Braveheart."

Brer Rabbit and the Wonderful Tar Baby

Preschool-Primary "Great-grandfather of Bugs Bunny" outwits Brer Fox again in this delightful classic American tale.
1991 30m/C VHS, LV *KUI, NLC*

Brer Rabbit Tales

Primary Story collection includes "Tar Baby" and "The Laughing Place."
1991 48m/C VHS *WEA, FHE*

Brewster's Millions 🦴 ♪

PG/Jr. High-Adult An aging minor league baseball player (Richard Pryor) must spend 30 million dollars in 30 days in order to collect an inheritance of 300 million dollars. (In the 1945 version, it was $1 million in a month.) Pryor just may find that money can't buy happiness. Sounds like it can't miss, but it does, despite added presence of John Candy, Hume Cronyn and Jerry Orbach. Ages 10 and up.

 Profanity.

1985 101m/C Richard Pryor, John Candy, Lonette McKee, Stephen Collins, Jerry Orbach, Pat Hingle, Tovah Feldshuh, Hume Cronyn, Rick Moranis; *D:* Walter Hill; *W:* Herschel Weingrod, Timothy Harris; *M:* Ry Cooder. **VHS, Beta, LV** *MCA*

Brian's Song 🦴 🦴 🦴 ♪

G/Family Affecting and warmly sentimental story of the unique relationship between Gale Sayers, the Chicago Bears' star running back, and his teammate Brian Piccolo. The friendship between the Bears' first interracial roommates ended suddenly when Brian lost his life to cancer. Made for television.

Terminal illness. A real tear jerker. At least three tissues.

1971 74m/C James Caan, Billy Dee Williams, Jack Warden, Shelley Fabares, Judy Pace; *D:* Buzz Kulik. **VHS, Beta, LV** *COL*

The Bridge on the River Kwai 🦴 🦴 🦴 🦴

Jr. High-Adult Powerful adaptation of the Pierre Bouelle novel about the folly of war focuses on the battle of wills between a Japanese POW camp commander and the prisoners' leader, a by-the-rules British colonel, portrayed brilliantly by Guinness. Conflict surrounds the construction of a rail bridge by the prisoners, and the parallel efforts by escaped prisoner Holden to destroy it. Holden's role was originally cast for Cary Grant. Memorable too for whistling "Colonel Bogey March." WWII adventure drama is superior on all fronts. Because Wilson and Foreman had been blacklisted, Boulle (who spoke no English) was credited as screenwriter.

 Wartime violence.

1957 161m/C William Holden, Alec Guinness, Jack Hawkins, Sessue Hayakawa, James Donald, Geoffrey Horne, Andre Morell, Ann Sears; **D:** David Lean; **W:** Michael Wilson, Carl Foreman; **M:** Malcolm Arnold. **Award Nominations:** Academy Awards '57: Best Supporting Actor (Hayakawa); **Awards:** Academy Awards '57: Best Actor (Guinness), Best Adapted Screenplay, Best Color Cinematography, Best Director (Lean), Best Film Editing, Best Picture, Best Original Score; British Academy Awards '57: Best Actor (Guinness), Best Film; Directors Guild of America Awards '57: Best Director (Lean); Golden Globe Awards '58: Best Actor—Drama (Guinness), Best Director (Lean), Best Film—Drama; National Board of Review Awards '57: 10 Best Films of the Year, Best Actor (Guinness), Best Director (Lean), Best Supporting Actor (Hayakawa). **VHS, Beta, LV** *COL, BTV, HMV*

Bridge to Terabithia

Family Schoolkids Jesse and Leslie strike up a friendship and create an imaginary fantasy world called Terabithia for themselves in a pine forest near their homes. When Leslie suddenly dies, Jesse is left with the memories and the strength to cope with the tragedy. "WonderWorks" short feature is based on the novel by Katherine Paterson.

1985 58m/C Annette O'Toole, Julian Coutts, Julie Beaulieu; **D:** Eric Till. **VHS** *PME, HMV, FCT*

A Bridge Too Far

PG/Family A meticulous recreation of one of the most disastrous battles of WWII, the Allied defeat at Arnhem in 1944. Misinformation, adverse conditions, and overconfidence combined to prevent the Allies from capturing six bridges that connected Holland to the German border.

 War violence.

1977 175m/C Sean Connery, Robert Redford, James Caan, Michael Caine, Elliott Gould, Gene Hackman, Laurence Olivier, Ryan O'Neal, Liv Ullmann, Dirk Bogarde, Hardy Kruger, Arthur Hill, Edward Fox, Anthony Hopkins; **D:** Richard Attenborough; **W:** William Goldman; **M:** John Addison. **VHS, Beta, LV** *MGM, FOX*

Bright Eyes

PG/Family Shirley stars as an adorable orphan caught between foster parents in a custody battle; in the meantime she has to live under the same roof with a spoiled brat (played by Withers, another popular kid star of the era). This is the one where Temple performed her signature tune "On the Good Ship Lollipop." Reissued version is rather mysteriously rated PG.

1934 84m/B Shirley Temple, James Dunn, Lois Wilson, Jane Withers, Judith Allen; **D:** David Butler. **VHS, Beta** *FOX, MLT*

Brighton Beach Memoirs

PG-13/Jr. High-Adult Popular (and autobiographical) Neil Simon play takes to the screen. Poignant comedy/drama about a young Jewish boy and his family in 1937 Brooklyn. Not exactly heavy on plot; teenager Eugene wants to see a naked woman at least once before he dies, 16-year old sister Nora wants to be a Broadway dancer etc., but Simon's script endows the characters with keen humanity, even if it worked better on stage. Eugene's story was continued in the plays (and the films) "Biloxi Blues" and "Broadway Bound."

 Curious youth sex talk and profanity.

1986 108m/C Blythe Danner, Bob Dishy, Judith Ivey, Jonathan Silverman, Brian Drillinger, Stacey Glick, Lisa Waltz, Jason Alexander; **D:** Gene Saks; **W:** Neil Simon; **M:** Michael Small. **VHS, Beta, LV** *MCA, FCT*

Bringing Up Baby

Family The quintessential screwball comedy, featuring Hepburn as a giddy socialite with a "baby" leopard, and Grant as the unwitting object of her affections. One ridiculous situation after another add up to high-speed entertainment. Hepburn looks lovely, the supporting actors are in fine form, and director Hawks manages the perfect balance of control and mayhem. From a story by Hagar Wilde, who helped Nichols with the screenplay. Also available in a colorized version.

1938 103m/B Katharine Hepburn, Cary Grant, May Robson, Charlie Ruggles, Walter Catlett, Fritz Feld, Jonathan Hale, Barry Fitzgerald, Ward Bond; **D:** Howard Hawks; **W:** Dudley Nichols. **VHS, Beta, LV** *TTC, HMV, BTV*

Broadway Danny Rose

PG/Sr. High-Adult One of Woody Allen's best films, a hilarious, heart-rending anecdotal comedy about a third-rate talent agent involved in one of his client's infidelities. The film magically unfolds as show business veterans swap Danny Rose stories at a delicatessen. Allen's Danny Rose is pathetically lovable.

 Brief violence, organized crime, and old comedians.

1984 85m/B Woody Allen, Mia Farrow, Nick Apollo Forte, Sandy Baron, Milton Berle, Howard Cosell; **D:** Woody Allen; **W:** Woody Allen. **VHS, Beta, LV** *VES*

Broken Arrow

R/Sr. High-Adult Air Force pilot Vic Deakins (Travolta) hijacks his own bomber, complete with nuclear missiles, and holds the weapons for ransom. Fellow pilot Riley Hale (Slater) bails out over the desert and, with the help of park ranger Terry Carmichael (Mathis), attempts to recover the missing missiles (broken arrows, in military parlance) before Travolta blows up all of Utah. (Up your nose with a thermonuclear hose?) Hong Kong action director Woo provides ceaseless fisticuffs, footsicuffs, shootings and explosions.

1995 108m/C John Travolta, Christian Slater, Samantha Mathis, Delroy Lindo, Bob Gunton, Frank Whaley, Howie Long; *D:* John Woo; *W:* Graham Yost; *C:* Peter Levy; *M:* Hans Zimmer. **VHS** *NYR*

Bronco Billy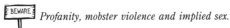

PG/Family Kinder, gentler Eastwood is New Jersey shoe clerk Billy McCoy, who dreams of being a cowboy. One day he fulfills his fantast by becoming the proprietor of a cheapo wild west show. Thin premise occasionally runs dry of charm, which is its chief asset, particularly when focusing on Locke's one-note performance as a spoiled rich girl who joins the show. On the other hand, it's a pleasant enough diversion for Clint and the viewer.

1980 117m/C Clint Eastwood, Sondra Locke, Bill McKinney, Scatman Crothers, Sam Bottoms, Geoffrey Lewis, Dan Vadis, Sierra Pecheur; *D:* Clint Eastwood; *M:* Stephen Dorff. **VHS, Beta, LV** *WAR, TLF, RXM*

A Bronx Tale

R/Sr. High-Adult Vivid snapshot of a young Italian-American boy growing up in the '60s among neighborhood small-time wiseguys. As a 9-year-old Calogero witnesses mobster Sonny kill a man but doesn't rat to the police, so Sonny takes the kid under his wing. His upright bus-driving father Lorenzo doesn't approve but the kid is drawn to Sonny's apparent glamour and power. At 17, he's gotten both an education in school and on the streets but he needs to make a choice. Good period detail and excellent performances. Palminteri shows both Sonny's charisma and violence and De Niro handles the less-showy father role with finesse. Based on Palminteri's one-man play; De Niro's directorial debut.

1993 122m/C Robert De Niro, Chazz Palminteri, Lillo Brancato, Frank Capra, Taral Hicks, Kathrine Narducci, Clem Caserta, Alfred Sauchelli Jr., Frank Pietrangolare; *Cameos:* Joe Pesci; *D:* Robert De Niro; *W:* Chazz Palminteri. **VHS, LV** *HBO*

The Brother from Another Planet

Sr. High-Adult A black man from outer space (Morton) crash lands a rocket ship—at Ellis Island, symbolically—and somehow makes his way to Harlem. He doesn't speak but manages to communicate with and endear himself to a variety of earthlings. Turns out he has a good reason for fleeing his planet and the white men from home who are looking for him. Morton is extraordinary in this film by the imaginative John Sayles who also plays one of the pursuers.

1984 109m/C Joe Morton, Dee Dee Bridgewater, Ren Woods, Steve James, Maggie Renzi, David Strathairn; *Cameos:* John Sayles; *D:* John Sayles; *W:* John Sayles; *M:* Mason Daring. **VHS, Beta** *FOX, FCT*

Brother Future

Family T.J., a black, streetsmart city kid who thinks school and helping others is all a waste of time gets knocked out in a car accident. As he's lying unconscious, he is transported back in time to a slave auction block in the Old South. There the displaced urbanite is forced to work on a cotton plantation, and watch the stirrings of a slave revolt. T.J. sees the light and realizes how much opportunity he's been wasting in his own life. He comes to just a few moments later, but worlds away from who he was before. Part of the "Wonderworks" series.

1991 110m/C Phill Lewis, Frank Converse, Carl Lumbly, Vonetta McGee. **VHS** *PME, HMV, BTV*

Brothers Lionheart

G/Primary-Jr. High Uneven Scandinavian fantasy about two warrior brothers fighting dragons and tyrants in a mystical Valhalla during the Middle Ages. Director Hellbron also gave the world the "Pippi Longstocking" series.

1985 120m/C Staffan Gotestam, Lars Soderdahl, Allan Edwall; *D:* Olle Hellbron. **VHS, Beta** *NO*

Brothers O'Toole

G/Family Repeated cases of mistaken identity plague two con-artist brothers in the Old West trying to bring prosperity to a luckless town. Episodic family comedy, atypical for relying on dialogue and characters for the attempted laughs, rather than standard slapstick. Good cast; Carroll later provided the voice of Ursula the Sea Witch in Disney's "The Little Mermaid."

1973 94m/C John Astin, Steve Carlson, Pat Carroll, Hans Conried, Lee Meriwether; *D:* Richard Erdman. **VHS, Beta** *VCI*

Bubbe's Boarding House: Chanukah at Bubbe's

Family Puppets populate Bubbe's Boarding House and help teach about the traditions of Chanukah and Passover.

1991 30m/C VHS *MON, MLT*

Buck and the Preacher

PG/Jr. High-Adult A trail guide and a con man preacher join forces to help a wagon train of former slaves who are seeking to homestead out West. Poitier's debut as a director.

1972 102m/C Sidney Poitier, Harry Belafonte, Ruby Dee, Cameron Mitchell, Denny Miller; *D:* Sidney Poitier. **VHS, Beta** *COL*

Buck Privates ♪♪ ▷

Jr. High-Adult The wartime comedy that made Abbott & Costello superstars still salutes smartly today. Two streetcorner tie salesmen mistakenly enlist in the army, are naturally assigned to a barracks full of misfits. Needless romantic subplot slows things down, but real fun is at the end when the platoon pulls together to compete in a practice wargame. A more family-friendly alternative to the lewd Bill Murray hit "Stripes."

1941 84m/B Bud Abbott, Lou Costello, Shemp Howard, Lee Norman, Alan Curtis, The Andrews Sisters; **D:** Arthur Lubin. **VHS, Beta, LV** *MCA*

Buck Privates Come Home ♪♪♪

Family Abbott and Costello return to their "Buck Privates" roles as two soldiers trying to adjust to civilian life after the war. They also try to help a French girl sneak into the United States. Funny antics culminate into a wild chase scene.

1947 77m/B Bud Abbott, Lou Costello, Tom Brown, Joan Shawlee, Nat Pendleton, Beverly Simmons, Don Beddoe, Don Porter, Donald MacBride; **D:** Charles T. Barton. **VHS** *MCA*

Buck Rogers Conquers the Universe ♪♪

Family Feature-film condensation of the vintage "Buck Rogers" serial, inspired by Phil Nolan's 25th-century comic-book hero. Buck helps a future Earth break the grasp of the evil Killer Kane, who saps the will of all who oppose him by putting shiny buckets over their heads. Retitled to recall Crabbe's better-known "Flash Gordon Conquers the Universe"; also known as "Buck Rogers: Planet Outlaws."

1939 91m/B Buster Crabbe, Constance Moore, Jackie Moran; **D:** Ford Beebe, Saul Goodkind. **VHS, Beta** *FOX*

Buck Rogers in the 25th Century ♪♪

PG/Family American astronaut preserved in space for 500 years is brought back to life by a passing Draconian flagship. Outer space adventures begin when he is accused of being a spy from Earth. Revival of the classic movie serial/'50s TV series/vintage comic strip never would have happened but for the success of "Star Wars" and it looks it, even indulging in the usual cute little robot (voice provided by Mel "Bugs Bunny" Blanc). Made-for-TV movie, subsequently released to theaters, that kicked off a weekly series. Additional series episodes available on tape.

 Violence.

1979 90m/C Gil Gerard, Pamela Hensley, Erin Gray, Henry Silva; **D:** Daniel Haller. **VHS, Beta, LV** *MCA, MOV*

Bucky O'Hare: Bye-Bye Berserker Baboon

Preschool-Primary Two episodes from the "Bucky O'Hare" series, which feature the rabbit captain of the space frigate Righteous Indignation and assorted space rip-offs. Additional volumes available.

1991 47m/C VHS

The Buddy Holly Story ♪♪♪ ▷

PG/Jr. High-Adult Busey, performing Holly's hits himself, lends a stellar performance as the famed 1950s pop icon. Story spans the years from Holly's meteoric career's beginnings in Lubbock to his tragic early death in the now famous plane crash. For that roots of rock 'n' roll double bill, see it with "La Bamba." ♪♪ Rock Around the Ollie Vee; That'll Be the Day; Oh, Boy; It's So Easy; Well All Right; Chantilly Lace; Peggy Sue.

BEWARE *For kids who don't know their rock n' roll history, the ending may be upsetting.*

1978 113m/C Gary Busey, Don Stroud, Charles Martin Smith, Conrad Janis, William Jordan; **D:** Steve Rash; **M:** Joe Renzetti. **Award Nominations:** Academy Awards '78: Best Actor (Busey), Best Sound; **Awards:** Academy Awards '78: Best Adapted Score; National Society of Film Critics Awards '78: Best Actor (Busey). **VHS, Beta, LV** *COL*

Buffy the Vampire Slayer ♪♪ ▷

PG-13/Jr. High-Adult Camp-oriented teen genre spoof about a Southern Cal valley girl reluctantly claiming her ancient destiny to slay vampires, specifically ones who have suddenly infested Los Angeles high school hangouts. Canned morality lesson: Buffy fights against the undead even though bimbo cheerleader friends declare her uncool and flee. "Pee Wee Herman" Reubens is unrecognizable and amusing as the vampire king's 1200-year-old henchman, engaging in one of the longer death scenes of film history.

BEWARE *Violence (the vampires get the sharper end of it, naturally), salty language, sex and drug talk.*

1992 98m/C Kristy Swanson, Donald Sutherland, Luke Perry, Paul (Pee Wee Herman) Reubens, Rutger Hauer, Michele Abrams, Randall Batinkoff, Hilary Swank, Paris Vaughan, David Arquette, Candy Clark, Natasha Gregson Wagner; **D:** Fran Rubel Kazui; **W:** Joss Whedon; **M:** Carter Burwell. **VHS, LV** *FXV, PMS*

Bugs & Daffy's Carnival of the Animals

Family A host of favorite animated critters are introduced by the wabbit and the duck—and conductor Michael Tilson-Thomas. All ages.

1989 26m/C D: Chuck Jones; **V:** Mel Blanc. **VHS** *WAR*

Bugs Bunny: All American Hero

Family Bugs takes a trip back through history, starting in 1492 when Columbus sailed the ocean blue and Bugs was his shipmate. Continues through the American Revo-

lution, WWI, and more with Yosemite Sam, Sylvester and all of your favorites.
1981 24m/C V: Mel Blanc. **VHS** *WAR*

Bugs Bunny Cartoon Festival

Family Four early cartoons starring the nefarious rabbit. One of nine volumes of Bugs and friends on the MGM video label.
1944 34m/C D: Bob Clampett, Chuck Jones, Isadore "Friz" Freleng. **VHS, Beta** *MGM*

Bugs Bunny: Festival of Fun

Family Five classic cartoons from the Bugsmeister. Includes "Hare Ribbin," "Rhapsody Rabbit," "Baseball Bugs," "The Wacky Wabbit," and "The Wabbit Who Came to Supper."
194? 35m/C VHS *MGM*

Bugs Bunny in King Arthur's Court

Family Bugs is Bugs and Arthur is Arthur and never the Twain shall meet—until now, in this spoof of a masterpiece of classic American literature. Ages 4 to 8.
1989 25m/C D: Chuck Jones; **W:** Chuck Jones; **V:** Mel Blanc. **VHS** *WAR*

The Bugs Bunny Mystery Special

Family Bugs Bunny and that hard-boiled detective Elmer Fudd tip their hats to the master of suspense Alfwed Hitchcock in this animated spoof. Ages 5 to 10.
19?? 24m/C VHS *WAR*

The Bugs Bunny/Road Runner Movie 🎵🎵🎵

G/Family Worthy compilation of classic Warner Brothers cartoons, starring Bugs Bunny, Daffy Duck, Elmer Fudd, the Road Runner, Wile E. Coyote, Porky Pig, and Pepe Le Pew, bookended by Bugs in some all-new animated narration sequences. Also available with Spanish dubbing.
1979 98m/C D: Chuck Jones, Phil Monroe; **V:** Mel Blanc. **VHS, Beta** *WAR, APD*

Bugs Bunny Superstar 🎵🎵 🎵

G/Family A look at the wild characters onscreen and off at the Warner Brothers cartoon studio that created the classic Looney Tunes/Merrie Melodies series in general and Bugs Bunny in particular. Bits and pieces from great cartoons are shown, along with some amazing home movies and behind-the-drawing-board footage, but the low-budget presentation leans toward the haphazard.
1975 91m/C D: Larry Jackson, Bob Clampett, Tex Avery, Isadore "Friz" Freleng; **V:** Mel Blanc. **VHS, LV** *MGM*

Bugs Bunny: Truth or Hare

Family It's Bugs Bunny vs. Marvin the Martian, Elmer Fudd, Yosemite Sam, and the Tasmanian Devil in "The Fair Haired Hare," "Dr. Devil and Mr. Hare," "Wideo Wabbit," "Hare-way to the Stars," and "Water, Water Every Hare." All ages.
198? 33m/C VHS *BTV, WAR*

Bugs Bunny's 3rd Movie: 1,001 Rabbit Tales 🎵🎵 🎵

G/Family Compilation of old and new classic cartoons featuring Bugs, Daffy, Sylvester, Porky, Elmer, Tweety, Speedy Gonzalez and Yosemite Sam. Favorites all, but a lot of this is better in small doses.
1982 74m/C D: Chuck Jones, Robert McKimson, Isadore "Friz" Freleng. **VHS, Beta** *WAR, FCT*

Bugs Bunny's Bustin' Out All Over

Family Three Bugs cartoons by animator Chuck Jones. Includes "Soup or Sonic," "Spaced Out Bunny" and "Portrait of the Artist as a Young Bunny." All ages.
1980 24m/C D: Chuck Jones; **V:** Mel Blanc. **VHS** *WAR*

Bugs Bunny's Creature Features

Family Join Bugs Bunny and Daffy Duck in three movie parodies "Invasion of the Bunny Snatchers," "The Duxorcist," and "Night of the Living Duck." All ages.
198? 33m/C VHS *WAR, BTV*

Bugs Bunny's Cupid Capers

Family Bugs and his pals are hit by a Cupid in the form of Elmer Fudd, who fires too many love arrows into Foghorn Leghorn, Yosemite Sam and others. All ages.
1979 24m/C V: Mel Blanc. **VHS** *WAR*

Bugs Bunny's Easter Funnies

Family Bugs helps the Easter Bunny deliver eggs. Originally a network special. Ages 4 to 8.
1977 50m/C V: Mel Blanc. **VHS** *WAR*

Bugs Bunny's Hare-Brained Hits

Family Five episodes from the classic cartoon series, including "My Bunny Lies Over the Sea," "Big House Bunny," "Baton Bunny," "Captain Hareblower," and "Hillbilly Hare." All ages.
19?? 35m/C VHS

Bugs Bunny's Hare-Raising Tales

Family Six standouts from the furry varmint's vault of classics; includes "Rabbitson Crusoe" and "Rabbit Hood." All ages.
1989 45m/C D: Chuck Jones, Robert McKimson, Abe Levitow; **W:** Chuck Jones, Robert McKimson, Isadore "Friz" Freleng; **V:** Mel Blanc. **VHS** *WAR*

Bugs Bunny's Howl-Oween Special

Family When Bugs dresses up as a witch for Halloween, he makes the mistake of knocking on Witch Hazel's door. She won't stand for any competition. The adventure unfolds as the witch tries to remove that unwanted hare. Ages 4 to 8.
1978 25m/C V: Mel Blanc. **VHS** *WAR, APD*

Bugs Bunny's Looney Christmas Tales

Family Join Bugs as he and his little nephew re-enact two of the world's most beloved Christmas stories; "A Christmas Carol" and "'Twas the Night Before Christmas." Ages 4 to 8.
1979 25m/C D: Chuck Jones, Isadore "Friz" Freleng; **V:** Mel Blanc. **VHS** *WAR, APD*

Bugs Bunny's Lunar Tunes

Family Bugs Bunny tries to prevent Marvin the Martian from blowing the Earth to smithereens. Ages 4 to 8.
19?? 24m/C VHS *WAR*

Bugs Bunny's Mad World of Television

Family Bugs does lunch as a slick network exec. Ages 4 to 8.
19?? 24m/C VHS *WAR*

Bugs Bunny's Mother's Day Special

Family Bugs and other Looney Tunes characters celebrate Mother's Day in their own wacky way. Ages 4 to 8.
1979 24m/C V: Mel Blanc. **VHS** *WAR*

Bugs Bunny's Overtures to Disaster

Family Bugs, who certainly has the ears for music, orchestrates a musical comedy. Ages 4 to 8.
19?? 24m/C VHS *WAR*

Bugs Bunny's Thanksgiving Diet

Family Spend everyone's favorite holiday with that wacky wabbit, Bugs Bunny. Ages 4 to 8.
1991 24m/C V: Mel Blanc. **VHS** *WAR*

Bugs Bunny's Wide World of Sports

Family Bugs shows his favorite sports cartoons. All ages.
1989 24m/C VHS *WAR*

Bugs vs. Daffy: Battle of the Music Video Stars

Family Radio stations "WABBIT" and "K-PUT" are battling for top rank in the ratings war, with Daffy and Bugs engaging in a no holds barred competition to get there. How dethpicable! Ages 4 to 8.
1988 24m/C VHS *WAR*

Bugs Malone 🎵🎵 ♭

G/Family Oddball musical spoof of 1930s mobster movies with an all-children cast. Plot loosely details a gangland war between sarsaparilla bootlegger Fat Sam and an upstart named Dandy Dan, who raids Sam's speakeasies with newfangled 'splurge guns' shooting whipped cream; evidently a pie in the face in this fantasy world is lethal, yet the what-do-we-do-now ending has the creamed casualties rising to sing together about love and brotherhood. It's hard to say what the point of it all is, but watch young Jodie Foster, as a vampy moll, acting circles around the rest of the cast. Fun but unmemorable songs by Paul Williams.

⚠ BEWARE *Cream-pie killings are so stylized and silly that it could be called violence.*

1976 94m/C Jodie Foster, Scott Baio, Florrie Augger, John Cassisi, Martin Lev; **D:** Alan Parker; **W:** Alan Parker; **M:** Paul Williams. **VHS, Beta, LV** *PAR*

Built for Speed

Preschool-Primary Stock car driver Julianne Seeley and her two young friends Max and Rebecca discuss automobile safety, as well as the differences between a race car and a standard automobile (one goes a lot faster). Julianne then takes the viewer for a ride on the racetrack. Ages 6 to 10.
1995 m/C VHS *AEL*

The Bulldozer Brigade 🎵🎵 ♭

Family Irish children's comedy (with serious undertones) set in Belfast; two schoolgirl friends, one Catholic, one Protestant, start a petition to save their secret wooded playground from land developers. But grownups misunderstand, and a simple kiddie protest snowballs into a terrorist scare. The low-budget yarn tends to meander, but offbeat settings and unforced good humor make it worth a look.

1985 86m/C VHS *FHE, BTV*

Bunnicula: Vampire Rabbit

Family Strange things happen after a family adopts a bunny. The other pets, a dog and a cat, team up to prove that their furry cohort is a vampire in disguise. "ABC Weekend Special" 'toon, based on the popular children's book by Deborah and James Howe.

1982 23m/C VHS, Beta *WOV, GKK*

The 'Burbs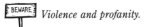

PG/Jr. High-Adult A tepid satire about suburbanites suspecting their creepy new neighbors of murderous activities. Slow and predictable despite interesting cast. Ages 11 and up.

BEWARE *Violence and profanity.*

1989 101m/C Tom Hanks, Carrie Fisher, Rick Ducommun, Corey Feldman, Brother Theodore, Bruce Dern, Gale Gordon, Courtney Gains; **D:** Joe Dante; **M:** Jerry Goldsmith. **VHS, Beta, LV** *MCA, CCB*

Burn 'Em Up Barnes

Family Mascot Studios was a serial-production outfit that later formed serial powerhouse Republic Pictures, but before that their output was generally unmemorable. This one depicts Barnes, the "Speed Racer" of the era, as he and a buddy battle gangsters. In twelve episodes.

1934 40m/B Frankie Darro, Lola Lane, Jack Mulhall. **VHS, Beta** *SNC, NOS, VCN*

The Bushbaby

Family Simple-minded stuff built around the title animal, a huge-eyed, raccoon-like denizen of the African jungle that's too cute for words. The little heroine is given a mischievous bush baby while visiting her father on the dark continent. When the critter makes her miss her ship home, she gets a ride with a former family servant (future Oscar-winner Louis Gossett Jr.), but authorities mistake him for a kidnapper, and the two—along with the trouble-causing pet—are pursued by cops.

1970 100m/C Margaret Brooks, Louis Gossett Jr., Donald Houston, Laurence Naismith, Marne Maitland, Geoffrey Bayldon, Jack Gwillim; **D:** John Trent. **VHS** *MGM, FCT*

Bushwhacked

PG-13/Family Crude, dim-witted, kid-hating Max Grabelski (Stern) is falsely accused of murder and forced to become a fugitive. He is mistaken for the leader of a group of scouts out on their first camping trip and soon finds himself in an unlikely partnership with the boys (and a token girl). They encounter everything from grizzly bears to the real killers, and become better people for it.

BEWARE *Crude dialogue, peeing off a cliff. Stern's character does a lot of yelling and kid-hating.*

1995 85m/C Daniel Stern, Jon Polito, Brad Sullivan, Ann Dowd, Anthony Heald, Thomas Wood; **D:** Greg Beeman; **W:** Tommy

Swerdlow, Michael Goldberg, John Jordan, Danny Byers; **M:** Bill Conti. **VHS** *FXV*

Bustin' Loose

R/Jr. High-Adult Con man on probation is ordered to drive a bus filled with problem children cross-country to a group home. Their comical and 'uplifting' misadventures on the way are standard stuff, improved immeasurably by the talented Pryor; it's no surprise when the star scores with the comedy, but he even makes the sentimental schmaltz seem better than it is.

BEWARE *The R rating is for Pryor's occasionally foul language—mild by 1994 standards, more like a PG13. Sex talk in a subplot about one of the kids having been a teen prostitute. Roughhousing.*

1981 94m/C Richard Pryor, Cicely Tyson, Robert Christian, George Coe, Bill Quinn; **D:** Oz Scott; **W:** Richard Pryor. **VHS, Beta, LV** *MCA*

Butch and Sundance: The Early Days

PG/Family Traces the origins of the famous outlaw duo. It contains the requisite shoot-outs, hold-ups, and escapes. A "prequel" to "Butch Cassidy and the Sundance Kid" is no match for the classic, but may prove of interest to fans of the original.

BEWARE *Western violence in the form of hold-ups and shoot-outs. Mild profanity.*

1979 111m/C Tom Berenger, William Katt, John Schuck, Jeff Corey, Jill Eikenberry, Brian Dennehy, Peter Weller; **D:** Richard Lester. **VHS, Beta** *FOX*

Butch Cassidy and the Sundance Kid

PG/Family Two legendary outlaws at the turn of the century take it on the lam with a beautiful, willing ex-school teacher. With a clever script, humanly fallible characters, and warm, witty dialogue, this film was destined to become a box-office classic. Featured the hit song, "Raindrops Keep Falling on My Head" and renewed the buddy film industry, as Newman and Redford trade insult for insult. Look for the great scene where Newman takes on giant Ted Cassidy in a fist fight.

BEWARE *Lots of shooting, hold-ups and other Western gunplay, as well as the occasional fist fight.*

1969 110m/C Paul Newman, Robert Redford, Katharine Ross, Jeff Corey, Strother Martin, Cloris Leachman, Kenneth Mars, Ted Cassidy, Henry Jones, George Furth, Sam Elliott; **D:** George Roy Hill; **W:** William Goldman; **M:** Burt Bacharach. **Award Nominations:** Academy Awards '69: Best Director (Hill), Best Picture, Best Sound; **Awards:** Academy Awards '69: Best Cinematography, Best Song ("Raindrops Keep Fallin' on My Head"), Best Story & Screenplay, Best Original Score; British Academy Awards '70: Best Actor (Redford), Best Actress (Ross), Best Director (Hill), Best Film; Golden Globe Awards '70: Best Score. **VHS, Beta, LV** *FOX, TLF*

The Butcher's Wife

PG-13/Jr. High-Adult Semi-charming tale of young psychic Moore who brings romance to a Greenwich Village neighborhood. As the clairvoyant married to butcher

Dzundza, Moore wields mystical powers that bring magic into the lives of everyone around her, though local psychiatrist Daniels has his doubts. Talented cast works above hamburger script.

BEWARE *Profanity.*

1991 107m/C Demi Moore, Jeff Daniels, George Dzundza, Frances McDormand, Margaret Colin, Mary Steenburgen, Max Perlich, Miriam Margolyes, Christopher Durang, Diane Salinger; **D:** Terry Hughes; **W:** Ezra Litwack, Marjorie Schwartz; **M:** Michael Gore. **VHS, Beta, LV** *PAR*

Butterflies Are Free 🎵🎵🎵

PG/Jr. High-Adult Fast-paced humor surrounds the Broadway play brought to the big screen. Blind youth Albert is determined to be self-sufficient. A next-door-neighbor actress helps him gain independence from his over-protective mother (Heckart).

1972 109m/C Goldie Hawn, Edward Albert, Eileen Heckart, Michael Glaser; **D:** Milton Katselas. **Award Nominations:** Academy Awards '72: Best Cinematography, Best Sound; **Awards:** Academy Awards '72: Best Supporting Actress (Heckart). **VHS, Beta** *GKK*

Buttons and Rusty Series

Family Selections from the popular children's animated show from the Disney Channel; Buttons the bear cub and Rusty the fox pup have comical adventures, usually with seasonal connections. Episodes include "The Easter Bunny," "The Turkey Gang," "The Halloween Party," "A Special Christmas," "The Adventure Machine," and "The Wildbird Caper."

1988 25m/C VHS, Beta *BFV*

Bye, Bye, Birdie 🎵🎵🎵

Family Energized and sweet film version of the Broadway musical about a teen rock and roll idol (Pearson doing Elvis) coming to a small town to see one of his fans (Ann Margret) in a public relations ploy before he leaves for the army. 22-year-old Ann-Margret emerged from role as a bonafide star, and it's easy to see why. 🎵 Bye Bye Birdie; The Telephone Hour; How Lovely to be a Woman; Honestly Sincere; One Boy; Put on a Happy Face; Kids; One Last Kiss; A Lot of Livin' to Do.

1963 112m/C Dick Van Dyke, Janet Leigh, Ann-Margret, Paul Lynde, Bobby Rydell, Maureen Stapleton, Ed Sullivan, Trudi Ames; **D:** George Sidney. **VHS, Beta, LV** *COL*

Bye Bye, Love 🎵🎵 🎵

PG-13/Jr. High-Adult A weekend in the lives of three divorced buddies starts at a McDonald's for the regular exchange of their kids. Comic, but just as often sadly poignant about the pain of divorce. The three leads are likeable enough, and Garofalo is a gem as one dad's blind date from hell.

BEWARE *Brief language; sensuality. A child stumbles upon his father in bed with a girlfriend.*

1994 107m/C Matthew Modine, Randy Quaid, Paul Reiser, Rob Reiner, Janeane Garofalo, Ed Flanders, Lindsay Crouse, James

Whitworth, Maria Pitillo; **D:** Sam Weisman; **W:** Gary David Goldberg, Brad Hall; **M:** J.A.C. Redford. **VHS, LV** *FXV*

The Cabbage Patch Kid's First Christmas

Family Hanna-Barbera cartoon TV special tied to the Cabbage Patch Kids dolls, who in their heyday caused near-riots at stores. The popular playthings learn the Christmas spirit when they befriend a disabled little girl (crippled in a stampede for toys, perhaps?).

1991 30m/C VHS, Beta *TTC*

Cabin Boy WOOF!

PG-13/Jr. High-Adult Obnoxious "fancy lad" Elliott mistakenly boards the wrong boat and becomes the new cabin boy for a ridiculous bunch of mean, smelly sailors who sail the dangerous seas on what looks to be a giant tank of water. Fish out of water saga sags from the start, so don't kid yourself that it will get better. Surprisingly produced by Tim Burton, who must have owed a favor to somebody. The good news is—it's mercifully short. Look for real-life dad Bob as the lad's dad; good friend Letterman appears briefly as nasty "Old Salt," but uses the alias Earl Hofert in the final credits. As usual, the acerbic Letterman gets the best line, one that viewers will understand all too well: "Man, oh, man do I hate them fancy lads."

BEWARE *Profanity, scatological humor, and suggested sex. Dumb meets dumbest.*

1994 80m/C Chris Elliott, Ann Magnuson, Ritch Brinkley, James Gammon, Brian Doyle-Murray, Russ Tamblyn, Brion James, Ricki Lake, Bob Elliott; **Cameos:** David Letterman; **D:** Adam Resnick; **W:** Adam Resnick; **M:** Steve Bartek. **VHS, LV** *TOU*

The Cable Guy 🎵🎵 🎵

PG-13/Jr. High-Adult A lonely cable TV installer (Jim Carrey), who calls himself Chip Douglas (after the character on "My Three Sons") installs himself into the life of a customer (Matthew Broderick). At first, he's genial and amusing, but soon reveals a darker, more intrusive side. It's a stretch for rubbery comic Carrey, but he plays the obsessive character well. There's a message here about the pervasive power of TV—as a little boy, Chip was "raised" by television while his mother went out—and there's lot to laugh at, too. Ages 14 and up. Not for Carrey's usual core of preteen fans.

BEWARE *A dirty word game ("Porno Password"), profanity, drugs and alcohol, obsession, sex talk, obtaining cable TV service without paying for it.*

1996 95m/C Jim Carrey, Matthew Broderick, Leslie Mann, George Segal, Diane Baker, Jack Black, Janeane Garofalo, Andy Dick, Charles Napier; **D:** Ben Stiller; **W:** Judd Apatow, Lou Holtz Jr.; **C:** Robert Brinkmann; **M:** John Ottman. **VHS** *NYR*

Cactus Swing and Other Tales

Preschool-Primary The National Film Board of Canada is at again, this time with a collection that features dancing cacti in red rock country; the enigmatic Oscar-win-

ning "The Sand Castle," cartoon about creatures made of sand; and the delightful "Every Dog's Guide to Complete Home Safety," about Wally, the safety dog, who tries to keep a very careless family intact. Ages 1 to 4.
199? 30m/C VHS *SMA*

Caddie Woodlawn

Family Title character is a tomboy in a pioneer family, building their homestead in 1864 Wisconsin. During that eventful year Caddie copes with school, resentful Dakota Indians, the tragic loss of a friend, and a visit from a snooty cousin from the East. She also tries to prevent her dad from hunting animals, a politically correct anachronism in this adaptation of the more realistic young adult novel by Carol Ryie Brink.
1988 104m/C Parker Stevenson, Emily Schulman, Season Hubley; **D:** George McQuilkin, Noel Resnick. **VHS, Beta** *CHF, RHU*

The Caddy 🦴🦴

Family Lewis plays frantic caddy prone to slapstick against Martin's smooth professional golfer with a bent toward singing. Mostly a series of Martin and Lewis sketches that frequently land in the rough. Introduces several songs, including a classic Martin and Lewis rendition of "That's Amore." Look for cameos by a host of professional golfers.
1953 95m/C Dean Martin, Jerry Lewis, Donna Reed, Barbara Bates, Joseph Calleia, Marshall Thompson, Fred Clark; **Cameos:** Ben Hogan, Sam Snead, Byron Nelson, Julius Boros, Jimmy Thomson, Harry E. Cooper; **D:** Norman Taurog. **VHS, Beta** *PAR*

Caddyshack 🦴🦴🦴 ᵛ

R/Sr. High-Adult Inspired performances by Murray and Dangerfield drive this sublimely moronic comedy onto the green. The action takes place at Bushwood Country Club, where caddy O'Keefe is bucking to win the club's college scholarship. Characters involved in various sophomoric set pieces include obnoxious club president Knight, a playboy who is too laid back to keep his score (Chase), a loud, vulgar, and extremely rich golfer (Dangerfield), and Murray as a filthy gopher-hunting groundskeeper. Occasional dry moments are followed by scenes of pure (and tasteless) anarchy, so watch with someone immature. Does for golf what "Major League" tried to do for baseball.
BEWARE *Nudity as Chase gives a massage and skinny dips, sex, profanity, and a possible pregnancy.*
1980 99m/C Chevy Chase, Rodney Dangerfield, Ted Knight, Michael O'Keefe, Bill Murray, Sarah Holcomb, Brian Doyle-Murray; **D:** Harold Ramis; **W:** Brian Doyle-Murray, Doug Kenney, Harold Ramis. **VHS, Beta, LV** *WAR*

Cadillacs and Dinosaurs

Preschool-Primary Two animated episodes from the syndicated television series. Includes "Rogue," and "Dino Drive." Ages 4 to 7.
1994 46m/C VHS *SKM*

Cahill: United States Marshal 🦴🦴

PG/Jr. High-Adult Graying Duke in one of his lesser moments, portraying a marshal who comes to the aid of his sons, mixed up with a gang of outlaws. Turns out that the boys harbor a grudge against pa Cahill due to years of neglect. Will Duke reconcile with the delinquents? Parenting skills mixed with traditional western gunplay.
BEWARE *Violence.*
1973 103m/C John Wayne, Gary Grimes, George Kennedy, Neville Brand, Marie Windsor, Harry Carey Jr.; **D:** Andrew V. McLaglen; **M:** Elmer Bernstein. **VHS, Beta, LV** *WAR, TLF*

Calendar Girl 🦴 ᵛ

PG-13/Jr. High-Adult In 1962 three high-school best friends borrow a convertible and travel from their Nevada homes to Hollywood to meet their pinup idol, Marilyn Monroe. Priestly portrays Roy the rebel, while Ned's (Olds, in his film debut) the sensitive one, and Scott (O'Connell) is just a regular guy. They stay with Roy's Uncle Harvey (Pantoliano), an aspiring actor, and work to meet their dream girl. Which they finally do, in a notably weak sequence which fits in with this notably uninspired effort basically directed at fans of Priestly. The three actors at least have enough comradery to make realistic buddies—one of the few true touches in the film.
BEWARE *Teen boy profanity and brief nudity.*
1993 86m/C Jason Priestley, Gabriel Olds, Jerry O'Connell, Joe Pantoliano, Stephen Tobolowsky, Kurt Fuller, Steve Railsback, Emily Warfield, Stephanie Anderson; **Cameos:** Chubby Checker; **D:** John Whitesell; **W:** Paul Shapiro; **M:** Hans Zimmer. **VHS, LV, 8mm** *COL*

The California Raisins: Meet the Raisins

Family Vinton's dancing, singing, rhythm'n'blues raisins became a hit with a series of cereal commercials and brought long-overdue appreciation of his Claymation art. Covers the Raisin characters (yes, they've all got names) and offers their best songs; continued in a followup video "Raisins Sold Out."
1989 30m/C VHS, Beta

Call of the Wild 🦴🦴

PG/Jr. High-Adult Parents who have never read Jack London's vivid Gold Rush tale may think it's a kiddies' animal adventure, but even this clunky European version (filmed cheaply in Finland) preserves the harshness and violence of a bloody novel. The Klondike sled dog Buck passes from one master to another, but fate returns him to the only good-hearted one, played nobly by Heston, until finally Buck must give in fully to his feral side.
BEWARE *Brutality among animals, profanity, alcohol use, offscreen sex.*

1972 105m/C Charlton Heston, Michele Mercier, George Eastman; **D:** Ken Annakin. **VHS, Beta** *KUI, SIM, MPI*

Call of the Wild ♪♪ ◌

Jr. High-Adult Jack London's most famous tale, dramatized for television. John Thornton (Rick Schroder) is a rich greenhorn seeking adventure during the 1897 Klondike gold rush. Buck is a German shepherd, sold as a sled dog, who finds adventures of his own in the frozen North until man and dog unite to search for a legendary gold mine. The book is more exciting but the film is more violent. Filmed on location in British Columbia, which is close. Ages 8 and up.

1993 97m/C Rick Schroder, Gordon Tootoosis, Mia Sara, Duncan Fraser, Richard Newman, Brent Stait. **VHS** *CAF*

Camel Boy ♪♪

Family Yoram Gross, better known for his endearing series of Australian cartoons starring the outback girl Dot, turned to a different part of the world for this animated feature about an Arabian lad and his camel pal who cross the deserts of the Mideast together.

1984 78m/C **D:** Yoram Gross; **V:** Michael Pate, Ron Haddrick, John Meillon. **VHS, Beta** *VES, LIV*

Camelot ♪♪

Family The long-running Lerner and Loewe Broadway musical about King Arthur, Guinevere, and Lancelot was adapted from T.H. White's book, "The Once and Future King." Redgrave and Nero have chemistry as the illicit lovers, Harris is strong as the king struggling to hold together his dream, but muddled direction undermines the effort. Laserdisc edition contains 28 minutes of previously edited footage, trailers and backstage info. ♫ I Wonder What the King is Doing Tonight; The Simple Joys of Maidenhood; Camelot; C'est Moi; The Lusty Month of May; Follow Me; How To Handle a Woman; Then You May Take Me to the Fair; If Ever I Would Leave You.

> **BEWARE** *Adultery and some pretty strong sorcery scenes.*

1967 150m/C Richard Harris, Vanessa Redgrave, David Hemmings, Franco Nero, Lionel Jeffries; **D:** Joshua Logan; **M:** Frederick Loewe, Alan Jay Lerner. **Award Nominations:** Academy Awards '67: Best Cinematography, Best Sound; **Awards:** Academy Awards '67: Best Art Direction/Set Decoration, Best Costume Design, Best Score; Golden Globe Awards '68: Best Actor—Musical/Comedy (Harris), Best Song ("If Ever I Should Leave You"), Best Score. **VHS, Beta, LV** *WAR, RDG, HMV*

Camp Nowhere ♪♪

PG/Family Bland Hollywood Pictures/Disney comedy in which enterprising youngsters, sick of being shipped to dull summer camps, concoct a phony camp of their own (renting an abandoned commune out in the countryside) and trick the dumb parents into sending them there instead. Funny idea, but when plot finally arrives at Camp Nowhere, it (like the kids) doesn't quite know what to do.

Lloyd is the token sympathetic adult, as a deadbeat drama teacher blackmailed into helping pull off the scam.

> **BEWARE** *Alcohol talk; sex talk; drug talk. All talk, no action.*

1994 95m/C Christopher Lloyd, Wendy Makkena, M. Emmet Walsh, Peter Scolari, Peter Onorati, Ray Baker, Kate Mulgrew, Jonathan Jackson, Romy Walthall, Maryedith Burrell, Tom Wilson, Nathan Cavaleri, Andrew Keegan, Melody Kay; **D:** Jonathan Prince; **W:** Andrew Kurtzman, Eliot Wald. **VHS** *NYR*

Canadian Bacon ♪♪

PG/Sr. High-Adult Feature film debut for director Michael Moore ("Roger and Me," "TV Nation") suggests, comically, that when America's military-industrial-political complex runs out of real enemies it will invent one. In this case, our friendly neighbor to the north becomes a sitting Canada goose for an unpopular president (Alda) who needs to distract voters' attention from the economy; Pollak is his adviser who mutters about Canadians "walking among us undetected." Filmed in Toronto. Candy in one of his last roles plays the sheriff of Niagara Falls, New York.

> **BEWARE** *Mild language and slapstick violence.*

1994 110m/C Alan Alda, Kevin Pollak, John Candy, Rhea Perlman, Rip Torn, Bill Nunn, Kevin J. O'Connor, Steven Wright, G.D. Spradlin; **Cameos:** Michael Moore; **D:** Michael Moore; **W:** Michael Moore; **C:** Haskell Wexler; **M:** Elmer Bernstein. **VHS** *PGV*

Cancel My Reservation ♪

G/Family New York talk show host Hope sets out for a vacation on an Arizona ranch, but winds up in trouble due to a mysterious corpse, a rich rancher, and an enigmatic mystic. Even more muddled than it sounds. Based on the novel "Broken Gun" by Louis L'Amour, with pointless cameos by Crosby, Wayne, and Wilson.

1972 99m/C Bob Hope, Eva Marie Saint, Ralph Bellamy, Anne Archer, Forrest Tucker, Keenan Wynn, Flip Wilson, Noriyuki "Pat" Morita, Chief Dan George; **Cameos:** John Wayne, Bing Crosby, Doodles Weaver; **D:** Paul Bogart; **W:** Arthur Marx. **VHS, Beta** *COL, FCT*

Candleshoe ♪♪♪

G/Family Noticing how much Los Angeles orphan Jodie Foster resembles the long-lost heiress to Candleshoe Manor, con man Leo McKern takes her back to England to pose as same. It seems there's a fortune hidden somewhere in the mansion, and McKern would have Foster find it and steal it. Great cast includes Helen Hayes as the kindly lady of the manor and David Niven as her resourceful butler. You can probably guess what happens, but it won't spoil anything. Based on "Christmas at Candleshoe" by Michael Innes. Ages 6 to 10.

1978 101m/C Vivian Pickles, Helen Hayes, David Niven, Jodie Foster, Leo McKern; **D:** Norman Tokar. **VHS, Beta** *DIS*

Canine Commando

G/Family Three wartime Pluto cartoons from Disney: "The Army Mascot," "Dog Watch" and "Canine Patrol."

1945 23m/C **VHS, Beta** *DIS*

Cannon Movie Tales: The Emperor's New Clothes 🦴🦴 ᵇ

Family Only mediocre but still probably the best of the terminally lame "Cannon Movie Tales" series of would-be Shelley Duvall rivals. Caesar is the vain, clotheshorse despot and Morse is the con-artist tailor who figures out how to swindle the royal treasury by weaving a nonexistent suit that 'only those fit for office can see.' Lively mugging by the talented stars keep this one going.

1989 85m/C Sid Caesar, Robert Morse, Clive Revill; **D:** David Irving. **VHS** *WAR*

Cannonball 🦴🦴

PG/Primary-Adult Assorted ruthless people leave patches of rubber across the country competing for grand prize in less than legal auto race. Not top drawer New World but nonetheless a cult fave. Inferior to Bartel's previous cult classic, "Death Race 2000." Most interesting for plethora of cult cameos, including Scorsese, Dante, and grandmaster Corman.

 Violence.

1976 93m/C David Carradine, Bill McKinney, Veronica Hamel, Gerrit Graham, Robert Carradine, Sylvester Stallone, Jonathan Kaplan; **Cameos:** Martin Scorsese, Roger Corman, Joe Dante; **D:** Paul Bartel. **VHS, Beta** *NO*

Cannonball Run 🦴 ᵇ

PG/Jr. High-Adult So many stars, so little plot. Reynolds and sidekick DeLuise disguise themselves as paramedics to foil cops while they compete in cross-country Cannonball race. Shows no sign of having been directed by an ex-stuntman. One of 1981's top grossers-go figure. Followed by equally languid sequel "Cannonball Run II."

BEWARE *Profanity and women running around in skimpy outfits. Sexual innuendos.*

1981 95m/C Burt Reynolds, Farrah Fawcett, Roger Moore, Dom DeLuise, Dean Martin, Sammy Davis Jr., Jack Elam, Adrienne Barbeau, Peter Fonda, Molly Picon, Bert Convy, Jamie Farr; **D:** Hal Needham. **VHS, Beta, LV** *VES*

Cannonball Run 2 🦴

PG/Jr. High-Adult More mindless cross-country wheel spinning with gratuitous star cameos. Director Needham apparently subscribes to the two wrongs make a right school of sequels.

1984 109m/C Burt Reynolds, Dom DeLuise, Jamie Farr, Marilu Henner, Shirley MacLaine, Jim Nabors, Frank Sinatra, Sammy Davis Jr., Dean Martin, Telly Savalas, Susan Anton, Catherine Bach, Jack Elam, Sid Caesar, Ricardo Montalban, Charles Nelson Reilly; **Cameos:** Henry Silva, Tim Conway, Don Knotts, Molly Picon; **D:** Hal Needham; **M:** Stephen Dorff. **VHS, Beta, LV** *WAR*

Can't Buy Me Love 🦴🦴

PG-13/Jr. High-Adult High school nerd Ronald buys a month of dates with teen babe Cindy for a grand, in order to win friends and influence people. The gambit works too well; Ronald turns into a popular party guy and ig-

nores his old pals including Cindy, who was falling for him. Youth morality play commits the cardinal sin of not offering believable situations or dialogue. Released through Disney's Touchstone division.

BEWARE *Sex talk that soon turns into the real thing, profanity.*

1987 94m/C Patrick Dempsey, Amanda Peterson, Dennis Dugan, Courtney Gains; **D:** Steve Rash; **M:** Robert Folk. **VHS, Beta, LV** *TOU*

The Canterville Ghost 🦴🦴

Jr. High-Adult Sir Simon de Canterville (Laughton) is a coward haunting his family home until a kinsman performs an act of bravery. After 300 years of successfully scaring Britons, Sir Simon faces a visiting platoon of brash American soldiers who aren't spooked by his moaning and groaning. Oscar Wilde's classic short story, in a way the original "Beetlejuice," was heavily padded here by styling it a WWII propaganda vehicle, as a yankee Canterville descendant gains courage to combat the Axis. Leading lady is the popular child star O'Brien, as the 6-year-old 'Lady Jessica,' mistress of the castle.

BEWARE *Brief battlefield violence.*

1944 95m/B Charles Laughton, Robert Young, Margaret O'Brien, William Gargan, Reginald Owen, Rags Ragland, Una O'Connor, Peter Lawford, Mike Mazurki; **D:** Jules Dassin. **VHS, Beta** *MGM*

The Canterville Ghost

Family Another version of Oscar Wilde's story about a ghost who tries to scare away a family that just moved in. This time Sir John Gielgud plays the ghost of Sir Simon De Canterville. Good and spooky. Ages 7 to 11.

1986 22m/C VHS, Beta *BAR*

The Canterville Ghost

Family During an American family's vacation in an old English manor, they run into an ineffective ghost, doomed to haunt the place until he can redeem himself. Mom and dad are unmoved by the spook and their son pulls pranks on him. Only daughter Virginia feels sorry for Simon de Canterville. Substandard entry in the "Wonderworks" series, hurt by fuzzy, cheap-looking cinematography and ill-conceived rewrites of the original Oscar Wilde tale.

1991 58m/C Richard Kiley, Mary Wickes. **VHS** *PME, FCT*

The Canterville Ghost 🦴🦴 ᵇ

PG/Family Another version of the Oscar Wilde short story features Stewart as the cursed Elizabethan spirit Sir Simon de Canterville, doomed to haunt the family mansion until a prophecy is fulfilled. The spirit is not happy, though, with the American Family that is currently renting his abode. That is until teenager Virginia (Campbell) discovers Sir Simon and realizes she may hold the key to freeing the unhappy ghost.

BEWARE *Some haunting moments, flying objects and ghostly aberrations. The story itself is a little spooky, too.*

1996 91m/C Patrick Stewart, Neve Campbell, Ed Wiley, Cherie Lunghi, Donald Sinden, Joan Sims, Leslie Phillips, Ciaran Fitzgerald, Daniel Betts, Raymond Pickard; **D:** Syd Macartney; **W:** Robert Benedetto; **C:** Denis Lewiston; **M:** Ernest Troost. **VHS** *HMK*

Cantinflas

Preschool-Primary Delightful cartoon character Cantinflas (based on the great Mexican comedian who co-starred in "Around the World in 80 Days") takes young viewers on a trip through history to meet King Tut, Daniel Boone, Madame Curie, and many other famous people.

1984 60m/C VHS, Beta *FHE*

Captain America

Family Republic serial that was the first film version of the patriotic comic-book character. May infuriate Marvel fans because the character here has no real superpowers. He's just a lawyer who, like Batman, adopts a disguise to fight crime—in this case an evil mastermind masquerading as a respected doctor. Plenty of action; in fact, one authority called this the most violent serial ever. In 15 chapters.

 Violence

1944 240m/B Dick Purcell, Adrian Booth, Lionel Atwill; **D:** John English; **W:** Elmer Clifton. **VHS, Beta** *VCN, MLB, VTR*

Captain America

PG-13/Jr. High-Adult The Marvel Comics superhero got his own movie (not counting previous made-for-TV incarnations) in time for his 50th anniversary, but this low-cost epic doesn't make the grade despite the wide ranging plot. In 1941 a secret serum turns polio-stricken Steve Rogers into a superstrong superhero, but he's matched by a Nazi counterpart known as the Red Skull. Their battle leaves Captain America frozen in the Arctic for 40 years, but he thaws out to battle the Red Skull again, now a world gangster and anti-environmental meanie. Possibly amusing for kids; adults may note ruefully that this Captain America movie was made in . . . Yugoslavia.

BEWARE *Violence (sometimes intense, even by comic-book standards). Profanity.*

1989 103m/C Matt Salinger, Scott Paulin, Ronny Cox, Ned Beatty, Darren McGavin, Melinda Dillon; **D:** Albert Pyun; **W:** Stephen Tolkin. **VHS, LV** *COL*

Captain America 2: Death Too Soon

Family Terrorists hit America where it hurts, threatening to use age accelerating drug. Sequelized superhero fights chronic crow lines and series dies slow, painful death. Made for TV.

1979 98m/C Reb Brown, Connie Sellecca, Len Birman, Christopher Lee, Katherine Justice, Lana Wood, Christopher Carey; **D:** Ivan Nagy. **VHS, Beta** *MCA*

Captain Blood

Family Adventure that launched then-unknown Flynn to fame is one of the best pirate swashbucklers ever. Exiled into slavery by a tyrannical governor, physician Peter Blood becomes a chivalrous buccaneer, a sort of seagoing Robin Hood. Finally, his heroics in battle against enemies of the Crown earn him a royal pardon. Based on the novel by Rafael Sabatini. Also available in a computer-colorized version.

BEWARE *Violence.*

1935 120m/B Errol Flynn, Olivia de Havilland, Basil Rathbone, J. Carrol Naish, Guy Kibbee, Lionel Atwill; **D:** Michael Curtiz. **VHS, Beta** *MGM, FCT, MLB*

Captain Harlock, Vol. 1

Primary Captain Harlock, the space pirate, is left alone to protect Earth from invasion by the queen of the marauding alien planet Millenia. Strung together episodes of a syndicated cartoon TV series. Additional volumes available.

1981 60m/C VHS, Beta *FHE, TPV*

Captain January

Family Crusty old lighthouse keeper rescues little orphan girl with curly hair from drowning, and everyone breaks into cutesy song and dance, interrupted only when the authorities try to separate the loving twosome. Popular Temple vehicle of the day, but check out her charming dance partner Ebsen, who was originally cast as Tin Man in "The Wizard of Oz"—but turned out to have a violent allergy to the makeup. At the Codfish Ball; Early Bird; The Right Somebody to Love.

1936 74m/B Shirley Temple, Guy Kibbee, Buddy Ebsen, Slim Summerville, Jane Darwell, June Lang, George Irving, Si Jenks; **D:** David Butler. **VHS, Beta** *FOX*

Captain Kangaroo & His Friends

Preschool-Primary Compilation of short segments from Captain Kangaroo's long-running TV show, with the Captain's favorite cohorts in kidvid and some surprising celebrity guests. Additional volumes available.

1985 60m/C Bob Keeshan, Phil Donahue, Joan Rivers, Dolly Parton. **VHS, Beta** *MPI*

Captain Kangaroo's Merry Christmas Stories

Preschool-Primary The Captain narrates a selection of animated and live-action tales to lift the Christmas spirits, including: "The Gift of the Little Juggler," "The Fir Tree," and Clement Moore's "A Christmas Carol."

1985 58m/C Bob Keeshan. **VHS, Beta** *MPI*

Captain Planet & the Planeteers: A Hero for Earth

Family Environmentally conscious TV cartoon launched with mighty fanfare by Ted Turner, though once you get past the eco-propaganda (which just about every kids' show since "Lassie's Rescue Rangers" has been pushing anyway) the Captain and his little buddies look a lot like any old superbunch. In this one they must keep the evil Dr. Blight and his cronies from polluting the Earth. Additional volumes available.
1990 45m/C VHS *TTC, WSH*

Captain Pugwash

Preschool-Primary Collection of animated shorts from English TV starring the bumbling pirate and his crew, aimed at a very young audience but worth a look for all animation fans; "Pugwash" is brought to life with stop-motion photography of cut-out paper characters, rather than drawings.
1975 80m/C VHS, Beta *FHE*

Captain Ron 🎵 ♪

PG-13/Jr. High-Adult The Harveys inherit a large boat docked in the West Indies, so they take a Caribbean vacation to pilot her back to the US. Knowing nothing about sailing, they hire the title character, a one-eyed, Long John Silver-talking sea dog whose salty manner hides the fact that he's an irresponsible bumbler. Numerous accidents, embarrassments, and navigational errors culminate in a battle with modern pirates. Pseudo-Disney comedy (through their more 'mature' Touchstone label) sinks instead of floats, and might be retitled "Captain Raunch" for a few of its gags.

⚠ **BEWARE** *Salty language, fittingly enough. Sex, nudity, and Captain Ron both boozes and gambles with the Harvey's adolescent son.*

1992 104m/C Kurt Russell, Martin Short, Mary Kay Place, Meadow Sisto, Benjamin Salisbury; **D:** Thom Eberhardt; **W:** Thom Eberhardt. **VHS, Beta, LV** *TOU*

Captain Scarlet vs. The Mysterons

Family When Captain Scarlet's expeditionary team mistakenly fires upon an extraterrestrial military complex, the humorless aliens retaliate by setting out to destroy the world. Feature-length compilation of episodes from Gerry Anderson's British TV series done in "Super Marionation," a technique using plastic models operated by very fine wires, matched with some dashing good spacecraft f/x.
1967 90m/C Alan Perry, Desmond Saunders, Ken Turner; **D:** David Lane. **VHS, Beta** *FHE*

Captains Courageous 🎵 🎵 🎵

Family Rich, spoiled Harvey falls over the side of a luxury ocean liner. Picked up by a Portuguese fishing boat, the boy has to spend three months at sea, enduring the same rigors as the humble sailors. Gradually he learns the value of hard work and friendship through service with the captain's young son (Rooney) and a fatherly crewman (Tracy, in an Oscar-winning performance). A fine voyage through adventure, triumph and tragedy, based on the Rudyard Kipling novel. Director Fleming went on to "Gone With the Wind" and "The Wizard of Oz." Recently very loosely remade with Chris Elliot in the eminently forgettable "Cabin Boy."
1937 116m/B Spencer Tracy, Lionel Barrymore, Freddie Bartholomew, Mickey Rooney, Melvyn Douglas, Charley Grapewin, John Carradine, Bobby Watson, Jack LaRue; **D:** Victor Fleming. **Award Nominations:** Academy Awards '37: Best Film Editing, Best Picture, Best Screenplay; **Awards:** Academy Awards '37: Best Actor (Tracy); National Board of Review Awards '37: 10 Best Films of the Year. **VHS, Beta** *MGM, BMV, BTV*

The Capture of Grizzly Adams 🎵 ♪

Family TV-movie reunion for the "Grizzly Adams" program, in which the mountain man is framed for murder. He and his bear companion must not only clear his name but outwit a band of outlaws holding Adams' young daughter captive.
1982 96m/C Dan Haggerty, Chuck Connors, June Lockhart, Kim Darby, Noah Beery Jr., Keenan Wynn. **VHS** *WOV*

Car 54, Where Are You? WOOF!

PG-13/Jr. High-Adult Exceedingly lame remake of the exceedingly lame (though strangely beloved) television series, which ran for only two seasons, 1961-63. This time, Toody (Johansen) and Muldoon (McGinley) are protecting a Mafia stool pigeon (Piven), while vampy Velma Velour (Drescher) sets her sights on Muldoon. Not many laughs and a waste of a talented cast. Sat on the shelf at Orion for three years (with good reason).

⚠ **BEWARE** *Profanity; sex talk.*

1994 89m/C David Johansen, Fran Drescher, Rosie O'Donnell, John C. McGinley, Nipsey Russell, Al Lewis, Daniel Baldwin, Jeremy Piven; **D:** Bill Fishman; **W:** Ebbe Roe Smith, Erik Tarloff, Peter McCarthy, Peter Crabbe; **M:** Bernie Worrell, Pray For Rain. **VHS, LV** *ORI*

Car Wash 🎵 🎵 ♪

PG/Jr. High-Adult L.A. carwash provides a soap-opera setting for disjointed comic bits about owners of dirty cars and people who hose them down for a living. Econo budget and lite plot, but serious comic talent. A sort of disco carwash version of "Grand Hotel."
1976 97m/C Franklin Ajaye, Sully Boyer, Richard Brestoff, George Carlin, Richard Pryor, Melanie Mayron, Ivan Dixon, Antonio Fargas; **D:** Michael A. Schultz; **W:** Joel Schumacher. **VHS, Beta** *MCA, FCT*

Carbon Copy 🎵 🎵

PG/Jr. High-Adult Successful white executive who's secretly a Jew has life turned inside out when his seventeen-year old illegitimate son, who happens to be black, decides it's time to look up dear old dad. Typical comedy-with-a-moral strains to state the obvious.

BEWARE *Profanity and sexual references. Interracial stereo-types.*

1981 92m/C George Segal, Susan St. James, Jack Warden, Paul Winfield, Dick Martin, Vicky Dawson, Tom Poston, Denzel Washington; **D:** Michael A. Schultz; **W:** Stanley Shapiro; **M:** Bill Conti. **VHS, Beta, LV** *COL*

Care Bears: Family Storybook

Preschool-Primary Collection of animated adventures featuring the huggable, buyable, toy-products bear clan. Additional volumes available.

1987 85m/C VHS, Beta *ORI*

The Care Bears Movie

G/Family Feature-length cartoon treacle to promote the Care Bears line of toys and tie-ins. Plot has the cuddly commodities leaving their cloud home in Care-a-lot to save Nicolas, a care-less boy magician under control of an evil spirit. Song contributions from the likes of Carole King, John Sebastian and NRBQ don't bring this respectability, though Rooney's narration almost does.

1984 75m/C D: Arna Selznick; **V:** Mickey Rooney, Georgia Engel, Harry Dean Stanton. **VHS, Beta** *LIV, VES, VTR*

The Care Bears Movie 2: A New Generation

G/Family More sugary Care Bear fare involving off-spring of the likes of Tender Heart Bear, Love-a-Lot Bear, Wish Bear, and Bedtime Bear. Too bad Script Bear never shows up.

1986 77m/C D: Dale Schott; **V:** Maxine Miller, Pam Hyatt, Hadley Key. **VHS, Beta** *COL*

Careful, He Might Hear You

PG/Family Abandoned by his widowed father, six-year-old P.S. becomes a prize in a tug-of-war custody fight between his two aunts, one working class and the other wealthy. The boy's world is further shaken by the sudden reappearance of that prodigal father. Set in Depression-era Australia, it's a touching and keenly observed child's-eye-sense of the adult world, its hypocrisies and often cruel manipulation. Hardly uplifting, but worthwhile. Based on a novel by Sumner Locke Elliott.

BEWARE *Emotional abuse of a child and profanity.*

1984 113m/C Nicholas Gledhill, Wendy Hughes, Robyn Nevin, John Hargreaves; **D:** Carl Schultz. **VHS, Beta** *FOX*

Carnival of the Animals

Family Poetry comes to life in this story of the animals at the zoo to the music of Saint-Saens. Performance filmed in 1984 features outstanding musicians and the narration of Close and Irons.

1984 30m/C D: Jon Stone. **VHS, Beta** *VAI, FCT, MVD*

Carousel

Family Much-loved Rodgers & Hammerstein musical based on Ferenc Molnar's play "Liliom" (filmed by Fritz Lang in 1935) about a swaggering carnival barker (Mac-Rae) who tries to change his life after he falls in love with a good woman. Killed while attempting to foil a robbery he was supposed to help commit, he begs his heavenly hosts for the chance to return to the mortal realm just long enough to sct things straight with his teenage daughter. Jones and MacRae never sounded better. Now indisputably a classic, the film lost $2 million when first released. ♫ If I Loved You; Soliloquy; You'll Never Walk Alone; What's the Use of Wond'rin; When I Marry Mister Snow; When the Children Are Asleep; A Real Nice Clambake; Carousel Ballet; Carousel Waltz.

1956 128m/C Gordon MacRae, Shirley Jones, Cameron Mitchell, Gene Lockhart, Barbara Ruick, Robert Rounseville, Richard Deacon, Tor Johnson; **D:** Henry King; **M:** Richard Rodgers, Oscar Hammerstein. **VHS, Beta, LV** *FOX, RDG, HMV*

The Carrot Highway

Family Another whimsical story about how it's done takes children into the world of carrot production. Includes visits with scientists, farmers, packing houses, workers, and grocery stores.

1996 40m/C VHS

Cartoons for Big Kids

Adult Movie historian and cartoon buff Leonard Maltin holds an animation appreciation collection for all ages, featuring the likes of Bugs Bunny and others.

1989 44m/C D: Mark Lamberti. **VHS** *TTC*

Casablanca

PG/Family Can you see George Raft as Rick? Jack Warner did, but producer Hal Wallis wanted Bogart. Considered by many to be the best film ever made and one of the most quoted movies of all time, it rocketed Bogart from gangster roles to romantic leads as he and Bergman (who never looked lovelier) sizzle on screen. Bogart runs a gin joint in Morocco during the Nazi occupation, and meets up with Bergman, an old flame, but romance and politics do not mix, especially in Nazi-occupied French Morocco. Greenstreet, Lorre, and Rains all create memorable characters, as does Wilson, the piano player to whom Bergman says the oft-misquoted, "Play it, Sam." Without a doubt, the best closing scene ever written; it was scripted on the fly during the end of shooting, and actually shot several ways. Written from an unproduced play. See it in the original black and white. Laserdisc edition features restored imaging and sound and commentary by film historian Ronald Haver about the production, the play it was based on, and the famed evolution of the screenplay on audio track two. 50th Anniversary Edition contains a restored and remastered print, the original 1942 theatrical trailer, a film documentary narrated by Lauren Bacall, and a booklet.

Meet the Star of *Casper,* Christina Ricci

Because she looked too much like a young Natalie Wood, Christina Ricci almost didn't get the part of the dour Wednesday in *The Addams Family*. But the 11-year-old actress almost stole the film, and the sequel was written to feature her. "We knew we had struck gold," said director Barry Sonnenfeld.

Ricci became a teenager while filming *Addams Family Values,* and Sonnenfeld had to tone down her emerging attitude. But puberty helped make a romantic subplot possible. "I don't want to be just another kid who did a couple of movies," says Ricci. There seems little chance of that. The daughter of a model and a lawyer, Ricci debuted on screen at age nine, playing the younger sister in *Mermaids*. On the set, she formed an enduring friendship with Cher, who played her mother. Ricci was 11 when she turned into the morbid Wednesday. At age 14, she starred in *Casper,* playing 12-year-old Kat Harvey, who befriends the friendless friendly ghost. And at 15, she played another 12-year-old in the coming-of-age film *Now and Then*.

Amazingly, Ricci has never taken an acting class and continues to study at a public high school in New Jersey. "I'm serious about acting," says the hardworking, determined Ricci. "I don't want to do cheesy films. I want to do things that have integrity."

BEWARE *Adultery acknowledged, gin joints glorified.*

1942 102m/B Humphrey Bogart, Ingrid Bergman, Paul Henreid, Claude Rains, Peter Lorre, Sydney Greenstreet, Conrad Veidt, S.Z. Sakall, Dooley Wilson, Marcel Dalio, John Qualen, Helmut Dantine; **D:** Michael Curtiz; **W:** Julius J. Epstein, Philip C. Epstein, Howard Koch; **M:** Max Steiner. **Award Nominations:** Academy Awards '43: Best Actor (Bogart), Best Black and White Cinematography, Best Film Editing, Best Supporting Actor (Rains), Best Original Score; **Awards:** Academy Awards '43: Best Director (Curtiz), Best Picture, Best Screenplay; National Board of Review Awards '45: 10 Best Films of the Year. **VHS, Beta, LV, 8mm** *MGM, FOX, TLF*

Casey at the Bat

Family From Shelley Duvall's made for cable television "Tall Tales and Legends" series, in which the immortal poem is brought to life. Rousing comedy for the whole family.

1985 52m/C Bill Macy, Hamilton Camp, Elliott Gould, Carol Kane, Howard Cosell; **D:** David Steinberg. **VHS, Beta** *FOX*

Casey's Shadow ♫♫

PG/Family Eight-year-old Casey is the youngest of three boys being raised by their impoverished horse-trainer dad after mom walks out. Then Casey raises a quarter horse with championship potential. Can a first-place finish at the world's richest race help this struggling family to survive? Can this plot be any more predictable?

BEWARE *Salty language.*

1978 116m/C Walter Matthau, Alexis Smith, Robert Webber, Murray Hamilton; **D:** Martin Ritt. **VHS, Beta** *COL*

Casper ♫♫♫

PG/Family A Casper the Friendly Ghost for the 90s—he's old enough to be interested in girls—haunts spooky old Whipstaff Manor, along with his less amicable uncles, Stinky, Fatso and Stretch (maybe if they had normal names they'd be nicer). Mansion owner Moriarty wants to get at the treasure she believes is hidden there and hires eccentric Dr. Harvey (Pullman) to get rid of the ghosts. Harvey's daughter (Ricci) and Casper become pals and set out to fix everything. Great animated special effects, but the live action is less, uh, animated.

BEWARE *Mild profanity. Dr. Harvey's "Lazarus Machine" will leave younger children thoroughly confused about death. But the kids will enjoy the prankish ghost uncles.*

1995 95m/C Christina Ricci, Bill Pullman, Cathy Moriarty, Eric Idle, Amy Brenneman; **Cameos:** Don Novello, Rodney Dangerfield, Clint Eastwood, Mel Gibson, Dan Aykroyd; **D:** Brad Silberling; **W:** Sherri Stoner, Deanna Oliver; **C:** Dean Cundey; **M:** James Horner; **V:** Malachi Pearson, Joe Nipote, Joe Alaskey, Brad Garrett. **VHS, LV** *MCA*

Casper's Halloween

Preschool-Primary The friendly ghost entertains with four Halloween treats: "To Boo or Not to Boo," "Which is Witch?," "Fright Day the 13th," and "The Witching Hour." Additional volumes available.

19?? 25m/C VHS *MCA*

The Castaway Cowboy 🦴🦴

G/Family Shanghaied cowboy becomes partners with a widow and helps turn her Hawaiian potato farm into a cattle ranch, but a bad guy wants the land for himself. Without the tropical settings it wouldn't be anything special. In fact, it's nothing special with them either.

1974 91m/C James Garner, Robert Culp, Vera Miles; **D:** Vincent McEveety. **VHS, Beta** *DIS, OM*

The Cat 🦴

Family Boy and tame cougar become friends while on the run from a murderous poacher. Simple-minded animal tale, as generic as the title.

1966 95m/C Peggy Ann Garner, Roger Perry, Barry Coe; **D:** Ellis Kadison. **VHS, Beta** *COL, NLC*

The Cat Came Back and Three Other Tales

Preschool-Primary Say you took in a stray kitty and it repaid you by destroying your whole house. You'd try anything to get rid of it. That's the premise of the song "The Cat Came Back" and of the title cartoon in this wonderful anthology from the National Film Board of Canada. There's a lilting singing cartoon (sung by Kate and Anna McGarrigle) about lumberjacks waltzing on logs floating down the river, a beautiful Mic Mac legend about the changing seasons, a story about an eccentric and her cats, and "Blackberry Sunday Jam" (reviewed separately). Ages 4 and up.

1992 30m/C VHS *SMA*

Cat City

Family Creative feature cartoon from Hungary, a rodent James Bond spoof in which heroic agent Grabowski is sent by the worldwide mouse intelligence organization ('Intermaus') to thwart a diabolical weapon developed by a cabal of evil cats. Dubbed into English.

1987 90m/C D: Bela Ternovsky. **VHS** *JTC*

The Cat from Outer Space 🦴🦴

G/Family Extraterrestrial cat crashes his spaceship on Earth and leads a group of civilians, military types and spies on merry chases. Unspectacular close encounter of the '70s Disney kind.

1978 103m/C Ken Berry, Sandy Duncan, Harry (Henry) Morgan, Roddy McDowall, McLean Stevenson; **D:** Norman Tokar. **VHS, Beta** *DIS, OM*

The Cat in the Hat

Primary Dr. Seuss classic about a feline freeloader who magically mess up the place and puts it back together in the nick of time. A simple TV cartoon that's great fun. Ages 1 to 8.

1972 25m/C VHS, Beta *BFA*

The Cat in the Hat Comes Back

Primary Dr Seuss' lovable cat makes another chaotic visit. Two other stories are included. Ages 1 to 8.

1990 30m/C VHS *RAN, VEC*

The Cat in the Hat Gets Grinched

Primary Two Dr. Seuss characters, the Cat in the Hat and the Grinch, meet on a summer's day and begin a crazy rivalry. Features music by Joe Raposo. Ages 1 to 8.

1991 30m/C VHS *RAN, BTV*

Catch Me . . . If You Can 🦴🦴

PG/Jr. High-Adult Here's school spirit for you: class president Melissa doesn't want the school torn down, so she enlists the homeroom rebel, a drag racer, to compete for cash in the local gambling syndicate. Don't expect greatness and you'll find this farfetched stuff entertaining. Director Sommers' touch with the youthful performers shows; he later did Disney's 1993 "Adventures of Huck Finn."

 *Salty language, reckless driving.*

1989 105m/C Matt Lattanzi, Loryn Locklin, M. Emmet Walsh, Geoffrey Lewis; **D:** Stephen Sommers. **VHS, LV** *MCG*

Cat's Eye 🦴 ▷

PG-13/Jr. High-Adult Lame anthology of three Stephen King short stories connected by a stray cat who wanders through each tale. Ages 13 and up.

 Violence.

1985 94m/C Drew Barrymore, James Woods, Alan King, Robert Hays, Candy Clark, Kenneth McMillan, James Naughton, Charles S. Dutton; **D:** Lewis Teague; **W:** Stephen King; **M:** Alan Silvestri. **VHS, Beta, LV** *FOX, FCT*

Celtic Pride 🦴🦴

PG-13/Jr. High-Adult There's a certain kind of sports fan, found only in Boston or Chicago, whose life is inextricably intertwined with the fate of his (or, rarely, her) city's professional sports teams. Aykroyd and Stern play such men, who if you cut them open would bleed Celtic green. These two nutballs kidnap a rival star player (Wayans) to ensure victory for Boston in a big playoff game. Trouble is there's nothing very interesting beyond that basic idea. Sports fans will relate, however.

BEWARE *Profanity. A scene in a public men's room. The lead characters get very drunk.*

1996 90m/C Damon Wayans, Daniel Stern, Dan Aykroyd, Gail O'Grady, Adam Hendershott, Paul Guilfoyle, Deion Sanders, Christopher McDonald, Gus Williams, Ted Rooney, Vladimir Cuk; **Cameos:** Bill Walton, Larry Bird; **D:** Tom DeCerchio; **W:** Judd Apatow; **C:** Oliver Wood; **M:** Basil Poledouris. **VHS** *NYR*

Christina Ricci meets the friendly ghost over breakfast in "Casper."

Challenge To Be Free 🦴🦴

G/Family Historical action adventure geared toward nature lovers. Depicts the struggles of a fugitive trapper and his wolf ally, pursued by 12 men and 100 dogs across a thousand miles of frozen wilderness. Made in 1972 (under the portentous title "Mad Trapper of the Yukon"), but released to the family marketplace in 1976.

 Violence.

1976 90m/C Mike Mazurki, Jimmy Kane; **Cameos:** Tay Garnett; **D:** Tay Garnett. **VHS, Beta** *MED, VTR*

Challenge to Lassie 🦴🦴 ◁

G/Family When Lassie's Scottish master dies, the faithful pup remains at his grave. An unsympathetic policeman orders Lassie to leave the premises, inspiring a debate among the townsfolk as to the dog's fate. Based on a true story (although the original hero was a Skye Terrier); remade by Disney as "Greyfriar's Bobby."

1949 76m/C Edmund Gwenn, Donald Crisp, Geraldine Brooks, Reginald Owen, Alan Webb, Henry Stephenson, Alan Napier, Sara Allgood; **D:** Richard Thorpe; **M:** Andre Previn. **VHS, Beta** *MGM, FCT*

Challenge to White Fang 🦴 ◁

PG/Jr. High-Adult Italian-made Jack London takeoff, no relation to the Disney "White Fang" pics. Courageous wolf-dog prevents a scheming businessman from taking over an old man's gold mine.

 *Roughhousing.*

1986 89m/C Harry Carey Jr., Franco Nero; **D:** Lucio Fulci. **VHS, Beta** *TWE*

Chances Are 🦴🦴🦴

PG/Jr. High-Adult After her loving husband dies in a chance accident, a pregnant woman remains unmarried, keeping her husband's best friend as her only close male companion. Years later, her now teenage daughter brings a friend home for dinner, but due to an error in heaven, the young man begins to realize that this may not be the first time he and this family have met. A wonderful love-story hampered only minimally by the unbelievable plot.

 *Mild profanity.*

1989 108m/C Cybill Shepherd, Robert Downey Jr., Ryan O'Neal, Mary Stuart Masterson, Josef Sommer, Christopher McDonald, Joe Grifasi, James Noble, Susan Ruttan, Fran Ryan; **D:** Emile Ardolino; **W:**

Perry Howze, Randy Howze; **M:** Maurice Jarre. **VHS, Beta, LV, 8mm**
COL, FCT

Change of Habit ♪♪

G/Family Three novitiates undertake to learn about the
world before becoming full-fledged nuns. While working
at a ghetto clinic a young doctor forms a strong, affectionate relationship with one of them. Presley's last feature
film. ♪♪ Change of Habit; Let Us Pray; Rubberneckin'.
1969 93m/C Elvis Presley, Mary Tyler Moore, Barbara McNair, Ed
Asner, Ruth McDevitt, Regis Toomey; **D:** William A. Graham; **M:** Billy
Goldenberg. **VHS, Beta** *MCA, GKK*

Chaplin ♪♪ ♪

PG-13/Jr. High-Adult The life and career of "The Little
Tramp" is chronicled by director Attenborough and brilliantly portrayed by Downey, Jr, as Chaplin. A flashback
format traces his life from its poverty-stricken Dickensian
origins in the London slums through his directing and
acting career, to his honorary Oscar in 1972. Slow-moving at parts, but captures Chaplin's devotion to his art and
also his penchant towards jailbait. In a clever casting
choice, Chaplin's own daughter from his fourth marriage
to Oona O'Neill, Geraldine Chaplin, plays her own grandmother who goes mad.

 Profanity, drinking and nudity.

1992 135m/C Robert Downey Jr., Dan Aykroyd, Geraldine Chaplin,
Kevin Dunn, Anthony Hopkins, Milla Jovovich, Moira Kelly, Kevin
Kline, Diane Lane, Penelope Ann Miller, Paul Rhys, John Thaw,
Marisa Tomei, Nancy Travis, James Woods, David Duchovny, Debo-
rah Maria Moore, Bill Paterson, John Standing, Robert Stephens; **D:**
Richard Attenborough; **W:** Bryan Forbes, William Boyd; **M:** John
Barry. **Award Nominations:** Academy Awards '92: Best Actor
(Downey), Best Art Direction/Set Decoration, Best Original Score;
Awards: British Academy Awards '93: Best Actor (Downey). **VHS, LV**
LIV, MOV, FCT

Charade ♪♪♪ ♪

Jr. High-Adult After her husband is murdered, a young
woman finds herself on the run from crooks and double
agents who want the $250,000 her husband stole during
WWII. Hepburn and Grant are charming and sophisti-
cated as usual in this stylish intrigue filmed in Paris.
Based on the story "The Unsuspecting Wife" by Marc
Behm and Peter Stone.
1963 113m/C Cary Grant, Audrey Hepburn, Walter Matthau, James
Coburn, George Kennedy; **D:** Stanley Donen; **W:** Peter Stone; **M:**
Henry Mancini. **Award Nominations:** Academy Awards '63: Best
Song ("Charade"); **Awards:** British Academy Awards '64: Best Actress
(Hepburn); Edgar Allan Poe Awards '63: Best Screenplay. **VHS, Beta**
CNG, MRV, MCA

The Charge of the Model T's ♪ ♪

G/Family Regionally made low-budgeter about a German spy during the First World War and his schemes to
derail the U.S. army using a souped-up automobile. Always knew we couldn't trust that Herbie in wartime.
1976 90m/C Louis Nye, John David Carson, Herb Edelman, Carol
Bagdasarian, Arte Johnson; **D:** Jim McCullough. **VHS, Beta**

Chariots of Fire ♪♪♪ ♪

PG/Family Lush, if slightly arcane telling of the parallel
stories of Harold Abraham and Eric Liddell, real-life English runners who competed in the 1924 Paris Olympics.
Abraham, a Jew, strove for excellence to defy widespread
bigotry, while the Christian Liddell sprints because he
believes he's following the will of God. Outstanding performances in a tale that addresses the universality (and
limitations) of sports, with memorable score by Vangelis.
1981 123m/C Ben Cross, Ian Charleson, Nigel Havers, Ian Holm,
Alice Krige, Brad Davis, Dennis Christopher, Patrick Magee, Cheryl
Campbell, John Gielgud, Lindsay Anderson, Nigel Davenport; **D:**
Hugh Hudson; **W:** Colin Welland; **M:** Vangelis. **Award Nominations:**
Academy Awards '81: Best Director (Hudson), Best Supporting Actor
(Holm); **Awards:** Academy Awards '81: Best Costume Design, Best
Original Screenplay, Best Picture, Best Score; British Academy
Awards '81: Best Film, Best Supporting Actor (Holm). **VHS, Beta, LV**
WAR, FCT, BTV

Charley and the Angel ♪♪

G/Family Heavily sentimental Disney comedy about
hardworking Charlie who tries to change his cold ways
with his family after being informed by an angel that he
hasn't long to live. Set in a warmly nostalgic version of the
Great Depression.
1973 93m/C Fred MacMurray, Cloris Leachman, Harry (Henry)
Morgan, Kurt Russell, Vincent Van Patten, Kathleen Cody; **D:** Vincent
McEveety. **VHS** *DIS, OM*

Charlie and the Great Balloon Chase ♪♪

Family When grandfather takes Charlie on a cross-country balloon trip to Virginia they're hotly pursued by
mom's stuffy fiancee, who wants to send the boy to mili-
tary-school, as well as by the FBI, a reporter, and the
Mafia. Airy made-for-TV movie.
1982 98m/C Jack Albertson, Adrienne Barbeau, Slim Pickens,
Moosie Drier; **D:** Larry Elikann. **VHS, Beta** *TLF*

The Charlie Brown and Snoopy Show

Family "Snoopy the Psychiatrist" finds Snoopy taking
over Lucy's job of listening to everyone's problems. Lucy
sets a new world record for crabbiness, 1000 days, in
"Lucy vs. the World." Several other volumes in the series.
Ages 5 to 11.
1995 46m/C VHS *PAR*

The Charlie Brown and Snoopy Show: Vol. 1

Family Video compilation from a mid-80s weekly TV
cartoon series, starring the "Peanuts" characters in various short subjects like "Snoopy and the Beanstalk." Vol. 2
includes the vintage prime-time special "It's the Great
Pumpkin, Charlie Brown."
1983 44m/C D: Bill Melendez, Sam Jaimes. **VHS, Beta** *BAR, KAR,
APD*

Two dedicated Boston fans hold the opposing team's star player hostage in "Celtic Pride."

A Charlie Brown Christmas

Family This is the one—the very first of the splendidly realized Lee Mendelson/Bill Melendez translations of Charles M. Schulz's "Peanuts" cartoons to prime-time TV in cartoon form. Virtually all of the "Peanuts" specials are now on video on various labels, in addition to the theatrical feature cartoons.

1965 30m/C D: Bill Melendez. **VHS, Beta** *MED, SHV, VTR*

A Charlie Brown Thanksgiving

Family Charlie Brown is so wishy-washy that he lets Peppermint Patty, Marcie and Franklin invite themselves to his house for Thanksgiving dinner (and where are their parents?) Meanwhile, Charlie knows full well that he won't be home; he's going to his grandmother's. Charlie and Snoopy improvise a feast for the friends (jelly beans, popcorn and don't ask). Somehow, they all arrive at the true meaning of the holiday. Ages 4 to 8.

1981 25m/C D: Bill Melendez, Phil Roman. **VHS, Beta** *BAR, KAR*

Charlie, the Lonesome Cougar

🎵🎵 🎬

G/Family Orphaned mountain lion finds a home with the rough-and-tumble loggers, and a dog named Chainsaw, in a timber camp. Enjoyable, if ambling, Disney nature drama. Ages 5 to 10.

1967 75m/C Linda Wallace, Jim Wilson, Ron Brown, Brian Russell, Clifford Peterson; **D:** Winston Hibler. **VHS, Beta** *DIS*

Charlie's Ghost: The Secret of Coronado 🎵🎵 🎬

PG/Jr. High-Adult Kid who has trouble fitting in is befriended by the ghost of a Spanish conquistador. Contains some rude language and bullying.

⚠️ BEWARE *Some rude language; bullying.*

1994 92m/C Richard "Cheech" Marin, Trenton Knight, Anthony Edwards, Linda Fiorentino, Daphne Zuniga. **VHS** *PSM*

Charlotte's Web 🎵🎵🎵

G/Family E.B. White's classic story (adapted by Earl Hamner Jr., creator of TV's "The Waltons") of a friendship between a spider named Charlotte and the pig she manages to save from being turned into bacon. In a touching finale Wilbur has to face the fact that pigs live a lot longer than spiders. This bigscreen treatment by Hanna-Barbera studios rates way above their TV cartoons, and the just-okay songs come to life when performed by Reynolds and other superb character voices.

1973 94m/C D: Charles A. Nichols; **V:** Debbie Reynolds, Agnes Moorehead, Paul Lynde, Henry Gibson. **VHS, Beta, LV** *KUI, PAR, FCT*

Charmkins

Primary-Jr. High Animated adventures of Lady Slipper and her friends in Charm World where they battle the evil Dragonweed. Designed to charm children into lusting after Charmkins-related toys.

1983 60m/C V: Ben Vereen, Sally Struthers, Aileen Quinn. **VHS, Beta** *FHE*

Chasing Dreams 🎵 🎬

PG/Jr. High-Adult Sickly melodrama about a farmboy who finds fulfillment as a baseball player. Lame, amateur family drama was widely revived on tape when supporting actor Costner became a star (he sued over the plastering of his face all over the video box). Not to be confused with "Field of Dreams," naturally.

1981 96m/C David G. Brown, John Fife, Jim Shane, Lisa Kingston, Matt Clark, Kevin Costner; **D:** Sean Roche, Therese Conte. **VHS, Beta** *PSM*

Chatterer the Squirrel

Preschool-Primary Two "Fables of the Green Forest," adapted from works of Thornton W. Burgess. Chatterer the Squirrel learns a much needed lesson in humility in "The Big Boast." In "Captive Chatterer," the farmer's son

tries to make a house pet out of Chatterer, but a new home and plenty of food are no substitute for freedom!
1983 60m/C VHS, Beta *FHE*

The Cheap Detective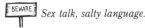

PG/Jr. High-Adult Neil Simon's parody of the "Maltese Falcon" gloriously exploits the resourceful Falk in a Bogart-like role. Vast supporting cast—notably Brennan, DeLuise, and Kahn—prove equally game for fun in this consistently amusing venture.
1978 92m/C Peter Falk, Ann-Margret, Eileen Brennan, Sid Caesar, Stockard Channing, James Coco, Dom DeLuise, Louise Fletcher, John Houseman, Madeline Kahn, Fernando Lamas, Marsha Mason, Phil Silvers, Vic Tayback, Abe Vigoda, Paul Williams, Nicol Williamson; *D:* Robert Moore; *W:* Neil Simon. **VHS** *CSM, COL*

Cheetah

G/Family California kids Ted and Susan, visiting their parents in Kenya, embark on the adventure of their lives when, with the help of a young Masai tribesman, they adopt and care for an orphaned cheetah. Based on "The Cheetahs" by Alan Caillou.
1989 80m/C Keith Coogan, Lucy Deakins, Collin Mothupi; *D:* Jeff Blyth. **VHS, LV** *DIS*

Chester the Earth Ant: Story Book Castle

Preschool-Primary Chester the Earth Ant and his friend the Princess embark on a magical adventure which encourages children to use their imagination through story and song. They learn about the 16th century and how insects have survived since then. Ages 4 to 9.
1994 30m/C VHS

The Chicken Chronicles

PG/Jr. High-Adult With only days before graduation and an uncertain future, a high school senior goes nuts with crazy pranks and a campaign to get horizontal with his dream girl. Set in the 1960s, with pretenses of insight into the teen mind, an indecipherable scientific puzzle.

 Sex talk, salty language.

1977 94m/C Phil Silvers, Ed Lauter, Steve Guttenberg, Lisa Reeves, Meredith Baer; *D:* Francis Simon. **VHS, Beta** *COL*

Child of Glass

G/Family Thirteen-year-old Alexander and his family move into a New Orleans mansion. Soon the boy encounters the spirit of a girl killed there during the Civil War, who puts Alexander on the trail of missing treasure. Disney feature, based on the novel "The Ghost Belonged to Me" by Richard Peck.
1978 93m/C Barbara Barrie, Biff McGuire, Anthony Zerbe, Nina Foch, Steve Shaw, Katy Kurtzman, Olivia Barash; *D:* John Erman. **VHS, Beta** *DIS*

The Children of Noisy Village

Preschool-Primary Noisy village is a small town in the Swedish countryside consisting of three red frame houses. In the town, six adventurous children discover a multitude of fantasy lands of imagination right in their own backyard—their backyard being the beautiful pastures, ponds, and fields of Sweden. From the author of "Pippi Longstocking" and the director of "My Life as a Dog."
1995 88m/C *D:* Lasse Hallstrom; *W:* Astrid Lindgren. **VHS** *ICA*

Children's Heroes of the Bible: Story of Jesus

Preschool-Primary Animated series depicting the lives of famous biblical figures. In this epiosde, the first in a two-part presentation, the actions and teachings of Jesus are chronicled. Additional volumes available.
1986 23m/C VHS, Beta *IGP*

Child's Christmas in Wales

Family Dylan Thomas' prose-poem of Christmas memories in his boyhood village is vividly dramatized in this lyrical, lightly plotted short feature. It doesn't have to be Noel (and you don't need to be Welsh) to savor the sights, sounds and flavors of a traditional British Christmas, circa 1910, recounted by a nice old chap to his grandson.

BEWARE *Alcohol use.*

1988 55m/C Mathonwy Reeves; *D:* Don McBrearty. **VHS, Beta** *LIV, VES, HMV*

A Child's Garden of Verses

Primary Fact-based animated short features the young Robert Louis Stevenson ill and bed-ridden, letting his imagination run free and composing the verses that are now familiar favorites among children.
1992 20m/C VHS *FHE, AMB*

Chip 'n' Dale Animated Antics Series

Preschool-Primary Chip 'n' Dale star with Donald Duck in a compilation of hilarious adventures from the Disney archives. Individual titles: "Chips Ahoy," "The Lone Chipmunks," "Out on a Limb," "Test Pilot Donald," "Three For Breakfast," and "Winter Storage."
1990 7m/C VHS, Beta *MTI, DSN*

Chip 'n' Dale Rescue Rangers: Crimebusters

Family Disney syndicated TV cartoon placing the two chipmunk favorites in a series of wild adventures with their squad of crime-fighting friends. Joining Chip 'n' Dale in this original episode are Zipper the housefly, Monterey Jack (an Australian mouse) and the inventor

Gadget. Together they form the Rescue Rangers. Additional volumes available.

1989 44m/C D: John Kimball, Bob Zamboni. **VHS, Beta** *DIS*

Chipmunk and His Bird Friends

Primary While a chipmunk is storing his winter supply of acorns, a chickadee and a pygmy nuthatch search in vain for insects. Suddenly they discover a feeding shelf which children have filled for them.

1967 10m/C VHS, Beta *BFA*

Chips the War Dog ♪♪

Family Disney made-for-TV movie about the friendship that develops under fire between a young soldier and the title canine during WWII.

1990 90m/C Brandon Douglas, Ned Vaughn, Paxton Whitehead, Ellie Cornell, Robert Miranda, William Devane; **D:** Ed Kaplan. **VHS** *DIS*

Chitty Chitty Bang Bang ♪♪

G/Family Eccentric inventor spruces up an old car and, in fantasy, takes his kids to a land where the evil rulers have forbidden children. Imitation-Disney cast and imitation-Disney charm is okay for a while, but certainly not for over two hours. Poor special effects and so-so musical numbers stall this vehicle. Loosely adapted by Roald Dahl and Hughes from an Ian Fleming story. ♪♪ Chitty Chitty Bang Bang; Hushabye Mountain; Truly Scrumptious; You Two; Toot Sweet; Me Ol' Bam-Boo; Lovely Lonely Man; Posh; The Roses of Success.

1968 142m/C Dick Van Dyke, Sally Ann Howes, Lionel Jeffries, Gert Frobe, Anna Quayle, Benny Hill; **D:** Ken Hughes; **W:** Ken Hughes, Roald Dahl. **VHS, Beta, LV** *FOX, MGM, TLF*

Chocolate Fever

Family Henry's lust for candy lands him in sickbay with a case of "measles" made of pure chocolate. Cartoon entry from the CBS "Storybreak" series, based on the book by Robert Kinnel Smith; nicely animated by Hanna-Barbera's Australian studios.

1985 25m/C VHS *FOX, KUI*

C.H.O.M.P.S. ♪ ♭

G/Family Comedy about a youthful inventor who builds a robot guard dog—the Canine Home Protection System—who performs super feats to save the town from burglars and win the girl for his master. Harmlessly unfunny, with a mechanical mutt that's a deliberate lookalike for B.E.N.J.I.

1979 90m/C Jim Backus, Valerie Bertinelli, Wesley Eure, Conrad Bain, Chuck McCann, Red Buttons; **D:** Don Chaffey. **VHS, Beta** *NO*

Christian the Lion ♪♪ ♭

G/Family Travers and McKenna, the stars of "Born Free," are committed animal-rights activists in real life. They portray themselves in this true story of an exploited zoo lion (shades of "Free Willy") and how two students,

the actors, and "Born Free" subject George Adamson, help send it to Africa to live with wild lions.

1976 87m/C Virginia McKenna, Bill Travers, George Adamson, James Hill; **D:** Bill Travers. **VHS, Beta** *UNI*

A Christmas Carol ♪♪♪

Family MGM version of Dickens' eternal tale of miserly Scrooge, instilled with the Christmas spirit of generosity after an evening with the ghosts of Christmas Past, Present and Future. Owen does a nice turn as Ebenezer, though overall production has a by-the-numbers feel. Unfortunate dialogue: Bob Crachit's line at dinner, "I don't think there's anyone who can touch my buns!"

1938 70m/B Reginald Owen, Gene Lockhart, Terence Kilburn, Leo G. Carroll, Lynne Carver, Ann Rutherford; **D:** Edwin L. Marin. **VHS, Beta, LV** *MGM*

A Christmas Carol ♪♪♪♪

Family If you weigh your "Christmas Carol" by the quality of its Scrooge, then this British retelling wins out over them all. Gaunt, glaring Alastair Sim, who could wither mistletoe with one scowl, portrays the penny-pinching holiday hater who learns appreciation of Christmas following a frightful, revealing evening with supernatural visitors; and he takes Ebenezer credibly from cruelty to contrition. "And God bless Tiny Tim!"

1951 86m/B Alastair Sim, Kathleen Harrison, Jack Warner, Michael Hordern, Patrick Macnee, Mervyn Johns, Hermione Baddeley, Clifford Mollison, George Cole, Carol Marsh, Miles Malleson, Ernest Thesiger, Hattie Jacques, Peter Bull, Hugh Dempster; **W:** Noel Langley; **M:** Richard Addinsell. **VHS, Beta, LV** *MLB, HMV*

A Christmas Carol ♪♪

Preschool Chuck Jones-style cartoon version of Charles Dickens' classic tale. The story of how Ebenezer Scrooge changed from a tyrant to a joyous human being one Christmas Eve.

1984 23m/C D: Chuck Jones. **VHS, Beta** *CHI*

Christmas Cartoons

Preschool-Primary Collection of children's favorite Christmas cartoons including "Rudolph the Red-Nosed Reindeer," "Santa's Surprise," "Christmas Comes But Once a Year," and more.

19?? 60m/C VHS *SIM*

The Christmas Collection

Primary Three-volume set of the best-known stories, folk songs, and hymns associated with the season.

1992 60m/C VHS *SVE, BTV*

Christmas Comes to Willow Creek ♪♪

Family Mutually antagonistic brothers are enlisted to deliver Christmas gifts to an isolated Alaskan community. Can brotherly love be far off? Made-for-TV holiday cheer taking advantage (if that's the word) of the fact that the leads played together in the rowdy series "Dukes of Hazzard."

1987 96m/C John Schneider, Tom Wopat, Hoyt Axton, Zachary Ansley, Kim Delaney; **D:** Richard Lang; **M:** Charles Fox. **VHS, Beta** *LIV, FHE*

Christmas Eve on Sesame Street

Family Particularly outstanding episode of the PBS series, lyrical, funny, and touching; Big Bird and the "Sesame Street" gang go ice skating, Ernie and Bert act out O. Henry's classic "Gift of the Magi," and Oscar the Grouch upsets everybody by posing the puzzle: How does Santa get down those skinny urban chimneys?

1990 60m/C VHS *RAN, MLT*

A Christmas Fantasy

Family Lonely old toymaker and two children take a magical journey on Christmas Eve. Featuring guest appearances by the miming team Shields and Yarnell, plus the music of the Vienna Boys Choir and Toller Cranston.

1989 50m/C VHS, Beta

The Christmas Messenger

Family Brilliantly colored animation in this tale of a young boy who realizes the true meaning of Christmas when joins a group of carolers with a secret identity. TV cartoon special produced in part by the Reader's Digest folks.

1975 25m/C V: Richard Chamberlain. **VHS, Beta** *PYR*

The Christmas Party

Primary The Little Dog and his friend Kitten must confront a greedy alley cat who has stolen Santa's bag of presents. From the "Little Dog" series.

1982 6m/C VHS, Beta *BFA*

Christmas Stories

Preschool-Primary Four animated Christmas stories for kids: "The Clown of God," "Morris's Disappearing Bag," "The Little Drummer Boy," and "The Twelve Days of Christmas." Part of the "Children's Circle" series from Weston Woods.

1986 100m/C VHS, Beta *FCT*

Christmas Stories

Family Four brief stories which highlight sharing and caring in the holiday season. In "Morris's Disappearing Bag" the title character discovers a very unusual Christmas gift. "The Clown of God" has an Italian juggler performing in front of baby Jesus. "Max's Christmas" details a child's curiosity about Santa. "The Little Drummer Boy" is highlighted by music by the St. Paul Choir School.

1992 30m/C VHS *WKV, CCC, BTV*

A Christmas Story

Family Hanna-Barbera Christmas 'toon in which Goober the mutt and Gumdrop the mouse embark on a quest to deliver young Timmy's errant letter to Santa. Yes, it's the same Goober who was recast as a cut-rate Scooby-Doo for the Saturday-morning series "Goober and the Ghost Chasers."

1971 30m/C VHS, Beta *TTC*

A Christmas Story

Family Fat Albert and the gang help new neighbors by giving them a temporary home in their clubhouse, forgetting about mean junkyard owner Tightwad Tyrone. Tyrone has other plans for the clubhouse and is about to demolish it until finally he has a change of heart.

1979 23m/C VHS, Beta, LV *BAR*

A Christmas Story 🎵🎵🎵 ♪

PG/Jr. High-Adult Unlikely but winning comedy centering around a boy's single-minded obsession to acquire a Red Ryder BB-gun for Christmas, woven in with nostalgic little vignettes about his eccentric 1940s family preparing for the holiday. Fun for everyone. Based on an autobiographical story by Jean Shepherd from his book "In God We Trust, All Others Pay Cash."

BEWARE *Glorification of BB guns. Father worships a rather unusual lamp and uses faked obscenities (really very funny).*

1983 95m/C Peter Billingsley, Darren McGavin, Melinda Dillon, Ian Petrella; **D:** Bob (Benjamin) Clark; **W:** Bob (Benjamin) Clark, Leigh Brown, Jean Shepherd. **VHS, Beta, LV** *MGM*

The Christmas That Almost Wasn't 🎵 ♪

G/Jr. High-Adult Scrooge-like Phineas T. Prune decides to destroy Christmas forever by evicting Santa Claus from the North Pole, where his rent payments have fallen behind. Crude Italian-made children's musical film makes one yearn for Ernest. 🎵 The Christmas That Almost Wasn't; Christmas is Coming; Hustle Bustle; I'm Bad; Kids Get All the Breaks; The Name of the Song is Prune; Nothing to do But Wait; Santa Claus; Time For Christmas.

1966 95m/C Rossano Brazzi, Paul Tripp, Lidia Brazzi, Sonny Fox, Mischa Auer; **D:** Rossano Brazzi. **VHS, Beta** *HBO*

A Christmas to Remember 🎵🎵 ♪

G/Family Depression-era Minnesota farmer who has lost his son in WWI is not too happy hosting his city-bred grandson, visiting the farm for the holidays. Gradually they reach an armistice. Somber, occasionally poignant made-for-TV film ornamented by the stars' presence.

1978 96m/C Jason Robards Jr., Eva Marie Saint, Joanne Woodward; **D:** George Englund. **VHS, Beta** *NO*

Dick Van Dyke shows off a new contraption to Sally-Ann Howes in "Chitty Chitty Bang Bang."

The Christmas Toy

Family Kermit the Frog hosts this Muppet tale about Christmas at the Joneses. All the toys in the playroom come alive to enjoy the holiday, even Rugby, a stuffed tiger who decides he wants to be Jamie's special present again. He sets out to find the family Christmas tree and all the gifts beneath it.
1993 50m/C VHS *JHV, BTV*

The Christmas Tree

Family Wordless pantomime story of a fir tree, played by mime Julian Chagrin, that gets cut down to be sold as a Christmas tree.
1975 12m/C Julian Chagrin. **VHS, Beta** *PYR*

The Christmas Tree

Family Yuletide cartoon about children at an orphanage who love a wondrous pine tree on the grounds, but the nasty superintendent plans to cut it down and spoil Christmas. Luckily Santa sides with the children.
1990 49m/C VHS *FHE*

A Christmas Tree/Puss-In-Boots

Preschool-Primary Animated TV double feature from the Rankin-Bass factory: "A Christmas Tree" features two young children who return a stolen Christmas tree from an evil giant. Magical cat helps his master woo a princess in "Puss-In-Boots."
1972 60m/C VHS, Beta *PSM*

Christmas Video Sing-Along

Preschool-Primary Sing along with children's favorite Christmas songs.
1992 30m/C VHS *SMV, MVD*

Christopher Columbus: The Discovery ♪

PG-13/Jr. High-Adult The 500th anniversary of Columbus' voyage was celebrated in this film. Though a less-than-perfect rendition of the story, it does serve as an educational diversion that does not glorify the Spaniards' oppression of the natives they discovered. Older children will appreciate the story of Columbus on-screen, but younger children will not care, nor will they sit through it.

BEWARE *Nudity in the form of bare-breasted native women and action violence. The Spaniards are killed by the revengeful natives and are shown hanging and mutilated.*

1992 120m/C Georges Corraface, Rachel Ward, Tom Selleck, Marlon Brando, Robert Davi, Oliver Cotton, Benicio Del Toro, Catherine Zeta Jones, Matthieu Carriere, Nigel Terry, Branscombe Richmond; **D:** John Glen; **W:** John Briley, Mario Puzo, Cary Bates; **M:** Cliff Eidelman. **VHS, Beta, LV** *WAR*

Christopher's Xmas Mission

Primary-Jr. High Satirical story of a wealthy young boy working in a post office who decides to play Robin Hood and redirect the gifts addressed to rich people to the poor. When the scheme is uncovered, the rich thank him and his parents praise him. Just like real life?

1992 23m/C VHS

Christy 🎵🎵 ♭

Family Pilot movie for the TV series finds 19-year-old Christy Huddleston (Martin) leaving her privileged Southern life to teach school in the Great Smoky Mountains. It's 1912 in Cutter Gap, Tennessee and her students are literally dirt poor, with ignorance and superstition the norm. Christy's inspiration is Miss Alice (Daly), a middle-aged Quaker who runs the mission school. And Christy needs encouragement as she struggles to cope with her new life and responsibilities. Based on the novel by Catherine Marshall, which is a fictional biography of her mother.

1994 90m/C Kellie Martin, Tyne Daly, Tess Harper, Randall Batinkoff, Annabelle Price, Stewart Finlay-McLennan; **D:** Michael Rhodes; **M:** Ron Ramin. **VHS** *GKK*

The Chronicles of Narnia 🎵🎵🎵

Family Multicassette BBC production of the C.S. Lewis fantasy series, spanning the first four of the seven interconnected books. Narnia is a country in parallel world of mythical beasts and talking animals, and a group of English children repeatedly find their way there at the right times to save Narnia from danger throughout its history. These scrupulously faithful adaptations sometimes mix animation jarringly with live-action while trying to bring Lewis' vision to life; to see how well an all-animated version would have worked, see the Bill Melendez production of the first book, "Lion, the Witch and the Wardrobe," also on tape. Titles in this BBC set, part of the "Wonderworks" series, include: "The Lion, the Witch and the Wardrobe," "Prince Caspian/Voyage of the Dawn Treader," and "The Silver Chair."

1989 180m/C Barbara Kellerman, Jeffery Perry, Richard Dempsey, Sophie Cook, Jonathan Scott, Sophie Wilcox, David Thwaites, Tom Baker; **D:** Alex Kirby. **VHS** *FCT, PME, TVC*

Chuck Amuck: The Movie

Family Made-for-video release chronicling the fifty-year career of Warner Brothers animator Chuck Jones, with highlights from his most famous Bugs Bunny/Daffy Duck cartoons.

1991 51m/C Chuck Jones. **VHS** *WAR, FCT*

Cinderella 🎵🎵🎵 ♭

Family Classic Disney animated fairytale about the slighted beauty who outshines her evil stepsisters at a royal ball, then returns to her grim existence before the handsome prince finds her again. Engaging film, with a wicked stepmother, kindly fairy godmother, and singing mice. Songs include: Cinderella; Bibbidy-Bobbidi-Boo; So This is Love; A Dream is a Wish Your Heart Makes; The Work Song; Oh Sing, Sweet Nightingale. 🎵 Cinderella; Bibbidy-Bobbidi-Boo; So This Is Love; A Dream Is a Wish Your Heart Makes; The Work Song; Oh Sing, Sweet Nightingale.

1950 76m/C D: Wilfred Jackson; **V:** Ilene Woods, William Phipps, Verna Felton, James MacDonald. **Award Nominations:** Academy Awards '50: Best Song ("Bibbidy-Bobbidi-Boo"), Best Sound, Best Original Score; **Awards:** Venice Film Festival '50: Special Jury Prize. **VHS, Beta** *DIS, KUI*

Cinderella 🎵🎵

Family Network TV special retelling the classic fairy tale of the girl with the mean stepsisters and the missing glass slipper, accompanied by original musical numbers from Broadway giants Richard Rodgers and Oscar Hammerstein. Without that asset it would be rather pedestrian.

1964 83m/C Lesley Ann Warren, Ginger Rogers, Walter Pidgeon, Stuart Damon, Celeste Holm; **D:** Charles S. Dubin; **M:** Richard Rodgers, Oscar Hammerstein. **VHS, Beta, LV** *FOX, FCT*

Cinderella

Family From "Faerie Tale Theatre" comes the classic tale of a poor girl who goes to a ball to meet the man of her dreams, despite her nasty stepmother and stepsisters. Jennifer Beals and Matthew Broderick are Cindy and the prince. Edie McClurg nearly steals the show as one of the stepsisters. Among the best in the "Faerie Tale Theatre" series. Ages 6 to 12.

1984 60m/C Jennifer Beals, Jean Stapleton, Matthew Broderick, Eve Arden; **D:** Mark Cullingham. **VHS, Beta, LV** *FOX, FCT, HMV*

Cinderella . . . Frozen in Time

Family Ice Capades spectacular starring Dorothy Hamill in the title role, with British pairs skating champ Andrew Naylor as the handsome Prince Charming. Good old-fashioned figure skating; nobody gets kneecapped. All ages.

1994 ?m/C VHS

Cinderfella 🎵🎵 ♭

Family This twist on the classic children's fairy tale features Lewis as the hapless, orphaned buffoon guided by his fairy godfather to win the hand of the fair, singing maiden over his selfish stepbrothers. Somewhat overdone, with extended talking sequences and gratuitous musical interludes. Lewis, though, mugs effectively, and kids will relate.

Cinderella's fairy godmother prepares to weave her magic in "Cinderella."

1960 88m/C Jerry Lewis, Ed Wynn, Judith Anderson, Anna Maria Alberghetti, Henry Silva, Count Basie, Robert Hutton; **D:** Frank Tashlin; **W:** Frank Tashlin. **VHS, Beta** *LIV*

Cindy Eller

Family ABC Afterschool Special does a cute job of modernizing the fairy tale of Cinderella, here a wallflower named Cindy who finally gets to meet the handsome "Greg Prince" thanks to her fairy godmother, a magical bag lady. In keeping with the political correctness, Cindy's stepmother is perfectly kind and understanding.

1991 44m/C Pearl Bailey, Jennifer Grey, Kyra Sedgwick, Melanie Mayron, Kelly Wolf; **D:** Lee Grant. **VHS** *VTR*

Cinema Paradiso 🎵🎵🎵

College-Adult Salvatore, a fatherless little boy in postwar Italy, spends all his time at his small village's movie palace, where Alfredo the projectionist is a surrogate papa. Salvatore becomes an apprentice projectionist himself, but Alfredo doesn't want the boy following in his lowly footsteps and urges Salvatore to leave and seek his fortune elsewhere. Story unreels in flashbacks as the adult Salvatore, a famous movie director, returns to his roots; it's partly an autobiographical effort by Tornatore, who captures both the sweep of the times and the poignancy of the central father-son relationship. Original

Italian version runs even longer, however, and calls into question whether Alfredo's actions enriched the boy's later life—or ruined it.

> 🚨 BEWARE 🚨 *Sex, alcohol use, brief nudity (in old movie clips), and profanity.*

1988 123m/C Philippe Noiret, Jacques Perrin, Salvatore Cascio, Marco Leonardi, Agnes Nano, Leopoldo Trieste; **D:** Giuseppe Tornatore; **W:** Giuseppe Tornatore; **M:** Ennio Morricone. **VHS, LV, 8mm** *HBO, APD, INJ*

Circle of Friends 🎵🎵 ♭

PG-13/Jr. High-Adult Three college women cope with romance, raging hormones and their strict Catholic upbringing in 1957 Ireland. Small-town teenager Benny (Driver), slightly overweight and awkward, falls for cute Jack Foley (O'Donnell) and wonders what sex is like. Nan (Burrows) pursues a rich young man, while Eve (O'Rawe) has plans of her own. Charming coming-of-age tale adapted from Maeve Binchy's novel.

> 🚨 BEWARE 🚨 *An attempted rape, some heavy petting, and a quick glimpse of a naked man from behind. A lot of blood is spilled when a character is accidently cut by a glass window.*

1994 96m/C Chris O'Donnell, Minnie Driver, Geraldine O'Rawe, Saffron Burrows, Colin Firth, Alan Cummings, Aidan Gillen; *D:* Pat O'Connor; *W:* Andrew Davies; *M:* Michael Kamen. **VHS** *HBO*

Circus Angel 🦴🦴🦴

Family Glorious, all-ages delight from French director Lamorisse, creator of "The Red Balloon." Petty thief hides in a circus where the ringmaster uses the fugitive in experiments to create a "birdman" act. With wings sewn in his back, the rogue learns to fly, and in a nightdress he looks positively angelic. Fluttering around the land, 'Fifi la Plume' (pic's original title) convinces folks he's indeed a heavenly visitor and performs dubious good deeds—like making a robber gang 'repent' and turn their loot over to him! It's all to win the love of a beautiful trapeze girl, and the hero has a hilarious fight with his romantic rival, the lion tamer, in which all weapons are ornamental clocks. A genuine treasure, long unseen in the US, a rewarding discovery on video. English-language dubbing is awkward, but much of the story needs no dialogue anyway.

⚠️ BEWARE *Slapstick roughhousing.*

1965 80m/B Philippe Avron, Mirielle Negre; *D:* Albert Lamorisse. **VHS, Beta** *NLC*

Citizen Kane 🦴🦴🦴🦴

Jr. High-Adult Extraordinary American tragedy of a newspaper tycoon (based loosely on William Randolph Hearst) from his humble beginnings to the solitude of his final years. Widely regarded as one of the greatest films ever made—a stunning tour-de-force in virtually every aspect, from the fragmented narration to breathtaking, deep-focus cinematography; from a vivid soundtrack to fabulous ensemble acting. Wonderkid Welles was only 25 when he co-wrote, directed, and starred. Three-disc laser edition was reproduced from a superior negative and features liner notes and running commentary from film historian Robert J. Carringer. Watch for Ladd and O'Connell as reporters.

1941 119m/B Orson Welles, Joseph Cotten, Everett Sloane, Dorothy Comingore, Ruth Warrick, George Couvlouris, Ray Collins, William Alland, Paul Stewart, Erskine Sanford, Agnes Moorehead, Alan Ladd, Gus Schilling, Philip Van Zandt, Harry Shannon, Sonny Bupp, Arthur O'Connell; *D:* Orson Welles; *W:* Orson Welles, Herman J. Mankiewicz; *M:* Bernard Herrmann. **Award Nominations:** Academy Awards '41: Best Actor (Welles), Best Black and White Cinematography, Best Director (Welles), Best Film Editing, Best Interior Decoration, Best Picture, Best Sound, Best Original Score; **Awards:** Academy Awards '41: Best Original Screenplay; National Board of Review Awards '41: 10 Best Films of the Year; New York Film Critics Awards '41: Best Film. **VHS, Beta, LV, 8mm** *CRC, FCT, TTC*

Citizens Band 🦴🦴🦴

PG/Jr. High-Adult Episodic, low-key comedy about people united by their CB use in a midwestern community. Notable performance from Clark as a soft-voiced guide for truckers passing through. Demme's first comedy is characteristically idiosyncratic.

1977 98m/C Paul LeMat, Candy Clark, Ann Wedgeworth, Roberts Blossom, Charles Napier, Marcia Rodd, Bruce McGill, Ed Begley Jr.,

Meet the Star of *Circle of Friends,* Minnie Driver

To get her break in film, Minnie Driver had to put on 25 pounds and stand in a ditch. The lithe, 5-foot-10 young British actress wanted so badly to be in *Circle of Friends* that she was willing to put on 20 pounds and go underground to play Benny Hogan, a dumpy Irish coed whose personality captures the heart of Chris O'Donnell. "I begged them to put the guy on a box, but no . . . they dug me a ditch every time," said Driver. "You try doing a love scene from a ditch. I felt like the biggest toad on earth."

For an actress trying to make a name for herself in America, playing dowdy was a risk. "When a man puts on weight for a part, he's called a great actor," Driver said. "When a woman puts on weight for a part, she's called fat." Not to worry. In her next role, in *Goldeneye,* Driver played a seductive Russian country-western singer.

Born in Barbados and raised in London, Driver is the daughter of a financier and an interior designer and one of five children. She had her own series on British TV and small parts on American TV before landing in *Circle of Friends.* She was in a rock band for awhile and she still writes music and plays guitar.

Alix Elias; *D:* Jonathan Demme; *W:* Paul Brickman; *M:* Bill Conti. **VHS, Beta** *PAR*

City Boy 🦴🦴

Family At the turn of the century, orphaned Nick goes from Chicago to the Pacific Northwest, takes a job guarding an old-growth forest, and is torn between the ideals of two new friends. Tom sees the forest as timber that will build homes and provide jobs, while Angelica sees the forest as an irreplaceable sanctuary. This adaptation of "Freckles" by Gene Stratton Porter is a sequel to "The

Minnie Driver speaks frankly to Chris O'Donnell in "Circle of Friends."

Girl of the Limberlost"; both done for the PBS collection "WonderWorks."

1993 120m/B Christian Campbell, James Brolin, Sarah Chalke, Wendel Meldrum, Christopher Bolton; **D:** John Kent Harrison; **W:** John Kent Harrison. **VHS** *PME, BTV, HMV*

City Lights ♪♪♪♪

Family Masterpiece that was Chaplin's last silent film is an eloquent and graceful romance, keenly balancing comedy and tragedy. The "Little Tramp" falls in love with a blind flower seller. A series of lucky accidents permits him to get the money she needs for a sight-restoring surgery.

1931 86m/B Charlie Chaplin, Virginia Cherrill, Florence Lee, Hank Mann, Harry Myers, Henry Bergman, Jean Harlow; **D:** Charlie Chaplin. **VHS, Beta, LV** *FOX*

City Slickers ♪♪♪

PG-13/Jr. High-Adult Box-office winner about three men with mid-life crises who leave NYC for a cattle-ranch vacation that turns into an arduous, sometimes dangerous character-building stint. Many hilarious (and some emotional) moments supplied by leads, but Palance steals the cattle drive as a crusty, wise cowpoke. Cuteness factor is provided by a newborn calf named Norman; on the other hand, black and female characters are tokens with nearly nothing to do. Followed by a sequel.

BEWARE! *Violence followed by rare cinematic regret: milquetoast Stern gets out of a scrape by pulling a gun, and breaks down about it afterwards. Salty language, sex talk.*

1991 114m/C Billy Crystal, Daniel Stern, Bruno Kirby, Patricia Wettig, Helen Slater, Jack Palance, Noble Willingham, Tracey Walter, Josh Mostel, David Paymer, Bill Henderson, Jeffrey Tambor, Phill Lewis, Kyle Secor, Yeardley Smith, Jayne Meadows; **D:** Ron Underwood; **W:** Lowell Ganz, Babaloo Mandel; **M:** Marc Shaiman. **VHS, Beta, LV, 8mm** *COL, NLC*

City Slickers 2: The Legend of Curly's Gold ♪♪ ♪

PG-13/Jr. High-Adult Mid-life crisis meets the wild west, part deux. Crystal and his fellow urban dudes discover a treasure map in the hat of departed trail boss Curly and decide to go a-huntin'. Palance is back as Curly's evil twin. Lovitz occupies the screen as Crystal's ne'er-do-well brother, replacing sidekick Bruno Kirby. A bit of a rehash, formulaic and occasionally straining for a punchline, it's still pretty darn funny, especially when the boys start to improvise.

BEWARE *Evil old cowpoke profanity and sex talk.*

1994 116m/C Billy Crystal, Daniel Stern, Jon Lovitz, Jack Palance, Patricia Wettig, Pruitt Taylor Vince, Bill McKinney, Lindsay Crystal, Noble Willingham, David Paymer, Josh Mostel; *D:* Paul Weiland; *W:* Billy Crystal, Lowell Ganz, Babaloo Mandel; *M:* Marc Shaiman. **VHS** *NYR*

Clara's Heart ♂

PG-13/Jr. High-Adult Jamaican maid enriches the lives of her insufferable, bourgeois employers and their particularly repellent son. Kinder, gentler waste of film proves that Goldberg continues to be better than her material. Sentimental clap-trap occasionally lapses into comedy. Young children may appreciate the simplistic message.

BEWARE *Profanity.*

1988 108m/C Whoopi Goldberg, Michael Ontkean, Kathleen Quinlan, Neil Patrick Harris, Spalding Gray, Beverly Todd, Hattie Winston; *D:* Robert Mulligan; *W:* Mark Medoff; *M:* Dave Grusin. **VHS, Beta, LV** *WAR, FCT*

Clarence ♂♂

G/Family "When you hear a bell, TV does a se-quel." But it can't make them as memorable; this would-be decades-late followup to "It's a Wonderful Life" finds Clarence the benevolent angel back on the job, risking his wings for a beautiful young woman. Made for cable.

1991 92m/C Robert Carradine, Kate Trotter; *D:* Eric Till. **VHS** *REP*

Clarence, the Cross-eyed Lion ♂♂

Family Widowed veterinarian and his critter-loving daughter work in the African bush, minister to the title feline and fight marauding poachers. Lighthearted, loosely plotted theatrical release from the creators of "Flipper" looks more like strung-together TV episodes. No wonder—it was the inspiration for the program "Daktari."

BEWARE *Violence, alcohol use.*

1965 98m/C Marshall Thompson, Betsy Drake, Richard Haydn, Cheryl Miller, Rockne Tarkington, Maurice Marsac; *D:* Andrew Marton. **VHS** *MGM, FCT*

Clash of the Titans ♂♂

PG/Primary-Adult Epic stew of Greek legends about heroic Perseus, who does mighty deeds to win a kingdom and the love of a princess, with the gods of Mt. Olympus observing and meddling. Deliberately, almost stubbornly old-fashioned adventure stuff, with plenty of slow stretches despite such creatures as the snake-haired Medusa, winged horse Pegasus and the sea monster Kraken. Ray Harryhausen's stop-motion visuals vary surprisingly in quality, sometimes good, sometimes wretched.

BEWARE *Violence, but the PG rating—rare in a Harryhausen fantasy—derives from brief nudity, sex talk.*

1981 118m/C Laurence Olivier, Maggie Smith, Claire Bloom, Ursula Andress, Burgess Meredith, Harry Hamlin, Sian Phillips, Judi Bowker; *D:* Desmond Davis; *W:* Beverley Cross. **VHS, Beta, LV** *MGM, MLB*

Class Act ♂♂ ♪

PG-13/Jr. High-Adult Rappers Kid 'N' Play team up once again in this role reversal comedy. A straight-laced brain and a partying, macho bully find their school records and identifications switched when they enroll in a new high school. This turns out to be good for the character of both young men, as the egghead learns to loosen up and the bully learns what it feels like to be respected for his ideas rather than a fierce reputation. Comedy is very uneven but the duo are energetic and likable.

BEWARE *High school profanity and sex talk.*

1991 98m/C Christopher Reid, Christopher Martin, Meshach Taylor, Karyn Parsons, Doug E. Doug, Rick Ducommun, Lamont Jackson, Rhea Perlman; *D:* Randall Miller; *M:* Vassal Benford. **VHS, LV** *WAR*

The Classic Tales Collection

Family Well-known works of literature are presented in animated form. See individual listings for details; titles include "Alice in Wonderland," "Around the World in 80 Days," "Black Beauty," "The Canterville Ghost," "Hiawatha," "Peter Pan," "The Prisoner of Zenda," "A Tale of Two Cities," "Treasure Island," and "The Wind in the Willows."

1988 51m/C VHS *FHE*

Clean Slate ♂♂

PG-13/Jr. High-Adult Private-eye Maurice Pogue (Carvey) sustains injuries that cause a rare type of amnesia making every day seem like the first day of his life. As the only witness to a crime, he bumbles through mix-ups with the mob and his job as a bodyguard. Lightweight comedy fare is good for a few yuks but doesn't work as well as the similar "Groundhog Day." Barkley the sight-impaired dog steals nearly every scene he's in; but then, he's a show-biz vet, having appeared in two "Ernest" adventures—knowwhatImean?.

BEWARE *Profanity, theft (the chief plot device is stolen from "Groundhog Day").*

1994 106m/C Dana Carvey, Valeria Golino, James Earl Jones, Kevin Pollak, Michael Murphy, Michael Gambon, Jayne Brook, Vyto Ruginis, Olivia D'Abo; *D:* Mick Jackson; *W:* Robert King; *M:* Alan Silvestri. **VHS, Beta, LV** *MGM*

Clear and Present Danger ♂♂

PG-13/Sr. High-Adult Ford returns as CIA agent Jack Ryan ("Patriot Games") in another Tom Clancy adventure. Here, Ryan discovers a link between a South American drug cartel and a Presidential advisor. Archer's back as Ryan's wife, and Birch and Jones also return. Complex plot becomes tedious, though. The clearest danger is to the audience's attention span.

BEWARE *Language and intense action and violence in the form of explosions and shootings.*

1994 141m/C Harrison Ford, Anne Archer, James Earl Jones, Willem Dafoe, Thora Birch, Henry Czerny, Harris Yulin, Raymond Cruz, Joaquim de Almeida, Miguel Sandoval, Donald Moffat, Theodore (Ted) Raimi; **D:** Phillip Noyce; **W:** Steven Zaillian, Donald Stewart, John Milius. **Award Nominations:** Academy Awards '94: Best Sound; MTV Movie Awards '95: Best Action Sequence; **Awards:** Blockbuster Entertainment Awards '95: Action Actor, Theatrical (Ford). **VHS, Beta** *PAR*

Clerks 🦴🦴🦴

R/College-Adult "What kind of convenience store do you run here?" Day in the life of a convenience store clerk is a lesson in the profane from first time writer/director Smith (who has a cameo as Silent Bob). Twenty-two-year-old Dante Hicks (O'Halloran) is a disaffected New Jersey Quick Stop employee who spends most of his time bored and dealing with borderline crazies. The next-door video store is clerked by his best friend Randal (Anderson), who derives equal delight from tormenting his customers and debating absolutely anything (especially anything sexual). Unless your teen is unusually mature, this movie is not family fare.

BEWARE *Most parents will blush at the explicit sex-related dialogue. The language and lingo walks hand-in-hand with the sex talk, using four-letter words like they were going out of style. Parents, beware when your teen asks to rent this one.*

1994 91m/B Brian O'Halloran, Jeff Anderson, Marilyn Ghigliotti, Lisa Spoonhauer, Jason Mewes; **Cameos:** Kevin Smith; **D:** Kevin Smith; **W:** Kevin Smith; **M:** Scott Angley. **Award Nominations:** Independent Spirit Awards '95: Best First Feature, Debut Performance (Anderson), First Screenplay; **Awards:** Sundance Film Festival '94: Filmmakers Trophy. **VHS, LV** *MAX*

The Client 🦴🦴 🦴

PG-13/Jr. High-Adult Another legal thriller from the Grisham factory. Sarandon is the troubled attorney hired by an 11-year-old boy who witnessed the suicide of a Mafia attorney and now knows more than he should. Jones is the ambitious federal prosecutor who's willing to risk the boy's life in exchange for career advancement. Lacks the mega-big Hollywood names of "The Firm" and "The Pelican Brief" but gains solid acting in return. No frills, near-faithful adaptation by Schumacher basically travels down the path of least resistance. Filmed on location in Memphis.

BEWARE *Profanity, alcohol use, a child is traumatized by seeing a suicide, his older brother is terrorized by mobsters.*

1994 120m/C Susan Sarandon, Tommy Lee Jones, Brad Renfro, Mary-Louise Parker, Anthony LaPaglia, Bradley Whitford, Anthony Edwards, Ossie Davis, Walter Olkewicz, J.T. Walsh, Will Patton, Anthony Heald; **D:** Joel Schumacher; **W:** Robert Getchell, Akiva Goldsman. **VHS**

Clifford WOOF!

PG/Family Short plays a 10-year-old in an effort delayed by Orion's financial crisis. Creepy little Clifford's uncle Martin (Grodin) rues the day he volunteered to babysit his nephew to prove to his girlfriend (Steenburgen) how much he likes kids. Clifford terrorizes Grodin in surprisingly nasty ways when their plans for visiting Dinosaurworld fall through, although Grodin sees to well-deserved revenge. Not just bad in the conventional sense, but bad in a bizarre sort of alien fashion that raises questions about who was controlling the bodies of the producers. To create the effect of Short really being short, other actors stood on boxes and sets were built slightly larger.

BEWARE *Profanity, comic violence. Clarence is a little monster and Grodin's character pays him back in a rather scary way.*

1992 90m/C Martin Short, Charles Grodin, Mary Steenburgen, Dabney Coleman, Sonia Jackson; **D:** Paul Flaherty; **W:** Bobby Von Hayes, Jay Dee Rock, Steven Kampmann; **M:** Richard Gibbs. **VHS, LV** *ORI*

Clifford's Fun with Numbers

Preschool-Primary That lovable red hound is back to entertain the kids and teach them about the numeric system in this fully animated instructional video. A workbook is part of the video package. Additional volumes available.

1988 30m/C VHS *FHE, FCT*

Clifford's Singalong Adventure

Preschool-Primary Made for video cartoon/live action film for children, leading them through 17 songs. A few of the many favorites included are, "Row, Row, Row Your Boat" and the ever-classic "Old McDonald."

1986 30m/C VHS, Beta *WAR*

Clipped Wings 🦴🦴 🦴

Family The Bowery Boys are at their best as they inadvertently join the army while visiting a friend and, in the process of their usual bumblings, uncover a Nazi plot.

1953 62m/B Leo Gorcey, Huntz Hall, Bernard Gorcey, David Condon, Bennie Bartlett, June Vincent, Mary Treen, Philip Van Zandt, Elaine Riley, Jeanne Dean, Lyle Talbot; **D:** Edward L. Bernds. **VHS** *WAR*

Cloak & Dagger 🦴🦴 🦴

PG/Family Thomas followed his starring role in "E.T." with this trifle about little David, a video-game fan who can't convince adults he's stumbled on a very real (and deadly) spy ring. Running for his life, the boy gets survival tips from his imaginary pal, a super-cool commando who's a lookalike for David's own joyless dad. Done like a mid-'70s Disney flick—no great compliment—with violence upped a notch.

BEWARE *Spy-like violence, including some shooting and stabbing.*

1984 101m/C Dabney Coleman, Henry Thomas, Michael Murphy, John McIntire, Jeanette Nolan; **D:** Richard Franklin; **W:** Tom Holland. **VHS, Beta, LV** *MCA*

Close Encounters of the Third Kind 🎵🎵🎵🎵

PG/Family Ordinary Americans are swept up in awesome, sometimes frightening phenomena—the result of benevolent aliens trying to contact earthlings. A forerunner to E.T., this Spielberg epic is a stirring achievement, studded with classic sequences, especially a subplot of a tiny boy the visitors want to abduct; he coos with delight as his mother cringes in uncomprehending terror. An exhilarating experience of majestic f/x and uplifting (literally!) themes. Laserdisc includes formerly edited scenes, live interviews with Spielberg and visual wizard Douglas Trumbull and publicity materials.

BEWARE *Very large spacecraft may frighten small children. Kids may be inspired to sculpt Devil's Tower with their mashed potatoes.*

1977 152m/C Richard Dreyfuss, Teri Garr, Melinda Dillon, Francois Truffaut, Bob Balaban, Cary Guffey; **D:** Steven Spielberg; **W:** Steven Spielberg; **M:** John Williams. **Award Nominations:** Academy Awards '77: Best Art Direction/Set Decoration, Best Director (Spielberg), Best Film Editing, Best Sound, Best Supporting Actress (Dillon), Best Original Score; **Awards:** Academy Awards '77: Best Cinematography, Best Sound Effects Editing; National Board of Review Awards '77: 10 Best Films of the Year. **VHS, Beta, LV** *COL, CRC, FUS*

Clowning Around 🎵🎵 🎵

Family Simon, who has lived in foster homes all his life, dreams of becoming a famous circus clown. When he's sent to a new home, his foster parents think his idea is silly, so he runs away and joins the circus. Part of the "Wonderworks" series.

1992 165m/C Clayton Williamson, Jean-Michel Dagory, Ernie Dingo. **VHS** *PME, HMV, BTV*

Clowning Around 2 🎵🎵 🎵

Family Continuing story of Sim, whose dream is to become a world-famous clown. Now a member of the Winter Circus in Paris, he is still training with his mentor Anatole. But Sim is dissatisfied and follows another greasepaint cohort Eve to her home in Montreal, then returns to his home in Australia where a surprise is in store.

1993 120m/C Clayton Williamson, Jean-Michel Dagory, Ernie Dingo, Frederique Fouche; **D:** George Whaley. **VHS** *PME, BTV*

Club Connect: Me and My Folks

Jr. High-College Episode of the PBS teen magazine show deals with young adults and their families. Interviews with rap groups Salt N Papa and Kriss Kross (yes, rappers have parents), and a story of a family who survived the Los Angeles earthquake. In another segment, a father and daughter compare growing up in the '50's and the '90's. Fast pacing will appeal to teens, but probably won't lead to meaningful discussion. Ages 12 and up.

1994 30m/C VHS *PBS*

Club Connect: The Hip-Hop Alternative 🎵🎵 🎵

Jr. High-College Episode of the PBS teen magazine show dealing with multiculturalism, individuality, and respect for others. Informal interviews with teens and designers, artists, and performers celebrate the hip-hop subculture and tolerance for different forms of expression. Ages 12 and up.

1994 30m/C VHS *PBS*

Club Med 🎵🎵

PG/Family An insecure comedian and his goofy friend try to make the most of a ski vacation. Perhaps your only chance to see Thicke, Killy, and Coolidge together.

1983 60m/C Alan Thicke, Jim Carrey, Jean-Claude Killy, Rita Coolidge, Ronnie Hawkins; **D:** David Mitchell, Bob Giraldi; **M:** Peter Bernstein. **VHS, Beta** *AHV*

Club Paradise 🎵🎵 🎵

PG-13/Jr. High-Adult Chicago fireman flees the big city for a faltering tropical resort and tries to develop some night life. Somewhat disappointing with Williams largely playing the straight man. Most laughs provided by Martin, particularly when she is assaulted by a shower, and Moranis, who gets lost while windsurfing.

BEWARE *Profanity and drug talk. You may need to explain what a coup is.*

1986 96m/C Robin Williams, Peter O'Toole, Rick Moranis, Andrea Martin, Jimmy Cliff, Brian Doyle-Murray, Twiggy, Eugene Levy, Adolph Caesar, Joanna Cassidy, Mary Gross, Carey Lowell, Robin Duke, Simon Jones; **D:** Harold Ramis; **W:** Harold Ramis, Brian Doyle-Murray; **M:** David Mansfield, Van Dyke Parks. **VHS, Beta, LV** *WAR*

Clue 🎵🎵

PG/Jr. High-Adult Enduring board game takes to the screen as characters must unravel a night of murder at a spooky Victorian mansion. Seemingly clueless as to how to overcome an uneven script, the cast resorts to wild eyes and frantic movements. Butler Curry best survives the evening, while Warren is appealing as well. Theatrical version played with three alternative endings, and the video version shows all three successively.

1985 96m/C Lesley Ann Warren, Tim Curry, Martin Mull, Madeline Kahn, Michael McKean, Christopher Lloyd, Eileen Brennan, Howard Hesseman, Lee Ving, Jane Wiedlin, Colleen Camp, Bill Henderson; **D:** Jonathan Lynn; **W:** Jonathan Lynn, John Landis; **M:** John Morris. **VHS, Beta, LV** *PAR*

Clue You In: The Case of the Mad Movie Mustacher

Primary-Jr. High Fran and Nick are two 13-year-olds who enter a movie screen to help the celluloid detective solve his case. Similarity to "The Last Action Hero" is purely coincidental. Additional volumes available.
19?? 28m/C VHS *CFV*

Clueless 🦴🦴🦴

PG-13/Jr. High-Adult Silverstone is adorable as pampered but kindhearted L.A. teen Cher whose vocabulary isn't really limited to "as if" and "what-EVER," although it seems that way. It's Cher's mission in life to make things better for those she knows, mostly by making them over. She takes under her wing a seemingly clueless newcomer to her high school and plays matchmaker to a couple of lonely teachers. All the while, Cher and her best friend, Dionne (they were both named after singers who now do infomercials), shop till they drop and talk about losing their virginity (which neither of them does). Loosely based on Jane Austen's "Emma."

BEWARE *Besides the usual sex related dialogue (the term "boinkfest"), teens use alcohol and marijuana at a party; kids may miss the satiric take on materialism and just envy the clothes and cars.*
1995 113m/C Alicia Silverstone, Stacey Dash, Paul Rudd, Brittany Murphy, Donald A. Faison, Julie Brown, Jeremy Sisto, Dan Hedaya, Wallace Shawn, Breckin Meyer, Elisa Donovan, Aida Linares; **D:** Amy Heckerling; **W:** Amy Heckerling; **C:** Bill Pope; **M:** David Kitay. **Award Nominations:** Writers Guild of America '95: Best Original Screenplay; **Awards:** National Society of Film Critics Awards '95: Best Screenplay. **VHS** *PAR*

The Clutching Hand 🦴🦴

Family The Clutching Hand seeks a formula that will turn metal into gold and detective Craig Kennedy is out to prevent him from doing so. Serial in 15 chapters on 3 cassettes.
1936 268m/B Jack Mulhall, Rex Lease. **VHS, Beta** *SNC, NOS, VDM*

C.L.U.T.Z.

Family Charming tale about a futuristic family with a slightly outdated robot. Meet George Jetson? No, it's part of the CBS/Storybreak TV specials hosted by Captain Kangaroo, Bob Keeshan.
1985 25m/C VHS *FOX, KUI*

Coach 🦴⸰

PG/Sr. High-Adult Sexy woman is unintentionally hired to coach a high school basketball team. Despite obvious temptations, her savvy and teamwork mold rookies into young champions. Low-grade roundball fever.

BEWARE *Salty language, sex.*
1978 100m/C Cathy Lee Crosby, Michael Biehn, Keenan Wynn, Sidney Wicks; **D:** Bud Townsend. **VHS, Beta** *MED*

Coal Miner's Daughter 🦴🦴🦴⸰

PG/Jr. High-Adult A strong bio of country singer Loretta Lynn, who rose from Appalachian poverty to Nashville riches. Spacek is perfect in the lead, and she even provides acceptable rendering of Lynn's tunes. Band drummer Helm shines as Lynn's father, and Jones is strong as Lynn's downhome husband. Uneven melodrama toward the end, but the film is still a good one.
🎵 Coal Miner's Daughter; Sweet Dreams of You; I'm a Honky-Tonk Girl; You're Lookin' at Country; One's On the Way; You Ain't Woman Enough to Take My Man; Back in My Baby's Arms.
1980 125m/C Sissy Spacek, Tommy Lee Jones, Levon Helm, Beverly D'Angelo; **D:** Michael Apted. **Award Nominations:** Academy Awards '80: Best Adapted Screenplay, Best Art Direction/Set Decoration, Best Cinematography, Best Film Editing, Best Picture; **Awards:** Academy Awards '80: Best Actress (Spacek); Golden Globe Awards '81: Best Actress—Musical/Comedy (Spacek), Best Film—Musical/Comedy; Los Angeles Film Critics Association Awards '80: Best Actress (Spacek); National Board of Review Awards '80: 10 Best Films of the Year, Best Actress (Spacek); National Society of Film Critics Awards '80: Best Actress (Spacek). **VHS, Beta, LV** *MCA, BTV*

The Cocoanuts 🦴🦴⸰

Family The Marx Brothers' first movie, an adaptation of the Broadway show that made them stars, with Groucho as a hotel manager in Florida trying to get rich through a real-estate deal. Technically crude early-sound film, hardly more than radio with pictures; most all the humor is dialogue. But with the Marx Brothers in their prime, the verbal gymnastics are still funnier than most any other picture from the era.
1929 96m/B Groucho Marx, Chico Marx, Harpo Marx, Zeppo Marx, Margaret Dumont, Kay Francis, Oscar Shaw, Mary Eaton; **D:** Robert Florey, Joseph Santley; **W:** George S. Kaufman, Morrie Ryskind; **M:** Irving Berlin. **VHS, Beta, LV** *MCA*

Cocoon 🦴🦴🦴

PG-13/Jr. High-Adult Sci-fi fantasy in which Florida senior citizens discover a watery nest of ancient, dormant aliens that serves effectively as the Fountain of Youth, restoring their health (and sexual virility). Warm-hearted and humane, even if the f/x-crammed finale rips off "Close Encounters of the Third Kind" in every way. Youngsters may want to watch it for the luminous E.T.s, but will also be charmed by elderly performers Ameche, Brimley, Gilford, Cronyn, and Tandy.

BEWARE *Sex talk, and an instance of alien-human lovemaking (with moans and glowing lights but apparently no touching). Salty language.*
1985 117m/C Wilford Brimley, Brian Dennehy, Steve Guttenberg, Don Ameche, Tahnee Welch, Jack Gilford, Hume Cronyn, Jessica Tandy, Gwen Verdon, Maureen Stapleton, Tyrone Power Jr., Barret Oliver, Linda Harrison, Herta Ware, Clint Howard; **D:** Ron Howard; **W:** Tom Benedek; **M:** James Horner. **VHS, Beta, LV** *FOX, FCT, BTV*

Cocoon: The Return 🦴

PG/Jr. High-Adult "Cocoon": The Rerun, as old timers who left with aliens revisit Earth and basically go through the same stuff all over again. Filmmakers desperately

push familiar emotional buttons in search of the fragile magic of the first film. You may find yourself fast-forwarding to the special f/x, or away from the schmaltz.

BEWARE *Sex talk, profanity, and alcohol use (but rather mild since most of the characters are over 60).*

1988 116m/C Don Ameche, Wilford Brimley, Steve Guttenberg, Maureen Stapleton, Hume Cronyn, Jessica Tandy, Gwen Verdon, Jack Gilford, Tahnee Welch, Courteney Cox, Brian Dennehy, Barret Oliver; *D:* Daniel Petrie; *M:* James Horner. **VHS, Beta, LV** *FOX*

Cold River 🎬🎬 ⌐

PG/Family Experienced guide takes his two children on an extended trip through the Adirondacks. For the children, it's a fantasy vacation—until their father succumbs to a heart attack and the boy and girl must fend for themselves in the chilly mountains. More hard-edged than the typical wilderness-family fare.

BEWARE *Profanity, youngsters in peril. Father has a heart attack.*

1981 94m/C Pat Petersen, Richard Jaeckel, Suzanne Weber; *D:* Fred G. Sullivan. **VHS, Beta** *FOX*

Collision Course 🎬🎬

PG/Family Wise-cracking cop from Detroit teams up with Japan's best detective to nail a ruthless gang leader. Release was delayed until 1992 due to a lawsuit, but it was resolved in time to coordinate the release with Leno's debut as the host of "The Tonight Show." Of marginal interest, though Leno fans may appreciate. Filmed on location in Motown.

1989 99m/C Noriyuki "Pat" Morita, Jay Leno, Chris Sarandon, Al Waxman. **VHS, Beta, LV** *HBO*

Colorforms Learn 'n Play VCR Adventures

Preschool-Primary Colorforms presents a program designed around the popular children's toy to teach vocabulary, problem solving skills and encourage creative thinking. Puppets and original music add to the Colorforms motif. Four volumes in the series, including "Journey to the Magic Jungle," "Voyage to Mermaid Island," "Blast Off to the Hidden Planet" and "Rescue at Glitter Palace."

1986 30m/C VHS, Beta *WAR*

Comeback Kid 🎬🎬

Family An ex-big league baseball player is conned into coaching an urban team of smarmy street youths, and falls for their playground supervisor. Made for TV.

1980 97m/C John Ritter, Susan Dey; *D:* Peter Levin. **VHS, Beta** *NLC*

Comfort and Joy 🎬🎬🎬 ⌐

PG/Sr. High-Adult After his kleptomaniac girlfriend deserts him, a Scottish disc jockey is forced to reevaluate his life. He becomes involved in an underworld battle between two mob-owned local ice cream companies. Another odd comedy gem from Forsyth, who did "Gregory's

Girl" and "Local Hero". Music by Dire Straits guitarist Knopfler.

1984 93m/C Bill Paterson, Eleanor David, C.P. Grogan, Alex Norton, Patrick Malahide, Rikki Fulton, Roberto Berrardi; *D:* Bill Forsyth; *M:* Mark Knopfler. **VHS, Beta** *MCA*

Comic Book Kids 🎬 ⌐

G/Family Two youngsters enjoy visiting their friend's comic strip studio, since they have the power to project themselves into the cartoon stories. It wasn't an outstanding premise in the blockbuster "Last Action Hero" and it isn't too impressive in this obscure production.

1982 90m/C Joseph Campanella, Mike Darnell, Robyn Finn, Jim Engelhardt, Fay De Witt. **VHS, Beta** *GEM*

The Commitments 🎬🎬🎬

R/Sr. High-Adult Convinced that they can bring soul music to Dublin, a group of working-class youth form a band. High-energy production paints an interesting, unromanticized picture of modern Ireland and refuses to follow standard showbiz cliches, even though its lack of resolution hurts. Honest, whimsical dialog laced with poetic obscenities, delivered by a cast of mostly unknowns. Very successful soundtrack features the music of Wilson Pickett, James Brown, Otis Redding, Aretha Franklin, Percy Sledge, and others, and received a Grammy nomination. Based on the book "The Commitments" by Roddy Doyle, part of a trilogy which includes "The Snapper" (also out on video) and "The Van."

BEWARE *Irish profanity.*

1991 116m/C Andrew Strong, Bronagh Gallagher, Glen Hansard, Michael Aberne, Dick Massey, Ken McCluskey, Robert Arkins, Dave Finnegan, Johnny Murphy, Angeline Ball, Felim Gormley, Maria Doyle, Colm Meaney; *D:* Alan Parker; *W:* Dick Clement, Ian LaFrenais. **Award Nominations:** Academy Awards '91: Best Film Editing; **Awards:** British Academy Awards '92: Best Director (Parker), Best Film. **VHS, Beta, LV** *FXV, CCB, IME*

Computer Wizard 🎬

G/Family Boy genius builds a powerful electronic device. His intentions are good, but the invention disrupts the town and lands him in big trouble. Not the "Thomas Edison Story."

1977 91m/C Henry Darrow, Kate Woodville, Guy Madison, Marc Gilpin; *D:* John Florea. **VHS, Beta** *NO*

The Computer Wore Tennis Shoes 🎬 ⌐

G/Family Slow-witted college student turns into a genius after a "shocking" encounter with the campus computer. His new brains give the local gangster headaches and help save the school. One of a series of awfully cloying Disney campus comedies that seemed singularly out of step with the times. Sequel: "Now You See Him, Now You Don't."

1969 87m/C Kurt Russell, Cesar Romero, Joe Flynn, William Schallert, Alan Hewitt, Richard Bakalayan; *D:* Robert Butler. **VHS, Beta** *DIS, OM*

Alicia Silverstone as Cher indulges in her favorite pastime in "Clueless."

Conan the Barbarian 🦴🦴🦴

R/Sr. High-Adult Vicious sword-and-sorcery tale, hearkening back to the original fantasy novels of Robert E. Howard—and not for kids despite the proliferation of Conan comics, cartoons, and of course, Uncle Arnold, ideally cast here as the young slave in an ancient land who embarks on a bloody path to avenge his murdered parents. Sequel, "Conan the Destroyer," is much better suited to the younger fans.

 Brutality and swordplay beyond what's suitable for youngsters. Sex and nudity.

1982 115m/C Arnold Schwarzenegger, James Earl Jones, Max von Sydow, Sandahl Bergman, Mako, Ben Davidson, Valerie Quennessen, Cassandra Gaviola, William Smith; **D:** John Milius; **W:** John Milius, Oliver Stone; **M:** Basil Poledouris. **VHS, Beta, LV** *MCA*

Conan the Destroyer 🦴🦴 ⌐

PG/Jr. High-Adult Conan is duped by sorceress Queen Tamaris into searching for a treasure and guarding a virgin maiden. In fact, the girl is to be a human sacrifice and Conan assassinated, but the muscleman acquires an Amazonian warrior ally (Jones) who helps out in their climactic battle against the forces of evil. Frequent action, excellent special f/x, monsters and a silly finale, with an cartoony campiness overall, in contrast to the darkness of the first film.

🔶 BEWARE 🔶 *Violence, mostly cartoony, with little or no blood, and sex talk.*

1984 101m/C Arnold Schwarzenegger, Grace Jones, Wilt Chamberlain, Sarah Douglas, Mako, Olivia D'Abo, Jeff Corey; **D:** Richard Fleischer; **M:** Basil Poledouris. **VHS, Beta, LV** *MCA*

Condorman 🦴🦴

PG/Family Woody Wilkins, an inventive comic book writer, adopts the identity of his own character, Condorman, in order to help a beautiful Russian spy defect. Disney strictly for the small fry.

🔶 BEWARE 🔶 *Roughhousing.*

1981 90m/C Michael Crawford, Oliver Reed, Barbara Carrera, James Hampton, Jean-Pierre Kalfon, Dana Elcar; **D:** Charles Jarrott; **M:** Henry Mancini. **VHS, Beta** *DIS*

The Coneheads

Family The popular Saturday Night Live skit comes alive with animation. Dan Ackroyd, Jane Curtin and Laraine Newman supply the voices for the family from Remulak in this cute made-for-kids copy of the original.

1983 23m/C VHS

Coneheads 🦴🦴

PG/Jr. High-Adult Comedy inspired by once popular characters from "Saturday Night Live" coasts in on the coattails of "Wayne's World." Aykroyd and Curtin reprise their roles as Beldar and Prymaat, the couple from the planet Remulak who are just trying to fit in on Earth. Newman, who created the role of teenage daughter Connie, appears as Beldar's sister, while Burke takes over as Connie (toddler Connie is Aykroyd's daughter, in her film debut). One-joke premise is a decade late and a dime short, though cast of comedy all-stars provides a lift.

> BEWARE *Alcohol use. Some kids may not remember the Saturday Night Live regulars.*

1993 86m/C Dan Aykroyd, Jane Curtin, Laraine Newman, Jason Alexander, Michelle Burke, Chris Farley, Michael Richards, Lisa Jane Persky, Sinbad, Shishir Kurup, Michael McKean, Phil Hartman, David Spade, Dave Thomas, Jan Hooks, Chris Rock, Adam Sandler, Julia Sweeney, Danielle Aykroyd; **D:** Steven Barron; **W:** Dan Aykroyd, Tom Davis, Bonnie Turner, Terry Turner. **VHS, Beta** *PAR, BTV*

Congo 🦴🦴

PG-13/Jr. High-Adult A lost diamond mine, killer gorillas, mysterious deaths, erupting volcanoes, an earthquake. It's no "Jurassic Park" but this adaptation of Michael Crichton's novel delivers all the cliches of the old B-movie jungle flicks which makes it sort of fun. You want art, go rent "Much Ado About Nothing."

> BEWARE *Jungle terror and action; following a gorilla attack, explorer finds his partner's eyeball; brief profanity. Warning: These monkeys are very scary!*

1995 109m/C Dylan Walsh, Laura Linney, Ernie Hudson, Tim Curry, Grant Heslov, Joe Don Baker; **D:** Frank Marshall; **W:** John Patrick Shanley; **C:** Allen Daviau; **M:** Jerry Goldsmith. **VHS, Beta** *NYR*

A Connecticut Yankee 🦴🦴🦴

Family Charming version of Twain's "A Connecticut Yankee in King Arthur's Court," adapted to the special talents of legendary American humorist Will Rogers. He even teaches King Arthur his famous rope tricks when he's transported back to the days of the Round Table. Humor is mostly verbal (Rogers tells the King of a new 'magic' called advertising: "It makes folks spend what they haven't got on things they don't want"), but the sight of telephones in Camelot and armored knights riding to the rescue in early automobiles make up for the slow spots.

> BEWARE *Violence, since the Connecticut Yankee gives the King's men machine guns.*

1931 96m/B Will Rogers, Myrna Loy, Maureen O'Sullivan, William Farnum; **D:** David Butler. **VHS** *FOX, FCT*

A Connecticut Yankee in King Arthur's Court 🦴🦴 ▹

Family Pleasant musicalized version of the Twain novel, here about a 1912 American blacksmith transported to Camelot of 538 A.D., where he passes himself off as a powerful wizard and tries to advise King Arthur about

democracy. Crosby is his own easygoing self, though the storyline (generally faithful to the original) stops in its tracks to accommodate the inevitable songs. 🎵 Once and For Always; Busy Doin' Nothin'; If You Stub Your Toe on the Moon; When Is Sometime?; Twixt Myself and Me.

1949 108m/C Bing Crosby, Rhonda Fleming, William Bendix, Cedric Hardwicke, Henry Wilcoxon, Murvyn Vye, Virginia Field; **D:** Tay Garnett. **VHS, Beta, LV** *MCA*

A Connecticut Yankee in King Arthur's Court 🦴🦴

Family Animated feature from Europe based on the classic Twain novel about an American transported to Camelot, where his modern inventions and Yankee ingenuity cause more problems than they solve. This version takes numerous liberties with Sam Clemens' story, including updating the tale to the space age rather than the original's Industrial Revolution era.

1970 74m/C D: Zoran Janjic. **VHS, Beta** *MGM*

Conquest of the Planet of the Apes 🦴🦴

PG/Jr. High-Adult More of a prequel than sequel as the simian series moves into film number four with a look back at how the Planet of the Apes developed. In the distant year of 1990, the apes turn the tables on the human Earth population when they lead a revolt against their cruel homo sapian masters. Trite and cliched at times, but of interest to fans of the series. Followed by "Battle for the Planet of the Apes."

> BEWARE *Violence.*

1972 87m/C Roddy McDowall, Don Murray, Ricardo Montalban, Natalie Trundy, Severn Darden, Hari Rhodes; **D:** J. Lee Thompson. **VHS, Beta, LV** *FOX*

Conrack 🦴🦴🦴

PG/Family True story of writer Pat Conroy, who tried to teach a group of illiterate black children, isolated and ignored on a South Carolina island. Through caring and common-sense teaching techniques, Mr. "Conrack" (how the kids pronounced his name) inspired the kids but rocked the boat too much for white authorities. Earnest, if a little bit formulaic. Based on Conroy's book "The Water Is Wide."

> BEWARE *Profanity and bigotry (which the title character tries to overcome).*

1974 111m/C Jon Voight, Paul Winfield, Madge Sinclair, Hume Cronyn, Martin Ritt; **D:** Martin Ritt; **W:** Harriet Frank Jr., Irving Ravetch; **M:** John Williams. **VHS, Beta** *FOX*

Conspiracy of Love 🦴

Jr. High-Adult TV drama about the strain of divorce within a family. The irresponsible husband walks out, though the careerist ex-wife still lives with his sympathetic parents. But she can't compete with an easygoing

Dylan Walsh shows gorilla Amy her jungle home in "Congo."

grandpa for the affections of her small daughter (Barrymore). Result: a court order to keep the old folks away. Good premise about how decent people can end up hurting each other, but not above sugary cliches.

1987 93m/C Robert Young, Drew Barrymore, Glynnis O'Connor, Elizabeth Wilson, Michael Laurence, John Fujioka, Alan Fawcett; **D:** Noel Black. **VHS** *VTR, NWV*

Cool As Ice

PG/Jr. High-Adult Creativity stopped with the apt casting of rapper Vanilla Ice (his 15 minutes are long gone) as a super-cool biker who motors into a conservative town, eventually winning a local girl's love via heroism. Several so-so musical segments in this mainly inoffensive juvenile exercise in wish-fulfillment, for teenage romantics only.

BEWARE *Roughhousing.*

1991 92m/C Vanilla Ice, Kristin Minter, Michael Gross, Sydney Lassick, Dody Goodman, Naomi Campbell, Candy Clark; **D:** David Kellogg; **M:** Stanley Clarke. **VHS, Beta, LV** *MCA*

Cool Change

PG/Jr. High-Adult Wonderfully scenic Australian drama from George Miller, the director of "The Man From Snowy River," about a young park ranger used as a

pawn in a government conspiracy to rob cattlemen of their land. It's been peddled as a family-oriented video, though between the politics and romance there seems little to really interest kids. Refreshing touch: environmentalists are bad guys, for once.

BEWARE *Sex, alcohol use.*

1986 79m/C VHS *FHE, BTV*

Cool Runnings

PG/Jr. High-Adult Bright, slapstick comedy based on the true story of the Jamaican bobsled team's quest to enter the 1988 Winter Olympics in Calgary. Candy is recruited to coach four unlikely athletes who don't quite exemplify the spirit of the Games. He accepts the challenge not only because of its inherent difficulty but because he needs to reconcile himself to past failures as a former sledder. When our heroes leave their sunny training ground for Calgary, their mettle is tested by serious sledders from more frigid climes who pursue the competition with a stern sense of mission. An upbeat story which will appeal to children, its target audience.

BEWARE *Mild profanity, fighting, and alcohol use (which can be dangerous when sledding).*

1993 98m/C Leon, Doug E. Doug, John Candy, Marco Brambilla, Malik Yoba, Rawle Lewis, Raymond J. Barry, Peter Outerbridge, Larry Gilman, Paul Coeur; **D:** Jon Turteltaub; **W:** Tommy Swerdlow, Lynn Siefert, Michael Goldberg; **M:** Hans Zimmer. **VHS, LV** *DIS*

Cooley High 🦴🦴🦴

PG/Jr. High-Adult Likeable comedy-drama about black high school students in Chicago experiencing the rites of passage in their senior year. Funny, streetwise, but with a tragic finale that prevents it from going sitcom. Set in the '60s (great soundtrack features Motown hits of the era) but very much a funky relic of the '70s, right down to a 1976 Godzilla flick playing at the heroes' cinema hangout.

🪧 BEWARE 🪧 *Violence and coming-of-age sex.*

1975 107m/C Glynn Turman, Lawrence-Hilton Jacobs, Garrett Morris, Cynthia Davis; **D:** Michael A. Schultz; **W:** Eric Monte. **VHS, LV** *ORI, FCT, PTB*

Cop and a Half 🦴🦴 🦴

PG/Family Eight-year-old cop groupie Devon witnesses a Miami mob murder and talks police into putting him on the force for a day—otherwise he'll withhold information. His short-term partner is kid-hating detective Reynolds, but bad guys are after Devon, and we know the action hero will adore his little pal by the end. Predictable comedy gets a bone for staying kid-friendly all the way (unlike the violent "Kindergarten Cop"), and Sharkey's ham villain is a treat. Grownup viewers will likely be bored.

🪧 BEWARE 🪧 *Roughhousing.*

1993 87m/C Norman D. Golden II, Burt Reynolds, Ruby Dee, Ray Sharkey, Holland Taylor, Frank Sivero, Marc Macaulay, Rocky Giordani, Sammy Hernandez; **D:** Henry Winkler; **W:** Arne Olsen; **M:** Alan Silvestri. **VHS, LV** *MCA*

Cops and Robbersons 🦴

PG/Jr. High-Adult Bored, dim-witted dad Chase, a TV cop-show junkie, wishes his life had a little more danger and excitement. How lucky for him when hard-nosed cop Palance sets up a command post in his house to stake out the mobster living next door (Davi). Predictable plot isn't funny and drags Chase's bumbling idiot persona on for too long. Wiest and Davi are two bright spots, but their talents are wasted, while Palance does little more than reincarnate his "City Slickers" character. Poor effort for otherwise notable director Ritchie.

🪧 BEWARE 🪧 *Profanity and brief nudity and Chase's typical pratfalls.*

1994 93m/C Chevy Chase, Jack Palance, Dianne Wiest, Robert Davi, Jason James Richter, Fay Masterson, Miko Hughes, Richard Romanus, David Barry Gray; **D:** Michael Ritchie; **W:** Bernie Somers; **M:** William Ross. **VHS** *NYR*

The Corn is Green 🦴🦴🦴

Family Touching story of a school teacher in a poor Welsh village who nurtures a clever boy from a mining family and eventually sends her pupil to a glorious future

at Oxford. Davis makes a fine teacher, though a little young, while the on-site photography provides atmosphere. Based on the play by Emlyn Williams.

1945 115m/B Bette Davis, John Dall, Nigel Bruce, Joan Lorring, Arthur Shields, Mildred Dunnock, Rhys Williams, Rosalind Ivan; **D:** Irving Rapper; **M:** Max Steiner. **VHS, Beta** *MGM, FCT*

The Corn is Green

Family Stirring second filming (for TV) of the Emlyn Williams play, with Hepburn well cast as the indomitable British schoolteacher determined to bring education and the promise of a better life to children of struggling miners in Wales.

🪧 BEWARE 🪧 *In this version the teacher's star pupil is imperiled by a pregnancy scare.*

1979 m/C Katharine Hepburn, Bill Fraser, Anna Massey; **D:** George Cukor; **M:** John Barry. *WEA*

Corrina, Corrina 🦴🦴 🦴

PG/Sr. High-Adult Whoopi brings humanity again to a white family struggling to find itself. Newly widowed jingle-writer Liotta needs someone to care for his withdrawn eight year-old daughter. Enter Whoopi, as housekeeper and eventual love interest. Sweet, nostalgic romance set in the 1950's rests squarely on the charm of its leads, with Liotta playing against type and Whoopi doing Whoopi. Goldberg also found off-screen romance (again), this time with the film's union organizer Lyle Trachtenberg. Last role for Ameche.

🪧 BEWARE 🪧 *Profanity (light), a fight in a restaurant, and a depiction of racism. The little girl has recently lost her mother and refuses to speak.*

1994 115m/C Whoopi Goldberg, Ray Liotta, Don Ameche, Tina Majorino, Wendy Crewson, Jenifer Lewis, Larry Miller, Erica Yohn; **Cameos:** Anita Baker; **D:** Jessie Nelson; **W:** Jessie Nelson. **VHS** *NYR*

The Cosmic Eye 🦴🦴🦴

Family Critically acclaimed, abstract cartoon about three musicians from outer space who come to Earth to spread messages of global peace and harmony. Much of the film consists of representations of various creation stories from different cultures, with tribal imagery (including human sacrifice) and music—great fun for kids who are budding anthropologists, arcane and confusing if they're not. Portions are really inserts from shorter pieces by animator Hubley, like "Moonbird," "Cockaboody" and "Voyage to Next," available on cassette by themselves and quite charming.

1971 71m/C **D:** Faith Hubley; **V:** Dizzy Gillespie, Maureen Stapleton, Benny Carter. **VHS, Beta, LV** *LTY, DIS, BTV*

The Count of Monte Cristo 🦴🦴 🦴

Family Alexander Dumas classic about an innocent man (Chamberlain) who is imprisoned, escapes, and finds the treasure of Monte Cristo, which he uses to bring down those who wronged him. Good version of the historical costumer. Originally shown in theaters in Europe, but broadcast on television in the U.S.

1974 104m/C Richard Chamberlain, Kate Nelligan, Donald Pleasence, Alessio Orano, Tony Curtis, Louis Jourdan, Trevor Howard, Taryn Power; **D:** David Greene. **VHS, Beta** *LIV, FUS*

Country 𝄢𝄢𝄢

PG/Family Strong story with a message about an Iowan farm family in crisis when the government attempts to foreclose on their land. Good performances all around and an excellent portrayal of the wife by Lange. "The River" and "Places In the Heart," both released in 1984, also dramatized the plight of many American farm families in the early 1980s.

1984 109m/C Jessica Lange, Sam Shepard, Wilford Brimley, Matt Clark, Therese Graham, Levi L. Knebel; **D:** Richard Pearce; **W:** William D. Wittliff. **VHS, Beta, LV** *TOU*

Country Girl 𝄢𝄢𝄢 ♭

Jr. High-Adult In the role that completely de-glamorized her (and won her an Oscar), Kelly plays the wife of alcoholic singer Crosby who tries to make a comeback with the help of director Holden. One of Crosby's four dramatic parts, undoubtedly one of his best. Seaton won an Oscar for his adaptation of the Clifford Odets play. Remade in 1982. ♫ The Search is Through; Dissertation on the State of Bliss; It's Mine, It's Yours; The Land Around Us.

 Alcohol use.

1954 104m/B Bing Crosby, Grace Kelly, William Holden, Gene Reynolds, Anthony Ross; **D:** George Seaton; **W:** George Seaton. **Award Nominations:** Academy Awards '54: Best Actor (Crosby), Best Black and White Cinematography, Best Director (Seaton), Best Picture; Academy Awards '56: Best Art Direction/Set Decoration (B & W); **Awards:** Academy Awards '54: Best Actress (Kelly), Best Screenplay; Golden Globe Awards '55: Best Actress—Drama (Kelly); National Board of Review Awards '54: 10 Best Films of the Year, Best Actress (Kelly). **VHS, Beta** *PAR, BTV*

The Country Mouse and the City Mouse: A Christmas Tale

Primary Well-animated fantasy tale tells the story of Emily, the country mouse and Alexander, the city mouse who lives in New York. Imaginative travel scenes involve a train, a milk wagon and more. Voices provided by Crystal Gayle and John Lithgow. Ages 3 to 7.

1994 25m/C V: John Lithgow, Crystal Gayle. **VHS** *RAN*

Country Music with the Muppets

Family Rowlf the Dog plays some of his favorite country music and stars in this collection of highlights from "The Muppet Show."

1985 55m/C Johnny Cash, Roy Clark, Crystal Gayle, Jim Henson, Frank Oz, Roger Miller. **VHS, Beta** *FOX*

Coupe de Ville 𝄢𝄢 ♭

PG-13/Jr. High-Adult Three very different, squabbling young brothers are ordered by their father to drive the title vehicle (mom's birthday gift), from Detroit to Florida in the summer of '63. By the journey's end, all three have grown up a little and come to appreciate each other better—and you've seen it coming from miles away. Convivial cast chauffeurs this sibling comedy-drama script with some panache.

BEWARE *Much sex talk on the road, plus profanity, roughhousing.*

1990 98m/C Patrick Dempsey, Daniel Stern, Arye Gross, Joseph Bologna, Alan Arkin, Annabeth Gish, Rita Taggart, James Gammon; **D:** Joe Roth; **W:** Mike Binder; **M:** James Newton Howard. **VHS, Beta, LV** *MCA*

Courage Mountain 𝄢 ♭

PG/Primary-Adult Would-be sequel to Johanna Spyri's classic "Heidi." Europe is on the brink of WWI when Heidi leaves her mountain for an exclusive boarding school in Italy. When armies take over, the kids are sent to an orphanage run by nasties. The girls escape to the mountains and are saved by Heidi's pal Peter (the twentysomething Sheen miscast as a teenager) Ridiculous sequel to the classic tale may appeal to kids, but postadolescents beware.

1989 92m/C Juliette Caton, Joanna Clarke, Nicola Stapleton, Charlie Sheen, Jan Rubes, Leslie Caron, Jade Magri, Kathryn Ludlow, Yorgo Voyagis; **D:** Christopher Leitch; **W:** Weaver Webb; **M:** Sylvester Levay. **VHS, Beta, LV** *COL, FCT*

Courage of Black Beauty 𝄢 ♭

Family If Black Beauty had real guts, he'd have trotted out of Hollywood before making this turkey about a horse and his boy. Ages 4 to 8.

1957 80m/C Johnny Crawford, Mimi Gibson, John Bryant, Diane Brewster, J. Pat O'Malley; **D:** Harold Schuster. **VHS, Beta** *LIV*

Courage of Lassie 𝄢𝄢 ♭

G/Family Fourteen-year-old Taylor is the heroine in this girl loves dog tale. In this case, the dog is actually called Bill, not Lassie, in spite of the film's title. Bill is found wounded by Taylor and she nurses him back to health. He proves to be loving, loyal, and useful, so much so that, through a complicated plotline, he winds up in the Army's K-9 division and returns home with the doggie version of shell-shock. Taylor's still there to nurse him back to his own kind self again.

1946 93m/C Elizabeth Taylor, Frank Morgan, Tom Drake, Selena Royle, Harry Davenport; **D:** Fred M. Wilcox. **VHS** *MGM*

The Court Jester 𝄢𝄢𝄢 ♭

Family Swashbuckling comedy stars Danny Kaye as a former circus clown who teams up with a band of outlaws trying to dethrone a tyrant king. Kaye poses as the court jester so he can learn more of the evil king's intentions. Filled with more color, more song, and more truly funny lines than any three comedies put together, this is Kaye's best performance. ♫ They'll Never Outfox the Fox; Baby, Let Me Take You Dreaming; My Heart Knows a Lovely Song; The Maladjusted Jester.

1956 101m/C Danny Kaye, Glynis Johns, Basil Rathbone, Angela Lansbury, Cecil Parker, John Carradine, Mildred Natwick, Robert Middleton; **D:** Norman Panama, Melvin Frank; **W:** Norman Panama. **VHS, Beta, LV** *PAR*

The Courtship of Eddie's Father ♫♫♫

Family Clever nine-year-old boy plays matchmaker for his widowed dad in this rewarding family comedy-drama, the inspiration for the TV series. Some plot elements are outdated, but young Howard's performance is terrific; he would later excel at direction. Based on the novel by Mark Toby.

1962 117m/C Glenn Ford, Shirley Jones, Stella Stevens, Dina Merrill, Ron Howard, Jerry Van Dyke; **D:** Vincente Minnelli; **W:** John Gay. **VHS** *MGM, FCT*

The Cowboys ♫♫♫

PG/Jr. High-Adult Wayne stars as an Old West cattle rancher who is forced to hire 11 schoolboys to help him drive his cattle 400 miles to market. The roughness—and violence—of the trail helps make men out of the kids, while a clever script makes this one of Duke's better late westerns. Laserdisc available in widescreen letterbox edition.

> ⚠ BEWARE *Violence, plus sex talk with a wagonload of prostitutes.*

1972 128m/C John Wayne, Roscoe Lee Browne, A. Martinez, Bruce Dern, Colleen Dewhurst, Slim Pickens, Robert Carradine; **D:** Mark Rydell; **W:** Harriet Frank Jr., Irving Ravetch; **M:** John Williams. **VHS, Beta, LV** *WAR, TLF*

Cracking Up ♫ ▷

PG/Jr. High-Adult Accident-prone misfit's mishaps on the road to recovery create chaos for everyone he meets. Lewis plays a dozen characters in this overboard comedy with few laughs.

1983 91m/C Jerry Lewis, Herb Edelman, Foster Brooks, Milton Berle, Sammy Davis Jr., Zane Buzby, Dick Butkus, Buddy Lester; **D:** Jerry Lewis. **VHS, Beta** *WAR*

Crazy Moon ♫♫ ▷

PG-13/Jr. High-Adult Eccentric high schooler Brooks falls in love with a deaf girl, and must struggle against his domineering father's and older brother's prejudices. The viewer must struggle against the romantic cliches and heavy-handed message to enjoy a basically tender tale of romance. Noteworthy for showcasing a fashion trend that didn't quite catch on in real life; Brooks is a 'retro' kid, dressing in 1930s fashions and relishing vintage music.

> ⚠ BEWARE *Salty language, mature themes.*

1987 89m/C Kiefer Sutherland, Vanessa Vaughan, Peter Spence, Ken Pogue, Eve Napier; **D:** Allan Eastman; **W:** Tom Berry, Stefan Wodoslowsky; **M:** Lou Forestieri. **VHS, Beta, LV** *NLC*

The Crazysitter ♫♫ ▷

PG-13/Jr. High-Adult Edie (D'Angelo), a petty thief recently released from jail, is hired as a sitter to the twins-from-hell. So, she decides to sell the little monsters. Crude humor.

> ⚠ BEWARE *Crude humor, thematic material.*

1994 92m/C Beverly D'Angelo, Ed Begley Jr., Carol Kane, Phil Hartman, Brady Bluhm, Rachel Duncan; **Cameos:** Nell Carter, Steve Landesburg; **D:** Michael James McDonald. **VHS, LV** *NHO*

Creatures of the Blue

Preschool-Jr. High From the well-filmed "Sierra Club" series. Meet underwater wildlife from the parrot fish of Australia's Great Barrier Reef to humpback whales on their journey home to the Caribbean. All ages.

1995 29m/C VHS

Creatures of the Wild

Preschool-Jr. High More from the "Sierra Club" series. Introduces children to animals in their natural habitat, including meerkats, lions, and mountain gorillas. All ages.

1995 29m/C VHS

Cria ♫♫♫

PG/Jr. High-Adult Award-winning story of 9-year-old Ana, who struggles to comprehend her mother's terminal cancer. Ultimately she holds her father responsible; later his death leaves her feeling like a murderer. No less an eminence than "Peanuts" creator Charles Schulz has recommended this somber drama for its portrayal of a child's mind. In Spanish with English subtitles.

> ⚠ BEWARE *Mature themes.*

1976 115m/C Geraldine Chaplin, Ana Torrent, Conchita Perez; **D:** Carlos Saura. **Award Nominations:** Cannes Film Festival '76: Best Film; **Awards:** National Board of Review Awards '77: 5 Best Foreign Films of the Year. **VHS, Beta, LV** *INT, TPV, APD*

The Cricket in Times Square

Primary Cat, mouse, boy, and cricket help revive a failing newsstand in this modern fantasy adapted for TV 'toons from George Selden's book.

1973 30m/C D: Chuck Jones. **VHS, Beta** *KUI, FHE, CHI*

The Crimson Ghost

Family Republic Pictures serial named after its villain, a respected university faculty member disguised in a robe and a skull mask (with bad teeth). With his gangster henchmen, the CG schemes to steal the newly invented 'cyclotrode' ray gun and hold the world hostage, unless a heroic criminologist can stop him. Silly chapter play antics, with the Ghost's identity revealed in the final of its 12 episodes. 93-minute colorized condensed version is also available.

Violence.

1946 100m/B Charles Quigley, Linda Stirling, I. Stanford Jolley, Clayton Moore, Kenne Duncan; **D:** William Witney, Fred Brannon. **VHS, Beta** *VCN, REP, MLB*

Crimson Tide 🎬🎬🎬

R/Sr. High-Adult With the future of the world at stake, mutiny erupts aboard the submarine USS Alabama as Captain Ramsey (Hackman) and his Executive Officer Hunter (Washington) clash over the validity of orders to launch the sub's missiles. Ramsey wants to fire the missiles, but Hunter refuses until the message can be verified. Suspenseful and well-paced thriller is a showcase for Hackman and Washington and could prompt a thoughtful discussion about whether it's OK to resist authority.

BEWARE *Profanity, but what would you expect from a group of sailors under stress and underwater.*

1995 116m/C Gene Hackman, Denzel Washington, George Dzundza, Viggo Mortensen, James Gandolfini, Matt Craven, Lillo Brancato, Danny Nucci, Steve Zahn, Rick Schroder, Vanessa Bell Calloway, Rocky Carroll; **Cameos:** Jason Robards Jr.; **D:** Tony Scott; **W:** Michael Schiffer, Richard P. Henrick; **C:** Dariusz Wolski; **M:** Hans Zimmer. **VHS, LV** *TOU*

Critters 🎬🎬♡

PG-13/Jr. High-Adult One of the better "Gremlins" clones. In fact, it's the only better "Gremlins" clone. Fast-growing, faster-eating little alien beasts crash to Earth with a pair of blast-'em-on-sight galactic bounty hunters right behind them. Both terrorize a farm family in a small Kansas community. Smart and sarcastic sci-fi action that doesn't push gore to extremes. Followed by several inferior sequels.

BEWARE *Violence, but mostly committed upon monsters and bowling alleys—and one E.T. doll, enthusiastically devoured in a priceless moment. One alien swear word, translated thanks to subtitles.*

1986 86m/C Dee Wallace Stone, M. Emmet Walsh, Billy Green Bush, Scott Grimes, Nadine Van Der Velde, Terrence Mann, Billy Zane; **D:** Stephen Herek; **W:** Stephen Herek; **M:** David Newman. **VHS, Beta, LV** *COL*

Cro: Adventures in Woollyville

Primary An unusually intelligent (and, need we add, short-lived) Saturday morning cartoon on ABC. At least it has a second life on video. Cro (as in Cro-magnon), is a prehistoric boy; Phil is his ultra-smart, time traveling woolly mammoth pal. Together they have adventures and learn a great deal about science in a comfortable way. Dr. C., a contemporary scientist character, and her young friends participate, too. On this installment, Phil's stuck in a tight spot in "Pulley for You" while "A Bridge Too Short" involves a bridge building attempt by the Neanderthals. Ages 5 to 12.

1994 60m/C V: Max Casella, Ruth Buzzi. **VHS** *REP*

Cro: Have Mammoths, Will Travel

Primary "No Way Up" finds Dr. C., Phil, and Mike in an out of control airborne adventure. In "Escape from Mung Island" Phil remembers a Woollyville adventure involving Nandy's cooking. Ages 5 to 12.

1994 60m/C V: Max Casella, Ruth Buzzi. **VHS** *REP*

Cro: It's a Woolly, Woolly World

Primary "Lever in a Million Years" finds Phil stuck in the bathroom and Mike trying to get him out. "Play it Again Cro . . . Not" finds Cro's music-making attempts unappreciated. Ages 5 to 12.

1994 60m/C V: Max Casella, Ruth Buzzi. **VHS** *REP*

Crocodile Dundee 🎬🎬🎬♡

PG-13/Jr. High-Adult New York reporter Sue Charlton is assigned to the Outback to interview living legend Mike Dundee. When she finally locates the man, she is so taken with him that she brings him back to New York with her. There, the naive Aussie wanders about, amazed at the wonders of the city and unwittingly charming everyone he comes in contact with, from high-society transvestites to street hookers. One of the surprise hits of 1986.

BEWARE *Fighting (even a little gator fighting), profanity, prostitutes, brief nudity, and a lot of very large knives.*

1986 98m/C Paul Hogan, Linda Kozlowski, John Meillon, David Gulpilil, Mark Blum; **D:** Peter Faiman. **Award Nominations:** Academy Awards '86: Best Original Screenplay; **Awards:** Golden Globe Awards '87: Best Actor—Musical/Comedy (Hogan). **VHS, Beta, LV, 8mm** *PAR*

Crocodile Dundee 2 🎬🎬♡

PG/Family Mike Dundee, the loveable rube, returns to his native Australia looking for new adventure, having "conquered" New York City. He inadvertently gets involved in stopping a gang of crooks active in Australia and New York. Sequel to original box office smash lacks its charm and freshness.

BEWARE *Violence in the Crocodile guy fashion and mild profanity.*

1988 110m/C Paul Hogan, Linda Kozlowski, Kenneth Welsh, John Meillon, Ernie Dingo, Juan Fernandez, Charles S. Dutton; **D:** John Cornell; **W:** Paul Hogan. **VHS, Beta, LV** *PAR*

Crooklyn 🎬🎬🎬

PG-13/Jr. High-Adult Director Lee turns from the life of Malcolm X to the early lives of Generation X in this profile of an African-American middle class family growing up in 1970's Brooklyn. Lee's least politically charged film to date is a joint effort between him and sibs Joie and Cinque, and profiles the only girl in a family of five children coming of age. Tender and real performances from all, especially newcomer Harris, propel the sometimes messy, music-laden trip to nostalgia land.

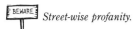 *Street-wise profanity.*

1994 112m/C Alfre Woodard, Delroy Lindo, Zelda Harris, David Patrick Kelly, Carlton Williams, Sharif Rashed, Tse-March Washington, Christopher Knowings, Jose Zuniga, Isaiah Washington, Ivelka Reyes, N. Jeremi Duru, Frances Foster, Norman Matlock, Patriece Nelson, Joie Lee, Vondie Curtis-Hall, Tiasha Reyes, Spike Lee; **D:** Spike Lee; **W:** Joie Lee, Cinque Lee; **M:** Terence Blanchard. **VHS, LV** *MCA*

Cross Creek 🎵🎵 🐾

PG/Family Based on the life of Marjorie Kinnan Rawlings, author of "The Yearling," who, after 10 years as a frustrated reporter/writer, moves to the remote and untamed Everglades. There she meets colorful local characters and receives the inspiration to write numerous bestsellers. Well acted though overtly sentimental at times. Produced by "Sounder" creator Robert B. Radnitz.

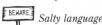 *Salty language; brief violence.*

1983 115m/C Mary Steenburgen, Rip Torn, Peter Coyote, Dana Hill, Alfre Woodard, Malcolm McDowell; **D:** Martin Ritt. **VHS, Beta** *REP*

Crossing Delancey 🎵🎵🎵 🐾

PG/Jr. High-Adult Jewish woman (Bozyk), in old world style, plays matchmaker to her independent thirtysomething granddaughter. Charming modern-day NYC fairy tale deftly manipulates cliches and stereotypes. Lovely performance from Irving as the woman whose heart surprises her. Riegert is swell playing the pickle vender who's the gentle but never wimpy suitor. Bozyk, a star on the Yiddish vaudeville stage, is perfectly cast in her film debut. Appealing music by the Roches, with Suzzy Roche giving a credible performance as Irving's friend. Adapted for the big screen by Sandler from her play of the same name.

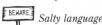 *Sex talk in lieu of matchmaking efforts.*

1988 97m/C Amy Irving, Reizl Bozyk, Peter Riegert, Jeroen Krabbe, Sylvia Miles, Suzzy Roche, George Martin, John Bedford Lloyd, Rosemary Harris, Amy Wright, Claudia Silver; **D:** Joan Micklin Silver; **W:** Suzzy Roche, Susan Sandler. **VHS, Beta, LV, 8mm** *WAR, FCT, JCF*

The Crow 🎵🎵 🐾

R/Sr. High-Adult Martial arts meets the supernatural, spawning a box office winner and a hit soundtrack. Revenge-fantasy finds Eric Draven (Lee) resurrected on Devil's Night, a year after his death, in order to avenge his own murder and that of his girlfriend. 90% of the scenes are at night, in the rain, or both, and it's not easy to tell what's going on (a blessing considering the violence level). Very dark, but with good performances, particularly from Lee (son of Bruce), in his last role before an unfortunate accident on the set killed him. That footage has been destroyed, but use of a stunt double and camera trickery allowed for the movie's completion. Film was dedicated to Lee and his fiance Eliza. Based on the comic strip by James O'Barr. The video release includes Lee's final interview.

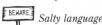 *Profanity, brutality, and drug use. Element of resurrection.*

1993 100m/C Brandon Lee, Ernie Hudson, Michael Wincott, David Patrick Kelly, Rochelle Davis, Angel David, Michael Massee, Bai Ling, Lawrence Mason, Bill Raymond, Marco Rodriguez, Anna Thomson, Sofia Shinas, Jon Polito, Tony Todd; **D:** Alex Proyas; **W:** David J. Schow, John Shirley; **M:** Graeme Revell. **VHS, LV** *TOU*

The Crush 🎵 🐾

R/Sr. High-Adult Wealthy 14-year-old temptress Silverstone (in her debut) develops an obsessive crush on handsome 28-year-old Elwes, who rents her family's guest house. In an attempt to win his heart, she rewrites his poorly composed magazine articles. This doesn't convince him they should mate for life, so she sabotages his apartment to vent her rage. Sound familiar? The plot's lifted right out of "Fatal Attraction" and Shapiro doesn't offer viewers anything inventively different. He does manage to substitute new methods for the spurned lover to snare her prey. Limp plot might have been exciting if we hadn't seen it so many times before.

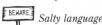 *Profanity, violence, and brief nudity. Silverstone's character is very deranged. She lets a hive of bees loose on another character.*

1993 89m/C Cary Elwes, Alicia Silverstone, Jennifer Rubin, Kurtwood Smith, Gwynyth Walsh, Amber Benson; **D:** Alan Shapiro; **W:** Alan Shapiro; **M:** Graeme Revell. **VHS, Beta, LV** *WAR*

Crusoe 🎵🎵 🐾

PG-13/Jr. High-Adult Lushly photographed version of the Daniel Defoe adventure classic that rethinks its title character; Crusoe is now an arrogant 1808 slave trader—disliked by even his own crew—who gets shipwrecked on an African island populated by unfriendly natives. When one warrior (not nicknamed Friday) saves his life, Crusoe adjusts his attitude a bit toward the darker-skinned races. With long, dialogue-free passages, it's a thoughtful, occasionally harsh spectacle. From the cinematographer of "The Black Stallion," but child viewers could be alternately bored or alarmed.

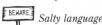 *Brutality, with human sacrifice (featuring slit throats and decapitation) are among the rituals of a hostile tribe.*

1989 94m/C Aidan Quinn, Ade Sapara, Jimmy Nail, Timothy Spall, Colin Bruce, Michael Higgins, Shane Rimmer, Hepburn Grahame; **D:** Caleb Deschanel; **W:** Walon Green, Christopher Logue; **M:** Michael Kamen. **VHS, Beta, LV** *NO*

Cry-Baby 🎵🎵🎵

PG-13/Jr. High-Adult Hilarious homage and spoof of "Grease"—stained '50s teen-rock-rebel melodramas. Waters made his name via strange cult faves rather than general audience efforts, but if you've got a weird and savvy family try this high-energy musical about the school delinquent (Depp, with a nearly full-scale electric chair tattooed on his chest) who romances a blonde debutante princess. Sure, the story's weak, but dig the dancing, cute/grotesque cast and the tribute to Elvis.

BEWARE *Sicko touches in the Waters manner, from a romantic opening set during a class vaccination to a finale that glorifies the deadly auto competition of 'chicken.' Loving teen couple has babies out of wedlock at awkward moments and the lone swear word is the centerpiece of a great gag.*

1990 85m/C Johnny Depp, Amy Locane, Polly Bergen, Traci Lords, Ricki Lake, Iggy Pop, Susan Tyrrell, Patty Hearst, Kim McGuire, Darren E. Burrows, Troy Donahue, Willem Dafoe, David Nelson, Mink Stole, Joe Dallesandro, Joey Heatherton, Robert Walsh; **D:** John Waters; **W:** John Waters; **M:** Patrick Williams. **VHS, Beta, LV** *MCA*

Cry from the Mountain 🎬🎬

PG/Family Family drama from the Billy Graham ministry shows a father and teen son on an Alaskan kayak trip so adulterous dad can break the news of his impending divorce. Mishap strands them with a mountain man who relies on his faith to get by in the wilderness. Meanwhile back in the city, bitter mom has her own turmoil. Truncated pic raises important issues, but leaves the resolution up to the viewer; instead of an ending, Graham appears with words of inspiration.

1985 78m/C James Cavan, Wes Parker, Rita Walter, Chris Kidd, Coleen Gray, Jerry Ballew, Allison Argo, Glen Alsworth, Myrna Kidd; **D:** James F. Collier. **VHS, Beta, LV** *LIV*

A Cry in the Wild 🎬🎬🎬

PG/Jr. High-Adult Fourteen-year-old Brian, still hurting from his parents' splitup, is about to visit his father when the chartered plane crashes, leaving the boy as the lone survivor. He must learn to sustain himself alone in the wilderness. Strong acting from Rushton, good pacing, and fine nature photography make a well-used story work again. Award-winning writer Gary Paulsen helped adapt his elemental novel "Hatchet." Sequel: "White Wolves: A Cry in the Wild 2."

BEWARE *Profanity, a plane crash, and a teenager lost in the wilderness. Character is dealing with his parents split-up.*

1990 93m/C Jared Rushton, Ned Beatty, Pamela Sue Martin, Stephen Meadows; **D:** Mark Griffiths. **VHS** *MGM*

Cry, the Beloved Country 🎬🎬🎬

PG-13/Jr. High-Adult First filmed in 1951, this adaptation of Alan Paton's classic South African apartheid novel finds a Zulu Christian pastor (Jones) and a wealthy white farmer (Harris) finding common ground through losing their sons to violence. Jones and Harris are excellent.

BEWARE *Realistic depiction of bigotry, brief profanity, and an execution by hanging.*

1995 112m/C James Earl Jones, Richard Harris, Charles S. Dutton, Leleti Khumalo, Dambisa Kente, Vusi Kunene, Eric Miyeni, Ian Robers; **D:** Darrell Roodt; **W:** Ronald Atwood; **C:** Paul Gilpin; **M:** John Barry. **VHS, LV** *TOU*

Crystalstone 🎬🎬

PG/Family In 1908 coastal Spain two kids seek a legendary gem but realize their long-lost father is their real treasure. Handsome but stiff children's adventure, sorely lacking in personality and spontaneity, with some real gloom and doom elements.

BEWARE *Violence, macabre stuff includes a shot of bugs erupting from the face of an exhumed corpse.*

1988 103m/C Frank Grimes, Kamlesh Gupta, Laura Jane Goodwin, Sydney Bromsley; **D:** Antonio Pelaez. **VHS, Beta** *MCG*

Culpepper Cattle Co. 🎬🎬 ◊

PG/Jr. High-Adult Sometimes harsh but instructive, realistic western adventure about a naive teenager who wants to be a cowboy. He gets his chance, joining a cattle drive as a cook's helper, but the truth about life on the range turns out to be rougher and less romantic than he expected. Compare/contrast with "City Slickers."

BEWARE *Violence; mature themes.*

1972 92m/C Gary Grimes, Billy Green Bush, Bo Hopkins, Charles Martin Smith, Geoffrey Lewis; **D:** Dick Richards; **M:** Jerry Goldsmith. **VHS, Beta** *FOX*

The Cure 🎬🎬🎬

PG-13/Jr. High-Adult Huckleberry Finn meets the H.I.V. virus in a most unusual movie. 11-year-old Erik (Renfro), the neighborhood bad kid with the mean, alcoholic mom, becomes friends with his new neighbor, 11-year-old Dexter (Mazzello), who has AIDS (the result of a blood transfusion). When the boys read about some quack in New Orleans with a cure for AIDS, they leave their Minnesota town and go rafting down the Mississippi to the Big Easy. It sounds ridiculous but the important thing is that it doesn't sound ridiculous to them. Young leads are excellent. There's plenty for parents and kids to discuss.

BEWARE *Themes include illness, alcoholism, divorce, death and prejudice. Some profanity.*

1995 99m/C Brad Renfro, Joseph Mazzello, Annabella Sciorra, Diana Scarwid, Bruce Davison; **D:** Peter Horton; **W:** Robert Kuhn; **C:** Andrew Dintenfass; **M:** Dave Grusin. **VHS, LV** *MCA*

Curious George

Primary Each of the two tapes in this set contain six five-minute stories featuring the lovable monkey created by H. A. and Margaret Rey. Additional volumes available including the memorable "Curious George Goes to the Hospital."

1988 30m/C VHS *RHU*

Curley 🎬🎬

Family After Hal Roach's "Our Gang" series was phased out in the early '40s (by new owners MGM), Roach launched another kiddie comedy team—in color now—with this very minor short feature in which Curley and his Little Rascals lookalikes play pranks on a teacher.

Also known as "The Adventures of Curley and His Gang"; follow-up "Curley and His Gang in the Haunted Mansion" is also on video as "Who Killed Doc Robbin?"

1947 53m/C Larry Olsen, Frances Rafferty, Eilene Janssen, Walter Abel; **D:** Bernard Carr. **VHS, Beta** *DVT, NOS, HHT*

Curly Sue 🦴🦴

PG/Family Adorable, homeless waif Curly Sue and her con-man guardian Bill plot to rip off a prosperous female attorney for extra cash. But all heartstrings are tugged, and the trio develop a warm, caring relationship. Throwback to the Depression era's Shirley Temple formula films, done by the very modern family filmmaker John Hughes ("Uncle Buck," "Home Alone"), whose wit trails off once the schmaltz starts showing. Available in widescreen format on laserdisc.

> 🪧BEWARE🪧 *Profanity, homelessness, and a rather sassy child participates in con games.*

1991 102m/C James Belushi, Kelly Lynch, Alison Porter, John Getz, Fred Dalton Thompson; **D:** John Hughes; **W:** John Hughes; **M:** Georges Delerue. **VHS, Beta, LV, 8mm** *WAR, CCB*

Curly Top 🦴🦴🦴

Family Aptly named title character is an orphan (no occupation was deadlier than being one of Shirley's biological parents in a '30s film) who charms a millionaire, then plays matchmaker between the rich man and her beautiful sister. Along the way the heroine sings one of her standards, "Animal Crackers in My Soup."

1935 74m/B Shirley Temple, John Boles, Rochelle Hudson, Jane Darwell, Esther Dale, Arthur Treacher, Rafaela Ottiano; **D:** Irving Cummings. **VHS, Beta** *FOX, MLT*

Curse of the Pink Panther 🦴🦴

PG/Jr. High-Adult Clifton Sleigh, an inept New York City detective played by Wass, is assigned to find the missing Inspector Clouseau. His efforts are complicated by an assortment of gangsters and aristocrats who cross paths with the detective. So-so attempt to keep popular series going after Seller's death. Niven's last film.

> 🪧BEWARE🪧 *Profanity, violence in the mostly innocent Clouseau pratfall fashion, and nudity.*

1983 110m/C Ted Wass, David Niven, Robert Wagner, Herbert Lom, Joanna Lumley, Capucine, Robert Loggia, Harvey Korman, Leslie Ash, Denise Crosby; **D:** Blake Edwards; **W:** Blake Edwards; **M:** Henry Mancini. **VHS, Beta** *MGM*

Cutthroat Island 🦴🦴

PG-13/Jr. High-Adult Who wants to see Geena Davis as a pirate? Not many, as this big-budget swashbuckler, long on action, short on plot and character, became the biggest flop in Hollywood history. Pirate captain Morgan Adams (Davis) is left part of a treasure map by her father and "persuades" educated slave/thief William Shaw (Modine) to assist her. Her double-crossing Uncle Dawg (Langella) also has a portion of the map, which leads to . . . Cutthroat Island. Director Harlin (Davis' husband in real life) likes lots of big, noisy explosions when he

Curious George Creator Turns 90

Curious George has delighted children for years. They can easily identify with his curious nature, which sometimes gets him into trouble. His creator, Margaret Rey, turns 90, quite a milestone for quite a remarkable woman. Rey, along with husband and illustrator Hans Augusto (H.A.), were born in Hamburg, Germany, but settled in the U.S. before the breakout of World War II. They carried the manuscript of the first Curious George book by bicycle from Paris just hours before the Nazis took occupation. That manuscript would later be published in the U.S.

The couple created the books for themselves—they never had children—and the writing was a result of the partnership of their marriage (H.A. died in 1977). Today Curious George is as popular as ever, with over 12.5 million copies in print and several videos on the market.

doesn't know what else to do. Film lost over $100 million and left Carolco Pictures drawn and quartered and beggin' for death, but every executive involved in it found high-paying employment elsewhere. Har har har.

> 🪧BEWARE🪧 *Some strong pirate action/violence and brief sensuality. Lots of alcohol consumption, but hey, they are pirates.*

1995 123m/C Geena Davis, Matthew Modine, Frank Langella, Patrick Malahide, Stan Shaw, Maury Chaykin, Harris Yulin, George Murcell; **D:** Renny Harlin; **W:** Robert King, Marc Norman; **C:** Peter Levy; **M:** John Debney. **VHS, LV** *LIV*

The Cutting Edge 🦴🦴🦴

PG/Jr. High-Adult Kate's a spoiled figure skater who can't keep a partner. Doug's a cocky ex-hockey player who thinks figure skating is for wimps. Naturally they team up together and fall in love. Plot's on thin ice as it revolves around their quest for Olympic gold, but the sparks fly between the actors, allowing the upbeat sports romance to work. You'll be tempted to utter "Toepick," at an appropriate moment.

1992 101m/C D.B. Sweeney, Moira Kelly, Roy Dotrice, Terry O'Quinn, Dwier Brown, Rachelle Ottley, Jo Jo Starbuck; **D:** Paul Michael Glaser; **W:** Tony Gilroy; **M:** Patrick Williams. **VHS, LV** *MGM*

Cyrano de Bergerac 🦴🦴🦴 ♭

PG/Jr. High-Adult Depardieu brings to exhilarating life Rostand's well-loved play about the brilliant but grotesque-looking swordsman/poet, afraid of nothing—except declaring his love to the beautiful Roxanne. One of France's costliest modern productions, a multi-award winner for its cast, costumes, music and sets. English subtitles (by Anthony Burgess) brilliantly capture the intricate rhymes of the original French dialogue. A rollicking, swashbuckling exploration of emotions at their most noble.

⚠ BEWARE *Violence and swashbuckling swordplay.*

1990 135m/C Gerard Depardieu, Jacques Weber, Anne Brochet, Vincent Perez, Roland Bertin, Josiane Stoleru, Phillipe Volter, Philippe Morier-Genoud, Pierre Maguelon; **D:** Jean-Paul Rappeneau; **W:** Jean-Claude Carriere, Jean-Paul Rappeneau. **Award Nominations:** Academy Awards '90: Best Actor (Depardieu), Best Art Direction/Set Decoration, Best Foreign Language Film, Best Makeup; **Awards:** Academy Awards '90: Best Costume Design; Cannes Film Festival '90: Best Actor (Depardieu); Cesar Awards '91: Best Actor (Depardieu), Best Director (Rappeneau), Best Film, Best Supporting Actor (Weber). **VHS, LV** *ORI, FCT, BTV*

D2: The Mighty Ducks 🦴🦴

PG/Jr. High-Adult When an injury forces Gordon (Estevez) out of the minor leagues, he is tapped by promotor Tibbles (Tucker) to coach Team U.S.A. in the Junior Goodwill Games. Upon arriving in LA, the coach's head is turned by the money to be made in endorsements, and he soon gets a lesson in character building (hey, it's Disney). The duck redux premise is lame, but kids will appreciate the hockey action that made the first "Bad News Bears" on ice a hit.

⚠ BEWARE *Hockey violence involving kids and mild profanity.*

1994 107m/C Emilio Estevez, Michael Tucker, Jan Rubes, Kathryn Erbe, Shaun Weiss, Kenan Thompson, Ty O'Neal; **Cameos:** Kristi Yamaguchi, Kareem Abdul-Jabbar, Wayne Gretzky; **D:** Sam Weisman; **W:** Steven Brill; **M:** J.A.C. Redford. **VHS** *DIS*

Dad 🦴🦴 ♭

PG/Jr. High-Adult Hoping to make up for lost time, a busy executive rushes home to take care of his father who has just had a heart attack. What could have easily become sappy is made bittersweet by the convincing performances of Lemmon and Danson. Based on the novel by William Wharton.

⚠ BEWARE *Terminal illness fortunately calls for major son-and-dad bonding.*

1989 117m/C Jack Lemmon, Ted Danson, Ethan Hawke, Olympia Dukakis, Kathy Baker, Zakes Mokae, J.T. Walsh, Kevin Spacey, Chris Lemmon; **D:** Gary David Goldberg; **W:** Gary David Goldberg; **M:** James Horner. **Award Nominations:** Academy Awards '89: Best

Makeup; **Awards:** National Media Owl Awards '90: First Prize. **VHS, Beta, LV** *MCA*

Daffy Duck: Tales from the Duckside

Family Daffy Duck stars in "Wise Quackers," "The Impatient Patient," "Porky and Daffy," "Porky Pig's Feat," and "Stork Naked." All ages.

198? 33m/C VHS *BTV, WAR*

Daffy Duck's Easter Egg-citement

Family A 1980 television special that featured three new Daffy Duck cartoons. Included are "The Yolks on You," "Chocolate Chase" and "Daffy Flies North." Ages 4 to 8.

1980 24m/C V: Mel Blanc. **VHS** *WAR*

Daffy Duck's Madcap Mania

Family Six of the billed-comedian's best. All ages.

1989 45m/C D: Robert McKimson, Chuck Jones; **W:** Robert McKimson. **VHS** *WAR*

Daffy Duck's Movie: Fantastic Island 🦴🦴

G/Family Fourth of a series of feature-length collections of classic Warner Brothers cartoons, starring Daffy Duck, Speedy Gonzales, Bugs Bunny, Porky Pig, Sylvester and Tweety, the Professor and Mary Anne—wait a minute, that's the wrong island. Daffy adopts the format of the TV show "Fantasy Island" to present these clips, but it's clear that the supply of above-average material is running dry.

1983 78m/C D: Isadore "Friz" Freleng. **VHS, Beta, LV** *WAR, FCT*

Daffy Duck's Quackbusters 🦴🦴🦴

G/Family Daffy, with help from pals Bugs and Porky, sets up his own "ghostbusting" service. Good compilation of old classics such as "Night of the Living Duck," plus a new feature, "The Duxcorcist," horror spoofs all, but never in bad taste. Video is also available in Spanish.

1989 79m/C D: Greg Ford, Terry Lennon; **V:** Mel Blanc. **VHS, Beta, LV** *WAR, FCT, APD*

Daffy Duck's Thanks-for-Giving Special

Family Daffy stars in a variety of cartoons, including "His Bitter Half," and "The Return of Duck Dodgers in the 24th-1/2 Century." Ages 4 to 8.

1980 33m/C VHS *BTV, WAR*

Daisy and Her Garden: A Dance Fantasy

Family Daisy lives happily in her enchanted garden until she and her animal friends are threatened with freezing by the Winter Witch. Made for Czech TV. Ages 2 to 6. **1994 38m/C VHS** *VWV*

Dakota

PG/Jr. High-Adult Trouble-prone teen biker is released to the custody of a farmer who needs extra help. Dakota proves his worth, fixing the car, romancing the daughter, and lending confidence to a crippled 12-year-old boy. Aspires to wholesome, positive values, but it's still bland melodrama.

BEWARE *Roughhousing, alcohol use.*

1988 96m/C Lou Diamond Phillips, Dee Dee Norton, Eli Cummins, Herta Ware; **D:** Fred Holmes. **VHS, Beta, LV** *HBO*

Dances with Wolves

PG-13/Jr. High-Adult The story of a U.S. Army soldier, circa 1870, whose heroism in battle allows him his pick of posts. His choice, to see the West before it disappears, changes his life. He meets, understands and eventually becomes a member of a Lakota Sioux tribe in the Dakotas. Costner's first directorial attempt proves him a talent of vision and intelligence. This sometimes too objective movie lacks a sense of definitive character, undermining its gorgeous scenery and interesting perspective on the plight of Native Americans. Lovely music and epic proportions. Adapted by Blake from his novel.

BEWARE *Massacres, bigotry toward Indians, cruel imprisonment, blood and gore in a Civil War field hospital.*

1990 181m/C Kevin Costner, Mary McDonnell, Graham Greene, Rodney Grant, Floyd "Red Crow" Westerman, Tantoo Cardinal, Robert Pastorelli, Charles Rocket, Maury Chaykin, Jimmy Herman, Nathan Lee Chasing His Horse, Wes Studi; **D:** Kevin Costner; **W:** Michael Blake; **M:** John Barry. **Award Nominations:** Academy Awards '90: Best Actor (Costner), Best Art Direction/Set Decoration, Best Costume Design, Best Supporting Actor (Greene), Best Supporting Actress (McDonnell), Best Original Score; **Awards:** Academy Awards '90: Best Adapted Screenplay, Best Cinematography, Best Director (Costner), Best Film Editing, Best Picture, Best Sound, Best Score; Directors Guild of America Awards '90: Best Director (Costner); Golden Globe Awards '91: Best Director (Costner), Best Film—Drama, Best Screenplay; National Board of Review Awards '90: 10 Best Films of the Year, Best Director (Costner). **VHS, Beta, LV** *ORI, FCT, IME*

The Dancing Princesses

Family "Faerie Tale Theatre" addresses the mystery of how the king's daughters' shoes wear out every night when the princesses are supposed to be sleeping. Peter Weller plays the resourceful soldier who cracks the case, thanks to a magic cloak that makes him invisible. Ages 8 to 12.
1984 60m/C Lesley Ann Warren, Peter Weller, Sachi Parker, Roy Dotrice; **D:** Peter Medak. **VHS, Beta** *FOX, FCT*

Danger Mouse, Vol. 1

Family British cartoon takeoff on the BBC secret-agent series of yore, "Danger Man." Here it's a fearless rodent (with an eyepatch) who matches wits against the wicked Baron Greenback. Additional volumes available.
1982 60m/C VHS, Beta *HBO*

Dangerous Minds

R/Sr. High-Adult Based on the autobiography of LouAnne Johnson (Pfeiffer), a former Marine turned inspirational inner-city high school English teacher. Naturally, Johnson has to take on the educational bureaucracy to fight for her kids. The kids are a fight in themselves; to get their attention, Johnson teaches them about drug imagery in Bob Dylan's "Mr. Tambourine Man" and bribes them with candy bars. Though laced with profanity, the movie does emphasize education.

BEWARE *Language and gang warfare. Messages about teen pregnancy and vendetta killings.*

1995 99m/C Michelle Pfeiffer, George Dzundza, Courtney B. Vance, Robin Bartlett, Renoly Santiago, Lorraine Toussaint; **Cameos:** John Neville; **D:** John N. Smith; **W:** Ronald Bass; **C:** Pierre Letarte. **VHS, LV** *TOU*

Daniel and the Towers

Family Part of the "Wonderworks" PBS TV series, this semi-factual tale spotlights the incredible, enigmatic glass towers built in Watts, California, by resident Sam Rodia. Through the device of a (fictional) boy Daniel who goes to work for Sam, the story teaches valuable lessons about beauty and determination—though not much about the real-life Rodia, who remains something of a mystery.

199? 58m/C Allan Arbus, Michael McKean, Carmen Zapata, Miguel Alamo. **VHS** *PME, BTV*

Danny

G/Family Predictable girl-and-her-horse drama with a few charms, as a lonely 12-year-old stable hand who cares for an injured show-jumping steed spurned by a spoiled rich child.

1979 90m/C Rebecca Page, Janet Zarish, Barbara Jean Earhardt, Gloria Maddox, George Luce; **D:** Gene Feldman. **VHS, Beta** *MON, WOM, HHE*

Danny and the Dinosaur and Other Stories

Preschool-Jr. High Four animated stories for children: "Danny and the Dinosaur," "The Camel Who Took a Walk," "The Happy Lion" and "The Island of the Skog." Ages 4 to 9.
1991 35m/C VHS, Beta *CCC, MLT, WKV*

The team faces their greatest competitors in "D2: The Mighty Ducks."

Darby O'Gill & the Little People 🦴 🦴 🦴 ◟

G/Family Roguish old Darby tumbles into a well and visits the King of the Leprechauns, who agrees to grant him three wishes. Wonderful Disney production, and the first done by longtime Disney live-action director Stevenson; he gives it a rich Irish flavor (leading man Sharpe was recruited from the Broadway cast of "Finian's Rainbow"), terrific special effects, wit, charm and an ounce or two of genuine chills.

⚠️ BEWARE *Alcohol use, and scary stuff—the Death Coach and the Banshee are not soon forgotten.*

1959 93m/C Albert Sharpe, Janet Munro, Sean Connery, Estelle Winwood; *D:* Robert Stevenson. **VHS, Beta, LV** *DIS*

Daredevils of the Red Circle

Family Three stunt flyers set out to free a man held captive by an escaped convict in this 12-episode Republic serial.

1938 195m/B Charles Quigley, Bruce (Herman Brix) Bennett, Carole Landis; *D:* John English, William Witney. **VHS** *REP, VCN, MLB*

Daring Dobermans 🦴 🦴

PG/Family In this sequel to "The Doberman Gang," the barking bank robbers have a new set of outlaw masters. Young Indian boy who loves the dogs enters the picture and may thwart their perfect crime. Dobermaniacs may also want to check out the G-rated "Amazing Dobermans."

1973 88m/C Charles Robinson, Tim Considine, David Moses, Claudio Martinez, Joan Caulfield; *D:* Byron Ross Chudnow. **VHS, Beta** *FOX*

The Dark Crystal 🦴 🦴 ◟

PG/Primary-Adult In the 1980s many filmmakers tried to do the ultimate fantasy epic set in a world like no other but combining the mythology of all others etc. Funny thing is, all ended up looking like "Star Wars" anyway. Here's the Jim Henson creature-factory contribution, acted entirely by original Muppets. To defeat the vulture-like Skesis, whose sorcery rules their land, the two surviving Gelflings (elf/fairy/Rebecca DeMornay lookalikes) must insert shard A in slot B on the title gem. An ancient prophecy tells you up front they'll succeed, so there's nothing to do but boggle at the imaginative sets and incredible creature designs by Brian Froud.

> **BEWARE** *Emphasis is on the strange and grotesque rather than the truly frightening. Various characters get killed but are magically resurrected straightaway.*

1982 93m/C D: Jim Henson; **M:** Trevor Jones. **VHS, Beta, LV** *NO*

Dark Horse

PG/Jr. High-Adult Gushy, sentimental family film about troubled teen Allison, sentenced after a reckless-driving mishap to community service on a horse farm. She enjoys it, and bonds with a seemingly untameable show-jumping steed. Midway through, however, tragedy strikes, and a girl-and-her-horse tale turns into a tearjerker about trauma and recovery. Meyers holds on gracefully astride the bucking bronco of a plot, playing a demanding (and sometimes unsympathetic) role.

> **BEWARE** *Salty language, alcohol use.*

1992 98m/C Ari Meyers, Mimi Rogers, Ed Begley Jr., Donovan Leitch, Samantha Eggar; **D:** David Hemmings. **VHS** *LIV, MOV, FCT*

Darkman

R/Sr. High-Adult Raimi's tale of a disfigured man who seeks revenge is comicbook kitsch cross-pollinated with a strain of gothic horror. Neeson plays a scientist who's on the verge of discovering the key to cloning body parts; brutally attacked by the henchmen of a crooked politico, his lab is destroyed and he's left for dead. Turns out he's not dead—just horribly disfigured and a wee bit chafed—and he stalks his deserving victims from the shadows, using his lab know-how to disguise his rugged bad looks. Exquisitely violent. Montage by Pablo Ferro.

> **BEWARE** *Brutality and other violence.*

1990 96m/C Liam Neeson, Frances McDormand, Larry Drake, Colin Friels, Nelson Mashita, Jenny Agutter, Rafael H. Robledo; **D:** Sam Raimi; **W:** Sam Raimi, Ivan Raimi; **M:** Danny Elfman. **VHS, Beta, LV** *MCA, CCB*

D.A.R.Y.L.

PG/Family Boy found by the side of the road is too polite, too honest, and too smart. Taken in by a childless couple, Daryl is told by a kid pal the necessities of imperfection (if you don't want the grownups to bother you too much), and he becomes more like a real child. But he's actually a lost top-secret military project, a computer brain in a cloned body. Intriguing parental "Twilight Zone" situation doesn't hold up to the finale, but offers some thrills thanks to straightfaced treatment by "Free Willy" director Wincer.

> **BEWARE** *Mild profanity and sex talk. Kinda scary when the military tries to recapture Daryl.*

1985 100m/C Mary Beth Hurt, Michael McKean, Barret Oliver, Colleen Camp; **D:** Simon Wincer; **W:** David Ambrose, Allan Scott; **M:** Marvin Hamlisch. **VHS, Beta, LV** *PAR*

Date with an Angel

PG/Jr. High-Adult Angel with busted wing crash lands into a swimming pool. Aspiring musician about to marry into rich stuffy family fishes her out and is soon overwhelmed by her grace and beauty, though certainly not by the manuscript masquerading as a script. Soon he finds himself questioning his upcoming wedding to Cates, a cosmetic mogul's daughter. Annoying surplus of sentiment and cuteness, though beauteous Beart is convincingly angelic.

> **BEWARE** *Profanity.*

1987 114m/C Emmanuelle Beart, Michael E. Knight, Phoebe Cates, David Dukes, Bibi Besch, Albert Macklin, David Hunt, Michael Goodwin; **D:** Tom McLoughlin. **VHS, Beta, LV** *HBO*

Dave

PG-13/Jr. High-Adult Regular guy Dave Kovic (Kline) is a dead ringer for hypocritical (politically sensitive) President (Kline), launching him into the White House after the prez suffers a stroke in embarrassing (adultery) circumstances. Langella is the evil political chief of staff who's arranged the switch and hopes to be the power behind the throne, while Grodin is the little guy accountant who helps Dave write the national budget. Weaver is just fine as the first lady hardened to her husband's personal and political deficiencies who is slowly attracted by his sudden aspirations to goodness. Timely fable is a seamless comedy prompting small chuckles and the occasional hearty laugh, inspiring the feel-good faith that as long as we subvert the standard political process, government works. Political cameos abound: look for real-life Senators Alan Simpson, Paul Simon, Howard Metzenbaum, Tom Harkin, and Christopher Dodd as well as the commentators from TV's "The McLaughlin Group," and Stone, poking fun at himself on "Larry King Live," as he tries to convince the public about the conspiracy.

> **BEWARE** *Profanity and brief nudity. President suffers stroke in a compromising position (if you know what I mean).*

1993 110m/C Kevin Kline, Sigourney Weaver, Frank Langella, Kevin Dunn, Ving Rhames, Ben Kingsley, Charles Grodin, Faith Prince, Laura Linney, Bonnie Hunt, Parley Baer, Stefan Gierasch, Anna Deavere Smith, Bonnie Bartlett; **Cameos:** Oliver Stone, Arnold Schwarzenegger, Jay Leno, Larry King; **D:** Ivan Reitman; **W:** Gary Ross; **M:** James Newton Howard. **VHS, Beta, LV** *WAR, BTV, FCT*

David and Goliath

Preschool-Primary Animated biblical tale of the young shepherd and future kind, and his battle with a giant is retold.

1992 30m/C VHS *MVD, BMG*

David and Lisa

Jr. High-Adult Director Perry won an Oscar for this sensitive independently produced adaption of Theodore

Michelle Pfeiffer instructs her class of tough kids in "Dangerous Minds."

Isaac Rubin's fact-based novel. In a halfway house for mentally ill kids, a schizophrenic young man and a childlike teenage girl form a delicate bond that strengthens each one on the path to recovery. Excellent performances throughout in this sleeper.

BEWARE *Mature themes, sex talk.*

1962 94m/B Keir Dullea, Janet Margolin, Howard da Silva, Neva Patterson, Clifton James; **D:** Frank Perry. **VHS, Beta, LV** *COL, MRV*

David Copperfield ♫♫♫♫

Family Superior and faithful adaptation of Charles Dickens' great novel. David, an orphan grows to manhood in Victorian England as a wide variety of mentors, friends and foes help and harm. Terrific acting by Bartholomew (one of the best child actors of the '30s), not to mention Fields, Rathbone, and all the rest. Lavish production, lovingly filmed—a fine example of what happens when the Hollywood system actually worked right.

1935 132m/B Lionel Barrymore, W.C. Fields, Freddie Bartholomew, Maureen O'Sullivan, Basil Rathbone, Lewis Stone, Frank Lawton, Madge Evans, Roland Young, Edna May Oliver, Lennox Pawle, Elsa Lanchester, Una O'Connor, Arthur Treacher; **D:** George Cukor; **W:** Howard Estabrook, Hugh Walpole; **M:** Herbert Stothart. **Award Nominations:** Academy Awards '35: Best Film Editing; Acad-

emy Awards '36: Best Picture; **Awards:** National Board of Review Awards '35: 10 Best Films of the Year. **VHS, Beta, LV** *MGM*

David Copperfield ♫♫ ♪

Family British made-for-TV production of the Dickens classic takes a more mature approach to the material. Begins with the melancholy, grownup David, then flashes back to the childhood friendships, rivalries, loves and disappointments that made him such a mopey young man. The added material, however, fails to highlight any one character as had the successful 1935 MGM version. Exceptional cast and photography do much to redeem the effort.

1970 118m/C Richard Attenborough, Cyril Cusack, Edith Evans, Pamela Franklin, Susan Hampshire, Wendy Hiller, Ron Moody, Laurence Olivier; **D:** Delbert Mann; **M:** Malcolm Arnold. **VHS** *FOX*

Davy Crockett

Family Tall tale about frontier hero Davy Crockett—half alligator, half snapping turtle, and a little bit of earthquake. Part of the "Rabbit Ears: American Heroes and Legends" storytelling series.

1992 30m/C VHS *RAB, BTV*

Davy Crockett and the River Pirates ♫♫♫ ♪

G/Family After "Davy Crockett, King of the Wild Frontier" became a surprise sensation Disney delivered a sequel (despite having killed off their hero in the original!) by splicing together more TV episodes covering Davy's life long before the Alamo. So maybe it's a prequel, but whatever adventure is a much more coherent and grandly entertaining effort, chronicling the friendly rivalry between our frontier hero and blustery Mike Fink, the King of the Ohio River. The bigger-than-life pair duel in a furious keelboat race, and then unite against a bandit gang masquerading as Indians and threatening the territories.

BEWARE *Western violence and alcohol use.*

1956 81m/C Fess Parker, Buddy Ebsen, Jeff York; **D:** Norman Foster. **VHS, Beta, LV** *DIS, OM*

Davy Crockett, King of the Wild Frontier ♫♫♫

PG/Family Walt Disney himself was surprised when special episodes of his TV show devoted to the life of Davy Crockett—technically, the very first miniseries— became a smash with '50s kids. Still rousing, this theatrical version blends the segments, covering Davy's days as an Indian fighter (some queasy moments, by modern standards, as the hero wipes out swarms of "those red hornets"), his days in Congress (fighting for, ironically, Indian rights), to his last gallant stand in defense of the Alamo (note how Davy's demise was edited out, by popular demand). Ebsen was to play the lead, then got reassigned to sidekick when Disney discovered the then-unknown Parker. Soundtrack includes the million-selling "Ballad of Davy Crockett," plus a lesser-known love song actually written by the frontiersman.

🎬 BEWARE 🎬 *Abundant violence makes the retroactive PG rating well-earned.*

1955 93m/C Fess Parker, Buddy Ebsen, Hans Conried, Ray Whiteside, Pat Hogan, William "Billy" Bakewell, Basil Ruysdael, Kenneth Tobey; *D:* Norman Foster. **VHS, Beta** *DIS, BTV*

A Day at the Circus: Alphabet Factory at the Circus

Family The Alphabet Factory gang takes children on a behind-the-scenes look at the events under the big top. Ages 1 to 4.
1995 25m/C VHS *ALP, TPV*

A Day at the Races ♪♪♪ ♭

Family Marx Brothers madness, with the congenitally lame and way overlong plot concerning veterinarian Groucho's attempt to buy his own hospital by making a fortune betting on the horse races. Some absolutely sidesplitting comic scenes, but also slow spots and numerous boring musical numbers that require the use of the fast-forward button. 🎵 A Message from the Man in the Moon; On Blue Venetian Waters; Tomorrow is Another Day; All God's Chillun Got Rhythm.

1937 111m/B Groucho Marx, Harpo Marx, Chico Marx, Sig Rumann, Douglass Dumbrille, Margaret Dumont, Allan Jones, Maureen O'Sullivan; *D:* Sam Wood. **VHS, Beta, LV** *MGM, CCB*

A Day at the Zoo: Alphabet Factory at the Zoo

Family The gang from the Alphabet Factory takes children on a trip to The Bronx Zoo and The Los Angeles Zoo. Ages 1 to 4.
1995 25m/C VHS *TPV, ALP*

A Day for Thanks on Walton's Mountain ♪♪

Family Ralph Waite, Ellen Corby and many other original television-show cast members returned for this sentimental Thanksgiving reunion on Walton's Mountain. Made for television. Ages 7 and up.
1982 97m/C Ralph Waite, Ellen Corby, Judy Norton-Taylor, Eric Scott, Jon Walmsley, Robert Wightman, Mary McDonough, David W. Harper, Kami Cotler, Joe Conley, Ronnie Clair Edwards, Richard Gilliland, Melinda Naud; *D:* Harry Harris. **VHS** *WAR*

A Day in October ♪♪ ♭

PG-13/Jr. High-Adult Niels Jensen (Sweeney) is a Danish resistance fighter fighting in Copenhagen as the Nazis prepare to invade Denmark in 1943. During a sabotage attempt he's injured and rescued by Sara, a young Jewish woman. Her family reluctantly hides the young man as they finally face up to the Nazi reality. Based on historical fact. Good performances help what is otherwise an average script. Filmed on location in Denmark.

The Amazing Creations of Jim Henson's Creature Shop

Not every Muppet you meet is a green felt frog or a glamour pig. The technology that helped Kermit ride a bicycle in *The Great Muppet Caper* helped found Jim Henson's Creature Shop. These days, the Shop is more than just a home for the Cookie Monster and Fozzie. It's a special effects lab that puts Muppet magic into a wide range of all-ages entertainment.

In 1979, Jim Henson's Creature Shop opened for business in London, where "The Muppet Show" was taped. In 1982 the Creature Shop was showcased by *The Dark Crystal*, a fantasy feature with no humans whatsoever, just a never-before-seen assembly of screen creatures utilizing Muppet techniques. The box-office winner proved that a feature motion picture could be 100% pure Muppet.

Soon, the Creature Shop was inventing new creations for other filmmakers, in such productions as *The Empire Strikes Back*, *Labyrinth*, the musical *Little Shop of Horrors*, the TV comedy "Dinosaurs," and most recently, the smash-hit *Babe* and *The Adventures of Pinocchio*. The common factor is Jim Henson's Creature Shop, now with branches in New York and Los Angeles, continuing the legacy that started with a green felt frog.

🎬 BEWARE 🎬 *Wartime violence and scary Nazis.*

1992 96m/C D.B. Sweeney, Kelly Wolf, Tovah Feldshuh, Daniel Benzali, Ole Lemmeke, Kim Romer, Anders Peter Bro, Lars Oluf

Larsen; *D:* Kenneth Madsen; *W:* Damian F. Slattery; *M:* Jens Lysdal. **VHS** *ACA, FOX*

The Day Jimmy's Boa Ate the Wash and Other Stories

Preschool-Primary Contains four animated stories adapted from popular children's books. The title story finds Jimmy bringing his favorite pet on a class trip. "Monty" features an overworked alligator who needs a rest from his taxi service. "The Great White Man-Eating Shark" and "Fourteen Rats and a Rat-Catcher" impart life's little lessons in a humorous way.
1992 35m/C VHS *CCC, WKV, BTV*

The Day of the Dolphin

PG/Family Research scientist, after successfully working out a means of teaching dolphins to talk, finds his animals kidnapped; espionage and assassination are involved. Dolphin voices by Henry, who also wrote the screenplay.

BEWARE *Salty language.*

1973 104m/C George C. Scott, Trish Van Devere, Paul Sorvino, Fritz Weaver, Jon Korkes, John Dehner, Edward Herrmann, Severn Darden; *D:* Mike Nichols; *W:* Buck Henry; *M:* Georges Delerue; *V:* Buck Henry. **Award Nominations:** Academy Awards '73: Best Sound; **Awards:** National Board of Review Awards '73: 10 Best Films of the Year. **VHS, Beta, LV** *NLC*

Daydreamer 🦴🦴🦴

Family Setting is 1801 Vienna, where young Hans Christian Anderson, always in trouble, runs away from home. In daydreams he imagines—and enters—the fairy tales he would later write down, like "Thumbelina" and "The Emperor's New Clothes." Early Arthur Rankin Jr./Jules Bass production, somewhat crudely integrating live-action and stop-motion animation. Puppet characters lack expression and humanity to match the celebrity voices. One nice touch: animated Hans takes unheroic parts in his fantasies (he's a faithless prince who jilts the Little Mermaid), confronting his own personal flaws.
1966 98m/C Paul O'Keefe, Ray Bolger, Jack Gilford, Margaret Hamilton; *D:* Jules Bass; *V:* Tallulah Bankhead, Boris Karloff, Burl Ives, Terry-Thomas, Ed Wynn, Victor Borge, Patty Duke. **VHS, Beta**

Dazed and Confused 🦴🦴🦴

R/Sr. High-Adult Day in the life of a bunch of high school seniors should prove to be a trip back in time for those coming of age in the 70's. Eight students faced with life after high school have one last hurrah, as they search for Aerosmith tickets and haze the incoming freshmen. Keen characterization by writer/director Linklater captures the spirit of a generation shaped by Watergate, the Vietnam War, feminism, and marijuana. Groovy soundtrack features Alice Cooper, Deep Purple, KISS, and Foghat.

BEWARE *Profanity; marijuana smoking (they inhale); alcohol use; poor role modeling; roughhousing.*

1993 97m/C Jason London, Rory Cochrane, Sasha Jensen, Wiley Wiggins, Michelle Burke, Adam Goldberg, Anthony Rapp, Marissa Ribisi; *D:* Richard Linklater; *W:* Richard Linklater. **VHS, LV** *MCA*

Dead Men Don't Wear Plaid 🦴🦴

PG/Primary-Adult Martin is frequently hilarious as a private detective who encounters a bizarre assortment of suspects while trying to find out the truth about a scientist's death. Ingeniously interspliced with clips from old Warner Brothers films, including snippets with Humphrey Bogart, Bette Davis, Alan Ladd, Burt Lancaster, Ava Gardner, Barbara Stanwyck, Ray Milland and others. With nowhere in particular to go, novel whodunit is lightweight amusement.

BEWARE *Comic violence in a bumbling detective sort of way.*

1982 89m/B Steve Martin, Rachel Ward, Reni Santoni, George Gaynes, Frank McCarthy, Carl Reiner; *D:* Carl Reiner; *W:* Steve Martin, Carl Reiner; *M:* Miklos Rozsa. **VHS, Beta, LV** *MCA, FCT, HMV*

Dead Poets Society 🦴🦴🦴 ⬙

PG/Jr. High-Adult Quirky English teacher inspires boys in a dry 1950s' prep school to pursue inner truth and beauty, resulting in clashes with administrative tyrants and hateful parents. Williams is offscreen more than you'd think; story belongs to the student characters. While their struggles with individuality and creative endeavor are enormously moving, pic sends some really mixed messages (advancing teen suicide as a preferable alternative to a military academy) that make this Disney/Touchstone release very iffy viewing for youngsters. On the other hand, what other pic even tries to show poetry class as interesting?

BEWARE *Profanity, sex talk, a rigidly insensitive parent. A teen commits suicide.*

1989 128m/C Robin Williams, Ethan Hawke, Robert Sean Leonard, Josh Charles, Gale Hansen, Kurtwood Smith, James Waterson, Dylan Kussman, Lara Flynn Boyle, Melora Hardin; *D:* Peter Weir; *W:* Tom Schulman; *M:* Maurice Jarre. **Award Nominations:** Academy Awards '89: Best Actor (Williams), Best Director (Weir), Best Picture; **Awards:** Academy Awards '89: Best Original Screenplay; British Academy Awards '89: Best Film; Cesar Awards '91: Best Foreign Film. **VHS, Beta, LV, 8mm** *TOU*

Dear Brigitte 🦴🦴

Family American boy genius ("Lost in Space" tyke Mumy) has a crush on international sex symbol Brigitte Bardot. He and his flustered family journey to Paris to meet her in person. Outdated early '60s screen sitcom/travelogue, putting a charming cast to a sore test. Based on the novel "Erasmus with Freckles" by John Haase.

1965 100m/C James Stewart, Billy Mumy, Glynis Johns, Fabian, Cindy Carol, John Williams, Jack Kruschen, Brigitte Bardot, Ed Wynn, Alice Pearce; *D:* Henry Koster; *W:* Hal Kanter. **VHS, Beta** *FOX*

Death Becomes Her 🦴🦴 ⬙

PG-13/Jr. High-Adult Aging actress Streep will do anything to stay young and beautiful, especially when childhood rival Hawn shows up, 200 pounds lighter and out to avenge the loss of her fiance, Streep's henpecked hubby. Doing anything arrives in the form of a Faustian pact and a potion that stops the aging process (and keeps her alive forever). Watch for the hilarious party filled with dead celebrities who all look as good as the day they died. Great special effects. Satirizes society's quest for youth and beauty, but you may have to point that out. Ages 10 and up.

BEWARE *Profanity, nudity, comic book violence, alcohol use, sex talk and living heads without bodies.*

1992 105m/C Meryl Streep, Bruce Willis, Goldie Hawn, Isabella Rosselini, Sydney Pollack, Michael Caine, Ian Ogilvy, Adam Storke, Nancy Fish, Alaina Reed Hall, Michelle Johnson, Mimi Kennedy, Jonathan Silverman; *Cameos:* Fabio Lanzoni; *D:* Robert Zemeckis; *W:* Martin Donovan, David Koepp; *M:* Alan Silvestri. **VHS, Beta, LV** *MGM, PMS*

Death of a Goldfish

Preschool-Primary Mister Rogers explores with children the difficult subject of death. In the Neighborhood of Make Believe, Lady Aberlin and Bob Dog learn that only living things die.

1974 30m/C VHS, Beta

Death of the Incredible Hulk

Jr. High-Adult Last of a series of TV movies based on the Marvel Comics superhero, aired after a "Hulk" TV series had run its course. Here scientist David Banner may have a cure to stop his periodic transformations into the big green guy (Ferrigno). But terrorists are also after the Hulk. Despite the portentous title there was to be a follow-up feature reviving the Hulk, but actor/director Bixby became a real-life casualty of terminal cancer.

BEWARE *Violence.*

1990 96m/C Bill Bixby, Lou Ferrigno, Elizabeth Gracen, Philip Sterling; *D:* Bill Bixby. **VHS** *RHI*

Death on the Nile

PG/Jr. High-Adult Agatha Christie's fictional detective, Hercule Poirot, interrupts his vacation to uncover who killed an heiress aboard a steamer cruising down the Nile. Scenic, but slow. Anthony Powell's costumes won an Oscar. Ages 11 and up.

1978 135m/C Peter Ustinov, Jane Birkin, Lois Chiles, Bette Davis, Mia Farrow, David Niven, Olivia Hussey, Angela Lansbury, Jack Warden, Maggie Smith, George Kennedy, Simon MacCorkindale, Harry Andrews, Jon Finch; *D:* John Guillermin; *W:* Anthony Shaffer; *M:* Nino Rota. **VHS, Beta, LV** *REP*

Deathcheaters

G/Family Proof that a tough-guy action-adventure need not be a profane bloodbath; two Aussie stuntmen accept a Secret Service mission to destroy a warlord's fortress in the Philippines. The twist; both heroes are Vietnam vets—and have since sworn never to kill again. So they don't, and the mission stays well within 'G' territory. Try

peddling that concept today! Repetitive, but the punchline is worth it.

BEWARE *Violence, only serious in one Vietnam flashback.*

1976 96m/C John Hargreaves, Grant Page, Noel Ferrer; *D:* Brian Trenchard-Smith; *W:* Michael Cove. **VHS, Beta** *VES*

A Decade of the Waltons

Family "The Waltons" creator Earl Hamner narrates this retrospective program which features poignant highlights from the series. Made for television. Ages 7 and up.

1985 120m/C Richard Thomas, Ellen Corby, Will Geer, Michael Learned, Ralph Waite. **VHS, Beta** *ORI, WAR, TVC*

December

PG/Jr. High-Adult Four prep-school boys in 1941 New Hampshire hear the first reports of Japanese bombing Pearl Harbor. In one night they debate loyalty, friendship, patriotism, censorship, etc. They never make it to national health policy and the ozone layer, but almost; this terribly stagy and earnestly unconvincing drama signals it's about Big Issues with every anachronistic line, and young protagonists are symbols more than people.

BEWARE *Profanity.*

1991 92m/C Wil Wheaton, Chris Young, Brian Krause, Balthazar Getty, Jason London; *D:* Gabe Torres; *W:* Gabe Torres. **VHS, LV** *NO*

Defenders of the Earth: The Story Begins

Preschool-Primary Saturday-morning cartoon compilation bringing together heroic characters from the classic newspaper comic-strip characters syndicated through King Features; Flash Gordon, Ming the Merciless, the Phantom, and Mandrake the Magician. Additional volumes available.

1986 90m/C VHS, Beta *FHE*

Defenders of the Vortex

Family Animated movie follows the Galaxy Legion as it tries to stop the evil Zoa from gaining control of the Vortex.

1990 92m/C VHS, Beta *JFK*

Defense Play

PG/Primary-Jr. High Espionage tale about two teens who uncover a Soviet agent stealing plans for advanced helicopter technology (with radio-controlled models as the prototypes; movie budget was cheaper that way). Fair throwback to the Hardy-Boys tradition.

BEWARE *Violence.*

1988 95m/C David Oliver, Susan Ursitti, Monte Markham, William Frankfather, Patch MacKenzie; *D:* Monte Markham. **VHS, Beta** *TWE*

The Delicate Delinquent

Family Lewis (in his first film without longtime partner Dean Martin) plays a naive young bumbler under heavy peer pressure to join the street hoods in his part of town. But with the guidance of a brotherly police officer, the delicate delinquent decides to become a cop instead. Message-laden comedy manages to deliver the laughs anyway; keep in mind this came out in the era of "Rebel Without a Cause," (back when gang members wore suits and ties) and its preachier moments can be forgiven.

BEWARE: *Roughhousing.*

1956 101m/B Jerry Lewis, Darren McGavin, Martha Hyer, Robert Ivers, Horace McMahon; **D:** Don McGuire; **W:** Don McGuire. **VHS, Beta, LV** *PAR*

Delirious

PG/Jr. High-Adult Cute idea, undone by a crummy script. A writer for a television soap opera (John Candy) gets bonked on the head and dreams he's inside the story where murder and mayhem are brewing. Can he write himself back to safety, and find romance along the way? Too bad filmmakers couldn't write their way out of a paper bag. Ages 10 and up.

1991 96m/C John Candy, Mariel Hemingway, Emma Samms, Raymond Burr, David Rasche, Dylan Baker, Charles Rocket, Jerry Orbach, Renee Taylor, Robert Wagner; **D:** Tom Mankiewicz; **M:** Cliff Eidelman. **VHS, Beta, LV, 8mm** *MGM*

Dennis the Menace

PG/Family John Hughes adaptation of the Hank Ketcham comic strip unfairly derided by critics as a "Home Alone" ripoff. Emphasis is instead on the relationship between crafty five-year-old Dennis Mitchell and his cranky neighbor Mr. Wilson (Matthau, perfectly cast), whose every pain and pratfall originates with the well-meaning tyke. This gets the epic treatment usually given Moby Dick and Ahab, and it's often hilarious. Dennis then turns his mischief against a nasty, knife-wielding burglar dubbed Switchblade Sam, featuring some really cruel slapstick of the "Home Alone" variety that's not quite as funny as the director would like it to be. Still better than either "Problem Child."

BEWARE: *Cartoonish violence; child kidnapping; sinister villain with dental problems.*

1993 96m/C Walter Matthau, Mason Gamble, Joan Plowright, Christopher Lloyd, Lea Thompson, Robert Stanton, Billie Bird, Paul Winfield, Amy Sakasitz, Kellen Hathaway, Arnold Stang; **D:** Nick Castle; **W:** John Hughes; **M:** Jerry Goldsmith. **VHS, Beta, LV, 8mm** *WAR*

Dennis the Menace: Dinosaur Hunter WOOF!

G/Family Opportunistic video distributors dug up a best-forgotten 1987 TV feature of Hank Ketchum's comic-strip character, tacked on the subtitle "Dinosaur Hunter," and released it on tape to rip off both "Jurassic Park" and John Hughes' "Dennis the Menace." Even without the deception (the listed running time is phony too!), this is still a loser, a dimwit sitcom with horrid kid actors and no dinosaurs—just prehistoric bones Dennis digs up that threaten to make his neighborhood an archaeological site.

1987 93m/C Victor Dimattia, William Windom, Pat Estrin, Jim Jansen, Patsy Garrett. **VHS, LV** *VMK*

Dennis the Menace in Mayday for Mother

Family Animated short that brought Hank Ketcham's comic strip to cartoon life for the first time, centering on Dennis' efforts to celebrate Mother's Day.

1980 24m/C VHS, Beta *MCA*

Dennis the Menace: Spies, Robbers and Ghosts

Family "Ghost Blusters" has Dennis wanting to make a club house out of a spooky old home. "The Monster of Mudville Flats" is tracked by Dennis, Tommy, and Margaret, and in "Young Sherlock Dennis," The Menace sets out to find who's been eating all the chocolates. "The Defective Detector" features Dennis and friends hunting treasure on the beach with a metal detector. Additionla volumes available.

1993 35m/C VHS *FOX*

Dennis the Movie Star

Family Dennis the Menace stars in his own group of movies when he is able to convince a director that his old star is no good.

1988 65m/C VHS, Beta *FOX*

Denver the Last Dinosaur

Family Magical, gentle dinosaur hatches from a giant egg into the 20th century and makes friends with some skateboarding kids who love rock music. Syndicated cartoon that scored big in the ratings and prompted a series. Additional volumes available.

1988 45m/C VHS *FRH*

Desert Bloom

PG/Sr. High-Adult On the eve of a nuclear bomb test nearby, an alcoholic veteran and his Las Vegas family struggle through tensions brought on by a promiscuous visiting aunt, a mother with a gambling habit, and the chaotic, rapidly changing world. Gish shines as Rose, the teenage daughter through whose eyes the story unfolds.

BEWARE: *Intense alcohol use, but lighter sex talk.*

1986 103m/C Jon Voight, JoBeth Williams, Ellen Barkin, Annabeth Gish, Allen (Goorwitz) Garfield, Jay Underwood; **D:** Eugene Corr; **W:** Eugene Corr; **M:** Brad Fiedel. **VHS, Beta, LV** *NO*

Mr. Wilson can barely enjoy his paper with "Dennis the Menace" around.

Desperately Seeking Susan 🦴🦴🦴

PG-13/Jr. High-Adult Bored New Jersey housewife Arquette gets her kicks reading the personals. She becomes obsessed with a relationship between two lovers who arrange their meetings through the columns, and goes to New York to find out who they are. But after a timely whack on the head, she takes on the identity of Susan, the free-spirited woman in the personals. Unfortunately, Susan (Madonna, of course) is in a lot of trouble with all sorts of unsavory folk. Will appeal to Madonna fans, and their parents. Ages 13 and up.

🚸 BEWARE *Violence, profanity, sex and brief nudity.*

1985 104m/C Rosanna Arquette, Madonna, Aidan Quinn, Mark Blum, Robert Joy, Laurie Metcalf, Steven Wright, John Turturro, Richard Hell, Annie Golden, Ann Magnuson; **D:** Susan Seidelman; **M:** Thomas Newman. **VHS, Beta, LV** *FCT*

Destroy All Monsters 🦴🦴 🦴

G/Jr. High-Adult When alien babes take control of Godzilla and his monstrous colleagues, it looks like all is lost for Earth. Adding insult to injury, Ghidra is sent in to take care of the loose ends. Can the planet possibly survive this madness? Classic Toho monster slugfest also features Mothra, Rodan, Son of Godzilla, Angila, Varan, Baragon, Spigas and others.

1968 88m/C Akira Kubo, Jun Tazaki, Yoshio Tsuchiya, Kyoko Ai, Yukiko Kobayashi, Kenji Sahara, Andrew Hughes; **D:** Inoshiro Honda. **VHS** *FRG*

The Devil & Max Devlin 🦴 🦴

PG/Family Recently deceased Max, a Scroogish landlord, strikes a hellish bargain to be restored to life if he gets three honest young folk to sell their souls to the devil. Targets are an aspiring singer, a motorbike racer, and a kid husband-hunting for his widow mom. But hanging with the goodie-goodies gives Max a change of heart. With a script by "Freaky Friday" author Mary Rodgers, a Disney pedigree and Cosby in a dual role (as a dapper demon and his satanic boss), this should have been fun but instead resides in lethargic limbo.

1981 95m/C Elliott Gould, Bill Cosby, Susan Anspach, Adam Rich, Julie Budd; **D:** Steven Hilliard Stern; **W:** Jimmy Sangster; **M:** Marvin Hamlisch, Buddy Baker. **VHS, Beta** *DIS, OM*

Devil Horse 🦴🦴

Family A boy's devotion to a wild horse marked for destruction as a killer leads him into trouble. A 12-chapter serial; 13 minutes each.

1932 156m/B Frankie Darro, Harry Carey Sr., Noah Beery Sr.; **D:** Otto Brower, Richard Talmadge. **VHS, Beta** *GPV, VCN, DVT*

Dial "M" for Murder 🦴🦴🦴

Jr. High-Adult An unfaithful husband devises an elaborate plan to murder his wife for her money, but when she accidentally stabs the killer-to-be, with scissors no less, he alters his methods. Part of the "A Night at the Movies" series, this tape simulates a 1954 movie evening with a Daffy Duck cartoon, "My Little Duckaroo," a newsreel, and coming attractions for "Them" and "A Star Is Born." Filmed in 3-D. Based on the play by Frederick Knotts.

🚸 BEWARE *Extreme spousal conflict.*

1954 123m/C Ray Milland, Grace Kelly, Robert Cummings, John Williams, Anthony (Antonio Margheriti) Dawson; **D:** Alfred Hitchcock; **M:** Dimitri Tiomkin. **VHS, Beta, LV** *WAR, TLF*

Diamonds are Forever 🦴🦴🦴

PG/Jr. High-Adult For a then record-setting salary of $1.25 million, Connery returned to his Bond role after a one-film absence, delivering an entertaining espionage epic. Agent 007 once again battles his nemesis Blofeld, this time in Las Vegas. Bond must prevent the implementation of a plot to destroy Washington through the use of a space-orbiting laser. Fabulous stunts include Bond's wild drive through the streets of Vegas in a '71 Mach 1. Theme sung by Shirley Bassey.

🚸 BEWARE *Violence, alcohol use, suggested sex, and sexism (you know, in the form of Bond girls).*

1971 120m/C Sean Connery, Jill St. John, Charles Gray, Bruce Cabot, Jimmy Dean, Lana Wood, Bruce Glover, Putter Smith, Norman Burton, Joseph Furst, Bernard Lee, Desmond Llewelyn, Laurence Naismith, Leonard Barr, Lois Maxwell, Margaret Lacey, Joe Robinson, Donna Garrat, Trina Parks; **D:** Guy Hamilton; **W:** Tom Mankiewicz; **M:** John Barry. **VHS, Beta, LV** *MGM, TLF*

Diamond's Edge 🦴🦴🦴

PG/Family Adolescent private eye and his brother snoop into the affairs of the late master criminal the Falcon, and find intrigue surrounding his box of malteser candies. Based on scripter Anthony Horowitz's book "The Falcon's Malteser" (ouch!), a sample of the puns and genre-parodying gags to be found in this sly English sendup of hardboiled detective tales, set somewhat jarringly in London and brimming with Briticisms despite the Bogart attitude. A real video hidden treasure, worth investigating. Watch the clue-packed, cartoon opening credits carefully. Originally titled "Just Ask For Diamond."

🚸 BEWARE *Roughhousing.*

1988 83m/C Susannah York, Peter Eyre, Patricia Hodge, Nickolas Grace; **D:** Stephen Bayly; **W:** Anthony Horowitz; **M:** Trevor Jones. **VHS, Beta** *HBO*

Diamonds on Wheels 🦴🦴

Family A Disney film about three British teenagers, amid a big road rally, discovering stolen diamonds and getting pursued by gangsters.

1973 84m/C VHS, Beta *DIS*

Dick Deadeye 🎬🎬◁

Family Offbeat animated feature from the creators of the "Charlie Brown" cartoons but based on the operas of Gilbert and Sullivan and drawings by Ronald Searle. Dick Deadeye sports an I.Q. of zero, but nevertheless is hired to wipe out pirates, thieves, and a sorcerer. Along the way, various G & S songs are presented in rock'n'roll arrangements.
1976 80m/C D: Bill Melendez. **VHS, Beta** *FHE, PRS*

Dick Tracy

Family Comic-strip detective first came to the screen in this early Republic serial, the studio's first of many raids on the funny pages. But they deliberately left out nearly all the supporting cast of Chester Gould's characters—even Tess Trueheart—and the results are mixed, as Tracy takes on a typical bizarrely costumed serial fiend called the Spider. Longer than usual in 15 episodes; exciting first chapter is 30 minutes, the tedious remainders are 20 minutes apiece. Hang on long enough to see the Spider's way-cool airplane.
1937 310m/B Ralph Byrd, Smiley Burnette, Irving Pichel, Jennifer Jones; **D:** John English. **VHS, Beta, LV** *SNC, VYY, VCI*

Dick Tracy 🎬🎬🎬

PG/Jr. High-Adult Beatty, as producer/director/star, brings Chester Gould's comic-strip detective to life, outdoing other recent megabucks funny-pages adaptations due to amazing art direction. Shot in only seven colors, using timeless sets that capture the printed page rather than the reality of the NYC setting, Beatty gives viewers a memorable spectacle. Alas, plot is a fairly ordinary feud between Tracy and crazed mobster Big Boy Caprice (other classic bad guys like Pruneface, Flattop and the Brow have bit parts). Villains are encased in exaggerated makeup, but Tracy isn't, guaranteeing that he's the least interesting guy onscreen—though a similarly unencumbered Madonna gives a fine performance as the femme fatale Breathless Mahoney, belting out Sondheim's musical numbers. Young Korsmo out acts them both as the nameless 'Kid' the hero adopts. Produced through Disney's Touchstone division. Ironically, though this strives for camp appeal, Gould's work was considered stark and realistic for its time, as the first comic strip to depict dead bodies.

BEWARE *Violence—gunfights and death, but not one drop of blood shown.*

1990 105m/C Warren Beatty, Madonna, Charlie Korsmo, Glenne Headly, Al Pacino, Dustin Hoffman, James Caan, Mandy Patinkin, Paul Sorvino, Charles Durning, Dick Van Dyke, R.G. Armstrong, Catherine O'Hara, Estelle Parsons, Seymour Cassel, Michael J. Pollard, William Forsythe, Kathy Bates, James Tolkan; **D:** Warren Beatty; **W:** Jim Cash, Jack Epps Jr.; **M:** Danny Elfman, Stephen Sondheim. **Award Nominations:** Academy Awards '90: Best Cinematography, Best Costume Design, Best Sound, Best Supporting Actor (Pacino); **Awards:** Academy Awards '90: Best Art Direction/Set Decoration, Best Makeup, Best Song ("Sooner or Later"). **VHS, Beta, LV** *TOU, FCT, IME*

Dick Tracy, Detective 🎬🎬

Family The first Dick Tracy feature film, in which Splitface is on the loose, a schoolteacher is murdered, the Mayor is threatened, and a nutty professor uses a crystal ball to give Tracy the clues needed to connect the crimes.
1945 62m/B Morgan Conway, Anne Jeffreys, Mike Mazurki, Jane Greer, Lyle Latell; **D:** William Burke. **VHS, Beta** *SNC, MED, VYY*

Dick Tracy Meets Gruesome 🎬🎬

Family Gruesome and his partner in crime, Melody, stage a bank robbery using the secret formula of Dr. A. Tomic. Tracy has to solve the case before word gets out and people rush to withdraw their savings, destroying civilization as we know it. One of the RKO "Dick Tracy" series that came closer than the serials to matching the comic strip.

 Violence.

1947 66m/B Boris Karloff, Ralph Byrd, Lyle Latell; **D:** John Rawlins. **VHS, Beta** *NOS, MRV, SNC*

Did I Ever Tell You How Lucky You Are?

Family Two Dr. Seuss stories narrated by John Cleese. Includes "Did I Ever Tell You How Lucky You Are?" and "Scrambled Eggs Super."
1993 30m/C VHS *BTV, RAN*

Die Hard 🎬🎬🎬

R/Sr. High-Adult High-voltage action thriller pits lone New York cop John McClane (Willis) against a band of ruthless high-stakes terrorists who attack and hold hostage the employees of a large corporation as they celebrate Christmas in a new Los Angeles high rise. You heard right. Don't ask. Rickman turns in a marvelous performance as the chief bad guy. Based on the novel "Nothing Lasts Forever" by Roderick Thorp.

BEWARE *Profanity, violence, explosions, all on a grand scale. When they say "Die Hard" they mean die hard! This guy limps around with glass in his feet and still won't give up.*

1988 114m/C Bruce Willis, Bonnie Bedelia, Alan Rickman, Alexander Godunov, Paul Gleason, William Atherton, Reginald Vel Johnson, Hart Bochner, James Shigeta, Mary Ellen Trainor, De'voreaux White, Robert Davi, Rick Ducommun; **D:** John McTiernan; **W:** Jeb Stuart, Steven E. de Souza; **C:** Jan De Bont; **M:** Michael Kamen. **VHS, Beta, LV** *FOX*

Die Hard 2: Die Harder 🎬🎬🎬

R/Sr. High-Adult Fast, well-done sequel brings another impossible situation before wise-cracking, tough-cookie cop Willis. Our hero tangles with a group of terrorists at an airport under siege, while his wife remains in a plane circling above as its fuel dwindles. Obviously a repeat of the plot and action of the first "Die Hard," with references to the former in the script. Fairly gory, especially the icicle-in-the-eyeball scene. Adapted from the novel "58 Minutes" by Walter Wager and characters created by Roderick Thorp.

BEWARE *More brutality, profanity and more explosions. If you liked the first, though, this stuff gets addicting.*

1990 124m/C Bruce Willis, William Atherton, Franco Nero, Bonnie Bedelia, John Amos, Reginald Vel Johnson, Dennis Franz, Art Evans, Fred Dalton Thompson, William Sadler, Sheila McCarthy, Robert Patrick, John Leguizamo, Robert Costanzo, Tom Verica; *D:* Renny Harlin; *W:* Doug Richardson, Steven E. de Souza; *M:* Michael Kamen. **VHS, LV** *FOX*

Die Hard: With a Vengeance 🦴🦴 ᗛ

R/Sr. High-Adult The series runs out of steam, with McClane (Willis) back home in the Big Apple and having another bad day. Brilliant and vengeful bomber Simon (Irons) blows up a department store and generally makes life miserable for McClane and his reluctant partner, a civilian (Jackson). The claustrophobic settings of the first two outings have been replaced by the expanse of New York City, to good effect, but frenetic action scenes and good chemistry between Willis and Jackson don't quite compensate for a lackluster script.

BEWARE *Strong violence; pervasive strong language, explosions and McClane gets blown all over New York. No, really, he does.*

1995 131m/C Bruce Willis, Samuel L. Jackson, Jeremy Irons, Graham Greene, Colleen Camp, Larry Bryggman, Tony Peck, Nick Wyman, Sam Phillips; *D:* John McTiernan; *W:* Jonathan Hensleigh; *M:* Michael Kamen. **VHS, LV** *FXV*

Die Laughing 🦴 ᗛ

PG/Jr. High-Adult Cab driver/aspiring rock musician unwittingly becomes involved in murder, intrigue, and the kidnapping of a monkey that has memorized a scientific formula capable of destroying the world. Benson wrote, produced, scored, and acted in lame comedy with supposed youth-appeal.

BEWARE *Violence, salty language, sex talk*

1980 108m/C Robby Benson, Charles Durning, Bud Cort, Elsa Lanchester, Peter Coyote; *D:* Jeff Werner; *W:* Robby Benson, Scott Parker; *M:* Robby Benson. **VHS, Beta** *WAR*

Dig Hole. Build House

Family Of course, there's more to it than that, and children will get a crash course on house building as Joe the builder takes them on a step by step process of turning an empty field into a new home (as opposed to an old home). Ages 3 to 9.

1994 30m/C VHS *TPV,*

Digby, the Biggest Dog in the World 🦴

G/Family Strained comedy-fantasy from Britain about Digby, an English sheepdog, who wanders around a scientific laboratory, drinks an experimental fluid, and

grows to giant size, bringing out the army. Even with hounds, bigger is not always better.

1973 88m/C Jim Dale, Angela Douglas, Spike Milligan, Dinsdale Landen; *D:* Joseph McGrath. **VHS, Beta** *PSM*

Digger 🦴🦴 ᗛ

PG/Primary-Adult Digger (Hann-Byrd) arrives at a Pacific Northwest island to stay with relatives, including his Grandma (Dukakis) who's being romanced by the fun-loving Arthur (Nielsen). He makes friends with another youth who turns out to have a terminal heart ailment.

BEWARE *Dying child.*

1994 92m/C Adam Hann-Byrd, Olympia Dukakis, Leslie Nielsen, Joshua Jackson, Barbara Williams, Timothy Bottoms; *D:* Robert Turner; *W:* Rodney Gibbons; *M:* Todd Boekelheide. **VHS** *PAR*

Digging Dinosaurs—2 Pack

Preschool-Jr. High Two-part set aimed at teaching younger audiences about dinosaurs. Covers different types of dinosaurs, as well as how and where dinosaur bones have been found. Includes computer animation, actual footage of dinosaur digs and visits to museums and paleontology labs. Ages 6 to 11.

1994 75m/C VHS *QVD*

Digging for Dinosaurs

Preschool-Primary There's nothing pale about paleontology as taught by jovial Professor Fossilworth, the very model of a dinosaur-digger with his shovel, pith helmet, khaki shirt and shorts and his dog, Rex. Fossilworth (played by Jerold Goldstein) sings, dances, climbs up a cliff, falls in a river and sits by the campfire (in his red pajamas), all the better to provide a wealth of information about dinosaurs. Highlight is footage of the prof cavorting with different kinds of dinos; to give this segment a genuine prehistoric look, it's in black-and-white. Ages 4 to 9.

199? ?m/C VHS *NYR*

Dimples 🦴🦴 ᗛ

PG/Family Shirley enlivens this Depression-era rags-to-riches tale as a singing and dancing orphan whose pickpocket grandfather, threatened with jail, gives her up to wealthy adoptive parents. But the girl misses the simple life and returns to the old man. ♬ Hey, What Did the Bluebird Say?; He Was a Dandy; Picture Me Without You; Oh Mister Man Up in the Moon; Dixie-Anna; Get On Board; Swing Low Sweet Chariot.

1936 78m/B Shirley Temple, John Carradine, Frank Morgan, Helen Westley, Berton Churchill, Robert Kent, Delma Byron; *D:* William A. Seiter. **VHS, Beta** *FOX*

Dinky: Dinky Finds a Home

Preschool-Primary Video reissue of Dinky Duck, a cartoon star of the Terrytoons series devised by classic animator Paul Terry; this example in glorious Technicolor.
1946 36m/C VHS *VTR*

Dinky: Much Ado About Nothing

Preschool-Primary Shakespeare doesn't have much in common with this wild and crazy duck from the Terrytoon archives.
1940 36m/C VHS *VTR*

Dinosaur Families

Preschool-Jr. High Part of the "Digging Dinosaurs" collection. This section covers the family structure of the dinosaurs and how paleontologists and children can dig for dinosaur bones. Ages 6 to 11.
1994 35m/C VHS *QVD*

Dinosaurs are Very Big

Preschool-Jr. High Winner of the Duh! Foundation Award for Video Naming. Part of the "Digging Dinosaurs" collection that takes a look at some of the dinosaurs that roamed the earth in the past. Uses computer animation with visits to digs and museums to help explain the differences between the various dinosaurs. Ages 6 to 11.
1994 35m/C VHS *QVD*

Dinosaurs, Dinosaurs, Dinosaurs

Family Overexposure to dinosaur lore is turning dino-fan Owens into a dinosaur, so partner Boardman must learn all he can in order to stop the changes. Entertaining, educational program which re-creates the world of dinosaurs.
1987 30m/C Gary Owens, Eric Boardman. **VHS, Beta** *MPI, KAR*

Dirt Bike Kid 🦴

PG/Primary-Sr. High Adolescent Jack buys a used motorbike with a mind of its own (a fact everyone accepts without question). Both battle a stuffy banker trying to close a favorite hot dog shop. Billingsley still shows the appeal he had in "A Christmas Story"; otherwise this moronic, low-budget comedy completely wipes out.

> **BEWARE** *Sex talk, drug talk, and alcohol use. At least Jack always wears his helmet.*

1986 91m/C Peter Billingsley, Anne Bloom, Stuart Pankin, Patrick Collins, Sage Parker, Chad Sheets; **D:** Hoite C. Caston; **W:** Lewis Colick, David Brandes. **VHS, Beta, LV, 8mm** *COL, NLC*

Dirty Dancing 🦴🦴🦴 ᵛ

PG-13/Jr. High-Adult Innocent 17-year-old Frances, tellingly nicknamed 'Baby,' is vacationing with her parents in the Catskills in 1963. Bored with the program at the hotel, she finds the real fun at the staff dances, falling for the sensitive-hunk dance instructor (Swayze). The same old story of bittersweet first love, jazzed by fun dance sequences, catchy music, and a terrifically likeable cast.

> **BEWARE** *Sex, provocative dancing, profanity. One character needs an abortion.*

1987 97m/C Patrick Swayze, Jennifer Grey, Cynthia Rhodes, Jerry Orbach, Jack Weston, Jane Brucker, Kelly Bishop, Lonny Price, Charles "Honi" Coles, Bruce Morrow; **D:** Emile Ardolino; **W:** Eleanor Bergstein; **M:** John Morris. **VHS, Beta, LV** *LIV, VES*

Dirty Rotten Scoundrels 🦴🦴🦴

PG/Jr. High-Adult A remake of the 1964 "Bedtime Story," in which two confidence tricksters on the Riviera endeavor to rip off a suddenly rich American woman, and each other. Caine and Martin are terrific, Martin has some of his best physical comedy ever, and Headly is charming as the prey who's always one step ahead of them. Fine direction from Oz, the man who brought us the voice of Yoda in "The Empire Strikes Back."

> **BEWARE** *Profanity. Devious con artist impersonates a crippled soldier.*

1988 112m/C Steve Martin, Michael Caine, Glenne Headly, Anton Rodgers, Barbara Harris, Dana Ivey; **D:** Frank Oz; **W:** Dale Launer, Stanley Shapiro; **M:** Miles Goodman. **VHS, Beta, LV** *ORI*

Disney's Adventures in Wonderland

Family Segments from the Disney Channel TV series featuring a new, hip Alice and friends in live-action musical adventures and sketches in Wonderland. Each video includes two exciting full episodes.
1993 58m/C VHS, Beta *TOU*

Disney's Darkwing Duck: His Favorite Adventures

Family Join Darkwing Duck on his favorite adventures from the 1991-92 Emmy nominated cartoon series. Each video includes an "MTV-style" Darkwing Duck music video plus feature presentations.
1993 48m/C VHS, Beta *TOU*

Disney's Greatest Lullabies

Family Each tape in this series includes five or so bedtime ballads, culled from classic Disney films, designed to bring somnolent bliss to the kiddies.
1986 25m/C VHS, Beta *DIS*

Disney's Haunted Halloween

Family Goofy helps students learn the origins of this crazy holiday. Superstitions and traditions are discussed. **1984 10m/C VHS, Beta** *MTI, DSN*

Disney's Sing-Along Songs: Circle of Life

Family Favorites from two Disney animated blockbusters, "The Lion King" and "Pocahontas." If your kids don't already know the words to all these songs, they will now! ♫ Circle of Life; I Just Can't Wait to Be King; Part of Your World; Belle; Prince Ali; When You Wish Upon a Star; Everybody Wants to Be a Cat. **1994 30m/C VHS** *DIS*

Disney's Sing-Along Songs: Pocahontas

Family Yet another sing-along video from Disney, this one focusing its efforts on the smash hit, "Pocahontas." At least your kids will get a little history exposure, right? **1995 35m/C VHS** *DIS*

Disney's Sing-Along Songs: Sebastian's Caribbean Jam

Family Sebastian, the musical crab from "The Little Mermaid" is back with another video. This time he co-hosts a travelogue through Walt Disney World with friend Sam Wright. **1991 30m/C VHS** *DIS*

Disney's Sing-Along Songs: Sebastian's Party Gras

Family Sebastian, the crab star of "The Little Mermaid," takes his friends on a reggae and calypso fest. **1991 30m/C VHS** *DIS*

Disney's Sing-Along Songs: The Hunchback of Notre Dame: Topsy Turvy

Family Another addition to the sing-along series, featuring songs "Topsy Turvy" and "Out There" from the newest Disney blockbuster, "The Hunchback of Notre Dame." Spotlights the unexpectedly cuddly Quasimodo. Also features numbers from "Toy Story," "James and the Giant Peach," "Oliver and Company," and Disney classics "Snow White and the Seven Dwarfs" and "Alice in Wonderland." **1996 30m/C VHS** *TOU*

Disney's Sing-Along Songs: The Twelve Days of Christmas

Family Get into the Christmas spirit with singing traditional holiday carols and new songs, too, with Mickey, Minnie, Donald, and all your favorite Disney pals. **1993 30m/C VHS** *DIS*

Disney's Sing-Along Songs, Vol. 1: Heigh-Ho

Family Musical moments from Disney classic movies with words on screen for viewers to sing-along with the characters. Professor Ludwig von Drake narrates many of the episodes in the series. This volume is one of the best, featuring "Heigh Ho" and "The Dwarfs' Yodel Song" from "Snow White and the Seven Dwarfs." Children can easily keep up and follow along with the large-size type on-screen of the wonderful Disney classics. **1988 28m/C VHS, Beta, LV** *DIS*

Disney's Sing-Along Songs, Vol. 2: Zip-A-Dee-Doo-Dah

Family Host Ludwig von Drake returns to take the kids through a musical tour of classic Disney movies. Includes selections from "Peter Pan," "Cinderella," "Song of the South," and others. **1988 26m/C VHS, Beta, LV** *DIS*

Disney's Sing-Along Songs, Vol. 3: You Can Fly!

Family Kids can join Peter Pan in NeverNeverland, too. Great addition to the series features the ever-present Professor Ludwig von Drake introducing popular songs from "Peter Pan," "Dumbo," "The Jungle Book," "Mary Poppins," and many others. **1988 28m/C VHS, Beta, LV** *DIS*

Disney's Sing-Along Songs, Vol. 4: The Bare Necessities

Family Children sing along with Mowgli, Baloo, and pals with songs featured from Disney's "The Jungle Book." **1988 27m/C VHS, Beta, LV** *DIS*

Disney's Sing-Along Songs, Vol. 5: Fun with Music

Family Sing-along fun from 12 Disney classics highlights this animated program narrated by Professor Ludwig von Drake. Guest star Billy Joel joins along to sing "Why Should I Worry," and selections from "Snow White and the Seven Dwarfs," "Alice in Wonderland," and the recently re-released "Oliver and Company" are included. **1988 28m/C M:** Billy Joel. **VHS, Beta** *DIS*

Disney's Sing-Along Songs, Vol. 6: Under the Sea

Family Professor Ludwig von Drake narrates another addition to the Sing-Along series. Featured are selections from "The Little Mermaid" (just can't get enough of that Sebastian!), "Twenty Thousand Leagues Under the Sea" and other Disney favorites.
1990 28m/C VHS, Beta, LV *DIS*

Disney's Sing-Along Songs, Vol. 7: Disneyland Fun

Family In this addition to the series, live actors appear for the first time, marching around the Disneyland amusement park with colorful favorite Disney characters in tow. More great fun for the kids.
1990 29m/C VHS, Beta *DIS*

Disney's Sing-Along Songs, Vol. 8: Very Merry Christmas Songs

Family Christmas fun as Professor Ludwig von Drake escorts the kids through a whirl of holiday songs. Disney characters perform in selected cartoons to the accompaniment of "Deck the Halls," "Silent Night," "The Twelve Days of Christmas," and other familiar favorites.
1988 27m/C VHS, Beta *DIS*

Disney's Sing-Along Songs, Vol. 9: I Love to Laugh!

Family Professor Ludwig von Drake and pals will have you floating on the ceiling in the "I Love to Laugh!" volume in this sing-along series. Features a variety of silly songs that will keep you in stitches set to classic Disney animation.
1988 29m/C VHS, Beta, LV *DIS*

Disney's Sing-Along Songs, Vol. 10: Be Our Guest

Family Hosted by Jiminy Cricket, this version captures the magic of Disney classics through songs like "Be Our Guest" from "Beauty and the Beast," "Chim Chim Cheree" from "Mary Poppins," and "Bella Notte" from "Lady and the Tramp." Also includes favorites like "Little Wooden Head" from "Pinocchio," "Once Upon a Dream" from "Sleeping Beauty," and "Hefalumps and Woozles" from "Winnie the Pooh and the Blustery Day."
1992 30m/C VHS, Beta *DIS*

Disney's Sing-Along Songs, Vol. 11: Friend Like Me

Family Another volume of musical moments from Disney movies, including "Aladdin," "The Fox and the Hound," "Song of the South," "Beauty and the Beast,"
"The Parent Trap," and "The Jungle Book." ♫ Friend Like Me; Best of Friends; How Do You Do; Something There; Friendship; In Harmony; Let's Get Together; That's What Friends Are For; A Whole New World.
1993 30m/C VHS, LV *DIS*

Disney's TaleSpin, Vol. 1: True Baloo

Family Acclaimed made-for-TV Disney cartoon show that revives the classic "Jungle Book" character Baloo the Bear as a daring courier pilot. He and his cohorts fly into adventure, danger, and fun. Additional volumes available.
1991 46m/C VHS, Beta *DIS, TOU*

Disney's Wonderful World of Winter

Family Stanley the Snowman, Professor of Winterology, teaches Goofy about Thanksgiving, Christmas, and New Years.
1990 10m/C VHS, Beta *MTI, DSN*

Disorderlies 🦴 🐾

PG/Jr. High-Adult Members of the popular rap group cavort as incompetent hospital orderlies assigned to care for a cranky millionaire. Fat jokes abound with performances by the Fat Boys.
1987 86m/C The Fat Boys, Ralph Bellamy; **D:** Michael A. Schultz; **M:** Anne Dudley. **VHS, Beta, LV** *WAR*

The Disorderly Orderly 🦴 🐾

Family When Lewis gets hired as a hospital orderly, nothing stands upright for long. Vintage slapstick with Lewis running amuck in a nursing home.
1964 90m/C Jerry Lewis, Glenda Farrell, Everett Sloane, Kathleen Freeman, Susan Oliver; **D:** Frank Tashlin. **VHS, Beta, LV** *PAR*

Diving In 🦴 🐾

PG-13/Jr. High-Adult Have you heard the one about the acrophobic diver? A paralyzing fear of heights is the only thing between Wayne and a gold medal. While facing his phobia, the teen hero endures romantic travails, bullying from meanie rival divers, and music videos. Cliched underdog jock drama was a longtime project for Indiana film producers, but it bellyflops.

🚫 BEWARE! *Teen hero has sex with his gorgeous (adult) lady phys.ed instructor. Profanity, nudity.*
1990 92m/C Burt Young, Matt Adler, Kristy Swanson, Matt Lattanzi, Richard Johnson, Carey Scott, Yolanda Jilot; **D:** Strathford Hamilton. **VHS, Beta** *PAR, FCT*

Divorce Can Happen to the Nicest People

Primary-Jr. High Gentle but honest animated program explains how nice people like Mom and Dad can want to be apart. Reassures children that nice people like themselves aren't to blame for parents' problems. Ages 6 to 10, but may also comfort older children.
1987 30m/C VHS, Beta *NWV*

The Doberman Gang 🦴🦴

PG/Family Criminal mastermind doesn't trust his cohorts, so for a string of bank robberies he turns to man's best friend, a sextet of trained dogs. The dogs steal the movie as well, and return for more Doberman drama in "The Daring Dobermans" and "The Amazing Dobermans."
1972 85m/C Byron Mabe, Hal Reed, Julie Parrish, Simmy Bow, JoJo D'Amore; **D:** Byron Ross Chudnow; **W:** Frank Ray Perilli. **VHS, Beta** *FOX*

Doc Hollywood 🦴🦴 ♬

PG-13/Sr. High-Adult Hotshot young physician (Michael J. Fox) on his way to a lucrative plastic surgery practice in California crashes his hotshot car in a small South Carolina town. He's sentenced to community service as a doctor, all the while longing to resume his life in the fast lane. You can guess what happens and you'd be right, but the performances are good and the lesson that there are things more important than wealth is taught well. Adapted from Neil B. Shulman's book "What? . . . Dead Again?" Ages 12 and up.

BEWARE *Brief nudity and profanity, but mostly a harmless small town story.*

1991 104m/C Michael J. Fox, Julie Warner, Woody Harrelson, Barnard Hughes, David Ogden Stiers, Frances Sternhagen, Bridget Fonda, George Hamilton, Roberts Blossom, Helen Martin, Macon McCalman, Barry Sobel; **D:** Michael Caton-Jones; **W:** Daniel Pyne, Jeffrey Price, Peter S. Seaman; **M:** Carter Burwell. **VHS, Beta, LV, 8mm** *WAR*

Doc Savage 🦴🦴

PG/Family Doc, superhero of a series of novels (by various authors under the pseudonym Kenneth Robeson) that excited boys since the '30s, finally came to the screen with the campy attitude of TV's "Batman." The muscular Doc and his Fabulous Five fight (without killing—that's a rule) an arch-villain out for gold. There had been 181 Doc Savage books, and the filmmakers announced plans to do all of them. That fell through when this bombed badly on first release, but it has its admirers.

BEWARE *Roughhousing.*

1975 100m/C Ron Ely, Pamela Hensley; **D:** Michael Anderson Sr. **VHS, Beta** *WAR*

Dr. Dad's PH3

Primary Twelve-part series showing kids that science can be fun and exciting. Emphasizes hands-on science exploration. PH3—it's is short for PHantastic PHysical PHenomenon—covers such topics as polymers, buoyancy, electromagnetism, radio broadcasting, alternative energy, oil spills, and optics. Ages 10 and up.
1994 180m/C VHS

Doctor Doolittle 🦴🦴

Family And it did do little, at the box office. All the sets and talent money could buy went into this big-budget musical version of Hugh Lofting's tale about the Victorian adventurer able to converse with the beasts, but the weak script mutes the entertainment value. Plot has to do with Dr. D pursuing a legendary giant snail to a remote floating island. Features one decent song, "Talk to the Animals." 🎵 Doctor Dolittle; My Friend the Doctor; Talk to the Animals; I've Never Seen Anything Like It; Beautiful Things; When I Look in Your Eyes; After Today; Fabulous Places; Where Are the Words?.
1967 144m/C Rex Harrison, Samantha Eggar, Anthony Newley, Richard Attenborough, Geoffrey Holder, Peter Bull; **D:** Richard Fleischer; **M:** Leslie Bricusse. **Award Nominations:** Academy Awards '66: Best Cinematography, Best Sound, Best Original Score; Academy Awards '67: Best Film Editing, Best Picture; **Awards:** Academy Awards '67: Best Song ("Talk to the Animals"), Best Visual Effects; Golden Globe Awards '68: Best Supporting Actor (Attenborough); National Board of Review Awards '67: 10 Best Films of the Year. **VHS, Beta, LV** *FOX, FCT, MLT*

Dr. Jekyll and Ms. Hyde 🦴 ♬

PG-13/Jr. High-Adult Perfume chemist Richard Jacks (Daly) stumbles across the secret formula of great-grandad Dr. Jekyll and, after trying to improve the potion, he finds himself transformed into wicked woman Helen Hyde (Young) who tries to steal his own job. He turns into her, and vice versa, at awkward moments.

BEWARE *Crude sex-related scenes and humor, nudity and brief strong language, smoking in bed after sex. The transformations are funny and "scary" at the same time.*

1995 89m/C Timothy Daly, Sean Young, Lysette Anthony, Stephen Tobolowsky, Harvey Fierstein, Polly Bergen, Stephen Shellan; **D:** David F. Price; **W:** William Davies, William Osborne, Tim John, Oliver Butcher; **C:** Tom Priestley; **M:** Mark McKenzie. **VHS** *HBO*

Dr. No 🦴🦴🦴

PG/Jr. High-Adult Bond, James Bond. The world is introduced to British secret agent 007 when it is discovered that a mad scientist is sabotaging rocket launchings from his hideout in Jamaica. Notable as the first of the Bond adventures, it's far less glitzy than any of its successors but boasts the sexiest "Bond girl" of them all in Andress, and promptly made stars of her and Connery. Laserdisc version includes interviews with principals as well as movie bills, publicity photos, location pictures, and the British and American trailers.

Violence, alcohol use (martinis), suggested sex, and sexism (hey, those girls are always in bikinis).

1962 111m/C Scan Connery, Ursula Andress, Joseph Wiseman, Jack Lord, Zena Marshall, Eunice Gayson, Margaret LeWars, John Kitzmiller, Lois Maxwell, Bernard Lee, Anthony (Antonio Margheriti) Dawson; **D:** Terence Young; **M:** John Barry. **VHS, Beta, LV** *MGM, CRC, TLF*

Dr. Otto & the Riddle of the Gloom Beam 🎵🎵

PG/Primary-Adult The first 'Ernest' epic, though Ernest P. Worrell only puts in a guest appearance. Instead comic-actor Varney plays Dr. Otto von Schnick, bizarre supervillain whose ray weapon can wreck the economy. Bankers hire an overconfident hero (his lady sidekick does all the work) to stop Otto, and the best scenes show how the two foes grew up side-by-side in the same town. Rest of the film is a way-weird combo of wacky sets, costumes, f/x, comic-book cliffhangers. Original, anyway, but very confusing for kids—or adults.

 *Roughhousing.*

1986 92m/C Jim Varney; **D:** John R. Cherry III. **VHS, Beta** *GKK*

Dr. Seuss' ABC

Family Dr. Seuss classic plus two more of his charming, discombobulating tales.

1990 30m/C VHS *KUI, RAN, VEC*

Dr. Seuss' Butter Battle Book

Family Durning narrates Seuss' socially conscious animated allegory of the nuclear arms race.

1989 30m/C VHS, Beta *GKK*

Dr. Seuss' Caldecotts

Family Three of Dr. Seuss's Caldecott Award books, "Bartholomew and the Oobleck," "If I Ran the Zoo," and "McElligot's Pool" are gathered together in read-along (rather than animated) form.

1988 90m/C VHS *RHU*

Dr. Seuss' Cat in the Hat

Family Everyone's favorite cat helps save two children from the boredom of a rainy day in this classic cartoon.

1971 30m/C VHS *TVC*

Dr. Seuss' Daisy-Head Mayzie

Family Hello, hello, it's Dr. Seuss, creator of Horton and Thidwick the Moose . . . Yes, it's Dr. Seuss calling from beyond the grave. The indefatigable author-artist continues to entertain his legions of fans. This 20-year-old story was discovered after he died. It's about a young girl who wakes up one morning to discover a daisy growing out of her head. Mayzie becomes a sensation, thanks to a clever agent, but she learns that love is more important than fame. Ages 5 to 10.

1994 40m/C VHS *TTC*

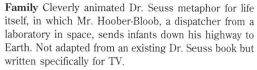

Dr. Seuss' Hoober-Bloob Highway

Family Cleverly animated Dr. Seuss metaphor for life itself, in which Mr. Hoober-Bloob, a dispatcher from a laboratory in space, sends infants down his highway to Earth. Not adapted from an existing Dr. Seuss book but written specifically for TV.

1975 24m/C VHS, Beta *TVC, BFA*

Dr. Seuss' Horton Hears a Who/How the Grinch Stole Christmas

Family Duo of animated Dr. Seuss classics.

1966 52m/C VHS, Beta, LV *MGM*

Dr. Seuss: I Am NOT Going to Get Up Today!

Family A young boy decides that NOTHING will force him out of bed! Also includes the stories "The Shape of Me and other Stuff," "Great Day for Up," and "In a People House."

1991 25m/C VHS, Beta *RAN*

Dr. Seuss on the Loose

Family Combines three short stories including "The Sneetches," "The Zax," and "Green Eggs and Ham," in a thematic trio which explores the often fickle and flexible world of attitudes.

1974 25m/C VHS, Beta *BFA*

Dr. Seuss Sleep Book

Family Animated tale of a long journey from day to night as well as the Seuss story "Hunches in Bunches."

1993 30m/C VHS *RAN, BTV*

Dr. Seuss' The Lorax

Family Environmentalist Dr. Seuss cartoon about a creature who emerges from a tree stump and tries to convince a voracious industrial society from greedily cutting down the last of the all-purpose Truffala trees. Strong stuff in kid terms; communities involved with the timber industry have even banned this video and the source book.

1971 48m/C D: Hawley Pratt; **V:** Bob Holt, Athena Lorde. **VHS** *FOX, TVC*

Dr. Strange 🎵 🕊

Jr. High-Adult One of numerous disappointing attempts to bring Marvel comic book characters to network TV; this time it's the turn of Dr. Strange, a playboy sorcerer who uses his magical powers to combat the malevolent witch Morgan Le Fey. Pilot for a "Dr. Strange" series that never materialized.

1978 94m/C Peter Hooten, Clyde Kusatsu, Jessica Walter, Eddie Benton, John Mills; **D:** Philip DeGuere. **VHS, Beta** *MCA*

Dr. Syn, Alias the Scarecrow 🦴🦴🦴

G/Family Mild-mannered clergyman is, in reality, a smuggler and pirate who dresses up in a creepy scarecrow outfit and avenges King George III's injustices upon the English people. Atmospheric Disney swashbuckler (an adaptation of an oft-filmed Russell Thorndyke novel) was originally a miniseries on the "Wonderful World of Disney" TV show.

1964 129m/C Patrick McGoohan, George Cole, Tony Britton, Michael Hordern, Geoffrey Keen, Kay Cole; **D:** James Neilson. **VHS, Beta** *DIS*

Doctor Who: An Unearthly Child

Family British sci-fi TV show is one of the longest continuously running programs in history. The title character is a whimsical time-traveller who, in this initial B&W episode from long ago, is a wizardlike old man who takes his granddaughter to prehistoric times to witness the discovery of fire. Though conceived as a kiddie show, "Doctor Who" evolved over two decades into a straightfaced sci-fi program for all ages, with enough aliens, planets, friends and enemies to match "Star Trek" trivia. With eight separate actors portraying the far-wandering Doctor, different editions of the Doctor would occasionally meet each other in the timestream. Apart from the two "Doctor Who" theatrical films, three dozen feature-length episodes of the TV program have been released to tape to date (they were originally aired a chapter at a time, with cliffhanger endings just like the great serials). While never graphically violent, some episodes dwell on grotesque mutations and fairly serious horror. The good news is that parents who preview the tapes beforehand may find themselves on the edge of their seats, just like the kids.

1963 98m/B William Hartnell, William Russell; **D:** Waris Hussein. **VHS** *FXV, MOV*

Doctor Who and the Daleks

Family First feature film based on the popular British TV character, in a broader vein than the BBC program. Though Cushing plays the time-travelling hero for the first time, the movie was done to showcase his most popular foes, a race of cruel, conquest-crazed cyborgs, shaped rather oddly like salt shakers rallying-cry of "Exterminate!" has been a catch phrase among Commonwealth kids for decades. If you can't get enough, the more lavish sequel "Daleks—Invasion Earth 2150 A.D." is also on cassette.

1965 78m/C Peter Cushing, Roy Castle; **D:** Gordon Flemyng. **VHS, Beta** *REP*

Doctor Zhivago 🦴🦴🦴 🦴

Sr. High-Adult Sweeping adaptation of the Nobel Prize-winning Boris Pasternak novel. Essentially a poignant love story filmed as a historical epic. Russian physician-poet-intellectual (Omar Sharif) is caught in the furor and chaos of the Bolshevik Revolution, World War I and beyond. Panoramic film popularized the song "Lara's Theme." Too long, but the scenery is beautiful and there's history to be learned amidst the borscht opera. Ages 12 and up.

1965 197m/C Omar Sharif, Julie Christie, Geraldine Chaplin, Rod Steiger, Alec Guinness, Klaus Kinski, Ralph Richardson, Rita Tushingham, Siobhan McKenna, Tom Courtenay; **D:** David Lean; **W:** Robert Bolt; **M:** Maurice Jarre. **Award Nominations:** Academy Awards '65: Best Director (Lean), Best Film Editing, Best Picture, Best Sound, Best Supporting Actor (Courtenay); **Awards:** Academy Awards '65: Best Adapted Screenplay, Best Art Direction/Set Decoration (Color), Best Color Cinematography, Best Costume Design (Color), Best Original Score; Golden Globe Awards '66: Best Actor—Drama (Sharif), Best Director (Lean), Best Film—Drama, Best Screenplay, Best Score; National Board of Review Awards '65: 10 Best Films of the Year, Best Actress (Christie). **VHS, Beta, LV** *MGM, RDG, HMV*

The Dog Days of Arthur Cane

Primary-Jr. High When spoiled, selfish Arthur Cane is transformed into a shaggy dog for a short time, he becomes a much better person for the experience. ABC-TV Weekend Special based on the book by T. Ernesto Bethancourt.

1992 29m/C VHS *AIM*

A Dog of Flanders 🦴🦴 🦴

Family Sentimental tale, based on an 1872 children's novel by Ouida, about a struggling Dutch milk-delivery boy and his grandfather, who find a severely beaten dog and restore it to health. The old man's demise leaves the dog and the kid to fend for themselves. If the canine hero looks familiar that's because it's the same animal thespian who acted in Disney's faithful "Old Yeller."

1959 96m/C David Ladd, Donald Crisp, Theodore Bikel, Max Croiset, Monique Ahrens; **D:** James B. Clark. **VHS, Beta** *PAR*

Dog Pound Shuffle 🦴🦴

PG/Primary-Adult Two drifters, a young man and old showbiz has-been, form a song-and-dance act in order to raise the funds necessary to win their dog's freedom from the pound. Unexceptional little Canadian production. Fans may remember Moody as Fagin from "Oliver!"

⚠️ **BEWARE** *Salty language, roughhousing, alcohol use.*

1975 98m/C Ron Moody, David Soul; **D:** Jeffrey Bloom; **W:** Jeffrey Bloom. **VHS, Beta** *FOX*

The Dog Who Dared

Primary Cautionary cartoon about Ralph the dog, who saves the day when troublemaker Darryl pressures his friends into trying drugs and alcohol. When Darryl laces Ralph's milk with booze, Ralph gets drunk and realizes

the dangers of substance abuse. His experience gets the kids to swear off intoxicants.
1992 25m/C VHS

The Dog Who Stopped the War 🦴🦴🦴🦴

G/Family Charming Canadian effort was the first of producer Rock Demers' acclaimed "Tales for All" series. Bunch of schoolkids spend Christmas break playing war; one side builds a giant snow fort, the other attacks it. Their tactics, weapons, and homemade battle armor grow more and more elaborate, until a fateful skirmish on the last day of vacation when one boy's St. Bernard gets involved and things turn serious. Even with the clear antiwar message tacked on, it's a captivating, credible look at childhood values and mischief. Dubbed from French into English.

⚠ BEWARE: *Despite the happy hound on the cassette box, Cleo the dog is more of a martyr than a heroine.*
1984 90m/C D: Andre Melancon. **VHS, Beta** *NO*

Doggy Faces

Preschool The idea is simple: Fill the screen, an animal at a time, with close-ups of appealing dogs. They gaze, they yawn, they stick their tongues out. Many breeds are shown, from fancy poodles to good old mongrels. The soundtrack is music, often English children singing nursery rhymes. Aww-some viewing. There's a companion video, Kitty Faces, about cats. Ages 1 to 4.
1995 30m/C VHS *NYR*

Doin' Time on Planet Earth 🦴🦴🦴

PG-13/Jr. High-Adult Grab bag of comic ideas, some wrongheaded, some on-target and even touching. Young Ryan feels out of place with his obnoxious family and tacky community. Two wacko UFO nuts give him an explanation; the kid is descended from a long-lost race of spacemen—teenage alienation, get it? If he can recall the right coordinates, Ryan and outcasts like him can blast off for their true home planet. The ending just doesn't follow through on one of the more intriguing ideas for a coming-of-age farce.

⚠ BEWARE: *Sex, profanity, the idea that parents and adolescents are literally from different planets.*
1988 83m/C Adam West, Candice Azzara, Hugh O'Brian, Matt Adler, Timothy Patrick Murphy, Roddy McDowall, Maureen Stapleton, Andrea Thompson; **D:** Charles Matthau. **VHS, Beta** *WAR*

Dolores Claiborne 🦴🦴🦴

R/Sr. High-Adult Successful New York journalist Selena (Leigh) returns to rural Maine when her coarse housekeeper mom Dolores (Bates) is accused of murdering her wealthy employer (Parfitt). Plummer is vengeful detective John Mackey who, like everyone else in town, believes Dolores murdered her husband 15

years before. Top-notch performances by Bates and Leigh. Strathairn is wonderfully despicable in flashback as the abusive husband and father. Film's overall message is that good mothers come in all economic and social varieties.

⚠ BEWARE: *Language, nudity and vivid accounts of domestic and sexual abuse.*
1994 132m/C Kathy Bates, Jennifer Jason Leigh, Christopher Plummer, Judy Parfitt, David Strathairn, John C. Reilly; **D:** Taylor Hackford; **W:** Tony Gilroy; **M:** Danny Elfman. **VHS, LV** *COL*

Dominick & Eugene 🦴🦴🦴

PG-13/Jr. High-Adult Dominick is a little slow, but he makes a fair living as a garbageman—good enough to put his brother through medical school. Both men struggle with the other's faults and weaknesses, as they learn the meaning of family and friendship. Well-acted, especially by Hulce, never melodramatic or weak.
1988 96m/C Ray Liotta, Tom Hulce, Jamie Lee Curtis, Todd Graff, Bill Cobbs, David Strathairn; **D:** Robert M. Young; **W:** Alvin Sargent, Corey Blechman; **M:** Trevor Jones. **VHS, Beta, LV** *ORI, FCT*

Don Cooper: Sing-Along Story Songs

Family Cooper sings about the Little Pigs and others in this animated, live action, puppet special.
1990 30m/C Don Cooper. **VHS** *RAN*

Don Winslow of the Coast Guard

Family 13-episode serial features comic-strip character Winslow as he strives to keep the waters of America safe for democracy.
1943 234m/B Don Terry, Elyse Knox; **D:** Ford Beebe, Ray Taylor. **VHS, Beta** *NOS, MED, VDM*

Don Winslow of the Navy

Family 13-episode serial centered around the evil Scorpion, who plots to attack the pacific Coast, but is thwarted by comic-strip hero Winslow.
1943 234m/B Don Terry, Walter Sande, Anne Nagel; **D:** Ford Beebe, Ray Taylor. **VHS, Beta** *VYY, MED, MLB*

Donald Duck in Mathmagic Land

Primary Donald Duck treks through the fantastic world of Mathmagic Land and learns about square roots, multiplication and fractions. Originally released theatrically, this short combines typical Disney humor with a healthy dose of math basics. Ages 5 to 10.
1959 27m/C VHS, Beta *DSN, MTI, APD*

Donny Deinonychus: The Educational Dinosaur, Vol. 1

Preschool-Primary Two debut episodes of a series which shares the story of prehistory while teaching basic morals, values, judgments, and courtesies. In "Donny Deinonychus," an experiment turns Donny the Parrot into his prehistoric ancestor, Donny Deinonychus (Dine-non-i-kus), whose bird memory is erased and replaced by that of a dinosaur. In "Stormy, the Long Lost Friend," Donny introduces Stormy the Triceratops and explains that even though someone may be scary looking, they may not necessarily be bad. Additional volumes available. **1993 30m/C VHS** *FHV*

Don't Change My World 🦴🦴

G/Family To preserve the natural beauty of the Appalachian Mountains, wildlife photographer Eric, along with his trusty dog and pet raccoon, oppose a villainous land developer and reckless poachers. Eco-correct. **1983 89m/C** Roy Tatum, Ben Jones. **VHS, Beta** *LIV*

Don't Eat the Pictures: Sesame Street at the Metropolitan Museum of Art

Family The Sesame Street Gang wind up locked in New York's Metropolitan Museum of Art after hours. While Cookie Monster learns that paintings of fruit are not for snacks, Big Bird helps the 4,000-year-old spirit of an Egyptian boy solve his ancient riddle. **1987 60m/C** Fritz Weaver, James Mason, Paul Dooley. **VHS** *AAI, KUI, RAN*

Don't Tell Mom the Babysitter's Dead 🦴🦴

PG-13/Jr. High-Adult Mom, travelling abroad, leaves a strict old lady in charge of the household. When she suddenly expires, the kids have the summer to themselves—if they can pay the bills. Daughter Sue Ellen cons her way into an office job and accidentally skyrockets to an exec-level position in the fashion biz, but she has to hide her true age and situation. Somewhere inside this wish-fulfillment comedy is a nice depiction of a teenage girl suddenly thrust into 'the Real World' (pic's original title) and finding she actually enjoys adult responsibility. But emphasis is on quick laughs, preposterous plot twists.

> ⚠️ BEWARE! *Sue Ellen's lazy brother just wants to relax with beer and pot. Profanity.*

1991 105m/C Christina Applegate, Keith Coogan, Joanna Cassidy, John Getz, Josh Charles, Concetta Tomei, Eda Reiss Merin; **D:** Stephen Herek. **VHS, Beta, LV, 8mm** *HBO*

Don't Wake Your Mom

Preschool-Primary Shari Lewis and her world famous puppets Lambchop, Charlie Horse, and Hush Puppy entertain children 3 to 8, so Mom can get her beauty sleep. **1988 43m/C VHS, Beta** *BAR, KAR*

The Donut Repair Club: On Tour

Preschool-Primary Donut Man (Rob Evans) and the lively Donut Repair Club engage in fun, music, and lessons about God. Additional volumes available. **1993 30m/C VHS** *SPW*

Dorothy in the Land of Oz

Preschool-Jr. High Province of Oz faces invasion by the Terrible Toy Maker in these further animated adventures of L. Frank Baum's characters from published sequels to the "Wizard of Oz." This particular one began life as a network TV special "Thanksgiving in the Land of Oz." **1981 60m/C VHS, Beta** *FHE, PMS*

Dot & Keeto 🦴🦴

Preschool-Primary Honey, they shrunk Dot! The star of the Australian cartoon features gets reduced to insect size and has exciting entomological adventures with her mosquito friend Keeto. **1986 73m/C** Robin Moore, Keith Scott. **VHS, Beta**

Dot & Santa Claus 🦴🦴 🕊

Preschool-Primary The cartoon heroine has lost her kangaroo. Suddenly a bush ranger turns into Santa Claus, and (with a sleigh pulled by kangaroos), they literally travel the world in search of the missing joey. An ambitious outing for Dot, including visits to the U.N. and the Moscow Circus, and twin tributes to Mickey Mouse and Henry Kissinger (!?). **1979 73m/C VHS, Beta** *FOX*

Dot & the Kangaroo 🦴🦴

Preschool-Primary First entry in the Australian "Dot," series of semi-musical cartoon features, quite unique in the way they put cleverly animated characters against filmed wildlife footage for nature-themed adventures. Here Dot, the small daughter of a settler, wanders into the outback and gets lost. She meets a friendly kangaroo who takes her on a fabulous journey. **1977 75m/C VHS, Beta** *FOX*

Dot & the Koala 🦴🦴

Preschool-Primary Another animated adventure finds young Dot teaming with cartoon animals from the outback to halt environmentally damaging progress. **1988 75m/C D:** Yoram Gross. **VHS, Beta** *FHE*

Dot & the Smugglers

Preschool-Primary Dot's Australian-made adventures continue. This time the cartoon outback girl and her animated animal friends stop a secret wildlife smuggling ring.
1987 75m/C VHS, Beta *FHE*

Dot & the Whale

Preschool-Primary Popular Australian theatrical feature for kids, about how Dot helps a stranded whale and gains a valuable lesson in marine life.
1987 75m/C VHS, Beta *FHE*

The Double McGuffin

PG/Jr. High-Adult So-so attempt by "Benji" creator Camp to do an equally smart flick with two-legged actors, specifically a group of mischievous schoolboys who discover a plot of international intrigue when a sexy prime minister and her security guard pay a visit to a small Virginia community. Vintage Disney in style—or should we say, out of style?

BEWARE *Salty language, sex talk, alcohol use.*

1979 100m/C Ernest Borgnine, George Kennedy, Elke Sommer, Ed "Too Tall" Jones, Lisa Whelchel, Vincent Spano; **D:** Joe Camp; **V:** Orson Welles. **VHS, Beta** *VES*

The Double O Kid

PG-13/Jr. High-Adult Lance, a 17-year-old office boy at the CIA, has to rush a package to Los Angeles, putting him in the midst of an evil scheme by a crazed computer virus designer. Aided by the prerequisite pretty girl, the boy must avoid all the hazards sent his way. You can safely avoid this worn-out teen-spy spoof, redeemed only by some cool computer graphics.

BEWARE *Salty language, violence.*

1992 95m/C Corey Haim, Wallace Shawn, Brigitte Nielsen, Nicole Eggert, John Rhys-Davies, Basil Hoffman, Karen Black; **Cameos:** Anne Francis; **D:** Duncan McLachlan; **W:** Andrea Buck, Duncan McLachlan. **VHS, Beta** *PSM*

Doug, Vol. 1: How Did I Get Into This Mess?

Primary-Jr. High Doug Funnie, age 11, encounters toothaches, power failures, and video-game addiction in "Doug's Lost Weekend," "Doug's Dental Disaster," and "Doug on His Own." Includes two original music videos based on the series. Additional volumes available.
1993 40m/C VHS *SMV, FCT*

The Dove

PG-13/Jr. High-Adult True story based on the popular book by Robin Lee Graham, of his adventures as a 16-year-old sailing around the world in a 23-foot sloop. The trip takes the boy not only to exotic locales but into manhood, and he falls in love with a girl and becomes a father. Lyrical, mellow, with magnificent photography and scenery.

BEWARE *Sex and nudity. Well, usually the two go hand-in-hand.*

1974 105m/C Joseph Bottoms, Deborah Raffin, Dabney Coleman, Peter Gwynne; **D:** Charles Jarrott. **VHS, Beta** *PAR, BMV*

Down Periscope

PG-13/Jr. High-Adult Modern-day Navy officer Grammar gets stuck with commanding an out-of-mothballs, rusting submarine on a training exercise with a crew of sub-standard goof-offs. Grammar is above average but uninspired comedy seldom rises above C level.

BEWARE *Some crude sailor language, talk of tattooed testicles, alcohol use.*

1996 92m/C Kelsey Grammer, Lauren Holly, Bruce Dern, Fred Schneider, Rip Torn, Harry Dean Stanton, William H. Macy, Ken Campbell, Toby Huss, Duane Martin, Jonathan Penner, Bradford Tatum, Hal Williams; **D:** David S. Ward; **W:** Hugh Wilson, Andrew Kurtzman, Eliot Wald; **C:** Victor Hammer; **M:** Randy Edelman. **VHS** *FXV*

Downhill Racer

PG/Jr. High-Adult An undisciplined American skier locks ski-tips with his coach and his new-found love while on his way to becoming an Olympic superstar. Character study on film. Beautiful ski and mountain photography keep it from sliding downhill.
1969 102m/C Robert Redford, Camilla Sparv, Gene Hackman, Dabney Coleman; **D:** Michael Ritchie. **VHS, Beta, LV** *PAR*

Dracula: Dead and Loving It

PG-13/Jr. High-Adult Brooks' weak take (dreck-ula?) on the ever-popular vampire, with Nielsen as the undead Count and Brooks himself as vampire-slayer Van Helsing.

BEWARE *Heaving bosoms, blood and gore.*

1995 90m/C Leslie Nielsen, Mel Brooks, Peter MacNicol, Lysette Anthony, Amy Yasbeck, Steven Weber, Harvey Korman, Anne Bancroft; **D:** Mel Brooks; **W:** Mel Brooks, Rudy DeLuca, Steve Haberman; **C:** Michael D. O'Shea; **M:** Hummie Mann. **VHS, LV** *COL*

Dragnet

PG-13/Jr. High-Adult Semi-parody of the vintage '50s television cop show. Sgt. Joe Friday's straight-laced nephew and his sloppy partner take on the seamy crime life of Los Angeles. Neither Aykroyd nor Hanks can save this big-budget but lackluster spoof that's full of holes.

BEWARE *Profanity and violence, disrespect for Jack Webb.*

1987 106m/C Dan Aykroyd, Tom Hanks, Christopher Plummer, Harry (Henry) Morgan, Elizabeth Ashley, Dabney Coleman; **D:** Tom Mankiewicz; **W:** Dan Aykroyd, Tom Mankiewicz, Alan Zweibel; **M:** Ira Newborn. **VHS, Beta, LV** *MCA*

Few dispute that suave Sean Connery was the best Bond ever, a sexy, manly yet gentle actor who defined the cool, ironic vigilante hero widely imitated since. Connery is also one of the few men to go from star to actor, forsaking Bond for a varied career of over 50 films, ranging from flops to epics.

Connery played Bond seven times, starting in 1961 with the original, *Dr. No*. But he didn't like being identified with the character and became bored when the Bond flicks turned high-tech. "When they started to do the stuff with the hardware, it began to lose it for me," Connery said. So the self-taught Scot sought more demanding roles in films like *The Man Who Would Be King, Robin and Marian,* and, much later, *The Untouchables* and *The Hunt for Red October*. His latest effort has been his contribution as the voice of Draco, the last living dragon in 1996's *Dragonheart*.

Born Thomas Connery in 1930 to a working-class Scot family, he started delivering milk at 9, and was at various times a seaman, coffin-polisher, cement mixer, truck driver, bodybuilder, lifeguard and model. Belying his playboy image, Connery has spent most of his adult life in two solid marriages. He and actress Diane Cilento produced a son, Jason, who is an actor. Connery has been married to French painter Micheline Roquebrune since 1975; they live in Spain and the Bahamas.

The Dragon That Wasn't (Or Was He?)

Family Animated full-length feature from the Netherlands finds Dexter the Dragon believing Ollie the Bear is his father. That's all right with kindhearted Ollie except that Dexter soon outgrows the house and Ollie must take Dexter to the land where dragons live, beyond the Misty Mountains. The journey is quite an adventure. A poignant lesson about the inevitability of growing up and leaving home. Ages 3 to 8.

1983 83m/C VHS, Beta *MCA*

Dragon: The Bruce Lee Story
♂♂♡

PG-13/Jr. High-Adult Entertaining, inspiring account of the life of Chinese-American martial-arts legend Bruce Lee. Jason Scott Lee (no relation) is great as the talented artist, exuding his joy of life and gentle spirit, before his mysterious death of a brain disorder at age 32. Ironically, this release coincided with son Brandon's accidental death on the set of "The Crow." The martial arts sequences in "Dragon" are extraordinary, but there's also romance as Lee meets and marries his wife (Holly, who acquits herself well). Based on the book "Bruce Lee: The Man Only I Knew" by his widow, Linda Lee Caldwell.

⚠ BEWARE *Martial arts violence and profanity.*

1993 121m/C Jason Scott Lee, Lauren Holly, Robert Wagner, Michael Learned, Nancy Kwan, Kay Tong Lim, Sterling Macer, Ric Young, Sven Ole-Thorsen; **D:** Rob Cohen; **W:** Edward Khmara, John Raffo, Rob Cohen; **M:** Randy Edelman. **VHS, LV** *MCA, BTV, FCT*

Dragonheart ♂♂♡

PG-13/Jr. High-Adult Middle Age fantasy finds a knight (Quaid) teaming up with an unlikely accomplice to battle the evil King Einon (Thewlis) to save their country. The other half of the duo is the knight's "natural" enemy, an 18-foot tall, 43-foot long last living dragon, known as Draco. Sean Connery loans his "kingly" voice to the beast, which appears more noble than the typical serpent of similar tales.

⚠ BEWARE *Action/violence in the form of the fire-breathing dragon and Middle Age battles and swordplay. The dragon looks pretty scary and will frighten young ones (and maybe even some older ones).*

1996 108m/C Dennis Quaid, David Thewlis, Pete Postlethwaite, Julie Christie, Dina Meyer, John Gielgud; **D:** Rob Cohen; **W:** Charles Edward Pogue; **V:** Sean Connery. **VHS** *NYR*

Dragonslayer ♂♂♂

PG/Jr. High-Adult Sorcerer's youthful apprentice is the only person who can save the kingdom of Urland from its last and worst fire-breathing dragon. Not a fairy-tale treatment, but a genuinely primordial and scary attempt at oft-told material, overlong but memorable. The Industrial Light and Magic f/x workshop created one of the screen's most fearsome dragons—plus gore that would have undoubtedly earned this at least a PG-13 today.

BEWARE *Brutality and gore during the fighting scenes. Nudity.*

1981 110m/C Peter MacNicol, Caitlin Clarke, Ralph Richardson, John Hallam, Albert Salmi, Chloe Salaman; **D:** Matthew Robbins; **W:** Matthew Robbins; **M:** Alex North. **VHS, Beta, LV** *PAR, COL*

Dragonworld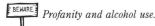

PG/Primary-Adult Creators of the direct-to-video family hit "Prehysteria" put extra effort into this fantasy and it shows. Five-year-old orphan Johnny McGowan, sent to remote Scottish Highlands to live with relatives, wishes for a friend and gets a baby dragon he names Yowler. Years later, outsiders discover the now giant-sized Yowler, and adult Johnny reluctantly rents his monster pal to an amusement park. But Dragonworld's owner has a Scrooge McDuck disposition, and Johnny and friends soon mount a "Free Willy" rescue of homesick Yowler. Cliches are bearable thanks to carefully calculated sentiment and an overriding gentleness. Dragon f/x are more whimsical than realistic.

BEWARE *Yowler breathes fire a little, but why this isn't rated G is as big a mystery as where the beast came from in the first place.*

1994 86m/C Sam Mackenzie, Courtland Mead, Brittney Powell, John Calvin, Andrew Keir, Lila Kaye, John Woodvine; **D:** Ted Nicolaou; **W:** Ted Nicolaou, Suzanne Glazener Naha; **M:** Richard Band. **VHS, Beta** *PAR*

Dream a Little Dream

PG-13/Jr. High-Adult If originality is what you're looking for, you must be dreaming. Elderly couple habitually meditate, trying mystically to regain their youth. When they collide bikes with the teenagers down the street, minds are exchanged, and the young folks with senior souls must figure out how to get back to their rightful bodies. Overly familiar brain exchange made bearable by cast.

BEWARE *Profanity and alcohol use.*

1989 114m/C Corey Feldman, Corey Haim, Meredith Salenger, Jason Robards Jr., Piper Laurie, Harry Dean Stanton, Victoria Jackson, Alex Rocco, Billy McNamara; **D:** Marc Rocco; **W:** Marc Rocco. **VHS, Beta, LV** *LIV, VES, HHE*

Dream a Little Dream 2

PG-13/Jr. High-Adult Friends Dinger Holefield (Haim) and Bobby Keller (Feldman) receive a mysterious package containing two pairs of sunglasses, which they discover have magic powers. The wearer of one pair is driven to do the bidding of the wearer of the second pair of specs—whether for good or evil. Movie bears The Curse of the Coreys and is as dumb as it sounds.

1994 91m/C Corey Haim, Corey Feldman, Stacie Randall, Michael Nicolosi, James Lemmo; **W:** David Weissman, Susan Forman. **VHS** *COL*

Dream Date

PG-13/Jr. High-Adult Race change doesn't improve the obsessed-dad comedy formula earlier attempted (and failed) in "She's Out of Control." When Danielle goes on a hot date with the high school football captain, her overly protective father Bill tags along to spy and gets caught in one disaster after another. Much of the humor has a surprisingly cruel edge in this TV movie.

BEWARE *Roughhousing, alcohol use.*

1993 96m/C Tempestt Bledsoe, Clifton Davis, Kadeem Hardison, Anne-Marie Johnson, Pauly Shore, Richard Moll; **D:** Anson Williams. **VHS** *TRI, PMS*

A Dream for Christmas

Family Earl Hamner Jr., best known for creating "The Waltons," wrote this moving TV drama of faith and family. Black minister moves with his wife, mother and children from their native rural Arkansas to sunny Los Angeles in December, 1950. Their difficulty in making the transition is capped by the belated discovery that the church the Rev. Douglas is to take over has been slated for demolition. He tries to boost church attendance by Noel.

1973 100m/C Hari Rhodes, Beah Richards, George Spell, Juanita Moore, Joel Fluellen, Robert DoQui, Clarence Muse; **D:** Ralph Senensky. **VHS** *LIV, HBO, WAR*

Dream Machine

PG/Jr. High-Adult Childish teen comedy with one of the Coreys is based on that old urban legend of the lucky kid given a free Porshe by the vengeful wife of a wealthy philanderer. The gimmick is that the husband's body is in the trunk; a murderer is in pursuit. Driver's Ed looms in near future as reckless motoring dominates action. To compensate for poor driving tips, the tape includes an anti-drug public service announcement.

BEWARE *Violence, salty language, bad driving.*

1991 88m/C Corey Haim, Evan Richards, Jeremy Slate, Randall England, Tracy Fraim, Brittney Lewis, Susan Seaforth Hayes; **D:** Lyman Dayton. **VHS, LV** *LIV*

The Dream Team

PG-13/Jr. High-Adult On their way to a ball game, four patients from a mental hospital find themselves lost in NYC after their doctor is knocked out by murderers. Scary enough for anyone in their right mind, but among the four of them, these guys lack a right mind. Even though you know the quartet will prove to be more sane than many of the people they encounter outside the hospital, effort still derives some fine moments from a cast of dependable comics. Watch for numerous nods to "One Flew Over the Cuckoo's Nest" (in which Lloyd had a memorable part). Maybe not the most authentic spin on the state of mental illness, but a lark nonetheless.

BEWARE *Profanity, violence, and vivid depictions of mental illness.*

1989 113m/C Michael Keaton, Christopher Lloyd, Peter Boyle, Stephen Furst, Lorraine Bracco, Milo O'Shea, Dennis Boutsikaris, Philip Bosco, James Remar, Cynthia Belliveau; **D:** Howard Zieff; **W:** Jon Connolly, David Loucka; **M:** David McHugh. **VHS, Beta, LV** *MCA*

Dreamchild 🐾🐾🐾

PG/Jr. High-Adult Poignant story of the autumn years of Alice Hargreaves, the model for Lewis Carroll's "Alice in Wonderland." As an old woman she makes a much-publicized visit to New York in the 1930s, where media attention inspires flashbacks to her childhood meetings with the eccentric, obsessive Reverend Dodgson (alias Carroll). Fantasy sequences feature Wonderland characters created by Jim Henson's Creature Shop. A most unusual approach to the "Through the Looking-Glass" material, perhaps better appreciated by grownups than kid viewers.

1985 94m/C Coral Browne, Ian Holm, Peter Gallagher, Jane Asher, Nicola Cowper, Amelia Shankley, Caris Corfman, Shane Rimmer, James Wilby; **D:** Gavin Millar; **W:** Dennis Potter; **M:** Max Harris, Stanley Myers. **VHS, Beta** *MGM*

Dreaming of Paradise 🐾🐾 🐾

Family Award-winning animated feature presents a tale of both caution and hope regarding Earth's future. Spike and her friends live below the planet's surface due to pollution and dream of a place with blue skies and green pastures. Environmentalism and children's cartoons are longtime (almost tiresome) companions, and with everyone from Aquaman to Widget evangelizing for The Cause, the topic weighs heavy. Imaginative animation makes this title distinct.

1987 75m/C VHS *JFK*

Driving Miss Daisy 🐾🐾🐾 🐾

PG/Jr. High-Adult When aging Daisy (Jessica Tandy) wrecks her car one too many times, her son (Dan Aykroyd) hires a chauffeur for her, Hoke, a black man (Morgan Freeman) who's almost as old as she is. In beautifully crafted vignettes spanning 25 years, Daisy and Hoke become close friends, though always at a certain psychological distance. It's the south (Atlanta) in the 50s and 60s; he's black, she's Jewish. More importantly, they're both human, both decent. Humorous and thought-provoking, skillfully acted and directed. Aykroyd plays it straight (and very well). Part of the fun is watching the changes in cars and clothes over the years. Adapted by Alfred Uhry from his Pulitzer Prize-winning play. Ages 10 and up.

BEWARE *Mild profanity. Issues of racial tension of the period.*

1989 99m/C Jessica Tandy, Morgan Freeman, Dan Aykroyd, Esther Rolle, Patti LuPone; **D:** Bruce Beresford; **W:** Alfred Uhry; **M:** Hans Zimmer. **Award Nominations:** Academy Awards '89: Best Actor (Freeman), Best Costume Design, Best Film Editing, Best Supporting

Actor (Aykroyd); **Awards:** Academy Awards '89: Best Actress (Tandy), Best Adapted Screenplay, Best Makeup, Best Picture; British Academy Awards '90: Best Actress (Tandy); Golden Globe Awards '90: Best Actor—Musical/Comedy (Freeman), Best Actress—Musical/Comedy (Tandy), Best Film—Musical/Comedy; National Board of Review Awards '89: 10 Best Films of the Year, Best Actor (Freeman). **VHS, Beta, LV, 8mm** *WAR, FCT, BTV*

Droopy & Company

Preschool-Jr. High Contains 6 cartoons starring Droopy the dog, including "Mutts About Racing," "Grin and Share It," "The Hungry Wolf," "Sheep Wrecked," "Officer Pooch," and "One Droopy Knight." Ages 4 to 8.

1958 44m/C VHS *NO*

Drop Dead Fred WOOF!

PG-13/Jr. High-Adult As a little girl, Lizzie had an impish imaginary playmate named Fred, who protected her from her domineering mother. When her husband dumps her twenty years later, Fred suddenly materializes to "help" as only he can. Misused cast, poor writing, and indifferent direction make this a truly dismal affair. Gutter humor and mean-spirited pranks throw the whole "heartwarming" premise out the window.

BEWARE *Salty language, roughhousing, general grossness with dog droppings, garbage, and worse.*

1991 103m/C Phoebe Cates, Rik Mayall, Tim Matheson, Marsha Mason, Carrie Fisher, Daniel Gerroll, Ron Eldard; **D:** Ate De Jong; **M:** Randy Edelman. **VHS, LV** *LIV*

Duck Soup 🐾🐾🐾🐾

Family Marx Brothers satiric masterpiece failed at the box office but remains a sterling achievement for the madcap brothers. Mrs. Teasdale (Dumont) promises $20 million to the duchy of Freedonia if Rufus T. Firefly (Groucho) becomes the dictator. His rival shows classic bad management tendencies and hires Chico and Harpo as spies. Jam-packed with the classic anarchic and irreverent Marx shtick; watch for the mirror scene. Zeppo plays a love-sick tenor, in this, his last film with the brothers.

1933 70m/B Groucho Marx, Chico Marx, Harpo Marx, Zeppo Marx, Louis Calhern, Margaret Dumont, Edgar Kennedy, Raquel Torres, Leonid Kinskey, Charles Middleton; **D:** Leo McCarey; **W:** Harry Ruby, Nat Perrin, Bert Kalmar, Arthur Sheekman; **M:** Harry Ruby, Bert Kalmar. **VHS, Beta, LV** *MCA, FCT*

DuckTales: Accidental Adventurers

Family Scrooge McDuck and his nephews Huey, Dewey, and Louie star in a series of cassette adventures excerpted from the Disney Studio's first daily TV cartoon series. Additional volumes available.

1989 44m/C VHS, Beta, LV *DIS*

DuckTales the Movie: Treasure of the Lost Lamp 🐾🐾 🐾

G/Family Uncle Scrooge and company embark on a lost-ark quest, ala Indiana Jones, for misplaced treasure (a lamp that can make the sky rain ice cream). Based on the daily Disney cartoon of the same name, it's more like an extended-version Saturday morning entertainment than bigscreen spectacle, but still worthy of the Disney name.

1990 74m/C D: Bob Hathcock; **W:** Alan Burnett; **M:** David Newman; **V:** Alan Young, Christopher Lloyd, Rip Taylor, June Foray, Chuck McCann, Richard Libertini, Russi Taylor, Joan Gerber, Terence McGovern. **VHS, Beta, LV** *DIS*

Dumb & Dumber ♪♪ ▷

PG-13/Jr. High-Adult There's the signpost up ahead. Next stop: The Toilet Zone. Bathroom humor abounds as idiotic limo driver Lloyd Christmas (Carrey) and his intellectual equal, dog groomer Harry Dunne (Daniels), travel across America in a van that looks like a dog. They head from Rhode Island to Colorado—at one point they go east—to return a briefcase full of cash to a beautiful socialite (Holly). Engaging in all sorts of gross-out, bodily function, and slapstick humor, they provide plenty of low-brow laughs. Daniels more than holds his own against over-the-top Carrey.

🚷 BEWARE 🚷 *Although written by guys who have the mind of a nine-year-old (and we wish they'd give it back), this is not for little kids. Jokes about peeing, diarrhea, dead pets and child molesters. Bare buttocks, plenty of dirty words.*

1994 110m/C Jim Carrey, Jeff Daniels, Lauren Holly, Teri Garr, Karen Duffy, Mike Starr, Charles Rocket, Victoria Rowell, Felton Perry; **D:** Peter Farrelly; **W:** Bennett Yellin, Bobby Farrelly, Peter Farrelly; **M:** Todd Rundgren. **Award Nominations:** MTV Movie Awards '95: Best On-Screen Duo (Jim Carrey/Jeff Daniels); **Awards:** MTV Movie Awards '95: Best Comedic Performance (Carrey), Best Kiss (Jim Carrey/Lauren Holly). **VHS, LV** *TTC, NLC*

Dumbo ♪♪♪♪

Family Disney classic about a baby elephant growing up in the circus who is ridiculed for his large ears, until he discovers he can fly. Then he becomes a circus star and, eventually, a hero. Expressively and imaginatively animated, highlighted by the hallucinatory dancing pink elephants sequence. Endearing songs by Frank Churchill, Oliver Wallace, and Ned Washington, including "Baby Mine," "Pink Elephants on Parade," and "I See an Elephant Fly."

1941 63m/C D: Ben Sharpsteen; **W:** Joe Grant, Dick Huemer; **M:** Frank Churchill, Oliver Wallace; **V:** Sterling Holloway, Edward Brophy, Verna Felton, Herman Bing, Cliff Edwards. **Award Nominations:** Academy Awards '41: Best Song ("Baby Mine"); **Awards:** Academy Awards '41: Best Score; National Board of Review Awards '41: 10 Best Films of the Year. **VHS, Beta, LV** *DIS, KUI, APD*

Duncan's World

G/Family Twelve-year-old Duncan helps dad run a wildlife museum and agonizes over who threw a cherry bomb into the duck pond. That's about it for plot in this slow-creeping kiddie obscurity, made on a low budget in North Carolina. Based on a book by Helen Masson Copeland.

1977 93m/C Larry Tobias, Billy Tobias, Calvin Brown Jr.; **D:** John Clayton. **VHS** *BFV*

Dunston Checks In ♪♪♪

PG/Primary-Adult A monkey, a posh hotel, a couple of cute kids. Can you say "high concept?" Yes, it's a monkey movie (technically, an orangutan movie) but "Dunston Checks In" is a comedy worth checking out. Robert Grant (Jason Alexander), the Hotel Majestic's live-in manager, has two sons, Kyle and Brian (Eric Lloyd and Graham Sack), who believe that the laundry chute falls under the category of recreational facilities. Enter Lord Rutledge (Rupert Everett), who has cruelly trained Dunston, the orangutan, to steal jewelry from guests' rooms. As Dunston and the boys discover each other, what follows is tasty simian cinema. Adding to the fun are Paul Reubens as a lunatic monkey exterminator, and Faye Dunaway who plays the hotel's owner a la Leona Helmsely.

🚷 BEWARE 🚷 *Some mild langauge and slapstick mayhem.*

1995 88m/C Jason Alexander, Faye Dunaway, Eric Lloyd, Rupert Everett, Graham Sack, Paul (Pee Wee Herman) Reubens, Glenn Shadix, Nathan Davis, Jennifer Bassey; **D:** Ken Kwapis; **W:** Bruce Graham, John Hopkins; **C:** Peter Collister; **M:** Miles Goodman. **VHS, LV** *FXV*

Dusty ♪♪

Family Touching story of a wild dingo dog raised by an Australian rancher and trained to herd sheep. Filmed in the Australian bush and based on the children's book by Frank Dalby Davison.

1985 89m/C Bill Kerr, Noel Trevarthen, Carol Burns, Nicholas Holland, John Stanton; **D:** John Richardson. **VHS, Beta** *MED, FCT, FHE*

Dutch ♪ ▷

PG-13/Jr. High-Adult Another suburban-contemporary family comedy scripted by John Hughes. Earthy, working-class guy picks up his girlfriend's stuck-up son from boarding school, and their trip together gives them plenty of chances to connect, if they don't kill each other first. Little innovation, obvious sentiment, and type-casting instead of acting.

🚷 BEWARE 🚷 *Sex talk, profanity, visit to a homeless shelter. Dutch and the kid are pretty cruel to each other.*

1991 107m/C Ed O'Neill, Ethan Randall, JoBeth Williams; **D:** Peter Faiman; **W:** John Hughes. **VHS** *FXV, IME*

Earth Tunes for Kids

Primary Songs and music videos from the World Patrol Kids that teach about the earth and its wildlife. Ages 4 to 8.

1994 30m/C VHS *TPV*

Earthling ♪♪ ▷

PG/Family Terminally ill old fellow helps a ten-year-old boy survive in the Australian wilderness after the kid's parents are killed in a tragic accident. Lessons of life and the power of the human heart are passed on in this panoramic, sentimental drama.

Jim Carrey is about to get his head stuck in "Dumb and Dumber."

1980 102m/C William Holden, Rick Schroder, Jack Thompson, Olivia Hamnett, Alwyn Kurts; **D:** Peter Collinson. **VHS, Beta** *LIV, VES*

EarthWorm Jim

Preschool-Primary Unusual superhero, Earthworm Jim, based on the popular video game and now star of the popular Warner Bros. Kids Network series ensues his battle against evil in a series of four tapes. Mild-mannered worm is transformed into the indestuctible hero when he dons the cyber-powered super suit. Along with trusty sidekicks Peter Puppy, Snott and Princess What's-Her-Name, he's out to conquer the dastardly villains like Psy-Crow, Henchrat, and Bob the Goldfish (all in the employ of Queen Slug-for-a-Butt, who wants the power suit all to herself). Ages 4 to 7.
1996 40m/C VHS *MCA*

East of Eden ♫♫♫♫

Family Steinbeck's contemporary retelling of the biblical Cain and Abel story receives superior treatment from Kazan and his excellent cast. Dean, in his first starring role, gives a reading of a young man's search for love and acceptance that defines adolescent pain. Though filmed in the 1950s, this story still rivets today's viewers with its emotional message.

 *Roughhousing.*

1954 115m/C James Dean, Julie Harris, Richard Davalos, Raymond Massey, Jo Van Fleet, Burl Ives, Albert Dekker; **D:** Elia Kazan; **W:** Paul Osborn; **M:** Leonard Rosenman. **Award Nominations:** Academy Awards '55: Best Actor (Dean), Best Director (Kazan), Best Screenplay; **Awards:** Academy Awards '55: Best Supporting Actress (Van Fleet); Golden Globe Awards '56: Best Film—Drama; National Board of Review Awards '55: 10 Best Films of the Year. **VHS, Beta, LV** *WAR, BTV, HMV*

East of the Sun, West of the Moon

Primary Beautifully illustrated storytelling adaptation of the traditional Norwegian folktale. Young girl leaves her family to go and live with a polar bear in his castle. The bear is really a bewitched handsome prince under the spell of a troll queen. The brave girl then seeks to break the spell. Part of the acclaimed "Rabbit Ears" series of tapes.
1991 28m/C VHS *RAB, MLT*

Easter Bunny is Coming to Town

Family Stop-motion animation TV special focusing on Sunny the Easter Bunny and how he got into the egg habit. Low cholesterol (it's only a video), but high sugar. Ages 3 to 6.

1977 50m/C VHS, Beta, LV *VES, IME, WAR*

Easter Egg Mornin'

Preschool-Primary It's up to Picasso "Speedy" Cottontail, the egg-painter, and his friends to save Easter as they go on various bunny adventures.

1993 27m/C VHS *FHE*

Easter Parade *♫♫♫*

Family Big musical star (Astaire) splits with his partner (Miller) claiming that he could mold any girl to replace her in the act. He tries and finally succeeds after much difficulty. Classic song and dance fest has numerous highlights, including "Drum Crazy" and "A Couple of Swells." Astaire, back after his first "retirement" (Gene Kelly was up first for the role, but broke an ankle and persuaded his reluctant friend to replace him), is in peak form with Garland, aided by a classic Irving Berlin score. ♪ Happy Easter; Drum Crazy; It Only Happens When I Dance With You; Everybody's Doin' It; I Want to Go Back to Michigan; Beautiful Faces Need Beautiful Clothes; A Fella With an Umbrella; I Love a Piano; Snookey Ookums.

1948 103m/C Fred Astaire, Judy Garland, Peter Lawford, Ann Miller, Jules Munshin, Joi Lansing; **D:** Charles Walters; **W:** Sidney Sheldon; **M:** Irving Berlin. **VHS, Beta, LV** *MGM, HMV*

Eat My Dust *♫♫*

PG/Jr. High-Adult Teenage son of a California sheriff steals the best stock cars from a race track to take the town's heartthrob for a joy ride. Subsequently he leads the town on a wild car chase. Brainless but fast-paced, serving as a demonstration on how to properly demolish a car. Plenty of Howards, with star Ron supported by dad Rance and brother Clint.

1976 89m/C Ron Howard, Christopher Norris, Warren Kemmerling, Rance Howard, Clint Howard, Corbin Bernsen; **D:** Charles B. Griffith. **VHS, Beta**

Ed *♫*

PG/Primary-Adult Two of filmdom's least cherished genres—the monkey movie and the woebegone sports team movie—meet, and the result is unbearable. The titular Ed is a chimpanzee acquired as a mascot by a bedraggled minor league baseball team. Matt LeBlanc (of TV's "Friends") is that team's star pitcher, or would be if he weren't so nervous in front of fans. Ed turns out to be a heckuva ballplayer (with the world's smallest strike zone) and leads the team of losers on a winning streak. Viewers don't fare as well, except for those who think scenes of passing gas are funny. Ed is a puppet (or sometimes a person in a monkey suit), and the film suffers from the same kind of artificiality.

BEWARE *Language, very crude humor and brief mild monkey violence. Food-throwing and they leave the kid with the monkey as babysitter!*

1996 94m/C Matthew LeBlanc, Jayne Brook, Bill Cobbs, Jack Warden, Doren Fein, Patrick Kerr, Charlie Schlatter, Carl Anthony Payne II, Curt Kaplan, Zack Ward, Mike McGlone, James Caviezel, Valente Rodriguez; **D:** Bill Couturie; **W:** David Mickey Evans; **C:** Alan Caso; **M:** Stephen Endelman. **VHS, LV** *MCA*

Eddie *♫♫ ◦*

PG-13/Jr. High-Adult Edwina (Eddie) Franklin (Whoopi Goldberg) is a New York limousine driver by occupation and a New York Knicks fan by pre-occupation—which means basketball comes before her job. One day she gets the Knicks' new owner as a passenger. Taken with her enthusiasm—and his current coach's dismal record—he makes her the new coach. Besides sexism, Whoopi's obstacles include the players, among them a lazy, ball-hogging superstar and a recalcitrant Russian from whom Coach Whoopi gets nothing but nyet. Not to worry. The value of teamwork prevails. In this Whoop dream, put your money on Goldberg. Real NBA players portray the movie's Knicks. Ages 9 and up.

BEWARE *The only profanity is mild, the only violence is on the court, and the only sex is foreplay (between a husband and wife, yet).*

1996 100m/C Whoopi Goldberg, Frank Langella, Dennis Farina, Richard Jenkins, Lisa Ann Walter, John Benjamin Hickey, John Salley; **D:** Steve Rash; **W:** Jon Connolly, David Loucka, Eric Champnella, Keith Mitchell, Steve Zacharias, Jeff Buhai; **C:** Victor Kemper; **M:** Stanley Clarke. **VHS** *NYR*

Eddie and the Cruisers *♫♫ ◦*

PG/Jr. High-Adult In the early 1960s, rockers Eddie and the Cruisers score with one hit album. Amid their success, lead singer Pare dies mysteriously in a car accident. Years later, a reporter decides to write a feature on the defunct group, prompting a former band member to begin a search for missing tapes of the Cruisers' unreleased second album. Questions posed at the end of the movie are answered in the sequel. Enjoyable soundtrack by John Cafferty and the Beaver Brown Band.

BEWARE *Profanity and a fateful car accident.*

1983 90m/C Tom Berenger, Michael Pare, Ellen Barkin, Joe Pantoliano, Matthew Laurance; **D:** Martin Davidson. **VHS, Beta, LV, 8mm** *MVD, NLC*

Edison Twins

Family The Edison twins, Tom and Annie (Andrew Sobiston and Marnie McPhail), aren't inventors but they are inventive as they delve into assorted mysteries. Kind of a coed Hardy boys, the scientifically-inclined teen siblings pursue such cases as the theft of a rock singer's favorite guitar, the mystery of an ancient South American figurine and whether a genial old gentleman with a pipe and deerstalker hat might really be Sherlock Holmes.

The mischievious orangutan looks down from a chandelier in "Dunston Checks In."

This terrific Canadian series (no violence, no car chases, a snowmobile chase or two) also aired on the Disney channel. Several volumes available. Ages 8 to 13.
1985 45m/C Andrew Sabiston, Marnie McPhail. **VHS, Beta** *COL*

Educating Rita 🦴🦴🦴 ◊

PG/Jr. High-Adult Walters and Caine team beautifully in this adaptation of the successful Willy Russell play which finds an uneducated hairdresser determined to improve her knowledge of literature. In so doing, she enlists the aid of a tutor: a disillusioned alcoholic, adeptly played by Caine. Together, the two find inspiration in one another's differences and experiences. Ultimately, the teacher receives a lesson in how to again appreciate his work and the classics as he observes his pupil's unique approach to her studies. Some deem this a "Pygmalion" for the '80s.

BEWARE *Profanity and depictions of alcoholism.*

1983 110m/C Michael Caine, Julie Walters, Michael Williams, Maureen Lipman; **D:** Lewis Gilbert; **W:** Willy Russell. **Award Nominations:** Academy Awards '83: Best Actor (Caine), Best Actress (Walters), Best Adapted Screenplay; **Awards:** British Academy Awards '83: Best Actor (Caine), Best Actress (Walters), Best Film; Golden Globe Awards '84: Best Actor—Musical/Comedy (Caine), Best Actress—Musical/Comedy (Walters). **VHS, Beta, LV, 8mm** *COL*

Edward Scissorhands 🦴🦴🦴

PG-13/Jr. High-Adult Edward's a synthetic teenager created by an eccentric inventor who dies before he can attach hands to his boy-creature. With scissors in place of hands, Edward is taken in by a sweetly oblivious Avon Lady but has more trouble fitting into suburbia than most new kids; his finger-blades can create delicate works of art, or maim and even kill. Visually captivating fairy tale full of splash and color, however predictable the Hollywood-prefab denouement.

BEWARE *Like many a classic fairy tale, this one has darker undertones, made manifest in violence, mature themes.*

1990 100m/C Johnny Depp, Winona Ryder, Dianne Wiest, Vincent Price, Anthony Michael Hall, Alan Arkin, Kathy Baker, Conchata Ferrell, Caroline Aaron, Dick Anthony Williams, Robert Oliveri, John Davidson; **D:** Tim Burton; **W:** Caroline Thompson, Tim Burton; **M:** Danny Elfman. **VHS, Beta, LV** *FOX, FCT*

Eek!Stravaganza: Catsanova and Hawaiieek 5-O

Family Two episodes from the Fox Kids Network cartoon series, "Eek!" In the first, "Catsanova," the Eekualizer and Cupid team up to win the heart of their new neighbor, Annabelle. In the second, "Hawaiieek 5-O," Eek enlists the aid of the famous undersea explorer, Jacques le Duck, to help rescue Annabelle from a mysterious island beneath her pool. Ages 5 to 8.

1995 50m/C VHS *TCF*

The Effect of Gamma Rays on Man-in-the-Moon Marigolds 🎵🎵🎵

PG/Jr. High-Adult Wonderful drama based on the Pulitzer-Prize winning play by Paul Zindel. Little Beatrice is preparing her experiment for the school science fair, showing how radiation sometimes kills the helpless marigolds and occasionally causes them to grow into even more beautiful mutations. This mirrors Beatrice, who flowers even amidst the drunkenness of her mother and the dullness of her sister.

⚠ BEWARE *Alcohol use and emotional abuse of child by mother.*

1973 100m/C Joanne Woodward, Nell Potts, Roberta Wallach, Judith Lowry, Richard Venture; **D:** Paul Newman. **Award Nominations:** Cannes Film Festival '73: Best Film; **Awards:** Cannes Film Festival '73: Best Actress (Woodward). **VHS** *NO*

Eight Men Out 🎵🎵🎵♪

PG/Jr. High-Adult Poignant, realistic (but fictional) account of the disgraced Chicago White Sox who took gamblers' money to throw the 1919 World Series. An eye-opening look at how poorly major league ballplayers were once treated. Players' humanity shines through, thanks to topnotch performances. Baseball scenes are superb, but non-fans will find much to enjoy, too. For a more fanciful take on the subject, watch "Field of Dreams."

1988 121m/C John Cusack, D.B. Sweeney, Perry Lang, Jace Alexander, Bill Irwin, Clifton James, Michael Rooker, Michael Lerner, Christopher Lloyd, Studs Terkel, David Strathairn, Charlie Sheen, Kevin Tighe, John Mahoney, John Sayles, Gordon Clapp, Richard Edson, James Reed, Don Harvey, John Anderson, Maggie Renzi; **D:** John Sayles; **W:** John Sayles; **C:** Robert Richardson; **M:** Mason Daring. **VHS, Beta, LV** *ORI, FCT*

8 Seconds 🎵🎵♪

PG-13/Jr. High-Adult Love, not sports, dominates the true-life story of rodeo star Lane Frost (Perry), a world champion bull rider killed in the ring at the age of 25 in 1990. A decent guy, he finds quick success on the rodeo circuit, marries (to Geary), and finds his career getting in the way of their happiness. Bull-riding sequences are genuinely stomach churning, the performances low-key. Title refers to the amount of time a rider must stay aboard his animal.

⚠ BEWARE *Profanity.*

1994 104m/C Luke Perry, Cynthia Geary, Stephen Baldwin, James Rebhorn, Carrie Snodgress, Red Mitchell, Ronnie Clair Edwards; **D:** John G. Avildsen; **W:** Monte Merrick; **M:** Bill Conti. **VHS, LV** *NLC*

18 Again! 🎵🎵♪

PG/Jr. High-Adult After a bump on the head, an 81-year-old man and his 18-year-old grandson mentally switch places, giving each a new look at his life. Lightweight romp with Burns in especially good form, but not good enough to justify redoing this tired theme.

1988 100m/C George Burns, Charlie Schlatter, Anita Morris, Jennifer Runyon, Tony Roberts, Red Buttons, Miriam Flynn, George DiCenzo; **D:** Paul Flaherty; **W:** Jonathan Prince, Josh Goldstein; **M:** Billy Goldenberg. **VHS, Beta, LV** *VTR, NWV*

Electric Dreams 🎵🎵♪

PG/Sr. High-Adult A young man buys a computer that yearns to do more than sit on a desk. First it takes over his apartment, then it sets its sights on the man's cello-playing neighbor—the same woman his owner is courting. To win her affections, the over-eager computer tries to dazzle her with a variety of musical compositions from his unique keyboard. Cort supplies the voice of Edgar the computer in this film that integrates a rock-music video format.

⚠ BEWARE *Profanity and horny microchips.*

1984 95m/C Lenny Von Dohlen, Virginia Madsen, Maxwell Caulfield, Bud Cort, Koo Stark; **D:** Steven Barron. **VHS, Beta, LV** *MGM*

The Electric Grandmother

Primary From the marvelous imagination of Ray Bradbury arises this excellent made-for-TV tale. A widower and his three children acquire a custom-made robot grandmother (Maureen Stapleton), sort of a Mary Poppins for the next century, who pours beverages from her fingertips, flies a kite to make a clothesline and teaches the children about enduring love and trust. Based on Bradbury's "I Sing the Body Electric." Ages 7 to 12.

1981 49m/C Maureen Stapleton, Edward Herrmann; **D:** Noel Black. **VHS, Beta** *BTV, LCA, NWV*

The Electric Horseman 🎵🎵🎵

PG/Jr. High-Adult Former champion cowboy Sonny Steele (Robert Redford), is now a boozing has-been who hawks breakfast cereal at third-rate rodeos and other public events. Scheduled to ride a $12 million thoroughbred across a stage at a Las Vegas hotel, Sonny instead steals the horse (which he sees as a kindred spirit) and rides away. Hallie Martin (Jane Fonda) is a TV reporter who follows the story, and Redford, out in the wild where Redford plans to return the horse, and himself, to a natural environment. Romance ensues, but film intelligently avoids the Hollywood ending it leads you to expect. Redford is a little too handsome as the dissipated cowpoke but gives it a good ride. Willie Nelson plays a friend and provides much of the very effective

Matt LeBlanc has his hands full with a new player in "Ed."

soundtrack. Fine scenery and a subtle animal-rights theme add to film's appeal. Ages 12 and up.

BEWARE *Brief profanity. Willie Nelson seeks a woman "who can suck the chrome off a trailer hitch."*

1979 120m/C Robert Redford, Jane Fonda, John Saxon, Willie Nelson, Valerie Perrine, Wilford Brimley, Nicolas Coster, James B. Sikking; **D:** Sydney Pollack; **M:** Dave Grusin. **VHS, Beta, LV** *MCA*

Elephant Boy 🦴🦴🦴

Family Triumphant British adaptation of Rudyard Kipling's "Toomai of the Elephants." Stay patient during child star Sabu's long, confusing speech at the start—his acting and diction improve straightaway, as he plays a boy taken on an wild elephant roundup in the jungles of India. Tragedy strikes, and the safari looks like a failure when Toomai runs away to the underbrush. There he finds a mythical haven of the great beasts, in astonishing nature scenes that probably couldn't be duplicated today at any cost. Minor classic, worth rediscovery on tape, even with its patronizing, colonial attitudes toward the natives.

1937 80m/B Sabu, Walter Hudd, W.E. Holloway; **D:** Robert Flaherty, Zoltan Korda. **VHS, Beta, LV** *HBO, WAR*

The Elephant Man 🦴🦴🦴 🦴

PG/Jr. High-Adult Based on the true story of John Merrick, an intelligent, but severely deformed man (John Hurt) who, with the help of a sympathetic doctor (Anthony Hopkins), moved from freak shows into posh London society. David Lynch's first mainstream film, shot in elegant black and white. Moving performance from Hurt. Grotesque makeup may terrify queasy souls. Ages 14 and up.

BEWARE *Hideous, historically accurate make-up.*

1980 125m/B Anthony Hopkins, John Hurt, Anne Bancroft, John Gielgud, Wendy Hiller, Freddie Jones, Kenny Baker; **D:** David Lynch; **W:** Eric Bergren, Christopher DeVore, David Lynch; **M:** John Morris, Samuel Barber. **Award Nominations:** Academy Awards '80: Best Actor (Hurt), Best Art Direction/Set Decoration, Best Costume Design, Best Director (Lynch), Best Film Editing, Best Picture, Best Original Score; **Awards:** British Academy Awards '80: Best Actor (Hurt), Best Film; Cesar Awards '82: Best Foreign Film; National Board of Review Awards '80: 10 Best Films of the Year. **VHS, Beta, LV** *PAR*

The ElmChanted Forest 🦴 🦴

Preschool-Primary Yugoslavian cartoon feature about how painter Peter Pallette sleeps under a mystical elm in the Fantasy Forest and gains the power to bring his art to

life. This annoys the local dictator (who's a cross between a circus clown and a cactus). Loud, off-putting mixture of old-style animation and frantic gag heroics.
1986 90m/C VHS, Beta *CEL*

Elmer Fudd's School of Hard Knocks

Family Five titles featuring the hunter extwaordinaiwee, Elmer Fudd. Ages 4 to 9.
19?? 35m/C VHS

Elmocize

Preschool Join Sesame Street's Elmo and the Elmocisizers at Elmo's Exercise Camp as he helps pre-schoolers to be fit with some easy and fun exercises. Any young fans of Elmo will be thrilled to have the "little red guy" leading them through fitness fun. Contains many segments, all in the Sesame Street tradition with animation and appearances by Sesame Street regulars, and even includes exercising for children with disabilities. Ages 2 to 5.
1996 35m/C VHS

Emil and the Detective 🦴🦴 ᗉ

Family A German ten-year-old is robbed of his grandmother's money by gangsters, and subsequently enlists the help of pre-adolescent detectives to retrieve it. Good Disney dramatization of the Erich Kastner children's novel. Remake of the 1931 German film starring Rolf Wenkhaus.
1964 99m/C Bryan Russell, Walter Slezak, Roger Mobley; *D:* Peter Tewkesbury. **VHS, Beta** *DIS*

Emma 🦴🦴🦴

Jr. High-Adult Jane Austen's 1816 novel about Emma Woodhouse (Paltrow) who makes it her goal to "fix" the lives of all her friends, while ignoring her own problems. Your kids will tell you "Sounds like Clueless'!" Yep, that was the modern version. This one's worth it, too, and it's a great period piece.
1996 111m/C Gwyneth Paltrow, Jeremy Northam, Greta Scacchi, Toni Collette, Alan Cummings, Juliet Stevenson, Polly Walker, Ewan McGregor, James Cosmo, Sophie Thompson, Phyllida Law; *D:* Douglas McGrath; *W:* Douglas McGrath. **VHS** *NYR*

Emmet Otter's Jug-Band Christmas

Family Emmet Otter and his Ma enter the Frog Town Hollow talent contest and try to beat out a rock group called the Riverbottom Nightmares for the prize money, which will enable them to have a merry Christmas.
1977 50m/C VHS, Beta *NO*

The Emperor's New Clothes

Family Hans Christian Andersen's story of the pretentious emperor, his yes-men and a couple of clever swindlers gets the "Faerie Tale Theatre" spin, with delightful results. Dick Shawn overacts delectably as the clothes-

If you like *Eddie* (1996), you'll love:

The Air Up There (1994)

The Bad News Bears (1976)

The Big Green (1995)

Blue Chips (1994)

D2: The Mighty Ducks (1994)

The Fish That Saved Pittsburgh (1979)

Hoosiers (1986)

Ladybugs (1992)

Little Big League (1994)

Major League (1989)

Major League 2 (1994)

The Mighty Ducks 2 (1994)

The Mighty Ducks 3 (1996)

Wildcats (1986)

crazed ruler, while Alan Arkin and Art Carney play tailors Morty and Rambo whose cloth can be seen only by intelligent people. A profound lesson about how the pressure to conform can cause us to ignore the truth. Ages 6 to 12.
1984 60m/C Art Carney, Alan Arkin, Dick Shawn; *D:* Peter Medak. **VHS, Beta** *KUI, FOX, FCT*

The Emperor's New Clothes

Preschool-Primary Classic tale from Hans Christian Andersen about two sly tailors and a vain king, read by master thespian Gielgud as part of the "Rabbit Ears: We All Have Tales" series.
1991 30m/C VHS, LV *KUI, NLC,*

The Emperor's New Clothes and Other Folktales

Preschool-Primary Two con-artists make the emperor a new set of clothes that nobody can see. Also includes "Why Mosquitoes Buzz in People's Ears" and "Suho and the White Horse," all from the "Children's Circle" series.
1992 30m/C VHS *CCC, WKV, BTV*

Meet the Star of Edward Scissorhands, Johnny Depp

Johnny Depp seems determined to be the outlaw movie star of his generation, the new Brando or James Dean. He's a rebel and he'll never, never be understood, he fondly hopes. A high-school dropout, he graduated from juvenile delinquent to rock guitarist. Turning actor, he became a teen idol and pouty magazine cover boy by playing a narc on Fox TV's "21 Jump Street." Now he has a reputation for trashing hotel rooms, fighting with high-profile girlfriends like Winona Ryder and Kate Moss and playing melancholic, marginal characters in quirky films such as *Benny and Joon* and *What's Eating Gilbert Grape?* A brooding, rebellious type who fancies himself a latter-day Beatnik, Depp counts Jack Kerouac and J.D. Salinger among his biggest heroes. His sensitive portrayals have earned him acclaim, particularly in the title role in *Edward Scissorhands*, where he deftly played a misfit with cutlery for fingers. One of the most sought-after actors in Hollywood, he's turned down many highly commercial roles in an effort to keep his rebel image intact. He constantly trashes his old teen-idol image, most notably by spoofing it in John Waters' *Cry-Baby*. He got to play opposite Brando in *Don Juan de Marco*, but so far has turned down all opportunities to play James Dean.

Empire of the Sun 🦴🦴🦴ᵛ

PG/Jr. High-Adult Extraordinarily vivid film of J.G. Ballard's autobiographical novel. Young, wealthy British boy is living in Shanghai when Japan invades China at the onset of World War II. Separated from his family, Jim adapts to a brutal (yet exhilarating) life of poverty, discomfort, betrayal, and survival at any cost when he is interred in a prison camp and befriends a scheming American black marketeer. A breathtaking work, in which Steven Spielberg's romantic child's-eye-view of the world has a heartrending context, as the sky fills with wonderful flying things—warplanes—and mysterious, mystical light—the atom bomb.

BEWARE *Brutality and poverty. Sex, kamikaze pilots, and war violence. For older children.*

1987 153m/C Christian Bale, John Malkovich, Miranda Richardson, Nigel Havers, Joe Pantoliano, Leslie Phillips, Rupert Frazer, Ben Stiller, Robert Stephens, Burt Kwouk, Masato Ibu, Emily Richard; **Cameos:** J.G. Ballard; **D:** Steven Spielberg; **W:** Tom Stoppard; **M:** John Williams. **Award Nominations:** Academy Awards '87: Best Art Direction/Set Decoration, Best Cinematography, Best Costume Design, Best Film Editing, Best Sound, Best Original Score; **Awards:** National Board of Review Awards '87: 10 Best Films of the Year, Best Director (Spielberg). **VHS, Beta, LV, 8mm** *WAR, INJ*

The Empire Strikes Back
🦴🦴🦴🦴

PG/Family Second in the "Star Wars" trilogy finds Luke Skywalker and the Rebel Alliance on the run from Darth Vader and the forces of the Dark Side. Luke learns the ways of a Jedi knight from master Yoda (a creation of Jim Henson's creature factory), while Han Solo and Princess Leia find romance and adventures of their own. Continues the excellent tradition set by 1977's "Star Wars" with the same superb special effects and a hearty plot, though viewers at the time were frustrated by the cliffhanger ending (followed up in "Return of the Jedi" in 1983). Also available on Laserdisc with "The Making of 'Star Wars'."

BEWARE *Galactic violence.*

1980 124m/C Mark Hamill, Carrie Fisher, Harrison Ford, Billy Dee Williams, Alec Guinness, David Prowse, Kenny Baker, Frank Oz, Anthony Daniels, Peter Mayhew, Clive Revill, Julian Glover, John Ratzenberger; **D:** Irvin Kershner; **W:** Leigh Brackett, Lawrence Kasdan; **M:** John Williams; **V:** James Earl Jones. **Award Nominations:** Academy Awards '80: Best Art Direction/Set Decoration, Best Original Score; **Awards:** Academy Awards '80: Best Sound, Best Visual Effects; People's Choice Awards '81: Best Film. **VHS, Beta, LV** *FOX, FCT, RDG*

Encino Man 🦴🦴

PG/Jr. High-Adult While excavating for a pool, two California high-school dudes dig up a 10,000-year old 'teenaged' caveman. After a makeover and teaching him the necessities like the four basic food groups (Milk Duds in the dairy group, Sweet Tarts in the fruit group), they take the bewildered guy to class where he becomes a hit, for some reason. Juvenile humor supposedly appealing to adolescents has its moments for adults, though the laughs are limited. Encino guy Fraser emotes little but somehow steals the show. Course, he's up against master thespians like Shore, so like, be forewarned, dude. Produced through Disney's Hollywood Pictures division.

1992 88m/C Sean Astin, Brendan Fraser, Pauly Shore, Megan Ward, Robin Tunney, Rick Ducommun, Mariette Hartley, Richard Masur, Michael DeLuise; **D:** Les Mayfield; **W:** Shawn Schepps. **VHS, Beta** *HPH*

Encyclopedia Brown: Case of the Missing Time Capsule

Family Before a precious time capsule can be opened during the centennial celebration of a small town, the container is stolen. The boy detective sets out to solve the case, in a tale that amalgamates several of Donald J. Sobol's "Encyclopedia Brown" stories (some better than others). Additional volumes available.

1988 55m/C Steve Holland, Scott Bremner, D. David Scheerer. **VHS** *VTR, MED*

The Endless Summer 🦴🦴🦴

Jr. High-Adult Classic surfing documentary about the freedom and sense of adventure that surfing symbolizes. Director Brown follows two young surfers around the world in search of the perfect wave. (They finally find it at a then-unknown break off Cape Saint Francis in South America.) Besides the excellent surfing photography, Big Kahuna Brown provides the amusing tongue-in-cheek narrative. Considered by many to be the best surf movie ever. Followed by a sequel nearly 30 years later.

1966 90m/C Mike Hynson, Robert August; **D:** Bruce Brown; **W:** Bruce Brown. **VHS, Beta, LV** *FCT, HMV, PBS*

The Endless Summer 2 🦴🦴🦴

PG/Jr. High-Adult You don't have to personally hang ten to get stoked about this long-awaited sequel that once again follows two surfer dudes in their quest for the perfect wave. This time out pro surfers O'Connell and Weaver circle the globe seeking adventure and the world's best waves. Traces the evolution of surfing, from the lazy, golden days of the '60s to the worldwide phenomenon it is today, complete with its own pro tour circuit. Breathtaking scenery and spectacular surfing sequences highlight this look at a unique subculture. Thirty years later and it's still a great ride, though the travelogue wears thin and the sub-culture's now fairly well exploited.

1994 107m/C Robert "Wingnut" Weaver, Pat O'Connell, Robert August; **D:** Bruce Brown; **W:** Bruce Brown, Dana Brown. **VHS, LV** *COL*

Enemy Mine 🦴🦴🦴

PG-13/Jr. High-Adult A space fantasy in which two pilots from warring planets, one an Earthling (Randy Quaid), the other a lizardlike being (Louis Gossett Jr.) crash land on a barren planet and must work together to survive. Ages 12 and up.

1985 108m/C Dennis Quaid, Louis Gossett Jr., Brion James, Richard Marcus, Lance Kerwin; **D:** Wolfgang Petersen; **M:** Maurice Jarre. **VHS, Beta, LV** *FOX*

EPIC: Days of the Dinosaurs 🦴🦴

Family From the creators of the Australian "Dot" series of cartoon movies comes this animated fable about two cave-kids separated from their prehistoric tribe, fighting for survival amidst savage dinosaurs. Animation is only slightly better than the prehistory.

1987 75m/C D: Yoram Gross. **VHS, Beta** *FHE*

Erik the Viking 🦴🦴

PG-13/Jr. High-Adult Mediocre farce about a Viking who grows dissatisfied with his barbaric way of life and sets out to find mythical Asgaard, where Norse gods dwell. Great cast of character actors in an insubstantial fairytale that flirts with the Monty Python style. That's no coincidence; script was loosely based on stories the director—Python alumnus Jones—wrote to amuse his small son. That this material could somehow wind up with a PG-13 is one of his better jokes.

1989 104m/C Tim Robbins, Terry Jones, Mickey Rooney, John Cleese, Imogen Stubbs, Anthony Sher, Gordon John Sinclair, Freddie Jones, Eartha Kitt; **D:** Terry Jones; **W:** Terry Jones. **VHS, Beta, LV** *ORI*

Ernest Goes to Camp 🦴🦴

PG/Jr. High-Adult The first Ernest hit (not counting cameos and video compilations) with Varney's TV commercial pitchman Ernest P. Worrell, here a fool handyman at a summer camp. For a gag he's promoted to counselor to a loser troop of juvenile delinquents, but of course the dope's upbeat attitude unites the boys to save Camp Kakakee from developers. Really, really poor jokes, with slobbery sentiment and quite a lesson at the climax for kid viewers: If you're unafraid of bullets, they won't hurt you.

1987 92m/C Jim Varney, Victoria Racimo, John Vernon, Iron Eyes Cody, Lyle Alzado, Gailard Sartain, Daniel Butler, Hakeem Abdul-Samad; **D:** John R. Cherry III. **VHS, Beta** *TOU*

Ernest Goes to Jail 🦴🦴

PG/Jr. High-Adult One of the better "Ernest" outings, thanks to creative gags and slam-bang plotting. Still, after 81 minutes you've had enough, knowwhutImean? Electromagnetized bank janitor Ernest P. Worrell gets switched for a lookalike hardcore convict and winds up in the felon's cell, while the bad guy, on the outside, schemes a heist. Get a load of Ernest's gadget-filled home—it looks like he inherited Pee Wee Herman's old place, as well as his audience.

1990 81m/C Jim Varney, Gailard Sartain, Randall "Tex" Cobb, Bill Byrge, Barry Scott, Charles Napier; **D:** John R. Cherry III. **VHS, LV** *TOU, TOU*

Ernest Goes to School

PG/Jr. High-Adult Ernest must finish high school if he wants to keep his job as school janitor. He's "aided" by two crazy science teachers who give him an experimental IQ booster.

1994 89m/C Jim Varney, Linda Kash, Bill Byrge; **D:** Coke Sams. **VHS** *MNC*

The Ernest Green Story

Jr. High-Adult One of the newer breed of Disney made-for-TV features, a true story of the racial hatred and rage endured by Green, the first black teenager to attend an all-white Arkansas high school in the 1950s. Well-acted and uncompromising in its subject matter, and ultimately optimistic and triumphant.

1993 92m/C Morris Chestnut, CCH Pounder, Gary Grubbs, Tina Lifford, Avery Brooks, Ruby Dee, Ossie Davis; **D:** Eric Laneuville. **VHS** *DIS*

Ernest Rides Again

PG/Jr. High-Adult Ernest P. "KnowwhutImean?" Worrell is now aiding a professor who thinks the British crown jewels (the real ones) were hidden in a Revolutionary War cannon. Ernest uncovers the massive wheeled weapon, and the plot is a long slapstick chase between him, British agents and a greedy antiquities collector. Redundant slapstick targeted strictly for Ernest fans in which the star gets comedically upstaged by a couple of goofball vacuum cleaner salesmen.

1993 93m/C Jim Varney, Ron James, Duke Ernsberger, Jeffrey Pillars, Linda Kash, Tom Butler; **D:** John Cherry; **W:** John Cherry, William M. Akers; **M:** Bruce Arntson, Kirby Shelstad. **VHS** *MNC*

Ernest Saves Christmas

PG/Jr. High-Adult Ernest P. Worrell is back in the second of the series. When Santa decides that it's time to retire, cabbie Ernest must help recruit a handpicked successor—a has-been children's show host who is a bit reluctant. Starts off with promise, then succumbs to the Ernest brand of slapstick tedium. For youngest fans only.

1988 91m/C Jim Varney, Douglas Seale, Oliver Clark, Noelle Parker, Billie Bird; **D:** John R. Cherry III. **VHS, Beta, LV** *TOU*

Ernest Scared Stupid

PG/Jr. High-Adult Pea-brained Ernest P. Worrell returns yet again in this silly comedy. When he accidentally releases a demon from a sacred tomb, a 200-year-old curse threatens to destroy his hometown, unless Ernest and a friendly witch-lady come to the rescue. Again, the Ernest level of slapstick crosses the line into being annoying, so ensure you're in the mood.

1991 93m/C Jim Varney, Eartha Kitt, Austin Nagler, Jonas Moscartolo, Shay Astar; **D:** John R. Cherry III; **M:** Bruce Arntson. **VHS, Beta** *TOU*

The Errand Boy

Family Lewis' distinct schnook character hits Hollywood in search of a job. He wins a position as a movie-studio errand boy, but his assignment is really to spy on other employees. That's the slender hook on which hangs some of the comic's brightest slapstick. Imagine the apocalypse if Jerry and Ernest P. Worrell ever met.

1961 92m/B Jerry Lewis, Brian Donlevy, Dick Wesson, Howard McNear, Felicia Atkins, Fritz Feld, Sig Rumann, Renee Taylor, Doodles Weaver, Mike Mazurki, Lorne Greene, Michael Landon, Dan Blocker, Pernell Roberts, Snub Pollard, Kathleen Freeman; **D:** Jerry Lewis; **W:** Jerry Lewis. **VHS, Beta, LV** *LIV*

Escapade in Florence

Family Two young art students practice their technique in Italy, only to discover that a criminal gang of forgers is passing on their classical-painting reproductions as the real thing. Generally artless Disney adventure.

1962 81m/C Tommy Kirk, Ivan Desny; **D:** Steve Previn. **VHS, Beta** *DIS*

Escape Artist

PG/Jr. High-Adult "Black Stallion" cinematographer Deschanel's first directorial effort was this quirky film about a teenage escape artist (played by the son of Ryan O'Neal, Tatum's brother) who sets out to uncover the identity of his magician-father's killers by using his own illusions and trickery. A more family-friendly alternative to the often rough "F/X" movies. Script co-authored by the writer of "E.T.," based on a novel by David Wagoner.

1982 96m/C Griffin O'Neal, Raul Julia, Teri Garr, Joan Hackett, Desi Arnaz Sr., Gabriel Dell, Huntz Hall, Jackie Coogan; **D:** Caleb Deschanel; **W:** Melissa Mathison; **M:** Georges Delerue. **VHS, Beta, LV** *LIV, VES*

Escape from the Planet of the Apes

G/Family Reprising their roles as intelligent, English-speaking apes, McDowall and Hunter flee their world before it's destroyed, and travel back in time to present-day America. In L.A. they become the subjects of a relentless search by the fearful population, much like humans Charlton Heston and James Franciscus were targeted for experimentation and destruction in simian society in the earlier "Planet of the Apes" and "Beneath the Planet of the Apes." Best of the "Planet of the Apes" sequels is followed by "Conquest of the Planet of the Apes."

 Violence.

1971 98m/C Roddy McDowall, Kim Hunter, Sal Mineo, Ricardo Montalban, William Windom, Bradford Dillman, Natalie Trundy, Eric (Hans Gudegast) Braeden; *D:* Don Taylor; *M:* Jerry Goldsmith. **VHS, Beta, LV** *FOX, FUS*

Escape of the One-Ton Pet

Preschool-Primary When her beloved calf grows into a full-grown steer, a young girl is ordered by her father to find a new pet.

1978 73m/C *D:* Richard Bennett; *V:* Stacy Swor, James Callahan, Michael Morgan, Richard Yniguez. **VHS, Beta** *FHE, TLF*

Escape to Witch Mountain
♫♫♫

G/Family Your ordinary youths might want to escape FROM a place called Witch Mountain, but siblings Tony and Tia are no ordinary kids. The have the power of telekinesis. They have the ability to see the future. They have a rich guardian who knows a good thing when he sees it and has sinister plans. The youngsters vaguely understand that the secret of their origins lies at Witch Mountain. They embark on an exciting and surprising journey, with the evil guardian in pursuit. One of the better 1970s live-action Disney features. Adapted from a novel by Alexander Key. Ages 6 to 11.

1975 97m/C Kim Richards, Ike Eisenmann, Eddie Albert, Ray Milland, Donald Pleasence; *D:* John Hough. **VHS, Beta, LV** *DIS, BTV*

E.T.: The Extra-Terrestrial
♫♫♫♫

PG/Family Spielberg's famous fantasy, one of the most popular films in history, portrays a homely, limpid-eyed little alien stranded on Earth. While trying desperately to signal to his mothership UFO, he forms a special relationship with Elliott, a young boy who literally stumbles across him. Modern fairy tale provides warmth, humor, pathos, and sheer wonder. Held first place as the highest grossing movie of all time for years until a new Spielberg hit replaced it—"Jurassic Park." Debra Winger contributed to the voice of E.T.

 Occasional salty language; death, dying and rejuvenation.

1982 115m/C Henry Thomas, Dee Wallace Stone, Drew Barrymore, Robert MacNaughton, Peter Coyote, C. Thomas Howell, Sean Frye, K.C. Martel; *D:* Steven Spielberg; *W:* Melissa Mathison; *M:* John Williams. **Award Nominations:** Academy Awards '81: Best Film Editing; Academy Awards '82: Best Cinematography, Best Director (Spielberg), Best Picture, Best Sound; **Awards:** Academy Awards '82: Best Sound, Best Visual Effects, Best Original Score; Golden Globe Awards '83: Best Film—Drama, Best Score; People's Choice Awards '83: Best Film. **VHS, Beta, LV** *MCA, APD, RDG*

If you like E.T.: The Extra-Terrestrial (1982), you'll love:

Battle Beyond the Stars (1980)

Battlestar Galactica (1978)

The Black Hole (1979)

Close Encounters of the Third Kind (1977)

Cocoon (1985)

Cocoon: The Return (1988)

The Empire Strikes Back (1980)

Enemy Mine (1985)

Independence Day (1996)

Invasion of the Body Snatchers (1978)

The Last Starfighter (1984)

Planet of the Apes (1968)

Return of the Jedi (1983)

Star Wars (1977)

Starman (1984)

2001: A Space Odyssey (1968)

2010: The Year We Make Contact (1984)

The War of the Worlds (1953)

Even More Baby Songs

Family Children and their parents will find even more fun with Hap Palmer and his finger-snapping tunes. Ages 1 to 5.

1990 32m/C VHS *MED*

Everyone Can Dance

Primary Dance instructor Linda Strickland exposes children to the art of dance while providing physical exercise and entertainment. She teaches three basic dance steps and takes children through an exercise routine starting with stretching and ending with a cool-down period.

1993 30m/C VHS

Evil Under the Sun 🎬🎬

PG/Jr. High-Adult Poor Agatha Christie outing in spite of all-star cast makes "Death on the Nile" look much better by comparison. An opulent beach resort is the setting as Hercule Poirot attempts to unravel a murder mystery.

BEWARE *Murder and mystery at the beach.*

1982 112m/C Peter Ustinov, Jane Birkin, Maggie Smith, Colin Blakely, Roddy McDowall, Diana Rigg, Sylvia Miles, James Mason, Nicholas Clay; **D:** Guy Hamilton; **W:** Anthony Shaffer. VHS, Beta, LV REP

The Ewok Adventure 🎬🎬

G/Family Those adorable, friendly creatures from "Return of the Jedi" go from film to made-for-TV in an utterly generic adventure by George Lucas. The teddy-bear Ewoks befriend two kids whose spaceship crashed, then journey to free their parents from "the dreaded giant Gorax." Little of the "Star Wars" lore is present, and the slow-moving plot may as well have taken place anywhere—but LucasFilm has the special-effects moxie like nobody else and the visuals, at least, do not disappoint. Followed by "Ewoks: The Battle for Endor."

BEWARE *Space violence and a spaceship crash.*

1984 96m/C Warwick Davis, Eric Walker, Aubree Miller, Fionnula Flanagan; **D:** John Korty; **M:** Elmer Bernstein. VHS, Beta, LV MGM, FCT

The Ewoks: Battle for Endor 🎬🎬 ▷

Family Made-for-TV follow-up to "The Ewok Adventure" is notably better, if you can get past the jolt at the start— the massacre of the happy human family so laboriously rescued in the last movie. Lone survivor, cute daughter Cindel, accompanies her furry friend Wicket (now speaking English) on a mission to free Ewoks from a monster warlord. They meet more creatures, allies and enemies. Ends with a thrilling battle, reminiscent of the Ewok skirmish at the end of "Return of the Jedi," which is praise indeed; it's the beginning of this that might upset tykes.

BEWARE *A family is killed, followed by Ewok violence.*

1985 98m/C Wilford Brimley, Warwick Davis, Aubree Miller, Sian Phillips, Paul Gleason, Eric Walker, Carel Struycken, Niki Botholo; **D:** Jim Wheat, Ken Wheat. VHS, Beta, LV MGM, FCT

Experience Preferred . . . But Not Essential 🎬🎬 ▷

PG/Jr. High-Adult English schoolgirl Annie gets her first job at a seaside resort where she meets assorted strange characters and learns about life. Gentle tale, often compared to "Gregory's Girl."

BEWARE *Nudity and sex talk.*

1983 77m/C Elizabeth Edmonds, Sue Wallace, Geraldine Griffith, Karen Meagher, Ron Bain, Alun Lewis, Robert Blythe; **D:** Peter Duffell; **W:** June Roberts. VHS, Beta MGM

Explorers 🎬🎬 ▷

PG/Family What if, in the middle of "E.T.," the classic alien suddenly took off his mask and revealed himself as . . . Mork from Ork? That's more or less what happens to this delicate, promising sci-fi tale that takes a galactic detour into gonzo comedy. Three boys, prompted by strange dreams, build a circuit that allows them to turn a scrapped carnival ride into a real spaceship. Zooming into space, they discover who invited them. Recommended more for kid viewers who may better appreciate—and forgive—the punchline. From the director of "Gremlins."

BEWARE *Salty language, roughhousing, alcohol use.*

1985 107m/C Ethan Hawke, River Phoenix, Jason Presson, Amanda Peterson, Mary Kay Place, Dick Miller, Robert Picardo, Dana Ivey, Meshach Taylor, Brooke Bundy; **D:** Joe Dante; **W:** Eric Luke; **M:** Jerry Goldsmith. VHS, Beta, LV PAR

The Extra-Special Substitute Teacher

Primary Effervescent singer Joanie Bartels takes over a classroom and whisks her youthful charges off to Mars, Mexico and the age of dinosaurs through the magic of music and imagination. Lively songs include "La Bamba," "The Martian Hop," "Dinosaur Rock and Roll," "Silly Pie," "The Locomotion" and "Would You Like To Swing on a Star." Ages 3 to 8.

1993 45m/C Joanie Bartels. VHS BMG

Eye on the Sparrow 🎬🎬 ▷

PG/Jr. High-Adult Winningham and Carradine are a couple who desperately want to raise a child of their own, but the system classifies them as unfit parents since they are both blind. Together they successfully fight the system in this inspiring made for television movie that was based on a true story.

1991 94m/C Mare Winningham, Keith Carradine, Conchata Ferrell, Sandy McPeak, Karen Lee, Bianca Rose; **D:** John Korty. VHS REP

The Ezra Jack Keats Library

Family The Children's Circle Studios present animated versions of six of Keats' children's books: "The Snowy Day," "Peter's Chair," "Goggles," "Apt. 3," "Pet Show," and "The Trip." Also included is an interview with Keats.

1992 45m/C Ezra Jack Keats. VHS CCC, MLT, WKV

F/X 🎬🎬🎬

R/Sr. High-Adult Hollywood special effects expert is contracted by the government to fake an assassination to protect a mob informer. After completing the assignment, he learns that he's become involved in a real crime and is forced to reach into his bag of F/X tricks to survive. Twists and turns abound in this fast-paced story that was the sleeper hit of the year. Followed by a sequel.

Profanity, violence and suggested sex. Lots of special effects, of course, and some scary.

1986 109m/C Bryan Brown, Cliff DeYoung, Diane Venora, Brian Dennehy, Jerry Orbach, Mason Adams, Joe Grifasi, Martha Gehman; **D:** Robert Mandel; **W:** Robert T. Megginson, Gregory Fleeman; **M:** Bill Conti. **VHS, Beta, LV** *HBO, FCT*

F/X 2: The Deadly Art of Illusion 🦴🦴

PG-13/Sr. High-Adult Weak follow-up finds the special-effects specialist set to pull off just one more illusion for the police. Once again, corrupt cops use him as a chump for their scheme, an over-complicated business involving a stolen Vatican treasure.

 Violence, nudity, and profanity.

1991 107m/C Bryan Brown, Brian Dennehy, Rachel Ticotin, Philip Bosco, Joanna Gleason; **D:** Richard Franklin. **VHS, LV** *ORI, IME*

The Fabulous World of Jules Verne 🦴🦴 🦴

Family Jules Verne pastiche by the Czech Zeman, filmed in "Mystimation"—a unique combo of set design and animation to reproduce the look of 19th-century engravings that illustrate Verne's works. Live actors seem to move in a storybook world, as a submarine pirate tricks a scientist into perfecting a new power source (atomic?) to make devastating bombs. The scientist's heroic colleague works to thwart the villain, in an adventuresome plot that doesn't have the full-throttle action of Disney's "20,000 Leagues Under the Sea" but rather an amused, ironic view of the incredible gizmos and technologies Verne predicted, whether they came true or not (note the underwater bicycles with bells on the handlebars!). Dubbed and re-edited for American release, with a classroom-style intro by Hugh Downs; get past that and you're in for a offbeat tale. Based mainly on a Verne novel "For the Flag," with a bit of Captain Nemo thrown in.

1958 83m/B Lubor Tolos, Arnost Navratil, Miroslav Holub, Zatloukalova; **D:** Karel Zeman. **VHS**

Face the Music 🦴 🦴

PG-13/Jr. High-Adult Ringwald and Dempsey were once stormily married and pursuing successful, collaborative careers as singer/songwriters for the movies. But they've abandoned the work, along with the marriage, until a movie producer makes them a very lucrative offer for a new song. Only Dempsey's new girlfriend has some voracious objections.

1992 93m/C Patrick Dempsey, Molly Ringwald, Lysette Anthony. **VHS** *LIV*

Faeries

Preschool-Primary The legendary hero Oisin finds himself enlisted in the fight to save the mystical inhabitants of faerie world from a tyrant king. Elaborate cartoon based on Brian Froud and Alan Lee's best-selling book.

1981 30m/C V: Morgan Brittany, Hans Conried, June Foray. **VHS, Beta** *FHE, PYR*

Fame 🦴🦴🦴

R/Sr. High-Adult The progress of eight talented teens, from freshmen year through graduation from New York's High School of Performing Arts. Untraditional plot opens with their audition, ends simply with their graduation; in between director Parker allows the students to mature on screen, revealing the pressures of constantly trying to prove themselves. A faultless parallel is drawn between these "special" kids and the pressures felt by high schoolers everywhere. Great dance and music sequences are skillfully woven into the realistic narrative, and you'd never detect the epic running time. Inspiration for the popular TV series. There's no shortage of profanity, lewdness and streetwise ambiance, and that R is well deserved. 🎵 Fame; Red Light; I Sing the Body Electric; Dogs in the Yard; Hot Lunch Jam; Out Here On My Own; Is It OK If I Call You Mine?.

 Streetwise profanity, nudity, violence, and a scene involving the filming of a skin flick.

1980 133m/C Irene Cara, Barry Miller, Paul McCrane, Anne Meara, Joanna Merlin, Richard Belzer, Maureen Teefy; **D:** Alan Parker; **M:** Michael Gore. **Award Nominations:** Academy Awards '80: Best Film Editing, Best Film Editing, Best Original Screenplay, Best Song ("Out Here on My Own"), Best Sound; **Awards:** Academy Awards '80: Best Song ("Fame"), Best Original Score; Golden Globe Awards '81: Best Song ("Fame"). **VHS, Beta, LV** *MGM, FCT*

A Family Circus Christmas

Family Characters of Bill Keane's comic strip, "Family Circus," celebrate Christmas in a cartoon approach. The hysterics begin when one of the children asks Santa for a very unusual present, which he delivers.

1984 30m/C D: Al Kouzel. **VHS, Beta** *FHE*

Family Circus Easter

Family "Family Circus" kids Billy, Dolly, and Jeffy celebrate Easter by trying to catch that celebrated bunny (whose voice is provided by jazz great Gillespie).

1980 30m/C VHS, Beta *FHE*

A Family Concert Featuring The Roches and The Music Workshop for Kids

Family Children will delight at the musical calvacade of live concert performances combined with animation and mime. Featuring music performed live by The Roches from their 1994 Parents' Choice Award winning album "Will You Be My Friend," and from The Music Workshop for Kids 1994 Parents' Choice Recommended Album "The Sky Blue Catfish."

1995 60m/C VHS *NYR*

Family Jewels 🎬🎬

Family Child heiress has to choose her adoptive father from among her six vastly different uncles, all played by Lewis. If you like Lewis you can't miss this. In addition to the six-pack of uncles, he's the chauffeur, plus (offscreen) producer, director, and co-author of the script. He may have also catered and provided transportation. Slapstick shtick and goofy guises will appeal to young viewers.
1965 100m/C Jerry Lewis, Donna Butterworth, Sebastian Cabot, Robert Strauss; **D:** Jerry Lewis; **W:** Jerry Lewis. **VHS, Beta** *PAR*

Family Prayers 🎬🎬 ♭

PG/Jr. High-Adult Coming-of-age drama, set in 1969 Los Angeles, about 13-year-old Andrew and his family troubles. Dad is a compulsive gambler which causes friction with his wife and the sister-in-law who has bailed the couple out of their money problems more than once. Meanwhile, Andrew tries to look out for his younger sister and prepare for his bar-mitzvah. A little too much of a nostalgic golden glow surrounds what is essentially a family tragedy.

> **BEWARE** *Gambling and family dysfunction (caused by, you guessed it, gambling).*

1991 109m/C Tzvi Ratner-Stauber, Joe Mantegna, Anne Archer, Patti LuPone, Paul Reiser, Allen (Goorwitz) Garfield, Conchata Ferrell, David Margulies; **D:** Scott Rosenfelt; **W:** Steven Ginsburg. **VHS** *COL*

A Family Thing 🎬🎬🎬

PG-13/Jr. High-Adult White southerner Earl Pilcher (Duvall) learns that his biological mother was black, after the only mother he's ever known dies and leaves him a letter. She also tells him he has a black half-brother (Jones) who is a policeman in Chicago, and urges Earl to reclaim his past. In Chicago, the brothers discover they have a lot in common, especially the simple fact that they are decent and human. Solid acting by Jones and Duvall and a terrific performance by Irma P. Hall as their aunt who is blind, but sees all.

> **BEWARE** *Some strong language, a violent carjacking, Duvall gets drunk at a bar, and a childbirth scene.*

1996 109m/C Robert Duvall, James Earl Jones, Irma P. Hall, Michael Beach, David Keith; **D:** Richard Pearce; **W:** Billy Bob Thornton, Tom Epperson. **VHS** *NYR*

Fandango 🎬🎬 ♭

PG/Sr. High-Adult Five college friends (including Costner in an early role) take a wild weekend drive across the Texas Badlands for one last fling before graduation and the prospect of military service. Expanded by Reynolds with assistance from Steven Spielberg, from his student film. Provides an interesting look at college and life during the '60s Vietnam crisis.

> **BEWARE** *Profanity and sex talk. A guy jumps out of a plane on a dare.*

1985 91m/C Judd Nelson, Kevin Costner, Sam Robards, Chuck Bush, Brian Cesak, Elizabeth Daily, Suzy Amis, Glenne Headly, Pepe Serna, Marvin J. McIntyre; **D:** Kevin Reynolds; **W:** Kevin Reynolds; **M:** Alan Silvestri. **VHS, Beta** *WAR*

Fangface

Family Scraps from old Saturday-morning network TV shows feature the adventures of Sherman Fangsworth, a teenager who changes into Fangface the werewolf and fights crime with friends Biff, Kim, and Puggsy. For what little it's worth, the premise actually predates the popular "Teen Wolf" movies and cartoon spinoffs.
1983 60m/C VHS, Beta *WOV*

Fangface Spooky Spoofs

Preschool-Primary Unearthed episodes of the teenage-werewolf TV cartoon, "Great Ape Escape" and "Dinosaur Daze."
1978 44m/C VHS

Fantasia 🎬🎬🎬🎬

Family An array of classic sequences, from Mickey Mouse as a sorcerer's apprentice to the life-cycle of dinosaurs set to Stravinsky concludes with the mighty occult visuals of "A Night on Bald Mountain." Walt Disney's most personal animation feature first bombed at the box office and irked purists who couldn't take the plotless, experimental mix of classical music and cartoons. It became a cult item, embraced by later, more liberal generations of filmgoers, particularly the Woodstock Nation. Video release was painstakingly restored to match the original version. That's the good news. Bad news is, Disney's distribution of it has ceased because of their planned remake. Note also the Italian "Allegro Non Troppo." 🎵 Toccata & Fugue in D; The Nutcracker Suite; The Sorcerer's Apprentice; The Rite of Spring; Pastoral Symphony; Dance of the Hours; Night on Bald Mountain; Ave Maria; The Cossack Dance.
1940 116m/C VHS, LV *DIS, FCT, RDG*

Fantastic Planet 🎬🎬🎬

PG/Family A critically acclaimed French, animated, sci-fi epic based on the drawings of Roland Topor. A race of small humanoids are enslaved and exploited by a race of giants on a savage planet, until one of the small creatures manages to unite his people and fight for equality.

> **BEWARE** *Mature themes, some violence.*

1973 68m/C D: Rene Laloux; **V:** Barry Bostwick. **VHS, Beta** *VYY, MRV, SNC*

The Fantastic World of D.C. Collins 🎬🎬

Jr. High-Adult Little D.C. constantly daydreams of action and adventure. Finally he gets to live out some TV-level James Bond exploits when he obtains a vital videotape lost by the bad guys. Mediocre telefilm designed as a vehicle for "Diff'rent Strokes" star Coleman.

1984 100m/C Gary Coleman, Bernie Casey, Shelley Smith, Fred Dryer, Marilyn McCoo, Philip Abbott, George Gobel, Michael Ansara; **D:** Leslie Martinson. **VHS** *VTR, NWV*

Far and Away 🦴🦴🦴

PG-13/Jr. High-Adult Meandering old-fashioned epic about immigrants, romance, and settling the American West. In the 1890s, Joseph Donelly (Cruise) is forced to flee his Irish homeland after threatening the life of his landlord, and emigrates to America in the company of the landlord's daughter, feisty Shannon Christie (Kidman). Particularly brutal scenes of Cruise earning his living as a bare-knuckled boxer contrast with the expansiveness of the land rush ending. Slow, spotty, and a little too slick for its own good, though real-life couple Cruise and Kidman are an attractive pair. Filmed in 70-mm Panavision on location in Ireland and Montana with a soundtrack contributed to by The Chieftains. Also available in a letter boxed version.

⚠️ BEWARE *Boxing violence and profanity. Tough living arrangements for the two main characters. A main character is shot and another falls from a horse.*

1992 140m/C Tom Cruise, Nicole Kidman, Thomas Gibson, Robert Prosky, Barbara Babcock, Colm Meaney, Eileen Pollock, Michelle Johnson, Cyril Cusack, Clint Howard, Rance Howard; **D:** Ron Howard; **W:** Bob Dolman; **M:** John Williams. **VHS, Beta, LV** *MCA*

Far from Home: The Adventures of Yellow Dog 🦴🦴🦴

PG/Family Resourceful 14-year-old Angus (Bradford) and his faithful pooch Yellow, shipwrecked on an uninhabited island in British Columbia, fight for survival and wait to be rescued. They face wolves and mountain lions, learn to live off the land, although the land sometimes plays rough. Good thing Dad (Davidson) gave them all those cool survival tips before they left, or else they never would've known that you can eat bugs. (Okay, the dog probably knew that already.) Mom (Rogers) does her bit by making sure the search mission stays focused.

⚠️ BEWARE *All sorts of danger. Dog battles wild animals.*

1994 81m/C Jesse Bradford, Bruce Davison, Mimi Rogers, Tom Bower; **D:** Phillip Borsos; **W:** Phillip Borsos. **VHS, LV** *FXV*

A Far Off Place 🦴🦴 🦴

PG-13/Jr. High-Adult In Africa two mismatched youngsters struggle to survive after poachers slaughter a herd of elephants, and then their parents. The boy and girl face peril during a trek across the Kalahari desert in the company of a teenage bushman. Witherspoon and Randall carry their end well, though Bok steals the show. Collaboration between Spielberg's Amblin Entertain and Disney studios is more violent that most productions bearing the Magic Kingdom stamp, though careful editing reduces the bloodshed. Based on the books "A Story Like the Wind" and "A Far Off Place" by Laurens van der Post.

⚠️ BEWARE *Elephants slaughtered, parents slaughtered, little blood shed.*

1993 107m/C Reese Witherspoon, Ethan Randall, Sarel Bok, Jack Thompson, Maximilian Schell, Robert Burke, Patricia Kalember, Daniel Gerroll, Miles Anderson; **D:** Mikael Salomon; **W:** Robert Caswell, Jonathan Hensleigh, Sally Robinson; **M:** James Horner. **VHS, Beta, LV** *DIS*

The Farmer's Daughter 🦴🦴🦴

Jr. High-Adult Young portrays Katrin Holmstrom, a Swedish farm girl who becomes a maid to Congressman Cotten and winds up running for office herself (not neglecting to find romance as well). The outspoken and multi-talented character charmed audiences and was the basis of a television series in the 1960s.

1947 97m/B Loretta Young, Joseph Cotten, Ethel Barrymore, Charles Bickford, Harry Davenport, Lex Barker, James Arness, Rose Hobart; **D:** H.C. Potter. **Award Nominations:** Academy Awards '47: Best Supporting Actor (Bickford); **Awards:** Academy Awards '47: Best Actress (Young). **VHS, Beta** *FOX, BTV*

Fast Break 🦴🦴

PG/Primary-Adult New York deli clerk who is a compulsive basketball fan talks his way into a college coaching job. He takes a team of street players (including a girl) with him, with predictable results on and off the court.

⚠️ BEWARE *Profanity, sex talk.*

1979 107m/C Gabe Kaplan, Harold Sylvester, Randee Heller; **D:** Jack Smight; **M:** David Shire. **VHS, Beta** *GKK*

Fast Forward 🦴 🦴

PG/Jr. High-Adult Group of eight teenagers from Ohio learn how to deal with success and failure when they enter a national dance contest in New York City. Breakdancing variation on the old show business chestnut.

🎵 Fast Forward; How Do You Do; As Long As We Believe; Pretty Girl; Mystery; Curves; Showdown; Do You Want It Right Now?; Hardrock.

1984 110m/C John Scott Clough, Don Franklin, Tracy Silver, Cindy McGee; **D:** Sidney Poitier; **W:** Richard Wesley; **M:** Tom Bahler. **VHS, Beta, LV** *COL*

Fast Getaway 🦴🦴

PG/Jr. High-Adult Chase scenes galore as a teen criminal mastermind plots bank heists for his outlaw father. But dad's karate-kicking new girlfriend/accomplice is jealous of the kid and schemes against him. Adolescent action-comedy, cleverly acted—but your enjoyment may be tempered by the portrayal of bank robbers as heroes.

⚠️ BEWARE *Profanity, robbery, fighting, and sex talk.*

1991 91m/C Corey Haim, Cynthia Rothrock, Leo Rossi, Ken Lerner, Marcia Strassman; **D:** Spiro Razatos. **VHS, LV, 8mm** *COL*

Jesse Bradford and Yellow Dog bond in "Far From Home: The Adventures of Yellow Dog."

Fast Getaway 2 🦴🦴 ◠

PG-13/Jr. High-Adult Ex-bank robber Nelson (Haim) has given up a life of crime to open a business with gal pal Beatrice (Buxton) while waiting for his partner/dad Sam (Rossi) to get out of jail. Then Nelson gets set up by Lily (Rothrock) and finds himself trying to convince an FBI agent of his innocence.

1994 90m/C Corey Haim, Sarah Buxton, Leo Rossi, Cynthia Rothrock, Peter Paul Liapis; **D:** Oley Sassone; **W:** Mark Sevi; **M:** David Robbins. **VHS** *LIV*

Fast Times at Ridgemont High 🦴🦴🦴 ◠

R/Sr. High-Adult Parents be forewarned: depicts high school as den of breeding anarchy. Teens at a Southern California high school revel in sex, drugs, and rock 'n' roll. A full complement of student types meet at the mall—that great suburban microcosm percolating with angst-ridden teen trials—to contemplate losing their virginity, plot skipping homeroom, and move inexorably closer to the end of their adolescence. Talented young cast became household names, led by Penn as the California surfer dude who antagonizes teacher, Walston, aka

"Aloha Mr. Hand." Based on the best-selling book by Crowe, who returned to high school to acquire necessary adolescent confidential. One of the best of the "escape from hell high school" genre, bettered only by "Rock 'N' Roll High School."

BEWARE *High school profanity and marijuana use. A nude girl dives into a pool. Two characters have sex in a cabana, she gets pregnant and needs an abortion. Roughhousing in the locker room.*

1982 91m/C Sean Penn, Jennifer Jason Leigh, Judge Reinhold, Robert Romanus, Brian Backer, Phoebe Cates, Ray Walston, Scott Thomson, Vincent Schiavelli, Amanda Wyss, Forest Whitaker, Kelli Maroney, Eric Stoltz, Pamela Springsteen, James Russo, Martin Brest, Anthony Edwards; **D:** Amy Heckerling; **W:** Cameron Crowe. **VHS, Beta, LV** *MCA*

Fat Albert & the Cosby Kids, Vol. 1

Primary-Jr. High The message of this Fat Albert series emphasizes communication: talking, listening, and sharing as important aspects of expression. The Cosby Kids develop these ideas through humorous situations. In this episode, two members of the gang drive an entire hospital crazy when they have to have their tonsils removed. Additional volumes available.

1973 60m/C V: Bill Cosby. **VHS, Beta** *BAR*

Fatal Instinct 🦴🦴

PG-13/Jr. High-Adult Spoof on erotic thrillers such as "Fatal Attraction" and "Basic Instinct" is sort of funny without really being funny. Suave Assante plays a guy with dual careers—he's both cop and attorney, defending the criminals he's arrested. Young plays a lovelorn psycho who's lost her panties. Plot is worth mentioning only in passing, since the point is to mercilessly skewer the entire film noir tradition. The gags occasionally hit deepchuckle level, though for every good joke there's at least three that misfire. Clemmons of "E Street Band" fame wanders around with sax for background music purposes, typical of the acute self-consciousness.

BEWARE *Profanity and sex talk. Requires knowledge of films being parodied.*

1993 90m/C Armand Assante, Sean Young, Sherilyn Fenn, Kate Nelligan, Christopher McDonald, James Remar, Tony Randall; **Cameos:** Clarence Clemmons, Doc Severinsen; **D:** Carl Reiner; **W:** David O'Malley; **M:** Richard Gibbs. **VHS, LV** *MGM*

Father and Scout 🦴🦴 ◠

PG/Primary-Adult Would-be Eagle Scout has a problem when he takes his city-bred, whiny, basically incompetent, dad (that would be Saget) on a camping trip. Get-um up, Scout. Saget is not exactly Sir Laurence Olivier. Made for TV.

BEWARE *Mild fisticuffs.*

1995 92m/C Bob Saget, Brian Bonsall, Heidi Swedberg, Stuart Pankin, David Graf, Troy Evans; **D:** Richard Michaels; **M:** David Kitay. **VHS, LV** *TTC*

Father Figure

Sr. High-Adult When a divorced man attends his ex-wife's funeral, he discovers that he must take care of his estranged sons. Based on young adult writer Richard Peck's novel; well-done made-for-TV movie.

1980 94m/C Hal Linden, Timothy Hutton, Cassie Yates, Martha Scott, Jeremy Licht; **D:** Jerry London; **M:** Billy Goldenberg. **VHS, Beta** *NO*

Father Hood

PG-13/Jr. High-Adult Family drama has Swayze playing a small-time criminal whose daughter tracks him down after leaving the foster-care shelter where she and her brother are being abused. The family takes to the road, running from both the police and a journalist (Berry) who wants to expose the corrupt foster-care system. The children are obnoxious, Swayze is miscast, and the entire film is a misfire.

BEWARE! *Roughhousing; salty language.*

1993 94m/C Patrick Swayze, Halle Berry, Sabrina Lloyd, Brian Bonsall, Diane Ladd, Michael Ironside, Bob Gunton; **D:** Darrell Roodt; **W:** Scott Spencer. **VHS, LV** *TOU*

Father of the Bride

Family Classic, quietly hilarious comedy about the tribulations of a father preparing for his only daughter's wedding. Tracy is suitably overwhelmed as the loving father and Taylor radiant as the bride. A warm vision of American family life, accompanied by the 1940 MGM short "Wedding Bills." Also available in a colorized version. Followed by "Father's Little Dividend" and later a television series. Remade in 1991.

1950 94m/C Spencer Tracy, Elizabeth Taylor, Joan Bennett, Billie Burke, Leo G. Carroll, Russ Tamblyn, Don Taylor, Moroni Olsen; **D:** Vincente Minnelli; **W:** Frances Goodrich, Albert Hackett. **VHS, Beta, LV** *MGM*

Father of the Bride

PG/Jr. High-Adult Remake of the 1950 comedy classic falls short of the original, but still manages to charm. Nice house, nice neighborhood, nice family. Martin is adequately confused about the upcoming nuptials and reluctant to cut the ties that bind with his daughter, played nicely by Williams in her film debut (later she appeared in a TV ad as a young bride-to-be calling her dad long distance to tell him she's engaged). Keaton is little more than attractive window dressing as the bride's mom, while Short gobbles up the screen and the first row of seats vamping as a pretentious wedding coordinator. Actual wedding is one of the more extravagant in recent film history. Adapted from a novel by Edward Streeter.

BEWARE! *Brief profanity.*

1991 105m/C Steve Martin, Diane Keaton, Kimberly Williams, Kieran Culkin, George Newbern, Martin Short, B.D. Wong, Peter Michael Goetz, Kate McGregor Stewart, Martha Gehman; **Cameos:** Eugene Levy; **D:** Charles Shyer; **W:** Charles Shyer, Nancy Meyer; **M:** Alan Silvestri. **VHS, Beta, LV** *TOU*

Father of the Bride Part II

PG/Jr. High-Adult First comes love, then comes marriage, then comes the sequel with the baby carriage. Doting dad George Banks (Martin) feels old when he learns he's about to become a grandfather. Ah, but not only is daughter Annie (Williams) pregnant, George's wife Nina (Keaton) is pregnant, too. It's all too much for George, which is good, because there's nothing youngsters like more than watching adults act sillier than children. Martin doesn't disappoint, especially when both women go into labor at the same time. Martin Short returns as party planner Franck (you know, FRONK) to add to the merriment. It's predictable but it's fun, and family does prevail.

BEWARE! *Be prepared to explain such concepts as menopause, midlife crisis and prostate exams. Some mild profanity.*

1995 106m/C Steve Martin, Diane Keaton, Kimberly Williams, Martin Short, George Newbern, Kieran Culkin, Peter Michael Goetz, Kate McGregor Stewart, Eugene Levy, B.D. Wong, Jane Adams; **D:** Charles Shyer; **W:** Nancy Myers, Charles Shyer; **C:** William A. Fraker; **M:** Alan Silvestri. **VHS** *NYR*

Father's Little Dividend

Family Tracy expects a little peace and quiet now that he's successfully married off Taylor in this charming sequel to "Father of the Bride." However, he's quickly disillusioned by the news he'll soon be a grandfather—a prospect that causes nothing but dismay. Reunited the stars, director, writers, and producer from the successful first film.

1951 82m/B Spencer Tracy, Joan Bennett, Elizabeth Taylor, Don Taylor, Billie Burke, Russ Tamblyn, Moroni Olsen; **D:** Vincente Minnelli; **W:** Frances Goodrich, Albert Hackett. **VHS, Beta, LV** *CNG, MRV, NOS*

Federal Agents vs. Underworld, Inc.

Family Super G-Man Dave Worth goes up against Nila, a greedy villainess bent on finding the golden hands of Kurigal so she may rule the world. 12-episode serial.

1949 167m/B Kirk Alyn, Rosemary La Planche, Roy Barcroft, Carol Forman, James Dale, Bruce Edwards; **D:** Fred Brannon. **VHS** *REP, MLB*

Felix the Cat: An Hour of Fun

Family The funny feline delves into his bag of tricks for a compilation of vintage cartoon adventures. Additional volumes available.

1989 60m/C VHS, LV *IME*

Felix the Cat: The Movie

Family Classic cartoon creation Felix returns in a trite feature. The feline and his bag of tricks enter a dimension

Martin and Keaton anxiously await the birth of their grandchild in "Father of the Bride Part 2."

filled with He-Man/Mutant Ninja Turtles leftovers; new-age princess, comic reptiles, robots and a Darth Vadar clone who's defeated with ridiculous ease. Strictly for undemanding kids. Numerous vintage "Felix" short subjects are also available on separate tapes.
1991 83m/C D: Tibor Hernadi; **V:** Chris Phillips, Alice Playten, Maureen O'Connell. **VHS, Beta** *TOU, FCT*

Ferdy

Family European cartoon based on the books by Ondrej Sekora, centering on the multi-legged inhabitants of Bugville.
1984 50m/C VHS, Beta *FHE*

Ferngully: The Last Rain Forest 🦴🦴🦴

G/Family Do fairies believe in human tales? "Humans don't have tails. They wear big bottoms with bad shorts." Thus speaks Robin Williams, as the voice of the wisecracking bat in "FernGully," an animated save-the-rain-forest film that has smart remarks for grownups, cute creatures for small children, action for older kids and plenty of songs for all. FernGully is the lush and unspoiled heart of the rain forest, where vegetation, wildlife and the fairylike tree spirits live in longstanding harmony. Along comes progress in the form of a logging crew with a monstrous tree-devouring machine. Ah, but a tree spirit named Crysta magically shrinks one of the loggers down to her size to convince him to spare the whole happy habitat. Lovely visuals, good character voices and singers (including Tim Curry, Tone-Loc, Christian Slater, Samantha Mathis, Grace Zabriskie, Cheech, Chong, and Raffi). If only the script had more zip. Ages 5 to 10.

🚨 BEWARE *Noisy, smoke-belching tree-destroying machine may frighten pre-schoolers.*

1992 72m/C D: Bill Kroyer; **M:** Alan Silvestri; **V:** Samantha Mathis, Christian Slater, Robin Williams, Tim Curry, Jonathan Ward, Grace Zabriskie, Richard "Cheech" Marin, Thomas Chong, Tone Loc, Jim Cox. **VHS** *FXV, MLT*

Ferris Bueller's Day Off 🦴🦴🦴

PG-13/Jr. High-Sr. High Writer/director/producer Hughes fashioned one of his most congenial screen teens in Ferris, a popular high school guy who knows all the angles and goes to elaborate lengths to cut class. Faking sickness, he sneaks his girlfriend and best buddy out of school to spend a grand day enjoying Chicago. Broderick is charming, sharing his philosophy of life with the viewer. Gray amuses as his tattle-tale sister doing everything she can to see him caught and getting Bueller's arch-enemy on the school faculty to hunt the renegade (he's a jerk, as are all the adults). Led to a Ferris Bueller TV series that quickly died and a shameless imitator, "Parker Lewis Can't Lose," that ran for years. Go figure.

 Roughhousing, certain anti-authoritarian flavor.

1986 103m/C Matthew Broderick, Mia Sara, Alan Ruck, Jeffrey Jones, Jennifer Grey, Cindy Pickett, Edie McClurg, Charlie Sheen, Del Close, Virginia Capers, Max Perlich, Louis Anderson; **D:** John Hughes; **W:** John Hughes; **M:** Ira Newborn. **VHS, Beta, LV, 8mm** *PAR, TLF*

Fiddler on the Roof 🦴🦴🦴 ♭

G/Family Poignant story of Tevye, a poor Jewish milkman at the turn of the century in a small Ukrainian village, and his five daughters, his lame horse, his wife, and his companionable relationship with God. Based on the long-running Broadway musical with finely detailed set decoration and choreography. Strong performances from the entire cast create a sense of intimacy in spite of near epic proportions of the production. The play was based on the stories of Sholem Aleichem. 🎵 Tradition; Matchmaker, Matchmaker; If I Were a Rich Man; Sabbath Prayer; To Life; Miracle of Miracles; Tevye's Dream; Sunrise, Sunset; Wedding Celebration.

 Persecution and soldiers spoil a wedding.

1971 184m/C Chaim Topol, Norma Crane, Leonard Frey, Molly Picon; **D:** Norman Jewison; **M:** John Williams. **Award Nominations:** Academy Awards '71: Best Actor (Topol), Best Art Direction/Set Decoration, Best Director (Jewison), Best Picture, Best Supporting Actor (Frey); **Awards:** Academy Awards '71: Best Cinematography, Best Sound, Best Score; Golden Globe Awards '72: Best Actor—Musical/Comedy (Topol), Best Film—Musical/Comedy. **VHS, Beta, LV** *FOX, MGM, TLF*

Field of Dreams 🦴🦴🦴 ♭

PG/Jr. High-Adult Based on W. P. Kinsella's novel "Shoeless Joe," this uplifting mythic fantasy depicts an Iowa corn farmer who, following the directions of a mysterious voice, cuts a baseball diamond in his crops. Neighbors doubt his sanity, but soon the ballfield hosts the spirit of Joe Jackson and other ballplayers who were caught up and disgraced in the notorious 1919 "Black Sox" World Series scandal. It's all about chasing a dream, paying debts, maintaining innocence in spite of adulthood, finding redemption, reconciling the child with the man, and of course, celebrating baseball; but avoids excess hokiness through Costner and Madigan's strong, believable characters.

1989 106m/C Kevin Costner, Amy Madigan, James Earl Jones, Burt Lancaster, Ray Liotta, Timothy Busfield, Frank Whaley, Gaby Hoffman; **D:** Phil Alden Robinson; **W:** Phil Alden Robinson; **M:** James Horner. **VHS, Beta, LV** *MCA, FCT, HMV*

The Fiendish Plot of Dr. Fu Manchu WOOF!

PG/Jr. High-Adult A sad farewell from Sellers, who in his last film portrays Dr. Fu in his desperate quest for the necessary ingredients for his secret life-preserving formula. Sellers portrays both Dr. Fu and the Scotland Yard detective on his trail, but it's not enough to save this picture, flawed by poor script and lack of direction.

1980 100m/C Peter Sellers, David Tomlinson, Sid Caesar, Helen Mirren; **D:** Piers Haggard. **VHS, Beta, LV** *WAR, FCT*

Fievel's American Tails: A Mouse Known as Zorrowitz/ Aunt Sophie's Visit

Preschool-Primary Two episodes from the animated television series featuring adventures in the Old West. In "A Mouse Known as Zorrowitz," Fievel foils the actions of a stagecoach heist and saves a cheese shipment. "Aunt Sophie's Visit" has Fievel thinking he'll have to miss the rodeo when Aunt Sophie shows up for a visit. Additional volumes available.

1994 48m/C D: Lawrence Jacobs; **V:** Dom DeLuise, Phillip Glasser, Dan Castellaneta, Cathy Cavadini, Kenneth Mars, Lloyd Baattista, Gemt Graham, Susan Silo. **VHS, LV** *MCA*

The Fifth Monkey 🦴 ♭

PG-13/Sr. High-Adult Brazilian man embarks on a journey to sell four monkeys in order to fill a dowry for his sexy bride, but throughout various obstacles and adventures he comes to view the captive beasts as more than mere property. Often dull, didactic lesson in animal rights that could have used a lighter touch and less raunchier elements. Based on a novel by Jacques Zibi.

 Raunchy nudity and violence.

1990 93m/C Ben Kingsley; **D:** Eric Rochant; **W:** Eric Rochant. **VHS, LV** *COL, FCT*

The Fifth Musketeer 🦴🦴

PG/Jr. High-Adult A campy adaptation of Dumas's "The Man in the Iron Mask," wherein a monarch's evil twin impersonates him while imprisoning the true king. A good cast and rich production shot in Austria make for a fairly entertaining swashbuckler.

1979 90m/C Beau Bridges, Sylvia Kristel, Ursula Andress, Cornel Wilde, Ian McShane, Alan Hale Jr., Helmut Dantine, Olivia de Havilland, Jose Ferrer, Rex Harrison, Helmut Dantine; **D:** Ken Annakin; **W:** David Ambrose. **Beta** *COL*

50 Classic All-Star Cartoons, Vol. 1

Family A feast for fans, a cassette collection totalling six hours worth of vintage cartoons featuring Popeye, Woody Woodpecker, Felix the Cat, Porky Pig, Casper,

Matthew Broderick skips school in "Ferris Bueller's Day Off."

Superman, and many more all time (non- Disney) favorites.
1991 60m/C VHS *VTR*

50 Classic All-Star Cartoons, Vol. 2

Family A second volume of great cartoon classics featuring Casper, Little Lulu, Superman, Popeye, Betty Boop, Daffy Duck, Bugs Bunny, and many others.
1991 60m/C VHS *VTR*

50 Degrees Below Zero

Primary Two wintery 'toons; in the title tale Jason finds creepy things happening in his house like objects getting moved and his father starting to sleepwalk. Jason wonders if everything is connected to his bad dreams. In "Thomas' Snow Suit," a young boy is teased at school for wearing a drab brown snow suit.
1993 25m/C VHS

50 Simple Things Kids Can Do to Save the Earth, Parts 1 & 2

Primary-Jr. High Children implementing the ideas listed in David Javna's book of the same title are the focus of this two-video set. Part one, "Water and Resources," explains how kids have cleaned up Pigeon Creek, and part two, "Greenlife, Wildlife, Energy and Air" answers questions kids have on a variety of environmental subjects.
1992 44m/C VHS *FHS*

The Fig Tree

Family After her mother passes away, grief-stricken Miranda is tormented by fear of death. A visit to her aunts helps her cope with this difficult stage of life. Introspective childhood drama from the "WonderWorks" series has little plot (it's based on a Katherine Anne Porter story, after all), but acting and mood are beyond reproach in this evocation of one girl's anguished state of mind.
1987 58m/C Olivia Cole, William Converse-Roberts, Doris Roberts, Teresa Wright, Karron Graves; *D:* Calvin Skaggs. **VHS** *PME, FCT, BTV*

Fighting Devil Dogs

Family Exciting Republic serial about two Marine officers roaming the globe as they unravel the identity of the masked evildoer known as the Lightning. In 12 chapters.

BEWARE *Violence.*

1938 195m/B Lee Powell, Bruce (Herman Brix) Bennett; *D:* John English, William Witney. **VHS** *REP, VCN, MLB*

Fighting Marines

Jr. High-Adult The last of the mostly mediocre serials made by the Mascot studio before they merged to form Republic. Throughout 12 episodes those Marines fight Tiger Shark, a modern-day pirate out to stop the leathernecks from establishing an airstrip on and island in the Pacific.

1936 69m/B Jason Robards Sr., Grant Withers, Ann Rutherford, Pat O'Malley; *D:* Joseph Kane, B. Reeves Eason. **VHS, Beta** *VYY, VCN, VDM*

The Fighting Prince of Donegal

Family Irish prince battles the invading British in 16th Century Ireland. Escaping their clutches, he leads his clan in rescuing his mother and his beloved in this Disney swashbuckler. Based on the novel "Red Hugh, Prince of Donegal" by Robert T. Reilly.

1966 110m/C Peter McEnery, Susan Hampshire, Tom Adams, Gordon Jackson, Andrew Keir; *D:* Michael O'Herlihy. **VHS, Beta** *DIS*

Fighting with Kit Carson

Family Famous guide and Indian fighter leads bands of settlers westward. 12-chapter serial.

BEWARE *Violence.*

1933 230m/B Johnny Mack Brown, Noah Beery Sr., Noah Beery Jr., Betsy King Ross; *D:* Armand Schaefer, Colbert Clark. **VHS, Beta** *VYY, VCN, VDM*

A Fine Mess

PG/Jr. High-Adult Two buffoons cash in when one overhears a plan to dope a racehorse, but they are soon fleeing the plotters' slapstick pursuit. The plot is further complicated by the romantic interest of a gangster's wife. The television popularity of the two stars did not translate to the big screen; perhaps it's Edwards' fault.

1986 100m/C Ted Danson, Howie Mandel, Richard Mulligan, Stuart Margolin, Maria Conchita Alonso, Paul Sorvino; *D:* Blake Edwards; *W:* Blake Edwards; *M:* Henry Mancini. **VHS, Beta, LV** *COL*

Finian's Rainbow

G/Family Og the leprechaun (Steele) comes to America to retrieve his pot of gold taken by Irish immigrant Finian; meanwhile the magic ore stirs up a southern community by changing a bigoted landowner black. Fanciful musical comedy based on a Broadway hit worked notably better onstage (and in 1947). The terrific cast heroically performs the overlong material with enough sheer zest to prevent this from becoming Finian's wake instead. ♫ How Are Things in Glocca Morra?; Look To the Rainbow; That Old Devil Moon; If This Isn't Love; Something Sort of Grandish; The Be-Gat; This Time of Year; The Great Come and Get It Day; When I'm Not Near the Girl I Love.

1968 141m/C Fred Astaire, Petula Clark, Tommy Steele, Keenan Wynn, Al Freeman Jr., Don Francks, Susan Hancock, Dolph Sweet; *D:* Francis Ford Coppola. **VHS, Beta, LV** *WAR, MVD*

Finn McCoul

Preschool-Primary Legendary Irish hero Finn McCoul and his wife Oonagh battle against the giant Cucullin. Part of the terrific "Rabbit Ears" series of video storybooks, with music by the Celtic band Boys of the Lough.

1992 30m/C VHS *RAB, MOV, BTV*

Fire and Ice

PG/Jr. High-Adult Cartoonist Bakshi collaborated with eminent fantasy and comic-book creators for this underimaginative animated fantasy about warriors fighting the evil conqueror Nekron, whose psychic control of glaciers is the script's one touch of originality. Devoid of humor, film's in a netherworld between adult and kiddie entertainment. Bakshi's rotoscope technique—tracing live, filmed actors—enables his human characters to move, fight, die and, in the case of the sexy, near-naked princess, jiggle realistically.

BEWARE *If this hadn't been a 'mere' cartoon, it would have gotten a stronger rating than PG for nonstop skull-bashing, slashing and spearing. Salty language; alcohol use.*

1983 81m/C Randy Norton, Cynthia Leake; *D:* Ralph Bakshi; *V:* Susan Tyrrell, William Ostrander. **VHS, Beta, LV** *COL*

Fire in the Sky

PG-13/Sr. High-Adult Mysterious disappearance of Sweeney sparks a criminal investigation, until he returns, claiming he was abducted by aliens. Though everybody doubts his story, viewers won't, since the alleged aliens have already made an appearance, shifting the focus to Sweeney as he tries to convince skeptics that his trauma is genuine. Perhaps this mirrors what director Lieberman went through while trying to convince backers the film should be made. He could have benefitted by understanding the difference between what he was telling viewers and what he was showing them. Captivating special effects are one of the few bright spots. Based on a story that might be true.

BEWARE *Profanity and nudity. Scary alien abduction. Gives credence to UFO abduction story.*

1993 98m/C D.B. Sweeney, Robert Patrick, Craig Sheffer, Peter Berg, James Garner, Henry Thomas; *D:* Robert Liebmann; *W:* Tracy Torme; *M:* Mark Isham. **VHS, Beta, LV** *PAR*

The Fire in the Stone 🎵🎵

Family A young boy discovers an opal mine and dreams of using the treasure to reunite his family. However, when the jewels are stolen from him, he enlists his friends to help get them back. Based on the novel by Colin Thiele.

1985 97m/C Paul Smith, Linda Hartley, Theo Pertsindis. **VHS, Beta** *WAR*

Fire Safety for Kids

Preschool-Primary Joins Beasel the Easel, Hector the Smoke Detector, and other characters as they teach children about fire safety. Ages 4 to 8.

1995 23m/C VHS *TPV*

Fireman Sam: Hero Next Door

Preschool-Primary British stop-motion animated short about how Fireman Sam does his best to keep the town of Pontypandy flame free, with the help of his truck, Jupiter.

1989 30m/C VHS *FHE*

First Born 🎵🎵 ♭

PG-13/Sr. High-Adult Divorced mother rushes blindly into romance with an intriguing stranger. Teen son Jake takes a stand when Prince Charming turns out to be a drug-pushing creep who gets mom hooked. Fresh, intriguing premise of a child having to take charge over a wayward parent, but eventually the patented Hollywood formula of chases and fights dilutes what should have been hard-hitting drama.

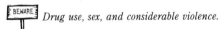 *Drug use, sex, and considerable violence.*

1984 100m/C Teri Garr, Peter Weller, Christopher Collet, Corey Haim, Sarah Jessica Parker, Robert Downey Jr.; **D:** Michael Apted. **VHS, Beta, LV** *PAR*

The First Christmas

Family Rankin-Bass TV holiday cartoon special, about a blind boy cared for by nuns in a small abbey in France, who is divinely rewarded for his kind heart.

1975 23m/C V: Angela Lansbury, Cyril Ritchard. **VHS, Beta** *WAR*

The First Easter Rabbit

Primary Rankin-Bass animated tale of a child's stuffed toy who, through magic, becomes the first Easter bunny. Very loose adaptation of the oft-told "Velveteen Rabbit" tale.

1982 25m/C VHS *WAR*

First Kid 🎵🎵 ♭

PG/Jr. High-Adult Sinbad stars as a secret service agent assigned to protect the President's teenage son, who's quite a handful. He needs to keep him out of trouble and help him to adjust to life in the public eye. Needless to say, the two become friends (in the tradition of "The Toy") and even manage to hinder a threat to the first family's security.

 Some violence, language, and brief partial nudity.

1996 ?m/C VHS *NYR*

First Knight 🎵🎵 ♭

PG-13/Jr. High-Adult King Arthur/Camelot legend comes to life again, as freelance lancer Lancelot (Gere) rescues beautiful Guinevere (Ormond), from would-be kidnapper (Cross). Guinevere is grateful, but she is betrothed to King Arthur (Connery). Hoo boy, here comes trouble. Big-scale battles, betrayals, passion, and fanciful sets make for a good, if overlong, time.

🛑 **BEWARE** *Some brutal medieval battles and the cave of the villain is dark and treacherous.*

1995 134m/C Sean Connery, Richard Gere, Julia Ormond, Ben Cross, John Gielgud, Liam Cunningham, Christopher Villiers, Valentine Pelka; **D:** Jerry Zucker; **W:** William Nicholson; **C:** Adam Greenberg; **M:** Jerry Goldsmith. **VHS, LV, 8mm** *COL*

First Men in the Moon 🎵🎵

Family Colorful, fun spectacle depicts a private 19th-century mission to the moon by British scientists who have a secret anti-gravity formula. They rise up through space in a sealed sphere, land on the moon and discover it inhabitant by a civilization of giant insects. Ray Harryhausen contributed the grandiose stop-motion f/x, including a giant caterpillar. Based on a novel by H.G. Wells.

1964 103m/C Martha Hyer, Edward Judd, Lionel Jeffries, Erik Chitty, Peter Finch; **D:** Nathan (Hertz) Juran; **W:** Nigel Kneale, Jan Read. **VHS, Beta, LV** *COL, MLB*

Fish Hawk 🎵 ♭

G/Family Canadian drama set at the turn of the century, about an alcoholic Indian named Fish Hawk befriending a young boy and going clean and sober. He gets a job at the boy's family's ranch, but finds winning the trust of white adults isn't so easy. While Fish Hawk defeats the bottle, this well-intentioned family film can't swear off the cliches. Based on a novel by Mitchell Jayne.

🛑 **BEWARE** *Alcohol use.*

1979 95m/C Will Sampson, Charlie Fields; **D:** Donald Shebib. **VHS, Beta** *MED, VTR*

The Fish that Saved Pittsburgh 🎵🎵

PG/Jr. High-Adult Sometimes you can tell just by the title. Lemon, of the Harlem Globetrotters, is among real-life basketball stars adding sparkle to a silly comedy about a loser team that hires an astrologer to change their luck. She makes sure all the team members' zodiac signs are compatible with Pisces (the fish).

 *Salty language.*

1979 104m/C Jonathan Winters, Stockard Channing, Flip Wilson, Julius Erving, Margaret Avery, Meadowlark Lemon, Nicholas Pryor, James Bond III, Kareem Abdul-Jabbar, Jack Kehoe, Debbie Allen; *D:* Gilbert Moses. **VHS, Beta** *ORI, WAR*

Fisher-Price Grimm's Fairy Tales: Briar Rose

Preschool-Primary The classic tale of Briar Rose is told here for two- to five-year-olds. Other volumes include "Frog Prince," "Hansel and Gretel," "Little Red Riding Hood," and "The Travelling Musicians of Bremen." 1990 25m/C **VHS** *MED*

Fisherman's Wharf

Jr. High-Adult Breen stars as an orphan adopted by a San Francisco fisherman who runs away when his aunt and bratty cousin come to live with them.
1939 72m/B Bobby Breen, Leo Carrillo, Henry Armetta, Lee Patrick, Rosina Galli, Leon Belasco; *D:* Bernard Vorhaus. **VHS** *NOS*

Five Lionni Classics

Preschool-Primary Children's writer Lionni and famed cut-out animator Giulio Gianini combine their talents to tell five original fairy tales for the young: "Frederick," "Fish Is Fish," "Swimmy," "Cornelius," and "It's Mine!"
1987 30m/C Leo Lionni. **VHS, Beta** *KUI, RAN, MLT*

Five Stories for the Very Young

Preschool-Primary Five excellent tales for kids are presented in various animated forms: "Caps for Sale," "Whistle for Willie," "Changes, Changes," "Drummer Hoff" and "Harold's Fairy Tale." Charming. Ages 2 to 6.
1986 33m/C *D:* Gene Deitch. **VHS, Beta** *CCC, FCT, MLT*

The 5000 Fingers of Dr. T

Family In Dr. Seuss's only non-animated movie, a boy tries to evade piano lessons and dreams of the surreal castle of Dr. Terwilliger, where hundreds of captive boys are held for piano practice and forced to wear silly beanies with "happy fingers" waving on top. Luckily, the trusted family plumber is on hand to save the day with an atom bomb. Marvelous anti-authoritarian satire may mean a bit more to adults than kids, but if only the music had been more memorable this would be in the top league with "The Wizard of Oz." As is, it's a weird, one-of-a-kind treat that, sadly, failed to score with '50s audiences.
1953 88m/C Peter Lind Hayes, Mary Healy, Tommy Rettig, Hans Conried; *D:* Roy Rowland; *W:* Theodore (Dr. Seuss) Geisel, Allan Scott. **VHS, Beta, LV** *COL, XVC, FCT*

The Flame Trees of Thika

Family In 1913, a British family relocates to East Africa to start a coffee plantation, and their struggles to adapt to the new environment are shown through the eyes of the youngest daughter. Her childhood includes the local Masai and Kikuyu tribes, plus eccentric and sometimes unhappy white neighbors, and the wild animals that roam the plains. Lovingly-made miniseries based on the memoirs of Elspeth Huxley. Originally broadcast on PBS-TV's "Masterpiece Theatre" and later The Disney Channel. On four cassettes.

BEWARE *Violence—some human, some animal.*

1981 366m/C Hayley Mills, Holly Aird, David Robb, Ben Cross. **VHS** *SIG, TVC*

Flaming Frontiers

Family Frontier scout matches wits against gold thieves and Indians in this Universal serial western, in 15 chapters.
1938 300m/B Johnny Mack Brown, Eleanor Hanson, Ralph Bowman; *D:* Ray Taylor. **VHS, Beta** *VYY, VCN, NOS*

The Flamingo Kid

PG-13/Sr. High-Adult Brooklyn teenager Jeffrey gets a summer job at a fancy beach club on Long Island. Suddenly making lots of easy money, the kid is attracted to the flashy style of the local car dealer/gin rummy king, and finds his plumber dad's solid life a bore. By the end of the season, Jeffrey's learned the true worth of both father figures, and the kind of adult he wants to be. Excellent performances all around in an intelligent coming-of-age comedy drama set in 1963, with a soundtrack of early '60s favorites.

BEWARE *Brief sex (overstressed in the ad campaign). Roughhousing, salty language, alcohol use.*

1984 100m/C Matt Dillon, Hector Elizondo, Molly McCarthy, Martha Gehman, Richard Crenna, Jessica Walter, Carole Davis, Janet Jones, Fisher Stevens, Bronson Pinchot; *D:* Garry Marshall. **VHS, Beta, LV** *LIV, VES*

The Flash

Jr. High-Adult Police scientist Barry Allen is doused with chemicals and struck by lightning, which turns him into a super strong, super speedy superhero. With the aid of a pretty researcher cohort, he uses his new identity to nail the biker gang leader who caused his brother's death. Based on a comic-book character from the same stable as Superman, this is the pilot episode for the short-lived network TV series. Obviously influenced by the Tim Burton "Batman" epics, the look is dark, stylized and not played for camp.

BEWARE *Violence.*

1990 94m/C John Wesley Shipp, Amanda Pays, Michael Nader; *M:* Danny Elfman. **VHS, Beta, LV** *WAR*

Flash Gordon

PG/Jr. High-Adult Gaudy candy-colored version of Flash Gordon's first adventure in outer space. His mission: go to far-off Mongo, where the tyrant Ming the Merciless is threatening the destruction of Earth. Deserves credit for aspiring to the 1930s flavor of the original "Flash" serials and Alex Raymond's comic strip rather

than being another "Star Wars" ripoff (like 1979's "Buck Rogers in the 25th Century"). One glaring anachronism: the pounding, glam-rock musical score by the group Queen.

BEWARE *Violence, salty language.*

1980 111m/C Sam Jones, Melody Anderson, Chaim Topol, Max von Sydow, Ornella Muti, Timothy Dalton, Brian Blessed; **D:** Mike Hodges; **M:** Howard Blake. **VHS, Beta, LV** *MCA*

Flash Gordon Conquers the Universe

Family Third and last of the hit "Flash Gordon" serials made by Universal Pictures, adapting Alex Raymond's famous comic-strip character. A plague called the purple death is devastating Earth. Flash Gordon and Dr. Zarkov discover that arch-villain Ming the Merciless is responsible. They follow his spaceship all the way back to Mars to put a stop to the interplanetary crime. Not quite as good as earlier adventures of the space hero, but diverting, and it does have those odd sets and curious touches peculiar to this series. The strange language of the Rock Men is really recorded English played backwards. In 12 chapters.

BEWARE *Roughhousing.*

1940 240m/B Buster Crabbe, Carol Hughes, Charles Middleton, Frank Shannon. **VHS, Beta** *VYY, MRV, SNC*

Flash Gordon: Rocketship

Family Re-edited from the original Flash Gordon serial in which Flash and company must prevent the planet Mongo from colliding with Earth. Good character acting and good clean fun.

1936 97m/B Buster Crabbe, Jean Rogers, Frank Shannon, Charles Middleton, Priscilla Lawson, Jack Lipson; **D:** Frederick Stephani. **VHS, Beta** *VYY, PSM, CAB*

Flash Gordon: Vol. 1

Family Three one-hour volumes of episodes from the cheapo 1950s Flash Gordon TV series are available on video, not to be confused with the classic serials.

1953 60m/B Steve Holland, Irene Champlin. **VHS, Beta** *DVT*

Flash, the Teenage Otter

Preschool-Primary The adventures of a teenaged (non-mutant, non-ninja) otter, as first televised on "The Wonderful World of Disney" TV program.

1976 48m/C VHS, Beta *MTI, DSN*

Flashdance

R/Sr. High-Adult 18-year-old Alex wants to dance classical ballet, even though she's from the blue-collar side of the tracks. Welder by day, exotic dancer by night (non-explicit), she tries to get up the confidence to audition for the stuffed shirts; complicating matters is her hot affair

with her young boss. Silly, souped-up music-video fairy tale, not to be confused with the superficially similar but far more realistic "Fame" (or for that matter, "It's Flashbeagle, Charlie Brown"). Made a mint at the box office anyway, and more off the hit soundtrack album. ♫ Flashdance . . . What a Feeling; I Love Rock 'n Roll; Manhunt; Gloria; Lady, Lady, Lady; Seduce Me Tonight.

BEWARE *Profanity; brief nudity; mature themes; sex. For what it's worth, Alex goes to confession regularly.*

1983 95m/C Jennifer Beals, Michael Nouri, Belinda Bauer, Lilia Skala, Cynthia Rhodes, Sunny Johnson, Lee Ving, Kyle T. Heffner, Ron Karabatsos, Robert Wuhl, Elizabeth Sagal; **D:** Franca Pasut. **Award Nominations:** Academy Awards '83: Best Cinematography, Best Film Editing, Best Song ("Maniac"); **Awards:** Academy Awards '83: Best Song ("Flashdance . . . What a Feeling"); Golden Globe Awards '84: Best Song ("Flashdance . . . What a Feeling"), Best Score. **VHS, Beta, LV, 8mm** *PAR*

Fletch

PG/Jr. High-Adult Newspaper journalist Fletch is a smart-mouthed guy with a talent for disguises. When he goes undercover to get the scoop on the local drug scene, a wealthy young businessman who claims to be dying enlists his help in helping him reach the here after. Something's rotten in Denmark when the man's doctor knows nothing of the illness and Fletch comes closer to the drug scene than he realizes. Charming comedy, particularly if you're a Chase fan. Based on Gregory McDonald's novel.

BEWARE *Violence and profanity, but most is pretty harmless.*

1985 98m/C Chevy Chase, Tim Matheson, Joe Don Baker, Dana Wheeler-Nicholson, M. Emmet Walsh, Kenneth Mars, Geena Davis, Richard Libertini, George Wendt, Kareem Abdul-Jabbar, Alison La Placa; **D:** Michael Ritchie; **W:** Andrew Bergman; **M:** Harold Faltermeyer. **VHS, Beta, LV** *MCA*

Fletch Lives

PG/Jr. High-Adult In this sequel to "Fletch," Chase is back again as the super-reporter. When Fletch learns of his inheritance of a Southern estate he is eager to claim it. During his down-home trip he becomes involved in a murder and must use his disguise skills to solve it before he becomes the next victim. Based on the novels of Gregory MacDonald.

1989 95m/C Chevy Chase, Hal Holbrook, Julianne Phillips, Richard Libertini, R. Lee Ermey, Cleavon Little; **D:** Michael Ritchie; **W:** Leon Capetanos; **M:** Harold Faltermeyer. **VHS, Beta, LV** *MCA*

Flight of Dragons

Primary Possibly the best of the many fantasies of Arthur Rankin Jr. and Jules Bass, this animated TV feature combines magical adventure with weighty themes on science and myth. Peter, a modern chemist fond of legendary lore, is magically transported to the world of his own D&D-style board game, where benign sorcery is losing out to logic, and a demon (yes, that's the voice of "Darth Vadar" Jones) schemes to take over. Complicated plot has Peter accidentally turned into a dragon himself, and we get an ingenious physiological explanation for the fire-breathing monsters. A fairy tale for bright kids and adults, it pretends to be based on its own hero's memoirs but is really from "The Dragon and the George," by Gordon R. Dickinson.

1982 98m/C D: Arthur Rankin Jr., Jules Bass; **V:** John Ritter, Victor Buono, James Earl Jones, Don Messick, Larry Storch. **VHS, Beta** *WAR*

Flight of the Grey Wolf ♫♫

Family Tame, innocent wolf is mistaken for a killer and must run for his life with the help of a boy owner. Standard Disney adventure, made for the Magic Kingdom's long-running weekly TV show.

1976 82m/C Bill Williams, Barbara Hale, Jeff East. **VHS, Beta** *DIS*

Flight of the Navigator ♫♫♫

PG/Family Twelve-year-old David comes back from a walk in the woods to find that eight years have passed for his family and the rest of the world. Meanwhile, NASA finds a parked UFO nearby but can't open it. The bewildered boy is the key and has an incredible adventure in time and space. Disney sci-fi starts with a real sense of awe and mystery, which it later abandons for comedy, as Reubens, in character as Pee Wee Herman, does the voice of the alien intelligence. Good fun nonetheless.

> ⚠ BEWARE *Salty language, without which this would have qualified for a G.*

1986 90m/C Joey Cramer, Veronica Cartwright, Cliff DeYoung, Sarah Jessica Parker, Matt Adler, Howard Hesseman; **D:** Randal Kleiser; **W:** Michael Burton, Matt MacManus; **M:** Alan Silvestri; **V:** Paul (Pee Wee Herman) Reubens. **VHS, Beta, LV** *DIS*

The Flintstone Kids

Preschool-Primary Collection of 12 episodes revealing the childhood antics of such prehistoric favorites as Fred, Barney, Wilma, Betty, and even Nick (as in Mr.) Slate.

1984 92m/C VHS, Beta *TTC*

The Flintstone Kids: "Just Say No"

Family Video adventures of the lead Flintstone characters as children, designed in this particular episode to teach young viewers the dangers of drugs. See also "What's Wrong with Wilma?"

1989 22m/C VHS, Beta *TTC*

The Flintstones

Family The foibles of the those modern Stone Age families (and blatant "Honeymooners" imitations, let's face it), the Flintstones and the Rubbles, are chronicled in these two animated episodes of the classic Hanna-Barbera series. Numerous other Flintstone deposits, both from the original series and later revivals, can be mined on tape.

1960 50m/C V: Alan Reed, Mel Blanc, Jean Vander Pyl, Bea Benadaret. **VHS, Beta** *TTC*

The Flintstones ♫♫ ♭

PG/Jr. High-Adult Preceded by massive hype, popular '60s cartoon comes to life thanks to a huge budget and creative sets and props. Seems that Fred's being set up by evil corporate types MacLachlan and Barry to take the fall for their embezzling scheme. Soon he gives up dining at RocDonald's for Cavern on the Green and cans best buddy Barney (Moranis). Forget the lame plot (32 writers took a shot at it) and sit back and enjoy the spectacle. Goodman's an amazingly true-to-type Fred, O'Donnell has Betty's giggle down pat, and Perkins looks a lot like Wilma. Wilma's original voice, VanderPyl, has a cameo; listen for Korman's voice as the Dictabird. Add half a bone if you're under 12.

> ⚠ BEWARE *Mild innuendos, but mostly a safe bet, even for youngsters.*

1994 92m/C John Goodman, Rick Moranis, Elizabeth Perkins, Rosie O'Donnell, Elizabeth Taylor, Kyle MacLachlan, Halle Berry, Jonathan Winters, Richard Moll, Irwin Keyes, Dann Florek; **Cameos:** Laraine Newman, Jean VanDerPyl, Jay Leno; **D:** Brian Levant; **W:** Tom S. Parker, Jim Jennewein, Steven E. de Souza; **M:** David Newman; **V:** Harvey Korman. **VHS, LV** *MCA*

A Flintstones Christmas Carol

Family Yabba dabba do we really need another version of "A Christmas Carol?" You decide. Fred has been cast as Scrooge in the Bedrock production but, dreaming of stardom, begins to take his role a little too seriously and causes trouble for his friends and family. Ages 6 to 9.

1995 90m/C VHS *TTC*

The Flintstones: Fred Flintstone Woos Again

Family Fred and Wilma take off on a second honeymoon in search of romance and adventure.

1989 60m/C V: Mel Blanc. **VHS, Beta** *TTC*

The Flintstones: Rappin' n' Rhymin'

Family Hanna-Barbera cartoon characters join real kids for an exciting thirty minutes of rappin' and dancin'!

1991 30m/C VHS, Beta *TTC*

Flipper ♫♫ ♭

Family The aquatic mammal that launched a thousand sequels. Sandy, a fisherman's 12-year-old son, saves an injured porpoise, earning the animal's gratitude. Flipper later repays the favor by rescuing Sandy from sharks. Pleasant for kids. Followed by the TV series and more. The theme song is repeated to distraction. Ages 4 to 9.

1963 87m/C Chuck Connors, Luke Halpin, Kathleen Maguire, Connie Scott; **D:** James B. Clark. **VHS, Beta** *MVD, MGM*

Elijah Wood's mother Debbie affectionately called her son her little "monkey" and for good reason. He was a normal, but energetic young child, and at the tender age of two, he accidently locked his mother out of the house. His talents became evident at an early age when he appeared in the school chorus for "The Sound of Music." He later moved onto modeling and before he knew it was appearing opposite Richard Gere in *Internal Affairs* at the age of eight. His big break came when he appeared in Barry Levinson's *Avalon* and the rest of the world got to see what his mom knew all along—he has talent.

Since then, he has appeared in several other films including *The Good Son* opposite another child prodigy Macaulay Culkin and *The War* opposite big-screen guru Kevin Costner. And he's held his own with these box office biggies. He even won the NATO/ShoWest award for Young Star of the Year after appearing in *The War*. His latest effort *Flipper* finds him the lead co-starring with a dolphin in the remake of the popular '60s TV show and his newest film *Ice Storm* directed by Ang Lee will be released Thanksgiving 1996.

Flipper

Family Widower Porter Ricks (Brian Kelly), chief ranger at Florida's Coral Key Park, lives with sons, 15-year-old Sandy (Luke Halpin) and 10-year-old Bud (Tommy Norden), and their pet dolphin Flipper. Good thing, because Flipper is always rescuing his trouble-prone charges from assorted aquatic dangers. The TV series ran from 1964-1968; two episodes are included per tape. Oh yes, the cetacean thespian who portrayed Flipper was

a girl dolphin named Suzy. Ages 4 to 11.
1964 60m/C Brian Kelly, Luke Halpin, Tommy Norden. **VHS** *HMK*

Flipper 🐬🐬 ᵛ

PG/Primary-Adult TV's dolphinitive marine mammal is up to his old heroics. Teen Sandy (Elijah Wood) is sent to visit his Uncle Porter (Paul Hogan, as sort of a Porpoise Dundee) on a tropical island. They don't get along at first—Sandy's royally ticked about missing a Red Hot Chili Peppers concert on the mainland—then they meet Flipper and things improve. But there's trouble in paradise. Some toxic meanie is dumping chemicals and poisoning dolphins, so it's up to Flipper and company to save the environment. They get help from law enforcer Isaac Hayes. He's the cop who won't cop out when there's danger all about. Terrific underwater photography saves the day for viewers.

⚠️ BEWARE *Flipper fights a shark. Another dolphin is shot and killed. Sandy smokes cigars, but learns a lesson (they make him sick) and there is some slight language.*
1996 94m/C Elijah Wood, Paul Hogan, Chelsea Field, Isaac Hayes, Jonathan Banks, Luke Halpin; **D:** Alan Shapiro; **W:** Alan Shapiro; **C:** Bill Butler; **M:** Joel McNeely. **VHS** *NYR*

Flipper's New Adventure 🐬🐬 ᵛ

Family Believing they are to be separated, Flipper and Sandy travel to a remote island. Little do they know, a British family is being held for ransom on the island they have chosen. It's up to the duo to save the day. Enjoyable, nicely done family adventure.
1964 103m/C Luke Halpin, Pamela Franklin, Tom Helmore, Francesca Annis, Brian Kelly, Joe Higgins, Ricou Browning; **D:** Leon Benson. **VHS, Beta** *MGM, FCT*

Flipper's Odyssey 🐬🐬

Family Flipper has disappeared and his adopted family goes looking for him, but when one of the boys gets trapped in a cave, the marine mammal is his only hope.
1966 77m/C Luke Halpin, Brian Kelly, Tommy Norden; **D:** Paul Landres. **VHS, Beta** *CNG, PSM*

Flirting 🐬🐬🐬

R/Sr. High-Adult In 1965 rural Australia, romantic misfit Danny Embling is enrolled at St. Albans boys boarding school next to a similar institution for girls. Male and female students are permitted to mix, under strict adult supervision, and Danny finds a soulmate in Thandi, bright, beautiful daughter of an African diplomat, whose black skin makes her as much of an outcast as Danny. Their defiant love affair is tender, amusing, sad and wise. Followup to "The Year My Voice Broke" is the second installment of director Duigan's coming-of-age trilogy, to be completed once actor Taylor is old enough for the concluding chapter.

⚠️ BEWARE *Sex, nudity, alcohol use, and fighting.*
1989 100m/C Noah Taylor, Thandie Newton, Nicole Kidman, Bartholomew Rose, Felix Nobis, Josh Picker, Kiri Paramore, Marc Gray,

Joshua Marshall, David Wieland, Craig Black, Leslie Hill; **D:** John Duigan; **W:** John Duigan. **VHS, LV** *VMK, BTV*

Flower Angel

Family Blue-eyed girl named Angel does good deeds during her globetrotting adventures in search of the Flower of Seven Colors. Dismal Japanese animation that makes the Care Bears look like Eugene O'Neill. Also available on tape with a compilation of Yankee cartoon castoffs, under the umbrella title "Angel."
1980 46m/C VHS, Beta *FHE*

Flower Drum Song ♫♫

Family Rodgers and Hammerstein musical played better on Broadway than in this overblown adaptation of life in San Francisco's Chinatown. Umeki plays the young girl who arrives from Hong Kong for an arranged marriage. Her intended (Soo) is a fast-living nightclub owner already enjoying the love of singer Kwan. Meanwhile Umeki falls for the handsome Shigeta. Naturally, everything comes together in a happy ending. ♫ I Enjoy Being A Girl; Don't Marry Me; Grant Avenue; You Are Beautiful; A Hundred Million Miracles; Fan Tan Fanny; Chop Suey; The Other Generation; I Am Going to Like It Here.
1961 133m/C Nancy Kwan, Jack Soo, James Shigeta, Miyoshi Umeki, Juanita Hall; **D:** Henry Koster; **M:** Richard Rodgers, Oscar Hammerstein. **VHS, Beta, LV** *MCA, FCT*

Fluke ♫♫

PG/Family "Ghost" meets "Oh, Heavenly Dog" as Tom (Modine) dies in a suspicious car accident and is reincarnated as a dog who remembers his past life. He returns to his former family (Travis and Pomeranc) to protect them from his former business partner (Stoltz), battling such puppy perils as cosmetic testing labs and dogcatchers along the way. While there's plenty of squishy sentimentality to go around, some of the scenes involving animal abuse may be a little much for the target audience of preteen kids. Jackson and Stoltz trade "Pulp Fiction" for pup fiction, but this dog won't hunt. It's too confusing for young children, too childish for the 12-and-up crowd. Based on the novel by James Herbert.

BEWARE *Be ready for dog attacks, a disturbing car crash, sad death scenes and an animal testing lab scene.*
1995 96m/C Matthew Modine, Nancy Travis, Eric Stoltz, Max Pomeranc, Ron Perlman, Jon Polito, Bill Cobbs, Frederico Pacifici, Collin Wilcox Paxton; **D:** Carlo Carlei; **W:** James Carrington, Carlo Carlei; **C:** Raffaele Mertes; **M:** Carlo Siliotto; **V:** Samuel L. Jackson. **VHS, LV** *MGM*

The Flying Deuces ♫♫♫

Family Ollie's broken heart lands Laurel and Hardy in the Foreign Legion. The comic pair escape a firing squad only to suffer a plane crash that results in Hardy's reincarnation as a horse. A musical interlude with a Laurel soft shoe while Hardy sings "Shine On, Harvest Moon" is one of the highlights.

1939 65m/B Stan Laurel, Oliver Hardy, Jean Parker, Reginald Gardiner, James Finlayson; **D:** Edward Sutherland. **VHS, Beta, LV** *CNG, MRV, NOS*

Follow Me, Boys! ♫♫♫

Family Disney film set in the 1930s about a simple man who decides to put down roots and enjoy the quiet life, after one year too many on the road with a ramshackle jazz band. That life is soon interrupted when he volunteers to lead a high-spirited boy scout troop. Effective mix of warmth, inspiration and rowdiness. Future adult star Russell plays a town delinquent reformed by the discipline of scouting.
1966 120m/C Fred MacMurray, Vera Miles, Lillian Gish, Charlie Ruggles, Elliott Reid, Kurt Russell, Luana Patten, Ken Murray; **D:** Norman Tokar. **VHS, Beta** *DIS*

Follow that Bunny!

Preschool-Primary Clay-animated musical about a magic egg stolen while on its way to the Easter Bunny. If the egg isn't found, spring will never arrive and the video will run eternally.
1993 27m/C VHS *FHE*

Follow That Sleigh!

Family Seasonal TV cartoon wherein Santa's sleigh is hijacked by two children, and Elf Control sends Elvis, the Rockin' Reindeer, to save the day. A hunka hunka burning snow.
1990 25m/C VHS *VTR*

Follow the Fleet ♫♫♫

Family Song-and-dance man joins the Navy and meets two sisters in need of help in this Rogers/Astaire bon-bon featuring a classic Berlin score. Look for Grable, Ball, and Martin in minor roles. Hilliard went on to be best known as the wife of Ozzie Nelson in TV's "The Adventures of Ozzie and Harriet." ♫ Let's Face the Music and Dance; We Saw the Sea; I'm Putting All My Eggs In One Basket; Get Thee Behind Me, Satan; But Where Are You?; I'd Rather Lead a Band; Let Yourself Go.
1936 110m/B Fred Astaire, Ginger Rogers, Randolph Scott, Harriet Hilliard Nelson, Betty Grable, Lucille Ball; **D:** Mark Sandrich; **M:** Irving Berlin, Max Steiner. **VHS, Beta, LV** *MED, TTC, IME*

Follow the Leader ♫♫

Jr. High-Adult Wartime "Bowery Boys" adventure. On leave from the Army, Slip and Satch discover that one of their pals has been jailed on a trumped-up charge and set about finding the real culprit. Also known as "East of the Bowery." ♫ Now and Then; All I Want to Do Play the Drums.
1944 65m/B Leo Gorcey, Huntz Hall, Gabriel Dell, Jack LaRue, Joan Marsh, Billy Benedict, Mary Gordon, Sammy Morrison; **D:** William Beaudine; **M:** Gene Austin, Sherrill Sisters. **VHS** *NOS*

Follow the River ♫♫ ♭

PG/Family It's 1775 and Mary Ingles (Lee) is living with her husband and family on a frontier farm in the Blue

Elijah Wood makes friends with a dolphin in "Flipper."

Ridge Mountains. The community is raided by the Shawnee, lead by Wildcat (Schweig), who take Mary and several other settlers away to their home camp. Once there,
Mary befriends another captive, the older Gretl
(Burstyn), proves her courage to the smitten Wildcat,
and plots to escape and find her way home. Based on the
1981 novel by James Alexander Thom; filmed in North
Carolina.

BEWARE *Some frontier violence, mild thematic material.*

1995 93m/C Sheryl Lee, Eric Schweig, Ellen Burstyn, Tim Guinee,
Renee O'Connor; **D:** Martin Davidson. **VHS** *HMK*

Foofur & His Friends

Preschool-Primary Leader of the pack Foofur gets into
trouble as usual in this animated compilation from the
Hanna-Barbera series. Additional volumes available.
1988 110m/C VHS, Beta *JFK*

Footloose ♫♫ ♪

PG/Jr. High-Adult When a city boy moves to a small
Midwestern town, he discovers some disappointing
news: rock music and dancing have been forbidden because parents blame such fun for a past drunk-driving
tragedy. Determined to bring some life into the place, he
enlists the help of the daughter of the minister responsible for the law. Rousing music, talented young cast, and
plenty of trouble make an entertaining musical drama.
♫ Footloose; Let's Hear it for the Boy; The Girl Gets
Around; Dancing in the Sheets; Somebody's Eyes;
Almost Paradise; I'm Free; Never; Holding Out for a
Hero.

BEWARE *Brief nudity, fighting, and profanity. But it seems
the sin of choice in this movie is dancing.*

1984 107m/C Kevin Bacon, Lori Singer, Christopher Penn, John
Lithgow, Dianne Wiest, John Laughlin, Sarah Jessica Parker; **D:** Herbert Ross; **M:** Miles Goodman. **VHS, Beta, LV, 8mm** *PAR*

For Better and For Worse ♫♫

PG/Jr. High-Adult Nice young couple is planning to
have your average nice wedding when one of their
friends gets hold of an invitation and decides to jokingly
invite the Pope to attend. But the joke is on them when
the Pope accepts. Talk about upstaging the bride.
1992 94m/C Patrick Dempsey, Kelly Lynch. **VHS, LV** *LIV*

For Better or For Worse: The Bestest Present

Family Fully animated Canadian TV special based on Lynn Johnston's popular and realistic newspaper comic strip, about a crusty widower who teaches the Patterson's boy the true meaning of Christmas.

1985 23m/C D: Lynn Johnston. **VHS, Beta** *FHE*

For Keeps

PG-13/Sr. High-Adult Two high school sweethearts on the verge of graduating get married after the girl becomes pregnant and rejects the option of abortion (that her own mother prefers). Ringwald was America's Sweetheart when this was made, and putting her through a realistic depiction of teenage parenthood and marital woes could have worked brilliantly. Alas, it's a muddled, missed opportunity, mixing cheap laughs with sentiment. The screenwriters later disavowed the heavily revamped script.

BEWARE *Sex, mature themes, alcohol use, salty language.*

1988 98m/C Molly Ringwald, Randall Batinkoff, Kenneth Mars; **D:** John G. Avildsen; **W:** Tim Kazurinsky, Denise DeClue; **M:** Bill Conti. **VHS, Beta, LV** *COL*

For Love or Money

PG/Jr. High-Adult Struggling hotel concierge with a heart of gold finds himself doing little "favors" for a slimy entrepreneur who holds the key to his dreams—the cash to open an elegant hotel of his own. Romantic comedy is reminiscent of the classic screwball comedies of the '30s and '40s, but lacks the trademark tight writing and impeccable timing. Fox is appealing and likable as the wheeling and dealing concierge, a role undermined by a mediocre script offering too few laughs and holes big enough for the entire cast to jump through. Anwar is effectively attractive.

BEWARE *Mild profanity and sex talk.*

1993 89m/C Michael J. Fox, Gabrielle Anwar, Isaac Mizrahi, Anthony Higgins, Michael Tucker, Bobby Short, Dan Hedaya, Bob Balaban, Udo Kier, Patrick Breen, Paula Laurence; **D:** Barry Sonnenfeld; **W:** Mark Rosenthal, Larry Konner; **M:** Bruce Broughton. **VHS, LV** *MCA*

For Our Children: The Concert

Family Disney music video that assembles a galaxy of star talent, performing children's music in a benefit for the Pediatric AIDS Foundation. Segments include Paula Abdul doing "Zip-A-Dee-Doo-Dah," Michael Bolton with "You Are My Sunshine," Salt'N'Pepa rapping "This Old Man," and Bobby McFerrin's a cappella "Wizard of Oz" medley.

1992 85m/C VHS *TOU*

For the Love of Benji

G/Family In the second "Benji" the small but clever dog accompanies his owners on a Greek vacation. Murky spy subplot has Benji dognapped for ready-made adventure involving a secret code, but never mind that; the brilliant move was putting Benji abroad without the benefit of English subtitles. Now the viewer sees the world from a canine perspective, as Benji sizes up various human friends and foes not on the basis of what they say (it's all Greek to him—and us) but what they do. Benji's expressive acting, if anything, has improved since last time.

1977 85m/C Benji, Patsy Garrett, Cynthia Smith, Allen Finzat, Ed Nelson; **D:** Joe Camp. **VHS, Beta** *FCT, APD, BFV*

For Your Eyes Only

PG/Jr. High-Adult In this James Bond adventure, 007 must keep the Soviets from getting hold of a valuable instrument aboard a sunken British spy ship. Sheds the gadgetry of its more recent predecessors in the series in favor of some spectacular stunt work and the usual beautiful girl and exotic locale. Glen's first outing as director, though he handled second units on previous Bond films. Sheena Easton sang the hit title tune.

BEWARE *Violence, alcohol use (another martini, James?) and suggested sex.*

1981 136m/C Roger Moore, Carole Bouquet, Chaim Topol, Lynn-Holly Johnson, Julian Glover, Cassandra Harris, Jill Bennett, Michael Gothard, John Wyman, Jack Hedley, Lois Maxwell, Desmond Llewelyn, Geoffrey Keen, Walter Gotell, Charles Dance; **D:** John Glen; **W:** Michael G. Wilson; **M:** Bill Conti. **VHS, Beta, LV** *MGM, FOX, TLF*

Forbidden Games

Family Excellent French antiwar drama about Paulette, a Parisian girl who sees her parents and dog killed during WWII air raid. Taken in by a well-meaning but rather petty farm family, she befriends their youngest son Michel. The two make a game of burying dead animals, in imitation of the constant war casualties around them, and soon have their own secret garden of crosses and memorials, borrowed from local cemeteries. Ultimately heartrending, but not the relentless downer it sounds; there's a lacing of ironic wit, coupled with the screen's shrewdest observation on how kids concoct their own fantasy worlds, and what happens when those clash with grownups. Winner of numerous awards; available in both subtitled and English-dubbed versions.

BEWARE *Profanity, alcohol use, and brief brutality when parents and a dog are killed.*

1952 90m/B Brigitte Fossey, Georges Poujouly, Amedee, Louis Herbert; **D:** Rene Clement. **Award Nominations:** Academy Awards '54: Best Story; **Awards:** Academy Awards '52: Best Foreign Language Film; British Academy Awards '53: Best Film; National Board of Review Awards '52: 5 Best Foreign Films of the Year; New York Film Critics Awards '52: Best Foreign Film; Venice Film Festival '52: Best Film. **VHS, Beta, LV** *NOS, APD, INJ*

Matthew Modine and dog share spirits and bodies in the story of "Fluke."

Forbidden Planet 🦴🦴🦴 ✧

Family Hollywood's first big-budget science fiction movie based on the Shakespearean classic "The Tempest." A rescue mission is sent to check on colonists on the planet Altair-4. They discover Robby the Robot and very few survivors (the rest were preyed upon by a terrible space monster).

🦴 BEWARE 🦴 *The story involves a young woman's coming-of-age and her father's inappropriate reaction.*

1956 98m/C Walter Pidgeon, Anne Francis, Leslie Nielsen, Warren Stevens, Jack Kelly, Richard Anderson, Earl Holliman, George Wallace; *D:* Fred M. Wilcox; *M:* Bebe Barron, Louis Barron. **VHS, Beta, LV** *MGM, CRC*

Force on Thunder Mountain 🦴

Family Father and son go camping and encounter peculiar stuff, the work of an old man from a flying saucer (the UFO looks just like clips from "Lost in Space"). Benign but dull mess of a family sci-fi flick that sometimes spontaneously turns into a nature documentary.

1977 93m/C Christopher Cain, Todd Dutson. **VHS, Beta** *VCI*

Foreign Correspondent 🦴🦴🦴🦴

Family Classic Hitchcock tale of espionage and derring-do. A reporter is sent to Europe during WWII to cover a pacifist conference in London, where he becomes romantically involved with the daughter of the group's founder and befriends an elderly diplomat. When the diplomat is kidnapped, the reporter uncovers a Nazi spy-ring headed by his future father-in-law.

1940 120m/B Joel McCrea, Laraine Day, Herbert Marshall, George Sanders, Robert Benchley, Albert Basserman, Edmund Gwenn, Eduardo Ciannelli, Harry Davenport, Martin Kosleck, Charles Halton; *D:* Alfred Hitchcock; *W:* Robert Benchley, Charles Bennett, Joan Harrison, James Hilton; *M:* Alfred Newman. **Award Nominations:** Academy Awards '40: Best Black and White Cinematography, Best Interior Decoration, Best Original Screenplay, Best Picture, Best Supporting Actor (Basserman); **Awards:** National Board of Review Awards '40: 10 Best Films of the Year. **VHS, Beta, LV** *WAR*

Forever Young 🦴🦴 ✧

PG/Jr. High-Adult When test pilot Gibson's girlfriend is hit by a car and goes into a coma, he volunteers to be cryogenically frozen for one year. As luck would have it, he's left frozen for fifty years, and when he finally thaws, he finds that he's a frozen fish out of water. He befriends a couple of kids, and the adventure begins. Predictable, though supported nicely by Wood, and designed to be a tear jerker, though it serves mostly as a star vehicle for Gibson who bumbles with 90s technology, finds his true love, and escapes from government heavies, adorable as ever. Schmaltzy but entertaining romantic drama.

🦴 BEWARE 🦴 *Mild profanity. And when Gibson wakes up and grabs Wood, your stomach will jump.*

1992 102m/C Mel Gibson, Jamie Lee Curtis, Elijah Wood, Isabel Glasser, George Wendt, Joe Morton, Nicolas Surovy, David Marshall Grant, Art LaFleur; *D:* Steve Miner; *W:* Jeffrey Abrams; *M:* Jerry Goldsmith. **VHS, LV, 8mm** *WAR, BTV*

Forget Paris 🦴🦴 ✧

PG-13/Sr. High-Adult Wisecracking pro basketball referee Mickey (Crystal) goes to Paris, a city slicker than most, and meets airline executive Ellen (Winger). He quips that the Swiss punched holes in his cheese. Who could resist? They get married, but once the honeymoon is over, the relationship unravels due to conflicting careers and the fact that her difficult father (the hilarious Hickey) moves in with them. The idea that marriage is hard work, but worth it, is unusually intelligent for Hollywood. In-joke: Kavner and Masur, who play another married couple, played boyfriend and girlfriend on TV's "Rhoda" in the '70s.

🦴 BEWARE 🦴 *Language, masturbation jokes, fertility clinic scene.*

1995 101m/C Billy Crystal, Debra Winger, Joe Mantegna, Cynthia Stevenson, Richard Masur, Julie Kavner, William Hickey, Cathy Moriarty, John Spencer; *D:* Billy Crystal; *W:* Billy Crystal, Lowell Ganz, Babaloo Mandel; *C:* Kent Beyda; *M:* Marc Shaiman. **VHS, LV** *COL*

Forrest Gump 🦴🦴🦴🦴

PG-13/Sr. High-Adult Director Zemeckis once again stretches the technological boundaries of film with this strange, satirically dark tale that became a smash at the box office. Intellectually challenged man from a small Southern town has a positive outlook on life so strong that he succeeds at whatever career he attempts, bringing him celebrity status over a span of four decades. Hanks turns in another great performance as the innocent Gump who becomes an All-American football player and decorated war hero, among other things. Historic events surround a tale of enduring love and friendship. Incredible special effects by Industrial Light & Magic put Forrest right into the footage of actual events. But while the special effects certainly entertain, it's Gump's good-heartedness and decency that stick with you. Hanks, in a role reminiscent of Peter Seller's simpleton in "Being There," manages to make Gump one of the great screen characters. Sinise offers stellar support as the disgruntled handicapped Vietnam vet, while Field is effective as Gump's beloved mother. From the novel by Winston Groom.

 Violence and gore during Vietnam episode; mature language and themes; brief nudity.

1994 142m/C Tom Hanks, Robin Wright, Sally Field, Gary Sinise, Mykelti Williamson; **D:** Robert Zemeckis; **W:** Eric Roth. **VHS** *NYR*

Foul Play 🦴🦴 ♡

PG/Jr. High-Adult Hawn is a librarian who picks up a hitchhiker which leads to nothing but trouble. She becomes involved with San Francisco detective Chase in an effort to expose a plot to kill the Pope during his visit to the city. Also involved is Moore as an English orchestra conductor with some kinky sexual leanings. Chase is charming (no mugging here) and Hawn both bubbly and brave. A big winner at the box office; features Barry Manilow's hit tune "Ready to Take a Chance Again."

 Odd sexual proclivities.

1978 116m/C Goldie Hawn, Chevy Chase, Dudley Moore, Burgess Meredith, Billy Barty, Rachel Roberts, Eugene Roche, Brian Dennehy, Chuck McCann, Bruce Solomon; **D:** Colin Higgins; **M:** Charles Fox. **VHS, Beta, LV, 8mm** *PAR*

Four Babar Classics

Family Babar, the witty, clever and charming elephant created by Jean de Brunhoff, is involved in four different engaging adventures on one cassette.
1987 60m/C VHS *RHU*

Four by Dr. Seuss

Primary Four Dr. Seuss classics, "Yertle the Turtle," "Gertrude McFuzz," "Thidwick, the Big-Hearted Moose," and "The Big Brag" are in this collection.
1987 46m/C VHS *RHU*

The 400 Blows 🦴🦴🦴🦴

Jr. High-Adult Truffaut created one of the most memorable alienated screen teens with this semi-autobiographical drama. Schoolboy Antoine Doinel cuts class, shoplifts, goes to movies, and does basically anything he can to help avoid his unhappy home life. Even when he seriously applies himself to studying for a vital exam, he fails anyway. Eventually he's sent to a seaside juvenile detention camp, supposedly escape-proof, where he gains an exhilarating sense of freedom. There are no easy solutions or convenient wrap-ups, and Truffaut was to follow the character into manhood in four later films (all done with Leaud). In French with English subtitles.

1959 97m/B Jean-Pierre Leaud, Claire Maurier, Albert Remy, Guy Decomble, Georges Flament, Patrick Auffay, Jeanne Moreau, Jean-Claude Brialy, Jacques Demy, Francois Truffaut; **D:** Francois Truffaut; **W:** Marcel Moussey, Francois Truffaut; **M:** Jean Constantin. **Award Nominations:** Academy Awards '59: Best Story & Screenplay; **Awards:** Cannes Film Festival '59: Best Director (Truffaut); New York Film Critics Awards '59: Best Foreign Film. **VHS, Beta, LV** *HMV, MRV, APD*

The Four Musketeers 🦴🦴🦴

PG/Jr. High-Adult Fun-loving continuation of Lester's "The Three Musketeers," filmed simultaneously. Lavish swashbuckler jaunts between France, England, and Italy, in following the adventures of D'Artagnan, Athos, Aramis and Porthos, fighting the treacheries of the seductive Milady DeWinter. Like its predecessor, a saucy and amusing romp, more for adults than other tellings of the Dumas classic. Gets serious near the end with the deaths of prominent characters. Followed, in 1989, by "The Return of the Musketeers."

 Swashbuckling violence, tipping of pints, medieval sex.

1975 108m/C Michael York, Oliver Reed, Richard Chamberlain, Frank Finlay, Raquel Welch, Christopher Lee, Faye Dunaway, Jean-Pierre Cassel, Geraldine Chaplin, Simon Ward, Charlton Heston, Roy Kinnear, Nicole Calfan; **D:** Richard Lester. **VHS, Beta** *LIV, OM*

Four Weddings and a Funeral 🦴🦴🦴 ♡

R/Sr. High-Adult Refreshing, intelligent adult comedy filled with upper-class sophistication and wit. Thirtyish Brit bachelor Charles (Grant) attends the weddings of his friends, but won't take the plunge himself-even as he falls in love with Carrie (MacDowell). Great beginning offers loads of laughs as the first two weddings unfold, then becomes decidedly bittersweet. Grant is terrific as the romantic bumbler, but MacDowell seems slightly out of place. Supporting characters are superb, especially Coleman as the "flirty" Scarlett and Atkinson as a new minister. Surprising box office hit found a broad audience.

 Mature teens may appreciate the charming love story, though film has fairly tame sexual situations and frequent usage of the "F" word.

1993 118m/C Hugh Grant, Andie MacDowell, Simon Callow, Kristin Scott Thomas, James Fleet, John Hannah, Charlotte Coleman, David Bower, Corin Redgrave, Rowan Atkinson; **D:** Mike Newell; **W:** Richard Curtis; **M:** Richard Rodney Bennett. **VHS, LV** *PGV*

1492: Conquest of Paradise
♫♫ ▷

PG-13/Jr. High-Adult Large-scale Hollywood production striving for political correctness is a drawn-out account of Columbus's (Depardieu) discovery and subsequent exploitation of the "New World." Skillful directing by Ridley Scott and impressive scenery add interest, yet don't make up for a script which chronicles events but tends towards trite dialogue and characterization. Available in both pan-and-scan and letterbox formats.

> **BEWARE** *Violence and nudity. Exploitation of New World inhabitants. (You know the story.)*

1992 142m/C Gerard Depardieu, Sigourney Weaver, Armand Assante, Frank Langella, Loren Dean, Angela Molina, Fernando Rey, Michael Wincott, Steven Waddington, Tcheky Karyo, Kario Salem; **D:** Ridley Scott; **W:** Roselyne Bosch; **M:** Vangelis. **VHS, Beta, LV** *PAR, BTV*

The Fourth King

Family Animated presentation in which animals of the world, seeing the Christmas Star, gather and choose one among them to represent the beasts to the Christ child. Italian-American TV cartoon co-production for Noel.

1977 24m/C **VHS** *JTC*

The Fourth Wish ♫♫ ▷

Family Australian father learns his 12-year-old son is dying of leukemia. He vows to make Sean's last months meaningful, quitting work to grant the lad's three wishes: owning a dog, reuniting with a divorced, drunkard mom, and meeting Queen Elizabeth. Bring lots of hankies; this effective tearjerker grips the heartstrings thanks to Meillon's prize-winning portrayal of a rough-hewn but devoted dad.

> **BEWARE** *Dying child, profanity (you'd curse too), and alcohol use.*

1975 107m/C John Meillon, Robert Bettles, Robyn Nevin; **D:** Don Chaffey. **VHS, Beta**

The Fox and the Hound ♫♫♫

G/Family Sweet story of the friendship shared by a fox and hound. Young and naive, the critters become pals, but a season later the hound has become his master's best hunting dog and may have to track down his former playmate. There's a convenient happy ending, though (for a lesson on how Disney sanitizes and homogenizes story material, read the original, grim novel by Daniel P. Mannix). Considered the final bow for remnants of the original Magic Kingdom animation team; it was the next generation who brought a new vigor with the likes of "The Little Mermaid" and "Beauty and the Beast."

1981 83m/C **D:** Art Stevens, Ted Berman, Richard Rich; **W:** Art Stevens, Peter Young, Steve Hulett, Earl Kress, Vance Gerry, Laury Clemmons, Dave Michener, Burny Mattinson; **M:** Buddy Baker; **V:**

Mickey Rooney, Kurt Russell, Pearl Bailey, Jack Albertson, Sandy Duncan, Jeanette Nolan, Pat Buttram, John Fiedler, John McIntire, Richard Bakalayan, Paul Winchell, Keith Mitchell, Corey Feldman. **VHS, Beta** *DIS, BTV*

Foxes ♫♫ ▷

R/Sr. High-Adult Four teenage California valley girls get by with little supervision from their divorced, distracted parents (still in need of maturity themselves). Awash in sex and drugs, the youthful quartet look for a good time and try—with varying degrees of success—to avoid tragic mistakes. Loose, not always clear storyline, but there's a sobering look at kids relying on each other in a world where they have to make adult choices, yet aren't considered grown up.

> **BEWARE** *Sex, profanity, drug use, violence, and, unfortunately, uninvolved parents.*

1980 106m/C Jodie Foster, Cherie Currie, Marilyn Kagan, Scott Baio, Sally Kellerman, Randy Quaid, Laura Dern; **D:** Adrian Lyne. **VHS, Beta** *MGM, FOX*

Fraggle Rock: A Festive Fraggle Holiday

Preschool-Primary Two holiday tales with the Fraggles. "The Bells of Fraggle Rock" features Gobo not believing the Great Bell used in the Festival of the Bells really exists, but he's proven wrong. In "Perfect Blue Rollie," Wembley and Boober find a riverbed full of smoothies and rollies and every Fraggle knows that a perfect blue rollie is the best gift you can give a friend.

199? 52m/C **VHS** *JHV*

Fraggle Rock, Vol. 1: Meet the Fraggles

Preschool-Primary Special series of Jim Henson's "Fraggle" videos with two episodes per tape. "Beginnings" introduces the playful Muppet characters, and "A Friend in Need" features Doc's misunderstood dog, and how a Fraggle comes to his rescue. Additional volumes available.

1993 ?m/C **VHS** *TOU*

Francis Goes to the Races
♫♫ ▷

Family The second in the talking-mule series finds O'Connor and Francis taking up residence on Kellaway's failing horse ranch. When mobsters seize control of the property to pay off a debt, Francis decides to check with the horses at the Santa Anita race track and find a sure winner to bet on.

1951 88m/B Donald O'Connor, Piper Laurie, Cecil Kellaway, Jesse White, Barry Kelley, Hayden Rorke, Vaughn Taylor, Larry Keating; **D:** Arthur Lubin; **W:** Oscar Brodney; **M:** Frank Skinner; **V:** Chill Wills. **VHS** *MCA*

Francis Joins the WACs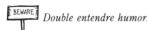

Family The fifth entry in the series finds O'Connor working as a bank clerk when he is mistakenly drafted back into the military-and sent to a WAC base. Francis tries to keep him out of trouble with the ladies. Wills, the voice of Francis, also turns up as a general.

1954 94m/B Donald O'Connor, Julie Adams, Chill Wills, Mamie Van Doren, Lynn Bari, ZaSu Pitts, Joan Shawlee, Mara Corday, Allison Hayes; **D:** Arthur Lubin; **V:** Chill Wills. **VHS** *MCA*

Francis the Talking Mule

Family The first of the silly but funny series about, what else, a talking mule. Peter Stirling (O'Connor) is the dim-bulb G.I. who hooks up with Francis while fighting in Burma. Francis helps Peter become a war hero but of course everyone thinks he's crazy when Peter insists the mule can talk. The joke is that Francis is smarter than any of the humans. O'Connor starred in six of the films, with Mickey Rooney taking over the final adventure. Director Lubin went on to create the television series "Mr. Ed," about a talking horse.

1949 91m/B Donald O'Connor, Patricia Medina, ZaSu Pitts, Ray Collins, Frank McIntire, Eduard Franz, Howland Chamberlin, Frank Faylen, Tony Curtis; **D:** Arthur Lubin; **M:** Frank Skinner; **V:** Chill Wills. **VHS** *MCA*

Frankenstein Sings ... The Movie

PG/Jr. High-Adult Musical horror spoof finds young couple seeking shelter in a creepy mansion that happens to belong to Dr. Frankenstein. Also visiting (it just happens to be Halloween) are Mr. and Mrs. Dracula, the Wolfman and his mother, and the mummified remains of Elvis and his agent. Hmmm. Sounds like the guest list from the song "Monster Mash" but it's not half as enjoyable.

Double entendre humor.

1995 83m/C Candace Cameron, Ian Bohen, Jimmie Walker, Anthony Crivello; **D:** Joel Cohen, Alec Sokolow. **VHS, LV** *TTC*

Frankenweenie

PG/Family Before he became a star director with "Pee Wee's Big Adventure," Burton made this offbeat short subject for Disney that went unreleased for years. Little Victor Frankenstein, a suburban science buff, is heartbroken when his dog is hit by a car. Boy resurrects pet through electricity, but neighborhood adults panic at the friendly but bolt-necked pooch. Affectionate, if mildly predictable parody of "Frankenstein" from a kid's eye view, with great B&W photography. Note the "Batman" kite and other elements prophetic of Burton's later career.

1984 27m/B Shelley Duvall, Daniel Stern, Barret Oliver, Paul Bartel; **D:** Tim Burton; **W:** Tim Burton. **VHS, Beta** *TOU*

Freaked

PG-13/Jr. High-Adult Bizarre little black comedy throws everything at the screen, hoping some of the gross-out humor will prove amusing (and some does). Greedy TV star Ricky Coogin (Winter) agrees to be the spokesman for E.E.S. Corporation, which markets a toxic green slime fertilizer to the Third World. He's sent to South America to promote the product and is captured by the mad scientist proprietor (Quaid) of a mysterious sideshow, who douses him with the fertilizer. Before you know it he's an oozing half-man, half-beast, perfect to join other freaks as the latest attraction. Lots of yucky makeup. Reeves has an uncredited cameo as the Dog Boy.

 Profanity, violence, and grotesque transformations.

1993 80m/C Alex Winter, Randy Quaid, Megan Ward, Michael Stoyanov, Brooke Shields, William Sadler, Derek McGrath, Mr. T, Alex Zuckerman, Karyn Malchus; **Cameos:** Keanu Reeves; **D:** Alex Winter, Tom Stern; **W:** Alex Winter, Tim Burns, Tom Stern; **M:** Kevin Kiner; **V:** Bob(cat) Goldthwait. **VHS** *FXV*

Freaky Friday

G/Family Here's a switch. Housewife (Barbara Harris) and her teenage daughter (Jodie Foster), each wishing for the other's "easy" life, inadvertently trade bodies on a memorable Friday the 13th. Mom's mind goes off to high school in daughter's body. Daughter's mind stays home in mom's body and tries to run the household. By the end of this slapstick-filled charmer, each character has come to appreciate the other. Based on Mary Rodgers' novel, brought to the screen by Disney, a decade ahead of "Big," and other brain-exchange movies, although "Freaky" itself was preceded by Peter Ustinov's 1948 "Vice Versa." Ages 5 to 11.

1976 95m/C Barbara Harris, Jodie Foster, Patsy Kelly, Dick Van Patten, Ruth Buzzi; **D:** Gary Nelson. **VHS, Beta** *DIS*

Fred Penner: A Circle of Songs

Preschool-Primary Engaging singer Penner, star of the TV show, "Fred Penner's Place" (seen on Nickelodeon and Canada's CBC), performs a concert for kids. Ages 3 to 9.

1991 40m/C VHS *SKM*

Fred Penner: The Cat Came Back—A Concert Video

Preschool-Primary This live performance includes "A House is a House for Me," "Holiday" and Penner's signature tune, the old folk tune "The Cat Came Back," about a most resilient kitty. Ages 3 to 9.

1986 ?m/C VHS *MVD*

Fred Penner: What A Day!

Preschool-Primary Fred is joined by fellow Canadian children's entertainers Al Simmons, Charlotte Diamond and Rocky Rolletti for musical adventures. At a railroad

If you like *Free Willy* (1993), you'll love:

Andre (1994)

The Day of the Dolphin (1973)

Flipper (1963)

Flipper (1996)

Free Willy 2: The Adventure Home (1995)

The Golden Seal (1983)

Sammy, the Way-Out Seal (1962)

Tarka the Otter (1978)

Whale of a Tale (1976)

The White Seal (1975)

station, Fred enters a magical photo booth and wait till you see what develops. Ages 3 to 9.
1993 28m/C VHS *BMG, BTV*

Free to Be . . . You and Me

Primary Marlo Thomas' all-star joyful animated celebration of childhood through song, story, comedy, and poetry. Like the book and record of the same name, video was created to let children feel "free to be who they are and who they want to be" without being stuck in a boys-don't-do-this, girls-don't-do-that mindset. There's a vignette about a boy who wants a doll, another in which Mel Brooks provides the voice of a baby who believes he's a girl. Ages 3 to 7.
1983 45m/C Marlo Thomas, Alan Alda, Harry Belafonte, Mel Brooks, Diana Ross, Roosevelt Grier. **VHS, Beta** *LIV*

Free Willy

PG/Family Hit film about 12-year-old runaway Jesse, sentenced to clean up his graffiti at an amusement park. Unexpectedly he befriends Willy, a moody, captive killer whale in a cramped tank. What eventually happens is as predictable as the title, and the same story's been done many times before (with every possible critter). What helps this is young Richter as the bad boy who makes good; Hollywood suits reportedly wanted the main character to be an angelic little girl, but the filmmakers went with a tough kid instead, and it made a difference. Madsen adds a nice touch as a concerned parent, while whales handle aquatic chores effortlessly. Closing theme performed by Michael Jackson.

 Touches lightly on juvenile delinquency, makes positive statement about self esteem and responsibility.

1993 112m/C Jason James Richter, Lori Petty, Jayne Atkinson, August Schellenberg, Michael Madsen; **D:** Simon Wincer; **W:** Keith A. Walker, Corey Blechman; **M:** Basil Poledouris. **Award Nominations:** MTV Movie Awards '94: Breakthrough Performance (Richter), Best Kiss (Jason James Richter/Willy); **Awards:** MTV Movie Awards '94: Best Song ("Will You Be There"). **VHS, LV, 8mm** *WAR, BTV*

Free Willy 2: The Adventure Home

PG/Family That darn whale! First he was penned up in a two-bit amusement park. Then he's free and Shamu-zing with his family in the ocean. Now, he gets separated from his family by an offshore oil spill that threatens them all. Good thing his human bud Jesse happens to be nearby on a camping trip and realizes the danger. All the principal characters are back, except for original Willy (real orca Keiko). Animatronic effects were used to replicate him.

 Mild profanity, the oil spill catches fire.

1995 98m/C Jason James Richter, Michael Madsen, Jayne Atkinson, August Schellenberg, Jon Tenney, Elizabeth Pena; **D:** Dwight Little; **W:** Corey Blechman, John Mattson; **C:** Laszlo Kovacs; **M:** Basil Poledouris. **VHS, LV** *WAR*

French Kiss 𝄢𝄢𝄢

PG-13/Jr. High-Adult When her fiance (Hutton) dumps her for a Frenchwoman, perky Kate (Ryan) overcomes her fear of flying and jets off to France to reclaim him. En route she meets Luc, a disreputable Gallic charmer (Kline, with an impeccable French accent). He steals her suitcase, she steals his heart. He agrees to 'elp 'er win back the cad she thinks she still loves. Good chemistry between Ryan and Kline, and lots of French atmosphere. Nice lesson about learning to recognize the possibilities life has to offer.

 Some sexuality, language, and drug references.

1995 111m/C Meg Ryan, Kevin Kline, Timothy Hutton, Jean Reno, Francois Cluzet, Renee Humphrey, Michael Riley, Susan Anbeh, Laurent Spielvogel; **D:** Lawrence Kasdan; **W:** Adam Brooks; **C:** Owen Roizman; **M:** James Newton Howard. **VHS, LV** *FXV*

French Postcards 𝄢𝄢 ♭

PG/Sr. High-Adult Misadventures of three American students studying all aspects of French culture during their junior year of college at the Institute of French Studies in Paris. By the same writers who penned "American Graffiti" a few years earlier, and like that classic, has its share of young soon-to-be stars.

1979 95m/C Miles Chapin, Blanche Baker, Valerie Quennessen, Debra Winger, Mandy Patinkin, Marie-France Pisier; **D:** Willard Huyck; **W:** Gloria Katz, Willard Huyck. **VHS, Beta** *PAR*

Jason James Richter says 'hello' to old pal Willy and his brother in "Free Willy 2: The Adventure Home."

The Freshman 🦴🦴 ▷

PG/Jr. High-Adult Brando, in an incredible parody of his Don Corleone character, makes this work. Broderick is a college student in need of fast cash, and innocent enough to believe that any work is honest. A good supporting cast and a twisty plot keep things interesting. Sometimes heavy handed with its sight gags, but Broderick and Brando push the movie to hilarious conclusion. Don't miss Burt Parks' musical extravaganza.

1990 102m/C Marlon Brando, Matthew Broderick, Penelope Ann Miller, Maximilian Schell, Bruno Kirby, Frank Whaley, Jon Polito, Paul Benedict, Richard Gant, B.D. Wong, Bert Parks; **D:** Andrew Bergman; **W:** Andrew Bergman; **M:** David Newman. **VHS, Beta, LV, 8mm** COL, FCT

Friendly Persuasion 🦴🦴🦴

Jr. High-Adult Earnest, solidly acted tale about a peaceful Quaker family struggling to remain true to its ideals in spite of the Civil War which touches their farm life in southern Indiana. Cooper and McGuire are excellent as the parents with Perkins fine as the son worried he's using his religion to hide his cowardice. Based on a novel by Jessamyn West.

1956 140m/C Gary Cooper, Dorothy McGuire, Anthony Perkins, Marjorie Main, Charles Halton; **D:** William Wyler; **M:** Dimitri Tiomkin. **Award Nominations:** Academy Awards '56: Best Adapted Screenplay, Best Director (Wyler), Best Picture, Best Song ("Friendly Persuasion (Thee I Love)"), Best Sound, Best Supporting Actor (Perkins); **Awards:** Cannes Film Festival '57: Best Film. **VHS, Beta, LV** FOX

A Friendship in Vienna 🦴🦴 ▷

Jr. High-Adult Serious-minded Disney TV drama set in Nazi-occupied Austria, about the daughter of a collaborator who struggles to help her friend, a Jewish teenager, escape to freedom with her family. Based on the book "Devil in Vienna" by Doris Orgel.

1988 100m/C Jenny Lewis, Ed Asner, Jane Alexander, Stephen Macht, Rosemary Forsyth, Ferdinand "Ferdy" Mayne, Kamie Harper; **D:** Arthur Seidelman; **W:** Richard Alfieri. **VHS** DIS

Frog 🦴🦴🦴

Family Fun tale of the nerdy Arlo who adds a frog to his reptile collection but finds it's really an enchanted Italian prince. With the help of the talkative frog, Arlo tries to ace his school science fair and get a fair maiden to kiss the creature. Duvall's Platypus Productions, responsible for her great "Faerie Tale Theatre" and other classics, contributed this to the PBS "Wonderworks" series. Followed by "Frogs!"

1989 55m/C Paul Williams, Scott Grimes, Shelley Duvall, Elliott Gould, David Grossman. **VHS, Beta, LV** ORI, IME

Frog and Toad are Friends

Preschool-Primary Animated film of Arnold Lobel's Caldecott Honor-winning children's book about Frog, who cheerfully welcomes each day, and his best friend Toad, who moans and groans each morning.

1985 30m/C VHS CHF

Frog and Toad Together

Primary Four of Arnold Lobel's classic children's stories are featured together.

1988 18m/C VHS, Beta CHF,

The Frog Prince

Family Delightful musical Muppet version, originally made for TV, of the classic fairy tale, abounding with frogs. Kermit discovers that the new frog at the pond is really a handsome prince who has been turned into an amphibian by a witch's spell, and only the kiss of a beautiful princess can cure him.

1981 54m/C V: Jim Henson, Frank Oz. **VHS, Beta** JHV, TOU

Frogs!

Family Lengthy "WonderWorks" sequel to "Frog" is one too many trips to the well, though it imaginatively inverts the plot of the earlier tale. Arlo is now the most popular (and conceited) kid in school. His plans to be prom king are interrupted when he and Gus are both reverted to froghood by a witch. When they discover the pond is being poisoned, their only hope is Hannah, a brainy classmate Arlo previously scorned as a nerd.

199? 55m/C Shelley Duvall, Elliott Gould, Paul Williams, Scott Grimes, Judith Ivey. **VHS** PME, HMV, BTV

From Russia with Love 🦴🦴🦴 ▷

PG/Jr. High-Adult Bond is back and on the loose in exotic Istanbul looking for a super-secret coding machine. He's involved with a beautiful Russian spy and has the SPECTRE organization after him, including villainess Rosa Klebb (she of the killer shoe). Lots of exciting escapes but no over-reliance on the gadgetry of the later films. Second 007 adventure is considered by many to be the best. Laserdisc edition includes interviews with director Terence Young and others on the creative staff.

⚠ BEWARE ⚠ *Violence, alcohol use, suggested sex, and switchblade shoes.*

1963 125m/C Sean Connery, Daniela Bianchi, Pedro Armendariz Sr., Lotte Lenya, Robert Shaw, Eunice Gayson, Walter Gotell, Lois Maxwell, Bernard Lee, Desmond Llewelyn, Nadja Regin, Alizia Gur, Martine Beswick, Leila; **D:** Terence Young; **M:** John Barry. **VHS, Beta, LV** MGM, CRC, TLF

From the Mixed-Up Files of Mrs. Basil E. Frankweiler 🦴🦴 ▷

PG/Family Runaway siblings (Barnwell and Lee) secretly hide out in a New York art museum. They get caught up in trying to determine the authenticity of a sculpture (could it be the work of Michelangelo?) and turn to the statue's last owner, elusive art patron Mrs. Basil E. Frankweiler (Bacall). Based on the Newberry Award-winning novel by E.L. Konigsburg. Made for TV.

1995 92m/C Lauren Bacall, Jean Marie Barnwell, Jesse Lee; **D:** Marcus Cole. **VHS** HMK

The Front Page

PG/Family A remake of the Hecht-MacArthur play about the managing editor of a 1920s Chicago newspaper who finds out his ace reporter wants to quit the business and get married. But first an escaped convicted killer offers the reporter an exclusive interview.

BEWARE *Profanity.*

1974 105m/C Jack Lemmon, Walter Matthau, Carol Burnett, Austin Pendleton, Vincent Gardenia, Charles Durning, Susan Sarandon; **D:** Billy Wilder; **W:** Billy Wilder, I.A.L. Diamond. **VHS, LV** *MCA*

Frosty Returns

Family Frosty the Snowman returns in another 'toon, befriending a little girl named Holly. But the evil Mr. Twitchell has an invention that sprays the snow away. Frosty and Holly must stop him if they want to save winter.

1992 25m/C V: John Goodman, Andrea Martin, Brian Doyle-Murray, Jan Hooks. **VHS** *FHE, MOV, BTV*

Frosty the Snowman

Family The original Rankin-Bass holiday classic cartoon about the snowman who comes to life when crowned with the hat of a magician, making him a friend to children.

1969 30m/C D: Arthur Rankin Jr., Jules Bass; **V:** Billy DeWolfe, Jackie Vernon. **VHS** *FHE, BTV*

Frosty's Winter Wonderland/ The Leprechauns' Christmas Gold

Preschool-Primary Features two Rankin-Bass holiday cartoons. In the first Jack Frost (no relation) threatens a certain Snowman and his newly-created wife, while in the second story a young boy discovers a magical island of leprechauns at Christmas.

1981 50m/C D: Arthur Rankin Jr., Jules Bass; **V:** Andy Griffith, Shelley Winters, Art Carney, Peggy Cass. **VHS, Beta** *LIV*

Fruit . . . Close Up and Very Personal

Preschool Orchards bloom, apples take a bath before being shipped, lemons cascade down a conveyer belt; "Fruit" is a video with appeal. Exceptionally well-photographed, with natural sounds but no narration. See how orange juice is processed, how pineapple tops are planted to grow into new trees and how blueberries are harvested by hand with a device that looks like a comb stuck to a box. "Fruit" is the berries. Ages 1 to 6.

1995 30m/C VHS *SFP, TPV*

The Fugitive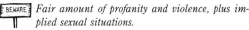

PG-13/Sr. High-Adult Exciting big-screen version of the '60s TV series with the same basic storyline: Dr. Richard Kimble's wife is murdered and he's implicated, so he goes on the lam to find the real killer, the mysteri-

ous one-armed man. Meanwhile, he's being pursued by relentless federal marshall Jones, who seems to have enormous fun throughout the show. Lots of mystery and action, particularly a spectacular train/bus crash sequence, keeps the tension high. Due to illness, Richard Jordan was replaced by Krabbe after production had begun. Alec Baldwin was originally slated to star as Kimble, but backed out and Ford was cast. Sound familiar? Ford also replaced Baldwin as Jack Ryan in "Patriot Games." The second highest grossing movie of 1993.

BEWARE *Fair amount of profanity and violence, plus implied sexual situations.*

1993 127m/C Harrison Ford, Tommy Lee Jones, Jeroen Krabbe, Julianne Moore, Sela Ward, Joe Pantoliano, Andreas Katsulas, Daniel Roebuck; **D:** Andrew Davis; **W:** David N. Twohy, Jeb Stuart; **M:** James Newton Howard. **Award Nominations:** Academy Awards '93: Best Cinematography, Best Film Editing, Best Original Screenplay, Best Picture, Best Sound, Best Sound Effects Editing; British Academy Awards '93: Best Supporting Actor (Jones); Directors Guild of America Awards '93: Best Director (Davis); Golden Globe Awards '94: Best Actor—Drama (Ford), Best Director (Davis); **Awards:** Academy Awards '93: Best Supporting Actor (Jones); Golden Globe Awards '94: Best Supporting Actor (Jones); Los Angeles Film Critics Association Awards '93: Best Supporting Actor (Jones); MTV Movie Awards '94: Best On-Screen Duo (Harrison Ford/Tommy Lee Jones), Best Action Sequence. **VHS** *WAR*

Fun & Fancy Free

Family Part-animated, part-live-action feature is split into two segments: "Bongo" with Dinah Shore narrating the story of a happy-go-lucky circus bear; and "Mickey and the Beanstalk"—a "new" version of an old fairly tale.

1947 96m/C Edgar Bergen, Charlie McCarthy, Dinah Shore. **VHS, Beta** *DIS*

Fun 'N Games

Preschool-Primary Field hockey, cross-country running and poetry—not your everyday triathlon, but that's how things go in the Hundred Acre Wood as Winnie the Pooh and his endearing pals romp and play through three animated stories. In the best one, "Tigger's Poohetry," effervescent Tigger makes up silly, imaginative rhymes which his friends act out, illustrating the magical power of words. Ages 2 to 6.

1995 33m/C VHS *TOU*

Funny Face 🎵🎵🎵

Jr. High-Adult Musical satire on beatniks and the fashion scene also features the May-December romance between Astaire and the ever-lovely Hepburn. He's a high-fashion photographer (based on Richard Avedon); she's a Greenwich Village bookseller fond of shapeless, drab clothing. He decides to take her to Paris and show her what modeling's all about. Elegant musical score features classic Gershwin. Laserdisc includes the original theatrical trailer and is available in widescreen. 🎵 Let's Kiss and Make Up; He Loves and She Loves; Funny Face; How Long Has This Been Going On?; Clap Yo' Hands; S'Wonderful; Bonjour Paris; On How To Be Lovely; Marche Funebre.

1957 103m/C Fred Astaire, Audrey Hepburn, Kay Thompson, Suzy Parker; *D:* Stanley Donen; *M:* George Gershwin, Ira Gershwin. **VHS, Beta, LV, 8mm** *PAR, FCT*

Funny Farm

PG/Jr. High-Adult Does "low-key Chevy Chase comedy" sound like an oxymoron? Think again, as Chase plays a New York sportswriter who seeks the country life. Sort of "Green Acres" with a few actual gags. Ages 8 and up.

BEWARE *Salty language.*

1988 101m/C Chevy Chase, Madolyn Smith, Joseph Maher, Jack Gilpin, Brad Sullivan, MacIntyre Dixon; *D:* George Roy Hill; *W:* Jeffrey Boam; *M:* Elmer Bernstein. **VHS, LV** *WAR, VTR*

Funny Girl 🎶🎶🎶

G/Family Follows the early career of comedian Fanny Brice, her rise to stardom with the Ziegfeld Follies and her stormy romance with gambler Nick Arnstein in a fun and funny look at back stage music hall life in the early 1900s. Streisand's film debut followed her auspicious performance of the role on Broadway. Score was augmented by several tunes sung by Brice during her performances. Excellent performances from everyone, captured beautifully by Wyler in his musical film debut. Followed by "Funny Lady." 🎵 My Man; Second Hand Rose; I'd Rather Be Blue Over You; People; Don't Rain On My Parade; I'm The Greatest Star; Sadie, Sadie; His Love Makes Me Beautiful; You Are Woman, I Am Man.

1968 151m/C Barbra Streisand, Omar Sharif, Walter Pidgeon, Kay Medford, Anne Francis; *D:* William Wyler. **Award Nominations:** Academy Awards '68: Best Cinematography, Best Film Editing, Best Picture, Best Song ("Funny Girl"), Best Sound, Best Supporting Actress (Medford), Best Original Score; **Awards:** Academy Awards '68: Best Actress (Streisand); Golden Globe Awards '69: Best Actress—Musical/Comedy (Streisand). **VHS, Beta, LV** *COL, BTV*

Funny Lady 🎶🎶 ♭

PG/Jr. High-Adult A continuation of "Funny Girl," recounting Fanny Brice's tumultuous marriage to showman Billy Rose in the 1930s and her lingering affection for first husband Nick Arnstein. One of the rare sequels which are just as good, or at least almost, as the original. 🎵 How Lucky Can You Get?; Great Day; More Than You Know; Blind Date; So Long, Honey Lamb; Isn't This Better; Let's Hear It For Me; I Like Him/I Like Her; It's Only a Paper Moon.

1975 137m/C Barbra Streisand, Omar Sharif, James Caan, Roddy McDowall, Ben Vereen, Carole Wells, Larry Gates, Heidi O'Rourke; *D:* Herbert Ross; *W:* Jay Presson Allen, Arnold Schulman. **VHS, Beta, LV** *COL, FCT*

Further Adventures of the Wilderness Family, Part 2 🎶🎶 ♭

G/Family More of the same scenic nature shots and low-intensity survival drama involving the Robinson clan of the Colorado wilderness, earlier depicted in "The Adventures of the Wilderness Family." Next sequel: "Mountain Family Robinson."

1977 104m/C Heather Rattray, Ham Larsen, George Flower, Robert F. Logan, Susan Damante Shaw; *D:* Frank Zuniga. **VHS, Beta** *MED, VTR*

The Further Adventures of Wil Cwac Cwac

Preschool-Primary Ten new episodes featuring the trouble-prone duckling and his farm-animal playmates from Welsh TV.

1987 40m/C VHS, Beta *LIV, FHE*

G-Men Never Forget

Family Moore, former stuntman and future Lone Ranger, stars in the 12-part serial about FBI agents battling the bad guys.

BEWARE *Violence.*

1948 167m/B Clayton Moore, Roy Barcroft, Ramsay Ames, Drew Allen, Tommy Steele, Eddie Acuff; *D:* Fred Brannon, Yakima Canutt. **VHS** *REP, MLB*

G-Men vs. the Black Dragon

Adult Re-edited serial of "Black Dragon of Manzanar" stars Cameron as a Fed who battle Asian Axis agents during WWII.

BEWARE *Violence.*

1943 244m/B Rod Cameron, Roland Got, Constance Worth, Nino Pipitone, Noel Cravat; *D:* William Witney. **VHS, LV** *REP, MED, MLB*

Gabby Cartoonies

Family Compilation of seven short Max Fleischer cartoons starring the determined but bumbling Gabby, first seen as the town crier in Fleischer's feature "Gulliver's Travels."

1941 49m/C VHS, LV

Galaxy High School: Welcome to Galaxy High

Family Melded-together episodes of the TV cartoon about the first two Earth kids to enroll in Galaxy High, meeting all manner of wacky, other-worldly creatures.

1988 91m/C VHS *FHE*

Gallavants 🎶🎶

Preschool-Primary Full-length animated fantasy about an ant society whose youngsters must demonstrate responsibility and maturity to earn their "kabumps"—bulges on their little ant rearends that prove they're adults and ready to take their places in insect society. Stop snickering, you.

1984 100m/C VHS, Beta *CEL*

Gandy Goose: One Man Navy

Preschool-Primary Video revival time for the vintage Terrytoons shorts about the silly goose and his Jimmy Durante-style companion Sourpuss the cat.
1941 38m/C VHS *VTR*

The Gang's All Here Series

Preschool-Primary Mickey Mouse, Donald Duck, and Goofy star together in some hilarious misadventures on separate tapes: "Lonesome Ghosts," "Mickey's Trailer," and "Tugboat Mickey."
1990 8m/C VHS, Beta *MTI, DSN*

Garbage Day!

Preschool Trash tidbits to help families recycle are offered by Gus the Garbage Man as he takes Billy and his dad on a trash tour—from the trucks to the recycling center to the landfill. Ages 3 to 7.
1994 30m/C VHS

The Garbage Pail Kids Movie WOOF!

PG/Jr. High-Adult Once upon a time there was a set of grotesque bubblegum cards that parodied the ever-so-cute Cabbage Patch Kids toys. The hit cards inspired this bad movie, with the Kids just little actors in stiff, ugly masks. Public reaction was, well ... TV stations subsequently refused to air a tie-in "Garbage Pail Kids" cartoon series. Any questions?
1987 100m/C Anthony Newley, MacKenzie Astin, Katie Barberi; **D:** Rod Amateau. **VHS, Beta, LV** *PAR, BAR, IME*

Garfield

Family Series of well-received prime-time animated specials featuring the cranky, self-possessed feline of comic strip fame. Episodes include "Here Comes Garfield," "Garfield on the Town," and "Garfield Goes Hollywood," all done by the "Peanuts" TV cartoon team.
1989 30m/C VHS, Beta *FOX*

A Garfield Christmas

Family The rotund feline spends Christmas down on the farm with Jon's family.
1991 24m/C VHS *FXV*

Garfield Goes Hollywood

Family Garfield tries out for Hollywood's TV show, "Pet Search." Under the name Johnny Bop and the Two-Steps, he, his owner Jon, and dog Odie have a shot at stardom.
1990 30m/C V: Lorenzo Music. **VHS, LV** *FOX*

Garfield: His 9 Lives

Family Litter of TV cartoons in which Garfield dreams about his past, present, and future lives, including his time as a Pharaoh's prized cat, a laboratory animal, and a space-age cat battling aliens.
1993 60m/C VHS *FOX*

Garfield in Paradise

Family Jon, Garfield, and Odie are on vacation at a cheap tropical resort where they meet a lost tribe who decides to sacrifice man and cat to their volcano god.
1986 30m/C VHS *FOX*

Garfield on the Town

Family Seeking refuge from a gang of cats ("The Claws"), Garfield hides in a restaurant. Lo and behold as luck and coincidence would have it, Garfield discovers his family owns the joint and that it is the site of his very own birth. All of this conspires to remind him of many of his past misdeeds.
1990 24m/C V: Lorenzo Music. **VHS** *FOX*

Garfield's Feline Fantasy

Family Animated spoof of Indiana Jones adventures with Garfield and Odie in search of the Banana of Bombay.
1993 35m/C VHS *FOX*

Garfield's Halloween Adventure

Family Garfield and Odie dress up as pirates for trick-or-treat fun but the trick may be on them when they find themselves at a haunted house.
1985 30m/C VHS *FOX*

Garfield's Thanksgiving

Family Garfield goes on a pre-Thanksgiving diet and Jon ruins dinner but Grandma arrives in time to save the day. Whew; what a relief.
1989 30m/C VHS *FOX*

Gargoyles, The Movie: The Heroes Awaken 🦴🦴 ᵈ

G/Family Mythical crimefighting creatures, trapped in stone by day thanks to a sorcerer's spell but released to live at night, are displaced in time from their medieval Scottish home, winding up in modern-day New York City. But they discover they still have old enemies to fight. First aired as a five-episode part of the animated TV series.
1994 80m/C V: Ed Asner, Keith David, Jonathon Frakes, Marina Sirtis, Bill Fagerbakke, Salli Richardson, Frank Welker, Thom Adcox, Jeff Bennett. **VHS** *TOU*

The Gate 🦴🦴

PG-13/Jr. High-Adult Left alone for the weekend (uh-oh!), youngster Glen and his playmates discover a large hole in the backyard that turns out to be the gateway to

Hell—and the natives are restless. Lowbrow but effective kids-eye-view horror indulges in wild special effect thrills rather than tasteless bloodletting and gore. Followed by a sequel.

🔖 BEWARE *Demon violence, but they're dead already, aren't they? Zero humans are killed, which could be a world's record for the genre.*

1987 85m/C Christa Denton, Stephen Dorff, Louis Tripp; **D:** Tibor Takacs. **VHS, Beta, LV** *LIV, VES*

Gateway to the Mind

Primary-Jr. High The five senses are explored in this animated video from "Bugs Bunny" animator Chuck Jones. Many revelations for children, including the ability of grasshoppers to hear with the stomach.

199? 58m/C D: Chuck Jones; **W:** Chuck Jones. **VHS** *FCT, RHI*

Gay Purr-ee 🦴🦴

Family Cartoon feature (co-written by Chuck Jones) in which provincial cat Mewsette goes to Paris in search of love and adventure. She winds up in the paws of suave scoundrel Meowrice and must be rescued by her tomcat boyfriend from home. Lushly animated parody of romantic melodramas, unevenly mixing kid stuff with clever touches for grownups. Gets an extra half-bone for the cast of voices, who make the songs much better than they are.

1962 85m/C D: Abe Levitow; **W:** Chuck Jones; **M:** Harold Arlen; **V:** Judy Garland, Robert Goulet, Red Buttons, Hermione Gingold, Mel Blanc. **VHS, LV** *WAR, FCT*

The Geisha Boy 🦴🦴 🦴

Family Jerry is a floundering magician who joins the USO and tours the Far East finding romance with a Japanese widow after her small son claims him as a father. But it's the slapstick that will win kid viewers over, much of it involving the conjuror's tricky white rabbit, one of the screen's most memorable bunnies since Bugs. Special appearance by the Los Angeles Dodgers.

1958 98m/C Jerry Lewis, Marie McDonald, Sessue Hayakawa, Barton MacLane, Suzanne Pleshette, Nobu McCarthy; **D:** Frank Tashlin. **VHS** *PAR*

General Spanky 🦴🦴

Family The only "Our Gang" feature with the original cast goofed by transplanting the Little Rascals from their accustomed 1920s/30s environment into a Civil War setting popular with Hollywood at the time. Spanky and Alfalfa are unlikely Confederate kids who play soldier, outsmarting Union troops. Some funny stuff, but Buckwheat's role as an eager slave is pretty disturbing today.

1936 73m/B George "Spanky" McFarland, Phillips Holmes, Ralph Morgan, Irving Pichel, Rosina Lawrence, Billie "Buckwheat" Thomas, Carl "Alfalfa" Switzer, Louise Beavers; **D:** Fred Newmeyer. **VHS, LV** *MGM, FCT*

Gentle Ben

Family Episodes from the late '60s television show about the a bear and the family he befriends, down in the Florida Everglades. Derived from the film "Gentle Giant," both from "Flipper" creator Ivan Tors.

1969 60m/C Dennis Weaver, Beth Brickell, Clint Howard, Rance Howard, Angelo Rutherford, Burt Reynolds. **VHS, Beta** *CNG*

Gentle Giant 🦴🦴

Family An orphaned bear is taken in by a boy and his family and grows to be a 750-pound giant who can sleep anywhere he wants and must be returned to the wild. Kids will love the bear. "Gentle Ben" TV series was derived from this feature. Ages 4 to 9.

1967 93m/C Dennis Weaver, Vera Miles, Ralph Meeker, Clint Howard, Huntz Hall; **D:** James Neilson. **VHS** *REP*

GeoKids: Camouflage, Cuttlefish, and Chameleons Changing Color

Preschool Ever meet a decorator crab? No, not a surly interior designer. A decorator crab lives undersea and disguises itself with bits of shell and rock to fool its predators. From the crab to the color-changing chameleon to insects that can look like leaves or sticks, this video is beautifully filmed and easily understood. Cute animal puppets are the narrators. Camouflage, they explain, is "like hide-and-seek without needing a hiding place." Ages 2 to 6.

1995 33m/C VHS *COL*

GeoKids: Chomping on Bugs, Swimming Sea Slugs, and Stuff That Makes Animals Special

Preschool Puppets Sunny Honeypossum and Bobby Bushbaby journey through the animal kingdom to see what makes each animal unique, including turtles, cheetahs, elephants, hedgehogs, and more. Beautifully filmed and easy to understand. Ages 2 to 6.

1995 33m/C VHS *COL*

GeoKids: Tadpoles, Dragonflies, and the Caterpillar's Big Change

Preschool Sunny, Bobby, and Uncle Balzac (a chameleon) learn about metamorphosis, including how caterpillars become butterflies and tadpoles turn into frogs. Another fine entry in National Geographic's GeoKids series. Ages 2 to 6.

1995 33m/C VHS *COL*

George! ♪ ♫

G/Family Carefree bachelor inherits the title St. Bernard and has to take both the clumsy 250-pound animal and his girlfriend on a Swiss Alps trip. George proves his worth when his new master gets caught in an avalanche. Low-budget ancestor of "Beethoven" combines unfunny gags with muddy travel footage. Originally 87 minutes.
1970 70m/C Marshall Thompson, Jack Mullaney, Inge Schoner; **D:** Wallace C. Bennett; **W:** Wallace C. Bennett. **VHS, Beta** *VCI*

George Balanchine's The Nutcracker ♪ ♪ ♫

G/Family Pas de deux redux. Tchaikovsky's classic ballet about the magic of Christmas and a little girl (Cohen) who dreams on Christmas Eve that she is in an enchanted kingdom. Culkin lamely grins through his wooden performance as the Nutcracker Prince, but the talent of the Sugarplum Fairy (Kistler) and the other dancers is such that conventional camera techniques sometimes fail to keep up with their exacting moves. Adapted from the 1816 book by E.T.A. Hoffmann.
1993 93m/C Macaulay Culkin, Jessica Lynn Cohen, Bart Robinson Cook, Darci Kistler, Damian Woetzel, Kyra Nichols, Wendy Whelan, Gen Horiuchi, Margaret Tracey; **D:** Emile Ardolino; **W:** Susan Cooper. **VHS, LV, 8mm** *WAR*

George of the Jungle

Family "Rocky and Bullwinkle" producer Jay Ward also created the inept animated TV hero "George of the Jungle" in these Tarzan spoofs that initially failed with audiences but have since become cult items for their snide humor (great moments in marketing: for video reissue they've been dubbed "greentoons" to catch the environmentalist wave). Also includes 'toons with the race-car driver Tom Slick and Super Chicken. Each tape is available individually: "Gullible Travels," "Jungle Mutants," "There's No Place Like Jungle," and "The World According to George."
1967 30m/C VHS *FXV*

George's Island ♪ ♪

PG/Family When young George is placed with the worst foster parents in the world, his eccentric grandfather helps him and a little girl escape. They wind up on an island where hammy ghosts of Captain Kidd and his crew still guard buried treasure. Canadian kids' film, cute in parts but too often scuttled by overacting and cheesy f/x. Filmed in Nova Scotia.
1991 89m/C Ian Bannen, Sheila McCarthy, Maury Chaykin, Nathaniel Moreau, Vicki Ridler, Brian Downey, Gary Reineke; **D:** Paul Donovan; **W:** J. William Ritchie; **M:** Marty Simon. **VHS, LV** *COL, NLC*

Gerald McBoing-Boing

Family Classic Dr. Seuss story of a boy who can only communicate through the title sound effect but finds fame, fortune, happiness, and self-fulfillment in spite of being "different." Considered in its day to be a break-

through of sorts in "sophisticated" cartoon style.
1950 55m/B VHS, Beta *CHF*

Gerald McBoing Boing, Vol. 1: Favorite Sing-Along Songs

Preschool-Jr. High Episodes from the first cartoon show made for television which includes educational aspects. Includes "Turned Around Clown," "The Unenchanted Princess," "The Freezee Yum Story," "The Little Boy Who Ran Away," and "Matador and the Troubador." Additional volumes available.
1956 20m/C D: Ernie Pintoff. **VHS** *PAR, FCT*

Geronimo ♪ ♪ ♪

Jr. High-Adult Not to be confused with the big screen version, this made for cable television drama uses three actors to portray the legendary Apache warrior (1829-1909) at various stages of his life. The intrepid teenager who leads attacks on Mexican troops, the adult fighting the duplicitous bluecoats, and the aged man witnessing the destruction of his way of life. The true story is told from the point of view of Native American culture and historical records.

 BEWARE *Western violence.*

1993 120m/C Joseph Runningfox, Jimmy Herman, Ryan Black, Nick Ramus, Michelle St. John, Michael Greyeyes, Tailinh Forest Flower, Kimberly Norris, August Schellenberg, Geno Silva, Harrison Lowe; **D:** Roger Young; **W:** J.T. Allen; **M:** Patrick Williams. **VHS** *TTC*

Geronimo: An American Legend ♪ ♪ ♫

PG-13/Jr. High-Adult Well-intentioned bio-actioner about the legendary Apache leader who fought the U.S. Army over forcing Native Americans onto reservations is often too noble for its own good, leading to some slow spots. Narrator is young Army officer Gatewood (Patric), whose division is to round up the renegades led by Geronimo (Studi), whom he naturally comes to admire. Hackman and Duvall (as a general and a scout respectively) steal any scene they're in although the leads manage to hold their own. Great location filming around Moab, Utah.

 BEWARE *Violence and profanity.*

1993 115m/C Wes Studi, Jason Patric, Robert Duvall, Gene Hackman, Matt Damon, Rodney Grant, Kevin Tighe, Carlos Palomino, Stephen McHattie; **D:** Walter Hill; **W:** John Milius, Larry Gross; **M:** Ry Cooder. **VHS, LV, 8mm** *COL*

The Get Along Gang, Vol. 1

Family Get Along Gang members are cartoon critters traveling the country in their Clubhouse Caboose, leaving worthwhile moral lessons in their wake. Additional volumes available.
198? 44m/C VHS *ORI, KAR*

Meet the Star of Getting Even With Dad, Macaulay Culkin

His hands squeezed his cheeks. His mouth opened in a terrorized "O." It's the lasting image of Macaulay Culkin. In the sleeper mega-hit *Home Alone,* Culkin was everyone's perfectly adorable, funny and pranksterish 10-year-old. In 1990, Macaulay starred in the most lucrative comedy film of all time (since surpassed by *Forrest Gump*). He'd been acting on stage and film since age 6. The idea of a kid left alone by adults was fleshed out by director John Hughes from a scene Macaulay played as John Candy's nephew in *Uncle Buck. Home Alone* made Macaulay a phenomenon. He starred in a Michael Jackson video, hosted "Saturday Night Live," and had his own Saturday morning cartoon series. By the time *Home Alone 2* hit the cineplexes, Macaulay was rich, famous and embattled. Named after British historian Thomas Babington Macaulay, "Mack" was born in 1980. He has four brothers and two sisters; three of them also act. His aunt is actress Bonnie Bedelia. His father, Kit Culkin, was a struggling actor and his mother, Patricia Brentrup, a phone operator when Mack hit the big time. Since, his career has taken a turn for the worse. "He's not growing up into a teen idol," one casting director noted. By his mid-teens Culkin was no longer making movies and his parents were locked in a nasty custody battle.

Getting Even with Dad 🎵 ♭

PG/Jr. High-Adult Crook Danson can't find the money he stole in his last heist. Why? because his precocious son has hidden it with the intention of blackmailing dear old dad into going straight and acting like a real father. Title is unintentionally funny in light of Mac's domineering dad Kit, who, as they say, drives a hard bargain. Fairly bland family film squanders charm of Danson and Culkin, running formulaic plot into ground. Headly is likewise wasted as district attorney who prosecutes and then falls for Pops, behaving like any good lawyer would. Macaulay's precocious days are down to a precious few.

🚨 BEWARE 🚨 *Fighting and profanity. Explain blackmail to your kids before watching this one.*

1994 108m/C Macaulay Culkin, Ted Danson, Glenne Headly, Hector Elizondo, Saul Rubinek, Gailard Sartain, Kathleen Wilhoite, Sam McMurray; **D:** Howard Deutch; **W:** Tom S. Parker, Jim Jennewein. **VHS** *NYR*

Gettysburg 🎵🎵🎵

PG/Jr. High-Adult Civil War buff Ted Turner (who has a cameo as a Confederate soldier) originally intended Michael Shaara's Pulitzer Prize-winning novel "The Killer Angels" to be adapted as a three-part miniseries for his "TNT" network, but the lure of the big screen prevailed, marking the first time the battle has been committed to film and the first time a film crew has been allowed to film battle scenes on the Gettysburg National Military Park battlefield. The greatest battle of the war and the bloodiest in U.S. history is realistically staged by more than 5,000 Civil War re-enactors. The all-male cast concentrates on presenting the human cost of the war, with Daniels particularly noteworthy as the scholarly Colonel Chamberlain, determined to hold Little Big Top for the Union. Last film role for Jordan, to whom the movie is co-dedicated. The full scale recreation of Pickett's Charge is believed to be the largest period scale motion-picture sequence filmed in North America since D.W. Griffith's "Birth of a Nation."

🚨 BEWARE 🚨 *Combat violence and bad fake beards.*

1993 254m/C Jeff Daniels, Martin Sheen, Tom Berenger, Sam Elliott, Richard Jordan, Stephen Lang, Kevin Conway, C. Thomas Howell, Maxwell Caulfield, Andrew Prine, James Lancaster, Royce D. Applegate, Brian Mallon; **Cameos:** Ken Burns, Ted Turner; **D:** Ronald F. Maxwell; **W:** Ronald F. Maxwell; **M:** Randy Edelman. **VHS** *TTC*

Ghost 🎵🎵🎵 ♭

PG-13/Sr. High-Adult Zucker, known for overboard comedies like "Airplane!" and "Ruthless People," changed tack and directed this undemanding romantic thriller, which was the surprising top grosser of 1990. Swayze is a murdered investment consultant attempting (from somewhere near the hereafter) to protect his lover, Moore, from imminent danger when he learns he was the victim of a hit gone afoul. Goldberg is the medium who suddenly discovers that the powers she's been faking are real. A winning blend of action, special effects (from Industrial Light and Magic) and romance.

🚨 BEWARE 🚨 *Main character is murdered by thugs. Violence, profanity, suggested sex, and scary demons come for dead bad guys.*

1990 127m/C Patrick Swayze, Demi Moore, Whoopi Goldberg, Tony Goldwyn, Rick Aviles, Vincent Schiavelli, Gail Boggs, Armelia McQueen, Phil Leeds; *D:* Jerry Zucker; *W:* Bruce Joel Rubin; *M:* Maurice Jarre. **Award Nominations:** Academy Awards '90: Best Film Editing, Best Picture, Best Original Score; **Awards:** Academy Awards '90: Best Original Screenplay, Best Supporting Actress (Goldberg); Golden Globe Awards '91: Best Supporting Actress (Goldberg); People's Choice Awards '91: Best Film—Drama. **VHS, Beta, LV, 8mm** *PAR, FCT, BTV*

The Ghost Belonged to Me

Primary-Sr. High Alexander Armsworth has an encounter with the spirit world and learns self-confidence. This live-action Walt Disney short was adapted for the Magic Kingdom's TV program from the book by Richard Peck. **1990 11m/C VHS, Beta** *MTI, DSN*

Ghost Chasers 🦴🦴

Family The Bowery Boys become mixed up in supernatural hijinks when a seance leads to the appearance of a ghost that only Sach can see.
1951 70m/B Leo Gorcey, Huntz Hall, Billy Benedict, David Gorcey, Buddy Gorman, Bernard Gorcey, Jan Kayne, Philip Van Zandt, Lloyd Corrigan; *D:* William Beaudine. **VHS** *WAR*

Ghost Dad 🦴🦴

PG/Primary-Adult Widowed workaholic Elliot Hopper dies in an auto mishap (well, not really, but that's getting ahead of ourselves). He returns in phantom form to help his kids prepare for life without him. The "Dad" theme of this movie is nice and sweet, as Cosby plays the belated family man. Alas, stress is on the "Ghost" part, with poor f/x trying to compete with "Beetlejuice" as Elliot masters walking through walls, flying, and general spooking. Booed at the box office, spectral flop might interest households with elementary fry.

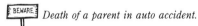 *Death of a parent in auto accident.*

1990 84m/C Bill Cosby, Denise Nicholas, Ian Bannen, Christine Ebersole, Dana Ashbrook, Arnold Stang; *D:* Sidney Poitier; *W:* S.S. Wilson, Brent Maddock; *M:* Henry Mancini. **VHS, Beta, LV** *MCA*

The Ghost Goes West 🦴🦴🦴

Family Antiquated but still fun fantasy about 200-year-old Murdoch Glourie cursed to haunt his Scottish castle. The kilt-clad ghost gets rattled when an American tycoon decides to buy Glourie Castle and move it brick-by-brick to Florida, turning the spook into a media gimmick for his grocery store chain. Special f/x are nothing special by modern standards, but overall pic is pleasant and satisfying. Available in digitally remastered stereo with the original theatrical trailer.

⚠️ **BEWARE** *Alcohol use.*

1936 85m/B Robert Donat, Jean Parker, Eugene Pallette, Elsa Lanchester; *D:* Rene Clair; *W:* Robert Sherwood. **VHS, Beta** *HBO*

The Ghost of Thomas Kempe

Primary-Jr. High When James Harrison unwittingly frees a mischievous ghost from a bottle, he's blamed for the many pranks pulled by the spook. Adaptation of the book by Penelope Lively.
1979 60m/C VHS, Beta *MTT, VTR*

Ghost Stories

Primary-Jr. High Three lesser-known Charles Dickens ghost stories, "The Ghost in the Wardrobe," "The Mail Coach Ghosts," and "The Goblin & The Gravedigger," (this last surprisingly reminiscent of "A Christmas Carol"), derived from Dickens' "Pickwick Papers." Quite spooky and entertaining, in spite of limited low-budget animation.
1988 60m/C VHS

Ghostbusters 🦴🦴🦴

PG/Family After losing their scholastic funding, a group of paranormal investigators go into business for themselves, aiding NYC citizens in removing ghosts, poltergeists, and other supernatural pests, climaxing in a titanic battle with an ancient demon-god. Comedy-thriller with great special effects, zany characters, and some of the best laughs of the decade. Also available in a laserdisc version with letterboxing, analysis of all special effects, complete screenplay, and original trailer. The inspiration for two competing cartoon shows also on video.

⚠️ **BEWARE** *Profanity, sex talk with the possessed, giant marshmallow man and some other scary effects.*

1984 103m/C Bill Murray, Dan Aykroyd, Harold Ramis, Rick Moranis, Sigourney Weaver, Annie Potts, Ernie Hudson, William Atherton; *D:* Ivan Reitman; *W:* Dan Aykroyd, Harold Ramis, Harold Ramis; *M:* Elmer Bernstein. **VHS, Beta, LV, 8mm** *COL, APD, CRC*

Ghostbusters 2 🦴🦴

PG/Family Fun opening finds the Ghostbusters out of work, reduced to doing Barney-the-Dinosaur-type birthday parties for kids. When a river of slime threatens NYC just so a long-dead baddie can reincarnate himself in Weaver's baby, the paranormal investigators are back in action. One priceless gag with the Statue of Liberty; otherwise a dispirited affair that offers music-videos in place of plot.

⚠️ **BEWARE** *Sex talk and profanity, and eeewwwww, don't forget the river of slime. Possessed people again.*

1989 102m/C Bill Murray, Dan Aykroyd, Sigourney Weaver, Harold Ramis, Rick Moranis, Ernie Hudson, Peter MacNicol, David Margulies, Wilhelm von Homburg, Harris Yulin, Annie Potts; *D:* Ivan Reitman; *W:* Harold Ramis; *M:* Randy Edelman. **VHS, Beta, LV, 8mm** *COL*

Dan Aykroyd, Bill Murray and Harold Ramis have a hair-raising experience in the library in "Ghostbusters."

Ghostbusters: Back to the Past

Family TV cartoon collection based not on the Bill Murray movies but an earlier Sid & Marty Krofft live-action kids' comedy that happened to bear that suddenly-sellable title "Ghostbusters." These 'toons cashed in on the name recognition by reviving the premise of two paranormal investigators and their gorilla friend, who can now travel back in time to take on ectoplasmic evildoers. Additional volumes available.
1991 75m/C VHS *JFK, CEL*

Ghostwriter, Vol. 1: Ghost Story

Primary-Jr. High Carefully conceived and quite enchanting educational series from PBS-TV; six urban children solve mysteries with the help of a special partner, an amnesiac ghost who can only communicate by reading and writing. Someone in the neighborhood is stealing backpacks, and clues point to a weird gang with monster masks, who leave coded messages. Lenni, Jamal, Alex, and Gaby, with a lesson in logic from their new friend Ghostwriter, crack the code and figure out what's up. Feature-length, five-episode compilation from the program, which is entertaining enough to give learning a good name. Supplementary materials, like exercise books and even a fan magazine, are also available. Additional volumes available.
1993 105m/C VHS *REP,*

Ghoulies 🦴

PG-13/Jr. High-Adult "Gremlins" recycled as young man gets more than he bargained for when he conjures up a batch of evil creatures when dabbling in the occult. Ridiculous but successful. Followed by two sequels.

🚸 BEWARE 🚸 *Violence and sex talk. Grotesque little creatures.*

1985 81m/C Lisa Pelikan, Jack Nance, Scott Thomson, Tamara DeTreaux, Mariska Hargitay, Bobbie Bresee; **D:** Luca Bercovici; **M:** Richard Band. **VHS, Beta** *LIV, VES, HHE*

G.I. Joe, Vol. 1: A Real American Hero

Family G.I. Joe and his army must fight off Cobra for control of a device that reduces people and objects to a molecular level. Additional volumes available.
1983 94m/C VHS, Beta *FHE*

Giant 🎵🎵🎵♭

Family Based on the Edna Ferber novel, this epic saga covers two generations of a wealthy Texas cattle baron (Hudson) who marries a strong-willed Virginia woman (Taylor) and takes her to live on his vast ranch. It explores the problems they have adjusting to life together, as well as the politics and prejudice of the time. Dean plays the resentful ranch hand (who secretly loves Taylor) who winds up striking oil and beginning a fortune to rival that of his former boss. Dean's last movie—he died in a car crash shortly before filming was completed.
1956 201m/C Elizabeth Taylor, Rock Hudson, James Dean, Carroll Baker, Chill Wills, Dennis Hopper, Rod Taylor, Earl Holliman, Jane Withers, Sal Mineo, Mercedes McCambridge; **D:** George Stevens. **Award Nominations:** Academy Awards '56: Best Actor (Dean), Best Actor (Hudson), Best Adapted Screenplay, Best Art Direction/Set Decoration (Color), Best Costume Design (Color), Best Film Editing, Best Picture, Best Supporting Actress (McCambridge), Best Original Score; **Awards:** Academy Awards '56: Best Director (Stevens); Directors Guild of America Awards '56: Best Director (Stevens). **VHS, Beta, LV** *WAR, BTV*

Gidget 🎵🎵

Family Plucky, boy-crazy teenage girl (whose nickname means girl midget) discovers romance and wisdom on the beaches of Malibu when she becomes involved with a group of college-aged surfers. First in a series of Gidget/surfer films also served as the basis for two television series. Based on a novel by Frederick Kohner about his daughter.
1959 95m/C Sandra Dee, James Darren, Cliff Robertson, Mary Laroche, Arthur O'Connell, Joby Baker; **D:** Paul Wendkos. **VHS, Beta, LV** *COL*

Gidget Goes Hawaiian 🎵🎵

Family Gidget is off to Hawaii with her parents and is enjoying the beach (and the boys) when she is surprised by a visit from boyfriend "Moondoggie." Sequel to "Gidget" and followed by "Gidget Goes to Rome."
1961 102m/C Deborah Walley, James Darren, Carl Reiner, Peggy Cass, Michael Callan, Eddie Foy Jr.; **D:** Paul Wendkos. **VHS, Beta** *COL*

Gidget Goes to Rome 🎵♭

Family Darren returns in his third outing as boyfriend "Moondoggie" to yet another actress playing "Gidget" as the two vacation in Rome and find themselves tempted by other romances. Second sequel to "Gidget."
1963 104m/C Cindy Carol, James Darren, Jeff Donnell, Cesare Danova, Peter Brooks, Jessie Royce Landis; **D:** Paul Wendkos; **M:** John Williams. **VHS, Beta** *COL*

The Gift of Amazing Grace

Family Twelve-year-old Grace Wheeler is the only member of her gospel-singing family without vocal talent. After much pain and frustration, she finally discovers how (besides lip-syncing) she can contribute to the act. ABC Afterschool Special is filled with great gospel tunes.
1986 48m/C Tempestt Bledsoe. **VHS** *VTR, FCT, MLT*

Gift of the Whales

Primary-Jr. High Makah Indian boy gains meaning in life by watching a pod of humpbacked whales frolic in the sea, their activities explained by a beachside researcher. One of the award-winning "Legend" videos from Miramar Home Video, concerned with wildlife and native culture of the Pacific Northwest. Others in the series: "Spirit of the Eagle" and "Winter Wolf."
1989 30m/C D: Kathleen Phelan. **VHS, Beta, LV** *BMG, AAI, MIR*

Gift of Winter

Preschool-Primary Canadian cartoon with future "Saturday Night Live" comics lending voiceovers to the tale of Mr. Winter taking complaints from some small town residents who feel he failed to deliver on a promise for snow.
1974 30m/C V: Gilda Radner, Dan Aykroyd. **VHS, Beta** *FHE, CVM*

Gigglesnort Hotel, Vol. 1

Preschool-Primary Puppets inhabiting the Gigglesnort Hotel teach kids to cope with the foibles of growing up. Two episodes here are "Puppy Parenthood" and "Tender is the Man." Additional volumes available.
1985 50m/C VHS, Beta *ORI, WAR*

Gilligan's Planet

Preschool-Primary Episode from the animated Saturday-morning cartoon of the well-known sitcom, finding the castaway gang stranded in outer space thanks to the Professor's rocket ship. Episode title: "Let Sleeping Minnows Lie."
1982 23m/C VHS, Beta *MGM*

A Gingerbread Christmas

Preschool-Primary As goodwill ambassadors from the North Pole, a gingerbread boy and girl are sent to bring the spirit of Christmas to Gloomsbury.
1992 30m/C VHS *UND, RAB*

The Gingerbread Man and Other Nursery Stories

Preschool-Primary The famed Gingerbread Man once again is on the run from those who seek only nourishment from his being. Also included are several other entertaining shorts.
1990 30m/C VHS

The Gingham Dog and the Calico Cat

Family The recording artist narrates the classic tale of antagonistic toyroom cohabitants, in this tape in the "Rabbit Ears" series, first aired on Showtime.
1991 30m/C M: Chet Atkins. **VHS** *RAB*

Girl Crazy 🦴🦴🦴

Family Wealthy young playboy is sent to an all-boy school in Arizona to get his mind off girls. Once there, he still manages to fall for a local girl who can't stand the sight of him. George and Ira Gershwin provide the tunes, while Rooney and Garland sing and dance up a storm in their eighth film pairing. Adapted from the Broadway hit starring Ethel Merman. 🎵 Sam and Delilah; Embraceable You; I Got Rhythm; Fascinating Rhythm; Treat Me Rough; Bronco Busters; Bidin' My Time; But Not For Me; Do.
1943 99m/B Mickey Rooney, Judy Garland, Nancy Walker, June Allyson; **D:** Norman Taurog; **M:** George Gershwin, Ira Gershwin. **VHS, Beta, LV** *MGM, TTC, FCT*

A Girl of the Limberlost

Family Teenage Elnora and her mother live on a farm in turn-of-the-century Indiana. To help pay for her schoolbooks, scholarly Elnora finds work catching butterflies and moths for a nature photographer. Meanwhile the farm work and expenses are piling up. And the mother-daughter relationship is stormy, at best. Well acted amidst beautiful scenery. Part of TV's "Wonderworks" family movie series. Adapted from Gene Stratton Porter's novel. Ages 11 and up.
1990 120m/C Annette O'Toole, Joanna Cassidy, Heather Fairfield. **VHS** *PME, HMV, FCT*

The Girl Who Spelled Freedom 🦴🦴🦴

Primary-Jr. High Cambodian war refugee girl, speaking little English, strives to adjust with her adoptive American family in Tennessee. She faces her challenges by becoming a national spelling bee champ. Genuinely inspirational Disney TV movie, handled without mawkishness by "Free Willy" director Wincer.
1986 90m/C Wayne Rogers, Mary Kay Place, Jade Chinn, Kieu Chinh, Kathleen Sisk; **D:** Simon Wincer. **VHS, Beta** *DIS*

Girlfriends 🦴🦴🦴

PG/Jr. High-Adult Bittersweet story of a young Jewish photographer learning to make it on her own. Directorial debut of Weill reflects her background in documentaries as the true-to-life episodes unfold.
1978 87m/C Melanie Mayron, Anita Skinner, Eli Wallach, Christopher Guest, Amy Wright, Viveca Lindfors, Bob Balaban; **D:** Claudia Weill; **W:** Vicki Polon. **VHS, Beta** *WAR*

Girls Just Want to Have Fun 🦴🦴

PG/Jr. High-Adult Teen army brat and her friends pull out all the stops and defy their parents for a chance to dance on a national TV program. Low-flying, but harmless; based loosely upon Cyndi Lauper's '80s hit song of the same name, so don't expect well-developed storyline.
1985 90m/C Sarah Jessica Parker, Helen Hunt, Ed Lauter, Holly Gagnier, Morgan Woodward, Lee Montgomery, Shannen Doherty, Biff Yeager; **D:** Alan Metter; **M:** Thomas Newman. **VHS, Beta, LV** *NWV, VTR*

The Glacier Fox

G/Preschool-Primary Feature nature documentary on the wild cousins of the domestic dog in their natural northern habitat.
1979 90m/C VHS, Beta *FHE*

Gleaming the Cube 🦴 ▷

PG-13/Jr. High-Adult Teenage Brian's brother's death is ruled a suicide by the cops, but Brian knows better. Using his skateboarding skills the rebellious young hero unmasks the murderer. Adolescent-minded action impresses with stunt footage only. Title is a fictional bit of kid slang dreamt up by the filmmakers, meaning 'way cool' or something.

⚠ **BEWARE** *Violence and profanity. Depiction of suicide.*

1989 102m/C Christian Slater, Steven Bauer, Min Luong, Art Chudabala, Le Tuan; **D:** Graeme Clifford; **W:** Michael Tolkin; **M:** Jay Michael Ferguson. **VHS, Beta, LV** *LIV, VES*

The Glenn Miller Story 🦴🦴🦴

G/Family The music of the Big Band Era lives again in this warm biography of the legendary Glenn Miller, following his life from the late '20s to his untimely death in a WWII plane crash. Stewart's likably convincing and even fakes the trombone playing well. 🎵 Moonlight Serenade; In the Mood; Tuxedo Junction; Little Brown Jug; Adios; String of Pearls; Pennsylvania 6-5000; Stairway to the Stars; American Patrol.
1954 113m/C James Stewart, June Allyson, Harry (Henry) Morgan, Gene Krupa, Louis Armstrong, Ben Pollack; **D:** Anthony Mann; **W:** Oscar Brodney; **M:** Henry Mancini. **Award Nominations:** Academy Awards '54: Best Story & Screenplay, Best Original Score; **Awards:** Academy Awards '54: Best Sound. **VHS, Beta, LV** *MCA, RDG*

Glory 🦴🦴🦴🦴

R/Sr. High-Adult Fighting Confederate forces on the battlefield and bigots back home, an all-black army unit from Massachusetts goes through the Civil War. Simultaneously beautiful, sweeping, brutal, stirring and heartwarming story focuses on the soldiers and the white man, Robert Gould Shaw (Broderick), who organized them amidst skepticism from his higher-ups. Wonderful performances by all, including Washington who won an Academy Award. Based on fact (including Shaw's letters).

BEWARE *Much violence and death, but that's what war is.*

1989 122m/C Matthew Broderick, Morgan Freeman, Denzel Washington, Cary Elwes, Jihmi Kennedy, Andre Braugher, John Finn, Donovan Leitch, John Cullum, Bob Gunton, Jane Alexander, Raymond St. Jacques; **D:** Edward Zwick; **W:** Kevin Jarre; **C:** Freddie Francis; **M:** James Horner. **Award Nominations:** Academy Awards '89: Best Film Editing; **Awards:** Academy Awards '89: Best Cinematography, Best Sound, Best Supporting Actor (Washington). **VHS, Beta, LV, 8mm** *COL, FCT, BTV*

The Gnome-Mobile 🦴🦴 ♪

Family Lumber baron and his two grandchildren attempt to free a pair of forest gnomes from a sideshow and return them to their gnome colony. Disney adventure filled with f/x is fun but no match for "Darby O'Gill and the Little People." Brennan has a dual role as both a human and a gnome grandfather. Based on a children's novel by Upton Sinclair.

1967 84m/C Walter Brennan, Richard Deacon, Ed Wynn, Karen Dotrice, Matthew Garber; **D:** Robert Stevenson; **M:** Buddy Baker. **VHS, Beta** *DIS, OM*

The Go-Between 🦴🦴🦴 ♪

PG/Jr. High-Adult Young boy acts as a messenger between an aristocratic beauty and her former lover, a mere farmer. But tragedy befalls them all when the lovers are discovered. The story is told as the elderly messenger (now played by Redgrave) recalls his younger days as this secret courier, himself secretly infatuated with the lady. Excellent, bittersweet tale of youthful innocence and loss, based on a story by L. P. Hartley and adapted by playwright Harold Pinter.

BEWARE *Lust, both young and old.*

1971 116m/C Julie Christie, Alan Bates, Dominic Guard, Margaret Leighton, Michael Redgrave, Michael Gough, Edward Fox; **D:** Joseph Losey; **W:** Harold Pinter. **Award Nominations:** Academy Awards '71: Best Supporting Actress (Leighton); **Awards:** British Academy Awards '71: Best Supporting Actor (Fox), Best Supporting Actress (Leighton). **VHS** *CSM, MGM*

Go Go Gophers: Up in the Air

Family Col. Coyote stars in this cartoon tape that includes episodes of "Underdog."

1966 60m/C VHS

Go West 🦴🦴🦴

Family The brothers Marx help in the making and unmaking of the Old West, with Groucho as swindler S. Quentin Quayle (the S. stands for San). It's no "Night at the Opera" or "Day at the Races" but it has its moments, especially in the train sequence, and it is the source of the classic line, "Didn't we meet in Monte Carlo the night you blew your brains out?" Ages 8 and up.

1940 80m/B Groucho Marx, Chico Marx, Harpo Marx, John Carroll, Diana Lewis; **D:** Edward Buzzell. **VHS, Beta, LV** *MGM, CCB*

Gobots

Family TV cartoon series in which the heroic Gobots battle the evil Renegades. Anyone here tell the difference between a Gobot and a Transformer?

1985 48m/C VHS

Gobots: Battle of the Rock Lords 🦴

Preschool-Jr. High Another theatrical cartoon designed to sell toys, in this case the mechanized Gobots. They strive to save the planet Quartex from the Rocklords and the Renegades. 75 minutes of merchandising may prove to be too much.

1985 75m/C D: Ray Patterson; **V:** Margot Kidder, Roddy McDowall, Michael Nouri, Telly Savalas. **VHS, LV** *BAR, IME*

The Gods Must Be Crazy 🦴🦴🦴 ♪

PG/Jr. High-Adult Charming comedy from South Africa that became a worldwide hit. Natives of the Kalihari desert make first contact with the 20th century via an empty Coke bottle dropped from a plane. The strange object "from the gods" sparks greed and envy in the tribe, so Xixo the bushman vows to walk to the edge of the world and throw the evil thing off. On the way he meets assorted representatives of civilization, including an oafish biologist, bureaucratic lawmen, and terrorists; soon their behavior seems as ridiculous to us as it is to the simple, sensible Xixo. Crammed with slapstick and broad humor of every sort, yet secretly gentle and profound.

BEWARE *Roughhousing, salty language. Native nudity and some risque stuff, but nothing distasteful at all.*

1984 109m/C N!xau, Marius Weyers, Sandra Prinsloo, Louw Verwey, Jamie Uys, Michael Thys, Nic de Jager; **D:** Jamie Uys. **VHS, Beta, LV** *FOX, FCT, TVC*

The Gods Must Be Crazy 2 🦴🦴🦴 ♪

PG/Jr. High-Adult Winning sequel to the 1981 hit, doesn't have the fable-like quality of the original—this is more like a string of gags—but what splendid gags! Children of Xixo accidentally stow away in a poacher's truck, and the heroic Kalihari bushman follows their trail to more slapstick encounters with so-called civilized people (including two opposing soldiers who repeatedly take each other hostage). Not as celebrated as its predecessor, but worthwhile nonetheless.

BEWARE *Salty language, roughhousing, alcohol use.*

1989 90m/C N!xau, Lena Farugia, Hans Strydom, Eiros Nadies, Eric Bowen; **D:** Jamie Uys; **M:** Charles Fox. **VHS, Beta, LV** *COL, TTC, FCT*

Godzilla vs. Megalon 🦴 ◔

G/Family Godzilla's creators show their gratitude to misguided but faithful American audiences by transforming the giant monster into a good guy. This time, the world is threatened by Megalon, the giant cockroach, and Gigan, a flying metal creature, simultaneously. Fortunately, the slippery hero's robot pal Jet Jaguar is on hand to slug it out side by side with Tokyo's ultimate defender. Dubbed in the usual incompetent manner.

> 🪧 *Mild salty language; monstrous roughhousing.*

1976 80m/C Katsuhiko Sasakai, Hiroyuki Kawase, Yutaka Hayashi, Robert Dunham; **D:** Jun Fukuda. **VHS** *NOS, MRV, NWV*

Godzilla vs. the Cosmic Monster 🦴🦴

G/Family Godzilla's worst nightmares become a reality as he is forced to take on the one foe he cannot defeat—a metal clone of himself! To make matters worse, Earth is in dire peril at the hands of cosmic apes. We all need friends, and Godzilla is never more happy to see his buddy King Seeser, who gladly lends a claw. Released originally as "Godzilla Vs. the Bionci Monster" until TV's "Bionic Man" served cease and desist papers.

1974 80m/C Masaki Daimon, Kazuya Aoyama, Reiko Tajima, Barbara Lynn, Akihiko Hirata; **D:** Jun Fukuda. **VHS** *NWV, MRV, VYY*

Godzilla vs. the Smog Monster 🦴

G/Preschool-Jr. High One of those campy Godzilla movies that reinvented the radioactive monster reptile (originally a metaphor for the devastating atom bomb) as a friend to all kids. Little Ken summons the Big G to battle a creature born of pollution, a 400-foot sludge blob named Hedora. Great (we're being sarcastic here) opening song: "Save the Earth" that you'll keep humming whether you want to or not.

> 🪧 *Monster violence, but some humans (including Ken's father) also wind up hurt by Hedora's acid-burning slime.*

1972 87m/C Akira Yamauchi, Hiroyuki Kawase, Toshio Shibaki; **D:** Yoshimitu Banno. **VHS, Beta** *ORI*

Goin' Coconuts 🦴

PG/Jr. High-Adult Donny and Marie play Donny and Marie in this smarmy comedy of crooks and jewels and Hawaiian travel scenes. Aimed at family audiences, and indeed on the level of a Saturday-morning cartoon—but without Scooby-Doo and a half-hour running time, it's a big bore on the big island.

1978 93m/C Donny Osmond, Marie Osmond, Herb Edelman, Kenneth Mars, Ted Cassidy, Marc Lawrence, Harold Sakata; **D:** Howard Morris. **VHS** *NO*

Goin' South 🦴🦴🦴

PG/Family An outlaw is saved from being hanged by a young woman who agrees to marry him in exchange for his help working a secret gold mine. They try to get the loot before his old gang gets wind of it. A tongue-in-cheek western that served as Nicholson's second directorial effort. Movie debuts of Steenburgen and Belushi.

> 🪧 *Salty language, violence.*

1978 109m/C Jack Nicholson, Mary Steenburgen, John Belushi, Christopher Lloyd, Veronica Cartwright, Richard Bradford, Danny DeVito, Luana Anders, Ed Begley Jr., Anne Ramsey; **D:** Jack Nicholson; **W:** Charles Shyer. **VHS, Beta, LV** *PAR*

Going Ape! 🦴

PG/Jr. High-Adult Tony Danza, not exactly the Laurence Olivier of his generation, can collect a $5 million inheritance if he takes good care of three orangutans. Moronic, even for a monkey movie. Ages 5 to 9.

1981 87m/C Tony Danza, Jessica Walter, Danny DeVito, Art Metrano, Rick Hurst; **D:** Jeremy Joe Kronsberg; **M:** Elmer Bernstein. **VHS, Beta** *PAR*

Going Bananas 🦴🦴

PG/Family Strictly-for-kids adventure about a talking chimp being chased throughout Africa by a villain who wants to sell the critter to the circus. To the monkey's aid comes a boy, his caretaker, and a guide.

> 🪧 *Salty language.*

1988 95m/C Dom DeLuise, Jimmie Walker, David Mendenhall, Herbert Lom; **D:** Boaz Davidson. **VHS, Beta** *MED, VTR*

Going in Style 🦴🦴🦴 ◔

PG/Family Three elderly gentlemen, tired of doing nothing, decide to liven up their lives by pulling a daylight bank stick-up. They don't care about the consequences because anything is better than sitting on a park bench all day long. The real fun begins when they get away with the robbery. Great cast makes this a winner.

> 🪧 *Depicts the dispiriting boredom of old age. A character dies.*

1979 91m/C George Burns, Art Carney, Lee Strasberg; **D:** Martin Brest. **VHS, Beta** *WAR*

Going My Way 🦴🦴🦴 ◔

Family Classic musical comedy about a progressive young Father O'Malley (the Bingster) assigned to a downtrodden parish. He works to get the parish out of debt, but clashes with his elderly curate Fitzgibbon (Fitzgerald, Oscar-nominated for both best actor and best supporting actor) who's set in his ways. A little music creates a lot of magic, however, helping O'Malley save the church and appease the cranky Fitzgibbon. Followed by "The Bells of St. Mary's." 🎵 The Day After Forever; Swingin' On a Star; Too-ra-loo-ra-loo-ra; Going My Way; Silent Night; Habanera; Ave Maria.

1944 126m/B Bing Crosby, Barry Fitzgerald, Rise Stevens, Frank McHugh, Gene Lockhart, Porter Hall; **D:** Leo McCarey; **W:** Frank Butler, Frank Cavett, Leo McCarey. **Award Nominations:** Academy Awards '44: Best Actor (Fitzgerald), Best Black and White Cinematography, Best Film Editing; **Awards:** Academy Awards '44: Best Actor (Crosby), Best Director (McCarey), Best Picture, Best Song ("Swinging on a Star"), Best Story & Screenplay, Best Supporting Actor (Fitzgerald); National Board of Review Awards '44: 10 Best Films of the Year; New York Film Critics Awards '44: Best Actor (Fitzgerald), Best Director (McCarey), Best Film. **VHS, Beta, LV** *MCA, IGP, BTV*

The Gold Bug 🦴

Family Young Frank searches for treasure on what he thought was a deserted island only to confront a mysterious recluse. Badly conceived and none-too-faithful adaptation of a classic Edgar Allan Poe adventure. Gone is the ingenious code-breaking subplot better explored in the PBS series "Ghostwriter."

1990 45m/C Roberts Blossom, Geoffrey Holder, Anthony Michael Hall; **D:** Robert Fuest. **VHS, Beta** *KUI, NWV, BTV*

Gold Diggers: The Secret of Bear Mountain 🦴🦴 ᵛ

PG/Primary-Adult Thirteen-year-old Beth (Ricci) moves to the small town in Washington. She misses the amenities of city life—cable, the mall—but becomes friends with adventurous Jody (Chlumsky), who tells her there's gold that was hidden in the mountain by a female prospector many years before. Together, the girls set out on a treasure hunt that takes them into a dangerous trek through sea-coast mountain terrain. The spirited girls will appeal strongly to pre-teen girls.

🪧 BEWARE 🪧 *Mild language, domestic abuse, an alcoholic parent, conversation about seeing boys naked and what sex must be like. A girl is caught in a rock slide as water rises around her.*

1995 94m/C Christina Ricci, Anna Chlumsky, Polly Draper, Brian Kerwin, Diana Scarwid, David Keith; **D:** Kevin J. Dobson; **W:** Barry Glasser; **C:** Ross Berryman; **M:** Joel McNeely. **VHS** *NYR*

The Gold Rush 🦴🦴🦴🦴

Family Chaplin's most critically acclaimed film and the best definition of his simple approach to film form: adept maneuvering of visual pathos. The "Little Tramp" searches for gold and romance in the Klondike in the mid-1800s. Includes the dance of the rolls, pantomime sequence of eating the shoe, and Chaplin's lovely music.

1925 85m/B Charlie Chaplin, Mack Swain, Tom Murray, Georgina Hale; **D:** Charlie Chaplin. **VHS, Beta, LV, 8mm** *CNG, NOS, CAB*

The Golden Child 🦴🦴

PG-13/Jr. High-Adult Title refers to a mystic Tibetan boy kidnapped by minions of Satan and transported to Los Angeles. The child's guardians contact a streetwise, ever-skeptical investigator to come to the rescue. Big-budget fantasy adventure was originally cast with Mel Gibson in mind; when Murphy took over aspects of his comic persona were plugged into the script, including sex talk, drug talk, and profanity. Result is a lively, but quite charmless escapist adventure.

Meet the Star of Gold Diggers, Anna Chlumsky

Fifteen-year-old Anna Chlumsky is not your average celebrity kid. Despite the fame that came with her debut film, *My Girl* (1991) and co-starring with mega-kid-star Macaulay Culkin, the young actress attempts to keep her life centered with good grades, church, and calm support from her mother, manager, and coach Nancy Chlumsky.

A model since she was 10 months old, Anna Chlumsky was chosen for the role of Vada Sultenfuss in *My Girl* from over 1,000 hopefuls. The role lead to a sequel, *My Girl 2* as well as roles in *Trading Mom* with Sissy Spacek and *Gold Diggers* with Christina Ricci. Anna, an only child, continues to live with her mother in a working-class suburb of her native Chicago. (Anna's father, Frank, from whom her mother is divorced, is a Wisconsin chef at whose restaurant Anna once ran the cash register and bussed tables.) A former airline reservation clerk and sometime actress, 40-year-old Nancy Chlumsky is determined to see that her famous daughter has a normal life, preferring to mail videotaped auditions to casting agents, rather than disrupting Anna's schedule with frequent trips to Los Angeles.

By all accounts, Anna does seem to be a normal kid: she loves dinosaurs ("I want to become a paleontologist," she says), she wants to attend college, and, like most girls her age, she is teased by boys—including her famous co-star, Mac Culkin, with whom, she asserts, she is "just friends."

Christina Ricci and Anna Chlumsky search for lost treasure in "Gold Diggers: The Secret of Bear Mountain."

BEWARE *Profanity, drug talk (no usage), sex talk. More than a little violent, but naturally the Golden Child can restore life to any important casualties.*

1986 94m/C Eddie Murphy, Charlotte Lewis, Charles Dance, Victor Wong, Randall "Tex" Cobb, James Hong; **D:** Michael Ritchie; **M:** Michel Colombier. **VHS, Beta, LV, 8mm** *PAR*

The Golden Seal 🦴🦴 🦴

PG/Family Well-meaning but somewhat facile tale of little Eric, dwelling on an island off Alaska, who finds a rare golden-haired seal and her pup animals prophesied by the native Aleuts as coming to bring peace and understanding. Trouble is, every adult (Eric's dad included) wants to shoot the seals for their hides, and the boy ends up throwing himself between gun and mammal so often that the drama loses its impact. Based on the novel "A River Ran From Eden," by Vance Marshall.

BEWARE *Animals are in danger and some fighting.*

1983 94m/C Steve Railsback, Michael Beck, Penelope Milford, Torquil Campbell; **D:** Frank Zuniga; **M:** John Barry. **VHS, Beta, LV, 8mm**

Golden Voyage of Sinbad 🦴🦴 🦴

G/Family Worthwhile high adventure, as Sinbad races the usual evil wizard to the mysterious land of Lemuria, where the power of ultimate good or evil can be had among the ruins. Along the way the valiant sailor combats the customary horde of magical creatures, from a ship's living figurehead to a giant one-eyed centaur, that rank among the best of Ray Harryhausen's stop-motion special effects.

BEWARE *Note to multiculturalists: this is one of the few Sinbad tales that makes any attempt to reflect Arab/Hindi civilization—and that includes a blink-and-you'll-miss-it reference to recreational hashish use. Violence, and a sexy slave girl who finds many excuses to bend over in her scant costume.*

1973 105m/C John Phillip Law, Caroline Munro, Tom Baker, Douglas Wilmer, Martin Shaw, John David Garfield, Gregoire Aslan; **D:** Gordon Hessler; **W:** Brian Clemens; **M:** Miklos Rozsa. **VHS, Beta, LV** *COL, MLB*

Goldeneye 🦴🦴 🦴

PG-13/Jr. High-Adult Gadgets, guns 'n gals—everything that made James Bond movies popular in the sixties and double-oh-seventies—take to the screen again. GoldenEye, a handheld item the size of an Etch-A-Sketch, controls a space-based weapon that can destroy any city on earth. Plus you've got your exploding pen and your BMW with a missile behind each headlight. The guns come in all varieties (hand-, machine-, mounted on tanks, etc.). The women include a good Russian, and a bad Russian who has the apparent ability to sexual intercourse a person to death. A spectacular opening finds Bond (suave Brosnan) plunging over a cliff in pursuit of a pilotless aircraft (talk about catching a plane). There isn't anything as exciting after that, just a lot of explosions.

BEWARE *Action/violence and some sexuality. The opening credits are typical Bond and features the naked silhouettes of beautiful women draped on guns, missiles, etc. (You get the point!)*

1995 130m/C Pierce Brosnan, Famke Janssen, Sean Bean, Izabela Scorupco, Joe Don Baker, Robbie Coltrane, Judi Dench, Tcheky Karyo, Gottfried John, Alan Cumming, Desmond Llewelyn, Michael Kitchen, Serena Gordon, Samantha Bond; **Cameos:** Minnie Driver; **D:** Martin Campbell; **W:** Michael France, Jeffrey Caine; **C:** Phil Meheux; **M:** Eric Serra. **VHS** *NYR*

Goldilocks & the Three Bears

Family One of the weaker entries in the "Faerie Tale Theatre" series, despite an intriguingly odd cast: Tatum O'Neal, Alex Karras and Carole King, to name three. But it's hard to wring a 50-minute video out of a three-minute tale. Ages 4 to 10.

1983 60m/C Tatum O'Neal, Alex Karras, Brandis Kemp, Donovan Scott, Hoyt Axton, John Lithgow, Carole King; **D:** Gilbert Cates. **VHS, Beta, LV** *KUI, FOX, FCT*

Pierce Brosnan as James Bond surveys the casino in "Goldeneye."

Goliath 2

Preschool-Primary The tiniest elephant in the world is the shame of his parents until he does a gigantic deed, showing that size isn't everything. A Disney short cartoon that earned an Oscar nomination.

1960 15m/C VHS, Beta *DSN, MTI*

Gone are the Days 🦴🦴

Family Government agent Korman is assigned to protect a family who witnessed an underworld shooting, but the family would like to get away from both the mob and the police. Made-for-cable Disney comedy is well-acted but done in by cliches.

1984 90m/C Harvey Korman, Susan Anspach, Robert Hogan; **D:** Gabrielle Beaumont. **VHS, Beta** *DIS*

Gone with the Wind 🦴🦴🦴🦴

Family Epic Civil War drama focuses on the life of petulant southern belle Scarlett O'Hara. Starting with her idyllic lifestyle on a sprawling plantation, the film traces her survival through the tragic history of the South during the Civil War and Reconstruction, and her tangled love affairs with Ashley Wilkes and Rhett Butler. Classic Hollywood doesn't get any better than this; one great scene after another, equally effective in intimate drama and sweeping spectacle. The train depot scene, one of the more technically adroit shots in movie history, involved hundreds of extras and dummies, and much of the MGM lot was razed to simulate the burning of Atlanta. Based on Margaret Mitchell's novel, screenwriter Howard was assisted by producer Selznick and novelist F. Scott Fitzgerald. For its 50th anniversary, a 231-minute restored version was released that included the trailer for "The Making of a Legend: GWTW." The laserdisc is available in a limited, numbered edition, fully restored to Technicolor from the original negative, with an enhanced soundtrack and seven minutes of rare footage, including the original trailer.

> **BEWARE** *Violence, the burning of Atlanta, and thousands of war wounded. And why is Scarlett so enamored with that weenie Ashley??*

1939 231m/C Clark Gable, Vivien Leigh, Olivia de Havilland, Leslie Howard, Thomas Mitchell, Hattie McDaniel, Butterfly McQueen, Evelyn Keyes, Harry Davenport, Jane Darwell, Ona Munson, Barbara O'Neil, William "Billy" Bakewell, Rand Brooks, Ward Bond, Laura Hope Crews, Yakima Canutt, George Reeves, Marjorie Reynolds, Ann Rutherford, Victor Jory, Carroll Nye, Paul Hurst, Isabel Jewell, Cliff Edwards, Eddie Anderson, Oscar Polk, Eric Linden, Violet Kemble-Cooper; **D:** Victor Fleming; **W:** Sidney Howard; **M:** Max Steiner. **Award Nominations:** Academy Awards '39: Best Actor (Gable), Best Sound, Best Special Effects, Best Supporting Actress (de Havilland), Best Original Score; **Awards:** Academy Awards '39: Best Actress (Leigh), Best Color Cinematography, Best Director (Fleming), Best Film Editing, Best Interior Decoration, Best Picture, Best Screenplay, Best Supporting Actress (McDaniel); New York Film Critics Awards '39: Best Actress (Leigh). **VHS, Beta, LV** *MGM, FUS, BTV*

Gonzo Presents Muppet Weird Stuff

Family Rare "Muppet Show" showcase for that strange but friendly turkey-creature Gonzo. With the dubious assistance of celebrity guest stars, he catches a cannonball and wrestles a brick blindfolded on a guided tour of his mansion.

1985 55m/C Frank Oz, Jim Henson, John Cleese, Julie Andrews, Vincent Price, Madeline Kahn. **VHS, Beta** *FOX*

Goober & the Ghost Chasers

Preschool-Primary Scrawny, semi-visible cartoon dog goes ghost-huntin' with his buddies in this short-lived Saturday-morning show that didn't give "Scooby-Doo" any serious competition, even with the Partridge Family as semi-regular guests. Both Goober and Scooby came from the Hanna-Barbera assembly line.

1974 50m/C VHS, Beta *WOV, GKK*

The Good Son 🦴🦴

R/Sr. High-Adult In a grand departure from cute, Culkin tackles evil as a 13-year-old obsessed with death and other unseemly hobbies. During a stay with his uncle, Mark (Wood) watches as his cousin (Culkin) gets creepier and creepier, and tries to alert the family. But will they listen? Nooo they, like most good Hollywood families, choose to ignore the little warning signs like the doll hanging by a noose in Culkin's room. And then there's the untimely death of a sibling. Hmmm. Culkin isn't as bad as expected, but doesn't quite get all the way down to bone-chilling terror either. Original star Jesse Bradford was dropped when Papa Culkin threatened to pull Mac off "Home Alone 2" if he wasn't cast in the lead.

> **BEWARE** *A vicious child, violence, profanity. And many scary scenes, including one where a girl plunges through the ice of a frozen pond.*

1993 87m/C Macaulay Culkin, Elijah Wood, Wendy Crewson, David Morse, Daniel Hugh-Kelly, Quinn Culkin; **D:** Joseph Ruben; **W:** Ian McEwan; **M:** Elmer Bernstein. **VHS, LV** *FXV*

The Goodbye Bird 🦴🦴

G/Family Frank is accused of stealing the school's prized talking parrot. With the aid of a kindly veterinarian, the boy tries to discover who the thief really is. Featherweight.

1993 91m/C Cindy Pickett, Concetta Tomei, Wayne Rogers, Christopher Pettiet; **D:** William Clark. **VHS** *WOV*

The Goodbye Girl 🦴🦴🦴 ♡

PG/Jr. High-Adult Top-notch original Neil Simon story of a divorced actress (Marsha Mason), her precocious nine-year-old daughter (Quinn Cummings) and the aspiring actor (Richard Dreyfuss) who moves in with them as a tenant (and who sleeps in the nude, naked, buff-o . . .) The little girl brings the adults together romantically.

Mason is believable in a tough role, while Dreyfuss' great performance won an Academy Award. Ages 12 and up.

BEWARE *Profanity and sex talk.*

1977 110m/C Richard Dreyfuss, Marsha Mason, Quinn Cummings, Barbara Rhoades, Marilyn Sokol; **D:** Herbert Ross; **W:** Neil Simon; **M:** Dave Grusin. **Award Nominations:** Academy Awards '76: Best Picture; Academy Awards '77: Best Actress (Mason), Best Original Screenplay, Best Supporting Actress (Cummings); **Awards:** Academy Awards '77: Best Actor (Dreyfuss); British Academy Awards '78: Best Actor (Dreyfuss); Golden Globe Awards '78: Best Actor—Musical/Comedy (Dreyfuss), Best Actress—Musical/Comedy (Mason), Best Film—Musical/Comedy, Best Screenplay; Los Angeles Film Critics Association Awards '77: Best Actor (Dreyfuss). **VHS, Beta, LV** *MGM, BTV*

Goodbye, Miss 4th of July

🐾🐾🐾

Family Disney TV-movie from "Man From Snowy River" director Miller about an American family who moves to Greece and must overcome the suspicion and mistrust the locals have for outsiders, especially Yankees. Based on the book by Christopher G. Janus.

1988 89m/C Roxana Zal, Louis Gossett Jr., Chris Sarandon, Chantal Contouri, Chynna Phillips, Mitchell Anderson, Conchata Ferrell, Ed Lauter; **D:** George Miller. **VHS** *DIS*

Goodtime Bedtime

Preschool-Primary Designed for parents to use with their children to help solve sleep problems. Instructs children to gain confidence in their ability to go to sleep more easily. Ages 2 to 7 and parents.

1994 27m/C VHS *TPV*

Goof Troop: Goin' Fishin'

Preschool-Primary Goofy and his friends go fishing in two episodes of TV's Disney kids' show. In "Slightly Dinghy," Max and Pete go fishing with their dads for sunken treasure. "Wrecks, Lies, and Videotape" features Max and P.J. trying to win a Hawaiian vacation for the best new home video by making Goofy their subject. Ah, you have to love the wordplay in those titles. Additional volumes available.

1992 ?m/C VHS *DIS*

A Goofy Look at Valentine's Day

Preschool-Primary The history and meaning of Valentine's Day is taught to Goofy by Cupid.

1990 10m/C VHS, Beta *MTI, DSN*

A Goofy Movie 🐾🐾🐾

G/Family For 63 years he's played second fiddle to a mouse with a squeaky voice. Now he's top dog and this time, it's personal . . . No, wait. It's not that kind of movie. Disney's Goofy (the voice of Bill Farmer) has his paws full with teenage son Max (voice of Jason Marsden) who goofs off in school, listens to rock music all day and is always trying to impress a certain girl. Goofy decides to

take Max on a cross-country trip for a little father-and-son bonding. Through lots of comic mishaps, Goofy and Max come to appreciate each other. The songs aren't bad, either. And ignore the New York Times' gripe that "the story is too rambling and emotionally diffuse for the title character to come fully alive." All together now: "It's a CARTOON!"

1994 78m/C D: Kevin Lima; **W:** Jymn Magon, Brian Pimental, Chris Matheson; **V:** Bill Farmer, Jason Marsden, Jim Cummings, Kellie Martin, Rob Paulsen, Wallace Shawn, Florence Stanley, Jo Anne Worley. **VHS** *DIS*

Goofy's Field Trip Series

Preschool-Primary Goofy teaches children the various parts of a plane, a ship and a train.

1989 15m/C VHS, Beta *MTI, DSN*

The Goonies 🐾🐾

PG/Family Two brothers, members of a band of outcast kids called the Goonies, are about to lose their family home to creditors but conveniently pick up an old pirate's treasure map. They muster the Goonies and head for the 'X,' finding caves filled with bones, ancient booby-traps and pursuing criminals. Producer Spielberg and "Superman" director Donner joined to do this high-energy action fantasy that shows what the Little Rascals might have looked like with million-dollar f/x and leftover sets and stunts from "Indiana Jones and the Temple of Doom" (which also starred Ke Huy Quan). Big, loud, dizzying, and not as cute as it thinks it is. Laserdisc edition comes in a widescreen format.

BEWARE *Profanity that would make a pirate blush. Violence continually threatened, seldom carried out.*

1985 114m/C Sean Astin, Josh Brolin, Jeff B. Cohen, Corey Feldman, Martha Plimpton, John Matuszak, Robert Davi, Anne Ramsey, Mary Ellen Trainor, Jonathan Ke Quan, Kerri Green, Joe Pantoliano; **D:** Richard Donner; **W:** Chris Columbus, Steven Spielberg; **M:** Dave Grusin. **VHS, Beta, LV** *WAR*

Goosebumps: A Night in Terror Tower

Primary-Jr. High While on vacation in London, a 12-year-old American girl and her younger brother find themselves trapped for the night in a wax museum's medieval torture chamber—with the wax figures coming to life. Based on the wildly popular horror books for pre-teens by R.L. Stine. Ages 10 and up.

1996 45m/C Kathryn Short, Corey Sevier, Diego Matamoros, Robert Collins. **VHS** *FXV*

The Goosehill Gang and the Gold Rush Treasure Map

Primary-Jr. High Goosehill Gang finds a treasure map hidden in an old diary. But instead of treasure, the Gang only finds greed, in this live-action morality tale. Additional volumes available.

1980 20m/C VHS, Beta *VBL, FFC*

Cool son Max is mortified by uncool dad Goofy in "The Goofy Movie."

Gordy

G/Family In a year when "Babe" hogged the spotlight, no other movie about a talking pig stood a chance. Certainly not this one, with its mediocre acting and awkwardly dubbed animal voices. On a quest to rescue his family from a future as breakfast links, Gordy winds up (A) in show business as part of a country music act and (B) in big business as head of a major corporation (no, not Swift & Co.) And you thought a pig who herds sheep sounded far-fetched.

1995 90m/C Doug Stone, Michael Roescher, Kristy Young, James Donadio, Deborah Hobart, Tom Lester, Ted Manson; **D:** Mark Lewis; **W:** Leslie Stevens; **C:** Richard Michalak; **M:** Tom Bahler; **V:** Justin Garms. **VHS** *TOU*

Gorillas in the Mist

PG-13/Jr. High-Adult The life of Dian Fossey, animal rights activist and world-renowned expert on the African Gorilla, from her pioneering contact with mountain gorillas to her murder at the hands of poachers. Weaver is totally appropriate as the increasingly obsessed Fossey, but the character moves away from us, just as we need to see and understand more about her. Excellent special effects.

BEWARE *Killing and mutilation of animals. Shot of gorilla body parts being sold in a market. Profanity, violence, and suggested sex.*

1988 117m/C Sigourney Weaver, Bryan Brown, Julie Harris, Iain Cuthbertson, John Omirah Miluwi, Constantin Alexandrov, Waigwa Wachira; **D:** Michael Apted; **W:** Anna Hamilton Phelan; **M:** Maurice Jarre. **Award Nominations:** Academy Awards '88: Best Actress (Weaver), Best Adapted Screenplay, Best Film Editing, Best Sound, Best Original Score; **Awards:** Golden Globe Awards '88: Best Actress—Drama (Weaver); Golden Globe Awards '89: Best Score. **VHS, Beta, LV** *MCA, HMV*

Gotcha!

PG-13/Jr. High-Adult The mock assassination game "Gotcha!" abounds on the college campus and sophomore Edwards is one of the best. What he doesn't know is that his "assassination" skills are about to take on new meaning when he meets up with a female Czech graduate student who is really an international spy.

BEWARE *Brief nudity, profanity, and assassination violence.*

1985 97m/C Anthony Edwards, Linda Fiorentino, Alex Rocco, Nick Corri, Marla Adams, Klaus Loewitsch, Christopher Rydell; **D:** Jeff Kanew; **W:** Dan Gordon; **M:** Bill Conti. **VHS, Beta, LV** *MCA*

Grandizer

Primary Japanese animation with toy connections, as a samurai-looking mechanical superhero tries to protect his adopted homeland, the planet Earth.
1982 101m/C VHS, Beta *FHE, TPV*

Grandpa Worked on the Railroad

Preschool-Primary Pictures in a magic scrapbook come alive and become film of steam locomotives as a father, played by Pete Shoemaker, helps four children learn about what it was like to working on the railroad in his grandfather's time. Folksinger Bruce (Utah) Phillips plays Grandpa. The children (and viewers) learn a lot about the days when steam was king they make up fun rhymes about what they've learned. No, they don't do the locomotion. Ages 2 to 9.
1994 30m/C VHS *FAF*

Granpa

Preschool-Primary A little girl and her grandfather spend a fun-filled day together. Based on the children's book by John Burningham.
1991 30m/C V: Peter Ustinov, Sarah Brightman. **VHS** *SMV, SIG, BTV*

Granpa

Preschool Peter Ustinov narrates this poignant and beautiful animated musical story of a grandfather's special relationship with his granddaughter, Emily. Everything they do together becomes a fantasy adventure: A rainy day turns into Noah's flood with its pairs of animals; a ride on a roller coaster becomes a flight in a World War II airplane. Then, one day, Emily comes in from playing and Granpa has died. Her memories of him live on. A British production based on the book of the same name by John Burningham. Ages 4 and up.
1992 27m/C VHS *MLT*

The Grass is Always Greener Over the Septic Tank 🦴🦴

Family Based on Erma Bombeck's best-seller. A city family's flight to the supposed peace of suburbia turns out to be a comic compilation of complications. Made for TV.
1978 98m/C Carol Burnett, Charles Grodin, Linda Gray, Alex Rocco, Robert Sampson, Vicki Belmonte, Craig Richard Nelson, Anrae Walterhouse, Eric Stoltz; **D:** Robert Day. **VHS, Beta** *NO*

The Grasshopper and the Ants

Preschool-Primary Animated Aesop fable pounds home the necessity of hard work.
1979 8m/C VHS, Beta *DSN,, MTI*

Grease 🦴🦴 🕊

PG/Jr. High-Adult Stage to screen musical sendup of '50s teens and rock'n'roll regarded by some as an unintentional camp classic. After a summer romance Danny and Sandy break up under high-school peer pressure; he's supposed to act macho and mean, she's urged to behave like a bad girl. Ultimately she does to get him back. There's also a makeout scene with an anti-condom punchline. With a likeable cast (all about ten years too old for their roles), and good dancing, this was a megahit among adolescent audiences in the '70s. That explains a lot. Dig that animated title sequence—this was once planned as a cartoon feature. 🎵 Grease; Summer Nights; Hopelessly Devoted To You; You're the One That I Want; Sandy; Beauty School Dropout; Look at Me, I'm Sandra Dee; Greased Lightnin'; It's Raining on Prom Night.

BEWARE *Alcohol use and much sex talk and sex songs. One character thinks she's pregnant. And why does Sandy have to dress trampy to get the guy??*

1978 110m/C John Travolta, Olivia Newton-John, Jeff Conaway, Stockard Channing, Eve Arden, Frankie Avalon, Sid Caesar; **D:** Randal Kleiser. **Award Nominations:** Academy Awards '78: Best Song ("Hopelessly Devoted to You"); **Awards:** People's Choice Awards '79: Best Film. **VHS, Beta, LV** *PAR, FCT*

Grease 2 🦴 🕊

PG/Jr. High-Adult There's no need for this Grease revival, a wretched sequel to the popular musical that spoofed the 1950s. Gone are Olivia Newton-John and John Travolta (they graduated). Michelle Pfeiffer and Maxwell Caulfield take their places. Adrian Zmed is there, too. A plot and decent tunes are, alas, absent. Ages 9 to 12.
1982 115m/C Maxwell Caulfield, Michelle Pfeiffer, Adrian Zmed, Lorna Luft, Didi Conn, Eve Arden, Sid Caesar, Tab Hunter; **D:** Patricia Birch. **VHS, Beta, LV** *PAR*

Greased Lightning 🦴🦴

PG/Jr. High-Adult The story of the first black auto racing champion, Wendell Scott, who had to overcome racial prejudice to achieve his success. Pryor's efforts are wasted. Richie Havens and Julian Bond put in an appearance. Ages 9 and up.
1977 95m/C Richard Pryor, Pam Grier, Beau Bridges, Cleavon Little, Vincent Gardenia; **D:** Michael A. Schultz; **W:** Leon Capetanos, Melvin Van Peebles. **VHS, Beta** *WAR*

Great Adventure 🦴🦴

PG/Jr. High-Adult In the severe environment of the gold rush days in the rugged Yukon territory, a touching tale unfolds of a young orphan boy and his eternal bond of friendship with a great northern dog. Italian-made adaption of a Jack London story.
1975 90m/C Jack Palance, Joan Collins, Fred Romer, Elisabetta Virgili, Remo de Angelis, Manuel de Blas; **D:** Paul Elliotts. **VHS, Beta** *MED, VTR*

Great Bible Stories: Abraham

Preschool-Primary One of a series of animated volumes relating well-known (and not so well-known) stories from the Bible in cartoon form; this tape covers the saga of

Abraham's unyielding faith, as well as the tale "Naaman and the Slave Girl." Additional volumes available.
1986 30m/C VHS, Beta *BFV*

The Great Cheese Conspiracy

Preschool-Primary Two mice plus one rat in a New York City cinema watch so many spy and gangster movies that they get the crime bug and plan a cheese-stealing caper. Animation based on a book by Jan van Leewen.
1991 60m/C D: Vaclav Bedrick. **VHS** *JFK*

The Great Land of Small

G/Preschool-Jr. High A rare misstep in the superb "Tales for All" series by Canadian producer Rock Demers; this is a strange mixture of dream imagery, circus stunts, and forced whimsy centering on a bag of magic gold stolen from a fairy kingdom. The elf responsible befriends two human children and takes them to visit the Great Land of Small, where a sad-eyed muck monster/mediator/god called Slimo both rewards and punishes the inhabitants by swallowing them. Huh? Maybe kids can explain it better.
1986 94m/C Karen Elkin, Michael Blouin, Michael Anderson Jr., Ken Roberts; **D:** Vojtech Jasny. **VHS, Beta** *VTR, NWV, HHE*

The Great Mike

Jr. High-Adult Unlikely but moving story of a young boy who convinces track management that his work horse has a chance against the touted thoroughbred. Sentimental, with little innovation, but generally well-acted.
1944 72m/B Stuart Erwin, Robert "Buzzy" Henry, Pierre Watkin, Gwen Kenyon, Carl "Alfalfa" Switzer, Edythe Elliott, Marion Martin; **D:** Wallace Fox. **VHS** *NOS*

The Great Mouse Detective

G/Family Disney animated version of the "Basil of Baker Street" stories by Eve Titus, with the exploits of a crime-fighting mouse who also resides at 221B Baker Street and styles himself as a Sherlock Holmes of the mouse world. Here he foils a plot against the rodent royal family. Not classic Disney—we defy you to remember one song afterwards—but Vincent Price lends terrific vocals to the insidious Professor Ratigan.
1986 74m/C D: John Musker, Ron Clements, Dave Michener, Burny Mattinson; **W:** Dave Michener; **M:** Henry Mancini; **V:** Vincent Price, Barrie Ingham, Val Bettin, Susanne Pollatschek, Candy Candido, Eve Brenner, Alan Young, Melissa Manchester. **VHS, Beta, LV** *DIS, OM*

The Great Muppet Caper

G/Family The followup to the original "Muppet Movie" is more like an extended musical parody skit from TV's "Muppet Show." And what's wrong with that? Writing is clever and filled with gag movie references for grownups, as Kermit the Frog and Fozzie Bear play twin brothers (!) investigating a jewel heist in London. Watch for Jim Henson's cameo in the supper club.

1981 95m/C Jim Henson's Muppets, Charles Grodin, Diana Rigg; *Cameos:* John Cleese, Robert Morley, Peter Ustinov, Peter Falk, Jack Warden; **D:** Jim Henson; **W:** Jack Rose; **V:** Frank Oz. **VHS, Beta, LV** *JHV, FOX*

The Great Outdoors

PG/Primary-Adult John "Home Alone" Hughes has a reputation for writing movies in a weekend. This one must have taken a lunch hour, as a family's peaceful summer vacation is disturbed by uninvited, trouble-making relatives. Aykroyd and Candy are two funny guys done in by a lame script that awkwardly examines friendship and growing up, then throws in a marauding bear when things get unbearably slow.

BEWARE *Salty language.*

1988 91m/C Dan Aykroyd, John Candy, Stephanie Faracy, Annette Bening, Chris Young, Lucy Deakins; **D:** Howard Deutch; **W:** John Hughes; **M:** Thomas Newman. **VHS, Beta, LV** *MCA*

Great Race

Family A dastardly villain, a noble hero and a spirited suffragette are among the competitors in an uproarious New York-to-Paris auto race circa 1908, complete with pie fights, saloon brawls, and a confrontation with a feisty polar bear. Road epic is jam-packed with stars but too long and only sporadically funny.
1965 160m/C Jack Lemmon, Tony Curtis, Natalie Wood, Peter Falk, Keenan Wynn, George Macready; **D:** Blake Edwards; **M:** Henry Mancini. **Award Nominations:** Academy Awards '65: Best Color Cinematography, Best Film Editing, Best Song ("The Sweetheart Tree"), Best Sound; **Awards:** Academy Awards '65: Best Sound Effects Editing. **VHS, Beta, LV** *WAR, FCT*

The Great Rupert

Family Few kids today have even heard of Jimmy Durante, and few parents have ever seen a Durante movie. This is one and it's good. A trained squirrel (a puppet) finds a large stash of money and brings it to down-and-out vaudeville performer Durante. Good fun. And good night, Mrs. Calabash, wherever you are. Ages 7 to 12.
1950 86m/B Jimmy Durante, Terry Moore, Tom Drake, Frank Orth, Sara Haden, Queenie Smith; **D:** Irving Pichel. **VHS, Beta** *DVT, HEG, VYY*

Great St. Trinian's Train Robbery

Jr. High-Adult Train robbers hide their considerable loot in an empty country mansion only to discover, upon returning years later, that the mansion has been converted into a girls' boarding school. When they try to recover the money, the thieves run up against a band of pestiferous adolescent girls, with hilarious results. Based on the cartoon by Ronald Searle. Sequel to "The Pure Hell of St. Trinian's."
1966 90m/C Dora Bryan, Frankie Howerd, Reg Varney, Desmond Walter Ellis; **D:** Sidney Gilliat, Frank Launder; **M:** Malcolm Arnold. **VHS, Beta** *NO*

John Travolta and pals dancing to "Greased Lightning" in "Grease."

The Great Santini 🐾🐾🐾

PG/Jr. High-Adult Lt. Col. Bull Meechum, a Marine pilot stationed stateside in a '60s southern town, fights private battles involving his frustrated career goals and repressed emotions. His kids become his platoon, as he abuses them in the name of discipline and allows himself no other way to show affection. Duvall stands out in successful blend of warm humor, tenderness, and the harsh cruelties inherent with dysfunctional families. Based on Pat Conroy's autobiographical novel, the movie was virtually undistributed at first, then re-released due to critical acclaim. Also known as "The Ace."

⚠ BEWARE *Child abuse, violence and frequent profanity. Pretend vomit.*

1980 118m/C Robert Duvall, Blythe Danner, Michael O'Keefe, Julie Ann Haddock, Lisa Jane Persky, David Keith; *D:* Lewis John Carlino; *M:* Elmer Bernstein. **Award Nominations:** Academy Awards '80: Best Actor (Duvall), Best Supporting Actor (O'Keefe); **Awards:** Montreal World Film Festival '80: Best Actor (Duvall); National Board of Review Awards '80: 10 Best Films of the Year. **VHS, Beta, 8mm** *WAR*

The Great Train Robbery 🐾🐾🐾

PG/Jr. High-Adult A dapper thief (Sean Connery) plots to heist a British train carrying gold in 1855, the first robbery from a moving train. Well-designed, fast-moving costume piece based on Michael Crichton's best-selling novel, which was based on a true story. Ages 9 and up.

1979 111m/C Sean Connery, Donald Sutherland, Lesley-Anne Down, Alan Webb; *D:* Michael Crichton; *W:* Michael Crichton; *M:* Jerry Goldsmith. **VHS, Beta, LV** *MGM, FCT, HMV*

The Great Waldo Pepper 🐾🐾🐾

PG/Family Low key (for Hill) film about a WWI pilot-turned-barnstormer (Robert Redford) who gets hired as a stuntman for the movies. Features spectacular vintage aircraft flying sequences. Can't decide if it wants to be comedy or straight drama. Watch for early career appearance by Susan Sarandon. Ages 10 and up.

1975 107m/C Robert Redford, Susan Sarandon, Margot Kidder, Bo Svenson, Scott Newman, Geoffrey Lewis, Edward Herrmann; *D:* George Roy Hill; *W:* William Goldman; *M:* Henry Mancini. **VHS, Beta, LV** *MCA*

The Great White Hope 🐾🐾 ᐟ

PG/Jr. High-Adult A semi-fictionalized biography of boxer Jack Johnson, played by Jones, who became the first black heavyweight world champion in 1910. Alexander makes her film debut as the boxer's white lover, as both battle the racism of the times. Two Oscar-nominated performances in what is essentially an "opened-out" version of the Broadway play.

1970 103m/C James Earl Jones, Jane Alexander, Lou Gilbert, Joel Fluellen, Chester Morris, Robert Webber, Hal Holbrook, R.G. Armstrong, Moses Gunn, Scatman Crothers; *D:* Martin Ritt. **VHS, Beta** *FOX, FCT*

The Greatest 🐾 ᐟ

PG/Family Autobiography of Cassius Clay, the fighter who could float like a butterfly and sting like a bee. Ali plays himself, and George Benson's hit "The Greatest Love of All" is introduced.

1977 100m/C Muhammad Ali, Robert Duvall, Ernest Borgnine, James Earl Jones, John Marley, Roger E. Mosley, Dina Merrill, Paul Winfield; *D:* Tom Gries; *W:* Ring Lardner Jr. **VHS, Beta** *COL*

The Greatest Show on Earth 🐾🐾🐾

Jr. High-Adult Hollywood's most lavish vision of the circus, a wildly melodramatic and kitschy spectacle that will nonetheless keep you watching as a love triangle develops between the no-nonsense ringmaster (Heston), his tightrope-walking girlfriend, and an arrogant new trapeze artist. Numerous subplots include a clown with a guilty past (Jimmy Stewart's underneath all that greasepaint), and a train wreck and spectacular fire. But no matter what, the show must go on. Emmett Kelly, one of the most celebrated big top clowns in real life, has a supporting role.

⚠ BEWARE *Roughhousing.*

1952 149m/C Betty Hutton, Cornel Wilde, James Stewart, Charlton Heston, Dorothy Lamour, Lawrence Tierney; *D:* Cecil B. DeMille. **Award Nominations:** Academy Awards '52: Best Costume Design (Color), Best Director (DeMille), Best Film Editing; **Awards:** Academy Awards '52: Best Picture, Best Story; Golden Globe Awards '53: Best Director (DeMille), Best Film—Drama. **VHS, Beta, LV** *PAR, BTV*

Greedy 🐾 ᐟ

PG-13/Jr. High-Adult Money-grubbing family suck up to elderly millionaire uncle Douglas when they fear he'll leave his money to d'Abo, the sexy, young former pizza delivery girl he's hired as his nurse. Fox is the long-lost nephew who comes to the rescue. Wicked comedy from veterans Ganz and Mandel should zing, but instead falls flat thanks to a descent into the maudlin. Fox bares his backside and Douglas has fun as the mean old miser, but check out Hartman, a riot as a snarky relative.

⚠ BEWARE *Profanity, brief nudity, suggested sex and, oh yeah, greed.*

1994 109m/C Kirk Douglas, Michael J. Fox, Olivia D'Abo, Phil Hartman, Nancy Travis, Ed Begley Jr., Bob Balaban, Colleen Camp, Jere Burns, Khandi Alexander; *Cameos:* Jonathan Lynn; *D:* Jonathan Lynn; *W:* Lowell Ganz, Babaloo Mandel; *M:* Randy Edelman. **VHS, LV** *MCA*

Green Archer

Family 15 episode serial featuring a spooky castle complete with secret passages and tunnels, trapdoors, and the mysterious masked figure of the Green Archer.

1940 283m/B Victor Jory, Iris Meredith, James Craven, Robert Fiske; *D:* James W. Horne. **VHS, Beta** *VYY, NOS, VCN*

Green Card 🐾🐾 ᐟ

PG-13/Jr. High-Adult Some marry for love, some for money, others for an apartment in the Big Apple. Refined, single MacDowell covets a rent-controlled apartment in Manhattan, but the lease stipulates that the apartment be let to a married couple. Enter brusque and burly Depardieu, a foreigner who covets the elusive green card from the government allowing him to permanently stay in the States. A marriage of convenience will give them both what they want. Will this practical arrangement between two distinctly different people turn into something more romantic? Engaging romantic comedy was written by Director Weir with Depardieu, making his English-language debut, in mind.

 Profanity.

1990 108m/C Gerard Depardieu, Andie MacDowell, Bebe Neuwirth, Gregg Edelman, Robert Prosky, Jessie Keosian, Ann Wedgeworth, Ethan Phillips, Mary Louise Wilson, Lois Smith, Simon Jones; **D:** Peter Weir; **W:** Peter Weir; **M:** Hans Zimmer. **Award Nominations:** Academy Awards '90: Best Original Screenplay; Golden Globe Awards '91: Best Actress—Musical/Comedy (MacDowell); **Awards:** Golden Globe Awards '91: Best Actor—Musical/Comedy (Depardieu), Best Film—Musical/Comedy. **VHS, Beta, LV** *TOU*

Green Eggs and Ham from Dr. Seuss on the Loose

Primary Story unfolds in classical cumulative rhyme as "Sam I Am" tries to share his "Green Eggs and Ham" with an unwilling acquaintance from the book by Dr. Seuss

1974 9m/C VHS, Beta *BFA*

The Green Hornet

Family Cheapo production values stung this fast-paced serial adaptation of the famous radio superhero—a blood relative of the Lone Ranger, no less—who made "Flight of the Bumblebee" famous as his theme song. News editor Britt Reid uses the Green Hornet disguise for the first time in his fight against racketeers, but cops initially think the masked avenger is a villain himself. Oriental valet Cato, who comes up with the Hornet's gadgets, is here loudly identified as Korean; his race kept changing depending on the war situation in the Pacific. In 13 episodes.

 Violence.

1939 100m/B Gordon Jones, Keye Luke, Anne Nagel, Wade Boteler, Walter McGrail, Douglas Evans, Cy Kendall. **VHS, Beta** *NOS, GKK, GPV*

Greenstone

G/Family Micro-budgeted obscurity about a 12-year-old boy who finds the title gem near a forbidden forest. Lots of pointless chases as assorted giants, dwarfs and leprechauns seek the Greenstone; they're all played by normal-sized actors in Merrie Men costumes. Orson Welles narrates in overly-poetic style.

1985 48m/C Joseph Corey, John Riley, Kathleen Irvine, Jack Mauck; **D:** Kevin Irvine. **VHS, Beta** *AHV*

Gregory's Girl 🎬🎬🎬♪

Jr. High-Adult Sweet, disarming comedy established Forsyth. An awkward young Scottish schoolboy falls in love with the female goalie of his soccer team. He turns to his ten-year-old sister for advice, but she's more interested in ice cream than love. His best friend is no help, either, since he has yet to fall in love. Perfect mirror of teen-agers and their instantaneous, raw, and all-consuming loves. Very sweet scene with Gregory and his girl lying on their backs in an open space illustrates the simultaneous simplicity and complexity of young love.

1980 91m/C Gordon John Sinclair, Dee Hepburn, Jake D'Arcy, Chic Murray, Alex Norton, John Bett, Clare Grogan; **D:** Bill Forsyth; **W:** Bill Forsyth. **VHS, Beta** *TVC*

Gremlins 🎬🎬🎬

PG/Jr. High-Adult Comedy horror with deft satiric edge, produced by Spielberg. Fumbling gadget salesman Rand Peltzer is looking for something really special to get his son Billy. He finds a small, adorable creature in Chinatown, but the "mogwai" mutates into a gang of nasty gremlins who tear up the town on Christmas Eve. The switch from cuteness to terror is jarring, but be ready for it and enjoy the ride.

 Violence (the worst committed against non-humans, of course), profanity, grotesque little creatures.

1984 106m/C Zach Galligan, Phoebe Cates, Hoyt Axton, Polly Holliday, Frances Lee McCain, Keye Luke, Dick Miller, Corey Feldman, Judge Reinhold; **D:** Joe Dante; **W:** Chris Columbus; **M:** Jerry Goldsmith. **VHS, Beta, LV, 8mm** *WAR, TLF*

Gremlins 2: The New Batch 🎬🎬🎬

PG-13/Jr. High-Adult Sequel to "Gremlins" sets the little monsters loose in a futuristic skyscraper in New York, where they overrun the empire and ambitions of a greedy real-estate/cable-TV magnate who plans to exploit them. Less violent and far more campy than the last infestations, with director Dante paying myriad surreal tributes to scores of movies, including "The Wizard of Oz" plus slams against modern urban living. Great fun, with Tony Randall as the voice of the Gremlin leader heading a long list of celebrity cameos.

 Gremlin violence similar to the original except mostly in a tall building, rather than the small town.

1990 107m/C Phoebe Cates, Christopher Lee, John Glover, Zach Galligan; **Cameos:** Jerry Goldsmith; **D:** Joe Dante; **M:** Jerry Goldsmith. **VHS, Beta, LV, 8mm** *WAR, HHE*

Grendel, Grendel, Grendel 🎬🎬

Family Urbane, ogre-like monster wants to be friends, but people are just terrified of Grendel. The tale sounds like "Casper the Friendly Ghost," but the intent is more serious (unfortunately, the animation is still Saturday-morning level) in this revision of the Beowulf legend, based on the novel by John Gardner.

1982 90m/C D: Alexander Stitt; **M:** Bruce Smeaton; **V:** Peter Ustinov, Arthur Dignam, Julie McKenna, Keith Michell. **VHS, Beta** *FHE*

The Grey Fox

PG/Jr. High-Adult A gentlemanly old stagecoach robber tries to pick up his life after thirty years in prison. Unable to resist another heist, he tries train robbery, and winds up hiding out in British Columbia where he meets an attractive photographer, come to document the changing West. Farnsworth is perfect as the man who suddenly finds himself in the 20th century trying to work at the only craft he knows. Based on the true story of Canada's most colorful and celebrated outlaw, Bill Miner.

 *Brief violence.*

1983 92m/C Richard Farnsworth, Jackie Burroughs, Wayne Robson, Timothy Webber, Ken Pogue; **D:** Phillip Borsos; **M:** Michael Conway Baker. **VHS, Beta, LV** *MED*

Greyfriars Bobby

Family True story of a Skye terrier named Bobby who, after his pauper master dies, refuses to leave the grave. Even after being coaxed by the local children into town, he still returns to the cemetery each evening. Eventually the loyal Bobby becomes the pet of 19th century Edinburgh. Nicely done by the Disney crew, with fine location photography and good acting. Great for children and animal lovers, and if you prefer collies, the same plot was used for earlier "Challenge to Lassie."

1961 91m/C Donald Crisp, Laurence Naismith, Kay Walsh; **D:** Don Chaffey. **VHS** *DIS*

Greystoke: The Legend of Tarzan, Lord of the Apes

PG/Jr. High-Adult The seventh Earl of Greystoke becomes a shipwrecked orphan and is raised by apes. Ruling the ape-clan in the vine-swinging persona of Tarzan, he is discovered by an anthropologist and returned to his ancestral home in Scotland, where he is immediately recognized by his grandfather. The contrast between the behavior of man and ape is interesting, and Tarzan's introduction to society is fun, but there's no melodrama or vine-hanging action, as we've come to expect of the Tarzan genre. Due to her heavy southern accent, MacDowell (as Jane) had her voice dubbed by Glenn Close.

BEWARE *Brief nudity and violence. A monkey is killed during a macho-monkey battle.*

1984 130m/C Christopher Lambert, Ralph Richardson, Ian Holm, James Fox, Andie MacDowell, Ian Charleson, Cheryl Campbell, Nigel Davenport; **D:** Hugh Hudson. **VHS, Beta, LV** *WAR*

Grimm's Fairy Tales: Beauty and the Beast

Preschool-Primary Animated retelling of the classic French story of the beautiful maiden and the fearsome beast, teaching "Don't judge a book by its cover." Additional fairytales available.

1990 27m/C VHS *VTR*

Grizzly Adams: The Legend Continues

Family Obscure attempt to revive the popular mountain man character but without original actor Dan Haggerty. A small town is saved from three desperadoes by Grizzly and his huge bear pet Martha.

1990 90m/C Gene Edwards, Link Wyler, Red West, Tony Caruso, Acquanetta, L.Q. Jones; **D:** Ken Kennedy. **VHS** *NO*

Gross Anatomy

PG-13/Sr. High-Adult Lightweight comedy/drama centers on the trials and tribulations of medical students. Modine is the very bright, but somewhat lazy, future doctor determined not to buy into the bitter competition among his fellow students. His lack of desire inflames Lahti, a professor dying of a fatal disease who nevertheless believes in modern medicine. She pushes and inspires him to focus on his potential, and his desire to help people. Worth watching, in spite of cheap laughs. Interesting cast of up-and-comers.

BEWARE *Profanity. Despite title, it's not "Police Academy Goes to Med School."*

1989 107m/C Matthew Modine, Daphne Zuniga, Christine Lahti, John Scott Clough, Alice Carter, Robert Desiderio, Zakes Mokae, Todd Field; **D:** Thom Eberhardt; **W:** Ron Nyswaner; **M:** David Newman. **VHS, Beta, LV** *TOU*

Groundhog Day

PG/Jr. High-Adult Phil, (Murray) an obnoxious weatherman, is in Punxatawney, PA to cover the annual emergence of the famous rodent from its hole. After he's caught in a blizzard that he didn't predict, he finds himself trapped in a time warp, doomed to relive the same day over and over again until he gets it right. Lighthearted romantic comedy takes a funny premise and manages to carry it through to the end. Murray has fun with the role, although he did get bitten by the groundhog during the scene where they're driving. Elliott, who has been missed since his days as the man under the seats on "Late Night with David Letterman" (forget "Cabin Boy") is perfectly cast as a smart-mouthed cameraman.

BEWARE *Profanity, a punch is thrown, dangerous driving and a snowball fight.*

1993 103m/C Bill Murray, Andie MacDowell, Chris Elliott, Stephen Tobolowsky, Brian Doyle-Murray, Marita Geraghty, Angela Paton; **D:** Harold Ramis; **W:** Harold Ramis, Daniel F. Rubin; **M:** George Fenton. **VHS, LV** *COL, FCT, BTV*

Grumpier Old Men

PG-13/Jr. High-Adult Max (Matthau) and John (Lemmon) are back at each other's throats. Of course, with John happily married to Ariel (Ann-Margret), what does he have to grump about? Enter Maria (Loren), who wants to turn the boys' favorite bait shop into an Italian restaurant. In a twist that should surprise no one, Max soon falls for the beautiful Maria, and she with him. Mama mia.

Sequel doesn't measure up to the original, but kids may find it reassuring that despite all that fighting people can remain friends forever.

BEWARE *Salty language, innuendos and marinara sauce abuse.*

1995 105m/C Jack Lemmon, Walter Matthau, Ann-Margret, Sophia Loren, Kevin Pollak, Burgess Meredith, Daryl Hannah, Ann Guilbert; **D:** Howard Deutch; **W:** Mark Steven Johnson; **C:** Tak Fujimoto; **M:** Alan Silvestri. **VHS** *NYR*

Grumpy Old Men 🦴🦴🦴

PG-13/Jr. High-Adult Lemmon and Matthau team for their seventh movie, in parts that seem written just for them. Boyhood friends and retired neighbors, they have been feuding for so long that neither of them can remember why. Doesn't matter much, when it provides a reason for them to spout off at each other every morning and play nasty practical jokes every night. This, and ice-fishing, is life as they know it, until feisty younger woman Ann-Margret moves into the neighborhood and lights some long dormant fires. Eighty-three-year old Meredith is a special treat playing Lemmon's extremely feisty ninetysomething father. Filmed in Wabasha, Minnesota, and grumpy, in the most pleasant way.

BEWARE *Profanity, fogey roughhousing, ice fishing. A character has a near-fatal scare.*

1993 104m/C Jack Lemmon, Walter Matthau, Ann-Margret, Burgess Meredith, Daryl Hannah, Kevin Pollak, Ossie Davis, Buck Henry, Christopher McDonald; **D:** Donald Petrie; **W:** Mark Steven Johnson; **M:** Alan Silvestri. **VHS, LV, 8mm** *WAR*

Gryphon

Family New substitute teacher at Ricky's inner-city school can do all sorts of magical things, like materializing angels and seeing dragons. Hidden among her tricks are lessons in creativity, beauty and imagination. New-Age spaciness intrudes in this family drama, aired on PBS as part of the "WonderWorks" series.

1988 58m/C Amanda Plummer, Sully Diaz, Alexis Cruz; **D:** Mark Cullingham. **VHS** *PME, FCT, BTV*

Guarding Tess 🦴🦴

PG-13/Jr. High-Adult Long-suffering Secret Service agent Cage is nearing the end of his three-year assignment to crotchety widowed First Lady MacLaine when the Prez extends his tour of duty. Feels like a TV movie, not surprising since writers Torokvei and Wilson have several sitcoms to their credit, including "WKRP in Cincinnati." Nice chemistry between Cage and MacLaine results in a few funny moments, but there are too many formulaic plot twists. A pleasant, if somewhat slow buddy comedy.

BEWARE *Some profanity and slight violence.*

1994 98m/C Shirley MacLaine, Nicolas Cage, Austin Pendleton, Edward Albert, Richard Griffiths; **D:** Hugh Wilson; **W:** Peter Torokvei, Hugh Wilson; **C:** Brian Reynolds; **M:** Michael Convertino. **VHS, LV, 8mm** *COL*

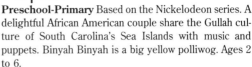

Gullah Gullah Island: Binyah's Surprise

Preschool-Primary Based on the Nickelodeon series. A delightful African American couple share the Gullah culture of South Carolina's Sea Islands with music and puppets. Binyah Binyah is a big yellow polliwog. Ages 2 to 6.

1995 m/C VHS

Gulliver in Lilliput 🦴🦴🦴

Family Live-action British TV adaptation of the Jonathan Swift classic that effectively preserves the stinging satire of the original, as gentleman castaway Gulliver deals with the petty rivalries rampant amidst the arrogant Lilliputian royalty. Tale is told largely from the point of the little people, who treat the giant Gulliver as a social inferior even as he defeats their enemies (scenes done through storybook illustrations rather than special f/x). Themes may be a bit complex for very young viewers, but those who stick with it will be rewarded.

BEWARE *Mildly risque, as a married lady in the palace makes the big guy the object of her (platonic) affections.*

1982 107m/C Andrew Burt, Linda Polan, Jonathan Cecil; **D:** Barry Letts. **VHS, Beta** *FOX*

Gulliver's Travels 🦴🦴 ◁

Family Max and Dave Fleischer, animation pioneers best known for "Popeye," tried to follow Walt Disney into the cartoon-feature arena with this version of castaway Gulliver's adventure in Lilliput, the island where the squabbling inhabitants average about two inches tall. Not up to "Snow White" standards, and certainly not Jonathan Swift, but still a 'toon treat thanks to glorious artwork. Gulliver, a live actor inked over in the rotoscope process, is awesome. The hilarious Gabby ("There's a giant on the beach!") was popular enough to get his own series of short subjects.

1939 74m/C D: Dave Fleischer; **V:** Lanny Ross, Jessica Dragonette. **VHS, LV** *CNG, MRV, NOS*

Gulliver's Travels 🦴🦴

G/Family Partially animated Commonwealth version of Jonathan Swift's classic finds Lemuel Gulliver shipwrecked in the miniature land of Lilliput, but in real life the movie was all at sea when the filmmakers ran out of money for a time. The low-budget blues show on-screen; see instead the all-animated 1939 feature or better still, "Gulliver in Lilliput."

1977 80m/C Richard Harris, Catherine Schell; **D:** Peter Hunt. **VHS, Beta** *VCI, VTR, HHE*

Gulliver's Travels

Family Jonathan Swift's tale about a sailor whose voyage takes him to an unusual island populated by tiny people. As with most kid-minded adaptations, it leaves out the majority of the book and sugars the abundantly sour elements of Swift's satire. This Hanna-Barbera retelling is still more accurate than their '60s Saturday-morning series "The Adventures of Gulliver."
1979 52m/C VHS, Beta *WOV, GKK, KUI*

Gulliver's Travels

Primary-Jr. High Yet another animated interpretation of Jonathan Swift's 18th century satire, done in "classics illustrated" fashion.
1992 47m/C VHS *BAR*

Gumball Rally

PG/Sr. High-Adult An unusual assortment of people converge upon New York for a cross country car race to Long Beach, California where breaking the rules is part of the game.

BEWARE *Salty language.*

1976 107m/C Michael Sarrazin, Gary Busey, Raul Julia, Nicholas Pryor, Tim McIntire, Susan Flannery; **D:** Chuck Bail; **W:** Leon Capetanos. **VHS, Beta** *WAR*

Gumby Adventures

Preschool-Primary Those timeless clay animation heroes, Gumby and Pokey, originally guests on the "Howdy Doody" program, battle evil and the Blockheads in this series of tapes. Each cassette includes 8 or 9 episodes of this TV staple.
1956 50m/C VHS, Beta *FHE*

Gumby and the Moon Boggles

Family Five episodes featuring the memorable green stop-motion character, in imaginative shorts that still stand up well today: "Indian Trouble," "Weight and See," "Mystic Magic," "Gabby Auntie," and the title episode.
1956 30m/C VHS, Beta *FHE*

Gumby: The Movie

G/Family Gumby may be flexible, but a full-length movie is stretching things too far. The Green One and his musical group, the Clayboys, seek to save their neighbors' farms from foreclosure by putting on a benefit concert (Gumb Aid?). And yes, horse pal Pokey is along to help out. An hour-and-a-half with our gentle clay hero, though, is a lot of time to kiln.
1995 90m/C D: Art Clokey; **W:** Art Clokey. **VHS** *KID*

Gumby, Vol. 1: The Return of Gumby

Family Nine episodes featuring the little green guy and his pal Pokey. Includes "Witty Witch," "Hot Rod Granny," and much more! Additional volumes available.
1956 50m/C VHS *FHE*

Gumby's Holiday Special

Family Gumby, Pokey, Prickle, and Goo celebrate the holidays in their own special way.
1956 60m/C VHS *FHE*

Gumby's Supporting Cast

Family Series featuring the clay-animated adventures of Gumby's buddies, with six 6-minute episodes per program.
1986 42m/C VHS, Beta *FHE*

Gung Ho

PG-13/Sr. High-Adult Ethnic stereotyping is the order of the day as a Japanese firm takes over a small-town U.S. auto factory, causing major cultural collisions. Keaton plays the go-between for employees and management while trying to keep both groups from killing each other. From the director of "Splash" and "Night Shift." Made into a short-lived television series.

BEWARE *Salty language.*

1985 111m/C Michael Keaton, Gedde Watanabe, George Wendt, Mimi Rogers, John Turturro, Clint Howard, Michelle Johnson, So Yamamura, Sab Shimono; **D:** Ron Howard; **W:** Babaloo Mandel, Lowell Ganz; **M:** Thomas Newman. **VHS, Beta, LV, 8mm** *PAR*

Guns of the Magnificent Seven

G/Jr. High-Adult The third remake of "The Seven Samurai." Action-packed western in which the seven free political prisoners and train them to kill. The war party then heads out to rescue a Mexican revolutionary being held in an impregnable fortress.
1969 106m/C George Kennedy, Monte Markham, James Whitmore, Reni Santoni, Bernie Casey, Joe Don Baker, Scott Thomas, Michael Ansara, Fernando Rey; **D:** Paul Wendkos; **M:** Elmer Bernstein. **VHS** *MGM*

Gus

G/Family The California Atoms football team has the worst record in the league until they begin winning games with the help of their field-goal kicking mule of a mascot, Gus. Gridiron rivals then plot a donkey-napping. Wackier than usual premise and a good comic ensemble breathe life into this predictable Disney farce.
1976 96m/C Ed Asner, Tim Conway, Dick Van Patten, Ronnie Schell, Bob Crane, Tom Bosley; **D:** Vincent McEveety. **VHS, Beta, LV** *COL, DIS*

Guys and Dolls 🦴🦴🦴

Family New York gambler Sky Masterson takes a bet that he can romance a Salvation Army lady. Based on the stories of Damon Runyon with Blaine, Kaye, Pully, and Silver recreating their roles from the Broadway hit. Brando's not-always-convincing musical debut. 🎵 More I Cannot Wish You; My Time of Day; Guys and Dolls; Fugue for Tinhorns; Follow the Fold; Sue Me; Take Back Your Mink; If I Were a Bell; Luck Be a Lady.

1955 150m/C Marlon Brando, Jean Simmons, Frank Sinatra, Vivian Blaine, Stubby Kaye, Sheldon Leonard, Veda Ann Borg; **D:** Joseph L. Mankiewicz; **W:** Joseph L. Mankiewicz; **M:** Frank Loesser. **Award Nominations:** Academy Awards '55: Best Art Direction/Set Decoration (Color), Best Color Cinematography, Best Costume Design (Color), Best Original Score; **Awards:** Golden Globe Awards '56: Best Actress—Musical/Comedy (Simmons), Best Film—Musical/Comedy. **VHS, Beta, LV** *FOX, FCT*

Gypsy Colt 🦴🦴🦴

G/Family "Lassie" with a species change; Gypsy is the horse beloved by the young Meg. But drought forces her family to sell the animal to a racing stable 500 miles away. Gypsy escapes and starts out on a journey to be reunited with Meg.

1954 72m/C Donna Corcoran, Ward Bond, Frances Dee, Lee Van Cleef, Larry Keating; **D:** Andrew Marton. **VHS** *MGM, FCT*

Hackers 🦴🦴

PG-13/Jr. High-Adult Dade Murphy, age 11, creates a computer virus that wreaks havoc on 1,500 corporations and causes a drop in the stock market. Heavily armed police surround Dade's peaceful Seattle home. What a great idea for a movie. So much for the first two minutes of "Hackers." It's repetitively downhill after that with Dade (Jonny Lee Miller), now 18, off probation, in high school. With his grungy cyber sidekicks, Dade matches wits with a murderous corporation. The tale of hacker vs. monsters of the microchip was told better in films from the computer Stone Age, "WarGames" (1983) and "Sneakers" (1993).

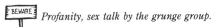 *Profanity, sex talk by the grunge group.*

1995 105m/C Jonny Lee Miller, Angelina Jolie, Fisher Stevens, Lorraine Bracco, Jesse Bradford, Wendell Pierce, Alberta Watson, Laurence Mason, Renoly Santiago, Matthew Lillard, Penn Jillette; **D:** Iain Softley; **W:** Rafael Moreu; **C:** Andrzej Sekula; **M:** Simon Boswell. **VHS, LV** *MGM*

Hadley's Rebellion 🦴🦴

PG/Jr. High-Adult Shy Georgia farm boy adjusts to life at an elitist California boarding school by flaunting his wrestling abilities. Eventually he realizes it takes more than that to be a man. Middling blend of low-key sports drama and coming-of-age tale.

 Salty language, roughhousing.

1984 96m/C Griffin O'Neal, Charles Durning, William Devane, Adam Baldwin, Dennis Hage, Lisa Lucas; **D:** Fred Walton; **W:** Fred Walton. **VHS, Beta** *FOX*

Hair Bear Bunch

Preschool-Primary Hanna-Barberian collection of five cartoons about a trio of bears who are always devising ways to escape from the zoo in which they live.

1984 85m/C VHS, Beta *TTC*

Hairspray 🦴🦴🦴

PG/Sr. High-Adult Waters, a cult filmmaker infamous for sleazo spoofs, pleased and surprised everyone with this wild comedy detailing 1962 Baltimore and teen rivals after the top spot in a local TV dance show. Deals with racism and stereotypes, as well as typical youth problems—like hair-do's and "hair-don'ts." Filled with refreshingly tasteful, subtle social satire, but not without demented touches. Only a movie rebel like Waters would create heroine like Ricki Lake's, an appealing girl who's fat and not ashamed by it. Her mom is played by a Waters mainstay, hefty transvestite actor Divine. Watch for the writer/director's cameo as a crazed shrink, listen for great 60s music.

 Profanity, transvestism, and Sonny Bono.

1988 94m/C Ricki Lake, Divine, Jerry Stiller, Colleen Fitzpatrick, Sonny Bono, Deborah Harry, Ruth Brown, Pia Zadora, Ric Ocasek, Michael St. Gerard, Leslie Ann Powers, Shawn Thompson; **Cameos:** John Waters; **D:** John Waters; **W:** John Waters. **VHS, Beta, LV** *COL, FCT*

The Halfback of Notre Dame 🦴🦴🦴

G/Family This story presents a little different twist on "The Hunchback of Notre Dame." The Quasimodo character takes on the form of star football player (and coach's son) Craig Modeau (Hogan), a lumbering misfit, constantly teased everywhere except on the field. French exchange student Esmerelda (Vaugier) thinks he's sweet—much to the dismay of current boyfriend, obnoxious quarterback Archie (Cutler). But when Craig quits the team right before the big game, it's up to Esmerelda to convince him to play.

1996 97m/C Gabriel Hogan, Emmanuelle Vaugier, Scott Hylands, Sandra Nelson, Allen Cutler; **D:** Rene Bonniere; **W:** Richard Clark, Mark Trafficante; **C:** Maris Jansons; **M:** George Blondheim. **VHS, LV** *HMK*

Halloween is Grinch Night

Family Dr. Seuss TV cartoon that serves as a follow-up to the classic "How the Grinch Stole Christmas." On Halloween night a lad named Eukariah saves Whoville from the schemes of the ever-unsociable Grinch.

1977 25m/C VHS

Hambone & Hillie 🦴🦴🦴

PG/Family Elderly woman traveller is separated from her dog during an airport transfer. Hambone makes a heroic 3000-mile trek across the United States to return to her. Sometimes entertaining, sometimes dull as the pooch stumbles into one subplot after another.

BEWARE *Brief and quite out-of-place violence.*

1984 97m/C Lillian Gish, Timothy Bottoms, Candy Clark, O.J. Simpson, Robert Walker Jr., Jack Carter, Alan Hale Jr., Anne Lockhart; *D:* Roy Watts. **VHS, Beta** *VTR*

Hang Your Hat on the Wind

Preschool-Primary A Navajo boy finds a renegade horse and is forced to choose whether to keep it or return it. The parish priest helps him to make the right choice in this episode from TV's "Wonderful World of Disney."
1990 46m/C VHS, Beta *MTI, DSN*

Hanna-Barbera Storybook Classics

Family Animated series of short features adapted from great works and characters of literature, given generally unspectacular renderings by the Hanna-Barbera 'toon factory. Individual titles: "Black Beauty," "The Count of Monte Cristo," "Cyrano," "Daniel Boone," "Davy Crockett on the Mississippi," "Gulliver's Travels," "Heidi's Song," "Jack and the Beanstalk," "Last of the Mohicans," "Oliver and the Artful Dodger," "The Three Musketeers," and "20,000 Leagues Under the Sea."
1973 50m/C VHS, Beta *TTC*

Hans Brinker 🎵🎵 ▷

Family Made-for-TV version of the 1865 novel by Mary Mapes Dodge, about Dutch youth Hans who enters an ice-skating race across Holland's frozen canals to earn money for his father's operation. Musical numbers don't add much, but the tale (nicely filmed in Amsterdam) comes to an exciting conclusion nonetheless.
1969 103m/C Robin Askwith, Eleanor Parker, Richard Basehart, Cyril Ritchard, John Gregson; *D:* Robert Scheerer. **VHS, Beta** *WAR, OM*

Hansel and Gretel

Family From Shelly Duvall's "Faerie Tale Theatre" comes the story of two young children who get more than they bargained for when they eat a gingerbread house. For one thing, they get Joan Collins as the witch. At least she doesn't force them to hear excerpts from her new novel. Ages 4 to 9.
1982 51m/C Rick Schroder, Joan Collins, Paul Dooley, Bridgette Anderson; *D:* James Frawley. **VHS, Beta, LV** *KUI, FOX, FCT*

Hansel & Gretel: An Opera Fantasy

Family Englebert Humperdinck's 1893 opera is re-created through hand-sculpted dolls and lavish sets. Ages 4 and up.
1994 72m/C VHS *VWV*

Hanukkah Tales & Tunes

Preschool-Primary Sing-along songs, stories, and games teach children the traditions surrounding the Festival of Lights. Includes "The Dreidel Song" and other tunes performed in Hebrew and English, a Menorah-lighting ceremony, and a story about a greedy goblin. Ages 3 to 10.
1994 30m/C VHS *VTR,*

Hap Palmer's Follow Along Songs

Preschool-Primary Young viewers are encouraged to sing along with their homemade musical instruments with "Baby Songs" singer Hap Palmer and his songs about colors and the alphabet.
1991 30m/C VHS *BTV*

The Happiest Millionaire 🎵🎵 ▷

Family Colorful period piece with musical interludes, about a newly immigrated lad who finds a job as butler in the home of an eccentric millionaire. Notable as the last Disney production personally okayed by Walt before his death, it's based on the book "My Philadelphia Father," by Kyle Chrichton. 🎵 What's Wrong With That?; Watch Your Footwork; Valentine Candy; Strengthen the Dwelling; I'll Always Be Irish; Bye-Yum Pum Pum; I Believe in This Country; Detroit; There Are Those.
1967 118m/C Fred MacMurray, Tommy Steele, Greer Garson, Geraldine Page, Lesley Ann Warren, John Davidson; *D:* Norman Tokar. **VHS, Beta** *DIS, OM*

Happily Ever After 🎵🎵

G/Family Non-Disney cartoon sequel to "Snow White" was long in the making, short in the theaters. Snow White and her Prince plan their wedding, but the Wicked Queen's brother, Lord Maliss, avenges his sister by kidnapping the groom. Because Disney has legal rights to the classic Seven Dwarfs, Snow White here seeks aid from their female cousins, the Dwarfelle. Matchless cast supplies voices to this tepid entertainment for the kiddies.
1993 80m/C *D:* John Howley; *W:* Martha Moran, Robby London; *V:* Dom DeLuise, Phyllis Diller, Zsa Zsa Gabor, Ed Asner, Sally Kellerman, Irene Cara, Carol Channing, Tracey Ullman. **VHS** *WOV*

Happy Birthday, Bugs: 50 Looney Years

Family The television special honoring the history and career of Bugs Bunny, including many old film clips. All ages.
1990 42m/C Milton Berle, Harry Anderson, Pierce Brosnan, Kirk Cameron, Phil Donahue, Joe Garagiola, Debbie Gibson, John Goodman, Valerie Harper, Chuck Norris, Fred Savage, Peter Scolari, Jane Seymour, William Shatner, Jon Voight, Cindy Williams, Dr. Ruth Westheimer, Vanna White, Geraldo Rivera, Pat Sajak, Tommy Lasorda, Whoopi Goldberg, Bill Cosby, Little Richard, Hulk Hogan, Mary Hart. **VHS, Beta** *WAR*

Happy Birthday, Moon and Other Stories

Preschool Four tales from children's literature come to life in this animated collection. Included are "Three Little Pigs," "The Napping House," "Peter's Chair" and the title tale about a little bear who wants to buy the moon a birthday present. Ages 2 to 6.
1989 35m/C VHS, Beta *CCC*

Happy Gilmore

PG-13/Jr. High-Adult Hockey player Gilmore (Sandler) has a wicked slap shot but can't skate worth a lick. He becomes a professional golfer and draws legions of working-class fans with his powerful drives. But, hoo boy, can he pitch a fit when he can't sink a putt. Speaking of putts, the tour's leading pro (McDonald) has it in for Happy, but never fear. Happy does seem to beat up (or try to beat up) 90% of the supporting cast, including aging game show host (and animal lover) Bob Barker in a charity pro-am.

> **BEWARE** *Frequent profanity, bare backsides, an abusive employee at a nursing home, and a character falls out a window. Happy autographs a woman's breasts (that must be why they call him Happy).*

1996 92m/C Adam Sandler, Christopher McDonald, Julie Bowen, Francis Bay, Ben Stiller, Richard Kiel, Joe Flaherty, Kevin Nealon, Alan Covert, Robert Smigel, Bob Barker, Dennis Dugan; **D:** Dennis Dugan; **W:** Adam Sandler, Tim Herlihy; **C:** Arthur Albert; **M:** Mark Mothersbaugh. **VHS** *NYR*

Happy Holidays with Darkwing Duck and Goofy

Family Two Christmas tales from recent made-for-TV Disney cartoons. Goofy gets carried away with decorations while son Max learns that silly family traditions really make the holiday special in "Have Yourself a Goofy Little Christmas." In "It's a Wonderful Leaf," Darkwing Duck saves Christmas for the citizens of St. Canard.
1993 47m/C VHS *DIS*

The Happy Prince

Primary There's nothing happy at all about Oscar Wilde's classic story of a prince and his friend, a stalwart little swallow, who sacrifice themselves for the poor. An uplifting tale for adults, but rare is the child who won't find it upsetting. An animated presentation from Reader's Digest, intended for preschoolers. Please don't let them see it. Ages 8 to 12.
1974 25m/C VHS, Beta *PYR, ECU*

Hard-Boiled Mahoney

Family Slip, Sach, and the rest of the Bowery Boys try to solve a mystery involving mysterious women and missing men. The last film in the series for Bobby Jordan, whose career was ended when he was injured in an accident involving a falling elevator.

1947 64m/B Leo Gorcey, Huntz Hall, Bobby Jordan, Billy Benedict, David Gorcey, Gabriel Dell, Teala Loring, Dan Seymour, Bernard Gorcey, Patti Brill, Betty Compson; **D:** William Beaudine. **VHS** *WAR*

A Hard Day's Night

Family On one hand, the Beatles' first film will reinforce your kids' belief that before they were born, everything was in black-and-white. On the other hand, it's proof that we had music videos, too. In this mockumentary John, George, Paul and Ringo are mobbed by fans, sing some hits, face the media, play with boats in the bathtub, crack wise and bubble over with charm and wit. But can you stand your kids walking around saying "Who's that lit'l old man?" ♫ A Hard Day's Night; Tell Me Why; I Should Have Known Better; She Loves You; I'm Happy Just To Dance With You; If I Fell; And I Love Her; This Boy; Can't Buy Me Love.
1964 90m/B John Lennon, Paul McCartney, George Harrison, Ringo Starr; **D:** Richard Lester. **VHS, Beta, LV, CD-I** *MVD, MPI, CRC*

Hardly Working

PG/Family Unemployed circus clown finds it difficult to adjust to real life, fumbling (well, he's a clown, right?) from one job to another. Continually threatens to dissolve into a disconnected series of skits, but some of them are funny, a few almost charming. Fans of Lewis and slapstick will appreciate it, but others need not bother.

> **BEWARE** *Alcohol use.*

1981 90m/C Jerry Lewis, Susan Oliver, Roger C. Carmel, Gary Lewis, Deanna Lund; **D:** Jerry Lewis; **W:** Jerry Lewis. **VHS, Beta** *FOX*

The Hare and the Hedgehog

Family One of the Grimm Brothers' lesser-known fairy tales, brought to animated life. One in a series of Grimm tales from the Nickelodeon cable TV channel.
1991 40m/C VHS *VTR*

Harley

PG/Jr. High-Adult Harley, an L.A. motorcycle delinquent, is sent to a Texas rehabilitation community. There, he bonds with an ex-biker, and may just find his way back down the straight and narrow path to virtue. But local citizens regard him with suspicion. Say, didn't Phillips do the same plot already as "Dakota?"
1990 80m/C Lou Diamond Phillips, Eli Cummins, DeWitt Jan, Valentine Kim; **D:** Fred Holmes; **W:** Frank Kuntz, Sandy Kuntz. **VHS** *VMK*

Harold and His Amazing Green Plants

Preschool-Primary This botanical bonanza explores the life cycle of the green plant, using a fun story line and bright animation.
1990 8m/C VHS, Beta *MTI, DSN*

Harold and the Purple Crayon and Other Harold Stories

Preschool-Primary Harold and his magic purple crayon in three animated adventures based on the books by author/illustrator George Crockett. Also includes a brief documentary about Crockett from animator Gene Deitch. **1993 27m/C VHS** *CCC, WKV, BTV*

Harper Valley P.T.A. 🦴🦴

PG/Jr. High-Adult A whole movie based on a Jeannie C. Riley song. Speaking of Jeannie, Barbara Eden stars as nonconformist housewife who takes on the Harper Valley PTA after it questions her parental capabilities. TV series followed. Ages 10 and up. **1978 93m/C** Barbara Eden, Nanette Fabray, Louis Nye, Pat Paulsen, Ronny Cox, Ron Masak, Audrey Christie, John Fiedler, Bob Hastings; **D:** Richard Bennett; **W:** Barry Schneider. **VHS, Beta** *VES*

Harriet the Spy 🦴🦴 ⌐

PG/Family Sixth-grader Harriet M. Welsh spies on everyone around her and encouraged by her nanny Golly, she writes down everything going on in her secret notebook, because she's determined to become a great writer. Unfortunately Harriet's imagination sometimes gets the best of her and when her notebook falls in the hands of family and friends, they are not too happy about the contents. Based on the award-winning novel by Louise Fitzhugh and presented by Nickelodeon Movies, this one is sure to please any young spy out there.

⚠️ BEWARE *Watch out—this one's not sugar-coated, because when Harriet gets mean, its pretty brutal.*

1996 101m/C Michelle Trachtenberg, Rosie O'Donnell, Vanessa Lee Chester, Gregory Edward Smith, Robert Joy, Eartha Kitt, J. Smith-Cameron; **D:** Bronwen Hughes; **W:** Douglas Petrie, Theresa Rebeck. **VHS** *NYR*

Harry & Son 🦴🦴

PG/Jr. High-Adult Crusty, widowed construction worker faces the problems of raising his teenaged offspring. Has Newman trademark all over it; he directed, co-wrote, and co-directed, making it a labor of love but less than stunning for all its parts and participants. Character-acting fest is potentially insightful; main complaint is we've seen this sort of plot plenty of times before.

⚠️ BEWARE *Profanity, sex talk, and father-son estrangement.*

1984 117m/C Paul Newman, Robby Benson, Ellen Barkin, Wilford Brimley, Judith Ivey, Ossie Davis, Morgan Freeman, Joanne Woodward; **D:** Paul Newman; **M:** Henry Mancini. **VHS, Beta, LV** *VES*

Harry and the Hendersons 🦴🦴 ⌐

PG/Jr. High-Adult Seattle family man accidentally runs down Bigfoot with his station wagon. Thinking the hairy giant dead, he brings home the body. But the man-beast revives, bewildered but friendly, though he's a tad rough on the furniture. Like any hairy, good-natured giant, he endears himself to the Hendersons, who do their best to conceal the big guy's presence from snoopy neighbors and a gun-toting hunter. Producer Steven Spielberg raided his own "E.T.," for this formula comedy about yet another middle-class household invaded by the fantastic. Well, better that Spielberg rip himself off than someone else, right? Nice little tale efficiently told, with Oscar-winning makeup and a fine performance from Lithgow as the frustrated dad. Eventually premise was used for a short-lived TV series.

⚠️ BEWARE *Sasquatch roughhousing.*

1987 111m/C John Lithgow, Melinda Dillon, Don Ameche, David Suchet, Margaret Langrick, Joshua Rudoy, Kevin Peter Hall, Lainie Kazan, M. Emmet Walsh; **D:** William Dear; **W:** William Dear, William E. Martin, Ezra D. Rappaport; **M:** Bruce Broughton. **VHS, Beta, LV** *MCA, APD*

Harry & Walter Go to New York 🦴🦴

PG/Family At the turn of the century, two vaudeville performers are hired by a crooked British entrepreneur for a wild crime scheme. The cast and crew try their hardest, but it's not enough to save this boring comedy. The vaudeville team of Caan and Gould perhaps served as a model for Beatty and Hoffman in "Ishtar." **1976 111m/C** James Caan, Elliott Gould, Michael Caine, Diane Keaton, Burt Young, Jack Gilford, Charles Durning, Lesley Ann Warren, Carol Kane; **D:** Mark Rydell; **M:** David Shire. **VHS, Beta, LV** *COL*

Hatari 🦴🦴🦴

Family Adventure-loving team of professional big game hunters ventures to East Africa to round up animals for zoos around the world. Led by Wayne, they get into a couple of scuffs along the way, including one with a lady photographer doing a story on the expedition. Extraordinary footage of Africa and the animals brought to life by a fantastic musical score, including the debut of Mancini's famous "Baby Elephant" tune. **1962 158m/C** John Wayne, Elsa Martinelli, Red Buttons, Hardy Kruger, Gerard Blain, Bruce Cabot; **D:** Howard Hawks; **M:** Henry Mancini. **VHS, Beta, LV** *PAR*

Haunted Mansion Mystery

Family ABC-TV production in which two children search for a million dollars in cash in a haunted mansion. **1983 42m/C VHS, Beta** *MTT, VTR*

The Haunting of Barney Palmer

Family New Zealand kid Barney fears he's inherited the family curse of magic powers after the death of a great-uncle, when he's suddenly tormented by eerie apparitions. Or something like that. This is surely the weirdest of the "WonderWorks" series, with some authentically chilling (non-gory) special f/x but a frantic, nearly incomprehensible plot, adapted by Margaret Mahy from her novel "The Haunting."

Adam Sandler as "Happy Gilmore" turns into an unlikely golf superstar.

You name the book—it's probably a movie. Well, not quite, but one thing is clear—books to film are all the rage. Take for instance the big screen releases of *The Secret Garden* and *The Adventures of Huck Finn* in 1993. And Disney has relied largely on print classics with *The Little Mermaid, The Jungle Book* and most recently, the adaptation of Victor Hugo's *The Hunchback of Notre Dame.*

But Disney is not alone on this boat. Remember Columbia Pictures' *Little Women* and Paramount Pictures' *The Indian in the Cupboard*? 1996 is no exception. Releases featuring Louise Fitzhugh's *Harriet the Spy* and Roald Dahl's *Matilda* graced the big screen in the summer months.

And Roald Dahl's stories are no stranger to the big screen. "Charlie and the Chocolate Factory" was adapted in 1971 as *Willy Wonka and the Chocolate Factory* and "The Witches" became a movie in 1990. Most recently "James and the Giant Peach" came to life through the work of director Henry Selick, "Matilda" through the eyes of Danny DeVito and "The BFG (The Big Friendly Giant)" arose from Dreamland. Obviously storytelling from books is here to stay in the film world.

199? 58m/C Ned Beatty, Alexis Banas, Eleanor Gibson. **VHS** *PME, FCT, BTV*

Have Picnic Basket, Will Travel

Preschool-Primary Vacation plans go haywire for Yogi Bear and the rest of the Hanna-Barbera gang.
19?? 90m/C VHS

Hawk of the Wilderness

Family A man, shipwrecked as an infant and reared on a remote island by native Indians, battle modern day pirates. 12-episode serial.
1938 195m/B Bruce (Herman Brix) Bennett, Mala, William Boyle; **D:** William Witney. **VHS, Beta** *VCN, MLB*

Hawmps! 🎬🎬

G/Family Old-west comedy from the makers of the "Benji" series focuses on a klutzy Civil War lieutenant ordered to try camels instead of horses in the American desert terrain. (You can hear the concept meeting on this one—we've done dogs to death; how about camels?) When the soldiers and animals begin to grow fond of each other, Congress orders the camels to be set free. Based on some sort of vague historical incident, and you'll quickly find out why there are a lot more movies about loyal dogs than camels. Course, it does have both Pickens and Pyle collaborating on old ham fest. Edited on video from an original length of 126 minutes.
1976 98m/C James Hampton, Christopher Connelly, Slim Pickens, Denver Pyle; **D:** Joe Camp. **VHS, Beta** *VES*

Hazel's People 🎬🎬 ♪

G/Family When a bitter student radical attends a friend's funeral in Mennonite country, the religious community's simple lifestyle soothes him and he tries to join. Despite a low budget approach and seriously dated 1960s elements, this drama of faith and doubt works more often than not, and it avoids simplifying a difficult subject. Based on the Merle Good novel "Happy as the Grass Was Green."
1975 105m/C Geraldine Page, Pat Hingle, Graham Beckel. **VHS, Beta** *VCI*

HBTV: Old Time Rock & Roll

Family Hanna-Barbera TV, get it? The Flintstones star in this animated music video for kids. Songs include Bob Seger's "Old Time Rock & Roll," "Teddy Bear" by Elvis, The Beach Boys' "Catch a Wave," "Da Doo Run Run" by Dave Edmunds, "See You Later Alligator" by Bill Haley & the Comets, and plenty more.
1986 30m/C VHS, Beta *TTC*

He-Man & the Masters of the Universe, Vol. 1

Primary-Jr. High He-Man and his friends from Eternia battle the evil Skeletor. "The Dragon Invasion" and "Curse of the Spellstone" are included. Additional volumes available.
1985 45m/C VHS, Beta, LV, 8mm *COL,*

Head 🎬🎬🎬

G/Family Infamously plotless musical comedy co-written by Nicholson starring the television fab four of the '60s, the Monkees, in their only film appearance. A number of guest stars appear and a collection of old movie clips are also included. ♫ Circle Sky; Can You Dig It; Long Title: Do I Have To Do This All Over Again; Daddy's Song; As We Go Along; The Porpoise Song.

1968 86m/C Peter Tork, Mickey Dolenz, Davy Jones, Michael Nesmith, Frank Zappa, Annette Funicello, Teri Garr; **D:** Bob Rafelson; **W:** Jack Nicholson, Bob Rafelson. **VHS, Beta, LV** *MVD, COL*

Heart and Souls ♫♫ ▷

PG-13/Jr. High-Adult Romantic comedy involving reincarnation casts Downey, Jr. as a mortal whose body is inhabited by four lost souls who died in a bus accident on the night he was born. Now a frustrated, self-centered adult, he must finish what they could not, no matter how outrageous the request. And his dead soulmates have only so much time before the big bus from the sky descends and takes them away. Talented cast carries the sometime creaky story (Sizemore particularly shines), creating a little magic amid the sentimentality. Downey, who demonstrated strong mimicry and physical comedy skills in "Chaplin," again displays his considerable talents.

> 🛑 BEWARE 🛑 *A fatal bus crash. Profanity, sex talk, and bizarre reincarnation, but mostly harmless fun.*

1993 104m/C Robert Downey Jr., Charles Grodin, Tom Sizemore, Alfre Woodard, Kyra Sedgwick, Elisabeth Shue, David Paymer; **D:** Ron Underwood; **W:** Brent Maddock, S.S. Wilson, Gregory Hansen, Erik Hansen; **M:** Marc Shaiman. **VHS, LV** *MCA, BTV*

Heart Like a Wheel ♫♫♫

PG/Jr. High-Adult The story of Shirley Muldowney, who rose from the daughter of a country-western singer to the leading lady in drag racing. The film follows her battles of sexism and choosing whether to have a career or a family. Bedelia's performance is outstanding. Fine showings from Bridges and Axton in supporting roles.

1983 113m/C Bonnie Bedelia, Beau Bridges, Bill McKinney, Leo Rossi, Hoyt Axton, Dick Miller, Anthony Edwards; **D:** Jonathan Kaplan; **W:** Ken Friedman. **VHS, Beta, LV** *FOX*

Heartbeeps ♫♫

PG/Jr. High-Adult Sci-fi fare set in 1995 (ha!), about two humanoid robot servants who fall in love at the factory and run off together. Listless and apparently aimed at the very young, though kids may enjoy the romantic electroplated duo (makeup effects by Stan Winston) of Kaufman and Peters.

1981 79m/C Andy Kaufman, Bernadette Peters, Randy Quaid, Kenneth McMillan, Christopher Guest, Melanie Mayron, Jack Carter; **D:** Allan Arkush; **M:** John Williams. **VHS, Beta** *MCA*

Heartbreak Hotel ♫♫ ▷

PG-13/Jr. High-Adult Johnny Wolfe kidnaps Elvis Presley from his show in Cleveland and drives him home to his mother, a die-hard Elvis fan. Completely unbelievable, utterly ridiculous, and still a lot of fun.

> 🛑 BEWARE 🛑 *Profanity and violence.*

If you like *Heart and Souls* (1993), you'll love:

Always (1989)

Angels in the Outfield (1994)

Chances Are (1989)

Clarence (1991)

Field of Dreams (1989)

Ghost (1990)

Ghost Dad (1990)

The Heavenly Kid (1985)

It's a Wonderful Life (1946)

Kiss Me Goodbye (1982)

Mr. Destiny (1990)

Oh God! (1977)

The Three Lives of Thomasina (1963)

1988 101m/C David Keith, Tuesday Weld, Charlie Schlatter, Angela Goethals, Jacque Lynn Colton, Chris Mulkey, Karen Landry, Tudor Sherrard, Paul Harkins; **D:** Chris Columbus; **W:** Chris Columbus; **M:** Georges Delerue. **VHS, Beta, LV** *TOU*

The Heartbreak Kid ♫♫♫

PG/Jr. High-Adult Director May's comic examination of love and hypocrisy. Grodin embroils himself in a triangle with his new bride and a woman he can't have, an absolutely gorgeous and totally unloving woman he shouldn't want. Walks the fence between tragedy and comedy, with an exceptional performance from Berlin. Based on Bruce Jay Friedman's story.

1972 106m/C Charles Grodin, Cybill Shepherd, Eddie Albert, Jeannie Berlin, Audra Lindley, Art Metrano; **D:** Elaine May; **W:** Neil Simon. **VHS, Beta, LV** *MED, VTR*

Heartland ♫♫♫ ▷

PG/Jr. High-Adult In 1910 a widow from Back East journeys west with her little daughter to a new life on the Wyoming frontier, working for (and eventually marrying) a laconic homesteader. The hazards she faces, her courage and spirit get an unprettified, stunningly realistic treatment, worth comparing to the later "Sarah, Plain and Tall." Based on the diaries of Elinore Randall Stewart.

1981 95m/C Conchata Ferrell, Rip Torn, Barry Primus, Lilia Skala, Megan Folson; **D:** Richard Pearce. **VHS, Beta** *HBO*

Hearts of the West 🎬🎬🎬 ◁

PG/Jr. High-Adult Fantasy-filled farm boy travels to Hollywood in the 1930s and seeks a writing career. Instead, he finds himself an ill-suited western movie star in this small offbeat comedy-drama that's a tribute to the cowboy serials and early "B" flicks. Under appreciated little gem is sure to charm.

1975 103m/C Jeff Bridges, Andy Griffith, Donald Pleasence, Alan Arkin, Blythe Danner; **D:** Howard Zieff; **W:** Rob Thompson. **VHS, Beta** *MGM*

Heathcliff & Cats & Co., Vol. 1

Primary-Jr. High Four cartoons from Heathcliff and the gang stitched together from TV episodes: "The Great Pussini," "Kitty Kat Kennels," "Chauncey's Big Escape," and "Carnival Caper." Additional volumes available.

1986 45m/C VHS, Beta

Heathcliff & Marmaduke

Family Saturday-morning animated adventures with the long-running comic-strip great dane Marmaduke sharing a time slot with his newspaper cohort Heathcliff the cat.

1983 60m/C VHS, Beta *WOV*

Heathcliff: The Movie 🎬 ◁

Family Title is a severe misnomer, as this full-length animated film, released to theaters, merely scrapes together episodes from the TV cartoon featuring the newspaper comic-strip cat. For more and better Heathcliff, see the various kidvid releases. Or read "Wuthering Heights."

1988 73m/C VHS, Beta, LV *BAR, IME*

Heathcliff's Double & Other Tails

Preschool-Primary Ten episodes from the animated series starring the hostile comic-strip feline.

1987 110m/C VHS, Beta

The Heavenly Kid 🎬

PG-13/Jr. High-Adult Leather-jacketed "cool" guy who died in a '60s hot rod crash can't get out of Purgatory until he teaches a dull 1980s teen on how to be a hip and worldly dude. Better he should teach the kid math or English. Tutorials include booze, marijuana, and behaving badly. It's supposed to be funny, but viewers can't get out of purgatory until they turn this off. Ages 14 and up.

🔔 BEWARE! *Marijuana use, brawling and profanity.*

1985 92m/C Lewis Smith, Jane Kaczmarek, Jason Gedrick, Richard Mulligan; **D:** Cary Medoway. **VHS, Beta** *NO*

Heavyweights 🎬

PG/Primary-Jr. High A low for Disney, there's nothing very original in story of overweight youngsters at a fat camp run by a sadistic fitness guru (Stiller). His boot camp methods cause the kids to band together and overthrow him—and eat!! Oh yes, there's a baseball game with the more athletic camp kids across the lake.

🔔 BEWARE! *Mild profanity. Butt jokes.*

1994 98m/C Jeffrey Tambor, Ben Stiller, Jerry Stiller, Anne Meara, Shaun Weiss, Kenan Thompson; **D:** Steven Brill; **W:** Judd Apatow, Steven Brill; **C:** Victor Hammer; **M:** J.A.C. Redford. **VHS, LV** *DIS*

Heck's Way Home 🎬🎬 ◁

Family Heck is the Neufeld family dog and best friend of 11-year-old Luke (Krowchuk). The family is moving from Winnipeg to Australia and have a three-day layover in Vancouver. Heck is supposed to come along but gets separated, and unbeknownst to the family, captured by the local dogcatcher (Arkin). The family is forced to leave without him. Naturally, Heck escapes and starts off on a 2000-mile journey to find his family before they fly away forever.

1995 92m/C Chad Krowchuk, Alan Arkin, Michael Riley, Shannon Lawson. **VHS** *HMK*

Hector's Bunyip

Family What's a bunyip? It's a traditional Australian bogeyman/dragon, and little Hector keeps an invisible one around as an imaginary friend. Welfare authorities are not amused, as they consider taking Hector from his large, eccentric family. Then Hector gets kidnapped—by his supposedly imaginary friend. A Down Under TV production aired on "WonderWorks," this veers toward sentimental slush, then turns around and becomes something absolutely fresh and delightful in the end, the hallmark of the justly acclaimed PBS series.

1986 58m/C Scott Bartle, Robert Coleby, Barbara Stephens, Tushka Hose; **D:** Mark Callan. **VHS** *PME, FCT, BTV*

Heidi 🎬🎬 ◁

Family Sentimental adaptation of German writer Johanna Spyri's 1881 novel. Heidi is an orphan shuttled from relative to relative until she happily ends up with her crotchety grandfather in his mountain cabin. But the child is taken off to the city to be a companion to an unpleasant invalid girl Klara. Will Heidi triumph over the household's mean governess and return to grandfather? Does Shirley have curls? Also available colorized. Available on laserdisc with another Temple treat, "Poor Little Rich Girl."

1937 88m/B Shirley Temple, Jean Hersholt, Helen Westley, Arthur Treacher; **D:** Allan Dwan. **VHS, Beta** *FXV, HMV, MLT*

Heidi 🎬🎬

Family Made-for-TV adaptation of the classic Johanna Spyri novel of an orphaned girl who goes to the Swiss Alps to live with her grandfather. This is the one that interrupted the Jets football game on TV.

1967 100m/C Maximilian Schell, Jennifer Edwards, Michael Redgrave, Jean Simmons; **D:** Delbert Mann; **M:** John Williams. **VHS, Beta** *LIV, VES, GLV*

Heidi 🎵🎵🎵

G/Family Made-for-TV Disney version of the children's classic by Johanna Spyri. Thornton is charming as the orphan shuttled from taken from her simple, mountain-dwelling grandfather and whisked off to the city to a rich relative's unhappy household. Seymour is the snobbish, scowling governess. This "Heidi" is spunky enough to keep the sugar level tolerable. Filmed on location in Austria.

1993 167m/C Noley Thornton, Jason Robards Jr., Jane Seymour, Lexi Randall, Sian Phillips, Patricia Neal, Benjamin Brazier, Michael Simkins, Andrew Bicknell, Jane Hazlegrove; **D:** Michael Rhodes; **W:** Jeanne Rosenberg; **M:** Lee Holdridge. **VHS** *DIS*

Hello Again 🎵🎵 ▷

PG/Primary-Adult A year after she chokes to death, Shelley Long is brought back to life by her delightful, witchy sister (Ivey). Discovering that her widowed plastic surgeon husband has taken up with a woman she never liked, Long seeks revenge—comically, of course.

1987 96m/C Shelley Long, Corbin Bernsen, Judith Ivey, Gabriel Byrne, Sela Ward, Austin Pendleton, Carrie Nye, Robert Lewis, Madeleine Potter; **D:** Frank Perry; **M:** William Goldstein. **VHS, Beta, LV** *TOU*

Hello, Dolly! 🎵🎵

G/Family "Hello, Dolly!" without Carol Channing is like New Year's Eve without Dick Clark. Barbara Streisand got the Channing role in the movie as widow Dolly Levi who, while matchmaking for her friends, finds a match for herself. Based on the hugely successful Broadway musical adapted from Thornton Wilder's play "The Matchmaker." Has one good song and not much else. Ages 5 to 12. 🎵 Hello Dolly; Just Leave Everything to Me; Love is Only Love; Dancing; Walter's Gavotte; It Only Takes a Moment; Ribbons Down My Back; Elegance; It Takes a Woman.

1969 146m/C Barbra Streisand, Walter Matthau, Michael Crawford, Louis Armstrong, E.J. Peaker, Marianne McAndrew, Tommy Tune; **D:** Gene Kelly; **W:** Ernest Lehman; **M:** Jerry Herman. **Award Nominations:** Academy Awards '69: Best Cinematography, Best Costume Design, Best Film Editing, Best Picture; **Awards:** Academy Awards '69: Best Art Direction/Set Decoration, Best Sound, Best Score. **VHS, Beta, LV** *FOX, FCT*

Hello Kitty: Cinderella

Preschool Animated character takes on the classic fairy ale to show that kindness and caring are rewarded. Also includes the story "Hello Kitty: Heidi." Ages 3 to 6.

1995 52m/C VHS *WEA*

Help! 🎵🎵🎵

G/Jr. High-Adult Ringo Starr's ruby ring is the object of a search by a human-sacrifice cult who chase the Beatles all over the globe in order to acquire the bauble. Zany, fun-filled satire pokes fun at the Fab Four's own superstardom with a mixture of satire and great music that still holds up. Tell the kids that if they enjoy "The Monkees" they'll like these foreign imitators. The laserdisc version

includes a wealth of Beatles memorabilia, rare footage behind the scenes and at the premiere, and extensive publicity material. 🎵 Help!; You're Gonna Lose That Girl; You've Got To Hide Your Love Away; The Night Before; Another Girl; Ticket To Ride; I Need You.

1965 90m/C John Lennon, Paul McCartney, Ringo Starr, George Harrison, Leo McKern, Eleanor Bron; **D:** Richard Lester; **W:** Charles Wood. **VHS, Beta, LV** *MPI, MVD, CRC*

Henry Hamilton: Graduate Ghost

Primary-Jr. High This junior specter of a Civil War soldier is too nice to haunt a modern family effectively, the way he was taught in ghost school. Instead he urges the mortals to believe in themselves and their dreams. Live-action comedy, based on a book by Marilyn Redmond.

1990 45m/C Larry Gelman, Stu Gilliam. **VHS** *VTR, AIM*

Henry's Cat

Primary-Jr. High TV's cartoon bear tells tales and conveys acceptable human principles in the process.

1986 60m/C VHS, Beta *HBO*

Her Alibi 🎵🎵

PG/Jr. High-Adult When successful murder-mystery novelist Phil Blackwood runs out of ideas for good books, he seeks inspiration in the criminal courtroom. There he discovers a beautiful Romanian immigrant named Nina who is accused of murder. He goes to see her in jail and offers to provide her with an alibi. Narrated by Blackwood in the tone of one of his thriller novels. Uneven comedy, with appealing cast and arbitrary plot.

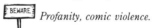 *Profanity, comic violence.*

1988 95m/C Tom Selleck, Paulina Porizkova, William Daniels, James Farentino, Hurd Hatfield, Patrick Wayne, Tess Harper, Joan Copeland; **D:** Bruce Beresford; **W:** Charlie Peters; **M:** Georges Delerue. **VHS, Beta, LV, 8mm** *WAR*

Herbie Goes Bananas 🎵 ▷

G/Family Last and least of the "Love Bug" film oeuvre. While Herbie the Volkswagen is racing in Brazil he is bugged by gangsters, a pickpocket, and a raging bull. The bullfighting scene isn't bad. Herbie later turned up in a TV series. Insider's note: By this point Herbie the car had become just too difficult to work with. Insisting that everyone now call him Herbert, or at least Herb, he developed a drinking problem and between takes would hide in his trailer, guzzling gasohol. The final straw was when he demanded that Disney hire a Renault Le Car to do his stunts. Although he dried out in Palm Springs (at the Henry Ford Clinic), Herbie's days in Hollywood were over. Ages 5 to 10.

1980 93m/C Cloris Leachman, Charles Martin Smith, Harvey Korman, John Vernon, Alex Rocco, Richard Jaeckel, Fritz Feld; **D:** Vincent McEveety. **VHS, Beta** *DIS*

Herbie Goes to Monte Carlo

G/Family Jewel thieves stash diamonds in Herbie's gas tank while the speedy Volkswagen is participating in a Paris-to-Monte Carlo auto race. Herbie also falls in love with a cute Lancia car. This is called auto eroticism (though not by anyone in the movie). Third in the Disney "Love Bug" series is a step down from the second. Ages 5 to 10.

1977 104m/C Dean Jones, Don Knotts, Julie Sommars, Roy Kinnear; **D:** Vincent McEveety. **VHS, Beta** *DIS*

Herbie Rides Again

G/Family In this "Love Bug" sequel, Herbie comes to the aid of elderly Widow Steinmetz (Helen Hayes), threatened by a ruthless tycoon determined to raise a skyscraper on her property (Herb-an renewal?) Humorous Disney fare with a rousing conclusion. Ages 5 to 10.

1974 88m/C Helen Hayes, Ken Berry, Stefanie Powers, John McIntire, Keenan Wynn; **D:** Robert Stevenson. **VHS, Beta, LV** *DIS*

Hercules

Family The one that started it all, Reeves is perfect as the mythical hero Hercules who encounters many dangerous situations while trying to win over his true love. Dubbed in English. Cinematography by Mario Bava.

BEWARE *Violence.*

1958 107m/C Steve Reeves, Sylva Koscina, Fabrizio Mioni, Gianna Maria Canale, Arturo Dominici; **D:** Pietro Francisci. **VHS, Beta, LV** *MRV, IME, VDM*

Hercules

PG/Primary-Adult Poor superhero saga finds legendary muscle guy Hercules in the person of TV's "Incredible Hulk" Ferrigno, fighting the evil King Minos for his own survival and the love of Cassiopeia, a rival king's daughter. The script makes a mess of the myths.

BEWARE *Muscle-stretching violence.*

1983 100m/C Lou Ferrigno, Sybil Danning, William Berger, Brad Harris, Ingrid Anderson; **D:** Lewis (Luigi Cozzi) Coates; **W:** Lewis (Luigi Cozzi) Coates; **M:** Pino Donaggio. **VHS, Beta, LV** *MGM, IME*

Hercules in New York

G/Family Cheapo motion picture debut of Schwarzenegger, here christened 'Arnold Strong' (with his voice terribly dubbed into English) resurfaced on home video to cash in on his action-hero superstardom. But Arnold's acting muscles in particular weren't developed when he did this charmless farce of the Greek demigod sent by Zeus to Manhattan, where he eventually becomes a professional wrestler. Also known as "Hercules Goes Bananas."

1970 93m/C Arnold Schwarzenegger, Arnold Stang, Deborah Loomis, James Karen, Ernest Graves; **D:** Arthur Seidelman. **VHS, Beta** *MPI*

Hercules Unchained

Jr. High-Adult Sequel to "Hercules" finds superhero Reeves must use all his strength to save the city of Thebes and the woman he loves from the giant Antaeus.

BEWARE *Violence.*

1959 101m/C Steve Reeves, Sylva Koscina, Silvia Lopel, Primo Carnera; **D:** Pietro Francisci. **VHS, Beta, LV** *VDM, MRV, SNC*

Here Comes Droopy

G/Family TV revival of the sad-eyed bloodhound sheriff created by Tex Avery, in which he once again saves the day in spite of himself. A little bit of Droopy-ness goes a long way.

1990 60m/C VHS *MGM*

Here Comes Garfield

G/Family Comic-strip cat Garfield's first step from newspaper to TV cartoon has the lazy feline rousing himself enough to save his dumb dog pal Odie from the pound. Animated by the same team responsible for the successful "Charlie Brown" series.

1990 24m/C V: Lorenzo Music. **VHS** *FOX*

Here Comes Peter Cottontail

Family Arthur Rankin-Jules Bass "Animagic" seasonal TV special that chronicles a scheme by an ambitious rabbit to dethrone Peter Cottontail, the reigning Head Easter Bunny.

1971 53m/C V: Danny Kaye, Casey Kasem, Vincent Price. **VHS** *FHE*

Here Comes Santa Claus

Family Yes, even the French can make crummy children's films. This slushy holiday tale involves two kids whose parents are held prisoner by African rebels. They visit the North Pole and get Santa's help. The sight of Pere Noel schlepping through the tropics is funny at first, but awful dialogue (English-dubbed) and production values melt any xmas spirit.

1984 78m/C Karen Cheryl, Armand Meffre; **D:** Christian Gion. **VHS, Beta** *NWV, VTR*

Here Comes the Cat! and Other Stories

Preschool-Primary All the mice in town are going about their business when someone sounds the cry: "Here comes the cat!" A lovely story with a great surprise. Three other animated stories about cats round out this video: "The Cat and the Collector," "Cat & Canary," and Wanda Gag's classic "Millions of Cats." Ages 3 to 10.

1992 30m/C VHS *WKV*

The Hero

PG/Jr. High-Adult Popular soccer player agrees to throw a game for big cash, and then worries about losing the respect of a young boy who idolizes him. Nothing new in this overly sentimental sports drama.

1971 97m/C Richard Harris, Romy Schneider, Kim Burfield, Maurice Kaufman; **D:** Richard Harris. **VHS, Beta**

Hero 🦴🦴ᵇ

PG-13/Jr. High-Adult Interesting twist on Cinderella fable and modern media satire has television reporter Davis looking for the man who saved her life, expecting a genuine hero, and accepting without question the one who fits her vision. Critically considered disappointing, but wait—Garcia and Hoffman make a great team, and Davis is fetching as the vulnerable media person. Strong language and dark edges may keep away some of the kids, but otherwise this is a fine fable.

⚠ BEWARE *A plane crash and heroic rescue. Deception and profanity.*

1992 116m/C Geena Davis, Dustin Hoffman, Andy Garcia, Joan Cusack, Kevin J. O'Connor, Chevy Chase, Maury Chaykin, Stephen Tobolowsky, Christian Clemenson, Tom Arnold, Janis Paige, Warren Berlinger, Susie Cusack, James Madio, Richard Riehle, Don Yesso, Darrell Larson; **D:** Stephen Frears; **W:** David Peoples; **M:** George Fenton. **VHS, LV, 8mm** *COL*

A Hero Ain't Nothin' But a Sandwich 🦴🦴🦴

PG/Jr. High-Adult The creators of the hit family film "Sounder" also made this under appreciated, ahead-of-its-time adaptation of Alice Childress' novel about Benjie, a smart, black 13-year-old in South Central L.A. who starts slipping into drugs. Teachers, preachers, counselors and family (especially his single mother's no-nonsense boyfriend) try to stop the boy's downward spiral, but in the end it's up to Benjie himself. Not a finger-wagging junkie horror story, but a sometimes wrenching drama that doesn't simplify either the rehab/recovery process or the alienation of its young main character. Though obviously meant to connect with younger viewers, there's much here of concern to grownups.

⚠ BEWARE *Sex, some very raw language, explicit drug use, nudity—when this came out the PG rating was considered a lot stronger than it is today—but none of it in an exploitive manner.*

1978 107m/C Cicely Tyson, Paul Winfield, Larry B. Scott, Helen Martin, Glynn Turman, David Groh; **D:** Ralph Nelson. **VHS, Beta** *PAR, FCT*

Hero at Large 🦴🦴ᵇ

PG/Jr. High-Adult Good-natured, unemployed actor foils a robbery while dressed in a promotional "Captain Avenger" suit, and instant celebrity follows, although he has no superpowers. When politicians exploit his popularity, Captain Avenger has to decide what he stands for. Lightweight, yet enjoyable tale with a moral.

⚠ BEWARE *Roughhousing.*

1980 98m/C John Ritter, Anne Archer, Bert Convy, Kevin McCarthy, Kevin Bacon; **D:** Martin Davidson. **VHS, Beta** *MGM*

Heroes on Hot Wheels, Vol. 1

Primary-Jr. High Animated series derived from a certain line of toy cars you may have heard of, with Michael Valiant and his racing team travelling the world in search of action-packed racing adventures. This video features the episodes "Valiant vs. Valiant" and "Highway Pirate." Additional volumes available.

1991 45m/C VHS *NO*

Hey, Cinderella!

Family One of the oldest Muppet presentations available on tape, this TV special displays all the characteristic sly wit and post-modern whimsy of the Jim Henson workshop, as Cinderella arrives at the ball in a coach pulled by a purple beast named Splurge (a Muppet character who never did quite catch on) and driven by Kermit the singing frog (one who did).

1969 54m/C V: Jim Henson, Frank Oz. **VHS, Beta** *JHV, TOU, BTV*

Hey There, It's Yogi Bear 🦴🦴

Family Bill Hanna and Joseph Barbera's first feature-length 'toon stars Yogi Bear, who comes out of hibernation and learns that his girlfriend Cindy has been taken away by the Chizzling Brothers Circus. With his pal Boo Boo, Yogi leaves Jellystone Park and journeys to the big city to rescue her. On the level of the TV show, with several musical numbers.

1964 98m/C D: William Hanna; **V:** Daws Butler, James Darren, Mel Blanc, J. Pat O'Malley, Julie Bennett. **VHS, Beta, LV** *WOV, IME*

The Hideaways 🦴🦴ᵇ

G/Family Twelve-year-old Claudia and her younger brother run away and hide in New York's Metropolitan Museum of Art, dodging night watchmen and living a seemingly grand adventure. Claudia ponders a marble angel that may or may not be a work by Michelangelo. Her search for the truth takes her to confront the wealthy, mysterious recluse who donated it. Only then does the issue of running away from home come up; previously it isn't even mentioned and hovers uneasily in the shadows of this sunny family tale. Based on the kids' novel "From the Mixed-Up Files of Mrs. Basel E. Frankweiler" by E.L. Konigsburg.

1973 105m/C Richard Mulligan, George Rose, Ingrid Bergman, Sally Prager, Johnny Doran, Madeline Kahn; **D:** Fielder Cook. **VHS, Beta** *WAR, VHE, FCT*

Hiding Out 🦴🦴

PG-13/Jr. High-Adult Young stockbroker testifies against the Mafia and must find a place to hide from their revenge. He winds up at his cousin's high school in Delaware, masquerading as an inmate, and reliving all the usual teenage troubles (repressive teachers, student cliques). Mediocre comedy that doesn't take too many opportunities for insight into youth culture.

⚠ BEWARE *Salty language, violence.*

1987 99m/C Jon Cryer, Keith Coogan, Gretchen Cryer, Annabeth Gish, Tim Quill; *D:* Bob Giraldi; *M:* Anne Dudley. **VHS, Beta** *HBO*

High Anxiety 🎵🎵

PG/Jr. High-Adult As always, Brooks tries hard to please in this low-brow parody of Hitchcock employing dozens of references to films like "Psycho," "Spellbound," "The Birds," and "Vertigo" (including the looping, revealing camera and the massive orchestral movements). Tells the tale of a height-fearing psychiatrist caught up in a murder mystery. The title song performed a la Sinatra by Brooks is one of the brighter moments in a uneven but generally amusing tribute.

BEWARE *Best for kids who know their films.*

1977 92m/C Mel Brooks, Madeline Kahn, Cloris Leachman, Harvey Korman, Ron Carey, Howard Morris, Dick Van Patten; *D:* Mel Brooks; *W:* Mel Brooks, Ron Clark, Barry Levinson, Rudy DeLuca. **VHS, Beta, LV** *FOX*

High Country Calling 🎵🎵

G/Family Wolf pups escape captivity and set off on a cross-country chase. Canine nature adventure narrated, suitably enough, by onetime Alpo representative Greene.
1975 84m/C VHS, Beta *GEM, CNG*

High Noon 🎵🎵🎵🎵

Jr. High-Adult Landmark western about Hadeyville town marshal Will Kane (Cooper) who faces four professional killers alone, after being abandoned to his fate by the gutless townspeople who profess to admire him. Cooper is the ultimate hero figure, his sheer presence overwhelming. Note the continuing use of the ballad written by Dimitri Tamkin, "Do Not Forsake Me, Oh My Darlin'" (sung by Tex Ritter) to heighten the tension and action. Laserdisc includes the original trailer, an essay by Howard Suber on audio 2, a photo essay of production stills, Carl Foreman's original notes of the film and the complete text of "The Tin Star," the story on which the film is based.

BEWARE *Violence.*

1952 85m/B Gary Cooper, Grace Kelly, Lloyd Bridges, Lon Chaney Jr., Thomas Mitchell, Otto Kruger, Katy Jurado, Lee Van Cleef, Harry (Henry) Morgan, Robert J. Wilke, Sheb Wooley; *D:* Fred Zinnemann; *W:* Carl Foreman; *M:* Dimitri Tiomkin. **Award Nominations:** Academy Awards '52: Best Director (Zinnemann), Best Picture, Best Screenplay; **Awards:** Academy Awards '52: Best Actor (Cooper), Best Film Editing, Best Song ("High Noon (Do Not Forsake Me, Oh My Darlin')"), Best Score; Golden Globe Awards '53: Best Actor—Drama (Cooper), Best Supporting Actress (Jurado), Best Score; National Board of Review Awards '52: 10 Best Films of the Year; New York Film Critics Awards '52: Best Director (Zinnemann), Best Film. **VHS, LV** *REP, TLF, BTV*

High School High 🎵🎵 ♭

Sr. High-Adult In this comedy, gung-ho and bright-sided teacher Richard C. Clark (Lovitz) leaves the safe and easy private school world for notorious inner city Marion Barry High. This high school is so bad, it has its

own cemetery, but Clark is determined to get through to these kids and with the help of a student (Phifer), he just might do it. This flick follows the tradition of all those other dedicated teacher flicks, but with a little more comedy thrown in.

1996 ?m/C Jon Lovitz, Tia Carrere, Mekhi Phifer, Louise Fletcher; *D:* Hart Bochner; *W:* David Zucker, Robert Locash. **VHS** *NYR*

High Society 🎵🎵 ♭

Jr. High-Adult Wealthy man attempts to win back his ex-wife who's about to be remarried in enjoyable remake of "The Philadelphia Story" that's most notable for the score by Cole Porter. Some memorable musical moments, including Frank, Bing, and Satchmo (playing himself) working together. Letterboxed laserdisc format also includes the original movie trailer. 🎵 High Society Calypso; Little One; Who Wants to Be a Millionaire?; True Love; You're Sensational; I Love You, Samantha; Now You Has Jazz; Well, Did You Evah?; Mind if I Make Love to You?.

1956 107m/C Frank Sinatra, Bing Crosby, Grace Kelly, Louis Armstrong, Celeste Holm, Sidney Blackmer, Louis Calhern; *D:* Charles Walters; *M:* Cole Porter. **VHS, Beta, LV, 8mm** *MGM*

Highlander 🎵🎵🎵

R/Sr. High-Adult Strange tale about an immortal 16th-century Scottish warrior who has had to battle his evil immortal enemy through the centuries. The feud comes to blows in modern-day Manhattan. Connery makes a memorable appearance as the good warrior's mentor. Spectacular battle and death scenes. A cult favorite which spawned a weak sequel and a television series. Based on a story by Gregory Widen.

BEWARE *Lots of supernatural violence, battle and death scenes.*

1986 110m/C Christopher Lambert, Sean Connery, Clancy Brown, Roxanne Hart, Beatie Edney, Alan North, Sheila Gish, Jon Polito; *D:* Russell Mulcahy; *W:* Gregory Widen, Peter Bellwood, Larry Ferguson; *M:* Michael Kamen. **VHS, Beta, LV** *REP*

Highlander 2: The Quickening 🎵 ♭

R/Sr. High-Adult The saga of Connor MacLeod and Juan Villa-Lobos continues in this sequel set in the year 2024. An energy shield designed to block out the sun's harmful ultraviolet rays has left planet Earth in perpetual darkness, but there is evidence that the ozone layer has repaired itself. An environmental terrorist and her group begin a sabotage effort and are joined by MacLeod and Villa-Lobos in their quest to save Earth. Stunning visual effects don't make up for ozone hole in script.

BEWARE *Supernatural violence and death. Same as the original.*

1991 90m/C Christopher Lambert, Sean Connery, Virginia Madsen, Michael Ironside, John C. McGinley; *D:* Russell Mulcahy; *W:* Peter Bellwood; *M:* Stewart Copeland. **VHS, LV, 8mm** *COL*

Highlander: The Adventure Begins

Family Animated TV series based on the movie finds the last highlander, Quentin MacLeod, battling the evil Kortaon for the future of mankind.
1994 77m/C VHS *LIV*

Highlander: The Adventure Begins

Primary Tells the story of good versus evil and the mythical battles the hero must engage in.
1996 ?m/C VHS *FHE, LIV*

Highlander: The Gathering 🦴🦴

PG-13/Jr. High-Adult Re-edited episodes from the syndicated television series finds good immortals Connor MacLeod (Lambert) and distant relative Duncan (Paul) battling against an evil immortal (Moll as a particularly nasty villain) and a misguided human (Vanity). Lots of sword-play and a little bit of romance (courtesy of Vandernoot).

 Violence. No magic in this gathering.

1993 98m/C Christopher Lambert, Adrian Paul, Richard Moll, Vanity, Alexandra Vandernoot, Stan Kirsh; **D:** Thomas J. Wright, Ray Austin; **W:** Lorain Despres, Dan Gordon. **VHS** *HMD*

Hillbilly Bears

Family Cartoon adventures of a backwoods clan of bruins, from the Hanna-Barbera territories.
197? 51m/C VHS, Beta *TTC*

Hiroshima Maiden

Family Idealistic family man in 1955 opens his house to a Japanese girl who survived the atom bomb, in the US for surgery to her radiation scars. But his son believes she's an enemy spy and won't be friends. Were American kids really this stupid? Maybe, but only the adult characters really come to life as sympathetic characters in this plea for tolerance from the "WonderWorks" series.
1988 58m/C Susan Blakely, Richard Masur, Tamlyn Tomita; **D:** Joan Darling. **VHS** *PME, WNE, HMV*

His Girl Friday 🦴🦴🦴🦴

Family Classic, unrelentingly hilarious war-between-the-sexes comedy in which a reporter and her ex-husband editor help a condemned man escape the law-while at the same time furthering their own ends as they try to get the big scoop on political corruption in the town. One of Hawks' most furious and inventive screen combats in which women are given uniquely equal (for Hollywood) footing, with staccato dialogue and wonderful performances. Based on the Hecht-MacArthur play "The Front Page," which was originally filmed in 1931. Remade again in 1974 as "The Front Page," and in 1988 as "Switching Channels." Also available colorized.

1940 92m/B Cary Grant, Rosalind Russell, Ralph Bellamy, Gene Lockhart, John Qualen, Porter Hall, Roscoe Karns, Abner Biberman, Cliff Edwards, Billy Gilbert, Helen Mack, Ernest Truex, Clarence Kolb, Frank Jenks; **D:** Howard Hawks; **W:** Charles Lederer; **M:** Morris Stoloff. **VHS, Beta** *CNG, MRV, NOS*

The Hobbit 🦴🦴🦴

Family Somewhat simplified but still the best animated interpretation of J.R.R. Tolkien. Hobbit Bilbo Baggins is persuaded to leave his comfortable Shire and help a tribe of dwarfs recover their gold from Smaug the evil dragon. In the process Bilbo discovers a magic Ring of Power, and its tale continues in Ralph Bakshi's "Lord of the Rings." This version can be enjoyed complete in itself, however. Good character voices, artwork, pleasant songs. Made for TV by Arthur Rankin Jr. and Jules Bass, who revisited Middle Earth with "The Return of the King."
1978 76m/C D: Arthur Rankin Jr., Jules Bass; **V:** Orson Bean, John Huston, Otto Preminger, Richard Boone. **VHS, Beta, 8mm** *WAR, CHI, FCT*

The Hoboken Chicken Emergency 🦴🦴 🦴

Family Arthur is sent to buy a holiday turkey, but a mad scientist instead persuades the boy to purchase a live, 6-foot tall 266-lb. chicken. Father won't have the friendly, freakish fowl around the house, but when Henrietta and

Arthur are separated the devoted bird runs wild throughout the town. Slight but funny "WonderWorks" adaptation of the absurdist kids' novel by D. Manus Pinkwater. The amusing Henrietta was fabricated by Sid & Marty Krofft puppeteers.

1984 55m/C Dick Van Patten, Peter Billingsley, Gabe Kaplan, Arlene Golonka; **D:** Peter Baldwin. **VHS** *PME, FCT, BTV*

Hockey Night

Primary-Jr. High Follows takes a break from her "Anne of Green Gables" persona to do a grittier Canadian-content drama, about hockey-loving Kathy who becomes the first girl on a kid's team in a provincial town. The team's offended adult sponsor turns up the heat to have her removed from the ice. Nice drama with superb young actors, but surprisingly dull hockey scenes, apparently filmed from the cheap seats.

🛑 BEWARE 🛑 *Alcohol use.*

1984 77m/C Megan Follows, Rick Moranis, Gail Youngs, Martin Harburg, Henry Ramer; **D:** Paul Shapiro. **VHS, Beta** *FHE*

Hocus Pocus

PG/Jr. High-Adult Midler, Najimy, and Parker are executed 17th-century witches accidentally conjured up by 20th century teenagers on Halloween in Salem, Massachusetts. They (the witches, that is) plot to take revenge on the town by sucking life from its children. Given the Disney label, pic is surprisingly gruesome (compare it with "Bedknobs and Broomsticks" to see how times change), but the pumpkin-pageant-performances of the three stars—they rant, rave, sing, fly—make up for the lack of substance with comedy sorcery. Production values and f/x are awesome even by lofty Magic Kingdom standards.

🛑 BEWARE 🛑 *Supernatural violence, including a comic zombie who gets temporarily dismembered (just like Scarecrow in "The Wizard of Oz"). Sex talk, since the witches need to kill a virgin—giggle, giggle.*

1993 95m/C Bette Midler, Kathy Najimy, Sarah Jessica Parker, Thora Birch, Doug Jones, Omri Katz, Vinessa Shaw, Stephanie Faracy, Charles Rocket; **Cameos:** Penny Marshall, Garry Marshall; **D:** Kenny Ortega; **W:** Neil Cuthbert, Mick Garris; **M:** John Debney. **VHS, Beta, LV** *DIS, TOU, BTV*

Hole in the Sky

PG/Jr. High-Adult Teenaged Mac (O'Connell) is working for the Montana forestry service in the summer of 1919 under the tutelage of taciturn legend Bill Bell (a mustache-less Elliott). Mac learns some lessons about growing up, first love, card-playing—and never to rile the camp cook. Based on an autobiographical story by Norman MacLean (who wrote "A River Runs Through It"). Made for TV; filmed on location in British Columbia.

🛑 BEWARE 🛑 *Barroom brawl with a little drinking and cussing.*

1995 94m/C Sam Elliott, Jerry O'Connell, Ricky Jay, Molly Parker; **D:** John Kent Harrison; **W:** Robert W. Lenski. **VHS** *HMK*

Holiday Facts & Fun: St. Patrick's Day

Preschool-Primary Part of the "Holiday Facts & Fun" series. Teaches the history, culture, and traditions associated with St. Patrick's Day. Contains scenes of an Irish-American family as they celebrate the holiday, complete with a look at the special foods, music, and remembrances of family vacations to Ireland. Also looks at the shamrock, leprechauns, the harp, and the shillelagh. Ages 5 and up.

1994 10m/C VHS

Holiday Inn

Family Astaire and Crosby are rival song-and-dance men who decide to work together to turn a Connecticut farm into an inn, open only on holidays. Remade (and improved) in 1954 as "White Christmas." 🎵 White Christmas; Be Careful, It's My Heart; Plenty to Be Thankful For; Abraham, Abraham; Let's Say It With Firecrackers; I Gotta Say I Love You Cause I Can't Tell A Lie; Let's Start the New Year Right; Happy Holidays; Song of Freedom.

1942 101m/B Bing Crosby, Fred Astaire, Marjorie Reynolds, Walter Abel, Virginia Dale; **D:** Mark Sandrich. **Award Nominations:** Academy Awards '42: Best Story, Best Original Score; **Awards:** Academy Awards '42: Best Song ("White Christmas"). **VHS, Beta, LV** *MCA*

Holidays for Children Video Series

Primary Six-part multicultural series for children which teaches about different holidays. Uses puppets, holiday-appropriate arts and crafts, music, dance, and an illustrated story to outline the traditions and history of each holiday. Ages 5 and up.

1994 180m/C VHS *LVC*

Hollywood on Parade

Family A collection of several "Hollywood on Parade" shorts produced by Paramount Studios between 1932 and 1934. Nearly every big star of the era is featured singing, dancing, or taking part in bizarre sketches.

1934 59m/B Fredric March, Ginger Rogers, Jean Harlow, Jeanette MacDonald, Maurice Chevalier, Mary Pickford, Jackie Cooper. **VHS, Beta** *NOS, HEG, DVT*

Hollywood or Bust

Family The zany comedy duo of Martin and Lewis (making the last of many successful appearances together) take off for the motion picture capital, where Jerry expects to meet his dream girl, screen siren Anita Ekberg. Lots of loose slapstick episodes ensue. Kid viewers will especially enjoy the antics of 'Mr. Bascombe,' Jerry's "Marmaduke"-sized great dane.

1956 95m/C Dean Martin, Jerry Lewis, Anita Ekberg, Pat Crowley, Maxie "Slapsie" Rosenbloom, Willard Waterman; **D:** Frank Tashlin. **VHS** *PAR, CCB*

Holt of the Secret Service

Family Secret Service agent runs afoul of saboteurs and fifth columnists in this 15-chapter serial.

1942 290m/B Jack Holt, Evelyn Brent, Montague Shaw, Tristram Coffin, John Ward, George Chesebro; **D:** James W. Horne. **VHS** *VYY, MED, DVT*

Holy Matrimony   🎷🎷 ♭

PG-13/Jr. High-Adult Mild-mannered and pleasant comedy in spite of its potentially salacious plot. Thieves Peter (Donovan) and Havana (Arquette) take off to Canada to hide out in the Hutterite religious community where Peter grew up and where he's welcomed as the prodigal son. Peter hides their stolen loot but neglects to pass the word on before he's killed in an accident. Wanting to stay and search for the money, Havana uses the colony's reliance on biblical law to marry Peter's brother, Zeke (Gordon-Levitt). Only problem is Zeke is 12 and doesn't even like girls. Strictly brother-sister affection develops between the two. Amusing performances by both.

> **BEWARE** *Profanity and sexual situations. Couple is chased by bad guys.*

1994 93m/C Patricia Arquette, Joseph Gordon-Levitt, Armin Mueller-Stahl, Tate Donovan, John Schuck, Lois Smith, Courtney B. Vance, Jeffrey Nordling, Richard Riehle; **D:** Leonard Nimoy; **W:** David Weisberg, Douglas S. Cook; **M:** Bruce Broughton. **VHS** *TOU*

Home Alone   🎷🎷🎷

PG/Family Eight-year-old Kevin is sent to his room for innocently misbehaving, and is forgotten the next day when his large family rushes to catch a plane to France. Left alone—and believing he somehow wished all his relatives into nonexistence—the tyke learns to survive on his own in a wintery suburban neighborhood haunted by suspicious grownups, a scary old man and two bumbling burglars planning to rob the house. One of John Hughes' most pleasing and successful films, thanks to Culkin's terrific, star-making performance and the slapstick siege pitting the crooks against the boy's many domestic booby-traps. Much-imitated; in fact Hughes reworked his earlier, more adult-oriented script "Career Opportunities" for the premise. Critics complained that the pratfalls bordered on real violence, but the main beef is the contrived Christmas sentiment.

> **BEWARE** *Cartoonish violence bordering on the severe but funny nonetheless.*

1990 105m/C Macaulay Culkin, Catherine O'Hara, Joe Pesci, Daniel Stern, John Heard, Roberts Blossom, John Candy, Catherine O'Hara, Billie Bird, Angela Goethals, Devin Ratray, Kieran Culkin; **D:** Chris Columbus; **W:** John Hughes; **M:** John Williams. **VHS, Beta, LV** *FXV, IME, RDG*

Home Alone 2: Lost in New York   🎷🎷

PG/Family Overlong, near-exact duplication of the original blockbuster. One year later the harebrained McCal-

listers again lose Kevin in the shuffle to catch a plane to Florida for their Yuletide vacation. The boy instead lands in NYC, scams his way into a luxury hotel, and goes through a rerun routine with returning burglars Pesci and Stern, who plot to steal a toy store's charity proceeds (you could call this "Kevin Saves Christmas"). Loaded with cartoon violence and shameless holiday pathos, all as fresh as December fruitcake in May. Culkin is as adorable, but his patented scream act wears out about the fiftieth time or so. Tape includes a banal breakfast cereal commercial, a fitting companion.

> **BEWARE** *Violence, bordering on brutality and Kevin hits the burglars with even nastier, bone-cracking booby-traps.*

1992 120m/C Macaulay Culkin, Joe Pesci, Daniel Stern, Catherine O'Hara, John Heard, Tim Curry, Brenda Fricker, Devin Ratray, Hillary Wolf, Eddie Bracken, Dana Ivey, Rob Schneider, Kieran Culkin, Gerry Bamman; **Cameos:** Donald Trump; **D:** Chris Columbus; **W:** John Hughes; **M:** John Williams. **VHS, LV** *FXV, BTV*

Home at Last

Family Billy, an orphaned street punk in turn-of-the-century New York, avoids jail by shipping to Nebraska and settles on the farm of a family whose own son has just died. After many difficulties the troublesome Billy and his Scandinavian foster father finally come to terms at a local horse-pulling contest. Somewhat plodding "Wonder-Works" entry that nonetheless has you caring for its characters by the close.

1988 58m/C Adrien Brody, Frank Converse, Caroline Lagerfelt, Sascha Radetsky. **VHS** *PME, HMV, FCT*

Home for Christmas   🎷🎷 ♭

Family An elderly homeless man, with the love of a young girl, teaches a wealthy family the spirit of Christmas.

1990 96m/C Mickey Rooney, Joel Kaiser; **D:** Peter McCubbin. **VHS** *RHI*

Home for the Holidays   🎷🎷 ♭

PG-13/Jr. High-Adult Single mom Claudia Larson (Hunter), just fired from her job in Chicago, heads to Baltimore to spend Thanksgiving with her family: eccentric parents (Bancroft and Durning); troubled siblings—frenzied gay brother Tommy (Downey, Jr.) and self-righteous sister Joanne (Stevenson)—as well as screwy, flatulent Aunt Glady (Chaplin) and Tommy's handsome friend Leo Fish (McDermott). Meanwhile Claudia worries about her teen daughter (Danes) back home who is intent on losing her virginity. None of which is as funny or endearing as it sounds. In fact, despite stellar cast, the film is draggy and squirm-inducing.

> **BEWARE** *Virginity as a conversation topic, a heavy make-out scene, profanity and brief drug use.*

1995 103m/C Holly Hunter, Anne Bancroft, Charles Durning, Robert Downey Jr., Dylan McDermott, Cynthia Stevenson, Geraldine Chaplin, Steve Guttenberg, Claire Danes; **Cameos:** David Strathairn, Austin Pendleton; **D:** Jodie Foster; **W:** W.D. Richter; **C:** Lajos Koltai; **M:** Mark Isham. **VHS, LV** *PGV*

If you like *Home Alone* (1990), you'll love:

Adventures in Babysitting (1987)

The Apple Dumpling Gang (1975)

Baby's Day Out (1994)

Blank Check (1993)

Camp Nowhere (1994)

Don't Tell Mom the Babysitter's Dead (1991)

The Goonies (1985)

Home Alone 2: Lost in New York (1992)

Honey I Blew Up the Kid (1989)

Honey I Shrunk the Kids (1992)

Hook (1991)

Monkey Trouble (1994)

Richie Rich (1994)

Home Movies

PG/Jr. High-Adult Blockbuster Hollywood director DePalma and his film students at Sarah Lawrence College devised this loose, sloppy comedy that got a theatrical release. Tells the story of a neurotic 16-year-old boy who uses moviemaking as a way to cope with (and wreak havoc on) his awful family. Pretty distasteful at times.

BEWARE *Profanity, mature themes, sex.*

1979 89m/C Kirk Douglas, Nancy Allen, Keith Gordon, Gerrit Graham, Vincent Gardenia, Harry Davenport; *D:* Brian DePalma; *W:* Brian DePalma; *M:* Pino Donaggio. **VHS, Beta, LV** *LIV, VES, IME*

A Home of Our Own

PG-13/Jr. High-Adult Semi-autobiographical tearjerker based on screenwriter Duncan's childhood. Widowed and poor mother of six is fired from her job at a Los Angeles potato chip factory. So she packs up the tribe and heads for a better life, landing in Idaho, in a ramshackle house owned by lonely Mr. Moon. What follows is a winter of discontent. Bates provides an intense performance as a poor but proud woman with a tough

exterior. Furlong supplies the story's narration as the eldest son.

1993 104m/C Kathy Bates, Edward Furlong, Soon-Teck Oh, Amy Sakasitz, Tony Campisi; *D:* Tony Bill; *W:* Patrick Duncan. **VHS, LV** *PGV*

Home to Stay

Jr. High-Adult Gentle, affecting made-for-TV family drama centered around a farm family whose aging patriarch Fonda insists on overseeing business affairs, even though his memory is clearly faltering. When the frustrated dad talks about putting the old man in a nursing home, the teenage daughter sneaks away with her beloved grandpa on an extended road trip so they can spend more time together. Based on the book "Grandpa and Frank" by Janet Marjerus.

1979 74m/C Henry Fonda, Frances Hyland, Michael McGuire; *D:* Delbert Mann; *M:* Hagood Hardy. **VHS, Beta** *TLF*

Homecoming

PG/Primary-Adult Disturbed mother abandons her four children at a Connecticut shopping mall in the care of 13-year-old eldest daughter Dicey (Peterson). The children slowly make their way to a relative's (Bedelia) home in Bridgeport, but when she proves equally uncaring, Dicey decides to continue the family trek to their maternal grandmother Ab's (Bancroft) house in Chrisfield, Maryland. No surprise when crazy grandma doesn't want them either, but this time Dicey is determined to make them all a home. Based on the Newberry Medal-winning children's novel by Cynthia Voight.

BEWARE *Themes of abandonment and hardship.*

1996 ?m/C Anne Bancroft, Kimberlee Peterson, Bonnie Bedelia, Trever O'Brien, Hanna Hall, William Greenblatt. **VHS** *HMK*

Homecoming: A Christmas Story

Family Made-for-television heart tugger that inspired the enduring television series "The Waltons." Depression-era Virginia mountain family struggles to celebrate Christmas although the whereabouts and safety of their father are unknown. Adapted by Earl Hamner, Jr. from his own autobiographical novel.

1971 98m/C Richard Thomas, Patricia Neal, Edgar Bergen, Cleavon Little, Ellen Corby; *D:* Fielder Cook. **VHS, Beta** *FOX*

Homer Price Stories

Primary Live-action filmizations of the popular children's stories.

1985 40m/C VHS, Beta *CCC, WKV, BTV*

Homeward Bound

G/Family Terminally ill teenager tries to reunite his long-estranged father and grandfather. Made-for-TV tearjerker with effective performances triumphing over formula script.

1980 96m/C David Soul, Moosie Drier, Barnard Hughes; *D:* Richard Michaels. **VHS, Beta** *HMV*

Homeward Bound: The Incredible Journey 🐾🐾🐾

G/Family Remake of the 1963 Disney flick tells the tried-and-true tale with a "Look Who's Talking" approach; now you can hear the lost animals talking, via celebrity voiceovers, as they try to find the way home after their owners relocate. The gimmick works (even though some of Fox's topical wisecracks may mean nothing to future generations), and it's hard not to shed a tear for the brave trio who develop a trusting bond through assorted misadventures. Stirring animalistic tale.

1993 85m/C Robert Hays, Kim Greist, Jean Smart, Benj Thall, Veronica Lauren, Kevin Timothy Chevalia; *D:* Duwayne Dunham; *W:* Linda Woolverton, Carolyn Thompson; *M:* Bruce Broughton; *V:* Don Ameche, Michael J. Fox, Sally Field. **VHS, LV** *DIS, BTV*

Homeward Bound 2: Lost in San Francisco 🐾🐾 ◁

G/Family Like Tony Bennett's heart, the winsome threesome from "Homeward Bound" get left in San Francisco. Chance the bulldog (voiced by Michael J. Fox), Sassy the Himalayan cat (Sally Field) and Shadow the wise old golden retriever (Ralph Waite, replacing the late Don Ameche) keep getting lost, but at least they have each other. They confront dognappers, a potentially deadly fire and other dangers, but always maintain their sense of humor, as they try to get home in this pretty good sequel to a very good original.

BEWARE *Dogfights, dog kissing, mean humans, a fire.*

1996 88m/C Robert Hays, Kim Greist, Veronica Lauren, Kevin Timothy Chevalia, Michael Rispoli, Max Perlich; *D:* David R. Ellis; *W:* Julie Hickson, Chris Hauty; *C:* Jack Conroy; *V:* Michael J. Fox, Sally Field, Ralph Waite, Al Michaels, Tommy Lasorda, Bob Uecker, Jon Polito, Adam Goldberg, Sinbad, Carla Gugino. **VHS** *TOU*

Honey, I Blew Up the Kid 🐾🐾 ◁

PG/Family Big-budget sequel to Disney's surprise hit "Honey, I Shrunk the Kids" cleverly turns the plot formula 180 degrees. Now screwball suburban inventor Wayne Szalinski works on an enlarging ray that accidentally zaps his two-year-old into a rambunctious, rampaging giant who gets bigger every time he comes in contact with electricity. Loaded with great f/x, tale gets a bit thin in places but remains charming and funny enough. Accompanied on cassette by a comic Little Richard music video "On Top of Spaghetti."

BEWARE *This could easily have been a G.*

1992 89m/C Rick Moranis, Marcia Strassman, Robert Oliveri, Daniel Shalikar, Joshua Shalikar, Lloyd Bridges, John Shea, Keri Russell, Gregory Sierra, Julia Sweeney, Kenneth Tobey, Peter Elbling; *D:* Randal Kleiser; *W:* Thom Eberhardt, Garry Goodrow; *M:* Bruce Broughton. **VHS, Beta, LV** *DIS*

If you like *Homeward Bound II: Lost in San Francisco* (1996), you'll love:

The Adventures of Milo and Otis (1989)

All Dogs Go to Heaven (1989)

All Dogs Go to Heaven 2 (1996)

Beethoven (1992)

Beethoven's 2nd (1993)

Benji (1974)

A Dog of Flanders (1959)

The Fox and the Hound (1981)

Heck's Way Home (1996)

Homeward Bound: The Incredible Journey (1993)

The Incredible Journey (1963)

Lady and the Tramp (1955)

Magic of Lassie (1978)

Old Yeller (1957)

101 Dalmatians (1961 & 1996)

Savage Sam (1953)

Honey, I Shrunk the Kids 🐾🐾 ◁

G/Family Not one of the greats, but an amicably gimmicky Disney fantasy that became a giant hit with audiences, about a suburban inventor whose raygun accidentally reduces his kids to 1/4 inch tall. When dad accidentally throws them out with the garbage, they must journey back to the house through the perilous jungle that was once the lawn. Accompanied by "Tummy Trouble," the first of a series of Roger Rabbit 'Maroon Cartoon' short subjects spun off from his own hit debut feature.

BEWARE *The shrunken kids befriend a loyal ant who dies defending them; not exactly "Old Yeller," but the filmmakers milk the sacrifice for all possible sentiment.*

Chance, Sassy and Shadow brave the streets to find their family in "Homeward Bound 2: Lost in San Francisco."

1989 101m/C Rick Moranis, Matt Frewer, Marcia Strassman, Kristine Sutherland, Thomas Wilson Brown, Jared Rushton, Amy O'Neill, Robert Oliveri; **D:** Joe Johnston, Rob Minkoff; **W:** Tom Schulman, Stuart Gordon; **M:** James Horner; **V:** Charles Fleischer, Kathleen Turner, Lou Hirsch, April Winchell. **VHS, Beta, LV** *DIS, MOV, RDG*

Honeymoon in Vegas 🎵🎵♭

PG-13/Jr. High-Adult Romantic comedy turns frantic after Cage loses his fiancee to wealthy but essentially criminal Caan in a high stakes Vegas poker game. So he has to get her back, providing Cage with more than an hour's worth of manic comedy in the classic Cage manic comedy vein. As the distraught young groom-to-be who encounters numerous obstacles on his way to the altar, Cage does his best to keep the juice going with basic economy script. Lightweight comedy features a bevy of Elvis impersonators in every size, shape, and color (including Elvis sky divers) and new versions of favorite Elvis tunes.

> ⚠ BEWARE ⚠ *Profanity; sexual situations and gambling for human stakes.*

1992 95m/C James Caan, Nicolas Cage, Sarah Jessica Parker, Noriyuki "Pat" Morita, John Capodice, Robert Costanzo, Anne Bancroft, Peter Boyle, Seymour Cassel, Tony Shalhoub; **D:** Andrew Bergman; **W:** Andrew Bergman; **M:** David Newman. **VHS, LV** *COL, NLC, IME*

Honkytonk Man 🎵🎵

PG/Jr. High-Adult Unsteady change-of-pace vehicle for action star Eastwood, set during the Depression. An aging, whoring, alcoholic country singer tries one last time to make it to Nashville, hoping to perform at the Grand Ole Opry. This time he takes his 14-year-old nephew (played by Eastwood's real-life son) with him, and a father-son relationship develops.

> ⚠ BEWARE ⚠ *Sex, alcohol use, profanity, hard life on the road, and terminal illness.*

1982 123m/C Clint Eastwood, Kyle Eastwood, John McIntire, Alexa Kenin, Verna Bloom; **D:** Clint Eastwood; **M:** Stephen Dorff. **VHS, Beta, LV** *WAR*

Hook 🎵🎵♭

PG/Jr. High-Adult Peter Banning, an uptight executive who puts work before family, is on a trip to London when his children are kidnapped by a supernatural force. This can happen on those transatlantic trips. However, it seems yuppie Banning is really Peter Pan, who did grow up and forgot Neverland. But his ancient enemy Captain

Hook remembers, and has the kids. Tinkerbell drags the frantic, nonbelieving Banning back to the fantasy realm for a showdown. Spielberg's take on the J.M. Barrie stories—what if they were true?—is a rich but unwieldy bag of treats, mixing action, huge sets, and superb f/x with serious themes of parenthood and rediscovery, literally, of one's inner child. But it's way too long, and the 'final' duel with the pompous Hook (Hoffman, in a dandy piece of ham acting) is unsatisfying and clearly open to a sequel. That proved wishful thinking; this was one of Stevie's few box-office disappointments. Still, there's a lot worthwhile here for youngsters and adults, especially when they can stop the VCR once or twice for a breather.

BEWARE *Lots of roughhousing between the pirates and the Lost Boys, and one of Peter's playmates is killed—but the plot soft pedals all violence.*

1991 142m/C Dustin Hoffman, Robin Williams, Julia Roberts, Bob Hoskins, Maggie Smith, Charlie Korsmo, Caroline Goodall, Amber Scott, Phil Collins, Arthur Malet, Dante Basco, Gwyneth Paltrow; **Cameos:** Glenn Close, David Crosby; **D:** Steven Spielberg; **W:** Nick Castle; **M:** John Williams. **VHS, Beta, LV, 8mm** *COL*

Hoop Dreams 🎷🎷🎷🎷

PG-13/Jr. High-Adult Exceptional documentary follows two inner-city basketball phenoms' lives through four years of high school as they chase their dreams of playing in the NBA. We meet Arthur Agee and William Gates as they prepare to enter St. Joseph, a predominantly white Catholic school that has offered them partial athletic scholarships. The coach tabs Gates as the next Isiah Thomas, the school's most famous alum. There's plenty of game footage, but the more telling and fascinating parts of the film deal with the kids' families and home life. Both players encounter dramatic reversals of fortune on and off the court. Terrific, thought-provoking look at the role sports plays in American life, at how families handle pressures, and the differences between expectations and reality.

BEWARE *No violence is shown, but Agee's account of being mugged at gunpoint is chilling. Williams and his girlfriend have a baby. The basketball coach gets profane when stressed.*

1994 169m/C Arthur Agee, William Gates; **D:** Steve James. **Award Nominations:** Academy Awards '94: Best Film Editing; **Awards:** Chicago Film Critics Awards '94: Best Film; Los Angeles Film Critics Association Awards '94: Best Feature Documentary; MTV Movie Awards '95: Best New Filmmaker Award (James); National Board of Review Awards '94: Best Feature Documentary; New York Film Critics Awards '94: Best Feature Documentary; National Society of Film Critics Awards '94: Best Feature Documentary; Sundance Film Festival '94: Audience Award. **VHS, LV** *NLC*

Hoosiers 🎷🎷🎷

PG/Jr. High-Adult In 1951 Indiana, a small-town high school basketball team gets a new, unorthodox coach. Despite public skepticism, he makes the team, and each person on it, better than they thought possible. Classic, uplifting plot rings true because of Hackman's complex and sensitive performance coupled with Hopper's touch-

ing portrait of an alcoholic ex-hoops star who becomes a winner again.

BEWARE *Alcohol use, salty language.*

1986 115m/C Gene Hackman, Barbara Hershey, Dennis Hopper, David Neidorf, Sheb Wooley, Fern Parsons, Brad Boyle, Steve Hollar, Brad Long; **D:** David Anspaugh; **W:** Angelo Pizzo; **M:** Jerry Goldsmith. **VHS, Beta, LV** *LIV*

Hop on Pop

Family Cartoon version of the Dr. Seuss classic plus two more, "Marvin K. Mooney Will You Please Go Now" and "Oh Say Can You Say?"

1990 30m/C VHS *RAN, VEC*

Hope and Glory 🎷🎷🎷 ᵇ

PG-13/Sr. High-Adult Boorman turns memories of WWII into a complex and sensitive family saga of suburban Londoners surviving the Battle of Britain. While father's away fighting, mother must cope with a mischief-prone son, the awakening sexuality of the teenage daughter, plus those pesky nightly air raids. Tale unfurls largely through the small boy's eyes, and such scenes are priceless: war becomes a giant, abstract game, sometimes tragic, but mostly an opportunity for grand fun. "Thank you Adolf!" shouts a child when a Nazi bomb levels their hated school. No real violence, but an abundance of mature themes (like the daughter's promiscuity and resulting pregnancy) skew this more toward adult viewers.

BEWARE *Mature themes, alcohol use, sex. The son joins a club of kid vandals in the bombed-out ruins; their admission ceremony is a recitation of swear words—all but one of which seems utterly inoffensive today.*

1987 97m/C Sebastian Rice Edwards, Geraldine Muir, Sarah Miles, Sammi Davis, David Hayman, Derrick O'Connor, Susan Wooldridge, Jean-Marc Barr, Ian Bannen, Jill Baker, Charley Boorman, Annie Leon, Katrine Boorman, Gerald James; **D:** John Boorman. **Award Nominations:** Academy Awards '87: Best Art Direction/Set Decoration, Best Cinematography, Best Director (Boorman), Best Original Screenplay, Best Picture; **Awards:** British Academy Awards '87: Best Film, Best Supporting Actress (Wooldridge); Los Angeles Film Critics Association Awards '87: Best Director (Boorman), Best Film; National Board of Review Awards '87: 10 Best Films of the Year. **VHS, Beta, LV, 8mm** *FCT, HMV, NLC*

Hoppity Goes to Town

Family Full-length animated feature from the Fleischer Brothers, the "Popeye" and "Betty Boop" animators, who sought to become cartoon tycoons on the scale of Disney but never earned "Snow White" scale profits at the box office. Their work is still well worth a look, and in this inventive modern tale the fun-loving inhabitants of Bugville, who live in a patch of weeds in NYC, try to avoid careless extermination by humans.

1941 77m/C D: Dave Fleischer; **M:** Frank Loesser, Hoagy Carmichael. **VHS, LV** *REP, MRV, FCT*

The Horn Blows at Midnight

🦴🦴🦴

Family Lavish comedy-fantasy starring comedian Benny as a band trumpeter who falls asleep and dreams he's an archangel, who must earn his wings not by helping some earthly soul like Clarence did in "It's a Wonderful Life"— but by sounding the mystical note that destroys the world. Sent to the doomed Earth on New Year's Eve, he's soon distracted by pretty faces and other temptations. Funny, and a little subversive; you really root for Benny and hope he'll blow that note to please his employers!

1945 78m/B Jack Benny, Alexis Smith, Dolores Moran, Allyn Joslyn, Reginald Gardiner, Guy Kibbee, John Alexander, Margaret Dumont; **D:** Raoul Walsh. **VHS** *MGM, FCT*

Horse Feathers 🦴🦴🦴 ⌐

Family Marx Brothers madness with Groucho sidesplitting as Professor Wagstaff, new president of Huxley College, who'll stop at nothing to win a big football match. He mistakes Harpo and Chico for championship athletic talent and recruits them as students. Terrific slapstick game finale that violates every known rule of sportsmanship, and a short running time that's just right.

 Alcohol use.

1932 67m/B Groucho Marx, Chico Marx, Harpo Marx, Zeppo Marx, Thelma Todd, David Landau, Nat Pendleton; **D:** Norman Z. McLeod. **VHS, Beta, LV** *MCA*

A Horse for Danny 🦴🦴 ⌐

G/Family First of all, Danny's an 11-year-old girl. She and her uncle, a hard-luck horse trainer (Robert Urich), find a thoroughbred named Tom Thumb, who may be their chance at the winners circle. TV movie. Ages 6 and up.

1995 92m/C Robert Urich, Leelee Sobieski, Ron Brice, Karen Carlson, Gary Basaraba; **D:** Dick Lowry. **VHS** *HMK*

The Horse in the Gray Flannel Suit 🦴🦴 ⌐

G/Family Disney diversion about a harried advertising man whose daughter wants a horse and whose client wants to boost sales of his aspirin pills. Our hero tries to combine the best of both worlds with an ad campaign built around a beer-drinking steed.

 Alcohol use.

1968 114m/C Dean Jones, Ellen Janov, Fred Clark, Diane Baker, Lloyd Bochner, Kurt Russell; **D:** Norman Tokar. **VHS, Beta** *DIS, OM*

The Horse That Played Center Field

Primary-Jr. High A horse is installed on the roster of a losing baseball team to motivate the players into performing up to their potential. The beast proves to be a phe-

nomenal fielder and leads the team to the World Series. An ABC Afterschool Special.

197? 48m/C VHS, Beta *MTT*

The Horse Without a Head

🦴🦴 ⌐

Family Stolen loot has been hidden in a discarded toy horse which is now the property of a group of poor children. The thieves, however, have different plans. Good family fare originally shown on the Disney television show.

1963 89m/C Jean-Pierre Aumont, Herbert Lom, Leo McKern, Pamela Franklin, Vincent Winter; **D:** Don Chaffey. **VHS, Beta** *DIS*

Horsemasters 🦴🦴

Family A group of young riders enter a special training program in England to achieve the ultimate equestrian title of horsemaster, with Annette having to overcome her fear of jumping. Originally a two-part Disney television show, and released as a feature film in Europe.

1961 85m/C Tommy Kirk, Annette Funicello, Janet Munro, Tony Britton, Donald Pleasence, Jean Marsh, John Fraser, Millicent Martin; **D:** William Fairchild. **VHS, Beta** *DIS*

Horses: Close Up and Very Personal

Preschool No words, but plenty of beautifully photographed Arabians, appaloosas, Clydesdales, quarter horses frolicking, running, jumping, learning to stand, switching their tails, walking on the beach, grazing in the Rockies, running at the race track, plowing on the farm, bucking at the rodeo, ambling at the dude ranch. Ages 1 to 7.

1994 30m/C VHS *SFP*

Horton Hatches the Egg

Primary Cartoon version of the Dr. Seuss tale of big-hearted Horton the Elephant who helps out a friend by sitting on the little egg in her nest. Also includes the story "If I Ran the Circus."

1991 30m/C VHS *RAN, BTV*

Horton Hears a Who!

Family Horton, the whimsical rhyming elephant, tries to rescue the tiny Whos of Whoville after realizing that their microscopic world resides on a dust speck, in this musicalized Dr. Seuss fable.

1970 26m/C VHS, Beta *MGM, KUI*

Hot Lead & Cold Feet 🦴🦴

G/Family In the Old West contrasting twin brothers (one a gunfighter, the other a missionary) compete in a train race where the winner will take ownership of a small western town. Dale plays both brothers and their curmudgeony father. Standard vintage-70s Disney comedy barely avoids Apple Dumpling gang territory.

1978 89m/C Jim Dale, Don Knotts, Karen Valentine; **D:** Robert Butler; **M:** Buddy Baker. **VHS, Beta** *DIS*

Hot Shot

PG/Primary-Sr. High Jimmy defies his wealthy parents to qualify as a soccer player. When his attitude threatens his pro career, though, the young man seeks training from a Brazilian champ, portrayed by Pele. Old story, different sport, new swear words, yellow cards.

BEWARE *Profanity.*

1986 90m/C Pele, Jim Youngs, Billy Warlock, Weyman Thompson, Mario Van Peebles, David Groh; **D:** Rick King. **VHS, Beta** *WAR, MVD*

Hot Shots! Part Deux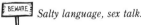

PG-13/Jr. High-Adult Second "Hot Shots" outing doesn't live up to the first, but it's not bad either. Admiral Tug Benson (Bridges) is elected President (yes, of the U.S.) and calls on Sheen's newly pumped-up Topper to take on Saddam Hussein Rambo-style. Love interest Ramada (Golino), returns but this time she's competing with Michelle (Bakke), a sexy CIA agent. Crenna spoofs his role in the "Rambo" films as Sheen's mentor; look for real-life dad Martin in a take-off of "Apocalypse Now." Shtick flies as fast and furious as the bullets and bodies, with Bridges getting a chance to reprise his glory days of "Sea Hunt." Don't miss the credits.

BEWARE *Brief nudity, profanity, violence, and sex talk, all done up in a farcical fashion.*

1993 89m/C Charlie Sheen, Lloyd Bridges, Valeria Golino, Brenda Bakke, Richard Crenna, Miguel Ferrer, Rowan Atkinson, Jerry Haleva, Mitchell Ryan, Gregory Sierra, Ryan Stiles, Michael Colyar; **Cameos:** Martin Sheen, Bob Vila; **D:** Jim Abrahams; **W:** Pat Proft, Jim Abrahams; **M:** Basil Poledouris. **VHS** *FXV, BTV*

Hot to Trot! 🦴

PG/Jr. High-Adult Babbling idiot inherits a talking horse who's full of stock-market tips, in an updated, downtrodden version of the "Francis, the Talking Mule" comedies, with a scent of Mr. Ed. The equine voice is provided by Candy. Some real funny guys are wasted here.

BEWARE *Salty language, sex talk.*

1988 90m/C Bob(cat) Goldthwait, Dabney Coleman, Virginia Madsen, Jim Metzler, Cindy Pickett, Tim Kazurinsky, Santos Morales, Barbara Whinnery, Garry Kluger; **D:** Michael Dinner; **W:** Charlie Peters; **M:** Danny Elfman; **V:** John Candy. **VHS, Beta, LV** *WAR*

The Hound that Thought He was a Raccoon

Preschool-Primary Nubbin the hound refuses to chase raccoons because he wants to be one. A live-action tale from the TV series "The Wonderful World of Disney."
1990 48m/C **VHS, Beta** *MTI, DSN*

House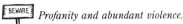

R/Sr. High-Adult Horror novelist moves into his dead aunt's supposedly haunted house only to find that the monsters don't necessarily stay in the closets. His worst nightmares come to life as he writes about his Vietnam experiences and is forced to relive the tragic events, but these aren't the only visions that start springing to life. It sounds depressing, but is actually a funny, intelligent "horror" flick. Followed by several lesser sequels.

BEWARE *Profanity and abundant violence.*

1986 93m/C William Katt, George Wendt, Richard Moll, Kay Lenz, Michael Ensign, Mary Stavin, Susan French; **D:** Steve Miner; **W:** Ethan Wiley; **M:** Harry Manfredini. **VHS, Beta, LV** *NWV, VTR*

House Arrest 🦴🦴

PG/Jr. High-Adult Kids lock their fighting parents in the basement so they'll be forced to sort things out. Kind of on the same lines as Disney's "Parent Trap." Most of the movie was actually shot in a basement, which could get a little claustrophobic, don't you think?? Watch for Jamie Lee Curtis hanging upside down in a laundry chute "True Lies" style.

BEWARE *Thematic material including divorce and language. And should kids really be locking their parents in basements??*

1996 107m/C Jamie Lee Curtis, Kevin Pollak, Jennifer Tilly, Ray Walston, Wallace Shawn. **VHS** *NYR*

House of Cards 🦴🦴

PG-13/Jr. High-Adult Six-year-old Sally suddenly stops talking and even reacting in normal ways after her father is killed in an accident at an archeological site in Mexico. Mom Ruth fights with conventional therapists to drag her daughter out of the fantasy realm, and her unorthodox treatment includes virtual-reality computer technology, Mexican mysticism, and an elaborate tower of cards. Coming out right after the thematically similar "Lorenzo's Oil," this couldn't help suffering by comparison; it's a melange of dubious psychology and arresting visual surprises, held together by Turner's intractable performance and little Menina's ethereal presence in her acting debut.

BEWARE *Child is greatly affected mentally by father's death. Profanity.*

1992 109m/C Kathleen Turner, Asha Menina, Tommy Lee Jones, Shiloh Strong, Esther Rolle, Park Overall, Michael Horse, Anne Pitoniak; **D:** Michael Lessac; **W:** Michael Lessac. **VHS, LV** *LIV, BTV, FCT*

The House of Dies Drear

Family A modern-day African American family moves into an old house that turns out to be haunted by the ghost of a long dead abolitionist. The family is transported back to the days of slavery as they interact with the ghost. Based on the story by Virginia Hamilton. Part of the "Wonderworks" series.

1988 107m/C Howard E. Rollins Jr., Moses Gunn, Shavar Ross, Gloria Foster, Clarence Williams III; **D:** Allan Goldstein. **VHS** *HMV, PME, FCT*

House of Wax 🎨🎨🎨

PG/Sr. High-Adult Deranged sculptor (Price, who else?) builds a sinister wax museum which showcases creations that were once alive. A remake of the early horror flick "Mystery of the Wax Museum," and one of the 50s' most popular 3-D films. This one still has the power to give the viewer the creeps, thanks to another chilling performance by Price. Look for a very young Bronson, as well as Carolyn "Morticia Addams" Jones as a victim.

> ⚠ BEWARE *Violence and grotesque wax figures. Wax figures and some humans are beheaded guillotine-style.*

1953 88m/C Vincent Price, Frank Lovejoy, Carolyn Jones, Phyllis Kirk, Paul Cavanagh, Charles Bronson; **D:** Andre de Toth. **VHS, Beta, LV** *WAR, MLB*

House Party 🎨🎨🎨

R/Sr. High-Adult Light-hearted, black hip-hop version of a '50s teen comedy with rap duo Kid 'n' Play. After his father grounds him for fighting, a high-schooler attempts all sorts of wacky schemes to get to his friend's party. Sleeper hit features real-life music rappers and some dynamite dance numbers.

> ⚠ BEWARE *Profanity and sex talk.*

1990 100m/C Christopher Reid, Christopher Martin, Martin Lawrence, Tisha Campbell, Paul Anthony, A.J. Johnson, Robin Harris; **D:** Reginald Hudlin; **W:** Reginald Hudlin; **M:** Marcus Miller. **VHS, Beta, LV** *COL, FCT, NLC*

House Party 2: The Pajama Jam 🎨🎨🎨

R/Sr. High-Adult Rap stars Kid 'N' Play are back in this hip-hop sequel to the original hit. At Harris University Kid 'N' Play hustle up overdue tuition by holding a campus "jammie jam jam." A stellar cast shines in this rap-powered pajama bash.

> ⚠ BEWARE *Profanity and sex talk, same as the first.*

1991 94m/C Christopher Reid, Christopher Martin, Tisha Campbell, Iman, Queen Latifah, Georg Stanford Brown, Martin Lawrence, Eugene Allen, George Anthony Bell, Kamron, Tony Burton, Helen Martin, William Schallert; **D:** Doug McHenry, George Jackson; **W:** Rusty Cundieff, Daryl G. Nickens; **M:** Vassal Benford. **VHS, LV** *COL, NLC*

House Party 3 🎨

R/Sr. High-Adult Kid is engaged to be married and Play tries to set up a blowout bachelor party. The duo are also working on their record producer careers by trying to sign a feisty female rap group (real life TLC). Strikes out early for easy profanity while never coming within spitting distance of first two flicks.

> ⚠ BEWARE *Profanity and sex talk again.*

1994 93m/C Christopher Reid, Christopher Martin, Angela Means, Tisha Campbell, Bernie Mac, Barbara Edwards, Michael Colyar, David Edwards, Betty Lester, Chris Tucker; **D:** Eric Meza; **W:** Takashi Bufford; **M:** David Allen Jones. **VHS, LV** *COL, IME*

The House with a Clock in Its Walls

Primary-Jr. High Eerie 'toon tale about a man with a plan to destroy the world. Lots of spooky imagery including a gothic house, a graveyard, an orphan, and magic. Based on the novel by John Bellairs.

1991 24m/C VHS *BAR*

A House Without a Christmas Tree 🎨🎨 🎨

Family Father with a sour attitude toward the holidays repeatedly denies his small daughter what she most desires—a real indoor Christmas tree. Will dad come around by fadeout? Charming, if slightly predictable, made-for-TV movie.

1972 90m/C Jason Robards Jr., Lisa Lucas, Mildred Natwick; **D:** Paul Bogart. **VHS, Beta** *FXV, FCT*

Houseguest 🎨🎨 🎨

PG/Primary-Adult Dumb but harmless comedy about mistaken identity finds hard luck dreamer Kevin Franklin (Sinbad) on the run from loan sharks. Fortunately, while trying to make a getaway at the airport, he's mistaken for the childhood buddy (who's now a dentist, prompting some hygiene humor) of family guy/lawyer Gary Young (Hartman), who opens his suburban home to his long lost pal. Street smart Kevin naturally manages to solve every family problem that arises while avoiding some inept Mafia thugs. Everyone is oh-so-good-natured and the importance of friendship over greed is emphasized.

> ⚠ BEWARE *Language, double entendre humor, and some comic violence. (Remember, he's hiding from loan sharks.)*

1994 109m/C Sinbad, Phil Hartman, Jeffrey Jones, Kim Greist, Stan Shaw, Tony Longo, Mason Adams, Paul Ben-Victor, Chauncey Leopardi, Ron Glass, Talia Seider, Kim Murphy; **D:** Randall Miller; **W:** Michael J. Di Gaetano, Laurence Gay; **C:** Jerzy Zielinski; **M:** John Debney. **VHS, LV** *TOU*

Housekeeping 🎨🎨🎨

PG/Jr. High-Adult Quiet, offbeat and sensitive comedy by "Gregory's Girl" Forsyth. Young sisters (orphaned by their mother's suicide) are cared for by their eccentric, free-spirited aunt in a small and small-minded '50s Oregon community. Soon it's clear that Aunt Sylvie is not only unorthodox but mentally ill, and the girls' relationship with her defies public disapproval. Acting showcase for Lahti receives generous support from young Walker and Burchill. Based on the novel "Sylvie's Ark" by Marilynne Robinson.

> ⚠ BEWARE *A bonkers adult is the primary caregiver of two young orphans.*

1987 117m/C Christine Lahti, Sarah Walker, Andrea Burchill; *D:* Bill Forsyth; *W:* Bill Forsyth; *M:* Michael Gibbs. **VHS, Beta** *COL*

Housesitter

PG/Jr. High-Adult Martin is an architect/dreamer who builds his high school sweetheart Delany a beautiful house and surprises her with a marriage proposal. After she says no, he has no choice but to have a one-night stand with Hawn, which changes his life. Hawn moves into Martin's empty dream house and assumes the position of his wife, unbeknownst to him. Soon she's spinning whoppers of lies and soon has the entire town, including Davis's parents and ex-girlfriend, believing her wacky stories, while she struggles to keep with the twists and turns of her story. Romantic screwball comedy is uneven and not exactly plotted with reality in mind, but Martin and Hawn give it a go.

> **BEWARE** *Sex talk and bad lesson that lying pays off.*

1992 102m/C Steve Martin, Goldie Hawn, Dana Delany, Julie Harris, Donald Moffat, Peter MacNicol, Richard B. Shull, Laurel Cronin, Christopher Durang; *D:* Frank Oz; *W:* Mark Stein, Brian Grazer; *M:* Miles Goodman. **VHS, Beta, LV** *MCA, PMS, BTV*

How a Car is Built

Primary A behind-the-scenes look at Dearborn, Michigan's Ford Mustang plant and assembly line. Cartoon character I.Q. Parrot tells how a car is made from cutting the steel for the body to driving off in a finished product. Includes commentary from workers, historic footage and a look at some amazing machinery. Ages 4 to 10.
1995 30m/C VHS

How a Car is Built with IQ Parrot

Preschool-Jr. High Animated character "I.Q.Parrot" takes a tour through the Ford Motor Comapny facilities, illustrating step-by-step how a Ford Mustang is built. Dad will probably like this one. too.
1995 30m/C VHS *TPV*

How a Tugboat Works with IQ Parrot

Preschool-Jr. High Emmy-Award winning producer Robert E. Frye and William K. Love follow the daily activities of a New York Harbor tugboat Miriam, and her crew. Contains actual footage of the various operations performed by a tugboat, including the steps taken when the Miriam helps the Queen Elizabeth 2 into dock. Also provides insight into the history of tugboats.
1995 ?m/C VHS

How Bugs Bunny Won the West

Family Cowpoke Bugs has a showdown against that ornery desperado Yosemite Sam. Ages 4 to 8.
19?? 24m/C VHS *WAR*

How Green was My Valley

Jr. High-Adult Saga of the triumphs and tribulations of a Welsh mining family, from the youthful perspective of the youngest child (played by a 13-year-old McDowall). Setting is turn of the century, when coal mining was a difficult but fair-paying way of life, and ends, after unionization, strikes, fatalities, romance, and the boy hero's ordeals at the hands of cruel schoolmaster. Splendid entertainment will leave you nostalgic for a time and place you never even knew. Based on the novel by Richard Llewellyn.

1941 118m/C Walter Pidgeon, Maureen O'Hara, Donald Crisp, Anna Lee, Roddy McDowall, John Loder, Sara Allgood, Barry Fitzgerald, Patric Knowles, Rhys Williams, Arthur Shields, Ann Todd, Mae Marsh; *D:* John Ford; *W:* Philip Dunne; *M:* Alfred Newman. **Award Nominations:** Academy Awards '41: Best Film Editing, Best Screenplay, Best Sound, Best Supporting Actress (Allgood), Best Original Score; **Awards:** Academy Awards '41: Best Black and White Cinematography, Best Director (Ford), Best Interior Decoration, Best Picture, Best Supporting Actor (Crisp). **VHS, Beta** *FOX, FUS, BTV*

How I Got into College

PG-13/Jr. High-Adult Underachieving but mainly inoffensive satire about a high school senior and the desperate measures he takes to qualify for admission to a ritzy local college (inspired by Wesleyan College) so he can pursue the girl of his dreams.

> **BEWARE** *Profanity.*

1989 87m/C Corey Parker, Lara Flynn Boyle, Christopher Rydell, Anthony Edwards, Phil Hartman, Brian Doyle-Murray, Nora Dunn, Finn Carter, Charles Rocket; *D:* Steve Holland; *W:* Terrel Seltzer. **VHS, Beta, LV** *FOX*

How It's Done: From Baseball Bats to Potato Chips

Preschool-Primary Detective Howie Dunn, private eye pelican, heads to south Florida to investigate a case of disappearing oranges. And what does he find? Why, a juice processing factory. Dunn also investigates a cherry plant, chocolate factory, and more. Ages 4 to 12.
1995 34m/C VHS *VTR*

How It's Done: From Roller Coasters to Ice Cream

Preschool-Primary Puppet pelican detective Howie Dunn likes to see how everyday items are made, including how roller coasters are designed, a trip to a softball

factory, an ice cream dairy, a pencil factory, and a TV newsroom. Ages 4 to 12.
1995 32m/C VHS *VTR*

How the Rhino Got His Skin/ How the Camel Got His Hump

Preschool-Primary Nicholson narrates these two tales from Kipling's Just So stories. Part of the "Rabbit Ears" series of marvelous storytelling videos.
1991 30m/C VHS *KUI, COL*

How the West Was Fun

Family The Olsen gals are visiting great godmother Natty's dude ranch, which is in financial difficulty, and must outsmart her greedy son Bart (Mull), a land grabber who wants to turn the ranch into an environmentally unfriendly western theme park. Made for TV, this one's sure to please fans of the Olsen twins.
1995 93m/C Mary-Kate Olsen, Ashley Olsen, Martin Mull, Michelle Greene, Patrick Cassidy, Leon Pownall, Peg Phillips; *D:* Stuart Margolin; *M:* Richard Bellis. **VHS** *WAR*

How the West was Won 🎬🎬🎬

G/Jr. High-Adult A panoramic view of the American West, focusing on the trials, tribulations and travels of three generations of one family, set against the background of wars and historical events. Particularly notable for its impressive cast list and expansive western settings.

🚨 **BEWARE** *Violence; alcohol use.*

1963 165m/C John Wayne, Carroll Baker, Lee J. Cobb, Spencer Tracy, Gregory Peck, Karl Malden, Robert Preston, Eli Wallach, Henry Fonda, George Peppard, Debbie Reynolds, Carolyn Jones, Richard Widmark, James Stewart, Walter Brennan, Andy Devine, Raymond Massey, Agnes Moorehead, Harry (Henry) Morgan, Thelma Ritter, Russ Tamblyn; *D:* John Ford, Henry Hathaway, George Marshall; *W:* James R. Webb. **Award Nominations:** Academy Awards '63: Best Art Direction/Set Decoration (Color), Best Color Cinematography, Best Costume Design (Color), Best Picture, Best Original Score; **Awards:** Academy Awards '63: Best Film Editing, Best Sound, Best Story & Screenplay; National Board of Review Awards '63: 10 Best Films of the Year. **VHS, Beta, LV** *MGM*

How the Whale Got His Throat

Primary-Jr. High From Kipling's "Just So Stories" comes this tale of what happens after a whale lets a man go free after he tried to eat him.
1984 10m/C VHS, Beta *MTI*

How to Be a Perfect Person in Just Three Days

Family Fun comedy for the whole family shows the efforts of a kid striving for perfection before realizing that individuality is more fun. Based on the book by Stephen Mane. Part of the "Wonderworks" series.
1984 58m/C Wallace Shawn, Ilan Mitchell-Smith, Hermione Gingold, Joan Micklin Silver. **VHS** *PME, FCT, HMV*

How to Eat Fried Worms

Preschool-Jr. High One of the CBS Storybreak series, an animated version of Thomas Rockwell's book about a boy named Billy who bets $50 that he can eat a worm a day for 15 days.
1985 25m/C VHS *KUI*

How to Make an American Quilt 🎬🎬 ♭

PG-13/Jr. High-Adult It takes all kinds of pieces to make a quilt, to make America, to make a slow and thoughtful movie. Perpetual grad student Finn (Ryder) spends the summer at her grandmother's (Burstyn's) big house in a small town. She's trying to avoid deciding whether or not to marry her boyfriend. Grandmother and friends tell stories (in flashback) of their lives and loves as they work on a wedding quilt for Finn. Rich in character, and the acting is fine, especially Bancroft as Finn's aunt, and Angelou as chief quilter, but there are many characters and stories to keep straight. Based on the novel by Whitney Otto.

🚨 **BEWARE** *Scene of drug use, some nudity, and heavy kissing.*

1995 109m/C Winona Ryder, Ellen Burstyn, Anne Bancroft, Lois Smith, Jean Simmons, Kate Nelligan, Maya Angelou, Alfre Woodard, Dermot Mulroney, Kate Capshaw, Rip Torn, Derrick O'Connor, Loren Dean, Samantha Mathis, Joanna Going, Tim Guinee, Johnathon Schaech, Claire Danes, Jared Leto, Esther Rolle, Melinda Dillon, Alicia (Lecy) Goranson, Maria Celedonio, Mykelti Williamson; *D:* Jocelyn Moorhouse; *W:* Jane Anderson; *C:* Janusz Kaminski; *M:* Thomas Newman. **VHS** *NYR*

How to Play Baseball

Preschool-Primary Disney cartoon comedy in which a whole team of Goofballs take to the field to play a hilarious game of baseball.
1977 8m/C VHS, Beta *MTI, DSN*

How to Stuff a Wild Bikini 🎬🎬

Family Tired next to last feature in the overlong tradition of Frankie and Annette doing the beach thing, featuring a pregnant Funicello (though this is hidden and not part of the plot). Avalon actually has only a small role as the jealous boyfriend trying to see if Annette will remain faithful while he's away on military duty. Keaton is the witch doctor who helps Frankie keep Annette true. "Playboy" playmates wander about in small swimsuits, garage band extraordinare "The Kingsmen" play themselves, and Brian Wilson of the "Beach Boys" makes a rare public appearance. Followed by "Ghost in the Invisible Bikini," the only movie in the series that isn't on video. 🎵 After the Party; Better Be Ready; Follow Your Leader; Give Her Lovin'; How About Us?; How to Stuff a Wild Bikini; I'm the Boy Next Door; Madison Avenue; The Perfect Boy.
1965 90m/C Annette Funicello, Dwayne Hickman, Frankie Avalon, Beverly Adams, Buster Keaton, Harvey Lembeck, Mickey Rooney, Brian Donlevy, Jody McCrea, John Ashley, Marianne Gaba, Len

Lesser, Irene Tsu, Bobbi Shaw, Luree Holmes; **D:** William Asher; **W:** William Asher, Leo Townsend; **M:** Les Baxter. **VHS, Beta** *NO*

How We Work: Building Construction

Preschool-Primary Foreman Scott shows how buildings are built and older buildings are demolished. Ages 5 to 9.
1994 35m/C VHS *QVD*

How We Work: Road Construction

Preschool-Primary Kids' Construction Company Foreman Scott introduces kids to earth moving and road construction equipment such as bulldozers, cranes, and trucks. Ages 4 to 9.
1994 35m/C VHS *QVD*

Howard the Duck 🦴

PG/Jr. High-Adult Quack if you've seen it. Megabucks Lucasfilm adaptation of a short-lived Marvel Comics superhero spoof. Alien resembling a talking duck accidentally beams to Earth—Cleveland, in fact. First half has Howard trying to fit into human society, and when those fowl gags run dry, the filmmakers give him space demons to fight in a climactic f/x barrage. Plus an all-girl rock band! Overstuffed screen turkey's premise has appeal for kids (it does have a talking duck) and a decent cast but it's feathered with birdbrained sex 'n' drug jokes. The stiff, mask-like duck face makes one appreciate the fine job the Jim Henson Creature Shop did for the Teenage Mutant Ninja Turtles.

> **BEWARE** *Sex talk, drug talk, violence, salty language, brief duck nudity (you think we're kidding?).*

1986 111m/C Lea Thompson, Jeffrey Jones, Tim Robbins; **D:** Willard Huyck; **W:** Willard Huyck, Gloria Katz; **M:** Sylvester Levay, John Barry. **VHS, Beta, LV** *MCA*

Howard's End 🦴🦴🦴🦴

PG/Jr. High-Adult E.M. Forster's 1910 novel about property, privilege, class differences, and Edwardian society is brought to enchanting life by the Merchant Ivory team. A tragic series of events occurs after two impulsive sisters become involved with a working class couple and a wealthy family. Tragedy aside, this is a visually beautiful effort with subtle performances where a glance or a gesture says as much as any dialog. The winner of numerous awards and wide critical acclaim. Thompson is especially notable as the compassionate Margaret, while Hopkins plays the repressed English gentleman brilliantly.

1992 143m/C Anthony Hopkins, Emma Thompson, Helena Bonham Carter, Vanessa Redgrave, James Wilby, Sam West, Jemma Redgrave, Nicola Duffett, Prunella Scales, Joseph Bennett; **Cameos:** Simon Callow; **D:** James Ivory; **W:** Ruth Prawer Jhabvala. **Award Nominations:** Academy Awards '92: Best Cinematography, Best Costume Design, Best Director (Ivory), Best Picture, Best Supporting Actress (Redgrave), Best Original Score; Cannes Film Festival '92: Best Film; **Awards:** Academy Awards '92: Best Actress (Thompson), Best Adapted Screenplay, Best Art Direction/Set Decoration; British

Academy Awards '93: Best Actress (Thompson); Chicago Film Critics Awards '92: Best Actress (Thompson); Golden Globe Awards '93: Best Actress—Drama (Thompson); Los Angeles Film Critics Association Awards '92: Best Actress (Thompson); National Board of Review Awards '92: 10 Best Films of the Year, Best Actress (Thompson), Best Director (Ivory); National Society of Film Critics Awards '92: Best Actress (Thompson). **VHS, LV, 8mm** *COL, CRC, MOV*

The Howdy Doody Show (Puppet Playhouse)/The Gabby Hayes Show

Preschool-Jr. High Buffalo Bill, Clarabell, and the Peanut Gallery help Howdy Doody with a nostalgic circus of fun in this popular and pioneering children's program. On the same tape, Gabby Hayes sings the Quaker Oats song and tells a tale of the old west.
1948 60m/B VHS, Beta *IHF, MVC*

The Howling 🦴🦴🦴

R/Sr. High-Adult Pretty television reporter takes a rest at a clinic and discovers slowly that its denizens are actually werewolves. Crammed with inside jokes, this horror comedy pioneered the use of the body-altering prosthetic make-up (by Rob Bottin) now essential for on-screen man-to-wolf transformations. At last count, followed by five sequels.

> **BEWARE** *Horror violence. Afraid of werewolves? Don't watch.*

1981 91m/C Dee Wallace Stone, Patrick Macnee, Dennis Dugan, Christopher Stone, Belinda Balaski, Kevin McCarthy, John Carradine, Slim Pickens, Elisabeth Brooks, Robert Picardo, Dick Miller; **D:** Joe Dante; **W:** John Sayles, Terence H. Winkless; **M:** Pino Donaggio. **VHS, Beta, LV** *COL*

H.R. Pufnstuf, Vol. 1

Primary-Jr. High Compilation of the famous surreal Sid & Marty Krofft production. The friendly dragon Mayor of Magic Island, H.R. Pufnstuf, and his friend Jimmy battle the evil Witchie-poo and her bumbling henchmen as they struggle to find the Secret Path of Escape. Additional volumes available.

1969 46m/C Billie Hayes, Jack Wild, Joan Gerber, Felix Silla, Jerry Landon. **VHS, Beta** *NLC*

Huck and the King of Hearts 🦴 ♪

PG/Jr. High-Adult Nice banter between the title characters is the best part of this trifle. Huck's a resourceful modern-day Hannibal boy fleeing a broken home to find his grandpa. He becomes buddies out west with a homeless Indian cardshark—named Jim, of course—who's (yawn) chased by gangsters. Insubstantial Twain takeoff, loses half a bone for the miserable, crotch-kicking finale.

> **BEWARE** *Roughhousing, salty language, alcohol use, (anti)drug talk.*

1993 103m/C Chauncey Leopardi, Graham Greene, Dee Wallace Stone, Joe Piscopo, John Astin, Gretchen Becker; **D:** Michael Keusch; **W:** Christopher Sturgeon; **M:** Chris Saranec. **VHS, Beta, LV** *PSM*

Winona Ryder listens to a story told by Anne Bancroft in "How to Make an American Quilt."

Huckleberry Finn 🦴🦴

G/Family Followup to the 1973 Readers Digest musical version of "Tom Sawyer" is a forgettable concoction, nowhere near as fun. East reprises his role as the adventurous Huck, and the storyline sticks to Mark Twain's novel of a boy and a runaway slave along the Mississippi, but tiresome songs stop the story deader'n'a riverboat on a sandbar.

1974 114m/C Jeff East, Paul Winfield, Harvey Korman, David Wayne, Arthur O'Connell, Gary Merrill, Natalie Trundy, Lucille Benson; **D:** J. Lee Thompson. **VHS, Beta, LV** *MGM, FOX, FCT*

Huckleberry Finn 🦴🦴

G/Family Whitewashed version of the Twain classic features Andy Griffith's onetime 'Opie' Howard among the miscastings as the footloose Huck. Stars three more members of the Howard clan; they should have let Ron direct instead. Made for TV.

1975 74m/C Ron Howard, Donny Most, Royal Dano, Antonio Fargas, Jack Elam, Merle Haggard, Rance Howard, Jean Howard, Clint Howard, Shug Fisher, Sarah Selby, Bill Erwin; **D:** Robert Totten. **VHS, Beta** *KUI, FXV, FCT*

Hugo the Hippo 🦴🦴

G/Family Animated feature from Hungary (with a plethora of Hollywood celebrity voices) about a fugitive baby hippo struggling to save his family from starvation in Zanzibar. Conservation-minded cartoon boasting songs by Donnie and Marie Osmond.

1976 90m/C V: Paul Lynde, Burl Ives, Robert Morley, Marie Osmond. **VHS, Beta** *FOX*

Hulk Hogan's Rock 'n' Wrestling

Primary Three episodes per tape of the World Wrestling Federation's cartoon counterparts as they battle evil and injustice. Lots of pro-wrestling stars are depicted, but all the voices are studio actors. Additional volumes available.

1987 50m/C VHS, Beta *ORI*

The Human Comedy 🦴🦴🦴 ♭

Family Straight, unapologetically sentimental version of the episodic William Saroyan novel. Focuses on Homer Macauley, messenger-boy son in a small-town family during WWII and how he and they cope with day-to-day life and an eventual battlefield tragedy. Well-acted and warm, but not a laugh riot; title is an allusion to Dante's "Divine Comedy."

1943 117m/B Mickey Rooney, Frank Morgan, James Craig, Fay Bainter, Ray Collins, Donna Reed, Van Johnson, Barry Nelson, Robert Mitchum, Jackie "Butch" Jenkins; **D:** Clarence Brown; **W:** William Saroyan. **Award Nominations:** Academy Awards '43: Best Actor (Rooney), Best Black and White Cinematography, Best Director (Brown), Best Picture; **Awards:** Academy Awards '43: Best Story. **VHS, Beta, LV** *MGM*

The Hunchback of Notre Dame 🐾🐾🐾

PG/Jr. High-Adult It's not often that a classic novel is remade into a classic movie that's remade into a made-for-TV reprise, and survives its multiple renderings. But it's not often a cast so rich in stage trained actors is assembled on the small screen. Hopkins gives a textured, pre-Hannibal Lecter interpretation of Quasimodo, the Hunchback in Hugo's eponymous novel. Impressive model of the cathedral by production designer John Stoll.

1982 102m/C Anthony Hopkins, Derek Jacobi, Lesley-Anne Down, John Gielgud, Tim Pigott-Smith, Rosalie Crutchley, Robert Powell; **D:** Michael Tuchner. **VHS** *VMK*

The Hunchback of Notre Dame 🐾🐾

Family Animated version of the Victor Hugo classic about the deformed bell-ringer in love with a gypsy girl.

1985 60m/C VHS, Beta *LIV, FHE*

The Hunchback of Notre Dame

Family Animated musical version of the familiar tale features the hunchbacked Quasimodo, who rings the bells of the cathedral of Notre Dame. He falls in love with the gypsy Melody but thinks he's too ugly to have her love him. But Melody sees his inner beauty (think "Beauty and the Beast").

1995 48m/C VHS

The Hunchback of Notre Dame 🐾🐾🐾 🐾

G/Family Nothing quasi here as Disney animation goes all out to make Victor Hugo's grim classic palatable to youngsters, without losing the book's message that one needn't be handsome, or even average looking, to be kind and courageous. Quasimodo (voiced by Tom Hulce) is the misshapen bell-ringer of Notre Dame who never strays far from the cathedral. Esmeralda (voiced by Demi Moore) is the Gypsy dancer who captures his fancy, but Quasimodo's evil guardian, Judge Frollo (Tony Jay), is a political demagogue who has all of Paris fired up against Gypsies and their sympathizers. Welcome comic relief comes from Quasimodo's friends Victor, Hugo and Laverne, three gargoyles. Actually, only one is a goil (Mary Wickes, the gravel-voiced nun from "Sister Act"), the other two are boys (Jason Alexander and Charles Kimbrough). There's no great hum-along toon tune, but

the songs complement the story, the artwork is stunning and the kids will cheer, cheer for old Notre Dame's bellboy. Ages 6 and up.

🐾 **BEWARE** *Deformed Quasimodo may frighten small children. Even scarier is the way he is subjected to ridicule by a mob. Movie could upset kids who are afraid of fire. Violence by sword and bow-and-arrow.*

1996 88m/C D: Kirk Wise, Gary Trousdale; **M:** Alan Menken, Stephen Schwartz; **V:** Tom Hulce, Demi Moore, Kevin Kline, Charles Kimbrough, Jason Alexander, Mary Wickes, David Ogden Stiers. **VHS** *NYR*

A Hungarian Fairy Tale 🐾🐾 🐾

College-Adult Title, packaging and plot outline makes this look likes a kids' picture, but it's a surreal, dense mass of symbolism about bureaucracy and Mozart's "The Magic Flute." After his single mother is killed, a boy searches for his real father, though the name and address he's got are fictions, concocted to satisfy government paperwork. For the art-film crowd. In Hungarian with English subtitles.

🐾 **BEWARE** *Violence; alcohol use.*

1987 97m/B Arpad Vermes, Maria Varga, Frantisek Husak, Eszter Csakanyi, Szilvia Toth, Judith Pogany, Geza Balkay; **D:** Gyula Gazdag. **VHS** *EVD, INJ*

The Hunt for Red October 🐾🐾🐾

PG/Jr. High-Adult Based on Tom Clancy's blockbuster novel, a high-tech Cold War yarn about a Soviet nuclear sub turning rogue and heading straight for U.S. waters, as both the U.S. and the U.S.S.R. try to stop it. Complicated, ill-plotted potboiler that succeeds breathlessly due to the cast and McTiernan's tommy-gun direction. Introduces the character of CIA analyst Jack Ryan who returns in "Patriot Games," though in the guise of Harrison Ford.

🐾 **BEWARE** *Brief violence and profanity at sea.*

1990 137m/C Sean Connery, Alec Baldwin, Richard Jordan, Scott Glenn, Joss Ackland, Sam Neill, James Earl Jones, Peter Firth, Tim Curry, Courtney B. Vance, Jeffrey Jones, Fred Dalton Thompson; **D:** John McTiernan; **W:** Larry Ferguson, Donald Stewart; **M:** Basil Poledouris. **Award Nominations:** Academy Awards '90: Best Film Editing, Best Sound; **Awards:** Academy Awards '90: Best Sound Effects Editing. **VHS, Beta, LV, 8mm, CD-I** *PAR*

Hurricane Express

Family One of the Wayne serials done by Mascot, a studio that later helped form Republic Pictures. But serial greatness was far away when Mascot did this tedious 12-chapter yarn in which the young Duke tries to find out the identity of The Wrecker, a villain whose acts of railroad sabotage cost the hero his father.

🐾 **BEWARE** *Violence.*

1932 223m/B John Wayne, Joseph Girard, Conway Tearle, Shirley Grey; **D:** J.P. McGowan, Armand Schaefer. **VHS, Beta** *SNC, NOS, RHI*

Toy Ploy

Entertainment tie-ins, souvenirs and promotional knick-knacks have been around for ages, from the first Mickey Mouse watch to the latest Hunchback meals at Burger King. And a new crop of summer movies calls for a new crop of summer toys. Last year entertainment tie-ins brought in over $16 billion dollars. And you ask what could replace my little darlings' *Pocahontas* thermos, *The Lion King* sleepwear, and *Babe* stuffed pig? What will you be buying to put under the Christmas tree this year?!?

Well, to start at the top, the newest Disney animated release, *The Hunchback of Notre Dame,* will undoubtedly have your kids scrambling to toy stores and fast food restaurants. There's a cuddly stuffed Quasimodo out there and replicas of his gargoyle sidekicks. And your little girl will definitely need a pair of Esmerelda shoes, as well as all the matching accessories.

Films like *Flipper, Dragonheart, Mission Impossible, Matilda,* and even *Independence Day* will feature toys marketed at your kids. From action figures to plush dolls to wristband walkie-talkies to swim gear, these films are capitalizing on the merchandising market in a big way. But, remember, this is nothing new. And as a parent, it is your duty to buy these things for your kid — right?!?

Hyper-Sapien: People from Another Star 🦴 🎵

PG/Family Two alien kids run away from UFO-sweet-UFO, accompanied by a space pal who looks like a big furry starfish. They befriend a Wyoming farmboy and get mistaken for assassins but don't worry, there's a happy—

and illogical—ending. Haphazard pic, dedicated "to the young in spirit throughout the Universe," had a messy production history and it shows.

1986 93m/C Sydney Penny, Keenan Wynn, Gail Strickland, Ricky Paull Goldin, Peter Jason, Talia Shire; **D:** Peter Hunt. **VHS, Beta, LV** *WAR*

I Am a Fugitive from a Chain Gang 🦴🦴🦴🦴

Jr. High-Adult WWI veteran Muni returns home with dreams of traveling across America. After a brief stint as a clerk, he strikes out on his own. Near penniless, Muni meets up with a tramp who takes him to get a hamburger. He becomes an unwilling accomplice when the bum suddenly robs the place. Convicted and sentenced to a Georgia chain gang, he's brutalized and degraded, though he eventually escapes and lives the life of a criminal on the run. Based on the autobiography by Robert E. Burns, timeless and thought-provoking classic combines brutal docu-details with powerhouse performances. Not a pretty picture and one that kids may have trouble hanging with, but an uncompromising expose worth the time for the mature.

1932 93m/B Paul Muni, Glenda Farrell, Helen Vinson, Preston Foster, Edward Ellis, Allen Jenkins; **D:** Mervyn LeRoy; **W:** Howard J. Green. **Award Nominations:** Academy Awards '33: Best Actor (Muni), Best Picture, Best Sound; **Awards:** National Board of Review Awards '32: 10 Best Films of the Year. **VHS, Beta** *MGM, FOX, CCB*

I am the Cheese 🦴🦴

Jr. High-Adult An institutionalized boy undergoes psychiatric treatment; with the aid of his therapist (Wagner) he relives his traumatic childhood and finds out the truth about the death of his parents. A bit muddled, but has its moments. Adapted from a Robert Cormier teen novel.

> **BEWARE!** *Profanity. Child must learn the truth about the death of his parents.*

1983 95m/C Robert MacNaughton, Hope Lange, Don Murray, Robert Wagner, Sudie Bond; **D:** Robert Jiras. **VHS, Beta** *LIV, VES*

I Can Dance

Primary An actual first ballet class, with a teacher and six students (there's one boy) who learn plies, the five basic positions and more. Ages 7 and up.

1989 29m/C VHS, Beta *MLT, MVD, STS*

I Confess 🦴🦴 🎵

Sr. High-Adult When a priest (Clift) hears a murderer's confession, the circumstances seem to point to him as the prime suspect. Tepid, overly serious and occasionally interesting mid-career Hitchcock. Adapted from Paul Anthelme's 1902 play.

1953 95m/B Montgomery Clift, Anne Baxter, Karl Malden, Brian Aherne; **D:** Alfred Hitchcock. **VHS, Beta, LV** *WAR, FCT, MLB*

I Dig Dirt

Preschool-Primary Grubby kids have fun in a huge dirt pile, leading to a look at some of the world's biggest earth-moving machines, used at the Black Thunder coal mine in Wyoming, including a machine that can scoop up 240 tons of dirt at one time. Ages 3 to 8.
1995 30m/C VHS

I Live with Me Dad 🦴 ▷

Family A vagrant drunk and his son fight the authorities for the right to be together.
1986 86m/C Peter Hehir, Haydon Samuels; **D:** Paul Maloney. **VHS, Beta** *FOX*

I Love Trouble 🦴🦴 ▷

PG/Sr. High-Adult Veteran reporter Peter Brackett (sexy veteran Nolte) and ambitious cub reporter Sabrina Petersen (young and sexy Roberts) are competitors working for rival Chicago newspapers. When they begin to secretly exchange information on a big story, they find their lives threatened and their rivalry turning to romance. Some action, simplistic retro script, one big star, one sorta big star, and you've got the perfect movie package for the Prozac decade. Written, produced and directed by husband/wife team Meyers and Shyer.

> ⚠ **BEWARE** *Violence, in the action-thriller sense. Nolte and Roberts are pursued by gangsters.*

1994 123m/C Julia Roberts, Nick Nolte, Saul Rubinek, Robert Loggia, James Rebhorn; **D:** Charles Shyer; **W:** Nancy Myers, Charles Shyer. **VHS** *NYR*

I Never Sang For My Father 🦴🦴🦴 ▷

PG/Jr. High-Adult A devoted son must choose between caring for his cantankerous but well-meaning father, and moving out West to marry the divorced doctor whom he loves. While his mother wants him to stay near home, his sister, who fell out of her father's favor by marrying out of the family faith, argues that he should do what he wants. An introspective, stirring story based on the Robert Anderson play.
1970 90m/C Gene Hackman, Melvyn Douglas, Estelle Parsons, Dorothy Stickney; **D:** Gilbert Cates; **W:** Robert Anderson. **Award Nominations:** Academy Awards '70: Best Actor (Douglas), Best Adapted Screenplay, Best Supporting Actor (Hackman); **Awards:** National Board of Review Awards '70: 10 Best Films of the Year. **VHS, Beta, LV** *COL*

I Ought to Be in Pictures 🦴🦴

PG/Jr. High-Adult After hitchhiking from New York to Hollywood to break into the movies, a teen-aged actress finds her father, a screenwriter, turned alcoholic and gambler. Far from the best Neil Simon comedies to hit the screen, but it does make points about the perils of parenthood.

> ⚠ **BEWARE** *Salty language, sex talk, alcohol use.*

1982 107m/C Walter Matthau, Ann-Margret, Dinah Manoff, Lance Guest, Michael Dudikoff; **D:** Herbert Ross; **W:** Neil Simon; **M:** Marvin Hamlisch. **VHS, Beta** *FOX*

I Remember Mama 🦴🦴🦴 ▷

Family True Hollywood heart tugger chronicling the life of a Norwegian immigrant family living in San Francisco during the early 1900s. Dunne triumphs as the self-sacrificing mother, providing her family with wisdom and inspiration. A kindly father, four children, three high-strung aunts and an eccentric doctor who treats a live-in uncle round out this nuclear family. Adapted from John Van Druten's stage play, based on Kathryn Forbes memoirs, "Mama's Bank Account." A TV series came later.
1948 95m/B Irene Dunne, Barbara Bel Geddes, Oscar Homolka, Ellen Corby, Cedric Hardwicke, Edgar Bergen, Rudy Vallee, Barbara O'Neil, Florence Bates; **D:** George Stevens. **Award Nominations:** Academy Awards '48: Best Actress (Dunne), Best Black and White Cinematography, Best Supporting Actor (Homolka), Best Supporting Actress (Corby, Bel Geddes); **Awards:** Golden Globe Awards '49: Best Supporting Actress (Corby). **VHS, Beta, LV** *CCB, TTC*

I Wanna Hold Your Hand 🦴🦴🦴

PG/Jr. High-Adult Funny slapstick recounting of the craziness surrounding the Beatle's first appearance on the "Ed Sullivan Show." Allen's about to be married but wants a night with one of the Liverpool lads, while Saldana is a photographer looking for the one great shot of the band to launch her career. Sperber and Deezen steal the show as groupies of the highest order. Warm and witty Spielberg production effectively captures craziness of the era.

> ⚠ **BEWARE** *Roughhousing.*

1978 104m/C Nancy Allen, Bobby DiCicco, Wendie Jo Sperber, Marc McClure, Susan Kendall Newman, Theresa Saldana, Eddie Deezen, William Jordan; **D:** Robert Zemeckis; **W:** Robert Zemeckis. **VHS, Beta, LV** *WAR, FCT*

I Want to be a Ballerina

Preschool-Jr. High For little girls who dream of becoming a ballerina, this video gives behind-the-scenes look at what it takes. Meet dancers from ages 4-17 to find out what it's like. Visit dancers in their classes and peek backstage as make-up and costumes transform children into real ballerinas. Also includes highlights from Tchaikovsky's "Nutcracker Ballet" as performed by the San Jose Dance Theatre.
19?? 30m/C VHS

Ice Castles 🦴🦴

PG/Family Affliction-of-the-week TV movie gets the big-screen treatment. Teen figure skater's Olympic dreams are dashed when she is blinded in an accident, but her boyfriend gives her the strength, encouragement, and love necessary to perform a small miracle. Way too schmaltzy, although lesson about persevering through adversity is sound. For a better film about an athletic young woman who deals with blindness, see "Wild Hearts Can't Be Broken." Ages 8 to 12.

1979 110m/C Robby Benson, Lynn-Holly Johnson, Tom Skerritt, Colleen Dewhurst, Jennifer Warren, David Huffman; **D:** Donald Wrye; **M:** Marvin Hamlisch. **VHS, Beta** *COL*

Ice Pirates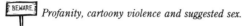

PG/Jr. High-Adult Kind of the flip side of "Waterworld," this one's set in a future where water, not dirt, is a precious commodity, and the title pirates zip through space stealing water in its frozen form. Ages 10 and up.

> **BEWARE** *Profanity, cartoony violence and suggested sex.*

1984 91m/C Robert Urich, Mary Crosby, Michael D. Roberts, John Matuszak, Anjelica Huston, Ron Perlman, John Carradine, Robert Symonds; **D:** Stewart Raffill; **W:** Stewart Raffill; **M:** Bruce Broughton. **VHS, Beta, LV** *MGM*

Ice Station Zebra

G/Family A nuclear submarine races Soviet seamen to find a downed Russian satellite under a polar ice cap. Suspenseful Cold War adventure based on the novel by Alistair MacLean.

1968 148m/C Rock Hudson, Ernest Borgnine, Patrick McGoohan, Jim Brown, Lloyd Nolan, Tony Bill; **D:** John Sturges; **M:** Michel Legrand. **VHS, Beta, LV** *MGM*

Iceman

PG/Jr. High-Adult Frozen prehistoric man is brought back to life, after which severe culture shock takes hold. Sympathetic scientist Hutton tries to help. Underwritten but nicely acted, especially by Lone as the primal man.

> **BEWARE** *Violence and profanity.*

1984 101m/C Timothy Hutton, Lindsay Crouse, John Lone, David Strathairn, Josef Sommer, Danny Glover; **D:** Fred Schepisi; **W:** Chip Proser; **M:** Bruce Smeaton. **VHS, Beta, LV** *MCA*

Ida Fanfanny and Three Magical Tales

Preschool-Primary Three animated children's tales: "Louis James Hates School," "The Lightning and Thunder Case," "How to Dig a Hole to the Other Side of the World," and the title short.

1981 49m/C **VHS, Beta** *NWV*

If Looks Could Kill

PG-13/Jr. High-Adult High school cutup travels to France with his class, gets mistaken for a CIA agent, and stumbles into a James-Bondish plot to take over all the money in the world. Much implausible action and I-was-a-teenaged-007 bits follow, but it's agreeably lightweight and leads to a rousing incendiary conclusion.

> **BEWARE** *Profanity, violence, and sex talk, but no extremes in those departments.*

1991 89m/C Richard Grieco, Linda Hunt, Roger Rees, Robin Bartlett, Gabrielle Anwar, Roger Daltrey, Geraldine James, Carole Davis; **D:** William Dear; **W:** Fred Dekker; **M:** David Foster. **VHS, Beta, LV, 8mm** *WAR*

If Lucy Fell

R/Sr. High-Adult Therapist Lucy Ackerman (Parker) and best friend, painter Joe MacGonaughbill (Schaeffer), made a pact to jump off the Brooklyn Bridge if they didn't find love before turning 30. Joe decides to talk to his gorgeous neighbor (Macpherson) and Lucy meets eccentric painter Bwick (Stiller) but with Lucy's 30th birthday a month away could true love prevent the big leap. You guess the ending. Like any rated-R romantic comedy, teens (especially of the girl kind) will be attracted to this film. It's mostly harmless.

> **BEWARE** *Mild language and some sexuality (hey, Elle Macpherson's bodacious bod is in it).*

1995 94m/C Sarah Jessica Parker, Eric Schaeffer, Ben Stiller, Elle Macpherson, James Rebhorn, Dominic Luchese; **D:** Eric Schaeffer; **W:** Eric Schaeffer, Tony Spiridakis; **C:** Ron Fortunato; **M:** Amanda Kravat, Charles Pettis. **VHS**

I'll Do Anything

PG-13/Jr. High-Adult Struggling actor lands a job as chauffeur to a powerful Hollywood producer, but even that doesn't seem to boost his thespian career. Meanwhile his small daughter—left with him when his ex-wife went to prison—gets a dream role as kiddie star of a TV sitcom. Sharply written comedy (which once was a musical with songs by the guy who used to be called Prince) suffers from a distinctly split personality; half is a satire of showbiz with a heavy 'insider' feel (and heavier profanity), while the rest is a truly touching picture of a man coping with emergency fatherhood, to a somewhat spooky girl trained since infancy by her unstable mother to distrust him. Uneven (it should be, having been completely recut after previews) but worthwhile.

> **BEWARE** *Profanity, brief nudity, and sex. Nolte's abandoned child is quite a little brat when she first appears.*

1993 115m/C Nick Nolte, Albert Brooks, Julie Kavner, Whittni Wright, Joely Richardson, Tracey Ullman; **D:** James L. Brooks; **W:** James L. Brooks; **M:** Hans Zimmer. **VHS, LV, 8mm** *COL*

I'm a Little Teapot

Preschool Includes the title song plus a host of other children's nursery songs and rhyme actions to encourage children to play along.

1993 40m/C **VHS** *FAF, VTR*

I'm Not Oscar's Friend Anymore . . . and Other Stories

Primary Animated tale of friendship and differences along with the stories "Creole," "Hug Me," and "Birds of a Feather."

1991 30m/C **VHS** *BTV*

Imaginary Crimes

PG/Jr. High-Adult Ray Weiler (Keitel) is a well-meaning salesman with dreams much bigger than his reach. After the death of his wife (Lynch), Ray tries to raise his two daughters, Sonya (Balk) and Greta (Moss). But gifted high school senior (in 1962) Sonya is resentful of being her sister's maternal anchor and having her father's schemes come to nothing even as she acknowledges how much Ray cares and how he wants to improve their lives. Remarkable performances by Keitel and Balk. From the novel by Sheila Ballantyne.

 *Mild language.*

1994 106m/C Harvey Keitel, Fairuza Balk, Kelly Lynch, Vincent D'Onofrio, Elissabeth Moss, Diane Baker, Christopher Penn, Seymour Cassel, Annette O'Toole; *D:* Tony Drazan; *W:* Kristine Johnson, Davia Nelson; *M:* Stephen Endelman. **VHS, LV** *WAR*

Immediate Family 🦴🦴 ᵇ

PG-13/Jr. High-Adult Childless couple contact a pregnant, unmarried girl and her boyfriend in hopes of adoption. As the pregnancy advances, the girl has doubts about giving up her baby. Good acting from a big screen cast elevates this to about the level of the usual surrogate-motherhood TV-movie.

 *Sex talk, profanity. Issues of infertility and surrogate motherhood.*

1989 112m/C Glenn Close, James Woods, Kevin Dillon, Mary Stuart Masterson, Kevin Dillon, Linda Darlow, Jane Greer, Jessica James, Mimi Kennedy; *D:* Jonathan Kaplan; *W:* Barbara Benedek; *M:* Brad Fiedel. **VHS, Beta, LV** *COL*

Improper Channels 🦴🦴

PG/Jr. High-Adult Mediocre comedy about a subject that's less and less a basis for family gags—child abuse. Zealous social worker snatches a six-year-old from the hospital, falsely thinking she's being beaten at home. Dad loses his job and his credit, and the lawyers smell blood. There's a point being made here about mindless bureaucracy, if you can get over the queasy premise.

BEWARE *Salty language.*

1982 91m/C Monica Parker, Alan Arkin, Mariette Hartley; *D:* Eric Till. **VHS, Beta, LV** *VES*

The In Crowd 🦴🦴 ᵇ

PG/Jr. High-Adult Bright high school guy crashes a Philadelphia TV dance-party show circa 1965, and must choose between uncertain broadcast fame and going to college. Rose-colored look at the era, with swell dancing but a central romance that sputters because the girl character gets a bimbo treatment. Nonetheless, a more wholesome alternative to "Grease." Leitch is the son of folk singer Donovan.

BEWARE *Mild roughhousing. Nice detail has feuding young men work out their differences not through fights but impromptu dance contest.*

1988 96m/C Donovan Leitch, Jennifer Runyon, Scott Plank, Joe Pantoliano; *D:* Mark Rosenthal; *W:* Mark Rosenthal. **VHS, Beta, LV** *ORI*

In Search of a Golden Sky 🦴🦴

PG/Jr. High-Adult Following their mother's death, a group of city-bred children move to the mountains and join their secluded, cabin-dwelling uncle, much to the righteous chagrin of the welfare department. Wholesome but unexceptional nature drama.

1984 94m/C Charles Napier, George Flower, Cliff Osmond; *D:* Jefferson Richard. **VHS, Beta** *FOX*

In Search of Dr. Seuss

Family In this tribute to children's author/illustrator extraordinaire, Theodor Seuss Geisel (1904-1991), Kathy Najimy serves as a newspaper reporter who's guided through Seuss-land with the help of the Cat in the Hat (Matt Frewer) and other characters. There are songs, readings from some of Seuss' best-known tales, and clips from animated favorites. All ages.

1994 90m/C Kathy Najimy, Matt Frewer, Christopher Lloyd, Patrick Stewart, Eileen Brennan, Robin Williams; *D:* Vincent Paterson; *W:* Keith R. Clarke; *M:* Steve Goldstein; *V:* Howie Mandel, Billy Crystal. **VHS** *TTC*

In Search of the Castaways 🦴🦴🦴

Family Stirring adventure tale of a teenage girl and her younger brother searching for their father, a ship's captain lost at sea years earlier. Powerful special effects and strong cast make this a winning Disney effort. Based on a story by Jules Verne.

1962 98m/C Hayley Mills, Maurice Chevalier, George Sanders, Wilfrid Hyde-White, Michael Anderson Jr.; *D:* Robert Stevenson. **VHS, Beta** *DIS*

In the Army Now 🦴 ᵇ

PG/Jr. High-Adult Strictly for Pauly Shore fans. Both of them. Pauly plays a slacker who joins the Army for the benefits but winds up in combat in the Sahara, and no, it's not a hotel in Las Vegas. Ages 13 and up.

BEWARE *Profanity, grossness, stupidity and sex talk.*

1994 93m/C Pauly Shore, Esai Morales, Lori Petty, David Alan Grier, Ernie Hudson, Andy Dick; *D:* Dan Petrie Jr.; *W:* Dan Petrie Jr., Ken Kaufman, Fax Bahr, Stu Krieger, Adam Small. **VHS**

Incident at Hawk's Hill

Preschool-Primary The Allen Eckert book comes to life in this TV drama from Disney about Ben, a lonely boy who finds it difficult to talk to people and finds peace, love and understanding as he befriends animals.

1990 29m/C VHS, Beta *MTI, DSN*

Incredible Agent of Stingray

Preschool-Primary Captain Troy Tempest and the Stingray crew take an underwater voyage to rescue a beautiful woman kept prisoner in Titanica. Compilation of the British "Stingray" puppet sci-fi series.

1980 93m/C VHS, Beta *FHE*

The Incredible Hulk

Family Bixby is a scientist who achieves superhuman strength after he is exposed to a massive dose of gamma rays. But his personal life suffers, as does his wardrobe. Ferrigno is the Hulkster. The pilot for the TV series is based on the Marvel Comics character. Later TV feature film specials were broadcast and released to video; they include "The Incredible Hulk Returns," "The Trial of the Incredible Hulk," and "The Death of the Incredible Hulk."

BEWARE *Violence.*

1977 94m/C Bill Bixby, Susan Sullivan, Lou Ferrigno, Jack Colvin; **D:** Kenneth Johnson. **VHS, Beta, LV** *MCA*

The Incredible Hulk Returns

Family The muscular green mutant is back, and in this TV movie he meets another of the Marvel Comics superheroes, the mild-mannered guy who changes into the Viking warrior named Thor. Paper-thin fantasy was designed as the pilot for a Thor TV series that never took flight on its own. The next feature, "The Trial of the Incredible Hulk," attempted to do the same for the comic character Daredevil.

BEWARE *Roughhousing.*

1988 100m/C Bill Bixby, Lou Ferrigno, Jack Colvin, Lee Purcell, Charles Napier, Steve Levitt; **D:** Nick Corea. **VHS, LV** *VTR, NWV*

The Incredible Journey

Family Labrador retriever, bull terrier and Siamese cat mistake their caretaker's intentions when he leaves for a hunting trip. Believing he's gone forever, the trio set out on a 250-mile, peril filled trek across Canada's rugged terrain to find their master. Told straightforwardly from the critters' point of view, this entertaining Disney adventure from Sheila Burnford's book suffers mainly from being copied and ripped off so often. Still stands up well, even next to the same studio's own clever remake "Homeward Bound."

1963 80m/C D: Fletcher Markle. **VHS, Beta** *DIS*

The Incredible Mr. Limpet

Family Reverse of "The Little Mermaid" has Knotts perfectly cast as a henpecked, nebbish bookkeeper who falls into the sea and transforms into a fish, fulfilling his aquatic dreams. Eventually he falls in love with another fish and helps the U.S. Navy find Nazi subs during WWII. Partially animated (by Warner Brothers), beloved by some, particularly those under the age of seven. Based on Theodore Pratt's novel.

1964 99m/C Don Knotts, Jack Weston, Carole Cook, Andrew Duggan, Larry Keating, Elizabeth McRae; **D:** Arthur Lubin. **VHS, Beta, LV** *WAR*

The Incredible Rocky Mountain Race

Family Townspeople of St. Joseph, fed up with Mark Twain's destructive feud with neighbor Mike Fink, devise a shrewd scheme to rid the town of the troublemakers by sending them on a road race through the west. A tall tale of short stature, made-for TV and starring recruits of the sitcom "F-Troop."

1977 97m/C Christopher Connelly, Forrest Tucker, Larry Storch, Mike Mazurki; **D:** James L. Conway. **VHS, Beta** *VTR*

The Incredible Shrinking Woman

PG/Jr. High-Adult "Kids, I shrunk Honey!" Inoffensive social satire finds household cleaners (that daddy advertises) producing some strange side effects on a housewife, slowly shrinking her to doll size. She tries to get on with life as normal, but gets kidnapped by evil scientists, befriends lab gorilla. Sight gags and fancy sets abound but the cuteness wears thin by the end.

BEWARE *Salty language, sex talk.*

1981 89m/C Lily Tomlin, Charles Grodin, Ned Beatty, Henry Gibson; **D:** Joel Schumacher; **W:** Jane Wagner. **VHS, Beta, LV** *MCA*

The Incredible Voyage of Stingray

Family A marionette adventure spinoff of Gerry Anderson's British "Thunderbirds" series, about the crew of the undersea vessel Stingray and their quest to save the beautiful Marina from captivity in the land of Titanica.

1980 93m/C VHS, Beta, LV *FHE*

Independence Day

PG-13/Jr. High-Adult This sci-fi thriller about aliens who are out to destroy the earth will definitely tantalize teens. They will be astounded as adults will by the more than 3,000 special effects shots. An unlikely trio, the U.S. President (Pullman), a computer expert (Goldblum), and a fighter pilot (Smith), must save the planet from a monstrous space crew that is out to create some fireworks on that all-American holiday, July 4th. Some effects will scare youngsters, thus, the PG13 rating.

BEWARE *Sci-fi destruction, including a lot of battle between huge spaceships and tiny jet fighters. Innocent people are killed, as well as some of the aliens, too.*

1996 ?m/C Bill Pullman, Will Smith, Jeff Goldblum, Brent Spiner, Judd Hirsch, Randy Quaid, Mary McDonnell, Harry Connick Jr., Robert Loggia, Harvey Fierstein; **D:** Roland Emmerich; **W:** Roland Emmerich, Dean Devlin; **C:** Karl Walter Lindenlaub; **M:** David Arnold. **VHS** *NYR*

The Indian in the Cupboard

♪♪♪

PG/Family A young boy named Omri (Scardino) receives a toy Indian as a birthday present, but when he puts the figure inside a tabletop cupboard, the Indian, named Little Bear, magically comes to life (but doesn't grow). The adult Little Bear has been transported from the year 1761 and yearns to return. Moreover, he informs Omri, "I'm not small. You are big." Through taking care of an adult, Omri, about 9 or 10, does get big, but it's the growth that comes from assuming responsibility for bringing a life into the world. Members of the Sandwich Generation, who must take care of parents and children, can relate. But they don't have quite the adventure Omri does as he, Little Bear and the living toy figures of a cowboy and a World War I medic travel through time and size. Based on the best-selling children's book by Lynne Reid Banks.

BEWARE *Some violence, not graphic and the term "horse's ass" is used.*

1995 97m/C Hal Scardino, Litefoot, Lindsay Crouse, Richard Jenkins, Rishi Bhat; **D:** Frank Oz; **W:** Melissa Mathison; **C:** Russell Carpenter; **M:** Miles Goodman. **VHS, LV, 8mm** *COL*

Indian Paint ♪♪

Primary Okay children's adventure set amid Plains Indian tribes before contact with the white man (though everybody speaks English anyway). Young brave Nishko forms a friendship with a newborn colt that later saves his life. Nishko's chieftain father is played by Silverheels, the great Native American actor who was Tonto in the "Lone Ranger" movies and TV show. Based on the novel by Glenn Balch.

BEWARE *Violence in battles with an enemy tribe.*

1964 90m/C Jay Silverheels, Johnny Crawford, Pat Hogan, Robert Crawford Jr., George Lewis; **D:** Norman Foster. **VHS, Beta** *VCI*

Indian Summer ♪♪ ♪

PG-13/Jr. High-Adult Yet another addition to the growing thirtysomething nostalgia genre. Delete the big house, add a crusty camp director (Arkin), change the characters' names (but not necessarily their lives) and you feel like you're experiencing deja vu. This time seven friends and the requisite outsider reconvene at Camp Tamakwa, the real-life summer camp to writer/director Binder. The former campers talk. They yearn. They save Camp Tamakwa and experience personal growth. A must see for those who appreciate listening to situational jokes that are followed by "I guess you had to be there." Good cast works hard, though the standout is probably Raimi as a camp maintenance guy.

BEWARE *Profanity, brief nudity, drug use, and sex. Kinda like "The Big Chill" of camp friends.*

1993 108m/C Alan Arkin, Matt Craven, Diane Lane, Bill Paxton, Elizabeth Perkins, Kevin Pollak, Sam Raimi, Vincent Spano, Julie

Warner, Kimberly Williams, Richard Chevolleau; **D:** Mike Binder; **W:** Mike Binder; **M:** Miles Goodman. **VHS, Beta, LV** *TOU, FCT*

Indiana Jones and the Last Crusade ♪♪♪

PG/Jr. High-Adult In the third Indiana Jones adventure, we find the fearless archaeologist once again up against the Nazis in a race to find a powerful religious artifact, this time the Holy Grail. Rerun syndrome is not entirely cured by the added attraction of Connery as Indy's domineering father. Splendid opening setup goes back to the hero's boyhood (he's played by Phoenix) and his first adventure; Indy fans even get the origin of the infamous fedora. More chases, exotic places, dastardly villains, and daring escapes.

BEWARE *Violence attached to the legend of the Holy Grail and many near escapes. Sex talk.*

1989 126m/C Harrison Ford, Sean Connery, Denholm Elliott, Alison Doody, Julian Glover, John Rhys-Davies, River Phoenix, Michael Byrne, Alex Hyde-White; **D:** Steven Spielberg; **W:** Jeffrey Boam; **M:** John Williams. **VHS, Beta, LV, 8mm** *PAR, TLF*

Indiana Jones and the Temple of Doom ♪♪♪ ♪

PG/Primary-Adult Daredevil archaeologist Jones is back and literally dropped into a quest for a magic stone and a ruthless cult in India that enslaves hundreds of children. Enough action for ten movies, f/x galore, and less regard for plot than original "Raiders of the Lost Ark." That actually helps the roller-coaster ride of nearly nonstop thrills. Stirred a debate over movie gore; nightmarish heart-removal/human-sacrifice scene is unrealistic but still too much for tot viewers. On the other hand, Indy has a terrific rapport with kid companion Quan, more believable than his romance with the prissy showgirl heroine.

BEWARE *Violence, occasional profanity, foreign stereotypes, alcohol use, and grossness.*

1984 118m/C Harrison Ford, Kate Capshaw, Ke Huy Quan, Amrish Puri; **D:** Steven Spielberg; **W:** Willard Huyck, Gloria Katz; **M:** John Williams. **Award Nominations:** Academy Awards '84: Best Original Score; **Awards:** Academy Awards '84: Best Visual Effects. **VHS, Beta, LV, 8mm** *PAR, APD*

Infantastic Lullabies II

Primary Animation set to children's songs; includes parents' guide. Ages 6 months to 3 years.
1993 25m/C VHS *VWV, BTV*

Infantastic Lullabyes on Video

Family Basic objects and shapes are presented in an animated format, set to music. Ages 6 months to 3 years.
1989 25m/C VHS, Beta *VWV, KAR, MBP*

The Inkwell ♪♪ ♪

R/Sr. High-Adult Quiet African-American teenager Drew (Tate) finds first love when his family spends a vacation with relatives on Martha's Vineyard. Drew is drawn into the party atmosphere of the Inkwell, the area where affluent black professionals have summered for decades. Meanwhile, differences between Drew's former Black Panther father and his conservative uncle threaten family harmony. Everything about the film has a sugary aura, with conflicts handled tastefully. Film is set in 1976.

BEWARE *Much explicit sex talk, but youngsters 13 and older won't be uncomfortable.*

1994 112m/C Larenz Tate, Joe Morton, Phyllis Stickney, Jada Pinkett; **D:** Matty Rich; **W:** Tom Ricostronza, Paris Qualles; **M:** Terence Blanchard. **VHS, LV** *TOU*

Innerspace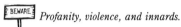

PG/Jr. High-Adult Space pilot, miniaturized for a journey through a lab rat a la "Fantastic Voyage," is accidentally injected into a nebbish supermarket clerk, and together they nab some bad guys and get the girl. Award-winning special effects support some funny moments between micro Quaid and nerdy Short, with Ryan producing the confused romantic interest.

BEWARE *Profanity, violence, and innards.*

1987 120m/C Dennis Quaid, Martin Short, Meg Ryan, Kevin McCarthy, Fiona Lewis, Henry Gibson, Robert Picardo, John Hora, Wendy Schaal, Orson Bean, Chuck Jones, William Schallert, Dick Miller, Vernon Wells, Harold Sylvester, Kevin Hooks, Kathleen Freeman, Kenneth Tobey; **D:** Joe Dante; **W:** Jeffrey Boam, Chip Proser; **M:** Jerry Goldsmith. **VHS, Beta, LV, 8mm** *WAR*

Inspector Clouseau: Ape Suzette

Family Five cartoons from the Pink Panther's peerless pursuer, an accident-prone French detective and his gendarme pal, Deaux-Deaux. Included are "Ape Suzette," "The Pique Poquette of Paris," "Sicque! Sicque! Sicque!," "Unsafe and Seine," and "That's No Lady, That's Notre Dame."

1966 35m/C V: Pat Harrington. **VHS** *MGM*

Inspector Clouseau: Napoleon Blown-Aparte

Family Four more cartoons from the bumbling French detective and his little Spanish buddy. Included are "Cirrhosis of the Louvre," "Napoleon Blown-Apart," "Reaux Reaux Reaux Your Boat," "Plastered in Paris," and "Cock-a-Doodle Deaux Deaux."

1966 35m/C V: Pat Harrington. **VHS** *MGM*

Inspector Gadget, Vol. 1

Preschool-Primary Comedian Adams lends his voice to the versatile cartoon Inspector Gadget, who, along with his trusted companions Penny and Brain, go up against the evil Dr. Claw. Additional volumes available.

1983 60m/C V: Don Adams. **VHS, Beta** *FHE, LIV*

International Velvet

PG/Primary-Adult In this belated sequel to "National Velvet," adult Velvet, with live-in companion, grooms her orphaned niece (O'Neal) to become an Olympic champion horsewoman. Good photography and performances by Plummer and Hopkins manage to keep the sentiment at a trot.

1978 126m/C Tatum O'Neal, Anthony Hopkins, Christopher Plummer; **D:** Bryan Forbes. **VHS, Beta** *MGM*

Into the West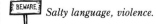

PG/Jr. High-Adult Seamless mix of magic and gritty reality in present-day Ireland. Shattered by his wife's death, gypsy Riley quits his caravan and moves with his small sons to a Dublin housing project, where the boys have a hard time hiding a mystical white horse that suddenly appears. Cops seize the champion-grade animal to sell to a businessman, but the children liberate the horse and hightail it on a wild cross-country chase. Outstanding all-ages entertainment, a hit in Britain that never found a proper audience in US theaters but was released widely on video through Disney.

BEWARE *Alcohol use and brawling. In the west, these two usually go together.*

1992 92m/C Gabriel Byrne, Ellen Barkin, Ciaran Fitzgerald, Ruaidhri Conroy, David Kelly, Colm Meaney; **D:** Mike Newell; **W:** Jim Sheridan; **M:** Patrick Doyle. **VHS, LV** *TOU*

Invaders from Mars

Jr. High-Adult Sci-fi juvie favorite about little David seeing a flying saucer bury itself behind his house. He can't convince grownups, though, and parents and playmates are soon possessed by the alien beings. Though a cheapo budget shows (note the balloons bobbing on walls of the Martians' 'glass' cave stronghold), this tale can be enjoyed as both a basic kid adventure and on a deeper level as a small boy's viewpoint of adult society—dominant, threatening and sometimes hostile as any green space invader. Video release includes previews of coming attractions from classic science fiction films.

BEWARE *Violence.*

1953 78m/C Helena Carter, Arthur Franz, Jimmy Hunt, Leif Erickson; **D:** William Cameron Menzies. **VHS, Beta** *MED, MLB*

Invaders from Mars

PG/Jr. High-Adult Adequate but pointless remake of the 1953 semi-classic about a Martian invasion perceived only by one young boy and a sympathetic school nurse (played by mother and son Black and Carson). Jimmy Hunt, child star of the first flick, cameos here as an adult cop; otherwise Stan Winston's colorful creature f/x are the attractions of this timekiller.

BEWARE *Salty language, violence.*

Hal Scardino holds miniature Litefoot in his hand in "The Indian in the Cupboard."

1986 102m/C Hunter Carson, Karen Black, Louise Fletcher, Laraine Newman, Timothy Bottoms, Bud Cort; **D:** Tobe Hooper; **W:** Dan O'Bannon, Don Jakoby. **VHS, Beta, LV** *MED, IME*

Invasion of the Body Snatchers

PG/Jr. High-Adult Aliens hatch from pods and replace humans in San Francisco in this remake of a sci-fi classic. Only a few people realize what's going on, but will they be able to stop the sinister takeover before it's too late? Very scary stuff. Fine performance by Sutherland. Ages 13 and up.

BEWARE *Creepy violence.*

1978 115m/C Donald Sutherland, Brooke Adams, Veronica Cartwright, Leonard Nimoy, Jeff Goldblum, Kevin McCarthy, Donald Siegel, Art Hindle; **D:** Philip Kaufman; **W:** W.D. Richter. **VHS, Beta, LV** *MGM*

The Invisible Boy

G/Family Vintage sci-fi was conceived as an encore for the 'Robby the Robot' character created for the sci-fi classic "Forbidden Planet." This is a more juvenile but still worthwhile adventure in which a kid named Timmie builds and befriends a mighty mechanical man. An evil supercomputer takes control of Robby, and the robot must decide whether to lead a machine takeover or defend his young master.

BEWARE *Roughhousing.*

1957 89m/C Richard Eyer, Diane Brewster, Philip Abbott, Harold J. Stone; **D:** Herman Hoffman; **W:** Cyril Hume; **M:** Les Baxter. **VHS** *MGM, FCT*

The Invisible Monster

Family Special investigators Lane Carlson and Carol Richards battle a mad scientist ready to take over the world with this invisible army. 12-episode serial.

1950 167m/B Richard Webb, Aline Towne, Lane Bradford, Stanley Price, John Crawford, George Meeker; **D:** Fred Brannon. **VHS** *REP*

Invitation to the Dance

Family The MGM musical studio gave Kelly free reign to make his dream project, and this is it; three exuberant, dialogue-free short pieces, pure dancing. First two are bittersweet love stories, one set in a circus, the other following a ring that passes between several sets of (unfaithful) partners. Kids may or may not get those, but viewers of all ages will be enthralled by the concluding "Sinbad the Sailor" segment, in which Kelly dances with two animated palace guards, fearsomely drawn by the Hanna-Barbera cartoonists. Colorful, vastly underrated film that was, sadly, a commercial disappointment in its day.

1956 93m/C Gene Kelly, Igor Youskevitch, Tamara Toumanova; **D:** Gene Kelly. **VHS, Beta** *MGM, CCB*

I.Q.

PG/Jr. High-Adult You don't have to be Einstein to see where this film is going. Walter Matthau, however, does have to be Einstein as the wise and kindly scientist plays Cupid, fixing up his brainy but lonely niece (Ryan) with an uneducated but bright and decent auto mechanic (Robbins). Film is long on charm, but short on logic; Einstein and his old prof buddies help the mechanic pass for a brilliant scientist. Matthau, Ryan and Robbins are convincing but the script doesn't do them justice. Einstein's sidekicks steal the show. Filmed in Princeton, New Jersey, where Einstein lived.

BEWARE *Mild language, otherwise pretty harmless.*

1994 95m/C Tim Robbins, Meg Ryan, Walter Matthau, Lou Jacobi, Gene Saks, Joseph Maher, Stephen Fry, Tony Shalhoub, Frank Whaley; **D:** Fred Schepisi; **W:** Michael Leeson, Andy Breckman; **M:** Jerry Goldsmith. **VHS, Beta** *PAR*

Ira Sleeps Over

Primary-Jr. High Young boy is invited to sleep over at his friend's house for the first time, and must decide whether to bring his teddy bear or brave it alone.
1988 13m/C **VHS** *FHE,*

Iron Will

PG/Jr. High-Adult Disney movie based on a true story and a script that had sat around since the early '70s. Maybe if they waited another 20 years its cliches would be back in style. In 1917 newly fatherless South Dakota teen Will Stoneman needs money for college. He enters a 500-mile dogsled race, becoming a nationwide media sensation as he mushes through a treacherous route that daunts professional racers. Successfully evokes the physical danger in dogsledding, but the canned sentiment, a villain seemingly inspired by Scrooge McDuck, and plenty of pilferings from other movies dog the plot all the way to the finish line.

BEWARE *Brawling, cold-weather hardship. One sledder is especially cruel, hitting dogs and sabotaging other sledders.*

1993 109m/C MacKenzie Astin, Kevin Spacey, David Ogden Stiers, August Schellenberg, George Gerdes, John Terry; **D:** Charles Haid; **W:** John Michael Hayes, Jeffrey Arch, Djordje Milicevic; **M:** Joel McNeely. **VHS, LV** *DIS*

Irreconcilable Differences

PG/Jr. High-Adult When her Beverly Hills parents spend more time working and fretting than giving hugs and love, a ten-year-old girl sues them for divorce on the grounds of "irreconcilable differences." Media has a field day when they hear that she would rather go live with the maid. Well cast, with solid characterizations, but goes for the humanely comical rather than uproarious gags.

1984 112m/C Ryan O'Neal, Shelley Long, Drew Barrymore, Sam Wanamaker, Allen (Goorwitz) Garfield, Sharon Stone, Luana Anders; **D:** Charles Shyer; **W:** Charles Shyer, Nancy Meyers. **VHS, Beta, LV** *LIV, VES*

The Island at the Top of the World 🦴🦴

G/Family Rich Englishman, in search of his missing son, travels to the Arctic Circle in 1908 via a fantastic balloon (the dirigible is the real star of the show). The rescue party discovers a lost Viking kingdom in a fairly workaday Jules Verne-style adventure from Disney. Based on the novel "The Lost Ones" by Ian Cameron.

⚠️ BEWARE *Viking roughhousing.*

1974 93m/C David Hartman, Donald Sinden, Jacques Marin, David Gwillim; **D:** Robert Stevenson; **M:** Maurice Jarre. **VHS, Beta** *DIS*

Island of Dr. Moreau 🦴🦴🦴

PG/Jr. High-Adult This remake of the "Island of the Lost Souls" (1933) is a bit disappointing but worth watching for Lancaster's solid performance as the scientist who has isolated himself on a Pacific island in order to continue his chromosome research-he can transform animals into near-humans and humans into animals. Neat-looking critters. Adaptation of the H.G. Wells novel of the same title.

1977 99m/C Burt Lancaster, Michael York, Nigel Davenport, Barbara Carrera, Richard Basehart; **D:** Don Taylor. **VHS, Beta** *WAR, OM*

Island of the Blue Dolphins 🦴🦴🦴

Family From the award-winning children's book by Scott O'Dell, this tells the tale of Karana, a young native girl left behind with her little brother on a Pacific island when their tribe abruptly leaves. The brother is killed by wild dogs, and Karana must survive on her own. Ironically, the leader of the dog pack becomes her loyal companion. Early production from Robert Radnitz, later to do "Sounder" and other fine family fare of the '70s. This isn't in that league due to stilted performances and conventional handling, but what remains of O'Dell's story is occasionally stirring.

⚠️ BEWARE *Violence.*

1964 99m/C Celia Kaye, Larry Domasin, Ann Daniel, George Kennedy; **D:** James B. Clark. **VHS, Beta** *MCA*

Islands 🦴🦴

Jr. High-Adult Minor Canadian made-for-TV short feature about trouble-prone teen punk Lacey left with motherly island-dweller Maureen, in hopes that a rustic lifestyle will teach the girl responsibility. They fight, they make up, and when you hear Lacey is adopted it's no brilliant deduction why Maureen is so interested in her. Broadcast on PBS-TV's "WonderWorks," but issued on a separate video label from the others in that exceptional series.

⚠️ BEWARE *Roughhousing, in a rather unnecessary subplot about an obsessed boy stalking Lacey.*

1987 55m/C Louise Fletcher. **VHS, Beta** *NWV*

It Came Upon a Midnight Clear 🦴🦴

Family A heavenly miracle enables a retired (and dead) New York policeman to keep a Christmas promise to his grandson. Made for TV.

1984 96m/C Mickey Rooney, Scott Grimes, George Gaynes, Annie Potts, Lloyd Nolan, Barrie Youngfellow; **D:** Peter Hunt. **VHS, Beta** *GKK*

It Could Happen to You 🦴🦴🦴

PG/Sr. High-Adult NYC cop Charlie Lang (Cage) doesn't have any change to leave coffee shop waitress Yvonne (Fonda) a tip, so he promises to drop by the next day and either double the tip or split his lottery ticket with her. When he nets four million dollars that evening, he makes good on the promise, much to the chagrin of his upwardly mobile wife (Perez). Feel-good romantic comedy is led by Cage's charm as the cop with a heart of gold and Fonda's winning waitress, but is nearly capsized by Perez's stereotypical Latin golddigger. Don't look for the diner on your next trip to NYC; it was specially built in TriBeCa and dismantled after the shoot.

⚠️ BEWARE *Profanity and a greedy, shrewish wife.*

1994 101m/C Bridget Fonda, Nicolas Cage, Rosie Perez, Red Buttons, Isaac Hayes, Seymour Cassel, Stanley Tucci, J.E. Freeman, Richard Jenkins, Ann Dowd, Wendell Pierce; **D:** Andrew Bergman; **W:** Jane Anderson, Andrew Bergman. **VHS** *NYR*

It Happened at the World's Fair 🦴🦴🦴

Family Fun and light romance comedy has Elvis and a companion (O'Brien) being escorted through the Seattle World's Fair by a fetching Chinese girl. 🎵 I'm Falling In Love Tonight; They Remind Me Too Much Of You; Take Me To The Fair; Relax; How Would You Like To Be; Beyond the Bend; One Broken Heart For Sale; Cotton Candy Land; A World Of Our Own.

1963 105m/C Elvis Presley, Joan O'Brien, Gary Lockwood, Kurt Russell, Edith Atwater, Yvonne Craig; **D:** Norman Taurog. **VHS, Beta** *MGM*

It Happened in New Orleans 🦴🦴

Family Vehicle for boy actor/singer Breen, regarded at the time as a sort of male counterpart to Shirley Temple. Except Breen's flicks haven't aged as well, and in this sentimental example he's cared for by a faithful former slave in post-Civil War New Orleans. His grandmother finally takes him to his resentful family in New York, but the kid's charm overcomes all hostilities.

1936 86m/B Bobby Breen, May Robson, Alan Mowbray, Benita Hume. **VHS, Beta** *VYY*

It Happened One Night 🎬🎬🎬🎬

Family Classic Capra comedy about an antagonistic couple determined to teach each other about life. Colbert is an unhappy heiress who runs away from her affluent home in search of contentment. On a bus she meets newspaper reporter Gable, who teaches her how "real" people live. She returns the favor in this first of the 1930s screwball comedies. The plot is a framework for an amusing examination of war between the sexes. Colbert and Gable are superb as affectionate foes. Remade as the musicals "Eve Knew Her Apples" and "You Can't Run Away From It."

1934 105m/B Clark Gable, Claudette Colbert, Roscoe Karns, Walter Connolly, Alan Hale, Ward Bond; **D:** Frank Capra; **W:** Robert Riskin. **VHS, Beta, LV** *COL, BTV, HMV*

It Takes Two 🎬

PG/Primary-Adult Vapid sugary comedy finds the nine-year-old Olsen twins playing a duo from opposite sides of the tracks who change identities in an effort to get their respective adults (Guttenberg and Alley) together. Young Olsen fans will want to see it. See "The Parent Trap" instead.

🚸 BEWARE *Some mild language.*

1995 100m/C Ashley Olsen, Mary-Kate Olsen, Kirstie Alley, Steve Guttenberg, Philip Bosco, Jane Sibbett, Lawrence Dane, Gerard Parkes; **D:** Andy Tennant; **W:** Deborah Dean Davis; **C:** Kenneth Zunder; **M:** Sherman Foote, Ray Foote. **VHS, LV** *WAR*

It's a Dog's Life 🎬🎬🎬

Family The hero and narrator of this story is a wily bull terrier called Wildfire. He's a tough dog on the mean streets of the Bowery in turn-of-the-century New York and his master has him in dog fights in the local saloon but then abandons him. Wildfire is taken in by the kindly employee of the rich and dog-hating Jagger but naturally manages to win the codger over. Based on the short story "The Bar Sinister" by Richard Harding Davis.

1955 87m/C Jeff Richards, Edmund Gwenn, Dean Jagger; **D:** Herman Hoffman; **W:** John Michael Hayes; **M:** Elmer Bernstein. **VHS** *FCT*

It's a Short Summer, Charlie Brown

Family Charlie, Lucy, Snoopy and the gang go off to camp for the summer. Ages 3 to 7.

19?? 25m/C VHS *VTR*

It's a Wonderful Life 🎬🎬🎬🎬

Family American classic about downtrodden George Bailey, saved from suicide by Clarence the Angel, who then shows the hero how secretly important he's been to his loved ones and community. Corny but inspirational and heartwarming, with endearing characters and performances. Christmas-themed, but perfect year-round for people who want to feel good, joyfully teetering on the border between Hollywood schmaltz and genuine heartbreak. Also available colorized. Laserdisc version includes production and publicity stills, the theatrical trailer, and commentary by film professor Jeanine Basinger. Also available in a 160-minute Collector's Edition with original preview trailer, "The Making of 'It's a Wonderful Life,'" and a new digital transfer from the original negative.

🚸 BEWARE *Alcohol use, roughhousing.*

1946 125m/B James Stewart, Donna Reed, Henry Travers, Thomas Mitchell, Lionel Barrymore, Samuel S. Hinds, Frank Faylen, Gloria Grahame, H.B. Warner, Ellen Corby, Sheldon Leonard, Beulah Bondi, Ward Bond, Frank Albertson, Todd Karns, Mary Treen, Charles Halton; **D:** Frank Capra; **W:** Frances Goodrich, Albert Hackett, Jo Swerling; **M:** Dimitri Tiomkin. **Award Nominations:** Academy Awards '46: Best Actor (Stewart), Best Director (Capra), Best Film Editing, Best Picture, Best Sound; **Awards:** Golden Globe Awards '47: Best Director (Capra). **VHS, LV** *IGP, MRV, CNG*

It's Not Easy Being Green

Preschool-Primary Children's sing-along presentation features Kermit, Miss Piggy, Fozzie, and Gonzo singing thirteen of the Muppets most popular tunes. 🎵 Kokomo; Splish Splash; Octopus' Garden; Pass It On; Movin' Right Along; Somewhere Over the Rainbow; Bein' Green; BBQ; Frog Talk.

1994 37m/C Jim Henson's Muppets. **VHS** *JHV, TOU*

It's Pat: The Movie WOOF!

PG-13/Jr. High-Adult Never released to theaters, this bloated "Saturday Night Skit" went straight to video. With good reason. A little of the guess-my-sex-character (Sweeney) goes a long way. The androgyne falls for equally gender-suspect Chris (Foley, from TV's "Kids in the Hall") and all sorts of embarrassing situations arise.

🚸 BEWARE *Bizarre gender-related humor. Try explaining androgyny to your kid.*

1994 78m/C Julia Sweeney, Dave Foley, Charles Rocket, Kathy Griffin, Julie Haydon, Tim Meadows, Arleen Sorkin; **Cameos:** Sally Jesse Raphael, Kathy Najimy; **D:** Adam Bernstein; **W:** Julia Sweeney, Jim Emerson, Stephen Hibbert. **VHS** *TOU*

It's the Easter Beagle, Charlie Brown

Family This Emmy Award Nominated episode finds the Peanut's gang anticipating the Easter holiday egg hunt. There's lots to do as Easter draws near, but not to worry, says Linus—the Easter Beagle will take care of everything. Looks like Snoopy has his work cut out for him. (Kinda reminds you of the mysterious Great Pumpkin, doesn't it?) Ages 4 to 8.

1974 30m/C D: Phil Roman; **V:** Lynn Mortensen, James Ahrens. **VHS** *MED, PAR*

It's the Great Pumpkin, Charlie Brown (triple feature)

Family In addition to Linus' telling of the "Great Pumpkin" legend, this three-episode collection includes "What a Nightmare Charlie Brown," and "It Was A Short Summer, Charlie Brown."
1966 77m/C VHS, Beta *SHV*

It's the Muppets, Vol. 1: Meet the Muppets

Family Comedy bits gathered from TV's "Muppet Show," including Kermit and Miss Piggy, Pigs in Space, piano-playing chickens, and lots of production numbers. Additional volumes available.
1992 37m/C VHS *JHV*

It's the Wolf

Preschool-Primary Collection of 12 cartoon episodes featuring Hanna-Barbera less-than-headliners like Lambsy, Mildew Wolf, and Bristle Hound.
1984 80m/C VHS, Beta *TTC*

Ivor the Engine & the Dragons

Preschool-Primary Ivor the locomotive and Jones, his engineer, operate a railway in Wales in this animated British TV series. In this episode, they meet some dragons who are small, and not very scary, but who do make pests of themselves. Ages 4 to 7.
19?? 59m/C VHS *VCO*

Ivor the Engine & the Elephants

Preschool-Primary What will Ivor the Engine do when an elephant blocks the train tracks? Ages 4 to 7.
19?? 60m/C VHS *VCO*

Jabberjaw

Preschool-Primary Four episodes from the Saturday-morning Hanna-Barbera cartoon about a friendly blue shark and his seagoing human friends in the year 2021.
1978 85m/C VHS, Beta *TTC*

Jabberwocky 🦴🦴

PG/Jr. High-Adult Chaos prevails in the medieval kingdom of King Bruno the Questionable, who rules with cruelty, stupidity, lust, and dust. Jabberwocky is the big dragon mowing everything down in its path until a hero decides to take it on. Uneven, undisciplined work by remnants of the Monty Python team who would subsequently do such wonderfully warped fairy tales as "Time Bandits" and "The Adventures of Baron Munchausen."

> ⚠ BEWARE *Violence, sex talk, pestilence, grotesque and ugly characters.*

1977 104m/C Michael Palin, Eric Idle, Max Wall, Deborah Fallender, Terry Jones, John Le Mesurier; *D:* Terry Gilliam; *W:* Terry Gilliam. **VHS, Beta, LV** *COL*

Jack 🦴🦴 ◟

Jr. High-Adult Ten-year-old Jack Powell (Williams) suffers from a rare genetic disorder that causes him to age at four times the normal rate so he looks like a 40-year-old. His family, fearing Jack would be ridiculed, has kept him at home with a tutor. But since Jack is so lonely and isolated, his tutor convinces his parents to let him attend school. This new fourth grader isn't the only one with a lot to learn. Touching story about what matters is what's on the inside.

> ⚠ BEWARE *Jack has heart problems when he falls in love with his new teacher.*

1996 ?m/C Robin Williams, Bill Cosby, Diane Lane, Brian Kerwin, Fran Drescher, Prof. Irwin Corey; *D:* Francis Ford Coppola. **VHS** *NYR*

Jack & the Beanstalk 🦴🦴

Family While babysitting, Costello falls asleep and dreams he's Jack in this weak spoof of the classic fairy tale. In keeping with the low budget, the 'giant' (Baer) seems unusually small for a member of the fe-fi-fo-fum crowd.
1952 78m/C Bud Abbott, Lou Costello, Buddy Baer; *D:* Jean Yarbrough. **VHS, Beta, LV** *NOS, VCI, VTR*

Jack & the Beanstalk 🦴🦴

Family Animated musical version of the familiar story of Jack, the young boy who climbs a magic beanstalk up into the clouds, where he meets a fearsome giant.
1976 80m/C *D:* Peter J. Solmo; *W:* Peter J. Solmo. **VHS, Beta** *COL*

Jack & the Beanstalk

Family From the "Faerie Tale Theatre" comes this classic tale of the boy who doesn't know beans. Or perhaps he does. Jack (Dennis Christopher) climbs the stalk and encounters giants Elliot Gould and Jean Stapleton. Ages 5 to 12.
1983 60m/C Dennis Christopher, Katherine Helmond, Elliott Gould, Jean Stapleton, Mark Blankfield; *D:* Lamont Johnson. **VHS, Beta, LV** *KUI, FOX, FCT*

Jack and the Beanstalk

Family Michael Palin (Monty Python, "A Fish Called Wanda") and the Eurythmics' own Dave Stewart team up for a memorable rendition of this classic tale. Fi, Fye, Fo, Fum! Part of the "Rabbit Ears" series of recited tales (against lush, painted illustrations) from different countries and cultures.
1991 30m/C *M:* Dave Stewart. **VHS, Beta** *RAB, MCA, FCT*

Jack Frost

Family Made-for-television Christmas special tells of the spritely Jack Frost's love for a human maiden via stop-motion model animation ("Animagic") perfected by the Rankin-Bass group.

Mary-Kate and Ashley Olsen play match-makers in "It Takes Two."

1979 48m/C V: Buddy Hackett, Robert Morse, Dave Garroway. **VHS, Beta, 8mm** *LIV*

Jack Houston's Imagineland: This is Imagineland

Preschool A country singer host in a cowboy hat and some beautifully designed puppets celebrate friendship, helpfulness and the importance of taking a bath. Ages 1 to 5.

199? ?m/C VHS *NYR*

Jack the Bear 🦴 🎵

PG-13/Jr. High-Adult Exercise in neuroses centering on a father and his two boys, trying to pick up the pieces after the death of mom. Dad, who hosts a late-night horror show, is cuddly as a bear—when he's not drinking. While the talent and circumstances might have been enough to create a sensitive study, the emotion is completely overwrought by contrived plot, including a kidnapping by the local Nazi. It's like a cement block dropped on a card house. Point made, but so much for subtlety. Based on a novel by Dan McCall.

BEWARE *Kidnaping, alcohol use, depression, violence, and neo-Nazism. The film took so long to make that child characters seem to age, then grow younger.*

1993 98m/C Danny DeVito, Robert J. Steinmiller Jr., Miko Hughes, Gary Sinise, Art LaFleur, Andrea Marcovicci, Julia Louis-Dreyfus, Reese Witherspoon; **D:** Marshall Herskovitz; **W:** Steven Zaillian; **M:** James Horner. **VHS, LV** *FXV*

Jack the Giant Killer 🦴 🦴

G/Family Brave young farmer, aided by a leprechaun, journeys to rescue a princess from an evil wizard. Along the way Jack fights giants and monsters, who unfortunately get cuter and cuddlier, not scarier, as the fairytale plot progresses. Economy-minded imitation of the classic Ray Harryhausen stop-motion adventures, this has school-pageant-level dialogue, costumes and mentality, with just adequate special effects from "Gumby" animator Jim Danforth. Filmed in 'Fantascope.' Right.

BEWARE *Monster roughhousing.*

1962 95m/C Kerwin Mathews, Judi Meredith, Torin Thatcher, Walter Burke, Roger Mobley, Barry Kelley, Don Beddoe, Anna Lee, Robert Gist; **D:** Nathan (Hertz) Juran. **VHS, Beta, LV** *MGM, FCT*

Jacob Have I Loved

Family Award-winning offering from PBS-TV's "Wonder-Works" vividly dramatizes the pain felt by Louise, a hardworking teenage girl in an isolated, deeply religious Chesapeake Bay community during WWII. All her life Louise has seen her simpering sister Caroline get all the attention and advantages. Then Louise takes a stand and befriends an outcast fisherman—and when he too seems to favor Caroline, the heroine feels more cheated than ever. Tale is flawed mainly by its short running time; you don't want this emotional family saga to end so suddenly. An abridgement of the source novel by Katherine Paterson.

1988 57m/C Bridget Fonda, Jenny Robertson, John Kellogg; *D:* Victoria Hochberg. **VHS** *PME, WNE, RHU*

Jacob Two-Two Meets the Hooded Fang

Primary Engaging, one-of-a-kind family film from Canada, based on a Mordechai Richter story. Jacob Two-Two (who has to say everything twice, since adults never listen to a kid the first time) dreams he's taken to a gloomy prison just for youngsters who give grief to grownups. The Hooded Fang is the bumbling, child-hating warden, an ex-pro wrestler. Fortunately Jacob has friends on the outside in the shape of zany superheroes who will rescue him if only he can get a message out. Production difficulties and deficiencies of a modest budget hold back tale somewhat, though it's still richly deserving and worth hunting up on tape.

1979 90m/C Alex Karras; *D:* Theodore J. Flicker. **VHS, Beta** *LIV*

Jamaica Inn 🦴🦴

Jr. High-Adult In old Cornwall, an orphan girl becomes involved with smugglers. Below-average Hitchcock, though stellar cast makes it interesting. Based on the story by Daphne Du Maurier and remade for British TV in 1982.

1939 98m/B Charles Laughton, Maureen O'Hara, Leslie Banks, Robert Newton; *D:* Alfred Hitchcock. **VHS, Beta** *SNC, NOS, CAB*

James and the Giant Peach 🦴🦴🦴

PG/Primary-Adult Roald Dahl's 1961 children's novel—a book kids actually like—gets a darkly imaginative and enjoyable treatment in the hands of stop-action animation master Selick ("The Nightmare Before Christmas"). It starts out with live actors. Orphaned James (his parents were eaten by a rhino) lives with his cruel aunts. One day a peach blooms on a tree in the yard and grows and grows and grows. When James crawls in he meets a cast of grotesque but friendly insects. He becomes a puppet, and all sail off to New York in the peach for further adventure. The bug voices—including Dreyfus as a Brooklynese centipede, Sarandon as a spider, and Leeves as a ladybug—are just peachy, and Randy Newman's songs are most pleasing.

> ⚠ BEWARE *Pre-schoolers may be scared by the mistreatment James gets from his aunts. A giant shark attacks the peach.*

1996 80m/C Paul Terry, Pete Postlethwaite, Joanna Lumley, Miriam Margolyes; *D:* Henry Selick; *C:* Pete Kozachik, Hiro Narita; *M:* Randy Newman; *V:* Richard Dreyfuss, Susan Sarandon, David Thewlis, Simon Callow, Jane Leeves. **VHS** *NYR*

James Bond, Jr.

Family The animated adventures of this young hero as he battles deranged criminals to save the world from disaster. Despite his name, the junior version of the suave James Bond is actually the nephew of the randy spy. James, Jr. attends a British boarding school with progeny of other characters from 007 movies and battles an evil organization known as S.C.U.M.

1992 ?m/C VHS *MGM*

James Hound: Give Me Liberty

Preschool-Primary Terrytoon series (created by Ralph Bakshi) in which a dog secret agent goes through James Bondesque perils and adventures.

1967 42m/C VHS *VTR*

James Hound: Mr. Winlucky

Preschool-Primary The cunning 007 of the dog world stars in another collection of TV episodes.

1967 30m/C VHS *VTR*

Jane & the Lost City 🦴🦴 ᗡ

PG/Jr. High-Adult A surprise, a comedy from a comic strip that could have been an ordeal but isn't. "Jane" was a British newspaper heroine meant to titillate WWII-era soldiers; during her adventures she constantly loses her clothes. This spritely, farcical version stays away from raunch (in her old-style undergarments Jane shows less skin than the Little Mermaid) and offers great spoofs of "Raiders"-type jungle flicks, as Jane races the Germans for African treasure.

1987 94m/C Kristen Hughes, Maud Adams, Sam Jones; *D:* Terry Marcel; *W:* Mervyn Haisman; *M:* Harry Robertson. **VHS, Beta** *NWV, VTR*

Jane Eyre 🦴🦴🦴

Jr. High-Adult Excellent adaptation of the Charlotte Bronte novel about the plain governess with the noble heart and her love for the mysterious and tragic Mr. Rochester. Fontaine has the proper backbone and yearning in the title role but to accommodate Welles' emerging popularity the role of Rochester was enlarged. Excellent bleak romantic-Gothic look. Taylor, in her third film role, is seen briefly in the early orphanage scenes.

1944 97m/B Joan Fontaine, Orson Welles, Margaret O'Brien, Peggy Ann Garner, John Sutton, Sara Allgood, Henry Daniell, Agnes Moorehead, Aubrey Mather, Edith Barrett, Barbara Everest, Hillary Brooke, Elizabeth Taylor; *D:* Robert Stevenson; *W:* John Houseman,

Jimmy Stewart surrounded by family and friends in "It's a Wonderful Life."

Aldous Huxley, Robert Stevenson; **M:** Bernard Herrmann. **VHS** *FXV, FCT, BTV*

Jane Eyre ♫♫♫

PG/Family Charlotte Bronte's story of plucky Jane, brooding Rochester and desolate mansion Thornfield Hall gets a fine production from director Zeffirelli, Charlotte Gainsbourg as the title character, and William Hurt as Mr. Rochester. Plucky orphan Jane (played as a child by Anna Paquin) takes a job as governess in the household where something isn't quite right. A true romance.

⚠ BEWARE *Mature themes and brief violence.*

1996 112m/C William Hurt, Anna Paquin, Charlotte Gainsbourg, Joan Plowright, Elle Macpherson, Geraldine Chaplin, Fiona Shaw, John Wood, Amanda Root, Marc Schneider, Josephine Serre; **D:** Franco Zeffirelli; **W:** Franco Zeffirelli, Hugh Whitemore; **C:** David Watkin; **M:** Alessio Vlad, Claudio Capponi. **VHS** *NYR*

Janosch: Fables from the Magic Forest

Family Storytelling bear spins a few more yarns about his mystical wooded homeland.
1990 115m/C VHS *JFK*

Jason and the Argonauts
♫♫♫ ◗

G/Family Jason, son of King of Thessaly, sails on the Argo to the land of Colchis. He and his valiant crew—including Hercules—encounter numerous perils and wonders during their quest for the magical Golden Fleece, guarded by a seven-headed hydra. Superb. Ray Harryhausen's special effects are at their best, and robust characters bring the classic figures of Greek legend to life, but myth buffs will note that the script brings the adventure to a close in time to skip the less-than-heroic tragedy of Jason and his lady love Medea.

⚠ BEWARE *Violence, alcohol use (or nectar of the gods, anyway, that gets the crew drunk). The famous battle between Jason and a horde of reanimated skeleton warriors blends horror, swashbuckling, and grisly humor.*

1963 104m/C Todd Armstrong, Nancy Kovack, Gary Raymond, Laurence Naismith, Nigel Green, Michael Gwynn, Honor Blackman; **D:** Don Chaffey; **W:** Jan Read, Beverley Cross. **VHS, Beta, LV, 8mm** *COL, MLB, FUS*

Jay Jay the Jet Plane

Preschool-Primary Thomas? No, tanks. Jay Jay is chubby and round-faced like Britain's Thomas the Tank Engine but he's American and he flies. With his similarly cute fellow aircraft, Jay Jay teaches entertaining life lessons, covering such subjects as doing what you're told, learning from mistakes, the difference between brave and being foolhardy and how practice leads to accomplishment. Ages 2 to 6.
1994 32m/C VHS *KID*

Jayce & the Wheeled Warriors, Vol. 1

Preschool-Jr. High Line of toy products provided this syndicated TV cartoon series with a reason for existing; Jayce, the son of a space scientist, and his gang of heroic freedom-fighters roll off on a long saga to overthrow a galactic vegetable tyrant. Episodes here are entitled "Ghostship" and "Escape from the Garden." Additional volumes available.
1985 45m/C VHS, Beta *COL*

Jazz Time Tale

Primary Funky, animated story of a young girl who meets jazz great Fats Waller.
19?? 29m/C D: Michael Sporn. **VHS** *LIV, FAF, BTV*

Jean de Florette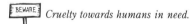

PG/Jr. High-Adult The first of two films (with "Manon of the Spring") based on Marcel Pagnol's novel. A single spring in drought-ridden Provence, France is blocked by two scheming countrymen (Montand and Auteuil). They await the imminent failure of the farm nearby, inherited by a city-born hunchback, whose chances for survival fade without water for his crops. A devastating story with a heartrending performance by Depardieu as the hunchback. Lauded and awarded; in French with English subtitles.

BEWARE *Cruelty towards humans in need.*

1987 122m/C Gerard Depardieu, Yves Montand, Daniel Auteuil, Elisabeth Depardieu, Ernestine Mazurowna; **D:** Claude Berri; **W:** Gerard Brach, Claude Berri. **VHS, Beta, LV** *ORI, IME, FCT*

Jefferson in Paris

PG-13/Jr. High-Adult Costume drama explores the impact Thomas Jefferson's (Nolte) five years in pre-revolutionary Paris (as American ambassador to Versailles) had on his private life. Jefferson confronts the personal and political issues of slavery in America, as well as his feelings for Sally Hemings (Newton), a Monticello slave brought to Paris by Jefferson's daughter. Long and boring, even for adults.

Meet the Star of James and the Giant Peach, Paul Terry

For such a little guy, Paul Terry had high aspirations at a very young age. The acting bug bit Terry when he was five-years-old, when the youngster convinced his mother, Gail (now his manager) to enroll him in a drama class in Hertfordshire, where the family resides. He made his stage debut at the age of six in a regional production of "A Month in the Country." Little did he know that he would later be dealing with a different kind of bug (or rather bugs).

His dad, Mark, heard about the auditions for *James and the Giant Peach* and thought his son would be perfect. He was right. Terry was picked by director Henry Selick from hundreds of applicants. Terry was given the chance to make his big screen debut, but the opportunity was not without its pitfalls. He had to act with a real-life tarantula that played Miss Spider during the live-action scenes. "I said to the spider, 'I'll be your friend,'" recalls the young Terry. "Then he bit me." Needless to say, Terry was a bit more leery of his co-stars after that.

But after all was said and done, Terry is as normal as every other kid out there. He's in his fifth year of school, he has a brother Matthew, and his chores are to empty the trash and feed the family dog Tom. For the next movie, he has but one demand, "No spiders this time. Absolutely not."

BEWARE *Contains mature themes including the interracial and forbidden relationship between Jefferson and Hemings, some images of violence, and a bawdy puppet show.*

James confers with his new insect friends in "James and the Giant Peach."

1994 139m/C Nick Nolte, Greta Scacchi, Gwyneth Paltrow, Thandie Newton, Jean-Pierre Aumont, Seth Gilliam, Todd Boyce, James Earl Jones; *D:* James Ivory; *W:* Ruth Prawer Jhabvala; *M:* Richard Robbins. **VHS, LV** *TOU*

Jem, Vol. 1: Truly Outrageous

Preschool-Primary Saturday-morning TV cartoon series from Hanna-Barbera about Jem, a futuristic rock star, who is also a superheroine/businesswoman/philanthropist/toy-store product. Additional volumes available.
1986 90m/C VHS, Beta *FHE*

Jeremiah Johnson ♫♫♫

PG/Jr. High-Adult Hollywood's concession to mountain man mania of the '70s is notably rougher than "Grizzly Adams" or the "Wilderness Family," but deserves mention for its sheer beauty and realistic portrayal of the American frontier. Based on a real character, Johnson turns his back on civilization, circa 1850, and learns a new code of survival amid isolated mountains, hostile Indians, and rival trappers.

 *Frontier violence.*

1972 107m/C Robert Redford, Will Geer; *D:* Sydney Pollack; *W:* Edward Anhalt, John Milius. **VHS, Beta, LV** *WAR, FCT*

The Jerky Boys WOOF!

R/Sr. High-Adult In childhood when you telephoned strangers and asked if their refrigerators were running, did you ever dream you could make a career of it? Well, the Jerky Boys (John Brennan and Kamal Ahmed) became professional prank callers, on recordings and on MTV. God bless America. Their idiotic movie is not so blessed, however. In the film's alleged plot, Johnny and Kamal prank call a mob boss (Arkin), pretending to be Chicago hitmen in need of a hideout. The gangsters catch on and come after them, but mostly the Boys are on the phone, making their revolting calls. It's enough to make Prince Albert get back in the can.

BEWARE *A nonstop profane-athon. If you dislike the "F word," stay away.*

1995 82m/C Johnny Brennan, Kamal Ahmed, Alan Arkin, William Hickey, Alan North, James Lorinz, Brad Sullivan, Vinny Pastore, Ozzy Osbourne, Paul Bartel, Suzanne Shepherd; *Cameos:* Tom Jones; *D:* James Melkonian; *W:* Johnny Brennan, Kamal Ahmed, Rich Wilkes, James Melkonian. **VHS, LV** *TOU*

Jersey Girl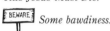

PG-13/Jr. High-Adult Toby Mastellone (Gertz) is a bright single gal from the Jersey shore who wants something better in her life. Her hard-working dad (Bologna) has fixed her up with an apprentice plumber but she wants a Manhattan guy. And then Toby meets cute Sal (McDermott), who seems just the ticket, but can you really take the Jersey out of the girl?

1992 95m/C Jami Gertz, Dylan McDermott, Joseph Bologna, Aida Turturro, Star Jasper, Sheryl Lee, Joseph Mazzello, Molly Price; **D:** David Burton Morris; **W:** Gina Wendkos. **VHS** *COL*

Jesse James Rides Again

Jr. High-Adult Republic serial giving the hero treatment to one of the west's most famous outlaws (played by "Lone Ranger" actor Moore), making him a sort of Robin Hood of the frontier.

1947 181m/B Clayton Moore, Linda Stirling, Roy Barcroft, Tristram Coffin; **D:** Fred Brannon, Thomas Carr. **VHS** *REP, MLB*

Jesus Christ, Superstar

G/Family A rock opera that portrays, in music, the last seven days in the earthly life of Christ, as reenacted by young tourists in Israel. Outstanding musical score was the key to the success of the film. Based on the stage play by Tim Rice and Andrew Lloyd Weber, film is sometimes stirring while exhibiting the usual heavy-handed Jewison approach. ♫ Jesus Christ, Superstar; I Don't Know How To Love Him; What's The Buzz?; Herod's Song; Heaven On Their Minds; Strange Thing, Mystifying; Then We Are Decided; Everything's Alright; This Jesus Must Die.

BEWARE *Some bawdiness.*

1973 108m/C Ted Neeley, Carl Anderson, Yvonne Elliman, Josh Mostel; **D:** Norman Jewison. **VHS, Beta, LV** *MCA*

Jesus of Nazareth

Family All-star cast vividly portrays the life of Christ in this made-for-television mini-series. Skillfully directed and sensitively acted. On three cassettes.

1977 371m/C Robert Powell, Anne Bancroft, Ernest Borgnine, Claudia Cardinale, James Mason, Laurence Olivier, Anthony Quinn; **D:** Franco Zeffirelli; **M:** Maurice Jarre. **VHS, Beta** *LIV, FOX, ECU*

A Jetson's Christmas Carol

Family Even Mr. Spacely gets into the spirit in this holiday special derived from the Hanna-Barbera cartoon series. Nine more volumes of Jetson flotsam are available on tape, plus the occasional feature-length production.

1989 30m/C V: George O'Hanlon, Penny Singleton, Daws Butler, Mel Blanc. **VHS, Beta, LV** *TTC, IME*

The Jetsons Meet the Flintstones

Family They said it couldn't be done: a melding of the space age with the stone age. Made-for-TV double-dose

If you like *Jane Eyre* (1996), you'll love:

The Age of Innocence (1993)

Amadeus (1984)

Anne of Avonlea (1987)

Anne of Green Gables (1934)

Anne of Green Gables (1985)

Emma (1996)

Howard's End (1992)

Much Ado About Nothing (1993)

Oliver! (1968)

Oliver Twist (1948)

Pollyanna (1960)

The Remains of the Day (1993)

Sarah, Plain and Tall (1991)

Sense and Sensibility (1995)

Shadowlands (1993)

of Hanna-Barbera franchises, when young Elroy Jetson's time machine takes him and his family back to the 25th century B.C. There they meet the Flintstones and the Rubbles, who accidentally get transported into the future. Will either family ever get back home?

1988 100m/C V: Mel Blanc, Daws Butler, Jean VanDerPyl, George O'Hanlon, Penny Singleton. **VHS, Beta, LV** *TTC, IME*

The Jetsons: The Movie

G/Family Ill-starred version of TV's outer space family is like an average episode with a half-hour plot stretched to feature length: George Jetson gets promoted in charge of an extraterrestrial factory that hurts the ecosystem of some furry Ewok lookalikes. 1990 environmental sermons make the 21st century story seem 100 years behind the times, and you might want to subtract a bone for the treatment of Janet Waldo, the original Judy Jetson, booted off the project at the last minute and replaced with the voice of teen crooner Tiffany. Other sad news: Mel Blanc (Mr. Spacely) and George O'Hanlon (George Jetson) died before the movie's release, and it's dedicated to them.

1990 82m/C **D:** William Hanna, Joseph Barbera; **M:** John Debney; **V:** George O'Hanlon, Mel Blanc, Penny Singleton, Tiffany, Patric Zimmerman, Don Messick, Jean VanDerPyl, Ronnie Schell, Patti Deutsch, Dana Hill, Russi Taylor, Paul Kreppel, Rick Dees. **VHS, Beta, LV** *MCA, APD*

The Jewel of the Nile 🦴🦴 ⌐

PG/Jr. High-Adult Sequel to "Romancing the Stone" with the same cast but new director. Romance novelist Joan thought she found her true love in Jack but finds that life doesn't always end happily ever. After they part ways, Jack realizes that she may be in trouble and endeavors to rescue her from the criminal hands of a charming North African president. Of course, he can always check out this "jewel" at the same time. Chemistry is still there, but the rest of the film isn't quite up to the "Stone's" charm.

> **BEWARE** *Violence, sex talk as the two try to rekindle an old flame, and profanity.*

1985 106m/C Michael Douglas, Kathleen Turner, Danny DeVito, Avner Eisenberg, The Flying Karamazov Brothers, Spiros Focas, Holland Taylor; **D:** Lewis Teague; **W:** Mark Rosenthal, Larry Konner; **M:** Jack Nitzsche. **VHS, Beta, LV** *FOX*

Jim Henson's Preschool Collection: Muppets on Wheels

Preschool-Primary Lindy, a new Muppet kid, joins Kermit the Frog on a journey through the world of wheels. They visit different locations ranging from the race track and amusement park, to a construction site. Along their way they meet children and a new clan of Muppet friends. Ages 2 to 6.
1995 30m/C **VHS** *TOU*

Jim Henson's Preschool Collection: Yes, I Can Help

Preschool-Primary Kermit the Frog helps his young nephew Robin learn about the world and how he fits in it. Ages 2 to 6.
1995 50m/C **VHS** *TOU*

Jim Henson's Preschool Collection: Yes, I Can Learn

Preschool-Primary Kermit gives nephew Robin advice about the world and how he can make a difference. Ages 2 to 6.
1995 50m/C **VHS** *TOU*

Jimbo and the Jet-Set, Vols. 1 & 2

Preschool-Primary A Jimbo jet, not a jumbo jet, he's a small plane who travels to far-away places. Each tape contains a dozen short adventures. Ages 3 to 7.
19?? 52m/C **VHS** *VCO*

Jiminy Cricket's Christmas

G/Family Yuletide collection of Disney cartoons, featuring Donald Duck, Chip 'n' Dale, Goofy, Jiminy Cricket; includes the rare "Mickey's Good Deed" (1932).
1932 47m/C **VHS, Beta, LV** *DIS*

Jimmy the Kid 🦴🦴

PG/Family Jimmy is kidnapped by a bumbling gang of crooks and held for ransom, but the clever tyke both befriends and outsmarts them. Screen vehicle for TV sitcom star Coleman ("Diff'rent Strokes"), based on a caper novel by Donald E. Westlake.

> **BEWARE** *Roughhousing, salty language.*

1982 95m/C Gary Coleman, Cleavon Little, Fay Hauser, Ruth Gordon, Dee Wallace Stone, Paul LeMat, Don Adams; **D:** Gary Nelson; **W:** Sam Bobrick. **VHS, Beta** *NO*

Jirimpimbira: An African Folktale

Family Animated tale follows Temba, a boy searching for food and water to rescue his village from a drought. But when an old man gives the boy some magic bones that will grant his every wish, Temba gets greedy and forgets his quest. Based on the book "Tales of Temba" by Kathleen Arnot.
1995 25m/C **VHS** *ABC*

Joe Panther 🦴🦴 ⌐

G/Family Well-intentioned family drama about a young Seminole Indian who wants to ship out on a fishing boat but instead stakes his claim in the white man's world by wrestling alligators.
1976 110m/C Brian Keith, Ricardo Montalban, Alan Feinstein, Cliff Osmond, A. Martinez, Robert Hoffman; **D:** Paul Krasny. **VHS** *WAR*

Joe Versus the Volcano 🦴🦴

PG/Jr. High-Adult The answer to the question: In what other movie besides "Sleepless in Seattle" have Hanks and Ryan co-starred? Shanley's directorial debut is an expressionistic goofball comedy about a dopey guy who, after finding out he has only months to live, contracts with a millionaire to leap into a volcano alive. Then of course, romance enters picture as Tom meets Meg, who plays not one, but three roles. Imaginatively styled farce displays great "Metropolis"-pastiche visuals but is undermined by a fairly stupid script caught between satire and sentiment, though youngsters seem to enjoy the fairy tale atmosphere and sheer charm of the stars. Special effects courtesy of Industrial Light and Magic.

> **BEWARE** *Slight salty language.*

1990 106m/C Tom Hanks, Meg Ryan, Lloyd Bridges, Robert Stack, Amanda Plummer, Abe Vigoda, Dan Hedaya, Barry McGovern, Ossie Davis; **D:** John Patrick Shanley; **W:** John Patrick Shanley; **M:** Georges Delerue. **VHS, Beta, LV, 8mm** *WAR*

Joey

PG/Primary-Adult Daddy, a former doo-wopper, looks back on his years of musical success as a waste of time. His son takes to the world of rock guitar with blind fervor. Their argument plays against the backdrop of the "Royal Doo-Wopp Show" at New York City's Radio Music Hall. Features multi-generational rock songs.
1985 90m/C Neill Barry, James Quinn. **VHS, Beta** *NO*

Joey Runs Away and Other Stories

Preschool-Primary Little Kangaroo Joey leaves his mother's pouch for better accommodations, but discovers that it really is hard to beat home. Selection of animated kids' books from the "Children's Circle" lineup also includes "The Cow Who Fell in the Canal," "The Bear and the Fly," and "The Most Wonderful Egg in the World."
1989 28m/C VHS *CCC, FCT, WKV*

Johann's Gift to Christmas

Preschool-Primary TV cartoon story of a young mouse who inspires the writing of the beloved Christmas carol "Silent Night." For a live action version, see "Silent Mouse."
1991 25m/C VHS *FHE, FAF*

John & Julie

Preschool-Primary Vintage British kids' film about two six-year-old children who set out by themselves on an eventful journey to London to see the coronation of the new Queen Elizabeth.
1957 82m/C Colin Gibson, Lesley Dudley. **VHS, Beta** *FHE*

John Henry

Primary Legend of John Henry, who singlehandedly defeats a steam drill in a steel driving competition, is illustrated in storybook fashion and read by thespian Washington as part of the "Rabbit Ears" collection of tall tales.
1993 30m/C M: B.B. King. **VHS** *RAB, PMS, BTV*

John the Fearless

Primary-Jr. High In Europe, 1410 A.D., John is a brawny young peasant, jobless because he refuses to cringe before any master (some things never change). Exiled from his hometown, John becomes a freelance hero, fighting deadly foes to see if he can ever truly experience fear. Belgian animated feature has a great premise (based on the novel by Constant De Kinder) and pro animation that looks like a medieval woodcut come to life. But after awhile the story gets very predictable and surprisingly short on action.

BEWARE *Roughhousing.*

1987 80m/C VHS

Johnny Appleseed

Preschool-Primary Recitation of the story of Johnny Appleseed, the American naturalist who roamed the Ohio Valley in the early 1800s, with artwork by Stan Olson. Part of the "Rabbit Ears: American Heroes and Legends" series.
1993 30m/C VHS *RAB,, BTV*

Johnny Dangerously

PG-13/Jr. High-Adult Gangster spoof about Johnny Dangerously, who turned to crime in order to pay his mother's medical bills. Now, Dangerously wants to go straight, but competitive crooks would rather see him dead than law-abiding and his mother requires more and more expensive operations. In spite of the talent, this crime only pays in near-comic ways.

BEWARE *Violence and profanity (though one character's profanity is garbled by his heavy accent).*

1984 90m/C Michael Keaton, Joe Piscopo, Danny DeVito, Maureen Stapleton, Marilu Henner, Peter Boyle, Griffin Dunne, Glynnis O'Connor, Dom DeLuise, Richard Dimitri, Ray Walston, Dick Butkus, Alan Hale Jr., Bob Eubanks; **D:** Amy Heckerling; **W:** Norman Steinberg. **VHS, Beta** *FOX*

Johnny Mnemonic

R/Sr. High-Adult Robo-yuppie data courier Johnny (Reeves), has over extended the storage capacity in his head and must download his latest job before his brain turns to applesauce. Aided by an implant-enhanced bodyguard (Meyer), underground hacker rebels called LoTeks, and a former doctor (Rollins) battling a technology-induced epidemic, Johnny is on the run from the corporation that wants his head (literally). Plot is a mess but action sequences and computer effects are done with panache.

BEWARE *Amputation by laser and other sci-fi violence and profanity.*

1995 98m/C Keanu Reeves, Dina Meyer, Ice-T, Takeshi, Dolph Lundgren, Henry Rollins, Udo Kier, Barbara Sukowa, Denis Akiyama; **D:** Robert Longo; **W:** William Gibson; **C:** Francois Protat; **M:** Brad Fiedel. **VHS, LV, 8mm** *COL*

Johnny Shiloh

Family Orphan youth becomes a heroic drummer during the Civil War. Originally a two-part Disney television show, somewhat lacking in spectacle.
1963 90m/C Kevin Corcoran, Brian Keith, Darryl Hickman, Skip Homeier; **D:** James Neilson. **VHS, Beta** *DIS*

Johnny the Giant Killer

Family When Johnny is reduced to miniature size by the giant, he befriends a bird and a queen bee who help him to even the score.
1954 68m/C VHS, Beta *DVT*

Johnny Tremain & the Sons of Liberty 🦴🦴

Family Disney adaptation of the Esther Forbes novel, depicting the beginnings of the American Revolution from the viewpoint of a teenage apprentice silversmith in 1773 Boston. Johnny eventually meets Paul Revere and Samuel Adams, joins the Boston Tea Party, and fights in the Battle of Lexington. Like the smash "Davy Crockett," this historical tale was made as a miniseries for Disney's network TV show and released to theaters. Scope, characters and production values remain small-screen-sized, however.

1958 85m/C Sebastian Cabot, Hal Stalmaster, Luana Patten, Richard Beymer; **D:** Robert Stevenson. **VHS, Beta** *DIS*

Johnny Woodchuck's Adventures

Preschool-Primary Little Johnny Woodchuck is more precocious than his well-behaved brothers. One day, he leaves home and family behind and sets out on an adventure.

1978 60m/C VHS, Beta *FHE*

Johnny's Girl 🦴🦴🕊

Family After her mom's death, a 16-year-old moves to Anchorage, Alaska to live with her wayward dad. He's a con man involved in shady deals, who tries to go legit in order to give his daughter a proper home. TV movie based on the novel by Kim Rich.

1995 92m/C Mia Kirshner, Treat Williams, Ron White, Gloria Reuben, Shirley Douglas, Janne Mortil; **D:** John Kent Harrison. **VHS** *HMK*

The Jolson Story 🦴🦴🦴

Family Smash Hollywood bio of Jolson, from his childhood to super-stardom, runs amuck with cliches but who cares? Parks, doing Jolson as seen by Jolson, delivers. Features dozens of vintage songs from Jolson's parade of hits. Jolson himself dubbed the vocals for Parks, rejuvenating his own career in the process. 🎵 Swanee; You Made Me Love You; By the Light of the Silvery Moon; I'm Sitting On Top of the World; There's a Rainbow Round My Shoulder; My Mammy; Rock-A-Bye Your Baby With a Dixie Melody; Liza; Waiting for the Robert E. Lee.

1946 128m/C Larry Parks, Evelyn Keyes, William Demarest, Bill Goodwin, Tamara Shayne, John Alexander, Jimmy Lloyd, Ludwig Donath, Scotty Beckett; **D:** Alfred E. Green; **M:** Morris Stoloff. **Award Nominations:** Academy Awards '46: Best Actor (Parks), Best Color Cinematography, Best Film Editing, Best Supporting Actor (Demarest); **Awards:** Academy Awards '46: Best Sound, Best Score. **VHS, Beta, LV** *COL*

Jonah and the Whale

Preschool-Primary Animated version of the biblical tale of Jonah, assigned by God to tell the people of Ninevah to renounce their evil ways, then swallowed by a whale. **1992 30m/C VHS** *MVD, RIN*

Jonathan Livingston Seagull 🦴🕊

G/Family Imagine how "Homeward Bound: The Incredible Journey" or "The Adventures of Milo and Otis" would have been if the animal characters mainly sat and talked philosophy all the time. Based on the best-seller by Richard Bach, this finds a vaguely Christlike nonconformist seabird banished by his flock for seeking a higher purpose. Hardly featherbrained, but the awkwardness of putting Bach's book on the screen made this a box-office turkey. Introspective songs on the soundtrack by Neil Diamond.

1973 99m/C James Franciscus, Juliet Mills; **D:** Hall Bartlett; **M:** Neil Diamond. **Award Nominations:** Academy Awards '73: Best Cinematography, Best Film Editing; **Awards:** Golden Globe Awards '74: Best Score. **VHS, Beta** *PAR, WSH*

Joni 🦴🦴🕊

G/Family Inspirational story based on the real life of Joni Tada (playing herself) who was severely paralyzed in a diving accident, but found the strength to cope. She took up painting, writing, and finally evangelizing her born again faith (Billy Graham helped produce the film and lends a Hitchcock-style cameo appearance). Wholesome drama based on the autobiography by Tada.

1979 75m/C Joni Eareckson Tada, Bert Remsen, Katherine De Hetre, Cooper Huckabee; **D:** James F. Collier. **VHS, Beta** *LIV*

Josh and S.A.M. 🦴🦴

PG-13/Jr. High-Adult Road movie with a twist: the driver can barely see over the dashboard. Josh and Sam are brothers whose parents are splitting. They cope by taking off on their own. Sam, meanwhile has been convinced by the older Josh that he's not a real boy at all, but rather a military S.A.M.: Strategically Altered Mutant (sounds like Josh saw "D.A.R.Y.L"). Lightweight tale in search of deeper significance will appeal to kids, but adults will see over the dashboard and through the transparent plot.

1993 97m/C Jacob Tierney, Noah Fleiss, Martha Plimpton, Joan Allen, Christopher Penn, Stephen Tobolowsky, Ronald Guttman; **D:** Billy Weber; **W:** Frank Deese; **M:** Thomas Newman. **VHS, LV** *NLC*

Josh Kirby . . . Time Warrior: Chapter 1, Planet of the Dino-Knights 🦴🦴🕊

PG/Primary-Adult Time-traveling 14-year-old Josh Kirby is accidently zapped to the 25th-century where fierce warriors ride dinosaurs and a madman is out to destroy the universe. The first tale in a fantasy series designed as an old-fashioned movie serial, complete with cliff-hanger ending. Five chapters in the series.

 Mild language and action violence.

1995 88m/C Corbin Allred, Jennifer Burns, Derek Webster, John De Mita; **D:** Ernest Farino; **W:** Ethan Reiff, Cyrus Voris, Paul Callisi. **VHS, Beta** *PAR*

Josie & the Pussycats in Outer Space

Family Three Saturday-morning episodes of the '70s all-girl cartoon rock group. None of the original, earthbound "Josie & the Pussycats" shows are currently available on tape (so suffer!), just this sci-fi spinoff in which the caterwaulers take off on a spaceship into the far corners of the galaxy. Additional volumes available.
197? 58m/C VHS, Beta *TTC*

Journey Back to Oz ♫♫

Preschool-Primary Animated musical sequel to "The Wizard of Oz" sat on the shelf for several years after its completion. Not bad, with some scenes quite nicely designed, but nothing is particularly magical about the story apart from the casting of Minelli (daughter of Judy Garland) to provide the voice for Dorothy. The Kansas girl and her little dog Toto return to visit their friends in the magical land of Oz, only to find the land hostage to the forces of evil witch Mombi.
1964 90m/C V: Liza Minnelli, Ethel Merman, Paul Lynde, Milton Berle, Mickey Rooney, Danny Thomas. **VHS, Beta** *FHE, KAR, HHE*

Journey for Margaret ♫♫♫

Family Young and Day star as an expectant American couple living in London during WWII. Day miscarries during an air raid and heads back to the States while Young stays in London where he meets two orphans and takes them under his wing. He decides to take them back to the U.S. but problems arise. Tearjerker with good story that shows the war through the eyes of children. O'Brien's first film. Based on the book by William L. White.
1942 81m/B Robert Young, Laraine Day, Fay Bainter, Signe Hasso, Margaret O'Brien, Nigel Bruce, G.P. Huntley Jr., William Severn, Doris Lloyd, Halliwell Hobbes, Jill Esmond; **D:** Woodbridge S. Van Dyke. **VHS** *MGM, FCT*

The Journey of August King ♫♫♫ ♪

PG-13/Jr. High-Adult August King (Jason Patric) is a widowed farmer in North Carolina in 1815, an ordinary man whose life changes when he crosses paths with Annalees, a runaway slave (Thandie Newton). It's illegal to help slaves escape, but Annalees's mean-looking owner (Larry Drake) arrives with his posse, August says he hasn't seen any runaway. Thus begins a journey that is harrowing, heartfelt and as much moral as it is physical. An outstanding and convincing work of historical fiction.

Patric is splendidly understated and Newton is simply smashing. Fine performances, too, from Sam Waterston, who co-produced, and narrator Maya Angelou. Ages 11 and up.

 Slavery, with its attendant violence and mistreatment of people.

1995 91m/C Jason Patric, Thandie Newton, Larry Drake, Sam Waterston; **D:** John Duigan; **W:** John Ehle; **C:** Slawomir Idziak; **M:** Stephen Endelman. **VHS, LV** *TOU*

The Journey of Natty Gann ♫♫♫ ♪

PG/Family With the help of a guardian wolf and a young hobo, 14-year-old Natalie travels across Depression-era America disguised as a boy to find her father. Warm and winning Disney family feature with memorable characters and an excellent sense of time and place. From the scriptwriter of "The Black Stallion."
1985 101m/C Meredith Salenger, John Cusack, Ray Wise, Scatman Crothers, Lainie Kazan, Verna Bloom; **D:** Jeremy Paul Kagan; **W:** Jeanne Rosenberg; **M:** James Horner. **VHS, Beta, LV** *DIS*

Journey to Spirit Island ♫♫♫

PG/Jr. High-Adult Maria, a present-day Makah Indian girl, has mysterious dreams of her ancestors buried on Spirit Island, now the potential site of a resort. Eventually she, a friend and two visiting Chicago boys are stranded on the island and try to save the sacred ground from underhanded developers. Not just a solid kiddie adventure but a fresh, stereotype-busting look at a modern Native American community, filled with nice little character surprises. Deserves more recognition. Filmed in the Neah Bay area of Washington state.
1992 93m/C Brandon Douglas, Gabriel Damon, Tony Acierto, Nick Ramus, Marie Antoinette Rodgers, Tarek McCarthy; **D:** Laszlo Pal. **VHS** *ACA*

Journey to the Center of the Earth ♫♫♫

Family Enjoyable fantasy based on the Jules Verne novel about a scientist who, following an ancient map, leads an expedition into the crater of an extinct Icelandic volcano and descends to a prehistoric world deep beneath the Earth, where both dinosaurs and the remains of Atlantis can be found. Dinos are just lizards filmed in closeup, and the romantic subplot is a silly trifle, but the sense of epic-scale adventure and discovery remain intact, though shrunken on video.

 Monsters and theme song sung by Pat Boone.

1959 132m/C James Mason, Pat Boone, Arlene Dahl, Diane Baker, Thayer David; **D:** Henry Levin. **VHS, Beta, LV** *FOX, FCT, FUS*

Journey to the Center of the Earth WOOF!

PG/Jr. High-Adult Young nanny and two teenage boys discover Atlantis while exploring a volcano. Embarrassment has next to nothing to do with Jules Verne and aborts itself in mid-plot, presumably when money ran out. MTV sets, costumes, film clips actually came from numerous other low-grade fantasies made around the same time.

BEWARE *Alcohol use, profanity, and fighting.*

1988 83m/C Nicola Cowper, Paul Carafotes, Ilan Mitchell-Smith; ***D:*** Rusty Lemorande; ***W:*** Rusty Lemorande, Kitty Chalmers. **VHS, Beta, LV** *CAN*

The Joy Luck Club ♫♫♫ ♭

R/Sr. High-Adult Universal themes in mother/daughter relationships are explored in a context Hollywood first rejected as too narrow, but which proved to be a modest sleeper hit. Tan skillfully weaves the plot of her 1989 bestseller into a screenplay which centers around young June's going-away party. Slowly the stories of four Chinese women, who meet weekly to play mah-jongg, are unraveled. Each vignette reveals life in China for the four women and the tragedies they survived, before reaching into the present to capture the relationships between the mothers and their daughters. Powerful, relevant, and moving.

BEWARE *Profanity, sex, and unhappy relationships. A lesson in the trials of family life.*

1993 136m/C Tsai Chin, Kieu Chinh, France Nuyen, Rosalind Chao, Tamlyn Tomita, Lisa Lu, Lauren Tom, Ming-Na Wen, Michael Paul Chan, Andrew McCarthy, Christopher Rich, Russell Wong, Victor Wong, Vivian Wu, Jack Ford, Diane Baker; ***D:*** Wayne Wang; ***W:*** Amy Tan. **VHS, LV** *TOU, HPH*

Judge Dredd ♫ ♭

R/Sr. High-Adult It's the year 2139 and Joseph Dredd (Stallone) is the latest in law enforcement: judge, jury, cop and executioner (whew! talk about your downsizing). He has it pretty good until someone accuses him of murder. Dredd is off to clear his name, and do a lot of damage along the way. including damage to the audience's intelligence. This movie would have been better with less violence and aimed at a younger audience with a more cartoony superhero feel.

BEWARE *Continuous violent action, including an impaling.*

1995 96m/C Sylvester Stallone, Armand Assante, Diane Lane, Rob Schneider, Joan Chen, Juergen Prochnow, Max von Sydow; ***D:*** Danny Cannon; ***W:*** Steven E. de Souza, Michael De Luca, William Wisher; ***M:*** Alan Silvestri. **VHS, LV** *TOU*

Judgment at Nuremberg ♫♫♫♫

Jr. High-Adult It's 1948 and a group of high-level Nazis are on trial for war crimes. Chief Justice Tracy must resist political pressures as he presides over the trials. Excellent performances throughout, especially by Dietrich and Garland. Considers to what extent an individual may be held accountable for actions committed under orders of a superior officer. Consuming account of the Holocaust

and WWII is deeply moving and powerful. Based on a "Playhouse 90" television program.

BEWARE *Graphic footage of concentration camp survivors, and those who didn't survive.*

1961 178m/B Spencer Tracy, Burt Lancaster, Richard Widmark, Montgomery Clift, Maximilian Schell, Judy Garland, Marlene Dietrich, William Shatner; ***D:*** Stanley Kramer; ***W:*** Abby Mann; ***M:*** Ernest Gold. **Award Nominations:** Academy Awards '61: Best Actor (Tracy), Best Art Direction/Set Decoration (B & W), Best Black and White Cinematography, Best Costume Design (B & W), Best Director (Kramer), Best Film Editing, Best Picture, Best Supporting Actor (Clift), Best Supporting Actress (Garland); **Awards:** Academy Awards '61: Best Actor (Schell), Best Adapted Screenplay; Golden Globe Awards '62: Best Actor—Drama (Schell), Best Director (Kramer); New York Film Critics Awards '61: Best Actor (Schell). **VHS, Beta, LV** *MGM, FOX, BTV*

Jumanji ♫♫ ♭

PG/Jr. High-Adult The title refers to an African safari board game, but Jumanji is no Candyland. Indeed when a couple of kids roll the dice they free a man (Williams) who's been trapped in the game for 26 years. They also unleash wild animals, armed hunters, giant mosquitoes and man-eating plants upon their small New England town. Based loosely on the children's book by Chris Van Allsburg. Action-packed return to childhood for Williams keeps you on the edge of your seat waiting for the next roll of the dice.

BEWARE *Menacing fantasy action makes film too frightening for pre-schoolers (and some older kids) and anybody who is afraid of bugs and spiders will cringe at the giant ones leaping out of this board game.*

1995 104m/C Robin Williams, Kirsten Dunst, Bonnie Hunt, Bradley Michael Pierce, Bebe Neuwirth, Jonathan Hyde, David Alan Grier; ***D:*** Joe Johnston; ***W:*** Jonathan Hensleigh; ***M:*** James Horner. **VHS, LV** *COL*

The Jungle Book ♫♫

Family Lavish, live-action British version of Rudyard Kipling's stories about Mowgli, the child raised by wolves in the jungles of India, who can talk to the beasts, both friendly and hostile, and develops a mortal enemy in Shere Khan the tiger. Animals are sometimes unconvincing puppets, but Sabu makes a fine boy hero and pic maintains a rich storybook flavor throughout. From the makers of another Kipling great, "Elephant Boy."

1942 109m/C Sabu, Joseph Calleia, Rosemary DeCamp, Ralph Byrd, John Qualen; ***D:*** Zoltan Korda; ***M:*** Miklos Rozsa. **VHS, LV** *CNG, MRV, REP*

The Jungle Book ♫♫♫

Family Based on Kipling's classic, a young boy raised by wolves must choose between his jungle friends and human "civilization." Along the way he meets a variety of jungle characters including zany King Louie, kindhearted Baloo, wise Bagheera and the evil Shere Khan. Great, classic songs including "Trust in Me," "I Wanna Be Like You," and Oscar-nominated "Bare Necessities." Last Disney feature overseen by Uncle Walt himself and a must for kids of all ages.

1967 78m/C **D:** Wolfgang Reitherman; **V:** Phil Harris, Sebastian Cabot, Louis Prima, George Sanders, Sterling Holloway, J. Pat O'Malley, Verna Felton, Darlene Carr. **VHS, Beta, LV** *DIS, TOU, FCT*

Jungle Book: Mowgli Comes to the Jungle

Family The first installment in the series of animated stories based on Rudyard Kipling's characters. This episode introduces Mowgli to green wilderness and his adoption by Alexander's wolf pack. Additional volumes available.
1990 30m/C VHS *VTR*

Jungle Drums of Africa

Family Dull Republic serial, one of their last. Moore, better known for portraying the Lone Ranger, encounters lions, wind tunnels, a heroine in jeopardy, voodoo and enemy agents in deepest Africa. 12 episodes, on two cassettes.
1953 167m/B Clayton Moore, Phyllis Coates, Roy Glenn, John Cason; **D:** Fred Brannon. **VHS** *REP, MLB*

A Jungle for Joey

Preschool-Primary Orangutan named Joey is separated from his family in Borneo.
1989 14m/C VHS, Beta *AIM*

The Jungle King

Preschool-Primary Animated tale of twin lions Max, the king, and Irwin, the shy and scholarly one, who switch identities in order to save the kingdom from its evil hyena chancellor. Borrows heavily from "The Lion King," "The Prince and the Pauper," and "Dave." Plus, the generic background music is relentless. And what kind of names are Max and Irwin for lions? Ages 3 to 7.
1994 48m/C VHS

Junior 🦴🦴

PG-13/Jr. High-Adult It's Conan the Caesarean, as Schwarzenegger plays a man who becomes pregnant. No, not in the usual way. He and DeVito are scientists testing a fertility drug, and being Schwarzenegger and DeVito they sort of mess things up. Emma Thompson, as another scientist, provides the egg. Film hits upon every pregnancy cliche in the book. It's all pretty grotesque.

> ⚐ BEWARE ⚐ *Sex-related humor and some profanity mar the otherwise innocent topics of babyland and motherhood, but hey, we all know babies really don't come from the stork.*

1994 109m/C Arnold Schwarzenegger, Danny DeVito, Emma Thompson, Frank Langella, Pamela Reed, Judy Collins, James Eckhouse, Aida Turturro; **D:** Ivan Reitman; **W:** Kevin Wade, Chris Conrad; **M:** James Newton Howard. **VHS, LV** *MCA*

Junior Bonner 🦴🦴🦴

PG/Jr. High-Adult A rowdy modern-day western about a young drifting rodeo star who decides to raise money

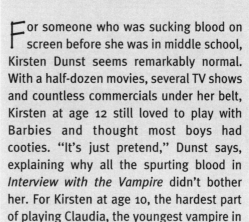

Meet the Star of Jumanji, Kirsten Dunst

For someone who was sucking blood on screen before she was in middle school, Kirsten Dunst seems remarkably normal. With a half-dozen movies, several TV shows and countless commercials under her belt, Kirsten at age 12 still loved to play with Barbies and thought most boys had cooties. "It's just pretend," Dunst says, explaining why all the spurting blood in *Interview with the Vampire* didn't bother her. For Kirsten at age 10, the hardest part of playing Claudia, the youngest vampire in a dysfunctional family, was kissing Brad Pitt. Working vampire hours to shoot night scenes also was tough, she says.

Dunst, whose mother was an art gallery owner and father a medical equipment salesman in New Jersey, started modeling as a toddler. She's appeared in over 70 television commercials. She played Mia Farrow's daughter in *New York Stories*, Tom Hanks' daughter in *Bonfire of the Vanities* and Susan Sarandon's daughter in *Little Women*, where she sold lemonade on the set between takes. Next she appeared with Robin Williams in *Jumanji*. In *Vampire*, her character ages while staying in a six—year-old's body. To her co-star Tom Cruise, that mirrored Dunst's uncanny acting maturity. "There seems to be the experience of a 35-year-old actress in the body of this little girl."

for his father's new ranch by challenging a formidable bull.

> *Alcohol use.*

Monkeys wreak havoc in the kitchen in "Jumanji."

1972 100m/C Steve McQueen, Robert Preston, Ida Lupino, Ben Johnson, Joe Don Baker, Barbara Leigh; *D:* Sam Peckinpah. **VHS, Beta** *FOX*

Junior Geologist: How Does the Land Wear Down?

Primary Part of the "Junior Geologist" series. Explains how different types of erosion affect the surface of the earth. Covers water, wind, and gravity erosion. Ages 10 and up.
1995 9m/C VHS

Junior Oceanographer

Primary Four-part series which explores the many oceans of the Earth. Combines footage of rare and unique ocean life, colorful graphics, and original music. Ages 10 and up.
1995 57m/C VHS

Junior Space Scientist

Primary Three-part series introduces kids to space and the universe. Helps teach the key concepts and terms associated with the solar system. Ages 10 and up.
1995 27m/C VHS

Jurassic Park 🦴🦴🦴 ᵇ

PG-13/Jr. High-Adult Michael Crichton's bestseller translates well to the big screen due to its main attraction: realistic, rampaging dinosaurs, brought to life with state-of-the-art special effects. In the plot, however, they're cloned from prehistoric cells, and all seems fine until the carnivores escape from their island pens and prove smarter and less controllable than expected. Spielberg's saurians knocked Spielberg's (!!) lovable alien E.T. out of first place as the highest grossing movie of all time, and launched a noisy debate over whether this was too intense for the kiddie viewers (whom advertisers and toy manufacturers mercilessly courted all the same). Our verdict: no problem. The script features two child characters—less bratty than the novel's, thankfully—who get chased, tossed, crushed, even electrocuted, and always bounce back, alive and well. Plenty of PG films put youngsters in worse danger than this blockbuster escapism.

BEWARE *Dinosaurs menace children, a man is devoured, idea that you're not safe even in the bathroom.*

1993 126m/C Sam Neill, Laura Dern, Jeff Goldblum, Richard Attenborough, Bob Peck, Martin Ferrero, B.D. Wong, Joseph Mazzello, Ariana Richards, Samuel L. Jackson, Wayne Knight; *D:* Steven Spielberg; *W:* David Koepp, Michael Crichton; *M:* John Williams; *V:* Richard Kiley. **Award Nominations:** MTV Movie Awards '94: Best

Film, Best Villain (T-Rex), Best Action Sequence; **Awards:** Academy Awards '93: Best Sound, Best Sound Effects Editing, Best Visual Effects. **VHS, LV** *MCA*

Jury Duty ⚐

PG-13/Jr. High-Adult In a film that should have been sequestered, loser Tommy Collins (Shore) gets jury duty in a serial-killer trial and tries to keep what seems to be an open-and-shut case going so he can continue to get free room and board. Shore is up to his wretchedly unintelligent standard.

⚑ BEWARE *Crude sex-related humor runs rampid as Shore is attracted (while she is repulsed) to jury member Carrere.*

1995 88m/C Pauly Shore, Tia Carrere, Shelley Winters, Brian Doyle-Murray, Abe Vigoda, Stanley Tucci, Charles Napier; **Cameos:** Andrew Dice Clay; **D:** John Fortenberry; **W:** Barbara Williams, Fax Bahr. **VHS, LV** *COL*

Just Around the Corner ⚐⚐

Family With the aid of song and dance, Temple helps her Depression-poor father get a job after she befriends a cantankerous millionaire. ♫ This Is A Happy Little Ditty; I'm Not Myself Today; I'll Be Lucky With You; Just Around the Corner; I Love To Walk in the Rain; Brass Buttons and Epaulets.

1938 70m/B Shirley Temple, Charles Farrell, Bert Lahr, Joan Davis, Bill Robinson, Cora Witherspoon, Franklin Pangborn; **D:** Irving Cummings. **VHS, Beta** *FOX*

Just Me & My Dad

Preschool-Primary Animated re-telling of Mercer Mayer's popular storybook about Little Critter and his dad on a camping trip. Ages 1 to 4.

1993 25m/C VHS

Just One of the Guys ⚐⚐⚐

PG-13/Jr. High-Adult When a high school newspaper refuses to accept the work of an attractive girl, she pulls a gender switch, dressing as a guy to prove her intrinsic worth. In this disguise she befriends a sensitive outcast boy and helps him outgrow his awkward stage, falling for him in the process. Very cute, but predictable tale.

⚑ BEWARE *Sex talk, fighting, and brief nudity.*

1985 100m/C Joyce Hyser, Clayton Rohner, Billy Jacoby, Toni Hudson, Leigh McCloskey, Sherilyn Fenn; **D:** Lisa Gottlieb. **VHS, Beta, LV** *COL*

Just Planes for Kids

Preschool-Primary Gives children a fun and educational look at the working of a modern jet airplane. Ages 3 to 8.

1994 30m/C VHS *TPV*

Just Tell Me You Love Me ⚐

PG/Family Unappealing youth-appeal tale about three runaway teens—two boys and a girl—on their own in

Hawaii and plotting to make money as con artists. Ages 10 and up.

1980 90m/C Robert Hegyes, Debralee Scott, Lisa Hartman Black, Ricci Martin, June Lockhart; **D:** Tony Mordente. **VHS, Beta** *LIV, VES*

Just the Way You Are ⚐⚐⚐

PG/Jr. High-Adult Kristy McNichol plays a handicapped musician who goes to a ski resort in the Alps and puts her leg in a cast to see how people will treat her when they don't know she has a disability. Intriguing idea, and not a bad romantic comedy. Ages 10 and up.

1984 96m/C Kristy McNichol, Robert Carradine, Kaki Hunter, Michael Ontkean, Alexandra Paul, Lance Guest, Timothy Daly, Patrick Cassidy; **D:** Edouard Molinaro; **M:** Vladimir Cosma. **VHS, Beta** *MGM*

Just William's Luck ⚐⚐

Family Precocious English brat sneaks into an old mansion, which happens to be the headquarters of a fur-thieving gang. Belated followup to 1939's "Just William" (not on video), the only two features based on Richmal Crompton's storybook hero, a sort of British Dennis the Menace. In fact, Dennis has been retitled "Just Dennis" for UK consumption.

1947 87m/B William A. Graham, Garry Marsh; **D:** Val Guest. **VHS, Beta** *VYY*

Justin Morgan Had a Horse ⚐⚐

Family True story of a colonial school teacher in post-Revolutionary War Vermont who first bred the Morgan horse, the first and most versatile American breed.

1981 91m/C Don Murray, Lana Wood, Gary Crosby; **D:** Hollingsworth Morse. **VHS, Beta** *DIS*

K-9 ⚐⚐

PG-13/Jr. High-Adult After having his car destroyed by a drug dealer, a lone-wolf cop is forced to take another type of canine as partner—a German Shepherd. Together they work to round up the bad guys and maybe chew on their shoes a little. Sometimes amusing one-joke comedy done in by a paper-thin script, though both the dog and Belushi are good.

⚑ BEWARE *Salty language and violence, barely worse than an average TV show.*

1989 111m/C James Belushi, Mel Harris, Kevin Tighe, Ed O'Neill, Cotter Smith, James Handy, Jerry Lee; **D:** Rod Daniel; **W:** Steven Siegel, Scott Myers; **M:** Miles Goodman. **VHS, Beta, LV** *MCA*

K-9000 ⚐⚐

Jr. High-Adult A cyberdog fights the forces of evil with the aid of a cop, a lady reporter, and the usual cliches. Made for TV.

1989 96m/C Chris Mulkey, Catherine Oxenberg; **D:** Kim Manners; **M:** Jan Hammer. **VHS** *FRH*

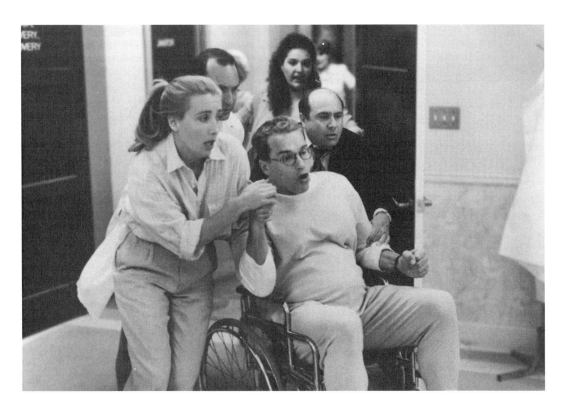

Dr. Alex Hesse suffers labor pains in "Junior."

The Karate Kat: Aristokratic Kapers

Family Spelling-impaired feline uses the ancient martial arts to take on bad guys in this cartoon.
1987 33m/C VHS, Beta *ORI, WAR*

The Karate Kid 🦴🦴🦴

PG/Family Cliches stack up like split bricks at a karate demo, but it's all done with grace and understated performances. New boy in town Danny is instantly victimized by sadistic bullies, because he's the new boy in town. As luck would have it, his apartment is blessed with a Japanese handyman/Zen master, who agrees to teach grasshopper martial arts. Hence, a friendship (and a movie) develops between boy and life tutor that is deep and sincere. The karate is really only an afterthought here; not so in the many sequels and ripoffs—including a Saturday-morning cartoon—that followed this popular crowd pleaser. From the director of the original "Rocky."

⚠️ BEWARE *Violence, drug use, salty language.*

1984 126m/C Ralph Macchio, Noriyuki "Pat" Morita, Elisabeth Shue, Randee Heller, Martin Kove, Chad McQueen; *D:* John G. Avildsen; *W:* Robert Mark Kamen; *M:* Bill Conti. **VHS, Beta, LV, 8mm** *COL*

The Karate Kid: Part 2 🦴🦴

PG/Jr. High Sequel in which Daniel accompanies his friend and teacher back to Japan. Instantly the two face Miyagi's old hometown enemy who holds a longstanding, dangerous grudge. Formula of the original is slavishly rerun; warm scenes between Macchio and Morita sandwiched between repetitive episodes of karate threats and revenge. Travelogues of Okinawa and Japanese culture are a minor bonus.

⚠️ BEWARE *Violence.*

1986 95m/C Ralph Macchio, Noriyuki "Pat" Morita, Danny Kamekona, Martin Kove, Tamlyn Tomita, Nobu McCarthy, Yuji Okumoto; *D:* John G. Avildsen; *W:* Robert Mark Kamen; *M:* Bill Conti. **VHS, Beta, LV, 8mm** *COL*

The Karate Kid: Part 3 🦴

PG/Jr. High-Sr. High The psycho Vietnam vet karate teacher from Part 1 teams up with a psycho Vietnam vet mobster to split up and smash Daniel and Miyagi. Somehow, bonsai trees are involved. Genuinely terrible sequel magnifies stupid elements of earlier chapters—overacting villains, asinine dialogue, violent revenge—

and what's with Macchio? Daniel babbles nearly nonstop (best line: "Why am I so stupid?"). Lone bone is for Morita maintaining serene dignity.

 Profanity (the worst in the series), violence.

1989 105m/C Ralph Macchio, Noriyuki "Pat" Morita, John G. Avildsen, Thomas Ian Griffith, Martin Kove, Sean Kanan, Robyn Elaine; *D:* John G. Avildsen; *W:* Robert Mark Kamen; *M:* Bill Conti. **VHS, Beta, LV, 8mm** *COL*

Katy and the Katerpillar Kids 🎵🎵

Preschool-Primary Cartoon feature about a beautiful butterfly named Katy who must deal with her two caterpillar children who are anxious to become butterflies and fly.

1987 85m/C *D:* Jose Luis, Santiago Moro. **VHS** *JFK*

Kavik, the Wolf Dog 🎵🎵

Family TV-movie spins a Yukon variant of "Lassie Come Home," with the bad guy taking loyal Kavik from his young master and transporting the canine to Alaska to pull a sled. Kavik escapes, and tries to return to his beloved boy in Seattle.

1984 99m/C Ronny Cox, Linda Sorensen, Andrew Ian McMillian, Chris Wiggins, John Ireland; *D:* Peter Carter. **VHS, Beta** *MED*

Kazaam 🎵🎵 ♭

PG/Family Twelve-year-old Max (Capra) is having problems—bullies are chasing him at school and his single mom's just found a new boyfriend. But his luck seems ready to change when a battered boombox reveals a seven-foot rappin' genie named Kazaam (O'Neal). Though the Shaq is not your typical thespian, your kids probably won't care. It's a nice, light-hearted film about friendship and family.

 Action violence and language.

1996 93m/C Francis Capra, Shaquille O'Neal; *D:* Paul Michael Glaser; *W:* Christian Ford, Roger Soffer. **VHS** *NYR*

Kermit and Piggy Story

Family Romantic story of how a pig rose from the chorus line to superstardom and finds the frog of her dreams along the way.

1985 57m/C Cheryl Ladd, Tony Randall, Loretta Swit, Raquel Welch, Jim Henson, Frank Oz. **VHS, Beta**

The Ketchup Vampires

Primary-Jr. High Elvira narrates this animated movie which features a group of kids and a kooky castle located in Transylvania. Ages 8 to 12.

1995 90m/C VHS *JFK*

Key Largo 🎵🎵🎵 ♭

Sr. High-Adult Gangster melodrama set in Key West, Florida, where hoods take over a hotel in the midst of a hurricane. Cynical WWII vet Frank McCloud (Bogart) visits the hotel owned by the family of a dead war buddy, and finds a tempest brewing both inside and out. Based on a play by Maxwell Anderson. Star-studded classic delivers great performances and a compelling story.

1948 101m/B Humphrey Bogart, Lauren Bacall, Claire Trevor, Edward G. Robinson, Lionel Barrymore; *D:* John Huston; *W:* Richard Brooks, John Huston; *M:* Max Steiner. **VHS, Beta, LV** *MGM, FOX, TLF*

Kid Colter 🎵🎵 ♭

Family 12-year-old Boston-bred Justin Colter goes to the Pacific Northwest to visit his divorced dad, played with great warmth by Stafford—who unfortunately drops from the story entirely when Justin gets kidnapped by "Home Alone"-style crooks (would you believe they're working for the Russians?). Abandoned in the wilderness, Justin has a mystic epiphany, becoming a junior mountain man. Messy family adventure never stays on one track long enough.

 Roughhousing, salty language.

1985 101m/C Jim Stafford, Jeremy Shamos, Hal Terrance, Greg Ward, Jim Turner; *D:* David O'Malley; *W:* David O'Malley. **VHS, Beta** *FOX*

Kid Dynamite

Family Boxer Gorcey is kidnapped to prevent his participation in a major fight. The real fighting occurs when his brother substitutes for him.

1943 73m/B Leo Gorcey, Huntz Hall, Bobby Jordan, Gabriel Dell, Pamela Blake; *D:* Wallace Fox. **VHS** *NOS, HEG*

A Kid for Two Farthings 🎵🎵 ♭

Preschool-Jr. High Episodic, sentimental portrait of life in the Jewish quarter of London's East End, centered on a little boy taught by his old-country grandfather about unicorns and their power to grant wishes. When the boy finds a malformed goat with only one horn, he uses his few coins to buy the animal in the hopes it will indeed bring his family what they most need—a steam press for their cleaning and tailoring business. Enjoyable but heavily sentimental family saga, adapted by scripter Wolf Mankowitz from his own novel. Severely condensed 30-minute version is also on tape under the title "The Unicorn."

1955 96m/C Jonathan Ashmore. **VHS** *HMV, FCT*

The Kid from Left Field 🎵🎵

Family Bat boy for the San Diego Padres transforms the team from losers to champions when he passes on the advice of his father, a has-been ballplayer, to the team members. A made-for-TV remake of the 1953 classic (not yet on video), here styled as a vehicle for prime-time child star Coleman.

1979 80m/C Gary Coleman, Robert Guillaume, Ed McMahon, Tab Hunter; *D:* Adell Aldrich. **VHS, Beta** *VES*

Kid from Not-So-Big 🦴🦴

G/Family Family film that was a foray into feature making by the Six Flags amusement park company. Title refers to Jenny, a young girl left to carry on her grandfather's frontier-town newspaper. When two con men come to town, the newskid sets out to expose them.

1978 87m/C Jennifer McAllister, Veronica Cartwright, Robert Viharo, Paul Tulley; **D:** Bill Crain. **VHS, Beta** *WAR, OM*

A Kid in King Arthur's Court 🦴🦴 ▷

PG/Primary-Adult A pleasant diversion for youngsters, film updates Mark Twain's "A Connecticut Yankee in King Arthur's Court." Where Twain had a man introducing baseball, bicycles and telephones to Camelot, we have a 14-year-old California boy offering up Big Macs and Rollerblades. A mysterious earthquake precipitates Calvin Fuller (Nicholas) into Arthur's times. As for old man Arthur (Ackland), he's not having such a hot time. An evil nobleman is threatening the realm. Calvin teams up with courageous Princess Katey to fight the good fight. The princess's older sister is Kate Winslet in her pre- "Sense and Sensibility" days.

BEWARE *Phrases such as "I'll kick thy butt."*

1995 91m/C Thomas Ian Nicholas, Joss Ackland, Art Malik, Paloma Baeza, Kate Winslet, Ron Moody, Daniel Craig; **D:** Michael Gottlieb; **W:** Michael Part, Robert L. Levy; **C:** Elemer Ragaly; **M:** J.A.C. Redford. **VHS** *TOU*

The Kid Who Loved Christmas 🦴🦴

Family After his adoptive mother is killed in a car crash, little Reggie is taken from his loving musician stepfather by a Scrooge-like social worker, who believes showbiz and parenthood don't mix. Reggie writes to Santa for help. Mushy Yuletide TV movie works hard to be touching, sometimes succeeds thanks to that once-in-a-lifetime ensemble cast gathered by producer Eddie Murphy. Last film for Sammy.

1990 118m/C Cicely Tyson, Michael Warren, Sammy Davis Jr., Gilbert Lewis, Ken Page, Della Reese, Esther Rolle, Ben Vereen, Vanessa Williams, John Beal, Trent Cameron, Arthur Seidelman. **VHS** *PAR*

The Kid with the 200 I.Q. 🦴🦴

Family When an earnest boy genius enters college at age 13, predictable comic situations arise that involve his attempts at impressing his idolized astronomy professor (Guillaume), as well as an equally unrequited bout of first love. Harmless comedy, one of a series of squeaky-clean made for TV family fare starring Coleman.

1983 96m/C Gary Coleman, Robert Guillaume, Harriet Hilliard Nelson, Dean Butler, Karli Michaelson, Christina Murrull, Mel Stewart; **D:** Leslie Martinson. **VHS, Beta** *LIV*

Kidco 🦴🦴 ▷

PG/Family Fact-based story of a toothpaste-making corporation headed and run by children ranging in age from nine to sixteen. Quite engaging, as the kids learn the ropes of capitalism, prosper—then get crushed by government regulations. Good Republican Party primer.

1983 104m/C Scott Schwartz, Elizabeth Gorcey, Cinnamon Idles, Tristine Skyler; **D:** Ronald F. Maxwell. **VHS, Beta** *FOX*

Kidnapped 🦴🦴 ▷

Family Scottish heir David Balfour is sold by his scheming uncle into servitude as a cabin boy to get him out of the way. By chance David meets Highland rebel Alan Stewart, who helps him regain his inheritance amidst much rather draggy historical background detail. Disney film based on the Robert Louis Stevenson classic, directed by no-relation namesake Robert Stevenson, long the Magic Kingdom's specialist in the production of live-action features.

1960 94m/C Peter Finch, James MacArthur, Peter O'Toole; **D:** Robert Stevenson. **VHS, Beta** *DIS*

Kidnapped 🦴🦴

Preschool-Jr. High Animated adaptation of the Robert Louis Stevenson adventure in which a young heir is kidnapped on the orders of a wicked uncle. Made for TV as part of the "Famous Classic Tales" series.

1973 49m/C VHS, Beta *MGM*

Kidsongs: A Day at Camp

Family Musical series provides instant acculturation for young children (or visitors from another planet who wish to learn our ways). Kids sing favorite songs in different settings. Clearly, the singing takes place in a studio, while the youngsters on-screen lip synch. There's nothing wrong with the series, except that all the songs are performed in a similar bland fashion. On this tape, the Kidsongs Kids are at a summer camp, singing such essential tunes as "The More We Get Together," "The Caissons Go Rolling Along," "On Top of Spaghetti," "Ninety-nine Bottles of Pop on the Wall," "Found a Peanut," "The Ants Go Marching," "Boom, Boom Ain't It Great to Be Crazy," "The Animal Fair," "Little Bunny Foo Foo," "Baa Baa Black Sheep" and more. Ages 3 to 8.

1990 25m/C VHS *MVD, WRV*

Kidsongs: A Day at Old MacDonald's Farm

Family More ever-popular children's songs, with friendly animals for visual appeal. Tunes includes "Old Mac-Donald Had a Farm," "Shortenin' Bread," "This Old Man," "Mary Had a Little Lamb," "Skip to My Lou," "Here We Go Round the Mulberry Bush," "Take Me Out to the Ball Game," "John Jacob Jingleheimer Schmidt" and more. Ages 3 to 6.

1986 25m/C VHS, Beta, LV *WRV, MLT*

Kidsongs: A Day at the Circus

Family Kids sing more fun songs, with the circus providing the visuals. Hear "Polly Wolly Doodle," "Put on a Happy Face," "If You're Happy and You Know It," "Strolling Through the Park," "The Ringmaster Song," "The Man on the Flying Trapeze," and more. Ages 3 to 6. **1988 25m/C VHS, Beta** *MVD, WRV, MLT*

Kidsongs: A Day with the Animals

Family More essential melodies sung by a group of children, this time at the zoo. Includes favorites "B.I.N.G.O.," "Do Your Ears Hang Low?," "Rockin' Robin," "How Much Is That Doggie in the Window?," "Little Bo Peep," "Little Duckie Duddle," "Hickory Dickory Dock," and "Itsy Bitsy Spider." Ages 3 to 6. **1986 25m/C VHS, Beta, LV** *WRV, MLT*

Kidsongs: Boppin' with the Biggles

Family Kids travel through time and visit Europe and Mexico along with the Biggles, who guide their fans into musical and magical situations. Ages 4 to 8. **1995 30m/C VHS** *WRV*

Kidsongs: Cars, Boats, Trains and Planes

Family Kids' songs about vehicles and traveling. Includes "Daylight Train," "Up, Up and Away," "Car Car Song," "Row, Row, Row Your Boat," "I Got Wheels," "I Like Trucks," "Wild Blue Yonder," and "The Bus Song." Ages 3 to 7. **1986 25m/C VHS, Beta** *WRV, MLT*

Kidsongs: Good Night, Sleep Tight

Family Grown-ups sing some favorite lullabies and other soothing songs for kids. Includes "The Unicorn," "St. Judy's Comet," "All the Pretty Little Horses," "Ring Around the Rosy," "Pat-A-Cake," "A Tisket, A Tasket," "Our House," "Tomorrow Is a Dream Away," "Hush, Little Baby," "Lullaby and Good Night." Ages 2 to 5. **1986 25m/C VHS** *WRV*

Kidsongs: Home on the Range

Family At a Fourth of July celebration, the kids sing favorite Western and patriotic songs. Includes "Deep in the Heart of Texas," "Turkey in the Straw," "If I Had a Hammer," "Yankee Doodle Dandy," "America's Heroes," "I've Been Working On the Railroad," "Oh Susanna," "You're a Grand Old Flag." Ages 3 to 8. **1986 25m/C VHS, Beta, LV** *WRV, MLT*

Kidsongs: I'd Like to Teach the World to Sing

Family Favorite children's songs from all over the globe, although the settings are obviously not the far-away places they purport to be. Includes "Funiculi, Funicula," "London Bridge," "Frere Jacques," "Waltzing Matilda," "Day-O," "I'd Like to Teach the World to Sing," "Did You Ever See a Lassie?," and "Sakura." Ages 3 to 8. **1986 25m/C VHS, Beta** *WRV, MLT*

Kidsongs: Let's Play Ball

Family Fun sports songs for kids, less familiar than most of the other Kidsongs. Includes "It's Not If you Win or Lose," "Practice Makes Perfect," "Bend Me, Shape Me," "I Get Around," "Catch a Wave," "Centerfield," and "You Know That You Can Do It." Ages 4 to 8. **1987 25m/C VHS, Beta, LV** *MVD, WRV*

Kidsongs: Ride the Roller Coaster

Family Rev your kids up with these fast-paced songs, plus see the Kidsongs Kids riding high on a zippy roller coaster! Songs include "Whole Lotta Shakin' Going On," "Little Deuce Coupe," "Fast Food," "1812 Overture" (sorry, no cannons), "Let's Twist Again," "Here We Go Loopty Loo" and "Splish Splash." Ages 4 to 8. **1990 25m/C VHS** *MVD, WRV*

Kidsongs: Very Silly Songs

Family Aha! So all those other Kidsongs tunes—"Do Your Ears Hang Low," "Found a Peanut," stuff like that— those were all SERIOUS songs. Okay. Now comes the silly material: "The Name Game," "Down by the Bay," "Purple People Eater," "Rig-a-Jig-Jig," "Mail Myself to You," "The Thing," "Michael Finnegan." Ages 3 to 8. **1991 25m/C VHS** *MVD, WRV, MLT*

Kidsongs: We Wish You a Merry Christmas

Family The Kidsongs Kids meet Santa Claus, Rudolph the Red Nosed Reindeer, and Frosty the Snowman on their Christmas adventure. Songs include "The Twelve Days of Christmas," "Silent Night," "Jingle Bells," and "Rockin' Around the Christmas Tree." Ages 3 to 8. **1992 ?m/C VHS** *WRV*

Kim 🎵🎵♪

Family Kim (Sheth) is a 15-year-old boy living by his wits on the streets of 1890s India. Trying to discover his true identity, Kim is befriended by a Buddhist monk, who wishes the boy to be his disciple, and a British spy, who trains him for a daring mission against the Russians. Rousing TV adaptation of Rudyard Kipling's novel.

Calvin Fuller chats with King Arthur in the mythical kingdom of Camelot.

1984 135m/C Ravi Sheth, Peter O'Toole, Bryan Brown, John Rhys-Davies, Julian Glover; **D:** John Davies. **VHS** *PME*

Kindergarten Cop 🦴🦴 ♭

PG-13/Jr. High-Adult Schwarzenegger spoofs his screen image (again) as one-man-army police officer Kimble, hunting a particularly vicious drug lord by staking out his ex-wife and six-year-old son. When Kimble's lady partner gets sick, he's forced to take her place masquerading as a kindergarten teacher in the school district where mother and son reside. Classroom of uncontrollable tykes (almost all of them the products of broken homes, by the way) manage to thoroughly unnerve the undercover tough man. Blockbuster hit covers all bases; it's got cutesy kiddie comedy and romance on one hand—and some really serious violence and killing on the other. Even Arnold called this unsuitable for very young viewers.

⚠ BEWARE *Profanity, violence bordering on brutality. Lots of gunplay and people, good and bad, getting shot. A young kid climbs a high tower in a storm. And a kindergartener uses some very anatomical language.*

1990 111m/C Arnold Schwarzenegger, Penelope Ann Miller, Pamela Reed, Linda Hunt, Richard Tyson, Carroll Baker, Cathy Moriarty, Park Overall, Richard Portnow, Jayne Brook; **D:** Ivan Reitman; **W:** Murray Salem, Herschel Weingrod, Timothy Harris; **M:** Randy Edelman. **VHS, Beta, LV** *MCA, CCB*

The King and I 🦴🦴🦴🦴

Family Wonderful adaptation of Rogers and Hammerstein's Broadway play based on the novel "Anna and the King of Siam" by Margaret Landon. English governess Kerr is hired to teach the King of Siam's many children and bring them into the 20th century. She has more of a job than she realizes, for this is a king, a country, and a people who value tradition above all else. Features one of Rodgers and Hammerstein's best-loved scores. Brynner made this role his, playing it over 4,000 times on stage and screen before his death. Kerr's voice was dubbed when she sang; the voice you hear is Marni Nixon, who also dubbed the star's singing voices in "West Side Story" and "My Fair Lady." ♫ Shall We Dance?; Getting To Know You; Hello, Young Lovers; We Kiss in a Shadow; I Whistle a Happy Tune; March of the Siamese Children; I Have Dreamed; A Puzzlement; Something Wonderful.

1956 133m/C Deborah Kerr, Yul Brynner, Rita Moreno, Martin Benson, Terry Saunders, Rex Thompson, Alan Mowbray, Carlos Rivas; **D:** Walter Lang; **W:** Ernest Lehman; **M:** Richard Rodgers, Oscar Hammerstein. **Award Nominations:** Academy Awards '56: Best Actress (Kerr), Best Color Cinematography, Best Director (Lang), Best

Picture; **Awards:** Academy Awards '56: Best Actor (Brynner), Best Art Direction/Set Decoration (Color), Best Costume Design (Color), Best Sound, Best Score; Golden Globe Awards '57: Best Actress—Musical/Comedy (Kerr), Best Film—Musical/Comedy. **VHS, Beta, LV** *FOX, BTV, RDG*

King Arthur & the Knights of the Round Table, Vol. 1

Family Tale of King Arthur is told beginning with his birth to the mighty sword Excalibur. Additional volumes available.

1981 60m/C VHS, Beta *FHE*

King Kong

Family Original beauty and beast classic tells the story of Kong, a giant ape captured in Africa and brought to New York as a sideshow attraction. Kong falls for Wray, escapes from his captors and rampages through the city, ending up on top of the newly built Empire State Building. Moody Steiner score adds color, and Willis O'Brien's stop-motion animation still holds up well. Remade numerous times.

> 🐾 BEWARE *Monster-movie destruction and cruelty to gorillas.*

1933 105m/B Fay Wray, Bruce Cabot, Robert Armstrong, Frank Reicher, Noble Johnson, Sam Hardy, James Flavin; **D:** Ernest B. Schoedsack; **M:** Max Steiner. **VHS, Beta, LV, 8mm** *TTC, MED, FUS*

King Kong

PG/Family Bloated, expensive remake of the 1933 classic, updates the storyline but otherwise follows it pretty closely, as an oil company discovering the fabled giant ape on a remote island. Kong becomes infatuated with a pretty shipwreck survivor, is captured and brought to New York, where he breaks loose and climbs the World Trade Center. The elaborate monkey suit, created and acted by makeup ace Rick Baker, is impressive, as are the sets, but the ponderous plot gains nothing from being a half-hour longer than the original. PG-13 sequel "King Kong Lives," from 1986, isn't worth anybody's time.

> 🐾 BEWARE *Violence, profanity, and alcohol use.*

1976 135m/C Jeff Bridges, Charles Grodin, Jessica Lange, Rene Auberjonois, John Randolph, Ed Lauter, Jack O'Halloran; **D:** John Guillermin; **M:** John Barry. **Award Nominations:** Academy Awards '76: Best Cinematography, Best Sound; **Awards:** Academy Awards '76: Best Visual Effects. **VHS, Beta, LV, 8mm** *PAR, HMV*

King of the Grizzlies 🦴🦴

G/Family Mystical relationship between a Cree Indian and a grizzly cub is put to the test when the full grown bear troubles a ranch at which the man is foreman. Just bear-able Disney nature drama, based on the book "Biography of a Grizzly" by Ernest Thompson Seton.

1969 93m/C Chris Wiggins, John Yesno; **D:** Ron Kelly. **VHS, Beta** *DIS*

King of the Hill 🦴🦴🦴 ◁

PG-13/Jr. High-Adult Excellent depression-era drama focuses on Aaron, a 12-year-old in St. Louis whose family is barely intact; mother is in a tuberculosis sanitarium, younger brother is with relatives, and the exceedingly self-centered father travels the countryside as a salesman. Left by himself, Aaron desperately guards the family's precious apartment and property, under ceaseless threat of eviction. Sadly overlooked at the box office, this suspenseful and exhilarating tale for all ages doesn't glorify its era but admires the main character's resourcefulness and imagination during hard times. Based on the book by A.E. Hochner describing his own childhood.

> 🐾 BEWARE *Violence, mature themes. As poverty closes in on Aaron and his neighbors, one commits suicide, another is engulfed in a police riot.*

1993 102m/C Jesse Bradford, Jeroen Krabbe, Lisa Eichhorn, Karen Allen, Spalding Gray, Elizabeth McGovern, Joseph Chrest, Adrien Brody, Cameron Boyd, Chris Samples, Katherine Heigl, Amber Benson, John McConnell, Ron Vawter, John Durbin, Lauryn Hill, David Jensen; **D:** Steven Soderbergh; **W:** Steven Soderbergh; **M:** Cliff Martinez. **VHS, LV** *MCA*

King of the Rocketmen

Family Republic serial that created their most emblematic character, Rocket Man. Mystery villain 'Dr. Vulcan' is knocking off eminent scientists, so researcher Jeff King (mustachioed actor Coffin, usually seen in bad-guy roles) fights back in disguise, using a newly invented jet backpack and metal mask to become the flying hero. In 12 chapters; first is 20 minutes long, the rest are 13 minutes each. The Rocket Man suit was re-used by Republic for two later, non-sequel serials, "Radar Men from the Moon" and "Zombies of the Stratosphere." And of course it inspired Disney's "The Rocketeer."

> 🐾 BEWARE *Roughhousing. More often than not, the Rocket Man and his allies will shoot the guns out of enemies' hands.*

1949 156m/B Tristram Coffin, Mae Clarke, I. Stanford Jolley; **D:** Fred Brannon. **VHS, LV** *MED, VCN, REP*

King of the Wind 🦴🦴 ◁

PG/Family Magnificent stallion is given as a gift by Arabs to the King of France in 1729. Agba, a mute stable boy, won't be parted from the horse; he and his beast pass from one mean-spirited owner to another throughout Europe. Based on Marguerite Henry's novel, this should be a stirring tale, but its episodic narrative grows repetitive, with poor Agba seeing the white infidels at their worst again and again. Gets an extra half-bone for being one of the few English-speaking family films (with "The Black Stallion Returns") to portray Arabs and Islam in a positive light.

1993 101m/C Richard Harris, Glenda Jackson. **VHS** *FHE*

King Ralph

PG/Jr. High-Adult When the rest of the royal family passes away in a freak accident, lounge lizard Ralph finds himself the only heir to the throne. O'Toole is the long-suffering valet who tries to train him for the job, while Hurt provides a certain touch of ham in cheek evil. Sporadically funny semi-satire flutters on the good graces of Goodman, making it a pleasant if not particularly memorable 96 minutes.

BEWARE *Brief profanity.*

1991 96m/C John Goodman, Peter O'Toole, Camille Coduri, Joely Richardson, John Hurt; *D:* David S. Ward; *W:* David S. Ward; *M:* James Newton Howard. **VHS, Beta, LV** *MCA, CCB*

Kingpin WOOF!

PG-13/Jr. High-Adult Another stupid (and we mean that in the nicest way) film from the Farrelly brothers, who brought you "Dumb and Dumber." Harrelson plays Roy Munson, a washed up former bowling phenom who discovers Ishmael (Quaid), an innocent Amish bowling natural who's about to be dragged to Reno for a bowling championship (and a lot of senseless debauchery). The two are up against bowling shark and Roy's old nemesis (Murray). Never underestimate the power of stupid movies.

BEWARE *Crude sex-related humor and a drug scene. Poor Ishmael is exposed to lots of beer, girls, and other sinful habits.*

1996 113m/C Woody Harrelson, Randy Quaid, Vanessa Angel, Bill Murray; *D:* Peter Farrelly, Bobby Farrelly; *W:* Bobby Farrelly, Mort Nathan; *C:* Mark Irwin; *M:* Freedy Johnston. **VHS** *NYR*

Kino's Storytime Vol. Three

Preschool-Primary Keen-o indeed is puppet Kino's neighborhood library, where every hour is story hour and amiable librarians are always willing to read aloud. But when they're not able, there's no shortage of volunteer celebrity readers, including Ellen DeGeneres, Patricia Richardson, John Goodman, Shari Belafonte and Meshach Taylor. Stories canter on family and friendship. Ages 3 to 8.

1995 ?m/C VHS *VTR*

Kipperbang

PG/Jr. High-Adult During the summer of 1948 a 13-year-old boy wishes he could kiss the girl of his dreams. He finally gets the chance in a school play. Not unsatisfying, but falls short of being the bittersweet comedy-drama it could have been. Title is a nonsense word the kids throw back and forth.

1982 85m/C John Albasiny, Abigail Cruttenden, Alison Steadman; *D:* Michael Apted. **VHS, Beta** *MGM*

Kismet

Family Big budget Arabian Nights musical drama of a Baghdad street poet who manages to infiltrate himself into the Wazir's harem. Based on the Broadway play (which was based on an earlier film version). Indifferently directed but still fun to watch. Music was adapted from Borodin by Robert Wright and George Forrest. Original trailer and letterboxed screen available in special laserdisc edition. ♫ Fate; Not Since Ninevah; Baubles, Bangles, and Beads; Stranger in Paradise; Bored; Night of My Nights; The Olive Tree; And This Is My Beloved; Sands of Time.

1955 113m/C Howard Keel, Ann Blyth, Dolores Gray, Vic Damone; *D:* Vincente Minnelli; *M:* Andre Previn. **VHS, Beta, LV** *MGM, FCT*

Kiss Me Goodbye

PG/Jr. High-Adult Young widow Fields can't shake the memory of her first husband, a charismatic but philandering Broadway choreographer, who's the antithesis of her boring but devoted professor fiance. She struggles with the charming ghost of her first husband, as well as her domineering mother, attempting to understand her own true feelings. Harmless but two-dimensional remake of "Dona Flor and Her Two Husbands."

BEWARE *Profanity and sexual situations.*

1982 101m/C Sally Field, James Caan, Jeff Bridges, Paul Dooley, Mildred Natwick, Claire Trevor; *D:* Robert Mulligan; *W:* Charlie Peters; *M:* Ralph Burns. **VHS, Beta** *FOX*

Kissyfur!: Hugs and Kissyfur

Preschool-Primary Animated antics of a pair of former circus bears, Kissyfur and his widowed papa bear Gus. Escapees from big top captivity, the two inhabit a marshful of wild characters, and the TV series placed an emphasis on a single parent raising a child—or cub, as the case may be. In this denful of episodes a vulture and a slithery snake try to corrupt the young animals. Will Kissyfur and friends be won over by their bad ways? Additional volumes available.

1991 75m/C VHS *JFK, CEL*

Kitty Faces

Preschool These cats don't sing "Memory" or spout the rhymes of T.S. Eliot. The idea here is simpler: Fill the screen, a beast at a time, with close-ups of appealing cats. They gaze, they yawn, they stick their tongues out. Many breeds are shown, from exotic Persians to good old alley cats. The soundtrack is music, often English children singing nursery rhymes. Aww-some viewing. There's a companion video, Doggy Faces, about dogs. Ages 1 to 4.

199? 30m/C VHS *NYR*

Kitty Love!

Preschool Adorable companion to "Puppy Love!" features dozens of kittens of various breeds pouncing around and being cute. Ages 6 months to 4 years.

1994 30m/C VHS *ABC*

Knights & Emeralds

PG/Jr. High-Adult In a modern British factory town, cross-cultural rivalries and romances develop between members of two high school marching bands, one all white and one black, as the national band championships draw near. Familiar but effective pleas for teen tolerance, mixed with mediocre music.

> **BEWARE** *Sex talk.*

1987 90m/C Christopher Wild, Beverly Hills, Warren Mitchell; **D:** Ian Emes; **M:** Colin Towns. **VHS, Beta** *WAR*

Knights of the Round Table

Family The story of the romantic triangle between King Arthur, Sir Lancelot and Guinevere, with Merlin, Mordred and Morgan le Fay along for the action. Filmed in England. Lots of jousting and swordplay and it just might pique a child's interest in reading all about it. Ages 7 and up.

1953 106m/C Robert Taylor, Ava Gardner, Mel Ferrer, Anne Crawford, Felix Aylmer, Stanley Baker; **D:** Richard Thorpe; **C:** Frederick A. (Freddie) Young; **M:** Miklos Rozsa. **VHS, Beta, LV** *MGM*

Knute Rockne: All American

Family Life story of Notre Dame football coach Knute Rockne, who inspired many victories with his powerful speeches. Reagan, as the dying George Gipp, utters that now-famous line, "Tell the boys to win one for the Gipper."

1940 96m/B Ronald Reagan, Pat O'Brien, Gale Page, Donald Crisp, John Qualen; **D:** Lloyd Bacon. **VHS, Beta** *MGM, FHE*

Koi and the Kola Nuts

Primary Koi, the son of an African chief, finds his place in the world with the help of a snake, an alligator and an army of ants in this African folktale from the "Rabbit Ears" series of recitations starring celebrity narrators and well-known musicians.

1992 30m/C M: Herbie Hancock. **VHS** *BTV, RAB*

Konrad

Family Prototype "instant" child, born and trained to perfection in a high-tech factory, is mistakenly delivered (in a can) to an eccentric woman. She makes room in her life for the unusual eight-year-old and grows to love him, and as Konrad attends school with real kids he learns that perfection isn't always appropriate. This is too much for the factory director, who tries to 'recall' the boy. Warm, witty and wry family satire, with a cast that's likewise perfect. Based on "Konrad oder Das Kind aus der Konservenbu echse" by Christine Noestlinger (but you knew that already, right?). Part of the "Wonderworks" series.

1985 110m/C Ned Beatty, Polly Holliday, Max Wright, Huckleberry Fox. **VHS** *PME, HMV, BTV*

Kotch

PG/Jr. High-Adult An elderly man resists his children's attempts to retire him. Warm detailing of old age with a splendid performance by Matthau. Lemmon's directorial debut.

1971 113m/C Walter Matthau, Deborah Winters, Felicia Farr; **D:** Jack Lemmon; **M:** Marvin Hamlisch. **Award Nominations:** Academy Awards '71: Best Actor (Matthau), Best Film Editing, Best Song ("Life Is What You MaKe It"), Best Sound; **Awards:** Golden Globe Awards '72: Best Song ("Life Is What You Make It"). **VHS** *FOX*

Kramer vs. Kramer

PG/Jr. High-Adult Highly acclaimed family drama about an ad executive husband and his small son left behind when the wife leaves on a quest to find herself. Formerly neglectful of his kid, Mr. Kramer wrestles with the newfound art of fatherhood—and the subsequent courtroom battle when Mrs. Kramer returns demanding custody. The entire cast gives exacting performances, successfully moving you from tears to laughter and back again. Based on the novel by Avery Corman.

> **BEWARE** *Child sees his father's girlfriend naked, sex talk, profanity, fiercely bickering parents.*

1979 105m/C Dustin Hoffman, Meryl Streep, Jane Alexander, Justin Henry, Howard Duff, JoBeth Williams; **D:** Robert Benton. **Award Nominations:** Academy Awards '79: Best Cinematography, Best Film Editing, Best Supporting Actor (Henry); **Awards:** Academy Awards '79: Best Actor (Hoffman), Best Adapted Screenplay, Best Director (Benton), Best Picture, Best Supporting Actress (Streep); Golden Globe Awards '80: Best Actor—Drama (Hoffman), Best Film—Drama, Best Screenplay, Best Supporting Actress (Streep); National Board of Review Awards '79: 10 Best Films of the Year, Best Supporting Actress (Streep); National Society of Film Critics Awards '79: Best Actor (Hoffman), Best Director (Benton), Best Supporting Actress (Streep). **VHS, Beta, LV** *COL, BTV*

Krull

PG/Jr. High-Adult Overly familiar mid-'80s attempt to do the Ultimate Fantasy Adventure Set in a World Peopled by Creatures of Myth and Magic. Prince embarks on a quest to find the Glaive (a magical weapon) and joins with Robin-Hood types to rescue his princess bride, taken by a giant Beast who travels in a spacegoing Black Fortress and controls endless hordes of "Star Wars" style armored stormtroopers. Wild special f/x, but the fun is labored.

> **BEWARE** *Supernatural violence.*

1983 121m/C Ken Marshall, Lysette Anthony, Freddie Jones, Francesca Annis, Liam Neeson; **D:** Peter Yates; **M:** James Horner. **VHS, Beta, LV** *GKK*

Kuffs

PG-13/Jr. High-Adult Slater stars as George Kuffs, a young guy who reluctantly joins his brother's highly respected private security team in this original action comedy. After his brother is gunned down in the line of duty, George finds himself the new owner of the business. Out to avenge his brother, George pursues a crooked art dealer as he battles crime on the streets of San Francisco. Thin on plot and with the predictable awaiting him at every turn, Slater mugs as best as can be expected.

BEWARE *Violence, profanity, man leaves pregnant girl-friend.*

1992 102m/C Christian Slater, Tony Goldwyn, Milla Jovovich, Bruce Boxleitner, Troy Evans, George de la Pena, Leon Rippy; **D:** Bruce A. Evans; **W:** Bruce A. Evans, Raynold Gideon; **M:** Harold Faltermeyer. **VHS, Beta, LV** *MCA*

La Bamba 🎵🎵🎵

PG-13/Jr. High-Adult Romantic biography of the late 1950s pop idol Ritchie Valens, concentrating on his stormy relationship with his half-brother, his love for his WASP girlfriend, and his tragic, sudden death in the famed plane crash that also took the lives of Buddy Holly and the Big Bopper. Soundtrack features Setzer, Huntsberry, Crenshaw, and Los Lobos as, respectively, Eddie Cochran, the Big Bopper, Buddy Holly, and a Mexican bordello band.

BEWARE *Serious domestic violence, profanity and drug talk.*

1987 99m/C Lou Diamond Phillips, Esai Morales, Danielle von Zerneck, Joe Pantoliano, Brian Setzer, Marshall Crenshaw, Howard Huntsberry, Rosana De Soto, Elizabeth Pena, Rick Dees; **D:** Luis Valdez; **W:** Luis Valdez; **M:** Carlos Santana, Miles Goodman. **VHS, Beta, LV, 8mm** *COL*

L.A. Story 🎵🎵🎵

PG-13/Sr. High-Adult Livin' ain't easy in the city of angels. Harris K. Telemacher (Martin), a weatherman in a city where the weather never changes, wrestles with emptiness while consorting with beautiful people, distancing from significant other Henner, cavorting with valley girl Parker, falling for newswoman Tennant (Martin's real-life wife), and taking messages from an electronic freeway information sign. Written by the comedian, the story's full of keen insights into the everyday problems and ironies of living in the Big Tangerine. (It's no wonder the script's full of so much thoughtful detail: Martin is said to have worked on it intermittently for seven years.) Charming story of life and love on the fault line and the semi-fast lane.

BEWARE *Profanity. Martin's character is confused about women.*

1991 98m/C Steve Martin, Victoria Tennant, Richard E. Grant, Marilu Henner, Sarah Jessica Parker, Sam McMurray, Patrick Stewart, Iman, Kevin Pollak; **D:** Mick Jackson; **W:** Steve Martin; **M:** Peter Melnick. **VHS, Beta, LV** *LIV, WAR*

Labyrinth 🎵🎵🎵

PG/Family Imaginative adventure directed by Muppeteer Henson, produced by "Star Wars" creator George Lucas, and written by Monty Python's Jones. While babysitting her baby brother, Sara, a modern teen absorbed in fairy-tale lore, gets frustrated and asks goblins to take the troublesome kid. The Goblin King (rock star Bowie) complies, and Sara can regain the tyke only by finding her way through the fantastic maze to the goblin castle. As she befriends odd creatures along the way, the narrative often loses momentum, but wild Muppet characters, production design, and musical numbers make this trip worth taking.

BEWARE *Solving the labyrinth is nothing compared with figuring out where the PG rating came from. Danger level is low, though creatures are often grotesque.*

1986 90m/C David Bowie, Jennifer Connelly, Toby Froud; **D:** Jim Henson; **W:** Terry Jones; **M:** David Bowie, Trevor Jones. **VHS, Beta, LV, 8mm** *NLC*

Lady and the Tramp 🎵🎵🎵🎵

G/Family Animated Disney classic about two dogs who fall in love. Tramp is wild and carefree; Lady is a spoiled pedigree who runs away from home after her owners have a baby. They just don't make dog romances like this one anymore, based on a novel by Ward Greene. Songs by Sonny Burke and Peggy Lee; decades later she sued and won a lucrative judgment against the Disney corporation for the royalties. 🎵 He's a Tramp; La La Lu; Siamese Cat Song; Peace on Earth; Bella Notte.

1955 76m/C D: Hamilton Luske; **M:** Peggy Lee, Sonny Burke; **V:** Larry Roberts, Peggy Lee, Barbara Luddy, Stan Freberg, Alan Reed, Bill Thompson, Bill Baucon, Verna Felton, George Givot, Dallas McKennon, Lee Millar. **VHS, Beta, LV** *DIS, APD*

The Lady in White 🎵🎵🎵

PG-13/Jr. High-Adult Small-town ghost story, nicely done from a kid's perspective. Schoolboy Frankie is accidentally locked in the classroom on Halloween and encounters the restless spirit of a murdered little girl. He sorts out clues to her killer, who's still very much at large. Well-developed characters, atmospheric style compensate for a whodunit plot that's almost as transparent as the spooks. A rarity among serious horror flicks: one suitable for the family.

BEWARE *Violence, alcohol use and scary situations*

1988 92m/C Lukas Haas, Len Cariou, Alex Rocco, Katherine Helmond, Jason Presson, Renata Vanni, Angelo Bertolini, Jared Rushton; **D:** Frank Laloggia; **W:** Frank Laloggia; **M:** Frank Laloggia. **VHS, Beta, LV** *NO*

Lady Jane 🎵🎵🎵

PG-13/Jr. High-Adult An accurate account of the life of 15-year-old Lady Jane Grey, who held the throne of England for 9 days in 1553 as a result of political maneuvering by noblemen and the Church-of-England. A wonderful film even for non-history buffs. Helena Bonham Carter's first movie. Could be slow for kids. Ages 11 and up.

BEWARE *Lady Jane and her husband are shown in bed naked from the waist up. Jane's mother beats her.*

1985 140m/C Helena Bonham Carter, Cary Elwes, Sara Kestelman, Michael Hordern, Joss Ackland, Richard Johnson, Patrick Stewart; **D:** Trevor Nunn. **VHS, Beta, LV** *PAR, TVC*

Lady Lovelylocks & the Pixietails, Vol. 1

Primary First of a mangy cartoon series pushing the Lady Lovelylocks toys onto brainwashable kids. Ms. Lovelylocks must save the inhabitants of her kingdom from villains Ravenwaves, Snarla, and Hairball. Additional volumes available.

1986 30m/C VHS, Beta

The Lady Vanishes 🦴🦴🦴🦴

Family When a kindly old lady disappears from a fast-moving train, her young friend finds an imposter in her place and a spiraling mystery to solve. Hitchcock's first real winner, a smarmy, wit-drenched British mystery that precipitated his move to Hollywood. Along with "39 Steps," considered an early Hitchcock classic. From the novel "The Wheel Spins," by Ethel Lina White. Special edition contains short subject on Hitchcock's cameos in his films. Remade in 1979.

1938 99m/B Margaret Lockwood, Paul Lukas, Michael Redgrave, May Whitty, Googie Withers, Basil Radford, Naunton Wayne, Cecil Parker, Linden Travers, Catherine Lacey, Sidney Gilliat; **Cameos:** Alfred Hitchcock; **D:** Alfred Hitchcock; **W:** Frank Launder, Louis Levy, Alma Reville. **VHS, Beta, LV** *SNC, NOS, MED*

Ladybugs 🦴 ᵛ

PG-13/Jr. High-Adult Hangdog salesman Dangerfield would like to move up the corporate ladder, but must first turn the company-sponsored girl's soccer team into winners. Routine Dangerfield vehicle exploits nearly everything for laughs, including dressing an athletic boy as a girl so he can play on the team. Obvious fluff that will likely engage the youngsters.

> 🚫 BEWARE 🚫 *Profanity, a boy in drag and crude sexual remarks. Remember, it's Dangerfield and he gets "no respect."*

1992 91m/C Rodney Dangerfield, Jackee, Jonathan Brandis, Ilene Graff, Vinessa Shaw, Tom Parks, Jeanetta Arnetta, Nancy Parsons, Blake Clark, Tommy Lasorda; **D:** Sidney J. Furie; **M:** Richard Gibbs. **VHS, Beta** *PAR*

Ladyhawke 🦴🦴🦴

PG-13/Jr. High-Adult In medieval France, a young pickpocket meets a nomadic warrior and his lady love, separated by a cruel spell. At night he turns into a wolf, while by day she is a hawk; they travel together, yet cannot meet in human form. More successful than many modern screen fantasies because it doesn't try to be the Ultimate Fairy Tale (f/x are virtually nonexistent), just a magically romantic adventure. Still, it's way too long, and Broderick unwisely falls back on his "Ferris Bueller" persona for the youthful knave.

> 🚫 BEWARE 🚫 *Medieval violence. Transformations from human forms to animal forms.*

1985 121m/C Matthew Broderick, Rutger Hauer, Michelle Pfeiffer, John Wood, Leo McKern, Alfred Molina, Ken Hutchison; **D:** Richard Donner; **W:** Edward Khmara, Michael Thomas, Tom Mankiewicz; **M:** Andrew Powell. **VHS, Beta, LV** *WAR*

Lamb Chop's Play Along: Action Songs

Preschool-Primary Shari Lewis and Lamb Chop sing songs that kids can interact with. Additional volumes available.

1992 ?m/C VHS *A&M, TVC, FAF*

Lamb Chop's Sing-Along Play-Along

Family Shari Lewis and her puppets joke and sing, and young viewers can join in.

1990 45m/C Shari Lewis. **VHS, Beta** *FRH*

The Land Before Time 🦴🦴🦴

G/Family Before his dinosaur tales "Jurassic Park" and "We're Back!," Steven Spielberg helped produce this lushly animated children's adventure about five orphaned baby dinos near the end of the Age of Reptiles. They band together and try to find the Great Valley, a green paradise where they can avoid extinction. Charming, coy, and often shamelessly tearjerking; for adult viewers who can't shake the idea that there was no Great Valley in real life, it's unusually melancholy. One of the more successful efforts from the Don Bluth Studios.

> 🚫 BEWARE 🚫 *Littlefoot, the baby brontosaurus hero, sees his mother die, though there's later a glimpse of her in dino-heaven.*

1988 70m/C D: Don Bluth; **W:** Stu Krieger; **M:** James Horner; **V:** Pat Hingle, Helen Shaver, Gabriel Damon, Candice Houston, Burke Barnes, Judith Barsi, Will Ryan. **VHS, LV** *MCA, FCT, APD*

The Land Before Time 2: The Great Valley Adventure 🦴🦴 ᵛ

G/Family Sequel to 1988's animated adventure finds dinosaur pals Littlefoot, Cera, Ducky, Petrie, and Spike happily settled in the Great Valley. But their adventures don't stop as they chase two egg-stealing Struthiomimuses (thank goodnees it's not a book) and retrieve an egg of unknown origin from the Mysterious Beyond.

1994 75m/C VHS, LV *MCA*

The Land Before Time 3: The Time of the Great Giving 🦴🦴 ᵛ

G/Family Littlefoot and his pals try to find a new source of water when the Great Valley experiences a severe water shortage.

1995 71m/C D: Roy Allen Smith. **VHS, LV** *MCA*

The Land of Faraway 🦴🦴

G/Family Mediocre international spectacle (dubbed into English) in which a boy is whisked from his dreary everyday existence to the magical Land of Faraway, where he does battle with evil knights and flies on winged horses. Based on a novel by Pippi Longstocking's creator Astrid Lindgren.

1987 95m/C Timothy Bottoms, Christian Bale, Susannah York, Christopher Lee, Nicholas Pickard; **D:** Vladimir Grammatikov. **VHS, Beta** *PSM*

Land of the Lost

Primary 1990s revival of one of the better Saturday-morning shows of the '70s. Tom Porter and his children Kevin and Annie are transported back to the prehistoric land, where they are joined by a mysterious jungle girl and a monkey-boy named Stink. They fight for survival against the familiar gigantic dinosaurs, evil lizard-men, and other dangers, with slightly upscale special f/x in this go-around. Two episodes per tape.

1992 ?m/C Timothy Bottoms. **VHS** *WOV*

Land of the Lost, Vol. 1

Family Forest ranger Rick Marshall and his two teenaged children Will and Holly become trapped in a strange prehistoric world populated by dinosaurs, "sleestax," futuristic ruins and other enigmas. Minor classic Saturday-morning kids' series with cool stop-motion animation dinosaurs and innovative, occasionally mind-expanding plot lines. No coincidence, because some classic "Star Trek" scriptwriters were contributors. The show was revived a decade later. Additional volumes available.

1974 46m/C Wesley Eure, Ron Harper, Kathy Coleman, Spencer Milligan, Phillip Paley. **VHS, Beta** *NLC*

Land That Time Forgot 🦴🦴

PG/Family Dinosaur adventure worth noting mainly for how much better special effects technology has improved in a few decades. WWI submarine goes off course into Antarctica and surfaces in a land outside time, filled with cavepersons and prehistoric monsters (mostly non-threatening puppets). Based on the 1918 novel by Tarzan's creator, Edgar Rice Burroughs. Followed in 1977 by "The People that Time Forgot."

> ⚠ BEWARE *Violence.*

1975 90m/C Doug McClure, John McEnery, Susan Penhaligon; **D:** Kevin Connor. **VHS, Beta** *LIV, VES*

Lantern Hill 🦴🦴🦴

G/Family During the Depression, 12-year-old Jane reluctantly goes to live with her long-absent father, liking him in spite of herself. She then attempts to reconcile both estranged parents. Gentle family drama from the pen of Lucy Maud Montgomery, done by the same high-quality Canadian filmmakers responsible for the "Anne of Green Gables" series. Released on tape in the US as part of the PBS Wonderworks series.

1990 112m/C Sam Waterston, Colleen Dewhurst, Sarah Polley, Marion Bennett, Zoe Caldwell; **D:** Kevin Sullivan. **VHS, LV** *TOU, FCT*

Lassie 🦴🦴🦴

PG/Family Everyone's favorite collie returns as the Turner family moves to Virginia's Shenandoah Valley to take up sheep ranching. However, because this is the '90s, Dad meets financial disaster, and junior can't stand his stepmom. Can Lassie meet the challenges of dysfunctional family living? "What is it girl? Call a therapist?" This Lassie is a direct descendant of Pal, the original 1943 star, and every bit as beautiful.

> ⚠ BEWARE *Mild profanity and family fiscal woes. And maybe one too many "What is it, girl?"*

1994 92m/C Helen Slater, Jon Tenney, Tom Guiry, Brittany Boyd, Richard Farnsworth, Frederic Forrest; **D:** Daniel Petrie; **W:** Matthew Jacobs, Gary Ross, Elizabeth Anderson. **VHS** *NYR*

Lassie, Come Home 🦴🦴🦴

G/Family In the first of the Lassie features, the famed collie is reluctantly sold by their impoverished owners to a rich guy. But the canine knows where she really belongs and makes an arduous treacherous cross-country journey back to her rightful family. Material has gotten a little familiar with the years, but you can't beat that cast. Nicely based on the novel by Eric Knight. Followup "Son of Lassie" is also on tape. Remade as both "The Magic of Lassie" and, with a species change, "The Gypsy Colt."

1943 90m/C Roddy McDowall, Elizabeth Taylor, Donald Crisp, Edmund Gwenn, May Whitty, Nigel Bruce, Elsa Lanchester, J. Pat O'Malley, Lassie; **D:** Fred M. Wilcox. **Award Nominations:** Academy Awards '43: Best Color Cinematography; **Awards:** National Board of Review Awards '43: 10 Best Films of the Year. **VHS, Beta, LV** *MGM*

Lassie: The Miracle 🦴

Primary Lassie's weekly TV show, which ran more or less continually for nearly 20 years, was barely retired when the heroic collie encored with this made-for-TV-movie featuring the photogenic canine saving newborn pups and befriending a mute boy.

1975 90m/C Lassie. **VHS, Beta** *MGM*

Lassie's Great Adventure 🦴🦴🦴

Family Lassie and her master Timmy are swept away from home by a runaway balloon. After they land in the Canadian wilderness, they learn to rely on each other through peril and adventure. Condensed from the long-running "Lassie" TV series.

1962 104m/C June Lockhart, Jon Provost, Hugh Reilly, Lassie; **D:** William Beaudine. **VHS, Beta** *MGM*

Lassie's Rescue Rangers

Preschool-Jr. High Cartoon version of the courageous collie, who tries to save the environment with the help of the brave Rescue Rangers animal friends. These repackaged Saturday-morning animated adventures are unrelated to the later Chip'n'Dale Rescue Rangers. Additional volumes available.

1973 60m/C D: Hal Sutherland; **V:** Ted Knight. **VHS, Beta** *FHE*

Last Action Hero

PG-13/Jr. High-Adult Adolescent boy addicted to action movies gets a magic movie ticket that lets him enter a bombastic Hollywood slam-bang sequel starring his idol Jack Slater, the kind of cop who never loses a fight, survives gunfire and explosions, has a cool car, and a great big gun. Expensive action/spoof of movies within a movie is tremendous fun for about the first half or so, then the not so original premise wears thin. Arnold possesses his usual self-mocking charm and exploits his rapport with the youngster to the fullest. Since the make-believe violence is really supposed to be make-believe violence (mostly, anyway), it's pretty inoffensive. Look for lots of big stars in small roles and cameos, plus tons of inside Hollywood gags.

BEWARE *Violence, but not realistic. Swearing, meanwhile, never exceeds a very soft PG-13 (the subject of a brilliant gag). Sex talk.*

1993 131m/C Arnold Schwarzenegger, Austin O'Brien, Mercedes Ruehl, F. Murray Abraham, Charles Dance, Anthony Quinn, Robert Prosky, Tommy Noonan, Frank McRae, Art Carney, Brigitte Wilson; **Cameos:** Sharon Stone, Hammer, Chevy Chase, Jean-Claude Van Damme, Tori Spelling, Joan Plowright, Adam Ant, James Belushi, James Cameron, Tony Curtis, Timothy Dalton, Tony Danza, Edward Furlong, Little Richard, Damon Wayans, Robert Patrick; **D:** John McTiernan; **W:** Shane Black, David Arnott; **M:** Michael Kamen. **VHS, Beta, LV, 8mm** *COL, BTV*

The Last American Hero

PG/Jr. High-Adult The true story of how former moonshine runner Junior Johnson became one of the fastest race car drivers in the history of the sport. Entertaining slice of life chronicling whiskey running and stock car racing, with Bridges superb in the lead. Based on a series of articles written by Tom Wolfe.

BEWARE *Profanity and sex.*

1973 95m/C Jeff Bridges, Valerie Perrine, Gary Busey, Art Lund, Geraldine Fitzgerald, Ned Beatty; **D:** Lamont Johnson; **W:** William Roberts; **M:** Charles Fox. **VHS, Beta** *FOX*

The Last Chance Detectives: Mystery Lights of Navajo Mesa

Family Action-packed mystery adventure, featuring the Last Chance Detectives, which teaches biblical life-lessons the whole family can enjoy. The detectives investigate a mystery in a small desert town which leads them to the conclusion that God is always with them. Ages 8 to 12.
1995 50m/C VHS *ECU*

The Last Flight of Noah's Ark

G/Family Disney adventure with story input from aviation novelist Ernest K. Gann. Result is a scenic diversion about an old B-29 bomber filled with animals and stowaway orphans that crash lands on a Pacific island, where two Japanese holdouts haven't yet heard that the war is over. Hey, it could happen. Major complaint is the high whine factor of the two obligatory kids.

1980 97m/C Elliott Gould, Genevieve Bujold, Rick Schroder, Vincent Gardenia, Tammy Lauren; **D:** Charles Jarrott; **M:** Maurice Jarre. **VHS, Beta** *DIS*

The Last of the Mohicans

Family The first talking pictures version of the famous James Fenimore Cooper novel was this stiff, low-budget serial from the Mascot studios, depicting the life-and-death struggle of the Mohican tribe during the French and Indian was in 12 chapters of 13 minutes each.

BEWARE *Violence.*

1932 230m/B Edwina Booth, Harry Carey Sr., Hobart Bosworth, Frank "Junior" Coghlan; **D:** Ford Beebe, B. Reeves Eason. **VHS, Beta** *VYY, VCN, NOS*

The Last of the Mohicans

Family So-so adaptation of the well-known novel, about the scout Hawkeye and his companions Natty Bumpo, Uncas and Chingachgook during the French and Indian Wars, done in unimaginative fashion for prime-time TV.

BEWARE *Violence.*

1985 97m/C Steve Forrest, Ned Romero, Andrew Prine, Don Shanks, Robert Tessier, Jane Actman; **D:** James L. Conway. **VHS, Beta** *VCI*

The Last of the Mohicans

R/Sr. High-Adult It's 1757, at the height of the French and English war in the American colonies, with native American tribes allied to each side. Hawkeye, a white frontiersman raised by the Mohicans, wants nothing to do with either side until he rescues Cora, an English officer's beautiful daughter, from the revenge-minded Huron Magua. The real pleasure in this adaptation, which draws from both the Cooper novel and the 1936 film, is in its lush look and attractive stars. Released in a letterbox format to preserve the original integrity of the film.

BEWARE *The Indian wars are dramatized in all their historically accurate brutality, and this gets an R for its violence.*

1992 114m/C Daniel Day-Lewis, Madeleine Stowe, Wes Studi, Russell Means, Eric Schweig, Jodhi May, Steven Waddington, Maurice Roeves, Colm Meaney, Patrice Chereau; **D:** Michael Mann; **W:** Christopher Crowe, Michael Mann; **M:** Trevor Jones, Randy Edelman. **VHS, LV** *FXV, BTV*

The Last Prostitute

PG-13/Sr. High-Adult Two teenage boys search for a legendary prostitute to initiate them into manhood, only to discover that she has retired. They hire on as workers on her horse farm, and one of them discovers the meaning of love. Well cast but somewhat labored coming-of-age saga, made for cable TV.

BEWARE *Mature themes, sex, profanity.*

1991 93m/C Sonia Braga, Wil Wheaton, David Kaufman, Woody Watson, Dennis Letts, Cotter Smith; *D:* Lou Antonio. **VHS** *MCA*

The Last Starfighter ♫♫ ♭

PG/Jr. High-Adult Bored with his small-town job at the family motel, teen Alex masters an arcade video game—then gets a visit from fast-talking "Music Man" type alien (Preston, of course), who informs him that he's just qualified to fight for the good guys in a distant intergalactic war. Infectiously high-spirited space adventure almost helps you forget the frequent "Star Wars" mimicry. Computer-generated f/x were considered revolutionary at the time.

BEWARE *Violence, salty language.*

1984 100m/C Lance Guest, Robert Preston, Barbara Bosson, Dan O'Herlihy, Catherine Mary Stewart, Cameron Dye, Kimberly Ross, Wil Wheaton; *D:* Nick Castle. **VHS, Beta, LV** *MCA*

Last Time Out ♫♫ ♭

PG-13/Jr. High-Adult Danny Dolan (Conrad) is a hard-partying college wide receiver who gets a shock when the father who abandoned him enrolls at his school to finish a college degree. Seems Joe (Beck) had his pro quarterback career cut short by a drinking problem and he's worried his son will follow in his unsteady footsteps.

BEWARE *Mild violence, alcohol abuse and drug content are major themes, but a valuable lesson is to be learned.*

1994 92m/C John Beck, Christian Conrad, Lori Werner, Gail Strickland, Betty Buckley; *D:* Don Fox Greene. **VHS, LV** *IMP*

The Last Unicorn ♫♫ ♭

G/Family Upon hearing she's the last of her kind in the world, Unicorn ventures forth with an incompetent magician and a bandit queen to find out what became of the rest. Too-literal adaptation of Peter S. Beagle dense fantasy novel (with a script by the author) has a great gallery of voices but its fragile spell is strained, though not broken, by budget-minded animation from Rankin-Bass studio. Unremarkable songs.

1982 95m/C *D:* Jules Bass; *M:* Jim Webb; *V:* Alan Arkin, Jeff Bridges, Tammy Grimes, Angela Lansbury, Mia Farrow, Robert Klein, Christopher Lee, Keenan Wynn. **VHS, Beta, LV** *FOX, KAR, LIV*

Law of the Wild

Family Mascot serial showcasing the son of the original movie dog hero Rin Tin Tin. Junior sniffs along the trail of a magnificent stallion, horsenapped by racketeers just before a championship sweepstakes race. In 12 chapters.

1934 230m/B Bob Custer, Ben Turpin, Lucille Browne, Lafe McKee; *D:* B. Reeves Eason, Armand Schaefer. **VHS** *GPV, NOS, VCN*

Lawrence of Arabia ♫♫♫♫

PG/Family Lean at the height of his epic period directs this exceptional biography of T.E. Lawrence, a British military "observer" who strategically helps the Bedouins battle the Turks during WWI. Lawrence, played masterfully by O'Toole in his first major film, is a hero consumed more by a need to reject British tradition than to save the Arab population. Stunning photography of the desert in all its harsh reality. Laser edition contains 20 minutes of restored footage and a short documentary about the making of the film. Available in letterboxed format.

BEWARE *Violence, a long, hard trek across the desert. Requires a long attention span. And you may get thirsty, too.*

1962 221m/C Peter O'Toole, Omar Sharif, Anthony Quinn, Alec Guinness, Jack Hawkins, Claude Rains, Anthony Quayle, Arthur Kennedy, Jose Ferrer; *D:* David Lean; *W:* Robert Bolt; *M:* Maurice Jarre. **Award Nominations:** Academy Awards '62: Best Actor (O'Toole), Best Adapted Screenplay, Best Supporting Actor (Sharif); **Awards:** Academy Awards '62: Best Art Direction/Set Decoration (Color), Best Color Cinematography, Best Director (Lean), Best Film Editing, Best Picture, Best Sound, Best Original Score; British Academy Awards '62: Best Actor (O'Toole), Best Film; Directors Guild of America Awards '62: Best Director (Lean); Golden Globe Awards '63: Best Director (Lean), Best Film—Drama, Best Supporting Actor (Sharif). **VHS, Beta, LV** *COL, CRC, BTV*

The Lawrenceville Stories ♫♫ ♭

Family Chronicles the life and times of a group of young men at the prestigious Lawrenceville prep school in 1905. Galligan plays William Hicks, alias "The Prodigious Hickey," the ringleader of their obnoxious stunts. Based on the stories of Owen Johnson, which originally ran in the Saturday Evening Post.

198? 180m/C Zach Galligan, Edward Herrmann, Nicholas Rowe, Allan Goldstein, Robert Joy, Stephen Baldwin; *D:* Robert Iscove. **VHS** *MON, BTV*

Lazer Tag Academy: The Movie

Family The toy line comes to animated life in this movie-length commercial, made of strung-together TV episodes from the short-lived cartoon series about present-day kids armed with futuristic weapons to make this a better world. Right.

1990 95m/C VHS, Beta *JFK*

Leader of the Band ♫♫

PG/Jr. High-Adult Wayward big-city musician takes a job in rural Georgia trying to train the world's worst high school band. The twist on the "Music Man" formula becomes evident in the farfetched finale. Good cast helps this comedy march along, if not always in step.

BEWARE *Profanity, sex.*

1987 90m/C Steve Landesburg, Gailard Sartain, Mercedes Ruehl, James Martinez, Calvert Deforest; *D:* Nessa Hyams; *M:* Dick Hyman. **VHS, Beta, LV** *LIV*

A League of Their Own 🎵🎵🎵

PG/Jr. High-Adult Charming segment of baseball history—the real-life All American Girls Professional Baseball League, formed in the 1940s when the men were off at war. Loose plot focuses on sibling rivalry between two farm-bred sisters; Dottie, a beautiful, crackerjack catcher wise enough to appreciate when the game is and isn't important, and Kit, the younger, insecure pitcher with a chance to shine outside her sister's shadow. A great cast of characters rounds out the film, including Hanks as a hard-drinking, reluctant coach and Madonna as a happily promiscuous wench. But director Marshall ("Big") keeps everything agreeably sunny, sweet, and nostalgic. Enjoyable family outing at the ballpark with a positive message for young girls.

BEWARE! *Ballpark-spiced pepper, sex talk, alcohol use, wads of chewing tobacco.*

1992 127m/C Tom Hanks, Geena Davis, Madonna, Lori Petty, Jon Lovitz, David Strathairn, Garry Marshall, Bill Pullman, Rosie O'Donnell, Megan Cavanagh, Tracy Reiner, Bitty Schram, Ann Cusack, Anne Elizabeth Ramsay, Freddie Simpson, Renee Coleman; *D:* Penny Marshall; *W:* Lowell Ganz, Babaloo Mandel; *M:* Hans Zimmer. **VHS, Beta, LV, 8mm** *COL*

Lean on Me 🎵🎵🎵

PG-13/Jr. High-Adult Dramatization of the true story of Joe Clark, a tough New Jersey teacher who takes charge as principal of the state's worst school and enforces strict discipline. He weeds out punk kids all right, but also fires teachers and insults even his supporters when they question his tactics. Well-acted and rousing, obviously favoring its controversial hero, yet doesn't hesitate in showing his tyrannical and egomaniac sides.

BEWARE! *Roughhousing, profanity, drug use, but nothing gratuitous as Mr. Clark cleans house.*

1989 109m/C Morgan Freeman, Robert Guillaume, Beverly Todd, Alan North, Lynne Thigpen, Robin Bartlett, Michael Beach, Ethan Phillips, Regina Taylor; *D:* John G. Avildsen; *W:* Michael Schiffer; *M:* Bill Conti. **VHS, Beta, LV, 8mm** *WAR, FCT*

Leap of Faith 🎵🎵🎵

PG-13/Jr. High-Adult Jonas Nightengale (Martin) is a traveling evangelist/scam artist whose tour bus is stranded in an impoverished farm town. Nevertheless he sets up his show and goes to work, aided by the technology utilized by accomplice Winger. Both Martin and Winger begin to have a change of heart after experiencing love-Winger with local sheriff Neeson and Martin after befriending a waitress (Davidovich) and her crippled brother (Haas). Martin is in his element as the slick revivalist with the hidden heart but the film is soft-headed as well as soft-hearted.

BEWARE! *Profanity and hypocrisy. Martin and gang try to fool innocent townsfolk and take advantage of a crippled boy.*

1992 110m/C Steve Martin, Debra Winger, Lolita Davidovich, Liam Neeson, Lukas Haas, Meat Loaf, Philip S. Hoffman, M.C. Gainey, La Chanze, Delores Hall, John Toles-Bey, Albertina Walker, Ricky Dil-lard; *D:* Richard Pearce; *W:* Janus Cercone; *M:* Cliff Eidelman. **VHS, Beta, LV** *PAR, BTV*

Leapin' Leprechauns 🎵🎵🎵

PG/Primary-Adult John Dennehy's dad Michael has arrived from Ireland for a visit, accompanied by some "wee folk" who are invisible to all non-believers. Seems the little leprechauns are just in time to rescue their ancestral home from a plot by John to turn their Irish land into a theme park. Too bad there aren't any leprechauns in France.

BEWARE! *Some frightening moments and mild language.*

1995 84m/C Grant Cramer, John Bluthal, Sharon Lee Jones, Gregory Edward Smith, Sylvester McCoy, James Ellis, Godfrey James, Tina Martin, Erica Nicole Hess; *D:* Ted Nicolaou; *W:* Ted Nicolaou, Michael McGann. **VHS, Beta** *PAR*

The Learning Tree 🎵🎵🎵

PG/Jr. High-Adult Uneven adaptation of Gordon Parks' autobiographical novel about Newton, a black teenager in 1930s Kansas, who matures while finding himself at the center of numerous racially-explosive situations, including witnessing a murder. Preachy but often hard-hitting. Major problem is that Johnson looks quite a bit older than Newt's 14 years.

BEWARE! *Brutality, profanity, alcohol use and racial tension.*

1969 107m/C Kyle Johnson, Alex Clarke, Estelle Evans, Dana Elcar; *D:* Gordon Parks. **VHS, Beta** *WAR, FCT, AFR*

The Left-Handed Gun 🎵🎵🎵

Family Offbeat version of the exploits of Billy the Kid, which portrays him as a 19th-century Wild West juvenile delinquent. Director Penn's movie debut is a psychological western that attempts to shed frontier myth and portray Billy as a dimwitted menace considerate of his few friends and deadly to his enemies. Stranger yet, The Kid was originally written for James Dean (who died before filming), and the screen version is based on a 1955 Philco teleplay written by Gore Vidal (and directed by Penn), which featured wild homosexual Billy.

1958 102m/B Paul Newman, Lita Milan, John Dehner; *D:* Arthur Penn. **VHS, Beta** *WAR, TLF*

Legend 🎵🎵🎵

PG/Family Epic fantasy evokes a rich visual landscape of unicorns, elves, goblins, fairies, swamps, mists, snows, forests, and castles. Too bad the Prince of Darkness (Curry, under awesome makeup) is the only character with personality, as he devilishly tilts the balance between good and evil. He also steals young Jack's girlfriend, and the nature-boy hero, accompanied by bumbling dwarfs, schleps to the rescue. Picture can't help looking impressive, but in the end it's just another pompous '80s try at the Ultimate Fairy Tale, never mind that one had already been done in 1977—"Star Wars."

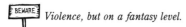 *Violence, but on a fantasy level.*

1986 89m/C Tom Cruise, Mia Sara, Tim Curry, David Bennent, Billy Barty, Alice Playten; *D:* Ridley Scott; *M:* Jerry Goldsmith. **VHS, Beta, LV** *MCA*

Legend of Billie Jean 🎷 ♭

PG-13/Jr. High-Adult Texas girl and her brother have some violent scrapes with thieving bullies and a would-be rapist. Now fugitives from the law, the pair become heroes to the local teen population. Likeable young actors, seen to better advantage elsewhere, make the most of this weightless brew of juvenile rebellion and sappy political symbolism.

 Violence and profanity. Billie Jean is man-handled and a character gets shot. An explosive ending.

1985 92m/C Helen Slater, Peter Coyote, Keith Gordon, Christian Slater, Richard Bradford, Yeardley Smith, Dean Stockwell; *D:* Matthew Robbins; *W:* Mark Rosenthal. **VHS, Beta** *FOX*

Legend of Boggy Creek 🎷 ♭

G/Family Peculiar mixture of fact, fiction and eerie ambiance, dramatizing various Arkansas Bigfoot sightings. Followed by a couple of sasquatch sequels that were entirely scripted kiddie-oriented adventures, like "Return to Boggy Creek"; stick with "Harry and the Hendersons."

Some scary moments, and visuals include cats and dogs allegedly slain by the Boggy Creek creature.

1975 87m/C Willie E. Smith, John P. Nixon, John W. Gates, Jeff Crabtree, Buddy Crabtree; *D:* Charles B. Pierce; *W:* Charles B. Pierce. **VHS, Beta** *LIV, MRV*

The Legend of Hiawatha

Family Hiawatha must confront a demon who casts a plague on his people. This animated program is loosely based on Henry Wadsworth Longfellow's poem.

1982 35m/C VHS, Beta *FHE*

Legend of Lobo 🎷🎷

Family Crafty wolf Lobo seeks to free his mate from the clutches of greedy hunters. A Disney wildlife adventure.

1962 67m/C VHS, Beta *DIS*

The Legend of Manxmouse 🎷🎷 ♭

Preschool-Primary Japanese-animated feature (based on a Paul Gallico story) looks childish and silly on the surface but addresses some deep philosophical concerns, as a Pinocchio-type mouse, who comes to life from a carved figurine, is told that by tradition he must be eaten in public by the last of the Manx cats. But Thomas J. Manxcat is a happy fellow, also troubled by the deadly ritual. Should the duo submit to destiny? Artwork is frankly crude at times, but this fate-vs-free-will fable is a lot easier to take than its literary soulmate, Shirley Jackson's "The Lottery."

 Violence

1991 85m/C VHS *JFK*

The Legend of Sleepy Hollow 🎷🎷

G/Family Washington Irving's classic tale of the Headless Horseman of Sleepy Hollow features Goldblum well cast as Ichabod Crane but otherwise stretches the short story to tedious length. Made for television.

Roughhousing. The legendary headless spook is unimpressive, scare-wise, compared to the Disney cartoon incarnation.

1979 100m/C Jeff Goldblum, Dick Butkus, Paul Sand, Meg Foster, James Griffith, John S. White. **VHS, Beta, LV** *VCI*

The Legend of Sleepy Hollow

Family Classic Washington Irving tale is given the classy Duvall treatment in her "Tall Tales and Legends" series. When a snooty teacher goes too far, the town blacksmith decides to play the ultimate Halloween trick on him. Made for cable television.

1986 51m/C Ed Begley Jr., Beverly D'Angelo, Charles Durning, Tim Thomerson. **VHS** *FOX*

Legend of the Lone Ranger 🎷 ♭

PG/Family Fabled Lone Ranger's first meeting with his Indian companion, Tonto, is brought almost to life in this weak and vapid version that tried to revive interest in the western hero. The narration by Merle Haggard leaves something to be desired as do most of the performances.

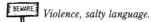 *Violence, salty language.*

1981 98m/C Klinton Spilsbury, Michael Horse, Jason Robards Jr., Richard Farnsworth, Christopher Lloyd, Matt Clark; *D:* William A. Fraker; *W:* William Roberts, Ivan Goff, Michael Kane; *M:* John Barry. **VHS, Beta** *FOX*

Legend of the Northwest 🎷🎷

G/Family The loyalty of a dog is evidenced in the fierce revenge he has for the drunken hunter who shot and killed his master. Jack London-esque wilderness adventure starring "Grizzly Adams" regular Pyle

Violence.

1978 83m/C Denver Pyle. **VHS, Beta** *GEM, HHE, VTR*

Legend of the White Horse 🎷 ♭

Family Scientist and his son travel to a faraway land where the magical white horse reigns. Botched internationally produced fantasy for the family market, with some past Spielberg thespians horsing around in the cast.

1985 91m/C Christopher Lloyd, Dee Wallace Stone, Allison Balson, Soon-Teck Oh, Luke Askew; *D:* Jerzy Domaradzki, Janusz Morgenstern. **VHS** *FXV*

The Legend of Wolf Mountain

PG/Jr. High-Adult Three kids are held hostage by prison escapees in the Utah mountains. But 11-year-old Kerry has a guardian angel in the form of a native medicine-man's ghost who helps the kids vanquish the bad guys. Terrible mixture of New-Age mysticism with a woodsy ripoff of "Home Alone." Wastes a decent cast of new and veteran performers, and Rooney's role is very small indeed.

BEWARE *Roughhousing.*

1992 91m/C Mickey Rooney, Bo Hopkins, Don Shanks, Vivian Schilling, Robert Z'Dar, David Shark, Nicole Lund, Natalie Lund, Matthew Lewis, Jonathan Best; **D:** Craig Clyde. **VHS, LV** *HMD*

The Legend of Young Robin Hood ♪♪

G/Family Dramatization on how the early life of the Sherwood Forest outlaw might have gone. He learns to use a longbow, and forms his convictions as his fellow Saxons struggle with their Norman conquerors.
197? 60m/C VHS, Beta *GEM*

The Legend of Zelda: Missing Link

Primary-Jr. High Nick and Zelda, teen adventurers, protect the kingdom of Hyrule from the evil wizard Ganon. The TV cartoon based on the Nintendo Game, originally paired on the tube with a "Super Mario Brothers" cartoon for maximum marketing. Additional volumes available.
1988 30m/C VHS *GKK*

Legends of the Fall ♪♪

R/Sr. High-Adult Sweeping, melodramatic family saga set in Montana (though filmed in Alberta, Canada). Patriarch William Ludlow (Hopkins) is raising three sons: reserved Alfred (Quinn), idealistic Samuel (Thomas), and wild middle son Tristan (Pitt). In 1913, Samuel returns from Boston with a fiancee, the lovely and refined Susannah (Ormond). Alfred and Tristan take one look and also desire her—a passion that will carry them through some 20 years of heartbreak.

BEWARE *Extreme violence: Scalping, gunplay, World War I combat. Nudity and sexual situations. Also consider gory Indian rituals when advising your teen Pitt fan on the content of this one.*

1994 134m/C Brad Pitt, Aidan Quinn, Julia Ormond, Anthony Hopkins, Henry Thomas, Gordon Tootoosis, Tantoo Cardinal, Karina Lombard, Paul Desmond, Kenneth Welsh; **D:** Edward Zwick; **W:** Susan Shilliday, William D. Wittliff; **C:** John Toll; **M:** James Horner. **Award Nominations:** Academy Awards '94: Best Art Direction/Set Decoration, Best Sound; Golden Globe Awards '95: Best Actor—Drama (Pitt), Best Director (Zwick), Best Film—Drama, Best Original Score; **Awards:** Academy Awards '94: Best Cinematography. **VHS, LV, 8mm** *COL*

Lend a Paw

Preschool-Primary One of those Academy Award-winning cartoon shorts that made Walt Disney owner of more Oscars than any other individual in history. Jealousy is overcome as Pluto deals with Mickey's newly adopted kitten.
1941 8m/C VHS, Beta *DSN, MTI*

Leonard Part 6 WOOF!

PG/Jr. High-Adult Expensive, inexplicable, ill-conceived 'family comedy' about super secret agent Leonard Parker (with five undiscussed missions behind him), who comes out of retirement to save San Francisco from killer animals controlled by an evil vegetarian, and patch up his collapsing personal life—not in that order. You're in trouble when the funniest actors are a trout and a bunch of frogs, rather than Cosby (who produced and co-scripted).

BEWARE *Superhero violence and sex talk.*

1987 83m/C Bill Cosby, Gloria Foster, Tom Courtenay, Joe Don Baker; **D:** Paul Weiland; **W:** Bill Cosby, Jonathan Reynolds; **M:** Elmer Bernstein. **VHS, Beta, LV** *COL*

The Leprechauns' Christmas Gold

Family An Irish lad lends a hand to a certain group of "wee people" (That's right! Leprechauns!) to help them find their pot of gold. Created in the magical stop-motion-animation technique of Rankin-Bass.
1981 24m/C V: Art Carney, Peggy Cass. **VHS** *WAR*

Les Miserables ♪♪

Family Victor Hugo's classic novel of injustice (the basis for the international hit musical) is adapted in this Japanese-animated family feature about Inspector Javert's long, pitiless pursuit of peasant petty thief Jean Valjean.
1979 70m/C VHS, Beta *FHE, APD*

Let the Balloon Go ♪♪

Preschool-Primary Based on the international children's bestseller by Ivan Southall, the story is set in the year 1917 and centers around the struggle of a handicapped boy in Australia to win independence and respect.
1976 92m/C Robert Bettles, Sally Whiteman, Matthew Wilson, Terry McQuillan. **VHS, Beta** *MCA*

Let's Be Friends

Primary Explores friendship, discussing how to make new friends, share feelings with established friends, and playing with more than one playmate at a time. Ages 5 to 8.
1994 14m/C VHS

Brad Pitt plays a free spirit in "Legends of the Fall."

Let's Create a Better World

Primary Children learn the importance of reducing, reusing, recycling and respect through music and special effects. Includes nine art projects using materials that would normally be thrown away. Ages 5 to 10.
1994 60m/C VHS *LET, CRY*

Let's Dance on the Farm with Miss Nola

Preschool-Primary Combines real farm animal footage, original music, and the "Storidance" techniques of Miss Nola to teach children to accept individuality and develop positive attitudes towards growing. Mis Nola leads children through the story of "The Rolling Eggs," in which children pretend to be eggs, rolling and bumping into different farm animal friends, which they then imitate. They dance with rabbits, big brown cows, and wooly sheep. Finally, near the end of the story, these "eggs" return to the nest, where they fall asleep, only to awaken to a new life as various types of farm birds.
1996 m/C VHS

Let's Explore ... Furry, Fishy, Feathery Friends

Preschool-Primary Captures children's imaginations while looking at different types of pets, including cats, dogs, birds, fish, lizards, frogs, and spiders. Ages 2 to 5.
1995 30m/C VHS *TPV*

Let's Go Camping

Preschool-Primary You don't have to be rugged to face the outdoors, but you'll need some essential gear, a sense of adventure and a sense of humor. That's the message here as a mom, a dad and their two children camp for a night at Smuggler's Notch State Park, in Vermont. With the help of friendly Ranger Ben, whose pancake flipping technique needs a lot of work, they learn about hanging their food out of animals' reach, and what to do if you get lost. They also discover that "bear right" doesn't mean a grizzly awaits in that direction. Ages 2 to 8.
1996 ?m/C VHS

Let's Go to the Farm

Preschool-Primary Storyteller Mac Parker takes kids on a behind-the-scenes look at a working farm in Vermont, including such activities as milking cows, riding tractors, harvesting crops, quilting, making maple syrup, and more. Ages 4 to 10.
1994 60m/C VHS

Let's Go to the Zoo with Captain Kangaroo

Preschool-Primary Composed of short clips from the Captain's Library of shows, this program features segments introducing youngsters to many great zoo beasts.
1985 60m/C Bob Keeshan. VHS, Beta *MPI*

Let's Pretend with Barney

Preschool Dinosaurs Barney and BJ use their imaginations to have adventures.
1994 30m/C VHS *LGV*

Let's Ride a Tractor

Preschool-Primary Farmer Paul takes the viewer behind the wheel of a tractor, explaining how it works and also explaining different aspects of dairy farming. Includes scenes of tractors at work plowing, planting and harvesting.
1995 30m/C VHS

Let's Sing Again ♩♩

Family Eight-year-old singing sensation Breen made his debut in this dusty musical vehicle, as a runaway orphan who becomes the pal of a washed-up opera star in a traveling show. ♫ Let's Sing Again; Lullaby; Farmer in the Dell; La Donna e Mobile.

1936 70m/B Bobby Breen, Henry Armetta, George Houston, Vivienne Osborne, Grant Withers, Inez Courtney, Lucien Littlefield; **D:** Kurt Neumann. **VHS** *NOS, LOO, DVT*

Liar's Moon

PG/Jr. High-Adult Local boy woos and weds the town's wealthiest young lady, only to be trapped in family intrigue. Standard soaper elevated by talented cast.

BEWARE *Salty language.*

1982 106m/C Cindy Fisher, Matt Dillon, Christopher Connelly, Susan Tyrrell; **D:** David Fisher. **VHS, Beta** *VES*

License to Drive

PG-13/Jr. High-Adult When Les fails his first driver's license test, the kid steals the family auto for a hot date with the girl of his dreams. Bad Example #1. The evening leads to slam-bang danger, including drunken driving. Bad Example #2. If you rented this inane teen-speed comedy instead of Haim's excellent "Lucas" make that Bad Example #3.

BEWARE *Alcohol use, profanity, roughhousing, extremely poor driving.*

1988 90m/C Corey Feldman, Corey Haim, Carol Kane, Richard Masur; **D:** Greg Beeman; **M:** Jay Michael Ferguson. **VHS, Beta, LV** *FOX*

The Life and Adventures of Santa Claus

Family Animated story of how Santa became the symbol of Christmas. Based on the story by L. Frank Baum.

1985 49m/C **W:** L. Frank Baum; **V:** Alfred Drake, Earle Hyman. **VHS, Beta** *WAR*

Life & Times of Grizzly Adams

G/Family Grizzly is mistakenly chased for a crime he didn't commit and along the way befriends a big bear. Lightweight family adventure based on the rugged life of legendary frontiersman, Grizzly Adams. Served as the launching pad for the TV series and locked the ursine Haggerty into a series of friendly mountain-man roles.

1974 93m/C Dan Haggerty, Denver Pyle, Lisa Jones, Marjorie Harper, Don Shanks; **D:** Richard Friedenberg. **VHS, Beta** *VCI*

Life Begins for Andy Hardy

Family Andy gets a job in New York before entering college and finds the working world to be a sobering experience. Surprisingly downbeat and hard-hitting for the Hardy series, and better for it. Garland's last appearance in the series.

1941 100m/B Mickey Rooney, Judy Garland, Lewis Stone, Ann Rutherford, Fay Holden, Gene Reynolds, Ralph Byrd; **D:** George B. Seitz. **VHS, Beta** *MGM*

Life on the Mississippi

Family Beautifully photographed production for PBS-TV based on selections from Mark Twain's memoir of the same title. Flavorful narrative follows the adolescent Samuel Clemens, already spinning tall tales during his pre-Civil War apprenticeship as a steamboat pilot on the mighty river; in his escapades and mischievous outlook we can see the roots of Tom Sawyer and Huck Finn. Preston is outstanding as usual as Mr. Bixby, the boy's mentor in navigating both sand bars and life. Introduction by novelist Kurt Vonnegut, who looks startlingly like Twain himself. An abridged 54-minute version is also available.

1980 120m/C Robert Lansing, David Knell, James Keane. **VHS, Beta** *KUI, MCA, FLI*

Life with Father

Family Based on the autobiographical writings of Clarence Day, Jr. and a long-running Broadway play, recalling a childhood spent in New York City during the 1880s. A delightful saga about stern but loving father Powell and his relationship with his knowing wife Dunne and four red-headed sons. Powell creates one of the great father figures of film in this heavily lauded classic that was followed by "Life with Mother."

1947 118m/C William Powell, Irene Dunne, Elizabeth Taylor, Edmund Gwenn, ZaSu Pitts, Jimmy Lydon, Martin Milner; **D:** Michael Curtiz; **M:** Max Steiner. **Award Nominations:** Academy Awards '47: Best Actor (Powell), Best Art Direction/Set Decoration (Color), Best Color Cinematography; **Awards:** Golden Globe Awards '48: Best Score; New York Film Critics Awards '47: Best Actor (Powell). **VHS, Beta** *CNG, MRV, NOS*

Life with Mikey

PG/Jr. High-Adult Fox is well cast as a once-beloved former TV child actor who as a grownup runs a struggling talent agency for other juvenile thespians. Looking for a new kid superstar to turn business around, he thinks he's found it in Angie, a 10-year-old Brooklyn pickpocket. Light comedy, low on urgency and generally predictable, but agreeably sweet-spirited.

BEWARE *Salty language.*

1993 92m/C Michael J. Fox, Christina Vidal, Cyndi Lauper, Nathan Lane, David Huddleston, Victor Garber, David Krumholtz, Tony Hendra; **Cameos:** Ruben Blades; **D:** James Lapine; **W:** Marc Lawrence; **M:** Alan Menken. **VHS, Beta, LV** *TOU, BTV*

The Light in the Forest

Family Disney adaptation of the Conrad Richter novel about a young man, kidnapped by Indians when he was a pioneer child and raised within the tribe. Years later he's forcibly returned to his original family. His problems coping with white society are a bit sentimentalized and familiar, but still effective drama.

1958 92m/C James MacArthur, Fess Parker, Carol Lynley, Wendell Corey, Joanne Dru, Jessica Tandy, Joseph Calleia, John McIntire; **D:** Herschel Daugherty. **VHS, Beta** *DIS*

Light of Day

PG-13/Sr. High-Adult Confused family drama with a rock 'n roll background. Working class siblings Joe and Patti escape their dreary lives through their bar band in Cleveland. Their parents disapprove, and Joe ends up torn between the prodigal sister and their sick mother. Script falls flat, although Jett is utterly believable (helps to have real-life experience) and Fox works up a sweat in uncharacteristic hard-edged role. Title song written by Bruce Springsteen.

BEWARE *Profanity, alcohol use and terminal illness.*

1987 107m/C Michael J. Fox, Joan Jett, Gena Rowlands, Jason Miller, Michael McKean, Michael Rooker, Michael Dolan; **D:** Paul Schrader; **W:** Paul Schrader; **M:** Thomas Newman. **VHS, Beta, LV** *LIV, VES*

The Light Princess

Family Charming British made-for-TV fairy tale fetchingly combines live actors with animated backgrounds and creatures in George MacDonald's 1862 story of how a wicked witch curses a princess, literally and figuratively, with lightness; she has zero gravity and never takes anything seriously, a trial for her royal parents who must keep her from floating away.

1979 56m/C Stacey Dorning, John Fortune; **D:** Andrew Gosling. **VHS, Beta** *FOX, HMV*

Lightning Jack

PG-13/Jr. High-Adult Alleged western comedy about Lightning Jack Kane (Hogan), an aging second-rate outlaw who desperately wants to become a western legend. Mute store clerk Ben (Gooding) winds up as his partner in crime, adept at rolling his eyes while running smack into criticism of Stepin Fetchitism. Saddlebags are full of cliches and the running gags (including Kane's surreptitious use of his eyeglasses so he can see his shooting targets) frequently fall flat.

BEWARE *Violence. Borderline stereotype performance by a black actor.*

1994 101m/C Paul Hogan, Cuba Gooding Jr., Beverly D'Angelo, Kamala Dawson, Pat Hingle, Richard Riehle, Frank McRae, Roger Daltrey, L.Q. Jones, Max Cullen; **D:** Simon Wincer; **W:** Paul Hogan; **M:** Bruce Rowland. **VHS** *HBO*

Lightning: The White Stallion

PG/Jr. High-Adult Can Mickey Rooney's megawatts of talent save a whole movie? The answer is . . . almost, but not quite, as he narrates this forgettable compendium of girl-and-her-horse cliches, right down to the heroine's urgent need for an operation. Meanwhile, she tries to train a racing steed to be a show-jumper, then has to reclaim the animal from thieves.

BEWARE *Alcohol use.*

1986 93m/C Mickey Rooney, Susan George, Isabel Lorca; **D:** William A. Levey. **VHS, Beta** *MED*

Like Father, Like Son

PG-13/Jr. High-Adult First and least of several body-switch movies that cluttered Hollywood in the late '80s. Magic potion makes Dr. Hammond and his small son Chris switch personalities, with predictable hijinks. The few good moments go to the impish Moore, at the top of his form as an adolescent spirit in a bigshot surgeon's body.

BEWARE *Profanity, sex.*

1987 101m/C Dudley Moore, Kirk Cameron, Catherine Hicks, Margaret Colin, Sean Astin; **D:** Rod Daniel; **M:** Miles Goodman. **VHS, Beta, LV** *COL*

Like Jake and Me

Primary-Jr. High Sensitive boy wonders what his new siblings will be like in this Mavis Jukes tale distributed through Disney.

1989 16m/C VHS, Beta *MTI, DSN*

Lili

Family Delightful musical romance about a 16-year-old orphan who joins a traveling carnival and falls in love with a crippled, embittered puppeteer. Heartwarming and charming, if occasionally cloying. Leslie Caron sings the films's song hit, "Hi-Lili, Hi-Lo."

1953 81m/C Leslie Caron, Jean-Pierre Aumont, Mel Ferrer, Kurt Kasznar, Zsa Zsa Gabor; **D:** Charles Walters; **M:** Bronislau Kaper. **Award Nominations:** Academy Awards '53: Best Actress (Caron), Best Art Direction/Set Decoration (Color), Best Color Cinematography, Best Director (Walters), Best Screenplay; **Awards:** Academy Awards '53: Best Score; British Academy Awards '53: Best Actress (Caron); Golden Globe Awards '54: Best Screenplay; National Board of Review Awards '53: 10 Best Films of the Year. **VHS, Beta** *MGM*

Lilies of the Field

Family Five East German nuns running a farm in the Southwest enlist the aid of a free-spirited U.S. Army veteran, persuading him to build a chapel for them and teach them English. As the itinerant laborer, Poitier helps limit the inherent saccharine, bringing an engaging honesty and strength to his role. Skala is fine as the mother superior; prior to this opportunity, she had been struggling to make ends meet in a variety of day jobs. Warm and engaging drama certified Poitier as a superstar, as he became the first black man to win an Oscar, and the first African American nominated since Hattie MacDaniel in 1939. Followed by "Christmas Lilies of the Field" (1979).

1963 94m/B Sidney Poitier, Lilia Skala, Lisa Mann, Isa Crino, Stanley Adams; **D:** Ralph Nelson; **M:** Jerry Goldsmith. **Award Nominations:** Academy Awards '63: Best Adapted Screenplay, Best Black and White Cinematography, Best Picture, Best Supporting Actress (Skala); **Awards:** Academy Awards '63: Best Actor (Poitier); Berlin International Film Festival '63: Best Actor (Poitier); Golden Globe Awards '64: Best Actor—Drama (Poitier); National Board of Review Awards '63: 10 Best Films of the Year. **VHS, Beta** *MGM, FOX, BTV*

Linnea in Monet's Garden

Primary Linnea and her friend Mr. Bloom travel from Sweden to Paris to visit the gardens that inspired the work of their favorite artist, Impressionist Claude Monet. From the children's book by Christina Bjork. A lovely, colorful introduction to a great artist's work. Ages 4 to 10. **1994 30m/C VHS** *ICA*

The Lion in Winter 🐾🐾🐾🐾

PG/Jr. High-Adult Medieval monarch Henry II and his wife, Eleanor of Aquitane, match wits over the succession to the English throne and much else in this fast-paced film version of James Goldman's play. The family, including three grown sons, and visiting royalty are united for the Christmas holidays fraught with tension, rapidly shifting allegiances, and layers of psychological manipulation. Superb dialogue and perfectly realized characterizations. O'Toole and Hepburn are triumphant. Screen debuts for Hopkins and Dalton. Shot on location, this literate costume drama surprised the experts with its box-office success.

1968 134m/C Peter O'Toole, Katharine Hepburn, Jane Merrow, Nigel Terry, Timothy Dalton, Anthony Hopkins, John Castle, Nigel Stock; **D:** Anthony Harvey; **W:** Jim Goldman; **M:** John Barry. **Award Nominations:** Academy Awards '68: Best Actor (O'Toole), Best Costume Design, Best Director (Harvey), Best Picture; **Awards:** Academy Awards '68: Best Actress (Hepburn), Best Adapted Screenplay, Best Score; Directors Guild of America Awards '68: Best Director (Harvey); Golden Globe Awards '69: Best Actor—Drama (O'Toole), Best Film—Drama; National Board of Review Awards '68: 10 Best Films of the Year; New York Film Critics Awards '68: Best Film. **VHS, LV** *COL, BTV, TVC*

The Lion King 🐾🐾🐾🐾

G/Family Epic animated African adventure once again does Disney proud. Lion cub Simba is destined to be king of the beasts, until evil uncle Scar (Irons) plots against him. Growing up in the jungles of Africa he learns about life and responsibility as he returns to reclaim his throne. Heartwarming combo of crowd-pleasing songs, a story with depth, emotion, and politically correct multiculturalism, and stunning animation created in painstaking detail with lifelike creatures and beautiful landscapes. 32nd Disney animated film is the first without human characters, the first based on an original story, and the first to use the voices of a well-known, ethnically diverse cast. Scenes of violence in the animal kingdom may be too much for younger viewers. 🎵 Can You Feel the Love Tonight; The Circle of Life; I Just Can't Wait to Be King; Be Prepared; Hakuna Matata.

> ⚠️ BEWARE *Simba's father dies tragically, a scene which may be too much for very young children.*

1994 87m/C Jim Cummings; **D:** Rob Minkoff, Roger Allers; **W:** Jonathan Roberts, Irene Mecchi; **M:** Elton John, Hans Zimmer, Tim Rice; **V:** Matthew Broderick, Jeremy Irons, James Earl Jones, Madge Sinclair, Robert Guillaume, Jonathan Taylor Thomas, Richard "Cheech" Marin, Whoopi Goldberg, Rowan Atkinson, Nathan Lane, Ernie Sabella, Niketa Calame, Moira Kelly. **VHS** *NYR*

The Lion, the Witch and the Wardrobe 🐾🐾🐾

Family The classic C.S. Lewis fantasy (with religious overtones) about four children who find a doorway to the mystical land of Narnia, under the icy spell of the White Witch. The animators of the TV "Peanuts" series and the Children's Television Workshop joined with the Episcopal Radio and TV Foundation to produce this made-for-TV cartoon adaptation (good news: the commercial-break blackouts are nearly unnoticeable) that starts off a little stiffly but improves and enchants as it goes along. Winner of an Emmy award for Best Animated Special.

1979 95m/C VHS *BTV, REP*

Lionheart 🐾🐾

PG/Primary-Adult Boy warrior in 12th-century France runs away from his first serious battle. Mistaken for one of Richard the Lionhearted noble Crusaders, the bland teen is joined by hundreds of orphaned and homeless children, seeking protection from the evil slave-trader known as the Black Prince. Played by Byrne, the BP's a terrific villain, and the major reason for watching this bogus, kiddie rewrite of medieval history, barely released in theaters.

> ⚠️ BEWARE *Violence.*

1987 105m/C Eric Stoltz, Talia Shire, Nicola Cowper, Dexter Fletcher, Nicholas Clay, Deborah Barrymore, Gabriel Byrne; **D:** Franklin J. Schaffner; **W:** Richard Outten; **M:** Jerry Goldsmith. **VHS, Beta, LV** *WAR*

Lisa 🐾

PG-13/Jr. High-Adult Teen psychothriller that almost works. Title character is a 14-year-old who plays prank phone calls on a handsome new guy in town, enticing him into a rendezvous. Little does Lisa realize he's a serial killer. Well-built suspense evaporates in violent climax, and the single mother/growing daughter relationship doesn't go very deep.

> ⚠️ BEWARE *Sex talk, profanity, violence and poor role models.*

1990 95m/C Staci Keanan, Cheryl Ladd, D.W. Moffett, Tanya Fenmore, Jeffrey Tambor, Julie Cobb; **D:** Gary Sherman. **VHS** *FOX*

Little Big League 🐾🐾

PG/Jr. High-Adult 12-year-old baseball nut inherits the Minnesota Twins baseball team from his grandfather, appoints himself manager when everyone else declines, and becomes the youngest owner-manager in history. He finds the sledding tough, losing contact with his friends and discovering the challenge of managing unruly pro ballplayers. Nothing new about the premise, but kids and America's favorite pastime add up to good clean family fun. Edwards is engaging as the mini exec. Features several real-life baseball players, including the Mariners' Griffey. Good cast features TV's Busfield at first base.

The jealous Uncle Scar checks out Simba in "The Lion King."

Screenwriting debut from Pincus, and directorial debut from the executive producer of "Seinfeld," Scheinman.

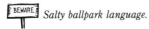 *Salty ballpark language.*

1994 119m/C Luke Edwards, Jason Robards Jr., Kevin Dunn, Dennis Farina, John Ashton, Jonathan Silverman, Wolfgang Bodison, Timothy Busfield, Ashley Crow, Scott Patterson, Billy L. Sullivan, Miles Feulner, Kevin Elster, Leon "Bull" Durham, Brad "The Animal" Lesley; *Cameos:* Don Mattingly, Ken Griffey Jr., Paul O'Neill; **D:** Andrew Scheinman; **W:** Gregory Pincus, Adam Scheinman. **VHS** *NYR*

Little Big Man 🦴🦴🦴🦴

PG/Jr. High-Adult Based on Thomas Berger's picaresque novel, this is the story of 121-year-old Jack Crabb and his quixotic life as gunslinger, charlatan, Indian, ally to George Custer, and the only white survivor of Little Big Horn. Told mainly through flashbacks. Hoffman provides a classic portrayal of Crabb, as fact and myth are jumbled and reshaped.

 *Violence, alcohol use and sex. Old West gunslinging and Indian battles.*

1970 135m/C Dustin Hoffman, Faye Dunaway, Chief Dan George, Richard Mulligan, Martin Balsam, Jeff Corey, Aimee Eccles; **D:** Arthur Penn; **W:** Calder Willingham. **VHS, Beta, LV** *FOX, HMV*

Little Buddha 🦴🦴

PG/Jr. High-Adult Tibetan Lama Norbu informs the Seattle Konrad family that their 10-year-old son Jesse may be the reincarnation of a respected monk. He wants to take the boy back to Tibet to find out and, with some apparently minor doubts, the family head off on their spiritual quest. In an effort to instruct Jesse in Buddhism, this journey is interspersed with the story of Prince Siddhartha, who will leave behind his worldly ways to follow the path towards enlightenment and become the Buddha. The two stories are an ill-fit, the acting awkward (with the exception of Ruocheng as the wise Norbu), but boy, does the film look good (from cinematographer Vittorio Storaro). Filmed on location in Nepal and Bhutan.

 *Salty language.*

1993 123m/C Keanu Reeves, Alex Wiesendanger, Ying Ruocheng, Chris Isaak, Bridget Fonda; **D:** Bernardo Bertolucci; **W:** Mark Peploe, Rudy Wurlitzer; **M:** Ryuichi Sakamoto. **VHS** *NYR*

Little Critter Series: Just Me and My Dad

Preschool-Primary Little Critter and his ever-patient father go on a camping trip, where dad rescues his son and teaches him the lessons of life. Based on the 1977 book by Mercer Mayer.

1993 25m/C VHS

The Little Crooked Christmas Tree

Family At a Christmas tree farm, one spruce grows crooked from bending branches to protect a mother dove and her babies. When the other trees are cut down at Christmastime, the little crooked tree is left behind, and the tree farmer has a special plan in mind. Holiday cartoon.

1993 30m/C *D:* Michael Cutting; *W:* Michael Cutting. **VHS** *BAR*

Little Darlings WOOF!

R/Sr. High-Adult A truly revolting film, with young stars but a plot completely inappropriate for youngsters. Summer campers Kristy McNichol and Tatum O'Neal see who'll be the first to lose her virginity. Does for the summer camp business what "Jaws" did for seaside resorts. Ages 15 and up.

> **BEWARE** *The whole movie is one long sexual situation. Profanity.*

1980 95m/C Tatum O'Neal, Kristy McNichol, Matt Dillon, Armand Assante, Margaret Blye; *D:* Ronald F. Maxwell; *M:* Charles Fox. **VHS, Beta, LV** *PAR*

Little Dog Lost

Preschool-Primary Abused dog Candy searches for and finally finds a kind master in this live-action adaptation of the book by Meindert de Jong. From TV's "Wonderful World of Disney" show.

1990 48m/C VHS, Beta *MTI, DSN*

Little Dorrit, Film 1: Nobody's Fault 🎜🎜🎜

Jr. High-Adult The mammoth version of the Dickens tome, about a father and daughter trapped interminably in the dreaded Marshalsea debtors' prison, and the good samaritan who works to free them. Told in two parts (on four tapes). Well-acted but dreadfully slow. Ages 12 and up.

1988 369m/C Alec Guinness, Derek Jacobi, Cyril Cusack, Sarah Pickering, Joan Greenwood, Max Wall, Amelda Brown, Daniel Chatto, Miriam Margolyes, Bill Fraser, Roshan Seth, Michael Elphick, Eleanor Bron, Patricia Hayes, Robert Morley, Sophie Ward; *D:* Christine Edzard; *W:* Christine Edzard; *M:* Giuseppe Verdi. **Award Nominations:** Academy Awards '88: Best Adapted Screenplay, Best Supporting Actor (Guinness); **Awards:** Los Angeles Film Critics Association Awards '88: Best Film, Best Supporting Actor (Guinness). **VHS, Beta, LV** *WAR, SIG, TVC*

Little Dorrit, Film 2: Little Dorrit's Story 🎜🎜🎜

Family The second half of the monumental adaptation of Dicken's most popular novel during his lifetime tells of Amy Dorrit's rise from debtor's prison to happiness. Well-acted but even slower than the first because it repeats much of it. Ages 12 and up.

1988 369m/C Alec Guinness, Derek Jacobi, Cyril Cusack, Sarah Pickering, Joan Greenwood, Max Wall, Amelda Brown, Daniel Chatto, Miriam Margolyes, Bill Fraser, Roshan Seth, Michael Elphick, Patricia Hayes, Robert Morley, Sophie Ward, Eleanor Bron; *D:* Christine Edzard; *W:* Christine Edzard; *M:* Giuseppe Verdi. **VHS, Beta, LV** *WAR, SIG, TVC*

The Little Drummer Boy

Family The classic Rankin-Bass rendering of the tale of the drummer who played for the Christ Child in the manger, one of their most successful stop-motion animated TV specials. Background vocals by the Vienna Boys Choir.

1968 30m/C *D:* Takeya Nakamura; *V:* Teddy Eccles, Jose Ferrer, Paul Frees. **VHS, Beta** *FHE*

The Little Engine That Could

Preschool-Primary Classic children's tale by Watty Piper comes to vivid animated life. The tiny engine comes upon the stranded Birthday Train and with a cheerful "I think I can . . . " refrain manages to haul the trainload of toys over a steep mountain pass.

1991 30m/C *D:* Dave Edwards. **VHS, LV** *MCA*

The Little Fox 🎜🎜

Preschool-Primary Cartoon feature from Europe following the adventures of an orphaned young fox named Vic, growing up in a forest.

1987 80m/C VHS, Beta *CEL*

Little Giants 🎜🎜🎜

PG/Primary-Adult Familiar kids/sport movie about the klutzy coach (Moranis) of an equally woeful pee-wee football team. Coach Danny is up against his overbearing big brother Kevin (O'Neill), former local football hero and the coach of the best team in town. You've seen it all before.

> **BEWARE** *Kids' rude language, gross pranks, and a kid blows snot bubbles.*

1994 106m/C Rick Moranis, Ed O'Neill, Shawna Waldron, Mary Ellen Trainor, Devon Sawa, Susanna Thompson, John Madden; *D:* Duwayne Dunham; *W:* Tommy Swerdlow, Michael Goldberg, James Ferguson, Robert Shallcross; *C:* Janusz Kaminski; *M:* John Debney. **VHS, LV** *WAR*

The Little Girl Who Lives Down the Lane 🎜🎜🎜

PG/Sr. High-Adult Engrossing, offbeat thriller about a strangely mature 13-year-old who apparently lives all by herself—her father never seems to be home, and she's

Meet the Star of *Little Giants*, Rick Moranis

Rick Moranis got his start in show business playing one of the beery, mock-Canadian McKenzie brothers on SCTV, the irreverent, innovative television series put together in the 1980s by members of the Toronto branch of the Second City comedy ensemble. Moranis, a short, sweet-faced fellow with glasses, did a fine send-up of Woody Allen in SCTV, and when the show went off the air, he got a successful movie career off the ground by continuing to play nebbishes.

Appearances in movies like *Ghostbusters, Little Shop of Horrors, and Spaceballs,* were followed by roles in some of the top grossing films of 1989, *Ghostbusters II, Parenthood* and the special effects showcase, *Honey, I Shrunk the Kids.* All of these film roles garnered Moranis an ardent following among children, who seemed especially to delight in the miniaturized children's encounters with insects in *Honey, I Shrunk the Kids.*

Moranis, who has two small children of his own, is pleased with this turn of events. *Honey, I Shrunk the Kids,* made with the Disney Studios is, Moranis says, like much of the solid, popular family fare Disney produced in the late 1950s. Moranis' experiences with the studio were good ones, and he says now that he would like to do a musical with Disney.

hiding something (guess what) in the basement. Foster is excellent, not playing a psycho but a sympathetic, self-possessed youngster who'll do anything, including murder, to maintain her independence in a world hostile to kids. Based on the novel by Laird Koenig.

BEWARE *Absent parent.*

1976 90m/C Jodie Foster, Martin Sheen, Alexis Smith, Scott Jacoby; **D:** Nicolas Gessner. **VHS, Beta, LV** *LIV, VES*

Little Heroes

G/Family Impoverished little girl gets through hard times with the aid of her loyal dog and eventually his memory helps her cope with tragedy. Low-budget family tearjerker that nonetheless works, it claims to be based on a true story.

1991 78m/C Raeanin Simpson, Katherine Willis, Keith Christensen; **D:** Craig Clyde; **W:** Craig Clyde; **M:** John McCallum. **VHS** *HMD*

Little Hiawatha

Preschool-Primary Playing fair is the name of the game as children win support and true friendship in this vintage Disney "Silly Symphony."

1937 8m/C VHS, Beta *DSN, MTI*

The Little House

Preschool-Primary The story of a house whose peace and quiet comes to an end when the city moves into its neighborhood. Disney adaptation of Virginia Lee Burton's book.

1988 8m/C VHS, Beta *DSN,, MTI*

Little House on the Prairie

Family Pilot for the fine network television series based on the life and books of Laura Ingalls Wilder and her family's struggles on the American plains in the 1860s. Other episodes are also available on tape, including Patricia Neal's Emmy-winning guest role as a dying widow seeking a home for her children. Rosy and warm, rendered with care by series creator Michael Landon.

1974 98m/C Michael Landon, Karen Grassle, Victor French, Melissa Gilbert, Melissa Sue Anderson; **D:** Michael Landon. **VHS, Beta** *WAR, OM*

Little Indian, Big City

PG/Primary-Adult French blockbuster dubbed over with "Americanized" English. Lhermitte travels to the Amazon to finalize the divorce of a long-dead marriage, only to find he has a 12-year-old son, Mimi-Siku (Briand). Father and son bond and Dad decides to bring the jungle-bred boy to his home in Paris. Dubbing process tomahawks this charming story as loin cloth meets Eiffel Tower, but Lhermitte, Briand and Miou-Miou (as estranged wife Patricia) shine through. Subplot of Russian mobsters who cut off the fingers of their victims gives an indication of the French definition of "family fare."

BEWARE *Crude language, adolescent sensuality and scenes of mild violence.*

1995 90m/C Thierry Lhermitte, Miou-Miou, Patrick Timsit, Arielle Dombasle, Ludwig Briand; **D:** Herve Palud; **W:** Thierry Lhermitte,

Herve Palud, Philippe Bruneau, Igor Aptekman; **C:** Pierre Lorraine; **M:** Manu Katche. **VHS** *NYR*

Little Lord Fauntleroy

Family The vintage Hollywood version of the Frances Hodgson Burnett story of fatherless Brooklyn boy Cedric Errol, who discovers he's the heir to a English dukedom and must win the affections of his nobleman grandfather. Charming and beautifully cast. Also available in a computer colorized edition. C. Aubrey Smith, the boy's crusty old guardian, was a grand British character actor who may be familiar to American audiences as a visual inspiration for the pipe-smoking, tale-telling Commander Mc-Bragg from the vintage "Tennessee Tuxedo" cartoon series.
1936 102m/B Freddie Bartholomew, Sir C. Aubrey Smith, Mickey Rooney, Dolores Costello, Jessie Ralph, Guy Kibbee; **D:** John Cromwell; **M:** Max Steiner. **VHS, Beta** *NOS, MRV, VEC*

Little Lord Fauntleroy

Family Poor boy in New York suddenly finds himself the heir to his grandfather's estate in England. Lavish remake of the 1936 classic, adapted from Frances Hodgson Burnett's novel. Guinness is his usual old-pro self; newcomer Schroder an appealing counterpoint as the Little Lord. Made for TV.
1980 98m/C Rick Schroder, Alec Guinness, Victoria Tennant, Eric Porter, Colin Blakely, Connie Booth, Rachel Kempson; **D:** Jack Gold. **VHS, Beta** *FHE*

Little Man Tate

PG/Jr. High-Adult Seven-year-old Fred Tate has a genius IQ and a close rapport with his streetwise, single parent Dede. But he's lonely and bored in school, so Dede reluctantly surrenders him to a (childless) woman academic specializing in gifted children. Enrolled in college and torn between competing mothers, the boy feels more of a misfit than ever. Compelling all-ages drama, thoughtful but never dry or dull; main complaint is it finishes with more than a few loose ends. Interesting to note Foster (making her directing debut) and musician/supporting actor Harry Connick, Jr. were both child prodigies themselves.

⚠ **BEWARE** *Fred catches a college-age pal in bed with a co-ed, and there's realistically salty language, alcohol talk.*
1991 99m/C Jodie Foster, Dianne Wiest, Harry Connick Jr., Adam Hann-Byrd, George Plimpton, Debi Mazar, Celia Weston, David Pierce, Danitra Vance, Josh Mostel, P.J. Ochlan; **D:** Jodie Foster; **W:** Scott Frank; **M:** Mark Isham. **VHS** *ORI, CCB*

The Little Match Girl

Family Adults more than small children should watch—and watch out for—this British TV redo of Hans Christian Andersen. Set in Victorian London, musical captures a "Les Miserables" sense of heroic melancholy with the story of a nameless urchin peddling matches in the icy streets on Christmas Eve. Unlike Andersen's sad waif, this match girl has a relatively stable home life, a rich

playmate and a gainfully employed boyfriend. But yearnings for her deceased mother drive her to the fate recounted in the original unhappy tale. Finale is rendered in theatrical, highly fantasized terms, and kid viewers may or may not sense the intimations of suicide. Recommended for grownup Andrew Lloyd-Webber fans; songs here derive from a Jeremy Paul/Leslie Stewart stage production "Scraps."

⚠ **BEWARE** *Alcohol use, mature themes, salty language.*
1987 90m/C John Rhys-Davies, Rue McClanahan, Roger Daltrey, Twiggy, Natalie Morse; **D:** Michael Lindsay-Hogg. **VHS, Beta** *ACA*

The Little Match Girl

Family Hans Christian Andersen goes politically correct in this jazzy cartoon adaptation, set in poverty-wracked NYC in 1899. Angela is a freezing street urchin peddling matches to rich snobs on New Year's Eve, and her bittersweet tale (still cheerier than the original) is heavy on help-the-homeless themes.
1990 30m/C VHS, Beta *FHE*

Little Men

Family Movie version of Louisa May Alcott's own sequel to her oft-filmed "Little Women" is a tepid tale that finds the grownup Jo March running an orphanage for boys.
1940 86m/B Jack Oakie, Jimmy Lydon, Kay Francis, George Bancroft; **D:** Norman Z. McLeod. **VHS, Beta** *NOS, MRV, VCN*

The Little Mermaid

G/Primary Animated version of Hans Christian Andersen's tale about a little mermaid who rescues a prince whose boat has capsized. She immediately falls in love and wishes that she could become a human girl. Not to be confused with the 1989 Disney version.
1978 71m/C D: Tim Reid. **VHS, Beta** *VTR, GEM*

The Little Mermaid

Family In this "Faerie Tale Theatre" production, Pam Dawber plays the mermaid who makes a big sacrifice to win the prince (Treat Williams) she loves. Ages 8 to 12.
1984 60m/C Karen Black, Brian Dennehy, Helen Mirren, Pam Dawber, Treat Williams; **D:** Robert Iscove. **VHS, Beta** *FOX, FCT*

The Little Mermaid

G/Family Teenage mermaid Ariel falls in love with a human prince and longs to be a land-dweller too. She makes a pact with Ursula the Sea Witch to trade her voice for a pair of legs. Charming family musical, which harks back to the days of classic Disney animation, and hailed a new era of superb Disney animated musicals. Sebastian the calypso crab nearly steals the show with his wit and musical numbers "Under the Sea" and "Kiss the Girl." Based on the Hans Christian Anderson fairy tale—but severely altering his original bittersweet ending.
♫ Under the Sea; Kiss the Girl; Daughters of Triton;

Ludwig Briand high above Paris in "Little Indian, Big City."

Part of Your World; Poor Unfortunate Souls; Les Poissons.

BEWARE! *Octopus-like Sea Witch may frighten small children.*

1989 82m/C D: John Musker, Ron Clements; **M:** Alan Menken, Howard Ashman; **V:** Jodi Benson, Christopher Daniel Barnes, Pat Carroll, Rene Auberjonois, Samuel E. Wright, Buddy Hackett, Jason Marin, Edie McClurg, Kenneth Mars, Nancy Cartwright. **Award Nominations:** Academy Awards '89: Best Song ("Kiss the Girl"); **Awards:** Academy Awards '89: Best Song ("Under the Sea"), Best Original Score; Golden Globe Awards '90: Best Song ("Under the Sea"), Best Score. **VHS, Beta, LV, 8mm** *DIS, OM*

Little Miss Broadway ♫♫

Family Orphan Temple brings the residents of a theatrical boarding house together in hopes of getting them into show business. Awfully cliched, but worth seeing just for Shirley and Jimmy combining talents. Also available in computer colorized version. ♫ Be Optimistic; How Can I Thank You; I'll Build a Broadway For You; If All the World Were Paper; Thank You For the Use of the Hall; We Should Be Together; Swing Me an Old-Fashioned Song; When You Were Sweet Sixteen; Happy Birthday to You.

1938 70m/B Shirley Temple, George Murphy, Jimmy Durante, Phyllis Brooks, Edna May Oliver, George Barbier, Donald Meek, Jane Darwell; **D:** Irving Cummings. **VHS, Beta** *FOX*

Little Miss Marker ♫♫♫

Family Heartwarming semi-musical based on the oft-filmed Damon Runyon tale. Little girl left with lowlifes as an IOU for a gambling debt charms her way into everyone's heart (always the hazard around Shirley), especially when her father's death makes her an orphan (always the hazard around Shirley). Great supporting cast.

1934 88m/B Adolphe Menjou, Shirley Temple, Dorothy Dell, Charles Bickford, Lynne Overman; **D:** Alexander Hall. **VHS** *MCA*

Little Miss Marker ♫ ♭

PG/Primary-Adult Star-studded cast can't do much with this mediocre remake of Damon Runyan's story of a bookie who accepts a little girl as an IOU for a $10 bet. Young Sara Stimson is no Shirley Temple, and the romantic combo of Walter Matthau and Julie Andrews never clicks. Talk about the odd couple. Ages 7 to 11.

BEWARE! *Profanity and gambling. You may need to explain what a marker is.*

1980 103m/C Walter Matthau, Julie Andrews, Tony Curtis, Bob Newhart, Lee Grant, Sara Stimson, Brian Dennehy; **D:** Walter Bernstein; **M:** Henry Mancini. **VHS, Beta** *MCA*

Little Miss Millions

PG/Jr. High-Adult Twelve-year-old heiress Heather has run away from the wicked stepmom who's siphoning off her fortune. Her family hires bounty hunter Nick Frost to bring her back. How much do you want to bet that cold-hearted Nick will warm to Heather before the movie's end? (Hint: plot takes place around Christmas.) Slow, sentimental timekiller with a good cast.

 Roughhousing, alcohol use.

1993 90m/C Howard Hesseman, Anita Morris, Love Hewitt; **D:** Roger Corman. **VHS** *NHO*

Little Monsters

PG/Jr. High-Sr. High Young Brian discovers that kid brother Eric's complaints are true: there really is a monster—named Maurice—under his bed. The blue-faced, horned prankster takes Brian on tours of the wild world beneath the bed in a plotline mildly reminiscent of Dr. Seuss but less successful, especially when it turns serious. But juvenile monster fest has its moments. Mandel plays Maurice; he and his creepy cohorts bear a more-than-coincident resemblance to the spooks in "Beetlejuice." Savage and Stern both served subsequent time on TV's "The Wonder Years" (Stern was the narrative voice).

 Profanity and monsters under the bed. May scare those who fear monsters under their own bed. Maurice is rather strange to look at.

1989 100m/C Fred Savage, Howie Mandel, Margaret Whitton, Ben Savage, Daniel Stern, Rick Ducommun, Frank Whaley; **D:** Richard Alan Greenberg; **W:** Ted Elliot, Terry Rossio; **M:** David Newman. **VHS, Beta, LV** *MGM*

Little Nemo: Adventures in Slumberland

G/Family Animators had planned for years to bring Winsor McKay's surreal turn-of-the-century comic strip to life, but this bland Japanese cartoon barely hints at the fun a truly inspired production might have been. Nemo is a young boy whose dreams take him to Slumberland. There, Nemo unwittingly unleashes a nightmare creature who kidnaps good King Morpheus. Nemo leads the rescue mission, but dull songs and tired gags don't save the film. Visually accomplished, but that's it.

1992 85m/C D: William T. Hurtz, Masami Hata; **W:** Chris Columbus, Richard Outten; **M:** Tom Chase, Steve Rucker; **V:** Gabriel Damon, Mickey Rooney, Rene Auberjonois, Daniel Mann, Laura Mooney, Bernard Erhard, William E. Martin. **VHS, LV** *HMD*

Little Nikita

PG/Jr. High-Adult California boy is shocked to learn that his parents are actually Soviet spies, planted long ago as American citizens to wait for an eventual call to duty. Now the FBI is closing in. What should the kid do? Poitier provides about the only spark in this somewhat incoherent thriller.

 Profanity, violence and parents with a dark secret.

1988 98m/C River Phoenix, Sidney Poitier, Richard Bradford, Richard Lynch, Caroline Kava, Lucy Deakins; **D:** Richard Benjamin; **W:** Bo Goldman; **M:** Marvin Hamlisch. **VHS, Beta, LV** *COL*

Little Orphan Annie

Family Long before she became a Broadway musical extravaganza, Annie went from Harold Gray's newspaper comic-strip to the silver screen with this unpretentious short feature, still worth a look for the curious.

1932 60m/B May Robson, Buster Phelps, Mitzie Green, Edgar Kennedy; **D:** John S. Robertson; **M:** Max Steiner. **VHS, Beta** *CCB*

The Little Prince

G/Family Antoine de Saint-Exupery's little book is a children's story that only adults love. This musical adaptation does nothing to change the situation. An aviator (Richard Kiley) stranded in the desert encounters a thoughtful little boy from asteroid B-612 longing away for his distant love, a rose. Interesting efforts by Gene Wilder (as a fox) and Bob Fosse (miming a snake). The forgettable score—by Lerner and Loewe, of all people—stands as a metaphor for the whole project. Ages 8 and up. ♫ It's a Hat; I Need Air; I'm On Your Side; Be Happy; You're a Child; I Never Met a Rose; Why Is the Desert (Lovely to See)?; Closer and Closer and Closer; Little Prince (From Who Knows Where).

1974 88m/C Richard Kiley, Bob Fosse, Steven Warner, Gene Wilder; **D:** Stanley Donen; **W:** Alan Jay Lerner; **M:** Frederick Loewe, Alan Jay Lerner. **Award Nominations:** Academy Awards '74: Best Song ("Little Prince"), Best Original Score; **Awards:** Golden Globe Awards '75: Best Score. **VHS, Beta, LV** *PAR*

The Little Prince & Friends

Family Will Vinton's wonderful Claymation tells Antoine de St. Exupery's story of the pilot who crashes in the desert, and the young prince from another planet who befriends him. Ages 5 to 9. Also includes Washington Irving's "Rip Van Winkle" and Leo Tolstoy's "Martin the Cobbler."

1987 90m/C VHS, Beta, LV *IME*

The Little Prince, Vols. 1-5

Primary-Jr. High Each program in this series adapts Antoine de Saint Exupery's beloved, thoughtful little character into different adventures designed to teach basic lessons and morals. Additional volumes available.

1985 60m/C VHS, Beta *LIV*

The Little Princess

Family Perhaps the best of Shirley's films and her first in color. The moppet's a schoolgirl in Victorian London sent to a harsh boarding school when her Army officer father is posted abroad. With dad missing in action, the penniless girl must work as a mistreated servant at the institution to pay her keep, all the while haunting the hospitals for her lost papa. Classic tearjerker, even with the obligatory song and dance numbers. Based on the Frances Hodgson Burnett children's classic.

BEWARE *A badly treated child.*

1939 91m/B Shirley Temple, Richard Greene, Anita Louise, Ian Hunter, Cesar Romero, Arthur Treacher, Sybil Jason, Miles Mander, Marcia Mae Jones, E.E. Clive; **D:** Walter Lang. **VHS, Beta, LV** *CNG, MRV, NOS*

The Little Princess 🎵🎵🎵

Family Multi-cassette adaptation of Frances Hodgson Burnett's book. In Victorian England, kind-hearted Sara is a star pupil (and thus much-resented) at Miss Minchin's Select Seminary for Young Ladies. She's forced into poverty when her father suddenly dies. Can his longtime friend find her and restore her happiness? British production originally aired in the US on PBS as part of the "Wonderworks" family movie series.

1987 180m/C Amelia Shankley, Nigel Havers, Maureen Lipman; **D:** Carol Wiseman. **VHS** *FCT, PME, SIG*

A Little Princess 🎵🎵🎵 ♭

G/Family Compelling fantasy, based on the children's book by Frances Hodgson Burnett, and previously best known for the 1939 Shirley Temple incarnation. Sara (Matthews), a young English girl raised in India, is deposited at a stuffy boarding school when her father goes off to fight World War I. Wealthy but fair—she dares to befriend a servant girl—Sara is also a captivating storyteller. The frosty headmistress, Miss Michin (Bron), will have none of that, especially after Sara's father is reported killed and her tuition payments stop. Miss Michin makes Sara a servant to pay her way, but Sara friends stick with her. Lively script and a welcome lack of sappiness create a winner. Bron was in the Beatles' movie "Help!"

1995 97m/C Liesl Matthews, Eleanor Bron, Liam Cunningham, Rusty Schwimmer, Arthur Malet, Vanessa Lee Chester, Errol Sitahal, Heather DeLoach, Taylor Fry; **D:** Alfonso Cuaron; **W:** Richard LaGravenese, Elizabeth Chandler; **C:** Emmanuel Lubezki; **M:** Patrick Doyle. **VHS, LV** *WAR*

The Little Rascals 🎵🎵 ♭

PG/Family Alfalfa runs afoul of the Rascals' "He-Man Woman Haters Club" when he starts to fall for Darla just at the time his mind should be on the upcoming go-kart race and the gang's entry, The Blur. Given the recent spate of disappointing films based on older movies and TV shows, this is surprisingly cute. Ages 4 to 9.

BEWARE *Bodily function jokes.*

1994 80m/C Daryl Hannah, Courtland Mead, Travis Tedford, Brittany Ashton Holmes, Bug Hall, Zachary Mabry, Kevin Jamal Woods, Ross Bagley, Sam Saletta, Blake Collins, Jordan Warkol, Blake Ewing, Juliette Brewer, Heather Karasek; *Cameos:* Whoopi Goldberg; **D:** Penelope Spheeris; **W:** Penelope Spheeris, Paul Guay, Steve Mazur; **M:** David Foster, Linda Thompson. **VHS** *NYR*

Little Rascals Christmas Special

Family Spanky and the "Our Gang" kids try to raise money to buy a winter coat for Spanky's mom and learn the true meaning of Christmas along the way. One-shot attempt to remake the vintage Little Rascals children in cartoon form (unrelated to a later Hanna-Barbera "Little Rascals" on Saturday-morning TV), even features two of the original performers, Darla and Stymie, lending their voiceovers to adult characters. Included on the cassette are also some brief 1930s Yuletide cartoons: "Jack Frost," "Rudolph the Red-Nosed Reindeer," "Christmas Comes But Once a Year," and "Somewhere in Dreamland."

1979 60m/C Darla Hood, Matthew "Stymie" Beard; **D:** Fred Wolf, Charles Swenson. **VHS, Beta** *FHE*

Little Red Riding Hood

Family From "Faerie Tale Theatre" comes the retelling of the story about a girl (Mary Steenburgen) off to give her grandmother a picnic basket, only to get stopped by wicked wolf Malcolm McDowell, Steenburgen's husband at the time. Not particularly faithful, but fun and scary. Ages 6 to 10.

1983 60m/C Mary Steenburgen, Malcolm McDowell; **D:** Graeme Clifford. **VHS, Beta, LV** *FOX, FCT*

A Little Romance 🎵🎵🎵

PG/Jr. High-Adult American girl living in Paris falls in love with a French boy; eventually they run away, to seal their love with a kiss beneath a bridge. Olivier gives a wonderful, if hammy, performance as the old pickpocket who encourages her. Gentle, agile comedy based on the novel by Patrick Cauvin.

BEWARE *Salty language.*

1979 110m/C Laurence Olivier, Diane Lane, Thelonious Bernard, Sally Kellerman, Broderick Crawford; **D:** George Roy Hill; **M:** Georges Delerue. **Award Nominations:** Academy Awards '79: Best Adapted Screenplay; **Awards:** Academy Awards '79: Best Original Score. **VHS, Beta, LV** *WAR, INJ*

Little Shop of Horrors 🎵🎵🎵

PG-13/Jr. High-Adult Screen version of the hit stage musical (based on a 1960 horror cheapie of the same title). Nerd florist Seymour finds a mystery plant that talks, sings like one of the Four Tops—and thrives on drops of human blood. As it gets bigger (and it does get bigger), the persuasive plant increasingly demands "Feed me!" so poor Seymour must turn to murder to appease his carnivorous green friend. Lively, darkly humorous, and not unduly gory. Trouble is, the storyline gets awfully thin for the big-budget Hollywood treatment. Kids will adore the voracious vegetable, brought to writhing, roaring life by the Jim Henson creature factory. In fact, a short-lived TV cartoon grew out of this. Songs by Alan Menken and Howard Ashman, who also collaborated on Disney classics like "Beauty and the Beast" and

"The Little Mermaid." ♫ Mean Green Mother From Outer Space; Some Fun Now; Your Day Begins Tonight.

🪧 BEWARE *Violence, serious gore only hinted. The stage production's original grim climax has been altered (rather awkwardly) into a cheery, upbeat finale.*

1986 94m/C Rick Moranis, Ellen Greene, Vincent Gardenia, Steve Martin, James Belushi, Christopher Guest, Bill Murray, John Candy; **D:** Frank Oz; **M:** Miles Goodman, Howard Ashman. **VHS, Beta, LV** *WAR, HMV, MVD*

Little Sister 🦴 ᵇ

PG-13/Jr. High-Adult Prankster Silverman, on a dare, dresses up as a girl and joins a sorority. Problems arise when he falls in love with his "big sister" (Milano) in the sorority. What will happen when she finds out the truth? Will we care?

🪧 BEWARE *Brief nudity and sexual situations.*

1992 94m/C Jonathan Silverman, Alyssa Milano. **VHS** *LIV*

Little Sister Rabbit

Primary Animated tale of Big Brother Rabbit left to babysit his little sister, demonstrating the responsibility of caring for a child. Adapted from the children's book by Ulf Nilsson and Eva Eriksson.

1992 23m/C VHS *LME*

The Little Thief 🦴🦴

PG-13/Sr. High-Adult Touted as Francois Truffaut's final legacy, this French drama is actually based on a story he co-wrote with Claude de Givray about a post-WWII adolescent girl who reacts to the world around her by stealing and getting involved in petty crime. The artistry of Truffaut's "The 400 Blows" and "Small Change" is markedly absent.

🪧 BEWARE *Mature themes, sex.*

1989 108m/C Charlotte Gainsbourg, Simon de la Brosse, Didier Bezace, Raoul Billerey, Nathalie Cardone; **D:** Claude Miller; **W:** Annie Miller, Claude Miller; **M:** Alain Jomy. **VHS, Beta, LV** *HBO, INJ*

Little Toot

Preschool-Primary Little Toot the tugboat welcomes Plato Pelican, Donna Dolphin, and temperamental waterspout, Typhoon Tina.

1992 52m/C VHS

Little Tough Guys 🦴🦴

Family The Little Tough Guys (AKA The Dead End Kids) come to the rescue of Halop, a young guy gone bad to avenge his father's unjust imprisonment. First of the series by the former Dead End Kids, who later become the East Side Kids before evolving into the Bowery Boys.

1938 84m/B Helen Parrish, Billy Halop, Leo Gorcey, Marjorie Main, Gabriel Dell, Huntz Hall; **D:** Harold Young. **VHS, Beta** *NOS, MRV, VYY*

The Little Troll Prince

Family Hanna-Barbera Christmas special produced in association with the Lutheran Laymen's League depicts Bu, prince of gnomes, saved from a dreary, backwards existence when he discovers God's love.

1990 46m/C V: Vincent Price, Jonathan Winters, Cloris Leachman, Don Knotts. **VHS, Beta** *TTC*

Little Wizards: The Singing Sword

Preschool-Primary First episode of in the Marvel network Saturday-morning cartoon fantasy: The Singing Sword could give Prince Dexter the magic he needs to reclaim his crown from the evil king.

1987 23m/C VHS

Little Women 🦴🦴🦴🦴

Family Louisa May Alcott's Civil War story of the four March sisters—Jo, Beth, Amy, and Meg—approaching womanhood who share their young loves, their joys, and their sorrows. Everything about this classic works, from the lavish period costumes to the excellent script, and particularly the captivating performances by the cast. A must-see for fans of Alcott and Hepburn, and others will find it enjoyable. Remade several times, but this version remains definitive.

1933 107m/B Katharine Hepburn, Joan Bennett, Paul Lukas, Edna May Oliver, Frances Dee, Spring Byington, Jean Parker, Douglass Montgomery; **D:** George Cukor; **W:** Andrew Solt, Sarah Y. Mason, Victor Heerman; **M:** Adolph Deutsch, Max Steiner. **Award Nominations:** Academy Awards '33: Best Director (Cukor), Best Picture; **Awards:** Academy Awards '33: Best Adapted Screenplay; Venice Film Festival '34: Best Actress (Hepburn). **VHS, Beta, 8mm** *MGM, KUI, IGP*

Little Women 🦴🦴🦴

Family Stylish, no-expense-spared color version of Louisa May Alcott's classic. Star power triumphs over genetics in casting the likes of Allyson, O'Brien, Taylor and Leigh as teenage sisters growing up against the backdrop of the Civil War.

1949 121m/C June Allyson, Peter Lawford, Margaret O'Brien, Elizabeth Taylor, Janet Leigh, Mary Astor; **D:** Mervyn LeRoy. **Award Nominations:** Academy Awards '49: Best Color Cinematography; **Awards:** Academy Awards '49: Best Art Direction/Set Decoration (Color). **VHS** *MGM*

Little Women 🦴🦴

Family Louisa May Alcott's classic tale of four loving sisters who face the joys and hardships of 19th-century America comes to life in this animated program hailing from Japan.

1983 60m/C VHS, Beta *LIV*

Little Women 🦴🦴🦴🦴

PG/Primary-Adult Authentic-looking and crafted with love and respect for the Louisa May Alcott book. The Marches are a close Civil-War era family in Massachu-

Shirley Temple in "The Little Princess."

setts. Marmee (Sarandon) and her daughters (Ryder, Alvarado, Danes, Dunst and Mathis) keep home fires burning while father is off fighting in the war. The delightful young women put on plays, make friends with a lonely young man, feed a starving family in town and generally grow up. Outstanding acting.

BEWARE *A beloved character dies. A beloved character falls through the ice. Depictions of poverty and illness. All this may upset young children, but shouldn't deter anyone over the age of 10.*

1994 118m/C Winona Ryder, Gabriel Byrne, Trini Alvarado, Samantha Mathis, Kirsten Dunst, Claire Danes, Christian Bale, Eric Stoltz, John Neville, Mary Wickes, Susan Sarandon; **D:** Gillian Armstrong; **W:** Robin Swicord; **C:** Geoffrey Simpson; **M:** Thomas Newman. **Award Nominations:** Academy Awards '94: Best Actress (Ryder), Best Costume Design, Best Original Score; **Awards:** Chicago Film Critics Awards '94: Most Promising Actress (Dunst). **VHS, LV, 8mm** *COL*

Little Women Series

Primary-Jr. High Seven episodes of an animated version of Louisa May Alcott's story about the four March sisters and their youth in Civil War New England.
1985 30m/C VHS, Beta, 8mm *KAR*

The Littlest Angel 🦴🦴

Family Well-cast but mediocre made-for-TV musical about a shepherd boy who dies falling off a cliff and wants to become an angel. He learns a valuable lesson in the spirit of giving.
1969 77m/C Johnny Whitaker, Fred Gwynne, E.G. Marshall, Cab Calloway, Connie Stevens, Tony Randall. **VHS, Beta** *CNG, KAR*

The Littlest Horse Thieves 🦴🦴🐾

G/Family Wholesome Disney film about three turn-of-the-century British children and their efforts to save 'pit ponies,' much-abused horses put to dangerous work in mines. Filmed on location in England, with the change of scenery doing well for the Magic Kingdom folks.
1976 109m/C Alastair Sim, Peter Barkworth; **D:** Charles Jarrott. **VHS, Beta** *DIS*

The Littlest Outlaw 🦴🦴🐾

Family Mexican peasant boy steals a beautiful stallion to save it from being destroyed. Together, they ride off on a series of adventures. Decent Disney effort filmed on location in Mexico.

Alfalfa sings his heart out in "The Little Rascals."

1954 73m/C Pedro Armendariz Sr., Joseph Calleia, Andres Velasquez; *D:* Roberto Gavaldon. **VHS, Beta** *DIS*

The Littlest Pet Shop

Primary-Primary Pets find their way out of their shop and engage in madcap adventure. Ages 5 to 10.

1996 ?m/C VHS *FHE, LIV*

The Littlest Rebel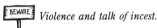

Family Shirley showcases this well-done piece set during the Civil War in the Old South. She befriends a Union officer while protecting her Confederate father at the same time. She even goes to Washington to plea with President Lincoln. Nice dance sequences by Temple and Robinson. Available in computer-colored version.

1935 70m/B Shirley Temple, John Boles, Jack Holt, Bill Robinson, Karen Morley, Willie Best; *D:* David Butler. **VHS, Beta** *FOX*

The Littlest Viking

PG/Primary-Adult Amidst sacred swords and fighting ships it's tough to be a pacifist in violent medieval Norway, but 12-year-old Prince Sigurd finds a way to prove his mettle, or at least his Norwegian wood. Scenic Scandinavian settings.

> **BEWARE** *Violence and talk of incest.*

1994 85m/C Kristian Tonby, Per Jansen, Terje Stromdahl; *D:* Knut W. Jorfald, Lars Rasmussen, Paul Trevor Bale. **VHS, LV** *HMD*

Littlest Warrior

Preschool-Primary Japanese cartoon feature in which Zooshio, the littlest warrior, is forced to leave his beloved forest and experiences many adventures before he is reunited with his family.

1975 70m/C VHS, Beta *FHE*

Live and Let Die

PG/Jr. High-Adult Roger Moore's debut as Agent 007, out to thwart the villainous Dr. Kananga, (Yaphet Kotto) a mastermind who plans to control the western powers with drugs. This Bond yields little interest. Moore makes you nostalgic for Sean Connery and title song by Paul McCartney makes you nostalgic for the Beatles. Ages 12 and up.

> **BEWARE** *Violence, alcohol use and suggested sex with Moore playing the secret agent.*

1973 131m/C Roger Moore, Jane Seymour, Yaphet Kotto, Clifton James, Julius W. Harris, Geoffrey Holder, David Hedison, Gloria Hendry, Bernard Lee, Lois Maxwell, Madeleine Smith, Roy Stewart; *D:* Guy Hamilton; *W:* Tom Mankiewicz; *M:* George Martin. **VHS, Beta, LV** *MGM, FOX, TLF*

The Living Desert

G/Family Life cycle of animals and plants in the American desert is shown through the seasons in this Disney documentary. The painstaking care that went into getting rare nature footage set a high mark that outdoor documentaries have tried to follow ever since.

1953 69m/C *D:* James Algar. **VHS, Beta** *DIS*

Living Free

G/Family Sequel to "Born Free," based on the nonfictional books by Joy Adamson. Recounts the travails of Elsa the lioness, who is now dying, with three young cubs that need care. Nice and pleasant, but could you pick up the pace?
1972 91m/C Susan Hampshire, Nigel Davenport; **D:** Jack Couffer. **VHS, Beta, LV** *COL, GKK*

Living God's Way

Primary Ralph Milton narrates six stories from his best-selling Bible storybook. Uses storytelling, animation, illustrations, puppetry, and drama. Stories include: God Makes a Promise (Noah's Ark); Miriam Saves her Brother (Miriam and Moses); The Loving Father (The Prodigal Son); Joseph's Coat of Many Colors; Two Brave Women (Naomi and Ruth); and David and Goliath. Ages 4 to 9.
1995 35m/C VHS *ECU*

Local Hero

PG/Jr. High-Adult Riegert is a yuppie representative of a huge oil company who endeavors to buy a sleepy Scottish fishing village for excavation, and finds himself hypnotized by the place and its crusty denizens. Back in Texas at company headquarters, tycoon Lancaster deals with a psycho therapist and gazes at the stars looking for clues. A low-key, charmingly offbeat Scottish comedy with its own sense of logic and quiet humor, poetic landscapes, and unique characters, epitomizing Forsyth's original style.

🚸 BEWARE 🚸 *Profanity.*

1983 112m/C Peter Riegert, Denis Lawson, Burt Lancaster, Fulton Mackay, Jenny Seagrove, Peter Capaldi, Norman Chancer; **D:** Bill Forsyth; **W:** Bill Forsyth; **M:** Mark Knopfler. **VHS, Beta, LV** *WAR*

Loch Ness

PG/Family Zoologist Danson actually finds Scottish legend Nessie but then must decide between fame, romance with innkeeper Richardson, and friendship with local Holm. Jim Henson's Creature Shop takes care of the monster's animatronics.

🚸 BEWARE 🚸 *Language, mild sensuality and a fist fight.*

1996 ?m/C Ted Danson, Ian Holm, Joely Richardson; **D:** John Henderson; **W:** John Fusco. **VHS** *NYR*

Locke the Superpower

Family Japanese-animated feature about male and female superheroes fighting an intergalactic war against each other.

🚸 BEWARE 🚸 *Violence.*

1986 92m/C VHS, Beta *JFK*

Lollipop Dragon: Magic Lollipop Adventure

Preschool-Primary Cartoon adventures of a kindly dragon opposing the evil Baron Bad Blood, who's dragon-napped three reptilian babies and taken them to Blood Castle.
1987 30m/C VHS, Beta *JFK*

Lollipop Dragon: The Great Christmas Race

Preschool-Primary Animated fantasy for the very young about a dragon and his buddies who battle Baron Bad Blood for the welfare of lollipopdom.
1985 25m/C VHS, Beta *JFK*

The Lone Ranger

Family Theatrical feature spun off into the TV series that made Moore the classic Kemosabe and Silverheels the definitive faithful Indian sidekick. And, of course, there's that "William Tell Overture." Still, it's pretty cliched stuff initially, as the Lone Ranger and Tonto try to prevent a war between ranchers and natives, with an outlaw gang behind all the trouble.

🚸 BEWARE 🚸 *Violence.*

1956 87m/C Clayton Moore, Jay Silverheels, Lyle Bettger, Bonita Granville; **D:** Stuart Heisler. **VHS, Beta** *MGM*

The Lone Ranger

Preschool-Jr. High Two volumes of three cartoons each depict the Saturday-morning TV adventures of the western hero. These episodes came from a "Tarzan/Lone Ranger Adventure Hour" 'toon show of the late '70s, rather than the "Lone Ranger" animated series of the 1960s.
1980 60m/C VHS, Beta *FHE*

The Lone Ranger: Code of the Pioneers

Family The Masked Man and Tonto hang around a town to make sure that local elections stay honest, in this B&W episode of the TV western series. Several other volumes of episodes are available; each tape in this series begins with a trivia quiz to test your knowledge of Lone Ranger-ology.
1955 55m/B Clayton Moore, Jay Silverheels. **VHS** *RHI*

Lone Star Kid

Family Eleven-year-old Brian realizes that his tiny community of Crabb, Texas, should incorporate as a town to survive. When no grownup is willing to push the idea, Brian runs for the (non-paying) job of mayor and learns a few important lessons. Slow-moving but pleasant "WonderWorks" drama based on a true story, done by "Happy Days" alumni Williams and exec producer Ron Howard.

Marmee and daughters read a letter in the Louisa May Alcott classic "Little Women."

Country-music star Daniels performs the soundtrack music and portrays Brian's loyal opposition.

1988 55m/C James Earl Jones, Chad Sheets; **M:** Charlie Daniels. **VHS** *PME, HMV, BTV*

The Lone Wolf

Family Boy learns kindness by befriending an old military dog which villagers think is mad and responsible for killing their sheep. After a brush with death, the boy convinces the villagers of the dog's good qualities.

1972 45m/C VHS, Beta

The Loneliest Runner ♫♫♫

Sr. High-Adult Writer/director Landon based this made-for-TV story on a wrenching true story—his own. Teenager with a miserable home life suffers humiliation as a bed-wetter. Nonetheless, he perseveres as an athlete, eventually becoming an Olympics track star. Touching and sensitive, and more effective than Landon's theatrical film "Sam's Son," with much the same story.

1976 74m/C Michael Landon, Lance Kerwin, DeAnn Mears, Brian Keith, Melissa Sue Anderson; **D:** Michael Landon. **VHS, Beta** *WAR, OM*

The Loneliness of the Long Distance Runner ♫♫♫

Jr. High-Adult Courtenay, in his film debut, turns in a powerful performance as an angry teenager, a hopeless product of the British slums. His first attempt at crime lands him in the reformatory, where the headmaster recruits him for the running team. The adult is obsessed with winning the big race, but the kid is indifferent, locking the two in a seemingly one-sided power struggle. One of the best teen-angst dramas of the '60s, a riveting depiction of one boy's difficult passage into manhood.

1962 104m/B Tom Courtenay, Michael Redgrave, Avis Bunnage, Peter Madden, James Bolam, Julia Foster, Topsy Jane, Frank Finlay; **D:** Tony Richardson; **M:** John Addison. **VHS, Beta** *WAR, SNC*

The Long Day Closes ♫♫♫

PG/Sr. High-Adult Not much plot, but a charming and lyrical memoir of England in the 1950s as seen from the viewpoint of 11-year-old Bud (standing in for writer-director Terence Davies). Bud enters a Liverpool parochial school (where all kids are beaten on the first day, as a warning of what will come if they really misbehave!), attends movies and church with equal devotion, and sadly leaves childhood behind. Nostalgic view of family life via sweet, small everyday moments in an impoverished postwar England made magical and musical in the dreamy youth's mind. Ages 11 and up.

BEWARE *Violence by adults against children.*

1992 84m/C Leigh McCormack, Marjorie Yates, Anthony Watson, Ayse Owens; **D:** Terence Davies; **W:** Terence Davies. **VHS** *COL*

Look What Happens . . . at the Carwash 🎵🎵🎵

Preschool-Primary Sort of a soap opera without the opera. Shows a red van driving on muddy roads and getting very dirty, then being washed in two ways: by hand and at an actual car wash. Teaches concepts like before and after, dirty and clean, and wash and dry. The van went through the car wash 16 times to make this video. There is natural sound, but no narration or dialogue. Ages 1 to 6.
1994 25m/C VHS

Look What I Found

Primary Children learn codes, how to identify and match fingerprints, and make a tin can telephone and a periscope from simple household materials. Amy Purcell does the teaching. Ages 6 to 12.
1993 45m/C VHS *PBS, BTV*

Look What I Grew: Windowsill Gardens

Primary A step-by-step demonstration of plant growing projects for kids, including learning to grow a sweet potato, avocado, and (mmm!) watercress. Amy Purcell does the teaching. Ages 6 to 12.
1992 45m/C VHS *BTV*

Look What I Made

Primary Amy Purcell, an elementary school teacher, demonstrates a number of crafts that children can learn to do on their own or with a little adult help, including paper hats, origami and pinatas. Ages 6 to 12.
1990 45m/C VHS, Beta *CRY, BTV*

Look Who's Talking 🎵🎵🎵

PG-13/Jr. High-Adult When a woman bears the child of a married man, she sets her sights elsewhere in search of the perfect stepfather; Travolta is the cabbie who tries to prove he's the best candidate. All the while, the baby gives us his views via the sarcastic voice of Willis. Disarming, often raunchy comedy that took a silly gimmick and made it thoroughly entertaining; two sequels and several TV imitations have failed to repeat the trick.

BEWARE *Bawdy stuff, including an early sex scene revealing the rock 'n' rolling action inside the woman's womb as the chatty tyke is conceived. Profanity.*

1989 90m/C John Travolta, Kirstie Alley, Olympia Dukakis, George Segal, Abe Vigoda; **D:** Amy Heckerling; **W:** Amy Heckerling; **M:** David Kitay; **V:** Bruce Willis. **VHS, Beta, LV** *COL, RDG*

Look Who's Talking Now 🎵🎵

PG-13/Jr. High-Adult Continuing to wring revenue from a tired premise, the family dogs throw in their two cents in the second sequel to "Look Who's Talking." Sparks, Alpo, and butt jokes fly as the dogs mark their territory. Meanwhile, dimwit wife Alley is worried that husband Travolta is having an affair, and is determined to get him back.

BEWARE *Sex talk, profanity.*

1993 95m/C John Travolta, Kirstie Alley, Olympia Dukakis, George Segal, Lysette Anthony; **D:** Tom Ropelewski; **W:** Tom Ropelewski, Leslie Dixon; **M:** William Ross; **V:** Diane Keaton, Danny DeVito. **VHS, LV, 8mm** *COL*

Look Who's Talking, Too 🎵

PG-13/Jr. High-Adult If Academy Awards for Stupidest Sequel and Lamest Dialogue existed, this diaper drama would have cleaned up. Second infant talkfest throws the now married accountant-cabbie duo into a marital tailspin and husband Travolta moves out. Meanwhile, the baby, still voiced by Willis, smartmouths incessantly. A once-clever gimmick now unencumbered by plot; not advised for linear thinkers. The voice of Arnold, though, is a guarantee you'll get one laugh for your rental.

BEWARE *Profanity galore and sex. Talking spermatozoa and general sleaziness.*

1990 81m/C Kirstie Alley, John Travolta, Olympia Dukakis, Elias Koteas; **D:** Amy Heckerling; **V:** Bruce Willis, Mel Brooks, Damon Wayans, Roseanne. **VHS, LV, 8mm** *COL*

Looking for Miracles 🎵🎵🎵

G/Family Sixteen-year-old Ryan lands a precious job at a summer camp during the Depression, but mom won't allow him to go unless he brings his kid brother along. In spite of themselves, the pair learn to get along. Fine Canadian TV production (released in the US through the PBS Wonderworks series) from the reliable "Anne of Green Gables" gang, based on the second volume of A.E. Hochner's fictionalized memoirs. The first book, "King of the Hill," was made into a splendid theatrical feature in 1993; these two are worth comparing.
1990 104m/C Zachary Bennett, Greg Spottiswood, Joe Flaherty. **VHS, LV** *TOU, DIS, FCT*

Looney Looney Looney Bugs Bunny Movie 🎵🎵🎵

G/Family Followup to "The Bugs Bunny/Road Runner Movie" does a more imaginative job of tying together a feature-length compilation of classic Warner Brothers cartoons. Watch for favorites Bugs Bunny, Elmer Fudd, Porky Pig, Yosemite Sam, Daffy Duck and Foghorn Leghorn.

1981 80m/C D: Isadore "Friz" Freleng, Chuck Jones, Bob Clampett; **V:** Mel Blanc, June Foray. **VHS, Beta** *WAR, FCT*

Looney Tunes Video Show, Vol. 1

Family Seven Warner Brothers cartoon classics of the 1940s and 50s: Bugs Bunny and the Tasmanian Devil in "Devil May Hare," Sylvester in "Birds of a Father," Daffy Duck and Porky Pig in "The Ducksters," the Road Runner and Wile E. Coyote in "Zipping Along," Sylvester and Tweety in "Room and Bird," Elmer Fudd in "Ant Pasted," and Speedy Gonzales in "Mexican Schmoes." All ages.
19?? 49m/C D: Chuck Jones, Bob Clampett, Isadore "Friz" Freleng. **VHS, Beta** *WAR*

Looney Tunes Video Show, Vol. 2

Family More Warner Brothers cartoon favorites: Daffy Duck in "Quackodile Tears," Porky Pig in "An Egg Scramble," Sylvester and Speedy Gonzales in "Cats and Bruises," Foghorn Leghorn in "All Fowled Up," Bugs Bunny and Yosemite Sam in "14 Carrot Rabbit," Professor Calvin Q. Calculus in "The Hole Idea," and Pepe Le Pew in "Two Scents Worth." All ages.
19?? 48m/C D: Chuck Jones, Isadore "Friz" Freleng, Bob Clampett. **VHS, Beta** *WAR*

Looney Tunes Video Show, Vol. 3

Family The Warner Brothers B-team join the regulars in seven cartoon shorts: Daffy Duck and Speedy Gonzales in "The Quacker Tracker," the Wolf and Sheepdog in "Double or Mutton," Claude Cat and Bulldog in "Feline Frameup," Bugs Bunny in "Eight Ball Bunny," Foghorn Leghorn in "A Featured Leghorn," Porky Pig and Sylvester in "Scaredy Cat" and Pepe Le Pew in "Louvre, Come Back to Me." All ages.
19?? 48m/C D: Chuck Jones, Bob Clampett, Isadore "Friz" Freleng. **VHS, Beta** *WAR*

Lord of the Flies 🦴🦴🦴 ▷

Sr. High-Adult In a society racked with gang violence and youth crime, William Golding's allegorical novel about castaway schoolboys, free from adult supervision, degenerating into barbarism is more relevant than ever. Not a children's film by any means, but since the novel is a fixture in many classrooms it warrants inclusion here. This stark, straightforward British adaptation is certainly the more faithful and tasteful version, though it makes no effort to humanize the characters, and the acting is subpar.

> **BEWARE** *Violence; mature themes.*

1963 91m/B James Aubrey, Tom Chapin, Hugh Edwards, Roger Elwin, Tom Gamen; **D:** Peter Brook. **VHS, Beta, LV** *HMV, FUS*

Lord of the Flies 🦴🦴

R/Sr. High-Adult Second filming of the harrowing novel tries to turn William Golding's highly symbolic characters into real people, as castaway boys on a deserted island split into factions—those who go savage, and the dwindling few determined to stay civilized. But the filmmakers give personalities to the kids by making them foulmouthed and sexually sophisticated (one brat even has a police record!), completely losing Golding's point about innocence gone bad. Violence also enters R territory.

> **BEWARE** *Brutality, profanity and sex talk. Parents be warned of intense scenes of savagery. And these kids are a little too "grown up" for their own good.*

1990 90m/C Balthazar Getty, Danuel Pipoly, Chris Furrh, Badgett Dale, Edward Taft, Andrew Taft; **D:** Harry Hook. **VHS, Beta, LV, 8mm** *COL, TVC, NLC*

The Lord of the Rings 🦴🦴

PG/Primary-Adult Murky—in more ways than one—interpretation of J.R.R. Tolkien's classic tale of the fantasy folk who inhabit Middle Earth. Animator Ralph Bakshi used rotoscoping (painting animated characters over live-action footage of actors, birds and horses) to give his characters lifelike motion and characteristics. Too bad nobody did the same for the script. Adapting Tolkien's highly detailed and lengthy works is a mighty task, and non-readers may feel confused by the beginning, confounded in the middle, and cheated at the ending, which leads straight to a next chapter, not yet filmed.

> **BEWARE** *Violence. Some very scary underworld creatures.*

1978 128m/C D: Ralph Bakshi; **V:** Christopher Guard, John Hurt. **VHS, Beta** *REP, FCT*

The Lords of Flatbush 🦴🦴 ▷

PG/Jr. High-Adult Four street toughs battle against their own maturation and responsibilities in 1950s Brooklyn. Winkler introduces the leather-clad hood he's made a career of and Stallone introduces a character not unlike Rocky. Interesting slice of life.

> **BEWARE** *Brief violence.*

1974 88m/C Sylvester Stallone, Perry King, Henry Winkler, Susan Blakely, Armand Assante, Paul Mace; **D:** Stephen Verona, Martin Davidson; **M:** Joseph Brooks. **VHS, Beta, LV** *COL*

Lords of Magick 🦴🦴

PG-13/Jr. High-Adult Medieval wizard brothers, disciples of Merlin the Magician himself, pursue an evil sorcerer with a kidnapped princess across time to 20th century L.A. Low-budget fantasy with a modest share of thrills and a climactic magical duel that's a hoot.

> **BEWARE** *Violence, profanity, alcohol use. The older brother is a lusty libertine, the younger chaste and virtuous, and much is made of the contrast.*

1988 98m/C Jarrett Parker, Matt Gauthier, Brendan Dillon Jr.; **D:** David Marsh. **VHS, Beta** *PSM*

Lorenzo's Oil 🦴🦴🦴

PG-13/Jr. High-Adult Wrenching family drama based on the true story of Augusto and Michaela Odone's efforts to cure their 5-year-old son, Lorenzo, diagnosed with a rare and incurable neurological disorder. Confronted by a medical community slow moving and clinically cold in character, the parents painstakingly research their own treatment. Sarandon delivers an outstanding and emotionally charged performance as Lorenzo's ferociously loving mother. The devastating disease is depicted in all its cruel progression, and Miller's operatic direction could never be described as subtle, but neither are any reason to pass up this emotional wringer of a film.

> **BEWARE** *Profanity, a horribly ill child and a desperate family guarantee to draw tears and fears.*

1992 135m/C Nick Nolte, Susan Sarandon, Zach O'Malley-Greenberg, Peter Ustinov, Kathleen Wilhoite, Gerry Bamman, Margo Martindale, James Rebhorn, Ann Hearn; **D:** George Miller; **W:** Nick Enright, George Miller. **VHS, Beta, LV** *MCA, MOV, BTV*

The Lost Boys 🦴🦴 ▷

R/Sr. High-Adult Teenaged Michael, new in town, falls for a pretty girl with some hard-living friends. These partying punks are actually a delinquent gang of kid vampires. And if Michael can't beat them, he'll have to join them. The R rating derives from blood-gushing violence—undead get the worst of it—but attitude overall is one of scary fun (including the pint-sized vampire-busting 'Frog Brothers'), making it acceptable for youngsters no longer afraid of the dark. The eerie Peter Pan parallel implied by the title is never really fleshed out.

> **BEWARE** *Carnage (though the recipients are already dead), profanity. Very scary and brutal vampire fight.*

1987 97m/C Jason Patric, Kiefer Sutherland, Corey Haim, Jami Gertz, Dianne Wiest, Corey Feldman, Barnard Hughes, Edward Herrmann, Billy Wirth; **D:** Joel Schumacher; **W:** Jeffrey Boam; **M:** Thomas Newman. **VHS, Beta, LV, 8mm** *WAR, FUS*

Lost in a Harem 🦴🦴 ▷

Family Abbott & Costello play magicians in a theatrical troupe stranded in a desert kingdom ruled by an evil sheik. The sheik's nephew (and rightful heir) hires the two to steal some magic rings and the pretty Maxwell to play footsie with his susceptible uncle in an attempt to regain his kingdom. Average comedy with musical numbers by Jimmy Dorsey and His Orchestra.

1944 89m/B Bud Abbott, Lou Costello, Marilyn Maxwell, John Conte, Douglass Dumbrille, Lottie Harrison; **D:** Charles Riesner. **VHS** *MGM*

Lost in Dinosaur World

Primary-Jr. High Ten-year old boy and his seven-year old sister have the experience of a lifetime when they get lost in a dinosaur park (where DO they get these clever story ideas?). Tension mounts as their parents are warned that it's almost feeding time for the dinosaurs. Strives to offer scientific facts about dinosaurs and the world in which they lived.

1993 30m/C VHS *PSS*

Lost in Yonkers 🦴🦴 ▷

PG/Jr. High-Adult Arty and Jay are two teenage brothers who, while their widowed father looks for work, are sent to live with their stern grandmother, small-time gangster uncle, and childlike aunt in 1942 New York. Ruehl reprises her Tony award-winning performance as Aunt Bella, who loses herself in the movies while trying to find a love of her own, out from under the oppressive thumb of her domineering mother (Worth). Performances by the adults are more theatrical than necessary but the teenagers do well in their observer roles. Based on the play by Neil Simon, which again chronicles his boyhood.

> **BEWARE** *Salty language.*

1993 114m/C Mercedes Ruehl, Irene Worth, Richard Dreyfuss, Brad Stoll, Mike Damus, David Strathairn, Robert Miranda, Jack Laufer, Susan Merson; **D:** Martha Coolidge; **W:** Neil Simon; **M:** Elmer Bernstein. **VHS, LV, 8mm** *COL, FCT*

The Lost Jungle

Family Circus legend Beatty searches for his girl and her dad in the jungle. Animal stunts keep it interesting. 12-chapter serial.

1934 156m/B Clyde Beatty, Cecilia Parker, Syd Saylor, Warner Richmond, Wheeler Oakman; **D:** Armand Schaefer, David Howard. **VHS, Beta** *NOS, VCN, VDM*

Lost Legacy: A Girl Called Hatter Fox 🦴🦴 ▷

Adult Tradition and technology are at odds in the life of a young Indian girl. Strong cast makes this work. Made for TV and better than average. Originally broadcast under the title "A Girl Called Hatter Fox."

1977 100m/C Ronny Cox, Joanelle Romero, Conchata Ferrell; **D:** George Schaefer. **VHS** *GEM*

Lots of Luck 🦴 ▷

Family Nice to see Annette working for the Magic Kingdom again, though this is a weak feature sitcom (with a good cast) for the Disney Channel. The hardworking Maris family goes on a nonstop winning streak, taking the prize in a million-dollar lottery. Their loser friends, peers and parasites are jealous and cause them much misery; somehow it all ends up in a car race featuring a "Love Bug" lookalike.

1985 88m/C Martin Mull, Annette Funicello, Fred Willard, Polly Holliday; **D:** Peter Baldwin; **M:** William Goldstein. **VHS, Beta** *DIS*

Love and Death 🦴🦴 ▷

PG/Jr. High-Adult Strictly for the youngster who knows enough of Russian literature to tell when it's being parodied. In 1812 Russia, a condemned man reviews the follies of his life. Woody Allen's satire on "War and Peace," and every other major Russian novel. Ages 15 and up, although there's little sex or violence.

1975 89m/C Woody Allen, Diane Keaton, Georges Adel, Despo Diamantidou, Frank Adu, Harold Gould; **D:** Woody Allen; **W:** Woody Allen. **VHS, Beta, LV** *MGM, FOX*

Love at First Bite 🦴🦴 ◁

PG/Jr. High-Adult Intentionally campy spoof of the vampire film. Dracula is forced to leave his Transylvanian home as the Rumanian government has designated his castle a training center for young gymnasts. Once in New York, the Count takes in the night life and falls in love with a woman whose boyfriend embarks on a campaign to warn the city of Dracula's presence. Hamilton of the never-fading tan is appropriately fang-in-cheek in a role which briefly resurrected his film career.

> ⚠ BEWARE *Sex talk and comic violence. Seems Dracula is hitting the singles' bars.*

1979 93m/C George Hamilton, Susan St. James, Richard Benjamin, Dick Shawn, Arte Johnson, Sherman Hemsley, Isabel Sanford; **D:** Stan Dragoti; **M:** Charles Bernstein. **VHS, Beta, LV** *ORI, WAR*

The Love Bug 🦴🦴🦴

G/Family Story of Herbie, a Volkswagen with a mind of its own, provides an adorable vehicle (sorry) for Dean Jones and the special effects wizards at Disney. Jones is a less-than-successful race car driver—his roommate, a sculptor, uses pieces of Jones's wrecked cars in his art—who buys Herbie, only to discover that Herbie decides when and where to drive. From a wild trip amidst the hills of San Francisco to victories at the race track, Herbie is one intriguing automobile. Led to three sequels. Ages 6 to 12.

> ⚠ BEWARE *Insensitive stereotyping of Asians*

1968 110m/C Dean Jones, Michele Lee, Hope Lange, Robert Reed, Bert Convy; **D:** Robert Stevenson. **VHS, Beta, LV** *DIS*

Love Finds Andy Hardy 🦴🦴🦴

Family Young Andy Hardy finds himself torn between three girls before returning to the girl next door. Garland's first appearance in the acclaimed Andy Hardy series features her singing "In Between" and "Meet the Best of my Heart." Also available with "Andy Hardy Meets Debutante" on laserdisc.

1938 90m/B Mickey Rooney, Judy Garland, Lana Turner, Ann Rutherford, Fay Holden, Lewis Stone, Marie Blake, Cecilia Parker, Gene Reynolds; **D:** George B. Seitz. **VHS, Beta, LV** *MGM*

Love Happy 🦴🦴

Family Impoverished troupe of actors accidentally gains possession of some stolen diamonds, and Groucho is the detective assigned to retrieve them. If the Marx Brothers had made this a decade or two earlier it might have been a classic, but this was late in their careers, and, except for the endearing pantomimes of Harpo, the comedy team

seems awfully tired. Young Monroe has Groucho drooling over her in a brief cameo.

1950 85m/B Groucho Marx, Harpo Marx, Chico Marx, Vera-Ellen, Ilona Massey, Marion Hutton, Raymond Burr, Marilyn Monroe; **D:** David Miller. **VHS, LV** *REP*

Love Laughs at Andy Hardy 🦴🦴

Family Andy Hardy, college boy, is in love and in trouble. Financial and romantic problems come to a head when Andy is paired with a six-foot tall blind date. Sixth in the series.

1946 93m/B Mickey Rooney, Lewis Stone, Sara Haden, Lina Romay, Bonita Granville, Fay Holden; **D:** Willis Goldbeck. **VHS, Beta** *NOS, MRV, HHT*

Love Leads the Way 🦴🦴

Family Disney TV movie retelling how Morris Frank established the Seeing-Eye Dog program for the blind in the 1930s. Heavily sentimentalized adaptation of Frank's own book "First Lady of the Seeing Eye."

1984 99m/C Timothy Bottoms, Eva Marie Saint, Arthur Hill, Susan Dey, Ralph Bellamy, Ernest Borgnine, Patricia Neal; **D:** Delbert Mann. **VHS, Beta** *DIS*

Love Your Mama 🦴🦴 ◁

PG-13/Jr. High-Adult Independently made, worthwhile urban family drama about the strong Lucia, whose religious faith and sheer refusal to give up help her bear many crosses, including a drunken husband, car thief son, and pregnant teenage daughter. Believable role models and uniquely good performances help out occasionally amateur film technique.

> ⚠ BEWARE *Profanity, alcohol use, sex talk.*

1989 93m/C Audrey Morgan, Carol E. Hall, Andre Robinson, Ernest Rayford, Kearo Johnson, Jacqueline Williams; **D:** Ruby L. Oliver; **W:** Ruby L. Oliver. **VHS** *HMD, BTV, FCT*

Lt. Robin Crusoe, U.S.N. 🦴

G/Family Navy pilot crash lands on a tropical island, falls hard for an island babe and schemes intensely against the local evil ruler. Lackluster Disney debacle.

1966 113m/C Dick Van Dyke, Nancy Kwan, Akim Tamiroff; **D:** Byron Paul. **VHS, Beta** *DIS, OM*

Lucas 🦴🦴🦴 ◁

PG-13/Jr. High-Adult Small but brainy Lucas is a classroom misfit, having skipped a few grades at high school. But when he falls in love with the new girl in town, the pint-sized hero tries to win her through the seemingly hopeless stunt of trying out for the football team. Humorous, sympathetic, and affectionate view of youthful infatuation and the perils of growing up. Outstanding performances and characterizations, with Sheen as the gridiron jock who's not a dumb villain but Lucas' close friend, even as he develops into a romantic rival.

Herbie's drivers in "The Love Bug."

> **BEWARE** *Salty language and sex talk, but there's not one swear word or locker-room jibe that's needless or gratuitous in context.*

1986 100m/C Corey Haim, Kerri Green, Charlie Sheen, Winona Ryder, Courtney Thorne-Smith, Thomas E. Hodges; **D:** David Seltzer; **W:** David Seltzer; **M:** Dave Grusin. **VHS, Beta** *FXV, FOX*

Lucky Luke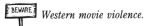

PG/Family Fastest gun in the west brings the law to Daisy Town, aided by his horse, Jolly Jumper—who can talk. Not exactly John Wayne material but amusing.

> **BEWARE** *Western movie violence.*

1994 91m/C Terence Hill, Roger Miller, Nancy Morgan, Ron Carey; **D:** Terence Hill. **VHS** *ACA*

Lucky Luke: Ballad of the Daltons

Family Easygoing cowboy hero Lucky Luke gets involved in a wild feud with the bumbling Dalton Brothers gang in this animated feature.

1978 82m/C D: Rene Goscinny. **VHS, Beta, LV** *DIS*

Lucky Luke: Daisy Town

Family Comic-strip cowboy Lucky Luke is virtually unknown in the US, but in France he's been a favorite for generations. In this rather spoofy feature cartoon from "Asterix" animator Goscinny, the all-American French cowboy saves the little community of Daisy Town from his perennial enemies, the hot-headed Dalton Gang. Dubbed into English.

1971 75m/C D: Rene Goscinny; **M:** Claude Bolling. **VHS, Beta, LV** *DIS*

Luggage of the Gods

G/Family Lost tribe of cave people are confronted with civilization when suitcases fall from an airplane. Low-budget comedy reminiscent of "The Gods Must Be Crazy" was filmed—and mainly seen—in upstate New York.

1987 78m/C Mark Stolzenberg, Gabriel Barre, Gwen Ellison; **D:** David Kendall. **VHS, Beta** *ACA*

Lumpkin the Pumpkin

Primary Animated Halloween tale of a witch and her friend, narrated by pop- and country-music star Goldsboro.

19?? 25m/C VHS *FHE*

Lyle, Lyle Crocodile: The Musical House on East 88th St.

Preschool-Primary Animated tale of a family who finds a surprise in the bathtub of their new home—a crocodile!

He's friendly, though, is quite a chef and heads for a career in show business. Ages 3 to 10.

19?? 25m/C VHS *SVE*

Mac and Me

PG/Primary-Sr. High Heavy backing by McDonalds created merchandising opportunity that turns out to be a subplot-by-subplot ripoff of "E.T." Here a whole family of Chaplinesque aliens are brought to Earth by a Mars probe. The tiniest escapes government captivity and befriends a wheelchair-bound boy. If you can forgive rampant Spielberg pillaging, some truly lively stuff occurs under guidance of "Wilderness Family" director Raffill that's sure to please young kids, and dig that wild final scene.

> **BEWARE** *Alcohol talk and an alien gets drunk. Whole movie is thinly disguised commercial.*

1988 94m/C Christine Ebersole, Jonathan Ward, Katrina Caspary, Lauren Stanley, Jade Calegory; **D:** Stewart Raffill; **W:** Stewart Raffill; **M:** Alan Silvestri. **VHS, Beta, LV** *ORI*

MacArthur

PG/Jr. High-Adult General Douglas MacArthur's life from Corregidor in 1942 to his dismissal a decade later in the midst of the Korean conflict. Episodic sage with forceful Peck but weak supporting characters. Fourteen minutes were cut from the original version; intended to be Peck's "Patton," it falls short of the mark.

1977 130m/C Gregory Peck, Ivan Bonar, Ward Costello, Nicolas Coster, Dan O'Herlihy; **D:** Joseph Sargent; **W:** Matthew Robbins; **M:** Jerry Goldsmith. **VHS, Beta, LV** *MCA, TLF*

Macron 1: Dark Discovery in a New World

Primary-Family Intergalactic animation! An unfortunate mishap switches the good and evil sides to opposite universes and the result is a battle to restore order. Major Chance and Dark Star fight to the end in this episode compilation. Additional volumes available.

1986 115m/C VHS, Beta *JFK*

Mad Max: Beyond Thunderdome

PG-13/Jr. High-Adult Max drifts into evil Barter Town ruled by Tina Turner, becomes a gladiator, fights in the Thunderdome, then gets dumped in desert and is rescued by band of feral orphans. Third in a bleak, extremely violent, but visually striking series. Ages 13 and up.

> **BEWARE** *Abundant violence and killing. Profanity and mature themes of the apocalypse. For older children only.*

1985 107m/C Mel Gibson, Tina Turner, Helen Buday, Frank Thring Jr., Bruce Spence, Robert Grubb, Angelo Rossitto, Angry Anderson, George Spartels, Rod Zuanic; **D:** George Miller, George Ogilvie; **W:** George Miller, Terry Hayes; **M:** Maurice Jarre. **VHS, Beta, LV, 8mm** *WAR*

Mad Monster Party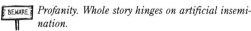

Family One of the cute but brittle stop-motion puppet animation features Arthur Rankin Jr. and Jules Bass did for theatrical release before turning their efforts primarily to TV. Aging Dr. Frankenstein wants to retire from being the senior monster, so he calls a convention of famous movie creatures to decide whether Mummy, Wolfman, Dracula or whatever should take his place. Rest assured that never have so many fiends been rendered in such a nonthreatening manner.

1968 94m/C D: Jules Bass; **V:** Boris Karloff, Ethel Ennis, Phyllis Diller. **VHS, Beta** *COL*

Mad Scientist

Family Mattel produced this 'toon about Dr. Sy N. Tist, who must eat his words when his Mad Lab is programmed to take his language seriously, even when it is figurative. Soon the Doctor learns to think before he talks. This might be educational.

1988 30m/C VHS, Beta *FHE*

Madame Rosa

PG/Sr. High-Adult Rosa (Simone Signoret), a retired hooker and Holocaust survivor, tends other prostitutes' offspring in Paris. Her spirit is revived by one of her charges—an abandoned Arab boy, and she determines to make a better life for him in the short time she has left. Warmhearted, though longish, Academy Award winner, in French with English subtitles. Ages 14 and up.

 Sex talk and prostitution.

1977 105m/C Simone Signoret, Claude Dauphin; **D:** Moshe Mizrahi. **VHS, Beta** *HTV, VES*

Madame Sousatzka

PG-13/Jr. High-Adult Eccentric, extroverted London piano teacher demands complete control over her students' lives, which is why they inevitably leave her. She meets her match in a strong-willed, ferociously talented Indian boy who seems destined for symphonic stardom. MacLaine's flamboyant acting helps carry this mixture of character study and coming-of-age drama.

 Salty language, sex, mature themes, alcohol use.

1988 113m/C Shirley MacLaine, Peggy Ashcroft, Shabana Azmi, Twiggy, Leigh Lawson, Geoffrey Bayldon, Navin Chowdhry, Lee Montague; **D:** John Schlesinger; **W:** Ruth Prawer Jhabvala, John Schlesinger; **M:** Gerald Gouriet. **VHS, Beta, LV** *MCA*

Made in America

PG-13/Jr. High-Adult High-energy, lightweight comedy stars Whoopi as a single mom whose daughter Long discovers her birth was the result of artificial insemination. More surprising is her biological dad: white, obnoxious, country-western car dealer Danson. Overwrought with obvious gags and basically a one-joke movie. Nonetheless, Goldberg and Danson chemically connect on-

screen (and for a short time offscreen as well) while supporting actor Smith grabs comedic attention as Teacake, Long's best friend.

1993 111m/C Whoopi Goldberg, Ted Danson, Will Smith, Nia Long, Paul Rodriguez, Jennifer Tilly, Peggy Rea, Clyde Kusatsu; **D:** Richard Benjamin; **W:** Holly Goldberg Sloan; **M:** Mark Isham. **VHS, Beta, LV** *WAR*

Madeline

Primary Musical cartoon adaptation of the classic Ludwig Bemelmans tale of the smallest, bravest, and wildest of a dozen French schoolgirls, and her friends' concern when Madeline has to have her appendix taken out. Simple but charming animation faithfully reproduces the original books' whimsical style, and it kicked off a series of "Madeline" shows first broadcast on HBO cable.

1989 30m/C VHS *KUI, VTR, SIG*

Madeline and the Toy Factory

Primary Madeline and the gang go on a tour of a toy factory and Madeline turns the outing into a real adventure. Madeline decides to pose as a doll herself, and she becomes the prize possession of a lonely little girl. Christopher Plummer narrates. Based on the books by Ludwig Bemelmans. Ages 2 to 7.

1994 26m/C VHS

Madeline at Cooking School

Primary Sacre bleu! Madeline and her schoolmates are enrolled at France's most famous cooking school where they fail to impress the picky Lord Koo-Kooface with their culinary abilities. Christopher Plummer narrates. Based on the books by Ludwig Bemelmans. Ages 2 to 7.

1994 25m/C VHS *WPC*

Madeline's Christmas

Family Madeline learns an important lesson about giving when she is forced to care for her sick friends on Christmas morning. Cartoon based on the books by Ludwig Bemelman. Additional volumes available.

1991 30m/C VHS, Beta *SIG, TVC*

Madeline's Rescue and Other Stories about Madeline

Primary Louise Roberts narrates the delightful story of Madeline's rescue of a dog named Genevieve. Other stories are "Madeline and the Bad Hat" and "Madeline and the Gypsies." Christopher Plummer narrates. Based on the books by Ludwig Bemelmans. Ages 2 to 7.

1990 23m/C VHS *FCT, MLT*

Madhouse

PG-13/Jr. High-Adult The beginning and, so far, end of John Larroquette's film career. Unfunny comedy finds him and Kirstie Alley as new homeowners plagued by guests who won't leave. Interestingly, Larroquette and guest Alison LaPlaca would later be reunited as lovers on Larroquette's TV sitcom. Ages 13 and up.

BEWARE *Profanity and sex.*

1990 90m/C John Larroquette, Kirstie Alley, Alison La Placa, John Diehl, Jessica Lundy, Bradley Gregg, Dennis Miller, Robert Ginty; **D:** Tom Ropelewski; **W:** Tom Ropelewski; **M:** David Newman. **VHS, Beta, LV** *ORI*

The Magic Flute

Primary Animated adventure, loosely based on the Mozart opera, with numerous contemporary original songs and an updated storyline. So much for Mozart. Dashing prince sets off to rescue beautiful princess from evil queen. Ages 5 to 9.
1994 45m/C VHS *ABC*

Magic in the Water

PG/Primary-Adult Hey, how's this for a movie? There's this guy and he's a psychologist giving advice on the radio, only his own life is a mess. He's divorced and unpleasant and he doesn't pay much attention to his kids. Anyway, he takes the kids on a vacation to this lake where's there's supposed to be like Canada's answer to the Loch Ness monster. And the guy doesn't believe it but then the monster, you know, takes over his body and makes him warn everybody about how pollution is destroying the lake. Yeah, sort of "E.T." meets "Free Willy" with a mild bit of "Invasion of the Body Snatchers." No, huh?

BEWARE *Moderate profanity and moments of peril.*

1995 100m/C Mark Harmon, Joshua Jackson, Harley Jane Kozak, Sarah Wayne, Willie Nark-Orn, Frank S. Salsedo; **D:** Rick Stevenson; **W:** Icel Dobell Massey, Rick Stevenson; **C:** Thomas Burstyn; **M:** David Schwartz. **VHS** *COL*

Magic Island

PG/Primary-Adult Thirteen-year-old Jack (Bryan) gets sucked into the pages of a pirate book and finds himself with Blackbeard and his scurvy crew. They're on a treasure hunt and figure Jack's book contains some missing clues. Naturally, Jack finds himself in lots of trouble.

BEWARE *Mild language and pirate roughhousing.*

1995 88m/C Zachery Ty Bryan, Edward Kerr, Lee Armstrong, French Stewart, Abraham Benrubi, Jessie-Ann Friend, Oscar Dillon, Sean O'Kane, Schae Harrison, Ja'net DuBois, Andrew Divoff; **D:** Sam Irvin; **W:** Neil Ruttenberg, Brent Friedman; **C:** James Lawrence Spencer; **M:** Richard Band. **VHS** *PAR*

Magic Kid

PG/Jr. High-Adult Filmmakers who usually do violent action B-pics tried a family feature with this. Don't quit your day jobs, fellas. Kevin, Michigan's youngest martial-arts champ, visits Uncle Bob, a shady L.A. talent agent in debt to the mob. Plot switches between Kevin kicking around bad guys, boring pep talks to boost Bob's self-

esteem, and lots of Hollywood travel footage (including a big promo for the Universal City Studios "Backdraft" tour).

BEWARE *Violence, sex talk, alcohol use. Also, coming-attractions for non-kiddie movies at the start of the tape contribute extra sex, brutality.*

1992 91m/C Ted Jan Roberts, Shonda Whipple, Stephen Furst, Joseph Campanella, Billy Hufsey, Sondra Kerns, Pamela Dixon, Lauren Tewes, Don "The Dragon" Wilson; **D:** Joseph Merhi; **W:** Stephen Smoke; **M:** Jim Halfpenny. **VHS, LV** *PMH*

Magic Kid 2

PG/Primary-Adult The young star of a popular martial arts program wants to quit and go to high school like a normal teenager. But the studio execs have other ideas.

BEWARE *Cartoon violence and adult business related stuff.*

1994 90m/C Ted Jan Roberts, Stephen Furst, Donald Gibb, Jennifer Savidge; **D:** Stephen Furst. **VHS, LV** *PMH*

Magic of Lassie

G/Family Attempt to revive the classic collie in the 1970s turned out to be a box office dog. Innocuous but simple-minded remake of 1943's "Lassie Come Home" has Jimmy Stewart as a singing grandpa who won't sell Lassie to an evil millionaire, so the bad guy dognaps the animal.

1978 100m/C James Stewart, Mickey Rooney, Stephanie Zimbalist, Alice Faye, Pernell Roberts, Lassie; **D:** Don Chaffey. **VHS, Beta** *MGM*

The Magic of the Golden Bear: Goldy 3

G/Family Down-on-his-luck magician (Marin) tries to buy Goldy to save his failing act and Jessie (Morgan) is torn between wanting to keep the bear or return her to the wild. An animal-loving holy man (Mr. T.) tries to help her decide.

1994 104m/C Bonnie Morgan, Richard "Cheech" Marin, Mr. T; **D:** John Quinn. **VHS** *FHE*

Magic Pony

Preschool-Primary Obscure US-Soviet cartoon co-production, blending Russian folklore with the voices of Yankee capitalist TV stars. With the help of a beautiful flying horse, Ivan battles a greedy emperor to become a kind-hearted prince and live happily ever after with a beautiful princess.

1978 80m/C D: Ivan Ivanov-vano; **V:** Jim Backus, Erin Moran, Hans Conried, Johnny Whitaker. **VHS, Beta, LV** *GEM*

The Magic School Bus for Lunch

Primary Miniaturized, science teacher Ms. Frizzle (the voice of Lily Tomlin) and the kids become Arnold's meal when he accidentally swallows them. Ms. Frizzle takes the opportunity to introduce everyone to the digestive system. We all know where the digestive system ends.

Mercifully, the video doesn't take us that far, though it acknowledges the truth. Ages 6 to 12.
1994 30m/C *V:* Lily Tomlin. **VHS** *KID*

The Magic School Bus Gets Eaten

Primary Science teacher Ms. Frizzle gives Arnold and Keesha an assignment to find two things that go together and shows how his soggy shoe and her tuna fish sandwich meet in the ocean food chain. Ages 6 to 12.
1995 30m/C *V:* Lily Tomlin. **VHS** *KID*

The Magic School Bus Gets Lost in Space

Primary Arnold's know-it-all cousin Janet has to prove she knows what's what when Ms. Frizzle gets lost in the solar system during a field trip. Trust the Frizz to get everyone home safely, and a little bit smarter. Ages 6 to 12.
1994 30m/C *V:* Lily Tomlin. **VHS** *KID*

The Magic School Bus Goes to Seed

Primary New episode from the popular series has the gang trying to plant a garden, and the bus shrinks them all down for a trip inside a flower. Ages 6 to 12.
1995 30m/C VHS *KID*

The Magic School Bus Hops Home

Primary Ms. Frizzle and the kids ribbit up as the class goes in search of a proper habitat for Wanda's pet frog. Ages 6 to 12.
1995 30m/C *V:* Lily Tomlin. **VHS** *KID*

The Magic School Bus Inside Ralphie

Primary Take a fantastic journey into Ralphie's body. He's got a fever and sore throat and can't go to school. So school comes to him. Sorry, Ralphie. Ages 6 to 12.
1995 30m/C *V:* Lily Tomlin. **VHS** *KID*

The Magic School Bus Inside the Earth

Primary Follows science teacher Ms. Frizzle and her students on an amazing adventure on board the magic school bus. Hosted by LeVar Burton, who embarks on his own adventure to the California Caverns and discusses stalagmites, stalactites, and other crystal formations found within the earth. Ages 6 to 12.
1994 30m/C VHS

The Magic School Bus Kicks Up a Storm

Primary Ms. Frizzle and the gang conjure up a thunderstorm. Ages 6 to 12.
1995 30m/C VHS *KID*

Magic School Bus Plays Ball

Primary Lily Tomlin, who supplies the voice of teacher Ms. Frizzle, certainly found signs of intelligent life in the universe on "The Magic School Bus." A series of science lessons disguised as a weekend TV cartoon, "School Bus" involves a class of inquisitive kids and their unpredictable teacher who takes them on the most extraordinary field trips. The bus can take them to a museum, all right, but it can also tour the solar system or shrink waaay down for a trip inside a flower. Every lesson comes with a heap of humor. In this episode the gang tries to create a baseball team out of a bumbling group of students. Ages 6 to 12.
1995 30m/C VHS *KID*

Magic Snowman 🎵 ♭

Family Young Jamie builds a snowman that starts talking, with the urbane voice of Roger Moore (yet with its spiky hair and glaring red eyes, the thing looks more like a snow-punk). The snowman tells Jamie where his fisherman father can find the best waters, but the boy misuses the information. Extremely awkward Yugoslavian fantasy slush, unconvincingly acted.

🚸 BEWARE *Roughhousing.*

1988 85m/C VHS *FHE, BTV*

The Magic Sword 🎵 🎵

Family Fantasy adventure about a young man raised by a doting sorceress stepmother, who sets out to rescue a beautiful princess from being the next meal for an evil wizard's dragon. Low-budget but fitfully imaginative tale that, in its better moments, achieves a smart mixture of fairy tale and satire.

🚸 BEWARE *The hero's magical posse of the six mightiest knights of all time get killed one by one. But hey, they were dead to begin with, and return unhurt at the finale.*
1962 80m/C Basil Rathbone, Estelle Winwood, Gary Lockwood; *D:* Bert I. Gordon. **VHS, Beta** *MGM, MRV, VYY*

The Magic Thinking Cap 🎵 🎵

Primary Mikey, pushed around by bullies, sets off the fire alarm at school to prove he's "cool." Judy, a marionette, shows him the error of his ways by having Mikey and his parents act out "The Boy Who Cried Wolf." Then, the magic thinking cap allows him to see his motives and intentions. Heavy-handed, with a family therapy session feel. Ages 7 to 11.
1994 30m/C VHS

The Magic Voyage 🦴🦴

G/Family Animated tale of a friendly woodworm named Pico who voyages with Columbus to the new world and convinces him that the world is indeed round. He then comes to the aid of a magical firefly named Marilyn who helps Columbus find gold to bring back to Spain.

1993 82m/C V: Dom DeLuise, Mickey Rooney, Corey Feldman, Irene Cara, Dan Haggerty, Samantha Eggar. **VHS, LV** *HMD*

Magical Mystery Tour 🦴🦴🦴

Jr. High-Adult Made for British TV. The Beatles, on the road in England, meet up with assorted odd folks and peculiar goings on, sing a few songs. 🎵 Magical Mystery Tour; Blue Jay Way; Your Mother Should Know; The Fool on the Hill.

1967 55m/C John Lennon, George Harrison, Ringo Starr, Paul McCartney, Victor Spinetti. **VHS, Beta, LV** *MPI, MED, WFV*

The Magical Princess Gigi

Family Spliced-together episodes from an imported Japanese cartoon from 1984, about an extraterrestrial princess coming to Earth disguised as an ordinary 12-year-old and working her magic to do good deeds.

1989 80m/C D: Hiroshi Watanabe. **VHS, Beta** *JFK*

Maid to Order 🦴 ⌐

PG/Jr. High-Adult Rich girl Sheedy's fairy godmother puts her in her place by turning her into a maid for a snooty Malibu couple. Good-natured and well-acted if rather mindless Cinderella story.

⚠️ BEWARE *Profanity and brief nudity.*

1987 92m/C Ally Sheedy, Beverly D'Angelo, Michael Ontkean, Dick Shawn, Tom Skerritt, Valerie Perrine; **D:** Amy Holden Jones; **W:** Perry Howze; **M:** Georges Delerue. **VHS, Beta, LV** *LIV*

The Main Event 🦴🦴

PG/Jr. High-Adult Streisand plays a wacky-and-bankrupt—cosmetic executive who must depend on the career of washed-up boxer O'Neal to rebuild her fortune. Desperate (and more than a little smitten), she badgers and bullies him back into the ring. Lame, derivative screwball comedy desperate to suggest chemistry of Streisand and O'Neal's "What's Up, Doc?" (1972). Streisand sings the title song.

1979 109m/C Barbra Streisand, Ryan O'Neal; **D:** Howard Zieff. **VHS, Beta** *WAR*

Major League 🦴🦴 ⌐

R/Sr. High-Adult Comedy about a pathetic major league baseball team whose new owner schemes to lose the season and relocate the team to Miami. Sheen is okay as the pitcher with control problems (both on and off the field), while Bernsen seems to be gazing affectionately at "L.A. Law" from a distance. Predictable sports spoof is good for a few laughs, particularly those scenes involving Haysbert as a slugger with voodoo on his mind (and in

his locker) and Snipes as a base stealer whose only problem is getting on base. Followed by a sequel outside the strike zone.

⚠️ BEWARE *Foul sportsman language and violence (some in the locker room). Not very good sports, you might say.*

1989 107m/C Tom Berenger, Charlie Sheen, Corbin Bernsen, James Gammon, Margaret Whitton, Bob Uecker, Rene Russo, Wesley Snipes, Dennis Haysbert, Charles Cyphers; **D:** David S. Ward; **W:** David S. Ward; **M:** James Newton Howard. **VHS, Beta, LV, 8mm** *PAR*

Major League 2 🦴

PG/Jr. High-Adult It's been five years since they won the series, and this plodding sequel finds the wacky championship Cleveland Indians ruined by success and once again struggling in last place. Limited charm of original is lost; dull and filled with such lame jokes that you won't care if they manage to make it to the top again. Cast returns with the exception of Wesley Snipes as Willie Mae Hays (now played by Epps).

⚠️ BEWARE *Profanity.*

1994 105m/C Charlie Sheen, Tom Berenger, Corbin Bernsen, James Gammon, Dennis Haysbert, Omar Epps, David Keith, Bob Uecker, Alison Doody, Michelle Burke, Margaret Whitton, Eric Bruskotter, Takaaki Ishibashi; **D:** David S. Ward; **W:** R.J. Stewart; **M:** Michel Colombier. **VHS, LV** *WAR*

Major Payne 🦴 ⌐

PG-13/Sr. High-Adult Aptly titled, this movie majors in stupidity. Benson Payne (Wains), a tough Marine with no war to fight, reluctantly agrees to train the inept junior ROTC cadets at a third-rate prep school. The usual gang of losers develops the usual self-esteem etc. Most of the jokes involve the humiliation of the kids, always a laugh-riot. This guy is just a little too rough around the edges. Remake of 1955's "The Private War of Major Benson."

⚠️ BEWARE *Lots and lots of vulgarity and crude behavior. Mistreatment of kids and scare tactics go a little overboard. One character is smacked by his abusive father.*

1995 97m/C Damon Wayans, Karyn Parsons, William Hickey, Albert Hall, Steven Martini, Andrew Harrison Leeds, Scott "Bam Bam" Bigelow; **D:** Nick Castle; **W:** Damon Wayans, Dean Lorey, Gary Rosen. **VHS, LV** *MCA*

Making Contact 🦴 ⌐

PG/Jr. High-Adult Oddball German production is one long tribute/ripoff of the imagery of George Lucas and Steven Spielberg. Joey (pic's original title), a small boy with a pet R2D2 robot, is assailed by poltergeists. Can his Jedi window curtains save him? How about his E.T. drinking glass? What about his Goonie friends? Harmless but annoyingly unoriginal.

⚠️ BEWARE *Fantasy violence. One death, followed by "E.T." style resurrection, amid much tears and pathos.*

1986 83m/C Joshua Morrell, Eve Kryll; **D:** Roland Emmerich. **VHS, Beta** *NWV, VTR*

Making Mr. Right ♪♪ ♭

PG-13/Jr. High-Adult Peculiar satire of image vs. reality. High-powered marketing consultant (Ann Magnuson) falls in love with the android (John Malkovich) that she's supposed to be promoting. An acquired taste. Ages 14 and up.

1986 95m/C John Malkovich, Ann Magnuson, Glenne Headly, Ben Masters, Laurie Metcalf, Polly Bergen, Hart Bochner, Polly Draper, Susan Anton; **D:** Susan Seidelman. **VHS, Beta, LV** *HBO*

Making the Grade ♪♪

PG/Jr. High-Adult Jersey tough kid owes the mob. For vital cash he attends prep school in place of a rich boy who can't be bothered, and shows preppie teens the view from the other side of the tracks. Better than similar '80s youth flicks, but not by much. Note the presence of actor Clay, before he assumed the persona of an ultra-offensive stand-up comic.

 *Salty language.*

1984 105m/C Judd Nelson, Joanna Lee, Dana Olsen, Ronald Lacey, Scott McGinnis, Gordon Jump, Carey Scott, Andrew Dice Clay; **D:** Dorian Walker; **W:** Gene Quintano; **M:** Basil Poledouris. **VHS, Beta** *MGM*

Malcolm X ♪♪♪♪

PG-13/Jr. High-Adult Stirring tribute to the controversial black activist, a leader in the struggle for black liberation. Hitting bottom during his imprisonment in the 50s, he became a Black Muslim and then a leader in the Nation of Islam. His assassination in 1965 left a legacy of black nationalism, self-determination, and racial pride. Marked by strong direction from Lee and good performances (notably Freeman Jr. as Elijah Muhammad), it is Washington's convincing performance in the title role that truly brings the film alive. Based on "The Autobiography of Malcolm X" by Malcolm X and Alex Haley.

 *Violence, profanity, drug use, suggested sex, and a Klan raid complete with burning cross.*

1992 201m/C Denzel Washington, Angela Bassett, Albert Hall, Al Freeman Jr., Delroy Lindo, Spike Lee, Theresa Randle, Kate Vernon, Lonette McKee, Tommy Hollis, James McDaniel, Ernest Thompson, Jean LaMarre, Giancarlo Esposito, Craig Wasson, John Ottavino, David Patrick Kelly, Shirley Stoler; **Cameos:** Christopher Plummer, Karen Allen, Peter Boyle, William Kunstler, Bobby Seale, Al Sharpton; **D:** Spike Lee; **W:** Spike Lee, Arnold Perl, James Baldwin; **M:** Terence Blanchard. **Award Nominations:** Academy Awards '92: Best Actor (Washington), Best Costume Design; **Awards:** Chicago Film Critics Awards '93: Best Actor (Washington), Best Film; MTV Movie Awards '93: Best Actor (Washington); New York Film Critics Awards '93: Best Actor (Washington). **VHS, Beta, LV, 8mm** *WAR, MOV, BTV*

Mallrats ♪♪ ♭

R/Sr. High-Adult Keep in mind, this is the follow-up to Smith's "Clerks," which means it deals with issues such as sex, drugs, and rock n' roll. (Not necessarily family issues.) But your teen may be attracted to the title and the young cast. This time Jersey slackers T.S. (London) and Brodie (Lee) get dumped by their girlfriends and head for the mall to wallow in food-court cookies and win back their chicks. While wandering the mall they encounter the usual band of bizarre characters, including Ivannah, the topless psychic. Plot is definitely not an issue here. The ensemble cast, featuring Shannon Doherty, is quite good, but tell your teen not to expect Brenda from 90210.

 *Strong language in the tradition of "Clerks," including sexual dialogue. Scenes of sexuality including an anonymous chick putting on some scanty panties in the middle of a store and the aforementioned topless psychic.*

1995 95m/C Shannen Doherty, Jeremy London, Jason Lee, Claire Forlani, Michael Rooker, Priscilla Barnes, Renee Humphrey, Ben Affleck, Joey Adams, Jason Mewes, Brian O'Halloran, David Brinkley, Kevin Smith; **Cameos:** Stan Lee; **D:** Kevin Smith; **W:** Kevin Smith; **C:** David Klein; **M:** Ira Newborn. **VHS, LV** *MCA*

The Maltese Falcon ♪♪♪♪

Sr. High-Adult After the death of his partner, detective Sam Spade finds himself enmeshed in a complicated, intriguing search for a priceless statuette. "It's the stuff dreams are made of," says Bogart of the Falcon. Excellent, fast-paced film noir with outstanding performances, great dialogue, and concentrated attention to details. Huston makes giant debut, Greenstreet appears in a nonsilent for the first time, and Bogart secures leading man status. First of several films by Bogart and Astor. Third version based on the novel by Dashiell Hammett. Also available colorized.

1941 101m/B Humphrey Bogart, Mary Astor, Peter Lorre, Sydney Greenstreet, Ward Bond, Barton MacLane, Gladys George, Lee Patrick, Elisha Cook Jr., Jerome Cowan; **Cameos:** Walter Huston; **D:** John Huston; **W:** John Huston; **M:** Adolph Deutsch. **VHS, Beta, LV** *MGM, FOX, TLF*

Man & Boy ♪♪

G/Family Delicate and beautiful family film goes very wrong in its third act. Cosby is a homesteader in old Arizona whose horse is stolen while in the care of his young son. Man and boy follow the trail of the lost animal, a thoughtful and seriocomic odyssey throughout the west that abruptly turns violent, with an ugly, bloody shootout between a black outlaw and a white sheriff bringing the tale to a pointless end. What were these filmmakers thinking? Don't trust the G rating.

 *Brutality during a terrible shoot-out and alcohol use.*

1971 98m/C Bill Cosby, Gloria Foster, George Spell, Henry Silva, Yaphet Kotto; **D:** E.W. Swackhamer; **M:** Quincy Jones. **VHS, Beta** *COL*

The Man Called Flintstone ♪♪

Family Long before "Stephen Spielrock's" mammoth-budget 1994 Flintstones epic, this feature-length theatrical release appeared in which Fred Flintstone spoofs James Bond cliches that were terribly in vogue in the mid-'60s (A.D.) and already getting stale. During the intrigues, Fred takes his family and the Rubbles to Paris and Rome.

1966 87m/C D: William Hanna, Joseph Barbera; **V:** Alan Reed, Mel Blanc, Jean VanDerPyl, Gerry Johnson, Don Messick, Janet Waldo, Paul Frees, Harvey Korman, John Stephenson, June Foray. **VHS, Beta, LV** *TTC, IME, APD*

A Man for All Seasons 🦴🦴🦴🦴

G/Family Sterling, heavily Oscar-honored biographical drama concerning the life and subsequent martyrdom of 16th-century Chancellor of England, Sir Thomas More (Scofield). Story revolves around his personal conflict when King Henry VIII (Shaw) seeks a divorce from his wife, Catherine of Aragon, so he can wed his mistress, Anne Boleyn—events that ultimately lead the King to bolt from the Pope and declare himself head of the Church of England. Remade for television in 1988 with Charlton Heston in the lead role.

1966 120m/C Paul Scofield, Robert Shaw, Orson Welles, Wendy Hiller, Susannah York, John Hurt, Nigel Davenport, Vanessa Redgrave; **D:** Fred Zinnemann; **W:** Constance Willis, Robert Bolt; **M:** Georges Delerue. **Award Nominations:** Academy Awards '66: Best Supporting Actor (Shaw), Best Supporting Actress (Hiller); **Awards:** Academy Awards '66: Best Actor (Scofield), Best Adapted Screenplay, Best Color Cinematography, Best Costume Design (Color), Best Director (Zinnemann), Best Picture; British Academy Awards '67: Best Actor (Scofield), Best Film; Directors Guild of America Awards '66: Best Director (Zinnemann); Golden Globe Awards '67: Best Actor—Drama (Scofield), Best Director (Zinnemann), Best Film—Drama, Best Screenplay; National Board of Review Awards '66: 10 Best Films of the Year, Best Actor (Scofield), Best Director (Zinnemann), Best Supporting Actor (Shaw). **VHS, Beta, LV** *COL, BTV, TVC*

Man from Clover Grove 🦴 ⍟

G/Family Nutty inventor stirs up the community with his supersonic gadgets and the spies they attract. Alternate title, "The Absent- Minded Man From Clover Grove," is a hint of where the filmmakers got their inspiration.

1978 96m/C Ron Masak, Cheryl Miller, Jed Allan, Rose Marie. **VHS, Beta** *MED*

The Man from Snowy River 🦴🦴 ⍟

PG/Family Stunning cinematography highlights this popular but otherwise fairly ordinary adventure story set in 1888 Australia's cowboy territory. Young Jim Craig tries to prove himself worthy while working on the ranch of a rich American and taming a destructive herd of wild horses ("brumbies"). Douglas plays a dual role as estranged twin brothers. Based on an epic Aussie poem by A.B. "Banjo" Paterson, and with enough loose ends left at the end for the sequel, "Return to Snowy River."

> ⚠ BEWARE *Fighting, profanity, alcohol use and a man slaps his daughter's face.*

1982 104m/C Kirk Douglas, Tom Burlinson, Sigrid Thornton, Terence Donovan, Tommy Dysart, Jack Thompson, Bruce Kerr; **D:** George Miller. **VHS, Beta, LV** *FOX, TVC, HMV*

The Man in the Iron Mask 🦴🦴🦴

Family Swashbuckling tale about twin brothers separated at birth. One turns out to be King Louis XIV of France, and the other a carefree wanderer and friend of the Three Musketeers. Their eventual clash leads to action-packed adventures and royal revenge.

1939 110m/B Louis Hayward, Alan Hale, Joan Bennett, Warren William, Joseph Schildkraut, Walter Kingsford, Marion Martin; **D:** James Whale. **VHS, Beta** *CCB, MED*

The Man in the Iron Mask 🦴🦴🦴

Jr. High-Adult Made for TV remake finds the tyrannical French king kidnapping his twin brother and imprisoning him on a remote island. Chamberlain, king of the miniseries, is excellent in the dual role. Adapted from the Dumas classic.

1977 105m/C Richard Chamberlain, Patrick McGoohan, Louis Jourdan, Jenny Agutter, Ian Holm, Ralph Richardson; **D:** Mike Newell. **VHS, Beta** *LIV, FUS, FOX*

The Man in the Moon 🦴🦴🦴 ⍟

PG-13/Jr. High-Adult Beautifully rendered coming-of-age tale. On a farm outside a small Louisiana town in the 1950s, 14 year-old Dani wonders if she will ever be as pretty and popular as her older sister Maureen. Dani is beginning to notice boys, particularly Court, a teenager she meets when swimming, and a rift develops between the sisters after Court meets Maureen. Intelligently written, excellent direction, lovely cinematography, and exceptional acting make this a particularly recommended film.

> ⚠ BEWARE *Sexual situations and sibling jealousy. A likable character is killed in an accident.*

1991 100m/C Reese Witherspoon, Emily Warfield, Jason London, Tess Harper, Sam Waterston, Gail Strickland; **D:** Robert Mulligan. **VHS** *MGM*

The Man in the Santa Claus Suit 🦴🦴

Family A costume shop owner has an effect on three people who rent Santa Claus costumes from him. Astaire plays seven different roles in this made for TV film. Average holiday feel-good movie.

1979 96m/C Fred Astaire, Gary Burghoff, John Byner, Nanette Fabray, Bert Convy; **D:** Corey Allen. **VHS, Beta** *MED*

Man of La Mancha 🦴 ⍟

PG/Jr. High-Adult Arrested by the Inquisition and thrown into prison, Miguel de Cervantes relates the story of Don Quixote. Not nearly as good as the Broadway musical it is based on. 🎵 It's All the Same; The Impossible Dream; Barber's Song; Man of La Mancha; Dulcinea; I'm Only Thinking of Him; Little Bird, Little Bird; Life as It Really Is; The Dubbing.

1972 129m/C Peter O'Toole, Sophia Loren, James Coco, Harry Andrews, John Castle, Brian Blessed; **D:** Arthur Hiller. **Award Nominations:** Academy Awards '72: Best Original Score; **Awards:** National Board of Review Awards '72: 10 Best Films of the Year, Best Actor (O'Toole). **VHS, Beta, LV** *FOX, FCT*

Man of the House 🦴🦴

PG/Primary-Adult Jack (Chase) has designs on a divorced woman (Fawcett) but there's a problem. His name is Ben (Thomas), he's 11, he's Farrah's son and he's gotten used to having mom all to himself. When Jack moves in, Ben tries everything (short of violence) to move him out, including the predictable rigors of a father-son camping trip. They eventually learn to like and respect each other, which isn't a bad lesson to learn.

🪧 BEWARE 🪧 *Bees are used as weapons and young Ben tries to keep the two adults from sleeping in the same room. Kids will laugh at the pranks and pratfalls, but parents may get bored. The mime is really annoying (Surprise!).*

1995 97m/C Chevy Chase, Farrah Fawcett, Jonathan Taylor Thomas, George Wendt, David Shiner, Art LaFleur, Richard Portnow, Richard Foronjy, Spencer Vrooman, John Disanti, Chief Leonard George, Peter Appel, George Greif, Chris Miranda, Ron Canada, Zachary Browne, Nicholas Garrett; **D:** James Orr; **W:** James Orr, Jim Cruickshank; **C:** Jamie Anderson; **M:** Mark Mancina. **VHS, LV** *DIS*

The Man Who Wagged His Tail 🦴🦴 ᵒ

Jr. High-Adult A mean slumlord is turned into a dog as the result of a curse cast upon him. In order to regain his human form, he must be loved by someone. Mildly amusing fantasy filmed in Spain and Brooklyn, New York.

1957 91m/B Peter Ustinov, Pablito Calvo, Aroldo Tieri, Silvia Marco; **D:** Ladislao Vajda. **VHS** *SNC, VYY*

The Man Who Would Be King 🦴🦴🦴🦴

PG/Jr. High-Adult Grand, old-fashioned adventure based on the classic story by Rudyard Kipling about two mercenary soldiers who travel from India to Kafiristan in order to conquer it and set themselves up as kings. Splendid characterizations by Connery and Caine, and Huston's royal directorial treatment provides it with adventure, majestic sweep, and well-developed characters.

🪧 BEWARE 🪧 *Violence.*

1975 129m/C Sean Connery, Michael Caine, Christopher Plummer, Saeed Jaffrey, Shakira Caine; **D:** John Huston; **W:** Gladys Hill, John Huston; **M:** Maurice Jarre. **VHS, Beta, LV** *FOX*

The Man with One Red Shoe 🦴 ᵒ

PG/Jr. High-Adult Hanks is a lovable clod of a violinist who ensnares himself in a web of intrigue when CIA agents, both good and evil, mistake him for a contact by his wearing one red shoe. Sporadically funny remake (even Hanks is not too crazy about this one) of the French "The Tall Blond Man with One Black Shoe."

🪧 BEWARE 🪧 *Profanity and violence.*

1985 92m/C Tom Hanks, Dabney Coleman, Lori Singer, Carrie Fisher, James Belushi, Charles Durning, Edward Herrmann, Tommy Noonan, Gerrit Graham, David Lander, David Ogden Stiers; **D:** Stan Dragoti; **M:** Thomas Newman. **VHS, Beta** *FXV, FOX*

The Man with the Golden Gun 🦴🦴 ᵒ

PG/Jr. High-Adult Moore is the debonair secret agent 007 in this ninth of the Bond series. Assigned to recover a small piece of equipment which can be utilized to harness the sun's energy, Bond engages the usual bevy of villains and beauties.

🪧 BEWARE 🪧 *Violence, alcohol use and suggested sex. Bizarre assassination games.*

1974 134m/C Roger Moore, Christopher Lee, Britt Ekland, Maud Adams, Herve Villechaize, Clifton James, Soon-Teck Oh, Richard Loo, Marc Lawrence, Bernard Lee, Lois Maxwell, Desmond Llewelyn; **D:** Guy Hamilton; **W:** Tom Mankiewicz; **M:** John Barry. **VHS, Beta, LV** *MGM, FOX*

The Man Without a Face 🦴🦴 ᵒ

PG-13/Jr. High-Adult In his directorial debut (before "Braveheart") Gibson plays McLeod, a badly scarred recluse with a cloudy past. Into his life comes a lonely, fatherless boy, Chuck (Nick Stahl), who wants to escape his all-female family by going away to military school. He asks former teacher McLeod to tutor him for the entrance exam. Ages 15 and up.

🪧 BEWARE 🪧 *Accusations of child abuse, sex talk, profanity and scary facial makeup.*

1993 115m/C Mel Gibson, Nick Stahl, Margaret Whitton, Fay Masterson, Richard Masur, Gaby Hoffman, Geoffrey Lewis, Jack DeMave; **D:** Mel Gibson; **W:** Malcolm MacRury; **M:** James Horner. **VHS, Beta, LV** *WAR*

Man, Woman & Child 🦴🦴

PG/Sr. High-Adult Close, upscale California family is shocked when a child from the husband's long-ago affair with a Frenchwoman appears at their door. Pure sentimentalism, as the family tries to do the right thing in confronting this unexpected development. Two hankies—one each for fine performances by Sheen and Danner. Based on a sentimental novel by Erich Segal of "Love Story" fame, who co-wrote the script.

1983 99m/C Martin Sheen, Blythe Danner, Craig T. Nelson, David Hemmings; **D:** Dick Richards; **W:** Erich Segal; **M:** Georges Delerue. **VHS, Beta** *PAR*

The Manhattan Project 🦴🦴

PG-13/Jr. High-Adult For a science fair project, a high school genius builds a functional nuclear bomb, complete with plutonium swiped from a government lab, and a manhunt for him begins. Lithgow is excellent as a flippant weapons scientist who belatedly realizes the destructive power held by the boy (and, by extension, anyone with nukes). Teen technothriller has a splendid concept, but too many implausibilities disarm it.

🪧 BEWARE 🪧 *Profanity, mild sex talk.*

1986 112m/C John Lithgow, Christopher Collet, Cynthia Nixon, Jill Eikenberry, John Mahoney, Sully Boyer, Richard Council, Robert

Ben Archer and dad-to-be spend quality time together at an Indian Guides' meeting.

Schenkkan, Paul Austin; **D:** Marshall Brickman; **W:** Marshall Brickman. **VHS, Beta, LV** *REP*

Mannequin

PG/Jr. High-Adult Nerd creates store window displays for a living. One plaster mannequin turns out to be an enchanted maiden of old, who comes to life only once she's alone with the hero. Whenever they start to kiss, someone walks in and catches the guy in a romantic embrace with a now-lifeless, life-size doll. Not as lewd as it sounds, but jokes and dialogue were written seemingly for . . . well, dummies.

 *Sex talk.*

1987 90m/C Andrew McCarthy, Kim Cattrall, Estelle Getty, James Spader, Meshach Taylor, Carole Davis, G.W. Bailey; **D:** Michael Gottlieb; **W:** Ed Rugoff. **VHS, Beta, LV** *CCB, MED, VTR*

Mannequin 2: On the Move WOOF!

PG/Jr. High-Adult Less of a sequel, more of a witless rerun, with yet another lovesick princess frozen for 1,000 years and reviving as a department store dummy. Wild overacting in the cast suggest that everyone is auditioning for the Cannon Movie Tales.

 *Roughhousing.*

1991 95m/C Kristy Swanson, William Ragsdale, Meshach Taylor, Terry Kiser, Stuart Pankin; **D:** Stewart Raffill; **W:** Ed Rugoff. **VHS, LV** *LIV*

The Manners Monster: Ruby Goes to Dinner

Family Mischievous, lovable Rudy the monster learns table manners from the Livingtons family. Includes over 60 manners pointers and contains two wild and wonderful songs that teach kids good table manners. Ages 4 to 8.

1995 30m/C Bill Farmer, Danny Breen, George de la Pena. **VHS** *TPV*

Manny's Orphans

PG/Family Out-of-work teacher takes on a lovable home for orphaned boys. Dull retread of "Bad News Bears"—from a director who later made his name with bloody horror flicks like "Friday the 13th."

1978 92m/C Richard Lincoln, Malachy McCourt, Sel Skolnick; **D:** Sean S. Cunningham. **VHS, Beta** *LIV, VES, CNG*

Manon of the Spring

PG/Jr. High-Adult Sequel to "Jean de Florette" is an outstanding morality play based on a Marcel Pagnol novel. The adult daughter of the dead hunchback, Jean, discovers who blocked up the spring on her father's land. She plots her revenge, which proves greater than she could ever imagine. As the villain of the piece, Montand is outstanding, while Beart brings a rare beauty to the screen. In French with English subtitles.

BEWARE *Nudity.*

1987 113m/C Yves Montand, Daniel Auteuil, Emmanuelle Beart, Hippolyte Girardot; **D:** Claude Berri; **W:** Gerard Brach, Claude Berri. **VHS, Beta, LV** *ORI, APD, INJ*

Man's Best Friend

Family Collection of nine cartoons, featuring such lovable but lesser-known cartoon canines like Cuddles, Snoozer, Duffy Dog and Dizzy, all from "Woody Woodpecker" creator Lantz.
1964 51m/C VHS, Beta *MCA*

Maple Town

Preschool-Primary Animated series about anthropomorphic animals living in a tiny town, acting out vital life lessons for kids. Based on a Tonka toy line, which is a lesson in itself. Episodes include "The Stolen Necklace," "The Pot That Wouldn't Hold Water," and "Welcome to Maple Town."
1987 86m/C VHS, Beta *FHE*

Maple Town: Case of the Missing Candy

Preschool-Primary Animated adventure featuring the toy-store figurines. When their parents come down hard on them, Bobby Bear, Patty Rabbit, and others decide to run away. Things are swell until Wilde Wolf turns up to make things interesting. Also included is the episode, "Teacher, Please Don't Go."
1987 51m/C VHS *FHE*

March of the Wooden Soldiers 🦴🦴🦴

Family Hal Roach produced this classic combo of Mother Goose tale and Victor Herbert musical about the secret life of Christmas toys, with clowns Laurel and Hardy as Santa's helpers, who must save Toyland and Bo Peep from the wicked Barnaby and his apelike Bogeymen. Less than grandiose, but still way charming by modern standards, and a Yuletide "must see." Don't be surprised if Barnaby looks familiar; actor Kleinbach (later Henry Brandon) was the model for Disney's Gepetto in "Pinocchio." Also known as "Babes in Toyland" and available in a colorized version.
1934 73m/B Stan Laurel, Oliver Hardy, Charlotte Henry, Henry Kleinbach (Brandon), Felix Knight, Jean Darling, Johnny Downs, Marie Wilson; **D:** Charles "Buddy" Rogers, Gus Meins. **VHS, LV** *NOS, GKK, IME*

Marco Polo, Jr. 🦴

Preschool-Jr. High Marco Polo, Jr., the daring descendant of the legendary explorer, travels to Xanadu himself in this song-filled but cheaply animated feature from Australia.
1972 82m/C D: Eric Porter; **V:** Bobby Rydell. **VHS, Beta** *FHE*

Maricela

Family Young Maricela Flores and her mother come to the US from El Salvador to escape the civil war that killed her brother. Living with a Southern California family, Maricela has a hard time adjusting to life in a free society. Another solid entry in the PBS "WonderWorks" anthology, this offers good, complicated characters and doesn't simplify the issues.
1988 55m/C Linda Lavin, Carlina Cruz. **VHS** *PME, HMV, BTV*

Mario

PG/Primary-Jr. High Autistic 10-year-old Mario can only be drawn out of catatonia by teen brother Simon, with whom he plays imagination games on their island home. When Simon finds first love with a tourist girl, the lifelong burden of caring for Mario becomes too clear. Dreamlike Canadian drama, more for adults than kids. Ending is pure tragedy, wrapped in a wishful fantasy sequence. Based on the novel "La Sabliere" by Claude Jasmin.

BEWARE *Salty language; mature themes.*

1974 98m/C Francis Reddy, Xavier Normann Petemann, Nathalie Chalifour; **D:** Jean Beudin. **VHS, Beta** *NFB, HHE*

Mark Twain and Me 🦴🦴 🦴

Family Disney TV movie in which Robards portrays the aging and irascible Samuel Clemens, attended by a devoted adult daughter who nonetheless seems distant to him. On a sea voyage the writer forms a closer attachment with an adolescent girl named Dorothy. Based on a true story, recounted by Dorothy Quick in her book "Enchantment."
1991 93m/C Jason Robards Jr., Talia Shire, Amy Stewart, Chris Wiggins, R.H. Thomson, Fiona Reid; **D:** Daniel Petrie. **VHS** *DIS, BTV*

Mark Twain's A Connecticut Yankee in King Arthur's Court

Family Low-budget (shot on videotape) but worthwhile TV version of the Mark Twain novel. New England industrialist is magically teleported from the 19th century back to Arthurian England, where he becomes a knight ("Sir Boss") and tries to put his all-American know-how to work in Camelot. Interesting revision: Merlin the Magician, a bad guy in the book, is here benevolent, wise— and African.
1978 60m/C Richard Basehart, Roscoe Lee Browne, Paul Rudd. **VHS, Beta, LV** *MAS*

Marsalis on Music Why Toes Tap: Wynton on Rhythm

Primary On this series of four tapes, trumpeter Wynton Marsalis helps youngsters appreciate all sorts of music with the assistance of conductor Seiji Ozawa and students from Tanglewood. Subjects include rhythm, melody, harmony and how different influences affect music. The "monster" in "Tackling the Monster" is . . . practicing! Cellist Yo-Yo Ma offers encouragement on this one. Ages 9 and up.

1995 ?m/C VHS *NYR*

Martin the Cobbler

Family Tolstoy's classic tale delightfully rendered in claymation by the master of the art, Will Vinton. When old and bitter Martin asks God to reveal himself, Martin meets a woman with a hungry child, a tired workman, and an old woman. Through caring for them, Martin realizes he is encountering God, and celebrates this revelation with his community in their winter festival.

1977 20m/C VHS *ECU*

Marvelous Land of Oz 🎵🎵 ♭

Family One of a series of cartoon Oz adventures generally faithful to the L. Frank Baum original novels, and amusing for young and old. Here Dorothy makes her first return visit to the magic land in time to foil an Emerald City takeover by General Ginger, her all-schoolgirl army, and bumbling witch Mombi. Canadian animation (oddly Japanese-looking) is simplistic but effective, though character voices tend to be dull.

1988 90m/C VHS, Beta *COL*

Marvin & Tige 🎵🎵 ♭

PG/Family Sentimental drama about the deep friendship that develops between an aging alcoholic and a streetwise 11-year-old black boy he talks out of committing suicide after they meet one night in an Atlanta park.

BEWARE *Salty language, mature themes.*

1984 104m/C John Cassavetes, Gibran Brown, Billy Dee Williams, Fay Hauser, Denise Nicholas-Hill; *D:* Eric Weston. **VHS, Beta**

Mary Kate and Ashley Olsen: Our First Video

Primary Those twin rascals, who play Michelle on TV's long-running "Full House," expand their entertainment horizons and hit the singing and dancing circuit. This video provides seven clips in a variety of musical settings and includes songs about selling their brother and about their love for their mom.

1993 30m/C VHS *BMG, MVD*

Mary Poppins 🎵🎵🎵 ♭

Family Wonder-working English nanny descends one day via the East Wind and takes over the household of stuffy Londoner Mr. Banks. She introduces the Banks kids to such characters as Bert, the chimney sweep (Van Dyke) and a host of cartoon penguins. From Mary Poppins (Andrews, in her movie debut) the entire family learns that life can always be happy and joyous—not to mention supercalifragilisticexpialidocious—if you take the proper perspective. Based on the books by P.L. Travers, this is a tuneful Disney perennial that hasn't lost any of its magic over the years. 🎵 Chim Chim Cheree; A Spoonful of Sugar; The Perfect Nanny; Sister Suffragette; The Life I Lead; Stay Awake; Feed the Birds; Fidelity Feduciary Bank; Let's Go Fly a Kite.

1964 139m/C Ed Wynn, Hermione Baddeley, Julie Andrews, Dick Van Dyke, David Tomlinson, Glynis Johns; *D:* Robert Stevenson. **Award Nominations:** Academy Awards '64: Best Adapted Screenplay, Best Art Direction/Set Decoration (Color), Best Color Cinematography, Best Costume Design (Color), Best Director (Stevenson), Best Picture, Best Sound, Best Original Score; **Awards:** Academy Awards '64: Best Actress (Andrews), Best Film Editing, Best Song ("Chim Chim Cher-ee"), Best Visual Effects, Best Score; Golden Globe Awards '65: Best Actress—Musical/Comedy (Andrews). **VHS, Beta, LV** *DIS, APD, BTV*

The Marzipan Pig

Family An animated children's story about a lovable swine who brings joy to a desolate mouse, a languishing owl, an exhausted flower, and a bee with a thirst for knowledge.

1990 30m/C VHS, Beta *FHE, FCT*

M*A*S*H 🎵🎵🎵🎵

R/Sr. High-Adult Hilarious, irreverent, and well-cast black comedy about a group of surgeons and nurses at a Mobile Army Surgical Hospital in Korea. The horror of war is set in counterpoint to their need to create havoc with episodic late-night parties, practical jokes, and sexual antics. An all-out anti-war festival, highlighted by scenes that starkly uncover the chaos and irony of war, and establish Altman's influential style. Watch for real-life football players Fran Tarkenton, Ben Davidson, and Buck Buchanan as they make an appearance in the squad football game. Loosely adapted from the novel by the pseudonymous Richard Hooker (Dr. H. Richard Hornberger and William Heinz). Subsequent hit TV series moved even further from the source novel.

BEWARE *Nudity, doctors and nurses sleeping together, profanity, drinking (usually when off-duty), wartime violence and hospital blood.*

1970 116m/C Donald Sutherland, Elliott Gould, Tom Skerritt, Sally Kellerman, JoAnn Pflug, Robert Duvall, Rene Auberjonois, Roger Bowen, Gary Burghoff, Fred Williamson, John Schuck, Bud Cort, G. Wood; *D:* Robert Altman; *W:* Ring Lardner Jr.; *M:* Johnny Mandel. **Award Nominations:** Academy Awards '70: Best Director (Altman), Best Film Editing, Best Picture, Best Supporting Actress (Kellerman); **Awards:** Academy Awards '70: Best Adapted Screenplay; Cannes Film Festival '70: Best Film; Golden Globe Awards '71: Best Film—Musical/Comedy. **VHS, Beta, LV** *FOX*

Mask

PG-13/Jr. High-Adult Fact-based story of Rocky Dennis, a bright teenager struck by a rare disease that grotesquely warped his head and face. Shunned by strangers, he's accepted and nurtured by the rambunctious motorcycle gang who hang out with his no-nonsense single mom, but her habitual drug use soon wears on him. Sounds gimmicky but it isn't thanks to Stoltz's magnificent performance and unintrusive direction by Bogdanovich that rarely slips into maudlin territory. Depiction of a rowdy biker gang as a bunch of cuddly aunts and uncles takes some getting used to.

BEWARE *Drug abuse is winked at by the bikers but opposed by Rocky, as is mom's promiscuity. She also brings home a young prostitute to make her son feel less lonely; Rocky and the girl just talk instead. Salty language.*

1985 120m/C Cher, Sam Elliott, Eric Stoltz, Estelle Getty, Richard Dysart, Laura Dern, Harry Carey Jr., Lawrence Monoson, Marsha Warfield, Barry Tubb, Andrew (Andy) Robinson, Alexandra Powers; **D:** Peter Bogdanovich; **W:** Anna Hamilton Phelan. **VHS, Beta, LV** *MCA*

The Mask

PG-13/Jr. High-Adult Rubbery comedian Carrey acquires even more flexibility with special effects that turn him into a comic book character with super-powers every time he puts on the titular mask. Carrey plays nebbish bank clerk Stanley Ipkiss whose life is dreary until he discovers the mask. Silly plot involves gangsters and cops, but pay it no mind. Highlight is mask-wearing Carrey singing "Cuban Pete" a la Desi Arnaz, before making his escape. Ages 11 and up.

BEWARE *Violence and sex talk. Shot-gun (and other guns) shooting. And threat of a huge explosion.*

1994 100m/C Jim Carrey, Peter Riegert, Peter Greene, Amy Yasbeck; **D:** Chuck Russell; **W:** Mike Werb. **VHS** *NYR*

The Mask: Baby's Wild Ride

Preschool-Primary Stanley gets into much trouble when a baby ends up with his mystical mask. From the Saturday morning animated TV series based on the Jim Carrey movie, but without Carrey. Ages 6 to 10.

1996 ?m/C VHS *NLC, TTC*

The Mask: S-S-S Somebody Stop Me!

Preschool-Primary One of the first episodes of this animated series on impish Stanley Ipkiss and the mystical mask that gets him into lots of trouble. Ages 6 to 10.

1996 ?m/C VHS *NLC, TTC*

The Masked Marvel

Family Wartime serial in which the title hero saves America's industries from Axis saboteur Sakima. Unusual gimmick in this one is that the identity of the Masked Marvel is a secret until the final chapter; usually that's how the serials treated their costumed bad guys. In 12 episodes.

BEWARE *Violence.*

1943 195m/B William Forrest, Louise Currie, Johnny Arthur; **D:** Spencer Gordon Bennet. **VHS** *VCN, REP, MLB*

Masters of the Universe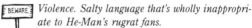

PG/Primary-Adult Action-choked movie of the cartoon character/toy franchise is of the it-could-have-been-worse variety; pitching it at a high school audience was a definite mistake. Muscular He-Man (actors actually say that name without giggling) and friends fight Skeletor for supremacy on the planet Eternia. A Cosmic Key teleports the heroes to Anytown USA, where they continue sword and laser battles in the conveniently deserted streets. Big-budget adventure wasn't Master of the Box Office, so you can disregard the promised sequel at the close.

BEWARE *Violence. Salty language that's wholly inappropriate to He-Man's rugrat fans.*

1987 109m/C Dolph Lundgren, Frank Langella, Billy Barty, Courteney Cox, Meg Foster; **D:** Gary Goddard; **M:** Bill Conti. **VHS, Beta, LV** *WAR*

Matewan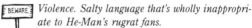

PG-13/Jr. High-Adult Sayles' gripping drama of a West Virginia coal miners' strike in the 1920's and the horrendous working conditions that brought on the strike. Good performances all around, particularly Jones, imposing yet understated as a union leader. Has the look and feel of the times; Sayles even wrote some authentic-sounding labor songs. Watch for Mary McDonnell and Gordon Clapp (Detective Medavoy on "NYPD Blue") in supporting roles. Hard-hitting, penetrating evocation of American labor history.

BEWARE *Strikers viciously attacked by goons.*

1987 130m/C Chris Cooper, James Earl Jones, Mary McDonnell, William Oldham, Kevin Tighe, David Strathairn; **D:** John Sayles; **W:** John Sayles; **C:** Haskell Wexler; **M:** Mason Daring. **Award Nominations:** Academy Awards '87: Best Cinematography; **Awards:** Independent Spirit Awards '88: Best Cinematography. **VHS, Beta, LV** *ORI, WAR*

Matilda

PG/Primary-Adult The only thing worse than a monkey movie is a boxing kangaroo movie, and the only thing worse than a boxing kangaroo movie is one in which the kangaroo is obviously a person in an animal costume. The roo is a ruse. The flick is a flop. Ages 4 to 8.

1978 103m/C Elliott Gould, Robert Mitchum, Harry Guardino, Clive Revill; **D:** Daniel Mann. **VHS, Beta** *LIV, VES*

Matilda

Family Intelligent child Matilda is misunderstood and oppressed by her moronic and monstrous parents and an awful school principal, but her first grade teacher, Miss

Mary Poppins, Bert and kids have fun being chimney sweeps in "Mary Poppins."

Honey (appropriately named!), believes in her. Matilda discovers she has hidden powers and begins to plot a way to get back at the miserable people in her life. Kids will enjoy the almost cartoon-like illusion of the film. Director DeVito even built a "Carrot-Cam" to capture the flight of the flying vegetable during a food fight. Based on the book by Roald Dahl.

BEWARE *Be wary of wretched parents and other mean adults who mentally abuse poor Matilda.*

1996 ?m/C Danny DeVito, Rhea Perlman, Embeth Davidtz, Mara Wilson, Pam Ferris; **D:** Danny DeVito; **W:** Robin Swicord, Nicholas Kazan. **VHS** *NYR*

Matinee 🎵🎵🎵

PG/Jr. High-Adult Comic look at fantasy/sci-fi cheapies and the youthful audiences raised on them in bygone days. Setting is Key West, Florida, during the 1962 Cuban Missile Crisis; while the rest of the country fears nuclear annihilation, a gimmick-crazed Hollywood producer (Goodman, based on more than one actual movie mogul) test screens his radioactive-monster movie "MANT: Half-man, Half-ant, All Terror!" for a teen audience. Meanwhile, kids in the crowd have their own little romantic subplots and intrigues going. Trouble is, none of that is ever as hip or funny as the too-brief "Mant" sequences, re-created in impeccable B&W by director Dante (who's had offers to finish "Mant" and release that on its own!). Note the brief coming-attractions spoof "The Screwy Shopping Cart," a poke at hopelessly square Disney flicks—like the "Herbie" series—that only drove smart kids to the creature features instead.

BEWARE *Monster movie within the movie may frighten small children.*

1992 98m/C John Goodman, Cathy Moriarty, Simon Fenton, Omri Katz, Lisa Jakub, Kellie Martin, Jesse Lee, Lucinda Jenney, James Villemaire, Robert Picardo, Dick Miller, John Sayles, Mark Mc-Cracken, Jesse White, David Clennon, Luke Halpin; **D:** Joe Dante; **M:** Jerry Goldsmith. **VHS, Beta, LV** *MCA, BTV*

Maurice Sendak Library

Family Three of Sendak's popular children's books are brought to the screen in animated form, plus an interview with Sendak himself in which he talks about his work.

1990 35m/C Maurice Sendak; **V:** Carole King, Prof. Peter Schickele. **VHS, Beta** *FCT, CCC, MLT*

Maurice Sendak's Really Rosie

Primary Animated tale of Rosie, who gets the entire neighborhood into her pretend movie and into her private spotlight. King provides the voice of Rosie and the songs.

1975 26m/C M: Carole King. **VHS, Beta** *CCC,, MVD*

Maverick 🎧🎧🎧

PG/Jr. High-Adult Entertaining remake of the popular ABC series is fresh and funny, with sharp dialogue and a good cast. Everybody looks like they're having a great time, not difficult for the charming Gibson, but a refreshing change of pace for the usually serious Foster and Greene. In a fun bit of casting, Garner, the original Maverick, shows up as Marshal Zane Cooper. Lightweight, fast-paced comedy was reportedly highly improvised, though Donner retained enough control to keep it coherent. The end is left wide open so a sequel seems likely. Keep your eyes peeled for cameos from country stars, old time Western actors, and an unbilled appearance from Glover.

> **BEWARE** *Profanity, people in bathtubs, gambling and alcohol.*

1994 129m/C Mel Gibson, Jodie Foster, James Garner, Graham Greene, James Coburn, Alfred Molina, Paul Smith, Geoffrey Lewis, Max Perlich; **Cameos:** Dub Taylor, Dan Hedaya, Robert Fuller, Doug McClure, Bert Remsen, Denver Pyle, Will Hutchins, Waylon Jennings, Kathy Mattea, Danny Glover, Clint Black; **D:** Richard Donner; **W:** William Goldman; **M:** Randy Newman. **VHS** *NYR*

Max Dugan Returns 🎧🎧

PG/Jr. High-Adult A Simon comedy about an ex-con trying to make up with his daughter by showering her with presents bought with stolen money. Sweet and light, with a good cast.

1983 98m/C Jason Robards Jr., Marsha Mason, Donald Sutherland, Matthew Broderick, Kiefer Sutherland; **D:** Herbert Ross; **W:** Neil Simon; **M:** David Shire. **VHS, Beta, LV** *FOX*

Max Fleischer's Cartoon Capers, Vol. 1: Playin' Around

Family Three vintage titles from the Fabulous Fleischer Studios: "Play Safe," "Small Fry," and "Ants in the Plants." Additional volumes available.

1941 25m/C VHS, Beta *DIS*

Max is Missing 🎧🎧 ♩

PG/Family Set in the ruins of Machu Picchu in the Peruvian Andes, an energetic 12-year-old is separated from his father and finds adventure in his mysterious surroundings. He is given a priceless Incan artifact by a dying man and teams up with a local lad to guard it from fortune hunters.

> **BEWARE** *Mild action violence and language.*

1995 95m/C Toran Caudell, Victor Rojas, Matthew Sullivan, Rick Dean, Charles Napier; **D:** Mark Griffiths. **VHS** *HMK*

Maxie's World: Dancin' & Romancin'

Preschool-Primary Antics of a modern teen queen, cartoon-style; fashionable Maxie has her own television program and leads a busy social life at Surfside High School. Such stuff as dreams are made of, repackaged for home video. Additional volumes available.

1989 120m/C VHS *JFK*

Max's Chocolate Chicken and Other Stories for Young Children

Preschool Three charming children's stories. "Max's Chocolate Chicken" by Rosemary Wells finds Max the bunny and his big sister Ruby in an Easter story which features a moral about playing fair. "Each Peach Pear Plum" by Janet and Allan Ahlberg has familiar Mother Goose and folklore characters hiding in colorful pictures and waiting to be found by eagle-eyed youngsters. "The Circus Baby" by Maud and Miska Petersham finds a baby elephant with bad manners learning a lesson from his mother.

1992 30m/C VHS *CCC, WKV, BTV*

Me and My Tugboat

Preschool-Primary Video stars the Margaret Moran, a sturdy little tug boat at work in New York Harbor, moving oil tankers and barges, escorting and docking giant ocean liners. Contributing a mega-dose of personality are the Margaret Moran's real-life skipper, Captain Bob (Robert Flannery), and deckhand, Big Mike (Michael Riordan), two knowing charmers with Big Apple accents as thick as those pretzels the street-corner vendors sell. Ages 4 to 9.

199? ?m/C VHS *NYR*

Meatballs 🎧🎧

PG/Jr. High-Adult The Activities Director at kiddie Camp North Star is a sarcastic goof, and . . . that's about it really, as Murray breezes through comic routines and a bit of sentimental schmaltz in the role that made him a sensation and inspired some many stinkaroo imitations—especially its own numerous sequels (all done without Murray or director Reitman).

> **BEWARE** *Brief nudity, sex, profanity and making fun of fat kids.*

1979 92m/C Bill Murray, Harvey Atkin, Kate Lynch; **D:** Ivan Reitman; **W:** Len Blum, Harold Ramis; **M:** Elmer Bernstein. **VHS, Beta, LV** *PAR*

Meet Me in St. Louis 🎧🎧🎧 ♩

Family Charming tale of a St. Louis family during the 1903 World's Fair has plenty of period detail. One of Garland's better musical performances as one of four daughters who become anxious when dad is told he

Jim Carrey as "The Mask" has a heart-pulsing moment.

needs to relocate to New York. Future husband Minnelli directs superbly. And the songs are great: "Meet Me in St. Louis" and "Have Yourself a Merry Christmas" among them. 🎵 You and I; Skip to My Lou; Over the Bannister; Meet Me In St. Louis; Brighten the Corner; Summer In St. Louis; All Hallow's Eve; Ah, Love; The Horrible One.

1944 113m/C Judy Garland, Margaret O'Brien, Mary Astor, Lucille Bremer, Tom Drake, June Lockhart, Harry Davenport; **D:** Vincente Minnelli. **Award Nominations:** Academy Awards '44: Best Color Cinematography, Best Screenplay, Best Song ("The Trolley Song"), Best Original Score; **Awards:** National Board of Review Awards '44: 10 Best Films of the Year. **VHS, Beta, LV, 8mm** *MGM, TLF, HMV*

Meet the Hollowheads 🦴 🕊

PG-13/Sr. High-Adult Miscalculated 'family' situation comedy set in a foul future society of tubes, drains, pipes and drippy conduits. There a harried father must prepare his awful, slime-ridden household for a visit from the tyrannical boss. Directorial debut of makeup expert Burnam not surprisingly emphasizes grossness and f/x.

⚠ BEWARE 🚩 *The Hollowhead daughter is a sex-crazed nymphet, and the boss who lusts after her gets what he deserves in a violent finale. Salty language.*

1989 89m/C John Glover, Nancy Mette, Richard Portnow, Matt Shakman, Juliette Lewis, Anne Ramsey; **D:** Tom Burman. **VHS, LV** *MED, IME*

Melody 🦴🦴 🕊

G/Family Melody is a 12-year-old girl in love with 11-year-old Daniel; so much so that they petition adults to allow them to marry. Sweet-natured British production (not at all the raunch it might have been a few decades later) slightly soured by slow narrative and severely outdated '60s-era 'Swinging London' ambiance. Frequent musical interludes by the Bee Gees.

1971 106m/C Tracy Hyde, Jack Wild, Mark Lester, Colin Barrie, Roy Kinnear; **D:** Waris Hussein; **W:** Alan Parker. **VHS, Beta**

Memoirs of an Invisible Man 🦴🦴

PG-13/Jr. High-Adult Nick Halloway, a slick and shallow stock analyst, is rendered invisible by a freak accident. When he is pursued by a CIA agent-hit man who wants to exploit him, Nick turns for help to Alice, a documentary filmmaker he has just met. Naturally, they fall in love along the way. Effective sight gags, hardworking cast can't overcome pitfalls in script, which indecisively meanders between comedy and thrills.

BEWARE *Comic violence. Not really as light as it should be.*

1992 99m/C Chevy Chase, Daryl Hannah, Sam Neill, Michael Mc-Kean, Stephen Tobolowsky, Jim Norton, Patricia Heaton, Rosalind Chao; *D:* John Carpenter. **VHS, LV** *WAR*

Men Don't Leave 🦴🦴🦴

PG-13/Jr. High-Adult Newly widowed, Beth has to sell her home and move to an urban apartment to take a full-time job. Her two sons start drifting away, the younger one staying with his best friend's family, the older a live-in lover for an older woman in the building. Muted, often painful family drama with a ring of truth—it doesn't tie up things neatly at the end and offers characters of unexpected depth and emotion. Great performances by all in drama deserving of more recognition.

BEWARE *Profanity, mature themes as Beth slips into pill-popping manic depression. Brief sex.*

1989 115m/C Jessica Lange, Arliss Howard, Joan Cusack, Kathy Bates, Charlie Korsmo, Corey Carrier, Chris O'Donnell, Tom Mason, Jim Haynie; *D:* Paul Brickman; *W:* Barbara Benedek, Paul Brickman; *M:* Thomas Newman. **VHS, Beta, LV, 8mm** *WAR*

Men of Boys Town 🦴🦴🦴

Family Sequel to 1938's "Boys Town" has the same sentimentality, even more if that's possible. Father Flanagan's reformatory faces closure, while the kids reach out to an embittered new inmate. Worth seeing for the cast reprising their roles.

1941 106m/B Spencer Tracy, Mickey Rooney, Darryl Hickman, Henry O'Neill, Lee J. Cobb, Sidney Miller; *D:* Norman Taurog. **VHS** *MGM, FCT*

Menace on the Mountain 🦴🦴

G/Family Family-oriented drama about a father and son facing hardship during the Civil War.

1970 89m/C Patricia Crowley, Albert Salmi, Charles Aidman. **VHS, Beta** *DIS*

Menace II Society 🦴🦴🦴🦴

R/Sr. High-Adult Portrayal of black teens lost in inner-city hell is realistically captured by 21-year-old twin directors, in their big-screen debut. Caine (Turner) lives with his grandparents and peddles drugs for spending money, from the eve of his high school graduation to his decision to escape south-central Los Angeles for Atlanta. Bleak and haunting, with unsettling, bloody violence at the core of this urban tragedy. Based on a story by the Hughes' and Tyger Williams.

BEWARE *Very mature teens may withstand the heavy violence, obscenity, drug taking, sexual situations, and so on that occur. On the other hand, lots of fairly mature adults have trouble sitting through this one.*

1993 104m/C Tyrin Turner, Larenz Tate, Samuel L. Jackson, Glenn Plummer, Julian Roy Doster, Bill Duke, Charles S. Dutton; *D:* Allen Hughes, Albert Hughes; *W:* Tyrin Turner. **Award Nominations:** Independent Spirit Awards '94: Best Actor (Turner), Best Cinematography, Best First Feature; **Awards:** MTV Movie Awards '94: Best Film. **VHS, LV** *COL, NLC, IME*

Meet the Star of Matilda, Mara Wilson

Mara Wilson is no stranger to the silver screen. She has starred in several feature films, including *Mrs. Doubtfire* with Robin Williams and *Miracle on 34th Street* with Richard Attenborough. But her latest effort as the lead character in *Matilda* is a bit more challenging. Not only is the story of Matilda, a little girl who is downtrodden by villainous parents, a tough story, but Wilson's real life has become tough over the past year. Her mother Suzie was diagnosed with cancer in 1995. As her mother underwent extreme therapy, Wilson was taken under the wings of *Matilda* co-stars Perlman and Devito, even spending the night at their home.

Like her character in *Matilda*, friends say Wilson seems mature beyond her years. She talks about what she'll do when she grows up. "I don't know if I'm always going to be acting," she says. "Maybe when I grow up, I will be a scriptwriter. I already have a few scripts in my head."

Born the fourth of five children to Mike and Suzie Wilson in the San Fernando Valley on July 24, 1987, Wilson was inspired by older brother Danny, who is also an actor. Mara showed her adult-like personality when she landed the role in *Mrs. Doubtfire* by impressing the producers by reading her own script.

Merlin and the Sword 🦴

Family Poor use of a good cast in this hokey, made-for-TV treatment of the legend of King Arthur, as a 20th-century gal tumbles back through time and finds herself in Camelot, caught up between intrigues with Merlin and the witch Morgan Le Fey.

1985 94m/C Malcolm McDowell, Edward Woodward, Candice Bergen, Dyan Cannon; *D:* Clive Donner. **VHS, Beta** *LIV, VES*

Mermaids 🎷🎷🎷

PG-13/Jr. High-Adult Mrs. Flax is a flamboyant single mother of two who leaves town every time a relationship threatens to turn serious. Having moved some eighteen times, her daughters, Charlotte, 15, and Kate, 8, are a little worse for the wear, psychologically. The former aspiring to be a nun though they're not Catholic. Amusing, well-acted comedy-drama of multi-generational maturity (or lack of it), based on a novel by Patty Dann.

> **BEWARE** *Sex talk and profanity. Charlotte almost loses virginity. Kate has a habit of submerging herself in the bathtub.*

1990 110m/C Cher, Winona Ryder, Bob Hoskins, Christina Ricci, Michael Schoeffling, Caroline McWilliams, Jan Miner; *D:* Richard Benjamin; *W:* June Roberts; *M:* Jack Nitzsche. **VHS, Beta, LV** *ORI*

A Merry Mirthworm Christmas

Family The animated annelids known as Mirthworms get together to celebrate Christmas and that's when the alleged fun begins.

1984 30m/C *V:* Rachel Rutledge, Jerry Reynolds, Peggy Nicholson. **VHS, Beta** *FHE*

The Meteor Man 🎷🎷 ♭

PG/Jr. High-Adult Initially gentle superhero spoof about a D.C. teacher acquiring semi-super powers after being hit by a meteor. Fun stuff; Meteor Man flies only four feet off the ground (because he's afraid of heights) and tries on ludicrous costumes sewn by his mother. Plot sags, though, in a prolonged knockabout showdown with a gang terrorizing the neighborhood. Theme of black citizens standing up against crime, but, as in the first Ninja Turtles feature, bad guys are ultra-cool, and one wonders what message kid viewers are getting. Special f/x by Industrial Light and Magic; interesting cameo by Cosby.

> **BEWARE** *Violence and street gang terrorism.*

1993 100m/C Robert Townsend, Robert Guillaume, Marla Gibbs, James Earl Jones, Frank Gorshin; *Cameos:* Bill Cosby, Sinbad, Luther Vandross, LaWanda Page; *D:* Robert Townsend; *W:* Robert Townsend. **VHS, LV** *MGM*

Metropolitan 🎷🎷🎷

PG-13/Sr. High-Adult Brittle comedy of manners among upper-class teenagers of Manhattan, during Christmas break. Middle-class Tom is drawn into a nightly circle of friends who debate socialism, Jane Austin heroines, the existence of God, and who's going out with whom with equal civility and precocious world-weary wit. After the monosyllabic grunts that pass for 'realistic' dialogue in other flirting-with-adulthood movies, this intelligent talkfest comes as a welcome change,

though viewers who aren't hooked right off will inevitably be bored. Released to theaters unrated; on video its PG-13 is inexplicable.

> **BEWARE** *Sex talk, with shades of drug use, and widely scattered profanity.*

1990 98m/C Carolyn Farina, Edward Clements, Taylor Nichols, Christopher Eigeman, Allison Rutledge-Parisi, Dylan Hundley, Isabel Gillies, Bryan Leder, Will Kempe, Elizabeth Thompson; *D:* Whit Stillman; *W:* Whit Stillman; *M:* Mark Suozzo. **Award Nominations:** Academy Awards '90: Best Original Screenplay; **Awards:** Independent Spirit Awards '91: Best First Feature; New York Film Critics Awards '90: Best Director (Stillman). **VHS, LV** *COL, FCT*

Mickey & the Beanstalk

Family Mickey, Donald and Goofy enact their version of "Jack and the Beanstalk" in this classic featurette which originally comprised one-half of the film "Fun and Fancy Free." Notable as the last film for which Disney provided the voice of Mickey Mouse. All ages.

1947 29m/C *V:* Walt Disney. **VHS, Beta** *DIS*

Mickey Mouse Club, Vol. 1

Preschool-Primary Each cassette in this series features three episodes from the popular 1950s' television series, with a newly filmed introduction by Annette Funicello. These lively programs, starring the "Mouseketeers," include song, dance, cartoons, documentary newsreels, and continuing serialized adventures. Additional volumes available.

195? 90m/B Annette Funicello. **VHS, Beta** *DIS*

Mickey Mouse: The Early Years Series

Preschool-Primary The world's best-loved animated mouse stars in some very early Disney adventures on separate tapes, including his very first, "Steamboat Willie" from 1928. Others are "The Band Concert" (1935) and "Thru the Mirror" (1936). In all three, Walt Disney himself lends his voice to the trademark creation.

1990 9m/C VHS, Beta *MTI, DSN*

Mickey's Birthday Party

Preschool-Primary It's Mickey's birthday, and the whole Disney cartoon gang celebrates with a cake made by Goofy.

1942 8m/C VHS, Beta *MTI, DSN*

Mickey's Christmas Carol 🎷🎷🎷

G/Family Mickey Mouse returns along with all the other Disney characters in this adaptation of the Charles Dickens classic that marked the legendary rodent's first all-new cartoon in decades; an added documentary describes how the featurette was made.

1983 25m/C VHS, Beta, LV *DIS, MTI, DSN*

Mickey's Crazy Careers

Family Outstanding collection from Disney with five bonafide classics, and one early black and white cartoon. The classics are Mickey's first Technicolor adventure "The Band Concert," plus "Clock Cleaners," "Tugboat Mickey," "Magician Mickey," and "Mickey's Fire Brigade."

1940 48m/C VHS, Beta *TOU*

Mickey's Field Trips Series

Preschool-Primary Mickey takes children on trips to a fire station, hospital, police station and the United Nations, where he teaches the importance of each and their various functions and value.

1988 12m/C VHS, Beta *MTI, DSN*

Mickey's Fun Songs: Campout at Walt Disney World

Preschool-Primary Go camping at Fort Wilderness in Orlando, Florida, and have a blast in relay races, boating games, a hayride and singing at a campfire. Among the songs: "Comin' Round the Mountain," "By the Sea," "The Happy Wanderer," "Don't Fence Me In," "Mountain Greenery" and "Jeepers Creepers." Ages 4 to 8. Comin' Round the Mountain; The Bare Necessities; The Caisons Go Rolling Along; The Happy Wanderer; Oh, Susanna!; Camptown Races; By the Beautiful Sea; Don't Fence Me In; Turkey in the Straw.

1994 40m/C VHS *TOU*

Mickey's Fun Songs: Let's Go to the Circus

Preschool-Primary Features the talents of "Children of the Rainbow," a circus troupe of young stars, who perform with Disney characters at the 200th anniversary celebration of the Ringling Brothers and Barnum & Bailey Circus. Plenty of rousing tunes and lyrics on the screen for kids of all ages to sing. Among the songs: "Aba Daba Honeymoon," "The Man on the Flying Trapeze," and "Be a Clown." Ages 4 to 8. Rainbow World; The Circus on Parade; Upside Down; Aba Daba Honeymoon; I Wanna Be Like You; The Man on the Flying Trapeze; Over and Over Again; Those Magnificent Men in their Flying Machines; Make 'Em Laugh.

1994 40m/C VHS *TOU*

Mickey's Magical World

Family A collection of excerpts and shorts from the golden era of Disney studios. Most of the excerpts are available in complete form in other collections. Included are "Gulliver Mickey," "Thru the Mirror" and part of "The Sorcerer's Apprentice," lifted from "Fantasia." Ages 5 to 10.

1988 27m/C VHS, Beta *TOU*

A Midnight Clear 🦴🦴🦴

PG/Sr. High-Adult Sensitive war drama takes place in the Ardennes Forest, near the French-German border in December 1944. It's Christmas time and six of the remaining members of a 12-member squad are sent on a dangerous mission to an abandoned house to locate the enemy. Filmed in a dreamy surreal style, the setting is somewhat reminiscent of a fairytale, although a sense of anguish is present throughout. Solid script, excellent direction, and a good cast make this more than another WWII fly by night. Adapted from the novel by William Wharton.

BEWARE *War violence and profanity.*

1992 107m/C Peter Berg, Kevin Dillon, Arye Gross, Ethan Hawke, Gary Sinise, Frank Whaley, John C. McGinley, Larry Joshua, Curt Lowens; **D:** Keith Gordon; **W:** Keith Gordon; **M:** Mark Isham. **VHS, LV** *COL, PMS*

Midnight Madness 🦴

PG/Family Five teams of college students chase all over the city of Los Angeles for clues in an all-night scavenger hunt. This insipid, no-brainer comedy's lone claim to fame (aside from an early Michael J. Fox appearance) was being among the Disney Studio's first PG-rated pics.

1980 110m/C David Naughton, Stephen Furst, Debra Clinger, Eddie Deezen, Michael J. Fox, Maggie Roswell; **D:** David Wechter; **W:** David Wechter. **VHS, Beta** *TOU, OM*

The Mighty Ducks 🦴🦴 🦴

PG/Jr. High-Adult Bad News Bears (Disney-style) on skates. Selfish lawyer Gordon Bombay is arrested for drunk driving, and his sentence is to coach juvenile hockey players, the usual misfits, slobs and underachievers. Dual themes of teamwork and redemption are hammered constantly and heavily, but there's exciting rink action and good ensemble work from the kids. Scored with young fans thanks to the phenomenon of peewee hockey, and a real-life team, the Mighty Ducks of Anaheim, was founded as a result/promo of this hit. Followed by more hockey shenanigans in "D2—The Mighty Ducks."

BEWARE *Alcohol use, fighting and hockey hijinks.*

1992 114m/C Emilio Estevez, Joss Ackland, Lane Smith, Heidi Kling, Josef Sommer, Matt Doherty, Steven Brill, Joshua Jackson, Elden Ratliff, Shaun Weiss; **D:** Stephen Herek; **W:** Steven Brill, Brian Hohlfield; **M:** David Newman. **VHS, Beta, LV** *TOU, BTV*

The Mighty Ducks 3 🦴🦴

PG/Jr. High-Adult After their victory in D2, the Mighty Ducks are hot and in demand and they're recruited by the snobby Eden Hall Academy to lock the state's championship for the school team. But, hold on! Dean Buckley doesn't believe in those mighty little hockey champs and he plans to revoke their scholarships and kick them out of school. To the rescue is their former coach Gordon Bombay, attempting to save the day with his legal expertise. Oh well, do you think we'll see these ducks through college?

BEWARE *Some hockey rough-housing and mild language.*

1996 ?m/C Emilio Estevez, Shaun Weiss, Matt Doherty. **VHS** *NYR*

Mighty Hercules: Champion of the People!

Family Hercules champions justice, fights for truth, and punishes evil-doers in these early '60s syndicated TV cartoons brought back from the Underworld.
1963 60m/C VHS *VMK*

Mighty Hercules: Conqueror of Evil!

Family When a magic ring is exposed to lightning it changes a mere mortal into . . . the Mighty Hercules!
1963 60m/C VHS *VMK*

The Mighty Hercules: Mightiest Mortal!

Family He's very mighty! But wait! If the Mighty Hercules is so great(!), why can't he do something about all these exclamation points?! Just asking!
1963 60m/C VHS *VMK*

Mighty Joe Young 🦴🦴🐾

Family Creators of the original "King Kong" and "Son of Kong" returned with more kid-friendly monkeyshines in this tale about yet another giant ape brought from the African wilds to civilization and exploited in a silly nightclub act. Bullied and gaining the key to the liquor cabinet, the sweet-tempered Joe goes on a drunken rampage but redeems himself by rescuing orphans from a convenient fire. Stop-motion special f/x courtesy of Willis O'Brien and the great Ray Harryhausen are probably the film's best feature. Also available colorized. Laserdisc includes commentary on the technical wizardry involved.

BEWARE *Roughhousing, primate alcohol use.*

1949 94m/B Terry Moore, Ben Johnson, Robert Armstrong, Frank McHugh; **D:** Ernest B. Schoedsack. **VHS, Beta, LV** *TTC*

Mighty Morphin Power Rangers: Alpha's Magical Christmas

Primary Alpha the Power Ranger robot celebrates Christmas with a group of children. Includes guest appearances by the Power Rangers and features 10 Christmas songs. Nobody gets karate-kicked. Ages 3 to 7.
1994 30m/C VHS *AVE*

Mighty Morphin Power Rangers: Green with Evil, Part 1

Preschool-Primary Rita Repulsa uses Green Ranger to weaken the rest of the team. Lots of karate kicks. Ages 3 to 7.
1994 25m/C VHS *PGV*

Mighty Morphin Power Rangers Karate Club

Primary Karate master Jason Frank, who plays Tommy on the popular series, introduces kids to the discipline of martial arts. Level one instruction with safety rules explained. Not an episode of the TV series. Ages 5 to 9.
1994 40m/C VHS *AVE*

Mighty Morphin Power Rangers: The Movie 🦴 🐾

PG/Family Teens with super powers (and swell-looking mechanical animals) save the world, before supper, from the evil Ivan Ooze. Ivan Ooze for you, too: you'll hate it, your six-year-old will love it.

BEWARE *Action violence—no blood.*

1995 93m/C Paul Freeman, Jason Harold Yost, Amy Jo Johnson, Jason David Frank, John Yong Bosch, Stephen Antonio Cardenas; **D:** Bryan Spicer; **W:** Arne Olsen, John Camps; **C:** Paul Murphy; **M:** Graeme Revell. **VHS** *FXV*

Mighty Mouse

Family Moon-dwelling mouse stars in this tape in a vintage Terrytoon, along with a few other animated creations. Titles include "Wolf! Wolf!," "Christmas Comes but Once a Year," "Porky's Railroad," and "Timid Toreador." Additional volumes available.
19?? 30m/C V: Tom Morrison. **VHS** *CNG*

Mighty Mouse in the Great Space Chase

Family Feature-length adventure starring the moon-dwelling rodent hero of Terrytoon fame, in which Mighty Mouse battles the nefarious Harry the Heartless in order to save Queen Pureheart and the galaxy. Additional volumes available.
1983 88m/C VHS, Beta

Mighty Orbots: Devil's Asteroid

Preschool-Primary Cartoon sci-fi; if you're old enough to decipher the anagram "orbot" you may be too old to watch. Evil lord creates an imposter killer Orbot, causing the real Orbots to be sentenced for murder to the Devil's Asteroid for 999 years.
1984 26m/C VHS, Beta *MGM*

The Mighty Pawns

Family To keep inner city junior-high kids off the streets, a progressive teacher starts a chess club and tricks some unruly students into joining. The logic and discipline of the ancient game motivates most of them to improve in and out of the classroom. Familiar but uplifting "Wonder-Works" episode, based on the true story of the "Bad Bishops" of Robert Vaux Junior High School in Philadelphia.

1987 58m/C Paul Winfield, Alfonso Ribeiro, Terence Knox, Rosalind Cash, Teddy Wilson; **D:** Eric Laneuville. **VHS** *PME, HMV, FCT*

Mighty Thor: Enter Hercules

Primary-Jr. High TV cartoons in which the Marvel Comics hero Thor fights for his girl in "Enter Hercules" and travels to the 30th Century in "The Tomorrow Man." Additional volumes available.

1966 35m/C VHS

Mike Mulligan and His Steam Shovel

Preschool-Primary Thanks to modern technology, Mike's trusty steamshovel Mary Anne is becoming obsolete. They still, however, manage to dig themselves into a number of dilemmas. A typically hip cartoon version of the Virginia Lee Burton book from animator Michael Sporn.

1992 25m/C VHS

Mikhail Baryshinikov's Stories from My Childhood

Preschool-Primary Presents fairy tales from around the world.

1996 ?m/C VHS *FHE, LIV*

Milk Money 🦴

PG-13/Jr. High-Adult Bunch of suburban 12-year-olds crack open their piggy banks and bike into the big city to find a woman they can pay to let them see her naked. They find a prostitute (Griffith) for the job, whom one boy decides would be perfect to bring home to his widower dad (Harris). Then things get far-fetched. Dad and the hooker fall for each other when they discover a mutual interest in ornithology. Indeed, this movie is for the birds. Hollywood seems to think that prostitution is an acceptable but slightly disreputable career choice, somewhere between lawyer and film critic. This may not be a seriously harmful message for children but it can't be doing them any good.

> **BEWARE** *Prostitution, sexual themes involving adolescents. Griffith in a bodysuit allows Frank to draw diagram of the female reproductive system on her in front of his class.*

1994 110m/C Michael Patrick Carter, Melanie Griffith, Ed Harris, Malcolm McDowell, Casey Siemaszko, Anne Heche, Philip Bosco; **D:**

Richard Benjamin; **W:** John Mattson; **M:** Michael Convertino. **VHS, Beta** *PAR*

Million Dollar Duck 🦴🦴

G/Family Hollywood lays an egg. Disney live action movie stars Dean Jones as a research scientist who can't afford to buy his son a dog (science pays better these days), so he brings home an irradiated duck from the lab. Turns out the duck lays golden eggs. This doesn't go unnoticed in the neighborhood and considerable silliness ensues. Ages 7 to 11.

1971 92m/C Dean Jones, Sandy Duncan, Joe Flynn, Tony Roberts; **D:** Vincent McEveety; **M:** Buddy Baker. **VHS, Beta** *DIS, OM*

Million Dollar Kid 🦴🦴

Jr. High-Adult When a group of thugs wreak havoc in the neighborhood, the East Side Kids try to help a wealthy man put a stop to it. They face an even greater dilemma when they discover that the man's son is part of the gang.

1944 65m/B Leo Gorcey, Huntz Hall, Gabriel Dell, Louise Currie, Noah Beery Jr., Iris Adrian, Mary Gordon; **D:** Wallace Fox. **VHS** *VYY, DVT, NOS*

The Mini-Monsters: Adventures at Camp Mini-Mon

Family Summer camp cartoon adventure for young monster admirers.

1987 33m/C VHS *ORI, WAR*

A Minor Miracle 🦴🦴

G/Family Minor movie about a group of orphaned children who band together under the loving guidance of a dying priest (famed movie director/actor Huston) to save St. Francis School from closure. Their plan: a big soccer match. And yes, that is soccer legend Pele in a supporting role. Also known as "Young Giants."

1983 100m/C John Huston, Pele, Peter Fox; **D:** Terrell Tannen. **VHS, Beta, LV** *COL*

The Miracle 🦴🦴🦴

PG/Jr. High-Adult Irish teens, whose strong friendship is based upon their equally unhappy home lives, find both tested when a secretive American woman turns up in town and intrigues the boy. Excellent debuts from the young actors, though the dreamy script tends to tell too much too soon.

> **BEWARE** *Roughhousing, alcohol use, Irish profanity, mature themes, sex talk.*

1991 97m/C Beverly D'Angelo, Donal McCann, Niall Byrne, Lorraine Pilkington, J.G. Devlin; **D:** Neil Jordan; **W:** Neil Jordan; **M:** Anne Dudley. **VHS, LV** *LIV*

Miracle at Moreaux

Family Three Jewish children fleeing from Nazis find sanctuary in a French convent school with a kindly nun. But some of the Catholic kids have been raised in anti-Semitic households and don't easily accept the newcom-

"The Mighty Morphin Power Rangers" ready to attack!

ers. Touching "WonderWorks" drama, based on Clare Huchet Bishop's book "Twenty and Ten."

 *Brief violence.*

1986 58m/C Loretta Swit, Marsha Moreau, Robert Joy, Ken Pogue, Robert Kosoy, Talya Rubin; **D:** Paul Shapiro. **VHS** *PME, HMV, IGP*

Miracle Down Under 🦴🦴 ♭

Family "Man from Snowy River" Miller (not fellow Australian "Mad Max" Miller) directs inoffensive Disney-produced drama. Family endures arduous times in 1890s Australia before a Christmas miracle changes their fortunes.

1987 101m/C Dee Wallace Stone, John Waters, Charles Tingwell, Bill Kerr, Andrew Ferguson; **D:** George Miller. **VHS, Beta** *TOU, IGP*

Miracle of Our Lady of Fatima 🦴🦴 ♭

Jr. High-Adult Lush, big-budget adaptation of the supposedly true events surrounding a vision of the Virgin Mary witnessed by three children in Portugal during WWI. Some of the pic's cliches owe more to the gods of Hollywood than the Catholic faith, but there are some undeniably touching and stirring moments.

1952 102m/C Gilbert Roland, Susan Whitney, Sherry Jackson, Sammy Ogg, Angela Clark, Frank Silvera, Jay Novello; **D:** John Brahm; **M:** Max Steiner. **VHS, Beta, LV** *WAR, IGP, KEP*

Miracle of the Heart: A Boys Town Story 🦴🦴

Family TV movie based on the story of Boys Town and an old priest who stick up for Boys Town's principles in the face of a younger priest with rigid ideas.

1986 100m/C Art Carney, Casey Siemaszko, Jack Bannon; **D:** Georg Stanford Brown. **VHS, Beta** *COL*

Miracle of the White Stallions 🦴 ♭

Family A disappointing Disney adventure about the director of a Viennese riding academy who guides his prized Lippizan stallions to safety when the Nazis occupy Austria in WWII.

1963 92m/C Robert Taylor, Lilli Palmer, Eddie Albert, Curt Jurgens; **D:** Arthur Hiller. **VHS, Beta** *DIS*

Miracle on 34th Street 🦴🦴🦴🦴

Family Nice old man named Kris Kringle is hired as Santa Claus for the Macy's Thanksgiving parade and claims to be the real thing. All New York is enchanted by the idea, but the parade sponsor's cynical little daughter refuses to be convinced. Eventually, Kringle goes on trial for his sanity and must prove himself to the law as well as the child. Hollywood classic that never fades, with terrific performances (especially by youngster Wood) and as satisfying an ending as has ever been done. Also available colorized.

1947 97m/B Maureen O'Hara, John Payne, Edmund Gwenn, Natalie Wood, William Frawley, Porter Hall, Gene Lockhart, Thelma Ritter, Jack Albertson; **D:** George Seaton; **W:** George Seaton; **M:** Cyril Mockridge. **Award Nominations:** Academy Awards '47: Best Picture; **Awards:** Academy Awards '47: Best Story & Screenplay, Best Supporting Actor (Gwenn). **VHS, Beta, LV** *CCB, FOX, HMV*

Miracle on 34th Street 🦴🦴 ᵛ

PG/Family Ho ho ho-ld everything! The 1947 "Miracle" wasn't broken so there was no need to fix it. This updated remake isn't bad, but it lacks the heart and soul of the original black-and-white classic. Attenborough and Wilson are fine in the Edmund Gwenn and Natalie Wood roles, but there's only one true "Miracle." And how do they manage to keep finding the only old-style Checker cab still operating in New York?

BEWARE *Contains scenes of drunkenness (you know, the drunk Santa Clause) and a reference to child molestation.*

1994 114m/C Richard Attenborough, Elizabeth Perkins, Dylan McDermott, J.T. Walsh, Mara Wilson, Joss Ackland, James Remar, Jane Leeves, Simon Jones, Robert Prosky, William Windom; **D:** Les Mayfield; **W:** John Hughes, George Seaton; **M:** Bruce Broughton. **VHS** *FXV*

The Miracle Worker 🦴🦴🦴 ᵛ

Family True story of the famous struggle by teacher Anne Sullivan to break through to the deaf, blind, mute girl Helen Keller. Helen's family allowed the (literally) senseless child to rampage willfully around the estate, until Sullivan took over and sought to communicate sign language to the crafty, but seemingly uncontrollable youngster—by force if necessary. An intense, moving experience adapted by William Gibson from his own play.

BEWARE *Roughhousing.*

1962 107m/B Anne Bancroft, Patty Duke, Victor Jory, Inga Swenson, Andrew Prine, Beah Richards; **D:** Arthur Penn. **Award Nominations:** Academy Awards '62: Best Adapted Screenplay, Best Costume Design (B & W), Best Director (Penn); **Awards:** Academy Awards '62: Best Actress (Bancroft), Best Supporting Actress (Duke); National Board of Review Awards '62: 10 Best Films of the Year, Best Actress (Bancroft). **VHS, Beta** *MGM, BTV, CCB*

The Miracle Worker 🦴🦴🦴

Family Remade for television story of blind, deaf and mute Helen Keller and her teacher, Annie Sullivan, whose patience, perseverance—and ability to swing with the punches—finally enables the child to learn to communicate with the world. Nice bit of casting has Duke, who played Keller in the 1962 original, as the teacher here. She teams splendidly with "Little House on the Prairie" pioneer Gilbert as Keller.

1979 98m/C Patty Duke, Melissa Gilbert; **D:** Paul Aaron; **M:** Billy Goldenberg. **VHS, Beta** *WAR, OM*

A Mirthworm Masquerade

Preschool Animated short from Hanna-Barbera featuring those "lovable" Mirthworms throwing Wormingham's annual costume ball. Who will win, Wormaline Wiggler or Crystal Crawler? Who wrote this stuff? Mirthworm fans will also want to see "A Merry Mirthworm Christmas."

1986 24m/C VHS, Beta *FHE*

The Misadventures of Merlin Jones 🦴🦴

G/Family Episodic comedy about college goof Merlin, who experiments with raising the intelligence of chimpanzees and athletes. Wacky adventures ensue. Some of the hardware is funny (like Merlin's wired-up football helmet) but most of this is bland, dated Disney. A sequel, "The Monkey's Uncle," followed.

1963 90m/C Tommy Kirk, Annette Funicello, Leon Ames, Stuart Erwin, Connie Gilchrist; **D:** Robert Stevenson; **M:** Buddy Baker. **VHS, Beta** *DIS*

Miss Annie Rooney 🦴🦴

G/Family Annie is a poor Irish girl who falls in love with a wealthy young man, with the usual family disapproval and ponderous plot twists. The maturing child starlet receives her first screen kiss.

1942 86m/B Shirley Temple, Dickie Moore, William Gargan, Guy Kibbee, Peggy Ryan, June Lockhart; **D:** Edwin L. Marin. **VHS, Beta** *LIV, MED*

Miss Firecracker 🦴🦴🦴

PG/Jr. High-Adult Longing for love and self-respect, Holly Hunter's character decides to change her promiscuous image (having a name like Carnelle doesn't help) by entering the local beauty pageant in her conservative southern town. She's a little wacko, and nutsy supporting characters add to the fun, including the bug-eyed woman who makes teeny tiny clothing for frogs. Adapted by Beth Henley from her off-Broadway play (which starred Hunter). Enjoyably funny. Christine Lahti, wife of director Thomas Schlamme, makes a brief appearance with their actual baby. Ages 12 and up.

BEWARE *Talk about sex.*

1989 102m/C Holly Hunter, Scott Glenn, Mary Steenburgen, Tim Robbins, Alfre Woodard, Trey Wilson, Bert Remsen, Ann Wedgeworth, Christine Lahti, Amy Wright; **D:** Thomas Schlamme; **W:** Beth Henley; **M:** David Mansfield. **VHS, Beta, LV** *HBO*

Mission: Impossible 🦴🦴🦴

PG-13/Jr. High-Adult With action, suspense, Tom Cruise and those nifty self-destructing tapes (video- these days, instead of audio-) "Mission: Impossible" is a good old-fashioned thriller. Old-fashioned, too, and most refreshing, is a total absence of sex or profanity. The plot is

Susan Walker is enchanted by Kris Kringle in "Miracle on 34th Street."

sometimes incomprehensible but it's clear that Cruise is the good guy trying to protect a list of America's secret agents from falling into the wrong hands. His heroic efforts include breaking into the highest security chamber at the CIA (suspended from the ceiling, a la "Topkapi") and pursuing a bad guy atop a high speed train. And don't forget the helicopter flying through the Chunnel. Ages 9 and up.

 A few explosions, some shooting, some blood, a man riding on top of an elevator gets squished (off-screen) against the roof.

1996 110m/C Tom Cruise, Jon Voight, Emmanuelle Beart, Ving Rhames, Henry Czerny, Emilio Estevez, Vanessa Redgrave; **D:** Brian DePalma; **W:** Robert Towne, David Koepp; **C:** Stephen Burum; **M:** Danny Elfman. **VHS** *NYR*

Mrs. Doubtfire 𝄞𝄞𝄞

PG-13/Jr. High-Adult Williams is an unemployed voiceover actor going through a messy divorce. When his wife gets custody, the distraught father dresses as a woman and become a nanny to his own children. He also has to deal with the old flame who re-enters his ex-wife's life. Vintage Williams shtick extraordinaire with more than a little sugary sentimentality. Based on the British children's book "Madame Doubtfire" by Anne Fine.

Sex talk.

1993 120m/C Robin Williams, Sally Field, Pierce Brosnan, Harvey Fierstein, Robert Prosky, Mara Wilson; **D:** Chris Columbus; **W:** Randi Mayem Singer, Leslie Dixon; **M:** Howard Shore. **Award Nominations:** MTV Movie Awards '94: Best Actor (Williams); **Awards:** Academy Awards '93: Best Makeup; Golden Globe Awards '94: Best Actor—Musical/Comedy (Williams), Best Film—Musical/Comedy; MTV Movie Awards '94: Best Comedic Performance (Williams). **VHS** *FXV*

Mrs. Winterbourne 𝄞𝄞 ♭

PG-13/Jr. High-Adult Down-and-out Connie Doyle is pregnant and broke. In a mishap and a case of mistaken identity, she is taken in by the Winterbourne family, who believe her to be their dead son's bride whom they never met. Finally, living a better life and beginning to fall for the twin brother, she decides to keep her identity concealed. But watch out, her old life shows up on her doorstep just when things seem to be going so well. Teens will probably like this one. The cast is funny and it has a sweet love story, not to mention heartthrob Fraser, as the surviving twin brother.

BEWARE *Brief strong language and death. Be ready to explain why keeping secrets can get you in trouble and even hurt people.*

1996 104m/C Ricki Lake, Brendan Fraser, Shirley MacLaine, Miguel Sandoval, Loren Dean, Susan Haskell; *D:* Richard Benjamin; *W:* Phoef Sutton, Lisa-Marie Rodano. **VHS** *NYR*

Mr. & Mrs. Bridge 🦴🦴

PG-13/Jr. High-Adult A potent soporific, even for adults, despite heartfelt performances by real-life married couple Newman and Woodward. Set in '30s and '40s in Kansas City, this adaptation of two overlapping Evan S. Connell novels painstakingly portrays an upper middle-class family. Father is stuffy and domineering; Mother has repressed all traces of personality in total submission to her husband. Ages 15 and up.

1991 127m/C Joanne Woodward, Paul Newman, Kyra Sedgwick, Blythe Danner, Simon Callow, Diane Kagan, Robert Sean Leonard, Saundra McClain, Margaret Welsh, Austin Pendleton, Gale Garnett, Remak Ramsay; *D:* James Ivory; *W:* Ruth Prawer Jhabvala. **VHS, LV** *HBO, FCT*

Mr. & Mrs. Condor

Preschool-Primary Life as a big bird in a big forest has its ups and downs. This cartoon series follows the fun-loving Condor family at work and play. Each tape includes three episodes.

1979 60m/C VHS, Beta *FHE*

Mr. & Mrs. Smith 🦴🦴🦴 🦴

Family Hitchcock's only screwball comedy, an underrated, endearing farce about a bickering but happy modern couple who discover their marriage isn't legitimate and go through courtship all over again. Vintage of its kind, with inspired performances and crackling dialogue.

1941 95m/B Carole Lombard, Robert Montgomery, Gene Raymond, Jack Carson, Lucile Watson, Charles Halton; *D:* Alfred Hitchcock; *W:* Norman Krasna. **VHS, Beta, LV** *MED, TTC*

Mr. Baseball 🦴🦴

PG-13/Jr. High-Adult Washed-up American baseball player tries to revive his career by playing in Japan and experiences cultures clashing under the ballpark lights. Semi-charmer swings and misses often enough to warrant return to minors. Film drew controversy during production when Universal was bought by the Japanese Matsushita organization and claims of both Japan- and America-bashing were thrown about.

BEWARE *Profanity and stereotyping of Asians .*

1992 109m/C Tom Selleck, Ken Takakura, Toshi Shioya, Dennis Haysbert, Aya Takanashi; *D:* Fred Schepisi; *W:* Gary Ross, Kevin Wade, Monte Merrick; *M:* Jerry Goldsmith. **VHS, Beta, LV** *MCA*

Mr. Bill's Real-Life Adventures

Jr. High-Adult One of Shelley Duvall's stranger productions, a gag that doesn't quite come off. Live-action sitcom (done for cable TV) with kiddie-show host Mr. Bill and his normally clay family impersonated by live actors, though they're still miniature people dwelling in a full-sized world. No serious violence or dismemberment, but flesh-and-blood Bill still takes a lot of slapstick abuse. A lengthy featurette hosted by Duvall shows how the f/x were done.

1986 43m/C Peter Scolari, Valerie Mahaffey, Lenore Kasdorf, Michael McManus; *D:* Jim Drake. **VHS, Beta** *PAR*

Mr. Bumpy's Karaoke Cafe

Primary The green and warty thing with the sousaphone eyes from the Saturday morning cartoon series has a sing-along with pals Molly and Squishington. A lyric sheet is enclosed. Ages 5 to 9.

1994 30m/C VHS *ABC*

Mr. Destiny 🦴🦴

PG-13/Sr. High-Adult Mid-level businessman Belushi has a mid-life crisis of sorts when his car dies. Wandering into an empty bar, he encounters bartender Caine who serves cocktails and acts omniscient before taking him on the ten-cent tour of life as it would've been if he hadn't struck out in a high school baseball game. Less than wonderful rehash of "It's a Wonderful Life."

BEWARE *Mild profanity.*

1990 110m/C James Belushi, Michael Caine, Linda Hamilton, Jon Lovitz, Bill McCutcheon, Hart Bochner, Rene Russo, Jay O. Sanders, Maury Chaykin, Pat Corley, Douglas Seale, Courteney Cox, Kathy Ireland; *D:* James Orr; *W:* James Orr, Jim Cruickshank. **VHS, Beta, LV** *TOU, FCT*

Mr. Holland's Opus 🦴🦴🦴

PG/Primary-Adult Promising composer Glenn Holland (Dreyfuss) takes a temporary teaching job when his wife (Headly) gets pregnant. He spends the next 30 years promising himself he'll compose his symphony. Meanwhile he educates, loves and inspires generations of high school students. A sad irony arises when the Hollands' only child, a son they name after Cole Porter, turns out to be deaf. A good, if overlong, film that says you don't have to be famous to be important.

BEWARE *Contains mild language. Observant youngsters can learn to express certain obscenities in sign language.*

1995 142m/C Richard Dreyfuss, Glenne Headly, Jay Thomas, Olympia Dukakis, William H. Macy, Alicia Witt, Jean Louisa Kelly, Anthony Natale; *D:* Stephen Herek; *W:* Patrick Sheane Duncan; *C:* Oliver Wood; *M:* Michael Kamen. **VHS** *TOU*

Mr. Hulot's Holiday 🦴🦴🦴 🦴

Family Superior slapstick details the misadventures of a dullard's sea-side holiday. Inventive French comedian Tati at his best. Light-hearted and natural, with magical mime sequences.

1953 86m/B Jacques Tati, Natalie Pascaud, Michelle Rolia; *D:* Jacques Tati. **Award Nominations:** Academy Awards '55: Best Story & Screenplay; **Awards:** National Board of Review Awards '54: 5 Best Foreign Films of the Year. **VHS, Beta, LV, 8mm** *NOS, MRV, VYY*

Richard Dreyfuss instructs Alicia Witt in "Mr. Holland's Opus."

Mr. Humdinger Goes Fishing

Preschool-Primary Mr. Humdinger and Mr. Fin have adventures as this video introduces kids to what it's like to be a commercial fisherman. Includes a tour of a fishing boat, a Coast Guard vessel, and a fire boat and a trip to a processing plant.

1996 ?m/C VHS *TPV*

Mr. Magoo: 1001 Arabian Night's Dream

Family Magoo appears as Aladdin's uncle, the lamp dealer, in this classic tale of genies and palaces.

1959 75m/C VHS

Mr. Magoo: Cyrano De Bergerac/A Midsummer Night's Dream

Primary-Jr. High The near-sighted Mr. Magoo stars in a compilation of theatrical cartoons that featured the character in whimsical (and sometimes quite straightforward) adaptations of great works of literature. Here he appears first as the large-nosed Cyrano De Bergerac, then as the silly Puck in the Shakespeare comedy. Others include

renditions of "Don Quixote de la Mancha," "Little Snow White," "The Three Musketeers," and "King Arthur."

1964 50m/C *V:* Jim Backus. **VHS** *PAR*

The Mr. Magoo Show, Vol. 1

Preschool-Jr. High Five episodes from the 1960 juvenile cartoon series. Included are "Magoo's Last Stand," "Short Order Magoo," "Lost Vegas," "Cupid Magoo," and "Cuckoo Magoo." Additional volumes available.

1960 25m/C *V:* Jim Backus. **VHS** *PAR, FCT*

Mr. Magoo's Christmas Carol ♪♪♪ ♪

Family Nearsighted Mr. Magoo, in character as Ebenezer Scrooge, receives Christmas visits from three ghosts in an entertaining and quite effective version of the classic tale. No less an authority than Sir Alistair Cooke has recommended this as one of the best of the many, many adaptations of the Charles Dickens original.

1962 52m/C *V:* Jim Backus. **VHS, Beta, LV** *PAR*

Mr. Mom ♪♪♪

PG/Jr. High-Adult Auto exec (Michael Keaton) loses his job and stays home with the kids while his wife (Teri

Garr) goes to work. Best scene involves Keaton being chased by a washing machine. You've seen it all before but your kids haven't. They should come away with a greater appreciation for housework and, who knows, maybe even a desire to pitch in. Written by John Hughes. Ages 5 to 10

> **BEWARE** *Dad copes with his deficiencies by drinking. Near sexual situations.*

1983 92m/C Michael Keaton, Teri Garr, Christopher Lloyd, Martin Mull, Ann Jillian, Jeffrey Tambor, Edie McClurg, Valri Bromfield; **D:** Stan Dragoti; **W:** John Hughes. **VHS, Beta, LV** *LIV, VES*

Mr. Nanny ♫♫

PG/Jr. High-Adult For those who fear change, this predictable plot should be comforting. Hulkster plays nanny/bodyguard to a couple of bratty kids. Meanwhile, his arch rival schemes to gain world dominance by holding the kids for the ransom of their father's top secret computer chip. Never fear—in this world, the good guys kick butt, naturally, and everyone learns a lesson.

> **BEWARE** *Fighting and children in danger. But Hulk's there to save the day. (Pretty scary, huh?)*

1993 85m/C Hulk Hogan, Sherman Hemsley, Austin Pendleton, Robert Gorman, Madeline Zima, Mother Love, David Johansen; **D:** Michael Gottlieb; **W:** Ed Rugoff, Michael Gottlieb; **M:** David Johansen, Brian Koonin. **VHS** *NLC, COL*

Mister Rogers: Music and Feelings

Preschool-Primary One in a series of specially edited Mr. Rogers program focusing on different children's topics, including the importance and enjoyment of music for kids. Others in the series include "Musical Stories," "When Parents Are Away," "Dinosaurs and Monsters."
1986 65m/C Fred Rogers. **VHS, Beta** *FOX*

Mr. Rossi's Dreams ♫♫

Family Mr. Rossi gets to act out his fantasies of being Tarzan, Sherlock Holmes, and a famous movie star in this cartoon feature from the "Allegro Non Troppo" animation maestro. Others in the series include "Mr. Rossi Looks For Happiness" and "Mr. Rossi's Vacation."
1983 80m/C D: Bruno Bozzetto. **VHS, Beta** *FHE*

Mr. Smith Goes to Washington ♫♫♫♫

Family Another classic from Hollywood's golden year of 1939. Jimmy Stewart is an idealistic and naive young man selected to fill in for an ailing Senator. Upon his arrival in Washington, he is inundated by a multitude of corrupt politicians. He takes a stand for his beliefs and tries to denounce many of those he feels are unfit for their positions, meeting with opposition from all sides. Great cast is highlighted by Stewart in one of his most endearing performances. Quintessential Capra tale sharply adapted from Lewis Foster's story. Outstanding in every regard.

1939 130m/B James Stewart, Jean Arthur, Edward Arnold, Claude Rains, Thomas Mitchell, Beulah Bondi, Eugene Pallette, Guy Kibbee, Harry Carey Sr., H.B. Warner, Porter Hall, Jack Carson, Charles Lane; **D:** Frank Capra; **W:** Sidney Buchman; **M:** Dimitri Tiomkin. **Award Nominations:** Academy Awards '39: Best Actor (Stewart), Best Director (Capra), Best Interior Decoration, Best Picture, Best Screenplay, Best Sound, Best Supporting Actor (Rains, Carey), Best Score; **Awards:** Academy Awards '39: Best Story; National Board of Review Awards '39: 10 Best Films of the Year; New York Film Critics Awards '39: Best Actor (Stewart). **VHS, Beta, LV** *COL, HMV*

Mr. Wise Guy ♫♫

Family The East Side Kids break out of reform school to clear one of the Kids' brother's of a murder charge. Typical pre-Bowery Boys vehicle.
1942 70m/B Leo Gorcey, Huntz Hall, Billy Gilbert, Guinn "Big Boy" Williams, Benny Rubin, Douglas Fowley, Ann Doran, Jack Mulhall, Warren Hymer, David Gorcey; **D:** William Nigh. **VHS, Beta** *NOS, DVT, HEG*

Mr. Wizard's World: Air and Water Wizardry

Family Before "Beakman's World" and Bill Nye the Science Guy there was Don Herbert, quintessential science instructor better known as Mr. Wizard. In a compilation from his Nickelodeon cable show, he conducts a slew of entertaining but simple experiments with air pressure and water. Companion tape, "Mr. Wizard's World: Puzzles, Problems & Impossibilities," is also available.
1983 44m/C VHS, Beta *FOX*

Mr. Wonderful ♫♫ ♪

PG-13/Jr. High-Adult Bittersweet (rather than purely romantic) look at love and romance. Divorced Con Ed worker Gus (Dillon) is hard up for cash and tries to marry off ex-wife Lee (Sciorra) so he can use her alimony to invest in a bowling alley with his buddies. Routine effort is elevated by the cast, who manage to bring a small measure of believability to a transparent plot. Minghella was a critical hit with his debut, "Truly, Madly, Deeply" but may find that fame can be fleeting.

> **BEWARE** *Profanity and sex.*

1993 99m/C Matt Dillon, Annabella Sciorra, William Hurt, Mary-Louise Parker, Luis Guzman, Dan Hedaya, Vincent D'Onofrio; **D:** Anthony Minghella; **W:** Amy Schor, Vicki Polon; **M:** Michael Gore. **VHS, Beta, LV** *WAR*

Mr. Wrong ♫ ♪

PG-13/Jr. High-Adult Whitman (Pullman) seemed like the perfect guy. Just how wrong could Martha (Ellen DeGeneres) be? Very. Wrong about the man. Wrong about this film as a vehicle for her feature debut. She's a talker, he's a stalker. Comedian DeGeneres doesn't display an abundance of acting talent in this poor excuse for a comedy.

> **BEWARE** *Crude language, sex related scenes, Whitman puts LSD in Martha's drink and shoots a former girl-friend.*

Life's no picnic for Ellen Degeneres with Bill Pullman in "Mr. Wrong."

1995 92m/C Ellen DeGeneres, Bill Pullman, Joan Cusack, Dean Stockwell, Joan Plowright, John Livingston, Robert Goulet, Ellen Cleghorne, Brad Henke, Polly Holliday, Briant Wells; *D:* Nick Castle; *W:* Chris Matheson, Kerry Ehrin, Craig Munson; *C:* John Schwartzman; *M:* Craig Safan. **VHS** *TOU*

Misunderstood 🦴🦴 ▷

PG/Jr. High-Adult Former black market merchant in Tunisia has to learn how to relate to his neglected sons after his wife dies. The father, now a legitimate business-man, is more concerned with running his shipping firm than growing closer to the boys. Fine acting by Hackman and "E.T.'"s Thomas grapples with a transparent tearjerker plot.

1984 92m/C Gene Hackman, Susan Anspach, Henry Thomas, Rip Torn, Huckleberry Fox; *D:* Jerry Schatzberg. **VHS, Beta** *MGM*

Mixed Nuts 🦴

PG-13/Jr. High-Adult Misfits staff a suicide hotline on Christmas Eve. Is anyone laughing yet? Director/writer Ephron (along with her co-writer sister Delia) tries way too hard to fashion a hip, racy, madcap farce reminiscent of the screwball comedies that Hollywood churned out in the 1930s and '40s. Hint: None of those films were about suicide hotlines. Film never finds its style and the story line is very weak. Ending is way too cheesy, even for a holiday film. Martin, Shandling, and Kahn are good for a few amusing scenes, but even they can't save this one.

> **BEWARE!** *Sex-related humor and profanity. Lewis is pregnant by her verbally abusive boyfriend and wields a gun at him when he won't let her leave him. Couples hook up in weird places—the bathroom, out on the street, etc.*

1994 97m/C Steve Martin, Madeline Kahn, Robert Klein, Anthony LaPaglia, Juliette Lewis, Rob Reiner, Adam Sandler, Rita Wilson, Garry Shandling, Liev Schreiber; *D:* Nora Ephron; *W:* Nora Ephron, Delia Ephron; *M:* George Fenton. **VHS, LV** *COL*

Modern Problems 🦴🦴

PG/Jr. High-Adult Chevy Chase is an air traffic control-ler who discovers he has acquired telekinetic powers. Ripe with potential, little of which is realized. Ages 8 to 12.

> **BEWARE!** *Brief nudity and suggested sex.*

1981 93m/C Chevy Chase, Patti D'Arbanville, Mary Kay Place, Brian Doyle-Murray, Nell Carter, Dabney Coleman; *D:* Ken Shapiro. **VHS, Beta** *FOX*

Moira's Birthday

Preschool-Primary Moira invites too many kids to her birthday party which makes for a lot of fun and confusion. And songs. On the same tape as "Blackberry Subway Jam." Ages 3 to 7.

19?? ?m/C VHS

Moll Flanders ♫♫♫

PG-13/Jr. High-Adult Loosely adapted from Daniel Defoe's 1722 novel is the tale of spirited heroine Moll Flanders, played skillfully by Wright. Related in flashback sequence, the story is told to Moll's daughter (newcomer Corcoran). Orphaned Moll is taken into a number of different homes and eventually into the brothel of greedy Mrs. Allworthy (Channing). Her life as a prostitute leads her to drink and near suicide—despite the unwavering friendship of Hibble (Freeman), Allworthy's dignified servant. She finally meets and falls in love with a seemingly impoverished artist (Lynch) and briefly finds happiness. See this one for the lovely storytelling and brilliant performances.

> **BEWARE** *Moll is beaten by attackers. She works in a brothel, which means there is nudity and sex (but not explicit). There is a sex scene with her husband and she poses partially nude for him to paint her. Two childbirth scenes.*

1996 123m/C Robin Wright, Morgan Freeman, Stockard Channing, John Lynch, Brenda Fricker, Aisling Corcoran, Geraldine James, Jim Sheridan, Jeremy Brett, Britta Smith, Ger Ryan; **D:** Pen Densham; **W:** Pen Densham; **C:** David Tattersall; **M:** Mark Mancina. **VHS** *NYR*

Mom and Dad Save the World ♫ ♭

PG/Primary-Adult Attempt to do "a so dumb it's funny" comedy for all ages only gets the dumb part right. Planet Spengo, populated entirely by idiots, plans to destroy Earth. But nasty King Tod spies through his telescope an average suburban housewife and falls in love. He teleports Mr. and Mrs. Nelson to Spengo, and postpones death-raying their world until he can marry Mom, dispose of Dad. Highlights are the goofy playpen sets; lowlight is the misuse of an excellent cast, especially Idle and Shawn. Very young kid viewers might be amused.

> **BEWARE** *Fighting and sex talk. Aliens are not scary.*

1992 87m/C Teri Garr, Jeffrey Jones, Jon Lovitz, Eric Idle, Wallace Shawn, Dwier Brown, Kathy Ireland, Thalmus Rasulala; **D:** Greg Beeman; **M:** Jerry Goldsmith. **VHS, LV** *HBO*

Mommie Dearest ♫ ♭

PG/Jr. High-Adult Based on Christina Crawford's memoirs of her incredibly abusive and violent childhood at the hands of her adoptive mother, actress Joan Crawford. More appreciated for its campiness than artistic merit, as Dunaway works up a lather in over-the-top performance as Lady Joan.

> **BEWARE** *Vivid depictions of child abuse, both verbal and physical.*

1981 129m/C Faye Dunaway, Diana Scarwid, Steve Forrest, Mara Hobel, Rutanya Alda, Harry Goz, Howard da Silva; **D:** Frank Perry; **W:** Robert Getchell; **M:** Henry Mancini. **VHS, Beta, LV** *PAR*

Mommy, Gimme a Drinka Water!

Preschool Didi Conn ("You Light Up My Life" and "Shining Time Station") performs droll tunes sung from a child's viewpoint of the world. Ages 3 to 8.

1994 35m/C VHS *WST*

The Money Pit ♫♫ ♭

PG/Jr. High-Adult Often hilarious urban nightmare comedy about a young yuppie couple encountering sundry problems when they attempt to renovate their newly purchased, seemingly self-destructive, Long Island home. Both home and relationship suffer in the ensuing domestic crisis. Never has a house fallen apart with such gusto. While the stunts tend to overwhelm the story and cast, both Hanks and Long are appealing as the young couple plunged into mortgage hell. A Spielberg production somewhat modeled after "Mr. Blandings Builds His Dream House."

> **BEWARE** *Profanity and suggested sex. A house literally falls apart, as does the couple's marriage.*

1986 91m/C Tom Hanks, Shelley Long, Alexander Godunov, Maureen Stapleton, Philip Bosco, Joe Mantegna, Josh Mostel; **D:** Richard Benjamin; **M:** Michel Colombier. **VHS, Beta, LV** *MCA*

Money Train ♫ ♭

R/Sr. High-Adult Snipes and Harrelson team up again, this time as New York City transit cops (and foster brothers) who decide to rob the money train—a subway car that collects all the cash accrued from the transit system each day. Oh yeah, and they're both in love with their new Latina partner (Lopez). Tries to capitalize on the Snipes and Harrelson chemistry, but falls short. Action-adventure-loving teens will want to see this one, but aren't most of us tired of violence on subways (and buses, and trains, and airplanes)?

> **BEWARE** *Contains strong language, violence, and a vivid sex scene.*

1995 103m/C Woody Harrelson, Wesley Snipes, Jennifer Lopez, Robert (Bobby) Blake, Chris Cooper, Joe Grifasi; **D:** Joseph Ruben; **W:** Doug Richardson, David Loughery; **C:** John Lindley; **M:** Mark Mancina. **VHS** *NYR*

Monkees, Volume 1

Family The notorious 'mod' '60s band, fabricated as a response to the Beatles, turned out to have undeniable and enduring appeal, and episodes of their anything-goes network comedy series have gained them a new generation of young viewers thanks to rebroadcasts on MTV. Monkee fans will flip for these six videocassette volumes, each holding two music-filled episodes each. The Monkees' daringly abstract (G-rated) feature film

"Head," as bizarre an experience as Hollywood ever produced, is also on tape, mainly of interest to film scholars and non-linear thinkers.

1966 50m/C Michael Nesmith, Davy Jones, Peter Tork, Mickey Dolenz. **VHS, Beta, LV** *MVD, COL*

Monkey Business

Family Before their antic ocean voyage in "A Night at The Opera," the Marx Brothers took to the seas as stowaways in "Monkey Business." Somehow, they get involved with a bunch of bootleggers, and Groucho gets involved with a bootlegger's wife. "You're a woman who's gotten nothing but dirty breaks," he tells her. "We can clean and tighten those brakes but you'll have to stay in the garage overnight." Harpo hilariously pretends he's a puppet in a puppet show, the boys wreak havoc on a gentleman's moustache in the ship's barbershop and they each try to convince a dubious Customs agent that they are Maurice Chevalier. Great fun. Ages 8 and up.

1931 77m/B Groucho Marx, Harpo Marx, Chico Marx, Zeppo Marx, Thelma Todd, Ruth Hall, Harry Woods; **D:** Norman Z. McLeod. **VHS, Beta, LV** *MCA*

Monkey Business 🦴🦴🦴

Family Scientist invents a fountain-of-youth potion, a lab chimpanzee mistakenly dumps it into a water cooler, and then grown-ups start turning into adolescents. Top-flight crew occasionally labors in this screwball comedy, though comic moments shine. Monroe is the secretary sans skills, while absent-minded Grant and sexy wife Rogers race hormonally as teens.

1952 97m/B Cary Grant, Ginger Rogers, Charles Coburn, Marilyn Monroe, Hugh Marlowe, Larry Keating, George Winslow; **D:** Howard Hawks; **W:** Ben Hecht, Charles Lederer, I.A.L. Diamond. **VHS, Beta, LV** *FOX*

The Monkey People

Primary South American folktale about a lazy village and an industrious boy who figures out a way to get work done. As a result of not working, the villagers become indistinguishable from animals, and the boy moves away to continue his trade. Great multicultural storytelling from the "Rabbit Ears: We All Have Tales" series.

1991 30m/C M: Lee Ritenour. **VHS** *UND, MCA,*

Monkey Trouble 🦴🦴🦴

PG/Primary-Adult Crummy title, surprisingly good movie. Girl feels abandoned when mom and stepdad shower attention on a new baby brother and won't let her get a pet. Then Dodger, a Capuchin monkey trained as a Venice Beach pickpocket, seeks refuge in her house from his conniving gypsy master. The little heroine goes to great lengths hiding Dodger from parent and gypsy alike, and the flick stakes a lot of its entertainment wallop on the talents of the slippery fingered simian, who steals the show (among other things). Formula abounds, but gags are fun and freshly paced, with a nice aside about

the divorced family conferring amicably over the daughter's welfare.

> **BEWARE** *Alcohol use.*

1994 95m/C Thora Birch, Harvey Keitel, Mimi Rogers, Christopher McDonald; **D:** Franco Amurri; **W:** Franco Amurri, Stu Krieger; **M:** Mark Mancina. **VHS** *NYR*

Monkeys, Go Home! 🦴

Family Dumb Disney yarn about young American who inherits a badly neglected French olive farm. When he brings in four chimpanzees to pick the olives, the local townspeople go on strike. First this, then Euro-Disneyland. Based on "The Monkeys" by G. K. Wilkinson.

1966 89m/C Dean Jones, Yvette Mimieux, Maurice Chevalier, Clement Harari, Yvonne Constant; **D:** Andrew V. McLaglen. **VHS, Beta** *DIS*

Monkey's Uncle 🦴🦴

Family Sequel to Disney's "The Misadventures of Merlin Jones" and featuring more bizarre antics and scientific hoopla, including teaching chimps with a flying machine.

1965 90m/C Tommy Kirk, Annette Funicello, Leon Ames, Arthur O'Connell; **D:** Robert Stevenson; **M:** Buddy Baker. **VHS, Beta** *DIS*

Monster Bash

Family Selection of Disney TV comedy cartoons parodying spooky plots. "Frankengoof" features Goofy inheriting a castle and encountering the Frankengoof monster. In "Ducky Horror Picture Show," the Monsters Unanimous Convention comes to Duckberg and Huey, Dewey, and Louie have a monstrously good time. Released along with two similar compilations, "Boo-Busters" and "Witcheroo."

1993 44m/C VHS *DIS*

Monster In My Pocket

Family Evil Transylvanian monsters try to escape from prison by shrinking themselves. They wind up shrinking their prison as well, which blows to L.A. where good monsters, aided by a little girl, try to track the evildoers down. Ages 5 to 9.

1995 30m/C VHS *VMK*

The Monster Squad 🦴🦴

PG-13/Jr. High School-age monster enthusiasts battle the real thing, the famous Universal Pictures horror icons, led by Dracula. Commanding the Wolf Man, Mummy and Black Lagoon gill-man, the vampire invades their community in search of a magic amulet, while the childlike Frankenstein monster becomes the kids' ally. Frank's also the only character with the right mix of innocence and menace. Meeting of classic creatures, high-tech special effects and typical foulmouthed movie youngsters is more of a collision than collusion.

> **BEWARE** *Salty language, violence (mostly against monsters), sex talk in abundance when the kids learn they need a virgin girl—giggle giggle—to recite a spell.*

1987 82m/C Andre Gower, Stephen Macht, Tommy Noonan, Duncan Regehr; **D:** Fred Dekker; **W:** Fred Dekker, Shane Black; **M:** Bruce Broughton. **VHS, Beta, LV** *LIV, VES*

Monty Python and the Holy Grail 🦴🦴🦴🦴

PG/Jr. High-Adult Britain's famed comedy band assaults the Arthurian legend in a cult classic replete with a Trojan rabbit and an utterly dismembered, but inevitably pugnacious, knight. Fans of manic comedy—and goofy but graphic violence—should get more than their fill here. Teens with mature funny bone may appreciate.

> **BEWARE** *Assault by killer rabbit; non-fatal dismemberment; salty language (though mostly in French).*

1975 90m/C Graham Chapman, John Cleese, Terry Gilliam, Eric Idle, Terry Jones, Michael Palin, Carol Cleveland, Connie Booth, Neil Innes, Patsy Kensit; **D:** Terry Gilliam, Terry Jones; **W:** Graham Chapman, John Cleese, Terry Gilliam, Eric Idle, Terry Jones, Michael Palin. **VHS, Beta, LV, 8mm** *COL, SIG, TVC*

Moon Pilot 🦴🦴

Family First astronaut scheduled to orbit the moon is followed prior to the launch by an enticing mystery woman. She turns out to be a (French-accented) alien who's only trying to help, but government security forces panic and chase them both. Outdated, rather dull Disney romantic comedy with no f/x whatsoever. Notable for inspiring a feud between Walt Disney and FBI Director J. Edgar Hoover, who was upset at the depiction of a federal agent character as a pompous blowhard. It's said Disney made sure the feds were bumbling boobs in all his subsequent productions.

1962 98m/C Tom Tryon, Brian Keith, Edmond O'Brien, Dany Saval, Tommy Kirk; **D:** James Neilson. **VHS, Beta** *DIS*

Moon-Spinners 🦴🦴

PG/Family Lightweight Disney mystery (based on a Mary Stewart novel) about a young Englishwoman travelling through Crete who meets up with a wounded man accused of being a jewel thief. The pair work together to unmask the real evildoers.

1964 118m/C Hayley Mills, Peter McEnery, Eli Wallach, Pola Negri; **D:** James Neilson. **VHS, Beta** *DIS, OM*

The Moon Stallion 🦴🦴▷

Family Professor Purwell leads an excavation to uncover evidence of the mythical King Arthur, but it's his daughter Diana, sightless and psychic, who holds the key to strange apparitions of a legendary white horse. Interesting British-German TV production of the novel by Brian Hayles, attempts to be a tale of fantasy and mystery for all ages.

1985 95m/C Sarah Sutton, David Haig, James Greene, John Abineri, Caroline Goodall; **D:** Dorothea Brooking. **VHS** *VCO, HMV*

Mooncussers 🦴🦴

Family Details the exploits of a precocious 12-year-old determined to exact revenge upon a band of ruthless pirates.

1962 85m/C Kevin Corcoran, Rian Garrick, Oscar Homolka; **D:** James Neilson. **VHS, Beta** *DIS*

Moonraker 🦴🦴

PG/Jr. High-Adult Uninspired Bond fare has 007 unraveling intergalactic hijinks. Bond is aided by a female CIA agent, assaulted by a giant with jaws of steel, and captured by Amazons when he sets out to protect the human race. Moore, Chiles, and Lonsdale all seem to be going through the motions only.

> **BEWARE** *Violence, alcohol use and suggested sex. Watch out for the tall guy with the steel mouth—scary even to look at.*

1979 136m/C Roger Moore, Lois Chiles, Richard Kiel, Michael Lonsdale, Corinne Clery, Geoffrey Keen, Emily Bolton, Walter Gotell, Bernard Lee, Lois Maxwell, Desmond Llewelyn; **D:** Lewis Gilbert; **M:** John Barry. **VHS, Beta, LV** *MGM, TLF*

Moonstruck 🦴🦴🦴▷

PG-13/Jr. High-Adult Winning romantic comedy about a widow engaged to one man but falling in love with his younger brother in Little Italy. Excellent performances all around, with Cher particularly fetching as attractive, hapless widow. Unlikely casting of usually dominating Aiello as unassuming mama's boy also works well, and Cage is at his best as a tormented one-handed opera lover/baker.

> **BEWARE** *Salty language and sexual situations. Cher's character spends the night with Cage's character.*

1987 103m/C Cher, Nicolas Cage, Olympia Dukakis, Danny Aiello, Vincent Gardenia, Julie Bovasso, Louis Guss, Anita Gillette, Feodor Chaliapin, John Mahoney; **D:** Norman Jewison; **W:** John Patrick Shanley. **Award Nominations:** Academy Awards '87: Best Director (Jewison), Best Picture, Best Supporting Actor (Gardenia); **Awards:** Academy Awards '87: Best Actress (Cher), Best Original Screenplay, Best Supporting Actress (Dukakis); Golden Globe Awards '88: Best Actress—Musical/Comedy (Cher), Best Supporting Actress (Dukakis). **VHS, Beta, LV** *MGM, BTV, HMV*

More Adventures of Roger Ramjet

Family Join Roger and his crew as they once again take on N.A.S.T.Y. Cartoons are "Monster Masquerade" and "Coffee House."

1965 30m/C **V:** Gary Owens. **VHS** *RHI*

More American Graffiti 🦴▷

PG/Jr. High-Adult George Lucas is not be found in this sequel to 1973's acclaimed early '60s homage "American Graffiti." Charts the various teenagers' experiences in the more radical late '60s. Gimmicky style shifts elaborately between the different guys and gals in different years (the nerdy Terry the Toad, for example, now bumbles through Vietnam). Sorely lacking the warmth and empathy of the first film; of interest only to fans desperate to see what became of the great characters.

> **BEWARE** *Violence and mature themes.*

1979 111m/C Candy Clark, Bo Hopkins, Ron Howard, Paul LeMat, MacKenzie Phillips, Charles Martin Smith, Anna Bjorn, Richard Bradford, Cindy Williams, Scott Glenn; **D:** Bill W.L. Norton. **VHS, LV** *MCA*

More Baby Songs

Family Presents traditional songs such as "Walking," "The Hammer Song," and "Sittin' in a High Chair." Lots of fun for the kids.
1987 30m/C VHS *MLT*

More Dinosaurs

Family Companion to other Owens/Boardman dinosaur videos like the aptly named "Dinosaurs, Dinosaurs, Dinosaurs." Our intrepid co-hosts go on an African safari to investigate reports of a living dinosaur and tour Dinosaur National Monument and the Smithsonian to learn more.
1985 30m/C VHS, Beta *MPI, KAR, MPI*

More Song City U.S.A.

Family Features rock videos for the kids such as "Clean Up My Room Blues" and "La Bamba."
1989 30m/C VHS, Beta *FHE*

More Stories for the Very Young

Preschool-Primary The Children's Circle Studios present five films animated from children's books. Includes "Max's Christmas," "The Little Red Hen," "Petunia," "Not So Fast, Songololo," and "The Napping House."
1992 36m/C VHS *CCC, MLT, WKV*

Morgan Stewart's Coming Home

PG-13/Jr. High-Adult When Dad needs to project a 'family values' image to the media in his political race, he brings son Morgan home from boarding school. But the boy doesn't approve of how his parents are using him as a prop and turns their lives upside down. Trite, sitcom-level stuff.
1987 96m/C Jon Cryer, Lynn Redgrave, Nicholas Pryor, Viveka Davis, Paul Gleason, Andrew Duncan, Savely Kramorov, John Cullum, Robert Sedgwick, Waweru Njenga, Sudhir Rad; **D:** Alan Smithee; **M:** Peter Bernstein. **VHS, Beta, LV** *HBO*

Mortal Kombat: The Journey Begins

Primary Animated adventure involving the origins of characters from the popular, violent video game, including Sonya Blade, Johnny Cage, and Lui Kang. Also has a featurette (in other words, a free ad) on the making of the Mortal Kombat movie. Ages 5 to 10.
1995 60m/C VHS *NLC*

Mortal Kombat: The Movie

PG-13/Jr. High-Sr. High Based on a grotesque, similarly misspelled video game, the movie is a non-stop karate-thon and worse. Good guys fight bad guys for the future of the world. Shameless nirvana for kids with permanent joystick scars on their hands. Grown-ups forced to sit through it may get into some of the eye-popping special effects and nifty martial arts sequences if they can block out the contrived plot, lame acting, and Lambert's presence as Thunder God. Basically, it's not worth the time.

BEWARE *Grotesque characters and violence, though not bloody, may be too intense for children 10 and under.*

1995 101m/C Christopher Lambert, Talisa Soto, Cary-Hiroyuki Tagawa, Brigitte Wilson; **D:** Paul Anderson. **VHS** *NLC*

Mosby's Marauders

Family Disney historical adventure about a boy during the Civil War who learns the meaning of courage, gallantry and love when he joins General Mosby's famous Confederate raiding company.

BEWARE *Violence.*

1966 79m/C Kurt Russell, James MacArthur, Jack Ging, Peggy Lipton, Nick Adams; **D:** Michael O'Herlihy. **VHS, Beta** *DIS*

Moschops: Adventures in Dinosaurland

Preschool-Primary British stop-motion animated series (from the animator of the puppet Paddington Bear) about a cute baby dinosaur who offers a whimsical lizard's-eye-view of the Age of Giant Reptiles. Four episodes lurk on the tape.
1983 44m/C D: Barry Leith. **VHS, Beta** *FHE*

Mother Goose Rock 'n' Rhyme

Family Another all-star kidvid romp with a cast that only Duvall could corral, as assorted prominent musicians and thespians hunt for a missing Mother Goose and return her to her rightful position in Rhymeland.
1990 96m/C Shelley Duvall, Teri Garr, Howie Mandel, Jean Stapleton, Ben Vereen, Bobby Brown, Art Garfunkel, Dan Gilroy, Deborah Harry, Cyndi Lauper, Little Richard, Paul Simon, Harry Anderson, Elayne Boosler, Woody Harrelson, Richard "Cheech" Marin, Garry Shandling. **VHS, Beta** *MED*

Mother Nature Tales of Discovery

Primary-Jr. High Footage of lots of woodland animals—deer, bears, beavers—and nobody gets eaten. From television's The Discovery Channel. Tapes are available individually or as a boxed set. Ages 4 to 10.
1991 28m/C VHS *DHE, SIG, BTV*

Mountain Family Robinson

G/Family Another retread of "The Adventures of the Wilderness Family," with the urban Robinsons trying to maintain their back-to-nature lifestyle in the Rockies despite multiple disasters and opposition from the US Forest Service. Scenic, though slow-moving.

1979 102m/C Robert F. Logan, Susan Damante Shaw, Heather Rattray, Ham Larsen, William Bryant, George Flower; **D:** John Cotter. **VHS, Beta** *MED, VTR*

Mountain Man

Family Historically accurate drama about Galen Clark's successful fight in the 1860s to save the magnificent wilderness area that is now Yosemite National Park. Together with naturalist John Muir, he fought a battle against the lumber companies who wanted the timber and won President Lincoln's support for his cause.

1977 96m/C Denver Pyle, John Dehner, Ken Berry, Cheryl Miller, Don Shanks, Cliff Osmond, Jack Kruschen, Ford Rainey; **D:** David O'Malley; **W:** David O'Malley. **VHS, Beta** *LME*

The Mouse and the Motorcycle

Family A double feature of TV specials based on Beverly Cleary's best-selling books about Ralph the talking (and motorcycle riding) mouse, who stars in "The Mouse and the Motorcycle" and its sequel "Runaway Ralph." Delightful stop-motion animation combined with well-known actors bring the unlikely rodent to life. For another Cleary classic, see the "Ramona" series.

198? 90m/C Fred Savage, Ray Walston, Sara Gilbert, Philip Waller; **V:** Billy Barty, Zelda Rubinstein. **VHS** *VTR*

Mouse on the Mayflower

Preschool-Primary William Mouse accompanies the Pilgrims on board the Mayflower to the New World in this Thanksgiving-related animated special from the Rankin-Bass TV show factory.

1968 48m/C V: Tennessee Ernie Ford, Eddie Albert, June Foray. **VHS** *FHE, BTV*

Mouse Soup

Preschool-Primary Think of Scheherazade as a mouse and you've got the concept of this animated cartoon based on Arnold Lobel's storybook. A bright little mouse saves himself from becoming mouse soup when a not-too-intelligent weasel takes him captive. Convincing the weasel that stories are essential ingredients in mouse soup, the little guy starts telling tales, eventually tricking the weasel into . . . oh, why spoil it. Buddy Hackett narrates. Most delicious. Ages 2 to 8.

1992 25m/C V: Buddy Hackett. **VHS** *WPC, CHF,*

The Mouse That Roared

Family With its wine export business going down the drain, tiny, desperate Grand Fenwick decides to declare war on the United States in hopes that the U.S., after its inevitable triumph, will revive the conquered nation with massive aid. So off to New York go 20 chain-mail clad warriors armed with bow and arrow. Off-the-wall farce features the great Sellers in three roles: army leader, Duchess of Grand Fenwick, and the prime minister. Based on "The Wrath of the Grapes" by Leonard Wib-

berley and followed by a humbler sequel, "Mouse on the Moon."

1959 83m/C Peter Sellers, Jean Seberg, Leo McKern, David Kossoff, William Hartnell, Timothy Bateson, MacDonald Parke, Monte Landis; **D:** Jack Arnold; **W:** Roger MacDougall, Stanley Mann; **M:** Edwin Astley. **VHS, Beta** *COL*

Movie, Movie

PG/Jr. High-Adult Acceptable spoof of 1930s films features Scott in twin-bill of black and white "Dynamite Hands," which lampoons boxing dramas, and "Baxter's Beauties," a color send-up of Busby Berkeley musicals. There's even a parody of coming attractions. Wholesome, mildly entertaining.

1978 107m/B Stanley Donen, George C. Scott, Trish Van Devere, Eli Wallach, Red Buttons, Barbara Harris, Barry Bostwick, Harry Hamlin, Art Carney; **D:** Stanley Donen; **W:** Larry Gelbart; **M:** Ralph Burns. **VHS** *FOX*

Moving Violations

PG-13/Jr. High-Adult This could be entitled "Adventures in Traffic Violations School." Wise-cracking tree planter is sent to traffic school after accumulating several moving violations issued to him by a morose traffic cop. Lightweight comedy has Bill Murray's little brother in feature role.

BEWARE *Profanity and suggested sex.*

1985 90m/C John Murray, Jennifer Tilly, James Keach, Brian Backer, Sally Kellerman, Fred Willard, Clara Peller, Wendie Jo Sperber; **D:** Neal Israel; **W:** Pat Proft; **M:** Ralph Burns. **VHS, Beta, LV** *FOX*

Mowgli's Brothers

Preschool-Primary Cartoon story, selected from Rudyard Kipling's "The Jungle Book," tells of a boy raised in jungle nobility by a pair of wolves. One of a trio of Kipling tales beautifully animated for TV by Chuck Jones; see also "Rikki-Tikki-Tavi" and "The White Seal."

1973 25m/C D: Chuck Jones. **VHS, Beta** *FHE, CHI*

Mozart's The Magic Flute Story: An Opera Fantasy

Family Abridged production with narration guides children through Mozart's comic opera. Performed by Germany's Gewandhaus Opera & Orchestra, with arias sung in the original German. Ages 5 to 10.

1994 42m/C VHS *VWV*

Much Ado About Nothing

PG-13/Sr. High-Adult Shakespeare for the masses details romance between two sets of would-be lovers—the battling Beatrice and Benedick (Thompson and Branagh) and the ingenuous Hero and Claudio (Beckinsale and Leonard). Washington is the noble warrior leader, Reeves his evil half-dressed half-brother, and Keaton serves brilliant comic relief as the officious, bum-

bling Dogberry. Sunlit, lusty, and revealing about all the vagaries of love, Branagh brings passion to his quest of making Shakespeare more approachable. His second attempt after "Henry V" at breaking the stuffy Shakespearean tradition. Filmed on location in Tuscany, Italy.

BEWARE *Brief nudity and suggested sex (in iambic pentameter). Some ethics of the period may need to be explained. Some men are flogged.*

1993 110m/C Kenneth Branagh, Emma Thompson, Robert Sean Leonard, Kate Beckinsale, Denzel Washington, Keanu Reeves, Michael Keaton, Brian Blessed, Phyllida Law, Imelda Staunton, Gerard Horan, Jimmy Yuill, Richard Clifford, Ben Elton; *D:* Kenneth Branagh; *W:* Kenneth Branagh; *M:* Patrick Doyle. **VHS, LV** *COL*

Multiplicity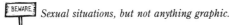

PG-13/Jr. High-Adult In "Multiplicity," Michael Keaton gets to play himself, himself, himself, and himself. Well, actually it's four different versions of the same character, an overworked and overly busy guy who attempts to juggle his schedule by cloning himself. And since the cloning process is far from perfect, each clone has a different dominant personality trait. Needless to say, things get a little hairy and his wife (MacDowell) has to deal with it all. Yes, Keaton is still funny—remember "Mr. Mom"?

BEWARE *Sexual situations, but not anything graphic.*

1996 110m/C Michael Keaton, Andie MacDowell; *D:* Harold Ramis; *W:* Harold Ramis, Chris Miller, Lowell Ganz, Babaloo Mandel. **VHS** *NYR*

Munchie

PG/Family A stiff-looking puppet—oops, we mean a magical dwarf creature, is discovered in a mine shaft by young Gage. Munchie turns out to be a friend, driving off bullies and an obnoxious potential stepfather. So-called sequel has nothing to do with 1987's "Munchies" (a dimwit "Gremlins" ripoff from the same filmmakers). That's the good news. Bad news is, it's uninspired and inane.

BEWARE *Alcohol use.*

1992 80m/C Loni Anderson, Andrew Stevens, Arte Johnson, Jamie McEnnan; *D:* Jim Wynorski; *V:* Dom DeLuise. **VHS** *NHO*

Munchies

PG/Jr. High-Adult "Gremlins" rip-off about tiny aliens who love beer and fast food, and invade a small town. Lewd and ribald.

BEWARE *Sex talk; alcohol use.*

1987 83m/C Harvey Korman, Charles Stratton, Nadine Van Der Velde; *D:* Bettina Hirsch. **VHS, Beta** *MGM*

Muppet Babies: Explore with Us

Preschool-Primary "The New Adventures of Kermo Polo" showcases the Muppet Babies on the high seas, discovering the Mountain of Youth and meeting the Great Gonzo Khan and Fozzie de Leon. "Transcontinental Whoo-Whoo" has the Muppet Babies helping to build the Transcontinental railroad. AGes 4 to 10.

1992 44m/C VHS *JHV*

Muppet Babies: Let's Build

Preschool-Primary In "Six to Eight Weeks," the Muppet Babies are expecting their new playhouse to come in the mail and dream about what it will be like. "Eight Flags Over the Nursery" features the Muppet Babies, using Scooter's computer, to build an amusement park called Babyland.

1992 44m/C VHS *JHV*

Muppet Babies: Time to Play

Preschool-Primary Two stories: "The Next Generation" has Baby Kermit commanding the Starship Booby Prize on a space adventure. In "Beauty and the Schnoz," Baby Gonzo and Baby Piggy act out their favorite fairy tales.

1992 44m/C VHS *JHV*

Muppet Babies Video Storybook, Vol. 1

Family Jim Henson's classic Muppet characters are depicted romping together as children. Or cubs. Or pups. Or whatever (especially Gonzo). Segments include: "Meet the Muppet Babies," "Baby Piggy and the Giant Bubble," and "What's a Gonzo?" Additional volumes available.

1988 30m/C VHS, LV *GKK*

The Muppet Christmas Carol

G/Family The Muppets take certain liberties with Charles Dickens, beginning with Mr. Dickens himself, herein played by long-snouted Gonzo, assisted by Rizzo the Rat as narrator. Most of the actors in this colorful, tuneful tale re-told are Muppets—Kermit as Bob Cratchit, Miss Piggy as his wife, Fozzie Bear as Mr., ahem, Fozziwig, manufacturer of rubber chickens. Statler and Waldorf show up as the ghosts of Jacob Marley and his brother, Robert (think about it). Human actor Michael Caine plays Scrooge somewhat short of the traditional heartless miser, but adequately. It's all quite enjoyable. Insider's note: In the last scene, Caine stands in front of a store labeled "Mickelwhite's." Caine's name at birth was Maurice Mickelwhite. Ages 6 to 11.

1992 120m/C Michael Caine; **D:** Brian Henson; **M:** Paul Williams, Miles Goodman; **V:** Dave Goelz, Steve Whitmire, Jerry Nelson, Frank Oz. **VHS, Beta** *JHV*

Muppet Family Christmas

Family Fozzie Bear invites all his friends to spend Christmas on his mom's farm where everyone has fun trimming the tree, cooking, and singing carols—and Miss Piggy traps Kermit under the mistletoe. Ages 4 to 10.

1995 47m/C **VHS** *TOU*

The Muppet Movie 🎵🎵🎵 🦴

G/Family Singer Kermit the Frog and his comedian pal Fozzie Bear leave their swamp to become rich and famous in Hollywood. Miss Piggy, Rowlf the Dog and other Muppet characters join them on their way. Meanwhile Kermit is pursued by restaurateur Doc Hopper (Charles Durning) whose specialte de la maison is (gasp!) frog legs. Delightful, with enough jokes and celebrity cameos to keep adults interested. Paul Williams contributes uniformly pleasant songs. Ages 3 and up. 🎵 The Rainbow Connection; Frog's Legs So Fine; Movin Right Along; Can You Picture That?; Never Before; Something Better; This Looks Familiar; I'm Going Back There Someday.

1979 94m/C Jim Henson's Muppets; **Cameos:** Edgar Bergen, Milton Berle, Mel Brooks, Madeline Kahn, Steve Martin, Carol Kane, Paul Williams, Charles Durning, Bob Hope, James Coburn, Dom DeLuise, Elliott Gould, Cloris Leachman, Telly Savalas, Orson Welles; **D:** James Frawley; **M:** Paul Williams; **V:** Jim Henson, Frank Oz. **VHS, Beta, LV** *JHV, FOX*

Muppet Musicians of Bremen

Family Kermit the Frog narrates this Muppet-ized Brothers Grimm story of a group of jazz-playing animals who want to escape from their masters and seek freedom and fame.

1982 50m/C **V:** Frank Oz, Jim Henson. **VHS, Beta, LV** *NO*

Muppet Revue

Family Join Kermit the Frog and Fozzie Bear as they go down Muppet Memory Lane to remember some of the best moments from "The Muppet Show."

1985 56m/C Frank Oz, Harry Belafonte, Linda Ronstadt, Paul Williams; **D:** Jim Henson. **VHS, Beta** *FOX*

Muppet Treasure Island 🦴🦴🦴

G/Family The Muppets take on Robert Louis Stevenson's tale of pirates and buried treasure with delightfully funny results. Kermit's the good Captain Smollett, Curry's the scurvy Long John Silver, and somehow a crowd of tourist rats is on board ship, dancing, water skiing and wearing loud Hawaiian shirts. Ben Gunn has become Benjamina Gunn, all the better to be played by Miss Piggy and to occasion the comment "Don't cry for me, Benjamina." An old-fashioned laff riot. Plus, it's a musical; not only do the Muppets sail the high seas, they hit them (or try).

1996 99m/C Tim Curry, Kevin Bishop, Billy Connolly, Jennifer Saunders; **D:** Brian Henson; **W:** Jerry Juhl, Jim V. Hart, Kirk R.

Thatcher; **C:** John Fenner; **M:** Hans Zimmer; **V:** Steve Whitmire, Frank Oz, Dave Goelz. **VHS** *TOU*

Muppet Treasure Island Sing-Alongs

Preschool-Primary This new sing along video from Jim Henson Productions features nine fun-filled Muppet songs, including two pirate tunes from the hit "Muppet Treasure Island," "Cabin Fever" and "Sailing For Adventure." Starring Kermit the Frog and a band of buccaneers.

1996 ?m/C **VHS** *JHV*

Muppet Treasures

Family Kermit and Fozzie discover some unexpected treasures in the "Muppet Show" attic archives, including cooking lessons with the Swedish Chef and episodes of "Pigs in Space" and "Veterinarian's Hospital."

1985 55m/C Frank Oz, Jim Henson, Peter Sellers, Zero Mostel, Buddy Rich, Paul Simon, Ethel Merman. **VHS, Beta** *FOX*

Muppet Video Series

Family Highlights of Muppet specials, including "Country Music with the Muppets," "Muppet Weird Stuff," and "Muppet Treasures."

1984 60m/C **V:** Jim Henson, Frank Oz. **VHS, Beta** *FOX*

Muppets Moments

Family Kermit and Fozzie uncover classic segments from "Veterinarian's Hospital" and "Pigs in Space" while doing their annual spring cleaning. Great stuff excerpted from "The Muppet Show" television series.

1985 55m/C Frank Oz, Jim Henson, Liza Minnelli, Zero Mostel, Lena Horne; **D:** Jim Henson. **VHS, Beta** *FOX*

Muppets Take Manhattan 🦴🦴🦴

G/Family Kermit and Miss Piggy and company take their college musical to Broadway, only to find that nobody's interested in producing it. They decide to take day jobs while composer Kermit works at selling the show. Unfortunately, he is struck by a car, suffers amnesia and ends up working in an all-frog ad agency. In true show biz fashion, the Muppets ... well, never mind. Great fun, lots of guest stars. Ages 4 to 8.

1984 94m/C Jim Henson's Muppets; **Cameos:** Dabney Coleman, James Coco, Art Carney, Joan Rivers, Gregory Hines, Linda Lavin, Liza Minnelli, Brooke Shields, John Landis; **D:** Frank Oz; **M:** Ralph Burns; **V:** Jim Henson, Frank Oz. **VHS, Beta, LV** *FOX, HMV*

Muriel's Wedding 🦴🦴🦴

R/Sr. High-Adult Muriel (Collette) can catch a bridal bouquet, but can she catch a husband? Her blond and shallow friends don't think so. But dowdy, pathetic, overweight Muriel dreams of a fairy tale wedding anyway. How she fulfills her obsessive fantasy is the basis for this quirky, hilarious, and often touchingly poignant ugly duckling tale with the occasional over-the-top satiric moment. Strong cast is led by sympathetic and engaging

Meet the Director of Muppet Treasure Island, Brian Henson

When Jim Henson died unexpectedly in May 1990 of a strep infection, his eldest son, Brian, was only twenty-six. Nonetheless, the employees of Jim Henson Productions, as well as Brian's four siblings, all looked to him as the heir apparent to the leadership of the industry created by his legendary puppeteer father. Brian Henson was indeed well-schooled in the business. Born in Manhattan and raised in Bedford, New York, he had long played with the denizens of his father's New York studio before he made his professional debut as a puppeteer in *The Great Muppet Caper.* Shortly thereafter he went off to study astrophysics at the University of Colorado, but finding college not to his liking, he dropped out and returned to puppeteering.

Part of what changed his mind about his career plans was meeting Ellis Flyte, a costume designer on the Jim Henson Productions film, *The Dark Crystal,* in 1983. They married in 1990. That year was a challenging one for Henson, who had to steer his family's company through the wreck of a proposed merger with Disney which fell apart in the wake of his father's death. Many observers felt that the company, too, would fall apart, but Henson as CEO has made Jim Henson Productions more profitable than ever—in part because of his own efforts as director of such films as *The Muppet Christmas Carol, Muppet Treasure Island* and development of such television shows as "Muppets Tonight."

performances from Collette (who gained 40-plus pounds for the role) and Griffiths as her best friend, Rhonda. '70s pop supergroup ABBA lends its kitschy but catchy tunes to the plot and soundtrack.

BEWARE *Contains profanity and sexual situations. For mature teens. Blond bimbo "friends" are overly cruel to Muriel and a catfight ensues. Muriel and friend Rhonda have sailors over to their new bachelorette pad.*

1994 105m/C Toni Collette, Bill Hunter, Rachel Griffiths, Jeanie Drynan, Gennie Nevinson Brice, Matt Day, Daniel Lapaine; **D:** P.J. Hogan; **W:** P.J. Hogan; **M:** Peter Best. **Award Nominations:** Australian Film Institute '94: Best Director (Hogan), Best Screenplay, Best Supporting Actor (Hunter), Best Supporting Actress (Drynan); Golden Globe Awards '96: Best Actress—Musical/Comedy (Collette); Writers Guild of America '95: Best Original Screenplay; **Awards:** Australian Film Institute '94: Best Actress (Collette), Best Film, Best Sound, Best Supporting Actress (Griffiths). **VHS, LV** *MAX*

Murmel, Murmel, Murmel

Preschool-Primary Contains two stories from popular children's author Robert Munsch. In "Murmel, Murmel, Murmel," Robin hears a noise coming from a hole in her sandbox and finds a baby. Robin must seek out the proper person to care for the baby. In the second, "The Boy in the Drawer," Shelley confronts the boy who lives in her sock drawer. Ages 4 to 8.
1994 25m/C VHS

Murphy's Romance

PG-13/Jr. High-Adult Young divorced mother with an urge to train horses pulls up the stakes and heads for Arizona with her son. There she meets a pharmacist who may be just what the doctor ordered to help her build a new life.

BEWARE *Sex.*

1985 107m/C James Garner, Sally Field, Brian Kerwin, Corey Haim, Dennis Burkley, Charles Lane, Georgann Johnson; **D:** Martin Ritt; **W:** Harriet Frank Jr., Irving Ravetch; **M:** Carole King. **VHS, Beta, LV** *COL, HMV*

Muscle Beach Party ♫♫

Jr. High-Adult Sequel to "Beach Party" finds Frankie and Annette romping in the sand again. Trouble invades teen nirvana when a new gym opens and the hardbodies try to muscle in on surfer turf. Meanwhile, Paluzzi tries to muscle in on Funicello's turf. Good clean corny fun, with the usual lack of script and plot. Lorre appeals in a cameo, his final screen appearance. Watch for "Little" Stevie Wonder in his debut. Rickles' first appearance in the "BP" series; Lupus was credited as Rock Stevens. Followed by "Bikini Beach." ♫ Muscle Beach Party; Runnin' Wild; Muscle Bustle; My First Love; Surfin' Woodie; Surfer's Holiday; Happy Street; A Girl Needs a Boy; A Boy Needs a Girl.

1964 94m/C Frankie Avalon, Annette Funicello, Buddy Hackett, Luciana Paluzzi, Don Rickles, John Ashley, Jody McCrea, Morey Amsterdam, Peter Lupus, Candy Johnson, Dolores Wells, Stevie Wonder, Donna Loren, Amadee Chabot; **Cameos:** Peter Lorre; **D:** William Asher; **W:** Robert Dillon; **M:** Les Baxter. **VHS, Beta, LV** *VTR*

The Music Factory

Primary Ten-part series featuring the fun-filled Musical Factory clubhouse and all the characters who reside there. Provides a strong foundation of musical knowledge; includes such topics as rhythm, tone, scales, melody, and accompaniment. Ages 8 and up.
1994 300m/C VHS

The Music Man 🦴🦴🦴🦴

G/Family Con man Henry Hill gets off the train in River City, Iowa, where there are plans to build a pool hall. Hill declares billiards would destroy family values (sound familiar?) and convinces adults to instead finance a wholesome children's marching band. Although the huckster plans to take their money and run before the instruments arrive, his love for the spinsterish town librarian makes him think twice about fleeing the Heartland. This musical isn't just a slice of Americana; it's a whole pie. Acting and singing are terrific "with a capital 'T' and that rhymes with 'P' and that stands for" Preston, who epitomizes the charismatic pitchman (for an encore, see "The Last Starfighter"). Future filmmaker Howard once again proves to be one of the screen's best child actors. Grabbed multiple Oscars, including Best Picture.
🎵 Seventy-six Trombones; Trouble; If You Don't Mind; Till There Way You; The Wells Fargo Wagon; Being in Love; Goodnight, My Someone; Rock Island; Iowa Stubborn.
1962 151m/C Robert Preston, Shirley Jones, Buddy Hackett, Hermione Gingold, Paul Ford, Pert Kelton, Ron Howard; **D:** Morton DaCosta; **W:** Marion Hargrove. **Award Nominations:** Academy Awards '62: Best Art Direction/Set Decoration (Color), Best Costume Design (Color), Best Film Editing, Best Picture, Best Sound; **Awards:** Academy Awards '62: Best Adapted Score; Golden Globe Awards '63: Best Film—Musical/Comedy. **VHS, Beta, LV** *WAR, MVD, TLF*

The Musical Universe of Nursery Rhymes, Vol. 1

Preschool-Primary Combines musical rhythm, whimsical sound effects, funny animation, and live action to help children learn Mother Goose nursery rhymes. Contains on-screen synchronized text. Ages 1 to 4.
1994 m/C VHS *TPV*

Mutant League

Family Mutant athletes vie for the Mutant League Championship trophy, displaying their super strength, speed, unusual abilities—and unsportsmanlike conduct. Adapted from the animated TV series. Quite wretched. Ages 5 to 8.
1995 69m/C VHS *COL*

My American Cousin 🦴🦴🦴

PG/Jr. High-Adult Canadian comedy-drama set in 1959. Bored 12-year-old Sandy and her girlfriends are excited by a surprise summer visit from Butch, a 17-year-old California cousin with a red sportscar and a James Dean attitude. Sandy figures out he's run away from home; she's had the same idea and hopes he'll take her away with him. Likeable and sympathetic, if mildly simplistic (who wouldn't flee from Butch's grotesque parents?). Sandy's romantic misadventures continued in sequel "American Boyfriends."

⚠️ BEWARE *Sex talk, salty language, mature themes, roughhousing, alcohol use.*

1985 94m/C Margaret Langrick, John Wildman, Richard Donat, Jane Mortifee; **D:** Sandy Wilson; **W:** Sandy Wilson. **VHS, Beta, LV** *MED, VTR*

My Best Friend Is a Vampire 🦴 🐾

PG/Jr. High-Adult Compare/contrast with "Buffy the Vampire Slayer." Average high schooler gets bitten, turns into a nice-guy vampire. It seems the undead are just another oppressed minority, and Leonard needs both his supernatural and normal pals to protect him when a fanatical vampire-exterminator shows up. Not exactly the most effective plea for social tolerance, but among the mildest teen-vampire fables you'll find.

⚠️ BEWARE *Salty language.*

1988 90m/C Robert Sean Leonard, Evan Mirand, Cheryl Pollak, Rene Auberjonois, Cecilia Peck, Fannie Flagg, Kenneth Kimmins, David Warner, Paul Wilson; **D:** Jimmy Huston; **M:** Stephen Dorff. **VHS** *HBO*

My Bodyguard 🦴🦴🦴

PG/Jr. High-Adult Undersized high school student fends off attacking bullies by hiring a hulking, withdrawn classmate as his bodyguard. Their "business" arrangement develops into true friendship. An acclaimed adolescent-underdog tale with realistic characters, intelligence, and sensitivity, even if a lot of the plot hinges on paybacks and revenge.

⚠️ BEWARE *Serious fistfighting, profanity and bullying.*

1980 96m/C Chris Makepeace, Adam Baldwin, Martin Mull, Ruth Gordon, Matt Dillon, John Houseman, Joan Cusack, Craig Richard Nelson; **D:** Tony Bill; **W:** Alan Ormsby; **M:** Dave Grusin. **VHS, Beta** *FOX*

My Boyfriend's Back 🦴

PG-13/Jr. High-Adult Embarrassingly dumb horror comedy about a teenage boy who wants to take the prettiest girl in the school to the prom. The only problem is that he's become a zombie. Bits of him keep falling off (she thoughtfully glues them back on) and if he wants to stay "alive" long enough to get to the dance he has to munch on human flesh. Distasteful. Director Balaban seems to have a fixation on cannibals and kids; he also did the adult-oriented "Parents."

⚠️ BEWARE *Violence juggles the gore quota within a PG-13 rating.*

1993 85m/C Andrew Lowery, Traci Lind, Edward Herrmann, Mary Beth Hurt, Danny Zorn, Austin Pendleton, Jay O. Sanders, Paul

Kermit and Sam the Eagle in "Muppet Treasure Island."

Dooley, Bob Dishy, Matthew Fox, Paxton Whitehead; *D:* Bob Balaban; *W:* Dean Lorey. **VHS, LV** *TOU*

My Dear Uncle Sherlock

Primary-Jr. High Little boy and his uncle enjoy playing detective. One day they get to solve a real-life mystery when a neighbor is robbed. ABC-TV kid-sized adaptation of a short story by thriller writer Hugh Pentacost.
197? 24m/C VHS, Beta *MTT*

My Dog, the Thief ♫♫

Family Disney's entry in the adorable St.Bernard sweepstakes is the story of a helicopter weatherman unaware that the pooch he has adopted is a kleptomaniac. When the beast steals a necklace from a gang of jewel thieves, the alleged fun begins.
1969 88m/C Joe Flynn, Elsa Lanchester, Roger C. Carmel, Mickey Shaughnessy, Dwayne Hickman, Mary Ann Mobley; *D:* Robert Stevenson. **VHS, Beta** *DVT*

My Father the Hero ♫♫

PG/Jr. High-Adult Another adaptation of a French film ("Mon Pere, Ce Heroes") finds 14-year-old Heigl on an island paradise with divorced dad Depardieu, passing him off as her boyfriend (without his knowledge) to impress a cute boy, causing obvious misunderstandings.

Depardieu shows a flair for physical comedy, but his talent is superior to a role that's vaguely disturbing; one of the funnier moments finds him unwittingly singing "Thank Heaven For Little Girls" to a horrified audience. Best for the pre-teen set. Top notch actress Thompson's surprising (uncredited) cameo is due to her friendship with Depardieu.

> **BEWARE** *Profanity and sex talk (some Depardieu's character would rather not hear from his daughter).*

1993 90m/C Gerard Depardieu, Katherine Heigl, Dalton James, Lauren Hutton, Faith Prince; *Cameos:* Emma Thompson; *D:* Steve Miner; *W:* Francis Veber, Charlie Peters; *M:* David Newman. **VHS, LV** *TOU*

My Father's Glory ♫♫♫

G/Jr. High-Adult Based on Marcel Pagnol's tales of his childhood, this is a sweet, beautiful memory of a young boy's favorite summer in the French countryside in the early 1900s. Not much happens, yet the film is such a perfect evocation of the place and time that you're carried into the dreams and thoughts of all the characters. One half of a duo, followed by "My Mother's Castle." In French with English subtitles.
1991 110m/C Julien Ciamaca, Philippe Caubere, Nathalie Roussel, Therese Liotard, Didier Pain; *D:* Yves Robert; *W:* Lucette Andrei; *M:* Vladimir Cosma. **VHS** *INJ, ORI, BTV*

My Favorite Brunette ♪♪ ♭

Family You may have wondered all your life what people like about Bob Hope. Your kids may wonder who he is. This funny movie may answer both questions. Hope plays a photographer turned private eye who gets involved with murder, mobsters (Peter Lorre and Lon Chaney) and a brown-haired femme fatale (Dorothy Lamour). Ages 10 and up.

1947 85m/B Bob Hope, Dorothy Lamour, Peter Lorre, Lon Chaney Jr., Alan Ladd, Reginald Denny, Bing Crosby; **D:** Elliott Nugent. **VHS, Beta, LV** *CNG, MRV, NOS*

My Favorite Year ♪♪♪

PG/Jr. High-Adult A young writer on a popular live television show in the 1950s is asked to keep a watchful eye on the week's guest star-his favorite swashbuckling movie hero. Through a series of misadventures, he discovers his matinee idol is actually a drunkard and womanizer who has trouble living up to his cinematic standards. Sterling performance from O'Toole, with memorable portrayal from Bologna as the show's host, King Kaiser (a take-off of Sid Caesar from "Your Show of Shows").

> ⚠ **BEWARE** *Profanity, sexual situations and gangsters. O'Toole's character has a severe drinking problem.*

1982 92m/C Peter O'Toole, Mark Linn-Baker, Joseph Bologna, Jessica Harper, Lainie Kazan, Bill Macy, Anne DeSalvo, Lou Jacobi, Adolph Green, Cameron Mitchell, Gloria Stuart; **D:** Richard Benjamin; **W:** Norman Steinberg; **M:** Ralph Burns. **VHS, Beta, LV** *MGM*

My First Magic

Preschool-Primary Offers magic tricks for children to perform at parties. Includes step-by-step instructions from a professional magician as he explains the secrets behind tricks with rings, rope, dancing matchboxes, and disappearing silk scarves. Ages 6 to 10.

1995 m/C VHS

My First Party

Preschool-Primary Offers tips that help children realize the fun involved in preparing for a party. Contains creative ideas for things to make in advance. Easy-to-follow instructions. Ages 6 to 10.

1995 m/C VHS

My Friend Flicka ♪♪♪

Family Colorado Rockies boy makes friends with a colt of dubious value. His rancher dad thinks the horse is full of wild oats, but young Roddie trains diligently until Flicka is the best gosh darned horse in pre-Disney family faredom. Based on Mary O'Hara's book, followed by "Thunderhead, Son of Flicka," and TV series.

1943 89m/C Roddy McDowall, Preston Foster, Rita Johnson, James Bell, Jeff Corey; **D:** Harold Schuster. **VHS, Beta** *FXV, FCT, HMV*

My Friend Walter ♪♪ ♭

Family Ten-year-old Bess Throckmorten is visiting the Tower of London when the 400-year old ghost of her distant ancestor, Sir Walter Raleigh, asks to follow her home to see how the family is doing. With the Throckmortens about to lose their farm, the gallant spook hatches a plan. Elements of this "WonderWorks Family Movie" seem overly familiar at first (only the charming little heroine can see the meddling ghost, etc.), but stick with it to the end and you'll be rewarded, and yankee kids unfamiliar with Sir Walter will gain a painless history lesson. Based on the book by Michael Morpurgo.

1993 87m/C Polly Grant, Ronald Pickup, Prunella Scales, Louise Jameson, James Hazeldine, Lawrence Cooper, Constance Chapman; **D:** Gavin Millar. **VHS** *PME, BTV*

My Girl ♪♪ ♭

PG/Primary-Adult Chlumsky is delightful in her debut as 11-year old tomboy Vada, who must come to grips with the realities of life—and death. Best friend Thomas (Culkin) understands her better than her widowed mortician father and his nice girlfriend, the new makeup artist at the funeral parlor, but the kids' budding romance is derailed by tragedy. Comedy-drama script battles between very real warmth and forced eccentricity, rewards the viewer in the end.

> ⚠ **BEWARE** *Salty language, sex talk. The demise of a certain lead character stirred a debate as to whether this was suitable for youngsters to see, but death is handled with dignity—and is no worse than any tearjerker of past eras anyway. Very young kids ought to be somewhat prepared.*

1991 102m/C Dan Aykroyd, Jamie Lee Curtis, Macaulay Culkin, Anna Chlumsky, Griffin Dunne, Raymond Buktenica, Richard Masur, Ann Nelson, Peter Michael Goetz, Tom Villard; **D:** Howard Zieff; **W:** Laurice Elehwany; **M:** James Newton Howard. **VHS, LV, 8mm** *COL*

My Girl 2 ♪♪ ♭

PG/Jr. High-Adult Chlumsky is back as Vada (this time without Culkin) in this innocent coming-of-ager. Portly Aykroyd and flaky Curtis return as parental window dressing who encourage Vada's search for information on her long-dead mother. She tracks down old friends of her mom's (Masur and Rose) who are having difficulties with their obnoxious adolescent son (O'Brien). Predictable, but enjoyable. Certain to fail the credibility test of nit-pickers who may wonder why the only thing Ackroyd can remember of his first wife is that she left behind a paper bag with a date scribbled on it. Set in 1974.

> ⚠ **BEWARE** *Dead parent.*

1994 99m/C Anna Chlumsky, Dan Aykroyd, Jamie Lee Curtis, Austin O'Brien, Richard Masur, Christine Ebersole; **D:** Howard Zieff; **W:** Janet Kovalcik; **M:** Cliff Eidelman. **VHS, LV, 8mm** *COL*

My Grandpa is a Vampire ♪

PG/Jr. High-Adult When 12 year-old Lonny and his pal visit nice old Grandpa Cooger in New Zealand, they dis-

Robert Preston leads a parade of kids in "The Music Man."

cover a long-hidden family secret—Grandpa's a vampire "of innocent origin." The boys help Grandpa elude some frightened locals, and that's about it. Also known as "Moonrise," uneventful tale needed to be "My Grandpa is a Scriptwriter." Terrible f/x; main attraction is Lewis recreating his character from TV's "The Munsters."

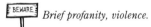 *Sex talk; alcohol use; salty language; roughhousing.*

1992 90m/C Al Lewis, Justin Gocke, Milan Borich, Noel Appleby; **D:** David Blyth. **VHS** *REP*

My Heroes Have Always Been Cowboys ♫♫ ♭

PG/Jr. High-Adult An aging rodeo rider returns to his hometown to recuperate and finds himself forced to confront his past. His ex-girlfriend, his dad and his sister all expect something from him. He learns how to give it, and gains the strength of purpose to get back on the bull that stomped him. Excellent rodeo footage, solid performances, but the story has been around the barn too many times to hold much interest.

Brief profanity, violence.

1991 106m/C Scott Glenn, Kate Capshaw, Ben Johnson, Balthazar Getty, Mickey Rooney, Gary Busey, Tess Harper, Clarence Williams III, Dub Taylor, Clu Gulager, Dennis Fimple; **D:** Stuart Rosenberg; **W:** Joel Don Humphreys; **M:** James Horner. **VHS, Beta, LV** *VTR, FXV, COL*

My Life ♫♫ ♭

PG-13/Jr. High-Adult Maudlin, sometimes depressing melodrama preaches the power of a well-examined life. Public relations exec Keaton is diagnosed with cancer and the doctors predict he will most likely die before the birth of his first child. Film follows his transition from uncommunicative and angry to acceptance, a role to which Keaton brings a sentimental strength. Kidman is window dressing as the ever-patient, nobly suffering wife, a cardboard character notable mainly for her beauty.

Dying parent and profanity. Guaranteed to draw tears and require several tissues.

1993 114m/C Michael Keaton, Nicole Kidman, Haing S. Ngor, Bradley Whitford, Queen Latifah, Michael Constantine, Toni Sawyer, Rebecca Schull, Lee Garlington; **D:** Bruce Joel Rubin; **W:** Bruce Joel Rubin; **M:** John Barry. **VHS, LV, 8mm** *COL*

My Life as a Dog 🦴🦴🦴🦴

Jr. High-Adult 12-year-old Ingmar doesn't mean to be troublesome, but calamities follow him everywhere. After he innocently burns down most of the neighborhood, his dying mother sends Ingmar to the country to live with an eccentric uncle's family, separating the boy from his beloved dog. Unhappy and confused, Ingmar gradually makes new friends as he struggles to find security, acceptance and love. Extraordinary, compassionate comedy drama, sometimes agonizing to watch, sometimes agonizingly funny as the hapless young hero faces a range of crushing disappointments and wild mishaps with the all-purpose attitude: "It could have been worse." Swedish film is geared to adults but by no means off limits to bright kid viewers who can take its rougher elements. Based on a novel by Reidar Jonsson, available in both subtitled and (badly) English-dubbed versions.

> 🚩BEWARE🚩 *Brief nudity, mature themes. If this were to be rated it would probably qualify as a PG13.*

1985 101m/C Anton Glanzelius, Tomas Van Bromssen, Anki Liden, Melinda Kinnaman, Kicki Rundgren, Ing-mari Carlsson; **D:** Lasse Hallstrom. **Award Nominations:** Academy Awards '87: Best Adapted Screenplay, Best Director (Hallstrom); **Awards:** Golden Globe Awards '88: Best Foreign Film; Independent Spirit Awards '88: Best Foreign Film. **VHS, Beta, LV** *PAR, INJ, HMV*

My Little Pony

Family My Little Pony is—guess what—a children's toy, here starring in a cartoon production pitting the adorable Ponyland playthings against the evil centaur Tirac. Additional volumes available.

1984 30m/C V: Tony Randall, Sandy Duncan. **VHS, Beta** *LIV*

My Little Pony: The Movie 🦴 🦴

Family One long animated toy commercial, all about the good little ponies, and a girl named Megan who helps them defend Phonyland—uh, Ponyland—from a wicked witch. And beware of the Smooze, a puddle of goo that gets bigger and bigger and bigger, not unlike the movie itself. Poor animation, but good voice acting by Madeline Kahn, Danny DeVito, Tony Randall and others. Ages 3 to 6.

1986 87m/C D: Michael Joens; **V:** Danny DeVito, Cloris Leachman, Tony Randall, Madeline Kahn. **VHS, Beta** *VTR*

My Mom's a Werewolf 🦴 🦴

PG/Jr. High-Adult Dizzy suburban housewife is bitten by a dashing pet-shop owner and soon begins to turn into a werewolf. Her teenage daughter must come up with a plan to regain dear, sweet mom. First-rate cast grapples with third-rate jokes and f/x. Werewolf faces are clearly store-bought masks; at least there's little chance of kid viewers being seriously scared.

1989 90m/C Susan Blakely, John Saxon, John Schuck, Katrina Caspary, Ruth Buzzi, Marilyn McCoo, Marcia Wallace, Diana Barrows; **D:** Michael Fischa; **W:** Mark Pirro. **VHS, Beta, LV** *PSM*

My Mother's Castle 🦴🦴🦴

PG/Jr. High-Adult Second half of the two-part French film series based on the boyhood memoirs of Marcel Pagnol that started with "My Father's Glory." Again, the story is loose, lyrical, and warm, as the Pagnol family spend free time at a home in the countryside. Some mild adventures confirm the young narrator's admiration for his father. Tenderly directed, charming, and suitable for the entire family, particularly if the kids are into subtitles (in French).

1991 98m/C Philippe Caubere, Nathalie Roussel, Didier Pain, Therese Liotard, Julien Ciamaca, Victorien Delmare; **D:** Yves Robert; **M:** Vladimir Cosma. **VHS** *INJ, ORI, BTV*

My Name is Nobody 🦴🦴 🦴

PG/Family Fast-paced spaghetti-western wherein a cocky, soft-hearted gunfighter is sent to kill the famous, retired outlaw he reveres, but instead they band together.

1974 115m/C Henry Fonda, Terence Hill, R.G. Armstrong; **D:** Tonino Valerii; **M:** Ennio Morricone. **VHS, Beta** *BAR, HHE*

My Neighbor Totoro 🦴🦴 🦴

G/Family Hit Japanese children's cartoon (dubbed into English) about two little girls who move to the countryside and meet magical forest denizens, especially the clan of furry Totoros, who look like a cross between the Tasmanian Devil and Barney the Dinosaur, though fortunately with the sweet temperament of the latter. Well-tuned to the bedtime-story crowd; animation is slow but pleasant, creatures fresh and endearing.

1993 76m/C D: Hayao Miyazaki; **W:** Hayao Miyazaki. **VHS** *FXV*

My Old Man 🦴🦴 🦴

Family Plucky teenaged girl and her seedy horsetrainer father come together over important horse race. Oates makes this one worth watching on a slow evening. A Hemingway story made for television.

> 🚩BEWARE🚩 *Alcohol use.*

1979 102m/C Kristy McNichol, Warren Oates, Eileen Brennan; **D:** John Erman. **VHS, Beta** *CAF*

My Pet Monster, Vol. 1

Preschool-Primary Another toy-inspired series of live-action fantasies about a boy who turns into a shaggy monster when he's hungry. From the same minds who brought you the Care Bears. Additional volumes available.

1986 60m/C VHS, Beta *MED*

My Science Project 🦴 🦴

PG/Jr. High-Adult Teenager Stockwell stumbles across a crystal sphere with a funky light. Unaware that it is an alien time-travel device, he takes it to school to use as a science project in a last-ditch effort to avoid failing his class. Chaos follows and Stockwell and his chums find themselves battling gladiators, mutants, and dinosaurs.

Plenty of special effects and a likeable enough, dumb teenage flick.

 Profanity.

1985 94m/C John Stockwell, Danielle von Zerneck, Fisher Stevens, Raphael Sbarge, Richard Masur, Barry Corbin, Ann Wedgeworth, Dennis Hopper, Candace Silvers, Beau Dremann, Pat Simmons, Pamela Springsteen; *D:* Jonathan Betuel; *M:* Peter Bernstein. **VHS, Beta, LV** *TOU*

My Side of the Mountain

G/Family Thirteen-year-old Teddy, at odds with his parents, decides to give up his home to live in the Canadian mountains. There a kindly folk-singer neighbor helps Teddy along with his unpracticed wilderness survival skills and eventual family reconciliation. Above-average adaptation of the novel by Jean Craighead George.

1969 100m/C Teddy Eccles, Theodore Bikel; *D:* James B. Clark. **VHS, Beta** *KUI, PAR*

My Stepmother Is an Alien

PG-13/Jr. High-Adult Eccentric astronomer sends a greeting to another galaxy on a stormy night; his answer is an inquisitive extraterrestrial in luscious human form. Of course, the scientist doesn't realize her origins (plot is rather farfetched) and courts the enticing visitor; only his young daughter notices the stepmom's strange ways. Fairly dim fantasy-comedy features a good cast and makes a very slight improvement over "My Mom's a Werewolf."

 *Salty language, sex talk, as alien has to learn all about human lovemaking.*

1988 108m/C Dan Aykroyd, Kim Basinger, Jon Lovitz, Alyson Hannigan, Joseph Maher, Seth Green, Wesley Mann, Adrian Sparks, Juliette Lewis, Tanya Fenmore; *D:* Richard Benjamin; *W:* Herschel Weingrod, Timothy Harris, Jonathan Reynolds; *M:* Alan Silvestri. **VHS, Beta, LV** *COL*

My Summer Story

PG/Family Writer Jean Shepherd and director Bob Clark created a big-screen winner and minor video classic in "A Christmas Story." Well, one out of two ain't so bad. "Summer Story" went straight to video. There's a reason. It's boring. Little Ralphie (Kieran Culkin) and the rest of his family find themselves battling their crazy new neighbors, the Bumpuses (Bumpi?) Meanwhile, Ralphie is hassled by a schoolyard bully and tries to bond with his dad (Grodin) while fishing, and mom (Steenburgen) becomes obsessed with gravy boats.

 Mild language and racy drawings.

1994 85m/C Charles Grodin, Mary Steenburgen, Kieran Culkin, Chris Culkin, Al Mancini, Troy Evans, Glenn Shadix, Dick O'Neill, Wayne Grace; *D:* Bob (Benjamin) Clark; *W:* Jean Shepherd, Bob (Benjamin) Clark, Leigh Brown; *C:* Stephen M. Katz; *M:* Paul Zaza. **VHS, LV** *MGM*

Mysterious Doctor Satan

Family Republic serial in which a mad scientist tries to conquer the world with his tin-can robots. Opposing him is Copperhead, a hero guy in a chain-mail mask and a business suit. If that sounds uninspired, there's a reason; this had been scripted as an Superman adventure, but Republic couldn't get legal rights to the Man of Steel, so writers hastily concocted Copperhead. Watch the 15 episodes and consider what might have been. Also available as an edited feature "Dr. Satan's Robot."

 Roughhousing.

1940 250m/B Eduardo Ciannelli, Robert Wilcox, Ella Neal; *D:* William Witney. **VHS** *REP, VCN, MLB*

Mysterious Island

Family Exhilarating sci-fi classic adapted from Jules Verne's novel about escaping Civil War soldiers who go up in a balloon and come down on a Pacific Island populated by giant animals. Adopting a Robinson Crusoe in Jurassic Park lifestyle, they encounter two shipwrecked English ladies (how very convenient), pirates, and eventually the notorious Captain Nemo and his sub. Ray Harryhausen's stop-motion animation brings mammoth crabs, turtles and bees to life.

 *Violence and giant animals may be scary for the young.*

1961 101m/C Michael Craig, Joan Greenwood, Michael Callan, Gary Merrill, Herbert Lom, Beth Rogan, Percy Herbert, Dan Jackson, Nigel Green; *D:* Cy Endfield; *M:* Bernard Herrmann. **VHS, Beta, LV** *COL, MLB*

Mysterious Tadpole and Other Stories

Preschool-Primary Louis gets a curious birthday gift from his uncle. The tape from Weston Woods' acclaimed "Children's Circle" series also includes "Five Chinese Brothers," "Jonah and the Great Fish," and "The Wizard."

1989 34m/C VHS *CCC, WKV*

Mystery Date

PG-13/Jr. High-Adult Another teen date-from-hell comedy, in which a shy college guy gets a date with the girl of his dreams, only to be mistaken for a master criminal and pursued by gangsters, police, and a crazed florist. Not terrible, but if you're old enough to drive, you're probably too old to watch with great amusement.

 Violence.

1991 98m/C Ethan Hawke, Teri Polo, Brian McNamara, Fisher Stevens, B.D. Wong; *D:* Jonathan Wacks; *W:* Terry Runte; *M:* John Du Prez. **VHS** *ORI*

Mystery Mansion

PG/Jr. High-Adult Made-in-Utah family film with a surprisingly dark undertone. Little girl exploring a spooky old house realizes she's the reincarnation of a pioneer child murdered a century ago, and thus knows where a fortune in gold is hidden.

> **BEWARE** *Violence is implied rather than shown, but it's still significant.*

1983 95m/C Dallas McKennon, Greg Wynne, Jane Ferguson. **VHS, Beta** *MED*

Mystery of the Million Dollar Hockey Puck 🏒🏒🏒

Family So you think you know movies? Name one that features the NHL Montreal Canadiens. "The Iceman Cometh?" No way. "My Dinner With Andre?" Not even close. It's this one, a little-known but worthwhile adventure about a hockey-loving orphan named Pierre who overhears a plot to smuggle diamonds inside a hockey puck. Pierre is spotted, however, and the chase is on as he and his sister, Catou, strive to elude capture and expose the smugglers. Part of the story involves a Canadiens' game. It's exciting but not violent (except perhaps for the hockey game). Ages 6 to 11.

198? 88m/C Michael MacDonald, Angele Knight; **D:** Jean LaFleur, Peter Svatek. **VHS, Beta** *NO*

Mystery Science Theater 3000: The Movie 🏒🏒🏒

PG-13/Jr. High-Adult The ultimate in laziness. Why rent a cheesy sci-fi flick and gather friends to jeer at it when this film does all the work for you? The sci-fi flick is "This Island Earth" (1955), the jeerers are a man and three robots who look like a gumball machine, a crow and a vacuum cleaner. The film rolls, the happy hecklers crack wise—they note, for instance, that the aliens with pulsing foreheads look suspiciously like Buddy Ebsen (who isn't in the movie). Like the TV version of "MST3K," there's no intellectual heavy lifting and many laughs. Not quite 3000, but many. Ages 12 and up.

> **BEWARE** *Rude remarks that people who know the TV series will already be familiar with.*

1996 73m/C Trace Beaulieu, James Mallon, Michael J. Nelson, Kevin Murphy, John Brady; **D:** James Mallon; **W:** Trace Beaulieu, James Mallon, Michael J. Nelson, Kevin Murphy, Mary Jo Pehl, Paul Chaplin, Bridget Jones; **C:** Jeff Stonehouse; **M:** Billy Barber. **VHS** *NYR*

The Naked Gun: From the Files of Police Squad 🏒🏒🏒

PG-13/Jr. High-Adult Good introduction for older kids to the most liberating of art forms—parody, the thing that's made Mad magazine popular with adolescents for years. A spoof of every cop and spy film ever made, and then some, beginning with Leslie Nielsen, deliciously mock serious as police Lt. Frank Drebin, singlehandedly beating up America's enemies (anyone remember Idi Amin?) and then driving insanely, through a car wash, a girls' dormitory and over the loops of a roller coaster . . .

to pick up some donuts. Jokes and physical gags are nonstop. And history has made O.J. Simpson's presence a warped joke of its own. Ages 13 and up.

> **BEWARE** *Profanity and sex talk and typical Nielsen spoof stupidity.*

1988 85m/C Leslie Nielsen, Ricardo Montalban, Priscilla Presley, George Kennedy, O.J. Simpson, Nancy Marchand, John Houseman; **Cameos:** Weird Al Yankovic, Reggie Jackson, Dr. Joyce Brothers; **D:** David Zucker; **W:** Jerry Zucker, Jim Abrahams, Pat Proft, David Zucker; **M:** Ira Newborn. **VHS, Beta, LV, 8mm** *PAR*

Naked Gun 33 1/3: The Final Insult 🏒🏒

PG-13/Jr. High-Adult Newly retired, but not for long, Lt. Frank Drebin (Leslie Nielsen) is up to his old jokes. "Why don't you want a child?" coos wife Jane (Priscilla Presley). "Didn't I try adopting that 18-year-old Korean girl," Frank responds. You may have to explain that one to the kids. You may have to remind yourself why it's funny. Funnier than intended is the continuing presence of O.J. Simpson as accident-prone cop Nordberg. Drebin and company are called upon to save Hollywood from terrorists. Strictly for fans of the series. Ages 13 and up.

> **BEWARE** *Vulgarity, sex talk, sperm bank jokes and urinal jokes.*

1994 90m/C Leslie Nielsen, Priscilla Presley, O.J. Simpson, Fred Ward, George Kennedy, Gary Cooper, Kathleen Freeman, Raquel Welch; **Cameos:** Pia Zadora, James Earl Jones, Weird Al Yankovic, Ann B. Davis; **D:** Peter Segal; **W:** Robert Locash, David Zucker, Pat Proft; **M:** Ira Newborn. **VHS, Beta** *PAR*

Naked Gun 2 1/2: The Smell of Fear 🏒🏒🏒

PG-13/Jr. High-Adult It starts off with Lt. Frank Drebin (Leslie Nielsen) racing to a White House dinner where 's he's being honored for shooting his 1000th drug dealer, and it only gets crazier. There are spoofs of other movies—notably, the pottery wheel scene in "Ghost"—and some nonsense about the Bush administration's energy policy. The send-up of John Sununu is sure to baffle everyone, but laughs fly furiously, and if you aren't chortling just wait a minute. O.J. Simpson and Priscilla Presley are on hand, and Robert Goulet is the chief baddie. Ages 13 and up.

> **BEWARE** *Profanity and adult humor.*

1991 85m/C Leslie Nielsen, Priscilla Presley, George Kennedy, O.J. Simpson, Robert Goulet, Richard Griffiths, Jacqueline Brookes, Lloyd Bochner, Tim O'Connor, Peter Mark Richman; **Cameos:** Mel Torme, Eva Gabor, Weird Al Yankovic; **D:** David Zucker; **W:** David Zucker, Pat Proft; **M:** Ira Newborn. **VHS, Beta, LV, 8mm, CD-I** *PAR*

Nancy Drew: Mystery of the Diamond Triangle

Family Teenage detective Nancy (Pamela Sue Martin) seldom draws a blank when it comes to solving baffling mysteries. And she's not a bad role model for girls. Eight separate episodes of the TV series are available on tape.

1978 47m/C Pamela Sue Martin, William Schallert, Susan Buckner, Ruth Cox. **VHS, Beta** *MCA*

Nancy Drew, Reporter 🦴🦴

Family The young sleuth gets to play reporter after winning a newspaper contest. In no time at all, she's involved in a murder mystery.
1939 68m/B Bonita Granville, John Litel, Frankie Thomas Jr., Mary Lee, Sheila Bromley, Betty Amann, Dick Jones, Olin Howlin, Charles Halton; **D:** William Clemens. **VHS** *HTV, NOS*

Napoleon and Samantha 🦴🦴🦴

Family Disney adventure written by "Wilderness Family" filmmaker Stewart Raffill. Napoleon is an orphan befriended by college guy Danny (Douglas, early in his career). After the death of his grandfather, Napoleon doesn't want to be locked in an institution, so he runs away, taking Major—an elderly pet lion—in pursuit of Danny, who like many college students on summer break, is goat herding in Oregon's mountain country. So who's Samantha? She's Major's co-owner, played by Foster, making her film debut and good as always. Pleasant and worth watching.
1972 91m/C Jodie Foster, Johnny Whitaker, Michael Douglas, Will Geer, Henry Jones; **D:** Bernard McEveety; **W:** Stewart Raffill; **M:** Buddy Baker. **VHS, Beta** *DIS*

Nate and Hayes 🦴🦴 ♭

PG/Sr. High-Adult Set during the mid-1800s in the South Pacific, the notorious real-life swashbuckler Captain "Bully" Hayes ("good pirate") helps young missionary Nate recapture his fiancee from a cutthroat gang of evil slave traders. Entertaining "jolly rogers" film.

 Violence.

1983 100m/C Tommy Lee Jones, Michael O'Keefe, Max Phipps, Jenny Seagrove; **D:** Ferdinand Fairfax; **M:** Trevor Jones. **VHS, Beta, LV** *PAR*

National Geographic: Really Wild Animals Series

Jr. High-Adult Series of documentaries spotlighting wild animals of various regions.
19?? 50m/C VHS

National Lampoon's Christmas Vacation 🦴🦴 ♭

PG-13/Jr. High-Adult On this vacation, the Griswolds don't go anywhere. Instead, obnoxious relatives come to visit them. Yule have a pretty good time. Despite predictable plot, the jokes do flow. Written by John Hughes. Ages 13 and up.

BEWARE *Profanity.*

1989 93m/C Chevy Chase, Beverly D'Angelo, Randy Quaid, Diane Ladd, John Randolph, E.G. Marshall, Doris Roberts, Julia Louis-Dreyfus, Mae Questel, William Hickey, Brian Doyle-Murray, Juliette Lewis, Johnny Galecki, Nicholas Guest, Miriam Flynn; **D:** Jeremiah S.

Chechik; **W:** John Hughes; **M:** Angelo Badalamenti. **VHS, Beta, LV, 8mm** *WAR*

National Lampoon's European Vacation 🦴 ♭

PG-13/Jr. High-Adult Idiotic, even for a Chevy Chase movie. Sequel to "Vacation" has the Griswolds traipsing about Europe in their usual witless manner. Stonehenge will never be the same. Ages 13 and up.

BEWARE *Profanity and sex jokes.*

1985 94m/C Chevy Chase, Beverly D'Angelo, Dana Hill, Jason Lively, Victor Lanoux, John Astin; **D:** Amy Heckerling; **W:** John Hughes, Robert Klane, Eric Idle; **M:** Charles Fox. **VHS, Beta, LV, 8mm** *WAR*

National Lampoon's Loaded Weapon 1 🦴 ♭

PG-13/Jr. High-Adult Cop Jack Colt (Estevez) and partner Wes Luger (Jackson) attempt to recover a microfilm which contains a formula for turning cocaine into cookies. Essentially a sendup of the popular "Lethal Weapon" series, although other movies and themes receive passing attention. Short on plot and long on slapstick as the jokes come fast and furious, but a tired formula creates nostalgia for the granddaddy of them all, "Airplane." Lots of cameos, including one from sibling spoof star Sheen. The magazine folded while the movie was in production, an ominous sign.

BEWARE *Profanity, violence and requires knowledge of other movies.*

1993 83m/C Emilio Estevez, Samuel L. Jackson, Jon Lovitz, Tim Curry, Kathy Ireland, William Shatner; **Cameos:** Dr. Joyce Brothers, James Doohan, Richard Moll, F. Murray Abraham, Denis Leary, Corey Feldman, Phil Hartman, J.T. Walsh, Erik Estrada, Larry Wilcox, Allyce Beasley, Charlie Sheen; **D:** Gene Quintano; **W:** Gene Quintano, Don Holley. **VHS, LV** *NLC, IME*

National Lampoon's Senior Trip 🦴

R/Sr. High-Adult Decidedly lesser "Lampoon" effort about Midwestern high school seniors who take a bus trip to Washington to meet the president. Frewer is Principal Moss, who leads the hopelessly cliched group of misfits who are used by a stereotypically corrupt senator to embarrass his political opponent. We knew "Animal House," and this is no "Animal House." They finally found a flick that even the Coreys wouldn't be caught dead in. The National Lampoon series stopped being funny when the Griswolds stopped taking vacations.

BEWARE *Continuous teenage alcohol and drug abuse when the kids steal some goods on a pit stop, leave the principal behind, and party with stoner veteran Chong, the bus driver. Crude sexual references.*

1995 91m/C Matt Frewer, Valerie Mahaffey, Lawrence Dane, Thomas Chong, Kevin McDonald; **D:** Kelly Makin; **W:** I. Marlene King, Roger Kumble. **VHS, LV** *NLC*

National Lampoon's Vacation ♫♫♫

R/Sr. High-Adult The original in the "Vacation" series, this one finds the Clark Griswold (Chase) clan headed west to visit the famous "Wally World" (yes, it is a take off of Disneyland!). Along the way, the family encounters ridiculous, yet hilarious adventures, including a falling asleep at the wheel sequence and the untimely death of Aunt Edna. Chase is at his pratfall best, however, this movie is not exactly wholesome family fun.

BEWARE *Watch out for the death of an aunt and a dog. Also, Chase seems to have a wandering eye, wandering towards Christie Brinkley. Pot smoking and girlie magazines are the activities of choice of the hillbilly cousins.*

1983 98m/C Chevy Chase, Beverly D'Angelo, Imogene Coca, Randy Quaid, Christie Brinkley, James Keach, Anthony Michael Hall, John Candy, Eddie Bracken, Brian Doyle-Murray, Eugene Levy; **D:** Harold Ramis; **W:** John Hughes, Harold Ramis; **M:** Ralph Burns. **VHS, Beta, LV** *WAR*

National Velvet ♫♫♫♫

Family 1920s English girl Velvet Brown wins a horse named Pie in a village raffle and is determined to enter it in the Grand National Steeplechase. Fortunately her family's tenant is a washed-up ex-jockey, and he helps train the animal for championship competition. The only question is, who will ride the Pie? 12-year-old Taylor is superb in her first starring role, and receives excellent supported from future "Black Stallion" co-star Rooney and the rest of the cast. Filmed with a loving eye for the bucolic locations, this inspirational story of a girl and her steed may have become cliched over the years but it still runs beautifully. Based on the novel by Enid Bagnold and followed many years later by "International Velvet" in 1978.

1944 124m/C Elizabeth Taylor, Mickey Rooney, Arthur Treacher, Donald Crisp, Anne Revere, Angela Lansbury, Reginald Owen, Norma Varden, Jackie "Butch" Jenkins, Terence Kilburn; **D:** Clarence Brown; **W:** Helen Deutsch, Theodore Reeves; **M:** Herbert Stothart. **Award Nominations:** Academy Awards '45: Best Color Cinematography, Best Director (Brown); **Awards:** Academy Awards '45: Best Film Editing, Best Supporting Actress (Revere). **VHS, Beta, LV, 8mm** *MGM, KUI, TLF*

The Natural ♫♫♫

PG/Jr. High-Adult A beautifully filmed movie about baseball as myth. A young man, whose gift for baseball sets him apart, finds that trouble dogs him, particularly with a woman. In time, as an aging rookie, he must fight against his past to lead his team to the World Series, and win the woman who is meant for him. From the Bernard Malamud story.

BEWARE *Brief violence.*

1984 134m/C Robert Redford, Glenn Close, Robert Duvall, Kim Basinger, Wilford Brimley, Barbara Hershey, Richard Farnsworth, Robert Prosky, Darren McGavin, Joe Don Baker, Michael Madsen; **D:** Barry Levinson; **M:** Randy Newman. **VHS, Beta, LV** *COL*

Nearly No Christmas

Preschool-Primary This bittersweet family tale depicts a Christmas that almost didn't come off.

1981 60m/C Michael Haigh, Mildred Woods, John Banas. **VHS, Beta** *FHE*

'Neath Brooklyn Bridge ♫♫

Jr. High-Adult The Bowery Boys get tangled up in crime when they try to help a young girl whose guardian was murdered.

1942 61m/B Leo Gorcey, Huntz Hall, Bobby Jordan, Sammy Morrison, Ann Gillis, Noah Beery Jr., Marc Lawrence, Gabriel Dell; **D:** Wallace Fox. **VHS** *NOS, MRV, PME*

Necessary Parties

Family Based on Barbara Dana's book that has a 15-year-old boy filing a lawsuit to stop his parents' divorce. Alan Arkin is the lawyer who takes the case. Part of the "Wonderworks" family movie series. Ages 11 and up.

1988 120m/C Alan Arkin, Mark Paul Gosselaar, Barbara Dana, Adam Arkin, Donald Moffat, Julie Hagerty, Geoffrey Pierson, Taylor Fry; **D:** Gwen Arner. **VHS** *PME, WNE, HMV*

Necessary Roughness ♫♫

PG-13/Sr. High-Adult The Texas Southern University (passing for the real Texas State) Armadillos football team looks like it's headed for disaster, made up of misfits and goofballs and not even having enough promising players to complete a line-up. But don't fret, help arrives in the form of a 34-year-old farmer with a golden arm, who's out to recapture some lost dreams as quarterback. It's all in the name of football, right?

BEWARE *Football roughhousing and a little blood on the field teams with some pretty graphic fighting off the field. A couple is shown in bed, implying sexual activity.*

1991 108m/C Scott Bakula, Robert Loggia, Harley Jane Kozak, Sinbad, Hector Elizondo, Kathy Ireland, Jason Bateman; **D:** Stan Dragoti; **M:** Bill Conti. **VHS, Beta, LV** *PAR*

Nell ♫♫ ♪

R/Sr. High-Adult Nell, a young woman (Foster) who appears to speak her own language, is discovered in an isolated cabin in North Carolina after her mother dies. The town doctor (Neeson) wants to do what's best for her and convinces authorities to leave Nell alone, at least for the time being. He and big city psychologist (Richardson) have different ideas about how Nell should join the rest of the world, though both have her interests at heart. When the media discover this "wild child," all hell breaks loose and plans must be changed. Fascinating story about how we come to understand and need each other. Beautifully photographed on location. Foster, Richardson and Neeson are outstanding. The Brits' American southern accents are very convincing. Based on the play "Idioglossia" (which means "a language unto itself") by Mark Handley.

Meet the Star of Nell, Jodie Foster

Jodie Foster is one of the most famous faces on the planet. She's a Yale grad, Academy Award-winning actress, producer, and critically acclaimed movie director. The youngest of four, Foster was born on November 19, 1962 in L.A., California, raised by her single mom. At three, she was the famous Coppertone girl, whose dog pulls down a corner of her pants. Foster first became a household name in the '70s, appearing in TV movies and films such as *Freaky Friday* and *The Girl Who Lives Down the Lane*. In 1975, she aced her role as a pre-teen prostitute in Scorsese's *Taxi Driver*. At 17, she entered the hollowed halls of Yale. Foster returned to the limelight when she gained her most infamous fan, John Hinckley Jr., who shot President Reagan in a twisted attempt to impress her.

Re-starting her movie career, she made all the right moves, choosing eclectic parts that enhanced her resume. Her big breakthrough came in the years most talked about movie *The Accused*. She pioneered her role as a rape victim, coming away with an Academy Award for best actress. Three years later she was up for the gold again, and got it, doubling her Oscar pleasure, this time for a fledgling FBI agent in *The Silence of the Lambs*. Her freshman directing effort was *Little Man Tate*, and she starred as a "wild" child in *Nell*. After *Sommersby* in 1993, she starred with Mel Gibson and James Garner in the creme puff Western comedy smash *Maverick*. Her encore directing effort was the recent *Home for the Holidays*.

BEWARE *Rated PG-13 for nudity. A lout in a bar induces Nell to pull her shirt up, exposing her breasts.*
1994 114m/C Jodie Foster, Liam Neeson, Natasha Richardson, Richard Libertini; **D:** Michael Apted; **W:** William Nicholson. **Award Nominations:** Academy Awards '94: Best Actress (Foster); Golden Globe Awards '95: Best Actress—Drama (Foster), Best Film—Drama, Best Original Score; MTV Movie Awards '95: Best Female Performance (Foster); **Awards:** Screen Actors Guild Award '94: Best Actress (Foster). **VHS** *FXV*

Neptune Factor 🐾

G/Family Scientists board a special new deep-sea sub to search for their colleagues lost in an undersea earthquake. Diving ever deeper into the abyss, they gawk at giant sea monsters—which anybody who's ever visited a pet shop will recognize as ordinary salt-water critters photographed in closeup. Underachieving, underwater, and undistinguished.
1973 94m/C Ben Gazzara, Yvette Mimieux, Walter Pidgeon, Ernest Borgnine; **D:** Daniel Petrie; **W:** Jack DeWitt. **VHS, Beta** *FOX*

Nestor the Long-Eared Christmas Donkey

Family Sort of a biblical variation of "Rudolph the Red-Nosed Reindeer" finds Nestor, the long-eared donkey scorned and unable to join in any donkey games. Then one foggy Christmas Eve, he's chosen to lead Mary and Joseph into Bethlehem. A Rankin-Bass production.
1977 23m/C V: Paul Frees, Brenda Vaccaro. **VHS, Beta** *WAR*

The Net 🐾🐾 🕊

PG-13/Jr. High-Adult The ever-spunky Bullock gets stuck behind a computer screen rather than the wheel of a bus as reclusive computer systems analyst Angela Bennett. She's puzzled by a mysterious Internet program, which Angela finds can easily access highly classified databases. And it's soon apparent that someone knows she knows because every record of her identity has been erased and the conspirators decide to eliminate her as well. Miller's the ex she turns to for help and Northam's a seductive British hacker. Encourages the suspicion that, thanks to computers, somebody somewhere knows all about you.
BEWARE *Violence, some sexuality and brief strong language. A scary scene in a hospital emergency room.*
1995 114m/C Sandra Bullock, Jeremy Northam, Dennis Miller, Diane Baker, Ken Howard, Wendy Gazelle, Ray McKinnon; **D:** Irwin Winkler; **W:** John Brancato, Michael Ferris; **C:** Jack N. Green; **M:** Mark Isham. **VHS, LV, 8mm** *COL*

Never a Dull Moment 🐾🐾

G/Family Disney comedy coasts along on the considerable charm of Van Dyke as an actor mistaken by mobsters for an accomplished assassin and thief. Naturally he has to play along with the heist of a valuable painting, and improvise wildly when the real crook shows up.
BEWARE *Roughhousing.*

1968 90m/C Dick Van Dyke, Edward G. Robinson, Dorothy Provine, Henry Silva, Joanna Moore, Tony Bill, Slim Pickens, Jack Elam; **D:** Jerry Paris. **VHS, Beta, LV** *DIS*

Never Cry Wolf 🐾🐾🐾 ▽

PG/Jr. High-Adult Tenderfoot biologist is dropped off alone in Arctic territory on an ill-conceived mission to study the behavior and habitation of wolves. As he adapts to the freezing climate and the ways of the wolf society, the assignment becomes a journey of self-discovery and awareness of nature. Beautifully photographed but unevenly paced adaptation of Farley Mowat's book. In one instant director Ballard will jolt your breath away, at another point he'll nearly lull you to sleep. Splendid scenery and images can never have impact on video that they do on the big screen, but this Disney release comes highly recommended all the same.

 *Non-exploitive nudity, as the hero literally runs naked with the wolf pack through a caribou herd. Alcohol talk.*

1983 105m/C Charles Martin Smith, Brian Dennehy, Samson Jorah; **D:** Carroll Ballard; **W:** Curtis Hanson, Sam Hamm. **VHS, Beta, LV** *DIS*

Never Say Never Again 🐾🐾 ▽

PG/Jr. High-Adult James Bond matches wits with a charming but sinister tycoon who is holding the world nuclear hostage as part of a diabolical plot by SPECTRE. Connery's return to the world of Bond after 12 years is smooth in this remake of "Thunderball" hampered by an atrocious musical score. Carrera is stunning as Fatima Blush.

 *James Bondish violence, sex and alcohol use.*

1983 134m/C Sean Connery, Klaus Maria Brandauer, Max von Sydow, Barbara Carrera, Kim Basinger, Edward Fox, Bernie Casey, Pamela Salem, Rowan Atkinson, Valerie Leon, Prunella Gee, Saskia Cohen Tanugi; **D:** Irvin Kershner. **VHS, Beta, LV** *WAR, TLF*

The NeverEnding Story 🐾🐾 ▽

PG/Family Dreamy schoolkid Bastian is roughed up daily by bullies, failing his classes, etc. He cowers and reads a magical storybook that lets him share adventures of a boy warrior on a quest to save the imaginary world of Fantasia from destruction by a creeping Nothingness. Big-scale f/x and wild characters in a thematically obscure European production (based on the novel by Michael Ende) that made the Hound recall that old Groucho joke: "It's so simple a ten-year-old child could figure it out . . . Somebody find me a ten-year-old child." In any case, it was popular enough with those ten-year-olds to spawn NeverEnding sequels.

 *Fantasy violence.*

1984 94m/C Barret Oliver, Noah Hathaway, Gerald McRaney, Moses Gunn, Tami Stronach, Patricia Hayes, Sydney Bromley; **D:** Wolfgang Petersen; **W:** Wolfgang Petersen; **M:** Klaus Doldinger, Giorgio Moroder. **VHS, Beta, LV, 8mm** *WAR, GLV, APD*

The NeverEnding Story 2: Next Chapter 🐾🐾

PG/Family Redundant-titled sequel to the first journey that didn't end suffers from rerun fatigue. Last time the land of Fantasia was threatened by the Nothing; now the menace is the Emptiness. Existential trauma like this is to be avoided. Only wimp kid Bastian can stop that empty feeling, so he enters the storybook realm again. Whimsical creatures and grandiose f/x return, and a witch villainess at least provides a more prosaic explanation for what's going on. The Warner Brothers videocassette also includes "Box Office Bunny," the first Bugs theatrical cartoon in 26 years.

 *Fantasy violence.*

1991 90m/C Jonathan Brandis, Kenny Morrison, Clarissa Burt, John Wesley Shipp, Martin Umbach; **D:** George Miller; **M:** Robert Folk. **VHS, LV, 8mm** *WAR, APD*

The Neverending Story 3 🐾🐾

G/Family The third time was not the charm in this case, but the kids may still find it dreamy. Bastian, on the edge of puberty, is being bullied by a group at school called the Nasties. He seeks refuge in the library and enters the world of Fantasia through the "Neverending Story" tome. When the book is stolen by the Nasties, it is up to Bastian to return it. Fantasia creatures are brought to life by Jim Henson's Creature Shop.

 *Bastian is pushed around by some kids and some of the Fantasia creatures may scare little ones.*

1994 95m/C Jason James Richter, Melody Kay, Freddie Jones, Jack Black, Ryan Bollman, Tracey Ellis, Kevin McNulty; **D:** Peter Macdonald. **VHS** *NYR*

The New Adventures of Peter Rabbit

Preschool-Primary Animated version of the Beatrix Potter children's tale follows Peter and his friends on a cross-country journey filled with adventure and songs. Ages 3 to 6.

1994 48m/C VHS

The New Adventures of Pippi Longstocking 🐾 ▽

G/Preschool-Primary Decent cast clowns in a buffoon musical rehash of Astrid Lindgren's children's books, no improvement over the Swedish-German "Pippi Longstocking" that it follows fairly closely. Separated in a storm from her sea-captain father, the spunky red-headed little girl returns to the deserted family mansion, where her spirited stunts and independent ways delight kids and outrage the grownups. Grates less as it goes on, but only slightly.

 *Roughhousing*

1988 100m/C Tami Erin, Eileen Brennan, Dennis Dugan, Dianne Hull, George DiCenzo, John Schuck, Dick Van Patten; **D:** Ken Annakin. **VHS, Beta, LV** *COL, TVC*

The New Adventures of Tom and Huck

Family An animated version of Mark Twain's classic following the adventures of Tom Sawyer and Huck Finn and what trouble they can find themselves in next.
1996 105m/C **VHS** *JFK*

The New Adventures of Winnie the Pooh, Vol. 1: Great Honey Pot Robbery

Family More adventures of A.A. Milne's Pooh and the other inhabitants of the 100-Acre Woods, from Disney but made for network Saturday mornings. Additional volumes available.
1987 44m/C **VHS, Beta** *DIS*

New Adventures of Zorro, Vol. 1

Preschool-Jr. High Daring swordplay highlights these three animated tales of the swashbuckling swordsman of Old California. He's foppish Don Diego one moment, fearless hero Zorro the other, and Saturday-morning TV leftovers always. Episodes are "Three's a Crowd," "Flash Flood," and "The Blockade." Additional volumes available.
1981 60m/C **VHS, Beta** *FHE*

New Zoo Revue, Vol. 1

Family Each episode of this entertaining, educational children's series stars costumed animals like Freddie the Frog and Henrietta Hippo teaching youngsters the importance of peace, friendship, and compassion in daily interaction with others. Additional volumes available.
1973 60m/C Emily Peden, Doug Momary. **VHS, Beta** *FHE*

Newsies 🦴🦴

PG/Jr. High-Adult Disney attempt at a grand-scale musical, but songs are forgettable and dance numbers just get in the way. Pic would have worked better straight, minus tunes, since it vividly evokes a true incident, the 1899 New York newsboys strike against newspaper baron Joseph Pulitzer (imagine Scrooge as a publisher) to get him to lower unfair prices. Lavish, turn-of-the-century NYC atmosphere, with much made of the city's immigrant kids overcoming their gang-like ethnic divisions.

⚑ BEWARE ⚑ *Some serious violence as Pulitzer lets his goons loose on the youthful picketers. Alcohol use.*
1992 121m/C Christian Bale, Bill Pullman, Robert Duvall, Ann-Margret, Michael Lerner, Kevin Tighe, Charles Cioffi, Luke Edwards, Max Casella, David Moscow; **D:** Kenny Ortega; **M:** Alan Menken, Jack Feldman. **VHS, Beta** *DIS*

The Next Karate Kid

PG/Jr. High-Adult Fourth installment in the "Kid" series finds martial arts expert Miyagi (Morita) training Julie Pierce (Swank), the orphaned tomboy daughter of an old war buddy who saved his life 50 years earlier. He even teaches her the waltz, just in time for the prom, but she's still tough enough to scrap with a guy. Must-see for "Karate Kid" fans, though many of them may now be too old to appreciate.

⚑ BEWARE ⚑ *Some mild language and violence.*
1994 104m/C Noriyuki "Pat" Morita, Hilary Swank; **D:** Christopher Cain; **W:** Mark Lee; **M:** Bill Conti. **VHS**

Nickelodeon: Frightfest

Primary Halloween episodes of three Nickelodeon animated series. Includes "Candy Bar Creep Show" from Rugrats, "Doug's Halloween Adventure," and "Haunted House" from Ren & Stimpy. Ages 8 to 12.
1994 50m/C **VHS**

A Night at the Opera 🦴🦴🦴🦴

Family The Marx Brothers get mixed up with grand opera in their first MGM-produced pic, their first without Zeppo, and perhaps their last truly great comedy, even with the usual romantic subplot about young lovers in a opera touring company. Groucho, Chico and Harpo try to get the kids a contract, and in the process they deflate and devastate a pompous production. Immortal comic moments include the famous scene aboard ship, in which the Marxes welcome more and more visitors to their small stateroom until it's literally packed to the ceiling with goofballs.
1935 92m/B Groucho Marx, Chico Marx, Harpo Marx, Allan Jones, Kitty Carlisle Hart, Sig Rumann, Margaret Dumont, Walter Woolf King; **D:** Sam Wood; **W:** George S. Kaufman, Morrie Ryskind, Bert Kalmar, Harry Ruby, Al Boasberg; **M:** Herbert Stothart. **VHS, Beta, LV** *MGM, CRC, CCB*

The Night Before 🦴

PG-13/Jr. High-Sr. High Snobby high school beauty Tara loses a bet and has to go to the prom with geek Winston. They get lost on the wrong side of the tracks and become involved with pimps, crime, and the police. Drunken Winston loses his virginity, as well as his father's car, but somehow wins Tara's heart, which is more than this obscure teen comedy will do with the viewer. Reeves later became a star in the "Bill & Ted" adventures.

⚑ BEWARE ⚑ *Sex, fighting and alcohol use. Street experiences by fish-out-of-water teens.*
1988 90m/C Keanu Reeves, Lori Loughlin, Trinidad Silva, Michael Greene, Theresa Saldana, Suzanne Snyder, Morgan Lofting, Gwil Richards; **D:** Thom Eberhardt; **W:** Gregory Scherick, Thom Eberhardt. **VHS, Beta** *HBO*

The Night Before Christmas

Family Christmas spirit is in the air in this Disney cartoon retelling of the eternal Clement Moore poem, complete with an appearance by Santa himself.
1933 9m/C VHS, Beta *MTI, DSN*

The Night Before Christmas and Best-Loved Yuletide Carols

Preschool-Primary Collection of Christmas classics combined with beautiful artwork and narration by Streep set the holiday spirit in this heartwarming program. Also featured are favorite Christmas carols performed by George Winston, the Edwin Hawkins Singers, and the Christ Church Cathedral Choir.
1992 30m/C VHS

Night Crossing 🎵🎵 🎵

PG/Family Fact-based Disney drama of two East German families who attempted a dangerous escape over the Berlin Wall to freedom in a homemade hot air balloon. Fairly exciting in spite of the bland dialogue and characters.

 Violence.

1981 106m/C John Hurt, Jane Alexander, Glynnis O'Connor, Doug McKeon, Beau Bridges; **D:** Delbert Mann; **W:** John McGreevey; **M:** Jerry Goldsmith. **VHS, Beta** *DIS*

Night of the Comet 🎵🎵 🎵

PG-13/Jr. High-Adult After surviving the explosion of a deadly comet, two California girls discover that they are the last people on Earth. When zombies begin to chase them, things begin to lose their charm. Cute and funny, but the script runs out before the movie does. Ages 13 and up.
1984 90m/C Catherine Mary Stewart, Kelli Maroney, Robert Beltran, Geoffrey Lewis, Mary Woronov, Sharon Farrell, Michael Bowen; **D:** Thom Eberhardt; **W:** Thom Eberhardt. **VHS, Beta** *FOX*

The Night the Lights Went Out in Georgia 🎵🎵

PG/Jr. High-Adult Very loosely based on the popular hit song, the film follows a brother and sister as they try to cash in on the country music scene in Nashville. McNichol is engaging. Ages 12 and up.
1981 112m/C Kristy McNichol, Dennis Quaid, Mark Hamill, Don Stroud; **D:** Ronald F. Maxwell; **M:** David Shire. **VHS, Beta** *TWE*

The Night They Saved Christmas 🎵 🎵

Family Made-for-TV musical in which Santa's North Pole headquarters is endangered by the progress of an expanding oil company. Will a petroleum geologist's children be able save the day? Carney is a treat as the businesslike Kris Kringle, but otherwise this stiff production would have worked better as a (shorter) Rankin/Bass animated special.
1987 94m/C Art Carney, Jaclyn Smith, Paul Williams, Paul LeMat; **D:** Jackie Cooper. **VHS, Beta** *CAF, PSM*

Nightingale

Preschool-Primary Animated version of the Hans Christian Andersen classic fairy tale of the Emperor of China and his little nightingale.
1988 30m/C VHS, Beta *HSE*

The Nightmare Before Christmas 🎵🎵🎵

PG/Jr. High-Adult Grandiose and grotesque tour de force of joyous stop-motion animation that manages to bag two holidays in one. Jack, the friendly but ghoulish Pumpkin King of Halloween Town, discovers neighboring Christmas Town for the first time and decides to put a fresh face on Noel by kidnapping Santa and take the old guy's place, delivering ghastly gifts to unsuspecting children on December 24. Outstanding modelwork, terrific Elfman musical score (Elfman also provide's Jack's singing voice), and a marvelously macabre sense of humor. This is the sort of kid movie the Addams Family would keep ready for a sunny day. Based on an idea (and co-produced) by Tim Burton. Distributed by Disney/Touchstone—but don't believe their advertising boast that this is the first ever puppet-animated theatrical feature; see 1954's "Hansel and Gretel."

 Halloween Town is a nonstop cavalcade of monsters and weirdos; still, that PG seems a little extreme.

1993 75m/C D: Henry Selick; **W:** Caroline Thompson; **M:** Danny Elfman; **V:** Danny Elfman, Chris Sarandon, Catherine O'Hara, William Hickey, Ken Page, Ed Ivory, Paul (Pee Wee Herman) Reubens, Glenn Shadix. **VHS** *TOU*

Nikki, the Wild Dog of the North 🎵🎵🎵

G/Family Malamute pup tethered to an orphaned bear cub are separated from their frontiersman master. In a charming series of semi-documentary scenes, the critters learn cooperation to survive. Second half of the story finds the dog, now fully grown, captured by an evil trapper. Swell Disney outdoor adventure set in 1890s Canada. Adapted from the novel "Nomads of the North" by James Oliver Curwood.

 Violence, especially when Nikki's nasty owner forces him into a dogfight.

1961 73m/C Jean Coutu; **D:** Jack Couffer, Don Haldane. **VHS, Beta** *DIS*

The Nine Lives of Elfego Baca 🎵🎵 🎵

Family Disney TV miniseries, part of a "True Heroes of the West" series done in the afterglow of the Davy

Crockett craze. Baca was a Mexican-American who became an instant legend when he survived an incredible 33-hour gun battle with a mob of galoots. The plot follows up his later career as New Mexico's numero uno lawman. Loggia is an ever-smiling and polite hero, and the action never gets unduly harsh.

BEWARE *Violence, alcohol use.*

1958 78m/C Robert Loggia, Robert Simon, Lisa Montell, Nestor Paiva; **D:** Norman Foster. **VHS, Beta** *DIS*

Nine Months

PG-13/Jr. High-Adult Happily single Samuel (Grant) gets girlfriend Rebecca (Moore) pregnant and promptly wigs out. He makes amends to the lovely Rebecca, they marry. Bachelor pal Sean (Goldblum) and an expectant couple (Arnold and Cusack) with three kids round out the cast, with Williams offering his usual manic flair as a Russian obstetrician, improvising his scenes with glee. Grant's knack for clumsy befuddlement fits well with the warm, fuzzy style of Columbus. Remake of the French film "Neuf Mois."

BEWARE *Much language during the hospital scenes. Mild violence when Grant hits a bicyclist with his Jeep on the way to the hospital and when Grant and Arnold get in a fight in the delivery room.*

1995 103m/C Hugh Grant, Julianne Moore, Tom Arnold, Joan Cusack, Jeff Goldblum; **Cameos:** Robin Williams; **D:** Chris Columbus; **W:** Chris Columbus; **C:** Donald McAlpine; **M:** Hans Zimmer. **VHS, LV** *TCF*

No Deposit, No Return

G/Family No awards either, but the cast does what they can with this Disney action comedy about rich brats who persuade bumbling crooks to kidnap them so they can all share a ransom from their irascible millionaire grandfather (Niven).

1976 115m/C David Niven, Don Knotts, Darren McGavin, Barbara Feldon, Charles Martin Smith; **D:** Norman Tokar; **M:** Buddy Baker. **VHS, Beta** *DIS*

No Dessert Dad, 'Til You Mow the Lawn

PG/Jr. High-Adult Suburban parents Ken and Carol Cochran (Robert Hays and Joanna Kerns) are harassed at home by their annoying offspring, Justin, Monica, and Tyler. When they try hypnosis tapes to quit smoking, the kids discover by doctoring the tapes, they can plant suggestions resulting in parental perks. Sounds cuter than it is.

1994 80m/C Robert Hays, Joanna Kerns, Joshua Schaefer, Allison Meek, Jimmy Marsden, Richard Moll, Larry Linville; **D:** Howard McCain. **VHS** *NHO*

No Drums, No Bugles

G/Family West Virginia farmer and conscientious objector leaves his family to live alone in a cave for three years

during the Civil War. Interesting decision but not particularly cinematic.

1971 85m/C Martin Sheen, Davey Davidson, Denine Terry, Rod McCary; **D:** Clyde Ware. **VHS, Beta** *CNG, VTR*

No Holds Barred

PG-13/Jr. High Cheesy camp about big-time professional wrestler Rip, who grapples not only with bestial opponents but an evil TV magnate who'll stop at nothing to make Rip do his wrestling show. The first feature to showcase WWF favorite 'Hulk' Hogan is obviously aimed at kids but went far enough with the violence that some commentators called foul. Fortunately, Hogan hasn't made that mistake in his subsequent vehicles like "Suburban Commando" and "Mr. Nanny."

BEWARE *Violence, alcohol use.*

1989 98m/C Hulk Hogan, Kurt Fuller, Joan Severance, Tiny Lister; **D:** Thomas J. Wright. **VHS, Beta, LV** *COL*

No Man's Valley

Preschool-Primary When the encroaching civilization endangers their homes, a flock of condors send a scout to find a safe place to colonize. Ecologically minded cartoon from the producer of TV's "Peanuts" series.

1981 30m/C V: Barney Phillips, Richard Deacon, Art Metrano, Arnold Stang, Joe E. Ross. **VHS, Beta** *FHE*

No Time for Sergeants

Family Young Griffith is excellent as the Georgia farm boy who gets drafted into the service during a war lull and creates mayhem among his superiors and colleagues. Hilarious film version written by John Lee Mahin from the Broadway play by Ira Levin, which was based on the novel by Mac Hyman and an earlier television special (and eventually became a TV series). Note eventual sidekick Knotts and Benny Baker in small roles along with Jameel Farah, who went on to star in TV's M*A*S*H after changing his name to Jamie Farr.

1958 119m/B Andy Griffith, Nick Adams, Murray Hamilton, Don Knotts, Jamie Farr, Myron McCormick; **D:** Mervyn LeRoy. **VHS, Beta, LV** *WAR*

Noah's Animals and Other Stories

Preschool-Primary Three animated children's tales, unrelated to the other "Noah's Animals." Segments include the title story, "King of the Beasts," and "Last of the Red Hot Dragons."

1986 78m/C VHS, Beta

Nobody's Boy

Preschool-Jr. High Japanese cartoon saga about an 8-year-old boy's search for his missing mother.

1971 80m/C D: Jim Flocker; **V:** Jim Backus. **VHS, Beta** *MPI*

Noel

Family Romer Muller's story about a Christmas ornament that comes to life.
1993 25m/C VHS *PGV*

Noisy Nora

Preschool-Primary Animated version of the 1973 Rosemary Well children's book. Nora tries to get attention in a family comprised of a bossy older sister, a needy younger brother, and preoccupied parents. She learns that sometimes being quiet can attract as much attention as being noisy. Ages 4 to 8.
1994 6m/C VHS

Nonsense and Lullabyes: Nursery Rhymes

Preschool-Primary Eighteen favorite nursery rhymes are presented in a quick, entertaining way, with songs, in 30 minutes. Among the rhymes are "The Crooked Man," "Little Miss Muffet," "The Queen of Hearts" and "Wynken, Blinken and Nod." Ages 1 to 4.
1992 27m/C VHS *LIV*

The Norfin Adventures: The Great Egg Robbery

Primary Magical trolls help a girl clear her father of stealing a golden egg.
1994 29m/C VHS *WEA*

Norma Rae 🦴🦴🦴

PG/Jr. High-Adult A poor, uneducated textile worker joins forces with a New York labor organizer to unionize the reluctant workers at a Southern mill. Field was a surprise with her fully developed character's strength, beauty, and humor; her Oscar was well-deserved. Ritt's direction is top-notch. Jennifer Warnes sings the theme song, "It Goes Like It Goes," which also won an Oscar.

BEWARE *Profanity, minor violence, mistreatment and intimidation of workers.*

1979 114m/C Sally Field, Ron Leibman, Beau Bridges, Pat Hingle; **D:** Martin Ritt; **W:** Harriet Frank Jr., Irving Ravetch; **M:** David Shire. **Award Nominations:** Academy Awards '79: Best Adapted Screenplay; Cannes Film Festival '79: Best Picture; **Awards:** Academy Awards '79: Best Actress (Field), Best Song ("It Goes Like It Goes"); Golden Globe Awards '80: Best Actress—Drama (Field); Los Angeles Film Critics Association Awards '79: Best Actress (Field); National Board of Review Awards '79: Best Actress (Field); New York Film Critics Awards '79: Best Actress (Field). **VHS, Beta, LV** *FOX, BTV*

Norman the Doorman and Other Stories

Family "Lentil," "Brave Irene," and "Norman the Doorman" are seen in their animated version from the "Children's Circle" collection.
1989 30m/C VHS *CCC, BTV*

North 🦴🦴

PG/Jr. High-Adult Some laughs with a message in disappointing family fare from Reiner. Eleven-year old Wood divorces his workaholic parents ("Seinfeld" costars Alexander and Louis-Dreyfus) and searches the world for a functional family (good luck). Instead, he becomes the poster boy for a fascist children's political organization while running into all manner of ethnic and class stereotypes (including Vigoda as an elderly Eskimo about to be set adrift at sea). Willis, who's a treat in a pink bunny suit among other costumes, acts as guardian angel/narrator and subtly helps the kid find what's the most important thing. Premise sags in spite of great sets and illustrious comedic cast. Based on a book by original "Saturday Night Live" screenwriter (and "Gary Shandling Show" co-creator) Zweibel, who put things in motion ten years ago when he asked Reiner to write a book jacket quote for the novel.

BEWARE *Profanity, stereotypes and neglectful parents. An elderly Eskimo is sent to meet his maker on a floating iceburg. Very disturbing.*

1994 88m/C Elijah Wood, Jason Alexander, Julia Louis-Dreyfus, Bruce Willis, Jon Lovitz, Alan Arkin, Dan Aykroyd, Kathy Bates, Faith Ford, Graham Greene, Reba McEntire, John Ritter, Abe Vigoda, Kelly McGillis, Alexander Godunov, Noriyuki "Pat" Morita; **D:** Rob Reiner; **W:** Andrew Scheinman, Alan Zweibel; **M:** Marc Shaiman. **VHS** *NYR*

The North Avenue Irregulars 🦴🦴🦴

G/Family A priest (Edward Herrmann) and three members of the local ladies' club try to bust a crime syndicate when the corrupt cops won't. Outstanding cast brings laughter to a silly Disney production. Based on a true story—probably without the big car pile-up—by the Rev. Albert Fay Hill. Ages 7 to 12.

1979 99m/C Edward Herrmann, Barbara Harris, Susan Clark, Karen Valentine, Michael Constantine, Cloris Leachman, Melora Hardin, Alan Hale Jr., Ruth Buzzi, Patsy Kelly, Virginia Capers; **D:** Bruce Bilson. **VHS** *DIS*

North by Northwest 🦴🦴🦴🦴

Jr. High-Adult The movie that put Mount Rushmore on the map. No, wait, it was already on the map, but it was never so much fun, as when Alfred Hitchcock sent Cary Grant and Eva Marie Saint clambering over it. Grant is terrific as a Madison Avenue advertising man who's being chased by spies (who mistake him for a double agent) and by the police (who believe he's a killer). Thriller with plenty of humor is one of Hitchcock's (and Hollywood's) best. You'll never again think of Mount Rushmore, or crop dusting airplanes, the same way. Ages 10 and up.

1959 136m/C Cary Grant, Eva Marie Saint, James Mason, Leo G. Carroll, Martin Landau, Jessie Royce Landis, Philip Ober, Adam Williams, Josephine Hutchinson, Edward Platt; **D:** Alfred Hitchcock; **W:** Ernest Lehman; **M:** Bernard Herrmann. **Award Nominations:** Academy Awards '59: Best Art Direction/Set Decoration (Color), Best Film Editing, Best Story & Screenplay; **Awards:** Edgar Allan Poe Awards '59: Best Screenplay. **VHS, Beta, LV** *MGM, CRC, TLF*

Bunny Bruce Willis counsels Elijah Wood in "North."

Not My Kid 🦴🦴🦴

Family The 15-year-old daughter of a surgeon brings turmoil to her family when she becomes heavily involved in drugs. Producer Polson, along with Dr. Miller Newton, wrote the original book for this emotional story. Made for TV.

 Drug use.

1985 120m/C George Segal, Stockard Channing, Viveka Davis, Andrew (Andy) Robinson, Gary Bayer, Nancy Cartwright, Tate Donovan; *D:* Michael Tuchner; *W:* Christopher Knopf. **VHS, Beta** *SVE*

Not Quite Human 🦴🦴

Family Okay but standard Disney TV comedy about an inventor who builds a robot teenage boy, named Chip, who's almost indistinguishable from the real thing. The doctor grows emotionally close to his creation as he tries to conceal Chip's secret from a rival. Based on a book series by Seth McEvoy, and followed by sequels "Not Quite Human II" and "Still Not Quite Human."

1987 91m/C Alan Thicke, Robin Lively, Robert Harper, Joseph Bologna, Jay Underwood; *D:* Steven Hilliard Stern. **VHS, Beta** *DIS*

Nothing in Common 🦴🦴🦴

PG/Sr. High-Adult In his last film, Gleason plays the abrasive, diabetic father of immature advertising agency worker Hanks. After his parents separate, Hanks learns to be more responsible and loving in caring for his father. Comedy and drama are blended well here with the help of satirical pokes at the ad business and Hanks turns in a fine performance, but the unorganized, lengthy plot may lose some viewers.

BEWARE *Profanity and suggested sex. Gleason's character drinks and lets his health deteriorate.*

1986 119m/C Tom Hanks, Jackie Gleason, Eva Marie Saint, Bess Armstrong, Hector Elizondo, Barry Corbin, Sela Ward, John Kapelos, Jane Morris, Dan Castellaneta, Tracy Reiner; *D:* Garry Marshall; *W:* Rick Podell; *M:* Patrick Leonard. **VHS, Beta, LV** *WAR, HBO*

Notorious 🦴🦴🦴🦴

Jr. High-Adult Post-WWII story of a beautiful playgirl sent by the US government to marry a suspected spy living in Brazil. Grant is the agent assigned to watch her. Duplicity and guilt are important factors in this brooding, romantic spy thriller. Suspenseful throughout, with a surprise ending. The acting is excellent all around and Hitchcock makes certain that suspense is maintained throughout this classy and complex thriller. Laser edition contains original trailer, publicity photos, and additional footage.

BEWARE *Implied sex.*

1946 101m/B Cary Grant, Ingrid Bergman, Claude Rains, Louis Calhern, Madame Konstantin, Reinhold Schunzel, Moroni Olsen; **D:** Alfred Hitchcock; **W:** Ben Hecht. **VHS, Beta, LV** *FOX, CRC, MLB*

Now and Then 🦴🦴

PG-13/Jr. High-Adult Playing the same characters as girls, young actresses steal the show from Griffith, O'Donnell, Moore and Wilson in this coming-of-age tale. The adults recall in flashback the summer when they were 12, hanging out at the swimming hole, watching boys, wondering about sex, holding seances in the cemetery and coping with divorce and the loss of a mother.

BEWARE *Contains strong language, brief nudity, and adolescent discussions about sex. Ricci slugs a guy in the nose, but he did deserve it.*

1995 97m/C Rosie O'Donnell, Melanie Griffith, Demi Moore, Rita Wilson, Christina Ricci, Thora Birch, Gaby Hoffman, Ashleigh Aston Moore, Cloris Leachman, Lolita Davidovich, Bonnie Hunt, Brendan Fraser; **D:** Lesli Linka Glatter; **W:** I. Marlene King; **C:** Ueli Steiger; **M:** Cliff Eidelman. **VHS, LV** *NLC*

Now You See Him, Now You Don't 🦴🦴

G/Family Featherweight Disney comedy involving a college guy who accidentally invents an invisibility formula to win a science fair and save his school. Of course, a gang of crooks want to use the stuff to rob a bank. Sequel to Disney's "The Computer Wore Tennis Shoes."

1972 85m/C Kurt Russell, Joe Flynn, Cesar Romero, Jim Backus; **D:** Robert Butler. **VHS, Beta** *DIS*

Nukie 🦴

PG/Family E.T. phone lawyer! European ripoff of the Spielberg favorite has not one, but two alien potato-heads crashing to Earth. One is tortured in the lab by heartless scientists, while his brother Nukie lands in Africa and spooks the silly natives. Don't worry, everyone utters their awful dialogue in English—even monkeys.

BEWARE *Alcohol use.*

1993 99m/C Glynis Johns, Steve Railsback; **D:** Sias Odendal. **VHS** *VMK*

Nursery Raps with Mama Goose

Preschool Mama Goose, complete with a flying pink Cadillac, travels to Hip Hop Land and does a rappin' update of some classic rhymes, including Old Mother Hubbard, Little Miss Muffett, Humpty Dumpty, and more. Ages 1 to 5.

1994 25m/C *V:* Natalie Cole. **VHS**

Nursery Rhymes

Preschool-Primary Pages of a nursery rhyme book come to cartoon life as a youngster leafs through them. Features all-time nursery rhyme favorites "Simple Simon," "Little Bo Peep," "Old King Cole," and many more.

1982 60m/C *V:* Isla St. Clair, Michael Berry, Valentine Dyall. **VHS, Beta** *FHE*

The Nutcracker

Preschool-Primary Animated version of the original story by E.T.A. Hoffman. Godfather Drosselmeier gives Fritz and Marie the story of the Nutcracker and the evil Mouse Queen as he gives them the gifts of a toy soldier and a nutcracker. The nutcracker comes to life. Ages 4 to 8.

1994 45m/C VHS *GKK*

Nutcracker Fantasy 🦴🦴

Family Rather confused Japanese stop-motion animated adaptation of E.T.A. Hoffman's classic tells the tale (using English-speaking actors) of little Clara, who must rescue a beautiful sleeping princess from wicked mice. Set to the music of Tchaikovsky.

1979 60m/C *V:* Melissa Gilbert, Roddy McDowall. **VHS, Beta** *COL*

The Nutcracker Prince 🦴🦴

Family Animated treatment of the E.T.A. Hoffman tale that inspired the classic ballet, but this Canadian cartoon feature has more in common with Tom & Jerry than Tchaikovsky as the enchanted Nutcracker Prince battles the thuglike Mouse King 'round and 'round the toyroom at Christmas. Good character voices.

BEWARE *Violence*

1991 75m/C D: Paul Schibli; *V:* Kiefer Sutherland, Megan Follows, Michael MacDonald, Phyllis Diller, Peter O'Toole. **VHS, LV, 8mm** *WAR*

The Nutty Professor 🦴🦴🦴

Family Clumsy scientist creates a potion that turns him from a homely but good-natured nerd-geek-dweeb into a handsome but cold-hearted ladies' man. One of Lewis' best comedies, though skewed more toward adult viewers; small kids accustomed to his goofy slapstick may want more of bumbling Professor Kelp and less of his subtle alter ego 'Buddy Love.'

1963 107m/C Jerry Lewis, Stella Stevens, Howard Morris, Kathleen Freeman; **D:** Jerry Lewis; **W:** Jerry Lewis. **VHS, Beta, LV** *PAR*

The Nutty Professor 🦴🦴🦴

PG-13/Jr. High-Adult Murphy takes on the ghost of Jerry Lewis with this remake of the 1963 comedy. He stars as Professor Sherman Klump, who takes a swig of his own secret potion and is transformed into the suave Buddy Love. Only the formula isn't perfect and has the nasty habit of wearing off at the worst possible times.

The girls cheer on their softball team in "Now and Then."

 *Crude humor and sexual references.*

1996 96m/C Eddie Murphy, Jada Pinkett, James Coburn, Dave Chappelle; *D:* Tom Shadyac; *W:* David Sheffield, Barry W. Blaustein, Steve Oedekerk, Tom Shadyac; *C:* Julio Macat; *M:* David Newman. **VHS** *NYR*

Nuzzling with the Noozles

Family Collection of Down Under TV cartoons starring koalas Blinky and Pinky, seen on American cable. They befriend Sandy, a little girl, and have many adventures.
1990 110m/C VHS, Beta *CEL*

Nyoka and the Tigermen

Family Adventurous scientist's daughter Nyoka, last seen (played by a different actress) in the serial "Jungle Girl," returns for more Republic action. This time evil princess Vultura and her pet gorilla Satan are seeking the fabled Lost Tablets of Hippocrates, artifacts of pure gold that hold a secret cancer cure. Loads of stunts and chases, and Nyoka is one vintage heroine who gets to use her fists. Elements of this serial in particular show exactly where George Lucas and Steven Spielberg got the notion

for Indiana Jones. Originally called "Perils of Nyoka." In 15 episodes.

 Violence.

1942 250m/B Kay Aldridge, Clayton Moore; *D:* William Witney. **VHS, LV** *VCN, REP, MLB*

Octopussy ♫ ♫

PG/Jr. High-Adult Bond, babes, booze, bombs. Roger Moore is Agent 007 on a mission to prevent a crazed Russian general from launching a nuclear attack against the NATO forces in Europe. Lots of special effects and gadgets. Ages 14 and up.

 Violence, sex and alcohol use.

1983 140m/C Roger Moore, Maud Adams, Louis Jourdan, Kristina Wayborn, Kabir Bedi; *D:* John Glen; *W:* Michael G. Wilson; *M:* John Barry. **VHS, Beta, LV** *MGM, FOX, TLF*

The Odd Couple ♫ ♫ ♫ ♪

G/Family Two divorced men with completely opposite personalities move in together. Lemmon's obsession with neatness drives slob Matthau up the wall, and their inability to see eye-to-eye results in many hysterical escapades. A Hollywood rarity, it is actually better in some ways than

VIDEOHOUND'S FAMILY VIDEO GUIDE

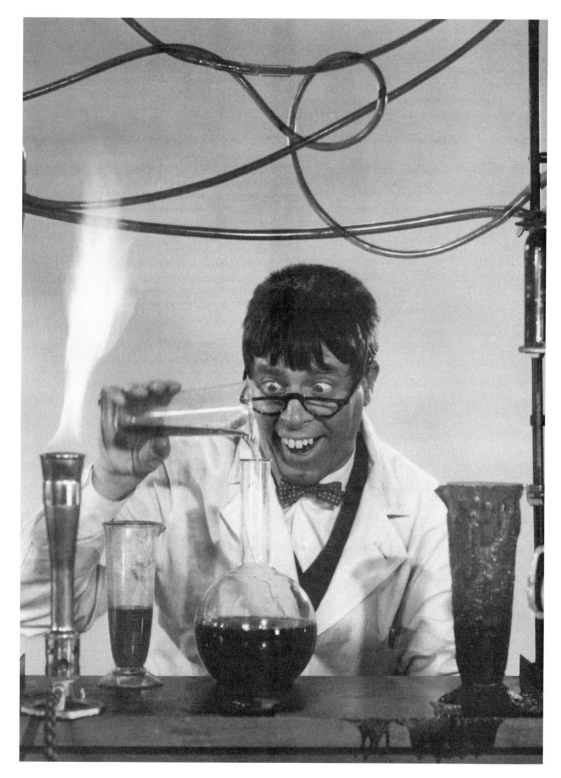

Jerry Lewis mixes a concoction in "The Nutty Professor."

If you like *The Nutty Professor* (1996), you'll love:

The Absent-Minded Professor (1961)

Back to the Future (1985)

Back to the Future, Part 2 (1989)

Back to the Future, Part 3 (1990)

Chitty Chitty Bang Bang (1968)

Leonard Part 6 (1987)

My Science Project (1985)

The Nutty Professor (1963)

Prehysteria (1993)

Real Genius (1985)

The Shaggy D.A. (1976)

The Shaggy Dog (1959)

Son of Flubber (1963)

Neil Simon's original Broadway version. Basis for the hit television series.
1968 106m/C Jack Lemmon, Walter Matthau; **D:** Gene Saks; **W:** Neil Simon. **VHS, Beta, LV** *PAR*

Odd Jobs 🎵🎵

PG-13/Jr. High-Adult When five college friends look for jobs during summer break, they wind up running their own moving business with the help of the mob. Good comic talent, but a silly slapstick script results in only a passable diversion.
1985 89m/C Paul Reiser, Scott McGinnis, Rick Overton, Robert Townsend; **D:** Mark Story; **M:** Robert Folk. **VHS, Beta** *HBO*

Ode to Billy Joe 🎵🎵

PG/Jr. High-Adult 1967 Bobby Gentry hit song of the same title is expanded to tell why a young man jumped to his death off the Tallahatchie Bridge. The problems of growing up in the rural South, sex and teenage romance don't match the mournful appeal (and brevity!) of the theme music, but the youthful leads work well together.

 Sex talk. Subject of the film is teenage suicide.

1976 106m/C Robby Benson, Glynnis O'Connor, Joan Hotchkis, Sandy McPeak, James Best; **D:** Max Baer Jr. **VHS, Beta** *CCB, WAR*

Of Mice and Men 🎵🎵🎵

PG-13/Jr. High-Adult Somber retelling of John Steinbeck's classic as adapted by Horton Foote. Set on the migratory farms of California, it follows the friendship of the simple-minded Lennie (Malkovich) with his reluctant protector George (Sinise). Interesting performances from both, well-supported by cinematographer Kenneth MacMillan. Director Sinise received permission from Steinbeck's widow to film the novel (actually the third adaptation).

BEWARE *Profanity, violence and unintentionally violent retarded man as a main character.*

1992 110m/C John Malkovich, Sherilyn Fenn, Casey Siemaszko, Joe Morton, Ray Walston, Gary Sinise, John Terry, Richard Riehle; **D:** Gary Sinise; **W:** Horton Foote. **VHS, LV** *MGM, PMS, BTV*

Off Beat 🎵🎵

PG/Sr. High-Adult Shy librarian unluckily wins a spot in a police benefit dance troupe, and then falls in love with a tough police woman. With a screenplay by playwright Medoff, and a good supporting cast, it still manages to miss the mark.
1986 92m/C Judge Reinhold, Meg Tilly, Cleavant Derricks, Fred Gwynne, John Turturro, Jacques D'Amboise, James Tolkan, Joe Mantegna, Harvey Keitel, Amy Wright; **D:** Michael Dinner; **W:** Mark Medoff; **M:** James Horner. **VHS, Beta, LV** *TOU*

An Officer and a Duck

Family Donald goes to war in this classic compilation of Donald Duck WWII episodes narrating his military adventures as a private, a paratrooper, and more. Component of Disney's Limited Gold Edition 2.
1943 45m/C VHS, Beta *DIS*

Oh, God! 🎵🎵🎵

PG/Family God, incarnated as a wizened, wisecracking senior citizen, recruits an average guy (Denver, in his film debut) as his herald in a plan to save the world. Society questions the man's sanity, but he keeps faith and is rewarded. It's not exactly a substitute for divinity school (the question of Jesus' parenthood is gingerly sidestepped), but sincere performances and optimism make for a satisfying, ecumenical parable. Based on the novel by Avery Corman.
1977 104m/C George Burns, John Denver, Paul Sorvino, Ralph Bellamy, Teri Garr, William Daniels, Donald Pleasence, Barnard Hughes, Barry Sullivan, Dinah Shore, Jeff Corey, David Ogden Stiers; **D:** Carl Reiner; **W:** Larry Gelbart. **VHS, Beta, LV** *WAR*

Oh, God! Book 2 🎵

PG/Family Burns returns as the "Almighty One" in strained sequel to "Oh God!" This time He enlists the help of a young girl to remind others of His existence. The slogan she concocts saves God's image, but not the movie. Followed by "Oh, God! You Devil."

1980 94m/C George Burns, Suzanne Pleshette, David Birney, Louanne, Conrad Janis, Wilfrid Hyde-White, Hans Conried, Howard Duff; *D:* Gilbert Cates; *M:* Charles Fox. **VHS, Beta** *WAR*

Oh, God! You Devil

PG/Family During his third trip to earth, Burns plays both the Devil and God as he first takes a struggling musician's soul, then gives it back. A few verbal zingers and light atmosphere spell salvation for an unoriginal plot.

BEWARE *Salty language.*

1984 96m/C George Burns, Ted Wass, Roxanne Hart, Ron Silver, Eugene Roche, Robert Desiderio; *D:* Paul Bogart; *W:* Andrew Bergman; *M:* David Shire. **VHS, Beta, LV** *WAR*

Oh, Heavenly Dog!

PG/Family Pairing of animal superstar Benji and 'sophisticated' comic Chase is an ungainly tale. Private eye returns from the dead as the dog and tries to solve his own murder. The canine is terrific, as ever, and kid viewers probably won't mind his use in such an inane gimmick.

BEWARE *Profanity and sex talk.*

1980 104m/C Chevy Chase, Jane Seymour, Omar Sharif, Robert Morley, Susan Kellerman; *D:* Joe Camp. **VHS, Beta** *FOX*

Oh, What a Night

PG-13/Jr. High-Adult Bittersweet coming of age tale about lonely 17-year-old Haim. He's moved with his father and stepmother to a chicken farm in 1955 Ontario, where he falls in love with an older woman who has a husband and two kids. Features a great fifties soundtrack and beautiful scenes of the Canadian countryside.

BEWARE *Sexual situations.*

1992 93m/C Corey Haim, Barbara Williams, Keir Dullea, Genevieve Bujold, Robbie Coltrane; *D:* Eric Till. **VHS, LV** *COL, NLC*

Oklahoma!

G/Family Cowboy and country girl fall in love, but she is tormented by another unwelcomed suitor. Throughout their travails, they sing, dance, and create a little movie magic. Arizona substitutes for Oklahoma in the screen adaptation of Rodgers and Hammerstein's Broadway hit, complete with original, culturally imprinted score. Agnes de Mille choreographed, replacing Jones and MacRae in the Dream Ballet with dancers Bambi Linn and James Mitchell. The 19-year-old Jones in her film debut is a must-see for musical fans. ♫ Oh, What a Beautiful Morning; Surrey with the Fringe on Top; I Cain't Say No; Many a New Day; People Will Say We're in Love; Poor Jud Is Dead; All 'Er Nuthin'; Everything's Up to Date in Kansas City; The Farmer and the Cowman.

1955 145m/C Gordon MacRae, Shirley Jones, Rod Steiger, Gloria Grahame, Eddie Albert, Charlotte Greenwood, James Whitmore, Gene Nelson, Barbara Lawrence, Jay C. Flippen; *D:* Fred Zinnemann; *W:* Sonya Levien, William Ludwig; *M:* Richard Rodgers, Oscar Ham-

merstein. **Award Nominations:** Academy Awards '55: Best Color Cinematography, Best Film Editing; **Awards:** Academy Awards '55: Best Sound, Best Score. **VHS, Beta, LV** *FOX, RDG, HMV*

Oklahoma Crude

PG/Jr. High-Adult Sadistic oil trust rep Palence battles man-hating Dunaway for her well. Drifter Scott helps her resist on the promise of shared profits. In this 1913 setting, Dunaway tells Scott she wishes she could avoid men altogether, but later settles for him.

1973 108m/C George C. Scott, Faye Dunaway, John Mills, Jack Palance, Harvey Jason, Woodrow Parfrey; *D:* Stanley Kramer; *W:* Marc Norman; *M:* Henry Mancini. **VHS** *FOX*

The Old Curiosity Shop

G/Family After plundering Mark Twain with mixed results for their musicals "Tom Sawyer" and "Huckleberry Finn," the Readers Digest group tried this British musicalization of Charles Dickens, in vain hopes of repeating the success of "Oliver!" Story concerns a Scroogish scoundrel who wants to take over a small antique shop run by an elderly man and his granddaughter. Also known as "Mr. Quilp." Songs written by Anthony Newley. ♫ When a Felon Needs a Friend; Somewhere; Love Has the Longest Memory; Happiness Pie; The Sport of Kings; What Shouldn't Happen to a Dog; Quilp.

1975 118m/C Anthony Newley, David Hemmings, David Warner, Jill Bennett, Peter Duncan, Michael Hordern; *D:* Michael Tuchner; *M:* Elmer Bernstein. **VHS, Beta** *REP*

The Old Curiosity Shop

G/Family Animated adaptation of the classic Dickens story about little Nell and her grandfather, who are evicted from their antique shop by evil landlord Quilp.

1984 72m/C VHS, Beta *LIV*

The Old Curiosity Shop

PG/Primary-Adult Another adaptation of Charles Dickens' 1840 tale about Grandfather Trent (Ustinov), an antiques dealer who has lost his fortune through gambling and makes matters worse by borrowing money from the miserable Mr. Quilp (Courtenay). Unable to repay the debt, Trent and young granddaughter Sally (Walsh) try to escape London, which turns Quilp's wrath upon them. Fine performances and a colorful production; made for cable TV.

BEWARE *Mild thematic elements regarding family and the evils of gambling.*

1994 280m/C Peter Ustinov, Tom Courtenay, James Fox, Sally Walsh, William Mannering, Christopher Ettridge, Julia McKenzie, Anne White, Jean Marlow, Cornelia Hayes O'Herlihy, Michael Mears; *D:* Kevin Connor; *W:* John Goldsmith; *C:* Doug Milsome; *M:* Mason Daring. **VHS** *HMK*

Old Enough

PG/Sr. High-Adult Slow-moving comedy-drama about the clique-crossing friendship of two NYC teenagers, one from a rich family, the other a streetwise Italian-American with plenty to teach about makeup, sex, and shoplifting. Independently made.

BEWARE *Sex talk, salty language.*

1984 91m/C Sarah Boyd, Rainbow Harvest, Neill Barry, Danny Aiello, Susan Kingsley, Roxanne Hart, Alyssa Milano, Fran Brill, Anne Pitoniak; **D:** Marisa Silver; **W:** Marisa Silver. **VHS, Beta** *MED*

The Old Mill

Preschool-Primary An Oscar-winning Disney "Silly Symphony": a run-down building, housing an array of animals, withstands a nasty storm and the animals learn the value of teamwork.

1937 9m/C VHS, Beta *DSN, MTI*

Old Yeller 🦴🦴🦴 🦴

G/Family Disney Studios' first and best boy-and-his-dog adventure. Fourteen-year-old Travis is left in charge of the family farm while Pa is away. When his younger brother brings home a stray dog, Travis is displeased but lets him stay. Yeller saves the boy's life, but contracts rabies in the process. Keep tissue handy, especially for the kids. Strong acting, effective scenery—all good stuff. Based on the novel by Fred Gipson. Sequel "Savage Sam" released in 1963.

BEWARE *Violence. Just about every Disney animal movie ever (even "The Shaggy Dog") has that scene in which someone threatens to shoot the dog/cow/deer/elephant, but this is the heartbreaker in which the deed is truly done.*

1957 84m/C Dorothy McGuire, Fess Parker, Tommy Kirk, Kevin Corcoran, Jeff York, Beverly Washburn, Chuck Connors; **D:** Robert Stevenson. **VHS, Beta, LV** *DIS*

Old Yeller

Preschool-Jr. High A condensed version of the heartbreaking 1957 Disney classic based on Fred Gipson's timeless tale; the ill-fated relationship between a boy and his mongrel dog cause the boy to become a man.

1990 28m/C VHS, Beta, LV *MTI, DSN*

The Olden Days Coat

Preschool-Primary "Anne of Green Gables" leading lady Follows stars in this minor Canadian time-travel short about a city girl who doesn't like visiting her grandmother for the holidays. Sally changes her attitude when a magical garment transports her to the old woman's own childhood.

1981 30m/C Megan Follows, Doris Petrie; **D:** Bruce Pittman. **VHS, Beta** *NWV*

Oliver! 🦴🦴🦴 🦴

G/Family Cinephiles were scandalized when this beat out "2001: A Space Odyssey" for a Best Picture Oscar, but face it—which movie made more people happy? Lush, big-budget musical adaptation of "Oliver Twist" does a grand job with London locations and a peerless cast in the classic story of the innocent orphan expelled from a Victorian workhouse and into a gang of boy pickpockets. Moody's Fagin is a more loveable rogue than Charles Dickens could ever have imagined. 🎵 Food, Glorious Food; Oliver; Boy For Sale; Where Is Love?; Consider Yourself; Pick a Pocket or Two; I'd Do Anything; Be Back Soon; As Long As He Needs Me.

BEWARE *Violence, alcohol use and exploited orphans who sing.*

1968 145m/C Mark Lester, Jack Wild, Ron Moody, Shani Wallis, Oliver Reed, Hugh Griffith; **D:** Carol Reed. **Award Nominations:** Academy Awards '68: Best Actor (Moody), Best Adapted Screenplay, Best Cinematography, Best Costume Design, Best Film Editing, Best Supporting Actor (Wild); **Awards:** Academy Awards '68: Best Art Direction/Set Decoration, Best Director (Reed), Best Picture, Best Sound, Best Score; Golden Globe Awards '69: Best Actor—Musical/Comedy (Moody), Best Film—Musical/Comedy; National Board of Review Awards '68: 10 Best Films of the Year. **VHS, Beta, LV** *COL, BTV, HMV*

Oliver & Company 🦴🦴🦴

Family Loosely based on "Oliver Twist," this animated Disney tale of a cute orphaned kitty and the gang of friendly dogs who take him in will charm the Dickens out of families. Nicely voiced by Joey Lawrence (when he was 12), Oliver meets singing streetwise terrier Dodger, voiced by Billy Joel (when he was, oh never mind), and his thieving band of bowsers. They work for Fagin (Dom DeLuise) who keeps them in dog food. There's a loan shark and a rich little girl, but never mind them. Enjoy Bette Midler as a pampered poodle, Roscoe Lee Browne as a Shakespeare-spouting bulldog, and Cheech Marin as a wisenheimer chihuahua.

BEWARE *A couple of scary Dobermans may be too much for children under 5. Also, there is some kitten kicking and little girl Jenny gets tied to a chair.*

1988 72m/C D: George Scribner; **W:** Jim Cox, James Mangold; **V:** Joey Lawrence, Billy Joel, Richard "Cheech" Marin, Bette Midler, Dom DeLuise, Roscoe Lee Browne, Richard Mulligan, Sheryl Lee Ralph, Robert Loggia, Taurean Blacque, Carl Weintraub, Natalie Gregory, William Glover. **VHS** *TOU*

Oliver Twist 🦴🦴

Family The first talking version of Dickens' classic (Jackie Coogan's 1922 silent is also on video), looks genuinely 19th-century and poverty-wracked—or is that a reflection of the primitive budget? English accents come and go, and Oliver's not even onscreen much in this one. Note Boyd, later a hero to millions as cowboy star Hopalong Cassidy, here cast as the murderous Bill Sykes.

BEWARE *Violence.*

1933 70m/B Dickie Moore, Irving Pichel, William Boyd, Barbara Kent; **D:** William J. Cowen. **VHS, Beta** *NOS, MRV, HHT*

Oliver Twist 🦴🦴🦴🦴

Family Charles Dickens' immortal story of a Victorian workhouse orphan, tricked into a life of crime with a gang of juvenile pickpockets, then finding a home with a wealthy Londoner. The best of the many film adaptations,

with excellent portrayals. But if you're expecting something fun and cuddly, try the musical "Oliver!"—this is a stark, deadly serious version of the novel, accurately reflecting the author's concern over poverty, cruel injustice and exploitation of children. And Fagin (Guinness) sure isn't the lovable rascal of the stage show. An earlier dramatization from 1933 is also on video.

BEWARE! *Violence, alcohol use and exploited orphans.*

1948 116m/C Robert Newton, John Howard Davies, Alec Guinness, Francis L. Sullivan, Anthony Newley, Kay Walsh, Diana Dors, Henry Stephenson; **D:** David Lean; **W:** David Lean. **VHS, Beta, LV** *PAR, DVT, FHS*

Oliver Twist 🎬🎬 ♭

Family Made-for-TV version of the classic tale of a Victorian orphan boy's rescue from a London pickpocket gang. Cut too short to capture Dicken's intricate narrative, and Scott's Fagin, though a treat, is of the heart-of-gold variety. Historical period details are on the mark.

1982 72m/C George C. Scott, Tim Curry, Michael Hordern, Timothy West, Lysette Anthony, Eileen Atkins, Cherie Lunghi; **D:** Clive Donner; **W:** James Goldman; **M:** Nick Bicat. **VHS, Beta** *REP, VES*

Oliver Twist

Family British TV miniseries adaptation crams more of Charles Dickens' original novel into its narrative than any other—you can do that when you're 5.5 hours long. Oliver the orphan boy plunges into the underworld of Victorian London and assorted villains seek to profit off the secret of his birth. On two tapes.

BEWARE! *Violence.*

1985 333m/C Ben Rodska, Eric Porter, Frank Middlemass, Gillian Martell. **VHS, Beta** *FOX, SIG, HMV*

Oliver Twist

Family Animated musical TV version of the Charles Dickens tale of the roguish Fagin, the Artful Dodger, and the orphaned Oliver (who has a pet toad named Squeaker in this none-too faithful adaptation).

19?? 95m/C V: Davy Jones, Larry Storch. **VHS** *WAR*

Ollie Hopnoodle's Haven of Bliss 🎬🎬 ♭

Family Jean Shepherd, the humorist whose work inspired "A Christmas Story," scripted and narrates this Disney made-for-TV comedy about a family man taking his unruly brood on an accident-fraught vacation.

1988 90m/C James B. Sikking, Dorothy Lyman, Jerry O'Connell; **D:** Dick Bartlett. **VHS, Beta** *DIS*

Olly Olly Oxen Free 🎬🎬

Family Junkyard owner Hepburn helps two boys fix up and fly a hot-air balloon, once piloted by McKenzie's grandfather, as a surprise for the man's birthday. Beautiful airborne scenes over California and a dramatic landing to the tune of the "1812 Overture," but not enough to make the whole film interesting.

1978 89m/C Katharine Hepburn, Kevin McKenzie, Dennis Dimster, Peter Kilman; **D:** Richard A. Colla. **VHS, Beta** *TLF*

The Olympic Champ

Preschool-Primary Walt Disney's Goofy is a contestant at the Olympic games where he proceeds to demonstrate his athletic prowess.

1981 8m/C VHS, Beta *MTI, DSN*

On a Clear Day You Can See Forever 🎬🎬

G/Family A psychiatric hypnotist helps a girl stop smoking and finds that in trances she remembers previous incarnations. He falls in love with one of the women she used to be. Alan Jay Lerner of "My Fair Lady" and "Camelot" wrote the lyrics and the book. Based on a musical by Lerner and Burton Lane. ♫ On a Clear Day, You Can See Forever; Come Back to Me; What Did I Have That I Don't Have?; He Isn't You; Hurry, It's Lovely Up Here; Go To Sleep; Love with All the Trimmings; Melinda.

1970 129m/C Barbra Streisand, Yves Montand, Bob Newhart, Jack Nicholson, Simon Oakland; **D:** Vincente Minnelli. **VHS, Beta, LV** *PAR*

On Golden Pond 🎬🎬🎬🎬

PG/Family A lake in New Hampshire that glimmers gold in the sun is a subtle metaphor for old age in this lovely movie adapted by Ernest Thompson from his play. 80-year-old retired professor Norman Thayer (Henry Fonda) and his wife, Ethel (Katharine Hepburn) have a summer house on the lake, and that's where their estranged daughter (Jane Fonda, Henry's real daughter) has dropped off her teenage son (Doug McKeon) as their guest for the summer. The affection between the witty old couple is charming, and gradually the teen and the grandparents draw touchingly close; and even Jane gets into the act. A beautiful film about affection and understanding across generations. Hepburn and Henry Fonda both won Oscars, as did Thompson's script. Dabney Coleman actually plays someone likable. Ages 11 and up.

BEWARE! *Nothing objectionable, except the phrases "suck face" and "old poop."*

1981 109m/C Henry Fonda, Jane Fonda, Katharine Hepburn, Dabney Coleman, Doug McKeon, William Lanteau; **D:** Mark Rydell; **W:** Ernest Thompson; **M:** Dave Grusin. **Award Nominations:** Academy Awards '81: Best Actor (Fonda), Best Cinematography, Best Director (Rydell), Best Film Editing, Best Sound, Best Supporting Actress (Fonda), Best Original Score; **Awards:** Academy Awards '81: Best Actor (Fonda), Best Actress (Hepburn), Best Adapted Screenplay; British Academy Awards '82: Best Actress (Hepburn); Golden Globe Awards '82: Best Actor—Drama (Fonda), Best Film—Drama, Best Screenplay. **VHS, Beta, LV** *FHE, KAR, BTV*

On Her Majesty's Secret Service 🎬🎬🎬

PG/Jr. High-Adult In the sixth 007 adventure, Bond again confronts the infamous Blofeld, who is planning a

Mark Lester asks "Please sir, may I have some more?" in "Oliver!"

germ-warfare assault on the entire world. Australian Lazenby took a crack at playing the super spy, with mixed results. Many feel this is the best-written of the Bond films and might have been the most famous, had Sean Connery continued with the series. Includes the song "We Have All the Time In the World," sung by Louis Armstrong.

BEWARE *Violence, alcohol use and sex (all in the James Bond tradition).*

1969 144m/C George Lazenby, Diana Rigg, Telly Savalas, Gabriele Ferzetti, Ilse Steppat, Bernard Lee, Lois Maxwell, Desmond Llewelyn, Catherine Schell, Julie Ege, Joanna Lumley, Mona Chong, Anouska Hempel, Jenny Hanley; **D:** Peter Hunt; **M:** John Barry. **VHS, Beta, LV** *MGM, FOX, TLF*

On the Comet 🦴🦴🦴

Family Lesser-known sci-fi fantasy by Jules Verne brought to life by Czech filmmaker Karl Zeman, with his trademark meld of whimsical animation and live action. Wandering planetoid brushes past 19th-century Earth and takes part of the Mediterranean coast with it. Drifting through the solar system, assorted Europeans, Arabs, soldiers, lovers and scalawags slowly realize their old nationalistic squabbles are pointless now that they're on

their own. Adults more than kid viewers may get the sly satire of human nature, though there are some memorable dinosaur f/x (stop motion and puppets) as well. English-language dubbing is on the clunky side.

BEWARE *Alcohol use.*

1968 76m/C Emil Horvath Jr., Magda Vasarykova, Frantisek Filipovsky; **D:** Karel Zeman. **VHS, Beta** *FCT, MRV*

On the Edge: The Survival of Dana 🦴

Family Hand-wringing TV-movie was intended in its day as a sincere examination of juvenile delinquency, but the results are maudlin and unintentionally silly. Anderson was also residing in "Little House on the Prairie" at the time she was calculatingly cast as Dana, new girl in town who falls in with a bad crowd of mean teens. Her concerned mom is played by Ross, Mrs. Cunningham from "Happy Days." See the similarly titled "Over the Edge" instead for a better treatment of the subject.

BEWARE *Drug use; sex talk; roughhousing.*

1979 92m/C Melissa Sue Anderson, Robert Carradine, Marion Ross, Talia Balsam, Michael Pataki, Kevin Breslin, Judge Reinhold, Barbara Babcock; **D:** Jack Starrett. **VHS, Beta** *GEM*

On the Move with Virgil

Primary Puppets, on-location filming, and music teach children different areas of American culture. Aimed at individuals who are new to the United States. Stresses school, cleanliness, food, pets, and times of the year. Also includes language and language development. Ages 4 to 10.
1994 280m/C VHS

On the Right Track 🎵 🦴

PG/Family Young orphan living in Chicago's Union Station has the gift of being able to pick winning race horses. May be appealing to fans of Coleman and "Different Strokes" television show, but lacks the momentum to keep most viewers from switching tracks.
1981 98m/C Gary Coleman, Lisa Eilbacher, Michael Lembeck, Norman Fell, Maureen Stapleton, Herb Edelman; **D:** Lee Philips. **VHS, Beta** *FOX*

On the Town 🎵🎵🎵 🦴

Family Kelly's directorial debut is a high-energy wonder about three sailors on a one-day leave searching for romance in the Big Apple. Notable for taking the musical from the soundstage to the street: filmed on location in New York City, with uncompromisingly authentic flavor. Based on the successful Broadway musical, with Leonard Bernstein's stage score modified by Roger Edens. Available in a deluxe collector's laserdisc edition. 🎵 New York, New York; I Feel Like I'm Not Out of Bed Yet; Come Up to My Place; Miss Turnstiles Ballet; Main Street; You're Awful; On the Town; You Can Count on Me; Pearl of the Persian Sea.
1949 98m/C Gene Kelly, Frank Sinatra, Vera-Ellen, Ann Miller, Betty Garrett; **D:** Gene Kelly, Stanley Donen; **W:** Betty Comden, Adolph Green. **VHS, Beta, LV** *MGM*

On Vacation with Mickey and Friends

Family Disney mouse and his pals star in a number of misadventures including, "Canine Caddy," "Bubble Bee," "Goofy and Wilbur," "Dude Duck," "Mickey's Trailer," and "Hawaiian Holiday."
19?? 47m/C VHS, Beta, LV *DIS*

Once a Hero 🎵🎵

Family Fictional Captain Justice's powers fade because readers are losing interest in his superhero comic book. He leaps out of the fantasy realm to complain to his human creator, and has to deal with the drawbacks and problems of dwelling in the real world. Fascinating, not entirely successful idea, slightly reminiscent of "The Last Action Hero," formed the pilot for a short-lived network TV series.

1988 74m/C Jeff Lester, Robert Forster, Milo O'Shea; **D:** Claudia Weill. **VHS** *NWV, VTR*

Once Upon a Brothers Grimm 🎵🎵

Family An original musical fantasy in which the Brothers Grimm meet a succession of their most famous storybook characters, including Hansel and Gretel, the Gingerbread Lady, Little Red Riding Hood, and Rumpelstiltskin.
1977 102m/C Dean Jones, Paul Sand, Cleavon Little, Ruth Buzzi, Chita Rivera, Teri Garr. **VHS, Beta** *VCI*

Once Upon a Crime 🎵 🦴

PG/Jr. High-Adult Extremely disappointing comedy featuring a high profile cast set in Europe. The plot centers around Young and Lewis finding a dachshund and traveling from Rome to Monte Carlo to return the stray and collect a $5,000 reward. Upon arrival in Monte Carlo, they find the dog's owner dead and are implicated for the murder. Other prime suspects include Belushi, Candy, Hamilton, and Shepherd. Weak script is made bearable only by the comic genius of Candy.

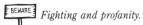 *Fighting and profanity.*

1992 94m/C John Candy, James Belushi, Cybill Shepherd, Sean Young, Richard Lewis, Ornella Muti, Giancarlo Giannini, George Hamilton, Joss Ackland, Elsa Martinelli; **D:** Eugene Levy; **M:** Richard Gibbs. **VHS** *MGM*

Once Upon a Forest 🎵🎵

G/Family Cartoon about young woodland creatures whose forest is slimed by a toxic spill. To save a chemically burned badger baby, the animals race to gather medicinal ingredients. Ecologically correct feature by Hanna-Barbera and "American Tail" creator David Kirschner is light on plot, heavy on sentiment about oppressive humans and their big, bad machines. Serviceable animation, undistinguished songs, put this well behind the similar "Ferngully."
1993 80m/C **D:** Charles Grosvenor; **W:** Mark Young, Kelly Ward; **V:** Michael Crawford, Ben Vereen. **VHS, LV** *FXV, FUS*

Once Upon a Scoundrel 🎵🎵 🦴

G/Family Mostel's delicious, larger-than-life luster brightens this tale of ruthless Mexican land baron whose villainy finally goes too far. Villagers stage a ghostly hoax to make him reform in Scrooge-like fashion. Ages 13 and up.
1973 90m/C Zero Mostel, Katy Jurado, Titos Vandis, Priscilla Garcia, A. Martinez; **D:** George Schaefer; **M:** Alex North. **VHS, Beta** *PSM*

Once Upon a Time in the West 🎵🎵🎵 🦴

PG/Jr. High-Adult The uncut version of Leone's sprawling epic about a band of ruthless gunmen who set out to murder a mysterious woman waiting for the railroad to

"Oliver and Company" hit the city streets.

come through. Filmed in John Ford's Monument Valley, it's a revisionist western with some of the longest opening credits in the history of the cinema. Fonda is cast against type as an extremely cold-blooded villain. Brilliant musical score.

1968 165m/C Henry Fonda, Jason Robards Jr., Charles Bronson, Claudia Cardinale, Keenan Wynn, Lionel Stander, Woody Strode, Jack Elam; **D:** Sergio Leone; **W:** Sergio Leone, Bernardo Bertolucci, Dario Argento; **M:** Ennio Morricone. **VHS, Beta, LV** *PAR*

Once Upon a Time . . . When We Were Colored 🦴🦴🦴

PG/Primary-Adult Just after World War II, just before sit-ins and bus boycotts. Those are the southern days recalled in this uplifting film by African-American director Tim Reid (better known as a TV actor, on "Frank's Place" and "WKRP.") Al Freeman and Phylicia Rashad stand out in this movie based on a memoir by Clifton Taulbert, that celebrates friendship, family and community. Ages 11 and up.

🚸 BEWARE *Segregation and bigotry.*

1995 112m/C Al Freeman Jr., Paula Kelly, Phylicia Rashad, Polly Bergen, Richard Roundtree, Charles Taylor, Willie Norwood, Jr.,

Damon Hines, Leon; **D:** Tim Reid; **W:** Paul Cooper; **C:** Johnny Simmons; **M:** Steve Tyrell. **VHS** *REP*

The One and Only, Genuine, Original Family Band 🦴🦴🦴

G/Family Harmonious musical family becomes divided when various members take sides in the 1888 presidential battle between Benjamin Harrison and Grover Cleveland. Semi-musical nostalgic Americana from Disney, best for those whose favorite section of Disney World is Main Street USA.

1968 110m/C Walter Brennan, Buddy Ebsen, Lesley Ann Warren, Kurt Russell, Goldie Hawn, Wally Cox, Richard Deacon, Janet Blair; **D:** Michael O'Herlihy. **VHS, Beta, LV** *DIS*

One Crazy Summer 🦴🦴🦴

PG/Jr. High-Adult Group of teens spend a fun-filled summer on Nantucket Island in New England. This follow-up to "Better Off Dead" is offbeat and fairly charming, led by Cusack's perplexed-about-his-future cartoonist (whose drawings come to animated life) and with comic moments delivered by Goldthwait.

🚸 BEWARE *Sex talk, profanity and fighting. Even some fighting among cartoon characters.*

1986 94m/C John Cusack, Demi Moore, William Hickey, Curtis Armstrong, Bob(cat) Goldthwait, Mark Metcalf, Joel Murray, Tom Villard, Joe Flaherty; *D:* Steve Holland; *W:* Steve Holland; *M:* Cory Lerios. VHS, Beta, LV *WAR*

One Fish, Two Fish, Red Fish, Blue Fish

Family The Dr. Seuss classic cartoon is paired with two other stories, "Oh, the Things You Can Think" and "The Foot Book" on one tape.
1990 30m/C VHS *VEC, RAN*

101 Dalmatians

G/Family Disney classic and one of the highest-grossing animated films in Hollywood history centers around Roger and Anita, and their respective dalmatians, Pongo and Perdita, whose purebred puppies are kidnapped by callous Cruella de Vil to make a spotted coat. When the canine parents go to the rescue, they find not only their own litter, but 84 more puppies. You can expect a happy ending in this adaptation of the children's book by Dodie Smith. Technically notable for the first time use of the Xerox process to transfer the animator's drawings onto celluloid, which made the opening sequence of dots evolving into 101 barking dogs possible and was a major step toward computerizing the Magic Kingdom's animation works. ♫ Remember When; Cruella de Vil; Dalmation Plantation; Kanine Krunchies Kommercial.

> **BEWARE** *Puppies in danger.*

1961 79m/C *D:* Clyde Geronomi, Wolfgang Reitherman, Hamilton Luske; *V:* Rod Taylor, Betty Lou Gerson, Lisa Davis, Ben Wright, Frederick Worlock, J. Pat O'Malley. VHS, Beta *DIS, OM*

101 Dalmatians 🐾🐾 ♭

Family Cruella DeVil is at it again, but this time in a live-action version of the Disney classic. She's out to get those cute, spotted pups with the help of her bumbling henchmen, Jaspar and Horace. You're kids will be clamoring to see this one, especially since it features so many real cuddly puppies. Be careful, they may want one for their own after seeing this flick.

> **BEWARE** *Puppy-napping may be hard on the littlest ones.*

1996 ?m/C Glenn Close, Joely Richardson, Jeff Daniels, Joan Plowright; *D:* Stephen Herek; *W:* John Hughes. VHS *NYR*

101 Problems of Hercules

Family Not a self-help tape; Disney version of the Hercules saga.
1966 50m/C VHS *DSN, DIS*

One Little Indian 🐾🐾

Family AWOL cavalry man and his 12-year-old Indian ward team up with a widow and her daughter in an attempt to cross the New Mexican desert via camel. Tepid presentation from the Disney studio.

1973 90m/C James Garner, Vera Miles, Jodie Foster, Clay O'Brien, Andrew Prine, Bernard McEveety; *D:* Bernard McEveety; *M:* Jerry Goldsmith. VHS, Beta *DIS*

One Magic Christmas 🐾🐾

G/Family Holiday tearjerker from Disney about a depressed lady hit with multiple calamities at Yuletime. Her little daughter restores her spirits with the help of Santa and a seedy-looking guardian angel. Jarring juxtaposition of fantasy and realistic elements—one moment a robbery and murder, the next moment the North Pole toy factory. It won't make anyone forget "Miracle on 34th Street."

> **BEWARE** *Crime and deprivation. Bad things happen at Christmastime.*

1985 88m/C Mary Steenburgen, Harry Dean Stanton, Gary Basaraba, Michelle Meyrink, Arthur Hill, Elisabeth Harnois, Robbie Magwood; *D:* Phillip Borsos; *M:* Michael Conway Baker. VHS, Beta, LV *DIS*

One of Our Dinosaurs Is Missing 🐾🐾

G/Family English nanny and her cohorts help British Intelligence retrieve a dinosaur skeleton from Red Chinese spies who stole it to obtain a secret microfilm formula. No "Jurassic Park," this calcified Disney comedy was shot on location in England. Based on the novel "The Great Dinosaur Robbery" by David Forrest.

1975 101m/C Peter Ustinov, Helen Hayes, Derek Nimmo, Clive Revill, Robert Stevenson, Joan Sims; *D:* Robert Stevenson. VHS, Beta *DIS*

One on One 🐾🐾 ♭

PG/Primary-Adult "Rocky"-esque story about a high school basketball star from the country who accepts an athletic scholarship to a big city university. He encounters a demanding coach and intense competition. Lightweight drama that occasionally scores, written by Benson and his own father.

> **BEWARE** *Salty language, sex talk.*

1977 100m/C Robby Benson, Annette O'Toole, G.D. Spradlin, Gail Strickland, Melanie Griffith; *D:* Lamont Johnson; *M:* Charles Fox. VHS, Beta *WAR*

Only the Lonely 🐾🐾 ♭

PG/Jr. High-Adult Danny Muldoon, a Chicago cop (John Candy) lives with his mother (Maureen O'Hara, in her first film role in 18 years). When he falls in love with Ally Sheedy, a shy undertaker's assistant he is torn between love and dear old Mom. Similar to the classic "Marty." Sentimental, tender, and uneven, supported by fine performances, particularly Candy's. Ages 13 and up.

> **BEWARE** *Profanity.*

1991 104m/C John Candy, Ally Sheedy, Maureen O'Hara, Anthony Quinn, Kevin Dunn, James Belushi, Milo O'Shea, Bert Remsen, Macaulay Culkin, Joe V. Greco; *D:* Chris Columbus; *W:* Chris Columbus; *M:* Maurice Jarre. VHS, Beta, LV *FXV*

Sergeant Tibs tries to rescue the pups from the evil Cruella De Vil in "101 Dalmatians."

Only You 🦴 🦴

PG-13/Jr. High-Adult Shy guy has always searched for true romance. But his cup runneth over when he meets, and must choose between, two beautiful women—your basic beach babe and a sensible beauty. What's a guy to do? Lightweight romantic comedy fails to satisfy.

BEWARE *Salty language.*

1992 85m/C Andrew McCarthy, Kelly Preston, Helen Hunt. **VHS** *LIV*

Only You 🦴🦴 🦴

PG/Sr. High-Adult According to her ouija board, young Faith's (Tomei) soul mate is named Damon Bradley. But as the years pass, Faith is about to settle for a podiatrist—until an old school friend of her fiance's calls from Venice, Italy, with best wishes. Guess what his name is. So Faith and best friend Kate (Hunt) hop on a plane in search of Mr. Right. Then Faith meets charming shoe salesman Peter Wright (Downey) and wonders if ouija got things wrong. Slight romantic comedy with Jason creating satisfactory chemistry with charming Downey

and the somewhat miscast Tomei (and the Venetian scenery is gorgeous).

BEWARE *Language and sexual innuendos. Married, but unhappy Hunt is romanced by a very suave Cassanova.*

1994 108m/C Marisa Tomei, Robert Downey Jr., Bonnie Hunt, Fisher Stevens, Billy Zane, Joaquim de Almeida; **D:** Norman Jewison; **W:** Diane Drake. **VHS, LV** *COL*

Open a Door

Primary Three-part series which follows a child through a world of adventures by visiting various countries. Visits includes: England, Cyprus, Holland, the Philippines, Dominica, Tanzania, New Zealand, Canada, Sweden, Poland, and Belarus. Ages 5 to 10.
1994 m/C VHS *BFI*

Operation Dumbo Drop 🦴🦴 🦴

PG/Jr. High-Adult It's 1968 and tough Green Beret captain (Glover), rescued by Vietnamese villagers, promises to replace their prized elephant, which was killed during his mission. He and a group of commandos use land, sea, and air to transport the reluctant beast, learning way more about elephant hygiene and eating habits than they ever wanted to know in the process. Wincer, who also directed "Free Willy," seems to be going for the title of "greatest large mammal director of all time." Anything with good-guy US troops, a paratrooper elephant, and a family-friendly plot should be a Bob Dole favorite.

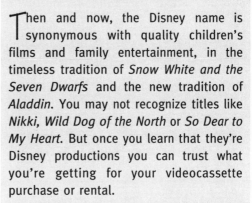

BEWARE *War action and language.*

1995 107m/C Danny Glover, Ray Liotta, Doug E. Doug, Denis Leary, Corin "Corky" Nemec, Thein Le Dihn; **D:** Simon Wincer; **W:** Jim Kouf, Gene Quintano; **C:** Russell Boyd; **M:** David Newman. **VHS, LV** *DIS*

Opportunity Knocks 🎵🎵 ♭

PG-13/Jr. High-Adult Dana's a small-time hood on the run from a vengeful gangster. Opportunity knocks and he begins impersonating a wealthy man, falls in tight with a rich suburbanite family, and has a go at romance with the comely daughter. Comedic capers then ensue. Basic sitcom is lightweight and obvious, but Carvey's first starring feature has its charms, particularly for young fans.

BEWARE *Salty language; violence.*

1990 105m/C Dana Carvey, Robert Loggia, Todd Graff, Milo O'Shea, Julia Campbell, James Tolkan, Doris Belack, Sally Gracie, Del Close; **D:** Donald Petrie; **W:** Mitchel Katlin, Nat Bernstein; **M:** Miles Goodman. **VHS, Beta, LV** *MCA*

The Original Fabulous Adventures of Baron Munchausen 🎵🎵🎵

Family To avoid mixups with a 1979 European cartoon (also on video, in a version that doesn't even spell "Munchausen" correctly) distributors retitled "The Fabulous Adventures of Baron Munchausen," from Czech animation master Karl Zeman. Under any name it's worth a search. Cosmonaut reaches the moon—only to find all the fictional greats who made the trip centuries ago, like Cyrano de Bergerac and Baron Munchausen. These legends mistake their visitor for an alien (!), and the slightly vain Baron volunteers to take 'moon man' on an explanatory tour of Earth, circa the 1700s. There follows familiar Munchausen escapades: rescuing a maiden from a sultan, riding through a battle on a cannonball, and circling the world inside a whale. Told with tinted live-action footage, stop-motion, and cutouts. Cumulative effect is lyrical, actually soothing—a true bedtime story in movie form.

1961 84m/C Milos Kopecky, Jana Brejchova, Rudolph Jelinek, Jan Werich; **D:** Karel Zeman. **VHS, LV** *NO*

Orphan Train 🎵🎵🎵

Family A woman realizes her New York soup kitchen can't do enough to help the neighborhood orphans, so she takes a group of children out West in hopes of finding families to adopt them. Their journey is chronicled by a newspaper photographer an a social worker. Based on

Disney: Still a Name to Depend On

Then and now, the Disney name is synonymous with quality children's films and family entertainment, in the timeless tradition of *Snow White and the Seven Dwarfs* and the new tradition of *Aladdin.* You may not recognize titles like *Nikki, Wild Dog of the North* or *So Dear to My Heart.* But once you learn that they're Disney productions you can trust what you're getting for your videocassette purchase or rental.

But when is Disney not Disney? In the 1980s, the Magic Kingdom staked out new realms in the territory of mass-audience motion pictures—more mature, even raw subjects far removed from Cinderella's Palace. Disney's two associated entities, Touchstone and Hollywood Pictures, with their own home video labels, acquired Miramax, and, after negotiations that make most peace treaties look like handshakes, Disney brought the Jim Henson Muppet catalogue into the fold with its very own label. And then there's Buena Vista Home Video, a regular catch-all of family titles. But the fact is that Disney Studios have shown a polished professionalism in everything they produce. Intentionally or not, a bit of the Disney spirit creeps in, and there are clearly Disney-less pics, like Touchstone's *Sister Act,* Hollywood's *Captain Ron,* or even the independently-made Miramax release *Into the West* that, with some adjustments, could conceivably have met the high standards of Uncle Walt himself.

Moving a heavy load in "Operation Dumbo Drop."

the orphans trains of the mid- to late 1800s. From the novel by Dorothea G. Petrie. Made for TV.

1979 150m/C Jill Eikenberry, Kevin Dobson, Glenn Close, Linda Manz; **D:** William A. Graham. **VHS** *PSM, KAR, HHE*

Oscar 𝄞𝄞

PG/Jr. High-Adult No Oscar bait here. A stretch for Stallone as Angelo Provolone, a gangster trying to go straight in this 1930s-style farce. Stallone has little to do as he plays the straight man to a stellar cast of character actors, including Chazz Palminteri, Marisa Tomei, Don Ameche and Tim Curry. Lots of slamming doors and mistaken identities. Based on a French play by Claude Magnier. Ages 12 and up.

🔖 BEWARE *Profanity.*

1991 109m/C Sylvester Stallone, Ornella Muti, Peter Riegert; **Cameos:** Tim Curry, Chazz Palminteri; **D:** John Landis; **M:** Elmer Bernstein. **VHS, LV** *COL, IME, TOU*

Othello 𝄞𝄞 ♭

R/Sr. High-Adult Fishburne stars as Shakespeare's tragically deceived Moor, with Branagh as silken agitator Iago, and Jacob as the tragic Desdemona. First time

director Oliver Parker (brother Nathaniel is also in the film) has drastically cut the play, rearranging scenes (and even adding material)—purists will no doubt scream but performances carry the production.

🔖 BEWARE *Contains violence, sexuality, and nudity, but in the Shakespearean tradition.*

1995 125m/C Laurence "Larry" Fishburne, Irene Jacob, Kenneth Branagh, Nathaniel Parker, Michael Maloney, Anna Patrick, Nicholas Farrell, Indra Ove, Michael Sheen, Andre Oumansky, Philip Locke, John Savident, Gabriele Ferzetti, Pierre Vaneck; **D:** Oliver Parker; **W:** Oliver Parker; **C:** David Johnson; **M:** Charlie Mole. **VHS** *NYR*

The Other Side of the Mountain 𝄞𝄞

PG/Jr. High-Adult Tear-jerking true story of Olympic hopeful skier Jill Kinmont, paralyzed in a fall. Bridges helps her pull her life together. A sequel followed two years later. Based on the book "A Long Way Up" by E. G. Valens.

1975 102m/C Marilyn Hassett, Beau Bridges, Dabney Coleman, John David Garfield, Griffin Dunne; **D:** Larry Peerce; **W:** David Seltzer; **M:** Charles Fox. **VHS, Beta** *MCA*

The Other Side of the Mountain, Part 2 🦴🦴

PG/Jr. High-Adult Quadriplegic Jill Kinmont, paralyzed in a skiing accident that killed her hopes for the Olympics, overcomes depression and the death of the man who helped her to recover. In this chapter, she falls in love again and finds happiness. More tears are jerked.

1978 99m/C Marilyn Hassett, Timothy Bottoms; **D:** Larry Peerce. **VHS, Beta** *MCA*

Our Little Girl 🦴🦴

Family Precocious little tyke tries to reunite her estranged parents by running away to their favorite vacation spot. Sure to please Temple fans, despite a lackluster script. Ages 6 to 12.

1935 63m/B Shirley Temple, Joel McCrea, Rosemary Ames, Lyle Talbot, Erin O'Brien Moore; **D:** John S. Robertson. **VHS, Beta** *FOX*

Out on a Limb 🦴

PG/Jr. High-Adult Lame comedy follows the misadventures of financial whiz Bill Campbell (Broderick). His young sister is convinced their stepfather is a criminal and persuades her brother to return home. On his way, Bill is robbed and abandoned by a woman hitchhiker, then found by two moronic brothers. It also turns out his stepfather has a twin brother who wants revenge for past crimes. Frantic chase scenes and lots of noise do not a comedy make. Broderick and Jones also appeared together in "Ferris Bueller's Day Off."

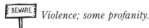 *Violence; some profanity.*

1992 82m/C Matthew Broderick, Jeffrey Jones, Heidi Kling, John C. Reilly, Marian Mercer, Larry Hankin, David Margulies; **D:** Francis Veber. **VHS, Beta, LV** *MGM*

Out There 🦴🦴 ᵛ

PG-13/Jr. High-Adult Cable sci-fi comedy finds photographer Delbert Mosley (Campbell) buying a Brownie camera at a garage sale and discovering the 25-year-old film shows pictures of a UFO encounter. Mosley then tries to verify the photos with a supermarket tabloid, the military, and UFO fanatics all on his trail. Fast-paced amusement with appealing performances.

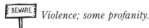 *Nude images and crude language.*

1995 98m/C Bill Campbell, Wendy Schaal, Julie Brown, David Rasche, Paul Dooley, Bill Cobbs, Bob(cat) Goldthwait, Rod Steiger, June Lockhart, Jill St. John, Carel Struycken, Billy Bob Thornton, P.J. Soles; **D:** Sam Irvin; **W:** Thomas Strelich, Alison Nigh; **C:** Gary Tieche; **M:** Deborah Holland, Frankie Blue. **VHS, Beta** *PAR*

Outbreak 🦴🦴🦴

R/Sr. High-Adult If TV gives us disease-of-the-week movies, this is a disease-of-the-decade movie, ripped from today's headlines (or maybe tomorrow's). A fatal and incurable virus travels from Africa to a pleasant town in northern California. It's up to disease-control experts Dr.

Sam Daniels (Hoffman) and Dr. Roberta Keough (Russo) to track down the illness's source and stop the virus from spreading, otherwise WE'RE ALL GOING TO DIE. If that's not bad enough, Hoffman's bosses (Freeman and Sutherland) don't want him to succeed for reasons of their own. Thrills, chills, lots of good actors in contamination suits. It makes epidemiology seem mighty exciting. Outbreak the popcorn and enjoy.

 *Profanity and people made hideous by illness.*

1994 128m/C Dustin Hoffman, Rene Russo, Morgan Freeman, Donald Sutherland, Cuba Gooding Jr., Kevin Spacey; **D:** Wolfgang Petersen; **W:** Laurence Dworet, Robert Roy Pool; **C:** Michael Ballhaus; **M:** James Newton Howard. **VHS, LV** *WAR*

The Outlaw Josey Wales 🦴🦴🦴 ᵛ

PG/Jr. High-Adult Eastwood plays a farmer with a motive for revenge—his family was killed and for years he was betrayed and hunted. His desire to play the lone killer is, however, tempered by his need for family and friends. He kills plenty, but in the end finds happiness. Considered one of the last great Westerns, with many superb performances. Eastwood took over directorial chores during filming from Kaufman, who co-scripted. Adapted from "Gone To Texas" by Forest Carter.

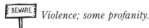 *Lots of violence. A man's family is brutally murdered and the man acts out an equally brutal revenge.*

1976 135m/C Clint Eastwood, Chief Dan George, Sondra Locke, Matt Clark, John Vernon, Bill McKinney, Sam Bottoms; **D:** Clint Eastwood, Philip Kaufman; **W:** Philip Kaufman. **VHS, Beta, LV** *WAR, TLF*

Outside Chance of Maximillian Glick 🦴🦴🦴

G/Jr. High-Adult Terrific, heartfelt comedy from Canada. Max Glick is a 12-year-old Jewish boy in the early 1960s who feels smothered by his tradition-bound family. He considers cancelling his bar mitzvah when they forbid his friendship with a gentile girl, but Max finds an unexpected ally in the free-thinking new rabbi who scandalizes the community. Viewers of any age—and any faith—will be rewarded by hunting up this delightful tale, based on a novel by Morley Torgov. Look closely at the cassette box art; ironically (for a film that celebrates ethnic identity), the video distributor retouched Max's yarmulke into a baseball cap. It's a shonda!

1988 94m/C Noam Zylberman, Fairuza Balk, Saul Rubinek; **D:** Allan Goldstein. **VHS, Beta** *HMD*

The Outsiders 🦴🦴

PG/Jr. High-Adult S.E. Hinton book (written when the author was just 17!) changed the tone of young adult fiction forever; still, it seems slender material smothered under this grandiose, melodramatic, all the talent money can buy treatment from Coppola. Simple story of a teen

gang from the wrong side of the tracks in 1966 Tulsa, and how their feuding with upper-class young hoods brings on both tragedy and heroism. Many characters are reduced to one-scene star cameos. Only Dillon has the chance to create a full personality as the hotheaded Dallas.

BEWARE *Brutality, alcohol use, sex talk and profanity. Gang fights. A character is severely burned.*

1983 91m/C C. Thomas Howell, Matt Dillon, Ralph Macchio, Patrick Swayze, Diane Lane, Tom Cruise, Emilio Estevez, Rob Lowe, Tom Waits, Leif Garrett; **D:** Francis Ford Coppola; **W:** Kathleen Rowell; **M:** Carmine Coppola. **VHS, Beta, LV** *WAR*

Over the Edge

PG/Jr. High-Adult Updated "Rebel Without a Cause" highlighted by music from 70's icons Cheap Trick, The Cars, and The Ramones. Realistic tale of bored, alienated suburban kids on violence and vandalism binges that escalate to tragedy. Intent is insight, not exploitation, and the dialogue is excellent. Shelved for several years and finally released after Dillon, making his screen debut, became a star.

BEWARE *Violence, drug use, sex and profanity. Kids commit crimes.*

1979 91m/C Michael Kramer, Matt Dillon, Pamela Ludwig, Vincent Spano; **D:** Jonathan Kaplan. **VHS, Beta** *WAR*

Over the Top

PG/Jr. High-Adult "Heavy handed" takes on a whole new meaning in this drama of parenthood and arm-wrestling. "Rocky"-type trucker (Stallone in a stretch) named Linc Hawk decides the only way he can gain custody of his little boy from a rich-creep stepfather, as well as win the boy's respect, is through triumph in big-time professional arm-wrestling. Contrived beyond belief, and an example of why arm-wrestling never edged out the World Wrestling Federation in terms of visual thrills.

BEWARE *Profanity, violence and arm wrestling taken seriously.*

1986 94m/C Sylvester Stallone, Susan Blakely, Robert Loggia, David Mendenhall; **D:** Menahem Golan; **W:** Sylvester Stallone, Gary Conway, Stirling Silliphant. **VHS, Beta, LV** *WAR*

Overboard

PG/Jr. High-Adult Spoiled heiress (Goldie Hawn) woman falls off of her yacht and suffers amnesia. A carpenter (Kurt Russell) claims her at the hospital and convinces her she is his wife, and mother to his four brats. She begins to like her new life, but further surprises await. The amnesia bit has done before (and since) but Hawn and Russell (a real life couple) are fun to watch. Insider's note: Watch for an uncredited Hector Elizondo as captain of a garbage scow. Ages 10 and up.

1987 112m/C Goldie Hawn, Kurt Russell, Katherine Helmond, Roddy McDowall, Edward Herrmann; **D:** Garry Marshall; **W:** Leslie Dixon; **M:** Alan Silvestri. **VHS, Beta, LV** *MGM, HMV, FOX*

Ovide and the Gang

Preschool-Primary Compilation of cartoon episodes featuring a cast of marsupials and other fantastic pals on their South Seas tropical island. Additional volumes available.

1987 120m/C VHS *JFK*

The Owl and the Pussycat

Family Animated version of Edward Lear's beloved children's poem with an original musical score.

19?? ?m/C VHS, Beta *COL, GKK*

Owl Moon and Other Stories

Preschool-Primary Collection of animated tales from the "Children's Circle" of books carefully and gracefully brought to cartoon life. Includes "Owl Moon" by Jane Yolen, "The Caterpillar and the Polliwog" by Jack Kent, "Hot Hippo" by Mwenye Hadithi, and "Time of Wonder" by Robert McCloskey.

1991 35m/C VHS *FCT, CCC*

Ox Tales

Preschool-Primary Another animal species proves that nobody is above TV animation, in this selection of Ollie the ox episodes. Additional volumes available.

1989 120m/C VHS *JFK*

Oxford Blues

PG-13/Sr. High-Adult Pursuing the girl of his dreams, an American (Rob Lowe) finagles his way into England's Oxford University and onto the rowing team. Which would make him a gentleman and a sculler. Beautiful scenery, but the plot is thin. Remake of "Yank at Oxford." Ages 12 an up.

BEWARE *Profanity and sexual situations.*

1984 98m/C Rob Lowe, Ally Sheedy, Amanda Pays, Julian Sands, Michael Gough, Gail Strickland; **D:** Robert Boris; **M:** John Du Prez. **VHS, Beta, LV** *FOX*

Ozma of Oz

Family Dorothy and her pals encounter Ozma, the beautiful Princess of Oz, and together they venture into Nomeland. Another in a worthwhile Canadian series that renders some of the many, many Oz books written by L. Frank Baum long after "The Wizard of Oz"; see also "The Marvelous Land of Oz" and "Emerald City of Oz."

1988 90m/C VHS, Beta *COL*

Paco

G/Family South American lad from the mountains of Columbia journeys alone to Bogota in hopes of retrieving his mule, gambled away by his shifty uncle. Potentially delightful material takes a wrong turn and shifts focus to a subplot about an actor forced by mobsters to participate in a jewel heist. Murky, low-cost look doesn't help either.

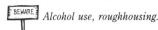 *Alcohol use, roughhousing.*

1975 89m/C Jose Ferrer, Panchito Gomez, Allen (Goorwitz) Garfield, Pernell Roberts, Andre Marquis; **D:** Robert Vincent O'Neil. **VHS, Beta** *GHV*

Paddington Bear

Family Michael Bond's internationally famous ursine creation gets into a variety of adventures after his adoption into the Brown family. Each volume of this two-dimensional and stop-motion animation production includes 11 vignettes.

1985 50m/C VHS, Beta *DIS*

Paddle to the Sea

Primary An Indian boy carves a toy canoe, names it Paddle-To-The-Sea and sets it loose in Lake Superior. Oscar-nominated short follows the canoe's journey to the Atlantic Ocean. Ages 3 to 10.

1966 28m/C VHS, Beta *NFB*

Paddy Beaver

Family Paddy Beaver teaches the residents of the Green Forest how to depend upon each other in this animated edition of Thornton Burgess' "Fables of the Green Forest."

1984 60m/C VHS, Beta *FHE*

The Pagemaster 🐾🐾

G/Family A timid boy named Richard (Macaulay Culkin) dashes into an empty public library to take refuge from a thunderstorm. Film switches from live action to animation in a wondrous riot of color. The boy becomes a cartoon and meets characters from famous books: Capt. Ahab, Long John Silver and many others, the Pagemaster himself (Christopher Lloyd), and books—Horror, Fantasy, Adventure—with their own personalities. All of them take part in adventures with Richard before he can return to the real world. If only the adventures were more original. But you can't argue with the idea that books open up a world of excitement.

 *A few scary creatures and situations.*

1994 76m/C Macaulay Culkin, Christopher Lloyd, Ed Begley Jr., Mel Harris; **D:** Joe Johnston, Maurice Hunt; **W:** David Casci, David Kirschner, Ernie Contreras; **M:** James Horner; **V:** Christopher Lloyd, Whoopi Goldberg, Patrick Stewart, Frank Welker, Leonard Nimoy. **VHS, LV** *FXV*

Paint Your Wagon 🐾🐾 ♪

PG/Family Big-budget western musical-comedy lurches about, occasionally providing stellar moments. In No-Name City, a gold mining boom town, two prospectors share the same Mormon wife while struggling with a classic Lerner and Loewe score. Marvin chews up the sagebrush and, along with Eastwood, attempts to sing,

although Seberg was mercifully dubbed. Presnell, who can sing, stands out. Overlong and occasionally engrossing, with pretty songs warbled plainly and plenty of panoramic scenery. Adapted from the Broadway play. 🎵 I Talk To the Trees; I Still See Elisa; I'm On My Way; Hand Me Down That Can O' Beans; Whoop-Ti-Ay; They Call the Wind Maria; There's a Coach Comin' In; Wandrin' Star; Best Things.

 Suggested sex.

1969 164m/C Lee Marvin, Clint Eastwood, Jean Seberg, Harve Presnell; **D:** Joshua Logan; **W:** Paddy Chayefsky; **M:** Frederick Loewe, Andre Previn, Alan Jay Lerner. **VHS, Beta, LV** *PAR*

Pajama Party 🐾🐾

Family Follow-up to "Bikini Beach" takes the party inside in this fourth entry in the popular "Beach Party" series. Plot is up to beach party realism. Funicello is Avalon-less (although he does have a cameo) so she falls for Martian Kirk instead. He's scouting for an alien invasion, but after he falls into Annette's lap decides to save the planet instead. Typical fluff with the usual beach movie faces present; look for a young Garr as a dancer. Followed by the classic "Beach Blanket Bingo." 🎵 It's That Kind of Day; There Has to Be a Reason; Where Did I Go Wrong?; Pajama Party; Beach Ball; Among the Young; Stuffed Animal.

1964 82m/C Tommy Kirk, Annette Funicello, Elsa Lanchester, Harvey Lembeck, Jesse White, Jody McCrea, Donna Loren, Susan Hart, Bobbi Shaw, Cheryl Sweeten, Luree Holmes, Candy Johnson, Dorothy Lamour, Toni Basil, Teri Garr, Ben Lessy; **Cameos:** Buster Keaton, Frankie Avalon, Don Rickles; **D:** Don Weis; **W:** Louis M. Heyward; **M:** Les Baxter. **VHS, LV** *NO*

The Pallbearer 🐾🐾 ♪

PG-13/Jr. High-Adult Tom Thompson (Schwimmer) is figuring out what he wants to do with his life (he still lives with his mom) when he agrees to be a pallbearer for a high school classmate he can't remember. He then runs into Julie (Paltrow), a beautiful classmate that he once had a crush on. There's also an affair with the dead guy's mother. Sound like "The Graduate" yet??? Well, this one will appeal to teen fans of the TV show "Friends," but keep in mind that the sexual content means it's better suited for older audiences.

 *Scenes in bed implying sex, mild language, and some drinking.*

1995 94m/C David Schwimmer, Gwyneth Paltrow, Barbara Hershey, Michael Rapaport, Carol Kane, Toni Collette, Michael Vartan; **D:** Matt Reeves; **W:** Matt Reeves, Jason Katims; **C:** Robert Elswit; **M:** Stewart Copeland. **VHS** *NYR*

Palooka 🐾🐾 ♪

G/Family Counterjab to night of watching "Rocky" numbers 1 through 33 is this movie version of Ham Fisher's long-running comic strip "Joe Palooka." Jimmy Durante is at his very best as the fast-talking boxing manager who discovers Joe and coaches him for the big fight against the champ. Dated, but Durante will never fade.

 *Roughhousing, alcohol use.*

1934 86m/B Jimmy Durante, Stuart Erwin, Lupe Velez, Robert Armstrong, Thelma Todd, William Cagney; **D:** Ben Stoloff. **VHS, Beta** *NOS, RXM, VYY*

Panda and the Magic Serpent 🦴🦴

Preschool-Primary Japanese cartoon feature based on a Chinese legend about a boy who finds a white snake his parents won't let him keep. The reptile is really an enchanted maiden, who falls in love with the boy when he grows up, though an evil wizard strives to keep them apart. Enter one heroic panda.

1975 78m/C VHS, Beta *FHE*

The Paper 🦴🦴🦴

R/Sr. High-Adult Another crowd pleaser from director Howard follows a red letter day in the life of an editor at the tabloid New York Sun (modeled on the trashy Post). Fresh, fast-moving script by the Koepp brothers (who appear as reporters) offers a fairly accurate portrayal of the business of journalism (including the "brisk" language), with a few Hollywood exceptions. Pace suffers from cutaways to life outside, while script and direction sometimes coast past targets. Propelled by a fine cast, with Keaton the focus as he juggles his personal and professional lives. Close is amusing as a managing editor married to her work, while Duvall is solid as the old newsroom warhorse. Tons of cameos, though those outside of the business may not notice them.

BEWARE *Profanity and brawling. Keaton and Close have a knockdown, drag-out fight. And a character is shot by a mad gunman.*

1994 112m/C Michael Keaton, Robert Duvall, Marisa Tomei, Glenn Close, Randy Quaid, Jason Robards Jr., Jason Alexander, Spalding Gray, Catherine O'Hara, Lynne Thigpen; **D:** Ron Howard; **W:** David Koepp, Steven Koepp; **M:** Randy Newman. **VHS, LV** *MCA*

The Paper Bag Princess

Preschool-Primary Animated tale of a young girl who sets out to rescue the neighboring prince from a fierce dragon. Only the dragon turns out to be a lot more likeable than the boy-prince. Gentle lesson in not judging people based on outward appearance.

1993 25m/C VHS

The Paper Chase 🦴🦴🦴

PG/Jr. High-Adult Students at Harvard Law School suffer and struggle through their first year. A realistic, sometimes acidly humorous look at Ivy League ambitions, with Houseman stealing the show as the tough professor. Wonderful adaptation of the John Jay Osborn novel which later became the basis for the acclaimed television series.

1973 111m/C Timothy Bottoms, Lindsay Wagner, John Houseman, Graham Beckel, Edward Herrmann, James Naughton, Craig Richard

Nelson, Bob Lydiard; **D:** James Bridges; **W:** James Bridges; **M:** John Williams. **Award Nominations:** Academy Awards '73: Best Adapted Screenplay, Best Sound; **Awards:** Academy Awards '73: Best Supporting Actor (Houseman); Golden Globe Awards '74: Best Supporting Actor (Houseman); National Board of Review Awards '73: Best Supporting Actor (Houseman). **VHS, Beta, LV** *FOX, BTV*

Paper Moon 🦴🦴🦴 🦴

PG/Jr. High-Adult Winning story set in 1930s Kansas, with Bible-wielding con artist Moses Pray stuck with a nine-year-old orphan who can see right through his scams. But little Addie (star O'Neal's daughter, Tatum) also watches out for him, and soon a paternal relationship develops in spite of their antagonism. Irresistible chemistry between the O'Neals helped Tatum grab the Oscar (she was the youngest actor at the time to take home a statue). Cinematically picturesque and cynical enough to keep overt sentimentalism away. Based on Joe David Brown's novel, "Addie Pray."

BEWARE *Addie chainsmokes; plus alcohol use, mature themes, offscreen sex, and violence.*

1973 102m/B Ryan O'Neal, Tatum O'Neal, Madeline Kahn, John Hillerman, Randy Quaid; **D:** Peter Bogdanovich; **W:** Alvin Sargent. **Award Nominations:** Academy Awards '73: Best Adapted Screenplay, Best Sound, Best Supporting Actress (Kahn); **Awards:** Academy Awards '73: Best Supporting Actress (O'Neal); National Board of Review Awards '73: 10 Best Films of the Year. **VHS, Beta, LV** *PAR, BTV*

Papillon 🦴🦴🦴

PG/Jr. High-Adult McQueen is a criminal sent to Devil's Island in the 1930s determined to escape from the Lemote prison. Hoffman is the swindler he befriends. A series of escapes and recaptures follow. Box-office winner based on the autobiographical writings of French thief Henri Charriere. Excellent portrayal of prison life and fine performances from the prisoners. Certain segments would have been better left on the cutting room floor. The film's title refers to the lead's butterfly tattoo.

1973 150m/C Steve McQueen, Dustin Hoffman, Victor Jory, George Coulouris, Anthony Zerbe; **D:** Franklin J. Schaffner; **M:** Jerry Goldsmith. **VHS, Beta, LV** *FOX, WAR*

Parade 🦴🦴🦴

Family French comic filmmaker and mime artist Jacques Tati fashioned this as a loving tribute to the circus that can be savored by all ages, though grownups might better appreciate the rhythms and magical transformations of its show-within-a-show format. A European troupe puts on a three-ring circus, with Tati (refreshingly agile and limber compared to his trudging Mr. Hulot character) as both ringmaster and performer in a series of acts. Highlight: a portly gentleman from the audience tries again and again to mount a bucking donkey.

1974 85m/C Jacques Tati; **D:** Jacques Tati; **W:** Jacques Tati. **VHS, LV** *HMV, CRC, FCT*

The Paradine Case 🦴🦴 🦴

Jr. High-Adult Passable Hitchcock romancer about a young lawyer who falls in love with the woman he's defending for murder, not knowing whether she is innocent or guilty. Script could be tighter and more cohesive. $70,000 of the $3 million budget were spent recreating the original Bailey courtroom. Based on the novel by Robert Hichens.

1947 125m/B Gregory Peck, Alida Valli, Ann Todd, Louis Jourdan, Charles Laughton, Charles Coburn, Ethel Barrymore, Leo G. Carroll; **D:** Alfred Hitchcock. **VHS, Beta, LV** *FOX*

Paradise 🦴🦴🦴

PG-13/Jr. High-Adult Ten-year-old Willard goes to the country to stay with his pregnant mother's married friends (real-life husband and wife Johnson and Griffith). From the outset it's clear that the couple's relationship is on the rocks, making the boy's assimilation all the more difficult, until he forms a charming relationship with a little girl who helps reconcile the adults. Largely predictable, this remake of the French film "Le Grand Chemin" works thanks to the surprisingly good work of its ensemble cast and gorgeous South Carolina scenery.

> 🐾 BEWARE 🐾 *Mature themes—source of the couple's unhappiness is the recent death of their own child.*

1991 112m/C Melanie Griffith, Don Johnson, Elijah Wood, Thora Birch, Sheila McCarthy, Eve Gordon, Louise Latham, Greg Travis, Sarah Trigger; **D:** Mary Agnes Donoghue; **W:** Mary Agnes Donoghue; **M:** David Newman. **VHS, Beta** *TOU*

The Parent Trap 🦴🦴 🦴

Family Mills plays twin sisters Susan and Sharon who have never met until an accidental reunion at summer camp in this heartwarming comedy. Posing as each other to visit the other's households, they conspire to bring their divorced parents together again. Well-known Disney fluff, overlong but a source of fond false hopes for a generation of kids from broken homes. Based on the novel by Eric Kastner. Followed by several made-for-TV sequels featuring the now grown-up twins.

1961 127m/C Hayley Mills, Maureen O'Hara, Brian Keith, Charlie Ruggles, Una Merkel, Leo G. Carroll; **D:** David Swift. **VHS, Beta, LV** *DIS*

Parenthood 🦴🦴🦴

PG-13/Jr. High-Adult Grown siblings struggle with various crises of parenthood in the same family; the nervous, newly divorced mother whose teenage daughter dates an irresponsible stock-car driver; a yuppie couple finding that their adolescent boy has deep psychological problems; a super dad who's a lousy husband; and the college drop-out who breezes into town towing a mixed-race son nobody knew about before. Genuinely warm ensemble comedy-drama that makes having children look like a nightmare, then a joy with a careful twist of storyline. Some of it treads sitcom territory (in fact it inspired a fast-faded network sitcom), but some fine family nuances and the life-affirming finale more than compensate.

> 🐾 BEWARE 🐾 *Profanity, mature themes, sex talk (including an incident with a vibrator), drug talk.*

If you like *Parenthood* (1989), you'll love:

Baby Boom (1987)

Father of the Bride (1950)

Father of the Bride (1991)

Father of the Bride, Part II (1996)

Father's Little Dividend (1951)

I'll Do Anything (1993)

Look Who's Talking (1989)

Look Who's Talking Now (1993)

Look Who's Talking, Too (1990)

Mr. Mom (1983)

North (1994)

Three Men and a Baby (1987)

Three Men and a Little Lady (1990)

Yours, Mine, Ours (1968)

1989 124m/C Steve Martin, Mary Steenburgen, Dianne Wiest, Martha Plimpton, Keanu Reeves, Tom Hulce, Jason Robards Jr., Rick Moranis, Harley Jane Kozak, Joaquin Rafael (Leaf) Phoenix, Paul Linke, Dennis Dugan; **D:** Ron Howard; **W:** Lowell Ganz, Babaloo Mandel, Ron Howard; **M:** Randy Newman. **VHS, Beta, LV** *MCA*

The Party 🦴🦴🦴

Jr. High-Adult Somewhat overlooked Peter Sellers vehicle that looks like a preview of the spectacular damage the star would wreak in Blake Edwards' "Pink Panther" pics of the 1970s. Here he plays an Indian (as in Bombay) movie actor of colossal clumsiness, who is mistakenly invited to a lavish Hollywood party. Some brilliantly choreographed slapstick occurs as he bumbles around the posh mansion, compensating for outdated hippie-era references and a general lack of any other sort of plot.

> 🐾 BEWARE 🐾 *Alcohol use.*

1968 99m/C Peter Sellers, Claudine Longet, Marge Champion, Sharron Kimberly, Denny Miller, Gavin MacLeod, Carol Wayne; **D:** Blake Edwards; **W:** Blake Edwards; **M:** Henry Mancini. **VHS** *MGM, TVC*

Past the Bleachers 🦴🦴 ⌐

PG/Family Sentimental TV movie finds Anderson starring as Bill Parish—a man still lost by the death of his 11-year-old son. Reluctantly, he agrees to coach the Little League team his son had played on, with the help of an opinionated senior citizen (scene-stealer Hughes), and is drawn to the boy who turns out to be the team's star player. The appropriately named Lucky Diamond (Fricke) is both mute and of a mysterious family background, and bonding proves therapeutic for both Bill and the youngster. Based on a novel by Christopher A. Bohjalian.

> **BEWARE** *Themes about death and how adults and children deal with it.*

1995 120m/C Richard Dean Anderson, Barnard Hughes, Grayson Fricke, Glynnis O'Connor, Ken Jenkins; **D:** Michael Switzer; **W:** Don Rhymer; **M:** Stewart Levin. **VHS, LV** *HMK*

Pastime 🦴🦴🦴

PG/Sr. High-Adult Bittersweet baseball elegy set in the minor leagues in 1957. Roy, a boyish 41-year-old pitcher, can't face his impending retirement and pals around with the team outcast, a 17-year-old rookie who's the franchise's first black player. The old pro ends up teaching the kid his championship moves. Beautifully written and acted, though quite sad as the likeable Roy enters his final inning.

> **BEWARE** *Ballpark profanity, alcohol use, roughhousing.*

1991 94m/C William Russ, Scott Plank, Glenn Plummer, Noble Willingham, Jeffrey Tambor, Deidre O'Connell; **D:** Robin B. Armstrong. **VHS, LV** *COL*

Pat and Mike 🦴🦴🦴

Family War of the sexes rages in this comedy about a leathery sports promoter who futilely attempts to train a woman for athletic competition. Tracy and Hepburn have fine chemistry, but supporting players contribute too. Watch for the first on-screen appearance of Bronson (then Charles Buchinski) as a crook.

1952 95m/B Spencer Tracy, Katharine Hepburn, Aldo Ray, Jim Backus, William Ching, Sammy White, Phyllis Povah, Charles Bronson, Chuck Connors, Mae Clarke, Carl "Alfalfa" Switzer; **D:** George Cukor; **W:** Ruth Gordon, Garson Kanin. **VHS, Beta, LV** *MGM*

Paul Bunyan

Primary-Jr. High Paul and his huge blue ox Babe were the greatest pair of loggers in the west. Here Disney animation retells their tall tale in appropriate larger-than-life fashion.

1958 17m/C VHS, Beta *DSN,, MTI*

P.C.U. 🦴🦴

PG-13/Sr. High-Adult Satire on campus political correctness follows freshman Tom Lawrence's (Young) adventures as he navigates the treacherous waters of Port Chester University (PCU). He falls in with the gang from the Pit, the militantly non-PC dorm, who encourage bizarre and offensive behavior. Essentially a modern update of "National Lampoon's Animal House," but without the brilliance; add half a bone for tackling the thorny sensitivity issue in a humorous way that parodies, but shouldn't offend. Actor Bochner's directorial debut.

> **BEWARE** *Profanity. Abuse of food, drugs and alcohol.*

1994 81m/C Jeremy Piven, Chris Young, David Spade, Sarah Trigger, Jessica Walter, Jon Favreau, Megan Ward, Jake Busey; **Cameos:** George Clinton; **D:** Hart Bochner; **W:** Adam Leff, Zak Penn; **M:** Steve Vai. **VHS** *FXV*

Peachboy

Family From Japan comes the story of the boy found living in a gigantic peach. A poor, barren couple discover Peachboy and raise him until he becomes a master warrior who conquers a clan of child-snatching ogres. Part of the "Rabbit Ears" series of worldwide stories read against glorious painted illustrations (rather than animation).

1991 30m/C M: Ryuichi Sakamoto. **VHS, Beta** *MVD, MCA, FCT*

The Peanut Butter Solution 🦴🦴🦴

PG/Family The second entry in Rock Demers' Tales for All is a wild piece of pure imagination that's slow to get started, then watch out! Eleven-year-old Michael looks in the window of a spooky house and sees something so frightful that his hair falls out. Helpful ghosts leave a recipe for a magical hair-replacement ointment, but Michael uses too much of the key ingredient—peanut butter—and his follicles sprout at an uncontrollable rate. And that's only the beginning; hop aboard this delightful, all-ages film and enjoy the ride.

> **BEWARE** *One off-color joke about a kid who applies the peanut-butter solution to a more private hairless area.*

1985 96m/C Matthew Mackay, Siluck Saysanasy, Alison Podbrey, Michael Maillot, Griffith Brewer, Michael Hogan, Helen Hughes; **D:** Michael Rubbo; **W:** Michael Rubbo; **M:** Lewis Furey. **VHS, Beta** *NWV, VTR, HHE*

The Pebble and the Penguin 🦴🦴 ⌐

G/Family It ain't the tuxedo, it's what's inside it. That's the message of this animated story of a shy penguin named Hubie (voiced by Martin Short). Hubie has the colds for Marina (Annie Golden) and finds the most beautiful stone to lay on her feet—not at, ON. That's the way Adeli penguins get engaged (this is a true fact). But there's a rival in the picture. Hubie falls into the sea and is swept away to Tahiti but, a fool for love, he must return to Antarctica before mating season ends. The songs are by Barry Manilow. It's pretty to look at, and adequately entertaining for people under 7.

1994 74m/C W: Rachel Koretsky, Steve Whitestone; **M:** Barry Manilow, Bruce Sussman, Mark Watters; **V:** Martin Short, Annie Golden, Tim Curry, James Belushi. **VHS, LV** *MGM*

Pecos Bill

Family Meet the man who used the Grand Canyon for a swimmin' hole, dug the Rio Grande and used the Texas panhandle for a fryin' pan. From Shelly Duvall's "Tall Tales and Legends" series. Originally made for cable television.

1986 50m/C Steve Guttenberg, Martin Mull, Claude Akins, Rebecca DeMornay. **VHS** *FOX, COL*

Pecos Bill

Preschool-Primary Disney cartoon version of the famous western folk hero raised by coyotes, narrated by another legend of the range. Bill manages to dig the Rio Grande and the Grand Canyon, and ride a cyclone.

1990 17m/C VHS, Beta *DSN, MTI*

Pecos Bill

Preschool-Primary Williams reads the text of the rollicking tall tales featuring frontier hero Pecos Bill roping cyclones and moving rivers. Musical accompaniment by Ry Cooder.

19?? 30m/C VHS *MLT, KUI*

Pee Wee's Big Adventure

PG/Primary-Adult Pee-wee (Paul Reubens), a childlike man with an innocent mien, sets off in search of his stolen bicycle. The pursuit is a hoot. A fortune teller advises Pee-wee that his bike is at the Alamo, and away Pee-wee hitchhikes. Best scenes involve Pee-wee in a biker bar dancing to "Tequila" and a tour of the Alamo with straight-faced guide Jan Hooks. There's no movie quite like this one. Tim Burton directed. Ages 8 and up.

BEWARE *Double entendres.*

1985 92m/C Paul (Pee Wee Herman) Reubens, Elizabeth Daily, Mark Holton, Diane Salinger, Judd Omen, Cassandra Peterson, James Brolin, Morgan Fairchild, Tony Bill, Jan Hooks; **D:** Tim Burton; **W:** Paul (Pee Wee Herman) Reubens, Phil Hartman, Michael Varhol; **M:** Danny Elfman. **VHS, Beta, LV** *WAR*

Pee Wee's Playhouse Festival of Fun

Family The TV series had a crazy brilliance all its own, as the man-child Pee Wee romps with such self-mocking characters as the King of Cartoons, grumpy Captain Carl, handsome hunk Tito and the beautiful Miss Yvonne. This tape compilation includes five episodes; 15 volumes of individual half-hour episodes are also available. Note however, that "The Pee Wee Herman Show" on HBO Video, is an early, more risque stand-up comedy special for adults rather than youngsters.

1988 123m/C Paul (Pee Wee Herman) Reubens. **VHS, Beta** *MED*

Peggy Sue Got Married

PG-13/Jr. High-Adult Uneven but entertaining comedy about an unhappily married middle-aged woman who takes a trip back in time. Turner's the Peggy Sue in question, and she's about to divorce her obnoxious hubby Cage. While attending her high school reunion, Turner falls unconscious and awakens to find herself back in school in 1960, with an opportunity to change her life. But will she? Film takes a fairly mature but entertaining look at the question, eschewing most of the ready-made time-traveling woman in a girl's body gimmicks. Turner shows considerable range in the dash from 43 to 17 and back again, while Cage is sufficiently annoying both as a teen and a middle-aged appliance salesman.

BEWARE *Profanity and suggested sex.*

1986 103m/C Kathleen Turner, Nicolas Cage, Catherine Hicks, Maureen O'Sullivan, John Carradine, Helen Hunt, Lisa Jane Persky, Barbara Harris, Joan Allen, Kevin J. O'Connor, Barry Miller, Don Murray, Leon Ames, Sofia Coppola, Sachi Parker, Jim Carrey; **D:** Francis Ford Coppola; **W:** Jerry Leichtling, Arlene Sarner; **M:** John Barry. **VHS, Beta, LV** *FOX*

The Pelican Brief

PG-13/Jr. High-Adult Tulane law student Darby Shaw (Roberts) writes a speculative brief on the murders of two Supreme Court justices that results in more murder and sends her running for her life. Fairly faithful to the Grisham bestseller, but the multitude of characters is confusing. Pakula adds style and star-power, but much will depend on your tolerance for paranoid political thrillers and ability to accept Roberts as the smart cookie who hits on the right answer and then manages to keep herself alive while bodies are dropping all around her. Washington is sharp as reporter Gray Grantham, the guy Roberts looks like she falls hard for (but the book's romance is nowhere to be seen).

BEWARE *Violence, explosions and harrowing pursuit.*

1993 141m/C Julia Roberts, Denzel Washington, John Heard, Tony Goldwyn, Stanley Tucci, James B. Sikking, William Atherton, Robert Culp, John Lithgow, Sam Shepard; **Cameos:** Hume Cronyn; **D:** Alan J. Pakula; **W:** Alan J. Pakula; **M:** James Horner. **VHS, LV, 8mm** *WAR*

Penny Serenade

Family Newlyweds adopt a child, but tragedy awaits. Simplistic story nonetheless proves to be a moving experience. They don't make 'em like this anymore, and no one plays Grant better than Grant. Dunne is adequate. Also available colorized.

1941 120m/B Cary Grant, Irene Dunne, Beulah Bondi, Edgar Buchanan; **D:** George Stevens. **VHS, LV** *CNG, NOS, PSM*

People

Primary Lively, lovely animated musical finds a girl named Cara who wishes that people were more alike so they wouldn't fight the way her parents do. Her grandfather (voiced by Hume Cronyn) takes Cara on a magical

Pals Hubie and Rocko in "The Pebble and the Penguin."

global tour to illustrate how differences make the world more interesting. Beautifully animated segments about sports, food, religion etc. help make the point. Musical performers include Lea Salonga and Chaka Khan. Ages 4 to 9.

1995 m/C VHS *AVE*

The People That Time Forgot

PG/Jr. High-Adult Sequel to "The Land That Time Forgot" has rescue team returning to a world of prehistoric monsters to bring back a man left there after the first film. Silly adventure; a case of the plot that time forgot.

⚠ BEWARE *Violence.*

1977 90m/C Doug McClure, Patrick Wayne, Sarah Douglas, Dana Gillespie, Thorley Walters, Shane Rimmer; **D:** Kevin Connor. **VHS, Beta**

Pepper and His Wacky Taxi ♫ ♭

G/Family Astin, a favorite character actor thanks to his TV role as Gomez Addams, plays a more conventional father of four who buys a '59 Cadillac and starts a cab company. Mild fun with a curious cast.

1972 79m/C John Astin, Frank Sinatra Jr., Jackie Gayle, Alan Sherman; **D:** Alex Grasshof. **VHS, Beta** *UNI*

A Perfect World ♫♫ ♭

PG-13/Sr. High-Adult Butch Haynes (Costner) is an escaped con who takes 8-year-old fatherless Phillip (who's also a Jehovah's Witness) as a hostage in 1963 Texas, becoming surrogate father to the lad as they attempt to evade the law on the backroads. Meanwhile, amid the man-boy bonding, crusty Texas Ranger Red Garnett (Eastwood) is hot on their trail in a trailer with Dern as a sidekick. Unusual premise is twist on standard fugitive road picture, as director Eastwood tries to bring something new to the genre. Butch, played with wooden intensity by Costner, is portrayed as a bad guy, though very intelligent, who's blessed with a sense of morality, though a wee bit twisted. He's also very sensitive to the issue of child abuse, based on his relationship with his own father. Lowther is convincing as the needy little boy, one of the drama's strengths. Ambitious, disjointed, but interesting, with one of the longer death scenes in recent film history. Eastwood also cowrote one of the songs.

⚠ BEWARE ⚠ *Violence; salty language; implied attempted child molestation.*

1993 138m/C Kevin Costner, T.J. Lowther, Clint Eastwood, Laura Dern, Keith Szarabajka, Leo Burmester, Paul Hewitt, Bradley Whitford, Ray McKinnon, Wayne Dehart, Jennifer Griffin, Linda Hart; **D:** Clint Eastwood; **W:** John Lee Hancock; **M:** Lennie Niehaus. **VHS, LV** *WAR*

The Perils of Penelope Pitstop

Family Convoy of old Saturday-morning cartoons starring animated motorist Penelope Pitstop, who has to ward off the villainous Sylvester Sneekly while she drives in races around the world. Additional volumes available.

1969 60m/C V: Janet Waldo, Paul Lynde, Mel Blanc, Paul Winchell, Don Messick. **VHS, Beta**

The Perils of Problemina 🦴🦴

Preschool-Primary Animated film about ants saving their families from a rampaging anteater.

19?? 90m/C VHS, Beta *LIV*

Permanent Record 🦴🦴🦴

PG-13/Jr. High-Adult Hyper-sincere drama about a popular high schooler's suicide and the emotional reactions of those he left behind. Great performance from Reeves. Be careful of touchy subject matter that may only be suitable for older children.

⚠ BEWARE ⚠ *Profanity, drugs, mature themes, but all for a noble cause.*

1988 92m/C Alan Boyce, Keanu Reeves, Michelle Meyrink, Jennifer Rubin, Pamela Gidley, Michael Elgart, Richard Bradford, Barry Corbin, Kathy Baker; **D:** Marisa Silver; **W:** Jarre Fees, Alice Liddle, Larry Ketron; **M:** Joe Strummer. **VHS, Beta, LV** *PAR*

Pete Seeger's Family Concert

Family At an outdoor concert, the world's pre-eminent folksinger performs sing-along favorites such as "Skip to My Lou," "Freight Train," "This Land Is Your Land," and "She'll Be Comin' Round the Mountain." He also tells the story of the fearsome giant AbiYoYo and the little boy with the ukulele who gets the better of him. A delight. Ages 3 and up.

1992 45m/C VHS *SMV, MVD, TVC*

Peter and the Magic Egg

Preschool-Primary Cartoon story of Amish farmers Mama and Papa Doppler who avoid losing their farm to greedy Tobias Tinwhiskers thanks to their mysterious foundling Peter Paas. Narrator Bolger was the Scarecrow from the classic "Wizard of Oz," is that why Tinwhiskers looks just like the Tin Woodman? Also on the tape with this animated TV special are two vintage Tex Avery 'toons, "Jerky Turkey" and Casper in "The Friendly Ghost."

1983 60m/C V: Ray Bolger. **VHS, Beta** *FHE, MTI, PMS*

Peter and the Wolf

Family The classic tale of the young woodsman is told Disney-style.

1946 30m/C VHS, Beta *DIS*

Peter and the Wolf

Preschool-Primary Puppeteer Jim Gamble uses a variety of marionettes to portray people, animals, and instruments in this tale based on Sergei Prokofiev's musical work. Prokofiev himself appears in puppet form to explain how a composer writes. Music performed by the Hamburg Symphony Orchestra.

1992 30m/C VHS *BOG, BTV*

Peter and the Wolf

Family Yes, the flute still represents the bird, the oboe stands for the duck and so on. But something's different in this fine new version of Prokofiev's musical tale: there's a story around the story. Kirstie Alley and young Ross Malinger are a mother and son visiting her father (Lloyd Bridges) in Switzerland—never mind that the story is Russian. Mom tells the story of Peter, which is shown as a cartoon with characters created by animation legend Chuck Jones. The boy is enthralled, and there's a nice surprise waiting for him when it's over. A filmed afterword explains about the different musical instruments. Ages 3 to 9.

1995 60m/C Lloyd Bridges, Kirstie Alley, Ross Malinger; **D:** George Daugherty. **VHS** *BMG*

Peter and the Wolf

Preschool-Jr. High Animated version of the classic tale, narrated by "Wizard of Oz" Scarecrow Ray Bolger.

19?? 82m/C VHS, Beta *VES*

Peter Cottontail: How He Got His Hop

Preschool-Primary Puppet tale in which Peter wants to enter the Meadowlands Spring Talent Show but can't figure out what he's good at. An assortment of animals try to help him out (most amusing is a Bob Dylanesque dog poet). Marionette production from Jim Gamble, whose string creations can ride skateboards and even juggle, making them more clever than most people we know.

1993 30m/C VHS *BOG*

Peter Cottontail's Adventures

Preschool-Primary Peter loves to play practical jokes until no one wants to be his friend anymore, teaching him the importance of his Green Forest cohorts like Johnny and Polly Woodchuck, Jimmy Skunk, Chatterer Chipmunk, Reddy and Granny Fox, and Sammy Bluejay, all cartoon adaptations of the classic characters from Thornton W. Burgess. See also "Fables of the Green Forest."

1978 70m/C VHS, Beta *FHE*

Peter Lundy and the Medicine Hat Stallion 🎵🎵 ▷

Family A teenaged Pony Express rider must outrun the Indians and battle the elements in order to carry mail from the Nebraska Territory to the West Coast in this made for TV film.

1977 85m/C Leif Garrett, Mitchell Ryan, Bibi Besch, John Quade, Milo O'Shea; **D:** Michael O'Herlihy. **VHS, Beta** *LIV, VES, VTR*

Peter-No-Tail 🎵🎵 ▷

Family Tail-less kitten wins the Cats Mastership and the heart of Molly Cream-Nose. Animation with an all-star gallery of voices.

1983 82m/C V: Ken Berry, Dom DeLuise, Richard Kline, Tina Louise, Larry Storch, June Lockhart. **VHS, Beta**

Peter Pan 🎵🎵🎵

G/Family Disney classic about the great Pan, the boy who never grew up, who takes the younger members of the Darling family to Never Never Land for perilous adventures fighting Captain Hook. Wonderful animation and action, forgettable tunes (not to be confused with the Mark Charlap-Jule Stein songs popularized by Mary Martin on Broadway). Based on J.M. Barrie's book and play.

1953 76m/C D: Hamilton Luske; **V:** Bobby Driscoll, Kathryn Beaumont, Hans Conried, Heather Angel, Candy Candido. **VHS, Beta, LV** *DIS, APD, HMV*

Peter Pan 🎵🎵🎵 ▷

Family A TV classic, this videotape of a performance of the 1954 Broadway musical, adapted from the J.M. Barrie classic, feature Martin in one of her most famous incarnations, as the boy who never wants to grow up. Songs include: "I'm Flying," "Neverland," and "I Won't Grow Up."

1960 100m/C Mary Martin, Cyril Ritchard, Sondra Lee, Heather Halliday, Luke Halpin; **D:** Vincent J. Donehue. **VHS, Beta, LV** *GKK, COL, MLT*

Peter Pan & the Pirates: Demise of Hook

Preschool-Primary In an attempt to cash in on Peter Pan-a-mania (which never quite happened) with the release of Spielberg's movie "Hook," the Fox Television Networks aired this cartoon adventure series based on the J.M. Barrie characters battling Captain Hook in Neverland.

1992 23m/C V: Tim Curry. **VHS** *FXV*

Peter Pan/Hiawatha

Family Two-volume set containing the classic fairy tales "Peter Pan" and "Hiawatha" in short animated form.

1990 63m/C VHS *FHE*

Peter, Paul and Mary: Peter, Paul and Mommy, Too

Family A mere 25 years after they recorded their first family concert album the folk trio recorded another, and by this time video had been invented—not to mention they could legitimately call themselves Peter, Paul and Grandma. PP&M remain highly entertaining. Tunes include "The Fox," "Day Is Done" "Pastures of Plenty," "Somos El Barco (We Are the Boat)," "Right Field," "Blowing in the Wind," "Day Is Done" and, of course, "Puff the Magic Dragon." Ages 4 and up.

1993 90m/C VHS *WRV, MVD, BTV*

Pete's Dragon 🎵🎵 ▷

G/Family Elliott, an enormous, sometimes-invisible dragon with a penchant for clumsy heroics, accompanies poor orphan Pete, newly arrived in a fishing village while on the run from his nasty stepfamily. Energetic but hopelessly juvenile Disney epic, crammed full of forgettable songs (and one not so forgettable—Reddy's hit "Candle on the Water") and large-scale slapstick. Elliott the dragon appears in cartoon form, while everything else is live-action, a technique perfected over a decade later with "Who Framed Roger Rabbit?" Main animator here is Disney dissident Don Bluth, who later formed his own 'toon studio.

⚠ BEWARE *Alcohol use—lots of it early on, apparently in the belief that public drunkenness is the cutest thing. Even Elliott drains a flask.*

1977 128m/C Helen Reddy, Shelley Winters, Mickey Rooney, Jim Dale, Red Buttons, Sean Marshall, Jim Backus, Jeff Conaway; **D:** Don Chaffey; **W:** Malcolm Marmorstein; **V:** Charlie Callas. **VHS, Beta, LV** *DIS, FCT*

The Phantom 🎵🎵 ▷

PG/Primary-Adult Ripsnorting Saturday matinee kind of adventure set in 1936 finds titular hero (Billy Zane) scampering around the jungle in purple tights riding his white horse, with his faithful wolf at his side, keeping the place safe from evildoers. The Phantom is actually a commuter, living part of the time in the jungle on the island of Bengalla, the rest of the time in the suburbs on the Island of Long. Enter bad Xander Drax (Treat Williams) who covets Bengalla's mystic skulls which hold the promise of superpowers. Williams is a treat as dastardly Drax, Zane does phine as the Phantom and a couple of adventurous women (Kristy Swanson and Catherine Zeta Jones) augment the fun. Ages 8 and up.

⚠ BEWARE *Violence of the Pow! Biff! kind; an oath or two.*

1996 100m/C Billy Zane, Kristy Swanson, Treat Williams, Catherine Zeta Jones, James Remar, Jon Tenney, Patrick McGoohan, Samantha Eggar, Cary-Hiroyuki Tagawa, Robert Coleby, David Proval; **D:** Simon Wincer; **W:** Jeffrey Boam; **C:** David Burr; **M:** David Newman. **VHS** *NYR*

Phantom 2040

Preschool-Primary New superhero that protects nature and life from evil.

1996 ?m/C VHS *FHE, LIV*

Phantom 2040 Movie: The Ghost Who Walks

Family Another version of The Phantom comic book series. Teenager Kit Walker discovers his destiny when a mysterious stranger tells him about his late father and how Kit must carry on his father's legacy as a superhero called the Phantom. A purple suit renders Kit invisible and he finds himself battling his dad's old nemesis, Rebecca Madison, who's out to destroy the Earth's resources.

1995 97m/C VHS *FHE*

The Phantom Creeps

Family Evil Dr. Zorka, armed with a meteorite chunk which can bring an army to a standstill, provides the impetus for this enjoyable 12-episode serial.

BEWARE *Violence.*

1939 235m/B Bela Lugosi, Dorothy Arnold, Robert Kent, Regis Toomey; ***D:*** Ford Beebe, Saul Goodkind. **VHS, Beta** *NOS, SNC, VCN*

The Phantom Empire

Family One of the strangest serials ever made. Publicity at the time claimed the writer dreamed up the story while doped with anesthesia at the dentist's! That's as good as any explanation, as singing cowboy Autry, playing himself, discovers that deep under his radio station/dude ranch is the lost kingdom of Murania, ruled by an evil queen and patrolled by robots (who look like the "Oz" Tin Man in aluminum stetsons). Gene fights life-or-death battles to prevent world conquest by the cloaked 'Thunder Riders'—but no matter how bad things get, Autry always manages to escape above ground in time for another song cue on his radio variety program. Really must be seen to be believed. In 12 episodes.

1935 245m/B Gene Autry, Frankie Darro, Betsy King Ross, Smiley Burnette; ***D:*** B. Reeves Eason, Otto Brower. **VHS, Beta** *NOS, SNC, VYY*

Phantom of the Opera

Family Deformed, skull-faced masked man who lives under the Paris Opera House wants a young soprano to sing just for him in a cut-rate cartoon adaptation of the oft-redone Gaston Leroux novel.

1987 60m/C VHS, Beta, LV *JFK*

Phantom Tollbooth

G/Family Milo, a live-action boy, drives his car into a cartoon world where the numbers are at war with the letters, and he has been chosen to save Rhyme and Reason to bring stability back to the Land of Wisdom. Completely unique; the first feature film from Warner Brothers animator Chuck Jones, it combines his Bugs-Bunny sense of mischief with more surreal and intellectual interests. Don't rule out adult viewers by any means. Based on Norman Justers' metaphorical novel.

1969 89m/C *D:* Chuck Jones; ***V:*** Mel Blanc, Hans Conried. **VHS, Beta** *MGM*

If you like *The Phantom* (1996), you'll love:

Batman (1989)
Batman Forever (1995)
Batman Returns (1992)
Blankman (1994)
Hero at Large (1980)
The Mask (1994)
The Meteor Man (1993)
The Shadow (1994)
Superman 1: The Movie (1978)
Superman 2 (1980)
Superman 3 (1983)
Superman 4: The Quest for Peace (1987)

Phar Lap

PG/Family "Free Willy" director Wincer made this factual saga of a legendary Australian racehorse who rose from obscurity to win nearly 40 races in just three years before tragically—and suspiciously—dying in 1932 (Aussies still blame American gambling syndicates for the deed).

BEWARE *Mature themes.*

1984 107m/C Ron Leibman, Tom Burlinson, Judy Morris, Celia de Burgh; ***D:*** Simon Wincer; ***W:*** David Williamson. **VHS, Beta** *FOX*

Phenomenon

PG/Primary-Adult Average nice guy George Malley (Travolta) is changed to a genius when he encounters a bright, white light on his 37th birthday. This development brings him to the attention of the scientific community and, of course, the military. But while others seek his counsel, the local folk, afraid of his newfound powers,

shun him. Good-natured weeper plays on the feel good strings of its viewers, which is a nice switch for Travolta.

> ⚠ BEWARE *Supernatural occurrences and an involved plot may not be suitable for youngsters.*

1996 117m/C John Travolta, Robert Duvall, Kyra Sedgwick, Forest Whitaker; *D:* Jon Turteltaub; *W:* Gerald DiPego. **VHS** *NYR*

Philadelphia 🎬🎬🎬 ◿

PG-13/Jr. High-Adult AIDS goes Hollywood as hotshot corporate attorney Andrew Beckett (Hanks), fired because he has the disease, hires brilliant but homophobic personal injury attorney Washington as his counsel when he sues for discrimination with the support of his mate and close-knit family. Hanks claims the title as hottest actor in America with his moving, dignified portrayal of a dying man denied his basic rights and determined to fight. Washington is superb as well as the lawyer forced to acknowledge his own prejudices in order to present his client's case. Woodward and Robards lead an expert supporting cast. Criticized by some for sterilizing its homosexual element, drama doesn't probe deeply into the gay lifestyle, focusing instead on the human search for justice and compassion. Emotional operatic set piece with Hanks and Washington will likely land in classic vault. Demme directs with confidence in taking AIDS issue into mainstream entertainment, complete with soundtrack contributions from Neil Young and Bruce Springsteen.

> ⚠ BEWARE *Derogatory slang for homosexuals. Graphic depiction (through makeup) of AIDS' effects on a person.*

1993 125m/C Tom Hanks, Denzel Washington, Antonio Banderas, Jason Robards Jr., Joanne Woodward, Mary Steenburgen, Ron Vawter, Robert Ridgely, Obba Babatunde, Robert Castle, Daniel Chapman, Roger Corman, John Bedford Lloyd, Roberta Maxwell, Warren Miller, Anna Deavere Smith, Kathryn Witt, Andre B. Blake, Ann Dowd, Bradley Whitford, Chandra Wilson, Charles Glenn, Peter Jacobs, Paul Lazar, Dan Olmstead, Joey Perillo, Lauren Roselli, Bill Rowe, Lisa Talerico, Daniel von Bargen, Tracey Walter; *Cameos:* Karen Finley, David Drake, Quentin Crisp; *D:* Jonathan Demme; *W:* Ron Nyswaner; *M:* Howard Shore. **Award Nominations:** Academy Awards '93: Best Makeup, Best Original Screenplay, Best Song ("Philadelphia"); MTV Movie Awards '94: Best Film, Best On-Screen Duo (Tom Hanks/ Denzel Washington), Best Song ("Streets of Philadelphia"); **Awards:** Academy Awards '93: Best Actor (Hanks), Best Song ("Streets of Philadelphia"); Golden Globe Awards '94: Best Actor—Drama (Hanks), Best Song ("Streets of Philadelphia"). **VHS, LV, 8mm** *COL*

The Philadelphia Story 🎬🎬🎬🎬

Family Woman's plans to marry again go awry when her dashing ex-husband arrives on the scene. Matters are further complicated when a loopy reporter—assigned to spy on the nuptials—falls in love with the blushing bride. Classic comedy, with trio of Hepburn, Grant, and Stewart all serving aces. Based on the hit Broadway play by Philip Barry, and remade as the musical "High Society" in 1956 (stick to the original). Also available colorized.

1940 112m/B Katharine Hepburn, Cary Grant, James Stewart, Ruth Hussey, Roland Young, John Howard, John Halliday, Virginia Weidler, Henry Daniell, Hillary Brooke, Mary Nash; *D:* George Cukor; *W:* Donald Ogden Stewart; *M:* Franz Waxman. **Award Nominations:**

Academy Awards '40: Best Actress (Hepburn), Best Director (Cukor), Best Picture, Best Supporting Actress (Hussey); **Awards:** Academy Awards '40: Best Actor (Stewart), Best Screenplay. **VHS, Beta, LV** *MGM, BTV, HMV*

The Phoenix and the Magic Carpet 🎬🎬 ◿

PG/Family Visiting England to settle her father's estate, Mrs. Wilson and her three children discover an egg from which a phoenix emerges. This mythical firebird proceeds to take the children on a magic adventure. Adapted from the book by Edith Nesbit.

> ⚠ BEWARE *Mild language.*

1995 80m/C Dee Wallace Stone, Timothy Hegeman, Nick Klein, Laura Kamrath, Peter Ustinov; *D:* Zoran Perisic; *W:* Florence Fox; *M:* Alan Parker. **VHS** *PAR*

The Pickwick Papers 🎬🎬 ◿

Family Feature-length TV cartoon version of the Charles Dickens novel about Samuel Pickwick, a wealthy talespinner who founds a club for similar eccentrics in Victorian England. Pickwick welcomes adventure, but has an undesired one when a lawsuit gets him abruptly thrown into jail. Much of the picture is devoted to recreations of the spooky tales members of the Pickwick Club tell each other; these have been excerpted and expanded for a separate video title "Ghost Stories" (aka "Charles Dickens' Ghost Stories").

1985 72m/C VHS, Beta *LIV*

Piece of the Action 🎬🎬 ◿

PG/Jr. High-Adult Good-natured comedy finds an excop tricking a safecracker and a con man (Cosby and Poitier) into supervising teen juvenile delinquents at a Chicago community center.

> ⚠ BEWARE *Salty language*

1977 135m/C Sidney Poitier, Bill Cosby, James Earl Jones, Denise Nicholas, Hope Clarke, Tracy Reed, Titos Vandis, Ja'net DuBois; *D:* Sidney Poitier; *M:* Curtis Mayfield. **VHS, Beta** *WAR*

The Pied Piper/Cinderella

Family Double-feature of short puppet-animated tales by British stop-motion specialists. First is an excellent adaptation of Robert Browning's poem about the mystery minstrel who rids Hamlin town of its rats, then exacts a terrible price. Next is an attempt to do "Cinderella" entirely in wordless puppet pantomime, but the puppets aren't expressive enough, and this seg comes truly to life only when the fairy godmother is at large.

1981 70m/C VHS, Beta *HBO*

The Pied Piper of Hamelin 🎬🎬 ◿

Family Television version of the evergreen classic about the magical piper who rids a village of rats and then disappears with the village children into a mountain when

the townspeople fail to keep a promise. Effective score and cast make it worthwhile.
1957 90m/C Van Johnson, Claude Rains, Jim Backus, Kay Starr, Lori Nelson; **D:** Bretaigne Windust. **VHS, Beta** *KAR, NOS, MED*

The Pied Piper of Hamelin

Family From Shelley Duvall's "Faerie Tale Theatre" comes the story of how a man (Eric Idle) with a magic flute charms the rats out of Hamelin, and what happens when he doesn't get paid. Ages 5 to 10.
1984 60m/C Eric Idle; **D:** Nicholas Meyer. **VHS, Beta** *FOX, FCT*

The Pied Piper of Hamelin

Family Animated version of the Robert Browning poem, recited by Orson Welles.
1985 18m/C VHS, Beta *CHF*

The Pigeon that Worked a Miracle

Preschool-Primary A pigeon is so loved by a boy that a miracle occurs when the bird forces him to walk again. A live-action episode of TV's "Wonderful World of Disney."
1990 47m/C VHS, Beta *MTI, DSN*

The Pigs' Wedding and Other Stories

Family Five stories from the acclaimed "Children's Circle" series, illustrated with non-animated drawings. Includes "Pig's Wedding," "The Selkie Girl," "A Letter to Amy," "The Happy Owls," and "The Owl and the Pussycat."
1991 39m/C VHS *CCC, FCT, BTV*

The Pinballs

Primary-Jr. High Three displaced youths, in the same foster home, come to learn about understanding themselves and caring for others. An "Afterschool Special" TV adaptation of the novel by Betsy Byars.
1990 31m/C Kristy McNichol. **VHS, Beta** *MTI, DSN*

Pink Cadillac 🦴🦴 ▷

PG-13/Jr. High-Adult A grizzled, middle-aged bondsman is on the road, tracking down bail-jumping crooks. He helps the wife and baby of his latest target escape from her husband's more evil associates. Eastwood's performance is good and fun to watch, in this otherwise lightweight film.

⚠ BEWARE *Violence, profanity, suggested sex.*

1989 121m/C Clint Eastwood, Bernadette Peters, Timothy Carhart, Michael Des Barres, William Hickey, John Dennis Johnston, Geoffrey Lewis, Jim Carrey, Tiffany Gail Robinson, Angela Louise Robinson; **D:** Buddy Van Horn; **W:** John Eskow; **M:** Stephen Dorff. **VHS, Beta, LV, 8mm** *WAR*

The Pink Panther 🦴🦴🦴

Family When the legendary Pink Panther diamond is stolen, disaster-prone Inspector Clouseau descends on a ski resort in search of the professional cat-burglar responsible. Fans of the slapstick epics of the 1970s will be disappointed that this opening installment is really a rather slow-paced romantic comedy, with more love triangles than sight gags. Sellers is a supporting character, with the spotlight on the charming Niven as the thief. Kids will likely be bored. Animated opening sequence originated the Pink Panther cartoon character.

⚠ BEWARE *Alcohol use and sex talk. Inspector Clouseau pratfalls and craziness.*

1964 113m/C Peter Sellers, David Niven, Robert Wagner, Claudia Cardinale, Capucine, Brenda de Banzie; **D:** Blake Edwards; **W:** Blake Edwards; **M:** Henry Mancini. **VHS, Beta, LV** *MGM, FOX, TVC*

The Pink Panther

Family The Pink Panther began life in the opening credits of a 1964 live-action caper comedy of the same name and was immediately judged popular enough for a series himself. This compilation includes his bigscreen outings like "Slink Pink," "Come On In! The Water's Pink," and more.
1988 60m/C VHS, Beta, LV *MGM*

Pink Panther: Fly in the Pink

Family Classic cartoons from the debonair Pink Panther include "Pink Flea," "A Fly in the Pink," "Keep our Forest Pink," and "Pink in the Clink."
1966 57m/C VHS, Beta, 8mm *MGM*

Pink Panther: Pink Christmas

Family TV cartoon Christmas special derived from O. Henry's tale "The Cop and the Anthem." This time the Pink Panther is cold and hungry on the streets of New York and, like many city residents, tries to get arrested to enjoy jailhouse food and shelter.
1989 23m/C VHS, Beta *MGM*

The Pink Panther Strikes Again 🦴🦴🦴

PG/Jr. High-Adult The wackiest and best in the "Pink Panther" series, and the closest to a live-action cartoon. Incompetent Inspector Clouseau now must fight his former boss from the police force, who has been driven insane thanks to the bumbling sleuth and menaces the entire planet with a death ray. A must for anyone who appreciates slapstick.

⚠ BEWARE *Fighting (Clouseau with trusty servant Kato) and sex talk.*

1976 103m/C Peter Sellers, Herbert Lom, Lesley-Anne Down, Colin Blakely, Leonard Rossiter, Burt Kwouk; **D:** Blake Edwards; **W:** Edwards Waldman, Frank Waldman; **M:** Henry Mancini. **VHS, Beta, LV** *FOX, TVC*

Pink Panther: Tickled Pink

Family Nine Pink Panther cartoons, including "Tickled Pink," "Pink 8-Ball," and "G.I. Pink" are featured.

1970 57m/C VHS, Beta *MGM*

Pinocchio 🎵🎵🎵🎵

G/Family Walt Disney's second animated film is considered by some to be his best. Pinocchio, a little wooden puppet made by the old woodcarver Geppetto, is brought to life by a good fairy. Except Pinocchio isn't content to be just a puppet—he wants to become a real boy. Lured by a sly fox, Pinocchio has a number of adventures as he tries to return safely home. Classic has held up over time, but don't let it make you skip Carlo Collodi's original, often satirical Pinocchio tales. 🎵 When You Wish Upon a Star; Give a Little Whistle; Turn on the Old Music Box; Hi-Diddle-Dee-Dee (An Actor's Life For Me); I've Got No Strings.

BEWARE *Several scenes that might chill the wee small ones, like the nightmarish Pleasure Island where naughty boys change into donkeys, and a close encounter with Monstro the Whale.*

1940 87m/C D: Ben Sharpsteen; **V:** Dick Jones, Cliff Edwards, Evelyn Venable, Walter Catlett, Frankie Darro, Charles Judels, Don Brodie, Christian Rub. **VHS, Beta, LV** *DIS*

Pinocchio

Family It took no genius to cast Paul Reubens (Pee-wee Herman) as the puppet Pinocchio in this "Faerie Tale Theatre" production—Reubens has always seemed three credits shy of being a real live boy. But casting Lainie Kazan as the Blue Fairy, was a masterstroke. Earthy and over-the-top, her character is called Sophia, the Fairy of Wooden Objects, and she says things like "Your nose, she's a-gonna grow, capisce?" Watch for Michael Richards (later Kramer on "Seinfeld") in a small role. Lots o' fun. Ages 4 to 8.

1983 60m/C Paul (Pee Wee Herman) Reubens, James Coburn, Carl Reiner, Lainie Kazan; **D:** Peter Medak. **VHS, Beta** *FOX, FCT*

Pinocchio

Family Lonely toymaker's finest creation is magically brought to life in this retelling of Carlo Collodi's story, animated with Brian Ajhar's illustrations. Music by the Les Miserables Brass Band. From the "Rabbit Ears: We All Have Tales" series.

1993 30m/C VHS *RAB, BTV, PMS*

Pinocchio and the Emperor of the Night 🎵🎵

Preschool-Primary Fast-forgotten theatrical cartoon sequel to the story of "Pinocchio," not from Disney but by an outfit responsible for plenty of bland Saturday-morning animation. It's Pinocchio's one-year anniversary as a real boy, and Gepetto sends him (and a Jiminy Cricket clone) on an errand. Just like last time, the little hero gets sidetracked, hoodwinked, and takes a long journey with a sinister circus. There are songs, but nothing that can touch "When You Wish Upon a Star."

1987 91m/C D: Hal Sutherland; **V:** William Windom, Tom Bosley, Ed Asner, Don Knotts, James Earl Jones, Rickie Lee Jones. **VHS, Beta, LV** *VTR, NWV*

Pinocchio in Outer Space

Family Dim-witted Belgian-American feature cartoon stars a blond Pinocchio, turned back into a puppet and sent on a musical, rocketship-age rerun of the original plot. Now for instance it's Astro the cosmic whale who swallows him, get it? Not exactly stellar entertainment.

1964 71m/C D: Ray Goosens; **V:** Arnold Stang, Minerva Pious, Peter Lazer, Conrad Jameson. **VHS, Beta** *COL*

Pinocchio's Christmas

Family Puppet-animated holiday TV special from the Rankin-Bass workshop, wherein Pinocchio finds romance and adventures while trying to raise money for a present for Geppetto.

1983 60m/C V: Alan King, George S. Irving. **VHS, Beta** *LIV, VES*

Pippi Goes on Board 🎵🎵

G/Family Fourth and final adventure in the popular Swedish-German series of Pippi Longstocking films of the 1970s finds Pippi's sea captain father arriving to take her to Taka-Kuka, his island kingdom. She can't bear to leave her landlubber friends and jumps ship to return home. Like all the features in the series, it's garishly photographed and poorly dubbed into English, but Pippi partisans probably won't notice; the films did well with small kids. Based on the books by Astrid Lindgren.

1971 83m/C Inger Nilsson; **D:** Olle Hellbron. **VHS, Beta** *GEM, MOV, TPV*

Pippi in the South Seas 🎵🎵

G/Family The indomitable Pippi Longstocking and her pals Tommy and Anneka journey to rescue Capt. Ephraim Longstocking, Pippi's father, a captive of pirates on a South Sea island. Naturally, clever Pippi saves the day. Badly dubbed and edited Swedish-German production that followed the first "Pippi Longstocking," redubbed for the poor English-speaking market in 1975.

1968 99m/C Inger Nilsson; **D:** Olle Hellbron. **VHS, Beta** *GEM, MOV, TPV*

Pippi Longstocking 🎵🎵

G/Family This little red-pigtailed tomboy became a favorite with kids thanks to the "Pippie Langstrumpf" books of Astrid Lindgren—and thanks to a garish series of Swedish-German kiddie pictures, released in the U.S. throughout the '70s. Separated from her seagoing father, Pippi descends on her hometown, creating havoc through her pets, pranks and feats of superhuman strength. The story is a rickety affair, f/x are terrible, and bad English dubbing hurts the ears, but one still sees why Pippi captivates kids—she lives just the way she wants and makes even household chores fun. Adults may just find her obnoxious. Followed by "Pippi in the South Seas," "Pippi on the Run," "Pippi Goes on Board," and the Yankee remake "New Adventures of Pippi Longstocking."

1968 99m/C Inger Nilsson; *D:* Olle Hellbron. **VHS, Beta** *GEM, MOV, TPV*

Pippi on the Run 🦴🦴

G/Family Third in the Swedish-German Astrid Lindgren adaptations finds Pippi Longstocking on the trail of two friends who have run away from home. The three have many poorly dubbed adventures before deciding home is best.

1970 99m/C VHS, Beta *GEM, MOV, TPV*

Pippin 🦴🦴🦴

Jr. High-Adult Video version of the stage musical about the adolescent son of Charlemagne finding true love as well as the perils of leadership. Adequate recording of Bob Fosse's Broadway smash features Vereen recreating his original Tony Award-winning role.

1981 120m/C Ben Vereen, William Katt, Martha Raye, Chita Rivera. **VHS, Beta, LV** *VCI, FHE, FCT*

Pirate Movie 🦴🦴

PG/Jr. High-Adult Gilbert and Sullivan's "The Pirates of Penzance" is combined with new pop songs in this tale of fantasy and romance. Feeble attempt to update a musical that was fine the way it was.

⚠️ BEWARE *Salty language; sex talk.*

1982 98m/C Kristy McNichol, Christopher Atkins, Ted Hamilton, Bill Kerr, Garry McDonald; *D:* Ken Annakin. **VHS, Beta** *FOX*

Pirates of Dark Water: The Saga Begins

Family Feature-length pilot of Hanna-Barbera's original cartoon series for the Fox Network, and it looks like this time they dreamt a fantastic world BEFORE planning the toys. Only Prince Ren and his bandit band can save the ocean-covered planet of Mer from the plague of Black Water (yes, more eco-propaganda), but to gather the antidote they combat the cruel pirate tyrant Bloth. Splendid production design (Asian animators helped out, natch), mediocre characters, pretty confusing story.

1991 90m/C VHS, Beta *TTC*

The Pirates of Penzance 🦴🦴

G/Family Gilbert and Sullivan's comic operetta is the story of a band of fun-loving pirates, their reluctant young apprentice, the "very model of a modern major general," and his lovely daughters. Less-than-inspired adaptation of Joseph Papp's award-winning Broadway play.

1983 112m/C Kevin Kline, Angela Lansbury, Linda Ronstadt, Rex Smith, George Rose; *D:* Wilford Leach. **VHS, Beta, LV** *MCA, FOX*

Pistol: The Birth of a Legend 🦴🦴◗

G/Family Wholesome, authorized biography of "Pistol" Pete Maravich, the basketball star who defied age limitations in the 1960s to play on his varsity team. Solidly told, though sadly, Maravich died unexpectedly soon after this was completed.

1990 104m/C Adam Guier, Nick Benedict, Boots Garland, Millie Perkins; *D:* Frank C. Schroeder. **VHS, Beta** *COL*

PJ's Unfunnybunny Christmas

Family Young PJ Funnybunny dreams Santa refuses to bring him any toys because he doesn't understand the true meaning of Christmas. So the rabbit tries to discover what the holiday is all about. Ages 2 to 6.

1994 25m/C VHS *ABC*

P.K. and the Kid 🦴🦴

Family A runaway kid meets up with a factory worker on his way to an arm wrestling competition and they become friends.

1985 90m/C Molly Ringwald, Paul LeMat, Alex Rocco, John Madden, Esther Rolle; *D:* Lou Lombardo; *M:* James Horner. **VHS, Beta, LV** *ORI, WAR*

Places in the Heart 🦴🦴🦴◗

PG/Jr. High-Adult After her lawman husband's sudden murder, a young widow strives to bring in her farm's vital cotton crop in Depression-era Texas. Support comes from her kids, a blind veteran, and a black drifter. Plot threatens to become just one disaster after another (including a scary tornado) but succeeds thanks to strong performances and an unforgettable final scene stressing love and Christian forgiveness.

⚠️ BEWARE *Violence and natural disasters.*

1984 113m/C Sally Field, John Malkovich, Danny Glover, Ed Harris, Lindsay Crouse, Amy Madigan, Terry O'Quinn; *D:* Robert Benton; *W:* Robert Benton; *M:* Howard Shore. **Award Nominations:** Academy Awards '84: Best Costume Design, Best Director (Benton), Best Picture, Best Supporting Actor (Malkovich), Best Supporting Actress (Crouse); **Awards:** Academy Awards '84: Best Actress (Field), Best Original Screenplay; Golden Globe Awards '85: Best Actress—Drama (Field). **VHS, Beta, LV** *FOX, BTV, HMV*

Plain Clothes 🦴

PG/Jr. High-Adult Though Coolidge directed the surprisingly empathetic teen flick "Valley Girl," this has none of that pic's redeeming qualities. Undercover cop masquerades as a high schooler to free his own kid brother from a charge of murdering a teacher. The student characters are just scenery, while the adult school faculty are crooks and loonies.

⚠️ BEWARE *The MPAA must have been cutting class the day of the screening, for they assigned a mild PG to this smarmy whodunit despite lots of profanity, sex talk, violence, mature themes.*

1988 98m/C Arliss Howard, George Wendt, Suzy Amis, Diane Ladd, Seymour Cassel, Larry Pine, Jackie Gayle, Abe Vigoda, Robert Stack; **D:** Martha Coolidge; **M:** Scott Wilk. **VHS, Beta** *PAR*

Planes, Trains & Automobiles

R/Sr. High-Adult A funny holiday treat from Hughes featuring laughmeisters Martin and Candy. An uptight businessman (played straight by Martin) is on his way home to Chicago for Thanksgiving and bumps into oafish, bad-luck-ridden Candy, who turns his efforts to get home upside down. Many hilarious misadventures ensue as the pair try every mode of transportation to get home (hence, the title!). Candy fans will really cherish this one. Fun for the entire family.

BEWARE *Some stinky feet and underwear may scare away the sqeamish, but be strong. Also, if you dislike the "F word", beware of the car rental scene.*

1987 93m/C Steve Martin, John Candy, Edie McClurg, Kevin Bacon, Michael McKean, William Windom, Laila Robins, Martin Ferrero, Charles Tyner, Dylan Baker; **D:** John Hughes; **W:** John Hughes; **M:** Ira Newborn. **VHS, Beta, LV, 8mm** *PAR*

Planet of the Apes

G/Family Astronauts crash land on a planet where apes are masters and humans are merely brute animals. Superior science fiction with sociological implications marred only by unnecessary humor. Heston delivers one of his more plausible performances. Superb ape makeup creates realistic pseudo-simians of McDowall, Hunter, Evans, Whitmore, and Daly. Adapted from Pierre Boulle's novel "Monkey Planet." Followed by four sequels and two television series.

BEWARE *Violence.*

1968 112m/C Charlton Heston, Roddy McDowall, Kim Hunter, Maurice Evans, Linda Harrison, James Whitmore, James Daly; **D:** Franklin J. Schaffner; **W:** Rod Serling, Michael G. Wilson; **M:** Jerry Goldsmith. **Award Nominations:** Academy Awards '68: Best Costume Design, Best Original Score; **Awards:** National Board of Review Awards '68: 10 Best Films of the Year. **VHS, Beta, LV** *FOX, FUS*

Planet of the Dinosaurs

PG/Family Spaceship crashes on a prehistoric planet, and the human survivors must put aside their considerable squabbles about what to do next to fight for survival against hungry Earth-style dinosaurs. Good stop-motion dinosaur f/x done on a minuscule budget; it's the acting and dialogue that seem fossilized.

BEWARE *Violence; alcohol use.*

1980 85m/C James Whitworth; **D:** James K. Shea. **VHS, Beta** *AHV, VTR*

Plastic Man

Preschool-Primary With his amazing ability to mold and stretch himself into any shape, Plastic Man stretches himself into new dimensions to fight evil and play with Baby Plas. Standard Saturday-morning cartoon stuff

adapted from a well-regarded satirical comic book.
1981 56m/C VHS, Beta *WOV*

Play-Along Video: Hey, You're as Funny as Fozzie Bear

Preschool-Primary Henson's Muppets star in one of a series of humorous, educational videos designed to capture the attention and imagination of pre-school and young children. This one offers a lesson in joketelling.
1989 30m/C Jim Henson's Muppets. **VHS** *ORI*

Play-Along Video: Mother Goose Stories

Preschool-Primary Muppet video for young children that both enlightens and entertains.
1989 30m/C Jim Henson's Muppets. **VHS** *ORI*

Play-Along Video: Sing-Along, Dance-Along, Do-Along

Preschool-Primary Music-oriented edition of the participatory Muppet videocassettes.
1989 30m/C Jim Henson's Muppets. **VHS** *ORI*

Play-Along Video: Wow, You're a Cartoonist!

Preschool-Primary Young children can have lots of fun learning how to draw with the Muppet gang. Basic animation using a flip-book is also covered.
1989 30m/C Jim Henson's Muppets. **VHS** *ORI*

Play It Again, Sam

PG/Jr. High-Adult Allen is—no surprise—a nerd, and this time he's in love with his best friend's wife. Modest storyline provides a framework of endless gags, with Allen borrowing heavily from "Casablanca." Bogey even appears periodically to counsel Allen on the ways of wooing women. Superior comedy isn't hurt by Ross directing instead of Allen, who adapted the script from his own play.
1972 85m/C Woody Allen, Diane Keaton, Tony Roberts, Susan Anspach, Jerry Lacy, Jennifer Salt, Joy Bang, Viva, Herbert Ross; **D:** Herbert Ross; **M:** Billy Goldenberg. **VHS, Beta, LV, 8mm** *PAR*

Playbox 1

Preschool-Primary Elementary entertainment for the very young, consisting of mime and live-action tricks mixed with animation of all shapes and styles.
1982 30m/C Brian Rix. **VHS, Beta** *FHE*

The Playboys

PG-13/Sr. High-Adult In 1957 in a tiny Irish village, unmarried Tara Maguire causes a scandal by having a baby. Her beauty attracts lots of men-there's a former beau who kills himself, the obsessive, middle-aged Sergeant Hegarty, and the newest arrival, Tom Castle, an actor with a rag-tag theatrical troupe called the Playboys. Slow-moving and simple story with particularly good performances by Wright as the strong-willed Tara and Finney as Hegarty, clinging to a last chance at love and family. The Playboys' hysterically hammy version of "Gone With the Wind" is a gem. Directorial debut of Mackinnon. Filmed in the village of Redhills, Ireland, the hometown of co-writer Connaughton.

 Profanity and violence.

1992 114m/C Albert Finney, Aidan Quinn, Robin Wright, Milo O'Shea, Alan Devlin, Niamh Cusack, Ian McElhinney, Niall Buggy, Adrian Dunbar; *D:* Gilles Mackinnon; *W:* Shane Connaughton, Kerry Crabbe; *M:* Jean-Claude Petit. **VHS** *HBO, FCT*

Playtime

Family Leisurely comedy in which bemused Frenchman Mr. Hulot goes to the city to meet relatives living in a see-through apartment, then tries to keep an appointment in a vast, impersonal office building. Mostly pantomime and slapstick, with a small amount of (English) dialogue. Quite slow-paced as it makes the point about an absurd concrete-and-glass modern civilization, and small viewers might be bored, but there are immortal comic whimsies. The traffic circle that turns into a merry-go-round is not to be missed. Third in Tati's Hulot series; see also "Mr. Hulot's Holiday" and "Mon Oncle."

BEWARE *Alcohol use.*

1967 108m/C Jacques Tati, Barbara Dennek, Jacqueline Lecomte, Jack Gautier; *D:* Jacques Tati. **VHS, Beta** *INJ, NLC*

Please Don't Eat the Daisies

Family Drama critic and family flee the Big Apple for the country and are traumatized by flora and fauna. Goofy sixties fluff taken from Jean Kerr's book and play and the basis for the eventual TV series.

1960 111m/C Doris Day, David Niven, Janis Paige, Spring Byington, Richard Haydn, Patsy Kelly, Jack Weston, Margaret Lindsay; *D:* Charles Walters. **VHS, Beta, LV** *MGM, FCT*

Pluto

Family Collection of Plutonian escapades with the Disney cartoon dog include "The Pointer," "Bone Trouble," "Private Pluto," "Camp Dog," and "The Legend of Coyote Rock."

1950 52m/C VHS, Beta *DIS*

Pluto (limited gold edition)

Family Pluto and pals Dinah the Dachshund and Butch the Bulldog star in a number of adventures including "Pluto at the Zoo" and "Pluto Junior."

1950 47m/C VHS, LV *DIS*

Pluto's Christmas Tree

Preschool-Primary Pluto is driven batty when the tree that Mickey Mouse chops down for Christmas turns out to be Chip 'n' Dale's home.

1952 7m/C VHS, Beta *MTI, DSN*

Pocahontas

Family Not the Disney version, and nowhere near as good. Animated musical tells the story of the beautiful Indian princess, dashing English colonist John Smith, and their undying love (along with comical animals and a talking canoe). Ages 4 to 9.

1995 48m/C VHS

Pocahontas

G/Family Everybody repeat: It's not history, it's a movie. It's not history, it's a movie. There. So much for the griping that befell Disney's animated look at the culture clash between English settlers and American Indians. Decent English Capt. John Smith (the voice of Mel Gibson) and strong Indian princess Pocahontas (spoken by Irene Bedard, sung by Judy Kuhn), fall in love despite the mistrust and outright prejudice their respective peoples feel toward one another. But this is more than "When Johnny Met Poca." The songs are excellent, though by now everyone is sick of "Colors of the Wind;" the story (it's not history, it's a movie) is intriguing, and, for the youngest viewers, cute threesome of raccoon Meeko, hummingbird Flit, and pug Percy practically steal the show.

BEWARE *One character dies, another is seriously hurt.*

1995 90m/C *D:* Mike Gabriel, Eric Goldberg; *W:* Carl Binder, Susannah Grant, Philip LaZebnik; *M:* Alan Menken, Stephen Schwartz; *V:* Irene Bedard, Judy Kuhn, Mel Gibson, Joe Baker, Christian Bale, Billy Connolly, James Apaumut Fall, Linda Hunt, John Kassir, Danny Mann, Bill Cobbs, David Ogden Stiers, Michelle St. John, Gordon Tootoosis, Frank Welker. **Award Nominations:** Academy Awards '95: Best Song ("Colors of the Wind"), Best Score; Golden Globe Awards '96: Best Score; **Awards:** Golden Globe Awards '96: Best Song ("Colors of the Wind"). **VHS** *DIS*

Poetic Justice

R/Sr. High-Adult Justice (Jackson in her movie debut, for better or worse) gives up college plans to follow a career in cosmetology after her boyfriend's brutal murder. She copes with her loss by dedicating herself to poetry writing (provided by no less than poet Maya Angelou) and meets postal worker Shakur. Singleton's second directorial effort is less bleak than his stunning debut but not as assured. Production stopped on the South Central L.A. set during the '92 riots, but the aftermath provided poignant pictures for later scenes.

BEWARE *Profanity, violence and sex.*

1993 109m/C Janet Jackson, Tupac Shakur, Tyra Ferrell, Regina King, Joe Torry; *D:* John Singleton; *W:* John Singleton; *M:* Stanley Clarke. **Award Nominations:** Academy Awards '93: Best Song

Steve Martin meets John Candy in the cross-country comedy "Planes, Trains and Automobiles."

("Again"); Golden Globe Awards '94: Best Song ("Again"); **Awards:** MTV Movie Awards '94: Best Actress (Jackson), Most Desirable Female (Jackson). **VHS, LV, 8mm** *COL, BTV*

Pogo for President: "I Go Pogo" 🦴🦴🦴

PG/Family Stop-motion animated feature of Walt Kelly's comic-strip character Pogo Possum. He becomes an unlikely and unwilling presidential candidate when ambitious Howland Owl proclaims him the winner of an election. Dull songs, fine cast of voices. Puppetry is exceptionally faithful to Kelly's concepts, but will kids comprehend the heavy-duty political satire? Exists on video in two versions, the original and a later re-edited edition with added narration. Either one could have been G-rated with no problems.

1980 84m/C V: Jonathan Winters, Vincent Price, Ruth Buzzi, Stan Freberg, Jimmy Breslin. **VHS, Beta** *DIS*

The Point 🦴🦴🦴🦴

Family Charming, lyrical, and timeless made-for-television animated fable, with a father reading his son the story of Oblio, a round-headed child who's a misfit in his world of pointy-headed people. Exiled to the Pointless

Forest, Oblio and his dog Arrow learn that "you don't have to have a point to have a point." Excellent score written and performed by Harry Nilsson.

1971 74m/C D: Fred Wolf; **M:** Harry Nilsson. **VHS, Beta, LV** *FHE, VES, MLT*

The Polar Bear King 🦴🦴

PG/Jr. High-Adult Prince refuses to marry the evil witch of Summerland, so she turns him into a polar bear. Only through the long-term love of a maiden can the Polar Bear King be restored to humanity. Jim Henson's workshop designed the title beast; too bad they didn't rewrite the script as well, a ponderous tale sorely lacking in traditional Muppet playfulness and humor. Scandinavian co-production based on Norse folklore.

🚸 BEWARE 🚸 *Alcohol use.*

1994 87m/C Maria Bonnerie, Jack Fjeldstad, Tobias Hoesl, Anna-Lotta Larsson; **D:** Ola Solum. **VHS, LV** *HMD*

Police Academy 🦴🦴

R/Sr. High-Adult In an attempt to recruit more cops, a big-city police department does away with all its job standards. The producers probably didn't know that they were introducing bad comedy's answer to the "Friday the 13th" series, but it's hard to avoid heaping the sins of its successors on this film. Besides, it's just plain dumb.

BEWARE *Fighting, profanity, sex talk and idiot cops.*

1984 96m/C Steve Guttenberg, Kim Cattrall, Bubba Smith, George Gaynes, Michael Winslow, Leslie Easterbrook, Georgina Spelvin, Debralee Scott; *D:* Hugh Wilson; *W:* Hugh Wilson, Pat Proft, Neal Israel; *M:* Robert Folk. **VHS, Beta, LV, 8mm** *WAR*

Police Academy 2: Their First Assignment 🦴

PG-13/Jr. High-Adult More predictable idiocy from the cop shop. This time they're determined to rid the precinct of some troublesome punks. No real story to speak of, just more high jinks in this mindless sequel.

BEWARE *Profanity and stupidity.*

1985 87m/C Steve Guttenberg, Bubba Smith, Michael Winslow, Art Metrano, Colleen Camp, Howard Hesseman, David Graf, George Gaynes; *D:* Jerry Paris; *W:* Barry W. Blaustein. **VHS, Beta, LV** *WAR*

Police Academy 3: Back in Training 🦴

PG/Jr. High-Adult In yet another sequel, the bumbling cops find their alma mater is threatened by a budget crunch and they must compete with a rival academy to see which school survives. The "return to school" plot allowed the filmmakers to add new characters to replace those who had some scruples about picking up yet another "Police Lobotomy" check. Followed by three more sequels.

BEWARE *Profanity and violence (and stupidity, of course).*

1986 84m/C Steve Guttenberg, Bubba Smith, David Graf, Michael Winslow, Marion Ramsey, Art Metrano, Bob(cat) Goldthwait, Leslie Easterbrook, Tim Kazurinsky, George Gaynes, Shawn Weatherly; *D:* Jerry Paris; *W:* Gene Quintano; *M:* Robert Folk. **VHS, Beta, LV** *WAR*

Police Academy 4: Citizens on Patrol 🦴

PG/Jr. High-Adult The comic cop cutups from the first three films aid a citizen's patrol group in their unnamed, but still wacky, hometown. Moronic high jinks ensue. Fourth in the series of five (or is it six?) that began with "Police Academy".

BEWARE *Mild profanity (and still stupid).*

1987 88m/C Steve Guttenberg, Bubba Smith, Michael Winslow, David Graf, Tim Kazurinsky, George Gaynes, Colleen Camp, Bob(cat) Goldthwait, Sharon Stone; *D:* Jim Drake; *W:* Gene Quintano; *M:* Robert Folk. **VHS, Beta, LV** *WAR*

Police Academy 5: Assignment Miami Beach WOOF!

PG/Jr. High-Adult The fourth sequel, wherein the misfits-with-badges go to Miami and bumble about in the

usual manner. It's about time these cops were retired from the force.

BEWARE *Profanity. (Aren't we tired of stupidity yet?)*

1988 89m/C Bubba Smith, David Graf, Michael Winslow, Leslie Easterbrook, Rene Auberjonois, Marion Ramsey, Janet Jones, George Gaynes, Matt McCoy; *D:* Alan Myerson; *M:* Robert Folk. **VHS, Beta, LV** *WAR*

Police Academy 6: City Under Siege 🦴

PG/Jr. High-Adult In what is hoped to be the last in a series of bad comedies, the distinguished graduates pursue three goofballs responsible for a crime wave.

BEWARE *Violence and profanity. (When will the madness and stupidity end?)*

1989 85m/C Bubba Smith, David Graf, Michael Winslow, Leslie Easterbrook, Marion Ramsey, Matt McCoy, Bruce Mahler, G.W. Bailey, George Gaynes; *D:* Peter Bonerz; *M:* Robert Folk. **VHS, LV** *WAR*

Police Academy: Mission to Moscow 🦴

PG/Jr. High-Adult Just when you think that humankind is on the road to a new millennium of enlightenment, comes this sobering speed bump: the seventh in the moronic comedy series of Police Academy movies. In this one, the twisted enforcers of the law extend their jurisdiction to Russia, where they take on a mobster. Winslow, man of a thousand voices (and other sounds), deserves a better vehicle for his talents but at least he's been eating well for more than a decade.

BEWARE *Profanity and typical "Police Academy" comic violence (you know, people falling down and crashing stuff for no apparent reason).*

1994 83m/C George Gaynes, Michael Winslow, David Graf, Leslie Easterbrook, G.W. Bailey, Charlie Schlatter, Ron Perlman, Christopher Lee; *D:* Alan Metter; *W:* Michele S. Chodos, Randolph Davis; *M:* Robert Folk. **VHS** *WAR*

Police Academy, the Series

Primary Purveyors of the animated "Rambo" also coughed up this TV cartoon series based on the profitable, mutton-headed comedy film franchise. Episodes include: "The Good, the Bad, and the Bogus" and "Cops and Robots." Additional volumes available.

1989 33m/C VHS, Beta *WAR*

Pollyanna 🦴🦴🦴 ♪

Family Based on the Eleanor Porter story about an enchanting young girl whose contagious enthusiasm and zest for life touches the hearts of all she meets in her all-American town in the early 1900s. Mills is perfect in the title role and was awarded a special Oscar for outstanding juvenile performance. Distinguished supporting cast is the icing on the cake in this delightful Disney confection.

"Pocahontas" finds herself attracted to handsome newcomer John Smith.

Silent version filmed in 1920 with Mary Pickford is also on tape.

1960 134m/C Hayley Mills, Jane Wyman, Richard Egan, Karl Malden, Nancy Olson, Adolphe Menjou, Donald Crisp, Agnes Moorehead, Kevin Corcoran; **D:** David Swift. **VHS, Beta, LV** *DIS, BTV*

Poltergeist 𝄢𝄢𝄢 ♭

PG/Jr. High-Adult He's listed only as co-writer and co-producer, but this production has Steven Spielberg written all over it. Young family's home becomes a house of horrors when menacing spirits contact, then abduct their five-year-old daughter ... through the TV screen! Rollercoaster thrills and chills, dazzling special effects, perfectly timed humor and a family you care about highlight this stupendous ghost story.

BEWARE *Spooky stuff successfully pushes every panic button ever, from tornadoes to rotting corpses to a child's fear of clowns, but no real casualties result. Mom and dad do smoke marijuana, though.*

1982 114m/C JoBeth Williams, Craig T. Nelson, Beatrice Straight, Heather O'Rourke, Zelda Rubinstein, Dominique Dunne, Oliver Robbins, Richard Lawson, James Karen; **D:** Tobe Hooper; **W:** Steven Spielberg, Michael Grais, Mark Victor; **M:** Jerry Goldsmith. **VHS, Beta, LV** *MGM*

Poltergeist 2: The Other Side 𝄢𝄢

PG-13/Jr. High-Adult Adequate sequel to the Spielberg-produced venture into the supernatural, where restless ghosts—explained in hackneyed terms as a 19th-century suicide cult—still hunt the Freelings to recapture the clairvoyant little daughter Carol Anne. In the climax, her family dives into the afterlife themselves to rescue her, encountering monsters galore. Script gets credit for attempting to depict the strain of demon attacks on family relationships, but visual effects and measured scares are the point here, not high drama.

BEWARE *Supernatural violence. Flick could actually put people off alcohol; Mr. Freeling swills tequila, and the worm in the bottle gets possessed, causing him to barf up a 'vomit creature.'*

1986 92m/C Craig T. Nelson, JoBeth Williams, Heather O'Rourke, Will Sampson, Julian Beck, Geraldine Fitzgerald, Oliver Robbins, Zelda Rubinstein; **D:** Brian Gibson; **W:** Mark Victor, Michael Grais; **M:** Jerry Goldsmith. **VHS, Beta, LV** *MGM*

Poltergeist 3 𝄢 ♭

PG-13/Jr. High-Adult Wrestling with the supernatural has unnerved little Carol Ann and she's sent to stay with her aunt and uncle in a modern high-rise apartment and attend a school for disturbed children. Evil ghosts follow her, and meanie psychotherapists don't believe her spook stories until it's too late. Flat acting, worn-out premise, paltry f/x finally exorcise the series. Dedicated to 12-year-old child actress O'Rourke, who died from an intestinal disorder before the theatrical release.

🖐 *BEWARE* *Violence, salty language. Climax features many of the supporting characters turned into rotting skeletons, but if they're good guys, they get to change back to normal.*

1988 97m/C Tom Skerritt, Nancy Allen, Heather O'Rourke, Lara Flynn Boyle, Zelda Rubinstein; **D:** Gary Sherman; **W:** Brian Taggert. **VHS, Beta, LV** *MGM*

Pontiac Moon 🎵 🎵

PG-13/Jr. High-Adult Danson plays a high school teacher who takes his son on a road trip to Spires of the Moon National Park hoping to arrive simultaneously with the astronauts' first lunar landing. His wife (Steenburgen) decides to follow them, although she's phobic about leaving the house and hasn't set foot outside in seven years. Sincere, tedious film about father-son bonding has a few heartfelt moments, but not enough to sustain interest for entire viewing period. Best (and only) reason for watching: Monument Valley scenery.

1994 108m/C Ted Danson, Mary Steenburgen, Ryan Todd, Eric Schweig, Cathy Moriarty, Max Gail, Lisa Jane Persky; **D:** Peter Medak; **W:** Finn Taylor, Jeffrey Brown; **M:** Randy Edelman. **VHS, Beta** *PAR*

Pontoffel Pock, Where Are You?

Primary Dr. Seuss cartoon features the hapless Pontoffel, whose magic piano can transport him though time and space.

1991 30m/C VHS *RAN, BTV*

Pony Express Rider 🎵🎵🎵

G/Family Young Jimmy joins up with the Pony Express hoping to bag the varmint responsible for killing his pa. Well-produced script boasts a bevy of veteran western character actors, all lending rugged performances. From the producers of "Where the Red Fern Grows."

1976 100m/C Stewart Peterson, Henry Wilcoxon, Buck Taylor, Maureen McCormick, Joan Caulfield, Ken Curtis, Slim Pickens, Dub Taylor, Jack Elam; **D:** Robert Totten. **VHS** *TPI*

Poochie

Preschool-Primary Toy-inspired cartoon. Poochie is a pink pup newspaper columnist who travels to Cairo with her robot sidekick Hermes to answer a young boy's distress call. Toy store receipts were apparently insufficient to justify a return visit from Poochie; even the last part of this cassette is devoted to some unrelated 'toons starring the winged horse Luna.

1984 30m/C VHS, Beta *LIV*

Pooh Learning: Helping Others

Preschool "Owl's Well That Ends Well" has Pooh and Piglet trying to teach Owl to sing. "A Very, Very Large Animal" turns out to be Piglet, at least to some very small ants. In "Caws and Effects," Pooh does his best to help Rabbit's harvest and in "To Dream the Impossible Scheme," Gopher and the gang learn dreams don't always have to come true.

1994 40m/C VHS *DIS*

Pooh Learning: Making Friends

Preschool In "Cloud, Cloud Go Away," Tigger makes friends with a lonely cloud and in "The Bug Stops Here," Christopher Robin discovers an irresistible insect. Piglet's good work turns out to be its own reward in "Tigger's the Mother of Invention."

1994 45m/C VHS *DIS*

Pooh Learning: Sharing and Caring

Preschool "Lights Out" has Rabbit borrowing Gopher's head lamp and learning a lesson about sharing. In "The Rats Who Came to Dinner," everyone turns to Pooh for help when there's a big rainstorm, and in "No Rabbit's a Fortress," Rabbit is taught a lesson about trusting his friends.

1994 45m/C VHS *DIS*

Pooh Playtime: Cowboy Pooh

Preschool "The Good, the Bad and the Tigger" is about a mysterious train robbery that causes Sheriff Piglet to round up some unusual suspects. In "Rabbit Marks the Spot," The Pooh Pirates are tricked into digging for buried treasure.

1993 46m/C VHS *DIS*

Pooh Playtime: Detective Tigger

Preschool In "Tigger Private Ear," Pooh realizes he's missing some of his honey pots, and Tigger investigates. "Sham Pooh" deals with a case of mistaken identity. "Invasion of the Pooh Snatcher" features more thrills with Pooh in peril and in "Eeyore's Tail Tale," Piglet comes to the rescue.

1993 52m/C VHS *DIS*

Pooh Playtime: Pooh Party

Preschool Three short tales featuring the A.A. Milne characters. "Party Poohper" features Rabbit finding too many relatives at his party. In "A Bird in the Hand," Pooh gets into trouble and "Pooh Day Afternoon" has Pooh appointed assistant dog-sitter by Christopher Robin.

1993 46m/C VHS *DIS*

Pooh's Great School Bus Adventure

Preschool-Primary Winnie, Piglet, Tigger, and the crowd sing songs about the safety rules for going to school that Christopher Robin has taught them.
1990 14m/C VHS, Beta *MTI, DSN*

The Poor Little Rich Girl ♫♫ ♭

Family Motherless rich girl wanders away from home and is "adopted" by a pair of struggling vaudevillians. With her help, they rise to the big time. Also available with "Heidi" on laserdisc. ♫ Oh My Goodness; Buy a Bar of Barry's; Wash Your Neck With a Cake of Peck's; Military Man; When I'm with You; But Definitely; You've Gotta Eat Your Spinach, Baby.
1936 79m/B Shirley Temple, Jack Haley, Alice Faye, Gloria Stuart, Michael Whalen, Sara Haden, Jane Darwell; *D:* Irving Cummings. **VHS, Beta** *FOX*

Popeye ♫♫

PG/Family Cartoon sailor is brought to life in a search to find his long-lost father. In a seaside town he meets Olive Oyl (Duvall) and adopts little Sweet Pea. Williams accomplishes the near-impossible feat of looking and sounding like the title character, Duvall and Dooley (as Bluto) are equally splendid—but the big mistake here is putting Popeye not into a great adventure but a landlocked domestic sitcom. Dull songs by Harry Nilsson don't spice up this stale spinach.
> **BEWARE** *Cartoony violence in the wind-up punching category. A baby is stolen.*

1980 114m/C Robin Williams, Shelley Duvall, Ray Walston, Paul Dooley, Bill Irwin, Paul Smith, Linda Hunt, Richard Libertini; *D:* Robert Altman; *W:* Jules Feiffer; *M:* Harry Nilsson. **VHS, Beta, LV** *PAR*

The Popples

Preschool-Primary Furry toys inspired these cartoon characters who star in a series of tapes, each featuring two short adventures.
1985 25m/C VHS, Beta *COL*

Porky Pig Tales

Family Six fabulous cartoons featuring that bumbling yet charming porker. You'll l-l-l-love it! All ages.
1989 45m/C V: Mel Blanc. **VHS** *WAR*

The Poseidon Adventure ♫♫ ♭

PG/Jr. High-Adult The cruise ship Poseidon is on its last voyage from New York to Athens on New Year's Eve when it is capsized by a tidal wave. The ten survivors struggle to escape the water-logged tomb. Oscar-winning special effects, such as Shelley Winters floating in a boiler room. Created an entirely new genre of film making-the big cast disaster flick.
> **BEWARE** *Don't see this if your family is planning a cruise.*

1972 117m/C Gene Hackman, Ernest Borgnine, Shelley Winters, Red Buttons, Jack Albertson, Carol Lynley, Roddy McDowall; *D:* Ronald Neame; *W:* Wendell Mayes, Stirling Silliphant; *M:* John Williams. **Award Nominations:** Academy Awards '72: Best Art Direction/Set Decoration, Best Cinematography, Best Costume Design, Best Film Editing, Best Sound, Best Supporting Actress (Winters), Best Original Score; **Awards:** Academy Awards '72: Best Song ("The Morning After"), Best Visual Effects; Golden Globe Awards '73: Best Supporting Actress (Winters). **VHS, Beta, LV** *FOX*

Posse Impossible

Preschool-Primary Hanna-Barbera reruns about a bungling group of good guys.
1984 81m/C VHS, Beta *TTC*

Possible Possum: Freight Fright

Preschool-Primary Terrytoon series spun off from "Deputy Dawg" and his associates, centering on a possum character dwelling in the same Happy Hollow. Additional volumes available.
1965 32m/C VHS *VTR*

Postman Pat

Preschool Thirteen-part animation puppet series from Britain aimed at teaching good values while entertaining children. Postman Pat is accompanied by a black and white cat named Jess as they teach about everyday courtesies and the need to help each other. Ages 1 to 4.
1991 182m/C VHS

Postman Pat's ABC Story

Preschool Learn about the alphabet from one of the most colorful cartoon figures in Europe, Postman Pat. Ages 1 to 4.
19?? 30m/C VHS *VTR, FAF*

Postman Pat's 123 Story

Preschool The postal one teaches numbers. Ages 1 to 4.
19?? 30m/C VHS *FAF, VTR*

Potato Head Kids, Vol. 1

Preschool-Primary A tater-rific time with the Potato Head Kids in this cartoon series that belatedly brought the toys to animated life for the first time. Additional volumes available.
1986 40m/C VHS, Beta *MCA*

Potsworth and the Midnight Patrol

Family Hanna-Barbera cartoon compilation about a heroic squad of dogs.
1991 84m/C VHS, Beta *TTC*

Pound Puppies

Preschool-Primary Saturday-morning cartoon canines organize and help other strays and lost dogs bust out of the prison known to humans as the City Pound. Hanna-

Barbera production is once again based on a line of ever-so-cute toy products. Additional volumes available.
1985 50m/C V: Ed Begley Jr., Jo Anne Worley, Jonathan Winters. **VHS, Beta** *FHE*

Powder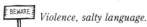

PG-13/Jr. High-Adult A la "Nell," film begins with police discovering albino boy Jeremy, aka Powder (Flanery), tucked away in a house after his grandfather dies. He's placed in a school for troubled boys, but the trouble is he's a genius who can also transmit electricity through his body. Other boys pick on him anyway. He bears it all stoically. Disney had to deal with unexpected controversy surrounding director Salva's prior criminal sexual conviction.

> **BEWARE** *Profanity, nudity, and sexual talk. A gripping scene with a dying deer may be hard for some.*

1995 111m/C Sean Patrick Flanery, Mary Steenburgen, Lance Henriksen, Jeff Goldblum, Brandon Smith, Bradford Tatum, Susan Tyrrell, Missy Crider, Ray Wise, Esteban Louis Powell; **D:** Victor Salva; **W:** Victor Salva; **C:** Jerzy Zielinski; **M:** Jerry Goldsmith. **VHS** *TOU*

The Power of One

PG-13/Jr. High-Adult Set in South Africa during the 1940s, the anti-apartheid drama depicts P.K., a white orphan of British descent sent to a boarding school run by Afrikaaners (South Africans of German descent). Humiliated and bullied, particularly when England and the Axis go to war, P.K. finds friends in a German pianist and a black coach who teach him to fight for rights of all races. Preachy, well-intentioned, and crammed with stereotypes, with "The Karate Kid" director giving it the usual triumphant young underdog treatment. Based on the novel by Bryce Courtenay.

> **BEWARE** *Violence, salty language.*

1992 126m/C Stephen Dorff, Armin Mueller-Stahl, Morgan Freeman, John Gielgud, Fay Masterson, Marius Weyers, Tracy Brooks Swope, John Osborne, Daniel Craig, Dominic Walker, Alois Mayo, Ian Roberts, Maria Marais; **D:** John G. Avildsen; **W:** Robert Mark Kamen. **VHS, LV** *WAR*

Prancer

G/Family Eight-year-old Jessica, motherless and facing a bleak winter in a recession-hit town, finds a sick, oddly docile reindeer. She decides he's one of Santa's flying deer gone astray, and tries to nurse 'Prancer' back to health. Recent revivals suggest this is evolving into a true holiday classic. Elliott's properly somber and gruff as the dad trying to do right, while Harrell is believable as the kid with a reindeer secret. Occasionally contrived and obvious, with an ending that steps too far over the line into fantasy. No wonder folks love it.
1989 102m/C Sam Elliott, Rebecca Harrell, Cloris Leachman, Rutanya Alda, John Joseph Duda, Abe Vigoda, Michael Constantine, Ariana Richards, Mark Rolston; **D:** John Hancock; **M:** Maurice Jarre. **VHS, Beta, LV, 8mm** *COL, ORI, FCT*

Precious Pupp

Family Cartoon compilation about the most charming dog alive and his owner, who enjoy some wacky adventures together, Hanna-Barbera style.
198? 51m/C VHS, Beta *TTC*

Prehysteria

PG/Primary-Adult Family flick deserves bones just for marketing savvy, arriving on tape while "Jurassic Park" cleaned up in theaters. But this dino-clone has 100% non-threatening monsters. Ancient eggs from South America hatch at the farm of a widower archaeologist. His kids are delighted at the resulting brood of tame, pygmy dinosaurs—cat-sized T.Rex, mini brachiosaur, etc.—each named for a different rock star. The puppet f/x beasts are cute, the villain is dumb, and rough stuff (when bumbling burglars go after the creatures) is minimal. Alas, the script is banal and boring, but it didn't prevent this trifle from being, until Disney's "The Return of Jafar," the most profitable straight-to-video feature ever.

> **BEWARE** *Roughhousing, sex talk.*

1993 86m/C Brett Cullen, Austin O'Brien, Samantha Mills, Colleen Morris, Tony Longo, Stuart Fratkin, Stephen Lee; **D:** Albert Band, Charles Band; **W:** Greg Suddeth, Mark Goldstein. **VHS, Beta** *PAR*

Prehysteria! 2

PG/Primary-Adult The original "Prehysteria" earned piles of money, but evidently none of it went to the f/x budget of this weak sequel, since the dwarf dinosaurs look even more like lifeless puppets. Talented kid actors can't help much with a plot about the monster midgets leaving their ranch and helping a poor little rich boy cope with a nasty nanny and an inattentive yuppie dad.

> **BEWARE** *Roughhousing.*

1994 81m/C Kevin R. Connors, Jennifer Harte, Dean Scofield, Bettye Ackerman, Larry Hankin, Greg Lewis, Alan Palo, Michael Hagiwara, Owen Bush; **D:** Albert Band; **W:** Brent Friedman, Michael Paul Davis; **M:** Richard Band. **VHS, Beta** *PAR*

Prehysteria 3

PG/Primary-Adult The mini-dinos take up miniature golf. Seems Thomas MacGregor's (Willard) putt-putt business is about to sink when his daughter Ella (Anderson) finds the pygmy dinosaurs and a promotional bonanza is born. But Thomas' evil brother Hal (Weitz) hatches a plot to take over the now-successful enterprise.

> **BEWARE** *Mild language and humorous mini pranks.*

1995 85m/C Fred Willard, Bruce Weitz, Whitney Anderson, Pam Matteson; **D:** Julian Breen; **W:** Michael Paul Davis, Neil Ruttenberg. **VHS** *PAR*

Prelude to a Kiss

PG-13/Jr. High-Adult Disappointing screen adaptation of Craig Lucas' hit play features Baldwin and Ryan as

Jeff Goldblum befriends outcast Sean Patrick Flanery in "Powder."

young lovers in this romantic fantasy. Ryan is Rita, a free-spirited bartender and Baldwin is Peter, a conservative writer, who decide to marry after a whirlwind courtship. At their wedding reception, Rita obligingly kisses one of their guests, an old man (Walker). Then, on their honeymoon, Peter begins to notice a number of changes to Rita's character and comes to realize this is truly not the girl he married. The delicate fantasy which worked on stage struggles to survive the "opening up" of the screen adaptation though Baldwin (who reprises his stage role) and Ryan are appealing. **1992 106m/C** Alec Baldwin, Meg Ryan, Sydney Walker, Ned Beatty, Patty Duke, Kathy Bates, Stanley Tucci; **D:** Norman Rene; **M:** Howard Shore. **VHS, LV** *FXV, PMS*

Pretty in Pink 🎵🎵 🎵

PG-13/Jr. High-Adult More teen pain from the pen of John Hughes. Working-class girl Andie falls for a rich guy. Their families fret, their friends are distressed particularly the boy's snobby clique and Andie's longtime steady. If you can buy into the themes of peer pressure and economic social classes flourishing in high school, then you may be able to accept the premise. Slickly done and adequately, if not enthusiastically, acted (watch for Clay, before his career as a hyper-offensive stand-up com-

ic). In 1987, Hughes remade this film and put himself in the director's chair with much of the same result: see "Some Kind of Wonderful."

> 🚸 BEWARE 🚸 *Profanity. Lots of teens cavorting and drinking at a party. Feelings get hurt.*

1986 96m/C Molly Ringwald, Andrew McCarthy, Jon Cryer, Harry Dean Stanton, James Spader, Annie Potts, Andrew Dice Clay, Margaret Colin, Alexa Kenin, Gina Gershon, Dweezil Zappa; **D:** Howard Deutch; **W:** John Hughes; **M:** Michael Gore. **VHS, Beta, LV, 8mm** *PAR*

The Pretty Piggies: The Adventure Begins

Family Four good-lookin' little pigs struggle for survival against pirates, dinosaurs, and a mean woman who acts like a queen. Additional volumes available.
1990 25m/C VHS *VTR*

The Prime of Miss Jean Brodie 🎵🎵🎵

PG/Jr. High-Adult Oscar-winning performance by Smith as a forward-thinking teacher in a Scottish girls' school during the 1920's. She captivates her impressionable young students with her fascist ideals and free-thinking attitudes in this adaptation of the play taken from Muriel Spark's novel.

 *Mature themes.*

1969 116m/C Maggie Smith, Pamela Franklin, Robert Stephens, Celia Johnson, Gordon Jackson, Jane Carr; *D:* Ronald Neame; *W:* Jay Presson Allen. **Award Nominations:** Academy Awards '69: Best Song ("Jean"); Cannes Film Festival '69: Best Film; **Awards:** Academy Awards '69: Best Actress (Smith); British Academy Awards '69: Best Actress (Smith), Best Supporting Actress (Johnson). **VHS, Beta** *FOX, BTV*

Primo Baby 🦴 🦴

Family A 15-year-old delinquent is placed with a foster father who happens to raise racehorses. The girl learns responsibility, discipline, and horse-movie cliches by caring for a vision-impaired thoroughbred and entering it in a championship race. Farfetched family horseventure from Canada.

1988 97m/C VHS *WOV*

The Prince and the Great Race 🦴 🦴

Family Three Australian children search the outback to find their kidnapped horse who is scheduled to run in the big New Year's Day Race.

1983 91m/C John Ewart, John Howard, Nicole Kidman. **VHS, Beta** *LIV*

The Prince and the Pauper 🦴 🦴 🦴

Family Satisfying version of the classic story of a young street urchin who trades places with the lookalike heir to the throne of England. Flynn's presence as the adult lead guarantees swashbuckling entertainment galore, though not the most accurate rendering of Mark Twain's class-boundary themes. Also available in a computer-colorized version.

1937 118m/B Errol Flynn, Claude Rains, Alan Hale, Billy Mauch, Montagu Love, Henry Stephenson, Barton MacLane; *D:* William Keighley; *M:* Erich Wolfgang Korngold. **VHS, Beta, LV** *FOX, MLB, CCB*

The Prince and the Pauper 🦴 🦴

Family Prince and a poor young boy swap their clothes and identities, thus causing understandable confusion in Merrie Englande. Minor-league Disney made-for-TV adaptation of the story by Mark Twain.

1962 93m/C Guy Williams, Laurence Naismith, Donald Houston, Jane Asher, Walter Hudd. **VHS, Beta** *DIS*

The Prince and the Pauper 🦴 🦴 🦴

PG/Family Large-scale redo of the Mark Twain classic, heavily indebted to the "Three Musketeers" swashbucklers of the '70s for its tongue-in-cheek attitude, as an English prince and a street urchin ("Oliver!" star Lester

If you like *The Prince and the Pauper (1937)*, you'll love:

Dave (1993)

Desperately Seeking Susan (1985)

18 Again! (1988)

Fluke (1995)

Freaky Friday (1976)

Hiding Out (1987)

It Takes Two (1996)

Just One of the Guys (1985)

Ladybugs (1992)

Like Father, Like Son (1987)

Monkey Business (1952)

Overboard (1987)

The Parent Trap (1961)

The Prince and Pauper (1978)

The Shaggy D.A. (1976)

The Shaggy Dog (1959)

Soul Man (1986)

Tootsie (1982)

Vice Versa (1988)

Yentl (1983)

was a bit old for the dual role) see that they have identical appearances and get switched with each other. Enjoyable, but still feels like a smug put-on from time to time. Also known as "Crossed Swords."

 Victorian roughhousing.

1978 113m/C Oliver Reed, Raquel Welch, Mark Lester, Ernest Borgnine, George C. Scott, Rex Harrison, Charlton Heston, Sybil Danning; *D:* Richard Fleischer; *M:* Maurice Jarre. **VHS, Beta** *MED*

The Prince and the Pauper

Family Mickey Mouse came out of nearly a decade's retirement to star in this cartoon version of the Twain classic about two lookalikes from opposite ends of the economic scale who trade places.
1991 24m/C VHS, Beta *DIS*

Prince Brat and the Whipping Boy 🎜🎜🎜

G/Family Orphaned Jemmy (Munro) is living on the streets of the 18th-century German town of Brattenburg with his younger sister Annyrose (Salt). Neglected, spoiled Prince Horace (Knight) has been causing mischief in the castle but instead of being punished himself, the king's men catch Jemmy and use him as a punishment stand-in. Jemmy escapes the castle to get back to his sister and the Prince decides to go along for the adventure. Filmed on location in North Rhine-Westphalia and Burgundy, Germany. Adventurous TV movie with spunky leads; adapted from Sid Fleischman's novella.
1995 96m/C Truan Munro, Nic Knight, Karen Salt, George C. Scott, Kevin Conway, Vincent Schiavelli, Andrew Bicknell, Jean Anderson, Mathilda May; *D:* Syd Macartney; *W:* Max Brindle; *M:* Lee Holdridge. **VHS, LV** *COL*

Prince Cinders

Family Title says it all. This twisted fairytale finds a prince who has to stay at home doing laundry while his macho brothers go to town. His fairy godmother tries to help but she winds up turning the young prince into an ape. Ages 5 to 9.
1994 30m/C VHS *ICA*

The Prince of Central Park 🎜🎜🎜

Jr. High-Adult Two young orphans are forced by circumstance to live in a tree In New York's Central Park until they are befriended by a lonely old woman. Above-average made for TV adaptation of the novel by Evan H. Rhodes; the story was later used for a Broadway play.
1977 76m/C Ruth Gordon, T.J. Hargrave, Lisa Richards, Brooke Shields, Marc Vahanian, Dan Hedaya; *D:* Harvey Hart. **VHS, Beta** *LIV*

Prince Valiant 🎜🎜 ♭

Family Uneven but entertaining swashbuckler based on Hal Foster's newspaper comic strip. Valiant is a Scandinavian prince who journey's to King Arthur's Court to learn to become a knight. First half of the picture gets sidetracked by silly romantic mixups (Princess: "I hate you! I love you!"), but it comes to rousing life in the action-packed second hour, when Val aids Christianized Vikings to rebel against a pagan tyrant. The use of Cinemascope filming suffers badly on the small screen, especially in the climactic duel.

BEWARE *Violence.*

1954 100m/C James Mason, Janet Leigh, Robert Wagner, Debra Paget, Sterling Hayden, Victor McLaglen, Donald Crisp, Brian Aherne, Barry Jones, Mary Philips; *D:* Henry Hathaway; *W:* Dudley Nichols. **VHS, Beta** *FXV, FCT*

Prince Valiant

Family Animated version of Hal Foster's comic strip, with Prince Valiant undertaking a dangerous journey to find the legendary land of Camelot.
199? 92m/C *V:* Robby Benson, Efrem Zimbalist Jr., Samantha Eggar, Tim Curry. **VHS**

Princes in Exile 🎜🎜 ♭

PG-13/Sr. High-Adult Made-for-TV movie about young people with life-threatening illnesses at a special summer camp. They find that love and friendship hold the key to dreams about the future. Excellent cast of newcomers. Based on a novel of the same name by Mark Schreiber.

BEWARE *Kids with terminal illnesses and tough situations.*

1990 103m/C Zachary Ansley, Nicholas Shields, Stacy Mistysyn, Alexander Chapman, Chuck Shamata; *D:* Giles Walker. **VHS, Beta, LV** *FRH, FCT*

Princess and the Goblin

PG/Primary-Jr. High Story based on the George MacDonald book combines illustration and closeups of Jackson reading. Complete with puzzle.
1992 60m/C VHS *DOV, HMD*

The Princess and the Goblin 🎜🎜

G/Family Smaller kiddies may enjoy this British-made animated adventure but it's a bland story with mediocre animation. Nasty, underground-dwelling goblins (portrayed as silly rather than scary) plot against the surface kingdom of humans, especially little Princess Irene. Brave boy miner Curdie helps save the day. Based on a book by George MacDonald that's been a favorite with English kids for a century.
1994 82m/C *V:* Sally Ann Marsh, Peter Murray, Claire Bloom. **VHS** *HMD*

The Princess and the Pea

Family "Faerie Tale Theatre" gives us Liza Minnelli in the title role (no, not the pea) in the story of a princess who tries to prove that she's a blueblood by feeling the bump of a tiny pea under the twenty mattresses. Ages 4 to 8.
1983 60m/C Liza Minnelli, Tom Conti, Tim Kazurinsky, Pat McCormick, Beatrice Straight; *D:* Tony Bill. **VHS, Beta, LV** *FOX, FCT*

The Princess Bride 🎜🎜🎜 ♭

PG/Family Smart spoof of the basic bedtime story, crammed with all the cliches. Beautiful maiden is carried off to the kingdom of Florin to be married to its prince, but he plans to do away with her in a diabolical plot. To the rescue comes her swashbuckling true love, at the head of an increasingly strange rescue party. Great dueling scenes and offbeat satire of fairy tales make this fun for adults as well as children. Based on William Goldman's cult novel—and without the book's infuriating open ending.

 Swashbuckling violence.

1987 98m/C Cary Elwes, Mandy Patinkin, Robin Wright, Wallace Shawn, Peter Falk, Andre the Giant, Chris Sarandon, Christopher Guest, Billy Crystal, Carol Kane, Fred Savage, Peter Cook, Mel Smith; **D:** Rob Reiner; **W:** William Goldman; **M:** Mark Knopfler. **VHS, Beta, LV, 8mm** *COL, HMV*

Princess Caraboo 🎵🎵🎵

PG/Jr. High-Adult Though based on a true story, film plays like pure fantasy. The year is 1817 and a young woman (Cates) who speaks a language nobody knows is taken for a shipwrecked princess from Java. She is taken in by an aristocratic family—or perhaps it's she who is taking them in. So suggests a skeptical reporter (Rea), while an even more skeptical language professor from Oxford (Lithgow) is convinced she's a phony. She could be the real thing, though. Charming and intelligent. Family films often pay lip service to the power of imagination but this one is about how imagination may truly change someone's life.

 The butler, who wants to see if Caraboo understands English, tells her he urinated in the soup.

1994 97m/C Phoebe Cates, Stephen Rea, John Lithgow, Kevin Kline, Jim Broadbent, Wendy Hughes, Peter Eyre, Jacqueline Pearce, John Lynch, John Sessions, Arkie Whiteley, John Wells; **D:** Michael Austin; **W:** John Wells, Michael Austin; **M:** Richard Hartley. **VHS, LV** *COL*

Princess Gwenevere and the Jewel Riders

Primary A band of three mythical females and their forest animal friends join forces to save their magical kingdom. Ages 3 to 6.

1996 ?m/C VHS *FHE, LIV*

Princess Jasmine: Magic and Mystery

Preschool-Primary From Disney's Princess Collection, this video features two episodes about spirited and loved heroine Princess Jasmine. "The Secret of Dagger Rock" finds Aladdin and Jasmine attacked by the evil Mozenrath who wants the Genie's lamp. Mozenrath keeps Aladdin hostage at Dagger Rock and his only chance is to be saved by beautiful Princess Jasmine. "Forget Me Lots" finds Jasmine under the spell of the Blue Rose of Forgetfulness.

1996 ?m/C VHS *DIS*

Princess Jasmine: True Hearts

Preschool-Primary Princess Jasmine appears in two exciting episodes. "Eye of the Beholder" Aladdin and Jasmine must find the cure for a terrible spell Jasmine has been put under. The evil Mirage has turned her into a hideous snake woman. True love prevails. In "Sandswitch," chaos ensues when Sadira, a female street rat, sets her sights on Aladdin.

1996 ?m/C VHS *DIS*

Princess Scargo and the Birthday Pumpkin

Preschool-Primary The "Rabbit Ears: We All Have Tales" series retells a Native American legend about a young girl who gives up a precious gift to aid her people.

1992 30m/C VHS *RAB, BTV, PMS*

The Princess Who Never Laughed

Family A stern king (Howard Hesseman) holds a laugh-off contest to make his morose daughter (Ellen Barkin) happy in this adaptation of the Brothers Grimm story from the "Faerie Tale Theatre" series. Howie Mandel is the successful candidate. Ages 4 to 10.

1984 60m/C Ellen Barkin, Howard Hesseman, Howie Mandel, Mary Woronov. **VHS, Beta** *FOX, FCT*

The Private Eyes 🎵 🎵

PG/Family Airheaded comedic romp with Knotts and Conway as bungling Scotland Yard sleuths investigating two deaths. They're led on a merry chase through secret passages to a meeting with a ghostly adversary in a spooky old house. Ages 6 to 10.

1980 91m/C Don Knotts, Tim Conway, Trisha Noble, Bernard Fox; **D:** Lang Elliott; **W:** Tim Conway, John Myhers. **VHS, Beta, LV** *VES*

Prize Fighter 🎵🎵

PG/Family The comedy team of Knotts and Conway take on the "Rocky" plot. Depression-era brawler Conway seems to be an underdog on a winning streak to the championship, but neither he nor his nitwit manager realize all their matches have been fixed by a gangster. Scripted by Conway and mainly enjoyable if intelligence is suspended at onset.

 *Roughhousing.*

1979 99m/C Tim Conway, Don Knotts; **D:** Michael Preece; **W:** Tim Conway. **VHS, Beta** *MED*

Problem Child 🎵 🎵

PG/Jr. High-Adult Way-obnoxious comedy that was a popular hit (so much for the Dignity of the Common Man). Junior is a destructive, sadistic brat, the terror of the orphanage. The Healys, childless yuppies, make a big mistake upon adopting Mr. Sweetness and Light. Meek stepdad Ben tries to reform the kid with love and

Cary Elwes protects Robin Wright in "The Princess Bride."

sweetness despite all the vicious pranks Junior and a repetitious, one-note script can unleash on him. In order to make Junior look 'cute,' every character but Ben is a cartoon creep, fully deserving of what they get.

BEWARE *Roughhousing, sex talk. Junior's no role model, that's for sure.*

1990 81m/C John Ritter, Michael Oliver, Jack Warden, Amy Yasbeck, Gilbert Gottfried, Michael Richards, Peter Jurasik; **D:** Dennis Dugan; **W:** Scott Alexander, Larry Karaszewski; **M:** Miles Goodman. **VHS, LV** *MCA*

Problem Child 2 ♫

PG-13/Jr. High-Adult Ben Healy and his nasty adopted son Junior move to another town, full of man-hungry divorcees. None is worse than wealthy, witchy Lawanda; in order to stop her marriage plans for Ben, Junior joins forces with his equal in malevolence, a little girl from school. Director Levant went on to do "Beethoven" and "The Flintstones," but he'll not escape responsibility for this lowly slapstick, with a marathon mass-vomiting scene setting a new high in depths.

BEWARE *Sex, slapstick violence, bad-taste gags involving urine and doggie dung, to name but a few.*

1991 91m/C John Ritter, Michael Oliver, Laraine Newman, Amy Yasbeck, Jack Warden, Ivyann Schwan, Gilbert Gottfried, James

Tolkan, Charlene Tilton, Alan Blumenfeld; **D:** Brian Levant; **W:** Scott Alexander, Larry Karaszewski. **VHS, Beta, LV** *MCA*

The Prodigal ♫♫

PG/Jr. High-Adult Born-again family drama in which a sundered family is brought together by the return of a once-estranged son. Filled with Hollywood celebrities, and the Rev. Billy Graham adding his own variation on star power.

1983 109m/C John Hammond, Hope Lange, John Cullum, Morgan Brittany, Ian Bannen, Arliss Howard, Joey Travolta, Billy Graham; **M:** Bruce Broughton. **VHS, Beta, LV** *LIV*

Professor Iris: Music Mania

Preschool Professor Iris teaches preschoolers all about music, song, and dance from around the world with his classroom orchestra. Additional volumes available.

1993 40m/C VHS *DHE, BTV*

The Program ♫♫ ♭

R/Sr. High-Adult Sensitive tearjerker about college football players getting caught up in the drive for a championship. As the season takes its toll on both mind and body, players prepare for the Big Game. Caan is the team's gruff coach, who's willing to look the other way as long as his boys are winning. Film sparked controversy when the Disney studio pulled and recut it after release because one scene, where Sheffer's character lies down in traffic, sparked copy-cat actions and several deaths. The scene was not restored for the video version.

 Profanity and a win-at-all-costs coach.

1993 110m/C James Caan, Craig Sheffer, Kristy Swanson, Halle Berry, Omar Epps, Duane Davis, Abraham Benrubi, Jon Maynard Pennell, Andrew Bryniarski; **D:** David S. Ward; **W:** Aaron Latham, David S. Ward; **M:** Michel Colombier. **VHS, Beta** *TOU*

Project X 🦮🦮🦮

PG/Jr. High-Adult Bemused young Air Force pilot gets a strange assignment—training chimpanzees to fly planes. He grows close to the appealing apes and is shocked to learn the true, cruel purpose of the experiments. High-tech tale falls somewhere between sci-fi and animal drama, but there's more than a touch of real wonder and an emotionally satisfying conclusion. Great performances by the primates.

BEWARE *Profanity and monkey casualties. Sensitive kids may be affected by experiments on monkeys.*

1987 107m/C Matthew Broderick, Helen Hunt, William Sadler, Johnny Rae McGhee, Jonathan Stark, Robin Gammell, Stephen Lang, Jean Smart, Dick Miller; **D:** Jonathan Kaplan; **W:** Stanley Weiser, Lawrence Lasker; **M:** James Horner. **VHS, Beta, LV** *FOX*

The Projectionist 🦮🦮🦮

PG/Jr. High-Adult Fetching and inventive low-budget tale about a misfit who works as a projectionist in a seedy New York movie house. In Walter Mitty-type fantasies, however, he's Captain Flash, a serial superhero who battles against a campy villain called The Bat (Dangerfield), aided by vintage clips of Hollywood heroes like Humphrey Bogart and John Wayne. Made when star McCann was a prominent NYC-area kiddie-show TV personality, though the intended audience is film buffs.

1971 84m/C Rodney Dangerfield, Chuck McCann, Ina Balin; **D:** Harry Hurwitz; **W:** Harry Hurwitz. **VHS, Beta** *LIV, VES*

Promises in the Dark 🦮🦮 ◦

PG/Jr. High-Adult Depressing drama focusing on the complex relationship between a woman doctor and her 17-year-old female patient who is terminally ill with cancer.

BEWARE *Dying teen.*

1979 118m/C Marsha Mason, Ned Beatty, Kathleen Beller, Susan Clark, Paul Clemens, Donald Moffat, Michael Brandon; **D:** Jerome Hellman. **VHS, Beta** *WAR*

Pssst! Hammerman's After You

Preschool-Primary A frail 11-year-old, Mouse, provokes the town bully and must face up to the consequences of his actions. Based on the Betsy Byars work

"The 18th Emergency," this was originally done for TV's "Afterschool Special."
1990 28m/C VHS, Beta *MTI, DSN*

Puff and the Incredible Mr. Nobody

Primary Cartoon compilation led by Puff the Magic Dragon and a little boy traveling through the Fantaverse to find an imaginary friend, Mr. Nobody. Does this mean that Nobody likes Puff? One of three TV specials recasting the folk-song dragon as a sort of guidance counselor to the young; musician Peter Yarrow (as in Peter, Paul and Mary) was one of the producers.
1982 45m/C V: Burgess Meredith. **VHS, Beta** *LIV, MTI*

Puff the Magic Dragon

Primary Animated adaptation of the song by Peter Yarrow (who contributes a voiceover) about little Jackie Paper and his friend Puff, The Magic Dragon. Except the boy is now called Jackie Draper (guess why) and Puff is a mentor figure who helps instill the lad with self-confidence through whimsical adventures. Taking up slack on the tape are three "Hector Heathcote" 'toons about a historical time-traveller.
1978 45m/C V: Burgess Meredith. **VHS, Beta** *LIV*

Puff the Magic Dragon in the Land of Living Lies

Primary Puff the Magic Dragon teaches a troubled little girl (caught in the throes of her parents' divorce) that there's a big difference between fantasy and telling a lie.
1979 24m/C V: Burgess Meredith. **VHS, Beta** *MTI*

Punky Brewster: Little Orphan Punky

Family Punky, Brandon, Cherie and the rest of the youthful ensemble from the short-lived network TV sitcom return for a not ready for prime-time adventure as globetrotting Saturday-morning cartoon kids. Additional volumes available.
1991 75m/C V: Soleil Moon Frye. **VHS** *JFK*

The Puppet Theater

Primary Three-part series, featuring Kansas City puppeteer Pal Mesner and company as they act out three fractured fairy tales. Emphasis is placed on teaching theatrical creation, literature, and the need to read. Ages 6 to 10.
1994 60m/C VHS

The Puppetoon Movie 🦮🦮

G/Family This begins by comparing stop-motion animation pioneer George Pal to Walt Disney, but when Pal's famous Puppetoon musical shorts from the '30s and '40s unreel it's clear they haven't held their charm like Uncle

Walt's cartoons. Included are "Tubby the Tuba," "Tulips Shall Grow" (an anti-Nazi allegory), and perhaps best of all, a modern Sleeping Beauty awakened by swing music. Outdated racial stereotypes too often predominate, though they're mercifully absent in the "John Henry" segment. Gumby, Pokey, Speedy Alka Seltzer and the Pillsbury Doughboy appear in too-brief prologue and epilogue scenes; for a career history of Pal himself, see "The Fantasy Film Worlds of George Pal."

1987 80m/C **D:** Arnold Leibovit; **M:** Buddy Baker. **VHS, Beta, LV** *FHE*

The Pure Hell of St. Trinian's

Jr. High-Adult Sequel to "Blue Murder at St. Trinian's" finds a sheik, desiring to fill out his harem, recruiting at the rowdy girls' school. Based on the Ronald Searle carton and followed by "The Great St. Trinian's Train Robbery."

1961 94m/B Cecil Parker, Joyce Grenfell, George Cole, Thorley Walters; **D:** Frank Launder; **M:** Malcolm Arnold. **VHS** *FCT*

Purple People Eater ♪ ▷

PG/Jr. High-Sr. High The alien of the title, a silly, shaggy cyclops with all the raw realism of Barney the Dinosaur, descends to Earth to mix with teen rock'n'rollers. Based on the novelty song of the same name whose performer, Sheb Wooley, has a small part. Harmless, stupid fun for the whole family.

1988 91m/C Ned Beatty, Shelley Winters, Neil Patrick Harris, Kareem Abdul-Jabbar, Little Richard, Chubby Checker, Peggy Lipton; **D:** Linda Shayne. **VHS, Beta, LV** *MED, VTR*

The Purple Rose of Cairo ♪♪♪

PG/Sr. High-Adult A diner waitress, disillusioned by the Depression and a lackluster life, escapes into a film playing at the local movie house where a blond film hero, tiring of the monotony of his role, makes a break from the celluloid to join her in the real world. The ensuing love story allows director-writer Allen to show his knowledge of old movies and provide his fans with a change of pace. Farrow's film sister is also her real-life sister Stephanie, who went on to appear in Allen's "Zelig."

◄BEWARE► *Violence.*

1985 82m/C Mia Farrow, Jeff Daniels, Danny Aiello, Dianne Wiest, Van Johnson, Zoe Caldwell, John Wood, Michael Tucker, Edward Herrmann, Milo O'Shea, Glenne Headly, Karen Akers, Deborah Rush; **D:** Woody Allen; **W:** Woody Allen; **M:** Dick Hyman. **Award Nominations:** Academy Awards '85: Best Original Screenplay; **Awards:** British Academy Awards '85: Best Film; Cesar Awards '86: Best Foreign Film; Golden Globe Awards '86: Best Screenplay. **VHS, Beta, LV** *LIV, VES, HMV*

Puss in Boots ♪♪

Family Children's Theater Company of Minneapolis presents a jazzed-up, New Orleans-style version of the "Puss in Boots" tale. VHS version is in stereo.

◄BEWARE► *Roughhousing.*

1982 89m/C VHS, Beta *FHE*

Puss in Boots ♪ ▷

Family Banal and overlong "Cannon Movie Tales" retelling of the famous cat tale, in which the well-meaning intentions of a mischievous feline get his master out of danger again and again. Several songs are yowled.

1988 96m/C Christopher Walken, Jason Connery; **D:** Eugene Marner. **VHS, Beta** *CAN*

Puss in Boots

Primary When a down-and-out man decides to eat his entire feline inheritance, the cat comes up with a plan to save himself by transforming his owner into a noble prince. Part of the "Rabbit Ears: We All Have Tales" series of great folktales told by terrific narrators against felicitous illustrations.

1992 30m/C M: Jean Luc Ponty. **VHS** *BTV*

Puss 'n Boots

Family From "Faerie Tale Theatre" comes the story of a clever cat who makes his poor master a rich land-owning nobleman. Ben Vereen and Gregory Hines play the cat and the man. Ages 5 to 9.

1984 60m/C Ben Vereen, Gregory Hines; **D:** Robert Iscove. **VHS, Beta** *FOX, FCT*

Puss 'n Boots Travels Around the World ♪♪

Family Fairy-tale adaptation of a certain Jules Verne tale finds the feline favorite on a bet to make his way around the globe before eighty days have passed. The evildoer, Rumblehog, tries at every turn to thwart his success.

1983 70m/C VHS, Beta *COL, GKK*

The Puzzle Place: Rock Dreams

Preschool Six ethnically diverse puppet kids—and a species-ly diverse dog and cat—help teach young children how to solve life's little dilemmas. On this tape, the puppets discover, with the help of the Boys Choir of Harlem, that you don't need a fancy instrument to make good music, you just need your voice. Meanwhile, Skye, the Apache puppet kid, wants to be a musician but he's afraid that Native Americans can't play rock 'n roll. Don't bet on it. Ages 3 to 7.

1995 60m/C VHS

The Puzzle Place: Tuned In

Preschool Skye wants his friends to join his party but all they ever want to do is watch TV. Meanwhile, Julie is so obsessed with meeting her favorite star that she ignores her friends only to find out that the star is not nearly as nice as she first seems. Ages 3 to 7.

1995 60m/C VHS

Quark the Dragon Slayer ♪♪

Preschool-Primary Python alumnus Cleese narrates this silly Norse animated feature about a baby giant called Quark (after his first word) who causes a lot of trouble for his adopted village.

1990 70m/C V: John Cleese. **VHS** *CEL*

Quarterback Princess ♪♪

Jr. High-Adult Workaday made-for-TV telling of the real-life girl who goes out for football and becomes homecoming queen. Heartwarming, if you like that kinda stuff, but not exciting.

1985 96m/C Helen Hunt, Don Murray, John Stockwell, Daphne Zuniga; **D:** Noel Black. **VHS, Beta** *FOX*

Queen of Hearts ♪♪♪ ♭

PG/Jr. High-Adult Whimsy set in early-'60s Britain, about an Italian couple who defied both their families to marry for love. Four children later they're running a diner in England, but the wife's old suitor arrives to launch a devious vendetta to split mama from papa. Told through the eyes of Eddie, the 10-year-old son, who lends the complicated saga a child's-eye-view quality, uniquely blending magic, laughter, tears and the everyday.

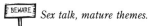 *Sex talk, mature themes.*

1989 112m/C Anita Zagaria, Joseph Long, Eileen Way, Vittorio Duse, Vittorio Amandola, Ian Hawkes; **D:** Jon Amiel; **M:** Michael Convertino. **VHS, Beta, LV** *NO*

The Quest ♪♪ ♭

PG/Jr. High-Adult Orphan Cody leads a carefree life in the Australian outback, under the hands-off parenting style of his adult guardian. Bright and brave, the boy builds wild inventions and investigates a local Aboriginal superstition about a monster in a lake. Sometimes dull, sometimes enthralling tale with an unsatisfying conclusion but an admirable young leading man in "E.T." star Thomas. Originally titled "Frog Dreaming."

BEWARE *Alcohol use, salty language.*

1986 94m/C Henry Thomas, Tony Barry, John Ewart, Rachel Friend, Tamsin West, Dennis Miller, Katya Manning; **D:** Brian Trenchard-Smith. **VHS, Beta** *NLC*

The Quiet Man ♪♪♪♪

Family Classic incarnation of Hollywood Irishness, and one of Ford's best. Wayne is Sean Thornton, a weary American ex-boxer who returns to the Irish hamlet of his childhood and tries to take a spirited lass (O'Hara, never lovelier) as his wife, despite the strenuous objections of her brawling brother (McLaglen). Thornton's aided by the leprechaun-like Fitzgerald and the local parish priest, Bond. High-spirited and memorable, brimming with stage Irish characters, witty banter, and shots of the lush countryside.

1952 129m/C John Wayne, Maureen O'Hara, Barry Fitzgerald, Victor McLaglen, Arthur Shields, Jack MacGowran, Ward Bond, Mildred Natwick, Ken Curtis, Mae Marsh, Sean McClory, Francis Ford; **D:** John Ford; **W:** Frank Nugent; **M:** Victor Young. **Award Nominations:** Academy Awards '52: Best Art Direction/Set Decoration (Color), Best Picture, Best Screenplay, Best Sound, Best Supporting Actor (McLaglen); **Awards:** Academy Awards '52: Best Color Cinematography, Best Director (Ford); National Board of Review Awards '52: 10 Best Films of the Year; Venice Film Festival '52: Best Director (Ford). **VHS, LV** *REP, TLF, CCB*

Quigley Down Under ♪♪ ♭

PG-13/Sr. High-Adult A Western sharpshooter moves to Australia to take a job. To his horror, he discovers that he has been hired to kill aboriginal people. Fine chemistry between Selleck and San Giacomo and the usual enjoyable theatrics from Rickman as the evil landowner who has hired Selleck. Ages 12 and up.

BEWARE *Violence and nudity.*

1990 121m/C Tom Selleck, Laura San Giacomo, Alan Rickman, Chris Haywood, Ron Haddrick, Tony Bonner, Roger Ward, Ben Mendelsohn, Jerome Ehlers, Conor McDermottroe; **D:** Simon Wincer; **W:** John Hill; **M:** Basil Poledouris. **VHS, Beta, LV, 8mm** *MGM*

Quiz Show ♪♪♪♪

PG-13/Sr. High-Adult Handsome college teacher Charles Van Doren (Fiennes) makes a bundle on the TV quiz show "Twenty-One" and becomes a national hero. Only one problem: The show was rigged. Not for action fans, but intellectual youngsters—the ones who call out the answers while you're watching "Jeopardy"—will appreciate a man of learning being treated like a rock star. Based on actual events. Depictions of greed, envy, corruption and that period of ancient history known as the 1950s are excellent. Exceptionally well-acted and thoughtfully directed.

BEWARE *Mild profanity and issues of moral ethics are questioned.*

1994 133m/C John Turturro, Rob Morrow, Ralph Fiennes, Paul Scofield, David Paymer, Hank Azaria, Christopher McDonald, Johann Carlo, Elizabeth Wilson, Mira Sorvino, Griffin Dunne, Martin Scorsese, Barry Levinson; **D:** Robert Redford; **W:** Paul Attanasio; **M:** Mark Isham. **Award Nominations:** Academy Awards '94: Best Adapted Screenplay, Best Director (Redford), Best Picture, Best Supporting Actor (Scofield); Golden Globe Awards '95: Best Director (Redford), Best Film—Drama, Best Screenplay, Best Supporting Actor (Turturro); **Awards:** British Academy Awards '94: Best Adapted Screenplay; New York Film Critics Awards '94: Best Film. **VHS, LV** *HPH*

Rabbit Ears Storybook Classics Collection

Family Acclaimed series of tapes in which well-known fairy tales are read by popular celebrities, while beautiful paintings (sometimes with limited animation) help bring the stories to life. See individual listings for details; titles include "The Emperor and His Nightingale," "The Fisherman and His Wife," "How the Leopard Got His Spots," "How the Rhinoceros Got His Skin," "How the Camel Got His Hump," "The Legend of Sleepy Hollow," "Pecos Bill,"

"The Tale of Gloucester," "The Tale of Mr. Jeremy Fisher," "The Tale of Peter Rabbit," "The Three Billy Goats Gruff," "The Three Little Pigs," "Thumbelina," "Bre'r Rabbit and the Wonderful Tar Baby," "Paul Bunyan," "Red Riding Hood," "Goldilocks," and "The Emperor's New Clothes."
1988 30m/C VHS, Beta COL, HMV

Raccoons: Let's Dance

Family Canadian TV cartoon characters Melissa, Ralph, and Bert Raccoon perform in six of their own original music videos, designed especially for children.
1984 30m/C Rita Coolidge, Leo Sayer, John Schneider, Dottie West. **VHS, Beta** NLC

Raccoons on Ice

Family Two Canadian cartoons featuring Ralph, Melissa, and Bert Raccoon. In "Raccoons on Ice," they play a hockey game against the Brutish Bears. "Christmas Raccoons" finds them fighting to protect Evergreen Forest and their "raccoondominium" home.
1982 49m/C M: Leo Sayer, Rita Coolidge. **VHS, Beta, LV**

Race for Your Life, Charlie Brown 🦴🦴 ▷

G/Family Third in the feature-length theatrical cartoons based on the "Peanuts" comic strip finds perennial loser Charlie Brown and his companions at summer camp long before Ernest ever set foot there. Traditionally loose plot concerns an anti-boy campaign (led by Lucy) and a whitewater raft race.
1977 76m/C W: Charles M. Schulz. **VHS, Beta, LV** PAR

Race the Sun 🦴🦴 ▷

PG/Family Your basic loser-kids-become-winners-through-bowling film, but substitute "solar-powered car" for the sport of your choice. Attractive science teacher (Berry) at a Hawaii high school, induces her class of scorned "lolos" (local lowlifes) to build a solar car and enter it in the World Solar Car Challenge, in Australia. Mmmm, that sounds easy. Now students, teacher and car must successfully cross the Australian desert. Win or lose, they're bound to learn the value of teamwork and perseverance. Nothing new, but the young actors are engaging and the Australian scenery is beautiful.

BEWARE *Mild language and a brief incident of teen drinking. Includes a scary scene when a driver is trapped in a burning car.*

1996 105m/C Halle Berry, James Belushi, Casey Affleck, Eliza Dushku, Kevin Tighe, Anthony Michael Ruivivar, J. Moki Cho, Dion Basco, Sara Tanaka, Nadja Pionilla, Steve Zahn, Bill Hunter; **D:** Charles Kanganis; **W:** Barry Morrow; **C:** David Burr; **M:** Graeme Revell. **VHS** NYR

Racing with the Moon 🦴🦴🦴

PG/Sr. High-Adult Sweet, nostalgic film about two buddies awaiting induction into the Marines in 1942.

They have their last chance at summer romance. Benjamin makes the most of skillful young actors and conventional story. Great period detail. Keep your eyes peeled for glimpses of many rising young stars including Hannah and Carvey.

BEWARE *Profanity, nudity, suggested sex, brief violence.*

1984 108m/C Sean Penn, Elizabeth McGovern, Nicolas Cage, John Karlen, Rutanya Alda, Max Casey Adams Showalter, Crispin Glover, Suzanne Adkinson, Page Hannah, Michael Madsen, Dana Carvey, Carol Kane, Michael Talbott; **D:** Richard Benjamin; **W:** Steven Kloves; **M:** Dave Grusin. **VHS, Beta, LV** PAR

Rad 🦴 ▷

PG/Jr. High-Adult Flat-tired teenage drama revolving around BMX bicycle racing from stuntmaster Needham. The kid hero neglects his paper route and endangers his SAT scores to show his stuff in the big competition. Real-life BMX Olympics star Bart Conner plays the nasty champ.

BEWARE *Salty junior biker language.*

1986 94m/C Bill Allen, Bart Conner, Talia Shire, Jack Weston, Lori Loughlin; **D:** Hal Needham. **VHS, Beta, LV** NLC

Radar Men from the Moon

Family Republic serial that reused both the Rocket Man costume (last seen in "King of the Rocketmen") and the alien suits (plus some of the plot) from "The Purple Monster Strikes." Space avenger Commando Cody flies into action against Retik, an invader from the moon who allies himself with Earth gangsters. An admirable example of recycling, but nothing special as a plot. In 12 episodes. Also known as "Commando Cody," after the hero who subsequently got his own network TV series.

BEWARE *Violence.*

1952 152m/B George Wallace, Aline Towne, Roy Barcroft, William "Billy" Bakewell, Clayton Moore; **D:** Fred Brannon. **VHS, LV** NOS, REP, SNC

Radio Days 🦴🦴🦴 ▷

PG/Sr. High-Adult Lovely, unpretentious remembrance of a NYC childhood during World War II. Allen fashions a series of comic vignettes centering around a youth in Brooklyn, his eccentric extended family, and the radio entertainers who held them spellbound in that pre-TV era. Not strong on plot, but many scenes (like the boy narrator's once-in-a- lifetime glimpse of an Axis submarine) won't soon be forgotten.

BEWARE *Sex talk.*

1987 96m/C Mia Farrow, Dianne Wiest, Julie Kavner, Michael Tucker, Wallace Shawn, Josh Mostel, Tony Roberts, Jeff Daniels, Kenneth Mars, Seth Green, William Magerman, Diane Keaton, Renee Lippin, Danny Aiello, Gina DeAngelis, Kitty Carlisle Hart, Mercedes Ruehl, Tito Puente; **D:** Woody Allen; **W:** Woody Allen. **VHS, Beta, LV** HBO

Radio Flyer

PG-13/Jr. High-Adult It's 1969 and Mike and Bobby have just moved to northern California with their divorced mom. All would be idyllic except mom marries a drunk who beats Bobby. Mike decides to help Bobby escape by turning their Radio Flyer wagon into a magic flying machine that will carry the boy beyond harm's reach. Infamous box-office flop offers a truly appealing version of childhood dreams and imagination, but its child abuse angle and darker aspects (some commentators interpret the Radio Flyer as a metaphor for suicide) were desperately rewritten and reshot. The unsatisfactory ending cops out with a flight into pure fantasy, followed by a child abuse public service announcement.

BEWARE *Salty language, brutality, mature themes (what's left of them).*

1992 114m/C Elijah Wood, Joseph Mazzello, Lorraine Bracco, Adam Baldwin, John Heard, Ben Johnson; **D:** Richard Donner. **VHS, LV** *COL*

Radio Patrol

Family Pinky Adams, radio cop, is assisted by his trusted canine partner Irish. A cop's best friend is his dog in this action-packed 12-chapter serial.

1937 235m/B Mickey Rentschler, Adrian Morris, Monte Montague, Jack Mulhall, Grant Withers, Catherine Hughes; **D:** Ford Beebe, Cliff Smith. **VHS, Beta** *NOS, VDM, MLB*

Radioland Murders

PG/Jr. High-Adult Looks overwhelm weak plot in this mystery-comedy about 1939 Chicago radio station WBN. Lots of stock types (befuddled director, preening announcer, lusty vamp) with Masterson as Penny, the secretary holding everything together except for her marriage to head writer Roger (Benben). Then bodies start piling up during the live broadcast and everyone runs around frantically trying to solve the crimes and keep the broadcast going. Tiring and cliched.

BEWARE *Mild language, brief nudity, and farcical violence.*

1994 112m/C Brian Benben, Mary Stuart Masterson, Ned Beatty, George Burns, Brion James, Michael Lerner, Michael McKean, Jeffrey Tambor, Scott Michael Campbell, Anita Morris, Stephen Tobolowsky, Christopher Lloyd, Larry Miller, Corbin Bernsen; **Cameos:** Robert Klein, Harvey Korman, Peter MacNicol, Joey Lawrence, Bob(cat) Goldthwait; **D:** Mel Smith; **W:** Willard Huyck, Gloria Katz, Jeff Reno, Ron Osborn; **C:** David Tattersall; **M:** Joel McNeely. **VHS, LV** *MCA*

Raffi in Concert with the Rise & Shine Band

Preschool-Primary Back by a four-piece band, favorite children's entertainer Raffi sings such kid-hits as "Baby Beluga," "Apples and Bananas," "All I Really Need," "Rise and Shine" "Shake My Sillies Out" and "Five Little Ducks." Lets kids feel like insiders with a bit of backstage, pre-concert footage showing Raffi and the band rehearsing "The More We Get Together." Ages 2 to 6.
1988 50m/C VHS, Beta, LV, 8mm *MVD, PGV, A&M*

Raffi on Broadway

Preschool-Primary Raffi goes uptown—or at least midtown—with a concert at the Gershwin Theater. Program of children songs includes "Day O," "This Little Light of Mine," "Down By the Bay," "Brush Your Teeth," "Evergreen Everblue" and his signature tune, the wonderful "Baby Beluga." Ages 2 to 6.
1994 63m/C VHS *MCA*

Raffi: Young Children's Concert with Raffi

Preschool-Primary The popular composer and singer of songs for kids performs his first videotaped concert, in Toronto. His standards include "Baby Beluga," "Shake My Sillies Out," "Wheels on a Bus." "You Gotta Sing when the Spirit Says Sing," "I've Been Working on the Railroad" and "The Corner Grocery Store." Ages 2 to 6.
1990 45m/C VHS, Beta, LV, 8mm *MVD, A&M, COL*

Raft Adventures of Huck & Jim

Preschool-Primary Loose adaptation of "Huckleberry Finn" puts Mark Twain's adventurous duo down the Mississippi River on a raft.
1978 72m/C Timothy Gibbs. **VHS, Beta** *FHE*

Raggedy Ann and Andy

Family Two cartoon Raggedy Ann and Andy TV specials from Chuck Jones. In "The Pumpkin Who Couldn't Smile," the pair aid a boy who lost his Halloween pumpkin. "The Great Santa Claus Caper" has them foiling a plot to turn Santa's workshop into a factory.
1979 52m/C D: Chuck Jones; **V:** June Foray, Daws Butler. **VHS, Beta** *MPI*

Raggedy Ann and Andy: A Musical Adventure

G/Family Cartoon feature adventure of the lookalike dolls Raggedy Ann and Andy, who embark on a song-filled quest to rescue a kidnapped plaything. Animation is lovely but the plot sags like a rag . . . well, you know. No fewer than 16 musical numbers ooze by.
1977 87m/C D: Richard Williams; **V:** Didi Conn, Joe Silver. **VHS, Beta** *FOX*

Rags to Riches

Family A wealthy Beverly Hills entrepreneur decides to improve his public image by adopting six teenage orphan girls. They have other ideas. TV pilot. Ages 8 to 12.
1987 96m/C Joseph Bologna, Tisha Campbell. **VHS, Beta** *VTR, NWV*

Raiders of the Lost Ark

PG/Family Breathless '30s-style adventure made Indiana Jones a household name. The intrepid archeologist

A group of misfit high schoolers build a solar car in "Race the Sun."

battles Nazis, decodes hieroglyphics and tries to avoid snakes in his search for the biblical Ark of the Covenant. Truly hair-raising opening scene starts an avalanche of f/x and fun (with a nagging feeling that the stunts are shaping the story instead of the other way around). Followed by the controversial "Indiana Jones and the Temple of Doom," and later a short-lived TV series.

BEWARE *Violence galore, including melting flesh that pushes the boundaries of a PG rating. Alcohol use, sex talk.*

1981 115m/C Harrison Ford, Karen Allen, Wolf Kahler, Paul Freeman, John Rhys-Davies, Denholm Elliott, Ronald Lacey, Anthony Higgins, Alfred Molina; **D:** Steven Spielberg; **W:** George Lucas, Philip Kaufman; **M:** John Williams. **Award Nominations:** Academy Awards '81: Best Cinematography, Best Director (Spielberg), Best Picture, Best Original Score; **Awards:** Academy Awards '81: Best Art Direction/Set Decoration, Best Film Editing, Best Sound, Best Visual Effects; People's Choice Awards '82: Best Film. **VHS, Beta, LV, 8mm** *PAR*

The Railway Dragon

Family Little Emily and her magical friend, a shy dragon who lives under the old railway tunnel, set off for a secret festival of the legendary reptiles in this well-animated adventure.

1988 30m/C VHS, Beta *FHE*

Rain Man 🎧🎧🎧🎧

R/Sr. High-Adult When his wealthy father dies, ambitious and self-centered Charlie Babbit finds he has Raymond, an older autistic brother who's been institutionalized for years. He's also something of a savant, having extraordinary math skills. Needing him to claim an inheritance, Charlie liberates Raymond from the institution and takes to the road, where both brothers undergo subtle changes. Vegas montage, with Raymond and his mathematical wizardry loose in the casinos, is special. Splendid from start to finish, with Hoffman providing a classic performance both funny and touching. Cruise supplies his best performance to date as he goes from cad to recognizing something wonderfully human in his brother and himself.

BEWARE *Profanity, subtle prostitution and sex.*

1988 128m/C Dustin Hoffman, Tom Cruise, Valeria Golino, Jerry Molen, Jack Murdock, Michael D. Roberts, Ralph Seymour, Lucinda Jenney, Bonnie Hunt, Kim Robillard, Beth Grant; **D:** Barry Levinson; **W:** Ronald Bass; **M:** Hans Zimmer. **Award Nominations:** Academy Awards '88: Best Art Direction/Set Decoration, Best Cinematography, Best Film Editing, Best Original Score; **Awards:** Academy Awards '88: Best Actor (Hoffman), Best Director (Levinson), Best Original Screenplay, Best Picture; Berlin International Film Festival '88: Golden Berlin Bear; Directors Guild of America Awards '88: Best Director

(Levinson); Golden Globe Awards '89: Best Actor—Drama (Hoffman), Best Film—Drama; People's Choice Awards '89: Best Film—Drama. **VHS, Beta, LV, 8mm** *MGM, BTV, JCF*

Rainbow Brite: A Horse of a Different Color

Family Episodes of a TV cartoon about a little girl whose magic rainbow belt allows here to spread joy and color everywhere; it's all sweetness and light and ruthless merchandising of the Rainbow Brite line of toys and accessories. Additional volumes available.
1986 42m/C VHS *LIV*

Rambling Rose ♂♂♂

R/Sr. High-Adult Dern is Rose, a free-spirited young woman in 1935 who's into free love several decades before everyone else. Taken in by a southern family, Rose immediately has an impact on the male members of the clan, father Duvall and son Haas, thanks to her insuppressible sexuality. This causes consternation with the strait-laced patriarch, who attempts to control his desire for the girl. Eventually Rose decides she must try to stick to one man, but this only causes further problems. Dern gives her best performance yet in this excellent period piece, and solid support is offered from the rest of the cast, in particular Duvall and Dern's real-life mother Ladd.

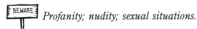 *Profanity; nudity; sexual situations.*

1991 115m/C Laura Dern, Diane Ladd, Robert Duvall, Lukas Haas, John Heard, Kevin Conway, Robert Burke, Lisa Jakub, Evan Lockwood; **D:** Martha Coolidge; **W:** Calder Willingham; **M:** Elmer Bernstein. **Award Nominations:** Academy Awards '91: Best Actress (Dern), Best Supporting Actress (Ladd); **Awards:** Independent Spirit Awards '92: Best Director (Coolidge), Best Film, Best Supporting Actress (Ladd). **VHS, LV** *LIV*

Rambo: Children for Peace

Preschool-Primary Two episodes of the movie-based children's animated series. On TV the Rambo character's explicit violence was toned down and the commando himself transformed into little more than G.I. Joe with long hair and less uniform. Episodes herein are "When S.A.V.A.G.E. Stole Santa" and the title segment. Additional volumes available.
1988 45m/C VHS, Beta *FHE*

Ramona

Preschool-Primary Series of live-action children's adventures starring the heroine from the famous Beverly Cleary children's books.
1987 60m/C VHS, Beta *ORI*

If you like *Raiders of the Lost Ark* (1981), you'll love:

Blackbeard's Ghost (1967)

City Slickers 2: The Legend of Curly's Gold (1994)

The Gold Bug (1990)

Gold Diggers: The Secret of Bear Mountain (1995)

Greedy (1994)

Hook (1991)

Indiana Jones and the Last Crusade (1989)

Indiana Jones and the Temple of Doom (1984)

The Jewel of the Nile (1985)

Muppet Treasure Island (1995)

Pirate Movie (1982)

The Pirates of Penzance (1983)

Romancing the Stone (1984)

Shipwrecked (1990)

Tom and Huck (1995)

Treasure Island (1934)

Treasure Island (1950)

Treasure Island (1989)

Ramona: Goodbye, Hello

Family Ramona and her sister deal with the death of the pet cat, but life goes on with Mrs. Quimby's pregnancy. Additional episodes featuring Beverly Cleary's heroine are also available.
1988 26m/C VHS *WAR*

Rapunzel

Family Unusually sad offering in the "Faerie Tale Theatre" series. Rapunzel (producer Shelley Duvall) is locked in a tower by an evil witch (Gena Rowlands). A prince (Jeff Bridges) discovers her, and climbs her long hair to reach her. When the witch discovers what's going on, she throws the prince from the tower, blinding him—graphically. This is not for the faint of heart. Happy ending fails to undo the damage for many viewers. Ages 10 and up.

1982 60m/C Shelley Duvall, Gena Rowlands, Jeff Bridges. **VHS, Beta, LV** *KUI, FOX, FCT*

A Rare Breed 🦴🦴

PG/Jr. High-Adult Adventure of a kidnapped horse in Italy and a young girl's quest to retrieve it. Directed by David Nelson, of television's "Ozzie and Harriet" fame, this one's cute and old fashioned, though decidedly on the bland side.

1981 94m/C George Kennedy, Forrest Tucker, Tracy Vaccaro, Tom Hallick, Don DeFore; **D:** David Nelson. **VHS, Beta** *VTR, LIV*

Rascal

Preschool-Primary Rascal the raccoon teaches a lonely boy responsibility and changes his life. Condensed adaption of the 1969 Disney feature based on the Sterling North book.

1990 15m/C VHS, Beta *MTI, DSN*

Rascals and Robbers

Family Subtitled "The Secret Adventures of Tom Sawyer and Huckleberry Finn," the secret being that this isn't taken from Mark Twain's writings but is a pretty standard TV adventure in which Tom and Huck are chased by a villainous embezzler.

1982 95m/C Anthony James. **VHS, Beta** *FOX*

Reading Rainbow: Abiyoyo

Family Award winning PBS-TV series is well represented on videocassette. Each episode uses a storytelling session (usually with a well-known celebrity reader) as a springboard for an informative segment hosted by actor LeVar Burton, with additional reading materials suggested at the program's conclusion. Here folk singing deity Pete Seeger relates a South African lullaby about a giant which threatens a town and the little boy who comes up with a plan to save his home. Burton reveals the way stories can be told through music. About 100 episodes available at last count.

1986 30m/C VHS

Real Genius 🦴🦴🦴

PG/Jr. High-Adult Socially awkward teen genius graduates high school early, then attends a technical college and finds friends among brilliant but wild young adults who use their scientific know-how for zany pranks and "Beakman's World"-style fun. When they learn their class-project laser is to be sold as a military weapon, the youths use their cleverness to thwart the illegal scheme. Nice to see a comedy that so clearly celebrates higher

intelligence; it's just too bad that the second half dwells on a basic revenge setup.

⚠ BEWARE *Sex, some of it quite touching (like the teen hero's affair with lonely girl nerd), some of it smarmy (a seductive blonde plots to sleep with the brightest man she can find). Salty language.*

1985 108m/C Val Kilmer, Gabe Jarret, Jonathan Gries, Michelle Meyrink, William Atherton, Patti D'Arbanville, Severn Darden; **D:** Martha Coolidge; **W:** Peter Torokvei, Neal Israel, Pat Proft; **M:** Thomas Newman. **VHS, Beta, LV** *COL*

The Real Ghostbusters

Preschool Cartoon series based on characters from the blockbuster '80s feature film comedies. Of special interest to kids whose parents want them to be copyright lawyers; it's called the "real" Ghostbusters to distinguish them from "The Original Ghostbusters," a mid-'70s live-action Saturday-morning Sid & Marty Krofft comedy that was later revived in cartoon form (as plain old "Ghostbusters") to take advantage of renewed ghost buster mania. All three titles haunt home video, if you need to compare. Additional volumes available.

1986 25m/C VHS, Beta *COL*

Real Life Boats & Ships for Kids

Family Led by genie Hard Hat Harry, children are taken on an introductory ride teaching them many sailing vessels including tugboats and hovercrafts. They are also taught applicable nautical terms. Ages 7 to 12.

1995 ?m/C VHS

The Real McCoy

PG-13/Jr. High-Adult Generally awful crime-caper film about female bank robber Karen McCoy (Basinger). Just out of prison, all Karen wants to do is go straight and raise her young son but her plans are thwarted by former associates who kidnap the child to force her into one last heist. Kilmer is the small-time thief, with a crush on Karen, who tries to help her out. Dumb, slow-moving story with a vapid performance by Basinger.

⚠ BEWARE *Violence and profanity.*

1993 104m/C Kim Basinger, Val Kilmer, Terence Stamp, Zach English, Gailard Sartain; **D:** Russell Mulcahy; **W:** William Davies. **VHS, LV** *MCA*

The Real Story of Humpty Dumpty

Preschool-Primary Animated story of good egg Humpty who rescues a princess from an evil witch but winds up scrambled.

1992 25m/C V: Glenda Jackson, Huey Lewis. **VHS** *BTV, WPC*

The Real Story of Oh Christmas Tree

Preschool-Primary Fable of why the pine tree stays green all year and how the tradition of Christmas trees got started.

1992 ?m/C *V:* John Ritter, Deborah Harry, Jason Ritter. **VHS** *FAF, WPC*

Reality Bites 🎜🎜🎜

PG-13/Jr. High-Adult Charming little story about life on the other side of college for four recent grads living, working, and slacking in Houston. Script by newcomer Childress is at its best when highlighting the Generation X artifacts: 7-Eleven Big Gulps, tacky '70s memorabilia, and games revolving around episodes of old TV shows like "Good Times," to name a few. Interesting story about the post-adolescent muddle, with strong performances by Ryder and Hawke as housemates fighting their attraction to each other, though newcomer Garofalo steals the show. Look for a nice bit by Mahoney as a cranky morning show host. Stiller proves adept both behind and in front of the camera.

> ⚠ BEWARE *Fairly tame stuff for mature teens, with a limited semi-sexual situation tastefully exploited. Should not be used as a teaching aid for credit card use. Some profanity; alcohol use; drug talk.*

1994 99m/C Winona Ryder, Ethan Hawke, Ben Stiller, Janeane Garofalo, Steve Zahn, Swoosie Kurtz, Joe Don Baker, John Mahoney; *Cameos:* David Pirner, Anne Meara, Jeanne Tripplehorn, Karen Duffy, Evan Dando; *D:* Ben Stiller; *W:* Helen Childress; *M:* Karl Wallinger. **VHS, LV** *MCA*

Really Wild Animals: Deep Sea Dive

Primary-Jr. High Neat new concept from the National Geographic Foundation makes their famed nature documentaries more accessible to MTV-generation kids through the use of animation, bright music, and graphics integrated with usual superb animal footage. Moore hosts (as a cartoon globe named Spin), and here he narrates amazing adventures with some of the ocean's remarkable denizens, including sharks, dolphins, and whales.

1994 45m/C **VHS** *COL, BTV*

Really Wild Animals: Swinging Safari

Primary-Jr. High National Geographic footage takes kids on an African safari from the Serengeti Plain to the Kalahari Desert, with looks at cheetahs, crocodiles, rhinos, and chimpanzees, both through Moore's witty narration and music-video montage. Child-friendly and notably absent of those standard scenes of lions disembowelling prey.

1994 44m/C **VHS** *COL, BTV*

Really Wild Animals: Wonders Down Under

Primary-Jr. High Series goes to Australia and reveals some of the country's strange creatures, including koalas, platypuses, and kangaroos. Moore does the marsupial rap.

1994 45m/C **VHS** *COL, BTV*

Rear Window 🎜🎜🎜🎜

Jr. High-Adult Newspaper photographer with a broken leg (Stewart) passes the time recuperating by observing his neighbors through the window. When he sees what he believes to be a murder, he decides to solve the crime himself. With help from his beautiful girlfriend and his nurse, he tries to catch the murderer without getting killed himself. Top-drawer Hitchcock blends exquisite suspense with occasional on-target laughs. Based on the story "It Had to Be Murder" by Cornell Woolrich.

1954 112m/C James Stewart, Grace Kelly, Thelma Ritter, Wendell Corey, Raymond Burr, Judith Evelyn; *D:* Alfred Hitchcock; *W:* John Michael Hayes; *M:* Franz Waxman. **Award Nominations:** Academy Awards '54: Best Director (Hitchcock), Best Screenplay, Best Sound; **Awards:** Edgar Allan Poe Awards '54: Best Screenplay. **VHS, Beta, LV** *MCA, TLF, HMV*

Rebecca 🎜🎜🎜 ♪

Jr. High-Adult Based on Daphne Du Maurier's best-selling novel about a young unsophisticated girl who marries a moody and prominent country gentleman haunted by the memory of his first wife, Rebecca. Fontaine and Olivier turn in fine performances as the unlikely couple. Suspenseful and surprising gothic romance was Hitchcock's first American film and earned his only "best picture" Oscar. Laserdisc features rare screen tests of Vivien Leigh, Anne Baxter, Loretta Young, and Joan Fontaine, footage from Rebecca's winning night at the Academy Awards, original radio broadcasts of film by Orson Welles and David O. Selznick, and commentary of film with interview excerpts with Hitchcock.

1940 130m/B Joan Fontaine, Laurence Olivier, Judith Anderson, George Sanders, Nigel Bruce, Florence Bates, Gladys Cooper, Reginald Denny, Leo G. Carroll, Sir C. Aubrey Smith, Melville Cooper; *D:* Alfred Hitchcock; *W:* Joan Harrison, Robert Sherwood; *M:* Franz Waxman. **Award Nominations:** Academy Awards '40: Best Actor (Olivier), Best Actress (Fontaine), Best Adapted Screenplay, Best Director (Hitchcock), Best Film Editing, Best Interior Decoration, Best Supporting Actress (Anderson), Best Original Score; **Awards:** Academy Awards '40: Best Black and White Cinematography, Best Picture; National Board of Review Awards '40: 10 Best Films of the Year. **VHS, Beta, LV** *FOX, HMV, BTV*

Rebecca of Sunnybrook Farm 🎜🎜 ♪

Family Farm girl Rebecca becomes a radio star over her aunt's objections, in this bouncy musical that has next to nothing to do with the famous Kate Douglas Wiggin novel of the title. The curly-topped one performs a medley of her song hits (including "On the Good Ship Lollipop") with future Tin Woodman Haley and dances the finale with Robinson. For purists, Mary Pickford's 1917 silent adaptation of "Rebecca of Sunnybrook Farm," more faithful to the book, is also on tape. ♫ On the Good Ship Lollipop/When I'm With You/Animal Crackers medley; Crackly Corn Flakes; Alone With You; Happy Ending; Au Revoir; An Old Straw Hat; Come and Get Your Happiness; Parade of the Wooden Soldiers.

1938 80m/B Shirley Temple, Randolph Scott, Jack Haley, Phyllis Brooks, Gloria Stuart, Slim Summerville, Bill Robinson, Helen Westley, William Demarest; **D:** Allan Dwan. **VHS, Beta, LV** *FOX, MLB, MLT*

Rebel Without a Cause ♪♪♪♪

Jr. High-Adult James Dean's most memorable screen appearance, as a troubled teen from the right side of the tracks. New kid in town Jim Stark is alienated from both his wealthy parents ("Mr. Magoo" Backus in a dramatic mien as Jim's weak-willed father) and high-school peers. One fateful night he competes with local punks over neighborhood bad girl Wood and tries to save a neurotic boy who trusts Jim as his only friend. Slang, hair and clothes may have changed since 1955, but this in-the-gut story of adolescence still packs a wallop. Peace's original widescreen format suffers severely on trimmed-down videocassette.

⚠️ BEWARE *Alcohol use, violence and very poor driving practices.*

1955 111m/C James Dean, Natalie Wood, Sal Mineo, Jim Backus, Nick Adams, Dennis Hopper, Ann Doran, William Hopper, Rochelle Hudson, Corey Allen, Edward Platt; **D:** Nicholas Ray; **W:** Stewart Stern; **M:** Leonard Rosenman. **VHS, Beta, LV** *WAR*

The Red Balloon ♪♪♪ ▷

Family The story of Pascal, a lonely French boy who befriends a wondrous red balloon which follows him everywhere. Lovely, finely done parable of childhood, imagination, and friendship.

1956 34m/C Pascal Lamorisse; **D:** Albert Lamorisse. **VHS, Beta, LV, 8mm** *COL, HHT, DVT*

The Red Pony ♪♪♪

Family Tommy, small son in a not-so-harmonious ranching family, feels closer to genial hired-hand Billy than to his moody father. Billy gives the boy his first pony to care for, but its tragic illness leaves Tommy feeling betrayed. Somewhat uneven in its mix of adult- and kid-level drama, but effectively tearjerking in the end, with a warm evocation of its time and place. Based on the novel by John Steinbeck.

1949 89m/C Myrna Loy, Robert Mitchum, Peter Miles, Louis Calhern, Shepperd Strudwick, Margaret Hamilton, Beau Bridges; **D:** Lewis Milestone; **M:** Aaron Copland. **VHS, LV** *REP, KUI*

The Red Pony ♪♪♪

Family Award-winning TV redo of the John Steinbeck novel about the troubled farm boy who spends time with a frail pony to help cope with his turbulent home life. Emphasis in this version is on the family's difficult father, portrayed superbly by Fonda.

⚠️ BEWARE *Violence.*

1976 101m/C Henry Fonda, Maureen O'Hara; **D:** Robert Totten. **VHS, Beta, LV** *BFA*

Red Riding Hood ♪ ▷

G/Family Cannon Movie Tale, which should be warning enough, stretches the story of the little girl in red and that nasty wolf to torturous feature length.

1989 84m/C Craig T. Nelson, Isabella Rossellini; **D:** Adam Brooks. **VHS** *WAR*

Red Riding Hood and Goldilocks

Preschool-Primary Two classic children's stories are read, not animated, against detailed illustrations and scintillating music, featuring actress Ryan as narrator. Part of the "Rabbit Ears: We All Have Tales" series.

1991 30m/C VHS, LV *KUI, COL*

The Red Shoes ♪♪♪♪

Family Beautifully filmed British classic about a young ballerina torn between love and her choreographer's demand that she devote herself completely to her work. What she primarily performs is, in fact, "The Red Shoes," the Hans Christian Andersen story about a pair of shoes that won't stop dancing even when the owner wants to, which is a metaphor for the heroine's dilemma. Only tangentially a children's film, and the climax is tragedy at its most dizzyingly romantic. The same filmmakers went on to do "The Tales of Hoffmann," arguably more kid-friendly.

⚠️ BEWARE *Mature themes of love and warped devotion to the arts.*

1948 136m/C Anton Walbrook, Moira Shearer, Marius Goring, Leonide Massine, Robert Helpmann, Albert Basserman, Ludmila Tcherina, Esmond Knight, Emeric Pressburger; **D:** Michael Powell; **W:** Emeric Pressburger, Michael Powell. **Award Nominations:** Academy Awards '48: Best Film Editing, Best Picture, Best Story; **Awards:** Academy Awards '48: Best Art Direction/Set Decoration (Color), Best Score; Golden Globe Awards '49: Best Score; National Board of Review Awards '48: 10 Best Films of the Year. **VHS, Beta, LV** *PAR, HMV*

The Red Shoes

Preschool-Primary An animated modernization of the Hans Christian Andersen tale, involving two present-day girls and a winning lottery ticket as well as that endlessly dancing footwear.

1990 30m/C D: Michael Sporn. **VHS, Beta** *FHE, TVC*

The Red Stallion ♪♪

Family A young boy raises his pony into an award-winning racehorse that saves the farm when it wins the big race. Good outdoor photography but loses something in the human relationships.

1947 82m/B Robert Paige, Noreen Nash, Ted Donaldson, Jane Darwell; **D:** Lesley Selander. **VHS** *NOS, MOV, HEG*

Reddy the Fox

Family Another cartoon character from "Fables of the Green Forest," an episode featuring the most cunning of all forest dwellers, Reddy, who's a sort of vulpine Wile E. Coyote eternally after Peter Cottontail. Available in Spanish as well as English.

1980 52m/C VHS *FHE*

Regarding Henry ♪♪♪

PG-13/Jr. High-Adult Cold-hearted successful lawyer gets shot in the head during a holdup and becomes warm-hearted unemployed lawyer with no memory of earlier life. During recovery the new Henry displays compassion and conscience the old one never had, bonding with lonely wife and daughter. Too calculated in its yuppie-bashing ironies, it's still a rather sweet good-feeler that works thanks to solid acting.

> **BEWARE** *Ford takes a bullet to the head in opening moments; otherwise, it's a fairly inoffensive affair.*

1991 107m/C Harrison Ford, Annette Bening, Bill Nunn, Mikki Allen, Elizabeth Wilson, Robin Bartlett, John Leguizamo, Donald Moffat, Nancy Marchand; **D:** Mike Nichols; **W:** Jeffrey Abrams; **M:** Hans Zimmer. **VHS, Beta, LV** *PAR*

Regl'ar Fellers ♪♪

Family Gang of kids save the town and soften the heart of their grandmother, too. Sloppy production redeemed by the presence of Little Rascal fave 'Alfalfa' Switzer. Not coincidentally, the short feature was based on a popular newspaper comic strip of the era that was itself inspired by "Our Gang."

1941 66m/B Billy Lee, Carl "Alfalfa" Switzer, Buddy Boles, Janet Dempsey, Sarah Padden, Roscoe Ates; **D:** Arthur Dreifuss. **VHS** *NOS, FMT, VYY*

The Reivers ♪♪♪

PG/Jr. High-Adult Young rich boy, his roguish chauffeur and another adult pal journey from small town Mississippi, circa 1905, to the big city of Memphis in a stolen car. Based on William Faulkner's last novel, it's an enjoyable, picaresque road trip.

> **BEWARE** *Alcohol use, sex talk, mature themes.*

1969 107m/C Steve McQueen, Sharon Farrell, Will Geer, Michael Constantine, Rupert Crosse; **D:** Mark Rydell; **W:** Harriet Frank Jr., Irving Ravetch; **M:** John Williams. **VHS, Beta** *FOX*

The Reluctant Astronaut ♪ ♪

Family Roy Fleming (Don Knotts) operates the spaceship ride at a carnival. His dad sends an application for Roy in to NASA. Roy gets accepted and he heads off to Florida but it turns out the job is janitorial. Somehow Roy makes friends with an astronaut (Leslie Nielsen), who persuades NASA that Roy would be the perfect civilian to send up in an experimental capsule. A not very funny comedy. Ages 4 to 8.

1967 103m/C Don Knotts, Leslie Nielsen, Joan Freeman, Arthur O'Connell, Jesse White, Jeanette Nolan, Joan Shawlee; **D:** Edward J.

Montagne; **W:** James Fritzell, Everett Greenbaum; **C:** Rexford Wimpy; **M:** Vic Mizzy. **VHS** *MCA*

The Reluctant Dragon

Preschool-Primary Sir Giles is called on to rid the town of its worst pest: a dragon who enjoys not fighting, but reading poetry. Abridged version of the Disney classic short.

1990 19m/C VHS, Beta *DSN, MTI, WPC*

The Remains of the Day ♪♪♪

PG/College-Adult If repression is your cup of tea then this is the film for you. Others may want to shake British butler par excellence Stevens (Hopkins) and tell him to express an emotion. In the 1930s, Stevens is the rigidly traditional butler to Lord Darlington (Fox). When Miss Kenton (Thompson) the almost vivacious new housekeeper expresses a quietly personal interest in Stevens his loyalty to an unworthy master prevents him from a chance at happiness. A quiet movie, told in flashback. Hopkins' impressive performance gets by strictly on nuance with Thompson at least allowed a small amount of natural charm. Based on the novel by Kazuo Ishiguro.

> **BEWARE** *Brief profanity.*

1993 135m/C Anthony Hopkins, Emma Thompson, James Fox, Christopher Reeve, Peter Vaughan, Hugh Grant, Michael Lonsdale, Tim Pigott-Smith; **D:** James Ivory; **W:** Ruth Prawer Jhabvala; **M:** Richard Robbins. **Award Nominations:** Academy Awards '93: Best Actor (Hopkins), Best Actress (Thompson), Best Adapted Screenplay, Best Art Direction/Set Decoration, Best Costume Design, Best Director (Ivory), Best Original Screenplay, Best Picture; British Academy Awards '94: Best Actress (Thompson), Best Adapted Screenplay, Best Director (Ivory), Best Film; Directors Guild of America Awards '93: Best Director (Ivory); Golden Globe Awards '94: Best Actor—Drama (Hopkins), Best Actress—Drama (Thompson), Best Director (Ivory), Best Film—Drama, Best Screenplay; **Awards:** British Academy Awards '94: Best Actor (Hopkins); Los Angeles Film Critics Association Awards '93: Best Actor (Hopkins); National Board of Review Awards '93: Best Actor (Hopkins). **VHS, LV, 8mm** *COL*

The Remarkable Rocket

Primary This is an animated version of Oscar Wilde's story about a conceited fireworks rocket. Features the voice of David Niven. A Reader's Digest presentation. Ages 4 to 7.

1975 25m/C VHS, Beta *PYR*

Remo Williams: The Adventure Begins ♪♪

PG-13/Jr. High-Adult Adaptation of "The Destroyer" adventure novel series with a Bond-like hero who can walk on water and dodge bullets after being instructed by a Korean martial arts master. Funny and diverting, and Grey is excellent (if a bit over the top) as the wizened oriental. The title's assumption is that the adventure will continue.

> **BEWARE** *Profanity and violence.*

1985 121m/C Fred Ward, Joel Grey, Wilford Brimley, Kate Mulgrew; **D:** Guy Hamilton. **VHS, Beta, LV** *HBO*

Remote 🎵🎵

PG/Jr. High-Adult Thirteen-year-old Randy is a whiz designing remote-control gadgets, but his parents have mixed feelings about his constant tinkering. The boy stashes his model planes, helicopters, robots, and cars in a home under construction, and when robbers invade the hideout, Randy fights back with his high-tech army. Innocuous but low-flying ripoff of "Home Alone," from the creators of "Prehysteria."

BEWARE *Roughhousing, though allegedly the PG rating was for salty language, which even the Hound's ears couldn't detect.*

1993 80m/C Chris Carrara, Jessica Bowman, John Diehl, Derya Ruggles, Tony Longo, Stuart Fratkin; **D:** Ted Nicolaou; **W:** Mike Farrow; **M:** Richard Band. **VHS, Beta** *PAR*

The Ren & Stimpy Show, Vol. 1: The Classics

Primary-Adult What is it about scrawny, apoplectic chihuahua Ren Hoek, and slow-witted litter-loving feline Stimpson J. Cat that makes them such favorites with children? Maybe it's their unstoppable joie de vivre, the way they laugh at adversity. Perhaps it's their friendship, which prevails through thick and thin. Or maybe it's the fact that they're heavily into saliva, "nose goblins," and bulging, bloodshot eyeballs. Or that their favorite game is "Don't Whiz on the Electric Fence." This animated series, well over the edge of good taste, lets nine- and ten-year-olds know there's room for subversiveness in a world run by adults. And Ren & Stimpy are a hoot. In the episodes here they travel to outer space and sing their immortal ditty "Happy Happy, Joy Joy." Ages 9 to 12.
1993 40m/C **VHS** *SMV*

The Ren & Stimpy Show, Vol. 2: The Stupidest Stories

Primary-Adult Stupid is as stupid does, as Forrest Gump said. He must have been thinking about Ren and Stimpy. This tape features "Ask Dr. Stupid" and an episode about Stimpy winning millions in a lottery. Ages 9 to 12.
1993 40m/C **VHS** *SMV*

The Ren & Stimpy Show, Vol. 3: The Stinkiest Stories

Primary-Adult Give the boys credit for honesty; this one gets pretty revolting. "Ren's Toothache" is a brutally graphic reminder of the importance of dental hygiene. As for "The Cat That Laid the Golden Hairball," it's better not to inquire. Ages 9 to 12.
1993 40m/C **VHS** *SMV*

Renaissance Man 🎵🎵 ♭

PG-13/Jr. High-Adult Skeptical new teacher inspires a classroom of underachievers and finds his true calling. Based loosely on the experiences of screenwriter Burnstein at a base in Michigan. Civilian Bill Rago (DeVito) is an unemployed ad exec assigned to teach Shakespeare to a group of borderline Army recruits led by Hardison. Add half a bone for the recruits and their Hamlet rap, a breath of fresh air in an otherwise stale plot. Some funny moments, reminiscent of "Stripes," but not quite as wacky. On the other hand, Marshall does endearing better than most. Shot with the cooperation of the Army.

BEWARE *Profanity.*

1994 124m/C Danny DeVito, Gregory Hines, James Remar, Stacey Dash, Ed Begley Jr., Mark Wahlberg, Lillo Brancato, Kadeem Hardison, Richard T. Jones, Khalil Kain, Peter Simmons, Jenifer Lewis; **Cameos:** Cliff Robertson; **D:** Penny Marshall; **W:** Jim Burnstein, Ned Mauldin; **M:** Hans Zimmer. **VHS** *NYR*

Renfrew of the Royal Mounted 🎵🎵

Family Canadian Mountie goes after counterfeiters and sings a few songs in this mild adaptation of a popular kid's radio serial. The original Dudley Do-Right, though humor here isn't quite so intentional. Perhaps Renfrew's dog Lightning should have been the star. Also on video: "Renfrew on the Great White Trail."
1937 57m/B Carol Hughes, James Newill, Kenneth Harlan; **D:** Al(bert) Herman. **VHS, Beta** *DVT, GPV, HEG*

Rent-A-Kid 🎵🎵 ♭

G/Family Businessman Harry Haber (Nielsen) is asked by his son to keep an eye out on the Mid-Valley Orphanage for a week. Then Harry meets a young couple who are unsure about having a family so, since Harry's business is renting all sorts of things, he decides to rent the couple three orphans so they can get a taste of parenting.
1995 89m/C Leslie Nielsen, Christopher Lloyd, Matt McCoy, Sherry Miller, Amos Crawley, Cody Jones, Tabitha Lupien, Tony Rosato; **D:** Fred Gerber; **W:** Paul Bernbaum; **C:** Rene Ohashi; **M:** Ron Ramin. **VHS, LV** *REP*

The Rescue 🎵 ♭

PG/Primary-Adult The Disney folks bought into the 1980s "Rambo" craze (through their Touchstone Pictures division) with this empty-headed mix of firefights and family values. When an elite team of U.S. Navy Seal commandoes is captured by the commies in North Korea, the U.S. government won't do a thing to save them. So their children decide to mount a rescue. Not for cynics.

BEWARE *Violence, salty language.*

1988 97m/C Marc Price, Charles Haid, Kevin Dillon, Christina Harnos, Edward Albert; **D:** Ferdinand Fairfax; **W:** Jim Thomas, John Thomas; **M:** Bruce Broughton. **VHS, Beta, LV** *TOU, HHE*

The Rescuers 🦴🦴🦴 🦴

G/Family Who could resist a movie that posits the existence of a parallel United Nations operated by mice in the basement of the real UN? This is the Rescue Aid Society. On its agenda is a note in a bottle and, no, it's not fan mail from some flounder but a plea for help from a girl named Penny who is held captive somewhere (part of the note has washed away.) Hmmm. Sounds like a job for Eva Gabor and Bob Newhart. OK, OK, it sounds like a job for James Bond but he was busy that year in "The Spy Who Loved Me." Gabor provides the voice of Miss Bianca, the delegate from Hungary, and Newhart is the voice of Bernard, the Rescue Aid Society's janitor. They trace Penny to a swamp where the evil Madame Medusa (Geraldine Page) is using her to search for a priceless diamond hidden by pirates. Speaking of which, this is an often overlooked gem of Disney animation. Ages 4 to 8. Scary alligators may be a little too much for the very young. Based on the stories of Margery Sharp.
1977 76m/C D: Wolfgang Reitherman, John Lounsbery; **V:** Bob Newhart, Eva Gabor, Geraldine Page, Jim Jordan, Joe Flynn, Jeanette Nolan, Pat Buttram. **VHS, LV** *DIS, OM*

The Rescuers Down Under 🦴🦴 🦴

G/Family Newhart and Gabor are again delightful as valiant mice Bernard and Bianca, but the story is a re-decorated re-hash of "The Rescuers." Again the assignment is to rescue a child (a boy this time) from a villain (George C. Scott this time) who is using the kid to obtain a treasure (this time a rare eagle). The animated Australian scenery is impressive and indigenous animals—kangaroo, kookaburra, frill-necked lizard—provide amusing authenticity. Film squanders its best moment—a glorious ride on an eagle's back—by showing it way too early. Ages 4 to 8.
1990 77m/C D: Hendel Butoy, Mike Gabriel; **W:** Jim Cox, Karey Kirkpatrick, Joe Ranft, Byron Simpson; **M:** Bruce Broughton; **V:** Bob Newhart, Eva Gabor, John Candy, Tristan Rogers, George C. Scott, Frank Welker, Adam Ryen. **VHS, Beta, LV** *DIS, OM*

Return from Witch Mountain 🦴 🦴

G/Family Sequel to the well-done "Escape to Witch Mountain" wastes a good cast in a rehash ranging from tepid to distressing. Two evil grownups use mind-control drugs to try and harness the psychic kids from the original and use their powers to place Los Angeles in nuclear jeopardy. Note the Disney-cute L.A. street gangs.
1978 93m/C Christopher Lee, Bette Davis, Ike Eisenmann, Kim Richards, Jack Soo; **D:** John Hough; **W:** Malcolm Marmorstein. **VHS, Beta** *DIS*

The Return of Jafar 🦴🦴🦴

G/Family Clumsy thief Abis Mal inadvertently releases evil sorcerer Jafar from his lamp prison and now the powerful "genie Jafar" plots his revenge. So it's up to Aladdin and friends to save the Sultan's kingdom once again. Contains five new songs. 🎵 Just Forget About Love; Nothing In the World (Quite Like a Friend); I'm Looking Out for Me; You're Only Second Rate; Arabian Nights.
1994 66m/C V: Scott Weinger, Linda Larkin, Gilbert Gottfried, Val Bettin, Dan Castellaneta. **VHS** *DIS*

The Return of Our Gang 🦴 🦴

Family Even kids who are longtime "Our Gang" fans may not be aware that the first Little Rascals adventures were made during the silent film era. This contains three silent Pathe shorts seldom seen today: "The School Play (Stage Fright)," "Summer Daze (The Cobbler)," and "Dog Days."
1925 57m/B Joe Cobb, Ernie Morrison, Mickey Daniels, Farina Hoskins, Mary Kornman, Jackie Condon, Jack Davis, Jannie Hoskins, Andy Samuels, Eugene Jackson. **VHS, Beta, 8mm** *VYY*

The Return of Roger Ramjet

Family More adventures of the well-remembered '60s animated camp hero, who could attain the power of 20 atom bombs in 20 seconds and fight evil with friends like Yank, Doodle, Dan, and Dee.
1966 30m/C V: Gary Owens. **VHS, Beta** *RHI*

The Return of Swamp Thing 🦴 🦴

PG-13/Jr. High-Adult The DC Comics creature rises again out of the muck to fight the same mad doctor he killed last time, now breeding a gallery of mutants. Don't ask how or why—it's all tongue-in-cheek, less serious than even the previous entry, let alone the cult comic book that inspired both. Brat alert: beware peripheral characters of two way-obnoxious kids trying to get a photo of Swamp Thing.

⚠ BEWARE *Violence, mainly between mutants and people-turned-mutants. Some of the monster designs are nightmarish indeed, but the filmmakers treat just about everything onscreen as a big joke.*
1989 95m/C Louis Jourdan, Heather Locklear, Sarah Douglas, Dick Durock; **D:** Jim Wynorski. **VHS, Beta, LV** *COL*

Return of the Jedi 🦴🦴🦴

PG/Family Third segment of George Lucas' original "Star Wars" trilogy is the weakest from the standpoint of storyline, but it does the job in wrapping up the space saga. Luke Skywalker and his allies first attempt to rescue the captive Han Solo, then again confront the forces of the Empire in essentially a mightier rerun of the first film's climactic battle, with truly awesome special effects. This introduces the cute-as-can-be Ewoks, teddy bearish forest creatures who were spun off in a cartoon series and made-for-TV features as well as into toy stores. May the force be with you.

⚠ BEWARE *Sci fi vi(olence).*

 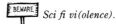

Bernard and Miss Bianca prepare to take flight in "The Rescuers."

1983 132m/C Mark Hamill, Carrie Fisher, Harrison Ford, Billy Dee Williams, David Prowse, James Earl Jones, Kenny Baker, Denis Lawson, Anthony Daniels, Peter Mayhew; **D:** Richard Marquand; **W:** George Lucas, Lawrence Kasdan; **M:** John Williams; **V:** Alec Guinness, Frank Oz. **Award Nominations:** Academy Awards '83: Best Art Direction/Set Decoration, Best Sound, Best Original Score; **Awards:** Academy Awards '83: Best Visual Effects; People's Choice Awards '84: Best Film. **VHS, Beta, LV** *FOX, RDG, HMV*

The Return of the King

Family The Rankin/Bass follow-up to their excellent TV feature cartoon adaptation of J.R.R. Tolkien's "The Hobbit," skips two whole books in the "Lord of the Rings" trilogy (Ralph Bakshi had already covered the same ground in his theatrical "Rings" movie) right to the final installment, as Samwise tries to rescue his friend Frodo from the orcs and destroy the One Ring in the forges of Mordor before the evil of Sauron conquers Middle Earth. Confused? It's all about as lucid as it could be, given the circumstances, with above-average animation and good character voices.

1980 120m/C D: Arthur Rankin Jr., Jules Bass; **V:** Orson Bean, Roddy McDowall, John Huston, Theodore Bikel, William Conrad, Glen Yarborough, Paul Frees, Casey Kasem, Sonny Melendrez. **VHS** *XVC, VTR, FAF*

The Return of the Musketeers

PG/Jr. High-Adult Lester's third Musketeers film (after his successful double-act in the '70s) is a good-natured but average costume/comedy/buddy film, based on Dumas' own literary sequel "Twenty Years After." Two decades passed since D'Artagnan, Athos, Porthos, and Aramis saved the French queen from scandal, but now Milady DeWinter's devious daughter Justine is here to take mama's scheming place, and just to add a little more excitement Athos' adopted son Raoul falls for the femme fatale.

BEWARE *Swashbuckling violence.*

1989 103m/C Michael York, Oliver Reed, Frank Finlay, Richard Chamberlain, Kim Cattrall, C. Thomas Howell, Geraldine Chaplin, Roy Kinnear, Christopher Lee, Philippe Noiret, Jean-Pierre Cassel, Billy Connolly, Eusebio Lazaro; **D:** Richard Lester; **W:** George MacDonald Fraser. **VHS, LV** *MCA, BTV, FCT*

Return of the Pink Panther

G/Family Bumbling Inspector Clouseau is called upon (again) to rescue the Pink Panther diamond stolen from a museum. Clouseau manages to produce mayhem with a vacuum cleaner and other devices that, in his accident-prone hands, become instruments of terror. While technically the fourth installment in the Pink Panther movie series, it revised and energized Clouseau to showcase nearly nonstop shtick and slapstick not seen since the glory days of Chaplin and Keaton.

1974 113m/C Peter Sellers, Christopher Plummer, Catherine Schell, Herbert Lom, Victor Spinetti; *D:* Blake Edwards; *W:* Frank Waldman, Blake Edwards; *M:* Henry Mancini. **VHS, Beta, LV** *FOX, FHE, FCT*

The Return of Tommy Tricker

Family Further philatelic thrills as Tommy, his sister and their friends work their magic to free Charles Meriweather from the Bluenose sailing ship stamp he's been imprisoned in for 60 years. But when they try to bring Charlie back, they rescue his younger sister Molly instead. Molly suddenly begins aging and Tommy must figure out how to save her (and still rescue Charlie). Ages 5 to 12.

1994 97m/C Michael Stevens, Joshawa Mathers, Heather Goodsell, Paul Nocholls, Andrew Bauer-Gador, Adele Gray; *D:* Michael Rubbo; *W:* Michael Rubbo. **VHS** *HMD*

Return to Boggy Creek ♫♫

G/Family Townspeople in a small fishing village learn from a photographer that a "killer" beast, whom they thought had disappeared, is back and living in Boggy Creek. Curious children follow the shutterbug into the marsh, despite hurricane warnings, and the bigfootish swamp monster reacts with kindliness and compassion. Kiddies-only sequel to allegedly fact-based "Legend of Boggy Creek."

1977 87m/C Dawn Wells, Dana Plato, Louise Belaire, John Hofeus; *D:* Tom Moore. **VHS, Beta** *FOX*

Return to Oz

Family Dorothy returns to you-know-where to find her friends in the wonderful land of Oz have lost their brain, heart, and courage, respectively, and once again she must demonstrate Kansas leadership qualities. Early Rankin-Bass animated TV special.

1964 60m/C VHS, Beta *PSM*

Return to Oz ♫♫ ♭

PG/Jr. High-Adult Disney and "Star Wars" producer Gary Kurtz united to pick up where "The Wizard of Oz" left off. Dorothy goes to a turn-of-the-century asylum for her "delusions" of a land called Oz. Then a natural disaster takes her back to Oz, where she has much to do—the Emerald City is ruined, Scarecrow is missing, and the Lion and Tin Man have turned to stone. Visually stunning adaptation of later L. Frank Baum books makes no effort to look (or sing) like the 1939 MGM classic. But premise is confused, and it's low on humor; except for a wisecracking hen, attitude is sober, even scary, as Doro-

thy meets the head-hunting witch Mombi and the rock giant Nome King (astonishing claymation technique by Will Vinton). Definitely worth a look for the curious. That's Jim Henson's son Brian as the voice of Jack Pumpkinhead.

1985 109m/C Fairuza Balk, Piper Laurie, Matt Clark, Nicol Williamson, Jean Marsh; *D:* Walter Murch; *M:* David Shire. **VHS, Beta, LV** *DIS*

Return to Snowy River ♫♫ ♭

PG/Jr. High-Adult Continues the scenic love story of the Australian buckaroo and the rancher's daughter that began in "The Man From Snowy River." Now Jim Craig has his own mountain spread, but city slickers and their roughriders plan to run him and the other mountain ranchers off their land. Sketchy plot indeed—part agriculture, part romance, mostly horses, horses, horses, beautifully filmed. Dennehy takes over from Kirk Douglas as the grouchy American. Distributed by Disney, but with a few harsh moments.

 Violence and profanity.

1988 99m/C Tom Burlinson, Sigrid Thornton, Brian Dennehy, Nicholas Eadie, Mark Hembrow, Bryan Marshall; *D:* Geoff Burrowes. **VHS, Beta, LV** *DIS, TVC*

Return to Treasure Island, Vol. 1

Family Disney-Channel TV Series based on the Robert Louis Stevenson classic with the continuing adventures of Jim Hawkins and encoring scoundrel Long John Silver. Five feature-length tapes of two episodes apiece are available.

1985 101m/C Brian Blessed, Kenneth Colley, Christopher Guard, Reiner Schoene; *D:* Piers Haggard. **VHS, Beta** *DIS*

Reunion ♫♫♫

PG-13/Jr. High-Adult Jewish businessman, living in the U.S., returns to his family home in Stuttgart, Germany. He hopes to find out what happened to a boyhood school friend, the son of a noble German family. Extensive flashbacks (in muted color; do not adjust your VCR) show the rise of anti-Semitism and how it affects the friendship of both youths. Thoughtful and well-acted though occasionally plodding drama, a more austere and dignified movie on the topic than "Swing Kids." Based on Fred Uhlman's autobiographical novella.

BEWARE *Nazisim, sex and nudity.*

1988 120m/C Jason Robards Jr., Christien Anholt, Sam West, Francoise Fabian, Maureen Kerwin, Barbara Jefford, Alexander Trauner; *D:* Jerry Schatzberg; *W:* Harold Pinter. **VHS, Beta, LV** *FRH, IME, FCT*

Revenge of Roger Ramjet

Family Campy-heroic adventures of the vintage TV good guy daredevil, who was using WHACK! and OUCH! title cards during his fights even before the live-action

"Batman." See also "The Return of Roger Ramjet" and "Roger Ramjet vs. N.A.S.T.Y."

1966 30m/C VHS, Beta *RHI*

Revenge of the Mysterons from Mars

Preschool-Primary Vicious plunderers arrive from the red planet, so Captain Scarlet and Spectrum rise to the battle. Adapted from the live-action galactic puppet adventure "Captain Scarlet and the Mysterons."

1981 91m/C VHS, Beta *FHE*

Revenge of the Nerds 🦴🦴 ᵛ

R/Sr. High-Adult Before he went to medical school and became a physician on TV's "ER" Anthony Edwards was a geeky college kid who, with co-star Robert Carradine and others, started a fraternity for guys tired of having campus sand kicked in their faces. They take on the school jocks, studs and lookers with amusing, if raunchy, results. Watch for early-career appearances by John Goodman and Timothy Busfield. Insider's note: Also watch for Matt Salinger, son of author J.D. Salinger. Led to several sequels, all of them worse. Ages 13 and up.

> ⚠ BEWARE *Profanity and sex talk. Jocks torture innocent "nerds."*

1984 89m/C Robert Carradine, Anthony Edwards, Timothy Busfield, Andrew Cassese, Curtis Armstrong, Larry B. Scott, Brian Tochi, Julia Montgomery, Michelle Meyrink, Ted McGinley, John Goodman, Bernie Casey; *D:* Jeff Kanew; *W:* Tim Metcalfe; *M:* Thomas Newman. **VHS, Beta, LV** *FOX*

Revenge of the Pink Panther 🦴🦴 ᵛ

PG/Jr. High-Adult Inspector Clouseau survives an assassination attempt, but allows the world to think he is dead in order to pursue an investigation of the culprits in his own unique, bumbling way. More laid-back than other "Pink Panther" romps of the '70s (and the last one made by Sellers when he was alive), breaking out with the full-fledged slapstick only in the fiery finale.

> ⚠ BEWARE *Comedy violence in the Pink Panther tradition and sex talk.*

1978 99m/C Peter Sellers, Herbert Lom, Dyan Cannon, Robert Webber, Burt Kwouk, Robert Loggia; *D:* Blake Edwards; *W:* Blake Edwards, Ron Clark, Frank Waldman; *M:* Henry Mancini. **VHS, Beta, LV** *FOX, FCT*

Rhinestone 🦴

PG/Jr. High-Adult A country singer claims she can turn anyone, even a cabbie, into a singing sensation. Stuck with Stallone, Parton prepares her protege to sing at New York City's roughest country-western club, The Rhinestone. Only die-hard Dolly and Rocky fans need bother with this bunk. Some may enjoy watching the thick, New York accented Stallone learn how to properly pronounce dog ("dawg") in country lingo. Yee-haw.

> ⚠ BEWARE *Profanity, violence, sex talk.*

1984 111m/C Sylvester Stallone, Dolly Parton, Ron Leibman, Richard Farnsworth, Tim Thomerson; *D:* Bob (Benjamin) Clark; *W:* Sylvester Stallone, Phil Alden Robinson. **VHS, Beta, LV** *FOX*

Rich in Love 🦴🦴 ᵛ

PG-13/Jr. High-Adult Lighthearted look at the changes in a Southern family after its matriarch leaves to pursue her own life. Seen through the eyes of 17-year-old daughter Lucille who assumes the role of "mother" for sister and father while trying to come to terms with her own confused feelings. Nice performances by newcomer Erbe and Finney can't overcome a mediocre script. Based on the novel by Josephine Humphreys.

1993 105m/C Albert Finney, Jill Clayburgh, Kathryn Erbe, Kyle MacLachlan, Piper Laurie, Ethan Hawke, Suzy Amis, Alfre Woodard; *D:* Bruce Beresford; *W:* Alfred Uhry; *M:* Georges Delerue. **VHS, LV** *MGM, BTV, FCT*

Rich Kids 🦴🦴 ᵛ

PG/Family Drama focusing on the children of divorce, specifically about a girl trying to cope with the split up of her parents, aided by a boyfriend whose parents have already called it quits. Somewhat simplistic screenplay tends to hang on the notion of middle-aged grownups as immature boobs, their kids as wise but vulnerable. Some touching moments nonetheless.

1979 97m/C John Lithgow, Kathryn Walker, Trini Alvarado, Paul Dooley, David Selby, Jill Eikenberry, Olympia Dukakis; *D:* Robert M. Young. **VHS, Beta** *MGM*

Richard Scarry's Best ABC Video Ever!

Family Huckle Cat and his school friends present the alphabet in 26 entertaining stories, each emphasizing a different letter.

1990 30m/C VHS *RAN, HMV, MLT*

Richard Scarry's Best Busy People Video Ever

Family Richard Scarry's animated characters illustrate for children the many jobs that people hold.

1993 30m/C VHS *BTV, RAB*

Richard Scarry's Best Counting Video Ever!

Family Learning to count can be darn fun. Lily Bunny counts from 1 to 20 in this numerical adventure. Huckle Cat, Lowly Worm, Bananas Gorilla, and more of the gang find things for Lily to count everywhere they go. Everyone: 1, 2, 3, 4 . . .

1990 30m/C VHS *RAN, HMV, MLT*

Richie Rich

Family World's wealthiest little boy, Richie Rich, with a weekly allowance of $100,000, and his girlfriend Gloria travel around the world to do good deeds. Cash becomes the equivalent of a super power in this Saturday-morning cartoon adaptation of a classic kiddie comic book; enough exposure to this stuff and Malcolm Forbes would've gone communist. A Hanna-Barbera production. **1980 50m/C VHS, Beta** *TTC*

Richie Rich 🎷🎷⬙

PG/Primary-Adult Money isn't everything, it's the only thing. Was it Vince Lombardi who said that? Donald Trump? Maybe it was Richie Rich, the wealthiest kid in the comics (Scrooge McDuck is a grown-up). When his parents mysteriously disappear, dauntless Richie (Culkin) tears himself away from his own roller coaster, his in-home McDonald's and his personal trainer, Claudia Schiffer, to take over the family business. What he doesn't have is friends. He manages to acquire some, and together they overcome a plot to take over the family fortune. Richie learns that his intelligence, kindness and bravery are more important than his wealth. Biltmore, the 8,000 acre Vanderbilt estate in Asheville, North Carolina, serves as the Rich family home.

> **BEWARE** *Mild violence and profanity. And try explaining what a kid is doing with all that great stuff!*

1994 94m/C Macaulay Culkin, John Larroquette, Edward Herrmann, Christine Ebersole, Jonathan Hyde, Micheal McShane, Stephi Lineburg; *Cameos:* Reggie Jackson, Claudia Schiffer; *D:* Donald Petrie; *W:* Tom S. Parker, Jim Jennewein; *C:* Don Burgess; *M:* Alan Silvestri. **VHS, LV** *WAR*

Ride a Wild Pony 🎷🎷⬙

G/Family In the early 1900s a poor Australian farmer's son is allowed to pick a horse of his own from a rancher's herd. After he trains and grows to love the pony, the rancher's daughter, a handicapped girl, decides to claim it for herself. Determining who should be the animal's master (or mistress) takes a courtroom wrangle and Solomon-like judgment in this slow-moving Disney feature, based on the tale "Sporting Proposition," by James Aldridge.

1975 86m/C John Meillon, Michael Craig, Robert Bettles, Eva Griffith, Graham Rouse; *D:* Don Chaffey; *M:* John Addison. **VHS, Beta** *DIS*

The Right Stuff 🎷🎷🎷⬙

PG/Jr. High-Adult Long, rambunctious adaptation of Tom Wolfe's long, rambunctious nonfiction bestseller about the beginnings of the U.S. space program, from Chuck Yeager's breaking of the sound barrier to the last of the Mercury missions. Featuring an all-star cast, sharp performances, and an ambitious script. Rowdy, imaginative, and thrilling, though broadly painted.

> **BEWARE** *Profanity. Not for most kids' attention spans.*

1983 193m/C Ed Harris, Dennis Quaid, Sam Shepard, Scott Glenn, Fred Ward, Charles Frank, William Russ, Kathy Baker, Barbara Hershey, Levon Helm, David Clennon, Kim Stanley, Mary Jo Deschanel, Veronica Cartwright, Pamela Reed, Jeff Goldblum, Harry Shearer, Donald Moffat, Scott Paulin, Lance Henriksen, Scott Wilson, John P. Ryan, Royal Dano; *D:* Philip Kaufman; *W:* Philip Kaufman; *M:* Bill Conti. **Award Nominations:** Academy Awards '83: Best Art Direction/Set Decoration, Best Cinematography, Best Picture, Best Supporting Actress (Shepard); **Awards:** Academy Awards '83: Best Film Editing, Best Sound, Best Original Score. **VHS, Beta, LV** *WAR*

Rikki-Tikki-Tavi

Preschool-Primary Derived from Rudyard Kipling's "The Jungle Book," this nicely animated story (directed by Chuck Jones) deals with a domesticated mongoose who saves his human family from two attacking cobras. Film features the voices of Orson Welles and June Foray; Citizen Kane meets Rocket J. Squirrel! Ages 3 to 7.

1975 30m/C *D:* Chuck Jones. **VHS, Beta** *FHE, MLT*

Rin Tin Tin, Hero of the West 🎷🎷

Family In one of his last adventures, the famous German Shepherd proves his courage and hyper-canine intelligence. Colorized.

1955 75m/C James Brown, Lee Aaker. **VHS, Beta** *MON*

Ring of Bright Water 🎷🎷🎷

G/Family Well-done story from Gavin Maxwell's nonfiction book, an endearing tale of a civil servant with a pet otter who moves to the country highlands of Scotland. Starring the "Born Free" acting team of Travers and McKenna, broadening their species experience.

1969 107m/C Bill Travers, Virginia McKenna, Peter Jeffrey, Archie Duncan; *D:* Charles Lamont. **VHS, Beta** *FCT, SIG, TVC*

Rip van Winkle

Primary-Jr. High Will Vinton's Claymation illustrates this version of Washington Irving's well-known tale about a man who sleeps for 20 years.

1979 30m/C VHS, Beta *BFA*

Rip van Winkle

Family Sleepy Francis Ford Coppola adaptation of the Washington Irving story about a man who falls asleep for twenty years after a ghostly Henry Hudson and crew get him drunk. From the "Faerie Tale Theatre" series. Could be a bit scary for youngsters. Ages 9 and up.

1985 60m/C Harry Dean Stanton, Talia Shire; *D:* Francis Ford Coppola. **VHS, Beta** *KUI, FOX, FCT*

Rip Van Winkle

Primary Washington Irving's tale of settler Van Winkle and his 20-year nap features delightful artwork and music, from the great "Rabbit Ears" series of storytelling videos.

1993 30m/C VHS *RAB, BTV*

The River 🦴🦴 ▷

PG/Family Hard-luck farmers battle a river whose flood threatens their farm, as well as the wealthy landowner hoping to scoop up their lots at discount prices. Spacek, is strong and believable as the wife and mother, but Gibson less so as the distressed husband and father. Beautiful photography by Vilmos Zsigmond highlights third (following "Country" and "Places in the Heart") in an onslaught of films in the early '80s that dramatized the plight of the small American farmer.

BEWARE *Brief nudity; violence; profanity.*

1984 124m/C Mel Gibson, Sissy Spacek, Scott Glenn, Billy Green Bush; **D:** Mark Rydell; **W:** Julian Barry, Robert Dillon; **M:** John Williams. **VHS, Beta, LV** *MCA*

The River Pirates 🦴🦴 ▷

PG/Family Mississippi boy discovers a lot about life over the summer of his 12th birthday in 1942. He finds the secret hiding place of a band of river thieves, endures a tornado, has some adventures with his friends, and finds out that his crush on the prettiest girl in town is reciprocated. Based on a novel by Willie Morris.

1994 108m/C Ryan Francis, Richard Farnsworth, Gennie James, Doug Emerson, Anne Ramsey, Maureen O'Sullivan; **D:** Tom G. Robertson. **VHS, LV** *VMK*

The River Rat 🦴🦴 ▷

PG/Family Ex-con is reunited with his 13-year-old daughter after spending that same number of years in prison, and they work together to restore an old Mississippi riverboat. Of course, there's a lesser storyline about stashed loot that should have been jettisoned in favor of more getting-to-know-you father-daughter drama.

BEWARE *Violence, salty language.*

1984 93m/C Tommy Lee Jones, Brian Dennehy, Martha Plimpton, Shawn Smith, Melissa Davis; **D:** Tom Rickman. **VHS, Beta, LV** *PAR*

A River Runs Through It 🦴🦴🦴

PG/Jr. High-Adult Contemplative exploration of family ties and growing up in Montana during the 1920s. Presbyterian minister raises two sons, trouble-prone and rebellious Paul, and Norman, equally strong-minded, but obedient. No matter how bad things get between the boys and their father, they join together on fly-fishing idylls that quietly relate to life, religion, and responsibility. Slow-moving philosophical fish story, but worthwhile. Based on the autobiographical novel by Norman Maclean. The laser disc version includes commentary by Redford.

BEWARE *Brawling, sex, destructive alcohol use and gambling. Disrespect of Native Americans (a problem of the era). A character dies.*

1992 123m/C Craig Sheffer, Brad Pitt, Tom Skerritt, Brenda Blethyn, Emily Lloyd, Edie McClurg, Stephen Shellan, Susan Taylor; **D:** Robert Redford; **W:** Richard Friedenberg; **M:** Mark Isham. **Award**

Nominations: Academy Awards '92: Best Adapted Screenplay, Best Original Score; **Awards:** Academy Awards '92: Best Cinematography. **VHS, LV, 8mm** *COL, CRC, BTV*

The River Wild 🦴🦴🦴 ▷

PG-13/Jr. High-Adult Urban mom Gail (Meryl Streep, with a side order of muscles), takes her husband, son and dog whitewater rafting in the western waters where she grew up and worked as a river guide. It's no day at the beach when vicious bank robbers in their own raft force Gail to help them escape. If the robbers don't get them, the deadly rapids will. But Gail and her nose-to-the-grindstone husband (Strathairn) are mighty resourceful. A highly contrived but highly exciting adventure, amidst beautiful Montana and Oregon settings. Bacon is supremely evil.

BEWARE *Violence, threatening moments and nice people get shot or shot at.*

1994 111m/C Meryl Streep, David Strathairn, Joseph Mazzello, Kevin Bacon, John C. Reilly, Benjamin Bratt; **D:** Curtis Hanson; **W:** Raynold Gideon; **M:** Jerry Goldsmith. **VHS, LV** *MCA*

Road Construction Ahead

Preschool-Primary Many children seem to be fascinated by the workings of heavy machinery, so this video should keep their attention. It shows every stage of road building from surveying to the first car driving on the completed highway. Machinery includes bulldozers, excavators, rock crushers, bucket loaders, and giant trucks, all explained by a friendly worker named George.

1992 30m/C VHS

The Road Home 🦴🦴 ▷

PG/Primary-Adult Depression-era heart-tugger features two orphaned brothers who ride the rails from New York to Nebraska in search of a new home at Father Flanagan's Boys Town.

BEWARE *Emotional death scene and some violence.*

1995 90m/C Keegan Macintosh, Will Estes, Kris Kristofferson, Charles Martin Smith, Danny Aiello, Dee Wallace Stone, Mickey Rooncy; **D:** Dean Hamilton. **VHS** *REP*

Road Runner & Wile E. Coyote: Scrapes of Wrath

Family The hapless Coyote chases his would-be dinner in "Whoa-Be Gone!," "Guided Muscle," "Hopalong Casualty," and "Stop! Look! and Hasten!" Ages 5 to 10.

198? 33m/C VHS *BTV, WAR*

Roald Dahl's: Dirty Beasts

Preschool-Primary Collection of comic verse from the author whose works inspired "Willy Wonka and the Chocolate Factory" and "The Witches." Dahl's ghastly menagerie of animals do crazy things in comic verse and animation based on the original illustrations by Quentin Blake.

19?? 30m/C V: Prunella Scales, Timothy West. **VHS** *FAF, VTR*

Macaulay Culkin stars as the richest kid in the world in "Richie Rich."

Roald Dahl's The Enormous Crocodile

Primary Crocodile's plot to have a child for lunch is foiled in typical Dahlesque fashion.
1993 25m/C VHS *VTR*

Rob Roy 🦴🦴🦴

R/Sr. High-Adult Kilt-raising though overlong tale of legendary Scot Robert Roy MacGregor mixes love and honor with bloodlust and revenge. Neeson's rugged clan leader fends off a band of dastardly nobles led by Cunningham (Roth), a foppish twit with an evil bent. Misty highland scenery and intense romantic interplay between Neeson and Lange as the spirited Mary MacGregor lend a passionate twist to an otherwise earthy, robust adventure of lore capped by one of the best sword fights in years. Visually stunning, with on-location shooting in the Scottish Highlands.

> **BEWARE** *Sexuality and violence, including a rape scene and a lot of bloody swordplay and separated body parts.*

1995 144m/C Liam Neeson, Jessica Lange, Tim Roth, John Hurt, Eric Stoltz, Andrew Keir, Brian Cox, Brian McCardie, Gilbert Martin, Vicki Masson, David Hayman; **D:** Michael Caton-Jones; **W:** Alan Sharp; **C:** Karl Walter Lindenlaub. **VHS, LV** *MGM*

Rob Roy—The Highland Rogue 🦴♡

Family In the early 18th century, Scottish Highlander Rob Roy must battle against the King of England's secretary, who would undermine the MacGregor clan to enact his evil deeds. Dull Disney drama.
1953 84m/C Richard Todd, Glynis Johns, James Robertson Justice, Michael Gough; **D:** Harold French. **VHS, Beta** *DIS*

The Robert McCloskey Library

Family Five delightful stories from writer-illustrator McCloskey, including "Lentil," "Make Way for Ducklings," "Blueberries for Sal," and "Time of Wonder." Also includes a 1964 interview with the author. Ages 2 to 8.
1990 55m/C VHS *CCC, MLT,*

Robin and Marian 🦴🦴

PG/Jr. High-Adult After a separation of twenty years, an aging, disillusioned Robin Hood is reunited with Maid Marian, who is now a nun. Their dormant feelings for each other are reawakened as Robin spirits her to Sherwood Forest for a reunion with old friends and enemies. Not really for kids, this "mature version" of the legend robs Robin of much magic, spontaneity, and fun (though there is swashbuckling violence). On the other hand, superior cast does what it can to bring some depth and charm to the endeavor.

> **BEWARE** *Violence.*

1976 106m/C Sean Connery, Audrey Hepburn, Robert Shaw, Richard Harris; **D:** Richard Lester; **M:** John Barry. **VHS, Beta, LV** *COL, FOX*

Robin Hood 🦴🦴🦴

Family Second-rate Disney—which means it's pretty good—animated tale of Robin (a fox), Little John (a bear) and the other merry, uh, men. Some catchy tunes by Roger Miller and quite possibly the only film to employ the vocal talents of Shakespearean actor Brian Bedford and non-Shakespearean actor Andy Devine. Ages 5 to 10.
1973 83m/C D: Wolfgang Reitherman; **M:** George Bruns; **V:** Roger Miller, Brian Bedford, Monica Evans, Phil Harris, Andy Devine, Carol Shelley, Peter Ustinov, Terry-Thomas, Pat Buttram, George Lindsey, Ken Curtis. **VHS, Beta, LV** *DIS, FCT, RDG*

Robin Hood: Men in Tights 🦴🦴

PG-13/Jr. High-Adult Brooksian rendition of the classic legend inspires guffaws, but doesn't hit the bullseye on all it promises. Hood aficionados will appreciate the painstaking effort taken to spoof the 1938 Errol Flynn classic while leaving plenty of room to poke fun at the more recent Costner non-classic "Robin Hood: Prince of Thieves." Elwes, last seen swinging swords in "The Princess Bride," is well cast as the Flynn look-alike. Expect the usual off-color humor that's so prevalent in all Brooks outings.

> **BEWARE** *Profanity, sex talk and risque jokes.*

1993 105m/C Cary Elwes, Richard Lewis, Roger Rees, Amy Yasbeck, Dave Chappelle, Isaac Hayes, Tracey Ullman, Mark Blankfield, Megan Cavanagh, Eric Allen Kramer, Tony Griffin, Dick Van Patten, Mel Brooks; **D:** Mel Brooks; **W:** Mel Brooks, J. David Shapiro; **M:** Hummie Mann. **VHS** *FXV*

Robin Hood: Prince of Thieves 🦴🦴♡

PG-13/Jr. High-Adult Revisionist retelling of the Sherwood Forest legends is a strange brew indeed; Costner's obviously American Robin Hood sorely lacks swashbuckling charisma, and Rickman easily overpowers him (dramatically, anyway) as the wicked, crazed Sheriff of Nottingham, just one of a memorable cast of character actors. Great action sequences, a gritty and credible picture of the Middle Ages (blown to shreds at the end when Bryan Adams and his band materialize in the heather to croon the hit music-video love theme!). Still has lots of fun for lovers of romance and fairy tales.

> **BEWARE** *Violence. The Sheriff of Nottingham worships Satan and nearly rapes Maid Marian (or is it the other way around?) but neither act is explicit.*

1991 144m/C Kevin Costner, Morgan Freeman, Mary Elizabeth Mastrantonio, Christian Slater, Alan Rickman, Geraldine McEwan, Micheal McShane, Brian Blessed, Michael Wincott, Nick Brimble, Jack Wild, Harold Innocent, Jack Wild; **Cameos:** Sean Connery; **D:** Kevin Reynolds; **W:** Pen Densham, John Watson; **M:** Michael Kamen. **Award Nominations:** Academy Awards '91: Best Song ("(Everything I Do) I Do It for You"); **Awards:** British Academy Awards '92: Best Supporting Actor (Rickman); MTV Movie Awards '92: Best Song ("(Everything I Do) I Do for You"). **VHS, LV** *WAR, RDG*

Robinson Crusoe

Family Animated adaptation of the classic Daniel Defoe story about a man marooned on a small island.
1978 86m/C VHS, Beta *FHE*

Robinson Crusoe & the Tiger 🎵 ♪

G/Family Ultra-cheapo version of Daniel Defoe's famous story of how Robinson Crusoe became stranded and survived on a desert island. Made in the Philippines.
1972 109m/C Hugo Stiglitz, Ahui; *D:* Rene Cardona Jr. **VHS, Beta**

Robocop 🎵🎵🎵

R/Sr. High-Adult Detroit cop killed in action is used as donor for the brain of a crime-fighting cyborg. Trouble begins when Robocop starts remembering his life as a human. Not just superhero action; there's a bleak, cynical view of the future, an acid satire of corporate America, and an underlying sadness about its main character. Though an inspiration for toys, comics and a later TV series, this one's not for children. Graphic gore nearly earned the picture an X rating.

⚠ BEWARE *Carnage, profanity, mature themes, alcohol use.*

1987 103m/C Peter Weller, Nancy Allen, Ronny Cox, Kurtwood Smith, Ray Wise, Miguel Ferrer, Dan O'Herlihy, Robert DoQui, Felton Perry, Paul McCrane, Del Zamora; *D:* Paul Verhoeven; *W:* Michael Miner, Edward Neumeier; *M:* Basil Poledouris. **VHS, Beta, LV** *ORI*

Robocop 2 🎵🎵

R/Sr. High-Adult Savagely violent sequel shows a new drug making future Detroit more dangerous yet. Robocop's corporate owners eventually build a bigger, stronger cyborg with the brain of a psycho pusher/addict/cult leader. It goes berserk, and the metal beings fight an epic battle, in between enough subplots for three movies. More comic-bookish than the previous entry, yet perversely unsuitable for kids. Besides gore, there's a sadistic boy drug lord and a scene of a little league team looting a store ("Harder!" orders one tyke as they beat an old man with a bat they're barely big enough to lift). Movies like this are aimed strictly and properly at jaded grownups, yet youngsters were obviously seen as consumers; note the finger-wagging antidrug PSA at the start of the tape.

⚠ BEWARE *Carnage, profanity, drug use.*

1990 117m/C Peter Weller, Nancy Allen, Belinda Bauer, Dan O'Herlihy, Tommy Noonan, Gabriel Damon, Galyn Gorg, Felton Perry, Patricia Charbonneau; *D:* Irvin Kershner; *W:* Walon Green. **VHS, Beta, LV** *ORI*

Robocop 3 🎵 ♪

PG-13/Jr. High-Adult Far from the best of the "Robocop" movies, but certainly the only kid-friendly one. There's a little orphan girl provided as partner and surrogate daughter for the metal hero when corporate mercenaries kill her parents to seize the real estate of

If you like *Robin Hood: Prince of Thieves* (1991), you'll love:

The Adventures of Robin Hood (1938)

Camelot (1967)

A Connecticut Yankee (1931)

A Connecticut Yankee in King Arthur's Court (1949)

Dragonheart (1996)

First Knight (1995)

A Kid in King Arthur's Court (1995)

Ladyhawke (1985)

Merlin and the Sword (1985)

Robin and Marian (1976)

The Sword in the Stone (1963)

Willow (1988)

their Detroit slum. Robocop joins with the citizens to protect their homes. Violence and swearing have been scaled down from the earlier films (so has the budget, obviously), in what could generally pass for an episode of the subsequent "Robocop" TV series.

⚠ BEWARE *Violence, profanity.*

1991 104m/C Robert Burke, Nancy Allen, John Castle, CCH Pounder, Bruce Locke, Rip Torn, Remi Ryan, Felton Perry; *D:* Fred Dekker; *W:* Fred Dekker, Frank Miller; *M:* Basil Poledouris. **VHS** *ORI*

Robocop, Vol. 1: Man in the Iron Suit

Primary-Jr. High Rebuilt episodes for the Marvel Comics TV cartoon series "Inhumanoids," based on the cyborg police officer from the ultraviolent movies. In this installment, a jealous villain tests a new powersuit against Robocop. Additional volumes available.
1989 22m/C VHS, LV

Robot Jox 🎵🎵

PG/Jr. High-Adult In the future, diplomacy means two lone gladiators fight to the finish inside giant robots. Will brotherhood and goodness prevail? Semi-meaningful, semi-ludicrous sci-fi (with uneven quality f/x) isn't strictly aimed at small fry but earns a mention here for the fighting machines' suspicious similarity to popular toys like the Transformers and the Gobots. At least it's better than their cartoons.

BEWARE *Profanity, violence, sex talk.*

1989 84m/C Gary Graham, Anne-Marie Johnson, Paul Koslo, Robert Sampson, Danny Kamekona, Hilary Mason, Michael Alldredge; **D:** Stuart Gordon; **W:** Stuart Gordon. **VHS, LV** *COL*

Robotech: Southern Cross

Primary-Jr. High The armies of the Southern Cross are left to defend Earth. Although inexperienced, they are smart and energetic. Eight volumes are available individually.
19?? 66m/C VHS

Robotech: The Macross Saga, Vol. 1

Family First in a series of six videos that recount the struggle of three generations of Earthlings who must fight off an invasion by the alien Zantraedi. Intricately plotted, character crammed, gadget-glutted Japanese TV cartoon adventure serial has a cult of admirers (plus various imitations and soundalikes) who consider it a cut above the usual toy-peddling 'toons. Additional volumes available.
1987 80m/C VHS, Beta *FHE, STP, TPV*

Robotech: The New Generation

Primary-Jr. High Contains eight more volumes of the popular Japanese-made space serial.
1985 66m/C VHS *STP, TPV*

Robotech, Vol. 1: Booby Trap

Family Rookie pilot in the elite Robotech Defense Force battles for his life against more experienced warriors. Ex-Yankees dominate cast. Additional volumes available.
1985 30m/C Roger Maris, Mickey Mantle, Whitey Ford, Elston Howard, Al Downing. **VHS, Beta** *FHE*

Robotman and Friends

Preschool-Primary Animated adventures with several episodes, detailing the TV escapades of Robotman and his pals Stellar and Oops, who repeatedly side with humanity against the evil forces of Roberon. Humanity was also the target for the Robotman line of toy products.
1984 48m/C VHS, Beta, LV *LIV*

Rock-a-Doodle ♫ ♪

G/Family A singing rooster (voice of Glen Campbell) leaves the barnyard and becomes an Elvis Presleyesque rock star. Animated entertainment for little children, but it's no "Follow That Bird." Speaking of which, this film is about animals searching for a large feathered friend,

Chanticleer the rooster. They are led by a little boy, Edmond, who while reading the story has been drawn into it as a kitten. There's little that will appeal to adults, except a chance to count how many other movies "Rock-A-Doodle" borrows from. And even children, may wince at Edmond, who says things like "The stowwy's twue." Apologies to Dorothy Parker, but that's the sort of thing that can make you fwow up. Insider's note: Singing backup behind Campbell are the Jordanaires, who sang backup on several of Elvis's hits. Ages 3-6.
1992 77m/C D: Don Bluth; **W:** David A. Weiss; **M:** Robert Folk; **V:** Glen Campbell, Christopher Plummer, Phil Harris, Sandy Duncan, Ellen Greene, Charles Nelson Reilly, Eddie Deezen, Toby Scott Granger, Sorrell Booke. **VHS, LV** *HBO, MVD*

Rock Music with the Muppets

Family The Muppets perform their own brand of rock and roll with their special musical guests. The songs featured include "Rock Around the Clock," "Call Me," "Rainbow Connection," and "Disco Frog."
1985 54m/C V: Frank Oz, Jim Henson, Alice Cooper, Deborah Harry, Paul Simon, Helen Reddy, Leo Sayer, Loretta Swit, Ben Vereen. **VHS, Beta** *FOX*

Rock 'n' Roll High School ♫♫♫

PG/Sr. High-Adult Music of the rockin' Ramones highlights this non-stop high-energy cult classic about high school kids out to thwart the rock-hating principal at every turn. If it had been made in 1957, it would have been the ultimate rock 'n' roll teen movie. The 1970s' milieu works against it, but the performances are perfect for the material, resembling a "Mad Magazine" parody (a good one) come to life. Songs include "Teenage Lobotomy," "Blitzkrieg Bop," "I Wanna Be Sedated," and the title track, among others. Followed far less successfully by "Rock 'n' Roll High School Forever."

BEWARE *Salty language.*

1979 94m/C The Ramones, P.J. Soles, Vincent Van Patten, Clint Howard, Dey Young, Mary Woronov, Alix Elias, Dick Miller, Paul Bartel; **D:** Allan Arkush. **VHS, Beta** *MVD*

Rock 'n' Roll High School Forever **WOOF!**

PG-13/Sr. High-Adult Jesse and his band just want to rock 'n' roll, but the new principal (Woronov, caricaturing her caricature from "Rock 'n' Roll High School") opposes them with terror tactics. Way late, way lame sequel misses by miles the spunk and wit that made the original a cult classic.

BEWARE *Profanity, and of course sex, drugs, and rock 'n' roll.*

1991 94m/C Corey Feldman, Mary Woronov, Mojo Nixon, Evan Richards, Michael Ceveris, Patrick Malone, Larry Linville, Sarah Buxton; **D:** Deborah Brock; **W:** Deborah Brock. **VHS, Beta, LV** *LIV, IME*

Rocket Gibraltar

PG/Jr. High-Adult Large family gathers to celebrate Levi Rockwell's 77th birthday, but his adult children seem preoccupied and awkward around the old guy. Only the grandkids realize what he wants and they conspire to grant his dying wish—a viking-style cremation at sea. Great when the juveniles (including "Home Alone's" Culkin, in his screen debut) and Lancaster are together. Nice little parable about family, inheritance, life, death, sex, and so on.

BEWARE: *Sex talk, profanity and dying as a theme.*

1988 92m/C Burt Lancaster, Bill Pullman, John Glover, Suzy Amis, Macaulay Culkin, Patricia Clarkson, Frances Conroy, Sinead Cusack, Bill Martin, Kevin Spacey; **D:** Daniel Petrie; **W:** Amos Poe; **M:** Andrew Powell. **VHS, Beta** *COL*

The Rocketeer

PG/Family Fun Disney adaptation of Dave Stevens' recent retro-style comic book. Stunt flyer in the 1930s finds a prototype jet backpack sought by Nazi spies. Donning a metal mask, he becomes a flying superhero. Breezy family entertainment with stupendous special effects; even better if you know movie trivia, as it brims with Hollywood references, like a great villain (Dalton) clearly based on Errol Flynn.

BEWARE: *Disney-style violence*

1991 109m/C Bill Campbell, Jennifer Connelly, Alan Arkin, Timothy Dalton, Paul Sorvino, Melora Hardin, Tiny Ron, Terry O'Quinn, Ed Lauter, James Handy; **D:** Joe Johnston; **W:** Danny Bilson, Paul DeMeo; **M:** James Horner. **VHS, Beta, LV** *DIS, CCB, IME*

Rockin' with Judy Jetson

Preschool-Primary Made-for-TV animated feature starring the Jetsons' teenage daughter, whose crush on future pop star Sky Rocker leads to her own bid for space-age music stardom. Fans of the Hanna-Barbera series will find this politically correct compared to "Jetsons: The Movie," which unceremoniously replaced the longstanding Judy vocalizer, Janet Waldo, with teen diva Tiffany.
1988 90m/C **VHS, Beta, LV** *TTC, IME*

Rocky

PG/Jr. High-Adult Surprising box office smash about a young man from the slums of Philadelphia who dreams of becoming a boxing champion. Then unknown Stallone wrote the script and stars as Rocky, the underdog who gets a shot at fame and self-respect when a conceited champ picks him as an easy opponent for a high-profile bout. Great rags-to-riches story that loses strength in the subsequent (and numerous) rerun sequels. Powerful score by Bill Conti.

BEWARE: *Brutality in the dynamic fight scenes. Alcohol use, occasional salty language.*

1976 125m/C Sylvester Stallone, Talia Shire, Burgess Meredith, Burt Young, Carl Weathers; **D:** John G. Avildsen; **W:** Sylvester Stal-

lone; **M:** Bill Conti. **Award Nominations:** Academy Awards '76: Best Actor (Stallone), Best Actress (Shire), Best Original Screenplay, Best Song ("Gonna Fly Now"), Best Sound, Best Supporting Actor (Meredith, Young); **Awards:** Academy Awards '76: Best Director (Avildsen), Best Film Editing, Best Picture; Directors Guild of America Awards '76: Best Director (Avildsen); Golden Globe Awards '77: Best Film—Drama; Los Angeles Film Critics Association Awards '76: Best Film; National Board of Review Awards '76: 10 Best Films of the Year, Best Supporting Actress (Shire). **VHS, Beta, LV, 8mm** *MGM, FOX, BTV*

Rocky 2

PG/Jr. High-Adult Time-marking sequel to the box office smash finds Rocky frustrated by the commercialism which followed his match to Apollo, but considering a return bout. Meanwhile, his wife fights for her life. Overall effect is to prepare you for the next sequel.

BEWARE: *Violence and profanity.*

1979 119m/C Sylvester Stallone, Talia Shire, Burt Young, Burgess Meredith, Carl Weathers; **D:** Sylvester Stallone; **W:** Sylvester Stallone; **M:** Bill Conti. **VHS, Beta, LV** *MGM, FOX*

Rocky 3

PG/Jr. High-Adult Rocky is beaten by big, mean Clubber Lang (played to a tee by Mr. T). He realizes success has made him soft, and has to dig deep to find the motivation to stay on top. Amazingly, Stallone regains his underdog persona here, looking puny next to Mr. T, who is the best thing about the second-best "Rocky" flick.

BEWARE: *Violence; salty language.*

1982 103m/C Sylvester Stallone, Talia Shire, Burgess Meredith, Carl Weathers, Mr. T, Leif Erickson, Burt Young; **D:** Sylvester Stallone; **W:** Sylvester Stallone; **M:** Bill Conti. **VHS, Beta, LV** *MGM, FOX*

Rocky 4

PG/Jr. High-Adult Rocky travels to Russia to fight the Soviet champ who killed his friend during a bout. Will Rocky knock the Russkie out? Will Rocky get hammered on the head a great many times and sag around the ring? Will Rocky ever learn? Lundgren isn't nearly as much fun as some of Rocky's former opponents and Stallone overdoes the hyper-patriotism and relies too heavily on uplifting footage from earlier "Rocky" movies.

BEWARE: *Violence and profanity.*

1985 91m/C Sylvester Stallone, Talia Shire, Dolph Lundgren, Brigitte Nielsen, Michael Pataki, Burt Young, Carl Weathers; **D:** Sylvester Stallone; **W:** Sylvester Stallone. **VHS, Beta, LV** *MGM, FOX*

Rocky 5

PG/Jr. High-Adult Brain damaged and broke, Rocky finds himself back where he started on the streets of Philadelphia. Boxing still very much in his blood, Rocky takes in a protege, training him in the style that made him a champ (take a lickin' and keep on tickin'). However an unscrupulous promoter has designs on the young fighter and seeks to wrest the lad from under the former champ's wing. This eventually leads to a showdown between Rocky and the young boxer in a brutal streetfight.

Supposedly the last "Rocky" film, it's clear the formula has run dry.
1990 105m/C Sylvester Stallone, Talia Shire, Burt Young, Sage Stallone, Tom Morrison, Burgess Meredith; **D:** John G. Avildsen; **W:** Sylvester Stallone; **M:** Bill Conti. **VHS, Beta, LV, 8mm** *MGM*

Roger Ramjet vs. N.A.S.T.Y.

Family Once again Roger must take on the fiendish bunch of N.A.S.T.Y. Cartoons are "Bank Robbers" and "Bathosphere."
1965 30m/C VHS *RHI*

Roman Holiday 🎬🎬🎬 ♭

Family Hepburn's first starring role is a charmer as a princess bored with her official visit to Rome who slips away and plays at being an "average Jane." A reporter discovers her little charade and decides to cash in with an exclusive story. Before they know it, love calls. Blacklisted screenwriter Trumbo was "fronted" by Ian McLellan Hunter, who accepted screen credit and the Best Story Oscar in Trumbo's stead. The Academy voted to posthumously award Trumbo his own Oscar in 1993.
1953 118m/B Audrey Hepburn, Gregory Peck, Eddie Albert, Tullio Carminati; **D:** William Wyler; **W:** Dalton Trumbo. **Award Nominations:** Academy Awards '53: Best Art Direction/Set Decoration (B & W), Best Black and White Cinematography, Best Director (Wyler), Best Film Editing, Best Picture, Best Screenplay, Best Supporting Actor (Albert); **Awards:** Academy Awards '53: Best Actress (Hepburn), Best Costume Design (B & W), Best Story; British Academy Awards '53: Best Actress (Hepburn); Golden Globe Awards '54: Best Actress—Drama (Hepburn); New York Film Critics Awards '53: Best Actress (Hepburn). **VHS, Beta, LV, 8mm** *PAR, BTV, HMV*

Romancing the Stone 🎬🎬🎬

PG/Family Uptight romance novelist Turner lives out her fantasies after she receives a mysterious map from her murdered brother-in-law and her sister is kidnapped in South America—the ransom being the map. Out to rescue her sister, she's helped and hindered by American soldier of fortune Douglas, whose main concern is himself and the hidden treasure described in the map. Great chemistry between the stars and loads of clever dialogue in this appealing adventure comedy. First outing with Turner, Douglas, and DeVito. Followed by "The Jewel of the Nile."
BEWARE *Action violence, brief nudity and profanity. Arguing between Turner's and Douglas' characters.*
1984 106m/C Michael Douglas, Kathleen Turner, Danny DeVito, Zack Norman, Alfonso Arau, Ron Silver; **D:** Robert Zemeckis; **M:** Alan Silvestri. **Award Nominations:** Academy Awards '84: Best Film Editing; **Awards:** Golden Globe Awards '85: Best Actress—Musical/Comedy (Turner), Best Film—Musical/Comedy. **VHS, Beta, LV** *FOX, HMV*

Romeo and Juliet 🎬🎬🎬 ♭

PG/Family Still one of the most heartbreaking and eloquent portrayals of young love ever, and the only one of many, many adaptations of Shakespeare's classic play to underscore such themes by casting actual teenagers as the adolescent leads. Also available in a 45-minute edited version.
BEWARE *Sex, violence, nudity, mature themes.*
1968 138m/C Olivia Hussey, Leonard Whiting, Michael York, Milo O'Shea; **D:** Franco Zeffirelli; **M:** Nino Rota. **Award Nominations:** Academy Awards '68: Best Director (Zeffirelli), Best Picture; **Awards:** Academy Awards '68: Best Cinematography, Best Costume Design; Golden Globe Awards '69: Best Foreign Film; National Board of Review Awards '68: 10 Best Films of the Year, Best Director (Zeffirelli). **VHS, Beta, LV** *PAR, HMV, PBC*

Romper Room and Friends: Explore Nature

Family Miss Molly and the Romper Room Gang learn all about nature, including animals and how they live, trees and how soil is made, how important every living thing is. Additional volumes available.
1985 32m/C VHS, Beta *FOX*

Roobarb

Preschool-Primary Collection of rambunctious cartoons from British TV about a mongrel named Roobarb and a cat named Custard.
1980 67m/C VHS, Beta *FHE*

Rookie of the Year 🎬🎬 ♭

PG/Primary-Adult Twelve-year-old Little Leaguer Henry breaks his arm, and when it heals askew he's blessed with a pitching arm so spectacular he's recruited for the Chicago Cubs, leading them to the World Series. Good-natured sports fantasy is a highly predictable but enjoyable family outing for first-time director Stern (who also plays a goofy, childlike teammate). Keep your eyes peeled for appearances by real-live sluggers Pedro Guerrero, Barry Bonds, and others.
BEWARE *One muffled word that might have been salty, but probably not. This could been a G with no problem.*
1993 103m/C Thomas Ian Nicholas, Daniel Stern, Gary Busey, Dan Hedaya; **D:** Daniel Stern; **W:** Sam Harper; **M:** Bill Conti. **VHS** *FXV*

Room for Heroes

Preschool-Primary Frontier favorites abound in this animated salute to Johnny Appleseed, Pecos Bill, Casey Jones, and Davey Crockett, with clips from past Disney classics.
1990 14m/C VHS, Beta *DSN, MTI*

Room Service 🎬🎬 ♭

Family Groucho plays a penniless Broadway producer who can't pay his hotel bill. With the help of cronies Harpo and Chico, he schemes to stay in the high-rise suite (staging a fake outbreak of measles, among other pranks) until he can secure funds for the next show. Not as funny as previous Marx Brothers comedies, mainly because it's based on a stage play of the era, with the Marxists following most of the script straight, imposing a minimum of their own personalities.

Thomas Ian Nicholas makes the leap from Little League to the Major Leagues in "Rookie of the Year."

1938 78m/B Groucho Marx, Harpo Marx, Chico Marx, Lucille Ball, Ann Miller, Frank Albertson, Donald MacBride, Charles Halton; **D:** William A. Seiter. **VHS, Beta, LV** *CCB, MED, TTC*

Rooster Cogburn

PG/Jr. High-Adult The sequel to "True Grit" pairs the hard-drinking, hard-fighting marshal with a straightlaced but equally spirited schoolmarm in order to capture a gang of outlaws who killed her father. Typical story, but the fireworks between Wayne and Hepburn are right on target.

BEWARE *Violence.*

1975 107m/C John Wayne, Katharine Hepburn, Richard Jordan, Anthony Zerbe, John McIntire, Strother Martin, Paul Koslo; **D:** Stuart Millar. **VHS, Beta, LV** *MCA, TLF*

Rose-Petal Place

Preschool Animated TV musical fantasy about flowers turning into young girls; foremost among the flower-fairies is Rose-Petal, voiced by Ms. Osmond.
1983 60m/C **V:** Marie Osmond. **VHS, Beta** *WOV*

Rosie's Walk

Primary Animated tale of little red hen Rosie, who struts across the barnyard keeping her cool while unknowingly leading a stalking fox into a series of disasters. Also includes "Charlie Needs a Cloak," "The Story about Ping," and "The Beast of Monsieur Racine." Part II of the "Children's Circle" series from Weston Woods.
1970 32m/C **VHS, Beta** *CCC,*

The Rousters

PG/Jr. High-Adult Descendants of Wyatt Earp run a carnival in a small Western town. Rambling, family-friendly made-for-TV movie that was a pilot for a short-lived TV series, this obscurity was released to home video to capitalize on the popularity of Jim Varney, playing a character almost identical (physically and intellectually) to his hit movie boob Ernest P. Worrell.

BEWARE *Roughhousing.*

1983 72m/C Jim Varney, Mimi Rogers, Chad Everett, Maxine Stuart, Hoyt Axton; **D:** E.W. Swackhamer; **W:** E.W. Swackhamer, Stephen J. Cannell. **VHS, LV** *VMK*

Rover Dangerfield

G/Family The "Brave Little Toaster" crew also did this cartoon vehicle for comic Rodney Dangerfield that cannily recasts him as the casino-wise pet hound of a Las Vegas showgirl. So far, so good, but then the plot unwisely dumps Rover in a farm setting, far from the glitter and gambling tables and into a worn-out farmboy-and-his-dog plot; you can imagine almost any animated character doing exactly the same tired tale. Dangerfield also wrote the script, incorporating characteristic catchphrases, mannerisms and fire-hydrant jokes.

BEWARE *Violence, surprisingly, in a wolf attack and miscellaneous mayhem.*

1991 78m/C **W:** Harold Ramis; **M:** David Newman; **V:** Rodney Dangerfield. **VHS, LV, 8mm** *WAR*

Roxanne

PG/Jr. High-Adult Modern comic retelling of "Cyrano de Bergerac" dwells on the romantic triangle between a small town fire chief with a very big nose and a fast tongue, a handsome, fairly stupid fireman, and the lovely astronomer they both love. In a complex, enjoyable performance, Martin is a hoot as Chief Bales, utilizing wit as his rapier and chivalrously assisting his dimwitted fireman's courtship of Roxanne while pining for her himself. Don't miss the bar scene where he gets back at a heckler. A wonderful adaptation for the modern age.

BEWARE *Profanity and suggested sex.*

1987 107m/C Steve Martin, Daryl Hannah, Rick Rossovich, Shelley Duvall, Michael J. Pollard, Fred Willard, John Kapelos, Max Alexander, Damon Wayans, Matt Lattanzi, Kevin Nealon; **D:** Fred Schepisi; **W:** Steve Martin; **M:** Bruce Smeaton. **VHS, Beta, LV, 8mm** *COL*

Rubber Tarzan

Family Ivan is a gentle, friendless, quiet (and possibly dyslexic) boy bullied daily at school and bossed at home by his workaholic dad, who wants him to be like Tarzan. But a sympathetic dockworker helps Ivan affirm his self-worth. Delicate little Danish film avoids gooey melodrama, but its slow pace and subtleties steer it more toward adult viewers than kids.
1983 75m/C **VHS, Beta** *NLC*

Rubik, the Amazing Cube, Vol. 1

Family One of the unlikeliest toy pandering Saturday-morning TV shows; here are two episodes from the animated series based upon the puzzle cube that became a commercial sensation too profitable for the networks to ignore, and originally broadcast together with a similar crossover concept, the cartoon edition of Pac-Man. "Welcome Back Kotter" character actor Palillo provides the voice of Rubik. Additional volumes available.
1984 45m/C **VHS, Beta** *COL*

Rudolph & Frosty's Christmas in July

Family Another adventure for "the most famous reindeer of all." This time Rudolph and pals find themselves on a sunny, tropical island for a magical visit, but tragedy is narrowly escaped when that famous nose stops shining. Another Rankin-Bass creation.
1982 97m/C **V:** Red Buttons, Ethel Merman, Mickey Rooney, Jackie Vernon, Shelley Winters. **VHS, Beta** *LIV, WAR, TLF*

Rudolph the Red-Nosed Reindeer 🦴🦴🦴

Family Durable Christmas story inspired by the Johnny Marks song about the nasally enhanced reindeer who saved the holiday. Colorful stop-motion animation and character voices bring it to life, with a memorable guest visit from an abominable snowman. Made for television by Arthur Rankin Jr. and Jules Bass.

1964 53m/C D: Larry Roemer. **VHS, Beta, LV, 8mm** *FHE, LME*

Rudolph's Shiny New Year

Family A made-for-TV Rankin-Bass production featuring that shiny-nosed reindeer everyone knows so well. Baby New Year is missing and Rudolph is recruited to lead the search.

1979 50m/C V: Red Skelton, Frank Gorshin. **VHS, Beta** *LIV*

Rudy 🦴🦴 ♡

PG/Jr. High-Adult Inspiring true story about an unlikely legend of Notre Dame football, the small-sized Daniel E. "Rudy" Ruettiger (onetime "Goonie" Astin). A mediocre student, the working-class youth dreams of playing for the prestigious school. Through determination and hard work he makes the practice squad, but still has his mind set on getting into a real game. Likeable sports drama with an engaging hero.

 *Football mayhem.*

1993 112m/C Sean Astin, Ned Beatty, Charles S. Dutton, Lili Taylor, Robert Prosky, Jason Miller, Ron Dean, Chelcie Ross, Jon Favreau, Greta Lind, Scott Benjaminson, Christopher Reed; **D:** David Anspaugh; **W:** Angelo Pizzo; **M:** Jerry Goldsmith. **VHS, LV, 8mm** *COL*

Rudyard Kipling's Just So Stories, Vol. 1

Family An animated adaptation of the Rudyard Kipling stories that explain "How the Camel Got His Hump" and "How the Elephant Got His Trunk." Animation is just so-so. Ages 8 to 12.

1982 34m/C VHS, Beta *VES*

Rudyard Kipling's Just So Stories, Vol. 2

Family Six animated adaptations of the famous tales, including "How the Rhinoceros Got His Skin," "The Crab that Played with the Sea" and "How the Whale Got His Throat." Just so-so animation. Ages 8 to 12.

1986 57m/C VHS, Beta *NO*

Rudyard Kipling's The Jungle Book 🦴🦴🦴

PG/Primary-Adult Rip-roaring live-action adventure filmed in India has little to do with the Kipling original or the Disney cartoon, and its dialogue, repeated out of context, sounds ridiculous: "I run with the wolf pack, you run with the man pack," says jungle-raised Mowgli (Lee) to proper Brit Kitty (Headey) whom he is just wild about. Yes, there are animals, and a beastly lot they are, especially snobbish Capt. Boone (Elwes) who wants Kitty for his own and would exploit Mowgli's knowledge of the treasure-rich lost monkey city. Much action ensues. Think of Mowgli as India Jones.

 *Beatings of prisoners and kicks in the crotch.*

1994 111m/C Jason Scott Lee, Cary Elwes, Sam Neill, Lena Headey, John Cleese; **D:** Stephen Sommers; **W:** Stephen Sommers. **VHS, LV** *DIS*

Rugrats: Passover

Family Baby Tommy Pickles and his friends interpret Passover in their own unique rugrattish way.

1995 25m/C VHS

Rugrats, Vol. 1: Tales from the Crib

Preschool-Primary Episodes of the award-winning Nickelodeon cable-TV 'toon show about mischievous toddlers. Tommy and his best friend, Chuckie, star in "Toy Palace," "Real or Robots," and "Beach Blanket Babies." Includes two claymation vignettes of Inside Out Boy, the superhero with the power to save kids by grossing out grownups. Additional volumes available.

1993 40m/C VHS *SMV*

Rumble Fish 🦴🦴🦴

R/Sr. High-Adult Rusty-James, a young street punk, idolizes his older brother, a cool but weary former gang leader who's become a slum legend known as the Motorcycle Boy. Coppola's second adaptation of a bestselling S.E. Hinton young-adult novel is a much more daring production than "The Outsiders," with stark B&W photography and occasionally muffled sound to reflect the Motorcycle Boy's view of the world (you have to pay close attention to catch the detail that he's color blind and partially deaf). Even with a musical score by rocker Stewart Copeland, this isn't at all a youth-pandering delinquent drama, but one that requires adult patience to get past the alienating style.

BEWARE *Mature themes; profanity; drug talk; alcohol use. Sex and nudity in a very brief but raw orgy scene.*

1983 94m/B Matt Dillon, Mickey Rourke, Dennis Hopper, Diane Lane, Vincent Spano, Nicolas Cage, Diana Scarwid, Christopher Penn, Tom Waits; **D:** Francis Ford Coppola; **W:** Francis Ford Coppola; **M:** Stewart Copeland. **VHS, Beta, LV** *MCA*

Rumpelstiltskin

Family From "Faerie Tale Theatre" comes the story of a woman who can spin straw into gold (Duvall) and the strange small man who saves her life (Villechaize) but demands much in return. Enjoyable for the whole family. Ages 4 and up.

1982 60m/C Bud Cort, Ned Beatty, Shelley Duvall, Herve Villechaize, Paul Dooley. **VHS, Beta, LV** *FOX, FCT*

Rumpelstiltskin

Family Canadian animated version of the classic Brothers Grimm fairy tale about the maiden ordered to spin straw into gold.
1985 24m/C **VHS, Beta** *FHE*

Rumpelstiltskin 🎵 ♭

G/Family First of the Cannon Movie Tales, musical retellings of classic fairy tales by the Cannon Film studio, is one of their better efforts, but that's not saying much. A miller brags that his daughter can spin straw into gold, so the greedy King and the scheming Queen (Irving's real-life mother Pointer) threaten to cut off her head unless she succeeds. Irving is lovely, and Barty is a mischievous delight as the rhyme-talking dwarf who helps her, but lackluster direction and uninspired songs make this a yawner; there just isn't enough story for feature length, as Shelley Duvall knew well.
1986 84m/C Amy Irving, Billy Barty, Robert Symonds, Priscilla Pointer, Clive Revill, John Moulder-Brown; **D:** David Irving. **VHS, Beta, LV** *MED*

Rumpelstiltskin

Primary Turner reads this classic tale from the Brothers Grimm about a girl who promises her first-born to a mysterious little man in exchange for a magical favor. Vividly illustrated by Peter Sis, with music by Tangerine Dream. A typically outstanding combo of sight and sound from the "Rabbit Ears: We All Have Tales" series.
1992 30m/C **M:** Tangerine Dream. **VHS** *BTV*

Run, Appaloosa, Run

Primary-Jr. High An Indian girl and Holy Smoke, her stallion, share happiness and tragedy in this adventure excerpted from the long-running Walt Disney TV program.
1966 48m/C **VHS, Beta** *MTI, DSN*

Run for Life: An Olympic Fable

Preschool-Primary Japanese animated feature delving into the origins of the Olympic Games; a young athlete running to restore support for his country's King in Ancient Greece.
1979 68m/C **VHS, Beta** *LIV*

Run for the Roses 🎵 ♭

PG/Family Young Puerto Rican boy living with a Kentucky step-family tries to make a racetrack winner out of a broken-down horse—not to mention the broken-down plot. Cliched underdog-horse tale, also known as "Thoroughbred."
1978 93m/C Lisa Eilbacher, Vera Miles, Stuart Whitman, Sam Groom; **D:** Henry Levin. **VHS, Beta** *LIV*

Runaway

Family A boy blames himself for his friend's accidental death and runs away to live in the subway tunnels of New York City. After four months of life underground, a disabled veteran and a waitress lend the boy a hand. Adapted from the novel "Slake's Limbo" by Felice Holman. Part of the "Wonderworks" series.
1989 58m/C Charles S. Dutton, Jasmine Guy, Gavin Allen; **D:** Gilbert Moses. **VHS** *PME, HMV, COL*

Runaway Ralph

Primary Ralph S. Mouse runs away from the Mountainview Inn so he won't have to share his motorcycle with the younger mice. He winds up at a summer camp, where he befriends a boy (Fred Savage), survives a cat, and plots his return home. Stop-motion and live action follow-up to "The Mouse and the Motorcycle," both based on Beverly Cleary books. Ages 5 to 10.
1989 40m/C Fred Savage; **D:** Ron Underwood. **VHS, Beta** *MLT, CHF*

The Runaways 🎵 🎵

Family TV movie about a troubled boy who runs away from an unhappy foster-home situation and finds a friend in a kindred spirit—a leopard that has similarly escaped from a zoo. Based on a novel by Victor Canning.
1975 76m/C Dorothy McGuire, John Randolph, Neva Patterson, Josh Albee; **D:** Harry Harris. **VHS, Beta** *NO*

Running Brave 🎵 🎵

PG/Family True story of Billy Mills, a South Dakota Sioux Indian who won the Gold Medal in the 10,000 meter run at the 1964 Tokyo Olympics. Not bad, but plodding and hokey in the way of many inspirational true-story flicks.

⚠ BEWARE *Brief nudity, mature themes, roughhousing.*

1983 90m/C Robby Benson, Claudia Cron, Pat Hingle, Denis Lacroix; **D:** D.S. Everett. **VHS, Beta, LV** *DIS*

Running Free 🎵 ♭

PG/Family Sullen Garrett joins his naturalist mother in the Alaskan wilderness and establishes a friendship with a wolverine cub (who's smarter than the kid). A rousing outdoor adventure.

⚠ BEWARE *Outdoor adventure violence.*

1994 90m/C Jesse Montgomery Sythe, Jayme Lee Misfeldt, Michael Pena; **D:** Steve Kroschel. **VHS, LV** *VMK*

Running Mates 🎵 🎵

PG-13/Jr. High-Adult Occasionally intriguing drama of two teens who fall in love, but are kept apart by their fathers' local political rivalry. Could have been better, but cardboard characters abound.
1986 90m/C Greg Webb, Barbara Howard, J. Don Ferguson, Clara Dunn; **D:** Thomas L. Neff. **VHS, Beta** *VTR, NWV*

Running on Empty 🦴🦴🦴 ▷

PG-13/Jr. High-Adult Two 1960s radicals are still on the run in 1988 for a long-ago bombing, changing their names and moving from place to place whenever they think the law is closing in. But now their teenage son wants a normal life, even if it means never seeing his parents again. Unimpeachable performances in a compelling, believable drama.

BEWARE *Profanity. Parents in trouble always having to pull up stakes.*

1988 116m/C Christine Lahti, River Phoenix, Judd Hirsch, Martha Plimpton, Jonas Arby, Ed Crowley, L.M. Kit Carson, Steven Hill, Augusta Dabney, David Margulies, Sidney Lumet; **D:** Sidney Lumet; **M:** Tony Mottola. **Award Nominations:** Academy Awards '88: Best Original Screenplay, Best Supporting Actor (Phoenix); **Awards:** Golden Globe Awards '89: Best Screenplay; National Board of Review Awards '88: Best Supporting Actor (Phoenix). **VHS, Beta, LV, 8mm** *WAR*

Running Wild 🦴🦴 ▷

G/Family Free-lance photographer on assignment in Colorado becomes personally involved in a dispute over the fate of a wild mustang herd. Easygoing, if vaguely dull story, enhanced by good performances, okay script, and modern Western backdrop.

1973 102m/C Lloyd Bridges, Dina Merrill, Pat Hingle, Gilbert Roland, Morgan Woodward; **D:** Robert McCahon; **W:** Robert McCahon. **VHS, Beta** *MED*

Rupert

Preschool Popular British character Rupert the Bear stars in 12 adventures told through storybook-style illustrations rather than animation. Rupert is joined by his friends Bill Badger, Tiger-Lily, and Jack Frost.

1988 57m/C VHS *FOX, FCT*

Rupert and the Frog Song

Preschool Paul and Linda McCartney produced this impressive music-video animation centered around the popular British cartoon bruin. Also on the tape: "Seaside Woman" and "Oriental Nightfish," two abstract 'toons based on Linda's compositions.

1985 22m/C VHS, Beta, LV *FHE*

Rupert and the Runaway Dragon

Preschool Join Rupert the Bear, Tiger-Lily, and Ping-Pong on a series of seven adventures in their magical wonderland.

1989 37m/C VHS *FOX, FCT*

Rupert: Caring and Sharing With Friends

Preschool Rupert, who first appeared in a cartoon strip in the United Kingdom in 1920, is back with adventures from around the world. He and his friends embark on magical journeys that encourage young imaginations and teach humorous lessons about growing up. From Nickel-

odeon's Nick Jr. preschool series.

1996 48m/C VHS

The Russians are Coming, the Russians are Coming 🦴🦴🦴

Family Cold War comedy still provokes chuckles. Russian submarine runs aground off the coast of New England. Townsfolk think it's an invasion, but the Soviet sailors just want assistance so they can leave. A crisis in town brings both sides together. Memorable moment has Russians helping authorities by calling out: "Ee-MAIR-gen-cy! Everybody to get from street!" A nice reminder that people should get to know each other before making judgements. Arkin is outstanding as Russian navy officer.

1966 126m/C Alan Arkin, Carl Reiner, Theodore Bikel, Eva Marie Saint, Brian Keith, Paul Ford, Jonathan Winters, Ben Blue, Tessie O'Shea, Doro Merande, John Phillip Law; **D:** Norman Jewison; **C:** Joseph Biroc. **Award Nominations:** Academy Awards '66: Best Actor (Arkin), Best Picture, Best Story & Screenplay; **Awards:** Golden Globe Awards '67: Best Actor—Musical/Comedy (Arkin), Best Film—Musical/Comedy; National Board of Review Awards '66: 10 Best Films of the Year. **VHS, Beta** *FOX, MLB*

Russkies 🦴 ▷

PG/Jr. High Tame, outdated comedy about three adorable Florida boys who capture, hide, and eventually grow to like a stranded young sailor off a Russian submarine. Politically correct villain is a meanie US serviceman in hot pursuit of the kids' pet Red.

BEWARE *Salty language.*

1987 98m/C Joaquin Rafael (Leaf) Phoenix, Whip Hubley, Peter Billingsley, Stefan DeSalle; **D:** Rick Rosenthal; **M:** James Newton Howard. **VHS, Beta, LV** *ORI, WAR*

Ryan's Daughter 🦴🦴 ▷

PG/Sr. High-Adult Irish woman (Miles) marries a man she does not love and then falls for a shell-shocked British major who arrives during the 1916 Irish uprising to keep the peace. Not surprisingly, she is accused of betraying the local IRA gunrunners to her British lover. Tasteful melodrama with lots of pretty scenery that goes on a bit too long.

1970 194m/C Sarah Miles, Robert Mitchum, John Mills, Trevor Howard, Christopher Jones, Leo McKern; **D:** David Lean; **W:** Robert Bolt; **M:** Maurice Jarre. **Award Nominations:** Academy Awards '70: Best Actress (Miles), Best Sound; **Awards:** Academy Awards '70: Best Cinematography, Best Supporting Actor (Mills); National Board of Review Awards '70: 10 Best Films of the Year. **VHS, Beta, LV** *MGM, BTV*

Saber Rider and the Star Sheriffs: All That Glitters

Family Japanese-made outer space western cartoon series, distinguished from any other Japanese-made outer space western cartoon series by being the first to use interactive technology; with proper toy equipment, kiddie viewers could supposedly play along with the action on-screen. In this particular episode, the evil, extradimensional Outriders tempt the good citizens with phony trinkets—sounds like an apt metaphor in there somewhere. Additional volumes available.

1990 45m/C VHS, Beta *FRH*

Saboteur 🎜🎜🎜

Family Man wrongly accused of sabotaging an American munitions plant during WWII sets out to find the traitor who framed him, meeting Lane along the way. Hitchcock uses his locations, including Boulder Dam, Radio City Music Hall, and the Statue of Liberty, to greatly intensify the action. Stunning resolution.

1942 108m/B Priscilla Lane, Robert Cummings, Otto Kruger, Alan Baxter, Norman Lloyd, Charles Halton; **D:** Alfred Hitchcock; **W:** Alfred Hitchcock, Peter Viertel. **VHS, Beta, LV** *MCA*

Sabrina 🎜🎜🎜

Jr. High-Adult Two wealthy brothers, one an aging businessman and the other a dissolute playboy, vie for the attention of their chauffeur's daughter, who has just returned from a French finishing school. Typically acerbic, in the Wilder manner, with Bogart and Holden cast interestingly against type. Based on the play "Sabrina Fair" by Samuel Taylor.

1954 113m/B Audrey Hepburn, Humphrey Bogart, William Holden, Walter Hampden, Francis X. Bushman, John Williams, Martha Hyer, Marcel Dalio; **D:** Billy Wilder; **W:** Billy Wilder, Ernest Lehman. **Award Nominations:** Academy Awards '54: Best Actress (Hepburn), Best Art Direction/Set Decoration (B & W), Best Black and White Cinematography, Best Director (Wilder), Best Screenplay; **Awards:** Academy Awards '54: Best Costume Design (B & W); Directors Guild of America Awards '54: Best Director (Wilder); Golden Globe Awards '55: Best Screenplay; National Board of Review Awards '54: 10 Best Films of the Year, Best Supporting Actor (Williams). **VHS, Beta, LV** *PAR*

Sabrina 🎜🎜 ♭

PG/Jr. High-Adult Updated version of Billy Wilder's 1954 fairytale. This time around the pretty Ormond is the chauffeur's daughter who gets closely involved with the wealthy Larrabees. And this time the emphasis is more on workaholic business mogul Linus (Ford), who plays a dangerous game when he decides to transfer Sabrina's affections from his engaged playboy brother David (Kinnear) to himself in order to protect a business merger. Ford's a little too stodgy but Kinnear's charming (in his film debut) and Marchand properly matriarchal. Girls may enjoy the love story and wishes-can-come-true storyline, but boys will definitely be turned off.

> **BEWARE** *Some mild language and mature talk about relationships. David's character is quite a playboy, ignoring his fiance to get Sabrina's attention.*

1995 127m/C Harrison Ford, Julia Ormond, Greg Kinnear, Nancy Marchand, John Wood, Richard Crenna, Angie Dickinson, Lauren Holly, Fanny Ardant, Dana Ivey, Patrick Bruel, Miriam Colon, Elizabeth Franz; **D:** Sydney Pollack; **W:** David Rayfiel, Barbara Benedek; **C:** Giuseppe Rotunno; **M:** John Williams. **VHS** *NYR*

Sabrina, the Teenaged Witch

Family Spinoff of the "Archie" TV cartoon series, in which one of the girls at Riverdale High is a fun-loving, non-wicked witch. Episodes feature appearances by those regulars Archie Andrews, Jughead, Betty, Veronica and Reggie.

1969 57m/C V: Jane Webb. **VHS, Beta**

Sad Cat: Apprentice Good Fairy

Preschool-Primary The backwoods adventures of a melancholy feline character created for Terrytoons by Ralph Bakshi. Additional volumes available.

1965 37m/C VHS *VTR*

Safe Passage 🎜🎜

PG-13/Jr. High-Adult The Persian Gulf war produced a lot of great TV but only this mediocre film. Sarandon and Shepherd are an estranged couple whose soldier son is missing and presumed dead. Their other grown children return home to share the watching and waiting and fight their old fights. TV news crews camp outside. Through it all, the family hangs together. Based on the novel by Ellyn Bache.

> **BEWARE** *Profanity and lots of family yelling. One scene of marijuana use.*

1994 98m/C Susan Sarandon, Sam Shepard, Robert Sean Leonard, Sean Astin, Marcia Gay Harden, Nick Stahl, Jason London, Philip Bosco, Matt Keeslar; **D:** Robert Ackerman; **W:** Deena Goldstone; **M:** Mark Isham. **VHS, LV** *TTC, NLC*

The Saga of Windwagon Smith

Preschool-Primary Disney cartoon short based on folklore about how inventor Smith embarks on a wacky trip across the prairie on his schooner fitted with sails and masts.

1961 13m/C VHS, Beta *DSN, MTI*

Salem's Lot 🎜🎜🎜

PG/Jr. High-Adult Based on Stephen King's novel about a sleepy New England village which is infiltrated by evil. Mysterious antiques dealer takes up residence in a forbidding hilltop house—and it becomes apparent that a vampire is on the loose. Generally creepy; Mason is good, but Soul only takes up space in the lead as a novelist returning home. Also available in the original television miniseries version at 190 minutes on two cassettes.

> **BEWARE** *Spooky violence. Can be very scary.*

1979 112m/C David Soul, James Mason, Lance Kerwin, Bonnie Bedelia, Lew Ayres, Bo Fanders, Elisha Cook Jr., Reggie Nalder, Fred Willard, Kenneth McMillan, Marie Windsor; **D:** Tobe Hooper. **VHS, Beta, LV** *WAR*

A Salute to Chuck Jones

Family One of a series of cassettes in the "24 Karat Collection," compiling some of the best of the Warner animation works. This tape contains some of the best-known productions by director Jones, including Daffy in "Duck Dodgers in the 24 1/4 Century," the Bugs-Bunny starrer "Rabbit Seasoning," plus the famous "One Froggy Evening" and more.
1960 56m/C D: Chuck Jones; **V:** Mel Blanc. **VHS, Beta** *WAR*

A Salute to Mel Blanc

Family This compilation of Warner Brothers animation pays tribute to Blanc, man of a thousand voices. Many of the all-time greatest cartoons would simply be un-imaginable without him, and Mel's memorable moments here include "The Rabbit of Seville," "Little Boy Boo" and "Robin Hood Daffy." Part of Warner's "24 Karat Collection."
1958 58m/C D: Chuck Jones, Isadore "Friz" Freleng, Bob Clampett; **V:** Mel Blanc. **VHS, Beta** *WAR*

Samantha 🎵🎵 ♭

PG/Jr. High-Adult Twenty-one year-old Samantha discovers she was left on her parents' doorstep in a basket and decides to find out where she came from. Good cast and high charm quotient help this film along.

 Profanity.

1992 101m/C Martha Plimpton, Dermot Mulroney, Hector Elizondo, Mary Kay Place, Ione Skye; **D:** Steven La Rocque; **W:** John Golden, Steven La Rocque. **VHS, Beta** *ACA*

Sammy Bluejay

Preschool-Primary Features two escapades from the world of author Thornton W. Burgess, "Brainy Bluejay" and "Sammy's Revenge," starring Sammy Bluejay, Peter Cottontail, and Reddy the Fox.
1983 60m/C VHS, Beta *FHE*

Sammy, the Way-Out Seal 🎵🎵 ♭

Family The first of several unrelated movies about seals or sea lions; "Salty" and "Andre" came later. (Ingmar Bergman's "The Seventh Seal" was earlier but it doesn't count). Notice how Disney, trying to be hip in the 60s, tosses the phrase "way out" into the title. Two young boys bring a mischievous seal to live in their beach house and try to keep it a secret from their parents. Robert Culp plays the dad. It's pretty cute. Ages 5 to 10.
1962 89m/C Michael McGreevey, Billy Mumy, Patricia Barry, Robert Culp; **D:** Norman Tokar. **VHS, Beta** *DIS*

Sam's Son 🎵🎵

PG/Family Writer/director Landon rehashed the sentimental themes he explored earlier in the 1979 TV movie "The Loneliest Runner" (also on video). Once again, it's

an autobiographical tale about a teen athlete—this time a javelin thrower—in a troubled relationship with his father.
1984 107m/C Eli Wallach, Anne Jackson, Timothy Patrick Murphy, Hallie Todd, James Karen, Allan Hayes, Joanna Lee, Michael Landon; **D:** Michael Landon; **W:** Michael Landon. **VHS, Beta** *WOV*

Samson and Sally: The Song of the Whales 🎵🎵🎵

Primary Two orphaned whales set off in search of Moby Dick; legend has it that the sea giant will save endangered whales from the "iron beasts"—predatory humans in their deadly whaling ships. Environmentally concerned animated feature stands out from the herd of eco-'toons with its well-rendered underwater settings and themes. Tellingly, it hails from Norway, one of the few nations to actively hunt whales in modern times. Based on the book "Song of the Whales" by Brent Haller.

 Violence.

1984 58m/C VHS, Beta *CEL, JFK, WSH*

The Sand Castle

Family Oscar-winning example of superb stop-motion animation shows the gentle Sandman and the whimsical creations and living animals he wordlessly sculpts out of the sand, plus "The Northwind and the Sun," "Alphabet," and "The Owl and the Lemming."
1977 30m/C VHS *SMA, NFB, SAL*

The Sandlot ♫♫♫

PG/Family Mom's remarriage takes non-athletic Scotty to a new town in California in 1962. He befriends local boys playing idle baseball at the local sandlot, and plot is a loose set of antics on and off the diamond. Finale is a long, crazy battle with "the Beast," a legendary junkyard dog (shown in glimpses as a monster-sized menace) lurking behind the fence, who's hoarded all their home-run balls. You don't have to be baseball fan—though it helps—to like this offbeat look at childhood, deliberately cast with newcomer young actors. Written and directed by the scripter of the ill-fated "Radio Flyer," in a gentler mode.

> **BEWARE** *Occasional lapses to near-ballpark grammar, mild sex talk.*

1993 101m/C Tom Guiry, Mike Vitar, Patrick Renna, Chauncey Leopardi, Marty York, Brandon Adams, Karen Allen, James Earl Jones, Maury Wills, Art LaFleur, Marlee Shelton; **Cameos:** Denis Leary, Brooke Adams; **D:** David Mickey Evans; **W:** Robert Gunter, David Mickey Evans; **M:** David Newman; **V:** Arliss Howard. **VHS, LV** *FXV*

Santa & the 3 Bears ♫♫

Preschool-Primary Holiday-oriented cartoon released to theaters. When a mother bear and her cubs discover the magic of Christmas in the forest, they decide to skip hibernation for the winter. Kindly park ranger decides to humor the cubs by impersonating Santa on the crucial night.
1979 60m/C VHS, Beta *PSM*

Santa & the Tooth Fairies

Preschool-Primary When Santa gets Hans' letter too late to deliver his gifts personally, he gives the job to the Tooth Fairies.
1992 ?m/C VHS

Santa Claus Conquers the Martians ♫

Family The green-faced Martian children are feeling blue, so to speak, and their parents decide it's because Earth has a Santa Claus and Mars doesn't. So the aliens invade the North Pole and abduct Kris Kringle. Fortunately human kids tag along for a rescue and some awful songs. Celebrated as one of the worst flicks ever made, but it's that kind of awfulness you can have fun with, if you're in the right mood.

1964 80m/C John Call, Pia Zadora, Leonard Hicks, Vincent Beck, Victor Stiles, Donna Conforti; **D:** Nicholas Webster. **VHS, Beta** *COL, SNC, MRV*

Santa Claus is Coming to Town ♫♫♫

Family Classic Arthur Rankin-Jules Bass TV-special biopic of Kris Kringle himself, taking you from his childhood to his marriage to Mrs. Claus to his destiny as the North Pole's magical purveyor of the Christmas spirit, as he give toys to the citizens of Sombertown. An "Animagic" tale done in stop-motion puppet animation.
1970 53m/C D: Arthur Rankin Jr., Jules Bass; **V:** Mickey Rooney, Keenan Wynn, Paul Frees. **VHS, Beta, LV** *FHE, LME*

Santa Claus: The Movie ♫♫

PG/Family Uneven holiday spectacle from the makers of the "Superman" pics; first part is a formal, stiff telling of how a child-loving old guy and his wife won the honor of being the immortal Mr. and Mrs. Claus. Rest is a fresher, amusing tale about a well-meaning elf who leaves the North Pole to work for a greedy toy tycoon and almost ruins Christmas. Good cast, tinsel-thin special f/x.

> **BEWARE** *Alcohol use, but nothing naughty enough to deserve that PG.*

1985 112m/C Dudley Moore, John Lithgow, David Huddleston, Judy Cornwell, Burgess Meredith; **D:** Jeannot Szwarc; **W:** David Newman; **M:** Henry Mancini. **VHS, Beta, LV** *MED*

The Santa Clause ♫♫♫

PG/Family Tim Allen goes to town as the man who's coming to town. A lightweight film about a heavyweight guy, "Clause" finds Tim Allen taking up Santa's burden after the jolly red one falls off Allen's roof. See, once you put on Santa's suit, you're stuck playing the part. You also acquire the beard and gain the weight. On the plus side, you get along much better with reindeer than you ever did before. Cute holiday film cashes in on the magic of the man in the red suit.

> **BEWARE** *Divorced spouses battle and Santa falls off the roof and vaporizes.*

1994 97m/C Tim Allen, Eric Lloyd, Judge Reinhold, Wendy Crewson, David Krumholtz, Mary Gross; **D:** John Pasquin; **W:** Leo Benvenuti, Steve Rudnick; **M:** Michael Convertino. **Award Nominations:** MTV Movie Awards '95: Breakthrough Performance (Allen), Best Comedic Performance (Allen); **Awards:** Blockbuster Entertainment Awards '95: Male Newcomer, Theatrical (Allen). **VHS** *TOU*

Santabear's First Christmas

Family That cuddly little fellow Santabear is back, and just in time for the holidays.
1989 25m/C VHS *VES*

Santabear's High Flying Adventure

Family Network TV cartoon finds Santabear saving Christmas when a rival steals toys from the real Santa Claus.

1987 23m/C **V:** John Malkovich, Kelly McGillis, Bobby McFerrin, Glenne Headly. **VHS, Beta** *LIV, VES*

Santa's First Christmas

Preschool-Primary Young Santa Claus trains reindeer and finds elves to help out as he begins his Christmas work.
1992 ?m/C VHS

Sarafina! 🦴🦴🦴

PG-13/Jr. High-Adult Part coming-of-age saga, part political drama, part musical, and all emotionally powerful. Sarafina is a young girl in a township school in Soweto, South Africa in the mid-'70s, gradually coming into a political awakening amid the Soweto riots. Khumalo recreates her stage role as the glowing and defiant Sarafina with both Goldberg and Makeba satisfying in their roles as Sarafina's outspoken and inspirational teacher and her long-suffering mother, respectively. Adapted from Ngema's stage musical.

> **BEWARE** *Graphic violence amid the riots.*

1992 98m/C Leleti Khumalo, Whoopi Goldberg, Miriam Makeba, John Kani, Mbongeni Ngema; **D:** Darrell Roodt; **W:** Mbongeni Ngema, William Nicholson; **M:** Stanley Myers. **VHS, Beta, LV** *TOU*

Sarah, Plain and Tall 🦴🦴🦴

G/Family New England schoolteacher Sarah travels to Kansas circa 1910 to care for the family of a widowed farmer who has advertised for a wife. Of course, a simple business arrangement soon blossoms into genuine love. Superior entertainment for the whole family. Adapted for television from Patricia MacLachlan's novel of the same name. Nominated for nine Emmy Awards.

1991 98m/C Glenn Close, Christopher Walken, Lexi Randall, Margaret Sophie Stein, Jon DeVries, Christopher Bell; **D:** Glenn Jordan. **VHS, LV** *REP*

Satisfaction 🦴

PG-13/Jr. High-Adult All-girl, high school rock band fool around with instruments the summer before college. The men, drugs and music they sample (and reject, eventually) is supposed to be a growing experience, but overall this teen-appeal tale is smarmy stuff.

> **BEWARE** *Sex, drugs, rock 'n roll and profanity. You won't get no satisfaction here.*

1988 93m/C Justine Bateman, Trini Alvarado, Britta Phillips, Julia Roberts, Scott Coffey, Liam Neeson, Deborah Harry; **D:** Joan Freeman; **W:** Charles Purpura; **M:** Michel Colombier. **VHS, Beta, LV** *FOX*

Saturday the 14th 🦴 🦴

PG/Jr. High-Adult Sloppy spoof of haunted houses and horror movies. Goofy family inherits a mansion where a black-magic book is hidden, copes with monster in the bathtub, mummy in refrigerator, cheapo special f/x. Kids might be amused, so were swear words really necessary? Followed by even worse in-name-only sequel: "Saturday the 14th Strikes Back".

If you like *The Santa Clause* (1994), you'll love:

All I Want for Christmas (1991)

The Berenstain Bears' Christmas (1990)

A Charlie Brown Christmas (1965)

A Christmas Carol (1951)

A Christmas Story (1983)

Frosty the Snowman (1969)

Holiday Inn (1942)

It's a Wonderful Life (1946)

The Man in the Santa Claus Suit (1979)

Miracle on 34th Street (1947)

Miracle on 34th Street (1994)

The Muppet Christmas Carol (1992)

National Lampoon's Christmas Vacation (1989)

Prancer (1989)

Santa Claus Is Coming to Town (1970)

Santa Claus: The Movie (1985)

White Christmas (1954)

The Year Without a Santa Claus (1974)

> **BEWARE** *Salty language, monster roughhousing.*

1981 91m/C Richard Benjamin, Paula Prentiss, Severn Darden; **D:** Howard R. Cohen. **VHS, Beta**

Savage Land 🦴🦴 🦴

PG/Primary-Adult Family western finds a young brother and sister traveling by stage to meet up with their father. The stage is robbed by some bumbling bad guys, who then pursue the kids and two other passengers across the frontier. The kids, of course, are smarter than most of the adults.

> **BEWARE** *Mild western violence and some frontier language.*

Santa and son deliver toys on Christmas Eve in "The Santa Clause."

1994 91m/C Graham Greene, Corbin Bernsen, Vivian Schilling, Mercedes McNab, Corey Carrier, Brion James, Bo Svenson, Charlotte Ross. **VHS, LV** *HMD*

Savage Sam 🦴🦴

Family Disney's sequel to their classic "Old Yeller" isn't anywhere near as effective. Sam is indeed the offspring of the loyal Old Yeller, and he proves his canine courage by assisting in the hunt for children kidnapped by hostile Apaches. Occasionally fun, but nothing more. Based on the novel by Fred Gipson.

1963 103m/C Tommy Kirk, Kevin Corcoran, Brian Keith, Dewey Martin, Jeff York, Marta Kristen; **D:** Norman Tokar. **VHS, Beta** *DIS*

Savannah Smiles 🦴🦴♭

PG/Family Poor little rich girl Savannah, frustrated by her neglectful, careerist parents, runs away. She hides in the car of two harmless escaped convicts, who are hunted as kidnappers. But while on the run the "captive" Savannah gets more love and caring attention than she did at home. Sweet-natured but much too long, sentimental family comedy.

🚫 BEWARE *Salty language, without which this could have earned an easy G rating.*

1982 104m/C Bridgette Anderson, Mark Miller, Donovan Scott, Peter Graves, Chris Robinson, Michael Parks; **D:** Pierre De Moro. **VHS, Beta, LV** *NLC*

Say Anything 🦴🦴🦴

PG-13/Jr. High-Adult Thoughtful, often sparkling, teen romance about a spirited loner who courts the beautiful, unapproachable valedictorian of his high school. Her father disapproves of their love affair, but he's got problems of his own. Smart comedy-drama works well on both the romantic and serious levels without getting too sticky, and offers young characters well worth your time.

🚫 BEWARE *Sex and profanity. Teen learns a dark secret about her doting father.*

1989 100m/C John Cusack, Ione Skye, John Mahoney, Joan Cusack, Lili Taylor, Richard Portnow, Pamela Segall, Jason Gould, Loren Dean, Bebe Neuwirth, Aimee Brooks, Eric Stoltz, Chynna Phillips, Joanna Frank; **D:** Cameron Crowe; **W:** Cameron Crowe; **M:** Anne Dudley, Richard Gibbs, Nancy Wilson. **VHS, Beta, LV** *FOX*

Scandalous John 🦴🦴♭

G/Family Disney comedy western about a last cattle drive devised by an aging rancher in order to save his spread from developers. Good acting carries this one; watch for a young John Ritter.

1971 113m/C Brian Keith, Alfonso Arau, Michele Carey, Rick Lenz, John Ritter, Harry (Henry) Morgan; **D:** Robert Butler. **VHS, Beta** *DIS*

The Scarlet Letter ♪♪

R/Sr. High-Adult There's nothing like a great American classic, and this film version of "The Scarlet Letter" is nothing like the great American classic. Onto Nathaniel Hawthorne's profound tale of spiritual corruption among the Puritans, filmmakers have grafted a war between settlers and Indians, an unsolved murder or two and a witchcraft trial. Hester Prynne (Moore) still becomes the town outcast because of her adulterous affair with Rev. Dimmesdale (Oldman), but her husband (Duvall) has been turned into sort of a middle-aged mutant ninja assassin. Oddly entertaining, but not for purists. Or Puritans. Or kids looking for video Cliffs Notes.

BEWARE *Violence, nudity and sex in the hay. Hester Prynne was never so lusty.*

1995 135m/C Demi Moore, Gary Oldman, Robert Duvall, Robert Prosky, Edward Hardwicke, Joan Plowright, Roy Dotrice, Dana Ivey, Sheldon Peters Wolfchild, Diane Salinger, Lisa Jolliff-Andoh, Amy Wright, Tim Woodward; **D:** Roland Joffe; **W:** Douglas Day Stewart; **C:** Alex Thomson; **M:** John Barry. **VHS, LV** *HPH*

The Scarlet Pimpernel ♪♪♪

Jr. High-Adult Remake of the classic about a British dandy who saved French aristocrats from the Reign of Terror guillotines during the French Revolution. Made for British television version is almost as good as the original 1935 film, with beautiful costumes and sets and strong performances from Seymour and Andrews.

1982 142m/C Anthony Andrews, Jane Seymour, Ian McKellen, James Villiers, Eleanor David; **D:** Clive Donner; **M:** Nick Bicat. **VHS, Beta, LV** *LIV, VES, FUS*

School Ties ♪♪♪

PG-13/Jr. High-Adult David is a talented, likeable quarterback who gets a scholarship to the elite St. Matthew prep school. To conform with the closed-mindedness of the 1950s, both his father and coach suggest that he hide his Jewish religion. David's a big man on campus until his secret comes out, creating an ugly rift in the school. What easily could have been just another teen hunk flick looks at much more than just Fraser's pretty face in successful, unflinching treatment of anti-Semitism.

BEWARE *Profanity and anti-Semitism.*

1992 110m/C Brendan Fraser, Matt Damon, Chris O'Donnell, Randall Batinkoff, Andrew Lowery, Cole Hauser, Ben Affleck, Anthony Rapp, Amy Locane, Peter Donat, Zeljko Ivanek, Kevin Tighe, Michael Higgins, Ed Lauter; **D:** Robert Mandel; **W:** Dick Wolf, Darryl Ponicsan; **M:** Maurice Jarre. **VHS, Beta, LV** *PAR*

Schoolhouse Rock: Grammar Rock

Primary Children get to learn grammar basics through timely rock music and animation in these nine segments from the award-winning network TV series of Saturday-

morning short subjects.
1974 28m/C VHS, Beta *KUI,, CHI*

Schoolhouse Rock: History Rock

Primary ABC-TV network's award-winning educational shorts that teach history using catchy songs and animation. This volume contains "Shot Heard 'Round the World," "Sufferin' Thru Suffrage," and the classic "I'm Just a Bill," plus more.
1974 32m/C VHS, Beta *KUI,, WPC*

Schoolhouse Rock: Science Rock

Primary Complicated scientific concepts are simplified in segments from the ABC-TV series.
1974 31m/C VHS, Beta *KUI,, CHI*

Scooby-Doo

Family Collection of the most mysterious adventures Hanna-Barbera's celebrated Scooby-Doo and his teen sidekicks (". . . those meddling kids!") have ever encountered. Take a ride in the Mystery Mobile as it takes the mongrel sleuth and his friends to all sorts of spooky venues, with periodic guest star voices. Additional volumes available.
1983 90m/C V: Sonny Bono, Cher, Don Messick, Casey Kasem, Frank Welker, Heather North. **VHS, Beta, LV** *TTC, IME*

The Scout ♪♪

PG-13/Sr. High-Adult Brooks is a luckless scout for the New York Yankees who discovers a weird, though genuine, phenom pitcher (Fraser) on a trip to Mexico. He convinces the Yankees to take the phenom, though he's not sure whether Fraser isn't a few innings shy of a complete game. But with a 109 mph fast ball and a bat that would have made Babe Ruth envious, who cares? Film straddles sports comedy and melodrama territories, satisfying in neither. Fraser plays variation on Encino Man. Real-life team owner Steinbrenner plays himself.

BEWARE *Sexual references and suggestions about child abuse in a character's past.*

1994 101m/C Albert Brooks, Brendan Fraser, Dianne Wiest, Lane Smith, Michael Rapaport, Steve Garvey, Bob Costas, Roy Firestone, Anne Twomey, Tony Bennett; **D:** Michael Ritchie; **W:** Albert Brooks, Andrew Bergman, Monica Johnson; **M:** Bill Conti. **VHS** *FXV*

Scrooge ♪♪ ♡

G/Family Lavish British musical version of Charles Dickens' classic "A Christmas Carol" obviously aimed to captivate audiences with the Victorian-England On-Broadway magic that "Oliver!" managed to work, but the songs aren't half as good. Still, production values and the energy levels run high, with Finney memorable as the title miser and Guiness a terrific Marley's Ghost. ♫ The Beautiful Day; Happiness; Thank You Very Much; A Christmas Carol; Christmas Children; I Hate People;

Albert Brooks plays father figure to Brendan Fraser in "The Scout."

Farver Chris'mas; See the Phantoms; December the 25th.

1970 86m/C Albert Finney, Alec Guinness, Edith Evans, Kenneth More; **D:** Ronald Neame; **M:** Leslie Bricusse. **Award Nominations:** Academy Awards '70: Best Art Direction/Set Decoration, Best Costume Design, Best Song ("Thank You Very Much"), Best Original Score; **Awards:** Golden Globe Awards '71: Best Actor—Musical/Comedy (Finney). **VHS, Beta, LV** *FOX, FUS*

Scrooge McDuck and Money

Preschool-Primary Children learn lessons in money and economics through song and dance.

1990 16m/C VHS, Beta *MTI, DSN*

Scrooged ♫♫ ♪

PG-13/Jr. High-Adult Big-budget but frequently leaden satire of the hallowed holiday classic finds maniacally callous TV executive Murray staging "A Christmas Carol." Suddenly he himself is visited by the traditional three ghosts, but with modern twists; Xmas Past is a ghoulish cabbie, Xmas Present is a sweet-looking fairy who's violently abusive, and Xmas Future is the usual ghoul. Starts on a hysterical pitch and stays there, leaving Murray to find any number of different ways to display cynicism and insincerity (he's very good at that, less believable upon transformation) and the rest of the all-star cast almost no room to develop their characters. Eye-poppin' f/x, nearly stinging satire in what is at least a fresh take on the Scrooge story.

🔲 BEWARE 🔲 *Sex talk, drug talk, salty language and lots of cartoony violence.*

1988 101m/C Bill Murray, Carol Kane, John Forsythe, David Johansen, Bob(cat) Goldthwait, Karen Allen, Michael J. Pollard, Brian Doyle-Murray, Alfre Woodard, John Glover, Robert Mitchum, Buddy Hackett, Robert Goulet, Jamie Farr, Mary Lou Retton, Lee Majors; **D:** Richard Donner; **W:** Mitch Glazer, Michael O'Donoghue; **M:** Danny Elfman. **VHS, Beta, LV, 8mm** *PAR*

Scruffy

Family Animated feature, actually a linked-together three-part TV special, sort of a mini-miniseries. Orphaned pooch Scruffy looks for a home, first with a vagrant Shakespearean actor, then a pack of other dogs, and finally a little boy.

1980 72m/C V: Alan Young, June Foray, Hans Conried, Nancy McKeon. **VHS, Beta** *WOV, GKK*

Sea Gypsies ♫♫ ♪

G/Family "Wilderness Family" crew set sail for a different sort of nature adventure in this passable effort about a handful of modern-day adults and kids who get shipwrecked off the Aleutian Islands, near Alaska. They must escape before winter or learn to survive attacks by wolves, bears and killer whales. Allegedly based on a true story.

1978 101m/C Robert F. Logan, Mikki Jamison-Olsen, Heather Rattray, Cjon Damitri; **D:** Stewart Raffill; **W:** Stewart Raffill. **VHS, Beta** *WAR*

Sea Hound

Family Actually, that's the name of the boat commanded by Captain Silver, a popular radio and comic-book hero of the era, who grapples with late-'40s pirates over a sunken treasure in this 15-part Columbia serial.

1947 ?m/B Buster Crabbe, Jimmy Lloyd, Pamela Blake, Ralph Hodges, Robert Barron; **D:** Walter B. Eason, Mack V. Wright. **VHS** *MLB, GPV*

Sea Prince and the Fire Child 🎵🎵

Family Japanese animated film follows two young lovers who set off on an adventure to escape the disapproval of their parents.

1982 70m/C VHS, Beta *COL*

Seabert: Good Guys Wear White

Primary Lovable Arctic white seal, accompanied by human friends Tommy and Aura, travel the world from their Greenland HQ to save endangered species and protect the ecosystem. Environmentally minded TV started out on a politically correct foot by recycling its own episodes for video. Additional volumes available.

1988 120m/C VHS, Beta *JFK*

Searching for Bobby Fischer 🎵🎵🎵🎵

PG/Jr. High-Adult Seven-year-old Josh Waitzkin (Pomeranc, in a terrific debut) shows an amazing gift for chess, stunning his parents, who must then try to strike the delicate balance of developing his abilities while also allowing him a "normal" childhood. Excellent cast features Mantegna and Allen as his parents, Kingsley as demanding chess teacher Pandolfini, and Fishburne as an adept speed-chess hustler. Pomeranc is great, and his knowledge of chess (he's a ranked player) brings authenticity to his role. Title comes from Pandolfini's belief that Josh may equal the abilities of chess whiz Bobby Fischer. Underrated little gem based on a true story and adapted from the book by Waitzkin's father. No automatic pull for the kids (unless they're into chess) but a sweet, worthy view.

⚠ BEWARE *Salty language.*

1993 111m/C Joe Mantegna, Max Pomeranc, Joan Allen, Ben Kingsley, Laurence "Larry" Fishburne, Robert Stephens, David Paymer, Robert Stephens, William H. Macy; **D:** Steven Zaillian; **W:** Steven Zaillian; **M:** James Horner. **Award Nominations:** Academy

Awards '93: Best Cinematography; **Awards:** MTV Movie Awards '94: Best New Filmmaker Award (Zaillian). **VHS, Beta** *PAR*

Secret Admirer 🎵 ♪

R/Sr. High-Adult When 16-year-old Michael is slipped an anonymous love letter, he replies with unsigned mash notes of his own. But all the messages go to the wrong people, resulting in car crashes, vandalism, marital infidelity, sexual dysfunction, police brutality, heavy drinking, heavier swearing. Maybe John Hughes could have done something sweet and human with the premise, but foulmouthed romantic farce isn't for kids and may not be of much interest to adults.

⚠ BEWARE *Profanity, alcohol use, sex, brief nudity, rough-housing.*

1985 98m/C C. Thomas Howell, Cliff DeYoung, Kelly Preston, Dee Wallace Stone, Lori Loughlin, Fred Ward, Casey Siemaszko, Corey Haim, Leigh Taylor-Young; **D:** David Greenwalt. **VHS, Beta, LV** *NO*

The Secret Garden 🎵🎵🎵

Family The beloved Frances Hodgson Burnett story has been remade and even revamped as a Broadway musical, but this early version is especially well-remembered. Orphan Mary Lennox arrives at her uncle's estate on the Yorkshire Moors and finds the household revolves around her screaming, spoiled invalid of a little cousin Colin. But Mary's discovery of a long-hidden garden—and her ability to scream right back—brings about a miraculous change in the boy. The cast is outstanding, and this telling of the tale concentrates more than the others on Colin's tormented father. Like the "Wizard of Oz," this starts out in beautifully photographed B&W before blazing into Technicolor for the scenes in the blooming garden.

1949 92m/B Margaret O'Brien, Herbert Marshall, Dean Stockwell, Gladys Cooper, Elsa Lanchester, Brian Roper; **D:** Fred M. Wilcox. **VHS, Beta, LV** *MGM*

The Secret Garden 🎵🎵🎵

PG/Family Effective made-for-TV adaptation of the Frances Hodgson Burnett story of the lonely orphan sent to live with her distant uncle in England, who warms up the chilly household—and her own selfish heart—through the discovery and nurturing of a long-neglected garden. A prologue and afterword to the story (depicting the characters as adults during the First World War) are unnecessary additions, but this is a class production with fine performances.

⚠ BEWARE *The deaths of the little heroine's parents from plague probably earned this the MPAA's PG. Either that or the coin came up heads.*

1987 100m/C Gennie James, Barret Oliver, Jadrien Steele, Michael Hordern, Derek Jacobi, Billie Whitelaw, Lucy Gutteridge, Julian Glover, Colin Firth, Alan Grint. **VHS, LV** *REP*

The Secret Garden 🎵🎵🎵

G/Family Renewed interest in Frances Hodgson Burnett's classic tale prompted a Broadway musical, two

TV movies, and this latest screen version about the orphaned Mary Lennox and the neglected garden she brings back to life, transforming a joyless cavern-like Yorkshire mansion. Stately and visually beautiful but thin on plot; trick the kids into watching this if you can, but it's skewed to adult emotions and attention spans.

1993 102m/C Kate Maberly, Maggie Smith, Haydon Prowse, Andrew Knott, John Lynch; **D:** Agnieszka Holland; **W:** Caroline Thompson; **M:** Zbigniew Preisner. **VHS, Beta, LV** *WAR, BTV*

Secret Life of Walter Mitty
🦴🦴🦴

Jr. High-Adult An entertaining adaptation of the James Thurber short story about a meek man (Kaye) who lives an unusual fantasy life. Henpecked by his fiancee and mother, oppressed at his job, Walter imagines himself in the midst of various heroic fantasies. Comedic romp for Kaye, though Thurber himself professed to hate the movie.

1947 110m/C Danny Kaye, Virginia Mayo, Boris Karloff, Ann Rutherford, Fay Bainter, Florence Bates; **D:** Norman Z. McLeod. **VHS, Beta, LV** *HBO*

Secret Lives of Waldo Kitty Volume 1

Family Saturday-morning TV show takeoff on the James Thurber character Walter Mitty, here re-imagined as a daydreaming cat in perpetual wrangles with a bulldog. The animals are live-action with voiceovers a la "Milo & Otis," while Waldo's fantasies are 'toons.

1975 48m/C VHS, Beta *NO*

The Secret of El Zorro 🦴 ♭

Family Compilation of Disney TV episodes concerning the swashbuckling swordsman of old California, secretly fighting for freedom while maintaining a deceptive identity as wimpy Don Diego. Here Don Diego's friend Don Ricardo unknowingly threatens to unmask the hero when he challenges the legendary Zorro to a duel. Also available: "The Sign of Zorro."

1957 75m/B Guy Williams. **VHS, Beta** *DIS*

The Secret of Navajo Cave 🦴🦴

G/Family Low budget adventure, narrated by cowboy star Allen, in which two young friends explore the mysterious title cavern.

1976 84m/C Holger Kasper, Steven Benally Jr., Johnny Guerro; **D:** James T. Flocker. **VHS** *XVC, VCI*

Secret of NIMH 🦴🦴🦴

G/Family Well-done animated tale, produced by a staff of former Disney artists led by Don Bluth. A newly widowed mouse, Mrs. Frisby, who discovers a secret agency of superintelligent rats (they've escaped from a science lab at the National Institute of Mental Health) who aid her in protecting her family. Animation is superb. Courage combined with intelligence carries the day.

Adapted from Robert C. O'Brien's "Mrs. Frisby and the Rats of N.I.M.H." Ages 6 to 11.

> **BEWARE** *Laboratory animals are given injections. There is a swordfight between rats that produces wounds.*

1982 84m/C D: Don Bluth; **W:** Don Bluth; **M:** Jerry Goldsmith; **V:** John Carradine, Derek Jacobi, Dom DeLuise, Elizabeth Hartman, Peter Strauss, Aldo Ray, Edie McClurg, Wil Wheaton. **VHS, Beta, LV, 8mm** *MGM*

The Secret of Roan Inish
🦴🦴🦴 ♭

PG/Jr. High-Adult The unpredictable, always intriguing John Sayles ("Eight Men Out," "Matewan," "Brother From Another Planet") turns his talents to Irish folklore. Young Fiona Conelly (Jeni Courtney) comes to live with her grandparents on the west coast of Ireland. Her grandfather (Mick Lally) tells her of the time when she and her parents moved from the island of Roan Inish and how her little brother was washed out to sea in his cradle. Fiona hears wild stories about her brother being raised by seals on Roan Inish. She decides to learn the truth. Fascinating and intelligent.

> **BEWARE** *A helpless baby floats away in a cradle.*

1994 102m/C Jeni Courtney, Michael Lally, Eileen Colgan, John Lynch, Richard Sheridan, Susan Lynch, Cillian Byrne; **D:** John Sayles; **W:** John Sayles; **C:** Haskell Wexler; **M:** Mason Daring. **VHS, LV** *COL*

The Secret of the Hunchback

Family Animated retelling of Victor Hugo's novel "The Hunchback of Notre Dame," which features a deformed bellringer for the Paris cathedral and his love for a gypsy girl. Ages 6 to 10.

1995 50m/C VHS *UAV*

Secret of the Ice Cave 🦴

PG-13/Jr. High-Adult Computer whiz kid, on a visit to his jungle-researcher mom, gets a hint of vast fortune hidden in nearby mountains. He ends up pursued by villains and mercenaries of all shapes but only one size—dumb and a half. Basically witless juvenile adventure.

> **BEWARE** *Violence, profanity.*

1989 106m/C Michael Moriarty, Sally Kellerman, David Mendenhall, Virgil Frye, Gerald Anthony, Norbert Weisser; **D:** Radu Gabrea. **VHS, Beta** *MOV*

Secret of the Seal 🦴🦴

Preschool-Primary Animated tale of young Tottoi who, while swimming around a beautiful Italian island, finds a mother Mediterranean seal (thought to be extinct) and her little cub. But Tottoi can't keep his discovery a secret and then must fight to save the seals lives.

1993 90m/C VHS *CEL, BTV, JFK*

Secret Places

PG/Jr. High-Adult During World War II a German refugee enrolled in an English girls' boarding school finds friendship with a popular classmate, who soon learns the causes of the new girl's unhappy home life. Touching, though not as involving as it could have been. Based on a novel by Janice Elliott.

BEWARE *Brief nudity, salty language, mature themes, drug use.*

1985 98m/C Maria Therese Relin, Tara MacGowran, Claudine Auger, Jenny Agutter; **D:** Zelda Barron. **VHS, Beta** *FOX*

See How They Grow

Preschool-Primary Introduces young children to new-born animals and insects and how they grow. Based on the best-selling Dorling Kindersley book series. This six-part series covers Pets, Farm Animals, Pond Animals, Forest Animals, Wild Animals, and Insects & Spiders.

1996 180m/C VHS *ENM*

See You in the Morning

PG-13/Jr. High-Adult Disappointing romantic comedy-drama about a divorced psychiatrist and a widow, both of whom had unhappy marriages, who meet and wed. They must cope with their respective children, family tragedies, and their own expectations in order to make this second chance work for both. About the level of an average TV show, despite the sterling cast and promises of psychological insight.

BEWARE *Mature themes, sex.*

1989 119m/C Jeff Bridges, Alice Krige, Farrah Fawcett, Drew Barrymore, Lukas Haas, Macaulay Culkin, David Dukes, Frances Sternhagen, Theodore Bikel, George Hearn, Linda Lavin; **D:** Alan J. Pakula; **W:** Alan J. Pakula. **VHS, Beta, LV** *WAR*

The Selfish Giant

Primary-Jr. High Animated version of Oscar Wilde's classic tale of a giant who builds a wall around his garden to keep the children out, only to find that his tress no longer blossoms and his flowers no longer grow. Ages 4 to 9.

1972 27m/C VHS, Beta *PYR, ECU*

Sense and Sensibility

PG/Jr. High-Adult A movie you wish your kids would love, "Sense and Sensibility" is based on Jane Austen's classic novel, is beautifully filmed (in England), wittily adapted (by star Thompson who won an Oscar for her screenplay), well-acted and contains nothing objectionable. Indeed, 'tis a fine film for adults and refined young ladies and gentlemen. So don't be surprised when your kids fall asleep. The Dashwood sisters and their mother are forced to move to a country cottage when father dies. Sensible Elinor Dashwood (Thompson) looks after the household while sensuous sister Marianne (Winslet) pines for passion. Men come and go. A good history lesson about how few options women had in the early 1800s (like why couldn't the Dashwood sisters get a job or something?)

BEWARE *Mild thematic elements.*

1995 135m/C Emma Thompson, Kate Winslet, Hugh Grant, Alan Rickman, Greg Wise, Robert Hardy, Elizabeth Spriggs, Emile Francois, Gemma Jones, James Fleet, Harriet Walter, Imogen Stubbs, Imelda Staunton, Hugh Laurie, Richard Lumsden; **D:** Ang Lee; **W:** Emma Thompson; **C:** Michael Coulter; **M:** Patrick Doyle. **Award Nominations:** Academy Awards '95: Best Actress (Thompson), Best Adapted Screenplay, Best Cinematography, Best Costume Design, Best Supporting Actress (Winslet), Best Score; Academy Awards '96: Best Picture; British Academy Awards '95: Best Actress (Thompson), Best Adapted Screenplay, Best Cinematography, Best Director (Lee), Best Film, Best Supporting Actor (Rickman), Best Supporting Actress (Winslet, Spriggs), Best Score; Directors Guild of America Awards '95: Best Director (Lee); Golden Globe Awards '96: Best Actress—Drama (Thompson), Best Director (Lee), Best Supporting Actress (Winslet), Best Score; Screen Actors Guild Award '95: Best Actress (Thompson), Cast; Writers Guild of America '95: Best Adapted Screenplay; **Awards:** Golden Globe Awards '96: Best Film—Drama, Best Screenplay; Los Angeles Film Critics Association Awards '95: Best Screenplay; National Board of Review Awards '95: Best Actress (Thompson), Best Director (Lee), Best Film; New York Film Critics Awards '95: Best Director (Lee); Screen Actors Guild Award '95: Best Supporting Actress (Winslet). **VHS** *NYR*

A Separate Peace

PG/Jr. High-Adult The John Knowles novel, a perpetual homework assignment for millions of high schoolers, gets a scrupulously faithful—though not terribly gripping—screen treatment. The quiet Gene and the athletic, boisterous Finny are roommates in a New England prep school during World War II. A tragic accident (or was it an accident?) shows the darker side of their apparent friendship.

BEWARE *Profanity.*

1973 104m/C John Heyl, Parker Stevenson, William Roerick; **D:** Larry Peerce; **M:** Charles Fox. **VHS, Beta** *PAR, HMV*

Serendipity the Pink Dragon

Preschool-Primary Boy gets stranded on Paradise Island and meets a gentle dragon.

1990 90m/C D: Jim Terry. **VHS, Beta** *JFK*

Sgt. Bilko

PG/Jr. High-Adult The '50s TV series gets the big screen treatment with Martin in the Phil Silvers role as wheeler-dealer master sergeant Ernie Bilko, who rents out Army trucks to private citizens and runs a clandestine casino right under the unknowing nose of commanding officer Col. Hall (Aykroyd). This time Ernie's up against Washington budget cutters who want to shut down Ft. Baxter and all Bilko's schemes along with it. That is, unless the secret weapon they've been working on—a tank that hovers—actually works. Run-of-the-mill script means that this, unfortunately, is not your father's Ernie Bilko.

A game of hide-and-go-seek from "The Secret Garden."

1995 92m/C Steve Martin, Dan Aykroyd, Phil Hartman, Glenne Headly, Daryl Mitchell, Max Casella, Brian Leckner, Pamela Segall, Eric Edwards, Dan Ferro, John Marshall Jones, Brian Ortiz; **D:** Jonathan Lynn; **W:** Andy Breckman; **C:** Peter Sova; **M:** Alan Silvestri. **VHS** *MCA*

Serial Mom 🎵🎵🎵

R/Sr. High-Adult June Cleaver-like housewife Turner is nearly perfect, except when someone disrupts her orderly life. Didn't rewind your videotape? Chose the white shoes after Labor Day? Uh oh. Stardom reigns after she's caught and the murderer-as-celebrity phenomenon is exploited to the fullest. Darkly funny Waters satire tends toward the mainstream and isn't as perverse as earlier efforts, but still maintains a shocking edge (vital organs are good for an appearance or two). Turner's chameleonic performance as the perfect mom/crazed killer is right on target, recalling "The War of the Roses." Waterston, Lake, and Lillard are terrific as her generic suburban family.

1994 93m/C Kathleen Turner, Ricki Lake, Sam Waterston, Matthew Lillard, Mink Stole, Traci Lords; **Cameos:** Suzanne Somers, Joan Rivers, Patty Hearst; **D:** John Waters; **W:** John Waters; **M:** Basil Poledouris. **VHS** *HBO*

Sesame Songs: Dance Along!

Family Big Bird, Oscar the Grouch, and the Count teach kids new dances and valuable lessons.
1990 30m/C VHS *RAN*

Sesame Songs: Elmo's Sing-Along Guessing Game

Family Elmo plays the host of a very silly game show. Kids will love to try to answer his questions while singing songs like "My Best Friend," "I Love My Elbows," "Eight Balls of Fur," and more.
1991 30m/C VHS, Beta *RAN*

Sesame Songs: Monster Hits!

Family Favorite monsters from "Sesame Street" sing the hits: "C is for Cookie," "Fuzzy and Blue," and many more.
1990 30m/C VHS *RAN*

Sesame Songs: Rock & Roll!

Family Your favorite Muppets from Sesame Street will have you rockin' and rollin' to the beat in this dynamic sing-a-long video. The Count sings his hit "Count Up to Nine" and Bert knows "It's Hip to Be Square." **1990 30m/C V:** Jim Henson. **VHS** *RAN*

Sesame Songs: Sing-Along Earth Songs

Family Sesame Street music videos featuring Grover and friends. ♫ Every Bit A'Litter Hurts; Just Throw it My Way; Air; Water Pollution; On My Pond; Little Plant; Box City Recycling Rap; Oscar's Junk Band; Keep the Parks Clean for the Pigeons. **1993 30m/C VHS** *RAN, BTV*

Sesame Songs: Sing, Hoot & Howl

Family Big Bird hosts this musical tribute to the animal world, where kids can sing songs like "Proud to Be a Cow," "The Insects in Your Neighborhood," "Cluck around the Clock," and nine more. **1991 30m/C VHS, Beta** *RAN*

Sesame Songs: Sing Yourself Silly!

Family Sesame Street stars and special guest stars Pee Wee Herman, Barbara Bush, and John Candy sing your favorites. **1990 30m/C VHS** *RAN*

Sesame Songs: We All Sing Together

Family From the Sesame Songs Home Video Series comes more delightful music for children to sing with their favorite Muppets: Elmo, the Count, and Telly. Emphasis is on tolerance and stresses that despite outward appearances, kids are basically the same. ♫ Skin; Fixin' My Hair; One Thousand Faces; I Want to be Me; Dancing Shoes; Mom and Me; Different Yet the Same; No Matter What; We All Sing With the Same Voice. **1993 30m/C VHS** *RAN*

Sesame Street: Bedtime Stories and Songs

Family Sesame Street characters read favorite bedtime stories. **1990 30m/C VHS** *KUI, RAN*

Sesame Street: Best of Ernie and Bert

Family Some of Ernie and Bert's best moments from the acclaimed children's TV series "Sesame Street." **1990 30m/C VHS** *RAN*

Sesame Street: Big Bird's Favorite Party Games

Family Big Bird shows children a number of fun and easy games they can play together. **1990 30m/C VHS** *RAN*

Sesame Street: Big Bird's Story Time

Family If childhood were a country, Big Bird would be on the stamps. Here, the yellow-feathered one is right on the money, reading stories. Ages 1 to 5. **1990 30m/C VHS** *RAN*

Sesame Street Celebrates Around the World

Family Originally a New Year's Eve 1993 PBS broadcast, that let kids say up late—until 9! The celebration moves from Sesame Street to countries where the new year is greeted in different ways. There is much fun, many songs, and an appreciation of different people from different places. Ages 3 to 9. **1994 60m/C VHS** *RAN*

Sesame Street: Count It Higher

Family Some of the best music videos from Sesame Street. **1990 30m/C VHS** *RAN*

Sesame Street: Developing Self-Esteem

Family The Sesame Street gang along with some special friends teach children to take pride in their accomplishments, aptitudes, and abilities. **1984 40m/C** Lily Tomlin, Marv Albert, Itzhak Perlman, Jim Henson's Muppets. **VHS, Beta** *CHI*

Sesame Street: Do the Alphabet

Family Baby Bear has trouble remembering his letters so he goes to Big Bird for some help. Clearly, he's come to the right guy. Ages 2 to 5. ♫ Alphabet Blues; Do the Alphabet; D (Dee Dee Dee); J Friends; Alpha-

The Dashwood women stand in the doorway of their new home in "Sense and Sensibility."

bet Song; Boogie Woogie Piggies; Alphabet Jungle Song; T Dance.
1995 45m/C VHS

Sesame Street: I'm Glad I'm Me

Family The PBS Muppets teach children the value of being themselves.
1990 30m/C VHS *KUI, RAN*

Sesame Street Kids' Guide to Life: Learning to Share

Family Elmo, with some help from his Sesame Street pals and guest Katie Couric, finds out that sharing his toys and taking turns makes playtime even more fun. Katie also provides parents with some tips for guiding kids in sharing. Now, Bryant, let Katie share the microphone. Ages 3 to 6. ♫ This Is My Train; Cooperation Station; Share; Two Heads Are Better Than One; Sharing; What Is a Friend.
1995 45m/C VHS

Sesame Street: Play-Along Games and Songs

Family Children learn while playing interesting games with all their favorite Sesame Street characters.
1990 30m/C VHS *KUI, RAN*

Sesame Street Presents: Follow That Bird 🦴🦴🦴

G/Family Television's Big Bird suffers an identity crisis, and leaves Sesame Street to join a family of real birds. He soon misses his home, and returns, in a danger-filled journey.
1985 92m/C Sandra Bernhard, John Candy, Chevy Chase, Joe Flaherty, Dave Thomas, Waylon Jennings, Jim Henson's Muppets; **D:** Ken Kwapis; **M:** Lennie Niehaus. **VHS, Beta, LV** *WAR*

Sesame Street Presents: Put Down the Duckie

Family Compiles some of the best bits from the long-running PBS children's series. Celebrity cameos and musical numbers abound as Kermit, Grover, Ernie, and more spoof opera, Hitchcock, TV news and Masterpiece

Theater, which becomes Monsterpiece Theater, with your furry blue host, Alistair Cookie. A major treat from the Street. Ages 4 to 8.

1994 45m/C Robert MacNeil; *Cameos:* Gladys Knight, Phil Donahue, Alistair Cooke, Martina Navratilova, Barbara Walters, Ralph Nader, John Candy, Jane Curtin, Andrea Martin, Madeline Kahn, Paul (Pee Wee Herman) Reubens, Paul Simon, Danny DeVito, Rhea Perlman, Itzhak Perlman, Pete Seeger, Jeremy Irons. **VHS** *RAN*

Sesame Street: Sing Along

Family Sing along with Sesame Street characters. Ages 2 to 6.

1990 30m/C VHS *RAN*

Sesame Street Visits the Firehouse

Family Big Bird, Elmo, and Gordon go to the fire station in this live action adventure. They learn about firefighters and their equipment and even see a real fire.

1990 30m/C V: Jim Henson. **VHS** *RAN, VEC*

Sesame Street Visits the Hospital

Family Reassuring video for children that joins Big Bird and his pals as they visit the sometimes very scary hospital. Ages 2 to 6.

1990 30m/C VHS *RAN*

Sesame Street's 25th Birthday: A Musical Celebration

Family The gang from "Sesame Street" performs some of their favorite songs. Wonderful stuff. All ages.

1993 60m/C VHS *RAN, BTV*

Seven Alone 🎬🎬▷

G/Family Fact-based adventure about a pioneer family on the treacherous 2000-mile journey from Missouri to the newly opened Oregon territory. When tragedy strikes, the trouble-prone eldest boy has to take charge of his brothers and sisters. Though performances teeter between adequate and amateurish, the young hero's change from wagon-train delinquent to fearless frontiersman is something to behold, and little sugarcoating the harsh 1842 wilderness occurs. The producers of the successful "Where the Red Fern Grows" adapted this from the memoir "On to Oregon" by Honore Morrow.

 Violence.

1975 85m/C Dewey Martin, Aldo Ray, Anne Collins, Dean Smith, Stewart Peterson; **D:** Earl Bellamy. **VHS, Beta** *NO*

Seven Brides for Seven Brothers 🎬🎬🎬▷

Family Eldest of seven fur-trapping brothers in the Oregon Territory brings home a wife. She begins to civilize the other six, who realize the merits of women and begin to look for romances of their own. Thrilling choreography by Michael Kidd—don't miss "The Barn Raising." Charming performances by Powell and Keel, both in lovely voice. Based on Stephen Vincent Benet's story. Thrills, chills, singin', and dancin'—a classic Hollywood good time. 🎵 When You're In Love; Spring, Spring, Spring; Sobbin' Women; Bless Your Beautiful Hide; Goin' Co'tin; Wonderful, Wonderful Day; June Bride; Lonesome Polecat Lament.

1954 103m/C Howard Keel, Jane Powell, Russ Tamblyn, Julie Newmar, Jeff Richards, Tommy Rall, Virginia Gibson; **D:** Stanley Donen. **Award Nominations:** Academy Awards '54: Best Color Cinematography, Best Film Editing, Best Picture, Best Screenplay; **Awards:** Academy Awards '54: Best Score; National Board of Review Awards '54: 10 Best Films of the Year. **VHS, Beta, LV, 8mm** *MGM, HMV*

Seven Faces of Dr. Lao 🎬🎬🎬

Family Dr. Lao is an old Chinese man who rides his mule into a town in the old west. Amazingly, he single-handedly sets up a full-fledged carnival, complete with monsters, marvels and magic that come to the aid of squabbling local citizens. Sunny flipside of "Something Wicked This Way Comes," with a heavily made-up Randall playing the buffoonish yet secretly wise Lao plus six other roles, from Merlin the Magician to the Abominable Snowman—admittedly with varied degrees of success (Peter Sellers was originally cast but backed out). Farfetched but winning fantasy, based on the novel by Charles Finney.

1963 101m/C Tony Randall, Barbara Eden, Arthur O'Connell, Lee Patrick, Noah Beery Jr., John Qualen; **D:** George Pal. **VHS, Beta, LV** *MGM*

The Seven Little Foys 🎬🎬🎬

Family Enjoyable musical about Eddie Foy, a turn-of-the-century vaudeville stage star whose wife's unexpected death (while he was away touring) leaves him father to seven kids he barely knows. He tries to be a dutiful dad by taking them on the road as his act. More time could have been spent on the parenthood theme—first hour is all romance and backstage stuff, pretty boring for young viewers—but overall pic is pleasant in the old-Hollywood style, and Hope is at his finest. Narrated by Charlie Foy, one of the real-life kids grown up. 🎵 Mary's a Grand Old Name; I'm a Yankee Doodle Dandy; I'm the Greatest Father of Them All; Nobody; Comedy Ballet; I'm Tired; Chinatown, My Chinatown.

▨BEWARE▨ *Alcohol use. Mr. and Mrs. Foy turned out to be unmarried during 16 years and seven kids together, a fact handled so gingerly you might miss it.*

1955 95m/C Bob Hope, Milly Vitale, George Tobias, Angela Clark, James Cagney; **D:** Melville Shavelson; **W:** Jack Rose, Melville Shavelson. **VHS, Beta** *COL*

Seven Minutes in Heaven 🎬🎬▷

PG/Jr. High-Adult Sensitive teen love story about a 15-year-old girl who invites her platonic male friend to live in

Steve Martin oversees the gambling cash in "Sgt. Bilko."

her house, and finds it disturbs her boyfriend, as these things will. Tastefully done, with gentle humor.

BEWARE *Sex talk.*

1986 90m/C Jennifer Connelly, Byron Thames, Maddie Corman; *D:* Linda Feferman. **VHS, Beta** *WAR*

7 Ninja Kids 𝄞

PG/Primary-Adult Unlike "3 Ninjas" and similar polished Hollywood fare, this is the real thing, a grungy, poorly dubbed Hong Kong production imported on videocassette to take advantage of American karatemania among the kidset. Seven Asian youngsters (who fight and even speak in unison) battle bad guys over a stolen jewel. Obnoxious stuff, but if you must know there are a whole series with this bunch, including "37 Ninja Kids."

BEWARE *Violence, needless profanity.*

1989 90m/C VHS *VTR, HHE, MTX*

1776 𝄞𝄞𝄞

G/Family Broadway musical comedy about America's first Continental Congress hits the screen straightaway, with many members of the original cast. Delegates battle the English and each other trying to establish a set of laws and the Declaration of Independence, all the while singing and dancing up a storm. Long and bellowing, but at the very least a novel faux-history lesson. Available in widescreen format on laserdisc with additional footage. 🎵 The Lees of Old Virginia; He Plays the Violin; But, Mr. Adams; Sit Down John; Till Then; Piddle, Twiddle and Resolve; Yours, Yours, Yours; Mama, Look Sharp; The Egg.

1972 141m/C William Daniels, Howard da Silva, Ken Howard, Donald Madden, Blythe Danner, Ronald Holgate, Virginia Vestoff, Stephen Nathan, Ralston Hill; *D:* Peter Hunt. **Award Nominations:** Academy Awards '72: Best Cinematography; **Awards:** National Board of Review Awards '72: 10 Best Films of the Year. **VHS, Beta, LV** *COL, FCT*

The Seventh Voyage of Sinbad
𝄞𝄞𝄞

G/Family Honey, he shrunk the Princess! When an evil magician reduces Sinbad's fiancee to tiny size (she hardly seems to object) the fearless sailor journeys to the monster-filled island of Colossa in search of a cure. Never mind that the plot has holes big enough for a cyclops, Ray Harryhausen created some of his best stop-motion animation creatures for this rousing adventure. See also "The Golden Voyage of Sinbad" and "Sinbad and the Eye of the Tiger."

BEWARE *Violence. A giant cyclops and a fearsome dragon.*

1958 94m/C Kerwin Mathews, Kathryn Grant, Torin Thatcher, Richard Eyer; *D:* Nathan (Hertz) Juran; *W:* Kenneth Kolb; *M:* Bernard Herrmann. **VHS, Beta, LV** *COL, MLB, CCB*

The Shadow 𝄞𝄞 ♪

PG-13/Jr. High-Adult Who knows what evil lurks in the hearts of men? Why "The Shadow" of course, as is shown in this highly stylized big screen version of the '30s radio show that once starred Orson Welles. Billionaire playboy Lamont Cranston (Baldwin) is a master of illusion and defender of justice thanks to his alter ego. Aided by companion Margo Lane (Miller), the Shadow battles super-criminal Shiwan Khan (Lone), the deadliest descendant of Ghenghis Khan. Story is not particularly enamoring, but you may not notice due to the wonderful sets. Numerous, elaborate special effects provide icing on the cake for those in the mood for a journey back to the radio past or a quick superhero fix.

BEWARE *Violence.*

1994 107m/C Alec Baldwin, John Lone, Penelope Ann Miller, Peter Boyle, Ian McKellen, Tim Curry, Jonathan Winters; *D:* Russell Mulcahy; *W:* David Koepp. **VHS** *NYR*

Shadow of a Doubt 𝄞𝄞𝄞 ♪

Jr. High-Adult Uncle Charlie has come to visit his relatives in Santa Rosa. Although he is handsome and charming, his young niece slowly comes to realize he is a wanted mass murderer—and he comes to recognize her suspicions. Hitchcock's personal favorite movie; a quietly creepy venture into Middle American menace based on a true story. Terrific performances throughout, distinguished by Cotten as the uncle with a problem and Cronyn as the oddball neighbor. Adapted by Wilder from the story by Gordon McConnell.

1943 108m/B Teresa Wright, Joseph Cotten, Hume Cronyn, MacDonald Carey, Henry Travers, Wallace Ford; **D:** Alfred Hitchcock; **W:** Thorton Wilder; **M:** Dimitri Tiomkin. **VHS, Beta, LV** *MCA*

Shadow of the Eagle

Family Wayne saves the day in more ways than one in this creaky Mascot serial. His winning star charisma is the main reason to watch, as members of an aviation corporation are blackmailed by a mystery villain called the Eagle. Suspicion points to a crippled fighter ace, now running a struggling carnival. His loyal stunt pilot Craig McCoy (Wayne) strives to unmask the lethal Eagle, in 12 chapters of 20 minutes each.

 *Roughhousing.*

1932 226m/B John Wayne, Dorothy Gulliver, Walter Miller; **D:** Ford Beebe. **VHS** *GPV, VYY, VCN*

Shadow of the Wolf 🐾🐾

PG-13/Jr. High-Adult Phillips is Agaguk, the son of the village leader, in this snowbound saga of survival set against the Arctic wilderness. Upset with the intrusion of white men onto his land, he decides to look for better accommodations elsewhere with Eskimo babe Tilly. Together they face the harsh tundra, struggling to stay alive in the Great White North. Big daddy, meanwhile, believes Agaguk's departure to be the ultimate betrayal and casts upon him the "curse of the white wolf." Sweeping cinematography helps make the adventure palatable, but first you must sled past the silliness of the casting (though if Abe Vigoda can play an Eskimo in "North," why not Phillips and Tilly as a cute Eskimo couple here?). Based on the novel "Agaguk" by Yves Theriault.

 *Violence and profanity.*

1992 108m/C Lou Diamond Phillips, Donald Sutherland, Jennifer Tilly, Toshiro Mifune; **D:** Jacques Dorfman; **W:** Rudy Wurlitzer, Evan Jones. **VHS, LV** *COL*

The Shadow Riders 🐾🐾

PG/Jr. High-Adult Two brothers who fought on opposite sides during the Civil War return home to find their brother's fiancee kidnapped by a renegade Confederate officer who plans to use her as ransom in a prisoner exchange, and they set out to rescue the woman. Preceded by "The Sacketts" and based on the works of Louis L'Amour. Made for television.

1982 96m/C Tom Selleck, Sam Elliott, Ben Johnson, Katharine Ross, Jeffery Osterhage, Gene Evans, R.G. Armstrong, Marshall Teague, Dominique Dunne, Jeanetta Arnetta; **D:** Andrew V. McLaglen. **VHS** *VMK*

Shadowlands 🐾🐾🐾

PG/Jr. High-Adult Touching, tragic story of the late-in-life romance between celebrated author and Christian theologian C.S. Lewis (Hopkins) and brash New York divorcee Joy Gresham (Winger). Attenborough's direction is rather stately and sweeping. Winger is good, Hopkins is excellent as (another) repressed man who finds more emotions than he can handle. Critically acclaimed adaptation of Nicholson's play will require lots of kleenex.

 *Brief profanity and a very sad situation develops.*

1993 130m/C Anthony Hopkins, Debra Winger, Edward Hardwicke, Joseph Mazzello, Michael Denison, John Wood, Peter Firth, Peter Howell; **D:** Richard Attenborough; **W:** William Nicholson; **M:** George Fenton. **Award Nominations:** Academy Awards '93: Best Actress (Winger), Best Adapted Screenplay; British Academy Awards '94: Best Actor (Hopkins), Best Actress (Winger), Best Adapted Screenplay, Best Director (Attenborough); **Awards:** British Academy Awards '94: Best Film; Los Angeles Film Critics Association Awards '93: Best Actor (Hopkins); National Board of Review Awards '93: Best Actor (Hopkins). **VHS** *HBO*

Shag: The Movie 🐾🐾🐾

PG/Jr. High-Adult The time is 1963, the setting Myrtle Beach, South Carolina, the latest craze shaggin' when four friends hit the beach for one last weekend together. Carson (Cates) is getting ready to marry staid Harley (Power); Melaina (Fonda) wants to be discovered in Hollywood; and Pudge (Gish) and Luanne (Hannah) are off to college. They encounter lots of music, boys, and dancing in affectionate nod to a more innocent time. Not to be confused with other "teen" movies, this one boasts a good script and an above average cast.

 *Brief nudity.*

1989 96m/C Phoebe Cates, Annabeth Gish, Bridget Fonda, Page Hannah, Scott Coffey, Robert Rusler, Tyrone Power Jr., Jeff Yagher, Carrie Hamilton, Shirley Anne Field, Leilani Sarelle Ferrer; **D:** Zelda Barron; **W:** Robin Swicord, Lanier Laney, Terry Sweeney. **VHS, Beta, LV** *HBO*

The Shaggy D.A. 🐾🐾🐾

G/Family The grownup Wilby Daniels is running for District Attorney when his old canine condition recurs. Ouch, did someone say 'curs?.' Fun next-generation sequel to Disney's "The Shaggy Dog" ranks a hair or two above the original.

1976 90m/C Dean Jones, Tim Conway, Suzanne Pleshette, Keenan Wynn; **D:** Robert Stevenson; **M:** Buddy Baker. **VHS, Beta** *DIS, OM*

The Shaggy Dog 🐾🐾🐾

G/Family When teenager Wilby Daniels utters some magical words from the inscription of an ancient ring he turns into a talking sheepdog. Little brother Moochie is delighted; dog-hating dad nearly goes over the edge. Disney slapstick is on target at times, though it drags in places and brings in a spy subplot even sillier than the one in "For Love of Benji." Tim Burton style stop-motion

Don't throw out this trash! Oscar the Grouch from "Sesame Street."

animation in the opening credits. Followed by "The Shaggy D.A." and "Return of the Shaggy Dog."

1959 101m/B Fred MacMurray, Jean Hagen, Tommy Kirk, Annette Funicello, Tim Considine, Kevin Corcoran; **D:** Charles T. Barton. **VHS, Beta, LV** *DIS, BTV*

Shakespeare: The Animated Tales

Primary-Sr. High Specially abridged versions (by author Leon Garfield) of Shakespeare's most accessible plays, designed as introductions to the author's timeless works. Plays are Hamlet, Romeo and Juliet, Macbeth, Twelfth Night, A Midsummer Night's Dream and The Tempest. Each play is reduced to 30 minutes, which isn't bad for a child's introduction to Willie the Shake. The intricate and beautiful animation was done in Russia and Armenia. Originally broadcast on HBO. Ages 8 and up.

1993 30m/C VHS *RAN, BTV*

The Shakiest Gun in the West 🎵🎵ᵖ

Family Don Knotts isn't Bob Hope, but he's pretty funny in the same bumbling way. Remake of Hope's "Paleface"

has Philadelphia dentist Knotts unwittingly taking on bad guys and sultry Rhoades.

1968 101m/C Don Knotts, Barbara Rhoades, Jackie Coogan, Donald (Don "Red") Barry, Ruth McDevitt; **D:** Alan Rafkin. **VHS, LV** *MCA*

Shall We Dance 🎵🎵🎵

Family And shall we ever! Seventh Astaire-Rogers pairing has a famous ballet dancer and a musical-comedy star embark on a promotional romance and marriage, to boost their careers, only to find themselves truly falling in love. Thin, formula plot is inconsequential, as Astaire and Rogers sing and dance their way to success. Score by the Gershwins includes lots of memorable songs. 🎵 Slap That Bass; Beginner's Luck; Let's Call the Whole Thing Off; Walking the Dog; They All Laughed; They Can't Take That Away From Me; Shall We Dance.

1937 116m/B Fred Astaire, Ginger Rogers, Edward Everett Horton, Eric Blore; **D:** Mark Sandrich; **M:** George Gershwin, Ira Gershwin. **VHS, Beta, LV** *TTC, CCB, MED*

Shalom Sesame

Family Engaging series of children's videos that provide an introduction to the land, people, and culture of Israel with the characters from the Israeli version of Sesame

Street. In English with an introduction to Hebrew songs, numbers, and letters.
1990 40m/C VHS *MLT, FAF, ADL*

Shamu & You: Exploring the World of Birds

Family With Shamu you'll take a look at such winged creatures as hummingbirds, parrots, owls, flamingos, vultures, oxpeckers, and eagles in a format which features songs, stories, animation, and wildlife footage. Others in the series include "Exploring the World of Fish," "Exploring the World of Mammals," and "Exploring the World of Reptiles."
1992 30m/C VHS *VTR*

Shane 🎵🎵🎵🎵

Family Retired gunfighter, now a drifter, comes to the aid of a homestead family threatened by a land baron and his hired gun. In the performance of his career, Ladd is the mystery man who becomes the idol of the family's young son, played with great sincerity by de Wilde. Classic, flawless archetypal western is long and stately and worth savoring. Pulitzer prize-winning western novelist A.B. Guthrie, Jr. adapted from the novel by Jack Schaefer.

 Violence. A child without a father.

1953 117m/C Alan Ladd, Jean Arthur, Van Heflin, Brandon de Wilde, Jack Palance, Ben Johnson, Elisha Cook Jr., Edgar Buchanan, Emile Meyer; **D:** George Stevens; **W:** Jack Sher; **M:** Victor Young. **Award Nominations:** Academy Awards '53: Best Director (Stevens), Best Picture, Best Screenplay, Best Supporting Actor (de Wilde, Palance); **Awards:** Academy Awards '53: Best Color Cinematography; National Board of Review Awards '53: 10 Best Films of the Year, Best Director (Stevens). **VHS, Beta, LV** *PAR, TLF*

Shari Lewis & Lamb Chop: In the Land of No Manners

Preschool-Primary Lewis and her puppet pal teach the value of good manners by visiting a horrible land where there are none.
1991 44m/C Shari Lewis. **VHS** *A&M, FCT, TVC*

Shari Lewis & Lamb Chop: One Minute Bible Stories, New Testament

Preschool-Primary Shari and her puppet friend present a number of Biblical tales for children.
1986 30m/C Shari Lewis, Florence Henderson. **VHS** *NO*

Shari Lewis: Don't Wake Your Mom

Preschool-Primary Lewis and her puppets Lamb Chop, Hush Puppy, and Charlie Horse sing and tell stories using the book "Is it Time Yet?"
1992 45m/C VHS *PGV, MVD, TVC*

Shari Lewis: Have I Got a Story for You

Preschool-Primary Lewis and her coterie of puppet characters tell classic stories, including "Rumpelstiltskin" and "The Sorcerer's Apprentice."
1984 59m/C Shari Lewis. **VHS, Beta** *MGM*

Shari Lewis: Kooky Classics

Preschool-Primary Lewis, Lambchop, and other puppets take children through the world of classical music, from Brahms to Mozart.
1984 59m/C Shari Lewis. **VHS, Beta** *MGM*

Shari Lewis: One Minute Bedtime Stories

Preschool-Primary Puppeteer and ventriloquist Lewis, aided by Lamb Chop and Hush Puppy, reads twenty-six popular children's stories.
1985 30m/C VHS, Beta *WOV, GKK*

Sharon, Lois & Bram at the Young People's Theatre

Preschool-Primary Three singers perform for and with children to help the youngsters develop an appreciation of music.
1983 30m/C VHS, Beta *BFI*

Sharon, Lois & Bram: Back by Popular Demand-Live

Preschool-Primary A live performance from the children's cable television stars. Songs include "Jelly Jelly in My Belly," "Chugga, Chugga" and more.
1990 30m/C VHS *MVD, A&M*

Sharon, Lois & Bram: Live in Your Living Room

Preschool-Primary A concert video from the beloved stars of the children's cable television program "Elephant Show."
1990 30m/C VHS, LV, 8mm *MVD, A&M*

Sharon, Lois & Bram: Sing A to Z

Preschool-Primary Trio of performers use songs, skits, and dances to entertain and teach the spelling and definition of new words.
1992 50m/C VHS *A&M, BTV*

Sharon, Lois & Bram's Elephant Show: Babysitting

Preschool-Primary Episodes from the popular Nickelodeon cable-TV show starring the three children's entertainers and their faithful pachyderm companion. Due to

Elephant's antics, Sharon, Lois & Bram end up babysitting a handful of kids. Juggling team Circus Shmirkus come over to help out. Additional volumes available.

1990 30m/C VHS *MOV*

The Shawshank Redemption

🦴🦴🦴 ♪

R/Sr. High-Adult Bank veep Andy (Robbins) is convicted of the murder of his wife and her lover and sentenced to the "toughest prison in the Northeast." While there he forms a friendship with lifer Red (Freeman), experiences the brutality of prison life, adapts, offers financial advice to the guards, and helps the warden (Gunton) cook the prison books. In his debut, director Darabont avoids belaboring most prison movie cliches while Robbins' talent for playing ambiguous characters is put to good use, and Freeman brings his usual grace to what could have been a thankless role. Adapted from the novella "Rita Hayworth and the Shawshank Redemption" by Stephen King.

🛑 BEWARE *Profanity, prison violence and implied brutality. For older teens only, and not all of them.*

1994 142m/C Tim Robbins, Morgan Freeman, Bob Gunton, William Sadler, Clancy Brown, Mark Rolston, Gil Bellows, James Whitmore; **D:** Frank Darabont; **W:** Frank Darabont; **C:** Roger Deakins. **VHS, LV** *COL*

Shazam!

Preschool-Jr. High Young Billy Batson says "shazam" and turns into the mighty Captain Marvel in this cheesy Saturday-morning live-action adaptation of the classic comic-book character whose popularity once exceeded Superman's. Additional episodes available.

1981 60m/C VHS, Beta *FHE*

Shazzan

Family Arabian adventures, Hanna-Barbera style; modern kids Chuck and Nancy are transported back in time by a magic ring and accompany Shazzan the genie through two tapes of excavated Saturday-morning cartoon adventures. Additional episodes available.

1967 60m/C V: Barney Phillips, Janet Waldo, Don Messick. **VHS, Beta** *TTC*

She-Devil 🦴🦴

PG-13/Jr. High-Adult Comic book version of the acidic Fay Weldon novel "The Life and Loves of a She-Devil." Fat, dowdy suburban wife (Arnold) becomes a vengeful beast when a smarmy romance novelist steals her husband. Uneven comedic reworking of a distinctly unforgiving feminist fiction. Arnold is given too much to handle (her role requires an actual range of emotions); Streep's role is too slight, though she displays a fine sense of comedic timing.

🛑 BEWARE *Profanity and sex. Main topic is revenge against an unfaithful husband.*

1989 100m/C Meryl Streep, Roseanne, Ed Begley Jr., Linda Hunt, Elizabeth Peters, Bryan Larkin, A. Martinez, Sylvia Miles; **D:** Susan Seidelman; **W:** Mark Burns, Barry Strugatz; **M:** Howard Shore. **VHS, Beta, LV** *ORI*

She-Ra, Vol. 1

Primary-Jr. High She-Ra is the twin sister of He-Man, of "Masters of the Universe" and toy store fame, and sometimes the big guy makes guest appearances in these episodes gathered from their cartoon TV series. In "Missing Axe," she saves a woodcutter from Mantenna and in "Crystal Castles," she saves Castle Bright Moon from the Shadow Weaver's energy blasts. Additional volumes available.

1985 45m/C VHS

Sheena 🦴

PG/Jr. High-Adult A sportscaster aids a jiggly jungle queen in defending her kingdom from an evil prince. Female Tarzan character (first a vintage comic book, then a '50s TV show) comes to the screen trapped in an ill-wrought effort somewhere between sexy satire and bubble-gum action.

🛑 BEWARE *Violence, salty language, and a surprising amount of nudity for a PG. One commentator sagely observed that this premiered just days before the initiation of the PG-13 rating, which it surely would have earned.*

1984 117m/C Tanya Roberts, Ted Wass, Donovan Scott, Elizabeth Toro; **D:** John Guillermin; **W:** David Newman. **VHS, Beta, LV** *GKK*

Shelley Duvall's Bedtime Stories

Preschool-Primary Another Shelley Duvall series of stories, here based on popular children's books and narrated by celebrities. Each tape is available individually and contains at least two stories. Originally produced for cable television. Additional episodes available.

1992 25m/C VHS, LV *MCA*

Shelley Duvall's Bedtime Stories: Moe the Dog in Tropical Paradise/Amos, the Story of an Old Dog and His Couch

Preschool-Primary Shelley Duvall hosts animated children's stories from her TV series; also features celebrity narrators, in this instance Richard Dreyfuss and Morgan Freeman. Ages 2 to 8.

1994 26m/C VHS *BTV*

Shelley Duvall's Bedtime Stories: My New Neighbors/ Rotten Island

Preschool-Primary Shelly Duvall hosts animated children's stories from her TV series. Celebrity narrators are Billy Crystal and Charles Grodin. Ages 2 to 8.
1994 26m/C VHS *BTV*

Shelley Duvall's Bedtime Stories: The Christmas Witch

Preschool-Primary Angela Lansbury narrates this enchanting story of a witch named Gloria who just wasn't any good at being bad and chose instead to use her magic to help spread the spirit of Christmas. Ages 4 to 10.
1994 27m/C VHS *MCA*

Shelley Duvall's Rock 'n' Rhymeland

Preschool-Primary Retelling of classic nursery rhymes done in Shelley Duvall's inimitable style, with guest stars from the pop-music scene.
1990 77m/C Shelley Duvall, Deborah Harry, Paul Simon, Cyndi Lauper, Bobby Brown, Little Richard. **VHS** *MVD*

Sherlock Hound: Dr. Watson I Presume?

Preschool-Primary Sherlock Hound searches for his arch-nemesis Professor Moriarty with the help of his pal, Dr. Watson. Additional volumes available.
1991 120m/C VHS *JFK*

Sherlock: Undercover Dog 🦴🦴 🦴

PG/Family Billy (Eroen) arrives on Catalina island to spend the summer with his father, an eccentric inventor. He makes a human friend in Emma (Cameron) and a canine companion in Sherlock, a police dog who's able to talk but naturally only to the two kids. Seems Sherlock's policeman master has been kidnapped by bumbling smugglers and it's up to the trio to save the day.
1994 80m/C Benjamin Eroen, Brynne Cameron, Anthony Simmons, Margy Moore, Barry Philips; **D:** Richard Harding Gardner; **W:** Richard Harding Gardner; **M:** Lou Forestieri. **VHS** *COL*

She's Having a Baby 🦴🦴 🦴

PG-13/Jr. High-Adult Newlyweds tread marital waters with difficulty, and an impending baby (after an infertility scare) further complicates their lives. Told from Bacon's viewpoint as the young writer and husband, still grappling with maturity and wondering if the suburban yuppie life traps him. Hughes' first venture into the adult world isn't as satisfying as his teen angst flicks, although the charming leads help. Major drawbacks are the arguably sexist premise and dull resolution. Great soundtrack.

🔺 BEWARE 🔺 *Sex, profanity and pregnancy.*

1988 106m/C Kevin Bacon, Elizabeth McGovern, William Windom, Paul Gleason, Alec Baldwin, Cathryn Damon, Holland Taylor, James Ray, Isabel Lorca, Dennis Dugan, Edie McClurg, John Ashton; **D:** John Hughes; **W:** John Hughes; **M:** Stewart Copeland. **VHS, Beta, LV, 8mm** *PAR*

Shinbone Alley 🦴🦴

G/Family Offbeat, loosely plotted musical hodgepodge about archy (who's name, like e.e. cummings, is never initially capped), a free-verse poet reincarnated as a cockroach, and his wayward lady friend Mehitabel, a loose-living alley cat. With uneven animation, the attractions are the great character voices and songs by "Man of La Mancha" composer Joe Darion. Adapted from a stage musical and a record album production based on the famous story-poems by Don Marquis—all aimed at and appreciated better by adults than small kids.

🔺 BEWARE 🔺 *Mature themes? Yes indeed—the morose archy is no stranger to suicide, and the irresponsible Mehitibel plans to drown her own kittens.*

1970 83m/C D: John D. Wilson; **V:** Carol Channing, Eddie Bracken, John Carradine, Alan Reed. **VHS, Beta** *SIM, GEM, KAR*

Shining Time Station: Singsongs, Vol. 1

Preschool-Primary Sixteen music videos written to enhance the themes of various "Shining Time Station" episodes.
1992 ?m/C VHS *FAF, FAF*

Shining Time Station: 'Tis a Gift Holiday Special

Preschool-Primary Whimsical Christmas tale about a mysterious bearded man named Mr. Nicholas who is waiting for a train a week before Christmas. From the acclaimed PBS series.
1992 51m/C Ringo Starr, Lloyd Bridges. **VHS** *AVE, FAF*

Shipwrecked 🦴🦴 🦴

PG/Family Disney-made kiddie swashbuckler based on an 1873 popular novel "Haakon Haakonsen." Title character is a cabin boy marooned on an island after pirates take over his ship. Familiar but pleasant enough seagoing adventure, with shades of "Home Alone" when the pirates come calling.

🔺 BEWARE 🔺 *Alcohol use, violence threatened but never really shown. The PG is pointless, unless someone at the MPAA thought this unfairly defamed pirates.*

1990 93m/C Gabriel Byrne, Stian Smestad, Louisa Haigh, Trond Munch, Bjorn Sundquist, Eva Von Hanno, Kjell Stormoen; **D:** Nils Gaup; **W:** Nick Thiel, Nils Gaup; **M:** Patrick Doyle. **VHS, LV** *TOU*

Shirley Temple Baby Berlesques

Family Before Shirley Temple became a 1930s mainstay in feature films, she started out in these curious short subjects that put all-toddler casts in short parodies of

standard Hollywood scenes (example: Shirley's a missionary in Africa, rescued by a pint-sized Tarzan from tiny cannibals). Unusual, sometimes in questionable taste, but entertaining, and even younger than usual, Shirley's star power shines through.

1933 60m/B Shirley Temple. **VHS, Beta** *MVC, VYY*

Shirley Temple Festival

Family Ramshackle assemblage of Temple material includes two "Baby Berlesks," plus a pair of unrelated comedy shorts in which Shirley has supporting parts (stealing the show, as always). Ends with a newsreel of her teenaged marriage to actor John Agar.

1933 55m/B Shirley Temple, Andy Clyde. **VHS, Beta** *MRV*

Shirley Temple Storybook Theater

Family Episodes of an irregularly broadcast network TV show hosted by the grownup Shirley, in one-hour re-enactments of classic fairy tales. As with Shelley Duvall, an amazing array of Hollywood celebrities appeared in the casts. 13 volumes are: "Ali Baba & the Forty Thieves," "Dick Whittington & His Cat," "Hiawatha," "Mother Goose," "Rapunzel," "Rip Van Winkle," "Sleeping Beauty," "The Emperor's New Clothes," "The Land of Green Ginger," "The Lame Little Prince," "The Magic Fishbone," "The Nightingale," and "The Wild Swan."

1960 60m/B Nehemiah Persoff, Sebastian Cabot, Pernell Roberts, Shirley Temple, Agnes Moorehead, E.G. Marshall, Nancy Marchand, Eli Wallach, Jack Albertson, Lorne Greene, Leo G. Carroll, Thomas Mitchell, Melville Cooper. **VHS, Beta** *WKV*

The Shootist 🎬🎬🎬 ▷

PG/Jr. High-Adult Wayne, in a supporting last role, plays a legendary gunslinger afflicted with cancer who seeks peace and solace in his final days. Town bad guys Boone and O'Brian aren't about to let him rest and are determined to gun him down to avenge past deeds. One of Wayne's best and most dignified performances about living up to a personal code of honor. Stewart and Bacall head excellent supporting cast. Based on Glendon Swarthout's novel.

1976 100m/C John Wayne, Lauren Bacall, Ron Howard, James Stewart, Richard Boone, Hugh O'Brian, Bill McKinney, Harry (Henry) Morgan, John Carradine, Sheree North, Scatman Crothers; **D:** Donald Siegel; **M:** Elmer Bernstein. **Award Nominations:** Academy Awards '76: Best Art Direction/Set Decoration; **Awards:** National Board of Review Awards '76: 10 Best Films of the Year. **VHS, Beta, LV** *PAR, TLF*

Short Circuit 🎬🎬

PG/Jr. High-Adult Advanced robot designed for the military is hit by lightning and begins to think for itself. The tin man is taken in by a spacey animal lover (who amusingly mistakes it for an "E.T."-style alien), then hides from the meanies at the weapons lab who want their hardware back. Intrinsically kid-friendly premise was apparently designed for short attention spans; every-

thing happens at ultra- high speed, and characters are needlessly lewd and obnoxious.

BEWARE *Profanity and sex talk.*

1986 98m/C Steve Guttenberg, Ally Sheedy, Austin Pendleton, Fisher Stevens, Brian McNamara; **D:** John Badham; **W:** S.S. Wilson, Brent Maddock; **M:** David Shire. **VHS, Beta, LV** *FOX*

Short Circuit 2 🎬🎬🎬 ▷

PG/Jr. High-Adult Sequel to the adorable-robot tale is actually an improvement, with better pacing and funnier gags. The cheerful metal hero, Number Five, arrives in the city to visit old friends, draws the attention of a toy merchant and gang of jewel thieves. Cute stuff; even Stevens' lead human character, a caricatured ethnic stereotype, has been toned down from last time.

BEWARE *Robot roughhousing, salty language.*

1988 95m/C Fisher Stevens, Cynthia Gibb, Michael McKean, Jack Weston, David Hemblen; **D:** Kenneth Johnson; **W:** S.S. Wilson, Brent Maddock; **M:** Charles Fox. **VHS, Beta, LV** *COL*

A Shot in the Dark 🎬🎬🎬 ▷

Family Second and possibly the best in the classic "Inspector Clouseau-Pink Panther" series of comedies. The bumbling Inspector Clouseau (Sellers, of course) investigates the case of a parlor maid (Sommer) accused of murdering her lover. Clouseau's libido convinces him she's innocent, even though all the clues point to her. Classic gags, wonderful music. After this film, Sellers as Clouseau disappears until 1975's "Return of the Pink Panther" (Alan Arkin played him in "Inspector Clouseau," made in 1968 by different folks.)

BEWARE *Sex talk; roughhousing; alcohol use.*

1964 101m/C Peter Sellers, Elke Sommer, Herbert Lom, George Sanders, Bryan Forbes; **D:** Blake Edwards; **W:** William Peter Blatty, Blake Edwards; **M:** Henry Mancini. **VHS, Beta, LV** *FOX, FCT*

Shout 🎬🎬

PG-13/Jr. High-Adult In a sleepy Texas town during the 1950s, Jesse's rebel ways land him in a work farm for delinquent boys. Then a hip new teacher (Travolta) turns the restless kids on to the new poetry called rock 'n' roll. It's all been done before and better. Note the anachronistic dance styles and MTV music videos, 30 years before their time.

BEWARE *Salty language, implied teen sex, roughhousing.*

1991 93m/C John Travolta, James Walters, Heather Graham, Richard Jordan, Linda Fiorentino, Scott Coffey; **D:** Jeffrey Hornaday; **M:** Randy Edelman. **VHS, Beta, LV** *MCA*

Sidekicks 🎬🎬

PG/Family Cutesy vehicle for action star/executive producer Norris. Barry has bully problems at school and an ineffectual dad at home. Barry instead worships movie hero Norris, who appears as himself in a series of daydream martial-arts sequences. Plot eventually evolves into a "Karate Kid" clone, predictable and sappy. Directed by the star's brother.

BEWARE *Roughhousing.*

1993 100m/C Chuck Norris, Jonathan Brandis, Beau Bridges, Mako, Julia Nickson-Soul, Danica McKellar, Richard Moll, Joe Piscopo; **D:** Aaron Norris; **W:** Donald W. Thompson, Lou Illar; **M:** Alan Silvestri, David Shire. **VHS, LV, 8mm** *COL*

Sigmund & the Sea Monsters, Vol. 1

Family Oceanside pals Johnny and Scott befriend a tentacled sea monster who's been disowned by his grumpy family for his inability to scare humans. Live-action Sid & Marty Krofft Saturday-morning show distinguished by its weird costumes. Additional volumes available.

1973 46m/C Billy Barty, Johnny Whitaker, Mary Wickes, Rip Torn, Margaret Hamilton, Fran Ryan. **VHS, Beta** *NLC*

The Sign of Zorro 🎞️🎞️

Family Adventures of the masked swordsman as he champions the cause of the oppressed in early California. Full-length version of the popular late-50s Disney TV series.

1960 89m/C Guy Williams, Henry Calvin, Gene Sheldon, Romney Brent, Britt Lomond, George Lewis, Lisa Gaye; **D:** Norman Foster, Lewis R. Foster. **VHS, Beta** *DIS*

Silence of the North 🎞️🎞️🐾

PG/Jr. High-Adult Widow with three children struggles to survive under rugged pioneer conditions on the Canadian frontier. The scenery is, not surprisingly, stunning. Based on a true but generic story.

1981 94m/C Ellen Burstyn, Tom Skerritt; **D:** Allan Winton King; **M:** Michael Conway Baker. **VHS, Beta** *MCA*

Silent Movie 🎞️🎞️🐾

PG/Family Dull execution of a terrific idea: a silent movie made in modern times. But this Mel Brooks clunker is no "Modern Times." Brooks also stars as a has-been movie director trying to save his studio from being taken over by a conglomerate. Has music and sound effects, but only one word of spoken dialogue—by Marcel Marceau! Ages 9 and up.

1976 88m/C Mel Brooks, Marty Feldman, Dom DeLuise, Burt Reynolds, Anne Bancroft, James Caan, Liza Minnelli, Paul Newman, Sid Caesar, Bernadette Peters, Harry Ritz, Marcel Marceau; **D:** Mel Brooks; **W:** Mel Brooks, Ron Clark, Rudy DeLuca, Barry Levinson. **VHS, Beta, LV** *FOX*

The Silver Fox and Sam Davenport

Preschool-Primary Man and beast come to a mutual respect when a farmer rescues a fox and nurtures it back to health. A live-action tale from TV's "Wonderful World of Disney."

1990 47m/C VHS, Beta *MTI, DSN*

Silver Stallion 🎞️🐾

Family Awe-inspiring all-ages spectacle from Australia tells of Thara, a mighty horse destined to rule a herd of mountain 'brumbies' (cowboy slang for wild horses). As in the "Man From Snowy River" adventures, one cowboy won't rest until he's caught and tamed the king of the brumbies. But this time their duel is told through the animal's eyes, and the result is a nature drama both mystical and heroic, combining "The Black Stallion" with "Prancer" but outdoing them both. Based on stories by Down Under author Elyne Mitchell, and taking place largely in the mind of her onscreen daughter, who checks the manuscript as mum types the tale of Thara and realizes it's more than fiction. Never got the major release on big theater screens a film this visionary deserves, but a must-see on video anyway.

BEWARE *Horse violence.*

1941 59m/C David Sharpe, Carol Hughes, Leroy Mason, Walter Long; **D:** Edward Finney. **VHS, Beta** *VYY, GPV*

The Silver Stallion: King of the Wild Brumbies 🎞️🎞️🐾

G/Family Adolescent Indi is enthralled as her writer-mother relates each new chapter in the saga of Thara, the amazing silver stallion. And she imagines each adventure as the horse triumphs over evil men, other horses, and the elements to become leader of the herd. Based on the Australian children's novel "The Silver Brumby" by Elyne Mitchell.

1994 93m/C Caroline Goodall, Ami Daemion, Russell Crowe; **D:** John Tatoulis; **W:** John Tatoulis, Jon Stephens; **M:** Tassos Ioannides. **VHS, Beta** *PAR*

The Silver Streak 🎞️🎞️🎞️

PG/Jr. High-Adult Pooped exec Wilder rides a train from L.A. to Chicago, planning to enjoy a leisurely, relaxing trip. Instead he becomes involved with murder, intrigue, and a beautiful woman. Energetic Hitchcock parody features successful first pairing of Wilder and Pryor.

1976 113m/C Gene Wilder, Richard Pryor, Jill Clayburgh, Patrick McGoohan, Ned Beatty, Ray Walston, Richard Kiel, Scatman Crothers; **D:** Arthur Hiller; **W:** Colin Higgins; **M:** Henry Mancini. **VHS, Beta, LV** *FOX*

Silverado 🎞️🎞️🎞️

PG-13/Jr. High-Adult Straightforward plot has four virtuous cowboys rise up against a crooked lawman in a blaze of six guns. Affectionate pastiche of western cliches is not subtle, with the meter running on deep background pieces that explain why our heroes came to be. But it's plenty of fun, with good clean frontier violence (shootings, knifings, etc.) and characters who have populated every western ever made. Laserdisc edition features a wide screen film-to-tape transfer monitored by the photography director, set photos, release trailers, and other publicity hoohah as well as a special time-lapse sequence of the set construction, and interviews with the stars and director Kasdan. Letterboxed laserdisc version is available with Dolby SurroundSound.

> 🔔 BEWARE 🔔 *Cowboy violence (lots of shootings and killings) and profanity.*

1985 132m/C Kevin Kline, Scott Glenn, Kevin Costner, Danny Glover, Brian Dennehy, Linda Hunt, John Cleese, Jeff Goldblum, Rosanna Arquette, Jeff Fahey; **D:** Lawrence Kasdan; **W:** Lawrence Kasdan; **M:** Bruce Broughton. **VHS, Beta, LV** *COL, CRC*

Silverhawks: Sky Shadows

Preschool-Primary Cartoon sci-fi series about law-enforcement officers on distant planets. The cyborg Silverhawks, under the command of Commander Stargazer, fight a continuing battle with the forces of Mon Star, Intergalactic Public Enemy 1. Not surprisingly, there was a toy-product tie-in. Additional volumes available.

1986 30m/C VHS, Beta *ORI*

Silverhawks: The Original Story

Preschool-Primary Full-length "debut film" (actually cobbled together from episodes of the series) delineating the first adventure of the part-metal, part-human, all-toy-promoting superheroes in the year 2839. A Rankin-Bass production.

1986 101m/C VHS, Beta *ORI, WAR*

Simon 🗡️🗡️ᵛ

PG/Jr. High-Adult Bored demented scientists looking for something to do brainwash a college professor, convincing him he's an alien from a distant galaxy. Whereupon he begins trying to correct the evil in America. Screwball comedy, or semi-serious satire of some kind? Hard to tell. Some terrific set pieces but as a whole it doesn't quite hold together. Directorial debut of Brickman, who previously worked as a scriptwriter with Woody Allen ("Sleeper," etc.).

1980 97m/C Alan Arkin, Madeline Kahn, Fred Gwynne, Adolph Green, Wallace Shawn, Austin Pendleton; **D:** Marshall Brickman; **W:** Marshall Brickman. **VHS, Beta** *WAR*

A Simple Twist of Fate 🗡️🗡️ᵛ

PG-13/Jr. High-Adult Comedy drama gives Martin chance to get serious with this update of George Eliot's "Silas Marner." He plays small-town cabinetmaker Michael McMann who adopts a little girl who enters his house when her mother dies outside. Eventually the girl's biological father (Byrne), a rich politician, enters the picture. McMann fights to keep his daughter Mathilda (played by adorable twins). Cuddly dad is hardly Martin's image (in spite of "Parenthood"), though strong cast limits the sugar. Slow-moving film sounds better than it is.

> 🔔 BEWARE 🔔 *A ·woman injects heroin and is frozen in a snowstorm; a lot of talk about sex and adultery.*

1994 106m/C Steve Martin, Gabriel Byrne, Catherine O'Hara, Stephen Baldwin, Alana Austin, Alyssa Austin, Laura Linney, Anne

Heche, Michael Des Barres, Byron Jennings; **D:** Gilles Mackinnon; **W:** Steve Martin; **M:** Cliff Eidelman. **VHS, LV** *TOU*

The Simpsons Christmas Special

Family The only episode of TV's hilarious, infamous "Simpsons" clan on video is one of the earliest, a holiday segment in which Bart gets a tattoo, Homer works as a mall Santa, and the unruly household gets the Christmas spirit thanks to the dog they adopt. Devotees of the series will have fun noting the changes made since this aired; mother Marge was subsequently written a lot smarter, dad Homer dumber.

1989 30m/C V: Dan Castellaneta, Julie Kavner, Harry Shearer, Maggie Roswell, Nancy Cartwright, Yeardley Smith. **VHS** *FXV*

Sinbad and the Eye of the Tiger 🗡️🗡️🗡️

G/Family Sinbad the Sailor voyages to the Polar regions to restore a prince transformed into a baboon, In pursuit is an evil sorceress, but as in every one of the these Sinbad adventures, the baddies' have a real quality control problem with those black magic spells. Forgive the clumsy opening and closing, and you'll be left with a fine, quite underrated adventure in the Sinbad series that showcased Ray Harryhausen's special effects skills.

> 🔔 BEWARE 🔔 *Violence, very brief nudity as a curious cave giant (who turns out to be a good guy) catches two girls bathing.*

1977 113m/C Patrick Wayne, Jane Seymour, Taryn Power, Margaret Whiting; **D:** Sam Wanamaker; **W:** Beverley Cross. **VHS, Beta, LV** *COL, CCB*

Sinbad the Sailor 🗡️🗡️🗡️

Family Old-style Hollywood retelling of Sinbad's eighth voyage—a joke, since the sailor of lore made only seven. Fans of the Ray Harryhausen fantasies will be disappointed, because this one has no magic or special effects, just Sinbad, a princess, and villains trying to outsmart each other over the location of a treasure isle. You can easily imagine crooks going through the same routine over the Maltese Falcon, though Fairbanks has one great swashbuckling chase/fight sequence through a palace.

> 🔔 BEWARE 🔔 *Violence.*

1947 117m/C Douglas Fairbanks Jr., Maureen O'Hara, Anthony Quinn, Walter Slezak, George Tobias, Jane Greer, Mike Mazurki, Sheldon Leonard; **D:** Richard Wallace. **VHS, Beta, LV** *MED, TTC*

Since You Went Away 🗡️🗡️🗡️ᵛ

Jr. High-Adult American family copes with the tragedy, heartache and shortages of wartime in classic megatribute to the home front. Be warned: very long and bring your hankies. Colbert is superb, as is the photography. John Derek unobtrusively made his film debut as an extra.

1944 172m/B Claudette Colbert, Jennifer Jones, Shirley Temple, Joseph Cotten, Agnes Moorehead, Monty Woolley, Guy Madison, Lionel Barrymore, Robert Walker, Hattie McDaniel, Keenan Wynn, Craig Stevens, Albert Basserman, Alla Nazimova, Lloyd Corrigan, Terry Moore, Florence Bates, Ruth Roman, Andrew V. McLaglen, Dorothy Dandridge, Rhonda Fleming; *D:* John Cromwell; *W:* David O. Selznick; *M:* Max Steiner. **Award Nominations:** Academy Awards '43: Best Supporting Actress (Jones); Academy Awards '44: Best Actress (Colbert), Best Black and White Cinematography, Best Film Editing, Best Interior Decoration, Best Picture, Best Supporting Actor (Woolley); **Awards:** Academy Awards '44: Best Score. **VHS, Beta, LV** *FOX*

Sing 🦴 ♭

PG-13/Jr. High-Adult The students in a Brooklyn public school endure the trials of adolescence while putting together a musical revue. Goes from the doubtful to the preposterous, with way too much cheesy music. From the creator of "Fame" and "Footloose."

⚠ BEWARE ⚠ *Profanity, mature themes.*

1989 111m/C Lorraine Bracco, Peter Dobson, Jessica Steen, Louise Lasser, George DiCenzo, Patti LaBelle; *D:* Richard Baskin; *M:* Jay Gruska. **VHS, Beta, LV** *COL*

Sing Along with Little Lulu

Family Vintage Little Lulu comic-book character stars in a special song-filled collection of her nostalgic cartoons.
1983 86m/C VHS *REP*

Singin' in the Rain 🦴🦴🦴🦴

Family One of the all-time great movie musicals—an affectionate spoof of the turmoil that afflicted the motion picture industry in the late 1920s during the changeover from silent films to sound. Co-director Kelly and Hagen lead a glorious cast. Music and lyrics by Arthur Freed and Nacio Herb Brown. Served as basis of story by Betty Comden and Adolph Green. Also available on laserdisc with the original trailer, outtakes, behind the scenes footage, and commentary by film historian Ronald Haver. Later a Broadway musical. 🎵 All I Do is Dream of You; Should I?; Singin' in the Rain; Wedding of the Painted Doll; Broadway Melody; Would You; I've Got a Feelin' You're Foolin'; You Are My Lucky Star; Broadway Rhythm.

1952 103m/C Gene Kelly, Donald O'Connor, Jean Hagen, Debbie Reynolds, Rita Moreno, King Donovan, Millard Mitchell, Cyd Charisse, Douglas Fowley, Madge Blake, Joi Lansing; *D:* Gene Kelly, Stanley Donen; *W:* Adolph Green, Betty Comden. **Award Nominations:** Academy Awards '52: Best Supporting Actress (Hagen), Best Original Score; **Awards:** Golden Globe Awards '53: Best Actor—Musical/Comedy (O'Connor); National Board of Review Awards '52: 10 Best Films of the Year. **VHS, Beta, LV** *MGM, TLF, CRC*

Singles 🦴🦴🦴

PG-13/Sr. High-Adult Seattle's music scene is the background for this lighthearted look at single twentysomethings in the '90s. Hits dead on thanks to Crowe's tight script and a talented cast, and speaks straight to its intended audience those fine young folks of the "Generation X" crowd. Real life band Pearl Jam portrays alternative band Citizen Dick (that's acting!) and

If you like *Singin' in the Rain* (1952), you'll love:

Anchors Aweigh (1945)

Babes in Arms (1939)

The Band Wagon (1953)

Dirty Dancing (1987)

Fame (1980)

Flashdance (1983)

Footloose (1984)

George Balanchine's The Nutcracker (1993)

Grease (1978)

The Red Shoes (1948)

Seven Brides for Seven Brothers (1954)

Shag: The Movie (1989)

Strictly Ballroom (1992)

Swing Kids (1993)

That's Dancing! (1985)

Yankee Doodle Dandy (1942)

sets the tone for a great soundtrack featuring the hot Seattle sounds of Alice in Chains, Soundgarden, and Mudhoney. The video contains six extra minutes of footage after the credits that was thankfully edited out of the final cut. Look for Horton, Stoltz (as a mime), Skerritt, and Burton in cameos.

⚠ BEWARE ⚠ *Profanity, suggested sex and drinking in bars based in the Seattle singles' scene. A character believes she's pregnant.*

1992 100m/C Matt Dillon, Bridget Fonda, Campbell Scott, Kyra Sedgwick, Sheila Kelley, Jim True, Bill Pullman, James LeGros, Ally Walker, Devon Raymond, Camillo Gallardo, Jeremy Piven; *Cameos:* Tom Skerritt, Peter Horton, Eric Stoltz, Tim Burton; *D:* Cameron Crowe; *W:* Cameron Crowe; *M:* Paul Westerberg. **VHS, Beta, LV** *WAR, PMS*

Sioux City 🦴🦴 ♭

PG-13/Jr. High-Adult Jesse Rainfeather Goldman (Phillips) is a Lakota Sioux adopted away from the reservation of his birth and raised in Beverly Hills by a Jewish family. Jesse's curious when his birth mother suddenly contacts him, but when he arrives at the Sioux reservation, he discovers she's suddenly died under mysterious circumstances. So Jesse sticks around to find out what's going on and discovers his heritage along the way. Well-meaning but dull.

BEWARE *Jesse is brutally beaten and left for dead. Mature issues about adoption.*

1994 102m/C Lou Diamond Phillips, Salli Richardson, Melinda Dillon, Ralph Waite, Adam Roarke, Bill Allen, Gary Farmer; **D:** Lou Diamond Phillips; **W:** L. Virginia Browne; **M:** Christopher Lindsey. **VHS** *CAF*

Sir Prancelot

Preschool-Jr. High Cartoon compilation about a medieval inventor and his wife, two children, butler, and others out to find adventure.

1970 94m/C VHS

Sister Act 🎵🎵🎵 ♭

PG/Jr. High-Adult Disney/Touchstone box office hit casts Goldberg as Deloris, a loose-living lounge singer who witnesses a mob murder and hides out in a convent where she's restless in a habit. Much to the dismay of the straightlaced Mother Superior, Deloris takes over the rag-tag choir and molds them into a swinging, religious version of a '60s girls group, singing "My God" to the tune of "My Guy." Predictable in the extreme, but sweet-natured and likeable.

BEWARE *Sex talk, comic violence and nuns in a bar.*

1992 100m/C Whoopi Goldberg, Maggie Smith, Harvey Keitel, Bill Nunn, Kathy Najimy, Wendy Makkena, Mary Wickes, Robert Miranda, Richard Portnow, Joseph Maher; **D:** Emile Ardolino; **W:** Joseph Howard; **M:** Marc Shaiman. **VHS, Beta, LV** *TOU, PMS*

Sister Act 2: Back in the Habit 🎵🎵

PG/Jr. High-Adult Her old convent friends convince Vegas singer Deloris to resume her nun identity to help bring order to a rough San Francisco parochial school. Even among lame excuses for sequels that's a weak one, but the movie improves when Deloris decides to revive the school's once-champion choir, and enters the kids in the World Series equivalent for gospel music. Forget the plot and turn up the soundtrack; Whoopi's opening medley is a hoot.

1993 107m/C Whoopi Goldberg, Kathy Najimy, James Coburn, Maggie Smith, Wendy Makkena, Barnard Hughes, Mary Wickes, Sheryl Lee Ralph, Michael Jeter, Robert Pastorelli, Thomas Gottschalk, Lauryn Hill, Brad Sullivan; **D:** Bill Duke; **W:** James Orr, Jim Cruickshank, Judi Ann Mason; **M:** Miles Goodman. **VHS, LV** *TOU*

Six Pack 🎵 ♭

PG/Jr. High-Adult Country-singer Rogers, in his theatrical debut, stars as Brewster Baker, a former stock car driver. When he finds six larcenous (and foulmouthed)

orphan kids trying to strip his car. Nevertheless, he becomes their pal and guardian, and they support his return to the racing circuit. A reminder of why it's bad to put sugar in a gas tank.

BEWARE *Profanity, sex talk.*

1982 108m/C Kenny Rogers, Diane Lane, Erin Gray, Barry Corbin, Anthony Michael Hall; **D:** Daniel Petrie; **M:** Charles Fox. **VHS, Beta** *FOX*

Six Weeks 🎵🎵

PG/Jr. High-Adult Young girl dying of leukemia brings together her work-driven mother and an aspiring married politician. Manipulative hanky-wringer has good acting from both Moores but oddly little substance.

BEWARE *Terminal illness. Tear jerker—at least three to four tissues.*

1982 107m/C Dudley Moore, Mary Tyler Moore, Katherine Healy; **D:** Tony Bill; **M:** Dudley Moore. **VHS, Beta, LV** *COL*

Sixteen Candles 🎵🎵🎵

PG/Jr. High-Adult Hughes, in his feature directing debut, gathers his stable of young stars again for one of his best films. Every girl's sixteenth birthday is supposed to be special, but in the rush of her sister's wedding nobody remembers Samantha's—and she had hoped the event would bring her together with the guy of her dreams. Instead a weirdo adolescent named Geek comes calling as part of a bet. Ringwald and Hall are especially charming in this humorous look at teenage traumas. Title song performed by The Stray Cats.

BEWARE *Profanity, sex talk, goofy Asian-American character, alcohol use and brief nudity. Teens have a huge party with lots of drinking.*

1984 93m/C Molly Ringwald, Justin Henry, Michael Schoeffling, Haviland Morris, Gedde Watanabe, Anthony Michael Hall, Paul Dooley, Carlin Glynn, Blanche Baker, Edward Andrews, Carole Cook, Max Casey Adams Showalter, Liane Curtis, John Cusack, Joan Cusack, Brian Doyle-Murray, Jami Gertz, Cinnamon Idles, Zelda Rubinstein; **D:** John Hughes; **W:** John Hughes; **M:** Ira Newborn. **VHS, Beta, LV** *MCA*

The Skateboard Kid WOOF!

PG/Jr. High-Adult Awful amalgam of two earlier lousy kid flicks, "The Dirt Bike Kid" and "Munchie," from the same filmmakers. When bullying bad guys break Jack's skateboard, the kid finds a magical replacement that can talk and fly (lousy f/x). Now the villains are in for it! And so are the viewers.

1993 90m/C Bess Armstrong, Timothy Busfield; **D:** Larry Swerdlove; **W:** Roger Corman; **V:** Dom DeLuise. **VHS** *NHO*

Skeezer 🎵🎵 ♭

Family Stray dog becomes a key factor in a sympathetic doctor's efforts to communicate with emotionally unstable children. Based on a true story, recounted in the book "Skeezer: Dog with a Mission" by Elizabeth Yates. Quality done-for-TV family fare, but don't be misled; emphasis is on the therapy rather than the mutt, making this nearer to "The Miracle Worker" than "Lassie."

 Roughhousing.

1982 100m/C Karen Valentine, Dee Wallace Stone, Tom Atkins, Mariclare Costello, Leighton Greer, Justine Lord; ***D:*** Peter Hunt. **VHS** *LIV*

Skeleton Warriors

Primary-Jr. High Another Saturday morning cartoon pits good guys against grotesque bad guys somewhere in the future. Ugh. Additional volumes available. Ages 6 to 10.

1995 30m/C VHS *BMG*

Ski Patrol ♫♫

PG/Jr. High-Adult Wacky ski groupies try to stop an evil developer. Good ski action in a surprisingly plotful effort from the crazy crew that brought the world "Police Academy."

 Profanity and sex talk.

1989 85m/C Roger Rose, Yvette Nipar, T.K. Carter, Leslie Jordan, Ray Walston, Martin Mull; ***D:*** Richard Correll. **VHS, Beta, LV** *COL*

Skylark ♫♫ ♭

G/Family In a sequel to television's hugely successful "Sarah, Plain and Tall," the whole Kansas crew returns for more of their little-farm-on-the-prairie life. After two years in America's squarest state, mail-order bride Sarah loves Jacob but not the scenery and still yearns for the lush greenery of Maine. When drought and fire threaten the farm, Jacob sends the family back east for their safety. Close's "tough Yankee" expression grows a bit tiresome in a plot that's a tad predictable, yet the simplistic charm and nostalgia work to propel this quality production.

1993 98m/C Glenn Close, Christopher Walken, Lexi Randall, Christopher Bell, Tresa Hughes, Lois Smith, Lee Richardson, Elizabeth Wilson, Margaret Sophie Stein, Jon DeVries, James Rebhorn, Woody Watson, Lois Smith; ***D:*** Joseph Sargent; ***W:*** Patricia MacLachlan. **VHS** *REP, BTV*

Slam Dunk Ernest ♫ ♭

PG-13/Jr. High-Adult Ernest (Varney) becomes a basketball star in a city league exhibition game when the Basketball Angel (Abdul-Jabbar) loans him his magic shoes. Really. The question is how many more of these Ernest films must we endure???

 Mild language and stupid Ernest tricks.

1995 93m/C Jim Varney, Kareem Abdul-Jabbar, Joy Brazeau; ***D:*** John R. Cherry III; ***W:*** Daniel Butler, John R. Cherry III; ***M:*** Mark Adler. **VHS, LV** *TOU*

Sleeper ♫♫♫ ♭

PG/Jr. High-Adult Hapless nerd Allen is revived two hundred years after an operation gone bad. Keaton por-

trays Allen's love interest in a futuristic land of robots and giant vegetables. He learns of the hitherto unknown health benefits of hot fudge sundaes; discovers the truth about the nation's dictator, known as The Leader; and gets involved with revolutionaries seeking to overthrow the government. Hilarious, fast-moving comedy, full of slapstick and satire. Don't miss the "orgasmatron."

 Sex talk. Awakened Allen cites the number of years he's gone without sex, adds a few to allow for his marriage.

1973 88m/C Woody Allen, Diane Keaton, John Beck, Howard Cosell; ***D:*** Woody Allen; ***W:*** Woody Allen, Marshall Brickman; ***M:*** Woody Allen. **VHS, Beta, LV** *MGM, FOX, FUS*

Sleeping Beauty ♫♫♫

G/Family Lavish Walt Disney cartoon feature wasn't just supposed to be any old 'toon; Walt himself promoted it as the most expensive and spectacular animated epic ever, about the handsome prince who must revive the enchanted princess and her frozen realm with a kiss. But the thin storyline and characters hold this back from being top-ranked. Still, the fiery climax doesn't Mickey Mouse around—the battle with Maleficent, the witch-turned-dragon, is one of those sequences that puts the magic into the Magic Kingdom.

 The demonic Maleficent rates as one of the scariest Disney villains of all time, without even the saving grace of humor.

1959 75m/C D: Clyde Geronomi, Eric Larson, Wolfgang Reitherman, Les Clark. **VHS, Beta, LV** *DIS, OM*

Sleeping Beauty

Family Bernadette Peters is the princess put to sleep by a jealous fairy. Christopher Reeve is the handsome prince. Both are a treat, as is Carol Kane as a good fairy. One of the best "Faerie Tale Theatre" episodes. Ages 5 to 12.

1983 60m/C Christopher Reeve, Bernadette Peters, Beverly D'Angelo. **VHS, Beta, LV** *FOX, FCT, WKV*

Sleeping Beauty ♫ ♭

Family "Cannon Movie Tales" treatment of the Grimm story features Baker, the dwarf actor inside R2D2 in "Star Wars," as a magic little man whose spell allows a childless Queen to bear a daughter at last. But a wicked witch curses the girl with a deep sleep, and only a handsome prince can revive her. Cannon's typically forgettable songs and dances curse the movie with its own brand of somnolence.

1989 92m/C Tahnee Welch, Morgan Fairchild, Nicholas Clay, Sylvia Miles, Kenny Baker. **VHS** *MGM, PSM, CVC*

Sleepless in Seattle ♫♫♫ ♭

PG/Jr. High-Adult Witty, sweet romantic comedy explores the differences between men and women when it comes to love and romance. When widower Hanks talks about his wife on a national talk show, recently engaged Ryan responds. Writer/director Ephron's humorous

Molly Ringwald finally gets her birthday wish in "Sixteen Candles."

screenplay is brought to life by a perfectly cast ensemble; it also breathed new life into the classic weepie "An Affair to Remember," comparing it to "The Dirty Dozen" in an unforgettable scene. Full of fine detail, from Sven Nykvist's camera work to the graphic layout of the opening credits to the great score. Captured millions at the box office, coming in as the fourth highest grossing movie of 1993.

BEWARE *Sex talk and mild profanity.*

1993 105m/C Tom Hanks, Meg Ryan, Bill Pullman, Ross Malinger, Rosie O'Donnell, Gaby Hoffman, Victor Garber, Rita Wilson, Barbara Garrick, Carey Lowell, Rob Reiner, Sarah Trigger; **D:** Nora Ephron; **W:** Jeffrey Arch, Larry Atlas, David S. Ward, Nora Ephron; **M:** Marc Shaiman. **VHS, LV, 8mm** *COL, BTV, FCT*

Sleuth ♫♫♫ ♭

PG/Jr. High-Adult A mystery novelist and his wife's lover face off in ever shifting, elaborate, and diabolical plots against each other, complete with red herrings, traps, and tricks. Playful, cerebral mystery thriller from top director Mankiewicz. Schaeffer also scripted "Frenzy" for Hitchcock, from his play.

1972 138m/C Laurence Olivier, Michael Caine; **D:** Joseph L. Mankiewicz; **W:** Anthony Shaffer; **M:** John Addison. **Award Nominations:** Academy Awards '72: Best Actor (Caine), Best Actor (Olivier),

Best Director (Mankiewicz), Best Original Score; **Awards:** Edgar Allan Poe Awards '72: Best Screenplay. **VHS, Beta, LV** *MED, HMV, VTR*

Slimey's World Games

Preschool-Primary Just in time for the Olympics, Sesame Street's Slimey the worm competes in the summer games (for worms, that is). Fans of Sesame Street will love watching the little worm compete and learn some lessons along the way. Activity book included.

1996 30m/C VHS

Small Change ♫♫♫♫

PG/Jr. High-Adult Sweet, nearly plotless record of a school year in a French town where students and instructors live virtually side-by-side in quaint tenements and courtyards. The mischief-prone kids disrupt class, tumble from windows, find first love, and assist their favorite teacher when he becomes a father himself. Ends with the news that one youngster is abused at home (sadly, not the shock today that it was back in 1976) and a direct plea for children's rights. A realistic and tender testament to the great director's belief in childhood as a "state of grace." Original title: "L'Argent de Poche"; on tape in French with English subtitles.

1976 104m/C Geory Desmouceaux, Philippe Goldman, Jean-Francois Stevenin, Chantal Mercier, Claudio Deluca, Frank Deluca, Richard Golfier, Laurent Devlaeminck, Francis Devlaeminck; **D:** Francois Truffaut; **W:** Suzanne Schiffman. **VHS, Beta, LV** *MGM, FCT, INJ*

The Small One

Family Poor boy must sell his beloved donkey, "Small One," on the eve of the first Christmas in Bethlehem. Holiday cartoon short from Disney.

1980 25m/C VHS, Beta *DIS, MTI, DSN*

Smart Alecks 🦴 ◌

Jr. High-Adult The Bowery Boys get involved with gangsters when Jordan helps capture a crook. The usual wise-cracking from Hall and Gorcey helps keep things moving.

1942 88m/B Leo Gorcey, Huntz Hall, Gabriel Dell, Gale Storm, Roger Pryor Jr., Walter Woolf King, Herbert Rawlinson, Joe Kirk, Marie Windsor; **D:** Wallace Fox. **VHS** *NOS*

Smile 🦴🦴🦴

PG/Jr. High-Adult Barbed, merciless send-up of small-town America focusing on a group of naive California girls who compete for the "Young American Miss" crown amid rampant commercialism, exploitation and pure middle-class idiocy. Hilarious neglected '70s-style satire. Early role for Griffith.

1975 113m/C Bruce Dern, Barbara Feldon, Michael Kidd, Nicholas Pryor, Geoffrey Lewis, Colleen Camp, Joan Prather, Annette O'Toole, Melanie Griffith, Denise Nickerson; **D:** Michael Ritchie; **W:** Jerry Belson. **VHS, Beta, LV** *MGM*

Smile for Auntie and Other Stories

Preschool-Primary Compilation of animated shorts based on famous children's stories, including the award-winning title segment, plus "Make Way for Ducklings," "The Snowy Day," and "Wynken, Blynken, and Nod." Volume III of the "Children's Circle" series from Weston Woods Studios.

1979 26m/C VHS, Beta *CCC, WKV, BTV*

Smith! 🦴🦴

G/Family Disney picture with a social conscience gets points for trying, but Davy Crockett enthusiastically killing off swarms of 'those red hornets' looms taller in the mind than this treatise on the sad circumstances of modern Indians. Headstrong rancher Smith takes the side of a native American accused of murdering a storekeeper, and it all boils down to courtroom drama. Based on Paul St. Pierre's novel "Breaking Smith's Quarter Horse."

1969 101m/C Glenn Ford, Frank Ramirez, Keenan Wynn; **D:** Michael O'Herlihy. **VHS, Beta** *DIS*

Smoke 🦴🦴 ◌

Family A young boy nurses a lost German shepherd back to health with the help of his new stepfather, whom he learns to trust. Then he runs away with the dog when the original owners show up. Made for television Disney fare starring Opie/Richie (and later successful director) Howard.

1970 89m/C Earl Holliman, Ron Howard, Andy Devine; **D:** Vincent McEveety. **VHS, Beta** *DIS*

Smokey and the Bandit 🦴🦴 ◌

PG/Jr. High-Adult If you don't know how to end a movie, you call for a car chase. The first and best of the horrible series about bootlegger Reynolds is one long car chase. Reynolds makes a wager that he can have a truck load of Coors beer-once unavailable east of Texas—delivered to Atlanta from Texas in 28 hours. Gleason is the "smokey" who tries to stop him. Field is the hitchhiker Reynolds picks up along the way. Great stunts; director Needham was a top stunt man.

1977 96m/C Burt Reynolds, Sally Field, Jackie Gleason, Jerry Reed, Mike Henry, Paul Williams, Pat McCormick; **D:** Hal Needham; **W:** Charles Shyer. **VHS, Beta, LV** *MCA*

Smokey and the Bandit, Part 2 🦴

PG/Jr. High-Adult Pathetic sequel to "Smokey and the Bandit" proved a box-office winner, grossing $40 million. The Bandit is hired to transport a pregnant elephant from Miami to the Republican convention in Dallas. Sheriff Buford T. Justice and family are in hot pursuit.

1980 101m/C Burt Reynolds, Sally Field, Jackie Gleason, Jerry Reed, Mike Henry, Dom DeLuise, Pat McCormick, Paul Williams; **D:** Hal Needham; **W:** Jerry Belson, Michael Kane. **VHS, Beta, LV** *MCA*

Smokey and the Bandit, Part 3 🦴

PG/Jr. High-Adult You thought the second one was bad? Another mega car chase, this time sans Reynolds and director Needham.

1983 88m/C Burt Reynolds, Jackie Gleason, Jerry Reed, Paul Williams, Pat McCormick, Mike Henry, Colleen Camp; **D:** Dick Lowry. **VHS, Beta, LV** *MCA*

Smokey the Bear: Founder's Day Folly

Preschool-Jr. High Episode from a Rankin-Bass TV cartoon show starring the furry mascot of the National Forest Fires Commission. Less strident in its environmental themes than later Saturday-morning fare.

1969 30m/C VHS

Smokey the Bear: Silliest Show on Earth

Preschool-Primary Smokey and friends have fun and occasionally teach the importance of wildlife and preventing forest fires.
1969 30m/C VHS

A Smoky Mountain Christmas 🎵🎵

Family Dolly gets away from it all in a secluded cabin that has been appropriated by a gang of orphans, and sings a half dozen songs. Innocuous seasonal country fun.
1986 94m/C Dolly Parton, Bo Hopkins, Dan Hedaya, Gennie James, David Ackroyd, Rene Auberjonois, John Ritter, Anita Morris, Lee Majors; **D:** Henry Winkler; **W:** Dolly Parton. **VHS, Beta** *FOX*

Smooth Talk 🎵🎵🎵

PG-13/Jr. High-Adult Flirtatious teenager Connie is determined to lose both her virginity and her mother's tight reins on her. A shady, possibly dangerous man looks like he may have the solution to at least one of her problems. Disturbing and thought-provoking maturity saga, with Dern giving a brilliant performance as the sheltered girl. Based on the Joyce Carol Oates story.

BEWARE *Profanity, alcohol use, mature themes. Frequent sex talk leads to more serious stuff offscreen.*
1985 92m/C Laura Dern, Treat Williams, Mary Kay Place, Levon Helm; **D:** Joyce Chopra. **VHS, Beta, LV** *LIV, VES*

Smurfs

Preschool-Primary These blue-hued forest-dwelling dwarfs started out as Disney-esque Belgian comic-strip characters (called 'Schtroumpfs, in Flemish) in the 1950s; only belatedly did American TV stumble across them, and Hanna-Barbera's first Smurf cartoon was a Saturday-morning ratings smash. Two volumes are available here, each containing six episodes per tape.
1984 90m/C VHS, Beta *TTC*

Smurfs & the Magic Flute 🎵🎵

G/Family The Smurfs, longtime Belgian comic-strip characters (known across the Atlantic as 'Schtroumpfs' by the way) were imported and mass-marketed in the U.S. as toys, as a Hanna-Barbera TV series, and as this mediocre feature cartoon, a musical tale about a flute with the magic power to make any listener dance.
1981 72m/C D: Jose Dutillieu, Jon Rust. **VHS, Beta, LV** *VTR*

The Snapper 🎵🎵🎵 ᵇ

R/Sr. High-Adult Originally made for BBC television, Frears creates a small comic gem based on the second novel of Doyle's Barrytown trilogy. Set in Dublin, 20-year-old Sharon Curley (Kellegher) finds herself unexpectedly pregnant and refuses to name the father. Family and friends are understanding—until they discover the man's identity. Affecting performances, particularly from Meany as Sharon's dad who takes a much greater interest in the birth of his grandchild than he ever did with his own children. Cheerful semi-sequel to "The Commitments" serves up domestic upheavals graced with humor and a strong sense of family loyalty.

BEWARE *Syntactically correct Irish profanity; sexual situations; alcohol use.*
1993 95m/C Tina Kellegher, Colm Meaney, Ruth McCabe, Colm O'Byrne, Pat Laffan, Eanna MacLiam, Ciara Duffy; **D:** Stephen Frears; **W:** Roddy Doyle. **VHS, LV** *TOU*

Sneakers 🎵🎵 ᵇ

PG-13/Jr. High-Adult Nearly competent thriller about five computer hackers with questionable pasts and an equally questionable government job. Of course, nothing is as it seems. Rather slow-going considering the talents and suspense involved and wildly off the map as to plausibility, but otherwise nearly entertaining. Aykroyd's handyman is a pleasant little gem.

BEWARE *Violence and profanity.*
1992 125m/C Robert Redford, Sidney Poitier, River Phoenix, Dan Aykroyd, Ben Kingsley, David Strathairn, Mary McDonnell, Timothy Busfield, George Hearn, Eddie Jones, James Earl Jones, Stephen Tobolowsky; **D:** Phil Alden Robinson; **W:** Lawrence Lasker, Walter F. Parkes, Phil Alden Robinson; **M:** James Horner, Branford Marsalis. **VHS, Beta, LV** *MCA, PMS*

The Sneetches from Dr. Seuss on the Loose

Primary Sneetches are Sneetches. Star-Belly Sneetches are no better or worse than Plain-Belly Sneetches, and Sylvester McMorkey, McBean's mechanical machine, helps to prove this point.
1974 14m/C VHS, Beta *BFA*

Sniffles Bells the Cat

Family Sniffles the Mouse (who never did quite catch on) stars in three of his classic Warner Brothers cartoons of the '40s.
1944 32m/C VHS, Beta *MGM*

Snoopy, Come Home 🎵🎵🎵

G/Family Snoopy leaves Charlie Brown to visit his former owner Lila in the hospital and returns with her to her apartment house. Will the Chaplinesque beagle ever return to the hapless boy? That question generates a bit more pathos than usual in this theatrical edition of Charles Schultz's popular comic strip "Peanuts." Director Bill Melendez also did the vocals for Snoopy's distinctive high-pitched barks and guffaws.
1972 80m/C D: Bill Melendez; **W:** Charles M. Schulz. **VHS, Beta, LV** *FOX*

Snoopy: The Musical

Family Clever revue features Peanuts characters in songs and skits; much like "You're a Good Man, Charlie Brown." Ages 5 and up.
1995 50m/C VHS *PAR*

Snorks

Preschool-Primary These snorkel-headed underwater creatures first came to prominence as a Belgian comic book, so it was only natural that when their countrymen, the Smurfs, made it big in America the Hanna-Barbera folks would import these for the standard Saturday-morning treatment too. Volume one and volume two are available and contain eight episodes per tape.
1984 90m/C VHS, Beta *TTC*

The Snow Queen

Family The "Faerie Tale Theatre" adaptation of a Hans Christian Andersen tale, narrated by producer Shelley Duvall. A boy and girl who grow up together are separated by evil when the boy is held captive in the icy palace of the Snow Queen (Lee Remick). The girl sets out to rescue him. It isn't easy. A fine story of courage and true friendship. Ages 6 to 11.
1983 60m/C Lauren Hutton, Linda Manz, David Hemmings, Melissa Gilbert, Lee Remick, Lance Kerwin; *D:* Peter Medak. **VHS, Beta** *FOX, FCT*

The Snow Queen

Preschool-Primary US-Russian animated version of the Hans Christian Andersen tale about Gerda, off to rescue her friend, Kay, from the icy grip of the Snow Queen. Story of friendship, courage and loyalty, but dark and brooding. Ages 8 to 12.
1992 30m/C VHS *MVD, BMG, PMS*

Snow Treasure 🎵🎵

G/Family With the help of an underground agent, Norwegian children smuggle gold out of the country right under the noses of the Nazis. Stiff and not terribly interesting international production. Based on the book by Marie McSwigan.
1967 96m/C James Franciscus, Paul Anstad; *D:* Irving Jacoby. **VHS, Beta** *LIV*

Snow White 🎵🎵

Family The incomparable Rigg brings some zest to her act as the jealous Evil Queen, who adopts numerous disguises to try to slay Snow White in this lackluster Cannon Movie Tales retelling of the Brothers Grimm story. Real star is Queen's spooky magic mirror, partly because it lends an eerie, "Dorian Grey" type ending, but mainly because it doesn't sing any of the dumb tunes.
1989 85m/C Diana Rigg, Sarah Patterson, Billy Barty; *D:* Michael Berz. **VHS** *WAR*

Snow White and Rose Red

Preschool-Primary Snow White and a fellow maiden encounter a prince transformed into a bear in this animated Grimm's tale.
19?? 30m/C VHS *VTR*

Snow White and the Seven Dwarfs 🎵🎵🎵🎵

G/Family Classic Disney adaptation of the Grimm Brothers fairy tale about the fairest of them all, who lives with seven hard-working little men ("heigh ho, heigh ho, it's off to work we go"). Beautiful animation, memorable characters, and wonderful songs mark this as the definitive "Snow White." Set the stage for other animated features after Uncle Walt took an unprecedented gamble by attempting the first animated feature-length film, a project which took over two years to create and $1.5 million to make, and made believers out of those who laughed at the concept. Lifelike animation was based on real stars; Margery Belcher (later Champion) posed for Snow, Louis Hightower was the Prince, and Lucille LaVerne gave the Queen her nasty look. As in most Disney animated films, evil is portrayed in a fairly intense way. Songs include "Whistle While You Work," "Heigh Ho," and "Some Day My Prince Will Come." 🎵 Some Day My Prince Will Come; One Song; With a Smile and a Song; Whistle While You Work; Bluddle-Uddle-Um-Dum; The Dwarfs' Yodel Song; Heigh Ho; I'm Wishing; Isn't This a Silly Song?.

BEWARE! *Hideous witch and titanic thunderstorm may terrify small children, although the small screen makes them less scary.*
1937 83m/C D: David Hand; *W:* Ted Sears, Otto Englander, Earl Hurd, Dorothy Blank, Richard Creedon, Dick Richard, Merrill De Maris, Webb Smith; *M:* Frank Churchill, Paul Smith, Larry Morey, Leigh Harline; *V:* Adriana Caseloti, Harry Stockwell, Lucille LaVerne, Moroni Olsen, Billy Gilbert, Pinto Colvig, Otis Harlan, Scotty Matraw, Roy Atwell, Stuart Buchanan, Marion Darlington, Jim Macdonald. **VHS** *DIS*

Snow White and the Seven Dwarfs

Family From cable television's "Faerie Tale Theatre" comes the story of a princess (Elizabeth McGovern) who befriends seven little men to protect her from the jealous evil queen (Vanessa Redgrave). Vincent Price is the mirror with the George Washington complex; he cannot tell a lie. Gruesome, as the Grimm fairy tales often are. Ages 9 and up.
1983 60m/C Elizabeth McGovern, Rex Smith, Vincent Price, Vanessa Redgrave; *D:* Peter Medak. **VHS, Beta, LV** *FOX, FCT, HMV*

Snow White and the Three Stooges 🎵

Family Explain this if you can: The aging Stooges, late in their careers, sub for the dwarfs as miners who discover and protect Snow White. She's played by champion fig-ure-skater Heiss, and much of her screen time involves ice-skating dream ballets of the Snow White saga. Good color photography; otherwise the words 'Dopey' and 'Sleepy' come to mind.

1961 107m/C Moe Howard, Curly Howard, Larry Fine, Carol Heiss, Patricia Medina; **D:** Walter Lang. **VHS, Beta** *FOX, FCT*

Snowball Express 🎵🎵

G/Family When the New Yorker Baxter family inherit a hotel in the Rocky Mountains, dad decides to move his family west to attempt to make a go of the defunct ski resort, only to find the place falling apart. Run of the mill, fish out of water Disney comedy, based on the novel "Chateau Bon Vivant" by Frankie and John O'Rear.

1972 120m/C Dean Jones, Nancy Olson, Harry (Henry) Morgan, Keenan Wynn; **D:** Norman Tokar. **VHS, Beta** *DIS*

The Snowman

Family A young boy makes his first snowman and at midnight it comes to life and takes the boy on wonderful adventures, including visiting Santa at the North Pole. A highly-rated cartoon without dialogue, based on the book by Raymond Briggs.

1978 30m/C VHS *COL,, MLT*

Snuffy the Elf Who Saved Christmas

Preschool-Primary Is there any animal/vegetable/min-eral out there who hasn't saved Christmas? It's Snuffy to the rescue when the Sandman puts all the other elves to sleep on the job.

1991 25m/C VHS *FHE, FAF*

So Dear to My Heart 🎵🎵🎵 ♪

Family Heartwarming Disney film about a farm boy determined to enter his black sheep at the county fair, who goes to great lengths to earn the entry fee. Several sequences combine live action with superb Disney ani-mation, and musical numbers include standards like "Lavender Blue." Straightforward and likeable but never sentimental. Great vintage Disney, not as well-remem-bered as some of their other classics but worth redis-covering on tape. Based on "Midnight and Jeremiah" by Sterling North. ♫ Sourwood Mountain; Billy Boy; So Dear To My Heart; County Fair; Stick-To-It-Ivity; Ol' Dan Patch; It's Whatcha Do With Watcha Got; Lavender Blue (Dilly Dilly).

1949 82m/C Bobby Driscoll, Burl Ives, Beulah Bondi, Harry Carey Sr., Luana Patten; **D:** Harold Schuster. **VHS, Beta, LV** *DIS*

So I Married an Axe Murderer 🎵🎵

PG-13/Jr. High-Adult Combination comedy/ro-mance/thriller that's fairly stupid while holding true to its own sense of parody. Charlie is a hip, angst-ridden book-store owner/poet with a commitment problem. When he finally falls in love with a butcher, he comes to suspect she's a serial killer and he's in line as her next victim. Myers has a dual role: as Charlie and as Scottish dad Stuart, who steals the show with his intense Scottish demeanor. Occasionally inspired, probably too self-con-scious, but there are worse ways to spend an evening.

BEWARE *Profanity, violence and brief nudity. Scenes in a butcher shop.*

1993 92m/C Mike Myers, Nancy Travis, Anthony LaPaglia, Amanda Plummer, Brenda Fricker, Matt Doherty, Charles Grodin; **Cameos:** Phil Hartman, Steven Wright, Alan Arkin; **D:** Thomas Schlamme; **W:** Mike Myers, Robbie Fox; **M:** Bruce Broughton. **VHS, LV, 8mm** *COL*

Solarbabies 🎵

PG-13/Jr. High-Adult Rollerskating youths in a drought-stricken future vie for a mysterious, friendly ball from the stars who can replenish the Earth's water. Juve-nile adventure is like an explosion in a mind-candy fac-tory, raining bits of every sci-fi movie from "Rollerball" to "E.T." Good sets and special effects wasted.

BEWARE *Mild violence, the worst of which is a pain device in the bad guys' torture chamber. But it only creates illusions of mutilating flesh.*

1986 95m/C Richard Jordan, Sarah Douglas, Charles Durning, Lukas Haas, Jami Gertz, Jason Patric; **D:** Alan Johnson; **W:** Walon Green; **M:** Maurice Jarre. **VHS, Beta, LV** *MGM*

Some Kind of Wonderful 🎵🎵

PG-13/Sr. High-Adult High school tomboy has a crush on a guy who also happens to be her best friend. Her feelings go unrequited as he falls for a rich girl with snobbish friends. Will true love win out in the end? Deutch also directed (and John Hughes also produced) the teen flick "Pretty in Pink," which had much the same plot, with the rich/outcast characters reversed by gen-der. OK, but completely predictable—whether you've seen its mirror-clone or not.

BEWARE *Profanity. Feelings are hurt.*

1987 93m/C Eric Stoltz, Lea Thompson, Mary Stuart Masterson, Craig Sheffer, John Ashton, Elias Koteas, Molly Hagan; **D:** Howard Deutch; **W:** John Hughes. **VHS, LV** *PAR*

Someday Me Series

Preschool-Primary Series of videotapes from Fisher-Price featuring the characters Max and Jennifer, who have fun experiencing what life is like in the adult world.

1988 30m/C VHS, Beta *HSE*

Something Good

Preschool-Primary Contains two stories from Robert Munsch. In the first, "Something Good," a little girl named Tyva goes shopping with her dad and when he tells her she can't have something, she embarks on a comical shopping spree of her own. In the second, "Mortimer," a little fellow is put in bed and told to be quiet by his mother. Yeah, right. Ages 3 to 8.

1994 25m/C VHS

Something to Talk About 🦴🦴 ᵇ

R/Sr. High-Adult Grace (Roberts) learns that her husband Eddie (the ever-charming Quaid) is tomcatting around. So Grace tosses him out and makes a temporary move with daughter Caroline (Aull) back home. Tart-tongued sister Emma Rae (Sedgwick) is sympathetic but long-suffering mama Georgia (Rowlands) thinks Grace should make the best of things (the way she's done). Between running her overbearing father Wyly's (Duvall) horsebreeding operation and coming to terms with what she wants out of life, she's got her hands full. Many funny moments keep the dark subject of divorce a little lighter. For teens and adults only.

BEWARE *Brief strong language and a kick in the crotch. Be prepared to talk about adultery, divorce and what may drive someone to poison their husband.*

1995 106m/C Julia Roberts, Dennis Quaid, Robert Duvall, Gena Rowlands, Kyra Sedgwick, Brett Cullen, Haley Aull, Muse Watson, Anne Shropshire; **D:** Lasse Hallstrom; **W:** Callie Khouri; **C:** Sven Nykvist; **M:** Hans Zimmer. **VHS, LV** *WAR*

Something Wicked This Way Comes 🦴🦴

PG/Jr. High-Adult Two boys discover the evil secret of Mr. Dark's traveling carnival that visits their town once a generation, wreaking havoc by granting folks their secret wishes. Ray Bradbury wrote the screenplay, adapting—and simplifying—his poetic horror novel for Disney, but results are severely stilted and slow-moving, with a storm of f/x at the end barely explained in terms of what it all means.

BEWARE *Some violence (including a severed head), but very stylized and hallucinatory.*

1983 94m/C Jason Robards Jr., Jonathan Pryce, Diane Ladd, Pam Grier, Richard Davalos, James Stacy; **D:** Jack Clayton; **W:** Ray Bradbury; **M:** James Horner. **VHS, Beta, LV** *DIS*

Somewhere in Time 🦴 ᵇ

PG/Jr. High-Adult Playwright Reeve (in his first post-Clark Kent role) falls in love with a beautiful woman in an old portrait. Through self-hypnosis he goes back in time to 1912 to discover what their relationship might have been. Drippy rip-off of the brilliant novel "Time and Again" by Jack Finney at least made a star of the Grand Hotel on Mackinac Island in Michigan, where romantic drama was shot. Probably best appreciated by Reeves fans with low expectations or friends of Mackinac Island.

1980 103m/C Christopher Reeve, Jane Seymour, Christopher Plummer, Teresa Wright; **D:** Jeannot Szwarc; **W:** Richard Matheson; **M:** John Barry. **VHS, Beta, LV** *MCA*

Somewhere Tomorrow 🦴🦴 ᵇ

PG/Jr. High-Adult Pleasant little romantic fantasy about a lonely, fatherless teenage girl trying to hold onto her horse farm. She receives assistance from the ghost of a young man. Works better than it sounds; charming and moving.

1985 91m/C Sarah Jessica Parker, Nancy Addison, Tom Shea; **D:** Robert Wiemer. **VHS, Beta** *MED*

Sommersby 🦴🦴 ᵇ

PG-13/Jr. High-Adult Too-good-to-be-true period romance based on the French "The Return of Martin Guerre." Civil War veteran Gere returns to his wife's Foster less-than-open arms. She soon warms up to his kind, sensitive and caring manner, but can't quite believe the change that the war has wrought. Neither can the neighbors, especially Pullman who has his own eye on Laurel Sommersby. So is he really Jack Sommersby or an all too clever imposter? Lots of hankies needed for the tender-hearted. Strong performance by Foster, while Gere's displays an acceptable level of narcissism (that's acting!). Filmed in Virginia (passing for the state of Tennessee.) The laserdisc version is available in letterbox format.

BEWARE *Nudity, violence and sex. Tough subjects of mistaken identity and ethics of the period.*

1993 114m/C Richard Gere, Jodie Foster, Bill Pullman, James Earl Jones, William Windom, Brett Kelley, Richard Hamilton, Maury Chaykin, Lanny Flaherty, Frankie Faison, Wendell Wellman, Clarice Taylor, R. Lee Ermey; **D:** Jon Amiel; **W:** Nicholas Meyer, Sarah Kernochan; **M:** Danny Elfman. **VHS, Beta, LV, 8mm** *WAR, FCT*

Son-in-Law 🦴🦴

PG-13/Jr. High-Adult Surfer-dude comic Shore's a laconic fish out of water as a city-boy rock 'n' roller who falls in love with a country beauty, marries her, and visits the family farm to meet the new in-laws. Once there, he weirds out family and neighbors before showing everyone how to live, Pauly style. Silly entertainment best appreciated by Shore fans.

BEWARE *Profanity and on-the-farm idiocy.*

1993 95m/C Pauly Shore, Carla Gugino, Lane Smith, Cindy Pickett, Mason Adams, Dennis Burkley, Dan Gauthier, Tiffani-Amber Thiessen; **D:** Steve Rash; **W:** Shawn Schepps, Fax Bahr, Adam Small; **M:** Richard Gibbs. **VHS, Beta** *HPH*

Son of Captain Blood 🦴 ᵇ

G/Family The son of the famous pirate meets up with his father's enemies on the high seas. The son of the famous actor Errol Flynn—Sean—plays the son of the character the elder Flynn played in "Captain Blood." Let's just say the gimmick didn't work.

1962 90m/C Sean Flynn, Ann Todd; **D:** Tulio Demicheli. **VHS, Beta** *PSM, MLB*

Son of Flubber 🦴🦴 ᵇ

Family Sequel to "The Absent Minded Professor" finds Professor Brainard still toying with his prodigious invention, Flubber, now in the form of Flubbergas, causes those who inhale it to float away (why didn't they Just Say No!). Disney's first-ever sequel is high family wackiness.

1963 96m/C Fred MacMurray, Nancy Olson, Tommy Kirk, Leon Ames, Joanna Moore, Keenan Wynn, Charlie Ruggles, Paul Lynde; **D:** Robert Stevenson. **VHS, Beta** *DIS*

Son of Kong

Family Expedition returns to King Kong's prehistoric island and discovers the great ape's descendant—smaller, cuter and albino. Kong 2 defends his human friends against rampaging dinosaurs, a bear, and other perils. Quickly minted sequel to take advantage of the smash success of the original isn't near as good but still has a spirit of fun and f/x by stop-motion pioneer Willis O'Brien.

BEWARE *Violence.*

1933 70m/B Robert Armstrong, Helen Mack; **D:** Ernest B. Schoedsack; **M:** Max Steiner. **VHS, Beta, LV** *NOS, MED, FCT*

Son of the Pink Panther

PG/Jr. High-Adult Lame leftover from the formerly popular comedy series. Director Edwards has chosen not to resurrect Inspector Clouseau, instead opting for his son (Benigni), who turns out to be just as much of a bumbling idiot as his father. Commissioner Dreyfus (Lom), the twitching, mouth-foaming former supervisor of the original Clouseau is looking for a kidnapped princess (Farentino) along with Clouseau, Jr., who himself does not know he is the illegitimate son of his partner's dead nemesis. Many of the sketches have been recycled from previous series entrants.

BEWARE *Violence.*

1993 115m/C Roberto Benigni, Herbert Lom, Robert Davi, Debrah Farentino, Claudia Cardinale, Burt Kwouk, Shabana Azmi; **D:** Blake Edwards; **W:** Blake Edwards; **M:** Henry Mancini. **VHS, LV** *MGM*

Son of Zorro

Family Zorro takes the law into his own hands to protect ranchers from bandits. A serial in thirteen chapters.

BEWARE *Violence.*

1947 164m/B George Turner, Peggy Stewart, Roy Barcroft, Edward Cassidy. **VHS** *REP, VCN, MLB*

Song City U.S.A.

Family The Song City crowd dazzles audiences with a slew of wild and wacky music videos down at the diner of the same name.

1989 30m/C Brian O'Connor. **VHS** *FHE, LIV*

The Song of Sacajawea

Preschool-Primary Story of the 17-year-old Shoshone woman, sister to her people's chief, who leads explorers Lewis and Clark to the Pacific Ocean. Beautifully animated by John Molloy; part of the "Rabbit Ears: American Heroes & Legends" series.

1993 30m/C **VHS** *RAB, UND, MVD*

Song Spinner

G/Family In a mysterious land, a stranger gives a young girl the power of music, which she hopes to share with the king. But first she must get past the kingdom's noise police. Good cast.

1995 95m/C Meredith Henderson, Patti LuPone, John Neville; **D:** Randy Bradshaw. **VHS** *HMK*

Songs for Us Series

Preschool-Primary This Disney series features songs that children can learn that relate to life in today's society. Tapes, available separately, are "Appreciating Differences," "Making Friends," and "Sharing and Cooperation."

1989 8m/C **VHS, Beta** *MTI, DSN*

Sorcerer's Apprentice

Preschool-Primary In this non-Disney animated version of Jacob Grimm's classic tale, young Hans realizes that his master plans to use magic for evil purposes and tries to motivate the old wizard towards more pleasant prestidigitation. Originally a syndicated TV special.

1985 22m/C **VHS, Beta** *ORI*

Sorrowful Jones

Family A "Little Miss Marker" remake, in which bookie Hope inherits a little girl as collateral for an unpaid bet. Good for a few yuks, but the original is much better.

1949 88m/B Bob Hope, Lucille Ball, William Demarest, Bruce Cabot, Thomas Gomez, Mary Jane Saunders; **D:** Sidney Lanfield; **W:** Jack Rose, Melville Shavelson. **VHS, Beta** *MCA*

Soul Man

PG-13/Sr. High-Adult Denied the funds he expected for his Harvard tuition, a young white student (Howell) masquerades as a black in order to get a minority scholarship. As a black student at Harvard, Howell learns about racism and bigotry. Pleasant lightweight comedy with romance thrown in (Chong is the black girl he falls for), and with pretensions to social satire that it never achieves.

BEWARE *Profanity, sex and violence. College antics.*

1986 101m/C C. Thomas Howell, Rae Dawn Chong, James Earl Jones, Leslie Nielsen, Arye Gross; **D:** Steve Miner. **VHS, Beta, LV** *NWV, VTR*

The Sound of Music

Family Classic film version of the Rodgers and Hammerstein musical based on the true story of the singing von Trapp family of Austria and their escape from the Nazis just before WWII. Beautiful Salzburg, Austria location photography and an excellent cast. Andrews, fresh from her Oscar for "Mary Poppins," is effervescent, in beautiful voice, but occasionally too good to be true. Not Rodgers & Hammerstein's most innovative score, but lovely to hear and see. Plummer's singing was dubbed by

Bill Lee. Marni Nixon, behind-the-scenes songstress for "West Side Story" and "My Fair Lady," makes her on-screen debut as one of the nuns. ♫ I Have Confidence In Me; Something Good; The Sound of Music; Preludium; Morning Hymn; Alleluia; How Do You Solve A Problem Like Maria?; Sixteen, Going on Seventeen; My Favorite Things.

1965 174m/C Julie Andrews, Christopher Plummer, Eleanor Parker, Peggy Wood, Charmian Carr, Heather Menzies, Marni Nixon, Richard Haydn, Anna Lee, Norma Varden, Nicholas Hammond, Angela Cartwright, Portia Nelson, Duane Chase, Debbie Turner, Kym Karath; **D:** Robert Wise; **W:** Ernest Lehman; **M:** Richard Rodgers, Oscar Hammerstein. **Award Nominations:** Academy Awards '65: Best Actress (Andrews), Best Art Direction/Set Decoration (Color), Best Color Cinematography, Best Costume Design (Color), Best Supporting Actress (Wood); **Awards:** Academy Awards '65: Best Adapted Score, Best Director (Wise), Best Film Editing, Best Picture, Best Sound; Directors Guild of America Awards '65: Best Director (Wise); Golden Globe Awards '66: Best Actress—Musical/Comedy (Andrews), Best Film—Musical/Comedy; National Board of Review Awards '65: 10 Best Films of the Year. **VHS, Beta, LV** *FOX, BTV, RDG*

Sounder 🐾🐾🐾🐾

G/Family The struggles of a family of black sharecroppers in rural Louisiana during the Depression. When David's father is sentenced to jail for stealing to feed his family, they work even harder to survive, and David finds education a path out of poverty. Moving and well made, with little sentimentality and superb acting. Script neatly expands and defines the short source novel by William Armstrong. Sequel, "Sounder, Part 2," is not yet available on tape.

⚠ BEWARE *Brief violence, with Sounder, the family hound, wounded by gunfire.*

1972 105m/C Paul Winfield, Cicely Tyson, Kevin Hooks, Taj Mahal, Carmen Mathews, James Best, Janet MacLachlan; **D:** Martin Ritt; **M:** Taj Mahal. **Award Nominations:** Academy Awards '72: Best Actor (Winfield), Best Actress (Tyson), Best Adapted Screenplay, Best Picture; **Awards:** National Board of Review Awards '72: 10 Best Films of the Year; National Society of Film Critics Awards '72: Best Actress (Tyson). **VHS, Beta, LV** *KUI, PAR, PTB*

Sounds Around

Preschool-Primary Stop. Hey, what's that sound? Entertaining tape helps children to be good listeners. Sounds include squeaks, snores, and noisy toys, household appliances, animals, people, plus music. Also shows children making the sounds they hear. Ages 2 to 6.

1994 27m/C VHS *BOP*

Sourdough 🐾🐾

Family Fur trapper Perry escapes the hustle and bustle of modern life by fleeing to the Alaskan wilderness. Near-plotless travelogue depends heavily on scenery—and there's plenty of that.

1977 94m/C Gil Perry, Charles Brock, Slim Carlson, Carl Clark; **D:** Martin J. Spinelli. **VHS, Beta, LV** *IMP*

South Pacific 🐾🐾🐾 ⌐

Family Young American Navy nurse and a Frenchman fall in love during WWII. Expensive production included much location shooting in Hawaii. Based on Rodgers and

Meet the Star of *The Sound of Music*, Julie Andrews

She made the hills come alive in *The Sound of Music* and made the musical scale come alive in *Mary Poppins*. Her recordings of her Broadway hit musicals "My Fair Lady" and "Camelot" were best-sellers. In the 1960s, no one except the Beatles made more popular music than Julie Andrews. Her prim and proper image, immortalized in her roles as Maria von Trapp, the *Poppins* nanny, Eliza Doolittle and Queen Guinevere, was the epitome of a culture that collapsed in the late 1960s, and Andrews never quite fit in with the new order. She has continued to appear on stage, screen and television. She received an Oscar nomination for her role as a cross-dressing singer in *Victor/Victoria* in 1982.

She was born Julia Elizabeth Wells in 1935 near London. Her mother, a pianist, divorced her father, a teacher, and remarried Canadian vaudeville singer Ted Andrews. Julie made her first stage appearance at age 3, and soon was touring with her parents. At 13, she was the youngest person ever to give a royal command performance. She came to Broadway at 19 to star in "The Boy Friend." She married British set designer Tony Walton in 1959; they divorced. In 1969, she married director Blake Edwards, who helped revive her film career in the 1980s. She has a daughter, two stepchildren, and two adopted Vietnamese children. She and Edwards live in Switzerland and Malibu.

Hammerstein's musical; not as good as the play, but still pretty darn entertaining. The play in turn was based on James Michener's novel "Tales of the South Pacific." 🎵 My Girl Back Home; Dites-Moi; Bali Ha'i; Happy Talk; A Cockeyed Optimist; Soliloquies; Some Enchanted Evening; Bloody Mary; I'm Gonna Wash That Man Right Out of My Hair.

1958 167m/C Mitzi Gaynor, Rossano Brazzi, Ray Walston, France Nuyen, John Kerr, Juanita Hall, Tom Laughlin; **D:** Joshua Logan; **M:** Richard Rodgers, Oscar Hammerstein; **V:** Giorgio Tozzi. **Award Nominations:** Academy Awards '56: Best Color Cinematography; Academy Awards '58: Best Original Score; **Awards:** Academy Awards '58: Best Sound. **VHS, Beta, LV** *FOX, RDG, HMV*

Space Angel, Vol. 1

Primary Some folks now look back with nostalgia on this ultra-cheap TV cartoon made with a process called 'Syncro-Vox': live actors' lips were filmed over the faces of the 'toon characters to save drawing the mouth movements when they talked. Similar money-saving touches pervade this tale of Space Agent Scott McCloud attempting to retrieve a solar panel stolen by aliens. Additional volumes available.

1964 50m/C VHS, Beta *FHE, STP, TPV*

Space Battleship Yamato

Preschool-Jr. High One of Japan's most popular cartoon TV shows is this lavishly animated saga, slightly reminiscent of "Battlestar Galactica," detailing the heroic star cruiser Yamato, in a running battle with alien blue meanies as they search for their lost homeworld of Earth. Available in 77 (aieeee!) half-hour cassettes, plus five two-hour theatrical feature spinoffs.

1983 30m/C VHS

Space Firebird 🎵🎵

Family Peculiar Japanese animated feature, a somewhat unpalatable mix of mysticism, mythology, and Lucasfilm. Greedy rulers of a dying Earth send star pilot Gordo off to capture a dangerous, shape-changing space phoenix, to exploit as an energy source. Some spectacular scenes of destruction, plus overly familiar environmental sermons. Loses half a bone for really lousy English dubbing.

 Violence.

1980 103m/C VHS, Beta *JFK*

Space Raiders 🎵

PG/Jr. High-Adult Plucky 10-year-old blasts off into a futuristic world of intergalactic desperados, crafty alien mercenaries, starship battles and cliff-hanging dangers. Recycled special effects (from producer Roger Corman's other, better "Battle Beyond the Stars") and plot (lifted near-whole from "Star Wars"). The same producer later filched scenes from this for "Andy and the Airwave Rangers!"

 Violence.

1983 84m/C Vince Edwards, David Mendenhall; **D:** Howard R. Cohen. **VHS, Beta** *WAR*

Space Warriors: Battle for Earth Station S/1

Family Animated space fantasy for kids, from Japanese TV.

1987 99m/C VHS, Beta *JFK*

Spaceballs 🎵🎵 ▷

PG/Jr. High-Adult Parody of sci-fi blockbusters, especially "Star Wars." The planet Spaceball needs air (so will you, after some of the jokes) and its forces, led by short bad guy Dark Helmet, try to conquer a neighboring world. Insubstantial and sometimes raunchy, but the plethora of sight gags will appeal to kids in "Mad Magazine" style. Crazy characters include Candy as the friendly "mog"—half man, half dog (a Chewbacca take-off) and Brooks in two roles, one of them puny wise man/ wise guy Yogurt.

BEWARE *Salty space/Brooks language, sex talk.*

1987 96m/C Mel Brooks, Rick Moranis, John Candy, Bill Pullman, Daphne Zuniga, Dick Van Patten, John Hurt, George Wyner, Joan Rivers, Lorene Yarnell, Sal Viscuso, Stephen Tobolowsky, Dom DeLuise, Michael Winslow; **D:** Mel Brooks; **W:** Mel Brooks, Ronny Graham, Thomas Meehan; **M:** John Morris. **VHS, Beta, LV** *MGM*

SpaceCamp 🎵🎵

PG/Primary-Adult Misfit kids and their adult instructor from the real-life NASA Space Camp in Alabama strap into a genuine space shuttle during a field trip. Suddenly the usual cute little robot friend tricks Ground Control into launching them into space, a field trip indeed. The kids must find the confidence and teamwork to return to Earth, a big challenge for anyone. Potentially exciting plot crashes thanks to hokey treatment, subpar special effects, predictably 'inspirational' moments, but younger kids might enjoy.

BEWARE *Salty space language.*

1986 115m/C Kate Capshaw, Tate Donovan, Joaquin Rafael (Leaf) Phoenix, Kelly Preston, Larry B. Scott, Tom Skerritt, Lea Thompson, Terry O'Quinn; **D:** Harry Winer; **M:** John Williams. **VHS, Beta, LV** *LIV, VES, IME*

Spaced Invaders 🎵🎵

PG/Primary-Adult Ship full of little green Martians is sent to an alien war but mistakenly lands in rural Illinois. It's Halloween, and the five bumbling would-be conquerors are mistaken for kiddie trick-or-treaters. Earth children know the truth: "They're not bad, just stupid." The same may be said for the film, a Disney co-production (through Touchstone) that undiscriminating kids might like but is just too loud and repetitive for anyone else.

BEWARE *Lots of bathroom/potty jokes; otherwise G-level. A Martian is hit by a truck, but he survives.*

1990 102m/C Douglas Barr, Royal Dano, Ariana Richards, Kevin Thompson, Jimmy Briscoe, Tony Cox, Debbie Lee Carrington, Tommy Madden; **D:** Patrick Read Johnson. **VHS, Beta, LV** *TOU, TOU*

Spaceketeers 🎵🎵

Family Japanese animation highlights this multi-cassette sci-fi saga in which an army of mutant invaders overrun a peaceful solar system. Opposing them are the lovely Princess Aurora (who looks about as oriental as General Douglas MacArthur) and her kung-fu cyborg sidekick Jesse Dart. Several volumes of individual episodes from the TV show are available.

 *Roughhousing.*

1982 100m/C **VHS, Beta** *FHE, TPV*

Spaceship 🎵 ♪

PG/Jr. High-Adult Misguided attempt to spoof creature-features. Mad scientist tries to protect kindly monster from crazed crew. Not very funny, with the exception of the song-and-dance routine by the monster.

1981 88m/C Cindy Williams, Bruce Kimmel, Leslie Nielsen, Gerrit Graham, Patrick Macnee, Ron Kurowski; **D:** Bruce Kimmel. **VHS** *LIV*

Sparky's Magic Piano

Family Cartoon (adapted from a famous kids' record) in which a magic piano grants a little boy who doesn't practice the ability to play like a master. But in the end Sparky learns a lesson in modesty and tact.

1988 51m/C **VHS, Beta** *FHE*

Speaking of Animals, Vol. 1

Family Modern compilation of vintage novelty shorts from the '30s and '40s, with different kinds of animals in funny situations—often singing and talking thanks to animated lips expertly superimposed and synced with recordings of famous celebrities. Still quite a riot.

1983 60m/C **VHS, Beta** *FHE*

Special Valentine with Family Circus

Family Cartoonist Bill Keane's comic-strip characters come to life in a special Valentine's Day program that has the kids trying to outdo each other for the best valentine. Also known as "A Family Circus Valentine."

1980 30m/C **VHS, Beta** *FHE*

Speechless 🎵🎵 ♪

PG-13/Jr. High-Adult Cute romantic comedy about sparring speechwriters who fall in love, and then briefly turn enemies when they discover they're working at professional odds. Although the film parallels the real-life romance of rival Bush-Clinton spin doctors Mary Matalin and James Carville, it was written prior to the 1992 presidential race. Davis is the idealistic liberal working for a senatorial candidate, while Keaton is a TV sitcom writer

doing a one-shot deal for a millionaire Republican. Stars are good; the supporting cast fares better with Reeve as an egotistical TV reporter, as well as Davis's fiance, and Bedelia as Keaton's ex-wife.

Mild profanity, adult talk about sex and adult sex. Kids may not understand why these two shouldn't date (the conflict of interest thing).

1994 99m/C Michael Keaton, Geena Davis, Christopher Reeve, Bonnie Bedelia, Ernie Hudson, Charles Martin Smith, Gailard Sartain, Ray Baker, Mitchell Ryan; **D:** Ron Underwood; **W:** Robert King; **M:** Marc Shaiman. **VHS, LV** *MGM*

Speed 🎵🎵🎵 ♪

R/Sr. High-Adult Excellent dude Reeves has grown up (and bulked up) as Los Angeles SWAT cop Jack Traven, up against bomb expert Howard Payne (Hopper, bringing a special glee to his usual mania) who's after major ransom money. First it's a rigged elevator in a very tall building. Then it's a rigged bus if it slows, it will blow, bad enough any day, but a nightmare in LA traffic. And that's still not the end. Terrific directorial debut for cinematographer De Bont, who certainly knows how to keep the adrenaline pumping. Fine support work by Daniels, Bullock, and Morton and enough wit in Yost's script to keep you chuckling. Great nonstop actioner from the "Die Hard" school.

Violence and profanity. Youngsters may never want to ride in an elevator again (or a bus).

1994 115m/C Keanu Reeves, Dennis Hopper, Sandra Bullock, Joe Morton, Jeff Daniels, Alan Ruck, Glenn Plummer, Richard Lineback, Beth Grant, Hawthorne James, David Kriegel, Carlos Carrasco, Natsuko Ohama, Daniel Villarreal; **D:** Jan De Bont; **W:** Graham Yost; **M:** Mark Mancina. **VHS** *FXV*

Speed Racer

Family Adult cult of admirers has lately joined the kiddie fans of this popular cartoon that originated in Japan. Speed Racer drives the fast, futuristic, jumping Mach-5 race car, and competes in various races that get them both in perilous escapades worldwide. Tapes are available individually.

1967 30m/C **VHS** *TPV*

Spellbound 🎵🎵🎵 ♪

Jr. High-Adult Psychological thriller stars Peck as an amnesia victim accused of murder. Bergman is the icy psychiatrist who uncovers his past through Freudian analysis and ends up falling in love with him. One of Hitchcock's finest films of the 1940s, with a riveting dream sequence designed by Salvador Dali. Full of classic Hitchcock plot twists and Freudian imagery. Based on Francis Bleeding's novel "The House of Dr. Edwardes."

1945 111m/B Ingrid Bergman, Gregory Peck, Leo G. Carroll, Michael Chekhov, Wallace Ford, Rhonda Fleming, Regis Toomey; **D:** Alfred Hitchcock; **M:** Miklos Rozsa. **Award Nominations:** Academy Awards '45: Best Actor (Chekhov), Best Black and White Cinematography, Best Director (Hitchcock), Best Picture; **Awards:** Academy Awards '45: Best Score. **VHS, Beta, LV** *FOX, IME, TLF*

Spencer's Mountain ♫♫ ᵛ

Family Henry Fonda plays the patriarch of 9 (with Maureen O'Hara as his wife), who's inherited his father's Wyoming mountain land. Fonda's dream is to build a new house for his big family but something always gets in his way. This time it's eldest son James MacArthur's dream of a college education (Book it, Dan-o). Sentimental family fare based on a novel by Earl Hamner, Jr., which also became the basis for TV's "The Waltons." Ages 8 and up.
1963 118m/C Henry Fonda, Maureen O'Hara, James MacArthur, Donald Crisp, Wally Cox, Mimsy Farmer, Virginia Gregg, Lillian Bronson, Whit Bissell, Hayden Rorke, Dub Taylor, Victor French, Veronica Cartwright; **D:** Delmer Daves; **W:** Delmer Daves; **M:** Max Steiner. **VHS** *WAR*

Spider-Woman

Family Stan Lee, creator of Spiderman, also came up with this, so that's why there's been no spider-lawsuit. Magazine editor Jessica Drew turns into the heroic Spider-Woman to take on a slew of criminals, super and otherwise, in these respun TV cartoons.
1985 60m/C VHS, Beta *MCA*

Spiderman

Family Two volumes of episodes from a brief prime-time TV series that brought the famous Marvel Comics superhero to very temporary life. Spidey saves the world from global terrorism and thwarts political plots in the sets "Night of the Clones/Escort to Danger" and "Con Caper/Curse of Rava."
1981 90m/C Nicholas Hammond, Morgan Fairchild, Lloyd Bochner, Barbara Luna, Theodore Bikel. **VHS, Beta** *PSM*

Spiderman & His Amazing Friends: Origin of the Spider Friends

Family Marvel superheroes meet as teenagers and form a crime-fighting alliance in this Saturday-morning TV cartoon.
1983 24m/C VHS

Spiderman: The Deadly Dust

Family Feature-length episode from the mediocre "Spiderman" live-action TV program, in which the Marvel Comics superhero tries to save New York from a city-destroying plutonium accident.
1978 93m/C Nicholas Hammond, Robert F. Simon, Chip Fields; **D:** Ron Satlof. **VHS, Beta** *FOX*

Spiderman, Vol. 1: Dr. Doom

Family Spiderman takes on the ultimate super villain, Dr. Doom, in this animated adventure. Additional volumes available.
1981 22m/C VHS, Beta *BFV*

Spies Like Us ♫♫ ᵛ

PG/Jr. High-Adult Chase and Aykroyd meet while taking the CIA entry exam. Caught cheating on the test, they seem the perfect pair for a special mission (one for bumbling idiots). Pursued by the Soviet government, they nearly start WWIII. Silly, fun homage to the Bing Crosby-Bob Hope "Road" movies that doesn't quite capture those classics' quota of guffaws, but comes moderately close. Kids will probably laugh at the pratfalling pair.

> **BEWARE** *Violence and profanity, but not much. There are some sexual innuendos when the foursome think they will be blown up by the nuclear weapon.*

1985 103m/C Chevy Chase, Dan Aykroyd, Steve Forrest, Bruce Davison, William Prince, Bernie Casey, Tom Hatton, Donna Dixon, Frank Oz; **Cameos:** Michael Apted, Constantin Costa-Gavras, Terry Gilliam, Ray Harryhausen, Joel Coen, Martin Brest, Bob Swaim; **D:** John Landis; **W:** Dan Aykroyd, Lowell Ganz, Babaloo Mandel; **M:** Elmer Bernstein. **VHS, Beta, LV** *WAR*

Spiral Zone: Ride the Whirlwind

Preschool-Primary Two episodes of the animated toy-inspired cartoon series, "The Unexploded Pod" and the title episode.
1987 45m/C VHS, Beta *FHE*

Spiral Zone: Zone of Darkness

Family The Spiral Force meets with corruption in sci-fi scoundrels. Includes "Small Packages," "King of the Skies," and "Holographic Zone Battles."
1987 86m/C VHS, Beta *FHE*

Spirit of the Eagle ♫♫

PG/Jr. High-Adult Man and young son wander in mountains and make friends with feathered creature. Then boy is kidnapped, creating problems for dad. Somnolent nature fare.
1990 93m/C Dan Haggerty, Bill Smith, Don Shanks, Jeri Arrendondo, Trever Yarrish; **D:** Boon Collins; **W:** Boon Collins. **VHS, LV** *SGE, IME*

Spirit of the Eagle

Primary-Sr. High In the wilds of Alaska a young boy and his pals witness the beauty and majesty of the American bald eagle. Part of the Miramar "Legends" series about fauna of the Pacific Northwest, accompanied by "Gift of the Whales" and "Winter Wolf."
1990 30m/C VHS, Beta *MIR, MLT, VPJ*

Splash ♫♫♫ ᵛ

PG/Family Beautiful mermaid ventures into New York City in search of the grown-up man she encountered at the seashore while they were both children. Growing legs, she seeks out lucky but bewildered Hanks, who can't figure out why his dream girl acts so odd—and eats raw lobsters whole at fancy restaurants. Charming, wide-eyed adult fairy tale (mildly racy content makes it an iffy choice for small kids), a winner that was among the first flicks from Disney's fledgling Touchstone division.

BEWARE *Sex, nudity (none of it truly vulgar), salty language.*

1984 109m/C Tom Hanks, Daryl Hannah, Eugene Levy, John Candy, Dody Goodman, Shecky Greene, Richard B. Shull, Bobby DiCicco, Howard Morris; **D:** Ron Howard; **W:** Babaloo Mandel, Lowell Ganz. **VHS, Beta, LV, 8mm** *TOU*

Spook Busters 🦴🦴 ᵕ

Family The Bowery Boys take jobs as exterminators, only to find themselves assigned the unenviable task of ridding a haunted house of ghosts. To make matters worse, the resident mad scientist wants to transplant Sach's brain into a gorilla. Essential viewing for anyone who thought "Ghostbusters" was an original story.

1946 68m/B Leo Gorcey, Huntz Hall, Douglass Dumbrille, Bobby Jordan, Gabriel Dell, Billy Benedict, David Gorcey, Bernard Gorcey, Tanis Chandler, Maurice Cass, Charles Middleton; **D:** William Beaudine. **VHS** *WAR, GPV*

Spooks Run Wild 🦴🦴 ᵕ

Family Early "Bowery Boys" comedy (back when the troupe was also known as the East Side Kids), with the comical band of overgrown urchins seeking refuge in an eerie mansion owned by Lugosi, secretly a Nazi spy. A fun horror-comedy, with the kids' antics playing off Lugosi's menace quite well.

1941 64m/B Huntz Hall, Leo Gorcey, Bobby Jordan, Sammy Morrison, Dave O'Brien, Dennis Moore, Bela Lugosi; **D:** Phil Rosen; **W:** Carl Foreman. **VHS, Beta** *NOS, SNC, VYY*

Sport Goofy

Family A half-dozen sport-themed cartoons starring that lovable mutt, Goofy, as he takes a swing at baseball, a whack at golf, and so on. Uh-hyuk, uh-hyuk, uh-hyuk. Ages 3 to 8.

1988 45m/C VHS, Beta *DIS*

Spot Goes to a Party

Preschool Five short, gentle stories about the lovable pup: "Spot Goes to a Party," "Spot Goes to the Fair," "Spot's First Picnic," "Spot Goes to the Beach," and "Spot Follows His Nose." Ages 1 to 5.

1994 30m/C VHS *TOU*

Spot Goes to School

Preschool Five short stories based on the puppy character by Eric Hill, including "Spot Goes to School," "Spot at the Playground," "Spot Makes a Cake," "Spot in the Woods," and "Spot's Winter Sports." No, there isn't one called "What's That Spot on the Rug?" Ages 1 to 5.

1994 30m/C V: Jonathan Taylor Thomas. **VHS** *TOU*

Spot Goes to the Farm

Preschool Features Spot the puppy, from the interactive book series by Eric Hill, in five fun stories including "Spot Goes to the Farm," "Spot Sleeps Over," "Spot Goes to the Circus," "Spot's Windy Day," and "Spot Goes to the

Park." The cassette box features the trademark hide-and-seek activities from the books. See also "Where's Spot?"
1993 30m/C VHS *TOU, BTV*

Spot's Magic Christmas

Preschool Spot and his friends have to help two reindeer find Santa's lost sleigh and Spot even gets to travel to the North Pole. Ages 1 to 5.

1995 30m/C VHS *TOU*

Spy Hard 🦴

PG-13/Jr. High-Adult This slapstick comedy starring the "king of spoofs," Leslie Nielsen, should entertain kids and keep teens and adults laughing. Agent WD-40, otherwise known as Dick Steele must stop his armless evil enemy, General Rancor, from taking over the world. Lots of mayhem and quick movie references keep this flick moving, but some of the satire may go over younger kids heads. Spoofs James Bond flicks mostly, with surprisingly enough, a little "Butch Cassidy and the Sundance Kid" thrown in for good measure.

BEWARE *Mostly slapstick violence, like a woman falling off a cliff and a runaway bus driven by a blind driver (Ray Charles), but nothing scary. There is some overacted kissing and a bedroom scene (only involves some lingerie, no nudity).*

1996 80m/C Leslie Nielsen, Nicolette Sheridan, Andy Griffith, Charles Durning, Marcia Gay Harden, Barry Bostwick; **D:** Rick Friedberg; **W:** Rick Friedberg, Dick Chudnow, Jason Friedberg, Aaron Seltzer; **C:** John R. Leonetti; **M:** Bill Conti. **VHS** *NYR*

Spy Smasher 🦴🦴🦴

Family Considered by serial fans to be one of the very finest, this stars a popular comic-book hero of the era, a war reporter who used his supposed death in a plane crash (and a convenient twin brother) to go underground and fight Nazi counterfeiters trying to wreck the economy. Most serials end with a cliffhanger; this 12-episode chapter play begins with one, and takes off from there. Fast and stylish, with "Beethoven's Fifth Symphony" as a theme song because the opening notes coincided with the Allied 'V for victory' Morse code signal. "Spy Smasher Returns," also on tape, isn't a sequel but a feature-length condensed version.

BEWARE *Violence.*

1942 185m/B Kane Richmond, Marguerite Chapman, Sam Flint, Hans Schumm, Tristram Coffin; **D:** William Witney. **VHS** *REP*

The Spy Who Loved Me 🦴🦴

PG/Jr. High-Adult James Bond teams up with female Russian Agent XXX to squash a villain's plan to use captured American and Russian atomic submarines in a plot to destroy the world. The villain's henchman, 7-foot, 2-inch Kiel, is the steel-toothed Jaws. Carly Simon sings the memorable, Marvin Hamlisch theme song, "Nobody Does It Better."

BEWARE *007-ish violence, alcohol use and suggested sex.*

1977 136m/C Roger Moore, Barbara Bach, Curt Jurgens, Richard Kiel, Caroline Munro, Walter Gotell, Geoffrey Keen, Valerie Leon, Bernard Lee, Lois Maxwell, Desmond Llewelyn; *D:* Lewis Gilbert; *M:* Marvin Hamlisch. **VHS, Beta, LV** *MGM, FOX, TLF*

Squanto: A Warrior's Tale 🎞🎞🎞

PG/Primary-Adult Squanto—it isn't just for Thanksgiving any more. More historically accurate than "Pocahontas," live action adventure chronicles 17th-century Massachusetts brave Squanto (Beach), who is captured by English traders and taken to England for display as a "savage." He escapes and stows away on a ship bound for home. Though he finds that his tribe has died off, he helps bring about a peace between fearful Pilgrims and a neighboring tribe, which results in the first Thanksgiving feast. It may be history lite but it's also a thoughtful, adventurous saga with good performances, and fine location filming in Nova Scotia and Cape Breton, Canada. And there's Mandy Patinkin as an English monk.

BEWARE *Action violence. Some is too brutal for very young children.*

1994 101m/C Adam Beach, Mandy Patinkin, Michael Gambon, Nathaniel Parker, Eric Schweig, Donal Donnelly, Stuart Pankin, Alex Norton, Irene Bedard; *D:* Xavier Koller; *W:* Darlene Craviotto; *M:* Joel McNeely. **VHS, LV** *DIS*

Squanto and the First Thanksgiving

Family More storybook-than-animated version of a true story about the Indian who was sold into slavery in Spain, returned to North America, and helped the Pilgrims survive their first severe years at the Plymouth colony. Narrated by Native American actor Greene.

1993 30m/C VHS *RAB, BTV,*

Stacking 🎞🎞

PG/Jr. High-Adult 1950s Montana family is threatened with losing their farm when father is injured. Mother struggles on, despite conflicting emotions, and the whole thing is told through the eyes of the 14-year-old daughter, played by "Anne of Green Gables" star Follows. Slow-paced agri-drama, aided by acting, blighted by boredom.

BEWARE *Mature themes, alcohol use, salty language.*

1987 111m/C Christine Lahti, Megan Follows, Frederic Forrest, Peter Coyote, Jason Gedrick; *D:* Martin Rosen; *M:* Patrick Gleeson. **VHS, Beta, LV** *NLC*

Stage Fright 🎞🎞🎞

Jr. High-Adult Wyman will stop at nothing to clear her old boyfriend, who has been accused of murdering the husband of his mistress, an actress (Dietrich). Disguised as a maid, she falls in love with the investigating detective, and discovers her friend's guilt. Dietrich sings "The Laziest Gal in Town" and "La Vie en Rose." The Master's last film made in England until "Frenzy" (1971).

1950 110m/B Jane Wyman, Marlene Dietrich, Alastair Sim, Sybil Thorndike, Michael Wilding, Kay Walsh; *D:* Alfred Hitchcock. **VHS, Beta, LV** *WAR, MLB*

Stand and Deliver 🎞🎞🎞 ♭

PG/Jr. High-Adult True story of Jaime Escalante, a tough but caring teacher who inspired hard-luck students in an East L.A. barrio to take the Advanced Placement Test in calculus. His ghetto pupils score so well that authorities suspect mass cheating, and the class must vindicate themselves. Not just a nudge to do your math homework but a clarion call to excellence and self-esteem, with a wonderful performance from Olmos.

BEWARE *Profanity. Depictions of poverty.*

1988 105m/C Edward James Olmos, Lou Diamond Phillips, Rosana De Soto, Andy Garcia, Will Gotay, Ingrid Oliu, Virginia Paris, Mark Eliot; *D:* Ramon Menendez; *W:* Tom Musca, Ramon Menendez; *M:* Craig Safan. **Award Nominations:** Academy Awards '88: Best Actor (Olmos); **Awards:** Independent Spirit Awards '89: Best Actor (Olmos), Best Director (Menendez), Best Film, Best Screenplay, Best Supporting Actor (Phillips), Best Supporting Actress (De Soto). **VHS, LV, 8mm** *WAR, HMV*

Stand By Me 🎞🎞🎞

R/Jr. High-Adult Observant adaptation of the Stephen King novella "The Body," one of the bestselling author's few well known non-horror tales. Four 12-year-olds in 1960 trek into the Oregon wilderness to find the body of a missing boy, learning about death and personal courage. Told as a reminiscence by narrator Dreyfuss with solid performances from all four child actors. Much R-rated obscene language may render this a turnoff for most families, which is too bad; there's some fine stuff here, like the riotous fireside discussion about the exact species of Disney's Goofy.

BEWARE *Profanity—loads of it—plus threatened violence, vomiting and a dead boy.*

1986 87m/C River Phoenix, Wil Wheaton, Jerry O'Connell, Corey Feldman, Kiefer Sutherland, Richard Dreyfuss, Casey Siemaszko, John Cusack; *D:* Rob Reiner; *W:* Raynold Gideon; *M:* Jack Nitzsche. **VHS, Beta, LV, 8mm** *COL*

Stand Up and Cheer 🎞🎞 ♭

Family The new federal Secretary of Entertainment organizes a huge show to raise the country's depressed spirits. Near-invisible plot, fantastic premise are an excuse for lots of imagery, dancing, and comedy, including four-year-old Temple singing "Baby Take a Bow." Also available colorized. 🎵 I'm Laughing; We're Out of the Red; Broadway's Gone Hillbilly; Baby Take a Bow; This Is Our Last Night Together; She's Way Up Thar; Stand Up and Cheer.

1934 80m/B Shirley Temple, Warner Baxter, Madge Evans, Nigel Bruce, Stepin Fetchit, Frank Melton, Lila Lee, James Dunn, John Boles, Scotty Beckett; *D:* Hamilton MacFadden; *W:* Will Rogers, Ralph Spence. **VHS, Beta** *FOX*

Stanley and the Dinosaurs

Primary Stanley the progressive caveman is banished from his tribe until they see the usefulness of his new inventions. Based on "Stanley" by Syd Hoff.
1989 16m/C VHS, Beta *CHF*

Stanley the Ugly Duckling

Preschool-Primary Stanley the aesthetically-challenged juvenile waterfowl and his fox friend Nathan learn that what is inside counts more than appearance in this cartoon variant of Hans Christian Andersen, from the portentously-named "I Like Myself Productions."
1982 27m/C V: Rick Dees, Wolfman Jack. **VHS** *FHE*

Star Fairies

Preschool Sickly sweet Hanna-Barbera cartoon about ethereal beings Spice, Nightsong, Jazz, True Love, and Whisper (sound like colognes) who grant children's wishes under the direction of Princess Sparkle.
1985 40m/C V: Jonathan Winters, Didi Conn, Howard Morris, Arte Johnson. **VHS, Beta** *FHE*

Star Street: Adventures of the Star Kids

Preschool-Primary The Star Kids embark on an exciting new adventure. Cosmic cartoon, not to be confused with either "Star Trek" or "Sesame Street."
1989 80m/C VHS

Star Street: The Happy Birthday Movie

Preschool-Primary The Star Kids star in a warmed-over cartoon collection.
1989 85m/C VHS *JFK, WSH*

Star Trek 2: The Wrath of Khan

PG/Family Picking up from the 1967 Star Trek episode "Space Seed," Admiral James T. Kirk and the crew of the Enterprise must battle Khan, an old foe out for revenge. Warm and comradly in the nostalgic mode of its successors. Introduced Kirk's former lover and unknown son to the series plot, as well as Mr. Spock's "death," which led to the next sequel (1984's "The Search for Spock"). Can be seen in widescreen format on laserdisc.

BEWARE *Violence and gore.*

1982 113m/C William Shatner, Leonard Nimoy, Ricardo Montalban, DeForest Kelley, Nichelle Nichols, James Doohan, George Takei, Walter Koenig, Kirstie Alley, Merritt Butrick, Paul Winfield; **D:** Nicholas Meyer; **M:** James Horner. **VHS, Beta, LV, 8mm** *PAR*

Star Trek 3: The Search for Spock

PG/Family Captain Kirk hijacks the USS Enterprise and commands the aging crew to go on a mission to the Genesis Planet to discover whether Mr. Spock still lives (supposedly he died in the last movie). Klingons threaten, as usual. Somewhat slow and humorless, but intriguing. Third in the series of six (so far) Star Trek movies. The laserdisc edition carries the film in widescreen format.

1984 105m/C William Shatner, Leonard Nimoy, DeForest Kelley, James Doohan, George Takei, Walter Koenig, Mark Lenard, Robin Curtis, Merritt Butrick, Christopher Lloyd, Judith Anderson, John Larroquette, James B. Sikking, Nichelle Nichols, Cathie Shirriff, Miguel Ferrer, Grace Lee Whitney; **D:** Leonard Nimoy; **M:** James Horner. **VHS, Beta, LV, 8mm** *PAR*

Star Trek 4: The Voyage Home

PG/Jr. High-Adult Kirk and the gang go back in time (to the 1980s, conveniently) to save the Earth of the future from destruction. Filled with hilarious moments and exhilarating action; great special effects enhance the timely conservation theme. Watch for the stunning going-back-in-time sequence. Spock is particularly funny as he tries to fit in and learn 80s lingo. Best of the "Trek" series is available in widescreen format on laserdisc and as part of Paramount's "director's series," in which Nimoy discusses various special effects aspects.

BEWARE *Salty language.*

1986 119m/C William Shatner, DeForest Kelley, Catherine Hicks, James Doohan, Nichelle Nichols, George Takei, Walter Koenig, Mark Lenard, Leonard Nimoy; **D:** Leonard Nimoy; **W:** Nicholas Meyer. **VHS, Beta, LV, 8mm** *PAR*

Star Trek 5: The Final Frontier

PG/Primary-Adult A renegade Vulcan kidnaps the Enterprise and takes it on a journey to the mythic center of the universe. Shatner's big-action directorial debut (he also co-wrote the script) is a poor follow-up to the Nimoy-directed fourth entry in the series. Heavy-handed and pretentiously pseudo-theological. Available in widescreen format on laserdisc.

BEWARE *Profanity, roughhousing.*

1989 107m/C William Shatner, Leonard Nimoy, DeForest Kelley, James Doohan, Laurence Luckinbill, Walter Koenig, George Takei, Nichelle Nichols, David Warner; **D:** William Shatner; **W:** William Shatner; **M:** Jerry Goldsmith. **VHS, Beta, LV, 8mm** *PAR*

Star Trek 6: The Undiscovered Country

PG/Jr. High-Adult The final chapter in the long running Star Trek series is finally here. The Federation and the Klingon Empire are preparing a much-needed peace summit but Captain Kirk has his doubts about the true intentions of the Federation's longtime enemies. When a Klingon ship is attacked, Kirk and the crew of the Enterprise, who are accused of the misdeed, must try to find the real perpetrator. Has an exciting, climactic ending. As is typical of the series, the film highlights current events-glasnost—in its plotlines. Meyer also directed Star Trek movies 2 ("The Wrath of Khan") and 4 ("The Voyage Home").

⚠ BEWARE *Violence.*

1991 110m/C William Shatner, Leonard Nimoy, DeForest Kelley, James Doohan, George Takei, Walter Koenig, Nichelle Nichols, Christopher Plummer, Kim Cattrall, Iman, David Warner, Mark Lenard, Grace Lee Whitney, Brock Peters, Kurtwood Smith, Rosana De Soto, John Schuck, Michael Dorn; **D:** Nicholas Meyer; **W:** Nicholas Meyer, Denny Martin Flinn; **M:** Cliff Eidelman. **VHS, Beta, CD-I** *PAR*

Star Trek: Animated, Vol. 1

Family Episodes of an Emmy-winning Saturday-morning cartoon revival of the classic "Star Trek" series, utilizing the voices of the original cast, with fair animation, literate scripts, and general quality control that made these respectable additions to Starfleet lore. Volume 1 includes "More Tribbles, More Troubles" and "The Infinite Vulcan." Additional volumes available.

1973 48m/C V: William Shatner, Leonard Nimoy, DeForest Kelley, James Doohan, Nichelle Nichols, George Takei, Walter Koenig, Majel Barrett. **VHS** *PAR*

Star Trek Generations ♪♪♪

PG/Primary-Adult No wonder they call it Enterprise. Based on the second "Star Trek" TV series, here's the seventh "Star Trek" movie. Everybody got that? The two splendid captains, Kirk (Shatner) and Picard (Stewart) team up in a time warp to take on evil Dr. Soren (Mc-Dowell) before he destroys an entire solar system. Among Picard's Starship Enterprise crew, the android Mr. Data gets an emotion implant. Appearing briefly from Kirk's era are Scotty and Chekhov. A good time (and space) for all Trek fans. By the way, they prefer to be called Trekkers these days. Trekkies sounded too geeky.

⚠ BEWARE *Sci-fi action; some mild language.*

1994 117m/C William Shatner, Patrick Stewart, Malcolm Mc-Dowell, Whoopi Goldberg, Jonathon Frakes, Brent Spiner, LeVar Burton, Michael Dorn, Gates McFadden, Marina Sirtis, James Doohan, Walter Koenig, Alan Ruck; **D:** David Carson; **W:** Ronald D. Moore, Brannon Braga; **M:** Dennis McCarthy. **VHS, Beta** *PAR*

Star Trek: The Motion Picture ♪♪☆

G/Family The Enterprise fights a strange alien force that threatens Earth in this first film adaptation of the famous television series. Slow cruise through the universe is best appreciated by fans of the TV series. Twelve additional minutes of previously unseen footage have been added to this home video version of the theatrical feature. Laserdisc edition in widescreen format is also available. Numerous sequels.

1980 143m/C William Shatner, Leonard Nimoy, DeForest Kelley, James Doohan, Stephen Collins, Persis Khambatta, Nichelle Nichols, Walter Koenig, George Takei; **D:** Robert Wise; **M:** Jerry Goldsmith. **VHS, Beta, LV** *PAR*

Star Trek the Next Generation Episode 1-2: Encounter at Farpoint

Family Gene Roddenberry, the creator of the original "Star Trek" television series, spearheaded this episodic reincarnation for network syndication. This series, set 80 or so years beyond the original, enjoys an entirely new crew and a modernized vessel. Also, the new series places less emphasis on violent solutions to conflicts than the original TV series. In this first installment, entitled "Encounter at Farpoint, Parts 1 and 2," a powerful life force named "Q" threatens the lives of Captain Jean-Luc Picard and his crew as they attempt to figure out what's going on at Farpoint Station. Look for a cameo appearance by DeForest Kelly, "Bones" from the original series, as a very old man waxing nostalgic about the old U.S.S. Enterprise. Excellent production values, including fine special effects. Additional episodes available. Further volumes of episodes are continually being released on video.

1987 96m/C Patrick Stewart, Michael Dorn, Jonathon Frakes, Gates McFadden, Marina Sirtis, Denise Crosby, Brent Spiner, Wil Wheaton, LeVar Burton; **Cameos:** DeForest Kelley; **W:** Gene Roddenberry. **VHS, LV** *PAR, MOV*

Star Wars ♪♪♪♪

PG/Family First of Lucas' "Star Wars" trilogy and one of the biggest box-office hits of all time, drawing successfully on both fairy tale and sci-fi traditions. Yarn looks for spins on the old cliches until it all clicks as an epic original: the young hero, captured princess, hot-shot pilot, cute robots, demonic villain, and a wizard-like old Jedi knight. Storyline and characterizations blend together with marvelous f/x to make you care about the rebel forces engaged in a life-or-death struggle with the tyrant leaders of the Galactic Empire. Followed by superior "The Empire Strikes Back" (1980) and "Return of the Jedi" (1983).

⚠ BEWARE *Battle scenes, other space-induced violence.*

1977 121m/C Mark Hamill, Carrie Fisher, Harrison Ford, Alec Guinness, Peter Cushing, Kenny Baker, James Earl Jones, David Prowse, Anthony Daniels; **D:** George Lucas; **W:** George Lucas; **M:** John Williams. **Award Nominations:** Academy Awards '77: Best Director (Lucas), Best Original Screenplay, Best Picture, Best Supporting Actor (Guinness); **Awards:** Academy Awards '77: Best Art Direction/Set Decoration, Best Costume Design, Best Film Editing, Best Sound, Best Visual Effects, Best Original Score; Golden Globe Awards '78: Best Score; Los Angeles Film Critics Association Awards '77: Best Film; National Board of Review Awards '77: 10 Best Films of the Year; People's Choice Awards '78: Best Film. **VHS, Beta, LV** *FOX, RDG, HMV*

Starbird and Sweet William 🎵🎵

G/Family On a solo plane flight, a young Native American crashes in the wilderness. He must fight for survival in the harsh woods with his only friend, a bear cub. Fair family nature adventure, also known as "The Adventures of Starbird."

1973 95m/C A. Martinez, Louise Fitch, Dan Haggerty, Skip Homeier; **D:** Jack B. Hively. **VHS** *VCI*

Starchaser: The Legend of Orin 🎵🎵

PG/Family Animated fantasy about heroic young cyborg Orin, who combats galactic pirates to save the world of the future. Strictly Saturday-morning TV-quality, but inexplicably released to theaters.

1985 107m/C D: Steven Hahn. **VHS, Beta, LV** *PAR*

Starcom: Galactic Adventures

Primary-Jr. High TV-cartoon adventures of future heroes fighting the antisocial Emperor Dark. In "Fire and Ice," Slim and Crowbar crash on the volcanic moon. A defense satellite malfunctions and turns deadly in "The Long Fall," and in "The Caverns of Mars," Slim's niece and nephew get trapped in an underground city on Mars.

1987 66m/C VHS

Stargate 🎵🎵

PG-13/Jr. High-Adult U.S. military probe of a ring-shaped ancient Egyptian artifact (your tax dollars at work) sends he-man colonel Russell and geeky Egyptologist Spader into a parallel universe. There they meet the builders of the pyramids who are enslaved by an evil despot (Davidson) posing as a sun god. Ambitious premise zapped from prepubescent imaginations gets an A for effort, but a silly plot that jumbles biblical epic panoramas and space odyssey special effects with otherworldly mysticism and needless emotional hang-ups trade shlock for style. Spader's shaggy scholar is neurotically fun, Russell's jarhead a bore, and Davidson's vampy villain an unintended hoot. Really only for the more mature crowd.

BEWARE *Sci-fi action violence and some strong language. The guardians of the pyramids are really scary and the bad guys metamorphosize from men to Egyptian figures.*

1994 119m/C Kurt Russell, James Spader, Jaye Davidson, Viveca Lindfors, Alexis Cruz, Leon Rippy, John Diehl, Erik Avari, Mili Avital; **D:** Roland Emmerich; **W:** Dean Devlin, Roland Emmerich; **C:** Jeff Okun. **VHS, LV** *LIV*

Starman 🎵🎵🎵 ♪

PG/Jr. High-Adult Peaceful alien from an advanced civilization lands in Wisconsin. Employing state-of-the-art alien analysis, he decides to hide beneath the guise of a grieving young widow's recently deceased husband. Pleased with that idea, star guy then makes the widow drive him across country with the government in pursuit so he can rendezvous with his spacecraft. On the road together, they get to know each other. Well-acted, carefully directed sci-fi romance with a road flick running through it (don't see too many of those) brings an interesting twist to the "Stranger in a Strange Land" theme. Bridges is engaging as the likeable starman in wonder at what Wisconsin (and the rest of the planet) has to offer, while Allen is lovely and earthy (just the thing for a guy from outer space), creating a one-of-a-kind romance. Available in widescreen format on laserdisc.

BEWARE *Sex, violence, profanity and misunderstanding of what yellow traffic light means.*

1984 115m/C Jeff Bridges, Karen Allen, Charles Martin Smith, Richard Jaeckel; **D:** John Carpenter; **W:** Bruce A. Evans, Raynold Gideon; **M:** Jack Nitzsche. **VHS, Beta, LV** *COL*

Starship 🎵

PG/Jr. High-Adult Lame British/Australian "Star Wars" ripoff is about underaged human freedom fighters on a planet run by evil robots. Lorca and the Outlaws (pic's original title) have help from one cute little mechanical man in their fight for truth, justice, and the Lucasfilm way. Okay special effects, and that's it.

BEWARE *Violence.*

1987 91m/C John Tarrant, Cassandra Webb, Donough Rees, Deep Roy, Ralph Cotterill; **D:** Roger Christian. **VHS, Beta** *HHE*

State Fair 🎵🎵🎵

Family The second version of the glossy slice of Americana about a family at the Iowa State Fair, featuring plenty of great songs by Rodgers and Hammerstein. The best of three versions, it was adapted by Hammerstein from the 1933 screen version of Phil Strong's novel. Remade again in 1962. It Might as Well Be Spring; It's a Grand Night for Singing; That's For Me; Isn't It Kinda Fun?; All I Owe Iowa; Our State Fair.

1945 100m/C Charles Winninger, Jeanne Crain, Dana Andrews, Vivian Blaine, Dick Haymes, Fay Bainter, Frank McHugh, Percy Kilbride, Donald Meek, William Marshall, Harry (Henry) Morgan; **D:** Walter Lang; **W:** Oscar Hammerstein; **M:** Richard Rodgers, Oscar Hammerstein. **Award Nominations:** Academy Awards '45: Best Original Score; **Awards:** Academy Awards '45: Best Song ("It Might as Well Be Spring"). **VHS, Beta** *FOX*

State Fair 🎵🎵

Family Third film version of the story of a farm family who travel to their yearly state fair and experience life. The original songs are still there, but otherwise this is a letdown. Texas setting required dropping the song "All I Owe Iowa." ♫ Our State Fair; It's a Grand Night for Singing; That's for Me; It Might as Well Be Spring; Isn't It Kinda Fun?; More Than Just a Friend; It's the Little Things in Texas; Willing and Eager; This Isn't Heaven.

1962 118m/C Pat Boone, Ann-Margret, Bobby Darin, Tom Ewell, Alice Faye, Pamela Tiffin, Wally Cox; **D:** Jose Ferrer. **VHS, Beta** *FOX*

Capt. Jean-Luc Picard and Capt. James T. Kirk try a different form of transportation in "Star Trek Generations."

Stay Tuned ♪

PG-13/Jr. High-Adult Suburban yuppie couple buys a large-screen TV and satellite dish from Hellvision salesman, are sucked into their dish, and wind up starring in hellish TV shows such as "Wayne's Underworld," "Northern Overexposure," "Sadistic Home Videos," and "My Three Sons of Bitches." If they can survive for 24 hours, they'll be able to return to their normal lives. Clever idea for a film is wasted as this one never experiences good reception; viewers may not want to stay tuned to the low comedy and frantic yucks.

1992 90m/C John Ritter, Pam Dawber, Jeffrey Jones, Eugene Levy, David Tom, Heather McComb; **D:** Peter Hyams; **W:** Tom S. Parker; **M:** Bruce Broughton. **VHS, LV** *WAR*

The Steadfast Tin Soldier

Preschool-Primary Beautifully illustrated (not animated) version of the classic Hans Christian Andersen fable, read aloud by British actor Irons as part of the "Rabbit Ears" series of videos from Random House.

1986 30m/C VHS, Beta *KUI, RAN, VEC*

Steel Magnolias ♪♪♪

PG/Jr. High-Adult Julia Roberts plays a young woman stricken with severe diabetes who chooses to live her life to the fullest despite her bad health. Much of the action centers around a Louisiana beauty shop where the women get together to discuss the goings-on of their lives. Screenplay by R. Harling, based on his partially autobiographical play. Sweet, poignant, and often hilarious, yet just as often overwrought. MacLaine is funny as a bitter divorcee, Parton is sexy and fun as the hairdresser. But Field and Roberts go off the deep end and make it all entirely too weepy.

BEWARE *Brief profanity and a seriously ill young woman. Scary diabetic episode.*

1989 118m/C Sally Field, Dolly Parton, Shirley MacLaine, Daryl Hannah, Olympia Dukakis, Julia Roberts, Tom Skerritt, Sam Shepard, Dylan McDermott, Kevin J. O'Connor, Bil McCurcheon, Ann Wedgeworth, Janine Turner; **D:** Herbert Ross; **W:** Robert Harling; **M:** Georges Delerue. **Award Nominations:** Academy Awards '89: Best Supporting Actress (Wiest); **Awards:** Golden Globe Awards '90: Best Supporting Actress (Roberts); People's Choice Awards '90: Best Film—Drama. **VHS, Beta, LV, 8mm** *COL*

Stepmonster

PG-13/Jr. High-Adult Twelve-year-old Todd tries to convince anyone who'll listen that his dumb father's fiancee can change into a scaly forest beast. Childish and predictable junk, with barely a cool creature costume to recommend it.

BEWARE *Profanity, violence (against monsters, mainly), sex talk.*

1992 84m/C Alan Thicke, Robin Riker, Corey Feldman, John Astin, Ami Dolenz, George Gaynes. **VHS** *NHO*

The Sting

PG/Jr. High-Adult Paul Newman and Robert Redford are con artists in 1930s Chicago who pull an elaborate scam on the gangster (Robert Shaw at his malevolent best) who's killed their friend. The plot is brilliant, full of surprises and the catharsis of sweet revenge. Excellent acting by stars and a large ensemble. The score is Scott Joplin's wonderful turn-of-the-century ragtime music adapted by Marvin Hamlisch. Joplin's music has been popular ever since. Ages 11 and up.

BEWARE *A likeable character is brutally killed, another is beaten. Sexual situations, nothing graphic.*

1973 129m/C Paul Newman, Robert Redford, Robert Shaw, Charles Durning, Eileen Brennan, Harold Gould, Ray Walston; **D:** George Roy Hill; **W:** David S. Ward; **M:** Marvin Hamlisch. **Award Nominations:** Academy Awards '73: Best Actor (Redford), Best Cinematography, Best Sound; **Awards:** Academy Awards '73: Best Adapted Score, Best Art Direction/Set Decoration, Best Costume Design, Best Director (Hill), Best Film Editing, Best Picture, Best Story & Screenplay; Directors Guild of America Awards '73: Best Director (Hill); People's Choice Awards '75: Best Film. **VHS, Beta, LV** *MCA, BTV*

The Sting 2 ♪ ♭

PG/Family Complicated comic plot concludes with the final con game, involving a fixed boxing match where the stakes top a million dollars and the payoff could be murder. Lame sequel to "The Sting."

BEWARE *Violence.*

1983 102m/C Jackie Gleason, Mac Davis, Teri Garr, Karl Malden, Oliver Reed; **D:** Jeremy Paul Kagan; **W:** David S. Ward. **VHS, Beta, LV** *MCA*

Stingiest Man in Town

Family The cartoon bear gets more than he bargained for in this birthday adventure. Additional volumes available.

1978 50m/C V: Tom Bosley, Walter Matthau, Paul Frees, Theodore Bikel, Robert Morse, Dennis Day. **VHS** *WAR*

Stingray: Invaders of the Deep

Preschool-Primary Spinoff of the popular British puppet TV adventure "Thunderbirds," this tale acted by marionettes depicts the fearless (and expressionless) Captain Tempest leading his futuristic submarine, "Stingray," against the aliens invading Marineville. More cool special f/x from Gerry Anderson.

1981 92m/C D: David Elliott, John Kelly, Desmond Saunders. **VHS, Beta, LV** *FHE*

The Stone Boy ♪♪♪ ♭

PG/Jr. High-Adult Boy accidentally shoots and kills his older brother in a hunting accident near their Montana farm. The family is torn apart by sadness and guilt. Sensitive, unflinching look at him and other family members reacting to the most personal of tragedies, with an excellent cast led by Duvall's crystal-clear performance. Script by Gina Berriault; based on her short story.

BEWARE *Violence and its attendant trauma.*

1984 93m/C Glenn Close, Robert Duvall, Jason Presson, Frederic Forrest, Wilford Brimley, Linda Hamilton; **D:** Christopher Cain; **M:** James Horner. **VHS, Beta** *FOX*

Stone Fox ♪♪

Family Wyoming, 1905. Following his grandfather's stroke, 12-year-old orphan Willy's only hope for saving the family farm is to win a dogsled race in which undefeated Indian champ Stone Fox is also entered. Good start, tearjerking finale, but terribly draggy in between. Somewhat softened made-for-TV version of the children's book by John Reynolds Gardiner.

1987 96m/C Buddy Ebsen, Joey Cramer, Belinda J. Montgomery, Gordon Tootoosis; **D:** Harvey Hart. **VHS** *WOV*

Stop! or My Mom Will Shoot ♪

PG-13/Jr. High-Adult Getty is an overbearing mother paying a visit to her cop son (Stallone) in Los Angeles. When mom witnesses a crime she has to stay in town longer than intended, which gives her time to meddle in her son's work and romantic lives. If Stallone wants to change his image this so-called comedy isn't the way to do it-because the joke is only on him. Viewers who rent this may find the joke is on them.

1992 87m/C Sylvester Stallone, Estelle Getty, JoBeth Williams, Roger Rees, Martin Ferrero, Gailard Sartain, Dennis Burkley; **D:** Roger Spottiswoode; **W:** William Osborne; **M:** Alan Silvestri. **VHS, Beta, LV** *MCA*

Stories and Fables, Vol. 1

Family Series of live-action stories for children. Each volume contains two tales about kings, emperors and warriors, filmed in exotic locales from around the world. Additional volumes available.

1985 50m/C VHS, Beta *DIS*

Stories from the Black Tradition

Primary-Jr. High A "Children's Circle" tape presenting five Caldecott award-winning classic children's books: "A Story—A Story" by Gail E. Haley, "Mufaro's Beautiful Daughters" by John Steptoe, "Why Mosquitoes Buzz in People's Ears" retold by Verna Aardema, "The Village of

Round and Square Houses" by Ann Grifalconi, and "Goggles!" by Ezra Jack Keats.
1992 52m/C VHS *CCC, MLT, WKV*

Stories to Remember: Baby's Morningtime

Preschool Award-winning animated versions of storybooks and fairy tales created for PBS's "Long Ago and Far Away" series. This video contains nineteen animated morning poems for children taken from illustrator Kay Chorao's "The Baby's Good Morning Book," including "Ducks at Dawn," "Getting Out of Bed," "The Year's at the Spring," and others. Also in the series are "Baby's Storytime," "Beauty and the Beast," "Noah's Ark" and others. The series is narrated by personalities such as James Earl Jones , Mia Farrow and Kevin Kline.
1992 25m/C *Performed by:* Judy Collins. **VHS** *LTY, BMG, FAF*

Stormalong

Preschool-Primary Comic actor Candy reads the tall tale of the New England sea captain in this installment of the "Rabbit Ears" storytelling series.
1992 30m/C VHS *MVD, RAB*

Storms

Preschool-Jr. High Clips from "Fantasia," "Bambi," and "The Old Mill" emphasize the power of storms. Demonstrations show their origins and safety measures for storms are examined.
1990 14m/C VHS, Beta *MTI, DSN*

Stormy, the Thoroughbred

Preschool-Primary Stormy, the pony not good enough for the game, is sold as a workhorse. Soon, however, he joins a string of polo ponies and proves his worth. A live-action episode of TV's "Wonderful World of Disney."
1990 46m/C VHS, Beta *MTI, DSN*

The Story Keepers: Breakout!

Primary Set in Rome 64 A.D., during the time of Nero's persecution of Christians, this animated tale follows the lives of Ben the baker, his wife, Helena, and the four children they adopt after their parents disappear during the burning of Rome. Ben tells the children the story of Jesus and other Gospel stories. Ages 5 to 9.
1995 30m/C VHS *ZON, FCS*

The Story Lady 🐾🐾 ▷

G/Family Retired widow's tale-spinning abilities get her a TV slot as hostess on a cable kids' program. She becomes so popular that network execs want to exploit her as a spokesperson for a toy company. Only a young girl can keep The Story Lady from selling out. Rosy, little, acclaimed made-for-TV tale.
1993 93m/C Jessica Tandy, Lisa Jakub, Ed Begley Jr., Charles Durning, Stephanie Zimbalist; **D:** Larry Elikann. **VHS** *UNT*

The Story of a Cowboy Angel 🐾

Family Rather than go to jail, a western desperado gets sentenced to work on a ranch belonging to a young widow. But he's still got a bad attitude until a wintery visitation from his deceased partner Murff, who must earn his angel's wings by spreading the holiday spirit.
1981 90m/C Slim Pickens. **VHS, Beta** *LIV, VES*

Story of Babar the Little Elephant

Family The tales of the lovable cartoon pachyderm, from jungle creature to well-dressed urbanite, to king of the elephants, are shown in this 30-minute musical feature. Features the voice of Peter Ustinov. Ages 3 to 7.
1968 30m/C VHS, Beta *NO*

The Story of 15 Boys 🐾🐾 ▷

Family After a shipwreck, 15 schoolmates cooperate to survive on a desert island in perilous, pirate-filled waters. Rousing Japanese-animated version of the only Jules Verne tale the great fantasy/adventure author penned expressly for young readers.
1990 80m/C VHS *JFK*

The Story of Seabiscuit 🐾🐾 ▷

Family The famous racing winner Seabiscuit is featured in a fluffy story of a racetrack romance. Temple is in love with a jockey but wants him to give up racing. Her uncle, who is Seabiscuit's trainer, has other things in mind.
1949 93m/C Shirley Temple, Barry Fitzgerald, Lon McCallister, Rosemary DeCamp; **D:** David Butler. **VHS** *MGM, BTV*

The Story of the Dancing Frog

Family Two very unusual frogs, George and Gertrude, dance around the globe in this cartoon narrated by Plummer.
1989 30m/C VHS, Beta *FHE*

Storybook 🐾🐾 ▷

G/Family Eight-year-old Brandon finds a magic storybook and enters into a realm of fantasy. He discovers the only way to return home from Storyland is to save the kingdom from the rule of Queen Evilia and along with Woody the Woodsman, Pouch the Boxing Kangaroo, and Hoot the Wise Owl, Brandon just may succeed.
1995 88m/C Sean Fitzgerald, William McNamara, Swoosie Kurtz, Robert Costanzo, James Doohan, Brenda Epperson, Gary Morgan, Richard Moll, Jack Scalia, Milton Berle; **D:** Lorenzo Doumani; **W:** Lorenzo Doumani, Susan Bowen. **VHS** *REP*

Stowaway 🐾🐾🐾

Family After her missionary parents are killed in a Chinese revolution, Shirley stows away on a line bound for San Francisco and plays cupid to a bickering couple who adopt her. 🎵 Good Night, My Love; One Never Knows, Does One; You Gotta S-M-I-L-E to Be H-A-P-P-Y; I Wanna Go To the Zoo; That's What I Want For Christmas.

1936 86m/B Shirley Temple, Robert Young, Alice Faye, Eugene Pallette, Helen Westley, Arthur Treacher, Astrid Allwyn; *D:* William A. Seiter. **VHS, Beta** *FOX*

Stowaways on the Ark

Preschool-Primary Clumps from the cartoon series featuring Willie the Woodworm, who gets himself into trouble by boring holes in the side of Noah's ark.
1989 90m/C VHS, Beta *CEL*

Straight Talk 🎵🎵 ♪

PG/Jr. High-Adult Shirlee is a down-home gal from Arkansas who heads for Chicago to start life anew. She finds a job as a receptionist at WNDY radio, but is mistaken for the new radio psychologist. Her homespun advice ("Get off the cross. Somebody needs the wood.") becomes hugely popular and soon "Dr." Shirlee is the toast of the town. Parton's advice is the funniest part of this flimsy comedy, but she is helped immensely by Dunne and Orbach. On the other hand, Woods as the love interest/journalist who's suspicious of the good Dr.'s credentials seems a mite underwhelmed by the proceedings.

 Profanity.

1992 91m/C Dolly Parton, James Woods, Griffin Dunne, Michael Madsen, Deidre O'Connell, John Sayles, Teri Hatcher, Spalding Gray, Jerry Orbach, Philip Bosco, Charles Fleischer, Jay Thomas; *D:* Barnet Kellman; *W:* Craig Bolotin, Patricia Resnick; *M:* Brad Fiedel. **VHS, Beta** *HPH*

Strange Brew 🎵🎵 ♪

PG/Jr. High-Adult Those that enjoy silly films and don't mind burping, beer drinking and other grotesque behavior will find this film worth a watch. The SCTV alumni character's Doug and Bob MacKenzie (of the Great White North) find themselves battling a powerful brewmeister who is trying to control the world by drugging Elsinore beer. The bumbling brothers, of course, save the day and manage to get a hockey game in, too!! Take off, eh!

 Burping and general stupidness galore. Young kids probaboly won't get it or care.

1983 91m/C Rick Moranis, Dave Thomas, Max von Sydow, Paul Dooley; *D:* Rick Moranis, Dave Thomas; *W:* Rick Moranis, Dave Thomas, Steve DeJarnatt; *M:* Charles Fox. **VHS, Beta, LV** *MGM*

Strange Invaders 🎵🎵🎵

PG/Jr. High-Adult Space folks have taken over a midwestern town in the '50s, assuming the locals' appearance and attire before returning to their ship. Seems one of them married an Earthling—but divorced and moved with her half-breed daughter to New York City. So the hicksters from space visit the Big Apple. Spoof of 50's sci-fi amusingly renders the story of confused alien body snatchers.

 Violence.

1983 94m/C Paul LeMat, Nancy Allen, Diana Scarwid, Michael Lerner, Louise Fletcher, Wallace Shawn, Fiona Lewis, Kenneth Tobey, June Lockhart, Charles Lane, Dey Young, Mark Goddard; *D:* Michael Laughlin. **VHS, Beta, LV** *VES*

Strangers in Good Company 🎵🎵🎵

PG/Jr. High-Adult Quiet little film about a bus load of elderly women lost in the Canadian wilderness. They wait for rescue without histrionics, using the opportunity instead to get to know each other and nature. Loving metaphor to growing older with non-actors in every role is beautifully made, intelligent, uncommon, and worthwhile.
1991 101m/C Alice Diabo, Mary Meigs, Cissy Meddings, Beth Webber, Winifred Holden, Constance Garneau, Catherine Roche, Michelle Sweeney; *D:* Cynthia Scott; *W:* Cynthia Scott, David Wilson, Gloria Demers, Sally Bochner; *M:* Marie Bernard. **VHS, Beta** *TOU*

Strangers on a Train 🎵🎵🎵🎵

Jr. High-Adult Long before there was "Throw Momma from the Train," there was this Hitchcock super-thriller about two passengers who accidentally meet and plan to "trade" murders. Amoral Walker wants the exchange and the money he'll inherit by his father's death; Granger would love to end his stifling marriage and wed Roman, a senator's daughter, but finds the idea ultimately sickening. What happens is pure Hitchcock. Screenplay co-written by murder mystery great Chandler. Patricia Hitchcock, the director's only child, plays Roman's sister. The concluding "carousel" scene is a masterpiece. From the novel by Patricia Highsmith.
1951 101m/B Farley Granger, Robert Walker, Ruth Roman, Leo G. Carroll, Patricia Hitchcock, Marion Lorne; *D:* Alfred Hitchcock; *W:* Raymond Chandler; *M:* Dimitri Tiomkin. **Award Nominations:** Academy Awards '51: Best Black and White Cinematography; **Awards:** National Board of Review Awards '51: 10 Best Films of the Year. **VHS, Beta, LV** *WAR, MLB*

Strawberry Shortcake and the Baby Without a Name

Family One of a series of cartoon specials promoting the ever-so-cute natives of Strawberry Land, really a merchandising blitz for "Strawberry Shortcake" greeting cards and toys. In this adventure (or is it just an ad?), the nefarious Purple Pieman, continuous villain of the series, comes home with something completely different: an affectionate monster and a baby without a name. What will Strawberry and the others do? Additional volumes available.
1984 60m/C VHS, Beta *FHE*

Street Fighter 🎵 ♪

PG-13/Jr. High-Adult While there have been decent video games based on movies, no movie based on a video game has ever been any good. In this one, Col. Guile (Van Damme) and his fighting force, the good guys, attempt to liberate a country from mad Gen. Bison (Julia in one of his last roles). It's all pretty dumb. Oh, there's a scene where a man becomes a monster with orange hair and big muscles and it isn't Dennis Rodman.

BEWARE! *Non-stop martial arts and action violence: electrocutions, broken necks, bloody gashes.*

1994 101m/C Jean-Claude Van Damme, Raul Julia, Wes Studi, Ming-Na Wen, Damian Chapa, Simon Callow, Roshan Seth, Kylie Minogue, Byrun Mann; **D:** Steven E. de Souza; **W:** Steven E. de Souza; **M:** Graeme Revell. **VHS, LV** *MCA*

Street Fighter 2: The Animated Movie

PG-13/Jr. High-Sr. High Based on the video game with non-stop animated martial arts violence.

BEWARE! *Non-stop animated martial arts violence.*

1995 96m/C VHS *SMV*

Street Frogs: Keep on Rappin'

Primary Street Frogs rap up a storm in this animated adventure.

1987 40m/C VHS, Beta *ORI, WAR*

Strega Nonna and Other Stories

Preschool-Primary Animated story of a man who unleashes a torrent of pasta from the pasta pot of Grandmother Witch that threatens to destroy the town. Also includes "The Foolish Frog," "A Story—a Story," and "Tikki Tikki Tembo." Volume IV of the "Children's Circle" series from Weston Woods.

1978 35m/C VHS, Beta *CCC,, FCT*

Strictly Ballroom 🦴🦴 ᵇ

PG/Jr. High-Adult Offbeat, cheerfully tacky dance/romance from Down Under amusingly turns every movie cliche it encounters slightly askew. Scott (Mercurio) has been in training for the Pan-Pacific ballroom championships since the age of six. While talented, he also refuses to follow convention and scandalizes the stuffy dance establishment with his new steps. When Scott takes up with a love-struck beginner (Morice), with some surprises of her own. Ballet dancer Mercurio (in his film debut) is appropriately arrogant yet vulnerable, while Morice is great as the plain Jane turned steel butterfly. One of a kind with a wonderful supporting cast is a substantial debut for director Luhrmann.

BEWARE! *Profanity and terminal eccentricity. Strictly for older kids.*

1992 94m/C Paul Mercurio, Tara Morice, Bill Hunter, Pat Thomsen, Barry Otto, Gia Carides, Peter Whitford, John Hannan, Sonia Kruger-Tayler, Kris McQuade, Pip Mushin, Leonie Page, Antonio Vargas, Armonia Benedito; **D:** Baz Luhrmann; **W:** Craig Pearce, Baz Luhrmann; **M:** David Hirshfelder. **Award Nominations:** Golden Globe Awards '94: Best Film—Musical/Comedy; **Awards:** Australian Film Institute '92: Best Costume Design, Best Director (Luhrmann), Best Film, Best Supporting Actor (Otto), Best Supporting Actress (Thomsen), Best Writing. **VHS, LV** *MAX, TOU, BTV*

Strike Up the Band 🦴🦴 ᵇ

Family High school band turns to hot swing music and enters a national radio contest. Rooney and Garland display their usual charm in this high-energy stroll down memory lane. 🎵 Over the Waves; The Light Cavalry Overture; Walkin Down Broadway; Five Foot Two, Eyes of Blue; After the Ball; Nobody; Strike Up the Band.

1940 120m/B Judy Garland, Mickey Rooney, Paul Whiteman, William Tracy, June Preisser; **D:** Busby Berkeley. **Award Nominations:** Academy Awards '40: Best Song ("Our Love Affair"), Best Score; **Awards:** Academy Awards '40: Best Sound. **VHS, Beta, LV** *MGM*

Stuart Saves His Family 🦴 ᵇ

PG-13/Jr. High-Adult Good thing Al Franken hit it big with his book, "Rush Limbaugh is a Big Fat Idiot." He sure wasn't going to make it as a movie star. In this bloated "Saturday Night Live" sketch, self-help advicemeister Stuart Smalley (Franken) helps his dysfunctional family deal with their pathetic problems.

BEWARE! *Profanity, alcoholism, marijuana smoking and binge eating.*

1994 97m/C Al Franken, Laura San Giacomo, Vincent D'Onofrio, Shirley Knight, Harris Yulin; **D:** Harold Ramis; **W:** Al Franken; **M:** Marc Shaiman. **VHS, Beta** *PAR*

The Stupids 🦴🦴 ᵇ

PG/Family Based on the best-selling children's book series, the aptly named Stupids—dad Stanley, mom Joan, brother Buster, and sis Petunia—blunder unwittingly into and out of life-and-death situations. The question is "how do they do it?" There's a plot involving space aliens and terrorists—yes, it is stupid, too. But that's the charm, isn't it? Keep a lookout for Captain Kangaroo (though only us older "kids" will recognize him).

BEWARE! *Some violence.*

1995 ?m/C Tom Arnold, Jessica Lundy, Bug Hall, Alex McKenna; **D:** John Landis; **W:** Brent Forrester. **VHS** *NYR*

Sub-Mariner: Atlantis Under Attack

Primary-Jr. High Marvel Comics characters in 'toon form star in these episodes. In the title feature Atuma kidnaps Lord Bashy and lures Sub-Mariner to the Forbidden Caverns. The superheroes reunite to fight Dr. Doom in "Dr. Doom's Day."

1966 35m/C VHS

Suburban Commando 🦴🦴

PG/Jr. High-Adult Muscular alien superhero (on steroids?) crashes to Earth while on a mission. He does his best to remain inconspicuous, renting a room with the suburban Wilcoxes and getting into goofy scrapes around the neighborhood. Wimpy family man Charlie Wilcox finally gains confidence from the big guy from beyond. Occasionally cute, lowbrow vehicle for wrestler Hogan, aimed at younger fans.

Typical World-Wrestling-Federation rough-housing, though care is taken that a space monster gets the worst of it. Salty language.

1991 88m/C Hulk Hogan, Christopher Lloyd, Shelley Duvall, Larry Miller, William Ball, JoAnn Dearing, Jack Elam, Roy Dotrice, Christopher Neame, Tony Longo; **D:** Burt Kennedy. **VHS, LV** *COL, NLC*

Sudden Terror 🐾🐾

PG/Family Murder of an African dignitary is witnessed by a young boy (Lester, of "Oliver!") who has trouble convincing his parents and the police about the incident. Pint-sized suspense, but less than original. Shot on location in Malta.

1970 95m/C Mark Lester, Lionel Jeffries, Susan George, Tony Bonner; **D:** John Hough. **VHS, Beta** *FOX*

Sudie & Simpson 🐾🐾 ♡

Jr. High-Adult Heart-tugging tale set in a viciously racist town in 1940s Georgia. Sudie, a 12-year-old white girl, forms a forbidden friendship with a gentle, educated black man secretly living in a shack in the woods, even though he could be lynched if they're found out. Superbly acted by Gilbert and Oscar-winner Gossett, but subplots about child molestation (graphically described) and sex education are more like encumbrances than assets. Made for cable TV, and based on the novel by Sara Flanagan Carter.

Sex talk, profanity and talk of child molestation.

1990 95m/C Sara Gilbert, Louis Gossett Jr., Frances Fisher, John M. Jackson, Paige Danahy, Ken Strong; **D:** Joan Tewkesbury; **W:** Sara Flanigan Carter, Ken Koser. **VHS** *WOV*

Sugar Cane Alley 🐾🐾🐾

PG/Family After the loss of his parents, an 11-year-old West Indian orphan goes to work with his grandmother on an island sugar plantation. She realizes that her boy's only hope to escape grinding poverty is an education. Set in Martinique in the 1930s. Poignant, memorable and too seldom seen.

1983 106m/C Garry Cadenat, Darling Legitimus, Douta Seck; **D:** Euzhan Palcy; **W:** Euzhan Palcy. **VHS, Beta, LV** *MED, FCT*

Summer Magic 🐾🐾

Family Impecunious recent widow is forced to leave Boston and settle her family in a small town in Maine. Typical, forgettable Disney drama served to showcase Mills early in her career. Remake of "Mother Carey's Chickens."

1963 116m/C Hayley Mills, Burl Ives, Dorothy McGuire, Deborah Walley, Una Merkel, Eddie Hodges; **D:** James Neilson; **M:** Buddy Baker. **VHS, Beta** *DIS*

Summer Rental 🐾🐾

PG/Jr. High-Adult Candy plays a harried air-traffic controller, trying to have a few days to relax with his family in sunny Florida. But a mean rich guy finally goads him and his kids into a machismo-flavored sailboat race. The star

could add something hefty to the limpest of plots, and does so here. Watch the first hour for yuks, then rewind.

Salty language, sex talk. Running joke about a woman who proudly asks everyone to inspect her newly augmented breasts.

1985 87m/C John Candy, Rip Torn, Richard Crenna, Karen Austin, Kerri Green, John Larroquette, Pierrino Mascarino; **D:** Carl Reiner; **M:** Alan Silvestri. **VHS, Beta, LV, 8mm** *PAR*

Summer School 🐾🐾 ♡

PG-13/Jr. High-Adult Semi-responsible high-school teacher's vacation plans are ruined when he gets stuck teaching remedial English to a bunch of party-hearty kids in California summer school. But our hero finds life is more than a beach, as he encounters romance, the kids bond, and classroom antics make a direct hit on the funny bone.

Sexual stuff, with an almost-funny/almost alarming subplot about a teen nymphet who constantly offers herself to her teacher (who resists). Drinking, salty language, and one teen pregnancy.

1987 98m/C Mark Harmon, Kirstie Alley, Nels Van Patten, Courtney Thorne-Smith, Lucy Lee Flippin, Shawnee Smith, Robin Thomas, Dean Cameron; **D:** Carl Reiner; **W:** Jeff Franklin; **M:** Danny Elfman. **VHS, Beta, LV** *PAR*

Summer Switch

Primary-Jr. High Mary Rodgers authored the famous "Freaky Friday" in which a mother and daughter switched bodies for the day. This ABC Afterschool Special takes its inspiration from an equal-time Rodgers book, in which a boy at summer camp wishes he could trade places with his executive dad. The two find themselves awkwardly in each other's places just before dad's vital business meeting. Two versions on video, one 46 minutes long, the other abridged to a half-hour.

1984 46m/C VHS, Beta *LCA, NWV*

A Summer to Remember 🐾🐾

PG/Family Deaf boy (played by Gerlis, himself deaf since birth) forms a friendship with an escaped lab orangutan through sign language. Becomes less-sophisticated simian "Free Willy" when carnival baddies abduct the ape. Parents depicted as morons while music seems to sample "Sesame Street." Made-for-TV monkeyshines whose cleverest touch isn't even in the movie—it's "Harry and the Hendersons," another primate title, as a coming attraction on the tape.

Roughhousing.

1984 93m/C Tess Harper, James Farentino, Burt Young, Louise Fletcher, Sean Gerlis, Bridgette Anderson; **D:** Robert Lewis; **M:** Charles Fox. **VHS, Beta** *MCA*

Summerdog 🐾🐾

G/Family Harmless but trite tale about a city family vacationing in Maine who adopt a stray mutt. Hobo the dog ends up saving them from numerous perils and even unmasks their evil landlord as a criminal fence.

1978 90m/C James Congdon, Elizabeth Eisenman, Oliver Zabriskie, Tavia Zabriskie; **D:** John Clayton. **VHS, Beta** *GEM*

The Sunshine Boys 🎵🎵🎵

PG/Jr. High-Adult Two veteran vaudeville partners, who have shared a love-hate relationship for decades, reunite for a television special. Adapted by Neil Simon from his play. Matthau was a replacement for Jack Benny, who died before the start of filming. Burns, for his first starring role since "Honolulu" in 1939, won an Oscar.

1975 111m/C George Burns, Walter Matthau, Richard Benjamin, Lee Meredith, F. Murray Abraham, Carol Arthur, Howard Hesseman; **D:** Herbert Ross; **W:** Neil Simon. **Award Nominations:** Academy Awards '75: Best Actor (Matthau), Best Adapted Screenplay, Best Art Direction/Set Decoration; **Awards:** Academy Awards '75: Best Supporting Actor (Burns); Golden Globe Awards '76: Best Actor—Musical/Comedy (Matthau), Best Film—Musical/Comedy, Best Supporting Actor (Benjamin). **VHS, Beta, LV** *MGM, BTV*

Sunshine Porcupine

Preschool-Primary In union with our star the Sun, the Sunshine Porcupine defeats the Ugli-Unks and saves Eggwood from a threatened loss of solar power. Animated production.

1979 45m/C VHS, Beta *MPI*

Super Fuzz 🎵🕊

PG/Jr. High-Adult Italian-made production (the easygoing Hill is a superstar over there) about a rookie policeman who develops super powers after being accidentally exposed to radiation. Somewhat ineptly, he uses his abilities to combat crime. Somewhat ineptly acted, written, and directed as well.

🚨 BEWARE 🚨 *Roughhousing, salty language.*

1981 97m/C Terence Hill, Joanne Dru, Ernest Borgnine; **D:** Sergio Corbucci. **VHS, Beta**

Super Mario Bros.

PG/Family Fantasy based on the hit Nintendo game series. Two Brooklyn plumbers discover a lost dimension, created when an asteroid struck Earth in dinosaur days. Its princess has been kidnapped and taken to Dinohattan, a fungi-infested underworld ruled by Koopa, a T.Rex evolved to human form. Mario and Luigi fight back, and about 100 elements of the video games show up. Lavish and gaudy mental junk food, harmless enough for kids—unless they happen to be young accountants; the $42 million epic was a big money-loser. Don't hold your breath waiting for the sequel the ending foretells (though there was a cartoon predecessor).

🚨 BEWARE 🚨 *Roughhousing; reptilian snarling; futuristic mayhem.*

1993 104m/C Bob Hoskins, John Leguizamo, Samantha Mathis, Fisher Stevens, Richard Edson, Dana Kaminsky, Dennis Hopper, Fiona Shaw, Mojo Nixon, Lance Henriksen; **D:** Rocky Morton, Annabel Jankel; **W:** Edward Solomon, Parker Bennett, Terry Runte; **M:** Alan Silvestri. **VHS, Beta, LV** *HPH, BTV, TOU*

Super Mario Bros. Super Show 1

Family Syndicated TV cartoon series based on the video-game characters Mario and Luigi, plumbers who battle evil King Koopa in a fantasy kingdom. Six cassettes of episode reruns are available.

1989 30m/C Captain Lou Albano, Danny Wells. **VHS** *GKK*

Super Seal 🎵🕊

G/Primary Injured seal pup disrupts a family's normal existence after the young daughter adopts him. Marine mush.

1977 95m/C Foster Brooks, Sterling Holloway, Sarah Brown; **D:** Michael Dugan. **VHS, Beta** *VCI*

Superboy

Family Join Superboy and his dog Krypto as they fight crime in this collection of eight animated adventures. Ages 5 to 10.

1966 60m/C VHS, Beta *WAR*

Superdad 🎵

G/Family Middle-aged dad is alarmed by his college-bound daughter's choice in boyfriends. Much to the girl's embarrassment, the overprotective parent tries joining her at various teenage activities. Dim Disney family sitcom about the Generation Gap that never bridges the credibility gap, let alone the joke gap.

1973 94m/C Bob Crane, Kurt Russell, Joe Flynn, Barbara Rush, Kathleen Cody, Dick Van Patten; **D:** Vincent McEveety; **M:** Buddy Baker. **VHS, Beta** *DIS*

Supergirl 🎵🕊

PG/Jr. High-Adult Unexciting and unsophisticated spinoff of the Christopher Reeve man of steel fests. Based on the comic books about the young cousin to Superman, similarly sent to Earth and in pursuit of a magic paperweight. But a carnival fortuneteller has used it to transform herself as an all-powerful sorceress. Dunaway is a terrifically vile villainess, Slater winsome, but the whole enterprise is dimwitted.

🚨 BEWARE 🚨 *Roughhousing.*

1984 114m/C Faye Dunaway, Helen Slater, Peter O'Toole, Mia Farrow, Brenda Vaccaro, Marc McClure, Simon Ward, Hart Bochner, Maureen Teefy, David Healy, Matt Frewer; **D:** Jeannot Szwarc; **M:** Jerry Goldsmith. **VHS, Beta, LV** *LIV*

Superman

Family Join Superman, who looks suspiciously like that reporter Clark Kent, as he foils crime in Metropolis in this collection of seven animated adventures. Ages 5 to 10.

1966 60m/C V: Bud Collyer, Joan Alexander, Jackson Beck. **VHS, Beta** *WAR*

Superman 1: The Movie

PG/Family The DC Comics legend comes alive in this wonderfully entertaining saga of Superman's life, from a baby on the doomed planet Krypton to Metropolis' own Man of Steel. Hackman and Beatty pair marvelously as super criminal Lex Luthor and his bumbling sidekick. Award winning special effects and a script that pays great respect to the Jerry Siegel/Joe Shuster comic-book character yet doesn't take itself too seriously; super-fun. Followed by three increasingly lesser sequels.

BEWARE *Superhero violence.*

1978 144m/C Christopher Reeve, Margot Kidder, Marlon Brando, Gene Hackman, Glenn Ford, Susannah York, Ned Beatty, Valerie Perrine, Jackie Cooper, Marc McClure, Trevor Howard, Sarah Douglas, Terence Stamp, Jack O'Halloran, Phyllis Thaxter; **D:** Richard Donner; **W:** Mario Puzo, Robert Benton, David Newman; **M:** John Williams. **Award Nominations:** Academy Awards '78: Best Film Editing, Best Sound, Best Original Score; **Awards:** Academy Awards '78: Best Visual Effects; National Board of Review Awards '78: 10 Best Films of the Year. **VHS, Beta, LV** *WAR*

Superman 2

PG/Family First sequel finds the Man of Steel with his powerful hands full fending off three super-powered villains from his home planet of Krypton (briefly glimpsed in the first film). The romance between reporter Lois Lane and our superhero heats up and the storyline has more pace than the original, making for an enjoyable part II.

BEWARE *Superhero violence, sex talk.*

1980 127m/C Christopher Reeve, Margot Kidder, Gene Hackman, Ned Beatty, Jackie Cooper, Sarah Douglas, Jack O'Halloran, Susannah York, Marc McClure, Terence Stamp, Valerie Perrine, E.G. Marshall; **D:** Richard Lester; **W:** Mario Puzo, David Newman; **M:** John Williams. **VHS, Beta, LV** *WAR*

Superman 3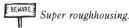

PG/Family Villainous businessman tries to conquer Superman via the expertise of bumbling computer expert Pryor and use of artificial Kryptonite. Superman explores his darker side after undergoing transformation into sleazy superbum. Promising, satirical start is ultimately defeated by uneven story and direction and often less-than-super f/x. Instead of Lois Lane, Clark Kent's long-lost love interest Lana Lang (O'Toole) pops up as the requisite heroine.

BEWARE *Super roughhousing.*

1983 123m/C Christopher Reeve, Richard Pryor, Annette O'Toole, Jackie Cooper, Margot Kidder, Marc McClure, Annie Ross, Robert Vaughn; **D:** Richard Lester; **W:** David Newman; **M:** John Williams. **VHS, Beta, LV** *WAR*

Superman 4: The Quest for Peace

PG/Family In answer to a child's wish, the Man of Steel endeavors to rid the world of all atomic weapons, thereby pitting himself against plutonium entrepreneur Lex Luthor and his superpowered creation, Nuclear Man. Special effects are dimestore quality and it seems that someone walked off with parts of the plot. Reeve deserves credit for remaining true to his classic character through good sequels and bad.

BEWARE *Salty language, superhero roughhousing.*

1987 90m/C Christopher Reeve, Gene Hackman, Jon Cryer, Marc McClure, Margot Kidder, Mariel Hemingway, Sam Wanamaker; **D:** Sidney J. Furie; **W:** Mark Rosenthal; **M:** John Williams; **V:** Susannah York. **VHS, Beta, LV** *WAR, APD*

Superman & the Mole Men

Family The cast of the 1950s TV show made this rarely seen feature as a pilot for the series. Superman faces the danger threatened by the invasion of radioactive molemen who make their way to the surface world from the bowels of the earth through an oil-well shaft. Simple fun.

1951 58m/C George Reeves, Phyllis Coates, Phyllis Coates, Jeff Corey; **D:** Lee Sholem. **VHS, Beta** *WAR*

Superman: The Serial, Vol. 1

Family The live-action Superman was first seen in this 15-chapter serial, tracing the Man of Steel from his origins on Krypton to his fight to save Metropolis from the evil Spider Lady and her ray gun. Columbia Pictures came up with an innovative way to avoid a big f/x budget: whenever Superman soars into action, he turns into a cartoon drawing!

BEWARE *Roughhousing.*

1948 248m/B Kirk Alyn, Noel Neill, Pierre Watkin, Tommy "Butch" Bond, Thomas Carr; **D:** Spencer Gordon Bennet. **VHS, Beta** *WAR*

SuperTed

Family Cartoon episodes from a popular British TV show about a toy stuffed bear transformed by an alien into a whimsical superhero. SuperTed now battles silly villains like Bulk, Skeleton, and Texas Pete. Lots better done than many toy product 'toons; additional volumes available.

1984 49m/C VHS, Beta *DIS*

Support Your Local Gunfighter

G/Family Western con man comes to the small town of Purgatory and is thought to be a notorious gunfighter. He decides to go with the mistaken identity and use it to his profitable advantage. A delightful, deliberately cliche-filled western that counts as a worthy follow-up, not a sequel, to "Support Your Local Sheriff" (1969).

1971 92m/C James Garner, Jack Elam, Suzanne Pleshette, Harry (Henry) Morgan, Dub Taylor, John Dehner, Joan Blondell, Ellen Corby, Henry Jones; **D:** Burt Kennedy. **VHS** *MGM*

Support Your Local Sheriff 🦴🦴🦴 ▷

G/Family Amiable, irreverent western spoof with more than its fair share of laughs. When a stranger stumbles into a gold rush town, he winds up becoming sheriff. Garner is perfect as the deadpan sheriff, particularly in the scene where he convinces Dern to remain in jail, in spite of the lack of bars. Neatly subverts every western cliche it encounters, yet keeps respect for formula western. Followed by "Support Your Local Gunfighter."

1969 92m/C James Garner, Joan Hackett, Walter Brennan, Bruce Dern, Jack Elam, Harry (Henry) Morgan; **D:** Burt Kennedy; **W:** William Bowers. **VHS, Beta, LV** *FOX, MGM*

The Sure Thing 🦴🦴🦴

PG-13/Jr. High-Adult Ivy League students who don't like each other end up travelling to California together, and of course, falling in love. Charming performances make up for predictability of comedic romance. Can't-miss director (and ex-Meathead) Reiner's second direct hit at the box office.

> 🔺 BEWARE 🔺 *PG-13 seems overstated; no explicit sex or nudity, mild language.*

1985 94m/C John Cusack, Daphne Zuniga, Anthony Edwards, Boyd Gaines, Lisa Jane Persky, Viveca Lindfors, Nicollette Sheridan, Tim Robbins; **D:** Rob Reiner; **W:** Jonathan Roberts. **VHS, Beta, LV, 8mm** *COL*

Surf Ninjas 🦴🦴

PG/Jr. High-Adult Martial-arts action comedy about two young California surfer dudes who are actually long-lost crown princes of the obscure nation of Patu San. The country's bionic bumbler warlord (Nielsen, hilarious but onscreen too briefly) wants the boys to stay lost. Frivolous tale, sort of a Teenage Mutant Ninja Turtle plot without Leonardo and co., has unexpectedly funny dialogue and situations early on, but gimmicky plot inevitably runs into shallow waters.

> 🔺 BEWARE 🔺 *Violence (largely non-serious), sex talk.*

1993 87m/C Ernie Reyes Jr., Nick Cowen, Rob Schneider, Leslie Nielsen, Tone Loc, John Karlen, Ernie Reyes Sr.; **D:** Neal Israel; **W:** Dan Gordon; **M:** David Kitay. **VHS, LV** *COL, NLC, IME*

Susannah of the Mounties 🦴🦴 ▷

Family Adorable young girl left orphaned after a wagon train massacre is adopted by a Mountie. An Indian squabble gives Shirley a chance to play little peacemaker and teach Scott how to tap dance, too. Could she be any cuter? Available colorized.

1939 78m/B Shirley Temple, Randolph Scott, Margaret Lockwood, J. Farrell MacDonald, Moroni Olsen, Victor Jory; **D:** William A. Seiter. **VHS, Beta** *FOX*

Susie, the Little Blue Coupe

Preschool-Primary A car ready to be junked is suddenly souped-up and revving to hit the road in this lesson of change and adaptation from Walt Disney's animation factory.

1952 8m/C VHS, Beta *DSN, MTI*

Suspicion 🦴🦴🦴 ▷

Jr. High-Adult Hitchcock's suspense thriller about a woman who gradually realizes she is married to a killer and may be next on his list. Excellent production unravels at the end due to RKO's insistence that Grant retain his "attractive" image, forcing the writers to leave his guilt or innocence undetermined. Available colorized.

1941 99m/B Cary Grant, Joan Fontaine, Cedric Hardwicke, Nigel Bruce, May Whitty, Leo G. Carroll, Heather Angel; **D:** Alfred Hitchcock. **Award Nominations:** Academy Awards '41: Best Picture; **Awards:** Academy Awards '41: Best Actress (Fontaine). **VHS, Beta, LV** *MED, MLB, BTV*

Swamp Thing 🦴🦴

PG/Jr. High-Adult Well-regarded comic book was the basis for this superhero/monster tale about a noble scientist accidentally turned into a lonely half-vegetable, half-man, all-cheapo-rubber-suit swamp creature. He fights an evil rival over a secret formula, with a sexy lady agent caught in the middle, occasionally topless. More silly than scary, but deemed worth a sequel, "The Return of Swamp Thing," and a TV series.

> 🔺 BEWARE 🔺 *Violence, nudity.*

1982 91m/C Adrienne Barbeau, Louis Jourdan, Ray Wise; **D:** Wes Craven; **W:** Wes Craven. **VHS, Beta, LV** *COL*

The Swan Princess 🦴🦴🦴

G/Family It's the old story: Boy meets gull (all right, boy meets swan), in this pleasant animated film loosely based on the tale that inspired Tchaikovsky's ballet "Swan Lake." Prince Derek (voiced by Howard McGillin) likes Princess Odette (Nicastro), mostly for her looks. Odette finds this appallingly shallow and tells him to go jump in the lake (figuratively). Enter evil sorcerer Rothbart (Palance) who wants Odette and the kingdom that comes with her. He spirits her away and turns Odette into a part-time swan. While repentant Derek searches for her, resourceful Odette plans her own escape with the show-stealing help of a frog (Cleese), a sl-o-o-o-w talking turtle (Wright) and a puffin (Vinovich). Director Richard Rich (yes!) fills the screen with colorful landscapes and sight gags: Watch for Palance's character doing a one-armed pushup. The songs are also good. Tell Tchaikovsky the news.

1994 90m/C D: Richard Rich; **W:** Richard Rich, Brian Nissen; **M:** Lex de Azevedo; **V:** Jack Palance, Michelle Nicastro, Howard McGillin, Liz Callaway, John Cleese, Steven Wright, Steve Vinovich, Dakin Matthews, Sandy Duncan, Mark Harelik, James Arrington, Davis Gaines, Joel McKinnon Miller. **VHS** *TTC*

Princess Odette and Prince Derek waltz the night away in "The Swan Princess."

The Swarm

PG/Jr. High-Adult Low-brow insect contest as scientist Caine fends off a swarm of killer bees when they attack metro Houston. The bees are really just black spots painted on the film. And the acting is terrible. "B" movie on bees, but it's still better than "The Bees."

1978 116m/C Michael Caine, Katharine Ross, Richard Widmark, Lee Grant, Richard Chamberlain, Olivia de Havilland, Henry Fonda, Fred MacMurray, Patty Duke, Ben Johnson, Jose Ferrer, Slim Pickens, Bradford Dillman, Cameron Mitchell; **D:** Irwin Allen; **W:** Stirling Silliphant; **M:** Jerry Goldsmith, John Williams. **VHS, Beta** *WAR*

The Sweater

Family Mail order mixup, a sweater, and a small boy and his passion for hockey all figure in the award-winning title short from Canada. Also includes "The Ride" and "Getting Started."

1982 30m/C VHS *FCT, NFB, INC*

Sweet 15

Family Marta Delacruz is approaching her 15th birthday—in Mexican-American culture a celebration that ushers her into adulthood. But plans of a lavish party and a dream date are displaced by more urgent matters when she finds her proud father never attained US citizenship despite his many years in the country. With immigration cops cracking down, Mr. Delacruz considers taking the family back south of the border. Marta tries to come up with a solution on her own, and does some real growing up in the process. Revealing and satisfying tale originally aired as part of PBS-TV's "WonderWorks" series.

1990 120m/C Karla Montana, Panchito Gomez, Tony Plana, Jenny Gago, Susan Ruttan; **D:** Victoria Hochberg. **VHS** *PME, HMV, FCT*

Sweet Honey in the Rock: Singing for Freedom

Family In this concert Sweet Honey in the Rock, five women who harmonize gloriously and without accompaniment, perform songs that reflect their African American heritage and invite-sometimes demand—audience involvement. Young listeners and their parents lock arms and sing and sway along to "We Shall Overcome" and join in on other numbers. Singing such tunes as "I Got Shoes" or "This Little Light of Mine," Sweet Honey is without peer. There's also much talk between songs and although the topics are important—for example, the history of the civil rights movement—the lectures sometimes make the concert seem less like honey and more like spinach. Ages 4 to 10.

1995 45m/C VHS *MLT*

Sweet Liberty 🎵🎵

PG/Jr. High-Adult Alda's hometown is overwhelmed by Hollywood chaos during the filming of a movie version of his novel about the American Revolution. Pleasant but predictable.

BEWARE *Mature themes; alcohol use; subtle sex scenes.*

1986 107m/C Alan Alda, Michael Caine, Michelle Pfeiffer, Bob Hoskins, Lillian Gish; **D:** Alan Alda; **W:** Alan Alda; **M:** Bruce Broughton. **VHS, Beta, LV** *MCA*

Swing Kids 🎵🎵

PG-13/Jr. High-Adult In 1939 Hamburg, big band "swing" music is used by a group of teenagers to rebel against conformity demanded by Hitler. Plot concentrates on three boys and the strains that Nazi power and propaganda put on their friendship. Although the premise is historically based, a disturbing wrong-end-of-the-telescope aspect affects the production; effective moments of searing drama and brutality get paired with youth-pandering visits to the dance floor or record den. Hopefully, the targeted young audience already knows that WWII was fought over larger issues than pop music and long hair. Made through Disney's Hollywood Pictures division.

BEWARE *Brutality, profane language, alcohol use, mature themes. One character commits suicide.*

1993 114m/C Robert Sean Leonard, Christian Bale, Frank Whaley, Barbara Hershey, Tushka Bergen, David Tom, Kenneth Branagh; **D:** Thomas Carter; **W:** Jonathan Marc Feldman; **M:** James Horner. **VHS, Beta, LV** *HPH*

Swing Shift 🎵🎵 🎵

PG/Jr. High-Adult When Hawn takes a job at an aircraft plant after husband Harris goes off to war, she learns more than riveting, courtesy of fellow worker Russell. Lahti steals the romantic comedy-drama as her friend and co-worker. In spite of performances, detailed reminiscence of the American home front during WWII never seems to gel. Produced by Hawn.

BEWARE *Profanity, sex and cheating on spouse.*

1984 100m/C Goldie Hawn, Kurt Russell, Ed Harris, Christine Lahti, Holly Hunter, Chris Lemmon, Belinda Carlisle, Fred Ward, Roger Corman, Lisa Pelikan; **D:** Jonathan Demme, **W:** Ron Nyswaner, Bo Goldman. **VHS, Beta, LV** *WAR*

The Swiss Family Robinson 🎵🎵🎵

Family Family seeking to escape Napoleon's war in Europe sets sail for New Guinea, but shipwrecks on a deserted tropical island. There they build an idyllic life, only to be confronted by a band of pirates. Lots of grandiose adventure for family viewing in the Disney tradition, even if some of it is farfetched at times. Filmed on location on the island of Tobago. Based on the novel by Johann Wyss.

1960 126m/C John Mills, Dorothy McGuire, James MacArthur, Tommy Kirk, Janet Munro, Sessue Hayakawa; **D:** Ken Annakin. **VHS, Beta, LV** *DIS, IGP*

The Sword & the Rose

Family Mary Tudor, widowed sister of King Henry VIII, shuns the advances of a power-hungry ignoble noblemen for the love of a valiant commoner, who swashbuckles to the rescue. Don't be surprised if you find none of this in the history books; adventure was the priority in this Disney production filmed in England and adapted from Charles Major's book "When Knighthood Was in Flower."

1953 91m/C Richard Todd, Glynis Johns, Michael Gough, Jane Barrett, James Robertson Justice; *D:* Ken Annakin. **VHS, Beta, LV** *DIS, HHE, BTV*

The Sword in the Stone

G/Family The Disney version of the first segment of T.H. White's "The Once and Future King" wherein King Arthur, as a 12-year-old boy, is instructed in the ways of the world by Merlin the Magician and Archimedes the owl. With a heavy emphasis on slapstick gags, it's short of the masterpiece rank—just compare Merlin's performing tableware with the delightful singing and dancing bric-a-brac in "Beauty and the Beast." But kids will be entertained.

1963 79m/C *D:* Wolfgang Reitherman, Wolfgang Reitherman; *V:* Ricky Sorenson, Sebastian Cabot, Karl Swenson, Junius Matthews, Alan Napier, Norman Alden, Martha Wentworth, Barbara Jo Allen. **VHS, Beta, LV** *DIS, KUI, HMV*

Sword of the Valiant

PG/Family Rattletrap filming of the poem "Sir Gawain And The Green Knight," based on a King Arthur legend of youthful Sir Gawain spending a year to prepare for a challenge by the supernatural, seemingly undefeatable Green Knight (Connery). Terrible f/x.

1983 102m/C Sean Connery, Miles O'Keeffe, Cyrielle Claire, Leigh Lawson, Trevor Howard, Peter Cushing, Wilfrid Brambell, Lila Kedrova, John Rhys-Davies; *D:* Stephen Weeks. **VHS, Beta** *MGM*

Sylvester

PG/Family A 16-year-old orphan girl and a cranky stockyard boss team up to train a battered horse named Sylvester for the National Equestrian trials. Nice riding sequences and good performances can't disguise a familiar plot, but kids will enjoy this one.

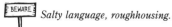 *Salty language, roughhousing.*

1985 104m/C Melissa Gilbert, Richard Farnsworth, Michael Schoeffling, Constance Towers; *D:* Tim Hunter. **VHS, Beta, LV** *COL*

Sylvester & Tweety: Best Yeows of our Lives

Family Tweety gets the better of Sylvester in "All A Bir-r-rd," "Tweet and Sour," "Tweet Tweet Tweety," "Home Tweet Home," and "A Bird in a Gilded Cage." Ages 4 to 8.

198? 33m/C VHS *BTV, WAR*

Sylvester and Tweety's Tale Feathers

Family Five episodes featuring dat cwazy putty tat and yellow bird. Ages 4 to 8.

19?? 34m/C VHS

Sylvia Anderson's The Animates

Preschool-Primary Thirteen mini-cartoons featuring British comic characters from one half of the Gerry and Sylvia Anderson team who devised "Thunderbirds" and "Captain Scarlet vs. the Mysterons" for British TV.

1978 57m/C VHS, Beta *FHE*

Table for Five

PG/Jr. High-Adult Divorced father takes his children on a Mediterranean cruise and while at sea, he learns that his ex-wife has died. The father and his ex-wife's husband struggle over who should raise the children. Sentimental and well-acted tale of an unbrady bunch.

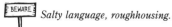 *Profanity, sex talk and a dead mother.*

1983 120m/C Jon Voight, Millie Perkins, Richard Crenna, Robbie Kiger, Roxana Zal, Son Hoang Bui, Marie-Christine Barrault, Kevin Costner; *D:* Robert Liebmann; *W:* David Seltzer; *M:* Miles Goodman. **VHS, Beta, LV** *FOX*

Tailor of Gloucester

Preschool-Primary Beatrix Potter's classic tale of sharing is narrated by Streep.

19?? 30m/C VHS *KUI, COL*

Tailspin Tommy

Family One of the first movie serials derived from a newspaper comic strip, this otherwise unremarkable Universal production stars the aviator hero performing airborne stunts (recycled scenes from other movies, actually). In 12 chapters. Followup, "Tailspin Tommy and the Great Air Mystery," is also available.

1934 ?m/B Maurice Murphy, Noah Beery Jr., Walter Miller, Patricia Farr, Grant Withers, John Davidson, William Desmond, Charles A. Browne. **VHS** *GPV*

Take Down

PG/Family Hermann is charming as a high-school English teacher who reluctantly takes charge as coach of a last-place student wrestling squad because nobody else wants the job. Through hard work and understanding, he turns the team into winners. Innocuous, though predictable on every count.

1979 96m/C Lorenzo Lamas, Kathleen Lloyd, Maureen McCormick, Edward Herrmann; *D:* Keith Merrill. **VHS, Beta** *UNI*

Take the Money and Run

PG/Jr. High-Adult Allen's directing debut; he also co-wrote and starred. "Documentary" follows a timid, would-

be bank robber who can't get his career off the ground and keeps landing in jail. Little plot, but who cares? Non-stop one-liners and slapstick.

1969 85m/C Woody Allen, Janet Margolin, Marcel Hillaire, Louise Lasser; *D:* Woody Allen; *W:* Woody Allen; *M:* Marvin Hamlisch. **VHS, Beta, LV** *FOX*

Taking Care of Terrific

Family A teenage babysitter takes the naive boy she is caring for to visit with a street musician. The trio plan an evening to help the homeless in this entry in the "Wonderworks" series. Ages 10 and up.

1988 55m/C Melvin Van Peebles, Joanne Vannicola, Jackie Burroughs. **VHS** *PME, HMV, BTV*

The Tale of Mr. Jeremy Fisher and the Tale of Peter Rabbit

Preschool-Primary Two more classic tales from Beatrix Potter narrated by Streep.

19?? 30m/C VHS *KUI, COL*

The Tale of Peter Rabbit

Preschool-Primary Another round of Beatrix Potter's rabbit vs. Mr. McGregor. Burnett narrates and sings in this animated special for HBO cable, with songs by Stephen Lawrence and Sheldon Harnick.

1991 27m/C V: Carol Burnett. **VHS** *FHE, LIV*

The Tale of Peter Rabbit and Benjamin Bunny

Preschool-Primary Released to commemorate the 100th anniversary of Beatrix Potter's series, this is a faithful translation of her classic story of two mischievous bunnies and their adventurous trip to Mr. MacGregor's garden. Potter's own watercolors are adapted to exceptional animation.

1993 30m/C VHS *GKK, ING*

The Tale of Samuel Whiskers

Preschool-Primary Released to commemorate the 100th anniversary of Beatrix Potter's series, this retells her story of cats and rats, with her watercolors faithfully translated to animation. See also "The Tale of Peter Rabbit and Benjamin Bunny."

1993 30m/C VHS *GKK*

The Tale of the Bunny Picnic

Preschool-Primary Muppet Bunnies prepare for their annual picnic but Bean, the smallest bunny, is too tiny to help. When he wanders off he finds the farmer's junkyard dog has a nasty surprise for his pals unless Bean can warn them first.

1992 50m/C VHS *JHV, BTV*

The Tale of the Frog Prince

Family Superb edition of Shelley Duvall's "Faerie Tale Theatre" finds Robin Williams the victim of an angry fairy's spell. Teri Garr to the rescue as the self-centered princess who saves him with a kiss. Directed and written by Eric Idle of Monty Python fame.

1983 60m/C Robin Williams, Teri Garr; *D:* Eric Idle; *W:* Eric Idle. **VHS, Beta, LV** *FOX*

A Tale of Two Chipmunks

G/Family Three Chip 'n' Dale Disney cartoons: "Chicken in the Rough," "The Lone Chipmunks" and "Chips Ahoy."

1953 24m/C VHS, Beta, LV *DIS*

A Tale of Two Critters

G/Preschool-Primary Young raccoon and a playful bear cub develop a rare friendship growing up in the wilderness.

1977 48m/C VHS, Beta *MTI, DSN*

Talent for the Game

PG/Jr. High-Family Minor-league baseball pleasantry about a talent scout who recruits a phenomenal young pitcher from rural Idaho, then sees the innocent kid unfairly pressured by the greedy team owner. Okay, with a fairy-tale ending that aims a little too hard to please.

BEWARE *Ballparkish language.*

1991 91m/C Edward James Olmos, Lorraine Bracco, Jeff Corbett, Jamey Sheridan, Terry Kinney; *D:* Robert M. Young; *W:* David Himmelstein, Tom Donnelly, Larry Ferguson; *M:* David Newman. **VHS, Beta, LV** *PAR*

Tales from Avonlea, Vol. 1: The Journey Begins

Family From the producer of "Anne of Green Gables" movie and its sequel comes this weekly TV series also set in Prince Edward Island, a collaboration of the Disney Channel and the Canadian Broadcasting Corporation. In "The Journey Begins," Sara meets her stuffy Aunt Hetty and her cousins Felix and Felicity. Unhappy with her life, she considers running away. "The Proof of the Pudding" finds the grownups away and Felicity in charge for the weekend. Fine attention to detail, particularly in the scenic views and costumes. Ages 8 and up.

1990 106m/C Sarah Polley, Jackie Burroughs, Gema Zamprogna. **VHS, Beta** *DIS, BTV*

Tales of Beatrix Potter

G/Family The Royal Ballet Company of England performs in this adaptation of the adventures of Beatrix Potter's colorful and memorable creatures. Beautifully done.

1971 90m/C *D:* Reginald Mills. **VHS** *REP, HMV*

Tales of Beatrix Potter

Preschool-Primary Six stories from Potter's canon, including "Peter Rabbit," "Two Bad Mice," "Miss Moppet," and "Jeremy Fisher," illustrated by Potter's original drawings and narrated by Sydney Walker.
1985 43m/C VHS, Beta *VES, RDG, HMV*

Tales of Deputy Dawg, Vol. 1

Family Terrytoons' pessimistic dawg rides again, undoing the bad guys in spite of himself. Additional volumes available.
196? 90m/C V: Dayton Allen. **VHS** *FOX*

The Tales of Hoffman 𝄪𝄪 ♭

Jr. High-Adult The British creators of the sentimental classic "The Red Shoes" followed up with this highly stylized ballet-opera, based on music and stories of Jacques Offenbach. Hoffman is a heartbroken poet who tells residents of an inn of his ill-fated romances, which all have a touch of the supernatural about them. Though innately tragic, the tales' fairy-tale quality that might be your best chance (other than "The Maestro's Company" and the Marx Brothers) to expose youngsters to a night at the opera. Standout: the "Dr. Coppelius" segment, about a doll-like mechanical girl who literally goes to pieces for love.

 Alcohol use.

1951 138m/C Robert Rounseville, Robert Helpmann, Moira Shearer; **D:** Michael Powell, Emeric Pressburger. **VHS** *HMV, PME*

Tales of Pluto Series

Preschool-Primary The inimitable hound stars in a collection of hilarious Disney cartoons. Available on separate tapes, they are "Wonder Dog," "Pluto's Surprise Package," and "Dog Watch."
1990 8m/C VHS, Beta *MTI, DSN*

Talespin

Family The Talespin adventures feature characters originally from Disney's "The Jungle Book," although it's doubtful Rudyard Kipling would recognize them. Baloo the bear now flies a plane, while the tiger Shere Khan is an industrialist. King Louie runs a nightclub. There are new bear characters: Rebecca, Kit, and Molly. It may not be the original move, but these 8 volumes of animated stories are entertaining. Ages 3 to 7.
19?? 46m/C VHS

The Talking Eggs

Preschool-Primary Animated version of the popular children's folktale features all African Americans, with narration by Danny Glover. Selina is invited to the home of a mysterious old woman who encourages her to take some eggs, but only the ones who speak to her. They are magical for Selina, but turn into a curse when her brother steals some for himself.
1992 25m/C VHS *CHF*

The Birth of Shelley Duvall's "Faerie Tale Theatre"

The big-budget 1980 live-action version of the classic cartoon *Popeye*, starring Robin Williams, may have been a disappointment at the box-office, but in one way it made history. During on-location shooting on the island of Malta, leading lady Shelley Duvall brought with her a set of children's tales for reading during the off hours. "I opened up to 'The Frog Prince' one day," she later recalled, "and thought, 'Wouldn't Robin make a great frog?'"

Williams agreed, and suggested British comic actor/director Eric Idle for the project as well. Their collaboration became the genesis of "Faerie Tale Theatre," an anthology of classic fairy tales Duvall produced between 1982 and 1985 for Showtime Cable, later widely released on Playhouse Video cassettes. The show's rare combination of storybook whimsy, childhood delight and occassional modern satire made it a hit.

Duvall, a college student planning to be a research scientist, was recruited into acting by Robert Altman, who would in fact later cast her as Olive Oyl in *Popeye*. For years the thin, toothy Texan played various dramatic, somewhat neurotic roles, like the frail-seeming wife of a maniac in the horror blockbuster *The Shining*. But since the age of 17 Shelley Duvall had been collecting antique storybooks and fairy tale lore. And now she's become Hollywood's resident Mother Goose.

The Tall Blond Man with One Black Shoe 🦴🦴🦴

PG/Jr. High-Adult A violinist is completely unaware that rival spies mistakenly think he is also a spy, and that he is the center of a plot to booby-trap an overly ambitious agent at the French Secret Service. A sequel followed called "Return of the Tall Blond Man with One Black Shoe" which was followed by a disappointing American remake, "The Man with One Red Shoe." In French with English subtitles or dubbed.

1972 90m/C Pierre Richard, Bernard Blier, Jean Rochefort, Mireille Darc, Jean Carmet; **D:** Yves Robert; **W:** Francis Veber; **M:** Vladimir Cosma. **VHS, Beta, 8mm** *CVC, COL, VYY*

Tall Tale: The Unbelievable Adventures of Pecos Bill 🦴🦴 🦴

PG/Family Take characters from American mythology—John Henry, Paul Bunyan, Pecos Bill—add a likable kid, and toss in a gen-u-ine movie star, Patrick Swayze, for good measure. It has all the ingredients, but someone forgot to stir. Performances are either lifeless or hammy (except Brown's John Henry), the dialogue trite ("You don't know what you can do until you try"). It's 1905 and greedy railroad barons are out for his pa's land, so young Daniel Hackett (Stahl) summons the help of the three folkloric heroes his father is always talking about. Trouble is Pecos Bill (Swayze) is supposed to be larger than two lives but comes off as just another good guy. At least there's Bill's big black horse and Bunyan's big blue ox. Lots of action, lots of jokes, and lots to say about the need to find heroes, including the heroes in your own family.

1995 98m/C Patrick Swayze, Oliver Platt, Roger Brown, Nick Stahl, Scott Glenn, Stephen Lang, Jared Harris, Catherine O'Hara; **D:** Jeremiah S. Chechik; **W:** Steven L. Bloom, Robert Rodat; **C:** Janusz Kaminski. **VHS, LV** *DIS*

Tall Tales and Legends: Johnny Appleseed

Family True story of the legendary American who spent his life planting apple trees across the country, with the accent on comedy as Short hilariously communes with nature and talks to animals (missing: the Swedenborgian religious motives that drove the real- life Appleseed).

1986 60m/C Martin Short, Rob Reiner, Molly Ringwald. **VHS** *FOX*

Tammy and the Bachelor 🦴🦴 🦴

Family Backwoods Southern girl becomes involved with a romantic pilot and his snobbish family. They don't quite know what to make of her but she wins them over with her down-home philosophy. Features the hit tune, "Tammy." Charming performance by Reynolds.

1957 89m/C Debbie Reynolds, Leslie Nielsen, Walter Brennan, Fay Wray, Sidney Blackmer, Mildred Natwick, Louise Beavers; **D:** Joseph Pevney, Oscar Brodney. **VHS, Beta** *MCA*

Tammy and the Doctor 🦴🦴

Family Dee reprises Debbie Reynolds's backwoods gal ("Tammy and the Bachelor"). Tammy becomes a nurse's aide, attracting the attention of young doctor Fonda, in his film debut.

1963 88m/C Sandra Dee, Peter Fonda, MacDonald Carey; **D:** Harry Keller; **W:** Oscar Brodney. **VHS, Beta** *MCA*

Tank 🦴 🦴

PG/Jr. High-Adult Retired Army officer Garner's son is thrown into jail on a trumped-up charge by a small town sheriff. Dad comes to the rescue with his restored Sherman tank. Trite and unrealistic portrayal of good versus bad made palatable by Garner's performance.

BEWARE *Violence and oppressive law enforcement.*

1983 113m/C James Garner, Shirley Jones, C. Thomas Howell, Mark Herrier, Sandy Ward, Jenilee Harrison, Dorian Harewood, G.D. Spradlin; **D:** Marvin J. Chomsky. **VHS, Beta, LV** *MCA*

Tanner's Growing Up in Alaska

Family Tanner, a small, blonde 3- or 4-year-old narrates his own story (or someone slightly older does off-screen) as he shows viewers around Homer, Alaska, where he lives. We get to see loggers with their massive machines, fishermen on their boats, and moose in Tanner's back yard. Tanner eats crabs and he goes dogsledding and snowmobiling by himself (he wears a helmet). It looks like Tanner is happy living in Alaska, and he's very nice to his little sister, Sasha. Ages 3 to 6.

199? ?m/C VHS *NYR*

Taps 🦴🦴 🦴

PG/Jr. High-Adult Military academy students (age 12 and up) learn their school is to be closed, so they grab the guns and turn the compound into an armed fortress against the outside world. Antiwar morality play about excesses of zeal and patriotism in youthful minds, aspiring to be another "Lord of the Flies." It doesn't quite make it, but still impressive at times.

BEWARE *Profanity, violence and kids with guns. Some kids are killed.*

1981 126m/C Timothy Hutton, George C. Scott, Ronny Cox, Sean Penn, Tom Cruise; **D:** Harold Becker; **W:** Darryl Ponicsan, Robert Mark Kamen; **M:** Maurice Jarre. **VHS, Beta** *FOX*

Tarka the Otter

Family Nicely done nature film from Britain, set in the 1920s. A young otter encounters danger as he pursued his favorite eel meals, and is captured by a well-meaning fellow who wants to turn Tarka into a pet. Based on the book by Henry Williamson.

1978 91m/C VHS, Beta *TWE*

Tarzan and His Mate 🦴🦴🦴

Family Second entry in the lavishly produced MGM Tarzan series. Weissmuller and O'Sullivan cohabit in

unmarried bliss before the Hays Code moved them to a tree house with twin beds. Many angry elephants, nasty white hunters, and hungry lions. Laserdisc includes the original trailer.
1934 93m/B Johnny Weissmuller, Maureen O'Sullivan, Neil Hamilton, Paul Cavanagh; **D:** Jack Conway. **VHS, LV** *MGM, FCT*

Tarzan Escapes 🎵🎵🎵

Family Jane is tricked by evil hunters into abandoning her fairy tale life with Tarzan, so the Ape Man sets out to reunite with his one true love. The third entry in MGM's Weissmuller/O'Sullivan series is still among the better Tarzan movies thanks to the leads, but the Hays Office made sure Jane was wearing a lot more clothes this time around.
1936 95m/B Johnny Weissmuller, Maureen O'Sullivan, John Buckler, Benita Hume, William Henry; **D:** Richard Thorpe. **VHS** *FOX, FCT*

Tarzan Finds a Son 🎵🎵🎵

Family Weissmuller and O'Sullivan returned to their roles after three years with the addition of the five-year-old Sheffield as Boy. He's an orphan whose awful relatives hope he stays lost so they can collect an inheritance. Jane and Tarzan fight to adopt the tyke and when the new family are captured by a wicked tribe only an elephant stampede can save them. More of what you expect in a Tarzan adventure.
1939 90m/B Johnny Weissmuller, Maureen O'Sullivan, Johnny Sheffield, Ian Hunter, Henry Stephenson, Frieda Inescort, Henry Wilcoxon; **D:** Richard Thorpe. **VHS** *MGM*

Tarzan, the Ape Man 🎵🎵🎵

Family The definitive Tarzan movie; the first Tarzan talkie; the original of the long series starring Weissmuller. Dubiously faithful to the Edgar Rice Burroughs story, but recent attempts to remake, update or improve it (notably the pretentious 1984 Greystoke) have failed to near the original's entertainment value or even its technical quality. O'Sullivan as Jane and Weissmuller bring style and wit to their classic roles.
1932 99m/B Johnny Weissmuller, Maureen O'Sullivan, Neil Hamilton; **D:** Woodbridge S. Van Dyke. **VHS, Beta, LV** *MGM, FCT*

Tarzan's New York Adventure 🎵🎵🎶

Family O'Sullivan's final appearance as Jane is a so-so adventure with some humorous moments when Tarzan meets the big city. When Boy is kidnapped by an evil circus owner, Tarzan, Jane, and Cheta head out to rescue him. Tarzan shows off his jungle prowess by climbing skyscrapers and diving off the Brooklyn Bridge into the Hudson River. Lincoln, the screen's first Tarzan, has a cameo.
1942 70m/B Johnny Weissmuller, Maureen O'Sullivan, Johnny Sheffield, Virginia Grey, Charles Bickford, Paul Kelly, Chill Wills, Russell Hicks, Cy Kendall; **Cameos:** Elmo Lincoln; **D:** Richard Thorpe. **VHS** *MGM*

Tarzan's Secret Treasure 🎵🎵🎶

Family Tarzan saves an expedition from a savage tribe only to be repaid by having the greedy hunters hold Jane and Boy hostage. They want Tarzan's help in finding a secret cache of gold. But Tarzan doesn't take kindly to threats to his family and teaches those evil-doers a lesson.
1941 81m/B Johnny Weissmuller, Maureen O'Sullivan, Johnny Sheffield, Reginald Owen, Barry Fitzgerald, Tom Conway, Philip Dorn; **D:** Richard Thorpe. **VHS** *MGM*

Tazmania: Taz-Maniac

Family Stars the Tazmanian Devil from the Saturday morning Fox Network cartoon series. Ages 4 to 8.
1993 34m/C VHS

Tazmania: Taz-Manimals

Family A collection of three animated episodes starring the Tazmanian Devil. Ages 4 to 8.
1993 34m/C VHS

Tazmania: Taz-Tronaut

Family Four more episodes from the animated devil from Tazmania. Ages 4 to 8.
1993 34m/C VHS

Techno Police 🎵🎵

Family Animated "Robocop" clone, but without that title's overwhelming live-action gore. Cyborg police officers patrol a futuristic urban landscape.
1987 77m/C VHS, Beta *JFK*

Ted E. Bear: The Bear Who Slept Through Christmas

Family Cartoon holiday TV special. As Christmas approaches, all the bears are getting ready to go to sleep for the winter, except Ted E. Bear, who wants to see the fat guy in the red suit. Additional volumes available.
1983 60m/C V: Tom Smothers, Arte Johnson, Barbara Feldon, Kelly Lange. **VHS, Beta** *FHE*

Teddy Bear Blues

Preschool Children can sing and dance along to this live-action video featuring dozens of favorite nursery rhymes and children's songs. Ages 1 to 4.
1994 60m/C VHS *KVI*

The Teddy Bears' Christmas

Preschool-Primary Teddy bear Ben goes on a quest to find his owner's little sister Sally a teddy bear of her own to love, just in time for Christmas.
1993 26m/C VHS *FHE*

Daniel Hackett meets Pecos Bill in "Tall Tale: The Unbelievable Adventures of Pecos Bill."

The Teddy Bears' Picnic

Family Little girl has the chance to find out what teddy bears do when they come to life one day per year in this cute cartoon.

1989 30m/C VHS, Beta *FHE*

Teen Alien WOOF!

PG/Jr. High-Adult On Halloween night some kids explore a spooky old house. Aliens are afoot, and the wrapup turns the thing into a subteen version of "Invasion of the Body Snatchers." Generally non-threatening thriller for juvie audiences in which the real horror is the acting and direction. Also known as "The Varrow Mission."

1988 88m/C Vern Adix, Michael Dunn. **VHS, Beta** *PSM*

Teen Witch &

PG-13/Jr. High-Adult Semi-musical, totally forgettable farce about a demure high school girl who inherits magic powers on her 16th birthday. Benign sorcery gets her good looks, popularity, and the dishiest guy in class. She also plays pranks on grouchy teachers, but nothing ex-

treme—or interesting. Note Sargent, of TV's "Bewitched," in a cameo.

1989 94m/C Robin Lively, Zelda Rubinstein, Dan Gauthier, Joshua Miller, Dick Sargent; **D:** Dorian Walker. **VHS, Beta** *MED, VTR*

Teen Wolf & & ˒

PG/Family Nice, average teenager begins to show were-wolf tendencies not part of usual adolescent transition—making him popular at high school when he leads the basketball team to victory. The underlying message is to be yourself, regardless of body hair. Lighthearted comedy, carried by the Fox charm, was made before "Back to the Future" but released afterwards to capitalize on his stardom. Inspired a sequel and a TV cartoon series, both also on video.

⚠ BEWARE *Salty wolfboy language, sex talk.*

1985 92m/C Michael J. Fox, James Hampton, Scott Paulin, Susan Ursitti; **D:** Rod Daniel; **M:** Miles Goodman. **VHS, Beta, LV, 8mm** *PAR*

Teen Wolf: All-American Werewolf

Family TV cartoon spinoff of the feature film. Young Scott Howard and his family seem normal enough by day but when the full moon hits, Scott and his family transform into wacky werewolves.
1986 120m/C VHS, Beta

Teen Wolf Too 🎵🎵

PG/Family Sequel to "Teen Wolf," without Michael J. Fox (surprise, surprise). Instead his character's cousin goes to college on a boxing scholarship and develops lycanthropy. More evidence that the sequel is rarely as good as the original.

BEWARE *Sex talk, full-moon roughhousing, salty language, growling.*

1987 95m/C Jason Bateman, Kim Darby, John Astin, Paul Sand; **D:** Christopher Leitch. **VHS, Beta** *PAR*

Teen Wolf: Wolf of My Dreams

Family Teen Wolf goes to Hollywood to meet his big screen werewolf idol and has a howl of a time.
1986 40m/C VHS, Beta *FHE*

Teenage Mutant Ninja Turtles 1: The Movie 🎵🎵🎶

PG/Primary-Adult Live-action hit about the four sewer-dwelling turtles turned into warrior ninja mutants due to radiation, who try to rid NYC of the evil samurai-masked gang chieftain Shredder. Brought to life by Jim Henson's studios, the mighty terrapins Donatello, Leonard, Michelangelo, and Raphael are wonderful creations. Muppet magic and some clever lines glide around minimalist plot. The much-discussed violence is a non-issue; fights with Shredder's minions are bloodless, very funny slapstick gymnastics. History does record, however, some young fans who tried to run away to the sewers after seeing this.

BEWARE *Much roughhousing. Every human kid in the movie belongs to Shredder's gang, a vast, ultra-cool tribe of urban Lost Boys whose criminal lifestyle is initially glamorized, though the message that juvenile delinquency leads to a certain emptiness (with allusions to Pinocchio) eventually is presented persuasively.*

1990 95m/C Judith Hoag, Elias Koteas; **D:** Steven Barron; **W:** Todd W. Langen; **M:** John Du Prez; **V:** Robbie Rist, Corey Feldman, Brian Tochi, Kevin Clash, David McCharen. **VHS, Beta, LV, 8mm** *FHE, LIV*

Teenage Mutant Ninja Turtles 2: The Secret of the Ooze 🎵🎵

PG/Primary-Adult The teen terrapins search for the toxic waste that turned them into marketable martial-artist kid idols, but their old enemy Shredder has similar notions to breed mutant monsters of his own. Same formula, same comic attitude, same story sloppiness as the first film; between the two flicks there's one good, whole feature waiting to be spliced together. Dedicated to the memory of the late Jim Henson.

BEWARE *Martial-arts roughhousing, again done as slapstick comedy.*

1991 88m/C Francois Chau, David Warner, Paige Turco, Ernie Reyes Jr., Vanilla Ice; **D:** Michael Pressman. **VHS, Beta** *COL, NLC*

Teenage Mutant Ninja Turtles 3 🎵🎵

PG/Primary-Adult The Turtles hit 17th-century Japan to rescue loyal friend, reporter April O'Neil, dragged back centuries by a magic scepter. More plot (and budget) than the mutant heroes' previous live-action shell games, but enthusiasm seems to be lagging. Martial arts remain blood-free gymnastics and swashbuckling, but they're not funny slapstick routines anymore. Better gags come from the parallel plight of several surprised samurai teleported to modern NYC.

BEWARE *Martial roughhousing.*

1993 95m/C Elias Koteas, Paige Turco, Stuart Wilson, Sab Shimono, Vivian Wu; **D:** Stuart Gillard; **W:** Stuart Gillard; **M:** John Du Prez; **V:** Randi Mayem Singer, Matt Hill, Jim Raposa, David Fraser. **VHS, LV** *NLC, COL, IME*

Teenage Mutant Ninja Turtles: The Epic Begins

Family Original tale of the hardshelled heroes and their mentor Splinter the Rat, and how the team started their mission to clean up the streets by battling reprobates left and right. Turtle fans will want to compare/contrast this with the first two Mutant Ninja Turtle live-action movies covering much the same ground (but with actually less violence than these cartoons). Additional volumes available.
1987 72m/C VHS, Beta, LV *FHE*

Teeny-Tiny and the Witch-Woman and Other Stories

Preschool-Primary A compilation of slightly scary children's animations, including "King of the Cats," "The Rainbow Serpent" and "A Dark, Dark Tale." Available separately from Weston Woods Studios. Ages 3 to 6.
1978 34m/C VHS, Beta *NO*

The Ten Commandments 🎵🎵🎵

G/Family Hollywood's garish Bible epics are mostly a motley bunch. On the short list of over-achievers is this stirring, mammoth-scale retelling of the life story of Moses, who turned his back on a privileged life to lead his enslaved people to freedom from Pharaoh and receive the title tablets. Exceptional cast, with Fraser Heston (son of Charlton) as the baby Moses at the beginning.

Parting of Red Sea rivals any modern special effects. Available in widescreen on laserdisc.

> **BEWARE!** *Original Sin of such religious epics was that they could depict all the violence and debauchery they wanted as long as Godliness prevailed in the last reel. This is no exception: brutality, mature themes, scary moments as the Ten Plagues ravage Egypt.*

1956 219m/C Charlton Heston, Yul Brynner, Anne Baxter, Yvonne De Carlo, Nina Foch, John Derek, H.B. Warner, Henry Wilcoxon, Judith Anderson, John Carradine, Douglass Dumbrille, Cedric Hardwicke, Martha Scott, Vincent Price, Debra Paget; **D:** Cecil B. DeMille; **M:** Elmer Bernstein. **Award Nominations:** Academy Awards '56: Best Art Direction/Set Decoration (Color), Best Color Cinematography, Best Costume Design (Color), Best Film Editing, Best Picture, Best Sound; **Awards:** Academy Awards '56: Best Special Effects. **VHS, Beta, LV** *PAR, FUS, IGP*

Ten Little Indians

PG/Jr. High-Adult Ten people are gathered in an isolated inn under mysterious circumstances. One by one they are murdered, each according to a verse from a children's nursery rhyme. Not-so-grand British adaptation of the novel and stage play by Agatha Christie.

> **BEWARE!** *Roughhousing.*

1975 98m/C Herbert Lom, Richard Attenborough, Oliver Reed, Elke Sommer, Charles Aznavour, Stephane Audran, Gert Frobe, Adolfo Celi, Orson Welles; **D:** Peter Collinson. **VHS, Beta, LV** *NLC*

Ten Who Dared

Family Fact-based tale of a team of Civil War vets braving the treacherous Colorado River in 1869 in an attempt to chart its course. Poorly paced tale from the Disney frontier-fun assembly line, sorely lacking even in the expected action.

1960 92m/C Brian Keith, John Beal, James Drury; **D:** William Beaudine. **VHS, Beta** *DIS*

Tender Mercies

PG/Jr. High-Adult Divorced, down-and-out country & western singer finds his life redeemed by the love of a young widow and her small son. He sobers up, gets Born Again, and is strong enough to survive when tragedy hits again. Wonderful, life-affirming, grassroots flick of the sort that Hollywood is always accused of never making anymore. Duvall does own warbling.

> **BEWARE!** *Alcohol use and death of a likeable character.*

1983 88m/C Robert Duvall, Tess Harper, Betty Buckley, Ellen Barkin, Wilford Brimley; **D:** Bruce Beresford; **W:** Horton Foote Jr.; **M:** George Dreyfus. **Award Nominations:** Academy Awards '83: Best Director (Beresford), Best Picture, Best Song ("Over You"); **Awards:** Academy Awards '83: Best Actor (Duvall), Best Original Screenplay; Golden Globe Awards '83: Best Actor—Drama (Duvall). **VHS, Beta, LV** *REP, BTV, HMV*

The Tender Tale of Cinderella Penguin

Family Five short animated tales retold through clever animation from Canada. In addition to the title story there's "Metamorphoses," "Froggie Went A' Courting," "The Sky Is Blue," and "The Owl and the Raven."

1991 30m/C VHS *FCT, SMA, NFB*

The Tender Warrior

G/Family Yet another animal adventure with "Grizzly Adams" star Haggerty as a woodsman; the twist is he's a grouchy moonshiner at odds with the nature-loving boy hero in the swamplands of Georgia.

1971 85m/C Dan Haggerty, Charles Lee, Liston Elkins; **D:** Stewart Raffill. **VHS, Beta** *VCD*

The Tender Years

Jr. High-Adult Sentimental drama of a minister trying to outlaw dog fighting, spurred on by his son's fondness for a particular dog.

1947 81m/B Joe E. Brown, Richard Lyon, Noreen Nash, Charles Drake, Josephine Hutchinson; **D:** Harold Schuster. **VHS, Beta** *TCF*

Tennessee Tuxedo in Brushing Off a Toothache

Family The wacky penguin joins his pal Chumly the walrus in episodes from the '60s TV cartoon series.

196? 60m/C VHS

Tennis Racquet

Preschool-Primary Walt Disney's Goofy plays one of the wackiest tennis games ever seen.

1977 8m/C VHS, Beta *DSN,*

Terminal Velocity

PG-13/Jr. High-Adult Skydiving instructor Ditch Brodie (Sheen) thinks he sees student Chris Morrow (Kinski) plummet to her death, only it turns out she's not dead and certainly not a beginner. Upon further investigation, he finds the usual web of international intrigue descending upon him, and that the KGB definitely wants him to mind his own business. (Don't they always.) Still, he pushes on. Another no-brainer actioner with few surprises satisfies the guilty pleasures of action addicts only.

> **BEWARE!** *Scenes of strong action/violence, including a woman being beaten to death.*

1994 132m/C Charlie Sheen, Nastassia Kinski, James Gandolfini, Melvin Van Peebles; **D:** Deran Sarafian; **W:** David N. Twohy; **M:** Joel McNeely. **VHS, LV** *HPH*

The Terminator

R/Sr. High-Adult Futuristic cyborg is sent to present-day Earth. His job: kill the woman who will conceive the child destined to become the great liberator and archenemy of the Earth's future rulers. The cyborg is also pursued by another futuristic visitor, who falls in love with the intended victim. Cameron's pacing is just right in this exhilarating, explosive thriller which displays Arnie as one cold-blooded villain who utters a now famous line: "I'll be back." Followed by "Terminator 2: Judgment Day."

 Brutality, profanity, brief nudity and sex.

1984 108m/C Arnold Schwarzenegger, Michael Biehn, Linda Hamilton, Paul Winfield, Lance Henriksen, Bill Paxton, Rick Rossovich, Dick Miller; **D:** James Cameron; **M:** Brad Fiedel. **VHS, Beta, LV** *NO*

Terminator 2: Judgment Day
🦴🦴🦴🦴

R/Sr. High-Adult He said he'd be back and he is, programmed to protect the boy who will be mankind's post-nuke resistance leader. But the T-1000, a shape-changing, ultimate killing machine, is also on the boy's trail. Twice the mayhem, five times the special effects, ten times the budget of the first, but without Arnold it'd be half the movie. The word hasn't been invented to describe the special effects, particularly THE scariest nuclear holocaust scene yet. Worldwide megahit, but the $100 million budget nearly ruined the studio; Arnold accepted his $12 million in the form of a jet. Laserdisc features include pan and scan, widescreen and a "Making of T-2" short.

 Brutality, profanity and terrifying violence.

1991 139m/C Arnold Schwarzenegger, Linda Hamilton, Edward Furlong, Robert Patrick, Earl Boen, Joe Morton; **D:** James Cameron; **M:** Brad Fiedel. **Award Nominations:** Academy Awards '91: Best Cinematography, Best Sound; **Awards:** Academy Awards '91: Best Makeup, Best Sound, Best Sound Effects Editing, Best Visual Effects; MTV Movie Awards '92: Best Actor (Schwarzenegger), Best Actress (Hamilton), Best Film, Breakthrough Performance (Furlong), Most Desirable Female (Hamilton), Best Action Sequence; People's Choice Awards '92: Best Film. **VHS, LV, 8mm** *LIV*

Terms of Endearment 🦴🦴🦴

PG/Jr. High-Adult Weeper follows the changing relationship between a young woman and her mother, over a thirty-year period. By turns comedy and high-level soap opera, this was Brooks' debut as screenwriter and director. Superb supporting cast headed by Nicholson's slyly charming neighbor/astronaut, with stunning performances by Winger and MacLaine as the two women who often know and love each other too well. Adapted from Larry McMurtry's novel.

 Profanity, sex and a seriously ill character.

1983 132m/C Shirley MacLaine, Jack Nicholson, Debra Winger, John Lithgow, Jeff Daniels, Danny DeVito; **D:** James L. Brooks; **W:** James L. Brooks; **M:** Michael Gore. **Award Nominations:** Academy Awards '83: Best Actress (Winger), Best Art Direction/Set Decoration, Best Film Editing, Best Sound, Best Supporting Actor (Lithgow), Best Original Score; **Awards:** Academy Awards '83: Best Actress (MacLaine), Best Adapted Screenplay, Best Director (Brooks), Best Picture, Best Supporting Actor (Nicholson); Golden Globe Awards '84: Best Actress—Drama (MacLaine), Best Film—Drama, Best Screenplay, Best Supporting Actor (Nicholson). **VHS, Beta, LV** *PAR, BTV, HMV*

Meet the Star of Terminator 2, Eddie Furlong

Eddie Furlong is a young Hollywood powerhouse known for his Byronic brooding. The self-described "half-Mexican, part Russian, and just American" kid came from a broken home who couldn't afford to see a movie let alone star in one. At 13 he fell into the Hollywood dream machine spotted by a casting director on the steps of the Pasadena boys club. Best known as Ahnuld's fiesty sidekick in *Terminator 2: The Judgement Day*, he rocketed to fame, starred in an Aerosmith video and is the current coverbabe of teen fanzines. Now, he's getting attention for his co-starring role with Meryl Streep and Liam Neeson in *Before and After*. T2 packed a punch at the box-office and Furlong caught Hollywood's eye. Before his career took off, he lived for a time with his aunt and uncle. In early '91 his mother, who won't say who Eddie's father is, sued them for custody. A family tug-of-war ensued which took years to resolve. During filming of *A Home of Our Own* Eddie, then 15, rocked the set by taking up with his tutor/stand-in Jackie Domac, then 29.

Furlong digs the vibes of the psychedelic '60s, especially the Beatles. Like his fab four-runners he was recently mobbed at a mall and had to make a run for it. Furlong and brand-new fiance Domac live in a picturesque L.A. house with lots of pets.

Terror in the Jungle 🦴

PG/Jr. High-Adult Plane crashes in Peruvian wilds and young boy survivor meets Jivaro Indians who think he's a god thanks to his golden hair. Cheapo jungle adventure, with horrible script—and a misleading video box cover depicting a sexy, scantily clad blonde. We won't get fooled again.

1968 95m/C Jimmy Angle, Robert Burns, Fawn Silver; **D:** Tom De Simone; **M:** Les Baxter. **VHS** *ACA*

Terrytoons Olympics

Preschool-Primary Collection of Terrytoon characters in Olympic-style events.

1966 42m/C VHS *VTR*

Tess

PG/Jr. High-Adult Sumptuous adaptation of the Thomas Hardy novel "Tess of the D'Ubervilles." Kinski is wonderful as an innocent farm girl who is seduced by the young aristocrat she works for and then finds marriage to a man of her own class only brings more grief. Polanski's direction is faithful and artful. Visually captivating, but plotted like a Victorian novel at nearly three hours (though essentially faithful to the book, if that matters).

BEWARE *Mature themes.*

1980 170m/C Nastassia Kinski, Peter Firth, Leigh Lawson, John Collin; **D:** Roman Polanski; **W:** Roman Polanski. **Award Nominations:** Academy Awards '80: Best Director (Polanski), Best Picture, Best Original Score; **Awards:** Academy Awards '80: Best Art Direction/Set Decoration, Best Cinematography, Best Costume Design; Cesar Awards '80: Best Director (Polanski), Best Film; Golden Globe Awards '81: Best Foreign Film; Los Angeles Film Critics Association Awards '80: Best Director (Polanski); National Board of Review Awards '80: 10 Best Films of the Year. **VHS, Beta, LV** *COL*

Tex

PG/Primary-Adult First and best movie inspired by S.E. Hinton's young-adult novels is a loosely plotted tale of Oklahoma boys trying to raise themselves while dad does the rodeo circuit. Older Mason develops an ulcer vying for a college scholarship while repeatedly bailing young, irresponsible Tex out of trouble. Excellent performances by all. Dillon makes his character understandable and sympathetic, even when blundering through booze, drugs, and pointless classroom pranks. Allegedly the first pic under the Disney banner to use four-letter words, but the Hound heard nothing foul, just credible teen talk.

BEWARE *Profanity, sex talk, drug use and violence.*

1982 103m/C Matt Dillon, Jim Metzler, Meg Tilly, Bill McKinney, Frances Lee McCain, Ben Johnson, Emilio Estevez; **D:** Tim Hunter; **M:** Pino Donaggio. **VHS, Beta, LV** *DIS, OM*

Tex Avery's Screwball Classics, Vol. 1

Family Collection of eight classic, and funny, cartoons by renowned director Avery. Ages 4 to 7.

194? 60m/C D: Tex Avery. **VHS, Beta, LV** *MGM*

Tex Avery's Screwball Classics, Vol. 2

Family More Averian cartoon classics, bearing the master's unmistakable stamp: "One Ham's Family," "Happy Go Nutty," "Slap Happy Lion," "Wild and Wolfy," "Ventriloquist Cat," "Big Heel Watha," "Northwest Hounded Police" and "Red Hot Riding Hood," which is pretty racy for a cartoon. Ages 4 to 7.

194? 60m/C D: Tex Avery. **VHS, Beta** *MGM*

Tex Avery's Screwball Classics, Vol. 3

Family More hilarious cartoons. Ages 4 to 7.

194? 60m/C VHS, Beta *MGM, FCT*

Tex Avery's Screwball Classics, Vol. 4

Family Includes "What Price Fleadom," "TV of Tomorrow," "The Counterfeit Cat," "Blitz Wolf," "The Cuckoo Clock," and "What's Buzzin' Buzzard?" Ages 4 to 7.

1953 46m/C VHS *NO*

That Darn Cat

G/Family Mediocre Disney comedy about a Siamese cat named D.C. ("Darned Cat," get it?) that provides enough clues for an allergy-afflicted FBI Agent to thwart kidnappers. Some funny slapstick and performances. Based on the book "Undercover Cat" by The Gordons.

1965 115m/C Hayley Mills, Dean Jones, Dorothy Provine, Neville Brand, Elsa Lanchester, Frank Gorshin, Roddy McDowall; **D:** Robert Stevenson. **VHS, Beta** *DIS*

That Darn Cat

PG/Family Disney remakes its 1965 favorite about a cat named D.C. that helps an FBI agent find a kidnapped woman.

1996 ?m/C Christina Ricci, Doug E. Doug; **D:** Bob Spiers. **VHS** *NYR*

That Gang of Mine

Family "East Side Kids" episode about gang member Mugg's ambition to be a jockey. Good racing scenes.

1940 62m/B Bobby Jordan, Leo Gorcey, Clarence Muse, Dave O'Brien; **D:** Joseph H. Lewis. **VHS, Beta** *NOS, DVT, HEG*

That Night

PG-13/Jr. High-Adult View of romance through the eyes of a young girl, circa 1961. Ten-year-old Alice is the confidant of rebellious 17-year-old neighbor Cheryl who enlists the young girl's aid as a go-between with her wrong side of the tracks boyfriend. Barely released to theaters, this sentimental tale gets a considerable lift from the cast. Based on a novel by Alice McDermott.

BEWARE *Sex, mature themes.*

1993 89m/C C. Thomas Howell, Juliette Lewis, Eliza Dushku, Helen Shaver, John Dossett; **D:** Craig Bolotin; **W:** Craig Bolotin. **VHS, Beta, LV** *WAR*

That Sinking Feeling 🎵🎵🎵

PG/Sr. High-Adult Group of bored Scottish teenagers decide to steal 90 sinks from a plumber's warehouse. After the success of Forsythe's "Gregory's Girl," this earlier effort from the filmmaker's career was released to his great (and needless) reluctance; despite rough edges it's genuinely funny as the boys try to get rid of the sinks and turn a profit.
1979 82m/C Robert Buchanan, John Hughes, Billy Greenlees, Alan Love; **D:** Bill Forsyth; **W:** Bill Forsyth. **VHS, Beta, LV**

That Was Then . . . This Is Now 🎵🎵

R/Sr. High-Adult Adaptation of S.E. Hinton's teen novel about two guys from the wrong side of the tracks. Bryan gradually matures and turns toward a responsible life, and away from his wild, adoptive brother Mark. Far from a success the scruffy Sheffer and "Mighty Duck" Estevez seem best suited to each other's roles instead of their respective Gallant and Goofus acts. And there's a silly finale contrived to end the tale on an upbeat note. But it does capture Hinton's moody mileau of young people fending for themselves in a hostile society where parents or other moral guardians are absent or ineffective.

BEWARE *Violence, profanity and drug use.*

1985 102m/C Emilio Estevez, Craig Sheffer, Kim Delaney, Jill Schoelen, Barbara Babcock, Frank Howard, Larry B. Scott, Morgan Freeman; **D:** Christopher Cain; **W:** Emilio Estevez. **VHS, Beta, LV** *PAR*

That's Dancing!

G/Family Anthology features some of film's finest moments in dance from classical ballet to break-dancing.
1985 104m/C Fred Astaire, Ginger Rogers, Ruby Keeler, Cyd Charisse, Gene Kelly, Shirley MacLaine, Liza Minnelli, Sammy Davis Jr., Mikhail Baryshnikov, Ray Bolger, Jennifer Beals, Dean Martin; **D:** Jack Haley Jr.; **M:** Henry Mancini. **VHS, Beta, LV** *MGM*

That's Entertainment

G/Family A compilation of scenes from the classic MGM musicals beginning with "The Broadway Melody" (1929) and ending with "Gigi" (1958). Great fun, especially for movie buffs.
1974 132m/C Judy Garland, Fred Astaire, Frank Sinatra, Gene Kelly, Esther Williams, Bing Crosby; **D:** Jack Haley Jr.; **M:** Henry Mancini. **VHS, Beta, LV** *MGM*

That's Entertainment, Part 2

G/Family Cavalcade of great musical and comedy sequences from MGM movies of the past. Also stars Jeanette MacDonald, Nelson Eddy, the Marx Brothers, Laurel and Hardy, Jack Buchanan, Ann Miller, Mickey Rooney, Louis Armstrong, Oscar Levant, Cyd Charisse, Elizabeth Taylor, Maurice Chavalier, Bing Crosby,

Jimmy Durante, Clark Gable, and the Barrymores. Not as unified as its predecessor, but priceless nonetheless.
1976 133m/C Fred Astaire, Gene Kelly. **VHS, Beta, LV** *MGM*

That's Entertainment, Part 3 🎵🎵♭

G/Family Third volume contains 62 MGM musical numbers from over 100 films, hosted by nine of the original stars, and is based on outtakes and unfinished numbers from studio archives. One new technique used here is a split-screen showing both the actual film with a behind-the-scenes shot that includes cameramen, set designers, and dancers scurrying around. Although it has its moments, TE3 doesn't generate the same reverence for Hollywood's Golden Age that its predecessors managed to do. That 18-year gap between sequels may say something about what the studio execs thought of their film vault's remainders.
1993 113m/C **D:** Bud Friedgen, Michael J. Sheridan; **W:** Bud Friedgen, Michael J. Sheridan; **M:** Marc Shaiman. **VHS, Beta, LV** *MGM*

That's My Hero!

Family Re-edited episodes of "The Secret Lives of Waldo Kitty," a Saturday-morning kids' show mixing live-action scenes of a daydreaming tabby cat with cartoon depictions of his fantasies, usually takeoffs on popular movie and TV adventures. Tapes of the original show are also available.
1975 72m/C **VHS, Beta** *NO*

Theodore Rex 🎵🎵♭

PG/Primary-Adult Goldberg plays a cynical cop who's teamed with an eight-foot-tall, three-ton, returned-from-extinction dinosaur (who has a taste for cookies). No, we're not making this up.

BEWARE *Sci-fi violence and language.*

1995 92m/C Whoopi Goldberg, Armin Mueller-Stahl, Richard Roundtree, Juliet Landau; **D:** Jonathan Betuel; **W:** Jonathan Betuel; **C:** David Tattersall; **M:** Robert Folk. **VHS, LV** *NLC*

There Goes a Boat

Preschool Hosts Becky and Dave explore tankers, freighters, and a submarine. Ages 4 to 8.
1994 35m/C **VHS** *KID*

There Goes a Race Car

Preschool Becky and Dave take a behind-the-scenes look at monster trucks, funny cars, and a demolition derby. Ages 4 to 8.
1994 35m/C **VHS** *KID*

There Goes a Spaceship

Preschool Becky and Dave explore being astronauts. Ages 4 to 8.
1994 35m/C **VHS** *KID*

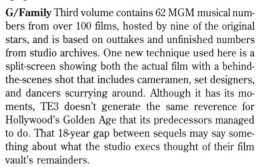

There Goes a Train

Preschool Engineer Dave explains in basic terms how diesel and steam engines work, while showing close-ups of trains in action. Ages 4 to 8.

1994 35m/C VHS *AVE*

They Went That-a-Way & That-a-Way 🦴 ᵇ

PG/Family Two bumbling deputies go undercover as convicts, then have to plan an escape when they realize nobody's going to let them out of prison. Lackluster family comedy, with a script by Conway.

1978 96m/C Tim Conway, Richard Kiel; *D:* Edward Montagne; *W:* Tim Conway. **VHS, Beta**

Thief of Baghdad 🦴🦴🦴 ᵇ

Family Fresh from "The Jungle Book," Sabu went on to play the nimble-witted young rogue Abu, who enlists the aid of a powerful genie to outwit the treacherous Grand Vizier of Baghdad and help a prince escape from a prison and realize his true love. Magnificent Arabian Nights spectacular, with lush Technicolor photography, epic special effects. Ingram makes the screen's greatest (non-animated) genie. The silent "Thief of Baghdad" (1924), with a superbly swashbuckling Douglas Fairbanks Sr., is also on cassette.

1940 106m/C Sabu, Conrad Veidt, June Duprez, Rex Ingram, Tim Whelan, Michael Powell; *D:* Ludwig Berger; *M:* Miklos Rozsa. **VHS, Beta, LV** *MLB, FUS*

Thief of Baghdad 🦴🦴

Family An Arabian Nights fantasy about a thief in love with a Sultan's daughter who has been poisoned. He seeks out the magical blue rose which is the antidote. Not as lavish as the previous two productions of this title, nor as much fun.

1961 89m/C Georgia Moll, Steve Reeves; *D:* Arthur Lubin. **VHS, Beta**

The Thief of Baghdad 🦴🦴 ᵇ

G/Family TV adaptation of the fantasy-adventure has special effects that don't quite make the grade but a cast that often does; McDowall is a delight as the wily thief who helps the rather stuffy prince win the hand of Princess Yasmine.

1978 101m/C Peter Ustinov, Roddy McDowall, Terence Stamp, Frank Finlay, Ian Holm; *D:* Clive Donner. **VHS, Beta** *GEM*

The Thin Man 🦴🦴🦴 ᵇ

Family Married sleuths Nick and Nora Charles investigate the mysterious disappearance of a wealthy inventor. Charming and sophisticated, this was the model for all husband-and-wife detective teams that followed. Don't miss Asta, their wire-hair terrier. Based on the novel by Dashiell Hammett. Its enormous popularity triggered five sequels, starting with "After the Thin Man."

1934 90m/B William Powell, Myrna Loy, Maureen O'Sullivan, Cesar Romero, Porter Hall, Nat Pendleton, Minna Gombell, Natalie Moorhead, Edward Ellis; *D:* Woodbridge S. Van Dyke. **VHS, Beta, LV** *MGM, HMV*

The Thing Called Love 🦴🦴 ᵇ

PG-13/Jr. High-Adult "Singles" takes to Nashville in this unsentimental tale of four twentysomething singles trying to make their mark in the world of country music. The idea for the plot comes from the real-life Bluebird Cafe—the place where all aspiring singers and songwriters want to perform. Phoenix, Mathis, Mulroney, and Bullock do their own singing; look for Oslin as the cafe owner. Phoenix's last completed film role.

⚠ BEWARE *Profanity and sex.*

1993 116m/C River Phoenix, Samantha Mathis, Sandra Bullock, Dermot Mulroney, K.T. Oslin, Anthony Clark, Webb Wilder; *Cameos:* Trisha Yearwood; *D:* Peter Bogdanovich; *W:* Allan Moyle, Carol Heikkinen. **VHS, Beta, LV** *PAR*

Things That Fly Sing Alongs

Preschool-Primary Kermit the Frog and friends explore different things that fly from hot air balloons to jet planes. Features seven Muppet originals including "Things That Go," "Up In the Air Without a Care," and "In the Wind."

1996 ?m/C VHS *JHV*

Things to Do On a Rainy Day

Primary Projects to keep kids entertained indoors, including making macaroni jewelry, having an indoor picnic, and playing sock toss. Suggestions are color-coded under topics such as "Cooking Fun" and "Creative Craft." Ages 5 to 10.

1995 40m/C VHS *LTY*

Think Big 🦴🦴 ᵇ

PG-13/Jr. High-Adult Twin bodybuilders, the Pauls (previously billed as 'The Barbarian Brothers'), are lunkhead truck drivers who pick up a brilliant teenage girl running from bad guys who want her revolutionary energy invention. Funnier than it sounds, with enjoyable goofing by the supporting cast. More than a spot of profanity.

⚠ BEWARE *Excessive profanity, slapstick violence, and just a hint of sex.*

1990 86m/C Peter Paul, David Paul, Martin Mull, Ari Meyers, Richard Kiel, David Carradine, Richard Moll, Peter Lupus; *W:* Jim Wynorski, R.J. Robertson. **VHS, Beta, LV** *LIV, VTR*

Third Man on the Mountain 🦴🦴 ᵇ

G/Family Thrilling Disney epic about mountain climbing, shot in Switzerland and based on James Ramsey Ullman's "Banner in the Sky" (another title by which the film is known). In 1865 Switzerland young Rudi is determined to ascend the same forbidding peak as his ancestors have. But, after he joins a British expedition, Rudi learns there's more to climbing than he imagined.

1959 106m/C James MacArthur, Michael Rennie, Janet Munro, James Donald, Herbert Lom, Laurence Naismith; **Cameos:** Helen Hayes; **D:** Ken Annakin. **VHS, Beta** *DIS*

13 Ghosts 🎵🎵♭

Jr. High-Adult Castle, gimmicky mogul who inspired "Matinee," did this fun spook story. Typical American family moves to a castle with a lost treasure and 12 grotesque specters who need just one more victim to make their quota. Naturally it's the family's little boy who's hip to what's going on, thanks to his special ghost-viewing eyeglasses; such 3D-type spectacles were made available to patrons when this played theaters. Allegedly, fearful moviegoers could choose to see or not to see the blurry, ghouls, depending on which lens they used, an effect missing on video. Hamilton, the Wicked Witch from "The Wizard of Oz," has a great role as the house-keeper.

1960 88m/C Charles Herbert, Jo Morrow, Martin Milner, Rosemary DeCamp, Donald Woods, Margaret Hamilton; **D:** William Castle. **VHS, Beta** *GKK*

The 39 Steps 🎵🎵🎵🎵

Jr. High-Adult Classic Hitchcock mistaken-man-caught-in-intrigue thriller, featuring some of his most often copied set pieces and the surest visual flair of his pre-war British period. Man on vacation in London meets a strange woman investigating a spy ring, who tells him a little something about what she knows. Soon she's dead and he's on the run to Scotland. The laserdisc version includes a twenty-minute documentary tracing the director's British period. Remade twice, in 1959 and 1979.

1935 81m/B Robert Donat, Madeleine Carroll, Godfrey Tearle, Lucie Mannheim, Peggy Ashcroft, John Laurie, Wylie Watson; **D:** Alfred Hitchcock; **W:** Charles Bennett, Alma Reville; **M:** Louis Levy. **VHS, Beta, LV, 8mm** *CNG, NOS, VHE*

This Boy's Life 🎵🎵🎵

R/Sr. High-Adult In the 1950s divorcee Carolyn and her troubled adolescent son Toby settle in the town of Concrete, outside Seattle. She's hitched with Dwight (De Niro), a slick but rough-edged mechanic who proves to be a domestic tyrant for the rebellious boy. Strong performances by all, but keep your eye on DiCaprio (great in his first major role) as the confused and abused Toby, divided between dreams of prep school and the allure of the going-nowhere crowd. Based on the memoirs of Tobias Wolff; director Caton-Jones sensitively illustrates the skewed understanding of masculinity in the 1950s.

🛑 **BEWARE** *Mature themes, domestic violence, profanity, juvenile drinking and smoking.*

1993 115m/C Robert De Niro, Ellen Barkin, Leonardo DiCaprio, Jonah Blechman, Eliza Dushku, Chris Cooper, Carla Gugino, Zachary Ansley, Tracey Ellis, Kathy Kinney, Gerrit Graham; **D:** Michael Caton-Jones; **W:** Robert Getchell; **M:** Carter Burwell. **VHS, Beta, LV** *WAR, FCT, BTV*

This Is America, Charlie Brown: The Birth of the Constitution

Family The nation's governing document is created with some help from the Peanuts gang. Ages 6 to 10.

1995 24m/C VHS *PAR*

This is America, Charlie Brown: The NASA Space Station

Family Charlie Brown and the rest of the gang, including Snoopy, become astronauts. Ages 6 to 10.

1995 25m/C VHS *PAR*

This is My Life 🎵🎵♭

PG-13/Jr. High-Adult Dottie is torn between her sky-rocketing career as a stand-up comic and her two small daughters. Immensely personable Kavner plays the divorced mom who is determined to chuck her cosmetic sales job for show business, but as offers pour in, she finds her girls suffering as a result of her success. Good performances highlight an otherwise average drama.

🛑 **BEWARE** *Profanity, sex, conflict of family vs. career, with family coming out second best, at least for a while.*

1992 105m/C Julie Kavner, Samantha Mathis, Carrie Fisher, Dan Aykroyd, Gaby Hoffman; **D:** Nora Ephron; **W:** Nora Ephron, Delia Ephron. **VHS** *FXV*

This Pretty Planet

Family Video captures the warm and playful pleasure of a Tom Chapin concert as the singer-songwriter performs some of his best material, including "Uh-Oh, Accident," "Good Garbage" . "Alphabet Soup" "Family Tree," "Cousins" and "Someone's Gonna Use It After You," most of which celebrate heredity and environment, all of which stand up to repeated hearings. Nobody writes better children's songs than Chapin and his collaborators John Forster and Michael Mark. Incidentally, that's Michael Mark accompanying Chapin on bass. Ages 5 and up.

1995 50m/C VHS

Thomas the Tank Engine: Better Late Than Never

Preschool-Primary Seven stories about Thomas and his choo-choo friends, including one where Thomas gets stuck underground in a mine. From the PBS program "Shining Time Station." Ringo Starr narrates. Ages 1 to 5.

1990 40m/C VHS *VTR*

Thomas the Tank Engine: James Goes Buzz Buzz and Other Thomas Stories

Preschool-Primary Seven figure- and model-animated stories about the adventures of the friendly engine and his Shining Time Station sidekicks. James goes buzz

buzz when a beehive breaks. George Carlin narrates. Ages 1 to 5.

1993 37m/C VHS *VTR*

Thomas the Tank Engine: James Learns a Lesson & Other Stories

Preschool-Primary James the Train, with the help of his pal Thomas, learns some valuable lessons about life. And what are those fish doing in Thomas boiler? From the PBS family program, "Shining Time Station." Ringo Starr narrates. Ages 1 to 5.

1990 40m/C VHS *VTR*

Thomas the Tank Engine: Tenders & Turntables & Other Stories

Preschool-Primary Join Thomas the Tank Engine from PBS' "Shining Time Station" in seven adventures, including finding out why Thomas is in the station master's dining room! Ringo Starr narrates. Ages 1 to 5.

1990 40m/C VHS *VTR*

Thomas the Tank Engine: Thomas Breaks the Rules & Other Stories

Preschool-Primary That wild man Thomas the Tank Engine learns the ramifications of breaking rules in this series of family stories from PBS' "Shining Time Station." And watch out, there are cows on the tracks. Ringo Starr narrates. Ages 1 to 5.

1990 40m/C VHS *VTR*

Thomas the Tank Engine: Thomas Gets Bumped

Preschool-Primary Percy and Duck go on strike. More pleasant tales from Thomas the Tank Engine and the Shining Time Station gang. Ages 1 to 5.

1992 40m/C VHS *VTR*

Thomas the Tank Engine: Thomas Gets Tricked & Other Stories

Preschool-Primary From the PBS childrens' series, "Shining Time Station" comes stories featuring Thomas, the little train engine from the land of Sodor. Henry refuses to work in the rain, afraid it will spoil his paint job. Ages 1 to 5.

1990 40m/C VHS *VTR*

Thomas the Tank Engine: Thomas, Percy and the Dragon & Other Stories

Preschool-Primary Thomas takes on a mysterious cargo, Percy learns everyone's afraid at some time, and other animated stories to keep the kiddies amused. Ages 1 to 5.

1993 37m/C VHS *VTR*

Thomas the Tank Engine: Trust Thomas & Other Stories

Preschool-Primary Seven more animated adventures with Thomas, Henry, James, and the others. From the PBS program "Shining Time Station." Ages 1 to 5.

199? 40m/C VHS *VTR*

Thoroughbreds Don't Cry 🦴🦴 ▷

Family There's no crying in horse racing. Future "National Velvet" and "Black Stallion" horseman Rooney plays a jockey who rides in a fixed race on the orders of his no-good father. The kid has guilty feelings about it later and tries to redeem himself, but his good intentions backfire. Well-acted equine melodrama, with Garland as the hero's girlfriend adding a few songs.

1937 80m/B Judy Garland, Mickey Rooney, Sophie Tucker, Sir C. Aubrey Smith, Ronald Sinclair, Forrester Harvey; *D:* Alfred E. Green. **VHS** *MGM, MVD*

Those Calloways 🦴🦴 ▷

PG/Family Those small-town Calloways attempt to establish a sanctuary for the flocks of wild geese who fly over the woods of Swiftwater, Maine. Okay Disney family fare, with good cast. Based on Paul Annixter's novel "Swiftwater."

1965 131m/C Brian Keith, Vera Miles, Brandon de Wilde, Walter Brennan, Ed Wynn, John Qualen, Linda Evans; *D:* Norman Tokar; *M:* Max Steiner. **VHS, Beta** *DIS*

Those Daring Young Men in Their Jaunty Jalopies 🦴🦴

G/Family Daring young 1920s drivers in noisy slow cars trek 1500 miles across country to a Monte Carlo finish line and call it a race. Sputtering attempt to conjure up the inspired zaniness of "Those Magnificent Men in Their Flying Machines."

1969 125m/C Tony Curtis, Susan Hampshire, Terry-Thomas, Eric Sykes, Gert Frobe, Peter Cook, Dudley Moore, Jack Hawkins; *D:* Ken Annakin. **VHS** *PAR, FCT*

A Thousand Clowns 🦴🦴🦴 ▷

Sr. High-Adult Loaded with laughs, and one of the best depictions ever of a parent's love for a child, though technically the man (Robards) and boy (Gordon) are uncle and nephew. Robards plays sharp-witted comedy writer Murray Burns, who can't stand working for an idiotic children's TV show. So he quits. Enter the child welfare people who threaten: no job, no kid. While he figures out his next move, Murray and precocious nephew Nick treat all of New York as their personal playground.

1965 118m/B Jason Robards Jr., Barry Gordon, William Daniels, Barbara Harris, Gene Saks, Martin Balsam; **D:** Fred Coe; **W:** Herb Gardner. **Award Nominations:** Academy Awards '65: Best Adapted Screenplay, Best Picture, Best Original Score; **Awards:** Academy Awards '65: Best Supporting Actor (Balsam); National Board of Review Awards '65: 10 Best Films of the Year. **VHS, Beta** *MGM, FOX, BTV*

Three Amigos 🎵🎵

PG/Jr. High-Adult Three out-of-work silent screen stars are asked to defend a Mexican town from bandits; they think it's a public appearance stint. Spoof of Three Stooges and Mexican bandito movies that at times falls short, given the enormous amount of comedic talent involved. Generally enjoyable with some very funny scenes. Co-written by former "Saturday Night Live" producer Michaels. Short's first major film appearance.

1986 105m/C Chevy Chase, Steve Martin, Martin Short, Joe Mantegna, Patrice Martinez, Jon Lovitz, Alfonso Arau, Randy Newman; **D:** John Landis; **W:** Steve Martin, Randy Newman, Lorne Michaels; **M:** Elmer Bernstein. **VHS, Beta, LV** *HBO*

The Three Billy Goats Gruff/ The Three Little Pigs

Preschool-Primary Hunter narrates these classic children's stories from the "Rabbit Ears" series.

1991 30m/C VHS, LV *KUI, NLC*

The Three Caballeros 🎵🎵🎵

Family Donald Duck stars in this journey through Latin America, where he falls in love with a local chick (so to speak) and tours the country on a flying serape. Full of music, variety, and live-action/animation segments. Stories include "Pablo the Penguin," "Little Gauchito," and adventures with Joe Carioca, who was first introduced in Disney's "Saludos Amigos." Produced initially for political reasons (to cement US relations with its southern neighbors during wartime), today this stands as one of their very best pieces of animation. 🎵 The Three Caballeros; Baia.

1945 71m/C V: Sterling Holloway, Aurora Miranda. **VHS, Beta, LV** *DIS, APD*

Three Decades of Donald Duck Series

Preschool-Primary Time-spanning Disney set of three separate Donald Duck tapes: "Donald's Nephews" (1938), "Fire Chief" (1940), and "Up a Tree" (1955).

1990 8m/C VHS, Beta *MTI, DSN*

Three Fugitives 🎵🎵

PG-13/Jr. High-Adult Ex-con determined to go straight is taken hostage by a bungling first-time bank robber, who is only attempting the holdup in order to support his withdrawn little girl. All three wind up hunted

by the cops, learn to like each other on the lam, etc. Comedy works, pathos is way too maudlin and slow. Like "Three Men and a Baby" and others, this is a calculated Disney/Touchstone remake of a French film; here "Les Fugitifs" done by the same director so you're not missing anything.

🔔 **BEWARE** *Violence, mainly slapstick.*

1989 96m/C Nick Nolte, Martin Short, James Earl Jones, Kenneth McMillan, Sarah Rowland Doroff, Alan Ruck; **D:** Francis Veber; **W:** Francis Veber. **VHS, Beta, LV** *TOU*

The Three Little Pigs

Preschool-Primary Walt Disney's "Silly Symphony" retelling of the famous pig tale that teaches the importance of careful planning is one of his very best shorts and took an Academy Award for Best Cartoon, Short Subject.

1933 13m/C VHS, Beta *DSN, MTI*

The Three Little Pigs

Family Jeff Goldblum is a fairly likeable Big Bad Wolf in this mostly comic "Faerie Tale Theatre" production. Did we say mostly comic? Consider this: The pigs are played by Billy Crystal, Fred Willard and Stephen Furst (remember the fat doctor from "St. Elsewhere?") And although the wolf gets it in the end, he lives to tell about it. Ages 6 to 11.

1984 60m/C Billy Crystal, Jeff Goldblum, Valerie Perrine; **D:** Howard Storm. **VHS, Beta** *KUI, FOX, FCT*

The Three Lives of Thomasina 🎵🎵🎵

PG/Family In turn-of-the-century Scotland, a veterinarian orders his daughter's beloved cat destroyed when the pet is diagnosed with tetanus. After Thomasina's death (with scenes of kitty heaven) a beautiful and mysterious healer from the woods is able to bring the animal back to life, restoring feline (with add-on bonus to standard nine lives) to the little girl mourning her previous demise. Lovely Disney fairy tale with good performances by all.

1963 95m/C Patrick McGoohan, Susan Hampshire, Karen Dotrice, Matthew Garber; **D:** Don Chaffey. **VHS, Beta** *DIS, TVC*

Three Men and a Baby 🎵🎵🎵

PG/Primary-Adult The lives of three swinging bachelors living in New York are shaken by the sudden arrival of a baby girl—possibly the daughter of one of them. The libertines take turns fathering the tyke under trying circumstances, especially when some crooks come sniffing around. Well-paced, charming and fun, with good acting from all. Remake of the French movie "Three Men and a Cradle," also on video and worth checking out in its own right.

🔔 **BEWARE** *Profanity, sex talk and excremental conversation.*

1987 102m/C Tom Selleck, Steve Guttenberg, Ted Danson, Margaret Colin, Nancy Travis, Philip Bosco, Celeste Holm, Derek De Lint,

Cynthia Harris, Lisa Blair, Michelle Blair; **D:** Leonard Nimoy; **W:** James Orr, Jim Cruickshank; **M:** Marvin Hamlisch. **VHS, Beta, LV, 8mm** *TOU*

Three Men and a Cradle 🦴🦴🦴 ⌐

PG-13/Sr. High-Adult Remade in the U.S. in 1987 as "Three Men and a Baby," this French film features the same plot about a bachelor trio living together who suddenly find themselves the guardians of a baby girl. After the initial shock wears off, they fall in love with her and won't let her go. Fans of the American version may like the original even more. In French with English subtitles. **1985 100m/C** Roland Giraud, Michel Boujenah, Andre Dussollier; **D:** Coline Serreau; **W:** Coline Serreau. **Award Nominations:** Academy Awards '85: Best Foreign Language Film; **Awards:** Cesar Awards '86: Best Film, Best Supporting Actor (Boujenah). **VHS, LV** *LIV, MGM, INJ*

Three Men and a Little Lady 🦴🦴 ⌐

PG/Primary-Adult In this lesser but still entertaining sequel to "Three Men and a Baby," the mother of the once-abandoned child decides that her daughter needs a legitimate father. Although she would prefer to marry Selleck's character, he doesn't get the message, so the mom chooses a snooty British film director. All comes out well in the end, though.

 *Profanity and sex talk.*

1990 100m/C Tom Selleck, Steve Guttenberg, Ted Danson, Nancy Travis, Robin Weisman, Christopher Cazenove, Fiona Shaw, Sheila Hancock, John Boswall, Jonathan Lynn, Sydney Walsh; **D:** Emile Ardolino; **W:** Charlie Peters, Sara Parriott, Josann McGibbon; **M:** James Newton Howard. **VHS, Beta, LV** *TOU*

Three Musketeers 🦴 ⌐

Family Very loose adaptation of Alexander Dumas, depicting the Musketeers in the form of a trio of American pals in the Foreign Legion, fighting against nefarious sheik El Shaitan. Wayne is the D'Artagnan equivalent, in the weakest of his serial efforts. In 12 chapters. **1933 215m/B** John Wayne, Raymond Hatton, Lon Chaney Jr. **VHS, Beta** *NOS, VCN, VDM*

The Three Musketeers 🦴🦴 ⌐

Family Three royal guards who are "all for one and one for all" join forces with rookie D'Artagnan to battle the power-hungry Cardinal Richelieu (portrayed by ace screen villain Price). Colorful edition of the adventure classic by Alexander Dumas, with an all-star cast and grand Hollywood production values. Singer/dancer Kelly seems overaged for the youthful hothead D'Artagnan, but his light-stepping moves suit the swordfights perfectly.

 Violence.

1948 126m/C Lana Turner, Gene Kelly, June Allyson, Gig Young, Angela Lansbury, Van Heflin, Keenan Wynn, Robert Coote, Reginald Owen, Frank Morgan, Vincent Price, Patricia Medina; **D:** George Sidney. **VHS, Beta, LV** *MGM, CCB*

Three Musketeers 🦴🦴

Family Hanna-Barbera cartoon TV version of the classic Alexander Dumas tale about three of the king's swordsmen and the upstart D'Artagnan pitted against the devious Cardinal Richelieu in France. **1973 74m/C VHS, Beta**

Three Musketeers 🦴🦴🦴

PG/Jr. High-Adult Extravagant, funny version of the Dumas classic, more for the young-at-heart than the very young. Three swashbucklers and newcomer D'Artagnan set out to save the honor of the French Queen. To do so they must oppose the evil cardinal who has his eyes on the power behind the throne. Winning combination of slapstick and high adventure throws some sexual bawdiness in for good measure. Followed by "The Four Musketeers" and "The Return of the Musketeers."

BEWARE *Swashbuckling violence, modest sex, alcohol use.*

1974 105m/C Richard Chamberlain, Oliver Reed, Michael York, Raquel Welch, Frank Finlay, Christopher Lee, Faye Dunaway, Charlton Heston, Geraldine Chaplin, Simon Ward, Jean-Pierre Cassel; **D:** Richard Lester. **VHS, Beta** *COL*

The Three Musketeers 🦴🦴 ⌐

PG/Jr. High-Adult Yet another version, this time from Disney, of the classic swashbuckler with Porthos, Athos, Aramis, and the youthful D'Artegnan banding together against the evil Cardinal Richelieu and the tempting Milady DeWinter to save France. Cute stars, a lot of action stunts and swordplay, a few jokes, and cartoon bad guys. Okay for the family crowd.

BEWARE *Swashbuckling MTV violence.*

1993 105m/C Kiefer Sutherland, Charlie Sheen, Chris O'Donnell, Oliver Platt, Rebecca DeMornay, Tim Curry, Gabrielle Anwar, Julie Delpy, Michael Wincott; **D:** Stephen Herek; **W:** David Loughery; **M:** Michael Kamen. **VHS, LV** *DIS*

The Three Musketeers: All for One and One for All! 🦴🦴

Family Animated adaptation of the legendary Dumas tale about D'Artagnan and his three swashbuckling friends fighting their honor and glory versus the plotters and pretenders against the throne of France. **1977 85m/C VHS** *JFK*

3 Ninjas 🦴🦴 ⌐

PG/Family There's barely an original moment in this lively cross between "Home Alone" and kung-fu pics, about three brothers who are trained as ninjas by their Japanese grandpa. When bad guys try to kidnap the boys, they're in for trouble. Likeable kids, funny action, short running time—all add up to surprisingly enjoyable, no-brainer family fun.

 Roughhousing—but with an emphasis on slapstick pratfalls and bumbling villains, no serious violence.

1992 84m/C Victor Wong, Michael Treanor, Max Elliott Slade, Chad Power, Rand Kingsley, Alan McRae, Margarita Franco, Toru Tanaka, Patrick Laborteaux; **D:** Jon Turteltaub; **W:** Edward Emanuel; **M:** Rick Marvin. **VHS, Beta, LV** *TOU, PMS*

3 Ninjas Kick Back 🦴🦴 ⌢

PG/Jr. High-Adult Sequel to the popular "3 Ninjas." Three brothers help their grandfather protect a ceremonial knife won in a ninja tournament in Japan 50 years earlier. Gramps' ancient adversary in that tournament, now an evil tycoon, wants the sword back and he's willing to enlist the aid of his three American grandchildren, members of garage band Teenage Vomit, to get it. The showdown eventually heads to Japan, where "Kick Back," unlike predecessors, dispenses with the Japan-bashing. High-spirited action fare that kids will enjoy.

 Roughhousing; beware tasteless gag about flatulence, fat women, and a garage band called Teenage Vomit.

1994 95m/C Victor Wong, Max Elliott Slade, Sean Fox, Evan Bonifant, Sab Shimono, Dustin Nguyen, Jason Schombing, Caroline Junko King, Angelo Tiffe; **D:** Charles Kanganis; **W:** Mark Saltzman; **M:** Rick Marvin. **VHS** *NYR*

Three O'Clock High 🦴🦴 ⌢

PG/Primary-Adult Nervous, nerdy Jerry stumbles into a 3 p.m. duel with the new bully in high school and tries every trick possible to avoid his fate, but naturally the ordeal turns out to be a growing experience for our student hero. Debuting director Joanou has fun with snazzy camera tricks and a high-school-as-Hell attitude.

 Roughhousing, salty language.

1987 97m/C Casey Siemaszko, Anne Ryan, Stacey Glick, Jonathan Wise, Richard Tyson, Jeffrey Tambor, Philip Baker Hall, John P. Ryan; **D:** Phil Joanou; **W:** Richard Christian Matheson, Thomas Szollosi; **M:** Tangerine Dream. **VHS, Beta, LV** *MCA*

The Three Robbers and Other Stories

Preschool-Primary A compilation of children's animated shorts including "Leopold and the See-Through Crumbpicker," "The Island of the Skog" and "Fourteen Rats & A Rat-Catcher." Ages 3 to 6.

1980 38m/C VHS, Beta *NO*

Three Sesame Street Stories

Preschool-Primary Jim Henson's muppets are set to animation in three tales based on the PBS children's series.

1990 30m/C VHS

Three Stooges

Family Long a fave with kids (and adult males), the slapstick Stooges are widely available in their original short subjects. Thirteen one-hour volumes are in this 1930s series; a separate "Other Nyuks" set from Columbia compiles Stooge offerings from the 1940s. Other titles like "The Lost Stooges" and "Medium Rare" concentrate mainly on Stooge cameo appearances and TV guest spots, mainly for hardcore Stoogephiles. Beware of a few tapes out there that are really episodes of a lame Stooges cartoon series, done when the original comedians got too old for roughhousing and head-bopping.

193? 60m/B Moe Howard, Shemp Howard, Larry Fine. **VHS, Beta, LV** *DVT*

Three Stooges: A Ducking They Will Go

Family Comedy trio nyuks it up in "Three Little Twirps" (1943), "Ants in the Pantry" (1936), and "A Ducking They Did Go" (1939), where they are conned into selling shares in a phony duck hunting club.

193? 50m/B Moe Howard, Curly Howard, Larry Fine. **VHS** *COL*

Three Stooges: A Plumbing We Will Go

Family Early Stooges episodes entitled "Violent is the Word for Curly" (1938), "Punch Drunks" (1934), and "A Plumbing We Will Go" (1940).

1934 60m/B Moe Howard, Curly Howard, Larry Fine. **VHS** *COL*

Three Stooges: Cash and Carry

Family Stooges comedy shorts include "Cash and Carry" (1937), "No Census, No Feeling" (1940), and "Some More of Samoa" (1941).

194? 56m/B Moe Howard, Curly Howard, Larry Fine. **VHS** *COL*

Three Stooges: If a Body Meets a Body

Family Stooges madness abounds in "Spook Louder" (1943), "Men in Black" (1934), and "If a Body Meets a Body" (1945).

1934 53m/B Moe Howard, Curly Howard, Larry Fine. **VHS** *COL*

Three Stooges: In the Sweet Pie and Pie

Family Wealthy Tiska, Taska, and Baska Jones need to marry three death row convicts in order to claim their inheritance "In the Sweet Pie and Pie" (1941), but then the Stooges are freed. Also features "Phony Express" (1943), and "Playing the Ponies" (1937).

194? 48m/B Moe Howard, Curly Howard, Larry Fine. **VHS** *COL*

Three Stooges Meet Hercules 🦴🦴 ⌢

Family In probably the best of their few feature films, the Stooges hop aboard a time machine and go from Ithaca, New York to Ithaca, ancient Greece, joining a wimpy scientist and his girlfriend. There the maiden is kidnapped by Hercules (a bad guy!), and the Stooges' brainy nerd friend must get pumped up to fight the muscleman.

1961 80m/B Moe Howard, Larry Fine, Joe DeRita, Vicki Trickett, Quinn Redeker; **D:** Edward L. Bernds. **VHS, Beta** *GKK*

Three Stooges: So Long Mr. Chumps

Family The boys blend violence and buffoonery as only they can in "So Long Mr. Chumps" (1941), which finds Larry, Moe, and Curly searching for an honest man. Also features "Three Loan Wolves" (1946), and "Even as I.O.U." (1942).

194? 50m/B Moe Howard, Curly Howard, Larry Fine. **VHS** *COL*

Three Stooges: What's the Matador?

Family The boys go for belly laughs in "Boob in Arms" (1940), "What's the Matador?" (1942), and "Mutts to You" (1938).

194? 60m/B Moe Howard, Curly Howard, Larry Fine. **VHS** *COL*

The Three Worlds of Gulliver
🎭🎭🎭

Family Colorful version of the Jonathan Swift classic that fits in more of the book than most adaptations. Here, after his tribulations with the small and small-minded Lilliputians, Gulliver and his fiancee drift to another island—Brobdingnag, inhabited by a superstitious race of giants. Now it's Gulliver's turn to view things from a tiny perspective. Occasional stop-motion f/x by Ray Harryhausen.

1959 100m/C Kerwin Mathews, Jo Morrow, Basil Sydney, Mary Ellis; **D:** Jack Sher; **W:** Arthur Ross, Jack Sher; **M:** Bernard Herrmann. **VHS, Beta, LV** *COL, MLB, CCB*

Threesome WOOF!

R/Sr. High-Adult Another Generation X movie that your teen may want to take a look at. It tries hard to be hip, but fails miserably. Due to a college administrative error, Alex (Boyle) winds up sharing a suite with two male roommates, Eddy (Charles) and Stuart (Baldwin). Despite having completely different personalities, they soon become best friends and form one cozy little group, with cozy being the key word. Sexual tension abounds— Alex wants Eddy who wants Stuart who wants Alex. So you see where this one is going. Down the Gen X tubes.

> ⚠ BEWARE ⚠ *Filled with pathetic dialogue (most of it relating to bodily functions and body parts) and shallow, obnoxious characters.*

1994 93m/C Lara Flynn Boyle, Stephen Baldwin, Josh Charles, Alexis Arquette, Mark Arnold, Martha Gehman, Michelle Matheson; **D:** Andrew Fleming; **W:** Andrew Fleming; **M:** Thomas Newman. **VHS, LV, 8mm** *COL*

Through the Looking Glass

Preschool-Primary Animated, contemporary version of the Alice in Wonderland story, with a wild assortment of celebrity voices.

1987 90m/C V: Leif Erickson, Phyllis Diller, Jonathan Winters, Mr. T. **VHS, Beta** *MED*

Throw Momma from the Train
🎭🎭🎭

PG-13/Jr. High-Adult DeVito plays a man, henpecked by his horrific mother, who tries to persuade his writing professor (Crystal) to exchange murders. DeVito will kill Crystal's ex-wife and Crystal will kill DeVito's mother. Only mama isn't going to be that easy to get rid of. Fast-paced and entertaining black comedy. Ramsey steals the film. Inspired by Hitchcock's "Strangers on a Train."

> ⚠ BEWARE ⚠ *Profanity and disrespect toward an aged parent.*

1987 88m/C Danny DeVito, Billy Crystal, Anne Ramsey, Kate Mulgrew, Kim Greist, Branford Marsalis, Rob Reiner, Bruce Kirby; **D:** Danny DeVito; **W:** Stu Silver; **M:** David Newman. **VHS, Beta, LV** *ORI*

Thumbelina

Family Carrie Fisher plays tiny Thumbelina in this version, from "Faerie Tale Theatre." She's kidnapped by a toad and a mole, but meets the man of her dreams in the nick of time. Ages 5 to 10.

1982 60m/C Carrie Fisher, William Katt, Burgess Meredith; **D:** Michael Lindsay-Hogg. **VHS, Beta, LV** *KUI, FOX, FCT*

Thumbelina

G/Family Japanese-made animation of the Hans Christian Andersen tale about a thumb-sized girl. While she searches for her prince's Tulip Kingdom, numerous friendly animals want her as a bride instead. A few genuinely funny bits make this easier to take, though songs are dreadful, and the picture looks elongated and weird; it seems they transferred a wide-screen cartoon (meant to project through a distorting lens) to video without image correction, so everything's tall and skinny.

1984 64m/C D: Y. Serigawa. **VHS, Beta** *COL*

Thumbelina 🎭🎭🎭

G/Family Bluth's long-in-production adaptation of Hans Christian Andersen's fable about a thumb-sized little girl searching for her handsome, and also miniature, prince. Subplot about Thumbelina being detoured into a concert career ("Rock-A-Doodle" all over again?) is a typical postmodern Bluth touch that seems jarring in its fairy-tale context. Blah songs by Barry Manilow.

1994 80m/C D: Don Bluth, Gary Goldman; **W:** Don Bluth; **M:** William Ross, Barry Manilow, Barry Manilow, Jack Feldman, Bruce Sussman; **V:** Jodi Benson, Gary Imhoff, Charo, Gilbert Gottfried, Carol Channing, John Hurt, Will Ryan, June Foray, Kenneth Mars. **VHS, Beta, LV** *WAR*

Thumpkin and the Easter Bunnies

Preschool-Primary When Johnny's eggs accidentally drop out of his bag, one by one they are retrieved and decorated by the animals who live in the meadow. **1992 26m/C VHS** *FHE*

Thundarr the Barbarian, Vol. 1

Preschool-Primary Outdated (we hope) Saturday-morning cartoon heroics set in a barbaric future world after a comet destroys civilization in 1994 (don't say nobody warned us). In this episode, Thundarr, Princess Ariel, and Ookla the Mot fight sorcery and slavery. Additional volumes available. **1980 57m/C VHS, Beta** *WOV*

Thunderball 🦴🦴

PG/Jr. High-Adult Fourth installment in Ian Fleming's James Bond series finds 007 on a mission to thwart SPECTRE, which has threatened to blow up Miami by atomic bomb if 100 million pounds in ransom is not paid. One of the more tedious Bond entries but a big box-office success. Tom Jones sang the title song. Remade as "Never Say Never Again" in 1983 with Connery reprising his role as Bond after a 12-year absence.

BEWARE *Violence, alcohol use and suggested sex in the spy fashion.*

1965 125m/C Sean Connery, Claudine Auger, Adolfo Celi, Luciana Paluzzi, Rik von Nutter, Martine Beswick, Molly Peters, Guy Doleman, Bernard Lee, Lois Maxwell, Desmond Llewelyn; *D:* Terence Young; *W:* John Hopkins, Richard Maibaum; *M:* John Barry. **VHS, Beta, LV** *MGM, TLF*

Thunderbirds

Preschool-Primary Popular sci-fi show from the British TV team of Gerry and Sylvia Anderson, this mixes terrific special effects and miniature sets with a cast composed entirely of marionette puppets, manipulated by electronics and invisible wires ("Super Marionation," they liked to call it). Yes, wooden acting triumphs in the sagas of the Tracy family, who run a high-tech interplanetary lifeguard agency called International Rescue and save the day anytime someone is plunging into the sun or drifting aimlessly in the ocean. Genuine cult item that has inspired spinoffs, feature films, and more than one rock band. Each tape in the series features one full-length adventure. **1966 92m/C VHS, Beta** *FHE*

Thundercats

Preschool-Primary Hailing from the planet Thundera (makes sense), these felines possess extraordinary intellectual and physical prowess far beyond those of ordinary kitties. Voyaging to Earth, where mankind is extinct, they use their advanced abilities to fight the villainous Mumma-Ra and start a brand new world. Rankin-Bass animated TV feature launching a "Thundercats" cartoon series for viewers who couldn't get enough of the T-cats and their line of toy action figures. **1985 80m/C VHS, Beta** *FHE*

Thundercats, Vol. 1: Exodus

Family Those unforgettable Thundercats rise to the occasion when they encounter sinister mutants. Additional volumes available. **1985 75m/C VHS, Beta** *FHE*

Thursday's Game 🦴🦴🦴

PG/Jr. High-Adult Two crisis-besieged businessmen meet every Thursday, using poker as a ruse to work on their business and marital problems. Wonderful cast; intelligently written. Made for television.

 **BEWARE** *Mature themes.*

1974 99m/C Gene Wilder, Ellen Burstyn, Bob Newhart, Cloris Leachman, Nancy Walker, Valerie Harper, Rob Reiner; *D:* James L. Brooks; *W:* James L. Brooks. **VHS, Beta, LV** *VMK*

The Tick: The Tick vs. The Idea Men and The Tick vs. Chairface Chippendale

Family Star of an animated cartoon TV series, The Tick is a crime-fighting insect but he's not as disgusting as he sounds. Fact is, if it weren't for a set of tasteful antennae, The Tick would look more or less human. With his sidekick, Arthur, who appears to be a moth; and American Maid, sort of Wonder Woman in an apron, The Tick fights a mostly funny battle against evildoers, as he does in these two episodes. Ages 5 to 10. **1995 50m/C VHS** *TCF*

The Tiger and the Brahmin

Family Kingsley, best known for his portrayal in "Gandhi," relates an Indian folktale against brilliant illustrations, from an episode of the acclaimed "Rabbit Ears" series first aired on Showtime cable TV. **1991 30m/C M:** Ravi Shankar. **VHS** *RAB, FCT, MLT*

Tiger Bay 🦴🦴🦴

Family Young Polish sailor, on leave in Cardiff, murders his unfaithful girlfriend. Lonely ten-year-old Gillie sees the crime and takes the murder weapon, thinking it will make her more popular with her peers. Confronted by a police detective, she convincingly lies but eventually the sailor finds Gillie and kidnaps her, hoping to keep her quiet until he can get aboard his ship. A delicate relationship evolves between the child and the killer as she tries to help him escape and the police close in. Marks Hayley Mills' first major role and one of her finest performances. **1959 107m/B** John Mills, Horst Buchholz, Hayley Mills, Yvonne Mitchell; *D:* J. Lee Thompson. **VHS, Beta** *PAR*

Tiger Town 🎵🎵🎵

G/Family Alex is a young Detroit Tigers baseball fan who fixates from afar on the team's oldest player Billy 'The Hawk' Young. Alex decides he's Billy's good luck charm, a la "Angels in the Outfield"; as long as the boy attends the game, the aging athlete will bat his way closer to a pennant victory. But how can Alex slip away from school to help his idol? A simple, unusually somber Disney drama (realistic, almost drab) made for the Magic Kingdom's cable channel.

1983 76m/C Roy Scheider, Justin Henry, Ron McLarty, Bethany Carpenter, Noah Moazezi; **D:** Alan Shapiro. **VHS, Beta** *DIS*

A Tiger Walks 🎵🎵🎵

Family Universal Pictures brought a number of newspaper comic strips to film as serials. This one features the title character, a heroic pilot, in battle against the oriental supervillain known as the Dragon, who wants to stop the formation of a worldwide airline. In 13 chapters.

1964 88m/C Sabu, Pamela Franklin, Brian Keith, Vera Miles, Kevin Corcoran, Peter Brown, Una Merkel, Frank McHugh, Edward Andrews; **D:** Norman Tokar; **M:** Buddy Baker. **VHS, Beta** *DIS*

Tigersharks: Power of the Shark

Family Undersea superheroes are challenged by the evil Mantanas and Captain Bizarrly in this animated adventure flotsam.

1987 40m/C VHS, Beta *ORI, WAR*

Till the Clouds Roll By 🎵🎵🎵

Family All-star, high-gloss musical biography of songwriter Jerome Kern, that, in typical Hollywood fashion, bears little resemblance to the composer's life. Filled with wonderful songs from his Broadway hit. 🎵 Showboat Medley; Till the Clouds Roll By; Howja Like to Spoon with Me?; The Last Time I Saw Paris; They Didn't Believe Me; I Won't Dance; Why Was I Born?; Who?; Sunny.

1946 137m/C Robert Walker, Van Heflin, Judy Garland, Frank Sinatra, Lucille Bremer, Kathryn Grayson, June Allyson, Dinah Shore, Lena Horne, Virginia O'Brien, Tony Martin; **D:** Richard Whorf. **VHS, Beta, LV** *CNG, NOS, MGM*

Tim Tyler's Luck

Family Well-remembered relic from when Universal Pictures was in the movie-serial business. This adaptation of Lyman Young's newspaper comic-strip follows Tim's African quest for his missing father. The hero must stay one step ahead of the evil ivory-hunter Spider Webb and his armored jungle tank. Good production values include a musical score Universal used again and again. In twelve chapters.

BEWARE *Violence.*

1937 235m/B Frankie Thomas Jr., Frances Robinson, Al Shear, Norman Willis, Earl Douglas, Jack Mulhall, Frank Mayo, Pat O'Brien; **D:** Ford Beebe, Wyndham Gittens. **VHS** *NOS, GPV, FCT*

Timberrr! From Logs to Lumber

Preschool-Primary When folks in timber country say "log on," they aren't talking about computers. Nor do they mean hatchets or handsaws. Modern logging is the province of massive machines. Take the all-in-one processor, which can pull up an entire tree like a weed, trim away its branches, saw off its ends and lay it on the ground. Equally impressive devices are in operation at the sawmill. Ages 3 to 9.

199? ?m/C VHS *NYR*

Time Bandits 🎵🎵🎵

PG/Family 11-year-old boy, neglected by his parents, takes off with a gang of time-travelling dwarfs using God's own map of holes in the Cosmos to commit robberies in the eras of Robin Hood, Napoleon, Agamemnon, and other legends. Epic fantasy-comedy from members of England's Monty Python team won comparisons with "The Wizard of Oz" when it first came out. Time has proven the Bandits to not be at Wizard's level, but it remains a frenetic mix of satire, amazing f/x, and high adventure. Produced by former Beatle George Harrison; the hit-hungry Disney company backed out of a chance to finance the offbeat tale, then had to watch as it became a surprise at the box office.

BEWARE *Violence, including a pitiless fate served up for the young hero's nitwit mom and dad.*

1981 110m/C John Cleese, Sean Connery, Shelley Duvall, Katherine Helmond, Ian Holm, Michael Palin, Ralph Richardson, Kenny Baker, Peter Vaughan, David Warner; **D:** Terry Gilliam; **W:** Michael Palin, Terry Gilliam. **VHS, Beta, LV** *PAR*

Time for Table Manners

Preschool-Primary Winnie the Pooh and friends teach the importance of washing hands before meals, saying please and thank you, cleanliness, and self-respect.

1990 6m/C VHS, Beta *MTI, DSN*

Time of Tears 🎵🎵

PG/Family Young boy has his first experience of grief when he befriends a nice old man who turns out to be a long-estranged relative, trying to reconcile with the family before he dies. Compassionate but no-frills kiddie tearjerker.

1985 95m/C VHS, Beta *VTR, NWV*

Timecop 🎵🎵

R/Sr. High-Adult "Terminator" rip-off is fodder for Van Damme followers, but not for the kiddies. 2004 policeman Max Walker (Van Damme) must travel back in time to prevent corrupt politician Aaron McComb (Silver) from altering history for personal gain. It's also Walker's chance to alter his personal history since his wife Melissa (Sara) was killed in an explosion he can now prevent. Futuristic thriller based on a Dark Horse comic, but this one is not for the young comic strip readers.

Extremely violent, including slayings by guns, knives, explosions, electrocutions and other horrific methods. A lot of gratuitous nudity and gratuitous sex means stay away—not much to see here.

1994 98m/C Jean-Claude Van Damme, Ron Silver, Mia Sara, Bruce McGill, Scott Lawrence, Kenneth Welsh, Gabrielle Rose, Duncan Fraser, Ian Tracey, Gloria Reuben, Scott Bellis, Jason Schombing, Kevin McNulty, Sean O'Byrne, Malcolm Stewart, Alfonso Quijada, Glen Roald, Theodore Thomas; **D:** Peter Hyams; **W:** Mark Verheiden, Gary De Vore. **VHS, LV** *MCA*

Timefighters in the Land of Fantasy

Family Cartoon team of time-travelers venture into the worlds of such classic fairy tales as Cinderella and Jack and the Beanstalk.

1984 94m/C VHS, Beta *PAR*

Timeless Tales from Hallmark

Family Collection of animated fairy tales from the Hanna-Barbera crew, sponsored by Hallmark Cards in their initial TV appearances. See individual titles for descriptions; programs include "The Elves and the Shoemaker," "The Emperor's New Clothes," "Puss in Boots," "Rapunzel," "Rumpelstiltskin," "The Steadfast Tin Soldier," "Thumbelina," and "The Ugly Duckling."

1990 30m/C VHS, Beta *TTC, IME*

Timemaster 🎵 🎶

PG-13/Jr. High-Adult Orphaned 12-year-old Jesse (Cameron-Glickenhaus) dreams his parents are alive in another time, so he asks inventor Isaiah (Morita) for help. The duo discover Jesse's parents are being held hostage by a galactic dictator (Dorn), who's using them in sinister virtual-reality games and Jesse must time-travel to rescue them.

 Some strong action-adventure violence.

1995 100m/C Jesse Cameron-Glickenhaus, Noriyuki "Pat" Morita, Joanna Pacula, Michael Dorn, Duncan Regehr, Michelle Williams; **D:** James Glickenhaus; **W:** James Glickenhaus. **VHS, LV** *MCA*

Timerider 🎵 🎵

PG/Jr. High-Adult Motorcyclist riding through the California desert is accidentally thrown back in time to 1877, the result of a scientific experiment gone awry. There he and his machine find no gas stations and lots of surprised cowboys. Not exactly "Back to the Future," but occasionally fun; director Dear went on to do "Harry and the Hendersons."

Violence, sex, salty language.

1983 93m/C Fred Ward, Belinda Bauer, Peter Coyote, Richard Masur, Ed Lauter, L.Q. Jones, Tracey Walter; **D:** William Dear. **VHS, Beta, LV** *NO*

Timmy's Gift: A Precious Moments Christmas

Family Holiday cartoon about a young angel who is given the monumental task of delivering a crown to the baby Jesus on the very first Christmas.

1991 23m/C VHS, Beta

Timon and Pumbaa's Wild Adventures: Don't Get Mad, Get Happy

Preschool-Primary Following the on-going antics of Timon and Pumbaa from Disney's smash hit, "The Lion King," these hilarious stories will keep youngsters laughing. Timon, the wise-cracking meerkat, and his pal Pumbaa the warthog will keep everyone in stitches. "Yosemite Remedy" finds the two searching for their lost suitcase full of valuables. "Kenya Be My Friend" tests the friendship of these two otherwise inseparable pals.

1996 31m/C VHS *DIS*

Timon and Pumbaa's Wild Adventures: Grub's On

Preschool-Primary Timon and Pumbaa are busy doing their favorite thing, insect hunting, when a lovestruck squirrel and Speedy the Snail ruin their plans. In another story, The Three Laughing Hyenas are in for a treat, but not what they expect, when a circus monkey falls from a train and into their lair.

1996 33m/C VHS *DIS*

Timon and Pumbaa's Wild Adventures: Hangin' With Baby

Preschool-Primary Timon and Pumbaa become babysitters when they must care for a baby alligator and a demanding baby eagle. And in another story, their friend Rafiki teaches a mouse that bigger doesn't always mean better.

1996 33m/C VHS *DIS*

Timon and Pumbaa's Wild Adventures: Live and Learn

Preschool-Primary Timon and Pumbaa are featured in two adventures. In "Law of the Jungle," Timon uses a "forbidden" stick to scratch his back and then must confront a judge who wants to send him to jungle jail. In "Uganda Be An Elephant," Pumbaa decides he'd like to be an elephant when he hears of the wondrous Ned the elephant.

1996 34m/C VHS *DIS*

Timon and Pumbaa's Wild Adventures: Quit Buggin' Me

Preschool-Primary Timon and Pumbaa catch the traveling bug. In "Frantic Atlantic," this crazy duo are disappointed when they find there are no ants to eat in Antarctica and in "Swiss Missed," the two munch on yummy chocolate-covered bugs, but find their surroundings a little hard to deal with.
1996 29m/C VHS *DIS*

Timon and Pumbaa's Wild Adventures: True Guts

Preschool-Primary Mistaken identity is the name of the game when Pumbaa is mistaken for a wild bull and Timon masquerades as a matador. Oops, guys, watch out for that real bull behind you! And in a second story, The Three Laughing Hyenas lock horns with several cheetahs.
1996 33m/C VHS *DIS*

The Tin Soldier

Family Canadian animated version of Hans Christian Andersen's "The Steadfast Tin Soldier," about a music-box ballerina and a toy soldier united by a pair of match-making mice.
1986 30m/C VHS *VTR*

The Tin Soldier

Primary-Jr. High Adaptation of Hans Christian Andersen's story using ballet scenes combined with animation and Sally Struthers' enthusiastic narration to introduce children to ballet. Costumes and lighting elements are designed to appeal to children. Features Canada's Ottawa Ballet. Ages 5 to 10.
1994 63m/C VHS *JFK*

The Tin Soldier ♫♫♪

PG/Family Updated version of the Hans Christian Andersen story finds 12-year-old Billy (Knight) moving with his widowed mom (Sheedy) to a tough L.A. neighborhood. He's intimidated by the school bully to join a gang and smitten by a pretty girl who doesn't like his new friends. What's a guy to do? Why meet a mysterious toy shop owner (DeLuise), who gives Billy a tin soldier that magically transforms into a very real medieval knight named Yarik (Voight). Good intentions—no subtlety. Voight's directorial debut; made for cable TV.

BEWARE! *Thematic elements, violence and language.*

1995 99m/C Trenton Knight, Ally Sheedy, Dom DeLuise, Jon Voight; **D:** Jon Voight. **VHS** *REP*

Tiny Toon Adventures: How I Spent My Vacation ♫♫♫

Family How the tiny toons of Acme Acres spend their summer vacation in this animated adventure that spoofs several popular films and amusements. Plucky Duck and Hampton Pig journey to "Happy World Land" (a takeoff on Walt Disney World), Babs and Buster Bunny's water adventure parodies "Deliverance," there's a spoof of "The Little Mermaid," and the Road Runner even makes a cameo appearance. Parents will be equally entertained by the level of humor and the fast-paced action. Based on the Steven Spielberg TV cartoon series, this is the first made-for-home-video animated feature ever released in the United States.
1991 80m/C VHS, Beta, LV, 8mm *WAR*

Tiny Toon Big Adventures

Family "Journey to the Center of Acme Acres" has Buster and Babs venturing where no rabbits have gone before. In "A Ditch in Time," a time-travelling Plucky Duck tries to get back to the present in order to complete a homework assignment.
1993 42m/C VHS *WAR, BTV*

Tiny Toon Fiendishly Funny Adventures

Family Cartoon collection from the TV series with spooky themes. "Duck in the Dark" has Plucky's imagination getting the best of him. In "Little Cake of Horrors," Hamton Pig's diet leads to extremes and in "The Night of the Living Pets," overaffectionate pet lover Elmyra goes too far. "Hare-Raising Night" features Babs and Buster tangling with a mad scientist.
1993 38m/C VHS *WAR, BTV*

Tiny Toon Island Adventures

Family Two tropical 'toons: "No Toon Is an Island" has The Acme Acres gang searching for lost treasure and in "Buster and Babs Go Hawaiian," Polynesian pleasures are apparent.
1993 42m/C VHS *WAR, BTV*

Tiny Toons in Two-Tone Town

Family "Two-Tone Town" has Buster and Babs helping two 1930s former cartoon stars get their flagging careers going again. "Fields of Honey" is a toon spoof of the movie "Field of Dreams."
1992 44m/C VHS, Beta *WAR*

Tiny Toons Music Television

Family In the TV episodes "TT Music Television" and "Toon TV," VJ's Buster and Babs do their own thing to the songs "Yakity-Yak" and "The Name Game."
1992 44m/C VHS, Beta *WAR*

Tiny Toons: The Best of Buster and Babs

Family Two episodes from the cable TV series. In "Promise Her Anything," Buster asks Babs to dance and in "Thirteensomething," Babs stars in her own TV show.
1993 44m/C VHS, Beta *WAR*

Tito and Me

College-Adult Uproarious all-ages film from Yugoslavia can be savored as both comedy and potent attack on political tyranny. It's 1954, and 10-year-old Zoran (a Spanky McFarland lookalike) is so bombarded by propaganda praising fearless leader Marshall Tito that he adopts Yugoslavia's dictator as his personal hero and imaginary pal. Zoran's classroom essay "Why I Love Marshall Tito" wins him a place in a junior Communist march to Tito's hometown, right alongside the girl of his dreams. But the adult guide is a fanatical taskmaster who bullies slowpoke Zoran during the hike, sparking the disaster that ends the child's Tito-worship. Smart, sharp and perceptive, but never dragged down by its weighty themes—and who could resist that carioca-beat soundtrack? In Serbo-Croatian with English subtitles.

BEWARE *Salty language.*

1992 104m/C Dimitrie Vojnov, Lazar Ristovski, Anica Dobra, Predrag Manojlovic, Olivera Markovic; *D:* Goran Markovic; *W:* Goran Markovic. **VHS** *FXL, FCT*

To Catch a Thief

Jr. High-Adult On the French Riviera, a reformed jewel thief falls for a wealthy American woman, who suspects he's up to his old tricks when a rash of jewel thefts occur. Oscar-winning photography by Robert Burks, a notable fireworks scene, and snappy dialogue. A change of pace for Hitchcock, this charming comedy-thriller proved to be as popular as his other efforts. Kelly met future husband Prince Ranier during shooting in Monaco. Based on the novel by David Dodge.

1955 103m/C Cary Grant, Grace Kelly, Jessie Royce Landis, John Williams, Charles Vanel, Brigitte Auber; *D:* Alfred Hitchcock; *W:* John Michael Hayes. **Award Nominations:** Academy Awards '55: Best Art Direction/Set Decoration (Color), Best Costume Design (Color); **Awards:** Academy Awards '55: Best Color Cinematography. **VHS, Beta, LV** *PAR, MLB, HMV*

To Kill a Mockingbird

Family Powerful, faithful adaptation of Pulitzer-winning Harper Lee novel by Horton Foote. It's both an evocative portrayal of childhood innocence and a denunciation of bigotry taking place in a small town in Alabama in the 1930s. Peck provides a career performance as Atticus Finch, a morally forthright lawyer (and a widower with two children) who takes on the unpopular defense of a black man accused of raping a white woman. His children, meanwhile, are fascinated with the mysterious but dimwitted Boo Radley, played by Duvall in his debut. Lee based her characterization of "Dill" on Truman Capote, a childhood friend.

BEWARE *Racism, vigilante justice and discussion of rape.*

1962 129m/B Gregory Peck, Brock Peters, Phillip Alford, Mary Badham, Robert Duvall, Rosemary Murphy, William Windom, Alice Ghostley, John Megna, Frank Overton, Paul Fix, Collin Wilcox; *D:* Robert Mulligan; *W:* Horton Foote; *M:* Elmer Bernstein. **Award Nominations:** Academy Awards '62: Best Black and White Cinematography, Best Director (Mulligan), Best Picture, Best Supporting Actress (Badham), Best Original Score; **Awards:** Academy Awards '62: Best Actor (Peck), Best Adapted Screenplay, Best Art Direction/Set Decoration (B & W); Golden Globe Awards '63: Best Actor—Drama (Peck), Best Score. **VHS, Beta, LV** *KUI, MCA, BTV*

To Sir, with Love

Family Teacher in London's tough East End tosses books in the wastebasket and proceeds to educate his class about life. Skillful and warm performance by Poitier as the idealistic instructor, and the supporting cast also performs nicely, though this sentimental favorite looks a bit corny today. And these 'bad kids' are teacher's pets compared to school youth in, for example, "Lean on Me." Based on the novel by E.R. Braithwaite. LuLu's title song made the hit parade in 1967-68.

1967 105m/C Sidney Poitier, Lulu, Judy Geeson, Christian Roberts, Suzy Kendall, Faith Brook; *D:* James Clavell; *W:* James Clavell. **VHS, Beta** *COL*

To the Last Man

Family An early Scott sagebrush epic, about two feuding families. Temple is seen in a small role. Based on Zane Grey's novel of the same name.

1933 70m/B Randolph Scott, Esther Ralston, Jack LaRue, Noah Beery Sr., Buster Crabbe, Gail Patrick, Barton MacLane, Fuzzy Knight, John Carradine, Jay Ward, Shirley Temple; *D:* Henry Hathaway. **VHS, Beta** *NOS, DVT, MLB*

To Wong Foo, Thanks for Everything, Julie Newmar

PG-13/Jr. High-Adult Three drag queens are headed to Hollywood when their 1967 Cadillac convertible inconveniently breaks down in a tiny Nebraska town. Den mother Vida (Swayze), tough beauty queen Noxeema (Snipes), and hot-blooded drag-queen-in-training Chi Chi (Leguizamo) fix most of the townspeople's problems, dealing with an abusive husband, straightening out juvenile delinquents, handling an obnoxious sheriff and giving the women makeovers. Inconsistent script undercuts exceptional efforts by Swayze and Leguizamo, but it's hard to argue with the film's message of tolerance.

BEWARE *Subject matter involving men living in drag will probably need to be explained. There is a brief scene of spousal abuse and profanity.*

1995 108m/C Wesley Snipes, Patrick Swayze, John Leguizamo, Stockard Channing, Blythe Danner, Melinda Dillon, Arliss Howard, Jason London, Christopher Penn; *Cameos:* Julie Newmar, Robin Williams; *D:* Beeban Kidron; *W:* Douglas Carter Beane; *M:* Rachel Portman. **VHS, LV** *MCA*

Tobor the Great ♫ ♪

Family Silly, overly juvenile vintage sci-fi about a boy, his inventor grandfather, and their pride and joy, Tobor the Robot. Villainous commie spies try to misuse Tobor, only to be thwarted in the end. Apparently aimed at viewers unable to figure out where the name 'Tobor' came from.

1954 77m/B Charles Drake, Billy Chapin, Karin Booth, Taylor Holmes, Joan Gerber, Steve Geray; *D:* Lee Sholem. **VHS, LV** *REP*

Toby McTeague ♫ ♫

PG/Jr. High-Adult Scenic but mediocre Canadian tale set in a snowy town where impulsive teen Toby and his widowed dad are constantly at odds. When the family's Siberian husky-breeding business is threatened, the only answer is for Toby to try for the cash prize in a regional dogsled race. Git along, doggies.

BEWARE *Salty language. One canine casualty.*

1987 94m/C Winston Rekert, Wannick Bisson, Timothy Webber; *D:* Jean-Claude Lord. **VHS, Beta, LV** *COL, NLC*

Toby Tyler ♫ ♫ ♫

G/Family Toby, a turn-of-the-century boy, realizes the perennial dream of running off to join the circus, and teams up with a chimpanzee. Highly enjoyable Disney film still appeals to circus-goers of all ages.

1959 93m/C Kevin Corcoran, Henry Calvin, Gene Sheldon, Bob Sweeney; *D:* Charles T. Barton. **VHS, Beta** *DIS*

Tom and Huck ♫ ♫ ♫

PG/Primary-Adult Tom Sawyer and pal Huck Finn are the only witnesses to a murder. Tom's friend Muff is framed for the crime and the boys are being tracked by the real killer. They must decide to come forward, expose the true fiend, and risk their own hides or run away and let an innocent man hang. The story keeps true to the original and Thomas is good as the mischievious Tom. Lots of child pranks and trouble-making ("Boy, painting this fence sure is fun!!") make for a good time for the youngsters, though parents may get a little bored (hey, the story is no surprise).

BEWARE *Not for kids under 8. There are stabbings, a near-drowning, and skeletons in a spooky cave. And Injun Joe is one mean and scary-looking fella (Bad teeth!).*

1995 91m/C Jonathan Taylor Thomas, Brad Renfro, Eric Schweig, Charles Rocket, Amy Wright, Micheal McShane, Marian Seldes, Rachel Leigh Cook, Lanny Flaherty, Courtland Mead, Peter M. Mac-Kenzie, Heath Lamberts; *D:* Pete Hewitt; *W:* Stephen Sommers, David Loughery; *C:* Bobby Bukowski; *M:* Stephen Endelman. **VHS** *TOU*

Tom & Jerry Kids: Out of This World Fun

Family Video repackaging of episodes from Hanna-Barbera's TV Tom & Jerry spinoff. Additional volumes available.

1991 43m/C VHS

Tom & Jerry On Parade

Family The cat and mouse are featured in "Cruise Cat," "Designs on Jerry," "His Mouse Friday," "Little School Mouse," "Pet Peeve," and "Pushbutton Kitty."
1954 41m/C VHS *NO*

Tom and Jerry: Starring

Family The real stuff from Hanna-Barbera's legendary cartoon cat and mouse team, not to be confused with "Tom and Jerry: The Movie."
1988 60m/C VHS, Beta *MGM*

Tom and Jerry: The Movie 🦴 ♬

G/Family Everybody's favorite cartoon cat/mouse duo (who began life in a 1940 MGM short "Puss Gets the Boot") have their own feature. And indeed, it opens with a wild chase that's pure T & J, until the plot turns into a hackneyed takeoff on "The Rescuers," with the battling pair now goody-goodies, saving a little girl heiress from evil relatives (and dig her father, a shameless Indiana Jones clone). Unlike their past work, Tom and Jerry speak and sing, both bad moves. True fans should stick to the original cartoons.
1993 84m/C D: Phil Roman; **W:** Dennis Marks; **M:** Henry Mancini, Leslie Bricusse; **V:** Richard Kind, Dana Hill, Charlotte Rae, Henry Gibson, Rip Taylor, Howard Morris, Edmund Gilbert, David Lander. **VHS** *FHE*

Tom & Jerry: The Very Best Of Tom & Jerry

Family Features Tom and Jerry in six favorite episodes.
19?? 44m/C VHS

Tom & Jerry's Cartoon Cavalcade

Family Features six vintage William Hanna-Joseph Barbera 'toons starring Tom and Jerry. Includes "Casanova Cat," "Jerry's Cousin," "Fine Feathered Friend," "Jerry & the Lion," "Mouse for Sale," and "Southbound Duckling."
1954 42m/C VHS *NO*

Tom & Jerry's Comic Capers

Family Tom and Jerry star in six more bigscreen cartoon shorts. Includes "Downhearted Duckling," "Fit to Be Tied," "The Flying Sorceress," "Hatch Up Your Troubles," "Polka Dot Puss," and "Puppy Tale."
1955 42m/C VHS *NO*

Tom & Jerry's Festival of Fun

Family More fun with that crazy cat and mouse. Includes "Blue Cat Blues," "Little Quacker," "Sufferin' Cats," "Tennis Chumps," "Touche Pussycat," and "The Truce Hurts."
1956 43m/C VHS *NO*

Tom & Jerry's 50th Birthday Classics

Family Anniversary compilation of the animated pair's best 'toons, including their 1940 debut "Puss Gets the Boot," as well as "Mouse in the House," "Dog Trouble," "Cat Fishin'," "Yankee Doodle Mouse," "Heavenly Puss" and "Part Time Pal."
19?? 57m/C VHS, Beta, LV *MGM*

Tom Brown's School Days 🦴 🦴 ♬

Family Adaptation on the classic book by Thomas Hughes, detailing the rigors of the Victorian British school system on a newcomer lad who suffers tribulations and adversity but ultimately perseveres under the direction of benevolent headmaster Dr. Arnold. British-made, but with a largely, and obviously, American cast that dispels some of the mood.
1940 86m/B Cedric Hardwicke, Jimmy Lydon, Freddie Bartholomew; **D:** Robert Stevenson. **VHS, Beta** *NOS, HHT, PSM*

Tom Brown's School Days 🦴 🦴 🦴

Family Nineteenth-century English boy Tom enrolls at Rugby School and is beset by bullies, but in the end he comes out a better, stronger young man for the harsh experience. Vivid and powerful recreation of the era and its values. Show it to kids today who complain about not enough arcade video games in the cafeteria.
1951 93m/B Robert Newton, John Howard Davies, James Hayter; **D:** Gordon Parry. **VHS, Beta** *VCI*

Tom Chapin: This Pretty Planet

Family Chapin's concert features songs about the environment, nature, and friends, and offers animation and spectacular nature footage. Songs include "Uh Oh Accident," "Alphabet Soup," "Family Tree," "Good Garbage," and "Sing a Whale Song."
1992 50m/C VHS *SMV, FAF*

Tom Sawyer 🦴 🦴 🦴

G/Family Readers Digest produced this flavorful account of the boisterous Tom, his superstitious friend Huck, and the choices they face when they accidentally witness a graveyard murder. Comes closer than most adaptations to capturing the flavor of the Mark Twain classic and you couldn't ask for a better cast, headed confidently by Whitaker as Tom and Foster as Becky

"Tom and Huck" plot to steal Injun Joe's buried treasure map.

Thatcher—with Hank just about the scariest Injun Joe ever. One big flaw: an ill-advised notion to turn this into a musical has left the story burdened with several forgettable songs. ♫ River Song; Gratification; Tom Sawyer; Freebootin'; Aunt Polly's Soliloquy; If'n I Was God; A Man's Gotta Be What He's Born To Be; How Come?; Hannibal, Mo.

 *Violence, alcohol use and a native American villain.*

1973 104m/C Johnny Whitaker, Jodie Foster, Celeste Holm, Warren Oates, Jeff East; *D:* Don Taylor; *M:* John Williams. **VHS, LV** *MGM*

tom thumb 🦴🦴 ᵇ

Family Fairy grants a childless couple's wish for a son, no matter how small. Tom arrives, thumb-sized but big in spirit, and he saves the village treasury from thieves (one of them, Sellers, pointlessly padded in a grotesque fat suit). Well-remembered children's film hasn't aged well over the years; satire and anachronisms clash with the Brothers Grimm material rather than enhance it. Undeniable highlight is the modish musical numbers, showcasing Tamblyn's dancing alongside the George Pal Puppetoons. An Oscar winner for special effects.

Roughhousing, alcohol use.

1958 92m/C Russ Tamblyn, Peter Sellers, Terry-Thomas; *D:* George Pal. **VHS, Beta, LV** *MGM*

Tom Thumb

Preschool-Primary This program from the "Grimm's Fairytale" series follows the adventures of tiny Mr. Thumb as he escapes from one danger after another.

1978 10m/C VHS, Beta *CHF*

Tomboy & the Champ 🦴 ᵇ

Family Sickly sweet family drama about a music-loving Angus bull and the adoring little girl who sees to it that 'Champy' enters and wins a stockyard blue ribbon. Only too late does the heroine realize this means her dear beast will be turned into steak. The solution to this dilemma is as sentimental and yucky as it gets.

1958 82m/C Candy Moore, Ben Johnson, Jesse White; *D:* Francis D. Lyon. **VHS, Beta** *VCI*

Tombstone 🦴🦴🦴

R/Sr. High-Adult Saga of Wyatt Earp and his band of law-abiding large moustaches beat the longer, slower

Kasdan/Costner vehicle to the big screen by several months. And yes, it is violent, with a band of sadistic villains running amuck. Legendary lawman Wyatt (Russell) moves to Tombstone, Arizona, aiming to start a new life with his brothers, but alas, that's not to be. The infamous gunfight at the OK Corral is here, Delany wanders about in period costume as Wyatt's romantic interest, the bad guys, led by Booth, Biehn, and Lange, are really bad, and best of all, Kilmer steals the show in a stand-out performance as the tubercular Doc Holliday, alcoholic, lover, gunslinger, and philosopher. You'll want to compare it with Dennis Quaid's emaciated Doc in Costner's epic. As the moralistic center of the sagebrush fable, Russell spends a lot of time looking troubled by the violence while adding to the body count. A mixed bag of western thrills that suffers some from '90s revisionism.

BEWARE *Violence (numerous shooting incidents, including a variety of ruthless killings); profanity; alcohol use.*

1993 130m/C Kurt Russell, Val Kilmer, Michael Biehn, Sam Elliott, Dana Delany, Bill Paxton, Powers Boothe, Stephen Lang, Jason Priestley, Dana Wheeler-Nicholson, Billy Zane, Thomas Haden Church, Joanna Pacula, Michael Rooker, Harry Carey Jr., Billy Bob Thornton, Charlton Heston, Robert Burke, John Corbett, Buck Taylor, Terry O'Quinn, Pedro Armendariz Jr., Chris Mitchum, Jon Tenney; **D:** George P. Cosmatos; **W:** Kevin Jarre; **M:** Bruce Broughton. **VHS, LV** HPH

The Tomi Ungerer Library

Preschool-Primary Four animated stories from the popular children's author/artist as well as a brief interview with the author about his work.

1993 35m/C VHS CCC,

Tommy ♪♪

PG/Jr. High-Adult Peter Townsend's rock opera (as imploded onto the screen in the usual laid-back Russell manner) about the deaf, dumb, and blind boy who becomes a celebrity due to his amazing skill at the pinball machines. Story is told entirely in song, as a parade of rock musicians perform throughout the affair, with varying degrees of success. Despite some good moments, bombastic vision ultimately falls prey to ill-conceived production concepts and miscasting. ♫ Underture; Captain Walker Didn't Come Home; It's A Boy; '51 is Going to Be A Good Year; What About the Boy?; The Amazing Journey; Christmas; See Me, Feel Me; Eyesight to the Blind.

BEWARE *Drug use and adultery and murder cause Tommy's trauma.*

1975 108m/C Ann-Margret, Elton John, Oliver Reed, Tina Turner, Roger Daltrey, Eric Clapton, Keith Moon, Pete Townshend, Jack Nicholson, Robert Powell; **D:** Ken Russell; **W:** Ken Russell. **Award Nominations:** Academy Awards '75: Best Actress (Ann-Margret), Best Original Score; **Awards:** Golden Globe Awards '76: Best Actress—Musical/Comedy (Ann-Margret). **VHS, Beta, LV** COL, MVD, WME

Tommy Boy ♪♪

PG-13/Jr. High-Adult Not-too-bright rich kid Tommy (Farley) teams up with snide, officious accountant Richard (Spade) to save the family auto parts business after Tommy's dad (Dennehy) dies. Tommy and Richard must deal with a conniving stepmom and stepbrother (Derek and Lowe), a ruthless rival (Aykroyd), and a long sales trip to drum up some new business. Not as bad as it sounds.

BEWARE *Sex-related humor, some drug content and nudity. Tommy's dad dies but you really won't miss him. Be warned that this movie contains the typical Farley nonsense, but it is funny.*

1995 98m/C Chris Farley, David Spade, Brian Dennehy, Bo Derek, Dan Aykroyd, Julie Warner, Rob Lowe; **D:** Peter Segal; **W:** Bonnie Turner, Terry Turner; **M:** David Newman. **VHS, Beta** PAR

Tommy Tricker & the Stamp Traveller ♪♪♪ ♭

Family In a mythical country where stamp collecting is the schoolyard rage (Canada), Tommy Tricker, 12-ish, helps support his fatherless family with philatelic scams. But when he cheats his friend Ralph out of his dad's prized stamp, it leads to the discovery of magical incantation that can make a child small enough to fit on a stamp and be mailed around the world. Ralph heads for Australia, where a young stamp traveler from the 1920s has stashed his collection of postal rarities, but if the letter doesn't get there he could remain stuck on the stamp forever. Wonderful story, though overlong at 101 minutes, with delightful special effects, good music (by the McGarrigle Sisters), a nice side trip to China, and endearing depictions of friendship and sibling relationships. This is one of the very best from Rock Demers' Les Productions la Fete. Insider's note: the boy singing in the shopping mall is Rufus Wainwright, son of Loudon Wainwright III and Kate McGarrigle. Ages 8 to 13.

1990 101m/C Lucas Evans, Anthony Rogers, Jill Stanley; **D:** Michael Rubbo. **VHS, Beta** FHE

Tony Draws a Horse ♪♪ ♭

Family An eight-year-old draws an anatomically correct stallion on the door of his father's office, leading to a rift between the parents on how to handle telling the boy the facts of life. Somewhat sitcommish but engaging picture based on the play by Lesley Storm.

BEWARE *Sex talk.*

1951 90m/B Cecil Parker, Anne Crawford, Derek Bond, Barbara Murray, Mervyn Johns, Barbara Everest, David Hurst; **D:** John Paddy Carstairs. **VHS** NOS

Too Smart for Strangers with Winnie the Pooh

Primary Winnie the Pooh and Tigger, along with Tyne Daly and Gavin MacLeod present tips on how children can defend themselves against strangers.

1985 40m/C VHS, Beta DIS

Toot, Whistle, Plunk & Boom

Primary Professor Owl traces the roots of musical instruments and keeps children alert with catchy tunes explaining all of it. An Oscar-winning short subject from Disney.

1953 10m/C VHS, Beta *MTI, DSN*

Tooter Turtle in Kink of Swat

Preschool-Primary Repackaged TV cartoons from yesteryear, in which Tooter, with the help of Wizard the Lizard, travels through time to become the next "Babe Rube." When he fails, he needs the Wizard to bring him home, as always.

1967 60m/C VHS

Tootsie 🦴🦴🦴🦴

PG/Jr. High-Adult Stubborn, unemployed actor disguises himself as a woman to secure a part on a soap opera. As his popularity on television mounts, his love life becomes increasingly soap operatic. Hoffman is delightful, as is the rest of the stellar cast. Debut of Davis; Murray's performance unbilled. Laserdisc version features audio commentary by director Sidney Pollack, behind the scenes footage and photographs, and complete coverage of Tootsie's production.

 *Sexual situations.*

1982 110m/C Dustin Hoffman, Jessica Lange, Teri Garr, Dabney Coleman, Bill Murray, Charles Durning, Geena Davis, George Gaynes, Estelle Getty, Christine Ebersole, Sydney Pollack; **D:** Sydney Pollack; **W:** Larry Gelbart, Murray Schisgal, Don McGuire; **M:** Dave Grusin. **Award Nominations:** Academy Awards '82: Best Actor (Hoffman), Best Cinematography, Best Director (Pollack), Best Film Editing, Best Original Screenplay, Best Picture, Best Song ("It Might Be You"), Best Sound, Best Supporting Actress (Garr); **Awards:** Academy Awards '82: Best Supporting Actress (Lange); British Academy Awards '83: Best Actor (Hoffman); Golden Globe Awards '83: Best Actor—Musical/Comedy (Hoffman), Best Film—Musical/Comedy, Best Supporting Actress (Lange). **VHS, Beta, LV** *COL, CRC, BTV*

Top Cat and the Beverly Hills Cats

Family Revival of the vintage Top Cat cartoon characters from Hanna-Barbera. Their lives take a twist when an inheritance moves them from alley to Beverly Hills estate.

1984 92m/C VHS, Beta *TTC*

Top Dog 🦴 ▽

PG-13/Family Another cop-and-dog-team-up flick, but it's no "Turner and Hooch." Jake Wilder (Norris), a beer-swillin' karate-choppin' loner cop, teams up with canine Reno, whose ex-partner was killed by neo-Nazi terrorists. Man and dog pursue the hate group. Weak script can't find a comfortable balance between the cute pooch scenes and the (admittedly toned-down) violence. Reno steals every scene he's in. Good dog.

 Shootings and martial arts violence. Strong language from the tough-guy cops.

1995 93m/C Chuck Norris, Clyde Kusatsu, Michele Lamar Richards, Carmine Caridi, Peter Savard Moore, Erik von Detten, Herta Ware, Kai Wulff, Francesco Quinn, Timothy Bottoms; **D:** Aaron Norris; **W:** Ron Swanson; **C:** Joao Fernandes. **VHS, LV** *LIV*

Top Gun 🦴🦴 ▽

PG/Jr. High-Adult Young Navy pilots compete against one another on the ground and in the air at the elite Fighter Weapons School. Cruise isn't bad as a maverick who comes of age in Ray Bans, but Edwards shines as his buddy. Awesome aerial photography and high-cal beefcake divert from the contrived plot and stock characters. The Navy subsequently noticed an increased interest in fighter pilots. If you're looking for slickness and action, seek no further. Features Berlin's Oscar-winning song "Take My Breath Away."

📛 BEWARE *Macho posturing, profanity, suggested sex, violence and alcohol use.*

1986 109m/C Tom Cruise, Kelly McGillis, Val Kilmer, Tom Skerritt, Anthony Edwards, Meg Ryan, Rick Rossovich, Michael Ironside, Barry Tubb, Whip Hubley, John Stockwell, Tim Robbins, Adrian Pasdar; **D:** Tony Scott; **W:** Jim Cash, Jack Epps Jr.; **M:** Harold Faltermeyer. **Award Nominations:** Academy Awards '86: Best Film Editing, Best Sound; **Awards:** Academy Awards '86: Best Song ("Take My Breath Away"); Golden Globe Awards '87: Best Song ("Take My Breath Away"); People's Choice Awards '87: Best Film. **VHS, Beta, LV, 8mm, CD-I** *PAR*

Top Rock

Preschool-Primary Compilation of Hanna-Barbera cartoon characters frolicking to upbeat songs from the 1980's.

1984 30m/C VHS, Beta *TTC*

Topper 🦴🦴🦴 ▽

Family George and Marion Kerby return as ghosts after a fatal car accident, determined to assist their pal Cosmo Topper. Producer Hal Roach's first big-budget effort is a sophisticated comedy led by a charming cast. Great script is complemented by trick photography and special effects. Immensely popular at the box office, inspiring two sequels ("Topper Takes a Trip" and "Topper Returns"), a television series, and a television remake in 1979. Also available colorized.

1937 97m/B Cary Grant, Roland Young, Constance Bennett, Billie Burke, Eugene Pallette, Hoagy Carmichael; **D:** Norman Z. McLeod. **VHS, Beta** *MED, CCB, VTR*

Topper Returns 🦴🦴🦴

Family Cosmo Topper helps ghostly Blondell find the man who mistakenly murdered her. Humorous conclusion to the trilogy preceded by "Topper" and "Topper Takes a Trip." Followed by a television series. Also available colorized.

1941 87m/B Roland Young, Joan Blondell, Dennis O'Keefe, Carole Landis, Eddie Anderson, H.B. Warner, Billie Burke; **D:** Roy Del Ruth. **VHS, Beta, LV** *SNC, NOS, CAB*

Topper Takes a Trip 🦴🦴🦴

Family Cosmo Topper and his wife have a falling out and ghost Marion Kerby helps them get back together. The special effects sequences are especially funny. Followed by "Topper Returns." Also available colorized.

1939 85m/B Constance Bennett, Roland Young, Billie Burke, Franklin Pangborn, Alan Mowbray; **D:** Norman Z. McLeod. **VHS, Beta** *MED, VTR*

Torn Curtain 🦴🦴 ᵒ

Jr. High-Adult American scientist poses as a defector to East Germany in order to uncover details of the Soviet missile program. He and his fiancee, who follows him behind the Iron Curtain, attempt to escape to freedom. Derivative and uninvolving.

1966 125m/C Paul Newman, Julie Andrews, Lila Kedrova, David Opatoshu; **D:** Alfred Hitchcock; **W:** Brian Moore; **M:** John Addison. **VHS, Beta, LV** *MCA*

The Tortoise and the Hare

Preschool-Primary This Academy Award winner for Best Cartoon Production relates the classic story of how the slow but determined reptile bested the overconfident mammal in a race. One of Disney's original "Silly Symphonies."

1935 8m/C VHS, Beta *DSN, MTI*

Toto le Heros 🦴🦴🦴

PG-13/Jr. High-Adult Thomas is a bitter old man who as a child fantasized that he was a secret agent named Toto. He harbors deep resentment over not living the life he should have, maintaining he and his rich neighbor were switched at birth in the maternity ward (Thomas even barges into his neighbor's birthday party demanding that he be given the boy's gifts). Flashbacks and fast forwards show glimpses of life, not necessarily as it was, but how the old man perceives it. Sounds complex but the story is actually clear and fluid thanks to precise, prophetic visuals. The script was conceived initially as a movie about kids; grownup segments were added later, but the childhood scenes retain a rare sense of tot logic, obsession, and vengeance. Belgian production is in French with English subtitles.

BEWARE *Violence, sex and nudity.*

1991 90m/C Michel Bouquet, Jo De Backer, Thomas Godet, Mireille Perrier, Sandrine Blancke, Didier Ferney, Hugo Harold Harrisson, Gisela Uhlen, Peter Bohlke; **D:** Jaco Van Dormael; **W:** Jaco Van Dormael. **VHS, Beta** *PAR, BTV*

Touched by Love 🦴🦴 ᵒ

PG/Jr. High-Adult True story of a handicapped child who begins to communicate when her teacher suggests she write to her idol, Elvis Presley. And he writes back. Sounds like a-hunk a-hunk o' hokum but it's a sincere and well-performed family drama; based on a true story. Ages 8 and up.

1980 95m/C Deborah Raffin, Diane Lane, Christina Raines, Clu Gulager, John Amos; **D:** Gus Trikonis; **W:** Hesper Anderson; **M:** John Barry. **VHS, Beta** *COL*

Tough Guys 🦴🦴 ᵒ

PG/Jr. High-Adult Two aging ex-cons, who staged America's last train robbery in 1961, try to come to terms with modern life after many years in prison. Amazed and hurt by the treatment of the elderly in the 1980s, frustrated with their inability to find something worthwhile to do, they begin to plan one last heist. Tailor-made for Lancaster and Douglas, who seem to enjoy each other's company but are not always strongly supported by the script.

BEWARE *Mild profanity, sex and violence.*

1986 103m/C Burt Lancaster, Kirk Douglas, Charles Durning, Eli Wallach, Lyle Alzado, Dana Carvey, Alexis Smith, Darlanne Fluegel, Billy Barty, Monty Ash; **D:** Jeff Kanew; **W:** James Orr, Jim Cruickshank; **M:** James Newton Howard. **VHS, Beta, LV** *TOU*

Toughlove 🦴🦴

Sr. High-Adult Gary's parents can't stop the rebellious teen's slide into drugs and delinquency, even though dad's an assistant high school principal himself. After much agony, the adults stop blaming themselves and decide on a 'tough love' approach to the kid, locking him out of the house until he behaves. Well-acted but didactic TV movie that dramatizes, but doesn't unduly glorify or simplify, the philosophy and methods of Toughlove International, a support group for families of problem kids.

BEWARE *Drug use.*

1985 100m/C Lee Remick, Bruce Dern, Piper Laurie, Louise Latham, Dana Elcar, Jason Patric, Eric Schiff, Dedee Pfeiffer; **D:** Glenn Jordan. **VHS, Beta** *FRH*

Touring the Firehouse

Preschool-Primary Jackie the Dalmatian provides the narration for this fun look at a fireman's day, including a look at the control center, how the equipment works, how firemen wash their trucks, putting out a small fire, and rescuing a cat from a tree.

1992 30m/C VHS *GKK*

The Toy 🦴 ᵒ

PG/Primary-Adult Janitor (Richard Pryor) is hired by a multimillionaire (Jackie Gleason) to be the new "toy" of the rich guy's spoiled nine-year-old son. Naturally Pryor softens the hearts of both these caricatures. Stresses the importance of friendship and kindness over money, but it's sooo preachy. Ages 11 and up.

BEWARE *Profanity, sex talk and brief nudity. Gleason's wife calls him "you aaasss" (U.S. with a Southern drawl).*

1982 99m/C Richard Pryor, Jackie Gleason, Ned Beatty, Wilfrid Hyde-White; **D:** Richard Donner. **VHS, Beta, LV, 8mm** *COL*

Toy Story 🎞🎞🎞🎞

G/Family Computer-animated winner about playthings that come to life is true family fare: safe for 3-year-olds, safe for grown-ups. The toys belong to a boy named Andy. Their leader is Woody (Hanks), a pull-string cowboy who drawls such tidbits as "Somebody's poisoned the water well." Woody's well gets poisoned, all right, when Andy acquires a new favorite toy on his birthday, cocky spaceman Buzz Lightyear (Allen) who doesn't realize he's a toy. Jealous Woody causes Buzz to suffer a grave mishap, then feels guilty and sets off to rescue Buzz. Supporting toys include Bo Peep (Potts), Slinky Dog (Varney, impressively understated) and, best of all, Mr. Potato Head played by Don Rickles; when he calls someone a hockey puck it's an actual hockey puck. Puckish humor pervades—the toys discuss a "plastic corrosion awareness session"—as do tugs at the heart. A truly wonderful film.

1995 80m/C D: John Lasseter; **W:** Joss Whedon, Joel Cohen, Alec Sokolow; **M:** Randy Newman; **V:** Tom Hanks, Tim Allen, Annie Potts, John Ratzenberger, Wallace Shawn, Jim Varney, Don Rickles, John Morris, R. Lee Ermey, Laurie Metcalf, Erik von Detten. **VHS** *TOU*

Toys 🎞🎞

PG-13/Jr. High-Adult Critics generally disliked this epic fable—just as many first scorned "The Wizard of Oz," "Fantasia," and "Willy Wonka and the Chocolate Factory." Difference is, those are timeless fantasies; this is a Cold-War era script that didn't get produced until its flower-power themes were long stale. Clownish son of a toy manufacturer tries to keep the playful spirit of the fantastic toy factory alive after it's taken over by his uncle, a crazed general with plans to retool the assembly line and make toy-sized automated weapons. Bizarre, visually captivating film holds one dumbstruck for about an hour, then succumbs to tedium with its hard-sell messages of military folly. Lack of any child characters should be noted, as should some unnecessary sex and profanity.

⚠ BEWARE *Salty language, one sex scene. Climactic violence tries to convey war's destruction via toy-on-toy massacres.*

1992 121m/C Robin Williams, Joan Cusack, Michael Gambon, L.L. Cool J., Robin Wright; **Cameos:** Donald O'Connor; **D:** Barry Levinson; **W:** Valerie Curtin, Barry Levinson. **VHS** *FXV*

Trader Tom of the China Seas

Family Heroic island merchant and a shipwrecked beauty get involved in espionage while helping the UN to safeguard the Asian front. A minor effort from the sunset of Republic's movie-serial era; from here on, television took over the weekly adventure format.

1954 167m/B Harry Lauter, Aline Towne, Lyle Talbot, Fred Graham. **VHS** *REP*

Trading Hearts 🎞🎞

PG/Jr. High-Adult Little girl plays matchmaker between an over-the-hill baseball player and her own single mom, an unsuccessful lounge singer. The two lovebirds detest each other immediately, and you can guess the rest. Set in 1957 and scripted by sportswriter Frank Deford. For more single mom meets over-the-hill baseball player romances, see "Rookie of the Year" and "Little Big League."

⚠ BEWARE *Salty language, alcohol use.*

1987 88m/C Beverly D'Angelo, Raul Julia, Jerry Lewis, Parris Buckner, Robert Gwaltney; **D:** Neil Leifer; **W:** Frank Deford. **VHS, Beta, LV** *LIV*

Trading Mom 🎞🎞

PG/Primary-Adult Mrs. Martin's kids are bummed out because the hardworking single mom seems to have no time for them. A magical neighbor introduces them to the Mommy Market, where they can pick a parent more to their liking, but predictably all the choices—a glamorous aristocrat, a hardy outdoorswoman, a circus performer go badly wrong. All moms are played by Spacek, a neat trick in a picture that never seems as fun as it should be and may remind you of 1994's "North" by Rob Reiner. Based on a British children's novel "The Mummy Market," written by Nancy Brelis—herself the mother of screenwriter/director Tia Brelis.

1994 82m/C Sissy Spacek, Anna Chlumsky, Aaron Michael Metchik, Asher Metchik, Maureen Stapleton; **D:** Tia Brelis; **M:** David Kitay. **VHS, LV** *VMK*

Trail of the Pink Panther WOOF!

PG/Jr. High-Adult The last and by far the least in Sellers' "Pink Panther" series. Inspector Clouseau disappears, and a lady TV reporter looks up his old enemies and associates while trying to find out why. Made after Sellers died; director Edwards did a Frankenstein job of pasting together old, unreleased (and unfunny) Sellers outtakes from other "Pink Panther" features, disguised here as flashbacks. It didn't work, and neither did subsequent "Curse of the Pink Panther" and "Son of the Pink Panther."

⚠ BEWARE *Salty language, nudity, sex talk.*

1982 97m/C Peter Sellers, David Niven, Herbert Lom, Capucine, Burt Kwouk, Robert Wagner, Robert Loggia; **D:** Blake Edwards; **W:** Blake Edwards, Frank Waldman; **M:** Henry Mancini. **VHS, Beta, LV** *MGM*

Transformers

Preschool-Primary Series of single-episode cartoon tapes derived, of course, from the toy product line, demonstrating the shape-changing robot warriors of Cybertron at their transforming best. Additional volumes available.

1986 30m/C VHS, Beta *FHE*

Transformers: The Movie 🎞

G/Primary Full-length cartoon with the universe-defending robots fighting the powers of evil. Speaking of evil, the Transformers started out as shape-changing toy robots on store shelves, so this waste of film amounts to a big fat commercial. Noted as maverick movie genius Welles' final bow; he provides the voice of a planet.

1986 85m/C D: Nelson Shin; **V:** Orson Welles, Eric Idle, Judd Nelson, Leonard Nimoy, Robert Stack. **VHS, Beta** *FHE*

Trap on Cougar Mountain

G/Family Young Erik crusades to save his cougar friend Jason from the snares and bullets of hunters. Another one-man nature effort from writer/actor/producer/director Larsen.

1972 97m/C Erik Larsen, Keith Larsen, Karen Steele; **D:** Keith Larsen. **VHS, Beta, LV** *NWV, VTR*

Trapped In Paradise

PG-13/Jr. High-Adult Three bungling brothers make off with a bundle of cash from the Paradise—the town not the afterlife—bank on Christmas Eve. When a blizzard blocks their escape, they take off their ski masks and pretend to be innocent travelers. The locals, naive refugees from a Rockwell painting, don't recognize the buffoons as criminals, and reward their crime with hospitality that would make Frank Capra proud. Chase scenes and subplots abound as the boys spend what seems an afterlife trying to make their getaway. Routine, humdrum comedy is hampered by an obvious plot. Watchable only because of Carvey, Lovitz, and Cage.

> *Profanity, shootings and a near-drowning. Cons kidnap the guys' mother and then hold a whole houseful hostage.*

1994 111m/C Nicolas Cage, Jon Lovitz, Dana Carvey, John Ashton, Madchen Amick, Donald Moffat, Richard Jenkins, Florence Stanley, Angela Paton, Vic Manni, Frank Pesce, Sean McCann, Paul Lazar, Richard B. Shull; **D:** George Gallo; **W:** George Gallo; **M:** Robert Folk. **VHS, LV** *FXV*

Travels of Marco Polo

Preschool-Jr. High Animated version of the adventurer's famed journeys.

1972 48m/C VHS, Beta *MGM*

Treasure Island

Family "Wizard of Oz" director Fleming's adaptation of Robert Louis Stevenson's 18th-century English pirate tale. Neither Cooper, as Jim Hawkins, the cabin boy who inspires the treasure hunt, or Beery as one-legged Long John Silver, seem very English, but the spirit of high-seas adventure fun survives. Also available colorized.

1934 102m/B Wallace Beery, Jackie Cooper, Lionel Barrymore, Lewis Stone, Otto Kruger, Douglass Dumbrille, Chic Sale, Nigel Bruce; **D:** Victor Fleming. **VHS, Beta, LV** *MGM, TLF, HMV*

Treasure Island

PG/Family Spine-tingling Robert Louis Stevenson tale of pirates and buried treasure, in which young cabin boy Jim Hawkins matches wits with the treacherous Long John Silver. Some editions excise extra violence, and

Stevenson's ending is revised, but this gets the rollicking, full Disney treatment. Excellent casting.

> *Piratical swashbuckling violence and swordplay.*

1950 96m/C Bobby Driscoll, Robert Newton, Basil Sydney, Walter Fitzgerald, Denis O'Dea, Ralph Truman, Finlay Currie; **D:** Byron Haskin. **VHS, Beta, LV** *DIS, IGP*

Treasure Island

Family Made-for-TV animated musical adaptation of the adventurous story of Long John Silver and young Jim Hawkins (who's accompanied by a tiny mouse friend named Hiccup in this version) of the novel by Robert Louis Stevenson.

1972 75m/C V: Richard Dawson, Davy Jones, Larry Storch. **VHS** *WAR*

Treasure Island

G/Family Unexceptional British reheat of familiar pirate tale, with Welles taking pseudonymous screenwriting credit as 'O.W. Jeeves.' He also mutteringly portrays Long John Silver, and for good or ill he's the most interesting thing onscreen.

1972 94m/C Orson Welles, Kim Burfield, Walter Slezak, Lionel Stander; **D:** John Hough; **W:** Orson Welles. **VHS** *BTV*

Treasure Island

Family Shiver me timbers, lad! Lengthy but excellent made-for-cable-TV version of the classic Robert Louis Stevenson pirate yarn. Innkeeper's boy is left with a treasure map that earns him a visit from the infamous Long John Silver, played with glee by Heston. His son Fraser wrote, produced and directed, while the Chieftains handle the soundtracking with Celtic abandon.

1989 131m/C Charlton Heston, Christian Bale, Julian Glover, Richard Johnson, Oliver Reed, Christopher Lee, Clive Wood, Nicholas Amer, Michael Halsey; **D:** Fraser Heston; **W:** Fraser Heston. **VHS** *TTC*

The Treasure of Matecumbe

G/Family Motley crew of adventurers led by a young boy search for buried pirate treasure in a remote part of the Florida Keys shortly after the Civil War. Mediocre Disney adventure comes across like a "Huckleberry Finn" knockoff; in fact it's based on Robert Lewis Taylor's acclaimed novel "A Journey to Matecumbe."

> *Violence.*

1976 107m/C Billy Attmore, Robert Foxworth, Joan Hackett, Peter Ustinov, Vic Morrow; **D:** Vincent McEveety; **M:** Buddy Baker. **VHS, Beta** *DIS*

The Treasure of Swamp Castle

Family In medieval times an exiled prince returns to claim his long-lost bride, his ancestral castle, and the treasure hidden within the ruins—not necessarily in that

Woody and Buzz race to catch up with their owner Andy in "Toy Story."

order. This English-dubbed Hungarian feature cartoon isn't the expected action fairy tale but a screwball comedy of errors, as both the villains and the clueless prince try to outwit each other. It's fun for kids and smart enough for grownups.

BEWARE! *Alcohol use, brief nudity.*

1990 80m/C VHS *JTC*

Treasure of the Sierra Madre
🦴🦴🦴🦴

Family Three prospectors in search of gold in Mexico find suspicion, treachery and greed. Bogart is superbly believable as the paranoid, and ultimately homicidal, Fred C. Dobbs. Huston directed his father and wrote the screenplay, based on a B. Traven story. Watch for a very young Baretta (Blake), still wet behind the ears after the "Our Gang" comedies. Both Hustons won an Oscar, the first and last time a father and son scored together.

1948 126m/B Humphrey Bogart, Walter Huston, Tim Holt, Bruce (Herman Brix) Bennett, Barton MacLane, Robert (Bobby) Blake, Alfonso Bedoya; **D:** John Huston; **W:** John Huston; **M:** Max Steiner. **Award Nominations:** Academy Awards '48: Best Picture; **Awards:** Academy Awards '48: Best Director (Huston), Best Screenplay, Best

Supporting Actor (Huston); National Board of Review Awards '48: 10 Best Films of the Year, Best Actor (Huston). **VHS, Beta, LV** *MGM, FOX, TLF*

A Tree Grows in Brooklyn
🦴🦴🦴▷

Family Sensitive young Irish lass growing up in turn-of-the-century Brooklyn tries to rise above her tenement existence. As the girl dreaming of a better life, Garner is wonderful, earning a special Oscar for her performance. Dunn, as the gentle alcoholic father who makes a slim living as a singing waiter, also stands out amid the generally superior performances. Kazan's impressive directorial debut used a script based on the novel by Betty Smith.

BEWARE! *Alcohol use; sex talk.*

1945 128m/B Peggy Ann Garner, James Dunn, Dorothy McGuire, Joan Blondell, Lloyd Nolan, Ted Donaldson, James Gleason, John Alexander, Charles Halton; **D:** Elia Kazan; **M:** Jerry Goldsmith. **Award Nominations:** Academy Awards '45: Best Screenplay; **Awards:** Academy Awards '45: Best Supporting Actor (Dunn); National Board of Review Awards '45: 10 Best Films of the Year. **VHS, Beta, LV** *KUI, FOX, BTV*

Trenchcoat 🐾 ◊

Family Made-for-TV adaptation of the first of British writer John Christopher's popular young adult sci-fi books. Alien invaders, in the form of towering three-legged machines, control humans through mind implants at the age of 16. Two boys try to escape Tripod captivity and join the resistance.

1983 95m/C Margot Kidder, Robert Hays; **D:** Michael Tuchner; **W:** Jeffrey Price, Peter S. Seaman; **M:** Charles Fox. **VHS, Beta** *DIS, OM*

The Trial of the Incredible Hulk 🐾🐾

Family Made-for-TV movie spun off from Ferrigno's "Incredible Hulk" TV series, although it really showcases another Marvel Comics character, Daredevil. A (blind) lawyer by day, Matt Murdock turns into an acrobatic ninja-type to battle gangsters; meanwhile the Hulk briefly becomes his client in the courtroom.

> 🪧 **BEWARE** *Violence.*

1989 96m/C Bill Bixby, Lou Ferrigno, Rex Smith, John Rhys-Davies, Marta DuBois, Nancy Everhard, Nicholas Hormann; **D:** Bill Bixby. **VHS** *VTR*

Trick or Treat

Preschool-Primary Vintage Disney cartoon in which Donald plays the gags on Halloween, only for them to backfire when his nephews and Witch Hazel reverse the tricks.

1952 8m/C VHS, Beta *MTI, DSN*

The Trip to Bountiful 🐾🐾🐾

PG/Jr. High-Adult An elderly widow, unhappy living in her son's fancy modern home, makes a pilgrimage back to her childhood home in Bountiful, Texas. Based on the Horton Foote play. Fine acting with Oscar-winning performance from Page.

1985 102m/C Geraldine Page, Rebecca DeMornay, John Heard, Carlin Glynn, Richard Bradford; **D:** Peter Masterson; **W:** Horton Foote. **Award Nominations:** Academy Awards '85: Best Adapted Screenplay; **Awards:** Academy Awards '85: Best Actress (Page); Independent Spirit Awards '86: Best Actress (Page), Best Screenplay; National Media Owl Awards '87: First Prize. **VHS, Beta, LV, 8mm** *COL, BTV, NLC*

Troll 🐾🐾

PG-13/Primary-Adult Mischievous troll haunts an urban apartment building, tries to make a little girl a princess, and turn all humans into mythical flora and fauna. The PG-13 rating is much too harsh for this mild fantasy, with charming creatures matched against some awfully embarrassing performances by most of the grownups (exception: "Lassie's" June Lockhart and her daughter Anne as the same sassy witch). The gorier "Troll 2" has nothing in common but the title.

> 🪧 **BEWARE** *The hairy old troll is meant to be a wicked soul, but he seems cute and mellow. Salty language, monster roughhousing, but nothing really scary.*

1985 86m/C Noah Hathaway, Gary Sandy, Anne Lockhart, Sonny Bono, Shelley Hack, June Lockhart, Michael Moriarty; **D:** John Carl Buechler; **M:** Richard Band. **VHS, Beta, LV** *LIV, VES*

Troll Classic Book Videos

Preschool-Primary Group of children's story programs based on fairy tales. Included are "The Bremen Town Musicians," "The Elves and the Shoemaker," "Gingerbread Boy," "The Golden Goose," "Henny Penny," "The House That Jack Built," "Jack and the Beanstalk," "Little Red Riding Hood," "Rumpelstiltskin," "Stone Soup," "Three Little Pigs," "The Twelve Days of Christmas," and "The Ugly Duckling."

1988 10m/C VHS

A Troll in Central Park 🐾🐾 ◊

G/Family That's a troll, not a stroll, in Central Park. Animated fantasy about Stanley the troll, who is cast out of his kingdom (because he's a good guy) and winds up in New York's Central Park. Talk about a punishment. There, Stanley brings happiness to a little girl and her skeptical brother, all the while battling the evil troll queen. Strictly average.

1994 76m/C **D:** Don Bluth, Gary Goldman; **W:** Stu Krieger; **M:** Robert Folk; **V:** Dom DeLuise, Cloris Leachman, Jonathan Pryce, Hayley Mills, Charles Nelson Reilly, Phillip Glasser, Robert Morley, Sy Goraleb, Tawney Sunshine Glover, Jordan Metzner. **VHS, LV** *WAR*

Trolls & the Christmas Express

Preschool Mischievous trolls threaten to keep Santa Claus from delivering his gifts in this whimsical cartoon originally broadcast on cable TV.

1981 25m/C V: Roger Miller, Hans Conried. **VHS, Beta** *PAR, MTI*

Tron 🐾🐾

PG/Primary-Adult Computer programmer is sucked into the memory banks of a giant mainframe, where he exists as a warrior in a virtual-reality civilization running parallel to the outside world. The bewildered hero fights video game-style battles against a rogue artificial intelligence seeking to dominate mankind. The sketchy plot of this much-anticipated Disney sci-fi sounds better than it plays; obviously more attention was paid to incredible computer-graphics f/x than the script.

> 🪧 **BEWARE** *Violence (clean and bloodless among nonhumans). Sex talk (human).*

1982 96m/C Jeff Bridges, Bruce Boxleitner, David Warner, Cindy Morgan, Barnard Hughes, Dan Shor; **D:** Steven Lisberger. **VHS, Beta, LV** *DIS*

Troop Beverly Hills 🐾🐾🐾

PG/Jr. High-Adult To be close to her daughter during a divorce, fashion-conscious, free-spending housewife Phyllis volunteers to lead a scout troop based in their

Rushing down the river in "A Troll in Central Park."

posh neighborhood of Beverly Hills. Result is a lot of wimp-out-of-water gags, as rich girls of Troop Beverly Hills compete in a survival hike. Long's perpetually upbeat personality propels this silly comedy mixing pratfalls and materialism.

BEWARE *Materialism, profanity, sex talk, alcohol use, pretty much in that order.*

1989 105m/C Shelley Long, Craig T. Nelson, Betty Thomas, Mary Gross, Stephanie Beacham, Audra Lindley, Edd Byrnes, Ami Foster, Jenny Lewis, Kellie Martin; *D:* Jeff Kanew; *W:* Pamela Norris, Margaret Grieco Oberman; *M:* Randy Edelman. **VHS, Beta, LV, 8mm** *COL*

The Trouble with Angels 🦴🦴 ⌐

Family Two young girls turn a convent upside down with their endless practical jokes. Eventually they do a bit of growing up when they're unwillingly left at school during the Christmas holiday and spend quality time with habit-clad Russell, who's everything a Mother Superior should be: understanding, wise, and graceful. Wholesome, if overlong, Catholic comedy. Followed by "Where Angels Go, Trouble Follows."

1966 112m/C Hayley Mills, June Harding, Rosalind Russell, Gypsy Rose Lee, Binnie Barnes; *D:* Ida Lupino; *M:* Jerry Goldsmith. **VHS, Beta, LV** *COL*

True Grit 🦴🦴🦴

G/Family Hard-drinking, one-eyed U.S. Marshal Rooster Cogburn is hired by a 14-year-old girl to find her father's killer. Wayne's rip-snortin' performance makes him the best saddle pal a kid could ever want and won him his only Oscar. Based on the Charles Portis novel. Followed by "Rooster Cogburn."

BEWARE *Violence, including scary moments in a snake pit. Alcohol use.*

1969 128m/C John Wayne, Glen Campbell, Kim Darby, Robert Duvall; *D:* Henry Hathaway; *M:* Elmer Bernstein. **Award Nominations:** Academy Awards '69: Best Song ("True Grit"); **Awards:** Academy Awards '69: Best Actor (Wayne); Golden Globe Awards '70: Best Actor—Drama (Wayne); National Board of Review Awards '69: 10 Best Films of the Year. **VHS, Beta, LV** *PAR, HHE, TLF*

True Lies 🦴🦴 ⌐

R/Sr. High-Adult Brain candy with a bang offers eye popping special effects and a large dose of unbelievability. Sort of like a big screen "Scarecrow and Mrs. King" as supposed computer salesman Ah-nuld keeps his spy work secret from mousy, neglected wife Curtis, who has a few secrets of her own and inadvertently ends up right in the thick of things. Raunchy and extremely sexist, but not without charm; the stupidity is part of the fun. Perfectly cast sidekick Arnold holds his own as a pig, but Heston is wasted as the head honcho. Tons of special effects culminate in a smashing finish. Very loosely adapted from the 1991 French comedy "La Total."

BEWARE *Violence; profanity; sex talk; Curtis does a strip tease in brief undergarments.*

1994 141m/C Arnold Schwarzenegger, Jamie Lee Curtis, Tom Arnold, Bill Paxton, Tia Carrere, Art Malik, Eliza Dushku, Charlton Heston, Grant Heslov; *D:* James Cameron; *W:* James Cameron. **VHS** *NYR*

Truly, Madly, Deeply

PG/Sr. High-Adult The recent death of her lover drives a young woman into despair and anger, until he turns up at her apartment one day. Tender and well written tale of love and the supernatural, with believable characters and plot-line. Playwright Minghella's directorial debut.

BEWARE *Brief profanity.*

1991 107m/C Juliet Stevenson, Alan Rickman, Bill Paterson, Michael Maloney, Christopher Rozycki, Keith Bartlett, David Ryall, Stella Maris; *D:* Anthony Minghella; *W:* Anthony Minghella. **VHS** *TOU*

The Truth About Cats and Dogs

PG-13/Jr. High-Adult Witty, but insecure Abby Barnes (Garofalo) hosts a radio-talk show for pet lovers. When handsome photographer Brian (Chaplin) calls in for help and becomes intrigued with her voice, he asks her out. She agrees, but she describes herself as a tall blond (Oops!). Since she isn't a tall blond, she must ask her dim-witted model girlfriend Noelle (Thurman) to stand in. Brian is increasingly smitten with Abby's voice, but with Noelle's everything else. Of course, both woman fall for Brian, which threatens their friendship. Oh yeah, and there's a cute dog in there, too. Teen girls will be attracted to the story, but younger kids just won't get it. Remember the message—it's what's inside that counts.

BEWARE *Sex-related scene and brief strong language.*

1996 97m/C Janeane Garofalo, Uma Thurman, Ben Chaplin, Jamie Foxx, Richard Coca, Stanley DeSantis; *D:* Michael Lehmann. **VHS** *NYR*

The Truth About Mother Goose

Preschool-Primary An Oscar-nominated Disney short that presents three Mother Goose classics, along with their backgrounds: "Jack Horner," "Mary, Mary Quite Contrary," and "London Bridge."
1957 15m/C VHS, Beta *DSN, MTI*

Tubby the Tuba

Family Tubby the Tuba searches for a melody he can call his own, in a cartoon remake of George Pal's Oscar-winning stop-motion short.

1977 81m/C Pearl Bailey, Jack Gilford, Hermione Gingold. **VHS, Beta** *VTR, LIV*

Tuck Everlasting

Family In the early 1900s, a little girl befriends a backwoods family with an incredible secret—they will never age or die. Brittle, low-budget adaptation of Natalie Babbitt's novel has definite charm and a good moral about mortality, but (like the Tucks themselves), it goes on way too long.

BEWARE *Brief violence*

1985 120m/C Fred A. Keller, James McGuire; *D:* Frederick King Keller. **VHS, Beta** *LIV, VES*

Tucker: The Man and His Dream

PG/Jr. High-Adult Portrait of Preston Tucker, entrepreneur and industrial idealist, who in 1946 tried to build the car of the future and was effectively run out of business by the powers-that-were. Ravishing, ultra-nostalgic lullaby to the American Dream. Watch for Jeff's dad, Lloyd, in a bit role.

BEWARE *Salty language.*

1988 111m/C Jeff Bridges, Martin Landau, Dean Stockwell, Frederic Forrest, Mako, Joan Allen, Christian Slater, Lloyd Bridges, Elias Koteas, Nina Siemaszko, Corin "Corky" Nemec, Marshall Bell, Don Novello, Peter Donat, Dean Goodman, Patti Austin; *D:* Francis Ford Coppola; *W:* Arnold Schulman, David Seidler; *M:* Joe Jackson, Carmine Coppola. **Award Nominations:** Academy Awards '88: Best Art Direction/Set Decoration, Best Costume Design, Best Supporting Actor (Landau); **Awards:** Golden Globe Awards '89: Best Supporting Actor (Landau). **VHS, Beta, LV, 8mm** *PAR*

Turf Boy

Jr. High-Adult Desperate for cash, a boy and his uncle try to get an old horse into prime condition for racing. A minor equine melodrama, just the right length for an old-time matinee double-feature.
1942 68m/B Robert "Buzzy" Henry, James Seay, Doris Day, William Halligan, Gavin Gordon; *D:* William Beaudine. **VHS** *NOS, LOO*

Turk 182!

PG-13/Jr. High-Adult Angry teen brother of a disabled, alcoholic fireman takes on local political bosses to win back the pension the firefighter deserves. The kid's weapon: a public graffiti campaign that plasters the title catch phrase all over town. Boy fights City Hall, audience loses, in this contrived, mostly silly feel-good plot.

BEWARE *Alcohol use, profanity, mature themes, including an attempted suicide.*

1985 96m/C Timothy Hutton, Robert Culp, Robert Urich, Kim Cattrall, Peter Boyle, Darren McGavin, Paul Sorvino; *D:* Bob (Benjamin) Clark. **VHS, Beta** *FOX*

Turner and Hooch

PG/Jr. High-Adult Slobbering pooch witnesses his master's murder, and a fussy police detective is partnered with the drooling, ugly mutt and a weak script in his search for the culprit. Hanks is his usual charming self, but even he can't wholly salvage this Touchstone effort. Came out not long after Universal's cop 'n' dog action/ comedy "K-9"; take your pick.

BEWARE *Violence and sex talk. Don't expect a happy ending.*

1989 99m/C Tom Hanks, Mare Winningham, Craig T. Nelson, Scott Paulin, J.C. Quinn; *D:* Roger Spottiswoode; *W:* Jim Cash, Jack Epps Jr., Michael Blodgett. **VHS, Beta, LV** *TOU*

Turtle Diary

PG/Sr. High-Adult "Free Willy" for grownups, though kids may be hooked by the premise and reeled in. Slow-paced but warm portrait of two lonely, bookish adult Londoners brought together in a scheme to secretly release giant turtles from the city aquarium into their rightful home, the sea. The animals' freedom somehow liberates the humans' spirits as well. Based on the Russell Hoban novel.

BEWARE *Salty language, mature themes.*

1986 90m/C Ben Kingsley, Glenda Jackson, Richard Johnson, Michael Gambon, Rosemary Leach, Jeroen Krabbe, Eleanor Bron; *D:* John Irvin; *W:* Harold Pinter. **VHS, Beta, LV** *LIV, VES*

Tut and Tuttle

Family Young dabbler in magic is transported to ancient Egypt, where he uses his wits against the evil Horemheb, who has kidnapped the child Prince Tut. Juvenile TV adventure, an early directorial effort for Ron Howard and broadcast as "Through the Magic Pyramid."

1982 97m/C Christopher Barnes, Eric Greene, Hans Conried, Vic Tayback. **VHS, Beta** *TLF*

TV's Best Adventures of Superman

Family This first package of episodes from the original television series, which ran from 1951-1957, contains "Superman on Earth," the black & white series pilot about the Man of Steel's childhood on Krypton and Earth, and "All That Glitters," the series final episode, wherein Lois Lane and Jimmy Olsen acquire super powers. Also includes the 1941 animated cartoon "Superman," the first-ever screen appearance of the superhero. Additional episodes available.

1951 62m/C George Reeves, Phyllis Coates, Noel Neill, Jack Larson, John Hamilton, Robert Shayne. **VHS, Beta** *WAR, MOV*

'Twas the Night Before Christmas

Family Santa Claus may not visit Junctionville because of an insulting letter printed in a local newspaper, so Joshua Trundle and Father Mouse look for a way to mend his hurt feelings. A Rankin-Bass cartoon adaptation of the classic Clement Moore poem.

1982 25m/C *V:* Joel Grey, George Gobel. **VHS, Beta** *MTI, WAR*

'Twas the Night Before Christmas

Preschool-Primary Clement Moore's poem is retold through animation.

1991 27m/C VHS *FHE, FAF*

Twelve Chairs

PG/Jr. High-Adult Take-off on Russian folktale first filmed in Yugoslavia in 1927. A rich matron admits on her deathbed that she has hidden her jewels in the upholstery of one of twelve chairs that are no longer in her home. A Brooksian treasure hunt ensues.

1970 94m/C Mel Brooks, Dom DeLuise, Frank Langella, Ron Moody, Bridget Brice; *D:* Mel Brooks; *W:* Mel Brooks. **VHS, Beta, LV** *MED*

12 Monkeys

R/Sr. High-Adult Forty years after a plague wipes out 99 percent of the human population and sends the survivors underground, scientists send prisoner James Cole (Willis) to the 1990s to investigate the connection between the virus and seriously deranged fanatic Jeffrey Goines (Pitt), whose father happens to be a renowned virologist. Convoluted plot and accumulated detail require a keen attention span, but as each piece of the puzzle falls into place the story becomes a fascinating sci-fi spectacle. Pitt drops the pretty-boy image with a nutzoid performance that'll make anybody stop swooning in a heartbeat.

BEWARE *Contains nudity and sadistic violence, including a rape (off camera). For high schoolers and up.*

1995 131m/C Bruce Willis, Madeleine Stowe, Brad Pitt, Christopher Plummer, David Morse, Frank Gorshin, John Seda; *D:* Terry Gilliam; *W:* David Peoples, Janet Peoples; *M:* Paul Buckmaster. **Award Nominations:** Academy Awards '95: Best Costume Design, Best Supporting Actor (Pitt); **Awards:** Golden Globe Awards '96: Best Supporting Actor (Pitt). **VHS** *MCA*

20,000 Leagues Under the Sea

Family Stout-hearted seafaring men of the 19th century investigate rumors of a monster sinking ships, discover it's actually a scientific genius named Nemo who's invented the atomic submarine a century early and uses the futuristic craft in a personal war against the surface world. One of Walt Disney's most celebrated and successful live actioners, with first-rate cast and f/x. Based on the novel by Jules Verne; for a non-Disney sequel, see "The Mysterious Island."

1954 127m/C Kirk Douglas, James Mason, Peter Lorre, Paul Lukas, Robert J. Wilke, Carleton Young; *D:* Richard Fleischer. **Award Nominations:** Academy Awards '54: Best Film Editing; **Awards:** Academy Awards '54: Best Art Direction/Set Decoration (Color), Best Special Effects; National Board of Review Awards '54: 10 Best Films of the Year. **VHS, Beta, LV** *DIS*

20,000 Leagues Under the Sea 🦴🦴

Family Straight animated retelling of the Jules Verne classic science fiction novel about two men and a boy held by the obsessed Captain Nemo aboard his fantastic submarine, as envisioned by the Hanna-Barbera studios.
1973 60m/C VHS, Beta *LIV, PSM, WOV*

20,000 Leagues Under the Sea

Family A lighthearted twist on the Verne tale happens when a cool kid and his weird friends go sailing to find a radical sea serpent.
1990 25m/C VHS *VTR*

20,000 Leagues Under the Sea 🦴🦴

Family Hanna-Barbera cartoon adaptation of the Jules Verne classic can't compare to the Disney version, as Captain Nemo reveals his submarine, the Nautilus, to an astounded world.
1990 47m/C VHS *VTR*

Twice Upon a Time 🦴🦴🦴 ▷

PG/Family George Lucas was executive producer for this one-of-a-kind cartoon fantasy that, shamefully, never got substantial theatrical release. Synonamess Botch, an incompetent villain who manufactures nightmares, sabotages the Cosmic Clock. To the rescue come occupants of Frivoli, the magical land where dreams originate. Heroes include the Chaplinesque mute Mumford and his shape-changing pal Ralph the All-Purpose Animal (voice by Lorenzo Music, who also does Garfield the Cat). Filmed in "lumage," an eye-catching style of cutout/collage animation, with sly dialogue to entertain young and old alike.

🦴 BEWARE 🦴 *The PG rating has no earthly explanation.*

1983 75m/C D: Charles Swenson, John Korty; **V:** Lorenzo Music, Marshall Efron, Paul Frees, Hamilton Camp. **VHS, Beta, LV** *WAR, FCT*

Twilight Zone: The Movie 🦴🦴 ▷

PG/Family Narrated by Meredith, four short horrific tales are anthologized as a tribute to Rod Serling and his popular television series. Three of the episodes, "Kick the Can," "It's a Good Life" and "Nightmare at 20,000 Feet," are based on original "Twilight Zone" scripts. Most effective of the four is the Miller-directed "Nightmare," with Lithgow as a terrified airplane passenger who spots a demon riding the wing. Morrow was killed during a helicopter stunt during filming.

🦴 BEWARE 🦴 *Old-fashioned Serling-esque scares.*

1983 101m/C Dan Aykroyd, Albert Brooks, Vic Morrow, Kathleen Quinlan, John Lithgow, Billy Mumy, Scatman Crothers, Kevin McCarthy, Bill Quinn, Selma Diamond, Abbe Lane, John Larroquette, Jeremy Licht, Patricia Barry, William Schallert, Burgess Meredith, Cherie Currie; **D:** John Landis, Steven Spielberg, George Miller, Joe Dante; **W:** John Landis; **M:** Jerry Goldsmith. **VHS, Beta, LV** *WAR*

Twins 🦴🦴 ▷

PG/Jr. High-Adult Funny teaming of Schwarzenegger and DeVito begins with the unlikely story of these two being twins. A genteics experiment goes awry producing one as a genetically-superior superman and the other a short, coniving petty criminal. Schwarzenegger learns he has a brother, sets out to find him and forces his brotherly affection on the ice-hearted Devito. The two find themselves wrapped up in a scandal and must work together to save the day. Funny premise with laughable moments. This one is OK for most young viewers.

🦴 BEWARE 🦴 *Sexual innuendos, but Schwarzenegger's character is too goody-goody to go through with anything. Mild language from the gruff DeVito.*

1988 107m/C Arnold Schwarzenegger, Danny DeVito, Kelly Preston, Hugh O'Brian, Chloe Webb, Bonnie Bartlett, Marshall Bell, Trey Wilson, Nehemiah Persoff; **D:** Ivan Reitman; **W:** William Davies, William Osborne, Timothy Harris, Herschel Weingrod; **M:** Georges Delerue, Randy Edelman. **VHS, Beta, LV** *MCA*

Twinsitters 🦴🦴 ▷

PG-13/Jr. High-Adult Twins Peter and David Falcone (Peter and David Paul) find themselves unexpectedly saving the life of corrupt businessman Frank Hillhurst (Martin). Hillhurst is turning state's evidence on his crooked operations and his disturbed partners have threatened both his life and the lives of his twin 10-year-old nephews. So Hillhurst hires the Falcones to protect his hellacious pint-sized relatives—who manage to get themselves kidnapped.

1995 93m/C Peter Paul, David Paul, Christian Cousins, Joseph Cousins, Jared Martin, George Lazenby, Rena Sofa, Mother Love; **D:** John Paragon; **W:** John Paragon. **VHS** *COL*

Twist 🦴🦴 ▷

PG/Jr. High-Adult Amusing documentary about the dance craze and American pop culture. Hank Ballard and the Midnighters first recorded "The Twist" in 1960 but it was Chubby Checker's cover version and Dick Clark's promotion of the record on "American Bandstand" that really started everyone moving—from kids to grandparents. Includes interviews, newsreel, and tv footage.
1993 78m/C D: Ron Mann. **VHS, LV** *COL, IME, MVD*

Twister 🦴🦴

PG-13/Jr. High-Adult Big-screen, big-sound special effects gave "Twister" its oomph, but even in the theater, when you'd seen one tornado you'd pretty much seen them all. Helen Hunt and Bill Paxton play a pair of dedicated almost-divorced meteorologists thrown together one last time when a plague of tornadoes threatens Oklahoma. When they refer to "the suck zone" they mean the area near a tornado, but when there's no tornado on screen, the film itself is pretty much in the suck zone. (Sample line: "You're still in love with him, aren't you?") If they can get their measuring instruments up into a funnel cloud, maybe they'll learn how to predict where a tornado will strike next. Thus, they must get close to vicious vortexes. Don't try this at home. On video, "Twister's" tornadoes lose their impact, while the plot and dialogue remain, alas, undiminished.

BEWARE *Conversation about genitalia. Scary cyclones. If you live in tornado country, be prepared for kids in your bed on stormy nights.*

1996 105m/C Bill Paxton, Helen Hunt, Cary Elwes, Jami Gertz, Cary Elwes; **D:** Jan De Bont; **W:** Michael Crichton, Anne-Marie Martin. **VHS** *WAR*

Two Bits

PG-13/Family A 12-year-old boy (Barone) is determined to find 25 cents for a ticket to the opening of a Depression-era Philadelphia movie palace. Mastrantonio is his mom and Pacino his grandpa who says he'll leave the boy a quarter when he dies.

BEWARE *Subjects include loss and sexuality.*

1996 85m/C Al Pacino, Gerlando Barone, Mary Elizabeth Mastrantonio, Joe Grifasi, Joanna Merlin, Andy Romano, Ron McLarty, Donna Mitchell, Patrick Borriello, Mary Lou Rosato, Rosemary DeAngelis; **D:** James Foley; **W:** Joseph Stefano; **C:** Juan Ruiz-Anchia; **M:** Jane Musky; **V:** Alec Baldwin. **VHS** *TOU*

Two Bits & Pepper

PG/Primary-Adult Bumbling criminals (both played by Piscopo) still manage to kidnap a young girl and her friend and it's up to the title characters, a pet horse and a pony, to attempt a daring rescue.

BEWARE *Mild violence and mild language.*

1995 90m/C Joe Piscopo, Lauren Eckstrom, Rachel Crane, Perry Stephens, Kathrin Lautner, Dennis Weaver; **D:** Corey Michael Eubanks; **W:** Corey Michael Eubanks; **C:** Jacques Haitkin; **M:** Louis Febre. **VHS** *REP*

Two If by Sea

R/Sr. High-Adult Take one petty thief whose about to pull his last scam (he promises) and his fed up girlfriend who wants to settle down and get on with their lives and you've got "Two If By Sea." Leary and Bullock are the couple who are hiding out on an upscale New England island waiting to make a deal for a painting he's stolen. And they try to fit in and, oh yeah, they really don't get along very well. Sound kinda boring? Well, it is, but they gave it a shot. Throw in a few FBI men and some would-be criminals for good measure. Some teens may be attracted to the "Speed"-popular Bullock, but this is not one of her best, to say the least. A simple romantic comedy, to say the most.

BEWARE *Criminal language.*

1995 96m/C Sandra Bullock, Denis Leary, Stephen Dillane, Yaphet Kotto, Wayne Robson, Jonathan Tucker, Mike Starr, Michael Badalucco, Lenny Clarke, John Friesen; **D:** Bill Bennett; **W:** Denis Leary, Michael Armstrong; **C:** Andrew Lesnie. **VHS, LV** *WAR*

Two of a Kind

Family In his television movie debut, Burns plays an elderly man whose mentally handicapped grandson helps him put the starch back in his shirt. Sensitively produced and performed.

1982 102m/C George Burns, Robby Benson, Cliff Robertson, Barbara Barrie, Frances Lee McCain, Geri Jewell, Ronny Cox; **D:** Roger Young. **VHS, Beta** *FOX*

2000 Year Old Man

G/Family Animated version of the classic Mel Brooks/Carl Reiner comedy routine, adapted as a network TV special complete with studio audience laughter and gags about the commercial breaks (nonexistent on tape). Neither detract from the wry hilarity as a 2,000 year old man recounts dating Joan of Arc, Robin Hood's press agent, what women are for, and Shakespeare's lost play "Queen Alexandra and Murray."

1982 25m/C D: Leo Salkin; **V:** Carl Reiner, Mel Brooks. **VHS, Beta** *MED*

2001: A Space Odyssey

Jr. High-Adult Space voyage to Jupiter turns chaotic when a computer, HAL 9000, takes over. Seen by some as a mirror of man's historical use of machinery and by others as a grim vision of the future, film scores with stunning storyline, special effects and music. A definitive sci-fi viewing experience. Martin Balsam originally recorded the voice of HAL, but was replaced by Raines. From Arthur C. Clarke's novel "The Sentinel." Followed by a sequel "2010: The Year We Make Contact." Laserdisc edition is presented in letterbox format and features a special supplementary section on the making of "2001," a montage of images from the film, production documents, memos and photos. Also included on the disc is a NASA film entitled "Art and Reality," which offers footage from the Voyager I and II flybys of Jupiter.

1968 139m/C Keir Dullea, Gary Lockwood, William Sylvester, Dan Richter; **D:** Stanley Kubrick; **W:** Arthur C. Clarke, Stanley Kubrick; **V:** Douglas Raines. **Award Nominations:** Academy Awards '68: Best Art Direction/Set Decoration, Best Director (Kubrick), Best Story & Screenplay; **Awards:** Academy Awards '68: Best Visual Effects; National Board of Review Awards '68: 10 Best Films of the Year. **VHS, Beta, LV** *MGM, CRC, FCT*

2010 : The Year We Make Contact

PG/Jr. High-Adult Sequel to "2001: A Space Odyssey" continues screen adaptation of Arthur C. Clarke's novel "The Sentinel" 16 years after the sci-fi classic was released. Americans and Russians unite to investigate the abandoned starship Discovery and its decaying orbit around Jupiter, trying to determine why the HAL 9000 computer sabotaged its mission years before, while signs of cosmic change are detected on and around the giant planet. Lacks the original's wallop, but worthy of a view.

BEWARE *Space violence.*

1984 116m/C Roy Scheider, John Lithgow, Helen Mirren, Bob Balaban, Keir Dullea, Madolyn Smith, Mary Jo Deschanel; ***D:*** Peter Hyams; ***W:*** Peter Hyams; ***M:*** David Shire; ***V:*** Douglas Raines. **VHS, Beta, LV** *MGM*

Ub Iwerks Cartoonfest

Family Iwerks was one of Walt Disney's original cohorts and even helped concoct Mickey Mouse. Later Iwerks went on to careers with several animation studios. Five volumes of Iwerks works (mostly adaptations of classic fairy tales), some B&W, some color, are available in this videocassette series.

193? 57m/C VHS, Beta *CCB*

The Ugly Dachshund 🦴🦴

Family Jones and Pleshette are married dog lovers breeding dachshunds. Then they take in a great dane puppy, who grows to massive full-size thinking he's a wiener dog because he's been raised with them. Just imagine what happens when such a large dog acts as if he's small and you've got the picture. Though it's a one-joke setup at best, small kids should enjoy this runt from the Disney film litter.

1965 93m/C Dean Jones, Suzanne Pleshette, Charlie Ruggles, Kelly Thordsen, Parley Baer; ***D:*** Norman Tokar. **VHS, Beta** *DIS, OM*

The Ugly Duckling

Preschool-Primary The Hans Christian Andersen story meets Disney animation and the result is 'toon magic in this Academy Award winner that teaches acceptance regardless of looks. It was also the last of the Disney's original cycle of "Silly Symphonies."

1939 8m/C VHS, Beta *DSN, MTI*

The Ugly Duckling

Preschool-Primary Paintings illustrate this version of the Hans Christian Andersen classic about the aesthetically challenged immature waterfowl; singer/actress Cher reads the text. Product of the distinguished "Rabbit Ears" video series from Random House.

1986 30m/C VHS, Beta *KUI, RAN, VEC*

The Ugly Duckling and other Classic Fairytales

Preschool-Primary Presentation of three classic stories in animated form, from the acclaimed "Children's Circle" series by Weston Woods.

1985 36m/C VHS, Beta *CCC,, BTV*

Ugly Little Boy

Primary Future scientists time-teleport a child from the Neanderthal age to the present for study. They treat the poor cave-kid like a specimen; only the nurse assigned to

him comes to view the boy as human. Strangely unmoving adaptation of one of Isaac Asimov's most famous sci-fi short stories.

1977 26m/C Kate Reid; ***D:*** Barry Morse, Don Thompson. **VHS, Beta** *LCA*

UHF 🦴🦴

PG-13/Jr. High-Adult Weird Al Yankovic is appointed manager of a woebegone UHF television station. He turns it around with bizarre programming ideas. Not much plot, but some fun parodies of TV. Ages 12 and up.

BEWARE *Profanity.*

1989 97m/C Weird Al Yankovic, Kevin McCarthy, Victoria Jackson, Michael Richards, David Bowie, Anthony Geary; ***D:*** Jay Levey; ***M:*** John Du Prez. **VHS, Beta, LV** *ORI*

Uncle Buck 🦴🦴 ♡

PG/Jr. High-Adult The Russells leave town and reluctantly put kids in the temporary care of good ol' Uncle Buck, a lovable slob who spends much of his time bowling, eating, and trying to make up with his girlfriend. The young children adore Buck, but moody punk teen Tia's disputes with him over her clothes and lifestyle cause real hurt on both sides. John Hughes wrote/directed this uneven comedy with its heart in the right place but seesawing between mean-spirited slapstick and intelligent drama. A hit with audiences thanks to the Candy man, then a short-lived TV series without him.

BEWARE *Profanity, sex talk and alcohol use. Teenager Tia hangs out with some rowdy teens.*

1989 100m/C John Candy, Amy Madigan, Jean Kelly, Macaulay Culkin, Jay Underwood, Gaby Hoffman, Laurie Metcalf, Elaine Bromka, Garrett M. Brown; ***D:*** John Hughes; ***W:*** John Hughes; ***M:*** Ira Newborn. **VHS, Beta, LV** *MCA*

Uncle Elephant

Preschool-Primary Arnie the elephant boy gets discouraged when his parents frown on his attempts at comedy. Then, his parents vanish on a sailing jaunt and he comes under the wing of his kindly Uncle Elephant. Deals with the concept that different emotions may be felt at the same time, and treats death in a touching manner. A 30-minute musical based on a story by Arnold Lobel. Ages 3 to 7.

1991 26m/C VHS *WPC, CHF,*

Uncle Nick and the Magic Forest

Preschool-Primary Uncle Nick is the friendly neighborhood storyteller who transports children into the exciting world of the magic forest. There the children can sing and dance along with various forest friends as well as sharpen their motor skills. Ages 2 to 7.

1995 30m/C VHS

Under Capricorn

Jr. High-Adult Bergman is an Irish lass who follows her convict husband Cotten out to 1830s Australia where he makes a fortune. She turns to drink, perhaps because of his neglect, and has her position usurped by a house-keeper with designs on her husband. When Bergman's cousin (Wilding) arrives, Cotten may have cause for his violent jealousy. There's a plot twist involving old family skeletons, but this is definitely lesser Hitchcock. Adapted from the Helen Simpson novel. Remade in 1982.

1949 117m/C Ingrid Bergman, Joseph Cotten, Michael Wilding, Margaret Leighton, Jack Watling, Cecil Parker, Denis O'Dea; **D:** Alfred Hitchcock. **VHS, Beta, LV** *VES*

Under the Rainbow WOOF!

PG/Primary-Adult "Comic" situations are encountered by a Hollywood talent scout and a secret service agent in a hotel filled with party-animal midget actors hired to portray Munchkins during the filming of "The Wizard of Oz." Nazi dwarf spy adds to prevailing lack of taste in this attempt at humor. Not really for kids. Or adults.

⚠ BEWARE ⚠ *Nudity, sex, alcohol use, profanity and unflattering depiction of little people.*

1981 97m/C Chevy Chase, Carrie Fisher, Eve Arden, Joseph Maher, Robert Donner, Mako, Pat McCormick, Billy Barty, Zelda Rubinstein; **D:** Steve Rash; **W:** Pat McCormick, Martin Smith, Harry Hurwitz. **VHS, Beta** *WAR*

Undercover Blues

PG-13/Jr. High-Adult Comedy-thriller starring Turner and Quaid as married spies Jane and Jeff Blue, on parental leave from the espionage biz, who are on vacation with their 11-month-old daughter in New Orleans. But the holiday is interrupted when they're recruited by their boss to stop an old adversary from selling stolen weapons. The leads play cute together and the baby is adorable but this is strictly routine escapism. Stick with "The Thin Man" instead.

⚠ BEWARE ⚠ *Profanity, spy-like violence and shooting and sex talk.*

1993 90m/C Kathleen Turner, Dennis Quaid, Fiona Shaw, Stanley Tucci, Larry Miller, Obba Babatunde, Park Overall, Tom Arnold, Saul Rubinek, Michelle Schuelke; **D:** Herbert Ross; **W:** Ian Abrams; **M:** David Newman. **VHS, LV** *MGM*

Underdog: The Tickle Feather Machine

Family Underdog comes up against Simon Bar Sinister's most fiendish plan. Also includes the comic misadventures of Tennessee Tuxedo and Chumly, Commander McBragg and the Go-Go Gophers.
1966 60m/C VHS *UAV*

Undergrads

Family Bright generational Disney comedy with Carney, estranged from his stick-in-the-mud son, deciding to at-

tend college with his free-thinking grandson. Made for television.
1985 102m/C Art Carney, Chris Makepeace, Jackie Burroughs, Len Birman; **D:** Steven Hilliard Stern. **VHS, Beta** *DIS*

Undersea Adventures of Captain Nemo: Vol. 1

Primary Not a "20,000 Leagues Under the Sea" adaptation, but a modern-day cartoon series with Captain Mark Nemo and his crew of the research submarine Nautilus on a series of daring voyages and rescues. Heavy on the ecological themes. Additional volumes available.
1975 60m/C VHS, Beta *FHE*

The Undersea Adventures of Snelgrove Snail

Primary Group of aquatic puppets sing songs and generally have all kinds of fun together.
1989 45m/C VHS, Beta *FHE*

Undersea Kingdom

Family One of the earlier Republic serials, but not one of the greats. Ray "Crash" Corrigan, usually seen above sea level as a cowboy hero, battles the tyrants in the lost city of Atlantis. In 12 chapters of 13 minutes each; first one runs 20 minutes. Later re-edited down into the feature "Sharad of Atlantis."
1936 226m/B Ray Corrigan, Lon Chaney Jr.; **D:** B. Reeves Eason. **VHS, LV** *NOS, SNC, VCN*

Unicorn Tales 1

Preschool-Primary Four stories for children, adapted from classic fairy tales, and told in a modern way, with music. Includes "The Magic Pony Ride" (based on the Ugly Duckling), "The Stowaway" (based on Pinocchio), "Carnival Circus" (based on Cinderella), and "The Maltese Unicorn" (based on The Boy Who Cried Wolf). Additional volumes available.
1980 90m/C VHS, Beta *FOX*

Unidentified Flying Oddball

G/Family Astronaut (Dennis Dugan) and his identical-twin robot co-pilot find their spaceship turning into a time machine that throws them back into Camelot and at the mercy of Merlin the magician. Farcical fantasy from Disney (with good special effects), based on Mark Twain's "A Connecticut Yankee at King Arthur's Court." Ages 8 to 12.
1979 92m/C Dennis Dugan, Jim Dale, Ron Moody, Kenneth More, Rodney Bewes; **D:** Russ Mayberry. **VHS, Beta** *DIS*

Unknown Island

Family The "Jurassic Park" of 1948, about an expedition to an remote island where dinosaurs still exist, though much screen time goes to a King Kong impersonator. Prehistoric special f/x all around.

Violence.

1948 76m/C Virginia Grey, Philip Reed, Richard Denning, Barton MacLane; **D:** Jack Bernhard. **VHS** *NOS, MOV, HEG*

Unsinkable Donald Duck with Huey, Dewey & Louie

G/Family Three vintage Disney cartoons featuring Donald and his nephews: "Sea Scouts," "Donald's Day Off" and "Lion Around."

1945 25m/C VHS, Beta, LV *DIS*

Unstrung Heroes 🦴🦴

PG/Jr. High-Adult Sort of a disease-of-the-week movie as if played by the Marx Brothers, but not nearly as appealing as that sounds. Semi-autobiographical tale of Steven Lidz (Watt), growing up in 1960s California with a mother who is dying of cancer (MacDowell) and an eccentric inventor father (Turturro) who refuses to accept her illness. Steven runs off to live with his uncles (Chaykin and Richards) at a seedy residential hotel. Their apartment is piled high with newspapers and salvaged trash; their minds are similarly cluttered. They believe, for instance, that "Idaho" mensa "Jew-hater" in Cherokee. But the uncles provide honesty and support to Steven. Despite good acting, the pathos and farce don't mesh well, and everything looks brown. And, hey, in only six years MacDowell has gone from hot new babe (in "sex, lies and videotape") to dying mother roles. That has to be a record, even by Hollywood's standards for women.

 Dying mother and mentally unbalanced uncles are a handful for young minds.

1995 93m/C Andie MacDowell, John Turturro, Michael Richards, Maury Chaykin, Nathan Watt, Kendra Krull; **D:** Diane Keaton; **W:** Richard LaGravenese; **C:** Phedon Papamichael; **M:** Thomas Newman. **VHS, LV** *HPH*

Untamed Heart 🦴🦴🦴

PG-13/Jr. High-Adult Adam (Slater), the painfully shy busboy with a heart condition, loves Caroline (Tomei), the bubbly waitress, from afar. She doesn't notice him until he saves her from some would-be rapists and their love blooms in the coffee shop where they both work. Tomei and Slater are both strong in the leads and Perez, as Caroline's best buddy Cindy, hurls comic barbs with ease. Charmingly familiar surroundings help set this formulaic romance apart. Filmed on location in Minneapolis. Laserdisc version is in letterbox format.

 Profanity and attempted rape. Slater's character is in a fight and stabbed.

1993 102m/C Christian Slater, Marisa Tomei, Rosie Perez, Kyle Secor, Willie Garson; **D:** Harold Ramis; **W:** Tom Sierchio; **M:** Cliff Eidelman. **VHS, Beta, LV** *MGM*

Up Against the Wall 🦴🦴

PG-13/Jr. High-Adult Black kid from the Chicago projects attends school in the affluent suburbs, but there too he must resist temptation, crime, and violence. Well-intentioned but didactic cautionary drama, adapted from the book by African-American author/commentator Dr. Jawanza Kunjufu.

 Violence, drug use, mature themes.

1991 103m/C Marla Gibbs, Stoney Jackson, Catero Colbert, Ron O'Neal, Salli Richardson; **D:** Ron O'Neal. **VHS** *BMG*

Up Close and Personal 🦴🦴 ⌐

PG-13/Jr. High-Adult Pfeiffer stars as Tally Atwater, a very ambitious would-be newscaster who's taken up by successful veteran Redford. They fall in love but clash about careers. Originally inspired by the tragic life of NBC reporter Jessica Savitch, but resemblance to Savitch is mostly gone. Teen girls will fall for the love story and chemistry between the couple and girls of all ages will fall for Redford.

 Off-screen sex. Tally gets trapped in a prison riot. A character is shot and killed.

1996 124m/C Michelle Pfeiffer, Robert Redford, Kate Nelligan, Stockard Channing, Joe Mantegna, Glenn Plummer, James Rebhorn, Noble Willingham, Scott Bryce, Raymond Cruz, Dedee Pfeiffer, Miguel Sandoval, James Karen; **D:** Jon Avnet; **W:** Joan Didion, John Gregory Dunne; **C:** Karl Walter Lindenlaub; **M:** Thomas Newman. **VHS** *NYR*

Up the Down Staircase 🦴🦴🦴

Jr. High-Adult Naive, newly trained New York public school teacher is determined to teach English literature to a group of poor students. In her first year she grapples not only with kids but also a bureaucratic faculty, a fragile romance, triumph and tragedy. Good production and acting in this straightforward adaptation of Bel Kaufman's celebrated scrapbook-style novel.

 Mature themes.

1967 124m/C Sandy Dennis, Patrick Bedford, Eileen Heckart, Ruth White, Jean Stapleton, Sorrell Booke; **D:** Robert Mulligan. **VHS** *WAR, OM*

The Usual Suspects 🦴🦴🦴 ⌐

R/Sr. High-Adult Twisted noir-thriller about some crooks, a $91 million heist, and a crime lord named Keyser Soze. Customs agent Kujan (Palminteri) is trying to get a straight story out of small-time con man "Verbal" Kint (Spacey). There's a burning tanker in the San Pedro harbor, 27 dead bodies, and a supposed cocaine shipment up in smoke, all related to five temperamental criminals. Forced into doing a job for the infamous Soze, nothing is as it seems, and the ending will leave you shaking your head (and not in dismay). Terrific performances and an Oscar-winning script may warrant viewing by mature

Andie MacDowell reassures son Nathan Watt in "Unstrung Heroes."

teens with a thrill for the twisted. Lots to keep track of, though, so some may get confused.

⚠ BEWARE *Violence, such as close range shootings with sawed-off shot guns; substantial amount of strong language, between criminals and between criminals and police.*

1995 105m/C Kevin Spacey, Gabriel Byrne, Chazz Palminteri, Kevin Pollak, Stephen Baldwin, Benicio Del Toro, Giancarlo Esposito, Pete Postlethwaite, Dan Hedaya, Suzy Amis, Paul Bartel; **D:** Bryan Singer; **W:** Christopher McQuarrie; **C:** Newton Thomas Sigel; **M:** John Ottman. **Award Nominations:** Academy Awards '95: Best Screenplay, Best Supporting Actor (Spacey); Golden Globe Awards '96: Best Supporting Actor (Spacey); Independent Spirit Awards '96: Best Cinematography, Best Screenplay, Best Supporting Actor (Del Toro); **Awards:** National Board of Review Awards '95: Best Supporting Actor (Spacey); New York Film Critics Awards '95: Best Supporting Actor (Spacey). **VHS, LV** *PGV*

Valley Girl 🦴🦴 🦴

R/Sr. High-Adult Teen romantic-comedy is not a film for the young ones, despite glowing reviews that might have made you think otherwise. Leather-jacketed rebel Randy falls for Julie, a trendy California high schooler. But her tightknit clique of friends don't approve. Will Julie drop Randy to keep her popularity? Julie has a nice, honest relationship with her (ex-hippie) parents, and

Cage is great in his first major role, but John Hughes would later do variations on this theme without the brief but exploitive nudity, drugs and sex titillation. Inspired by the popularity of Frank Zappa's novelty tune "Valley Girl," which is just about the only song not heard on the hit-heavy soundtrack.

⚠ BEWARE *Exploitive nudity, sex, profanity, drug use and fighting. Not for kids.*

1983 95m/C Nicolas Cage, Deborah Foreman, Colleen Camp, Frederic Forrest; **D:** Martha Coolidge. **VHS, Beta, LV** *VES*

The Valley of Gwangi 🦴🦴🦴

G/Family "Jurassic Park" goes west, as cowboys discover a lost valley of dinosaurs and try to capture a vicious, carnivorous allosaurus for a carnival. The creatures (including an adorable, miniature prehistoric horse) move via the stop-motion model animation by f/x maestro Ray Harryhausen, here at his finest.

⚠ BEWARE *Dinosaur roughhousing.*

1969 95m/C James Franciscus, Gila Golan, Richard Carlson, Laurence Naismith, Freda Jackson; **D:** James O'Connolly. **VHS, Beta, LV** *WAR*

Velveteen Rabbit

Preschool-Primary Discarded stuffed toy rabbit finds the meaning of love and receives a fabulous gift. Beautifully told Canadian version of the classic Margery Williams fairy tale.

1985 30m/C VHS, Beta *FHE*

Velveteen Rabbit

Family Classic Margery Williams story of a toy rabbit that wants to be real, presented by the Enchanted Musical Playhouse.

1985 60m/C Marie Osmond. **VHS** *VTR*

The Velveteen Rabbit

Preschool-Primary Margery Williams' well-known children's story gets a new rendering in this cassette.

1988 30m/C VHS *RAN, KUI, VEC*

Vengeance of the Space Pirate

Family Fully animated space fantasy for kids, from the Japanese creators of the similar "Space Warriors: Battle for Earth Station S/1."

1987 102m/C Beta *JFK*

A Very Brady Sequel

PG-13/Family They're back! The cast from the surprise hit "The Brady Bunch Movie" returns and if you dug the first flick, you'll probably think this one is pretty groovy, too. Brady mom Carol is shocked when her presumed dead first husband suddenly appears on their doorstep and could possibly shake up the perfect sunshine world of the Bradys. They must travel to Hawaii in an attempt to save the family, and along the way they experience tikis and tarantulas (and that spooky background music!). Based on a three-part episode from the original TV series, this one's sure to please Brady fans of all shapes and sizes.

> **BEWARE** *Sex-related humor and drug content. Watch out for innuendos about Greg and Marcia.*

1996 ?m/C Shelley Long, Gary Cole, Tim Matheson, Christopher Daniel Barnes, Christine Taylor, Paul Sutera, Jennifer Elise Cox, Henriette Mantel, Olivia Hack, Jesse Lee; **D:** Arlene Sanford; **W:** Harry Elfont, Deborah Kaplan, Stan Zimmerman, James Berg. **VHS** *NYR*

A Very Merry Cricket

Family Cartoon in which the adventurous Chester C. Cricket sets out to rescue the real spirit of Christmas from rampant commercialism. Sequel to "The Cricket in Times Square."

1973 30m/C D: Chuck Jones; **V:** Mel Blanc. **VHS, Beta** *FHE*

Vice Versa

PG/Jr. High-Adult Another oft-rerun '80s comedy plot about a workaholic father and his 11-year-old son who switch bodies, with predictable slapstick results. Reinhold and Savage carry this, appearing to have a great time in spite of secondhand story.

> **BEWARE** *Profanity and sex talk.*

1988 97m/C Judge Reinhold, Fred Savage, Swoosie Kurtz, David Proval, Corinne Bohrer, Jane Kaczmarek, William Prince, Gloria Gifford; **D:** Brian Gilbert; **W:** Dick Clement, Ian LaFrenais; **M:** David Shire. **VHS, Beta, LV** *COL*

Victory

PG/Jr. High-Adult Soccer match between WWII prisoners of war and their captors, a German team, gives the players a chance to escape through the sewer tunnels. But the game's heating up; should the Allied athletes bolt to freedom or stay to beat the Nazis on the field? Not particularly believable as either a sports flick (even with Pele and other soccer stars) or a great escape, but watchable.

> **BEWARE** *Violence, but not as bad as you might expect.*

1981 116m/C Sylvester Stallone, Michael Caine, Max von Sydow, Pele, Carole Laure, Bobby Moore, Daniel Massey; **D:** John Huston; **W:** Jeff Maguire, Djordje Milicevic; **M:** Bill Conti. **VHS, Beta** *FOX, WAR*

A View to a Kill

PG/Jr. High-Adult This James Bond mission takes him to the United States, where he must stop the evil Max Zorin from destroying California's Silicon Valley. Feeble and unexciting plot with unscary villain. Duran Duran performs the catchy title tune. Moore's last appearance as 007.

> **BEWARE** *Spy-style violence, sex and alcohol use (shaken, not stirred).*

1985 131m/C Roger Moore, Christopher Walken, Tanya Roberts, Grace Jones, Patrick Macnee, Lois Maxwell, Dolph Lundgren, Desmond Llewelyn; **D:** John Glen; **W:** Michael G. Wilson; **M:** John Barry. **VHS, Beta, LV** *FOX, TLF*

The Villain

PG/Jr. High-Adult Labored spoof of westerns that gets its gags from the "Roadrunner" cartoons. Douglas plays Cactus Jack, a bandit who keeps trying to kidnap a fair damsel or wipe out the simple-minded cowboy hero "Handsome Stranger" (early Schwarzenegger) accompanying her. But the pair ride on obliviously as Jack knocks himself off cliffsides, blows himself up, etc. This worked in a 10-minute Chuck Jones 'toon, but here it's slowed to feature length. Kids might be amused.

> **BEWARE** *Roughhousing, cartoon violence.*

1979 93m/C Kirk Douglas, Ann-Margret, Arnold Schwarzenegger, Paul Lynde, Foster Brooks, Ruth Buzzi, Jack Elam, Strother Martin, Robert Tessier, Mel Tillis; **D:** Hal Needham. **VHS** *COL*

Vip, My Brother Superman

Family The Vips are modern-day descendants of superbeings about to become legends in their own times. SuperVip is broad of chest and pure in spirit while his brother MiniVip possesses only limited powers. From the

creator of "Allegro Non Troppo" comes this enticing, amusing piece of animation.
1990 90m/C D: Bruno Bozzetto. **VHS** *EXP, TPV*

Visionaries, Vol. 1: The Age of Magic Begins

Family Through an inexplicable turn of the planets, Prysmos is left in the dark. The sorcery of the middle ages prevails in this stricken land, and the visionaries, with their feel for the future, must restore the universe to proper balance . . . oh yes, and Visionaries action figures with real holographs were available at shopping centers everywhere. Additional volumes available.
1987 30m/C VHS, Beta

Voyage to the Bottom of the Sea 🦴🦴🦴

Family Crew of an atomic submarine must destroy a deadly radiation belt which has set the polar ice cap ablaze. Fun stuff, with good special effects and photography. Later became a television show.
1961 106m/C Walter Pidgeon, Joan Fontaine, Barbara Eden, Peter Lorre, Robert Sterling, Michael Ansara, Frankie Avalon; **D:** Irwin Allen; **W:** Irwin Allen, Charles Bennett. **VHS, Beta, LV** *FOX, FCT*

Voyager from the Unknown

Family Feature-length compilation from the short-lived TV series "Voyagers." Phineas Boggs is a time-traveller with a mission to fix any details of history that go astray. A little orphan named Jeffrey (who's considerably smarter) gets to accompany the hapless hero.
1983 91m/C Jon-Erik Hexum, Meeno Peluce, Ed Begley Jr., Faye Grant, Fionnula Flanagan. **VHS, Beta** *MCA*

Vrrrooommm! Farming for Kids

Preschool-Primary Farmer Bill visits a 7000-acre family-run vegetable and grain farm in Upstate New York to educate children on how the nation's food supply is produced. Tractors, combines and cultivators are shown in action planting and harvesting wheat, sweet corn, beans, carrots and cabbage. Farmer Bill shows how farming is like everyday family activities to help explain the processes. Was a finalist in the 1995 Telly Awards.
1995 30m/C VHS

Wackiest Wagon Train in the West 🦴

G/Family Hapless wagon master is saddled with a dummy assistant as they guide a party of five characters across the West. Based on the short-lived TV sitcom "Dusty's Trail." Produced by the same folks who delivered the series "Gilligan's Island," which this closely resembles.
1977 86m/C Bob Denver, Forrest Tucker, Jeannine Riley. **VHS, Beta** *MED*

Wacky & Packy

Family Cartoon series collection about a caveman and his woolly mammoth in the modern world, causing trouble wherever they go.
1975 70m/C VHS, Beta *PSM*

The Wacky World of Mother Goose

Preschool-Primary Rankin-Bass production for small fry, featuring their distinct stop-motion animation previously seen in the likes of "Daydreamer" and "Mad Monster Party." Storybook characters like Tom Thumb, Mother Hubbard, Sleeping Beauty, Jack Horner and even the Three Men in a Tub figure in a conspiracy by Count Warptwist to take the place of Mother Goose.
1967 81m/C V: Margaret Rutherford. **VHS, Beta** *COL*

Wagons East 🦴 ˒

PG-13/Jr. High-Adult Pioneers head west and then change their minds. Candy (who died during filming) plays the drunken former wagonmaster hired to get them back home, but he's oddly underused. Script does little in the way of original or inventively recycled humor, making genre parody head east slowly.

 Fighting and off-color humor

1994 100mm/C John Candy, Richard Lewis, Ellen Greene, John C. McGinley, Robert Picardo, William Sanderson, Thomas F. Duffy, Russell Means, Rodney Grant, Michael Horse, Gailard Sartain, Lochlyn Munro, Stuart Proud Eagle Grant; **D:** Peter Markle; **W:** Matthew Carlson. **VHS** *NYR*

Waif Goodbye to the Paw Paws

Family Aunt Pruney dresses up as a waif to trick the Paw Paws, but her plan is nipped in the bud by Dark Paw. He conjures up a terrible lightning storm to teach her a lesson she'll never forget. Ripped from today's headlines, this obscure 'toon comes from Hanna-Barbera.
1990 30m/C VHS, Beta *TTC*

Wait Till Your Mother Gets Home 🦴🦴

Family "Mr. Mom"-like zaniness abounds as a football coach cares for the kids and does chores while his wife takes her first job in 15 years. Almost too darn cute, but well written. Made for TV.
1983 97m/C Paul Michael Glaser, Dee Wallace Stone, Peggy McKay, David Doyle, Raymond Buktenica, James Gregory, Joey Lawrence, Lynne Moody; **D:** Bill Persky. **VHS, Beta** *PSM*

Wait Until Spring, Bandini 🦴🦴 ˒

PG-13/Jr. High-Family Flavorful immigrant tale about a transplanted Italian family weathering the winter in 1925 Colorado, as seen through the eyes of a young son. Alternately funny and moving, with one of Dunaway's scenery-chewing performances as a local temptation for the father. Based on the autobiographical novel by John Fante, co-produced by Francis Ford Coppola.

 Mature themes, mainly brief marital straying.

1990 104m/C Joe Mantegna, Faye Dunaway, Burt Young, Ornella Muti, Alex Vincent, Renata Vanni, Michael Bacall, Daniel Wilson; ***D:*** Dominique Deruddere; ***M:*** Angelo Badalamenti. **VHS** *WAR*

Waiting for the Light 🦴🦴ᵛ

PG/Jr. High-Adult Lightweight comedy set amid small-town panic during the Cuban missile crisis. Chicago-transplant Garr and her two kids inherit a diner in the Pacific Northwest. Aunt Zena (MacLaine), a magician, arrives and after some unlikely events, is mistaken for an angel by the gullible townspeople. The divine sighting becomes a boost for restaurant business. Professional troupe keeps the less-than-heavenly story flying.

 Profanity.

1990 94m/C Shirley MacLaine, Teri Garr, Vincent Schiavelli, John Bedford Lloyd; ***D:*** Christopher Monger; ***W:*** Christopher Monger. **VHS, LV, 8mm** *COL*

Waiting to Exhale 🦴🦴🦴

R/Sr. High-Adult Four upper middle class African-American women complain incessantly about men and their lousy love lives in this adaptation of Terry McMillan's bestselling novel. Sexually explicit, filled with profanity and bearing the message "men bad, women good," this is no film for children, except the most mature high school students.

 Serious sex and profanity. Themes of divorce and extramarital affairs.

1995 120m/C Whitney Houston, Angela Bassett, Loretta Devine, Lela Rochon, Gregory Hines, Dennis Haysbert, Mykelti Williamson, Michael Beach, Leon, Wendell Pierce, Donald A. Faison, Jeffrey D. Sams, Toyomichi Kurita; ***Cameos:*** Wesley Snipes; ***D:*** Forest Whitaker; ***W:*** Ronald Bass; ***M:*** Babyface. **Award Nominations:** MTV Movie Awards '96: Breakthrough Performance (Rochon), Best Song ("Exhale (Shoop Shoop)"); **Awards:** MTV Movie Awards '96: Best Song ("Sittin' Up in My Room"). **VHS** *TCF*

A Walk in the Clouds 🦴🦴ᵛ

PG-13/Jr. High-Adult Set in the 1940s, when one could still find romance on a bus trip. Keanu Reeves is a veteran home from the war who befriends a young woman (Aitana Sanchez-Gijon) on a bus. Turns out she's a college student who's been impregnated by a married professor. She's returning home to her strict and wealthy wine-making family and, boy, are they going to be mad. He has a wife, but Reeves agrees to pose as her husband long enough for her to get settled at home. Complications ensue, the biggest one being that Reeves and Sanchez-Gijon fall in love. Beautiful to look at, especially the nighttime scene in which everyone dons a pair of wings to wave fires' warmth at frost-threatened grapevines. Predictable, but well-acted and romantic. Ages 12 and up.

 Pre-marital pregnancy. Sex. (Sort of figures, no?)

1995 103m/C Keanu Reeves, Aitana Sanchez-Gijon, Giancarlo Giannini, Anthony Quinn, Angelica Aragon, Evangelina Elizondo, Freddy Rodriguez, Debra Messing; ***D:*** Alfonso Arau; ***W:*** Robert Mark Kamen; ***C:*** Emmanuel Lubezki; ***M:*** Leo Brower. **Award Nominations:** MTV Movie Awards '96: Most Desirable Male (Reeves), Best Kiss (Keanu Reeves/Aitana Sanchez-Gijon); **Awards:** Golden Globe Awards '96: Best Score. **VHS** *FXV*

Walk Like a Man 🦴ᵛ

PG/Jr. High-Adult In a take-off of Tarzan movies, Mandel is a man raised by wolves. Comic problems arise when he is found by his mother and the family attempts to civilize him. Juvenile script wastes fine cast.

1987 86m/C Howie Mandel, Christopher Lloyd, Cloris Leachman, Colleen Camp, Amy Steel, George DiCenzo; ***D:*** Melvin Frank. **VHS, Beta** *MGM*

Walking on Air

Family In the near future, paralyzed adolescent Danny realizes that he and his wheelchair-bound friends are prisoners of gravity; in the weightlessness of space they would have full mobility. He campaigns to allow disabled kids into the space program. Uplifting (in more ways than one) "WonderWorks" story, based on an idea by sci-fi author Ray Bradbury, which explains why a "Bradbury Science Museum" figures prominently in the plot.

1987 60m/C Lynn Redgrave, Jordan Marder, James Treuer, Katheryn Trainor; ***D:*** Ed Kaplan. **VHS** *PME, FCT, BTV*

Walking Tall 🦴🦴ᵛ

R/Sr. High-Adult Tennessee sheriff takes a stand against syndicate-run gambling and his wife is murdered in response. Ultra-violent crime saga wowed the movie going public and spawned several sequels and a TV series. Based on the true story of folk-hero Buford Pusser, admirably rendered by Baker.

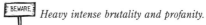 *Heavy intense brutality and profanity.*

1973 126m/C Joe Don Baker, Elizabeth Hartman, Noah Beery Jr., Gene Evans, Rosemary Murphy, Felton Perry; ***D:*** Phil Karlson. **VHS, Beta, LV** *LIV*

Wally Gator

Preschool-Primary Count 'em: 17 episodes from the Hanna-Barbera show about the alligator who resides at the zoo.

1984 80m/C VHS, Beta *TTC*

A Walt Disney Christmas

Family Six classic cartoons with a wintry theme are combined for this program: "Pluto's Christmas Tree" (1952), "On Ice," "Donald's Snowball Fight;" two Silly Symphonies from 1932-33: "Santa's Workshop" and "The Night Before Christmas;" and an excerpt from the 1948

feature "Melody Time," entitled "Once Upon a Wintertime."
1982 46m/C VHS, Beta *DIS*

Walt Disney Films in French

G/Family Exclusive release of well-known Disney films for the French, without English subtitles, recommended for fun language training.
1986 100m/C VHS, Beta *INJ*

The Waltons: A Thanksgiving Story

Family As the Walton family anticipates the Thanksgiving holiday, John-Boy prepares for college entrance exams and Jenny Pendleton's visit. Then John-Boy suffers a head injury and is faced with a risky operation. A holiday special from the television series. Ages 8 and up.
1973 100m/C Richard Thomas, Ralph Waite, Michael Learned, Will Geer, Ellen Corby, Judy Norton-Taylor, Kami Cotler, Jon Walmsley, Mary McDonough, Eric Scott, David W. Harper; *D:* Philip Leacock. **VHS** *IGP*

The Waltons: The Children's Carol 🎵🎵

Family The winter solstice brings no special joy to Walton's Mountain; WWII has taken many men, with short wave reports indicating the Nazi terror spreading across Europe. But huddled in the glow of Walton's barn, the children rediscover the true meaning of Christmas.
1980 94m/C Judy Norton-Taylor, Jon Walmsley, Mary McDonough, Eric Scott, Kami Cotler, Joe Conley, Ronnie Clare, Leslie Winston, Peggy Rea; *D:* Lawrence Dobkin. **VHS, Beta** *ORI*

Waltz King 🎵🎵

Family Typically hokey Disney biography of the young composer Johann Strauss during his old Viennese heyday. Fine music, pretty German locations.
1963 94m/C Kerwin Mathews, Senta Berger, Brian Aherne; *D:* Steve Previn. **VHS, Beta** *DIS*

A Waltz Through the Hills

Family Two orphans head into the Australian outback and experience many adventures en route to the coast where they can set sail for England and their grandparents. Part of the "Wonderworks" series.
1988 116m/C Tina Kemp, Andre Jansen, Ernie Dingo, Dan O'Herlihy; *D:* Frank Arnold. **VHS** *PME, HMV, FCT*

War Games 🎵🎵🎵

PG/Jr. High-Adult Teen computer hacker, thinking that he's sneaking an advance look at a new line of video games, breaks into the US missile-defense system and challenges it to a game of Global Thermonuclear Warfare. The game might just turn out to be the real thing if the boy can't stop it. Oft-imitated formula of high-tech whiz kids getting into trouble has seldom been better; plot moves like gangbusters, though it slackens toward the end.

🚫 BEWARE 🚫 *Profanity and potential apocalypse.*

1983 110m/C Matthew Broderick, Dabney Coleman, John Wood, Ally Sheedy; *D:* John Badham; *W:* Walter F. Parkes, Lawrence Lasker. **VHS, Beta, LV** *FOX*

War of the Buttons 🎵🎵 ♭

PG/Primary-Adult Two sleepy Irish fishing villages provide childish battle grounds for two groups of local lads. The Ballys (Ballydowse village), lead by Fergus (Fitzgerald), and the Carricks (Carrickdowse), with leader Geronimo (Coffey), have an intense rivalry and capture by the other gang leads to the removal of every clothing button for the unfortunate captive. When Fergus becomes a Carrick victim, he organizes a retaliatory strike, and emotions threaten to overwhelm all concerned. Based on the French novel "La Guerre des Boutons" by Louis Pergaud. Filmed on location in West Cork, Ireland.

🚫 BEWARE 🚫 *Some mild language.*

1995 94m/C Gregg Fitzgerald, John Coffey, Liam Cunningham, Paul Batt, Eveanna Ryan, Colm Meaney, Johnny Murphy; *D:* John Roberts; *W:* Colin Welland; *C:* Bruno de Keyzer; *M:* Rachel Portman. **VHS** *WAR*

The War of the Worlds 🎵🎵🎵 ♭

Family H.G. Wells's classic novel of the invasion of Earth by Martians, updated to 1950s California, with spectacular special effects of destruction caused by the Martian war machines. Pretty scary and tense; based more on Orson Welles's radio broadcast than on the book. Still very popular; hit the top 20 in sales when released on video. Classic thriller later made into a TV series. Produced by George Pal (appearing in cameo as a street person), who brought the world much sci-fi, including "The Time Machine," "Destination Moon," and "When Worlds Collide."
1953 85m/C Gene Barry, Ann Robinson, Les Tremayne, Lewis Martin, Robert Cornthwaite, Sandro Giglio; *D:* Byron Haskin. **Award Nominations:** Academy Awards '53: Best Film Editing, Best Sound; **Awards:** Academy Awards '53: Best Special Effects. **VHS, Beta, LV** *PAR*

Warriors of the Wind 🎵🎵

PG/Jr. High-Adult Re-edited American release of the Japanese animated feature "Nausicaa," about a fantasy world where kingdoms fight their petty wars in the shadow of the dominant life form—enormous, vaguely godlike caterpillar insects. As always, there's one of those prophecies promising that a human messiah will bring peace to people and bugs alike; best to ignore the story and marvel at the creature designs.

🚫 BEWARE 🚫 *Violence.*

1985 85m/C *D:* Kazuo Komatsubara. **VHS, Beta** *NWV, VTR*

Watcher in the Woods 🎔 ♭

PG/Family American family rents an English country house, and their children are haunted by blue lights and ghostly visions of a long-missing young girl. Ill-fated early excursion by Disney into PG territory; after a few good scares the story builds to a sloppy, unsatisfying conclusion, hastily re-edited from an original aha!-it-was-aliens cop-out that bombed with preview audiences. Based on a novel by Florence Engel Randall.

1981 83m/C Bette Davis, Carroll Baker, David McCallum, Ian Bannen, Lynn-Holly Johnson; **D:** John Hough; **W:** Brian Clemens. **VHS, Beta** *DIS*

Water Babies 🎔🎔

G/Family When a chimney sweep's 12-year-old apprentice is wrongly accused of stealing silver, the boy and his dog fall into a pond and eventually rescue some of the characters they find there. Combination of live-action and animated fairytale story set in 19th-century London. Based on the book by Charles Kingsley. Boring, unless you're a young child with equivalent standards.

1979 93m/C James Mason, Billie Whitelaw, David Tomlinson, Paul Luty, Sammantha Coates; **D:** Lionel Jeffries. **VHS, Beta**

Watership Down 🎔🎔🎔

PG/Jr. High-Adult Although it's an animated cartoon about rabbits, this is no kiddie movie. Wonderfully animated story based on Richard Adams' novel about rabbits displaced when their den is destroyed. The survivors find fear and oppression in other bunny societies while searching for a new and better home. Ages 10 and up.

🟦 BEWARE 🟦 *Animal violence and cruelty by animals towards other animals.*

1978 92m/C D: Martin Rosen; **W:** Martin Rosen; **V:** Ralph Richardson, Zero Mostel, John Hurt, Denholm Elliott, Harry Andrews, Michael Hordern, Joss Ackland. **VHS, Beta, 8mm** *WAR, TVC*

Waterworld 🎔🎔 ♭

PG-13/Jr. High-Adult Despite jokesters' calling this $150 million film "Fishtar" and "Kevin's Gate," the Kevins (star Costner and director Reynolds) had the last laugh. When American and overseas (sorry) receipts were totaled, the movie made a profit. Costner is Mariner, a man with a little fish in his bloodline who reluctantly helps humans search for the possibly mythical Dryland in a world flooded when the polar ice caps melt. The bad guys, who have oil and thus vessels with engines, are led by Hopper, who can play these roles in his sleep. Entertaining, but long.

🟦 BEWARE 🟦 *Some intense scenes of action violence, brief nudity and profanity. Costner's character is pretty mean to a little girl.*

1995 135m/C Kevin Costner, Dennis Hopper, Jeanne Tripplehorn, Tina Majorino, Michael Jeter, R.D. Call, Robert Joy; **D:** Kevin Reynolds; **W:** Peter Rader, Marc Norman, David N. Twohy; **C:** Dean Semler; **M:** James Newton Howard. **VHS, LV** *MCA*

The Way We Were 🎔🎔🎔

PG/Jr. High-Adult Big box-office hit follows a love story between opposites from the 1930s to the 1950s. Streisand is a Jewish political radical who meets the handsome WASP Redford at college. They're immediately attracted to one another, but it takes years before they act on it and eventually marry. They move to Hollywood where Redford is a screenwriter and left-wing Streisand becomes involved in the Red scare and the blacklist, much to Redford's dismay. Will their obvious differences drive them apart? Old-fashioned and sweet romance, with much gloss. Hit title song sung by Streisand. Adapted by Arthur Laurents from his novel.

 *Mature themes.*

1973 118m/C Barbra Streisand, Robert Redford, Bradford Dillman, Viveca Lindfors, Herb Edelman, Murray Hamilton, Patrick O'Neal, James Woods, Sally Kirkland; **D:** Sydney Pollack; **W:** Arthur Laurents; **M:** Marvin Hamlisch. **Award Nominations:** Academy Awards '73: Best Actress (Streisand), Best Art Direction/Set Decoration, Best Cinematography; Academy Awards '76: Best Costume Design; **Awards:** Academy Awards '73: Best Song ("The Way We Were"), Best Original Score; Golden Globe Awards '74: Best Song ("The Way We Were"); National Board of Review Awards '73: 10 Best Films of the Year. **VHS, Beta, LV, 8mm** *COL*

Wayne's World 🎔🎔 ♭

PG-13/Jr. High-Adult Surprise-hit comedy based on a "Saturday Night Live" sketch about two rock-loving Illinois teen guys who have their own basement cable-TV show, which they make entertaining by sheer force of their ebullient personalities. Joke is that both Wayne and Garth are played by adult comics, their teenspeak slang and trend-spoofing adventures an affectionate parody of modern youth culture. Good-natured but probably not destined to last; this film's references to early '90s topics already makes it look like a relic. "Wayne's World 2," released a year later, is more of the same, no more and no less. A video compilation of original "Wayne's World" sketches from "Saturday Night Live" is also available.

🟦 BEWARE 🟦 *Horny guys, profanity, crudity and playing with food.*

1992 93m/C Mike Myers, Dana Carvey, Rob Lowe, Tia Carrere, Brian Doyle-Murray, Lara Flynn Boyle, Kurt Fuller, Colleen Camp, Donna Dixon, Ed O'Neill; **Cameos:** Alice Cooper, Meat Loaf; **D:** Penelope Spheeris; **W:** Mike Myers, Bonnie Turner, Terry Turner; **M:** J. Peter Robinson. **VHS, LV** *PAR, FCT*

Wayne's World 2 🎔🎔

PG-13/Jr. High-Adult Good-natured rerun of the original has plenty of sophomoric gags, but feels tired. Wayne and Garth are on their own, planning a major concert, Waynestock. "If you book them they will come," Jim Morrison says in a dream. Meanwhile, Wayne's girlfriend (Carrere) is falling for slimeball record promoter Walken. Offers a few brilliantly funny segments. If you liked the "Bohemian Rhapsody" spot in the original, get ready for the Village People here. Heston has a funny

The boys square off in "War of the Buttons."

cameo, and Walken and Basinger push the limits without going over the top. Feature film debut for director Surjik.

 Sex talk.

1993 94m/C Mike Myers, Dana Carvey, Tia Carrere, Christopher Walken, Ralph Brown, Kim Basinger, James Hong, Chris Farley, Ed O'Neill, Olivia D'Abo, Kevin Pollak, Drew Barrymore; ***Cameos:*** Charlton Heston, Rip Taylor; **D:** Stephen Surjik; **W:** Mike Myers, Bonnie Turner, Terry Turner; **M:** Carter Burwell. **VHS, Beta** *PAR*

We All Have Tales

Primary Rabbit Ears, the media outfit noted for combining celebrity narrators and musicians with good scripts and beautiful fade-in animation, offers entertaining tales from around the world and closer to home. Here is a sampling: Denzel Washington tells "Anansi," from Jamaica; William Hurt tells "The Boy Who Drew Cats," from Japan; Danny Glover tells the African-American story, "Bre'r Rabbit;" Max Von Sydow tells "East of the Sun, West of the Moon," from Scandinavia; Catherine O'Hara tells "Finn McCoul," from Ireland; Robin Williams has a ball with "The Fool and the Flying Ship," from Russia; Michael Palin tells "Jack and the Beanstalk," from England; Michael Caine tells "King Midas," from ancient Greece; Whoopi Goldberg tells "Koi and the Kola Nuts,"

from Africa; Raul Julia tells "The Monkey People," from South America; Sigourney Weaver tells "Peachboy," from Japan; Danny Aiello tells "Pinocchio," from Italy; Tracey Ullman has fun with French accents as she tells "Puss In Boots;" Kathleen Turner tells "Rumpelstiltskin," from Germany, and Ben Kingsley tells "The Tiger and the Brahmin," from India. Ages 4 to 11.

1991 30m/C VHS *SVE, RAB,*

We of the Never Never 🦴🦴🦴

G/Family The Rescuers may have had to go Down Under but the Wilderness Family were saved the trip by this sincere and well-done drama based on the memoirs of Jeannie Gunn, a pioneer woman in turn-of-the-century Australia. The city-bred heroine marries a rancher and moves from civilized Melbourne to the barren outback of the Northern Territory. There she must fight for her rights as well as for those of the aborigines.

1982 136m/C Angela Punch McGregor, Arthur Dignam, Tony Barry; **D:** Igor Auzins. **VHS, Beta** *COL*

We Think the World is Round

Preschool-Primary Animated adventure about Christopher Columbus's voyage to the new world. Only this time the story is told by his three sailing ships, the Nina, the

Pinta, and the Santa Maria. "Look Who's Talking," 1492 style.
1992 30m/C VHS *TTC, BTV*

Wee Sing: Grandpa's Magical Toys

Preschool-Primary Filled with songs, the Wee Sing series of live action videos also offers a decent narrative framework on which to hang its tunes, plus colorful costumes and fanciful sets. In this one, a playful grandfather leads children through a special fantasy wonderland where toys come to life and the songs are singable. Ages 1 to 6.
1988 60m/C VHS *PSS, MLT, THP*

Wee Sing in Sillyville

Preschool-Primary Two children visit the land of Sillyville where the townspeople teach them the meaning of friendship. Silly songs include "The Little Green Frog," "I'm a Nut" and "Roll over." Ages 1 to 6.
1990 60m/C VHS *MLT, THP*

Wee Sing in the Big Rock Candy Mountains

Preschool-Primary When Lisa's friends leave her to go play, her two stuffed Snoodle Doodles (bears) come to life, and together they all go to the magical Big Rock Candy Mountain. There Lisa meets characters in traditional children's songs who sing and play with her. Ages 1 to 6.
1991 60m/C VHS *PSS*

Wee Sing: In the Marvelous Musical Mansion

Preschool-Primary Three children learn about music and self-esteem as they explore a mansion and try to solve a mystery. Songs include "My Hat It Has Three Corners," "Reuben and Rachel," and "When the Saints Go Marching In." Ages 1 to 6.
1992 72m/C VHS *PSS, MLT*

Wee Sing: The Best Christmas Ever!

Preschool-Primary Popular Christmas songs are here for kids to sing along with, from "Deck the Halls" to "We Wish You a Merry Christmas." Ages 1 to 6.
1990 60m/C VHS *PSS, THP*

Wee Sing Together

Preschool-Primary An enchanting mixture of live-action and special effects, encourages kids to sing along with "Old Macdonald," "I'm A Little Teapot," "B-I-N-G-O" and other songs. Ages 1 to 6.
1985 60m/C VHS *PSS, MLT, THP*

Meet the Star of Waterworld, Tina Majorino

Tina Majorino made her acting debut at age two and one-half, playing an oyster in a local production of "Alice in Wonderland." She loved the experience, and today at ten, Majorino is one of the most sought after child actors around.

After much begging on Tina's part in the wake of her stage debut, her mother permitted her to take on other acting jobs. She began, like many actors, by appearing in commercials, then she landed a role on a short-lived television series. At eight, she beat out 500 competitors to land the role in *When a Man Loves a Woman*, her big screen breakthrough, and in *Corrina, Corrina*, she got a chance to sing with co-star Whoopi Goldberg. The same year she appeared opposite a sea lion—playing a character whose personality strongly resembles her own—in *Andre*. Next, in 1994, she landed a part playing an orphan taken in by Kevin Costner in the notoriously problem-plagued *Waterworld*.

Majorino lives in Southern California's San Fernando Valley with her real estate broker father, her mother, and a fifteen-year-old brother, as well as a menagerie of animals that includes a parakeet and a cockatoo she acquired on the set of *Waterworld*. She attends the local public school, where she is a sixth grader, and she claims that her extracurricular interests include karate, hiking, climbing trees, and making forts.

Wee Sing Train

Preschool-Primary Casey and Carter imagine themselves as passengers aboard their toy train, along with Tusky the elephant, Chug-a-long the Engine, and Cubby the Caboose. You bet, they sing "I've Been Working on the Railroad." Also "Down By the Station," "Get On Board" and more. Ages 1 to 6.
1993 58m/C VHS *PSS, BTV*

Wee Sing Under the Sea

Preschool-Primary A boy and his artist grandmother dive into her undersea-scape and sing along with friendly, colorful creatures like Spike the beret-wearing puffer fish, Weeber the penguin and Stella the stuck-up starfish. Features more than 20 original and classic songs all about the ocean.
1994 60m/C VHS *PSS*

Wee Wendy

Family Wee Wendy and her people are aliens who land on earth and set up a village on an island in a lake, in this children's animated movie.
1989 100m/C VHS, Beta *CEL*

Wee Willie Winkie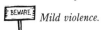

PG/Family Precocious little girl is taken in by a British regiment in India and manages to resolve conflict between the colonials and the rebels. Although directed by Ford in a departure from his usual rugged western, it's still a sugar-coated treat; if you're a cinematic diabetic, be forewarned. Inspired by the Rudyard Kipling story.

> [BEWARE] *Mild violence.*

1937 99m/B Shirley Temple, Victor McLaglen, Sir C. Aubrey Smith, June Lang, Michael Whalen, Cesar Romero, Constance Collier; **D:** John Ford. **VHS, Beta** *FOX*

Weekend at Bernie's

PG-13/Jr. High-Adult Two computer nerds discover embezzlement at their workplace after being invited to their boss's beach house for a weekend party. They find their host murdered. They endeavor to keep up appearances by (you guessed it) dressing and strategically posing the corpse during the party. Kiser as the dead man is memorable, and the two losers gamely keep the silliness flowing. Lots of fun.

> [BEWARE] *Profanity, drug overdose and wild parties at the beach. Woman has sex with a corpse off-screen. Lots of shooting.*

1989 101m/C Andrew McCarthy, Jonathan Silverman, Catherine Mary Stewart, Terry Kiser, Don Calfa, Louis Giambalvo; **D:** Ted Kotcheff; **W:** Robert Klane; **M:** Andy Summers. **VHS, VHS, Beta** *LIV*

Weekend at Bernie's 2

PG/Jr. High-Adult Unlikely but routine sequel to the original's cavorting cadaver slapstick, except now McCarthy and Silverman are frantically hunting for Bernie's (Kiser) cash stash, a quest that takes them and poor dead Bernie to the Caribbean. See Bernie get stuffed in a suitcase, see Bernie hang glide, see Bernie tango, see Bernie attract the opposite sex. Thin script with one-joke premise done to death but fun for those in the mood for the postmortem antics of a comedic stiff. Plenty of well-executed gags involving the well-preserved corpse (particularly one that's been dead for two films now) should lure back fans of the 1989 original.

> [BEWARE] *Profanity. More stiff dead jokes.*

1993 89m/C Andrew McCarthy, Jonathan Silverman, Terry Kiser, Tom Wright, Steve James, Troy Beyer, Barry Bostwick; **D:** Robert Klane; **W:** Robert Klane; **M:** Peter Wolf. **VHS, LV** *COL*

Weird Science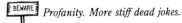

PG-13/Jr. High-Adult Two sex-starved high school computer geeks use their software skills to materialize the ideal woman. Acting as a sort of seductive fairy godmother, she wreaks 'zany' havoc in their lives from the outset. The actors are sometimes appealing, and even with this lame-o plot Hughes can write teen dialogue with the best of them, but many of the jokes are in poor taste, and the gaudy comic tale seems to go on forever.

> [BEWARE] *Much talk of sex and body functions. Roughhousing, nudity.*

1985 94m/C Kelly Le Brock, Anthony Michael Hall, Ilan Mitchell-Smith, Robert Downey Jr., Bill Paxton; **D:** John Hughes; **W:** John Hughes; **M:** Ira Newborn. **VHS, Beta, LV** *MCA*

Welcome Back Wil Cwac Cwac

Family Ten more short TV cartoons for the very young, with the hapless duckling from Welsh TV.
1990 43m/C VHS, Beta *FHE*

Welcome Home, Roxy Carmichael

PG-13/Preschool-Jr. High Caustic satire of teen angst and small-town society in a vapid Ohio community eagerly awaiting a visit by Hollywood superstar Carmichael, a local vixen who cleared out years ago. Soulful 15-year-old misfit named Dinky—loathed and mistreated by most everyone—decides she's Roxy's long-lost daughter, but if anything, Ryder's moody performance suggests blood ties to the Addams Family. Offbeat material definitely strikes a nerve or two, but "Roxy's" relentless bitterness and hateful characters soon wear out welcome.

> [BEWARE] *Profanity, sex talk, mature themes. The legendary Roxy is constantly discussed but never clearly seen, except for her bare backside during a nude swim.*

1990 98m/C Winona Ryder, Jeff Daniels, Laila Robins, Dinah Manoff, Ava Fabian, Robbie Kiger, Sachi Parker; **D:** Jim Abrahams. **VHS, Beta, LV, 8mm** *PAR*

Kevin Costner as the Mariner in "Waterworld."

Welcome to Pooh Corner: Vol. 1

Family Disney's series of made-for-video episodes use Winnie the Pooh's misadventures in the Hundred Acre Wood to instruct children, both directly and by example, using all Pooh's cronies like Tigger, Christopher Robin, and Eeyore. Additional volumes available.

1984 111m/C VHS, Beta *DIS*

We're Back! A Dinosaur's Story 🎵🎵

G/Family Steven Spielberg put this dinosaur cartoon in theaters at the same time as "Jurassic Park," offering an alternative for young viewers easily scared by the PG-13 monster blockbuster. Commendable idea; disappointing movie, as a talking, time-traveling T.Rex and his prehistoric posse visit modern NYC. Kids befriend the gentle giants, but they're captured by an evil carnival owner (right out of "Something Wicked This Way Comes") intent on returning the reptiles to savagery. Overplotted and disorganized, with merely adequate animation (it seems the smarter dinosaurs are, the simpler they look), adapted and inflated from a children's picture-book by Hudson Talbott.

1993 78m/C D: Dick Zondag, Ralph Zondag, Phil Nibbelink, Simon Wells; **W:** John Patrick Shanley; **V:** John Goodman, Felicity Kendal, Walter Cronkite, Joey Shea, Jay Leno, Julia Child, Kenneth Mars, Martin Short, Rhea Perlman, Rene LeVant, Blaze Berdahl, Charles Fleischer, Yeardley Smith. **VHS** *MCA*

We're Goin' to the Farm with Father Dan

Preschool-Primary Father Dan and his friends take a magical musical journey to the farm to explore the world of farm animals. They feed the animals, herd the cows, bail the hay, and go to the county fair. Ages 3 to 8.

1994 30m/C VHS *TPV*

West Side Story 🎵🎵🎵 ♭

Jr. High-Adult Gang rivalry and ethnic tension on New York's West Side erupts in a ground-breaking musical. Loosely based on Shakespeare's "Romeo and Juliet," the story follows the Jets and the Sharks as they fight for their turf while Tony and Maria fight for love. Features frenetic and brilliant choreography by co-director Robbins, who also directed the original Broadway show, and a high-caliber score by Bernstein and Sondheim. Wood's voice was dubbed by Marni Nixon and Jimmy Bryant dubbed Beymer's. Laserdisc version includes the complete storyboards, production sketches, re-issue trailer, and an interview with Wise in a letterbox format with digital stereo surround sound. 🎵 Prologue; Jet Song; Something's Coming; Dance at the Gym; Maria; America; Tonight; One Hand, One Heart; Gee, Officer Krupke.

1961 151m/C Natalie Wood, Richard Beymer, Russ Tamblyn, Rita Moreno, George Chakiris, Simon Oakland, Ned Glass; **D:** Robert Wise, Jerome Robbins; **W:** Ernest Lehman; **M:** Leonard Bernstein, Stephen Sondheim. **Award Nominations:** Academy Awards '61: Best Adapted Screenplay; **Awards:** Academy Awards '61: Best Art Direction/Set Decoration (Color), Best Color Cinematography, Best Costume Design (Color), Best Director (Wise), Best Film Editing, Best Picture, Best Sound, Best Supporting Actor (Chakiris), Best Supporting Actress (Moreno), Best Score; Directors Guild of America Awards '61: Best Director (Wise), Best Director (Robbins). **VHS, Beta, LV** *MGM, KUI, FOX*

Westward Ho, the Wagons! 🎵🎵

Family Promised land lies west, but to get there America's homesteaders have to cross the arduous Oregon Trail, facing starvation, bandits and Indians both hostile and benign. Overly familiar pioneer yarn from Disney, featuring "Davy Crockett" Parker and four Mouseketeers in the cast. Based on the novel by Mary Jane Carr.

1956 94m/B Fess Parker, Kathleen Crowley, Jeff York, Sebastian Cabot, George Reeves; **D:** William Beaudine. **VHS, Beta** *DIS*

Whale for the Killing 🎵🎵 ♭

Jr. High-Adult Eco-minded TV movie, based on the book by "Never Cry Wolf" author Farley Mowat. Naturalist in a Newfoundland fishing community cares for a stranded humpbacked whale, and confronts locals who want to sell the giant sea creature to Russian whalers. Heavy on the sermonizing, but effective.

1981 145m/C Richard Widmark, Peter Strauss, Dee Wallace Stone, Bruce McGill, Kathryn Walker; **D:** Richard T. Heffron; **M:** Basil Poledouris. **VHS, Beta** *FOX*

Whale of a Tale 🎵🎵

G/Family Young boy trains a killer whale to do tricks in the big show at a Marineland amusement park, in this obscure ancestor of "Free Willy."

1976 90m/C William Shatner, Marty Allen, Abby Dalton, Andy Devine, Nancy O'Conner; **D:** Ewing Miles Brown. **VHS, Beta** *VCI*

What About Bob? 🎵🎵🎵

PG/Jr. High-Adult Neurotic, hypochondriac Bob can barely make a move without his new psychiatrist. When the doctor takes his family to their New England cottage for a vacation, Bob follows, refusing to leave the poor shrink alone. The joke is that the doctor's wife and children find Bob an ideal pal and playmate, just the opposite of dry old dad. Appealing all-ages comedy from veteran Muppeteer Frank Oz.

🍷 BEWARE 🍷 *Alcohol use. Very funny profanity as Bob experiments with the notion that he has Tourette's syndrome (uncontrollable swearing).*

1991 99m/C Richard Dreyfuss, Bill Murray, Julie Hagerty, Charlie Korsmo, Tom Aldredge, Roger Bowen, Fran Brill, Kathryn Erbe, Doris Belack, Susan Willis; **D:** Frank Oz; **W:** Tom Schulman, Alvin Sargent; **M:** Miles Goodman. **VHS, Beta, LV** *TOU*

What Do You Tell a Phone?

Primary-Jr. High Rules for answering the door and telephone, focusing on safety and courtesy. Includes presentations by young hosts Joel and Jennifer, and Professor Manners. Common sense rules are presented in a humorous and musical format that kids will enjoy. Ages 3 to 7.

1994 20m/C VHS

What Do You Want to Be When You Grow Up: Railroaders

Preschool-Primary Two youngsters hop a ride on a train and begin an odyssey where they learn about all the different types of jobs fulfilled in order to keep a train running smoothly and safely. Ages 4 to 8.

1994 30m/C VHS *TPV*

What Do You Want to be When You Grow Up?—Zoo Crew

Preschool-Primary Visits the world famous Cincinnati, San Antonio, and Fort Worth Zoos, centering on the people who work there. Ages 4 to 8.

1995 30m/C VHS *TPV*

What the Moon Saw 🦴🦴🦴

Family What a sweet little movie. Steven spends a season with his grandmother in the city. She works at a theater putting on "Sinbad's Last Adventure," a somewhat threadbare children's play. But Steven's mind magnifies the show into a lavish, magical spectacle that helps the boy deal with assorted real-life tribulations. It rambles a bit, but this Australian-made family treat is really worth seeking out.

1990 86m/C VHS *FHE, BTV*

What's Eating Gilbert Grape 🦴🦴🦴

PG-13/Sr. High-Adult Offbeat is mildly descriptive. Depp stars as Gilbert Grape, the titular head of a very dysfunctional family living in a big house in a small Iowa town. His Momma (Cates) weighs more than 500 pounds and hasn't left the house in 7 years, he has two squabbling teenage sisters, he's having an affair with an older married woman (Steenburgen), and 17-year-old brother Arnie (DiCaprio) is mentally retarded, requiring constant supervision or he'll climb the water tower. What's a good-hearted grocery clerk to do? Well, when free-spirited Becky (Lewis) is momentarily marooned in town, Gilbert may have found a true soulmate. Performances, especially DiCaprio's, make this a keeper, though scenes between Lewis and Depp tend to stall. Cates came to the attention of filmmakers while on a guest on a TV talk show. Based on the novel by Hedges, who adapted for the screen.

🪧 BEWARE 🪧 *Grotesque people, profanity and sexual situations.*

1993 118m/C Johnny Depp, Leonardo DiCaprio, Juliette Lewis, Mary Steenburgen, Darlene Cates, Laura Harrington, Mary Kate Schellhardt, Kevin Tighe, John C. Reilly, Crispin Glover, Penelope Branning; **D:** Lasse Hallstrom; **W:** Peter Hedges; **M:** Alan Parker, Bjorn Isfalt. **Award Nominations:** Academy Awards '93: Best Sup-

porting Actor (DiCaprio); Golden Globe Awards '94: Best Supporting Actor (DiCaprio); **Awards:** National Board of Review Awards '93: Best Supporting Actor (DiCaprio). **VHS, Beta, LV** *PAR*

What's Love Got to Do With It? 🦴🦴 🦴

R/Sr. High-Adult Energetic biopic of powerhouse songstress Tina Turner. Short sequences cover her early life before moving into her abusive relationship with Ike and solo comeback success. Bassett may not look like Tina, but her exceptionally strong performance leaves no question as to who she's supposed to be, even during on-stage Tina sequences. Some credibility is lost when the real Tina is shown in the final concert sequence. Fishburne is a sympathetic but still chilling Ike, rising to the challenge of showing both Ike's initial charm and longtime cruelty. Based on "I, Tina" by Turner and Kurt Loder.

🪧 BEWARE 🪧 *Intense domestic violence, drug use and profanity.*

1993 118m/C Angela Bassett, Laurence "Larry" Fishburne, Vanessa Bell Calloway, Jenifer Lewis, Phyllis Stickney, Khandi Alexander, Pamela Tyson, Penny Johnson, Rae'ven Kelly, Robert Miranda, Chi; **D:** Brian Gibson; **W:** Kate Lanier; **M:** Stanley Clarke. **Award Nominations:** Academy Awards '93: Best Actor (Fishburne), Best Actress (Bassett); **Awards:** Golden Globe Awards '94: Best Actress—Musical/Comedy (Bassett). **VHS, LV** *TOU*

What's New Mr. Magoo?, Vol. 1

Preschool-Jr. High Four episodes from a 1970s resurrection of the classic Magoo series. Includes "What's Zoo Magoo," "Museum Magoo," "Magoo's Monster Mansion," and "Mountain Man Magoo." Additional volumes available.

1978 42m/C VHS *PAR, FCT*

What's Under My Bed? and Other Creepy Stories

Family Four scary (but not too scary) stories for children from part of the "Children's Circle" series from Weston Woods. "What's Under my Bed?" lets children know that even grown-ups get scared. "The Three Robbers" provides an excellent role model in the form of a brave and bright little girl. "Teeny-tiny and the Witch Woman" is a version of the Grimm Brothers' "Hansel and Gretel." Least scary is "Georgie the Ghost." Excellent production values, from sound to graphics.

1990 30m/C Rosanna Arquette, Bruce Spence; **D:** Michael Pattinson. **VHS** *CCC, FCT, WKV*

What's Up, Doc? 🦴🦴🦴

G/Family Shy musicologist Ryan travels from Iowa to San Francisco with his fiance Kahn for a convention. He meets the eccentric Streisand at his hotel and becomes involved in a chase to recover four identical flight bags containing top secret documents, a wealthy woman's jewels, the professor's musical rocks, and Streisand's clothing. Bogdanovich's homage to the screwball come-

dies of the '30s is not quite up to the level of the classics it honors, though still highly entertaining. Kahn's feature film debut.

1972 94m/C Barbra Streisand, Ryan O'Neal, Kenneth Mars, Austin Pendleton, Randy Quaid; **D:** Peter Bogdanovich; **W:** David Newman, Buck Henry. **VHS, Beta** *WAR*

What's Wrong with Wilma?

Preschool-Primary "Flintstones" video release that focuses on Fred and Barney as youngsters and their campaign against drugs in the stone age. See also "The Flintstone Kids: Just Say No." Another artifact of the Reagan Years.

1984 22m/C VHS, Beta *TTC*

When Dinosaurs Ruled the Earth 🦴🦴

G/Family This gets a plug in "Jurassic Park"; its title appears on a banner torn down by the T.Rex at the climax. Sort of a follow-up to the Raquel Welch version of "One Million Years B.C." (not on video), it repeats the mix of bikini-clad cavegirls and cool dinosaur f/x. Plot sees a superstitious tribe in a series of natural disasters caused by the sudden formation of Earth's moon. They blame a blonde cutie, who, in the silliest subplot, takes a nap in a giant eggshell and is mistakenly adopted by the loving dinosaur mama. Fast-paced but about as scientifically accurate as "The Flintstones." Dinosaurs are a combination of Jim Danforth's stop-motion work and live lizards filmed in closeup.

 Violence, alcohol use and skimpy attire.

1970 96m/C Victoria Vetri, Robin Hawdon, Patrick Allen, Drewe Henley, Sean Caffrey, Magda Konopka, Imogen Hassall, Patrick Holt, Jan Rossini; **D:** Val Guest; **W:** Val Guest. **VHS, Beta, LV** *WAR, FCT, MLB*

When Every Day was the Fourth of July 🦴🦴

Jr. High-Adult Made-for-TV nostalgia piece, clumsily derivative of "To Kill a Mockingbird." In a New England town in the '30s a nine-year-old girl asks her lawyer father to defend a pal, a mute handyman accused of murder. Meanwhile her brothers turn pint-sized sleuths to unmask the real culprit. Well-received enough to inspire a sequel, "The Long Days of Summer," also available on tape.

 Violence. Accusations of child-molestation in the courtroom.

1978 100m/C Katy Kurtzman, Dean Jones, Louise Sorel, Harris Yulin, Chris Petersen, Geoffrey Lewis, Scott Brady, Henry Wilcoxon, Michael Pataki; **D:** Dan Curtis. **VHS, Beta** *LIV*

When Magoo Flew

Family When Mr. Magoo decides to go to the movies, he ends up on an airplane and gets chased by police over a stolen briefcase. Nominated for an Oscar for Best Short Subject.

1954 7m/C V: Jim Backus. **VHS, Beta** *CHF*

When Mom and Dad Break Up

Family Introduces the concept of divorce to children ages four to twelve and offers methods of coping.

1989 32m/C VHS, Beta *PAR*

When the North Wind Blows 🦴🦴

G/Family Old trapper on the run from the law befriends a snow tiger in the Alaskan wilderness. Scenic nature adventure from "Wilderness Family" writer/director Raffil.

1974 113m/C Henry Brandon, Herbert Nelson, Dan Haggerty; **D:** Stewart Raffill. **VHS, Beta** *VCI*

When the Whales Came 🦴🕊

PG/Jr. High-Adult Ineffective conservationist fable about two children in a WWI-era fishing village on a remote British isle. Weak story has Gracie and Daniel befriending a shunned old codger who says the community was cursed for killing narwhal whales long ago. When more narwhals (finally) appear, will grouchy grownups listen this time and spare them? Nice music, interesting locale, but a dull, preachy plot merely inspires a whale of a slumber. Scripter Michael Morpurgo adapted his own novel "Why the Whales Came."

 Alcohol use.

1989 100m/C Paul Scofield, Helen Mirren, David Threlfall, David Suchet, Jeremy Kemp, Max Rennie, Helen Pearce, Barbara Jefford; **D:** Clive Rees; **W:** Michael Morpugo; **M:** Christopher Gunning, Ruth Rennie. **VHS, Beta, LV** *FOX*

When Wolves Cry 🦴🕊

G/Family Ill-conceived French tearjerker with an international cast mixes terminal illness, family drama, and antinuke politics. And, yes, wolves. Estranged dad and young son reunite on a Corsican vacation. Then a radiation leak from stray nuclear warheads gives the lad leukemia just in time for Christmas. Based on a novel by Michel Bataille. Also known as "The Christmas Tree."

1969 108m/C William Holden, Virna Lisi, Brook Fuller, Andre Bourvil; **D:** Terence Young. **VHS, Beta** *GEM, VCI*

Where Angels Go, Trouble Follows 🦴🦴

Family Followup to "The Trouble with Angels," with Russell reprising her role as the wise Mother Superior challenged by her mischief loving students. Younger, 'mod' nun Sister George urges her to change with the times and take the convent students on a bus trip to a California peace rally. Very dated and contrived, but still mildly amusing. Note that Wickes also dons a habit in both the "Sister Act" flicks.

1968 94m/C Rosalind Russell, Stella Stevens, Binnie Barnes, Mary Wickes, Susan St. James, Dolores Sutton, Alice Rawlings; *Cameos:* Milton Berle, Arthur Godfrey, Van Johnson, Robert Taylor; *D:* James Neilson; *W:* Blanche Hanalis. **VHS** *COL*

Where on Earth is Carmen Sandiego? Vol. I : A Date with Carmen (Parts One and Two)

Family Contains two episodes from the animated show. In "A Date with Carmen," Zack and Ivy go back to Boston in 1775 and meet Paul Revere. They discover that due to Carmen's dumbfoolery, Paul has missed his famous midnight ride. The second feature, finds Zack and Ivy trying to keep the history of the American Revolution as it was originally, including the Boston Tea Party and the kite-flying of Ben Franklin. Ages 6 to 11.

1995 50m/C VHS *TCF*

Where on Earth is Carmen Sandiego? Vol. II: By a Whisker and Dinosaur Delirium

Family "By a Whisker," follows Zack and Ivy as they trace clues from Carmen's theft of the Tower of London and an entire black sand beach in Hawaii. They finally uncover her scheme as they travel on the Siberian Express. "Dinosaur Delirium," finds the Acme detectives trying to figure out how Carmen is recreating prehistoric times as they journey from India to Indonesia, finally ending up in Washington, D.C.'s famous Smithsonian. Ages 6 to 11.

1995 50m/C VHS *TCF*

Where on Earth is Carmen Sandiego? Vol. III: The Good Old Bad Old Days and The Stolen Smile

Family "The Good Old Bad Old Days," finds Zack and Ivy stumped over what Carmen is doing until they enlist the aid of the famous gaucho detective, Armando, who uses a few old fashioned tricks to help track her down. "The Stolen Smile," has Zack and Ivy tracking Carmen in Europe when they discover that she has stolen parts of some famous works of art, including eyes from a Van Gogh, a nose from a Picasso, and the smile from the Mona Lisa. At least she kept her hands off Michelangelo's "David." Ages 6 to 11.

1995 50m/C VHS *TCF*

Where on Earth is Carmen Sandiego? Vol. IV: Split Up and Moondreams

Family "Split Up," finds Zack and Ivy in competition with each other as they try to prove which method of investigation is better, the computerized approach or good old-fashioned legwork. "Moondreams," follows the escapades of Carmen as she steals a toy in New York, a rocket in China, and the space shuttle in Florida, and then tries to become the first woman on the moon. Ages 6 to 11.

1995 50m/C VHS *TCF*

Where the Lilies Bloom 🦴🦴🦴

G/Family Touching story of four backwoods children left orphans when their father dies. They don't report his death to authorities out of fear the family will be separated into institutions. Stanton is great as the crusty landlord the children gradually accept as a friend. Based on the book by Vera and Bill Cleaver.

1974 96m/C Julie Gholson, Jan Smithers, Matthew Burrill, Helen Harmon, Harry Dean Stanton, Rance Howard, Sudie Bond, Tom Spratley, Helen Bragdon, Alice Beardsley; *D:* William A. Graham. **VHS** *MGM*

Where the Red Fern Grows 🦴🦴🦴

G/Family Young Billy Coleman, dwelling in the Ozarks during the Depression, learns maturity from his love and responsibility for two redbone hounds. Well produced, if sentimental, boy-and-his-dogs family fare works despite a surplus of Andy Williams songs. The ending is guaranteed to bring a tear or two. Based on the novel by Wilson Rawls, who also narrates.

⚠ BEWARE *Violence, both in cougar attacks and the sudden, shocking death of a child.*

1974 97m/C James Whitmore, Beverly Garland, Jack Ging, Lonny Chapman, Stewart Peterson; *D:* Norman Tokar. **VHS, Beta** *FHE, VES, HHE*

Where the Red Fern Grows: Part 2 🦴🦴

G/Family Sequel to the popular '70s family movie finds Billy Coleman returning from WWII with an artificial leg and a case of malaise that his dying Grandpa tries to cure by bringing him two additional 'coon dog pups. After more cutesy closeups of puppies than even "Beethoven's 2nd" dared, the story settles down into soap opera and maudlin dialogue. Though the actors give it their best, tale told once frustrates everyone's attempt to do it again.

⚠ BEWARE *Roughhousing.*

1992 105m/C Wilford Brimley, Doug McKeon, Lisa Whelchel, Chad McQueen; *D:* Jim McCullough. **VHS** *VCI*

Where the River Runs Black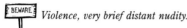

PG/Jr. High-Adult In the remote Brazilian jungle a baby results from the (discreet) encounter between a young missionary and a native woman. When both parents get killed, river dolphins become the boy's guardians. Kindly priest eventually finds Lazaro and introduces him to the modern world, where the kid beholds intolerance, corruption—and the man who murdered his mother. Offbeat, but too slow and self-important to evoke the childlike sense of wonder required by this plot.

BEWARE *Violence, very brief distant nudity.*

1986 96m/C Charles Durning, Peter Horton, Ajay Naidu, Conchata Ferrell, Alessandro Rabelo, Castulo Guerra; **D:** Christopher Cain; **M:** James Horner. **VHS, Beta** *FOX*

Where the Spirit Lives

PG/Jr. High-Adult Historical drama about Indian children kidnapped by Canadian government agents and forced to live in dreadful boarding schools where they are abused emotionally and physically. New arrival refuses to put up with it and tries to escape. Engrossing and vivid, with a good sense of the era.

BEWARE *Mature themes.*

1989 97m/C Michelle St. John; **D:** Bruce Pittman. **VHS** *BTV, HHE, UWA*

Where the Toys Come From

Family Stop-motion Disney creation in which two Christmas toys, a camera and a pair of binoculars, take a trip around the world in order to find out where they came from.

1984 58m/C VHS, Beta *DIS*

Where the Wild Things Are

Preschool-Primary Animated version of the classic Maurice Sendak story of Max, the small boy who reigns over a fantasy kingdom inhabited by weird and delightful monsters.

1976 8m/C VHS, Beta

Where Time Began

G/Family Antique manuscript details a route to an amazing world far below the Earth's surface. A professor and his friends decide to follow directions and see the wonders for themselves. Cheap, Spanish-made redo of Jules Verne's "Journey to the Center of the Earth," with a good cast but goofy dinosaur f/x.

1977 87m/C Kenneth More, Pep Munne, Jack Taylor; **D:** J. Piquer Simon. **VHS, Beta**

Where's Spot?

Preschool Features Eric Hill's adorable puppy Spot in five stories for the very young: "Where's Spot?," "Spot's First Walk," "Spot's Birthday Party," "Spot Goes Splash," and "Spot Finds a Key." Like the Hill books, the video box features trademark hide-and-seek activities for toddlers. See also "Spot Goes to the Farm."

1993 30m/C VHS *TOU, BTV*

Which Way Weather?

Preschool Everybody talks about the weather. This video talks about it, sings about it and tells what to do with it. Covers activities such as swimming, sailing, kite flying, ice skating, sledding, pumpkin picking and puddle jumping. Lively music. Ages 3 to 7.

1995 30m/C VHS *TPV*

While You Were Sleeping

PG/Jr. High-Adult Chicago subway cashier (Bullock) has more than a token interest in a handsome commuter (Gallagher) but he barely notices her. When he is mugged on the platform she steps in and rescues him. He's unconscious; she rides along to the hospital where she is mistaken for his fiancee. While he remains comatose, she is warmly welcomed by his family, except for his suspicious brother (Pullman). However, it doesn't take long for them to fall for each other. Endearing comedy graced by fine performance from Bullock and Pullman. And Gallagher, when he wakes up.

BEWARE *Some crude language.*

1995 103m/C Sandra Bullock, Bill Pullman, Peter Gallagher, Jack Warden, Peter Boyle, Glynis Johns, Micole Mercurio, Jason Bernard, Michael Rispoli, Ally Walker, Monica Keena; **D:** Jon Turteltaub; **W:** Fred Lebow, Daniel G. Sullivan; **C:** Phedon Papamichael; **M:** Randy Edelman. **VHS, LV** *TOU*

Whistle Down the Wind

Jr. High-Adult Three motherless children of strict religious upbringing find a murderer hiding in their family's barn and believe him to be Jesus Christ. A well done and hardly grim or dull allegory of childhood innocence based on a novel by Mills's mother, Mary Hayley Bell. Relying heavily on child characters, it portrays childhood well and realistically, with Mills perfect in her role as the eldest child. Forbes's directorial debut uses religious symbolism judiciously; Richard Attenborough's second production.

1962 98m/B Hayley Mills, Bernard Lee, Alan Bates; **D:** Bryan Forbes; **M:** Malcolm Arnold. **VHS, Beta** *NLC*

White Christmas

Family Two ex-army buddies become a popular comedy team and play at a financially unstable Vermont inn at Christmas for charity's sake. Many swell Irving Berlin songs rendered with zest. Paramount's first Vista Vision film. Presented in widescreen on laserdisc. ♫ The Best Things Happen While You're Dancing; Love, You Didn't Do Right By Me; Choreography; Count Your Blessings Instead of Sheep; What Can You Do With a General; Mandy; The Minstrel Show; Sisters; Heat Wave.

1954 120m/C Bing Crosby, Danny Kaye, Rosemary Clooney, Vera-Ellen, Dean Jagger; **D:** Michael Curtiz; **W:** Norman Panama. **VHS, Beta, LV, 8mm, CD-I** *PAR, FUS*

White Fang 🐾🐾🐾

PG/Family Spectacular adventure manages to stay true to both the Disney family-movie style and writer Jack London's unsentimental depiction of Gold Rush days. Tenderfoot miner Jack Casey befriends a heroic wolf-dog and they struggle, together and separately, to survive both human and natural dangers in Alaska. Gets gooey just near the end. Beautiful cinematography.

>  *Violence (animals get the worst of it), alcohol use and c-c-c-cold.*

1991 109m/C Klaus Maria Brandauer, Ethan Hawke, Seymour Cassel, James Remar, Susan Hogan; **D:** Randal Kleiser; **W:** Jeanne Rosenberg, Nick Thiel, David Fallon; **M:** Basil Poledouris. **VHS, LV** *TOU, DIS, TVC*

White Fang 2: The Myth of the White Wolf 🐾🐾

PG/Family White boy and his wolf-dog lead starving Native American tribe to caribou during the Alaskan Gold Rush. Simplistic story with obvious heroes and villains, yes, but this is also wholesome (and politically correct) family fare compliments of Disney. Sequel to "White Fang" with Ethan Hawke focuses less on the wolf, a flaw, and more on Bairstow and his love interest Craig, a Haida Indian princess, while exploring Native American mythology and dreams in sequences that tend to stop the action cold. Still, kids will love it, and there are plenty of puppies to achieve required awwww factor. Beautiful scenery filmed on location in Colorado and British Columbia.

>  *Roughhousing*

1994 106m/C Scott Bairstow, Alfred Molina, Geoffrey Lewis, Charmaine Craig, Victoria Racimo, Paul Coeur, Anthony Michael Ruivivar, Al Harrington; **Cameos:** Ethan Hawke; **D:** Ken Olin; **W:** David Fallon; **M:** John Debney. **VHS** *NYR*

White Fang and the Hunter 🐾🐾

G/Family Adventures of a boy and his dog who survive an attack from wild wolves and then help to solve a murder mystery. Loosely based on the novel by Jack London; no relation to the Disney "White Fang" sagas.
1985 87m/C Pedro Sanchez, Robert Wood; **D:** Alfonso Brescia. **VHS, Beta** *VTR, HHE*

White Mama 🐾🐾🐾

Family A poor widow (Davis, in a splendid role) takes in a street-wise black kid (Harden) in return for protection from the neighborhood's dangers, and they discover friendship. Poignant drama, capably directed by Cooper, featuring sterling performances all around. Made-for-TV drama at its best.
1980 96m/C Bette Davis, Ernest Harden, Eileen Heckart, Virginia Capers, Lurene Tuttle, Anne Ramsey; **D:** Jackie Cooper. **VHS, Beta** *LIV*

The White Seal

Preschool-Primary Man's presence in the Bering Sea poses a threat to Kitock's safety. The little white seal searches the frigid waters for a new home in this environmentally themed TV cartoon.
1975 30m/C **V:** Roddy McDowall, June Foray. **VHS, Beta** *FHE*

White Squall 🐾🐾

PG-13/Jr. High-Adult Based on the 1960 true story of 13 young men who become students at Ocean Academy, a year-long school adventure spent aboard the brigantine Albatross (unfortunate name). In the Caribbean, the crew hits a storm that puts everyone in danger. Robinson adapted a 1961 "Boys' Life" magazine story.

>  *Drownings, shootings, dolphin mistreatment and a traumatic shipwreck. The boys hire a prostitute (though nothing happens).*

1996 128m/C Jeff Bridges, Scott Wolf, Caroline Goodall, Balthazar Getty, John Savage, Jeremy Sisto, Jason Marsden, David Selby, Zeljko Ivanek, Ryan Phillippe, David Lascher, Eric Michael Cole, Julio Mechoso, Ethan Embry; **D:** Ridley Scott; **W:** Todd Robinson; **C:** Hugh Johnson; **M:** Jeff Rona. **VHS** *TOU*

White Water Summer 🐾🐾

PG/Jr. High-Adult Four mismatched teen campers trek into the Sierras, and find themselves struggling through dangerous rapids and rock climbs. Bacon seems miscast as a rugged outdoorsman who shows the tenderfoots how to survive, if they don't kill each other first. Great nature scenery, anyway.

>  *Salty language, roughhousing.*

1987 90m/C Kevin Bacon, Sean Astin, Jonathan Ward, Matt Adler; **D:** Jeff Bleckner; **M:** Michael Boddicker. **VHS, Beta, LV** *COL*

Whitewater Sam 🐾

G/Family In the 1820s mountain man Sam and his wonder husky Sybar survive one peril after another in the hostile wilds of the Great Northwest. Clumsy, virtually plotless nature adventure with blurry visuals; either writer/producer/director/star Larsen used soft focus a lot or Sybar kept licking the lens.

>  *Violence, in savage cougar, bear and Indian attacks (that Sam seems to survive with barely a scratch).*

1978 87m/C Keith Larsen; **D:** Keith Larsen; **W:** Keith Larsen. **VHS, Beta** *MON*

Who Framed Roger Rabbit? 🐾🐾🐾♡

PG/Jr. High-Adult Technically marvelous, cinematically hilarious, eye-popping combo of cartoon and live-action creates a Hollywood of the 1940s where animated characters are alive and a repressed minority, working in films and dwelling in their own Toontown ghetto. A 'toon-hating detective is hired to trail the sexy wife of comedy star Roger Rabbit and instead uncovers

Bridges teaches a student a lesson in "White Squall."

murder, mayhem, and a multi-zillion dollar conspiracy. Special appearances by famous cartoon characters from the past, with one major absentee—legal rights to Popeye and his friends couldn't be secured. Coproduced by Touchstone (Disney) and Amblin (Spielberg). A complete rethinking of the source novel, "Who Censored Roger Rabbit?" by Gary K. Wolf, which dealt not with cartoons but comic-strips.

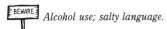 *Reports of nude scenes involving Roger Rabbit's humanoid wife Jessica are wildly exaggerated. There's violence—95% of it against 'toons, who are virtually indestructible anyway—plus salty language, alcohol use, sex puns that will easily elude toddler viewers.*

1988 104m/C Bob Hoskins, Christopher Lloyd, Joanna Cassidy, Alan Tilvern, Stubby Kaye; **D:** Robert Zemeckis; **W:** Jeffrey Price, Peter S. Seaman; **M:** Alan Silvestri; **V:** Charles Fleischer, Mae Questel, Kathleen Turner, Amy Irving, Mel Blanc, June Foray, Frank Sinatra. **Award Nominations:** Academy Awards '88: Best Art Direction/Set Decoration, Best Cinematography, Best Sound; **Awards:** Academy Awards '88: Best Film Editing, Best Visual Effects; National Board of Review Awards '88: 10 Best Films of the Year. **VHS, Beta, LV** *TOU*

Who Has Seen the Wind? ♪♪

Family Two boys grow up in Saskatchewan during the Depression. So-so family viewing drama. Ferrer as a bootlegger steals the otherwise small-paced show.

Alcohol use; salty language.

1977 102m/C Jose Ferrer, Brian Painchaud, Charmion King, Helen Shaver. **VHS, Beta**

Who Is Healthy Herb?—Food, Fitness, and Fun!

Preschool-Primary Healthy Herb, the zany ambassador of children's fitness, teaches about the benefits of proper nutrition and exercise. He leads kids through various quizzes and exercise routines. Ages 4 to 9.
1995 m/C VHS

Who'll Save Our Children? ♪♪♪

Jr. High-Adult Two kids are abandoned on the doorstep of a middle-aged, childless couple, who care for the foundlings for years and are on the point of adopting then when the real parents reappear and sue for custody. Superior, sometimes painful family drama, made for TV. Based on "The Orchard Children" by Rachel Maddox.

1982 96m/C Shirley Jones, Len Cariou, Conchata Ferrell, Frances Sternhagen, Cassie Yates, David Hayward; **D:** George Schaefer. **VHS, Beta** *TLF*

Who's Who at the Zoo?

Preschool-Primary Timmy the Angel tries to save the zoo in a dingy little town by trying to show people the color in their lives. Ages 3 to 6.
1994 25m/C VHS *WPC*

Why Christmas Trees Aren't Perfect

Family Animated holiday tale of kindness and its reward. Sweetly told until a fairly heavy-handed finale.
1990 25m/C VHS

Why Shoot the Teacher?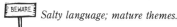

Family Novice teacher takes charge of a proverbial one-room schoolhouse in an isolated prairie town in 1930s Saskatchewan. The chilly reception he gets matches the weather, but eventually he warms up to the hardworking farm kids that comprise his pupils. Don't be put off by the dire title; this is a sweet-spirited comedy-drama with heart, adapted from the novel by Max Braithwaite.

BEWARE *Salty language; mature themes.*

1979 101m/C Bud Cort, Samantha Eggar, Chris Wiggins; *D:* Silvio Narizzano. **VHS, Beta**

Widget of the Jungle

Preschool-Jr. High Episodes from the cartoon TV series starring the little shape-changing alien Widget, a "world-watcher" fighting on behalf of the environment. Here he goes to Africa to foil some elephant ivory poachers. Also contains an extremely "Free Willy"-ish story entitled "Kona, The Captive Whale."
1990 47m/C VHS, Beta *FHE*

Widget's Great Whale Adventure

Preschool-Jr. High The delightful alien's power to talk with animals helps him prevent lawless hunters from capturing immature whales. Also includes another animated story entitled "Gorilla My Dream."
1990 47m/C VHS, Beta *FHE*

Wil Cwac Cwac: Vol. 1

Preschool Wil Cwac Cwac is a mischief-prone duckling living in a village of farm animals in this set of ten cute short cartoons from Welsh TV (dubbed over with American voices) for the very young. Also available: "The Further Adventures of Wil Cwac Cwac" and "Welcome Back, Wil Cwac Cwac."
1983 50m/C VHS, Beta *FHE*

Wild and Woody

Family Find out how Woody Woodpecker won the West in this collection of nine Lantz cartoons from the 50s and the 60s.
1965 51m/C V: Grace Stafford. **VHS, Beta** *MCA*

The Wild Child

G/Sr. High-Adult Brilliant film based on the journal of a 19th century physician who attempted to educate and civilize a young feral boy who had been found dwelling like a wild beast by himself in a French forest. Not gimmicky in the least, with director Truffaut as the doctor trying to reach the boy's dormant intellect. Tenderly told, the perfect antidote to the "Problem Child" pictures. In French with English subtitles.
1970 85m/B D: Francois Truffaut; **W:** Jean Gruault; **M:** Antoine Duhamel. **VHS** *MGM, INJ, FCT*

The Wild Country

G/Family Disney fare detailing the trials and tribulations of a Pittsburgh family moving into an inhospitable Wyoming ranch in the 1880s. Ronny Howard acts alongside real life father Rance and brother Clint. Based on the novel "Little Britches" by Ralph Moody.

BEWARE *Violence.*

1971 92m/C Steve Forrest, Ron Howard, Clint Howard, Rance Howard; **D:** Robert Totten. **VHS, Beta** *DIS*

Wild Geese Calling

Preschool-Primary Dan Tolliver rescues a Canada gander, nurses it back to health and, once he realizes he is unable to control it he releases the bird into the wild. A live-action tale from TV's "Wonderful World of Disney."
1990 33m/C VHS, Beta *MTI, DSN*

Wild Hearts Can't Be Broken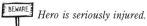

G/Family True story of Sonora Webster, a 1930s Georgia teen who runs away from a foster home to a carnival. She becomes a stunt horse rider, specializing in jumping with the animal 40 feet into a pool of water (just when you thought movies had exploited every sporting event ever known). Diving injury threatens her career, but she persists and rides and dives again. Storyline has little tension, but that doesn't detract from this fresh, well-written Disney film with a feisty heroine and a novel sport.

BEWARE *Hero is seriously injured.*

1991 89m/C Gabrielle Anwar, Cliff Robertson, Dylan Kussman, Michael Schoeffling, Kathleen York, Frank Renzulli; **D:** Steve Miner; **W:** Oley Sassone; **M:** Mason Daring. **VHS, Beta** *DIS*

Wild Horse Hank

Family A young woman risks everything to save a herd of wild mustangs from being slaughtered for use as dog food. Crenna's good; otherwise, it's sentimental family fare. Based on the novel "The Wild Horse Killers" by Mel Ellis.

1979 94m/C Linda Blair, Richard Crenna, Michael Wincott, Al Waxman; **D:** Eric Till. **VHS, Beta** *LIV, VES*

Wild Pony

Family Compelling frontier family drama with as much to interest adults as kids. Hot-headed young farmer dies after a drunken fight with an innocent rancher. The widow, facing a harsh winter alone with two kids, proposes the only logical move—a marriage of convenience to the guilt-ridden rancher. How these characters interact is unpredictable and the stuff of truly great drama, and no surprise; director Sullivan later went on to steer Canada's successful "Anne of Green Gables" series.

BEWARE *Violence and alcohol use.*

1983 87m/C Marilyn Lightstone, Art Hindle, Josh Byrne; **D:** Kevin Sullivan; **M:** Hagood Hardy. **VHS, Beta** *FHE, VES, LIV*

The Wild Puffalumps

Preschool-Primary Animated fantasy adventure about two kids entering a land of weird animals.

1987 22m/C VHS, Beta *FHE*

Wild Swans

Primary Danish fairy tale about eleven princes turned into wild swans by an evil queen. Only their sister's hard work and devotion can return them to human form.

1980 11m/C VHS, Beta *MTI*

Wild Swans

Family Young girl must save her six brothers, who have been turned into swans by an evil witch. Cartoon adaptation of the classic fairy tale.

198? 62m/C VHS, Beta *COL, WKV*

Wildcats

R/Sr. High-Adult Naive lady phys. ed instructor is saddled with the job of coaching a completely undisciplined inner-city high-school football team. Formulaic connect-the-dots comedy, shares both the premise and the director of the original "Bad News Bears." Hawn is winning as her character gains confidence both on the field and off—in a custody battle with an ex-husband over her daughters—but it all feels like a long sitcom episode.

BEWARE *Profanity, sex talk and brief nudity. A minor gets drunk at a school dance.*

1986 106m/C Goldie Hawn, James Keach, Swoosie Kurtz, Bruce McGill, M. Emmet Walsh, Woody Harrelson, Wesley Snipes, Tab Thacker; **D:** Michael Ritchie; **M:** James Newton Howard. **VHS, Beta, LV** *WAR*

Wildlife Tales: The Legend of the Bison

Family Program follows the bison at Yellowstone National Park as they breed, forage, and struggle for survival. Ages 7 to 11.

1995 25m/C VHS *PAR*

Will Vinton's Claymation Comedy of Horrors

Family Halloween fantasy wherein Wilshire Pig and Sheldon Snail are after the powers of the legendary Frankenswine, so they set out for the Doctor's spooky castle. Very funny TV special showcasing Vinton's brand of stop-motion animation magic and wild humor.

1992 27m/C VHS *MOV, LIV*

Will Vinton's Claymation Easter

Family Claymation brings to life the story of the Easter Bunny and Vinton's perennial troublemaker, Wilshire Pig. The pig tries to take the place of the E.B. through a series of underhanded tricks, but justice wins out in the end. Clever and entertaining for all ages.

1992 27m/C VHS *FHE*

The William Steig Library

Preschool-Primary "Children's Circle" animated adaptations of author-illustrator Steig's childrens' books centering on humor, adventure and fear. Includes the stories "Sylvester and the Magic Pebble," "The Amazing Bone," "Doctor De Soto," and "Brave Irene." Also has an interview from the famous storybook creator himself. Ages 4 to 9.

1995 ?m/C VHS *CCC*

Willie Mays & The Say-Hey Kid

Preschool-Primary In return for making a great catch and saving the pennant, baseball great Mays (doing his own 'toon voice) must provide a home for Veronica, a lonely orphan. Condensed version of a one-hour Rankin-Bass cartoon done for Saturday-morning TV.

1972 30m/C VHS

Willie, the Operatic Whale

Family Willie the whale has dreams of singing opera at the Met, including Figaro, Pagliacci, Tristan and Isolde, and Mephistopheles, but a maestro brought out to sea to hear him badly misunderstands. A classic Disney short cartoon with all the voices (not to mention the singing) performed by the legendary Eddy.

1946 29m/C VHS, Beta *DIS, MTI, DSN*

The Willies WOOF!

PG-13/Jr. High-Adult Three youngsters attempt to outdo each other with juvenile tales of horror and scariness while camping in the backyard. Pointless, doltish, and terribly acted. Watch closely—if you watch at all—and you'll hear a poke at Astin's role in "The Goonies."

BEWARE *Violence and grossness, including a poodle cooked in a microwave, monsters snatching children, children eating flies.*

1990 120m/C James Karen, Sean Astin, Kathleen Freeman, Jeremy Miller; *D:* Brian Peck. **VHS, LV** *PSM*

Willow 🦴🦴 🦴

PG/Jr. High-Adult Blockbuster fantasy combined the talents of writer/producer George Lucas with director Ron Howard, but results are disappointing. Recycled plotline filches from stories of Moses, Peter Pan, Ulysses and many others as Willow, a friendly dwarf and aspiring wizard, becomes guardian of an infant princess. Every ten minutes or so we're reminded of a prophecy that the baby will successfully end the tyranny of evil queen Bavmorda (thanks, there goes the suspense), and the plot is one chase/fight after another as the Queen's imperial stormtroopers try to seize the tyke. Superb special effects (including a memorable dragon), but only small kids unfamiliar with Myths 101 will be enthralled.

BEWARE *Violence, sometimes intense.*

1988 118m/C Warwick Davis, Val Kilmer, Jean Marsh, Joanne Whalley, Billy Barty, Pat Roach, Ruth Greenfield, Patricia Hayes, Gavan O'Herlihy, Kevin Pollak; *D:* Ron Howard; *W:* Bob Dolman; *M:* James Horner. **VHS, Beta, LV, 8mm** *COL*

Willy McBean & His Magic Machine

Family Early Arthur Rankin Jr./Jules Bass production done entirely through stop-motion animation, long before "A Nightmare Before Christmas." Inventor Rasputin von Rotten wants to become the greatest man in history, so he goes back in time to upstage Columbus, Merlin the Magician, and others. Boy named Willy races after him, trying to unmask the imposter at every step. Somewhat tedious, and the puppet characters lack personality, but with enough fun touches (like a T.Rex mysteriously wearing sneakers) to keep you watching. Nice ending points out a real-life 'magic machine'—movies.

BEWARE *It would take a greater genius than von Rotten to figure out why the cassette distributor has put a PG on this kiddie fare.*

1959 94m/C *D:* Arthur Rankin Jr. **VHS, Beta** *PSM*

Willy Wonka & the Chocolate Factory 🦴🦴🦴🦴

G/Family Charlie, a poor English boy, wins a tour of the most wonderfully strange candy factory in the world, run by mysterious man-child recluse Willy Wonka. He leads Charlie and four other kids on a thrilling tour of the complex, but hidden traps wait for each child who misbehaves. In theaters for only about a week, this box-office

disappointment was rescued by TV rebroadcasts (just like "The Wizard of Oz") and has earned its reputation as a top-quality children's film with much to engage the adult intellect as well. Wilder's ever-so-demented Wonka is a delight; listen close to his slightly off-color mutterings. Adapted from "Charlie and the Chocolate Factory" by Roald Dahl (who hated this movie) with a memorable musical score by Anthony Newley and Leslie Bricusse.
🎵 Willy Wonka, the Candy Man; Cheer Up, Charlie; I've Got a Golden Ticket; Oompa-Loompa-Doompa-Dee-Doo; Pure Imagination.

BEWARE *Some mildly gruesome imagery if you freeze-frame during Willy Wonka's psychedelic high-speed boat trip.*

1971 100m/C Gene Wilder, Jack Albertson, Denise Nickerson, Peter Ostrum, Roy Kinnear, Aubrey Woods, Michael Bollner, Ursula Reit, Leonard Stone, Dodo Denney; *D:* Mel Stuart; *M:* Leslie Bricusse. **VHS, Beta, LV** *WAR, APD, HMV*

Wind 🦴🦴 🦴

PG-13/Jr. High-Adult Fairly routine romance on the water/sports drama gains buoyancy via good performances and scenic crashing waves. Sailor Will Parker (Modine) chooses the opportunity to be on the America's Cup team over opportunity of being with girlfriend Grey. Then he has the dubious honor of making a technical error that causes the team to lose. Undaunted, he locates Grey and her new engineer boyfriend (Skarsgard) and convinces them to design the ultimate boat for the next set of races. When ESPN carried extensive coverage of the America's Cup races for the first time in the summer of '92, viewers discovered that a little goes a long way. The same holds true here, though the race footage is stunning.

BEWARE *Salty language.*

1992 123m/C Matthew Modine, Jennifer Grey, Cliff Robertson, Jack Thompson, Stellan Skarsgard, Rebecca Miller, Ned Vaughn; *D:* Carroll Ballard; *W:* Rudy Wurlitzer, Mac Gudgeon; *M:* Basil Poledouris. **VHS, LV, 8mm** *COL*

The Wind and the Lion 🦴🦴🦴

PG/Jr. High-Adult In turn-of-the-century Morocco, a sheik (Connery) kidnaps a feisty American woman (Bergen) and her children and holds her as a political hostage. President Teddy Roosevelt (Keith) sends in the Marines to free the captives, who are eventually released by their captor. Directed with venue and style by Milius. Highly entertaining, if heavily fictionalized. Based very loosely on a historical incident.

1975 120m/C Sean Connery, Candice Bergen, Brian Keith, John Huston, Geoffrey Lewis; *D:* John Milius; *W:* John Milius; *M:* Jerry Goldsmith. **VHS, Beta, LV** *MGM*

The Wind in the Willows

Family "The Wind in the Willows," originally a part of the 1950 Disney feature "Ichabod and Mr. Toad," is the tale of J. Thaddeus Toad, of Toad Hall, who has a strange mania for fast cars. Based on a story by Kenneth Grahame. Also

Charlie redeems his winning golden ticket in "Willy Wonka and the Chocolate Factory."

on this tape are two Disney cartoons with similar automotive themes, "Motor Mania" with Goofy and "Trailer Horn" with Donald Duck and Chip 'n' Dale. Ages 5 to 10. **1949 34m/C** Eric Blore; **D:** Wolfgang Reitherman. **VHS, Beta** *DIS, HMV, WAR*

The Wind in the Willows

Preschool-Primary A chapter from Kenneth Grahame's children's classic that follows the adventures of Mr. Toad and his passion for motorcars, which gets him thrown into jail.
1966 34m/C VHS *DIS*

The Wind in the Willows

Family The Children's Theatre Company and School of Minneapolis perform their own unique interpretation of the Kenneth Grahame story.
1983 75m/C VHS, Beta *MCA*

Wind in the Willows, Vol. 1

Family Delightful and intricate stop-motion animation brings Kenneth Grahame's animal characters Mole, Ratty, Badger, and Toad of Toad Hall to life in this multivolume British series, boasting voices by eminent

character actors and a literate script. Additional volumes available.
1983 60m/C V: Ian Carmichael, Beryl Reid. **VHS** *HBO*

The Window 🦴🦴🦴 ▷

Jr. High-Adult A little boy has a reputation for telling lies, so no one believes him when he says he witnessed a murder—except the killers. Almost unbearably tense, claustrophobic thriller about the helplessness of childhood. Based on "The Boy Who Cried Murder" by Cornell Woolrich. Driscoll was awarded a special miniature Oscar as Outstanding Juvenile for his performance.

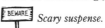 *Scary suspense.*

1949 73m/B Bobby Driscoll, Barbara Hale, Arthur Kennedy, Ruth Roman; **D:** Ted Tetzlaff. **Award Nominations:** Academy Awards '49: Best Film Editing; **Awards:** Edgar Allan Poe Awards '49: Best Screenplay. **VHS, Beta, LV** *MED*

Windrunner 🦴🦴 ▷

PG/Primary-Adult Angry at his football-star dad and rejected by the local high school team, Greg Cima (Wiles) finds an unlikely ally in the spirit of Native American Olympic hero Jim Thorpe (Means). Seems Thorpe needs some aid to return to the spirit world and, by coaching Cima, he'll also get the help he needs. Believable performances and an exploration of the power of Native American mysticism help the unlikely premise along.

BEWARE *Mild thematic elements regarding family relationships and feelings of rejection.*

1994 110m/C Russell Means, Jason Wiles, Amanda Peterson, Margot Kidder, Jake Busey, Max Casella, Bruce Weitz; *D:* William Clark; *W:* Mitch Davis; *M:* Arthur Kempel. **VHS** *AVE*

Wings of Desire 𝄞𝄞𝄞 ♭

PG-13/Sr. High-Adult An ethereal, haunting modern fable about one of many angels observing human life in and above the broken existence of Berlin, and how he begins to long to experience life as humans do. A moving, unequivocable masterpiece, with as many beautiful things to say about spiritual need as about the schizophrenic emptiness of contemporary Germany; Wenders' magnum opus. In German with English subtitles, and with black-and-white sequences. Magnificent cinematography by Henri Alekan.

BEWARE *Not for most kids, but teen cinephiles should appreciate it.*

1988 130m/C Bruno Ganz, Peter Falk, Solveig Dommartin, Otto Sander, Curt Bois; *D:* Wim Wenders; *W:* Wim Wenders, Peter Handke. **VHS, Beta, LV** *ORI, GLV, INJ*

A Winner Never Quits 𝄞𝄞 ♭

PG/Jr. High-Adult True story based on the life of 1940s baseball player Pete Gray, who lost his right arm in a boyhood accident. He's determined to prove himself on the diamond during WWII. Though teammates consider him a sideshow freak, he becomes an inspiration to fans. Properly wholesome, made-for-TV effort. Cynics can see Woody Allen's "Radio Days" for a hilarious spoof of a Pete Gray-type ballplayer.

1986 96m/C Keith Carradine, Mare Winningham, Huckleberry Fox, Dennis Weaver, Dana Delany, G.W. Bailey, Charles Hallahan, Fionnula Flanagan, Jack Kehoe; *D:* Mel Damski; *W:* Burt Prelutsky. **VHS** *COL*

Winners of the West

Family A landowner schemes to prevent a railroad from running through his property. The railroad's chief engineer leads the good guys in an attempt to prevent sabotage. A fun serial in thirteen chapters, full of shooting, blown-up bridges, locomotives afire, etc.; and of course, the requisite damsel in distress.

1940 250m/B Anne Nagel, Dick Foran, James Craig, Harry Woods; *D:* Ray Taylor, Ford Beebe. **VHS** *GPV, VCN, NOS*

Winnie the Pooh

Preschool One of the Disney Video-A-Long books on videocassette, this tape features Winnie telling three favorite stories: "Winnie the Pooh and Tigger, Too," "Win-

nie the Pooh and the Honey Tree," and "Winnie the Pooh and the Blustery Day."

1985 30m/C VHS, Beta *DIS, APD*

Winnie the Pooh

Family Four original, non-Disney stories starring the A.A. Milne favorite bear and all his friends. Stories include "Kanga and Roo Come to the Forest," "Pooh Invents a New Game and Eeyore Joins In," "Rabbit Has a Busy Day and Learns What Christopher Robin Does in the Morning," and "Christopher Robin and Pooh Discover an Enchanted Place."

1989 60m/C VHS *FOX, FCT*

Winnie the Pooh and a Day for Eeyore 𝄞𝄞𝄞

G/Family The fourth in the Disney animated series sees Pooh, Tigger and their friends throw a birthday party for Eeyore, the depressed donkey.

1973 25m/C *V:* Sterling Holloway, Sebastian Cabot. **VHS, Beta, LV** *DIS, MTI, DSN*

Winnie the Pooh and Christmas Too

Preschool Winnie and his friends write their Christmas lists for Santa, but Pooh fails to get them to the North Pole. So Pooh dresses up as St. Nick and, with Piglet as a reindeer, works to bring some holiday magic (with a little help from Christopher Robin). Ages 3 to 7.

1994 38m/C VHS *DIS*

Winnie the Pooh & Friends

Family Winnie the Pooh and his friends from the Hundred Acre Wood are trying to arrange a birthday party for Eeyore the mule.

1984 46m/C *V:* Sterling Holloway, Sebastian Cabot, John Fiedler. **VHS, Beta** *DIS*

Winnie the Pooh and the Blustery Day

Family Another classic A.A. Milne tale about Pooh, the Hundred Acre Woods and Tigger, this time caught in a galestorm.

1968 24m/C *D:* Wolfgang Reitherman; *V:* Sterling Holloway, John Fiedler, Paul Winchell, Hal Smith, Ralph Wright. **VHS, Beta** *DIS, MTI, DSN*

Winnie the Pooh and the Honey Tree

Family Pooh becomes stuck in Rabbit's hole after attempting to steal some honey from a beehive. The first of Disney's Pooh features.

1965 25m/C *D:* Wolfgang Reitherman; *V:* Sterling Holloway, Ralph Wright, Hal Smith, Barbara Luddy, Clint Howard, Junius Matthews, Howard Morris, Bruce Reitherman. **VHS, Beta, LV** *DIS, DSN, MTI*

Winnie the Pooh falls asleep in "Winnie the Pooh and the Blustery Day."

Winnie the Pooh and Tigger Too

G/Family A.A. Milne's classic characters—as animated by Disney—encounter Tigger and his irascible bouncing, find it intolerable, and discover a questionable cure involving circular logic. "The wonderful thing about tiggers is tiggers are wonderful things . . . "

1974 25m/C D: John Lounsbery; **V:** Sterling Holloway, Paul Winchell, Junius Matthews, John Fiedler, Timothy Turner, Dori Whitaker. **VHS, Beta, LV** *DIS, MTI, DSN*

Winnie the Pooh Discovers the Seasons

Preschool-Primary Winnie and friends learn some basic science vocabulary and concepts, while exploring animal habitats.

1990 8m/C VHS, Beta *MTI, DSN*

Winnie the Pooh Un-Valentine's Day

Preschool-Primary Rabbit wants to cancel Valentine's day because last year's celebration caused too much trash in the Hundred Acre Wood. But someone secretly sends Pooh a jar of honey and then he tries to find out who the gift-giver was and everyone decides to put on a holiday show to celebrate instead. Good idea. Ages 3 to 7.

1995 30m/C VHS *DIS*

Winsome Witch

Family Compilation of Hanna-Barbera's "Winsome Witch" cartoons, in which a good-natured dropout from the Fairy Godmother School freelances as a witch and steps into some amusing retellings of "Snow White" and other tales. Additional volumes available.

1965 55m/C VHS, Beta *TTC*

Winter of the Witch

Primary-Jr. High Tame kiddie short, produced by the folks behind Parents Magazine, about what happens when Nicky and her mother discover a witch in the attic. The not-so-wicked witch helps them make magic pancakes that bring joy and simple f/x to all.

1970 25m/C Hermione Gingold. VHS, Beta *LCA*

Winter Wolf

Family Excellent entry in the "Legends" series imparts much information in a brief plot about a part-Indian girl caught in the public panic when wolves appear on the outskirts of her ranching community. Nature expert visits and teaches about wolves in fact and lore, and why they need not be feared.

1992 30m/C D: Kathleen Phelan; **W:** Kathleen Phelan. **VHS** *BMG, MIR*

Wishbone: A Tail in Twain

Family You may have read "Tom Sawyer" or seen a movie but have you ever seen Tom played by a dog dressed in straw hat, corduroy slacks, suspenders and shirt? That'd be Wishbone, the story-telling terrier (affably voiced by Larry Brantley) who portrays characters in classic tales on his own PBS series. With humans as supporting actors, Wishbone appears in two parallel stories—a famous one like "Tom Sawyer" and a contemporary one that leads into and out of the classic.In this one, the contemporary story concerns a stranger seen digging up what looks like a grave. Good humor, excellent sets and a charming canine actor (and charming human voice) make "Wishbone" highly entertaining. Other episodes available. Ages 6 to 12.

1996 30m/C VHS *PGV*

Wishbone: Homer Sweet Homer

Family The kids must protect their favorite playground, Jackson Park, and their favorite tree when developers come to destroy them. Meanwhile, Wishbone is lured far from home and must journey on a heroic quest to save it as Odysseus in Homer's "The Odyssey." Encourages literature appreciation by creating a fantasy world that the little Jack Russell terrier enters and lives out classic stories.

1996 30m/C VHS *PGV*

Wishbone: Salty Dog

Family Ahoy there mateys! It's Wishbone on the high seas. Samantha leads the gang into a dangerous adventure searching for Blackbeard's horseshoe in a condemned barn. Meanwhile, Wishbone races a mutinied crew as Jim Hawkins in a crazed search for gold in Robert Louis Stevenson's "Treasure Island."

1996 30m/C VHS *PGV*

Wishbone: Terrified Terrier

Family This episode of the award-winning PBS series finds Wishbone and friends left home alone when Joe begins playing basketball with some new older friends. Meanwhile, the daydreaming pooch pictures himself as Henry Fleming from Steven Crain's "The Red Badge of Courage" skipping out on friends on the battlefield.

1996 30m/C VHS *PGV*

Wishbone: The Prince and the Pooch

Family Joe gets his wish to become a coach when he takes the job for Emily's tee-ball team, but it may be a wish he regrets. In daydream world, Wishbone becomes both the Prince of Wales and and pauper Tom Canty in

Mark Twain's "The Prince and the Pauper." He learns that switching places can lead to big trouble.

1996 30m/C VHS *PGV*

Wishbone: The Slobbery Hound

Family A mystery dog terrorizes Oakdale and Wishbone is falsely accused. He must team up with the gang to take the case and prove his innocence. Meanwhile, the daydreaming guy finds himself as Sherlock Holmes, investigating an alleged canine criminal in Sir Arthur Conan Doyle's "The Hound of the Baskervilles."

1996 30m/C VHS *PGV*

Wishbone: Twisted Tail

Family Joe's house is hit by burglars and a crime wave sweeps Oakdale. Fingers start pointing at the new kid Max. And in Wishbone's world, the pooch finds himself as the orphan Oliver from Charles Dickens' novel "Oliver Twist," where he becomes trapped in another web of crime, but in London.

1996 30m/C VHS *PGV*

The Witch Who Turned Pink

Family When a green witch turns pink, she and the scandalized inhabitants of her woods desperately seek the means to regain her original shade. Colorful cartoon.

198? 30m/C VHS *KAR*

Witcheroo

Family Selection of all-new Disney cartoons (excerpted from TV shows) with Halloween themes. "Ghoul of My Dreams" features Darkwing Duck who must come to the rescue of the citizens of St. Canard when an evil spell puts everyone to sleep. In "Good Times, Bat Times," Chip 'n' Dale befriend an apprentice witch with a lovesick bat. Disney also issued two similar spooky collections on tape at the same time, "Boo-Busters" and "Monster Bash."

1993 44m/C VHS *DIS*

The Witches 🎵🎵🎵 ♭

PG/Jr. High-Adult Nine-year-old Luke, at a seaside resort with his grandmother, discovers that the Royal Society for the Prevention of Cruelty to Children meeting there is really a witch convention to launch the Grand High Witch's scheme to turn all England's children into mice. How can he stop them? Top-notch fantasy from the tart pen of "Willy Wonka" creator Roald Dahl (who, of course, hated this adaptation of his book), blends delightful f/x with a funny, imaginative adventure storyline. The final project of executive producer Jim Henson.

⚠ BEWARE ⚠ *Fantasy violence in the witch-busting finale. Fundamentalists and neo-pagans (both of whom have complained against Roald Dahl's book for different reasons) may or may not care that these bald, purple-eyed movie witches are pure invention, with all the reality of Margaret Hamilton in "The Wizard of Oz."*

1990 92m/C Anjelica Huston, Mai Zetterling, Jasen Fisher, Rowan Atkinson, Charlie Potter, Bill Paterson, Brenda Blethyn, Jane Horrocks; **D:** Nicolas Roeg; **W:** Allan Scott; **M:** Stanley Myers. **VHS, Beta, LV, 8mm** *WAR, FCT, ORI*

Witches' Brew 🎵🎵

PG/Jr. High-Adult Three young women try to use their undeveloped skills in witchcraft and black magic to help Garr's husband get a prestigious position at a university, with calamitous results. Oft-funny spoof is silly and oft-predictable. Turner's role is small as an older, experienced witch.

1979 98m/C Teri Garr, Richard Benjamin, Lana Turner, Kathryn Leigh Scott; **D:** Richard Shorr, Herbert L. Strock. **VHS, Beta**

The Witching of Ben Wagner 🎵🎵 ♭

G/Family Strange occurrences have Ben believing his friend Regina and her grandmother may be witches. But,

if so, they're friendly ones as they help Ben adjust to a new home and neighborhood.

1995 96m/C Justin Gocke, Harriet Hall, Sam Bottoms; **D:** Paul Annett. **VHS** *AVE*

Witch's Night Out

Preschool-Primary Rankin-Bass cartoon for the Halloween season on TV, in which a broom-riding mama takes a night on the town. She meets two children who ask to be transformed into their favorite monsters.

1979 30m/C V: Gilda Radner. **VHS, Beta** *FHE, CVM*

With Honors 🎵🎵 ♭

PG-13/Jr. High-Adult Pesci is a bum who finds desperate Harvard student Fraser's honors thesis, and, like any quick-witted bum with a yen for literature, holds it for ransom. Desperate to salvage his future gold card, Fraser and his roommates agree to fix Joe's homeless state. Self-involved students learn something about love and life while Madonna drones on the soundtrack. Fraser is believable as the ambitious student about to endure Pesci's enlightenment. Pesci is Pesci, doing his best to overcome numerous script cliches.

🚫 BEWARE 🚫 *Profanity and homelessness.*

1994 100m/C Joe Pesci, Brendan Fraser, Moira Kelly, Patrick Dempsey, Josh Hamilton, Gore Vidal; **D:** Alek Keshishian; **W:** William Mastrosimone; **M:** Patrick Leonard. **VHS** *WAR*

With Six You Get Eggroll 🎵🎵

G/Family Widow with three sons and a widower with a daughter elope and then must deal with the antagonism of their children and even their dogs. Brady Bunch-esque comedy about a blended family means well, but doesn't cut it. Hershey's debut. Farr, Christopher, and Tayback have small parts. To date, Doris Day's last big-screen appearance. Ages 7 to 12.

1968 95m/C Doris Day, Brian Keith, Pat Carroll, Alice Ghostley, Vic Tayback, Jamie Farr, William Christopher, Barbara Hershey; **D:** Howard Morris. **VHS, Beta** *FOX*

The Wiz 🎵🎵

G/Family Based on the black-oriented Broadway version of the long-time favorite "The Wizard of Oz," with Charlie Smalls' original score augmented by Quincy Jones. Waiflike Ross is Dorothy, a Harlem schoolteacher whisked to a fantasy version of New York City in a search for her identity. Stupendous sets, crazy costumes and memorable makeup effects (by Stan Winston and Albert Whitlock) tend to overwhelm the characterizations that were so crucial to the 1939 Judy Garland classic. One exception: Jackson's sweetly hapless scarecrow. Much of the dialogue and details (like the Wicked Witch's sweatshop) are very specific to the New York urban African American experience—if you don't know the history and geography it's more puzzling than fun. 🎵 The Feeling That We Have; Can I Go On Not Knowing; Glinda's Theme; He's the Wizard; Soon as I Get Home;

You Can't Win; Ease on Down the Road; What Would I Do If I Could Feel?; Slide Some Oil to Me.

1978 133m/C Diana Ross, Michael Jackson, Nipsey Russell, Ted Ross, Mabel King, Thelma Carpenter, Richard Pryor, Lena Horne; **D:** Sidney Lumet; **W:** Joel Schumacher; **M:** Quincy Jones. **VHS, Beta, LV** *MCA, FCT*

The Wizard WOOF!

PG/Family Autistic little Jimmy's been a handful, so mom and stepdad dump him in an institution. To the rescue comes brother Corey, who snatches the boy and races for California, where Jimmy can prove his hidden genius as a game wizard at 'Video Armageddon,' a Nintendo championship at the Universal Studios theme park. Yechh! There's more, like a sassy little girl who cries rape to get her way, but it adds up to a feature-length promo for that aforementioned game company and amusement park. Nothing kid or adult characters say or do is remotely credible, and dramatic highlight is the debut of . . . Super Mario 3. Game Over!

BEWARE *Profanity, fighting, alcohol talk and robbery (of the plot from "The Rain Man.")*

1989 99m/C Fred Savage, Beau Bridges, Christian Slater, Luke Edwards, Jenny Lewis; **D:** Todd Holland; **W:** David Chisholm. **VHS, Beta, LV** *MCA*

The Wizard of Loneliness 🎵🎵♭

PG-13/Jr. High-Adult Alienated 12-year-old Wendell goes to live with his grandparents during WWII, and slowly uncovers family secrets centering on his pretty young war-widow aunt. Excellent performances boost a moody, distracted, coming-of-age plot with a violent denouement. Based on the novel by John Nichols.

BEWARE *Violence, profanity and sex.*

1988 110m/C Lukas Haas, Lea Thompson, John Randolph, Lance Guest, Anne Pitoniak, Jeremiah Warner, Dylan Baker; **D:** Jenny Bowen; **W:** Nancy Larson; **M:** Michel Colombier. **VHS, Beta, LV** *NO*

The Wizard of Oz 🎵🎵🎵🎵

Family We won't dwell on those interpretations of L. Frank Baum tale as metaphor for the political-economic situation at the turn of the century. MGM didn't, and the result was pure entertainment. Farm girl Dorothy rides a tornado from B&W Kansas to a brightly colored world over the rainbow, full of munchkins, flying monkeys, a talking scarecrow, a tin man and a cowardly lion. She must appease the Oz the Great and Powerful and outwit the Wicked Witch if she is ever to go home. Delightful vaudeville performances from Lahr, Bolger, and Hamilton. Director Fleming originally wanted Shirley Temple (see "The Blue Bird") for the role of Dorothy, but settled for the overaged Garland, who made the song "Somewhere Over the Rainbow" her own and earned a special Academy Award. 50th anniversary edition is repackaged with rare clips of Bolger's "Scarecrow Dance" and the cut "Jitterbug" number, and shots of Buddy Ebsen as the Tin Man before he left the production due to an allergy to the

makeup. Laserdisc edition has digital sound, commentary by film historian Ronald Haver, test footage, trailers and stills, as well as Jerry Maren's memories as a Munchkin. Yet another special release, "The Ultimate Oz," adds a documentary, a reproduction of the original script, still photos, and liner notes. The sequel-interested should see also Disney's "Return to Oz."

🎵🎵 Munchkinland; Ding Dong the Witch is Dead; Follow the Yellow Brick Road; If I Only Had a Brain/a Heart/the Nerve; If I Were the King of the Forest; The Merry Old Land of Oz; Threatening Witch; Into the Forest of the Wild Beast; The City Gates are Open.

1939 101m/C Judy Garland, Margaret Hamilton, Ray Bolger, Jack Haley, Bert Lahr, Frank Morgan, Charley Grapewin, Clara Blandick, Mitchell Lewis, Billie Burke; **D:** Victor Fleming; **W:** Noel Langley; **M:** Herbert Stothart. **Award Nominations:** Academy Awards '39: Best Color Cinematography, Best Interior Decoration, Best Picture, Best Special Effects; **Awards:** Academy Awards '39: Best Song ("Over the Rainbow"), Best Original Score. **VHS, Beta, LV** *MGM, APD, TLF*

The Wizard of Oz 🎵🎵

Family All-animated version of the L. Frank Baum classic "The Wizard of Oz," more ideally suited for young children. Featured is the voice of Quinn, who played "Annie" on Broadway.

1982 78m/C V: Lorne Greene, Aileen Quinn. **VHS, Beta** *PAR*

The Wizard of Oz: Danger in a Strange Land

Family Cartoon takeoff on the L. Frank Baum "Oz" characters, produced by Ted Turner's company, not terribly faithful to the original books and stories. Two episodes here: "Time Town" and "The Day the Music Died." Additional volumes available.

1991 44m/C VHS, Beta *TTC*

The Wizard of Speed and Time 🎵🎵🎵

PG/Jr. High-Adult Ambitious, self-taught young movie-f/x master is hired by a greedy producer to jazz up a TV show with his gags and gadgets. But he doesn't know the exec is secretly out to stop him at all costs. Jittlov, a true special-effects expert who's done work for Disney, plays himself in this personally financed all-ages comedy. Though brimming with inside jokes and occasional self-pity, this indulgence succeeds. Its zippy, joyful style evokes a Pee Wee Herman-esque vision of Hollywood and a sincere plea for dreamers everywhere to persevere despite the odds (and unions). Constant visual trickery incorporates footage from Jittlov's many stop-motion and complex collage short subjects; be quick with the FREEZE and REWIND buttons to appreciate it all.

BEWARE *Roughhousing and minor double entendres, but nothing that would merit a PG. Maybe it's a conspiracy by the unions.*

1988 95m/C Mike Jittlov, Richard Kaye, Page Moore, David Conrad, Steve Brodie, John Massari, Frank Laloggia, Philip Michael Thomas, Angelique Pettyjohn, Arnetia Walker, Paulette Breen; **D:** Mike Jittlov;

Dorothy, the Tin Man and Scarecrow happen upon the Cowardly Lion in "The Wizard of Oz."

W: Mike Jittlov, Richard Kaye, Deven Chierighino; M: John Massari. **VHS, LV**

Wizards

PG/Jr. High-Adult After doing a series of taboo-breaking adults-only animated features, Bakshi softened—just a little—with this odd mixture of Tolkien satire and political cynicism. In a magic land (evolved after our civilization is nuked), a Skeletor lookalike uses an old projector and rediscovered Nazi propaganda newsreels to incite his armies and conquer peaceful kingdoms. His good-guy brother, the dwarfish wizard Avatar, reluctantly schleps to the rescue. Not for all tastes, but genuinely thought-provoking.

 *Violence, salty language, mature themes.*

1977 81m/C *D:* Ralph Bakshi. **VHS, Beta, LV** *FOX*

Wizards of the Lost Kingdom

PG/Jr. High-Adult Boy magician, aided by genial swordmaster Kor the Conqueror, battles a powerful wiz-ard for control of a kingdom. Harmless, brainless fairy tale fare. Poor f/x and halfhearted performances by all but roguish Svenson, whose modern-slang wisecracks strike the right campy note.

BEWARE *Fantasy violence.*

1985 76m/C Bo Svenson, Vidal Peterson, Thom Christopher; *D:* Hector Olivera. **VHS, Beta** *MED*

Wizards of the Lost Kingdom 2

PG/Jr. High-Adult Boy wizard is charged with vanquishing the evil tyrants from three kingdoms. Barely a sequel; no plot continuation or cast from earlier kiddie sword epic.

BEWARE *Fantasy violence.*

1989 80m/C David Carradine, Bobby Jacoby, Lana Clarkson, Mel Welles, Susan Lee Hoffman, Sid Haig; *D:* Charles B. Griffith. **VHS, Beta** *MED*

The Woman Who Raised a Bear as Her Son

Preschool-Primary Old woman adopts an orphaned polar bear cub who must learn lessons about how to treat others.

1990 27m/C VHS *FHE*

The Wombles

Preschool-Primary Series for children based on the British TV show about a race of adorable subterranean creatures who live in a London park and care for the environment.

1986 60m/C VHS, Beta *COL*

Wonder Man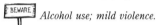

Family Wartime fantasy diversion starring Kaye in dual roles. As nightclub entertainer Buzzy he witnesses a murder and gets killed by gangsters to ensure his silence. But you can't keep Buzzy down; he returns as a ghost, possessing his studious twin brother (Kaye again) to give evidence to police. Heavier on the song-and-dance comedy than the supernatural elements, though the brief, Oscar-winning ghost f/x are good even by modern standards, and Kaye is a delight throughout. Watch for Schafer, Mrs. Howell from "Gilligan's Island." Tape includes the original theatrical trailer. ♫ So In Love; Bali Boogie; Ortchi Chornya; Opera Number.

BEWARE *Alcohol use; mild violence.*

1945 98m/C Danny Kaye, Virginia Mayo, Vera-Ellen, Steve Cochran, S.Z. Sakall, Otto Kruger; **D:** H. Bruce Humberstone. **Award Nominations:** Academy Awards '45: Best Song ("So in Love"), Best Sound, Best Original Score; **Awards:** Academy Awards '45: Best Special Effects. **VHS, Beta** *HBO*

Wonderful Wizard of Oz

Family Another version of Frank Baum's classic story, this time part of a Canadian cartoon series (though suspiciously Japanese-looking in design and voices) that's nonetheless faithful to the original "Oz" books. Others in the series: "The Marvelous Land of Oz," "Emerald City of Oz," and "Ozma of Oz."

1987 93m/C VHS

Wonderful World of Puss 'N Boots

Preschool-Primary Japanese-animated version of the classic fairy tale about the brave, clever cat who helps out his master.

1970 80m/C VHS, Beta *MED, VES*

The Wonderful World of the Brothers Grimm

Family Big-budget musical fantasy based very loosely on the lives of those famous fairy-tale mongers, the Grimm brothers. Hokey made in Hollywood romantic and business conflicts come between dreamer Wilhelm and the more pragmatic Jacob. Highlights are adaptations of three Grimm stories, "The Dancing Princesses," "The Cobbler and the Elves" and "The Singing Bone" (featuring a notably fearsome dragon), done using George Pal's stop-motion Puppetoon f/x. Originally a showcase for the new Cinerama widescreen process; both that and the cliches suffer on home video. ♫ The Theme From the Wonderful World of the Brothers Grimm; Gypsy Rhapsody; Christmas Land; Ah-Oom; Above the Stars; Dee-Are-A-Gee-O-En (Dragon).

1962 134m/C Laurence Harvey, Karl-Heinz Boehm, Claire Bloom, Buddy Hackett, Terry-Thomas, Russ Tamblyn, Yvette Mimieux, Oscar Homolka, Walter Slezak, Beulah Bondi, Martita Hunt, Otto Kruger, Barbara Eden, Jim Backus, Arnold Stang; **D:** Henry Levin, George Pal; **W:** William Roberts. **Award Nominations:** Academy Awards '62: Best Art Direction/Set Decoration (Color), Best Color Cinematography, Best Original Score; **Awards:** Academy Awards '62: Best Costume Design (Color). **VHS, Beta, LV** *MGM*

The Wonderful World of Wombles

Preschool-Primary Adventure starring the adorable animated Womble characters from Britain, underground critters on a mission against pollution. See also "Wombling Free" and "The Wombles."

1987 60m/C VHS, Beta *COL*

Wonderland Cove

Family The five MacKenzie orphans of Hawaii don't want to be scattered in foster homes, so they create a fictitious guardian uncle on paper. When a social worker gets suspicious, the kids hire a grouchy neighbor to impersonate Uncle. He's played with believable salt by Gulager, who's the best thing about this TV pilot for the short-lived series "The MacKenzies of Paradise Cove."

BEWARE *Alcohol use.*

1975 78m/C Clu Gulager, Sean Marshall, Randi Kiger, Lori Walsh; **D:** Jerry Thorpe. **Beta** *PSM*

Wonders of Aladdin

Family Feeble Italian-American co-production of the genie-in-the-lamp saga, with song-and-dance man O'Connor decidedly overaged (and a few continents off) as the title Arabian hero, putting the emphasis on slapstick. Tiny kids may love it, adults will yawn.

1961 93m/C Donald O'Connor, Vittorio De Sica; **D:** Henry Levin, Mario Bava. **VHS, Beta** *NLC*

Woody Woodpecker & His Friends: Vol. 1

Family Ten favorite 1940-1955 Walter Lantz "cartunes" were chosen for this tape: "Knock," "Bandmaster," "Ski for Two," "Hot Noon," "The Legend of Rockabye Point," "Wet Blanket Policy," "To Catch a Woodpecker," "Musi-

cal Moments from Chopin," "Bats in the Belfry," and "Crazy Mixed-Up Pup." Additional volumes available.
1982 80m/C VHS, Beta, LV *MCA*

Woody Woodpecker Collector's Edition, Vol. 1

Family Collection of the hilarious bird's greatest cartoons. "Woody Woodpecker (Cracked Nut)" is the very first Woody appearance. "Banquet Busters"—Woody and Andy Panda crash Mrs. Van Glutton's dinner party. Woody also stars in "Born to Peck" and "The Redwood Sap." Additional volumes available.
1990 30m/C VHS, Beta, LV *MCA*

Woof! 🦴🦴🦴

Family Charming British TV movie about young Eric, a boy with an uncontrollable tendency to turn into a dog and back again. With the help of school buddy he tackles this little problem with common sense and a quick change of clothes. Based on the book by Allan Ahlberg.
1990 82m/C VHS *FHE, UND, BTV*

Words by Heart

Family An African American family in turn of the century Missouri faces issues of discrimination and prejudice. Twelve-year-old Lena wins a speech contest and begins to question their place in the community and their aspirations for a better life. Based on a book by Ouida Sebestyen. Aired by PBS as part of the "Wonderworks" family movie series.
1984 116m/C Charlotte Rae, Robert Hooks, Alfre Woodard; **D:** Robert Thompson. **VHS** *PME, FCT, HMV*

Workin' on the Railroad: Alphabet Factory on the Railroad

Preschool The Alphabet Factory takes the kids on various train rides. Children can sing along to six all-time great railroad songs. Ages 2 to 6.
1995 25m/C VHS *TPV, ALP*

The World According to Gumby

Family Another collection of episodes from the original Gumby series spun off from "Howdy Doody." Segments include "The Big Eye," "Outcast Marbles," "Tail Tale," "Haunted Hot Dog," and "Indian Challenge."
1956 30m/C VHS, Beta

A World Apart 🦴🦴🦴 🐾

PG/Jr. High-Adult Blistering drama told from the view of a 13-year-old white girl in South Africa, resentful that her crusading journalist mother tirelessly fights against the racist government but makes no time for her family. Not just a political morality tale, but a look at the personal sacrifices activists must make in their private lives. Heavily lauded, with good reason. The autobiographical script is based on writer Slovo's parents, apartheid fighters Joe Slovo and Ruth First.

BEWARE *Apartheid, profanity and violence.*

1988 114m/C Barbara Hershey, Jodhi May, Linda Mvusi, David Suchet, Jeroen Krabbe, Paul Freeman, Tim Roth; **D:** Chris Menges; **W:** Shawn Slovo; **M:** Hans Zimmer. **VHS, Beta, LV** *MED*

A World is Born

Preschool-Primary Evolution of the world from prehistoric times is set to music by Igor Stravinsky, and glorious animation in this excerpt from Walt Disney's 1940 "Fantasia."
1990 20m/C VHS, Beta *MTI, DSN*

The World of Andy Panda

Family Collection of nine Andy Panda cartoons done by Lantz in the 1940s, featuring "Apple Andy," "Crow Crazy," and "Meatless Tuesday."
1946 62m/C VHS, Beta *MCA*

World of David the Gnome: Kangaroo Adventure

Family Cartoon adventure series based on the bestselling gnome tomes by Rien Poortvliet and Wil Huygen. In this one the main character, a globetrotting gnome named David, must aid some Australian birds when they are captured by a mean hunter. Additional volumes available.
1987 45m/C V: Tom Bosley. **VHS, Beta** *FHE, LIV*

World of Hans Christian Andersen

Preschool-Primary Animated Hans Christian Andersen relates the delightful tales that made him a legend in the storytelling business.
1985 73m/C VHS, Beta *COL*

The World of Henry Orient 🦴🦴🦴 🐾

Family Charming, eccentric comedy about two 15-year-old girls who, madly in love with an egotistical concert pianist, pursue him all around New York City. Sellers is hilarious, Walker and Spaeth are adorable as his teen groupies; Bosley and Lansbury are great as Walker's indulgent parents. For anyone who has ever been uncontrollably infatuated. Screenplay by the father/daughter team, Nora and Nunnally Johnson, based on Nora Johnson's novel. Music by Elmer Bernstein.
1964 106m/C Peter Sellers, Tippy Walker, Merrie Spaeth, Tom Bosley, Angela Lansbury, Paula Prentiss; **D:** George Roy Hill; **W:** Nunnally Johnson, Nora Johnson; **M:** Elmer Bernstein. **VHS, Beta, LV** *MGM, FCT*

A World of Stories with Katharine Hepburn

Primary Venerable actress tells six of her favorite fairy tales. Includes illustrations from the stories.
1993 78m/C VHS *WST, KUL*

World of Strawberry Shortcake

Preschool-Primary The Peculiar Purple Pieman of Porcupine Peak poses pitfalls aplenty for Ms. Shortcake and pals. Pernicious tape peddling pointless playthings to preschoolers.
1980 60m/C VHS, Beta *FHE*

The World's Greatest Athlete 🦴🦴

G/Family Lame Disney comedy about Tarzan-like jungle-man Vincent recruited by unsuccessful American college coach Amos and his bumbling assistant Conway. Fun special effects, weak script add up to mediocre family fare. Cameo by Howard Cosell as—who else?—himself.
1973 89m/C Jan-Michael Vincent, Tim Conway, John Amos, Roscoe Lee Browne, Dayle Haddon; **Cameos:** Howard Cosell; **D:** Robert Scheerer; **M:** Marvin Hamlisch. **VHS, Beta** *DIS, OM*

The Worst Witch 🦴🦴 ▷

G/Family Well-cast British TV fantasy (with songs) about Miss Cackle's Academy for Witches, where newcomer Mildred can never get her magic straight but winds up a hero anyway. Adapted from the children's book series by Jill Murphy.
1986 70m/C Diana Rigg, Charlotte Rae, Tim Curry, Fairuza Balk; **D:** Robert Young. **VHS, Beta** *PSM*

Wowser: Wow-Wow Wowser

Preschool-Primary Helpful dog aids his master by trying out a group of inventions. Additional volumes available.
1989 110m/C VHS, Beta *CEL*

Wrinkles: In Need of Cuddles

Preschool Another popular toy bites the dust in a Saturday-morning TV adaptation.
1986 48m/C Ami Foster; **D:** Lee Mendelson. **VHS, Beta** *LIV*

The Wrong Man 🦴🦴🦴 ▷

Sr. High-Adult Nightclub musician Fonda is falsely accused of a robbery and his life is destroyed. Taken almost entirely from the real-life case of mild-mannered bass player "Manny" Balestrero; probes his anguish at being wrongly accused; and showcases Miles (later to appear in "Psycho") and her character's agony. Harrowing, especially following more lighthearted Hitchcock fare such as "The Trouble with Harry." Part of the "A Night at the Movies" series, this tape simulates a 1956 movie evening with a color Bugs Bunny cartoon, "A Star Is Bored," a newsreel and coming attractions for "Toward the Unknown."
1956 126m/B Henry Fonda, Vera Miles, Anthony Quayle, Nehemiah Persoff; **D:** Alfred Hitchcock. **VHS, Beta, LV** *WAR, MLB*

Wuthering Heights 🦴🦴 ▷

G/Jr. High-Adult The third screening of the classic Emily Bronte romance about two doomed lovers. Fuest's version features excellent photography, and Calder-Marshall's and Dalton's performances are effective, but fail even to approach the intensity and pathos of the 1939 film original (or of the book). Filmed on location in Yorkshire, England.
1970 105m/C Anna Calder-Marshall, Timothy Dalton, Harry Andrews, Pamela Brown, Judy Cornwell, James Cossins, Rosalie Crutchley, Hilary Dwyer, Hugh Griffith, Ian Ogilvy; **D:** Robert Fuest. **VHS, Beta** *CNG, KAR, TVC*

X-Men: Deadly Reunions

Primary-Jr. High TV episode of the cartoon series bringing to animated life the wildly popular Marvel Comics superhero troupe. While Rogue and Cyclops do battle with the ever-menacing Magento, Wolverine is confronted by his ancient arch-rival, Sabertooth. Can you tell the players without a scorecard? Additional episodes available.
1993 25m/C VHS *PGV*

Xanadu WOOF!

PG/Jr. High-Adult Dorky star-vehicle remake (of 1947's "Down to Earth") eminently of the disco era, which is now better forgotten. Newton-John is a mystical muse who descends to Earth to help two friends open a roller disco. In the process she proves that as an actor, she's a singer. Kelly attempts to soft shoe some grace into the proceedings, though he seems mystified as anyone as to why he's on the set. Don Bluth adds an animated sequence. 🎵 I'm Alive; The Fall; Don't Walk Away; All Over the World; Xanadu; Magic; Suddenly; Dancing; Suspended in Time.
1980 96m/C Olivia Newton-John, Michael Beck, Gene Kelly, Sandahl Bergman; **D:** Robert Greenwald. **VHS, Beta, LV** *MCA, MLB*

Xuxa: Funtastic Birthday Party

Primary-Jr. High Xuxa, the superstar Latin-American children's entertainer watches a magic show, sings, and dances with friends.
1994 40m/C VHS *SKM*

Yanco 🦴🦴

Family A young Mexican boy makes visits to an island where he plays his homemade violin. Unfortunately, no one can understand or tolerate his love for music, save for an elderly violinist, who gives him lessons on an instrument known as "Yanco." No dialogue. Not exactly riveting, but sensitively played.
1964 95m/B Ricardo Ancona, Jesus Medina, Maria Bustamante. **VHS, Beta** *WFV, DVT, INJ*

Yankee Doodle Cricket

Primary Follow-up to "The Cricket in Times Square" finds animated animals present to compose "Yankee Doodle Dandy," help Thomas Jefferson write The Declaration of Independence, and assist Paul Revere.
1976 26m/C VHS, Beta *CHI, FHE*

Yankee Doodle Dandy

Family Nostalgic view of the Golden Era of show business and the man who made it glitter—George M. Cohan. His early days, triumphs, songs, musicals and romances are brought to life by the inexhaustible Cagney in a rare and wonderful song-and-dance performance. Told in flashback, covering the Irishman's struggling days as a young song writer and performer to his salad days as the toast of Broadway. Cagney, never more charismatic, dances up a storm, reportedly inventing most of the steps on the spot. ♫ Give My Regards to Broadway; Yankee Doodle Dandy; You're a Grand Old Flag; Over There; I Was Born in Virginia; Off the Record; You're a Wonderful Girl; Blue Skies, Grey Skies; Oh You Wonderful Girl.
1942 126m/B James Cagney, Joan Leslie, Walter Huston, Richard Whorf, Irene Manning, Rosemary DeCamp, Jeanne Cagney, S.Z. Sakall, Walter Catlett, Frances Langford, Eddie Foy Jr., George Tobias, Michael Curtiz; **D:** Michael Curtiz; **W:** Robert Buckner. **Award Nominations:** Academy Awards '42: Best Director (Curtiz), Best Picture, Best Story, Best Supporting Actor (Huston); **Awards:** Academy Awards '42: Best Actor (Cagney), Best Sound, Best Score. **VHS, Beta, LV** *MGM, FOX, FCT*

The Year My Voice Broke ♫♫♫

PG-13/Sr. High-Adult Danny is an undersized, thoughtful boy in an Australian outback town, deeply infatuated with childhood playmate Freya, an orphan teen now gaining a reputation as the village tramp. While Freya considers Danny her best friend, she keeps their relationship platonic—and gets pregnant by a tougher, older guy. An overflow of melodrama in the second half is the only false note in this bluesy portrait of first love at its most bittersweet. Writer/director Duigan followed unlucky-in-love Danny's further romantic mishaps in "Flirting."

BEWARE *Sex, implied more than shown. Mature themes, alcohol use.*

1987 103m/C Noah Taylor, Leone Carmen, Ben Mendelsohn, Graeme Blundell, Lynette Curran, Malcolm Robertson, Judi Farr; **D:** John Duigan; **W:** John Duigan; **M:** Christine Woodruff. **VHS, Beta, LV** *LIV*

Year of the Comet ♫♫

PG-13/Jr. High-Adult Amusing adventure/romantic comedy throws straightlaced Maggie (Miller) together with carefree Oliver (Daly) in a quest for a rare bottle of wine. Fine wine is Maggie's passion, and snagging this particular bottle will boost her status in the family business. Oliver is a pretzels and beer kind of guy, but his boss wants this bottle and will pay a lot to get it. Wants to be another "Romancing the Stone," but plot and characters are too thin. Nice chemistry between Miller and Daly sort of saves this one despite a disappointing script. Beautiful location shots of Scotland.

BEWARE *Profanity and violence.*

1992 135m/C Penelope Ann Miller, Timothy Daly, Louis Jourdan, Art Malik, Ian Richardson, Ian McNeice, Timothy Bentinck, Julia McCarthy, Jacques Mathou; **D:** Peter Yates; **W:** William Goldman; **M:** Hummie Mann. **VHS, LV** *NLC*

The Year Without a Santa Claus

Family Hip, funny, stop-motion-animated TV special shows the panic that hits the North Pole when a tired Santa decides to take December 25th off for once. A stylish standout in the children's Christmas parade from the Rankin-Bass Animagic works. Great musical numbers are fun for adults, too, especially Heatmiser and Coldmiser. Based on the award-winning book by Phyllis McGinley.
1974 50m/C V: Mickey Rooney, Shirley Booth. **VHS, Beta** *LIV, TVC*

The Yearling ♫♫♫♪

Family Tearjerking adaptation of the Marjorie Kinnan Rawlings novel about how a young boy's love for a yearling fawn during the post Civil War era. His father's encouragement and his mother's bitterness play against the story of unqualified love amid poverty and the boy's coming of age. Evocative recreation of wilderness Florida of another era. Jarman was awarded a special Oscar as outstanding child actor.

BEWARE *The title deer distinguishes itself as one of the least heroic animal stars in history, but it still must share Old Yeller's fate.*

1946 128m/C Gregory Peck, Jane Wyman, Claude Jarman Jr., Chill Wills, Henry Travers, Jeff York, Forrest Tucker, June Lockhart, Margaret Wycherly; **D:** Clarence Brown. **Award Nominations:** Academy Awards '46: Best Actor (Peck), Best Actress (Wyman), Best Director (Brown), Best Film Editing, Best Picture; **Awards:** Academy Awards '46: Best Color Cinematography, Best Interior Decoration; Golden Globe Awards '47: Best Actor—Drama (Peck). **VHS, Beta, LV** *KUI, MGM, TLF*

Yellow Submarine ♫♫♫♪

G/Family Acclaimed all-ages animated phantasmagoria based on a plethora of mid-career Beatles songs. The Fab Four fight the music-hating Blue Meanies to save Sgt. Pepper, the Nowhere Man, Strawberry Fields, and Pepperland. The first full-length British animated feature in 14 years features a host of talented cartoonists pulling out all the stops with wild op-art animation and imagery. Speaking voices were NOT provided by the Beatles themselves but rather sound-alikes John Clive (John), Geoff Hughes (Paul), Peter Batten (George), and Paul Angelis (Ringo). The group themselves do appear in a short scene at the end of the film. ♫ Yellow Submarine; All You Need is Love; Hey, Bulldog; When I'm Sixty Four;

Nowhere Man; Lucy in the Sky With Diamonds; Sgt. Pepper's Lonely Hearts Club Band; A Day in the Life; All Together Now.

1968 87m/C D: George Duning, Dick Emery; **W:** Erich Segal; **M:** George Martin. **VHS, Beta, LV** *MVD, MGM*

Yellowstone Cubs

Preschool-Primary Disney live-action nature footage allows the viewer to share in the misadventures of Tuffy and Tubby, a pair of cute bears who always manage to find trouble.

1976 45m/C VHS, Beta *MTI, DSN*

Yentl

PG/Jr. High-Adult The famous Barbra adaptation of Isaac Bashevis Singer's story set in 1900s Eastern Europe about a Jewish girl who masquerades as a boy in order to study the Talmud, and who becomes enmeshed in romantic miscues. Lushly photographed, with a repetitive score that nevertheless won an Oscar. Singer was reportedly appalled by the results of Streisand's hyper-controlled project. ♫ A Piece of Sky; No Matter What Happens; This Is One of Those Moments; Tomorrow Night; Where Is It Written; No Wonder; The Way He Makes Me Feel; Papa, Can You Hear Me; Will Someone Ever Look at Me That Way?.

⚠ BEWARE *Brief nudity.*

1983 134m/C Barbra Streisand, Mandy Patinkin, Amy Irving, Nehemiah Persoff, Steven Hill, Allan Corduner, Ruth Goring, David DeKeyser, Bernard Spear; **D:** Barbra Streisand; **M:** Michel Legrand, Alan Bergman, Marilyn Bergman. **Award Nominations:** Academy Awards '83: Best Art Direction/Set Decoration, Best Song ("Papa, Can You Hear Me?", "The Way He Makes Me Feel"), Best Supporting Actress (Irving); **Awards:** Academy Awards '83: Best Original Score; Golden Globe Awards '84: Best Director (Streisand), Best Film—Musical/Comedy. **VHS, Beta, LV** *MGM, IME*

Yes, Virginia, There is a Santa Claus

Family Realistic cartoon retelling the true story of little Virginia O'Hanlon, whose belief in Santa Claus inspired that most famous column in the New York Sun newspaper in 1897. Award-winning animation courtesy of the Bill Melendez team otherwise responsible for "Peanuts" in prime time.

1974 30m/C V: Jim Backus, Courtney Lemmon, Louis Nye. **VHS, Beta** *PAR*

Yogi and the Invasion of the Space Bears

Family Yogi Bear and Boo Boo are kidnapped by aliens who threaten to clone them thousands of times, posing a threat to picnic baskets throughout Jellystone Park and the rest of the world. Hanna-Barbera made-for-TV cartoon feature.

1991 90m/C V: Daws Butler, Don Messick, Sorrell Booke, Julie Bennett. **VHS, Beta** *TTC*

Yogi and the Magical Flight of the Spruce Goose

Family Yogi and other Hanna-Barbera characters visit Long Beach and Howard Hughes' famous wooden airliner the Spruce Goose. They manage to use the craft in a fantasy voyage to rescue trapped animals. Made-for-TV cartoon feature.

1984 96m/C V: Daws Butler, Don Messick, Paul Winchell, John Stephenson. **VHS, Beta** *TTC*

Yogi, the Easter Bear

Preschool-Primary Yogi can't resist eating all the goodies Ranger Smith brought for the Easter Jamboree. Now, he and Boo-Boo must search for the Easter Bunny to get more treats for the children at Jellystone Park. Ages 2 to 6.

1995 55m/C VHS *TTC*

Yogi's First Christmas

Family Made-for-TV cartoon feature in which Hanna-Barbera characters like Huckleberry Hound, Snagglepuss, Auggie Doggie and others convene at Jellystone Park for Noel with the title bear. Complications arise with the revelation that their lodge is to be bulldozed for a freeway. Can Santa save the day?

1980 100m/C D: Ray Patterson; **V:** Daws Butler, Don Messick, John Stephenson, Janet Waldo, Hal Smith. **VHS, Beta, LV** *TTC, IME*

Yogi's Great Escape

Family Yogi learns that Jellystone Park is to be closed down and the bear population moved to zoos. He, Boo Boo and three cubs go on the run with Ranger Smith in a cross-country pursuit. Made-for-TV cartoon feature.

1984 96m/C V: Daws Butler, Don Messick, Susan Blu, Frank Welker. **VHS, Beta** *TTC*

Yogi's Treasure Hunt: Heavens to Planetoid!

Family Yogi ventures farther and wide in these recyclings from a recent syndicated TV series finding him and other Hanna-Barbera characters aboard the S.S. Jolly Roger, roaming the globe in search of treasure for charitable causes (like the salaries of cut-rate animators?). In these three adventures, the gang explores outer-space, the mountains of Peru, and below the earth's crust. Additional volumes available.

1985 80m/C VHS, Beta *TTC*

Yosemite Sam: The Good, the Bad, and the Ornery

Family Yosemite Sam and friends are featured in several cartoon shorts.

198? 33m/C VHS *WAR, BTV*

Claude Jarman Jr. cares for a little fawn in "The Yearling."

You Can Ride a Horse

Preschool-Primary When it comes to horseback riding there's no substitute for seat-on experience, but this video does provide the flavor without the, uh, aroma. It shows very young children mounting up and riding, and older kids a-gallop. Plus, see how to give a horse a bath, watch a blacksmith at work, and see examples of vaulting and grooming. Ages 3 to 7.
1995 30m/C VHS

You Only Live Twice 🦴🦴 ᵇ

PG/Jr. High-Adult Agent 007 (Sean Connery) travels to Japan to take on arch-nemesis Blofeld, who has been capturing Russian and American spacecraft in an attempt to start WWIII. Great location photography, but implausible plot defies even Bond standard. Theme sung by Nancy Sinatra. Script by Roald Dahl, but it's nothing to write home about. Ages 12 and up.

🐾 BEWARE 🐾 *More violence, alcohol use and suggested sex in the James Bond style.*

1967 125m/C Sean Connery, Mie Hama, Akiko Wakabayashi, Tetsuro Tamba, Karin Dor, Charles Gray, Donald Pleasence, Tsai Chin, Bernard Lee, Lois Maxwell, Desmond Llewelyn; *D:* Lewis Gilbert; *M:* John Barry. **VHS, Beta, LV** *MGM, TLF*

Young & Free 🦴 ᵇ

Sr. High-Adult Following the death of his parents, a young man must learn to face the perils of an unchartered wilderness alone. Ultimately he must choose between returning to civilization, or remain with his beloved wife and life in the wild.
1978 87m/C Erik Larsen; *D:* Keith Larsen. **VHS, Beta** *MON*

A Young Children's Concert with Raffi

Preschool Concert starring the famed Canadian children's entertainer.
1985 50m/C VHS, Beta *MLT, A&M*

The Young Detectives on Wheels 🦴🦴 ᵇ

Family Sandra and Mark find stolen emeralds in their backyard, and their father is arrested for the theft. The kids turn to a neighborhood assortment of BMX bike riders and young computer hackers to solve the crime and unmask the true criminals. Fun, if somewhat overlong New Zealand family film. Mystery is foggy in parts, but Sandra makes a nicely untypical and spunky heroine.

 Roughhousing.

1987 107m/C VHS *VMK, FHE, BTV*

Young Eagles

Family Low-budget vintage serial devoted to the exploits of an adventurous Boy Scout troop. In 12 chapters, lasting 13 minutes each. What Merit Badge will you earn for sitting through the whole thing?

1934 156m/B Bobby Cox, Jim Vance, Carter Dixon. **VHS, Beta** *VYY, VCN, MLB*

Young Einstein

PG/Jr. High-Adult Goofy, irreverent Australian farce starring, directed, co-scripted and co-produced by Serious, depicting Einstein as a young Outback clod who splits beer atoms and invents rock and roll. Mysterious winner of several Aussie awards will likely prove fun for the kids.

 Profanity.

1989 91m/C Yahoo Serious, Odile Le Clezio, John Howard, Pee Wee Wilson, Su Cruickshank; **D:** Yahoo Serious; **W:** Yahoo Serious. **VHS, Beta, LV** *WAR*

Young Frankenstein

PG/Jr. High-Adult Young Dr. Frankenstein (Wilder), a brain surgeon, inherits the family castle back in Transylvania. He's skittish about the family business, but upon learning his grandfather's secrets, he becomes obsessed with making his own monster. Once a Frankensteen, always a Frankensteen. Hilarious parody is crowded with numerous classic moments in faithful black and white, including Wilder and monster Boyle singing and dancing to Irving Berlin's "Puttin' on the Ritz," and Hackman's cameo as a blind man who befriends young Franky.

 Vulgarity, suggested sex and weird science.

1974 108m/B Peter Boyle, Gene Wilder, Marty Feldman, Madeline Kahn, Cloris Leachman, Teri Garr, Kenneth Mars, Richard Haydn; **Cameos:** Gene Hackman; **D:** Mel Brooks; **W:** Gene Wilder, Mel Brooks; **M:** John Morris. **VHS, Beta, LV** *FOX, HMV*

Young Guns

R/Sr. High-Adult Sophomoric Wild Bunch look-alike that ends up resembling a western version of the Bowery Boys with lots of guns, bullets, and bodies. Ensemble of semi-hip young stars provides an MTV portrait of Billy the Kid (Emilio Estevez) and his gang as they move from prairie trash to demi-legends. Followed by Young Guns II. Ages 15 and up.

 Profanity and extreme violence and gunplay. Lots of useless killing.

1988 107m/C Emilio Estevez, Kiefer Sutherland, Lou Diamond Phillips, Charlie Sheen, Casey Siemaszko, Dermot Mulroney, Terence Stamp, Terry O'Quinn, Jack Palance, Brian Keith, Patrick Wayne,

Sharon Thomas; **D:** Christopher Cain; **W:** John Fusco; **M:** Anthony Marinelli, Brian Backus. **VHS, Beta, LV** *LIV, VES*

Young Magician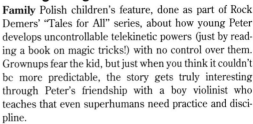

Family Polish children's feature, done as part of Rock Demers' "Tales for All" series, about how young Peter develops uncontrollable telekinetic powers (just by reading a book on magic tricks!) with no control over them. Grownups fear the kid, but just when you think it couldn't bc more predictable, the story gets truly interesting through Peter's friendship with a boy violinist who teaches that even superhumans need practice and discipline.

1988 99m/C Rusty Jedwab, Natasza Maraszek, Edward Garson; **D:** Waldemar Dziki. **VHS, Beta** *FHE*

Young Robin Hood

Family The Hanna-Barbera folks took advantage of the recently hip Robin Hood legend to issue this feature-length cartoon knockoff. This time "The Prince of Thieves" is 14 years old and, with his band of youthful Merry Men, intends to besiege Nottingham Castle.

1991 90m/C VHS, Beta *TTC*

Young Sherlock Holmes

PG-13/Jr. High-Adult Can't-miss premise does: Holmes and Watson meet as schoolboys in London and join on their first case, a series of bizarre murders committed by an Egyptian cult (who look like Hare Krishnas). You're in trouble when not one, but two on-screen disclaimers declare this is based on NO work by Sir Arthur Conan Doyle; inspiration instead comes from the hi-tech f/x department of Steven Spielberg's production company, with cult-induced hallucinations spawning unreal monsters and a climax ripped off from "Indiana Jones and the Temple of Doom." In there somewhere is a melancholy turn by Rowe as the lonely adolescent Sherlock.

 Violence, but not as bad as the PG-13 rating would suggest.

1985 109m/C Nicholas Rowe, Alan Cox, Sophie Ward, Freddie Jones, Michael Hordern; **D:** Barry Levinson; **W:** Chris Columbus; **M:** Bruce Broughton. **VHS, Beta, LV, 8mm** *PAR*

You're a Good Man, Charlie Brown

Preschool-Jr. High Not a cartoon, but a straight, filmed version of Charles Schulz's stage musical (originally a record album, then a Broadway hit), bringing to life his immortal "Peanuts" characters in a series of true-to-the-comic-strip sketches and songs.

1987 60m/C VHS, Beta *BAR, KAR*

You're Invited to Mary-Kate & Ashley's Sleep Over Party

Primary Mary-Kate and Ashley take a break from solving mysteries and throw a slumber party. The fun starts when the two girls prevent any boys from coming to the party. Ages 4 to 8.
1996 ?m/C VHS *KID, AVE*

You're Not Elected, Charlie Brown!/A Charlie Brown Christmas

Family Peanuts doubleheader, including Charlie Brown and Linus running against each other for the office of student body president. "A Charlie Brown Christmas," dating from 1965, is one of the first of the animated "Peanuts" specials, and features Charlie Brown worrying that the holiday has become over-commercialized.
1965 50m/C D: Bill Melendez; **W:** Charles M. Schulz. **VHS, Beta** *SHV, VTR*

Yours, Mine & Ours 🦴🦴🦴

Family Bigger, better, big screen version of "The Brady Bunch." It's the story of a lovely lady (Ball) with eight kids who marries a widower (Fonda) who has ten. Imagine the zany shenanigans! Family comedy manages to be both wholesome and funny. Based on a true story.
1968 114m/C Lucille Ball, Henry Fonda, Van Johnson, Tim Matheson, Tom Bosley, Tracy Nelson; **D:** Melville Shavelson; **W:** Melville Shavelson. **VHS, Beta, LV** *MGM*

Yukon Flight 🦴🦴

Family A Renfrew of the Mounties adventure. The hero finds illegal gold mining operations and murder in the Yukon.
1940 57m/B James Newill, Dave O'Brien. **VHS, Beta** *NOS, VCN*

The Zax From Dr. Seuss on the Loose

Primary North-going Zax and a south-going Zax meet face-to-face midway on their journeys; neither is willing to budge to let the other through.
1974 5m/C W: Theodore (Dr. Seuss) Geisel. **VHS, Beta** *BFA*

Zebra in the Kitchen 🦴🦴 ◗

Family Critter comedy from "Flipper" creator Tors takes the "Free Willy" concept to its extremes. Little Chris is so upset by the way his pet cougar gets treated in a bleak zoo that he liberates the big cat, and in the process unlocks the whole menagerie. For much of the remaining run time, townsfolk are spooked by stray ostriches, monkeys, elephants, and that zebra (it looks weird because none of the 'terrified' human extras ever make a sound or even a facial expression). It does get boring and repetitious very quickly.

1965 92m/C Jay North, Martin Milner, Andy Devine, Joyce Meadows, Jim Davis; **D:** Ivan Tors. **VHS** *MGM, BTV*

Zebrahead 🦴🦴🦴

R/Sr. High-Adult Zack and Nikki are two high schoolers in love—which would be okay except Zack's white and Nikki's black. Will their romance succumb to the pressures of society, family, and friends? With mature theme, urban violence, sexual situations, and drugs, it won't be everyone's cup of tea. But writer/director Drazan's expressive debut is a small gem featuring one of the last appearances by Sharkey (as Zack's dad) and outstanding performances by the young and largely unknown cast, particularly Rappaport and Wright. Great musical score enriches the action. Filmed on location in Detroit, with plenty of authentic Motown scenery displayed. Developed with assistance by the Sundance Institute.

🔔 BEWARE 🔔 *Violence, profanity, drug use and sexual situations.*

1992 102m/C Michael Rapaport, N'Bushe Wright, Ray Sharkey, DeShonn Castle, Ron Johnson, Marsha Florence, Paul Butler, Abdul Hassan Sharif, Dan Ziskie, Candy Ann Brown, Helen Shaver, Luke Reilly, Martin Priest; **D:** Tony Drazan; **W:** Tony Drazan; **M:** Taj Mahal. **VHS, LV, 8mm** *COL*

Zelly & Me 🦴🦴🦴

PG/Jr. High-Adult Psychological drama about a young orphan living with her possessive grandmother. Granny forces the child to become a participant in her own somewhat twisted version of reality (including an obsession with Joan of Arc) through humiliation and isolation from anyone she cares for. Written by Rathborne, this is well-acted and interesting despite the introspective plot and confusing gaps in the narrative.

🔔 BEWARE 🔔 *Mature themes.*

1988 87m/C Isabella Rossellini, Alexandra Johnes, David Lynch, Glynis Johns, Kaiulani Lee, Joe Morton; **D:** Tina Rathborne; **W:** Tina Rathborne; **M:** Pino Donaggio. **VHS, Beta, LV** *COL*

Zero to Sixty 🦴

PG/Jr. High-Adult Newly divorced man finds his car has been repossessed for nonpayment. Seeking out the manager of the finance company, he gets a job as a repo man with a sassy 16-year-old girl as his assistant. Repartee develops, stuff happens, and the movie ends.
1978 96m/C Darren McGavin, Sylvia Miles, Denise Nickerson, Joan Collins; **D:** Don Weis. **VHS, Beta**

Ziggy's Gift

Family Ziggy, the lovable cartoon character created by Tom Wilson, stars (but never speaks) in this TV Christmas program. Recruited as a street-corner Santa by what turns out to be a criminal gang, the hapless Ziggy nonetheless spreads holiday kindness and good cheer.
1983 30m/C M: Harry Nilsson. **VHS, Beta** *LIV, VES*

Zillion

Primary-Jr. High Five-part cartoon miniseries featuring the White Knights who will battle until the death for their planet called Maris.
1990 30m/C VHS *STP, TPV*

Zombies of the Stratosphere

Family The heyday of the movie serial was long past when Republic released this 12-chapter revival of their "Rocket Man" character for silly but undeniable fun. He fights not zombies but meanies from Mars, in cahoots with Earth gangsters to hijack our whole planet. Yes, that is Nimoy, later to be Mr. Spock, as a rookie Martian, complete with pointy ears.

 Violence.

1952 152m/B Judd Holdren, Aline Towne, Leonard Nimoy, John Crawford, Ray Boyle; **D:** Fred Brannon. **VHS, Beta, LV** *REP, VCN, MLB*

The Zoo Gang

PG-13/Jr. High-Adult Group of teens want to open a nightclub but meet opposition from a mean rival gang and a stupid youth-comedy script. Vereen's dignity barely survives his thankless role as a vagrant ex-wrestler who helps out.

 Roughhousing, salty language, alcohol use.

1985 96m/C Jackie Earle Haley, Tiffany Helm, Ben Vereen, Jason Gedrick, Eric Gurry; **D:** John Watson, Pen Densham; **W:** John Watson, Pen Densham; **M:** Patrick Gleeson. **VHS, Beta** *NWV, VTR*

Zoobilee Zoo, Vol. 1: Land of Rhymes & Other Stories

Primary A special fantasy/educational program for children in which the residents of a magical zoo are portrayed by various dancers and actors. This volume is entitled "Land of Rhymes and Other Stories" and includes "Land of Rhymes," "Singalong 1," and "Bravo's Puppets." Additional volumes available.
1987 70m/C Ben Vereen. **VHS, Beta** *COL*

Zoofari

Preschool-Primary A visit to a the zoo and a look at the wonders of the animal kingdom. Ages 2 to 7.
1995 ?m/C VHS *AEL*

Zoom the White Dolphin

Primary Sunny but basic cartoon feature about a family on a tropical island who befriend their watery neighbors, a clan of porpoises led by the albino Zoom.
1974 94m/C VHS, Beta

Zorro Rides Again

Family Fast-moving, fun serial in which Zorro, here placed in 'present-day' (1930s) California, risks his life to outwit enemy agents and make sure the railroad goes through. The first chapter runs 30 minutes, the rest 17.

 *Roughhousing.*

1937 217m/B John Carroll, Helen Christian, Noah Beery Sr., Duncan Renaldo; **D:** William Witney, John English. **VHS, Beta** *NOS, VCN, MED*

Zorro, Vol. 1

Family In addition to the two Disney "Zorro" movies, six feature-length volumes of the TV series are on video starring Madison as the masked avenger of old California.

1958 75m/B Guy Williams, Gene Sheldon, Britt Lomond, Henry Calvin, Jan Avran, Eugenia Paul, Annette Funicello, Richard Anderson, Jolene Brand. **VHS, Beta** *DIS*

Zorro's Black Whip

Family Lady crime reporter dons the mask of her slain crime-fighting brother (not Zorro, incidentally; he really has nothing to do with it) to continue the struggle for truth and justice. Makers of this okay 12-episode Republic serial brainstormed for a method of hand-to-hand combat that was 'ladylike,' so they settled for the whip.

 *Roughhousing.*

1944 182m/B George Lewis, Linda Stirling, Lucien Littlefield, Francis McDonald, Tom London; **D:** Spencer Gordon Bennet; **W:** Wallace Grissell. **VHS, LV** *NOS, GPV, MED*

Zorro's Fighting Legion

Family Zorro forms a legion to help the president of Mexico fight a band of outlaws endeavoring to steal gold shipments. A serial in 12 chapters.

 *Roughhousing.*

1939 215m/B Reed Hadley; **D:** William Witney, John English. **VHS, LV** *NOS, VCN, VDM*

Alternate Titles Index

The **ALTERNATE TITLES INDEX** lists variant titles for movies, including foreign titles. Titles are listed in alphabetical order followed by a cross-reference to the appropriate title as listed in the main video review section.

Abbott and Costello Meet the Ghosts *See* Abbott and Costello Meet Frankenstein (1948)

Ace *See* The Great Santini (1980)

Ace Ventura Goes to Africa *See* Ace Ventura: When Nature Calls (1995)

The Adventure of Lyle Swan *See* Timerider (1983)

Adventures at Rugby *See* Tom Brown's School Days (1940)

The Adventures of Chatran *See* The Adventures of Milo & Otis (1989)

The Adventures of the Great Mouse Detective *See* The Great Mouse Detective (1986)

The Amazing Panda Rescue *See* The Amazing Panda Adventure (1995)

Amelia and the King of Plants *See* Bed of Roses (1995)

And Then There Were None *See* Ten Little Indians (1975)

Andy Colby's Incredibly Awesome Adventure *See* Andy and the Airwave Rangers (1989)

An Angel Passed Over Brooklyn *See* The Man Who Wagged His Tail (1957)

Anne of Green Gables: The Sequel *See* Anne of Avonlea (1987)

Arthur the King *See* Merlin and the Sword (1985)

Atomic Rocketship *See* Flash Gordon: Rocketship (1936)

Avonlea *See* Tales from Avonlea, Vol. 1: The Journey Begins (1990)

Babe, the Gallant Pig *See* Babe (1995)

Babes in Toyland *See* March of the Wooden Soldiers (1934)

Bach et Bottine *See* Bach & Broccoli (1987)

Bachelor Knight *See* The Bachelor and the Bobby-Soxer (1947)

Banner in the Sky *See* Third Man on the Mountain (1959)

The Bar Sinister *See* It's a Dog's Life (1955)

Batman: The Animated Movie *See* Batman: Mask of the Phantasm (1993)

Behind the Iron Mask *See* The Fifth Musketeer (1979)

The Big Heart *See* Miracle on 34th Street (1947)

Birds of a Feather *See* The Birdcage (1995)

Blake Edwards' Son of the Pink Panther *See* Son of the Pink Panther (1993)

Blood Thirst *See* Salem's Lot (1979)

Bloomfield *See* The Hero (1971)

Blue Sierra *See* Courage of Lassie (1946)

Bruce Brown's The Endless Summer 2 *See* The Endless Summer 2 (1994)

Buckaroo Banzai *See* The Adventures of Buckaroo Banzai Across the Eighth Dimension (1984)

Cactus Jack *See* The Villain (1979)

California Man *See* Encino Man (1992)

Carlo Collodi's Pinocchio *See* The Adventures of Pinocchio (1996)

Carquake *See* Cannonball (1976)

Charlie's Ghost Story *See* Charlie's Ghost: The Secret of Coronado (1994)

The Christmas Tree *See* When Wolves Cry (1969)

Christmas Vacation *See* National Lampoon's Christmas Vacation (1989)

Code 645 *See* G-Men Never Forget (1948)

The Company of Strangers *See* Strangers in Good Company (1991)

Cop Tips Waitress $2 Million *See* It Could Happen to You (1994)

The Courage of Kavik, the Wolf Dog *See* Kavik, the Wolf Dog (1984)

The Creature Wasn't Nice *See* Spaceship (1981)

Cria Cuervos *See* Cria (1976)

Crossed Swords *See* The Prince and the Pauper (1978)

A Day to Remember *See* Two Bits (1996)

Der Himmel Uber Berlin *See* Wings of Desire (1988)

Dick Tracy Meets Karloff *See* Dick Tracy Meets Gruesome (1947)

Dick Tracy's Amazing Adventure *See* Dick Tracy Meets Gruesome (1947)

Die Hard 3 *See* Die Hard: With a Vengeance (1995)

Disney's Blank Check *See* Blank Check (1993)

Double Trouble *See* No Deposit, No Return (1976)

Dumbo Drop *See* Operation Dumbo Drop (1995)

East of the Bowery *See* Follow the Leader (1944)

Emil Und Die Detektive *See* Emil and the Detective (1964)

Ercole e la Regina de Lidia *See* Hercules Unchained (1959)

Escape from the Dark *See* The Littlest Horse Thieves (1976)

European Vacation *See* National Lampoon's European Vacation (1985)

Evil Dead 3 *See* Army of Darkness (1992)
Except For Me and Thee *See* Friendly Persuasion (1956)
Eyewitness *See* Sudden Terror (1970)
The Fabulous Baron Munchausen *See* The Original Fabulous Adventures of Baron Munchausen (1961)
The First Great Train Robbery *See* The Great Train Robbery (1979)
The Flight of the White Stallions *See* Miracle of the White Stallions (1963)
Flipper and the Pirates *See* Flipper's New Adventure (1964)
Flying Aces *See* The Flying Deuces (1939)
Follow That Bird *See* Sesame Street Presents: Follow That Bird (1985)
Francis *See* Francis the Talking Mule (1949)
Friz Freleng's Looney Looney Looney Bugs Bunny Movie *See* Looney Looney Looney Bugs Bunny Movie (1981)
From the Mixed-Up Files of Mrs. Basil E. Frankweiler *See* The Hideaways (1973)
The Ghost Creeps *See* Boys of the City (1940)
Gilbert Grape *See* What's Eating Gilbert Grape (1993)
Girl in Pawn *See* Little Miss Marker (1934)
Godzilla vs. Hedora *See* Godzilla vs. the Smog Monster (1972)
Godzilla vs. Mechagodzilla *See* Godzilla vs. the Cosmic Monster (1974)
Godzilla vs. the Bionic Monster *See* Godzilla vs. the Cosmic Monster (1974)
Gojira Tai Hedora *See* Godzilla vs. the Smog Monster (1972)
Gojira Tai Megaro *See* Godzilla vs. Megalon (1976)
Gojira Tai Meka-Gojira *See* Godzilla vs. the Cosmic Monster (1974)
Golden Hands of Kurigal *See* Federal Agents vs. Underworld, Inc. (1949)
Goldy 3 *See* The Magic of the Golden Bear: Goldy 3 (1994)
Goodbye, Children *See* Au Revoir Les Enfants (1987)
Grace Under Pressure *See* Something to Talk About (1995)
Great American Bugs Bunny-Road Runner Chase *See* The Bugs Bunny/Road Runner Movie (1979)
The Great Balloon Adventure *See* Olly Olly Oxen Free (1978)
The Great Schnozzle *See* Palooka (1934)
Guardian of the Wilderness *See* Mountain Man (1977)
Haakon Haakonsen *See* Shipwrecked (1990)
Handle With Care *See* Citizens Band (1977)
Hans Christian Andersen's Thumbelina *See* Thumbelina (1994)
Hard Driver *See* The Last American Hero (1973)
Hector Servadac's Ark *See* On the Comet (1968)
Hercules Goes Bananas *See* Hercules in New York (1970)
Hercules: The Movie *See* Hercules in New York (1970)
Here Come the Tigers *See* Manny's Orphans (1978)
Him *See* Only You (1994)
Hol Volt, Hol Nem Volt *See* A Hungarian Fairy Tale (1987)
Hollywood Cowboy *See* Hearts of the West (1975)
Home Front *See* Morgan Stewart's Coming Home (1987)
Hot and Cold *See* Weekend at Bernie's (1989)
House Without Windows *See* Seven Alone (1975)
Huggers *See* Crazy Moon (1987)
Hunchback *See* The Hunchback of Notre Dame (1982)
I Am a Fugitive from the Chain Gang *See* I Am a Fugitive from a Chain Gang (1932)
I Was a Teenage Teenager *See* Clueless (1995)
Il Figlio del Capitano Blood *See* Son of Captain Blood (1962)
Il Ladro Di Bagdad *See* Thief of Baghdad (1961)
Il Mio Nome e Nessuno *See* My Name is Nobody (1974)

Il Natale Che Quasi Non Fu *See* The Christmas That Almost Wasn't (1966)
An Indian in the City *See* Little Indian, Big City (1995)
It Happened One Summer *See* State Fair (1945)
It Runs in the Family *See* My Summer Story (1994)
Jean de Florette 2 *See* Manon of the Spring (1987)
Joe Palooka *See* Palooka (1934)
Johnny Zombie *See* My Boyfriend's Back (1993)
The Jungle Book *See* Rudyard Kipling's The Jungle Book (1994)
Just Ask for Diamond *See* Diamond's Edge (1988)
Just in Time *See* Only You (1994)
Kaiju Soshingeki *See* Destroy All Monsters (1968)
Koneko Monogatari *See* The Adventures of Milo & Otis (1989)
La Belle et Laete *See* Beauty and the Beast (1946)
La Gloire de Mon Pere *See* My Father's Glory (1991)
La Isla Del Tersoro *See* Treasure Island (1972)
La Planete Sauvage *See* Fantastic Planet (1973)
La Tatiche de Ercole *See* Hercules (1958)
La Vie Devant Soi *See* Madame Rosa (1977)
The Lane Frost Story *See* 8 Seconds (1994)
Le Chateau de Ma Mere *See* My Mother's Castle (1991)
Le Grand Blond Avec Une Chassure Noire *See* The Tall Blond Man with One Black Shoe (1972)
Le Meraviglie Di Aladino *See* Wonders of Aladdin (1961)
Le Voleur De Bagdad *See* Thief of Baghdad (1961)
Legend of Cougar Canyon *See* The Secret of Navajo Cave (1976)
L'Enfant Sauvage *See* The Wild Child (1970)
Les Jeux Interdits *See* Forbidden Games (1952)
Les Mille Et Une Nuits *See* Wonders of Aladdin (1961)
Les Quartre Cents Coups *See* The 400 Blows (1959)
Les Vacances de Monsieur Hulot *See* Mr. Hulot's Holiday (1953)
Lifesavers *See* Mixed Nuts (1994)
Little Panda *See* The Amazing Panda Adventure (1995)
Loaded Weapon 1 *See* National Lampoon's Loaded Weapon 1 (1993)
Louis L'Amour's "The Shadow Riders" *See* The Shadow Riders (1982)
Macskafogo *See* Cat City (1987)
Mad Trapper of the Yukon *See* Challenge To Be Free (1976)
A Man in Mommy's Bed *See* With Six You Get Eggroll (1968)
Manhattan Project: The Deadly Game *See* The Manhattan Project (1986)
Manon des Sources *See* Manon of the Spring (1987)
Mark Twain *See* The Adventures of Mark Twain (1985)
The Marx Brothers at the Circus *See* At the Circus (1939)
Mauri *See* Big Mo (1973)
The Medicine Hat Stallion *See* Peter Lundy and the Medicine Hat Stallion (1977)
Men in Tights *See* Robin Hood: Men in Tights (1993)
The Mighty Ducks 2 *See* D2: The Mighty Ducks (1994)
The Miracle of Fatima *See* Miracle of Our Lady of Fatima (1952)
Mr. Bug Goes to Town *See* Hoppity Goes to Town (1941)
Mr. Celebrity *See* Turf Boy (1942)
Mr. Quilp *See* The Old Curiosity Shop (1975)
Mitt Liv Som Hund *See* My Life as a Dog (1985)
A Modern Hero *See* Knute Rockne: All American (1940)
Monsieur Hulot's Holiday *See* Mr. Hulot's Holiday (1953)
Monte Carlo or Bust *See* Those Daring Young Men in Their Jaunty Jalopies (1969)

MPAA/Age Group Index

The **MPAA INDEX** lists the titles of videos with their respective MPAA Rating, whether it be a G, PG, PG-13, or R-rated film. A list of Unrated features is also included following the individual ratings.

G RATED

Across the Great Divide
The Adventures of
  Mark Twain
The Adventures of Milo
  & Otis
The Adventures of
  Pinocchio
The Adventures of the
  Wilderness Family
Against A Crooked Sky
Airport
Aladdin
Alice in Wonderland
All Dogs Go to Heaven
All Dogs Go to Heaven
  2
All I Want for
  Christmas
Almos' a Man
The Amazing
  Dobermans
Amazing Mr. Blunden
An American Tail
An American Tail:
  Fievel Goes West
Amy
Andre
The Andromeda Strain
Animal Crackers
The Apple Dumpling
  Gang
The Apple Dumpling
  Gang Rides Again
Arabian Knight
Around the World in 80
  Days
Babar: The Movie
Babe
Balto
Bambi
The Barefoot Executive
Battle for the Planet of
  the Apes
Battle of Britain
The Bears & I

Beauty and the Beast
Bedknobs and
  Broomsticks
Beneath the Planet of
  the Apes
The Beniker Gang
Benji
Benji the Hunted
Bernard and the Genie
Big Mo
The Billion Dollar Hobo
Black Beauty
The Black Hole
The Boatniks
Bon Voyage, Charlie
  Brown
The Boy Friend
Boy of Two Worlds
The Brave Little Frog
Brian's Song
Brothers Lionheart
Brothers O'Toole
The Bugs Bunny/Road
  Runner Movie
Bugs Bunny Superstar
Bugs Bunny's 3rd
  Movie: 1,001 Rabbit
  Tales
Bugsy Malone
Cancel My Reservation
Candleshoe
Canine Commando
The Care Bears Movie
The Care Bears Movie
  2: A New Generation
The Castaway Cowboy
The Cat from Outer
  Space
Challenge To Be Free
Challenge to Lassie
Change of Habit
The Charge of the
  Model T's
Charley and the Angel
Charlie, the Lonesome
  Cougar

Charlotte's Web
Cheetah
Child of Glass
Chitty Chitty Bang
  Bang
C.H.O.M.P.S.
Christian the Lion
The Christmas That
  Almost Wasn't
A Christmas to
  Remember
Clarence
Comic Book Kids
Computer Wizard
The Computer Wore
  Tennis Shoes
Courage of Lassie
Daffy Duck's Movie:
  Fantastic Island
Daffy Duck's
  Quackbusters
Danny
Darby O'Gill & the
  Little People
Davy Crockett and the
  River Pirates
Deathcheaters
Dennis the Menace:
  Dinosaur Hunter
Destroy All Monsters
Digby, the Biggest Dog
  in the World
Dr. Syn, Alias the
  Scarecrow
The Dog Who Stopped
  the War
Don't Change My World
DuckTales the Movie:
  Treasure of the Lost
  Lamp
Duncan's World
Escape from the Planet
  of the Apes
Escape to Witch
  Mountain
The Ewok Adventure

Ferngully: The Last
  Rain Forest
Fiddler on the Roof
Finian's Rainbow
Fish Hawk
For the Love of Benji
The Fox and the Hound
Freaky Friday
Funny Girl
Further Adventures of
  the Wilderness
  Family, Part 2
Gargoyles, The Movie:
  The Heroes Awaken
George!
George Balanchine's
  The Nutcracker
The Glacier Fox
The Glenn Miller Story
Godzilla vs. Megalon
Godzilla vs. the Cosmic
  Monster
Godzilla vs. the Smog
  Monster
Golden Voyage of
  Sinbad
The Goodbye Bird
A Goofy Movie
Gordy
The Great Land of
  Small
The Great Mouse
  Detective
The Great Muppet
  Caper
Greenstone
Gulliver's Travels
Gumby: The Movie
Guns of the
  Magnificent Seven
Gus
Gypsy Colt
The Halfback of Notre
  Dame
Happily Ever After
Hawmps!

Hazel's People
Head
Heidi
Hello, Dolly!
Help!
Herbie Goes Bananas
Herbie Goes to Monte
  Carlo
Herbie Rides Again
Hercules in New York
Here Comes Droopy
Here Comes Garfield
The Hideaways
High Country Calling
Homeward Bound
Homeward Bound 2:
  Lost in San Francisco
Homeward Bound: The
  Incredible Journey
Honey, I Shrunk the
  Kids
A Horse for Danny
The Horse in the Gray
  Flannel Suit
Hot Lead & Cold Feet
How the West was
  Won
Huckleberry Finn
Hugo the Hippo
The Hunchback of
  Notre Dame
Ice Station Zebra
The Invisible Boy
The Island at the Top
  of the World
Jack the Giant Killer
Jason and the
  Argonauts
Jesus Christ, Superstar
The Jetsons: The Movie
Jiminy Cricket's
  Christmas
Joe Panther
Jonathan Livingston
  Seagull
Joni

Kid from Not-So-Big
King of the Grizzlies
Lady and the Tramp
The Land Before Time
The Land Before Time
2: The Great Valley
Adventure
The Land Before Time
3: The Time of the
Great Giving
The Land of Faraway
Lantern Hill
Lassie, Come Home
The Last Flight of
Noah's Ark
The Last Unicorn
Legend of Boggy Creek
The Legend of Sleepy
Hollow
Legend of the
Northwest
The Legend of Young
Robin Hood
Life & Times of Grizzly
Adams
The Lion King
Little Heroes
The Little Mermaid
Little Nemo:
Adventures in
Slumberland
The Little Prince
A Little Princess
The Littlest Horse
Thieves
The Living Desert
Living Free
Looking for Miracles
Looney Looney Looney
Bugs Bunny Movie
The Love Bug
Lt. Robin Crusoe,
U.S.N.
Luggage of the Gods
Magic of Lassie
The Magic of the
Golden Bear: Goldy 3
The Magic Voyage
Man & Boy
A Man for All Seasons
Man from Clover Grove
Melody
Menace on the
Mountain
Mickey's Christmas
Carol
Million Dollar Duck
A Minor Miracle
The Misadventures of
Merlin Jones
Miss Annie Rooney
Mountain Family
Robinson
The Muppet Christmas
Carol
The Muppet Movie
Muppet Treasure Island
Muppets Take
Manhattan
The Music Man
My Father's Glory

My Neighbor Totoro
My Side of the
Mountain
Neptune Factor
Never a Dull Moment
The Neverending Story
3
The New Adventures of
Pippi Longstocking
Nikki, the Wild Dog of
the North
No Deposit, No Return
No Drums, No Bugles
The North Avenue
Irregulars
Now You See Him, Now
You Don't
The Odd Couple
Oklahoma!
The Old Curiosity Shop
Old Yeller
Oliver!
On a Clear Day You
Can See Forever
Once Upon a Forest
Once Upon a Scoundrel
The One and Only,
Genuine, Original
Family Band
101 Dalmatians
One Magic Christmas
One of Our Dinosaurs
Is Missing
Outside Chance of
Maximillian Glick
Paco
The Pagemaster
Palooka
The Pebble and the
Penguin
Pepper and His Wacky
Taxi
Peter Pan
Pete's Dragon
Phantom Tollbooth
Pinocchio
Pippi Goes on Board
Pippi in the South Seas
Pippi Longstocking
Pippi on the Run
The Pirates of
Penzance
Pistol: The Birth of a
Legend
Planet of the Apes
Pocahontas
Pony Express Rider
Prancer
Prince Brat and the
Whipping Boy
The Princess and the
Goblin
The Puppetoon Movie
Race for Your Life,
Charlie Brown
Raggedy Ann and
Andy: A Musical
Adventure
Red Riding Hood
Rent-A-Kid
The Rescuers

The Rescuers Down
Under
Return from Witch
Mountain
The Return of Jafar
Return of the Pink
Panther
Return to Boggy Creek
Ride a Wild Pony
Ring of Bright Water
Robinson Crusoe & the
Tiger
Rock-a-Doodle
Rover Dangerfield
Rumpelstiltskin
Running Wild
Sarah, Plain and Tall
Scandalous John
Scrooge
Sea Gypsies
The Secret Garden
The Secret of Navajo
Cave
Secret of NIMH
Sesame Street
Presents: Follow
That Bird
Seven Alone
1776
The Seventh Voyage of
Sinbad
The Shaggy D.A.
The Shaggy Dog
Shinbone Alley
The Silver Stallion:
King of the Wild
Brumbies
Sinbad and the Eye of
the Tiger
Skylark
Sleeping Beauty
Smith!
Smurfs & the Magic
Flute
Snoopy, Come Home
Snow Treasure
Snow White and the
Seven Dwarfs
Snowball Express
Son of Captain Blood
Song Spinner
Sounder
Star Trek: The Motion
Picture
Starbird and Sweet
William
The Story Lady
Storybook
Summerdog
Super Seal
Superdad
Support Your Local
Gunfighter
Support Your Local
Sheriff
The Swan Princess
The Sword in the Stone
A Tale of Two
Chipmunks
A Tale of Two Critters
Tales of Beatrix Potter

The Ten
Commandments
The Tender Warrior
That Darn Cat
That's Dancing!
That's Entertainment
That's Entertainment,
Part 2
That's Entertainment,
Part 3
The Thief of Baghdad
Third Man on the
Mountain
Those Daring Young
Men in Their Jaunty
Jalopies
Thumbelina
Tiger Town
Toby Tyler
Tom and Jerry: The
Movie
Tom Sawyer
Toy Story
Transformers: The
Movie
Trap on Cougar
Mountain
Treasure Island
The Treasure of
Matecumbe
A Troll in Central Park
True Grit
2000 Year Old Man
Unidentified Flying
Oddball
Unsinkable Donald
Duck with Huey,
Dewey & Louie
The Valley of Gwangi
Wackiest Wagon Train
in the West
Walt Disney Films in
French
Water Babies
We of the Never Never
We're Back! A
Dinosaur's Story
Whale of a Tale
What's Up, Doc?
When Dinosaurs Ruled
the Earth
When the North Wind
Blows
When Wolves Cry
Where the Lilies Bloom
Where the Red Fern
Grows
Where the Red Fern
Grows: Part 2
Where Time Began
White Fang and the
Hunter
Whitewater Sam
The Wild Child
The Wild Country
Wild Hearts Can't Be
Broken
Willy Wonka & the
Chocolate Factory
Winnie the Pooh and a
Day for Eeyore

Winnie the Pooh and
Tigger Too
The Witching of Ben
Wagner
With Six You Get
Eggroll
The Wiz
The World's Greatest
Athlete
The Worst Witch
Wuthering Heights
Yellow Submarine

PG RATED
Adios Amigo
Adventures in Dinosaur
City
The Adventures of a
Gnome Named
Gnorm
The Adventures of
Baron Munchausen
The Adventures of
Buckaroo Banzai
Across the Eighth
Dimension
The Adventures of
Huck Finn
The Adventures of
Sherlock Holmes'
Smarter Brother
The Age of Innocence
The Air Up There
Airborne
Airplane!
Airplane 2: The Sequel
Airport '75
Airport '77
Aladdin
Alan & Naomi
Alaska
All the President's Men
Allan Quartermain and
the Lost City of Gold
Allegro Non Troppo
Almost an Angel
Aloha, Bobby and Rose
Aloha Summer
Always
Amadeus
Amazing Grace &
Chuck
The Amazing Panda
Adventure
American Dreamer
American Graffiti
And Now for
Something
Completely Different
And You Thought Your
Parents Were Weird!
Angels in the Outfield
Animal Behavior
Anne Frank
Remembered
Annie
Annie Hall
Annie O
Any Which Way You
Can
Apollo 13

The Great Train Robbery
The Great Waldo Pepper
The Great White Hope
The Greatest
Gremlins
The Grey Fox
Greystoke: The Legend of Tarzan, Lord of the Apes
Groundhog Day
Gumball Rally
Hadley's Rebellion
Hairspray
Hambone & Hillie
Hardly Working
Harley
Harper Valley P.T.A.
Harriet the Spy
Harry & Son
Harry and the Hendersons
Harry & Walter Go to New York
Heart Like a Wheel
Heartbeeps
The Heartbreak Kid
Heartland
Hearts of the West
Heavyweights
Hello Again
Her Alibi
Hercules
The Hero
A Hero Ain't Nothin' But a Sandwich
Hero at Large
High Anxiety
Hocus Pocus
Hole in the Sky
Home Alone
Home Alone 2: Lost in New York
Home Movies
Homecoming
Honey, I Blew Up the Kid
Honkytonk Man
Hook
Hoosiers
Hot Shot
Hot to Trot!
House Arrest
House of Wax
Houseguest
Housekeeping
Housesitter
Howard the Duck
Howard's End
Huck and the King of Hearts
The Hunchback of Notre Dame
The Hunt for Red October
Hyper-Sapien: People from Another Star
I Love Trouble
I Never Sang For My Father

I Ought to Be in Pictures
I Wanna Hold Your Hand
Ice Castles
Ice Pirates
Iceman
Imaginary Crimes
Improper Channels
The In Crowd
In Search of a Golden Sky
In the Army Now
The Incredible Shrinking Woman
The Indian in the Cupboard
Indiana Jones and the Last Crusade
Indiana Jones and the Temple of Doom
Innerspace
International Velvet
Into the West
Invaders from Mars
Invasion of the Body Snatchers
I.Q.
Iron Will
Irreconcilable Differences
Island of Dr. Moreau
It Could Happen to You
It Takes Two
Jabberwocky
James and the Giant Peach
Jane & the Lost City
Jane Eyre
Jean de Florette
Jeremiah Johnson
The Jewel of the Nile
Jimmy the Kid
Joe Versus the Volcano
Joey
Josh Kirby . . . Time Warrior: Chapter 1, Planet of the Dino-Knights
The Journey of Natty Gann
Journey to Spirit Island
Journey to the Center of the Earth
Jumanji
Junior Bonner
Just Tell Me You Love Me
Just the Way You Are
The Karate Kid
The Karate Kid: Part 2
The Karate Kid: Part 3
Kazaam
A Kid in King Arthur's Court
Kidco
King Kong
King of the Wind
King Ralph
Kipperbang
Kiss Me Goodbye

Knights & Emeralds
Kotch
Kramer vs. Kramer
Krull
Labyrinth
Land That Time Forgot
Lassie
The Last American Hero
The Last Starfighter
Lawrence of Arabia
Leader of the Band
A League of Their Own
Leapin' Leprechauns
The Learning Tree
Legend
Legend of the Lone Ranger
The Legend of Wolf Mountain
Leonard Part 6
Liar's Moon
Life with Mikey
Lightning: The White Stallion
The Lion in Winter
Lionheart
Little Big League
Little Big Man
Little Buddha
Little Giants
The Little Girl Who Lives Down the Lane
Little Indian, Big City
Little Man Tate
Little Miss Marker
Little Miss Millions
Little Monsters
Little Nikita
The Little Rascals
A Little Romance
Little Women
The Littlest Viking
Live and Let Die
Local Hero
Loch Ness
The Long Day Closes
The Lord of the Rings
The Lords of Flatbush
Lost in Yonkers
Love and Death
Love at First Bite
Lucky Luke
Mac and Me
MacArthur
Madame Rosa
Magic in the Water
Magic Island
Magic Kid
Magic Kid 2
Maid to Order
The Main Event
Major League 2
Making Contact
Making the Grade
The Man from Snowy River
Man of La Mancha
Man of the House
The Man Who Would Be King

The Man with One Red Shoe
The Man with the Golden Gun
Man, Woman & Child
Mannequin
Mannequin 2: On the Move
Manny's Orphans
Manon of the Spring
Mario
Marvin & Tige
Masters of the Universe
Matilda
Matinee
Maverick
Max Dugan Returns
Max is Missing
Meatballs
The Meteor Man
A Midnight Clear
Midnight Madness
The Mighty Ducks
The Mighty Ducks 3
Mighty Morphin Power Rangers: The Movie
The Miracle
Miracle on 34th Street
Miss Firecracker
Mr. Holland's Opus
Mr. Mom
Mr. Nanny
Misunderstood
Modern Problems
Mom and Dad Save the World
Mommie Dearest
The Money Pit
Monkey Trouble
Monty Python and the Holy Grail
Moon-Spinners
Moonraker
More American Graffiti
Movie, Movie
Munchie
Munchies
My American Cousin
My Best Friend Is a Vampire
My Bodyguard
My Father the Hero
My Favorite Year
My Girl
My Girl 2
My Grandpa is a Vampire
My Heroes Have Always Been Cowboys
My Mom's a Werewolf
My Mother's Castle
My Name Is Nobody
My Science Project
My Summer Story
Mystery Mansion
Nate and Hayes
The Natural
Never Cry Wolf
Never Say Never Again

The NeverEnding Story
The NeverEnding Story 2: Next Chapter
Newsies
The Next Karate Kid
Night Crossing
The Night the Lights Went Out in Georgia
The Nightmare Before Christmas
No Dessert Dad, 'Til You Mow the Lawn
Norma Rae
North
Nothing in Common
Nukie
Octopussy
Ode to Billy Joe
Off Beat
Oh, God!
Oh, God! Book 2
Oh, God! You Devil
Oh, Heavenly Dog!
Oklahoma Crude
The Old Curiosity Shop
Old Enough
On Golden Pond
On Her Majesty's Secret Service
On the Right Track
Once Upon a Crime
Once Upon a Time in the West
Once Upon a Time . . . When We Were Colored
One Crazy Summer
One on One
Only the Lonely
Only You
Operation Dumbo Drop
Oscar
The Other Side of the Mountain
The Other Side of the Mountain, Part 2
Out on a Limb
The Outlaw Josey Wales
The Outsiders
Over the Edge
Over the Top
Overboard
Paint Your Wagon
The Paper Chase
Paper Moon
Papillon
Past the Bleachers
Pastime
The Peanut Butter Solution
Pee Wee's Big Adventure
The People That Time Forgot
The Phantom
Phar Lap
The Phoenix and the Magic Carpet
Piece of the Action

The Pink Panther
  Strikes Again
Pirate Movie
Places in the Heart
Plain Clothes
Planet of the Dinosaurs
Play It Again, Sam
Pogo for President: "I
  Go Pogo"
The Polar Bear King
Police Academy 3: Back
  in Training
Police Academy 4:
  Citizens on Patrol
Police Academy 5:
  Assignment Miami
  Beach
Police Academy 6: City
  Under Siege
Police Academy:
  Mission to Moscow
Poltergeist
Popeye
The Poseidon
  Adventure
Prehysteria
Prehysteria 3
The Prime of Miss Jean
  Brodie
The Prince and the
  Pauper
Princess and the Goblin
The Princess Bride
Princess Caraboo
The Private Eyes
Prize Fighter
Problem Child
The Prodigal
Project X
The Projectionist
Promises in the Dark
Purple People Eater
The Purple Rose of
  Cairo
Queen of Hearts
The Quest
Race the Sun
Racing with the Moon
Rad
Radio Days
Radioland Murders
Raiders of the Lost Ark
A Rare Breed
Real Genius
The Reivers
The Remains of the
  Day
Remote
The Rescue
Return of the Jedi
The Return of the
  Musketeers
Return to Oz
Return to Snowy River
Revenge of the Pink
  Panther
Rhinestone
Rich Kids
Richie Rich
The Right Stuff
The River

The River Pirates
The River Rat
A River Runs Through
  It
The Road Home
Robin and Marian
Robot Jox
Rock 'n' Roll High
  School
Rocket Gibraltar
The Rocketeer
Rocky
Rocky 2
Rocky 3
Rocky 4
Rocky 5
Romancing the Stone
Romeo and Juliet
Rookie of the Year
Rooster Cogburn
The Rousters
Roxanne
Rudy
Rudyard Kipling's The
  Jungle Book
Run for the Roses
Running Brave
Running Free
Splash
Russkies
Ryan's Daughter
Sabrina
Salem's Lot
Samantha
Sam's Son
The Sandlot
Santa Claus: The Movie
The Santa Clause
Saturday the 14th
Savage Land
Savannah Smiles
Searching for Bobby
  Fischer
The Secret Garden
The Secret of Roan
  Inish
Secret Places
Sense and Sensibility
A Separate Peace
Sgt. Bilko
Seven Minutes in
  Heaven
7 Ninja Kids
The Shadow Riders
Shadowlands
Shag: The Movie
Sheena
Sherlock: Undercover
  Dog
Shipwrecked
The Shootist
Short Circuit
Short Circuit 2
Sidekicks
Silence of the North
Silent Movie
The Silver Streak
Simon
Sister Act
Sister Act 2: Back in
  the Habit
Six Pack

Six Weeks
Sixteen Candles
The Skateboard Kid
Ski Patrol
Sleeper
Sleepless in Seattle
Sleuth
Small Change
Smile
Smokey and the Bandit
Smokey and the
  Bandit, Part 2
Smokey and the
  Bandit, Part 3
Something Wicked This
  Way Comes
Somewhere in Time
Somewhere Tomorrow
Son of the Pink
  Panther
Space Raiders
Spaceballs
SpaceCamp
Spaced Invaders
Spaceship
Spies Like Us
Spirit of the Eagle
Splash
The Spy Who Loved Me
Squanto: A Warrior's
  Tale
Stacking
Stand and Deliver
Star Trek 2: The Wrath
  of Khan
Star Trek 3: The Search
  for Spock
Star Trek 4: The
  Voyage Home
Star Trek 5: The Final
  Frontier
Star Trek 6: The
  Undiscovered
  Country
Star Trek Generations
Star Wars
Starchaser: The Legend
  of Orin
Starman
Starship
Steel Magnolias
The Sting
The Sting 2
The Stone Boy
Straight Talk
Strange Brew
Strange Invaders
Strangers in Good
  Company
Strictly Ballroom
The Stupids
Suburban Commando
Sudden Terror
Sugar Cane Alley
Summer Rental
A Summer to
  Remember
The Sunshine Boys
Super Fuzz
Super Mario Bros.

Super Mario Bros.
  Super Show 1
Supergirl
Superman 1: The Movie
Superman 2
Superman 3
Superman 4: The Quest
  for Peace
Surf Ninjas
Swamp Thing
The Swarm
Sweet Liberty
Swing Shift
Sword of the Valiant
Sylvester
Table for Five
Take Down
Take the Money and
  Run
Talent for the Game
The Tall Blond Man
  with One Black Shoe
Tall Tale: The
  Unbelievable
  Adventures of Pecos
  Bill
Tank
Taps
Teen Alien
Teen Wolf
Teen Wolf Too
Teenage Mutant Ninja
  Turtles 1: The Movie
Teenage Mutant Ninja
  Turtles 2: The Secret
  of the Ooze
Teenage Mutant Ninja
  Turtles 3
Ten Little Indians
Tender Mercies
Terms of Endearment
Terror in the Jungle
Tess
Tex
That Darn Cat
That Sinking Feeling
Theodore Rex
They Went That-a-Way
  & That-a-Way
Those Calloways
Three Amigos
The Three Lives of
  Thomasina
Three Men and a Baby
Three Men and a Little
  Lady
Three Musketeers
The Three Musketeers
3 Ninjas
3 Ninjas Kick Back
Three O'Clock High
Thunderball
Thursday's Game
Time Bandits
Time of Tears
Timerider
The Tin Soldier
Toby McTeague
Tom and Huck
Tommy
Tootsie

Top Gun
Touched by Love
Tough Guys
The Toy
Trading Hearts
Trading Mom
Trail of the Pink
  Panther
Treasure Island
The Trip to Bountiful
Tron
Troop Beverly Hills
Truly, Madly, Deeply
Tucker: The Man and
  His Dream
Turner and Hooch
Turtle Diary
Twelve Chairs
Twice Upon a Time
Twilight Zone: The
  Movie
Twins
Twist
Two Bits & Pepper
2010 : The Year We
  Make Contact
Uncle Buck
Under the Rainbow
Unstrung Heroes
Vice Versa
Victory
A View to a Kill
The Villain
Waiting for the Light
Walk Like a Man
War Games
War of the Buttons
Warriors of the Wind
Watcher in the Woods
Watership Down
The Way We Were
Wee Willie Winkie
Weekend at Bernie's 2
What About Bob?
When the Whales Came
Where the River Runs
  Black
Where the Spirit Lives
While You Were
  Sleeping
White Fang
White Fang 2: The
  Myth of the White
  Wolf
White Water Summer
Who Framed Roger
  Rabbit?
Willow
The Wind and the Lion
Windrunner
A Winner Never Quits
The Witches
Witches' Brew
The Wizard
The Wizard of Speed
  and Time
Wizards
Wizards of the Lost
  Kingdom
Wizards of the Lost
  Kingdom 2

A World Apart
Xanadu
Yentl
You Only Live Twice
Young Einstein
Young Frankenstein
Zelly & Me
Zero to Sixty

PG13 RATED
Ace Ventura: Pet
    Detective
Ace Ventura: When
    Nature Calls
Across the Tracks
The Addams Family
Addams Family Values
Adventures in
    Babysitting
Adventures in Spying
Airheads
American Anthem
American Boyfriends
American Flyers
The American President
Amos and Andrew
Angus
Another Stakeout
Arachnophobia
Arena
Aspen Extreme
Awakenings
Back to School
Bad Medicine
Batman
Batman Forever
Batman Returns
Beastmaster 2:
    Through the Portal of
    Time
Bebe's Kids
Before and After
Being Human
Beverly Hills Brats
Big Shots
Big Trouble in Little
    China
Billy Madison
Bio-Dome
Black Magic
Black Sheep
Blame It on the Night
Blankman
Blue Chips
Book of Love
Bopha!
Boys
The Brady Bunch Movie
Breaking the Rules
Brighton Beach
    Memoirs
Buffy the Vampire
    Slayer
Bushwhacked
The Butcher's Wife
Bye Bye, Love
Cabin Boy
The Cable Guy
Calendar Girl
Can't Buy Me Love
Captain America

Captain Ron
Car 54, Where Are You?
Cat's Eye
Celtic Pride
Chaplin
Christopher Columbus:
    The Discovery
Circle of Friends
City Slickers
City Slickers 2: The
    Legend of Curly's
    Gold
Clara's Heart
Class Act
Clean Slate
Clear and Present
    Danger
The Client
Club Paradise
Clueless
Cocoon
Congo
Coupe de Ville
Crazy Moon
The Crazysitter
Critters
Crocodile Dundee
Crooklyn
Crusoe
Cry-Baby
Cry, the Beloved
    Country
The Cure
Cutthroat Island
Dances with Wolves
Dave
A Day in October
Death Becomes Her
Desperately Seeking
    Susan
Dirty Dancing
Diving In
Doc Hollywood
Dr. Jekyll and Ms. Hyde
Doin' Time on Planet
    Earth
Dominick & Eugene
Don't Tell Mom the
    Babysitter's Dead
The Double O Kid
The Dove
Down Periscope
Dracula: Dead and
    Loving It
Dragnet
Dragon: The Bruce Lee
    Story
Dragonheart
Dream a Little Dream
Dream a Little Dream 2
Dream Date
The Dream Team
Drop Dead Fred
Dumb & Dumber
Dutch
Eddie
Edward Scissorhands
8 Seconds
Enemy Mine
Erik the Viking

F/X 2: The Deadly Art
    of Illusion
Face the Music
A Family Thing
Far and Away
A Far Off Place
Fast Getaway 2
Fatal Instinct
Father Hood
Ferris Bueller's Day Off
The Fifth Monkey
Fire in the Sky
First Born
First Knight
The Flamingo Kid
For Keeps
Forget Paris
Forrest Gump
1492: Conquest of
    Paradise
Freaked
French Kiss
The Fugitive
The Gate
Geronimo: An American
    Legend
Ghost
Ghoulies
Gleaming the Cube
The Golden Child
Goldeneye
Gorillas in the Mist
Gotcha!
Greedy
Green Card
Gremlins 2: The New
    Batch
Gross Anatomy
Grumpier Old Men
Grumpy Old Men
Guarding Tess
Gung Ho
Hackers
Happy Gilmore
Heart and Souls
Heartbreak Hotel
The Heavenly Kid
Hero
Hiding Out
Highlander: The
    Gathering
Holy Matrimony
Home for the Holidays
A Home of Our Own
Honeymoon in Vegas
Hoop Dreams
Hope and Glory
Hot Shots! Part Deux
House of Cards
How I Got into College
How to Make an
    American Quilt
If Looks Could Kill
I'll Do Anything
Immediate Family
Independence Day
Indian Summer
It's Pat: The Movie
Jack the Bear
Jefferson in Paris
Jersey Girl

Johnny Dangerously
Josh and S.A.M.
The Journey of August
    King
Junior
Jurassic Park
Jury Duty
Just One of the Guys
K-9
Kindergarten Cop
King of the Hill
Kingpin
Kuffs
La Bamba
L.A. Story
The Lady in White
Lady Jane
Ladybugs
Ladyhawke
Last Action Hero
The Last Prostitute
Last Time Out
Lean on Me
Leap of Faith
Legend of Billie Jean
License to Drive
Light of Day
Lightning Jack
Like Father, Like Son
Lisa
Little Shop of Horrors
Little Sister
The Little Thief
Look Who's Talking
Look Who's Talking
    Now
Look Who's Talking,
    Too
Lords of Magick
Lorenzo's Oil
Love Your Mama
Lucas
Mad Max: Beyond
    Thunderdome
Madame Sousatzka
Made in America
Madhouse
Major Payne
Making Mr. Right
Malcolm X
The Man in the Moon
The Man Without a
    Face
The Manhattan Project
Mask
The Mask
Matewan
Meet the Hollowheads
Memoirs of an Invisible
    Man
Men Don't Leave
Mermaids
Metropolitan
Milk Money
Mission: Impossible
Mrs. Doubtfire
Mrs. Winterbourne
Mr. & Mrs. Bridge
Mr. Baseball
Mr. Destiny
Mr. Wonderful

Mr. Wrong
Mixed Nuts
Moll Flanders
The Monster Squad
Moonstruck
Morgan Stewart's
    Coming Home
Mortal Kombat: The
    Movie
Moving Violations
Much Ado About
    Nothing
Multiplicity
Murphy's Romance
My Boyfriend's Back
My Life
My Stepmother Is an
    Alien
Mystery Date
Mystery Science
    Theater 3000: The
    Movie
The Naked Gun: From
    the Files of Police
    Squad
Naked Gun 33 1/3: The
    Final Insult
Naked Gun 2 1/2: The
    Smell of Fear
National Lampoon's
    Christmas Vacation
National Lampoon's
    European Vacation
National Lampoon's
    Loaded Weapon 1
Necessary Roughness
The Net
The Night Before
Night of the Comet
Nine Months
No Holds Barred
Now and Then
The Nutty Professor
Odd Jobs
Of Mice and Men
Oh, What a Night
Only You
Opportunity Knocks
Out There
Oxford Blues
The Pallbearer
Paradise
Parenthood
P.C.U.
Peggy Sue Got Married
The Pelican Brief
A Perfect World
Permanent Record
Philadelphia
Pink Cadillac
The Playboys
Police Academy 2:
    Their First
    Assignment
Poltergeist 2: The
    Other Side
Poltergeist 3
Pontiac Moon
Powder
The Power of One
Prelude to a Kiss

Pretty in Pink
Princes in Exile
Problem Child 2
Quigley Down Under
Quiz Show
Radio Flyer
The Real McCoy
Reality Bites
Regarding Henry
Remo Williams: The
   Adventure Begins
Renaissance Man
The Return of Swamp
   Thing
Reunion
Rich in Love
The River Wild
Robin Hood: Men in
   Tights
Robin Hood: Prince of
   Thieves
Robocop 3
Rock 'n' Roll High
   School Forever
Running Mates
Running on Empty
Safe Passage
Sarafina!
Satisfaction
Say Anything
School Ties
The Scout
Scrooged
Secret of the Ice Cave
See You in the Morning
The Shadow
Shadow of the Wolf
She-Devil
She's Having a Baby
Shout
Silverado
A Simple Twist of Fate
Sing
Singles
Sioux City
Slam Dunk Ernest
Smooth Talk
Sneakers
So I Married an Axe
   Murderer
Solarbabies
Some Kind of
   Wonderful
Sommersby
Son-in-Law
Soul Man
Speechless
Spy Hard
Stargate
Stay Tuned
Stepmonster
Stop! or My Mom Will
   Shoot
Street Fighter
Street Fighter 2: The
   Animated Movie
Stuart Saves His Family
Summer School
The Sure Thing
Swing Kids
Teen Witch

Terminal Velocity
That Night
The Thing Called Love
Think Big
This is My Life
Three Fugitives
Three Men and a
   Cradle
Throw Momma from
   the Train
Timemaster
To Wong Foo, Thanks
   for Everything, Julie
   Newmar
Tommy Boy
Top Dog
Toto le Heros
Toys
Trapped In Paradise
Troll
The Truth About Cats
   and Dogs
Turk 182!
Twinsitters
Twister
Two Bits
UHF
Undercover Blues
Untamed Heart
Up Against the Wall
Up Close and Personal
A Very Brady Sequel
Wagons East
Wait Until Spring,
   Bandini
A Walk in the Clouds
Waterworld
Wayne's World
Wayne's World 2
Weekend at Bernie's
Weird Science
Welcome Home, Roxy
   Carmichael
What's Eating Gilbert
   Grape
White Squall
The Willies
Wind
Wings of Desire
With Honors
The Wizard of
   Loneliness
The Year My Voice
   Broke
Year of the Comet
Young Sherlock Holmes
The Zoo Gang

R RATED
Above the Rim
Alive
All the Right Moves
Alligator
American Heart
Angelo My Love
Army of Darkness
Backbeat
Bad Boys
The Basketball Diaries
The Bay Boy
Beautiful Girls

Before Sunrise
Beverly Hills Cop
Beverly Hills Cop 2
Beverly Hills Cop 3
The Birdcage
Boys on the Side
Boyz N the Hood
Braveheart
The Breakfast Club
Broken Arrow
A Bronx Tale
Bustin' Loose
Caddyshack
Clerks
The Commitments
Conan the Barbarian
Crimson Tide
The Crow
The Crush
Dangerous Minds
Darkman
Dazed and Confused
Die Hard
Die Hard 2: Die Harder
Die Hard: With a
   Vengeance
Dolores Claiborne
F/X
Fame
Fast Times at
   Ridgemont High
Flashdance
Flirting
Four Weddings and a
   Funeral
Foxes
Glory
The Good Son
Highlander
Highlander 2: The
   Quickening
House
House Party
House Party 2: The
   Pajama Jam
House Party 3
The Howling
If Lucy Fell
The Inkwell
The Jerky Boys
Johnny Mnemonic
The Joy Luck Club
Judge Dredd
The Last of the
   Mohicans
Legends of the Fall
Little Darlings
Lord of the Flies
The Lost Boys
Major League
Mallrats
M*A*S*H
Menace II Society
Money Train
Muriel's Wedding
National Lampoon's
   Senior Trip
National Lampoon's
   Vacation
Nell
Othello

Outbreak
The Paper
Planes, Trains &
   Automobiles
Poetic Justice
Police Academy
The Program
Rain Man
Rambling Rose
Revenge of the Nerds
Rob Roy
Robocop
Robocop 2
Rumble Fish
The Scarlet Letter
Secret Admirer
Serial Mom
The Shawshank
   Redemption
The Snapper
Something to Talk
   About
Speed
Stand By Me
The Terminator
Terminator 2: Judgment
   Day
That Was Then. . .This
   Is Now
This Boy's Life
Threesome
Timecop
Tombstone
True Lies
12 Monkeys
Two If by Sea
The Usual Suspects
Valley Girl
Waiting to Exhale
Walking Tall
What's Love Got to Do
   With It?
Wildcats
Young Guns
Zebrahead

UNRATED
Abbott and Costello
   Cartoon Festival
Abbott and Costello
   Meet Captain Kidd
Abbott and Costello
   Meet Dr. Jekyll and
   Mr. Hyde
Abbott and Costello
   Meet Frankenstein
Abel's Island
The Absent-Minded
   Professor
Adam's Rib
Adventures in
   Dinosaurland
Adventures in Odyssey:
   The Knight Travellers
Adventures in
   Wonderland: Hare-
   Raising Magic
The Adventures of a
   Two-Minute
   Werewolf

The Adventures of an
   American Rabbit
The Adventures of
   Babar
The Adventures of
   Batman & Robin:
   Robin
The Adventures of
   Batman & Robin: The
   Joker
The Adventures of
   Batman & Robin: The
   Riddler
The Adventures of
   Batman & Robin:
   Two-Face
Adventures of Black
   Beauty
The Adventures of
   Blinky Bill
The Adventures of
   Bullwhip Griffin
Adventures of Buster
   the Bear
The Adventures of
   Captain Marvel
The Adventures of
   Curious George
Adventures of Droopy
The Adventures of
   Dudley the Dragon:
   Dudley and the
   Genie
The Adventures of
   Dudley the Dragon:
   Dudley Finds His
   Home
The Adventures of
   Dudley the Dragon:
   Dudley's Tea Party
The Adventures of
   Dudley the Dragon:
   Mr. Crabby Tree
The Adventures of
   Frank and Jesse
   James
The Adventures of
   Frontier Fremont
The Adventures of
   Huckleberry Finn
The Adventures of
   Mary-Kate & Ashley:
   The Case of the Fun
   House Mystery
The Adventures of
   Mary-Kate & Ashley:
   The Case of the
   Logical Ranch
The Adventures of
   Mary-Kate & Ashley:
   The Case of the
   Mystery Cruise
The Adventures of
   Mary-Kate & Ashley:
   The Case of the Sea
   World Adventure
The Adventures of
   Mary-Kate & Ashley:
   The Case of the
   Shark Encounter

The Adventures of
Mary-Kate & Ashley:
The Case of the U.S.
Space Camp Mission
The Adventures of
Mary-Kate & Ashley:
The Case of Thorn
Mansion
The Adventures of
Mary-Kate & Ashley:
The Christmas Caper
Adventures of Mighty
Mouse, Vol. 1
The Adventures of
Oliver Twist
The Adventures of
Peter Cottontail
The Adventures of
Peter Cottontail and
His Friends of the
Green Forest
Adventures of
Pinocchio
The Adventures of
Raggedy Ann &
Andy: Pirate
Adventure
Adventures of Red
Ryder
Adventures of Reddy
the Fox
The Adventures of
Robin Hood
The Adventures of
Rocky & Bullwinkle:
Birth of Bullwinkle
The Adventures of
Sinbad the Sailor
Adventures of Smilin'
Jack
The Adventures of
SuperTed
The Adventures of
Teddy Ruxpin
The Adventures of the
Little Koala and
Friends
The Adventures of
Timmy the Tooth:
Big Mouth Gulch
The Adventures of
Timmy the Tooth:
Lost My Brush
The Adventures of
Timmy the Tooth:
Molar Island
The Adventures of
Timmy the Tooth:
Operation: Secret
Birthday Surprise!
The Adventures of
Timmy the Tooth:
Timmy in Space
The Adventures of Tom
Sawyer
The Adventures of
Ultraman
The Adventures of Walt
Disney's Alice
Aesop's Fables

Aesop's Fables, Vol. 1:
The Hen with the
Golden Egg
Africa Screams
Africa Texas Style
African Journey
The African Queen
African Story Magic
Ah, Wilderness!
Aladdin and His Magic
Lamp
Aladdin and His
Wonderful Lamp
Aladdin and the King of
Thieves
Aladdin and the
Wonderful Lamp
Alakazam the Great!
Alex
Alex Mack: In the Nick
of Time
Ali Baba and the Forty
Thieves
Ali Baba's Revenge
Alice in Wonderland
Alice's Adventures in
Wonderland
All New Adventures of
Tom Sawyer:
Mischief on the
Mississippi
All This and Tex Avery
Too!
Alligator Pie
Almost Angels
Almost Partners
Alvin & the Chipmunks:
A Chipmunk
Christmas
Alvin & the Chipmunks:
A Christmas
Celebration
Alvin & the Chipmunks:
Alvin's Christmas
Carol
Alvin & the Chipmunks:
Batmunk
Amahl and the Night
Visitors
Amazing Adventures of
Joe 90
Amazing Bone and
Other Stories
The Amazing Spider-
Man
An American Christmas
Carol
An American in Paris
An American Summer
Anansi
Anchors Aweigh
And Baby Makes Six
And Now Miguel
And the Children Shall
Lead
Androcles and the Lion
Andy and the Airwave
Rangers
Andy Hardy Gets
Spring Fever

Andy Hardy Meets
Debutante
Andy Hardy's Double
Life
Andy Hardy's Private
Secretary
The Angel and the
Soldier Boy
Angel Square
Angela's Airplane
Animal Alphabet
Animal Babies in the
Wild
Animal Farm
Animal Stories
Animals Are Beautiful
People
Animalympics: Winter
Games
Anne of Avonlea
Anne of Green Gables
Annie Oakley
The Ant and the
Aardvark
Antarctica
Aquaman
Ariel's Undersea
Adventure, Vol. 1:
Whale of a Tale
Ariel's Undersea
Adventure, Vol. 2:
Stormy the Wild
Seahorse
Ariel's Undersea
Adventure, Vol. 3:
Double Bubble
Ariel's Undersea
Adventure, Vol. 4: In
Harmony
Ariel's Undersea
Adventure, Vol. 5:
Ariel's Gift
The Aristocats
Arnold of the Ducks
Around the World in 80
Days
Astronomy 101: A
Beginner's Guide to
the Night Sky
At the Circus
Atom Man vs.
Superman
Attic In the Blue
Away We Go!
Babar and Father
Christmas
Babar Comes to
America
Babar: Monkey
Business
Babar Returns
Babar the Elephant
Comes to America
Babar the Little
Elephant
Babar's First Step
Babar's Triumph
Babes in Arms
Babes in Toyland
Babes on Broadway
Babies at Play

Baby Animals
Baby Animals Just
Want to Have Fun
Baby, It's You: Dirty
Diaper Dancing
Baby, It's You: Giggles
and Gurgles
Baby, It's You: Multiple
Madness
The Baby-Sitter's Club
Baby Songs
Baby Songs Christmas
Baby Songs: Follow
Along Songs
Baby Songs Presents:
Baby Rock
Baby Songs Presents:
John Lithgow's Kid-
Size Concert
Baby Songs: Sing
Together
Baby Songs: Turn on
the Music
Baby, Take a Bow
BabyMugs
Baby's First Workout:
The Gerard Method
Bach & Broccoli
The Bachelor and the
Bobby-Soxer
Bach's Flight to
Freedom
Back Home
Back to Hannibal: The
Further Adventures
of Tom Sawyer and
Huckleberry Finn
The Bad Seed
The Ballad of Paul
Bunyan
Ballet Shoes
The Band Wagon
Barnaby and Me
Barney & Friends:
Barney Rhymes with
Mother Goose
Barney & Friends:
Barney's Best
Manners
Barney & Friends:
Families are Special
Barney Live in New
York City
Barney's Alphabet Zoo
Barney's Christmas
Surprise
Barney's Imagination
Island
Baron Munchausen
Basil Hears a Noise
Batman
Battle for Moon Station
Dallos
Battle of the Bullies
B.C.: A Special
Christmas
B.C.: The First
Thanksgiving

Be My Valentine,
Charlie Brown/Is
This Goodbye,
Charlie Brown?
Beach Blanket Bingo
Beach Party
Bear's Barnyard: It's a
Dog's Life
Bear's Big Lake
Beauty and the Beast
Bedrock Wedlock
Bedrockin' and Rappin'
Bedtime for Bonzo
Beethoven Lives
Upstairs
Beetle Bailey: Military
Madness
Beetlejuice, Vol. 1
The Bellboy
The Belle of New York
The Belles of St.
Trinian's
The Bells of St. Mary's
The Belstone Fox
Ben and Me
Benji at Work
Benji's Very Own
Christmas Story
The Berenstain Bears'
Christmas
Berenstain Bears'
Comic Valentine
Berenstain Bears'
Easter Surprise
Berenstain Bears Meet
Big Paw
The Best Christmas
Pageant Ever
The Best of Betty
Boop, Vol. 1
The Best of Betty
Boop, Vol. 2
Best of Bugs Bunny &
Friends
The Best of Gumby
The Best of Roger
Rabbit
Bethie's Really Silly
Clubhouse
Betty Boop
Betty Boop Special
Collector's Edition:
Volume 1
Beverly Hills Teens
Beyond the Stars
The B.F.G. (Big Friendly
Giant)
Big Bird in China
Big Bird in Japan
Big Cable Bridges
The Big Plane Trip
Big Red
The Big Store
Bigfoot and Wildboy
Bikini Beach
Bill
Bill and Coo
Bill: On His Own
Billie
A Billion for Boris

A Day for Thanks on
Walton's Mountain
The Day Jimmy's Boa
Ate the Wash and
Other Stories
Daydreamer
Dear Brigitte
Death of a Goldfish
Death of the Incredible
Hulk
A Decade of the
Waltons
Defenders of the Earth:
The Story Begins
Defenders of the
Vortex
The Delicate
Delinquent
Dennis the Menace in
Mayday for Mother
Dennis the Menace:
Spies, Robbers and
Ghosts
Dennis the Movie Star
Denver the Last
Dinosaur
Devil Horse
Dial "M" for Murder
Diamonds on Wheels
Dick Deadeye
Dick Tracy
Dick Tracy, Detective
Dick Tracy Meets
Gruesome
Did I Ever Tell You How
Lucky You Are?
Dig Hole. Build House
Digging Dinosaurs - 2
Pack
Digging for Dinosaurs
Dinky: Dinky Finds a
Home
Dinky: Much Ado About
Nothing
Dinosaur Families
Dinosaurs are Very Big
Dinosaurs, Dinosaurs,
Dinosaurs
Disney's Adventures in
Wonderland
Disney's Darkwing
Duck: His Favorite
Adventures
Disney's Greatest
Lullabies
Disney's Haunted
Halloween
Disney's Sing-Along
Songs: Circle of Life
Disney's Sing-Along
Songs: Pocahontas
Disney's Sing-Along
Songs: Sebastian's
Caribbean Jam
Disney's Sing-Along
Songs: Sebastian's
Party Gras
Disney's Sing-Along
Songs: The
Hunchback of Notre
Dame: Topsy Turvy

Disney's Sing-Along
Songs: The Twelve
Days of Christmas
Disney's Sing-Along
Songs, Vol. 1: Heigh-
Ho
Disney's Sing-Along
Songs, Vol. 2: Zip-A-
Dee-Doo-Dah
Disney's Sing-Along
Songs, Vol. 3: You
Can Fly!
Disney's Sing-Along
Songs, Vol. 4: The
Bare Necessities
Disney's Sing-Along
Songs, Vol. 5: Fun
with Music
Disney's Sing-Along
Songs, Vol. 6: Under
the Sea
Disney's Sing-Along
Songs, Vol. 7:
Disneyland Fun
Disney's Sing-Along
Songs, Vol. 8: Very
Merry Christmas
Songs
Disney's Sing-Along
Songs, Vol. 9: I Love
to Laugh!
Disney's Sing-Along
Songs, Vol. 10: Be
Our Guest
Disney's Sing-Along
Songs, Vol. 11:
Friend Like Me
Disney's TaleSpin, Vol.
1: True Baloo
Disney's Wonderful
World of Winter
The Disorderly Orderly
Divorce Can Happen to
the Nicest People
Dr. Dad's PH3
Doctor Doolittle
Dr. Seuss' ABC
Dr. Seuss' Butter Battle
Book
Dr. Seuss' Caldecotts
Dr. Seuss' Cat in the
Hat
Dr. Seuss' Daisy-Head
Mayzie
Dr. Seuss' Hoober-
Bloob Highway
Dr. Seuss' Horton
Hears a Who/How
the Grinch Stole
Christmas
Dr. Seuss: I Am NOT
Going to Get Up
Today!
Dr. Seuss on the Loose
Dr. Seuss Sleep Book
Dr. Seuss' The Lorax
Dr. Strange
Doctor Who: An
Unearthly Child
Doctor Who and the
Daleks

Doctor Zhivago
The Dog Days of Arthur
Cane
A Dog of Flanders
The Dog Who Dared
Doggy Faces
Don Cooper: Sing-
Along Story Songs
Don Winslow of the
Coast Guard
Don Winslow of the
Navy
Donald Duck in
Mathmagic Land
Donny Deinonychus:
The Educational
Dinosaur, Vol. 1
Don't Eat the Pictures:
Sesame Street at the
Metropolitan
Museum of Art
Don't Wake Your Mom
The Donut Repair Club:
On Tour
Dorothy in the Land of
Oz
Dot & Keeto
Dot & Santa Claus
Dot & the Kangaroo
Dot & the Koala
Dot & the Smugglers
Dot & the Whale
Doug, Vol. 1: How Did I
Get Into This Mess?
The Dragon That
Wasn't (Or Was He?)
A Dream for Christmas
Dreaming of Paradise
Droopy & Company
Duck Soup
DuckTales: Accidental
Adventurers
Dumbo
Dusty
Earth Tunes for Kids
EarthWorm Jim
East of Eden
East of the Sun, West
of the Moon
Easter Bunny is Coming
to Town
Easter Egg Mornin'
Easter Parade
Edison Twins
Eek!Stravaganza:
Catsanova and
Hawaiieek 5-O
The Electric
Grandmother
Elephant Boy
The ElmChanted Forest
Elmer Fudd's School of
Hard Knocks
Elmocize
Emil and the Detective
Emma
Emmet Otter's Jug-
Band Christmas
The Emperor's New
Clothes

The Emperor's New
Clothes and Other
Folktales
Encyclopedia Brown:
Case of the Missing
Time Capsule
The Endless Summer
EPIC: Days of the
Dinosaurs
The Ernest Green Story
The Errand Boy
Escapade in Florence
Escape of the One-Ton
Pet
Even More Baby Songs
Everyone Can Dance
The Ewoks: Battle for
Endor
The Extra-Special
Substitute Teacher
The Ezra Jack Keats
Library
The Fabulous World of
Jules Verne
Faeries
A Family Circus
Christmas
Family Circus Easter
A Family Concert
Featuring The Roches
and The Music
Workshop for Kids
Family Jewels
Fangface
Fangface Spooky
Spoofs
Fantasia
The Fantastic World of
D.C. Collins
The Farmer's Daughter
Fat Albert & the Cosby
Kids, Vol. 1
Father Figure
Father of the Bride
Father's Little Dividend
Federal Agents vs.
Underworld, Inc.
Felix the Cat: An Hour
of Fun
Felix the Cat: The
Movie
Ferdy
Fievel's American Tails:
A Mouse Known as
Zorrowitz/Aunt
Sophie's Visit
50 Classic All-Star
Cartoons, Vol. 1
50 Classic All-Star
Cartoons, Vol. 2
50 Degrees Below Zero
50 Simple Things Kids
Can Do to Save the
Earth, Parts 1 & 2
The Fig Tree
Fighting Devil Dogs
Fighting Marines
The Fighting Prince of
Donegal
Fighting with Kit
Carson

Finn McCoul
The Fire in the Stone
Fire Safety for Kids
Fireman Sam: Hero
Next Door
The First Christmas
The First Easter Rabbit
First Men in the Moon
Fisher-Price Grimm's
Fairy Tales: Briar
Rose
Fisherman's Wharf
Five Lionni Classics
Five Stories for the
Very Young
The 5000 Fingers of Dr.
T
The Flame Trees of
Thika
Flaming Frontiers
The Flash
Flash Gordon Conquers
the Universe
Flash Gordon:
Rocketship
Flash Gordon: Vol. 1
Flash, the Teenage
Otter
Flight of Dragons
Flight of the Grey Wolf
The Flintstone Kids
The Flintstone Kids:
"Just Say No"
The Flintstones
A Flintstones Christmas
Carol
The Flintstones: Fred
Flintstone Woos
Again
The Flintstones:
Rappin' n' Rhymin'
Flipper
Flipper's New
Adventure
Flipper's Odyssey
Flower Angel
Flower Drum Song
The Flying Deuces
Follow Me, Boys!
Follow that Bunny!
Follow That Sleigh!
Follow the Fleet
Follow the Leader
Foofur & His Friends
For Better or For
Worse: The Bestest
Present
For Our Children: The
Concert
Forbidden Games
Forbidden Planet
Force on Thunder
Mountain
Foreign Correspondent
Four Babar Classics
Four by Dr. Seuss
The 400 Blows
The Fourth King
The Fourth Wish
Fraggle Rock: A Festive
Fraggle Holiday

How the Rhino Got His
Skin/How the Camel
Got His Hump
How the West Was Fun
How the Whale Got His
Throat
How to Be a Perfect
Person in Just Three
Days
How to Eat Fried
Worms
How to Play Baseball
How to Stuff a Wild
Bikini
How We Work: Building
Construction
How We Work: Road
Construction
The Howdy Doody
Show (Puppet
Playhouse)/The
Gabby Hayes Show
H.R. Pufnstuf, Vol. 1
Hulk Hogan's Rock 'n'
Wrestling
The Human Comedy
The Hunchback of
Notre Dame
A Hungarian Fairy Tale
Hurricane Express
I Am a Fugitive from a
Chain Gang
I am the Cheese
I Can Dance
I Confess
I Dig Dirt
I Live with Me Dad
I Remember Mama
I Want to be a
Ballerina
Ida Fanfanny and Three
Magical Tales
I'm a Little Teapot
I'm Not Oscar's Friend
Anymore...and Other
Stories
In Search of Dr. Seuss
In Search of the
Castaways
Incident at Hawk's Hill
Incredible Agent of
Stingray
The Incredible Hulk
The Incredible Hulk
Returns
The Incredible Journey
The Incredible Mr.
Limpet
The Incredible Rocky
Mountain Race
The Incredible Voyage
of Stingray
Indian Paint
Infantastic Lullabies II
Infantastic Lullabyes on
Video
Inspector Clouseau:
Ape Suzette
Inspector Clouseau:
Napoleon Blown-
Aparte

Inspector Gadget, Vol.
1
Invaders from Mars
The Invisible Monster
Invitation to the Dance
Ira Sleeps Over
Island of the Blue
Dolphins
Islands
It Came Upon a
Midnight Clear
It Happened at the
World's Fair
It Happened in New
Orleans
It Happened One Night
It's a Dog's Life
It's a Short Summer,
Charlie Brown
It's a Wonderful Life
It's Not Easy Being
Green
It's the Easter Beagle,
Charlie Brown
It's the Great Pumpkin,
Charlie Brown (triple
feature)
It's the Muppets, Vol.
1: Meet the Muppets
It's the Wolf
Ivor the Engine & the
Dragons
Ivor the Engine & the
Elephants
Jabberjaw
Jack
Jack & the Beanstalk
Jack and the Beanstalk
Jack Frost
Jack Houston's
Imagineland: This is
Imagineland
Jacob Have I Loved
Jacob Two-Two Meets
the Hooded Fang
Jamaica Inn
James Bond, Jr.
James Hound: Give Me
Liberty
James Hound: Mr.
Winlucky
Jane Eyre
Janosch: Fables from
the Magic Forest
Jay Jay the Jet Plane
Jayce & the Wheeled
Warriors, Vol. 1
Jazz Time Tale
Jem, Vol. 1: Truly
Outrageous
Jesse James Rides
Again
Jesus of Nazareth
A Jetson's Christmas
Carol
The Jetsons Meet the
Flintstones
Jim Henson's Preschool
Collection: Muppets
on Wheels

Jim Henson's Preschool
Collection: Yes, I Can
Help
Jim Henson's Preschool
Collection: Yes, I Can
Learn
Jimbo and the Jet-Set,
Vols. 1 & 2
Jirimpimbira: An African
Folktale
Joey Runs Away and
Other Stories
Johann's Gift to
Christmas
John & Julie
John Henry
John the Fearless
Johnny Appleseed
Johnny Shiloh
Johnny the Giant Killer
Johnny Tremain & the
Sons of Liberty
Johnny Woodchuck's
Adventures
Johnny's Girl
The Jolson Story
Jonah and the Whale
Josie & the Pussycats
in Outer Space
Journey Back to Oz
Journey for Margaret
Journey to the Center
of the Earth
Judgment at
Nuremberg
The Jungle Book
Jungle Book: Mowgli
Comes to the Jungle
Jungle Drums of Africa
A Jungle for Joey
The Jungle King
Junior Geologist: How
Does the Land Wear
Down?
Junior Oceanographer
Junior Space Scientist
Just Around the Corner
Just Me & My Dad
Just Planes for Kids
Just William's Luck
Justin Morgan Had a
Horse
K-9000
The Karate Kat:
Aristocratic Kapers
Katy and the
Katerpillar Kids
Kavik, the Wolf Dog
Kermit and Piggy Story
The Ketchup Vampires
Key Largo
Kid Colter
Kid Dynamite
A Kid for Two Farthings
The Kid from Left Field
The Kid Who Loved
Christmas
The Kid with the 200
I.Q.
Kidnapped

Kidsongs: A Day at
Camp
Kidsongs: A Day at Old
MacDonald's Farm
Kidsongs: A Day at the
Circus
Kidsongs: A Day with
the Animals
Kidsongs: Boppin' with
the Biggles
Kidsongs: Cars, Boats,
Trains and Planes
Kidsongs: Good Night,
Sleep Tight
Kidsongs: Home on the
Range
Kidsongs: I'd Like to
Teach the World to
Sing
Kidsongs: Let's Play
Ball
Kidsongs: Ride the
Roller Coaster
Kidsongs: Very Silly
Songs
Kidsongs: We Wish You
a Merry Christmas
Kim
The King and I
King Arthur & the
Knights of the Round
Table, Vol. 1
King Kong
King of the Rocketmen
Kino's Storytime Vol.
Three
Kismet
Kissyfur!: Hugs and
Kissyfur
Kitty Faces
Kitty Love!
Knights of the Round
Table
Knute Rockne: All
American
Koi and the Kola Nuts
Konrad
Lady Lovelylocks & the
Pixietails, Vol. 1
The Lady Vanishes
Lamb Chop's Play
Along: Action Songs
Lamb Chop's Sing-
Along Play-Along
Land of the Lost
Land of the Lost, Vol. 1
Lassie: The Miracle
Lassie's Great
Adventure
Lassie's Rescue
Rangers
The Last Chance
Detectives: Mystery
Lights of Navajo
Mesa
The Last of the
Mohicans
Law of the Wild
The Lawrenceville
Stories

Lazer Tag Academy:
The Movie
The Left-Handed Gun
The Legend of
Hiawatha
Legend of Lobo
The Legend of
Manxmouse
The Legend of Sleepy
Hollow
Legend of the White
Horse
The Legend of Zelda:
Missing Link
Lend a Paw
The Leprechauns'
Christmas Gold
Les Miserables
Let the Balloon Go
Let's Be Friends
Let's Create a Better
World
Let's Dance on the
Farm with Miss Nola
Let's Explore . . . Furry,
Fishy, Feathery
Friends
Let's Go Camping
Let's Go to the Farm
Let's Go to the Zoo
with Captain
Kangaroo
Let's Pretend with
Barney
Let's Ride a Tractor
Let's Sing Again
The Life and
Adventures of Santa
Claus
Life Begins for Andy
Hardy
Life on the Mississippi
Life with Father
The Light in the Forest
The Light Princess
Like Jake and Me
Lili
Lilies of the Field
Linnea in Monet's
Garden
The Lion, the Witch
and the Wardrobe
Little Critter Series:
Just Me and My Dad
The Little Crooked
Christmas Tree
Little Dog Lost
Little Dorrit, Film 1:
Nobody's Fault
Little Dorrit, Film 2:
Little Dorrit's Story
The Little Drummer Boy
The Little Engine That
Could
The Little Fox
Little Hiawatha
The Little House
Little House on the
Prairie
Little Lord Fauntleroy
The Little Match Girl

Little Men
The Little Mermaid
Little Miss Broadway
Little Miss Marker
Little Orphan Annie
The Little Prince & Friends
The Little Prince, Vols. 1-5
The Little Princess
Little Rascals Christmas Special
Little Red Riding Hood
Little Sister Rabbit
Little Toot
Little Tough Guys
The Little Troll Prince
Little Wizards: The Singing Sword
Little Women
Little Women Series
The Littlest Angel
The Littlest Outlaw
The Littlest Pet Shop
The Littlest Rebel
Littlest Warrior
Living God's Way
Locke the Superpower
Lollipop Dragon: Magic Lollipop Adventure
Lollipop Dragon: The Great Christmas Race
The Lone Ranger
The Lone Ranger: Code of the Pioneers
Lone Star Kid
The Lone Wolf
The Loneliest Runner
The Loneliness of the Long Distance Runner
Look What Happens . . . at the Carwash
Look What I Found
Look What I Grew: Windowsill Gardens
Look What I Made
Looney Tunes Video Show, Vol. 1
Looney Tunes Video Show, Vol. 2
Looney Tunes Video Show, Vol. 3
Lord of the Flies
Lost in a Harem
Lost in Dinosaur World
The Lost Jungle
Lost Legacy: A Girl Called Hatter Fox
Lots of Luck
Love Finds Andy Hardy
Love Happy
Love Laughs at Andy Hardy
Love Leads the Way
Lucky Luke: Ballad of the Daltons
Lucky Luke: Daisy Town
Lumpkin the Pumpkin

Lyle, Lyle Crocodile: The Musical House on East 88th St.
Macron 1: Dark Discovery in a New World
Mad Monster Party
Mad Scientist
Madeline
Madeline and the Toy Factory
Madeline at Cooking School
Madeline's Christmas
Madeline's Rescue and Other Stories about Madeline
The Magic Flute
Magic Pony
The Magic School Bus for Lunch
The Magic School Bus Gets Eaten
The Magic School Bus Gets Lost in Space
The Magic School Bus Goes to Seed
The Magic School Bus Hops Home
The Magic School Bus Inside Ralphie
The Magic School Bus Inside the Earth
The Magic School Bus Kicks Up a Storm
Magic School Bus Plays Ball
Magic Snowman
The Magic Sword
The Magic Thinking Cap
Magical Mystery Tour
The Magical Princess Gigi
The Maltese Falcon
The Man Called Flintstone
The Man in the Iron Mask
The Man in the Santa Claus Suit
The Man Who Wagged His Tail
The Manners Monster: Ruby Goes to Dinner
Man's Best Friend
Maple Town
Maple Town: Case of the Missing Candy
March of the Wooden Soldiers
Marco Polo, Jr.
Maricela
Mark Twain and Me
Mark Twain's A Connecticut Yankee in King Arthur's Court
Marsalis on Music Why Toes Tap: Wynton on Rhythm

Martin the Cobbler
Marvelous Land of Oz
Mary Kate and Ashley Olsen: Our First Video
Mary Poppins
The Marzipan Pig
The Mask: Baby's Wild Ride
The Mask: S-S-S Somebody Stop Me!
The Masked Marvel
Matilda
Maurice Sendak Library
Maurice Sendak's Really Rosie
Max Fleischer's Cartoon Capers, Vol. 1: Playin' Around
Maxie's World: Dancin' & Romancin'
Max's Chocolate Chicken and Other Stories for Young Children
Me and My Tugboat
Meet Me in St. Louis
Men of Boys Town
Merlin and the Sword
A Merry Mirthworm Christmas
Mickey & the Beanstalk
Mickey Mouse Club, Vol. 1
Mickey Mouse: The Early Years Series
Mickey's Birthday Party
Mickey's Crazy Careers
Mickey's Field Trips Series
Mickey's Fun Songs: Campout at Walt Disney World
Mickey's Fun Songs: Let's Go to the Circus
Mickey's Magical World
Mighty Hercules: Champion of the People!
Mighty Hercules: Conqueror of Evil!
The Mighty Hercules: Mightiest Mortal!
Mighty Joe Young
Mighty Morphin Power Rangers: Alpha's Magical Christmas
Mighty Morphin Power Rangers: Green with Evil, Part 1
Mighty Morphin Power Rangers Karate Club
Mighty Mouse
Mighty Mouse in the Great Space Chase
Mighty Orbots: Devil's Asteroid
The Mighty Pawns
Mighty Thor: Enter Hercules

Mike Mulligan and His Steam Shovel
Mikhail Baryshinikov's Stories from My Childhood
Million Dollar Kid
The Mini-Monsters: Adventures at Camp Mini-Mon
Miracle at Moreaux
Miracle Down Under
Miracle of Our Lady of Fatima
Miracle of the Heart: A Boys Town Story
Miracle of the White Stallions
Miracle on 34th Street
The Miracle Worker
A Mirthworm Masquerade
Mr. & Mrs. Condor
Mr. & Mrs. Smith
Mr. Bill's Real-Life Adventures
Mr. Bumpy's Karaoke Cafe
Mr. Hulot's Holiday
Mr. Humdinger Goes Fishing
Mr. Magoo: 1001 Arabian Night's Dream
Mr. Magoo: Cyrano De Bergerac/A Midsummer Night's Dream
The Mr. Magoo Show, Vol. 1
Mr. Magoo's Christmas Carol
Mister Rogers: Music and Feelings
Mr. Rossi's Dreams
Mr. Smith Goes to Washington
Mr. Wise Guy
Mr. Wizard's World: Air and Water Wizardry
Moira's Birthday
Mommy, Gimme a Drinka Water!
Monkees, Volume 1
Monkey Business
The Monkey People
Monkeys, Go Home!
Monkey's Uncle
Monster Bash
Monster In My Pocket
Moon Pilot
The Moon Stallion
Mooncussers
More Adventures of Roger Ramjet
More Baby Songs
More Dinosaurs
More Song City U.S.A.
More Stories for the Very Young
Mortal Kombat: The Journey Begins

Mosby's Marauders
Moschops: Adventures in Dinosaurland
Mother Goose Rock 'n' Rhyme
Mother Nature Tales of Discovery
Mountain Man
The Mouse and the Motorcycle
Mouse on the Mayflower
Mouse Soup
The Mouse That Roared
Mowgli's Brothers
Mozart's The Magic Flute Story: An Opera Fantasy
Muppet Babies: Explore with Us
Muppet Babies: Let's Build
Muppet Babies: Time to Play
Muppet Babies Video Storybook, Vol. 1
Muppet Family Christmas
Muppet Musicians of Bremen
Muppet Revue
Muppet Treasure Island Sing-Alongs
Muppet Treasures
Muppet Video Series
Muppets Moments
Murmel, Murmel, Murmel
Muscle Beach Party
The Music Factory
The Musical Universe of Nursery Rhymes, Vol. 1
Mutant League
My Dear Uncle Sherlock
My Dog, the Thief
My Favorite Brunette
My First Magic
My First Party
My Friend Flicka
My Friend Walter
My Life as a Dog
My Little Pony
My Little Pony: The Movie
My Old Man
My Pet Monster, Vol. 1
Mysterious Doctor Satan
Mysterious Island
Mysterious Tadpole and Other Stories
Mystery of the Million Dollar Hockey Puck
Nancy Drew: Mystery of the Diamond Triangle
Nancy Drew, Reporter

Napoleon and
  Samantha
National Geographic:
  Really Wild Animals
  Series
National Velvet
Nearly No Christmas
'Neath Brooklyn Bridge
Necessary Parties
Nestor the Long-Eared
  Christmas Donkey
The New Adventures of
  Peter Rabbit
The New Adventures of
  Tom and Huck
The New Adventures of
  Winnie the Pooh,
  Vol. 1: Great Honey
  Pot Robbery
New Adventures of
  Zorro, Vol. 1
New Zoo Revue, Vol. 1
Nickelodeon: Frightfest
A Night at the Opera
The Night Before
  Christmas
The Night Before
  Christmas and Best-
  Loved Yuletide
  Carols
The Night They Saved
  Christmas
Nightingale
The Nine Lives of
  Elfego Baca
No Man's Valley
No Time for Sergeants
Noah's Animals and
  Other Stories
Nobody's Boy
Noel
Noisy Nora
Nonsense and
  Lullabyes: Nursery
  Rhymes
The Norfin Adventures:
  The Great Egg
  Robbery
Norman the Doorman
  and Other Stories
North by Northwest
Not My Kid
Not Quite Human
Notorious
Nursery Raps with
  Mama Goose
Nursery Rhymes
The Nutcracker
Nutcracker Fantasy
The Nutcracker Prince
The Nutty Professor
Nuzzling with the
  Noozles
Nyoka and the
  Tigermen
An Officer and a Duck
The Old Mill
Old Yeller
The Olden Days Coat
Oliver & Company
Oliver Twist

Ollie Hopnoodle's
  Haven of Bliss
Olly Olly Oxen Free
The Olympic Champ
On the Comet
On the Edge: The
  Survival of Dana
On the Move with Virgil
On the Town
On Vacation with
  Mickey and Friends
Once a Hero
Once Upon a Brothers
  Grimm
One Fish, Two Fish,
  Red Fish, Blue Fish
101 Dalmatians
101 Problems of
  Hercules
One Little Indian
Open a Door
The Original Fabulous
  Adventures of Baron
  Munchausen
Orphan Train
Our Little Girl
Ovide and the Gang
The Owl and the
  Pussycat
Owl Moon and Other
  Stories
Ox Tales
Ozma of Oz
Paddington Bear
Paddle to the Sea
Paddy Beaver
Pajama Party
Panda and the Magic
  Serpent
The Paper Bag Princess
Parade
The Paradine Case
The Parent Trap
The Party
Pat and Mike
Paul Bunyan
Peachboy
Pecos Bill
Pee Wee's Playhouse
  Festival of Fun
Penny Serenade
People
The Perils of Penelope
  Pitstop
The Perils of
  Problemina
Pete Seeger's Family
  Concert
Peter and the Magic
  Egg
Peter and the Wolf
Peter Cottontail: How
  He Got His Hop
Peter Cottontail's
  Adventures
Peter Lundy and the
  Medicine Hat Stallion
Peter-No-Tail
Peter Pan

Peter Pan & the
  Pirates: Demise of
  Hook
Peter Pan/Hiawatha
Peter, Paul and Mary:
  Peter, Paul and
  Mommy, Too
Phantom 2040
Phantom 2040 Movie:
  The Ghost Who
  Walks
The Phantom Creeps
The Phantom Empire
Phantom of the Opera
Phenomenon
The Philadelphia Story
The Pickwick Papers
The Pied Piper/
  Cinderella
The Pied Piper of
  Hamelin
The Pigeon that
  Worked a Miracle
The Pigs' Wedding and
  Other Stories
The Pinballs
The Pink Panther
Pink Panther: Fly in the
  Pink
Pink Panther: Pink
  Christmas
Pink Panther: Tickled
  Pink
Pinocchio
Pinocchio and the
  Emperor of the Night
Pinocchio in Outer
  Space
Pinocchio's Christmas
Pippin
Pirates of Dark Water:
  The Saga Begins
PJ's Unfunnybunny
  Christmas
P.K. and the Kid
Plastic Man
Play-Along Video: Hey,
  You're as Funny as
  Fozzie Bear
Play-Along Video:
  Mother Goose
  Stories
Play-Along Video: Sing-
  Along, Dance-Along,
  Do-Along
Play-Along Video: Wow,
  You're a Cartoonist!
Playbox 1
Playtime
Please Don't Eat the
  Daisies
Pluto
Pluto (limited gold
  edition)
Pluto's Christmas Tree
Pocahontas
The Point
Police Academy, the
  Series
Pollyanna

Pontoffel Pock, Where
  Are You?
Poochie
Pooh Learning: Helping
  Others
Pooh Learning: Making
  Friends
Pooh Learning: Sharing
  and Caring
Pooh Playtime: Cowboy
  Pooh
Pooh Playtime:
  Detective Tigger
Pooh Playtime: Pooh
  Party
Pooh's Great School
  Bus Adventure
The Poor Little Rich
  Girl
The Popples
Porky Pig Tales
Posse Impossible
Possible Possum:
  Freight Fright
Postman Pat
Postman Pat's ABC
  Story
Postman Pat's 123
  Story
Potato Head Kids, Vol.
  1
Potsworth and the
  Midnight Patrol
Pound Puppies
Precious Pupp
Prehysteria! 2
The Pretty Piggies: The
  Adventure Begins
Primo Baby
The Prince and the
  Great Race
The Prince and the
  Pauper
Prince Cinders
The Prince of Central
  Park
Prince Valiant
The Princess and the
  Pea
Princess Gwenevere
  and the Jewel Riders
Princess Jasmine:
  Magic and Mystery
Princess Jasmine: True
  Hearts
Princess Scargo and
  the Birthday
  Pumpkin
The Princess Who
  Never Laughed
Professor Iris: Music
  Mania
Pssst! Hammerman's
  After You
Puff and the Incredible
  Mr. Nobody
Puff the Magic Dragon
Puff the Magic Dragon
  in the Land of Living
  Lies

Punky Brewster: Little
  Orphan Punky
The Puppet Theater
The Pure Hell of St.
  Trinian's
Puss in Boots
Puss 'n Boots
Puss 'n Boots Travels
  Around the World
The Puzzle Place: Rock
  Dreams
The Puzzle Place:
  Tuned In
Quark the Dragon
  Slayer
Quarterback Princess
The Quiet Man
Rabbit Ears Storybook
  Classics Collection
Raccoons: Let's Dance
Raccoons on Ice
Radar Men from the
  Moon
Radio Patrol
Raffi in Concert with
  the Rise & Shine
  Band
Raffi on Broadway
Raffi: Young Children's
  Concert with Raffi
Raft Adventures of
  Huck & Jim
Raggedy Ann and Andy
Rags to Riches
The Railway Dragon
Rainbow Brite: A Horse
  of a Different Color
Rambo: Children for
  Peace
Ramona
Ramona: Goodbye,
  Hello
Rapunzel
Rascal
Rascals and Robbers
Reading Rainbow:
  Abiyoyo
The Real Ghostbusters
Real life Boats & Ships
  for Kids
The Real Story of
  Humpty Dumpty
The Real Story of Oh
  Christmas Tree
Really Wild Animals:
  Deep Sea Dive
Really Wild Animals:
  Swinging Safari
Really Wild Animals:
  Wonders Down
  Under
Rear Window
Rebecca
Rebecca of Sunnybrook
  Farm
Rebel Without a Cause
The Red Balloon
The Red Pony
Red Riding Hood and
  Goldilocks
The Red Shoes

Sniffles Bells the Cat
Snoopy: The Musical
Snorks
The Snow Queen
Snow White
Snow White and Rose Red
Snow White and the Seven Dwarfs
Snow White and the Three Stooges
The Snowman
Snuffy the Elf Who Saved Christmas
So Dear to My Heart
Someday Me Series
Something Good
Son of Flubber
Son of Kong
Son of Zorro
Song City U.S.A.
The Song of Sacajawea
Songs for Us Series
Sorcerer's Apprentice
Sorrowful Jones
The Sound of Music
Sounds Around
Sourdough
South Pacific
Space Angel, Vol. 1
Space Battleship Yamato
Space Firebird
Space Warriors: Battle for Earth Station S/1
Spaceketeers
Sparky's Magic Piano
Speaking of Animals, Vol. 1
Special Valentine with Family Circus
Speed Racer
Spellbound
Spencer's Mountain
Spider-Woman
Spiderman
Spiderman & His Amazing Friends: Origin of the Spider Friends
Spiderman: The Deadly Dust
Spiderman, Vol. 1: Dr. Doom
Spiral Zone: Ride the Whirlwind
Spiral Zone: Zone of Darkness
Spirit of the Eagle
Spook Busters
Spooks Run Wild
Sport Goofy
Spot Goes to a Party
Spot Goes to School
Spot Goes to the Farm
Spot's Magic Christmas
Spy Smasher
Squanto and the First Thanksgiving
Stage Fright
Stand Up and Cheer

Stanley and the Dinosaurs
Stanley the Ugly Duckling
Star Fairies
Star Street: Adventures of the Star Kids
Star Street: The Happy Birthday Movie
Star Trek: Animated, Vol. 1
Star Trek the Next Generation Episode 1-2: Encounter at Farpoint
Starcom: Galactic Adventures
State Fair
The Steadfast Tin Soldier
Stingiest Man in Town
Stingray: Invaders of the Deep
Stone Fox
Stories and Fables, Vol. 1
Stories from the Black Tradition
Stories to Remember: Baby's Morningtime
Stormalong
Storms
Stormy, the Thoroughbred
The Story Keepers: Breakout!
The Story of a Cowboy Angel
Story of Babar the Little Elephant
The Story of 15 Boys
The Story of Seabiscuit
The Story of the Dancing Frog
Stowaway
Stowaways on the Ark
Strangers on a Train
Strawberry Shortcake and the Baby Without a Name
Street Frogs: Keep on Rappin'
Strega Nonna and Other Stories
Strike Up the Band
Sub-Mariner: Atlantis Under Attack
Sudie & Simpson
Summer Magic
Summer Switch
Sunshine Porcupine
Superboy
Superman
Superman & the Mole Men
Superman: The Serial, Vol. 1
SuperTed
Susannah of the Mounties

Susie, the Little Blue Coupe
Suspicion
The Sweater
Sweet 15
Sweet Honey in the Rock: Singing for Freedom
The Swiss Family Robinson
The Sword & the Rose
Sylvester & Tweety: Best Yeows of our Lives
Sylvester and Tweety's Tale Feathers
Sylvia Anderson's The Animates
Tailor of Gloucester
Tailspin Tommy
Taking Care of Terrific
The Tale of Mr. Jeremy Fisher and the Tale of Peter Rabbit
The Tale of Peter Rabbit
The Tale of Peter Rabbit and Benjamin Bunny
The Tale of Samuel Whiskers
The Tale of the Bunny Picnic
The Tale of the Frog Prince
Tales from Avonlea, Vol. 1: The Journey Begins
Tales of Beatrix Potter
Tales of Deputy Dawg, Vol. 1
The Tales of Hoffman
Tales of Pluto Series
Talespin
The Talking Eggs
Tall Tales and Legends: Johnny Appleseed
Tammy and the Bachelor
Tammy and the Doctor
Tanner's Growing Up in Alaska
Tarka the Otter
Tarzan and His Mate
Tarzan Escapes
Tarzan Finds a Son
Tarzan, the Ape Man
Tarzan's New York Adventure
Tarzan's Secret Treasure
Tazmania: Taz-Maniac
Tazmania: Taz-Manimals
Tazmania: Taz-Tronaut
Techno Police
Ted E. Bear: The Bear Who Slept Through Christmas
Teddy Bear Blues

The Teddy Bears' Christmas
The Teddy Bears' Picnic
Teen Wolf: All-American Werewolf
Teen Wolf: Wolf of My Dreams
Teenage Mutant Ninja Turtles: The Epic Begins
Teeny-Tiny and the Witch-Woman and Other Stories
Ten Who Dared
The Tender Tale of Cinderella Penguin
The Tender Years
Tennessee Tuxedo in Brushing Off a Toothache
Tennis Racquet
Terrytoons Olympics
Tex Avery's Screwball Classics, Vol. 1
Tex Avery's Screwball Classics, Vol. 2
Tex Avery's Screwball Classics, Vol. 3
Tex Avery's Screwball Classics, Vol. 4
That Gang of Mine
That's My Hero!
There Goes a Boat
There Goes a Race Car
There Goes a Spaceship
There Goes a Train
Thief of Baghdad
The Thin Man
Things That Fly Sing Alongs
Things to Do On a Rainy Day
13 Ghosts
The 39 Steps
This Is America, Charlie Brown: The Birth of the Constitution
This is America, Charlie Brown: The NASA Space Station
This Pretty Planet
Thomas the Tank Engine: Better Late Than Never
Thomas the Tank Engine: James Goes Buzz Buzz and Other Thomas Stories
Thomas the Tank Engine: James Learns a Lesson & Other Stories
Thomas the Tank Engine: Tenders & Turntables & Other Stories

Thomas the Tank Engine: Thomas Breaks the Rules & Other Stories
Thomas the Tank Engine: Thomas Gets Bumped
Thomas the Tank Engine: Thomas Gets Tricked & Other Stories
Thomas the Tank Engine: Thomas, Percy and the Dragon & Other Stories
Thomas the Tank Engine: Trust Thomas & Other Stories
Thoroughbreds Don't Cry
A Thousand Clowns
The Three Billy Goats Gruff/The Three Little Pigs
The Three Caballeros
Three Decades of Donald Duck Series
The Three Little Pigs
Three Musketeers
The Three Musketeers
Three Musketeers
The Three Musketeers: All for One and One for All!
The Three Robbers and Other Stories
Three Sesame Street Stories
Three Stooges
Three Stooges: A Ducking They Will Go
Three Stooges: A Plumbing We Will Go
Three Stooges: Cash and Carry
Three Stooges: If a Body Meets a Body
Three Stooges: In the Sweet Pie and Pie
Three Stooges Meet Hercules
Three Stooges: So Long Mr. Chumps
Three Stooges: What's the Matador?
The Three Worlds of Gulliver
Through the Looking Glass
Thumbelina
Thumpkin and the Easter Bunnies
Thundarr the Barbarian, Vol. 1
Thunderbirds
Thundercats
Thundercats, Vol. 1: Exodus

The Tick: The Tick vs. The Idea Men and The Tick vs. Chairface Chippendale
The Tiger and the Brahmin
Tiger Bay
A Tiger Walks
Tigersharks: Power of the Shark
Till the Clouds Roll By
Tim Tyler's Luck
Timberrr! From Logs to Lumber
Time for Table Manners
Timefighters in the Land of Fantasy
Timeless Tales from Hallmark
Timmy's Gift: A Precious Moments Christmas
Timon and Pumbaa's Wild Adventures: Don't Get Mad, Get Happy
Timon and Pumbaa's Wild Adventures: Grub's On
Timon and Pumbaa's Wild Adventures: Hangin' With Baby
Timon and Pumbaa's Wild Adventures: Live and Learn
Timon and Pumbaa's Wild Adventures: Quit Buggin' Me
Timon and Pumbaa's Wild Adventures: True Guts
The Tin Soldier
Tiny Toon Adventures: How I Spent My Vacation
Tiny Toon Big Adventures
Tiny Toon Fiendishly Funny Adventures
Tiny Toon Island Adventures
Tiny Toons in Two-Tone Town
Tiny Toons Music Television
Tiny Toons: The Best of Buster and Babs
Tito and Me
To Catch a Thief
To Kill a Mockingbird
To Sir, with Love
To the Last Man
Tobor the Great
Tom & Jerry Kids: Out of This World Fun
Tom & Jerry On Parade
Tom and Jerry: Starring Tom & Jerry
Tom & Jerry: The Very Best Of Tom & Jerry

Tom & Jerry's Cartoon Cavalcade
Tom & Jerry's Comic Capers
Tom & Jerry's Festival of Fun
Tom & Jerry's 50th Birthday Classics
Tom Brown's School Days
Tom Chapin: This Pretty Planet
tom thumb
Tom Thumb
Tomboy & the Champ
The Tomi Ungerer Library
Tommy Tricker & the Stamp Traveller
Tony Draws a Horse
Too Smart for Strangers with Winnie the Pooh
Toot, Whistle, Plunk & Boom
Tooter Turtle in Kink of Swat
Top Cat and the Beverly Hills Cats
Top Rock
Topper
Topper Returns
Topper Takes a Trip
Torn Curtain
The Tortoise and the Hare
Toughlove
Touring the Firehouse
Trader Tom of the China Seas
Transformers
Travels of Marco Polo
Treasure Island
The Treasure of Swamp Castle
Treasure of the Sierra Madre
A Tree Grows in Brooklyn
Trenchcoat
The Trial of the Incredible Hulk
Trick or Treat
Troll Classic Book Videos
Trolls & the Christmas Express
The Trouble with Angels
The Truth About Mother Goose
Tubby the Tuba
Tuck Everlasting
Turf Boy
Tut and Tuttle
TV's Best Adventures of Superman
'Twas the Night Before Christmas
20,000 Leagues Under the Sea

Two of a Kind
2001: A Space Odyssey
Ub Iwerks Cartoonfest
The Ugly Dachshund
The Ugly Duckling
The Ugly Duckling and other Classic Fairytales
Ugly Little Boy
Uncle Elephant
Uncle Nick and the Magic Forest
Under Capricorn
Underdog: The Tickle Feather Machine
Undergrads
Undersea Adventures of Captain Nemo: Vol. 1
The Undersea Adventures of Snelgrove Snail
Undersea Kingdom
Unicorn Tales 1
Unknown Island
Up the Down Staircase
Velveteen Rabbit
The Velveteen Rabbit
Vengeance of the Space Pirate
A Very Merry Cricket
Vip, My Brother Superman
Visionaries, Vol. 1: The Age of Magic Begins
Voyage to the Bottom of the Sea
Voyager from the Unknown
Vrrrooommm! Farming for Kids
Wacky & Packy
The Wacky World of Mother Goose
Waif Goodbye to the Paw Paws
Wait Till Your Mother Gets Home
Walking on Air
Wally Gator
A Walt Disney Christmas
The Waltons: A Thanksgiving Story
The Waltons: The Children's Carol
Waltz King
A Waltz Through the Hills
The War of the Worlds
We All Have Tales
We Think the World is Round
Wee Sing: Grandpa's Magical Toys
Wee Sing in Sillyville
Wee Sing in the Big Rock Candy Mountains

Wee Sing: In the Marvelous Musical Mansion
Wee Sing: The Best Christmas Ever!
Wee Sing Together
Wee Sing Train
Wee Sing Under the Sea
Wee Wendy
Welcome Back Wil Cwac Cwac
Welcome to Pooh Corner: Vol. 1
We're Goin' to the Farm with Father Dan
West Side Story
Westward Ho, the Wagons!
Whale for the Killing
What Do You Tell a Phone?
What Do You Want to Be When You Grow Up: Railroaders
What Do You Want to be When You Grow Up? - Zoo Crew
What the Moon Saw
What's New Mr. Magoo?, Vol. 1
What's Under My Bed? and Other Creepy Stories
What's Wrong with Wilma?
When Every Day was the Fourth of July
When Magoo Flew
When Mom and Dad Break Up
Where Angels Go, Trouble Follows
Where on Earth is Carmen Sandiego? Vol. I : A Date with Carmen (Parts One and Two)
Where on Earth is Carmen Sandiego? Vol. II: By a Whisker and Dinosaur Delirium
Where on Earth is Carmen Sandiego? Vol. III: The Good Old Bad Old Days and The Stolen Smile
Where on Earth is Carmen Sandiego? Vol. IV: Split Up and Moondreams
Where the Toys Come From
Where the Wild Things Are
Where's Spot?
Which Way Weather?
Whistle Down the Wind
White Christmas
White Mama

The White Seal
Who Has Seen the Wind?
Who Is Healthy Herb? - Food, Fitness, and Fun!
Who'll Save Our Children?
Who's Who at the Zoo?
Why Christmas Trees Aren't Perfect
Why Shoot the Teacher?
Widget of the Jungle
Widget's Great Whale Adventure
Wil Cwac Cwac: Vol. 1
Wild and Woody
Wild Geese Calling
Wild Horse Hank
Wild Pony
The Wild Puffalumps
Wild Swans
Wildlife Tales: The Legend of the Bison
Will Vinton's Claymation Comedy of Horrors
Will Vinton's Claymation Easter
The William Steig Library
Willie Mays & The Say-Hey Kid
Willie, the Operatic Whale
Willy McBean & His Magic Machine
The Wind in the Willows
Wind in the Willows, Vol. 1
The Window
Winners of the West
Winnie the Pooh
Winnie the Pooh and Christmas Too
Winnie the Pooh & Friends
Winnie the Pooh and the Blustery Day
Winnie the Pooh and the Honey Tree
Winnie the Pooh Discovers the Seasons
Winnie the Pooh Un-Valentine's Day
Winsome Witch
Winter of the Witch
Winter Wolf
Wishbone: A Tail in Twain
Wishbone: Homer Sweet Homer
Wishbone: Salty Dog
Wishbone: Terrified Terrier
Wishbone: The Prince and the Pooch

Wishbone: The
Slobbery Hound
Wishbone: Twisted Tail
The Witch Who Turned
Pink
Witcheroo
Witch's Night Out
The Wizard of Oz
The Wizard of Oz:
Danger in a Strange
Land
The Woman Who
Raised a Bear as Her
Son
The Wombles
Wonder Man
Wonderful Wizard of Oz
Wonderful World of
Puss 'N Boots
The Wonderful World
of the Brothers
Grimm
The Wonderful World
of Wombles
Wonderland Cove
Wonders of Aladdin

Woody Woodpecker &
His Friends: Vol. 1
Woody Woodpecker
Collector's Edition,
Vol. 1
Woof!
Words by Heart
Workin' on the
Railroad: Alphabet
Factory on the
Railroad
The World According to
Gumby
A World is Born
The World of Andy
Panda
World of David the
Gnome: Kangaroo
Adventure
World of Hans Christian
Andersen
The World of Henry
Orient
A World of Stories with
Katharine Hepburn

World of Strawberry
Shortcake
Wowser: Wow-Wow
Wowser
Wrinkles: In Need of
Cuddles
The Wrong Man
X-Men: Deadly
Reunions
Xuxa: Funtastic
Birthday Party
Yanco
Yankee Doodle Cricket
Yankee Doodle Dandy
The Year Without a
Santa Claus
The Yearling
Yellowstone Cubs
Yes, Virginia, There is a
Santa Claus
Yogi and the Invasion
of the Space Bears
Yogi and the Magical
Flight of the Spruce
Goose
Yogi, the Easter Bear

Yogi's First Christmas
Yogi's Great Escape
Yogi's Treasure Hunt:
Heavens to
Planetoid!
Yosemite Sam: The
Good, the Bad, and
the Ornery
You Can Ride a Horse
Young & Free
A Young Children's
Concert with Raffi
The Young Detectives
on Wheels
Young Eagles
Young Magician
Young Robin Hood
You're a Good Man,
Charlie Brown
You're Invited to Mary-
Kate & Ashley's
Sleep Over Party
You're Not Elected,
Charlie Brown!/A
Charlie Brown
Christmas

Yours, Mine & Ours
Yukon Flight
The Zax From Dr. Seuss
on the Loose
Zebra in the Kitchen
Ziggy's Gift
Zillion
Zombies of the
Stratosphere
Zoobilee Zoo, Vol. 1:
Land of Rhymes &
Other Stories
Zoofari
Zoom the White
Dolphin
Zorro Rides Again
Zorro, Vol. 1
Zorro's Black Whip
Zorro's Fighting Legion

Cast/Director Index

The **CAST/DIRECTOR INDEX** lists the video accomplishments of thousands of actors and directors in straight alphabetical format by last name (names are presented in first name, last name format, but alphabetization begins with the last name). Directors are indicated by a black triangular symbol (dingbat) next to their name. Every cast member credited in the main review section is indexed here, creating an intriguing array of videographies for the famous and not-so-famous.

Lee Aaker
Rin Tin Tin, Hero of the
   West '55

Caroline Aaron
Edward Scissorhands '90

Paul Aaron ▲
The Miracle Worker '79

Bud Abbott
Abbott and Costello Meet
   Captain Kidd '52
Abbott and Costello Meet Dr.
   Jekyll and Mr. Hyde '52
Abbott and Costello Meet
   Frankenstein '48
Africa Screams '49
Buck Privates '41
Buck Privates Come Home '47
Jack & the Beanstalk '52
Lost in a Harem '44

Philip Abbott
The Fantastic World of D.C.
   Collins '84
The Invisible Boy '57

Kareem Abdul-Jabbar
The Fish that Saved
   Pittsburgh '79
Fletch '85
Purple People Eater '88
Slam Dunk Ernest '95

Hakeem Abdul-Samad
Ernest Goes to Camp '87

Walter Abel
Curley '47
Holiday Inn '42

Ian Abercrombie
Army of Darkness '92

Michael Aberne
The Commitments '91

John Abineri
The Moon Stallion '85

F. Murray Abraham
All the President's Men '76
Amadeus '84
Beyond the Stars '89
Last Action Hero '93
The Sunshine Boys '75

Jim Abrahams ▲
Airplane! '80
Big Business '88
Hot Shots! Part Deux '93
Welcome Home, Roxy
   Carmichael '90

Michele Abrams
Buffy the Vampire Slayer '92

Tony Acierto
Journey to Spirit Island '92

Bettye Ackerman
Prehysteria! 2 '94

Leslie Ackerman
Blame It on the Night '84

Robert Ackerman ▲
Safe Passage '94

Joss Ackland
Bill & Ted's Bogus
   Journey '91
The Hunt for Red October '90
A Kid in King Arthur's
   Court '95
Lady Jane '85
The Mighty Ducks '92
Miracle on 34th Street '94
Once Upon a Crime '92

David Ackroyd
A Smoky Mountain
   Christmas '86

Acquanetta
Grizzly Adams: The Legend
   Continues '90

Jane Actman
The Last of the Mohicans '85

Eddie Acuff
G-Men Never Forget '48

Beverly Adams
How to Stuff a Wild Bikini '65

Brandon Adams
The Sandlot '93

Brooke Adams
The Baby-Sitters Club '95
Invasion of the Body
   Snatchers '78

Don Adams
Back to the Beach '87
Jimmy the Kid '82

Jane Adams
Father of the Bride Part II '95

Joey Adams
Bio-Dome '96
Mallrats '95

Julie Adams
Francis Joins the WACs '54

Marla Adams
Gotcha! '85

Mason Adams
F/X '86
Houseguest '94
Son-in-Law '93

Maud Adams
Jane & the Lost City '87
The Man with the Golden
   Gun '74
Octopussy '83

Nick Adams
Mosby's Marauders '66
No Time for Sergeants '58
Rebel Without a Cause '55

Stanley Adams
Lilies of the Field '63

Tom Adams
The Fighting Prince of
   Donegal '66

George Adamson
Christian the Lion '76

Nancy Addison
Somewhere Tomorrow '85

Georges Adel
Love and Death '75

Vern Adix
Teen Alien '88

Suzanne Adkinson
Racing with the Moon '84

Matt Adler
Diving In '90
Doin' Time on Planet
   Earth '88
Flight of the Navigator '86
White Water Summer '87

Percy Adlon ▲
Bagdad Cafe '88

Edvin Adolphson
Boy of Two Worlds '70

Iris Adrian
Million Dollar Kid '44

Max Adrian
The Boy Friend '71

Frank Adu
Love and Death '75

Ben Affleck
Mallrats '95
School Ties '92

Casey Affleck
Race the Sun '96

Janet Agren
Aladdin '86

Jenny Agutter
Amy '81
Darkman '90
The Man in the Iron Mask '77
Secret Places '85

Brian Aherne
I Confess '53
Prince Valiant '54
Waltz King '63

Kamal Ahmed
The Jerky Boys '95

Monique Ahrens
A Dog of Flanders '59

Ahui
Robinson Crusoe & the
   Tiger '72

Kyoko Ai
Destroy All Monsters '68

Charles Aidman
Menace on the Mountain '70

Danny Aiello
Bang the Drum Slowly '73
Moonstruck '87
Old Enough '84
The Purple Rose of Cairo '85
Radio Days '87
The Road Home '95

Holly Aird
The Flame Trees of Thika '81

Franklin Ajaye
Car Wash '76

Karen Akers
The Purple Rose of Cairo '85

Claude Akins
Battle for the Planet of the
   Apes '73
Pecos Bill '86

Denis Akiyama
Johnny Mnemonic '95

Marc Alaimo
Arena '88

Miguel Alamo
Daniel and the Towers '90s

John Albasiny
Kipperbang '82

Josh Albee
The Adventures of Tom
   Sawyer '73
The Runaways '75

Anna Maria Alberghetti
Cinderfella '60

Hans Albers
Baron Munchausen '43

Eddie Albert
The Birch Interval '78
Brenda Starr '86
Escape to Witch Mountain '75
The Heartbreak Kid '72
Miracle of the White
   Stallions '63
Oklahoma! '55
Roman Holiday '53

Edward Albert
Butterflies Are Free '72
Guarding Tess '94
The Rescue '88

Frank Albertson
Ah, Wilderness! '35
It's a Wonderful Life '46
Room Service '38

Jack Albertson
Charlie and the Great Balloon
   Chase '82
Miracle on 34th Street '47
The Poseidon Adventure '72
Shirley Temple Storybook
   Theater '60
Willy Wonka & the Chocolate
   Factory '71

Alan Alda
Canadian Bacon '94
Sweet Liberty '86

Alan Alda ▲
Sweet Liberty '86

Rutanya Alda
Mommie Dearest '81
Prancer '89
Racing with the Moon '84

Tom Aldredge
The Adventures of Huck
   Finn '93
What About Bob? '91

Adell Aldrich ▲
The Kid from Left Field '79

Kay Aldridge
Nyoka and the Tigermen '42

Jace Alexander
Eight Men Out '88

Jane Alexander
All the President's Men '76
A Friendship in Vienna '88
Glory '89
The Great White Hope '70
Kramer vs. Kramer '79
Night Crossing '81

Jason Alexander
Blankman '94
Brighton Beach Memoirs '86
Coneheads '93

Dunston Checks In '95
North '94
The Paper '94

John Alexander
The Horn Blows at
   Midnight '45
The Jolson Story '46
A Tree Grows in Brooklyn '45

Khandi Alexander
Greedy '94
What's Love Got to Do With
   It? '93

Max Alexander
Roxanne '87

Spike Alexander
Brain Donors '92

Constantin Alexandrov
Gorillas in the Mist '88

Phillip Alford
To Kill a Mockingbird '62

James Algar ▲
The Living Desert '53

Muhammad Ali
The Greatest '77

Jed Allan
Man from Clover Grove '78

William Alland
Citizen Kane '41

Michael Alldredge
Robot Jox '89

Bill Allen
Rad '86
Sioux City '94

Corey Allen
Rebel Without a Cause '55

Corey Allen ▲
Avalanche '78
The Man in the Santa Claus
   Suit '79

Debbie Allen
The Fish that Saved
   Pittsburgh '79

Eugene Allen
House Party 2: The Pajama
   Jam '91

Gavin Allen
Runaway '89

Irwin Allen ▲
The Swarm '78
Voyage to the Bottom of the
   Sea '61

Joan Allen
Josh and S.A.M. '93
Peggy Sue Got Married '86
Searching for Bobby
   Fischer '93

Tucker: The Man and His
   Dream '88

Judith Allen
Bright Eyes '34

Karen Allen
Animal Behavior '89
King of the Hill '93
Raiders of the Lost Ark '81
The Sandlot '93
Scrooged '88
Starman '84

Marty Allen
Whale of a Tale '76

Mikki Allen
Regarding Henry '91

Nancy Allen
Home Movies '79
I Wanna Hold Your Hand '78
Poltergeist 3 '88
Robocop '87
Robocop 2 '90
Robocop 3 '91
Strange Invaders '83

Patrick Allen
When Dinosaurs Ruled the
   Earth '70

Steve Allen
Alice in Wonderland '85

Tim Allen
The Santa Clause '94

Woody Allen
Annie Hall '77
Bananas '71
Broadway Danny Rose '84
Love and Death '75
Play It Again, Sam '72
Sleeper '73
Take the Money and Run '69

Woody Allen ▲
Annie Hall '77
Bananas '71
Broadway Danny Rose '84
Love and Death '75
The Purple Rose of Cairo '85
Radio Days '87
Sleeper '73
Take the Money and Run '69

Roger Allers ▲
The Lion King '94

Kirstie Alley
It Takes Two '95
Look Who's Talking '89
Look Who's Talking Now '93
Look Who's Talking, Too '90
Madhouse '90
Peter and the Wolf '95
Star Trek 2: The Wrath of
   Khan '82
Summer School '87

Sara Allgood
Challenge to Lassie '49

How Green was My Valley '41
Jane Eyre '44

Corbin Allred
Josh Kirby . . . Time Warrior:
   Chapter 1, Planet of the
   Dino-Knights '95

Astrid Allwyn
Stowaway '36

June Allyson
Girl Crazy '43
The Glenn Miller Story '54
Little Women '49
The Three Musketeers '48
Till the Clouds Roll By '46

Maria Conchita Alonso
A Fine Mess '86

Glen Alsworth
Cry from the Mountain '85

Robert Altman ▲
M*A*S*H '70
Popeye '80

Trini Alvarado
The Babe '92
Little Women '94
Rich Kids '79
Satisfaction '88

Kirk Alyn
Atom Man vs. Superman '50
Federal Agents vs.
   Underworld, Inc. '49
Superman: The Serial, Vol.
   1 '48

Lyle Alzado
Ernest Goes to Camp '87
Tough Guys '86

Vittorio Amandola
Queen of Hearts '89

Betty Amann
Nancy Drew, Reporter '39

Rod Amateau ▲
The Garbage Pail Kids
   Movie '87

Don Ameche
The Boatniks '70
Cocoon '85
Cocoon: The Return '88
Corrina, Corrina '94
Harry and the Hendersons '87

Amedee
Forbidden Games '52

Nicholas Amer
Treasure Island '89

Leon Ames
The Absent-Minded
   Professor '61
The Misadventures of Merlin
   Jones '63
Monkey's Uncle '65
Peggy Sue Got Married '86

Son of Flubber '63

Rosemary Ames
Our Little Girl '35

Trudi Ames
Bye, Bye, Birdie '63

Madchen Amick
Trapped In Paradise '94

Jon Amiel ▲
Queen of Hearts '89
Sommersby '93

Suzy Amis
Fandango '85
Plain Clothes '88
Rich in Love '93
Rocket Gibraltar '88
The Usual Suspects '95

John Amos
American Flyers '85
Beastmaster '82
Die Hard 2: Die Harder '90
Touched by Love '80
The World's Greatest
   Athlete '73

Morey Amsterdam
Beach Party '63
Muscle Beach Party '64

Franco Amurri ▲
Monkey Trouble '94

Susan Anbeh
French Kiss '95

Ricardo Ancona
Yanco '64

Luana Anders
Goin' South '78
Irreconcilable Differences '84

Angry Anderson
Mad Max: Beyond
   Thunderdome '85

Bridgette Anderson
Hansel and Gretel '82
Savannah Smiles '82
A Summer to Remember '84

Carl Anderson
Jesus Christ, Superstar '73

Eddie Anderson
Gone with the Wind '39
Topper Returns '41

Harry Anderson
Happy Birthday, Bugs: 50
   Looney Years '90

Ingrid Anderson
Hercules '83

Jean Anderson
Back Home '90
Prince Brat and the Whipping
   Boy '95

Jeff Anderson
Clerks '94

John Anderson
Eight Men Out '88

Judith Anderson
Cinderfella '60
Rebecca '40
Star Trek 3: The Search for
   Spock '84
The Ten Commandments '56

Lindsay Anderson
Chariots of Fire '81

Loni Anderson
Munchie '92

Louis Anderson
Ferris Bueller's Day Off '86

Melissa Sue Anderson
Little House on the Prairie '74
The Loneliest Runner '76
On the Edge: The Survival of
   Dana '79

Melody Anderson
Flash Gordon '80

Michael Anderson Sr. ▲
Around the World in 80
   Days '56
Doc Savage '75

Michael Anderson Jr.
The Great Land of Small '86
In Search of the
   Castaways '62

Miles Anderson
A Far Off Place '93

Mitchell Anderson
Back to Hannibal: The Further
   Adventures of Tom Sawyer
   and Huckleberry Finn '90
Goodbye, Miss 4th of July '88

Paul Anderson ▲
Mortal Kombat: The
   Movie '95

Richard Anderson
Forbidden Planet '56
Zorro, Vol. 1 '58

Richard Dean Anderson
Past the Bleachers '95

Stephanie Anderson
Calendar Girl '93

Whitney Anderson
Prehysteria 3 '95

Marcel Andre
Beauty and the Beast '46

Andre the Giant
The Princess Bride '87

Ursula Andress
Clash of the Titans '81
Dr. No '62

The Fifth Musketeer '79

Anthony Andrews
The Scarlet Pimpernel '82

Dana Andrews
Airport '75 '75
State Fair '45

David Andrews
Apollo 13 '95

Edward Andrews
Sixteen Candles '84
A Tiger Walks '64

Harry Andrews
Death on the Nile '78
Man of La Mancha '72
Wuthering Heights '70

Julie Andrews
Gonzo Presents Muppet Weird
   Stuff '85
Little Miss Marker '80
Mary Poppins '64
The Sound of Music '65
Torn Curtain '66

Stanley Andrews
The Adventures of Frank and
   Jesse James '48

Heather Angel
Suspicion '41

Vanessa Angel
Kingpin '96

Maya Angelou
How to Make an American
   Quilt '95

Jimmy Angle
Terror in the Jungle '68

Christien Anholt
Reunion '88

Evelyn Ankers
Black Beauty '46

Ann-Margret
Bye, Bye, Birdie '63
The Cheap Detective '78
Grumpier Old Men '95
Grumpy Old Men '93
I Ought to Be in Pictures '82
Newsies '92
State Fair '62
Tommy '75
The Villain '79

Ken Annakin ▲
Call of the Wild '72
The Fifth Musketeer '79
The New Adventures of Pippi
   Longstocking '88
Pirate Movie '82
The Swiss Family
   Robinson '60
The Sword & the Rose '53
Third Man on the
   Mountain '59

Those Daring Young Men in
Their Jaunty Jalopies '69

Jean-Jacques Annaud ▲
The Bear '89

Paul Annett ▲
The Witching of Ben
Wagner '95

Francesca Annis
Flipper's New Adventure '64
Krull '83

Michael Ansara
And Now Miguel '66
The Bears & I '74
The Fantastic World of D.C.
Collins '84
Guns of the Magnificent
Seven '69
Voyage to the Bottom of the
Sea '61

Zachary Ansley
Christmas Comes to Willow
Creek '87
Princes in Exile '90
This Boy's Life '93

Susan Anspach
The Devil & Max Devlin '81
Gone are the Days '84
Misunderstood '84
Play It Again, Sam '72

David Anspaugh ▲
Hoosiers '86
Rudy '93

Paul Anstad
Snow Treasure '67

Gerald Anthony
Secret of the Ice Cave '89

Lysette Anthony
Dr. Jekyll and Ms. Hyde '95
Dracula: Dead and Loving
It '95
Face the Music '92
Krull '83
Look Who's Talking Now '93
Oliver Twist '82

Paul Anthony
House Party '90

Susan Anton
The Boy Who Loved Trolls '84
Cannonball Run 2 '84
Making Mr. Right '86

Lou Antonio ▲
The Last Prostitute '91

Gabrielle Anwar
For Love or Money '93
If Looks Could Kill '91
The Three Musketeers '93
Wild Hearts Can't Be
Broken '91

Kazuya Aoyama
Godzilla vs. the Cosmic
Monster '74

Peter Appel
Man of the House '95

Noel Appleby
My Grandpa is a Vampire '92

Christina Applegate
Don't Tell Mom the
Babysitter's Dead '91

Royce D. Applegate
Gettysburg '93

Michael Apted ▲
Coal Miner's Daughter '80
First Born '84
Gorillas in the Mist '88
Kipperbang '82
Nell '94

Amy Aquino
Alan & Naomi '92

Angelica Aragon
A Walk in the Clouds '95

Alfonso Arau
Romancing the Stone '84
Scandalous John '71
Three Amigos '86

Alfonso Arau ▲
A Walk in the Clouds '95

Allan Arbus
Daniel and the Towers '90s

Jonas Arby
Running on Empty '88

Anne Archer
Cancel My Reservation '72
Clear and Present Danger '94
Family Prayers '91
Hero at Large '80

Fanny Ardant
Sabrina '95

Eve Arden
At the Circus '39
Cinderella '84
Grease '78
Grease 2 '82
Under the Rainbow '81

Emile Ardolino ▲
Chances Are '89
Dirty Dancing '87
George Balanchine's The
Nutcracker '93
Sister Act '92
Three Men and a Little
Lady '90

Allison Argo
Cry from the Mountain '85

David Argue
BMX Bandits '83

Yareli Arizmendi
The Big Green '95

Adam Arkin
Necessary Parties '88

Alan Arkin
Bad Medicine '85
Coupe de Ville '90
Edward Scissorhands '90
The Emperor's New
Clothes '84
Hearts of the West '75
Heck's Way Home '95
Improper Channels '82
Indian Summer '93
The Jerky Boys '95
Necessary Parties '88
North '94
The Rocketeer '91
The Russians are Coming, the
Russians are Coming '66
Simon '80

Robert Arkins
The Commitments '91

Allan Arkush ▲
Heartbeeps '81
Rock 'n' Roll High School '79

Pedro Armendariz Sr.
From Russia with Love '63
The Littlest Outlaw '54

Pedro Armendariz Jr.
Tombstone '93

Henry Armetta
Fisherman's Wharf '39
Let's Sing Again '36

Alun Armstrong
Black Beauty '94

Bess Armstrong
Nothing in Common '86
The Skateboard Kid '93

Curtis Armstrong
The Adventures of Huck
Finn '93
Bad Medicine '85
Better Off Dead '85
Big Bully '95
One Crazy Summer '86
Revenge of the Nerds '84

Gillian Armstrong ▲
Little Women '94

Lee Armstrong
Magic Island '95

Louis Armstrong
The Glenn Miller Story '54
Hello, Dolly! '69
High Society '56

R.G. Armstrong
Dick Tracy '90
The Great White Hope '70
My Name is Nobody '74
The Shadow Riders '82

Robert Armstrong
King Kong '33
Mighty Joe Young '49
Palooka '34
Son of Kong '33

Robin B. Armstrong ▲
Pastime '91

Todd Armstrong
Jason and the Argonauts '63

Desi Arnaz Sr.
Escape Artist '82

Gwen Arner ▲
Necessary Parties '88

James Arness
The Farmer's Daughter '47

Jeanetta Arnetta
Ladybugs '92
The Shadow Riders '82

Dorothy Arnold
The Phantom Creeps '39

Edward Arnold
Mr. Smith Goes to
Washington '39

Frank Arnold ▲
A Waltz Through the Hills '88

Jack Arnold ▲
The Mouse That Roared '59

Mark Arnold
Threesome '94

Tom Arnold
Big Bully '95
Hero '92
Nine Months '95
The Stupids '95
True Lies '94
Undercover Blues '93

Alexis Arquette
Threesome '94

David Arquette
Beautiful Girls '96
Buffy the Vampire Slayer '92

Lewis Arquette
Book of Love '91

Patricia Arquette
Holy Matrimony '94

Rosanna Arquette
Desperately Seeking
Susan '85
Silverado '85

Jeri Arrendondo
Spirit of the Eagle '90

Carol Arthur
The Sunshine Boys '75

Jean Arthur
Mr. Smith Goes to
Washington '39

Shane '53

Johnny Arthur
The Masked Marvel '43

Leslie Ash
Curse of the Pink Panther '83

Monty Ash
Tough Guys '86

Dana Ashbrook
Ghost Dad '90

Hal Ashby ▲
Being There '79
Bound for Glory '76

Peggy Ashcroft
Madame Sousatzka '88
The 39 Steps '35

Jane Asher
Dreamchild '85
The Prince and the
    Pauper '62

William Asher ▲
Beach Blanket Bingo '65
Beach Party '63
Bikini Beach '64
How to Stuff a Wild Bikini '65
Muscle Beach Party '64

Elizabeth Ashley
Dragnet '87

John Ashley
Beach Blanket Bingo '65
Beach Party '63
Bikini Beach '64
How to Stuff a Wild Bikini '65
Muscle Beach Party '64

Jonathan Ashmore
A Kid for Two Farthings '55

John Ashton
Beverly Hills Cop '84
Beverly Hills Cop 2 '87
Little Big League '94
She's Having a Baby '88
Some Kind of Wonderful '87
Trapped In Paradise '94

Luke Askew
Legend of the White
    Horse '85

Robin Askwith
Hans Brinker '69

Gregoire Aslan
Golden Voyage of Sinbad '73

Ed Asner
Change of Habit '69
A Friendship in Vienna '88
Gus '76

Armand Assante
Animal Behavior '89
Fatal Instinct '93
1492: Conquest of
    Paradise '92

Judge Dredd '95
Little Darlings '80
The Lords of Flatbush '74

Fred Astaire
The Amazing Dobermans '76
The Band Wagon '53
The Belle of New York '52
Easter Parade '48
Finian's Rainbow '68
Follow the Fleet '36
Funny Face '57
Holiday Inn '42
The Man in the Santa Claus
    Suit '79
Shall We Dance '37
That's Dancing! '85
That's Entertainment '74
That's Entertainment, Part
    2 '76

Shay Astar
Ernest Scared Stupid '91

John Astin
Brothers O'Toole '73
Huck and the King of
    Hearts '93
National Lampoon's European
    Vacation '85
Pepper and His Wacky
    Taxi '72
Stepmonster '92
Teen Wolf Too '87

MacKenzie Astin
The Garbage Pail Kids
    Movie '87
Iron Will '93

Sean Astin
Encino Man '92
The Goonies '85
Like Father, Like Son '87
Rudy '93
Safe Passage '94
White Water Summer '87
The Willies '90

Mary Astor
Little Women '49
The Maltese Falcon '41
Meet Me in St. Louis '44

Roscoe Ates
Regl'ar Fellers '41

William Atherton
Bio-Dome '96
Die Hard '88
Die Hard 2: Die Harder '90
Ghostbusters '84
The Pelican Brief '93
Real Genius '85

Harvey Atkin
Meatballs '79

Christopher Atkins
Pirate Movie '82

Eileen Atkins
Oliver Twist '82

Felicia Atkins
The Errand Boy '61

Tom Atkins
Skeezer '82

Jayne Atkinson
Free Willy '93
Free Willy 2: The Adventure
    Home '95

Rowan Atkinson
Bernard and the Genie '91
Four Weddings and a
    Funeral '93
Hot Shots! Part Deux '93
Never Say Never Again '83
The Witches '90

Richard Attenborough
David Copperfield '70
Doctor Doolittle '67
Jurassic Park '93
Miracle on 34th Street '94
Ten Little Indians '75

Richard Attenborough ▲
A Bridge Too Far '77
Chaplin '92
Shadowlands '93

Billy Attmore
The Treasure of
    Matecumbe '76

Edith Atwater
It Happened at the World's
    Fair '63

Lionel Atwill
Captain America '44
Captain Blood '35

Brigitte Auber
To Catch a Thief '55

Rene Auberjonois
King Kong '76
M*A*S*H '70
My Best Friend Is a
    Vampire '88
Police Academy 5: Assignment
    Miami Beach '88
A Smoky Mountain
    Christmas '86

Lenore Aubert
Abbott and Costello Meet
    Frankenstein '48

James Aubrey
Lord of the Flies '63

Danielle Aubry
Bikini Beach '64

Michel Auclair
Beauty and the Beast '46

Stephane Audran
Ten Little Indians '75

Mischa Auer
The Christmas That Almost
    Wasn't '66

Patrick Auffay
The 400 Blows '59

Claudine Auger
Secret Places '85
Thunderball '65

Florrie Augger
Bugsy Malone '76

Robert August
The Endless Summer '66
The Endless Summer 2 '94

Haley Aull
Something to Talk About '95

Jean-Pierre Aumont
The Horse Without a
    Head '63
Jefferson in Paris '94
Lili '53

Georges Auric
Beauty and the Beast '46

Alana Austin
A Simple Twist of Fate '94

Alyssa Austin
A Simple Twist of Fate '94

Karen Austin
Summer Rental '85

Michael Austin ▲
Princess Caraboo '94

Patti Austin
Tucker: The Man and His
    Dream '88

Paul Austin
The Manhattan Project '86

Ray Austin ▲
Highlander: The Gathering '93

Daniel Auteuil
Jean de Florette '87
Manon of the Spring '87

Gene Autry
The Phantom Empire '35

Igor Auzins ▲
We of the Never Never '82

Frankie Avalon
Back to the Beach '87
Beach Blanket Bingo '65
Beach Party '63
Bikini Beach '64
Grease '78
How to Stuff a Wild Bikini '65
Muscle Beach Party '64
Voyage to the Bottom of the
    Sea '61

Erik Avari
Stargate '94

James Avery
Beastmaster 2: Through the
    Portal of Time '91

Margaret Avery
The Fish that Saved
   Pittsburgh '79

Tex Avery ▲
Adventures of Droopy '55
All This and Tex Avery Too!
   '92
Bugs Bunny Superstar '75
Tex Avery's Screwball
   Classics, Vol. 1 '40s
Tex Avery's Screwball
   Classics, Vol. 2 '40s

John G. Avildsen
The Karate Kid: Part 3 '89

John G. Avildsen ▲
8 Seconds '94
For Keeps '88
The Karate Kid '84
The Karate Kid: Part 2 '86
The Karate Kid: Part 3 '89
Lean on Me '89
The Power of One '92
Rocky '76
Rocky 5 '90

Rick Aviles
Ghost '90

Mili Avital
Stargate '94

Jon Avnet ▲
Up Close and Personal '96

Jan Avran
Zorro, Vol. 1 '58

Philippe Avron
Circus Angel '65

Hoyt Axton
Christmas Comes to Willow
   Creek '87
Goldilocks & the Three
   Bears '83
Gremlins '84
Heart Like a Wheel '83
The Rousters '83

Dan Aykroyd
Celtic Pride '96
Chaplin '92
Coneheads '93
Dragnet '87
Driving Miss Daisy '89
Ghostbusters '84
Ghostbusters 2 '89
The Great Outdoors '88
My Girl '91
My Girl 2 '94
My Stepmother Is an
   Alien '88
North '94
Sgt. Bilko '95
Sneakers '92
Spies Like Us '85
This is My Life '92
Tommy Boy '95
Twilight Zone: The Movie '83

Danielle Aykroyd
Coneheads '93

Felix Aylmer
Alice in Wonderland '50
Knights of the Round
   Table '53

Lew Ayres
Battle for the Planet of the
   Apes '73
Salem's Lot '79

Hank Azaria
The Birdcage '95
Quiz Show '94

Annette Azcuy
Bill & Ted's Bogus
   Journey '91

Shabana Azmi
Madame Sousatzka '88
Son of the Pink Panther '93

Charles Aznavour
Ten Little Indians '75

Candice Azzara
Doin' Time on Planet
   Earth '88

Obba Babatunde
Philadelphia '93
Undercover Blues '93

Barbara Babcock
Far and Away '92
On the Edge: The Survival of
   Dana '79
That Was Then. . .This Is
   Now '85

Lauren Bacall
All I Want for Christmas '91
From the Mixed-Up Files of
   Mrs. Basil E.
   Frankweiler '95
Key Largo '48
The Shootist '76

Michael Bacall
Wait Until Spring, Bandini '90

Barbara Bach
The Spy Who Loved Me '77

Catherine Bach
Cannonball Run 2 '84

Brian Backer
Fast Times at Ridgemont
   High '82
Moving Violations '85

Jim Backus
Billie '65
C.H.O.M.P.S. '79
Now You See Him, Now You
   Don't '72
Pat and Mike '52
Pete's Dragon '77
The Pied Piper of Hamelin '57
Rebel Without a Cause '55

The Wonderful World of the
   Brothers Grimm '62

Kevin Bacon
The Air Up There '94
Apollo 13 '95
Footloose '84
Hero at Large '80
Planes, Trains &
   Automobiles '87
The River Wild '94
She's Having a Baby '88
White Water Summer '87

Lloyd Bacon ▲
Knute Rockne: All
   American '40

Michael Badalucco
Two If by Sea '95

Hermione Baddeley
The Belles of St. Trinian's '53
A Christmas Carol '51
Mary Poppins '64

Diedrich Bader
The Beverly Hillbillies '93

John Badham ▲
American Flyers '85
Another Stakeout '93
Bingo Long Traveling All-Stars
   & Motor Kings '76
Short Circuit '86
War Games '83

Mary Badham
To Kill a Mockingbird '62

Buddy Baer
Jack & the Beanstalk '52

Max Baer Jr. ▲
Ode to Billy Joe '76

Meredith Baer
The Chicken Chronicles '77

Parley Baer
The Adventures of Huckleberry
   Finn '60
Dave '93
The Ugly Dachshund '65

Paloma Baeza
A Kid in King Arthur's
   Court '95

Carol Bagdasarian
The Aurora Encounter '85
The Charge of the Model
   T's '76

Ross Bagley
The Little Rascals '94

Chuck Bail ▲
Gumball Rally '76

G.W. Bailey
Mannequin '87
Police Academy 6: City Under
   Siege '89

Police Academy: Mission to
   Moscow '94
A Winner Never Quits '86

Conrad Bain
Bananas '71
C.H.O.M.P.S. '79

Ron Bain
Experience Preferred. . . But
   Not Essential '83

Fay Bainter
Babes on Broadway '41
The Human Comedy '43
Journey for Margaret '42
Secret Life of Walter Mitty '47
State Fair '45

Jimmy Baio
The Bad News Bears in
   Breaking Training '77

Scott Baio
Bugsy Malone '76
Foxes '80

Scott Bairstow
White Fang 2: The Myth of the
   White Wolf '94

Richard Bakalayan
The Computer Wore Tennis
   Shoes '69

Blanche Baker
French Postcards '79
Sixteen Candles '84

Carroll Baker
Giant '56
How the West was Won '63
Kindergarten Cop '90
Watcher in the Woods '81

Diane Baker
The Cable Guy '96
The Horse in the Gray Flannel
   Suit '68
Imaginary Crimes '94
Journey to the Center of the
   Earth '59
The Joy Luck Club '93
The Net '95

Dylan Baker
Delirious '91
Planes, Trains &
   Automobiles '87
The Wizard of Loneliness '88

Jill Baker
Hope and Glory '87

Joby Baker
Gidget '59

Joe Don Baker
Congo '95
Fletch '85
Goldeneye '95
Guns of the Magnificent
   Seven '69
Junior Bonner '72
Leonard Part 6 '87

The Natural '84
Reality Bites '94
Walking Tall '73

Kathy Baker
Dad '89
Edward Scissorhands '90
Permanent Record '88
The Right Stuff '83

Kenny Baker
The Elephant Man '80
The Empire Strikes Back '80
Return of the Jedi '83
Sleeping Beauty '89
Star Wars '77
Time Bandits '81

Kenny L. Baker
Amadeus '84
At the Circus '39

Ray Baker
Camp Nowhere '94
Speechless '94

Stanley Baker
Knights of the Round
    Table '53

Tom Baker
The Chronicles of Narnia '89
Golden Voyage of Sinbad '73

Gary Bakewell
Backbeat '94

**William "Billy"
    Bakewell**
Davy Crockett, King of the
    Wild Frontier '55
Gone with the Wind '39
Radar Men from the
    Moon '52

Brenda Bakke
Hot Shots! Part Deux '93

Ralph Bakshi ▲
Fire and Ice '83
The Lord of the Rings '78
Wizards '77

Scott Bakula
Necessary Roughness '91

Bob Balaban
Amos and Andrew '93
Close Encounters of the Third
    Kind '77
For Love or Money '93
Girlfriends '78
Greedy '94
2010 : The Year We Make
    Contact '84

Bob Balaban ▲
My Boyfriend's Back '93

Belinda Balaski
The Howling '81

Adam Baldwin
Hadley's Rebellion '84
My Bodyguard '80

Radio Flyer '92

Alec Baldwin
Beetlejuice '88
The Hunt for Red October '90
Prelude to a Kiss '92
The Shadow '94
She's Having a Baby '88

Daniel Baldwin
Car 54, Where Are You? '94

Peter Baldwin ▲
The Hoboken Chicken
    Emergency '84
Lots of Luck '85

Stephen Baldwin
Bio-Dome '96
8 Seconds '94
The Lawrenceville
    Stories '80s
A Simple Twist of Fate '94
Threesome '94
The Usual Suspects '95

Christian Bale
Empire of the Sun '87
The Land of Faraway '87
Little Women '94
Newsies '92
Swing Kids '93
Treasure Island '89

Paul Trevor Bale ▲
The Littlest Viking '94

Ina Balin
The Projectionist '71

Fairuza Balk
Imaginary Crimes '94
Outside Chance of Maximillian
    Glick '88
Return to Oz '85
The Worst Witch '86

Geza Balkay
A Hungarian Fairy Tale '87

Angeline Ball
The Commitments '91

Lucille Ball
Follow the Fleet '36
Room Service '38
Sorrowful Jones '49
Yours, Mine & Ours '68

William Ball
Suburban Commando '91

Carroll Ballard ▲
The Black Stallion '79
Never Cry Wolf '83
Wind '92

Kaye Ballard
Ava's Magical Adventure '94

Jerry Ballew
Cry from the Mountain '85

Martin Balsam
All the President's Men '76

Little Big Man '70
A Thousand Clowns '65

Talia Balsam
On the Edge: The Survival of
    Dana '79

Allison Balson
Legend of the White
    Horse '85

Gerry Bamman
Home Alone 2: Lost in New
    York '92
Lorenzo's Oil '92

Alexis Banas
The Haunting of Barney
    Palmer '90s

Anne Bancroft
Dracula: Dead and Loving
    It '95
The Elephant Man '80
Home for the Holidays '95
Homecoming '96
Honeymoon in Vegas '92
How to Make an American
    Quilt '95
Jesus of Nazareth '77
The Miracle Worker '62
Silent Movie '76

George Bancroft
Little Men '40

Albert Band ▲
Prehysteria '93
Prehysteria! 2 '94

Charles Band ▲
Prehysteria '93

Antonio Banderas
Philadelphia '93

Joy Bang
Play It Again, Sam '72

Jonathan Banks
Beverly Hills Cop '84
Flipper '96

Leslie Banks
Jamaica Inn '39

Ian Bannen
George's Island '91
Ghost Dad '90
Hope and Glory '87
The Prodigal '83
Watcher in the Woods '81

Yoshimitu Banno ▲
Godzilla vs. the Smog
    Monster '72

Jack Bannon
Miracle of the Heart: A Boys
    Town Story '86

Christine Baranski
Addams Family Values '93
The Birdcage '95

Olivia Barash
Child of Glass '78

Adrienne Barbeau
Back to School '86
Cannonball Run '81
Charlie and the Great Balloon
    Chase '82
Swamp Thing '82

Joseph Barbera ▲
The Jetsons: The Movie '90

Katie Barberi
The Garbage Pail Kids
    Movie '87

George Barbier
Little Miss Broadway '38

Joan Barclay
Blake of Scotland Yard '36

Roy Barcroft
Federal Agents vs.
    Underworld, Inc. '49
G-Men Never Forget '48
Jesse James Rides Again '47
Radar Men from the
    Moon '52
Son of Zorro '47

Brigitte Bardot
Dear Brigitte '65

Lynn Bari
Francis Joins the WACs '54

Bob Barker
Happy Gilmore '96

Lex Barker
The Farmer's Daughter '47

Ellen Barkin
The Adventures of Buckaroo
    Banzai Across the Eighth
    Dimension '84
Desert Bloom '86
Eddie and the Cruisers '83
Harry & Son '84
Into the West '92
The Princess Who Never
    Laughed '84
Tender Mercies '83
This Boy's Life '93

Peter Barkworth
The Littlest Horse Thieves '76

Binnie Barnes
The Trouble with Angels '66
Where Angels Go, Trouble
    Follows '68

Christopher Barnes
Battle of the Bullies '85
Tut and Tuttle '82

**Christopher Daniel
    Barnes**
The Brady Bunch Movie '95
A Very Brady Sequel '96

Priscilla Barnes
Ava's Magical Adventure '94
Mallrats '95

Jean Marie Barnwell
Born to Be Wild '95
From the Mixed-Up Files of
Mrs. Basil E.
Frankweiler '95

Sandy Baron
Broadway Danny Rose '84

Gerlando Barone
Two Bits '96

Douglas Barr
Spaced Invaders '90

Jean-Marc Barr
Hope and Glory '87

Leonard Barr
Diamonds are Forever '71

Marie-Christine Barrault
Table for Five '83

Gabriel Barre
Luggage of the Gods '87

Edith Barrett
Jane Eyre '44

Jane Barrett
The Sword & the Rose '53

Barbara Barrie
Breaking Away '79
Child of Glass '78
Two of a Kind '82

Colin Barrie
Melody '71

Robert Barron
Bill & Ted's Excellent
Adventure '89
Sea Hound '47

Steven Barron ▲
The Adventures of
Pinocchio '96
Coneheads '93
Electric Dreams '84
Teenage Mutant Ninja Turtles
1: The Movie '90

Zelda Barron ▲
Secret Places '85
Shag: The Movie '89

Diana Barrows
My Mom's a Werewolf '89

**Donald (Don "Red")
Barry**
Adventures of Red Ryder '40
The Shakiest Gun in the
West '68

Gene Barry
The War of the Worlds '53

Neill Barry
Joey '85

Old Enough '84

Patricia Barry
Sammy, the Way-Out Seal '62
Twilight Zone: The Movie '83

Raymond J. Barry
Cool Runnings '93

Tony Barry
The Quest '86
We of the Never Never '82

Deborah Barrymore
Lionheart '87

Drew Barrymore
Babes in Toyland '86
Batman Forever '95
Boys on the Side '94
Cat's Eye '85
Conspiracy of Love '87
E.T.: The Extra-Terrestrial '82
Irreconcilable Differences '84
See You in the Morning '89
Wayne's World 2 '93

Ethel Barrymore
The Farmer's Daughter '47
The Paradine Case '47

Lionel Barrymore
Ah, Wilderness! '35
Captains Courageous '37
David Copperfield '35
It's a Wonderful Life '46
Key Largo '48
Since You Went Away '44
Treasure Island '34

Paul Bartel
Frankenweenie '84
The Jerky Boys '95
Rock 'n' Roll High School '79
The Usual Suspects '95

Paul Bartel ▲
Cannonball '76

Joanie Bartels
The Extra-Special Substitute
Teacher '93

Freddie Bartholomew
Captains Courageous '37
David Copperfield '35
Little Lord Fauntleroy '36
Tom Brown's School Days '40

Scott Bartle
Hector's Bunyip '86

Bennie Bartlett
Clipped Wings '53

Bonnie Bartlett
Dave '93
Twins '88

Dick Bartlett ▲
Ollie Hopnoodle's Haven of
Bliss '88

Hall Bartlett ▲
Jonathan Livingston
Seagull '73

Keith Bartlett
Truly, Madly, Deeply '91

Robin Bartlett
Baby Boom '87
Dangerous Minds '95
If Looks Could Kill '91
Lean on Me '89
Regarding Henry '91

Robyn Barto
Blue Skies Again '83

Charles T. Barton ▲
Abbott and Costello Meet
Frankenstein '48
Africa Screams '49
Buck Privates Come Home '47
The Shaggy Dog '59
Toby Tyler '59

Billy Barty
The Amazing Dobermans '76
Foul Play '78
Legend '86
Masters of the Universe '87
Rumpelstiltskin '86
Snow White '89
Tough Guys '86
Under the Rainbow '81
Willow '88

Mikhail Baryshnikov
That's Dancing! '85

Gary Basaraba
A Horse for Danny '95
One Magic Christmas '85

Dante Basco
Hook '91

Dion Basco
Race the Sun '96

Richard Basehart
Being There '79
Hans Brinker '69
Island of Dr. Moreau '77
Mark Twain's A Connecticut
Yankee in King Arthur's
Court '78

Blake Bashoff
Big Bully '95

Count Basie
Cinderfella '60

Toni Basil
Pajama Party '64

Kim Basinger
Batman '89
My Stepmother Is an
Alien '88
The Natural '84
Never Say Never Again '83
The Real McCoy '93
Wayne's World 2 '93

Richard Baskin ▲
Sing '89

Jules Bass ▲
The Ballad of Paul
Bunyan '72
Daydreamer '66
Flight of Dragons '82
Frosty the Snowman '69
The Hobbit '78
The Last Unicorn '82
Mad Monster Party '68
The Return of the King '80
Santa Claus is Coming to
Town '70

Albert Basserman
Foreign Correspondent '40
The Red Shoes '48
Since You Went Away '44

Angela Bassett
Boyz N the Hood '91
Malcolm X '92
Waiting to Exhale '95
What's Love Got to Do With
It? '93

Jennifer Bassey
Dunston Checks In '95

Michal Bat-Adam ▲
Boy Takes Girl '83

Joy Batchelor ▲
Animal Farm '55

Jason Bateman
Breaking the Rules '92
Necessary Roughness '91
Teen Wolf Too '87

Justine Bateman
Satisfaction '88

Kent Bateman
Breaking the Rules '92

Alan Bates
The Go-Between '71
Whistle Down the Wind '62

Barbara Bates
The Caddy '53

Florence Bates
I Remember Mama '48
Rebecca '40
Secret Life of Walter Mitty '47
Since You Went Away '44

Kathy Bates
Angus '95
Dick Tracy '90
Dolores Claiborne '94
A Home of Our Own '93
Men Don't Leave '89
North '94
Prelude to a Kiss '92

Timothy Bateson
The Mouse That Roared '59

Randall Batinkoff
Buffy the Vampire Slayer '92

Christy '94
For Keeps '88
School Ties '92

Paul Batt
War of the Buttons '95

Belinda Bauer
Flashdance '83
Robocop 2 '90
Timerider '83

Steven Bauer
Gleaming the Cube '89

Andrew Bauer-Gador
The Return of Tommy
    Tricker '94

Mario Bava ▲
Wonders of Aladdin '61

Alan Baxter
Saboteur '42

Anne Baxter
I Confess '53
The Ten Commandments '56

Warner Baxter
Stand Up and Cheer '34

Francis Bay
Happy Gilmore '96

Michael Bay ▲
Bad Boys '95

Gary Bayer
Not My Kid '85

Geoffrey Bayldon
The Bushbaby '70
Madame Sousatzka '88

Stephen Bayly ▲
Diamond's Edge '88

Adam Beach
Squanto: A Warrior's Tale '94

Michael Beach
A Family Thing '96
Lean on Me '89
Waiting to Exhale '95

Stephanie Beacham
Troop Beverly Hills '89

John Beal
The Kid Who Loved
    Christmas '90
Ten Who Dared '60

Jennifer Beals
Cinderella '84
Flashdance '83
That's Dancing! '85

Orson Bean
Innerspace '87

Sean Bean
Black Beauty '94
Goldeneye '95

**Matthew "Stymie"
    Beard**
Little Rascals Christmas
    Special '79

Alice Beardsley
Where the Lilies Bloom '74

Emmanuelle Beart
Date with an Angel '87
Manon of the Spring '87
Mission: Impossible '96

Clyde Beatty
Africa Screams '49
The Lost Jungle '34

Ned Beatty
Angel Square '92
Back to Hannibal: The Further
    Adventures of Tom Sawyer
    and Huckleberry Finn '90
Back to School '86
The Big Bus '76
Captain America '89
A Cry in the Wild '90
The Haunting of Barney
    Palmer '90s
The Incredible Shrinking
    Woman '81
Konrad '85
The Last American Hero '73
Prelude to a Kiss '92
Promises in the Dark '79
Purple People Eater '88
Radioland Murders '94
Rudy '93
Rumpelstiltskin '82
The Silver Streak '76
Superman 1: The Movie '78
Superman 2 '80
The Toy '82

Warren Beatty
Dick Tracy '90

Warren Beatty ▲
Dick Tracy '90

William Beaudine ▲
Blues Busters '50
Bowery Buckaroos '47
Follow the Leader '44
Ghost Chasers '51
Hard-Boiled Mahoney '47
Spook Busters '46
Ten Who Dared '60
Turf Boy '42
Westward Ho, the Wagons!
    '56

Julie Beaulieu
Bridge to Terabithia '85

Trace Beaulieu
Mystery Science Theater
    3000: The Movie '96

Gabrielle Beaumont ▲
Gone are the Days '84

Louise Beavers
General Spanky '36
Tammy and the Bachelor '57

John Beck
Audrey Rose '77
The Big Bus '76
Last Time Out '94
Sleeper '73

Julian Beck
Poltergeist 2: The Other
    Side '86

Michael Beck
The Golden Seal '83
Xanadu '80

Vincent Beck
Santa Claus Conquers the
    Martians '64

Graham Beckel
Hazel's People '75
The Paper Chase '73

Gretchen Becker
Huck and the King of
    Hearts '93

Harold Becker ▲
Taps '81

Scotty Beckett
Ali Baba and the Forty
    Thieves '43
The Jolson Story '46
Stand Up and Cheer '34

Kate Beckinsale
Much Ado About Nothing '93

Irene Bedard
Squanto: A Warrior's Tale '94

Don Beddoe
Buck Privates Come Home '47
Jack the Giant Killer '62

Bonnie Bedelia
The Boy Who Could Fly '86
Die Hard '88
Die Hard 2: Die Harder '90
Heart Like a Wheel '83
Homecoming '96
Salem's Lot '79
Speechless '94

Patrick Bedford
Up the Down Staircase '67

Kabir Bedi
Octopussy '83

Alfonso Bedoya
Treasure of the Sierra
    Madre '48

Ford Beebe ▲
Buck Rogers Conquers the
    Universe '39
Don Winslow of the Coast
    Guard '43
Don Winslow of the Navy '43
The Last of the Mohicans '32
The Phantom Creeps '39
Radio Patrol '37
Shadow of the Eagle '32
Tim Tyler's Luck '37

Winners of the West '40

Greg Beeman ▲
Bushwhacked '95
License to Drive '88
Mom and Dad Save the
    World '92

Noah Beery Sr.
Adventures of Red Ryder '40
Devil Horse '32
Fighting with Kit Carson '33
To the Last Man '33
Zorro Rides Again '37

Noah Beery Jr.
The Capture of Grizzly
    Adams '82
Fighting with Kit Carson '33
Million Dollar Kid '44
'Neath Brooklyn Bridge '42
Seven Faces of Dr. Lao '63
Tailspin Tommy '34
Walking Tall '73

Wallace Beery
Ah, Wilderness! '35
Treasure Island '34

Ed Begley Jr.
Citizens Band '77
The Crazysitter '94
Dark Horse '92
Goin' South '78
Greedy '94
The Legend of Sleepy
    Hollow '86
The Pagemaster '94
Renaissance Man '94
She-Devil '89
The Story Lady '93
Voyager from the
    Unknown '83

Sam Behrens
Alive '93
And You Thought Your
    Parents Were Weird! '91

Barbara Bel Geddes
I Remember Mama '48

Doris Belack
Opportunity Knocks '90
What About Bob? '91

Harry Belafonte
Buck and the Preacher '72
Free to Be. . .You and Me '83
Muppet Revue '85

Louise Belaire
Return to Boggy Creek '77

Leon Belasco
Fisherman's Wharf '39

Christopher Bell
Sarah, Plain and Tall '91
Skylark '93

George Anthony Bell
House Party 2: The Pajama
    Jam '91

James Bell
My Friend Flicka '43

Marshall Bell
Tucker: The Man and His
   Dream '88
Twins '88

Martin Bell ▲
American Heart '92

Earl Bellamy ▲
Against A Crooked Sky '75
Seven Alone '75

Ralph Bellamy
Cancel My Reservation '72
Disorderlies '87
His Girl Friday '40
Love Leads the Way '84
Oh, God! '77

Kathleen Beller
Promises in the Dark '79

Scott Bellis
Timecop '94

Cynthia Belliveau
The Dream Team '89

Gil Bellows
The Shawshank
   Redemption '94

Vicki Belmonte
The Grass is Always Greener
   Over the Septic Tank '78

Robert Beltran
Night of the Comet '84

Mark Beltzman
Billy Madison '94

James Belushi
Curly Sue '91
K-9 '89
Little Shop of Horrors '86
The Man with One Red
   Shoe '85
Mr. Destiny '90
Once Upon a Crime '92
Only the Lonely '91
Race the Sun '96

John Belushi
Goin' South '78

Richard Belzer
Fame '80

Paul Ben-Victor
Houseguest '94

Steven Benally Jr.
The Secret of Navajo Cave '76

Brian Benben
Radioland Murders '94

Robert Benchley
Foreign Correspondent '40

William Bendix
A Connecticut Yankee in King
   Arthur's Court '49

Billy Benedict
Bowery Buckaroos '47
Follow the Leader '44
Ghost Chasers '51
Hard-Boiled Mahoney '47
Spook Busters '46

Dirk Benedict
Alaska '96
Battlestar Galactica '78

Nick Benedict
Pistol: The Birth of a
   Legend '90

Paul Benedict
The Addams Family '91
The Freshman '90

Armonia Benedito
Strictly Ballroom '92

Roberto Benigni
Son of the Pink Panther '93

Annette Bening
The American President '95
The Great Outdoors '88
Regarding Henry '91

Richard Benjamin
Love at First Bite '79
Saturday the 14th '81
The Sunshine Boys '75
Witches' Brew '79

Richard Benjamin ▲
Little Nikita '88
Made in America '93
Mermaids '90
Milk Money '94
Mrs. Winterbourne '96
The Money Pit '86
My Favorite Year '82
My Stepmother Is an
   Alien '88
Racing with the Moon '84

Scott Benjaminson
Rudy '93

Benji
Benji '74
Benji the Hunted '87
For the Love of Benji '77

David Bennent
Legend '86

**Spencer Gordon
   Bennet ▲**
Atom Man vs. Superman '50
The Black Widow '47
The Masked Marvel '43
Superman: The Serial, Vol.
   1 '48
Zorro's Black Whip '44

Bill Bennett ▲
Two If by Sea '95

**Bruce (Herman Brix)
   Bennett**
Daredevils of the Red
   Circle '38
Fighting Devil Dogs '38
Hawk of the Wilderness '38
Treasure of the Sierra
   Madre '48

Constance Bennett
Topper '37
Topper Takes a Trip '39

Jill Bennett
For Your Eyes Only '81
The Old Curiosity Shop '75

Joan Bennett
Father of the Bride '50
Father's Little Dividend '51
Little Women '33
The Man in the Iron Mask '39

Joseph Bennett
Howard's End '92

Marion Bennett
Lantern Hill '90

Richard Bennett ▲
Harper Valley P.T.A. '78

Tony Bennett
The Scout '94

Wallace C. Bennett ▲
George! '70

Zachary Bennett
Looking for Miracles '90

Jack Benny
The Horn Blows at
   Midnight '45

Abraham Benrubi
Magic Island '95
The Program '93

Amber Benson
The Crush '93
King of the Hill '93

Leon Benson ▲
Flipper's New Adventure '64

Lucille Benson
Huckleberry Finn '74

Martin Benson
The King and I '56

Robby Benson
Die Laughing '80
Harry & Son '84
Ice Castles '79
Ode to Billy Joe '76
One on One '77
Running Brave '83
Two of a Kind '82

Timothy Bentinck
Year of the Comet '92

Eddie Benton
Dr. Strange '78

Robert Benton ▲
Bad Company '72
Kramer vs. Kramer '79
Places in the Heart '84

Daniel Benzali
A Day in October '92

Luca Bercovici
American Flyers '85

Luca Bercovici ▲
Ghoulies '85

Tom Berenger
Butch and Sundance: The
   Early Days '79
Eddie and the Cruisers '83
Gettysburg '93
Major League '89
Major League 2 '94

Bruce Beresford ▲
Driving Miss Daisy '89
Her Alibi '88
Rich in Love '93
Tender Mercies '83

Peter Berg
Aspen Extreme '93
Fire in the Sky '93
A Midnight Clear '92

Candice Bergen
Merlin and the Sword '85
The Wind and the Lion '75

Edgar Bergen
Fun & Fancy Free '47
Homecoming: A Christmas
   Story '71
I Remember Mama '48

Polly Bergen
Cry-Baby '90
Dr. Jekyll and Ms. Hyde '95
Making Mr. Right '86
Once Upon a Time . . . When
   We Were Colored '95

Tushka Bergen
Swing Kids '93

Ludwig Berger ▲
Thief of Baghdad '40

Senta Berger
Waltz King '63

William Berger
Hercules '83

Andrew Bergman ▲
The Freshman '90
Honeymoon in Vegas '92
It Could Happen to You '94

Henry Bergman
City Lights '31

Ingrid Bergman
The Bells of St. Mary's '45

Bill Bixby
The Apple Dumpling Gang '75
Death of the Incredible
   Hulk '90
The Incredible Hulk '77
The Incredible Hulk
   Returns '88
The Trial of the Incredible
   Hulk '89

Bill Bixby ▲
Death of the Incredible
   Hulk '90
The Trial of the Incredible
   Hulk '89

Anna Bjorn
More American Graffiti '79

Craig Black
Flirting '89

Jack Black
The Cable Guy '96
The Neverending Story 3 '94

Karen Black
Airport '75 '75
The Double O Kid '92
Invaders from Mars '86
The Little Mermaid '84

Noel Black ▲
Conspiracy of Love '87
The Electric Grandmother '81
Quarterback Princess '85

Royana Black
Almost Partners '87

Ryan Black
Geronimo '93

Honor Blackman
Jason and the Argonauts '63

Sidney Blackmer
High Society '56
Tammy and the Bachelor '57

Gerard Blain
Hatari '62

Vivian Blaine
Guys and Dolls '55
State Fair '45

Bre Blair
The Baby-Sitters Club '95

Janet Blair
The One and Only, Genuine,
   Original Family Band '68

Linda Blair
Airport '75 '75
Wild Horse Hank '79

Lisa Blair
Three Men and a Baby '87

Michelle Blair
Three Men and a Baby '87

Andre B. Blake
Philadelphia '93

Madge Blake
Singin' in the Rain '52

Marie Blake
Love Finds Andy Hardy '38

Pamela Blake
Kid Dynamite '43
Sea Hound '47

Robert (Bobby) Blake
Andy Hardy's Double Life '42
Money Train '95
Treasure of the Sierra
   Madre '48

Colin Blakely
Evil Under the Sun '82
Little Lord Fauntleroy '80
The Pink Panther Strikes
   Again '76

Susan Blakely
Hiroshima Maiden '88
The Lords of Flatbush '74
My Mom's a Werewolf '89
Over the Top '86

Jewel Blanch
Against A Crooked Sky '75

Sandrine Blancke
Toto le Heros '91

Clara Blandick
The Wizard of Oz '39

Mark Blankfield
Jack & the Beanstalk '83
Robin Hood: Men in
   Tights '93

Jonah Blechman
This Boy's Life '93

Jeff Bleckner ▲
White Water Summer '87

Tempestt Bledsoe
Dream Date '93

Brian Blessed
Flash Gordon '80
Man of La Mancha '72
Much Ado About Nothing '93
Return to Treasure Island, Vol.
   1 '85
Robin Hood: Prince of
   Thieves '91

Brenda Blethyn
A River Runs Through It '92
The Witches '90

Jason Blicker
African Journey '89
American Boyfriends '89

Bernard Blier
The Tall Blond Man with One
   Black Shoe '72

Dan Blocker
The Errand Boy '61

Dirk Blocker
Bonanza: The Return '93

Joan Blondell
Support Your Local
   Gunfighter '71
Topper Returns '41
A Tree Grows in Brooklyn '45

Anne Bloom
Dirt Bike Kid '86

Claire Bloom
Clash of the Titans '81
The Wonderful World of the
   Brothers Grimm '62

Jason Bloom ▲
Bio-Dome '96

Jeffrey Bloom ▲
Dog Pound Shuffle '75

Verna Bloom
Honkytonk Man '82
The Journey of Natty
   Gann '85

Eric Blore
Shall We Dance '37
The Wind in the Willows '49

Roberts Blossom
Always '89
Citizens Band '77
Doc Hollywood '91
Home Alone '90

Michael Blouin
The Great Land of Small '86

Ben Blue
The Russians are Coming, the
   Russians are Coming '66

Brady Bluhm
The Crazysitter '94

Mark Blum
Crocodile Dundee '86
Desperately Seeking
   Susan '85

Alan Blumenfeld
Problem Child 2 '91

Graeme Blundell
The Year My Voice Broke '87

Don Bluth ▲
All Dogs Go to Heaven '89
An American Tail '86
The Land Before Time '88
Rock-a-Doodle '92
Secret of NIMH '82
Thumbelina '94
A Troll in Central Park '94

John Bluthal
Leapin' Leprechauns '95

Margaret Blye
Little Darlings '80

Ann Blyth
Kismet '55

David Blyth ▲
My Grandpa is a Vampire '92

Jeff Blyth ▲
Cheetah '89

Robert Blythe
Experience Preferred. . . But
   Not Essential '83

Anne Bobby
Beautiful Girls '96

Hart Bochner
Die Hard '88
Making Mr. Right '86
Mr. Destiny '90
Supergirl '84

Hart Bochner ▲
High School High '96
P.C.U. '94

Lloyd Bochner
The Horse in the Gray Flannel
   Suit '68
Naked Gun 2 1/2: The Smell
   of Fear '91
Spiderman '81

Wolfgang Bodison
Little Big League '94

Karl-Heinz Boehm
The Wonderful World of the
   Brothers Grimm '62

Earl Boen
Terminator 2: Judgment
   Day '91

Dirk Bogarde
A Bridge Too Far '77

Humphrey Bogart
The African Queen '51
Casablanca '42
Key Largo '48
The Maltese Falcon '41
Sabrina '54
Treasure of the Sierra
   Madre '48

Paul Bogart ▲
Cancel My Reservation '72
A House Without a Christmas
   Tree '72
Oh, God! You Devil '84

Peter Bogdanovich ▲
Mask '85
Paper Moon '73
The Thing Called Love '93
What's Up, Doc? '72

Gail Boggs
Ghost '90

Ian Bohen
Frankenstein Sings . . . The
Movie '95

Peter Bohlke
Toto le Heros '91

Corinne Bohrer
Vice Versa '88

Curt Bois
Wings of Desire '88

Sarel Bok
A Far Off Place '93

James Bolam
The Loneliness of the Long
Distance Runner '62

Buddy Boles
Regl'ar Fellers '41

John Boles
Curly Top '35
The Littlest Rebel '35
Stand Up and Cheer '34

Ray Bolger
Babes in Toyland '61
Daydreamer '66
That's Dancing! '85
The Wizard of Oz '39

Ryan Bollman
The Neverending Story 3 '94

Michael Bollner
Willy Wonka & the Chocolate
Factory '71

Joseph Bologna
The Big Bus '76
Coupe de Ville '90
Jersey Girl '92
My Favorite Year '82
Not Quite Human '87
Rags to Riches '87

Craig Bolotin ▲
That Night '93

Christopher Bolton
City Boy '93

Emily Bolton
Moonraker '79

Fortunio Bonanova
Ali Baba and the Forty
Thieves '43

Ivan Bonar
MacArthur '77

Derek Bond
Tony Draws a Horse '51

James Bond III
The Fish that Saved
Pittsburgh '79

Samantha Bond
Goldeneye '95

Sudie Bond
I am the Cheese '83
Where the Lilies Bloom '74

Tommy "Butch" Bond
Atom Man vs. Superman '50
Superman: The Serial, Vol.
1 '48

Ward Bond
Bringing Up Baby '38
Gone with the Wind '39
Gypsy Colt '54
It Happened One Night '34
It's a Wonderful Life '46
The Maltese Falcon '41
The Quiet Man '52

Beulah Bondi
It's a Wonderful Life '46
Mr. Smith Goes to
Washington '39
Penny Serenade '41
So Dear to My Heart '49
The Wonderful World of the
Brothers Grimm '62

Peter Bonerz ▲
Police Academy 6: City Under
Siege '89

Helena Bonham Carter
Howard's End '92
Lady Jane '85

Evan Bonifant
3 Ninjas Kick Back '94

Tony Bonner
Quigley Down Under '90
Sudden Terror '70

Maria Bonnerie
The Polar Bear King '94

Rene Bonniere ▲
The Halfback of Notre
Dame '96

Sonny Bono
Airplane 2: The Sequel '82
Hairspray '88
Troll '85

Brian Bonsall
Blank Check '93
Father and Scout '95
Father Hood '93

Bonzo the Chimp
Bedtime for Bonzo '51

Sorrell Booke
Up the Down Staircase '67

Pat Boone
Journey to the Center of the
Earth '59
State Fair '62

Richard Boone
Against A Crooked Sky '75
Big Jake '71
The Shootist '76

Charley Boorman
Hope and Glory '87

John Boorman ▲
Hope and Glory '87

Katrine Boorman
Hope and Glory '87

Adrian Booth
Captain America '44

Connie Booth
Little Lord Fauntleroy '80
Monty Python and the Holy
Grail '75

Edwina Booth
The Last of the Mohicans '32

Karin Booth
Tobor the Great '54

Powers Boothe
Tombstone '93

Veda Ann Borg
The Bachelor and the Bobby-
Soxer '47
Guys and Dolls '55

Ernest Borgnine
The Black Hole '79
The Double McGuffin '79
The Greatest '77
Ice Station Zebra '68
Jesus of Nazareth '77
Love Leads the Way '84
Neptune Factor '73
The Poseidon Adventure '72
The Prince and the
Pauper '78
Super Fuzz '81

Milan Borich
My Grandpa is a Vampire '92

Robert Boris ▲
Oxford Blues '84

Patrick Borriello
Two Bits '96

Phillip Borsos ▲
Far from Home: The
Adventures of Yellow
Dog '94
The Grey Fox '83
One Magic Christmas '85

John Yong Bosch
Mighty Morphin Power
Rangers: The Movie '95

Philip Bosco
The Dream Team '89
F/X 2: The Deadly Art of
Illusion '91
It Takes Two '95
Milk Money '94
The Money Pit '86
Safe Passage '94
Straight Talk '92
Three Men and a Baby '87

Tom Bosley
Gus '76
The World of Henry Orient '64
Yours, Mine & Ours '68

Barbara Bosson
The Last Starfighter '84

Barry Bostwick
Movie, Movie '78
Spy Hard '96
Weekend at Bernie's 2 '93

John Boswall
Three Men and a Little
Lady '90

Hobart Bosworth
The Last of the Mohicans '32

Wade Boteler
The Green Hornet '39

Niki Bothelo
The Ewoks: Battle for
Endor '85

Joseph Bottoms
The Black Hole '79
The Dove '74

Sam Bottoms
Bronco Billy '80
The Outlaw Josey Wales '76
The Witching of Ben
Wagner '95

Timothy Bottoms
Ava's Magical Adventure '94
Digger '94
Hambone & Hillie '84
Invaders from Mars '86
The Land of Faraway '87
Love Leads the Way '84
The Other Side of the
Mountain, Part 2 '78
The Paper Chase '73
Top Dog '95

Michel Boujenah
Three Men and a Cradle '85

Carole Bouquet
For Your Eyes Only '81

Michel Bouquet
Toto le Heros '91

Andre Bourvil
When Wolves Cry '69

Dennis Boutsikaris
*batteries not included '87
The Dream Team '89

Julie Bovasso
Moonstruck '87

Simmy Bow
The Doberman Gang '72

Eric Bowen
The Gods Must Be Crazy
2 '89

Jenny Bowen ▲
Animal Behavior '89
The Wizard of Loneliness '88

Julie Bowen
Happy Gilmore '96

Michael Bowen
Night of the Comet '84

Roger Bowen
M*A*S*H '70
What About Bob? '91

Malick Bowens
Bopha! '93

Dallas Bower ▲
Alice in Wonderland '50

David Bower
Four Weddings and a
Funeral '93

Tom Bower
Far from Home: The
Adventures of Yellow
Dog '94

David Bowie
Labyrinth '86
UHF '89

Judi Bowker
Clash of the Titans '81

Jessica Bowman
Remote '93

Ralph Bowman
Flaming Frontiers '38

Rob Bowman ▲
Airborne '93

Bruce Boxleitner
The Babe '92
Kuffs '92
Tron '82

Alan Boyce
Permanent Record '88

Todd Boyce
Jefferson in Paris '94

Brittany Boyd
Lassie '94

Cameron Boyd
King of the Hill '93

Sarah Boyd
Old Enough '84

William Boyd
Oliver Twist '33

Sally Boyden
Barnaby and Me '77

Charles Boyer
Around the World in 80
Days '56

Sully Boyer
Car Wash '76
The Manhattan Project '86

Brad Boyle
Hoosiers '86

Lara Flynn Boyle
Baby's Day Out '94
Dead Poets Society '89
How I Got into College '89
Poltergeist 3 '88
Threesome '94
Wayne's World '92

Peter Boyle
Born to Be Wild '95
The Dream Team '89
Honeymoon in Vegas '92
Johnny Dangerously '84
The Shadow '94
Turk 182! '85
While You Were Sleeping '95
Young Frankenstein '74

Ray Boyle
Zombies of the
Stratosphere '52

William Boyle
Hawk of the Wilderness '38

Reizl Bozyk
Crossing Delancey '88

Bruno Bozzetto ▲
Allegro Non Troppo '76
Mr. Rossi's Dreams '83
Vip, My Brother
Superman '90

Lorraine Bracco
The Basketball Diaries '94
Being Human '94
The Dream Team '89
Hackers '95
Radio Flyer '92
Sing '89
Talent for the Game '91

Eddie Bracken
Home Alone 2: Lost in New
York '92
National Lampoon's
Vacation '83

Jesse Bradford
Far from Home: The
Adventures of Yellow
Dog '94
Hackers '95
King of the Hill '93

Lane Bradford
The Invisible Monster '50

Richard Bradford
Goin' South '78
Legend of Billie Jean '85
Little Nikita '88
More American Graffiti '79
Permanent Record '88
The Trip to Bountiful '85

Benjamin C. Bradlee
Born Yesterday '93

Randy Bradshaw ▲
Song Spinner '95

John Brady
Mystery Science Theater
3000: The Movie '96

Scott Brady
When Every Day was the
Fourth of July '78

**Eric (Hans Gudegast)
Braeden**
Escape from the Planet of the
Apes '71

Sonia Braga
The Last Prostitute '91

Helen Bragdon
Where the Lilies Bloom '74

John Brahm ▲
Miracle of Our Lady of
Fatima '52

Wilfrid Brambell
Sword of the Valiant '83

Marco Brambilla
Cool Runnings '93

Kenneth Branagh
Much Ado About Nothing '93
Othello '95
Swing Kids '93

Kenneth Branagh ▲
Much Ado About Nothing '93

Lillo Brancato
A Bronx Tale '93
Crimson Tide '95
Renaissance Man '94

Jolene Brand
Zorro, Vol. 1 '58

Neville Brand
The Adventures of Huckleberry
Finn '60
Cahill: United States
Marshal '73
That Darn Cat '65

Klaus Maria Brandauer
Never Say Never Again '83
White Fang '91

Jonathan Brandis
Ladybugs '92
The NeverEnding Story 2: Next
Chapter '91
Sidekicks '93

Marlon Brando
Christopher Columbus: The
Discovery '92
The Freshman '90
Guys and Dolls '55
Superman 1: The Movie '78

Henry Brandon
When the North Wind
Blows '74

Michael Brandon
Promises in the Dark '79

Penelope Branning
What's Eating Gilbert
Grape '93

Fred Brannon ▲
The Crimson Ghost '46
Federal Agents vs.
Underworld, Inc. '49
G-Men Never Forget '48
The Invisible Monster '50
Jesse James Rides Again '47
Jungle Drums of Africa '53
King of the Rocketmen '49
Radar Men from the
Moon '52
Zombies of the
Stratosphere '52

Benjamin Bratt
The River Wild '94

Andre Braugher
Glory '89

Joy Brazeau
Slam Dunk Ernest '95

Benjamin Brazier
Heidi '93

Lidia Brazzi
The Christmas That Almost
Wasn't '66

Rossano Brazzi
The Christmas That Almost
Wasn't '66
South Pacific '58

Rossano Brazzi ▲
The Christmas That Almost
Wasn't '66

Peter Breck
Benji '74

Bobby Breen
Breaking the Ice '38
Fisherman's Wharf '39
It Happened in New
Orleans '36
Let's Sing Again '36

Danny Breen
The Manners Monster: Ruby
Goes to Dinner '95

Julian Breen ▲
Prehysteria 3 '95

Patrick Breen
For Love or Money '93

Paulette Breen
The Wizard of Speed and
Time '88

Jana Brejchova
The Original Fabulous
    Adventures of Baron
    Munchausen '61

Tia Brelis ▲
Trading Mom '94

Lucille Bremer
Meet Me in St. Louis '44
Till the Clouds Roll By '46

Eileen Brennan
Babes in Toyland '86
The Cheap Detective '78
Clue '85
In Search of Dr. Seuss '94
My Old Man '79
The New Adventures of Pippi
    Longstocking '88
The Sting '73

Johnny Brennan
The Jerky Boys '95

Walter Brennan
The Gnome-Mobile '67
How the West was Won '63
The One and Only, Genuine,
    Original Family Band '68
Support Your Local Sheriff '69
Tammy and the Bachelor '57
Those Calloways '65

Amy Brenneman
Casper '95

Dori Brenner
Baby Boom '87

Evelyn Brent
Holt of the Secret Service '42

Romney Brent
The Sign of Zorro '60

Alfonso Brescia ▲
White Fang and the
    Hunter '85

Bobbie Bresee
Ghoulies '85

Kevin Breslin
On the Edge: The Survival of
    Dana '79

Martin Brest
Fast Times at Ridgemont
    High '82

Martin Brest ▲
Beverly Hills Cop '84
Going in Style '79

Richard Brestoff
Car Wash '76

Jeremy Brett
Moll Flanders '96

Griffith Brewer
The Peanut Butter
    Solution '85

Juliette Brewer
The Little Rascals '94

Diane Brewster
Courage of Black Beauty '57
The Invisible Boy '57

Maia Brewton
Adventures in Babysitting '87
Back to the Future '85

Kevin Breznahan
Alive '93

Jean-Claude Brialy
The 400 Blows '59

Ludwig Briand
Little Indian, Big City '95

Bridget Brice
Twelve Chairs '70

Gennie Nevinson Brice
Muriel's Wedding '94

Ron Brice
A Horse for Danny '95

Beth Brickell
Gentle Ben '69

Marshall Brickman ▲
The Manhattan Project '86
Simon '80

Paul Brickman ▲
Men Don't Leave '89

Beau Bridges
The Fifth Musketeer '79
Greased Lightning '77
Heart Like a Wheel '83
Night Crossing '81
Norma Rae '79
The Other Side of the
    Mountain '75
The Red Pony '49
Sidekicks '93
The Wizard '89

James Bridges ▲
The Paper Chase '73

Jeff Bridges
American Heart '92
Bad Company '72
Hearts of the West '75
King Kong '76
Kiss Me Goodbye '82
The Last American Hero '73
Rapunzel '82
See You in the Morning '89
Starman '84
Tron '82
Tucker: The Man and His
    Dream '88
White Squall '96

Lloyd Bridges
Airplane! '80
Airplane 2: The Sequel '82
High Noon '52
Honey, I Blew Up the Kid '92
Hot Shots! Part Deux '93

Joe Versus the Volcano '90
Peter and the Wolf '95
Running Wild '73
Tucker: The Man and His
    Dream '88

Dee Dee Bridgewater
The Brother from Another
    Planet '84

Julie Briggs
Bowery Buckaroos '47

Richard Bright
Beautiful Girls '96

Fran Brill
Old Enough '84
What About Bob? '91

Patti Brill
Hard-Boiled Mahoney '47

Steven Brill
The Mighty Ducks '92

Steven Brill ▲
Heavyweights '94

Nick Brimble
Robin Hood: Prince of
    Thieves '91

Wilford Brimley
Cocoon '85
Cocoon: The Return '88
Country '84
The Electric Horseman '79
The Ewoks: Battle for
    Endor '85
Harry & Son '84
The Natural '84
Remo Williams: The Adventure
    Begins '85
The Stone Boy '84
Tender Mercies '83
Where the Red Fern Grows:
    Part 2 '92

Christie Brinkley
National Lampoon's
    Vacation '83

David Brinkley
Mallrats '95

Ritch Brinkley
Cabin Boy '94

Jimmy Briscoe
Spaced Invaders '90

Morgan Brittany
The Prodigal '83

Pamela Britton
Anchors Aweigh '45

Tony Britton
Dr. Syn, Alias the
    Scarecrow '64
Horsemasters '61

Anders Peter Bro
A Day in October '92

Jim Broadbent
Princess Caraboo '94

Anne Brochet
Cyrano de Bergerac '90

Charles Brock
Sourdough '77

Deborah Brock ▲
Andy and the Airwave
    Rangers '89
Rock 'n' Roll High School
    Forever '91

Roy Brocksmith
Arachnophobia '90
Big Business '88
Bill & Ted's Bogus
    Journey '91

Matthew Broderick
The Cable Guy '96
Cinderella '84
Ferris Bueller's Day Off '86
The Freshman '90
Glory '89
Ladyhawke '85
Max Dugan Returns '83
Out on a Limb '92
Project X '87
War Games '83

Steve Brodie
The Wizard of Speed and
    Time '88

Adrien Brody
Home at Last '88
King of the Hill '93

James Brolin
City Boy '93
Pee Wee's Big Adventure '85

Josh Brolin
Bed of Roses '95
The Goonies '85

Valri Bromfield
Mr. Mom '83

Elaine Bromka
Uncle Buck '89

Sheila Bromley
Nancy Drew, Reporter '39

Sydney Bromley
Crystalstone '88
The NeverEnding Story '84

Eleanor Bron
Black Beauty '94
Help! '65
Little Dorrit, Film 1: Nobody's
    Fault '88
Little Dorrit, Film 2: Little
    Dorrit's Story '88
A Little Princess '95
Turtle Diary '86

Charles Bronson
House of Wax '53

Once Upon a Time in the
West '68
Pat and Mike '52

Lillian Bronson
Spencer's Mountain '63

Faith Brook
To Sir, with Love '67

Jayne Brook
Clean Slate '94
Ed '96
Kindergarten Cop '90

Peter Brook ▲
Lord of the Flies '63

Hillary Brooke
Abbott and Costello Meet
Captain Kidd '52
Africa Screams '49
Jane Eyre '44
The Philadelphia Story '40

Jacqueline Brookes
Naked Gun 2 1/2: The Smell
of Fear '91

Dorothea Brooking ▲
The Moon Stallion '85

Adam Brooks ▲
Red Riding Hood '89

Aimee Brooks
Say Anything '89

Albert Brooks
I'll Do Anything '93
The Scout '94
Twilight Zone: The Movie '83

Avery Brooks
The Ernest Green Story '93

Elisabeth Brooks
The Howling '81

Foster Brooks
Cracking Up '83
Super Seal '77
The Villain '79

Geraldine Brooks
Challenge to Lassie '49

James L. Brooks ▲
I'll Do Anything '93
Terms of Endearment '83
Thursday's Game '74

Margaret Brooks
The Bushbaby '70

Mel Brooks
Dracula: Dead and Loving
It '95
Free to Be. . .You and Me '83
High Anxiety '77
Robin Hood: Men in
Tights '93
Silent Movie '76
Spaceballs '87
Twelve Chairs '70

Mel Brooks ▲
Dracula: Dead and Loving
It '95
High Anxiety '77
Robin Hood: Men in
Tights '93
Silent Movie '76
Spaceballs '87
Twelve Chairs '70
Young Frankenstein '74

Peter Brooks
Gidget Goes to Rome '63

Phyllis Brooks
Little Miss Broadway '38
Rebecca of Sunnybrook
Farm '38

Rand Brooks
Gone with the Wind '39

Pierce Brosnan
Goldeneye '95
Happy Birthday, Bugs: 50
Looney Years '90
Mrs. Doubtfire '93

Otto Brower ▲
Devil Horse '32
The Phantom Empire '35

Amelda Brown
Little Dorrit, Film 1: Nobody's
Fault '88
Little Dorrit, Film 2: Little
Dorrit's Story '88

Barry Brown
Bad Company '72

Bruce Brown ▲
The Endless Summer '66
The Endless Summer 2 '94

Bryan Brown
F/X '86
F/X 2: The Deadly Art of
Illusion '91
Gorillas in the Mist '88
Kim '84

Candy Ann Brown
Zebrahead '92

Clancy Brown
Highlander '86
The Shawshank
Redemption '94

Clarence Brown ▲
Ah, Wilderness! '35
The Human Comedy '43
National Velvet '44
The Yearling '46

David G. Brown
Chasing Dreams '81

Dwier Brown
The Cutting Edge '92
Mom and Dad Save the
World '92

Ewing Miles Brown ▲
Whale of a Tale '76

Garrett M. Brown
Uncle Buck '89

Georg Stanford Brown
Ava's Magical Adventure '94
House Party 2: The Pajama
Jam '91

Georg Stanford Brown ▲
Miracle of the Heart: A Boys
Town Story '86

Gibran Brown
Marvin & Tige '84

James Brown
Adios Amigo '75
Rin Tin Tin, Hero of the
West '55

Jim Brown
Ice Station Zebra '68

Joe E. Brown
Around the World in 80
Days '56
The Tender Years '47

Johnny Mack Brown
Fighting with Kit Carson '33
Flaming Frontiers '38

Julie Brown
Clueless '95
Out There '95

Pamela Brown
Alice in Wonderland '50
Wuthering Heights '70

Peter Brown
The Aurora Encounter '85
A Tiger Walks '64

Ralph Brown
Wayne's World 2 '93

Reb Brown
Captain America 2: Death Too
Soon '79

Roger Brown
Tall Tale: The Unbelievable
Adventures of Pecos
Bill '95

Ron Brown
Charlie, the Lonesome
Cougar '67

Ruth Brown
Hairspray '88

Sarah Brown
Super Seal '77

Thomas Wilson Brown
Honey, I Shrunk the Kids '89

Tom Brown
Adventures of Smilin' Jack '43
Anne of Green Gables '34
Buck Privates Come Home '47

Charles A. Browne
Tailspin Tommy '34

Coral Browne
American Dreamer '84
Dreamchild '85

Lucille Browne
Law of the Wild '34

Roscoe Lee Browne
The Cowboys '72
Mark Twain's A Connecticut
Yankee in King Arthur's
Court '78
The World's Greatest
Athlete '73

Zachary Browne
Man of the House '95

Ricou Browning
Flipper's New Adventure '64

Brenda Bruce
Back Home '90

Colin Bruce
Crusoe '89

Nigel Bruce
The Blue Bird '40
The Corn is Green '45
Journey for Margaret '42
Lassie, Come Home '43
Rebecca '40
Stand Up and Cheer '34
Suspicion '41
Treasure Island '34

Jane Brucker
Dirty Dancing '87

Patrick Bruel
Sabrina '95

Eric Bruskotter
Major League 2 '94

Dora Bryan
Great St. Trinian's Train
Robbery '66

Zachery Ty Bryan
Bigfoot: The Unforgettable
Encounter '94
Magic Island '95

John Bryant
Courage of Black Beauty '57

William Bryant
Mountain Family
Robinson '79

Scott Bryce
Up Close and Personal '96

Larry Bryggman
Die Hard: With a
Vengeance '95

Andrew Bryniarski
Batman Returns '92
The Program '93

 584

Yul Brynner
The King and I '56
The Ten Commandments '56

Edgar Buchanan
Penny Serenade '41
Shane '53

Jack Buchanan
The Band Wagon '53

Robert Buchanan
That Sinking Feeling '79

Horst Buchholz
Tiger Bay '59

John Buckler
Tarzan Escapes '36

Betty Buckley
Last Time Out '94
Tender Mercies '83

Parris Buckner
Trading Hearts '87

Susan Buckner
Nancy Drew: Mystery of the
Diamond Triangle '78

Helen Buday
Mad Max: Beyond
Thunderdome '85

Julie Budd
The Devil & Max Devlin '81

John Carl Buechler ▲
Troll '85

Niall Buggy
The Playboys '92

Son Hoang Bui
Table for Five '83

Genevieve Bujold
The Last Flight of Noah's
Ark '80
Oh, What a Night '92

Raymond Buktenica
My Girl '91
Wait Till Your Mother Gets
Home '83

Peter Bull
The African Queen '51
A Christmas Carol '51
Doctor Doolittle '67

Sandra Bullock
The Net '95
Speed '94
The Thing Called Love '93
Two If by Sea '95
While You Were Sleeping '95

Alan Bunce ▲
Babar: The Movie '88

Brooke Bundy
Explorers '85

Avis Bunnage
The Loneliness of the Long
Distance Runner '62

Victor Buono
Beneath the Planet of the
Apes '70

Sonny Bupp
Citizen Kane '41

Andrea Burchill
Housekeeping '87

Kim Burfield
The Hero '71
Treasure Island '72

Gary Burghoff
The Man in the Santa Claus
Suit '79
M*A*S*H '70

Billie Burke
Father of the Bride '50
Father's Little Dividend '51
Topper '37
Topper Returns '41
Topper Takes a Trip '39
The Wizard of Oz '39

Michelle Burke
Coneheads '93
Dazed and Confused '93
Major League 2 '94

Robert Burke
A Far Off Place '93
Rambling Rose '91
Robocop 3 '91
Tombstone '93

Walter Burke
Jack the Giant Killer '62

William Burke ▲
Dick Tracy, Detective '45

Dennis Burkley
Murphy's Romance '85
Son-in-Law '93
Stop! or My Mom Will
Shoot '92

Tom Burlinson
The Man from Snowy
River '82
Phar Lap '84
Return to Snowy River '88

Tom Burman ▲
Meet the Hollowheads '89

Leo Burmester
A Perfect World '93

Carol Burnett
Annie '82
The Front Page '74
The Grass is Always Greener
Over the Septic Tank '78

Smiley Burnette
Dick Tracy '37
The Phantom Empire '35

Carol Burns
Dusty '85

George Burns
18 Again! '88
Going in Style '79
Oh, God! '77
Oh, God! Book 2 '80
Oh, God! You Devil '84
Radioland Murders '94
The Sunshine Boys '75
Two of a Kind '82

Jennifer Burns
Josh Kirby . . . Time Warrior:
Chapter 1, Planet of the
Dino-Knights '95

Jere Burns
Greedy '94

Robert Burns
Terror in the Jungle '68

Raymond Burr
Airplane 2: The Sequel '82
Delirious '91
Love Happy '50
Rear Window '54

Maryedith Burrell
Camp Nowhere '94

Matthew Burrill
Where the Lilies Bloom '74

Jackie Burroughs
Anne of Green Gables '85
The Grey Fox '83
Taking Care of Terrific '88
Tales from Avonlea, Vol. 1:
The Journey Begins '90
Undergrads '85

Geoff Burrowes ▲
Return to Snowy River '88

Darren E. Burrows
Cry-Baby '90

Saffron Burrows
Circle of Friends '94

Ellen Burstyn
The Baby-Sitters Club '95
Follow the River '95
How to Make an American
Quilt '95
Silence of the North '81
Thursday's Game '74

Clarissa Burt
The NeverEnding Story 2: Next
Chapter '91

Kate Burton
Big Trouble in Little China '86

LeVar Burton
Almos' a Man '78
And the Children Shall
Lead '85
Star Trek Generations '94

Star Trek the Next Generation
Episode 1-2: Encounter at
Farpoint '87

Norman Burton
Diamonds are Forever '71

Tim Burton ▲
Aladdin and His Wonderful
Lamp '84
Batman '89
Batman Returns '92
Beetlejuice '88
Edward Scissorhands '90
Frankenweenie '84
Pee Wee's Big Adventure '85

Tony Burton
House Party 2: The Pajama
Jam '91

Steve Buscemi
Airheads '94

Gary Busey
Barbarosa '82
Black Sheep '96
The Buddy Holly Story '78
Gumball Rally '76
The Last American Hero '73
My Heroes Have Always Been
Cowboys '91
Rookie of the Year '93

Jake Busey
P.C.U. '94
Windrunner '94

Timothy Busfield
Field of Dreams '89
Little Big League '94
Revenge of the Nerds '84
The Skateboard Kid '93
Sneakers '92

Billy Green Bush
Critters '86
Culpepper Cattle Co. '72
The River '84

Chuck Bush
Fandango '85

Owen Bush
Prehysteria 2 '94

Francis X. Bushman
Sabrina '54

Ricky Busker
Big Shots '87

Maria Bustamante
Yanco '64

Dick Butkus
Cracking Up '83
Johnny Dangerously '84
The Legend of Sleepy
Hollow '79

Daniel Butler
Ernest Goes to Camp '87

David Butler ▲
Bright Eyes '34
Captain January '36
A Connecticut Yankee '31
The Littlest Rebel '35
The Story of Seabiscuit '49

Dean Butler
The Kid with the 200 I.Q. '83

Paul Butler
Zebrahead '92

Robert Butler ▲
The Barefoot Executive '71
The Computer Wore Tennis
 Shoes '69
Hot Lead & Cold Feet '78
Now You See Him, Now You
 Don't '72
Scandalous John '71

Tom Butler
Ernest Rides Again '93

Hendel Butoy ▲
The Rescuers Down Under '90

Merritt Butrick
Star Trek 2: The Wrath of
 Khan '82
Star Trek 3: The Search for
 Spock '84

Donna Butterworth
Family Jewels '65

Red Buttons
Alice in Wonderland '85
C.H.O.M.P.S. '79
18 Again! '88
Hatari '62
It Could Happen to You '94
Movie, Movie '78
Pete's Dragon '77
The Poseidon Adventure '72

Pat Buttram
Back to the Future, Part 3 '90

Sarah Buxton
Fast Getaway 2 '94
Rock 'n' Roll High School
 Forever '91

Zane Buzby
Cracking Up '83

Edward Buzzell ▲
At the Circus '39
Go West '40

Ruth Buzzi
Freaky Friday '76
My Mom's a Werewolf '89
The North Avenue
 Irregulars '79
Once Upon a Brothers
 Grimm '77
The Villain '79

Spring Byington
Ah, Wilderness! '35
The Blue Bird '40

Little Women '33
Please Don't Eat the
 Daisies '60

John Byner
The Man in the Santa Claus
 Suit '79

Ralph Byrd
Blake of Scotland Yard '36
Dick Tracy '37
Dick Tracy Meets
 Gruesome '47
The Jungle Book '42
Life Begins for Andy
 Hardy '41

Bill Byrge
Ernest Goes to Jail '90
Ernest Goes to School '94

Cillian Byrne
The Secret of Roan Inish '94

Gabriel Byrne
Hello Again '87
Into the West '92
Lionheart '87
Little Women '94
Shipwrecked '90
A Simple Twist of Fate '94
The Usual Suspects '95

Josh Byrne
Wild Pony '83

Michael Byrne
Indiana Jones and the Last
 Crusade '89

Niall Byrne
The Miracle '91

Edd Byrnes
Back to the Beach '87
Troop Beverly Hills '89

Delma Byron
Dimples '36

James Caan
Brian's Song '71
A Bridge Too Far '77
Dick Tracy '90
Funny Lady '75
Harry & Walter Go to New
 York '76
Honeymoon in Vegas '92
Kiss Me Goodbye '82
The Program '93
Silent Movie '76

Bruce Cabot
Diamonds are Forever '71
Hatari '62
King Kong '33
Sorrowful Jones '49

Sebastian Cabot
Family Jewels '65
Johnny Tremain & the Sons of
 Liberty '58
Shirley Temple Storybook
 Theater '60

Westward Ho, the Wagons!
 '56

Garry Cadenat
Sugar Cane Alley '83

Adolph Caesar
Club Paradise '86

Sid Caesar
Airport '75 '75
Barnaby and Me '77
Cannon Movie Tales: The
 Emperor's New Clothes '89
Cannonball Run 2 '84
The Cheap Detective '78
The Fiendish Plot of Dr. Fu
 Manchu '80
Grease '78
Grease 2 '82
Silent Movie '76

Sean Caffrey
When Dinosaurs Ruled the
 Earth '70

Stephen Caffrey
The Babe '92

Nicolas Cage
Amos and Andrew '93
Guarding Tess '94
Honeymoon in Vegas '92
It Could Happen to You '94
Moonstruck '87
Peggy Sue Got Married '86
Racing with the Moon '84
Rumble Fish '83
Trapped In Paradise '94
Valley Girl '83

James Cagney
The Seven Little Foys '55
Yankee Doodle Dandy '42

Jeanne Cagney
Yankee Doodle Dandy '42

William Cagney
Palooka '34

Christopher Cain
Force on Thunder
 Mountain '77

Christopher Cain ▲
The Amazing Panda
 Adventure '95
The Next Karate Kid '94
The Stone Boy '84
That Was Then. . .This Is
 Now '85
Where the River Runs
 Black '86
Young Guns '88

Michael Caine
Battle of Britain '69
A Bridge Too Far '77
Death Becomes Her '92
Dirty Rotten Scoundrels '88
Educating Rita '83
Harry & Walter Go to New
 York '76

The Man Who Would Be
 King '75
Mr. Destiny '90
The Muppet Christmas
 Carol '92
Sleuth '72
The Swarm '78
Sweet Liberty '86
Victory '81

Shakira Caine
The Man Who Would Be
 King '75

Anna Calder-Marshall
Wuthering Heights '70

Zoe Caldwell
Lantern Hill '90
The Purple Rose of Cairo '85

Jade Calegory
Mac and Me '88

Don Calfa
Weekend at Bernie's '89

Nicole Calfan
The Four Musketeers '75

Louis Calhern
Duck Soup '33
High Society '56
Notorious '46
The Red Pony '49

Monica Calhoun
Bagdad Cafe '88

John Call
Santa Claus Conquers the
 Martians '64

R.D. Call
Waterworld '95

Mark Callan ▲
Hector's Bunyip '86

Michael Callan
Gidget Goes Hawaiian '61
Mysterious Island '61

Joseph Calleia
The Caddy '53
The Jungle Book '42
The Light in the Forest '58
The Littlest Outlaw '54

Simon Callow
Ace Ventura: When Nature
 Calls '95
Amadeus '84
Four Weddings and a
 Funeral '93
Mr. & Mrs. Bridge '91
Street Fighter '94

Cab Calloway
The Littlest Angel '69

Vanessa Bell Calloway
Crimson Tide '95
What's Love Got to Do With
 It? '93

Henry Calvin
The Sign of Zorro '60
Toby Tyler '59
Zorro, Vol. 1 '58

John Calvin
Dragonworld '94

Pablito Calvo
The Man Who Wagged His
Tail '57

Brynne Cameron
Sherlock: Undercover Dog '94

Candace Cameron
Frankenstein Sings . . . The
Movie '95

Dean Cameron
Summer School '87

James Cameron ▲
The Terminator '84
Terminator 2: Judgment
Day '91
True Lies '94

Kirk Cameron
The Best of Times '86
Happy Birthday, Bugs: 50
Looney Years '90
Like Father, Like Son '87

Rod Cameron
G-Men vs. the Black
Dragon '43

Trent Cameron
The Kid Who Loved
Christmas '90

**Jesse Cameron-
Glickenhaus**
Timemaster '95

Tony Camilieri
Bill & Ted's Excellent
Adventure '89

Colleen Camp
Clue '85
D.A.R.Y.L. '85
Die Hard: With a
Vengeance '95
Greedy '94
Police Academy 2: Their First
Assignment '85
Police Academy 4: Citizens on
Patrol '87
Smile '75
Smokey and the Bandit, Part
3 '83
Valley Girl '83
Walk Like a Man '87
Wayne's World '92

Hamilton Camp
Arena '88
Casey at the Bat '85

Joe Camp ▲
Benji '74
Benji the Hunted '87

The Double McGuffin '79
For the Love of Benji '77
Hawmps! '76
Oh, Heavenly Dog! '80

Joseph Campanella
Comic Book Kids '82
Magic Kid '92

Bill Campbell
Out There '95
The Rocketeer '91

Bruce Campbell
Army of Darkness '92

Cheryl Campbell
Chariots of Fire '81
Greystoke: The Legend of
Tarzan, Lord of the
Apes '84

Christian Campbell
City Boy '93

Glen Campbell
True Grit '69

Julia Campbell
Opportunity Knocks '90

Ken Campbell
Down Periscope '96

Martin Campbell ▲
Goldeneye '95

Naomi Campbell
Cool As Ice '91

Neve Campbell
The Canterville Ghost '96

Scott Michael Campbell
Radioland Murders '94

Tisha Campbell
House Party '90
House Party 2: The Pajama
Jam '91
House Party 3 '94
Rags to Riches '87

Torquil Campbell
The Golden Seal '83

Tony Campisi
A Home of Our Own '93

Ron Canada
Man of the House '95

Gianna Maria Canale
Hercules '58

John Candy
Brewster's Millions '85
Canadian Bacon '94
Cool Runnings '93
Delirious '91
The Great Outdoors '88
Home Alone '90
Little Shop of Horrors '86
National Lampoon's
Vacation '83
Once Upon a Crime '92

Only the Lonely '91
Planes, Trains &
Automobiles '87
Sesame Street Presents:
Follow That Bird '85
Spaceballs '87
Splash '84
Summer Rental '85
Uncle Buck '89
Wagons East '94

Danny Cannon ▲
Judge Dredd '95

Dyan Cannon
Author! Author! '82
Merlin and the Sword '85
Revenge of the Pink
Panther '78

Judy Canova
The Adventures of Huckleberry
Finn '60

Cantinflas
Around the World in 80
Days '56

Yakima Canutt
Gone with the Wind '39

Yakima Canutt ▲
The Adventures of Frank and
Jesse James '48
G-Men Never Forget '48

Peter Capaldi
Local Hero '83

Virginia Capers
Ferris Bueller's Day Off '86
The North Avenue
Irregulars '79
White Mama '80

John Capodice
Honeymoon in Vegas '92

Francis Capra
Kazaam '96

Frank Capra
A Bronx Tale '93

Frank Capra ▲
It Happened One Night '34
It's a Wonderful Life '46
Mr. Smith Goes to
Washington '39

Kate Capshaw
How to Make an American
Quilt '95
Indiana Jones and the Temple
of Doom '84
My Heroes Have Always Been
Cowboys '91
SpaceCamp '86

Capucine
Curse of the Pink Panther '83
The Pink Panther '64
Trail of the Pink Panther '82

Irene Cara
Fame '80

Paul Carafotes
Journey to the Center of the
Earth '88

**Stephen Antonio
Cardenas**
Mighty Morphin Power
Rangers: The Movie '95

Pat Cardi
And Now Miguel '66

Tantoo Cardinal
Dances with Wolves '90
Legends of the Fall '94

Claudia Cardinale
Jesus of Nazareth '77
Once Upon a Time in the
West '68
The Pink Panther '64
Son of the Pink Panther '93

Rene Cardona Jr. ▲
Robinson Crusoe & the
Tiger '72

Nathalie Cardone
The Little Thief '89

Christopher Carey
Captain America 2: Death Too
Soon '79

Harry Carey Sr.
Devil Horse '32
The Last of the Mohicans '32
Mr. Smith Goes to
Washington '39
So Dear to My Heart '49

Harry Carey Jr.
Back to the Future, Part 3 '90
Bandolero! '68
Cahill: United States
Marshal '73
Challenge to White Fang '86
Mask '85
Tombstone '93

MacDonald Carey
Shadow of a Doubt '43
Tammy and the Doctor '63

Michele Carey
Scandalous John '71

Ron Carey
High Anxiety '77
Lucky Luke '94

Timothy Carey
Beach Blanket Bingo '65
Bikini Beach '64

Timothy Carhart
Beverly Hills Cop 3 '94
Black Sheep '96
Pink Cadillac '89

Gia Carides
Strictly Ballroom '92

Carmine Caridi
Top Dog '95

Len Cariou
The Lady in White '88
Who'll Save Our Children?
'82

Carlo Carlei ▲
Fluke '95

George Carlin
Bill & Ted's Bogus
Journey '91
Bill & Ted's Excellent
Adventure '89
Car Wash '76

Lewis John Carlino ▲
The Great Santini '80

Belinda Carlisle
Swing Shift '84

Kitty Carlisle Hart
A Night at the Opera '35
Radio Days '87

Johann Carlo
Quiz Show '94

Karen Carlson
A Horse for Danny '95

Linda Carlson
The Beverly Hillbillies '93

Richard Carlson
The Valley of Gwangi '69

Slim Carlson
Sourdough '77

Steve Carlson
Brothers O'Toole '73

Ing-mari Carlsson
My Life as a Dog '85

Roger C. Carmel
Hardly Working '81
My Dog, the Thief '69

Leone Carmen
The Year My Voice Broke '87

Jean Carmet
The Tall Blond Man with One
Black Shoe '72

Hoagy Carmichael
Topper '37

Tullio Carminati
Roman Holiday '53

Michael Carmine
*batteries not included '87

Primo Carnera
Hercules Unchained '59

Art Carney
The Blue Yonder '86
The Emperor's New
Clothes '84

Going in Style '79
Last Action Hero '93
Miracle of the Heart: A Boys
Town Story '86
Movie, Movie '78
The Night They Saved
Christmas '87
Undergrads '85

Cindy Carol
Dear Brigitte '65
Gidget Goes to Rome '63

Martine Carol
Around the World in 80
Days '56

Leslie Caron
An American in Paris '51
Courage Mountain '89
Lili '53

Bethany Carpenter
Tiger Town '83

Jake Carpenter
Alive '93

John Carpenter ▲
Big Trouble in Little China '86
Memoirs of an Invisible
Man '92
Starman '84

Thelma Carpenter
The Wiz '78

Bernard Carr ▲
Curley '47

Charmian Carr
The Sound of Music '65

Hayley Carr
Back Home '90

Jane Carr
The Prime of Miss Jean
Brodie '69

Thomas Carr
Superman: The Serial, Vol.
1 '48

Thomas Carr ▲
Jesse James Rides Again '47

David Carradine
Bound for Glory '76
Cannonball '76
Think Big '90
Wizards of the Lost Kingdom
2 '89

John Carradine
The Adventures of Huckleberry
Finn '60
Around the World in 80
Days '56
Captains Courageous '37
The Court Jester '56
Dimples '36
The Howling '81
Ice Pirates '84
Peggy Sue Got Married '86

The Shootist '76
The Ten Commandments '56
To the Last Man '33

Keith Carradine
Andre '94
Eye on the Sparrow '91
A Winner Never Quits '86

Robert Carradine
Aladdin and His Wonderful
Lamp '84
Aloha, Bobby and Rose '74
Cannonball '76
Clarence '91
The Cowboys '72
Just the Way You Are '84
On the Edge: The Survival of
Dana '79
Revenge of the Nerds '84

Chris Carrara
Remote '93

Carlos Carrasco
Speed '94

Barbara Carrera
Condorman '81
Island of Dr. Moreau '77
Never Say Never Again '83

Tia Carrere
Aloha Summer '88
High School High '96
Jury Duty '95
True Lies '94
Wayne's World '92
Wayne's World 2 '93

Jim Carrey
Ace Ventura: Pet
Detective '93
Ace Ventura: When Nature
Calls '95
Batman Forever '95
The Cable Guy '96
Club Med '83
Dumb & Dumber '94
The Mask '94
Peggy Sue Got Married '86
Pink Cadillac '89

Corey Carrier
Men Don't Leave '89
Savage Land '94

Matthieu Carriere
The Bay Boy '85
Christopher Columbus: The
Discovery '92

Leo Carrillo
Fisherman's Wharf '39

Debbie Lee Carrington
Spaced Invaders '90

John Carroll
Go West '40
Zorro Rides Again '37

Leo G. Carroll
A Christmas Carol '38

Father of the Bride '50
North by Northwest '59
The Paradine Case '47
The Parent Trap '61
Rebecca '40
Shirley Temple Storybook
Theater '60
Spellbound '45
Strangers on a Train '51
Suspicion '41

Madeleine Carroll
The 39 Steps '35

Pat Carroll
Brothers O'Toole '73
With Six You Get Eggroll '68

Rocky Carroll
Crimson Tide '95

David Carson ▲
Star Trek Generations '94

Hunter Carson
Invaders from Mars '86

Jack Carson
Mr. & Mrs. Smith '41
Mr. Smith Goes to
Washington '39

John David Carson
The Charge of the Model
T's '76

L.M. Kit Carson
Running on Empty '88

John Paddy Carstairs ▲
Tony Draws a Horse '51

Alice Carter
Gross Anatomy '89

Finn Carter
How I Got into College '89

Helena Carter
Invaders from Mars '53

Jack Carter
Alligator '80
The Amazing Dobermans '76
Arena '88
Hambone & Hillie '84
Heartbeeps '81

Jim Carter
Black Beauty '94

Michael Patrick Carter
Milk Money '94

Nell Carter
Modern Problems '81

Peter Carter ▲
Kavik, the Wolf Dog '84

Terry Carter
Battlestar Galactica '78

Thomas Carter ▲
Swing Kids '93

T.K. Carter
Ski Patrol '89

Angela Cartwright
The Sound of Music '65

Nancy Cartwright
Not My Kid '85

Veronica Cartwright
The Birds '63
Flight of the Navigator '86
Goin' South '78
Invasion of the Body
    Snatchers '78
Kid from Not-So-Big '78
The Right Stuff '83
Spencer's Mountain '63

Tony Caruso
Grizzly Adams: The Legend
    Continues '90

Lynne Carver
The Adventures of Huckleberry
    Finn '39
A Christmas Carol '38

Dana Carvey
Clean Slate '94
Opportunity Knocks '90
Racing with the Moon '84
Tough Guys '86
Trapped In Paradise '94
Wayne's World '92
Wayne's World 2 '93

Salvatore Cascio
Cinema Paradiso '88

Max Casella
Newsies '92
Sgt. Bilko '95
Windrunner '94

Clem Caserta
A Bronx Tale '93

Bernie Casey
Big Mo '73
Bill & Ted's Excellent
    Adventure '89
The Fantastic World of D.C.
    Collins '84
Guns of the Magnificent
    Seven '69
Never Say Never Again '83
Revenge of the Nerds '84
Spies Like Us '85

Rosalind Cash
The Adventures of Buckaroo
    Banzai Across the Eighth
    Dimension '84
The Mighty Pawns '87

John Cason
Jungle Drums of Africa '53

Katrina Caspary
Mac and Me '88
My Mom's a Werewolf '89

Maurice Cass
Spook Busters '46

Peggy Cass
Gidget Goes Hawaiian '61

John Cassavetes
Marvin & Tige '84

Jean-Pierre Cassel
The Four Musketeers '75
The Return of the
    Musketeers '89
Three Musketeers '74

Seymour Cassel
Adventures in Spying '92
Dick Tracy '90
Honeymoon in Vegas '92
Imaginary Crimes '94
It Could Happen to You '94
Plain Clothes '88
White Fang '91

Andrew Cassese
Revenge of the Nerds '84

Edward Cassidy
Son of Zorro '47

Joanna Cassidy
Club Paradise '86
Don't Tell Mom the
    Babysitter's Dead '91
A Girl of the Limberlost '90
Who Framed Roger Rabbit?
    '88

Patrick Cassidy
How the West Was Fun '95
Just the Way You Are '84

Ted Cassidy
Butch Cassidy and the
    Sundance Kid '69
Goin' Coconuts '78

John Cassisi
Bugsy Malone '76

Dan Castellaneta
Nothing in Common '86

Christopher Castile
Beethoven '92
Beethoven's 2nd '93

DeShonn Castle
Zebrahead '92

John Castle
The Lion in Winter '68
Man of La Mancha '72
Robocop 3 '91

Nick Castle ▲
The Boy Who Could Fly '86
Dennis the Menace '93
The Last Starfighter '84
Major Payne '95
Mr. Wrong '95

Robert Castle
Philadelphia '93

Roy Castle
Doctor Who and the
    Daleks '65

William Castle ▲
13 Ghosts '60

Hoite C. Caston ▲
Dirt Bike Kid '86

Darlene Cates
What's Eating Gilbert
    Grape '93

Gilbert Cates ▲
Goldilocks & the Three
    Bears '83
I Never Sang For My
    Father '70
Oh, God! Book 2 '80

Phoebe Cates
Date with an Angel '87
Drop Dead Fred '91
Fast Times at Ridgemont
    High '82
Gremlins '84
Gremlins 2: The New
    Batch '90
Princess Caraboo '94
Shag: The Movie '89

Walter Catlett
Bringing Up Baby '38
Yankee Doodle Dandy '42

Juliette Caton
Courage Mountain '89

Michael Caton-Jones ▲
Doc Hollywood '91
Rob Roy '95
This Boy's Life '93

Kim Cattrall
Big Trouble in Little China '86
Mannequin '87
Police Academy '84
The Return of the
    Musketeers '91
Star Trek 6: The Undiscovered
    Country '91
Turk 182! '85

Philippe Caubere
My Father's Glory '91
My Mother's Castle '91

Toran Caudell
Max is Missing '95

Joan Caulfield
Daring Dobermans '73
Pony Express Rider '76

Maxwell Caulfield
Electric Dreams '84
Gettysburg '93
Grease 2 '82

Nathan Cavaleri
Camp Nowhere '94

James Cavan
Cry from the Mountain '85

Megan Cavanagh
A League of Their Own '92
Robin Hood: Men in
    Tights '93

Paul Cavanagh
House of Wax '53
Tarzan and His Mate '34

Dick Cavett
Beetlejuice '88

James Caviezel
Ed '96

Christopher Cazenove
Three Men and a Little
    Lady '90

Larry Cedar
Boris and Natasha: The
    Movie '92

Maria Celedonio
How to Make an American
    Quilt '95

Adolfo Celi
Ten Little Indians '75
Thunderball '65

Brian Cesak
Fandango '85

Michael Ceveris
Rock 'n' Roll High School
    Forever '91

Amadee Chabot
Muscle Beach Party '64

Don Chaffey ▲
C.H.O.M.P.S. '79
The Fourth Wish '75
Greyfriars Bobby '61
The Horse Without a
    Head '63
Jason and the Argonauts '63
Magic of Lassie '78
Pete's Dragon '77
Ride a Wild Pony '75
The Three Lives of
    Thomasina '63

Julian Chagrin
The Christmas Tree '75

George Chakiris
West Side Story '61

Feodor Chaliapin
Moonstruck '87

Nathalie Chalifour
Mario '74

Sarah Chalke
City Boy '93

Richard Chamberlain
Allan Quartermain and the
    Lost City of Gold '86
The Count of Monte Cristo '74
The Four Musketeers '75
The Man in the Iron Mask '77

The Return of the
Musketeers '89
The Swarm '78
Three Musketeers '74

Wilt Chamberlain
Conan the Destroyer '84

Howland Chamberlin
Francis the Talking Mule '49

Marge Champion
The Party '68

Irene Champlin
Flash Gordon: Vol. 1 '53

Michael Paul Chan
The Joy Luck Club '93

Norman Chancer
Local Hero '83

Tanis Chandler
Spook Busters '46

Lon Chaney Jr.
Abbott and Costello Meet
Frankenstein '48
High Noon '52
My Favorite Brunette '47
Three Musketeers '33
Undersea Kingdom '36

Stockard Channing
The Big Bus '76
The Cheap Detective '78
The Fish that Saved
Pittsburgh '79
Grease '78
Moll Flanders '96
Not My Kid '85
To Wong Foo, Thanks for
Everything, Julie
Newmar '95
Up Close and Personal '96

Rosalind Chao
The Joy Luck Club '93
Memoirs of an Invisible
Man '92

Damian Chapa
Street Fighter '94

Billy Chapin
Tobor the Great '54

Miles Chapin
Bless the Beasts and
Children '71
French Postcards '79

Tom Chapin
Lord of the Flies '63

Ben Chaplin
The Truth About Cats and
Dogs '96

Charlie Chaplin
City Lights '31
The Gold Rush '25

Charlie Chaplin ▲
City Lights '31
The Gold Rush '25

Geraldine Chaplin
The Age of Innocence '93
Chaplin '92
Cria '76
Doctor Zhivago '65
The Four Musketeers '75
Home for the Holidays '95
Jane Eyre '96
The Return of the
Musketeers '89
Three Musketeers '74

Alexander Chapman
Princes in Exile '90

Constance Chapman
My Friend Walter '93

Daniel Chapman
Philadelphia '93

Graham Chapman
And Now for Something
Completely Different '72
Monty Python and the Holy
Grail '75

Lonny Chapman
Where the Red Fern
Grows '74

Marguerite Chapman
Spy Smasher '42

Michael Chapman ▲
All the Right Moves '83

Dave Chappelle
The Nutty Professor '96
Robin Hood: Men in
Tights '93

Patricia Charbonneau
Robocop 2 '90

Jon Chardiet
Beat Street '84

Cyd Charisse
The Band Wagon '53
Singin' in the Rain '52
That's Dancing! '85

Josh Charles
Dead Poets Society '89
Don't Tell Mom the
Babysitter's Dead '91
Threesome '94

Ian Charleson
Chariots of Fire '81
Greystoke: The Legend of
Tarzan, Lord of the
Apes '84

Chevy Chase
Benji at Work '93
Caddyshack '80
Cops and Robbersons '94
Fletch '85
Fletch Lives '89

Foul Play '78
Funny Farm '88
Hero '92
Man of the House '95
Memoirs of an Invisible
Man '92
Modern Problems '81
National Lampoon's Christmas
Vacation '89
National Lampoon's European
Vacation '85
National Lampoon's
Vacation '83
Oh, Heavenly Dog! '80
Sesame Street Presents:
Follow That Bird '85
Spies Like Us '85
Three Amigos '86
Under the Rainbow '81

Duane Chase
The Sound of Music '65

Stephan Chase
The Black Arrow '84

**Nathan Lee Chasing His
Horse**
Dances with Wolves '90

Daniel Chatto
Little Dorrit, Film 1: Nobody's
Fault '88
Little Dorrit, Film 2: Little
Dorrit's Story '88

Francois Chau
Teenage Mutant Ninja Turtles
2: The Secret of the
Ooze '91

Maury Chaykin
Cutthroat Island '95
Dances with Wolves '90
George's Island '91
Hero '92
Mr. Destiny '90
Sommersby '93
Unstrung Heroes '95

Jeremiah S. Chechik ▲
Benny & Joon '93
National Lampoon's Christmas
Vacation '89
Tall Tale: The Unbelievable
Adventures of Pecos
Bill '95

Chubby Checker
Purple People Eater '88

Michael Chekhov
Spellbound '45

Joan Chen
Judge Dredd '95

Cher
Mask '85
Mermaids '90
Moonstruck '87

Patrice Chereau
The Last of the Mohicans '92

Virginia Cherrill
City Lights '31

John Cherry ▲
Ernest Rides Again '93

John R. Cherry III ▲
Dr. Otto & the Riddle of the
Gloom Beam '86
Ernest Goes to Camp '87
Ernest Goes to Jail '90
Ernest Saves Christmas '88
Ernest Scared Stupid '91
Slam Dunk Ernest '95

Karen Cheryl
Here Comes Santa Claus '84

George Chesebro
Holt of the Secret Service '42

Vanessa Lee Chester
Harriet the Spy '96
A Little Princess '95

Morris Chestnut
Boyz N the Hood '91
The Ernest Green Story '93

Kevin Timothy Chevalia
Homeward Bound 2: Lost in
San Francisco '96
Homeward Bound: The
Incredible Journey '93

Maurice Chevalier
In Search of the
Castaways '62
Monkeys, Go Home! '66

Richard Chevolleau
Indian Summer '93

Chi
What's Love Got to Do With
It? '93

Lois Chiles
Death on the Nile '78
Moonraker '79

Tsai Chin
The Joy Luck Club '93
You Only Live Twice '67

William Ching
Pat and Mike '52

Kieu Chinh
The Girl Who Spelled
Freedom '86
The Joy Luck Club '93

Jade Chinn
The Girl Who Spelled
Freedom '86

Michael Chinyamurindi
Bopha! '93

Erik Chitty
First Men in the Moon '64

Anna Chlumsky
Gold Diggers: The Secret of
   Bear Mountain '95
My Girl '91
My Girl 2 '94
Trading Mom '94

J. Moki Cho
Race the Sun '96

Marvin J. Chomsky ▲
Tank '83

Mona Chong
On Her Majesty's Secret
   Service '69

Rae Dawn Chong
American Flyers '85
Beat Street '84
Soul Man '86

Thomas Chong
National Lampoon's Senior
   Trip '95

Joyce Chopra ▲
Smooth Talk '85

Navin Chowdhry
Madame Sousatzka '88

Joseph Chrest
King of the Hill '93

Keith Christensen
Little Heroes '91

Claudia Christian
Arena '88

Helen Christian
Zorro Rides Again '37

Robert Christian
Bustin' Loose '81

Roger Christian ▲
Starship '87

Audrey Christie
Harper Valley P.T.A. '78

Julie Christie
Doctor Zhivago '65
Dragonheart '96
The Go-Between '71

Dennis Christopher
Breaking Away '79
Chariots of Fire '81
Jack & the Beanstalk '83

Thom Christopher
Wizards of the Lost
   Kingdom '85

William Christopher
With Six You Get Eggroll '68

Art Chudabala
Gleaming the Cube '89

Byron Ross Chudnow ▲
The Amazing Dobermans '76
Daring Dobermans '73

The Doberman Gang '72

Thomas Haden Church
Tombstone '93

Berton Churchill
Dimples '36

Julien Ciamaca
My Father's Glory '91
My Mother's Castle '91

Eduardo Ciannelli
Foreign Correspondent '40
Mysterious Doctor Satan '40

Charles Cioffi
Newsies '92

Rene Clair ▲
The Ghost Goes West '36

Cyrielle Claire
Sword of the Valiant '83

Bob Clampett ▲
Bugs Bunny Cartoon
   Festival '44
Bugs Bunny Superstar '75
Looney Looney Looney Bugs
   Bunny Movie '81
Looney Tunes Video Show,
   Vol. 1
Looney Tunes Video Show,
   Vol. 2
Looney Tunes Video Show,
   Vol. 3
A Salute to Mel Blanc '58

Gordon Clapp
Eight Men Out '88

Eric Clapton
Tommy '75

Ronnie Clare
The Waltons: The Children's
   Carol '80

Angela Clark
Miracle of Our Lady of
   Fatima '52
The Seven Little Foys '55

Anthony Clark
The Thing Called Love '93

Blake Clark
Ladybugs '92

Bob (Benjamin) Clark ▲
A Christmas Story '83
My Summer Story '94
Rhinestone '84
Turk 182! '85

Candy Clark
American Graffiti '73
Buffy the Vampire Slayer '92
Cat's Eye '85
Citizens Band '77
Cool As Ice '91
Hambone & Hillie '84
More American Graffiti '79

Carl Clark
Sourdough '77

Colbert Clark ▲
Fighting with Kit Carson '33

Fred Clark
The Caddy '53
The Horse in the Gray Flannel
   Suit '68

George Clark
Back Home '90

James B. Clark ▲
And Now Miguel '66
A Dog of Flanders '59
Flipper '63
Island of the Blue
   Dolphins '64
My Side of the Mountain '69

Les Clark ▲
Sleeping Beauty '59

Matt Clark
Back to the Future, Part 3 '90
Chasing Dreams '81
Country '84
Legend of the Lone
   Ranger '81
The Outlaw Josey Wales '76
Return to Oz '85

Oliver Clark
Ernest Saves Christmas '88

Petula Clark
Finian's Rainbow '68

Susan Clark
Airport '75 '75
The Apple Dumpling Gang '75
The North Avenue
   Irregulars '79
Promises in the Dark '79

William Clark ▲
The Goodbye Bird '93
Windrunner '94

Alex Clarke
The Learning Tree '69

Caitlin Clarke
Dragonslayer '81

Hope Clarke
Piece of the Action '77

Joanna Clarke
Courage Mountain '89

Lenny Clarke
Two If by Sea '95

Mae Clarke
King of the Rocketmen '49
Pat and Mike '52

Lana Clarkson
Wizards of the Lost Kingdom
   2 '89

Patricia Clarkson
Rocket Gibraltar '88

James Clavell ▲
To Sir, with Love '67

Andrew Dice Clay
Making the Grade '84
Pretty in Pink '86

Nicholas Clay
Evil Under the Sun '82
Lionheart '87
Sleeping Beauty '89

Jill Clayburgh
Rich in Love '93
The Silver Streak '76

Bob Clayton
The Bellboy '60

Jack Clayton ▲
Something Wicked This Way
   Comes '83

John Clayton ▲
Duncan's World '77
Summerdog '78

Merry Clayton
Blame It on the Night '84

John Cleese
And Now for Something
   Completely Different '72
Erik the Viking '89
Gonzo Presents Muppet Weird
   Stuff '85
Monty Python and the Holy
   Grail '75
Rudyard Kipling's The Jungle
   Book '94
Silverado '85
Time Bandits '81

Ellen Cleghorne
Mr. Wrong '95

Paul Clemens
Promises in the Dark '79

William Clemens ▲
Nancy Drew, Reporter '39

Christian Clemenson
Hero '92

Rene Clement ▲
Forbidden Games '52

Edward Clements
Metropolitan '90

Ron Clements ▲
Aladdin '92
The Great Mouse
   Detective '86
The Little Mermaid '89

David Clennon
Matinee '92
The Right Stuff '83

Corinne Clery
Moonraker '79

Carol Cleveland
Monty Python and the Holy
 Grail '75

Jimmy Cliff
Club Paradise '86

Graeme Clifford ▲
The Boy Who Left Home to
 Find Out About the
 Shivers '81
Gleaming the Cube '89
Little Red Riding Hood '83

Richard Clifford
Much Ado About Nothing '93

Montgomery Clift
I Confess '53
Judgment at Nuremberg '61

Debra Clinger
Midnight Madness '80

E.E. Clive
The Little Princess '39

Art Clokey ▲
Gumby: The Movie '95

Rosemary Clooney
White Christmas '54

Del Close
Ferris Bueller's Day Off '86
Opportunity Knocks '90

Glenn Close
Immediate Family '89
The Natural '84
101 Dalmatians '96
Orphan Train '79
The Paper '94
Sarah, Plain and Tall '91
Skylark '93
The Stone Boy '84

John Scott Clough
Fast Forward '84
Gross Anatomy '89

Francois Cluzet
French Kiss '95

Andy Clyde
Shirley Temple Festival '33

Craig Clyde ▲
The Legend of Wolf
 Mountain '92
Little Heroes '91

**Lewis (Luigi Cozzi)
 Coates** ▲
Hercules '83

Phyllis Coates
Blues Busters '50
Jungle Drums of Africa '53
Superman & the Mole
 Men '51

Sammantha Coates
Water Babies '79

Joe Cobb
The Return of Our Gang '25

Julie Cobb
Lisa '90

Lee J. Cobb
How the West was Won '63
Men of Boys Town '41

Randall "Tex" Cobb
Ernest Goes to Jail '90
The Golden Child '86

Bill Cobbs
Dominick & Eugene '88
Ed '96
Fluke '95
Out There '95

Charles Coburn
Around the World in 80
 Days '56
Monkey Business '52
The Paradine Case '47

James Coburn
Charade '63
Maverick '94
The Nutty Professor '96
Pinocchio '83
Sister Act 2: Back in the
 Habit '93

Imogene Coca
National Lampoon's
 Vacation '83

Richard Coca
The Truth About Cats and
 Dogs '96

Stacy Cochran ▲
Boys '96

Steve Cochran
Wonder Man '45

Rory Cochrane
Dazed and Confused '93

James Coco
The Cheap Detective '78
Man of La Mancha '72

Jean Cocteau ▲
Beauty and the Beast '46

Camille Coduri
King Ralph '91

Iron Eyes Cody
Bowery Buckaroos '47
Ernest Goes to Camp '87

Kathleen Cody
Charley and the Angel '73
Superdad '73

Barry Coe
The Cat '66

Fred Coe ▲
A Thousand Clowns '65

George Coe
Bustin' Loose '81

Paul Coeur
Cool Runnings '93
White Fang 2: The Myth of the
 White Wolf '94

John Coffey
War of the Buttons '95

Scott Coffey
Satisfaction '88
Shag: The Movie '89
Shout '91

Tristram Coffin
Holt of the Secret Service '42
Jesse James Rides Again '47
King of the Rocketmen '49
Spy Smasher '42

Frank "Junior" Coghlan
The Adventures of Captain
 Marvel '41
The Last of the Mohicans '32

Howard R. Cohen ▲
Saturday the 14th '81
Space Raiders '83

Jeff B. Cohen
The Goonies '85

Jessica Lynn Cohen
George Balanchine's The
 Nutcracker '93

J.J. Cohen
Back to the Future '85
Back to the Future, Part 2 '89
Back to the Future, Part 3 '90

Joel Cohen ▲
Frankenstein Sings . . . The
 Movie '95

Rob Cohen ▲
Dragon: The Bruce Lee
 Story '93
Dragonheart '96

Saskia Cohen Tanugi
Never Say Never Again '83

Catero Colbert
Up Against the Wall '91

Claudette Colbert
It Happened One Night '34
Since You Went Away '44

Eric Michael Cole
White Squall '96

Gary Cole
The Brady Bunch Movie '95
A Very Brady Sequel '96

George Cole
The Belles of St. Trinian's '53

Blue Murder at St.
 Trinian's '56
A Christmas Carol '51
Dr. Syn, Alias the
 Scarecrow '64
The Pure Hell of St.
 Trinian's '61

Kay Cole
Dr. Syn, Alias the
 Scarecrow '64

Marcus Cole ▲
From the Mixed-Up Files of
 Mrs. Basil E.
 Frankweiler '95

Olivia Cole
The Fig Tree '87

Robert Coleby
Hector's Bunyip '86
The Phantom '96

Charlotte Coleman
Four Weddings and a
 Funeral '93

Dabney Coleman
Amos and Andrew '93
The Beverly Hillbillies '93
Clifford '92
Cloak & Dagger '84
The Dove '74
Downhill Racer '69
Dragnet '87
Hot to Trot! '88
The Man with One Red
 Shoe '85
Modern Problems '81
On Golden Pond '81
The Other Side of the
 Mountain '75
Tootsie '82
War Games '83

Gary Coleman
The Fantastic World of D.C.
 Collins '84
Jimmy the Kid '82
The Kid from Left Field '79
The Kid with the 200 I.Q. '83
On the Right Track '81

Renee Coleman
A League of Their Own '92

Charles "Honi" Coles
Dirty Dancing '87

Eileen Colgan
The Secret of Roan Inish '94

John Colicos
Battlestar Galactica '78

Margaret Colin
Amos and Andrew '93
The Butcher's Wife '91
Like Father, Like Son '87
Pretty in Pink '86
Three Men and a Baby '87

Richard A. Colla
Battlestar Galactica '78

Richard A. Colla ▲
Battlestar Galactica '78
Olly Olly Oxen Free '78

Christopher Collet
First Born '84
The Manhattan Project '86

Toni Collette
Emma '96
Muriel's Wedding '94
The Pallbearer '95

Kenneth Colley
Return to Treasure Island, Vol.
1 '85

Constance Collier
Wee Willie Winkie '37

James F. Collier ▲
Cry from the Mountain '85
Joni '79

John Collin
Tess '80

Albert Collins
Adventures in Babysitting '87

Anne Collins
Seven Alone '75

Blake Collins
The Little Rascals '94

Boon Collins ▲
Spirit of the Eagle '90

Eddie Collins
The Blue Bird '40

Joan Collins
Great Adventure '75
Hansel and Gretel '82
Zero to Sixty '78

Judy Collins
Junior '94

Patrick Collins
Dirt Bike Kid '86

Phil Collins
Hook '91

Ray Collins
The Bachelor and the Bobby-
Soxer '47
Citizen Kane '41
Francis the Talking Mule '49
The Human Comedy '43

Robert Collins
Goosebumps: A Night in
Terror Tower '96

Stephen Collins
All the President's Men '76
Brewster's Millions '85
Star Trek: The Motion
Picture '80

Peter Collinson ▲
Earthling '80
Ten Little Indians '75

Ronald Colman
Around the World in 80
Days '56

Miriam Colon
Sabrina '95

Jacque Lynn Colton
Heartbreak Hotel '88

Robbie Coltrane
The Adventures of Huck
Finn '93
Goldeneye '95
Oh, What a Night '92

Chris Columbus ▲
Adventures in Babysitting '87
Heartbreak Hotel '88
Home Alone '90
Home Alone 2: Lost in New
York '92
Mrs. Doubtfire '93
Nine Months '95
Only the Lonely '91

Jack Colvin
The Incredible Hulk '77
The Incredible Hulk
Returns '88

Michael Colyar
Hot Shots! Part Deux '93
House Party 3 '94

Dorothy Comingore
Citizen Kane '41

Betty Compson
Hard-Boiled Mahoney '47

Cristi Conaway
Batman Returns '92

Jeff Conaway
Grease '78
Pete's Dragon '77

David Condon
Clipped Wings '53

Jackie Condon
The Return of Our Gang '25

Donna Conforti
Santa Claus Conquers the
Martians '64

James Congdon
Summerdog '78

Joe Conley
A Day for Thanks on Walton's
Mountain '82
The Waltons: The Children's
Carol '80

Didi Conn
Grease 2 '82

Christopher Connelly
Benji '74
Hawmps! '76
The Incredible Rocky
Mountain Race '77
Liar's Moon '82

Jennifer Connelly
Labyrinth '86
The Rocketeer '91
Seven Minutes in Heaven '86

Bart Conner
Rad '86

Sean Connery
A Bridge Too Far '77
Darby O'Gill & the Little
People '59
Diamonds are Forever '71
Dr. No '62
First Knight '95
From Russia with Love '63
The Great Train Robbery '79
Highlander '86
Highlander 2: The
Quickening '91
The Hunt for Red October '90
Indiana Jones and the Last
Crusade '89
The Man Who Would Be
King '75
Never Say Never Again '83
Robin and Marian '76
Sword of the Valiant '83
Thunderball '65
Time Bandits '81
The Wind and the Lion '75
You Only Live Twice '67

Harry Connick Jr.
Independence Day '96
Little Man Tate '91

Billy Connolly
Muppet Treasure Island '96
The Return of the
Musketeers '89

Kevin Connolly
Alan & Naomi '92
The Beverly Hillbillies '93

Walter Connolly
The Adventures of Huckleberry
Finn '39
It Happened One Night '34

Kevin Connor ▲
At the Earth's Core '76
Land That Time Forgot '75
The Old Curiosity Shop '94
The People That Time
Forgot '77

Chuck Connors
Airplane 2: The Sequel '82
The Capture of Grizzly
Adams '82
Flipper '63
Old Yeller '57
Pat and Mike '52

Kevin R. Connors
Prehysteria! 2 '94

Christian Conrad
Last Time Out '94

David Conrad
The Wizard of Speed and
Time '88

Shane Conrad
The Brady Bunch Movie '95

Hans Conried
Brothers O'Toole '73
Davy Crockett, King of the
Wild Frontier '55
The 5000 Fingers of Dr. T '53
Oh, God! Book 2 '80
Tut and Tuttle '82

Frances Conroy
The Adventures of Huck
Finn '93
Rocket Gibraltar '88

Ruaidhri Conroy
Into the West '92

Tim Considine
Daring Dobermans '73
The Shaggy Dog '59

Yvonne Constant
Monkeys, Go Home! '66

Michael Constantine
My Life '93
The North Avenue
Irregulars '79
Prancer '89
The Reivers '69

John Conte
Lost in a Harem '44

Therese Conte ▲
Chasing Dreams '81

Tom Conti
American Dreamer '84
The Princess and the Pea '83

Chantal Contouri
Goodbye, Miss 4th of July '88

Frank Converse
Anne of Avonlea '87
Brother Future '91
Home at Last '88

**William Converse-
Roberts**
The Fig Tree '87

Bert Convy
Cannonball Run '81
Hero at Large '80
The Love Bug '68
The Man in the Santa Claus
Suit '79

Jack Conway ▲
Tarzan and His Mate '34

James L. Conway ▲
The Incredible Rocky
   Mountain Race '77
The Last of the Mohicans '85

Kevin Conway
Gettysburg '93
Prince Brat and the Whipping
   Boy '95
Rambling Rose '91

Morgan Conway
Dick Tracy, Detective '45

Tim Conway
The Apple Dumpling Gang '75
The Apple Dumpling Gang
   Rides Again '79
The Billion Dollar Hobo '78
Gus '76
The Private Eyes '80
Prize Fighter '79
The Shaggy D.A. '76
They Went That-a-Way & That-
   a-Way '78
The World's Greatest
   Athlete '73

Tom Conway
Tarzan's Secret Treasure '41

Jackie Coogan
Escape Artist '82
The Shakiest Gun in the
   West '68

Keith Coogan
Adventures in Babysitting '87
Book of Love '91
Cheetah '89
Don't Tell Mom the
   Babysitter's Dead '91
Hiding Out '87

Bart Robinson Cook
George Balanchine's The
   Nutcracker '93

Carole Cook
The Incredible Mr. Limpet '64
Sixteen Candles '84

Elisha Cook Jr.
The Maltese Falcon '41
Salem's Lot '79
Shane '53

Fielder Cook ▲
The Hideaways '73
Homecoming: A Christmas
   Story '71

Peter Cook
Black Beauty '94
The Princess Bride '87
Those Daring Young Men in
   Their Jaunty Jalopies '69

Rachel Leigh Cook
The Baby-Sitters Club '95
Tom and Huck '95

Sophie Cook
The Chronicles of Narnia '89

Tony Cookson ▲
And You Thought Your
   Parents Were Weird! '91

Martha Coolidge ▲
Lost in Yonkers '93
Plain Clothes '88
Rambling Rose '91
Real Genius '85
Valley Girl '83

Rita Coolidge
Club Med '83

Chris Cooper
Matewan '87
Money Train '95
This Boy's Life '93

Gary Cooper
Naked Gun 33 1/3: The Final
   Insult '94

Gary Cooper
Friendly Persuasion '56
High Noon '52

Gladys Cooper
Rebecca '40
The Secret Garden '49

Jackie Cooper
Superman 1: The Movie '78
Superman 2 '80
Superman 3 '83
Treasure Island '34

Jackie Cooper ▲
The Night They Saved
   Christmas '87
White Mama '80

Lawrence Cooper
My Friend Walter '93

Maggie Cooper
And Baby Makes Six '79

Melville Cooper
The Adventures of Robin
   Hood '38
Rebecca '40
Shirley Temple Storybook
   Theater '60

Robert Coote
The Three Musketeers '48

Joan Copeland
Her Alibi '88

Teri Copley
Brain Donors '92

Francis Ford Coppola ▲
Finian's Rainbow '68
Jack '96
The Outsiders '83
Peggy Sue Got Married '86
Rip van Winkle '85
Rumble Fish '83
Tucker: The Man and His
   Dream '88

Sofia Coppola
Peggy Sue Got Married '86

Jeff Corbett
Talent for the Game '91

John Corbett
Tombstone '93

Barry Corbin
My Science Project '85
Nothing in Common '86
Permanent Record '88
Six Pack '82

Bruno Corbucci ▲
Aladdin '86

Sergio Corbucci ▲
Super Fuzz '81

Ellen Corby
A Day for Thanks on Walton's
   Mountain '82
A Decade of the Waltons '85
Homecoming: A Christmas
   Story '71
I Remember Mama '48
It's a Wonderful Life '46
Support Your Local
   Gunfighter '71
The Waltons: A Thanksgiving
   Story '73

Aisling Corcoran
Moll Flanders '96

Donna Corcoran
Gypsy Colt '54

Kevin Corcoran
Johnny Shiloh '63
Mooncussers '62
Old Yeller '57
Pollyanna '60
Savage Sam '63
The Shaggy Dog '59
A Tiger Walks '64
Toby Tyler '59

Mara Corday
Francis Joins the WACs '54

Allan Corduner
Yentl '83

Nick Corea ▲
The Incredible Hulk
   Returns '88

Prof. Irwin Corey
Jack '96

Jeff Corey
Beneath the Planet of the
   Apes '70
Butch and Sundance: The
   Early Days '79
Butch Cassidy and the
   Sundance Kid '69
Conan the Destroyer '84
Little Big Man '70
My Friend Flicka '43
Oh, God! '77

Superman & the Mole
   Men '51

Joseph Corey
Greenstone '85

Wendell Corey
The Light in the Forest '58
Rear Window '54

Caris Corfman
Dreamchild '85

Pat Corley
Mr. Destiny '90

Maddie Corman
Seven Minutes in Heaven '86

Roger Corman
Philadelphia '93
Swing Shift '84

Roger Corman ▲
Little Miss Millions '93

Ellie Cornell
Chips the War Dog '90

John Cornell ▲
Almost an Angel '90
Crocodile Dundee 2 '88

Robert Cornthwaite
The War of the Worlds '53

Judy Cornwell
Santa Claus: The Movie '85
Wuthering Heights '70

Eugene Corr ▲
Desert Bloom '86

Georges Corraface
Christopher Columbus: The
   Discovery '92

Richard Correll ▲
Ski Patrol '89

Nick Corri
Gotcha! '85

Lloyd Corrigan
Ghost Chasers '51
Since You Went Away '44

Ray Corrigan
Undersea Kingdom '36

Bud Cort
Die Laughing '80
Electric Dreams '84
Invaders from Mars '86
M*A*S*H '70
Rumpelstiltskin '82
Why Shoot the Teacher? '79

Valentina Cortese
The Adventures of Baron
   Munchausen '89

Bill Cosby
Bill Cosby, Himself '81
The Devil & Max Devlin '81
Ghost Dad '90

Happy Birthday, Bugs: 50
 Looney Years '90
Jack '96
Leonard Part 6 '87
Man & Boy '71
Piece of the Action '77

Bill Cosby ▲
Bill Cosby, Himself '81

Don A. Coscarelli ▲
Beastmaster '82

Howard Cosell
Bananas '71
Broadway Danny Rose '84
Casey at the Bat '85
Sleeper '73

Brian Cosgrove ▲
The B.F.G. (Big Friendly
 Giant) '90

George P. Cosmatos ▲
Tombstone '93

James Cosmo
Braveheart '95
Emma '96

James Cossins
Wuthering Heights '70

Robert Costanzo
Die Hard 2: Die Harder '90
Honeymoon in Vegas '92
Storybook '95

Bob Costas
The Scout '94

Dolores Costello
Breaking the Ice '38
Little Lord Fauntleroy '36

Lou Costello
Abbott and Costello Meet
 Captain Kidd '52
Abbott and Costello Meet Dr.
 Jekyll and Mr. Hyde '52
Abbott and Costello Meet
 Frankenstein '48
Africa Screams '49
Buck Privates '41
Buck Privates Come Home '47
Jack & the Beanstalk '52
Lost in a Harem '44

Mariclare Costello
Skeezer '82

Ward Costello
MacArthur '77

Nicolas Coster
The Electric Horseman '79
MacArthur '77

Kevin Costner
American Flyers '85
Chasing Dreams '81
Dances with Wolves '90
Fandango '85
Field of Dreams '89
A Perfect World '93

Robin Hood: Prince of
 Thieves '91
Silverado '85
Table for Five '83
Waterworld '95

Kevin Costner ▲
Dances with Wolves '90

Kami Cotler
A Day for Thanks on Walton's
 Mountain '82
The Waltons: A Thanksgiving
 Story '73
The Waltons: The Children's
 Carol '80

Joseph Cotten
Airport '77 '77
Citizen Kane '41
The Farmer's Daughter '47
Shadow of a Doubt '43
Since You Went Away '44
Under Capricorn '49

John Cotter ▲
Mountain Family
 Robinson '79

Ralph Cotterill
Starship '87

Oliver Cotton
Christopher Columbus: The
 Discovery '92

Jack Couffer ▲
Living Free '72
Nikki, the Wild Dog of the
 North '61

George Coulouris
Citizen Kane '41
Papillon '73

Bernie Coulson
Adventures in Spying '92

Richard Council
The Manhattan Project '86

Tom Courtenay
Doctor Zhivago '65
Leonard Part 6 '87
The Loneliness of the Long
 Distance Runner '62
The Old Curiosity Shop '94

Inez Courtney
Let's Sing Again '36

Jeni Courtney
The Secret of Roan Inish '94

Christian Cousins
Twinsitters '95

Joseph Cousins
Twinsitters '95

Julian Coutts
Bridge to Terabithia '85

Jean Coutu
Nikki, the Wild Dog of the
 North '61

Bill Couturie ▲
Ed '96

Alan Covert
Happy Gilmore '96

Hil Covington ▲
Adventures in Spying '92

Jerome Cowan
The Maltese Falcon '41

Nick Cowen
Surf Ninjas '93

William J. Cowen ▲
Oliver Twist '33

Nicola Cowper
Dreamchild '85
Journey to the Center of the
 Earth '88
Lionheart '87

Alan Cox
Young Sherlock Holmes '85

Bobby Cox
Young Eagles '34

Brian Cox
Rob Roy '95

Courteney Cox
Ace Ventura: Pet
 Detective '93
Cocoon: The Return '88
Masters of the Universe '87
Mr. Destiny '90

Jennifer Elise Cox
The Brady Bunch Movie '95
A Very Brady Sequel '96

Ronny Cox
Beverly Hills Cop '84
Beverly Hills Cop 2 '87
Bound for Glory '76
Captain America '89
Harper Valley P.T.A. '78
Kavik, the Wolf Dog '84
Lost Legacy: A Girl Called
 Hatter Fox '77
Robocop '87
Taps '81
Two of a Kind '82

Ruth Cox
Nancy Drew: Mystery of the
 Diamond Triangle '78

Tony Cox
Spaced Invaders '90

Wally Cox
The Barefoot Executive '71
The Boatniks '70
The One and Only, Genuine,
 Original Family Band '68
Spencer's Mountain '63
State Fair '62

Peter Coyote
The Blue Yonder '86
Cross Creek '83
Die Laughing '80
E.T.: The Extra-Terrestrial '82
Legend of Billie Jean '85
Stacking '87
Timerider '83

Buster Crabbe
Buck Rogers Conquers the
 Universe '39
Flash Gordon Conquers the
 Universe '40
Flash Gordon: Rocketship '36
Sea Hound '47
To the Last Man '33

Buddy Crabtree
Legend of Boggy Creek '75

Jeff Crabtree
Legend of Boggy Creek '75

Charmaine Craig
White Fang 2: The Myth of the
 White Wolf '94

Daniel Craig
A Kid in King Arthur's
 Court '95
The Power of One '92

James Craig
The Human Comedy '43
Winners of the West '40

Michael Craig
Mysterious Island '61
Ride a Wild Pony '75

Yvonne Craig
It Happened at the World's
 Fair '63

Bill Crain ▲
Kid from Not-So-Big '78

Jeanne Crain
State Fair '45

William Crain ▲
Blacula '72

Grant Cramer
Leapin' Leprechauns '95

Joey Cramer
Flight of the Navigator '86
Stone Fox '87

Bob Crane
Gus '76
Superdad '73

Norma Crane
Fiddler on the Roof '71

Rachel Crane
Two Bits & Pepper '95

Noel Cravat
G-Men vs. the Black
 Dragon '43

James Craven
Green Archer '40

Matt Craven
Crimson Tide '95
Indian Summer '93

Wes Craven ▲
Swamp Thing '82

Anne Crawford
Knights of the Round
Table '53
Tony Draws a Horse '51

Broderick Crawford
A Little Romance '79

John Crawford
The Invisible Monster '50
Zombies of the
Stratosphere '52

Johnny Crawford
Courage of Black Beauty '57
Indian Paint '64

Michael Crawford
Condorman '81
Hello, Dolly! '69

Robert Crawford Jr.
Indian Paint '64

Amos Crawley
Rent-A-Kid '95

Richard Crenna
The Flamingo Kid '84
Hot Shots! Part Deux '93
Sabrina '95
Summer Rental '85
Table for Five '83
Wild Horse Hank '79

Marshall Crenshaw
La Bamba '87

Laura Hope Crews
Gone with the Wind '39

Wendy Crewson
Corrina, Corrina '94
The Good Son '93
The Santa Clause '94

Michael Crichton ▲
The Great Train Robbery '79

Missy Crider
Powder '95

Isa Crino
Lilies of the Field '63

Donald Crisp
Challenge to Lassie '49
A Dog of Flanders '59
Greyfriars Bobby '61
How Green was My Valley '41
Knute Rockne: All
American '40
Lassie, Come Home '43
National Velvet '44
Pollyanna '60

Prince Valiant '54
Spencer's Mountain '63

Anthony Crivello
Frankenstein Sings . . . The
Movie '95

Max Croiset
A Dog of Flanders '59

Jonathan Crombie
Anne of Avonlea '87
Anne of Green Gables '85

James Cromwell
The Babe '92
Babe '95

John Cromwell ▲
Little Lord Fauntleroy '36
Since You Went Away '44

Claudia Cron
Running Brave '83

Laurel Cronin
Beethoven '92
Housesitter '92

Hume Cronyn
*batteries not included '87
Brewster's Millions '85
Cocoon '85
Cocoon: The Return '88
Conrack '74
Shadow of a Doubt '43

Bing Crosby
The Bells of St. Mary's '45
A Connecticut Yankee in King
Arthur's Court '49
Country Girl '54
Going My Way '44
High Society '56
Holiday Inn '42
My Favorite Brunette '47
That's Entertainment '74
White Christmas '54

Cathy Lee Crosby
Coach '78

Denise Crosby
Curse of the Pink Panther '83
Star Trek the Next Generation
Episode 1-2: Encounter at
Farpoint '87

Gary Crosby
Justin Morgan Had a
Horse '81

Mary Crosby
Ice Pirates '84

Ben Cross
Chariots of Fire '81
First Knight '95
The Flame Trees of Thika '81

Rupert Crosse
The Reivers '69

Scatman Crothers
Bronco Billy '80

The Great White Hope '70
The Journey of Natty
Gann '85
The Shootist '76
The Silver Streak '76
Twilight Zone: The Movie '83

Lindsay Crouse
All the President's Men '76
Being Human '94
Bye Bye, Love '94
Iceman '84
The Indian in the
Cupboard '95
Places in the Heart '84

Ashley Crow
Little Big League '94

Cameron Crowe ▲
Say Anything '89
Singles '92

Russell Crowe
The Silver Stallion: King of
the Wild Brumbies '94

Ed Crowley
Running on Empty '88

Kathleen Crowley
Westward Ho, the Wagons!
'56

Pat Crowley
Hollywood or Bust '56

Patricia Crowley
Menace on the Mountain '70

Su Cruickshank
Young Einstein '89

Tom Cruise
All the Right Moves '83
Far and Away '92
Legend '85
Mission: Impossible '96
The Outsiders '83
Rain Man '88
Taps '81
Top Gun '86

Rosalie Crutchley
The Hunchback of Notre
Dame '82
Wuthering Heights '70

Abigail Cruttenden
Kipperbang '82

Alexis Cruz
Gryphon '88
Stargate '94

Carlina Cruz
Maricela '88

Raymond Cruz
Clear and Present Danger '94
Up Close and Personal '96

Gretchen Cryer
Hiding Out '87

Jon Cryer
Hiding Out '87
Morgan Stewart's Coming
Home '87
Pretty in Pink '86
Superman 4: The Quest for
Peace '87

Billy Crystal
City Slickers '91
City Slickers 2: The Legend of
Curly's Gold '94
Forget Paris '95
The Princess Bride '87
The Three Little Pigs '84
Throw Momma from the
Train '87

Billy Crystal ▲
Forget Paris '95

Lindsay Crystal
City Slickers 2: The Legend of
Curly's Gold '94

Eszter Csakanyi
A Hungarian Fairy Tale '87

Alfonso Cuaron ▲
A Little Princess '95

Vladimir Cuk
Celtic Pride '96

George Cukor ▲
Adam's Rib '50
The Corn is Green '79
David Copperfield '35
Little Women '33
Pat and Mike '52
The Philadelphia Story '40

Chris Culkin
My Summer Story '94

Kieran Culkin
Father of the Bride '91
Father of the Bride Part II '95
Home Alone '90
Home Alone 2: Lost in New
York '92
My Summer Story '94

Macaulay Culkin
George Balanchine's The
Nutcracker '93
Getting Even with Dad '94
The Good Son '93
Home Alone '90
Home Alone 2: Lost in New
York '92
My Girl '91
Only the Lonely '91
The Pagemaster '94
Richie Rich '94
Rocket Gibraltar '88
See You in the Morning '89
Uncle Buck '89

Quinn Culkin
The Good Son '93

Brett Cullen
Apollo 13 '95

VIDEOHOUND'S FAMILY VIDEO GUIDE

Prehysteria '93
Something to Talk About '95

Max Cullen
Lightning Jack '94

Mark Cullingham ▲
Cinderella '84
Gryphon '88

John Cullum
Glory '89
Morgan Stewart's Coming
  Home '87
The Prodigal '83

Robert Culp
The Castaway Cowboy '74
The Pelican Brief '93
Sammy, the Way-Out Seal '62
Turk 182! '85

Alan Cumming
Bernard and the Genie '91
Goldeneye '95

Alan Cummings
Circle of Friends '94
Emma '96

Irving Cummings ▲
Curly Top '35
Just Around the Corner '38
Little Miss Broadway '38
The Poor Little Rich Girl '36

Jim Cummings
The Lion King '94

Quinn Cummings
The Goodbye Girl '77

Robert Cummings
Beach Party '63
Dial "M" for Murder '54
Saboteur '42

Eli Cummins
Dakota '88
Harley '90

Peter Cummins
Blue Fire Lady '78

Liam Cunningham
First Knight '95
A Little Princess '95
War of the Buttons '95

Sean S. Cunningham ▲
Manny's Orphans '78

Lynette Curran
The Year My Voice Broke '87

Cherie Currie
Foxes '80
Twilight Zone: The Movie '83

Finlay Currie
The Adventures of Huckleberry
  Finn '60
Treasure Island '50

Louise Currie
The Adventures of Captain
  Marvel '41
The Masked Marvel '43
Million Dollar Kid '44

Tim Curry
Annie '82
Clue '85
Congo '95
Home Alone 2: Lost in New
  York '92
The Hunt for Red October '90
Legend '86
Muppet Treasure Island '96
National Lampoon's Loaded
  Weapon 1 '93
Oliver Twist '82
The Shadow '94
The Three Musketeers '93
The Worst Witch '86

Jane Curtin
Coneheads '93

Alan Curtis
Buck Privates '41

Dan Curtis ▲
When Every Day was the
  Fourth of July '78

Jamie Lee Curtis
The Adventures of Buckaroo
  Banzai Across the Eighth
  Dimension '84
Amazing Grace & Chuck '87
Annie Oakley '85
Dominick & Eugene '88
Forever Young '92
House Arrest '96
My Girl '91
My Girl 2 '94
True Lies '94

Ken Curtis
Pony Express Rider '76
The Quiet Man '52

Liane Curtis
Sixteen Candles '84

Robin Curtis
Star Trek 3: The Search for
  Spock '84

Tony Curtis
The Bad News Bears Go to
  Japan '78
The Count of Monte Cristo '74
Francis the Talking Mule '49
Great Race '65
Little Miss Marker '80
Those Daring Young Men in
  Their Jaunty Jalopies '69

Vondie Curtis-Hall
Crooklyn '94

Michael Curtiz
Yankee Doodle Dandy '42

Michael Curtiz ▲
The Adventures of Huckleberry
  Finn '60
The Adventures of Robin
  Hood '38
Captain Blood '35
Casablanca '42
Life with Father '47
White Christmas '54
Yankee Doodle Dandy '42

Ann Cusack
A League of Their Own '92

Cyril Cusack
David Copperfield '70
Far and Away '92
Little Dorrit, Film 1: Nobody's
  Fault '88
Little Dorrit, Film 2: Little
  Dorrit's Story '88

Joan Cusack
Addams Family Values '93
Hero '92
Men Don't Leave '89
Mr. Wrong '95
My Bodyguard '80
Nine Months '95
Say Anything '89
Sixteen Candles '84
Toys '92

John Cusack
Better Off Dead '85
Eight Men Out '88
The Journey of Natty
  Gann '85
One Crazy Summer '86
Say Anything '89
Sixteen Candles '84
Stand By Me '86
The Sure Thing '85

Niamh Cusack
The Playboys '92

Sinead Cusack
Rocket Gibraltar '88

Susie Cusack
Hero '92

Peter Cushing
At the Earth's Core '76
Doctor Who and the
  Daleks '65
Star Wars '77
Sword of the Valiant '83

Bob Custer
Law of the Wild '34

Iain Cuthbertson
Gorillas in the Mist '88

Allen Cutler
The Halfback of Notre
  Dame '96

Michael Cutting ▲
The Little Crooked Christmas
  Tree '93

Charles Cyphers
Major League '89

Henry Czerny
Clear and Present Danger '94
Mission: Impossible '96

Howard da Silva
David and Lisa '62
Mommie Dearest '81
1776 '72

Augusta Dabney
Running on Empty '88

Olivia D'Abo
Beyond the Stars '89
The Big Green '95
Clean Slate '94
Conan the Destroyer '84
Greedy '94
Wayne's World 2 '93

Morton DaCosta ▲
The Music Man '62

Ami Daemion
The Silver Stallion: King of
  the Wild Brumbies '94

Willem Dafoe
Clear and Present Danger '94
Cry-Baby '90

Jean-Michel Dagory
Clowning Around '92
Clowning Around 2 '93

Arlene Dahl
Journey to the Center of the
  Earth '59

Elizabeth Daily
Fandango '85
Pee Wee's Big Adventure '85

Masaki Daimon
Godzilla vs. the Cosmic
  Monster '74

Badgett Dale
Lord of the Flies '90

Dick Dale
Back to the Beach '87

Esther Dale
Curly Top '35

James Dale
Federal Agents vs.
  Underworld, Inc. '49

Jim Dale
The Adventures of Huckleberry
  Finn '85
Digby, the Biggest Dog in the
  World '73
Hot Lead & Cold Feet '78
Pete's Dragon '77
Unidentified Flying
  Oddball '79

Virginia Dale
Holiday Inn '42

Marcel Dalio
Casablanca '42
Sabrina '54

John Dall
The Corn is Green '45

Joe Dallesandro
Cry-Baby '90

Abby Dalton
Whale of a Tale '76

Timothy Dalton
Brenda Starr '86
Flash Gordon '80
The Lion in Winter '68
The Rocketeer '91
Wuthering Heights '70

Roger Daltrey
If Looks Could Kill '91
Lightning Jack '94
The Little Match Girl '87
Tommy '75

Robert Dalva ▲
The Black Stallion
   Returns '83

James Daly
Planet of the Apes '68

Timothy Daly
Dr. Jekyll and Ms. Hyde '95
Just the Way You Are '84
Year of the Comet '92

Tyne Daly
Christy '94

Jacques D'Amboise
Off Beat '86

Cjon Damitri
Sea Gypsies '78

Cathryn Damon
She's Having a Baby '88

Gabriel Damon
Journey to Spirit Island '92
Robocop 2 '90

Matt Damon
Geronimo: An American
   Legend '93
School Ties '92

Stuart Damon
Cinderella '64

Vic Damone
Kismet '55

JoJo D'Amore
The Doberman Gang '72

Mel Damski ▲
A Winner Never Quits '86

Mike Damus
Lost in Yonkers '93

Barbara Dana
Necessary Parties '88

Paige Danahy
Sudie & Simpson '90

Charles Dance
For Your Eyes Only '81
The Golden Child '86
Last Action Hero '93

Dorothy Dandridge
Since You Went Away '44

Lawrence Dane
It Takes Two '95
National Lampoon's Senior
   Trip '95

Claire Danes
Home for the Holidays '95
How to Make an American
   Quilt '95
Little Women '94

Angelo D'Angelo
BMX Bandits '83

Beverly D'Angelo
Annie Hall '77
Coal Miner's Daughter '80
The Crazysitter '94
The Legend of Sleepy
   Hollow '86
Lightning Jack '94
Maid to Order '87
The Miracle '91
National Lampoon's Christmas
   Vacation '89
National Lampoon's European
   Vacation '85
National Lampoon's
   Vacation '83
Sleeping Beauty '83
Trading Hearts '87

Rodney Dangerfield
Back to School '86
Caddyshack '80
Ladybugs '92
The Projectionist '71

Ann Daniel
Island of the Blue
   Dolphins '64

Rod Daniel ▲
Beethoven's 2nd '93
K-9 '89
Like Father, Like Son '87
Teen Wolf '85

Henry Daniell
Jane Eyre '44
The Philadelphia Story '40

Anthony Daniels
The Empire Strikes Back '80
Return of the Jedi '83
Star Wars '77

J.D. Daniels
Beanstalk '94

Jeff Daniels
Arachnophobia '90
The Butcher's Wife '91

Dumb & Dumber '94
Gettysburg '93
101 Dalmatians '96
The Purple Rose of Cairo '85
Radio Days '87
Speed '94
Terms of Endearment '83
Welcome Home, Roxy
   Carmichael '90

Mickey Daniels
The Return of Our Gang '25

William Daniels
Her Alibi '88
Oh, God! '77
1776 '72
A Thousand Clowns '65

Blythe Danner
Brighton Beach Memoirs '86
The Great Santini '80
Hearts of the West '75
Man, Woman & Child '83
Mr. & Mrs. Bridge '91
1776 '72
To Wong Foo, Thanks for
   Everything, Julie
   Newmar '95

Sybil Danning
Battle Beyond the Stars '80
Hercules '83
The Prince and the
   Pauper '78

Royal Dano
The Adventures of Huckleberry
   Finn '60
Huckleberry Finn '75
The Right Stuff '83
Spaced Invaders '90

Cesare Danova
Gidget Goes to Rome '63

Ted Danson
Dad '89
A Fine Mess '86
Getting Even with Dad '94
Loch Ness '96
Made in America '93
Pontiac Moon '94
Three Men and a Baby '87
Three Men and a Little
   Lady '90

Joe Dante ▲
The 'Burbs '89
Explorers '85
Gremlins '84
Gremlins 2: The New
   Batch '90
The Howling '81
Innerspace '87
Matinee '92
Twilight Zone: The Movie '83

Helmut Dantine
Casablanca '42
The Fifth Musketeer '79

Tony Danza
Angels in the Outfield '94

Going Ape! '81

Frank Darabont ▲
The Shawshank
   Redemption '94

Patti D'Arbanville
Modern Problems '81
Real Genius '85

Kim Darby
Better Off Dead '85
The Capture of Grizzly
   Adams '82
Teen Wolf Too '87
True Grit '69

Mireille Darc
The Tall Blond Man with One
   Black Shoe '72

Jake D'Arcy
Gregory's Girl '80

Severn Darden
Back to School '86
Battle for the Planet of the
   Apes '73
Conquest of the Planet of the
   Apes '72
The Day of the Dolphin '73
Real Genius '85
Saturday the 14th '81

Bobby Darin
State Fair '62

Jean Darling
March of the Wooden
   Soldiers '34

Joan Darling ▲
Hiroshima Maiden '88

Linda Darlow
Immediate Family '89

Mike Darnell
Comic Book Kids '82

Steve Darrell
The Adventures of Frank and
   Jesse James '48

James Darren
Gidget '59
Gidget Goes Hawaiian '61
Gidget Goes to Rome '63

Frankie Darro
Burn 'Em Up Barnes '34
Devil Horse '32
The Phantom Empire '35

Henry Darrow
Computer Wizard '77

Jane Darwell
Captain January '36
Curly Top '35
Gone with the Wind '39
Little Miss Broadway '38
The Poor Little Rich Girl '36
The Red Stallion '47

Stacey Dash
Clueless '95
Renaissance Man '94

Jules Dassin ▲
The Canterville Ghost '44

George Daugherty ▲
Peter and the Wolf '95

Herschel Daugherty ▲
The Light in the Forest '58

Claude Dauphin
Madame Rosa '77

Richard Davalos
East of Eden '54
Something Wicked This Way
    Comes '83

Harry Davenport
The Bachelor and the Bobby-
    Soxer '47
Courage of Lassie '46
The Farmer's Daughter '47
Foreign Correspondent '40
Gone with the Wind '39
Home Movies '79
Meet Me in St. Louis '44

Nigel Davenport
Chariots of Fire '81
Greystoke: The Legend of
    Tarzan, Lord of the
    Apes '84
Island of Dr. Moreau '77
Living Free '72
A Man for All Seasons '66

Delmer Daves ▲
Spencer's Mountain '63

Robert Davi
Christopher Columbus: The
    Discovery '92
Cops and Robbersons '94
Die Hard '88
The Goonies '85
Son of the Pink Panther '93

Angel David
The Crow '93

Eleanor David
Comfort and Joy '84
The Scarlet Pimpernel '82

Keith David
Always '89

Lolita David
Adventures in Babysitting '87

Thayer David
Journey to the Center of the
    Earth '59

Lolita Davidovich
Leap of Faith '92
Now and Then '95

Ben Davidson
Conan the Barbarian '82

Boaz Davidson ▲
Going Bananas '88

Davey Davidson
No Drums, No Bugles '71

Jaye Davidson
Stargate '94

John Davidson
Edward Scissorhands '90
The Happiest Millionaire '67
Tailspin Tommy '34

Martin Davidson ▲
Eddie and the Cruisers '83
Follow the River '95
Hero at Large '80
The Lords of Flatbush '74

Tommy Davidson
Ace Ventura: When Nature
    Calls '95

Embeth Davidtz
Army of Darkness '92
Matilda '96

John Davies ▲
Kim '84

John Howard Davies
Oliver Twist '48
Tom Brown's School Days '51

Terence Davies ▲
The Long Day Closes '92

Andrew Davis ▲
The Fugitive '93

Bette Davis
The Corn is Green '45
Death on the Nile '78
Return from Witch
    Mountain '78
Watcher in the Woods '81
White Mama '80

Brad Davis
Chariots of Fire '81

Carole Davis
The Flamingo Kid '84
If Looks Could Kill '91
Mannequin '87

Clifton Davis
Dream Date '93

Cynthia Davis
Cooley High '75

Desmond Davis ▲
Clash of the Titans '81

Duane Davis
The Program '93

Geena Davis
Beetlejuice '88
Cutthroat Island '95
Fletch '85
Hero '92
A League of Their Own '92

Speechless '94
Tootsie '82

Guy Davis
Beat Street '84

Jack Davis
The Return of Our Gang '25

Jim Davis
Bad Company '72
Zebra in the Kitchen '65

Joan Davis
Just Around the Corner '38

Mac Davis
The Sting 2 '83

Melissa Davis
The River Rat '84

Michael Paul Davis ▲
Beanstalk '94

Nathan Davis
Dunston Checks In '95

Ossie Davis
The Client '94
The Ernest Green Story '93
Grumpy Old Men '93
Harry & Son '84
Joe Versus the Volcano '90

Philip Davis
The Bounty '84

Rochelle Davis
The Crow '93

Sammi Davis
Hope and Glory '87

Sammy Davis Jr.
Alice in Wonderland '85
Cannonball Run '81
Cannonball Run 2 '84
Cracking Up '83
The Kid Who Loved
    Christmas '90
That's Dancing! '85

Tamra Davis ▲
Billy Madison '94

Viveka Davis
Morgan Stewart's Coming
    Home '87
Not My Kid '85

Warwick Davis
The Ewok Adventure '84
The Ewoks: Battle for
    Endor '85
Willow '88

Bruce Davison
The Baby-Sitters Club '95
The Cure '95
Far from Home: The
    Adventures of Yellow
    Dog '94
Spies Like Us '85

Peter Davison
Black Beauty '94

Pam Dawber
The Little Mermaid '84
Stay Tuned '92

**Anthony (Antonio
    Margheriti) Dawson**
Dial "M" for Murder '54
Dr. No '62

Kamala Dawson
Lightning Jack '94

Vicky Dawson
Carbon Copy '81

Doris Day
Please Don't Eat the
    Daisies '60
Turf Boy '42
With Six You Get Eggroll '68

Josette Day
Beauty and the Beast '46

Laraine Day
Foreign Correspondent '40
Journey for Margaret '42

Matt Day
Muriel's Wedding '94

Patrick Day
The Adventures of Huckleberry
    Finn '85

Robert Day ▲
The Grass is Always Greener
    Over the Septic Tank '78

Daniel Day-Lewis
The Age of Innocence '93
The Bounty '84
The Last of the Mohicans '92

Lyman Dayton ▲
Dream Machine '91

Joaquim de Almeida
Clear and Present Danger '94
Only You '94

Remo de Angelis
Great Adventure '75

Jo De Backer
Toto le Heros '91

Brenda de Banzie
The Pink Panther '64

Manuel de Blas
Great Adventure '75

Jan De Bont ▲
Speed '94
Twister '96

Celia de Burgh
Phar Lap '84

Yvonne De Carlo
The Ten Commandments '56

Fred de Cordova ▲
Bedtime for Bonzo '51

Olivia de Havilland
The Adventures of Robin
    Hood '38
Airport '77 '77
Captain Blood '35
The Fifth Musketeer '79
Gone with the Wind '39
The Swarm '78

Katherine De Hetre
Joni '79

Nic de Jager
The Gods Must Be Crazy '84

Ate De Jong ▲
Drop Dead Fred '91

Simon de la Brosse
The Little Thief '89

George de la Pena
Brain Donors '92
Kuffs '92
The Manners Monster: Ruby
    Goes to Dinner '95

Derek De Lint
Three Men and a Baby '87

**Stanislas Carre de
    Malberg**
Au Revoir Les Enfants '87

John De Mita
Josh Kirby . . . Time Warrior:
    Chapter 1, Planet of the
    Dino-Knights '95

Pierre De Moro ▲
Savannah Smiles '82

Robert De Niro
Awakenings '90
Bang the Drum Slowly '73
A Bronx Tale '93
This Boy's Life '93

Robert De Niro ▲
A Bronx Tale '93

Joe De Santis
And Now Miguel '66

Vittorio De Sica
Wonders of Aladdin '61

Tom De Simone ▲
Terror in the Jungle '68

Rosana De Soto
La Bamba '87
Stand and Deliver '88
Star Trek 6: The Undiscovered
    Country '91

Steven E. de Souza ▲
Street Fighter '94

Andre de Toth ▲
House of Wax '53

Brandon de Wilde
Shane '53
Those Calloways '65

Fay De Witt
Comic Book Kids '82

Richard Deacon
Billie '65
Blackbeard's Ghost '67
Carousel '56
The Gnome-Mobile '67
The One and Only, Genuine,
    Original Family Band '68

Lucy Deakins
The Boy Who Could Fly '86
Cheetah '89
The Great Outdoors '88
Little Nikita '88

James Dean
East of Eden '54
Giant '56
Rebel Without a Cause '55

Jeanne Dean
Clipped Wings '53

Jimmy Dean
Diamonds are Forever '71

Loren Dean
1492: Conquest of
    Paradise '92
How to Make an American
    Quilt '95
Mrs. Winterbourne '96
Say Anything '89

Rick Dean
Max is Missing '95

Ron Dean
Rudy '93

Gina DeAngelis
Radio Days '87

Rosemary DeAngelis
Two Bits '96

William Dear ▲
Angels in the Outfield '94
Harry and the Hendersons '87
If Looks Could Kill '91
Timerider '83

JoAnn Dearing
Suburban Commando '91

John DeBello ▲
Attack of the Killer
    Tomatoes '77

Rosemary DeCamp
The Jungle Book '42
The Story of Seabiscuit '49
13 Ghosts '60
Yankee Doodle Dandy '42

Tom DeCerchio ▲
Celtic Pride '96

Guy Decomble
The 400 Blows '59

Frances Dee
Gypsy Colt '54
Little Women '33

Ruby Dee
Buck and the Preacher '72
Cop and a Half '93
The Ernest Green Story '93

Sandra Dee
Gidget '59
Tammy and the Doctor '63

Rick Dees
La Bamba '87

Eddie Deezen
I Wanna Hold Your Hand '78
Midnight Madness '80

Don DeFore
A Rare Breed '81

Calvert Deforest
Leader of the Band '87

Ellen DeGeneres
Mr. Wrong '95

Philip DeGuere ▲
Dr. Strange '78

Wayne Dehart
A Perfect World '93

John Dehner
The Day of the Dolphin '73
The Left-Handed Gun '58
Mountain Man '77
Support Your Local
    Gunfighter '71

Gene Deitch ▲
Five Stories for the Very
    Young '86

David DeKeyser
Yentl '83

Albert Dekker
East of Eden '54

Fred Dekker ▲
The Monster Squad '87
Robocop 3 '91

Pilar Del Rey
And Now Miguel '66

Roy Del Ruth ▲
Topper Returns '41

Benicio Del Toro
Christopher Columbus: The
    Discovery '92
The Usual Suspects '95

Kim Delaney
Christmas Comes to Willow
    Creek '87
That Was Then. . .This Is
    Now '85

Dana Delany
Housesitter '92
Tombstone '93
A Winner Never Quits '86

Dorothy Dell
Little Miss Marker '34

Gabriel Dell
Blues Busters '50
Bowery Buckaroos '47
Escape Artist '82
Follow the Leader '44
Hard-Boiled Mahoney '47
Kid Dynamite '43
Little Tough Guys '38
Million Dollar Kid '44
'Neath Brooklyn Bridge '42
Smart Alecks '42
Spook Busters '46

Victorien Delmare
My Mother's Castle '91

Heather DeLoach
A Little Princess '95

Julie Delpy
Before Sunrise '94
The Three Musketeers '93

Claudio Deluca
Small Change '76

Frank Deluca
Small Change '76

Dom DeLuise
The Adventures of Sherlock
    Holmes' Smarter
    Brother '78
Cannonball Run '81
Cannonball Run 2 '84
The Cheap Detective '78
Going Bananas '88
Johnny Dangerously '84
Silent Movie '76
Smokey and the Bandit, Part
    2 '80
Spaceballs '87
The Tin Soldier '95
Twelve Chairs '70

Michael DeLuise
Encino Man '92

William Demarest
The Jolson Story '46
Rebecca of Sunnybrook
    Farm '38
Sorrowful Jones '49

Jack DeMave
The Man Without a Face '93

Tulio Demicheli ▲
Son of Captain Blood '62

Cecil B. DeMille ▲
The Greatest Show on
    Earth '52
The Ten Commandments '56

Jonathan Demme ▲
Citizens Band '77
Philadelphia '93
Swing Shift '84

Ted Demme ▲
Beautiful Girls '96

Rebecca DeMornay
Pecos Bill '86
The Three Musketeers '93
The Trip to Bountiful '85

Janet Dempsey
Regl'ar Fellers '41

Patrick Dempsey
Ava's Magical Adventure '94
Can't Buy Me Love '87
Coupe de Ville '90
Face the Music '92
For Better and For Worse '92
With Honors '94

Patrick Dempsey ▲
Ava's Magical Adventure '94

Richard Dempsey
The Chronicles of Narnia '89

Hugh Dempster
A Christmas Carol '51

Jacques Demy
The 400 Blows '59

Judi Dench
Goldeneye '95

Michael Denison
Shadowlands '93

Brian Dennehy
Annie Oakley '85
Butch and Sundance: The
    Early Days '79
Cocoon '85
Cocoon: The Return '88
F/X '86
F/X 2: The Deadly Art of
    Illusion '91
Foul Play '78
The Little Mermaid '84
Little Miss Marker '80
Never Cry Wolf '83
Return to Snowy River '88
The River Rat '84
Silverado '85
Tommy Boy '95

Barbara Dennek
Playtime '67

Dodo Denney
Willy Wonka & the Chocolate
    Factory '71

Richard Denning
Black Beauty '46
Unknown Island '48

Sandy Dennis
Up the Down Staircase '67

Reginald Denny
Abbott and Costello Meet Dr.
    Jekyll and Mr. Hyde '52
My Favorite Brunette '47
Rebecca '40

Pen Densham ▲
Moll Flanders '96
The Zoo Gang '85

Christa Denton
The Gate '87

Bob Denver
Back to the Beach '87
Wackiest Wagon Train in the
    West '77

John Denver
Oh, God! '77

Brian DePalma ▲
Home Movies '79
Mission: Impossible '96

Elisabeth Depardieu
Jean de Florette '87

Gerard Depardieu
Cyrano de Bergerac '90
1492: Conquest of
    Paradise '92
Green Card '90
Jean de Florette '87
My Father the Hero '93

Johnny Depp
Benny & Joon '93
Cry-Baby '90
Edward Scissorhands '90
What's Eating Gilbert
    Grape '93

Bo Derek
Tommy Boy '95

John Derek
The Ten Commandments '56

Joe DeRita
Three Stooges Meet
    Hercules '61

Bruce Dern
The 'Burbs '89
The Cowboys '72
Down Periscope '96
Smile '75
Support Your Local Sheriff '69
Toughlove '85

Laura Dern
Foxes '80
Jurassic Park '93
Mask '85
A Perfect World '93
Rambling Rose '91
Smooth Talk '85

Cleavant Derricks
Off Beat '86

Dominique Deruddere ▲
Wait Until Spring, Bandini '90

Michael Des Barres
Pink Cadillac '89
A Simple Twist of Fate '94

Stefan DeSalle
Russkies '87

Anne DeSalvo
My Favorite Year '82

Stanley DeSantis
The Truth About Cats and
    Dogs '96

Caleb Deschanel ▲
Crusoe '89
Escape Artist '82

Mary Jo Deschanel
The Right Stuff '83
2010 : The Year We Make
    Contact '84

Robert Desiderio
Gross Anatomy '89
Oh, God! You Devil '84

Paul Desmond
Legends of the Fall '94

William Desmond
Tailspin Tommy '34

Geory Desmouceaux
Small Change '76

Ivan Desny
Escapade in Florence '62

Tamara DeTreaux
Ghoulies '85

Howard Deutch ▲
Getting Even with Dad '94
The Great Outdoors '88
Grumpier Old Men '95
Pretty in Pink '86
Some Kind of Wonderful '87

William Devane
The Bad News Bears in
    Breaking Training '77
Chips the War Dog '90
Hadley's Rebellion '84

Andy Devine
The Adventures of Huckleberry
    Finn '60
Ali Baba and the Forty
    Thieves '43
How the West was Won '63
Smoke '70
Whale of a Tale '76
Zebra in the Kitchen '65

David Devine ▲
Beethoven Lives Upstairs '92

Loretta Devine
Waiting to Exhale '95

Danny DeVito
Batman Returns '92
Goin' South '78
Going Ape! '81

Jack the Bear '93
The Jewel of the Nile '85
Johnny Dangerously '84
Junior '94
Matilda '96
Renaissance Man '94
Romancing the Stone '84
Terms of Endearment '83
Throw Momma from the
    Train '87
Twins '88

Danny DeVito ▲
Matilda '96
Throw Momma from the
    Train '87

Francis Devlaeminck
Small Change '76

Laurent Devlaeminck
Small Change '76

Alan Devlin
The Playboys '92

J.G. Devlin
The Miracle '91

Jon DeVries
Sarah, Plain and Tall '91
Skylark '93

Colleen Dewhurst
And Baby Makes Six '79
Anne of Avonlea '87
Anne of Green Gables '85
Annie Hall '77
The Boy Who Could Fly '86
The Cowboys '72
Ice Castles '79
Lantern Hill '90

Billy DeWolfe
Billie '65

Susan Dey
Comeback Kid '80
Love Leads the Way '84

Cliff DeYoung
Annie Oakley '85
F/X '86
Flight of the Navigator '86
Secret Admirer '85

Alice Diabo
Strangers in Good
    Company '91

Despo Diamantidou
Love and Death '75

Selma Diamond
Bang the Drum Slowly '73
Twilight Zone: The Movie '83

Sully Diaz
Gryphon '88

Leonardo DiCaprio
The Basketball Diaries '94
This Boy's Life '93
What's Eating Gilbert
    Grape '93

George DiCenzo
Back to the Future '85
18 Again! '88
The New Adventures of Pippi
    Longstocking '88
Sing '89
Walk Like a Man '87

Bobby DiCicco
I Wanna Hold Your Hand '78
Splash '84

Andy Dick
The Cable Guy '96
In the Army Now '94

Angie Dickinson
Sabrina '95

John Diehl
Madhouse '90
Remote '93
Stargate '94

Marlene Dietrich
Judgment at Nuremberg '61
Stage Fright '50

Arthur Dignam
We of the Never Never '82

Thein Le Dihn
Operation Dumbo Drop '95

Matt Dill
The Boy Who Loved Trolls '84

Stephen Dillane
Two If by Sea '95

Ricky Dillard
Leap of Faith '92

Bradford Dillman
Escape from the Planet of the
    Apes '71
The Swarm '78
The Way We Were '73

Brendan Dillon Jr.
Lords of Magick '88

Kevin Dillon
Immediate Family '89
A Midnight Clear '92
The Rescue '88

Matt Dillon
Beautiful Girls '96
The Flamingo Kid '84
Liar's Moon '82
Little Darlings '80
Mr. Wonderful '93
My Bodyguard '80
The Outsiders '83
Over the Edge '79
Rumble Fish '83
Singles '92
Tex '82

Melinda Dillon
Bound for Glory '76
Captain America '89
A Christmas Story '83

Close Encounters of the Third
    Kind '77
Harry and the Hendersons '87
How to Make an American
    Quilt '95
Sioux City '94
To Wong Foo, Thanks for
    Everything, Julie
    Newmar '95

Oscar Dillon
Magic Island '95

Victor Dimattia
Dennis the Menace: Dinosaur
    Hunter '87

Richard Dimitri
Johnny Dangerously '84

Dennis Dimster
Olly Olly Oxen Free '78

Alan Dinehart
Baby, Take a Bow '34

Yi Ding
The Amazing Panda
    Adventure '95

Ernie Dingo
Clowning Around '92
Clowning Around 2 '93
Crocodile Dundee 2 '88
A Waltz Through the Hills '88

Michael Dinner ▲
Hot to Trot! '88
Off Beat '86

John Disanti
Man of the House '95

Bob Dishy
Brighton Beach Memoirs '86
My Boyfriend's Back '93

Divine
Hairspray '88

Andrew Divoff
Magic Island '95

Carter Dixon
Young Eagles '34

Donna Dixon
Spies Like Us '85
Wayne's World '92

Ivan Dixon
Car Wash '76

MacIntyre Dixon
Funny Farm '88

Pamela Dixon
Magic Kid '92

Lawrence Dobkin ▲
The Waltons: The Children's
    Carol '80

Anica Dobra
Tito and Me '92

Kevin Dobson
Orphan Train '79

Kevin J. Dobson ▲
Gold Diggers: The Secret of
    Bear Mountain '95

Peter Dobson
Sing '89

Robert Dogui
Almos' a Man '78

Matt Doherty
The Mighty Ducks '92
The Mighty Ducks 3 '96
So I Married an Axe
    Murderer '93

Shannen Doherty
Girls Just Want to Have
    Fun '85
Mallrats '95

Michael Dolan
Light of Day '87

Guy Doleman
Thunderball '65

Ami Dolenz
Stepmonster '92

Mickey Dolenz
Head '68
Monkees, Volume 1 '66

Jerzy Domaradzki ▲
Legend of the White
    Horse '85

Larry Domasin
Island of the Blue
    Dolphins '64

Arielle Dombasle
Little Indian, Big City '95

Arturo Dominici
Hercules '58

Solveig Dommartin
Wings of Desire '88

James Donadio
Gordy '95

Phil Donahue
Happy Birthday, Bugs: 50
    Looney Years '90

Troy Donahue
Cry-Baby '90

James Donald
The Bridge on the River
    Kwai '57
Third Man on the
    Mountain '59

Juli Donald
Brain Donors '92

Roger Donaldson ▲
The Bounty '84

Ted Donaldson
The Red Stallion '47
A Tree Grows in Brooklyn '45

Peter Donat
The Babe '92
The Bay Boy '85
School Ties '92
Tucker: The Man and His
    Dream '88

Richard Donat
My American Cousin '85

Robert Donat
The Ghost Goes West '36
The 39 Steps '35

Ludwig Donath
The Jolson Story '46

Vincent J. Donehue ▲
Peter Pan '60

Stanley Donen
Movie, Movie '78

Stanley Donen ▲
Charade '63
Funny Face '57
The Little Prince '74
Movie, Movie '78
On the Town '49
Seven Brides for Seven
    Brothers '54
Singin' in the Rain '52

Brian Donlevy
The Errand Boy '61
How to Stuff a Wild Bikini '65

Jeff Donnell
Gidget Goes to Rome '63

Donal Donnelly
Squanto: A Warrior's Tale '94

Clive Donner ▲
Babes in Toyland '86
Merlin and the Sword '85
Oliver Twist '82
The Scarlet Pimpernel '82
The Thief of Baghdad '78

Richard Donner ▲
The Goonies '85
Ladyhawke '85
Maverick '94
Radio Flyer '92
Scrooged '88
Superman 1: The Movie '78
The Toy '82

Robert Donner
Under the Rainbow '81

Vincent D'Onofrio
Adventures in Babysitting '87
Being Human '94
Imaginary Crimes '94
Mr. Wonderful '93
Stuart Saves His Family '94

602   VIDEOHOUND'S FAMILY VIDEO GUIDE

Mary Agnes Donoghue ▲
Paradise '91

Jack Donohue ▲
Babes in Toyland '61

Elisa Donovan
Clueless '95

King Donovan
Singin' in the Rain '52

Paul Donovan ▲
George's Island '91

Tate Donovan
Holy Matrimony '94
Not My Kid '85
SpaceCamp '86

Terence Donovan
The Man from Snowy
River '82

Alison Doody
Indiana Jones and the Last
Crusade '89
Major League 2 '94

James Doohan
Star Trek 2: The Wrath of
Khan '82
Star Trek 3: The Search for
Spock '84
Star Trek 4: The Voyage
Home '86
Star Trek 5: The Final
Frontier '89
Star Trek 6: The Undiscovered
Country '91
Star Trek Generations '94
Star Trek: The Motion
Picture '80
Storybook '95

Paul Dooley
Breaking Away '79
Hansel and Gretel '82
Kiss Me Goodbye '82
My Boyfriend's Back '93
Out There '95
Popeye '80
Rich Kids '79
Rumpelstiltskin '82
Sixteen Candles '84
Strange Brew '83

Robert DoQui
A Dream for Christmas '73
Robocop '87

Karin Dor
You Only Live Twice '67

Ann Doran
Mr. Wise Guy '42
Rebel Without a Cause '55

Johnny Doran
The Hideaways '73

Stephen Dorff
Backbeat '94

The Gate '87
The Power of One '92

Jacques Dorfman ▲
Shadow of the Wolf '92

Michael Dorn
Star Trek 6: The Undiscovered
Country '91
Star Trek Generations '94
Star Trek the Next Generation
Episode 1-2: Encounter at
Farpoint '87
Timemaster '95

Philip Dorn
Tarzan's Secret Treasure '41

Sarah Rowland Doroff
Three Fugitives '89

Diana Dors
Amazing Mr. Blunden '72
Oliver Twist '48

John Dossett
That Night '93

Julian Roy Doster
Menace II Society '93

Karen Dotrice
The Gnome-Mobile '67
The Three Lives of
Thomasina '63

Roy Dotrice
Amadeus '84
The Cutting Edge '92
The Dancing Princesses '84
The Scarlet Letter '95
Suburban Commando '91

Doug E. Doug
Class Act '91
Cool Runnings '93
Operation Dumbo Drop '95
That Darn Cat '96

Angela Douglas
Digby, the Biggest Dog in the
World '73

Brandon Douglas
Chips the War Dog '90
Journey to Spirit Island '92

Earl Douglas
Tim Tyler's Luck '37

Illeana Douglas
Alive '93

Kirk Douglas
Greedy '94
Home Movies '79
The Man from Snowy
River '82
Tough Guys '86
20,000 Leagues Under the
Sea '54
The Villain '79

Melvyn Douglas
Being There '79

Captains Courageous '37
I Never Sang For My
Father '70

Michael Douglas
The American President '95
The Jewel of the Nile '85
Napoleon and Samantha '72
Romancing the Stone '84

Sarah Douglas
Beastmaster 2: Through the
Portal of Time '91
Conan the Destroyer '84
The People That Time
Forgot '77
The Return of Swamp
Thing '89
Solarbabies '86
Superman 1: The Movie '78
Superman 2 '80

Shirley Douglas
Johnny's Girl '95

Lorenzo Doumani ▲
Storybook '95

Brad Dourif
Amos and Andrew '93

Tony Dow
Back to the Beach '87

Ann Dowd
Bushwhacked '95
It Could Happen to You '94
Philadelphia '93

Lesley-Anne Down
The Great Train Robbery '79
The Hunchback of Notre
Dame '82
The Pink Panther Strikes
Again '76

Brian Downey
George's Island '91

Robert Downey Jr.
Back to School '86
Chances Are '89
Chaplin '92
First Born '84
Heart and Souls '93
Home for the Holidays '95
Only You '94
Weird Science '85

Johnny Downs
March of the Wooden
Soldiers '34

Denise Dowse
Bio-Dome '96

David Doyle
Wait Till Your Mother Gets
Home '83

Maria Doyle
The Commitments '91

Tony Doyle
Adventures in Dinosaur
City '92

Brian Doyle-Murray
Cabin Boy '94
Caddyshack '80
Club Paradise '86
Groundhog Day '93
How I Got into College '89
Jury Duty '95
Modern Problems '81
National Lampoon's Christmas
Vacation '89
National Lampoon's
Vacation '83
Scrooged '88
Sixteen Candles '84
Wayne's World '92

Stan Dragoti ▲
Love at First Bite '79
The Man with One Red
Shoe '85
Mr. Mom '83
Necessary Roughness '91

Betsy Drake
Clarence, the Cross-eyed
Lion '65

Charles Drake
The Tender Years '47
Tobor the Great '54

Jim Drake ▲
Mr. Bill's Real-Life
Adventures '94
Police Academy 4: Citizens on
Patrol '87

Larry Drake
Darkman '90
The Journey of August
King '95

Tom Drake
Courage of Lassie '46
The Great Rupert '50
Meet Me in St. Louis '44

Polly Draper
Gold Diggers: The Secret of
Bear Mountain '95
Making Mr. Right '86

Tony Drazan ▲
Imaginary Crimes '94
Zebrahead '92

Arthur Dreifuss ▲
Regl'ar Fellers '41

Beau Dremann
My Science Project '85

Fran Drescher
Car 54, Where Are You? '94
Jack '96

Richard Dreyfuss
Always '89
American Graffiti '73
The American President '95

Another Stakeout '93
The Apprenticeship of Duddy
   Kravitz '74
Close Encounters of the Third
   Kind '77
The Goodbye Girl '77
Lost in Yonkers '93
Mr. Holland's Opus '95
Stand By Me '86
What About Bob? '91

Moosie Drier
Charlie and the Great Balloon
   Chase '82
Homeward Bound '80

Brian Drillinger
Brighton Beach Memoirs '86

Bobby Driscoll
So Dear to My Heart '49
Treasure Island '50
The Window '49

Minnie Driver
Circle of Friends '94

Joanne Dru
The Light in the Forest '58
Super Fuzz '81

James Drury
Ten Who Dared '60

Fred Dryer
The Fantastic World of D.C.
   Collins '84

Jeanie Drynan
Muriel's Wedding '94

Charles S. Dubin ▲
Cinderella '64

Ja'net DuBois
Magic Island '95
Piece of the Action '77

Marta DuBois
The Trial of the Incredible
   Hulk '89

David Duchovny
Beethoven '92
Chaplin '92

Rick Ducommun
Blank Check '93
The 'Burbs '89
Class Act '91
Die Hard '88
Encino Man '92
Little Monsters '89

John Joseph Duda
Prancer '89

Michael Dudikoff
I Ought to Be in Pictures '82

Lesley Dudley
John & Julie '57

Howard Duff
Kramer vs. Kramer '79

Oh, God! Book 2 '80

Peter Duffell ▲
Experience Preferred. . . But
   Not Essential '83

Nicola Duffett
Howard's End '92

Ciara Duffy
The Snapper '93

Karen Duffy
Blank Check '93
Dumb & Dumber '94

Thomas F. Duffy
Wagons East '94

Dennis Dugan
Can't Buy Me Love '87
Happy Gilmore '96
The Howling '81
The New Adventures of Pippi
   Longstocking '88
Parenthood '89
She's Having a Baby '88
Unidentified Flying
   Oddball '79

Dennis Dugan ▲
Brain Donors '92
Happy Gilmore '96
Problem Child '90

Michael Dugan ▲
Super Seal '77

Andrew Duggan
The Bears & I '74
The Incredible Mr. Limpet '64

John Duigan ▲
Flirting '89
The Journey of August
   King '95
The Year My Voice Broke '87

Olympia Dukakis
Dad '89
Digger '94
Look Who's Talking '89
Look Who's Talking Now '93
Look Who's Talking, Too '90
Mr. Holland's Opus '95
Moonstruck '87
Rich Kids '79
Steel Magnolias '89

Bill Duke
Menace II Society '93

Bill Duke ▲
Sister Act 2: Back in the
   Habit '93

Patty Duke
Billie '65
The Miracle Worker '62
The Miracle Worker '79
Prelude to a Kiss '92
The Swarm '78

Robin Duke
Club Paradise '86

David Dukes
Date with an Angel '87
See You in the Morning '89

Keir Dullea
David and Lisa '62
Oh, What a Night '92
2001: A Space Odyssey '68
2010 : The Year We Make
   Contact '84

Douglass Dumbrille
A Day at the Races '37
Lost in a Harem '44
Spook Busters '46
The Ten Commandments '56
Treasure Island '34

Margaret Dumont
Animal Crackers '30
At the Circus '39
The Big Store '41
The Cocoanuts '29
A Day at the Races '37
Duck Soup '33
The Horn Blows at
   Midnight '45
A Night at the Opera '35

Dennis Dun
Big Trouble in Little China '86

Faye Dunaway
Dunston Checks In '95
The Four Musketeers '75
Little Big Man '70
Mommie Dearest '81
Oklahoma Crude '73
Supergirl '84
Three Musketeers '74
Wait Until Spring, Bandini '90

Adrian Dunbar
The Playboys '92

Andrew Duncan
Morgan Stewart's Coming
   Home '87

Archie Duncan
Ring of Bright Water '69

Kenne Duncan
The Crimson Ghost '46

Peter Duncan
The Old Curiosity Shop '75

Rachel Duncan
The Crazysitter '94

Sandy Duncan
The Cat from Outer Space '78
Million Dollar Duck '71

Jennie Dundas
The Beniker Gang '83

Duwayne Dunham ▲
Homeward Bound: The
   Incredible Journey '93
Little Giants '94

Robert Dunham
Godzilla vs. Megalon '76

George Duning ▲
Yellow Submarine '68

Clara Dunn
Running Mates '86

James Dunn
Baby, Take a Bow '34
Bright Eyes '34
Stand Up and Cheer '34
A Tree Grows in Brooklyn '45

Kevin Dunn
Chaplin '92
Dave '93
Little Big League '94
Only the Lonely '91

Michael Dunn
Teen Alien '88

Nora Dunn
Born Yesterday '93
How I Got into College '89

Dominique Dunne
Poltergeist '82
The Shadow Riders '82

Griffin Dunne
Big Girls Don't Cry. . .They
   Get Even '92
Johnny Dangerously '84
My Girl '91
The Other Side of the
   Mountain '75
Quiz Show '94
Straight Talk '92

Irene Dunne
I Remember Mama '48
Life with Father '47
Penny Serenade '41

Mildred Dunnock
And Baby Makes Six '79
The Corn is Green '45

Rosemary Dunsmore
Anne of Avonlea '87

Kirsten Dunst
Jumanji '95
Little Women '94

June Duprez
Thief of Baghdad '40

Christopher Durang
The Butcher's Wife '91
Housesitter '92

Jimmy Durante
The Great Rupert '50
Little Miss Broadway '38
Palooka '34

John Durbin
King of the Hill '93

Leon "Bull" Durham
Little Big League '94

Charles Durning
Brenda Starr '86

Dick Tracy '90
Die Laughing '80
The Front Page '74
Hadley's Rebellion '84
Harry & Walter Go to New York '76
Home for the Holidays '95
The Legend of Sleepy Hollow '86
The Man with One Red Shoe '85
Solarbabies '86
Spy Hard '96
The Sting '73
The Story Lady '93
Tootsie '82
Tough Guys '86
Where the River Runs Black '86

Dick Durock
The Return of Swamp Thing '89

N. Jeremi Duru
Crooklyn '94

Vittorio Duse
Queen of Hearts '89

Eliza Dushku
Race the Sun '96
That Night '93
This Boy's Life '93
True Lies '94

Andre Dussollier
Three Men and a Cradle '85

Jose Dutillieu ▲
Smurfs & the Magic Flute '81

Todd Dutson
Force on Thunder Mountain '77

Charles S. Dutton
Cat's Eye '85
Crocodile Dundee 2 '88
Cry, the Beloved Country '95
Menace II Society '93
Rudy '93
Runaway '89

Robert Duvall
A Family Thing '96
Geronimo: An American Legend '93
The Great Santini '80
The Greatest '77
M*A*S*H '70
The Natural '84
Newsies '92
The Paper '94
Phenomenon '96
Rambling Rose '91
The Scarlet Letter '95
Something to Talk About '95
The Stone Boy '84
Tender Mercies '83
To Kill a Mockingbird '62
True Grit '69

Robert Duvall ▲
Angelo My Love '83

Shelley Duvall
Annie Hall '77
Frankenweenie '84
Frog '89
Frogs! '90s
Popeye '80
Rapunzel '82
Roxanne '87
Rumpelstiltskin '82
Suburban Commando '91
Time Bandits '81

Allan Dwan ▲
Heidi '37
Rebecca of Sunnybrook Farm '38

Hilary Dwyer
Wuthering Heights '70

Cameron Dye
The Last Starfighter '84

Richard Dysart
Back to the Future, Part 3 '90
Being There '79
Mask '85

Tommy Dysart
The Man from Snowy River '82

George Dzundza
The Butcher's Wife '91
Crimson Tide '95
Dangerous Minds '95

Nicholas Eadie
Return to Snowy River '88

Barbara Jean Earhardt
Danny '79

B. Reeves Eason ▲
Fighting Marines '36
The Last of the Mohicans '32
Law of the Wild '34
The Phantom Empire '35
Undersea Kingdom '36

Walter B. Eason ▲
Sea Hound '47

Jeff East
Flight of the Grey Wolf '76
Huckleberry Finn '74
Tom Sawyer '73

Leslie Easterbrook
Police Academy '84
Police Academy 3: Back in Training '86
Police Academy 5: Assignment Miami Beach '88
Police Academy 6: City Under Siege '89
Police Academy: Mission to Moscow '94

Allan Eastman ▲
Crazy Moon '87

George Eastman
Call of the Wild '72

Clint Eastwood
Any Which Way You Can '80
Bronco Billy '80
Honkytonk Man '82
The Outlaw Josey Wales '76
Paint Your Wagon '69
A Perfect World '93
Pink Cadillac '89

Clint Eastwood ▲
Bronco Billy '80
Honkytonk Man '82
The Outlaw Josey Wales '76
A Perfect World '93

Kyle Eastwood
Honkytonk Man '82

Mary Eaton
The Cocoanuts '29

Thom Eberhardt ▲
Captain Ron '92
Gross Anatomy '89
The Night Before '88
Night of the Comet '84

Christine Ebersole
Amadeus '84
Black Sheep '96
Ghost Dad '90
Mac and Me '88
My Girl 2 '94
Richie Rich '94
Tootsie '82

Buddy Ebsen
The Adventures of Tom Sawyer '73
Captain January '36
Davy Crockett and the River Pirates '56
Davy Crockett, King of the Wild Frontier '55
The One and Only, Genuine, Original Family Band '68
Stone Fox '87

Aimee Eccles
Little Big Man '70

Teddy Eccles
My Side of the Mountain '69

James Eckhouse
Junior '94

Lauren Eckstrom
Two Bits & Pepper '95

Gregg Edelman
Green Card '90

Herb Edelman
The Charge of the Model T's '76
Cracking Up '83
Goin' Coconuts '78
On the Right Track '81
The Way We Were '73

Barbara Eden
The Amazing Dobermans '76
Harper Valley P.T.A. '78
Seven Faces of Dr. Lao '63
Voyage to the Bottom of the Sea '61
The Wonderful World of the Brothers Grimm '62

Elizabeth Edmonds
Experience Preferred. . . But Not Essential '83

Beatie Edney
Highlander '86

Richard Edson
Eight Men Out '88
Super Mario Bros. '93

Allan Edwall
Brothers Lionheart '85

Anthony Edwards
Charlie's Ghost: The Secret of Coronado '94
The Client '94
Fast Times at Ridgemont High '82
Gotcha! '85
Heart Like a Wheel '83
How I Got into College '89
Revenge of the Nerds '84
The Sure Thing '85
Top Gun '86

Barbara Edwards
House Party 3 '94

Blake Edwards ▲
Curse of the Pink Panther '83
A Fine Mess '86
Great Race '65
The Party '68
The Pink Panther '64
The Pink Panther Strikes Again '76
Return of the Pink Panther '74
Revenge of the Pink Panther '78
A Shot in the Dark '64
Son of the Pink Panther '93
Trail of the Pink Panther '82

Bruce Edwards
The Black Widow '47
Federal Agents vs. Underworld, Inc. '49

Cliff Edwards
Gone with the Wind '39
His Girl Friday '40

David Edwards
House Party 3 '94

Eric Edwards
Sgt. Bilko '95

Gene Edwards
Grizzly Adams: The Legend Continues '90

Hugh Edwards
Lord of the Flies '63

Jennifer Edwards
Heidi '67

Luke Edwards
Little Big League '94
Newsies '92
The Wizard '89

Ronnie Clair Edwards
A Day for Thanks on Walton's
Mountain '82
8 Seconds '94

Sebastian Rice Edwards
Hope and Glory '87

Stephanie Edwards
Big Mo '73

Vince Edwards
Andy and the Airwave
Rangers '89
Space Raiders '83

Christine Edzard ▲
Little Dorrit, Film 1: Nobody's
Fault '88
Little Dorrit, Film 2: Little
Dorrit's Story '88

Aeryk Egan
Book of Love '91

Richard Egan
Pollyanna '60

Julie Ege
On Her Majesty's Secret
Service '69

Samantha Eggar
Dark Horse '92
Doctor Doolittle '67
The Phantom '96
Why Shoot the Teacher? '79

Nicole Eggert
The Double O Kid '92

Jennifer Ehle
Backbeat '94

Jerome Ehlers
Quigley Down Under '90

Lisa Eichhorn
King of the Hill '93

Christopher Eigeman
Metropolitan '90

Jill Eikenberry
Arthur '81
Butch and Sundance: The
Early Days '79
The Manhattan Project '86
Orphan Train '79
Rich Kids '79

Lisa Eilbacher
Beverly Hills Cop '84
On the Right Track '81

Run for the Roses '78

Avner Eisenberg
The Jewel of the Nile '85

Elizabeth Eisenman
Summerdog '78

Ike Eisenmann
Escape to Witch Mountain '75
Return from Witch
Mountain '78

Anita Ekberg
Hollywood or Bust '56

Britt Ekland
The Man with the Golden
Gun '74

Robyn Elaine
The Karate Kid: Part 3 '89

Jack Elam
The Apple Dumpling Gang
Rides Again '79
The Aurora Encounter '85
Bonanza: The Return '93
Cannonball Run '81
Cannonball Run 2 '84
Huckleberry Finn '75
Never a Dull Moment '68
Once Upon a Time in the
West '68
Pony Express Rider '76
Suburban Commando '91
Support Your Local
Gunfighter '71
Support Your Local Sheriff '69
The Villain '79

Peter Elbling
Honey, I Blew Up the Kid '92

Dana Elcar
Blue Skies Again '83
Condorman '81
The Learning Tree '69
Toughlove '85

Ron Eldard
Drop Dead Fred '91

Gabi Eldor
Boy Takes Girl '83

Erika Eleniak
The Beverly Hillbillies '93

Michael Elgart
Permanent Record '88

Alix Elias
Citizens Band '77
Rock 'n' Roll High School '79

Larry Elikann ▲
Charlie and the Great Balloon
Chase '82
The Story Lady '93

Mark Eliot
Stand and Deliver '88

Evangelina Elizondo
A Walk in the Clouds '95

Hector Elizondo
Being Human '94
Beverly Hills Cop 3 '94
The Flamingo Kid '84
Getting Even with Dad '94
Necessary Roughness '91
Nothing in Common '86
Samantha '92

Karen Elkin
The Great Land of Small '86

Liston Elkins
The Tender Warrior '71

Yvonne Elliman
Jesus Christ, Superstar '73

Bob Elliott
Cabin Boy '94

Chris Elliott
Cabin Boy '94
Groundhog Day '93

Denholm Elliott
The Apprenticeship of Duddy
Kravitz '74
Indiana Jones and the Last
Crusade '89
Raiders of the Lost Ark '81

Edythe Elliott
The Great Mike '44

Lang Elliott ▲
The Private Eyes '80

Sam Elliott
Butch Cassidy and the
Sundance Kid '69
Gettysburg '93
Hole in the Sky '95
Mask '85
Prancer '89
The Shadow Riders '82
Tombstone '93

Stephen Elliott
Arthur '81
Arthur 2: On the Rocks '88
Beauty and the Beast '83
Beverly Hills Cop '84

Paul Elliotts ▲
Great Adventure '75

David R. Ellis ▲
Homeward Bound 2: Lost in
San Francisco '96

Desmond Walter Ellis
Great St. Trinian's Train
Robbery '66

Edward Ellis
I Am a Fugitive from a Chain
Gang '32
The Thin Man '34

James Ellis
Leapin' Leprechauns '95

Mary Ellis
The Three Worlds of
Gulliver '59

Tracey Ellis
The Neverending Story 3 '94
This Boy's Life '93

Gwen Ellison
Luggage of the Gods '87

Michael Elphick
Little Dorrit, Film 1: Nobody's
Fault '88
Little Dorrit, Film 2: Little
Dorrit's Story '88

Kevin Elster
Little Big League '94

Ben Elton
Much Ado About Nothing '93

Cary Elwes
The Crush '93
Glory '89
Lady Jane '85
The Princess Bride '87
Robin Hood: Men in
Tights '93
Rudyard Kipling's The Jungle
Book '94
Twister '96

Roger Elwin
Lord of the Flies '63

Ron Ely
Doc Savage '75

Ethan Embry
White Squall '96

Doug Emerson
The River Pirates '94

Hope Emerson
Adam's Rib '50

Dick Emery ▲
Yellow Submarine '68

Ian Emes ▲
Knights & Emeralds '87

Michael Emil
Adventures in Spying '92

Noah Emmerich
Beautiful Girls '96

Roland Emmerich ▲
Independence Day '96
Making Contact '86
Stargate '94

Cy Endfield ▲
Mysterious Island '61

Jim Engelhardt
Comic Book Kids '82

Randall England
Dream Machine '91

 606

Alex English
Amazing Grace & Chuck '87

John English ▲
Captain America '44
Daredevils of the Red
Circle '38
Dick Tracy '37
Fighting Devil Dogs '38
Zorro Rides Again '37
Zorro's Fighting Legion '39

Zach English
The Real McCoy '93

George Englund ▲
A Christmas to Remember '78

Michael Ensign
Born Yesterday '93
House '86

Nora Ephron ▲
Mixed Nuts '94
Sleepless in Seattle '93
This is My Life '92

Brenda Epperson
Storybook '95

Omar Epps
Major League 2 '94
The Program '93

Kathryn Erbe
D2: The Mighty Ducks '94
Rich in Love '93
What About Bob? '91

Richard Erdman ▲
Brothers O'Toole '73

Leif Erickson
Abbott and Costello Meet
Captain Kidd '52
Invaders from Mars '53
Rocky 3 '82

Tami Erin
The New Adventures of Pippi
Longstocking '88

John Erman ▲
Child of Glass '78
My Old Man '79

R. Lee Ermey
Fletch Lives '89
Sommersby '93

Duke Ernsberger
Ernest Rides Again '93

Benjamin Eroen
Sherlock: Undercover Dog '94

Chester Erskine ▲
Androcles and the Lion '52

Julius Erving
The Fish that Saved
Pittsburgh '79

Bill Erwin
Huckleberry Finn '75

Stuart Erwin
The Great Mike '44
The Misadventures of Merlin
Jones '63
Palooka '34

Jill Esmond
Journey for Margaret '42

Giancarlo Esposito
Amos and Andrew '93
Malcolm X '92
The Usual Suspects '95

Will Estes
The Road Home '95

Emilio Estevez
Another Stakeout '93
The Breakfast Club '85
D2: The Mighty Ducks '94
The Mighty Ducks '92
The Mighty Ducks 3 '96
Mission: Impossible '96
National Lampoon's Loaded
Weapon 1 '93
The Outsiders '83
Tex '82
That Was Then. . .This Is
Now '85
Young Guns '88

Erik Estrada
Andy and the Airwave
Rangers '89

Pat Estrin
Dennis the Menace: Dinosaur
Hunter '87

Christopher Ettridge
The Old Curiosity Shop '94

Bob Eubanks
Johnny Dangerously '84

**Corey Michael
Eubanks** ▲
Bigfoot: The Unforgettable
Encounter '94
Two Bits & Pepper '95

Wesley Eure
C.H.O.M.P.S. '79

Angelo Evans
Angelo My Love '83

Art Evans
Die Hard 2: Die Harder '90

Bruce A. Evans ▲
Kuffs '92

David Mickey Evans ▲
The Sandlot '93

Douglas Evans
The Green Hornet '39

Edith Evans
David Copperfield '70
Scrooge '70

Estelle Evans
The Learning Tree '69

Gene Evans
The Shadow Riders '82
Walking Tall '73

Linda Evans
Beach Blanket Bingo '65
Those Calloways '65

Madge Evans
David Copperfield '35
Stand Up and Cheer '34

Maurice Evans
Androcles and the Lion '52
Beneath the Planet of the
Apes '70
Planet of the Apes '68

Michael Evans
Angelo My Love '83

Troy Evans
Father and Scout '95
Kuffs '92
My Summer Story '94

Judith Evelyn
Rear Window '54

Barbara Everest
Jane Eyre '44
Tony Draws a Horse '51

Chad Everett
Airplane 2: The Sequel '82
The Rousters '83

D.S. Everett ▲
Running Brave '83

Rupert Everett
Dunston Checks In '95

Nancy Everhard
The Trial of the Incredible
Hulk '89

John Ewart
The Prince and the Great
Race '83
The Quest '86

Tom Ewell
Adam's Rib '50
State Fair '62

Blake Ewing
The Little Rascals '94

Richard Eyer
The Invisible Boy '57
The Seventh Voyage of
Sinbad '58

Peter Eyre
Diamond's Edge '88
Princess Caraboo '94

Maynard Eziashi
Ace Ventura: When Nature
Calls '95
Bopha! '93

Shelley Fabares
Brian's Song '71

Fabian
Dear Brigitte '65

Ava Fabian
Welcome Home, Roxy
Carmichael '90

Francoise Fabian
Reunion '88

Nanette Fabray
Amy '81
The Band Wagon '53
Harper Valley P.T.A. '78
The Man in the Santa Claus
Suit '79

Jeff Fahey
Silverado '85

Peter Faiman ▲
Crocodile Dundee '86
Dutch '91

Douglas Fairbanks Jr.
Sinbad the Sailor '47

Morgan Fairchild
Pee Wee's Big Adventure '85
Sleeping Beauty '89
Spiderman '81

William Fairchild ▲
Horsemasters '61

Ferdinand Fairfax ▲
Nate and Hayes '83
The Rescue '88

Heather Fairfield
A Girl of the Limberlost '90

Donald A. Faison
Clueless '95
Waiting to Exhale '95

Frankie Faison
Sommersby '93

Peter Falk
The Cheap Detective '78
Great Race '65
The Princess Bride '87
Wings of Desire '88

Deborah Fallender
Jabberwocky '77

Bo Fanders
Salem's Lot '79

Lou Fant
Amy '81

Stephanie Faracy
The Great Outdoors '88
Hocus Pocus '93

Debrah Farentino
Son of the Pink Panther '93

James Farentino
Her Alibi '88

A Summer to Remember '84

Antonio Fargas
Car Wash '76
Huckleberry Finn '75

Carolyn Farina
Metropolitan '90

Dennis Farina
Another Stakeout '93
Eddie '96
Little Big League '94

Ernest Farino ▲
Josh Kirby . . . Time Warrior:
Chapter 1, Planet of the
Dino-Knights '95

Chris Farley
Airheads '94
Black Sheep '96
Coneheads '93
Tommy Boy '95
Wayne's World 2 '93

Bill Farmer
The Manners Monster: Ruby
Goes to Dinner '95

Gary Farmer
Sioux City '94

Mimsy Farmer
Spencer's Mountain '63

Richard Farnsworth
Anne of Green Gables '85
The Grey Fox '83
Lassie '94
Legend of the Lone
Ranger '81
The Natural '84
Rhinestone '84
The River Pirates '94
Sylvester '85

William Farnum
A Connecticut Yankee '31

Felicia Farr
Kotch '71

Jamie Farr
Cannonball Run '81
Cannonball Run 2 '84
No Time for Sergeants '58
Scrooged '88
With Six You Get Eggroll '68

Judi Farr
The Year My Voice Broke '87

Patricia Farr
Tailspin Tommy '34

Charles Farrell
Just Around the Corner '38

Glenda Farrell
The Disorderly Orderly '64
I Am a Fugitive from a Chain
Gang '32

Nicholas Farrell
Othello '95

Sharon Farrell
Night of the Comet '84
The Reivers '69

Terry Farrell
Back to School '86

Bobby Farrelly ▲
Kingpin '96

Peter Farrelly ▲
Dumb & Dumber '94
Kingpin '96

Mia Farrow
Avalanche '78
Broadway Danny Rose '84
Death on the Nile '78
The Purple Rose of Cairo '85
Radio Days '87
Supergirl '84

Lena Farugia
The Gods Must Be Crazy
2 '89

The Fat Boys
Disorderlies '87

Jon Favreau
P.C.U. '94
Rudy '93

Alan Fawcett
Conspiracy of Love '87

Farrah Fawcett
Cannonball Run '81
Man of the House '95
See You in the Morning '89

Alice Faye
Magic of Lassie '78
The Poor Little Rich Girl '36
State Fair '62
Stowaway '36

Frank Faylen
Francis the Talking Mule '49
It's a Wonderful Life '46

Linda Feferman ▲
Seven Minutes in Heaven '86

Wang Fei
The Amazing Panda
Adventure '95

Doren Fein
Ed '96

Alan Feinstein
Joe Panther '76

Raphael Fejto
Au Revoir Les Enfants '87

Fritz Feld
At the Circus '39
Bringing Up Baby '38
The Errand Boy '61
Herbie Goes Bananas '80

Corey Feldman
The 'Burbs '89
Dream a Little Dream '89
Dream a Little Dream 2 '94
The Goonies '85
Gremlins '84
License to Drive '88
The Lost Boys '87
Rock 'n' Roll High School
Forever '91
Stand By Me '86
Stepmonster '92

Gene Feldman ▲
Danny '79

Marty Feldman
The Adventures of Sherlock
Holmes' Smarter
Brother '78
Silent Movie '76
Young Frankenstein '74

Barbara Feldon
No Deposit, No Return '76
Smile '75

Tovah Feldshuh
Brewster's Millions '85
A Day in October '92

Norman Fell
The Boatniks '70
On the Right Track '81

Julian Fellowes
Baby. . .Secret of the Lost
Legend '85

Tanya Fenmore
Lisa '90
My Stepmother Is an
Alien '88

Sherilyn Fenn
Fatal Instinct '93
Just One of the Guys '85
Of Mice and Men '92

Simon Fenton
Matinee '92

Andrew Ferguson
Miracle Down Under '87

J. Don Ferguson
Running Mates '86

Jane Ferguson
Mystery Mansion '83

Juan Fernandez
Crocodile Dundee 2 '88

Didier Ferney
Toto le Heros '91

Conchata Ferrell
Edward Scissorhands '90
Eye on the Sparrow '91
Family Prayers '91
Goodbye, Miss 4th of July '88
Heartland '81
Lost Legacy: A Girl Called
Hatter Fox '77

Where the River Runs
Black '86
Who'll Save Our Children?
'82

Tyra Ferrell
Boyz N the Hood '91
Poetic Justice '93

Jose Ferrer
The Big Bus '76
The Fifth Musketeer '79
Lawrence of Arabia '62
Paco '75
The Swarm '78
Who Has Seen the Wind? '77

Jose Ferrer ▲
State Fair '62

Leilani Sarelle Ferrer
Shag: The Movie '89

Mel Ferrer
Knights of the Round
Table '53
Lili '53

Miguel Ferrer
Another Stakeout '93
Blank Check '93
Hot Shots! Part Deux '93
Robocop '87
Star Trek 3: The Search for
Spock '84

Noel Ferrer
Deathcheaters '76

Martin Ferrero
Jurassic Park '93
Planes, Trains &
Automobiles '87
Stop! or My Mom Will
Shoot '92

Lou Ferrigno
Death of the Incredible
Hulk '90
Hercules '83
The Incredible Hulk '77
The Incredible Hulk
Returns '88
The Trial of the Incredible
Hulk '89

Pam Ferris
Matilda '96

Dan Ferro
Sgt. Bilko '95

Gabriele Ferzetti
On Her Majesty's Secret
Service '69
Othello '95

Stepin Fetchit
Stand Up and Cheer '34

Miles Feulner
Little Big League '94

John Fiedler
Harper Valley P.T.A. '78

Chelsea Field
Andre '94
Flipper '96

Sally Field
Forrest Gump '94
Kiss Me Goodbye '82
Mrs. Doubtfire '93
Murphy's Romance '85
Norma Rae '79
Places in the Heart '84
Smokey and the Bandit '77
Smokey and the Bandit, Part 2 '80
Steel Magnolias '89

Shirley Anne Field
Shag: The Movie '89

Todd Field
Gross Anatomy '89

Virginia Field
A Connecticut Yankee in King Arthur's Court '49

Charlie Fields
The Beniker Gang '83
Fish Hawk '79

Chip Fields
Spiderman: The Deadly Dust '78

W.C. Fields
David Copperfield '35

Robert Fieldsteel
Beastmaster 2: Through the Portal of Time '91

Ralph Fiennes
Quiz Show '94

Harvey Fierstein
Dr. Jekyll and Ms. Hyde '95
Independence Day '96
Mrs. Doubtfire '93

John Fife
Chasing Dreams '81

Frantisek Filipovsky
On the Comet '68

Dennis Fimple
My Heroes Have Always Been Cowboys '91

Jon Finch
Death on the Nile '78

Peter Finch
First Men in the Moon '64
Kidnapped '60

Larry Fine
Snow White and the Three Stooges '61
Three Stooges '30s
Three Stooges: A Ducking They Will Go '30s
Three Stooges: A Plumbing We Will Go '34

Three Stooges: Cash and Carry '40s
Three Stooges: If a Body Meets a Body '34
Three Stooges: In the Sweet Pie and Pie '40s
Three Stooges Meet Hercules '61
Three Stooges: So Long Mr. Chumps '40s
Three Stooges: What's the Matador? '40s

Ken Finkleman
Airplane 2: The Sequel '82

Ken Finkleman ▲
Airplane 2: The Sequel '82

Frank Finlay
The Four Musketeers '75
The Loneliness of the Long Distance Runner '62
The Return of the Musketeers '89
The Thief of Baghdad '78
Three Musketeers '74

Stewart Finlay-McLennan
Christy '94

James Finlayson
The Flying Deuces '39

John Finn
Glory '89

Robyn Finn
Comic Book Kids '82

Dave Finnegan
The Commitments '91

Albert Finney
Annie '82
The Playboys '92
Rich in Love '93
Scrooge '70

Edward Finney ▲
Silver Stallion '41

Allen Finzat
For the Love of Benji '77

Linda Fiorentino
Charlie's Ghost: The Secret of Coronado '94
Gotcha! '85
Shout '91

Roy Firestone
The Scout '94

Colin Firth
Circle of Friends '94
The Secret Garden '87

Peter Firth
The Hunt for Red October '90
Shadowlands '93
Tess '80

Michael Fischa ▲
My Mom's a Werewolf '89

Nancy Fish
Death Becomes Her '92

Laurence "Larry" Fishburne
Boyz N the Hood '91
Othello '95
Searching for Bobby Fischer '93
What's Love Got to Do With It? '93

Carrie Fisher
The 'Burbs '89
Drop Dead Fred '91
The Empire Strikes Back '80
The Man with One Red Shoe '85
Return of the Jedi '83
Star Wars '77
This is My Life '92
Thumbelina '82
Under the Rainbow '81

Cindy Fisher
Liar's Moon '82

David Fisher ▲
Liar's Moon '82

Frances Fisher
Sudie & Simpson '90

Jasen Fisher
The Witches '90

Shug Fisher
Huckleberry Finn '75

Tricia Leigh Fisher
Book of Love '91

Bill Fishman ▲
Car 54, Where Are You? '94

Scuyler Fisk
The Baby-Sitters Club '95

Robert Fiske
Green Archer '40

Louise Fitch
Starbird and Sweet William '73

Peter Fitz
Au Revoir Les Enfants '87

Barry Fitzgerald
Bringing Up Baby '38
Going My Way '44
How Green was My Valley '41
The Quiet Man '52
The Story of Seabiscuit '49
Tarzan's Secret Treasure '41

Ciaran Fitzgerald
The Canterville Ghost '96
Into the West '92

Geraldine Fitzgerald
Arthur '81

Arthur 2: On the Rocks '88
The Last American Hero '73
Poltergeist 2: The Other Side '86

Gregg Fitzgerald
War of the Buttons '95

Sean Fitzgerald
Storybook '95

Walter Fitzgerald
Treasure Island '50

Colleen Fitzpatrick
Hairspray '88

Paul Fix
The Bad Seed '56
To Kill a Mockingbird '62

Jack Fjeldstad
The Polar Bear King '94

Darron Flagg
Bagdad Cafe '88

Fannie Flagg
My Best Friend Is a Vampire '88

Joe Flaherty
Back to the Future, Part 2 '89
Happy Gilmore '96
Looking for Miracles '90
One Crazy Summer '86
Sesame Street Presents: Follow That Bird '85

Lanny Flaherty
Sommersby '93
Tom and Huck '95

Paul Flaherty ▲
Clifford '92
18 Again! '88

Robert Flaherty ▲
Elephant Boy '37

Georges Flament
The 400 Blows '59

Fionnula Flanagan
The Ewok Adventure '84
Voyager from the Unknown '83
A Winner Never Quits '86

Ed Flanders
Bye Bye, Love '94

Sean Patrick Flanery
Powder '95

Susan Flannery
Gumball Rally '76

James Flavin
King Kong '33

Flea
Back to the Future, Part 2 '89

James Fleet
Four Weddings and a
　Funeral '93
Sense and Sensibility '95

Charles Fleischer
Back to the Future, Part 2 '89
Straight Talk '92

Dave Fleischer ▲
Betty Boop Special Collector's
　Edition: Volume 1 '35
Gulliver's Travels '39
Hoppity Goes to Town '41

Max Fleischer ▲
Betty Boop Special Collector's
　Edition: Volume 1 '35

Richard Fleischer ▲
Conan the Destroyer '84
Doctor Doolittle '67
The Prince and the
　Pauper '78
20,000 Leagues Under the
　Sea '54

Noah Fleiss
Josh and S.A.M. '93

Andrew Fleming ▲
Threesome '94

Rhonda Fleming
A Connecticut Yankee in King
　Arthur's Court '49
Since You Went Away '44
Spellbound '45

Victor Fleming ▲
Captains Courageous '37
Gone with the Wind '39
Treasure Island '34
The Wizard of Oz '39

Gordon Flemyng ▲
Doctor Who and the
　Daleks '65

Dexter Fletcher
Lionheart '87

Louise Fletcher
The Boy Who Could Fly '86
The Cheap Detective '78
High School High '96
Invaders from Mars '86
Islands '87
Strange Invaders '83
A Summer to Remember '84

Sam Flint
Spy Smasher '42

Jay C. Flippen
Oklahoma! '55

Lucy Lee Flippin
Summer School '87

James T. Flocker ▲
The Secret of Navajo Cave '76

Calista Flockhart
The Birdcage '95

John Florea ▲
Computer Wizard '77

Dann Florek
The Flintstones '94

Marsha Florence
Zebrahead '92

Robert Florey ▲
The Cocoanuts '29

George Flower
Across the Great Divide '76
Further Adventures of the
　Wilderness Family, Part
　2 '77
In Search of a Golden Sky '84
Mountain Family
　Robinson '79

Darlanne Fluegel
Battle Beyond the Stars '80
Tough Guys '86

Joel Fluellen
A Dream for Christmas '73
The Great White Hope '70

**The Flying Karamazov
　Brothers**
The Jewel of the Nile '85

Errol Flynn
The Adventures of Robin
　Hood '38
Captain Blood '35
The Prince and the
　Pauper '37

Joe Flynn
The Computer Wore Tennis
　Shoes '69
Million Dollar Duck '71
My Dog, the Thief '69
Now You See Him, Now You
　Don't '72
Superdad '73

Miriam Flynn
18 Again! '88
National Lampoon's Christmas
　Vacation '89

Sean Flynn
Son of Captain Blood '62

Spiros Focas
The Jewel of the Nile '85

Nina Foch
An American in Paris '51
Child of Glass '78
The Ten Commandments '56

Dave Foley
It's Pat: The Movie '94

James Foley ▲
Two Bits '96

Alison Folland
Before and After '95

Megan Follows
Anne of Avonlea '87
Anne of Green Gables '85
Back to Hannibal: The Further
　Adventures of Tom Sawyer
　and Huckleberry Finn '90
Hockey Night '84
The Olden Days Coat '81
Stacking '87

Megan Folson
Heartland '81

Bridget Fonda
Doc Hollywood '91
It Could Happen to You '94
Jacob Have I Loved '88
Little Buddha '93
Shag: The Movie '89
Singles '92

Henry Fonda
Home to Stay '79
How the West was Won '63
My Name is Nobody '74
On Golden Pond '81
Once Upon a Time in the
　West '68
The Red Pony '76
Spencer's Mountain '63
The Swarm '78
The Wrong Man '56
Yours, Mine & Ours '68

Jane Fonda
The Electric Horseman '79
On Golden Pond '81

Peter Fonda
Cannonball Run '81
Tammy and the Doctor '63

Joan Fontaine
Jane Eyre '44
Rebecca '40
Suspicion '41
Voyage to the Bottom of the
　Sea '61

Dick Foran
Winners of the West '40

Bryan Forbes
A Shot in the Dark '64

Bryan Forbes ▲
International Velvet '78
Whistle Down the Wind '62

Faith Ford
North '94

Francis Ford
The Quiet Man '52

Glenn Ford
The Courtship of Eddie's
　Father '62
Smith! '69
Superman 1: The Movie '78

Greg Ford ▲
Daffy Duck's
　Quackbusters '89

Harrison Ford
American Graffiti '73
Clear and Present Danger '94
The Empire Strikes Back '80
The Fugitive '93
Indiana Jones and the Last
　Crusade '89
Indiana Jones and the Temple
　of Doom '84
Raiders of the Lost Ark '81
Regarding Henry '91
Return of the Jedi '83
Sabrina '95
Star Wars '77

Jack Ford
The Joy Luck Club '93

John Ford ▲
How Green was My Valley '41
How the West was Won '63
The Quiet Man '52
Wee Willie Winkie '37

Paul Ford
The Music Man '62
The Russians are Coming, the
　Russians are Coming '66

Wallace Ford
Shadow of a Doubt '43
Spellbound '45

Whitey Ford
Robotech, Vol. 1: Booby
　Trap '85

Deborah Foreman
Valley Girl '83

Tailinh Forest Flower
Geronimo '93

Claire Forlani
Mallrats '95

Carol Forman
The Black Widow '47
Federal Agents vs.
　Underworld, Inc. '49

Milos Forman ▲
Amadeus '84

Richard Foronjy
Man of the House '95

Frederic Forrest
The Adventures of Huckleberry
　Finn '85
Lassie '94
Stacking '87
The Stone Boy '84
Tucker: The Man and His
　Dream '88
Valley Girl '83

Steve Forrest
The Last of the Mohicans '85
Mommie Dearest '81
Spies Like Us '85
The Wild Country '71

William Forrest
The Masked Marvel '43

Robert Forster
Alligator '80
Avalanche '78
The Black Hole '79
Once a Hero '88

Bill Forsyth ▲
Being Human '94
Comfort and Joy '84
Gregory's Girl '80
Housekeeping '87
Local Hero '83
That Sinking Feeling '79

Bruce Forsyth
Bedknobs and
  Broomsticks '71

Rosemary Forsyth
A Friendship in Vienna '88

John Forsythe
Scrooged '88

William Forsythe
Dick Tracy '90

Nick Apollo Forte
Broadway Danny Rose '84

John Fortenberry ▲
Jury Duty '95

Bob Fosse
The Little Prince '74

Brigitte Fossey
Forbidden Games '52

Ami Foster
Troop Beverly Hills '89

Frances Foster
Crooklyn '94

Gloria Foster
The House of Dies Drear '88
Leonard Part 6 '87
Man & Boy '71

Jodie Foster
Bugsy Malone '76
Candleshoe '78
Foxes '80
Freaky Friday '76
The Little Girl Who Lives
  Down the Lane '76
Little Man Tate '91
Maverick '94
Napoleon and Samantha '72
Nell '94
One Little Indian '73
Sommersby '93
Tom Sawyer '73

Jodie Foster ▲
Home for the Holidays '95
Little Man Tate '91

Julia Foster
The Loneliness of the Long
  Distance Runner '62

Lewis R. Foster ▲
The Sign of Zorro '60

Meg Foster
The Legend of Sleepy
  Hollow '79
Masters of the Universe '87

Norman Foster ▲
Davy Crockett and the River
  Pirates '56
Davy Crockett, King of the
  Wild Frontier '55
Indian Paint '64
The Nine Lives of Elfego
  Baca '58
The Sign of Zorro '60

Phil Foster
Bang the Drum Slowly '73

Preston Foster
I Am a Fugitive from a Chain
  Gang '32
My Friend Flicka '43

Frederique Fouche
Clowning Around 2 '93

Douglas Fowley
Mr. Wise Guy '42
Singin' in the Rain '52

Bernard Fox
The Private Eyes '80

Edward Fox
Battle of Britain '69
The Bounty '84
A Bridge Too Far '77
The Go-Between '71
Never Say Never Again '83

Huckleberry Fox
The Blue Yonder '86
Konrad '85
Misunderstood '84
A Winner Never Quits '86

James Fox
Greystoke: The Legend of
  Tarzan, Lord of the
  Apes '84
The Old Curiosity Shop '94
The Remains of the Day '93

Matthew Fox
My Boyfriend's Back '93

Michael J. Fox
The American President '95
Back to the Future '85
Back to the Future, Part 2 '89
Back to the Future, Part 3 '90
Doc Hollywood '91
For Love or Money '93
Greedy '94
Life with Mikey '93
Light of Day '87
Midnight Madness '80
Teen Wolf '85

Peter Fox
A Minor Miracle '83

Sean Fox
3 Ninjas Kick Back '94

Sonny Fox
The Christmas That Almost
  Wasn't '66

Wallace Fox ▲
Bowery Blitzkrieg '41
The Great Mike '44
Kid Dynamite '43
Million Dollar Kid '44
'Neath Brooklyn Bridge '42
Smart Alecks '42

Robert Foxworth
Beyond the Stars '89
The Treasure of
  Matecumbe '76

Jamie Foxx
The Truth About Cats and
  Dogs '96

Eddie Foy Jr.
Gidget Goes Hawaiian '61
Yankee Doodle Dandy '42

Tracy Fraim
Dream Machine '91

William A. Fraker ▲
Legend of the Lone
  Ranger '81

Jonathon Frakes
Star Trek Generations '94
Star Trek the Next Generation
  Episode 1-2: Encounter at
  Farpoint '87

Anne Francis
Forbidden Planet '56
Funny Girl '68

Kay Francis
The Cocoanuts '29
Little Men '40

Ryan Francis
The River Pirates '94

Pietro Francisci ▲
Hercules '58
Hercules Unchained '59

James Franciscus
The Amazing Dobermans '76
Beneath the Planet of the
  Apes '70
Jonathan Livingston
  Seagull '73
Snow Treasure '67
The Valley of Gwangi '69

Don Francks
Finian's Rainbow '68

Margarita Franco
3 Ninjas '92

Emile Francois
Sense and Sensibility '95

Charles Frank
The Right Stuff '83

Jason David Frank
Mighty Morphin Power
  Rangers: The Movie '95

Joanna Frank
Say Anything '89

Melvin Frank ▲
The Court Jester '56
Walk Like a Man '87

Al Franken
Stuart Saves His Family '94

William Frankfather
Born Yesterday '93
Defense Play '88

Diane Franklin
Better Off Dead '85

Don Franklin
Fast Forward '84

John Franklin
The Addams Family '91

Pamela Franklin
David Copperfield '70
Flipper's New Adventure '64
The Horse Without a
  Head '63
The Prime of Miss Jean
  Brodie '69
A Tiger Walks '64

Richard Franklin ▲
Cloak & Dagger '84
F/X 2: The Deadly Art of
  Illusion '91

Arthur Franz
Invaders from Mars '53

Dennis Franz
Die Hard 2: Die Harder '90

Eduard Franz
Francis the Talking Mule '49

Elizabeth Franz
Sabrina '95

Bill Fraser
The Corn is Green '79
Little Dorrit, Film 1: Nobody's
  Fault '88
Little Dorrit, Film 2: Little
  Dorrit's Story '88

Brendan Fraser
Airheads '94
Encino Man '92
Mrs. Winterbourne '96
Now and Then '95
School Ties '92
The Scout '94
With Honors '94

Duncan Fraser
Call of the Wild '93
Timecop '94

John Fraser
Horsemasters '61

Moyra Fraser
The Boy Friend '71

Stuart Fratkin
Prehysteria '93
Remote '93

James Frawley ▲
The Big Bus '76
Hansel and Gretel '82
The Muppet Movie '79

William Frawley
The Adventures of Huckleberry
    Finn '39
Miracle on 34th Street '47

Rupert Frazer
Back Home '90
Empire of the Sun '87

Stephen Frears ▲
Hero '92
The Snapper '93

Lynne Frederick
Amazing Mr. Blunden '72

Al Freeman Jr.
Finian's Rainbow '68
Malcolm X '92
Once Upon a Time . . . When
    We Were Colored '95

J.E. Freeman
It Could Happen to You '94

Joan Freeman
The Reluctant Astronaut '67

Joan Freeman ▲
Satisfaction '88

Kathleen Freeman
The Disorderly Orderly '64
The Errand Boy '61
Innerspace '87
Naked Gun 33 1/3: The Final
    Insult '94
The Nutty Professor '63
The Willies '90

Mona Freeman
Black Beauty '46

Morgan Freeman
Driving Miss Daisy '89
Glory '89
Harry & Son '84
Lean on Me '89
Moll Flanders '96
Outbreak '94
The Power of One '92
Robin Hood: Prince of
    Thieves '91
The Shawshank
    Redemption '94
That Was Then. . .This Is
    Now '85

Morgan Freeman ▲
Bopha! '93

Paul Freeman
Mighty Morphin Power
    Rangers: The Movie '95
Raiders of the Lost Ark '81
A World Apart '88

Isadore "Friz" Freleng ▲
Best of Bugs Bunny &
    Friends '40
Bugs Bunny Cartoon
    Festival '44
Bugs Bunny Superstar '75
Bugs Bunny's 3rd Movie:
    1,001 Rabbit Tales '82
Bugs Bunny's Looney
    Christmas Tales '79
Daffy Duck's Movie: Fantastic
    Island '83
Looney Looney Looney Bugs
    Bunny Movie '81
Looney Tunes Video Show,
    Vol. 1
Looney Tunes Video Show,
    Vol. 2
Looney Tunes Video Show,
    Vol. 3
A Salute to Mel Blanc '58

David French
Bingo '91

Harold French ▲
Rob Roy - The Highland
    Rogue '53

Leigh French
Aloha, Bobby and Rose '74

Susan French
House '86

Victor French
Little House on the Prairie '74
Spencer's Mountain '63

Matt Frewer
Honey, I Shrunk the Kids '89
In Search of Dr. Seuss '94
National Lampoon's Senior
    Trip '95
Supergirl '84

Leonard Frey
Fiddler on the Roof '71

Grayson Fricke
Past the Bleachers '95

Brenda Fricker
Angels in the Outfield '94
Home Alone 2: Lost in New
    York '92
Moll Flanders '96
So I Married an Axe
    Murderer '93

Rick Friedberg ▲
Spy Hard '96

Richard Friedenberg ▲
The Adventures of Frontier
    Fremont '75
Life & Times of Grizzly
    Adams '74

Bud Friedgen ▲
That's Entertainment, Part
    3 '93

William Friedkin ▲
Blue Chips '94

Colin Friels
Darkman '90

Jessie-Ann Friend
Magic Island '95

Rachel Friend
The Quest '86

John Friesen
Two If by Sea '95

Gert Frobe
Chitty Chitty Bang Bang '68
Ten Little Indians '75
Those Daring Young Men in
    Their Jaunty Jalopies '69

Toby Froud
Labyrinth '86

Stephen Fry
I.Q. '94

Taylor Fry
A Little Princess '95
Necessary Parties '88

E. Max Frye ▲
Amos and Andrew '93

Sean Frye
E.T.: The Extra-Terrestrial '82

Virgil Frye
Secret of the Ice Cave '89

Leo Fuchs
Avalon '90

Robert Fuest ▲
Wuthering Heights '70

John Fujioka
Conspiracy of Love '87

Jun Fukuda ▲
Godzilla vs. Megalon '76
Godzilla vs. the Cosmic
    Monster '74

Lucio Fulci ▲
Challenge to White Fang '86

Brook Fuller
When Wolves Cry '69

Kurt Fuller
Bingo '91
Calendar Girl '93
No Holds Barred '89
Wayne's World '92

Penny Fuller
The Beverly Hillbillies '93

Rikki Fulton
Comfort and Joy '84

Annette Funicello
Babes in Toyland '61
Back to the Beach '87
Beach Blanket Bingo '65
Beach Party '63
Bikini Beach '64
Head '68
Horsemasters '61
How to Stuff a Wild Bikini '65
Lots of Luck '85
The Misadventures of Merlin
    Jones '63
Monkey's Uncle '65
Muscle Beach Party '64
Pajama Party '64
The Shaggy Dog '59
Zorro, Vol. 1 '58

Sidney J. Furie ▲
Ladybugs '92
Superman 4: The Quest for
    Peace '87

Edward Furlong
American Heart '92
Before and After '95
A Home of Our Own '93
Terminator 2: Judgment
    Day '91

Chris Furrh
Lord of the Flies '90

Joseph Furst
Diamonds are Forever '71

Stephen Furst
The Dream Team '89
Magic Kid '92
Magic Kid 2 '94
Midnight Madness '80

Stephen Furst ▲
Magic Kid 2 '94

George Furth
Butch Cassidy and the
    Sundance Kid '69

Dan Futterman
The Birdcage '95

Marianne Gaba
How to Stuff a Wild Bikini '65

Christopher Gable
The Boy Friend '71

Clark Gable
Gone with the Wind '39
It Happened One Night '34

June Gable
Brenda Starr '86

Zsa Zsa Gabor
Lili '53

Radu Gabrea ▲
Secret of the Ice Cave '89

Mike Gabriel ▲
Pocahontas '95
The Rescuers Down Under '90

Holly Gagnier
Girls Just Want to Have
Fun '85

Jenny Gago
Sweet 15 '90

Max Gail
Pontiac Moon '94

Boyd Gaines
The Sure Thing '85

M.C. Gainey
Leap of Faith '92

Courtney Gains
Back to the Future '85
The 'Burbs '89
Can't Buy Me Love '87

Charlotte Gainsbourg
Jane Eyre '96
The Little Thief '89

Johnny Galecki
National Lampoon's Christmas
Vacation '89

Anna Galiena
Being Human '94

Bronagh Gallagher
The Commitments '91

Megan Gallagher
Breaking Free '95

Peter Gallagher
Dreamchild '85
While You Were Sleeping '95

Camillo Gallardo
Singles '92

Rosina Galli
Fisherman's Wharf '39

Zach Galligan
Gremlins '84
Gremlins 2: The New
Batch '90
The Lawrenceville
Stories '80s

George Gallo ▲
Trapped In Paradise '94

Mason Gamble
Dennis the Menace '93

Michael Gambon
Clean Slate '94
Squanto: A Warrior's Tale '94
Toys '92
Turtle Diary '86

Tom Gamen
Lord of the Flies '63

Robin Gammell
Project X '87

James Gammon
The Adventures of Huck
Finn '93

Cabin Boy '94
Coupe de Ville '90
Major League '89
Major League 2 '94

James Gandolfini
Crimson Tide '95
Terminal Velocity '94

Richard Gant
The Freshman '90

Bruno Ganz
Wings of Desire '88

Joe Garagiola
Happy Birthday, Bugs: 50
Looney Years '90

Matthew Garber
The Gnome-Mobile '67
The Three Lives of
Thomasina '63

Victor Garber
Life with Mikey '93
Sleepless in Seattle '93

Andy Garcia
Blue Skies Again '83
Hero '92
Stand and Deliver '88

Priscilla Garcia
Once Upon a Scoundrel '73

Vincent Gardenia
Bang the Drum Slowly '73
The Front Page '74
Greased Lightning '77
Home Movies '79
The Last Flight of Noah's
Ark '80
Little Shop of Horrors '86
Moonstruck '87

Reginald Gardiner
The Flying Deuces '39
The Horn Blows at
Midnight '45

Ava Gardner
Knights of the Round
Table '53

**Richard Harding
Gardner ▲**
Sherlock: Undercover Dog '94

Allen (Goorwitz) Garfield
Beverly Hills Cop 2 '87
Desert Bloom '86
Family Prayers '91
Irreconcilable Differences '84
Paco '75

John David Garfield
Golden Voyage of Sinbad '73
The Other Side of the
Mountain '75

William Gargan
The Canterville Ghost '44
Miss Annie Rooney '42

Beverly Garland
Where the Red Fern
Grows '74

Boots Garland
Pistol: The Birth of a
Legend '90

Judy Garland
Andy Hardy Meets
Debutante '40
Babes in Arms '39
Babes on Broadway '41
Easter Parade '48
Girl Crazy '43
Judgment at Nuremberg '61
Life Begins for Andy
Hardy '41
Love Finds Andy Hardy '38
Meet Me in St. Louis '44
Strike Up the Band '40
That's Entertainment '74
Thoroughbreds Don't Cry '37
Till the Clouds Roll By '46
The Wizard of Oz '39

Lee Garlington
My Life '93

Constance Garneau
Strangers in Good
Company '91

James Garner
The Castaway Cowboy '74
Fire in the Sky '93
Maverick '94
Murphy's Romance '85
One Little Indian '73
Support Your Local
Gunfighter '71
Support Your Local Sheriff '69
Tank '83

Peggy Ann Garner
The Cat '66
Jane Eyre '44
A Tree Grows in Brooklyn '45

Gale Garnett
Mr. & Mrs. Bridge '91

Tay Garnett ▲
Challenge To Be Free '76
A Connecticut Yankee in King
Arthur's Court '49

Janeane Garofalo
Bye Bye, Love '94
The Cable Guy '96
Reality Bites '94
The Truth About Cats and
Dogs '96

Teri Garr
The Black Stallion '79
The Black Stallion
Returns '83
Close Encounters of the Third
Kind '77
Dumb & Dumber '94
Escape Artist '82
First Born '84

Head '68
Mr. Mom '83
Mom and Dad Save the
World '92
Oh, God! '77
Once Upon a Brothers
Grimm '77
Pajama Party '64
The Sting 2 '83
The Tale of the Frog
Prince '83
Tootsie '82
Waiting for the Light '90
Witches' Brew '79
Young Frankenstein '74

Donna Garrat
Diamonds are Forever '71

Betty Garrett
On the Town '49

Leif Garrett
The Outsiders '83
Peter Lundy and the Medicine
Hat Stallion '77

Nicholas Garrett
Man of the House '95

Patsy Garrett
Benji '74
Dennis the Menace: Dinosaur
Hunter '87
For the Love of Benji '77

Barbara Garrick
Sleepless in Seattle '93

Rian Garrick
Mooncussers '62

Greer Garson
The Happiest Millionaire '67

Willie Garson
Untamed Heart '93

Steve Garvey
The Scout '94

John W. Gates
Legend of Boggy Creek '75

Larry Gates
Funny Lady '75

Nils Gaup ▲
Shipwrecked '90

Dan Gauthier
Son-in-Law '93
Teen Witch '89

Matt Gauthier
Lords of Magick '88

Jack Gautier
Playtime '67

Roberto Gavaldon ▲
The Littlest Outlaw '54

Cassandra Gaviola
Conan the Barbarian '82

Lisa Gaye
The Sign of Zorro '60

Crystal Gayle
Country Music with the
Muppets '85

Jackie Gayle
Pepper and His Wacky
Taxi '72
Plain Clothes '88

Mitch Gaylord
American Anthem '86

George Gaynes
Dead Men Don't Wear
Plaid '82
It Came Upon a Midnight
Clear '84
Police Academy '84
Police Academy 2: Their First
Assignment '85
Police Academy 3: Back in
Training '86
Police Academy 4: Citizens on
Patrol '87
Police Academy 5: Assignment
Miami Beach '88
Police Academy 6: City Under
Siege '89
Police Academy: Mission to
Moscow '94
Stepmonster '92
Tootsie '82

Mitzi Gaynor
South Pacific '58

Eunice Gayson
Dr. No '62
From Russia with Love '63

Gyula Gazdag ▲
A Hungarian Fairy Tale '87

Wendy Gazelle
The Net '95

Ben Gazzara
Neptune Factor '73

Anthony Geary
UHF '89

Cynthia Geary
8 Seconds '94

Jason Gedrick
The Heavenly Kid '85
Stacking '87
The Zoo Gang '85

Prunella Gee
Never Say Never Again '83

Will Geer
Bandolero! '68
The Billion Dollar Hobo '78
A Decade of the Waltons '85
Jeremiah Johnson '72
Napoleon and Samantha '72
The Reivers '69

The Waltons: A Thanksgiving
Story '73

Judy Geeson
To Sir, with Love '67

Martha Gehman
F/X '86
Father of the Bride '91
The Flamingo Kid '84
Threesome '94

Grant Gelt
Avalon '90

Chief Dan George
The Bears & I '74
Cancel My Reservation '72
Little Big Man '70
The Outlaw Josey Wales '76

Gladys George
The Maltese Falcon '41

Chief Leonard George
Man of the House '95

Susan George
Lightning: The White
Stallion '86
Sudden Terror '70

Marita Geraghty
Groundhog Day '93

Gil Gerard
Buck Rogers in the 25th
Century '79

Steve Geray
Tobor the Great '54

Fred Gerber ▲
Rent-A-Kid '95

Joan Gerber
Tobor the Great '54

George Gerdes
Iron Will '93

Richard Gere
First Knight '95
Sommersby '93

Sean Gerlis
A Summer to Remember '84

Nane Germon
Beauty and the Beast '46

Clyde Geronomi ▲
Alice in Wonderland '51
101 Dalmatians '61
Sleeping Beauty '59

Daniel Gerroll
Big Business '88
Drop Dead Fred '91
A Far Off Place '93

Alex Gerry
The Bellboy '60

Gina Gershon
Pretty in Pink '86

Jami Gertz
Jersey Girl '92
The Lost Boys '87
Sixteen Candles '84
Solarbabies '86
Twister '96

Nicolas Gessner ▲
The Little Girl Who Lives
Down the Lane '76

Balthazar Getty
December '91
Lord of the Flies '90
My Heroes Have Always Been
Cowboys '91
White Squall '96

Estelle Getty
Mannequin '87
Mask '85
Stop! or My Mom Will
Shoot '92
Tootsie '82

John Getz
Curly Sue '91
Don't Tell Mom the
Babysitter's Dead '91

Marilyn Ghigliotti
Clerks '94

Julie Gholson
Where the Lilies Bloom '74

Alice Ghostley
To Kill a Mockingbird '62
With Six You Get Eggroll '68

Louis Giambalvo
Weekend at Bernie's '89

Giancarlo Giannini
American Dreamer '84
Once Upon a Crime '92
A Walk in the Clouds '95

Cynthia Gibb
Short Circuit 2 '88

Donald Gibb
Magic Kid 2 '94

Marla Gibbs
The Meteor Man '93
Up Against the Wall '91

Susan Gibney
And You Thought Your
Parents Were Weird! '91

Brian Gibson ▲
Poltergeist 2: The Other
Side '86
What's Love Got to Do With
It? '93

Colin Gibson
John & Julie '57

Debbie Gibson
Happy Birthday, Bugs: 50
Looney Years '90

Eleanor Gibson
The Haunting of Barney
Palmer '90s

Henry Gibson
Bio-Dome '96
Brenda Starr '86
The Incredible Shrinking
Woman '81
Innerspace '87

Mel Gibson
The Bounty '84
Braveheart '95
Forever Young '92
Mad Max: Beyond
Thunderdome '85
The Man Without a Face '93
Maverick '94
The River '84

Mel Gibson ▲
Braveheart '95
The Man Without a Face '93

Mimi Gibson
Courage of Black Beauty '57

Thomas Gibson
Far and Away '92

Virginia Gibson
Seven Brides for Seven
Brothers '54

Pamela Gidley
Permanent Record '88

John Gielgud
Arthur '81
Arthur 2: On the Rocks '88
Chariots of Fire '81
Dragonheart '96
The Elephant Man '80
First Knight '95
The Hunchback of Notre
Dame '82
The Power of One '92

Stefan Gierasch
Dave '93

Gloria Gifford
Vice Versa '88

Sandro Giglio
The War of the Worlds '53

Billy Gilbert
Breaking the Ice '38
His Girl Friday '40
Mr. Wise Guy '42

Brian Gilbert ▲
Vice Versa '88

Helen Gilbert
Andy Hardy Gets Spring
Fever '39

Lewis Gilbert ▲
Educating Rita '83
Moonraker '79
The Spy Who Loved Me '77
You Only Live Twice '67

Lou Gilbert
The Great White Hope '70

Marcus Gilbert
Army of Darkness '92

Melissa Gilbert
Little House on the Prairie '74
The Miracle Worker '79
The Snow Queen '83
Sylvester '85

Sara Gilbert
The Mouse and the
Motorcycle '80s
Sudie & Simpson '90

Connie Gilchrist
The Misadventures of Merlin
Jones '63

Jack Gilford
Arthur 2: On the Rocks '88
Cocoon '85
Cocoon: The Return '88
Daydreamer '66
Harry & Walter Go to New
York '76

Stuart Gillard ▲
Teenage Mutant Ninja Turtles
3 '93

Aidan Gillen
Circle of Friends '94

Dana Gillespie
The People That Time
Forgot '77

Anita Gillette
Boys on the Side '94
Moonstruck '87

Seth Gilliam
Jefferson in Paris '94

Terry Gilliam
And Now for Something
Completely Different '72
Monty Python and the Holy
Grail '75

Terry Gilliam ▲
The Adventures of Baron
Munchausen '89
Jabberwocky '77
Monty Python and the Holy
Grail '75
Time Bandits '81
12 Monkeys '95

Sidney Gilliat
The Lady Vanishes '38

Sidney Gilliat ▲
Great St. Trinian's Train
Robbery '66

Isabel Gillies
Metropolitan '90

Richard Gilliland
A Day for Thanks on Walton's
Mountain '82

Ann Gillis
'Neath Brooklyn Bridge '42

Larry Gilman
Cool Runnings '93

Jack Gilpin
Funny Farm '88

Marc Gilpin
Computer Wizard '77

Jack Ging
Mosby's Marauders '66
Where the Red Fern
Grows '74

Hermione Gingold
How to Be a Perfect Person in
Just Three Days '84
The Music Man '62

Robert Ginty
Madhouse '90

Christian Gion ▲
Here Comes Santa Claus '84

Rocky Giordani
Cop and a Half '93

Bob Giraldi ▲
Club Med '83
Hiding Out '87

Joseph Girard
Hurricane Express '32

Hippolyte Girardot
Manon of the Spring '87

Roland Giraud
Three Men and a Cradle '85

Annabeth Gish
Beautiful Girls '96
Coupe de Ville '90
Desert Bloom '86
Hiding Out '87
Shag: The Movie '89

Lillian Gish
The Adventures of Huckleberry
Finn '85
Follow Me, Boys! '66
Hambone & Hillie '84
Sweet Liberty '86

Sheila Gish
Highlander '86

Robert Gist
Jack the Giant Killer '62

Wyndham Gittens ▲
Tim Tyler's Luck '37

Robin Givens
Blankman '94

Anton Glanzelius
My Life as a Dog '85

Darel Glaser
Bless the Beasts and
Children '71

Michael Glaser
Butterflies Are Free '72

Paul Michael Glaser
Wait Till Your Mother Gets
Home '83

Paul Michael Glaser ▲
The Air Up There '94
The Cutting Edge '92
Kazaam '96

Ned Glass
West Side Story '61

Ron Glass
Houseguest '94

Isabel Glasser
Forever Young '92

Lesli Linka Glatter ▲
Now and Then '95

Matthew Glave
Baby's Day Out '94

Jackie Gleason
Nothing in Common '86
Smokey and the Bandit '77
Smokey and the Bandit, Part
2 '80
Smokey and the Bandit, Part
3 '83
The Sting 2 '83
The Toy '82

James Gleason
A Tree Grows in Brooklyn '45

Joanna Gleason
F/X 2: The Deadly Art of
Illusion '91

Paul Gleason
The Breakfast Club '85
Die Hard '88
The Ewoks: Battle for
Endor '85
Morgan Stewart's Coming
Home '87
She's Having a Baby '88

Nicholas Gledhill
Careful, He Might Hear
You '84

Brendan Gleeson
Braveheart '95

John Glen ▲
Christopher Columbus: The
Discovery '92
For Your Eyes Only '81
Octopussy '83
A View to a Kill '85

Charles Glenn
Philadelphia '93

Roy Glenn
Jungle Drums of Africa '53

Scott Glenn
The Hunt for Red October '90

Miss Firecracker '89
More American Graffiti '79
My Heroes Have Always Been
Cowboys '91
The Right Stuff '83
The River '84
Silverado '85
Tall Tale: The Unbelievable
Adventures of Pecos
Bill '95

Stacey Glick
Brighton Beach Memoirs '86
Three O'Clock High '87

James Glickenhaus ▲
Timemaster '95

Bruce Glover
Diamonds are Forever '71

Crispin Glover
Back to the Future '85
Back to the Future, Part 2 '89
Racing with the Moon '84
What's Eating Gilbert
Grape '93

Danny Glover
And the Children Shall
Lead '85
Angels in the Outfield '94
Bopha! '93
Iceman '84
Operation Dumbo Drop '95
Places in the Heart '84
Silverado '85

John Glover
Annie Hall '77
Gremlins 2: The New
Batch '90
Meet the Hollowheads '89
Rocket Gibraltar '88
Scrooged '88

Julian Glover
The Empire Strikes Back '80
For Your Eyes Only '81
Indiana Jones and the Last
Crusade '89
Kim '84
The Secret Garden '87
Treasure Island '89

Carlin Glynn
Sixteen Candles '84
The Trip to Bountiful '85

George Gobel
The Fantastic World of D.C.
Collins '84

Justin Gocke
My Grandpa is a Vampire '92
The Witching of Ben
Wagner '95

Catherine Godbold
Alex '92

Gary Goddard ▲
Masters of the Universe '87

Mark Goddard
Strange Invaders '83

Thomas Godet
Toto le Heros '91

Alexander Godunov
Die Hard '88
The Money Pit '86
North '94

Angela Goethals
Heartbreak Hotel '88
Home Alone '90

Peter Michael Goetz
Father of the Bride '91
Father of the Bride Part II '95
My Girl '91

Joanna Going
How to Make an American
    Quilt '95

Gila Golan
The Valley of Gwangi '69

Menahem Golan ▲
Over the Top '86

Jack Gold ▲
Little Lord Fauntleroy '80

Willis Goldbeck ▲
Love Laughs at Andy
    Hardy '46

Adam Goldberg
Dazed and Confused '93

Eric Goldberg ▲
Pocahontas '95

Gary David Goldberg ▲
Dad '89

Whoopi Goldberg
Boys on the Side '94
Clara's Heart '88
Corrina, Corrina '94
Eddie '96
Ghost '90
Happy Birthday, Bugs: 50
    Looney Years '90
Made in America '93
Sarafina! '92
Sister Act '92
Sister Act 2: Back in the
    Habit '93
Star Trek Generations '94
Theodore Rex '95

Jeff Goldblum
The Adventures of Buckaroo
    Banzai Across the Eighth
    Dimension '84
Annie Hall '77
Independence Day '96
Invasion of the Body
    Snatchers '78
Jurassic Park '93
The Legend of Sleepy
    Hollow '79
Nine Months '95

Powder '95
The Right Stuff '83
Silverado '85
The Three Little Pigs '84

Annie Golden
Baby Boom '87
Desperately Seeking
    Susan '85

Norman D. Golden II
Cop and a Half '93

Michael Goldenberg ▲
Bed of Roses '95

Ricky Paull Goldin
Hyper-Sapien: People from
    Another Star '86

Gary Goldman ▲
Thumbelina '94
A Troll in Central Park '94

Philippe Goldman
Small Change '76

Allan Goldstein
The Lawrenceville
    Stories '80s

Allan Goldstein ▲
The House of Dies Drear '88
Outside Chance of Maximilian
    Glick '88

Bob(cat) Goldthwait
Hot to Trot! '88
One Crazy Summer '86
Out There '95
Police Academy 3: Back in
    Training '86
Police Academy 4: Citizens on
    Patrol '87
Scrooged '88

Tony Goldwyn
Ghost '90
Kuffs '92
The Pelican Brief '93

Richard Golfier
Small Change '76

Valeria Golino
Clean Slate '94
Hot Shots! Part Deux '93
Rain Man '88

Arlene Golonka
The Hoboken Chicken
    Emergency '84

Minna Gombell
The Thin Man '34

Panchito Gomez
Paco '75
Sweet 15 '90

Thomas Gomez
Sorrowful Jones '49

Caroline Goodall
Hook '91

The Moon Stallion '85
The Silver Stallion: King of
    the Wild Brumbies '94
White Squall '96

Cuba Gooding Jr.
Boyz N the Hood '91
Lightning Jack '94
Outbreak '94

Saul Goodkind ▲
Buck Rogers Conquers the
    Universe '39
The Phantom Creeps '39

Dean Goodman
Tucker: The Man and His
    Dream '88

Dody Goodman
Cool As Ice '91
Splash '84

John Goodman
Always '89
Arachnophobia '90
The Babe '92
Born Yesterday '93
The Flintstones '94
Happy Birthday, Bugs: 50
    Looney Years '90
King Ralph '91
Matinee '92
Revenge of the Nerds '84

Heather Goodsell
The Return of Tommy
    Tricker '94

Bill Goodwin
The Jolson Story '46

Laura Jane Goodwin
Crystalstone '88

Michael Goodwin
Date with an Angel '87

Ray Goosens ▲
Pinocchio in Outer Space '64

Alicia (Lecy) Goranson
How to Make an American
    Quilt '95

Bernard Gorcey
Blues Busters '50
Bowery Buckaroos '47
Clipped Wings '53
Ghost Chasers '51
Hard-Boiled Mahoney '47
Spook Busters '46

David Gorcey
Blues Busters '50
Bowery Buckaroos '47
Ghost Chasers '51
Hard-Boiled Mahoney '47
Mr. Wise Guy '42
Spook Busters '46

Elizabeth Gorcey
Kidco '83

Leo Gorcey
Blues Busters '50
Bowery Blitzkrieg '41
Bowery Buckaroos '47
Boys of the City '40
Clipped Wings '53
Follow the Leader '44
Ghost Chasers '51
Hard-Boiled Mahoney '47
Kid Dynamite '43
Little Tough Guys '38
Million Dollar Kid '44
Mr. Wise Guy '42
'Neath Brooklyn Bridge '42
Smart Alecks '42
Spook Busters '46
Spooks Run Wild '41
That Gang of Mine '40

Barry Gordon
A Thousand Clowns '65

Bert I. Gordon ▲
The Magic Sword '62

Eve Gordon
Avalon '90
Paradise '91

Gale Gordon
The 'Burbs '89

Gavin Gordon
Turf Boy '42

Keith Gordon
Back to School '86
Home Movies '79
Legend of Billie Jean '85

Keith Gordon ▲
A Midnight Clear '92

Mary Gordon
Follow the Leader '44
Million Dollar Kid '44

Ruth Gordon
Any Which Way You Can '80
The Big Bus '76
Jimmy the Kid '82
My Bodyguard '80
The Prince of Central Park '77

Serena Gordon
Goldeneye '95

Steve Gordon ▲
Arthur '81

Stuart Gordon ▲
Robot Jox '89

Joseph Gordon-Levitt
Angels in the Outfield '94
Holy Matrimony '94

Galyn Gorg
Robocop 2 '90

Marius Goring
The Red Shoes '48

Ruth Goring
Yentl '83

Buddy Gorman
Ghost Chasers '51

Robert Gorman
Mr. Nanny '93

Eydie Gorme
Alice in Wonderland '85

Felim Gormley
The Commitments '91

Frank Gorshin
The Meteor Man '93
That Darn Cat '65
12 Monkeys '95

Rene Goscinny ▲
Lucky Luke: Ballad of the
    Daltons '78
Lucky Luke: Daisy Town '71

Mark Paul Gosselaar
Necessary Parties '88

Louis Gossett Jr.
The Bushbaby '70
Enemy Mine '85
Goodbye, Miss 4th of July '88
Sudie & Simpson '90

Roland Got
G-Men vs. the Black
    Dragon '43

Will Gotay
Stand and Deliver '88

Walter Gotell
The African Queen '51
For Your Eyes Only '81
From Russia with Love '63
Moonraker '79
The Spy Who Loved Me '77

Staffan Gotestam
Brothers Lionheart '85

Michael Gothard
For Your Eyes Only '81

Gilbert Gottfried
Bad Medicine '85
Problem Child '90
Problem Child 2 '91

Lisa Gottlieb ▲
Just One of the Guys '85

Michael Gottlieb ▲
A Kid in King Arthur's
    Court '95
Mannequin '87
Mr. Nanny '93

Thomas Gottschalk
Sister Act 2: Back in the
    Habit '93

Michael Gough
The Age of Innocence '93
Batman '89
Batman Forever '95
Batman Returns '92
The Go-Between '71

Oxford Blues '84
Rob Roy - The Highland
    Rogue '53
The Sword & the Rose '53

Elliott Gould
A Bridge Too Far '77
Casey at the Bat '85
The Devil & Max Devlin '81
Frog '89
Frogs! '90s
Harry & Walter Go to New
    York '76
Jack & the Beanstalk '83
The Last Flight of Noah's
    Ark '80
M*A*S*H '70
Matilda '78

Harold Gould
Love and Death '75
The Sting '73

Jason Gould
Say Anything '89

Robert Goulet
Mr. Wrong '95
Naked Gun 2 1/2: The Smell
    of Fear '91
Scrooged '88

Andre Gower
The Monster Squad '87

Harry Goz
Bill '81
Bill: On His Own '83
Mommie Dearest '81

Betty Grable
Follow the Fleet '36

Nickolas Grace
Diamond's Edge '88

Wayne Grace
My Summer Story '94

Elizabeth Gracen
Death of the Incredible
    Hulk '90

Sally Gracie
Opportunity Knocks '90

David Graf
The Brady Bunch Movie '95
Father and Scout '95
Police Academy 2: Their First
    Assignment '85
Police Academy 3: Back in
    Training '86
Police Academy 4: Citizens on
    Patrol '87
Police Academy 5: Assignment
    Miami Beach '88
Police Academy 6: City Under
    Siege '89
Police Academy: Mission to
    Moscow '94

Ilene Graff
Ladybugs '92

Todd Graff
Dominick & Eugene '88
Opportunity Knocks '90

Aimee Graham
Amos and Andrew '93

Billy Graham
The Prodigal '83

Fred Graham
Trader Tom of the China
    Seas '54

Gary Graham
Robot Jox '89

Gerrit Graham
Cannonball '76
Home Movies '79
The Man with One Red
    Shoe '85
Spaceship '81
This Boy's Life '93

Heather Graham
Shout '91

Therese Graham
Country '84

William A. Graham
Just William's Luck '47

William A. Graham ▲
Change of Habit '69
Orphan Train '79
Where the Lilies Bloom '74

Gloria Grahame
It's a Wonderful Life '46
Oklahoma! '55

Hepburn Grahame
Crusoe '89

Vladimir Grammatikov ▲
The Land of Faraway '87

Kelsey Grammer
Down Periscope '96

Farley Granger
Strangers on a Train '51

Marc Granger
Amazing Mr. Blunden '72

Beth Grant
Rain Man '88
Speed '94

Cary Grant
The Bachelor and the Bobby-
    Soxer '47
Bringing Up Baby '38
Charade '63
His Girl Friday '40
Monkey Business '52
North by Northwest '59
Notorious '46
Penny Serenade '41
The Philadelphia Story '40
Suspicion '41
To Catch a Thief '55

Topper '37

David Marshall Grant
American Flyers '85
Forever Young '92

Faye Grant
Voyager from the
    Unknown '83

Hugh Grant
Four Weddings and a
    Funeral '93
Nine Months '95
The Remains of the Day '93
Sense and Sensibility '95

Kathryn Grant
The Seventh Voyage of
    Sinbad '58

Lee Grant
Airport '77 '77
A Billion for Boris '90
Little Miss Marker '80
The Swarm '78

Leon Grant
Beat Street '84

Polly Grant
My Friend Walter '93

Richard E. Grant
The Age of Innocence '93
L.A. Story '91

Rodney Grant
Dances with Wolves '90
Geronimo: An American
    Legend '93
Wagons East '94

Schuyler Grant
Anne of Avonlea '87
Anne of Green Gables '85

**Stuart Proud Eagle
    Grant**
Wagons East '94

Bonita Granville
The Lone Ranger '56
Love Laughs at Andy
    Hardy '46
Nancy Drew, Reporter '39

Charley Grapewin
Ah, Wilderness! '35
Captains Courageous '37
The Wizard of Oz '39

Alex Grasshof ▲
Pepper and His Wacky
    Taxi '72

Karen Grassle
The Best Christmas Pageant
    Ever '86
Little House on the Prairie '74

Ernest Graves
Hercules in New York '70

Karron Graves
The Fig Tree '87

Peter Graves
Airplane! '80
Airplane 2: The Sequel '82
Savannah Smiles '82

Adele Gray
The Return of Tommy
Tricker '94

Charles Gray
Diamonds are Forever '71
You Only Live Twice '67

Coleen Gray
Cry from the Mountain '85

David Barry Gray
Cops and Robbersons '94

Dolores Gray
Kismet '55

Erin Gray
Buck Rogers in the 25th
Century '79
Six Pack '82

John Gray ▲
Billy Galvin '86
Born to Be Wild '95

Linda Gray
Bonanza: The Return '93
The Grass is Always Greener
Over the Septic Tank '78

Marc Gray
Flirting '89

Spalding Gray
Clara's Heart '88
King of the Hill '93
The Paper '94
Straight Talk '92

Kathryn Grayson
Anchors Aweigh '45
Andy Hardy's Private
Secretary '41
Till the Clouds Roll By '46

Joe V. Greco
Only the Lonely '91

Adolph Green
My Favorite Year '82
Simon '80

Alfred E. Green ▲
The Jolson Story '46
Thoroughbreds Don't Cry '37

Brian Austin Green
An American Summer '90

Kerri Green
The Goonies '85
Lucas '86
Summer Rental '85

Mitzie Green
Little Orphan Annie '32

Nigel Green
Africa Texas Style '67
Jason and the Argonauts '63
Mysterious Island '61

Seth Green
Airborne '93
My Stepmother Is an
Alien '88
Radio Days '87

**Richard Alan
Greenberg ▲**
Little Monsters '89

William Greenblatt
Homecoming '96

David Greene ▲
The Count of Monte Cristo '74

Don Fox Greene ▲
Last Time Out '94

Ellen Greene
Little Shop of Horrors '86
Wagons East '94

Eric Greene
Tut and Tuttle '82

Graham Greene
The Adventures of Dudley the
Dragon: Mr. Crabby
Tree '94
Dances with Wolves '90
Die Hard: With a
Vengeance '95
Huck and the King of
Hearts '93
Maverick '94
North '94
Savage Land '94

James Greene
The Moon Stallion '85

Lorne Greene
Battlestar Galactica '78
The Errand Boy '61
Shirley Temple Storybook
Theater '60

Michael Greene
The Night Before '88

Michelle Greene
How the West Was Fun '95

Peter Greene
The Mask '94

Richard Greene
The Little Princess '39

Shecky Greene
Splash '84

Ruth Greenfield
Willow '88

Billy Greenlees
That Sinking Feeling '79

Sydney Greenstreet
Casablanca '42
The Maltese Falcon '41

Robert Greenwald ▲
Xanadu '80

David Greenwalt ▲
Secret Admirer '85

Charlotte Greenwood
Oklahoma! '55

Joan Greenwood
Little Dorrit, Film 1: Nobody's
Fault '88
Little Dorrit, Film 2: Little
Dorrit's Story '88
Mysterious Island '61

Jane Greer
Billie '65
Dick Tracy, Detective '45
Immediate Family '89
Sinbad the Sailor '47

Leighton Greer
Skeezer '82

Bradley Gregg
Madhouse '90

Virginia Gregg
Spencer's Mountain '63

Andre Gregory
Author! Author! '82

James Gregory
Beneath the Planet of the
Apes '70
Wait Till Your Mother Gets
Home '83

John Gregson
Hans Brinker '69

George Greif
Man of the House '95

Richard Greig
Animal Crackers '30

Kim Greist
Homeward Bound 2: Lost in
San Francisco '96
Homeward Bound: The
Incredible Journey '93
Houseguest '94
Throw Momma from the
Train '87

Joyce Grenfell
The Belles of St. Trinian's '53
Blue Murder at St.
Trinian's '56
The Pure Hell of St.
Trinian's '61

Googy Gress
Babes in Toyland '86

Jennifer Grey
American Flyers '85
Dirty Dancing '87

Ferris Bueller's Day Off '86
Wind '92

Joel Grey
Remo Williams: The Adventure
Begins '85

Shirley Grey
Hurricane Express '32

Virginia Grey
The Big Store '41
Tarzan's New York
Adventure '42
Unknown Island '48

Michael Greyeyes
Geronimo '93

Richard Grieco
If Looks Could Kill '91

David Alan Grier
Blankman '94
In the Army Now '94
Jumanji '95

Pam Grier
Bill & Ted's Bogus
Journey '91
Greased Lightning '77
Something Wicked This Way
Comes '83

Jonathan Gries
Real Genius '85

Tom Gries ▲
The Greatest '77

Joe Grifasi
Bad Medicine '85
Benny & Joon '93
Chances Are '89
F/X '86
Money Train '95
Two Bits '96

Jennifer Griffin
A Perfect World '93

Kathy Griffin
It's Pat: The Movie '94

Lorie Griffin
Aloha Summer '88

Tony Griffin
Robin Hood: Men in
Tights '93

Andy Griffith
Hearts of the West '75
No Time for Sergeants '58
Spy Hard '96

Charles B. Griffith ▲
Eat My Dust '76
Wizards of the Lost Kingdom
2 '89

Eva Griffith
Ride a Wild Pony '75

Geraldine Griffith
Experience Preferred. . . But
Not Essential '83

Hugh Griffith
Oliver! '68
Wuthering Heights '70

James Griffith
The Legend of Sleepy
Hollow '79

Melanie Griffith
Born Yesterday '93
Milk Money '94
Now and Then '95
One on One '77
Paradise '91
Smile '75

Thomas Ian Griffith
The Karate Kid: Part 3 '89

Mark Griffiths ▲
A Cry in the Wild '90
Max is Missing '95

Rachel Griffiths
Muriel's Wedding '94

Richard Griffiths
Guarding Tess '94
Naked Gun 2 1/2: The Smell
of Fear '91

Frank Grimes
Crystalstone '88

Gary Grimes
Cahill: United States
Marshal '73
Culpepper Cattle Co. '72

Scott Grimes
Critters '86
Frog '89
Frogs! '90s
It Came Upon a Midnight
Clear '84

Alan Grint
The Secret Garden '87

Charles Grodin
Beethoven '92
Beethoven's 2nd '93
Clifford '92
Dave '93
The Grass is Always Greener
Over the Septic Tank '78
The Great Muppet Caper '81
Heart and Souls '93
The Heartbreak Kid '72
The Incredible Shrinking
Woman '81
King Kong '76
My Summer Story '94
So I Married an Axe
Murderer '93

Clare Grogan
Gregory's Girl '80

C.P. Grogan
Comfort and Joy '84

David Groh
A Hero Ain't Nothin' But a
Sandwich '78
Hot Shot '86

Sam Groom
Run for the Roses '78

Arye Gross
Boris and Natasha: The
Movie '92
Coupe de Ville '90
A Midnight Clear '92
Soul Man '86

Edan Gross
And You Thought Your
Parents Were Weird! '91

Mary Gross
Baby Boom '87
Big Business '88
Club Paradise '86
The Santa Clause '94
Troop Beverly Hills '89

Michael Gross
Alan & Naomi '92
Big Business '88
Cool As Ice '91

Paul Gross
Aspen Extreme '93

Yoram Gross ▲
Camel Boy '84
EPIC: Days of the
Dinosaurs '87

David Grossman
Frog '89

Charles Grosvenor ▲
Once Upon a Forest '93

Richard Grove
Army of Darkness '92

Robert Grubb
Mad Max: Beyond
Thunderdome '85

Gary Grubbs
The Ernest Green Story '93

Christopher Guard
Return to Treasure Island, Vol.
1 '85

Dominic Guard
The Go-Between '71

Harry Guardino
The Adventures of Bullwhip
Griffin '66
Any Which Way You Can '80
Matilda '78

Castulo Guerra
Where the River Runs
Black '86

Johnny Guerro
The Secret of Navajo Cave '76

Christopher Guest
Girlfriends '78
Heartbeeps '81
Little Shop of Horrors '86
The Princess Bride '87

Lance Guest
I Ought to Be in Pictures '82
Just the Way You Are '84
The Last Starfighter '84
The Wizard of Loneliness '88

Nicholas Guest
National Lampoon's Christmas
Vacation '89

Val Guest ▲
Just William's Luck '47
When Dinosaurs Ruled the
Earth '70

Georges Guetary
An American in Paris '51

Cary Guffey
Close Encounters of the Third
Kind '77

Carla Gugino
Son-in-Law '93
This Boy's Life '93

Adam Guier
Pistol: The Birth of a
Legend '90

Ann Guilbert
Grumpier Old Men '95

Paul Guilfoyle
Billy Galvin '86
Celtic Pride '96

Robert Guillaume
The Kid from Left Field '79
The Kid with the 200 I.Q. '83
Lean on Me '89
The Meteor Man '93

John Guillermin ▲
Death on the Nile '78
King Kong '76
Sheena '84

Tim Guinee
Follow the River '95
How to Make an American
Quilt '95

Alec Guinness
The Bridge on the River
Kwai '57
Doctor Zhivago '65
The Empire Strikes Back '80
Lawrence of Arabia '62
Little Dorrit, Film 1: Nobody's
Fault '88
Little Dorrit, Film 2: Little
Dorrit's Story '88
Little Lord Fauntleroy '80
Oliver Twist '48

Scrooge '70
Star Wars '77

Tom Guiry
Lassie '94
The Sandlot '93

Clu Gulager
And Now Miguel '66
My Heroes Have Always Been
Cowboys '91
Touched by Love '80
Wonderland Cove '75

Dorothy Gulliver
Shadow of the Eagle '32

David Gulpilil
Crocodile Dundee '86

Moses Gunn
The Great White Hope '70
The House of Dies Drear '88
The NeverEnding Story '84

Bob Gunton
Ace Ventura: When Nature
Calls '95
Broken Arrow '95
Father Hood '93
Glory '89
The Shawshank
Redemption '94

Kamlesh Gupta
Crystalstone '88

Alizia Gur
From Russia with Love '63

Eric Gurry
The Zoo Gang '85

Louis Guss
Moonstruck '87

Steve Guttenberg
Bad Medicine '85
The Big Green '95
The Chicken Chronicles '77
Cocoon '85
Cocoon: The Return '88
Home for the Holidays '95
It Takes Two '95
Pecos Bill '86
Police Academy '84
Police Academy 2: Their First
Assignment '85
Police Academy 3: Back in
Training '86
Police Academy 4: Citizens on
Patrol '87
Short Circuit '86
Three Men and a Baby '87
Three Men and a Little
Lady '90

Lucy Gutteridge
The Secret Garden '87

Ronald Guttman
Josh and S.A.M. '93

Jasmine Guy
Runaway '89

Joe Guzaldo
Bingo '91

Luis Guzman
Mr. Wonderful '93

Robert Gwaltney
Trading Hearts '87

Edmund Gwenn
Challenge to Lassie '49
Foreign Correspondent '40
It's a Dog's Life '55
Lassie, Come Home '43
Life with Father '47
Miracle on 34th Street '47

David Gwillim
The Island at the Top of the
    World '74

Jack Gwillim
The Bushbaby '70

Michael Gwynn
Jason and the Argonauts '63

Fred Gwynne
The Boy Who Could Fly '86
The Littlest Angel '69
Off Beat '86
Simon '80

Peter Gwynne
The Dove '74

Lukas Haas
Alan & Naomi '92
Boys '96
The Lady in White '88
Leap of Faith '92
Rambling Rose '91
See You in the Morning '89
Solarbabies '86
The Wizard of Loneliness '88

Olivia Hack
The Brady Bunch Movie '95
A Very Brady Sequel '96

Shelley Hack
Annie Hall '77
Troll '85

Buddy Hackett
Muscle Beach Party '64
The Music Man '62
Scrooged '88
The Wonderful World of the
    Brothers Grimm '62

Joan Hackett
Escape Artist '82
Support Your Local Sheriff '69
The Treasure of
    Matecumbe '76

Taylor Hackford ▲
Dolores Claiborne '94

Gene Hackman
The Birdcage '95
A Bridge Too Far '77
Crimson Tide '95
Downhill Racer '69

Geronimo: An American
    Legend '93
Hoosiers '86
I Never Sang For My
    Father '70
Misunderstood '84
The Poseidon Adventure '72
Superman 1: The Movie '78
Superman 2 '80
Superman 4: The Quest for
    Peace '87

Julie Ann Haddock
The Great Santini '80

Dayle Haddon
The World's Greatest
    Athlete '73

Ron Haddrick
Quigley Down Under '90

Sara Haden
Andy Hardy Gets Spring
    Fever '39
Andy Hardy Meets
    Debutante '40
Andy Hardy's Double Life '42
Andy Hardy's Private
    Secretary '41
The Great Rupert '50
Love Laughs at Andy
    Hardy '46
The Poor Little Rich Girl '36

Reed Hadley
Zorro's Fighting Legion '39

Molly Hagan
Some Kind of Wonderful '87

Dennis Hage
Hadley's Rebellion '84

Jean Hagen
Adam's Rib '50
The Shaggy Dog '59
Singin' in the Rain '52

Julie Hagerty
Airplane! '80
Airplane 2: The Sequel '82
Bad Medicine '85
Necessary Parties '88
What About Bob? '91

Merle Haggard
Huckleberry Finn '75

Piers Haggard ▲
Back Home '90
The Fiendish Plot of Dr. Fu
    Manchu '80
Return to Treasure Island, Vol.
    1 '85

Dan Haggerty
The Adventures of Frontier
    Fremont '75
Blood Brothers '77
The Capture of Grizzly
    Adams '82
Life & Times of Grizzly
    Adams '74

Spirit of the Eagle '90
Starbird and Sweet
    William '73
The Tender Warrior '71
When the North Wind
    Blows '74

Michael Hagiwara
Prehysteria! 2 '94

Larry Hagman
The Big Bus '76

Steven Hahn ▲
Starchaser: The Legend of
    Orin '85

Charles Haid
The Rescue '88

Charles Haid ▲
Iron Will '93

David Haig
The Moon Stallion '85

Sid Haig
Wizards of the Lost Kingdom
    2 '89

Louisa Haigh
Shipwrecked '90

Corey Haim
The Double O Kid '92
Dream a Little Dream '89
Dream a Little Dream 2 '94
Dream Machine '91
Fast Getaway '91
Fast Getaway 2 '94
First Born '84
License to Drive '88
The Lost Boys '87
Lucas '86
Murphy's Romance '85
Oh, What a Night '92
Secret Admirer '85

John Halas ▲
Animal Farm '55

Don Haldane ▲
Nikki, the Wild Dog of the
    North '61

Alan Hale
The Adventures of Robin
    Hood '38
It Happened One Night '34
The Man in the Iron Mask '39
The Prince and the
    Pauper '37

Alan Hale Jr.
The Fifth Musketeer '79
Hambone & Hillie '84
Johnny Dangerously '84
The North Avenue
    Irregulars '79

Barbara Hale
The Boy with the Green
    Hair '48
Flight of the Grey Wolf '76
The Window '49

Georgina Hale
The Boy Friend '71
The Gold Rush '25

Jonathan Hale
Bringing Up Baby '38

Jerry Haleva
Hot Shots! Part Deux '93

Brian Haley
Baby's Day Out '94

Jack Haley
The Poor Little Rich Girl '36
Rebecca of Sunnybrook
    Farm '38
The Wizard of Oz '39

Jack Haley Jr. ▲
That's Dancing! '85
That's Entertainment '74

Jackie Earle Haley
The Bad News Bears '76
The Bad News Bears Go to
    Japan '78
The Bad News Bears in
    Breaking Training '77
Breaking Away '79
The Zoo Gang '85

Alaina Reed Hall
Death Becomes Her '92

Albert Hall
Major Payne '95
Malcolm X '92

Alexander Hall ▲
Little Miss Marker '34

Anthony Michael Hall
The Breakfast Club '85
Edward Scissorhands '90
National Lampoon's
    Vacation '83
Six Pack '82
Sixteen Candles '84
Weird Science '85

Bug Hall
The Big Green '95
The Little Rascals '94
The Stupids '95

Carol E. Hall
Love Your Mama '89

Christopher John Hall
Bopha! '93

Delores Hall
Leap of Faith '92

Hanna Hall
Homecoming '96

Harriet Hall
The Witching of Ben
    Wagner '95

Huntz Hall
Blues Busters '50
Bowery Blitzkrieg '41

Glen Hansard
The Commitments '91

Gale Hansen
Dead Poets Society '89

Curtis Hanson ▲
The River Wild '94

Eleanor Hanson
Flaming Frontiers '38

Clement Harari
Monkeys, Go Home! '66

Martin Harburg
Hockey Night '84

Ernest Harden
White Mama '80

Marcia Gay Harden
Safe Passage '94
Spy Hard '96

Melora Hardin
Dead Poets Society '89
The North Avenue
  Irregulars '79
The Rocketeer '91

June Harding
The Trouble with Angels '66

Kadeem Hardison
Beat Street '84
Dream Date '93
Renaissance Man '94

Cedric Hardwicke
A Connecticut Yankee in King
  Arthur's Court '49
I Remember Mama '48
Suspicion '41
The Ten Commandments '56
Tom Brown's School Days '40

Edward Hardwicke
The Scarlet Letter '95
Shadowlands '93

Oliver Hardy
The Flying Deuces '39
March of the Wooden
  Soldiers '34

Robert Hardy
Sense and Sensibility '95

Sam Hardy
King Kong '33

Dorian Harewood
An American Christmas
  Carol '79
Tank '83

Mariska Hargitay
Ghoulies '85

T.J. Hargrave
The Prince of Central Park '77

John Hargreaves
Careful, He Might Hear
  You '84

Deathcheaters '76

Paul Harkins
Heartbreak Hotel '88

Kenneth Harlan
Renfrew of the Royal
  Mounted '37

Renny Harlin ▲
Cutthroat Island '95
Die Hard 2: Die Harder '90

Jean Harlow
City Lights '31

Helen Harmon
Where the Lilies Bloom '74

Mark Harmon
Magic in the Water '95
Summer School '87

Elisabeth Harnois
One Magic Christmas '85

Christina Harnos
The Rescue '88

David W. Harper
A Day for Thanks on Walton's
  Mountain '82
The Waltons: A Thanksgiving
  Story '73

Jessica Harper
My Favorite Year '82

Kamie Harper
A Friendship in Vienna '88

Marjorie Harper
Life & Times of Grizzly
  Adams '74

Robert Harper
Not Quite Human '87

Tess Harper
Christy '94
Her Alibi '88
The Man in the Moon '91
My Heroes Have Always Been
  Cowboys '91
A Summer to Remember '84
Tender Mercies '83

Valerie Harper
Happy Birthday, Bugs: 50
  Looney Years '90
Thursday's Game '74

Rebecca Harrell
Prancer '89

Woody Harrelson
Doc Hollywood '91
Kingpin '96
Money Train '95
Wildcats '86

Al Harrington
White Fang 2: The Myth of the
  White Wolf '94

Laura Harrington
What's Eating Gilbert
  Grape '93

Barbara Harris
Dirty Rotten Scoundrels '88
Freaky Friday '76
Movie, Movie '78
The North Avenue
  Irregulars '79
Peggy Sue Got Married '86
A Thousand Clowns '65

Brad Harris
Hercules '83

Cassandra Harris
For Your Eyes Only '81

Cynthia Harris
Three Men and a Baby '87

Ed Harris
Apollo 13 '95
Milk Money '94
Places in the Heart '84
The Right Stuff '83
Swing Shift '84

Harry Harris ▲
Alice in Wonderland '85
A Day for Thanks on Walton's
  Mountain '82
The Runaways '75

Jared Harris
Tall Tale: The Unbelievable
  Adventures of Pecos
  Bill '95

Julie Harris
East of Eden '54
Gorillas in the Mist '88
Housesitter '92

Julius W. Harris
Live and Let Die '73

Mel Harris
K-9 '89
The Pagemaster '94

Neil Patrick Harris
Clara's Heart '88
Purple People Eater '88

Richard Harris
Camelot '67
Cry, the Beloved Country '95
Gulliver's Travels '77
The Hero '71
King of the Wind '93
Robin and Marian '76

Richard Harris ▲
The Hero '71

Robin Harris
House Party '90

Rosemary Harris
Crossing Delancey '88

Zelda Harris
The Baby-Sitters Club '95

Crooklyn '94

Cathryn Harrison
Blue Fire Lady '78

George Harrison
A Hard Day's Night '64
Help! '65
Magical Mystery Tour '67

Jenilee Harrison
Tank '83

John Kent Harrison ▲
City Boy '93
Hole in the Sky '95
Johnny's Girl '95

Kathleen Harrison
A Christmas Carol '51

Linda Harrison
Beneath the Planet of the
  Apes '70
Cocoon '85
Planet of the Apes '68

Lottie Harrison
Lost in a Harem '44

Rex Harrison
Doctor Doolittle '67
The Fifth Musketeer '79
The Prince and the
  Pauper '78

Schae Harrison
Magic Island '95

Hugo Harold Harrisson
Toto le Heros '91

Deborah Harry
Hairspray '88
Satisfaction '88

Christopher Hart
The Addams Family '91
Addams Family Values '93

Harvey Hart ▲
The Prince of Central Park '77
Stone Fox '87

Ian Hart
Backbeat '94

Linda Hart
A Perfect World '93

Mary Hart
Happy Birthday, Bugs: 50
  Looney Years '90

Roxanne Hart
Highlander '86
Oh, God! You Devil '84
Old Enough '84

Susan Hart
Pajama Party '64

Jennifer Harte
Prehysteria! 2 '94

Linda Hartley
The Fire in the Stone '85

Mariette Hartley
Encino Man '92
Improper Channels '82

Lisa Hartman Black
Just Tell Me You Love Me '80

David Hartman
The Island at the Top of the
World '74

Elizabeth Hartman
Walking Tall '73

Phil Hartman
Coneheads '93
The Crazysitter '94
Greedy '94
Houseguest '94
How I Got into College '89
Sgt. Bilko '95

William Hartnell
The Mouse That Roared '59

Rainbow Harvest
Old Enough '84

Anthony Harvey ▲
The Lion in Winter '68

Don Harvey
American Heart '92
Eight Men Out '88

Forrester Harvey
Thoroughbreds Don't Cry '37

Laurence Harvey
The Wonderful World of the
Brothers Grimm '62

Patrick Hasburgh ▲
Aspen Extreme '93

Susan Haskell
Mrs. Winterbourne '96

Byron Haskin ▲
Treasure Island '50
The War of the Worlds '53

Imogen Hassall
When Dinosaurs Ruled the
Earth '70

Marilyn Hassett
The Other Side of the
Mountain '75
The Other Side of the
Mountain, Part 2 '78

Signe Hasso
Journey for Margaret '42

Bob Hastings
Harper Valley P.T.A. '78

Masami Hata ▲
Little Nemo: Adventures in
Slumberland '92

Masanori Hata ▲
The Adventures of Milo &
Otis '89

Richard Hatch
Battlestar Galactica '78

Teri Hatcher
Straight Talk '92

Hurd Hatfield
Her Alibi '88

Henry Hathaway ▲
How the West was Won '63
Prince Valiant '54
To the Last Man '33
True Grit '69

Kellen Hathaway
Dennis the Menace '93

Noah Hathaway
The NeverEnding Story '84
Troll '85

Bob Hathcock ▲
DuckTales the Movie:
Treasure of the Lost
Lamp '90

Raymond Hatton
Three Musketeers '33

Tom Hatton
Spies Like Us '85

Rutger Hauer
Buffy the Vampire Slayer '92
Ladyhawke '85

Cole Hauser
School Ties '92

Fay Hauser
Jimmy the Kid '82
Marvin & Tige '84

Wings Hauser
Beastmaster 2: Through the
Portal of Time '91

Nigel Havers
Chariots of Fire '81
Empire of the Sun '87
The Little Princess '87

Robin Hawdon
When Dinosaurs Ruled the
Earth '70

Ethan Hawke
Alive '93
Before Sunrise '94
Dad '89
Dead Poets Society '89
Explorers '85
A Midnight Clear '92
Mystery Date '91
Reality Bites '94
Rich in Love '93
White Fang '91

Ian Hawkes
Queen of Hearts '89

Jack Hawkins
The Bridge on the River
Kwai '57
Lawrence of Arabia '62
Those Daring Young Men in
Their Jaunty Jalopies '69

Ronnie Hawkins
Club Med '83

Howard Hawks ▲
Bringing Up Baby '38
Hatari '62
His Girl Friday '40
Monkey Business '52

Goldie Hawn
Butterflies Are Free '72
Death Becomes Her '92
Foul Play '78
Housesitter '92
The One and Only, Genuine,
Original Family Band '68
Overboard '87
Swing Shift '84
Wildcats '86

Elizabeth Hawthorne
Alex '92

Sessue Hayakawa
The Bridge on the River
Kwai '57
The Geisha Boy '58
The Swiss Family
Robinson '60

Yutaka Hayashi
Godzilla vs. Megalon '76

Sterling Hayden
Prince Valiant '54

Richard Haydn
Clarence, the Cross-eyed
Lion '65
Please Don't Eat the
Daisies '60
The Sound of Music '65
Young Frankenstein '74

Julie Haydon
It's Pat: The Movie '94

Allan Hayes
Sam's Son '84

Allison Hayes
Francis Joins the WACs '54

Helen Hayes
Airport '70
Candleshoe '78
Herbie Rides Again '74
One of Our Dinosaurs Is
Missing '75

Isaac Hayes
Flipper '96
It Could Happen to You '94
Robin Hood: Men in
Tights '93

Patricia Hayes
Little Dorrit, Film 1: Nobody's
Fault '88
Little Dorrit, Film 2: Little
Dorrit's Story '88
The NeverEnding Story '84
Willow '88

Peter Lind Hayes
The 5000 Fingers of Dr. T '53

David Hayman
Hope and Glory '87
Rob Roy '95

Dick Haymes
State Fair '45

Jim Haynie
Men Don't Leave '89

Robert Hays
Airplane! '80
Airplane 2: The Sequel '82
Cat's Eye '85
Homeward Bound 2: Lost in
San Francisco '96
Homeward Bound: The
Incredible Journey '93
No Dessert Dad, 'Til You Mow
the Lawn '94
Trenchcoat '83

Dennis Haysbert
Major League '89
Major League 2 '94
Mr. Baseball '92
Waiting to Exhale '95

James Hayter
Tom Brown's School Days '51

David Hayward
Who'll Save Our Children?
'82

Louis Hayward
The Man in the Iron Mask '39

Chris Haywood
Alex '92
Quigley Down Under '90

James Hazeldine
My Friend Walter '93

Jane Hazlegrove
Heidi '93

Lena Headey
Rudyard Kipling's The Jungle
Book '94

Glenne Headly
Dick Tracy '90
Dirty Rotten Scoundrels '88
Fandango '85
Getting Even with Dad '94
Making Mr. Right '86
Mr. Holland's Opus '95
The Purple Rose of Cairo '85
Sgt. Bilko '95

Anthony Heald
Bushwhacked '95

The Client '94

David Healy
Supergirl '84

Katherine Healy
Six Weeks '82

Mary Healy
The 5000 Fingers of Dr. T '53

John Heard
Awakenings '90
Before and After '95
Big '88
Home Alone '90
Home Alone 2: Lost in New
   York '92
The Pelican Brief '93
Radio Flyer '92
Rambling Rose '91
The Trip to Bountiful '85

Ann Hearn
Lorenzo's Oil '92

George Hearn
See You in the Morning '89
Sneakers '92

Patty Hearst
Cry-Baby '90

Joey Heatherton
Cry-Baby '90

Patricia Heaton
Beethoven '92
Memoirs of an Invisible
   Man '92

Anne Heche
The Adventures of Huck
   Finn '93
Milk Money '94
A Simple Twist of Fate '94

Eileen Heckart
The Bad Seed '56
Butterflies Are Free '72
Up the Down Staircase '67
White Mama '80

Amy Heckerling ▲
Clueless '95
Fast Times at Ridgemont
   High '82
Johnny Dangerously '84
Look Who's Talking '89
Look Who's Talking, Too '90
National Lampoon's European
   Vacation '85

Dan Hedaya
The Addams Family '91
The Adventures of Buckaroo
   Banzai Across the Eighth
   Dimension '84
Benny & Joon '93
Clueless '95
For Love or Money '93
Joe Versus the Volcano '90
Mr. Wonderful '93
The Prince of Central Park '77

Rookie of the Year '93
A Smoky Mountain
   Christmas '86
The Usual Suspects '95

David Hedison
Live and Let Die '73

Jack Hedley
For Your Eyes Only '81

Tippi Hedren
The Birds '63

Victor Heerman ▲
Animal Crackers '30

Kyle T. Heffner
Flashdance '83

Richard T. Heffron ▲
Whale for the Killing '81

Van Heflin
Airport '70
Shane '53
The Three Musketeers '48
Till the Clouds Roll By '46

Timothy Hegeman
The Phoenix and the Magic
   Carpet '95

O.P. Heggie
Anne of Green Gables '34

Robert Hegyes
Just Tell Me You Love Me '80

Peter Hehir
I Live with Me Dad '86

Katherine Heigl
King of the Hill '93
My Father the Hero '93

Stuart Heisler ▲
The Lone Ranger '56

Carol Heiss
Snow White and the Three
   Stooges '61

Marg Helgenberger
Always '89
Bad Boys '95

Richard Hell
Desperately Seeking
   Susan '85

Olle Hellbron ▲
Brothers Lionheart '85
Pippi Goes on Board '71
Pippi in the South Seas '68
Pippi Longstocking '68

Randee Heller
Fast Break '79
The Karate Kid '84

Jerome Hellman ▲
Promises in the Dark '79

Levon Helm
Coal Miner's Daughter '80

The Right Stuff '83
Smooth Talk '85

Tiffany Helm
The Zoo Gang '85

Katherine Helmond
Jack & the Beanstalk '83
The Lady in White '88
Overboard '87
Time Bandits '81

Tom Helmore
Flipper's New Adventure '64

Robert Helpmann
The Red Shoes '48
The Tales of Hoffman '51

David Hemblen
Short Circuit 2 '88

Mark Hembrow
Return to Snowy River '88

Mariel Hemingway
Delirious '91
Superman 4: The Quest for
   Peace '87

David Hemmings
Camelot '67
Man, Woman & Child '83
The Old Curiosity Shop '75
The Snow Queen '83

David Hemmings ▲
Dark Horse '92

Anouska Hempel
On Her Majesty's Secret
   Service '69

Sherman Hemsley
Love at First Bite '79
Mr. Nanny '93

Adam Hendershott
Celtic Pride '96

Bill Henderson
City Slickers '91
Clue '85

John Henderson ▲
Loch Ness '96

Meredith Henderson
Song Spinner '95

Tony Hendra
Life with Mikey '93

Gloria Hendry
Live and Let Die '73

Brad Henke
Mr. Wrong '95

Drewe Henley
When Dinosaurs Ruled the
   Earth '70

Marilu Henner
Cannonball Run 2 '84
Johnny Dangerously '84

L.A. Story '91

Paul Henreid
Casablanca '42

Lance Henriksen
Powder '95
The Right Stuff '83
Super Mario Bros. '93
The Terminator '84

Buck Henry
Grumpy Old Men '93

Charlotte Henry
Bowery Blitzkrieg '41
March of the Wooden
   Soldiers '34

Justin Henry
Kramer vs. Kramer '79
Sixteen Candles '84
Tiger Town '83

Lenny Henry
Bernard and the Genie '91

Mike Henry
Adios Amigo '75
Smokey and the Bandit '77
Smokey and the Bandit, Part
   2 '80
Smokey and the Bandit, Part
   3 '83

Robert "Buzzy" Henry
The Great Mike '44
Turf Boy '42

William Henry
Tarzan Escapes '36

Pamela Hensley
Buck Rogers in the 25th
   Century '79
Doc Savage '75

Brian Henson ▲
The Muppet Christmas
   Carol '92
Muppet Treasure Island '96

Jim Henson
Country Music with the
   Muppets '85
Muppets Moments '85

Jim Henson ▲
The Dark Crystal '82
The Great Muppet Caper '81
Labyrinth '86
Muppets Moments '85

Audrey Hepburn
Always '89
Charade '63
Funny Face '57
Robin and Marian '76
Roman Holiday '53
Sabrina '54

Dee Hepburn
Gregory's Girl '80

Katharine Hepburn
Adam's Rib '50
The African Queen '51
Bringing Up Baby '38
The Corn is Green '79
The Lion in Winter '68
Little Women '33
Olly Olly Oxen Free '78
On Golden Pond '81
Pat and Mike '52
The Philadelphia Story '40
Rooster Cogburn '75

Charles Herbert
13 Ghosts '60

Louis Herbert
Forbidden Games '52

Percy Herbert
Mysterious Island '61

Stephen Herek ▲
Bill & Ted's Excellent
   Adventure '89
Critters '86
Don't Tell Mom the
   Babysitter's Dead '91
The Mighty Ducks '92
Mr. Holland's Opus '95
101 Dalmatians '96
The Three Musketeers '93

Al(bert) Herman ▲
Renfrew of the Royal
   Mounted '37

Jimmy Herman
Dances with Wolves '90
Geronimo '93

Tibor Hernadi ▲
Felix the Cat: The Movie '91

Sammy Hernandez
Cop and a Half '93

Mark Herrier
Tank '83

Edward Herrmann
Big Business '88
Born Yesterday '93
The Day of the Dolphin '73
The Electric Grandmother '81
The Great Waldo Pepper '75
The Lawrenceville
   Stories '80s
The Lost Boys '87
The Man with One Red
   Shoe '85
My Boyfriend's Back '93
The North Avenue
   Irregulars '79
Overboard '87
The Paper Chase '73
The Purple Rose of Cairo '85
Richie Rich '94
Take Down '79

Barbara Hershey
Hoosiers '86
The Natural '84
The Pallbearer '95

The Right Stuff '83
Swing Kids '93
With Six You Get Eggroll '68
A World Apart '88

Jean Hersholt
Heidi '37

Marshall Herskovitz ▲
Jack the Bear '93

Jason Hervey
Back to School '86
Back to the Future '85

Grant Heslov
Black Sheep '96
Congo '95
True Lies '94

Erica Nicole Hess
Leapin' Leprechauns '95

Howard Hesseman
The Big Bus '76
Clue '85
Flight of the Navigator '86
Little Miss Millions '93
Police Academy 2: Their First
   Assignment '85
The Princess Who Never
   Laughed '84
The Sunshine Boys '75

Gordon Hessler ▲
Golden Voyage of Sinbad '73

Charlton Heston
Airport '75 '75
Alaska '96
Almost an Angel '90
Beneath the Planet of the
   Apes '70
Call of the Wild '72
The Four Musketeers '75
The Greatest Show on
   Earth '52
Planet of the Apes '68
The Prince and the
   Pauper '78
The Ten Commandments '56
Three Musketeers '74
Tombstone '93
Treasure Island '89
True Lies '94

Fraser Heston ▲
Alaska '96
Treasure Island '89

Alan Hewitt
The Computer Wore Tennis
   Shoes '69

Love Hewitt
Little Miss Millions '93

Paul Hewitt
A Perfect World '93

Pete Hewitt ▲
Bill & Ted's Bogus
   Journey '91
Tom and Huck '95

Jon-Erik Hexum
Voyager from the
   Unknown '83

John Heyl
A Separate Peace '73

Barton Heyman
Billy Galvin '86

Winston Hibler ▲
Charlie, the Lonesome
   Cougar '67

John Benjamin Hickey
Eddie '96

William Hickey
Forget Paris '95
The Jerky Boys '95
Major Payne '95
National Lampoon's Christmas
   Vacation '89
One Crazy Summer '86
Pink Cadillac '89

Darryl Hickman
Johnny Shiloh '63
Men of Boys Town '41

Dwayne Hickman
How to Stuff a Wild Bikini '65
My Dog, the Thief '69

Catherine Hicks
Like Father, Like Son '87
Peggy Sue Got Married '86
Star Trek 4: The Voyage
   Home '86

Leonard Hicks
Santa Claus Conquers the
   Martians '64

Russell Hicks
Tarzan's New York
   Adventure '42

Taral Hicks
A Bronx Tale '93

Anthony Higgins
For Love or Money '93
Raiders of the Lost Ark '81

Colin Higgins ▲
Foul Play '78

Joe Higgins
Flipper's New Adventure '64

Michael Higgins
Crusoe '89
School Ties '92

Arthur Hill
The Andromeda Strain '71
A Bridge Too Far '77
Love Leads the Way '84
One Magic Christmas '85

Benny Hill
Chitty Chitty Bang Bang '68

Bernard Hill
The Bounty '84

Dana Hill
Cross Creek '83
National Lampoon's European
   Vacation '85

George Roy Hill ▲
Butch Cassidy and the
   Sundance Kid '69
Funny Farm '88
The Great Waldo Pepper '75
A Little Romance '79
The Sting '73
The World of Henry Orient '64

James Hill
Christian the Lion '76

James Hill ▲
The Belstone Fox '73
Black Beauty '71
Born Free '66

Lauryn Hill
King of the Hill '93
Sister Act 2: Back in the
   Habit '93

Leslie Hill
Flirting '89

Ralston Hill
1776 '72

Robert F. "Bob" Hill ▲
Blake of Scotland Yard '36

Steven Hill
Running on Empty '88
Yentl '83

Terence Hill
Lucky Luke '94
My Name is Nobody '74
Super Fuzz '81

Terence Hill ▲
Lucky Luke '94

Teresa Hill
Bio-Dome '96

Walter Hill ▲
Brewster's Millions '85
Geronimo: An American
   Legend '93

Marcel Hillaire
Take the Money and Run '69

Arthur Hiller ▲
Author! Author! '82
The Babe '92
Man of La Mancha '72
Miracle of the White
   Stallions '63
The Silver Streak '76

Bernard Hiller
Avalon '90

Wendy Hiller
Anne of Avonlea '87

David Copperfield '70
The Elephant Man '80
A Man for All Seasons '66

John Hillerman
Audrey Rose '77
Paper Moon '73

Beverly Hills
Knights & Emeralds '87

Art Hindle
Invasion of the Body
    Snatchers '78
Wild Pony '83

Samuel S. Hinds
It's a Wonderful Life '46

Damon Hines
Once Upon a Time . . . When
    We Were Colored '95

Gregory Hines
Puss 'n Boots '84
Renaissance Man '94
Waiting to Exhale '95

Pat Hingle
Baby Boom '87
Batman '89
Batman Forever '95
Batman Returns '92
Brewster's Millions '85
Hazel's People '75
Lightning Jack '94
Norma Rae '79
Running Brave '83
Running Wild '73

Akihiko Hirata
Godzilla vs. the Cosmic
    Monster '74

Bettina Hirsch ▲
Munchies '87

Judd Hirsch
Independence Day '96
Running on Empty '88

Alfred Hitchcock ▲
The Birds '63
Dial "M" for Murder '54
Foreign Correspondent '40
I Confess '53
Jamaica Inn '39
The Lady Vanishes '38
Mr. & Mrs. Smith '41
North by Northwest '59
Notorious '46
The Paradine Case '47
Rear Window '54
Rebecca '40
Saboteur '42
Shadow of a Doubt '43
Spellbound '45
Stage Fright '50
Strangers on a Train '51
Suspicion '41
The 39 Steps '35
To Catch a Thief '55
Torn Curtain '66
Under Capricorn '49

The Wrong Man '56

Patricia Hitchcock
Strangers on a Train '51

Jack B. Hively ▲
The Adventures of Huckleberry
    Finn '78
Starbird and Sweet
    William '73

Judith Hoag
Teenage Mutant Ninja Turtles
    1: The Movie '90

Deborah Hobart
Gordy '95

Rose Hobart
The Farmer's Daughter '47

Halliwell Hobbes
Journey for Margaret '42

Lyndall Hobbs ▲
Back to the Beach '87

Mara Hobel
Mommie Dearest '81

Victoria Hochberg ▲
Jacob Have I Loved '88
Sweet 15 '90

Patricia Hodge
Diamond's Edge '88

Eddie Hodges
The Adventures of Huckleberry
    Finn '60
Summer Magic '63

Mike Hodges ▲
Flash Gordon '80

Ralph Hodges
Sea Hound '47

Thomas E. Hodges
Lucas '86

Tobias Hoesl
The Polar Bear King '94

John Hofeus
Return to Boggy Creek '77

Basil Hoffman
The Double O Kid '92

Dustin Hoffman
All the President's Men '76
Dick Tracy '90
Hero '92
Hook '91
Kramer vs. Kramer '79
Little Big Man '70
Outbreak '94
Papillon '73
Rain Man '88
Tootsie '82

Gaby Hoffman
Field of Dreams '89
The Man Without a Face '93
Now and Then '95

Sleepless in Seattle '93
This is My Life '92
Uncle Buck '89

Herman Hoffman ▲
The Invisible Boy '57
It's a Dog's Life '55

Philip S. Hoffman
Leap of Faith '92

Robert Hoffman
Joe Panther '76

Shawn Hoffman
Adventures in Dinosaur
    City '92

Susan Lee Hoffman
Wizards of the Lost Kingdom
    2 '89

Gabriel Hogan
The Halfback of Notre
    Dame '96

Hulk Hogan
Happy Birthday, Bugs: 50
    Looney Years '90
Mr. Nanny '93
No Holds Barred '89
Suburban Commando '91

Michael Hogan
The Peanut Butter
    Solution '85

Pat Hogan
Davy Crockett, King of the
    Wild Frontier '55
Indian Paint '64

Paul Hogan
Almost an Angel '90
Crocodile Dundee '86
Crocodile Dundee 2 '88
Flipper '96
Lightning Jack '94

P.J. Hogan ▲
Muriel's Wedding '94

Robert Hogan
Gone are the Days '84

Susan Hogan
White Fang '91

Hal Holbrook
All the President's Men '76
Fletch Lives '89
The Great White Hope '70

Sarah Holcomb
Caddyshack '80

Fay Holden
Andy Hardy Gets Spring
    Fever '39
Andy Hardy Meets
    Debutante '40
Andy Hardy's Double Life '42
Andy Hardy's Private
    Secretary '41

Life Begins for Andy
    Hardy '41
Love Finds Andy Hardy '38
Love Laughs at Andy
    Hardy '46

Mark Holden
Blue Fire Lady '78

William Holden
The Bridge on the River
    Kwai '57
Country Girl '54
Earthling '80
Sabrina '54
When Wolves Cry '69

Winifred Holden
Strangers in Good
    Company '91

Geoffrey Holder
Doctor Doolittle '67
Live and Let Die '73

Judd Holdren
Zombies of the
    Stratosphere '52

Ronald Holgate
1776 '72

Agnieszka Holland ▲
The Secret Garden '93

Nicholas Holland
Dusty '85

Steve Holland
Flash Gordon: Vol. 1 '53

Steve Holland ▲
Better Off Dead '85
How I Got into College '89
One Crazy Summer '86

Todd Holland ▲
The Wizard '89

Steve Hollar
Hoosiers '86

Judy Holliday
Adam's Rib '50

Polly Holliday
Gremlins '84
Konrad '85
Lots of Luck '85
Mr. Wrong '95

Earl Holliman
Forbidden Planet '56
Giant '56
Smoke '70

Tommy Hollis
Malcolm X '92

Sterling Holloway
The Adventures of Huckleberry
    Finn '60
Super Seal '77

W.E. Holloway
Elephant Boy '37

Lauren Holly
Beautiful Girls '96
Down Periscope '96
Dragon: The Bruce Lee
    Story '93
Dumb & Dumber '94
Sabrina '95

Celeste Holm
Cinderella '64
High Society '56
Three Men and a Baby '87
Tom Sawyer '73

Ian Holm
Chariots of Fire '81
Dreamchild '85
Greystoke: The Legend of
    Tarzan, Lord of the
    Apes '84
Loch Ness '96
The Man in the Iron Mask '77
The Thief of Baghdad '78
Time Bandits '81

Brittany Ashton Holmes
The Little Rascals '94

Fred Holmes ▲
Dakota '88
Harley '90

Luree Holmes
How to Stuff a Wild Bikini '65
Pajama Party '64

Phillips Holmes
General Spanky '36

Taylor Holmes
Tobor the Great '54

Hans Holt
Almost Angels '62

Jack Holt
Holt of the Secret Service '42
The Littlest Rebel '35

Patrick Holt
When Dinosaurs Ruled the
    Earth '70

Tim Holt
Treasure of the Sierra
    Madre '48

Mark Holton
Pee Wee's Big Adventure '85

Miroslav Holub
The Fabulous World of Jules
    Verne '58

Skip Homeier
Johnny Shiloh '63
Starbird and Sweet
    William '73

Oscar Homolka
I Remember Mama '48
Mooncussers '62
The Wonderful World of the
    Brothers Grimm '62

Inoshiro Honda ▲
Destroy All Monsters '68

James Hong
Big Trouble in Little China '86
The Golden Child '86
Wayne's World 2 '93

Darla Hood
Little Rascals Christmas
    Special '79

Harry Hook ▲
Lord of the Flies '90

Jan Hooks
Batman Returns '92
Coneheads '93
Pee Wee's Big Adventure '85

Kevin Hooks
Innerspace '87
Sounder '72

Robert Hooks
Words by Heart '84

Kaitlyn Hooper
Addams Family Values '93

Kristen Hooper
Addams Family Values '93

Tobe Hooper ▲
Invaders from Mars '86
Poltergeist '82
Salem's Lot '79

Peter Hooten
Dr. Strange '78

Bob Hope
Cancel My Reservation '72
My Favorite Brunette '47
The Seven Little Foys '55
Sorrowful Jones '49

Anthony Hopkins
Audrey Rose '77
The Bounty '84
A Bridge Too Far '77
Chaplin '92
The Elephant Man '80
Howard's End '92
The Hunchback of Notre
    Dame '82
International Velvet '78
Legends of the Fall '94
The Lion in Winter '68
The Remains of the Day '93
Shadowlands '93

Bo Hopkins
American Graffiti '73
Culpepper Cattle Co. '72
The Legend of Wolf
    Mountain '92
More American Graffiti '79
A Smoky Mountain
    Christmas '86

Dennis Hopper
Giant '56
Hoosiers '86

My Science Project '85
Rebel Without a Cause '55
Rumble Fish '83
Speed '94
Super Mario Bros. '93
Waterworld '95

William Hopper
Rebel Without a Cause '55

John Hora
Innerspace '87

Gerard Horan
Much Ado About Nothing '93

Michael Hordern
A Christmas Carol '51
Dr. Syn, Alias the
    Scarecrow '64
Lady Jane '85
The Old Curiosity Shop '75
Oliver Twist '82
The Secret Garden '87
Young Sherlock Holmes '85

Gen Horiuchi
George Balanchine's The
    Nutcracker '93

Nicholas Hormann
The Trial of the Incredible
    Hulk '89

Jeffrey Hornaday ▲
Shout '91

Geoffrey Horne
The Bridge on the River
    Kwai '57

James W. Horne ▲
Green Archer '40
Holt of the Secret Service '42

Lena Horne
Till the Clouds Roll By '46
The Wiz '78

Wil Horneff
Born to Be Wild '95

Jane Horrocks
The Witches '90

Michael Horse
House of Cards '92
Legend of the Lone
    Ranger '81
Wagons East '94

Edward Everett Horton
Shall We Dance '37

Peter Horton
The Baby-Sitters Club '95
Where the River Runs
    Black '86

Peter Horton ▲
The Cure '95

Emil Horvath Jr.
On the Comet '68

Tushka Hose
Hector's Bunyip '86

Bob Hoskins
Hook '91
Mermaids '90
Super Mario Bros. '93
Sweet Liberty '86
Who Framed Roger Rabbit?
    '88

Farina Hoskins
The Return of Our Gang '25

Jannie Hoskins
The Return of Our Gang '25

Joan Hotchkis
Ode to Billy Joe '76

John Hough ▲
The Black Arrow '84
Escape to Witch Mountain '75
Return from Witch
    Mountain '78
Sudden Terror '70
Treasure Island '72
Watcher in the Woods '81

John Houseman
The Cheap Detective '78
My Bodyguard '80
The Naked Gun: From the
    Files of Police Squad '88
The Paper Chase '73

Donald Houston
The Bushbaby '70
The Prince and the
    Pauper '62

George Houston
Let's Sing Again '36

Renee Houston
The Belles of St. Trinian's '53

Whitney Houston
Waiting to Exhale '95

Arliss Howard
Men Don't Leave '89
Plain Clothes '88
The Prodigal '83
To Wong Foo, Thanks for
    Everything, Julie
    Newmar '95

Barbara Howard
Running Mates '86

Clint Howard
Bigfoot: The Unforgettable
    Encounter '94
Cocoon '85
Eat My Dust '76
Far and Away '92
Gentle Ben '69
Gentle Giant '67
Gung Ho '85
Huckleberry Finn '75
Rock 'n' Roll High School '79
The Wild Country '71

Curly Howard
Snow White and the Three
   Stooges '61
Three Stooges: A Ducking
   They Will Go '30s
Three Stooges: A Plumbing
   We Will Go '34
Three Stooges: Cash and
   Carry '40s
Three Stooges: If a Body
   Meets a Body '34
Three Stooges: In the Sweet
   Pie and Pie '40s
Three Stooges: So Long Mr.
   Chumps '40s
Three Stooges: What's the
   Matador? '40s

David Howard ▲
The Lost Jungle '34

Elston Howard
Robotech, Vol. 1: Booby
   Trap '85

Frank Howard
That Was Then. . .This Is
   Now '85

Jean Howard
Huckleberry Finn '75

Jean Speegle Howard
Apollo 13 '95

John Howard
The Philadelphia Story '40
Young Einstein '89

Ken Howard
The Net '95
1776 '72

Leslie Howard
Gone with the Wind '39

Moe Howard
Snow White and the Three
   Stooges '61
Three Stooges '30s
Three Stooges: A Ducking
   They Will Go '30s
Three Stooges: A Plumbing
   We Will Go '34
Three Stooges: Cash and
   Carry '40s
Three Stooges: If a Body
   Meets a Body '34
Three Stooges: In the Sweet
   Pie and Pie '40s
Three Stooges Meet
   Hercules '61
Three Stooges: So Long Mr.
   Chumps '40s
Three Stooges: What's the
   Matador? '40s

Rance Howard
Bigfoot: The Unforgettable
   Encounter '94
Eat My Dust '76
Far and Away '92
Gentle Ben '69

Huckleberry Finn '75
Where the Lilies Bloom '74
The Wild Country '71

Ron Howard
American Graffiti '73
The Courtship of Eddie's
   Father '62
Eat My Dust '76
Huckleberry Finn '75
More American Graffiti '79
The Music Man '62
The Shootist '76
Smoke '70
The Wild Country '71

Ron Howard ▲
Apollo 13 '95
Cocoon '85
Far and Away '92
Gung Ho '85
The Paper '94
Parenthood '89
Splash '84
Willow '88

Shemp Howard
Africa Screams '49
Buck Privates '41
Three Stooges '30s

Trevor Howard
Battle of Britain '69
The Count of Monte Cristo '74
Ryan's Daughter '70
Superman 1: The Movie '78
Sword of the Valiant '83

Clark Howat
Billy Jack '71

C. Thomas Howell
Breaking the Rules '92
E.T.: The Extra-Terrestrial '82
Gettysburg '93
The Outsiders '83
The Return of the
   Musketeers '89
Secret Admirer '85
Soul Man '86
Tank '83
That Night '93

Peter Howell
Shadowlands '93

Frankie Howerd
Great St. Trinian's Train
   Robbery '66

Sally Ann Howes
Chitty Chitty Bang Bang '68

John Howley ▲
Happily Ever After '93

Olin Howlin
Nancy Drew, Reporter '39

Faith Hubley ▲
The Cosmic Eye '71

Season Hubley
Caddie Woodlawn '88

Whip Hubley
Russkies '87
Top Gun '86

Cooper Huckabee
Joni '79

Walter Hudd
Elephant Boy '37
The Prince and the
   Pauper '62

David Huddleston
Life with Mikey '93
Santa Claus: The Movie '85

Reginald Hudlin ▲
House Party '90

Ernie Hudson
Airheads '94
The Basketball Diaries '94
Congo '95
The Crow '93
Ghostbusters '84
Ghostbusters 2 '89
In the Army Now '94
Speechless '94

Hugh Hudson ▲
Chariots of Fire '81
Greystoke: The Legend of
   Tarzan, Lord of the
   Apes '84

Rochelle Hudson
Curly Top '35
Rebel Without a Cause '55

Rock Hudson
Avalanche '78
Giant '56
Ice Station Zebra '68

Toni Hudson
Just One of the Guys '85

David Huffman
Ice Castles '79

Billy Hufsey
Magic Kid '92

Daniel Hugh-Kelly
The Good Son '93

Albert Hughes ▲
Menace II Society '93

Allen Hughes ▲
Menace II Society '93

Andrew Hughes
Destroy All Monsters '68

Barnard Hughes
The Adventures of Huckleberry
   Finn '85
Doc Hollywood '91
Homeward Bound '80
The Lost Boys '87
Oh, God! '77
Past the Bleachers '95
Sister Act 2: Back in the
   Habit '93

Tron '82

Bronwen Hughes ▲
Harriet the Spy '96

Carol Hughes
Flash Gordon Conquers the
   Universe '40
Renfrew of the Royal
   Mounted '37
Silver Stallion '41

Catherine Hughes
Radio Patrol '37

Finola Hughes
Aspen Extreme '93

Helen Hughes
The Peanut Butter
   Solution '85

John Hughes
That Sinking Feeling '79

John Hughes ▲
The Breakfast Club '85
Curly Sue '91
Ferris Bueller's Day Off '86
Planes, Trains &
   Automobiles '87
She's Having a Baby '88
Sixteen Candles '84
Uncle Buck '89
Weird Science '85

Ken Hughes ▲
Chitty Chitty Bang Bang '68

Kristen Hughes
Jane & the Lost City '87

Lloyd Hughes
Blake of Scotland Yard '36

Megan Hughes
Adventures in Dinosaur
   City '92

Miko Hughes
Apollo 13 '95
Cops and Robbersons '94
Jack the Bear '93

Terry Hughes ▲
The Butcher's Wife '91

Tresa Hughes
Skylark '93

Wendy Hughes
Careful, He Might Hear
   You '84
Princess Caraboo '94

Tom Hulce
Amadeus '84
Dominick & Eugene '88
Parenthood '89

Dianne Hull
Aloha, Bobby and Rose '74
The New Adventures of Pippi
   Longstocking '88

Cast/Director Index

Kurt Ida
The Adventures of Huckleberry Finn '78

Eric Idle
The Adventures of Baron Munchausen '89
And Now for Something Completely Different '72
Casper '95
Jabberwocky '77
Mom and Dad Save the World '92
Monty Python and the Holy Grail '75
The Pied Piper of Hamelin '84

Eric Idle ▲
The Tale of the Frog Prince '83

Cinnamon Idles
Kidco '83
Sixteen Candles '84

Jean Image ▲
Aladdin and His Magic Lamp '69

Iman
House Party 2: The Pajama Jam '91
L.A. Story '91
Star Trek 6: The Undiscovered Country '91

Michael Imperioli
The Basketball Diaries '94

Frieda Inescort
Tarzan Finds a Son '39

Sarah Inglis
Battle of the Bullies '85

Rex Ingram
The Adventures of Huckleberry Finn '39
Thief of Baghdad '40

Frank Inn
Benji the Hunted '87

Neil Innes
Monty Python and the Holy Grail '75

Harold Innocent
Robin Hood: Prince of Thieves '91

John Ireland
Kavik, the Wolf Dog '84

Kathy Ireland
Mr. Destiny '90
Mom and Dad Save the World '92
National Lampoon's Loaded Weapon 1 '93
Necessary Roughness '91

Jeremy Irons
Die Hard: With a Vengeance '95

Michael Ironside
Father Hood '93
Highlander 2: The Quickening '91
Top Gun '86

John Irvin ▲
Turtle Diary '86

Sam Irvin ▲
Magic Island '95
Out There '95

Kathleen Irvine
Greenstone '85

Kevin Irvine ▲
Greenstone '85

Amy Irving
Crossing Delancey '88
Rumpelstiltskin '86
Yentl '83

David Irving ▲
Cannon Movie Tales: The Emperor's New Clothes '89
Rumpelstiltskin '86

George Irving
Captain January '36

Bill Irwin
Eight Men Out '88
Popeye '80

Chris Isaak
Little Buddha '93

Robert Iscove ▲
The Lawrenceville Stories '80s
The Little Mermaid '84
Puss 'n Boots '84

Takaaki Ishibashi
Major League 2 '94

Neal Israel ▲
Breaking the Rules '92
Moving Violations '85
Surf Ninjas '93

Robert Ito
The Adventures of Buckaroo Banzai Across the Eighth Dimension '84

Jose Iturbi
Anchors Aweigh '45

Rosalind Ivan
The Corn is Green '45

Zeljko Ivanek
School Ties '92
White Squall '96

Robert Ivers
The Delicate Delinquent '56

Burl Ives
East of Eden '54
So Dear to My Heart '49
Summer Magic '63

Dana Ivey
The Addams Family '91
Addams Family Values '93
The Adventures of Huck Finn '93
Dirty Rotten Scoundrels '88
Explorers '85
Home Alone 2: Lost in New York '92
Sabrina '95
The Scarlet Letter '95

Judith Ivey
Brighton Beach Memoirs '86
Frogs! '90s
Harry & Son '84
Hello Again '87

James Ivory ▲
Howard's End '92
Jefferson in Paris '94
Mr. & Mrs. Bridge '91
The Remains of the Day '93

Jackee
Ladybugs '92

Anne Jackson
Sam's Son '84

Dan Jackson
Mysterious Island '61

Eugene Jackson
The Return of Our Gang '25

Freda Jackson
The Valley of Gwangi '69

George Jackson ▲
House Party 2: The Pajama Jam '91

Glenda Jackson
King of the Wind '93
Turtle Diary '86

Gordon Jackson
The Fighting Prince of Donegal '66
The Prime of Miss Jean Brodie '69

Janet Jackson
Poetic Justice '93

John M. Jackson
Sudie & Simpson '90

Jonathan Jackson
Camp Nowhere '94

Joshua Jackson
Digger '94
Magic in the Water '95
The Mighty Ducks '92

Lamont Jackson
Class Act '91

Larry Jackson ▲
Bugs Bunny Superstar '75

Lauren Jackson
Alex '92

Michael Jackson
The Wiz '78

Mick Jackson ▲
Clean Slate '94
L.A. Story '91

Samuel L. Jackson
Amos and Andrew '93
Die Hard: With a Vengeance '95
Jurassic Park '93
Menace II Society '93
National Lampoon's Loaded Weapon 1 '93

Sherry Jackson
The Adventures of Huckleberry Finn '60
Miracle of Our Lady of Fatima '52

Sonia Jackson
Clifford '92

Stoney Jackson
Up Against the Wall '91

Victoria Jackson
Baby Boom '87
Dream a Little Dream '89
UHF '89

Wilfred Jackson ▲
Cinderella '50

Irene Jacob
Au Revoir Les Enfants '87
Othello '95

Derek Jacobi
The Hunchback of Notre Dame '82
Little Dorrit, Film 1: Nobody's Fault '88
Little Dorrit, Film 2: Little Dorrit's Story '88
The Secret Garden '87

Lou Jacobi
Arthur '81
Avalon '90
I.Q. '94
My Favorite Year '82

Lawrence Jacobs ▲
Fievel's American Tails: A Mouse Known as Zorrowitz/Aunt Sophie's Visit '94

Lawrence-Hilton Jacobs
Cooley High '75

Manny Jacobs
Battle of the Bullies '85

Peter Jacobs
Philadelphia '93

Billy Jacoby
Beastmaster '82
Just One of the Guys '85

Bobby Jacoby
Wizards of the Lost Kingdom
2 '89

Irving Jacoby ▲
Snow Treasure '67

Scott Jacoby
The Little Girl Who Lives
Down the Lane '76

Hattie Jacques
A Christmas Carol '51

Richard Jaeckel
Cold River '81
Herbie Goes Bananas '80
Starman '84

Sam Jaffe
Battle Beyond the Stars '80
Bedknobs and
Broomsticks '71

Saeed Jaffrey
The Man Who Would Be
King '75

Dean Jagger
Alligator '80
It's a Dog's Life '55
White Christmas '54

Sam Jaimes ▲
The Charlie Brown and
Snoopy Show: Vol. 1 '83

Lisa Jakub
Matinee '92
Rambling Rose '91
The Story Lady '93

Brion James
Black Magic '92
Cabin Boy '94
Enemy Mine '85
Radioland Murders '94
Savage Land '94

Clifton James
The Bad News Bears in
Breaking Training '77
David and Lisa '62
Eight Men Out '88
Live and Let Die '73
The Man with the Golden
Gun '74

Dalton James
My Father the Hero '93

Gennie James
The River Pirates '94
The Secret Garden '87
A Smoky Mountain
Christmas '86

Gerald James
Hope and Glory '87

Geraldine James
If Looks Could Kill '91
Moll Flanders '96

Godfrey James
Leapin' Leprechauns '95

Hawthorne James
Speed '94

Jessica James
Immediate Family '89

Ron James
Ernest Rides Again '93

Steve James
The Brother from Another
Planet '84
Weekend at Bernie's 2 '93

Steve James ▲
Hoop Dreams '94

Louise Jameson
My Friend Walter '93

Mikki Jamison-Olsen
Sea Gypsies '78

DeWitt Jan
Harley '90

Topsy Jane
The Loneliness of the Long
Distance Runner '62

Conrad Janis
The Buddy Holly Story '78
Oh, God! Book 2 '80

Zoran Janjic ▲
A Connecticut Yankee in King
Arthur's Court '70

Annabel Jankel ▲
Super Mario Bros. '93

Ellen Janov
The Horse in the Gray Flannel
Suit '68

Andre Jansen
A Waltz Through the Hills '88

Jim Jansen
Dennis the Menace: Dinosaur
Hunter '87

Per Jansen
The Littlest Viking '94

Eilene Janssen
Curley '47

Famke Janssen
Goldeneye '95

Claude Jarman Jr.
The Yearling '46

Gabe Jarret
Real Genius '85

Charles Jarrott ▲
Condorman '81
The Dove '74
The Last Flight of Noah's
Ark '80
The Littlest Horse Thieves '76

Vojtech Jasny ▲
The Great Land of Small '86

Harvey Jason
Oklahoma Crude '73

Peter Jason
Arachnophobia '90
Hyper-Sapien: People from
Another Star '86

Sybil Jason
The Blue Bird '40
The Little Princess '39

Star Jasper
Jersey Girl '92

Ricky Jay
Hole in the Sky '95

Barbara Jefford
Reunion '88
When the Whales Came '89

Peter Jeffrey
The Adventures of Baron
Munchausen '89
Ring of Bright Water '69

Anne Jeffreys
Dick Tracy, Detective '45

Lionel Jeffries
Blue Murder at St.
Trinian's '56
Camelot '67
Chitty Chitty Bang Bang '68
First Men in the Moon '64
Sudden Terror '70

Lionel Jeffries ▲
Amazing Mr. Blunden '72
Water Babies '79

Rudolph Jelinek
The Original Fabulous
Adventures of Baron
Munchausen '61

Allen Jenkins
I Am a Fugitive from a Chain
Gang '32

Jackie "Butch" Jenkins
The Human Comedy '43
National Velvet '44

Ken Jenkins
Past the Bleachers '95

Richard Jenkins
Eddie '96
The Indian in the
Cupboard '95
It Could Happen to You '94
Trapped In Paradise '94

Frank Jenks
His Girl Friday '40

Si Jenks
Captain January '36

Lucinda Jenney
American Heart '92
Matinee '92
Rain Man '88

Byron Jennings
A Simple Twist of Fate '94

Waylon Jennings
Sesame Street Presents:
Follow That Bird '85

Astrid Henning Jensen ▲
Boy of Two Worlds '70

David Jensen
King of the Hill '93

Karen Jensen
Battlestar Galactica '78

Sasha Jensen
Dazed and Confused '93

Adele Jergens
Blues Busters '50

Michael Jeter
Sister Act 2: Back in the
Habit '93
Waterworld '95

Joan Jett
Light of Day '87

Geri Jewell
Two of a Kind '82

Isabel Jewell
Gone with the Wind '39

Norman Jewison ▲
Fiddler on the Roof '71
Jesus Christ, Superstar '73
Moonstruck '87
Only You '94
The Russians are Coming, the
Russians are Coming '66

Penn Jillette
Hackers '95

Ann Jillian
Mr. Mom '83

Yolanda Jilot
Diving In '90

Robert Jiras ▲
I am the Cheese '83

Mike Jittlov
The Wizard of Speed and
Time '88

Mike Jittlov ▲
The Wizard of Speed and
Time '88

Phil Joanou ▲
Three O'Clock High '87

Tricia Joe
The Baby-Sitters Club '95

Michael Joens ▲
My Little Pony: The Movie '86

Roland Joffe ▲
The Scarlet Letter '95

David Johansen
Car 54, Where Are You? '94
Mr. Nanny '93
Scrooged '88

Elton John
Tommy '75

Gottfried John
Goldeneye '95

Alexandra Johnes
Zelly & Me '88

Glynis Johns
The Court Jester '56
Dear Brigitte '65
Mary Poppins '64
Nukie '93
Rob Roy - The Highland
   Rogue '53
The Sword & the Rose '53
While You Were Sleeping '95
Zelly & Me '88

Mervyn Johns
A Christmas Carol '51
Tony Draws a Horse '51

A.J. Johnson
House Party '90

Alan Johnson ▲
Solarbabies '86

Amy Jo Johnson
Mighty Morphin Power
   Rangers: The Movie '95

Anne-Marie Johnson
Dream Date '93
Robot Jox '89

Arte Johnson
The Charge of the Model
   T's '76
Love at First Bite '79
Munchie '92

Ben Johnson
Angels in the Outfield '94
Bonanza: The Return '93
Junior Bonner '72
Mighty Joe Young '49
My Heroes Have Always Been
   Cowboys '91
Radio Flyer '92
The Shadow Riders '82
Shane '53
The Swarm '78
Tex '82
Tomboy & the Champ '58

Brad Johnson
Always '89

Candy Johnson
Beach Party '63
Bikini Beach '64

Muscle Beach Party '64
Pajama Party '64

Celia Johnson
The Prime of Miss Jean
   Brodie '69

Don Johnson
Born Yesterday '93
Paradise '91

Georgann Johnson
Murphy's Romance '85

Kearo Johnson
Love Your Mama '89

Kenneth Johnson ▲
The Incredible Hulk '77
Short Circuit 2 '88

Kyle Johnson
The Learning Tree '69

Lamont Johnson ▲
Jack & the Beanstalk '83
The Last American Hero '73
One on One '77

Lynn-Holly Johnson
For Your Eyes Only '81
Ice Castles '79
Watcher in the Woods '81

Michelle Johnson
Death Becomes Her '92
Far and Away '92
Gung Ho '85

Noble Johnson
King Kong '33

Patrick Read Johnson ▲
Angus '95
Baby's Day Out '94
Spaced Invaders '90

Penny Johnson
What's Love Got to Do With
   It? '93

Richard Johnson
Diving In '90
Lady Jane '85
Treasure Island '89
Turtle Diary '86

Rita Johnson
My Friend Flicka '43

Ron Johnson
Zebrahead '92

Sunny Johnson
Flashdance '83

Tor Johnson
Carousel '56

Van Johnson
The Human Comedy '43
The Pied Piper of Hamelin '57
The Purple Rose of Cairo '85
Yours, Mine & Ours '68

Joe Johnston ▲
Honey, I Shrunk the Kids '89
Jumanji '95
The Pagemaster '94
The Rocketeer '91

John Dennis Johnston
Pink Cadillac '89

Angelina Jolie
Hackers '95

I. Stanford Jolley
The Crimson Ghost '46
King of the Rocketmen '49

Lisa Jolliff-Andoh
The Scarlet Letter '95

Allan Jones
A Day at the Races '37
A Night at the Opera '35

Amy Holden Jones ▲
Maid to Order '87

Barry Jones
Prince Valiant '54

Ben Jones
Don't Change My World '83

Carolyn Jones
House of Wax '53
How the West was Won '63

Catherine Zeta Jones
Christopher Columbus: The
   Discovery '92
The Phantom '96

Christopher Jones
Ryan's Daughter '70

Chuck Jones
Chuck Amuck: The Movie '91
Innerspace '87

Chuck Jones ▲
Best of Bugs Bunny &
   Friends '40
Bugs & Daffy's Carnival of the
   Animals '89
Bugs Bunny Cartoon
   Festival '44
Bugs Bunny in King Arthur's
   Court '89
The Bugs Bunny/Road Runner
   Movie '79
Bugs Bunny's 3rd Movie:
   1,001 Rabbit Tales '82
Bugs Bunny's Bustin' Out All
   Over '80
Bugs Bunny's Hare-Raising
   Tales '89
Bugs Bunny's Looney
   Christmas Tales '79
A Christmas Carol '84
Daffy Duck's Madcap
   Mania '89
Looney Looney Looney Bugs
   Bunny Movie '81
Looney Tunes Video Show,
   Vol. 1

Looney Tunes Video Show,
   Vol. 2
Looney Tunes Video Show,
   Vol. 3
Phantom Tollbooth '69
A Salute to Chuck Jones '60
A Salute to Mel Blanc '58
A Very Merry Cricket '73

Cody Jones
Rent-A-Kid '95

Davy Jones
Head '68
Monkees, Volume 1 '66

Dean Jones
Beethoven '92
Blackbeard's Ghost '67
Herbie Goes to Monte
   Carlo '77
The Horse in the Gray Flannel
   Suit '68
The Love Bug '68
Million Dollar Duck '71
Monkeys, Go Home! '66
Once Upon a Brothers
   Grimm '77
The Shaggy D.A. '76
Snowball Express '72
That Darn Cat '65
The Ugly Dachshund '65
When Every Day was the
   Fourth of July '78

Dick Jones
Nancy Drew, Reporter '39

Doug Jones
Hocus Pocus '93

Duane Jones
Beat Street '84

Ed "Too Tall" Jones
The Double McGuffin '79

Eddie Jones
Sneakers '92

Freddie Jones
The Elephant Man '80
Erik the Viking '89
Krull '83
The Neverending Story 3 '94
Young Sherlock Holmes '85

Gemma Jones
Sense and Sensibility '95

Gordon Jones
The Green Hornet '39

Grace Jones
Conan the Destroyer '84
A View to a Kill '85

Henry Jones
Arachnophobia '90
The Bad Seed '56
Butch Cassidy and the
   Sundance Kid '69
Napoleon and Samantha '72

Support Your Local
    Gunfighter '71

James Earl Jones
Aladdin and His Wonderful
    Lamp '84
Allan Quartermain and the
    Lost City of Gold '86
Bingo Long Traveling All-Stars
    & Motor Kings '76
Clean Slate '94
Clear and Present Danger '94
Conan the Barbarian '82
Cry, the Beloved Country '95
A Family Thing '96
Field of Dreams '89
The Great White Hope '70
The Greatest '77
The Hunt for Red October '90
Jefferson in Paris '94
Lone Star Kid '88
Matewan '87
The Meteor Man '93
Piece of the Action '77
Return of the Jedi '83
The Sandlot '93
Sneakers '92
Sommersby '93
Soul Man '86
Star Wars '77
Three Fugitives '89

Janet Jones
American Anthem '86
The Flamingo Kid '84
Police Academy 5: Assignment
    Miami Beach '88

Jeffrey Jones
Amadeus '84
Beetlejuice '88
Ferris Bueller's Day Off '86
Houseguest '94
Howard the Duck '86
The Hunt for Red October '90
Mom and Dad Save the
    World '92
Out on a Limb '92
Stay Tuned '92

Jennifer Jones
Dick Tracy '37
Since You Went Away '44

John Marshall Jones
Sgt. Bilko '95

Lisa Jones
Life & Times of Grizzly
    Adams '74

L.Q. Jones
Grizzly Adams: The Legend
    Continues '90
Lightning Jack '94
Timerider '83

Marcia Mae Jones
The Little Princess '39

Nicholas Jones
Black Beauty '94

Richard T. Jones
Renaissance Man '94

Sam Jones
Flash Gordon '80
Jane & the Lost City '87

Sharon Lee Jones
Leapin' Leprechauns '95

Shirley Jones
Carousel '56
The Courtship of Eddie's
    Father '62
The Music Man '62
Oklahoma! '55
Tank '83
Who'll Save Our Children?
    '82

Simon Jones
Club Paradise '86
Green Card '90
Miracle on 34th Street '94

Terry Jones
And Now for Something
    Completely Different '72
Erik the Viking '89
Jabberwocky '77
Monty Python and the Holy
    Grail '75

Terry Jones ▲
Erik the Viking '89
Monty Python and the Holy
    Grail '75

Tommy Lee Jones
Batman Forever '95
The Client '94
Coal Miner's Daughter '80
The Fugitive '93
House of Cards '92
Nate and Hayes '83
The River Rat '84

Samson Jorah
Never Cry Wolf '83

Bobby Jordan
Bowery Blitzkrieg '41
Bowery Buckaroos '47
Boys of the City '40
Hard-Boiled Mahoney '47
Kid Dynamite '43
'Neath Brooklyn Bridge '42
Spook Busters '46
Spooks Run Wild '41
That Gang of Mine '40

Glenn Jordan ▲
Sarah, Plain and Tall '91
Toughlove '85

Leslie Jordan
Ski Patrol '89

Neil Jordan ▲
The Miracle '91

Richard Jordan
Gettysburg '93
The Hunt for Red October '90

Rooster Cogburn '75
Shout '91
Solarbabies '86

William Jordan
The Buddy Holly Story '78
I Wanna Hold Your Hand '78

Knut W. Jorfald ▲
The Littlest Viking '94

Victor Jory
Gone with the Wind '39
Green Archer '40
The Miracle Worker '62
Papillon '73
Susannah of the Mounties '39

Larry Joshua
A Midnight Clear '92

Allyn Joslyn
The Horn Blows at
    Midnight '45

Louis Jourdan
The Count of Monte Cristo '74
The Man in the Iron Mask '77
Octopussy '83
The Paradine Case '47
The Return of Swamp
    Thing '89
Swamp Thing '82
Year of the Comet '92

Milla Jovovich
Chaplin '92
Kuffs '92

Robert Joy
Big Shots '87
Desperately Seeking
    Susan '85
Harriet the Spy '96
The Lawrenceville
    Stories '80s
Miracle at Moreaux '86
Waterworld '95

Edward Judd
First Men in the Moon '64

Raul Julia
The Addams Family '91
Addams Family Values '93
Escape Artist '82
Gumball Rally '76
Street Fighter '94
Trading Hearts '87

Gordon Jump
Making the Grade '84

Katy Jurado
High Noon '52
Once Upon a Scoundrel '73

Nathan (Hertz) Juran ▲
First Men in the Moon '64
Jack the Giant Killer '62
The Seventh Voyage of
    Sinbad '58

Peter Jurasik
Problem Child '90

Curt Jurgens
Battle of Britain '69
Miracle of the White
    Stallions '63
The Spy Who Loved Me '77

James Robertson Justice
Rob Roy - The Highland
    Rogue '53
The Sword & the Rose '53

Katherine Justice
Captain America 2: Death Too
    Soon '79

Kaethe Kaack
Baron Munchausen '43

Jane Kaczmarek
The Heavenly Kid '85
Vice Versa '88

Ellis Kadisan ▲
The Cat '66

Diane Kagan
Mr. & Mrs. Bridge '91

Jeremy Paul Kagan ▲
The Journey of Natty
    Gann '85
The Sting 2 '83

Marilyn Kagan
Foxes '80

Wolf Kahler
Raiders of the Lost Ark '81

Madeline Kahn
The Adventures of Sherlock
    Holmes' Smarter
    Brother '78
The Cheap Detective '78
Clue '85
The Hideaways '73
High Anxiety '77
Mixed Nuts '94
Paper Moon '73
Simon '80
Young Frankenstein '74

Khalil Kain
Renaissance Man '94

Joel Kaiser
Home for Christmas '90

Toni Kalem
Billy Galvin '86

Patricia Kalember
Big Girls Don't Cry. . .They
    Get Even '92
A Far Off Place '93

Jean-Pierre Kalfon
Condorman '81

Scott Kalvert ▲
The Basketball Diaries '94

Danny Kamekona
The Karate Kid: Part 2 '86
Robot Jox '89

Dana Kaminsky
Super Mario Bros. '93

Laura Kamrath
The Phoenix and the Magic
Carpet '95

Kamron
House Party 2: The Pajama
Jam '91

Sean Kanan
The Karate Kid: Part 3 '89

Carol Kane
Addams Family Values '93
Annie Hall '77
Baby on Board '92
Big Bully '95
Casey at the Bat '85
The Crazysitter '94
Harry & Walter Go to New
York '76
License to Drive '88
The Pallbearer '95
The Princess Bride '87
Racing with the Moon '84
Scrooged '88

Jimmy Kane
Challenge To Be Free '76

Joseph Kane ▲
Fighting Marines '36

Jeff Kanew ▲
Gotcha! '85
Revenge of the Nerds '84
Tough Guys '86
Troop Beverly Hills '89

Charles Kanganis ▲
Race the Sun '96
3 Ninjas Kick Back '94

John Kani
Sarafina! '92

John Kapelos
The Breakfast Club '85
Nothing in Common '86
Roxanne '87

Tracey Kapisky
American Heart '92

Curt Kaplan
Ed '96

Ed Kaplan ▲
Chips the War Dog '90
Walking on Air '87

Gabe Kaplan
Fast Break '79
The Hoboken Chicken
Emergency '84

Jonathan Kaplan
Cannonball '76

Jonathan Kaplan ▲
Heart Like a Wheel '83
Immediate Family '89
Over the Edge '79

Project X '87

Marvin Kaplan
Adam's Rib '50

Ron Karabatsos
Flashdance '83

Heather Karasek
The Little Rascals '94

Kym Karath
The Sound of Music '65

James Karen
Hercules in New York '70
Poltergeist '82
Sam's Son '84
Up Close and Personal '96
The Willies '90

John Karlen
Racing with the Moon '84
Surf Ninjas '93

Boris Karloff
Abbott and Costello Meet Dr.
Jekyll and Mr. Hyde '52
Dick Tracy Meets
Gruesome '47
Secret Life of Walter Mitty '47

Phil Karlson ▲
Walking Tall '73

Roscoe Karns
His Girl Friday '40
It Happened One Night '34

Todd Karns
It's a Wonderful Life '46

Sarah Rose Karr
Beethoven '92
Beethoven's 2nd '93

Alex Karras
Goldilocks & the Three
Bears '83

Vincent Kartheiser
Alaska '96

Tcheky Karyo
Bad Boys '95
The Bear '89
1492: Conquest of
Paradise '92
Goldeneye '95

Lawrence Kasdan ▲
French Kiss '95
Silverado '85

Lenore Kasdorf
Mr. Bill's Real-Life
Adventures '86

Linda Kash
Ernest Goes to School '94
Ernest Rides Again '93

Holger Kasper
The Secret of Navajo Cave '76

Kurt Kasznar
Lili '53

Kurt Katch
Ali Baba and the Forty
Thieves '43

Bernard Kates
The Babe '92

Milton Katselas ▲
Butterflies Are Free '72

Andreas Katsulas
The Fugitive '93

William Katt
Baby. . .Secret of the Lost
Legend '85
Butch and Sundance: The
Early Days '79
House '86
Pippin '81
Thumbelina '82

Omri Katz
Adventures in Dinosaur
City '92
Hocus Pocus '93
Matinee '92

Andy Kaufman
Heartbeeps '81

David Kaufman
The Last Prostitute '91

Maurice Kaufman
The Hero '71

Philip Kaufman ▲
Invasion of the Body
Snatchers '78
The Outlaw Josey Wales '76
The Right Stuff '83

Christine Kaufmann
Bagdad Cafe '88

Caroline Kava
Little Nikita '88

Julie Kavner
Awakenings '90
Bad Medicine '85
Forget Paris '95
I'll Do Anything '93
Radio Days '87
This is My Life '92

Hiroyuki Kawase
Godzilla vs. Megalon '76
Godzilla vs. the Smog
Monster '72

Dianne Kay
Andy and the Airwave
Rangers '89

Melody Kay
Camp Nowhere '94
The Neverending Story 3 '94

Celia Kaye
Island of the Blue
Dolphins '64

Danny Kaye
The Court Jester '56
Secret Life of Walter Mitty '47
White Christmas '54
Wonder Man '45

Lila Kaye
Dragonworld '94

Richard Kaye
The Wizard of Speed and
Time '88

Stubby Kaye
Guys and Dolls '55
Who Framed Roger Rabbit?
'88

Jan Kayne
Ghost Chasers '51

Elia Kazan ▲
East of Eden '54
A Tree Grows in Brooklyn '45

Lainie Kazan
Harry and the Hendersons '87
The Journey of Natty
Gann '85
My Favorite Year '82
Pinocchio '83

Fran Rubel Kazui ▲
Buffy the Vampire Slayer '92

Tim Kazurinsky
A Billion for Boris '90
Hot to Trot! '88
Police Academy 3: Back in
Training '86
Police Academy 4: Citizens on
Patrol '87
The Princess and the Pea '83

James Keach
Moving Violations '85
National Lampoon's
Vacation '83
Wildcats '86

Staci Keanan
Lisa '90

James Keane
Life on the Mississippi '80

Larry Keating
Francis Goes to the Races '51
Gypsy Colt '54
The Incredible Mr. Limpet '64
Monkey Business '52

Buster Keaton
The Adventures of Huckleberry
Finn '60
Beach Blanket Bingo '65
How to Stuff a Wild Bikini '65

Diane Keaton
Annie Hall '77
Baby Boom '87

Father of the Bride '91
Father of the Bride Part II '95
Harry & Walter Go to New
    York '76
Love and Death '75
Play It Again, Sam '72
Radio Days '87
Sleeper '73

Diane Keaton ▲
Unstrung Heroes '95

Michael Keaton
Batman '89
Batman Returns '92
Beetlejuice '88
The Dream Team '89
Gung Ho '85
Johnny Dangerously '84
Mr. Mom '83
Much Ado About Nothing '93
Multiplicity '96
My Life '93
The Paper '94
Speechless '94

Lila Kedrova
Sword of the Valiant '83
Torn Curtain '66

Andrew Keegan
Camp Nowhere '94

Howard Keel
Kismet '55
Seven Brides for Seven
    Brothers '54

Ruby Keeler
That's Dancing! '85

Geoffrey Keen
Dr. Syn, Alias the
    Scarecrow '64
For Your Eyes Only '81
Moonraker '79
The Spy Who Loved Me '77

Monica Keena
While You Were Sleeping '95

Matt Keeslar
Safe Passage '94

Jack Kehoe
The Fish that Saved
    Pittsburgh '79
A Winner Never Quits '86

William Keighley ▲
The Prince and the
    Pauper '37

Andrew Keir
Dragonworld '94
The Fighting Prince of
    Donegal '66
Rob Roy '95

Harvey Keitel
Imaginary Crimes '94
Monkey Trouble '94
Off Beat '86
Sister Act '92

Brian Keith
Joe Panther '76
Johnny Shiloh '63
The Loneliest Runner '76
Moon Pilot '62
The Parent Trap '61
The Russians are Coming, the
    Russians are Coming '66
Savage Sam '63
Scandalous John '71
Ten Who Dared '60
Those Calloways '65
A Tiger Walks '64
The Wind and the Lion '75
With Six You Get Eggroll '68
Young Guns '88

David Keith
Born Wild '95
A Family Thing '96
Gold Diggers: The Secret of
    Bear Mountain '95
The Great Santini '80
Heartbreak Hotel '88
Major League 2 '94

Cecil Kellaway
Francis Goes to the Races '51

Tina Kellegher
The Snapper '93

Harry Keller ▲
Tammy and the Doctor '63

Barbara Kellerman
The Chronicles of Narnia '89

Sally Kellerman
Back to School '86
The Big Bus '76
Boris and Natasha: The
    Movie '92
Foxes '80
A Little Romance '79
M*A*S*H '70
Moving Violations '85
Secret of the Ice Cave '89

Susan Kellerman
Oh, Heavenly Dog! '80

Barry Kelley
Francis Goes to the Races '51
Jack the Giant Killer '62

Brett Kelley
Sommersby '93

DeForest Kelley
Star Trek 2: The Wrath of
    Khan '82
Star Trek 3: The Search for
    Spock '84
Star Trek 4: The Voyage
    Home '86
Star Trek 5: The Final
    Frontier '89
Star Trek 6: The Undiscovered
    Country '91
Star Trek: The Motion
    Picture '80

Sheila Kelley
Singles '92

Barnet Kellman ▲
Straight Talk '92

David Kellogg ▲
Cool As Ice '91

John Kellogg
Jacob Have I Loved '88

Brian Kelly
Flipper '64
Flipper's New Adventure '64
Flipper's Odyssey '66

David Kelly
Into the West '92

David Patrick Kelly
Crooklyn '94
The Crow '93
Malcolm X '92

Gene Kelly
An American in Paris '51
Anchors Aweigh '45
Invitation to the Dance '56
On the Town '49
Singin' in the Rain '52
That's Dancing! '85
That's Entertainment '74
That's Entertainment, Part
    2 '76
The Three Musketeers '48
Xanadu '80

Gene Kelly ▲
Hello, Dolly! '69
Invitation to the Dance '56
On the Town '49
Singin' in the Rain '52

Grace Kelly
Country Girl '54
Dial "M" for Murder '54
High Noon '52
High Society '56
Rear Window '54
To Catch a Thief '55

Jack Kelly
Forbidden Planet '56

Jean Kelly
Uncle Buck '89

Jean Louisa Kelly
Mr. Holland's Opus '95

Moira Kelly
Chaplin '92
The Cutting Edge '92
With Honors '94

Nancy Kelly
The Bad Seed '56

Patsy Kelly
Freaky Friday '76
The North Avenue
    Irregulars '79
Please Don't Eat the
    Daisies '60

Paul Kelly
Tarzan's New York
    Adventure '42

Paula Kelly
The Andromeda Strain '71
Once Upon a Time . . . When
    We Were Colored '95

Rae'ven Kelly
What's Love Got to Do With
    It? '93

Ron Kelly ▲
King of the Grizzlies '69

Pert Kelton
The Music Man '62

Violet Kemble-Cooper
Gone with the Wind '39

Warren Kemmerling
Eat My Dust '76

Brandis Kemp
Goldilocks & the Three
    Bears '83

Jeremy Kemp
The Belstone Fox '73
When the Whales Came '89

Martin Kemp
Aspen Extreme '93

Tina Kemp
A Waltz Through the Hills '88

Will Kempe
Metropolitan '90

Rachel Kempson
Little Lord Fauntleroy '80

Cy Kendall
The Green Hornet '39
Tarzan's New York
    Adventure '42

David Kendall ▲
Luggage of the Gods '87

Suzy Kendall
To Sir, with Love '67

Alexa Kenin
Honkytonk Man '82
Pretty in Pink '86

Arthur Kennedy
Lawrence of Arabia '62
The Window '49

Burt Kennedy ▲
Suburban Commando '91
Support Your Local
    Gunfighter '71
Support Your Local Sheriff '69

Edgar Kennedy
Duck Soup '33
Little Orphan Annie '32

George Kennedy
Airport '70

Airport '75 '75
Airport '77 '77
Bandolero! '68
Cahill: United States
 Marshal '73
Charade '63
Death on the Nile '78
The Double McGuffin '79
Guns of the Magnificent
 Seven '69
Island of the Blue
 Dolphins '64
The Naked Gun: From the
 Files of Police Squad '88
Naked Gun 33 1/3: The Final
 Insult '94
Naked Gun 2 1/2: The Smell
 of Fear '91
A Rare Breed '81

Jihmi Kennedy
Glory '89

Ken Kennedy ▲
Grizzly Adams: The Legend
 Continues '90

Mimi Kennedy
Death Becomes Her '92
Immediate Family '89

Patsy Kensit
Monty Python and the Holy
 Grail '75

Barbara Kent
Oliver Twist '33

Robert Kent
Dimples '36
The Phantom Creeps '39

Dambisa Kente
Cry, the Beloved Country '95

Gwen Kenyon
The Great Mike '44

Jessie Keosian
Green Card '90

Joanna Kerns
An American Summer '90
No Dessert Dad, 'Til You Mow
 the Lawn '94

Sondra Kerns
Magic Kid '92

Bill Kerr
Dusty '85
Miracle Down Under '87
Pirate Movie '82

Bruce Kerr
The Man from Snowy
 River '82

Deborah Kerr
The King and I '56

Edward Kerr
Magic Island '95

John Kerr
South Pacific '58

Patrick Kerr
Ed '96

Irvin Kershner ▲
The Empire Strikes Back '80
Never Say Never Again '83
Robocop 2 '90

Brian Kerwin
Gold Diggers: The Secret of
 Bear Mountain '95
Jack '96
Murphy's Romance '85

Lance Kerwin
Enemy Mine '85
The Loneliest Runner '76
Salem's Lot '79
The Snow Queen '83

Maureen Kerwin
Reunion '88

Alek Keshishian ▲
With Honors '94

Sara Kestelman
Lady Jane '85

Michael Keusch ▲
Huck and the King of
 Hearts '93

Evelyn Keyes
Gone with the Wind '39
The Jolson Story '46

Irwin Keyes
The Flintstones '94

Persis Khambatta
Star Trek: The Motion
 Picture '80

Leleti Khumalo
Cry, the Beloved Country '95
Sarafina! '92

Guy Kibbee
Babes in Arms '39
Captain Blood '35
Captain January '36
The Horn Blows at
 Midnight '45
Little Lord Fauntleroy '36
Miss Annie Rooney '42
Mr. Smith Goes to
 Washington '39

Chris Kidd
Cry from the Mountain '85

Michael Kidd
Smile '75

Myrna Kidd
Cry from the Mountain '85

Margot Kidder
Beanstalk '94
The Great Waldo Pepper '75
Superman 1: The Movie '78

Superman 2 '80
Superman 3 '83
Superman 4: The Quest for
 Peace '87
Trenchcoat '83
Windrunner '94

Nicole Kidman
Batman Forever '95
BMX Bandits '83
Far and Away '92
Flirting '89
My Life '93
The Prince and the Great
 Race '83

Beeban Kidron ▲
To Wong Foo, Thanks for
 Everything, Julie
 Newmar '95

Richard Kiel
Happy Gilmore '96
Moonraker '79
The Silver Streak '76
The Spy Who Loved Me '77
They Went That-a-Way & That-
 a-Way '78
Think Big '90

Udo Kier
The Adventures of
 Pinocchio '96
For Love or Money '93
Johnny Mnemonic '95

Randi Kiger
Wonderland Cove '75

Robbie Kiger
Table for Five '83
Welcome Home, Roxy
 Carmichael '90

Percy Kilbride
State Fair '45

Terence Kilburn
A Christmas Carol '38
National Velvet '44

Richard Kiley
The Adventures of Huckleberry
 Finn '85
The Canterville Ghost '91
The Little Prince '74

Jean-Claude Killy
Club Med '83

Peter Kilman
Olly Olly Oxen Free '78

Val Kilmer
Batman Forever '95
Real Genius '85
The Real McCoy '93
Tombstone '93
Top Gun '86
Willow '88

Valentine Kim
Harley '90

Sharron Kimberly
The Party '68

Bruce Kimmel
Spaceship '81

Bruce Kimmel ▲
Spaceship '81

Kenneth Kimmins
My Best Friend Is a
 Vampire '88

Alan King
Author! Author! '82
Cat's Eye '85

Allan Winton King ▲
Silence of the North '81

Carole King
Goldilocks & the Three
 Bears '83

Caroline Junko King
3 Ninjas Kick Back '94

Charmion King
Anne of Green Gables '85
Who Has Seen the Wind? '77

Henry King ▲
Carousel '56

Mabel King
The Wiz '78

Perry King
The Lords of Flatbush '74

Regina King
Poetic Justice '93

Rick King ▲
Hot Shot '86

Walter Woolf King
A Night at the Opera '35
Smart Alecks '42

Alan Kingsberg ▲
Almost Partners '87

Walter Kingsford
The Man in the Iron Mask '39

Ben Kingsley
Dave '93
The Fifth Monkey '90
Searching for Bobby
 Fischer '93
Sneakers '92
Turtle Diary '86

Rand Kingsley
3 Ninjas '92

Susan Kingsley
Old Enough '84

Lisa Kingston
Chasing Dreams '81

Sam Kinison
Back to School '86

Melinda Kinnaman
My Life as a Dog '85

Greg Kinnear
Sabrina '95

Roy Kinnear
The Adventures of Sherlock
 Holmes' Smarter
 Brother '78
The Four Musketeers '75
Herbie Goes to Monte
 Carlo '77
Melody '71
The Return of the
 Musketeers '89
Willy Wonka & the Chocolate
 Factory '71

Jack Kinney ▲
Bongo '47

Kathy Kinney
This Boy's Life '93

Terry Kinney
Talent for the Game '91

Leonid Kinskey
Duck Soup '33

Klaus Kinski
Beauty and the Beast '83
Doctor Zhivago '65

Nastassia Kinski
Terminal Velocity '94
Tess '80

Alex Kirby ▲
The Chronicles of Narnia '89

Bruce Kirby
Throw Momma from the
 Train '87

Bruno Kirby
The Basketball Diaries '94
City Slickers '91
The Freshman '90

Joe Kirk
Smart Alecks '42

Phyllis Kirk
House of Wax '53

Tommy Kirk
The Absent-Minded
 Professor '61
Babes in Toyland '61
Escapade in Florence '62
Horsemasters '61
The Misadventures of Merlin
 Jones '63
Monkey's Uncle '65
Moon Pilot '62
Old Yeller '57
Pajama Party '64
Savage Sam '63
The Shaggy Dog '59
Son of Flubber '63
The Swiss Family
 Robinson '60

Sally Kirkland
The Way We Were '73

Stan Kirsh
Highlander: The Gathering '93

Mia Kirshner
Johnny's Girl '95

Terry Kiser
Mannequin 2: On the
 Move '91
Weekend at Bernie's '89
Weekend at Bernie's 2 '93

Darci Kistler
George Balanchine's The
 Nutcracker '93

Cathy Kitchen
Angelo My Love '83

Michael Kitchen
Goldeneye '95

Eartha Kitt
Erik the Viking '89
Ernest Scared Stupid '91
Harriet the Spy '96

John Kitzmiller
Dr. No '62

Robert Klane ▲
Weekend at Bernie's 2 '93

Nick Klein
The Phoenix and the Magic
 Carpet '95

Robert Klein
Mixed Nuts '94

**Henry Kleinbach
 (Brandon)**
March of the Wooden
 Soldiers '34

Randal Kleiser ▲
Big Top Pee Wee '88
Flight of the Navigator '86
Grease '78
Honey, I Blew Up the Kid '92
White Fang '91

Kevin Kline
Chaplin '92
Dave '93
French Kiss '95
The Pirates of Penzance '83
Princess Caraboo '94
Silverado '85

Heidi Kling
The Mighty Ducks '92
Out on a Limb '92

Garry Kluger
Hot to Trot! '88

Levi L. Knebel
Country '84

David Knell
Life on the Mississippi '80

Angele Knight
Mystery of the Million Dollar
 Hockey Puck '80s

Esmond Knight
The Red Shoes '48

Felix Knight
March of the Wooden
 Soldiers '34

Fuzzy Knight
To the Last Man '33

Michael E. Knight
Date with an Angel '87

Nic Knight
Prince Brat and the Whipping
 Boy '95

Shirley Knight
Stuart Saves His Family '94

Ted Knight
Caddyshack '80

Trenton Knight
Charlie's Ghost: The Secret of
 Coronado '94
The Tin Soldier '95

Wayne Knight
Jurassic Park '93

Andrew Knott
Black Beauty '94
The Secret Garden '93

Don Knotts
The Apple Dumpling Gang '75
The Apple Dumpling Gang
 Rides Again '79
Big Bully '95
Herbie Goes to Monte
 Carlo '77
Hot Lead & Cold Feet '78
The Incredible Mr. Limpet '64
No Deposit, No Return '76
No Time for Sergeants '58
The Private Eyes '80
Prize Fighter '79
The Reluctant Astronaut '67
The Shakiest Gun in the
 West '68

Christopher Knowings
Crooklyn '94

Patric Knowles
The Adventures of Robin
 Hood '38
How Green was My Valley '41

Elyse Knox
Don Winslow of the Coast
 Guard '43

Terence Knox
The Mighty Pawns '87

Yukiko Kobayashi
Destroy All Monsters '68

Pete Koch
Adventures in Dinosaur
 City '92

Walter Koenig
Star Trek 2: The Wrath of
 Khan '82
Star Trek 3: The Search for
 Spock '84
Star Trek 4: The Voyage
 Home '86
Star Trek 5: The Final
 Frontier '89
Star Trek 6: The Undiscovered
 Country '91
Star Trek Generations '94
Star Trek: The Motion
 Picture '80

Clarence Kolb
His Girl Friday '40

Xavier Koller ▲
Squanto: A Warrior's Tale '94

Kazuo Komatsubara ▲
Warriors of the Wind '85

Magda Konopka
When Dinosaurs Ruled the
 Earth '70

Madame Konstantin
Notorious '46

Milos Kopecky
The Original Fabulous
 Adventures of Baron
 Munchausen '61

Zoltan Korda ▲
Elephant Boy '37
The Jungle Book '42

Jon Korkes
The Day of the Dolphin '73

Harvey Korman
Curse of the Pink Panther '83
Dracula: Dead and Loving
 It '95
Gone are the Days '84
Herbie Goes Bananas '80
High Anxiety '77
Huckleberry Finn '74
Munchies '87

Mary Kornman
The Return of Our Gang '25

Charlie Korsmo
Dick Tracy '90
Hook '91
Men Don't Leave '89
What About Bob? '91

John Korty ▲
The Ewok Adventure '84
Eye on the Sparrow '91
Twice Upon a Time '83

Sylva Koscina
Hercules '58
Hercules Unchained '59

Martin Kosleck
Foreign Correspondent '40

Paul Koslo
Robot Jox '89
Rooster Cogburn '75

Robert Kosoy
Miracle at Moreaux '86

David Kossoff
The Mouse That Roared '59

Henry Koster ▲
Dear Brigitte '65
Flower Drum Song '61

Sho Kosugi
Aloha Summer '88

Ted Kotcheff ▲
The Apprenticeship of Duddy
  Kravitz '74
Weekend at Bernie's '89

Elias Koteas
Almost an Angel '90
Look Who's Talking, Too '90
Some Kind of Wonderful '87
Teenage Mutant Ninja Turtles
  1: The Movie '90
Teenage Mutant Ninja Turtles
  3 '93
Tucker: The Man and His
  Dream '88

Yaphet Kotto
Live and Let Die '73
Man & Boy '71
Two If by Sea '95

Al Kouzel ▲
A Family Circus Christmas '84

Nancy Kovack
Jason and the Argonauts '63

Geza Kovacs
Baby on Board '92

Martin Kove
The Karate Kid '84
The Karate Kid: Part 2 '86
The Karate Kid: Part 3 '89

Harley Jane Kozak
All I Want for Christmas '91
Arachnophobia '90
Magic in the Water '95
Necessary Roughness '91
Parenthood '89

Linda Kozlowski
Almost an Angel '90
Crocodile Dundee '86
Crocodile Dundee 2 '88

Jeroen Krabbe
Crossing Delancey '88
The Fugitive '93
King of the Hill '93
Turtle Diary '86
A World Apart '88

Bob Kramer
Bless the Beasts and
  Children '71

Eric Allen Kramer
Robin Hood: Men in
  Tights '93

Michael Kramer
Over the Edge '79

Stanley Kramer ▲
Bless the Beasts and
  Children '71
Judgment at Nuremberg '61
Oklahoma Crude '73

Savely Kramorov
Morgan Stewart's Coming
  Home '87

Paul Krasny ▲
Back to Hannibal: The Further
  Adventures of Tom Sawyer
  and Huckleberry Finn '90
Joe Panther '76

Brian Krause
December '91

Lee Kresel ▲
Alakazam the Great! '61

David Kriegel
Alive '93
Speed '94

Alice Krige
Chariots of Fire '81
See You in the Morning '89

Sylvia Kristel
The Fifth Musketeer '79

Marta Kristen
Beach Blanket Bingo '65
Savage Sam '63

Kris Kristofferson
Big Top Pee Wee '88
The Road Home '95

Jeremy Joe Kronsberg ▲
Going Ape! '81

Steve Kroschel ▲
Running Free '94

Chad Krowchuk
Heck's Way Home '95

Bill Kroyer ▲
Ferngully: The Last Rain
  Forest '92

Hardy Kruger
Blue Fin '78
A Bridge Too Far '77
Hatari '62

Otto Kruger
High Noon '52
Saboteur '42
Treasure Island '34
Wonder Man '45

The Wonderful World of the
  Brothers Grimm '62

Sonia Kruger-Tayler
Strictly Ballroom '92

Kendra Krull
Unstrung Heroes '95

David Krumholtz
Addams Family Values '93
Life with Mikey '93
The Santa Clause '94

Gene Krupa
The Glenn Miller Story '54

Jack Kruschen
Dear Brigitte '65
Mountain Man '77

Eve Kryll
Making Contact '86

Akira Kubo
Destroy All Monsters '68

Stanley Kubrick ▲
2001: A Space Odyssey '68

Buzz Kulik ▲
Brian's Song '71

Vusi Kunene
Cry, the Beloved Country '95

Koreyoshi Kurahara ▲
Antarctica '84

Ron Kurowski
Spaceship '81

Alwyn Kurts
Earthling '80

Swoosie Kurtz
Reality Bites '94
Storybook '95
Vice Versa '88
Wildcats '86

Katy Kurtzman
Child of Glass '78
When Every Day was the
  Fourth of July '78

Shishir Kurup
Coneheads '93

Clyde Kusatsu
Dr. Strange '78
Made in America '93
Top Dog '95

Dylan Kussman
Dead Poets Society '89
Wild Hearts Can't Be
  Broken '91

Nancy Kwan
Dragon: The Bruce Lee
  Story '93
Flower Drum Song '61
Lt. Robin Crusoe, U.S.N. '66

Ken Kwapis ▲
The Beniker Gang '83
Dunston Checks In '95
Sesame Street Presents:
  Follow That Bird '85

Burt Kwouk
Empire of the Sun '87
The Pink Panther Strikes
  Again '76
Revenge of the Pink
  Panther '78
Son of the Pink Panther '93
Trail of the Pink Panther '82

La Chanze
Leap of Faith '92

Alison La Placa
Fletch '85
Madhouse '90

Rosemary La Planche
Federal Agents vs.
  Underworld, Inc. '49

Steven La Rocque ▲
Samantha '92

Patti LaBelle
Sing '89

Patrick Laborteaux
3 Ninjas '92

Catherine Lacey
The Lady Vanishes '38

Margaret Lacey
Diamonds are Forever '71

Ronald Lacey
Making the Grade '84
Raiders of the Lost Ark '81

Harry Lachman ▲
Baby, Take a Bow '34

Andre Lacombe
The Bear '89

Denis Lacroix
Running Brave '83

Jerry Lacy
Play It Again, Sam '72

Alan Ladd
Citizen Kane '41
My Favorite Brunette '47
Shane '53

Cheryl Ladd
Lisa '90

David Ladd
A Dog of Flanders '59

Diane Ladd
Father Hood '93
National Lampoon's Christmas
  Vacation '89
Plain Clothes '88
Rambling Rose '91

Something Wicked This Way
    Comes '83

Pat Laffan
The Snapper '93

Art LaFleur
Forever Young '92
Jack the Bear '93
Man of the House '95
The Sandlot '93

Jean LaFleur ▲
Mystery of the Million Dollar
    Hockey Puck '80s

Caroline Lagerfelt
Home at Last '88

Bert Lahr
Just Around the Corner '38
The Wizard of Oz '39

Christine Lahti
Gross Anatomy '89
Housekeeping '87
Miss Firecracker '89
Running on Empty '88
Stacking '87
Swing Shift '84

Harvey Laidman ▲
The Boy Who Loved Trolls '84

Ricki Lake
Cabin Boy '94
Cry-Baby '90
Hairspray '88
Mrs. Winterbourne '96
Serial Mom '94

Michael Lally
The Secret of Roan Inish '94

Frank Laloggia
The Wizard of Speed and
    Time '88

Frank Laloggia ▲
The Lady in White '88

Rene Laloux ▲
Fantastic Planet '73

Jean LaMarre
Malcolm X '92

Fernando Lamas
The Cheap Detective '78

Lorenzo Lamas
Take Down '79

Christopher Lambert
Greystoke: The Legend of
    Tarzan, Lord of the
    Apes '84
Highlander '86
Highlander 2: The
    Quickening '91
Highlander: The Gathering '93
Mortal Kombat: The
    Movie '95

Mark Lamberti ▲
Cartoons for Big Kids '89

Heath Lamberts
Tom and Huck '95

Charles Lamont ▲
Abbott and Costello Meet
    Captain Kidd '52
Abbott and Costello Meet Dr.
    Jekyll and Mr. Hyde '52
Ring of Bright Water '69

Albert Lamorisse ▲
Circus Angel '65
The Red Balloon '56

Pascal Lamorisse
The Red Balloon '56

Dorothy Lamour
The Greatest Show on
    Earth '52
My Favorite Brunette '47
Pajama Party '64

Zohra Lampert
Alan & Naomi '92

Burt Lancaster
Airport '70
Field of Dreams '89
Island of Dr. Moreau '77
Judgment at Nuremberg '61
Local Hero '83
Rocket Gibraltar '88
Tough Guys '86

James Lancaster
Gettysburg '93

Elsa Lanchester
Blackbeard's Ghost '67
David Copperfield '35
Die Laughing '80
The Ghost Goes West '36
Lassie, Come Home '43
My Dog, the Thief '69
Pajama Party '64
The Secret Garden '49
That Darn Cat '65

Micheline Lanctot
The Apprenticeship of Duddy
    Kravitz '74

Geoffrey Land
Against A Crooked Sky '75

David Landau
Horse Feathers '32

Juliet Landau
Theodore Rex '95

Martin Landau
The Adventures of
    Pinocchio '96
North by Northwest '59
Tucker: The Man and His
    Dream '88

Dinsdale Landen
Digby, the Biggest Dog in the
    World '73

David Lander
Ava's Magical Adventure '94
The Man with One Red
    Shoe '85

Michael Landes
An American Summer '90

Steve Landesburg
Leader of the Band '87

Carole Landis
Daredevils of the Red
    Circle '38
Topper Returns '41

Jessie Royce Landis
Gidget Goes to Rome '63
North by Northwest '59
To Catch a Thief '55

John Landis ▲
Beverly Hills Cop 3 '94
Oscar '91
Spies Like Us '85
The Stupids '95
Three Amigos '86
Twilight Zone: The Movie '83

Monte Landis
The Mouse That Roared '59

Hal Landon Jr.
Bill & Ted's Bogus
    Journey '91

Michael Landon
The Errand Boy '61
Little House on the Prairie '74
The Loneliest Runner '76
Sam's Son '84

Michael Landon ▲
Little House on the Prairie '74
The Loneliest Runner '76
Sam's Son '84

Michael Landon Jr.
Bonanza: The Return '93

Paul Landres ▲
Flipper's Odyssey '66

Karen Landry
Heartbreak Hotel '88

Abbe Lane
Twilight Zone: The Movie '83

Charles Lane
Billie '65
Mr. Smith Goes to
    Washington '39
Murphy's Romance '85
Strange Invaders '83

Diane Lane
Chaplin '92
Indian Summer '93
Jack '96
Judge Dredd '95
A Little Romance '79
The Outsiders '83
Rumble Fish '83
Six Pack '82

Touched by Love '80

Lola Lane
Burn 'Em Up Barnes '34

Nathan Lane
The Birdcage '95
Life with Mikey '93

Priscilla Lane
Saboteur '42

Eric Laneuville ▲
The Ernest Green Story '93
The Mighty Pawns '87

Sidney Lanfield ▲
Sorrowful Jones '49

Doreen Lang
Almost an Angel '90

June Lang
Captain January '36
Wee Willie Winkie '37

Perry Lang
Eight Men Out '88

Richard Lang ▲
Christmas Comes to Willow
    Creek '87

Stephen Lang
The Amazing Panda
    Adventure '95
Gettysburg '93
Project X '87
Tall Tale: The Unbelievable
    Adventures of Pecos
    Bill '95
Tombstone '93

Walter Lang ▲
The Blue Bird '40
The King and I '56
The Little Princess '39
Snow White and the Three
    Stooges '61
State Fair '45

Hope Lange
I am the Cheese '83
The Love Bug '68
The Prodigal '83

Jessica Lange
Country '84
King Kong '76
Men Don't Leave '89
Rob Roy '95
Tootsie '82

Frank Langella
Cutthroat Island '95
Dave '93
Eddie '96
1492: Conquest of
    Paradise '92
Junior '94
Masters of the Universe '87
Twelve Chairs '70

Frances Langford
Yankee Doodle Dandy '42

Margaret Langrick
American Boyfriends '89
Harry and the Hendersons '87
My American Cousin '85

Victor Lanoux
National Lampoon's European
    Vacation '85

Angela Lansbury
Bedknobs and
    Broomsticks '71
The Court Jester '56
Death on the Nile '78
National Velvet '44
The Pirates of Penzance '83
The Three Musketeers '48
The World of Henry Orient '64

Joi Lansing
Easter Parade '48
Singin' in the Rain '52

Robert Lansing
Life on the Mississippi '80

William Lanteau
On Golden Pond '81

Anthony LaPaglia
Black Magic '92
The Client '94
Mixed Nuts '94
So I Married an Axe
    Murderer '93

Daniel Lapaine
Muriel's Wedding '94

James Lapine ▲
Life with Mikey '93

Bryan Larkin
She-Devil '89

Mary Laroche
Gidget '59

John Larroquette
Madhouse '90
Richie Rich '94
Star Trek 3: The Search for
    Spock '84
Summer Rental '85
Twilight Zone: The Movie '83

Erik Larsen
Trap on Cougar Mountain '72
Young & Free '78

Ham Larsen
Further Adventures of the
    Wilderness Family, Part
    2 '77
Mountain Family
    Robinson '79

Keith Larsen
Trap on Cougar Mountain '72
Whitewater Sam '78

Keith Larsen ▲
Trap on Cougar Mountain '72
Whitewater Sam '78
Young & Free '78

Lars Oluf Larsen
A Day in October '92

Darrell Larson
Hero '92

Eric Larson ▲
Sleeping Beauty '59

Anna-Lotta Larsson
The Polar Bear King '94

Jack LaRue
Captains Courageous '37
Follow the Leader '44
To the Last Man '33

David Lascher
White Squall '96

Tommy Lasorda
Happy Birthday, Bugs: 50
    Looney Years '90
Ladybugs '92

Louise Lasser
Bananas '71
Sing '89
Take the Money and Run '69

John Lasseter ▲
Toy Story '95

Sydney Lassick
The Billion Dollar Hobo '78
Cool As Ice '91

Lyle Latell
Dick Tracy, Detective '45
Dick Tracy Meets
    Gruesome '47

Louise Latham
Paradise '91
Toughlove '85

Stan Lathan ▲
Beat Street '84

Matt Lattanzi
Catch Me. . .If You Can '89
Diving In '90
Roxanne '87

Jack Laufer
Lost in Yonkers '93

John Laughlin
Footloose '84

Michael Laughlin ▲
Strange Invaders '83

Tom Laughlin
Billy Jack '71
South Pacific '58

Tom Laughlin ▲
Billy Jack '71

Charles Laughton
Abbott and Costello Meet
    Captain Kidd '52
The Canterville Ghost '44
Jamaica Inn '39
The Paradine Case '47

Frank Launder ▲
The Belles of St. Trinian's '53
Blue Murder at St.
    Trinian's '56
Great St. Trinian's Train
    Robbery '66
The Pure Hell of St.
    Trinian's '61

Cyndi Lauper
Life with Mikey '93

Matthew Laurance
Eddie and the Cruisers '83

Carole Laure
Victory '81

Stan Laurel
The Flying Deuces '39
March of the Wooden
    Soldiers '34

Tammy Lauren
The Last Flight of Noah's
    Ark '80

Veronica Lauren
Homeward Bound 2: Lost in
    San Francisco '96
Homeward Bound: The
    Incredible Journey '93

Michael Laurence
Conspiracy of Love '87

Paula Laurence
For Love or Money '93

Hugh Laurie
Sense and Sensibility '95

John Laurie
The 39 Steps '35

Piper Laurie
Dream a Little Dream '89
Francis Goes to the Races '51
Return to Oz '85
Rich in Love '93
Toughlove '85

Ed Lauter
The Chicken Chronicles '77
Girls Just Want to Have
    Fun '85
Goodbye, Miss 4th of July '88
King Kong '76
The Rocketeer '91
School Ties '92
Timerider '83

Harry Lauter
Trader Tom of the China
    Seas '54

Kathrin Lautner
Two Bits & Pepper '95

Linda Lavin
Maricela '88
See You in the Morning '89

John Phillip Law
Golden Voyage of Sinbad '73

The Russians are Coming, the
    Russians are Coming '66

Phyllida Law
Emma '96
Much Ado About Nothing '93

Peter Lawford
The Canterville Ghost '44
Easter Parade '48
Little Women '49

Barbara Lawrence
Oklahoma! '55

Joey Lawrence
Wait Till Your Mother Gets
    Home '83

Marc Lawrence
Goin' Coconuts '78
The Man with the Golden
    Gun '74
'Neath Brooklyn Bridge '42

Martin Lawrence
Bad Boys '95
House Party '90
House Party 2: The Pajama
    Jam '91

Rosina Lawrence
General Spanky '36

Scott Lawrence
Timecop '94

Steve Lawrence
Alice in Wonderland '85

Denis Lawson
Local Hero '83
Return of the Jedi '83

Leigh Lawson
Madame Sousatzka '88
Sword of the Valiant '83
Tess '80

Priscilla Lawson
Flash Gordon: Rocketship '36

Richard Lawson
Poltergeist '82

Shannon Lawson
Heck's Way Home '95

Frank Lawton
David Copperfield '35

Paul Lazar
Philadelphia '93
Trapped In Paradise '94

Eusebio Lazaro
The Return of the
    Musketeers '89

George Lazenby
On Her Majesty's Secret
    Service '69
Twinsitters '95

Kelly Le Brock
Weird Science '85

Cast/Director Index

Ole Lemmeke
A Day in October '92

James Lemmo
Dream a Little Dream 2 '94

Chris Lemmon
Dad '89
Swing Shift '84

Jack Lemmon
Airport '77 '77
Dad '89
The Front Page '74
Great Race '65
Grumpier Old Men '95
Grumpy Old Men '93
The Odd Couple '68

Jack Lemmon ▲
Kotch '71

Rusty Lemorande ▲
Journey to the Center of the
    Earth '88

Mark Lenard
Star Trek 3: The Search for
    Spock '84
Star Trek 4: The Voyage
    Home '86
Star Trek 6: The Undiscovered
    Country '91

John Lennon
A Hard Day's Night '64
Help! '65
Magical Mystery Tour '67

Terry Lennon ▲
Daffy Duck's
    Quackbusters '89

Jay Leno
Collision Course '89

Lotte Lenya
From Russia with Love '63

Kay Lenz
House '86

Rick Lenz
Scandalous John '71

Leon
Above the Rim '94
Cool Runnings '93
Once Upon a Time . . . When
    We Were Colored '95
Waiting to Exhale '95

Annie Leon
Hope and Glory '87

Valerie Leon
Never Say Never Again '83
The Spy Who Loved Me '77

Robert Sean Leonard
The Age of Innocence '93
Dead Poets Society '89
Mr. & Mrs. Bridge '91
Much Ado About Nothing '93

My Best Friend Is a
    Vampire '88
Safe Passage '94
Swing Kids '93

Sheldon Leonard
Guys and Dolls '55
It's a Wonderful Life '46
Sinbad the Sailor '47

Marco Leonardi
Cinema Paradiso '88

Sergio Leone ▲
Once Upon a Time in the
    West '68

Al Leong
Bill & Ted's Excellent
    Adventure '89

Tea Leoni
Bad Boys '95

Chauncey Leopardi
The Big Green '95
Houseguest '95
Huck and the King of
    Hearts '93
The Sandlot '93

Ken Lerner
Fast Getaway '91

Michael Lerner
Amos and Andrew '93
Blank Check '93
Eight Men Out '88
Newsies '92
Radioland Murders '94
Strange Invaders '83

Mervyn LeRoy ▲
The Bad Seed '56
I Am a Fugitive from a Chain
    Gang '32
Little Women '49
No Time for Sergeants '58

Brad "The Animal"
    Lesley
Little Big League '94

Joan Leslie
Yankee Doodle Dandy '42

Michael Lessac ▲
House of Cards '92

Len Lesser
How to Stuff a Wild Bikini '65

Ben Lessy
Pajama Party '64

Betty Lester
House Party 3 '94

Buddy Lester
Cracking Up '83

Jeff Lester
Once a Hero '88

Mark Lester
Black Beauty '71
Melody '71
Oliver! '68
The Prince and the
    Pauper '78
Sudden Terror '70

Richard Lester ▲
Butch and Sundance: The
    Early Days '79
The Four Musketeers '75
A Hard Day's Night '64
Help! '65
The Return of the
    Musketeers '89
Robin and Marian '76
Superman 2 '80
Superman 3 '83
Three Musketeers '74

Tom Lester
Gordy '95

Jared Leto
How to Make an American
    Quilt '95

Dennis Letts
The Last Prostitute '91

Martin Lev
Bugsy Malone '76

Brian Levant ▲
Beethoven '92
The Flintstones '94
Problem Child 2 '91

Oscar Levant
An American in Paris '51
The Band Wagon '53

Calvin Levels
Adventures in Babysitting '87

Jay Levey ▲
UHF '89

William A. Levey ▲
Lightning: The White
    Stallion '86

Henry Levin ▲
Journey to the Center of the
    Earth '59
Run for the Roses '78
The Wonderful World of the
    Brothers Grimm '62
Wonders of Aladdin '61

Peter Levin ▲
Comeback Kid '80

Barry Levinson
Quiz Show '94

Barry Levinson ▲
Avalon '90
The Natural '84
Rain Man '88
Toys '92
Young Sherlock Holmes '85

Abe Levitow ▲
Bugs Bunny's Hare-Raising
    Tales '89
Gay Purr-ee '62

Steve Levitt
The Incredible Hulk
    Returns '88

Eugene Levy
Club Paradise '86
Father of the Bride Part II '95
National Lampoon's
    Vacation '83
Splash '84
Stay Tuned '92

Eugene Levy ▲
Once Upon a Crime '92

Margaret LeWars
Dr. No '62

Al Lewis
Car 54, Where Are You? '94
My Grandpa is a Vampire '92

Alun Lewis
Experience Preferred. . . But
    Not Essential '83

Brittney Lewis
Dream Machine '91

Charlotte Lewis
The Golden Child '86

Diana Lewis
Andy Hardy Meets
    Debutante '40
Go West '40

Fiona Lewis
Innerspace '87
Strange Invaders '83

Gary Lewis
Hardly Working '81

Geoffrey Lewis
Bronco Billy '80
Catch Me. . .If You Can '89
Culpepper Cattle Co. '72
The Great Waldo Pepper '75
The Man Without a Face '93
Maverick '94
Night of the Comet '84
Pink Cadillac '89
Smile '75
When Every Day was the
    Fourth of July '78
White Fang 2: The Myth of the
    White Wolf '94
The Wind and the Lion '75

George Lewis
Indian Paint '64
The Sign of Zorro '60
Zorro's Black Whip '44

Gilbert Lewis
The Kid Who Loved
    Christmas '90

Greg Lewis
Prehysteria! 2 '94

Jenifer Lewis
Corrina, Corrina '94
Renaissance Man '94
What's Love Got to Do With
   It? '93

Jenny Lewis
A Friendship in Vienna '88
Troop Beverly Hills '89
The Wizard '89

Jerry Lewis
The Bellboy '60
The Caddy '53
Cinderfella '60
Cracking Up '83
The Delicate Delinquent '56
The Disorderly Orderly '64
The Errand Boy '61
Family Jewels '65
The Geisha Boy '58
Hardly Working '81
Hollywood or Bust '56
The Nutty Professor '63
Trading Hearts '87

Jerry Lewis ▲
The Bellboy '60
Cracking Up '83
The Errand Boy '61
Family Jewels '65
Hardly Working '81
The Nutty Professor '63

Joseph H. Lewis ▲
Boys of the City '40
That Gang of Mine '40

Juliette Lewis
The Basketball Diaries '94
Meet the Hollowheads '89
Mixed Nuts '94
My Stepmother Is an
   Alien '88
National Lampoon's Christmas
   Vacation '89
That Night '93
What's Eating Gilbert
   Grape '93

Mark Lewis ▲
Gordy '95

Matthew Lewis
The Legend of Wolf
   Mountain '92

Mitchell Lewis
The Wizard of Oz '39

Phill Lewis
Brother Future '91
City Slickers '91

Rawle Lewis
Cool Runnings '93

Richard Lewis
Once Upon a Crime '92
Robin Hood: Men in
   Tights '93

Wagons East '94

Robert Lewis
Hello Again '87

Robert Lewis ▲
A Summer to Remember '84

John Ley
BMX Bandits '83

Thierry Lhermitte
Little Indian, Big City '95

Peter Paul Liapis
Fast Getaway 2 '94

Richard Libertini
Animal Behavior '89
Fletch '85
Fletch Lives '89
Nell '94
Popeye '80

Jeremy Licht
Father Figure '80
Twilight Zone: The Movie '83

G. Gordon Liddy
Adventures in Spying '92

Anki Liden
My Life as a Dog '85

Robert Liebmann ▲
All I Want for Christmas '91
Fire in the Sky '93
Table for Five '83

Tina Lifford
The Ernest Green Story '93

Marilyn Lightstone
Anne of Green Gables '85
Wild Pony '83

Matthew Lillard
Hackers '95
Serial Mom '94

Kay Tong Lim
Dragon: The Bruce Lee
   Story '93

Kevin Lima ▲
A Goofy Movie '94

Dina Limon
Boy Takes Girl '83

Aida Linares
Clueless '95

Richard Lincoln
Manny's Orphans '78

Greta Lind
Rudy '93

Traci Lind
My Boyfriend's Back '93

Eric Linden
Ah, Wilderness! '35
Gone with the Wind '39

Hal Linden
Father Figure '80

Viveca Lindfors
Girlfriends '78
Stargate '94
The Sure Thing '85
The Way We Were '73

Audra Lindley
The Heartbreak Kid '72
Troop Beverly Hills '89

Delroy Lindo
Broken Arrow '95
Crooklyn '94
Malcolm X '92

Margaret Lindsay
Please Don't Eat the
   Daisies '60

Michael Lindsay-Hogg ▲
Annie Oakley '85
The Little Match Girl '87
Thumbelina '82

Richard Lineback
Speed '94

Stephi Lineburg
Richie Rich '94

Bai Ling
The Crow '93

Paul Linke
Parenthood '89

Richard Linklater ▲
Before Sunrise '94
Dazed and Confused '93

Mark Linn-Baker
My Favorite Year '82

Laura Linney
Congo '95
Dave '93
A Simple Twist of Fate '94

Larry Linville
No Dessert Dad, 'Til You Mow
   the Lawn '94
Rock 'n' Roll High School
   Forever '91

Therese Liotard
My Father's Glory '91
My Mother's Castle '91

Ray Liotta
Corrina, Corrina '94
Dominick & Eugene '88
Field of Dreams '89
Operation Dumbo Drop '95

Maureen Lipman
Educating Rita '83
The Little Princess '87

Renee Lippin
Radio Days '87

Jack Lipson
Flash Gordon: Rocketship '36

Peggy Lipton
Mosby's Marauders '66
Purple People Eater '88

Steven Lisberger ▲
Tron '82

Virna Lisi
When Wolves Cry '69

Tiny Lister
No Holds Barred '89

Litefoot
The Indian in the
   Cupboard '95

John Litel
Nancy Drew, Reporter '39

John Lithgow
The Adventures of Buckaroo
   Banzai Across the Eighth
   Dimension '84
Baby Songs Presents: John
   Lithgow's Kid-Size
   Concert '90
Footloose '84
Goldilocks & the Three
   Bears '83
Harry and the Hendersons '87
The Manhattan Project '86
The Pelican Brief '93
Princess Caraboo '94
Rich Kids '79
Santa Claus: The Movie '85
Terms of Endearment '83
Twilight Zone: The Movie '83
2010 : The Year We Make
   Contact '84

Cleavon Little
Fletch Lives '89
Greased Lightning '77
Homecoming: A Christmas
   Story '71
Jimmy the Kid '82
Once Upon a Brothers
   Grimm '77

Dwight Little ▲
Free Willy 2: The Adventure
   Home '95

Michelle Little
Apollo 13 '95

Little Richard
Happy Birthday, Bugs: 50
   Looney Years '90
Purple People Eater '88

Lucien Littlefield
Let's Sing Again '36
Zorro's Black Whip '44

Jason Lively
National Lampoon's European
   Vacation '85

Robin Lively
Not Quite Human '87
Teen Witch '89

John Livingston
Mr. Wrong '95

L.L. Cool J.
Toys '92

Desmond Llewelyn
Diamonds are Forever '71
For Your Eyes Only '81
From Russia with Love '63
Goldeneye '95
The Man with the Golden
    Gun '74
Moonraker '79
On Her Majesty's Secret
    Service '69
The Spy Who Loved Me '77
Thunderball '65
A View to a Kill '85
You Only Live Twice '67

Christopher Lloyd
The Addams Family '91
Addams Family Values '93
The Adventures of Buckaroo
    Banzai Across the Eighth
    Dimension '84
Angels in the Outfield '94
Back to the Future '85
Back to the Future, Part 2 '89
Back to the Future, Part 3 '90
Camp Nowhere '94
Clue '85
Dennis the Menace '93
The Dream Team '89
Eight Men Out '88
Goin' South '78
In Search of Dr. Seuss '94
Legend of the Lone
    Ranger '81
Legend of the White
    Horse '85
Mr. Mom '83
The Pagemaster '94
Radioland Murders '94
Rent-A-Kid '95
Star Trek 3: The Search for
    Spock '84
Suburban Commando '91
Walk Like a Man '87
Who Framed Roger Rabbit?
    '88

Doris Lloyd
Journey for Margaret '42

Emily Lloyd
A River Runs Through It '92

Emily Ann Lloyd
Apollo 13 '95

Eric Lloyd
Dunston Checks In '95
The Santa Clause '94

Jimmy Lloyd
The Jolson Story '46
Sea Hound '47

John Bedford Lloyd
Crossing Delancey '88
Philadelphia '93
Waiting for the Light '90

Kathleen Lloyd
Take Down '79

Norman Lloyd
Saboteur '42

Sabrina Lloyd
Father Hood '93

Amy Locane
Airheads '94
Cry-Baby '90
School Ties '92

Bruce Locke
Robocop 3 '91

Philip Locke
Othello '95

Sondra Locke
Any Which Way You Can '80
Bronco Billy '80
The Outlaw Josey Wales '76

Anne Lockhart
Hambone & Hillie '84
Troll '85

Gene Lockhart
Carousel '56
A Christmas Carol '38
Going My Way '44
His Girl Friday '40
Miracle on 34th Street '47

June Lockhart
The Capture of Grizzly
    Adams '82
Just Tell Me You Love Me '80
Lassie's Great Adventure '62
Meet Me in St. Louis '44
Miss Annie Rooney '42
Out There '95
Strange Invaders '83
Troll '85
The Yearling '46

Heather Locklear
The Return of Swamp
    Thing '89

Loryn Locklin
Catch Me. . .If You Can '89

Evan Lockwood
Rambling Rose '91

Gary Lockwood
It Happened at the World's
    Fair '63
The Magic Sword '62
2001: A Space Odyssey '68

Margaret Lockwood
The Lady Vanishes '38
Susannah of the Mounties '39

John Loder
How Green was My Valley '41

Klaus Loewitsch
Gotcha! '85

Morgan Lofting
The Night Before '88

Joshua Logan ▲
Camelot '67
Paint Your Wagon '69
South Pacific '58

Ricky Dean Logan
Back to the Future, Part 2 '89
Back to the Future, Part 3 '90

Robert F. Logan
Across the Great Divide '76
The Adventures of the
    Wilderness Family '76
Further Adventures of the
    Wilderness Family, Part
    2 '77
Mountain Family
    Robinson '79
Sea Gypsies '78

Robert Loggia
Big '88
Curse of the Pink Panther '83
I Love Trouble '94
Independence Day '96
Necessary Roughness '91
The Nine Lives of Elfego
    Baca '58
Opportunity Knocks '90
Over the Top '86
Revenge of the Pink
    Panther '78
Trail of the Pink Panther '82

Herbert Lom
Curse of the Pink Panther '83
Going Bananas '88
The Horse Without a
    Head '63
Mysterious Island '61
The Pink Panther Strikes
    Again '76
Return of the Pink
    Panther '74
Revenge of the Pink
    Panther '78
A Shot in the Dark '64
Son of the Pink Panther '93
Ten Little Indians '75
Third Man on the
    Mountain '59
Trail of the Pink Panther '82

Carole Lombard
Mr. & Mrs. Smith '41

Karina Lombard
Legends of the Fall '94

Lou Lombardo ▲
P.K. and the Kid '85

Britt Lomond
The Sign of Zorro '60
Zorro, Vol. 1 '58

Jason London
Dazed and Confused '93

December '91
The Man in the Moon '91
Safe Passage '94
To Wong Foo, Thanks for
    Everything, Julie
    Newmar '95

Jeremy London
Breaking Free '95
Mallrats '95

Jerry London ▲
Father Figure '80

Rosalyn London
Amazing Mr. Blunden '72

Tom London
Zorro's Black Whip '44

John Lone
Iceman '84
The Shadow '94

Brad Long
Hoosiers '86

Howie Long
Broken Arrow '95

Jodi Long
Amos and Andrew '93

Joseph Long
Queen of Hearts '89

Nia Long
Boyz N the Hood '91
Made in America '93

Shelley Long
The Brady Bunch Movie '95
Hello Again '87
Irreconcilable Differences '84
The Money Pit '86
Troop Beverly Hills '89
A Very Brady Sequel '96

Walter Long
Silver Stallion '41

Claudine Longet
The Party '68

Robert Longo ▲
Johnny Mnemonic '95

Tony Longo
Houseguest '94
Prehysteria '93
Remote '93
Suburban Commando '91

Michael Lonsdale
Moonraker '79
The Remains of the Day '93

Richard Loo
The Man with the Golden
    Gun '74

Deborah Loomis
Hercules in New York '70

Rod Loomis
Bill & Ted's Excellent
Adventure '89

Silvia Lopel
Hercules Unchained '59

Jennifer Lopez
Money Train '95

Isabel Lorca
Lightning: The White
Stallion '86
She's Having a Baby '88

Jack Lord
Dr. No '62

Jean-Claude Lord ▲
Toby McTeague '87

Justine Lord
Skeezer '82

Traci Lords
Cry-Baby '90
Serial Mom '94

Donna Loren
Bikini Beach '64
Muscle Beach Party '64
Pajama Party '64

Sophia Loren
Grumpier Old Men '95
Man of La Mancha '72

Teala Loring
Hard-Boiled Mahoney '47

James Lorinz
The Jerky Boys '95

Marion Lorne
Strangers on a Train '51

Peter Lorre
Casablanca '42
The Maltese Falcon '41
My Favorite Brunette '47
20,000 Leagues Under the
Sea '54
Voyage to the Bottom of the
Sea '61

Joan Lorring
The Corn is Green '45

Joseph Losey ▲
The Boy with the Green
Hair '48
The Go-Between '71

Louanne
Oh, God! Book 2 '80

Lori Loughlin
Back to the Beach '87
The Night Before '88
Rad '86
Secret Admirer '85

Julia Louis-Dreyfus
Jack the Bear '93

National Lampoon's Christmas
Vacation '89
North '94

Anita Louise
The Little Princess '39

John Lounsbery ▲
The Rescuers '77
Winnie the Pooh and Tigger
Too '74

Alan Love
That Sinking Feeling '79

Montagu Love
The Adventures of Robin
Hood '38
The Prince and the
Pauper '37

Mother Love
Mr. Nanny '93
Twinsitters '95

Frank Lovejoy
House of Wax '53

Jon Lovitz
Big '88
City Slickers 2: The Legend of
Curly's Gold '94
High School High '96
A League of Their Own '92
Mr. Destiny '90
Mom and Dad Save the
World '92
My Stepmother Is an
Alien '88
National Lampoon's Loaded
Weapon 1 '93
North '94
Three Amigos '86
Trapped In Paradise '94

Harrison Lowe
Geronimo '93

Rob Lowe
The Outsiders '83
Oxford Blues '84
Tommy Boy '95
Wayne's World '92

Carey Lowell
Club Paradise '86
Sleepless in Seattle '93

Curt Lowens
A Midnight Clear '92

Andrew Lowery
My Boyfriend's Back '93
School Ties '92

Dick Lowry ▲
A Horse for Danny '95
Smokey and the Bandit, Part
3 '83

Judith Lowry
The Effect of Gamma Rays on
Man-in-the-Moon
Marigolds '73

T.J. Lowther
A Perfect World '93

Myrna Loy
Airport '75 '75
The Bachelor and the Bobby-
Soxer '47
A Connecticut Yankee '31
The Red Pony '49
The Thin Man '34

Lisa Lu
The Joy Luck Club '93

Arthur Lubin ▲
Ali Baba and the Forty
Thieves '43
Buck Privates '41
Francis Goes to the Races '51
Francis Joins the WACs '54
Francis the Talking Mule '49
The Incredible Mr. Limpet '64
Thief of Baghdad '61

George Lucas ▲
American Graffiti '73
Star Wars '77

Lisa Lucas
Hadley's Rebellion '84
A House Without a Christmas
Tree '72

George Luce
Danny '79

Dominic Luchese
If Lucy Fell '95

Laurence Luckinbill
Star Trek 5: The Final
Frontier '89

Kathryn Ludlow
Courage Mountain '89

Pamela Ludwig
Over the Edge '79

Lorna Luft
Grease 2 '82

Bela Lugosi
Abbott and Costello Meet
Frankenstein '48
The Phantom Creeps '39
Spooks Run Wild '41

Baz Luhrmann ▲
Strictly Ballroom '92

Paul Lukas
The Lady Vanishes '38
Little Women '33
20,000 Leagues Under the
Sea '54

Keye Luke
Bowery Blitzkrieg '41
The Green Hornet '39
Gremlins '84

Lulu
To Sir, with Love '67

Carl Lumbly
Brother Future '91

Sidney Lumet
Running on Empty '88

Sidney Lumet ▲
Running on Empty '88
The Wiz '78

Joanna Lumley
Curse of the Pink Panther '83
James and the Giant
Peach '96
On Her Majesty's Secret
Service '69

Richard Lumsden
Sense and Sensibility '95

Barbara Luna
Spiderman '81

Art Lund
The Last American Hero '73

Deanna Lund
Hardly Working '81

Natalie Lund
The Legend of Wolf
Mountain '92

Nicole Lund
The Legend of Wolf
Mountain '92

Dolph Lundgren
Johnny Mnemonic '95
Masters of the Universe '87
Rocky 4 '85
A View to a Kill '85

William Lundigan
Andy Hardy's Double Life '42

Jessica Lundy
Madhouse '90
The Stupids '95

Cherie Lunghi
The Canterville Ghost '96
Oliver Twist '82

Min Luong
Gleaming the Cube '89

Tabitha Lupien
Rent-A-Kid '95

Ida Lupino
Junior Bonner '72

Ida Lupino ▲
The Trouble with Angels '66

Patti LuPone
Driving Miss Daisy '89
Family Prayers '91
Song Spinner '95

Peter Lupus
Muscle Beach Party '64
Think Big '90

Hamilton Luske
Bongo '47

Hamilton Luske ▲
Lady and the Tramp '55
101 Dalmatians '61
Peter Pan '53

Paul Luty
Water Babies '79

Bob Lydiard
The Paper Chase '73

Jimmy Lydon
Life with Father '47
Little Men '40
Tom Brown's School Days '40

Dorothy Lyman
Ollie Hopnoodle's Haven of
Bliss '88

David Lynch
Zelly & Me '88

David Lynch ▲
The Elephant Man '80

John Lynch
Moll Flanders '96
Princess Caraboo '94
The Secret Garden '93
The Secret of Roan Inish '94

Kate Lynch
Meatballs '79

Kelly Lynch
Curly Sue '91
For Better and For Worse '92
Imaginary Crimes '94

Richard Lynch
Little Nikita '88

Susan Lynch
The Secret of Roan Inish '94

Paul Lynde
Beach Blanket Bingo '65
Bye, Bye, Birdie '63
Son of Flubber '63
The Villain '79

Adrian Lyne ▲
Foxes '80

Carol Lynley
The Light in the Forest '58
The Poseidon Adventure '72

Barbara Lynn
Godzilla vs. the Cosmic
Monster '74

Diana Lynn
Bedtime for Bonzo '51

Jonathan Lynn
Three Men and a Little
Lady '90

Jonathan Lynn ▲
Clue '85
Greedy '94

Sgt. Bilko '95

Francis D. Lyon ▲
Tomboy & the Champ '58

Richard Lyon
The Tender Years '47

Byron Mabe
The Doberman Gang '72

Kate Maberly
The Secret Garden '93

Zachary Mabry
The Little Rascals '94

Bernie Mac
Above the Rim '94
House Party 3 '94

James MacArthur
Kidnapped '60
The Light in the Forest '58
Mosby's Marauders '66
Spencer's Mountain '63
The Swiss Family
Robinson '60
Third Man on the
Mountain '59

Syd Macartney ▲
The Canterville Ghost '96
Prince Brat and the Whipping
Boy '95

Marc Macaulay
Cop and a Half '93

Donald MacBride
Buck Privates Come Home '47
Room Service '38

Ralph Macchio
The Karate Kid '84
The Karate Kid: Part 2 '86
The Karate Kid: Part 3 '89
The Outsiders '83

Simon MacCorkindale
Death on the Nile '78

J. Farrell MacDonald
Susannah of the Mounties '39

Michael MacDonald
Mystery of the Million Dollar
Hockey Puck '80s

Norm MacDonald
Billy Madison '94

Peter Macdonald ▲
The Neverending Story 3 '94

Ray Macdonald
Babes on Broadway '41

Alistair MacDougall
Bonanza: The Return '93

Andie MacDowell
Four Weddings and a
Funeral '93
Green Card '90

Greystoke: The Legend of
Tarzan, Lord of the
Apes '84
Groundhog Day '93
Multiplicity '96
Unstrung Heroes '95

Paul Mace
The Lords of Flatbush '74

Sterling Macer
Dragon: The Bruce Lee
Story '93

Hamilton MacFadden ▲
Stand Up and Cheer '34

Jack MacGowran
The Quiet Man '52

Tara MacGowran
Secret Places '85

Stephen Macht
A Friendship in Vienna '88
The Monster Squad '87

Keegan Macintosh
The Road Home '95

Helen Mack
His Girl Friday '40
Son of Kong '33

Fulton Mackay
Local Hero '83

Matthew Mackay
The Peanut Butter
Solution '85

Patch MacKenzie
Defense Play '88

Peter M. MacKenzie
Tom and Huck '95

Sam Mackenzie
Dragonworld '94

Gilles Mackinnon ▲
The Playboys '92
A Simple Twist of Fate '94

Albert Macklin
Date with an Angel '87

Janet MacLachlan
Big Mo '73
Sounder '72

Kyle MacLachlan
The Flintstones '94
Rich in Love '93

Shirley MacLaine
Around the World in 80
Days '56
Being There '79
Cannonball Run 2 '84
Guarding Tess '94
Madame Sousatzka '88
Mrs. Winterbourne '96
Steel Magnolias '89
Terms of Endearment '83
That's Dancing! '85

Waiting for the Light '90

Barton MacLane
The Geisha Boy '58
The Maltese Falcon '41
The Prince and the
Pauper '37
To the Last Man '33
Treasure of the Sierra
Madre '48
Unknown Island '48

Gavin MacLeod
The Party '68

Eanna MacLiam
The Snapper '93

Aline MacMahon
Ah, Wilderness! '35

Fred MacMurray
The Absent-Minded
Professor '61
Charley and the Angel '73
Follow Me, Boys! '66
The Happiest Millionaire '67
The Shaggy Dog '59
Son of Flubber '63
The Swarm '78

Robert MacNaughton
E.T.: The Extra-Terrestrial '82
I am the Cheese '83

Patrick Macnee
Battlestar Galactica '78
A Christmas Carol '51
The Howling '81
Spaceship '81
A View to a Kill '85

Robert MacNeil
Sesame Street Presents: Put
Down the Duckie '94

Peter MacNicol
Addams Family Values '93
The Boy Who Left Home to
Find Out About the
Shivers '81
Dracula: Dead and Loving
It '95
Dragonslayer '81
Ghostbusters 2 '89
Housesitter '92

Elle Macpherson
If Lucy Fell '95
Jane Eyre '96

Joe MacPherson
The Bay Boy '85

Gordon MacRae
Carousel '56
Oklahoma! '55

Heather MacRae
Bang the Drum Slowly '73

Meredith MacRae
Bikini Beach '64

George Macready
Great Race '65

Bill Macy
Bad Medicine '85
Casey at the Bat '85
My Favorite Year '82

William H. Macy
Being Human '94
Benny & Joon '93
Down Periscope '96
Mr. Holland's Opus '95
Searching for Bobby
   Fischer '93

Donald Madden
1776 '72

John Madden
Little Giants '94
P.K. and the Kid '85

Peter Madden
The Loneliness of the Long
   Distance Runner '62

Tommy Madden
Spaced Invaders '90

Gloria Maddox
Danny '79

Amy Madigan
Field of Dreams '89
Places in the Heart '84
Uncle Buck '89

James Madio
The Basketball Diaries '94
Hero '92

Guy Madison
Computer Wizard '77
Since You Went Away '44

Madonna
Desperately Seeking
   Susan '85
Dick Tracy '90
A League of Their Own '92

Kenneth Madsen ▲
A Day in October '92

Michael Madsen
Free Willy '93
Free Willy 2: The Adventure
   Home '95
The Natural '84
Racing with the Moon '84
Straight Talk '92

Virginia Madsen
Electric Dreams '84
Highlander 2: The
   Quickening '91
Hot to Trot! '88

Patrick Magee
Chariots of Fire '81

William Magerman
Radio Days '87

Albert Magnoli ▲
American Anthem '86

Ann Magnuson
Before and After '95
Cabin Boy '94
Desperately Seeking
   Susan '85
Making Mr. Right '86

Jade Magri
Courage Mountain '89

Pierre Maguelon
Cyrano de Bergerac '90

Kathleen Maguire
Flipper '63

Robbie Magwood
One Magic Christmas '85

Valerie Mahaffey
Mr. Bill's Real-Life
   Adventures '86
National Lampoon's Senior
   Trip '95

Joseph Maher
Funny Farm '88
I.Q. '94
My Stepmother Is an
   Alien '88
Sister Act '92
Under the Rainbow '81

Grace Mahlaba
Being Human '94
Bopha! '93

Bruce Mahler
Police Academy 6: City Under
   Siege '89

John Mahoney
The American President '95
Eight Men Out '88
The Manhattan Project '86
Moonstruck '87
Reality Bites '94
Say Anything '89

Michael Maillot
The Peanut Butter
   Solution '85

Marjorie Main
The Belle of New York '52
Friendly Persuasion '56
Little Tough Guys '38

Charles Gitona Maina
The Air Up There '94

Marne Maitland
The Bushbaby '70

Tina Majorino
Andre '94
Corrina, Corrina '94
Waterworld '95

Lee Majors
Scrooged '88

A Smoky Mountain
   Christmas '86

Miriam Makeba
Sarafina! '92

Chris Makepeace
Aloha Summer '88
My Bodyguard '80
Undergrads '85

Kelly Makin ▲
National Lampoon's Senior
   Trip '95

Wendy Makkena
Camp Nowhere '94
Sister Act '92
Sister Act 2: Back in the
   Habit '93

Mako
Conan the Barbarian '82
Conan the Destroyer '84
The Island at the Top of the
   World '74
Sidekicks '93
Tucker: The Man and His
   Dream '88
Under the Rainbow '81

Mala
Hawk of the Wilderness '38

Patrick Malahide
Comfort and Joy '84
Cutthroat Island '95

Karyn Malchus
Freaked '93

Karl Malden
The Adventures of Bullwhip
   Griffin '66
Billy Galvin '86
How the West was Won '63
I Confess '53
Pollyanna '60
The Sting 2 '83

Arthur Malet
Beastmaster 2: Through the
   Portal of Time '91
Hook '91
A Little Princess '95

Wendie Malick
The American President '95

Art Malik
A Kid in King Arthur's
   Court '95
True Lies '94
Year of the Comet '92

Judith Malina
The Addams Family '91

Ross Malinger
Peter and the Wolf '95
Sleepless in Seattle '93

John Malkovich
Empire of the Sun '87
Making Mr. Right '86

Of Mice and Men '92
Places in the Heart '84

Louis Malle ▲
Au Revoir Les Enfants '87

Miles Malleson
A Christmas Carol '51

Brian Mallon
Gettysburg '93

James Mallon
Mystery Science Theater
   3000: The Movie '96

James Mallon ▲
Mystery Science Theater
   3000: The Movie '96

Dorothy Malone
Beach Party '63

Patrick Malone
Rock 'n' Roll High School
   Forever '91

Michael Maloney
Othello '95
Truly, Madly, Deeply '91

Paul Maloney ▲
I Live with Me Dad '86

Al Mancini
My Summer Story '94

Nick Mancuso
Blame It on the Night '84

Howie Mandel
A Fine Mess '86
Little Monsters '89
The Princess Who Never
   Laughed '84
Walk Like a Man '87

Robert Mandel ▲
Big Shots '87
F/X '86
School Ties '92

Miles Mander
The Little Princess '39

Luis Mandoki ▲
Born Yesterday '93

Gaspard Manesse
Au Revoir Les Enfants '87

Joseph L. Mankiewicz ▲
Guys and Dolls '55
Sleuth '72

Tom Mankiewicz ▲
Delirious '91
Dragnet '87

Anthony Mann ▲
The Glenn Miller Story '54

Byrun Mann
Street Fighter '94

Daniel Mann ▲
Big Mo '73
Matilda '78

Delbert Mann ▲
The Birch Interval '78
David Copperfield '70
Heidi '67
Home to Stay '79
Love Leads the Way '84
Night Crossing '81

Hank Mann
City Lights '31

Leslie Mann
The Cable Guy '96

Lisa Mann
Lilies of the Field '63

Michael Mann ▲
The Last of the Mohicans '92

Ron Mann ▲
Twist '93

Terrence Mann
Critters '86

Wesley Mann
My Stepmother Is an
   Alien '88

William Mannering
The Old Curiosity Shop '94

Kim Manners ▲
K-9000 '89

Lucie Mannheim
The 39 Steps '35

Vic Manni
Trapped In Paradise '94

Irene Manning
Yankee Doodle Dandy '42

Katya Manning
The Quest '86

Dinah Manoff
I Ought to Be in Pictures '82
Welcome Home, Roxy
   Carmichael '90

Predrag Manojlovic
Tito and Me '92

Peter Manoogian ▲
Arena '88

Ted Manson
Gordy '95

Joe Mantegna
Airheads '94
Baby's Day Out '94
Family Prayers '91
Forget Paris '95
The Money Pit '86
Off Beat '86
Searching for Bobby
   Fischer '93
Three Amigos '86

Up Close and Personal '96
Wait Until Spring, Bandini '90

Henriette Mantel
The Brady Bunch Movie '95
A Very Brady Sequel '96

Mickey Mantle
Robotech, Vol. 1: Booby
   Trap '85

Linda Manz
Orphan Train '79
The Snow Queen '83

Jean Marais
Beauty and the Beast '46

Maria Marais
The Power of One '92

Marcel Marceau
Silent Movie '76

Sophie Marceau
Braveheart '95

Terry Marcel ▲
Jane & the Lost City '87

Nancy Marchand
Brain Donors '92
The Naked Gun: From the
   Files of Police Squad '88
Regarding Henry '91
Sabrina '95
Shirley Temple Storybook
   Theater '60

Silvia Marco
The Man Who Wagged His
   Tail '57

Andrea Marcovicci
Jack the Bear '93

Richard Marcus
Enemy Mine '85

Jordan Marder
Walking on Air '87

Janet Margolin
Annie Hall '77
David and Lisa '62
Take the Money and Run '69

Stuart Margolin
The Big Bus '76
A Fine Mess '86

Stuart Margolin ▲
How the West Was Fun '95

Miriam Margolyes
The Age of Innocence '93
The Butcher's Wife '91
James and the Giant
   Peach '96
Little Dorrit, Film 1: Nobody's
   Fault '88
Little Dorrit, Film 2: Little
   Dorrit's Story '88

David Margulies
Family Prayers '91

Ghostbusters 2 '89
Out on a Limb '92
Running on Empty '88

Edwin L. Marin ▲
A Christmas Carol '38
Miss Annie Rooney '42

Jacques Marin
The Island at the Top of the
   World '74

Richard "Cheech" Marin
Charlie's Ghost: The Secret of
   Coronado '94
The Magic of the Golden Bear:
   Goldy 3 '94

Dan Marino
Ace Ventura: Pet
   Detective '93

Stella Maris
Truly, Madly, Deeply '91

Monte Markham
Defense Play '88
Guns of the Magnificent
   Seven '69

Monte Markham ▲
Defense Play '88

Fletcher Markle ▲
The Incredible Journey '63

Peter Markle ▲
Wagons East '94

Goran Markovic ▲
Tito and Me '92

Olivera Markovic
Tito and Me '92

John Marley
The Greatest '77

Jean Marlow
The Old Curiosity Shop '94

Hugh Marlowe
Monkey Business '52

Kelli Maroney
Fast Times at Ridgemont
   High '82
Night of the Comet '84

Richard Marquand ▲
Return of the Jedi '83

Andre Marquis
Paco '75

Kenneth Mars
The Apple Dumpling Gang
   Rides Again '79
Butch Cassidy and the
   Sundance Kid '69
Fletch '85
For Keeps '88
Goin' Coconuts '78
Radio Days '87
What's Up, Doc? '72
Young Frankenstein '74

Maurice Marsac
Clarence, the Cross-eyed
   Lion '65

Branford Marsalis
Throw Momma from the
   Train '87

Jason Marsden
White Squall '96

Jimmy Marsden
No Dessert Dad, 'Til You Mow
   the Lawn '94

Carol Marsh
Alice in Wonderland '50
A Christmas Carol '51

David Marsh ▲
Lords of Magick '88

Garry Marsh
Just William's Luck '47

Jean Marsh
Horsemasters '61
Return to Oz '85
Willow '88

Joan Marsh
Follow the Leader '44

Mae Marsh
How Green was My Valley '41
The Quiet Man '52

Bryan Marshall
Return to Snowy River '88

E.G. Marshall
The Littlest Angel '69
National Lampoon's Christmas
   Vacation '89
Shirley Temple Storybook
   Theater '60
Superman 2 '80

Frank Marshall ▲
Alive '93
Arachnophobia '90
Congo '95

Garry Marshall
A League of Their Own '92

Garry Marshall ▲
The Flamingo Kid '84
Nothing in Common '86
Overboard '87

George Marshall ▲
How the West was Won '63

Herbert Marshall
Foreign Correspondent '40
The Secret Garden '49

Joshua Marshall
Flirting '89

Ken Marshall
Krull '83

Penny Marshall ▲
Awakenings '90

Big '88
A League of Their Own '92
Renaissance Man '94

Sean Marshall
Pete's Dragon '77
Wonderland Cove '75

William Marshall
Blacula '72
State Fair '45

Zena Marshall
Dr. No '62

K.C. Martel
E.T.: The Extra-Terrestrial '82

Gillian Martell
Oliver Twist '85

Lisa Repo Martell
American Boyfriends '89

Andrea Martin
All I Want for Christmas '91
Boris and Natasha: The
    Movie '92
Club Paradise '86

Barney Martin
Arthur 2: On the Rocks '88

Bill Martin
Rocket Gibraltar '88

Christopher Martin
Class Act '91
House Party '90
House Party 2: The Pajama
    Jam '91
House Party 3 '94

Dean Martin
Airport '70
Bandolero! '68
The Caddy '53
Cannonball Run '81
Cannonball Run 2 '84
Hollywood or Bust '56
That's Dancing! '85

Dewey Martin
Savage Sam '63
Seven Alone '75

Dick Martin
Carbon Copy '81

Duane Martin
Above the Rim '94
Down Periscope '96

George Martin
Crossing Delancey '88

Gilbert Martin
Rob Roy '95

Helen Martin
Doc Hollywood '91
A Hero Ain't Nothin' But a
    Sandwich '78
House Party 2: The Pajama
    Jam '91

Jared Martin
Twinsitters '95

Kellie Martin
Christy '94
Matinee '92
Troop Beverly Hills '89

Lewis Martin
The War of the Worlds '53

Marion Martin
The Great Mike '44
The Man in the Iron Mask '39

Mary Martin
Peter Pan '60

Millicent Martin
Horsemasters '61

Pamela Sue Martin
A Cry in the Wild '90
Nancy Drew: Mystery of the
    Diamond Triangle '78

Ricci Martin
Just Tell Me You Love Me '80

Steve Martin
Dead Men Don't Wear
    Plaid '82
Dirty Rotten Scoundrels '88
Father of the Bride '91
Father of the Bride Part II '95
Housesitter '92
L.A. Story '91
Leap of Faith '92
Little Shop of Horrors '86
Mixed Nuts '94
Parenthood '89
Planes, Trains &
    Automobiles '87
Roxanne '87
Sgt. Bilko '95
A Simple Twist of Fate '94
Three Amigos '86

Strother Martin
Butch Cassidy and the
    Sundance Kid '69
Rooster Cogburn '75
The Villain '79

Tina Martin
Leapin' Leprechauns '95

Tony Martin
The Big Store '41
Till the Clouds Roll By '46

Margo Martindale
Lorenzo's Oil '92

Elsa Martinelli
Hatari '62
Once Upon a Crime '92

A. Martinez
The Cowboys '72
Joe Panther '76
Once Upon a Scoundrel '73
She-Devil '89

Starbird and Sweet
    William '73

Claudio Martinez
Daring Dobermans '73

James Martinez
Leader of the Band '87

Patrice Martinez
Three Amigos '86

Steven Martini
Major Payne '95

Leslie Martinson ▲
The Fantastic World of D.C.
    Collins '84
The Kid with the 200 I.Q. '83

Andrew Marton ▲
Africa Texas Style '67
Clarence, the Cross-eyed
    Lion '65
Gypsy Colt '54

Lee Marvin
Paint Your Wagon '69

Chico Marx
Animal Crackers '30
At the Circus '39
The Big Store '41
The Cocoanuts '29
A Day at the Races '37
Duck Soup '33
Go West '40
Horse Feathers '32
Love Happy '50
Monkey Business '31
A Night at the Opera '35
Room Service '38

Groucho Marx
Animal Crackers '30
At the Circus '39
The Big Store '41
The Cocoanuts '29
A Day at the Races '37
Duck Soup '33
Go West '40
Horse Feathers '32
Love Happy '50
Monkey Business '31
A Night at the Opera '35
Room Service '38

Harpo Marx
Animal Crackers '30
At the Circus '39
The Big Store '41
The Cocoanuts '29
A Day at the Races '37
Duck Soup '33
Go West '40
Horse Feathers '32
Love Happy '50
Monkey Business '31
A Night at the Opera '35
Room Service '38

Zeppo Marx
Animal Crackers '30
The Cocoanuts '29

Duck Soup '33
Horse Feathers '32
Monkey Business '31

Ron Masak
Harper Valley P.T.A. '78
Man from Clover Grove '78

Pierrino Mascarino
Summer Rental '85

Nelson Mashita
Darkman '90

Hilary Mason
Robot Jox '89

James Mason
Evil Under the Sun '82
Jesus of Nazareth '77
Journey to the Center of the
    Earth '59
North by Northwest '59
Prince Valiant '54
Salem's Lot '79
20,000 Leagues Under the
    Sea '54
Water Babies '79

Laurence Mason
Hackers '95

Lawrence Mason
The Crow '93

Leroy Mason
Silver Stallion '41

Marsha Mason
Audrey Rose '77
The Cheap Detective '78
Drop Dead Fred '91
The Goodbye Girl '77
Max Dugan Returns '83
Promises in the Dark '79

Tom Mason
Men Don't Leave '89

John Massari
The Wizard of Speed and
    Time '88

Michael Massee
The Crow '93

Anna Massey
The Corn is Green '79

Daniel Massey
Victory '81

Dick Massey
The Commitments '91

Ilona Massey
Love Happy '50

Raymond Massey
East of Eden '54
How the West was Won '63

Leonide Massine
The Red Shoes '48

Vicki Masson
Rob Roy '95

Ben Masters
Making Mr. Right '86

Fay Masterson
Cops and Robbersons '94
The Man Without a Face '93
The Power of One '92

Mary Stuart Masterson
Bed of Roses '95
Benny & Joon '93
Chances Are '89
Immediate Family '89
Radioland Murders '94
Some Kind of Wonderful '87

Peter Masterson ▲
The Trip to Bountiful '85

Mary Elizabeth Mastrantonio
Robin Hood: Prince of Thieves '91
Two Bits '96

Richard Masur
Encino Man '92
Forget Paris '95
Hiroshima Maiden '88
License to Drive '88
The Man Without a Face '93
My Girl '91
My Girl 2 '94
My Science Project '85
Timerider '83

Diego Matamoros
Goosebumps: A Night in Terror Tower '96

Aubrey Mather
Jane Eyre '44

Jerry Mathers
Back to the Beach '87

Joshawa Mathers
The Return of Tommy Tricker '94

Michelle Matheson
Threesome '94

Tim Matheson
The Apple Dumpling Gang Rides Again '79
Black Sheep '96
Drop Dead Fred '91
Fletch '85
A Very Brady Sequel '96
Yours, Mine & Ours '68

Carmen Mathews
Sounder '72

Kerwin Mathews
Jack the Giant Killer '62
The Seventh Voyage of Sinbad '58
The Three Worlds of Gulliver '59

Waltz King '63

Samantha Mathis
The American President '95
Broken Arrow '95
How to Make an American Quilt '95
Little Women '94
Super Mario Bros. '93
The Thing Called Love '93
This is My Life '92

Jacques Mathou
Year of the Comet '92

Norman Matlock
Crooklyn '94

Pam Matteson
Prehysteria 3 '95

Charles Matthau ▲
Doin' Time on Planet Earth '88

Walter Matthau
The Bad News Bears '76
Casey's Shadow '78
Charade '63
Dennis the Menace '93
The Front Page '74
Grumpier Old Men '95
Grumpy Old Men '93
Hello, Dolly! '69
I Ought to Be in Pictures '82
I.Q. '94
Kotch '71
Little Miss Marker '80
The Odd Couple '68
The Sunshine Boys '75

Liesl Matthews
A Little Princess '95

Burny Mattinson ▲
The Great Mouse Detective '86

Victor Mature
Androcles and the Lion '52

John Matuszak
The Goonies '85
Ice Pirates '84

Billy Mauch
The Prince and the Pauper '37

Jack Mauck
Greenstone '85

Claire Maurier
The 400 Blows '59

Lois Maxwell
Diamonds are Forever '71
Dr. No '62
For Your Eyes Only '81
From Russia with Love '63
Live and Let Die '73
The Man with the Golden Gun '74
Moonraker '79

On Her Majesty's Secret Service '69
The Spy Who Loved Me '77
Thunderball '65
A View to a Kill '85
You Only Live Twice '67

Marilyn Maxwell
Lost in a Harem '44

Roberta Maxwell
Philadelphia '93

Ronald F. Maxwell ▲
Kidco '83
Little Darlings '80
The Night the Lights Went Out in Georgia '81

Elaine May ▲
The Heartbreak Kid '72

Jodhi May
The Last of the Mohicans '92
A World Apart '88

Mathilda May
Prince Brat and the Whipping Boy '95

Rik Mayall
Drop Dead Fred '91

Russ Mayberry ▲
Unidentified Flying Oddball '79

Les Mayfield ▲
Encino Man '92
Miracle on 34th Street '94

Peter Mayhew
The Empire Strikes Back '80
Return of the Jedi '83

Mimi Maynard
Adventures in Dinosaur City '92

Ferdinand "Ferdy" Mayne
A Friendship in Vienna '88

Alois Mayo
The Power of One '92

Frank Mayo
Tim Tyler's Luck '37

Virginia Mayo
Secret Life of Walter Mitty '47
Wonder Man '45

Melanie Mayron
Car Wash '76
Cindy Eller '91
Girlfriends '78
Heartbeeps '81

Melanie Mayron ▲
The Baby-Sitters Club '95

Debi Mazar
Batman Forever '95
Beethoven's 2nd '93

Little Man Tate '91

Mike Mazurki
The Adventures of Huckleberry Finn '78
The Canterville Ghost '44
Challenge To Be Free '76
Dick Tracy, Detective '45
The Errand Boy '61
The Incredible Rocky Mountain Race '77
Sinbad the Sailor '47

Ernestine Mazurowna
Jean de Florette '87

Joseph Mazzello
The Cure '95
Jersey Girl '92
Jurassic Park '93
Radio Flyer '92
The River Wild '94
Shadowlands '93

Jennifer McAllister
Kid from Not-So-Big '78

Marianne McAndrew
Hello, Dolly! '69

Cathy McAuley
Beanstalk '94

Don McBrearty ▲
Child's Christmas in Wales '88

Ruth McCabe
The Snapper '93

Robert McCahon ▲
Running Wild '73

Frances Lee McCain
Gremlins '84
Tex '82
Two of a Kind '82

Howard McCain ▲
No Dessert Dad, 'Til You Mow the Lawn '94

Lon McCallister
The Story of Seabiscuit '49

David McCallum
Watcher in the Woods '81

Macon McCalman
Doc Hollywood '91

Mercedes McCambridge
Giant '56

Chuck McCann
C.H.O.M.P.S. '79
Foul Play '78
The Projectionist '71

Donal McCann
The Miracle '91

Sean McCann
The Air Up There '94
Trapped In Paradise '94

Brian McCardie
Rob Roy '95

Leo McCarey ▲
The Bells of St. Mary's '45
Duck Soup '33
Going My Way '44

Andrew McCarthy
The Beniker Gang '83
The Joy Luck Club '93
Mannequin '87
Only You '92
Pretty in Pink '86
Weekend at Bernie's '89
Weekend at Bernie's 2 '93

Charlie McCarthy
Fun & Fancy Free '47

Frank McCarthy
Dead Men Don't Wear
Plaid '82

Julia McCarthy
Year of the Comet '92

Kevin McCarthy
Hero at Large '80
The Howling '81
Innerspace '87
Invasion of the Body
Snatchers '78
Twilight Zone: The Movie '83
UHF '89

Molly McCarthy
The Flamingo Kid '84

Nobu McCarthy
The Geisha Boy '58
The Karate Kid: Part 2 '86

Sheila McCarthy
Beethoven Lives Upstairs '92
Die Hard 2: Die Harder '90
George's Island '91
Paradise '91

Tarek McCarthy
Journey to Spirit Island '92

Paul McCartney
A Hard Day's Night '64
Help! '65
Magical Mystery Tour '67

Rod McCary
No Drums, No Bugles '71

Saundra McClain
Mr. & Mrs. Bridge '91

Rue McClanahan
The Little Match Girl '87

Michael McClary ▲
Annie O '95

Sean McClory
The Quiet Man '52

Leigh McCloskey
Just One of the Guys '85

Doug McClure
At the Earth's Core '76
Land That Time Forgot '75
The People That Time
Forgot '77

Marc McClure
Back to the Future '85
Back to the Future, Part 3 '90
I Wanna Hold Your Hand '78
Supergirl '84
Superman 1: The Movie '78
Superman 2 '80
Superman 3 '83
Superman 4: The Quest for
Peace '87

Edie McClurg
Airborne '93
Back to School '86
Ferris Bueller's Day Off '86
Mr. Mom '83
Planes, Trains &
Automobiles '87
A River Runs Through It '92
She's Having a Baby '88

Ken McCluskey
The Commitments '91

Heather McComb
Stay Tuned '92

Matthew McConaughey
Boys on the Side '94

John McConnell
King of the Hill '93

Marilyn McCoo
The Fantastic World of D.C.
Collins '84
My Mom's a Werewolf '89

Catherine McCormack
Braveheart '95

Leigh McCormack
The Long Day Closes '92

Patty McCormack
The Adventures of Huckleberry
Finn '60
The Bad Seed '56

Maureen McCormick
Pony Express Rider '76
Take Down '79

Myron McCormick
No Time for Sergeants '58

Pat McCormick
The Princess and the Pea '83
Smokey and the Bandit '77
Smokey and the Bandit, Part
2 '80
Smokey and the Bandit, Part
3 '83
Under the Rainbow '81

Malachy McCourt
Manny's Orphans '78

Alec McCowen
The Age of Innocence '93

Matt McCoy
Bigfoot: The Unforgettable
Encounter '94
Police Academy 5: Assignment
Miami Beach '88
Police Academy 6: City Under
Siege '89
Rent-A-Kid '95

Sylvester McCoy
Leapin' Leprechauns '95

Mark McCracken
Matinee '92

Paul McCrane
Fame '80
Robocop '87

Darius McCrary
Big Shots '87

Jody McCrea
Beach Blanket Bingo '65
Beach Party '63
Bikini Beach '64
How to Stuff a Wild Bikini '65
Muscle Beach Party '64
Pajama Party '64

Joel McCrea
Foreign Correspondent '40
Our Little Girl '35

Peter McCubbin ▲
Home for Christmas '90

Jim McCullough ▲
The Aurora Encounter '85
The Charge of the Model
T's '76
Where the Red Fern Grows:
Part 2 '92

Bil McCurcheon
Steel Magnolias '89

Bill McCutcheon
Mr. Destiny '90

Hattie McDaniel
Gone with the Wind '39
Since You Went Away '44

James McDaniel
Malcolm X '92

Dylan McDermott
Home for the Holidays '95
Jersey Girl '92
Miracle on 34th Street '94
Steel Magnolias '89

Shane McDermott
Airborne '93

Conor McDermottroe
Quigley Down Under '90

Ruth McDevitt
Change of Habit '69

The Shakiest Gun in the
West '68

Christopher McDonald
Celtic Pride '96
Chances Are '89
Fatal Instinct '93
Grumpy Old Men '93
Happy Gilmore '96
Monkey Trouble '94
Quiz Show '94

Francis McDonald
Zorro's Black Whip '44

Garry McDonald
Pirate Movie '82

Kevin McDonald
National Lampoon's Senior
Trip '95

Marie McDonald
The Geisha Boy '58

**Michael James
McDonald** ▲
The Crazysitter '94

Mary McDonnell
Blue Chips '94
Dances with Wolves '90
Independence Day '96
Matewan '87
Sneakers '92

Mary McDonough
A Day for Thanks on Walton's
Mountain '82
The Waltons: A Thanksgiving
Story '73
The Waltons: The Children's
Carol '80

Frances McDormand
The Butcher's Wife '91
Darkman '90

Roddy McDowall
The Adventures of Bullwhip
Griffin '66
Battle for the Planet of the
Apes '73
Bedknobs and
Broomsticks '71
The Cat from Outer Space '78
Conquest of the Planet of the
Apes '72
Doin' Time on Planet
Earth '88
Escape from the Planet of the
Apes '71
Evil Under the Sun '82
Funny Lady '75
How Green was My Valley '41
Lassie, Come Home '43
My Friend Flicka '43
Overboard '87
Planet of the Apes '68
The Poseidon Adventure '72
That Darn Cat '65
The Thief of Baghdad '78

Malcolm McDowell
Bopha! '93
Cross Creek '83
Little Red Riding Hood '83
Merlin and the Sword '85
Milk Money '94
Star Trek Generations '94

Ian McElhinney
The Playboys '92

John McEnery
Black Beauty '94
Land That Time Forgot '75

Peter McEnery
The Fighting Prince of
 Donegal '66
Moon-Spinners '64

Jamie McEnnan
Munchie '92

Reba McEntire
North '94

Bernard McEveety
One Little Indian '73

Bernard McEveety ▲
The Bears & I '74
Napoleon and Samantha '72
One Little Indian '73

Vincent McEveety ▲
Amy '81
The Apple Dumpling Gang
 Rides Again '79
The Castaway Cowboy '74
Charley and the Angel '73
Gus '76
Herbie Goes Bananas '80
Herbie Goes to Monte
 Carlo '77
Million Dollar Duck '71
Smoke '70
Superdad '73
The Treasure of
 Matecumbe '76

Geraldine McEwan
Robin Hood: Prince of
 Thieves '91

Gates McFadden
Star Trek Generations '94
Star Trek the Next Generation
 Episode 1-2: Encounter at
 Farpoint '87

Angus McFadyen
Braveheart '95

**George "Spanky"
 McFarland**
The Aurora Encounter '85
General Spanky '36

Darren McGavin
Airport '77 '77
Billy Madison '94
Captain America '89
A Christmas Story '83
The Delicate Delinquent '56

The Natural '84
No Deposit, No Return '76
Turk 182! '85
Zero to Sixty '78

Patrick McGaw
The Basketball Diaries '94

Cindy McGee
Fast Forward '84

Vonetta McGee
Blacula '72
Brother Future '91

Johnny Rae McGhee
Project X '87

Bruce McGill
Black Sheep '96
Citizens Band '77
Timecop '94
Whale for the Killing '81
Wildcats '86

Kelly McGillis
The Babe '92
North '94
Top Gun '86

John C. McGinley
Born to Be Wild '95
Car 54, Where Are You? '94
Highlander 2: The
 Quickening '91
A Midnight Clear '92
Wagons East '94

Ted McGinley
Revenge of the Nerds '84

Scott McGinnis
Making the Grade '84
Odd Jobs '85

John McGiver
The Adventures of Tom
 Sawyer '73

Mike McGlone
Ed '96

Patrick McGoohan
Baby. . .Secret of the Lost
 Legend '85
Braveheart '95
Dr. Syn, Alias the
 Scarecrow '64
Ice Station Zebra '68
The Man in the Iron Mask '77
The Phantom '96
The Silver Streak '76
The Three Lives of
 Thomasina '63

Barry McGovern
Joe Versus the Volcano '90

Elizabeth McGovern
King of the Hill '93
Racing with the Moon '84
She's Having a Baby '88
Snow White and the Seven
 Dwarfs '83

J.P. McGowan ▲
Hurricane Express '32

Stuart E. McGowan ▲
The Billion Dollar Hobo '78

Tom McGowan
The Birdcage '95

Michael McGrady
The Babe '92

Walter McGrail
The Green Hornet '39

Derek McGrath
Freaked '93

Douglas McGrath ▲
Emma '96

Joseph McGrath ▲
Digby, the Biggest Dog in the
 World '73

Michael McGreevey
Sammy, the Way-Out Seal '62

Angela Punch McGregor
We of the Never Never '82

Ewan McGregor
Emma '96

Biff McGuire
Child of Glass '78

Don McGuire ▲
The Delicate Delinquent '56

Dorothy McGuire
Friendly Persuasion '56
Old Yeller '57
The Runaways '75
Summer Magic '63
The Swiss Family
 Robinson '60
A Tree Grows in Brooklyn '45

Kim McGuire
Cry-Baby '90

Michael McGuire
Home to Stay '79

Stephen McHattie
Beverly Hills Cop 3 '94
Geronimo: An American
 Legend '93

Doug McHenry ▲
House Party 2: The Pajama
 Jam '91

Frank McHugh
Going My Way '44
Mighty Joe Young '49
State Fair '45
A Tiger Walks '64

John McIntire
Cloak & Dagger '84
Francis the Talking Mule '49
Herbie Rides Again '74
Honkytonk Man '82
The Light in the Forest '58

Rooster Cogburn '75

Tim McIntire
Aloha, Bobby and Rose '74
Gumball Rally '76

Marvin J. McIntyre
Born to Be Wild '95
Fandango '85

Peggy McKay
Wait Till Your Mother Gets
 Home '83

Michael McKean
Airheads '94
Book of Love '91
The Brady Bunch Movie '95
Clue '85
Coneheads '93
Daniel and the Towers '90s
D.A.R.Y.L. '85
Light of Day '87
Memoirs of an Invisible
 Man '92
Planes, Trains &
 Automobiles '87
Radioland Murders '94
Short Circuit 2 '88

Donna McKechnie
Breakin' Through '84

Lafe McKee
Law of the Wild '34

Lonette McKee
Brewster's Millions '85
Malcolm X '92

Danica McKellar
Sidekicks '93

Ian McKellen
The Scarlet Pimpernel '82
The Shadow '94

Alex McKenna
The Stupids '95

Siobhan McKenna
Doctor Zhivago '65

Virginia McKenna
Born Free '66
Christian the Lion '76
Ring of Bright Water '69

Dallas McKennon
Mystery Mansion '83

Julia McKenzie
The Old Curiosity Shop '94

Kevin McKenzie
Olly Olly Oxen Free '78

Doug McKeon
Night Crossing '81
On Golden Pond '81
Where the Red Fern Grows:
 Part 2 '92

Charles McKeown
The Adventures of Baron
  Munchausen '89

Leo McKern
The Adventures of Sherlock
  Holmes' Smarter
  Brother '78
Candleshoe '78
Help! '65
The Horse Without a
  Head '63
Ladyhawke '85
The Mouse That Roared '59
Ryan's Daughter '70

Robert McKimson ▲
Best of Bugs Bunny &
  Friends '40
Bugs Bunny's 3rd Movie:
  1,001 Rabbit Tales '82
Bugs Bunny's Hare-Raising
  Tales '89
Daffy Duck's Madcap
  Mania '89

Bill McKinney
Bronco Billy '80
Cannonball '76
City Slickers 2: The Legend of
  Curly's Gold '94
Heart Like a Wheel '83
The Outlaw Josey Wales '76
The Shootist '76
Tex '82

Ray McKinnon
The Net '95
A Perfect World '93

Duncan McLachlan ▲
Born Wild '95
The Double O Kid '92

Andrew V. McLaglen
Since You Went Away '44

Andrew V. McLaglen ▲
Bandolero! '68
Cahill: United States
  Marshal '73
Monkeys, Go Home! '66
The Shadow Riders '82

Victor McLaglen
Prince Valiant '54
The Quiet Man '52
Wee Willie Winkie '37

Ron McLarty
Tiger Town '83
Two Bits '96

Norman Z. McLeod ▲
Horse Feathers '32
Little Men '40
Monkey Business '31
Secret Life of Walter Mitty '47
Topper '37
Topper Takes a Trip '39

Allyn Ann McLerie
And Baby Makes Six '79

Tom McLoughlin ▲
Date with an Angel '87

Marshall McLuhan
Annie Hall '77

Ed McMahon
The Kid from Left Field '79

Horace McMahon
The Delicate Delinquent '56

Michael McManus
Mr. Bill's Real-Life
  Adventures '86

Sharon McManus
Anchors Aweigh '45

Kenneth McMillan
Blue Skies Again '83
Cat's Eye '85
Heartbeeps '81
Salem's Lot '79
Three Fugitives '89

Andrew Ian McMillian
Kavik, the Wolf Dog '84

Sam McMurray
Getting Even with Dad '94
L.A. Story '91

Mercedes McNab
Addams Family Values '93
Savage Land '94

Barbara McNair
Change of Habit '69

Billy McNamara
Dream a Little Dream '89

Brian McNamara
Arachnophobia '90
Mystery Date '91
Short Circuit '86

William McNamara
Storybook '95

Ian McNaughton ▲
And Now for Something
  Completely Different '72

Howard McNear
The Errand Boy '61

Ian McNeice
Ace Ventura: When Nature
  Calls '95
Year of the Comet '92

Kristy McNichol
Just the Way You Are '84
Little Darlings '80
My Old Man '79
The Night the Lights Went Out
  in Georgia '81
Pirate Movie '82

Kevin McNulty
The Neverending Story 3 '94
Timecop '94

Sandy McPeak
Eye on the Sparrow '91
Ode to Billy Joe '76

Kris McQuade
Strictly Ballroom '92

Armelia McQueen
Ghost '90

Butterfly McQueen
The Adventures of Huckleberry
  Finn '85
Gone with the Wind '39

Chad McQueen
The Karate Kid '84
Where the Red Fern Grows:
  Part 2 '92

Steve McQueen
Junior Bonner '72
Papillon '73
The Reivers '69

George McQuilkin ▲
Caddie Woodlawn '88

Alan McRae
3 Ninjas '92

Elizabeth McRae
The Incredible Mr. Limpet '64

Frank McRae
*batteries not included '87
Last Action Hero '93
Lightning Jack '94

Gerald McRaney
The NeverEnding Story '84

Ian McShane
The Fifth Musketeer '79

Micheal McShane
Richie Rich '94
Robin Hood: Prince of
  Thieves '91
Tom and Huck '95

John McTiernan ▲
Die Hard '88
Die Hard: With a
  Vengeance '95
The Hunt for Red October '90
Last Action Hero '93

Caroline McWilliams
Mermaids '90

Courtland Mead
Dragonworld '94
The Little Rascals '94
Tom and Huck '95

Jayne Meadows
City Slickers '91

Joyce Meadows
Zebra in the Kitchen '65

Stephen Meadows
A Cry in the Wild '90

Tim Meadows
It's Pat: The Movie '94

Karen Meagher
Experience Preferred. . . But
  Not Essential '83

Colm Meaney
The Commitments '91
Far and Away '92
Into the West '92
The Last of the Mohicans '92
The Snapper '93
War of the Buttons '95

Angela Means
House Party 3 '94

Russell Means
The Last of the Mohicans '92
Wagons East '94
Windrunner '94

Anne Meara
Awakenings '90
Fame '80
Heavyweights '94

DeAnn Mears
The Loneliest Runner '76

Michael Mears
The Old Curiosity Shop '94

Meat Loaf
Leap of Faith '92

Julio Mechoso
White Squall '96

Peter Medak ▲
Breakin' Through '84
The Dancing Princesses '84
The Emperor's New
  Clothes '84
Pinocchio '83
Pontiac Moon '94
The Snow Queen '83
Snow White and the Seven
  Dwarfs '83

Cissy Meddings
Strangers in Good
  Company '91

Kay Medford
Funny Girl '68

Jesus Medina
Yanco '64

Patricia Medina
Francis the Talking Mule '49
Snow White and the Three
  Stooges '61
The Three Musketeers '48

Cary Medoway ▲
The Heavenly Kid '85

Allison Meek
No Dessert Dad, 'Til You Mow
  the Lawn '94

Donald Meek
Little Miss Broadway '38
State Fair '45

George Meeker
The Invisible Monster '50

Ralph Meeker
Gentle Giant '67

Armand Meffre
Here Comes Santa Claus '84

John Megna
To Kill a Mockingbird '62

Shane Meier
Andre '94

Mary Meigs
Strangers in Good
  Company '91

John Meillon
Crocodile Dundee '86
Crocodile Dundee 2 '88
The Fourth Wish '75
Ride a Wild Pony '75

Gus Meins ▲
March of the Wooden
  Soldiers '34

Isabelle Mejias
The Bay Boy '85

Andre Melancon ▲
The Dog Who Stopped the
  War '84

Wendel Meldrum
City Boy '93

Bill Melendez ▲
Bon Voyage, Charlie
  Brown '80
The Charlie Brown and
  Snoopy Show: Vol. 1 '83
A Charlie Brown
  Christmas '65
A Charlie Brown
  Thanksgiving '81
Dick Deadeye '76
Snoopy, Come Home '72
You're Not Elected, Charlie
  Brown!/A Charlie Brown
  Christmas '65

John Melendez
Airheads '94

James Melkonian ▲
The Jerky Boys '95

Frank Melton
Stand Up and Cheer '34

Ben Mendelsohn
Quigley Down Under '90
The Year My Voice Broke '87

David Mendenhall
Going Bananas '88
Over the Top '86
Secret of the Ice Cave '89

Space Raiders '83

Ramon Menendez ▲
Stand and Deliver '88

Chris Menges ▲
A World Apart '88

Asha Menina
House of Cards '92

Adolphe Menjou
Little Miss Marker '34
Pollyanna '60

Heather Menzies
The Sound of Music '65

**William Cameron
  Menzies ▲**
Invaders from Mars '53

Christian Meoli
Alive '93

Doro Merande
The Russians are Coming, the
  Russians are Coming '66

Marian Mercer
Out on a Limb '92

Chantal Mercier
Small Change '76

Michele Mercier
Call of the Wild '72

Micole Mercurio
While You Were Sleeping '95

Paul Mercurio
Strictly Ballroom '92

Burgess Meredith
Clash of the Titans '81
Foul Play '78
Grumpier Old Men '95
Grumpy Old Men '93
Rocky '76
Rocky 2 '79
Rocky 3 '82
Rocky 5 '90
Santa Claus: The Movie '85
Thumbelina '94
Twilight Zone: The Movie '83

Iris Meredith
Green Archer '40

Judi Meredith
Jack the Giant Killer '62

Lee Meredith
The Sunshine Boys '75

Joseph Merhi ▲
Magic Kid '92

Eda Reiss Merin
Don't Tell Mom the
  Babysitter's Dead '91

Lee Meriwether
Brothers O'Toole '73

Una Merkel
The Parent Trap '61
Summer Magic '63
A Tiger Walks '64

Joanna Merlin
Fame '80
Two Bits '96

Ethel Merman
Airplane! '80

Dina Merrill
The Courtship of Eddie's
  Father '62
The Greatest '77
Running Wild '73

Gary Merrill
Huckleberry Finn '74
Mysterious Island '61

Keith Merrill ▲
Take Down '79

Theresa Merritt
Billy Madison '94

Jane Merrow
The Lion in Winter '68

Susan Merson
Lost in Yonkers '93

Debra Messing
A Walk in the Clouds '95

Laurie Metcalf
Desperately Seeking
  Susan '85
Making Mr. Right '86
Uncle Buck '89

Mark Metcalf
One Crazy Summer '86

Aaron Michael Metchik
The Baby-Sitters Club '95
Trading Mom '94

Asher Metchik
Trading Mom '94

Art Metrano
Going Ape! '81
The Heartbreak Kid '72
Police Academy 2: Their First
  Assignment '85
Police Academy 3: Back in
  Training '86

Nancy Mette
Meet the Hollowheads '89

Alan Metter ▲
Back to School '86
Girls Just Want to Have
  Fun '85
Police Academy: Mission to
  Moscow '94

Jim Metzler
Hot to Trot! '88
Tex '82

Jason Mewes
Clerks '94
Mallrats '95

Breckin Meyer
Clueless '95

Dina Meyer
Dragonheart '96
Johnny Mnemonic '95

Emile Meyer
Shane '53

Nicholas Meyer ▲
The Pied Piper of Hamelin '84
Star Trek 2: The Wrath of
  Khan '82
Star Trek 6: The Undiscovered
  Country '91

Ari Meyers
Dark Horse '92
Think Big '90

Michelle Meyrink
One Magic Christmas '85
Permanent Record '88
Real Genius '85
Revenge of the Nerds '84

Eric Meza ▲
House Party 3 '94

Richard Michaels ▲
Blue Skies Again '83
Father and Scout '95
Homeward Bound '80

Karli Michaelson
The Kid with the 200 I.Q. '83

Dave Michener ▲
The Great Mouse
  Detective '86

Frank Middlemass
Oliver Twist '85

Charles Middleton
Duck Soup '33
Flash Gordon Conquers the
  Universe '40
Flash Gordon: Rocketship '36
Spook Busters '46

Robert Middleton
The Court Jester '56

Bette Midler
Big Business '88
Hocus Pocus '93

Toshiro Mifune
Shadow of the Wolf '92

Lita Milan
The Left-Handed Gun '58

Alyssa Milano
Little Sister '92
Old Enough '84

Peter Miles
The Red Pony '49

Sarah Miles
Hope and Glory '87
Ryan's Daughter '70

Sylvia Miles
Crossing Delancey '88
Evil Under the Sun '82
She-Devil '89
Sleeping Beauty '89
Zero to Sixty '78

Vera Miles
The Castaway Cowboy '74
Follow Me, Boys! '66
Gentle Giant '67
One Little Indian '73
Run for the Roses '78
Those Calloways '65
A Tiger Walks '64
The Wrong Man '56

Lewis Milestone ▲
The Red Pony '49

Penelope Milford
The Golden Seal '83

John Milius ▲
Conan the Barbarian '82
The Wind and the Lion '75

Ray Milland
Dial "M" for Murder '54
Escape to Witch Mountain '75

Gavin Millar ▲
Dreamchild '85
My Friend Walter '93

Stuart Millar ▲
Rooster Cogburn '75

Ann Miller
Easter Parade '48
On the Town '49
Room Service '38

Aubree Miller
The Ewok Adventure '84
The Ewoks: Battle for
    Endor '85

Barry Miller
Fame '80
Peggy Sue Got Married '86

Charles Miller
Being Human '94

Cheryl Miller
Clarence, the Cross-eyed
    Lion '65
Man from Clover Grove '78
Mountain Man '77

Claude Miller ▲
The Little Thief '89

David Miller ▲
Love Happy '50

Dennis Miller
Madhouse '90
The Net '95
The Quest '86

Denny Miller
Buck and the Preacher '72
The Party '68

Dick Miller
Explorers '85
Gremlins '84
Heart Like a Wheel '83
The Howling '81
Innerspace '87
Matinee '92
Project X '87
Rock 'n' Roll High School '79
The Terminator '84

Garry Miller
Amazing Mr. Blunden '72

George Miller ▲
Andre '94
Goodbye, Miss 4th of July '88
The Man from Snowy
    River '82
The NeverEnding Story 2: Next
    Chapter '91

George Miller ▲
Lorenzo's Oil '92
Mad Max: Beyond
    Thunderdome '85
Miracle Down Under '87
Twilight Zone: The Movie '83

Harvey Miller ▲
Bad Medicine '85

Helen Miller
Being Human '94

Jason Miller
Light of Day '87
Rudy '93

Jeremy Miller
The Willies '90

Jonny Lee Miller
Hackers '95

Joshua Miller
And You Thought Your
    Parents Were Weird! '91
Teen Witch '89

Larry Miller
Corrina, Corrina '94
Radioland Murders '94
Suburban Commando '91
Undercover Blues '93

Mark Miller
Savannah Smiles '82

Penelope Ann Miller
Adventures in Babysitting '87
Awakenings '90
Big Top Pee Wee '88
Chaplin '92
The Freshman '90
Kindergarten Cop '90
The Shadow '94
Year of the Comet '92

Randall Miller ▲
Class Act '91
Houseguest '94

Rebecca Miller
Wind '92

Robert Ellis Miller ▲
Brenda Starr '86

Roger Miller
Lucky Luke '94

Sherry Miller
Rent-A-Kid '95

Sidney Miller
Boys Town '38
Men of Boys Town '41

Walter Miller
Shadow of the Eagle '32
Tailspin Tommy '34

Warren Miller
Philadelphia '93

Spike Milligan
Digby, the Biggest Dog in the
    World '73

Hayley Mills
Back Home '90
The Flame Trees of Thika '81
In Search of the
    Castaways '62
Moon-Spinners '64
The Parent Trap '61
Pollyanna '60
Summer Magic '63
That Darn Cat '65
Tiger Bay '59
The Trouble with Angels '66
Whistle Down the Wind '62

John Mills
Africa Texas Style '67
Dr. Strange '78
Oklahoma Crude '73
Ryan's Daughter '70
The Swiss Family
    Robinson '60
Tiger Bay '59

Juliet Mills
Barnaby and Me '77
Jonathan Livingston
    Seagull '73

Reginald Mills ▲
Tales of Beatrix Potter '71

Samantha Mills
Prehysteria '93

Martin Milner
Life with Father '47
13 Ghosts '60
Zebra in the Kitchen '65

Josh Milrad
Beastmaster '82

Ernest Milton
Alice in Wonderland '50

John Omirah Miluwi
Gorillas in the Mist '88

Yvette Mimieux
The Black Hole '79
Monkeys, Go Home! '66
Neptune Factor '73
The Wonderful World of the
    Brothers Grimm '62

Sal Mineo
Escape from the Planet of the
    Apes '71
Giant '56
Rebel Without a Cause '55

Jan Miner
Mermaids '90

Steve Miner ▲
Big Bully '95
Forever Young '92
House '86
My Father the Hero '93
Soul Man '86
Wild Hearts Can't Be
    Broken '91

Anthony Minghella ▲
Mr. Wonderful '93
Truly, Madly, Deeply '91

Rob Minkoff ▲
Honey, I Shrunk the Kids '89
The Lion King '94

Liza Minnelli
Arthur '81
Arthur 2: On the Rocks '88
Muppets Moments '85
The Princess and the Pea '83
Silent Movie '76
That's Dancing! '85

Vincente Minnelli ▲
An American in Paris '51
The Band Wagon '53
The Courtship of Eddie's
    Father '62
Father of the Bride '50
Father's Little Dividend '51
Kismet '55
Meet Me in St. Louis '44
On a Clear Day You Can See
    Forever '70

Kylie Minogue
Bio-Dome '96
Street Fighter '94

Kristin Minter
Cool As Ice '91

Fabrizio Mioni
Hercules '58

Miou-Miou
Little Indian, Big City '95

Evan Mirand
My Best Friend Is a
    Vampire '88

Chris Miranda
Man of the House '95

Robert Miranda
Chips the War Dog '90
Lost in Yonkers '93
Sister Act '92
What's Love Got to Do With
It? '93

Helen Mirren
The Fiendish Plot of Dr. Fu
Manchu '80
The Little Mermaid '84
2010 : The Year We Make
Contact '84
When the Whales Came '89

Jayme Lee Misfeldt
Running Free '94

Mr. T
Freaked '93
The Magic of the Golden Bear:
Goldy 3 '94
Rocky 3 '82

Stacy Mistysyn
Princes in Exile '90

Cameron Mitchell
Buck and the Preacher '72
Carousel '56
My Favorite Year '82
The Swarm '78

Daryl Mitchell
Sgt. Bilko '95

David Mitchell ▲
Club Med '83

Donna Mitchell
Two Bits '96

John Cameron Mitchell
Book of Love '91

Millard Mitchell
Singin' in the Rain '52

Red Mitchell
8 Seconds '94

Thomas Mitchell
Gone with the Wind '39
High Noon '52
It's a Wonderful Life '46
Mr. Smith Goes to
Washington '39
Shirley Temple Storybook
Theater '60

Warren Mitchell
Knights & Emeralds '87

Yvonne Mitchell
Tiger Bay '59

Ilan Mitchell-Smith
How to Be a Perfect Person in
Just Three Days '84
Journey to the Center of the
Earth '88
Weird Science '85

Chris Mitchum
Big Jake '71
Tombstone '93

Robert Mitchum
The Human Comedy '43
Matilda '78
The Red Pony '49
Ryan's Daughter '70
Scrooged '88

Hayao Miyazaki ▲
My Neighbor Totoro '93

Eric Miyeni
Cry, the Beloved Country '95

Isaac Mizrahi
For Love or Money '93

Moshe Mizrahi ▲
Madame Rosa '77

Noah Moazezi
Tiger Town '83

Mary Ann Mobley
My Dog, the Thief '69

Roger Mobley
Emil and the Detective '64
Jack the Giant Killer '62

Matthew Modine
Bye Bye, Love '94
Cutthroat Island '95
Fluke '95
Gross Anatomy '89
Wind '92

Donald Moffat
The Best of Times '86
Clear and Present Danger '94
Housesitter '92
Necessary Parties '88
Promises in the Dark '79
Regarding Henry '91
The Right Stuff '83
Trapped In Paradise '94

D.W. Moffett
Lisa '90

Zakes Mokae
Dad '89
Gross Anatomy '89

Jerry Molen
Rain Man '88

Alfred Molina
Before and After '95
Ladyhawke '85
Maverick '94
Raiders of the Lost Ark '81
White Fang 2: The Myth of the
White Wolf '94

Angela Molina
1492: Conquest of
Paradise '92

Edouard Molinaro ▲
Just the Way You Are '84

Georgia Moll
Thief of Baghdad '61

Richard Moll
Beanstalk '94
Dream Date '93
The Flintstones '94
Highlander: The Gathering '93
House '86
No Dessert Dad, 'Til You Mow
the Lawn '94
Sidekicks '93
Storybook '95
Think Big '90

Clifford Mollison
A Christmas Carol '51

Christopher Monger ▲
Waiting for the Light '90

Debra Monk
Bed of Roses '95

Lawrence Monoson
Mask '85

Marilyn Monroe
Love Happy '50
Monkey Business '52

Phil Monroe ▲
The Bugs Bunny/Road Runner
Movie '79

Edward Montagne ▲
They Went That-a-Way & That-
a-Way '78

Edward J. Montagne ▲
The Reluctant Astronaut '67

Lee Montague
Madame Sousatzka '88

Monte Montague
Radio Patrol '37

Carlos Montalban
Bananas '71

Ricardo Montalban
Cannonball Run 2 '84
Conquest of the Planet of the
Apes '72
Escape from the Planet of the
Apes '71
Joe Panther '76
The Naked Gun: From the
Files of Police Squad '88
Star Trek 2: The Wrath of
Khan '82

Karla Montana
Sweet 15 '90

Yves Montand
Jean de Florette '87
Manon of the Spring '87
On a Clear Day You Can See
Forever '70

Lisa Montell
The Nine Lives of Elfego
Baca '58

Maria Montez
Ali Baba and the Forty
Thieves '43

Belinda J. Montgomery
Stone Fox '87

Douglass Montgomery
Little Women '33

Julia Montgomery
Revenge of the Nerds '84

Lee Montgomery
Girls Just Want to Have
Fun '85

Robert Montgomery
Mr. & Mrs. Smith '41

Lynne Moody
Wait Till Your Mother Gets
Home '83

Ron Moody
David Copperfield '70
Dog Pound Shuffle '75
A Kid in King Arthur's
Court '95
Oliver! '68
Twelve Chairs '70
Unidentified Flying
Oddball '79

Keith Moon
Tommy '75

Archie Moore
The Adventures of Huckleberry
Finn '60

Ashleigh Aston Moore
Now and Then '95

Bobby Moore
Victory '81

Candy Moore
Tomboy & the Champ '58

Clayton Moore
The Adventures of Frank and
Jesse James '48
The Crimson Ghost '46
G-Men Never Forget '48
Jesse James Rides Again '47
Jungle Drums of Africa '53
The Lone Ranger '56
The Lone Ranger: Code of the
Pioneers '55
Nyoka and the Tigermen '42
Radar Men from the
Moon '52

Constance Moore
Buck Rogers Conquers the
Universe '39

Deborah Maria Moore
Chaplin '92

Demi Moore
The Butcher's Wife '91
Ghost '90
Now and Then '95

Sammy Morrison
Follow the Leader '44
'Neath Brooklyn Bridge '42
Spooks Run Wild '41

Tom Morrison
Rocky 5 '90

Bruce Morrow
Dirty Dancing '87

Jo Morrow
13 Ghosts '60
The Three Worlds of
Gulliver '59

Rob Morrow
Quiz Show '94

Vic Morrow
The Adventures of Tom
Sawyer '73
The Bad News Bears '76
The Treasure of
Matecumbe '76
Twilight Zone: The Movie '83

Barry Morse ▲
Ugly Little Boy '77

David Morse
The Good Son '93
12 Monkeys '95

Hollingsworth Morse ▲
Justin Morgan Had a
Horse '81

Natalie Morse
The Little Match Girl '87

Robert Morse
The Boatniks '70
Cannon Movie Tales: The
Emperor's New Clothes '89

Viggo Mortensen
Crimson Tide '95

Jane Mortifee
My American Cousin '85

Janne Mortil
Johnny's Girl '95

Joe Morton
The Brother from Another
Planet '84
Forever Young '92
The Inkwell '94
Of Mice and Men '92
Speed '94
Terminator 2: Judgment
Day '91
Zelly & Me '88

Rocky Morton ▲
Super Mario Bros. '93

Jonas Moscartolo
Ernest Scared Stupid '91

David Moscow
Big '88
Newsies '92

David Moses
Daring Dobermans '73

Gilbert Moses ▲
The Fish that Saved
Pittsburgh '79
Runaway '89

Rick Moses
Avalanche '78

Roger E. Mosley
The Greatest '77

Elissabeth Moss
Imaginary Crimes '94

Donny Most
Huckleberry Finn '75

Josh Mostel
Animal Behavior '89
The Basketball Diaries '94
Billy Madison '94
City Slickers '91
City Slickers 2: The Legend of
Curly's Gold '94
Jesus Christ, Superstar '73
Little Man Tate '91
The Money Pit '86
Radio Days '87

Zero Mostel
Muppet Treasures '85
Muppets Moments '85
Once Upon a Scoundrel '73

Collin Mothupi
Cheetah '89

John Moulder-Brown
Rumpelstiltskin '86

Alan Mowbray
It Happened in New
Orleans '36
The King and I '56
Topper Takes a Trip '39

Armin Mueller-Stahl
Avalon '90
Holy Matrimony '94
The Power of One '92
Theodore Rex '95

Nino Muhlach
The Boy God '86

Geraldine Muir
Hope and Glory '87

Russell Mulcahy ▲
Highlander '86
Highlander 2: The
Quickening '91
The Real McCoy '93
The Shadow '94

Kate Mulgrew
Camp Nowhere '94
Remo Williams: The Adventure
Begins '85
Throw Momma from the
Train '87

Jack Mulhall
Burn 'Em Up Barnes '34
The Clutching Hand '36
Mr. Wise Guy '42
Radio Patrol '37
Tim Tyler's Luck '37

Chris Mulkey
Heartbreak Hotel '88
K-9000 '89

Martin Mull
Clue '85
How the West Was Fun '95
Lots of Luck '85
Mr. Mom '83
My Bodyguard '80
Pecos Bill '86
Ski Patrol '89
Think Big '90

Jack Mullaney
George! '70

Richard Mulligan
Babes in Toyland '86
The Big Bus '76
A Fine Mess '86
The Heavenly Kid '85
The Hideaways '73
Little Big Man '70

Robert Mulligan ▲
Clara's Heart '88
Kiss Me Goodbye '82
The Man in the Moon '91
To Kill a Mockingbird '62
Up the Down Staircase '67

Dermot Mulroney
How to Make an American
Quilt '95
Samantha '92
The Thing Called Love '93
Young Guns '88

Billy Mumy
Bless the Beasts and
Children '71
Dear Brigitte '65
Sammy, the Way-Out Seal '62
Twilight Zone: The Movie '83

Trond Munch
Shipwrecked '90

Herbert Mundin
The Adventures of Robin
Hood '38

Paul Muni
I Am a Fugitive from a Chain
Gang '32

Pep Munne
Where Time Began '77

Caroline Munro
At the Earth's Core '76
Golden Voyage of Sinbad '73
The Spy Who Loved Me '77

Janet Munro
Darby O'Gill & the Little
People '59
Horsemasters '61
The Swiss Family
Robinson '60
Third Man on the
Mountain '59

Lochlyn Munro
Wagons East '94

Neil Munro
Beethoven Lives Upstairs '92

Truan Munro
Prince Brat and the Whipping
Boy '95

Jules Munshin
Easter Parade '48

Ona Munson
Gone with the Wind '39

Jim Henson's Muppets
The Great Muppet Caper '81
The Muppet Movie '79
Muppets Take Manhattan '84
Sesame Street Presents:
Follow That Bird '85

Jimmy T. Murakami ▲
Battle Beyond the Stars '80

George Murcell
Cutthroat Island '95

Walter Murch ▲
Return to Oz '85

Jack Murdock
Rain Man '88

Brittany Murphy
Clueless '95

Eddie Murphy
Beverly Hills Cop '84
Beverly Hills Cop 2 '87
Beverly Hills Cop 3 '94
The Golden Child '86
The Nutty Professor '96

George Murphy
Little Miss Broadway '38

Johnny Murphy
The Commitments '91
War of the Buttons '95

Kevin Murphy
Mystery Science Theater
3000: The Movie '96

Kim Murphy
Houseguest '94

Maurice Murphy
Tailspin Tommy '34

Michael Murphy
Batman Returns '92
Clean Slate '94
Cloak & Dagger '84

Rosemary Murphy
To Kill a Mockingbird '62
Walking Tall '73

Timothy Patrick Murphy
Doin' Time on Planet
   Earth '88
Sam's Son '84

Barbara Murray
Tony Draws a Horse '51

Bill Murray
Caddyshack '80
Ghostbusters '84
Ghostbusters 2 '89
Groundhog Day '93
Kingpin '96
Little Shop of Horrors '86
Meatballs '79
Scrooged '88
Tootsie '82
What About Bob? '91

Chic Murray
Gregory's Girl '80

Don Murray
Conquest of the Planet of the
   Apes '72
I am the Cheese '83
Justin Morgan Had a
   Horse '81
Peggy Sue Got Married '86
Quarterback Princess '85

Joel Murray
One Crazy Summer '86

John Murray
Moving Violations '85

Ken Murray
Follow Me, Boys! '66

Stephen Murray
Alice in Wonderland '50

Tom Murray
The Gold Rush '25

Christina Murrull
The Kid with the 200 I.Q. '83

Clarence Muse
The Black Stallion '79
A Dream for Christmas '73
That Gang of Mine '40

Pip Mushin
Strictly Ballroom '92

John Musker ▲
Aladdin '92
The Great Mouse
   Detective '86
The Little Mermaid '89

Ornella Muti
Flash Gordon '80
Once Upon a Crime '92
Oscar '91
Wait Until Spring, Bandini '90

Floyd Mutrux ▲
Aloha, Bobby and Rose '74

Linda Mvusi
A World Apart '88

Harry Myers
City Lights '31

Mike Myers
So I Married an Axe
   Murderer '93
Wayne's World '92
Wayne's World 2 '93

Alan Myerson ▲
Police Academy 5: Assignment
   Miami Beach '88

Jim Nabors
Cannonball Run 2 '84

Michael Nader
The Flash '90

Eiros Nadies
The Gods Must Be Crazy
   2 '89

Anne Nagel
Don Winslow of the Navy '43
The Green Hornet '39
Winners of the West '40

Austin Nagler
Ernest Scared Stupid '91

Ivan Nagy ▲
Captain America 2: Death Too
   Soon '79

Ajay Naidu
Where the River Runs
   Black '86

Jimmy Nail
Crusoe '89

J. Carrol Naish
Captain Blood '35

Laurence Naismith
Amazing Mr. Blunden '72
The Bushbaby '70
Diamonds are Forever '71
Greyfriars Bobby '61
Jason and the Argonauts '63
The Prince and the
   Pauper '62
Third Man on the
   Mountain '59
The Valley of Gwangi '69

Kathy Najimy
Hocus Pocus '93
In Search of Dr. Seuss '94
Sister Act '92
Sister Act 2: Back in the
   Habit '93

Takeya Nakamura ▲
The Little Drummer Boy '68

Reggie Nalder
Salem's Lot '79

Jack Nance
Ghoulies '85

Agnes Nano
Cinema Paradiso '88

Alan Napier
Challenge to Lassie '49

Charles Napier
The Cable Guy '96
Citizens Band '77
Ernest Goes to Jail '90
In Search of a Golden Sky '84
The Incredible Hulk
   Returns '88
Jury Duty '95
Max is Missing '95

Eve Napier
Crazy Moon '87

Tom Nardini
Africa Texas Style '67

Kathrine Narducci
A Bronx Tale '93

Silvio Narizzano ▲
Why Shoot the Teacher? '79

Willie Nark-Orn
Magic in the Water '95

Mary Nash
The Philadelphia Story '40

Noreen Nash
The Red Stallion '47
The Tender Years '47

Anthony Natale
Mr. Holland's Opus '95

Stephen Nathan
1776 '72

Masako Natsume
Antarctica '84

Mildred Natwick
The Court Jester '56
A House Without a Christmas
   Tree '72
Kiss Me Goodbye '82
The Quiet Man '52
Tammy and the Bachelor '57

Melinda Naud
A Day for Thanks on Walton's
   Mountain '82

David Naughton
Beanstalk '94
Midnight Madness '80

James Naughton
Cat's Eye '85
The Paper Chase '73

Erastheo J. Navda ▲
The Boy God '86

Arnost Navratil
The Fabulous World of Jules
   Verne '58

Alla Nazimova
Since You Went Away '44

Ella Neal
Mysterious Doctor Satan '40

Patricia Neal
Heidi '93
Homecoming: A Christmas
   Story '71
Love Leads the Way '84

Tom Neal
Andy Hardy Meets
   Debutante '40

Kevin Nealon
All I Want for Christmas '91
Happy Gilmore '96
Roxanne '87

Christopher Neame
Boris and Natasha: The
   Movie '92
Suburban Commando '91

Ronald Neame ▲
The Poseidon Adventure '72
The Prime of Miss Jean
   Brodie '69
Scrooge '70

Hal Needham ▲
Cannonball Run '81
Cannonball Run 2 '84
Rad '86
Smokey and the Bandit '77
Smokey and the Bandit, Part
   2 '80
The Villain '79

Ted Neeley
Jesus Christ, Superstar '73

Hillel Neeman
Boy Takes Girl '83

Liam Neeson
Before and After '95
The Bounty '84
Darkman '90
Krull '83
Leap of Faith '92
Nell '94
Rob Roy '95
Satisfaction '88

Thomas L. Neff ▲
Running Mates '86

Mirielle Negre
Circus Angel '65

Francois Negret
Au Revoir Les Enfants '87

Pola Negri
Moon-Spinners '64

Taylor Negron
Bad Medicine '85
Better Off Dead '85

David Neidorf
Hoosiers '86

Noel Neill
The Adventures of Frank and
 Jesse James '48
Atom Man vs. Superman '50
Superman: The Serial, Vol.
 1 '48

Sam Neill
The Hunt for Red October '90
Jurassic Park '93
Memoirs of an Invisible
 Man '92
Rudyard Kipling's The Jungle
 Book '94

James Neilson ▲
The Adventures of Bullwhip
 Griffin '66
Dr. Syn, Alias the
 Scarecrow '64
Gentle Giant '67
Johnny Shiloh '63
Moon Pilot '62
Moon-Spinners '64
Mooncussers '62
Summer Magic '63
Where Angels Go, Trouble
 Follows '68

Kate Nelligan
The Count of Monte Cristo '74
Fatal Instinct '93
How to Make an American
 Quilt '95
Up Close and Personal '96

Ann Nelson
My Girl '91

Barry Nelson
Airport '70
The Human Comedy '43

Bob Nelson
Brain Donors '92

Craig Richard Nelson
The Grass is Always Greener
 Over the Septic Tank '78
My Bodyguard '80
The Paper Chase '73

Craig T. Nelson
All the Right Moves '83
Man, Woman & Child '83
Poltergeist '82
Poltergeist 2: The Other
 Side '86
Red Riding Hood '89
Troop Beverly Hills '89
Turner and Hooch '89

David Nelson
Cry-Baby '90

David Nelson ▲
A Rare Breed '81

Ed Nelson
Brenda Starr '86
For the Love of Benji '77

Gary Nelson ▲
Allan Quartermain and the
 Lost City of Gold '86
The Black Hole '79
Freaky Friday '76
Jimmy the Kid '82

Gene Nelson
Oklahoma! '55

Harriet Hilliard Nelson
Follow the Fleet '36
The Kid with the 200 I.Q. '83

Herbert Nelson
When the North Wind
 Blows '74

Jessie Nelson ▲
Corrina, Corrina '94

Judd Nelson
Airheads '94
The Breakfast Club '85
Fandango '85
Making the Grade '84

Lori Nelson
The Pied Piper of Hamelin '57

Michael J. Nelson
Mystery Science Theater
 3000: The Movie '96

Patriece Nelson
Crooklyn '94

Portia Nelson
The Sound of Music '65

Ralph Nelson ▲
A Hero Ain't Nothin' But a
 Sandwich '78
Lilies of the Field '63

Sandra Nelson
The Halfback of Notre
 Dame '96

Tracy Nelson
Yours, Mine & Ours '68

Willie Nelson
Barbarosa '82
The Electric Horseman '79

Corin "Corky" Nemec
Operation Dumbo Drop '95
Tucker: The Man and His
 Dream '88

Franco Nero
Camelot '67
Challenge to White Fang '86
Die Hard 2: Die Harder '90

Michael Nesmith
Head '68
Monkees, Volume 1 '66

Kurt Neumann ▲
Let's Sing Again '36

Bebe Neuwirth
The Adventures of
 Pinocchio '96
Green Card '90
Jumanji '95
Say Anything '89

John Neville
The Adventures of Baron
 Munchausen '89
Baby's Day Out '94
Little Women '94
Song Spinner '95

Robyn Nevin
Careful, He Might Hear
 You '84
The Fourth Wish '75

George Newbern
Adventures in Babysitting '87
Father of the Bride '91
Father of the Bride Part II '95

Mike Newell ▲
Amazing Grace & Chuck '87
Four Weddings and a
 Funeral '93
Into the West '92
The Man in the Iron Mask '77

Bob Newhart
Little Miss Marker '80
On a Clear Day You Can See
 Forever '70
Thursday's Game '74

James Newill
Renfrew of the Royal
 Mounted '37
Yukon Flight '40

Anthony Newley
Alice in Wonderland '85
Boris and Natasha: The
 Movie '92
Doctor Doolittle '67
The Garbage Pail Kids
 Movie '87
The Old Curiosity Shop '75
Oliver Twist '48

Barry Newman
Amy '81

Laraine Newman
Coneheads '93
Invaders from Mars '86
Problem Child 2 '91

Paul Newman
Butch Cassidy and the
 Sundance Kid '69
Harry & Son '84
The Left-Handed Gun '58
Mr. & Mrs. Bridge '91
Silent Movie '76
The Sting '73
Torn Curtain '66

Paul Newman ▲
The Effect of Gamma Rays on
 Man-in-the-Moon
 Marigolds '73

Harry & Son '84

Randy Newman
Three Amigos '86

Richard Newman
Call of the Wild '93

Scott Newman
The Great Waldo Pepper '75

Susan Kendall Newman
I Wanna Hold Your Hand '78

Julie Newmar
Seven Brides for Seven
 Brothers '54

Fred Newmeyer ▲
General Spanky '36

John Haymes Newton
Alive '93

Robert Newton
Androcles and the Lion '52
Around the World in 80
 Days '56
Jamaica Inn '39
Oliver Twist '48
Tom Brown's School Days '51
Treasure Island '50

Thandie Newton
Flirting '89
Jefferson in Paris '94
The Journey of August
 King '95

Olivia Newton-John
Grease '78
Xanadu '80

Mbongeni Ngema
Sarafina! '92

Haing S. Ngor
My Life '93

Dustin Nguyen
3 Ninjas Kick Back '94

Phil Nibbelink ▲
An American Tail: Fievel Goes
 West '91
We're Back! A Dinosaur's
 Story '93

Maurizio Nichetti
Allegro Non Troppo '76

Denise Nicholas
And the Children Shall
 Lead '85
Blacula '72
Ghost Dad '90
Piece of the Action '77

Denise Nicholas-Hill
Marvin & Tige '84

Thomas Ian Nicholas
A Kid in King Arthur's
 Court '95
Rookie of the Year '93

George Nicholls Jr. ▲
Anne of Green Gables '34

Charles A. Nichols ▲
Charlotte's Web '73

Kyra Nichols
George Balanchine's The
Nutcracker '93

Mike Nichols ▲
The Birdcage '95
The Day of the Dolphin '73
Regarding Henry '91

Nichelle Nichols
Star Trek 2: The Wrath of
Khan '82
Star Trek 3: The Search for
Spock '84
Star Trek 4: The Voyage
Home '86
Star Trek 5: The Final
Frontier '89
Star Trek 6: The Undiscovered
Country '91
Star Trek: The Motion
Picture '80

Taylor Nichols
Metropolitan '90

Jack Nicholson
Batman '89
Goin' South '78
On a Clear Day You Can See
Forever '70
Terms of Endearment '83
Tommy '75

Jack Nicholson ▲
Goin' South '78

Denise Nickerson
Smile '75
Willy Wonka & the Chocolate
Factory '71
Zero to Sixty '78

Julia Nickson-Soul
Sidekicks '93

Ted Nicolaou ▲
Dragonworld '94
Leapin' Leprechauns '95
Remote '93

Michael Nicolosi
Dream a Little Dream 2 '94

Brigitte Nielsen
Beverly Hills Cop 2 '87
The Double O Kid '92
Rocky 4 '85

Leslie Nielsen
Airplane! '80
All I Want for Christmas '91
Digger '94
Dracula: Dead and Loving
It '95
Forbidden Planet '56
The Naked Gun: From the
Files of Police Squad '88

Naked Gun 33 1/3: The Final
Insult '94
Naked Gun 2 1/2: The Smell
of Fear '91
The Reluctant Astronaut '67
Rent-A-Kid '95
Soul Man '86
Spaceship '81
Spy Hard '96
Surf Ninjas '93
Tammy and the Bachelor '57

William Nigh ▲
Mr. Wise Guy '42

Inger Nilsson
Pippi Goes on Board '71
Pippi in the South Seas '68
Pippi Longstocking '68

Derek Nimmo
One of Our Dinosaurs Is
Missing '75

Leonard Nimoy
Aladdin and His Wonderful
Lamp '84
Invasion of the Body
Snatchers '78
Star Trek 2: The Wrath of
Khan '82
Star Trek 3: The Search for
Spock '84
Star Trek 4: The Voyage
Home '86
Star Trek 5: The Final
Frontier '89
Star Trek 6: The Undiscovered
Country '91
Star Trek: The Motion
Picture '80
Zombies of the
Stratosphere '52

Leonard Nimoy ▲
Holy Matrimony '94
Star Trek 3: The Search for
Spock '84
Star Trek 4: The Voyage
Home '86
Three Men and a Baby '87

Yvette Nipar
Ski Patrol '89

David Niven
Around the World in 80
Days '56
Candleshoe '78
Curse of the Pink Panther '83
Death on the Nile '78
No Deposit, No Return '76
The Pink Panther '64
Please Don't Eat the
Daisies '60
Trail of the Pink Panther '82

Cynthia Nixon
Amadeus '84
The Manhattan Project '86

John P. Nixon
Legend of Boggy Creek '75

Marni Nixon
The Sound of Music '65

Mojo Nixon
Rock 'n' Roll High School
Forever '91
Super Mario Bros. '93

Waweru Njenga
Morgan Stewart's Coming
Home '87

Felix Nobis
Flirting '89

James Noble
Chances Are '89

Trisha Noble
The Private Eyes '80

Paul Nocholls
The Return of Tommy
Tricker '94

Philippe Noiret
Cinema Paradiso '88
The Return of the
Musketeers '89

Jeanette Nolan
Cloak & Dagger '84
The Reluctant Astronaut '67

Kathleen Nolan
Amy '81

Lloyd Nolan
Airport '70
Ice Station Zebra '68
It Came Upon a Midnight
Clear '84
A Tree Grows in Brooklyn '45

Nick Nolte
Blue Chips '94
I Love Trouble '94
I'll Do Anything '93
Jefferson in Paris '94
Lorenzo's Oil '92
Three Fugitives '89

Chris Noonan ▲
Babe '95

John Ford Noonan
Adventures in Babysitting '87

Tommy Noonan
Adam's Rib '50
Last Action Hero '93
The Man with One Red
Shoe '85
The Monster Squad '87
Robocop 2 '90

Tommy Norden
Flipper '64
Flipper's Odyssey '66

Jeffrey Nordling
Holy Matrimony '94

Lee Norman
Buck Privates '41

Zack Norman
Romancing the Stone '84

Aaron Norris ▲
Sidekicks '93
Top Dog '95

Christopher Norris
Eat My Dust '76

Chuck Norris
Happy Birthday, Bugs: 50
Looney Years '90
Sidekicks '93
Top Dog '95

Kimberly Norris
Geronimo '93

Alan North
Billy Galvin '86
Highlander '86
The Jerky Boys '95
Lean on Me '89

Heather North
The Barefoot Executive '71

Jay North
Zebra in the Kitchen '65

Sheree North
The Shootist '76

Jeremy Northam
Emma '96
The Net '95

Alex Norton
Comfort and Joy '84
Gregory's Girl '80
Squanto: A Warrior's Tale '94

Bill W.L. Norton ▲
Baby. . .Secret of the Lost
Legend '85
More American Graffiti '79

Dee Dee Norton
Dakota '88

Jim Norton
Memoirs of an Invisible
Man '92

Randy Norton
Fire and Ice '83

Judy Norton-Taylor
A Day for Thanks on Walton's
Mountain '82
The Waltons: A Thanksgiving
Story '73
The Waltons: The Children's
Carol '80

Willie Norwood, Jr.
Once Upon a Time . . . When
We Were Colored '95

Jack Noseworthy
Alive '93
The Brady Bunch Movie '95

Max Nosseck ▲
Black Beauty '46

Christopher Noth
Baby Boom '87

Michael Nouri
Flashdance '83

Don Novello
Tucker: The Man and His
   Dream '88

Jay Novello
Miracle of Our Lady of
   Fatima '52

Phillip Noyce ▲
Clear and Present Danger '94

Danny Nucci
Book of Love '91
Crimson Tide '95

Elliott Nugent ▲
My Favorite Brunette '47

Bill Nunn
Canadian Bacon '94
Regarding Henry '91
Sister Act '92

Trevor Nunn ▲
Lady Jane '85

France Nuyen
The Joy Luck Club '93
South Pacific '58

N!xau
The Gods Must Be Crazy '84
The Gods Must Be Crazy
   2 '89

Carrie Nye
Hello Again '87

Carroll Nye
Gone with the Wind '39

Louis Nye
The Charge of the Model
   T's '76
Harper Valley P.T.A. '78

Jack Oakie
Little Men '40

Simon Oakland
On a Clear Day You Can See
   Forever '70
West Side Story '61

Wheeler Oakman
The Lost Jungle '34

Warren Oates
And Baby Makes Six '79
My Old Man '79
Tom Sawyer '73

Philip Ober
North by Northwest '59

Hugh O'Brian
Africa Texas Style '67

Doin' Time on Planet
   Earth '88
The Shootist '76
Twins '88

Austin O'Brien
The Baby-Sitters Club '95
Last Action Hero '93
My Girl 2 '94
Prehysteria '93

Clay O'Brien
One Little Indian '73

Dave O'Brien
Spooks Run Wild '41
That Gang of Mine '40
Yukon Flight '40

Edmond O'Brien
Moon Pilot '62

Joan O'Brien
It Happened at the World's
   Fair '63

Margaret O'Brien
Amy '81
The Canterville Ghost '44
Jane Eyre '44
Journey for Margaret '42
Little Women '49
Meet Me in St. Louis '44
The Secret Garden '49

Pat O'Brien
Airborne '93
The Boy with the Green
   Hair '48
Knute Rockne: All
   American '40
Tim Tyler's Luck '37

Trever O'Brien
Homecoming '96

Virginia O'Brien
The Big Store '41
Till the Clouds Roll By '46

Colm O'Byrne
The Snapper '93

Sean O'Byrne
Timecop '94

Ric Ocasek
Hairspray '88

P.J. Ochlan
Little Man Tate '91

Arthur O'Connell
Citizen Kane '41
Gidget '59
Huckleberry Finn '74
Monkey's Uncle '65
The Reluctant Astronaut '67
Seven Faces of Dr. Lao '63

Deidre O'Connell
Pastime '91
Straight Talk '92

Jerry O'Connell
Calendar Girl '93
Hole in the Sky '95
Ollie Hopnoodle's Haven of
   Bliss '88
Stand By Me '86

Pat O'Connell
The Endless Summer 2 '94

Nancy O'Conner
Whale of a Tale '76

James O'Connolly ▲
The Valley of Gwangi '69

Brian O'Connor
Song City U.S.A. '89

Derrick O'Connor
Hope and Glory '87
How to Make an American
   Quilt '95

Donald O'Connor
Francis Goes to the Races '51
Francis Joins the WACs '54
Francis the Talking Mule '49
Singin' in the Rain '52
Wonders of Aladdin '61

Glynnis O'Connor
Conspiracy of Love '87
Johnny Dangerously '84
Night Crossing '81
Ode to Billy Joe '76
Past the Bleachers '95

Kevin J. O'Connor
Canadian Bacon '94
Hero '92
Peggy Sue Got Married '86
Steel Magnolias '89

Pat O'Connor ▲
Circle of Friends '94

Renee O'Connor
Follow the River '95

Tim O'Connor
Naked Gun 2 1/2: The Smell
   of Fear '91

Una O'Connor
The Adventures of Robin
   Hood '38
The Canterville Ghost '44
David Copperfield '35

Denis O'Dea
Treasure Island '50
Under Capricorn '49

Sias Odendal ▲
Nukie '93

Chris O'Donnell
Batman Forever '95
Circle of Friends '94
Men Don't Leave '89
School Ties '92
The Three Musketeers '93

Rosie O'Donnell
Another Stakeout '93
Beautiful Girls '96
Car 54, Where Are You? '94
The Flintstones '94
Harriet the Spy '96
A League of Their Own '92
Now and Then '95
Sleepless in Seattle '93

Steve Oedekerk ▲
Ace Ventura: When Nature
   Calls '95

Sammy Ogg
Miracle of Our Lady of
   Fatima '52

George Ogilvie ▲
Mad Max: Beyond
   Thunderdome '85

Ian Ogilvy
Death Becomes Her '92
Wuthering Heights '70

Keiko Oginome
Antarctica '84

Gail O'Grady
Celtic Pride '96

Soon-Teck Oh
A Home of Our Own '93
Legend of the White
   Horse '85
The Man with the Golden
   Gun '74

Brian O'Halloran
Clerks '94
Mallrats '95

Jack O'Halloran
King Kong '76
Superman 1: The Movie '78
Superman 2 '80

Natsuko Ohama
Speed '94

Catherine O'Hara
Beetlejuice '88
Dick Tracy '90
Home Alone '90
Home Alone 2: Lost in New
   York '92
The Paper '94
A Simple Twist of Fate '94
Tall Tale: The Unbelievable
   Adventures of Pecos
   Bill '95

David O'Hara
Braveheart '95

Maureen O'Hara
Big Jake '71
How Green was My Valley '41
Jamaica Inn '39
Miracle on 34th Street '47
Only the Lonely '91
The Parent Trap '61
The Quiet Man '52

The Red Pony '76
Sinbad the Sailor '47
Spencer's Mountain '63

**Cornelia Hayes
O'Herlihy**
The Old Curiosity Shop '94

Dan O'Herlihy
The Last Starfighter '84
MacArthur '77
Robocop '87
Robocop 2 '90
A Waltz Through the Hills '88

Gavan O'Herlihy
Willow '88

Michael O'Herlihy ▲
The Fighting Prince of
Donegal '66
Mosby's Marauders '66
The One and Only, Genuine,
Original Family Band '68
Peter Lundy and the Medicine
Hat Stallion '77
Smith! '69

Sean O'Kane
Magic Island '95

Dennis O'Keefe
Topper Returns '41

Michael O'Keefe
Caddyshack '80
The Great Santini '80
Nate and Hayes '83

Paul O'Keefe
Daydreamer '66

Miles O'Keeffe
Sword of the Valiant '83

Sophie Okonedo
Ace Ventura: When Nature
Calls '95

Yuji Okumoto
Aloha Summer '88
The Karate Kid: Part 2 '86

William Oldham
Matewan '87

Gary Oldman
The Scarlet Letter '95

Gabriel Olds
Calendar Girl '93

Sven Ole-Thorsen
Dragon: The Bruce Lee
Story '93

Larisa Oleynik
The Baby-Sitters Club '95

Ken Olin ▲
White Fang 2: The Myth of the
White Wolf '94

Ingrid Oliu
Stand and Deliver '88

Barret Oliver
Cocoon '85
Cocoon: The Return '88
D.A.R.Y.L. '85
Frankenweenie '84
The NeverEnding Story '84
The Secret Garden '87

David Oliver
Defense Play '88

Edna May Oliver
David Copperfield '35
Little Miss Broadway '38
Little Women '33

Michael Oliver
Problem Child '90
Problem Child 2 '91

Ruby L. Oliver ▲
Love Your Mama '89

Susan Oliver
The Disorderly Orderly '64
Hardly Working '81

Hector Olivera ▲
Wizards of the Lost
Kingdom '85

Robert Oliveri
Edward Scissorhands '90
Honey, I Blew Up the Kid '92
Honey, I Shrunk the Kids '89

Laurence Olivier
Battle of Britain '69
The Bounty '84
A Bridge Too Far '77
Clash of the Titans '81
David Copperfield '70
Jesus of Nazareth '77
A Little Romance '79
Rebecca '40
Sleuth '72

Walter Olkewicz
The Client '94

Edward James Olmos
Aloha, Bobby and Rose '74
Stand and Deliver '88
Talent for the Game '91

Dan Olmstead
Philadelphia '93

Ashley Olsen
How the West Was Fun '95
It Takes Two '95

Dana Olsen
Making the Grade '84

Larry Olsen
Curley '47

Mary-Kate Olsen
How the West Was Fun '95
It Takes Two '95

Moroni Olsen
Ali Baba and the Forty
Thieves '43

Father of the Bride '50
Father's Little Dividend '51
Notorious '46
Susannah of the Mounties '39

James Olson
The Andromeda Strain '71

Nancy Olson
The Absent-Minded
Professor '61
Pollyanna '60
Snowball Express '72
Son of Flubber '63

David O'Malley ▲
Kid Colter '85
Mountain Man '77

J. Pat O'Malley
Courage of Black Beauty '57
Lassie, Come Home '43

Pat O'Malley
Fighting Marines '36

**Zach O'Malley-
Greenberg**
Lorenzo's Oil '92

Judd Omen
Pee Wee's Big Adventure '85

Griffin O'Neal
Escape Artist '82
Hadley's Rebellion '84

Patrick O'Neal
The Way We Were '73

Ron O'Neal
Up Against the Wall '91

Ron O'Neal ▲
Up Against the Wall '91

Ryan O'Neal
A Bridge Too Far '77
Chances Are '89
Irreconcilable Differences '84
The Main Event '79
Paper Moon '73
What's Up, Doc? '72

Shaquille O'Neal
Blue Chips '94
Kazaam '96

Tatum O'Neal
The Bad News Bears '76
Goldilocks & the Three
Bears '83
International Velvet '78
Little Darlings '80
Paper Moon '73

Ty O'Neal
D2: The Mighty Ducks '94

Barbara O'Neil
Gone with the Wind '39
I Remember Mama '48

Robert Vincent O'Neil ▲
Paco '75

Amy O'Neill
Honey, I Shrunk the Kids '89

Chris O'Neill
Backbeat '94

Dick O'Neill
My Summer Story '94

Ed O'Neill
Blue Chips '94
Dutch '91
K-9 '89
Little Giants '94
Wayne's World '92
Wayne's World 2 '93

Henry O'Neill
Men of Boys Town '41

Peter Onorati
Camp Nowhere '94

Michael Ontkean
Clara's Heart '88
Just the Way You Are '84
Maid to Order '87

David Opatoshu
Torn Curtain '66

Terry O'Quinn
The Cutting Edge '92
Places in the Heart '84
The Rocketeer '91
SpaceCamp '86
Tombstone '93
Young Guns '88

Alessio Orano
The Count of Monte Cristo '74

Geraldine O'Rawe
Circle of Friends '94

Jerry Orbach
Brewster's Millions '85
Delirious '91
Dirty Dancing '87
F/X '86
Straight Talk '92

Julia Ormond
First Knight '95
Legends of the Fall '94
Sabrina '95

Heather O'Rourke
Poltergeist '82
Poltergeist 2: The Other
Side '86
Poltergeist 3 '88

Heidi O'Rourke
Funny Lady '75

James Orr ▲
Man of the House '95
Mr. Destiny '90

Kenny Ortega ▲
Hocus Pocus '93
Newsies '92

Frank Orth
The Great Rupert '50

Brian Ortiz
Sgt. Bilko '95

John Osborne
The Power of One '92

Vivienne Osborne
Let's Sing Again '36

Ozzy Osbourne
The Jerky Boys '95

Milo O'Shea
The Dream Team '89
Once a Hero '88
Only the Lonely '91
Opportunity Knocks '90
Peter Lundy and the Medicine
   Hat Stallion '77
The Playboys '92
The Purple Rose of Cairo '85
Romeo and Juliet '68

Tessie O'Shea
The Russians are Coming, the
   Russians are Coming '66

Mamoru Oshii ▲
Battle for Moon Station
   Dallos '86

K.T. Oslin
The Thing Called Love '93

Cliff Osmond
In Search of a Golden Sky '84
Joe Panther '76
Mountain Man '77

Donny Osmond
Goin' Coconuts '78

Marie Osmond
Goin' Coconuts '78

Jeffery Osterhage
The Shadow Riders '82

Peter Ostrum
Willy Wonka & the Chocolate
   Factory '71

Maureen O'Sullivan
A Connecticut Yankee '31
David Copperfield '35
A Day at the Races '37
Peggy Sue Got Married '86
The River Pirates '94
Tarzan and His Mate '34
Tarzan Escapes '36
Tarzan Finds a Son '39
Tarzan, the Ape Man '32
Tarzan's New York
   Adventure '42
Tarzan's Secret Treasure '41
The Thin Man '34

Annette O'Toole
Bridge to Terabithia '85
A Girl of the Limberlost '90
Imaginary Crimes '94
One on One '77

Smile '75
Superman 3 '83

Peter O'Toole
Club Paradise '86
Kidnapped '60
Kim '84
King Ralph '91
Lawrence of Arabia '62
The Lion in Winter '68
Man of La Mancha '72
My Favorite Year '82
Supergirl '84

John Ottavino
Malcolm X '92

Rafaela Ottiano
Curly Top '35

Rachelle Ottley
The Cutting Edge '92

Barry Otto
Strictly Ballroom '92

Andre Oumansky
Othello '95

Peter Outerbridge
Cool Runnings '93

Indra Ove
Othello '95

Park Overall
House of Cards '92
Kindergarten Cop '90
Undercover Blues '93

Lynne Overman
Little Miss Marker '34

Frank Overton
To Kill a Mockingbird '62

Rick Overton
Beverly Hills Cop '84
Odd Jobs '85

Chris Owen
Angus '95

Reginald Owen
The Canterville Ghost '44
Challenge to Lassie '49
A Christmas Carol '38
National Velvet '44
Tarzan's Secret Treasure '41
The Three Musketeers '48

Ayse Owens
The Long Day Closes '92

Catherine Oxenberg
K-9000 '89

Frank Oz
The Empire Strikes Back '80
Spies Like Us '85

Frank Oz ▲
Dirty Rotten Scoundrels '88
Housesitter '92
The Indian in the
   Cupboard '95

Little Shop of Horrors '86
Muppets Take Manhattan '84
What About Bob? '91

Judy Pace
Brian's Song '71

Frederico Pacifici
Fluke '95

Al Pacino
Author! Author! '82
Dick Tracy '90
Two Bits '96

Joanna Pacula
Timemaster '95
Tombstone '93

Sarah Padden
Regl'ar Fellers '41

Anthony Page ▲
Bill '81
Bill: On His Own '83

Gale Page
Knute Rockne: All
   American '40

Geraldine Page
The Adventures of Huckleberry
   Finn '85
The Happiest Millionaire '67
Hazel's People '75
The Trip to Bountiful '85

Grant Page
Deathcheaters '76

Ken Page
The Kid Who Loved
   Christmas '90

Leonie Page
Strictly Ballroom '92

Rebecca Page
Danny '79

Debra Paget
Prince Valiant '54
The Ten Commandments '56

Suzze Pai
Big Trouble in Little China '86

Janis Paige
Hero '92
Please Don't Eat the
   Daisies '60

Robert Paige
The Red Stallion '47

Didier Pain
My Father's Glory '91
My Mother's Castle '91

Brian Painchaud
Who Has Seen the Wind? '77

Nestor Paiva
The Nine Lives of Elfego
   Baca '58

Alan J. Pakula ▲
All the President's Men '76
The Pelican Brief '93
See You in the Morning '89

George Pal ▲
Seven Faces of Dr. Lao '63
tom thumb '58
The Wonderful World of the
   Brothers Grimm '62

Laszlo Pal ▲
Journey to Spirit Island '92

Holly Palance
The Best of Times '86

Jack Palance
Bagdad Cafe '88
Batman '89
City Slickers '91
City Slickers 2: The Legend of
   Curly's Gold '94
Cops and Robbersons '94
Great Adventure '75
Oklahoma Crude '73
Shane '53
Young Guns '88

Euzhan Palcy ▲
Sugar Cane Alley '83

Michael Palin
And Now for Something
   Completely Different '72
Jabberwocky '77
Monty Python and the Holy
   Grail '75
Time Bandits '81

Eugene Pallette
The Adventures of Robin
   Hood '38
The Ghost Goes West '36
Mr. Smith Goes to
   Washington '39
Stowaway '36
Topper '37

Lilli Palmer
Miracle of the White
   Stallions '63

Chazz Palminteri
A Bronx Tale '93
The Usual Suspects '95

Alan Palo
Prehysteria! 2 '94

Carlos Palomino
Geronimo: An American
   Legend '93

Gwyneth Paltrow
Emma '96
Hook '91
Jefferson in Paris '94
The Pallbearer '95

Herve Palud ▲
Little Indian, Big City '95

Johnny Tremain & the Sons of
  Liberty '58
So Dear to My Heart '49

Neva Patterson
David and Lisa '62
The Runaways '75

Ray Patterson ▲
Yogi's First Christmas '80

Sarah Patterson
Snow White '89

Scott Patterson
Little Big League '94

Will Patton
The Client '94

Adrian Paul
Highlander: The Gathering '93

Alexandra Paul
American Flyers '85
Just the Way You Are '84

Byron Paul ▲
Lt. Robin Crusoe, U.S.N. '66

David Paul
Think Big '90
Twinsitters '95

Don Michael Paul
Aloha Summer '88

Eugenia Paul
Zorro, Vol. 1 '58

Peter Paul
Think Big '90
Twinsitters '95

Richard Paul
Beanstalk '94

Scott Paulin
Captain America '89
The Right Stuff '83
Teen Wolf '85
Turner and Hooch '89

Pat Paulsen
Harper Valley P.T.A. '78

Lennox Pawle
David Copperfield '35

Bill Paxton
Apollo 13 '95
Indian Summer '93
The Terminator '84
Tombstone '93
True Lies '94
Twister '96
Weird Science '85

Collin Wilcox Paxton
Fluke '95

Gilles Payant
Big Red '62

David Paymer
The American President '95

City Slickers '91
City Slickers 2: The Legend of
  Curly's Gold '94
Heart and Souls '93
Quiz Show '94
Searching for Bobby
  Fischer '93

Carl Anthony Payne II
Ed '96

John Payne
Miracle on 34th Street '47

Amanda Pays
The Flash '90
Oxford Blues '84

E.J. Peaker
Hello, Dolly! '69

Alice Pearce
The Belle of New York '52
Dear Brigitte '65

Helen Pearce
When the Whales Came '89

Jacqueline Pearce
Princess Caraboo '94

Richard Pearce ▲
Country '84
A Family Thing '96
Heartland '81
Leap of Faith '92

Sierra Pecheur
Bronco Billy '80

Bob Peck
Jurassic Park '93

Brian Peck ▲
The Willies '90

Cecilia Peck
My Best Friend Is a
  Vampire '88

Gregory Peck
Amazing Grace & Chuck '87
How the West was Won '63
MacArthur '77
The Paradine Case '47
Roman Holiday '53
Spellbound '45
To Kill a Mockingbird '62
The Yearling '46

Tony Peck
Brenda Starr '86
Die Hard: With a
  Vengeance '95

Sam Peckinpah ▲
Junior Bonner '72

Larry Peerce ▲
The Other Side of the
  Mountain '75
The Other Side of the
  Mountain, Part 2 '78
A Separate Peace '73

Antonio Pelaez ▲
Crystalstone '88

Pele
Hot Shot '86
Victory '81

Lisa Pelikan
Ghoulies '85
Swing Shift '84

Valentine Pelka
First Knight '95

Clara Peller
Moving Violations '85

Meeno Peluce
Voyager from the
  Unknown '83

Elizabeth Pena
*batteries not included '87
Free Willy 2: The Adventure
  Home '95
La Bamba '87

Michael Pena
Running Free '94

Austin Pendleton
The Front Page '74
Guarding Tess '94
Hello Again '87
Mr. & Mrs. Bridge '91
Mr. Nanny '93
My Boyfriend's Back '93
Short Circuit '86
Simon '80
What's Up, Doc? '72

Nat Pendleton
At the Circus '39
Buck Privates Come Home '47
Horse Feathers '32
The Thin Man '34

Susan Penhaligon
Land That Time Forgot '75

Arthur Penn ▲
The Left-Handed Gun '58
Little Big Man '70
The Miracle Worker '62

Christopher Penn
All the Right Moves '83
Beethoven's 2nd '93
Footloose '84
Imaginary Crimes '94
Josh and S.A.M. '93
Rumble Fish '83
To Wong Foo, Thanks for
  Everything, Julie
  Newmar '95

Sean Penn
Fast Times at Ridgemont
  High '82
Racing with the Moon '84
Taps '81

Jon Maynard Pennell
The Program '93

Jonathan Penner
Down Periscope '96

Sydney Penny
Hyper-Sapien: People from
  Another Star '86

George Peppard
Battle Beyond the Stars '80
How the West was Won '63

Conchita Perez
Cria '76

Rosie Perez
It Could Happen to You '94
Untamed Heart '93

Vincent Perez
Cyrano de Bergerac '90

Joey Perillo
Philadelphia '93

Zoran Perisic ▲
The Phoenix and the Magic
  Carpet '95

Anthony Perkins
The Black Hole '79
Friendly Persuasion '56

Elizabeth Perkins
Avalon '90
Big '88
The Flintstones '94
Indian Summer '93
Miracle on 34th Street '94

Millie Perkins
Pistol: The Birth of a
  Legend '90
Table for Five '83

Max Perlich
Beautiful Girls '96
Born Yesterday '93
The Butcher's Wife '91
Ferris Bueller's Day Off '86
Homeward Bound 2: Lost in
  San Francisco '96
Maverick '94

Rhea Perlman
Canadian Bacon '94
Class Act '91
Matilda '96

Ron Perlman
The Adventures of Huck
  Finn '93
Fluke '95
Ice Pirates '84
Police Academy: Mission to
  Moscow '94

Mireille Perrier
Toto le Heros '91

Jacques Perrin
Cinema Paradiso '88

Valerie Perrine
The Electric Horseman '79
The Last American Hero '73

Raymond Pickard
The Canterville Ghost '96

Slim Pickens
The Apple Dumpling Gang '75
Charlie and the Great Balloon
  Chase '82
The Cowboys '72
Hawmps! '76
The Howling '81
Never a Dull Moment '68
Pony Express Rider '76
The Story of a Cowboy
  Angel '81
The Swarm '78

Josh Picker
Alex '92
Flirting '89

Sarah Pickering
Little Dorrit, Film 1: Nobody's
  Fault '88
Little Dorrit, Film 2: Little
  Dorrit's Story '88

Cindy Pickett
Ferris Bueller's Day Off '86
The Goodbye Bird '93
Hot to Trot! '88
Son-in-Law '93

Vivian Pickles
Candleshoe '78

Ronald Pickup
My Friend Walter '93

Molly Picon
Cannonball Run '81
Fiddler on the Roof '71

Walter Pidgeon
Big Red '62
Cinderella '64
Forbidden Planet '56
Funny Girl '68
How Green was My Valley '41
Neptune Factor '73
Voyage to the Bottom of the
  Sea '61

Bradley Michael Pierce
Jumanji '95

Charles B. Pierce ▲
Legend of Boggy Creek '75

David Pierce
Little Man Tate '91

Tony Pierce
Big Bully '95

Wendell Pierce
Hackers '95
It Could Happen to You '94
Waiting to Exhale '95

Geoffrey Pierson
Necessary Parties '88

Frank Pietrangolare
A Bronx Tale '93

Tim Pigott-Smith
The Hunchback of Notre
  Dame '82
The Remains of the Day '93

Lorraine Pilkington
The Miracle '91

Jeffrey Pillars
Ernest Rides Again '93

Bronson Pinchot
Beverly Hills Cop '84
Beverly Hills Cop 3 '94
The Flamingo Kid '84

Larry Pine
Plain Clothes '88

Jada Pinkett
The Inkwell '94
The Nutty Professor '96

Tonya Pinkins
Above the Rim '94

Leah K. Pinsent
The Bay Boy '85

Danny Pintauro
The Beniker Gang '83

Nadja Pionilla
Race the Sun '96

Nino Pipitone
G-Men vs. the Black
  Dragon '43

Danuel Pipoly
Lord of the Flies '90

Joe Piscopo
Huck and the King of
  Hearts '93
Johnny Dangerously '84
Sidekicks '93
Two Bits & Pepper '95

Marie-France Pisier
French Postcards '79

Maria Pitillo
Bye Bye, Love '94

Anne Pitoniak
House of Cards '92
Old Enough '84
The Wizard of Loneliness '88

Brad Pitt
Across the Tracks '89
Legends of the Fall '94
A River Runs Through It '92
12 Monkeys '95

Bruce Pittman ▲
The Olden Days Coat '81
Where the Spirit Lives '89

ZaSu Pitts
Francis Joins the WACs '54
Francis the Talking Mule '49
Life with Father '47

Jeremy Piven
Car 54, Where Are You? '94
P.C.U. '94
Singles '92

Mary Kay Place
Captain Ron '92
Explorers '85
The Girl Who Spelled
  Freedom '86
Modern Problems '81
Samantha '92
Smooth Talk '85

Michele Placido
Big Business '88

Tony Plana
Sweet 15 '90

Scott Plank
The In Crowd '88
Pastime '91

Dana Plato
Return to Boggy Creek '77

Edward Platt
North by Northwest '59
Rebel Without a Cause '55

Oliver Platt
Beethoven '92
Benny & Joon '93
Tall Tale: The Unbelievable
  Adventures of Pecos
  Bill '95
The Three Musketeers '93

Alice Playten
Legend '86

Donald Pleasence
The Black Arrow '84
The Count of Monte Cristo '74
Escape to Witch Mountain '75
Hearts of the West '75
Horsemasters '61
Oh, God! '77
You Only Live Twice '67

Suzanne Pleshette
The Adventures of Bullwhip
  Griffin '66
The Birds '63
Blackbeard's Ghost '67
The Geisha Boy '58
Oh, God! Book 2 '80
The Shaggy D.A. '76
Support Your Local
  Gunfighter '71
The Ugly Dachshund '65

George Plimpton
Little Man Tate '91

Martha Plimpton
Beautiful Girls '96
The Goonies '85
Josh and S.A.M. '93
Parenthood '89
The River Rat '84
Running on Empty '88
Samantha '92

Joan Plowright
Avalon '90
Dennis the Menace '93
Jane Eyre '96
Mr. Wrong '95
101 Dalmatians '96
The Scarlet Letter '95

Amanda Plummer
Gryphon '88
Joe Versus the Volcano '90
So I Married an Axe
  Murderer '93

Christopher Plummer
Battle of Britain '69
Dolores Claiborne '94
Dragnet '87
International Velvet '78
The Man Who Would Be
  King '75
Return of the Pink
  Panther '74
Somewhere in Time '80
The Sound of Music '65
Star Trek 6: The Undiscovered
  Country '91
12 Monkeys '95

Glenn Plummer
Menace II Society '93
Pastime '91
Speed '94
Up Close and Personal '96

Alison Podbrey
The Peanut Butter
  Solution '85

Judith Pogany
A Hungarian Fairy Tale '87

Ken Pogue
Crazy Moon '87
The Grey Fox '83
Miracle at Moreaux '86

Eric Pohlmann
The Belles of St. Trinian's '53

Priscilla Pointer
Rumpelstiltskin '86

Sidney Poitier
Buck and the Preacher '72
Lilies of the Field '63
Little Nikita '88
Piece of the Action '77
Sneakers '92
To Sir, with Love '67

Sidney Poitier ▲
Buck and the Preacher '72
Fast Forward '84
Ghost Dad '90
Piece of the Action '77

Roman Polanski ▲
Tess '80

Jon Polito
Blankman '94
Bushwhacked '95
The Crow '93

Fluke '95
The Freshman '90
Highlander '86

Oscar Polk
Gone with the Wind '39

Ben Pollack
The Glenn Miller Story '54

Jeff Pollack ▲
Above the Rim '94

Sydney Pollack
Death Becomes Her '92
Tootsie '82

Sydney Pollack ▲
The Electric Horseman '79
Jeremiah Johnson '72
Sabrina '95
Tootsie '82
The Way We Were '73

Cheryl Pollak
My Best Friend Is a
    Vampire '88

Kevin Pollak
Avalon '90
Canadian Bacon '94
Clean Slate '94
Grumpier Old Men '95
Grumpy Old Men '93
House Arrest '96
Indian Summer '93
L.A. Story '91
The Usual Suspects '95
Wayne's World 2 '93
Willow '88

Michael J. Pollard
Dick Tracy '90
Roxanne '87
Scrooged '88

Snub Pollard
The Errand Boy '61

Sarah Polley
The Adventures of Baron
    Munchausen '89
Lantern Hill '90
Tales from Avonlea, Vol. 1:
    The Journey Begins '90

Eileen Pollock
Far and Away '92

Teri Polo
Aspen Extreme '93
Mystery Date '91

Max Pomeranc
Fluke '95
Searching for Bobby
    Fischer '93

Paulina Porizkova
Her Alibi '88

Alison Porter
Curly Sue '91

Don Porter
Buck Privates Come Home '47

Eric Porter
The Belstone Fox '73
Little Lord Fauntleroy '80
Oliver Twist '85

Eric Porter ▲
Marco Polo, Jr. '72

Natalie Portman
Beautiful Girls '96

Richard Portnow
Kindergarten Cop '90
Man of the House '95
Meet the Hollowheads '89
Say Anything '89
Sister Act '92

Ted Post ▲
Beneath the Planet of the
    Apes '70

Pete Postlethwaite
Dragonheart '96
James and the Giant
    Peach '96
The Usual Suspects '95

Tiffanie Poston
Adventures in Dinosaur
    City '92

Tom Poston
Carbon Copy '81

Pam Potillo
And the Children Shall
    Lead '85

Charlie Potter
The Witches '90

H.C. Potter ▲
The Farmer's Daughter '47

Madeleine Potter
Hello Again '87

Annie Potts
Breaking the Rules '92
Ghostbusters '84
Ghostbusters 2 '89
It Came Upon a Midnight
    Clear '84
Pretty in Pink '86

Nell Potts
The Effect of Gamma Rays on
    Man-in-the-Moon
    Marigolds '73

Georges Poujouly
Forbidden Games '52

CCH Pounder
Bagdad Cafe '88
Benny & Joon '93
The Ernest Green Story '93
Robocop 3 '91

Phyllis Povah
Pat and Mike '52

Brittney Powell
Airborne '93
Dragonworld '94

Esteban Louis Powell
Powder '95

Jane Powell
Seven Brides for Seven
    Brothers '54

Lee Powell
Fighting Devil Dogs '38

Michael Powell
Thief of Baghdad '40

Michael Powell ▲
The Red Shoes '48
The Tales of Hoffman '51

Robert Powell
The Hunchback of Notre
    Dame '82
Jesus of Nazareth '77
Tommy '75

William Powell
Life with Father '47
The Thin Man '34

Chad Power
3 Ninjas '92

Taryn Power
The Count of Monte Cristo '74
Sinbad and the Eye of the
    Tiger '77

Tyrone Power Jr.
Cocoon '85
Shag: The Movie '89

Alexandra Powers
Mask '85

Leslie Ann Powers
Hairspray '88

Stefanie Powers
The Boatniks '70
Herbie Rides Again '74

Leon Pownall
How the West Was Fun '95

Sally Prager
The Hideaways '73

Joan Prather
Smile '75

Michael Preece ▲
Prize Fighter '79

June Preisser
Babes in Arms '39
Strike Up the Band '40

Paula Prentiss
Saturday the 14th '81
The World of Henry Orient '64

Elvis Presley
Change of Habit '69

It Happened at the World's
    Fair '63

Priscilla Presley
The Naked Gun: From the
    Files of Police Squad '88
Naked Gun 33 1/3: The Final
    Insult '94
Naked Gun 2 1/2: The Smell
    of Fear '91

Harve Presnell
Paint Your Wagon '69

Emeric Pressburger
The Red Shoes '48

Emeric Pressburger ▲
The Tales of Hoffman '51

Lawrence Pressman
Angus '95

Michael Pressman ▲
And the Children Shall
    Lead '85
The Bad News Bears in
    Breaking Training '77
Teenage Mutant Ninja Turtles
    2: The Secret of the
    Ooze '91

Jason Presson
Explorers '85
The Lady in White '88
The Stone Boy '84

Billy Preston
Blame It on the Night '84

Kelly Preston
Only You '92
Secret Admirer '85
SpaceCamp '86
Twins '88

Robert Preston
How the West was Won '63
Junior Bonner '72
The Last Starfighter '84
The Music Man '62

Steve Previn ▲
Almost Angels '62
Escapade in Florence '62
Waltz King '63

Annabelle Price
Christy '94

David F. Price ▲
Dr. Jekyll and Ms. Hyde '95

Lonny Price
Dirty Dancing '87

Marc Price
The Rescue '88

Molly Price
Jersey Girl '92

Stanley Price
The Invisible Monster '50

Vincent Price
The Boy Who Left Home to
Find Out About the
Shivers '81
Edward Scissorhands '90
House of Wax '53
Snow White and the Seven
Dwarfs '83
The Ten Commandments '56
The Three Musketeers '48

Martin Priest
Zebrahead '92

Jason Priestley
The Boy Who Could Fly '86
Calendar Girl '93
Tombstone '93

Barry Primus
Big Business '88
Heartland '81

Faith Prince
Big Bully '95
Dave '93
My Father the Hero '93

Jonathan Prince ▲
Camp Nowhere '94

William Prince
Spies Like Us '85
Vice Versa '88

Andrew Prine
And the Children Shall
Lead '85
Bandolero! '68
Gettysburg '93
The Last of the Mohicans '85
The Miracle Worker '62
One Little Indian '73

Sandra Prinsloo
The Gods Must Be Crazy '84

Juergen Prochnow
Beverly Hills Cop 2 '87
Judge Dredd '95

Robert Prosky
Big Shots '87
Far and Away '92
Green Card '90
Last Action Hero '93
Miracle on 34th Street '94
Mrs. Doubtfire '93
The Natural '84
Rudy '93
The Scarlet Letter '95

David Proval
The Phantom '96
Vice Versa '88

Dorothy Provine
Never a Dull Moment '68
That Darn Cat '65

Jon Provost
Lassie's Great Adventure '62

David Prowse
The Empire Strikes Back '80
Return of the Jedi '83
Star Wars '77

Haydon Prowse
The Secret Garden '93

Alex Proyas ▲
The Crow '93

Jonathan Pryce
The Adventures of Baron
Munchausen '89
The Age of Innocence '93
Something Wicked This Way
Comes '83

Nicholas Pryor
The Fish that Saved
Pittsburgh '79
Gumball Rally '76
Morgan Stewart's Coming
Home '87
Smile '75

Richard Pryor
Adios Amigo '75
Bingo Long Traveling All-Stars
& Motor Kings '76
Brewster's Millions '85
Bustin' Loose '81
Car Wash '76
Greased Lightning '77
The Silver Streak '76
Superman 3 '83
The Toy '82
The Wiz '78

Roger Pryor Jr.
Smart Alecks '42

Tito Puente
Radio Days '87

Frank Puglia
Ali Baba and the Forty
Thieves '43

Bill Pullman
Casper '95
Independence Day '96
A League of Their Own '92
Mr. Wrong '95
Newsies '92
Rocket Gibraltar '88
Singles '92
Sleepless in Seattle '93
Sommersby '93
Spaceballs '87
While You Were Sleeping '95

Dick Purcell
Captain America '44

Lee Purcell
The Incredible Hulk
Returns '88

Amrish Puri
Indiana Jones and the Temple
of Doom '84

Jack Purvis
The Adventures of Baron
Munchausen '89

Denver Pyle
The Adventures of Frontier
Fremont '75
Blood Brothers '77
Hawmps! '76
Legend of the Northwest '78
Life & Times of Grizzly
Adams '74
Mountain Man '77

Albert Pyun ▲
Captain America '89

John Quade
And You Thought Your
Parents Were Weird! '91
Peter Lundy and the Medicine
Hat Stallion '77

Dennis Quaid
Bill '81
Bill: On His Own '83
Breaking Away '79
Dragonheart '96
Enemy Mine '85
Innerspace '87
The Night the Lights Went Out
in Georgia '81
The Right Stuff '83
Something to Talk About '95
Undercover Blues '93

Randy Quaid
The Apprenticeship of Duddy
Kravitz '74
Bound for Glory '76
Bye Bye, Love '94
Foxes '80
Freaked '93
Heartbeeps '81
Independence Day '96
Kingpin '96
National Lampoon's Christmas
Vacation '89
National Lampoon's
Vacation '83
The Paper '94
Paper Moon '73
What's Up, Doc? '72

John Qualen
Casablanca '42
His Girl Friday '40
The Jungle Book '42
Knute Rockne: All
American '40
Seven Faces of Dr. Lao '63
Those Calloways '65

Jonathan Ke Quan
The Goonies '85

Ke Huy Quan
Indiana Jones and the Temple
of Doom '84

Anna Quayle
Chitty Chitty Bang Bang '68

Anthony Quayle
Lawrence of Arabia '62
The Wrong Man '56

Queen Latifah
House Party 2: The Pajama
Jam '91
My Life '93

Valerie Quennessen
Conan the Barbarian '82
French Postcards '79

Mae Questel
National Lampoon's Christmas
Vacation '89

Charles Quigley
The Crimson Ghost '46
Daredevils of the Red
Circle '38

Alfonso Quijada
Timecop '94

Tim Quill
Army of Darkness '92
Hiding Out '87

Richard Quine
Babes on Broadway '41

Kathleen Quinlan
Airport '77 '77
American Graffiti '73
Apollo 13 '95
Clara's Heart '88
Twilight Zone: The Movie '83

Aidan Quinn
Avalon '90
Benny & Joon '93
Crusoe '89
Desperately Seeking
Susan '85
Legends of the Fall '94
The Playboys '92

Aileen Quinn
Annie '82

Anthony Quinn
Jesus of Nazareth '77
Last Action Hero '93
Lawrence of Arabia '62
Only the Lonely '91
Sinbad the Sailor '47
A Walk in the Clouds '95

Bill Quinn
Bustin' Loose '81
Twilight Zone: The Movie '83

Francesco Quinn
Top Dog '95

James Quinn
Joey '85

J.C. Quinn
The Babe '92
Turner and Hooch '89

John Quinn ▲
The Magic of the Golden Bear:
Goldy 3 '94

Sally Quinn
Born Yesterday '93

Gene Quintano ▲
National Lampoon's Loaded
Weapon 1 '93

Alessandro Rabelo
Where the River Runs
Black '86

Francine Racette
Au Revoir Les Enfants '87

Victoria Racimo
Ernest Goes to Camp '87
White Fang 2: The Myth of the
White Wolf '94

Sudhir Rad
Morgan Stewart's Coming
Home '87

Rosemary Radcliffe
Anne of Green Gables '85

Sascha Radetsky
Home at Last '88

Basil Radford
The Lady Vanishes '38

Eric Radomski ▲
Batman: Mask of the
Phantasm '93

Charlotte Rae
Bananas '71
Words by Heart '84
The Worst Witch '86

Bob Rafelson ▲
Head '68

Frances Rafferty
Curley '47

Stewart Raffill ▲
Across the Great Divide '76
The Adventures of the
Wilderness Family '76
Ice Pirates '84
Mac and Me '88
Mannequin 2: On the
Move '91
Sea Gypsies '78
The Tender Warrior '71
When the North Wind
Blows '74

Deborah Raffin
The Dove '74
Touched by Love '80

Alan Rafkin ▲
The Shakiest Gun in the
West '68

Rags Ragland
The Canterville Ghost '44

Joe Ragno
The Babe '92

William Ragsdale
Mannequin 2: On the
Move '91

Umberto Raho
Aladdin '86

Steve Railsback
Calendar Girl '93
The Golden Seal '83
Nukie '93

Ivan Raimi
Army of Darkness '92

Sam Raimi
Indian Summer '93

Sam Raimi ▲
Army of Darkness '92
Darkman '90

Theodore (Ted) Raimi
Army of Darkness '92
Clear and Present Danger '94

Christina Raines
Touched by Love '80

Ford Rainey
Mountain Man '77

Claude Rains
The Adventures of Robin
Hood '38
Casablanca '42
Lawrence of Arabia '62
Mr. Smith Goes to
Washington '39
Notorious '46
The Pied Piper of Hamelin '57
The Prince and the
Pauper '37

Tommy Rall
Seven Brides for Seven
Brothers '54

Jessie Ralph
The Blue Bird '40
Little Lord Fauntleroy '36

Sheryl Lee Ralph
Sister Act 2: Back in the
Habit '93

Esther Ralston
To the Last Man '33

Henry Ramer
Hockey Night '84

Carlos Ramirez
Anchors Aweigh '45

Frank Ramirez
Smith! '69

Harold Ramis
Baby Boom '87
Ghostbusters '84
Ghostbusters 2 '89

Harold Ramis ▲
Caddyshack '80
Club Paradise '86
Groundhog Day '93
Multiplicity '96
National Lampoon's
Vacation '83
Stuart Saves His Family '94
Untamed Heart '93

Anne Elizabeth Ramsay
A League of Their Own '92

Bruce Ramsay
Alive '93

Remak Ramsay
Mr. & Mrs. Bridge '91

Anne Ramsey
Goin' South '78
The Goonies '85
Meet the Hollowheads '89
The River Pirates '94
Throw Momma from the
Train '87
White Mama '80

Marion Ramsey
Police Academy 3: Back in
Training '86
Police Academy 5: Assignment
Miami Beach '88
Police Academy 6: City Under
Siege '89

Nick Ramus
Geronimo '93
Journey to Spirit Island '92

Ethan Randall
All I Want for Christmas '91
Dutch '91
A Far Off Place '93

Lexi Randall
Heidi '93
Sarah, Plain and Tall '91
Skylark '93

Stacie Randall
Dream a Little Dream 2 '94

Tony Randall
The Adventures of Huckleberry
Finn '60
Fatal Instinct '93
The Littlest Angel '69
Seven Faces of Dr. Lao '63

Theresa Randle
Bad Boys '95
Beverly Hills Cop 3 '94
Malcolm X '92

Jane Randolph
Abbott and Costello Meet
Frankenstein '48

John Randolph
King Kong '76
National Lampoon's Christmas
Vacation '89
The Runaways '75

The Wizard of Loneliness '88

Arthur Rankin Jr. ▲
The Ballad of Paul
Bunyan '72
Flight of Dragons '82
Frosty the Snowman '69
The Hobbit '78
The Return of the King '80
Santa Claus is Coming to
Town '70

Stacey Linn Ransower
The Baby-Sitters Club '95

Michael Rapaport
The Basketball Diaries '94
Beautiful Girls '96
The Pallbearer '95
The Scout '94
Zebrahead '92

Anthony Rapp
Adventures in Babysitting '87
Dazed and Confused '93
School Ties '92

Jean-Paul Rappeneau ▲
Cyrano de Bergerac '90

Irving Rapper ▲
The Corn is Green '45

David Rasche
Bigfoot: The Unforgettable
Encounter '94
Bingo '91
Delirious '91
Out There '95

Steve Rash ▲
The Buddy Holly Story '78
Can't Buy Me Love '87
Eddie '96
Son-in-Law '93
Under the Rainbow '81

Phylicia Rashad
Once Upon a Time . . . When
We Were Colored '95

Sharif Rashed
Crooklyn '94

Lars Rasmussen ▲
The Littlest Viking '94

Thalmus Rasulala
Adios Amigo '75
Blacula '72
Mom and Dad Save the
World '92

Basil Rathbone
The Adventures of Robin
Hood '38
Captain Blood '35
The Court Jester '56
David Copperfield '35
The Magic Sword '62

Tina Rathborne ▲
Zelly & Me '88

Elden Ratliff
The Mighty Ducks '92

Tzvi Ratner-Stauber
Family Prayers '91

Devin Ratray
Home Alone '90
Home Alone 2: Lost in New
    York '92

Heather Rattray
Across the Great Divide '76
Further Adventures of the
    Wilderness Family, Part
    2 '77
Mountain Family
    Robinson '79
Sea Gypsies '78

John Ratzenberger
The Empire Strikes Back '80

Alice Rawlings
Where Angels Go, Trouble
    Follows '68

John Rawlins ▲
Dick Tracy Meets
    Gruesome '47

Herbert Rawlinson
Blake of Scotland Yard '36
Smart Alecks '42

Aldo Ray
Pat and Mike '52
Seven Alone '75

James Ray
She's Having a Baby '88

Nicholas Ray ▲
Rebel Without a Cause '55

Martha Raye
Pippin '81

Ernest Rayford
Love Your Mama '89

Bill Raymond
The Crow '93

Devon Raymond
Singles '92

Gary Raymond
Jason and the Argonauts '63

Gene Raymond
Mr. & Mrs. Smith '41

Paula Raymond
Adam's Rib '50

Spiro Razatos ▲
Fast Getaway '91

Peggy Rea
Made in America '93
The Waltons: The Children's
    Carol '80

Stephen Rea
Princess Caraboo '94

Ronald Reagan
Bedtime for Bonzo '51
Knute Rockne: All
    American '40

James Rebhorn
8 Seconds '94
I Love Trouble '94
If Lucy Fell '95
Lorenzo's Oil '92
Skylark '93
Up Close and Personal '96

Francis Reddy
Mario '74

Helen Reddy
Airport '75 '75
Pete's Dragon '77

Quinn Redeker
Three Stooges Meet
    Hercules '61

Robert Redford
All the President's Men '76
A Bridge Too Far '77
Butch Cassidy and the
    Sundance Kid '69
Downhill Racer '69
The Electric Horseman '79
The Great Waldo Pepper '75
Jeremiah Johnson '72
The Natural '84
Sneakers '92
The Sting '73
Up Close and Personal '96
The Way We Were '73

Robert Redford ▲
Quiz Show '94
A River Runs Through It '92

Corin Redgrave
Four Weddings and a
    Funeral '93

Jemma Redgrave
Howard's End '92

Lynn Redgrave
The Big Bus '76
Morgan Stewart's Coming
    Home '87
Walking on Air '87

Michael Redgrave
Battle of Britain '69
The Go-Between '71
Heidi '67
The Lady Vanishes '38
The Loneliness of the Long
    Distance Runner '62

Vanessa Redgrave
Camelot '67
Howard's End '92
A Man for All Seasons '66
Mission: Impossible '96
Snow White and the Seven
    Dwarfs '83

Carol Reed ▲
Oliver! '68

Christopher Reed
Rudy '93

Donna Reed
The Caddy '53
The Human Comedy '43
It's a Wonderful Life '46

James Reed
Eight Men Out '88

Jerry Reed
Smokey and the Bandit '77
Smokey and the Bandit, Part
    2 '80
Smokey and the Bandit, Part
    3 '83

Oliver Reed
The Adventures of Baron
    Munchausen '89
The Black Arrow '84
Condorman '81
The Four Musketeers '75
Oliver! '68
The Prince and the
    Pauper '78
The Return of the
    Musketeers '89
The Sting 2 '83
Ten Little Indians '75
Three Musketeers '74
Tommy '75
Treasure Island '89

Pamela Reed
The Best of Times '86
Junior '94
Kindergarten Cop '90
The Right Stuff '83

Philip Reed
Unknown Island '48

Robert Reed
The Love Bug '68

Tracy Reed
Piece of the Action '77

Clive Rees ▲
When the Whales Came '89

Donough Rees
Starship '87

Roger Rees
If Looks Could Kill '91
Robin Hood: Men in
    Tights '93
Stop! or My Mom Will
    Shoot '92

Della Reese
The Kid Who Loved
    Christmas '90

Christopher Reeve
The Remains of the Day '93
Sleeping Beauty '83
Somewhere in Time '80
Speechless '94
Superman 1: The Movie '78
Superman 2 '80

Superman 3 '83
Superman 4: The Quest for
    Peace '87

George Reeves
Gone with the Wind '39
Superman & the Mole
    Men '51
Westward Ho, the Wagons!
    '56

Keanu Reeves
Babes in Toyland '86
Bill & Ted's Bogus
    Journey '91
Bill & Ted's Excellent
    Adventure '89
Johnny Mnemonic '95
Little Buddha '93
Much Ado About Nothing '93
The Night Before '88
Parenthood '89
Permanent Record '88
Speed '94
A Walk in the Clouds '95

Lisa Reeves
The Chicken Chronicles '77

Mathonwy Reeves
Child's Christmas in
    Wales '88

Matt Reeves ▲
The Pallbearer '95

Steve Reeves
Hercules '58
Hercules Unchained '59
Thief of Baghdad '61

Duncan Regehr
The Monster Squad '87
Timemaster '95

Nadja Regin
From Russia with Love '63

Frank Reicher
King Kong '33

Beryl Reid
The Belles of St. Trinian's '53

Christopher Reid
Class Act '91
House Party '90
House Party 2: The Pajama
    Jam '91
House Party 3 '94

Elliott Reid
Follow Me, Boys! '66

Fiona Reid
Beethoven Lives Upstairs '92
Mark Twain and Me '91

Kate Reid
The Andromeda Strain '71
Ugly Little Boy '77

Michael Earl Reid
Army of Darkness '92

Tim Reid ▲
The Little Mermaid '78
Once Upon a Time . . . When
We Were Colored '95

Charles Nelson Reilly
Cannonball Run 2 '84

Hugh Reilly
Lassie's Great Adventure '62

John C. Reilly
Boys '96
Dolores Claiborne '94
Out on a Limb '92
The River Wild '94
What's Eating Gilbert
Grape '93

Luke Reilly
Zebrahead '92

Gary Reineke
George's Island '91

Carl Reiner
Dead Men Don't Wear
Plaid '82
Gidget Goes Hawaiian '61
Pinocchio '83
The Russians are Coming, the
Russians are Coming '66

Carl Reiner ▲
Dead Men Don't Wear
Plaid '82
Fatal Instinct '93
Oh, God! '77
Summer Rental '85
Summer School '87

Rob Reiner
Bye Bye, Love '94
Mixed Nuts '94
Sleepless in Seattle '93
Tall Tales and Legends:
Johnny Appleseed '86
Throw Momma from the
Train '87
Thursday's Game '74

Rob Reiner ▲
The American President '95
North '94
The Princess Bride '87
Stand By Me '86
The Sure Thing '85

Tracy Reiner
Apollo 13 '95
A League of Their Own '92
Nothing in Common '86

Judge Reinhold
Baby on Board '92
Beverly Hills Cop '84
Beverly Hills Cop 2 '87
Beverly Hills Cop 3 '94
Black Magic '92
Fast Times at Ridgemont
High '82
Gremlins '84
Off Beat '86

On the Edge: The Survival of
Dana '79
The Santa Clause '94
Vice Versa '88

Ann Reinking
Annie '82

Irving Reis ▲
The Bachelor and the Bobby-
Soxer '47

Paul Reiser
Beverly Hills Cop '84
Beverly Hills Cop 2 '87
Bye Bye, Love '94
Family Prayers '91
Odd Jobs '85

Ursula Reit
Willy Wonka & the Chocolate
Factory '71

Wolfgang Reitherman ▲
The Aristocats '70
The Jungle Book '67
101 Dalmatians '61
The Rescuers '77
Robin Hood '73
Sleeping Beauty '59
The Sword in the Stone '63
The Wind in the Willows '49
Winnie the Pooh and the
Blustery Day '68
Winnie the Pooh and the
Honey Tree '65

Ivan Reitman ▲
Dave '93
Ghostbusters '84
Ghostbusters 2 '89
Junior '94
Kindergarten Cop '90
Meatballs '79
Twins '88

Winston Rekert
Toby McTeague '87

Maria Therese Relin
Secret Places '85

James Remar
Boys on the Side '94
The Dream Team '89
Fatal Instinct '93
Miracle on 34th Street '94
The Phantom '96
Renaissance Man '94
White Fang '91

Lee Remick
The Snow Queen '83
Toughlove '85

Bert Remsen
Joni '79
Miss Firecracker '89
Only the Lonely '91

Albert Remy
The 400 Blows '59

Duncan Renaldo
Zorro Rides Again '37

Norman Rene ▲
Prelude to a Kiss '92

Brad Renfro
The Client '94
The Cure '95
Tom and Huck '95

Patrick Renna
Beanstalk '94
The Big Green '95
The Sandlot '93
Son-in-Law '93

Max Rennie
When the Whales Came '89

Michael Rennie
Third Man on the
Mountain '59

Jean Reno
French Kiss '95

Kelly Reno
The Black Stallion '79
The Black Stallion
Returns '83

Mickey Rentschler
Radio Patrol '37

Maggie Renzi
The Brother from Another
Planet '84
Eight Men Out '88

Frank Renzulli
Wild Hearts Can't Be
Broken '91

Adam Resnick ▲
Cabin Boy '94

Noel Resnick ▲
Caddie Woodlawn '88

Tommy Rettig
The 5000 Fingers of Dr. T '53

Mary Lou Retton
Scrooged '88

Gloria Reuben
Johnny's Girl '95
Timecop '94

**Paul (Pee Wee Herman)
Reubens**
Back to the Beach '87
Batman Returns '92
Big Top Pee Wee '88
Buffy the Vampire Slayer '92
Dunston Checks In '95
Pee Wee's Big Adventure '85
Pee Wee's Playhouse Festival
of Fun '88
Pinocchio '83

Anne Revere
National Velvet '44

Clive Revill
Cannon Movie Tales: The
Emperor's New Clothes '89
The Empire Strikes Back '80
Matilda '78
One of Our Dinosaurs Is
Missing '75
Rumpelstiltskin '86

Fernando Rey
1492: Conquest of
Paradise '92
Guns of the Magnificent
Seven '69

Ernie Reyes Sr.
Surf Ninjas '93

Ernie Reyes Jr.
Surf Ninjas '93
Teenage Mutant Ninja Turtles
2: The Secret of the
Ooze '91

Ivelka Reyes
Crooklyn '94

Tiasha Reyes
Crooklyn '94

Burt Reynolds
Cannonball Run '81
Cannonball Run 2 '84
Cop and a Half '93
Gentle Ben '69
Silent Movie '76
Smokey and the Bandit '77
Smokey and the Bandit, Part
2 '80
Smokey and the Bandit, Part
3 '83

Debbie Reynolds
How the West was Won '63
Singin' in the Rain '52
Tammy and the Bachelor '57

Gene Reynolds
Andy Hardy's Private
Secretary '41
Boys Town '38
Country Girl '54
Life Begins for Andy
Hardy '41
Love Finds Andy Hardy '38

Kevin Reynolds ▲
Fandango '85
Robin Hood: Prince of
Thieves '91
Waterworld '95

Marjorie Reynolds
Gone with the Wind '39
Holiday Inn '42

Ving Rhames
Dave '93
Mission: Impossible '96

Barbara Rhoades
The Goodbye Girl '77
The Shakiest Gun in the
West '68

Cynthia Rhodes
Dirty Dancing '87
Flashdance '83

Hari Rhodes
Conquest of the Planet of the
 Apes '72
A Dream for Christmas '73

Michael Rhodes ▲
Christy '94
Heidi '93

Paul Rhys
Chaplin '92

John Rhys-Davies
The Double O Kid '92
Indiana Jones and the Last
 Crusade '89
Kim '84
The Little Match Girl '87
Raiders of the Lost Ark '81
Sword of the Valiant '83
The Trial of the Incredible
 Hulk '89

Alfonso Ribeiro
The Mighty Pawns '87

Marissa Ribisi
Dazed and Confused '93

Christina Ricci
The Addams Family '91
Addams Family Values '93
Casper '95
Gold Diggers: The Secret of
 Bear Mountain '95
Mermaids '90
Now and Then '95
That Darn Cat '96

Florence Rice
At the Circus '39

Adam Rich
The Devil & Max Devlin '81

Christopher Rich
The Joy Luck Club '93

Matty Rich ▲
The Inkwell '94

Richard Rich ▲
The Fox and the Hound '81
The Swan Princess '94

Emily Richard
Empire of the Sun '87

Jefferson Richard ▲
In Search of a Golden Sky '84

Pierre Richard
The Tall Blond Man with One
 Black Shoe '72

Ariana Richards
Angus '95
Jurassic Park '93
Prancer '89
Spaced Invaders '90

Beah Richards
A Dream for Christmas '73
The Miracle Worker '62

Dick Richards ▲
Culpepper Cattle Co. '72
Man, Woman & Child '83

Evan Richards
Dream Machine '91
Rock 'n' Roll High School
 Forever '91

Gwil Richards
The Night Before '88

Jeff Richards
It's a Dog's Life '55
Seven Brides for Seven
 Brothers '54

Kim Richards
Escape to Witch Mountain '75
Return from Witch
 Mountain '78

Lisa Richards
The Prince of Central Park '77

Michael Richards
Airheads '94
Coneheads '93
Problem Child '90
UHF '89
Unstrung Heroes '95

Michele Lamar Richards
Top Dog '95

Ian Richardson
Year of the Comet '92

Joely Richardson
I'll Do Anything '93
King Ralph '91
Loch Ness '96
101 Dalmatians '96

John Richardson ▲
Dusty '85

Lee Richardson
Skylark '93

Miranda Richardson
Empire of the Sun '87

Natasha Richardson
Nell '94

Ralph Richardson
Battle of Britain '69
Doctor Zhivago '65
Dragonslayer '81
Greystoke: The Legend of
 Tarzan, Lord of the
 Apes '84
The Man in the Iron Mask '77
Time Bandits '81

Salli Richardson
Sioux City '94
Up Against the Wall '91

Tony Richardson ▲
The Loneliness of the Long
 Distance Runner '62

Peter Mark Richman
Naked Gun 2 1/2: The Smell
 of Fear '91

Branscombe Richmond
Christopher Columbus: The
 Discovery '92

Kane Richmond
Spy Smasher '42

Warner Richmond
The Lost Jungle '34

Dan Richter
2001: A Space Odyssey '68

Jason James Richter
Cops and Robbersons '94
Free Willy '93
Free Willy 2: The Adventure
 Home '95
The Neverending Story 3 '94

W.D. Richter ▲
The Adventures of Buckaroo
 Banzai Across the Eighth
 Dimension '84

Don Rickles
Beach Blanket Bingo '65
Bikini Beach '64
Muscle Beach Party '64

Alan Rickman
Die Hard '88
Quigley Down Under '90
Robin Hood: Prince of
 Thieves '91
Sense and Sensibility '95
Truly, Madly, Deeply '91

Tom Rickman ▲
The River Rat '84

Robert Ridgely
Philadelphia '93

Vicki Ridler
George's Island '91

Peter Riegert
Crossing Delancey '88
Local Hero '83
The Mask '94
Oscar '91

Richard Riehle
Hero '92
Holy Matrimony '94
Lightning Jack '94
Of Mice and Men '92

Charles Riesner ▲
The Big Store '41
Lost in a Harem '44

Dean Riesner ▲
Bill and Coo '47

Diana Rigg
Evil Under the Sun '82
The Great Muppet Caper '81
On Her Majesty's Secret
 Service '69
Snow White '89
The Worst Witch '86

Robin Riker
Alligator '80
Stepmonster '92

Elaine Riley
Clipped Wings '53

Jeannine Riley
Wackiest Wagon Train in the
 West '77

John Riley
Greenstone '85

Michael Riley
French Kiss '95
Heck's Way Home '95

Shane Rimmer
Crusoe '89
Dreamchild '85
The People That Time
 Forgot '77

Molly Ringwald
The Breakfast Club '85
Face the Music '92
For Keeps '88
P.K. and the Kid '85
Pretty in Pink '86
Sixteen Candles '84
Tall Tales and Legends:
 Johnny Appleseed '86

Leon Rippy
Kuffs '92
Stargate '94

Michael Rispoli
Homeward Bound 2: Lost in
 San Francisco '96
While You Were Sleeping '95

Lazar Ristovski
Tito and Me '92

Cyril Ritchard
Hans Brinker '69
Peter Pan '60

Clint Ritchie
Against A Crooked Sky '75

Michael Ritchie ▲
The Bad News Bears '76
Cops and Robbersons '94
Downhill Racer '69
Fletch '85
Fletch Lives '89
The Golden Child '86
The Scout '94
Smile '75
Wildcats '86

Martin Ritt
Conrack '74

Martin Ritt ▲
Casey's Shadow '78
Conrack '74
Cross Creek '83
The Great White Hope '70
Murphy's Romance '85
Norma Rae '79
Sounder '72

John Ritter
The Barefoot Executive '71
Comeback Kid '80
Hero at Large '80
North '94
Problem Child '90
Problem Child 2 '91
Scandalous John '71
A Smoky Mountain
   Christmas '86
Stay Tuned '92

Thelma Ritter
How the West was Won '63
Miracle on 34th Street '47
Rear Window '54

Harry Ritz
Silent Movie '76

Carlos Rivas
The King and I '56

Chita Rivera
Once Upon a Brothers
   Grimm '77
Pippin '81

Geraldo Rivera
Happy Birthday, Bugs: 50
   Looney Years '90

Joan Rivers
Spaceballs '87

Pat Roach
Willow '88

Glen Roald
Timecop '94

Adam Roarke
Sioux City '94

Jason Robards Sr.
Fighting Marines '36

Jason Robards Jr.
The Adventures of Huck
   Finn '93
All the President's Men '76
A Christmas to Remember '78
Dream a Little Dream '89
Heidi '93
A House Without a Christmas
   Tree '72
Legend of the Lone
   Ranger '81
Little Big League '94
Mark Twain and Me '91
Max Dugan Returns '83
Once Upon a Time in the
   West '68
The Paper '94
Parenthood '89

Philadelphia '93
Reunion '88
Something Wicked This Way
   Comes '83
A Thousand Clowns '65

Sam Robards
Beautiful Girls '96
Fandango '85

David Robb
The Flame Trees of Thika '81

Gale Robbins
The Belle of New York '52

Jerome Robbins ▲
West Side Story '61

Matthew Robbins ▲
*batteries not included '87
Bingo '91
Dragonslayer '81
Legend of Billie Jean '85

Oliver Robbins
Poltergeist '82
Poltergeist 2: The Other
   Side '86

Tim Robbins
Erik the Viking '89
Howard the Duck '86
I.Q. '94
Miss Firecracker '89
The Shawshank
   Redemption '94
The Sure Thing '85
Top Gun '86

Ian Robers
Cry, the Beloved Country '95

Yves Robert ▲
My Father's Glory '91
My Mother's Castle '91
The Tall Blond Man with One
   Black Shoe '72

Bill Roberts
Bongo '47

Christian Roberts
To Sir, with Love '67

Doris Roberts
The Fig Tree '87
National Lampoon's Christmas
   Vacation '89

Ian Roberts
The Power of One '92

John Roberts ▲
War of the Buttons '95

Julia Roberts
Hook '91
I Love Trouble '94
The Pelican Brief '93
Satisfaction '88
Something to Talk About '95
Steel Magnolias '89

Ken Roberts
The Great Land of Small '86

Michael D. Roberts
Ice Pirates '84
Rain Man '88

Pernell Roberts
The Errand Boy '61
Magic of Lassie '78
Paco '75
Shirley Temple Storybook
   Theater '60

Rachel Roberts
The Belstone Fox '73
Foul Play '78

Tanya Roberts
Beastmaster '82
Sheena '84
A View to a Kill '85

Ted Jan Roberts
Magic Kid '92
Magic Kid 2 '94

Tony Roberts
Annie Hall '77
18 Again! '88
Million Dollar Duck '71
Play It Again, Sam '72
Radio Days '87

Cliff Robertson
Gidget '59
Two of a Kind '82
Wild Hearts Can't Be
   Broken '91
Wind '92

Jenny Robertson
Jacob Have I Loved '88

John S. Robertson ▲
Little Orphan Annie '32
Our Little Girl '35

Malcolm Robertson
The Year My Voice Broke '87

Tom G. Robertson ▲
The River Pirates '94

Kim Robillard
Rain Man '88

Barry Robins
Bless the Beasts and
   Children '71

Laila Robins
Planes, Trains &
   Automobiles '87
Welcome Home, Roxy
   Carmichael '90

Andre Robinson
Love Your Mama '89

Andrew (Andy) Robinson
Mask '85
Not My Kid '85

Angela Louise Robinson
Pink Cadillac '89

Ann Robinson
The War of the Worlds '53

Bill Robinson
Just Around the Corner '38
The Littlest Rebel '35
Rebecca of Sunnybrook
   Farm '38

Charles Robinson
Daring Dobermans '73

Chris Robinson
Amy '81
Savannah Smiles '82

Edward G. Robinson
Key Largo '48
Never a Dull Moment '68

Frances Robinson
Tim Tyler's Luck '37

Joe Robinson
Diamonds are Forever '71

Phil Alden Robinson ▲
Field of Dreams '89
Sneakers '92

Tiffany Gail Robinson
Pink Cadillac '89

Rafael H. Robledo
Darkman '90

May Robson
Bringing Up Baby '38
It Happened in New
   Orleans '36
Little Orphan Annie '32

Wayne Robson
The Grey Fox '83
Two If by Sea '95

Alex Rocco
Boris and Natasha: The
   Movie '92
Dream a Little Dream '89
Gotcha! '85
The Grass is Always Greener
   Over the Septic Tank '78
Herbie Goes Bananas '80
The Lady in White '88
P.K. and the Kid '85

Marc Rocco ▲
Dream a Little Dream '89

Eric Rochant ▲
The Fifth Monkey '90

Catherine Roche
Strangers in Good
   Company '91

Eugene Roche
Foul Play '78
Oh, God! You Devil '84

Sean Roche ▲
Chasing Dreams '81

Suzzy Roche
Crossing Delancey '88

Jean Rochefort
The Tall Blond Man with One Black Shoe '72

Lela Rochon
Waiting to Exhale '95

Chris Rock
Coneheads '93

Charles Rocket
Dances with Wolves '90
Delirious '91
Dumb & Dumber '94
Hocus Pocus '93
How I Got into College '89
It's Pat: The Movie '94
Tom and Huck '95

Marcia Rodd
Citizens Band '77

Anton Rodgers
Dirty Rotten Scoundrels '88

Marie Antoinette Rodgers
Journey to Spirit Island '92

Freddy Rodriguez
A Walk in the Clouds '95

Marco Rodriguez
The Crow '93

Paul Rodriguez
Made in America '93

Valente Rodriguez
Ed '96

Ben Rodska
Oliver Twist '85

Daniel Roebuck
The Fugitive '93

Nicolas Roeg ▲
The Witches '90

Larry Roemer ▲
Rudolph the Red-Nosed Reindeer '64

William Roerick
A Separate Peace '73

Michael Roescher
Gordy '95

Maurice Roeves
The Last of the Mohicans '92

Beth Rogan
Mysterious Island '61

Charles "Buddy" Rogers ▲
March of the Wooden Soldiers '34

Ginger Rogers
Cinderella '64
Follow the Fleet '36
Monkey Business '52
Shall We Dance '37
That's Dancing! '85

Jean Rogers
Flash Gordon: Rocketship '36

Kenny Rogers
Six Pack '82

Mimi Rogers
Blue Skies Again '83
Dark Horse '92
Far from Home: The Adventures of Yellow Dog '94
Gung Ho '85
Monkey Trouble '94
The Rousters '83

Wayne Rogers
The Girl Who Spelled Freedom '86
The Goodbye Bird '93

Will Rogers
A Connecticut Yankee '31

Clayton Rohner
Just One of the Guys '85

Victor Rojas
Max is Missing '95

Gilbert Roland
Barbarosa '82
Miracle of Our Lady of Fatima '52
Running Wild '73

Michelle Rolia
Mr. Hulot's Holiday '53

Esther Rolle
Driving Miss Daisy '89
House of Cards '92
How to Make an American Quilt '95
The Kid Who Loved Christmas '90
P.K. and the Kid '85

Henry Rollins
Johnny Mnemonic '95

Howard E. Rollins Jr.
The House of Dies Drear '88

Mark Rolston
Prancer '89
The Shawshank Redemption '94

Phil Roman ▲
A Charlie Brown Thanksgiving '81
It's the Easter Beagle, Charlie Brown '74
Tom and Jerry: The Movie '93

Ruth Roman
Since You Went Away '44

Strangers on a Train '51
The Window '49

Andy Romano
Two Bits '96

Richard Romanus
Cops and Robbersons '94

Robert Romanus
Bad Medicine '85
Fast Times at Ridgemont High '82

Lina Romay
Love Laughs at Andy Hardy '46

Fred Romer
Great Adventure '75

Kim Romer
A Day in October '92

Cesar Romero
The Computer Wore Tennis Shoes '69
The Little Princess '39
Now You See Him, Now You Don't '72
The Thin Man '34
Wee Willie Winkie '37

Joanelle Romero
Lost Legacy: A Girl Called Hatter Fox '77

Ned Romero
The Last of the Mohicans '85

Tiny Ron
The Rocketeer '91

Linda Ronstadt
Muppet Revue '85
The Pirates of Penzance '83

Darrell Roodt ▲
Cry, the Beloved Country '95
Father Hood '93
Sarafina! '92

Michael Rooker
Eight Men Out '88
Light of Day '87
Mallrats '95
Tombstone '93

Mickey Rooney
The Adventures of Huckleberry Finn '39
Ah, Wilderness! '35
Andy Hardy Gets Spring Fever '39
Andy Hardy Meets Debutante '40
Andy Hardy's Double Life '42
Andy Hardy's Private Secretary '41
Babes in Arms '39
Babes on Broadway '41
Bill '81
Bill: On His Own '83
The Black Stallion '79
Boys Town '38

Captains Courageous '37
Erik the Viking '89
Girl Crazy '43
Home for Christmas '90
How to Stuff a Wild Bikini '65
The Human Comedy '43
It Came Upon a Midnight Clear '84
The Legend of Wolf Mountain '92
Life Begins for Andy Hardy '41
Lightning: The White Stallion '86
Little Lord Fauntleroy '36
Love Finds Andy Hardy '38
Love Laughs at Andy Hardy '46
Magic of Lassie '78
Men of Boys Town '41
My Heroes Have Always Been Cowboys '91
National Velvet '44
Pete's Dragon '77
The Road Home '95
Strike Up the Band '40
Thoroughbreds Don't Cry '37

Ted Rooney
Celtic Pride '96

Amanda Root
Jane Eyre '96

Tom Ropelewski ▲
Look Who's Talking Now '93
Madhouse '90

Brian Roper
The Secret Garden '49

Hayden Rorke
Francis Goes to the Races '51
Spencer's Mountain '63

Mary Lou Rosato
Two Bits '96

Tony Rosato
Rent-A-Kid '95

Bartholomew Rose
Flirting '89

Bianca Rose
Eye on the Sparrow '91

Gabrielle Rose
Timecop '94

George Rose
The Hideaways '73
The Pirates of Penzance '83

Rose Marie
Man from Clover Grove '78

Roger Rose
Ski Patrol '89

Roseanne
She-Devil '89

Lauren Roselli
Philadelphia '93

Martin Rosen ▲
Stacking '87
Watership Down '78

Phil Rosen ▲
Spooks Run Wild '41

Stuart Rosenberg ▲
My Heroes Have Always Been
Cowboys '91

**Maxie "Slapsie"
Rosenbloom**
Hollywood or Bust '56

Scott Rosenfelt ▲
Family Prayers '91

Mark Rosenthal ▲
The In Crowd '88

Rick Rosenthal ▲
American Dreamer '84
Russkies '87

Mark Rosman ▲
The Blue Yonder '86

Annie Ross
Superman 3 '83

Anthony Ross
Country Girl '54

Betsy King Ross
Fighting with Kit Carson '33
The Phantom Empire '35

Charlotte Ross
Savage Land '94

Chelcie Ross
Amos and Andrew '93
Bill & Ted's Bogus
Journey '91
Rudy '93

Diana Ross
The Wiz '78

Herbert Ross
Play It Again, Sam '72

Herbert Ross ▲
Boys on the Side '94
Footloose '84
Funny Lady '75
The Goodbye Girl '77
I Ought to Be in Pictures '82
Max Dugan Returns '83
Play It Again, Sam '72
Steel Magnolias '89
The Sunshine Boys '75
Undercover Blues '93

Katharine Ross
Butch Cassidy and the
Sundance Kid '69
The Shadow Riders '82
The Swarm '78

Kimberly Ross
The Last Starfighter '84

Marion Ross
On the Edge: The Survival of
Dana '79

Shavar Ross
The House of Dies Drear '88

Ted Ross
Arthur 2: On the Rocks '88
The Wiz '78

Isabella Rossellini
Death Becomes Her '92
Red Riding Hood '89
Zelly & Me '88

Leo Rossi
Fast Getaway '91
Fast Getaway 2 '94
Heart Like a Wheel '83

Jan Rossini
When Dinosaurs Ruled the
Earth '70

Leonard Rossiter
The Pink Panther Strikes
Again '76

Angelo Rossitto
Mad Max: Beyond
Thunderdome '85

Rick Rossovich
Roxanne '87
The Terminator '84
Top Gun '86

Maggie Roswell
Midnight Madness '80

Joe Roth ▲
Coupe de Ville '90

Lillian Roth
Animal Crackers '30

Tim Roth
Rob Roy '95
A World Apart '88

Cynthia Rothrock
Fast Getaway '91
Fast Getaway 2 '94

Richard Roundtree
Bonanza: The Return '93
Once Upon a Time . . . When
We Were Colored '95
Theodore Rex '95

Robert Rounseville
Carousel '56
The Tales of Hoffman '51

Mickey Rourke
Rumble Fish '83

Graham Rouse
Ride a Wild Pony '75

Nathalie Roussel
My Father's Glory '91
My Mother's Castle '91

Bill Rowe
Philadelphia '93

Greg Rowe
Blue Fin '78

Nicholas Rowe
The Lawrenceville
Stories '80s
Young Sherlock Holmes '85

Victoria Rowell
Dumb & Dumber '94

Roy Rowland ▲
The 5000 Fingers of Dr. T '53

Gena Rowlands
Light of Day '87
Rapunzel '82
Something to Talk About '95

Deep Roy
Starship '87

Selena Royle
Courage of Lassie '46

Christopher Rozycki
Truly, Madly, Deeply '91

Michael Rubbo ▲
The Peanut Butter
Solution '85
The Return of Tommy
Tricker '94
Tommy Tricker & the Stamp
Traveller '90

Joseph Ruben ▲
The Good Son '93
Money Train '95

Jan Rubes
Courage Mountain '89
D2: The Mighty Ducks '94

Benny Rubin
Mr. Wise Guy '42

Bruce Joel Rubin ▲
My Life '93

Jennifer Rubin
The Crush '93
Permanent Record '88

Talya Rubin
Miracle at Moreaux '86

Israel Rubinek
Avalon '90

Saul Rubinek
Getting Even with Dad '94
I Love Trouble '94
Outside Chance of Maximillian
Glick '88
Undercover Blues '93

John Rubinstein
Another Stakeout '93

Zelda Rubinstein
Poltergeist '82

Poltergeist 2: The Other
Side '86
Poltergeist 3 '88
Sixteen Candles '84
Teen Witch '89
Under the Rainbow '81

Alan Ruck
Ferris Bueller's Day Off '86
Speed '94
Star Trek Generations '94
Three Fugitives '89

Paul Rudd
Clueless '95
Mark Twain's A Connecticut
Yankee in King Arthur's
Court '78

Joshua Rudoy
Harry and the Hendersons '87

Mercedes Ruehl
Big '88
Last Action Hero '93
Leader of the Band '87
Lost in Yonkers '93
Radio Days '87

Charlie Ruggles
Breaking the Ice '38
Bringing Up Baby '38
Follow Me, Boys! '66
The Parent Trap '61
Son of Flubber '63
The Ugly Dachshund '65

Derya Ruggles
Remote '93

Vyto Ruginis
Clean Slate '94

Barbara Ruick
Carousel '56

**Anthony Michael
Ruivivar**
Race the Sun '96
White Fang 2: The Myth of the
White Wolf '94

Janice Rule
American Flyers '85

Sig Rumann
A Day at the Races '37
The Errand Boy '61
A Night at the Opera '35

Kicki Rundgren
My Life as a Dog '85

Joseph Runningfox
Geronimo '93

Jennifer Runyon
18 Again! '88
The In Crowd '88

Ying Ruocheng
Little Buddha '93

RuPaul
The Brady Bunch Movie '95

Barbara Rush
Superdad '73

Deborah Rush
The Purple Rose of Cairo '85

Jared Rushton
Big '88
A Cry in the Wild '90
Honey, I Shrunk the Kids '89
The Lady in White '88

Robert Rusler
Shag: The Movie '89

William Russ
Aspen Extreme '93
Pastime '91
The Right Stuff '83

Brian Russell
Charlie, the Lonesome
Cougar '67

Bryan Russell
Emil and the Detective '64

Chuck Russell ▲
The Mask '94

John Russell
The Blue Bird '40

Ken Russell ▲
The Boy Friend '71
Tommy '75

Keri Russell
Honey, I Blew Up the Kid '92

Kurt Russell
The Barefoot Executive '71
The Best of Times '86
Big Trouble in Little China '86
Captain Ron '92
Charley and the Angel '73
The Computer Wore Tennis
Shoes '69
Follow Me, Boys! '66
The Horse in the Gray Flannel
Suit '68
It Happened at the World's
Fair '63
Mosby's Marauders '66
Now You See Him, Now You
Don't '72
The One and Only, Genuine,
Original Family Band '68
Overboard '87
Stargate '94
Superdad '73
Swing Shift '84
Tombstone '93

Nipsey Russell
Car 54, Where Are You? '94
The Wiz '78

Rosalind Russell
His Girl Friday '40
The Trouble with Angels '66
Where Angels Go, Trouble
Follows '68

Theresa Russell
Being Human '94

James Russo
Beverly Hills Cop '84
Fast Times at Ridgemont
High '82

Rene Russo
Major League '89
Mr. Destiny '90
Outbreak '94

Jon Rust ▲
Smurfs & the Magic Flute '81

Angelo Rutherford
Gentle Ben '69

Ann Rutherford
Andy Hardy Gets Spring
Fever '39
Andy Hardy Meets
Debutante '40
Andy Hardy's Double Life '42
A Christmas Carol '38
Fighting Marines '36
Gone with the Wind '39
Life Begins for Andy
Hardy '41
Love Finds Andy Hardy '38
Secret Life of Walter Mitty '47

Allison Rutledge-Parisi
Metropolitan '90

Susan Ruttan
Chances Are '89
Sweet 15 '90

Basil Ruysdael
Davy Crockett, King of the
Wild Frontier '55

David Ryall
Truly, Madly, Deeply '91

Anne Ryan
Three O'Clock High '87

Eileen Ryan
Benny & Joon '93

Eveanna Ryan
War of the Buttons '95

Fran Ryan
Chances Are '89

Ger Ryan
Moll Flanders '96

John P. Ryan
The Right Stuff '83
Three O'Clock High '87

Meg Ryan
French Kiss '95
Innerspace '87
I.Q. '94
Joe Versus the Volcano '90
Prelude to a Kiss '92
Sleepless in Seattle '93
Top Gun '86

Mitchell Ryan
Hot Shots! Part Deux '93
Peter Lundy and the Medicine
Hat Stallion '77
Speechless '94

Peggy Ryan
Miss Annie Rooney '42

Remi Ryan
Ava's Magical Adventure '94
Robocop 3 '91

Robert Ryan
The Boy with the Green
Hair '48

Bobby Rydell
Bye, Bye, Birdie '63

Christopher Rydell
Gotcha! '85
How I Got into College '89

Mark Rydell ▲
The Cowboys '72
Harry & Walter Go to New
York '76
On Golden Pond '81
The Reivers '69
The River '84

Winona Ryder
The Age of Innocence '93
Beetlejuice '88
Boys '96
Edward Scissorhands '90
How to Make an American
Quilt '95
Little Women '94
Lucas '86
Mermaids '90
Reality Bites '94
Welcome Home, Roxy
Carmichael '90

Paul Sabella ▲
All Dogs Go to Heaven 2 '95

Sabu
Elephant Boy '37
The Jungle Book '42
Thief of Baghdad '40
A Tiger Walks '64

Graham Sack
Dunston Checks In '95

William Sadler
Bill & Ted's Bogus
Journey '91
Die Hard 2: Die Harder '90
Freaked '93
Project X '87
The Shawshank
Redemption '94

Elizabeth Sagal
Flashdance '83

William Sage
Boys '96

Marianne Sagebrecht
Bagdad Cafe '88

Bob Saget
Father and Scout '95

Kenji Sahara
Destroy All Monsters '68

Eva Marie Saint
Cancel My Reservation '72
A Christmas to Remember '78
Love Leads the Way '84
North by Northwest '59
Nothing in Common '86
The Russians are Coming, the
Russians are Coming '66

Michael St. Gerard
Hairspray '88

Raymond St. Jacques
Glory '89

Susan St. James
Carbon Copy '81
Love at First Bite '79
Where Angels Go, Trouble
Follows '68

Jill St. John
Diamonds are Forever '71
Out There '95

Michelle St. John
Geronimo '93
Where the Spirit Lives '89

Pat Sajak
Happy Birthday, Bugs: 50
Looney Years '90

S.Z. Sakall
Casablanca '42
Wonder Man '45
Yankee Doodle Dandy '42

Amy Sakasitz
Dennis the Menace '93
A Home of Our Own '93

Harold Sakata
Goin' Coconuts '78

Gene Saks
I.Q. '94
A Thousand Clowns '65

Gene Saks ▲
Brighton Beach Memoirs '86
The Odd Couple '68

Chloe Salaman
Dragonslayer '81

Theresa Saldana
I Wanna Hold Your Hand '78
The Night Before '88

Chic Sale
Treasure Island '34

Kario Salem
1492: Conquest of
Paradise '92

Pamela Salem
Never Say Never Again '83

Meredith Salenger
Dream a Little Dream '89
The Journey of Natty
  Gann '85

Sam Saletta
The Little Rascals '94

Diane Salinger
The Butcher's Wife '91
Pee Wee's Big Adventure '85
The Scarlet Letter '95

Matt Salinger
Captain America '89

Benjamin Salisbury
Captain Ron '92

Leo Salkin ▲
2000 Year Old Man '82

John Salley
Eddie '96

Albert Salmi
Dragonslayer '81
Menace on the Mountain '70

Mikael Salomon ▲
A Far Off Place '93

Frank S. Salsedo
Magic in the Water '95

Jennifer Salt
Play It Again, Sam '72

Karen Salt
Prince Brat and the Whipping
  Boy '95

Victor Salva ▲
Powder '95

Emma Samms
Delirious '91

Chris Samples
King of the Hill '93

Robert Sampson
The Grass is Always Greener
  Over the Septic Tank '78
Robot Jox '89

Will Sampson
Fish Hawk '79
Poltergeist 2: The Other
  Side '86

Coke Sams ▲
Ernest Goes to School '94

Jeffrey D. Sams
Waiting to Exhale '95

Andy Samuels
The Return of Our Gang '25

Haydon Samuels
I Live with Me Dad '86

Laura San Giacomo
Quigley Down Under '90
Stuart Saves His Family '94

Pedro Sanchez
White Fang and the
  Hunter '85

Aitana Sanchez-Gijon
A Walk in the Clouds '95

Paul Sand
The Legend of Sleepy
  Hollow '79
Once Upon a Brothers
  Grimm '77
Teen Wolf Too '87

Walter Sande
Don Winslow of the Navy '43

Otto Sander
Wings of Desire '88

Deion Sanders
Celtic Pride '96

George Sanders
Foreign Correspondent '40
In Search of the
  Castaways '62
Rebecca '40
A Shot in the Dark '64

Jay O. Sanders
Angels in the Outfield '94
The Big Green '95
Mr. Destiny '90
My Boyfriend's Back '93

William Sanderson
Wagons East '94

Adam Sandler
Airheads '94
Billy Madison '94
Coneheads '93
Happy Gilmore '96
Mixed Nuts '94

Miguel Sandoval
Clear and Present Danger '94
Mrs. Winterbourne '96
Up Close and Personal '96

Mark Sandrich ▲
Follow the Fleet '36
Holiday Inn '42
Shall We Dance '37

Julian Sands
Arachnophobia '90
Oxford Blues '84

Sonny Sands
The Bellboy '60

Tommy Sands
Babes in Toyland '61

Gary Sandy
Troll '85

Arlene Sanford ▲
A Very Brady Sequel '96

Erskine Sanford
Citizen Kane '41

Isabel Sanford
Love at First Bite '79

Renoly Santiago
Dangerous Minds '95
Hackers '95

Saundra Santiago
Beat Street '84

Joseph Santley ▲
The Cocoanuts '29

Reni Santoni
Dead Men Don't Wear
  Plaid '82
Guns of the Magnificent
  Seven '69

Ade Sapara
Crusoe '89

David Saperstein ▲
Beyond the Stars '89

Mia Sara
Call of the Wild '93
Ferris Bueller's Day Off '86
Legend '86
Timecop '94

Deran Sarafian ▲
Terminal Velocity '94

Chris Sarandon
Collision Course '89
Goodbye, Miss 4th of July '88
The Princess Bride '87

Susan Sarandon
Beauty and the Beast '83
The Client '94
The Front Page '74
The Great Waldo Pepper '75
Little Women '94
Lorenzo's Oil '92
Safe Passage '94

Dick Sargent
Billie '65
Teen Witch '89

Joseph Sargent ▲
MacArthur '77
Skylark '93

Michael Sarrazin
Gumball Rally '76

Gailard Sartain
Ernest Goes to Camp '87
Ernest Goes to Jail '90
Getting Even with Dad '94
Leader of the Band '87
The Real McCoy '93
Speechless '94
Stop! or My Mom Will
  Shoot '92
Wagons East '94

Katsuhiko Sasakai
Godzilla vs. Megalon '76

Oley Sassone ▲
Fast Getaway 2 '94

Ron Satlof ▲
Spiderman: The Deadly
  Dust '78

Paul Satterfield
Arena '88

Alfred Sauchelli Jr.
A Bronx Tale '93

Jennifer Saunders
Muppet Treasure Island '96

Mary Jane Saunders
Sorrowful Jones '49

Terry Saunders
The King and I '56

Carlos Saura ▲
Cria '76

Ben Savage
Big Girls Don't Cry. . .They
  Get Even '92
Little Monsters '89

Fred Savage
The Boy Who Could Fly '86
Happy Birthday, Bugs: 50
  Looney Years '90
Little Monsters '89
The Princess Bride '87
Vice Versa '88
The Wizard '89

John Savage
Bad Company '72
White Squall '96

Dany Saval
Moon Pilot '62

Telly Savalas
Alice in Wonderland '85
Cannonball Run 2 '84
On Her Majesty's Secret
  Service '69

John Savident
Brain Donors '92
Othello '95

Jennifer Savidge
Magic Kid 2 '94

Devon Sawa
Little Giants '94

Toni Sawyer
My Life '93

John Saxon
Battle Beyond the Stars '80
Beverly Hills Cop 3 '94
The Electric Horseman '79
My Mom's a Werewolf '89

John Sayles
Eight Men Out '88
Matinee '92
Straight Talk '92

John Sayles ▲
The Brother from Another
  Planet '84
Eight Men Out '88
Matewan '87
The Secret of Roan Inish '94

Syd Saylor
The Lost Jungle '34

Siluck Saysanasy
The Peanut Butter
  Solution '85

Raphael Sbarge
Back to Hannibal: The Further
  Adventures of Tom Sawyer
  and Huckleberry Finn '90
My Science Project '85

Greta Scacchi
Emma '96
Jefferson in Paris '94

Prunella Scales
Howard's End '92
My Friend Walter '93

Jack Scalia
Storybook '95

Hal Scardino
The Indian in the
  Cupboard '95

Alan Scarfe
The Bay Boy '85

Diana Scarwid
Brenda Starr '86
The Cure '95
Gold Diggers: The Secret of
  Bear Mountain '95
Mommie Dearest '81
Rumble Fish '83
Strange Invaders '83

Wendy Schaal
Innerspace '87
Out There '95

Johnathon Schaech
How to Make an American
  Quilt '95

Armand Schaefer ▲
Fighting with Kit Carson '33
Hurricane Express '32
Law of the Wild '34
The Lost Jungle '34

George Schaefer ▲
Lost Legacy: A Girl Called
  Hatter Fox '77
Once Upon a Scoundrel '73
Who'll Save Our Children?
  '82

Joshua Schaefer
No Dessert Dad, 'Til You Mow
  the Lawn '94

Eric Schaeffer
If Lucy Fell '95

Eric Schaeffer ▲
If Lucy Fell '95

Francis Schaeffer ▲
Baby on Board '92

Franklin J. Schaffner ▲
Lionheart '87
Papillon '73
Planet of the Apes '68

William Schallert
The Computer Wore Tennis
  Shoes '69
House Party 2: The Pajama
  Jam '91
Innerspace '87
Nancy Drew: Mystery of the
  Diamond Triangle '78
Twilight Zone: The Movie '83

Jerry Schatzberg ▲
Misunderstood '84
Reunion '88

Robert Scheerer ▲
Hans Brinker '69
The World's Greatest
  Athlete '73

Roy Scheider
Tiger Town '83
2010 : The Year We Make
  Contact '84

Andrew Scheinman ▲
Little Big League '94

Catherine Schell
Gulliver's Travels '77
On Her Majesty's Secret
  Service '69
Return of the Pink
  Panther '74

Maximilian Schell
The Black Hole '79
A Far Off Place '93
The Freshman '90
Heidi '67
Judgment at Nuremberg '61

Ronnie Schell
Gus '76

August Schellenberg
Free Willy '93
Free Willy 2: The Adventure
  Home '95
Geronimo '93
Iron Will '93

Mary Kate Schellhardt
Apollo 13 '95
What's Eating Gilbert
  Grape '93

Robert Schenkkan
The Manhattan Project '86

Fred Schepisi ▲
Barbarosa '82
Iceman '84
I.Q. '94

Mr. Baseball '92
Roxanne '87

Vincent Schiavelli
The Adventures of Buckaroo
  Banzai Across the Eighth
  Dimension '84
Amadeus '84
Batman Returns '92
Better Off Dead '85
Fast Times at Ridgemont
  High '82
Ghost '90
Prince Brat and the Whipping
  Boy '95
Waiting for the Light '90

Paul Schibli ▲
The Nutcracker Prince '91

Eric Schiff
Toughlove '85

Joseph Schildkraut
The Man in the Iron Mask '39

Gus Schilling
Citizen Kane '41

Vivian Schilling
The Legend of Wolf
  Mountain '92
Savage Land '94

Thomas Schlamme ▲
Miss Firecracker '89
So I Married an Axe
  Murderer '93

Charlie Schlatter
Ed '96
18 Again! '88
Heartbreak Hotel '88
Police Academy: Mission to
  Moscow '94

John Schlesinger ▲
Madame Sousatzka '88

Dan Schneider
Better Off Dead '85

Fred Schneider
Down Periscope '96

John Schneider
Christmas Comes to Willow
  Creek '87

Marc Schneider
Jane Eyre '96

Rob Schneider
The Adventures of
  Pinocchio '96
The Beverly Hillbillies '93
Home Alone 2: Lost in New
  York '92
Judge Dredd '95
Surf Ninjas '93

Romy Schneider
The Hero '71

Ernest B. Schoedsack ▲
King Kong '33
Mighty Joe Young '49
Son of Kong '33

Michael Schoeffling
Mermaids '90
Sixteen Candles '84
Sylvester '85
Wild Hearts Can't Be
  Broken '91

Jill Schoelen
Adventures in Spying '92
Babes in Toyland '86
That Was Then. . .This Is
  Now '85

Reiner Schoene
Return to Treasure Island, Vol.
  1 '85

Jason Schombing
3 Ninjas Kick Back '94
Timecop '94

Inge Schoner
George! '70

Dale Schott ▲
The Care Bears Movie 2: A
  New Generation '86

Paul Schrader ▲
Light of Day '87

Bitty Schram
A League of Their Own '92

Liev Schreiber
Mixed Nuts '94

Rick Schroder
Across the Tracks '89
Call of the Wild '93
Crimson Tide '95
Earthling '80
Hansel and Gretel '82
The Last Flight of Noah's
  Ark '80
Little Lord Fauntleroy '80

Barbet Schroeder ▲
Before and After '95

Frank C. Schroeder ▲
Pistol: The Birth of a
  Legend '90

John Schuck
Butch and Sundance: The
  Early Days '79
Holy Matrimony '94
M*A*S*H '70
My Mom's a Werewolf '89
The New Adventures of Pippi
  Longstocking '88
Star Trek 6: The Undiscovered
  Country '91

Michelle Schuelke
Undercover Blues '93

Rebecca Schull
My Life '93

Emily Schulman
Caddie Woodlawn '88

Albert Schultz
Beethoven Lives Upstairs '92

Carl Schultz ▲
Blue Fin '78
Careful, He Might Hear
You '84

Michael A. Schultz ▲
Car Wash '76
Carbon Copy '81
Cooley High '75
Disorderlies '87
Greased Lightning '77

Joel Schumacher ▲
Batman Forever '95
The Client '94
The Incredible Shrinking
Woman '81
The Lost Boys '87

Hans Schumm
Spy Smasher '42

Reinhold Schunzel
Notorious '46

Harold Schuster ▲
Courage of Black Beauty '57
My Friend Flicka '43
So Dear to My Heart '49
The Tender Years '47

Ivyann Schwan
Problem Child 2 '91

Scott Schwartz
Kidco '83

Arnold Schwarzenegger
Conan the Barbarian '82
Conan the Destroyer '84
Hercules in New York '70
Junior '94
Kindergarten Cop '90
Last Action Hero '93
The Terminator '84
Terminator 2: Judgment
Day '91
True Lies '94
Twins '88
The Villain '79

Eric Schweig
Follow the River '95
The Last of the Mohicans '92
Pontiac Moon '94
Squanto: A Warrior's Tale '94
Tom and Huck '95

David Schwimmer
The Pallbearer '95

Rusty Schwimmer
A Little Princess '95

Annabella Sciorra
The Cure '95
Mr. Wonderful '93

Dean Scofield
Prehysteria! 2 '94

Paul Scofield
A Man for All Seasons '66
Quiz Show '94
When the Whales Came '89

Peter Scolari
Camp Nowhere '94
Happy Birthday, Bugs: 50
Looney Years '90
Mr. Bill's Real-Life
Adventures '86

Martin Scorsese
Quiz Show '94

Martin Scorsese ▲
The Age of Innocence '93

Nicolette Scorsese
Aspen Extreme '93

Izabela Scorupco
Goldeneye '95

Amber Scott
Hook '91

Barry Scott
Ernest Goes to Jail '90

Campbell Scott
Singles '92

Carey Scott
Diving In '90
Making the Grade '84

Connie Scott
Flipper '63

Cynthia Scott ▲
Strangers in Good
Company '91

Debralee Scott
Just Tell Me You Love Me '80
Police Academy '84

Donovan Scott
Goldilocks & the Three
Bears '83
Savannah Smiles '82
Sheena '84

Eric Scott
A Day for Thanks on Walton's
Mountain '82
The Waltons: A Thanksgiving
Story '73
The Waltons: The Children's
Carol '80

George C. Scott
Angus '95
The Day of the Dolphin '73
Movie, Movie '78
Oklahoma Crude '73
Oliver Twist '82
The Prince and the
Pauper '78
Prince Brat and the Whipping
Boy '95

Taps '81

Jonathan Scott
The Chronicles of Narnia '89

Kathryn Leigh Scott
Witches' Brew '79

Larry B. Scott
A Hero Ain't Nothin' But a
Sandwich '78
Revenge of the Nerds '84
SpaceCamp '86
That Was Then. . .This Is
Now '85

Martha Scott
Father Figure '80
The Ten Commandments '56

Oz Scott ▲
Bustin' Loose '81

Randolph Scott
Follow the Fleet '36
Rebecca of Sunnybrook
Farm '38
Susannah of the Mounties '39
To the Last Man '33

Ridley Scott ▲
1492: Conquest of
Paradise '92
Legend '86
White Squall '96

Kristin Scott Thomas
Four Weddings and a
Funeral '93

Tony Scott ▲
Beverly Hills Cop 2 '87
Crimson Tide '95
Top Gun '86

George Scribner ▲
Oliver & Company '88

Susan Seaforth Hayes
Billie '65
Dream Machine '91

Jenny Seagrove
Local Hero '83
Nate and Hayes '83

Douglas Seale
Ernest Saves Christmas '88
Mr. Destiny '90

Ann Sears
The Bridge on the River
Kwai '57

George Seaton ▲
Airport '70
Country Girl '54
Miracle on 34th Street '47

James Seay
Turf Boy '42

Jean Seberg
Airport '70
The Mouse That Roared '59

Paint Your Wagon '69

Douta Seck
Sugar Cane Alley '83

Kyle Secor
City Slickers '91
Untamed Heart '93

John Seda
12 Monkeys '95

Kyra Sedgwick
Cindy Eller '91
Heart and Souls '93
Mr. & Mrs. Bridge '91
Phenomenon '96
Singles '92
Something to Talk About '95

Robert Sedgwick
Morgan Stewart's Coming
Home '87

George Segal
The Cable Guy '96
Carbon Copy '81
Look Who's Talking '89
Look Who's Talking Now '93
Not My Kid '85

Peter Segal ▲
Naked Gun 33 1/3: The Final
Insult '94
Tommy Boy '95

Pamela Segall
Bed of Roses '95
Say Anything '89
Sgt. Bilko '95

Arthur Seidelman
The Kid Who Loved
Christmas '90

Arthur Seidelman ▲
A Friendship in Vienna '88
Hercules in New York '70

Susan Seidelman ▲
Desperately Seeking
Susan '85
Making Mr. Right '86
She-Devil '89

Talia Seider
Houseguest '94

William A. Seiter ▲
Dimples '36
Room Service '38
Stowaway '36
Susannah of the Mounties '39

George B. Seitz ▲
Andy Hardy Meets
Debutante '40
Andy Hardy's Double Life '42
Andy Hardy's Private
Secretary '41
Life Begins for Andy
Hardy '41
Love Finds Andy Hardy '38

Lesley Selander ▲
The Red Stallion '47

David Selby
Rich Kids '79
White Squall '96

Sarah Selby
Huckleberry Finn '75

Marian Seldes
Tom and Huck '95

Henry Selick ▲
James and the Giant
Peach '96
The Nightmare Before
Christmas '93

Connie Sellecca
Captain America 2: Death Too
Soon '79

Tom Selleck
Christopher Columbus: The
Discovery '92
Her Alibi '88
Mr. Baseball '92
Quigley Down Under '90
The Shadow Riders '82
Three Men and a Baby '87
Three Men and a Little
Lady '90

Peter Sellers
Being There '79
The Fiendish Plot of Dr. Fu
Manchu '80
The Mouse That Roared '59
The Party '68
The Pink Panther '64
The Pink Panther Strikes
Again '76
Return of the Pink
Panther '74
Revenge of the Pink
Panther '78
A Shot in the Dark '64
tom thumb '58
Trail of the Pink Panther '82
The World of Henry Orient '64

David Seltzer ▲
Lucas '86

Arna Selznick ▲
The Care Bears Movie '84

Ralph Senensky ▲
A Dream for Christmas '73

Y. Serigawa ▲
Thumbelina '84

Yahoo Serious
Young Einstein '89

Yahoo Serious ▲
Young Einstein '89

Pepe Serna
The Adventures of Buckaroo
Banzai Across the Eighth
Dimension '84

Fandango '85

Nestor Serrano
Brenda Starr '86

Josephine Serre
Jane Eyre '96

Coline Serreau ▲
Three Men and a Cradle '85

John Sessions
Princess Caraboo '94

Roshan Seth
Little Dorrit, Film 1: Nobody's
Fault '88
Little Dorrit, Film 2: Little
Dorrit's Story '88
Street Fighter '94

Brian Setzer
La Bamba '87

Joan Severance
No Holds Barred '89

William Severn
Journey for Margaret '42

Corey Sevier
Goosebumps: A Night in
Terror Tower '96

Dan Seymour
Hard-Boiled Mahoney '47

Jane Seymour
Battlestar Galactica '78
Benji at Work '93
Happy Birthday, Bugs: 50
Looney Years '90
Heidi '93
Live and Let Die '73
Oh, Heavenly Dog! '80
The Scarlet Pimpernel '82
Sinbad and the Eye of the
Tiger '77
Somewhere in Time '80

Ralph Seymour
Rain Man '88

Glenn Shadix
Bingo '91
Dunston Checks In '95
My Summer Story '94

Tom Shadyac ▲
Ace Ventura: Pet
Detective '93
The Nutty Professor '96

Matt Shakman
Meet the Hollowheads '89

Tupac Shakur
Above the Rim '94
Poetic Justice '93

Tony Shalhoub
Honeymoon in Vegas '92
I.Q. '94

Daniel Shalikar
Honey, I Blew Up the Kid '92

Joshua Shalikar
Honey, I Blew Up the Kid '92

Chuck Shamata
Princes in Exile '90

Jeremy Shamos
Kid Colter '85

Garry Shandling
Mixed Nuts '94

Jim Shane
Chasing Dreams '81

Amelia Shankley
Dreamchild '85
The Little Princess '87

Don Shanks
Blood Brothers '77
The Last of the Mohicans '85
The Legend of Wolf
Mountain '92
Life & Times of Grizzly
Adams '74
Mountain Man '77
Spirit of the Eagle '90

John Patrick Shanley ▲
Joe Versus the Volcano '90

Frank Shannon
Flash Gordon Conquers the
Universe '40
Flash Gordon: Rocketship '36

Harry Shannon
Citizen Kane '41

Alan Shapiro ▲
The Crush '93
Flipper '96
Tiger Town '83

Ken Shapiro ▲
Modern Problems '81

Paul Shapiro ▲
Hockey Night '84
Miracle at Moreaux '86

Abdul Hassan Sharif
Zebrahead '92

Omar Sharif
Doctor Zhivago '65
Funny Girl '68
Funny Lady '75
Lawrence of Arabia '62
Oh, Heavenly Dog! '80

David Shark
The Legend of Wolf
Mountain '92

Ray Sharkey
Cop and a Half '93
Zebrahead '92

Albert Sharpe
Darby O'Gill & the Little
People '59

David Sharpe
Silver Stallion '41

Ben Sharpsteen ▲
Dumbo '41
Pinocchio '40

William Shatner
Airplane 2: The Sequel '82
Bill & Ted's Bogus
Journey '91
Happy Birthday, Bugs: 50
Looney Years '90
Judgment at Nuremberg '61
National Lampoon's Loaded
Weapon 1 '93
Star Trek 2: The Wrath of
Khan '82
Star Trek 3: The Search for
Spock '84
Star Trek 4: The Voyage
Home '86
Star Trek 5: The Final
Frontier '89
Star Trek 6: The Undiscovered
Country '91
Star Trek Generations '94
Star Trek: The Motion
Picture '80
Whale of a Tale '76

William Shatner ▲
Star Trek 5: The Final
Frontier '89

Shari Shattuck
Arena '88

Mickey Shaughnessy
The Adventures of Huckleberry
Finn '60
My Dog, the Thief '69

Melville Shavelson ▲
The Seven Little Foys '55
Yours, Mine & Ours '68

Helen Shaver
Born to Be Wild '95
That Night '93
Who Has Seen the Wind? '77
Zebrahead '92

Bobbi Shaw
Beach Blanket Bingo '65
How to Stuff a Wild Bikini '65
Pajama Party '64

Fiona Shaw
Jane Eyre '96
Super Mario Bros. '93
Three Men and a Little
Lady '90
Undercover Blues '93

Martin Shaw
Golden Voyage of Sinbad '73

Montague Shaw
Holt of the Secret Service '42

Oscar Shaw
The Cocoanuts '29

Robert Shaw
Battle of Britain '69
From Russia with Love '63
A Man for All Seasons '66
Robin and Marian '76
The Sting '73

Stan Shaw
Bingo Long Traveling All-Stars
    & Motor Kings '76
Cutthroat Island '95
Houseguest '94

Steve Shaw
Child of Glass '78

Susan Damante Shaw
The Adventures of the
    Wilderness Family '76
Further Adventures of the
    Wilderness Family, Part
    2 '77
Mountain Family
    Robinson '79

Vinessa Shaw
Hocus Pocus '93
Ladybugs '92

Joan Shawlee
Buck Privates Come Home '47
Francis Joins the WACs '54
The Reluctant Astronaut '67

Dick Shawn
The Emperor's New
    Clothes '84
Love at First Bite '79
Maid to Order '87

Wallace Shawn
Clueless '95
The Double O Kid '92
House Arrest '96
How to Be a Perfect Person in
    Just Three Days '84
Mom and Dad Save the
    World '92
The Princess Bride '87
Radio Days '87
Simon '80
Strange Invaders '83

Robert Shaye ▲
Book of Love '91

Linda Shayne ▲
Purple People Eater '88

Tamara Shayne
The Jolson Story '46

James K. Shea ▲
Planet of the Dinosaurs '80

John Shea
Honey, I Blew Up the Kid '92

Tom Shea
Somewhere Tomorrow '85

Al Shear
Tim Tyler's Luck '37

Harry Shearer
The Right Stuff '83

Moira Shearer
The Red Shoes '48
The Tales of Hoffman '51

Donald Shebib ▲
Fish Hawk '79

Ally Sheedy
The Breakfast Club '85
Maid to Order '87
Only the Lonely '91
Oxford Blues '84
Short Circuit '86
The Tin Soldier '95
War Games '83

Charlie Sheen
Courage Mountain '89
Eight Men Out '88
Ferris Bueller's Day Off '86
Hot Shots! Part Deux '93
Lucas '86
Major League '89
Major League 2 '94
Terminal Velocity '94
The Three Musketeers '93
Young Guns '88

Martin Sheen
The American President '95
Beverly Hills Brats '89
Beyond the Stars '89
Born Wild '95
Gettysburg '93
The Little Girl Who Lives
    Down the Lane '76
Man, Woman & Child '83
No Drums, No Bugles '71

Michael Sheen
Othello '95

Chad Sheets
Dirt Bike Kid '86
Lone Star Kid '88

Craig Sheffer
Fire in the Sky '93
The Program '93
A River Runs Through It '92
Some Kind of Wonderful '87
That Was Then. . .This Is
    Now '85

Johnny Sheffield
Tarzan Finds a Son '39
Tarzan's New York
    Adventure '42
Tarzan's Secret Treasure '41

Gene Sheldon
The Sign of Zorro '60
Toby Tyler '59
Zorro, Vol. 1 '58

Stephen Shellan
Dr. Jekyll and Ms. Hyde '95
A River Runs Through It '92

Adrienne Shelly
Big Girls Don't Cry. . .They
    Get Even '92

Marlee Shelton
The Sandlot '93

Reid Shelton
Breakin' Through '84

Sam Shepard
Baby Boom '87
Country '84
The Pelican Brief '93
The Right Stuff '83
Safe Passage '94
Steel Magnolias '89

Cybill Shepherd
Chances Are '89
The Heartbreak Kid '72
Once Upon a Crime '92

Suzanne Shepherd
The Jerky Boys '95

Anthony Sher
Erik the Viking '89

Jack Sher ▲
The Three Worlds of
    Gulliver '59

Jamey Sheridan
All I Want for Christmas '91
Talent for the Game '91

Jim Sheridan
Moll Flanders '96

Michael J. Sheridan ▲
That's Entertainment, Part
    3 '93

Nicolette Sheridan
Spy Hard '96
The Sure Thing '85

Richard Sheridan
The Secret of Roan Inish '94

Alan Sherman
Pepper and His Wacky
    Taxi '72

Gary Sherman ▲
Lisa '90
Poltergeist 3 '88

George Sherman ▲
Big Jake '71

Tudor Sherrard
Heartbreak Hotel '88

Ravi Sheth
Kim '84

Vladek Sheybal
The Boy Friend '71

Toshio Shibaki
Godzilla vs. the Smog
    Monster '72

Arthur Shields
The Corn is Green '45
How Green was My Valley '41
The Quiet Man '52

Brooke Shields
Born Wild '95
Brenda Starr '86
Freaked '93
The Prince of Central Park '77

Nicholas Shields
Princes in Exile '90

James Shigeta
Die Hard '88
Flower Drum Song '61

Armin Shimerman
Arena '88

Sab Shimono
Gung Ho '85
Teenage Mutant Ninja Turtles
    3 '93
3 Ninjas Kick Back '94

Nelson Shin ▲
Transformers: The Movie '86

Sofia Shinas
The Crow '93

David Shiner
Man of the House '95

Toshi Shioya
Mr. Baseball '92

John Wesley Shipp
The Flash '90
The NeverEnding Story 2: Next
    Chapter '91

Talia Shire
Hyper-Sapien: People from
    Another Star '86
Lionheart '87
Mark Twain and Me '91
Rad '86
Rip van Winkle '85
Rocky '76
Rocky 2 '79
Rocky 3 '82
Rocky 4 '85
Rocky 5 '90

Anne Shirley
Anne of Green Gables '34

Bill Shirley
Abbott and Costello Meet
    Captain Kidd '52

Cathie Shirriff
Star Trek 3: The Search for
    Spock '84

Lee Sholem ▲
Superman & the Mole
    Men '51
Tobor the Great '54

Dan Shor
Bill & Ted's Excellent
 Adventure '89
Tron '82

Dinah Shore
Fun & Fancy Free '47
Oh, God! '77
Till the Clouds Roll By '46

Pauly Shore
Bio-Dome '96
Dream Date '93
Encino Man '92
In the Army Now '94
Jury Duty '95
Son-in-Law '93

Richard Shorr ▲
Witches' Brew '79

Bobby Short
For Love or Money '93

Kathryn Short
Goosebumps: A Night in
 Terror Tower '96

Martin Short
Captain Ron '92
Clifford '92
Father of the Bride '91
Father of the Bride Part II '95
Innerspace '87
Tall Tales and Legends:
 Johnny Appleseed '86
Three Amigos '86
Three Fugitives '89

**Max Casey Adams
 Showalter**
Racing with the Moon '84
Sixteen Candles '84

Anne Shropshire
Something to Talk About '95

Elisabeth Shue
Adventures in Babysitting '87
Back to the Future, Part 2 '89
Back to the Future, Part 3 '90
Heart and Souls '93
The Karate Kid '84

Richard B. Shull
The Big Bus '76
Housesitter '92
Splash '84
Trapped In Paradise '94

Charles Shyer ▲
Baby Boom '87
Father of the Bride '91
Father of the Bride Part II '95
I Love Trouble '94
Irreconcilable Differences '84

Jane Sibbett
It Takes Two '95

George Sidney ▲
Anchors Aweigh '45
Bye, Bye, Birdie '63
The Three Musketeers '48

Sylvia Sidney
Beetlejuice '88

Donald Siegel
Invasion of the Body
 Snatchers '78

Donald Siegel ▲
The Shootist '76

Casey Siemaszko
Back to the Future '85
Back to the Future, Part 2 '89
Milk Money '94
Miracle of the Heart: A Boys
 Town Story '86
Of Mice and Men '92
Secret Admirer '85
Stand By Me '86
Three O'Clock High '87
Young Guns '88

Nina Siemaszko
Airheads '94
The American President '95
Tucker: The Man and His
 Dream '88

Gregory Sierra
Honey, I Blew Up the Kid '92
Hot Shots! Part Deux '93

Simone Signoret
Madame Rosa '77

James B. Sikking
The Electric Horseman '79
Ollie Hopnoodle's Haven of
 Bliss '88
The Pelican Brief '93
Star Trek 3: The Search for
 Spock '84

Brad Silberling ▲
Casper '95

Geno Silva
Geronimo '93

Henry Silva
Alligator '80
Buck Rogers in the 25th
 Century '79
Cinderfella '60
Man & Boy '71
Never a Dull Moment '68

Trinidad Silva
The Night Before '88

Claudia Silver
Crossing Delancey '88

Fawn Silver
Terror in the Jungle '68

Joan Micklin Silver
How to Be a Perfect Person in
 Just Three Days '84

Joan Micklin Silver ▲
Big Girls Don't Cry. . .They
 Get Even '92
Crossing Delancey '88

Joe Silver
The Apprenticeship of Duddy
 Kravitz '74

Marisa Silver ▲
Old Enough '84
Permanent Record '88

Ron Silver
Oh, God! You Devil '84
Romancing the Stone '84
Timecop '94

Tracy Silver
Fast Forward '84

Frank Silvera
Miracle of Our Lady of
 Fatima '52

Jay Silverheels
Indian Paint '64
The Lone Ranger '56
The Lone Ranger: Code of the
 Pioneers '55

Jonathan Silverman
Breaking the Rules '92
Brighton Beach Memoirs '86
Death Becomes Her '92
Little Big League '94
Little Sister '92
Weekend at Bernie's '89
Weekend at Bernie's 2 '93

Candace Silvers
My Science Project '85

Phil Silvers
The Boatniks '70
The Cheap Detective '78
The Chicken Chronicles '77

Alicia Silverstone
Clueless '95
The Crush '93

Alastair Sim
The Belles of St. Trinian's '53
Blue Murder at St.
 Trinian's '56
A Christmas Carol '51
The Littlest Horse Thieves '76
Stage Fright '50

Michael Simkins
Heidi '93

Anthony Simmons
Sherlock: Undercover Dog '94

Beverly Simmons
Buck Privates Come Home '47

Jean Simmons
Androcles and the Lion '52
Guys and Dolls '55
Heidi '67
How to Make an American
 Quilt '95

Pat Simmons
My Science Project '85

Peter Simmons
Renaissance Man '94

Francis Simon ▲
The Chicken Chronicles '77

J. Piquer Simon ▲
Where Time Began '77

Paul Simon
Annie Hall '77

Robert Simon
The Nine Lives of Elfego
 Baca '58

Robert F. Simon
Spiderman: The Deadly
 Dust '78

Freddie Simpson
A League of Their Own '92

Megan Simpson ▲
Alex '92

O.J. Simpson
Hambone & Hillie '84
The Naked Gun: From the
 Files of Police Squad '88
Naked Gun 33 1/3: The Final
 Insult '94
Naked Gun 2 1/2: The Smell
 of Fear '91

Raeanin Simpson
Little Heroes '91

Joan Sims
The Canterville Ghost '96
One of Our Dinosaurs Is
 Missing '75

Frank Sinatra
Anchors Aweigh '45
Cannonball Run 2 '84
Guys and Dolls '55
High Society '56
On the Town '49
That's Entertainment '74
Till the Clouds Roll By '46

Frank Sinatra Jr.
Pepper and His Wacky
 Taxi '72

Sinbad
Coneheads '93
Houseguest '94
Necessary Roughness '91

Gordon John Sinclair
Erik the Viking '89
Gregory's Girl '80

Madge Sinclair
Almos' a Man '78
Conrack '74

Ronald Sinclair
Thoroughbreds Don't Cry '37

Donald Sinden
The Canterville Ghost '96

The Island at the Top of the
World '74

Bryan Singer ▲
The Usual Suspects '95

Lori Singer
Footloose '84
The Man with One Red
Shoe '85

Marc Singer
Beastmaster '82
Beastmaster 2: Through the
Portal of Time '91

John Singleton ▲
Boyz N the Hood '91
Poetic Justice '93

Gary Sinise
Apollo 13 '95
Forrest Gump '94
Jack the Bear '93
A Midnight Clear '92
Of Mice and Men '92

Gary Sinise ▲
Of Mice and Men '92

Marina Sirtis
Star Trek Generations '94
Star Trek the Next Generation
Episode 1-2: Encounter at
Farpoint '87

Kathleen Sisk
The Girl Who Spelled
Freedom '86

Jeremy Sisto
Clueless '95
White Squall '96

Meadow Sisto
Captain Ron '92

Errol Sitahal
A Little Princess '95

Pedzisai Sithole
African Journey '89

Frank Sivero
Cop and a Half '93

Eva Six
Beach Party '63

Tom Sizemore
Heart and Souls '93

Calvin Skaggs ▲
The Fig Tree '87

Lilia Skala
Flashdance '83
Heartland '81
Lilies of the Field '63

Stellan Skarsgard
Wind '92

Tom Skerritt
Ice Castles '79
Maid to Order '87

M*A*S*H '70
Poltergeist 3 '88
A River Runs Through It '92
Silence of the North '81
SpaceCamp '86
Steel Magnolias '89
Top Gun '86

Anita Skinner
Girlfriends '78

Jerzy Skolimowski
Big Shots '87

Sel Skolnick
Manny's Orphans '78

Ione Skye
Samantha '92
Say Anything '89

Tristine Skyler
Kidco '83

Demian Slade
Better Off Dead '85

Max Elliott Slade
Apollo 13 '95
3 Ninjas '92
3 Ninjas Kick Back '94

Jeremy Slate
Dream Machine '91

Christian Slater
Bed of Roses '95
Beyond the Stars '89
Broken Arrow '95
Gleaming the Cube '89
Kuffs '92
Legend of Billie Jean '85
Robin Hood: Prince of
Thieves '91
Tucker: The Man and His
Dream '88
Untamed Heart '93
The Wizard '89

Helen Slater
City Slickers '91
Lassie '94
Legend of Billie Jean '85
Supergirl '84

Ryan Slater
The Amazing Panda
Adventure '95

Leo Slezak
Baron Munchausen '43

Walter Slezak
Bedtime for Bonzo '51
Black Beauty '71
Emil and the Detective '64
Sinbad the Sailor '47
Treasure Island '72
The Wonderful World of the
Brothers Grimm '62

Holly Goldberg Sloan ▲
The Big Green '95

Everett Sloane
Citizen Kane '41
The Disorderly Orderly '64

Georgia Slowe
The Black Arrow '84

Errol Slue
Baby on Board '92

Jean Smart
The Brady Bunch Movie '95
Homeward Bound: The
Incredible Journey '93
Project X '87

Stian Smestad
Shipwrecked '90

Robert Smigel
Happy Gilmore '96

Jack Smight ▲
Airport '75 '75
Airport '77 '77
Fast Break '79

Yakov Smirnoff
The Adventures of Buckaroo
Banzai Across the Eighth
Dimension '84

Alexis Smith
The Age of Innocence '93
Casey's Shadow '78
The Horn Blows at
Midnight '45
The Little Girl Who Lives
Down the Lane '76
Tough Guys '86

Anna Deavere Smith
The American President '95
Dave '93
Philadelphia '93

Bill Smith
Spirit of the Eagle '90

Brandon Smith
Powder '95

Britta Smith
Moll Flanders '96

Bruce Smith ▲
Bebe's Kids '92

Bubba Smith
Police Academy '84
Police Academy 2: Their First
Assignment '85
Police Academy 3: Back in
Training '86
Police Academy 4: Citizens on
Patrol '87
Police Academy 5: Assignment
Miami Beach '88
Police Academy 6: City Under
Siege '89

Sir C. Aubrey Smith
Little Lord Fauntleroy '36
Rebecca '40
Thoroughbreds Don't Cry '37

Wee Willie Winkie '37

Charles Martin Smith
American Graffiti '73
The Buddy Holly Story '78
Culpepper Cattle Co. '72
Herbie Goes Bananas '80
More American Graffiti '79
Never Cry Wolf '83
No Deposit, No Return '76
The Road Home '95
Speechless '94
Starman '84

Charles Martin Smith ▲
Boris and Natasha: The
Movie '92

Cliff Smith ▲
Radio Patrol '37

Cotter Smith
K-9 '89
The Last Prostitute '91

Cynthia Smith
Benji '74
For the Love of Benji '77

Dean Smith
Seven Alone '75

Gregory Edward Smith
Harriet the Spy '96
Leapin' Leprechauns '95

Jaclyn Smith
The Night They Saved
Christmas '87

John N. Smith ▲
Dangerous Minds '95

Kevin Smith
Mallrats '95

Kevin Smith ▲
Clerks '94
Mallrats '95

Kurtwood Smith
The Crush '93
Dead Poets Society '89
Robocop '87
Star Trek 6: The Undiscovered
Country '91

Lane Smith
The Mighty Ducks '92
The Scout '94
Son-in-Law '93

Lewis Smith
The Adventures of Buckaroo
Banzai Across the Eighth
Dimension '84
The Heavenly Kid '85

Lois Smith
Green Card '90
Holy Matrimony '94
How to Make an American
Quilt '95
Skylark '93

Madeleine Smith
Live and Let Die '73

Madolyn Smith
Funny Farm '88
2010 : The Year We Make
  Contact '84

Maggie Smith
Clash of the Titans '81
Death on the Nile '78
Evil Under the Sun '82
Hook '91
The Prime of Miss Jean
  Brodie '69
The Secret Garden '93
Sister Act '92
Sister Act 2: Back in the
  Habit '93

Mel Smith
Brain Donors '92
The Princess Bride '87

Mel Smith ▲
Radioland Murders '94

Paul Smith
The Fire in the Stone '85
Maverick '94
Popeye '80

Putter Smith
Diamonds are Forever '71

Queenie Smith
The Great Rupert '50

Rex Smith
The Pirates of Penzance '83
Snow White and the Seven
  Dwarfs '83
The Trial of the Incredible
  Hulk '89

Robin Smith
Bopha! '93

Roy Allen Smith ▲
The Land Before Time 3: The
  Time of the Great
  Giving '95

Shawn Smith
The River Rat '84

Shawnee Smith
Summer School '87

Shelley Smith
The Fantastic World of D.C.
  Collins '84

Will Smith
Bad Boys '95
Independence Day '96
Made in America '93

William Smith
Conan the Barbarian '82

Willie E. Smith
Legend of Boggy Creek '75

Yeardley Smith
City Slickers '91
Legend of Billie Jean '85

J. Smith-Cameron
Harriet the Spy '96

Alan Smithee ▲
Morgan Stewart's Coming
  Home '87

Jan Smithers
Where the Lilies Bloom '74

Wesley Snipes
Major League '89
Money Train '95
To Wong Foo, Thanks for
  Everything, Julie
  Newmar '95
Wildcats '86

Carrie Snodgress
Across the Tracks '89
8 Seconds '94

Suzanne Snyder
The Night Before '88

Barry Sobel
Doc Hollywood '91

Leelee Sobieski
A Horse for Danny '95

Steven Soderbergh ▲
King of the Hill '93

Lars Soderdahl
Brothers Lionheart '85

Rena Sofa
Twinsitters '95

Iain Softley ▲
Backbeat '94
Hackers '95

Marilyn Sokol
The Goodbye Girl '77

Alec Sokolow ▲
Frankenstein Sings . . . The
  Movie '95

Paul Soles
Beethoven Lives Upstairs '92

P.J. Soles
Out There '95
Rock 'n' Roll High School '79

Peter J. Solmo ▲
Jack & the Beanstalk '76

Bruce Solomon
Foul Play '78

Ola Solum ▲
The Polar Bear King '94

Suzanne Somers
American Graffiti '73

Julie Sommars
Herbie Goes to Monte
  Carlo '77

Elke Sommer
The Double McGuffin '79
A Shot in the Dark '64
Ten Little Indians '75

Josef Sommer
Chances Are '89
Iceman '84
The Mighty Ducks '92

Stephen Sommers ▲
The Adventures of Huck
  Finn '93
Catch Me. . .If You Can '89
Rudyard Kipling's The Jungle
  Book '94

Gale Sondergaard
The Blue Bird '40

Barry Sonnenfeld ▲
The Addams Family '91
Addams Family Values '93
For Love or Money '93

Jack Soo
Flower Drum Song '61
Return from Witch
  Mountain '78

Louise Sorel
When Every Day was the
  Fourth of July '78

Linda Sorensen
Kavik, the Wolf Dog '84

Louis Sorin
Animal Crackers '30

Arleen Sorkin
It's Pat: The Movie '94

Mira Sorvino
Beautiful Girls '96
Quiz Show '94

Paul Sorvino
Almost Partners '87
The Day of the Dolphin '73
Dick Tracy '90
A Fine Mess '86
Oh, God! '77
The Rocketeer '91
Turk 182! '85

Dimitri Sotirakis ▲
Beverly Hills Brats '89

Talisa Soto
Mortal Kombat: The
  Movie '95

David Soul
Dog Pound Shuffle '75
Homeward Bound '80
Salem's Lot '79

Sissy Spacek
Coal Miner's Daughter '80
The River '84

Trading Mom '94

Kevin Spacey
Dad '89
Iron Will '93
Outbreak '94
Rocket Gibraltar '88
The Usual Suspects '95

David Spade
Black Sheep '96
Coneheads '93
P.C.U. '94
Tommy Boy '95

James Spader
Baby Boom '87
Mannequin '87
Pretty in Pink '86
Stargate '94

Merrie Spaeth
The World of Henry Orient '64

Timothy Spall
Crusoe '89

Laurette Spang
Battlestar Galactica '78

Joe Spano
American Graffiti '73

Vincent Spano
Alive '93
The Black Stallion
  Returns '83
The Double McGuffin '79
Indian Summer '93
Over the Edge '79
Rumble Fish '83

Adrian Sparks
My Stepmother Is an
  Alien '88

George Spartels
Mad Max: Beyond
  Thunderdome '85

Camilla Sparv
Downhill Racer '69

Bernard Spear
Yentl '83

Hermann Speelmanns
Baron Munchausen '43

George Spell
A Dream for Christmas '73
Man & Boy '71

Georgina Spelvin
Police Academy '84

Bruce Spence
Mad Max: Beyond
  Thunderdome '85

Peter Spence
Crazy Moon '87

Bud Spencer
Aladdin '86

John Spencer
Forget Paris '95

Wendie Jo Sperber
Back to the Future '85
Back to the Future, Part 3 '90
I Wanna Hold Your Hand '78
Moving Violations '85

Penelope Spheeris ▲
The Beverly Hillbillies '93
Black Sheep '96
The Little Rascals '94
Wayne's World '92

Bryan Spicer ▲
Mighty Morphin Power
    Rangers: The Movie '95

Steven Spielberg ▲
Always '89
Close Encounters of the Third
    Kind '77
Empire of the Sun '87
E.T.: The Extra-Terrestrial '82
Hook '91
Indiana Jones and the Last
    Crusade '89
Indiana Jones and the Temple
    of Doom '84
Jurassic Park '93
Raiders of the Lost Ark '81
Twilight Zone: The Movie '83

Laurent Spielvogel
French Kiss '95

Bob Spiers ▲
That Darn Cat '96

Klinton Spilsbury
Legend of the Lone
    Ranger '81

Martin J. Spinelli ▲
Sourdough '77

Brent Spiner
Independence Day '96
Star Trek Generations '94
Star Trek the Next Generation
    Episode 1-2: Encounter at
    Farpoint '87

Victor Spinetti
Magical Mystery Tour '67
Return of the Pink
    Panther '74

Lisa Spoonhauer
Clerks '94

Michael Sporn ▲
Abel's Island '88
Jazz Time Tale

Greg Spottiswood
Looking for Miracles '90

Roger Spottiswoode ▲
The Best of Times '86
Stop! or My Mom Will
    Shoot '92
Turner and Hooch '89

G.D. Spradlin
Canadian Bacon '94
One on One '77
Tank '83

Tom Spratley
Where the Lilies Bloom '74

Elizabeth Spriggs
Sense and Sensibility '95

Pamela Springsteen
Fast Times at Ridgemont
    High '82
My Science Project '85

Robert Stack
Airplane! '80
Joe Versus the Volcano '90
Plain Clothes '88

James Stacy
Something Wicked This Way
    Comes '83

Jim Stafford
Kid Colter '85

Nick Stahl
The Man Without a Face '93
Safe Passage '94
Tall Tale: The Unbelievable
    Adventures of Pecos
    Bill '95

Brent Stait
Call of the Wild '93

James Staley
American Dreamer '84

Sage Stallone
Rocky 5 '90

Sylvester Stallone
Cannonball '76
Judge Dredd '95
The Lords of Flatbush '74
Oscar '91
Over the Top '86
Rhinestone '84
Rocky '76
Rocky 2 '79
Rocky 3 '82
Rocky 4 '85
Rocky 5 '90
Stop! or My Mom Will
    Shoot '92
Victory '81

Sylvester Stallone ▲
Rocky 2 '79
Rocky 3 '82
Rocky 4 '85

Hal Stalmaster
Johnny Tremain & the Sons of
    Liberty '58

Terence Stamp
The Real McCoy '93
Superman 1: The Movie '78
Superman 2 '80
The Thief of Baghdad '78

Young Guns '88

Lionel Stander
Once Upon a Time in the
    West '68
Treasure Island '72

John Standing
Chaplin '92

Arnold Stang
Dennis the Menace '93
Ghost Dad '90
Hercules in New York '70
The Wonderful World of the
    Brothers Grimm '62

Florence Stanley
Trapped In Paradise '94

Kim Stanley
The Right Stuff '83

Lauren Stanley
Mac and Me '88

Harry Dean Stanton
The Adventures of Huckleberry
    Finn '60
Down Periscope '96
Dream a Little Dream '89
One Magic Christmas '85
Pretty in Pink '86
Rip van Winkle '85
Where the Lilies Bloom '74

John Stanton
Dusty '85

Robert Stanton
Dennis the Menace '93

Jean Stapleton
Cinderella '84
Jack & the Beanstalk '83
Up the Down Staircase '67

Maureen Stapleton
Airport '70
Bye, Bye, Birdie '63
Cocoon '85
Cocoon: The Return '88
Doin' Time on Planet
    Earth '88
The Electric Grandmother '81
Johnny Dangerously '84
The Money Pit '86
On the Right Track '81
Trading Mom '94

Nicola Stapleton
Courage Mountain '89

Alex Stapley
Baby on Board '92

Holly Stapley
Baby on Board '92

Jo Jo Starbuck
The Cutting Edge '92

Jonathan Stark
Project X '87

Koo Stark
Electric Dreams '84

Kay Starr
The Pied Piper of Hamelin '57

Mike Starr
Dumb & Dumber '94
Two If by Sea '95

Ringo Starr
Alice in Wonderland '85
A Hard Day's Night '64
Help! '65
Magical Mystery Tour '67

Jack Starrett ▲
On the Edge: The Survival of
    Dana '79

Imelda Staunton
Much Ado About Nothing '93
Sense and Sensibility '95

Mary Stavin
House '86

Alison Steadman
The Adventures of Baron
    Munchausen '89
Kipperbang '82

Red Steagall
Benji the Hunted '87

Ted Steedman
Bill & Ted's Excellent
    Adventure '89

Amy Steel
Walk Like a Man '87

Jadrien Steele
The Secret Garden '87

Karen Steele
Trap on Cougar Mountain '72

Tommy Steele
Finian's Rainbow '68
G-Men Never Forget '48
The Happiest Millionaire '67

Jessica Steen
Sing '89

Mary Steenburgen
Back to the Future, Part 3 '90
The Butcher's Wife '91
Clifford '92
Cross Creek '83
Goin' South '78
Little Red Riding Hood '83
Miss Firecracker '89
My Summer Story '94
One Magic Christmas '85
Parenthood '89
Philadelphia '93
Pontiac Moon '94
Powder '95
What's Eating Gilbert
    Grape '93

Rod Steiger
Doctor Zhivago '65

Oklahoma! '55
Out There '95

Margaret Sophie Stein
Sarah, Plain and Tall '91
Skylark '93

David Steinberg ▲
Casey at the Bat '85

Robert J. Steinmiller Jr.
Bingo '91
Jack the Bear '93

Frederick Stephani ▲
Flash Gordon: Rocketship '36

Barbara Stephens
Hector's Bunyip '86

Perry Stephens
Two Bits & Pepper '95

Robert Stephens
Chaplin '92
Empire of the Sun '87
The Prime of Miss Jean
    Brodie '69
Searching for Bobby
    Fischer '93

Henry Stephenson
Challenge to Lassie '49
Oliver Twist '48
The Prince and the
    Pauper '37
Tarzan Finds a Son '39

Ilse Steppat
On Her Majesty's Secret
    Service '69

Philip Sterling
Death of the Incredible
    Hulk '90

Robert Sterling
Voyage to the Bottom of the
    Sea '61

William Sterling ▲
Alice's Adventures in
    Wonderland '72

Daniel Stern
Breaking Away '79
Bushwhacked '95
Celtic Pride '96
City Slickers '91
City Slickers 2: The Legend of
    Curly's Gold '94
Coupe de Ville '90
Frankenweenie '84
Home Alone '90
Home Alone 2: Lost in New
    York '92
Little Monsters '89
Rookie of the Year '93

Daniel Stern ▲
Rookie of the Year '93

Steven Hilliard Stern ▲
The Devil & Max Devlin '81
Not Quite Human '87

Undergrads '85

Tom Stern ▲
Freaked '93

Frances Sternhagen
Doc Hollywood '91
See You in the Morning '89
Who'll Save Our Children?
    '82

Jimmy Sternman
Boy of Two Worlds '70

Jean-Francois Stevenin
Small Change '76

Andrew Stevens
Munchie '92

Art Stevens ▲
The Fox and the Hound '81

Becca Stevens
Boyd's Shadow '92

Bill Stevens
Boyd's Shadow '92

Carolyn Stevens
Boyd's Shadow '92

Connie Stevens
Back to the Beach '87
The Littlest Angel '69

Craig Stevens
Abbott and Costello Meet Dr.
    Jekyll and Mr. Hyde '52
Blues Busters '50
Since You Went Away '44

Fisher Stevens
The Flamingo Kid '84
Hackers '95
My Science Project '85
Mystery Date '91
Only You '94
Short Circuit '86
Short Circuit 2 '88
Super Mario Bros. '93

George Stevens ▲
Giant '56
I Remember Mama '48
Penny Serenade '41
Shane '53

John Stevens ▲
Boyd's Shadow '92

Katie Stevens
Boyd's Shadow '92

Michael Stevens
The Return of Tommy
    Tricker '94

Rise Stevens
Going My Way '44

Scooter Stevens
Better Off Dead '85

Stella Stevens
The Courtship of Eddie's
    Father '62
The Nutty Professor '63
Where Angels Go, Trouble
    Follows '68

Warren Stevens
Forbidden Planet '56

William Stevens
Boyd's Shadow '92

Adam Stevenson
Back Home '90

Cynthia Stevenson
Forget Paris '95
Home for the Holidays '95

Juliet Stevenson
Emma '96
Truly, Madly, Deeply '91

McLean Stevenson
The Cat from Outer Space '78

Parker Stevenson
Caddie Woodlawn '88
A Separate Peace '73

Rick Stevenson ▲
Magic in the Water '95

Robert Stevenson
One of Our Dinosaurs Is
    Missing '75

Robert Stevenson ▲
The Absent-Minded
    Professor '61
Bedknobs and
    Broomsticks '71
Blackbeard's Ghost '67
Darby O'Gill & the Little
    People '59
The Gnome-Mobile '67
Herbie Rides Again '74
In Search of the
    Castaways '62
The Island at the Top of the
    World '74
Jane Eyre '44
Johnny Tremain & the Sons of
    Liberty '58
Kidnapped '60
The Love Bug '68
Mary Poppins '64
The Misadventures of Merlin
    Jones '63
Monkey's Uncle '65
My Dog, the Thief '69
Old Yeller '57
One of Our Dinosaurs Is
    Missing '75
The Shaggy D.A. '76
Son of Flubber '63
That Darn Cat '65
Tom Brown's School Days '40

Amy Stewart
Mark Twain and Me '91

Catherine Mary Stewart
The Last Starfighter '84
Night of the Comet '84
Weekend at Bernie's '89

French Stewart
Magic Island '95

James Stewart
Airport '77 '77
Bandolero! '68
Dear Brigitte '65
The Glenn Miller Story '54
The Greatest Show on
    Earth '52
How the West was Won '63
It's a Wonderful Life '46
Magic of Lassie '78
Mr. Smith Goes to
    Washington '39
The Philadelphia Story '40
Rear Window '54
The Shootist '76

Kate McGregor Stewart
Father of the Bride '91
Father of the Bride Part II '95

Malcolm Stewart
Timecop '94

Mel Stewart
The Kid with the 200 I.Q. '83

Patrick Stewart
The Canterville Ghost '96
In Search of Dr. Seuss '94
L.A. Story '91
Lady Jane '85
Star Trek Generations '94
Star Trek the Next Generation
    Episode 1-2: Encounter at
    Farpoint '87

Paul Stewart
Citizen Kane '41

Peggy Stewart
Son of Zorro '47

Robert Stewart
Annie O '95

Roy Stewart
Live and Let Die '73

Dorothy Stickney
I Never Sang For My
    Father '70

Phyllis Stickney
The Inkwell '94
What's Love Got to Do With
    It? '93

David Ogden Stiers
Better Off Dead '85
Doc Hollywood '91
Iron Will '93
The Man with One Red
    Shoe '85
Oh, God! '77

Hugo Stiglitz
Robinson Crusoe & the
 Tiger '72

Ryan Stiles
Hot Shots! Part Deux '93

Victor Stiles
Santa Claus Conquers the
 Martians '64

Ben Stiller
Empire of the Sun '87
Happy Gilmore '96
Heavyweights '94
If Lucy Fell '95
Reality Bites '94

Ben Stiller ▲
The Cable Guy '96
Reality Bites '94

Jerry Stiller
Hairspray '88
Heavyweights '94

Whit Stillman ▲
Metropolitan '90

Sara Stimson
Little Miss Marker '80

Sting
The Adventures of Baron
 Munchausen '89

Linda Stirling
The Crimson Ghost '46
Jesse James Rides Again '47
Zorro's Black Whip '44

Alexander Stitt ▲
Grendel, Grendel, Grendel '82

Nigel Stock
The Lion in Winter '68

Amy Stock-Poynton
Beanstalk '94
Bill & Ted's Bogus
 Journey '91
Bill & Ted's Excellent
 Adventure '89

Dean Stockwell
Anchors Aweigh '45
Beverly Hills Cop 2 '87
Bonanza: The Return '93
The Boy with the Green
 Hair '48
Legend of Billie Jean '85
Mr. Wrong '95
The Secret Garden '49
Tucker: The Man and His
 Dream '88

Guy Stockwell
And Now Miguel '66

John Stockwell
My Science Project '85
Quarterback Princess '85
Top Gun '86

Mink Stole
Cry-Baby '90
Serial Mom '94

Shirley Stoler
Malcolm X '92

Josiane Stoleru
Cyrano de Bergerac '90

Brad Stoll
Lost in Yonkers '93

Ben Stoloff ▲
Palooka '34

Eric Stoltz
Fast Times at Ridgemont
 High '82
Fluke '95
The Grass is Always Greener
 Over the Septic Tank '78
Lionheart '87
Little Women '94
Mask '85
Rob Roy '95
Say Anything '89
Some Kind of Wonderful '87

Mark Stolzenberg
Luggage of the Gods '87

Christopher Stone
The Howling '81

Doug Stone
Gordy '95

Harold J. Stone
The Invisible Boy '57

Leonard Stone
Willy Wonka & the Chocolate
 Factory '71

Lewis Stone
Andy Hardy Gets Spring
 Fever '39
Andy Hardy Meets
 Debutante '40
Andy Hardy's Double Life '42
Andy Hardy's Private
 Secretary '41
David Copperfield '35
Life Begins for Andy
 Hardy '41
Love Finds Andy Hardy '38
Love Laughs at Andy
 Hardy '46
Treasure Island '34

Sharon Stone
Allan Quartermain and the
 Lost City of Gold '86
Beyond the Stars '89
Irreconcilable Differences '84
Police Academy 4: Citizens on
 Patrol '87

Larry Storch
The Adventures of Huckleberry
 Finn '78
The Incredible Rocky
 Mountain Race '77

Adam Storke
Death Becomes Her '92

Gale Storm
Smart Alecks '42

Howard Storm ▲
The Three Little Pigs '84

Kjell Stormoen
Shipwrecked '90

Mark Story ▲
Odd Jobs '85

Madeleine Stowe
Another Stakeout '93
The Last of the Mohicans '92
12 Monkeys '95

Michael Stoyanov
Freaked '93

Beatrice Straight
Poltergeist '82
The Princess and the Pea '83

Glenn Strange
Abbott and Costello Meet
 Frankenstein '48

Lee Strasberg
Going in Style '79

Marcia Strassman
And You Thought Your
 Parents Were Weird! '91
Another Stakeout '93
Fast Getaway '91
Honey, I Blew Up the Kid '92
Honey, I Shrunk the Kids '89

David Strathairn
Big Girls Don't Cry. . .They
 Get Even '92
The Brother from Another
 Planet '84
Dolores Claiborne '94
Dominick & Eugene '88
Eight Men Out '88
Iceman '84
A League of Their Own '92
Lost in Yonkers '93
Matewan '87
The River Wild '94
Sneakers '92

Charles Stratton
Munchies '87

Peter Strauss
Whale for the Killing '81

Robert Strauss
Family Jewels '65

Meryl Streep
Before and After '95
Death Becomes Her '92
Kramer vs. Kramer '79
The River Wild '94
She-Devil '89

Barbra Streisand
Funny Girl '68

Funny Lady '75
Hello, Dolly! '69
The Main Event '79
On a Clear Day You Can See
 Forever '70
The Way We Were '73
What's Up, Doc? '72
Yentl '83

Barbra Streisand ▲
Yentl '83

Gail Strickland
Hyper-Sapien: People from
 Another Star '86
Last Time Out '94
The Man in the Moon '91
One on One '77
Oxford Blues '84

Herbert L. Strock ▲
Witches' Brew '79

Woody Strode
Once Upon a Time in the
 West '68

Terje Stromdahl
The Littlest Viking '94

Tami Stronach
The NeverEnding Story '84

Andrew Strong
The Commitments '91

Ken Strong
Sudie & Simpson '90

Shiloh Strong
House of Cards '92

Don Stroud
The Buddy Holly Story '78
The Night the Lights Went Out
 in Georgia '81

Shepperd Strudwick
The Red Pony '49

Carel Struycken
The Addams Family '91
Addams Family Values '93
The Ewoks: Battle for
 Endor '85
Out There '95

Hans Strydom
The Gods Must Be Crazy
 2 '89

Gloria Stuart
My Favorite Year '82
The Poor Little Rich Girl '36
Rebecca of Sunnybrook
 Farm '38

Maxine Stuart
The Rousters '83

Mel Stuart ▲
Willy Wonka & the Chocolate
 Factory '71

Imogen Stubbs
Erik the Viking '89
Sense and Sensibility '95

Stephen Stucker
Airplane! '80
Airplane 2: The Sequel '82

Wes Studi
Dances with Wolves '90
Geronimo: An American
   Legend '93
The Last of the Mohicans '92
Street Fighter '94

John Sturges ▲
Ice Station Zebra '68

David Suchet
Harry and the Hendersons '87
When the Whales Came '89
A World Apart '88

Barbara Sukowa
Johnny Mnemonic '95

Barry Sullivan
Oh, God! '77

Billy L. Sullivan
The Big Green '95
Little Big League '94

Brad Sullivan
Bushwhacked '95
Funny Farm '88
The Jerky Boys '95
Sister Act 2: Back in the
   Habit '93

Ed Sullivan
Bye, Bye, Birdie '63

Francis L. Sullivan
Oliver Twist '48

Fred G. Sullivan ▲
Cold River '81

Kevin Sullivan ▲
Anne of Avonlea '87
Anne of Green Gables '85
Lantern Hill '90
Wild Pony '83

Matthew Sullivan
Max is Missing '95

Susan Sullivan
The Incredible Hulk '77

Slim Summerville
Captain January '36
Rebecca of Sunnybrook
   Farm '38

Clinton Sundberg
The Belle of New York '52

Bjorn Sundquist
Shipwrecked '90

Stephen Surjik ▲
Wayne's World 2 '93

Nicolas Surovy
Forever Young '92

Paul Sutera
The Brady Bunch Movie '95
A Very Brady Sequel '96

Donald Sutherland
Buffy the Vampire Slayer '92
The Great Train Robbery '79
Invasion of the Body
   Snatchers '78
M*A*S*H '70
Max Dugan Returns '83
Outbreak '94
Shadow of the Wolf '92

Edward Sutherland ▲
The Flying Deuces '39

Hal Sutherland ▲
Pinocchio and the Emperor of
   the Night '87

Kiefer Sutherland
The Bay Boy '85
Crazy Moon '87
The Lost Boys '87
Max Dugan Returns '83
Stand By Me '86
The Three Musketeers '93
Young Guns '88

Kristine Sutherland
Honey, I Shrunk the Kids '89

Dolores Sutton
Where Angels Go, Trouble
   Follows '68

John Sutton
Jane Eyre '44

Sarah Sutton
The Moon Stallion '85

Peter Svatek ▲
Mystery of the Million Dollar
   Hockey Puck '80s

Bo Svenson
Andy and the Airwave
   Rangers '89
Big Mo '73
The Great Waldo Pepper '75
Savage Land '94
Wizards of the Lost
   Kingdom '85

E.W. Swackhamer ▲
Man & Boy '71
The Rousters '83

Mack Swain
The Gold Rush '25

Hilary Swank
Buffy the Vampire Slayer '92
The Next Karate Kid '94

Gloria Swanson
Airport '75 '75

Kristy Swanson
Buffy the Vampire Slayer '92

Diving In '90
Mannequin 2: On the
   Move '91
The Phantom '96
The Program '93

Patrick Swayze
Dirty Dancing '87
Father Hood '93
Ghost '90
The Outsiders '83
Tall Tale: The Unbelievable
   Adventures of Pecos
   Bill '95
To Wong Foo, Thanks for
   Everything, Julie
   Newmar '95

Heidi Swedberg
Father and Scout '95

Bob Sweeney
Toby Tyler '59

D.B. Sweeney
The Cutting Edge '92
A Day in October '92
Eight Men Out '88
Fire in the Sky '93

Julia Sweeney
Coneheads '93
Honey, I Blew Up the Kid '92
It's Pat: The Movie '94

Michelle Sweeney
Strangers in Good
   Company '91

Dolph Sweet
Finian's Rainbow '68

Barbara Willis Sweete
Bigfoot: The Unforgettable
   Encounter '94

Cheryl Sweeten
Pajama Party '64

Charles Swenson ▲
Little Rascals Christmas
   Special '79
Twice Upon a Time '83

Inga Swenson
The Miracle Worker '62

Larry Swerdlove ▲
The Skateboard Kid '93

David Swift ▲
The Parent Trap '61
Pollyanna '60

Loretta Swit
Kermit and Piggy Story '85
Miracle at Moreaux '86

Carl "Alfalfa" Switzer
General Spanky '36
The Great Mike '44
Pat and Mike '52
Regl'ar Fellers '41

Michael Switzer ▲
Past the Bleachers '95

Ken Swofford
Bless the Beasts and
   Children '71

Tracy Brooks Swope
The Power of One '92

Basil Sydney
The Three Worlds of
   Gulliver '59
Treasure Island '50

Eric Sykes
Those Daring Young Men in
   Their Jaunty Jalopies '69

Harold Sylvester
Fast Break '79
Innerspace '87

William Sylvester
2001: A Space Odyssey '68

Robert Symonds
Ice Pirates '84
Rumpelstiltskin '86

Jesse Montgomery Sythe
Running Free '94

Keith Szarabajka
Andre '94
Billy Galvin '86
A Perfect World '93

Magna Szubanski
Babe '95

Jeannot Szwarc ▲
Santa Claus: The Movie '85
Somewhere in Time '80
Supergirl '84

Sylvio Tabet ▲
Beastmaster 2: Through the
   Portal of Time '91

Joni Eareckson Tada
Joni '79

Andrew Taft
Lord of the Flies '90

Edward Taft
Lord of the Flies '90

Gene Taft ▲
Blame It on the Night '84

Cary-Hiroyuki Tagawa
Mortal Kombat: The
   Movie '95
The Phantom '96

Rita Taggart
Coupe de Ville '90

Taj Mahal
Bill & Ted's Bogus
   Journey '91
Sounder '72

Reiko Tajima
Godzilla vs. the Cosmic
    Monster '74

Tibor Takacs ▲
The Gate '87

Ken Takakura
Antarctica '84
Mr. Baseball '92

Aya Takanashi
Mr. Baseball '92

George Takei
Star Trek 2: The Wrath of
    Khan '82
Star Trek 3: The Search for
    Spock '84
Star Trek 4: The Voyage
    Home '86
Star Trek 5: The Final
    Frontier '89
Star Trek 6: The Undiscovered
    Country '91
Star Trek: The Motion
    Picture '80

Takeshi
Johnny Mnemonic '95

Charlie Talbert
Angus '95

Lyle Talbot
Atom Man vs. Superman '50
Clipped Wings '53
Our Little Girl '35
Trader Tom of the China
    Seas '54

Michael Talbott
Racing with the Moon '84

Lisa Talerico
Philadelphia '93

Patricia Tallman
Army of Darkness '92

Richard Talmadge ▲
Devil Horse '32

Tetsuro Tamba
You Only Live Twice '67

Russ Tamblyn
Cabin Boy '94
Father of the Bride '50
Father's Little Dividend '51
How the West was Won '63
Seven Brides for Seven
    Brothers '54
tom thumb '58
West Side Story '61
The Wonderful World of the
    Brothers Grimm '62

Jeffrey Tambor
Big Bully '95
Brenda Starr '86
City Slickers '91
Heavyweights '94
Lisa '90

Mr. Mom '83
Pastime '91
Radioland Murders '94
Three O'Clock High '87

Akim Tamiroff
Lt. Robin Crusoe, U.S.N. '66

Sara Tanaka
Race the Sun '96

Toru Tanaka
3 Ninjas '92

Jessica Tandy
*batteries not included '87
The Birds '63
Cocoon '85
Cocoon: The Return '88
Driving Miss Daisy '89
The Light in the Forest '58
The Story Lady '93

Terrell Tannen ▲
A Minor Miracle '83

Daniel Taplitz ▲
Black Magic '92

Rockne Tarkington
Clarence, the Cross-eyed
    Lion '65

John Tarrant
Starship '87

Frank Tashlin ▲
Cinderfella '60
The Disorderly Orderly '64
The Geisha Boy '58
Hollywood or Bust '56

Larenz Tate
The Inkwell '94
Menace II Society '93

Jacques Tati
Mr. Hulot's Holiday '53
Parade '74
Playtime '67

Jacques Tati ▲
Mr. Hulot's Holiday '53
Parade '74
Playtime '67

John Tatoulis ▲
The Silver Stallion: King of
    the Wild Brumbies '94

Bradford Tatum
Down Periscope '96
Powder '95

Roy Tatum
Don't Change My World '83

Norman Taurog ▲
Boys Town '38
The Caddy '53
Girl Crazy '43
It Happened at the World's
    Fair '63
Men of Boys Town '41

Vic Tayback
The Cheap Detective '78
Tut and Tuttle '82
With Six You Get Eggroll '68

Benedict Taylor
The Black Arrow '84

Buck Taylor
And Now Miguel '66
Pony Express Rider '76
Tombstone '93

Charles Taylor
Once Upon a Time . . . When
    We Were Colored '95

Christine Taylor
The Brady Bunch Movie '95
Breaking Free '95
A Very Brady Sequel '96

Clarice Taylor
Sommersby '93

Delores Taylor
Billy Jack '71

Don Taylor
Father of the Bride '50
Father's Little Dividend '51

Don Taylor ▲
Escape from the Planet of the
    Apes '71
Island of Dr. Moreau '77
Tom Sawyer '73

Dub Taylor
Back to the Future, Part 3 '90
My Heroes Have Always Been
    Cowboys '91
Pony Express Rider '76
Spencer's Mountain '63
Support Your Local
    Gunfighter '71

Elizabeth Taylor
Courage of Lassie '46
Father of the Bride '50
Father's Little Dividend '51
The Flintstones '94
Giant '56
Jane Eyre '44
Lassie, Come Home '43
Life with Father '47
Little Women '49
National Velvet '44

Holland Taylor
Cop and a Half '93
The Jewel of the Nile '85
She's Having a Baby '88

Jack Taylor
Where Time Began '77

Lili Taylor
Rudy '93
Say Anything '89

Mark L. Taylor
Arachnophobia '90

Meshach Taylor
Class Act '91
Explorers '85
Mannequin '87
Mannequin 2: On the
    Move '91

Noah Taylor
Flirting '89
The Year My Voice Broke '87

Ray Taylor ▲
Adventures of Smilin' Jack '43
Don Winslow of the Coast
    Guard '43
Don Winslow of the Navy '43
Flaming Frontiers '38
Winners of the West '40

Regina Taylor
Lean on Me '89

Renee Taylor
Delirious '91
The Errand Boy '61

Robert Taylor
Knights of the Round
    Table '53
Miracle of the White
    Stallions '63

Rod Taylor
The Birds '63
Giant '56

Susan Taylor
A River Runs Through It '92

Vaughn Taylor
Francis Goes to the Races '51

Leigh Taylor-Young
Secret Admirer '85

Jun Tazaki
Destroy All Monsters '68

Ludmila Tcherina
The Red Shoes '48

Lewis Teague
Alligator '80

Lewis Teague ▲
Alligator '80
Cat's Eye '85
The Jewel of the Nile '85

Marshall Teague
The Shadow Riders '82

Conway Tearle
Hurricane Express '32

Godfrey Tearle
The 39 Steps '35

Travis Tedford
The Little Rascals '94

Maureen Teefy
Fame '80
Supergirl '84

Shirley Temple
Baby, Take a Bow '34
The Bachelor and the Bobby-
    Soxer '47
The Blue Bird '40
Bright Eyes '34
Captain January '36
Curly Top '35
Dimples '36
Heidi '37
Just Around the Corner '38
Little Miss Broadway '38
Little Miss Marker '34
The Little Princess '39
The Littlest Rebel '35
Miss Annie Rooney '42
Our Little Girl '35
The Poor Little Rich Girl '36
Rebecca of Sunnybrook
    Farm '38
Shirley Temple Baby
    Berlesques '33
Shirley Temple Festival '33
Shirley Temple Storybook
    Theater '60
Since You Went Away '44
Stand Up and Cheer '34
The Story of Seabiscuit '49
Stowaway '36
Susannah of the Mounties '39
To the Last Man '33
Wee Willie Winkie '37

Andy Tennant ▲
It Takes Two '95

Victoria Tennant
L.A. Story '91
Little Lord Fauntleroy '80

Jon Tenney
Free Willy 2: The Adventure
    Home '95
Lassie '94
The Phantom '96
Tombstone '93

Studs Terkel
Eight Men Out '88

Bela Ternovsky ▲
Cat City '87

Hal Terrance
Kid Colter '85

Denine Terry
No Drums, No Bugles '71

Don Terry
Don Winslow of the Coast
    Guard '43
Don Winslow of the Navy '43

John Terry
The Big Green '95
Iron Will '93
Of Mice and Men '92

Nigel Terry
Christopher Columbus: The
    Discovery '92
The Lion in Winter '68

Paul Terry
James and the Giant
    Peach '96

Terry-Thomas
Blue Murder at St.
    Trinian's '56
Those Daring Young Men in
    Their Jaunty Jalopies '69
tom thumb '58
The Wonderful World of the
    Brothers Grimm '62

Robert Tessier
The Last of the Mohicans '85
The Villain '79

Ted Tetzlaff ▲
The Window '49

Lauren Tewes
Magic Kid '92

Joan Tewkesbury ▲
Sudie & Simpson '90

Peter Tewkesbury ▲
Emil and the Detective '64

Tab Thacker
Wildcats '86

Benj Thall
Homeward Bound: The
    Incredible Journey '93

Byron Thames
Blame It on the Night '84
Seven Minutes in Heaven '86

Torin Thatcher
Jack the Giant Killer '62
The Seventh Voyage of
    Sinbad '58

John Thaw
Chaplin '92

Phyllis Thaxter
Superman 1: The Movie '78

Brother Theodore
The 'Burbs '89

Ernest Thesiger
A Christmas Carol '51

David Thewlis
Black Beauty '94
Dragonheart '96

Alan Thicke
Club Med '83
Not Quite Human '87
Stepmonster '92

Tiffani-Amber Thiessen
Son-in-Law '93

Lynne Thigpen
Lean on Me '89
The Paper '94

Betty Thomas
Troop Beverly Hills '89

Betty Thomas ▲
The Brady Bunch Movie '95

**Billie "Buckwheat"
    Thomas**
General Spanky '36

Dave Thomas
Boris and Natasha: The
    Movie '92
Coneheads '93
Sesame Street Presents:
    Follow That Bird '85
Strange Brew '83

Dave Thomas ▲
Strange Brew '83

Frankie Thomas Jr.
Boys Town '38
Nancy Drew, Reporter '39
Tim Tyler's Luck '37

Henry Thomas
Cloak & Dagger '84
E.T.: The Extra-Terrestrial '82
Fire in the Sky '93
Legends of the Fall '94
Misunderstood '84
The Quest '86

Jay Thomas
Mr. Holland's Opus '95
Straight Talk '92

Jonathan Taylor Thomas
The Adventures of
    Pinocchio '96
Man of the House '95
Tom and Huck '95

Philip Michael Thomas
The Wizard of Speed and
    Time '88

Richard Thomas
Andy and the Airwave
    Rangers '89
Battle Beyond the Stars '80
A Decade of the Waltons '85
Homecoming: A Christmas
    Story '71
The Waltons: A Thanksgiving
    Story '73

Robin Thomas
Summer School '87

Scott Thomas
Guns of the Magnificent
    Seven '69

Sharon Thomas
Young Guns '88

Theodore Thomas
Timecop '94

Tim Thomerson
The Legend of Sleepy
    Hollow '86
Rhinestone '84

Andrea Thompson
Doin' Time on Planet
    Earth '88

Anna Thompson
Angus '95

Brett Thompson ▲
Adventures in Dinosaur
    City '92

Caroline Thompson ▲
Black Beauty '94

Don Thompson ▲
Ugly Little Boy '77

Elizabeth Thompson
Metropolitan '90

Emma Thompson
Howard's End '92
Junior '94
Much Ado About Nothing '93
The Remains of the Day '93
Sense and Sensibility '95

Ernest Thompson
Malcolm X '92

Fred Dalton Thompson
Baby's Day Out '94
Born Yesterday '93
Curly Sue '91
Die Hard 2: Die Harder '90
The Hunt for Red October '90

Hal Thompson
Animal Crackers '30

J. Lee Thompson ▲
Battle for the Planet of the
    Apes '73
Conquest of the Planet of
    the Apes '72
Huckleberry Finn '74
Tiger Bay '59

Jack Thompson
Earthling '80
A Far Off Place '93
The Man from Snowy
    River '82
Wind '92

Kay Thompson
Funny Face '57

Kenan Thompson
D2: The Mighty Ducks '94
Heavyweights '94

Kevin Thompson
Spaced Invaders '90

Lea Thompson
All the Right Moves '83
Back to the Future '85
Back to the Future, Part 2 '89
Back to the Future, Part 3 '90
The Beverly Hillbillies '93
Dennis the Menace '93
Howard the Duck '86
Some Kind of Wonderful '87
SpaceCamp '86

David Tomlinson
Bedknobs and
  Broomsticks '71
The Fiendish Plot of Dr. Fu
  Manchu '80
Mary Poppins '64
Water Babies '79

Kristian Tonby
The Littlest Viking '94

Tone Loc
Ace Ventura: Pet
  Detective '93
Blank Check '93
Surf Ninjas '93

Regis Toomey
Change of Habit '69
The Phantom Creeps '39
Spellbound '45

Gordon Tootoosis
Call of the Wild '93
Legends of the Fall '94
Stone Fox '87

Chaim Topol
Fiddler on the Roof '71
Flash Gordon '80
For Your Eyes Only '81

Peter Tork
Head '68
Monkees, Volume 1 '66

Rip Torn
Airplane 2: The Sequel '82
Beastmaster '82
The Birch Interval '78
Canadian Bacon '94
Cross Creek '83
Down Periscope '96
Heartland '81
How to Make an American
  Quilt '95
Misunderstood '84
Robocop 3 '91
Summer Rental '85

Giuseppe Tornatore ▲
Cinema Paradiso '88

Elizabeth Toro
Sheena '84

Ana Torrent
Cria '76

Gabe Torres ▲
December '91

Raquel Torres
Duck Soup '33

Joe Torry
Poetic Justice '93

Ivan Tors ▲
Zebra in the Kitchen '65

Szilvia Toth
A Hungarian Fairy Tale '87

Robert Totten ▲
Huckleberry Finn '75
Pony Express Rider '76
The Red Pony '76
The Wild Country '71

Tamara Toumanova
Invitation to the Dance '56

Lorraine Toussaint
Dangerous Minds '95

Constance Towers
Sylvester '85

Aline Towne
The Invisible Monster '50
Radar Men from the
  Moon '52
Trader Tom of the China
  Seas '54
Zombies of the
  Stratosphere '52

Bud Townsend ▲
Coach '78

Robert Townsend
American Flyers '85
The Meteor Man '93
Odd Jobs '85

Robert Townsend ▲
The Meteor Man '93

Pete Townshend
Tommy '75

Ian Tracey
Timecop '94

Margaret Tracey
George Balanchine's The
  Nutcracker '93

Michelle Trachtenberg
Harriet the Spy '96

Spencer Tracy
Adam's Rib '50
Boys Town '38
Captains Courageous '37
Father of the Bride '50
Father's Little Dividend '51
How the West was Won '63
Judgment at Nuremberg '61
Men of Boys Town '41
Pat and Mike '52

William Tracy
Strike Up the Band '40

Katheryn Trainor
Walking on Air '87

Mary Ellen Trainor
Die Hard '88
The Goonies '85
Little Giants '94

Alexander Trauner
Reunion '88

Bill Travers
Born Free '66

Christian the Lion '76
Ring of Bright Water '69

Bill Travers ▲
Christian the Lion '76

Henry Travers
The Bells of St. Mary's '45
It's a Wonderful Life '46
Shadow of a Doubt '43
The Yearling '46

Linden Travers
The Lady Vanishes '38

Greg Travis
Paradise '91

Nancy Travis
Chaplin '92
Fluke '95
Greedy '94
So I Married an Axe
  Murderer '93
Three Men and a Baby '87
Three Men and a Little
  Lady '90

Joey Travolta
The Prodigal '83

John Travolta
Broken Arrow '95
Grease '78
Look Who's Talking '89
Look Who's Talking Now '93
Look Who's Talking, Too '90
Phenomenon '96
Shout '91

Arthur Treacher
Curly Top '35
David Copperfield '35
Heidi '37
The Little Princess '39
National Velvet '44
Stowaway '36

Michael Treanor
3 Ninjas '92

Mary Treen
Clipped Wings '53
It's a Wonderful Life '46

Les Tremayne
The War of the Worlds '53

Brian Trenchard-Smith ▲
BMX Bandits '83
Deathcheaters '76
The Quest '86

John Trent ▲
The Bushbaby '70

James Treuer
Walking on Air '87

Noel Trevarthen
Dusty '85

Claire Trevor
Baby, Take a Bow '34
Key Largo '48

Kiss Me Goodbye '82

Vicki Trickett
Three Stooges Meet
  Hercules '61

Leopoldo Trieste
Cinema Paradiso '88

Sarah Trigger
Bill & Ted's Bogus
  Journey '91
Paradise '91
P.C.U. '94
Sleepless in Seattle '93

Gus Trikonis ▲
Touched by Love '80

Louis Tripp
The Gate '87

Paul Tripp
The Christmas That Almost
  Wasn't '66

Jeanne Tripplehorn
Waterworld '95

Kate Trotter
Clarence '91

Gary Trousdale ▲
Beauty and the Beast '91
The Hunchback of Notre
  Dame '96

Jim True
Singles '92

Ernest Truex
His Girl Friday '40

Francois Truffaut
Close Encounters of the Third
  Kind '77
The 400 Blows '59

Francois Truffaut ▲
The 400 Blows '59
Small Change '76
The Wild Child '70

Ralph Truman
Treasure Island '50

Natalie Trundy
Battle for the Planet of the
  Apes '73
Beneath the Planet of the
  Apes '70
Conquest of the Planet of the
  Apes '72
Escape from the Planet of the
  Apes '71
Huckleberry Finn '74

Tom Tryon
Moon Pilot '62

Millie Tsiginoff
Angelo My Love '83

Steve "Patalay" Tsiginoff
Angelo My Love '83

Irene Tsu
How to Stuff a Wild Bikini '65

Yoshio Tsuchiya
Destroy All Monsters '68

Le Tuan
Gleaming the Cube '89

Barry Tubb
Mask '85
Top Gun '86

Stanley Tucci
Beethoven '92
It Could Happen to You '94
Jury Duty '95
The Pelican Brief '93
Prelude to a Kiss '92
Undercover Blues '93

Michael Tuchner ▲
The Hunchback of Notre Dame '82
Not My Kid '85
The Old Curiosity Shop '75
Trenchcoat '83

Chris Tucker
House Party 3 '94

Forrest Tucker
The Adventures of Huckleberry Finn '78
Cancel My Reservation '72
The Incredible Rocky Mountain Race '77
A Rare Breed '81
Wackiest Wagon Train in the West '77
The Yearling '46

Jonathan Tucker
Two If by Sea '95

Michael Tucker
D2: The Mighty Ducks '94
For Love or Money '93
The Purple Rose of Cairo '85
Radio Days '87

Sophie Tucker
Thoroughbreds Don't Cry '37

Paul Tulley
Kid from Not-So-Big '78

Tommy Tune
The Boy Friend '71
Hello, Dolly! '69

Sandy Tung ▲
Across the Tracks '89

Robin Tunney
Encino Man '92

Paige Turco
Teenage Mutant Ninja Turtles 2: The Secret of the Ooze '91

Teenage Mutant Ninja Turtles 3 '93

Glynn Turman
Cooley High '75
A Hero Ain't Nothin' But a Sandwich '78

Debbie Turner
The Sound of Music '65

George Turner
Son of Zorro '47

Janine Turner
Steel Magnolias '89

Jim Turner
Kid Colter '85

Kathleen Turner
House of Cards '92
The Jewel of the Nile '85
Peggy Sue Got Married '86
Romancing the Stone '84
Serial Mom '94
Undercover Blues '93

Lana Turner
Love Finds Andy Hardy '38
The Three Musketeers '48
Witches' Brew '79

Robert Turner ▲
Digger '94

Tina Turner
Mad Max: Beyond Thunderdome '85
Tommy '75

Tyrin Turner
Menace II Society '93

Ben Turpin
Law of the Wild '34

Jon Turteltaub ▲
Cool Runnings '93
Phenomenon '96
3 Ninjas '92
While You Were Sleeping '95

Aida Turturro
Jersey Girl '92
Junior '94

John Turturro
Being Human '94
Brain Donors '92
Desperately Seeking Susan '85
Gung Ho '85
Off Beat '86
Quiz Show '94
Unstrung Heroes '95

Rita Tushingham
Doctor Zhivago '65

Lurene Tuttle
White Mama '80

Twiggy
The Boy Friend '71

Club Paradise '86
The Little Match Girl '87
Madame Sousatzka '88

Anne Twomey
The Scout '94

Jeff Tyler
The Adventures of Tom Sawyer '73

Tom Tyler
The Adventures of Captain Marvel '41

Charles Tyner
Planes, Trains & Automobiles '87

Susan Tyrrell
Big Top Pee Wee '88
Cry-Baby '90
Liar's Moon '82
Powder '95

Cicely Tyson
Bustin' Loose '81
A Hero Ain't Nothin' But a Sandwich '78
The Kid Who Loved Christmas '90
Sounder '72

Pamela Tyson
What's Love Got to Do With It? '93

Richard Tyson
The Babe '92
Kindergarten Cop '90
Three O'Clock High '87

Bob Uecker
Major League '89
Major League 2 '94

Gisela Uhlen
Toto le Heros '91

Tracey Ullman
I'll Do Anything '93
Robin Hood: Men in Tights '93

Liv Ullmann
The Bay Boy '85
A Bridge Too Far '77

Skeet Ulrich
Boys '96

Martin Umbach
The NeverEnding Story 2: Next Chapter '91

Miyoshi Umeki
Flower Drum Song '61

Jay Underwood
The Boy Who Could Fly '86
Desert Bloom '86
Not Quite Human '87
Uncle Buck '89

Ron Underwood ▲
City Slickers '91
Heart and Souls '93
Speechless '94

Robert Urich
A Horse for Danny '95
Ice Pirates '84
Turk 182! '85

Susan Ursitti
Defense Play '88
Teen Wolf '85

Peter Ustinov
Blackbeard's Ghost '67
Death on the Nile '78
Evil Under the Sun '82
Lorenzo's Oil '92
The Man Who Wagged His Tail '57
The Old Curiosity Shop '94
One of Our Dinosaurs Is Missing '75
The Phoenix and the Magic Carpet '95
The Thief of Baghdad '78
The Treasure of Matecumbe '76

Jamie Uys
The Gods Must Be Crazy '84

Jamie Uys ▲
The Gods Must Be Crazy '84
The Gods Must Be Crazy 2 '89

Brenda Vaccaro
Airport '77 '77
Supergirl '84

Tracy Vaccaro
A Rare Breed '81

Roger Vadim ▲
Beauty and the Beast '83

Dan Vadis
Bronco Billy '80

Marc Vahanian
The Prince of Central Park '77

Ladislao Vajda ▲
The Man Who Wagged His Tail '57

Luis Valdez ▲
La Bamba '87

Karen Valentine
Hot Lead & Cold Feet '78
The North Avenue Irregulars '79
Skeezer '82

Tonino Valerii ▲
My Name is Nobody '74

Rudy Vallee
The Bachelor and the Bobby-Soxer '47
I Remember Mama '48

Alida Valli
The Paradine Case '47

Tomas Van Bromssen
My Life as a Dog '85

Lee Van Cleef
Gypsy Colt '54
High Noon '52

Jean-Claude Van Damme
Street Fighter '94
Timecop '94

James Van Der Beek
Angus '95

Nadine Van Der Velde
Critters '86
Munchies '87

Trish Van Devere
The Day of the Dolphin '73
Movie, Movie '78

Mamie Van Doren
Francis Joins the WACs '54

Jaco Van Dormael ▲
Toto le Heros '91

Dick Van Dyke
Bye, Bye, Birdie '63
Chitty Chitty Bang Bang '68
Dick Tracy '90
Lt. Robin Crusoe, U.S.N. '66
Mary Poppins '64
Never a Dull Moment '68

Jerry Van Dyke
The Courtship of Eddie's
Father '62

Woodbridge S. Van Dyke ▲
Andy Hardy Gets Spring
Fever '39
Journey for Margaret '42
Tarzan, the Ape Man '32
The Thin Man '34

Jo Van Fleet
East of Eden '54

Buddy Van Horn ▲
Any Which Way You Can '80
Pink Cadillac '89

Dick Van Patten
Freaky Friday '76
Gus '76
High Anxiety '77
The Hoboken Chicken
Emergency '84
The New Adventures of Pippi
Longstocking '88
Robin Hood: Men in
Tights '93
Spaceballs '87
Superdad '73

Joyce Van Patten
The Bad News Bears '76
Billy Galvin '86

Nels Van Patten
Summer School '87

Vincent Van Patten
Charley and the Angel '73
Rock 'n' Roll High School '79

Mario Van Peebles
Hot Shot '86

Melvin Van Peebles
Taking Care of Terrific '88
Terminal Velocity '94

Sterling Van Wagenen ▲
Alan & Naomi '92

Philip Van Zandt
Citizen Kane '41
Clipped Wings '53
Ghost Chasers '51

Courtney B. Vance
The Adventures of Huck
Finn '93
Dangerous Minds '95
Holy Matrimony '94
The Hunt for Red October '90

Danitra Vance
Little Man Tate '91

Jim Vance
Young Eagles '34

Alexandra Vandernoot
Highlander: The Gathering '93

Titos Vandis
Once Upon a Scoundrel '73
Piece of the Action '77

Pierre Vaneck
Othello '95

Charles Vanel
To Catch a Thief '55

Vanilla Ice
Cool As Ice '91
Teenage Mutant Ninja Turtles
2: The Secret of the
Ooze '91

Vanity
Highlander: The Gathering '93

Renata Vanni
The Lady in White '88
Wait Until Spring, Bandini '90

Joanne Vannicola
Taking Care of Terrific '88

Evelyn Varden
The Bad Seed '56

Norma Varden
National Velvet '44
The Sound of Music '65

Maria Varga
A Hungarian Fairy Tale '87

Antonio Vargas
Strictly Ballroom '92

Jim Varney
The Beverly Hillbillies '93
Dr. Otto & the Riddle of the
Gloom Beam '86
Ernest Goes to Camp '87
Ernest Goes to Jail '90
Ernest Goes to School '94
Ernest Rides Again '93
Ernest Saves Christmas '88
Ernest Scared Stupid '91
The Rousters '83
Slam Dunk Ernest '95

Reg Varney
Great St. Trinian's Train
Robbery '66

Michael Vartan
The Pallbearer '95

John Varty
Born Wild '95

Magda Vasarykova
On the Comet '68

Paris Vaughan
Buffy the Vampire Slayer '92

Peter Vaughan
The Remains of the Day '93
Time Bandits '81

Vanessa Vaughan
Crazy Moon '87

Ned Vaughn
Chips the War Dog '90
Wind '92

Robert Vaughn
Battle Beyond the Stars '80
Superman 3 '83

Emmanuelle Vaugier
The Halfback of Notre
Dame '96

Ron Vawter
King of the Hill '93
Philadelphia '93

Francis Veber ▲
Out on a Limb '92
Three Fugitives '89

Isela Vega
Barbarosa '82

Conrad Veidt
Casablanca '42
Thief of Baghdad '40

Reginald Vel Johnson
Die Hard '88
Die Hard 2: Die Harder '90

Andres Velasquez
The Littlest Outlaw '54

Lupe Velez
Palooka '34

Luca Venantini
Aladdin '86

Diane Venora
F/X '86

Richard Venture
The Effect of Gamma Rays on
Man-in-the-Moon
Marigolds '73

Vera-Ellen
The Belle of New York '52
Love Happy '50
On the Town '49
White Christmas '54
Wonder Man '45

Gwen Verdon
Cocoon '85
Cocoon: The Return '88

Ben Vereen
Breakin' Through '84
Funny Lady '75
The Kid Who Loved
Christmas '90
Pippin '81
Puss 'n Boots '84
The Zoo Gang '85

Paul Verhoeven ▲
Robocop '87

Tom Verica
Die Hard 2: Die Harder '90

Arpad Vermes
A Hungarian Fairy Tale '87

John Vernon
Ernest Goes to Camp '87
Herbie Goes Bananas '80
The Outlaw Josey Wales '76

Kate Vernon
Malcolm X '92

Stephen Verona ▲
The Lords of Flatbush '74

Louw Verwey
The Gods Must Be Crazy '84

Virginia Vestoff
1776 '72

Victoria Vetri
When Dinosaurs Ruled the
Earth '70

Yvette Vickers
Beach Party '63

Christina Vidal
Life with Mikey '93

Gore Vidal
With Honors '94

Abe Vigoda
The Cheap Detective '78
Joe Versus the Volcano '90
Jury Duty '95
Look Who's Talking '89
North '94
Plain Clothes '88
Prancer '89

Robert Viharo
Kid from Not-So-Big '78

Tom Villard
My Girl '91
One Crazy Summer '86

Daniel Villarreal
Speed '94

Herve Villechaize
The Man with the Golden
Gun '74
Rumpelstiltskin '82

James Villemaire
Matinee '92

Christopher Villiers
First Knight '95

James Villiers
The Scarlet Pimpernel '82

Pruitt Taylor Vince
Beautiful Girls '96
City Slickers 2: The Legend of
Curly's Gold '94

Alex Vincent
Wait Until Spring, Bandini '90

Jan-Michael Vincent
The World's Greatest
Athlete '73

June Vincent
Clipped Wings '53

Lee Ving
Clue '85
Flashdance '83

Helen Vinson
I Am a Fugitive from a Chain
Gang '32

Gustav Vintas
And You Thought Your
Parents Were Weird! '91

Bobby Vinton
Big Jake '71

Will Vinton ▲
The Adventures of Mark
Twain '85

Elisabetta Virgili
Great Adventure '75

Sal Viscuso
Spaceballs '87

Milly Vitale
The Seven Little Foys '55

Mike Vitar
The Sandlot '93

Viva
Play It Again, Sam '72

Darlene Vogel
Back to the Future, Part 2 '89

Jon Voight
Conrack '74
Desert Bloom '86
Happy Birthday, Bugs: 50
Looney Years '90
Mission: Impossible '96
Table for Five '83
The Tin Soldier '95

Jon Voight ▲
The Tin Soldier '95

Dimitrie Vojnov
Tito and Me '92

Julian Voloshin
Aladdin '86

Phillipe Volter
Cyrano de Bergerac '90

Josef von Baky ▲
Baron Munchausen '43

Daniel von Bargen
Before and After '95
Philadelphia '93

Erik von Detten
Top Dog '95

Lenny Von Dohlen
Billy Galvin '86
Electric Dreams '84

Eva Von Hanno
Shipwrecked '90

Wilhelm von Homburg
Ghostbusters 2 '89

Rik von Nutter
Thunderball '65

Max von Sydow
Awakenings '90
Conan the Barbarian '82
Flash Gordon '80
Judge Dredd '95
Never Say Never Again '83
Strange Brew '83
Victory '81

Danielle von Zerneck
La Bamba '87
My Science Project '85

Kurt Vonnegut Jr.
Back to School '86

Bernard Vorhaus ▲
Fisherman's Wharf '39

Yorgo Voyagis
Courage Mountain '89

Spencer Vrooman
Man of the House '95

Murvyn Vye
A Connecticut Yankee in King
Arthur's Court '49

Waigwa Wachira
Gorillas in the Mist '88

Jonathan Wacks ▲
Mystery Date '91

Steven Waddington
1492: Conquest of
Paradise '92
The Last of the Mohicans '92

Lindsay Wagner
The Paper Chase '73

**Natasha Gregson
Wagner**
Buffy the Vampire Slayer '92

Robert Wagner
Curse of the Pink Panther '83
Delirious '91
Dragon: The Bruce Lee
Story '93
I am the Cheese '83
The Pink Panther '64
Prince Valiant '54
Trail of the Pink Panther '82

Mark Wahlberg
The Basketball Diaries '94
Renaissance Man '94

Rupert Wainwright ▲
Blank Check '93

Ralph Waite
A Day for Thanks on Walton's
Mountain '82
A Decade of the Waltons '85
Sioux City '94
The Waltons: A Thanksgiving
Story '73

Tom Waits
The Outsiders '83
Rumble Fish '83

Akiko Wakabayashi
You Only Live Twice '67

Tomisaburo Wakayama
The Bad News Bears Go to
Japan '78

Anton Walbrook
The Red Shoes '48

Shawna Waldron
The American President '95
Little Giants '94

Christopher Walken
Annie Hall '77
Batman Returns '92
Sarah, Plain and Tall '91
Skylark '93
A View to a Kill '85
Wayne's World 2 '93

Albertina Walker
Leap of Faith '92

Ally Walker
Bed of Roses '95
Singles '92
While You Were Sleeping '95

Arnetia Walker
The Wizard of Speed and
Time '88

Dominic Walker
The Power of One '92

Dorian Walker ▲
Making the Grade '84
Teen Witch '89

Eric Walker
And You Thought Your
Parents Were Weird! '91
The Ewok Adventure '84
The Ewoks: Battle for
Endor '85

Giles Walker ▲
Princes in Exile '90

Jimmie Walker
Frankenstein Sings . . . The
Movie '95
Going Bananas '88

Kathryn Walker
Rich Kids '79
Whale for the Killing '81

Nancy Walker
Girl Crazy '43
Thursday's Game '74

Polly Walker
Emma '96

Robert Walker
Since You Went Away '44
Strangers on a Train '51
Till the Clouds Roll By '46

Robert Walker Jr.
Hambone & Hillie '84

Sarah Walker
Housekeeping '87

Sydney Walker
Prelude to a Kiss '92

Tippy Walker
The World of Henry Orient '64

Max Wall
Jabberwocky '77
Little Dorrit, Film 1: Nobody's
Fault '88
Little Dorrit, Film 2: Little
Dorrit's Story '88

George Wallace
Forbidden Planet '56
Radar Men from the
Moon '52

Jack Wallace
The Bear '89

Linda Wallace
Charlie, the Lonesome
Cougar '67

Marcia Wallace
My Mom's a Werewolf '89

Richard Wallace ▲
Sinbad the Sailor '47

Sue Wallace
Experience Preferred. . . But
  Not Essential '83

Tommy Lee Wallace ▲
Aloha Summer '88

Dee Wallace Stone
Critters '86
E.T.: The Extra-Terrestrial '82
The Howling '81
Huck and the King of
  Hearts '93
Jimmy the Kid '82
Legend of the White
  Horse '85
Miracle Down Under '87
The Phoenix and the Magic
  Carpet '95
The Road Home '95
Secret Admirer '85
Skeezer '82
Wait Till Your Mother Gets
  Home '83
Whale for the Killing '81

Eli Wallach
Girlfriends '78
How the West was Won '63
Moon-Spinners '64
Movie, Movie '78
Sam's Son '84
Shirley Temple Storybook
  Theater '60
Tough Guys '86

Roberta Wallach
The Effect of Gamma Rays on
  Man-in-the-Moon
  Marigolds '73

Philip Waller
The Mouse and the
  Motorcycle '80s

Deborah Walley
Beach Blanket Bingo '65
Benji '74
Gidget Goes Hawaiian '61
Summer Magic '63

Shani Wallis
Oliver! '68

Jon Walmsley
A Day for Thanks on Walton's
  Mountain '82
The Waltons: A Thanksgiving
  Story '73
The Waltons: The Children's
  Carol '80

Dylan Walsh
Congo '95

Gwynyth Walsh
The Crush '93

J.T. Walsh
Blue Chips '94
The Client '94

Dad '89
Miracle on 34th Street '94

Kay Walsh
Greyfriars Bobby '61
Oliver Twist '48
Stage Fright '50

Lori Walsh
Wonderland Cove '75

M. Emmet Walsh
Back to School '86
The Best of Times '86
Camp Nowhere '94
Catch Me. . .If You Can '89
Critters '86
Fletch '85
Harry and the Hendersons '87
Wildcats '86

Raoul Walsh ▲
The Horn Blows at
  Midnight '45

Robert Walsh
Cry-Baby '90

Sally Walsh
The Old Curiosity Shop '94

Sydney Walsh
Three Men and a Little
  Lady '90

Ray Walston
Fast Times at Ridgemont
  High '82
House Arrest '96
Johnny Dangerously '84
Of Mice and Men '92
Popeye '80
The Silver Streak '76
Ski Patrol '89
South Pacific '58
The Sting '73

Harriet Walter
Sense and Sensibility '95

Jessica Walter
Dr. Strange '78
The Flamingo Kid '84
Going Ape! '81
P.C.U. '94

Lisa Ann Walter
Eddie '96

Rita Walter
Cry from the Mountain '85

Tracey Walter
Batman '89
City Slickers '91
Philadelphia '93
Timerider '83

Anrae Walterhouse
The Grass is Always Greener
  Over the Septic Tank '78

Charles Walters ▲
The Belle of New York '52
Easter Parade '48

High Society '56
Lili '53
Please Don't Eat the
  Daisies '60

James Walters
Shout '91

Julie Walters
Educating Rita '83

Thorley Walters
The Adventures of Sherlock
  Holmes' Smarter
  Brother '78
Blue Murder at St.
  Trinian's '56
The People That Time
  Forgot '77
The Pure Hell of St.
  Trinian's '61

Romy Walthall
Camp Nowhere '94

Fred Walton ▲
Hadley's Rebellion '84

Lisa Waltz
Brighton Beach Memoirs '86

Sam Wanamaker
Baby Boom '87
Irreconcilable Differences '84
Superman 4: The Quest for
  Peace '87

Sam Wanamaker ▲
Sinbad and the Eye of the
  Tiger '77

Wayne Wang ▲
The Joy Luck Club '93

David S. Ward ▲
Down Periscope '96
King Ralph '91
Major League '89
Major League 2 '94
The Program '93

Fred Ward
Big Business '88
Naked Gun 33 1/3: The Final
  Insult '94
Remo Williams: The Adventure
  Begins '85
The Right Stuff '83
Secret Admirer '85
Swing Shift '84
Timerider '83

Greg Ward
Kid Colter '85

Jay Ward
To the Last Man '33

John Ward
Holt of the Secret Service '42

Jonathan Ward
Mac and Me '88
White Water Summer '87

Megan Ward
Encino Man '92
Freaked '93
P.C.U. '94

Rachel Ward
Black Magic '92
Christopher Columbus: The
  Discovery '92
Dead Men Don't Wear
  Plaid '82

Roger Ward
Quigley Down Under '90

Sandy Ward
Tank '83

Sela Ward
The Fugitive '93
Hello Again '87
Nothing in Common '86

Simon Ward
The Four Musketeers '75
Supergirl '84
Three Musketeers '74

Sophie Ward
Little Dorrit, Film 1: Nobody's
  Fault '88
Little Dorrit, Film 2: Little
  Dorrit's Story '88
Young Sherlock Holmes '85

Zack Ward
Ed '96

Anthony Warde
The Black Widow '47

Jack Warden
The Apprenticeship of Duddy
  Kravitz '74
Being There '79
Brian's Song '71
Carbon Copy '81
Death on the Nile '78
Ed '96
Problem Child '90
Problem Child 2 '91
While You Were Sleeping '95

Clyde Ware ▲
No Drums, No Bugles '71

Herta Ware
Cocoon '85
Dakota '88
Top Dog '95

Emily Warfield
Bonanza: The Return '93
Calendar Girl '93
The Man in the Moon '91

Marsha Warfield
Mask '85

Jordan Warkol
The Little Rascals '94

Billy Warlock
Hot Shot '86

Suzanne Weber
Cold River '81

Derek Webster
Josh Kirby . . . Time Warrior:
Chapter 1, Planet of the
Dino-Knights '95

Nicholas Webster ▲
Santa Claus Conquers the
Martians '64

David Wechter ▲
Midnight Madness '80

Peter Weck
Almost Angels '62

Ann Wedgeworth
Bang the Drum Slowly '73
The Birch Interval '78
Citizens Band '77
Green Card '90
Miss Firecracker '89
My Science Project '85
Steel Magnolias '89

Stephen Weeks ▲
Sword of the Valiant '83

Virginia Weidler
Babes on Broadway '41
The Philadelphia Story '40

Paul Weiland ▲
Bernard and the Genie '91
City Slickers 2: The Legend of
Curly's Gold '94
Leonard Part 6 '87

Claudia Weill ▲
Girlfriends '78
Once a Hero '88

Peter Weir ▲
Dead Poets Society '89
Green Card '90

Don Weis ▲
Billie '65
Pajama Party '64
Zero to Sixty '78

Robin Weisman
Three Men and a Little
Lady '90

Sam Weisman ▲
Bye Bye, Love '94
D2: The Mighty Ducks '94

Shaun Weiss
D2: The Mighty Ducks '94
Heavyweights '94
The Mighty Ducks '92
The Mighty Ducks 3 '96

Norbert Weisser
Secret of the Ice Cave '89

Jeffrey Weissman
Back to the Future, Part 2 '89
Back to the Future, Part 3 '90

Johnny Weissmuller
Tarzan and His Mate '34
Tarzan Escapes '36
Tarzan Finds a Son '39
Tarzan, the Ape Man '32
Tarzan's New York
Adventure '42
Tarzan's Secret Treasure '41

Bruce Weitz
Prehysteria 3 '95
Windrunner '94

Raquel Welch
Bandolero! '68
The Four Musketeers '75
Kermit and Piggy Story '85
Naked Gun 33 1/3: The Final
Insult '94
The Prince and the
Pauper '78
Three Musketeers '74

Tahnee Welch
Cocoon '85
Cocoon: The Return '88
Sleeping Beauty '89

Tuesday Weld
Author! Author! '82
Heartbreak Hotel '88

Julia Weldon
Before and After '95

Peter Weller
The Adventures of Buckaroo
Banzai Across the Eighth
Dimension '84
Butch and Sundance: The
Early Days '79
The Dancing Princesses '84
First Born '84
Robocop '87
Robocop 2 '90

Mel Welles
Wizards of the Lost Kingdom
2 '89

Orson Welles
Citizen Kane '41
Jane Eyre '44
A Man for All Seasons '66
Ten Little Indians '75
Treasure Island '72

Orson Welles ▲
Citizen Kane '41

Wendell Wellman
Sommersby '93

Briant Wells
Mr. Wrong '95

Carole Wells
Funny Lady '75

Claudia Wells
Back to the Future '85

Dawn Wells
Return to Boggy Creek '77

Dolores Wells
Beach Party '63
Bikini Beach '64
Muscle Beach Party '64

John Wells
Princess Caraboo '94

Simon Wells ▲
An American Tail: Fievel Goes
West '91
Balto '95
We're Back! A Dinosaur's
Story '93

Vernon Wells
Innerspace '87

Kenneth Welsh
Crocodile Dundee 2 '88
Legends of the Fall '94
Timecop '94

Margaret Welsh
American Heart '92
Mr. & Mrs. Bridge '91

Ming-Na Wen
The Joy Luck Club '93
Street Fighter '94

Wim Wenders ▲
Wings of Desire '88

Paul Wendkos ▲
Gidget '59
Gidget Goes Hawaiian '61
Gidget Goes to Rome '63
Guns of the Magnificent
Seven '69

George Wendt
Fletch '85
Forever Young '92
Gung Ho '85
House '86
Man of the House '95
Plain Clothes '88

Jan Werich
The Original Fabulous
Adventures of Baron
Munchausen '61

Jeff Werner ▲
Die Laughing '80

Lori Werner
Last Time Out '94

Dick Wesson
The Errand Boy '61

Adam West
Doin' Time on Planet
Earth '88

Dottie West
The Aurora Encounter '85

Kevin West
Bio-Dome '96

Red West
Grizzly Adams: The Legend
Continues '90

Sam West
Howard's End '92
Reunion '88

Tamsin West
The Quest '86

Timothy West
Oliver Twist '82

Helen Westcott
Abbott and Costello Meet Dr.
Jekyll and Mr. Hyde '52

**Floyd "Red Crow"
Westerman**
Dances with Wolves '90

Dr. Ruth Westheimer
Happy Birthday, Bugs: 50
Looney Years '90

Helen Westley
Dimples '36
Heidi '37
Rebecca of Sunnybrook
Farm '38
Stowaway '36

Celia Weston
Little Man Tate '91

Eric Weston
The Billion Dollar Hobo '78

Eric Weston ▲
Marvin & Tige '84

Jack Weston
Dirty Dancing '87
The Incredible Mr. Limpet '64
Please Don't Eat the
Daisies '60
Rad '86
Short Circuit 2 '88

Patricia Wettig
City Slickers '91
City Slickers 2: The Legend of
Curly's Gold '94

Marius Weyers
Bopha! '93
The Gods Must Be Crazy '84
The Power of One '92

James Whale ▲
The Man in the Iron Mask '39

Michael Whalen
The Poor Little Rich Girl '36
Wee Willie Winkie '37

Frank Whaley
Broken Arrow '95
Field of Dreams '89
The Freshman '90
I.Q. '94
Little Monsters '89
A Midnight Clear '92
Swing Kids '93

George Whaley ▲
Clowning Around 2 '93

Joanne Whalley
Willow '88

Jim Wheat ▲
The Ewoks: Battle for
Endor '85

Ken Wheat ▲
The Ewoks: Battle for
Endor '85

Wil Wheaton
December '91
The Last Prostitute '91
The Last Starfighter '84
Stand By Me '86
Star Trek the Next Generation
Episode 1-2: Encounter at
Farpoint '87

Anne Wheeler ▲
Angel Square '92

Dana Wheeler-Nicholson
Fletch '85
Tombstone '93

Tim Whelan
Thief of Baghdad '40

Wendy Whelan
George Balanchine's The
Nutcracker '93

Lisa Whelchel
The Double McGuffin '79
Where the Red Fern Grows:
Part 2 '92

Barbara Whinnery
Hot to Trot! '88

Shonda Whipple
Magic Kid '92

Forest Whitaker
Fast Times at Ridgemont
High '82
Phenomenon '96

Forest Whitaker ▲
Waiting to Exhale '95

Johnny Whitaker
The Littlest Angel '69
Napoleon and Samantha '72
Tom Sawyer '73

Anne White
The Old Curiosity Shop '94

De'voreaux White
Die Hard '88

Jesse White
Bedtime for Bonzo '51
Bless the Beasts and
Children '71
Francis Goes to the Races '51
Matinee '92
Pajama Party '64
The Reluctant Astronaut '67

Tomboy & the Champ '58

John S. White
The Legend of Sleepy
Hollow '79

Ron White
Johnny's Girl '95

Ruth White
Up the Down Staircase '67

Sammy White
Pat and Mike '52

Vanna White
Happy Birthday, Bugs: 50
Looney Years '90

Paxton Whitehead
The Adventures of Huck
Finn '93
Baby Boom '87
Back to School '86
Boris and Natasha: The
Movie '92
Chips the War Dog '90
My Boyfriend's Back '93

Billie Whitelaw
The Secret Garden '87
Water Babies '79

Arkie Whiteley
Princess Caraboo '94

Paul Whiteman
Strike Up the Band '40

John Whitesell ▲
Calendar Girl '93

Ray Whiteside
Davy Crockett, King of the
Wild Frontier '55

Bradley Whitford
Billy Madison '94
The Client '94
My Life '93
A Perfect World '93
Philadelphia '93

Peter Whitford
Strictly Ballroom '92

Leonard Whiting
Romeo and Juliet '68

Margaret Whiting
Sinbad and the Eye of the
Tiger '77

Stuart Whitman
Run for the Roses '78

James Whitmore
Guns of the Magnificent
Seven '69
Oklahoma! '55
Planet of the Apes '68
The Shawshank
Redemption '94
Where the Red Fern
Grows '74

Grace Lee Whitney
Star Trek 3: The Search for
Spock '84
Star Trek 6: The Undiscovered
Country '91

Susan Whitney
Miracle of Our Lady of
Fatima '52

Margaret Whitton
The Best of Times '86
Big Girls Don't Cry. . .They
Get Even '92
Little Monsters '89
Major League '89
Major League 2 '94
The Man Without a Face '93

May Whitty
The Lady Vanishes '38
Lassie, Come Home '43
Suspicion '41

James Whitworth
Bye Bye, Love '94
Planet of the Dinosaurs '80

Richard Whorf
Yankee Doodle Dandy '42

Richard Whorf ▲
Till the Clouds Roll By '46

Mary Wickes
Almost Partners '87
The Canterville Ghost '91
Little Women '94
Sister Act '92
Sister Act 2: Back in the
Habit '93
Where Angels Go, Trouble
Follows '68

Sidney Wicks
Coach '78

Richard Widmark
How the West was Won '63
Judgment at Nuremberg '61
The Swarm '78
Whale for the Killing '81

Jane Wiedlin
Clue '85

David Wieland
Flirting '89

Robert Wiemer ▲
Somewhere Tomorrow '85

Alex Wiesendanger
Little Buddha '93

Kai Wiesinger
Backbeat '94

Dianne Wiest
The Birdcage '95
Cops and Robbersons '94
Edward Scissorhands '90
Footloose '84
Little Man Tate '91
The Lost Boys '87

Parenthood '89
The Purple Rose of Cairo '85
Radio Days '87
The Scout '94

Chris Wiggins
The Bay Boy '85
Kavik, the Wolf Dog '84
King of the Grizzlies '69
Mark Twain and Me '91
Why Shoot the Teacher? '79

Wiley Wiggins
Dazed and Confused '93

Robert Wightman
A Day for Thanks on Walton's
Mountain '82

James Wilby
Dreamchild '85
Howard's End '92

Collin Wilcox
To Kill a Mockingbird '62

Fred M. Wilcox ▲
Courage of Lassie '46
Forbidden Planet '56
Lassie, Come Home '43
The Secret Garden '49

Robert Wilcox
Mysterious Doctor Satan '40

Sophie Wilcox
The Chronicles of Narnia '89

Henry Wilcoxon
A Connecticut Yankee in King
Arthur's Court '49
Pony Express Rider '76
Tarzan Finds a Son '39
The Ten Commandments '56
When Every Day was the
Fourth of July '78

Christopher Wild
Knights & Emeralds '87

Jack Wild
Melody '71
Oliver! '68
Robin Hood: Prince of
Thieves '91

Cornel Wilde
The Fifth Musketeer '79
The Greatest Show on
Earth '52

Billy Wilder ▲
The Front Page '74
Sabrina '54

Gene Wilder
The Adventures of Sherlock
Holmes' Smarter
Brother '78
The Little Prince '74
The Silver Streak '76
Thursday's Game '74
Willy Wonka & the Chocolate
Factory '71
Young Frankenstein '74

Gene Wilder ▲
The Adventures of Sherlock
　Holmes' Smarter
　Brother '78

Webb Wilder
The Thing Called Love '93

Michael Wilding
Stage Fright '50
Under Capricorn '49

John Wildman
American Boyfriends '89
My American Cousin '85

Jason Wiles
Windrunner '94

Ed Wiley
The Canterville Ghost '96

Kathleen Wilhoite
Getting Even with Dad '94
Lorenzo's Oil '92

Robert J. Wilke
High Noon '52
20,000 Leagues Under the
　Sea '54

Fred Willard
Lots of Luck '85
Moving Violations '85
Prehysteria 3 '95
Roxanne '87
Salem's Lot '79

Chad Willet
Annie O '95

Warren William
The Man in the Iron Mask '39

Adam Williams
North by Northwest '59

Anson Williams ▲
Dream Date '93

Barbara Williams
Digger '94
Oh, What a Night '92

Bill Williams
Flight of the Grey Wolf '76

Billy Dee Williams
Batman '89
Bingo Long Traveling All Stars
　& Motor Kings '76
Brian's Song '71
The Empire Strikes Back '80
Marvin & Tige '84
Return of the Jedi '83

Carlton Williams
Crooklyn '94

Cindy Williams
American Graffiti '73
Bingo '91
Happy Birthday, Bugs: 50
　Looney Years '90
More American Graffiti '79

Spaceship '81

Clarence Williams III
The House of Dies Drear '88
My Heroes Have Always Been
　Cowboys '91

Dick Anthony Williams
Edward Scissorhands '90

Esther Williams
Andy Hardy's Double Life '42
That's Entertainment '74

**Guinn "Big Boy"
　Williams**
Mr. Wise Guy '42

Gus Williams
Celtic Pride '96

Guy Williams
The Prince and the
　Pauper '62
The Secret of El Zorro '57
The Sign of Zorro '60
Zorro, Vol. 1 '58

Hal Williams
Down Periscope '96

Jacqueline Williams
Love Your Mama '89

JoBeth Williams
American Dreamer '84
Desert Bloom '86
Dutch '91
Kramer vs. Kramer '79
Poltergeist '82
Poltergeist 2: The Other
　Side '86
Stop! or My Mom Will
　Shoot '92

John Williams
Dear Brigitte '65
Dial "M" for Murder '54
Sabrina '54
To Catch a Thief '55

Kimberly Williams
Father of the Bride '91
Father of the Bride Part II '95
Indian Summer '93

Michael Williams
Educating Rita '83

Michelle Williams
Timemaster '95

Paul Williams
Battle for the Planet of the
　Apes '73
The Cheap Detective '78
Frog '89
Frogs! '90s
Muppet Revue '85
The Night They Saved
　Christmas '87
Smokey and the Bandit '77
Smokey and the Bandit, Part
　2 '80

Smokey and the Bandit, Part
　3 '83

Paul Williams ▲
The Black Planet '82

Rhys Williams
The Corn is Green '45
How Green was My Valley '41

Richard Williams ▲
Arabian Knight '95
Raggedy Ann and Andy: A
　Musical Adventure '77

Robin Williams
Awakenings '90
Being Human '94
The Best of Times '86
The Birdcage '95
Club Paradise '86
Dead Poets Society '89
Hook '91
In Search of Dr. Seuss '94
Jack '96
Jumanji '95
Mrs. Doubtfire '93
Popeye '80
The Tale of the Frog
　Prince '83
Toys '92

Samm-Art Williams
The Adventures of Huckleberry
　Finn '85

Scot Williams
Backbeat '94

Treat Williams
Johnny's Girl '95
The Little Mermaid '84
The Phantom '96
Smooth Talk '85

Vanessa Williams
The Kid Who Loved
　Christmas '90

Clayton Williamson
Clowning Around '92
Clowning Around 2 '93

Fred Williamson
Adios Amigo '75
M*A*S*H '70

Fred Williamson ▲
Adios Amigo '75

Mykelti Williamson
Forrest Gump '94
How to Make an American
　Quilt '95
Waiting to Exhale '95

Nicol Williamson
The Cheap Detective '78
Return to Oz '85

Noble Willingham
City Slickers '91
City Slickers 2: The Legend of
　Curly's Gold '94
Pastime '91

Up Close and Personal '96

Bruce Willis
Death Becomes Her '92
Die Hard '88
Die Hard 2: Die Harder '90
Die Hard: With a
　Vengeance '95
North '94
12 Monkeys '95

Katherine Willis
Little Heroes '91

Norman Willis
Tim Tyler's Luck '37

Susan Willis
What About Bob? '91

Chill Wills
Francis Joins the WACs '54
Giant '56
Tarzan's New York
　Adventure '42
The Yearling '46

Maury Wills
The Sandlot '93

Douglas Wilmer
The Adventures of Sherlock
　Holmes' Smarter
　Brother '78
Golden Voyage of Sinbad '73

Brigitte Wilson
Billy Madison '94
Last Action Hero '93
Mortal Kombat: The
　Movie '95

Chandra Wilson
Philadelphia '93

Daniel Wilson
Wait Until Spring, Bandini '90

**Don "The Dragon"
　Wilson**
Magic Kid '92

Dooley Wilson
Casablanca '42

Earl Wilson
Beach Blanket Bingo '65

Elizabeth Wilson
The Addams Family '91
Conspiracy of Love '87
Quiz Show '94
Regarding Henry '91
Skylark '93

Flip Wilson
Cancel My Reservation '72
The Fish that Saved
　Pittsburgh '79

Hugh Wilson ▲
Guarding Tess '94
Police Academy '84

 702

Cast/Director Index

Nyoka and the Tigermen '42
Spy Smasher '42
Zorro Rides Again '37
Zorro's Fighting Legion '39

Alicia Witt
Mr. Holland's Opus '95

Kathryn Witt
Philadelphia '93

Meg Wittner
Born Yesterday '93

Damian Woetzel
George Balanchine's The
  Nutcracker '93

Fred Wolf ▲
Little Rascals Christmas
  Special '79
The Point '71

Hillary Wolf
Big Girls Don't Cry. . .They
  Get Even '92
Home Alone 2: Lost in New
  York '92

Kelly Wolf
A Day in October '92

Scott Wolf
White Squall '96

**Sheldon Peters
  Wolfchild**
The Scarlet Letter '95

Wolfman Jack
American Graffiti '73

Illya Woloshyn
Beethoven Lives Upstairs '92

Stevie Wonder
Bikini Beach '64
Muscle Beach Party '64

B.D. Wong
Father of the Bride '91
Father of the Bride Part II '95
The Freshman '90
Jurassic Park '93
Mystery Date '91

Russell Wong
The Joy Luck Club '93

Victor Wong
Big Trouble in Little China '86
The Golden Child '86
The Joy Luck Club '93
3 Ninjas '92
3 Ninjas Kick Back '94

John Woo ▲
Broken Arrow '95

Clive Wood
Treasure Island '89

Elijah Wood
The Adventures of Huck
  Finn '93

Avalon '90
Flipper '96
Forever Young '92
The Good Son '93
North '94
Paradise '91
Radio Flyer '92

G. Wood
M*A*S*H '70

John Wood
Jane Eyre '96
Ladyhawke '85
The Purple Rose of Cairo '85
Sabrina '95
Shadowlands '93
War Games '83

Lana Wood
Captain America 2: Death Too
  Soon '79
Diamonds are Forever '71
Justin Morgan Had a
  Horse '81

Natalie Wood
Great Race '65
Miracle on 34th Street '47
Rebel Without a Cause '55
West Side Story '61

Peggy Wood
The Sound of Music '65

Robert Wood
White Fang and the
  Hunter '85

Sam Wood ▲
A Day at the Races '37
A Night at the Opera '35

Thomas Wood
Bushwhacked '95

Alfre Woodard
Blue Chips '94
Bopha! '93
Crooklyn '94
Cross Creek '83
Heart and Souls '93
How to Make an American
  Quilt '95
Miss Firecracker '89
Rich in Love '93
Scrooged '88
Words by Heart '84

Largo Woodruff
Bill '81
Bill: On His Own '83

Aubrey Woods
Willy Wonka & the Chocolate
  Factory '71

Donald Woods
13 Ghosts '60

Harry Woods
Monkey Business '31
Winners of the West '40

James Woods
Cat's Eye '85
Chaplin '92
Immediate Family '89
Straight Talk '92
The Way We Were '73

Kevin Jamal Woods
The Little Rascals '94

Ren Woods
The Brother from Another
  Planet '84

Kate Woodville
Computer Wizard '77

John Woodvine
Dragonworld '94

Edward Woodward
Merlin and the Sword '85

Joanne Woodward
A Christmas to Remember '78
The Effect of Gamma Rays on
  Man-in-the-Moon
  Marigolds '73
Harry & Son '84
Mr. & Mrs. Bridge '91
Philadelphia '93

Morgan Woodward
Girls Just Want to Have
  Fun '85
Running Wild '73

Tim Woodward
The Scarlet Letter '95

Susan Wooldridge
Hope and Glory '87

Sheb Wooley
High Noon '52
Hoosiers '86

Monty Woolley
Since You Went Away '44

Tom Wopat
Christmas Comes to Willow
  Creek '87

Jimmy Workman
The Addams Family '91
Addams Family Values '93

Mary Woronov
Night of the Comet '84
The Princess Who Never
  Laughed '84
Rock 'n' Roll High School '79
Rock 'n' Roll High School
  Forever '91

Constance Worth
G-Men vs. the Black
  Dragon '43

Irene Worth
Lost in Yonkers '93

Adam Worton
Baby's Day Out '94

Jacob Worton
Baby's Day Out '94

Fay Wray
King Kong '33
Tammy and the Bachelor '57

Amy Wright
Breaking Away '79
Crossing Delancey '88
Girlfriends '78
Miss Firecracker '89
Off Beat '86
The Scarlet Letter '95
Tom and Huck '95

Mack V. Wright ▲
Sea Hound '47

Max Wright
Konrad '85

N'Bushe Wright
Zebrahead '92

Robin Wright
Forrest Gump '94
Moll Flanders '96
The Playboys '92
The Princess Bride '87
Toys '92

Steven Wright
Canadian Bacon '94
Desperately Seeking
  Susan '85

Teresa Wright
Bill: On His Own '83
The Fig Tree '87
Shadow of a Doubt '43
Somewhere in Time '80

Thomas J. Wright ▲
Highlander: The Gathering '93
No Holds Barred '89

Tom Wright
Weekend at Bernie's 2 '93

Whittni Wright
I'll Do Anything '93

Donald Wrye ▲
Ice Castles '79

Vivian Wu
The Joy Luck Club '93
Teenage Mutant Ninja Turtles
  3 '93

Robert Wuhl
Batman '89
Flashdance '83

Kari Wuhrer
Beastmaster 2: Through the
  Portal of Time '91

Kai Wulff
Top Dog '95

Jane Wyatt
The Adventures of Tom
  Sawyer '73

Margaret Wycherly
The Yearling '46

Link Wyler
Grizzly Adams: The Legend
    Continues '90

William Wyler ▲
Friendly Persuasion '56
Funny Girl '68
Roman Holiday '53

Jane Wyman
Pollyanna '60
Stage Fright '50
The Yearling '46

John Wyman
For Your Eyes Only '81

Nick Wyman
Die Hard: With a
    Vengeance '95

George Wyner
The Bad News Bears Go to
    Japan '78
Spaceballs '87

Ed Wynn
The Absent-Minded
    Professor '61
Babes in Toyland '61
Cinderfella '60
Dear Brigitte '65
The Gnome-Mobile '67
Mary Poppins '64
Those Calloways '65

Keenan Wynn
The Absent-Minded
    Professor '61
The Belle of New York '52
Bikini Beach '64
Cancel My Reservation '72
The Capture of Grizzly
    Adams '82
Coach '78
Finian's Rainbow '68
Great Race '65
Herbie Rides Again '74
Hyper-Sapien: People from
    Another Star '86
Once Upon a Time in the
    West '68
The Shaggy D.A. '76
Since You Went Away '44
Smith! '69
Snowball Express '72
Son of Flubber '63
The Three Musketeers '48

Greg Wynne
Mystery Mansion '83

Jim Wynorski ▲
Munchie '92
The Return of Swamp
    Thing '89

Amanda Wyss
Better Off Dead '85
Fast Times at Ridgemont
    High '82

Jeff Yagher
Shag: The Movie '89

So Yamamura
Gung Ho '85

Akira Yamauchi
Godzilla vs. the Smog
    Monster '72

Weird Al Yankovic
UHF '89

Jean Yarbrough ▲
Jack & the Beanstalk '52

Coco Yares
Annie O '95

Celeste Yarnall
Born Yesterday '93

Lorene Yarnell
Spaceballs '87

Trever Yarrish
Spirit of the Eagle '90

Amy Yasbeck
Dracula: Dead and Loving
    It '95
The Mask '94
Problem Child '90
Problem Child 2 '91
Robin Hood: Men in
    Tights '93

Cassie Yates
Father Figure '80
Who'll Save Our Children?
    '82

Marjorie Yates
The Long Day Closes '92

Peter Yates ▲
Breaking Away '79
Krull '83
Year of the Comet '92

Biff Yeager
Girls Just Want to Have
    Fun '85

John Yesno
King of the Grizzlies '69

Don Yesso
Hero '92

Malik Yoba
Cool Runnings '93

Erica Yohn
Corrina, Corrina '94

Jeff York
Davy Crockett and the River
    Pirates '56
Old Yeller '57
Savage Sam '63
Westward Ho, the Wagons!
    '56
The Yearling '46

Kathleen York
Wild Hearts Can't Be
    Broken '91

Marty York
The Sandlot '93

Michael York
The Four Musketeers '75
Island of Dr. Moreau '77
The Return of the
    Musketeers '89
Romeo and Juliet '68
Three Musketeers '74

Susannah York
Battle of Britain '69
Diamond's Edge '88
The Land of Faraway '87
A Man for All Seasons '66
Superman 1: The Movie '78
Superman 2 '80

Bud Yorkin ▲
Arthur 2: On the Rocks '88

Jason Harold Yost
Mighty Morphin Power
    Rangers: The Movie '95

Alan Young
Androcles and the Lion '52
Beverly Hills Cop 3 '94

Burt Young
Back to School '86
Beverly Hills Brats '89
Diving In '90
Harry & Walter Go to New
    York '76
Rocky '76
Rocky 2 '79
Rocky 3 '82
Rocky 4 '85
Rocky 5 '90
A Summer to Remember '84
Wait Until Spring, Bandini '90

Carleton Young
20,000 Leagues Under the
    Sea '54

Chris Young
Book of Love '91
December '91
The Great Outdoors '88
P.C.U. '94

Dey Young
Rock 'n' Roll High School '79
Strange Invaders '83

Gig Young
The Three Musketeers '48

Harold Young ▲
Little Tough Guys '38

Kristy Young
Gordy '95

Loretta Young
The Farmer's Daughter '47

Ric Young
Dragon: The Bruce Lee
    Story '93

Robert Young
The Canterville Ghost '44
Conspiracy of Love '87
Journey for Margaret '42
Stowaway '36

Robert Young ▲
The Worst Witch '86

Robert M. Young ▲
Dominick & Eugene '88
Rich Kids '79
Talent for the Game '91

Roger Young ▲
Geronimo '93
Two of a Kind '82

Roland Young
David Copperfield '35
The Philadelphia Story '40
Topper '37
Topper Returns '41
Topper Takes a Trip '39

Sean Young
Ace Ventura: Pet
    Detective '93
Baby. . .Secret of the Lost
    Legend '85
Dr. Jekyll and Ms. Hyde '95
Fatal Instinct '93
Once Upon a Crime '92

Terence Young ▲
Dr. No '62
From Russia with Love '63
Thunderball '65
When Wolves Cry '69

Barrie Youngfellow
It Came Upon a Midnight
    Clear '84

Gail Youngs
Hockey Night '84

Jim Youngs
Hot Shot '86

Igor Youskevitch
Invitation to the Dance '56

Chief Yowlachie
Bowery Buckaroos '47

Jimmy Yuill
Much Ado About Nothing '93

Harris Yulin
Clear and Present Danger '94
Cutthroat Island '95
Ghostbusters 2 '89
Stuart Saves His Family '94
When Every Day was the
    Fourth of July '78

Oliver Zabriskie
Summerdog '78

Tavia Zabriskie
Summerdog '78

Pia Zadora
Hairspray '88
Santa Claus Conquers the
  Martians '64

Anita Zagaria
Queen of Hearts '89

Steve Zahn
Crimson Tide '95
Race the Sun '96
Reality Bites '94

Steven Zaillian ▲
Searching for Bobby
  Fischer '93

Roxana Zal
Goodbye, Miss 4th of July '88
Table for Five '83

Del Zamora
Robocop '87

Gema Zamprogna
Tales from Avonlea, Vol. 1:
  The Journey Begins '90

Billy Zane
Back to the Future '85
Back to the Future, Part 2 '89
Critters '86
Only You '94
The Phantom '96
Tombstone '93

Vanessa Zaoui
Alan & Naomi '92

Carmen Zapata
Daniel and the Towers '90s

Dweezil Zappa
Pretty in Pink '86

Frank Zappa
Head '68

Janet Zarish
Danny '79

Zatloukalova
The Fabulous World of Jules
  Verne '58

Robert Z'Dar
Beastmaster 2: Through the
  Portal of Time '91
The Legend of Wolf
  Mountain '92

Franco Zeffirelli ▲
Jane Eyre '96
Jesus of Nazareth '77
Romeo and Juliet '68

Karel Zeman ▲
The Fabulous World of Jules
  Verne '58
On the Comet '68
The Original Fabulous
  Adventures of Baron
  Munchausen '61

Robert Zemeckis ▲
Back to the Future '85
Back to the Future, Part 2 '89
Back to the Future, Part 3 '90
Death Becomes Her '92
Forrest Gump '94
I Wanna Hold Your Hand '78
Romancing the Stone '84
Who Framed Roger Rabbit?
  '88

Anthony Zerbe
Child of Glass '78

Papillon '73
Rooster Cogburn '75

Mai Zetterling
The Witches '90

Howard Zieff ▲
The Dream Team '89
Hearts of the West '75
The Main Event '79
My Girl '91
My Girl 2 '94

Madeline Zima
Mr. Nanny '93

Efrem Zimbalist Jr.
Airport '75 '75

Stephanie Zimbalist
Magic of Lassie '78
The Story Lady '93

Fred Zinnemann ▲
High Noon '52
A Man for All Seasons '66
Oklahoma! '55

Dan Ziskie
Zebrahead '92

Adrian Zmed
Grease 2 '82

Dick Zondag ▲
We're Back! A Dinosaur's
  Story '93

Ralph Zondag ▲
We're Back! A Dinosaur's
  Story '93

Danny Zorn
My Boyfriend's Back '93

Rod Zuanic
Mad Max: Beyond
  Thunderdome '85

David Zucker ▲
Airplane! '80
The Naked Gun: From the
  Files of Police Squad '88
Naked Gun 2 1/2: The Smell
  of Fear '91

Jerry Zucker ▲
Airplane! '80
First Knight '95
Ghost '90

Alex Zuckerman
Freaked '93

Joshua Zuehlke
Amazing Grace & Chuck '87

Daphne Zuniga
Charlie's Ghost: The Secret of
  Coronado '94
Gross Anatomy '89
Quarterback Princess '85
Spaceballs '87
The Sure Thing '85

Frank Zuniga ▲
Further Adventures of the
  Wilderness Family, Part
  2 '77
The Golden Seal '83

Jose Zuniga
Crooklyn '94

Edward Zwick ▲
Glory '89
Legends of the Fall '94

Noam Zylberman
Outside Chance of Maximillian
  Glick '88

Category List

The **CATEGORY LIST** contains the fanciful and fantastical subjects by which the main reviews are categorized, ranging from the very general (such as drama) to the more particular (such as genies). While we've done our best to provide serious subject references, we've also had a bit of fun in the making of the various lists and definitions. No one list is inclusive; we're continually reclassifying, adding and subtracting. We've tried to select categories that would be of interest to children and parents, and in some cases these lists represent only a beginning. *VideoHound* would like to invite you to join in the fun by sending in suggestions for new titles for existing categories, as well as suggestions for brand-new categories (including a few movies that fit the subject). Following the "Category List" is the "Category Index," listing movies for each subject.

Adapted from a Cartoon: Movies that imitate popular cartoons, like "Batman."

Adapted from the Radio: Movies that borrow plots from old radio shows, like "The Phantom."

Adapted from TV: Movies borrowing storylines from popular TV series or TV shows, and sometimes remakes of a TV icon, like "The Brady Bunch."

Africa: Tales from the Banana Republic.

African America: Dominant African American themes.

AIDS: The disease that frightens us all. Usually a tearjerker.

Airborne: Those amazing flying machines.

Aliens-Nasty: Mean space visitors with ray guns and stuff.

Aliens-Nice: Friendly visitors from outer space, like E.T.

Amazing Adventures: Adventures ranging from treasure hunts to long arduous journeys.

Amazing Animals Those amazing beasts of the wild kingdom and some from the not-so-wild kingdom.

Amnesia: Who am I? Where am I? Who are you?

Amusement Parks: Roller coasters, cotton candy and Ferris wheels. What more could a kid want?

Andy Hardy: Mickey Rooney stars as the hero of this charming series.

Angels: Our winged guardians from above.

Apartheid: Afrikaans term for racial segregation in South Africa.

Asia: Tales from the continent of pandas and mysticism of the East.

At the Movies: The movie within a movie or movies about watching the movies.

Baby Talk: Can you say "goo goo"?

Babysitters: We've all had one of these, but how many are like the ones in the movies?

Ballet: On your toes.

Ballooning: Up, up, and away.

Baseball: America's favorite pastime.

Basketball: On the court hoop-la.

Beach Blanket Bingo: Annette, Frankie, sand, surf, bikinis.

Bedtime Stories: Night-ty night favorites.

Bereavement: Grieving for the loss of another.

Best Friends: These can be childhood friends, animal friends, or any other kind of friend you may have.

The Big Sting: The perfect con job (and sometimes not-so-perfect).

Bigfoot: Large, hairy beast with big feet.

Biking: Kids on bikes.

Biopics: True life tales.

Birds: Our feathered friends from the sky.

Blindness: Sight-impaired.

Books: The joy of reading.

Books to Film: Louisa May Alcott: From the author of "Little Women."

Books to Film: J.M. Barrie: From the author of "Peter Pan."

Books to Film: Frances Hodgson Burnett: From the author of "The Secret Garden."

Books to Film: Rudyard Kipling: From the author of "The Jungle Book."

Books to Film: Astrid Lindgren: From the author of "Pippi Longstocking."

Books to Film: Jack London: From the author of "Call of the Wild."

Books to Film: L.M. Montgomery: From the author of "Anne of Avonlea."

Books to Film: Mark Twain: From the author of "Tom Sawyer."

Bowling: Fred and Barney's favorite pastime.

Boxing: A few bouts in the ring.

Boy Meets Girl: Billy and Susie sitting in a tree K-I-S-S-I-N-G . . .

Buses Public transportation, usually out of control.

Business Gone Berserk: Executives and the like lose control.

Canada: America's neighbor to the North.

Cartoon Classics: Everyone's old animated favorites.

Cartoon Tunes: Girls, boys, ducks, mice, birds, and monkeys croon. Many of the Disney variety.

Cartoonmercials: Animated shorts, usually based on popular toys or television characters.

Cats: Felines are the center of attention, which is how they like it.

Cave People: The primitive precursor to modern humans.

Charlie Brown and the Peanuts: Everyone's favorite round-headed kid and his beagle.

Chases: Someone's after someone else, usually at high-speed, and may involve horses, autos, bikes, trains or other movable transportation.

Child Abuse: Not funny at all — children are in pain.

Childhood Visions: Stories told from a kid point of view or an adult flashing back to childhood.

China: Tales from the Far East.

Christmas: Stories surrounding that Santa Claus holiday.

Circuses & Carnivals: Send in the clowns.

Civil Rights: Fighting for equality.

Civil War: The Yankees against the Confederates or the Blue vs. the Gray.

Classics: Those golden oldies.

Clowning Around: Those circus regulars with the big red noses.

Cold Spots: Set in the regions of the world where shivering is a sport.

College Capers: What really goes on at school.

Comedy with an Edge: Comedy that's a little on the dark side.

Coming to America: Chasing the dream of becoming a citizen.

Computers: Bits and bytes play major role.

Cool Cars: The love affair with the automobile.

Courtroom Capers: Order in the court.

Cowboys & Indians: Not the kind you played as kids.

Crime Doesn't Pay: Bad guys and gals turning their noses up at the law.

Dads: Fathers are the topic here. (You may call him Daddy.)

Deafness: Can't hear or hearing impaired.

Demons & Wizards: Swords, sorcery, and wrinkled old men with magic wands.

Detectives: Those guys at the crime scene sniffing out the clues.

Dinos: Thundering lizards from the Jurassic Age.

Disaster Strikes!: Natural and man-made calamities.

Disney Animated Movies: A staple in the Disney tradition of family entertainment and always a safe bet for family viewing.

Disney Family Movies: All those wonderful classics you can watch over and over again, and if you have young children, you will.

Divorce: Breaking up is hard to do.

Dr. Seuss: From the man who brought you "The Cat in the Hat."

Doctors & Nurses: Men and women in white that you meet in the hospital or other medical venue.

Documentaries: Real life portrayed on film.

Down Under: Life in Australia and New Zealand.

Drama: Conflict, tension, climax, resolution.

Eco-Vengeance!: Never underestimate the power of Mother Nature.

Ecotoons: Animated environmental tales.

Elementary School Escapades: School days, wonderful golden rule days.

Explorers: Going boldly where no man or woman has gone before.

Fairy Tales: Classic tales passed on through the years.

Family Ties: The ties that bind.

Fantasy: Tales from the imagination.

Fast Cars: Racing in the streets or on the track.

Film Noir: Dark and moody or tributes to the dark and moody.

Film Stars: Movies or bios about film celebs, real or make-believe.

Firemen: Brave people who look fire in the eye.

Folk Tales: Age-old tales passed down through the years.

Football: On the gridiron or just a game of touch.

France: That country where they speak French.

Funny Adventures: Escapades you can laugh at.

Gangs: Criminally motivated people running in packs.

Garfield: The adventures of a fat, lasagna-loving cat.

Genies: They grant wishes and fly on magic carpets and stuff.

Ghosts, Ghouls, & Goblins: Sometimes they float and fly through walls, sometimes they don't.

Giants: Really, really, really, really, really, really tall people.

Gifted Children: Kids with amazing abilities astound adults.

Go Fish: Not the card game, but the sport of fishing.

Godzilla & Friends: Very large monster who attacks cities and fights other monsters.

Going Native: Outsiders try to blend in.

Golf: Slow stick and ball game played by people with weird tastes in clothes.

Gory Stories: Yucky movies.

Gotta Dance!: Put on your dancing shoes and get down.

Gotta Sing!: Ok, the same thing except you don't necessarily need shoes and you sing songs.

Grand Hotel: Check out time is noon.

Great Britain: Kings and queens, tea and crumpets, the Brontes and Dickens.

Great Death Scenes: Signing off with style or great elaboration.

Great Depression: The 1930s, following the stock market crash.

Great Escapes: Reaching for freedom.

Growing Older: The Golden Years.

Growing Pains: Coming of age can be a bummer.

Gymnastics: Human acrobats like Nadia and Mary Lou.

Hallmark Hall of Fame: Tales produced by Hallmark.

Heaven Sent: Visits or returns from the place where good souls and all dogs go.

Heists: The big lift.

High School Hijinks: Life in the classroom and out of the classroom.

High Seas Adventure: Takes place on large bodies of water.

Historical Happenings: Usually loosely based on real incidents or personalities.

Hockey: Icy tales of passing the puck.

Holidays: Easter, Thanksgiving, New Year's, Halloween, but generally not Christmas.

Home Alone: Kids left home without adult supervision.

Homeless: Street people with no homes.

Horses: You know, like Black Beauty.

Hospitals: Big buildings that you go to when you're sick.

Hunting: Where's dat wascally wabbit?

In Concert: Live performances of performers and singers.

Inventors: Those wacky folk who work in labs and create newfangled stuff.

Ireland: The Emerald Isle. Leprechauns and the wearing o' the green.

Islands in the Sea: Isolated land surrounded by water, where people usually get shipwrecked.

Italy: Passion, vino, lust, vino, Sophia Loren, vino . . . oh yeah, it's a beautiful country, too.

It's the Mob: Gangsters , godfathers, and really good pasta.

It's True!: Movies fashioned after real-life adventures.

James Bond: I'll take my martini shaken, not stirred.

Japan: From the Land of the Rising Sun.

Judaism: In the Jewish tradition.

Jungle Stories: Tarzan, tribes, trees, treasure, temperature, temptresses, and tigers.

Kidnapped!: Held for ransom or just for the heck of it.

A Kid's Best Friend: Animals and kids bonding.

Kindness of Strangers: When someone you've never met helps.

King of Beasts (Dogs): You know, Snoopy, Lassie, Rin Tin Tin, and the list goes on.

Korean War: Follow the trials of a M*A*S*H unit.

Labor Unions: Look for the union label.

Lassie: What's the matter, girl?

Laugh Riots: Get ready to yuk it up!

Lawyers: Legal adventures through the eyes of attorneys.

Life in the 'Burbs: These are the days of the lives of the people in your neighborhood.

Live Action/Animation Combos: Mixing cartoons and real people.

Lost Worlds: Lost cities, lost islands, lost people — they're all lost.

Macho Men: Severe cases of excessive testosterone.

Mad Scientists: Scientists with wild hair whose experiments usually get the best of them.

Magic: Hocus pocus and all that jazz.

Magic Carpet Rides: Flying carpets. They save fossil fuels.

Marriage: Wedding bells, honeymoons, affairs, divorce and growing old together.

Martial Arts: Head-kicking, rib-crunching, chop-socky action.

The Meaning of Life: The search for the elusive answer to a really big question.

Medieval Romps: Flashback to a time of royalty, knights in shining armor, peasants and castles. (And your occasional dragon or two.)

Mental Retardation: Themes of the mentally challenged.

Mickey Mouse & Friends: Your favorite mouse and mine and his many adventures.

Miners: Helmets with the little flashlights are nifty, but going in those dark tunnels isn't.

Missing Persons: People who disappear for a variety of reasons.

Misspelled Titles: Not proper Anglish.

Mistaken Identity: You mean to say you're not the King of France?

Modern Cowboys: Cowpokes doing what they do in modern days.

Moms: Maternal figures take the spotlight.

Monsters, General: Generally scary, that is.

Mountains: Very large hills. Sometimes people get stuck on them or ski down them.

The Muppets: Jim Henson's cuddly creations.

Music: Anything that sets your toes to tappin'.

Musician Biopics: Real-life musicians get the Hollywood treatment.

Mysteries: Thrillers, chillers and whodunnits.

Nashville Narratives: Country stories from the town of country music.

Nasty Nazis: Self-explanatory.

Native America: Tales from the world of Native Americans.

Newsroom Notes: Stop the presses.

Nifty '50s: Poodle skirts, Rock 'n' Roll, and "Grease Is the Word."

Nuclear War: Big bombs that blow up everything.

Nuns & Priests: Collars and habits.

The Olympics: Tales of athletic discipline and overcoming the odds to reach a dream.

On the Farm: Old MacDonald had a farm . . .

On the Run: Running away, usually from the law.

Only the Lonely: Things to do when you're all alone.

Ooooh...That's Scary!: Creepy tales that'll make your skin crawl and your heart leap.

Opera: Shouting in a melodic way while in costume.

Orphans: Cute kids without permanent authority figures.

Our Gang: Those little rascals!!!

Over the Airwaves: Turn up the radio.

Overlooked Gems: No box office to speak of, but worth a rent.

Parades: People gather, floats and bands go by, people go home.

Parenthood: Moms, dads and parental substitutes.

Period Piece: Costume epics or tales evocative of a certain time and place.

Physical Problems: Physically challenged people overcoming the odds.

Poetry: Poems, nursery rhymes and other tales about rhyming.

Policemen: To serve and protect. Police and pseudo-police work.

Postwar: After effects of war.

POW/MIA: Captured by the enemy.

Presidential Pics: That man in the Oval Office.

Price of Fame: It's not all it's cracked up to be.

Puppets: Usually with strings.

Race Against Time: Tick, tock, tick, tock.

Rags to Riches: Grit, determination and hustling (or just pure dumb luck) lead to fortune.

Raiders of the Lost Ark: The earth-shaking Indiana Jones series.

Rebel With a Cause: Bucking the establishment for a reason.

Rebel Without a Cause: Bucking the establishment just because it's the establishment.

Red Scare: Cold War and Communism.

Repressed Men: Often British, always with plenty of stiffness in the upper lip.

Rescue Missions: I'll save you!!

Revolutionary War: That darned tea tax.

The Right Choice: Making the decision to do what's right.

Robots: Mechanical and technological creations that can do neat things.

Rodeos: Rope tricks with steers and horses.

Royalty: Emperors, kings, queens, princes, princesses, crowns, and scepters.

Running: Long distance running, cross country running . . .

Savants: Half-minded geniuses.

Scary Beasties: Monsters that are out to get ya.

Scary Bugs: Giant and/or mean spiders, ants, bees and other creepy crawlers.

Scary Plants: Too much fertilizer produces killer tomatoes and other scary flora.

Sci Fi: Imagination fueled by science and a vision of the future.

Scientists: The guys and gals in the lab coats.

Scotland: Lush hills, thick brogues, kilts and bagpipes.

Scuba Diving: Wet suits and fins and underwater adventures.

Serial Adventures: Segmented adventures that had their heyday in the 1930s.

Sesame Street: Can you tell me how to get to Sesame Street?

Shutterbugs: Photographers and their work.

Silence is Golden: No small talk. No big talk. No talk talk.

Silly Detectives: Bumbling private eyes.

Silly Spoofs: Laughable parodies of real-life or other movies.

Sing-Alongs: Follow the bouncing ball . . . well, kind of.

Sixties Sagas: The era of love and peace (and sit-ins and drugs and Woodstock).

Skateboarding: Teens on boards on wheels.

Skating: Roller, ice and in-line.

Skiing: Grab your skis, grab your poles and hit the slopes.

Slavery: Imprisoned servants.

Soccer: Known as football outside the USA.

Southern Belles: Southern gals sippin' mint juleps and oozin' charm.

Southern Sagas: Tales from below the Mason-Dixon Line.

Special F/X Extravaganzas: Explosions, burning buildings, fantastic stunts and incredible make-up.

Sports Comedies: Humorous athletic tales, usually not based on a true story.

Sports Dramas: Intense athletic tales, often based on a true story.

Spy Stories: Double agents and James Bond compare notes and spy gadgets.

Star Wars: The George Lucas extravaganza.

Stepparents: New spouse greets unprepared family.

Storytelling: Told before bedtime, told around the campfire, told on road trips.

Struggling Musicians: Talented and reaching for the top.

Stupid Crime: Bumbling criminals usually meet equally bumbling lawmen.

Submarines: Dive, dive, dive . . .

Subways: The Underground, the Metro, the Loop . . .

Summer Camp: Where children go to misbehave.

Super Heroes: Men and women of extraordinary strength and abilities wearing silly looking costumes.

Supernatural Tales: Stories about the forces from beyond.

Surfing: Awesome wave, dude!

Survival: Overcoming the odds to make it out alive.

Swashbucklers: Sword-wielding heroes and various Musketeers.

Table Manners: Teaching the finer virtues of good manners.

Tall Tales & Legends Series: Stories about legendary folk.

Teacher, Teacher: An apple for the teacher.

Team Efforts: Throwing aside our differences and working together pays off.

Tearjerkers: Better grab a hankie.

Technological Nightmares: Machines that wreak havoc.

Teen Tribulations: Adolescent anxieties.

That's Showbiz: Hollywood stories.

Three Stooges: Larry, Moe and Curly (oh yeah, and Shemp).

Time Travel: Fast forward or reverse. (Remember not to mess up destiny.)

Tom & Jerry: Cat and mouse battle.

Toys: Those childhood (and for some, adulthood) playthings.

Trading Places: Switching lives or souls with someone else.

Trains: All aboard!

Treasure Hunt: Dig on the spot marked "X."

Trees: Lots of these make a forest.

TV Movies: First shown on broadcast, cable or foreign television.

TV Series: Collections, anthologies and individual episodes of memorable shows.

TV Tales: The media rage.

Twins: A double take.

Vacations: As the British say, "On holiday."

Vampires: Blood sucking guys from Transylvania.

Viva Las Vegas!: The lights, the casinos, the wedding chapels, Wayne Newton.

Volcanoes: Mountain blowing off some steam.

Voodoo: Do that voodoo that you do so well.

Waitresses: Just a job to pass the time before my acting career takes off.

War, General: Generally any conflict that defies other classification.

Wedding Bells: Here comes the bride.

Werewolves: When the moon is full, I feel kind of funny.

Winnie the Pooh: That pot-bellied, honey-loving bear.

Witches' Brew: Hocus-pocus and toil and trouble.

WonderWorks Movies: Tales from the PBS series.

World War I: The First Big One.

World War II: The Last Big One.

Wrestling: Choreographed sport that may involve men or women, but usually not a combo of the two.

Wrong Side of the Tracks: Often involves relationship with someone from the right side.

Category Index

The **CATEGORY INDEX** includes terms ranging from the serious to the silly, allowing you to search for genres (Drama), themes (Family Ties), events (the Olympics), places (Scotland), people (Babysitters) and more. Category definitions and cross references are contained in the "Category List" preceding the index; category terms and movie titles are listed alphabetically.

Adapted from a Cartoon

Ace Ventura: Pet Detective
The Addams Family
Addams Family Values •
The Adventures of Captain Marvel
Adventures of Red Ryder
Adventures of Smilin' Jack
Annie
Baby's Day Out
Batman •
Batman Forever
Batman Returns
The Belles of St. Trinian's •
Brenda Starr
Captain America
Casper •
The Crow
Dennis the Menace
Dennis the Menace: Dinosaur Hunter
Dick Tracy
Dick Tracy •
Dr. Strange
The Flash
Flash Gordon
The Flintstones
Great St. Trinian's Train Robbery
Howard the Duck
The Incredible Hulk
Judge Dredd
Little Nemo: Adventures in Slumberland
Little Orphan Annie
The Mask •
Mighty Morphin Power Rangers: The Movie
Phantom 2040 Movie: The Ghost Who Walks
The Pink Panther •
Prince Valiant
The Pure Hell of St. Trinian's
Regl'ar Fellers

The Return of Swamp Thing
Richie Rich
Skeleton Warriors
Superman 1: The Movie •
Superman 2 •
Superman 3
Superman 4: The Quest for Peace
Teenage Mutant Ninja Turtles 1: The Movie
Teenage Mutant Ninja Turtles 2: The Secret of the Ooze
Teenage Mutant Ninja Turtles 3
Timecop
Tom and Jerry: The Movie

Adapted from the Radio

Renfrew of the Royal Mounted
The Shadow
The War of the Worlds •

Adapted from TV

The Addams Family
Addams Family Values •
Batman: Mask of the Phantasm
The Beverly Hillbillies
Bonanza: The Return
Boris and Natasha: The Movie
The Brady Bunch Movie •
Car 54, Where Are You?
Coneheads
Cooley High •
Dennis the Menace
Dragnet
The Flintstones
Flipper
The Fugitive •
Gargoyles, The Movie: The Heroes Awaken
It's Pat: The Movie
The Jetsons: The Movie
Lassie

The Left-Handed Gun •
Maverick •
Mission: Impossible •
Mystery Science Theater 3000: The Movie •
The Naked Gun: From the Files of Police Squad •
Naked Gun 33 1/3: The Final Insult
Naked Gun 2 1/2: The Smell of Fear
Phantom 2040 Movie: The Ghost Who Walks
Sgt. Bilko
Sesame Street's 25th Birthday: A Musical Celebration
Star Trek 2: The Wrath of Khan •
Star Trek 3: The Search for Spock
Star Trek 4: The Voyage Home •
Star Trek 5: The Final Frontier
Star Trek 6: The Undiscovered Country
Star Trek Generations •
Star Trek: The Motion Picture
Stuart Saves His Family
A Very Brady Sequel
Wackiest Wagon Train in the West
Wayne's World
Wayne's World 2

Adolescence
see Growing Pains; High School Hijinks; Summer Camp; Teen Tribulations

Africa
see also Apartheid
Ace Ventura: When Nature Calls

Africa Screams
African Journey
The African Queen •
The Air Up There
Allan Quartermain and the Lost City of Gold
Animals Are Beautiful People
Bopha! •
Born Wild
The Bushbaby
Cheetah
Congo
A Far Off Place
The Flame Trees of Thika •
The Gods Must Be Crazy •
The Gods Must Be Crazy 2 •
Hatari •
In the Army Now
The Jewel of the Nile
Jirimpimbira: An African Folktale
Jungle Drums of Africa
King Kong •
Koi and the Kola Nuts
Mighty Joe Young
Really Wild Animals: Swinging Safari
Sarafina! •
A World Apart •

African America
Above the Rim
African Story Magic
Almos' a Man
Anansi
Bebe's Kids
Bingo Long Traveling All-Stars & Motor Kings •
Bopha! •
Boyz N the Hood •
Club Connect: The Hip-Hop Alternative
Crooklyn •
A Dream for Christmas •
The Ernest Green Story
A Family Thing •

Glory •
The Great White Hope
Gullah Gullah Island: Binyah's Surprise
A Hero Ain't Nothin' But a Sandwich •
Hoop Dreams •
House Party •
House Party 2: The Pajama Jam
House Party 3
The Inkwell
Jazz Time Tale
Love Your Mama
Malcolm X •
Menace II Society •
The Meteor Man
Once Upon a Time . . . When We Were Colored •
Piece of the Action
Poetic Justice
Sarafina! •
Sounder •
Stories from the Black Tradition
The Talking Eggs
Waiting to Exhale •
Words by Heart
Zebrahead •

AIDS
Boys on the Side
The Cure •
For Our Children: The Concert
Forrest Gump •
Philadelphia •

Airborne
Adventures of Smilin' Jack
Airplane! •
Airplane 2: The Sequel
Airport •
Airport '75
Airport '77
Alaska
Alive
Always

 Bullets (•) indicate 3 bones or above

Angela's Airplane
Apollo 13 •
Battle of Britain
The Big Plane Trip
Broken Arrow
The Buddy Holly Story •
Die Hard 2: Die Harder •
Dumbo •
The Flying Deuces •
Forget Paris
French Kiss •
The Great Waldo
    Pepper •
Hero
The Island at the Top of
    the World
It Happened at the
    World's Fair
Jay Jay the Jet Plane
Just Planes for Kids
La Bamba •
Look Who's Talking Now
The Man with the Golden
    Gun
Moon Pilot
Operation Dumbo Drop
The Phantom
The Right Stuff •
Shadow of the Eagle
Terminal Velocity
Top Gun

Airplanes
see Airborne

Aliens — Nasty
see also Aliens — Nice
The Adventures of
    Buckaroo Banzai
    Across the Eighth
    Dimension •
Battle Beyond the Stars
Battlestar Galactica
Captain Scarlet vs. The
    Mysterons
Critters
Destroy All Monsters
Doctor Who: An
    Unearthly Child
Doctor Who and the
    Daleks
The Empire Strikes
    Back •
Godzilla vs. the Cosmic
    Monster
Gremlins •
Gremlins 2: The New
    Batch •
Independence Day •
Invaders from Mars
Invasion of the Body
    Snatchers •
Mom and Dad Save the
    World
Munchies
Radar Men from the
    Moon
Return of the Jedi •
Revenge of the
    Mysterons from Mars
Space Angel, Vol. 1
Star Trek 3: The Search
    for Spock
Star Trek: The Motion
    Picture
Star Wars •

Stargate
Strange Invaders •
Super Mario Bros.
Superman 1: The Movie •
Teen Alien
The War of the Worlds •
Zombies of the
    Stratosphere

Aliens — Nice
see also Aliens —
    Nasty
The Aurora Encounter
*batteries not included
The Brother from Another
    Planet •
The Cat from Outer
    Space
Close Encounters of the
    Third Kind •
Cocoon •
Cocoon: The Return
Coneheads
The Cosmic Eye •
Dr. Seuss' Hoober-Bloob
    Highway
Doin' Time on Planet
    Earth
The Empire Strikes
    Back •
Enemy Mine
Escape to Witch
    Mountain •
E.T.: The Extra-
    Terrestrial •
The Ewok Adventure
The Ewoks: Battle for
    Endor
Fire in the Sky
Flight of the Navigator •
Gremlins •
Gremlins 2: The New
    Batch •
Howard the Duck
Hyper-Sapien: People
    from Another Star
Labyrinth •
The Last Starfighter
Mac and Me
Munchie
My Stepmother Is an
    Alien
Nukie
Pajama Party
Purple People Eater
Return of the Jedi •
Simon
Spaced Invaders
Star Trek 3: The Search
    for Spock
Star Trek 4: The Voyage
    Home •
Star Wars •
Starman •
Suburban Commando
Super Mario Bros.
Supergirl
Superman 1: The Movie •
Superman 2 •
Superman 3
Superman 4: The Quest
    for Peace
Teenage Mutant Ninja
    Turtles 2: The Secret
    of the Ooze
Wee Wendy

Widget of the Jungle

Amazing Adventures
see also Disaster
    Strikes!; Funny
    Adventures; Martial
    Arts;
    Swashbucklers
Across the Great Divide
The Adventures of
    Captain Marvel
The Adventures of Frank
    and Jesse James
The Adventures of
    Frontier Fremont
The Adventures of Huck
    Finn •
The Adventures of
    Huckleberry Finn
The Adventures of
    Huckleberry Finn •
The Adventures of Milo &
    Otis •
Adventures of Red Ryder
The Adventures of Robin
    Hood •
Adventures of Smilin'
    Jack
The Adventures of
    SuperTed
The Adventures of the
    Wilderness Family
The Adventures of Tom
    Sawyer
The Adventures of
    Ultraman
Aladdin and the
    Wonderful Lamp
Alaska
Ali Baba and the Forty
    Thieves
Allan Quartermain and
    the Lost City of Gold
Aloha, Bobby and Rose
The Amazing Panda
    Adventure
The Amazing Spider-Man
Antarctica
Apollo 13 •
Around the World in 80
    Days •
Atom Man vs. Superman
Bad Boys
Batman •
Batman Forever
Batman Returns
Beetlejuice, Vol. 1
The Belstone Fox
Benji the Hunted
Bigfoot: The
    Unforgettable
    Encounter
The Black Arrow
The Black Stallion •
The Black Stallion
    Returns
The Black Widow
Blood Brothers
Blue Fin
BMX Bandits
Born Wild
The Bounty
Boy of Two Worlds
Broken Arrow
Brothers Lionheart

The Bulldozer Brigade
Burn 'Em Up Barnes
The Bushbaby
Call of the Wild
Camel Boy
Candleshoe •
Cannonball
Captain America
Captain America 2: Death
    Too Soon
Captain Blood •
Captain Harlock, Vol. 1
Captain Planet & the
    Planeteers: A Hero for
    Earth
The Cat
Catch Me. . .If You Can
Challenge To Be Free
Challenge to White Fang
Charlie and the Great
    Balloon Chase
Charlie, the Lonesome
    Cougar
Cheetah
Child of Glass
Clarence, the Cross-eyed
    Lion
Clear and Present Danger
Cloak & Dagger
Conan the Barbarian •
Conan the Destroyer
Congo
Cool As Ice
The Count of Monte
    Cristo
Courage Mountain
Courage of Black Beauty
The Crimson Ghost
Crimson Tide •
Crusoe
A Cry in the Wild •
Crystalstone
Cutthroat Island
Danger Mouse, Vol. 1
Daredevils of the Red
    Circle
Daring Dobermans
Davy Crockett and the
    River Pirates •
Davy Crockett, King of
    the Wild Frontier •
The Day of the Dolphin
Death of the Incredible
    Hulk
Diamonds are Forever •
Dick Deadeye
Dick Tracy
Dick Tracy, Detective
Dick Tracy Meets
    Gruesome
Die Hard •
Die Hard 2: Die Harder •
Die Hard: With a
    Vengeance
The Doberman Gang
Doc Savage
Dr. No •
Dr. Syn, Alias the
    Scarecrow
Don Winslow of the
    Coast Guard
Don Winslow of the Navy
Don't Change My World
The Dove
Dragonheart
Duncan's World

Edison Twins
Elephant Boy •
Emil and the Detective
Escape to Witch
    Mountain •
F/X 2: The Deadly Art of
    Illusion
Far from Home: The
    Adventures of Yellow
    Dog •
A Far Off Place
Fast Getaway 2
Federal Agents vs.
    Underworld, Inc.
Fighting Devil Dogs
Fighting Marines
The Fighting Prince of
    Donegal
The Fire in the Stone
Fish Hawk
The Flash
Flight of Dragons
Flight of the Grey Wolf
Flipper
Flipper's New Adventure
Flipper's Odyssey
For Your Eyes Only •
Free Willy 2: The
    Adventure Home
From Russia with Love •
The Fugitive •
Further Adventures of the
    Wilderness Family,
    Part 2
G-Men Never Forget
G-Men vs. the Black
    Dragon
Gentle Giant
The Ghost of Thomas
    Kempe
Goin' Coconuts
The Gold Bug
Gold Diggers: The Secret
    of Bear Mountain
Golden Voyage of Sinbad
Goldeneye
The Goonies
Great Adventure
The Great Train
    Robbery •
The Great Waldo
    Pepper •
The Green Hornet
Greenstone
Greystoke: The Legend of
    Tarzan, Lord of the
    Apes
Hackers
Harley
Hatari •
Hawk of the Wilderness
Heck's Way Home
Hercules
Hercules in New York
Hercules Unchained
High Country Calling
Highlander •
Highlander: The
    Gathering
Holt of the Secret Service
Homeward Bound 2: Lost
    in San Francisco
Homeward Bound: The
    Incredible Journey •
Huck and the King of
    Hearts

Elephant Boy •
Far from Home: The
    Adventures of Yellow
    Dog •
The Fifth Monkey
Flash, the Teenage Otter
Flight of the Grey Wolf
Flipper
The Fox and the Hound •
Francis Goes to the
    Races
Francis Joins the WACs
Francis the Talking
    Mule •
Free Willy
Gentle Ben
Gentle Giant
GeoKids: Camouflage,
    Cuttlefish, and
    Chameleons Changing
    Color
GeoKids: Tadpoles,
    Dragonflies, and the
    Caterpillar's Big
    Change
Gift of the Whales
The Glacier Fox
Going Ape!
Going Bananas
The Golden Seal
Gordy
Gorillas in the Mist •
The Great Cheese
    Conspiracy
The Great Rupert •
Grizzly Adams: The
    Legend Continues
Gus
Harry and the
    Hendersons
Hatari •
Hawmps!
High Country Calling
Homeward Bound 2: Lost
    in San Francisco
The Hound that Thought
    He was a Raccoon
Incident at Hawk's Hill
Island of the Blue
    Dolphins
Johann's Gift to
    Christmas
Jumanji
The Jungle Book •
Jungle Drums of Africa
A Jungle for Joey
The Jungle King
Kidsongs: A Day with the
    Animals
King of the Grizzlies
Lassie, Come Home •
Lassie: The Miracle
Legend of Lobo
Leonard Part 6
Let's Dance on the Farm
    with Miss Nola
Let's Explore . . . Furry,
    Fishy, Feathery Friends
The Lion King •
The Littlest Pet Shop
Living Free
The Magic of the Golden
    Bear: Goldy 3
The Marzipan Pig
Matilda

The Misadventures of
    Merlin Jones
Monkeys, Go Home!
Monkey's Uncle
Mountain Family
    Robinson
Mountain Man
Mowgli's Brothers
Napoleon and
    Samantha •
Never Cry Wolf •
Nikki, the Wild Dog of
    the North •
Once Upon a Forest
Operation Dumbo Drop
Ovide and the Gang
Pippi Longstocking
Planet of the Apes •
The Polar Bear King
The Pretty Piggies: The
    Adventure Begins
Project X •
Rascal
Really Wild Animals:
    Swinging Safari
Really Wild Animals:
    Wonders Down Under
Reddy the Fox
The Rescuers •
The Rescuers Down
    Under
Rikki-Tikki-Tavi
Ring of Bright Water •
Rock-a-Doodle
Rudyard Kipling's The
    Jungle Book •
The Runaways
Running Free
Sammy, the Way-Out
    Seal
Seabert: Good Guys
    Wear White
Secret of NIMH •
See How They Grow
Sesame Songs: Sing,
    Hoot & Howl
The Silver Fox and Sam
    Davenport
The Silver Streak •
Speaking of Animals, Vol.
    1
A Summer to Remember
Super Seal
A Tale of Two Critters
Tarka the Otter
The Tender Warrior
Those Calloways
The Three Little Pigs
Thumbelina
Thumpkin and the Easter
    Bunnies
A Tiger Walks
Tomboy & the Champ
The Tortoise and the
    Hare
Trap on Cougar Mountain
Walk Like a Man
Watership Down •
We're Goin' to the Farm
    with Father Dan
Whale of a Tale
When the North Wind
    Blows
When the Whales Came
The White Seal

Wildlife Tales: The
    Legend of the Bison
Wind in the Willows, Vol.
    1
Winter Wolf
The Yearling •
Yogi and the Invasion of
    the Space Bears
Yogi and the Magical
    Flight of the Spruce
    Goose
Yogi's Great Escape
Zebra in the Kitchen
Zoofari

American Indians
see Native America

Amnesia
Clean Slate
Overboard
Regarding Henry •
Spellbound •

Amusement Parks
*see also Circuses &
    Carnivals*
The Adventures of Mary-
    Kate & Ashley: The
    Case of the Fun House
    Mystery
Bebe's Kids
Beverly Hills Cop 3
My Life
National Lampoon's
    Vacation •
Strangers on a Train •

Andy Hardy
Andy Hardy Gets Spring
    Fever
Andy Hardy Meets
    Debutante
Andy Hardy's Double Life
Andy Hardy's Private
    Secretary
Life Begins for Andy
    Hardy •
Love Finds Andy Hardy •
Love Laughs at Andy
    Hardy

Angels
see also Heaven Sent
Always
Angels in the Outfield
Clarence
Date with an Angel
Field of Dreams •
Heart and Souls
The Heavenly Kid
The Horn Blows at
    Midnight •
It Came Upon a Midnight
    Clear
It's a Wonderful Life •
The Littlest Angel
One Magic Christmas
Slam Dunk Ernest
Waiting for the Light
Who's Who at the Zoo?
Wings of Desire •

Animals
*see Amazing Animals;
    Birds; Cats; Horses;
    King of Beasts
    (Dogs)*

Apartheid
*see also Africa; Civil
    Rights*
Bopha! •
Cry, the Beloved
    Country •
The Power of One
Sarafina! •
A World Apart •

Asia
see also China
The Amazing Panda
    Adventure
Flower Drum Song
Little Buddha
The Man with the Golden
    Gun

At the Movies
Cinema Paradiso •
Last Action Hero
The Long Day Closes •
Matinee •
The Projectionist •
The Purple Rose of
    Cairo •
Two Bits

Australia
see Down Under

Baby Talk
see also Parenthood
Addams Family Values •
And Baby Makes Six
Baby Boom
Baby's Day Out
Enemy Mine
Eye on the Sparrow
Father's Little Dividend •
For Keeps
Funny Girl •
Immediate Family
In Search of a Golden
    Sky
Little Man Tate •
Look Who's Talking •
Look Who's Talking, Too
My Life
Parenthood •
Penny Serenade •
Problem Child 2
Rumpelstiltskin
She's Having a Baby
The Snapper •
Table for Five
The Tender Years
The Terminator •
Three Men and a Baby •
Three Men and a
    Cradle •

Babysitters
*see also Baby Talk;
    Parenthood*
Addams Family Values •
Adventures in Babysitting •
The Baby-Sitters Club

Bebe's Kids
The Crazysitter
Look Who's Talking •
Mr. Nanny
Uncle Buck

Ballet
see also Gotta Dance!
Brain Donors
George Balanchine's The
    Nutcracker
I Want to be a Ballerina
Nine Months
The Red Shoes •
Shall We Dance •
Tales of Beatrix Potter •
The Tales of Hoffman
The Tin Soldier

Ballooning
Around the World in 80
    Days •
Around the World in 80
    Days
Charlie and the Great
    Balloon Chase
Mysterious Island •
Night Crossing
Olly Olly Oxen Free
The Red Balloon •

Baseball
Amazing Grace & Chuck
Angels in the Outfield
The Babe
The Bad News Bears •
The Bad News Bears Go
    to Japan
The Bad News Bears in
    Breaking Training
Bang the Drum Slowly •
Big Mo
Bingo Long Traveling All-
    Stars & Motor Kings •
Blue Skies Again
Brewster's Millions
Casey at the Bat
Chasing Dreams
Comeback Kid
Ed
Eight Men Out •
Field of Dreams •
How to Play Baseball
The Kid from Left Field
A League of Their Own •
Little Big League
Major League
Major League 2
Mr. Baseball
Mr. Destiny
The Natural •
Past the Bleachers
Pastime •
Rookie of the Year
The Sandlot •
The Scout
Talent for the Game
Tiger Town
Trading Hearts
Wait Until Spring,
    Bandini
A Winner Never Quits

Basketball
Above the Rim

The Absent-Minded
  Professor ●
The Air Up There
Annie O
The Basketball Diaries
Blue Chips
Celtic Pride
Coach
Eddie
Fast Break
The Fish that Saved
  Pittsburgh
Forget Paris
Hoop Dreams ●
Hoosiers ●
One on One
Pistol: The Birth of a
  Legend
Slam Dunk Ernest
Teen Wolf

Beach Blanket Bingo
see also Surfing
Back to the Beach
Beach Blanket Bingo ●
Beach Party
Bikini Beach
How to Stuff a Wild
  Bikini
Muscle Beach Party
Pajama Party
Shag: The Movie ●

Bedtime Stories
*see also Fairy Tales;
  Storytelling*
Abel's Island
Adventures in
  Dinosaurland
Adventures of Buster the
  Bear
The Adventures of
  Curious George
The Adventures of Mark
  Twain ●
The Adventures of Oliver
  Twist
The Adventures of Peter
  Cottontail
The Adventures of Peter
  Cottontail and His
  Friends of the Green
  Forest
Adventures of Reddy the
  Fox
Aesop's Fables
Aesop's Fables, Vol. 1:
  The Hen with the
  Golden Egg
All New Adventures of
  Tom Sawyer: Mischief
  on the Mississippi
Anansi
Animal Farm ●
Around the World in 80
  Days
Babar and Father
  Christmas
Babar Comes to America
Babar: Monkey Business
Babar Returns
Babar the Elephant
  Comes to America
Babar the Little Elephant
Babar: The Movie ●
Babar's First Step

Babar's Triumph
The Baby-Sitter's Club
Berenstain Bears' Comic
  Valentine
Berenstain Bears' Easter
  Surprise
Berenstain Bears Meet
  Big Paw
Billy Possum
The Black Tulip
Bob the Quail
The Bollo Caper
The Boy Who Drew Cats
Brer Rabbit Tales
Bunnicula: Vampire
  Rabbit
Chatterer the Squirrel
The Classic Tales
  Collection
A Connecticut Yankee in
  King Arthur's Court
The Cricket in Times
  Square
David and Goliath
Davy Crockett
The Day Jimmy's Boa Ate
  the Wash and Other
  Stories
Dick Deadeye
Dorothy in the Land of
  Oz
The Ezra Jack Keats
  Library
Faeries
Flight of Dragons
Frog and Toad are
  Friends
The Grasshopper and the
  Ants
Great Bible Stories:
  Abraham
Gulliver's Travels
Hanna-Barbera Storybook
  Classics
Harold and the Purple
  Crayon and Other
  Harold Stories
The Hobbit ●
How to Eat Fried Worms
The Hunchback of Notre
  Dame
Jack & the Beanstalk
Jack and the Beanstalk
Joey Runs Away and
  Other Stories
Jonah and the Whale
Journey Back to Oz
Jungle Book: Mowgli
  Comes to the Jungle
Kidnapped
King Arthur & the
  Knights of the Round
  Table, Vol. 1
Koi and the Kola Nuts
The Last Unicorn
The Legend of Hiawatha
The Legend of
  Manxmouse
Les Miserables
The Lion, the Witch and
  the Wardrobe ●
The Little Engine That
  Could
The Little House
The Little Match Girl
The Little Prince

Little Sister Rabbit
Little Women ●
Little Women
Little Women Series
The Lord of the Rings
Madeline
Marvelous Land of Oz
Maurice Sendak Library
Maurice Sendak's Really
  Rosie
Max's Chocolate Chicken
  and Other Stories for
  Young Children
Mike Mulligan and His
  Steam Shovel
More Stories for the Very
  Young
Mowgli's Brothers
Nursery Rhymes
Paddington Bear
The Paper Bag Princess
Peachboy
Peter and the Wolf
Peter Pan ●
Phantom of the Opera
Phantom Tollbooth ●
The Pickwick Papers
The Pigs' Wedding and
  Other Stories
The Prince and the
  Pauper ●
The Prince and the
  Pauper
Princess and the Goblin
The Princess and the
  Goblin
Reading Rainbow:
  Abiyoyo
Return to Oz
Richard Scarry's Best
  ABC Video Ever!
Richard Scarry's Best
  Busy People Video
  Ever
Rikki-Tikki-Tavi
Rip Van Winkle
Robinson Crusoe
Shari Lewis & Lamb
  Chop: One Minute
  Bible Stories, New
  Testament
Shari Lewis: Don't Wake
  Your Mom
Shirley Temple
  Storybook Theater
Stories and Fables, Vol. 1
Stories to Remember:
  Baby's Morningtime
The Tender Tale of
  Cinderella Penguin
Tommy Tricker & the
  Stamp Traveller ●
The Tortoise and the
  Hare
The Truth About Mother
  Goose
20,000 Leagues Under
  the Sea
Velveteen Rabbit
The Velveteen Rabbit
The Willies
Wind in the Willows, Vol.
  1
The Wizard of Oz

The Wizard of Oz:
  Danger in a Strange
  Land
Wonderful Wizard of Oz
World of Hans Christian
  Andersen
A World of Stories with
  Katharine Hepburn

Bereavement
The Addams Family
Always
Audrey Rose
Babar's First Step
Beetlejuice ●
Bill & Ted's Bogus
  Journey
Black Magic
Boys on the Side
Breaking the Rules
The Canterville Ghost
Carousel ●
Chances Are ●
A Christmas Carol
A Christmas Carol
The Crow
Death of a Goldfish
The Devil & Max Devlin
Earthling
The Fig Tree
First Knight
Fluke
Four Weddings and a
  Funeral ●
Ghost ●
Granpa
Heart and Souls
The Heavenly Kid
Hello Again
Hocus Pocus
Homeward Bound
Into the West ●
It Came Upon a Midnight
  Clear
It's a Wonderful Life ●
Kiss Me Goodbye
The Lady in White ●
Mannequin
My Girl
My Girl 2
My Life
Oh, Heavenly Dog!
Only the Lonely
The Pallbearer
The Peanut Butter
  Solution ●
Poltergeist ●
Poltergeist 2: The Other
  Side
Poltergeist 3
Promises in the Dark
Scrooge
Scrooged
Sleepless in Seattle ●
Somewhere Tomorrow
Stand By Me ●
Star Trek 3: The Search
  for Spock
Terms of Endearment ●
13 Ghosts
Tom and Huck ●
Topper ●
Topper Returns ●
Topper Takes a Trip ●
Truly, Madly, Deeply ●
Uncle Elephant

Unstrung Heroes
Weekend at Bernie's
Weekend at Bernie's 2
What's Eating Gilbert
  Grape ●
Where the Lilies Bloom ●

Best Friends
Abbott and Costello Meet
  Frankenstein ●
Adios Amigo
The Adventures of Huck
  Finn ●
The Adventures of
  Huckleberry Finn
The Adventures of Milo &
  Otis ●
The Baby-Sitters Club
Backbeat ●
Bad Boys
Bad Company ●
The Basketball Diaries
The Bear ●
Beautiful Girls
Big Mo
Big Shots
Bigfoot: The
  Unforgettable
  Encounter
Bill & Ted's Bogus
  Journey
Black Beauty
Born to Be Wild
The Boy Who Could Fly
Breaking the Rules
Butch Cassidy and the
  Sundance Kid ●
The Cable Guy
The Caddy
Calendar Girl
The Cat
Celtic Pride
Charlie's Ghost: The
  Secret of Coronado
Circle of Friends
City Slickers ●
City Slickers 2: The
  Legend of Curly's Gold
Class Act
Clerks ●
Courage of Black Beauty
The Cure ●
December
Die Hard: With a
  Vengeance
Digger
Dream a Little Dream 2
Driving Miss Daisy ●
Drop Dead Fred
Dumb & Dumber
Dunston Checks In ●
Enemy Mine
F/X 2: The Deadly Art of
  Illusion
Far from Home: The
  Adventures of Yellow
  Dog ●
First Kid
The Flintstones
Flipper
Free Willy
Free Willy 2: The
  Adventure Home
Gold Diggers: The Secret
  of Bear Mountain
Gordy

Grumpier Old Men
Grumpy Old Men •
Guarding Tess
Gumby and the Moon
  Boggles
Hollywood or Bust
Homeward Bound 2: Lost
  in San Francisco
Huck and the King of
  Hearts
If Lucy Fell
Indian Summer
K-9000
The Karate Kid •
The Karate Kid: Part 2
The Karate Kid: Part 3
Kingpin
Little Rascals Christmas
  Special
The Littlest Outlaw
Looking for Miracles
The Lords of Flatbush
Madeline
Mallrats
The Man Who Would Be
  King •
My Girl
Now and Then
The Odd Couple •
Oliver & Company •
One Crazy Summer
Papillon •
Past the Bleachers
P.K. and the Kid
Racing with the Moon •
The Red Balloon •
The Reivers •
The Return of the
  Musketeers
Revenge of the Nerds
Russkies
The Sandlot •
Shag: The Movie •
Snow White and the
  Seven Dwarfs
Spies Like Us
Stand By Me •
Star Trek 4: The Voyage
  Home •
Starbird and Sweet
  William
The Sunshine Boys •
Ten Who Dared
That Sinking Feeling •
Three Amigos
Three Men and a Baby •
Three Men and a
  Cradle •
Three Musketeers
The Three Musketeers
Three Musketeers
Three Musketeers •
The Three Musketeers
Thursday's Game •
To Wong Foo, Thanks for
  Everything, Julie
  Newmar
Tombstone •
Top Dog
Top Gun
Tough Guys
Toy Story •
Wayne's World
Wayne's World 2
Where the River Runs
  Black

Where the Toys Come
  From
White Christmas •
White Mama •
Winnie the Pooh &
  Friends

The Big Sting
see also Heists
Adios Amigo
Barnaby and Me
Blue Murder at St.
  Trinian's •
Candleshoe •
Curly Sue
Dirty Rotten Scoundrels •
F/X •
F/X 2: The Deadly Art of
  Illusion
Federal Agents vs.
  Underworld, Inc.
Green Card
Harry & Walter Go to
  New York
Housesitter
Kid from Not-So-Big
Leap of Faith
Maverick •
Never Say Never Again
Opportunity Knocks
Paper Moon •
Piece of the Action
Quiz Show •
Sgt. Bilko
The Sting •
The Sting 2
Support Your Local
  Gunfighter •
Tootsie •

Bigfoot
Bigfoot: The
  Unforgettable
  Encounter
Harry and the
  Hendersons
Legend of Boggy Creek
Return to Boggy Creek

Biking
American Flyers
BMX Bandits
Breaking Away •
Pee Wee's Big
  Adventure •
Rad

Biography
see Biopics

Biopics
*see also Musician
  Biopics; Nashville
  Narratives*
Amadeus •
American Graffiti •
Annie Oakley
Au Revoir Les Enfants •
The Babe
Backbeat •
Beethoven Lives
  Upstairs •
Big Mo
Bound for Glory •
The Buddy Holly Story •
Chaplin

Chariots of Fire •
Christopher Columbus:
  The Discovery
Coal Miner's Daughter •
Conrack •
Cross Creek
Davy Crockett
Dragon: The Bruce Lee
  Story
Dreamchild •
8 Seconds
The Elephant Man •
1492: Conquest of
  Paradise
Funny Girl •
Funny Lady
Geronimo •
The Glenn Miller Story •
Gorillas in the Mist •
Greased Lightning
The Great White Hope •
The Greatest
Heart Like a Wheel •
I Am a Fugitive from a
  Chain Gang •
In Search of Dr. Seuss
Jefferson in Paris
Jesus Christ, Superstar •
The Jolson Story •
Joni
Knute Rockne: All
  American •
La Bamba •
Lady Jane •
Lawrence of Arabia •
The Learning Tree
The Left-Handed Gun •
The Loneliest Runner •
MacArthur
Malcolm X •
The Miracle Worker •
Mommie Dearest •
My Father's Glory •
Pistol: The Birth of a
  Legend
Ring of Bright Water •
The Seven Little Foys •
The Ten
  Commandments •
This Boy's Life •
Till the Clouds Roll By •
Wait Until Spring,
  Bandini
Waltz King
What's Love Got to Do
  With It? •
Wild Hearts Can't Be
  Broken •
A Winner Never Quits
The Wonderful World of
  the Brothers Grimm
Yankee Doodle Dandy •

Birds
Bill and Coo
The Birds •
Chipmunk and His Bird
  Friends
The Goodbye Bird
High Anxiety •
Howard the Duck
Million Dollar Duck
Mr. & Mrs. Condor
The Pebble and the
  Penguin

The Pigeon that Worked
  a Miracle
Sesame Street Presents:
  Follow That Bird •
Shamu & You: Exploring
  the World of Birds
Spirit of the Eagle
Unsinkable Donald Duck
  with Huey, Dewey &
  Louie
Wild Geese Calling
Woody Woodpecker
  Collector's Edition, Vol.
  1

Blindness
*see also Physical
  Problems*
Amy •
Breaking Free
Butterflies Are Free •
City Lights •
Eye on the Sparrow •
Ice Castles
Love Leads the Way •
The Miracle Worker •
Places in the Heart •

Boating
*see High Seas
  Adventure*

Books
*see also Bedtime
  Stories; Storytelling*
Cross Creek
Crossing Delancey •
The Joy Luck Club •
The NeverEnding Story
The Paper Chase •

Books to Film: Louisa
  May Alcott
Little Men
Little Women •
Little Women
Little Women •
Little Women Series

Books to Film: J.M.
  Barrie
Hook
Peter Pan •
Peter Pan •
Peter Pan & the Pirates:
  Demise of Hook

Books to Film:
  Frances Hodgson
  Burnett
Little Lord Fauntleroy •
The Little Princess •
A Little Princess •
The Secret Garden •

Books to Film:
  Rudyard Kipling
Captains Courageous •
The Jungle Book •
Kim
The Man Who Would Be
  King •
Rudyard Kipling's The
  Jungle Book •
Wee Willie Winkie •

Books to Film: Astrid
  Lindgren
The Land of Faraway
The New Adventures of
  Pippi Longstocking
Pippi Goes on Board
Pippi in the South Seas
Pippi Longstocking
Pippi on the Run

Books to Film: Jack
  London
Call of the Wild
Great Adventure
White Fang •
White Fang and the
  Hunter

Books to Film: L.M.
  Montgomery
Anne of Avonlea •
Anne of Green Gables •
Lantern Hill
Tales from Avonlea, Vol.
  1: The Journey Begins

Books to Film: Mark
  Twain
The Adventures of Huck
  Finn •
The Adventures of
  Huckleberry Finn
The Adventures of
  Huckleberry Finn •
The Adventures of Tom
  Sawyer
Ava's Magical Adventure
A Connecticut Yankee •
A Connecticut Yankee in
  King Arthur's Court
Huck and the King of
  Hearts
Huckleberry Finn •
A Kid in King Arthur's
  Court
Mark Twain's A
  Connecticut Yankee in
  King Arthur's Court
The New Adventures of
  Tom and Huck
The Prince and the
  Pauper •
The Prince and the
  Pauper
Tom and Huck •
Tom Sawyer •
Unidentified Flying
  Oddball
Wishbone: A Tail in
  Twain

Bowling
Grease 2
Kingpin
Mr. Wonderful

Boxing
Any Which Way You Can
Arena
Bowery Blitzkrieg
Far and Away •
The Great White Hope •
The Greatest
Kid Dynamite
The Main Event
Matilda

Josie & the Pussycats in
  Outer Space
Little Nemo: Adventures
  in Slumberland
The Lone Ranger
The Man Called
  Flintstone
Max Fleischer's Cartoon
  Capers, Vol. 1: Playin'
  Around
Mighty Hercules:
  Champion of the
  People!
Mighty Hercules:
  Conqueror of Evil!
The Mighty Hercules:
  Mightiest Mortal!
Mighty Mouse
Mighty Mouse in the
  Great Space Chase
Mighty Thor: Enter
  Hercules
Mr. Magoo: 1001 Arabian
  Night's Dream
Mr. Magoo: Cyrano De
  Bergerac/A
  Midsummer Night's
  Dream
The Mr. Magoo Show,
  Vol. 1
The Pink Panther •
The Pink Panther
Pink Panther: Fly in the
  Pink
Pink Panther: Tickled
  Pink
Pogo for President: "I Go
  Pogo"
Precious Pupp
Schoolhouse Rock:
  Grammar Rock
Schoolhouse Rock:
  History Rock
Schoolhouse Rock:
  Science Rock
Scooby-Doo
Speed Racer
Thunderbirds
Underdog: The Tickle
  Feather Machine
Winnie the Pooh
Winnie the Pooh and a
  Day for Eeyore
Winnie the Pooh &
  Friends
Winnie the Pooh and
  Tigger Too

Cartoon Tunes
Aladdin •
All Dogs Go to Heaven
All Dogs Go to Heaven 2
An American Tail •
An American Tail: Fievel
  Goes West •
Beauty and the Beast •
Charlotte's Web •
Cinderella •
Disney's Sing-Along
  Songs: The Hunchback
  of Notre Dame: Topsy
  Turvy
Gay Purr-ee
The Hunchback of Notre
  Dame •
Jack & the Beanstalk

The Jungle Book •
Lady and the Tramp •
The Lion King •
Little Critter Series: Just
  Me and My Dad
The Little Mermaid •
The Magic Voyage
The New Adventures of
  Peter Rabbit
The Nutcracker
The Pebble and the
  Penguin
People
Pinocchio •
Pocahontas
Pocahontas •
Robin Hood •
Rock-a-Doodle
Shinbone Alley
Sleeping Beauty •
Snow White and the
  Seven Dwarfs •
The Swan Princess •
Thumbelina
Treasure Island
Tubby the Tuba
Water Babies
Yellow Submarine •
You're a Good Man,
  Charlie Brown

Cartoonmercials
Abbott and Costello
  Cartoon Festival
The Adventures of Teddy
  Ruxpin
Blackstar
The Cabbage Patch Kid's
  First Christmas
The California Raisins:
  Meet the Raisins
Care Bears: Family
  Storybook
The Care Bears Movie
The Care Bears Movie 2:
  A New Generation
Charmkins
G.I. Joe, Vol. 1: A Real
  American Hero
Gobots
Gobots: Battle of the
  Rock Lords
He-Man & the Masters of
  the Universe, Vol. 1
Heroes on Hot Wheels,
  Vol. 1
Lady Lovelylocks & the
  Pixietails, Vol. 1
Lazer Tag Academy: The
  Movie
The Legend of Zelda:
  Missing Link
Maple Town
Maple Town: Case of the
  Missing Candy
My Little Pony: The
  Movie
Potato Head Kids, Vol. 1
Pound Puppies
Rainbow Brite: A Horse
  of a Different Color
The Real Ghostbusters
Rubik, the Amazing
  Cube, Vol. 1

Strawberry Shortcake
  and the Baby Without
  a Name
Super Mario Bros. Super
  Show 1
Transformers
Transformers: The Movie
World of Strawberry
  Shortcake

Cats
The Adventures of Milo &
  Otis •
The Aristocats •
Baby Animals Just Want
  to Have Fun
Batman Returns
Bunnicula: Vampire
  Rabbit
The Cat
Cat City
The Cat from Outer
  Space
Cat's Eye
Felix the Cat: An Hour of
  Fun
Felix the Cat: The Movie
A Garfield Christmas
Garfield: His 9 Lives
Garfield in Paradise
Garfield's Feline Fantasy
Garfield's Halloween
  Adventure
Garfield's Thanksgiving
Gay Purr-ee
Heathcliff & Marmaduke
Here Comes Garfield
Here Comes the Cat! and
  Other Stories
Homeward Bound 2: Lost
  in San Francisco
Homeward Bound: The
  Incredible Journey
The Incredible Journey •
Kitty Faces
Kitty Love!
Oliver & Company •
Puss in Boots
Puss 'n Boots
Secret Lives of Waldo
  Kitty Volume 1
That Darn Cat
That's My Hero!
The Three Lives of
  Thomasina •
Tom and Jerry: Starring
Tom and Jerry: The
  Movie
Tom & Jerry's 50th
  Birthday Classics
Top Cat and the Beverly
  Hills Cats

Cave People
Being Human
Encino Man
The Flintstones
When Dinosaurs Ruled
  the Earth

Charlie Brown & the
Peanuts
Be My Valentine, Charlie
  Brown/Is This
  Goodbye, Charlie
  Brown?

Bon Voyage, Charlie
  Brown
The Charlie Brown and
  Snoopy Show
The Charlie Brown and
  Snoopy Show: Vol. 1
A Charlie Brown
  Christmas
A Charlie Brown
  Thanksgiving
It's a Short Summer,
  Charlie Brown
It's the Easter Beagle,
  Charlie Brown
It's the Great Pumpkin,
  Charlie Brown (triple
  feature)
Race for Your Life,
  Charlie Brown
Snoopy, Come Home •
Snoopy: The Musical
This Is America, Charlie
  Brown: The Birth of
  the Constitution
This is America, Charlie
  Brown: The NASA
  Space Station
You're a Good Man,
  Charlie Brown
You're Not Elected,
  Charlie Brown!/A
  Charlie Brown
  Christmas

Chases
American Graffiti •
At the Circus
Baby on Board
Bad Boys
Beverly Hills Cop
Beverly Hills Cop 3
Born to Be Wild
Broken Arrow
Buck Privates Come
  Home •
Butch Cassidy and the
  Sundance Kid •
Charlie and the Great
  Balloon Chase
Diamonds are Forever •
Dick Tracy •
Dr. No •
Dumb & Dumber
Eat My Dust
E.T.: The Extra-
  Terrestrial •
For Your Eyes Only •
Foul Play
From Russia with Love •
The Fugitive •
The Golden Child
Goldeneye
Honeymoon in Vegas
The Hunt for Red
  October •
Indiana Jones and the
  Temple of Doom •
The Jewel of the Nile •
Jurassic Park •
License to Drive
Live and Let Die
The Man from Snowy
  River •
Man of the House
The Man with the Golden
  Gun

Memoirs of an Invisible
  Man
Money Train
Monkey Trouble •
North by Northwest •
Octopussy
On Her Majesty's Secret
  Service •
Outbreak •
Pee Wee's Big
  Adventure •
The Pelican Brief
A Perfect World
Planet of the Apes •
Raiders of the Lost Ark •
Return of the Jedi •
Romancing the Stone •
Savage Land
Smokey and the Bandit
Smokey and the Bandit,
  Part 2
Smokey and the Bandit,
  Part 3
The Spy Who Loved Me
Star Wars •
The Sting •
The Terminator •
Thunderball
Tom and Jerry: The
  Movie
Tom & Jerry: The Very
  Best Of Tom & Jerry
Tom & Jerry's 50th
  Birthday Classics
Top Gun
Toy Story •
Trapped In Paradise
True Lies
What's Up, Doc? •
Who Framed Roger
  Rabbit? •
Year of the Comet
You Only Live Twice

Child Abuse
Dolores Claiborne •
Father Hood
Mommie Dearest
Radio Flyer •
This Boy's Life •
Too Smart for Strangers
  with Winnie the Pooh
Where the Spirit Lives

Childhood Visions
see also Home Alone
All I Want for Christmas
American Heart •
And Now Miguel
Angels in the Outfield
Au Revoir Les Enfants •
The Baby-Sitters Club
Beethoven Lives
  Upstairs •
The Beniker Gang
Big •
Big Bully
The Black Stallion •
Blankman
Born to Run
Boyd's Shadow
The Cable Guy
Camp Nowhere
Captain January
Careful, He Might Hear
  You •

Casey's Shadow
Casper •
The Cat
A Christmas Story •
Cinema Paradiso •
Cria •
Crooklyn •
David Copperfield •
Desert Bloom •
Digger
Empire of the Sun •
E.T.: The Extra-
    Terrestrial •
The Flame Trees of
    Thika •
Flight of the Grey Wolf
Forbidden Games •
A Girl of the Limberlost
The Golden Seal
Heavyweights
Heidi
Heidi
Heidi •
Home Alone •
Home for Christmas
Hook
Hope and Glory •
The Indian in the
    Cupboard •
Into the West •
Invaders from Mars
Ira Sleeps Over
Jack
Josh and S.A.M.
Journey for Margaret •
The Kid from Left Field
King of the Hill •
The Lady in White •
Lassie's Great Adventure
Last Action Hero
Little Buddha •
Little Man Tate •
Little Monsters
The Little Princess •
A Little Princess •
The Little Rascals
The Littlest Horse
    Thieves
Look Who's Talking •
Look Who's Talking, Too
Lord of the Flies •
Lord of the Flies
Lost in Yonkers
Magic in the Water
Magic of Lassie
Magic Snowman
Man of the House
Matilda
Mommie Dearest
Mosby's Marauders
My Friend Flicka •
My Life as a Dog •
My Mother's Castle •
My Summer Story
National Velvet •
Nobody's Boy
Now and Then
Oliver! •
Pollyanna •
Poltergeist •
Poltergeist 2: The Other
    Side
The Poor Little Rich Girl
Radio Flyer •
Real Genius •
The Red Balloon •

The Red Pony •
Return from Witch
    Mountain
Richie Rich
Rock-a-Doodle
Running Free
Savage Sam
Searching for Bobby
    Fischer •
The Secret Garden •
Sidekicks
Small Change •
Sudden Terror
Sudie & Simpson
Taking Care of Terrific
Taps
Tito and Me •
To Kill a Mockingbird •
Toto le Heros •
Toy Story •
Treasure Island •
Turf Boy
12 Monkeys •
Wait Until Spring,
    Bandini
Wee Sing in the Big Rock
    Candy Mountains
What the Moon Saw •
Whistle Down the Wind •
White Fang •
The Wild Country
The Witching of Ben
    Wagner
The Wizard of Loneliness
A World Apart •
The Yearling •

China
see also Asia
Adventures of Smilin'
    Jack
The Amazing Panda
    Adventure
Big Bird in China
Empire of the Sun •
The Joy Luck Club •

Christmas
see also Holidays
All I Want for Christmas
Alvin & the Chipmunks: A
    Chipmunk Christmas
Alvin & the Chipmunks:
    Alvin's Christmas Carol
Amahl and the Night
    Visitors
An American Christmas
    Carol
The Angel and the
    Soldier Boy
Babar and Father
    Christmas
Babes in Toyland
Baby Songs Christmas
Barney's Christmas
    Surprise
B.C.: A Special Christmas
Benji's Very Own
    Christmas Story
The Berenstain Bears'
    Christmas
Bernard and the Genie
The Best Christmas
    Pageant Ever
Bluetoes the Christmas
    Elf

Bugs Bunny's Looney
    Christmas Tales
The Cabbage Patch Kid's
    First Christmas
Captain Kangaroo's
    Merry Christmas
    Stories
A Charlie Brown
    Christmas
Child's Christmas in
    Wales
A Christmas Carol •
A Christmas Carol
Christmas Cartoons
The Christmas Collection
Christmas Comes to
    Willow Creek
Christmas Eve on
    Sesame Street
A Christmas Fantasy
The Christmas
    Messenger
The Christmas Party
Christmas Stories
A Christmas Story
A Christmas Story •
The Christmas That
    Almost Wasn't
A Christmas to
    Remember
The Christmas Toy
The Christmas Tree
A Christmas Tree/Puss-
    In-Boots
Christmas Video Sing-
    Along
Christopher's Xmas
    Mission
The Country Mouse and
    the City Mouse: A
    Christmas Tale
Disney's Sing-Along
    Songs: The Twelve
    Days of Christmas
Disney's Sing-Along
    Songs, Vol. 8: Very
    Merry Christmas Songs
Dot & Santa Claus
Ernest Saves Christmas
A Family Circus
    Christmas
The First Christmas
A Flintstones Christmas
    Carol
Follow That Sleigh!
For Better or For Worse:
    The Bestest Present
The Fourth King
Frosty Returns
Frosty the Snowman
Frosty's Winter
    Wonderland/The
    Leprechauns'
    Christmas Gold
A Garfield Christmas
George Balanchine's The
    Nutcracker
A Gingerbread Christmas
Gremlins •
Gumby's Holiday Special
Happy Holidays with
    Darkwing Duck and
    Goofy
Here Comes Santa Claus
Holiday Inn
Home Alone •

Home Alone 2: Lost in
    New York
Home for Christmas
Homecoming: A
    Christmas Story •
A House Without a
    Christmas Tree
It Came Upon a Midnight
    Clear
It's a Wonderful Life •
Jack Frost
A Jetson's Christmas
    Carol
Jiminy Cricket's
    Christmas
Johann's Gift to
    Christmas
The Kid Who Loved
    Christmas
Kidsongs: We Wish You a
    Merry Christmas
The Life and Adventures
    of Santa Claus
The Lion in Winter •
The Little Crooked
    Christmas Tree
The Little Drummer Boy
The Little Match Girl •
Little Rascals Christmas
    Special
The Little Troll Prince
Lollipop Dragon: The
    Great Christmas Race
Madeline's Christmas
Magic Snowman
The Man in the Santa
    Claus Suit
March of the Wooden
    Soldiers •
A Merry Mirthworm
    Christmas
Mickey's Christmas
    Carol •
Mighty Morphin Power
    Rangers: Alpha's
    Magical Christmas
Miracle Down Under
Miracle on 34th Street •
Miracle on 34th Street
Mr. Magoo's Christmas
    Carol •
Mixed Nuts
The Muppet Christmas
    Carol •
Muppet Family Christmas
National Lampoon's
    Christmas Vacation
Nearly No Christmas
Nestor the Long-Eared
    Christmas Donkey
The Night Before
    Christmas
The Night Before
    Christmas and Best-
    Loved Yuletide Carols
The Night They Saved
    Christmas
The Nightmare Before
    Christmas •
Noel
The Nutcracker
The Nutcracker Prince
One Magic Christmas
Pink Panther: Pink
    Christmas
Pinocchio's Christmas

PJ's Unfunnybunny
    Christmas
Pluto's Christmas Tree
Prancer
Raggedy Ann and Andy
The Real Story of Oh
    Christmas Tree
Rudolph & Frosty's
    Christmas in July
Rudolph the Red-Nosed
    Reindeer •
Rudolph's Shiny New
    Year
Santa & the 3 Bears
Santa & the Tooth Fairies
Santa Claus Conquers
    the Martians
Santa Claus is Coming to
    Town •
Santa Claus: The Movie
The Santa Clause •
Santabear's First
    Christmas
Santabear's High Flying
    Adventure
Santa's First Christmas
Scrooge
Scrooged
Shelley Duvall's Bedtime
    Stories: The Christmas
    Witch
Shining Time Station:
    'Tis a Gift Holiday
    Special
The Simpsons Christmas
    Special
The Small One
A Smoky Mountain
    Christmas
Snuffy the Elf Who Saved
    Christmas
Spot's Magic Christmas
Stingiest Man in Town
Ted E. Bear: The Bear
    Who Slept Through
    Christmas
The Teddy Bears'
    Christmas
Timmy's Gift: A Precious
    Moments Christmas
Tommy Tricker & the
    Stamp Traveller •
Trapped In Paradise
Trolls & the Christmas
    Express
'Twas the Night Before
    Christmas
A Very Merry Cricket
A Walt Disney Christmas
Walt Disney Films in
    French
The Waltons: The
    Children's Carol
Wee Sing: The Best
    Christmas Ever!
Where the Toys Come
    From
While You Were
    Sleeping •
White Christmas •
Why Christmas Trees
    Aren't Perfect
Winnie the Pooh and
    Christmas Too
The Year Without a Santa
    Claus

Yes, Virginia, There is a Santa Claus
Yogi's First Christmas
You're Not Elected, Charlie Brown!/A Charlie Brown Christmas
Ziggy's Gift

Circuses & Carnivals
see also Amusement Parks; Clowning Around
At the Circus
Ava's Magical Adventure
Big Top Pee Wee
Bongo
Bozo the Clown: Ding Dong Dandy Adventures
Carousel •
Clowning Around
Clowning Around 2
The Court Jester •
A Day at the Circus: Alphabet Factory at the Circus
Dumbo •
Freaked
The Greatest Show on Earth •
Kidsongs: A Day at the Circus
Lili •
Mickey's Fun Songs: Let's Go to the Circus Parade •
The Rousters
Seven Faces of Dr. Lao •
So Dear to My Heart •
Something Wicked This Way Comes
State Fair •
Toby Tyler •
Wild Hearts Can't Be Broken •

Civil Rights
see also Apartheid; Slavery
And the Children Shall Lead
Driving Miss Daisy •
The Ernest Green Story
Hawmps!
We of the Never Never •

Civil War
see also Southern Relics; Southern Sagas
Bad Company •
Friendly Persuasion •
General Spanky
Gettysburg •
Glory •
Gone with the Wind •
Henry Hamilton: Graduate Ghost
How the West was Won •
It Happened in New Orleans
Johnny Shiloh
Little Women •
The Littlest Rebel

Menace on the Mountain
Mosby's Marauders
Mysterious Island •
No Drums, No Bugles
The Shadow Riders

Classics
Adam's Rib •
The Adventures of Robin Hood •
The African Queen •
Airplane! •
Alice in Wonderland •
American Graffiti •
An American in Paris •
Anchors Aweigh •
Animal Crackers •
Annie Hall •
At the Circus
Bambi •
Beauty and the Beast •
Black Beauty •
Bowery Blitzkrieg
Boys Town •
The Bridge on the River Kwai •
Butch Cassidy and the Sundance Kid •
Caddyshack •
Casablanca •
Challenge to Lassie
A Christmas Carol •
Cinderella •
Citizen Kane •
City Lights •
Curly Top
Dial "M" for Murder •
Dimples
Duck Soup •
Dumbo •
East of Eden •
Easter Parade •
E.T.: The Extra-Terrestrial •
Fantasia •
Father of the Bride •
Forbidden Games •
Forbidden Planet •
Foreign Correspondent •
The 400 Blows •
Giant •
Going My Way •
The Gold Rush •
Gone with the Wind •
Grease
High Noon •
His Girl Friday •
Horse Feathers •
How Green was My Valley •
I Am a Fugitive from a Chain Gang •
I Remember Mama •
Invaders from Mars
Invasion of the Body Snatchers •
It Happened One Night •
It's a Wonderful Life •
Judgment at Nuremberg •
Key Largo •
The King and I •
King Kong •
Lady and the Tramp •
The Lady Vanishes •
Lassie, Come Home •
Lawrence of Arabia •

Little Women •
The Maltese Falcon •
The Man Who Would Be King •
M*A*S*H •
Mickey's Crazy Careers
Mighty Joe Young
Miracle on 34th Street •
Mr. Hulot's Holiday •
Mr. Smith Goes to Washington •
Monkey Business •
Moonstruck •
The Muppet Movie •
Mysterious Island •
National Velvet •
A Night at the Opera •
North by Northwest •
The Nutcracker
Old Yeller •
Oliver Twist •
Once Upon a Time in the West •
101 Dalmatians •
The Philadelphia Story •
Pinocchio •
Planet of the Apes •
The Quiet Man •
Rebel Without a Cause •
The Red Pony •
The Red Shoes •
Shadow of a Doubt •
Shane •
Singin' in the Rain •
Sleeping Beauty •
The Sound of Music •
Star Wars •
Strangers on a Train •
Suspicion •
Tarzan, the Ape Man •
The Ten Commandments •
Thief of Baghdad •
The Thin Man •
The Three Musketeers
To Kill a Mockingbird •
Topper •
Treasure of the Sierra Madre •
The War of the Worlds •
West Side Story •
White Christmas •
The Wizard of Oz •
Yankee Doodle Dandy •
The Yearling •

Clowning Around
see also Circuses & Carnivals
Clowning Around
Clowning Around 2
The Court Jester •
Poltergeist •

Cold Spots
Alaska
Antarctica
Balto
Call of the Wild
Challenge To Be Free
Christmas Comes to Willow Creek
Cool Runnings •
Doctor Zhivago •
Ice Station Zebra
Kavik, the Wolf Dog

Never Cry Wolf •
The Pebble and the Penguin
Shadow of the Wolf
White Fang 2: The Myth of the White Wolf

College Capers
see also Elementary School Escapades; High School Hijinks; Teacher, Teacher
Adventures in Spying
Animal Behavior
Back to School
Blue Chips
Catch Me. . .If You Can
Circle of Friends
The Computer Wore Tennis Shoes
Ernest Rides Again
Escapade in Florence
The Freshman
Girl Crazy
Gotcha!
Gross Anatomy
Horse Feathers •
House Party 2: The Pajama Jam
How I Got into College
I.Q.
The Kid with the 200 I.Q.
Little Sister
Making the Grade
Midnight Madness
The Misadventures of Merlin Jones
Monkey's Uncle
Odd Jobs
The Paper Chase •
P.C.U.
The Program
Revenge of the Nerds
Rudy
Soul Man
The Sure Thing •
Teen Wolf Too
Threesome
Undergrads •
Witches' Brew
With Honors

Comedy with an Edge
see also Laugh Riots
The Addams Family
Addams Family Values •
Battle of the Bullies
The Cable Guy
Canadian Bacon
Clerks •
Death Becomes Her
Freaked
I Ought to Be in Pictures
Muriel's Wedding •
Serial Mom •
She-Devil
So I Married an Axe Murderer
Throw Momma from the Train •
Toto le Heros •

Coming to America
Avalon •

Buck Privates Come Home •
Far and Away
Green Card
Maricela
Monkey Business •
Wait Until Spring, Bandini

Computers
see also Robots; Technological Nightmares
The Computer Wore Tennis Shoes
The Double O Kid
Electric Dreams
The Electric Grandmother
Hackers
Johnny Mnemonic
Mission: Impossible •
The Net
Superman 3
War Games •

Cool Cars
see also Fast Cars
American Graffiti •
Back to the Future •
Built for Speed
Car Wash
Chitty Chitty Bang Bang
Coupe de Ville
Dream Machine
Dumb & Dumber
Ferris Bueller's Day Off •
Gung Ho
Herbie Rides Again
How a Car is Built
How a Car is Built with IQ Parrot
License to Drive
Look What Happens . . . at the Carwash
The Love Bug •
Moving Violations
National Lampoon's Vacation •
Pepper and His Wacky Taxi
Susie, the Little Blue Coupe
There Goes a Race Car
Tucker: The Man and His Dream •
Zero to Sixty

Courtroom Capers
see also Lawyers
Adam's Rib •
Before and After
The Client
Ernest Goes to Jail
Judgment at Nuremberg •
Jury Duty
Miracle on 34th Street
The Paradine Case
Philadelphia •
A Simple Twist of Fate
To Kill a Mockingbird •
Tom and Huck •
When Every Day was the Fourth of July
White Squall

Cowboys & Indians

Adios Amigo
Adventures of Red Ryder
Against A Crooked Sky
The Apple Dumpling Gang
The Apple Dumpling Gang Rides Again
Bad Company •
Bandolero!
Barbarosa •
Big Jake
Bonanza: The Return
Bowery Buckaroos
Bravestarr: The Legend Returns
Bronco Billy
Brothers O'Toole
Buck and the Preacher
Butch and Sundance: The Early Days
Butch Cassidy and the Sundance Kid •
Cahill: United States Marshal
City Slickers •
City Slickers 2: The Legend of Curly's Gold
The Cowboys •
Culpepper Cattle Co.
Devil Horse
The Electric Horseman •
Fievel's American Tails: A Mouse Known as Zorrowitz/Aunt Sophie's Visit
Fighting with Kit Carson
Flaming Frontiers
Geronimo: An American Legend
Go West •
Goin' South •
Guns of the Magnificent Seven
Hearts of the West •
High Noon •
Hole in the Sky
How the West Was Fun
How the West was Won •
Hurricane Express
The Incredible Rocky Mountain Race
Indian Paint
Jeremiah Johnson •
Jesse James Rides Again
Junior Bonner •
King of the Grizzlies
The Last of the Mohicans
The Left-Handed Gun •
Legend of the Lone Ranger
Lightning Jack
Little Big Man •
The Lone Ranger
The Lone Ranger: Code of the Pioneers
Lucky Luke
Lucky Luke: Ballad of the Daltons
Lucky Luke: Daisy Town
Man & Boy
The Man from Snowy River
Maverick •
Mosby's Marauders

My Heroes Have Always Been Cowboys
My Name is Nobody
The Nine Lives of Elfego Baca
Once Upon a Time in the West •
One Little Indian
The Outlaw Josey Wales •
Peter Lundy and the Medicine Hat Stallion
The Phantom Empire
Pony Express Rider
Quigley Down Under
Renfrew of the Royal Mounted
Return to Snowy River
Rin Tin Tin, Hero of the West
Rooster Cogburn
Running Wild
Savage Land
Scandalous John
The Shadow Riders
The Shakiest Gun in the West
Shane •
The Shootist •
Silver Stallion
Silverado •
Support Your Local Gunfighter •
Support Your Local Sheriff •
Tales of Deputy Dawg, Vol. 1
Tall Tale: The Unbelievable Adventures of Pecos Bill
To the Last Man
Tombstone •
True Grit •
The Villain
Wackiest Wagon Train in the West
Wagons East
Westward Ho, the Wagons!
The Wild Country
Winners of the West
Young Guns
Yukon Flight
Zorro Rides Again
Zorro, Vol. 1
Zorro's Black Whip
Zorro's Fighting Legion

Crime Doesn't Pay

see also It's the Mob; On the Run; Stupid Crime
All Dogs Go to Heaven
Almost an Angel
Bad Boys
Batman •
Batman Forever
Batman Returns
The Bay Boy
Before and After
Beverly Hills Cop
Beverly Hills Cop 2
Beverly Hills Cop 3
Boys Town •
Bugsy Malone

The Cat
Charade •
Crocodile Dundee 2
The Crow
Cry, the Beloved Country •
Dead Men Don't Wear Plaid
Diamonds on Wheels
Dick Tracy
Dick Tracy •
Dick Tracy, Detective
The Doberman Gang
The Dream Team •
Emil and the Detective
Escapade in Florence
Fast Getaway
The Fire in the Stone
Flipper's New Adventure
Follow the Leader
The Goonies
The Grey Fox •
Johnny Dangerously
The Meteor Man
Moonraker
The Naked Gun: From the Files of Police Squad •
'Neath Brooklyn Bridge
Never a Dull Moment
No Deposit, No Return
The North Avenue Irregulars
Oliver! •
Oliver & Company •
Oliver Twist
Oliver Twist
A Perfect World
The Real McCoy
Rear Window •
Savannah Smiles
The Shadow
Shadow of a Doubt •
Shadow of the Eagle
Spy Hard
Stage Fright •
Superman 3
Take the Money and Run •
Ten Little Indians
That Darn Cat
That Was Then. . .This Is Now
Three Fugitives
Tiger Bay •
Tim Tyler's Luck
Trenchcoat
Two If by Sea
The Usual Suspects •
Walking Tall
Weekend at Bernie's
Where on Earth is Carmen Sandiego? Vol. I : A Date with Carmen (Parts One and Two)
Where on Earth is Carmen Sandiego? Vol. II: By a Whisker and Dinosaur Delirium
Where on Earth is Carmen Sandiego? Vol. III: The Good Old Bad Old Days and The Stolen Smile

Where on Earth is Carmen Sandiego? Vol. IV: Split Up and Moondreams

Dads

see also Moms; Parenthood
The Brady Bunch Movie •
Father of the Bride •
Father of the Bride Part II •
Getting Even with Dad •
Ghost Dad
A Goofy Movie •
Imaginary Crimes •
Life with Father •
Magic in the Water
Mom and Dad Save the World
My Father the Hero
National Lampoon's Christmas Vacation
National Lampoon's European Vacation
National Lampoon's Vacation •
Parenthood •
Sleepless in Seattle •
So I Married an Axe Murderer
Superdad
Three Men and a Baby •
Three Men and a Cradle •
Three Men and a Little Lady
A Very Brady Sequel
Wait Till Your Mother Gets Home

Deafness

see also Physical Problems
Amy •
Crazy Moon
The Miracle Worker •
Mr. Holland's Opus •
A Summer to Remember

Death

see Bereavement

Demons & Wizards

Army of Darkness •
Conan the Barbarian •
Conan the Destroyer
Ernest Scared Stupid
Fire and Ice
The Hobbit •
Krull
Ladyhawke •
The Return of the King
Supergirl
The Sword in the Stone •
Troll
Warriors of the Wind
Willow
Wizards of the Lost Kingdom
Wizards of the Lost Kingdom 2

Detectives

see also Policemen; Silly Detectives
Ace Ventura: Pet Detective
Ace Ventura: When Nature Calls
The Adventures of Sherlock Holmes' Smarter Brother •
Another Stakeout
The Big Store
The Cheap Detective •
Clean Slate
Clue You In: The Case of the Mad Movie Mustacher
Curse of the Pink Panther
Dead Men Don't Wear Plaid
Death on the Nile
Dick Tracy •
Dick Tracy, Detective
Dick Tracy Meets Gruesome
Dragnet
Emil and the Detective
Encyclopedia Brown: Case of the Missing Time Capsule
Evil Under the Sun
The Great Mouse Detective
Hard-Boiled Mahoney
Inspector Clouseau: Ape Suzette
Inspector Clouseau: Napoleon Blown-Aparte
K-9
The Last Chance Detectives: Mystery Lights of Navajo Mesa
Little Miss Millions
Love Happy
The Maltese Falcon •
My Favorite Brunette
The Naked Gun: From the Files of Police Squad •
Naked Gun 33 1/3: The Final Insult
Nancy Drew, Reporter
The Pink Panther •
The Pink Panther Strikes Again •
The Private Eyes
Return of the Pink Panther
Revenge of the Pink Panther
A Shot in the Dark •
The Thin Man •
Top Dog
Trail of the Pink Panther
Who Framed Roger Rabbit? •
The Young Detectives on Wheels
Young Sherlock Holmes

Bullets (•) indicate 3 bones or above

Dinos

see also Scary Beasties

Adventures in Dinosaur City
Adventures in Dinosaurland
At the Earth's Core
Baby. . .Secret of the Lost Legend
Barney & Friends: Barney Rhymes with Mother Goose
Barney & Friends: Barney's Best Manners
Barney & Friends: Families are Special
Barney's Imagination Island
Clifford
Dennis the Menace: Dinosaur Hunter
Denver the Last Dinosaur
Digging Dinosaurs - 2 Pack
Digging for Dinosaurs
Dinosaur Families
Dinosaurs are Very Big
Dinosaurs, Dinosaurs, Dinosaurs
Donny Deinonychus: The Educational Dinosaur, Vol. 1
EPIC: Days of the Dinosaurs
Josh Kirby . . . Time Warrior: Chapter 1, Planet of the Dino-Knights
Jurassic Park •
The Land Before Time •
The Land Before Time 2: The Great Valley Adventure
The Land Before Time 3: The Time of the Great Giving
Land of the Lost
Land of the Lost, Vol. 1
Land That Time Forgot
Let's Pretend with Barney
Lost in Dinosaur World
More Dinosaurs
My Science Project
One of Our Dinosaurs Is Missing
The People That Time Forgot
Planet of the Dinosaurs
Prehysteria
Prehysteria! 2
Prehysteria 3
Super Mario Bros.
Theodore Rex
Toy Story •
Unknown Island
The Valley of Gwangi •
We're Back! A Dinosaur's Story
When Dinosaurs Ruled the Earth

Where on Earth is Carmen Sandiego? Vol. II: By a Whisker and Dinosaur Delirium

Disaster Strikes!

see also Amazing Adventures; Nuclear War

Airport •
Airport '75
Airport '77
Alive
Apollo 13 •
Avalanche
The Big Bus
Independence Day •
The Poseidon Adventure
Twister
White Squall

Disney Animated Movies

Aladdin •
Alice in Wonderland •
The Aristocats •
Bambi •
Beauty and the Beast •
The Brave Little Toaster •
Cinderella •
Donald Duck in Mathmagic Land
DuckTales the Movie: Treasure of the Lost Lamp
Dumbo •
Fantasia •
The Fox and the Hound •
Fun N Games
A Goofy Movie •
The Great Mouse Detective
The Hunchback of Notre Dame •
The Jungle Book •
Lady and the Tramp •
The Lion King •
The Little Mermaid •
The Nightmare Before Christmas •
Oliver & Company •
101 Dalmatians •
Peter Pan •
Pinocchio •
Pocahontas •
Princess Jasmine: Magic and Mystery
Princess Jasmine: True Hearts
The Rescuers •
The Rescuers Down Under
The Return of Jafar •
Robin Hood •
Sleeping Beauty •
Snow White and the Seven Dwarfs •
The Sword in the Stone •
The Three Caballeros •
Timon and Pumbaa's Wild Adventures: Don't Get Mad, Get Happy
Timon and Pumbaa's Wild Adventures: Grub's On

Timon and Pumbaa's Wild Adventures: Hangin' With Baby
Timon and Pumbaa's Wild Adventures: Live and Learn
Timon and Pumbaa's Wild Adventures: Quit Buggin' Me
Timon and Pumbaa's Wild Adventures: True Guts
Toy Story •

Disney Family Movies

The Absent-Minded Professor •
The Adventures of Bullwhip Griffin
The Adventures of Huck Finn •
The Air Up There •
Almost Angels
Amy •
Angels in the Outfield
The Apple Dumpling Gang
The Apple Dumpling Gang Rides Again
Babes in Toyland
The Barefoot Executive
The Bears & I
Bedknobs and Broomsticks
Benji the Hunted
Big Red
The Black Arrow
The Black Hole
Blackbeard's Ghost
Blank Check
The Blue Yonder
Born to Run
Breakin' Through
Candleshoe •
The Castaway Cowboy
The Cat from Outer Space
Charley and the Angel
Charlie, the Lonesome Cougar
Cheetah
Child of Glass
The Computer Wore Tennis Shoes
Condorman
Darby O'Gill & the Little People •
Davy Crockett and the River Pirates •
Davy Crockett, King of the Wild Frontier •
The Devil & Max Devlin
Diamonds on Wheels
Dr. Syn, Alias the Scarecrow
Emil and the Detective
Escapade in Florence
Escape to Witch Mountain •
A Far Off Place
The Fighting Prince of Donegal
Flight of the Grey Wolf
Flight of the Navigator •
Freaky Friday •
Fun & Fancy Free

The Girl Who Spelled Freedom •
The Gnome-Mobile
Gone are the Days
A Goofy Movie •
Greyfriars Bobby •
Gus
Heavyweights
Herbie Goes Bananas
Herbie Goes to Monte Carlo
Herbie Rides Again
Homeward Bound: The Incredible Journey •
Honey, I Blew Up the Kid
Honey, I Shrunk the Kids
The Horse in the Gray Flannel Suit
The Horse Without a Head
Horsemasters
Hot Lead & Cold Feet
The Hunchback of Notre Dame •
In Search of the Castaways •
The Incredible Journey •
Iron Will
The Island at the Top of the World
Johnny Shiloh
Johnny Tremain & the Sons of Liberty
The Journey of Natty Gann •
Justin Morgan Had a Horse
King of the Grizzlies
The Last Flight of Noah's Ark
The Light in the Forest
The Littlest Horse Thieves
The Littlest Outlaw
Lots of Luck
The Love Bug •
Love Leads the Way
Lt. Robin Crusoe, U.S.N.
Mary Poppins •
Menace on the Mountain
Mickey's Christmas Carol •
Million Dollar Duck
Miracle Down Under
Miracle of the White Stallions
The Misadventures of Merlin Jones
Monkeys, Go Home!
Monkey's Uncle
Moon Pilot
Moon-Spinners
Mooncussers
Mosby's Marauders
My Dog, the Thief
Napoleon and Samantha •
Never a Dull Moment
Newsies
Night Crossing
Nikki, the Wild Dog of the North •
The Nine Lives of Elfego Baca
No Deposit, No Return

The North Avenue Irregulars
Now You See Him, Now You Don't
Old Yeller •
The One and Only, Genuine, Original Family Band
101 Dalmatians •
One Little Indian
One Magic Christmas
One of Our Dinosaurs Is Missing
The Parent Trap
Pete's Dragon
Pocahontas •
Pollyanna •
Return from Witch Mountain
Return to Oz
Ride a Wild Pony
Rob Roy - The Highland Rogue
The Rocketeer •
Sammy, the Way-Out Seal
Savage Sam
Scandalous John
The Secret of El Zorro
The Shaggy D.A.
The Shaggy Dog
The Sign of Zorro
Smith!
Smoke
Snowball Express
So Dear to My Heart •
Son of Flubber
Summer Magic
Superdad
The Swiss Family Robinson •
The Sword & the Rose
Tall Tale: The Unbelievable Adventures of Pecos Bill
Ten Who Dared
That Darn Cat
Third Man on the Mountain
Those Calloways
The Three Lives of Thomasina •
3 Ninjas
3 Ninjas Kick Back
A Tiger Walks
Toby Tyler •
Tom and Huck •
Toy Story •
Treasure Island •
The Treasure of Matecumbe
20,000 Leagues Under the Sea •
The Ugly Dachshund
Undergrads •
Unidentified Flying Oddball
Waltz King
Watcher in the Woods
Westward Ho, the Wagons!
White Fang •
White Fang 2: The Myth of the White Wolf
The Wild Country

Wild Hearts Can't Be
Broken •
The World's Greatest
Athlete

Divorce
see also Marriage
All I Want for Christmas
Bye Bye, Love
Clara's Heart
Conspiracy of Love
Divorce Can Happen to
the Nicest People
E.T.: The Extra-
Terrestrial •
Face the Music
Father Figure
High Society
House Arrest
Irreconcilable Differences
Kramer vs. Kramer •
Mrs. Doubtfire •
Mr. Wonderful
Necessary Parties
Nothing in Common
The Odd Couple •
Peggy Sue Got Married
People
Play It Again, Sam •
Rich Kids
The Santa Clause •
See You in the Morning
Something to Talk About
Table for Five
Twister
When Mom and Dad
Break Up

Dr. Seuss
The Cat in the Hat
The Cat in the Hat
Comes Back
The Cat in the Hat Gets
Grinched
Did I Ever Tell You How
Lucky You Are?
Dr. Seuss' ABC
Dr. Seuss' Butter Battle
Book
Dr. Seuss' Cat in the Hat
Dr. Seuss' Daisy-Head
Mayzie
Dr. Seuss' Hoober-Bloob
Highway
Dr. Seuss' Horton Hears
a Who/How the Grinch
Stole Christmas
Dr. Seuss: I Am NOT
Going to Get Up
Today!
Dr. Seuss on the Loose
Dr. Seuss Sleep Book
Dr. Seuss' The Lorax
The 5000 Fingers of Dr.
T •
Halloween is Grinch
Night
Hop on Pop
Horton Hatches the Egg
Horton Hears a Who!
In Search of Dr. Seuss
One Fish, Two Fish, Red
Fish, Blue Fish
The Zax From Dr. Seuss
on the Loose

Doctors & Nurses
see also AIDS;
Hospitals
Awakenings •
Bad Medicine
Death Becomes Her
Doc Hollywood
Doctor Doolittle
The Elephant Man •
Gross Anatomy
Junior
M*A*S*H •
Nell
Nine Months
Outbreak •
Promises in the Dark
Skeezer

Documentaries
Animals Are Beautiful
People
Anne Frank
Remembered •
Blackberry Subway Jam
Chuck Amuck: The Movie
Don't Eat the Pictures:
Sesame Street at the
Metropolitan Museum
of Art
The Endless Summer •
The Endless Summer 2
The Glacier Fox
Hoop Dreams •
I Want to be a Ballerina
Kidco
The Living Desert •
National Geographic:
Really Wild Animals
Series
Twist

Dogs
see King of Beasts
(Dogs)

Down Under
Born to Run
Cool Change
Dusty
The Man from Snowy
River
Miracle Down Under
Muriel's Wedding •
Phar Lap
The Prince and the Great
Race
The Quest
Quigley Down Under
Race the Sun
Really Wild Animals:
Wonders Down Under
The Rescuers Down
Under
Return to Snowy River
Ride a Wild Pony
The Silver Stallion: King
of the Wild Brumbies
Strictly Ballroom
Under Capricorn
A Waltz Through the Hills
We of the Never Never •

Drama
see also Historical
Happenings;
Tearjerkers
Above the Rim
Across the Tracks
Africa Texas Style
African Journey
Airborne
Alan & Naomi •
Alex
All the President's Men •
All the Right Moves
Amazing Grace & Chuck
American Anthem
An American Christmas
Carol
American Flyers
American Heart •
The American President •
An American Summer
Amy •
And Now Miguel
Andre
Angelo My Love •
Anne Frank
Remembered •
Anne of Green Gables •
Annie O
Au Revoir Les Enfants •
The Babe
Bach & Broccoli •
Bach's Flight to Freedom
Back Home
Backbeat •
Ballet Shoes
The Basketball Diaries
The Bay Boy
The Bear •
The Bears & I
Beethoven Lives
Upstairs •
Before and After
The Beniker Gang
The Best Christmas
Pageant Ever
Big Mo
Big Red
Bill •
Bill: On His Own •
Billy Galvin
Billy Jack
The Birch Interval •
Black Beauty
Black Beauty •
Blake of Scotland Yard
Bless the Beasts and
Children
Blue Chips
Blue Fire Lady
Bopha! •
Born Free •
Born to Run
Bound for Glory •
The Boy Who Could Fly
The Boy with the Green
Hair
Boys
Boys on the Side
Boys Town •
Boyz N the Hood •
Breaking Free
Brenda Starr
The Bridge on the River
Kwai •

A Bronx Tale •
Brother Future
The Canterville Ghost
Captains Courageous •
The Capture of Grizzly
Adams
Careful, He Might Hear
You •
Challenge to Lassie
Change of Habit
Chaplin
Chariots of Fire •
Chasing Dreams
A Christmas Carol •
Christmas Comes to
Willow Creek
A Christmas to
Remember
The Christmas Tree
Christy
Cinema Paradiso •
Citizen Kane •
City Boy
The Client
Clowning Around
Clowning Around 2
Coach
Cold River
The Commitments •
Conrack •
Conspiracy of Love
Cooley High •
The Corn is Green •
Country •
Country Girl •
Courage of Lassie
Cria •
Cross Creek
Cry from the Mountain
Cry, the Beloved
Country •
The Cure •
Cyrano de Bergerac •
Dad
Dakota
Daniel and the Towers
Danny
Dark Horse
David and Lisa •
A Day for Thanks on
Walton's Mountain
A Day in October
Dead Poets Society •
A Decade of the Waltons
December
Desert Bloom •
Dirty Dancing •
Diving In
Dr. Strange
A Dog of Flanders
The Dog Who Stopped
the War •
Dominick & Eugene •
Downhill Racer
Dragon: The Bruce Lee
Story
A Dream for Christmas •
Dreamchild •
Driving Miss Daisy •
Dusty
Earthling
East of Eden •
The Effect of Gamma
Rays on Man-in-the-
Moon Marigolds •
Eight Men Out •

The Electric Grandmother
The Elephant Man •
Empire of the Sun •
The Ernest Green Story
Escape Artist •
Eye on the Sparrow
Family Prayers
Fandango
Father Figure
Father Hood
The Fig Tree
First Born
The Flame Trees of
Thika •
Follow the River
Forbidden Games •
The 400 Blows •
Foxes
Friendly Persuasion •
A Friendship in Vienna
Gentle Ben
Geronimo •
Giant •
The Gift of Amazing
Grace
A Girl of the Limberlost
The Girl Who Spelled
Freedom •
Gleaming the Cube
The Golden Seal
The Good Son
Goodbye, Miss 4th of
July
Gorillas in the Mist •
The Great Mike
The Great Santini •
The Great White Hope
The Greatest
The Greatest Show on
Earth •
The Grey Fox •
Greyfriars Bobby •
Grizzly Adams: The
Legend Continues
Gypsy Colt
Hadley's Rebellion
Hansel and Gretel
Harry & Son
Hazel's People
Heart Like a Wheel •
Heartland •
Heidi
Heidi
Heidi •
The Hero
A Hero Ain't Nothin' But
a Sandwich •
Hiroshima Maiden
Hockey Night
A Home of Our Own
Home to Stay •
Homecoming
Homecoming: A
Christmas Story •
Homeward Bound
Honkytonk Man
Hoosiers •
Hope and Glory •
A Horse for Danny
House of Cards
The House of Dies Drear
A House Without a
Christmas Tree
How Green was My
Valley •

How to Make an American Quilt
Howard's End •
The Human Comedy •
I Am a Fugitive from a Chain Gang •
I Remember Mama •
Imaginary Crimes •
The Inkwell
International Velvet
Into the West •
It Came Upon a Midnight Clear
It Happened in New Orleans
It's a Dog's Life
Jacob Have I Loved
Jean de Florette •
Joe Panther
Joey
Johnny's Girl
Joni
The Journey of August King •
Journey to Spirit Island •
The Joy Luck Club •
Judgment at Nuremberg •
A Kid for Two Farthings •
Kid from Not-So-Big
The Kid Who Loved Christmas
King of the Hill •
King of the Wind •
Knute Rockne: All American •
Kramer vs. Kramer •
Lantern Hill
Lassie •
Lassie's Great Adventure •
Last Time Out
Lawrence of Arabia •
The Lawrenceville Stories •
Lean on Me •
The Learning Tree •
The Legend of Sleepy Hollow
The Legend of Young Robin Hood
Let the Balloon Go
Liar's Moon
Lightning: The White Stallion
Lilies of the Field •
Little Buddha
Little Dorrit, Film 1: Nobody's Fault •
Little Heroes
Little House on the Prairie •
Little Lord Fauntleroy •
Little Man Tate •
Little Men
Little Orphan Annie
The Little Princess •
Little Tough Guys
Little Women •
The Littlest Outlaw
Lone Star Kid
The Lone Wolf
The Loneliest Runner •
The Loneliness of the Long Distance Runner •
The Long Day Closes •
Looking for Miracles
Lord of the Flies •

Lord of the Flies •
The Lords of Flatbush •
Lorenzo's Oil •
Lost Legacy: A Girl Called Hatter Fox •
Love Leads the Way
Love Your Mama
MacArthur
Madame Rosa •
Magic of Lassie •
The Magic of the Golden Bear: Goldy 3
Malcolm X •
The Man Without a Face •
Man, Woman & Child •
Manon of the Spring •
Maricela
Mark Twain and Me •
Marvin & Tige
Mask •
Matewan •
Men of Boys Town •
Menace II Society •
A Midnight Clear •
The Mighty Pawns •
A Minor Miracle
The Miracle •
Miracle at Moreaux •
Miracle Down Under •
Miracle of Our Lady of Fatima
Miracle of the Heart: A Boys Town Story •
Miracle of the White Stallions •
Miracle on 34th Street •
The Miracle Worker •
Mr. & Mrs. Bridge •
Mr. Smith Goes to Washington •
Misunderstood
Mommie Dearest •
My Father's Glory •
My Life
My Mother's Castle •
My Old Man
My Side of the Mountain •
National Velvet •
The Natural •
Nearly No Christmas
Necessary Parties
Nell
Never Cry Wolf •
The Next Karate Kid •
The Night the Lights Went Out in Georgia
No Drums, No Bugles
Norma Rae •
Not My Kid
Now and Then
Ode to Billy Joe
Of Mice and Men •
Oklahoma Crude
The Old Curiosity Shop •
Oliver Twist •
Oliver Twist •
Oliver Twist •
On Golden Pond •
On the Edge: The Survival of Dana
One on One
Othello
The Outsiders •
Over the Edge •
Over the Top •
Paradise •

Past the Bleachers •
Pastime •
A Perfect World
Permanent Record •
Phar Lap
Phenomenon
Philadelphia •
Pistol: The Birth of a Legend
Places in the Heart •
Primo Baby
The Prince and the Great Race
The Prince and the Pauper •
The Prince and the Pauper •
The Prince of Central Park •
Princes in Exile
The Prodigal
The Program
Promises in the Dark •
Quiz Show •
Race the Sun
Rad
Radio Flyer •
Rain Man •
Rambling Rose •
A Rare Breed
Rebel Without a Cause •
The Red Pony •
The Red Stallion •
Regarding Henry •
The Remains of the Day •
Reunion •
Rich Kids
Ride a Wild Pony •
Ring of Bright Water •
The River •
The River Rat •
A River Runs Through It •
The Road Home
Rocky •
Rocky 2 •
Rocky 3 •
Rocky 4 •
Rocky 5 •
Rubber Tarzan •
Rudy •
Rumble Fish •
Run, Appaloosa, Run •
Run for the Roses •
Runaway
The Runaways •
Running Brave •
Running Free
Running Mates •
Running on Empty •
Safe Passage
Sam's Son
Savannah Smiles •
The Scarlet Pimpernel •
School Ties •
Searching for Bobby Fischer •
The Secret Garden •
The Secret of Roan Inish •
Secret Places •
A Separate Peace •
Shadowlands •
The Shawshank Redemption •
Silence of the North •

Skeezer •
Skylark
Smith! •
Smoke
A Smoky Mountain Christmas
Smooth Talk •
Snow Treasure
So Dear to My Heart •
Sounder •
Stacking
Stand and Deliver •
Stand By Me •
The Stone Boy •
Stone Fox •
The Story Lady •
Strangers in Good Company •
Sudie & Simpson •
Sugar Cane Alley •
Summer Magic •
A Summer to Remember •
Susannah of the Mounties •
Sweet 15
Swing Kids •
Sylvester •
Table for Five
Taking Care of Terrific •
Talent for the Game •
Tales from Avonlea, Vol. 1: The Journey Begins •
The Tender Years •
Tess •
Tex •
That Was Then. . .This Is Now •
This Boy's Life •
Thoroughbreds Don't Cry •
The Three Lives of Thomasina •
Tiger Town •
Time of Tears •
The Tin Soldier •
To Kill a Mockingbird •
To Sir, with Love •
Tomboy & the Champ •
Touched by Love •
Toughlove •
A Tree Grows in Brooklyn •
The Trip to Bountiful •
Tucker: The Man and His Dream •
Turf Boy •
Turtle Diary •
Two Bits •
Two of a Kind •
Unstrung Heroes •
Up Against the Wall •
Victory •
Waiting to Exhale •
Walking on Air •
Walking Tall •
The Waltons: The Children's Carol •
War Games •
War of the Buttons •
We of the Never Never •
Wee Willie Winkie •
Whale for the Killing •
Whale of a Tale •
What the Moon Saw •
What's Eating Gilbert Grape •

When Every Day was the Fourth of July •
When the Whales Came •
When Wolves Cry
Where the Lilies Bloom •
Where the Red Fern Grows: Part 2
Whistle Down the Wind •
White Mama •
Who'll Save Our Children? •
Why Shoot the Teacher? •
The Wild Child •
Wild Horse Hank
Wild Pony •
Windrunner
A Winner Never Quits •
The Wizard of Loneliness •
Words by Heart •
A World Apart •
Yanco
Zelly & Me •
The Zoo Gang •

Eco-Vengeance!
see also Scary Bugs
Alligator •
Arachnophobia •
The Birds •
Jurassic Park •
Magic in the Water
Phantom 2040 Movie: The Ghost Who Walks •
The Swarm •

Ecotoons
Captain Planet & the Planeteers: A Hero for Earth
The Cosmic Eye •
Dreaming of Paradise
Ferngully: The Last Rain Forest •
The Land Before Time •
Lassie's Rescue Rangers
No Man's Valley
Once Upon a Forest •

Elementary School Escapades
see also College Capers; High School Hijinks; Teacher, Teacher
Amy •
Au Revoir Les Enfants •
Back to School
The Belles of St. Trinian's •
The Bells of St. Mary's •
Billy Madison
Chester the Earth Ant: Story Book Castle
Christy
Clifford's Fun with Numbers
The Corn is Green •
Dangerous Minds
Dead Poets Society •
Disney's Haunted Halloween
Dr. Dad's PH3
Doctor Doolittle
Educating Rita •

Encino Man
The Ernest Green Story
Fame •
The Flintstone Kids: "Just
 Say No"
Flirting •
French Postcards
Fruit . . . Close Up and
 Very Personal
Fun N Games
Gerald McBoing Boing,
 Vol. 1: Favorite Sing-
 Along Songs
Ghostwriter, Vol. 1: Ghost
 Story
The Girl Who Spelled
 Freedom •
The Goodbye Bird
Grease
The Halfback of Notre
 Dame
High School High
Horsemasters
How I Got into College
Jack
Jim Henson's Preschool
 Collection: Muppets on
 Wheels
Jim Henson's Preschool
 Collection: Yes, I Can
 Help
Jim Henson's Preschool
 Collection: Yes, I Can
 Learn
Jungle Book: Mowgli
 Comes to the Jungle
The Kid with the 200 I.Q.
Kindergarten Cop
Last Time Out
Leader of the Band
Lean on Me •
Let's Dance on the Farm
 with Miss Nola
The Little Princess •
A Little Princess •
The Magic School Bus
 for Lunch
The Magic School Bus
 Gets Eaten
The Magic School Bus
 Gets Lost in Space
The Magic School Bus
 Goes to Seed
The Magic School Bus
 Hops Home
The Magic School Bus
 Inside Ralphie
The Magic School Bus
 Inside the Earth
The Magic School Bus
 Kicks Up a Storm
Magic School Bus Plays
 Ball
The Magic Thinking Cap
Major Payne
The Manners Monster:
 Ruby Goes to Dinner
Matilda
Mickey's Field Trips
 Series
A Minor Miracle
The Music Factory
The Musical Universe of
 Nursery Rhymes, Vol. 1
My First Party

National Lampoon's
 Senior Trip
The NeverEnding Story
On the Move with Virgil
Oxford Blues
Postman Pat
Postman Pat's ABC Story
Postman Pat's 123 Story
Powder
The Prime of Miss Jean
 Brodie •
The Puppet Theater
The Pure Hell of St.
 Trinian's
Real Genius •
Renaissance Man
Romper Room and
 Friends: Explore
 Nature
Schoolhouse Rock:
 History Rock
Secret Places
See How They Grow
A Separate Peace
Sesame Street Visits the
 Firehouse
Shout
Sing
Something Good
Songs for Us Series
Sounds Around
Stand and Deliver •
Summer School
To Sir, with Love
Tom Brown's School
 Days
Tom Brown's School
 Days •
Tommy Boy
The Trouble with Angels
Undergrads •
Up the Down Staircase •
When Mom and Dad
 Break Up
Which Way Weather?
Who Is Healthy Herb? -
 Food, Fitness, and Fun!
Why Shoot the
 Teacher? •
With Honors
The Worst Witch
Yentl
Zebrahead •
Zoofari

Explorers
Apollo 13 •
Christopher Columbus:
 The Discovery
Congo
1492: Conquest of
 Paradise
The Magic Voyage
The Song of Sacajawea
We Think the World is
 Round

Fairy Tales
*see also Bedtime
 Stories*
Adventures of Pinocchio
The Adventures of
 Pinocchio
The Adventures of
 Sinbad the Sailor

The Adventures of Walt
 Disney's Alice
Aesop's Fables
Aesop's Fables, Vol. 1:
 The Hen with the
 Golden Egg
Aladdin
Aladdin •
Aladdin and His Magic
 Lamp
Aladdin and His
 Wonderful Lamp
Aladdin and the
 Wonderful Lamp
Ali Baba and the Forty
 Thieves
Alice in Wonderland
Alice in Wonderland •
Alice's Adventures in
 Wonderland
Arabian Knight
Beanstalk
Beauty and the Beast •
Beauty and the Beast
Beauty and the Beast •
Black Beauty
Blackberry Subway Jam
The Boy Who Drew Cats
The Boy Who Left Home
 to Find Out About the
 Shivers
Cannon Movie Tales: The
 Emperor's New Clothes
Casey at the Bat
A Christmas Fantasy
Cinderella •
Cinderella
Cinderella . . . Frozen in
 Time
Cinderfella
Cindy Eller
The Classic Tales
 Collection
Colorforms Learn 'n Play
 VCR Adventures
Curious George
The Dancing Princesses
Daydreamer •
The Emperor's New
 Clothes
The Emperor's New
 Clothes and Other
 Folktales
Fisher-Price Grimm's
 Fairy Tales: Briar Rose
Five Lionni Classics
Flower Angel
Frog •
The Frog Prince
Fun & Fancy Free
George Balanchine's The
 Nutcracker
The Gingerbread Man
 and Other Nursery
 Stories
Goldilocks & the Three
 Bears
Grimm's Fairy Tales:
 Beauty and the Beast
Hanna-Barbera Storybook
 Classics
Hansel and Gretel
Happily Ever After
Happy Birthday, Moon
 and Other Stories
The Happy Prince

The Hare and the
 Hedgehog
Hello Kitty: Cinderella
Hey, Cinderella!
How the Whale Got His
 Throat
A Hungarian Fairy Tale
Jack & the Beanstalk
Jack and the Beanstalk
Janosch: Fables from the
 Magic Forest
Johnny the Giant Killer
The Little Match Girl •
The Little Match Girl
The Little Mermaid
The Little Mermaid •
The Little Prince &
 Friends
Little Red Riding Hood
The Magic Flute
The Magic Sword
March of the Wooden
 Soldiers •
The Marzipan Pig
Mickey & the Beanstalk
Mikhail Baryshinikov's
 Stories from My
 Childhood
Mother Goose Rock 'n'
 Rhyme •
Muppet Musicians of
 Bremen
The Musical Universe of
 Nursery Rhymes, Vol. 1
My Little Pony
The NeverEnding Story
The Neverending Story 3
Nightingale
Noah's Animals and
 Other Stories
The Norfin Adventures:
 The Great Egg Robbery
Nutcracker Fantasy
The Nutcracker Prince
Once Upon a Brothers
 Grimm
The Owl and the
 Pussycat
The Paper Bag Princess
Peter and the Wolf
Peter Cottontail: How He
 Got His Hop
Peter Cottontail's
 Adventures
Peter Pan •
Peter Pan •
Peter Pan/Hiawatha
The Pied Piper/Cinderella
The Pied Piper of
 Hamelin
Pinocchio •
Pinocchio
Prince Cinders
Prince Valiant
The Princess and the Pea
The Princess Bride •
The Princess Who Never
 Laughed
Puss in Boots
Puss 'n Boots
Puss 'n Boots Travels
 Around the World
Rabbit Ears Storybook
 Classics Collection
Rapunzel

The Real Story of
 Humpty Dumpty
Red Riding Hood
The Red Shoes
Rip van Winkle
Rudyard Kipling's Just So
 Stories, Vol. 1
Rumpelstiltskin
The Selfish Giant
Shari Lewis: Have I Got a
 Story for You
Shari Lewis: One Minute
 Bedtime Stories
Shelley Duvall's Rock 'n'
 Rhymeland
Shirley Temple
 Storybook Theater
Sleeping Beauty •
Sleeping Beauty
The Snow Queen
Snow White
Snow White and Rose
 Red
Snow White and the
 Seven Dwarfs
Snow White and the
 Three Stooges
Stanley the Ugly
 Duckling
The Steadfast Tin Soldier
Strega Nonna and Other
 Stories
The Swan Princess •
The Tale of the Frog
 Prince •
Tales of Beatrix Potter
The Three Little Pigs
Thumbelina
The Tiger and the
 Brahmin
Timeless Tales from
 Hallmark
The Tin Soldier
tom thumb
Tom Thumb
Troll Classic Book Videos
The Ugly Duckling
The Ugly Duckling and
 other Classic Fairytales
Unicorn Tales 1
Velveteen Rabbit
The Wacky World of
 Mother Goose
What's Under My Bed?
 and Other Creepy
 Stories
Wild Swans
The Wind in the Willows
The Witches •
The Wonderful World of
 the Brothers Grimm
Wonders of Aladdin
A World of Stories with
 Katharine Hepburn
Wrinkles: In Need of
 Cuddles

Family Ties
see also Parenthood
Above the Rim
The Addams Family
Addams Family Values •
The Adventures of the
 Wilderness Family
Alaska

Alex Mack: In the Nick of
  Time
All I Want for Christmas
An American Christmas
  Carol
American Flyers
American Heart •
And Baby Makes Six
And You Thought Your
  Parents Were Weird!
Andy Hardy Gets Spring
  Fever
Andy Hardy Meets
  Debutante
Andy Hardy's Double Life
Andy Hardy's Private
  Secretary
Angus
Anne of Green Gables •
The Apprenticeship of
  Duddy Kravitz •
Author! Author!
Avalon •
The Baby-Sitters Club
Bach & Broccoli •
Back Home
Back to the Beach
Back to the Future •
The Bad Seed
Beethoven
Beethoven's 2nd
Before and After
Being Human
Benny & Joon •
The Best Christmas
  Pageant Ever
The Beverly Hillbillies
Beverly Hills Brats
Big Business •
Big Girls Don't Cry. .
  .They Get Even
Billy Galvin
Billy Madison
The Birch Interval •
The Birdcage •
Black Sheep
Blue Fin
The Blue Yonder
Bonanza: The Return
Bopha! •
Boyd's Shadow
The Brady Bunch Movie •
A Bronx Tale •
Bye Bye, Love
Cahill: United States
  Marshal
Candleshoe •
Captain Ron
The Capture of Grizzly
  Adams
Carbon Copy
Careful, He Might Hear
  You •
Carousel •
Casey's Shadow
Casper •
Chances Are •
Charley and the Angel
Cheetah
Christmas Comes to
  Willow Creek
A Christmas Story •
A Christmas to
  Remember
Clifford

Club Connect: Me and
  My Folks
Conspiracy of Love
Country •
Country Girl •
Coupe de Ville
The Courtship of Eddie's
  Father •
Crooklyn •
Crossing Delancey •
Cry from the Mountain
Cry, the Beloved
  Country •
Curly Top
Dad
Dark Horse
D.A.R.Y.L.
A Day for Thanks on
  Walton's Mountain
Desert Bloom •
Dick Tracy
Digger
Dimples
Doctor Who and the
  Daleks
Doin' Time on Planet
  Earth
Dolores Claiborne •
Dominick & Eugene •
Dumbo •
East of Eden •
18 Again!
The Electric Grandmother
The Empire Strikes
  Back •
Escape Artist •
Family Prayers
A Family Thing •
A Far Off Place
Fast Getaway 2
Father and Scout
Father Figure
Father Hood
Father of the Bride •
Father of the Bride
Father of the Bride Part
  II •
Father's Little Dividend •
Field of Dreams •
First Born
The Flame Trees of
  Thika •
The Flintstones
Flipper
Flower Angel
Force on Thunder
  Mountain
The Fourth Wish
Friendly Persuasion •
Further Adventures of the
  Wilderness Family,
  Part 2
Getting Even with Dad
The Gift of Amazing
  Grace
The Good Son
Goodbye, Miss 4th of
  July
A Goofy Movie •
Granpa
The Grass is Always
  Greener Over the
  Septic Tank
The Great Outdoors
The Great Santini •
Greedy

Greenstone
Gypsy Colt
Harry & Son
Harry and the
  Hendersons
The Haunting of Barney
  Palmer
Heidi
Heidi
Heidi •
Henry Hamilton:
  Graduate Ghost
Hero
Holy Matrimony
Home at Last
Home for the Holidays
A Home of Our Own
Home to Stay •
Homecoming
Homecoming: A
  Christmas Story •
Homeward Bound
Homeward Bound: The
  Incredible Journey •
Honey, I Blew Up the Kid
Honey, I Shrunk the Kids
Hope and Glory •
A Horse for Danny
The Horse in the Gray
  Flannel Suit
Hot Lead & Cold Feet
House Arrest
House of Cards
A House Without a
  Christmas Tree
Houseguest
Housekeeping •
How Green was My
  Valley •
How the West was Won •
Huck and the King of
  Hearts
I Live with Me Dad
I Never Sang For My
  Father •
I Ought to Be in Pictures
I'll Do Anything
Imaginary Crimes •
Immediate Family
In Search of a Golden
  Sky
In Search of the
  Castaways •
Indiana Jones and the
  Last Crusade •
The Inkwell
Into the West •
It Takes Two
It's a Wonderful Life •
Jack the Bear
Jacob Have I Loved
Joey
Johnny's Girl
Josh and S.A.M.
The Joy Luck Club •
The Kid Who Loved
  Christmas
King of the Hill •
Kotch •
Kramer vs. Kramer •
Kuffs
La Bamba •
Labyrinth •
Lantern Hill
Last Time Out
The Last Unicorn

Leapin' Leprechauns
Legends of the Fall
Liar's Moon
Life with Father •
Light of Day
Like Jake and Me
The Lion in Winter •
The Lion King •
Little Buddha
Little Critter Series: Just
  Me and My Dad
Little Dorrit, Film 1:
  Nobody's Fault •
Little Dorrit, Film 2: Little
  Dorrit's Story •
Little Giants
Little House on the
  Prairie •
Little Indian, Big City
A Little Princess •
Little Sister Rabbit
Little Women •
The Littlest Viking
The Long Day Closes •
Look Who's Talking Now
Looking for Miracles
Lorenzo's Oil •
The Lost Boys
Lost in Yonkers
Lots of Luck
Love Finds Andy Hardy •
Love Laughs at Andy
  Hardy
Love Your Mama
Made in America
Magic Kid
Man & Boy
The Man in the Iron
  Mask •
The Man in the Moon •
The Man in the Santa
  Claus Suit
Man of the House
Man, Woman & Child
The Manners Monster:
  Ruby Goes to Dinner
Maverick •
Meet Me in St. Louis •
Meet the Hollowheads
Menace on the Mountain
Milk Money
Miracle Down Under
Miracle on 34th Street •
Miracle on 34th Street •
Mrs. Doubtfire •
Mr. & Mrs. Bridge
Misunderstood
Monkey Trouble •
Moonstruck •
Mowgli's Brothers
My Father the Hero
My Father's Glory •
My Friend Walter
My Girl 2
My Grandpa is a Vampire
My Heroes Have Always
  Been Cowboys
My Life
My Mother's Castle •
My Old Man
My Summer Story
National Lampoon's
  Christmas Vacation
National Lampoon's
  European Vacation

Nearly No Christmas
Night Crossing
Nine Months
Noisy Nora
North
Not My Kid
Not Quite Human
Nothing in Common
The Nutty Professor •
The Old Curiosity Shop
The Old Mill
Old Yeller •
Ollie Hopnoodle's Haven
  of Bliss
Olly Olly Oxen Free
On Golden Pond •
Once Upon a Time . . .
  When We Were
  Colored •
The One and Only,
  Genuine, Original
  Family Band
Only the Lonely
Only You
Our Little Girl
Out on a Limb
Outside Chance of
  Maximillian Glick •
Over the Top
Overboard
Paco
Paradise •
The Parent Trap
Parenthood •
Peggy Sue Got Married
Penny Serenade •
Phar Lap
Philadelphia •
Places in the Heart •
Please Don't Eat the
  Daisies
Pollyanna •
Pontiac Moon
Prehysteria
Prehysteria 3
The Prodigal
Queen of Hearts •
The Quiet Man •
Quiz Show •
Radio Flyer
Rain Man •
A Rare Breed
The Real McCoy
Rebecca of Sunnybrook
  Farm
The Red Pony •
Regarding Henry •
Rich in Love
Richie Rich
The River Rat
A River Runs Through It •
The River Wild •
The Road Home
Rocket Gibraltar
Romeo and Juliet •
Rumble Fish •
Running Mates
Running on Empty •
Sabrina
Safe Passage
Samantha
The Santa Clause •
Searching for Bobby
  Fischer •
The Secret Garden •

The Secret of Roan Inish •
See You in the Morning
Sense and Sensibility •
Sesame Songs: Monster Hits!
Seven Alone
Seven Faces of Dr. Lao •
Shadow of a Doubt •
The Shadow Riders
The Silver Stallion: King of the Wild Brumbies
Since You Went Away •
Sioux City
Sixteen Candles •
Skylark
Smoke
The Snapper •
Something to Talk About
Son-in-Law
Son of Flubber
The Sound of Music •
Spencer's Mountain
State Fair •
State Fair
Stepmonster
The Stone Boy •
Stop! or My Mom Will Shoot
The Stupids
Sugar Cane Alley •
Summer Magic
The Swiss Family Robinson •
Sylvester
Tales from Avonlea, Vol. 1: The Journey Begins
Tank
Terms of Endearment •
Tex •
That Was Then. . .This Is Now
This Boy's Life •
This is My Life
A Thousand Clowns •
The Three Lives of Thomasina •
Three Men and a Cradle •
3 Ninjas
3 Ninjas Kick Back
Timemaster
Tito and Me •
Toby McTeague
Tommy Boy
Toughlove
Toys
Trading Mom
Trapped In Paradise
Treasure of the Sierra Madre •
The Trip to Bountiful •
Two Bits
The Ugly Dachshund
Uncle Buck
Uncle Elephant
Undergrads •
Unstrung Heroes
A Very Brady Sequel
Wait Till Your Mother Gets Home
A Walk in the Clouds •
The Waltons: A Thanksgiving Story
The Waltons: The Children's Carol

What About Bob? •
What's Eating Gilbert Grape •
When Mom and Dad Break Up
When Wolves Cry
Where the Lilies Bloom •
While You Were Sleeping •
The Wild Country
Wild Pony •
Wild Swans
Winnie the Pooh & Friends
With Six You Get Eggroll
The Wizard
The Wizard of Loneliness
A World Apart •
The Young Detectives on Wheels
Yours, Mine & Ours •

Fantasy
see also Folk Tales
Adventures in Dinosaur City
Adventures in Wonderland: Hare-Raising Magic
The Adventures of a Gnome Named Gnorm
The Adventures of Babar
The Adventures of Baron Munchausen •
Adventures of Black Beauty
The Adventures of Dudley the Dragon: Dudley and the Genie
The Adventures of Dudley the Dragon: Dudley Finds His Home
The Adventures of Dudley the Dragon: Dudley's Tea Party
The Adventures of Dudley the Dragon: Mr. Crabby Tree
The Adventures of Mark Twain •
The Adventures of Pinocchio
Aladdin
Aladdin and His Wonderful Lamp
Alice in Wonderland
Alice's Adventures in Wonderland
Alligator Pie
Amazing Mr. Blunden
Babar: Monkey Business
Babar the Elephant Comes to America
Babar's Triumph
Babe •
Baby. . .Secret of the Lost Legend
Baron Munchausen •
Batman •
Batman Forever
Batman Returns
*batteries not included
Battle for Moon Station Dallos
Beanstalk
Beastmaster

Beastmaster 2: Through the Portal of Time
Benji's Very Own Christmas Story
Bernard and the Genie
The B.F.G. (Big Friendly Giant)
Big •
Big Top Pee Wee
Big Trouble in Little China
Bigfoot and Wildboy
Bill and Coo
Bill & Ted's Excellent Adventure
The Blue Bird •
Box of Delights
The Boy God
The Boy Who Could Fly
The Boy Who Loved Trolls
Bridge to Terabithia
Brothers Lionheart
The Canterville Ghost
The Cat from Outer Space
Charley and the Angel
Child's Christmas in Wales
The Christmas Party
The Christmas That Almost Wasn't
The Chronicles of Narnia •
Circus Angel •
Clarence
Clash of the Titans
Cocoon •
Cocoon: The Return
Conan the Barbarian •
Conan the Destroyer
A Connecticut Yankee •
The Crow
Daisy and Her Garden: A Dance Fantasy
Darby O'Gill & the Little People •
The Dark Crystal
Daydreamer •
The Devil & Max Devlin
Digby, the Biggest Dog in the World
Disney's Adventures in Wonderland
Disney's TaleSpin, Vol. 1: True Baloo
Dr. Seuss' ABC
Dr. Seuss' Hoober-Bloob Highway
Dr. Seuss on the Loose
Dr. Seuss' The Lorax
Donald Duck in Mathmagic Land
Dragonheart
Dragonslayer •
Dragonworld •
Dream a Little Dream
Dream a Little Dream 2
Dreamchild •
DuckTales: Accidental Adventurers
Edward Scissorhands •
The ElmChanted Forest
EPIC: Days of the Dinosaurs

E.T.: The Extra-Terrestrial •
The Ewok Adventure
The Ewoks: Battle for Endor
Explorers
The Fabulous World of Jules Verne
Field of Dreams •
Fire and Ice
Flight of Dragons
Flight of the Navigator •
Flower Angel
Fluke
Francis Goes to the Races
Francis Joins the WACs
Francis the Talking Mule •
Frogs!
George's Island
Ghostbusters: Back to the Past
The Gnome-Mobile
Golden Voyage of Sinbad
The Great Cheese Conspiracy
The Great Land of Small
Green Eggs and Ham from Dr. Seuss on the Loose
Greenstone
Grendel, Grendel, Grendel
Grimm's Fairy Tales: Beauty and the Beast
Gryphon
Gulliver in Lilliput •
Gulliver's Travels
He-Man & the Masters of the Universe, Vol. 1
Heartbreak Hotel
Hector's Bunyip
Henry Hamilton: Graduate Ghost
Herbie Rides Again
Hercules
Hey There, It's Yogi Bear
Highlander 2: The Quickening
The Hobbit •
Hook
Hoppity Goes to Town
The Horse That Played Center Field
H.R. Pufnstuf, Vol. 1
A Hungarian Fairy Tale
Hyper-Sapien: People from Another Star
The Incredible Mr. Limpet
The Indian in the Cupboard •
Indiana Jones and the Last Crusade •
It's a Wonderful Life •
Jack Frost
Jack the Giant Killer
James and the Giant Peach •
Jason and the Argonauts •
Jonathan Livingston Seagull

Josh Kirby . . . Time Warrior: Chapter 1, Planet of the Dino-Knights
Journey to the Center of the Earth •
Jumanji
The Jungle Book
Kazaam
A Kid for Two Farthings
King Kong •
King Kong
Kiss Me Goodbye
Kissyfur!: Hugs and Kissyfur
Krull
L.A. Story •
Ladyhawke •
The Land of Faraway
Land of the Lost
The Last Unicorn
Leapin' Leprechauns
Legend
Legend of the White Horse
The Light Princess
Like Father, Like Son
The Lion, the Witch and the Wardrobe •
The Little Mermaid
Little Monsters
Little Nemo: Adventures in Slumberland
Little Red Riding Hood
Loch Ness
Locke the Superpower
The Lord of the Rings
Lords of Magick
Magic in the Water
Magic Island
The Magical Princess Gigi
Making Contact
The Man in the Santa Claus Suit
The Man Who Wagged His Tail
Mannequin 2: On the Move
Maple Town: Case of the Missing Candy
Marco Polo, Jr.
Mario
Marvelous Land of Oz
Masters of the Universe
Maurice Sendak Library
Maurice Sendak's Really Rosie
Merlin and the Sword
Mighty Joe Young
Mighty Morphin Power Rangers: The Movie
Million Dollar Duck
Mr. Destiny
The Moon Stallion
Mortal Kombat: The Movie
Munchie
My Friend Walter
My Neighbor Totoro
My Pet Monster, Vol. 1
My Science Project
My Stepmother Is an Alien
The NeverEnding Story
The NeverEnding Story 2: Next Chapter

The Neverending Story 3
The New Adventures of Winnie the Pooh, Vol. 1: Great Honey Pot Robbery
The Nightmare Before Christmas •
The Nutcracker
The Olden Days Coat
Once a Hero
One Magic Christmas
The Original Fabulous Adventures of Baron Munchausen •
Ozma of Oz
The Pagemaster
Panda and the Magic Serpent
The Peanut Butter Solution •
Peter-No-Tail
Peter Pan •
Peter Pan & the Pirates: Demise of Hook
Pete's Dragon
Phantom Tollbooth •
The Phoenix and the Magic Carpet
Pinocchio's Christmas
The Point •
The Polar Bear King
Powder
Prancer
Prehysteria
Prehysteria! 2
Prehysteria 3
Prelude to a Kiss
Puff and the Incredible Mr. Nobody
Puff the Magic Dragon in the Land of Living Lies
The Puppetoon Movie
Raccoons on Ice
Radio Flyer
The Railway Dragon
Rainbow Brite: A Horse of a Different Color
The Red Balloon •
The Reluctant Dragon
The Rescuers Down Under
Return from Witch Mountain
The Return of Jafar •
The Return of the King
The Return of Tommy Tricker •
Return to Oz
The Robert McCloskey Library
Robotman and Friends
Rookie of the Year
Rose-Petal Place
Rosie's Walk
Rudolph & Frosty's Christmas in July
Rumpelstiltskin
Rupert
Rupert and the Runaway Dragon
Samson and Sally: The Song of the Whales •
Santa Claus Conquers the Martians
Santa Claus: The Movie

Santabear's First Christmas
Santabear's High Flying Adventure
Seabert: Good Guys Wear White
Secret of NIMH •
The Secret of Roan Inish •
Serendipity the Pink Dragon
Seven Faces of Dr. Lao •
The Seventh Voyage of Sinbad •
The Shaggy Dog
Sherlock Hound: Dr. Watson I Presume?
Shirley Temple Storybook Theater
Sigmund & the Sea Monsters, Vol. 1
Sinbad and the Eye of the Tiger •
The Sneetches from Dr. Seuss on the Loose
Solarbabies
Something Wicked This Way Comes
Somewhere in Time
Son of Flubber
Son of Kong
Song Spinner
Space Firebird
Space Raiders
Space Warriors: Battle for Earth Station S/1
Splash •
Stand Up and Cheer
The Story of a Cowboy Angel
Storybook
Stowaways on the Ark
Street Fighter 2: The Animated Movie
Super Mario Bros.
Supergirl
Superman
Superman 1: The Movie •
Superman 2 •
Superman 3
Superman 4: The Quest for Peace
Superman & the Mole Men
Superman: The Serial, Vol. 1
The Sword in the Stone •
Sword of the Valiant
Tales of Beatrix Potter •
Tall Tale: The Unbelievable Adventures of Pecos Bill
Ted E. Bear: The Bear Who Slept Through Christmas
Teenage Mutant Ninja Turtles 1: The Movie
Teenage Mutant Ninja Turtles: The Epic Begins
Thief of Baghdad •
Thief of Baghdad •
The Thief of Baghdad
The Three Worlds of Gulliver

Through the Looking Glass
Thumbelina
Thundercats, Vol. 1: Exodus
Time Bandits •
Timefighters in the Land of Fantasy
Tobor the Great
tom thumb
Tommy Tricker & the Stamp Traveller •
Toy Story •
Trading Mom
Transformers: The Movie
A Troll in Central Park
20,000 Leagues Under the Sea •
20,000 Leagues Under the Sea
The Undersea Adventures of Snelgrove Snail
Undersea Kingdom
Unidentified Flying Oddball
The Valley of Gwangi •
The Velveteen Rabbit
Vengeance of the Space Pirate
Vice Versa •
Visionaries, Vol. 1: The Age of Magic Begins
Walking on Air
Warriors of the Wind
Watership Down •
Wee Sing: Grandpa's Magical Toys
Wee Sing in the Big Rock Candy Mountains
Welcome to Pooh Corner: Vol. 1
Where the Wild Things Are
Willow
Willy McBean & His Magic Machine
Wind in the Willows, Vol. 1
Wings of Desire •
Winnie the Pooh and the Blustery Day
Winnie the Pooh and the Honey Tree
Winter of the Witch
The Witching of Ben Wagner
The Wizard of Oz
The Wizard of Oz: Danger in a Strange Land
The Wizard of Speed and Time •
Wizards
Wizards of the Lost Kingdom
Wizards of the Lost Kingdom 2
The Wonderful World of the Brothers Grimm
Woof! •
World of David the Gnome: Kangaroo Adventure
The Worst Witch
Young Magician •

The Zax From Dr. Seuss on the Loose

Farming
see On the Farm

Fast Cars
see also Cool Cars
Built for Speed
Burn 'Em Up Barnes
Cannonball
Cannonball Run
Cannonball Run 2
Catch Me. . .If You Can
Eat My Dust
Greased Lightning
Great Race
Gumball Rally
Heart Like a Wheel •
The Heavenly Kid
Herbie Goes Bananas
Herbie Goes to Monte Carlo
Heroes on Hot Wheels, Vol. 1
The Last American Hero •
The Perils of Penelope Pitstop
Race the Sun
Rebel Without a Cause •
Six Pack
Smokey and the Bandit
Those Daring Young Men in Their Jaunty Jalopies

Fifties
see Nifty '50s

Film Noir
Key Largo •
The Maltese Falcon •
The Window •
The Wrong Man •

Film Stars
see also Price of Fame
Calendar Girl
Chaplin
Dear Brigitte
Hurricane Express
My Favorite Year •
Play It Again, Sam •
The Purple Rose of Cairo •
That's Entertainment
That's Entertainment, Part 2
That's Entertainment, Part 3

Firemen
see also Policemen
Always
Angela's Airplane
Club Paradise
Fire Safety for Kids
Mighty Joe Young
Roxanne •
Sesame Street Visits the Firehouse
Touring the Firehouse
Turk 182!

Flight
see Airborne

Flying Saucer
see Aliens — Nasty; Aliens — Nice

Folk Tales
see also Fairy Tales
African Story Magic
Ali Baba and the Forty Thieves
Anansi
The Ballad of Paul Bunyan
Brer Rabbit and Boss Lion
Clash of the Titans
Darby O'Gill & the Little People •
Dragonheart
East of the Sun, West of the Moon
Erik the Viking
Field of Dreams •
Finn McCoul
Force on Thunder Mountain
Golden Voyage of Sinbad
Grendel, Grendel, Grendel
Hercules
Hercules Unchained
Into the West •
Invitation to the Dance
Jason and the Argonauts •
Jirimpimbira: An African Folktale
John Henry
Johnny Appleseed
King Arthur & the Knights of the Round Table, Vol. 1
Koi and the Kola Nuts
Leapin' Leprechauns
The Legend of Sleepy Hollow
Magic in the Water
Merlin and the Sword
Mighty Hercules: Champion of the People!
Mighty Hercules: Conqueror of Evil!
The Mighty Hercules: Mightiest Mortal!
The Monkey People
Monty Python and the Holy Grail •
The Owl and the Pussycat
Paul Bunyan
Pecos Bill
Peter and the Wolf
The Phoenix and the Magic Carpet
Princess Scargo and the Birthday Pumpkin
Rip Van Winkle
Room for Heroes
The Secret of Navajo Cave
The Secret of Roan Inish •

Baby, It's You: Multiple Madness
The Band Wagon •
Beat Street
The Belle of New York
Breakin' Through
Captain January
Daisy and Her Garden: A Dance Fantasy
Dirty Dancing •
The Extra-Special Substitute Teacher
Fame •
Fast Forward
Flashdance
Flower Drum Song
Follow the Fleet •
Footloose
Girls Just Want to Have Fun
Grease
Grease 2
The In Crowd
Invitation to the Dance
Let's Dance on the Farm with Miss Nola
Sesame Songs: Dance Along!
Seven Brides for Seven Brothers •
Shag: The Movie
Shall We Dance •
Singin' in the Rain •
Strictly Ballroom
Swing Kids
That's Dancing!
That's Entertainment, Part 2
That's Entertainment, Part 3
Twist
Yankee Doodle Dandy •

Gotta Sing!
see also Cartoon Tunes; Gotta Dance!
Almost Angels
An American in Paris •
Anchors Aweigh •
Andy Hardy Meets Debutante
Annie
Babes in Arms
Babes in Toyland
Babes on Broadway
The Band Wagon •
Beach Blanket Bingo •
Beach Party
Beat Street
Bedknobs and Broomsticks
The Belle of New York
Bikini Beach
Bizet's Dreams
Blame It on the Night
The Boy Friend •
Breakin' Through
Breaking the Ice
The Buddy Holly Story •
Bugsy Malone
Bye, Bye, Birdie •
Camelot
Captain January
Car Wash
Carousel •

Chitty Chitty Bang Bang
Cinderella
Coal Miner's Daughter •
The Cocoanuts
Comic Book Kids
A Connecticut Yankee in King Arthur's Court
The Court Jester •
Cry-Baby •
Curly Top
Dimples
Disorderlies
Doctor Doolittle
Easter Parade •
Eddie and the Cruisers
Fame •
Fast Forward
Fiddler on the Roof •
Finian's Rainbow
Fisherman's Wharf
The 5000 Fingers of Dr. T •
Flashdance
Flower Drum Song
Follow the Fleet •
Footloose
Frankenstein Sings . . . The Movie
Funny Face •
Funny Girl •
Funny Lady
George Balanchine's The Nutcracker
Girl Crazy
The Glenn Miller Story •
Going My Way •
Grease
Grease 2
Guys and Dolls •
Hairspray •
Hans Brinker
The Happiest Millionaire
Head •
Hello, Dolly! •
Help! •
High Society
Holiday Inn
How to Stuff a Wild Bikini
Huckleberry Finn
The In Crowd
Invitation to the Dance
It Happened at the World's Fair
Jesus Christ, Superstar •
The Jolson Story •
Just Around the Corner
The King and I •
Kismet
La Bamba •
Labyrinth •
Let's Sing Again
Life Begins for Andy Hardy •
Light of Day
Lili •
Little Miss Broadway
The Little Prince
Little Shop of Horrors •
The Littlest Angel
The Littlest Rebel
Magical Mystery Tour •
Man of La Mancha
March of the Wooden Soldiers •
Mary Poppins •

Meet Me in St. Louis •
The Muppet Christmas Carol •
The Muppet Movie •
Muppets Take Manhattan •
Muscle Beach Party
The Music Man •
The New Adventures of Pippi Longstocking
Newsies
Oklahoma! •
The Old Curiosity Shop
Oliver! •
On a Clear Day You Can See Forever
Once Upon a Brothers Grimm
The One and Only, Genuine, Original Family Band
Paint Your Wagon •
Pajama Party
Peter Pan •
Pippin •
Pirate Movie
The Pirates of Penzance
The Poor Little Rich Girl
Popeye
Rebecca of Sunnybrook Farm
The Red Shoes •
Rock 'n' Roll High School •
Rock 'n' Roll High School Forever
Rumpelstiltskin
Sarafina! •
Satisfaction
Scrooge
Seven Brides for Seven Brothers •
The Seven Little Foys •
1776 •
Shall We Dance •
Shout
Sing
Singin' in the Rain •
Sleeping Beauty
Song City U.S.A.
The Sound of Music •
South Pacific •
State Fair •
State Fair
Stowaway
Strike Up the Band
That's Dancing!
That's Entertainment
That's Entertainment, Part 2
That's Entertainment, Part 3
Till the Clouds Roll By
Tommy
Waltz King
West Side Story •
What's Love Got to Do With It?
White Christmas •
Willy Wonka & the Chocolate Factory •
The Wiz
The Wizard of Oz •
Wonder Man
Xanadu
Yankee Doodle Dandy •

Yentl

Grand Hotel
Billy Madison
Dirty Dancing •
Dunston Checks In •
For Love or Money
French Kiss •
Holiday Inn
Room Service
Snowball Express

Great Britain
see also Ireland; Scotland
Amazing Mr. Blunden
Back Home
Camelot
The Canterville Ghost
The Corn is Green •
Diamonds on Wheels
Emma •
Four Weddings and a Funeral •
The Great Muppet Caper •
How Green was My Valley •
Jack and the Beanstalk
King Ralph
Lady Jane •
The Lion in Winter •
The Long Day Closes •
A Man for All Seasons •
Princess Caraboo •
The Secret Garden •
Sense and Sensibility •
Shadowlands •
That Sinking Feeling •
Year of the Comet

Great Death Scenes
Buffy the Vampire Slayer
Butch Cassidy and the Sundance Kid •
Die Hard: With a Vengeance
Gettysburg •
Glory •
Highlander •
Highlander: The Gathering
Johnny Mnemonic
Jurassic Park •
Monty Python and the Holy Grail •
Shadowlands •
The Wizard of Oz •

Great Depression
see also Homeless
Bound for Glory •
Charley and the Angel
A Christmas to Remember
Homecoming: A Christmas Story •
Honkytonk Man
It Happened One Night •
The Journey of Natty Gann •
Just Around the Corner
King of the Hill •
Of Mice and Men •
Paper Moon •
Places in the Heart •

Rambling Rose •
The Road Home
Sounder •
Two Bits
Who Has Seen the Wind?
Why Shoot the Teacher? •
Wild Hearts Can't Be Broken •

Great Escapes
see also POW/MIA; War, General
Born to Be Wild
Butch Cassidy and the Sundance Kid •
A Day in October
Die Hard •
Die Hard: With a Vengeance
Escape Artist •
Escape to Witch Mountain •
Follow the River
The Great Train Robbery •
Ladyhawke •
Mysterious Island •
Night Crossing
North by Northwest •
Papillon •
A Perfect World
Raiders of the Lost Ark •
Rob Roy •
Romancing the Stone •
The Sound of Music •
To Catch a Thief •
Torn Curtain
Toy Story •
Victory
Zebra in the Kitchen

Growing Older
*batteries not included
The Best of Times
Citizen Kane •
City Slickers •
Cocoon •
Cocoon: The Return
Dad
Dream a Little Dream •
Driving Miss Daisy •
Father of the Bride Part II •
Going in Style •
Greedy
Grumpier Old Men •
Grumpy Old Men •
Home to Stay •
Ira Sleeps Over
Kotch •
Lightning Jack
Miss Firecracker •
My Heroes Have Always Been Cowboys
On Golden Pond •
Pastime •
Rocket Gibraltar •
The Shootist •
Strangers in Good Company •
The Sunshine Boys •
Toto le Heros •
Tough Guys
Two of a Kind

Category Index

Geronimo: An American
  Legend
Gettysburg •
Glory •
The Hunchback of Notre
  Dame •
Jefferson in Paris
Jesus of Nazareth •
Johnny Tremain & the
  Sons of Liberty
Justin Morgan Had a
  Horse
Lady Jane •
The Last of the Mohicans
The Lion in Winter •
Lionheart
Little House on the
  Prairie •
A Man for All Seasons •
Moll Flanders •
Mountain Man
Once Upon a Time . . .
  When We Were
  Colored •
Orphan Train •
The Power of One
The Right Stuff •
Rob Roy - The Highland
  Rogue
Robin and Marian
The Scarlet Letter
The Scarlet Pimpernel •
The Ten
  Commandments •
Ten Who Dared
Who Has Seen the Wind?

Hockey
see also Skating
The Cutting Edge
D2: The Mighty Ducks
Happy Gilmore
Hockey Night
The Mighty Ducks
The Mighty Ducks 3
Mystery of the Million
  Dollar Hockey Puck •
Raccoons on Ice

Holidays
see also Christmas
B.C.: The First
  Thanksgiving
Bobby Goldsboro's
  Easter Egg Mornin'
Bubbe's Boarding House:
  Chanukah at Bubbe's
Bugs Bunny's Easter
  Funnies
Bugs Bunny's Mother's
  Day Special
Bugs Bunny's
  Thanksgiving Diet
Casper's Halloween
A Charlie Brown
  Thanksgiving
Daffy Duck's Easter Egg-
  citement
A Day for Thanks on
  Walton's Mountain
Disney's Haunted
  Halloween
Disney's Wonderful
  World of Winter
Easter Bunny is Coming
  to Town

Easter Egg Mornin'
Easter Parade •
Family Circus Easter
The First Easter Rabbit
Follow that Bunny!
Frankenstein Sings . . .
  The Movie
Frosty Returns
Groundhog Day
Gumby's Holiday Special
Hanukkah Tales & Tunes
Happy Holidays with
  Darkwing Duck and
  Goofy
Here Comes Peter
  Cottontail
The Hoboken Chicken
  Emergency
Hocus Pocus
Holiday Facts & Fun: St.
  Patrick's Day
Holidays for Children
  Video Series
Home for the Holidays
It's the Easter Beagle,
  Charlie Brown
The Legend of Sleepy
  Hollow
Lumpkin the Pumpkin
Mouse on the Mayflower
PJ's Unfunnybunny
  Christmas
Planes, Trains &
  Automobiles
Rugrats: Passover
Sesame Street
  Celebrates Around the
  World
Spaced Invaders
Special Valentine with
  Family Circus
Squanto: A Warrior's
  Tale •
Squanto and the First
  Thanksgiving
Thumpkin and the Easter
  Bunnies
Trick or Treat
The Waltons: A
  Thanksgiving Story
Will Vinton's Claymation
  Comedy of Horrors
Will Vinton's Claymation
  Easter
Winnie the Pooh and
  Christmas Too
Winnie the Pooh Un-
  Valentine's Day
Witch's Night Out
Yogi, the Easter Bear

Home Alone
*see also Childhood
  Visions*
Adventures in Babysitting
And You Thought Your
  Parents Were Weird!
The Apple Dumpling
  Gang
Baby's Day Out
Blank Check
Bless the Beasts and
  Children
Camp Nowhere
Cloak & Dagger
Courage Mountain

Dirt Bike Kid
Don't Tell Mom the
  Babysitter's Dead
Explorers
A Far Off Place
Gleaming the Cube
The Goonies
Home Alone •
Home Alone 2: Lost in
  New York
Honey, I Shrunk the Kids
Hook
The Horse Without a
  Head
Invaders from Mars
Just William's Luck
Legend of Billie Jean
The Littlest Horse
  Thieves
Lord of the Flies
Lord of the Flies
Mr. Wise Guy
Monkey Trouble
The Monster Squad
The Rescue
Shipwrecked
Snow Treasure
3 Ninjas
3 Ninjas Kick Back
A Waltz Through the Hills
The Window •
Young Sherlock Holmes

Homeless
*see also Great
  Depression*
The Billion Dollar Hobo
City Lights •
Curly Sue
Home for Christmas
Homecoming
Into the West •
Little Dog Lost
Sounder •
Summer Magic
Taking Care of Terrific
With Honors

Horses
Black Beauty
Black Beauty •
The Black Stallion •
The Black Stallion
  Returns
Blue Fire Lady
Born to Run
Casey's Shadow
City Slickers 2: The
  Legend of Curly's Gold
Courage of Black Beauty
Danny
Dark Horse
Devil Horse
The Electric Horseman •
The Flying Deuces •
The Great Mike
Gypsy Colt
The Horse in the Gray
  Flannel Suit
Horsemasters
Horses: Close Up and
  Very Personal
Hot to Trot!
Indian Paint
International Velvet
Into the West •

Justin Morgan Had a
  Horse
King of the Wind
Legend of the White
  Horse
The Littlest Horse
  Thieves
The Littlest Outlaw
Lucky Luke
The Man from Snowy
  River
Miracle of the White
  Stallions
My Friend Flicka •
Primo Baby
The Prince and the Great
  Race
The Quiet Man •
A Rare Breed
The Red Pony •
Return to Snowy River
Ride a Wild Pony
Run, Appaloosa, Run
Running Wild
Silver Stallion
The Silver Stallion: King
  of the Wild Brumbies
Something to Talk About
Stormy, the
  Thoroughbred
Two Bits & Pepper
Wild Hearts Can't Be
  Broken •
Wild Horse Hank
Wild Pony •
You Can Ride a Horse

Hospitals
*see also Doctors &
  Nurses*
The Adventures of
  Curious George
Disorderlies
The Disorderly Orderly
Gross Anatomy
Junior
Nine Months
12 Monkeys •
While You Were
  Sleeping •

Hunting
see also Go Fish
The Amazing Panda
  Adventure
The Bear •
The Belstone Fox
Caddyshack •
The Silver Fox and Sam
  Davenport
Those Calloways

In Concert
For Our Children: The
  Concert
Sharon, Lois & Bram at
  the Young People's
  Theatre
Sharon, Lois & Bram:
  Back by Popular
  Demand-Live
Sharon, Lois & Bram:
  Live in Your Living
  Room
Sharon, Lois & Bram:
  Sing A to Z

Tom Chapin: This Pretty
  Planet

Inventors
*see also Mad
  Scientists;
  Scientists*
Chitty Chitty Bang Bang
C.H.O.M.P.S.
Honey, I Blew Up the Kid
Honey, I Shrunk the Kids
Not Quite Human
The Nutty Professor •
The Saga of Windwagon
  Smith
Wowser: Wow-Wow
  Wowser

Ireland
see also Great Britain
Circle of Friends
The Commitments •
Darby O'Gill & the Little
  People •
Far and Away
The Fighting Prince of
  Donegal
Holiday Facts & Fun: St.
  Patrick's Day
Into the West •
Leapin' Leprechauns
The Playboys •
The Quiet Man •
Ryan's Daughter
The Secret of Roan
  Inish •
The Snapper •
War of the Buttons

Islands in the Sea
Aloha Summer
Cabin Boy
Captain Ron
The Castaway Cowboy
Club Paradise
Crusoe
Cutthroat Island
Fighting Marines
Flipper
Hawk of the Wilderness
Island of Dr. Moreau
Island of the Blue
  Dolphins
Joe Versus the Volcano
Jurassic Park •
The Last Flight of Noah's
  Ark
Lt. Robin Crusoe, U.S.N.
My Father the Hero
Mysterious Island •
Pippi in the South Seas
Robinson Crusoe
South Pacific •
A Very Brady Sequel

Italy
Cinema Paradiso •
Escapade in Florence
Only You
A Rare Breed

It's the Mob

see also Crime Doesn't Pay; Gangs; Stupid Crime

Another Stakeout
Baby on Board
Blank Check
A Bronx Tale •
Bugsy Malone
Car 54, Where Are You?
The Client
Comfort and Joy •
Cops and Robbersons
Dick Tracy •
Ernest Goes to Jail
The Freshman
Goldeneye
Hiding Out
Johnny Mnemonic
Magic Kid
Making the Grade
Odd Jobs
Police Academy: Mission to Moscow
7 Ninja Kids

It's True!

see also Biopics

Alive
All the President's Men •
Andre
Apollo 13 •
Au Revoir Les Enfants •
Awakenings •
Backbeat •
Balto
The Basketball Diaries
Big Mo
Bill •
Bill: On His Own •
Camel Boy
Chariots of Fire •
Christian the Lion
Conrack •
Cool Runnings •
Dangerous Minds
David and Lisa •
The Dove
Eight Men Out •
The Elephant Man •
Empire of the Sun •
The Ernest Green Story
Eye on the Sparrow
Fire in the Sky
Geronimo •
The Girl Who Spelled Freedom •
Goodbye, Miss 4th of July
The Great Train Robbery •
The Grey Fox •
Heart Like a Wheel •
Heartland •
A Home of Our Own
I Am a Fugitive from a Chain Gang •
Iron Will
Island of the Blue Dolphins
Jesus Christ, Superstar •
Joni
Justin Morgan Had a Horse

Kidco
King of the Wind
Knute Rockne: All American •
Lady Jane •
The Last American Hero •
Lean on Me •
Legend of Boggy Creek
Life & Times of Grizzly Adams
Little Heroes
Lone Star Kid
Lorenzo's Oil •
Love Leads the Way
Mark Twain and Me •
Mask •
Matewan •
Miracle of Our Lady of Fatima
The Miracle Worker •
Mountain Man
Night Crossing
Norma Rae •
The Other Side of the Mountain
Phar Lap
Princess Caraboo •
Quarterback Princess
Ring of Bright Water •
Rudy
Running Brave
Sea Gypsies
Searching for Bobby Fischer •
Shadowlands •
Silence of the North
Skeezer
The Sound of Music •
Squanto and the First Thanksgiving
Stand and Deliver •
Ten Who Dared
Till the Clouds Roll By
Touched by Love
Walking Tall
What's Love Got to Do With It? •
The Wild Child •
Wild Hearts Can't Be Broken •
A Winner Never Quits •
A World Apart •
The Wrong Man •
Yours, Mine & Ours •

James Bond

Diamonds are Forever •
Dr. No •
For Your Eyes Only •
From Russia with Love •
Goldeneye
Live and Let Die
The Man with the Golden Gun
Moonraker
Never Say Never Again
Octopussy
On Her Majesty's Secret Service •
The Spy Who Loved Me
Thunderball
A View to a Kill
You Only Live Twice

Japan

see also Asia

Big Bird in Japan
Hiroshima Maiden
Mr. Baseball
Peachboy
3 Ninjas Kick Back
You Only Live Twice

Journalism

see Newsroom Notes

Judaism

The Apprenticeship of Duddy Kravitz •
Au Revoir Les Enfants •
Crossing Delancey •
Fiddler on the Roof •
A Friendship in Vienna
Funny Girl •
Hanukkah Tales & Tunes
Miracle at Moreaux
Outside Chance of Maximillian Glick •
Radio Days •
Rugrats: Passover
School Ties •
Unstrung Heroes
Yentl

Jungle Stories

see also Treasure Hunt

Ace Ventura: When Nature Calls
Africa Screams
Baby. . .Secret of the Lost Legend
Congo
Disney's Sing-Along Songs, Vol. 4: The Bare Necessities
Elephant Boy •
George of the Jungle
Greystoke: The Legend of Tarzan, Lord of the Apes
Jane & the Lost City
Jumanji
The Jungle Book
The Jungle Book
Jungle Book: Mowgli Comes to the Jungle
Jungle Drums of Africa
Land of the Lost
The Lion King •
The Lost Jungle
Mowgli's Brothers
Operation Dumbo Drop
The Phantom
Rikki-Tikki-Tavi
Romancing the Stone •
Rudyard Kipling's The Jungle Book •
Sheena
Son of Kong
Tarzan and His Mate •
Tarzan Escapes •
Tarzan Finds a Son •
Tarzan, the Ape Man •
Tarzan's Secret Treasure
Terror in the Jungle
Where the River Runs Black
Widget of the Jungle

The World's Greatest Athlete

Kidnapped!

see also Missing Persons

Ace Ventura: Pet Detective
Against A Crooked Sky
Baby's Day Out
Beach Blanket Bingo •
Beethoven's 2nd
Benji •
Beverly Hills Brats
Celtic Pride
Dumb & Dumber
Fire in the Sky
Follow the River
Guarding Tess
Kid Colter
The Light in the Forest
Mr. Nanny
The Nightmare Before Christmas •
No Deposit, No Return
101 Dalmatians
A Perfect World
The Real McCoy
Son of the Pink Panther
Street Fighter
Tarzan's New York Adventure
3 Ninjas
Twinsitters
Two Bits & Pepper

A Kid's Best Friend

Andre
Black Beauty •
Flipper
Free Willy
Iron Will
Lassie
Lassie, Come Home •
Lassie: The Miracle
Monkey Trouble •

Kindness of Strangers

Forrest Gump •
Lilies of the Field •
Powder
While You Were Sleeping •

King of Beasts (Dogs)

The Adventures of Milo & Otis •
All Dogs Go to Heaven •
All Dogs Go to Heaven 2
The Amazing Dobermans
Antarctica
Baby Animals Just Want to Have Fun
Balto
Barney's Christmas Surprise
Bear's Big Lake
Beethoven
Beethoven's 2nd
Benji •
Benji the Hunted
Benji's Very Own Christmas Story
Big Red

Bingo
Bunnicula: Vampire Rabbit
Call of the Wild
Canine Commando
Challenge To Be Free
Challenge to Lassie
Challenge to White Fang
The Charlie Brown and Snoopy Show: Vol. 1
Chips the War Dog
C.H.O.M.P.S.
Clean Slate
Courage of Lassie
Daring Dobermans
Digby, the Biggest Dog in the World
The Doberman Gang
A Dog of Flanders
Dog Pound Shuffle
The Dog Who Dared
The Dog Who Stopped the War •
Doggy Faces
Dumb & Dumber
Dusty
Far from Home: The Adventures of Yellow Dog •
Fluke
For the Love of Benji •
The Fox and the Hound •
Frankenweenie
George!
Goober & the Ghost Chasers
A Goofy Movie •
Great Adventure
Greyfriars Bobby •
Hambone & Hillie
Heathcliff & Marmaduke
Heck's Way Home
Here Comes Droopy
Homeward Bound 2: Lost in San Francisco
Homeward Bound: The Incredible Journey
The Incredible Journey •
Iron Will
It's a Dog's Life
K-9
K-9000
Kavik, the Wolf Dog •
Lady and the Tramp •
Lassie
Lassie, Come Home •
Lassie: The Miracle
Lassie's Great Adventure
Lassie's Rescue Rangers
Legend of the Northwest
Little Dog Lost
Little Heroes
The Lone Wolf
Look Who's Talking Now
Love Leads the Way
Magic of Lassie
The Man Who Wagged His Tail
Man's Best Friend
My Dog, the Thief
Nikki, the Wild Dog of the North •
Oh, Heavenly Dog!
Old Yeller •
Old Yeller
Oliver & Company •

101 Dalmatians ●
101 Dalmatians
Potsworth and the
    Midnight Patrol
Pound Puppies
Precious Pupp
The Return of Our Gang
Rin Tin Tin, Hero of the
    West
Rover Dangerfield
The Sandlot ●
Savage Sam
Scooby-Doo
Scruffy
The Shaggy D.A.
The Shaggy Dog
Sherlock: Undercover
    Dog
Silver Stallion
Skeezer
Smoke
Sport Goofy
Spot Goes to School
Spot's Magic Christmas
Summerdog
The Tender Years
The Thin Man ●
Toby McTeague
Tom and Jerry: The
    Movie
Top Dog
The Truth About Cats
    and Dogs ●
Turner and Hooch
The Ugly Dachshund
Where the Red Fern
    Grows ●
Where the Red Fern
    Grows: Part 2
White Fang 2: The Myth
    of the White Wolf
White Fang and the
    Hunter
Whitewater Sam
Wishbone: A Tail in
    Twain
Wishbone: Homer Sweet
    Homer
Wishbone: Salty Dog
Wishbone: Terrified
    Terrier
Wishbone: The Prince
    and the Pooch
Wishbone: The Slobbery
    Hound
Wishbone: Twisted Tail
The Wizard of Oz ●
Woof! ●
Wowser: Wow-Wow
    Wowser

Kings
see Royalty

Korean War
MacArthur
M*A*S*H ●

Kung Fu
see Martial Arts

Labor Unions
see also Miners
Gung Ho
Matewan ●
Newsies

Norma Rae ●

Lassie
Challenge to Lassie
Courage of Lassie
Lassie, Come Home ●
Lassie: The Miracle
Lassie's Great Adventure
Lassie's Rescue Rangers
Magic of Lassie

Laugh Riots
*see also Boy Meets
    Girl; Comedy with
    an Edge; Funny
    Adventures; Silly
    Spoofs; Sports
    Comedies*
Abbott and Costello Meet
    Captain Kidd
Abbott and Costello Meet
    Dr. Jekyll and Mr. Hyde
Abbott and Costello Meet
    Frankenstein ●
Ace Ventura: Pet
    Detective
Ace Ventura: When
    Nature Calls
The Adventures of a
    Gnome Named Gnorm
The Adventures of a Two-
    Minute Werewolf
The Adventures of
    Buckaroo Banzai
    Across the Eighth
    Dimension ●
Africa Screams
Ah, Wilderness! ●
The Air Up There
Airheads
All I Want for Christmas
Aloha Summer
American Boyfriends
American Graffiti ●
Amos and Andrew
And Baby Makes Six
Androcles and the Lion
Andy Hardy Gets Spring
    Fever
Andy Hardy's Double Life
Andy Hardy's Private
    Secretary
Angus
Animal Crackers ●
Any Which Way You Can
The Apprenticeship of
    Duddy Kravitz ●
At the Circus
Author! Author!
Avalon ●
Ava's Magical Adventure
Awakenings ●
The Baby-Sitters Club
Baby, Take a Bow
Baby's Day Out
The Bachelor and the
    Bobby-Soxer ●
Back to School
The Bad News Bears ●
The Bad News Bears Go
    to Japan
The Bad News Bears in
    Breaking Training
The Ballad of Paul
    Bunyan

The Barefoot Executive
B.C.: A Special Christmas
Beautiful Girls
Bedtime for Bonzo
Beethoven
Beethoven's 2nd
Beetle Bailey: Military
    Madness
Being Human
The Bellboy
The Belles of St.
    Trinian's ●
The Bells of St. Mary's ●
Benji ●
Better Off Dead
The Beverly Hillbillies
Beverly Hills Brats
Big ●
Big Bully
Big Business ●
Big Girls Don't Cry. .
    .They Get Even
The Big Green
Big Shots
The Big Store
Big Top Pee Wee
Billie
The Billion Dollar Hobo
A Billion for Boris
Billy Madison
Bio-Dome
The Birdcage ●
Black Sheep
Blank Check
Blankman
Blue Murder at St.
    Trinian's ●
Blues Busters
The Boatniks
Book of Love
Born to Be Wild
Boys of the City
Brain Donors
The Breakfast Club ●
Breaking Away ●
Breaking the Rules
Brewster's Millions
Bright Eyes
Brighton Beach Memoirs
Bringing Up Baby ●
Broadway Danny Rose ●
Buck Privates
Buck Privates Come
    Home ●
Buffy the Vampire Slayer
Bushwhacked
Bustin' Loose
Butterflies Are Free ●
Bye Bye, Love
Cabin Boy
The Caddy
Caddyshack ●
Calendar Girl
Camp Nowhere
Cancel My Reservation
Candleshoe ●
The Canterville Ghost
Captain Ron
Car 54, Where Are You?
Carbon Copy
Casey's Shadow
Casper ●
Celtic Pride
The Charge of the Model
    T's
Charley and the Angel

Charlie and the Great
    Balloon Chase
Charlie's Ghost: The
    Secret of Coronado
The Chicken Chronicles
Chips the War Dog
Chocolate Fever
C.H.O.M.P.S.
A Christmas Story ●
Cinderfella
Citizens Band ●
City Lights ●
Clara's Heart
Clarence
Class Act
Clean Slate
Clifford
Clipped Wings
Club Paradise
Clue
Cocoon ●
Cocoon: The Return
Comfort and Joy ●
Computer Wizard
The Computer Wore
    Tennis Shoes
Condorman
Coneheads
A Connecticut Yankee ●
Cool Runnings ●
Cop and a Half
Cops and Robbersons
Coupe de Ville
The Courtship of Eddie's
    Father ●
Cracking Up
The Crazysitter
Crooklyn ●
Curley
Curse of the Pink
    Panther
D2: The Mighty Ducks
Daffy Duck's
    Quackbusters ●
Dave ●
A Day at the Races ●
Dazed and Confused ●
The Delicate Delinquent
Delirious
Dennis the Menace
Dennis the Menace:
    Dinosaur Hunter
The Devil & Max Devlin
Die Laughing
Digby, the Biggest Dog
    in the World
Digger
The Disorderly Orderly
Dr. Jekyll and Ms. Hyde
Dr. Otto & the Riddle of
    the Gloom Beam
Doin' Time on Planet
    Earth
Donald Duck in
    Mathmagic Land
Don't Tell Mom the
    Babysitter's Dead
Dream a Little Dream
Dream a Little Dream 2
Dream Machine
The Dream Team ●
Drop Dead Fred
Duck Soup ●
Dumb & Dumber
Dunston Checks In ●
Dutch

Eat My Dust
Ed
Eddie
Educating Rita ●
18 Again!
Encino Man
Ernest Goes to Camp
Ernest Goes to Jail
Ernest Goes to School
Ernest Rides Again
Ernest Saves Christmas
Ernest Scared Stupid
The Errand Boy
Experience Preferred. . .
    But Not Essential
Explorers
Family Jewels
A Family Thing ●
The Fantastic World of
    D.C. Collins
Fast Times at Ridgemont
    High ●
Fat Albert & the Cosby
    Kids, Vol. 1
Fatal Instinct
Father and Scout
Father of the Bride ●
Father of the Bride
Father of the Bride Part
    II ●
Father's Little Dividend ●
Felix the Cat: The Movie
Ferris Bueller's Day Off ●
The Fiendish Plot of Dr.
    Fu Manchu
The Fifth Monkey
A Fine Mess
First Kid
The Flamingo Kid ●
Flash, the Teenage Otter
Fletch
Fletch Lives
The Flintstones
Flirting ●
The Flying Deuces ●
Follow Me, Boys! ●
Follow the Leader
For Better and For Worse
For Keeps
For the Love of Benji ●
Forrest Gump ●
The Four Musketeers ●
Francis Goes to the
    Races
Francis Joins the WACs
Francis the Talking
    Mule ●
Freaky Friday ●
Frog ●
Frogs!
From the Mixed-Up Files
    of Mrs. Basil E.
    Frankweiler
The Front Page
Funny Farm
The Garbage Pail Kids
    Movie
The Geisha Boy
General Spanky
George!
Gerald McBoing-Boing
Getting Even with Dad
Ghost Chasers
Girlfriends ●
Girls Just Want to Have
    Fun

Shag: The Movie •
The Shaggy D.A.
The Shaggy Dog
Shirley Temple Baby
    Berlesques
Short Circuit 2
A Shot in the Dark •
Simon
A Simple Twist of Fate
Sister Act •
Sister Act 2: Back in the
    Habit
Six Weeks
Slam Dunk Ernest
Small Change •
Smart Alecks
The Snapper •
Snoopy, Come Home •
Snow White and the
    Three Stooges
Snowball Express
Some Kind of Wonderful
Something to Talk About
Son-in-Law
Son of Flubber
Son of the Pink Panther
Sorrowful Jones
Soul Man
Spaceballs
Spaced Invaders
Speaking of Animals, Vol.
    1
Spencer's Mountain
Spies Like Us
Splash •
Spook Busters
Sport Goofy
Spy Hard
The Story of Seabiscuit
Strange Brew
Stuart Saves His Family
The Stupids
Summer Rental
Summer School
The Sunshine Boys •
Super Seal
Superdad
The Sure Thing •
Sweet Liberty
Swing Shift
Take Down
Take the Money and
    Run •
Teen Witch
Teen Wolf
Teen Wolf Too
Tex Avery's Screwball
    Classics, Vol. 3
That Darn Cat
That Gang of Mine
That's Entertainment,
    Part 2
They Went That-a-Way &
    That-a-Way
This is My Life
A Thousand Clowns •
Three Men and a Baby •
Three Men and a
    Cradle •
Three Men and a Little
    Lady
Three O'Clock High
Three Stooges
Three Stooges: A
    Ducking They Will Go

Three Stooges: A
    Plumbing We Will Go
Three Stooges: Cash and
    Carry
Three Stooges: If a Body
    Meets a Body
Three Stooges: In the
    Sweet Pie and Pie
Three Stooges Meet
    Hercules
Three Stooges: So Long
    Mr. Chumps
Three Stooges: What's
    the Matador?
Thursday's Game •
Tito and Me •
To Wong Foo, Thanks for
    Everything, Julie
    Newmar
Toby Tyler •
Tom Brown's School
    Days
Tom Brown's School
    Days •
Tommy Boy
Tony Draws a Horse
Tootsie •
Topper •
Topper Returns •
Topper Takes a Trip •
The Toy
Toy Story •
Toys
Trading Hearts
Trail of the Pink Panther
Trapped In Paradise
Troop Beverly Hills •
The Trouble with Angels
Truly, Madly, Deeply •
Turk 182!
Turner and Hooch
Twelve Chairs •
Twinsitters
Two Bits & Pepper
2000 Year Old Man •
The Ugly Dachshund
Uncle Buck
Undercover Blues
Undergrads •
Unidentified Flying
    Oddball
Up the Down Staircase •
A Very Brady Sequel
Vice Versa •
Wait Until Spring,
    Bandini
Walk Like a Man
Walt Disney Films in
    French
Wayne's World
Wayne's World 2
Weekend at Bernie's
Weekend at Bernie's 2
Weird Science
Welcome Home, Roxy
    Carmichael
What About Bob? •
What's Up, Doc? •
Where Angels Go,
    Trouble Follows
Who Framed Roger
    Rabbit? •
Witches' Brew
With Honors
The Wizard
Wonders of Aladdin

Woody Woodpecker
    Collector's Edition, Vol.
    1
Woof! •
The World of Henry
    Orient •
The Year My Voice
    Broke •
Young Einstein
Zebra in the Kitchen
Zero to Sixty

Lawyers

*see also Courtroom
    Capers*
Adam's Rib •
Before and After
Brain Donors
The Client
Judge Dredd
Jury Duty
Legend of Billie Jean
Man of the House
North
The Paper Chase •
The Pelican Brief
Philadelphia •
Regarding Henry •
A Simple Twist of Fate
To Kill a Mockingbird •

Life in the 'Burbs

Adventures in Spying
Amos and Andrew
The Brady Bunch Movie •
The 'Burbs
Coneheads
Dennis the Menace
Don't Tell Mom the
    Babysitter's Dead
Edward Scissorhands •
The Grass is Always
    Greener Over the
    Septic Tank
Hocus Pocus
House •
Madhouse
The Money Pit
Opportunity Knocks
Over the Edge •
Please Don't Eat the
    Daisies
Serial Mom •
The Simpsons Christmas
    Special
A Very Brady Sequel
When Every Day was the
    Fourth of July

Live Action/
    Animation Combos

Alice in Wonderland
Anchors Aweigh •
Bedknobs and
    Broomsticks
Daydreamer •
Fun & Fancy Free
The Incredible Mr. Limpet
James and the Giant
    Peach •
Mary Poppins •
The Pagemaster
So Dear to My Heart •
The Three Caballeros •
Who Framed Roger
    Rabbit? •

Xanadu

Loneliness

see Only the Lonely

Lost Worlds

At the Earth's Core
Jane & the Lost City
Journey to the Center of
    the Earth •
Jumanji
Land That Time Forgot
Mysterious Island •
The People That Time
    Forgot
When Dinosaurs Ruled
    the Earth
Where Time Began

Macho Men

*see also Amazing
    Adventures*
The Adventures of
    Captain Marvel
Atom Man vs. Superman
A Bridge Too Far
Buck Rogers in the 25th
    Century
Cannonball Run
Cannonball Run 2
Captain America
Conan the Barbarian •
Diamonds are Forever •
Dick Tracy •
Dick Tracy, Detective
Dick Tracy Meets
    Gruesome
Dr. No •
First Knight
For Your Eyes Only •
G.I. Joe, Vol. 1: A Real
    American Hero
Giant •
Gone with the Wind •
The Green Hornet
Greystoke: The Legend of
    Tarzan, Lord of the
    Apes
Hercules
Hercules in New York
Hot Shots! Part Deux
Kindergarten Cop
Last Action Hero
Legend of the Lone
    Ranger
The Man with the Golden
    Gun
The Masked Marvel
Never Say Never Again
No Holds Barred
Rocky •
Rocky 2
Rocky 3
Rocky 4
Rocky 5
The Seventh Voyage of
    Sinbad •
The Shadow
Speed •
Street Fighter
Suburban Commando
Superman 1: The Movie •
Superman 2 •
Superman 3
Superman 4: The Quest
    for Peace

Superman & the Mole
    Men
Tarzan, the Ape Man •
Thunderball

Mad Scientists

*see also Inventors;
    Scientists*
Brenda Starr
Captain America
Dr. No •
The Double O Kid
Freaked
Island of Dr. Moreau
Jurassic Park •
Mystery Science Theater
    3000: The Movie •
The Pink Panther Strikes
    Again •
Star Trek Generations •

Made for Television

*see TV Movies; TV
    Series*

Mafia

see It's the Mob

Magic

*see also Genies;
    Magic Carpet Rides*
Aladdin and His Magic
    Lamp
Bedknobs and
    Broomsticks
The Butcher's Wife
Dream a Little Dream 2
Escape to Witch
    Mountain •
Gryphon
The Man in the Santa
    Claus Suit
My First Magic
Sorcerer's Apprentice
Teen Witch
Tut and Tuttle
Xuxa: Funtastic Birthday
    Party

Magic Carpet Rides

Aladdin •
Golden Voyage of Sinbad
The Phoenix and the
    Magic Carpet
The Seventh Voyage of
    Sinbad •
Sinbad and the Eye of
    the Tiger
Sinbad the Sailor •
Thief of Baghdad •
Thief of Baghdad
The Thief of Baghdad

Marriage

*see also Divorce;
    Wedding Bells*
The Age of Innocence •
Bill Cosby, Himself
Country Girl •
Dial "M" for Murder •
Father of the Bride •
For Keeps
Forget Paris
Giant •
Grumpier Old Men

The Heartbreak Kid •
High Society
Holy Matrimony
How to Make an
    American Quilt
Liar's Moon
Man of the House
Mr. & Mrs. Smith •
Mr. Mom •
Mr. Wonderful
The Money Pit
Moonstruck •
Muriel's Wedding •
On Golden Pond •
On Her Majesty's Secret
    Service •
Paint Your Wagon
Paradise •
Peggy Sue Got Married
The Philadelphia Story •
Prelude to a Kiss
Rebecca •
Rocky 2
Ryan's Daughter
Safe Passage
Shadowlands •
She-Devil
She's Having a Baby
Something to Talk About
Son-in-Law
Suspicion •
Thursday's Game •
True Lies
Under Capricorn
Undercover Blues
A Walk in the Clouds
Yours, Mine & Ours •

Martial Arts
Aloha Summer
Big Trouble in Little
    China
Dragon: The Bruce Lee
    Story
The Karate Kid •
The Karate Kid: Part 2
The Karate Kid: Part 3
Magic Kid
Magic Kid 2
Mighty Morphin Power
    Rangers Karate Club
Mortal Kombat: The
    Movie
The Next Karate Kid
Remo Williams: The
    Adventure Begins
7 Ninja Kids
Sidekicks
Surf Ninjas
Teenage Mutant Ninja
    Turtles: The Epic
    Begins
3 Ninjas
3 Ninjas Kick Back
Timecop
Top Dog

The Meaning of Life
Being Human
Funny Face
Love and Death
My Life
The Remains of the
    Day •
Shadowlands •

Medieval Romps
*see also Historical
    Happenings; Period
    Piece;
    Swashbucklers*
The Adventures of Robin
    Hood •
Being Human
Braveheart •
Camelot
A Connecticut Yankee •
A Connecticut Yankee in
    King Arthur's Court
Dragonheart
Dragonslayer •
The Fighting Prince of
    Donegal
First Knight
Jabberwocky
Jack the Giant Killer
A Kid in King Arthur's
    Court
Knights of the Round
    Table
Ladyhawke •
Legend
The Legend of Young
    Robin Hood
The Lion in Winter •
Lionheart
The Magic Sword
Mark Twain's A
    Connecticut Yankee in
    King Arthur's Court
Merlin and the Sword
Monty Python and the
    Holy Grail •
Pippin •
Robin and Marian
Robin Hood •
Robin Hood: Men in
    Tights
Robin Hood: Prince of
    Thieves
The Secret of El Zorro
Sir Prancelot
The Sword in the Stone •
Sword of the Valiant
Time Bandits •
Unidentified Flying
    Oddball
Wizards of the Lost
    Kingdom

Mental Retardation
*see also Physical
    Problems; Savants*
Bill •
Bill: On His Own •
Dominick & Eugene •
Of Mice and Men •
Rain Man •
Two of a Kind
What's Eating Gilbert
    Grape •
The Wizard

**Mickey Mouse &
    Friends**
Boo-Busters
Canine Commando
Chip 'n' Dale Animated
    Antics Series
Chip 'n' Dale Rescue
    Rangers: Crimebusters

Disney's Darkwing Duck:
    His Favorite
    Adventures
Disney's Haunted
    Halloween
Disney's TaleSpin, Vol. 1:
    True Baloo
Disney's Wonderful
    World of Winter
DuckTales: Accidental
    Adventurers
DuckTales the Movie:
    Treasure of the Lost
    Lamp
The Gang's All Here
    Series
Goof Troop: Goin' Fishin'
A Goofy Look at
    Valentine's Day
Lend a Paw
Mickey Mouse: The Early
    Years Series
Mickey's Birthday Party
Mickey's Crazy Careers
Monster Bash
An Officer and a Duck
On Vacation with Mickey
    and Friends
Pluto
Pluto (limited gold
    edition)
Three Decades of Donald
    Duck Series
Unsinkable Donald Duck
    with Huey, Dewey &
    Louie

Miners
The Adventures of
    Bullwhip Griffin
Challenge to White Fang
Flaming Frontiers
How Green was My
    Valley •
Matewan •
Paint Your Wagon

Missing Persons
see also Kidnapped!
Big Jake
Curse of the Pink
    Panther
The Island at the Top of
    the World
The Lady Vanishes •
Little Miss Millions
Romancing the Stone •

Misspelled Titles
The 'Burbs
C.H.O.M.P.S.
Doin' Time on Planet
    Earth
I Live with Me Dad
Puss 'n Boots
Regl'ar Fellers
Singin' in the Rain •

Mistaken Identity
*see also Amnesia;
    Trading Places*
The Adventures of
    Bullwhip Griffin
Amos and Andrew
Being There •
Bushwhacked

Charade •
The Court Jester •
Dave •
Ernest Goes to Jail
F/X 2: The Deadly Art of
    Illusion
Hero
Houseguest
If Looks Could Kill
Invasion of the Body
    Snatchers •
It Takes Two
The Legend of
    Manxmouse
Lisa
Little Sister
Made in America
The Man with One Red
    Shoe
Mrs. Winterbourne
Mystery Date
Never a Dull Moment
North by Northwest •
Only You
Opportunity Knocks
Oscar
Out on a Limb
Prelude to a Kiss
The Reluctant Astronaut
The Santa Clause •
Sister Act •
Sister Act 2: Back in the
    Habit
Smokey and the Bandit,
    Part 3
Straight Talk
Support Your Local
    Gunfighter •
The 39 Steps •
Toto le Heros •
The Truth About Cats
    and Dogs •
While You Were
    Sleeping •

Modern Cowboys
*see also Cowboys &
    Indians*
Barbarosa •
Bronco Billy
City Slickers •
City Slickers 2: The
    Legend of Curly's Gold
The Electric Horseman •
My Heroes Have Always
    Been Cowboys
Rhinestone
Toy Story •

Moms
*see also Dads;
    Parenthood*
Baby Boom
The Brady Bunch Movie •
The Incredible Shrinking
    Woman
Little Women •
Made in America
Mermaids •
Mrs. Winterbourne
Mom and Dad Save the
    World
Only the Lonely
The River Wild •
She-Devil
She's Having a Baby

So I Married an Axe
    Murderer
Stop! or My Mom Will
    Shoot
Throw Momma from the
    Train •
Troop Beverly Hills •
A Very Brady Sequel

Monsters, General
*see also Ghosts,
    Ghouls, & Goblins;
    Giants; Mad
    Scientists; Robots;
    Scary Beasties;
    Scary Bugs; Scary
    Plants; Vampires;
    Werewolves*
The Boy Who Loved
    Trolls
Destroy All Monsters
Dragonheart
Forbidden Planet •
Gargoyles, The Movie:
    The Heroes Awaken
Godzilla vs. Megalon
Godzilla vs. the Cosmic
    Monster
Godzilla vs. the Smog
    Monster
The Invisible Monster
Island of Dr. Moreau
Jack the Giant Killer
Jason and the
    Argonauts •
Labyrinth •
Legend of Boggy Creek
Little Monsters
Loch Ness
Mad Monster Party
The Monster Squad
My Pet Monster, Vol. 1
The Phantom Creeps
The Quest
The Return of Swamp
    Thing
Return to Boggy Creek
Stepmonster
20,000 Leagues Under
    the Sea

Mountains
Bushwhacked
Heidi
My Side of the Mountain
Third Man on the
    Mountain

The Muppets
The Adventures of a
    Gnome Named Gnorm
Basil Hears a Noise
Billy Bunny's Animal
    Song
The Christmas Toy
Country Music with the
    Muppets
Fraggle Rock: A Festive
    Fraggle Holiday
Fraggle Rock, Vol. 1:
    Meet the Fraggles
The Frog Prince
The Great Muppet
    Caper •
Hey, Cinderella!

It's Not Easy Being Green
It's the Muppets, Vol. 1: Meet the Muppets
Jim Henson's Preschool Collection: Muppets on Wheels
Jim Henson's Preschool Collection: Yes, I Can Help
Jim Henson's Preschool Collection: Yes, I Can Learn
Kermit and Piggy Story
Labyrinth •
Muppet Babies: Explore with Us
Muppet Babies: Let's Build
Muppet Babies: Time to Play
The Muppet Christmas Carol •
Muppet Family Christmas
The Muppet Movie •
Muppet Revue
Muppet Treasure Island •
Muppet Treasure Island Sing-Alongs
Muppet Video Series
Muppets Moments
Muppets Take Manhattan •
Rock Music with the Muppets
Sesame Street: Do the Alphabet
Sesame Street Kids' Guide to Life: Learning to Share
Sesame Street Presents: Follow That Bird •
Sesame Street Presents: Put Down the Duckie: An All-Star Musical Special
Sesame Street's 25th Birthday: A Musical Celebration
Shirley Temple Baby Berlesques
The Tale of the Bunny Picnic
Things That Fly Sing Alongs

Music

see also Musician Biopics; Nashville Narratives; Struggling Musicians
Airheads
Allegro Non Troppo •
Amadeus •
Baby Songs: Turn on the Music
Bach's Flight to Freedom
Backbeat •
Beat Street
Bedrockin' and Rappin'
Beethoven Lives Upstairs •
Blame It on the Night
Club Connect: The Hip-Hop Alternative

Coal Miner's Daughter •
The Commitments •
Cool As Ice
Eddie and the Cruisers
Face the Music
Fantasia •
The Flintstones: Rappin' n' Rhymin'
Follow Me, Boys! •
The Glenn Miller Story •
Gullah Gullah Island: Binyah's Surprise
A Hard Day's Night •
Heartbreak Hotel
House Party •
House Party 2: The Pajama Jam
House Party 3
I Wanna Hold Your Hand •
I Want to be a Ballerina
Jazz Time Tale
Joey
Johann's Gift to Christmas
Kidsongs: A Day at Camp
Knights & Emeralds
Marsalis on Music Why Toes Tap: Wynton on Rhythm
Mr. Holland's Opus •
Peter and the Wolf
Professor Iris: Music Mania
Rock 'n' Roll High School •
Rock 'n' Roll High School Forever
Satisfaction
Shout
Song Spinner
Sparky's Magic Piano
Toot, Whistle, Plunk & Boom
A World is Born
Yanco

Musician Biopics

see also Nashville Narratives
Amadeus •
Bound for Glory •
The Buddy Holly Story •
Coal Miner's Daughter •
The Glenn Miller Story •
La Bamba •
Waltz King
What's Love Got to Do With It?

Mysteries

Almost Partners
Amazing Mr. Blunden
The Andromeda Strain
Back to Hannibal: The Further Adventures of Tom Sawyer and Huckleberry Finn
Charade •
Child of Glass
Clue
The Clutching Hand
Death on the Nile •
Desperately Seeking Susan •
Dial "M" for Murder •

Diamond's Edge •
Diamonds on Wheels
Dick Tracy •
Dick Tracy, Detective
Dick Tracy Meets Gruesome
The Double McGuffin
Emil and the Detective
Escapade in Florence
Evil Under the Sun •
F/X •
Foreign Correspondent •
Green Archer
Hard-Boiled Mahoney
Haunted Mansion Mystery
The Haunting of Barney Palmer
Help! •
The Horse Without a Head
I am the Cheese
I Confess
The Lady in White •
The Lady Vanishes •
The Last Chance Detectives: Mystery Lights of Navajo Mesa
Lisa
The Little Girl Who Lives Down the Lane •
Little Nikita
The Lost Jungle
The Maltese Falcon •
The Manhattan Project
Mysterious Doctor Satan
Mystery Mansion
Nancy Drew: Mystery of the Diamond Triangle
Nancy Drew, Reporter
North by Northwest •
Notorious •
Octopussy
The Pelican Brief •
The Phantom Creeps
Plain Clothes
Project X •
Radioland Murders •
Rear Window •
Rebecca •
Saboteur •
Shadow of a Doubt •
Sherlock Hound: Dr. Watson I Presume?
Sioux City
Sleuth •
Sneakers
Spellbound •
Stage Fright •
Strangers on a Train •
Sudden Terror
Suspicion •
Swamp Thing
The Tall Blond Man with One Black Shoe •
Ten Little Indians
That Darn Cat •
The Thin Man •
The 39 Steps •
Tiger Bay •
To Catch a Thief •
Torn Curtain
Twice Upon a Time •
Under Capricorn •
The Usual Suspects •
The Window •

The Wrong Man •
The Young Detectives on Wheels
Young Sherlock Holmes

Nashville Narratives

see also Musician Biopics; Southern Belles; Southern Sagas
Coal Miner's Daughter •
Honkytonk Man •
Jack Houston's Imagineland: This is Imagineland
The Night the Lights Went Out in Georgia
Rhinestone
A Smoky Mountain Christmas
Tender Mercies •
The Thing Called Love

Nasty Nazis

see also Judaism; World War II
Bedknobs and Broomsticks •
Casablanca •
Clipped Wings
A Day in October
Foreign Correspondent •
A Friendship in Vienna
The Incredible Mr. Limpet
Indiana Jones and the Last Crusade •
Indiana Jones and the Temple of Doom •
Judgment at Nuremberg •
Madame Rosa •
Miracle at Moreaux
Notorious •
Raiders of the Lost Ark •
The Rocketeer •
Snow Treasure
The Sound of Music •
Swing Kids
Top Dog
Wizards

Native America

The Bears & I
Billy Jack
Dances with Wolves •
Fish Hawk
Follow the River
Geronimo •
Geronimo: An American Legend
The Indian in the Cupboard •
Island of the Blue Dolphins •
Joe Panther
Journey to Spirit Island •
The Last of the Mohicans •
The Last of the Mohicans •
The Legend of Hiawatha
The Legend of Wolf Mountain
The Light in the Forest •
Little Big Man •
Lost Legacy: A Girl Called Hatter Fox

Man of the House
Pocahontas
Pocahontas •
Poltergeist 2: The Other Side
Princess Scargo and the Birthday Pumpkin
Run, Appaloosa, Run
Running Brave
Savage Sam
The Secret of Navajo Cave
Sioux City
Smith! •
The Song of Sacajawea
Squanto: A Warrior's Tale •
Squanto and the First Thanksgiving
Terror in the Jungle
The Villain
Where the Spirit Lives •
White Fang 2: The Myth of the White Wolf
Windrunner
Winter Wolf

Newspapers

see Newsroom Notes

Newsroom Notes

see also Shutterbugs; TV Tales
All the President's Men •
The Beniker Gang
Blankman
Brenda Starr
Citizen Kane •
Delirious
Father Hood
Fletch
Fletch Lives
Foreign Correspondent •
The Great Muppet Caper •
Hero
His Girl Friday •
I Love Trouble
Journey for Margaret •
Just One of the Guys •
Kid from Not-So-Big
Newsies
The Paper •
The Pelican Brief •
The Philadelphia Story •
Roman Holiday •
Straight Talk
Three O'Clock High •
A World Apart •

Nifty '50s

Alex
Back to the Future •
Back to the Future, Part 2
Book of Love
The Buddy Holly Story •
Bye, Bye, Birdie •
Circle of Friends
Cry-Baby •
Dead Poets Society •
Dirty Dancing •
Father of the Bride •
Grease
Grease 2
Housekeeping •

I.Q.
La Bamba •
The Long Day Closes •
The Lords of Flatbush
The Man in the Moon •
Matinee •
My Favorite Year •
Oh, What a Night
Peggy Sue Got Married
The Playboys •
Quiz Show •
School Ties •
Shag: The Movie •
Shout
Stacking
Strange Invaders •
Superdad
This Boy's Life •
Trading Hearts
The War of the Worlds •
The Way We Were •

Nuclear War
see also Disaster
Strikes!
Amazing Grace & Chuck
Broken Arrow
The Crimson Ghost
Crimson Tide •
Desert Bloom •
Dr. Seuss' Butter Battle
Book
Hiroshima Maiden
The Manhattan Project
Modern Problems
The Spy Who Loved Me
Superman 4: The Quest
for Peace
True Lies
Voyage to the Bottom of
the Sea •
War Games •

Nuns & Priests
The Bells of St. Mary's •
Change of Habit
Cry, the Beloved
Country •
For Better and For Worse
Going My Way •
I Confess
Lilies of the Field •
Sister Act •
Sister Act 2: Back in the
Habit
The Sound of Music •
The Trouble with Angels
Where Angels Go,
Trouble Follows

Oceans
see Go Fish; Scuba
Diving; Submarines

The Olympics
see also Sports
Dramas
Alex
Animalympics: Winter
Games
Chariots of Fire •
Cool Runnings •
International Velvet
The Olympic Champ
Running Brave
Terrytoons Olympics

On the Farm
Babe •
Boy Takes Girl
The Carrot Highway
The Castaway Cowboy
Country •
Doc Hollywood •
Giant •
Jean de Florette •
Let's Go to the Farm
Let's Ride a Tractor
Places in the Heart •
The River
Rock-a-Doodle
The Silver Fox and Sam
Davenport
Skylark
Son-in-Law
Sounder •
Stacking
The Stone Boy •
Tomboy & the Champ
Vrrrooommm! Farming for
Kids
We're Goin' to the Farm
with Father Dan

On the Run
Boys on the Side
Bushwhacked
Butch and Sundance: The
Early Days
Butch Cassidy and the
Sundance Kid •
Father Hood
The Fugitive •
A Perfect World

Only the Lonely
Bed of Roses
Citizen Kane •
Cyrano de Bergerac •
Desperately Seeking
Susan •
Doin' Time on Planet
Earth
E.T.: The Extra-
Terrestrial •
Men Don't Leave •
Only the Lonely
Only You
The Prime of Miss Jean
Brodie •
The Prince of Central
Park •
Richie Rich
Sleepless in Seattle •
Stuart Saves His Family
Turtle Diary •
While You Were
Sleeping •
Zelly & Me •

Oooh...That's Scary!
see also Gory Stories;
Mad Scientists;
Monsters, General;
Scary Beasties;
Scary Bugs; Scary
Plants; Vampires;
Werewolves
Alligator
Arachnophobia •
Army of Darkness •

Attack of the Killer
Tomatoes
Beetlejuice •
The Birds •
Black Magic
Blacula
Cat's Eye
Critters
The Crow
Dracula: Dead and Loving
It
Frankenstein Sings . . .
The Movie
Ghoulies
Goosebumps: A Night in
Terror Tower
Gremlins •
Gremlins 2: The New
Batch •
House •
House of Wax •
The House with a Clock
in Its Walls
Island of Dr. Moreau
The Ketchup Vampires
Legend of Boggy Creek
Little Shop of Horrors •
The Lost Boys
The Mask •
Matinee •
The Monster Squad •
Munchies
My Boyfriend's Back
My Grandpa is a Vampire
My Mom's a Werewolf
Return to Boggy Creek
Salem's Lot •
Saturday the 14th
Spooks Run Wild
The Swarm
Troll
Twilight Zone: The Movie
Watcher in the Woods
The Willies

Opera
see also Gotta Sing!
Amahl and the Night
Visitors
Hansel & Gretel: An
Opera Fantasy
Mozart's The Magic Flute
Story: An Opera
Fantasy
A Night at the Opera •

Orphans
see also Only the
Lonely
Across the Great Divide
The Adventures of Oliver
Twist
Aladdin •
Anne of Green Gables •
Annie
Babes on Broadway
The Beniker Gang
Big Red
Born Free •
The Boy with the Green
Hair
City Boy
Crystalstone
D.A.R.Y.L.
David Copperfield •
David Copperfield

Dick Tracy •
Earthling
Escape to Witch
Mountain •
A Family Thing •
A Far Off Place
Free Willy •
Hector's Bunyip
Home at Last
Immediate Family
James and the Giant
Peach •
Jane Eyre •
The Kid Who Loved
Christmas
The Land Before Time •
Little Orphan Annie
The Little Princess •
Mad Max: Beyond
Thunderdome
Major Payne
Man, Woman & Child
Manny's Orphans
Mighty Joe Young
Moll Flanders •
Mystery of the Million
Dollar Hockey Puck •
Napoleon and
Samantha •
Oliver! •
Oliver & Company •
Oliver Twist
Oliver Twist •
Oliver Twist
On the Right Track
Orphan Train •
Paper Moon •
Penny Serenade •
Pollyanna •
The Poor Little Rich Girl
The Prince of Central
Park •
Problem Child
Rags to Riches
Rent-A-Kid
The Road Home
Samantha
A Simple Twist of Fate
Sioux City
Snow White and the
Seven Dwarfs •
Sugar Cane Alley •
Superman 1: The Movie •
Susannah of the
Mounties
Tarzan Finds a Son •
Where the River Runs
Black
Who'll Save Our
Children? •
Wild Hearts Can't Be
Broken •
The Woman Who Raised
a Bear as Her Son
Young & Free

Our Gang
General Spanky
The Little Rascals
Little Rascals Christmas
Special
The Return of Our Gang

Over the Airwaves
see also TV Tales
Airheads

Citizens Band •
Comfort and Joy •
Radio Days •
Radioland Murders
Rebecca of Sunnybrook
Farm
Sleepless in Seattle •
Straight Talk
Strike Up the Band
The Truth About Cats
and Dogs •

Overlooked Gems
Cross Creek
Crossing Delancey •
Dazed and Confused •
Housekeeping •
The Joy Luck Club •
Local Hero
Matewan •
Metropolitan •
Miss Firecracker •
Searching for Bobby
Fischer •
Shag: The Movie •
Strictly Ballroom

Parades
see also Circuses &
Carnivals
Easter Parade •
Ferris Bueller's Day Off •
Miracle on 34th Street •
Miracle on 34th Street

Parenthood
see also Baby Talk;
Stepparents
Addams Family Values •
American Heart •
Baby Boom •
Big Girls Don't Cry. .
.They Get Even
Boys Town •
Bye Bye, Love
Cahill: United States
Marshal
Careful, He Might Hear
You •
Cold River
Crooklyn •
Dutch
East of Eden •
Father Figure
Father of the Bride •
Father of the Bride Part
II •
Forbidden Planet •
Ghost Dad
Goodtime Bedtime
A Goofy Movie •
Harry & Son
A Home of Our Own •
I Live with Me Dad
I Never Sang For My
Father •
I Remember Mama •
I'll Do Anything
Immediate Family
Irreconcilable Differences
Journey for Margaret •
Magic in the Water
Matilda
Max Dugan Returns
Miracle on 34th Street
Mr. Mom •

Bullets (•) indicate 3 bones or above

Misunderstood
My Life
My Mom's a Werewolf
National Lampoon's
  European Vacation
No Dessert Dad, 'Til You
  Mow the Lawn
Nobody's Boy
North
Nothing in Common
On Golden Pond •
Only the Lonely
Parenthood •
Rent-A-Kid
The River Rat
A River Runs Through It •
The Santa Clause •
Sesame Street Kids'
  Guide to Life: Learning
  to Share
The Shaggy D.A.
A Simple Twist of Fate
Superdad
Terms of Endearment •
Three Fugitives
Three Men and a Baby •
Three Men and a
  Cradle •
Throw Momma from the
  Train •
Trading Mom
Undercover Blues
When Wolves Cry
Yours, Mine & Ours •

Period Piece
see also Historical
  Happenings;
  Medieval Romps;
  Royalty
The Age of Innocence •
Amadeus •
American Graffiti •
Anne of Avonlea •
Anne of Green Gables •
The Babe
Back Home
Back to Hannibal: The
  Further Adventures of
  Tom Sawyer and
  Huckleberry Finn
Backbeat •
Balto
Batman: Mask of the
  Phantasm
The Bay Boy
Beauty and the Beast •
Bopha! •
Brenda Starr
A Bronx Tale •
Brothers Lionheart
Calendar Girl
Call of the Wild
Chips the War Dog
A Christmas Carol •
Christy
City Boy
Courage Mountain
Crooklyn •
Dazed and Confused •
Doctor Zhivago •
Eight Men Out •
The Elephant Man •
Emma •
Empire of the Sun •

The Ernest Green Story
Family Prayers
Far and Away
Fiddler on the Roof •
First Knight
The Flame Trees of
  Thika •
Follow the River
The Four Musketeers •
Geronimo •
Geronimo: An American
  Legend
Gettysburg •
Glory •
The Go-Between •
Goodbye, Miss 4th of
  July
The Great Train
  Robbery •
The Great Waldo
  Pepper •
Greyfriars Bobby •
Heartland •
Hole in the Sky
Home at Last
Howard's End •
I Remember Mama •
Imaginary Crimes
The Inkwell
Iron Will
It Happened in New
  Orleans
It's a Dog's Life
Jamaica Inn
Jane Eyre •
Jefferson in Paris
The Journey of August
  King •
Kim
The King and I •
King of the Hill •
The Last of the
  Mohicans •
The Lawrenceville Stories
A League of Their Own •
Legends of the Fall
Life with Father •
The Lion in Winter •
Little Dorrit, Film 1:
  Nobody's Fault •
Little House on the
  Prairie •
The Little Princess •
A Little Princess •
Little Women •
The Littlest Viking
The Long Day Closes •
The Lords of Flatbush
Lost in Yonkers •
Love and Death
Malcolm X •
A Man for All Seasons •
The Man from Snowy
  River
The Man in the Iron
  Mask •
The Man in the Moon •
Matinee •
Meet Me in St. Louis •
Moll Flanders •
Much Ado About
  Nothing •
The Music Man •
My Summer Story
Newsies •
No Drums, No Bugles

Oliver! •
Oliver Twist •
Oliver Twist •
Oliver Twist
On a Clear Day You Can
  See Forever
Once Upon a Time . . .
  When We Were
  Colored •
Oscar
Othello
A Perfect World
The Playboys •
Pollyanna •
The Power of One
Prince Brat and the
  Whipping Boy •
Prince Valiant
Princess Caraboo •
Racing with the Moon •
Radioland Murders
Rambling Rose •
The Remains of the
  Day •
The Return of the
  Musketeers
A River Runs Through It •
Rob Roy •
Robin Hood: Prince of
  Thieves
The Rocketeer •
The Sandlot •
Sarah, Plain and Tall •
School Ties •
The Secret Garden •
Sense and Sensibility •
Shadowlands •
Shag: The Movie •
Skylark
Sommersby
Squanto: A Warrior's
  Tale •
Sudie & Simpson
Swing Kids
Swing Shift
Tales from Avonlea, Vol.
  1: The Journey Begins
Tess •
That Night
The Three Musketeers •
Tito and Me •
Tom and Huck •
Tom Sawyer •
Trading Hearts
20,000 Leagues Under
  the Sea •
Two Bits
Under Capricorn
We of the Never Never •
Wild Hearts Can't Be
  Broken •
A Winner Never Quits
Yentl
Young Sherlock Holmes

Photography
see Shutterbugs

Physical Problems
see also Blindness;
  Deafness; Mental
  Retardation;
  Savants
Amy •
The Elephant Man •

Jack
Joni
Lightning Jack
Mac and Me
The Man Without a Face
Mask •
The Miracle Worker •
The Other Side of the
  Mountain
The Other Side of the
  Mountain, Part 2
Powder
Rear Window •
Ride a Wild Pony
Songs for Us Series
Untamed Heart
Walking on Air
What's Eating Gilbert
  Grape •
A Winner Never Quits

Poetry
A Child's Garden of
  Verses
The Night Before
  Christmas
Poetic Justice
Stories to Remember:
  Baby's Morningtime

Policemen
see also Detectives;
  Firemen
The Adventures of a
  Gnome Named Gnorm
Bad Boys
Beverly Hills Cop
Beverly Hills Cop 2
Beverly Hills Cop 3
Bopha! •
Car 54, Where Are You?
Cop and a Half
Cops and Robbersons
The Crow
The Delicate Delinquent
Die Hard •
Die Hard 2: Die Harder •
Die Hard: With a
  Vengeance
Gone are the Days
It Could Happen to You •
Judge Dredd
K-9
K-9000
Kuffs
Money Train
Moving Violations
Mystery Date
The Naked Gun: From
  the Files of Police
  Squad •
Naked Gun 33 1/3: The
  Final Insult
Naked Gun 2 1/2: The
  Smell of Fear
National Lampoon's
  Loaded Weapon 1
Piece of the Action
Police Academy
Police Academy 2: Their
  First Assignment
Police Academy 3: Back
  in Training
Police Academy 4:
  Citizens on Patrol

Police Academy 5:
  Assignment Miami
  Beach
Police Academy 6: City
  Under Siege
Police Academy: Mission
  to Moscow
Police Academy, the
  Series
Renfrew of the Royal
  Mounted
Robocop •
Son of the Pink Panther
Speed •
Stop! or My Mom Will
  Shoot
Super Fuzz
Techno Police
Theodore Rex
Timecop
Top Dog
Turner and Hooch
The Usual Suspects •

Postwar
Back Home
Cinema Paradiso •
House •
I Am a Fugitive from a
  Chain Gang •
It Happened in New
  Orleans
Judgment at Nuremberg •
Lilies of the Field •
Notorious •
Reunion •
Sommersby
A Walk in the Clouds

POW/MIA
see also War,
  General; World War
  II
Au Revoir Les Enfants •
The Bridge on the River
  Kwai •
Empire of the Sun •
Victory

Presidential Pics
All the President's Men •
The American President •
Canadian Bacon
Dave •
First Kid
Forrest Gump •
Guarding Tess
Independence Day •
Jefferson in Paris

Price of Fame
see also Rags to
  Riches
The Buddy Holly Story •
Citizen Kane •
Coal Miner's Daughter •
The Commitments •
Eddie and the Cruisers
Fame •
Flashdance
A Hard Day's Night •
Hero at Large
I Ought to Be in Pictures
Irreconcilable Differences
La Bamba •
Lady Jane •

The Main Event
The Man Who Would Be
    King •
Mommie Dearest
My Favorite Year •
Oh, God! You Devil
Rocky •
Rocky 2
Rocky 3
Rocky 4
Rocky 5
The Thing Called Love
Tucker: The Man and His
    Dream •
What's Love Got to Do
    With It?

Princes/Princesses
see Fairy Tales;
    Royalty

Puppets
see also Toys
The Adventures of
    Dudley the Dragon:
    Dudley and the Genie
The Adventures of
    Dudley the Dragon:
    Dudley Finds His Home
The Adventures of
    Dudley the Dragon:
    Dudley's Tea Party
The Adventures of
    Dudley the Dragon:
    Mr. Crabby Tree
The Adventures of
    Pinocchio
The Adventures of Timmy
    the Tooth: Big Mouth
    Gulch
The Adventures of Timmy
    the Tooth: Lost My
    Brush
The Adventures of Timmy
    the Tooth: Molar
    Island
The Adventures of Timmy
    the Tooth: Operation:
    Secret Birthday
    Surprise!
The Adventures of Timmy
    the Tooth: Timmy in
    Space
Alice in Wonderland
Alligator Pie
Amazing Adventures of
    Joe 90
The Dark Crystal
Don't Wake Your Mom
Gigglesnort Hotel, Vol. 1
The Great Rupert •
Gullah Gullah Island:
    Binyah's Surprise
How It's Done: From
    Baseball Bats to
    Potato Chips
How It's Done: From
    Roller Coasters to Ice
    Cream
The Howdy Doody Show
    (Puppet Playhouse)/
    The Gabby Hayes
    Show
The Incredible Voyage of
    Stingray
Jack Frost

Jack Houston's
    Imagineland: This is
    Imagineland
Kino's Storytime Vol.
    Three
Lamb Chop's Play Along:
    Action Songs
Lamb Chop's Sing-Along
    Play-Along
Lili •
The Magic Thinking Cap
Muppet Babies Video
    Storybook, Vol. 1
Peter and the Wolf
Peter Cottontail: How He
    Got His Hop
Pinocchio •
Pinocchio
Pinocchio and the
    Emperor of the Night
Play-Along Video: Hey,
    You're as Funny as
    Fozzie Bear
Play-Along Video: Mother
    Goose Stories
Play-Along Video: Sing-
    Along, Dance-Along,
    Do-Along
Play-Along Video: Wow,
    You're a Cartoonist!
Professor Iris: Music
    Mania
The Puppet Theater
The Puzzle Place: Rock
    Dreams
The Puzzle Place: Tuned
    In
Rudolph's Shiny New
    Year
Shari Lewis & Lamb
    Chop: In the Land of
    No Manners
Shari Lewis & Lamb
    Chop: One Minute
    Bible Stories, New
    Testament
Shari Lewis: Don't Wake
    Your Mom
Shari Lewis: Have I Got a
    Story for You
Shari Lewis: Kooky
    Classics
Shining Time Station:
    'Tis a Gift Holiday
    Special
Slimey's World Games
Willy McBean & His
    Magic Machine
The Year Without a Santa
    Claus
Zoobilee Zoo, Vol. 1:
    Land of Rhymes &
    Other Stories

Queens
see Royalty

Race Against Time
The Andromeda Strain
Apollo 13 •
Broken Arrow
Free Willy 2: The
    Adventure Home
Lorenzo's Oil •
Once Upon a Forest
Outbreak •

War Games •

Rags to Riches
see also Price of
    Fame; Wrong Side
    of the Tracks
Aladdin •
Annie
The Beverly Hillbillies
Blank Check
Brewster's Millions
The Buddy Holly Story •
Citizen Kane •
Coal Miner's Daughter •
The Great Rupert •
Hero
It Could Happen to You •
A Kid for Two Farthings
The Last American Hero •
Lili •
Little Lord Fauntleroy •
Lots of Luck
Mrs. Winterbourne
The Prince and the
    Pauper •
The Prince and the
    Pauper
Rocky •
Straight Talk

Raiders of the Lost
Ark
Indiana Jones and the
    Last Crusade •
Indiana Jones and the
    Temple of Doom •
Raiders of the Lost Ark •

Rebel With a Cause
see also Rebel
    Without a Cause
The Adventures of Robin
    Hood •
Billy Jack
Boyz N the Hood •
Braveheart •
Dead Poets Society •
Die Hard •
Die Hard 2: Die Harder •
A Dream for Christmas •
East of Eden •
Gorillas in the Mist •
The Last American Hero •
Lawrence of Arabia •
Legend of Billie Jean
Legend of the Lone
    Ranger
Little Tough Guys
The Loneliness of the
    Long Distance
    Runner •
The Manhattan Project
Mr. Smith Goes to
    Washington •
Mountain Man
Norma Rae •
Outbreak •
Project X •
Rob Roy •
Robin Hood: Prince of
    Thieves
The Scarlet Pimpernel •
War Games •

Rebel Without a
Cause
see also Rebel With a
    Cause
Across the Tracks
Cool As Ice
The Electric Horseman •
Ferris Bueller's Day Off •
On the Edge: The
    Survival of Dana
Over the Edge •
Rebel Without a Cause •
Rocky 4
That Was Then. . .This Is
    Now
Top Gun
West Side Story •

Red Scare
Night Crossing
Tito and Me •
Tobor the Great

Repressed Men
The Age of Innocence •
The Remains of the
    Day •
Shadowlands •

Rescue Missions
see also Rescue
    Missions Involving
    Time Travel
Alaska
The Amazing Panda
    Adventure
Apollo 13 •
Balto
Born to Be Wild
Daredevils of the Red
    Circle
Die Hard •
Die Hard 2: Die Harder •
Die Hard: With a
    Vengeance •
Dragonworld •
Ernest Scared Stupid
The Ewok Adventure
Far from Home: The
    Adventures of Yellow
    Dog •
Free Willy •
Free Willy 2: The
    Adventure Home
Oliver & Company •
Operation Dumbo Drop
Outbreak •
The Rescue
Street Fighter
Toy Story •
Two Bits & Pepper

Rescue Missions
Involving Time
Travel
see also Rescue
    Missions
Back to the Future •
Back to the Future, Part
    2
Back to the Future, Part
    3
Bill & Ted's Excellent
    Adventure
Jumanji

Star Trek 4: The Voyage
    Home •
Superman 1: The Movie •
The Terminator •
Terminator 2: Judgment
    Day •
Timemaster

Revolutionary War
Johnny Tremain & the
    Sons of Liberty
1776 •
Sweet Liberty
Where on Earth is
    Carmen Sandiego? Vol.
    I : A Date with Carmen
    (Parts One and Two)

The Right Choice
The Adventures of Teddy
    Ruxpin
Blue Chips
The Boy with the Green
    Hair
Dr. Seuss' Butter Battle
    Book
The Elephant Man •
Fat Albert & the Cosby
    Kids, Vol. 1
The Ghost Belonged to
    Me
Hang Your Hat on the
    Wind
It Could Happen to You •
Judgment at Nuremberg •
Mr. Smith Goes to
    Washington •
Quiz Show •
The Shootist •
Soul Man
The Toy
Welcome Back Wil Cwac
    Cwac
With Honors

Robots
see also
    Technological
    Nightmares
And You Thought Your
    Parents Were Weird!
Bill & Ted's Bogus
    Journey
Doctor Who: An
    Unearthly Child
Doctor Who and the
    Daleks
The Empire Strikes
    Back •
Forbidden Planet •
The Invisible Boy
K-9000
Mighty Morphin Power
    Rangers: Alpha's
    Magical Christmas
Mystery Science Theater
    3000: The Movie •
Not Quite Human
Return of the Jedi •
Robocop
Robocop 2
Robocop 3
Robot Jox
Short Circuit
Star Wars •
The Terminator •

Terminator 2: Judgment
Day •
Tobor the Great
Transformers

Rodeos
*see also Cowboys &
Indians*
8 Seconds
Junior Bonner •
My Heroes Have Always
Been Cowboys

Romance
see Boy Meets Girl

Royalty
*see also Historical
Happenings;
Medieval Romps;
Period Piece*
Aladdin •
Ali Baba and the Forty
Thieves
The Court Jester •
Dr. Syn, Alias the
Scarecrow
Dragonheart
The Emperor's New
Clothes
The Fifth Musketeer
The Fighting Prince of
Donegal
First Knight
A Kid in King Arthur's
Court
The King and I •
King Ralph
Lady Jane •
The Lion in Winter •
Lost in a Harem
A Man for All Seasons •
The Man in the Iron
Mask •
The Man Who Would Be
King •
Mannequin 2: On the
Move
Mom and Dad Save the
World
The Polar Bear King
The Prince and the
Pauper •
The Prince and the
Pauper
Prince Brat and the
Whipping Boy •
The Princess and the Pea
Princess Caraboo •
The Return of the
Musketeers
Return to Oz
Roman Holiday •
Snow White and the
Seven Dwarfs •
Snow White and the
Seven Dwarfs
Song Spinner
Storybook
Surf Ninjas
The Sword & the Rose
Three Musketeers •
Willow

Running
Across the Tracks
Billie
Forrest Gump •
The Loneliest Runner •
The Loneliness of the
Long Distance
Runner •
Running Brave
Sam's Son

Savants
*see also Mental
Retardation*
Being There •
Doctor Doolittle
Forrest Gump •
Rain Man •
Tony Draws a Horse

Scary Beasties
Alligator
Battle for the Planet of
the Apes
Beneath the Planet of
the Apes
Bunnicula: Vampire
Rabbit
Congo
Conquest of the Planet of
the Apes
Dragonslayer •
Godzilla vs. Megalon
Godzilla vs. the Cosmic
Monster
Jabberwocky
Jurassic Park •
King Kong •
King Kong
Mighty Joe Young
Monty Python and the
Holy Grail •
Mysterious Island •
Planet of the Apes •
Return to Boggy Creek
Son of Kong

Scary Bugs
Arachnophobia •
Man of the House
The Swarm

Scary Plants
Attack of the Killer
Tomatoes
Invasion of the Body
Snatchers •
Little Shop of Horrors •

Sci Fi
see also Fantasy
The Adventures of
Ultraman
Arena
At the Earth's Core
Atom Man vs. Superman
Attack of the Killer
Tomatoes
The Aurora Encounter
*batteries not included
Battle Beyond the Stars
Battle for Moon Station
Dallos
Battle for the Planet of
the Apes
Battlestar Galactica

Beneath the Planet of
the Apes
Beyond the Stars
The Black Hole
The Black Planet
Blake of Scotland Yard
Brain 17
The Brother from Another
Planet •
Buck Rogers Conquers
the Universe
Buck Rogers in the 25th
Century
Captain Harlock, Vol. 1
Captain Scarlet vs. The
Mysterons
Close Encounters of the
Third Kind •
Cocoon •
Conquest of the Planet of
the Apes
Darkman •
D.A.R.Y.L.
Destroy All Monsters
Doc Savage
Doctor Who: An
Unearthly Child
Doctor Who and the
Daleks
Doin' Time on Planet
Earth
The Empire Strikes
Back •
Enemy Mine
Escape from the Planet
of the Apes •
E.T.: The Extra-
Terrestrial •
Explorers
The Fabulous World of
Jules Verne
Fantastic Planet •
Fire in the Sky
First Men in the Moon
Flash Gordon •
Flash Gordon Conquers
the Universe
Flash Gordon: Rocketship
Flash Gordon: Vol. 1
Forbidden Planet •
Force on Thunder
Mountain
Gobots: Battle of the
Rock Lords
Godzilla vs. Megalon
Godzilla vs. the Cosmic
Monster
Godzilla vs. the Smog
Monster
Grandizer
Heartbeeps
Highlander 2: The
Quickening
Howard the Duck
Hyper-Sapien: People
from Another Star
Iceman •
Incredible Agent of
Stingray
Independence Day •
Innerspace
Invaders from Mars
Invasion of the Body
Snatchers •
The Invisible Boy
Johnny Mnemonic

Journey to the Center of
the Earth •
Journey to the Center of
the Earth
Krull
Land That Time Forgot
The Last Starfighter
Locke the Superpower
Macron 1: Dark Discovery
in a New World
Making Mr. Right
Meet the Hollowheads
Mighty Orbots: Devil's
Asteroid
Moon Pilot
Mysterious Island •
Mystery Science Theater
3000: The Movie •
The Olden Days Coat
On the Comet •
The Original Fabulous
Adventures of Baron
Munchausen •
Out There
Outbreak •
The People That Time
Forgot
The Phantom Empire
Pirates of Dark Water:
The Saga Begins
Planet of the Apes •
Planet of the Dinosaurs
Purple People Eater
Puss in Boots
Radar Men from the
Moon
Return from Witch
Mountain
The Return of Swamp
Thing
Return of the Jedi •
Robot Jox
Robotech: The Macross
Saga, Vol. 1
Robotech, Vol. 1: Booby
Trap
Saber Rider and the Star
Sheriffs: All That
Glitters
Silverhawks: Sky
Shadows
Silverhawks: The Original
Story
Skeleton Warriors
Sleeper •
Solarbabies
Space Angel, Vol. 1
Space Battleship Yamato
Space Firebird
Space Raiders
Space Warriors: Battle
for Earth Station S/1
Spaceballs
SpaceCamp
Spaced Invaders
Spaceketeers
Spaceship
Spiral Zone: Zone of
Darkness
Star Trek 2: The Wrath of
Khan •
Star Trek 3: The Search
for Spock
Star Trek 4: The Voyage
Home •

Star Trek 5: The Final
Frontier
Star Trek 6: The
Undiscovered Country
Star Trek: Animated, Vol.
1
Star Trek Generations •
Star Trek: The Motion
Picture
Star Trek the Next
Generation Episode 1-
2: Encounter at
Farpoint
Star Wars •
Starchaser: The Legend
of Orin
Stargate
Starman •
Starship
Superman: The Serial,
Vol. 1
Teen Alien
Terminator 2: Judgment
Day •
The Three Worlds of
Gulliver
Timecop
Timefighters in the Land
of Fantasy
Timemaster
Timerider
Tobor the Great
The Trial of the
Incredible Hulk
Tron
12 Monkeys •
2001: A Space Odyssey •
2010 : The Year We
Make Contact •
Ugly Little Boy
Undersea Kingdom
The Valley of Gwangi •
Vengeance of the Space
Pirate
Voyage to the Bottom of
the Sea •
Voyager from the
Unknown
The War of the Worlds •
Waterworld
Weird Science
When Dinosaurs Ruled
the Earth
Where Time Began
Zombies of the
Stratosphere

Scientists
*see also Inventors;
Mad Scientists*
The Andromeda Strain •
Beach Party
Darkman •
The Day of the Dolphin
Dead Men Don't Wear
Plaid
Die Laughing
Dr. Dad's PH3
Doctor Doolittle
Dr. Jekyll and Ms. Hyde
The Incredible Hulk
Returns
I.Q.
Junior

Disney's Sing-Along
Songs: Pocahontas
Disney's Sing-Along
Songs: The Hunchback
of Notre Dame: Topsy
Turvy
Disney's Sing-Along
Songs: The Twelve
Days of Christmas
Disney's Sing-Along
Songs, Vol. 1: Heigh-
Ho
Disney's Sing-Along
Songs, Vol. 2: Zip-A-
Dee-Doo-Dah
Disney's Sing-Along
Songs, Vol. 3: You Can
Fly!
Disney's Sing-Along
Songs, Vol. 4: The
Bare Necessities
Disney's Sing-Along
Songs, Vol. 5: Fun with
Music
Disney's Sing-Along
Songs, Vol. 6: Under
the Sea
Disney's Sing-Along
Songs, Vol. 7:
Disneyland Fun
Disney's Sing-Along
Songs, Vol. 8: Very
Merry Christmas Songs
Disney's Sing-Along
Songs, Vol. 9: I Love
to Laugh!
Disney's Sing-Along
Songs, Vol. 10: Be Our
Guest
Disney's Sing-Along
Songs, Vol. 11: Friend
Like Me
Don Cooper: Sing-Along
Story Songs
The Donut Repair Club:
On Tour
Earth Tunes for Kids
Even More Baby Songs
The Extra-Special
Substitute Teacher
A Family Concert
Featuring The Roches
and The Music
Workshop for Kids
The Flintstones: Rappin'
n' Rhymin'
Fred Penner: A Circle of
Songs
Fred Penner: The Cat
Came Back — A Concert
Video
Fred Penner: What A
Day!
Gerald McBoing Boing,
Vol. 1: Favorite Sing-
Along Songs
Granpa
Hap Palmer's Follow
Along Songs
HBTV: Old Time Rock &
Roll
Infantastic Lullabies II
Infantastic Lullabyes on
Video
It's Not Easy Being Green
Kidsongs: A Day at Camp

Kidsongs: A Day at Old
MacDonald's Farm
Kidsongs: A Day at the
Circus
Kidsongs: A Day with the
Animals
Kidsongs: Boppin' with
the Biggles
Kidsongs: Cars, Boats,
Trains and Planes
Kidsongs: Good Night,
Sleep Tight
Kidsongs: Home on the
Range
Kidsongs: I'd Like to
Teach the World to
Sing
Kidsongs: Let's Play Ball
Kidsongs: Ride the Roller
Coaster
Kidsongs: Very Silly
Songs
Kidsongs: We Wish You a
Merry Christmas
Lamb Chop's Play Along:
Action Songs
Lamb Chop's Sing-Along
Play-Along
Marsalis on Music Why
Toes Tap: Wynton on
Rhythm
Mary Kate and Ashley
Olsen: Our First Video
Mickey's Fun Songs:
Campout at Walt
Disney World
Mickey's Fun Songs:
Let's Go to the Circus
Mr. Bumpy's Karaoke
Cafe
Mister Rogers: Music and
Feelings
Mommy, Gimme a Drinka
Water!
More Baby Songs
More Song City U.S.A.
Muppet Treasure Island
Sing-Alongs
The Night Before
Christmas and Best-
Loved Yuletide Carols
On the Move with Virgil
Pete Seeger's Family
Concert
Peter and the Wolf
Peter, Paul and Mary:
Peter, Paul and
Mommy, Too
The Pied Piper of
Hamelin
Puff the Magic Dragon
Raffi in Concert with the
Rise & Shine Band
Raffi on Broadway
Raffi: Young Children's
Concert with Raffi
Raggedy Ann and Andy:
A Musical Adventure
Schoolhouse Rock:
Grammar Rock
Schoolhouse Rock:
History Rock
Schoolhouse Rock:
Science Rock

Sesame Songs: Elmo's
Sing-Along Guessing
Game
Sesame Songs: Monster
Hits!
Sesame Songs: Rock &
Roll!
Sesame Songs: Sing-
Along Earth Songs
Sesame Songs: Sing,
Hoot & Howl
Sesame Songs: Sing
Yourself Silly!
Sesame Songs: We All
Sing Together
Sesame Street: Bedtime
Stories and Songs
Sesame Street: Count It
Higher
Sesame Street: Play-
Along Games and
Songs
Sesame Street Presents:
Put Down the Duckie:
An All-Star Musical
Special
Sesame Street: Sing
Along
Sesame Street's 25th
Birthday: A Musical
Celebration
Sharon, Lois & Bram at
the Young People's
Theatre
Sharon, Lois & Bram:
Back by Popular
Demand-Live
Sharon, Lois & Bram:
Live in Your Living
Room
Sharon, Lois & Bram:
Sing A to Z
Sharon, Lois & Bram's
Elephant Show:
Babysitting
Shining Time Station:
Singsongs, Vol. 1
Shining Time Station:
'Tis a Gift Holiday
Special
Songs for Us Series
Sweet Honey in the
Rock: Singing for
Freedom
Teddy Bear Blues
Things That Fly Sing
Alongs
This Pretty Planet
Tom Chapin: This Pretty
Planet
Uncle Elephant
Uncle Nick and the Magic
Forest
Wee Sing: Grandpa's
Magical Toys
Wee Sing in Sillyville
Wee Sing in the Big Rock
Candy Mountains
Wee Sing: In the
Marvelous Musical
Mansion
Wee Sing: The Best
Christmas Ever!
Wee Sing Together
Wee Sing Train
Wee Sing Under the Sea

You're Invited to Mary-
Kate & Ashley's Sleep
Over Party

Sixties Sagas
Hair Bear Bunch
Head •
More American Graffiti
Where Angels Go,
Trouble Follows
Yellow Submarine •

Skateboarding
Gleaming the Cube

Skating
see also Hockey
Airborne
Breaking the Ice
Cinderella . . . Frozen in
Time
The Cutting Edge
Hans Brinker
Ice Castles
Xanadu

Skiing
Aspen Extreme
Avalanche
Better Off Dead
Club Med
Downhill Racer
Dumb & Dumber
For Your Eyes Only •
On Her Majesty's Secret
Service •
The Other Side of the
Mountain
The Other Side of the
Mountain, Part 2
Ski Patrol
Snowball Express

Slavery
see also Civil Rights
The Adventures of
Huckleberry Finn •
Brother Future
Buck and the Preacher
The House of Dies Drear
Jefferson in Paris
The Journey of August
King •

Soccer
The Big Green
Gregory's Girl
The Hero
Hot Shot
Ladybugs
Victory

Southern Belles
see also Nashville
Narratives;
Southern Sagas
Driving Miss Daisy •
Gone with the Wind •
Miss Firecracker •
Rich in Love
Steel Magnolias •
The Trip to Bountiful •

Southern Sagas
see also Nashville
Narratives;
Southern Belles
Boyd's Shadow
Brer Rabbit and the
Wonderful Tar Baby
Driving Miss Daisy •
Fletch Lives
Forrest Gump •
Gettysburg •
Gone with the Wind •
The Great Santini
The Journey of August
King •
Miss Firecracker •
Norma Rae •
Once Upon a Time . . .
When We Were
Colored •
Paradise •
Rambling Rose •
Rich in Love
Running Mates
Shag: The Movie •
Something to Talk About
Sounder •
Tammy and the Bachelor
Tammy and the Doctor
Tank
To Kill a Mockingbird •
The Trip to Bountiful •
Walking Tall
Where the Lilies Bloom •

Special F/X
Extravaganzas
Alice in Wonderland
Batman
Batman Forever
Beetlejuice •
Big Trouble in Little
China
The Black Hole
The Ewok Adventure
Forbidden Planet •
Independence Day •
Innerspace
Judge Dredd
Jurassic Park •
The Mask •
Poltergeist •
Return of the Jedi •
The Shadow
Star Trek 2: The Wrath of
Khan •
Star Trek 4: The Voyage
Home •
Star Trek Generations •
Star Wars •
Superman 2 •
The Terminator •
Terminator 2: Judgment
Day •
Twister
2001: A Space Odyssey •
2010 : The Year We
Make Contact •
Who Framed Roger
Rabbit? •

Sports

*see Baseball;
Basketball; Biking;
Boxing; Fast Cars;
Football; Golf;
Hockey; The
Olympics; Scuba
Diving; Skating;
Skiing; Soccer;
Sports Comedies;
Sports Dramas;
Surfing; Tennis*

Sports Comedies
The Air Up There
Angels in the Outfield
The Bad News Bears •
The Bad News Bears Go
  to Japan
The Bad News Bears in
  Breaking Training
The Best of Times
The Big Green
Billie
Bingo Long Traveling All-
  Stars & Motor Kings •
Blue Skies Again
Bowery Blitzkrieg
Celtic Pride
Comeback Kid
Cool Runnings •
D2: The Mighty Ducks
Ed
Eddie
Fast Break
The Fish that Saved
  Pittsburgh
Happy Gilmore
Kingpin
Ladybugs
A League of Their Own •
Little Big League
Little Giants
Major League
Major League 2
The Mighty Ducks
The Mighty Ducks 3
Mr. Baseball
Necessary Roughness
Pat and Mike •
Prehysteria 3
Prize Fighter
Rookie of the Year
The Sandlot •
The Scout
Slam Dunk Ernest
Trading Hearts
Wildcats
The World's Greatest
  Athlete

Sports Dramas
Above the Rim
Airborne
Alex
All the Right Moves
American Anthem
American Flyers
The Babe
Bang the Drum Slowly •
Big Mo
Blue Chips
Breaking Away •
Brian's Song •

Chariots of Fire •
Chasing Dreams
Coach
The Cutting Edge
Diving In
Downhill Racer
Eight Men Out •
8 Seconds
Field of Dreams •
Heart Like a Wheel •
The Hero
Hockey Night
Hoosiers •
Hot Shot
Ice Castles
International Velvet
Knute Rockne: All
  American •
The Last American Hero •
Last Time Out
The Loneliest Runner •
The Natural •
One on One
Over the Top
Pastime •
Pistol: The Birth of a
  Legend
The Program
Rocky •
Rocky 2
Rocky 3
Rocky 4
Rocky 5
Rudy
Running Brave
Talent for the Game
Tiger Town
Victory
Wind
A Winner Never Quits

Spy Stories
Adventures in Spying
Boris and Natasha: The
  Movie
Casablanca •
The Charge of the Model
  T's
Clear and Present Danger
Clipped Wings
Cloak & Dagger
Condorman
A Day in October
The Day of the Dolphin
Deathcheaters
Defense Play
Diamonds are Forever •
Dr. No •
The Double O Kid
Duck Soup •
The Fantastic World of
  D.C. Collins
For Your Eyes Only •
Foreign Correspondent •
From Russia with Love •
Goldeneye
Gotcha!
Harriet the Spy
Holt of the Secret Service
The Hunt for Red
  October •
Ice Station Zebra •
If Looks Could Kill
Jungle Drums of Africa
Kim
Live and Let Die

The Man with One Red
  Shoe
The Man with the Golden
  Gun
Mission: Impossible •
Moonraker
My Favorite Brunette
Never Say Never Again
North by Northwest •
Notorious •
Octopussy
On Her Majesty's Secret
  Service •
One of Our Dinosaurs Is
  Missing
Saboteur •
Sneakers
Spy Hard
Spy Smasher •
The Spy Who Loved Me
The Tall Blond Man with
  One Black Shoe
Terminal Velocity
The 39 Steps •
Thunderball
Torn Curtain
Trenchcoat
True Lies
Under the Rainbow
Undercover Blues
A View to a Kill
You Only Live Twice

Star Wars
The Empire Strikes
  Back •
The Ewok Adventure
The Ewoks: Battle for
  Endor
Return of the Jedi •
Star Wars •

Stepparents
*see also Family Ties;
Parenthood*
Big Girls Don't Cry. .
  .They Get Even
Cinderella •
Cinderella
Lassie
Out on a Limb
This Boy's Life •

Storytelling
*see also Bedtime
Stories*
Amazing Bone and Other
  Stories
Danny and the Dinosaur
  and Other Stories
The Gingham Dog and
  the Calico Cat
Here Comes the Cat! and
  Other Stories
Just Me & My Dad
Kino's Storytime Vol.
  Three
A Little Princess •
Living God's Way
Mouse Soup
The Neverending Story 3
Noisy Nora
The Pagemaster
The Princess Bride •
The Puppet Theater

The Robert McCloskey
  Library
Sesame Street: Big Bird's
  Story Time
The Story Lady
Tall Tale: The
  Unbelievable
  Adventures of Pecos
  Bill
Thomas the Tank Engine:
  Better Late Than Never
Thomas the Tank Engine:
  James Goes Buzz Buzz
  and Other Thomas
  Stories
Thomas the Tank Engine:
  James Learns a Lesson
  & Other Stories
Thomas the Tank Engine:
  Tenders & Turntables
  & Other Stories
Thomas the Tank Engine:
  Thomas Breaks the
  Rules & Other Stories
Thomas the Tank Engine:
  Thomas Gets Tricked &
  Other Stories
Thomas the Tank Engine:
  Trust Thomas & Other
  Stories

Struggling Musicians
see also Music
Backbeat •
The Brady Bunch Movie •
Eddie and the Cruisers
Light of Day
Oh, God! You Devil
Rhinestone
Satisfaction
Singles •
Tender Mercies •

Stupid Crime
*see also Crime
Doesn't Pay; It's
the Mob*
Airheads
Amos and Andrew
The Apple Dumpling
  Gang
The Apple Dumpling
  Gang Rides Again
Baby on Board
Baby's Day Out
Cop and a Half
Dr. Otto & the Riddle of
  the Gloom Beam
Ernest Goes to Jail
A Fine Mess
Her Alibi
Herbie Goes Bananas
Home Alone •
Home Alone 2: Lost in
  New York
The Jerky Boys
Man of the House
Mixed Nuts
Once Upon a Crime
Oscar
Out on a Limb
Sister Act •
Stop! or My Mom Will
  Shoot
Trapped In Paradise
Two If by Sea

Submarines
Crimson Tide •
Down Periscope
For Your Eyes Only •
The Hunt for Red
  October •
Mysterious Island •
The Spy Who Loved Me
20,000 Leagues Under
  the Sea •
Voyage to the Bottom of
  the Sea •
You Only Live Twice

Subways
see also Trains
Adventures in Babysitting
The Fugitive •
Highlander 2: The
  Quickening
Money Train
Speed •

Summer Camp
Addams Family Values •
Bushwhacked
Camp Nowhere
Cry from the Mountain
Ernest Goes to Camp
Father and Scout
The Great Outdoors
Heavyweights
Indian Summer
Let's Go Camping
Little Critter Series: Just
  Me and My Dad
Little Darlings
Man of the House
Meatballs
Mickey's Fun Songs:
  Campout at Walt
  Disney World
Princes in Exile
The River Wild •
Troop Beverly Hills •
The Willies

Super Heroes
The Adventures of
  Batman & Robin:
  Robin
The Adventures of
  Batman & Robin: The
  Joker
The Adventures of
  Batman & Robin: The
  Riddler
The Adventures of
  Batman & Robin: Two-
  Face
The Amazing Spider-Man
Batman
Batman •
Batman Forever
Batman: Mask of the
  Phantasm
Batman Returns
Blankman
Captain America
Captain America 2: Death
  Too Soon
Cloak & Dagger
Death of the Incredible
  Hulk
Dr. Strange
EarthWorm Jim

The Flash
Flash Gordon
Highlander: The
Adventure Begins
The Incredible Hulk
The Incredible Hulk
Returns
The Mask •
The Meteor Man
Mighty Morphin Power
Rangers: Green with
Evil, Part 1
Mighty Morphin Power
Rangers: The Movie
Mighty Mouse in the
Great Space Chase
The Phantom
Phantom 2040
Phantom 2040 Movie:
The Ghost Who Walks
Plastic Man
Princess Gwenevere and
the Jewel Riders
The Shadow
Spider-Woman
Spiderman & His
Amazing Friends:
Origin of the Spider
Friends
Spiderman: The Deadly
Dust
Spiderman, Vol. 1: Dr.
Doom
Sub-Mariner: Atlantis
Under Attack
Super Fuzz
Supergirl
Superman 1: The Movie •
Superman 2 •
Superman 3
Superman 4: The Quest
for Peace
Superman & the Mole
Men
The Tick: The Tick vs.
The Idea Men and The
Tick vs. Chairface
Chippendale
The Trial of the
Incredible Hulk
TV's Best Adventures of
Superman
Vip, My Brother
Superman
X-Men: Deadly Reunions

Supernatural Tales
Angels in the Outfield
Audrey Rose
Back to the Future, Part
3
Beetlejuice •
Bernard and the Genie
Blackbeard's Ghost
The Crow
The Devil & Max Devlin
The Gate
Ghost Chasers
Ghost Dad
The Ghost Goes West •
Ghostbusters •
Ghostbusters 2
Heart and Souls
Hocus Pocus
The Howling •

The Man in the Santa
Claus Suit
Matilda
My Best Friend Is a
Vampire
Oh, God! •
Oh, God! Book 2
Oh, God! You Devil
Poltergeist •
Poltergeist 2: The Other
Side
Poltergeist 3
Remo Williams: The
Adventure Begins
Saturday the 14th
She-Devil
Spook Busters
Spooks Run Wild
Teen Wolf
Teen Wolf Too
13 Ghosts
Timerider
Topper •
Topper Returns •
Topper Takes a Trip •

Surfing
*see also Beach
Blanket Bingo*
Aloha Summer
Beach Blanket Bingo •
Beach Party
Bikini Beach
The Endless Summer •
The Endless Summer 2
Gidget
How to Stuff a Wild
Bikini
Muscle Beach Party

Survival
Alaska
Alive
Antarctica
Born Wild
The Bridge on the River
Kwai •
Captain January
Challenge To Be Free
Cold River
Earthling
Empire of the Sun •
Enemy Mine
Far from Home: The
Adventures of Yellow
Dog •
Heck's Way Home
High Noon •
The Incredible Journey •
The Island at the Top of
the World
Island of the Blue
Dolphins
Jeremiah Johnson •
Land of the Lost
Land That Time Forgot
The Last Flight of Noah's
Ark
The Legend of Wolf
Mountain
Little Dorrit, Film 1:
Nobody's Fault •
Little Dorrit, Film 2: Little
Dorrit's Story •
Lord of the Flies •
Lord of the Flies

Melody
My Side of the Mountain
Mysterious Island •
The Poseidon Adventure
Return of the Jedi •
Sea Gypsies
Shadow of the Wolf
Silence of the North
Sourdough
SpaceCamp
Starbird and Sweet
William
The Swiss Family
Robinson •
Waterworld
White Fang and the
Hunter
White Water Summer

Swashbucklers
*see also Amazing
Adventures;
Medieval Romps*
Abbott and Costello Meet
Captain Kidd
The Adventures of
Raggedy Ann & Andy:
Pirate Adventure
The Adventures of Robin
Hood •
Ali Baba and the Forty
Thieves
Blackbeard's Ghost
Captain Blood •
Captain Ron
The Count of Monte
Cristo
The Court Jester •
Cutthroat Island
Dick Deadeye
Dr. Syn, Alias the
Scarecrow
The Fifth Musketeer
Fighting Marines
The Fighting Prince of
Donegal
First Knight
The Four Musketeers •
Hawk of the Wilderness
Highlander: The
Gathering
Hook
Magic Island
The Man in the Iron
Mask •
Mooncussers
Muppet Treasure Island •
My Favorite Year •
Nate and Hayes
Peter Pan & the Pirates:
Demise of Hook
The Phantom
Pirate Movie
The Pirates of Penzance
The Princess Bride •
The Return of the
Musketeers
Return to Treasure
Island, Vol. 1
Robin Hood •
The Scarlet Pimpernel •
Sea Hound
The Secret of El Zorro
Shipwrecked
The Sign of Zorro

Sinbad and the Eye of
the Tiger •
Sinbad the Sailor •
Son of Captain Blood
Son of Zorro
The Swiss Family
Robinson •
Three Amigos
Three Musketeers
The Three Musketeers
Three Musketeers
Three Musketeers
The Three Musketeers
Treasure Island •
Treasure Island
Vengeance of the Space
Pirate

Table Manners
Educating Rita •
The Manners Monster:
Ruby Goes to Dinner
Shari Lewis & Lamb
Chop: In the Land of
No Manners
Time for Table Manners

Tall Tales & Legends
Series
Annie Oakley
Casey at the Bat
The Legend of Sleepy
Hollow
Pecos Bill
Tall Tales and Legends:
Johnny Appleseed

Teacher, Teacher
*see also Elementary
School Escapades;
High School Hijinks*
Amy •
Born Yesterday
Conrack •
The Corn is Green •
Dangerous Minds
Dead Poets Society •
Educating Rita •
High School High
If Lucy Fell
Kindergarten Cop
Lean on Me •
Madame Sousatzka •
Matilda
The Miracle Worker •
Mr. Holland's Opus •
The Paper Chase •
Powder
The Prime of Miss Jean
Brodie •
Race the Sun
Renaissance Man
Stand and Deliver •
To Sir, with Love
Up the Down Staircase •
White Squall

Team Efforts
The Bad News Bears Go
to Japan
The Bad News Bears in
Breaking Training
The Big Green
Breaking Away •
Coach
The Cutting Edge

D2: The Mighty Ducks
Dragonheart
Hoosiers •
Ladybugs
The Mighty Ducks
The Mighty Ducks 3
Race the Sun
Renaissance Man
Silverado •
Victory
Wind

Tearjerkers
All Dogs Go to Heaven
Bang the Drum Slowly •
Breaking the Rules
Brian's Song •
Christmas Comes to
Willow Creek
Curly Sue
A Dog of Flanders •
Dog Pound Shuffle
The Fourth Wish
Free Willy •
Ghost •
A Home of Our Own
Ice Castles
Jack the Bear
Journey for Margaret •
Legends of the Fall
The Little Princess •
A Little Princess •
Look Who's Talking Now
Lorenzo's Oil •
Mr. Holland's Opus •
My Life
Old Yeller •
The Other Side of the
Mountain
The Other Side of the
Mountain, Part 2
Penny Serenade •
Philadelphia •
Princes in Exile
Promises in the Dark
Shadowlands •
Since You Went Away •
Six Weeks
Sommersby
Steel Magnolias •
Terms of Endearment •
This Boy's Life •
Untamed Heart
When Wolves Cry
Where the Red Fern
Grows •
The Yearling •

Technological
Nightmares
*see also Computers;
Robots*
Back to the Future •
The Black Hole
Computer Wizard
Defense Play
Diamonds are Forever •
Electric Dreams
Gobots: Battle of the
Rock Lords
Goldeneye
Hackers
Improper Channels
Johnny Mnemonic
Judge Dredd

Lost Legacy: A Girl Called Hatter Fox
Moonraker
The Net
Remote
Robocop •
Robocop 2
Robocop 3
Robot Jox
Short Circuit
Short Circuit 2
Sneakers
Space Firebird
The Spy Who Loved Me
Stay Tuned
Techno Police
The Terminator •
Tron
2001: A Space Odyssey •
War Games •
Weird Science
Where on Earth is Carmen Sandiego? Vol. IV: Split Up and Moondreams

Teen Tribulations
see also Growing Pains; High School Hijinks
Above the Rim
Across the Tracks
Adventures in Dinosaur City
Ah, Wilderness! •
Airborne
Alex
Almos' a Man
American Graffiti •
An American Summer
Andy Hardy Gets Spring Fever
Andy Hardy Meets Debutante
Andy Hardy's Double Life
Andy Hardy's Private Secretary
Angus
Annie O
The Baby-Sitters Club
The Bachelor and the Bobby-Soxer •
The Basketball Diaries
Battle of the Bullies
The Bay Boy
Beach Blanket Bingo •
Beach Party
Before and After
The Beniker Gang
Better Off Dead
Big Bully
Big Girls Don't Cry. . .They Get Even
Bikini Beach
Bill & Ted's Excellent Adventure
BMX Bandits
Book of Love
Born to Be Wild
Boys
Boyz N the Hood •
The Brady Bunch Movie •
The Breakfast Club •
Breaking Away •
Breaking Free
Buffy the Vampire Slayer

Bye, Bye, Birdie •
Can't Buy Me Love
The Canterville Ghost
The Chicken Chronicles
Club Connect: Me and My Folks
Club Connect: The Hip-Hop Alternative
Clueless •
Coneheads
The Crush
Cry-Baby
A Cry in the Wild •
The Cure •
Dangerous Minds
Dark Horse
Dazed and Confused •
Dead Poets Society •
Defense Play
Desert Bloom •
Diving In
Doin' Time on Planet Earth
Don't Tell Mom the Babysitter's Dead
Dream Date
Dream Machine
Dutch
East of Eden •
The Effect of Gamma Rays on Man-in-the-Moon Marigolds •
Emma •
Encino Man
The Ernest Green Story
Escape Artist •
E.T.: The Extra-Terrestrial •
Fame •
Fast Times at Ridgemont High •
Ferris Bueller's Day Off •
The Flamingo Kid •
Flipper
Flirting •
Footloose
For Keeps
Foxes
A Friendship in Vienna •
A Girl of the Limberlost
Girls Just Want to Have Fun
Gleaming the Cube
The Goodbye Bird
Goodbye, Miss 4th of July
A Goofy Movie •
Grease
Grease 2
Hackers
Hadley's Rebellion
Hairspray •
Harley
The Heavenly Kid
Heavyweights
A Home of Our Own
Hoop Dreams •
Hoosiers •
How I Got into College
How to Stuff a Wild Bikini
I am the Cheese
I Wanna Hold Your Hand •
If Looks Could Kill
Imaginary Crimes •

The In Crowd
The Inkwell
Kid Dynamite
A Kid in King Arthur's Court
Kim
Knights & Emeralds
La Bamba •
Lantern Hill
The Lawrenceville Stories
License to Drive
Life Begins for Andy Hardy •
Lisa
Little Darlings
A Little Romance •
The Little Thief
The Loneliest Runner •
The Loneliness of the Long Distance Runner •
Looking for Miracles
The Lost Boys
Love Laughs at Andy Hardy
Lucas •
Magic Kid 2
Major Payne
Making the Grade
The Man in the Moon •
The Manhattan Project
Meatballs
Mermaids •
Metropolitan •
The Miracle
Miss Annie Rooney
Monkey Business •
Morgan Stewart's Coming Home
Muscle Beach Party
My American Cousin •
My Best Friend Is a Vampire
My Boyfriend's Back
My Father the Hero
My Girl 2
My Science Project
Mystery Date
National Lampoon's Senior Trip
The Night Before
Not My Kid
Now and Then
On the Edge: The Survival of Dana
One Crazy Summer
Outside Chance of Maximillian Glick •
The Outsiders
Over the Edge •
Pajama Party
Parenthood •
Peggy Sue Got Married •
Phantom 2040 Movie: The Ghost Who Walks
Pippin •
Pretty in Pink
The Prime of Miss Jean Brodie •
Primo Baby
Princes in Exile
Quarterback Princess
Race the Sun
Racing with the Moon •
Rad
Rambling Rose •

Rebel Without a Cause •
Rock 'n' Roll High School Forever
Romeo and Juliet •
Running Mates
Say Anything •
Secret Admirer
Seven Minutes in Heaven
Shag: The Movie •
Shout
Sing
Sixteen Candles •
Solarbabies
Some Kind of Wonderful •
Stand and Deliver •
Starchaser: The Legend of Orin
Summer School
Swing Kids
Teen Wolf
Teenage Mutant Ninja Turtles 2: The Secret of the Ooze
Tex •
That Night
That Was Then. . .This Is Now
This Boy's Life •
Three O'Clock High
Tom Brown's School Days •
Toughlove
Treasure Island
Troop Beverly Hills •
The Trouble with Angels •
Uncle Buck
Unstrung Heroes
Up Against the Wall
Valley Girl
A Very Brady Sequel •
Weird Science
Welcome Home, Roxy Carmichael
Where Angels Go, Trouble Follows
White Squall
Wild Pony •
Windrunner
The Year My Voice Broke •
Young Guns
Zebrahead •
The Zoo Gang

Tennis
Tennis Racquet

That's Showbiz
The Boy Friend •
Bugs Bunny Superstar
Chaplin
A Decade of the Waltons
Delirious
Dog Pound Shuffle
The Errand Boy
F/X •
F/X 2: The Deadly Art of Illusion
Face the Music
Fame •
Funny Girl •
Funny Lady
Help! •
I'll Do Anything
Last Action Hero
Life with Mikey

Matinee •
Mommie Dearest
The Muppet Movie •
Muppets Take Manhattan
My Favorite Year •
The Party •
Pastime •
The Purple Rose of Cairo •
Sam's Son
Silent Movie
Sweet Liberty
Tootsie •
Under the Rainbow
What's Love Got to Do With It?
Who Framed Roger Rabbit? •
The Wizard of Speed and Time •

3 Stooges
Snow White and the Three Stooges
Three Stooges
Three Stooges: A Ducking They Will Go
Three Stooges: A Plumbing We Will Go
Three Stooges: Cash and Carry
Three Stooges: If a Body Meets a Body
Three Stooges: In the Sweet Pie and Pie
Three Stooges Meet Hercules
Three Stooges: So Long Mr. Chumps
Three Stooges: What's the Matador?

Time Travel
see also Rescue Missions Involving Time Travel
Adventures in Dinosaur City
The Adventures of Dudley the Dragon: Mr. Crabby Tree
Amazing Mr. Blunden
Army of Darkness •
Back to the Future •
Back to the Future, Part 2
Back to the Future, Part 3
Beastmaster 2: Through the Portal of Time
Being Human
Bill & Ted's Bogus Journey
Bill & Ted's Excellent Adventure
The Blue Yonder
Brother Future
Buck Rogers in the 25th Century
Doctor Who: An Unearthly Child
Doctor Who and the Daleks
Escape from the Planet of the Apes •

Category Index

Groundhog Day
Hercules in New York
Highlander 2: The
    Quickening
The Indian in the
    Cupboard •
The Jetsons Meet the
    Flintstones
Josh Kirby . . . Time
    Warrior: Chapter 1,
    Planet of the Dino-
    Knights
Land of the Lost, Vol. 1
Lords of Magick
Mannequin 2: On the
    Move
Peggy Sue Got Married
Stargate
Teenage Mutant Ninja
    Turtles 3
Terminator 2: Judgment
    Day •
Three Stooges Meet
    Hercules
Time Bandits •
Timecop
Timefighters in the Land
    of Fantasy
Timemaster
12 Monkeys •
Unidentified Flying
    Oddball
Voyager from the
    Unknown

Tom & Jerry

Tom & Jerry Kids: Out of
    This World Fun
Tom & Jerry On Parade
Tom and Jerry: Starring
Tom and Jerry: The
    Movie
Tom & Jerry: The Very
    Best Of Tom & Jerry
Tom & Jerry's Cartoon
    Cavalcade
Tom & Jerry's Comic
    Capers
Tom & Jerry's Festival of
    Fun
Tom & Jerry's 50th
    Birthday Classics

Toys

Babes in Toyland
The Indian in the
    Cupboard •
Jumanji
Madeline and the Toy
    Factory
Not Quite Human
The Tin Soldier
The Toy
Toy Story •
Toys
Where the Toys Come
    From

Trading Places

Babe •
Big •
Billy Madison
Cinderfella
Class Act
Condorman
Dave •

Desperately Seeking
    Susan •
Doctor Doolittle
Dr. Jekyll and Ms. Hyde
Dream a Little Dream
18 Again!
Fluke
Freaky Friday •
Greystoke: The Legend of
    Tarzan, Lord of the
    Apes
Heart Like a Wheel •
Hiding Out
The Incredible Mr. Limpet
It Takes Two
Junior
Just One of the Guys
The Lady Vanishes •
Ladybugs
Like Father, Like Son
Maid to Order
The Man Who Wagged
    His Tail
Mrs. Winterbourne
Monkey Business •
Overboard
The Prince and the
    Pauper •
The Prince and the
    Pauper
Roman Holiday •
The Scarlet Pimpernel •
The Shaggy D.A.
The Shaggy Dog
The Shakiest Gun in the
    West
Soul Man
Tootsie •
Vice Versa •
Wait Till Your Mother
    Gets Home
Wonder Man
Yentl

Trains

see also Subways

Before Sunrise
Broken Arrow
From Russia with Love •
The Fugitive •
Grandpa Worked on the
    Railroad
The Great Train
    Robbery •
The Grey Fox •
Hot Lead & Cold Feet
The Lady Vanishes •
The Little Engine That
    Could
Mrs. Winterbourne
Once Upon a Time in the
    West •
Planes, Trains &
    Automobiles
The Road Home
Shining Time Station:
    Singsongs, Vol. 1
Shining Time Station:
    'Tis a Gift Holiday
    Special
The Silver Streak •
Strangers on a Train •
There Goes a Train
Thomas the Tank Engine:
    Thomas Gets Bumped

Thomas the Tank Engine:
    Thomas, Percy and the
    Dragon & Other
    Stories
Throw Momma from the
    Train •
Tough Guys
What Do You Want to Be
    When You Grow Up:
    Railroaders
Workin' on the Railroad:
    Alphabet Factory on
    the Railroad

Treasure Hunt

Call of the Wild
City Slickers 2: The
    Legend of Curly's Gold
Cutthroat Island
Ernest Rides Again
The Gold Bug
Gold Diggers: The Secret
    of Bear Mountain
Greedy
The Jewel of the Nile
Max is Missing
Muppet Treasure Island •
Romancing the Stone •
Rudyard Kipling's The
    Jungle Book •
Secret of the Ice Cave
Tarzan's Secret Treasure
Tom and Huck •
Treasure Island •
Treasure Island
The Treasure of
    Matecumbe
Treasure of the Sierra
    Madre •

Trees

Hole in the Sky
The Little Crooked
    Christmas Tree
Princess Gwenevere and
    the Jewel Riders
Reddy the Fox
Timberrr! From Logs to
    Lumber
The Wizard of Oz •

TV Movies

The Adventures of a Two-
    Minute Werewolf
The Adventures of
    Huckleberry Finn
The Adventures of
    Huckleberry Finn •
The Adventures of Tom
    Sawyer
African Journey
Almost Partners
An American Christmas
    Carol
And Baby Makes Six
And the Children Shall
    Lead
Anne of Avonlea •
Anne of Green Gables •
Annie O
Annie Oakley
Babes in Toyland
Back Home

Back to Hannibal: The
    Further Adventures of
    Tom Sawyer and
    Huckleberry Finn
Battle of the Bullies
Beauty and the Beast
The Beniker Gang
Bill •
Bill: On His Own •
The Black Arrow
Black Magic
Bon Voyage, Charlie
    Brown
The Boy Who Left Home
    to Find Out About the
    Shivers
The Boy Who Loved
    Trolls
Brian's Song •
Bridge to Terabithia •
Brother Future
Buck Rogers in the 25th
    Century
Call of the Wild
The Canterville Ghost
Captain America 2: Death
    Too Soon
Captain Kangaroo & His
    Friends
Captain Kangaroo's
    Merry Christmas
    Stories
The Capture of Grizzly
    Adams
Casey at the Bat
Charlie and the Great
    Balloon Chase
Child of Glass
Chips the War Dog
Christmas Comes to
    Willow Creek
A Christmas to
    Remember
The Chronicles of
    Narnia •
Cinderella
Clarence
Clowning Around
Comeback Kid
Conspiracy of Love
The Dancing Princesses
Daniel and the Towers
David Copperfield
A Day for Thanks on
    Walton's Mountain
Death of the Incredible
    Hulk
Dr. Syn, Alias the
    Scarecrow
A Dream for Christmas •
The Electric Grandmother
The Emperor's New
    Clothes
The Ernest Green Story
The Ewok Adventure
The Ewoks: Battle for
    Endor
Experience Preferred. . .
    But Not Essential
Eye on the Sparrow
The Fantastic World of
    D.C. Collins
Father and Scout
Father Figure
The Fig Tree

The Flame Trees of
    Thika •
Follow the River
A Friendship in Vienna
Frog •
Frogs!
From the Mixed-Up Files
    of Mrs. Basil E.
    Frankweiler
Geronimo •
A Girl of the Limberlost
The Girl Who Spelled
    Freedom •
Gone are the Days
Goodbye, Miss 4th of
    July
The Grass is Always
    Greener Over the
    Septic Tank
Gryphon
Gulliver in Lilliput •
The Halfback of Notre
    Dame
Happy Birthday, Bugs: 50
    Looney Years
The Haunting of Barney
    Palmer
Heck's Way Home
Hector's Bunyip
Heidi
Heidi •
Here Comes Garfield
Hiroshima Maiden
The Hobbit •
The Hoboken Chicken
    Emergency
Hole in the Sky
Home at Last
Home for Christmas
Home to Stay •
Homecoming
Homecoming: A
    Christmas Story •
Homeward Bound
A Horse for Danny
The Horse Without a
    Head
Horsemasters
The House of Dies Drear
A House Without a
    Christmas Tree
How the West Was Fun
How to Be a Perfect
    Person in Just Three
    Days
Huckleberry Finn
The Hunchback of Notre
    Dame •
The Incredible Hulk
    Returns
The Incredible Rocky
    Mountain Race
Islands
It Came Upon a Midnight
    Clear
It's the Muppets, Vol. 1:
    Meet the Muppets
Jack Frost
Jacob Have I Loved
Jem, Vol. 1: Truly
    Outrageous
Jesus of Nazareth •
Johnny Shiloh
Johnny's Girl
K-9000
Kavik, the Wolf Dog

Kermit and Piggy Story
The Kid from Left Field
The Kid Who Loved
Christmas
The Kid with the 200 I.Q.
Kim
Konrad •
Lantern Hill
Lassie: The Miracle
Lassie's Great Adventure
The Last of the Mohicans
The Last Prostitute
The Lawrenceville Stories
The Legend of Sleepy
Hollow
Little Lord Fauntleroy •
The Little Mermaid
The Little Princess •
Little Red Riding Hood
The Littlest Angel
The Loneliest Runner •
The Lord of the Rings
Lost Legacy: A Girl Called
Hatter Fox
Lots of Luck
Magical Mystery Tour •
The Man in the Iron
Mask •
The Man in the Santa
Claus Suit
Maricela
Mark Twain and Me
Max is Missing
The Mighty Pawns
Miracle at Moreaux
Miracle of the Heart: A
Boys Town Story
The Miracle Worker •
Mr. Bill's Real-Life
Adventures
Mother Nature Tales of
Discovery
My Old Man
Necessary Parties
Not My Kid
Not Quite Human
The Old Curiosity Shop
Oliver Twist
Ollie Hopnoodle's Haven
of Bliss
On the Edge: The
Survival of Dana
Orphan Train •
Out There
Past the Bleachers
Pecos Bill
Pee Wee's Playhouse
Festival of Fun
Peter Lundy and the
Medicine Hat Stallion
Peter Pan •
The Pied Piper of
Hamelin
Pinocchio
The Point •
Prince Brat and the
Whipping Boy •
The Prince of Central
Park •
The Princess and the Pea
The Princess Who Never
Laughed
Puss 'n Boots
Quarterback Princess
The Red Pony •
The Return of the King

The Rousters
Rudolph the Red-Nosed
Reindeer •
Rudolph's Shiny New
Year
Runaway
Sarah, Plain and Tall •
The Scarlet Pimpernel •
The Secret Garden •
The Shadow Riders
Shakespeare: The
Animated Tales
Skeezer
Smoke
A Smoky Mountain
Christmas
Smooth Talk •
The Snow Queen
Snow White and the
Seven Dwarfs
Spiderman
Spiderman: The Deadly
Dust
Stone Fox
Sudie & Simpson
A Summer to Remember
Sweet 15
Taking Care of Terrific
Tall Tales and Legends:
Johnny Appleseed
The Thief of Baghdad
The Three Little Pigs
Thumbelina
Thursday's Game •
Tiger Town
The Tin Soldier
Toughlove
Treasure Island
The Trial of the
Incredible Hulk
Two of a Kind
Undergrads •
Voyager from the
Unknown
Wait Till Your Mother
Gets Home
Walking on Air
The Waltons: The
Children's Carol
A Waltz Through the Hills
Whale for the Killing
When Every Day was the
Fourth of July
Where the Spirit Lives
White Mama •
Who'll Save Our
Children? •
A Winner Never Quits
Words by Heart
The Year Without a Santa
Claus

TV Series
The Adventures of Rocky
& Bullwinkle: Birth of
Bullwinkle
Africa Texas Style
And Now for Something
Completely Different •
Battlestar Galactica
Bedrock Wedlock
Bigfoot and Wildboy
Buck Rogers in the 25th
Century
Cadillacs and Dinosaurs
Cartoons for Big Kids

Christy
Davy Crockett and the
River Pirates •
Davy Crockett, King of
the Wild Frontier •
A Decade of the Waltons
Dr. Strange
Doctor Who: An
Unearthly Child
The Flash
Flipper
Gentle Ben
George of the Jungle
Ghostwriter, Vol. 1: Ghost
Story
Happy Birthday, Bugs: 50
Looney Years
Highlander: The
Gathering
The Howdy Doody Show
(Puppet Playhouse)/
The Gabby Hayes
Show
H.R. Pufnstuf, Vol. 1
The Incredible Hulk
Land of the Lost
Land of the Lost, Vol. 1
Little House on the
Prairie •
The Lone Ranger: Code
of the Pioneers
The Man Called
Flintstone
Mickey Mouse Club, Vol.
1
Mr. Magoo: Cyrano De
Bergerac/A
Midsummer Night's
Dream
Monkees, Volume 1
Muppet Revue
Muppet Video Series
Muppets Moments
Nancy Drew: Mystery of
the Diamond Triangle
The Perils of Penelope
Pitstop
Rags to Riches
Return to Treasure
Island, Vol. 1
Scooby-Doo
Sigmund & the Sea
Monsters, Vol. 1
Star Trek the Next
Generation Episode 1-
2: Encounter at
Farpoint
Superman & the Mole
Men
Tales from Avonlea, Vol.
1: The Journey Begins
Tales of Deputy Dawg,
Vol. 1
Tiny Toons in Two-Tone
Town
Tiny Toons Music
Television
Tiny Toons: The Best of
Buster and Babs
TV's Best Adventures of
Superman
The Waltons: A
Thanksgiving Story
Yogi and the Invasion of
the Space Bears

Yogi and the Magical
Flight of the Spruce
Goose
Yogi's Great Escape
Zorro, Vol. 1

TV Tales
*see also Newsroom
Notes; Over the
Airwaves*
Bigfoot: The
Unforgettable
Encounter
Groundhog Day
Hero
My Favorite Year •
Quiz Show •
Scrooged
UHF
Up Close and Personal

Twins
Big Business •
The Crazysitter
How the West Was Fun
It Takes Two
The Man in the Iron
Mask •
Nukie
Out on a Limb
The Parent Trap
Twins
Twinsitters

UFOs
*see Aliens — Nasty;
Aliens — Nice*

Vacations
Cabin Boy
Cancel My Reservation
Dirty Dancing •
A Far Off Place
Gidget Goes Hawaiian
Gidget Goes to Rome
Goosebumps: A Night in
Terror Tower
Home Alone •
The Inkwell
Magic in the Water
Mr. Hulot's Holiday •
My Father the Hero
My Grandpa is a Vampire
National Lampoon's
Christmas Vacation
National Lampoon's
European Vacation
National Lampoon's
Vacation •
Ollie Hopnoodle's Haven
of Bliss
The River Wild •
Two If by Sea

Vampires
Blacula
Buffy the Vampire Slayer
Bunnicula: Vampire
Rabbit
Dracula: Dead and Loving
It
The Ketchup Vampires
The Lost Boys
Love at First Bite
The Monster Squad

My Best Friend Is a
Vampire
My Grandpa is a Vampire
Salem's Lot •

Viva Las Vegas!
Honeymoon in Vegas
Kingpin
Rock-a-Doodle
Sister Act •

Volcanos
*see also Disaster
Strikes!*
Joe Versus the Volcano

Voodoo
How to Stuff a Wild
Bikini
Jungle Drums of Africa
Live and Let Die
Weekend at Bernie's 2

Waitresses
It Could Happen to You •
Untamed Heart

War, General
*see also Civil War;
Korean War;
Postwar; POW/MIA;
Revolutionary War;
World War I; World
War II*
Braveheart •
Dr. Seuss' Butter Battle
Book
Doctor Zhivago •
Fighting Marines
The Fighting Prince of
Donegal
The Last of the Mohicans
The Last of the
Mohicans •
The Mouse That Roared •
An Officer and a Duck
Revenge of the
Mysterons from Mars
Ryan's Daughter

Wedding Bells
see also Marriage
Father of the Bride •
Father of the Bride
For Better and For Worse
Forget Paris
Four Weddings and a
Funeral •
Honeymoon in Vegas
House Party 3
Housesitter
The Jewel of the Nile
Muriel's Wedding •
Nine Months
Only You
The Philadelphia Story •
Prelude to a Kiss
She's Having a Baby

Werewolves
The Adventures of a Two-
Minute Werewolf
The Howling •
The Monster Squad
My Mom's a Werewolf
Teen Wolf

Category Index

Teen Wolf: All-American
  Werewolf
Teen Wolf Too
Teen Wolf: Wolf of My
  Dreams

Westerns
*see Cowboys &
  Indians*

Winnie the Pooh
The New Adventures of
  Winnie the Pooh, Vol.
  1: Great Honey Pot
  Robbery
Pooh Learning: Helping
  Others
Pooh Learning: Making
  Friends
Pooh Learning: Sharing
  and Caring
Pooh Playtime: Cowboy
  Pooh
Pooh Playtime: Detective
  Tigger
Pooh Playtime: Pooh
  Party
Winnie the Pooh and the
  Blustery Day
Winnie the Pooh and the
  Honey Tree

Witches' Brew
*see also Demons &
  Wizards*
Black Magic
Dr. Strange
Hocus Pocus
Lost Legacy: A Girl Called
  Hatter Fox
Lumpkin the Pumpkin
My Little Pony: The
  Movie

The Polar Bear King
Return to Oz
Sabrina, the Teenaged
  Witch
Shelley Duvall's Bedtime
  Stories: The Christmas
  Witch
The Witch Who Turned
  Pink
The Witches •
Witches' Brew
The Witching of Ben
  Wagner
Witch's Night Out
The Wizard of Oz •
The Worst Witch

Wonderworks Movies
African Journey
Almost Partners
And the Children Shall
  Lead
Anne of Avonlea •
Anne of Green Gables •
The Boy Who Loved
  Trolls
Bridge to Terabithia
Brother Future
The Canterville Ghost
The Chronicles of
  Narnia •
City Boy
Clowning Around
Clowning Around 2
Daniel and the Towers
The Fig Tree
Frog •
Frogs!
A Girl of the Limberlost
Gryphon
The Haunting of Barney
  Palmer
Hector's Bunyip

Hiroshima Maiden
The Hoboken Chicken
  Emergency
Home at Last
The House of Dies Drear
How to Be a Perfect
  Person in Just Three
  Days
Jacob Have I Loved
Konrad •
Lantern Hill
The Little Princess •
Lone Star Kid
Looking for Miracles
Maricela
The Mighty Pawns
Miracle at Moreaux
My Friend Walter
Necessary Parties
Runaway
Sweet 15
Taking Care of Terrific
Walking on Air
A Waltz Through the Hills
Words by Heart

World War I
The African Queen •
The Charge of the Model
  T's
Courage Mountain
Land That Time Forgot
Lawrence of Arabia •
Miracle of Our Lady of
  Fatima
When the Whales Came

World War II
*see also Postwar;
  POW/MIA*
Adventures of Smilin'
  Jack
Alan & Naomi •

Au Revoir Les Enfants •
Back Home
Battle of Britain
Bedknobs and
  Broomsticks
The Bridge on the River
  Kwai •
A Bridge Too Far
Canine Commando
The Canterville Ghost
Casablanca •
Chips the War Dog
A Day in October
December
Empire of the Sun •
Forbidden Games •
Foreign Correspondent •
A Friendship in Vienna
G-Men vs. the Black
  Dragon
Hiroshima Maiden
Hope and Glory •
The Human Comedy •
The Incredible Mr. Limpet
Journey for Margaret •
Judgment at Nuremberg •
A League of Their Own •
The Little Thief
MacArthur
A Midnight Clear •
Miracle at Moreaux
Miracle of the White
  Stallions
An Officer and a Duck
Racing with the Moon •
Reunion •
Saboteur •
Since You Went Away •
Snow Treasure
The Sound of Music •
South Pacific •
Swing Shift
Victory

The Wizard of Loneliness

Wrestling
Hadley's Rebellion
No Holds Barred
Take Down

Wrong Side of the
  Tracks
*see also Rags to
  Riches*
Breaking Away •
Captains Courageous •
Carbon Copy
Careful, He Might Hear
  You •
Cool As Ice
Cry-Baby •
Dirty Dancing •
Far and Away
The Flamingo Kid •
Grease
It Happened One Night •
Jersey Girl
King Ralph
Liar's Moon
The Man from Snowy
  River
Off Beat
Pretty in Pink •
Return to Snowy River •
Rocky •
Rumble Fish •
Some Kind of Wonderful
That Night
A Tree Grows in
  Brooklyn •
Valley Girl

Distributor Index

The **DISTRIBUTOR INDEX** is a list of the distributor codes that appear at the end of each movie review. You can find the addresses, phone numbers and fax numbers for those distributors in the "Distributor Guide" following this index.

A&M — A & M Video
AAI — Arts America, Inc.
ABC — ABC Video
ACA — Academy Entertainment
ADL — Anti-Defamation League of B'nai B'rith
AEL — Atlantic Entertainment Ltd.
AFR — Afro-Am Distributing Company
AHV — Active Home Video
AIM — AIMS Media
ALP — Alphabet Factory
AMB — Ambrose Video Publishing, Inc.
AOV — Admit One Video
APD — Applause Productions, Inc.
AUD — Audio-Forum
AVE — WarnerVision
BAR — Barr Films
BFA — Phoenix/BFA Films
BFI — Beacon Films
BFV — Best Film & Video Corporation
BMG — BMG
BMV — Bennett Marine Video
BOG — Bogner Entertainment Inc.
BOP — Bo-Peep Productions
BPG — Bridgestone Multimedia
BTV — Baker & Taylor Video
CAB — Cable Films & Video
CAF — Cabin Fever Entertainment
CAN — Cannon Video

CCB — Critics' Choice Video, Inc.
CCC — Children's Circle Westwoods Studios/ Childrens Circle
CEL — Celebrity Home Entertainment
CFV — Carousel Film & Video
CHF — Churchill Media
CHI — Center for Humanities, Inc.
CNG — Congress Entertainment, Ltd.
COL — Columbia Tristar Home Video
CRC — Criterion Collection
CRY — Crystal Productions
CSM — Coliseum Video
CTW — Children's Television Workshop (CTW)
CVC — Connoisseur Video Collection
CVM — Crest Video Marketing
DHE — Discovery Home Entertainment
DIS — Walt Disney Home Video
DOV — Dove Kids
DSN — Disney Educational Productions
DVT — Discount Video Tapes, Inc.
ECU — EcuFilm
ENM — Environmental Media
EVD — European Video Distributor
EXP — Expanded Entertainment
FAF — Fast Forward

FCS — Focus on the Family
FCT — Facets Multimedia, Inc.
FFC — Family Films/ Concordia
FHE — Family Home Entertainment
FHS — Films for the Humanities & Sciences
FHV — Falcon Home Video
FLI — Films Inc. Video
FMT — Format International
FOC — Focus on Animals
FOX — CBS/Fox Video
FRG — Fright Video
FRH — Fries Home Video
FUS — Fusion Video
FXL — Fox/Lorber Home Video
FXV — FoxVideo
GEM — Video Gems
GHV — Genesis Home Video
GKK — Goodtimes Entertainment
GLV — German Language Video Center
GPV — Grapevine Video
GVV — Glenn Video Vistas, Ltd.
HBO — HBO Home Video
HEG — Horizon Entertainment
HHE — Hollywood Home Entertainment
HHT — Hollywood Home Theatre

HMD — Hemdale Home Video
HMK — Hallmark Home Entertainment
HMV — Home Vision Cinema
HPH — Hollywood Pictures Home Video
HSE — High/Scope Educational Research Foundation
HTV — Hen's Tooth Video
ICA — First Run Features/Icarus Films
IGP — Ignatius Press
IHF — International Historic Films, Inc. (IHF)
IME — Image Entertainment
IMP — Imperial Entertainment Corp.
INC — Increase/ SilverMine Video
ING — Ingram Entertainment
INJ — Ingram International Films
INT — Interama, Inc.
JCF — Judaica Captioned Film Center, Inc.
JEF — JEF Films, Inc.
JFK — Just for Kids Home Video
JHV — Jim Henson Productions
JTC — J2 Communications
KAR — Karol Video
KEP — Keep the Faith Inc.
KID — Kid Vision
KUI — Knowledge Unlimited, Inc.
KUL — Kultur Video

KVI — Dream Video Productions/Kid-VID
LCA — Modern Curriculum Press - MCP
LET — Let's Create
LGV — Lyons Group
LIV — Live Entertainment
LME — Lucerne Media
LOO — Loonic Video
LSV — LSVideo, Inc.
LTY — Lightyear Entertainment
LVC — Library Video Company
MAS — Mastervision, Inc.
MAX — Miramax Pictures Home Video
MAZ — Mazon Productions
MBP — Moonbeam Publications, Inc.
MCA — MCA/Universal Home Video
MCG — Management Company Entertainment Group (MCEG), Inc.
MED — Media Home Entertainment
MGM — MGM/UA Home Entertainment
MIR — Miramar Productions
MLB — Mike LeBell's Video
MLT — Music for Little People
MNC — Monarch Home Video
MON — Monterey Home Video
MOV — Movies Unlimited

MPI — MPI Home Video
MRV — Moore Video
MTI — Coronet/MTI Film & Video
MTT — Coronet-MTI Film & Video International
MTX — MNTEX Entertainment, Inc.
MVC — Moviecraft, Inc.
MVD — Music Video Distributors
NFB — National Film Board of Canada
NHO — New Horizons Home Video
NLC — New Line Home Video
NOS — Nostalgia Family Video
NWV — New World Entertainment
NYR — Not Yet Released
ORI — Orion Home Video
PAR — Paramount Home Video
PBC — Princeton Book Co. Publishers
PBS — PBS Home Video
PGV — Polygram Video (PV)
PIC — Videos.com, Inc.
PME — Public Media Video
PMH — PM Entertainment Group, Inc.

PMS — Professional Media Service Corp.
PRS — Proscenium Entertainment
PSM — Prism Entertainment
PSS — Price Stern Sloan, Inc.
PTB — Proud To Be . . . A Black Video Collection
PYR — Pyramid Film & Video
QVD — Quality Video
RAB — Rabbit Ears Home Video
RAN — Random House Home Video
RDG — Reader's Digest Home Video
REP — Republic Pictures Home Video
RHI — Rhino Home Video
RHU — Random House Media
RHV — Regency Home Video
RIN — Rincon Children's Entertainment/BMG Kidz
RXM — Rex #Miller
SAL — Salenger Films, Inc.
SCH — Schoolmasters Video
SFP — Stage Fright Productions

SGE — SGE Entertainment Corp.
SHV — Snoopy's Home Video Library
SIG — Signals
SIM — Simitar Entertainment
SKM — Sony Kids Music
SMA — Super Management
SMV — Sony Music Video Enterprises
SNC — Sinister Cinema
SPW — Chordant Distribution Group
STP — Streamline Pictures
STS — Stagestep
SVE — Society for Visual Education, Inc. (SVE)
SWC — Simon Wiesenthal Center
TCF — 20th Century Fox Film Corporation
THP — Tyndale House Publishers
TIM — Timeless Video Inc.
TLF — Time-Life Video and Television
TOU — Buena Vista Home Video
TPI — Thomson Productions, Inc.
TPV — Tapeworm Video Distributors
TRI — Triboro Entertainment Group

TTC — Turner Home Entertainment Company
TVC — The Video Catalog
TWE — Trans-World Entertainment
UAV — UAV Corporation
UND — Uni Distribution
UNI — Unicorn Video, Inc.
UNT — Unity Productions
UWA — University of Washington Educational Media Collection
VAI — Video Artists International, Inc.
VAN — Vantage Communications, Inc.
VBL — Video Bible Library, Inc.
VCD — Video City Productions/ Distributing
VCI — Video Communications, Inc. (VCI)
VCN — Video Connection
VCO — Video Collectibles/BFS Video
VDC — Vidcrest
VDM — Video Dimensions
VEC — Valencia Entertainment Corp.

VES — Vestron Video
VHE — VCII Home Entertainment, Inc.
VMK — Vidmark Entertainment
VPJ — The Video Project
VTR — Anchor Bay
VWV — V.I.E.W. Video
VYY — Video Yesteryear
WAR — Warner Home Video, Inc.
WEA — Warner/Elektra/ Atlantic (WEA) Corporation
WFV — Western Media Systems
WKV — Wood Knapp & Company, Inc.
WME — Warren Miller Entertainment
WNE — WNET/Thirteen Non-Broadcast
WOM — Wombat Film and Video
WOV — Worldvision Home Video, Inc.
WPC — Western Publishing Co., Inc.
WRV — Warner Reprise Video
WSH — Wishing Well Distributing
WST — White Star
XVC — Xenon
ZON — Zondervan

Distributor Guide

The **DISTRIBUTOR GUIDE** alphabetically lists the full address, phone, toll-free, and fax numbers of the distributors listed in the movie reviews. The key to the codes are listed in the "Distributor Index" preceding this guide. Those reviews with the code **OM** are on moratorium (distributed at one time, but not currently). Since a title enjoying such status was once distributed, it may well linger on your local video store shelf. When the distributor is not known, the code **NO** appears in the review. For new releases to the theater that have not yet made it to video (but likely will in the coming year), the code **NYR** (not yet released) appears.

ABC VIDEO *(ABC)*
Capital Cities/ABC
Video Enterprises
1200 High Ridge Rd.
Stamford, CT 06905
203-968-9100
Fax: 203-329-6464

ACADEMY ENTERTAINMENT *(ACA)*
9250 Wilshire Blvd.,
Ste. 400
Beverly Hills, CA 90212
Fax: 310-275-2195

ACTIVE HOME VIDEO *(AHV)*
12121 Wilshire Blvd.,
No. 401
Los Angeles, CA 90025
310-447-6131
800-824-6109
Fax: 310-207-0411

ADMIT ONE VIDEO *(AOV)*
PO Box 66, Sta. O
Toronto, ON, Canada
M4A 2M8
416-463-5714
Fax: 416-463-5714

AFRO-AM DISTRIBUTING COMPANY *(AFR)*
1909 W. 95th St.
Chicago, IL 60643-1105
312-235-4504

AIMS MEDIA *(AIM)*
9710 DeSoto Ave.
Chatsworth, CA 91311-4409
818-773-4300
800-367-2467
Fax: 818-341-6700

ALPHABET FACTORY *(ALP)*
43 W. 85th St., Ste. 2A
New York, NY 10024
212-787-3459
Fax: 212-787-5426

AMBROSE VIDEO PUBLISHING, INC. *(AMB)*
1290 Avenue of the
Americas, Ste. 2245
New York, NY 10104
212-265-7272
800-526-4663
Fax: 212-265-8088

ANCHOR BAY *(VTR)*
500 Kirts Blvd.
Troy, MI 48084
810-362-9660
800-786-8777
Fax: 810-362-4454

A & M VIDEO *(A&M)*
1416 N. LaBrea Ave.
Hollywood, CA 90028
213-469-2411
Fax: 213-856-2778

ANTI-DEFAMATION LEAGUE OF B'NAI B'RITH *(ADL)*
Audio-Visual Dept.
823 United Nations
Plaza
New York, NY 10017
212-490-2525
Fax: 212-867-0779

APPLAUSE PRODUCTIONS, INC. *(APD)*
85 Longview Rd.
Port Washington, NY
11050

516-883-2825
800-278-7326
Fax: 516-883-7460

ARTS AMERICA, INC. *(AAI)*
9 Benedict Pl.
Greenwich, CT 06830-5321
203-869-4694
800-553-5278
Fax: 203-869-3075

ATLANTIC ENTERTAINMENT LTD. *(AEL)*
1111 Rte. 110, Ste. 324
E. Farmingdale, NY
11735
Fax: 516-249-1690

AUDIO-FORUM *(AUD)*
96 Broad St.
Guilford, CT 06437
203-453-9794
800-243-1234
Fax: 203-453-9774

BAKER & TAYLOR VIDEO *(BTV)*
501 S. Gladiolus
Momence, IL 60954
815-472-2444
800-775-2300
Fax: 800-775-3500

BARR FILMS *(BAR)*
12801 Schabarum
Irwindale, CA 91706
818-338-7878
800-234-7878
Fax: 818-814-2672

BEACON FILMS *(BFI)*
1560 Sherman Ave.,
Ste. 100
Evanston, IL 60201

708-328-6700
800-323-9084
Fax: 708-328-6706

BENNETT MARINE VIDEO *(BMV)*
8436 W. 3rd St., Ste.
740
Los Angeles, CA 90048
213-951-7570
800-733-8862
Fax: 213-957 — 595

BEST FILM & VIDEO CORPORATION *(BFV)*
108 New South Rd.
Hicksville, NY 11801-5223
516-931-6969
800-527-2189
Fax: 516-931-5959

BMG *(BMG)*
6363 Sunset Blvd., 6th
Fl.
Hollywood, CA 90028-7318

BO-PEEP PRODUCTIONS *(BOP)*
PO Box 982
Eureka, MT 59917
406-889-3225
800-532-0420
Fax: 406-889-3225

BOGNER ENTERTAINMENT INC. *(BOG)*
PO Box 641428
Los Angeles, CA 90064
310-473-0139
800-264-6375
Fax: 310-473-6417

BRIDGESTONE MULTIMEDIA *(BPG)*
300 N. McKemy Ave.
Chandler, AZ 85226
602-940-5771
800-523-0988
Fax: 602-940-8924

BUENA VISTA HOME VIDEO *(TOU)*
350 S. Buena Vista St.
Burbank, CA 91521-7145
818-562-3568

CABIN FEVER ENTERTAINMENT *(CAF)*
100 W. Putnam Ave.
Greenwich, CT 06830
203-661-1100
Fax: 203-863-5258

CABLE FILMS & VIDEO *(CAB)*
Country Club Sta.
PO Box 7171
Kansas City, MO 64113
816-362-2804
800-514-2804
Fax: 816-341-7365

CANNON VIDEO *(CAN)*
PO Box 17198
Beverly Hills, CA 90290
310-772-7765

CAROUSEL FILM & VIDEO *(CFV)*
260 5th Ave., Rm. 405
New York, NY 10001
212-683-1660
800-683-1660
Fax: 212-683-1662

CBS/FOX VIDEO
(FOX)
PO Box 900
Beverly Hills, CA 90213
562-373-4800
800-800-2369
Fax: 562-373-4803

CELEBRITY HOME ENTERTAINMENT
(CEL)
22025 Ventura Blvd.,
Ste. 200
PO Box 4112
Woodland Hills, CA
91365-4112
818-595-0666
Fax: 818-716-0168

CENTER FOR HUMANITIES, INC.
(CHI)
Communications Park
Box 1000
Mount Kisco, NY 10549
914-666-4100
800-431-1242
Fax: 914-666-5319

CHILDREN'S CIRCLE WESTWOODS STUDIOS/ CHILDRENS CIRCLE
(CCC)
389 Newtown Tpke.
Weston, CT 06883
203-222-0002
800-KIDS-VID
Fax: 203-226-3818

CHILDREN'S TELEVISION WORKSHOP (CTW)
(CTW)
1 Lincoln Plaza
New York, NY 10023
212-595-3456
Fax: 212-875-6104

CHORDANT DISTRIBUTION GROUP (SPW)
101 Winners Circle
Brentwood, TN 37027
615-371-6800
800-877-4443
Fax: 615-371-6980

CHURCHILL MEDIA
(CHF)
6901 Woodley Ave.
Van Nuys, CA 91406
818-778-1978
800-334-7830
Fax: 818-778-1994

COLISEUM VIDEO
(CSM)
430 W. 54th St.
New York, NY 10019
212-489-8130
800-288-8130
Fax: 212-582-5690

COLUMBIA TRISTAR HOME VIDEO (COL)
Sony Pictures Plaza
10202 W. Washington
Blvd.
Culver City, CA 90232
310-280-8000
Fax: 310-280-2485

CONGRESS ENTERTAINMENT, LTD. (CNG)
Learn Plaza, Ste. 6
PO Box 845
Tannersville, PA 18372-0845
717-620-9001
800-847-8273
Fax: 717-620-9278

CONNOISSEUR VIDEO COLLECTION (CVC)
1575 Westwood Blvd.,
Ste. 305
Los Angeles, CA 90024
310-231-1350
800-529-2300
Fax: 310-231-1359

CORONET/MTI FILM & VIDEO (MTI)
4350 Equity Dr.
PO Box 2649
Columbus, OH 43216
614-876-0371
800-777-8100
Fax: 614-771-5841

CORONET-MTI FILM & VIDEO INTERNATIONAL (MTT)
PO Box 2649
Colombus, OH 43216
800-777-8100

CREST VIDEO MARKETING (CVM)
415 N. Figueroa St.
Wilmington, CA 90744
800-682-7378
Fax: 310-835-7892

CRITERION COLLECTION (CRC)
c/o The Voyager
Company
1 Bridge St.
Irvington, NY 10533-1543

CRITICS' CHOICE VIDEO, INC. (CCB)
PO Box 749
Itasca, IL 60143-0749
708-775-3300
800-367-7765
Fax: 708-775-3355

CRYSTAL PRODUCTIONS
(CRY)
1812 Johns Dr.

Box 2159
Glenview, IL 60025
708-657-8144
800-255-8629
Fax: 708-657-8149

DISCOUNT VIDEO TAPES, INC. (DVT)
PO Box 7122
Burbank, CA 91510
818-843-3366
Fax: 818-843-3821

DISCOVERY HOME ENTERTAINMENT
(DHE)
7700 Wisconsin Ave.
Bethesda, MD 20814-3579
301-986-1999
800-813-7409
Fax: 301-986-4827

DISNEY EDUCATIONAL PRODUCTIONS
(DSN)
4350 Equity
Columbus, OH 43228
800-621-2131
Fax: 614-771-7362

DOVE KIDS (DOV)
301 N. Canon Dr., Ste. 203
Beverly Hills, CA 90210

DREAM VIDEO PRODUCTIONS/ KID-VID (KVI)
479 N. Santa Cruz Ave.
Los Gatos, CA 95030
408-395-3190
800-4-KIDVID
Fax: 408-395-5117

ECUFILM (ECU)
810 12th Ave. S.
Nashville, TN 37203
615-242-6277
800-251-4091
Fax: 615-742-5125

ENVIRONMENTAL MEDIA (ENM)
Marketing and Catalog
PO Box 99
Beaufort, SC 29901-0099
803-933-3003
800-368-3382
Fax: 803-986-9093

EUROPEAN VIDEO DISTRIBUTOR
(EVD)
2402 W. Olive Ave.
Burbank, CA 91506
818-848-5902
800-423-6752
Fax: 818-848-1965

EXPANDED ENTERTAINMENT
(EXP)
28024 Dorothy Dr.
Agoura Hills, CA 91301-2635
818-991-2884
800-996-TOON
Fax: 818-991-3773

FACETS MULTIMEDIA, INC. (FCT)
1517 W. Fullerton Ave.
Chicago, IL 60614
312-281-9075
800-331-6197
Fax: 312-929-5437

FALCON HOME VIDEO
(FHV)
12124 Sherman Way
North Hollywood, CA 91605
818-765-1777
800-422-6484
Fax: 818-503-5282

FAMILY FILMS/ CONCORDIA (FFC)
3558 S. Jefferson Ave.
St. Louis, MO 63118-9988
314-268-1000
800-325-3040
Fax: 314-268-1329

FAMILY HOME ENTERTAINMENT
(FHE)
c/o Live Home Video
15400 Sherman Way
PO Box 10124
Van Nuys, CA 91410-0124
818-908-0303
800-677-0789
Fax: 818-778-3259

FAST FORWARD (FAF)
3420 Ocean Park Blvd.,
Ste. 3075
Santa Monica, CA 90405
310-396-4434
Fax: 310-396-2292

FILMS FOR THE HUMANITIES & SCIENCES (FHS)
PO Box 2053
Princeton, NJ 08543-2053
609-275-1400
800-257-5126
Fax: 609-275-3767

FILMS INC. VIDEO
(FLI)
5547 N. Ravenswood
Ave.
Chicago, IL 60640-1199

312-878-2600
800-323-4222
Fax: 312-878-0416

FIRST RUN FEATURES/ICARUS FILMS (ICA)
153 Waverly Pl.
New York, NY 10014
212-727-1711
800-876-1710
Fax: 212-989-7649

FOCUS ON ANIMALS
(FOC)
Fay Spring Center-
Humane Education
Center
534 Red Bud Rd.
Winchester, VA 22603
703-665-2827

FOCUS ON THE FAMILY (FCS)
8605 Exployer Dr.
Colorado Springs, CO 80920
719-531-3400
800-932-9123
Fax: 719-548-4652

FORMAT INTERNATIONAL
(FMT)
2421 E. Washington St.
Indianapolis, IN 46201-4123

FOX/LORBER HOME VIDEO (FXL)
419 Park Ave., S., 20th
Fl.
New York, NY 10016
212-532-3392
Fax: 212-685-2625

FOXVIDEO (FXV)
2121 Avenue of the
Stars, 25th Fl.
Los Angeles, CA 90067
310-369-3900
800-800-2FOX
Fax: 310-369-5811

FRIES HOME VIDEO
(FRH)
6922 Hollywood Blvd.,
12th Fl.
Hollywood, CA 90028
213-466-2266
Fax: 213-466-2126

FRIGHT VIDEO (FRG)
16 Kenmar Dr., Ste. 141
Billerica, MA 01821-4788

FUSION VIDEO (FUS)
100 Fusion Way
Country Club Hills, IL 60478
708-799-2073
Fax: 708-799-8375

GENESIS HOME VIDEO *(GHV)*
15820 Arminta St.
Van Nuys, CA 91406

GERMAN LANGUAGE VIDEO CENTER *(GLV)*
7625 Pendleton Pike
Indianapolis, IN 46226-5298
317-547-1257
800-252-1957
Fax: 317-547-1263

GLENN VIDEO VISTAS, LTD. *(GVV)*
6924 Canby Ave., Ste. 103
Reseda, CA 91335
818-881-8110
Fax: 818-981-5506

GOODTIMES ENTERTAINMENT *(GKK)*
16 E. 40th St., 8th Fl.
New York, NY 10016-0113
212-951-3000
Fax: 212-213-9319

GRAPEVINE VIDEO *(GPV)*
PO Box 46161
Phoenix, AZ 85063
602-973-3661
Fax: 602-973-0060

HALLMARK HOME ENTERTAINMENT *(HMK)*
6100 Wilshire Blvd., Ste. 1400
Los Angeles, CA 90048
213-549-3790
Fax: 213-549-3760

HBO HOME VIDEO *(HBO)*
1100 6th Ave.
New York, NY 10036
212-512-7400
Fax: 212-512-7498

HEMDALE HOME VIDEO *(HMD)*
7966 Beverly Blvd.
Los Angeles, CA 90048
213-966-3700
Fax: 213-653-5452

HEN'S TOOTH VIDEO *(HTV)*
2805 E. State Blvd.
Fort Wayne, IN 46805
219-471-4332
Fax: 219-471-4449

HIGH/SCOPE EDUCATIONAL RESEARCH FOUNDATION *(HSE)*
600 N. River St.
Ypsilanti, MI 48198-2898
313-485-2000
800-40-PRESS
Fax: 313-485-0704

HOLLYWOOD HOME ENTERTAINMENT *(HHE)*
6165 Crooked Creek Rd., Ste. B
Norcross, GA 30092-3105

HOLLYWOOD HOME THEATRE *(HHT)*
1540 N. Highland Ave., Ste. 110
Hollywood, CA 90028
213-466-0127

HOLLYWOOD PICTURES HOME VIDEO *(HPH)*
Fairmont Bldg. 526
500 S. Buena Vista St.
Burbank, CA 91505-9842

HOME VISION CINEMA *(HMV)*
5547 N. Ravenswood Ave.
Chicago, IL 60640-1199
312-878-2600
800-826-3456
Fax: 312-878-8648

HORIZON ENTERTAINMENT *(HEG)*
45030 Trevor Ave.
Lancaster, CA 93534
805-940-1040
800-323-2061
Fax: 805-940-8511

IGNATIUS PRESS *(IGP)*
33 Oakland Ave.
Harrison, NY 10528-9974
914-835-4216
Fax: 914-835-8406

IMAGE ENTERTAINMENT *(IME)*
9333 Oso Ave.
Chatsworth, CA 91311
818-407-9100
800-473-3475
Fax: 818-407-9111

IMPERIAL ENTERTAINMENT CORP. *(IMP)*
4640 Lankershim Blvd., Ste. 201
North Hollywood, CA 91602
818-762-0005
800-888-5826
Fax: 818-762-0006

INCREASE/ SILVERMINE VIDEO *(INC)*
6860 Canby Ave., Ste. 118
Reseda, CA 91335
818-342-2880
800-233-2880
Fax: 818-342-4029

INGRAM ENTERTAINMENT *(ING)*
2 Ingram Blvd.
La Vergne, TN 37086-7006
615-287-4000
800-759-5000
Fax: 615-287-4992

INGRAM INTERNATIONAL FILMS *(INJ)*
7900 Hickman Rd.
Des Moines, IA 50322
515-254-7000
800-621-1333
Fax: 515-254-7021

INTERAMA, INC. *(INT)*
301 W. 53rd St., Ste. 19E
New York, NY 10019
212-977-4830
Fax: 212-581-6582

INTERNATIONAL HISTORIC FILMS, INC. (IHF) *(IHF)*
PO Box 29035
Chicago, IL 60629
312-927-2900
Fax: 312-927-9211

JEF FILMS, INC. *(JEF)*
Film House
143 Hickory Hill Circle
Osterville, MA 02655-1322
508-428-7198
Fax: 508-428-7198

JIM HENSON PRODUCTIONS *(JHV)*
5358 Melrose Ave., Ste. 300W
Los Angeles, CA 90038
818-953-3030

J2 COMMUNICATIONS *(JTC)*
10850 Wilshire Blvd., Ste. 1000
Los Angeles, CA 90024
310-474-5252
800-521-8273
Fax: 310-474-1219

JUDAICA CAPTIONED FILM CENTER, INC. *(JCF)*
United States

JUST FOR KIDS HOME VIDEO *(JFK)*
6320 Canoga Ave., Penthouse Ste.
PO Box 4112
Woodland Hills, CA 91365-4112
818-715-1980
800-445-8210
Fax: 818-716-0168

KAROL VIDEO *(KAR)*
PO Box 7600
Wilkes Barre, PA 18773
717-822-8899
Fax: 717-822-8226

KEEP THE FAITH INC. *(KEP)*
PO Box 10544
10 Audrey Pl.
Fairfield, NJ 07004
201-244-1990
Fax: 201-244-1990

KID VISION *(KID)*
75 Rockefeller Plaza
New York, NY 10019
212-275-2900
800-3KID-VID
Fax: 212-765-0899

KNOWLEDGE UNLIMITED, INC. *(KUI)*
Box 52
Madison, WI 53701-0052
608-836-6660
800-356-2303
Fax: 608-831-1570

KULTUR VIDEO *(KUL)*
195 Hwy. No. 36
West Long Branch, NJ 07764
908-229-2343
800-458-5887
Fax: 908-229-0066

LET'S CREATE *(LET)*
50 Cherry Hill Rd.
Parsippany, NJ 07054
201-299-0633
800-790-6655
Fax: 201-402-0264

LIBRARY VIDEO COMPANY *(LVC)*
PO Box 1110
Bala Cynwyd, PA 19004
610-667-0200
800-843-3620
Fax: 610-667-3425

LIGHTYEAR ENTERTAINMENT *(LTY)*
350 5th Ave., Ste. 5101
New York, NY 10118
212-563-4610
800-229-7867
Fax: 212-563-1932

LIVE ENTERTAINMENT *(LIV)*
15400 Sherman Way
PO Box 10124
Van Nuys, CA 91410-0124
818-988-5060

LOONIC VIDEO *(LOO)*
2022 Taraval St., Ste. 6427
San Francisco, CA 94116
510-526-5681

LSVIDEO, INC. *(LSV)*
PO Box 415
Carmel, IN 46032

LUCERNE MEDIA *(LME)*
37 Ground Pine Rd.
Morris Plains, NJ 07950
201-538-1401
800-341-2293
Fax: 201-538-0855

LYONS GROUP *(LGV)*
2435 N. Central Expy., Ste. 1600
Richardson, TX 75080-3884
214-390-6000
800-418-2371
Fax: 214-390-6066

MANAGEMENT COMPANY ENTERTAINMENT GROUP (MCEG), INC. *(MCG)*
1888 Century Park, E., Ste. 1777
Los Angeles, CA 90067-1721
310-282-0871
Fax: 310-282-8303

MASTERVISION, INC. *(MAS)*
969 Park Ave.
New York, NY 10028
212-879-0448
Fax: 212-744-3560

MAZON PRODUCTIONS *(MAZ)*
PO Box 2427
Northbrook, IL 60065-2427

MCA/UNIVERSAL HOME VIDEO *(MCA)*
100 Universal City Plaza
Universal City, CA 91608-9955
818-777-1000
Fax: 818-733-1483

MEDIA HOME ENTERTAINMENT *(MED)*
510 W. 6th St., Ste. 1032
Los Angeles, CA 90014
213-236-1336
Fax: 213-236-1346

MGM/UA HOME ENTERTAINMENT *(MGM)*
2500 Broadway
Santa Monica, CA 90404-6061
310-449-3000
Fax: 310-449-3100

MIKE LEBELL'S VIDEO *(MLB)*
75 Freemont Pl.
Los Angeles, CA 90005
213-938-3333
Fax: 213-938-3334

REX MILLER *(RXM)*
Rte. 1, Box 457-D
East Prairie, MO 63845
314-649-5048

MIRAMAR PRODUCTIONS *(MIR)*
200 2nd Ave., W.
Seattle, WA 98119
206-284-4700
800-245-6472
Fax: 206-286-4433

MIRAMAX PICTURES HOME VIDEO *(MAX)*
500 S. Buena Vista St.
Burbank, CA 91521

MNTEX ENTERTAINMENT, INC. *(MTX)*
500 Kirts Dr.
Troy, MI 48084-5225

MODERN CURRICULUM PRESS - MCP *(LCA)*
PO Box 70935
108 Wilmot Rd.

Chicago, IL 60673-0933
800-777-8100

MONARCH HOME VIDEO *(MNC)*
Two Ingram Blvd.
La Vergne, TN 37086-7006
615-287-4632
Fax: 615-287-4992

MONTEREY HOME VIDEO *(MON)*
28038 Dorothy Dr., Ste. 1
Agoura Hills, CA 91301
818-597-0047
800-424-2593
Fax: 818-597-0105

MOONBEAM PUBLICATIONS, INC. *(MBP)*
836 Hastings St.
Traverse City, MI 49686
616-922-0533
800-445-2391
Fax: 616-922-0544

MOORE VIDEO *(MRV)*
PO Box 5703
Richmond, VA 23220
804-745-9785
Fax: 804-745-9785

MOVIECRAFT, INC. *(MVC)*
PO Box 438
Orland Park, IL 60462
708-460-9082
Fax: 708-460-9099

MOVIES UNLIMITED *(MOV)*
6736 Castor Ave.
Philadelphia, PA 19149
215-722-8298
800-466-8437
Fax: 215-725-3683

MPI HOME VIDEO *(MPI)*
16101 S. 108th Ave.
Orland Park, IL 60462
708-460-0555
Fax: 708-873-3177

MUSIC FOR LITTLE PEOPLE *(MLT)*
Box 1460
Redway, CA 95560
707-923-3991
800-346-4445
Fax: 707-923-3241

MUSIC VIDEO DISTRIBUTORS *(MVD)*
O'Neill Industrial Center
1210 Standbridge St.
Norristown, PA 19401

610-272-7771
800-888-0486
Fax: 610-272-6074

NATIONAL FILM BOARD OF CANADA *(NFB)*
1251 Avenue of the Americas, 16th Fl.
New York, NY 10020-1173
212-596-1770
800-542-2164
Fax: 212-596-1779

NEW HORIZONS HOME VIDEO *(NHO)*
2951 Flowers Rd., S., Ste. 237
Atlanta, GA 30341
404-458-3488
800-854-3323
Fax: 404-458-2679

NEW LINE HOME VIDEO *(NLC)*
116 N. Robertson Blvd.
Los Angeles, CA 90048
310-967-6670
Fax: 310-854-0602

NEW WORLD ENTERTAINMENT *(NWV)*
1440 S. Sepulveda Blvd.
Los Angeles, CA 90025
310-444-8100
Fax: 310-444-8101

NOSTALGIA FAMILY VIDEO *(NOS)*
PO Box 606
Baker City, OR 97814
503-523-9034
800-784-8362
Fax: 503-523-7115

ORION HOME VIDEO *(ORI)*
1888 Century Park E.
Los Angeles, CA 90067
310-282-0550
Fax: 310-282-9902

PARAMOUNT HOME VIDEO *(PAR)*
Bluhdorn Bldg.
5555 Melrose Ave.
Los Angeles, CA 90038
213-956-8090
Fax: 213-862-1100

PBS HOME VIDEO *(PBS)*
Catalog Fulfillment Center
PO Box 4030
Santa Monica, CA 90411
800-531-4727
800-645-4PBS

PHOENIX/BFA FILMS *(BFA)*
2349 Chaffee Dr.
St. Louis, MO 63146
314-569-0211
800-221-1274
Fax: 314-569-2834

PM ENTERTAINMENT GROUP, INC. *(PMH)*
9450 Chivers Ave.
Sun Valley, CA 91352
818-504-6332
800-934-2111
Fax: 818-504-6380

POLYGRAM VIDEO (PV) *(PGV)*
825 8th Ave.
New York, NY 10019
212-333-8000
800-825-7781
Fax: 212-603-7960

PRICE STERN SLOAN, INC. *(PSS)*
11835 Olympic Blvd., East Bldg., 5th Fl.
Los Angeles, CA 90064-5006
310-477-6100
800-421-0892
Fax: 310-445-3933

PRINCETON BOOK CO. PUBLISHERS *(PBC)*
PO Box 57
Pennington, NJ 08534
609-737-8177
800-220-7149
Fax: 609-737-1869

PRISM ENTERTAINMENT *(PSM)*
1888 Century Park, E., Ste. 350
Los Angeles, CA 90067
310-277-3270
Fax: 310-203-8036

PROFESSIONAL MEDIA SERVICE CORP. *(PMS)*
19122 S. Vermont Ave.
Gardena, CA 90248
310-532-9024
800-223-7672
Fax: 800-253-8853

PROSCENIUM ENTERTAINMENT *(PRS)*
PO Box 909
Hightstown, NJ 08520
800-222-6260
Fax: 609-448-9499

PROUD TO BE**A BLACK VIDEO COLLECTION** *(PTB)*
1235-E East Blvd., Ste. 209
Charlotte, NC 28203
704-523-2227

PUBLIC MEDIA VIDEO *(PME)*
5547 N. Ravenswood Ave.
Chicago, IL 60640-1199
312-878-2600
800-826-3456
Fax: 312-878-8406

PYRAMID FILM & VIDEO *(PYR)*
2801 Colorado Ave.
Santa Monica, CA 90404
310-828-7577
800-421-2304
Fax: 310-453-9083

QUALITY VIDEO *(QVD)*
7399 Bush Lake Rd.
Minneapolis, MN 55439-2027
612-893-0903
Fax: 612-893-1585

RABBIT EARS HOME VIDEO *(RAB)*
131 Rowayton Ave.
Rowayton, CT 06853
203-857-3760
800-800 EARS
Fax: 203-857-3777

RANDOM HOUSE HOME VIDEO *(RAN)*
201 E. 50th St.
New York, NY 10022
212-751-2600
800-733-3000
Fax: 212-572-8700

RANDOM HOUSE MEDIA *(RHU)*
400 Hahn Rd.
Westminster, MD 21157
410-848-1900
800-726-0600
Fax: 800-632-9242

READER'S DIGEST HOME VIDEO *(RDG)*
Reader's Digest Rd.
Pleasantville, NY 10570

REGENCY HOME VIDEO *(RHV)*
9911 W. Pico Blvd.
Los Angeles, CA 90035
310-552-2660
Fax: 310-552-9039

REPUBLIC PICTURES HOME VIDEO *(REP)*
5700 Wilshire Blvd.,
Ste. 525
Los Angeles, CA 90036
213-965-6900
Fax: 213-965-6963

RHINO HOME VIDEO *(RHI)*
10635 Santa Monica
Blvd., 2nd Fl.
Los Angeles, CA 90025-4900
310-828-1980
800-843-3670
Fax: 310-453-5529

RINCON CHILDREN'S ENTERTAINMENT/ BMG KIDZ *(RIN)*
1525 Crossroads of the
World
Hollywood, CA 90028

SALENGER FILMS, INC. *(SAL)*
1635 12th St.
Santa Monica, CA
90404-9988
310-450-1300
800-775-5025
Fax: 310-450-1010

SCHOOLMASTERS VIDEO *(SCH)*
745 State Circle
PO Box 1941
Ann Arbor, MI 48106
313-761-5175
800-521-2832
Fax: 313-761-8711

SGE ENTERTAINMENT CORP. *(SGE)*
12001 Ventura Pl., 4th
Fl., Ste. 404
Studio City, CA 91604
818-766-8500
Fax: 818-766-7873

SIGNALS *(SIG)*
PO Box 64428
St. Paul, MN 55164-0428
612-659-4738
800-669-5225
Fax: 612-659-4320

SIMITAR ENTERTAINMENT *(SIM)*
3850 Annapolis Ln.,
Ste. 140
Plymouth, MN 55447
612-559-6660
800-486-TAPE
Fax: 612-559-0210

SIMON WIESENTHAL CENTER *(SWC)*
9760 W. Pico Blvd.

Los Angeles, CA 90035-4792
310-553-9036
Fax: 310-553-8007

SINISTER CINEMA *(SNC)*
PO Box 4369
Medford, OR 97501-0168
503-773-6860
Fax: 503-779-8650

SNOOPY'S HOME VIDEO LIBRARY *(SHV)*
c/o Media Home
Entertainment
510 W. 6th St., Ste.
1032
Los Angeles, CA 90014-1311
213-236-1336
Fax: 818-992-6520

SOCIETY FOR VISUAL EDUCATION, INC. (SVE) *(SVE)*
6677 N. NW Hwy.
Chicago, IL 60631
312-775-9550
800-829-1900
Fax: 312-775-5091

SONY KIDS MUSIC *(SKM)*
550 Madison Ave.
New York, NY 10022
212-833-8000

SONY MUSIC VIDEO ENTERPRISES *(SMV)*
550 Madison Ave.
New York, NY 10022
212-833-7095

STAGE FRIGHT PRODUCTIONS *(SFP)*
11 S. 2nd St.
PO Box 373
Geneva, IL 60134
708-208-9845
800-979-6800
Fax: 708-232-6206

STAGESTEP *(STS)*
PO Box 328
Philadelphia, PA 19105
215-829-9800
800-523-0961
Fax: 215-829-0508

STREAMLINE PICTURES *(STP)*
PO Box 691418
W. Hollywood, CA
90069
310-998-0070
Fax: 310-998-1145

SUPER MANAGEMENT *(SMA)*
15104 Detroit Ave., Ste.
2
Lakewood, OH 44107-3916
216-221-5300
Fax: 216-221-5348

TAPEWORM VIDEO DISTRIBUTORS *(TPV)*
27833 Hopkins Ave.,
Unit 6
Valencia, CA 91355
805-257-4904
Fax: 805-257-4820

THOMSON PRODUCTIONS, INC. *(TPI)*
PO Box 1225
Orem, UT 84059
801-226-0155
Fax: 801-226-0166

TIME-LIFE VIDEO AND TELEVISION *(TLF)*
1450 E. Parham Rd.
Richmond, VA 23280
804-266-6330
800-621-7026

TIMELESS VIDEO INC. *(TIM)*
9943 Canoga Ave., Ste.
B2
Chatsworth, CA 91311
818-773-0284
800-478-6734
Fax: 818-773-0176

TRANS-WORLD ENTERTAINMENT *(TWE)*
8899 Beverly Blvd., 8th
Fl.
Los Angeles, CA 90048-2412

TRIBORO ENTERTAINMENT GROUP *(TRI)*
12 W. 27th St., 15th Fl.
New York, NY 10001
212-686-6116
Fax: 212-686-6178

TURNER HOME ENTERTAINMENT COMPANY *(TTC)*
Box 105366
Atlanta, GA 35366
404-827-3066
800-523-0823
Fax: 404-827-3266

20TH CENTURY FOX FILM CORPORATION *(TCF)*
PO Box 900
Beverly Hills, CA 90213
310-369-1000
Fax: 310-369-3318

TYNDALE HOUSE PUBLISHERS *(THP)*
351 Executive Dr.
PO Box 80
Wheaton, IL 60189
708-668-8300
800-323-9400
Fax: 708-668-9092

UAV CORPORATION *(UAV)*
PO Box 5497
Fort Mill, SC 29715
803-548-7300
800-486-6782
Fax: 803-548-3335

UNI DISTRIBUTION *(UND)*
60 Universal City Plaza
Universal City, CA
91608
818-777-4400
Fax: 818-766-5740

UNICORN VIDEO, INC. *(UNI)*
9025 Eton Ave., Ste. D.
Canoga Park, CA 91304
818-407-1333
800-528-4336
Fax: 818-407-8246

UNITY PRODUCTIONS *(UNT)*
4007 Willowwood Ln.
Aberdeen, SD 57401-9544

UNIVERSITY OF WASHINGTON EDUCATIONAL MEDIA COLLECTION *(UWA)*
Kane Hall
Box 353090
Seattle, WA 98195
206-543-9909
Fax: 206-685-7892

VALENCIA ENTERTAINMENT CORP. *(VEC)*
45030 Trevor Ave.
Lancaster, CA 93534-2648
805-940-1040
800-323-2061
Fax: 805-940-8511

VANTAGE COMMUNICATIONS, INC. *(VAN)*
PO Box 546-G

Nyack, NY 10960
914-268-0715
800-872-0068
Fax: 914-268-3429

VCII HOME ENTERTAINMENT, INC. *(VHE)*
13418 Wyandotte St.
North Hollywood, CA
91605
818-764-1777
800-350-1931
Fax: 818-764-0231

VESTRON VIDEO *(VES)*
c/o Live Home Video
15400 Sherman Way
PO Box 10124
Van Nuys, CA 91410-0124
818-988-5060
800-367-7765
Fax: 818-778-3125

VIDCREST *(VDC)*
PO Box 69642
Los Angeles, CA 90069
213-650-7310
Fax: 213-654-4810

VIDEO ARTISTS INTERNATIONAL, INC. *(VAI)*
158 Linwood Plaza, Ste.
301
Fort Lee, NJ 07024
201-944-0099
800-477-7146
Fax: 201-947-8850

VIDEO BIBLE LIBRARY, INC. *(VBL)*
Box 17515
Portland, OR 97217
360-892-7707
Fax: 360-254-8318

THE VIDEO CATALOG *(TVC)*
PO Box 64267
Saint Paul, MN 55164-0267
612-659-4312
800-733-6656
Fax: 612-659-4320

VIDEO CITY PRODUCTIONS/ DISTRIBUTING *(VCD)*
4266 Broadway
Oakland, CA 94611
510-428-0202
Fax: 510-654-7802

VIDEO COLLECTIBLES/BFS VIDEO *(VCO)*
1500 Clinton St.
Buffalo, NY 14206-9911

800-268-3891
Fax: 800-269-8877

**VIDEO
COMMUNICATIONS,
INC. (VCI)** *(VCI)*
11333 E. 60th Pl.
Tulsa, OK 74146
918-254-6337
800-331-4077
Fax: 918-254-6117

VIDEO CONNECTION
(VCN)
3123 W. Sylvania Ave.
Toledo, OH 43613
419-472-7727
800-365-0449
Fax: 419-472-2655

VIDEO DIMENSIONS
(VDM)
322 8th Ave., 4th Fl.
New York, NY 10001
212-929-6135
Fax: 212-929-6135

VIDEO GEMS *(GEM)*
12228 Venice Blvd., No.
504
Los Angeles, CA 90066

THE VIDEO PROJECT
(VPJ)
5332 College Ave., Ste.
101
Oakland, CA 94618
510-655-9050
800-4-PLANET
Fax: 510-655-9115

VIDEO YESTERYEAR
(VYY)
Box C
Sandy Hook, CT 06482
203-426-2574
800-243-0987
Fax: 203-797-0819

VIDEOS.COM, INC.
(PIC)
1725 W. Catalpa Ave.,
3rd Fl.
Chicago, IL 60640
312-878-9282
800-670-9282
Fax: 800-308-5003

**VIDMARK
ENTERTAINMENT**
(VMK)
2644 30th St.
Santa Monica, CA
90405-3009
310-314-2000
Fax: 310-392-0252

V.I.E.W. VIDEO *(VWV)*
34 E. 23rd St.
New York, NY 10010
212-674-5550
800-843-9843
Fax: 212-979-0266

**WALT DISNEY HOME
VIDEO** *(DIS)*
500 S. Buena Vista St.
Burbank, CA 91521
818-562-3560

**WARNER/ELEKTRA/
ATLANTIC (WEA)
CORPORATION**
(WEA)
9451 LBJ Fwy., Ste. 107
Dallas, TX 75243
214-234-6200
Fax: 214-699-9343

**WARNER HOME
VIDEO, INC.** *(WAR)*
4000 Warner Blvd.
Burbank, CA 91522
818-954-6000

**WARNER REPRISE
VIDEO** *(WRV)*
3300 Warner Blvd.
Burbank, CA 91505-
4694
818-846-9090
Fax: 818-953-3329

WARNERVISION
(AVE)
A Time Warner
Company
75 Rockefeller Plaza
New York, NY 10019
212-275-2900
800-95-WARNER
Fax: 212-765-0899

**WARREN MILLER
ENTERTAINMENT**
(WME)
2540 Frontier Ave., Ste.
104
Boulder, CO 80301
303-442-3430
800-523-7117
Fax: 303-442-3402

**WESTERN MEDIA
SYSTEMS** *(WFV)*
30941 W. Agoura Rd.,
Ste. 302
Westlake Village, CA
91361
818-889-7350
Fax: 818-889-7350

**WESTERN
PUBLISHING CO.,
INC.** *(WPC)*
1220 Mound Ave.
Racine, WI 53404
414-633-2431

WHITE STAR *(WST)*
195 Hwy. 36
West Long Branch, NJ
07764
908-229-2343
800-458-5887
Fax: 908-229-0066

**WISHING WELL
DISTRIBUTING**
(WSH)
PO Box 1008
Silver Lake, WI 53170
414-889-8501
800-888-9355
Fax: 414-889-8591

**WNET/THIRTEEN
NON-BROADCAST**
(WNE)
356 W. 58th St.
New York, NY 10019
212-560-2000
Fax: 212-582-3297

**WOMBAT FILM AND
VIDEO** *(WOM)*
1560 Sherman Ave.,
Ste. 100
Evanston, IL 60201
708-328-6700
800-323-9084
Fax: 708-328-6706

**WOOD KNAPP &
COMPANY, INC.**
(WKV)
Knapp Press
5900 Wilshire Blvd.
Los Angeles, CA 90036
800-521-2666
Fax: 213-930-2742

**WORLDVISION HOME
VIDEO, INC.** *(WOV)*
1700 Broadway
New York, NY 10019-
5905
212-261-2700
Fax: 212-261-2950

XENON *(XVC)*
211 Arizona Ave.
Santa Monica, CA
90401

ZONDERVAN *(ZON)*
ZPH New Media
5300 Patterson Ave.,
SE
Grand Rapids, MI
49530
616-698-3465
800-925-0316
Fax: 616-698-3454